You will need this registration code to access parts of wwnorton.com/literature:

VYKA-RWCF

# The Norton Anthology
# of American Literature

## SEVENTH EDITION

### VOLUME C

*1865–1914*

# The Norton Anthology
# of American Literature

## SEVENTH EDITION

### Nina Baym, *General Editor*

SWANLUND CHAIR AND CENTER FOR
ADVANCED STUDY PROFESSOR EMERITA OF ENGLISH
JUBILEE PROFESSOR OF LIBERAL ARTS AND SCIENCES
UNIVERSITY OF ILLINOIS AT URBANA-CHAMPAIGN

### VOLUME C

*1865–1914*

Jeanne Campbell Reesman
Arnold Krupat

W • W • NORTON & COMPANY • *New York* • *London*

W. W. Norton & Company has been independent since its founding in 1923, when William Warder Norton and Mary D. Herter Norton first published lectures delivered at the People's Institute, the adult education division of New York City's Cooper Union. The Nortons soon expanded their program beyond the Institute, publishing books by celebrated academics from America and abroad. By mid-century, the two major pillars of Norton's publishing program—trade books and college texts—were firmly established. In the 1950s, the Norton family transferred control of the company to its employees, and today—with a staff of four hundred and a comparable number of trade, college, and professional titles published each year—W. W. Norton & Company stands as the largest and oldest publishing house owned wholly by its employees.

*Editor:* Julia Reidhead
*Manuscript Editors:* Kurt Wildermuth, Michael Fleming,
Katharine Ings, Candace Levy, Pam Lawson
*Electronic Media Editor:* Eileen Connell
*Editorial Assistants:* Ann Abrams, Catherine Spencer
*Production Manager:* Diane O'Connor
*Permissions Manager:* Nancy Rodwan
*Permissions Clearing:* Margaret Gorenstein
*Text Design:* Antonina Krass
*Art Research:* Neil Ryder Hoos
*Managing Editor, College:* Marian Johnson

*Composition:* Binghamton Valley Composition
*Manufacturing:* RR Donnelley

Copyright © 2007, 2003, 1998, 1994, 1989, 1985, 1979
by W. W. Norton & Company, Inc.

ISBN 10: 0-393-92741-5
ISBN 13: 978-0-393-92741-2

W. W. Norton & Company, Inc., 500 Fifth Avenue, New York, NY 10110
www.wwnorton.com

W. W. Norton & Company Ltd., Castle House, 75/76 Wells Street, London W1T 3QT

7 8 9 0

# Contents

# Preface to the Seventh Edition

In this Seventh Edition of *The Norton Anthology of American Literature*, we offer the most extensive revision in our long publishing history. Three new section editors have joined the team, working with each other and the General Editor to consider afresh each selection and rethink the entire apparatus, from headnotes to footnotes to section introductions to bibliographies. These editors are Robert S. Levine, Professor of English at the University of Maryland, College Park, who succeeds Hershel Parker as editor of "American Literature 1820–1865"; Jeanne Campbell Reesman, Ashbel Smith Professor of English at the University of Texas at San Antonio, who succeeds Ronald Gottesman as editor of "American Literature 1865–1914"; and Mary Loeffelholz, Professor of English at Northeastern University, who succeeds Nina Baym as editor of "American Literature 1914–1945." Each editor, new or continuing, is a well-known expert in the relevant field or period and had ultimate responsibility for his or her section of the anthology, but we have worked together closely from first to last. We are excited about the outcome of our collaboration and anticipate that, like the previous six editions, this edition of *The Norton Anthology of American Literature* will lead the field among American literature anthologies.

From the anthology's inception in 1979, the editors have had three main aims: first, to present a rich and substantial enough variety of works to enable teachers to build courses according to their own ideals (thus, teachers are offered more authors and more selections than they will probably use in any one course); second, to make the anthology self-sufficient by featuring many works in their entirety along with extensive selections for individual authors; third, to balance traditional interests with developing critical concerns in a way that points to a coherent literary history. As early as 1979, we anthologized work by Anne Bradstreet, Mary Rowlandson, Sarah Kemble Knight, Phillis Wheatley, Margaret Fuller, Harriet Beecher Stowe, Frederick Douglass, Sarah Orne Jewett, Kate Chopin, Mary E. Wilkins Freeman, Booker T. Washington, Charles Chesnutt, Edith Wharton, W. E. B. Du Bois, and other writers who were not yet part of a standard canon. Yet we never shortchanged writers like Franklin, Emerson, Whitman, Hawthorne, Melville, Dickinson, Hemingway, Fitzgerald, and Faulkner, whose work students expected to read in their American literature courses, and whom teachers then and now would not think of doing without.

Although the so-called "canon wars" of the 1980s and 1990s appear to have subsided, it is clear that the number and diversity of authors now recognized as contributors to the totality of American literature have expanded dramatically since 1979. The traditional writers look different in this expanded context; they also change according to which of their works are selected. Teachers and students remain committed to the idea of the literary—that writers strive to produce artifacts that are both intellectually serious and formally skillful—but believe more than ever that writers should be understood in relation to their cultural and historical situations. In endeavoring to do justice to these complex realities, we have worked, as in previous editions, with detailed suggestions from many teachers and, through those teachers, the students who use the anthology. Thanks to questionnaires, comment cards, face-to-face and phone discussions, letters, and email, we have been able to listen to those for whom this book is intended. For this Seventh Edition, we have drawn on the careful commentary of 101 reviewers.

Our new materials have thoughtfully broadened the canon by representing 34 new writers in depth, without sacrificing widely assigned writers, many of whose selections have been reconsidered, reselected, and expanded. Our aim is always to provide extensive enough selections to do the writers justice, including complete works wherever possible. To the 36 complete longer texts already in the anthology we have added Benjamin Franklin's *Autobiography* (restored by popular demand); Hannah Foster's *The Coquette*; Frederick Douglass's novella *The Heroic Slave* (never before in a survey anthology); Stephen Crane's *Maggie: A Girl of the Streets*; Abraham Cahan's novella of immigrant New York City, *The Imported Bridegroom*; Willa Cather's *My Ántonia*; Raymond Chandler's hard-boiled detective story *Red Wind*; Sam Shepard's play *True West*; Louise Glück's *October*; and more. The Seventh Edition has expanded and in some cases reconfigured such central figures as Emerson, Hawthorne, Melville, Dickinson, and Twain, emphasizing new approaches in the headnotes and section introductions. The Seventh Edition likewise expands its representation of women writers and writers of diverse ethnic, racial, and regional origins—African Americans, Native Americans, Latina/os, and Asian Americans—whose critically acclaimed works have contributed to the American literary record. Under Arnold Krupat's editorship, Native American materials throughout the Seventh Edition have been rethought. New writers such as Sarah Winnemucca and Jane Johnston Schoolcraft, more selections from writers such as Zitkala Ša, and two new clusters (described below) enable teachers to bring early Native American writing and oratory into their syllabus or, should they prefer, to focus on these selections as a free-standing unit leading toward the moment after 1945 when Native writers fully entered the mainstream of literary activity.

In an innovation new to the Seventh Edition, each editor has gathered short texts that illuminate the cultural, historical, intellectual, and literary concerns of the period. The resulting clusters bring together markedly diverse voices—48 new to the anthology—in selections that highlight the range of views on a key issue or topic. For example, in "Slavery, Race, and the Making of American Literature," texts by David Walker, William Lloyd Garrison, Angelina Grimke, Sojourner Truth, and Martin R. Delany speak to the great paradox of pre–Civil War America: the rupture between the realities of slavery and the ideals of freedom. Or, in an example close to our own experience, "Writing in a Time of Terror: September 11, 2001" gathers verse and prose—from an excerpt from the collaboratively written official account, *The 9/11 Commission Report*, to selections by John Updike, Kimiko Hahn, Naomi Shahib Nye, and others—that show the range of powerful responses, written and visual, evoked by times of terror. Designed to be taught in a class period or two, or used as context, each of the twelve clusters consists of brief, carefully excerpted primary texts (about 6–10 per cluster) and an introduction.

Visual media, so central in contemporary American culture as well as in the classroom, has a prominent place in the Seventh Edition, which features forty pages of color plates in five new color inserts. In selecting our color plates—from Charles Wilson Peale's *Exhuming the Mastodon* at the beginning of the nineteenth century to *The Gates* by Christo and Jeanne-Claude at the beginning of the twenty-first—the editors aimed to provide images relevant to literary works in the anthology while depicting arts and artifacts typical of each era. We have looked for visually striking images that will provoke discussion, and our captions draw attention to important details and cross-reference authors and related literary texts. In addition, new graphic works—segments from Art Spiegelman's canonical graphic novel *Maus* and from the colonial children's classic *The New-England Primer*, a facsimile page of Emily Dickinson manuscript, an original illustration from Twain's *Roughing It*—open possibilities for teaching visual texts.

## Period-by-Period Revisions

*Volume A, Beginnings to 1820.* "Beginnings to 1700," edited by Wayne Franklin, continues to feature narratives by a range of early European explorers of the North American continent. Along with a cluster on the much-recounted story of Hannah Dustan's captivity—which intensified European fear of Native populations and was used to rationalize stern measures against them—the section adds material from *The Bay Psalm Book*, Roger Williams, Edward Taylor, Robert Calef, and *The New-England Primer*, and retains the complete text of Mary Rowlandson's captivity narrative. The heightened attention in this section to the combined religious and territorial aspirations of the Anglo settlers gives students a fuller sense of the conflicts that ensued when the North American continent was perceived, by Europeans, as a "New World." We note, too, the important role of the experiences of, and narratives by, women in the early European settlement of the future United States.

In "American Literature 1700–1820," edited by Philip Gura, we distinguish the eighteenth century as a period of consolidation and development in an emergent American literature. Work by the political Founders is augmented by Benjamin Franklin's *Autobiography*, included complete by teacher request, and Royall Tyler's play *The Contrast*. Newly added is the complete text of Hannah Foster's novel *The Coquette*, which uses a real-life tragedy to meditate on the proper role of well-bred women in the new republic and testifies to the formation of a female audience. A segment from Tabitha Tenney's satiric novel *Female Quixotism* helps extend student awareness of literary activity among women, as does the cluster "Women's Poetry: From Manuscript to Print," with verse by six poets—among them Mercy Otis Warren, Sarah Wentworth Morton, and Annis Boudinot Stockton—whose work contributed to the civil and political discourse of the early republic. A second new cluster, prepared by Arnold Krupat, "Native Americans: Contact and Conflict," highlights speeches and accounts by Pontiac, Samson Occom, Chief Logan (as cited by Thomas Jefferson), Red Jacket, and Tecumseh that underscore a centuries-long pattern of initial friendly contact mutating into bitter and violent conflict between Native Americans and whites.

*Volume B, American Literature 1820–1865.* Under the editorship of Robert S. Levine, this volume is now much more diverse. Teachers will still find Emerson's *Nature*, Hawthorne's *Scarlet Letter*, Thoreau's *Walden*, Douglass's *Narrative*, and Whitman's *Song of Myself* complete, as well as novellas by Melville, Davis's *Life in the Iron Mills*, and other frequently assigned works. But, aware of the important role of African American writers in the period and the omnipresence of race and slavery as literary and political themes, we have added two major African American writers, William Wells Brown and Frances E. W. Harper, as well as Douglass's novella *The Heroic Slave*, Thoreau's "Plea for Captain John Brown," more chapters from Stowe's *Uncle Tom's Cabin*, and the cluster "Slavery, Race, and the Making of American Literature." The section also includes two other new clusters: "Section, Region, Nation," in which writers from varying regions—Daniel Webster, William Gilmore Simms, Richard Henry Dana, John Louis O'Sullivan, Francis Parkman, Louise Amelia Clappe Smith, Mary Boykin Miller Chesnut—challenge the notion of consensus on a "national" literature while reflecting the extraordinary enlargement of territory included within the national boundaries; "Native Americans: Resistance and Removal," prepared by Arnold Krupat, gathers oratory and writings—by Native Americans such as Black Hawk, Petelasharo, Elias Boudinot, and the collective authors of the Cherokee Memorials as well as by whites such as Ralph Waldo Emerson—protesting Andrew Jackson's ruthless national policy of Indian removal.

New women writers in this period include Lydia Huntley Sigourney, Elizabeth Stoddard, and the Native American writer Jane Johnston Schoolcraft, who is represented by authoritative texts established in Robert Dale Parker's new edition of her complete works. Added prose fiction includes chapters from Cooper's *Last of the Mohicans*, Sedgwick's *Hope Leslie*, Kirkland's *A New Home—Who'll Follow?* and Melville's *Moby-Dick*, along with Poe's "The Black Cat" and Hawthorne's "Wakefield." Nonfiction prose offerings have been expanded with several of Lydia Maria Child's letters and new selections by Fanny Fern and Margaret Fuller. By instructors' request, we have increased the representation of poems by Emerson, Longfellow, and Whittier; poetry by Emily Dickinson has been reselected, using the newly established texts by Franklin (we retain the Johnson numbers in brackets for reference), and now includes a facsimile page from Fascicle 10. Finally, the section introduction has been entirely recast; author headnotes have been updated to reflect the latest biographies and critical discussions; and the selected bibliographies have been completely revised and updated.

*Volume C, American Literature 1865–1914.* Edited by Jeanne Campbell Reesman, this section has taken on a striking new look. To our well-received complete longer works—Twain's *Adventures of Huckleberry Finn*, Chopin's *The Awakening*, and James's *Daisy Miller*—we add complete texts of Stephen Crane's *Maggie: A Girl of the Streets* and Abraham Cahan's *The Imported Bridegroom*, as well as chapters from Theodore Dreiser's *Sister Carrie* and Twain's *Roughing It*. Also new is a selection from Twain's *Letters from the Earth*. Short fiction throughout the section has been reconsidered; new selections include James's "The Figure in the Carpet," Edith Wharton's "The Other Two" and "Roman Fever," and works by Jack London, Sui Sin Far, Bret Harte (notably the ground-breaking "Miggles" and "Tennessee's Partner"), Zitkala

Ša, Joel Chandler Harris, and Ambrose Bierce. New poets James Weldon Johnson and Paul Laurence Dunbar, Emma Lazarus (moved from Volume B to this volume, where she belongs chronologically), the anonymous authors of *corridos*, and new prose writers Maria Ruíz de Burton, Anna Julia Cooper, Pauline Hopkins, Sarah Winnemucca, Mary Austin (restored by instructors' request), and Ida Wells-Barnett underscore that writers—male and female— from diverse ethnic, racial, and regional origins assumed the right and felt inspired to represent the American scene in the late nineteenth century. Finally, two clusters take up important political and literary disputes from the era: "Debates over 'Americanization' " considers internal divisions on policy toward the huge number of immigrants, toward Native Americans in the path of "manifest destiny," on the education of African Americans after the Civil War, and on hemispheric ideas of "America" in an age of imperialist expansion. Texts by Frederick Jackson Turner, Theodore Roosevelt, José Martí, Charles W. Chesnutt, Jane Addams, and Anna Julia Cooper consider these issues as they relate to the perennial question, Who is an American? Literary movements attuned to these divisions are considered in "Realism and Naturalism," where critical writings by William Dean Howells, Henry James, Frank Norris, Theodore Dreiser, and Jack London illuminate the turn to realism and naturalism as styles developed to represent an era of rapid modernization.

*Volume D, American Literature 1914–1945.* Newly edited by Mary Loeffelholz, Volume D expands its offering of complete longer works—O'Neill's *Long Day's Journey into Night* (exclusive to the Norton Anthology), Larsen's eminently teachable *Quicksand*, Faulkner's *As I Lay Dying*—with Cather's *My Ántonia*, returned by popular demand, and Raymond Chandler's hard-boiled detective story *Red Wind*, which introduces students to the fact that stylish writing has long found a home among popular genres. Other new prose texts are "Hands" from Sherwood Anderson's *Winesburg, Ohio* and "The White Horses of Vienna" by Kay Boyle, an author new to the anthology. The poet Mina Loy also appears for the first time. Loy's experimental work, as well as reconsidered selections by Ezra Pound, T. S. Eliot, Marianne Moore, Hart Crane, and Langston Hughes, encourages students and teachers to contemplate the interrelation of modernist aesthetics with ethnic, regional, and popular writing. Two new clusters address central events of the modern period. In "World War I and Its Aftermath," writings by John Reed, Ernest Hemingway, Gertrude Stein, Jessie Redmon Fauset, and others explore sharply divided views on the U.S. role in World War I, as well as the radicalizing effect of modern warfare—with 365,000 American casualties—on contemporary writing. And in "Modernist Manifestos," F. T. Marinetti, Mina Loy, Ezra Pound, Willa Cather, William Carlos Williams, and Langston Hughes show how the manifesto as a form exerted a powerful influence on international modernism in all arts.

*Volume E, American Literature since 1945.* In Volume E, prose and poetry, previously separately edited by Jerome Klinkowitz and Patricia B. Wallace, have been brought together in a mutually reinforcing collaboration. The result is a richer representation of the period's literary activity, and a more accurate presentation of the writers themselves, many of whom write in multiple genres. The collaboratively rewritten period introduction and headnotes provide a more nuanced, vital picture of the postwar literary scene and individual writers' contributions to it. The section continues to feature complete texts of Tennessee Williams's *A Streetcar Named Desire* (exclusive to this anthology), Amiri Baraka's *Dutchman*, Arthur Miller's *Death of a Salesman*, David Mamet's *Glengarry Glen Ross*, and Allen Ginsberg's *Howl*; to this group we add Sam Shepard's *True West* and Louise Glück's long poem *October*. Poets Lucille Clifton, Fanny Howe, and Yusef Komunyakaa have been added, as have new poems by Lorraine Niedecker, Theodore Roethke, Frank O'Hara, Adrienne Rich, Gary Snyder, James Merrill, Billy Collins, Charles Simic, Joy Harjo, and Rita Dove. Prose fiction has been enriched with short stories by newly added contemporary authors Max Apple, Amy Tan, Julia Alvarez, and Jhumpa Lahiri and new selections by Richard Powers, Annie Dillard, and Sandra Cisneros. In addition, Louise Erdrich and Sherman Alexie, two writers who work in multiple genres, are represented by selections from their poetry and prose. Appearing for the first time, a free-standing segment from Art Spiegelman's prize-winning *Maus* opens possibilities for teaching the graphic novel. Another innovation is the introduction of teachable stand-alone segments from important novels by Saul Bellow (*The Adventures of Augie March*), Kurt Vonnegut (*Slaughterhouse-Five*), Rudolfo Anaya (*Bless Me, Ultima*), and Jack Kerouac (*Big Sur*). Two new clusters add literary and topical context to this diverse section: "Postmodernist Manifestos" by Ronald Sukenick, William H. Gass, Hunter S. Thompson, Charles Olson, Frank O'Hara, Elizabeth Bishop, A. R. Ammons, and Audre Lorde show how many literary artists saw experimentation in poetry and fiction as the best way to register politics and culture in the postwar era. Finally, in "Writing in a Time of Terror: September 11, 2001," ten prose and verse selections show the powerful literary responses evoked by times of terror.

## Additional Resources from the Publisher

The Seventh Edition retains the paperback splits format introduced in the Sixth Edition, which was welcomed by instructors and students for its flexibility and portability. This format accommodates the many instructors who use the anthology in a two-semester survey, but allows for mixing and matching the five volumes in a variety of courses organized by period or topic, at levels from introductory to advanced. To give instructors even more flexibility, the publisher is making available the full list of 180 Norton Critical Editions, including such frequently assigned novels as Harriet Beecher Stowe's *Uncle Tom's Cabin*, Herman Melville's *Moby-Dick*, Edith Wharton's *The House of Mirth*, and William Faulkner's *The Sound and the Fury*, among many others. A Norton Critical Edition can be included with Package 1 or 2 of the Seventh Edition for free. Each Norton Critical Edition gives students an authoritative, carefully annotated text accompanied by rich contextual and critical materials prepared by an expert in the subject.

With the Seventh Edition of *The Norton Anthology of American Literature*, the publisher expands its already extensive online resource, Norton Literature Online (wwnorton.com/literature). Students who activate the free password included in each new copy of the anthology gain access to an array of general resources, among them a glossary of literary terms, advice on writing about literature and using MLA documentation style, study aids and quizzes, an author portrait gallery featuring 380 authors, more than 100 maps, and over 90 minutes of recorded readings and musical selections. With their passwords, students also gain access to a site specifically developed to support *The Norton Anthology of American Literature*. Redesigned for easier navigation, this student website (wwnorton.com/naal), prepared by Bruce Michelson, offers timelines, outlines of the period introductions, over 400 annotated links, resource pages for 160 of the writers in the anthology, and searchable "Explorations" with questions and research projects. Also on the site are new self-grading quizzes, prepared by Jason Coats, on thirty of the most widely taught works in the anthology.

*Teaching with* The Norton Anthology of American Literature: *A Guide for Instructors* has been expanded and updated by Bruce Michelson. This much-praised guide offers extensive help, from developing a syllabus to preparing exams. The guide entries suggest approaches to each author and provide questions for class discussion. Finally, the Norton Resource Library (wwnorton .com/nrl) offers instructors the Course Guide and student website content in PDF format as well as a WebCT/BlackBoard coursepack featuring tests and quizzes on the period introductions and individual works, lecture outlines, maps, and timelines, among other resources.

Instructors who adopt *The Norton Anthology of American Literature* have access to an extensive array of films and videos. In addition to videos of the plays by O'Neill, Williams, Miller, and Mamet in the anthology, segments of the award-winning video series *American Passages: A Literary Survey* are available without charge on orders of specified quantities of the Norton Anthology. Funded by Annenberg/CPB, produced by Oregon Public Broadcasting, and developed with the Norton Anthology as its exclusive companion anthology, *American Passages* contains sixteen segments, each covering a literary movement or period by exploring two or three authors in depth. A website (learner.org/amerpass), instructor's guide, and student guide are also available. For information about the videos, contact your Norton representative.

### Editorial Procedures

As in past editions, editorial features—period introductions, headnotes, annotations, and bibliographies—are designed to be concise yet full and to give students necessary information without imposing an interpretation. For long-time users, the familiar format may obscure the breadth of revisions in this edition, in which the editors have updated all apparatus in response to new scholarship and new ways of thinking about the literature of the United States: period introductions have been entirely or substantially rewritten, as have dozens of headnotes. All Selected Bibliographies have been thoroughly updated and augmented with new general-resources bibliographies categorized by Reference Works, Histories, and Literary Criticism for each period. The Seventh Edition retains three editorial features that help students place their reading in historical and cultural context—a Texts/Contexts timeline following each period introduction, a map on the front endpaper of each volume, and a chronological chart, on the back endpaper, showing the lifespans of many of the writers anthologized.

Our policy has been to reprint each text in the form that accords, as far as it is possible to determine, to the intention of its author. There is one exception: we have modernized most spellings and (very sparingly) the punctuation in Volume A on the principle that archaic spellings and typography pose unnecessary problems for beginning students. We have used square brackets to indicate titles supplied by the editors for the convenience of students. Whenever a portion of a text has been omitted, we have indicated that omission with three asterisks. If the omitted portion is important for following the plot or argument, we give a brief summary within the text or in a footnote. After each work, we cite (when known) the date of composition on the left and the date of first publication on the right; in some instances, the latter is followed by the date of a revised edition for which the author was responsible.

With the three additions to our editorial team, we offer an editorial line-up of experienced, active, expert classroom teachers and scholars. All of us have benefited from commentary offered by hundreds of teachers throughout the country. Those teachers who prepared detailed critiques, or who offered special help in preparing texts, are listed under Acknowledgments, on a separate page. The editors would like to express appreciation for their assistance to Kenneth L. Baughman, Genevieve Burger-Weiser, John Bryant, Lawrence I. Berkove, Kirby Brown, Lawrence Buell, Brad Campbell, Russ Castronovo, Granville Ganter, Samuel L. Gladden, Ivy Goodman, Vince Gotera, Ezra Greenspan, Tim Gustafson, Katrina Huffman, Julie Huffman-Klinkowitz, Julie Husband, Daniel Heath Justice, Carolyn Karcher, Virginia Kennedy, Judith Kicinski, Maurice Lee, David Wei Li, Joseph R. McElrath Jr., Anne Myles, James O'Laughlin, Samuel Otter, Kenneth Price, Sally Promey, Julian Rice, Alan Shucard, Martha Nell Smith, Paul Sorrentino, Julia Stern, Jesse Swan, John Swope, Heidi Shira Tannenbaum, Karen Tracey, Jennie Wang, Edward Whitley, Thomas Wolfe, and Christina Zwarg. We also thank the many people at Norton who contributed to the Seventh Edition: Julia Reidhead, who supervised the Seventh Edition; Marian Johnson, Managing Editor, College; Kurt Wildermuth, manuscript and project editor; Mike Fleming, Katharine Ings, Candace Levy, and Pam Lawson, manuscript editors; Catherine Spencer and Ann Abrams, editorial assistants; Eileen Connell, electronic media editor; Diane O'Connor, production manager; Toni Krass, designer; Neil Ryder Hoos, art researcher; Debra Morton Hoyt, art director; Nancy Rodwan, permissions manager; and Margaret Gorenstein, who cleared permissions. We also wish to acknowledge our debt to the late George P. Brockway, former president and chairman at Norton, who invented this anthology, and to M. H. Abrams, Norton's advisor on English texts. All have helped us to create an anthology that, more than ever, is testimony to the continuing richness of American literary traditions.

NINA BAYM

# Acknowledgments

Among our many critics, advisors, and friends, the following were of especial help toward the preparation of the Seventh Edition, either with advice or by providing critiques of particular periods of the anthology: Jose Amaya (Iowa State University); Marilyn J. Atlas (Ohio University); Debra Bailey (Brazosport College); Peter J. Bailey (St. Lawrence University); Craig Barrett (Brescia College); Dale M. Bauer (University of Illinois, Urbana-Champaign); Alfred Bendixen (Texas A&M University); Nancy Bentley (University of Pennsylvania); Jill Bergman (University of Montana, Missoula); Bruce Bickley (Florida State University); Sarah Blair (University of Michigan); Tamara Ponzo Brattoli (Joliet Junior College); Jennifer Brezina (College of the Canyons); Patricia Brooke (Fontbonne College); Lawrence Buell (Harvard University); Keen Butterworth (University of South Carolina, Columbia); Russ Castronovo (University of Wisconsin); Charles Chappell (Hendrix College); Jeff Cofer (Belleune Community College); Robert M. Como (Northern Virginia Community College); Marc Conner (Washington and Lee University); G. T. Couser (Hofstra University); Robert W. Croft (Gainesville College); Andrew Delbanco (Columbia University); Matthew DeVold (University of Alabama, Birmingham); Steven Fink (The Ohio State University); Granville Ganter (St. John's University); Richard Gaughran (James Madison University); James Gifford (Mohawk Valley Community College); Ivy Goodman; Lisa Gordis (Barnard College, Columbia University); Ezra Greenspan (Southern Methodist University); Jay Grossman (Northwestern University); Andrew Gutteridge (University College of the Fraser Valley); Sally Harvey (Yuba College); Stephen Hathaway (Wichita State University); Susan Henry (Glendale Community College); Avis Hewitt (Grand Valley State University); Andrew Higgins (Louisiana Tech University); Susanna Hoeness-Krupsaw (University of Southern Indiana); James Hutchinson (The Citadel); Maggie Jaffe (San Diego State University); Ben Jennings (Virginia Highlands Community College); Gwendolyn Jones (Clayton College and State University); Daniel Heath Justice (University of Toronto); Carolyn Karcher (Temple University); Carla Kaplan (Northeastern University); Virginia Kennedy (Cornell University); Christopher Knight (University of Montana); Denise D. Knight (State University of New York, Cortland); Bill Koon (Clemson University); Donald D. Kummings (University of Wisconsin, Parkside); Peter J. Kvidera (John Carroll University); John Lang (Emory and Henry College); Caroline F. Levander (Rice University); Anna Lillios (University of Central Florida); Helen Lojek (Boise State University); Steven Mailloux (University of California, Irvine); Michael Marzelli (Florida Atlantic University); Tim Melley (Miami University); Jon

Miller (University of Akron); Clay Motley (Charleston Southern University); Peter F. Murphy (Murray State University); Lance Newman (California State University, San Marcos); Michael North (University of California, Los Angeles); Patricia Okker (University of Missouri, Columbia); Samuel Otter (University of California, Berkeley); Jennifer Parchesky (Arizona State University); Jeanne Perreault (University of Calgary); Kenneth M. Price (University of Nebraska); Sally Promey (University of Maryland); Ken Rayes (University of New Orleans); Elizabeth Renker (Ohio State University); David Reynolds (The Graduate Center, The City University of New York); Todd R. Richardson (University of Texas, Permian Basin); Debby Rosenthal (John Carroll University); David Rota (University of Missouri, St. Louis); Elizabeth Sachs (Niagara County Community College); Charles Scarborough (Northern Virginia Community College); John Schaffer (Blinn College); Gary Scharnhorst (University of New Mexico); Bill Schlientz (Philander Smith College); Lissa Schneider (University of Miami); Richard Schneider (Wartburg College); Dorothy U. Seyler (Northern Virginia Community College); Mark Silverberg (Cape Breton University); Ernest Smith (University of Central Florida); John J. Smith (United States Military Academy, West Point); Martha Nell Smith (University of Maryland); Jeffrey Steele (University of Wisconsin, Madison); Julia Stern (Northwestern University); Jenny Sullivan (Northern Virginia Community College); Carole S. Tabor (Louisiana Tech University); Cynthia Van Sickle (McHenry County College); Kathryn Van Spancheren (University of Tampa); Kenneth Warren (University of Chicago); Cindy Weinstein (California Institute of Technology); Norman Weinstein (Boise State University); John Wenke (Salisbury University); Patrick Allen Wright (Lamar University); Dale G. Yerpe (Jamestown Community College).

# American Literature
# 1865–1914

### THE TRANSFORMATION OF A NATION

From the earliest moment in their nation's history, Americans had been pushing westward. Thomas Jefferson's Louisiana Purchase (1803) had added a huge swath of territory west of the Alleghenies; the outcome of the Mexican War (1846–48) brought the entire Southwest, including California, into the nation; and the discovery of gold in California late in 1848 increased the pace of westward movement beyond anything that could have been imagined even one year earlier. The westward settlement by Americans—most of them of Northern European ancestry—from the older parts of the country displaced Native American cultures and Spanish settlements, and the process became more intense and systematic as these whites settled on more and more terrain west of the Mississippi River.

The Civil War, which began in 1861 and lasted for four years, was the ultimate result of economic, political, social, and cultural divisions between North and South—above all, the division between an economy and way of life based on wage labor and one based on slavery. The war cost 8 billion dollars and claimed over six hundred thousand American lives, more than any other war in U.S. history. Nevertheless, the country prospered materially over the following five decades. The war effort had stimulated innovations in methods of efficiently moving large numbers of people, raw materials, and goods. The first transcontinental railroad, completed in 1869, made it possible to cross the country cheaply in just a few days, whereas covered wagon processions on the overland trail (expensive to outfit and difficult to organize) required two or three months. The railroad took settlers west from the eastern seaports, and also allowed for rapid, inexpensive shipments of goods, thereby transporting the American economy itself into the industrial age, once and for all. But the railroad also disrupted the migration of the buffalo herds on which Native peoples of the Plains depended. The telegraph, introduced in the 1840s, now ran into small towns (many of them newly settled) everywhere; electricity was introduced on a large scale; the telephone began to revolutionize daily life; coal, oil, iron, gold, silver, and other kinds of mineral wealth were discovered and extracted, producing many individual fortunes that allowed the nation for the first time to capitalize its own further development. All this development required more people, preferably (from the point of view of employers) in numbers sufficient to keep the cost of labor cheap. Often lured by advertisements from railroad and land companies, immigrants arrived in the United States from the Scandinavian countries and from Italy, Poland, Czechoslovakia, Lithuania, Russia, and more. Many European newcomers, taking advantage of the railroad's cheap passenger fares, went on to the plains to farm; but most became urban dwellers, causing enormous population growth in such cities as New York, Boston, and Chicago at the same time that Chinese and then Japanese immigrants hastened the growth of San Francisco and other western cities.

The historian Frederick Jackson Turner declared in 1893 that the frontier in which many Americans had believed for so long was now closed, basing his analysis on the census of 1890, which found no place in the United States with fewer than two people per square mile. Now the United States, eager to join the European imperialist nations, turned to imperialist ventures of its own, including expansion into the former Spanish possessions of Cuba, Puerto Rico, and the Philippines following the Spanish-American War in 1898. U.S. colonization also included Hawai'i. The expanding power of American capitalism and imperialism had long been experienced by indigenous peoples, whose populations suffered enormous declines in the last few decades of the nineteenth century, especially when tribes were assigned to reservations. Along with Native American reservations came a new desire to "study" the tribes—always with the expectation that their members would "vanish." Anthropologists—most of them originally students of Franz Boas— began to study Native American oral productions, even as Euro-American authors such as Helen Hunt Jackson (1830–1885) wrote book-length denunciations of the treatment of Native Americans. While the Lakota writer Zitkala-Ša (Gertrude Simmons Bonnin) (1876–1938) published prose accounts of her life toward the end of the nineteenth century, it was not until the twentieth century, with the work of Native writers such as Charles Alexander Eastman (Ohiyesa) (1858–1939), also a Lakota, among others, that a "modern" Indian literature began to be produced.

With the end of the frontier era, industrialization on a scale unprecedented in Great Britain and Europe came to the fore in the United States. Between 1850 and 1880, capital invested in manufacturing industries more than quadrupled and factory employment nearly doubled. By 1885 four transcontinental railroad lines had been completed, using in their own construction and carrying to manufacturing centers in Cleveland and Detroit the nation's quintupled output of steel from Pittsburgh and Chicago. As major industries were consolidated into monopolies, a small number of men came to control such enormously profitable enterprises as steel, oil, railroads, meat packing, banking, and finance, among them Jay Gould, Jim Hill, Leland Stanford, Cornelius Vanderbilt, Andrew Carnegie, J. P. Morgan, and John D. Rockefeller. Robber barons to some, captains of industry to others, these men successfully squeezed out competitors and accumulated vast wealth and power, social, political, and economic; whereas there had been only a handful of millionaires before the Civil War, now there were hundreds, and they formed a class whose wealth and the styles of life associated with what the sociologist Thorstein Veblen called "conspicuous consumption" had not been seen before in American life.

In 1865 the United States, except for the manufacturing centers of the northeastern seaboard, was a country of farms, villages, and small towns. Manufacturing was more a matter of workshops than factories. In 1870 the U.S. population was 38.5 million; by 1910, 92 million; by 1920, 123 million.

This increase in population was due almost entirely to immigration, as was the shift in the percentages of dwellers in the country and the city. For example, the population of New York City grew sevenfold, from half a million to nearly 3.5 million between 1865 and the turn of the twentieth century, while Chicago, with a population of only 29,000 in 1850, had more than 2 million inhabitants by 1910. These immigrants and their descendants enabled the United States to become an urban, industrial, international, capitalist power while altering the ethnic composition of the still mostly white population and contributing immeasurably to the democratization of the nation's cultural life. By 1890, New Englanders and their descendents were no longer numerically dominant. Long-settled white Americans faced newly arrived white people across divides of power, income, and privilege—worker against owner, farm against city, immigrant against native-born, leading to suspicion and social turbulence on a scale that the nation had not seen.

The transformation of an entire continent involved suffering for millions even as others prospered. Farmers in the Midwest and high plains depended on the railroads for transport of their crops but were squeezed off the land by the pricing policies of these very same railroads—what the novelist Frank Norris characterized as the giant "octopus" of corporate power, especially the Southern Pacific Railroad. Though the Homestead Act of 1862 promised free or cheap acreage to every individual or family who would settle and "improve" land according to a set formula, much available land was donated to railroads to encourage their growth, while speculators bought up much land as well by various subterfuges. It is estimated that only 10 percent of the land opened by the Homestead Act actually went to would-be independent farmers. Buying at high prices, or forced to rent, everywhere such farmers were "under the lion's paw," as the midwestern writer Hamlin Garland put it, of land speculators and absentee landlords, or faced with mortgage payments they could not make. Large-scale farming quickly began to squeeze out such small family farms as had been able to develop—even as it increased agricultural yields. And for many, the great cities were also, as the socialist novelists Jack London and Upton Sinclair argued, jungles where only the strongest, most ruthless, and luckiest survived. An oversupply of labor brought about by immigration campaigns kept wages low, and—in the absence of laws regulating factory conditions and working hours—workers faced inhumane and dangerous working conditions.

Neither farmers nor urban laborers organized effectively to pursue their own interests. Legislators usually served the interests of business and industry—sometimes in the honest belief that a healthy economy required capitalism, sometimes via bribery and kickbacks, as in President Ulysses S. Grant's administration, or the looting of the New York City treasury by William Marcy ("Boss") Tweed in the 1870s, or municipal corruption cases exposed by the journalist Lincoln Steffens and other "muckrakers," including the writers Stephen Crane and Frank Norris. Early attempts by labor to organize were often violent, and such groups as the terroristic "Molly Maguires," active in the 1870s and 1880s in the coal-mining area of northeastern Pennsylvania, bolstered the conviction of those who believed in open markets and free enterprise that labor organizations were un-American. Industrial workers had little significant political leverage until the 1880s, when the American Federation of Labor emerged as the first unified national voice of workers. But not until collective bargaining legislation was enacted in the 1930s did labor acquire the right to strike. As for farmers, their organizing efforts involved experiments in cooperative farming and storage, which usually failed—partly for lack of funds but also because of the long tradition of independence among agricultural people. It was exactly to own one's own land that immigrants and native-born white people had moved to the prairies in the first place. On the other hand, individual ownership of land parcels was forced on the Native people through the Dawes Allotment Act of 1887, fragmenting the collectively held Native land base and resulting in the loss of some 60 million acres from Native possession.

## THE LITERARY MARKETPLACE

Rapid transcontinental settlement and new urban industrial conditions were accompanied by the development of a national literature of great abundance and variety. New themes, new forms, new subjects, new regions, new authors, new audiences—all emerged in the literature of this half century. Inevitably, Americans new and old were drawn into more complex social and cultural engagements as citizens of a nation still largely composed of dispossessed and otherwise "marginalized" people. In literature, realism, naturalism, and regionalism strove to express the challenges and rewards of what President Theodore Roosevelt called—from his perspective as a wealthy and entitled New Yorker—"the winning of the west." The notion of what makes one an American was defined from diverse points of view. Fictionalized representations of characters rarely encountered before the Civil War became familiar: industrial workers, the rural poor, ambitious business leaders and downcast vagrants, prostitutes and unheroic soldiers, as described by Ambrose Bierce, Bret Harte, Jack London, and Stephen Crane. Women from many social groups, African Americans, Native Americans, Mexican Americans, Asian Americans, and immigrants began to write for publication, and a rapidly growing market for their work helped confirm authorship as a possible career.

Literature in the sense of fine writing figured at the top of a market that began with newspapers, which had been important to the political, social, and cultural life of America since colonial times. After the Civil War their numbers and influence grew. Joseph Pulitzer established the St. Louis Post-Dispatch in 1878, and in 1883 he bought the New York World; both papers were hugely successful. William Randolph Hearst, a Californian who inherited a fortune from his mining entrepreneur father, made the San Francisco Examiner the dominant newspaper in the Far West, then bought the New York Journal in 1895 to compete with Pulitzer's World, and gradually acquired newspapers across the country. In 1897 the Jewish Daily Forward, in Yiddish, was founded by Abraham Cahan; its circulation eventually reached 250,000, and it was read by three or four times that number. Many "writers" who went on to become "authors" started as newspaper journalists: Ambrose Bierce, Abraham Cahan, Stephen Crane, Theodore Dreiser, Jack London, Sui Sin Far, Joel Chandler Harris, William Dean Howells, Frank Norris, and Mark Twain among them. Perhaps of equal importance to the development of literary careers and literature as an American institution was the establishment of newspaper syndicates in the 1880s by Irving Bachellor and S. S. McClure. These syndicates, which distributed material to newspapers and magazines in all sections of the country, published humor, news, and novels—Crane's *The Red Badge of Courage*, for example—in installments.

Magazines became another feature of American life as early as the mid-eighteenth century. After the Civil War, East Coast magazines such as *Harper's New Monthly Magazine* (1850), *Scribner's Monthly* (1870), *Century Illustrated Monthly Magazine* (1881), the *Atlantic Monthly* (1857), and the *Galaxy* (1866) provided outlets for such figures as Kate Chopin, Sarah Orne Jewett, Henry James, William Dean Howells, Sui Sin Far, and Mark Twain. On the West Coast, the *Overland Monthly* (1868) emerged as the leading literary periodical; designed to showcase western-themed writing, it published Bret Harte, Ambrose Bierce, London, Mary Austin, Sui Sin Far, and Twain among others. Without the periodicals, many writers would not have been able to support themselves; the income and audiences these magazines provided were crucial to the further formation of the complex literary tradition of a vast nation undergoing modernization.

Periodicals also contributed to the emergence toward the end of the nineteenth century of what the critic Warner Berthoff calls "the literature of argument"—powerful works in sociology, philosophy, and psychology, many of them impelled by the spirit of exposure and reform. It would be hard to exaggerate the influence—on other writers as well as on the educated public—of works such as Henry George's *Progress and Poverty* (1879), Henry Demarest Lloyd's *Wealth against Commonwealth* (1894), Charlotte Perkins Gilman's *Women and Economics* (1898), Thorstein Veblen's *The Theory of the Leisure Class* (1899), and William James's *The Varieties of Religious Experience* (1902). For many women writers, magazines provided an important public forum in which to explore new views of women and women's rights.

In short, as the United States became an international political, economic, and military power during this half century, its literary production kept pace, and it welcomed (in translation) works by the leading European figures of the time, such as Leo Tolstoy, Henrik Ibsen, Anton Chekhov, and Émile Zola. American writers in this period, like most writers of other times and places, wrote to earn money, gain fame, change the world, and express themselves in a permanent art form. The nature of that form—what might be called the "realistic international art story"—was itself a product of the interplay of historical forces and aesthetic developments apparent, in retrospect, since the publication of the French writer Gustave Flaubert's *Madame Bovary* (1856). Among the most critically praised American writers of the period were Mark Twain, Henry James, Edith Wharton, and William Dean Howells, two of them from the Midwest and two of them easterners, whose literary styles encompassed the comic vernacular, ordinary discourse, and impressionistic subjectivity. These writers recorded life on the vanishing frontier, in the village, small town, and turbulent metropolis, as well as in European resorts and capitals. They established the literary identity of distinctively American protagonists, specifically the vernacular boy hero and the "American Girl," the baffled and strained middle-class family, the businessman, the psychologically complicated citizens of a new international culture. They set the example and charted the future course for the subjects, themes, techniques, and styles of fiction we still call modern.

## FORMS OF REALISM

The term *realism* labels a movement in English, European, and American literature that gathered force from the 1830s to the end of the century. Realists attempted to record life as it was lived rather than life as it ought to be lived (the term used for this at the time was *idealism*) or had been lived in times past (the term used for this at the time was *romance*). As defined by William Dean Howells (1837–1920), the magazine editor who was for some decades the chief American advocate of realist aesthetics as well as author of over thirty novels, realism "is nothing more and nothing less than the truthful treatment of material." Henry James spoke of the "documentary" value of Howells's work, thereby calling attention to realism's preoccupation with the physical surfaces, the particularities of the sensate world in which fictional characters lived. Characters in Howell's novels were "representative" or ordinary characters—people much like the readers themselves, without fame or huge fortunes, without startling accomplishments or immense abilities. Realism, as practiced by Howells, particularly in *The Rise of Silas Lapham* (1885), the novel many literary historians have identified as the epitome of American realism, seeks to convince readers that the life in the book's pages is true to ordinary people in familiar surroundings.

Edith Wharton's realism, like Henry James's, is less about middle-class people than about characters' psychological and moral interiors. Wharton (1862–1937) holds a mirror up to New York high society, especially as its dramas of human consciousness play out; the achievement of what might be called upper-class realism is to convince readers that the inner lives of these wealthy people accord with the truth of human nature. In novels such as *The House of Mirth* (1905), *The Custom of the Country* (1913), and *The Age of Innocence* (1920), Wharton's primary concerns are with the intangible—thwarted desire, self-betrayal, murderous emotion, repressed voices. In this sense, her depiction of the struggles of individuals such as Lily Bart of *The House of Mirth* to survive in a seemingly pleasant but actually hostile society goes beyond realism to reflect an almost Darwinian view of upper-class life.

In fact, it proved impossible for any realist to represent things exactly as they were. Present-day literary theorists are probably more aware of what may be called "the crisis of representation"—the difference between the representation and the thing represented—than were these realists of the late nineteenth and early twentieth centuries. But whether they could actually duplicate "reality" or not, these writers insisted that their work called attention to areas of experience that literature had not dealt with before and made such areas legitimate subjects for serious writing. The two most acclaimed artists of the era—Mark Twain and Henry James—understood that language was an interpretation of the real rather than the real thing itself. Twain's work was realistic in its use of colloquial and vernacular speech and its parade of characters from ordinary walks of life. For many later writers, the simple language of *Adventures of Huckleberry Finn* (1884) signified the beginning of a truly American style. But Twain (1835–1910) is also a comic genius whose language goes well beyond the demands of realism. The author of *Huckleberry Finn* is funny in ways that Huck could never be—Twain's writing resembles performance art, and, indeed, he achieved enormous success as a public reader of his own work. (At the same time, readers misinterpret Twain if they read him only for his jokes and do not sense the pessimism about humankind that lies not far beneath the surface.) He was, as a western writer, ambiguously attached to an oral tradition of vernacular speech. At the other extreme, Henry James (1843–1916) worked his way from recognizably realistic fiction, with a large cast of socially specified (typically upper-class) characters described by an all-knowing narrator, as in *The American* (1876), toward increasingly subtle metaphorical representations of the flow of a character's inner thought, as in *The Golden Bowl* (1904). All strong realist writers believed in the power of language to represent reality in ways that were aesthetically satisfying and thus demanded the skill of a literary artist as well as the observational precision of a journalist.

*Naturalism* is understood by some as an extension or intensification of realism; it introduces characters from the fringes and depths of society whose fates are determined by degenerate heredity, a sordid environment, and/or a good deal of bad luck. Stephen Crane, Theodore Dreiser, Jack London, and Frank Norris are usually identified as the leading American naturalists of this period, but before we turn to their work, the philosophic and scientific backgrounds of naturalism require some attention.

One of the most far-reaching intellectual events of the last half of the nineteenth century was the publication in 1859 of Charles Darwin's *Origin of Species*. This book, together with his *Descent of Man* (1870), hypothesized on the basis of massive physical evidence that over the millennia humans had evolved from "lower" forms of life. Humans were special, not—as the Bible taught—because God had created them in his image, but because as a species they had successfully adapted to changing environmental conditions and had passed on their survival-making characteristics. Indigenous Native traditions were consistent with Darwinism in their sense that humans were, indeed, the last creatures to develop, but Native traditions also saw the last formed as handicapped by their belatedness, needing the wisdom derived from their winged and four-legged brothers and sisters, beings that had been on this earth for a great deal longer. In the 1870s, the English philosopher Herbert Spencer's application of Darwin's theory of evolution to social relations, applying the concept of "survival of the fittest" to human groups, was enthusiastically welcomed by many leading American businessmen. Andrew Carnegie was only one of the successful industrialists who argued that unrestrained competition was the equivalent of a law of nature designed to eliminate those unfit for the new economic order.

Another response to Darwin was to accept the deterministic implications of evolutionary theory and to use them to explain the behavior of characters in literary works. As Émile Zola (1840–1902), the influential French theorist and novelist, put the matter in his essay "The Experimental Novel" (1880):

> [W]e must operate with characters, passions, human and social data as the chemist and the physicist work on inert bodies, as the physiologist works on living bodies. Determinism governs everything. It is scientific investigation . . . and will replace novels of pure imagination by novels of observation and experiment.

A number of American writers adopted aspects of this form of naturalism, though each brought naturalism into his or her work in individual ways. For Frank Norris, naturalism was not a "realistic" genre or "an inner circle of realism." To be a naturalist, Norris believed, was to enter the zone of romance:

> [W]e must leave the rank and file . . . [and] separate ourselves; we must become individual, unique. The naturalist takes no note of common people, common as far as their interests, their lives, and the things that occur in them are common, are ordinary. Terrible things must happen to the characters of the naturalistic tale. They must be twisted from the ordinary, wrenched out from the quiet, uneventful round of every-day life, and flung into the throes of a vast and terrible drama that works itself out in unleashed passions, in blood, and in sudden death.

Characters may be "common," but what happens to them cannot be: "These great, terrible dramas no longer happen among the personnel of a feudal and Renaissance nobility . . . but among the lower—almost the lowest—classes; those who have been thrust or wrenched from the ranks who are falling by the roadway." Certainly the slum families in Norris's "Fantaisie Printanière" and Stephen Crane's *Maggie: A Girl of the Streets* (1893) experience "terrible things" and react in predictable "terrible" ways. Though American naturalists were concerned on the one hand to explore the new territories opened up by Darwin, Spencer, and Zola—the pressures of biology, environment, and other material forces—in depicting people, particularly lower-class people, they allowed in different degrees for the value of human beings, for their potential to make some sense out of their experience, and for their capacity to act compassionately—even altruistically—under the most adverse circumstances. Even though these writers were challenging conventional wisdom about human motivation and causality in the natural world, the bleakness and pessimism sometimes found in their fiction are not the same as despair and cynicism.

Stephen Crane (1871–1900) believed, as he said of his pitiful protagonist in *Maggie*, that environments such as slums count for a great deal in determining human fate. In the wild, nature is not hostile, he observes in "The Open Boat," only "indifferent, flatly indifferent." Crane, like most naturalists, is ambiguous, accepting of paradoxes. In his *Red Badge of Courage* (1895), the soldier Henry Fleming responds to the chaos and violence that surround him with alternating surges of panic and self-congratulation, never fully understanding himself and his place in the world. After granting an apparently naturalistic perspective to Crane, we are left with his distinctiveness, especially his use of impressionistic literary techniques to present incomplete characters in a broken world—a world more random than scientifically predictable. We are also left, however, with the hardly pessimistic implication of "The Open Boat": that precisely because human beings are exposed to a world of chance where death is always imminent, they would do well to learn the arts of sympathetic identification and solidarity, arts often learned at the price of death. Jack London's "To Build a Fire" (1908) illustrates the fate of those who decide to do without trail mates.

Theodore Dreiser (1871–1945) did not share Crane's tendency to use words and images as if he were a composer or a painter; his sense of the solidity of the real world called out a heavily solid prose. But he did share, at least early in his career, Crane's skepticism; like Crane, he was inclined to see men and women as moths drawn to flame rather than as lords of creation. Still, it is not Dreiser's beliefs that make him significant in American letters: it is what his imagination and literary technique do with a rich set of ideas, experiences, and emotions to create the "color of life" in his fiction. If Crane gave American readers a new sense of human consciousness under conditions of extreme pressure, Dreiser gave them in novels such as *Sister Carrie* (1900) and *Jennie Gerhardt* (1911) a sense of the fumbling, yearning, confused response to the simultaneously enchanting, exciting, ugly, and dangerous metropolis that had become home to such large numbers of Americans by the turn of the century.

Jack London (1876–1916) is also far from a "pure" naturalist or determinist; a powerful current of myth and romance underlies his most successful works, such as *The Call of the Wild* (1903) and *The Sea-Wolf* (1904), and most of his nearly two hundred short stories. London is a writer notorious for his contradictions, at once a socialist and an individualist, a believer in Anglo-Saxon superiority who attacked white racism and colonialism. As the critic Earle Labor has noted, "[T]he essential creative tension for [London's] literary artistry is the opposition of materialism versus spiritualism—that is, the tension between the logical and the scientific on the one hand and the irrational and mystical on the other." In "The Law of Life" (1901) Old Koskoosh—an imagined not a realistic representation of an indigenous person—when about to be left to die by his tribe, thinks: "Nature did not care. To life she set one task, gave one law. To perpetuate was the task of life, its law is death." This thought suggests a deterministic view of life—that nothing individuals do is of real significance. Yet the bulk of the story is given over to Old Koskoosh's memories, particularly to the re-creation of a formative moment from his youth when he and a companion came upon an old moose struggling against the wolves that have wounded and will soon devour him. In re-creating this extraordinary moment in all of its vivid, dramatic power, and in identifying with the totemic figure of the moose, Koskoosh, it might be argued, has erased his earlier generalization about evolutionary necessity and the meaninglessness of the individual.

In sum, despite a residual insistence on humanity's elevated place in the universe and a middle-class readership that disliked ugliness and "immorality," urban America and the sparsely populated hinterland offered much material for realistic and naturalistic literary techniques and ideas. The "Realism and Naturalism" cluster in this volume together diverse voices to debate these important terms of late-nineteenth- and early-twentieth-century American literature.

## WRITING

...ion of the realist impulse, resulted from the ...d of distinctive ways of life before industrialized them and to come to terms with the harsh Regional writing ... replacing these early and allegedly happier times. desire both ... azines, much of the regional writing was a response to the ization d ... with opportunities, which created a new, largely female market for reali... ury, virtually every region of the country, from Maine to California, from the northern plains to the Louisiana bayous, had a "local colorist" (the implied comparison is to painters of so-called genre scenes) to immortalize its natural, social, and linguistic features. Though often suffused with nostalgia, the best work of the regionalists both renders a convincing surface of a particular time and location and investigates psychological character traits from a more universal perspective. This mélange may be seen in such an early example of regional writing as Bret Harte's "The Luck of Roaring Camp," which, when it was published in 1868, made Harte a national celebrity. The story is locally specific as well as entertaining, and it created mythic types as well as offered realistic depictions of frontier characters, though these depictions were later called into question by Ambrose Bierce, among others.

One school of regionalist writing that developed quickly, once the "West" was "won," was the "Western." Although the origins of this type go back to James Fenimore Cooper's tales of the frontier when it was located in western New York State, the addition of gold mines and cowboys to the formula identified the genre with the Far West. Diverse writers such as Owen Wister, author of the popular novel *The Virginian* (1902), Mark Twain, Bret Harte, Ambrose Bierce, Mary Austin, and Jack London all contributed to the work of depicting the West as a legendary region—or (as in the case of Twain and Bierce) to the work of debunking the legends. Native Americans also described their lives and traditions—especially as these were imperiled by white advances into their territories. Navajo chants and Chippewa songs; the native oratory of Cochise, Charlot, and Wovoka; and the writings of Zitkala-Ša, Sarah Winnemucca, and Charles Alexander Eastman (Ohiyesa) have not only been increasingly added to the discourse of the West but have challenged the Euro-American identification of the West with the moving line of the frontier as it incorporated territory for that particular ethnic group. One of the great themes of Native American literary work is the land and the people's relation to it, whether in oratorical performances that dramatize this relation or in chants and tales about its sacredness. But Native American conceptions about land were radically at odds with the profit-oriented conceptions of the settlers and the railroads. "With beauty all around me, may I walk" is the pra.. of the Navajo Night Chant, but though these traditional songs and other co of in N.nal and artistic practices are kept alive today, a new theme emerged in writes American cultures in general: loss of the beloved land. Zitkala-Ša missionaries, izen of the modern age, educated in eastern schools by Western plains. till laments the vision of "my mother far away on the "corridos," or border ly, the voices of Mexican Americans, as in the understood as important to an the Mexican Revolution, are now West. derstanding of the U.S. literary

Hamlin Garland (1860–1940), destroy one. Like many writers of th William Dean Howells to write about w ating a myth, set out to farmers of the upper Midwest. As he late d was encouraged by ries was to show that the "mystic quality co st—in his case the myth." Garland's farmers are not the vigoro in his early sto yeomen of Crèvecoeur's *Letters from an America*, nd . . . was a drab figures. In Garland's "Under the Lion's Paw," houghtful t bent, ain-

*Travelled Roads* (1891), local color is not nostalgia but realism deployed for social protest—another way in which realism could never be only "realistic" but was always something more.

Regional writers created not only places but also themes that assumed increasing importance in the twentieth century. The work of Harriet Beecher Stowe, Sarah Orne Jewett, Mary E. Wilkins Freeman, Sui Sin Far, Charlotte Perkins Gilman, Winnemucca, and others may be seen as considering the world from the perspective of women awakening to, protesting against, and offering alternatives to a world dominated by men and male interests and values. Mary Austin was a feminist, and much of her writing, including her classic *Land of Little Rain* (1903), invites readers to see the world from a woman's perspective. But Austin's larger claim on literary history is to have made the deserts of southern California palpable for the first time in literature, as in "The Walking Woman" and other sketches. The marginal characters that people this inhospitable terrain cannot be imagined as existing anywhere else. Stowe, Jewett, and Freeman do more than lament the postwar economic and spiritual decline of New England; their female characters suggest the capacity of human beings to live independently and with dignity in the face of community pressures, patriarchal power over women, including women artists and writers, and material deprivation.

Kate Chopin (1850–1904) may be thought of as a regional writer interested in the customs, language, and landscapes of the northern Louisiana countryside and, downriver, New Orleans. But in addition to preserving local color, Chopin wrote probing psychological fiction. Edna Pontellier of *The Awakening* (1899) looks back to Flaubert's Madame Bovary and forward to Virginia Woolf's Mrs. Dalloway. Chopin began her writing career only after she returned to her native St. Louis from a long sojourn in Louisiana, and in her narratives she memorializes the relaxed and sensuous way of life of the Creole population. As an urban outsider, Chopin was perhaps all the more sensitive to the nuances of Louisiana country life. Perhaps, too, as a woman, she was attracted to a way of life that centered on families and small communities. In any case, her treatment of New Orleans and of Natchitoches Parish provides a fine example of the literary portrayal of a distinctive region—one less severe and less repressed than the towns and villages portrayed by the New England regionalists. Yet Chopin, especially in *The Awakening*, with its portrayal of the interior life of a Protestant woman in a conservative Catholic community, gives the ugly side as well. That *The Awakening* has served to crystallize many women's issues of the turn of the nineteenth century, and since, shows that regional realism, even if its settings and characters are marginal to modern life, is by no means a marginal genre.

## REALISM AS SOCIAL ARGUMENT

Between the end of the Civil War and the outbreak of World War I, a vast body of nonfiction prose was devoted to the description, analysis, and critique of social, economic, and political institutions and to the unsolved social problems that were one consequence of rapid growth and change. Women's rights, political corruption, the degradation of the natural world, economic inequity, business deceptions, the exploitation of labor—these became the subjects of articles and books by numerous journalists, historians, social critics, and economists. Much of this writing had literary ambitions, survives as literature, and continues to have genuine power. In his ambitious work of moral exhortation, *The Education of Henry Adams* (1918), Henry Adams registers through a literary sensibility a historian's sense of the disorientation that accompanies rapid and continuous change. Among the most significant and influential voices of the period were those of African Americans speaking out against racism, including W. E. B. Du Bois, Booker T. Washington, Ida B. Wells-Barnett, and Anna Julia Cooper.

Several selections in this volume address the long, shameful history of white injustices against black Americans, as the shift from Reconstruction to Jim Crow laws and the "separate but equal" decision in *Plessy v. Ferguson* (1896) defined and redefined racial inequalities in America. Two works by black writers and leaders from the turn of the century have a special claim on our attention: the widely admired autobiography of Washington, *Up from Slavery* (1900) and the richly imagined *The Souls of Black Folk* (1903) by Du Bois, with its brilliantly argued rejection of Washington's philosophy. The Washington–Du Bois controversy set the major terms of the continuing debate between black leaders and in the black community: which strategies will most effectively hasten equality for blacks educationally, socially, politically, and economically? It is fair to say that in very different ways *Up from Slavery* and *The Souls of Black Folk*—admirable literary achievements in themselves—carried forward the antebellum traditions of such writers as Frederick Douglass and Harriet Jacobs and helped encourage other African American writers of the era such as Wells-Barnett and Cooper, leading eventually to the powerful statements of Harlem Renaissance modernism. In fiction, characters in Pauline Hopkins's novel *Contending Forces* take opposite sides of this argument, while its various implications are also addressed by Charles Chesnutt and James Weldon Johnson in their work. In poetry, authors such as Paul Laurence Dunbar gave voice to African American identities. Their interrelated perspectives on race and national identity are among those in our cluster on "Americanization."

This volume begins with perhaps the two most fundamental American writers of their time and subsequent decades, Walt Whitman and Emily Dickinson. These poets, whose roots are in the antebellum period, continued their work into the 1880s. Though their influence would be felt most strongly after World War II, in hindsight they can be seen as the fountainheads of two major strains in modern poetry: the expansive, gregarious open form of the self-celebratory Whitman and the concise, compact idiosyncratic verse of the radically private Dickinson. Whitman especially, with his interest in the city, prefigures realism and naturalism in surprising ways, while Dickinson focuses on the inner life of the psyche.

In the half century from 1865 to 1914, material, intellectual, social, and psychological changes in the lives of many Americans went forward at such extreme speed and on such a massive scale that the diverse writing of the time registers, at its core, shocked recognition of the human consequences of these radical transformations. Sometimes the shock is expressed in recoil and denial—thus the persistence, in the face of the apparent triumph of realism, of the literature of diversion: nostalgic poetry, sentimental and melodramatic drama, and swashbuckling historical novels. The more enduring fictional and nonfictional prose forms of the era, however, try to come to terms imaginatively with the individual and collective dislocations and discontinuities associated with the closing of the frontier, urbanization, unprecedented immigration, the surge of national wealth unequally distributed, revised conceptions of human nature and destiny, the increasing assertion of the full rights of humanity and citizenship by marginalized minorities, the reordering of family and civil life, and the pervasive spread of mechanical and organizational technologies.

# AMERICAN LITERATURE 1865–1914

| TEXTS | CONTEXTS |
|---|---|
| 1855   Walt Whitman, *Leaves of Grass* | |
| 1860–65   Emily Dickinson writes several hundred poems | 1860   Short-lived Pony Express runs from Missouri to California |
| | 1861   South Carolina batteries fire on Fort Sumter, initiating the Civil War • Southern states secede from the Union and found the Confederate States of America |
| | 1865   Civil War ends • Reconstruction begins • Lincoln assassinated • Thirteenth Amendment ratified, prohibiting slavery |
| | 1867   United States purchases Alaska from Russia • Jesse Chisholm maps out the Chisholm Trail, connecting Texas cattle ranches to railheads in Kansas City, Cheyenne, Dodge City, and Abilene |
| | 1868   Fourteenth Amendment passed, guaranteeing citizenship to all peoples born in the United States (exclusive of Native peoples) • Congress institutes eight-hour workday for federal employees • sweatshops, using mostly immigrant labor, begin to proliferate in cities |
| | 1869   First transcontinental railroad completed by construction crews composed largely of Chinese laborers • Susan B. Anthony elected president of American Equal Rights Association; Elizabeth Cady Stanton elected president of National Women's Suffrage Association |
| 1870   Bret Harte, *The Luck of Roaring Camp and Other Sketches* | 1870   Fifteenth Amendment, giving African American men the right to vote, ratified |
| | 1871   Indian Appropriation Act deems Native peoples wards of the state |
| 1872   Mark Twain, *Roughing It*; Cochise, "I am alone" | 1872   Yellowstone, first U.S. national park, established |
| | 1874   Women's Christian Temperance Union founded in Cleveland • invention of barbed wire effectively ends the open range |
| 1876   Charlot, "[**He has filled graves with our bones**]" | 1876   Custer's regiment defeated by the Sioux and Cheyenne at Little Big Horn River, Montana • Alexander Graham Bell invents the telephone |
| | 1877   Reconstruction ends • segregationist Jim Crow laws begin |

Boldface titles indicate works in the anthology.

| TEXTS | CONTEXTS |
|---|---|
| 1878 Henry James, "Daisy Miller" | |
| | 1879 Thomas Edison invents the electric light bulb • female lawyers permitted to argue before Supreme Court |
| 1880 Joel Chandler Harris, *Uncle Remus: His Songs and Sayings* | 1880–1910 Massive immigration from Europe |
| 1881 Helen Hunt Jackson, *A Century of Dishonor* | 1881 Tuskegee Institute founded |
| | 1882 J. D. Rockefeller organizes Standard Oil Trust • Chinese Exclusion Act instituted |
| 1883 Emma Lazarus, "**The New Colossus**" | |
| 1884 Twain, *Adventures of Huckleberry Finn* | 1884 Tailor's strike in New York City brings national attention to sweatshops |
| 1885 María Amparo Ruiz de Burton, *The Squatter and the Don* | |
| | 1886 Statue of Liberty dedicated • Haymarket Square labor riot leaves eleven dead • American Federation of Labor organized |
| | 1887 General Allotment Act (Dawes Act) passed, limiting the amount of tribally held land |
| 1889 Theodore Roosevelt, *The Winning of the West* • Hamlin Garland, "**Under the Lion's Paw**" | 1889 Violating treaties with Native peoples, Congress opens Indian Territory to settlement, giving rise to the "Oklahoma Land Rush" |
| 1890 Ambrose Bierce, "**An Occurrence at Owl Creek Bridge**" | 1890 Census Bureau declares frontier "closed" • Seventh Cavalry massacre at Wounded Knee ends Native American armed resistance to U.S. government • Ellis Island Immigration Station opens |
| 1891 José Martí, "**Our America**" • Mary E. Wilkins Freeman, "**A New England Nun**" • Wovoka, "**The Messiah Letter**" | |
| 1892 Anna Julia Cooper, *A Voice from the South* • Charlotte Perkins Gilman, "**The Yellow Wall-Paper**" | |
| 1893 Stephen Crane, *Maggie: A Girl of the Streets* • Frederick Jackson Turner, *The Significance of the Frontier* | 1893 World's Columbian Exposition held in Chicago |
| 1895 Crane, *Black Riders* and *The Red Badge of Courage* | |
| 1896 Paul Laurence Dunbar, *Lyrics of a Lowly Life* • James Mooney publishes *Ghost Dance Songs* | 1896 *Plessy v. Ferguson* upholds segregated transportation |

| TEXTS | CONTEXTS |
|---|---|
| 1897   Crane, *The Open Boat and Other Tales of Adventure* | |
| 1898   Abraham Cahan, *The Imported Bridegroom and Other Stories* | 1898   United States annexes Hawai'i |
| | 1898–99   Spanish-American War |
| 1899   Charles Chesnutt, *The Conjure Woman* and *The Life of His Youth and Other Stories of the Color Line* • Kate Chopin, *The Awakening* • Frank Norris, *McTeague* | |
| 1900   Theodore Dreiser, *Sister Carrie* • Ida B. Wells-Barnett, *Mob-Rule in New Orleans* • Pauline Hopkins, *Contending Forces* | 1900   U.S. population exceeds seventy-five million |
| 1901   Zitkala-Ša, *Impressions of an Indian Childhood, The School Days of an Indian Girl*, and *An Indian Teacher Among Indians* • Norris, *The Octopus* • London, "The Law of Life" • Booker T. Washington, *Up From Slavery* | 1901   J. P. Morgan founds U.S. Steel Corporation • first transatlantic radio • oil discovered in Spindletop, Texas |
| 1903   W. E. B. Du Bois, *The Souls of Black Folks* • London, *The Call of the Wild* • Washington Matthews edits *The Night Chant: A Navajo Ceremony* | 1903   Henry Ford founds Ford Motor Co. • Wright brothers make the first successful airplane flight • *The Great Train Robbery* is first U.S. cinematic narrative |
| 1904   Edith Wharton, "The Other Two" | 1904   National Child Labor Committee formed |
| | 1905   Industrial Workers of the World (the Wobblies) founded |
| | 1906   April 18: San Francisco earthquake and fire |
| 1907   Henry Adams, *The Education of Henry Adams*, privately printed | |
| 1909   Mary Austin, *Lost Borders* | 1909   National Association for the Advancement of Colored People (NAACP) founded |
| 1910   Jane Addams, *Twenty Years at Hull-House* • Sui Sin Far, *Mrs. Spring Fragrance* • Francis Densmore publishes *Chippewa Songs* | 1910   Mexican Revolution |
| 1912   James Weldon Johnson • *The Autobiography of an Ex-Coloured Man* | |
| | 1914   U.S. Marines invade and occupy Vera Cruz, Mexico • Panama Canal opens |

# WALT WHITMAN
## 1819–1892

Walt Whitman revolutionized American poetry. Responding to Emerson's call in "The Poet" (1842) for an American bard who would address all "the facts of the animal economy, sex, nutriment, gestation, birth," he put the living, breathing, sexual body at the center of much of his poetry, challenging conventions of the day. Responding also to Emerson's call for a "metre-making argument" rather than mere meters, he rejected traditions of poetic scansion and elevated diction, improvising the form that has came to be known as free verse, while adopting a wide-ranging vocabulary opening new possibilities for poetic expression. A poet of democracy, Whitman celebrated the mystical, divine potential of the individual; a poet of the urban, he wrote about the sights, sounds, and energies of the modern metropolis. In his 1855 preface to *Leaves of Grass*, he declared that "the proof of a poet is that his country absorbs him as affectionately as he has absorbed it." On the evidence of his enormous influence on later poets—Hart Crane, Langston Hughes, Robert Lowell, Allen Ginsberg, Cherrie Moraga, and countless others, including Spain's Federico García Lorca and Chile's Pablo Neruda—Whitman not only was affectionately absorbed by his own country but remains a persistent presence who continues to influence poetic traditions throughout the world.

Whitman was born on May 31, 1819, in West Hills, Long Island (New York), the second of eight surviving children of the Quakers Louisa Van Velsor and Walter Whitman. In 1823, Whitman's father, a farmer turned carpenter, sought to take advantage of a building boom by moving the family to Brooklyn—then a town at the western and most urbanized part of Long Island. The Whitmans' ancestors were early settlers of Long Island, and stories survived of some forceful characters among them. Whitman left school at eleven to become an office boy in a law firm, and then briefly worked for a doctor. By the age of twelve he was employed in the printing office of a newspaper, reading the novels of Sir Walter Scott and contributing short items; and when his family moved east on Long Island in 1833, he remained in Brooklyn on his own. In his midteens he contributed pieces to one of the best Manhattan papers, the *Mirror*, and often crossed the East River on the ferry from Brooklyn to Manhattan to attend debating societies and the theater. He was hired as a compositor in Manhattan in 1835, but two fires later that year disrupted the printing industry, and he rejoined his family. For five years Whitman taught at country and small-town schools at East Norwich, Long Swamp, and other towns on Long Island, interrupting his teaching to start a newspaper of his own in 1838 and to work briefly on another Long Island paper. By early 1840 he had started the series "Sun-Down Papers from the Desk of a School-Master" for the Jamaica, New York, *Democrat* and was writing poems and fiction. One of his stories prophetically culminated with the dream of writing "a wonderful and ponderous book."

Just before he turned twenty-one Whitman stopped teaching, went back to Manhattan, and began work at Park Benjamin's *New World*, a literary weekly that pirated British novels; he also began a political career by speaking at Democratic rallies. Simultaneously, he published stories in the *Democratic Review*, the foremost magazine of the Democratic Party, which was also Hawthorne's main publishing venue during the 1840s. Before he was twenty-three, Whitman became editor of a Manhattan daily, the *Aurora*. He exulted in the extremes of the city, where street-gang violence was countered by the lectures of Emerson and where even a young editor could get to know the poet William Cullen Bryant, editor of the *Evening Post*. Fired from the *Aurora*, which publicly charged him with laziness, he wrote a temperance novel, *Franklin Evans, or the Inebriate*, for a one-issue extra of the *New World* late in 1842. After three years of various literary and political jobs, he returned to Brooklyn in 1845, becoming a special contributor to the Long Island *Star*, assigned to Manhattan events, including theatrical and musical performances. All through the 1840s he attended operas on his journalist's passes, hearing the greatest singers of the time, and he would later say that without the "emotions, raptures, uplifts" of opera he could never have written *Leaves of Grass*. Just before he was twenty-seven he took over the editorship of the Brooklyn *Eagle*, writing most of the literary reviews, which included books by Carlyle, Emerson, Melville, Fuller, and Goethe, among others. Like most Democrats, he was able to justify the Mexican War (1846–48) by linking territorial acquisition to personal and civic betterment, and by hailing the great American mission of "peopling the New World with a noble race." Yet at the beginning of 1848 he was fired from the *Eagle* because, like Bryant, he had become a Free-Soiler, opposed to the acquisition of more territory for slavery. Taking a chance offer of newspaper work, he traveled to New Orleans, his only extensive journey until late in life, when in 1879 and 1880 he made trips as far west as Colorado and north to Canada.

By the summer of 1848, Whitman was back in Brooklyn, serving as a delegate to the Buffalo Free-Soil convention and helping to found the Free-Soil newspaper the *Brooklyn Freeman*. Around this time he began writing poetry in a serious way, experimenting with form and prosody; he published several topical poems in 1850, including "Europe," which would appear in *Leaves of Grass*. He also started a house-building business in Brooklyn, acting as a contractor and sometimes hiring himself out as a carpenter, while continuing to read, study, and write. He became a student of astronomy, attending lectures and reading recent books; some of this material, along with other scientific information, appears in the poetry. Cutting articles out of the great British quarterlies and monthlies, he annotated them and argued with them in the margins, developing in the process clear ideas about aesthetics, such as his distrust of "fine" or what he termed "artificial" poetry. Around the end of 1854 he gave up carpentry and committed himself to writing. He also enjoyed sessions with literary, publishing, and theatrical people in such bohemian spots as the famous Pfaff's saloon on lower Broadway.

Whitman's notebook fragments suggest that he envisioned the overall shape for his first volume of poetry in 1853 and 1854. On May 15, 1855, he took out a copyright for *Leaves of Grass*, and he spent the spring and early summer seeing his book through the press, probably setting some of the type himself. Published in Brooklyn, New York, during the first week of July, the volume, bound in dark green cloth with a sprig of grass in gilt on the cover, contained twelve untitled poems (including the initial version of "Song of Myself") along with an exuberant preface declaring his ambition to be *the* American bard. In the image of Whitman on the book's frontispiece, which was based on an 1854 daguerreotype, the bearded Whitman—rejecting the conventional suit jacket, buttoned-up shirt, and high collar of the formal studio portrait—stands with one arm akimbo, one hand in a pocket, workingman's hat on slightly cocked head, shirt unbuttoned at the collar, looking directly at the reader. The image, like the poetry itself, defied convention by aligning the poet with working people rather than the educated classes. The poems, with their absence of standard verse and stanza patterns (although strongly rhythmic and controlled by numerous poetic devices of repetition and variation), also introduced his use of "catalogs"—journalistic and encyclopedic listings—that were to become a hallmark of his style, turning poetry toward realism. In "The Poet," Emerson had called for a poetry of logrolling, political stump speeches, northern trade, southern planting, and western clearing; "America is a poem in our eyes," he said. This was the challenge that Whitman initially sought to answer by producing national, and nationalistic, poetry from a democratic perspective. Appearing in 1855 during a time of increasing sectional conflict, the volume was offered as a statement of "union." But ordinary people were less drawn to Whitman's poetry than to that of the Harvard professor Longfellow, the era's most popular poet by far; in his lifetime, Whitman fell short of achieving his goal of being regarded as the writer for (or representative of) the masses.

Whitman's father died just after *Leaves of Grass* appeared, and Whitman became mostly responsible for support of his mother and a mentally slow younger brother. He sent out numerous presentation and review copies of his book, receiving an immediate response from Emerson, who greeted him "at the beginning of a great career," but met mostly silence. As weeks passed with few reviews, Whitman chose to write a few himself to be published anonymously, praising *Leaves of Grass* in the *American Phrenological Journal*, for instance, as one of "the most glorious triumphs, in the known history of literature." In October he let Horace Greeley's *New York Tribune* print Emerson's private letter of praise, and he put clippings of the letter in presentation copies to Longfellow, among others. Emerson termed Whitman's appropriation of the letter "a strange, rude thing," but he remained interested in meeting the poet. While Whitman was angling for reviews in England and working on expanding his book, Emerson visited him in December of 1855. Thoreau, who admired *Leaves of Grass* but found several of its poems "simply sensual," visited him later in 1856. That year also saw the appearance of the second edition of *Leaves of Grass*, now with thirty-three poems, including "Crossing Brooklyn Ferry" under the title "Sundown Poem." Returning to miscellaneous journalism, Whitman edited the Brooklyn *Times* from 1857 to 1859 and published several pieces in the *Times* affirming his Free-Soiler hopes for a continued national expansion into the western territories that would not entail the expansion of slavery.

During the late 1850s Whitman wrote a group of twelve poems, "Live Oak, with Moss," that seems to recount his passionate love for another man. Had he printed it, the sequence would have constituted a public declaration of the pleasures, but also the ordinariness, of same-sex love—a stunning challenge to the conventional norms of the time. He chose instead to disperse these poems among others treating bodily and romantic attractions, and including in the third (1860) edition of *Leaves of Grass* a cluster (he had begun to break his poems into clusters) called "Enfans d'Adam," for which he wrote fifteen poems focused on what he termed the "amative" love of man for woman in contrast to the "adhesive" love of man for man. Adhesive love figured in forty-five poems under the heading "Calamus," among which he distributed (or concealed) his "Live Oak" poems. The two clusters as printed in 1860 differ from the poems in the now-familiar 1891–92 "Children of Adam" (as "Enfans d'Adam" was retitled in 1867) and "Calamus" sections, for in the intervening editions (1867, 1871, 1881) Whitman revised poems and moved some poems out of and into the clusters, as he did with all the poems in the expanded editions he published. For him, *Leaves of Grass* was an organic creation responsive to the fluctuations of his life, so that really to read him would require comprehending all the editions at once. Inevitably, editors and anthologists have been forced to make choices, as we do here.

With the outbreak of the Civil War, Whitman turned his attention to the wounded. Having visited prisoners and the sick for years, this role merged almost imperceptibly into Civil War service as a hospital attendant. He started at New-York Hospital; but in early 1863, after visiting with his wounded brother George in an army camp in Virginia, he moved to Washington, D.C., and began to work at the huge open-air military hospitals there. Nursing gave Whitman a profound sense of vocation. As he wrote a friend in 1863: "I am very happy . . . I was never so beloved. I am running over with health, fat, red & sunburnt in face. I tell thee I am just the one to go to our sick boys." But ministering to tens of thousands of maimed and dying young men took its toll, and eventually contributed to undercutting his previously buoyant physical health. He succinctly voiced his despair in a notebook entry of 1864: "the dead, the dead, the dead, *our* dead." At the same time, he worked on a series of war poems, tracing his changed attitudes toward the conflict, from his early jingoistic celebrations of impending battles to starkly realistic depictions of the ravages of warfare. He later wrote a section in his prose work *Specimen Days* (1882) titled "The Real War Will Never Get in the Books"; but to incorporate the "real war" into a book of poetry became one of the dominant impulses of the *Drum-Taps* collection, which he published in 1865. After Lin-

coln's assassination, Whitman reissued the volume with a sequel including "O Captain! My Captain!" and "When Lilacs Last in the Dooryard Bloom'd," his famous elegy for the murdered president.

As he prepared *Drum-Taps and Sequel* for publication in late 1865, Whitman was also revising a copy of the Boston edition (1860) of *Leaves of Grass* at his desk in the Department of the Interior, where he had obtained a position as clerk to support himself while doing his hospital work. The new secretary of the interior, James Harlan, read the annotated copy and abruptly fired Whitman on the grounds that he was writing an obscene book, objecting to Whitman's frankness about bodily functions and heterosexual love; the erotic same-sex implications of some of the poems remained uncommented upon. Whitman's friend William O'Connor quickly got him a new position as clerk in the attorney general's office; and in his rage at the firing (and with significant help from Whitman), he wrote *The Good Gray Poet* (1866), a piece of pure hero worship in which Whitman was identified with Jesus and Harlan with the forces of evil. O'Connor's book appeared shortly after the publication of *Drum-Taps*, and only strengthened Whitman's determination not to yield to censorship or to apologize for his earlier poems. He continued to rework *Leaves of Grass*, incorporating *Drum-Taps* into it in 1867, and with his friends' help continued to propagandize for its recognition as a landmark in the history of poetry. Ruminations that in earlier years might have gone into editorials went into essays in 1867 and 1868 numbers of the New York periodical *Galaxy*, and then (in expanded form) into his book *Democratic Vistas* (1870), a disquisition on democracy and democratic literature in the United States, based on his sometimes condemnatory but always hopeful appraisal of the possibilities of postwar culture.

The Washington years ended early in 1873 when Whitman suffered a paralytic stroke. His mother died a few months later, and Whitman joined his brother George's household in Camden, New Jersey, to recuperate. During the second year of his illness, the government ceased to hold his clerk job open for him, and he became dependent for a living on occasional publication in newspapers and magazines. The 1867 edition of *Leaves of Grass* had involved much reworking and rearrangement, and the fifth edition (1871) continued that process, with many of the original *Drum-Taps* poems distributed throughout the book and with an assemblage of old and new poems in a large new section, "Passage to India." In 1876 he privately published a prose work, *Memoranda during the War*, and six years later he brought out *Specimen Days*, which has affinities with his early editorial accounts of strolls through the city but is even more intensely personal, the record of representative days in the life of a poet who had lived in the midst of great national events.

Throughout the 1870s and early 1880s, Whitman was increasingly noticed by the leading writers of the time, especially in England. The English poet Algernon Swinburne sent him a poem, the Poet Laureate Alfred, Lord Tennyson sent him an admiring letter, and both Longfellow and Oscar Wilde visited him in Camden. Despite his frail health, he lectured on Thomas Paine in Philadelphia in 1877 and on Abraham Lincoln in New York in 1879 (he would continue to deliver occasional public lectures on Lincoln until 1890). Opposition to his poetry because of its supposed immorality began to dissipate, and readers, having become accustomed over time to Whitman's poetic devices, began to recognize the poet as an artist. Still, in 1881, when the reputable Boston firm of James R. Osgood & Co. printed the sixth edition of *Leaves of Grass*, the Boston district attorney threatened to prosecute on the grounds of obscenity. Ironically, when the Philadelphia firm of Rees Welsh and Co. reprinted this edition in 1882, the publicity contributed to Whitman's greatest sales in his lifetime: he earned nearly $1,500 in royalties from that edition (around $50,000 in today's value), compared to the $25 he had earned from the Osgood edition before the publisher withdrew it.

In 1884, the still infirm Whitman moved to a cottage at 328 Mickle Street in Camden, which he purchased for $1,750. A year later friends and admirers, including Mark

Twain and John Greenleaf Whittier, presented him with a horse and buggy for local travel. He had another stroke in 1888 and in 1890 made preparations for his death by signing a $4,000 contract for the construction in Camden's Harleigh Cemetery of a granite mausoleum, or what he termed a "burial house," suitable for a national bard. In 1891 he did the final editing of *Complete Prose Works* (1892) and oversaw the preparations of the "deathbed" edition of the now more than three hundred poems in *Leaves of Grass* (1891–92), which was in fact a reissue of the 1881 edition with the addition of two later groups of poems, "Sands at Seventy" (from *November Boughs* [1888]) and *Good-bye My Fancy* (1891). Whitman died at Camden on March 26, 1892, and was buried in Harleigh Cemetery in the mausoleum he had helped design.

The Whitman poems reprinted here, regardless of when they were first composed and printed, are given in their final form: that of the 1891–92 edition of *Leaves of Grass*.

## Crossing Brooklyn Ferry[1]

### 1

Flood-tide below me! I see you face to face!
Clouds of the west—sun there half an hour high—I see you also face to
    face.

Crowds of men and women attired in the usual costumes, how curious you
    are to me!
On the ferry-boats the hundreds and hundreds that cross, returning home,
    are more curious to me than you suppose,
And you that shall cross from shore to shore years hence are more to me,
    and more in my meditations, than you might suppose.    5

### 2

The impalpable sustenance of me from all things at all hours of the day,
The simple, compact, well-join'd scheme, myself disintegrated, every one
    disintegrated yet part of the scheme,
The similitudes of the past and those of the future,
The glories strung like beads on my smallest sights and hearings, on the
    walk in the street and the passage over the river,
The current rushing so swiftly and swimming with me far away,    10
The others that are to follow me, the ties between me and them,
The certainty of others, the life, love, sight, hearing of others.

Others will enter the gates of the ferry and cross from shore to shore,
Others will watch the run of the flood-tide,
Others will see the shipping of Manhattan north and west, and the heights
    of Brooklyn to the south and east,    15
Others will see the islands large and small;
Fifty years hence, others will see them as they cross, the sun half an hour
    high,

---

1. First published as "Sun-Down Poem" in the 2nd edition of *Leaves of Grass* (1856), "Crossing Brooklyn Ferry" was given its final title in 1860.

A hundred years hence, or ever so many hundred years hence, others will
    see them,
Will enjoy the sunset, the pouring-in of the flood-tide, the falling-back to
    the sea of the ebb-tide.

3

It avails not, time nor place—distance avails not,                   20
I am with you, you men and women of a generation, or ever so many
    generations hence,
Just as you feel when you look on the river and sky, so I felt,
Just as any of you is one of a living crowd, I was one of a crowd,
Just as you are refresh'd by the gladness of the river and the bright flow, I
    was refresh'd,
Just as you stand and lean on the rail, yet hurry with the swift current, I
    stood yet was hurried,                                      25
Just as you look on the numberless masts of ships and the thick-stemm'd
    pipes of steamboats, I look'd.

I too many and many a time cross'd the river of old,
Watched the Twelfth-month[2] sea-gulls, saw them high in the air floating
    with motionless wings, oscillating their bodies,
Saw how the glistening yellow lit up parts of their bodies and left the rest in
    strong shadow,
Saw the slow-wheeling circles and the gradual edging toward the south,   30
Saw the reflection of the summer sky in the water,
Had my eyes dazzled by the shimmering track of beams,
Look'd at the fine centrifugal spokes of light round the shape of my head in
    the sunlit water,
Look'd on the haze on the hills southward and south-westward,
Look'd on the vapor as it flew in fleeces tinged with violet,              35
Look'd toward the lower bay to notice the vessels arriving,
Saw their approach, saw aboard those that were near me,
Saw the white sails of schooners and sloops, saw the ships at anchor,
The sailors at work in the rigging or out astride the spars,
The round masts, the swinging motion of the hulls, the slender serpentine
    pennants,                                           40
The large and small steamers in motion, the pilots in their pilot-houses,
The white wake left by the passage, the quick tremulous whirl of the
    wheels,
The flags of all nations, the falling of them at sunset.
The scallop-edged waves in the twilight, the ladled cups, the frolicsome
    crests and glistening,
The stretch afar growing dimmer and dimmer, the gray walls of the granite
    storehouses by the docks,                               45
On the river the shadowy group, the big steam-tug closely flank'd on each
    side by the barges, the hay-boat, the belated lighter,[3]
On the neighboring shore the fires from the foundry chimneys burning
    high and glaringly into the night,

---

2. December.                                 3. Barge used to load or unload a cargo ship.

Casting their flicker of black contrasted with wild red and yellow light over
   the tops of houses, and down into the clefts of streets.

4

These and all else were to me the same as they are to you,
I loved well those cities, loved well the stately and rapid river,                    50
The men and women I saw were all near to me,
Others the same—others who looked back on me because I look'd forward
   to them,
(The time will come, though I stop here to-day and to-night.)

5

What is it then between us?
What is the count of the scores or hundreds of years between us?          55

Whatever it is, it avails not—distance avails not, and place avails not,
I too lived, Brooklyn of ample hills was mine,
I too walk'd the streets of Manhattan island, and bathed in the waters
   around it,
I too felt the curious abrupt questionings stir within me,
In the day among crowds of people sometimes they came upon me,          60
In my walks home late at night or as I lay in my bed they came upon me,
I too had been struck from the float forever held in solution,
I too had receiv'd identity by my body,
That I was I knew was of my body, and what I should be I knew I should be
   of my body.

6

It is not upon you alone the dark patches fall,                                        65
The dark threw its patches down upon me also,
The best I had done seem'd to me blank and suspicious,
My great thoughts as I supposed them, were they not in reality meagre?
Nor is it you alone who know what it is to be evil,
I am he who knew what it was to be evil,                                               70
I too knitted the old knot of contrariety,
Blabb'd, blush'd, resented, lied, stole, grudg'd,
Had guile, anger, lust, hot wishes I dared not speak,
Was wayward, vain, greedy, shallow, sly, cowardly, malignant,
The wolf, the snake, the hog, not wanting in me,                                      75
The cheating look, the frivolous word, the adulterous wish, not wanting,
Refusals, hates, postponements, meanness, laziness, none of these
   wanting,
Was one with the rest, the days and haps of the rest,
Was call'd by my nighest name by clear loud voices of young men as they
   saw me approaching or passing,
Felt their arms on my neck as I stood, or the negligent leaning of their flesh
   against me as I sat,                                                               80

Saw many I loved in the street or ferry-boat or public assembly, yet never
    told them a word,
Lived the same life with the rest, the same old laughing, gnawing, leeping,
Play'd the part that still looks back on the actor or actress,
The same old role, the role that is what we make it, as great as we like,
Or as small as we like, or both great and small.        85

### 7

Closer yet I approach you,
What thought you have of me now, I had as much of you—I laid in my
    stores in advance,
I consider'd long and seriously of you before you were born.

Who was to know what should come home to me?
Who knows but I am enjoying this?        90
Who knows, for all the distance, but I am as good as looking at you now, for
    all you cannot see me?

### 8

Ah, what can ever be more stately and admirable to me than mast-hemm'd
    Manhattan?
River and sunset and scallop-edg'd waves of flood-tide?
The sea-gulls oscillating their bodies, the hay-boat in the twilight, and the
    belated lighter?
What gods can exceed these that clasp me by the hand, and with voices I
    love call me promptly and loudly by my nighest name as I approach?  95
What is more subtle than this which ties me to the woman or man that
    looks in my face?
Which fuses me into you now, and pours my meaning into you?

We understand then do we not?
What I promis'd without mentioning it, have you not accepted?
What the study could not teach—what the preaching could not accomplish
    is accomplish'd, is it not?        100

### 9

Flow on, river! flow with the flood-tide, and ebb with the ebb-tide!
Frolic on, crested and scallop-edg'd waves!
Gorgeous clouds of the sunset! drench with your splendor me, or the men
    and women generations after me!
Cross from shore to shore, countless crowds of passengers!
Stand up, tall masts of Mannahatta!⁴ stand up, beautiful hills
    of Brooklyn!        105
Throb, baffled and curious brain! throw out questions and answers!
Suspend here and everywhere, eternal float of solution!
Gaze, loving and thirsting eyes, in the house or street or public assembly!

---

4. Variant of the American Indian word normally spelled "Manhattan."

Sound out, voices of young men! loudly and musically call me by my
    nighest name!
Live, old life! play the part that looks back on the actor or actress!     110
Play the old role, the role that is great or small according as one makes it!
Consider, you who peruse me, whether I may not in unknown ways be
    looking upon you;
Be firm, rail over the river, to support those who lean idly, yet haste with
    the hasting current;
Fly on, sea-birds! fly sideways, or wheel in large circles high in the air;
Receive the summer sky, you water, and faithfully hold it till all downcast
    eyes have time to take it from you!     115
Diverge, fine spokes of light, from the shape of my head, or any one's head,
    in the sunlit water!
Come on, ships from the lower bay! pass up or down, white-sail'd
    schooners, sloops, lighters!
Flaunt away, flags of all nations! be duly lower'd at sunset!
Burn high your fires, foundry chimneys! cast black shadows at nightfall!
    cast red and yellow light over the tops of the houses!
Appearances, now or henceforth, indicate what you are,     120
You necessary film, continue to envelop the soul,
About my body for me, and your body for you, be hung our divinest aromas,
Thrive, cities—bring your freight, bring your shows, ample and sufficient
    rivers,
Expand, being than which none else is perhaps more spiritual,
Keep your places, objects than which none else is more lasting.     125

You have waited, you always wait, you dumb, beautiful ministers,
We receive you with free sense at last, and are insatiate henceforward,
Not you any more shall be able to foil us, or withhold yourselves from us,
We use you, and do not cast you aside—we plant you permanently within
    us,
We fathom you not—we love you—there is perfection in you also,     130
You furnish your parts toward eternity,
Great or small, you furnish your parts toward the soul.

                              1856, 1881


## Out of the Cradle Endlessly Rocking[1]

Out of the cradle endlessly rocking,
Out of the mocking-bird's throat, the musical shuttle,
Out of the Ninth-month midnight,
Over the sterile sands and the fields beyond, where the child leaving his
    bed wander'd alone, bareheaded, barefoot,

---

1. First published as "A Child's Reminiscence" in the *New York Saturday Press* of December 24, 1859, this poem was incorporated into the 1860 *Leaves of Grass* as "A Word Out of the Sea." Whit- man continued to revise it until it reached the present form in the *Sea-Drift* section of the 1881 edition.

Down from the shower'd halo, 5
Up from the mystic play of shadows twining and twisting as if they were
    alive,
Out from the patches of briers and blackberries,
From the memories of the bird that chanted to me,
From your memories sad brother, from the fitful risings and fallings I
    heard,
From under that yellow half-moon late-risen and swollen as if with tears, 10
From those beginning notes of yearning and love there in the mist,
From the thousand responses of my heart never to cease,
From the myriad thence-arous'd words,
From the word stronger and more delicious than any,
From such as now they start the scene revisiting, 15
As a flock, twittering, rising, or overhead passing,
Borne hither, ere all eludes me, hurriedly,
A man, yet by these tears a little boy again,
Throwing myself on the sand, confronting the waves,
I, chanter of pains and joys, uniter of here and hereafter, 20
Taking all hints to use them, but swiftly leaping beyond them,
A reminiscence sing.

Once Paumanok,[2]
When the lilac-scent was in the air and Fifth-month grass was growing,
Up this seashore in some briers, 25
Two feather'd guests from Alabama, two together,

And their nest, and four light-green eggs spotted with brown,
And every day the he-bird to and fro near at hand,
And every day the she-bird crouch'd on her nest, silent, with bright eyes,
And every day I, a curious boy, never too close, never disturbing them, 30
Cautiously peering, absorbing, translating.

*Shine! shine! shine!*
*Pour down your warmth, great sun!*
*While we bask, we two together.*

*Two together!* 35
*Winds blow south, or winds blow north,*
*Day come white, or night come black,*
*Home, or rivers and mountains from home,*
*Singing all time, minding no time,*
*While we two keep together.* 40

Till of a sudden,
May-be kill'd, unknown to her mate,
One forenoon the she-bird crouch'd not on the nest,
Nor return'd that afternoon, nor the next
Nor ever appear'd again. 45

2. Long Island.

And thenceforward all summer in the sound of the sea,
And at night under the full of the moon in calmer weather,
Over the hoarse surging of the sea,
Or flitting from brier to brier by day,
I saw, I heard at intervals the remaining one, the he-bird,    50
The solitary guest from Alabama.

*Blow! blow! blow!*
*Blow up sea-winds along Paumanok's shore;*
*I wait and I wait till you blow my mate to me.*

Yes, when the stars glisten'd,    55
All night long on the prong of a moss-scallop'd stake,
Down almost amid the slapping waves,
Sat the lone singer wonderful causing tears.

He call'd on his mate,
He pour'd forth the meanings which I of all men know.    60

Yes my brother I know,
The rest might not, but I have treasur'd every note,
For more than once dimly down to the beach gliding,
Silent, avoiding the moonbeams, blending myself with the shadows,
Recalling now the obscure shapes, the echoes, the sounds and sights after
    their sorts,    65
The white arms out in the breakers tirelessly tossing,
I, with bare feet, a child, the wind wafting my hair,
Listen'd long and long.

Listen'd to keep, to sing, now translating the notes.
Following you my brother.    70

*Soothe! soothe! soothe!*
*Close on its wave soothes the wave behind,*
*And again another behind embracing and lapping, every one close,*
*But my love soothes not me, not me.*

*Low hangs the moon, it rose late,*    75
*It is lagging—O I think it is heavy with love, with love.*

*O madly the sea pushes upon the land,*
*With love, with love.*

*O night! do I not see my love fluttering out among the breakers?*
*What is that little black thing I see there in the white?*    80

*Loud! loud! loud!*
*Loud I call to you, my love!*

*High and clear I shoot my voice over the waves,*
*Surely you must know who is here, is here,*
*You must know who I am, my love.*    85

*Low-hanging moon!*
*What is that dusky spot in your brown yellow?*
*O it is the shape, the shape of my mate!*
*O moon do not keep her from me any longer.*

*Land! land! O land!*                                                              90
*Whichever way I turn, O I think you could give me my mate back again if*
      *you only would,*
*For I am almost sure I see her dimly whichever way I look.*

*O rising stars!*
*Perhaps the one I want so much will rise, will rise with some of you.*

*O throat! O trembling throat!*                                                    95
*Sound clearer through the atmosphere!*
*Pierce the woods, the earth,*
*Somewhere listening to catch you must be the one I want.*

*Shake out carols!*
*Solitary here, the night's carols!*                                              100
*Carols of lonesome love! death's carols!*
*Carols under that lagging, yellow, waning moon!*
*O under that moon where she droops almost down into the sea!*
*O reckless despairing carols.*

*But soft! sink low!*                                                             105
*Soft! let me just murmur,*
*And do you wait a moment you husky-nois'd sea,*
*For somewhere I believe I heard my mate responding to me,*
*So faint, I must be still, be still to listen,*
*But not altogether still, for then she might not come immediately to me.*   110

*Hither my love!*
*Here I am! here!*
*With this just-sustain'd note I announce myself to you,*
*This gentle call is for you my love, for you.*

*Do not be decoy'd elsewhere,*                                                    115
*That is the whistle of the wind, it is not my voice,*
*That is the fluttering, the fluttering of the spray,*
*Those are the shadows of leaves.*

*O darkness! O in vain!*
*O I am very sick and sorrowful.*                                                 120

*O brown halo in the sky near the moon, drooping upon the sea!*
*O troubled reflection in the sea!*
*O throat! O throbbing heart!*
*And I singing uselessly, uselessly all the night.*

*O past! O happy life! O songs of joy!*                                           125
*In the air, in the woods, over fields,*

*Loved! loved! loved! loved! loved!*
*But my mate no more, no more with me!*
*We two together no more.*

The aria sinking,        130
All else continuing, the stars shining,
The winds blowing, the notes of the bird continuous echoing,
With angry moans the fierce old mother incessantly moaning,
On the sands of Paumanok's shore gray and rustling,

The yellow half-moon enlarged, sagging down, drooping, the face of the sea
    almost touching,      135
The boy ecstatic, with his bare feet the waves, with his hair the atmosphere
    dallying,
The love in the heart long pent, now loose, now at last tumultuously
    bursting,
The aria's meaning, the ears, the soul, swiftly depositing,
The strange tears down the cheeks coursing,
The colloquy there, the trio, each uttering,    140
The undertone, the savage old mother incessantly crying,
To the boy's soul's questions sullenly timing, some drown'd secret hissing,
To the outsetting bard.

Demon or bird! (said the boy's soul,)
Is it indeed toward your mate you sing? or is it really to me?    145
For I, that was a child, my tongue's use sleeping, now I have heard you,
Now in a moment I know what I am for, I awake,
And already a thousand singers, a thousand songs, clearer, louder and more
    sorrowful than yours,
A thousand warbling echoes have started to life within me, never to die.

O you singer solitary, singing by yourself, projecting me,    150
O solitary me listening, never more shall I cease perpetuating you,
Never more shall I escape, never more the reverberations,
Never more the cries of unsatisfied love be absent from me,
Never again leave me to be the peaceful child I was before what there in
    the night,
By the sea under the yellow and sagging moon,    155
The messenger there arous'd, the fire, the sweet hell within,
The unknown want, the destiny of me.

O give me the clew! (it lurks in the night here somewhere,)
O if I am to have so much, let me have more!

A word then, (for I will conquer it,)    160
The word final, superior to all,
Subtle, sent up—what is it?—I listen;
Are you whispering it, and have been all the time, you sea-waves?
Is that it from your liquid rims and wet sands?

Whereto answering, the sea,    165
Delaying not, hurrying not,

Whisper'd me through the night, and very plainly before daybreak,
Lisp'd to me the low and delicious word death,
And again death, death, death, death,
Hissing melodious, neither like the bird nor like my arous'd child's heart, 170
But edging near as privately for me rustling at my feet,
Creeping thence steadily up to my ears and laving me softly all over,
Death, death, death, death, death.

Which I do not forget,
But fuse the song of my dusky demon and brother, 175
That he sang to me in the moonlight on Paumanok's gray beach,
With the thousand responsive songs at random,
My own songs awaked from that hour,
And with them the key, the word up from the waves,
The word of the sweetest song and all songs, 180
That strong and delicious word which, creeping to my feet,
(Or like some old crone rocking the cradle, swathed in sweet garments,
    bending aside,)
The sea whisper'd me.

1859, 1881

# Song of Myself[1]

## 1

*[handwritten margin note: We are all one? We share same virtues of the country etc]*

I celebrate myself, and sing myself,
And what I assume you shall assume,
For every atom belonging to me as good belongs to you.

I loafe and invite my soul,
I lean and loafe at my ease observing a spear of summer grass. 5

*[handwritten margin note: Part of surroundings.]*

My tongue, every atom of my blood, form'd from this soil, this air, *[handwritten margin note: Literally, blood taking in O₂ from surrounding.]*
Born here of parents born here from parents the same, and their parents
    the same,
I, now thirty-seven years old in perfect health begin, *[handwritten margin note: Begin @ 37.]*
Hoping to cease not till death.

Creeds and schools in <u>abeyance</u>, 10
Retiring back a while sufficed at what they are, but never forgotten,
I harbor for good or bad, I permit to speak at every hazard,
Nature without check with original energy.

1. In the 1855 first edition of *Leaves of Grass*, the poem that has come to be known as "Song of Myself" appeared without a title and without numbered subdivisions or stanzas. For the 1856 edition, Whitman titled it "Poem of Walt Whitman, an American," and in the 1860 edition he titled it "Walt Whitman"; it retained that title in the 1867 and 1871 editions. Whitman first gave the title "Song of Myself" to this, his most famous and influential poem, in the 1881 edition of *Leaves of Grass*. In addition to the change of title and use of numbered subdivisions, Whitman made numerous other changes in the poem from the first 1855 printing to the 1881 final version.

2

Houses and rooms are full of perfumes, the shelves are crowded with
  perfumes,
I breathe the fragrance myself and know it and like it,
The distillation would intoxicate me also, but I shall not let it.

The atmosphere is not a perfume, it has no taste of the distillation, it is
  odorless,
It is for my mouth forever, I am in love with it,
I will go to the bank by the wood and become undisguised and naked,
I am mad for it to be in contact with me.                                    20

The smoke of my own breath,
Echoes, ripples, buzz'd whispers, love-root, silk-thread, crotch and vine,
My respiration and inspiration, the beating of my heart, the passing of
  blood and air through my lungs,
The sniff of green leaves and dry leaves, and of the shore and dark-color'd
  sea-rocks, and of hay in the barn,
The sound of the belch'd words of my voice loos'd to the eddies of the
  wind,                                                                       25
A few light kisses, a few embraces, a reaching around of arms,
The play of shine and shade on the trees as the supple boughs wag,
The delight alone or in the rush of the streets, or along the fields and
  hill-sides,
The feeling of health, the full-noon trill, the song of me rising from bed and
  meeting the sun.

Have you reckon'd a thousand acres much? have you reckon'd the earth
  much?                                                                       30
Have you practis'd so long to learn to read?
Have you felt so proud to get at the meaning of poems?

Stop this day and night with me and you shall possess the origin of all
  poems,
You shall possess the good of the earth and sun, (there are millions of suns
  left,)
You shall no longer take things at second or third hand, nor look through
  the eyes of the dead, nor feed on the spectres in books,                    35
You shall not look through my eyes either, nor take things from me,
You shall listen to all sides and filter them from your self.

3

I have heard what the talkers were talking, the talk of the beginning and
  the end,
But I do not talk of the beginning or the end.

There was never any more inception than there is now,                         40
Nor any more youth or age than there is now,
And will never be any more perfection than there is now,

Nor any more heaven or hell than there is now.
Urge and urge and urge,
Always the procreant urge of the world.                                     45

Out of the dimness opposite equals advance, always substance and
    increase, always sex,
Always a knit of identity, always distinction, always a breed of life.

To elaborate is no avail, learn'd and unlearn'd feel that it is so.

Sure as the most certain sure, plumb in the uprights, well entretied,[2]
    braced in the beams,
Stout as a horse, affectionate, haughty, electrical,                        50
I and this mystery here we stand.

Clear and sweet is my soul, and clear and sweet is all that is not my soul.

Lack one lacks both, and the unseen is proved by the seen,
Till that becomes unseen and receives proof in its turn.

Showing the best and dividing it from the worst age vexes age,              55
Knowing the perfect fitness and equanimity of things, while they discuss I
    am silent, and go bathe and admire myself.

Welcome is every organ and attribute of me, and of any man hearty and
    clean,
Not an inch nor a particle of an inch is vile, and none shall be less familiar
    than the rest.

I am satisfied—I see, dance, laugh, sing;
As the hugging and loving bed-fellow sleeps at my side through the night,
    and withdraws at the peep of the day with stealthy tread,              60
Leaving me baskets cover'd with white towels swelling the house with their
    plenty,
Shall I postpone my acceptation and realization and scream at my eyes,
That they turn from gazing after and down the road,
And forthwith cipher[3] and show me to a cent,
Exactly the value of one and exactly the value of two, and which is
    ahead?                                                                  65

4

Trippers and askers surround me,
People I meet, the effect upon me of my early life or the ward and city I live
    in, or the nation,
The latest dates, discoveries, inventions, societies, authors old and new,
My dinner, dress, associates, looks, compliments, dues,
The real or fancied indifference of some man or woman I love,              70
The sickness of one of my folks or of myself, or ill-doing or loss or lack of
    money, or depressions or exaltations,

2. Cross-braced.                              3. Calculate.

*[handwritten margin notes: "Previously are the distractions that divert attention from the fact that we have frightening brothers"]*

Battles, the horrors of fratricidal war, the fever of doubtful news, the fitful events;
These come to me days and nights and go from me again,
But they are not the Me myself.

Apart from the pulling and hauling stands what I am,                              75
Stands amused, complacent, compassionating, idle, unitary, *[handwritten: why?]*
Looks down, is erect, or bends an arm on an impalpable certain rest,
Looking with side-curved head curious what will come next,
Both in and out of the game and watching and wondering at it.

Backward I see in my own days where I sweated through fog with linguists
    and contenders,
I have no mockings or arguments, I witness and wait.                            80

*[handwritten: Not involved in politics?]*

5

I believe in you my soul, the other I am must not abase itself to you,
And you must not be abased to the other.

Loafe with me on the grass, loose the stop from your throat,
Not words, not music or rhyme I want, not custom or lecture, not even the
    best,                                                                        85
Only the lull I like, the hum of your valvèd voice.

*[handwritten: his soul?]*

I mind how once we lay such a transparent summer morning,
How you settled your head athwart my hips and gently turn'd over upon me,
And parted the shirt from my bosom-bone, and plunged your tongue to my
    bare-stript heart,
And reach'd till you felt my beard, and reach'd till you held my feet.         90

Swiftly arose and spread around me the peace and knowledge that pass all
    the argument of the earth,
And I know that the hand of God is the promise of my own,
And I know that the spirit of God is the brother of my own,
And that all the men ever born are also my brothers, and the women my
    sisters and lovers,
And that a kelson[4] of the creation is love,                                   95
And limitless are leaves stiff or drooping in the fields,
And brown ants in the little wells beneath them,
And mossy scabs of the worm fence,[5] heap'd stones, elder, mullein and
    poke-weed.

6

A child said *What is the grass?* fetching it to me with full hands;
How could I answer the child? I do not know what it is any more than
    he.                                                                         100

4. A basic structural unit; a reinforcing timber     5. Zigzag fence of split rails.
bolted to the keel (backbone) of a ship.

I guess it must be the flag of my disposition, out of hopeful green stuff
    woven.

Or I guess it is the handkerchief of the Lord,
A scented gift and remembrancer designedly dropt,
Bearing the owner's name someway in the corners, that we may see and
    remark, and say *Whose?*

Or I guess the grass is itself a child, the produced babe of the vegetation.    105

Or I guess it is a uniform hieroglyphic,
And it means, Sprouting alike in broad zones and narrow zones,
Growing among black folks as among white,
Kanuck, Tuckahoe, Congressman, Cuff,[6] I give them the same, I receive
    them the same.

And now it seems to me the beautiful uncut hair of graves.    110

Tenderly will I use you curling grass,
It may be you transpire from the breasts of young men,
It may be if I had known them I would have loved them,
It may be you are from old people, or from offspring taken soon out of their
    mothers' laps,
And here you are the mothers' laps.    115

This grass is very dark to be from the white heads of old mothers,
Darker than the colorless beards of old men,
Dark to come from under the faint red roofs of mouths.

O I perceive after all so many uttering tongues,
And I perceive they do not come from the roofs of mouths for nothing.    120

I wish I could translate the hints about the dead young men and women,
And the hints about old men and mothers, and the offspring taken soon out
    of their laps.

What do you think has become of the young and old men?
And what do you think has become of the women and children?

They are alive and well somewhere,    125
The smallest sprout shows there is really no death,
And if ever there was it led forward life, and does not wait at the end to
    arrest it,
And ceas'd the moment life appear'd.

All goes onward and outward, nothing collapses,
And to die is different from what any one supposed, and luckier.    130

6. Black, from the African word *cuffee* (name for a black male born on a Friday). "Kanuck": French Canadian (now considered pejorative). "Tuckahoe": Virginian, from eaters of the American Indian food plant Tuckahoe.

*(handwritten: If lucky to exist, why not to die. lucky to die. Praise in both directions)*

7

Has any one supposed it lucky to be born?
I hasten to inform him or her it is just as lucky to die, and I know it.

I pass death with the dying and birth with the new-wash'd babe, and am
    not contain'd between my hat and boots,
And peruse manifold objects, no two alike and every one good,
The earth good and the stars good, and their adjuncts all good.          135

I am not an earth nor an adjunct of an earth,
I am the mate and companion of people, all just as immortal and
    fathomless as myself,
(They do not know how immortal, but I know.)

Every kind for itself and its own, for me mine male and female,
For me those that have been boys and that love women,          140
For me the man that is proud and feels how it stings to be slighted,
For me the sweet-heart and the old maid, for me mothers and the mothers
    of mothers,
For me lips that have smiled, eyes that have shed tears,
For me children and the begetters of children.

*(handwritten: Similarities of all men. common experiences they all share.)*

Undrape! you are not guilty to me, nor stale nor discarded,
I see through the broadcloth and gingham whether or no,          145
And am around, tenacious, acquisitive, tireless, and cannot be shaken
    away.

8

*(handwritten: DARK)*

The little one sleeps in its cradle,
I lift the gauze and look a long time, and silently brush away flies with my
    hand.

The youngster and the red-faced girl turn aside up the bushy hill,          150
I peeringly view them from the top.

The suicide sprawls on the bloody floor of the bedroom,
I witness the corpse with its dabbled hair, I note where the pistol has fallen.

The blab of the pave, tires of carts, sluff of boot-soles, talk of the
    promenaders,
The heavy omnibus, the driver with his interrogating thumb, the clank of
    the shod horses on the granite floor,          155
The snow-sleighs, clinking, shouted jokes, pelts of snow-balls,
The hurrahs for popular favorites, the fury of rous'd mobs,
The flap of the curtain'd litter, a sick man inside borne to the hospital,
The meeting of enemies, the sudden oath, the blows and fall,
The excited crowd, the policeman with his star quickly working his passage
    to the centre of the crowd,          160
The impassive stones that receive and return so many echoes,

*(handwritten: energetic imagery.)*

What groans of over-fed or half-starv'd who fall sunstruck or in fits,
What exclamations of women taken suddenly who hurry home and give
    birth to babes,
What living and buried speech is always vibrating here, what howls
    restrain'd by decorum,
Arrests of criminals, slights, adulterous offers made, acceptances,
    rejections with convex lips,                                          165
I mind them or the show or resonance of them—I come and I depart.

### 9

The big doors of the country barn stand open and ready,
The dried grass of the harvest-time loads the slow-drawn wagon,
The clear light plays on the brown gray and green intertinged,
The armfuls are pack'd to the sagging mow.                               170

I am there, I help, I came stretch'd atop of the load,
I felt its soft jolts, one leg reclined on the other,
I jump from the cross-beams and sieze the clover and timothy,
And roll head over heels and tangle my hair full of wisps.

### 10

Alone far in the wilds and mountains I hunt,                             175
Wandering amazed at my own lightness and glee,
In the late afternoon choosing a safe spot to pass the night,
Kindling a fire and broiling the fresh-kill'd game,
Falling asleep on the gather'd leaves with my dog and gun by my side.

The Yankee clipper is under her sky-sails, she cuts the sparkle and scud,  180
My eyes settle the land, I bend at her prow or shout joyously from the deck.

The boatmen and clam-diggers arose early and stopt for me,
I tuck'd my trowser-ends in my boots and went and had a good time;
You should have been with us that day round the chowder-kettle.

I saw the marriage of the trapper in the open air in the far west, the bride
    was a red girl,                                                      185
Her father and his friends sat near cross-legged and dumbly smoking, they
    had moccasins to their feet and large thick blankets hanging from their
    shoulders,
On a bank lounged the trapper, he was drest mostly in skins, his luxuriant
    beard and curls protected his neck, he held his bride by the hand,
She had long eyelashes, her head was bare, her coarse straight locks
    descended upon her voluptuous limbs and reach'd to her feet.

The runaway slave came to my house and stopt outside,
I heard his motions crackling the twigs of the woodpile,                 190
Through the swung half-door of the kitchen I saw him limpsy[7] and weak,
And went where he sat on a log and led him in and assured him,

7. Limping or swaying.

And brought water and fill'd a tub for his sweated body and bruis'd feet,
And gave him a room that enter'd from my own, and gave him some coarse
    clean clothes,
And remember perfectly well his revolving eyes and his awkwardness,     195
And remember putting plasters on the galls of his neck and ankles;
He staid with me a week before he was recuperated and pass'd north,
I had him sit next me at table, my fire-lock lean'd in the corner.

*11*

*in the water → being enveloped by nature.*

Twenty-eight young men bathe by the shore,
Twenty-eight young men and all so friendly;     200
Twenty-eight years of womanly life and all so lonesome.

*Her body is impacted even though she's just watching.*

She owns the fine house by the rise of the bank,
She hides handsome and richly drest aft the blinds of the window.

Which of the young men does she like the best?
Ah the homeliest of them is beautiful to her.     205

Where are you off to, lady? for I see you,
You splash in the water there, yet stay stock still in your room.

Dancing and laughing along the beach came the twenty-ninth bather,
The rest did not see her, but she saw them and loved them.

The beards of the young men glisten'd with wet, it ran from their long
    hair,     210
Little streams pass'd over their bodies.

An unseen hand also pass'd over their bodies,
It descended tremblingly from their temples and ribs.

*Homoerotic?*

The young men float on their backs, their white bellies bulge to the sun,
    they do not ask who seizes fast to them,
They do not know who puffs and declines with pendant and
    bending arch,     215
They do not think whom they souse with spray.

*12*

The butcher-boy puts off his killing-clothes, or sharpens his knife at the
    stall in the market,
I loiter enjoying his repartee and his shuffle and break-down.[8]

Blacksmiths with grimed and hairy chests environ the anvil,
Each has his main-sledge, they are all out, there is a great heat in the
    fire.     220

---

8. Dances familiar in popular entertainment and minstrelsy. The "shuffle" involves the sliding of feet
across the floor, and the "break-down" is faster and noisier.

From the cinder-strew'd threshold I follow their movements,
The lithe sheer of their waists plays even with their massive arms,
Overhand the hammers swing, overhand so slow, overhand so sure,
They do not hasten, each man hits in his place.

### 13

The negro holds firmly the reins of his four horses, the block swags
    underneath on its tied-over chain,                                                225
The negro that drives the long dray of the stone-yard, steady and tall he
    stands pois'd on one leg on the string-piece,[9]
His blue shirt exposes his ample neck and breast and loosens over his
    hip-band,
His glance is calm and commanding, he tosses the slouch of his hat away
    from his forehead,
The sun falls on his crispy hair and mustache, falls on the black of his
    polish'd and perfect limbs.

I behold the picturesque giant and love him, and I do not stop there,      230
I go with the team also.

In me the caresser of life wherever moving, backward as well as forward
    sluing,[1]
To niches aside and junior[2] bending, not a person or object missing,
Absorbing all to myself and for this song.

Oxen that rattle the yoke and chain or halt in the leafy shade, what is that
    you express in your eyes?                                                235
It seems to me more than all the print I have read in my life.

My tread scares the wood-drake and wood-duck on my distant and day-long
    ramble.
They rise together, they slowly circle around.

I believe in those wing'd purposes,
And acknowledge red, yellow, white, playing within me,                     240
And consider green and violet and the tufted crown[3] intentional,
And do not call the tortoise unworthy because she is not something else,
And the jay in the woods never studied the gamut,[4] yet trills pretty well to
    me,
And the look of the bay mare shames silliness out of me.

### 14

The wild gander leads his flock through the cool night,                    245
*Ya-honk* he says, and sounds it down to me like an invitation,
The pert may suppose it meaningless, but I listening close,
Find its purpose and place up there toward the wintry sky.

9. Long, heavy timber used to keep a load in place.    3. Of the wood drake.
1. Twisting.    4. Here, the series of recognized musical notes.
2. Smaller.

*[handwritten: (everything has a place.)]*

The sharp-hoof'd moose of the north, the cat on the house-sill, the
    chickadee, the prairie-dog,
The litter of the grunting sow as they tug at her teats,          250
The brood of the turkey-hen and she with her half-spread wings,
I see in them and myself the same old law.
The press of my foot to the earth springs a hundred affections,
They scorn the best I can do to relate them.

I am enamour'd of growing out-doors,          255
Of men that live among cattle or taste of the ocean or woods,
Of the builders and steerers of ships and the wielders of axes and mauls,
    and the drivers of horses,
I can eat and sleep with them week in and week out.

What is commonest, cheapest, nearest, easiest, is Me,
Me going in for my chances, spending for vast returns,          260
Adorning myself to bestow myself on the first that will take me,
Not asking the sky to come down to my good will,
Scattering it freely forever.

### 15

The pure contralto sings in the organ loft,
The carpenter dresses his plank, the tongue of his foreplane whistles its
    wild ascending lisp,          265
The married and unmarried children ride home to their Thanksgiving *[handwritten: innocense]*
    dinner,
The pilot seizes the king-pin,[5] he heaves down with a strong arm, *[handwritten: Controling]*
The mate stands braced in the whale-boat, lance and harpoon are ready,
The duck-shooter walks by silent and cautious stretches,
The deacons are ordain'd with cross'd hands at the altar,          270
The spinning-girl retreats and advances to the hum of the big wheel,
The farmer stops by the bars as he walks on a First-day[6] loafe and looks at
    the oats and rye,
The lunatic is carried at last to the asylum a confirm'd case,
(He will never sleep any more as he did in the cot in his mother's
    bed-room;) *[handwritten: Impermenence.]*
The jour printer[7] with gray head and gaunt jaws works at his case,         275
He turns his quid of tobacco while his eyes blurr with the manuscript;
The malform'd limbs are tied to the surgeon's table,
What is removed drops horribly in a pail;
The quadroon[8] girl is sold at the auction-stand, the drunkard nods by the
    bar-room stove,
The machinist rolls up his sleeves, the policeman travels his beat, the gate-
    keeper marks who pass,         280

---

5. The extended spoke of the pilot wheel, used to maintain leverage during storms.
6. Sunday. Whitman frequently uses the numerical Quaker designations for the names of days and months. "Bars": i.e., of a rail fence.
7. I.e., a journeyman printer, or one who has passed an apprenticeship and is fully qualified for all professional work.
8. One quarter black.

The young fellow drives the express-wagon, (I love him, though I do not know him;)
The half-breed straps on his light boots to compete in the race,
The western turkey-shooting draws old and young, some lean on their rifles, some sit on logs,
Out from the crowd steps the marksman, takes his position, levels his piece;
The groups of newly-come immigrants cover the wharf or levee,          285
As the woolly-pates[9] hoe in the sugar-field, the overseer views them from his saddle,
The bugle calls in the ball-room, the gentlemen run for their partners, the dancers bow to each other,
The youth lies awake in the cedar-roof'd garret and harks to the musical rain,
The Wolverine[1] sets traps on the creek that helps fill the Huron,
The squaw wrapt in her yellow-hemm'd cloth is offering moccasins and bead-bags for sale,          290
The connoisseur peers along the exhibition-gallery with half-shut eyes bent sideways,
As the deck-hands make fast the steamboat the plank is thrown for the shore-going passengers,
The young sister holds out the skein while the elder sister winds it off in a ball, and stops now and then for the knots,
The one-year wife is recovering and happy having a week ago borne her first child,
The clean-hair'd Yankee girl works with her sewing-machine or in the factory or mill,          295
The paving-man[2] leans on his two-handed rammer, the reporter's lead flies swiftly over the note-book, the sign-painter is lettering with blue and gold,
The canal boy trots on the tow-path, the book-keeper counts at his desk, the shoemaker waxes his thread,
The conductor beats time for the band and all the performers follow him,
The child is baptized, the convert is making his first professions,
The regatta is spread on the bay, the race is begun, (how the white sails sparkle!)          300
The drover watching his drove sings out to them that would stray,
The pedler sweats with his pack on his back, (the purchaser higgling about the odd cent;)
The bride unrumples her white dress, the minute-hand of the clock moves slowly,
The opium-eater reclines with rigid head and just-open'd lips,
The prostitute draggles her shawl, her bonnet bobs on her tipsy and pimpled neck,          305
The crowd laugh at her blackguard oaths, the men jeer and wink to each other,
(Miserable! I do not laugh at your oaths nor jeer you;)
The President holding a cabinet council is surrounded by the great Secretaries,

9. Black slaves (with stereotypical emphasis on the "woolly" hair on their heads).

1. Inhabitant of Michigan.
2. Man building or repairing streets.

On the piazza walk three matrons stately and friendly with twined arms,
The crew of the fish-smack pack repeated layers of halibut in the hold,   310
The Missourian crosses the plains toting his wares and his cattle,
As the fare-collector goes through the train he gives notice by the jingling
    of loose change,
The floor-men are laying the floor, the tinners are tinning the roof, the
    masons are calling for mortar,
In single file each shouldering his hod pass onward the laborers;
Seasons pursuing each other the indescribable crowd is gather'd, it is the
    fourth of Seventh-month,[3] (what salutes of cannon and small arms!) 315
Seasons pursuing each other the plougher ploughs, the mower mows, and
    the winter-grain falls in the ground;
Off on the lakes the pike-fisher watches and waits by the hole in the frozen
    surface,
The stumps stand thick round the clearing, the squatter strikes deep with
    his axe,
Flatboatmen make fast towards dusk near the cotton-wood or pecan-trees,
Coon-seekers go through the regions of the Red river or through those
    drain'd by the Tennessee, or through those of the Arkansas,   320
Torches shine in the dark that hangs on the Chattahooch or Altamahaw,[4]
Patriarchs sit at supper with sons and grandsons and great-grandsons
    around them,
In walls of adobie, in canvas tents, rest hunters and trappers after their
    day's sport,
The city sleeps and the country sleeps,
The living sleep for their time, the dead sleep for their time,   325
The old husband sleeps by his wife and the young husband sleeps by his
    wife;
And these tend inward to me, and I tend outward to them,
And such as it is to be of these more or less I am,
And of these one and all I weave the song of myself.

### 16

*Paradoxical.*

I am of old and young, of the foolish as much as the wise,   330
Regardless of others, ever regardful of others,
Maternal as well as paternal, a child as well as a man,
Stuff'd with the stuff that is coarse and stuff'd with the stuff that is fine,
One of the Nation of many nations, the smallest the same and the largest
    the same,
A Southerner soon as a Northerner, a planter nonchalant and hospitable
    down by the Oconee[5] I live,   335
A Yankee bound my own way ready for trade, my joints the limberest joints
    on earth and the sternest joints on earth,
A Kentuckian walking the vale of the Elkhorn[6] in my deer-skin leggings, a
    Louisianian or Georgian,
A boatman over lakes or bays or along coasts, a Hoosier, Badger, Buckeye;[7]

---

3. I.e., the Fourth of July.
4. Georgia rivers.
5. River in central Georgia.

6. River in Nebraska.
7. Inhabitants of Indiana, Wisconsin, and Ohio,
respectively.

At home on Kanadian[8] snow-shoes or up in the bush, or with fishermen off
    Newfoundland,
At home in the fleet of ice-boats, sailing with the rest and tacking,     340
At home on the hills of Vermont or in the woods of Maine, or the Texan
    ranch,
Comrade of Californians, comrade of free North-Westerners, (loving their
    big proportions,)
Comrade of raftsmen and coalmen, comrade of all who shake hands and
    welcome to drink and meat,
A learner with the simplest, a teacher of the thoughtfullest,
A novice beginning yet experient of myriads of seasons,     345
Of every hue and caste am I, of every rank and religion,
A farmer, mechanic, artist, gentleman, sailor, quaker,
Prisoner, fancy-man, rowdy, lawyer, physician, priest.

I resist any thing better than my own diversity,
Breathe the air but leave plenty after me,     350
And am not stuck up, and am in my place.

(The moth and the fish-eggs are in their place,
The bright suns I see and the dark suns I cannot see are in their place,
The palpable is in its place and the impalpable is in its place.)

## 17

These are really the thoughts of all men in all ages and lands, they are not
    original with me,     355
If they are not yours as much as mine they are nothing, or next to nothing,
If they are not the riddle and the untying of the riddle they are nothing,
If they are not just as close as they are distant they are nothing.

This is the grass that grows wherever the land is and the water is,
This the common air that bathes the globe.     360

## 18

With music strong I come, with my cornets and my drums,
I play not marches for accepted victors only, I play marches for conquer'd
    and slain persons.

Have you heard that it was good to gain the day?
I also say it is good to fall, battles are lost in the same spirit in which they
    are won.

I beat and pound for the dead,     365
I blow through my embouchures[9] my loudest and gayest for them.

Vivas to those who have fail'd!
And to those whose war-vessels sank in the sea!

8. Canadian.
9. Mouthpieces of musical instruments such as the cornet.

And to those themselves who sank in the sea!
And to all generals that lost engagements, and all overcome heroes!   370
And the numberless unknown heroes equal to the greatest heroes known!

### 19

This is the meal equally set, this the meat for natural hunger,
It is for the wicked just the same as the righteous, I make appointments
    with all,
I will not have a single person slighted or left away,
The kept-woman, sponger, thief, are hereby invited,   375
The heavy-lipp'd slave is invited, the venerealee[1] is invited;
There shall be no difference between them and the rest.

This is the press of a bashful hand, this the float and odor of hair,
This is the touch of my lips to yours, this the murmur of yearning,
This the far-off depth and height reflecting my own face,   380
This the thoughtful merge of myself, and the outlet again.

Do you guess I have some intricate purpose?
Well I have, for the Fourth-month showers have, and the mica on the side
    of a rock has.

Do you take it I would astonish?
Does the daylight astonish? does the early redstart twittering through the
    woods?   385
Do I astonish more than they?

This hour I tell things in confidence,
I might not tell everybody, but I will tell you.

### 20

Who goes there? hankering, gross, mystical, nude;
How is it I extract strength from the beef I eat?   390

What is a man anyhow? what am I? what are you?

All I mark as my own you shall offset it with your own,
Else it were time lost listening to me.

I do not snivel that snivel the world over,
That months are vacuums and the ground but wallow and filth.   395

Whimpering and truckling fold with powders for invalids, conformity goes
    to the fourth-remov'd,[2]
I wear my hat as I please indoors or out.

---

1. Someone afflicted with a venereal (sexually transmitted) disease.
2. Those very remote in relationship; from the genealogical use such as "third cousin, fourth removed." "Fold with powders": a reference to the custom of a physician's wrapping up a dose of medicine in a piece of paper.

Why should I pray? why should I venerate and be ceremonious?

Having pried through the strata, analyzed to a hair, counsel'd with doctors
    and calculated close,
I find no sweeter fat than sticks to my bones. 400

In all people I see myself, none more and not one a barley-corn[3] less,
And the good or bad I say of myself I say of them.

I know I am solid and sound,
To me the converging objects of the universe perpetually flow,
All are written to me, and I must get what the writing means. 405

I know I am deathless,
I know this orbit of mine cannot be swept by a carpenter's compass,
I know I shall not pass like a child's carlacue[4] cut with a burnt stick at
    night.

I know I am august,
I do not trouble my spirit to vindicate itself or be understood, 410
I see that the elementary laws never apologize,
(I reckon I behave no prouder than the level I plant my house by, after all.)

I exist as I am, that is enough,
If no other in the world be aware I sit content,
And if each and all be aware I sit content. 415

One world is aware and by far the largest to me, and that is myself,
And whether I come to my own to-day or in ten thousand or ten million
    years,
I can cheerfully take it now, or with equal cheerfulness I can wait.

My foothold is tenon'd and mortis'd[5] in granite,
I laugh at what you call dissolution, 420
And I know the amplitude of time.

## 21

I am the poet of the Body and I am the poet of the Soul,
The pleasures of heaven are with me and the pains of hell are with me,
The first I graft and increase upon myself, the latter I translate into a new
    tongue.

I am the poet of the woman the same as the man, 425
And I say it is as great to be a woman as to be a man,
And I say there is nothing greater than the mother of men.

---

3. The seed or grain of barley, but also a unit of
measure equal to about one-third inch.
4. Or *curlicue*, a fancy flourish made with a writing implement, here made in the dark with a
lighted stick.

5. Carpenter's terms for a particular way of joining
two boards together. A mortise is a cavity in a piece
of wood into which is placed the projection (tenon)
from another piece of wood.

I chant the chant of dilation or pride,
We have had ducking and deprecating about enough,
I show that size is only development.                                            430

Have you outstript the rest? are you the President?
It is a trifle, they will more than arrive there every one, and still pass on.

I am he that walks with the tender and growing night,
I call to the earth and sea half-held by the night.

Press close bare-bosom'd night—press close magnetic nourishing night!   435
Night of south winds—night of the large few stars!
Still nodding night—mad naked summer night.

Smile O voluptuous cool-breath'd earth!
Earth of the slumbering and liquid trees!
Earth of departed sunset—earth of the mountains misty-topt!              440
Earth of the vitreous pour of the full moon just tinged with blue!
Earth of shine and dark mottling the tide of the river!
Earth of the limpid gray of clouds brighter and clearer for my sake!
Far-swooping elbow'd earth—rich apple-blossom'd earth!
Smile, for your lover comes.                                                    445

Prodigal, you have given me love—therefore I to you give love!
O unspeakable passionate love.


22

You sea! I resign myself to you also—I guess what you mean,
I behold from the beach your crooked inviting fingers,
I believe you refuse to go back without feeling of me,                   450
We must have a turn together, I undress, hurry me out of sight of the land,
Cushion me soft, rock me in billowy drowse,
Dash me with amorous wet, I can repay you.

Sea of stretch'd ground-swells,
Sea breathing broad and convulsive breaths,                              455
Sea of the brine of life and of unshovell'd yet always-ready graves,
Howler and scooper of storms, capricious and dainty sea,
I am integral with you, I too am of one phase and of all phases.

Partaker of influx and efflux I, extoller of hate and conciliation,
Extoller of amies[6] and those that sleep in each others' arms.          460

I am he attesting sympathy,
(Shall I make my list of things in the house and skip the house that
     supports them?)

I am not the poet of goodness only, I do not decline to be the poet of
     wickedness also.

6. Friends (French).

What blurt is this about virtue and about vice?
Evil propels me and reform of evil propels me, I stand indifferent,               465
My gait is no fault-finder's or rejecter's gait,
I moisten the roots of all that has grown.

Did you fear some scrofula[7] out of the unflagging pregnancy?
Did you guess the celestial laws are yet to be work'd over and rectified?

I find one side a balance and the antipodal side a balance,                        470
Soft doctrine as steady help as stable doctrine,
Thoughts and deeds of the present our rouse and early start.

This minute that comes to me over the past decillions,[8]
There is no better than it and now.
What behaved well in the past or behaves well to-day is not such a
    wonder,                                                                        475
The wonder is always and always how there can be a mean man or an
    infidel.

### 23

Endless unfolding of words of ages!
And mine a word of the modern, the word En-Masse.

A word of the faith that never balks,
Here or henceforward it is all the same to me, I accept Time absolutely.           480

*Time is deity?*

It alone is without flaw, it alone rounds and completes all,
That mystic baffling wonder alone completes all.

I accept Reality and dare not question it.
Materialism first and last imbuing.

Hurrah for positive science! long live exact demonstration!                        485
Fetch stonecrop mixt with cedar and branches of lilac,
This is the lexicographer, this the chemist, this made a grammar of the old
    cartouches,[9]
These mariners put the ship through dangerous unknown seas,
This is the geologist, this works with the scalpel, and this is a
    mathematician.

Gentlemen, to you the first honors always!                                         490
Your facts are useful, and yet they are not my dwelling,
I but enter by them to an area of my dwelling.

---

7. Form of tuberculosis characterized by swelling of the lymph glands.
8. The number 1 followed by thirty-three zeroes.
9. Scroll-like tablet with space for an inscription.

Whitman knew the Egyptian cartouches with hieroglyphics, the deciphering of which contributed to knowledge of ancient life. "Stonecrop": a fleshy-leafed plant.

Less the reminders of properties told my words,
And more the reminders they of life untold, and of freedom and extrication,
And make short account of neuters and geldings, and favor men and
women fully equipt,                                                          495
And beat the gong of revolt, and stop with fugitives and them that plot and
conspire.

## 24

Walt Whitman, a kosmos, of Manhattan the son,
Turbulent, fleshy, sensual, eating, drinking and breeding,
No sentimentalist, no stander above men and women or apart from them,
No more modest than immodest.                                                500

Unscrews the locks from the doors!
Unscrews the doors themselves from their jambs!

Whoever degrades another degrades me,
And whatever is done or said returns at last to me.

Through me the afflatus[1] surging and surging, through me the current and
index.                                                                       505

I speak the pass-word primeval, I give the sign of democracy,
By God! I will accept nothing which all cannot have their counterpart of on
the same terms.

Through me many long dumb voices,
Voices of the interminable generations of prisoners and slaves,
Voices of the diseas'd and despairing and of thieves and dwarfs,             510

Voices of cycles of preparation and accretion,
And of the threads that connect the stars, and of wombs and of the
fatherstuff,
And of the rights of them the others are down upon,
Of the deform'd, trivial, flat, foolish, despised,
Fog in the air, beetles rolling balls of dung.                              515

Through me forbidden voices,
Voices of sexes and lusts, voices veil'd and I remove the veil,
Voices indecent by me clarified and transfigur'd.

I do not press my fingers across my mouth,
I keep as delicate around the bowels as around the head and heart,          520
Copulation is no more rank to me than death is.

I believe in the flesh and the appetites,
Seeing, hearing, feeling, are miracles, and each part and tag of me is a
miracle.

---

1. Divine wind or spirit.

Divine am I inside and out, and I make holy whatever I touch or am
    touch'd from,
The scent of these arm-pits aroma finer than prayer,            525
This head more than churches, bibles, and all the creeds.

If I worship one thing more than another it shall be the spread of my own
    body, or any part of it,
Translucent mould of me it shall be you!
Shaded ledges and rests it shall be you!
Firm masculine colter[2] it shall be you!            530
Whatever goes to the tilth[3] of me it shall be you!
You my rich blood! your milky stream pale strippings of my life!
Breast that presses against other breasts it shall be you!
My brain it shall be your occult convolutions!
Root of wash'd sweet-flag! timorous pond-snipe! nest of guarded duplicate
    eggs! it shall be you!            535
Mix'd tussled hay of head, beard, brawn, it shall be you!
Trickling sap of maple, fibre of manly wheat, it shall be you!
Sun so generous it shall be you!
Vapors lighting and shading my face it shall be you!
You sweaty brooks and dews it shall be you!            540
Winds whose soft-tickling genitals rub against me it shall be you!
Broad muscular fields, branches of live oak, loving lounger in my winding
    paths, it shall be you!
Hands I have taken, face I have kiss'd, mortal I have ever touch'd, it shall
    be you.

I dote on myself, there is that lot of me and all so luscious,
Each moment and whatever happens thrills me with joy,           545
I cannot tell how my ankles bend, nor whence the cause of my faintest
    wish,
Nor the cause of the friendship I emit, nor the cause of the friendship I
    take again.

That I walk up my stoop, I pause to consider if it really be,
A morning-glory at my window satisfies me more than the metaphysics of
    books.

To behold the day-break!           550
The little light fades the immense and diaphanous shadows,
The air tastes good to my palate.

Hefts[4] of the moving world at innocent gambols silently rising freshly
    exuding,
Scooting obliquely high and low.

Something I cannot see puts upward libidinous prongs,          555
Seas of bright juice suffuse heaven.

---

2. This phallic passage begins with reference to the blade at the front of a plow.

3. Cultivation or tillage of the soil.
4. Something being heaved or raised upward.

The earth by the sky staid with, the daily close of their junction,
The heav'd challenge from the east that moment over my head,
The mocking taunt, See then whether you shall be master!

### 25

Dazzling and tremendous how quick the sun-rise would kill me,                    560
If I could not now and always send sun-rise out of me.

We also ascend dazzling and tremendous as the sun,
We found our own O my soul in the calm and cool of the day-break.

My voice goes after what my eyes cannot reach,
With the twirl of my tongue I encompass worlds and volumes of worlds.   565

Speech is the twin of my vision, it is unequal to measure itself,
It provokes me forever, it says sarcastically,
*Walt you contain enough, why don't you let it out then?*

Come now I will not be tantalized, you conceive too much of articulation,
Do you not know O speech how the buds beneath you are folded?            570
Waiting in gloom, protected by frost,
The dirt receding before my prophetical screams,
I underlying causes to balance them at last,
My knowledge my live parts, it keeping tally with the meaning of all things,
Happiness, (which whoever hears me let him or her set out in search of
      this day.)                                                         575

My final merit I refuse you, I refuse putting from me what I really am,
Encompass worlds, but never try to encompass me.
I crowd your sleekest and best by simply looking toward you.

Writing and talk do not prove me,
I carry the plenum[5] of proof and every thing else in my face,          580
With the hush of my lips I wholly confound the skeptic.

### 26

Now I will do nothing but listen,
To accrue what I hear into this song, to let sounds contribute toward it.

I hear bravuras of birds, bustle of growing wheat, gossip of flames, clack of
      sticks cooking my meals,
I hear the sound I love, the sound of the human voice,                   585
I hear all sounds running together, combined, fused or following,
Sounds of the city and sounds out of the city, sounds of the day and night,
Talkative young ones to those that like them, the loud laugh of work-people
      at their meals,
The angry base of disjointed friendship, the faint tones of the sick,

5. Fullness.

The judge with hands tight to the desk, his pallid lips pronouncing a
    death-sentence,    590
The heave'e'yo of stevedores unlading ships by the wharves, the refrain of
    the anchor-lifters,
The ring of alarm-bells, the cry of fire, the whirr of swift-streaking engines
    and hose-carts with premonitory tinkles and color'd lights,
The steam-whistle, the solid roll of the train of approaching cars,
The slow march play'd at the head of the association marching two and
    two,
(They go to guard some corpse, the flag-tops are draped with black muslin.) 595

I hear the violoncello ('tis the young man's heart's complaint,)
I hear the key'd cornet, it glides quickly in through my ears,
It shakes mad-sweet pangs through my belly and breast.

I hear the chorus, it is a grand opera,
Ah this indeed is music—this suits me.    600

A tenor large and fresh as the creation fills me,
The orbic flex of his mouth is pouring and filling me full.

I hear the train'd soprano (what work with hers is this?)
The orchestra whirls me wider than Uranus[6] flies,
It wrenches such ardors from me I did not know I possess'd them,    605
It sails me, I dab with bare feet, they are lick'd by the indolent waves,
I am cut by bitter and angry hail, I lose my breath,
Steep'd amid honey'd morphine, my windpipe throttled in fakes[7] of death,
At length let up again to feel the puzzle of puzzles,
And that we call Being.    610

### 27

To be in any form, what is that?
(Round and round we go, all of us, and ever come back thither,)
If nothing lay more develop'd the quahaug[8] in its callous shell were
    enough.

Mine is no callous shell,
I have instant conductors all over me whether I pass or stop,    615
They seize every object and lead it harmlessly through me.

I merely stir, press, feel with my fingers, and am happy,
To touch my person to some one else's is about as much as I can stand.

### 28

Is this then a touch? quivering me to a new identity,
Flames and ether making a rush for my veins,    620

6. The seventh planet from the sun; at that time it
was thought to be the most remote planet in the
solar system.

7. Coils of rope.
8. Edible clam of the Atlantic coast.

Treacherous tip of me reaching and crowding to help them,
My flesh and blood playing out lightning to strike what is hardly different
    from myself,
On all sides prurient provokers stiffening my limbs,
Straining the udder of my heart for its withheld drip,
Behaving licentious toward me, taking no denial,             625
Depriving me of my best as for a purpose,
Unbuttoning my clothes, holding me by the bare waist,
Deluding my confusion with the calm of the sunlight and pasture-fields,
Immodestly sliding the fellow-senses away,
They bribed to swap off with touch and go and graze at the edges of me,  630
No consideration, no regard for my draining strength or my anger,
Fetching the rest of the herd around to enjoy them a while,
Then all uniting to stand on a headland and worry me.

The sentries desert every other part of me,
They have left me helpless to a red marauder,              635
They all come to the headland to witness and assist against me.

I am given up by traitors,
I talk wildly, I have lost my wits, I and nobody else am the greatest traitor,
I went myself first to the headland, my own hands carried me there.

You villain touch! what are you doing? my breath is tight in its throat,   640
Unclench your floodgates, you are too much for me.


29

Blind loving wrestling touch, sheath'd hooded sharp-tooth'd touch!
Did it make you ache so, leaving me?

Parting track'd by arriving, perpetual payment of perpetual loan,
Rich showering rain, and recompense richer afterward.         645

Sprouts take and accumulate, stand by the curb prolific and vital,
Landscapes projected masculine, full-sized and golden.


30

All truths wait in all things,
They neither hasten their own delivery nor resist it,
They do not need the obstetric forceps of the surgeon,         650
The insignificant is as big to me as any,
(What is less or more than a touch?)

Logic and sermons never convince,
The damp of the night drives deeper into my soul.

(Only what proves itself to every man and woman is so,         655
Only what nobody denies is so.)

A minute and a drop of me settle my brain,
I believe the soggy clods shall become lovers and lamps,
And a compend[9] of compends is the meat of a man or woman,
And a summit and flower there is the feeling they have for each other,    660
And they are to branch boundlessly out of that lesson until it becomes
    omnific,[1]
And until one and all shall delight us, and we them.

### 31

I believe a leaf of grass is no less than the journey-work of the stars,
And the pismire[2] is equally perfect, and a grain of sand, and the egg of the
    wren,
And the tree-toad is a chief-d'œuvre for the highest,    665
And the running blackberry would adorn the parlors of heaven,
And the narrowest hinge in my hand puts to scorn all machinery,
And the cow crunching with depress'd head surpasses any statue,
And a mouse is miracle enough to stagger sextillions of infidels.

I find I incorporate gneiss,[3] coal, long-threaded moss, fruits, grains,
    esculent roots,    670
And am stucco'd with quadrupeds and birds all over,
And have distanced what is behind me for good reasons,
But call any thing back again when I desire it.
In vain the speeding or shyness,
In vain the plutonic rocks[4] send their old heat against my approach,    675
In vain the mastodon retreats beneath its own powder'd bones,
In vain objects stand leagues off and assume manifold shapes,
In vain the ocean settling in hollows and the great monsters lying low,
In vain the buzzard houses herself with the sky,
In vain the snake slides through the creepers and logs,    680
In vain the elk takes to the inner passes of the woods,
In vain the razor-bill'd auk sails far north to Labrador,
I follow quickly, I ascend to the nest in the fissure of the cliff.

### 32

I think I could turn and live with animals, they are so placid and self-
    contain'd,
I stand and look at them long and long.    685

They do not sweat and whine about their condition,
They do not lie awake in the dark and weep for their sins,
They do not make me sick discussing their duty to God,
Not one is dissatisfied, not one is demented with the mania of owning
    things,

---

9. I.e., a compendium, in which something is
reduced to a short, essential summary.
1. All-encompassing.
2. Ant.
3. Metamorphic rock in which minerals are
arranged in layers.
4. Rock of igneus (fire created) or magmatic
(molten) origin; from Pluto, ruler of infernal
regions.

Not one kneels to another, nor to his kind that lived thousands of years
    ago,                                          690
Not one is respectable or unhappy over the whole earth.

So they show their relations to me and I accept them,
They bring me tokens of myself, they evince them plainly in their
    possession.

I wonder where they get those tokens,
Did I pass that way huge times ago and negligently drop them?    695

Myself moving forward then and now and forever,
Gathering and showing more always and with velocity,
Infinite and omnigenous,[5] and the like of these among them,
Not too exclusive toward the reachers of my remembrancers,
Picking out here one that I love, and now go with him on brotherly
    terms.                                    700

A gigantic beauty of a stallion, fresh and responsive to my caresses,
Head high in the forehead, wide between the ears,
Limbs glossy and supple, tail dusting the ground,
Eyes full of sparkling wickedness, ears finely cut, flexibly moving.

His nostrils dilate as my heels embrace him,    705
His well-built limbs tremble with pleasure as we race around and return.

I but use you a minute, then I resign you, stallion,
Why do I need your paces when I myself out-gallop them?
Even as I stand or sit passing faster than you.

### 33

Space and Time! now I see it is true, what I guess'd at,    710
What I guess'd when I loaf'd on the grass,
What I guess'd while I lay alone in my bed,
And again as I walk'd the beach under the paling stars of the morning.

My ties and ballasts leave me, my elbows rest in sea-gaps,[6]
I skirt sierras, my palms cover continents,    715
I am afoot with my vision.

By the city's quadrangular houses—in log huts, camping with lumbermen,
Along the ruts of the turnpike, along the dry gulch and rivulet bed,
Weeding my onion-patch or hoeing rows of carrots and parsnips, crossing
    savannas,[7] trailing in forests,
Prospecting, gold-digging, girdling the trees of a new purchase,    720
Scorch'd ankle-deep by the hot sand, hauling my boat down the shallow
    river,

5. Belonging to every form of life.          7. Flat, treeless, tropical grasslands.
6. Estuaries or bays.

Where the panther walks to and fro on a limb overhead, where the buck
    turns furiously at the hunter,
Where the rattlesnake suns his flabby length on a rock, where the otter is
    feeding on fish,
Where the alligator in his tough pimples sleeps by the bayou,
Where the black bear is searching for roots or honey, where the beaver pats
    the mud with his paddle-shaped tail;             725
Over the growing sugar, over the yellow-flower'd cotton plant, over the rice
    in its low moist field,
Over the sharp-peak'd farm house, with its scallop'd scum and slender
    shoots from the gutters,[8]

Over the western persimmon, over the long-leav'd corn, over the delicate
    blue-flower flax,
Over the white and brown buckwheat, a hummer and buzzer there with the
    rest,
Over the dusky green of the rye as it ripples and shades in the breeze;   730
Scaling mountains, pulling myself cautiously up, holding on by low
    scragged limbs,
Walking the path worn in the grass and beat through the leaves of the
    brush,
Where the quail is whistling betwixt the woods and the wheat-lot,
Where the bat flies in the Seventh-month eve, where the great gold-bug[9]
    drops through the dark,
Where the brook puts out of the roots of the old tree and flows to the
    meadow,             735
Where cattle stand and shake away flies with the tremulous shuddering of
    their hides,
Where the cheese-cloth hangs in the kitchen, where andirons straddle the
    hearth-slab, where cobwebs fall in festoons from the rafters;
Where trip-hammers crash, where the press is whirling its cylinders,
Wherever the human heart beats with terrible throes under its ribs,
Where the pear-shaped balloon is floating aloft, (floating in it myself and
    looking composedly down,)          740
Where the life-car[1] is drawn on the slip-noose, where the heat hatches
    pale-green eggs in the dented sand,
Where the she-whale swims with her calf and never forsakes it,
Where the steam-ship trails hind-ways its long pennant of smoke,
Where the fin of the shark cuts like a black chip out of the water,
Where the half-burn'd brig is riding on unknown currents,      745
Where shells grow to her slimy deck, where the dead are corrupting below;
Where the dense-star'd flag is borne at the head of the regiments,
Approaching Manhattan up by the long-stretching island,
Under Niagara, the cataract falling like a veil over my countenance,
Upon a door-step, upon the horse-block of hard wood outside,    750
Upon the race-course, or enjoying picnics or jigs or a good game of
    baseball,

---

8. Presumably debris washed or blown down
roofs, settling into scalloplike shapes in the gutter
and providing nutrients for grasses or weeds.
9. Beetle.

1. Watertight compartment for lowering passengers from a ship when emergency evacuation is
required.

At he-festivals, with blackguard gibes, ironical license, bull-dances,[2]
    drinking, laughter,
At the cider-mill tasting the sweets of the brown mash, sucking the juice
    through a straw,
At apple-peelings wanting kisses for all the red fruit I find,
At musters, beach-parties, friendly bees,[3] huskings, house-raisings;    755
Where the mocking-bird sounds his delicious gurgles, cackles, screams,
    weeps,
Where the hay-rick[4] stands in the barn-yard, where the dry-stalks are
    scatter'd, where the brood-cow waits in the hovel,
Where the bull advances to do his masculine work, where the stud to the
    mare, where the cock is treading the hen,
Where the heifers browse, where geese nip their food with short jerks,
Where sun-down shadows lengthen over the limitless and lonesome prairie,    760
Where herds of buffalo make a crawling spread of the square miles far and
    near,
Where the humming-bird shimmers, where the neck of the long-lived swan
    is curving and winding,
Where the laughing-gull scoots by the shore, where she laughs her near-
    human laugh,
Where bee-hives range on a gray bench in the garden half hid by the high
    weeds,
Where band-neck'd partridges roost in a ring on the ground with their
    heads out,    765
Where burial coaches enter the arch'd gates of a cemetery,
Where winter wolves bark amid wastes of snow and icicled trees,
Where the yellow-crown'd heron comes to the edge of the marsh at night
    and feeds upon small crabs,
Where the splash of swimmers and divers cools the warm noon,
Where the katy-did works her chromatic[5] reed on the walnut-tree over the
    well,    770
Through patches of citrons[6] and cucumbers with silver-wired leaves,
Through the salt-lick or orange glade, or under conical firs,
Through the gymnasium, through the curtain'd saloon, through the office
    or public hall;
Pleas'd with the native and pleas'd with the foreign, pleas'd with the new
    and old,
Pleas'd with the homely woman as well as the handsome,    775
Pleas'd with the quakeress as she puts off her bonnet and talks melodiously,
Pleas'd with the tune of the choir of the whitewash'd church,
Pleas'd with the earnest words of the sweating Methodist preacher,
    impress'd seriously at the camp-meeting;
Looking in at the shop-windows of Broadway the whole forenoon, flatting
    the flesh of my nose on the thick plate glass,

---

2. Rowdy backwoods dances for which, in the absence of women, men took male partners.
3. Gatherings where people work while socializing with their neighbors. "Musters": assemblages of people, particularly gatherings of military troops for drill.
4. Hayracks, from which livestock eat hay.
5. Consisting of chords or harmonies based on nonharmonic tones.
6. Here, small, hard-skinned watermelons.

Wandering the same afternoon with my face turn'd up to the clouds, or
    down a lane or along the beach,       780
My right and left arms round the sides of two friends, and I in the middle;
Coming home with the silent and dark-cheek'd bush-boy, (behind me he
    rides at the drape of the day,)
Far from the settlements studying the print of animals' feet, or the
    moccasin print,
By the cot in the hospital reaching lemonade to a feverish patient,
Nigh the coffin'd corpse when all is still, examining with a candle;   785
Voyaging to every port to dicker and adventure,
Hurrying with the modern crowd as eager and fickle as any,
Hot toward one I hate, ready in my madness to knife him,
Solitary at midnight in my back yard, my thoughts gone from me a long
    while,
Walking the old hills of Judæa with the beautiful gentle God by my side,  790
Speeding through space, speeding through heaven and the stars,
Speeding amid the seven satellites[7] and the broad ring, and the diameter of
    eighty thousand miles,
Speeding with tail'd meteors, throwing fire-balls like the rest,
Carrying the crescent child that carries its own full mother in its belly,[8]
Storming, enjoying, planning, loving, cautioning,   795
Backing and filling, appearing and disappearing,
I tread day and night such roads.

I visit the orchards of spheres and look at the product,
And look at quintillions ripen'd and look at quintillions green.

I fly those flights of a fluid and swallowing soul,   800
My course runs below the soundings of plummets.

I help myself to material and immaterial,
No guard can shut me off, no law prevent me.

I anchor my ship for a little while only,
My messengers continually cruise away or bring their returns to me.   805

I go hunting polar furs and the seal, leaping chasms with a pike-pointed
    staff, clinging to topples of brittle and blue.[9]

I ascend to the foretruck,[1]
I take my place late at night in the crow's-nest,
We sail the arctic sea, it is plenty light enough,
Through the clear atmosphere I stretch around on the wonderful
    beauty,   810
The enormous masses of ice pass me and I pass them, the scenery is plain
    in all directions,
The white-topt mountains show in the distance, I fling out my fancies
    toward them,

---

7. The then-known moons of Saturn.
8. Image of a crescent moon, with the full moon also palely visible.

9. Toppled pieces of ice.
1. Platform of a foremast.

We are approaching some great battle-field in which we are soon to be
    engaged,
We pass the colossal outposts of the encampment, we pass with still feet
    and caution,
Or we are entering by the suburbs some vast and ruin'd city,       815
The blocks and fallen architecture more than all the living cities of the
    globe.

I am a free companion, I bivouac by invading watchfires,
I turn the bridegroom out of bed and stay with the bride myself,
I tighten her all night to my thighs and lips.

My voice is the wife's voice, the screech by the rail of the stairs,    820
They fetch my man's body up dripping and drown'd.

I understand the large hearts of heroes,
The courage of present times and all times,
How the skipper saw the crowded and rudderless wreck of the steam-ship,
    and Death chasing it up and down the storm,
How he knuckled tight and gave not back an inch, and was faithful of days
    and faithful of nights,    825
And chalk'd in large letters on a board, *Be of good cheer, we will not desert
    you;*
How he follow'd with them and tack'd with them three days and would not
    give it up,
How he saved the drifting company at last,
How the lank loose-gown'd women look'd when boated from the side of
    their prepared graves,
How the silent old-faced infants and the lifted sick, and the sharp-lipp'd
    unshaved men;    830
All this I swallow, it tastes good, I like it well, it becomes mine,
I am the man, I suffer'd, I was there.[2]

The disdain and calmness of martyrs,
The mother of old, condemn'd for a witch, burnt with dry wood, her
    children gazing on,
The hounded slave that flags in the race, leans by the fence, blowing,
    cover'd with sweat,    835
The twinges that sting like needles his legs and neck, the murderous
    buckshot and the bullets,
All these I feel or am.

I am the hounded slave, I wince at the bite of the dogs,
Hell and despair are upon me, crack and again crack the marksmen,
I clutch the rails of the fence, my gore dribs, thinn'd with the ooze of my
    skin,[3]    840
I fall on the weeds and stones,

2. Whitman describes the wreck of the *San Francisco*, which sailed from New York on December 22, 1853, bound for South America, and was caught in a storm a day later. The ship drifted help- lessly until early January. Over 150 died in the disaster, which was reported widely in the New York papers.

3. Dribbles down, diluted with sweat.

The riders spur their unwilling horses, haul close,
Taunt my dizzy ears and beat me violently over the head with whip-stocks.

Agonies are one of my changes of garments,
I do not ask the wounded person how he feels, I myself become the
    wounded person,                                                    845
My hurts turn livid upon me as I lean on a cane and observe.

I am the mash'd fireman with breast-bone broken,
Tumbling walls buried me in their debris,
Heat and smoke I inspired, I heard the yelling shouts of my comrades,
I heard the distant click of their picks and shovels,                 850
They have clear'd the beams away, they tenderly lift me forth.

I lie in the night air in my red shirt, the pervading hush is for my sake,
Painless after all I lie exhausted but not so unhappy,
White and beautiful are the faces around me, the heads are bared of their
    fire-caps,
The kneeling crowd fades with the light of the torches.               855

Distant and dead resuscitate,
They show as the dial or move as the hands of me, I am the clock myself.

I am an old artillerist, I tell of my fort's bombardment,
I am there again.

Again the long roll of the drummers,                                  860
Again the attacking cannon, mortars,
Again to my listening ears the cannon responsive.

I take part, I see and hear the whole,
The cries, curses, roar, the plaudits of well-aim'd shots,
The ambulanza slowly passing trailing its red drip,                  865
Workmen searching after damages, making indispensable repairs,
The fall of grenades through the rent roof, the fan-shaped explosion,
The whizz of limbs, heads, stone, wood, iron, high in the air.

Again gurgles the mouth of my dying general, he furiously waves with his
    hand,
He gasps through the clot *Mind not me—mind—the entrenchments.*      870

## 34

Now I tell what I knew in Texas in my early youth,
(I tell not the fall of Alamo,[4]
Not one escaped to tell the fall of Alamo,

---

4. During the Texan Revolution of 1835–36, emigrants from the United States to Texas—at the
time part of Mexico—attempted to make Texas
into a separate republic. Among battles fought in
what is now the state of Texas were the defense of
the Alamo, which fell on March 6, 1836, after a
siege by Mexican forces beginning on February 23,
when around two hundred men were killed, and
the battle of Goliad, when some four hundred
secessionist troops were killed after surrendering
to the Mexicans on March 19 of the same year.

The hundred and fifty are dumb yet at Alamo,)
'Tis the tale of the murder in cold blood of four hundred and twelve young
    men.       875

Retreating they had form'd in a hollow square with their baggage for
    breastworks,
Nine hundred lives out of the surrounding enemy's, nine times their
    number, was the price they took in advance,
Their colonel was wounded and their ammunition gone,
They treated for an honorable capitulation, receiv'd writing and seal, gave
    up their arms and march'd back prisoners of war.

They were the glory of the race of rangers,      880
Matchless with horse, rifle, song, supper, courtship,
Large, turbulent, generous, handsome, proud, and affectionate,
Bearded, sunburnt, drest in the free costume of hunters,
Not a single one over thirty years of age.

The second First-day morning they were brought out in squads and
    massacred, it was beautiful early summer,      885
The work commenced about five o'clock and was over by eight.

None obey'd the command to kneel,
Some made a mad and helpless rush, some stood stark and straight,
A few fell at once, shot in the temple or heart, the living and dead lay
    together,
The maim'd and mangled dug in the dirt, the new-comers saw
    them there,      890
Some half-kill'd attempted to crawl away,
These were despatch'd with bayonets or batter'd with the blunts of
    muskets,
A youth not seventeen years old seiz'd his assassin till two more came to
    release him,
The three were all torn and cover'd with the boy's blood.

At eleven o'clock began the burning of the bodies;      895
That is the tale of the murder of the four hundred and twelve young men.

## 35

Would you hear of an old-time sea-fight?[5]
Would you learn who won by the light of the moon and stars?
List to the yarn, as my grandmother's father the sailor told it to me.

Our foe was no skulk in his ship I tell you, (said he,)      900
His was the surly English pluck, and there is no tougher or truer, and never
    was, and never will be;
Along the lower'd eve he came horribly raking us.

5. The famous Revolutionary sea battle on September 23, 1779, between the American *Bon-Homme Richard*, commanded by John Paul Jones, and the British *Serapis* off the coast of Yorkshire. When Jones was asked to surrender, he famously declared, "I have not yet begun to fight." He eventually defeated the *Serapis*.

We closed with him, the yards entangled, the cannon touch'd,
My captain lash'd fast with his own hands.

We had receiv'd some eighteen pound shots under the water,                905
On our lower-gun-deck two large pieces had burst at the first fire, killing all
    around and blowing up overhead.

Fighting at sun-down, fighting at dark,
Ten o'clock at night, the full moon well up, our leaks on the gain, and five
    feet of water reported,
The master-at-arms loosing the prisoners confined in the after-hold to give
    them a chance for themselves.

The transit to and from the magazine[6] is now stopt by the sentinels,                910
They see so many strange faces they do not know whom to trust.

Our frigate takes fire,
The other asks if we demand quarter?
If our colors are struck and the fighting done?

Now I laugh content, for I hear the voice of my little captain,                915
*We have not struck,* he composedly cries, *we have just begun our part of the*
    *fighting.*

Only three guns are in use,
One is directed by the captain himself against the enemy's mainmast,
Two well serv'd with grape and canister[7] silence his musketry and clear his
    decks.

The tops[8] alone second the fire of this little battery, especially the
    main-top,                920
They hold out bravely during the whole of the action.

Not a moment's cease,
The leaks gain fast on the pumps, the fire eats toward the powder-
    magazine.

One of the pumps has been shot away, it is generally thought we are
    sinking.

Serene stands the little captain,                925
He is not hurried, his voice is neither high nor low,
His eyes give more light to us than our battle-lanterns.

Toward twelve there in the beams of the moon they surrender to us.


### 36

Stretch'd and still lies the midnight,
Two great hulls motionless on the breast of the darkness,                930

6. Storeroom for ammunition.
7. Grapeshot ("grape"), clusters of small iron balls, was packed inside a metal cylinder ("canister") and used to charge a cannon.
8. Platforms enclosing the heads of each mast; here, the sailors manning the tops.

Our vessel riddled and slowly sinking, preparations to pass to the one we
　　have conquer'd,
The captain on the quarter-deck coldly giving his orders through a
　　countenance white as a sheet,
Near by the corpse of the child that serv'd in the cabin,
The dead face of an old salt with long white hair and carefully curl'd
　　whiskers,
The flames spite of all that can be done flickering aloft and below,　　935
The husky voices of the two or three officers yet fit for duty,
Formless stacks of bodies and bodies by themselves, dabs of flesh upon the
　　masts and spars,
Cut of cordage, dangle of rigging, slight shock of the soothe of waves,
Black and impassive guns, litter of powder-parcels, strong scent,
A few large stars overhead, silent and mournful shining,　　940
Delicate sniffs of sea-breeze, smells of sedgy grass and fields by the shore,
　　death-messages given in charge to survivors,
The hiss of the surgeon's knife, the gnawing teeth of his saw,
Wheeze, cluck, swash of falling blood, short wild scream, and long, dull,
　　tapering groan,
These so, these irretrievable.


### 37

You laggards there on guard! look to your arms!　　945
In at the conquer'd doors they crowd! I am possess'd!
Embody all presences outlaw'd or suffering,
See myself in prison shaped like another man,
And feel the dull unintermitted pain.

For me the keepers of convicts shoulder their carbines and keep watch,　　950
It is I let out in the morning and barr'd at night.

Not a mutineer walks handcuff'd to jail but I am handcuff'd to him and
　　walk by his side,
(I am less the jolly one there, and more the silent one with sweat on my
　　twitching lips.)

Not a youngster is taken for larceny but I go up too, and am tried and
　　sentenced.

Not a cholera patient lies at the last gasp but I also lie at the last gasp,　　955
My face is ash-color'd, my sinews gnarl, away from me people retreat.

Askers embody themselves in me and I am embodied in them,
I project my hat, sit shame-faced, and beg.


### 38

Enough! enough! enough!
Somehow I have been stunn'd. Stand back!　　960
Give me a little time beyond my cuff'd head, slumbers, dreams, gaping,
I discover myself on the verge of a usual mistake.

That I could forget the mockers and insults!
That I could forget the trickling tears and the blows of the bludgeons and
    hammers!
That I could look with a separate look on my own crucifixion and bloody
    crowning.                                                                    965

I remember now,
I resume the overstaid fraction,
The grave of rock multiplies what has been confided to it, or to any graves,
Corpses rise, gashes heal, fastenings roll from me.

I troop forth replenish'd with supreme power, one of an average unending
    procession,                                                                 970
Inland and sea-coast we go, and pass all boundary lines,
Our swift ordinances on their way over the whole earth,
The blossoms we wear in our hats the growth of thousands of years.

Eleves,[9] I salute you! come forward!
Continue your annotations, continue your questionings.                          975

39

The friendly and flowing savage, who is he?
Is he waiting for civilization, or past it and mastering it?

Is he some Southwesterner rais'd out-doors? is he Kanadian?
Is he from the Mississippi country? Iowa, Oregon, California?
The mountains? prairie-life, bush-life? or sailor from the sea?                 980

Wherever he goes men and women accept and desire him,
They desire he should like them, touch them, speak to them, stay with
    them.

Behavior lawless as snow-flakes, words simple as grass, uncomb'd head,
    laughter, and naivetè,
Slow-stepping feet, common features, common modes and emanations,
They descend in new forms from the tips of his fingers,                         985
They are wafted with the odor of his body or breath, they fly out of the
    glance of his eyes.

40

Flaunt of the sunshine I need not your bask—lie over!
You light surfaces only, I force surfaces and depths also.

Earth! you seem to look for something at my hands,
Say, old top-knot,[1] what do you want?                                         990

---

9. Students (French).
1. An epithet common in frontier humor, deriving
from the fact that some Native Americans gathered
their hair into tufts at the top of the head. The poet
seems to be addressing an older Indian, perhaps
picking up on the reference to "the friendly and
flowing savage" of the previous stanza.

Man or woman, I might tell how I like you, but cannot,
And might tell what it is in me and what it is in you, but cannot,
And might tell that pining I have, that pulse of my nights and days.

Behold, I do not give lectures or a little charity,
When I give I give myself.                                          995

You there, impotent, loose in the knees,
Open your scarf'd chops till I blow grit² within you,
Spread your palms and lift the flaps of your pockets,
I am not to be denied, I compel, I have stores plenty and to spare,
And any thing I have I bestow.                                     1000

I do not ask who you are, that is not important to me,
You can do nothing and be nothing but what I will infold you.

To cotton-field drudge or cleaner of privies I lean,
On his right cheek I put the family kiss,
And in my soul I swear I never will deny him.                     1005

On women fit for conception I start bigger and nimbler babes,
(This day I am jetting the stuff of far more arrogant republics.)

To any one dying, thither I speed and twist the knob of the door,
Turn the bed-clothes toward the foot of the bed,
Let the physician and the priest go home.                         1010

I seize the descending man and raise him with resistless will,
O despairer, here is my neck,
By God, you shall not go down! hang your whole weight upon me.

I dilate you with tremendous breath, I buoy you up,
Every room of the house do I fill with an arm'd force,            1015
Lovers of me, bafflers of graves.

Sleep—I and they keep guard all night,
Not doubt, not decease shall dare to lay finger upon you,
I have embraced you, and henceforth possess you to myself,
And when you rise in the morning you will find what I tell you is so.   1020

### 41

I am he bringing help for the sick as they pant on their backs,
And for strong upright men I bring yet more needed help.

I heard what was said of the universe,
Heard it and heard it of several thousand years;
It is middling well as far as it goes—but is that all?            1025

---

2. Courage. "Scarf'd chops": lined, worn-down jaw or face.

Magnifying and applying come I,
Outbidding at the start the old cautious hucksters,
Taking myself the exact dimensions of Jehovah,[3]
Lithographing Kronos, Zeus his son, and Hercules[4] his grandson,
Buying drafts of Osiris, Isis, Belus, Brahma, Buddha,[5]                    1030
In my portfolio placing Manito loose, Allah[6] on a leaf, the crucifix
    engraved,
With Odin and the hideous-faced Mexitli[7] and every idol and image,
Taking them all for what they are worth and not a cent more,
Admitting they were alive and did the work of their days,
(They bore mites as for unfledg'd birds who have now to rise and fly and
    sing for themselves,)                                      1035
Accepting the rough deific sketches to fill out better in myself, bestowing
    them freely on each man and woman I see,
Discovering as much or more in a framer framing a house,
Putting higher claims for him there with his roll'd-up sleeves driving the
    mallet and chisel,
Not objecting to special revelations, considering a curl of smoke or a hair
    on the back of my hand just as curious as any revelation,
Lads ahold of fire-engines and hook-and-ladder ropes no less to me than
    the gods of the antique wars,                                  1040
Minding their voices peal through the crash of destruction,
Their brawny limbs passing safe over charr'd laths, their white foreheads
    whole and unhurt out of the flames;
By the mechanic's wife with her babe at her nipple interceding for every
    person born,
Three scythes at harvest whizzing in a row from three lusty angels with
    shirts bagg'd out at their waists,
The snag-tooth'd hostler with red hair redeeming sins past and to come, 1045
Selling all he possesses, traveling on foot to fee lawyers for his brother and
    sit by him while he is tried for forgery;
What was strewn in the amplest strewing the square rod about me, and not
    filling the square rod then,
The bull and the bug never worshipp'd half enough,[8]
Dung and dirt more admirable than was dream'd,
The supernatural of no account, myself waiting my time to be one of the
    supremes,                                                     1050
The day getting ready for me when I shall do as much good as the best, and
    be as prodigious;
By my life-lumps![9] becoming already a creator,
Putting myself here and now to the ambush'd womb of the shadows.

---

3. God of the Jews and Christians.
4. Kronos (or Cronus), in Greek mythology, was the Titan who ruled the universe until dethroned by Zeus, his son, the chief of the Olympian gods. Hercules was the son of Zeus and the mortal Alcmene, won immortality by performing twelve supposedly impossible feats.
5. The Indian philosopher Gautama Siddhartha, founder of Buddhism. Osiris was the Egyptian god who annually died and was reborn, symbolizing the fertility of nature. Isis was the Egyptian goddess of fertility and the sister and wife of Osiris. Belus was a legendary god-king of Assyria. Brahma, in Hinduism, was the divine reality in the role of creator.
6. The supreme being in Islam. Manito was the nature god of the Algonquian Indians.
7. An Aztec war god. Odin was the chief Norse god.
8. As Whitman implies, the bull and the bug had in fact been worshiped in earlier religions, the bull in several, the scarab beetle as an Egyptian symbol of the soul; but they had been worshiped wrongly, as supernatural objects.
9. Testicles.

## 42

A call in the midst of the crowd,
My own voice, orotund sweeping and final.                    1055

Come my children,
Come my boys and girls, my women, household and intimates,
Now the performer launches his nerve, he has pass'd his prelude on the
    reeds within.

Easily written loose-finger'd chords—I feel the thrum of your climax and
    close.

My head slues round on my neck,                              1060
Music rolls, but not from the organ,
Folks are around me, but they are no household of mine.

Ever the hard unsunk ground,
Ever the eaters and drinkers, ever the upward and downward sun, ever the
    air and the ceaseless tides,
Ever myself and my neighbors, refreshing, wicked, real,      1065
Ever the old inexplicable query, ever that thorn'd thumb, that breath of
    itches and thirsts,
Ever the vexer's *hoot! hoot!* till we find where the sly one hides and bring
    him forth,
Ever love, ever the sobbing liquid of life,
Ever the bandage under the chin, ever the trestles[1] of death.

Here and there with dimes on the eyes[2] walking,            1070
To feed the greed of the belly the brains liberally spooning,
Tickets buying, taking, selling, but in to the feast never once going,
Many sweating, ploughing, thrashing, and then the chaff for payment
    receiving,
A few idly owning, and they the wheat continually claiming.

This is the city and I am one of the citizens,               1075
Whatever interests the rest interests me, politics, wars, markets,
    newspapers, schools,
The mayor and councils, banks, tariffs, steamships, factories, stocks, stores,
    real estate and personal estate.

The little plentiful manikins skipping around in collars and tail'd coats,
I am aware who they are, (they are positively not worms or fleas,)
I acknowledge the duplicates of myself, the weakest and shallowest is
    deathless with me,                                        1080
What I do and say the same waits for them,
Every thought that flounders in me the same flounders in them.

---

1. Sawhorses or similar supports holding up a coffin.

2. Coins were placed on eyelids to hold them closed until burial.

I know perfectly well my own egotism,
Know my omnivorous lines and must not write any less,
And would fetch you whoever you are flush with myself.                    1085
Not words of routine this song of mine,
But abruptly to question, to leap beyond yet nearer bring;
This printed and bound book—but the printer and the printing-office boy?
The well-taken photographs—but your wife or friend close and solid in
    your arms?
The black ship mail'd with iron, her mighty guns in her turrets—but the
    pluck of the captain and engineers?                                    1090
In the houses the dishes and fare and furniture—but the host and hostess,
    and the look out of their eyes?
The sky up there—yet here or next door, or across the way?
The saints and sages in history—but you yourself?
Sermons, creeds, theology—but the fathomless human brain,
And what is reason? and what is love? and what is life?                    1095


### 43

I do not despise you priests, all time, the world over,
My faith is the greatest of faiths and the least of faiths,
Enclosing worship ancient and modern and all between ancient and
    modern,
Believing I shall come again upon the earth after five thousand years,
Waiting responses from oracles, honoring the gods, saluting the sun,       1100
Making a fetich of the first rock or stump, powowing with sticks in the
    circle of obis.[3]
Helping the llama or brahmin[4] as he trims the lamps of the idols,
Dancing yet through the streets in a phallic procession, rapt and austere in
    the woods a gymnosophist,[5]
Drinking mead from the skull-cup, to Shastas and Vedas admirant, minding
    the Koran,[6]
Walking the teokallis,[7] spotted with gore from the stone and knife, beating
    the serpent-skin drum,                                                 1105
Accepting the Gospels,[8] accepting him that was crucified, knowing
    assuredly that he is divine,
To the mass kneeling or the puritan's prayer rising, or sitting patiently in a
    pew,
Ranting and frothing in my insane crisis, or waiting dead-like till my spirit
    arouses me,
Looking forth on pavement and land, or outside of pavement and land,
Belonging to the winders of the circuit of circuits.                       1110

---

3. Magical charms, such as shells, used in African and West Indian religious practices. "Fetich": i.e., fetish; object of worship.
4. Here, also a Buddhist priest. "Llama": i.e., lama; a Buddhist monk of Tibet or Mongolia.
5. Members of an ancient Hindu ascetic sect.
6. The other worshipers include old Teutonic drinkers of mead (an alcoholic beverage made of fermented honey), admiring or wondering readers of the sastras (or shastras or shasters, books of Hindu law) or of the Vedas (the oldest sacred writings of Hinduism), those attentive to the Koran (the sacred book of Islam, containing Allah's revelations to Muhammad).
7. An ancient Central American temple built on a pyramidal mound.
8. Of the New Testament of the Bible.

One of that centripetal and centrifugal gang I turn and talk like a man
    leaving charges before a journey.

Down-hearted doubters dull and excluded,
Frivolous, sullen, moping, angry, affected, dishearten'd, atheistical,
I know every one of you, I know the sea of torment, doubt, despair and
    unbelief.

How the flukes[9] splash!        1115
How they contort rapid as lightning, with spasms and spouts of blood!

Be at peace bloody flukes of doubters and sullen mopers,
I take my place among you as much as among any,
The past is the push of you, me, all, precisely the same,
And what is yet untried and afterward is for you, me, all, precisely the
    same.        1120

I do not know what is untried and afterward,
But I know it will in its turn prove sufficient, and cannot fail.

Each who passes is consider'd, each who stops is consider'd, not a single
    one can it fail.

It cannot fail the young man who died and was buried,
Nor the young woman who died and was put by his side,    1125
Nor the little child that peep'd in at the door, and then drew back and was
    never seen again,
Nor the old man who has lived without purpose, and feels it with bitterness
    worse than gall,
Nor him in the poor house tubercled by rum and the bad disorder,[1]

Nor the numberless slaughter'd and wreck'd, nor the brutish koboo[2] call'd
    the ordure of humanity,
Nor the sacs merely floating with open mouths for food to slip in,    1130
Nor any thing in the earth, or down in the oldest graves of the earth,
Nor any thing in the myriads of spheres, nor the myriads of myriads that
    inhabit them,
Nor the present, nor the least wisp that is known.

### 44

It is time to explain myself—let us stand up.

What is known I strip away,    1135
I launch all men and women forward with me into the Unknown.

The clock indicates the moment—but what does eternity indicate?

We have thus far exhausted trillions of winters and summers,
There are trillions ahead, and trillions ahead of them.

---

9. The flat parts on either side of a whale's tail;
here used figuratively.

1. Syphilis.
2. Native of Sumatra.

Births have brought us richness and variety,                                          1140
And other births will bring us richness and variety.

I do not call one greater and one smaller,
That which fills its period and place is equal to any.

Were mankind murderous or jealous upon you, my brother, my sister?
I am sorry for you, they are not murderous or jealous upon me,                         1145
All has been gentle with me, I keep no account with lamentation,
(What have I to do with lamentation?)

I am an acme of things accomplish'd, and I an encloser of things to be.

My feet strike an apex of the apices[3] of the stairs,
On every step bunches of ages, and larger bunches between the steps,                   1150
All below duly travel'd, and still I mount and mount.

Rise after rise bow the phantoms behind me,
Afar down I see the huge first Nothing, I know I was even there,
I waited unseen and always, and slept through the lethargic mist,
And took my time, and took no hurt from the fetid carbon.[4]                           1155

Long I was hugg'd close—long and long.

Immense have been the preparations for me,
Faithful and friendly the arms that have help'd me.

Cycles[5] ferried my cradle, rowing and rowing like cheerful boatmen,
For room to me stars kept aside in their own rings,                                    1160
They sent influences to look after what was to hold me.

Before I was born out of my mother generations guided me,
My embryo has never been torpid, nothing could overlay it.

For it the nebula cohered to an orb,
The long slow strata piled to rest it on,                                              1165
Vast vegetables gave it sustenance,
Monstrous sauroids[6] transported it in their mouths and deposited it with
    care.

All forces have been steadily employ'd to complete and delight me,
Now on this spot I stand with my robust soul.

### 45

O span of youth! ever-push'd elasticity!                                              1170
O manhood, balanced, florid and full.

---

3. The highest points (variant plural of *apex*).
4. The "lethargic mist" (line 1154) and "fetid carbon" suggest a time before the appearance of human beings on earth.

5. Centuries.
6. Prehistoric mammoth reptiles or dinosaurs, thought to have carried their eggs in their mouths.

My lovers suffocate me,
Crowding my lips, thick in the pores of my skin,
Jostling me through streets and public halls, coming naked to me at night,
Crying by day *Ahoy!* from the rocks of the river, swinging and chirping over
    my head,          1175
Calling my name from flower-beds, vines, tangled underbrush,
Lighting on every moment of my life,
Bussing[7] my body with soft balsamic busses,
Noiselessly passing handfuls out of their hearts and giving them to be
    mine.

Old age superbly rising! O welcome, ineffable grace of dying days!    1180

Every condition promulges[8] not only itself, it promulges what grows after
    and out of itself,
And the dark hush promulges as much as any.

I open my scuttle[9] at night and see the far-sprinkled systems,
And all I see multiplied as high as I can cipher edge but the rim of the
    farther systems.

Wider and wider they spread, expanding, always expanding,    1185
Outward and outward and forever outward.

My sun has his sun and round him obediently wheels,
He joins with his partners a group of superior circuit,
And greater sets follow, making specks of the greatest inside them.

There is no stoppage and never can be stoppage,    1190
If I, you, and the worlds, and all beneath or upon their surfaces, were this
    moment reduced back to a pallid float,[1] it would not avail in the long
    run,
We should surely bring up again where we now stand,
And surely go as much farther, and then farther and farther.

A few quadrillions of eras, a few octillions of cubic leagues, do not hazard[2]
    the span or make it impatient,
They are but parts, any thing is but a part.    1195

See ever so far, there is limitless space outside of that,
Count ever so much, there is limitless time around that.

My rendezvous is appointed, it is certain,
The Lord will be there and wait till I come on perfect terms,
The great Camerado, the lover true for whom I pine will be there.    1200

### 46

I know I have the best of time and space, and was never measured and
    never will be measured.

---

7. Kissing.
8. Promulgates, officially announces.
9. Roof hatch.

1. That period before the solar system had defined
itself.
2. Imperil, make hazardous.

I tramp a perpetual journey, (come listen all!)
My signs are a rain-proof coat, good shoes, and a staff cut from the woods,
No friend of mine takes his ease in my chair,
I have no chair, no church, no philosophy,                                    1205
I lead no man to a dinner-table, library, exchange,[3]
But each man and each woman of you I lead upon a knoll,
My left hand hooking you round the waist,
My right hand pointing to landscapes of continents and the public road.

Not I, not any one else can travel that road for you,                         1210
You must travel it for yourself.

It is not far, it is within reach,
Perhaps you have been on it since you were born and did not know,
Perhaps it is everywhere on water and on land.

Shoulder your duds dear son, and I will mine, and let us hasten forth,        1215
Wonderful cities and free nations we shall fetch as we go.

If you tire, give me both burdens, and rest the chuff[4] of your hand on my
     hip,
And in due time you shall repay the same service to me,
For after we start we never lie by again.

This day before dawn I ascended a hill and look'd at the crowded
     heaven,                                                                  1220
And I said to my spirit *When we become the enfolders of those orbs,
     and the pleasure and knowledge of every thing in them, shall we be
     fill'd and satisfied then?*
And my spirit said *No, we but level that lift to pass and continue beyond.*

You are also asking me questions and I hear you,
I answer that I cannot answer, you must find out for yourself.

Sit a while dear son,                                                         1225
Here are biscuits to eat and here is milk to drink,
But as soon as you sleep and renew yourself in sweet clothes, I kiss you
     with a good-by kiss and open the gate for your egress hence.

Long enough have you dream'd contemptible dreams,
Now I wash the gum from your eyes,
You must habit yourself to the dazzle of the light and of every moment of
     your life.                                                              1230

Long have you timidly waded holding a plank by the shore,
Now I will you to be a bold swimmer,
To jump off in the midst of the sea, rise again, nod to me, shout, and
     laughingly dash with your hair.

---

3. Stock exchange.                          4. The fleshy part of the palm.

47

I am the teacher of athletes,
He that by me spreads a wider breast than my own proves the width of my
    own,                                                                                    1235
He most honors my style who learns under it to destroy the teacher.

The boy I love, the same becomes a man not through derived power, but in
    his own right,
Wicked rather than virtuous out of conformity or fear,
Fond of his sweetheart, relishing well his steak,
Unrequited love or a slight cutting him worse than sharp steel cuts,        1240
First-rate to ride, to fight, to hit the bull's eye, to sail a skiff, to sing a song
    or play on the banjo,
Preferring scars and the beard and faces pitted with small-pox over all
    latherers,
And those well-tann'd to those that keep out of the sun.

I teach straying from me, yet who can stray from me?
I follow you whoever you are from the present hour,                         1245
My words itch at your ears till you understand them.

I do not say these things for a dollar or to fill up the time while I wait for a
    boat,
(It is you talking just as much as myself, I act as the tongue of you,
Tied in your mouth, in mine it begins to be loosen'd.)

I swear I will never again mention love or death inside a house,            1250
And I swear I will never translate myself at all, only to him or her who
    privately stays with me in the open air.

If you would understand me go to the heights or water-shore,
The nearest gnat is an explanation, and a drop or motion of waves a key,
The maul, the oar, the hand-saw, second my words.

No shutter'd room or school can commune with me,                           1255
But roughs and little children better than they.

The young mechanic is closest to me, he knows me well,
The woodman that takes his axe and jug with him shall take me with him
    all day,
The farm-boy ploughing in the field feels good at the sound of my voice,
In vessels that sail my words sail, I go with fishermen and seamen and love
    them.                                                                                  1260

The soldier camp'd or upon the march is mine,
On the night ere the pending battle many seek me, and I do not fail them,
On that solemn night (it may be their last) those that know me seek me.

My face rubs to the hunter's face when he lies down alone in his blanket,
The driver thinking of me does not mind the jolt of his wagon,             1265
The young mother and old mother comprehend me,

The girl and the wife rest the needle a moment and forget where they are,
They and all would resume what I have told them.

### 48

I have said that the soul is not more than the body,
And I have said that the body is not more than the soul,                    1270
And nothing, not God, is greater to one than one's self is,
And whoever walks a furlong without sympathy walks to his own funeral
    drest in his shroud,
And I or you pocketless of a dime may purchase the pick of the earth,
And to glance with an eye or show a bean in its pod confounds the learning
    of all times,
And there is no trade or employment but the young man following it may
    become a hero,                    1275
And there is no object so soft but it makes a hub for the wheel'd universe,
And I say to any man or woman, Let your soul stand cool and composed
    before a million universes.

And I say to mankind, Be not curious about God,
For I who am curious about each am not curious about God,
(No array of terms can say how much I am at peace about God and about
    death.)                    1280

I hear and behold God in every object, yet understand God not in the least,
Nor do I understand who there can be more wonderful than myself.

Why should I wish to see God better than this day?
I see something of God each hour of the twenty-four, and each moment
    then,
In the faces of men and women I see God, and in my own face in
    the glass,                    1285
I find letters from God dropt in the street, and every one is sign'd by God's
    name,
And I leave them where they are, for I know that wheresoe'er I go,
Others will punctually come for ever and ever.

### 49

And as to you Death, and you bitter hug of mortality, it is idle to try to
    alarm me.

To his work without flinching the accoucheur[5] comes,                    1290
I see the elder-hand pressing receiving supporting,
I recline by the sills of the exquisite flexible doors,
And mark the outlet, and mark the relief and escape.

And as to you Corpse I think you are good manure, but that does not
    offend me,
I smell the white roses sweet-scented and growing,                    1295
I reach to the leafy lips, I reach to the polish'd breasts of melons.

5. Midwife.

And as to you Life I reckon you are the leavings of many deaths,
(No doubt I have died myself ten thousand times before.)

I hear you whispering there O stars of heaven,
O suns—O grass of graves—O perpetual transfers and promotions,    1300
If you do not say any thing how can I say any thing?
Of the turbid pool that lies in the autumn forest,
Of the moon that descends the steeps of the soughing twilight,
Toss, sparkles of day and dusk—toss on the black stems that decay in the
    muck,
Toss to the moaning gibberish of the dry limbs.    1305

I ascend from the moon, I ascend from the night,
I perceive that the ghastly glimmer is noonday sunbeams reflected,
And debouch[6] to the steady and central from the offspring great or small.

## 50

There is that in me—I do not know what it is—but I know it is in me.

Wrench'd and sweaty—calm and cool then my body becomes, I sleep—I
    sleep long.    1310

I do not know it—it is without name—it is a word unsaid,
It is not in any dictionary, utterance, symbol.

Something it swings on more than the earth I swing on,
To it the creation is the friend whose embracing awakes me.

Perhaps I might tell more. Outlines! I plead for my brothers and sisters.    1315
Do you see O my brothers and sisters?
It is not chaos or death—it is form, union, plan—it is eternal life—it is
    Happiness.

## 51

The past and present wilt—I have fill'd them, emptied them,
And proceed to fill my next fold of the future.

Listener up there! what have you to confide to me?    1320
Look in my face while I snuff the sidle[7] of evening,
(Talk honestly, no one else hears you, and I stay only a minute longer.)

Do I contradict myself?
Very well then I contradict myself,
(I am large, I contain multitudes.)    1325

I concentrate toward them that are nigh, I wait on the door-slab.

6. Pour forth.
7. To snuff is to put out, as in extinguishing a can-

dle; here the light is the hesitant last light of day,
sidling or moving along sideways.

Who has done his day's work? who will soonest be through with his supper?
Who wishes to walk with me?

Will you speak before I am gone? will you prove already too late?

### 52

The spotted hawk swoops by and accuses me, he complains of my gab and
    my loitering.        1330

I too am not a bit tamed, I too am untranslatable.
I sound my barbaric yawp over the roofs of the world.

The last scud of day[8] holds back for me,
It flings my likeness after the rest and true as any on the shadow'd wilds,
It coaxes me to the vapor and the dusk.        1335

I depart as air, I shake my white locks at the runaway sun,
I effuse my flesh in eddies,[9] and drift it in lacy jabs.

I bequeath myself to the dirt to grow from the grass I love,
If you want me again look for me under your boot-soles.

You will hardly know who I am or what I mean,        1340
But I shall be good health to you nevertheless,
And filter and fibre your blood.

Failing to fetch me at first keep encouraged,
Missing me one place search another,
I stop somewhere waiting for you.        1345

                            1855, 1881

8. Wind-driven clouds, or merely the last rays of the sun.    9. Air currents. "Effuse": pour forth.

---

# EMILY DICKINSON
## 1830–1886

With her formal experimentation and bold thematic ambitions, Emily Dickinson is recognized as one of the greatest American poets, a poet who continues to exert an enormous influence on the way writers think about the possibilities of poetic craft and vocation. Little known in her own lifetime, she was first publicized in almost mythic terms as a reclusive, eccentric, death-obsessed spinster who wrote in fits and starts as the spirit moved her—the image of the woman poet at her oddest. As with all myths, this one has some truth in it, but the reality is more interesting and complicated. Though she lived in her parents' homes for all but a year of her life, she was acutely aware of current events and drew on them for some of her poetry. Her dazzlingly complex lyrics—compressed statements abounding in startling imagery and marked by an extraordinary vocabulary—explore a wide range of subjects: psychic pain and joy, the relationship of self to nature, the intensely spiritual, and the intensely ordinary. Her poems about death confront its grim reality with honesty, humor, curiosity, and above all a refusal to be comforted. In her poems about religion, she expressed piety and hostility, and she was fully capable of moving within the same poem from religious consolation to a rejection of doctrinal piety and a querying of God's plans for the universe. Her many love poems seem to have emerged in part from close relationships with at least one woman and several men. It is sometimes possible to extract autobiography from her poems, but she was not a confessional poet; rather, she used personae— invented first-person speakers—to dramatize the various situations, moods, and perspectives she explored in her lyrics. Though each of her poems is individually short, when collected in one volume, her nearly eighteen hundred surviving poems (she probably wrote hundreds more that were lost) have the feel of an epic produced by a person who devoted much of her life to her art.

Emily Elizabeth Dickinson was born on December 10, 1830, in Amherst, Massachusetts, the second child of Emily Norcross Dickinson and Edward Dickinson. Economically, politically, and intellectually, the Dickinsons were among Amherst's most prominent families. Edward Dickinson, a lawyer, served as a state representative and a state senator. He helped found Amherst College as a Calvinist alternative to the more liberal Harvard and Yale, and was its treasurer for thirty-six years. During his term in the national House of Representatives (1853–54), Emily visited him in Washington and stayed briefly in Philadelphia on her way home, but travel of any kind was unusual for her. She lived most of her life in the spacious Dickinson family house in Amherst called the Homestead. Among her closest friends and lifelong allies were her brother, Austin, a year and a half older than she, and her younger sister, Lavinia. In 1856, when her brother married Emily's close friend Susan Gilbert, the couple moved into what was called the Evergreens, a house next door to the Homestead, built for the newlyweds by Edward Dickinson. Neither Emily nor Lavinia married. The two women stayed with their parents, as was typical of unmarried middle- and upper-class women of the time. New England in this period had many more women than men in these groups, owing to the male population exodus during the gold rush years (1849 and after) and the carnage of the Civil War. For Dickinson, home was a place of "Infinite power."

Dickinson attended Amherst Academy from 1840 through 1846, and then boarded for less than a year at the Mount Holyoke Female Seminary in South Hadley, ten miles from Amherst. She quickly became intensely homesick for her *"own* DEAR HOME" and never completed the three-year course of study, dropping out in less than a year. Her stay at Mount Holyoke was not just a time of homesickness but of religious crisis. The school, presided over by the energetic Mary Lyon, sought to develop women intellectually and spiritually so that some might one day serve as Christian missionaries. In line with the Seminary's Calvinist expectations that individuals would experience a religious awakening as a sign of divine favor, students were regularly queried as to whether they "professed faith," had "hope," or were resigned to "no hope." Dickinson remained adamantly among the small group of "no hopes." Arguably, her assertion of no hope was a matter of defiance, a refusal to capitulate to the demands of orthodoxy. A year after leaving Mount Holyoke, Dickinson, in a letter to a friend, described her failure to convert with darkly comic glee: "*I am one of the lingering bad ones,*" she said. But she went on to assert that it was her very "failure" to conform to the conventional expectations of her evangelical culture that helped to liberate her to think on her own—to "pause," as she put it, "and ponder, and ponder."

Once back at home, Dickinson embarked on a lifelong course of reading. Her deepest literary debts were to the Bible and classic English authors, such as Shakespeare and Milton. Through the national magazines the family subscribed to and books ordered from Boston, she encountered the full range of the English and American literature of her time, including among Americans Longfellow, Holmes, Lowell, Hawthorne, and Emerson. Characteristically, however, she did not go next door to meet Emerson in 1857 when he stayed at the Evergreens during a lecture tour—preferring the Emerson she could imagine to the actual presence. She read the novels of

Charles Dickens as they appeared and knew the poems of Robert Browning and the poet laureate Tennyson. But the English contemporaries who mattered most to her were the Brontë sisters, George Eliot, and above all, as an example of a successful contemporary woman poet, Elizabeth Barrett Browning.

No one has persuasively traced the precise stages of Dickinson's artistic growth from this supposedly "somber Girl" to the young woman who, within a few years of her return from Mount Holyoke, began writing a new kind of poetry, with its distinctive voice, style, and transformation of traditional form. She found a paradoxical poetic freedom within the confines of the meter of the "fourteener"—seven-beat lines usually broken into stanzas alternating four and three beats—familiar to her from earliest childhood. This is the form of nursery rhymes, ballads, church hymns, and some classic English poetry—strongly rhythmical, easy to memorize and recite. But Dickinson veered sharply from this form's expectations. If Walt Whitman at this time was heeding Emerson's call for a "metre-making argument" by turning to an open form—as though rules did not exist—Dickinson made use of this and other familiar forms only to break their rules. She used dashes and syntactical fragments to convey her pursuit of a truth that could best be communicated indirectly; these fragments dispensed with prosy verbiage and went directly to the core. Her use of enjambment (the syntactical technique of running past the conventional stopping place of a line or a stanza break) forced her reader to learn where to pause to collect the sense before reading on, often creating dizzying ambiguities. She multiplied aural possibilities by making use of what later critics termed "off" or "slant" rhymes that, as with her metrical and syntactical experimentations, contributed to the expressive power of her poetry. In short, poetic forms thought to be simple, predictable, and safe were altered irrevocably by Dickinson's language experiments with the lyric. Along with its opposite, free verse, the compressed lyric flaunting its refusal to conform became a hallmark of modernist poetry in the twentieth century.

Writing about religion, science, music, nature, books, and contemporary events both national and local, Dickinson often presented her poetic ideas as terse, striking definitions or propositions, or dramatic narrative scenes, in a highly abstracted moment, or setting, often at the boundaries between life and death. The result was a poetry that, as is typical of the lyric tradition, focused on the speaker's response to a situation rather than the details of the situation itself. Her "nature" poems offer sharp, precise observations but, infused with mingled ecstasy and pain, are often as much about psychological and spiritual matters as about the specifics of nature. The sight of a familiar bird—the robin—in the poem beginning "A bird came down the walk" leads to a statement about nature's strangeness rather than the expected statement about friendly animals. Whitman generally seems intoxicated by his ability to appropriate nature for his own purposes; Dickinson's nature is much more resistant to human schemes, and the poet's experiences of nature range from a sense of its hostility to an ability to become an "Inebriate of Air" and "Debauchee of Dew." Openly expressive of sexual and romantic longings, her personae reject conventional gender roles. In one of her most famous poems, for instance, she imagines herself as a "Loaded Gun" with "the power to kill."

Dickinson's private letters, in particular three drafts of letters to an unidentified "Master," and dozens of love poems have convinced biographers that she fell in love a number of times; candidates include Benjamin Newton, a law clerk in her father's office; one or more married men; and above all, Susan Gilbert Dickinson, the friend who became her sister-in-law. The exact nature of any of these relationships is hard to determine, in part because Dickinson's letters and poems could just as easily be taken as poetic meditations on desire as writings directed to specific people. On the evidence of the approximately five hundred letters that Dickinson wrote Susan, many of which contained drafts or copies of her latest poems, that relationship would appear to have been the most passionate (and long-lived) of Dickinson's life. Whatever the nature of their relationship, it melded love, friendship, intellectual exchange, and art.

One of the men she was involved with was Samuel Bowles, editor of the Springfield *Republican*, whom Dickinson described (in a letter to Bowles himself) as having "the most triumphant face out of paradise"; another was the Reverend Charles Wadsworth, whom she met in Philadelphia in 1855 and who visited her in Amherst in 1860. Evidence suggests that she was upset by his decision to move to San Francisco in 1862, but none of her letters to Wadsworth survive.

Knowing her powers as a poet, Dickinson wanted to be published, but only around a dozen poems appeared during her lifetime. She sent many poems to Bowles, perhaps hoping he would publish them in the *Republican*. Although he did publish a few, he also edited them into more conventional shape. She also sent poems to editor Josiah Holland at *Scribner's*, who chose not to publish her. She sent a few poems to Thomas Wentworth Higginson, editor at the *Atlantic Monthly*, after he printed "Letter to a Young Contributor" in the April 1862 issue. Her cover letter of April 15, 1862, asked him, "Are you too deeply occupied to say if my Verse is alive?" Higginson, like other editors, saw her formal innovations as imperfections. But he remained intrigued by Dickinson and in 1869 invited her to visit him in Boston. When she refused, he visited her in 1870. He would eventually become one of the editors of her posthumously published poetry.

But if Dickinson sought publication, she also regarded it as "the Auction / Of the Mind of Man," as she put it in poem 788; at the very least, she was unwilling to submit to the touching-up operations editors performed on her poems. Some critics have argued that Dickinson's letters constituted a form of publication, for Dickinson included poems in many of her letters. Even more intriguing, beginning around 1858 Dickinson began to record her poems on white, unlined paper, in some cases marking moments of textual revision, and then folded and stacked the sheets and sewed groups of them together in what are called fascicles. She created thirty such fascicles, ranging in length from sixteen to twenty-four pages; and there is considerable evidence that she worked diligently at the groupings, thinking about chronology, subject matter, and specific thematic orderings within each. These fascicles were left for others to discover after her death, neatly stacked in a drawer. It can be speculated that Dickinson, realizing that her unconventional poetry would not be published in her own lifetime as written, became a sort of self-publisher. Critics remain uncertain, however, about just how self-conscious her arrangements were and argue over what is lost and gained by considering individual poems in the context of their fascicle placement. There is also debate about whether the posthumous publication of Dickinson's manuscript poetry violates the visual look of the poems—their inconsistent dashes and even some of the designs that Dickinson added to particular poems. The selections printed here include a photographic reproduction of poem 269, which can be compared to the now-standard printed version, also included.

Dickinson's final decades were marked by health problems and a succession of losses. Beginning in the early 1860s she suffered from eye pain. She consulted with an ophthalmologist in Boston in 1864 and remained concerned about losing her vision. In 1874 her father died in a Boston hotel room after taking an injection of morphine for his pain, and one year later her mother had a stroke and would remain bedridden until her death in 1882. Her beloved eight-year-old nephew Gilbert died of typhoid fever in 1883, next door at the Evergreens; and in 1885, her close friend from childhood, Helen Hunt Jackson, who had asked to be Dickinson's literary executor, died suddenly in San Francisco. Dickinson's seclusion late in life may have been a response to her grief at these losses or a concern for her own health, but ultimately a focus on the supposed eccentricity of her desire for privacy draws attention away from the huge number of poems she wrote—she may well have secluded herself so that she could follow her vocation. Emily Dickinson died on May 15, 1886, perhaps from a kidney disorder called "Bright's Disease," the official diagnosis, but just as likely from hypertension.

In 1881 the astronomer David Todd, with his young wife, Mabel Loomis Todd, arrived in Amherst to direct the Amherst College Observatory. The next year, Austin Dickinson and Mabel Todd began an affair that lasted until Austin's death in 1895. Despite this turn of events Mabel Todd and Emily Dickinson established a friendship without actually meeting (Todd saw Dickinson once, in her coffin), and Todd decided that the poet was "in many respects a genius." Soon after Dickinson's death, Mabel Todd (at Emily's sister Lavinia's invitation) painstakingly transcribed many of her poems. The subsequent preservation and publication of her poetry and letters were initiated and carried forth by Todd. She persuaded Higginson to help her see a posthumous collection of poems into print in 1890 and a second volume of poems in 1891; she went on to publish a collection of Dickinson's letters in 1894 and a third volume of poems in 1896. In the 1890s some critics reacted patronizingly toward what they saw as verse that violated the laws of meter, and even Todd and Higginson edited some of the poems to make them more conventional. The three volumes were popular, going through several printings and selling over ten thousand copies. During the 1890s, Susan Dickinson and her daughter, Martha Dickinson Bianchi, also published a few of Dickinson's poems in journals such as *The Century*. By 1900 or so, however, Dickinson's work had fallen out of favor, and had Martha Dickinson Bianchi not resumed publication of her aunt's poetry in 1914 (she published eight volumes of Dickinson's work between 1914 and 1937), Dickinson's writings might never have achieved the audience they have today. Taken together, the editorial labors of Todd, Susan Dickinson, and Bianchi set in motion the critical and textual work that would help establish Dickinson as one of the great American poets. They also made her poetry available to the American modernists, poets such as Hart Crane and Marianne Moore; Dickinson and Whitman are the nineteenth-century poets who exerted the greatest influence on American poetry to come.

The texts of the poems, and the numbering, are from R. W. Franklin's one-volume edition, *The Poems of Emily Dickinson: Reading Edition* (1999), which draws on his three-volume variorum, *The Poems of Emily Dickinson* (1998). Bracketed numbers refer to the numbering of Thomas Johnson's *The Poems of Emily Dickinson* (1955), for many years the standard edition. The dating of Dickinson's poetry remains uncertain, though Franklin is more accurate than Johnson. The date following each poem corresponds to Franklin's estimate of Dickinson's first finished draft; if the poem was published in Dickinson's lifetime, that date is supplied as well.

## 39

[49]

I never lost as much but twice -
And that was in the sod.
Twice have I stood a beggar
Before the door of God!

Angels - twice descending                    5
Reimbursed my store -
Burglar! Banker - Father!
I am poor once more!

1858

# 112[1]

## [67]

Success is counted sweetest
By those who ne'er succeed. *waste not*
To comprehend a nectar *want not.*
Requires sorest need.

Not one of all the purple Host                                         5
Who took the Flag[2] today
Can tell the definition
So clear of Victory

As he defeated - dying -
On whose forbidden ear                                                 10
The distant strains of triumph
Burst agonized and clear!

1859, 1864

# 124[1]

## [216]

Safe in their Alabaster[2] Chambers -
Untouched by Morning -
And untouched by noon -                          *preservation*
Sleep the meek members of the Resurrection,
Rafter of Satin and Roof of Stone -                                    5

Grand go the Years,
In the Crescent above them -
Worlds scoop their Arcs -
And Firmaments - row -
Diadems - drop -                                                       10
And Doges[3] - surrender -
Soundless as Dots,
On a Disc of Snow.

1859, 1862

---

1. Dickinson published a version of this poem in the *Brooklyn Daily Union*, April 27, 1864, and it was republished in *A Masque of Poets* (1878), edited by her friend Helen Hunt Jackson. When printed in *Masque*, most reviewers thought it was by Emerson.

2. Triumphed.
1. Dickinson published a version of this poem in the *Springfield Daily Republican*, March 1, 1862.
2. Translucent, white chalky material.
3. Chief magistrates in the republics of Venice and Genoa from the 11th through the 16th centuries.

# 202

## [*185*]

*irony*

"Faith" is a fine invention
For Gentlemen who *see*!
But Microscopes are prudent
In an Emergency!

1861

# 207

## [*214*]

*drunk / enveloped by surroundings*

I taste a liquor never brewed -
From Tankards scooped in Pearl -
Not all the Frankfort Berries
Yield such an Alcohol!

Inebriate of air - am I -                                          5
And Debauchee of Dew -
Reeling - thro' endless summer days -
From inns of molten Blue -

When "Landlords" turn the drunken Bee
Out of the Foxglove's door -                                      10
When Butterflies - renounce their "drams" -
I shall but drink the more!

Till Seraphs[1] swing their snowy Hats -
And Saints - to windows run -
To see the little Tippler                                         15
Leaning against the - Sun!

1861

---

1. Angels.

## 225

### [199]

I'm "wife" - I've finished that -
That other state -
I'm Czar - I'm "Woman" now -
It's safer so -

How odd the Girl's life looks                                    5
Behind this soft Eclipse -
I think that Earth feels so
To folks in Heaven - now -

This being comfort - then
That other kind - was pain -                                    10
But Why compare?
I'm "Wife"! Stop there!

1861

## 236

### [324]

*reflective of the book of Genesis?*

Some keep the Sabbath going to Church -          *she doesn't reject God. She's just fed up w/ the rules.*
I keep it, staying at Home -                                    *Personal spin on religion.*
With a Bobolink for a Chorister -
And an Orchard, for a Dome -

Some keep the Sabbath in Surplice[1]              *She thinks some regard it as a social experience.*    5
I, just wear my Wings -
And instead of tolling the Bell, for Church,
Our little Sexton[2] - sings.

God preaches, a noted Clergyman -                  *some feel the need to impress God. She doesn't.*
And the sermon is never long,                                                         10
So instead of getting to Heaven, at last -          *experience.*
I'm going, all along.   *Heaven is an earthly experience.*
*Here is heaven. Not somewhere else to go to.*          1861

---

1. Open-sleeved gown worn by clergymen.          2. Church custodian.

## 269

[249]

Wild nights - Wild nights!
Were I with thee
Wild nights should be
Our luxury!

Futile - the winds -                                    5
To a Heart in port -
Done with the Compass -
Done with the Chart!

Rowing in Eden -
Ah - the Sea!                                          10
Might I but moor - tonight -
In thee!

1861

## 320

[258]

There's a certain Slant of light,
Winter Afternoons -
That oppresses, like the Heft
Of Cathedral Tunes -

Heavenly Hurt, it gives us -                            5
We can find no scar,
But internal difference -
Where the Meanings, are -

None may teach it - Any -
'Tis the Seal Despair -                                 10
An imperial affliction
Sent us of the Air -

When it comes, the Landscape listens -
Shadows - hold their breath -
When it goes, 'tis like the Distance                   15
On the look of Death -

1862

## 339

[241]

I like a look of Agony,
Because I know it's true -
Men do not sham Convulsion,
Nor simulate, a Throe -

Poem 269 [249] of Fascicle 11, from vol. 1 of *The Manuscript Books of Emily Dickinson* (1981), ed. R. W. Franklin, reproduced with the permission of Harvard University Press. Dickinson's handwriting, which changed over the years, can be dated by comparison with her letters. Ambiguities of punctuation are typical. Line 1, for instance, may or may not end with a dash and an exclamation point; Dickinson's modern editors use the exclamation point only.

The eyes glaze once - and that is Death -                                    5
Impossible to feign
The Beads opon the Forehead
By homely Anguish strung.

                                                                        1862


## 340

### [280]

I felt a Funeral, in my Brain,
And Mourners to and fro
Kept treading - treading - till it seemed
That Sense was breaking through -

And when they all were seated,                                              5
A Service, like a Drum -
Kept beating - beating - till I thought
My mind was going numb -

And then I heard them lift a Box
And creak across my Soul                                                   10
With those same Boots of Lead, again,
Then Space - began to toll,

As all the Heavens were a Bell,
And Being, but an Ear,
And I, and Silence, some strange Race                                      15
Wrecked, solitary, here -

And then a Plank in Reason, broke,
And I dropped down, and down -
And hit a World, at every plunge,
And Finished knowing - then -                                              20

                                                                        1862

*Narrator has different identities "persona poems"*

*Bird is harsh +"big man" until he feels something bigger than him. Bird evolves.*

*comments on nature as a natural post process.*

## 359

### [328]

*capital letters describing nature. Regarding nature on same level as her or above. respecting it.*

A Bird, came down the Walk -
He did not know I saw -
He bit an Angle Worm in halves
And ate the fellow, raw,

And then, he drank a Dew                                                    5
From a convenient Grass -
And then hopped sidewise to the Wall
To let a Beetle pass -

He glanced with rapid eyes,
That hurried all abroad - 10
They looked like frightened Beads, I thought,
He stirred his Velvet Head. -

Like one in danger, Cautious, *She approves of the bird.*
I offered him a Crumb,
And he unrolled his feathers, 15
And rowed him softer Home -

*mixing imagery.*

Than Oars divide the Ocean, *Human interaction w/ nature?*
Too silver for a seam, *Sky becomes the ocean.*
Or Butterflies, off Banks of Noon, *Bird "rowing" through*
Leap, plashless[1] as they swim. *the sky.* 20
*He leaves no trace. No "seam"/plashless →*
*So no wake.* 1862
*Nothing left of that encounter.*

372 *can't step in the same river twice*
*Something important about*
[341] *the momentary. Be here to*
*experience it + then*
After great pain, a formal feeling comes - *leave.*
The Nerves sit ceremonious, like Tombs - *(like her poetry).*
The stiff Heart questions 'was it He, that bore,'
And 'Yesterday, or Centuries before'?

The Feet, mechanical, go round - 5
A Wooden way
Of Ground, or Air, or Ought -
Regardless grown,
A Quartz contentment, like a stone -

This is the Hour of Lead - 10
Remembered, if outlived,
As Freezing persons, recollect the Snow -
First - Chill - then Stupor - then the letting go -

1862

409

[303]

The Soul selects her own Society -
Then - shuts the Door -
To her divine Majority -
Present no more -

Unmoved - she notes the Chariots - pausing - 5
At her low Gate -
Unmoved - an Emperor be kneeling
Opon her Mat -

---

1. I.e., splashless.

I've known her - from an ample nation -
Choose One -                                                                          10
Then - close the Valves of her attention -
Like Stone -

1862

## 448

### [449]

I died for Beauty - but was scarce
Adjusted in the Tomb
When One who died for Truth, was lain
In an adjoining Room -

He questioned softly "Why I failed"?                                        5
"For Beauty", I replied -
"And I - for Truth - Themself are One -
We Bretheren, are", He said -

And so, as Kinsmen, met a Night -
We talked between the Rooms -                                                10
Until the Moss had reached our lips -
And covered up - Our names -

1862

## 479

### [712]

Because I could not stop for Death -
He kindly stopped for me -
The Carriage held but just Ourselves -
And Immortality.

We slowly drove - He knew no haste                                          5
And I had put away
My labor and my leisure too,
For His Civility -

We passed the School, where Children strove
At Recess - in the Ring -                                                            10
We passed the Fields of Gazing Grain -
We passed the Setting Sun -

Or rather - He passed Us -
The Dews drew quivering and Chill -
For only Gossamer,[1] my Gown -                                              15
My Tippet - only Tulle[2] -

1. Delicate, light fabric.
2. Thin silk. "Tippet": scarf for covering neck and shoulders.

We paused before a House that seemed
A Swelling of the Ground -
The Roof was scarcely visible -
The Cornice[3] - in the Ground -                    20

Since then - 'tis Centuries - and yet
Feels shorter than the Day
I first surmised the Horses' Heads
Were toward Eternity -

1862


## 519

### [441]

This is my letter to the World
That never wrote to Me -
The simple News that Nature told -
With tender Majesty

Her Message is committed                    5
To Hands I cannot see -
For love of Her - Sweet - countrymen -
Judge tenderly - of Me

1863


## 591

### [465]

I heard a Fly buzz - when I died -
The Stillness in the Room
Was like the Stillness in the Air -
Between the Heaves of Storm -

The Eyes around - had wrung them dry -                    5
And Breaths were gathering firm
For that last Onset - when the King
Be witnessed - in the Room -

I willed my Keepsakes - Signed away
What portion of me be                    10
Assignable - and then it was
There interposed a Fly -

3. Decorative molding beneath a roof.

With Blue - uncertain - stumbling Buzz -
Between the light - and me -
And then the Windows failed - and then                    15
I could not see to see -

                                                              1863


## 598

### [632]

The Brain - is wider than the Sky -
For - put them side by side -
The one the other will contain
With ease - and You - beside -

The Brain is deeper than the sea -                          5
For - hold them - Blue to Blue -
The one the other will absorb -
As Sponges - Buckets - do -

The Brain is just the weight of God -
For - Heft them - Pound for Pound -                        10
And they will differ - if they do -
As Syllable from Sound -

                                                              1863


## 620

### [435]

Much Madness is divinest Sense -
To a discerning Eye -
Much Sense - the starkest Madness -
'Tis the Majority
In this, as all, prevail -                                  5
Assent - and you are sane -
Demur - you're straightway dangerous -
And handled with a Chain -

                                                              1863


## 656

### [520]

I started Early - Took my Dog -
And visited the Sea -
The Mermaids in the Basement
Came out to look at me -

And Frigates - in the Upper Floor                    5
Extended Hempen Hands -
Presuming Me to be a Mouse -
Aground - opon the Sands - *She's small by comparison*

But no Man moved Me - till the Tide
Went past my simple Shoe -                    *overarching*    10
And past my Apron - and my Belt
And past my Boddice - too -

And made as He would eat me up -    *potential threat.*
As wholly as a Dew
Opon a Dandelion's Sleeve -                    15
And then - I started - too -    *Its all about a wave.
could be about love?*

And He - He followed - close behind -
I felt His Silver Heel
Opon my Ancle - Then My Shoes
Would overflow with Pearl - *offering her something.*    20
*gentleness / awesomeness
Juxtaposed.*

Until We met the Solid Town - *distinct*
No One He seemed to know - *from the*
And bowing - with a Mighty look - *ocean.*
At me - The Sea withdrew -

                                                   1863


## 764
### [754]          *reflective of the ideologies
of the civil war.*

My Life had stood - a Loaded Gun -    *She seems powerful
In Corners - till a Day    bc she is a weapon,
The Owner passed - identified -    but really she has no
And carried Me away -    power bc he decides
where to go +*

And now We roam in Sovreign Woods -    *what to do etc.*    5
And now We hunt the Doe -
And every time I speak for Him
The Mountains straight reply - *echo.  Reflective of
feminism? Women
is regarded as extention
of man - sarcasm.*

And do I smile, such cordial light
Opon the Valley glow -                    10
It is as a Vesuvian[1] face
Had let it's pleasure through *Destruction*

And when at Night - Our good Day done -
I guard My Master's Head -
'Tis better than the Eider Duck's                    15
Deep Pillow - to have shared -

---

1. Reference to Mount Vesuvius, the active volcano in southern Italy that destroyed Pompeii (79 C.E.).

To foe of His - I'm deadly foe -
None stir the second time -
On whom I lay a Yellow Eye -
Or an emphatic Thumb -                                        20

Though I than He - may longer live
He longer must - than I -
For I have but the power to kill,
Without - the power to die -

*The two*
*Seperately are*
*powerless*

*men of the country are powerless, divided.*                  1863


## 1096

### [986]

A narrow Fellow in the Grass
Occasionally rides -
You may have met him? Did you not
His notice instant is -

The Grass divides as with a Comb -                            5
A spotted Shaft is seen,
And then it closes at your Feet
And opens further on -

He likes a Boggy Acre -
A Floor too cool for Corn -                                   10
But when a Boy and Barefoot
I more than once at Noon

Have passed I thought a Whip Lash
Unbraiding in the Sun
When stooping to secure it                                    15
It wrinkled And was gone -

Several of Nature's People
I know and they know me
I feel for them a transport
Of Cordiality                                                 20

But never met this Fellow
Attended or alone
Without a tighter Breathing
And Zero at the Bone.

1865

## 1263

[*1129*]

Tell all the truth but tell it slant -
Success in Circuit lies
Too bright for our infirm Delight
The Truth's superb surprise
As Lightning to the Children eased          5
With explanation kind
The Truth must dazzle gradually
Or every man be blind -

1872

## 1668

[*1624*]

*[handwritten left margin: Pondering of pain + agony of death in a bubbly way. Poking fun @ what humans approve of? W/ every death there becomes new life. Is the frost playing or is the flower playing? Two very different readings. Sun doesn't care. Just pervades cycle of life. This is all part of God's plan? Or is God malicious.]*

*[handwritten right/top: Changing of seasons. Interesting juxtaposition of language. Harsh words but playful, bouncy feel. Sarcasm?]*

Apparently with no surprise
To any happy Flower
The Frost beheads it at it's play -
In accidental power -
The blonde Assassin passes on -     *[handwritten: very matter of fact. Cycle of life.]*
The Sun proceeds unmoved     5
To measure off another Day     *[handwritten: Bouncy rythm to poem.]*
For an Approving God -     *[handwritten: Illustrating a cycle, but she breaks her cycle w/ the last line.]*

1884

*[handwritten: Dealing w/ greater issues of life + death. Immortality or does it end when you die.]*

**IRONY**     *[handwritten: Sarcastic tone towards religion? She didn't strongly connect to God.]*

## 1773[1]

[*1732*]

My life closed twice before it's close;
It yet remains to see
If Immortality unveil
A third event to me,

So huge, so hopeless to conceive          5
As these that twice befell.
Parting is all we know of heaven,
And all we need of hell.

---

1. The poem was transcribed by Mabel Loomis Todd, and there is no surviving manuscript; it is difficult to determine a probable date of composition.

# MARÍA AMPARO RUIZ DE BURTON
## 1832–1895

Since republication of *The Squatter and the Don* (1885) in 1992, María Amparo Ruiz de Burton has become a key figure in the recovery of nineteenth-century Mexican American literature. Her two novels, both published anonymously (the first, satirizing East Coast attitudes toward race during the Civil War, is *Who Would Have Thought It?* [1872]), are the earliest written in English by a Mexican American in the United States. Born in either La Paz or Loreto in Baja California (there are conflicting accounts), Ruiz de Burton was by all accounts a well-educated woman of great personal charm. Raised an heiress, she was the granddaughter of Don José Manuel Ruiz, commandant of the presidio in Baja California and *padron* of the vast Rancho Ensenada de Todos Santos. Ruiz de Burton was a hostess to and friend of the politically powerful, especially after her marriage to a prominent army officer, Henry Stanton Burton, later General Burton, whom she met in La Paz and who helped evacuate her and other Baja Californios to Monterey after California became a U.S. territory following the Mexican War of 1846–48. After the death of her husband from malaria during the Civil War, Ruiz de Burton directed multiple activities at each of her two ranches, including running cattle; growing wheat, barley, and castor beans; tending beehives; burning limestone to make lime; and advocating a scheme to produce water for San Diego. Attempts to secure her claims to her land involved long, expensive legal struggles and were ongoing when she died.

The Californios—native-born Californians of Spanish descent—ruled the Southwest for many generations; but by the 1880s, due to the land "reforms" that followed the U.S. victory in the Mexican War, the Treaty of Guadalupe Hidalgo, which granted the United States the Mexican territories of present-day Arizona, California, New Mexico, and Texas as well as parts of other states, and an 1851 Land Act designed to unseat Mexicans from land owned by their families, this group found itself cheated out of its land by Anglos and demoted to the level of common laborers. They also found that they had lost the privileges of "whiteness." *The Squatter and the Don* protests both losses. Among the novel's characters are genteel Californios, crude and rapacious Anglo squatters, mercenary Yankee businessmen, and a younger generation that includes the Don's daughter Mercedes, who enters into a romance with the son of a squatter, Clarence Darrell. Despite the romance's happy ending, both families lose their land through the workings of U.S. capitalism and corruption, particularly the government's vulnerability to the bribery of railroad barons. The chapter included here presents a highly ironic scene in which the Spanish landowner Don Mariano negotiates with his new neighbors, Anglo "squatters" intent on claiming land, about using cheap Indian labor to benefit himself and them.

Ruiz de Burton clearly identifies with the landed class and did not produce social protest fiction on behalf of the poor. Her work offers a complicating set of identities and values for the study of Mexican American literature and Anglo narratives of "democracy" couched in terms of "Manifest Destiny" and Western expansionism and imperialism. *The Squatter and the Don* invites the reader to identify with multiple groups under attack by white, capitalist corporate entities. That Ruiz de Burton's work accepts many racial stereotypes even while arguing against others is a marker not only of her own times but of the difficulty of articulating an ethos completely free of derogatory assumptions about racial or ethnic "others."

# The Squatter and the Don[1]

## Chapter V. The Don in His Broad Acres

"The one great principle of English law,"—Charles Dickens[2] says, "is to make business for itself. There is no other principle distinctly, certainly and consistently maintained through all its narrow turnings. Viewed by this light, it becomes a coherent scheme, and not the monstrous maze the laity are apt to think it. Let them but once clearly perceive that its grand principle is to make business for itself at their expense, and surely they will cease to grumble."

The one great principle of American law is very much the same; our law-givers keep giving us laws and then enacting others to explain them. The lawyers find plenty of occupation, but what becomes of the laity?

"No. 189. *An Act to ascertain and settle the private land claims in the State of California,*" says the book.[3]

And by a sad subversion of purposes, all the private land titles became *unsettled*. It ought to have been said, "An Act to *unsettle* land titles, and to upset the rights of the Spanish population of the State of California."

It thus became not only necessary for the Spanish people to present their titles for revision, and litigate to maintain them (in case of anyone contesting their validity, should the least irregularity be discovered, and others covet their possession), but to maintain them against the government before several tribunals; for the government, besides making its own laws, *appeals to itself* as against the land-owners, after their titles might have been *approved*. But this benign Act says (in "Sec. II"), "That the Commissioners, the District and Supreme Courts, in deciding on the validity of any claim, shall be governed by the treaty of Guadalupe Hidalgo; the law of nations; the laws, usages, and customs of the government *from which the claim is derived;* the principles of equity, and the decisions of the Supreme Court of the United States, etc., etc."

Thus the government washes its hands clean, liberally providing plenty of tribunals, plenty of crooked turnings through which to scourge the wretched land-owners.

Don Mariano had been for some years under the lash of the maternal government, whom he had found a cruel stepmother, indeed.

As it was arranged with Clarence, the meeting would take place that day

---

1. First published in San Francisco in 1885 by "C. Loyal," the pen name of Ruiz de Burton and an abbreviated form of *Ciudadano Leal,* "Loyal Citizen," a conventional method of closing official letters in 19th-century Mexico. The name signals both her loyalty to Mexico and her disdain for what she saw as corrupt American politics. In 1992 Arte Público Press in Houston reprinted the novel, edited by Rosaura Sánchez and Beatrice Pita, the source of the present text.

2. English novelist (1812–1870) whose works attack social evils, injustice, and hypocrisy. The quotation is from *Bleak House* (1852–53).

3. The Land Act of 1851 created a Land Commission to determine the validity of the large Spanish-Mexican grants to Californios; though the Treaty of Guadalupe Hidalgo, which ended the 1846–48 Mexican War and ceded 55 percent of Mexico's territory (present-day Arizona, California, New Mexico, Texas, and parts of Colorado, Nevada, and Utah) to the United States for fifteen million dollars, initially gave Mexicans who remained in the Southwest citizenship and title to their property, the Land Act placed the burden on landowners to prove their claims against those of squatters, in many cases forcing Mexicans off their land through extensive litigation fees and protracted tribunals. When the U.S. Senate ratified the treaty in 1848, it deleted an article guaranteeing the protection of Mexican land grants.

on the broad piazza of John Gasbang's house, this being the most central point in the rancho.

The heads of families all came—the male heads, be it understood—as the squatters did not make any pretense to regard female opinion with any more respect than other men.

All the benches and chairs that the house contained, with the exception of Mrs. Gasbang's sewing rocker, had been brought to the porch, which was quite roomy and airy.

At ten minutes before two, all the settlers were there, that is to say, all the old men, with their elder sons.

Clarence, Romeo, Tom and Jack sat together in a corner, conversing in low tones, while Gasbang was entertaining his guests with some broad anecdotes, which brought forth peals of laughter.

At five minutes to two, Señor Alamar, accompanied by Mr. Mechlin, arrived in a buggy; his two sons followed on horseback.

Clarence had time to look at them leisurely, while they dismounted, and tied their horses to a hitching post.

"They are gentlemen, no doubt," observed Clarence.

"You bet they are," Romeo coincided. Evidently he admired and liked them.

"How much the boys look like the old man," Tom said.

"They look like Englishmen," was Clarence's next observation.

"Yes, particularly Victoriano; he is so light he looks more like a German, I think," said Romeo.

"I think Gabriel is very handsome," Tom said, "only of late he seems always so sad or thoughtful."

"That won't do for a man who is to marry soon," said Romeo. "I think he has always been rather reserved. He has only a cold salutation to give, while Victoriano will be laughing and talking to everybody. But, perhaps, you are right, and he is changed. I think he is less reconciled than others, to have us, settlers, helping ourselves to what they consider their land. He certainly was far more talkative four or five years ago. I used to work with them in plough- ing and harvesting time, and both boys, and the Don, were always very kind to me, and I can't help liking them."

"The ladies, though, ain't so affable. They are very proud," said Tom; "they walk like queens."

"They didn't seem proud to me, but I never spoke to them," said Romeo.

Gasbang went forward to meet his guests, and all came into the porch.

"Good afternoon, gentlemen," said Don Mariano to the settlers, lifting his hat and bowing. His sons and Mr. Mechlin did the same. Clarence arose, and so did the other young men with him, returning their salutation. The elder Darrell, Pittikin and Hughes followed this example; the other settlers nodded only, and remained sitting with their hats on, looking with affected indiffer- ence at the trees beyond.

"I thank you for your courtesy in complying with my request to have this meeting," he said. Some nodded, others grinned and winked, others smiled silently.

"Take this chair, Señor, and you, Mr. Mechlin, take this one. They are the best in my establishment," said Gasbang. "The young gentlemen will find seats somewhere on the benches."

Clarence came forward and offered three chairs. Mr. Mechlin took his arm and presented him to the Alamars.

"I take pleasure in making your acquaintance, and I hope to have the opportunity to thank you for your kind co-operation more appropriately afterward," said Don Mariano. His sons shook hands with Clarence cordially, and accepted the proffered chairs.

Don Mariano excused himself for not speaking English more fluently.

"If you don't understand me I will repeat my words until I make my meaning clear, but I hope you will ask me to repeat them; or perhaps, some one of these young gentlemen will do me the kindness to be my interpreter," said he.

"Romeo talks Spanish; he can interpret for you," said Victoriano.

"You talk English better," Romeo proudly replied, thinking he could tell his wife that the Don had asked him to be his interpreter.

"Perhaps Mr. Clarence Darrell would do me the favor," said Don Mariano.

"You speak very good English, Señor. We understand you perfectly. You do not require an interpreter," Clarence said.

"That is so; you speak very well," said Mr. Mechlin.

Gasbang and Pittikin added: "Certainly, we understand him very well."

"Of course we do," said Darrell and others.

"You are very kind," said the Don, smiling, "and I will try to be brief, and not detain you long."

"We have all the afternoon," said Hughes.

"That's so, we ain't in a hurry," said several.

"Only let us out in time to bring the milch cows home, before night comes on," said old Miller, dryly.

"Exactly, we want to look after our cows, too," said the Don, laughing.

All saw the fine irony of the rejoinder, and laughed heartily. Miller scratched his ear, as if he had felt the retort there, knowing well, that with the exception of Mathews and Gasbang, he had killed and "corralled" more of the Don's cattle than any other settler.

"Speaking about cows, brings us at once to the object of this meeting,"— Don Mariano, still smiling, went on, saying: "You know that I have lost many, and that it is natural I should wish to save those I have left. To do this, and yet not ask that you give up your claims, I have one or two propositions to make to you. The reason why you have taken up land here is because you want homes. You want to make money. Isn't that the reason? Money! money!"

"That's it, exactly," said many voices, and all laughed.

"Well, I can show you how you may keep your homes and make more money than you can by your present methods, while at the same time, I also save my cattle. That little point, you know, I must keep in view."

All laughed again.

"To fence your fields, you have said, is too expensive, particularly as the rainy seasons are too uncertain to base upon them any calculations for getting crops to pay for fencing. I believe this is what most of you say; is it not?"

"We could have raised better crops if your cattle hadn't damaged them," said Mathews.

"I beg to differ; but supposing that you are right, do you think you could be sure of good crops if you killed all my stock, or if I took them all away to the mountains? No, most assuredly. The rainy season would still be irregular and unreliable, I think. Yes, I may say, I feel sure, it is a mistake to try to make San Diego County a grain-producing county. It is not so, and I feel certain it never will be, to any great extent. This county is, and has been and will be always, a good grazing county—one of the best counties for cattle-raising on this coast, and the very best for fruit-raising on the face of the earth. God intended it should be. Why, then, not devote your time, your labor and your money to raising vineyards, fruits and cattle, instead of trusting to the uncertain rains to give you grain crops?"

"It takes a long time to get fruit trees to bearing. What are we to do for a living in the meantime?" asked Miller.

"Begin raising cattle—that will support you," the Don replied.

"Where is the capital to buy cattle with?" Gasbang asked.

"You don't require any more capital than you already have. I can let each of you have a number of cows to begin with, and give you four or five years' time to pay me. So you see, it will be with the increase of these cattle you will pay, for I shall charge you no interest."

"What do you expect us to do in return? To give back to you our homesteads?" asked Hughes.

"No, sir; I have said, and repeat again, you will retain your homesteads."[4]

"And will you stop contesting our claims?" asked Mathews.

"I will, and will give each one a quit-claim deed."[5]

"You will not fight our claims, but you don't want us to plant grain on our land," said Gasbang.

"You can plant grain, if you like, but to do so you must fence your land so, as you all say, that fencing is expensive, I suggest your fencing orchard and vineyards only, but no grain fields—I mean large fields?"

"Pshaw! I knew there was to be something behind all that display of generosity," muttered Mathews.

Don Mariano reddened with a thrill of annoyance, but quietly answered.

"You are too good business men to suppose that I should not reserve some slight advantage for myself, when I am willing you should have many more yourselves. All I want to do is to save the few cattle I have left. I am willing to quit-claim to you the land you have taken, and give you cattle to begin the stock business, and all I ask you in return is to put a fence around whatever land you wish to cultivate, so that my cattle cannot go in there. So I say, plant vineyards, plant olives, figs, oranges; make wines and oil and raisins; export olives and dried and canned fruits. I had some very fine California canned fruit sent to me from San Francisco. Why could we not can fruits as well, or better? Our olives are splendid—the same our figs, oranges, apricots, and truly all semi-tropical fruits are of a superior quality. When this fact becomes generally known, I feel very sure that San Diego County will be selected for

---

4. The Homestead Act, signed into law in 1862 by Abraham Lincoln, turned over vast amounts of the public domain to private citizens. Two hundred seventy million acres, or 10 percent of the area of the United States, were claimed and settled under this act. A "homesteader" had only to be the head of a household and at least twenty-one years old to claim a 160-acre parcel of land. Settlers from all walks of life, including newly arrived immigrants, farmers from the East, single women, and former slaves, met the challenge of "proving up" (living on the land, building a home, making improvements, and farming for five years) to keep the free land. 5. Type of deed in which a person who owns an interest in a property transfers it to someone else without guarantees about the title.

fruit and grape-growing. In two years grape vines begin to bear; the same with figs, peaches and other fruits. At three years old they bear quite well, and all without irrigation. So you would not have to wait so very long to begin getting a return from your labor and capital. Moreover, an orchard of forty acres or vineyard of twenty will pay better after three years' growth than one hundred and sixty acres of wheat or barley in good seasons, and more than three hundred acres of any grain in moderately good seasons, or one thousand acres in bad seasons. You can easily fence twenty or forty or sixty acres for a vineyard or orchard, but not so easily fence a field of one hundred and sixty, and the grain crop would be uncertain, depending on the rains, but not so the trees, for you can irrigate them, and after the trees are rooted that is not required."

"Where is the water to irrigate?" asked Miller.

"The water is in the sea now, for there we let it go every year; but if we were sensible, judicious men, we would not let it go to waste—we would save it. This rancho has many deep ravines which bring water from hills and sierras. These ravines all open into the valleys, and run like so many little rivers in the rainy season. By converting these ravines into reservoirs we could have more water than would be needed for irrigating the fruit trees on the foothills. In the low valleys no irrigation would be needed. If we all join forces to put up dams across the most convenient of the ravines, we will have splendid reservoirs. I will defray half the expense if you will get together and stand the other half. Believe me, it will be a great god-send to have a thriving, fruit-growing business in our county. To have the cultivated land well fenced, and the remainder left out for grazing. Then there would not be so many thousands upon thousands of useless acres as now have to be. For every ten acres of cultivated land (not fenced) there are ten thousand, yes, twenty thousand, entirely idle, useless. Why? Because those ten acres of growing grain must be protected, and the cattle which don't know the 'no fence law,'[6] follow their inclination to go and eat the green grass. Then they are 'corralled' or killed. Is it not a pity to kill the poor dumb brutes, because we can't make them understand the law, and see the wisdom of our Sacramento legislators who enacted it? And is it not a pity to impoverish our county by making the bulk of its land useless? The foolishness of letting all of the rainfall go to waste, is an old time folly with us. Still, in old times, we had, at least, the good excuse that we raised all the fruits we needed for our use, and there was no market for any more. But we were not then, as now, guilty of the folly of making the land useless. We raised cattle and sold hides and tallow every year, and made money. When gold was discovered, we drove our stock north, got a good price for it, and made money. But now no money will be made by anybody out of cattle, if they are to be destroyed, and no money made out of land, for the grazing will be useless, when there will be no stock left to eat it. Thus, the county will have no cattle, and the crops be always uncertain. Believe me, in years to come, you will see that the county

6. The "No-Fence Law" of 1872 repealed the Trespass Act of 1850, which had required farmers to build fences to protect planted fields from free-ranging cattle if they wished to receive payment for damage done to crops by such cattle. The repeal of the act required that the stockman fence his stock in, rather than the farmer fence stock out. Counties that depended greatly on stock raising were exempt.

will have no cattle, and the crops be always uncertain. Believe me, in years to come, you will see that the county was impoverished by the 'no fence law,' unless we try to save our county, in spite of foolish legislation. If our wise legislators could enact a law obliging rain to come, so that we could have better chances to raise grain, then there would be some show of excuse for the 'no fence law,' perhaps. I say PERHAPS, because, in my humble opinion, we ought to prefer cattle raising and fruit growing for our county. We should make these our specialty."

"I think it would be much more foolish to trust to a few cows to make out a living while trees grow," said Miller, "than to the seasons to give us grain crops."

"No, sir; because cattle are sure to increase, if they are not killed, and you could make cheese and butter, and sell your steers every year, while trees grow. You have been seven years a settler on this rancho. In these seven years you have raised two good crops; three poor, or only middling, and two, no crops at all."

"Yes, because your cattle destroyed them," said Mathews.

"No, sir, my cattle were not all over California; but the bad seasons were, and only in few places, moderately good crops were harvested; in the southern counties none at all. We had rains enough to get sufficiently good grazing, but not to raise grain."

"I think you are right about the uncertainty of our seasons, and I think a good dairy always pays well, also a good orchard and vineyard." said Darrell. "But the question is, whether we can adopt some feasible plan to put your idea into practice."

"Yes, how many cows will you let us have?" asked Hager.

"I will divide with you. Next week I shall have my 'rodeo.' We can see then the number of cattle I have left. We shall count them. I shall take half, the other half you divide pro rata; each head of a family taking a proportionate number of cattle."

"That is fair," Darrell said.

"I don't want any cattle. I ain't no 'vaquero' to go 'busquering'[7] around and lassoing cattle. I'll lasso myself; what do I know about whirling a lariat?" said Mathews.

"Then, don't take cattle. You can raise fruit trees and vineyards," said Darrell.

"Yes, and starve meantime," Mathews replied.

"You will not have to be a vaquero. I don't go 'busquering' around lassoing, unless I wish to do so," said the Don. "You can hire an Indian boy to do that part. They know how to handle la reata and echar el lazo[8] to perfection. You will not starve, either, for if you wish, you can make butter and cheese enough to help to pay expenses. I think this State ought to make and export as good cheese as it now imports, and some day people will see it, and do it, too. Thus, with the produce of your dairies, at first, and afterward with your fruits, you will do far better than with grain crops, and not work as hard. Let the northern counties raise grain, while we raise fruits and make wine, butter and

---

7. From the Spanish buscar, meaning "to search for." "Vaquero": Spanish for "cowboy."

8. Spanish for "to rope" or "to lasso." "La reata": Spanish for "the rope."

cheese. You must not forget, either, that every year you can sell a number of cattle, besides keeping as many milch cows as you need."

"Where can we sell our cattle?" asked Hancock.

"Cattle-buyers will come to buy from you. But if you prefer it, you can drive your stock north yourselves, and make a good profit. Since 1850, I have sent nine times droves of cattle to the northern counties, and made a handsome profit every time. The first time we took stock north, was in '50; I took nearly six thousand head—three thousand were mine—and the others belonged to my brothers. We lost very few, and sold at a good price—all the way from eighteen to twenty-five dollars per head. About five hundred of mine I sold as high as thirty dollars per head. I made sixty thousand dollars by this operation. Then out of the next lot I made twenty-seven thousand dollars. Then I made twenty-two thousand, and so on, until my tame cows began to disappear, as you all know. In four years after my cows began to get shot, my cattle decreased more than half. Now I don't think I have many more than three thousand head. So you cannot blame me for wishing to save these few. But believe me, the plan I propose will be as beneficial to you as to me, and also to the entire county, for as soon as it is shown that we can make a success of the industries I propose, others will follow our example."

"If you have only three thousand head, you can't spare many to us, and it will hardly be worth while to stop planting crops to get a few cows," said Gasbang.

"I think I will be able to spare five or six hundred cows. I don't know how many I have left."

"We will buy from somebody else, if we want more," said Darrell. "We won't want many to begin with; it will be something of an experiment for some of us."

"For all of us here. Perhaps you understand *vaquering*;[9] we don't," said Hancock; all laughed.

"Then fence your claim and plant grain," Darrell retorted.

"I am not so big a fool as to spend money in fences. The 'no fence law' is better than all the best fences," Mathews said.

"But what if you make more money by following other laws that are more just, more rational?" said the Don.

"The 'no fence law' is rational enough for me," said Miller.

"And so say I," said Mathews.

"And I," said Gasbang.

Hughes nodded approvingly, but he was too much of a hypocrite to commit himself in words.

"We did not come to discuss the 'no fence law,' but only to propose something that will put more money in your pockets than killing dumb beasts," said Mr. Mechlin.

"Then propose something practicable," said Mathews.

"I think what has been proposed is practicable enough," Darrell said.

"Certainly it is," Mr. Mechlin added.

"I don't see it," said Mathews.

"Nor I, either," added Gasbang.

9. Spanish for "cowboy's work."

"Nor I, neither," said Hughes.

"Well, gentlemen," said Don Mariano, rising, "I shall leave you now; you know my views, and you perhaps prefer to discuss them, and discuss your own among yourselves, and not in my presence. Take your time, and when you come to a final decision let me know. Perhaps I can advance the money to those of you who do not have it ready to purchase fencing lumber. I shall charge no interest, and give you plenty of time to pay."

"I will do that, Señor Alamar," Clarence said; "if the settlers agree to fence their lands, I will advance the money to them to put up their fences."

"Yes, and if our crops fail, we will be in debt to the ears, with a chain around our necks," Mathews growled.

"I thought you said that if it were not for my cattle, your crops would not have failed," said Don Mariano, smiling.

"I said so, and it is so. But you see, that was before we had the 'no fence law,'" answered he, grinning.

Don Mariano shook hands with Clarence, whom he invited to call at his house—this invitation Clarence accepted with warm thanks—and followed by his sons and his friend Mr. Mechlin, Don Mariano took his leave, bowing to the settlers, who nodded and grinned in return.

"I suppose you, too, think the 'no fence law' iniquitous, as you appear to favor the aristocracy," said Gasbang to Clarence.

"It is worse than that, it is stupid. Now it kills the cattle, afterwards it will kill the county," Clarence answered.

"Shall we plant no wheat, because the Spaniards want to raise cattle?" Mathews asked.

"Plant wheat, if you can do so without killing cattle. But do not destroy the larger industry with the smaller. If, as the Don very properly says, this is a grazing county, no legislation can change it. So it would be wiser to make laws to suit the county, and not expect that the county will change its character to suit absurd laws," Clarence replied.

1880                                                                                      1885

---

# MARK TWAIN (SAMUEL L. CLEMENS)
## 1835–1910

Samuel Langhorne Clemens, the third of five children, was born on November 30, 1835, in the village of Florida, Missouri, and grew up in the somewhat larger river town of Hannibal, Missouri, that place of idylls and also dangers he called St. Petersburg in his writings, home to his two most famous characters, Tom Sawyer and Huck Finn. Twain's father, a justice of the peace who had unsuccessfully tried to become a storekeeper and clerk, died when Twain was twelve, and from that time on Twain worked to support himself and the rest of the family. He seems to have acquired his dry sense of humor and love for literature from his mother, Jane Lampton Clemens, to whom he was very close. After his father's death, Twain was apprenticed to a printer, and in 1851, when his brother Orion became a publisher in Hannibal, Twain went to work for him. In 1853 he began three years of travel, stopping in St. Louis, New York,

Philadelphia, Keokuk (Iowa), and Cincinnati, in each place earning his living as printer hired by the day. In 1856 he left Cincinnati for New Orleans by steamboat, intending to go to the Amazon. He changed his plans, however, and instead apprenticed himself to Horace Bixby, a Mississippi riverboat pilot. After training for eighteen months, Twain satisfied a boyhood ambition by becoming a pilot himself, and he practiced this lucrative and prestigious trade until 1861, when the Civil War virtually ended commercial river traffic. During this time he began to write humorous accounts of his activities for the *Keokuk Saturday Post*; though only three of these articles were published (under the pseudonym Thomas Jefferson Snodgrass), they introduced him to journalism, his occupation for much of the next ten years. Twain never forgot the inspiration of his time on the Mississippi; as he remarked, "When I find a well-drawn character in fiction or biography I generally take a warm personal interest in him, for the reason that I have known him before—met him on the river."

Slavery was legal in Missouri, though the state did not join the Confederacy, and Twain may have seen brief service in a woefully unorganized Confederate militia, an experience that he later fictionalized in "The Private History of a Campaign That Failed" (1885). In 1861 he went west with his brother Orion, who had been appointed secretary of the Nevada Territorial government. This move started him on the path toward his life as a humorist, lecturer, journalist, and author. In *Roughing It* (1872), written a decade later, Twain fictionally elaborated the brothers' stagecoach adventures on the way to Carson City and recounted his unsuccessful schemes for making money (including mining the Comstock lode in Virginia City) once he got there. Throughout *Roughing It*, which also covers his stint in San Francisco as a reporter and his half-hearted gold-mining in the Sierras, as well as his trip to Hawai'i, Twain's project is to debunk the sentimental idea of the West as a place where fortunes could be easily made and show its disappointing and even brutal side.

In the West, Twain began writing for newspapers, first the *Territorial Enterprise* in Virginia City and then, after 1864, the *Californian*. The fashion of the time called for a pen name, and so from a columnist for the New Orleans *Times-Picayune*, he borrowed "Mark Twain," which means in riverboat terms "two fathoms deep," or "safe water." His early writing was modeled on the humorous journalism of the day, especially that practiced by his friend and roommate in Nevada, who wrote under the penname Dan De Quille. Also important to his development during these years were friendships with the western writer Bret Harte, the famous professional lecturer and comic Artemus Ward, and the obscure amateur raconteur Jim Gillis. Twain's reputation as a lecturer and his first success as a writer lay in his skillful retelling of a well-known tall tale, "The Notorious Jumping Frog of Calaveras County," first published in 1865.

In this same year Twain signed with the *Sacramento Union* to write a series of letters covering the newly opened steamboat passenger service between San Francisco and Honolulu. In these letters he used a fictitious character, Mr. Brown, to present inelegant ideas and unorthodox views, attitudes, and information, often in impolite language. This device allowed him to say just about anything he wanted, provided he could convincingly claim he was simply reporting what others said and did. The refinement of this deadpan technique made it a staple of his lectures. Twain's first book of this period, and still one of his most popular, was *Innocents Abroad* (1869), consisting of a revised form of the letters he wrote for the *Alta California* and *New York Tribune* during his 1867 excursion on the *Quaker City* to the Mediterranean and Holy Land. Led by the pious Henry Ward Beecher, the passengers were a group of largely New England and Midwestern Protestants, and at the last moment Twain was hired to entertain them. What a mismatch it was! Twain wrote hilarious satires of his fellow passengers as well as the pretentious, decadent, and undemocratic Old World as viewed by a citizen of a young country on the rise. A characteristically impertinent note was sounded in a remark upon disembarking in New York: When Twain was asked for his impressions of the Holy Land, he said he knew for a fact there would be no Second Coming, for if Jesus had been there once he certainly wouldn't go back. Such scoffing drew angry editorials and speeches, publicity that helped make *Innocents Abroad* successful.

Twain's many travels, including lecture tours around the globe, did not erase the rich material of his Missouri boyhood, which ran deep in his memory and imagination. To get to it, he had, in effect, to work chronologically backward and psychically inward. He tentatively probed this material as early as 1870 in an early version of *The Adventures of Tom Sawyer* called *A Boy's Manuscript*. In 1875 he wrote *Old Times on the Mississippi* in seven installments for the *Atlantic Monthly* (edited by his friend William Dean Howells, who tirelessly promoted Twain's career), arriving at the place that many critics see as his imaginative home. In this work, an account of Twain's adventures as an apprentice to the pilot Horace Bixby, he evokes not only "the great Mississippi, the majestic, the magnificent Mississippi, rolling its mile-wide tide along, shining in the sun," but also his sense of the inner life of what took place on the river's surface and shores. These sketches were later incorporated into *Life on the Mississippi* (1883), written after Twain took a monthlong steamboat trip on the Mississippi, stopping along the way to visit Hannibal. The added material—part history, part memoir, part travelogue—offers, among other things, a scathing critique of the southern romanticism Twain believed had made the Civil War inevitable, a theme that would reappear in his masterpiece, *Adventures of Huckleberry Finn*.

Twain had married Olivia Langdon, genteel and devout daughter of a wealthy coal dealer from Buffalo, New York, in 1870. This entry into a higher stratum of society than he had previously known, along with his increasing fascination with wealth, created a constant struggle in his work between the conventional and the disruptive, which is typical of much of the best American humor. In the perennially popular *The Adventures of Tom Sawyer* (1876), the struggle emerges in the contrast between the entrepreneurial but entirely respectable Tom and his disreputable friend Huck. In this narrative, Twain also mingles childhood pleasures with childhood fears of the violence, terror, and death lurking at the edges of the village. This book has long been recognized as an adult classic as well as a children's book, and its publication established Twain as a popular writer of fiction.

Twain's marriage was a happy one. He went to such lengths as (for a time) attending church and quitting smoking and drinking. His wife read his manuscripts, occasionally noting unseemly material; though she has been criticized for censoring him, this is what Twain wanted her to do. Her unquestioned love and respect for him gave him the security he needed, especially when his fiery personality caused him to become frustrated or depressed.

Twain began *Adventures of Huckleberry Finn* in 1876 and, after several stops and starts, published it in 1884 and 1885. In recent years the racial (and racist) implications of every aspect of the novel have been the subjects of critical debate, as have questions about the racial beliefs of the author. Similar questions have been raised about gender and sexuality in Twain's life and work. In Twain's own day *Huck* was banned in many libraries and schools around the country and denounced in pulpits not for its racial content but for its supposedly encouraging boys to swear, smoke, and run away. Nevertheless, *Huck Finn* has enjoyed extraordinary popularity since its publication. It broke literary ground as a novel written entirely in the vernacular and established the vernacular's capacity to result in high art. Its unpretentious, colloquial, yet poetic style, its wide-ranging humor, its embodiment of the enduring and widely shared dream of innocence and freedom, and its recording of a vanished way of life in the pre–Civil War Mississippi Valley have instructed and moved people of all ages and conditions all over the world. *Huck* sold 51,000 copies in its first fourteen months, compared to *Tom Sawyer's* 25,000 in the same period. Ernest Hemingway once called it the source of "all modern American literature."

Twain wrote another successful and memorable book in this period, the bitter *A*

*Connecticut Yankee in King Arthur's Court* (1889). The novel seems to be a satire on sixth-century Arthurian England seen through the eyes of a crafty "Yankee," Hank Morgan, who is transported back thirteen centuries and tries to "introduce," in Twain's words, the "great and beneficent civilization of the nineteenth century" into the chivalric and decidedly undemocratic world of Camelot. But Hank's "Gilded Age" schemes end in their own destruction and the massacre of thousands of knights. *The Tragedy of Pudd'nhead Wilson* (1894), though a confusing mishmash of separate storylines, is also a dark and troubling view of nineteenth-century American values, set in a Mississippi river town of the 1830s and centered on the switching of two babies born the same day—one the result of miscegenation, the other the legitimate son of a white slave owner. The book painfully reveals the absurdities of slavery and its terrible effects on victims and victimizers alike—the undeserved self-hate of slaves and the unearned pride of whites. The way in which Twain portrays the twinning of law and custom in sustaining the institution of slavery (the book is full of such doublings) indicates his despair over prospects for true racial equality, a despair supported by the realities of Jim Crow laws and the escalation of lynchings in the post-Reconstruction period.

In the decade after *Pudd'nhead Wilson* was published, Twain experienced a series of calamities. Suddenly, his health became bad; poor investments led to bankruptcy in the panic of 1893; his youngest daughter, Jean, was diagnosed as epileptic; his oldest daughter, Susy, died of meningitis while he was away; and his wife, Livy, began to decline into permanent invalidism. Twain's grief for a time threatened his sanity; for several years writing was both agonized labor and necessary therapy. The results of these circumstances were a travel book, *Following the Equator* (1897), which records the round-the-world lecture tour that Twain undertook to pay off debts; a sardonically brilliant interrogation of middle-class American morality, "The Man That Corrupted Hadleyburg" (1900); an embittered treatise on humanity's foibles, follies, and venality, *What Is Man?* (1906); and the bleakly despairing *The Mysterious Stranger*, first published in an inaccurate and unauthorized version by Albert Bigelow Paine, Twain's first biographer, in 1916. Scholars continue to study the large bulk of Twain's unfinished or (until recently) unpublished writings and have called for reevaluation of his work from the decade after 1895. But Lawrence I. Berkove, among others, has emphasized that the notion of a sudden turn to bleak pessimism in his later work, especially the pieces included by Bernard De Voto in the posthumously published *Letters from the Earth* (1961), is incorrect. Twain, argues Berkove, was from the beginning a pessimist, an unorthodox Calvinist who hated God for his malice toward humanity, especially his duplicity in commanding humans to be moral, when he had predestined them to be as they were, and in urging humans to seek salvation, when he had predestined most of them to Hell. Twain was also disgusted with his fellow humans and found the world intolerable. He did not believe that things were meant to turn out right. This can be clearly seen even in such seemingly upbeat earlier works as *Roughing It* and *Huck Finn*. Many humorists have been deeply pessimistic, and Twain fits this mold.

Twain became a revered public institution in his last years, his opinions sought by the press on every subject of general interest. Though his views on political, military, and social subjects were often acerbic, it was only to his best friends that he confessed the depth of his disillusionment. Much of this bitterness informs such published works as "To a Person Sitting in Darkness" (1901), "The United States of Lyncherdom" (1901), and "King Leopold's Soliloquy" (1905), as well as other writings unpublished in his lifetime, such as *Letters from the Earth*, in which he skewers religion from the skeptical and irreverent perspective of Satan, who was punished by being cast down to earth, and who writes letters back to his friend Gabriel.

Twain maintained his magical power with language throughout his career. What he said of one of his characters explains a large part of his permanent appeal: "He could curl his tongue around the bulliest words in the language when he was a mind to, and lay them before you without a jint started, anywheres" (*Life on the Mississippi* [1883], Chapter 3). His love of language informs his hilarious attack on the novels of James Fenimore Cooper, "Fenimore Cooper's Literary Offences" (printed here). As his friend Howells observed, Twain was unlike any of his contemporaries in American letters: "Emerson, Longfellow, Lowell, Holmes—I knew them all and all the rest of our sages, poets, seers, critics, humorists; they were like one another and like other literary men; but Clemens was sole, incomparable, the Lincoln of our literature."

## The Notorious Jumping Frog of Calaveras County[1]

In compliance with the request of a friend of mine, who wrote me from the East, I called on good-natured, garrulous old Simon Wheeler, and inquired after my friend's friend, Leonidas W. Smiley, as requested to do, and I hereunto append the result. I have a lurking suspicion that *Leonidas W.* Smiley is a myth; that my friend never knew such a personage; and that he only conjectured that if I asked old Wheeler about him, it would remind him of his infamous *Jim* Smiley, and he would go to work and bore me to death with some exasperating reminiscence of him as long and as tedious as it should be useless to me. If that was the design, it succeeded.

I found Simon Wheeler dozing comfortably by the barroom stove of the dilapidated tavern in the decayed mining camp of Angel's, and I noticed that he was fat and bald-headed, and had an expression of winning gentleness and simplicity upon his tranquil countenance. He roused up, and gave me goodday. I told him a friend of mine had commissioned me to make some inquiries about a cherished companion of his boyhood named *Leonidas W.* Smiley— *Rev. Leonidas W.* Smiley, a young minister of the Gospel, who he had heard was at one time a resident of Angel's Camp. I added that if Mr. Wheeler could tell me anything about this Rev. Leonidas W. Smiley, I would feel under many obligations to him.

Simon Wheeler backed me into a corner and blockaded me there with his chair, and then sat down and reeled off the monotonous narrative which follows this paragraph. He never smiled, he never frowned, he never changed his voice from the gentle-flowing key to which he tuned his initial sentence, he never betrayed the slightest suspicion of enthusiasm; but all through the interminable narrative there ran a vein of impressive earnestness and sincerity, which showed me plainly that, so far from his imagining that there was anything ridiculous or funny about his story, he regarded it as a really important matter, and admired its two heroes as men of transcendent genius in *finesse.* I let him go on in his own way, and never interrupted him once.

Rev. Leonidas W. H'm, Reverend Le—well, there was a feller here once by the name of *Jim* Smiley, in the winter of '49—or may be it was the spring of '50—I don't recollect exactly, somehow, though what makes me think it was one or the other is because I remember the big flume warn't finished when he first come to the camp; but any way, he was the curiosest man about

---

1. The story first appeared in the *New York Saturday Press* of November 18, 1865, and was subsequently revised several times. The source of the text is the version published in *Mark Twain's Sketches, New and Old* (1875). In a note, Twain instructs his readers that "Calaveras" is pronounced *Cal-e-va'-ras.*

always betting on anything that turned up you ever see, if he could get any-body to bet on the other side; and if he couldn't he'd change sides. Any way that suited the other man would suit *him*—any way just so's he got a bet, *he* was satisfied. But still he was lucky, uncommon lucky; he most always come out winner. He was always ready and laying for a chance; there couldn't be no solit'ry thing mentioned but that feller'd offer to bet on it, and take ary side you please, as I was just telling you. If there was a horse-race, you'd find him flush or you'd find him busted at the end of it; if there was a dog-fight, he'd bet on it; if there was a cat-fight, he'd bet on it; if there was a chicken-fight, he'd bet on it; why, if there was two birds setting on a fence, he would bet you which one would fly first; or if there was a camp-meeting, he would be there reg'lar to bet on Parson Walker, which he judged to be the best exhorter about here, and so he was too, and a good man. If he even see a straddle-bug start to go anywheres, he would bet you how long it would take him to get to—to wherever he was going to, and if you took him up, he would foller that straddle-bug to Mexico but what he would find out where he was bound for and how long he was on the road. Lots of the boys here has seen that Smiley, and can tell you about him. Why, it never made no difference to *him*—he'd bet on *any* thing—the dangdest feller. Parson Walker's wife laid very sick once, for a good while, and it seemed as if they warn't going to save her; but one morning he come in, and Smiley up and asked him how she was, and he said she was considable better—thank the Lord for his inf'nite mercy—and coming on so smart that with the blessing of Prov'dence she'd get well yet; and Smiley, before he thought says, "Well, I'll resk two-and-a-half she don't anyway."

Thish-yer Smiley had a mare—the boys called her the fifteen-minute nag, but that was only in fun, you know, because of course she was faster than that—and he used to win money on that horse, for all she was so slow and always had the asthma, or the distemper, or the consumption, or something of that kind. They used to give her two or three hundred yards start, and then pass her under way; but always at the fag end of the race she'd get excited and desperate-like, and come cavorting and straddling up, and scattering her legs around limber, sometimes in the air, and sometimes out to one side among the fences, and kicking up m-o-r-e dust and raising m-o-r-e racket with her coughing and sneezing and blowing her nose—and *always* fetch up at the stand just about a neck ahead, as near as you could cipher it down.

And he had a little small bull-pup, that to look at him you'd think he warn't worth a cent but to set around and look ornery and lay for a chance to steal something. But as soon as money was up on him he was a different dog; his under-jaw'd begin to stick out like the fo'castle of a steamboat, and his teeth would uncover and shine like the furnaces. And a dog might tackle him and bully-rag him, and bite him, and throw him over his shoulder two or three times, and Andrew Jackson—which was the name of the pup—Andrew Jack-son would never let on but what *he* was satisfied, and hadn't expected noth-ing else—and the bets being doubled and doubled on the other side all the time, till the money was all up; and then all of a sudden he would grab that other dog jest by the j'int of his hind leg and freeze to it—not chaw, you understand, but only just grip and hang on till they throwed up the sponge, if it was a year. Smiley always come out winner on that pup, till he harnessed a dog once that didn't have no hind legs, because they'd been sawed off in a circular saw, and when the thing had gone along far enough, and the money was all up, and he come to make a snatch for his pet holt, he see in a minute how he's been imposed on, and how the other dog had him in the door, so to speak, and he 'peared surprised, and then he looked sorter discouraged-like, and didn't try no more to win the fight, and so he got shucked out bad. He give Smiley a look, as much as to say his heart was broke, and it was *his* fault, for putting up a dog that hadn't no hind legs for him to take holt of, which was his main dependence in a fight, and then he limped off a piece and laid down and died. It was a good pup, was that Andrew Jackson, and would have made a name for hisself if he'd lived, for the stuff was in him and he had genius—I know it, because he hadn't no opportunities to speak of, and it don't stand to reason that a dog could make such a fight as he could under them circumstances if he hadn't no talent. It always makes me feel sorry when I think of that last fight of his'n, and the way it turned out.

Well, thish-yer Smiley had rat-tarriers, and chicken cocks, and tomcats and all them kind of things, till you couldn't rest, and you couldn't fetch nothing for him to bet on but he'd match you. He ketched a frog one day, and took him home, and said he cal'lated to educate him; and so he never done nothing for three months but set in his back yard and learn that frog to jump. And you bet you he *did* learn him, too. He'd give him a little punch behind, and the next minute you'd see that frog whirling in the air like a doughnut—see him turn one summerset, or may be a couple, if he got a good start, and come down flat-footed and all right, like a cat. He got him up so in the matter of ketching flies, and kep' him in practice so constant, that he'd nail a fly every time as fur as he could see him. Smiley said all a frog wanted was education, and he could do 'most anything—and I believe him. Why, I've seen him set Dan'l Webster down here on this floor—Dan'l Webster was the name of the frog—and sing out, "Flies, Dan'l, flies!" and quicker'n you could wink he'd spring straight up and snake a fly off'n the counter there, and flop down on the floor ag'in as solid as a gob of mud, and fall to scratching the side of his head with his hind foot as indifferent as if he hadn't no idea he'd been doin' any more'n any frog might do. You never see a frog so modest and straight-for'ard as he was, for all he was so gifted. And when it come to fair and square jumping on a dead level, he could get over more ground at one straddle than any animal of his breed you ever see. Jumping on a dead level was his strong suit, you understand; and when it come to that, Smiley would ante up money on him as long as he had a red. Smiley was monstrous proud of his frog, and well he might be, for fellers that had traveled and been everywheres all said he laid over any frog that ever *they* see.

Well, Smiley kep' the beast in a little lattice box, and he used to fetch him down town sometimes and lay for a bet. One day a feller—a stranger in the camp, he was—come acrost him with his box, and says:

"What might it be that you've got in the box?"

And Smiley says, sorter indifferent-like, "It might be a parrot, or it might be a canary, maybe, but it ain't—it's only just a frog."

And the feller took it, and looked at it careful, and turned it round this way and that, and says, "H'm—so 'tis. Well, what's *he* good for?"

"Well," Smiley says, easy and careless, "he's good enough for *one* thing, I should judge—he can outjump any frog in Calaveras county."

The feller took the box again, and took another long, particular look, and give it back to Smiley, and says, very deliberate, "Well," he says, "I don't see no p'ints about that frog that's any better'n any other frog."

"Maybe you don't," Smiley says. "Maybe you understand frogs and maybe you don't understand 'em; maybe you've had experience, and maybe you ain't only an amature, as it were. Anyways, I've got *my* opinion and I'll resk forty dollars that he can outjump any frog in Calaveras county."

And the feller studied a minute, and then says, kinder sad like, "Well, I'm only a stranger here, and I ain't got no frog; but if I had a frog, I'd bet you."

And then Smiley says, "That's all right—that's all right—if you'll hold my box a minute, I'll go and get you a frog." And so the feller took the box, and put up his forty dollars along with Smiley's, and set down to wait.

So he set there a good while thinking and thinking to hisself, and then he got the frog out and prized his mouth open and took a teaspoon and filled him full of quail shot—filled him pretty near up to his chin—and set him on the floor. Smiley he went to the swamp and slopped around in the mud for a long time, and finally he ketched a frog, and fetched him in, and give him to this feller, and says:

"Now, if you're ready, set him alongside of Dan'l, with his forepaws just even with Dan'l's, and I'll give the word." Then he says, "One—two—three—*git!*" and him and the feller touched up the frogs from behind, and the new frog hopped off lively, but Dan'l give a heave, and hysted up his shoulders—so—like a Frenchman, but it warn't no use—he couldn't budge; he was planted as solid as a church, and he couldn't no more stir than if he was anchored out. Smiley was a good deal surprised, and he was disgusted too, but he didn't have no idea what the matter was, of course.

The feller took the money and started away; and when he was going out at the door, he sorter jerked his thumb over his shoulder—so—at Dan'l, and says again, very deliberate, "Well," he says, "*I* don't see no p'ints about that frog that's any better'n any other frog."

Smiley he stood scratching his head and looking down at Dan'l a long time, and at last he says, "I do wonder what in the nation that frog throw'd off for—I wonder if there ain't something the matter with him—he 'pears to look mighty baggy, somehow." And he ketched Dan'l by the nap of the neck, and hefted him, and says, "Why blame my cats if he don't weigh five pound!" and turned him upside down and he belched out a double handful of shot. And then he see how it was, and he was the maddest man—he set the frog down and took out after that feller, but he never ketched him. And——"

[Here Simon Wheeler heard his name called from the front yard, and got up to see what was wanted.] And turning to me as he moved away, he said: "Just set where you are, stranger, and rest easy—I ain't going to be gone a second."

But, by your leave, I did not think that a continuation of the history of the enterprising vagabond *Jim* Smiley would be likely to afford me much information concerning the *Rev. Leonidas W.* Smiley, and so I started away.

At the door I met the sociable Wheeler returning, and he button-holed me and recommenced:

"Well, thish-yer Smiley had a yaller one-eyed cow that didn't have no tail, only jest a short stump like a bannanner, and——"

However, lacking both time and inclination, I did not wait to hear about the afflicted cow, but took my leave.

1865, 1867

# Adventures of Huckleberry Finn[1]

*(Tom Sawyer's Comrade)*

*Scene: The Mississippi Valley*

*Time: Forty to Fifty Years Ago*[2]

---

NOTICE
Persons attempting to find a motive in this narrative will be prosecuted; persons attempting to find a moral in it will be banished; persons attempting to find a plot in it will be shot.

BY ORDER OF THE AUTHOR
PER G. G., CHIEF OF ORDNANCE.

---

*Explanatory*

In this book a number of dialects are used, to wit: the Missouri negro dialect; the extremest form of the backwoods South-Western dialect; the ordinary "Pike-County"[3] dialect; and four modified varieties of this last. The shadings have not been done in a hap-hazard fashion, or by guess-work; but pains-takingly, and with the trustworthy guidance and support of personal familiarity with these several forms of speech.

I make this explanation for the reason that without it many readers would suppose that all these characters were trying to talk alike and not succeeding.

THE AUTHOR

## Chapter I

You don't know about me, without you have read a book by the name of "The Adventures of Tom Sawyer,"[4] but that ain't no matter. That book was made by Mr. Mark Twain, and he told the truth, mainly. There was things which he stretched, but mainly he told the truth. That is nothing. I never seen anybody but lied, one time or another, without it was Aunt Polly, or the widow, or maybe Mary. Aunt Polly—Tom's Aunt Polly, she is—and Mary, and the Widow Douglas, is all told about in that book—which is mostly a true book; with some stretchers, as I said before.

---

1. *Adventures of Huckleberry Finn* was first published in England in December 1884. The text printed here is a corrected version of the first American edition of 1885.

2. I.e., in 1835 or 1845—well before the Civil War.

3. Pike County, Missouri.

4. Published in 1876.

Now the way that the book winds up, is this: Tom and me found the money that the robbers hid in the cave, and it made us rich. We got six thousand dollars apiece—all gold. It was an awful sight of money when it was piled up. Well, Judge Thatcher, he took it and put it out at interest, and it fetched us a dollar a day apiece, all the year round—more than a body could tell what to do with. The Widow Douglas, she took me for her son, and allowed she would sivilize me; but it was rough living in the house all the time, considering how dismal regular and decent the widow was in all her ways; and so when I couldn't stand it no longer, I lit out. I got into my old rags, and my sugar-hogshead[5] again, and was free and satisfied. But Tom Sawyer, he hunted me up and said he was going to start a band of robbers, and I might join if I would go back to the widow and be respectable. So I went back.

The widow she cried over me, and called me a poor lost lamb, and she called me a lot of other names, too, but she never meant no harm by it. She put me in them new clothes again, and I couldn't do nothing but sweat and sweat, and feel all cramped up. Well, then, the old thing commenced again. The widow rung a bell for supper, and you had to come to time. When you got to the table you couldn't go right to eating, but you had to wait for the widow to tuck down her head and grumble a little over the victuals, though there warn't really anything the matter with them. That is, nothing only everything was cooked by itself. In a barrel of odds and ends it is different; things get mixed up, and the juice kind of swaps around, and the things go better.

After supper she got out her book and learned me about Moses and the Bulrushers;[6] and I was in a sweat to find out all about him; but by-and-by she let it out that Moses had been dead a considerable long time; so then I didn't care no more about him; because I don't take no stock in dead people.

Pretty soon I wanted to smoke, and asked the widow to let me. But she wouldn't. She said it was a mean practice and wasn't clean, and I must try to not do it any more. That is just the way with some people. They get down on a thing when they don't know nothing about it. Here she was a bothering about Moses, which was no kin to her, and no use to anybody, being gone, you see, yet finding a power of fault with me for doing a thing that had some good in it. And she took snuff too; of course that was all right, because she done it herself.

Her sister, Miss Watson, a tolerable slim old maid, with goggles on, had just come to live with her, and took a set at me now, with a spelling-book. She worked me middling hard for about an hour, and then the widow made her ease up. I couldn't stood it much longer. Then for an hour it was deadly dull, and I was fidgety. Miss Watson would say, "Don't put your feet up there, Huckleberry"; and "don't scrunch up like that, Huckleberry—set up straight"; and pretty soon she would say, "Don't gap and stretch like that, Huckleberry—why don't you try to behave?" Then she told me all about the bad place, and I said I wished I was there. She got mad, then, but I didn't mean no harm. All I wanted was to go somewheres; all I wanted was a change, I warn't particular. She said it was wicked to say what I said; said she wouldn't say it for the whole world; *she* was going to live so as to go to the good place. Well, I couldn't see no advantage in going where she was going, so I made up

---

5. A large barrel.
6. Pharaoh's daughter discovered the infant Moses floating in the Nile in a basket woven from bulrushes (Exodus 2). She adopted him into the royal family just as the widow has adopted Huck.

my mind I wouldn't try for it. But I never said so, because it would only make trouble, and wouldn't do no good.

Now she had got a start, and she went on and told me all about the good place. She said all a body would have to do there was to go around all day long with a harp and sing, forever and ever.[7] So I didn't think much of it. But I never said so. I asked her if she reckoned Tom Sawyer would go there, and, she said, not by a considerable sight. I was glad about that, because I wanted him and me to be together.

Miss Watson she kept pecking at me, and it got tiresome and lonesome. By-and-by they fetched the niggers[8] in and had prayers, and then everybody was off to bed. I went up to my room with a piece of candle and put it on the table. Then I set down in a chair by the window and tried to think of something cheerful, but it warn't no use. I felt so lonesome I most wished I was dead. The stars was shining, and the leaves rustled in the woods ever so mournful; and I heard an owl, away off, who-whooing about somebody that was dead, and a whippowill and a dog crying about somebody that was going to die; and the wind was trying to whisper something to me and I couldn't make out what it was, and so it made the cold shivers run over me. Then away out in the woods I heard that kind of a sound that a ghost makes when it wants to tell about something that's on its mind and can't make itself understood, and so can't rest easy in its grave and has to go about that way every night grieving. I got so down-hearted and scared, I did wish I had some company. Pretty soon a spider went crawling up my shoulder, and I flipped it off and it lit in the candle; and before I could budge it was all shriveled up. I didn't need anybody to tell me that that was an awful bad sign and would fetch me some bad luck, so I was scared and most shook the clothes off of me. I got up and turned around in my tracks three times and crossed my breast every time; and then I tied up a little lock of my hair with a thread to keep witches away. But I hadn't no confidence. You do that when you've lost a horse-shoe that you've found, instead of nailing it up over the door, but I hadn't ever heard anybody say it was any way to keep off bad luck when you'd killed a spider.

I set down again, a shaking all over, and got out my pipe for a smoke; for the house was all as still as death, now, and so the widow wouldn't know. Well, after a long time I heard the clock away off in the town go boom—boom—boom—twelve licks—and all still again—stiller than ever. Pretty soon I heard a twig snap, down in the dark amongst the trees—something was a stirring. I set still and listened. Directly I could just barely hear a *"me-yow! me-yow!"* down there. That was good! Says I, *"me-yow! me-yow!"* as soft as I could, and then I put out the light and scrambled out of the window onto the shed. Then I slipped down to the ground and crawled in amongst the trees, and sure enough there was Tom Sawyer waiting for me.

## Chapter II

We went tip-toeing along a path amongst the trees back towards the end of the widow's garden, stooping down so as the branches wouldn't scrape our

*[Handwritten margin notes: "Creepy", "Sad / depressing", "Spider", "out of all the creepiness comes good. It's almost like hell bc it was outside. no prayers cared when Tom was there"]*

7. Conventional conceptions of the Christian heaven were satirized early and late in Twain's writings.
8. Huck appropriately speaks the colloquial word used in the South to describe black slaves; it is not used derisively or contemptuously by him, though for much of the narrative Huck expresses the racial prejudices of his time and place.

heads. When we was passing by the kitchen I fell over a root and made a noise. We scrouched down and laid still. Miss Watson's big nigger, named Jim, was setting in the kitchen door; we could see him pretty clear, because there was a light behind him. He got up and stretched his neck out about a minute, listening. Then he says,

"Who dah?"

He listened some more; then he come tip-toeing down and stood right between us; we could a touched him, nearly. Well, likely it was minutes and minutes that there warn't a sound, and we all there so close together. There was a place on my ankle that got to itching; but I dasn't scratch it; and then my ear begun to itch; and next my back, right between my shoulders. Seemed like I'd die if I couldn't scratch. Well, I've noticed that thing plenty of times since. If you are with the quality, or at a funeral, or trying to go to sleep when you ain't sleepy—if you are anywheres where it won't do for you to scratch, why you will itch all over in upwards of a thousand places. Pretty soon Jim says:

"Say—who is you? Whar is you? Dog my cats ef I didn' hear sumf'n. Well, I knows what I's gwyne to do. I's gwyne to set down here and listen tell I hears it agin."

So he set down on the ground betwixt me and Tom. He leaned his back up against a tree, and stretched his legs out till one of them most touched one of mine. My nose begun to itch. It itched till the tears come into my eyes. But I dasn't scratch. Then it begun to itch on the inside. Next I got to itching underneath. I didn't know how I was going to set still. This miserableness went on as much as six or seven minutes; but it seemed a sight longer than that. I was itching in eleven different places now. I reckoned I couldn't stand it more'n a minute longer, but I set my teeth hard and got ready to try. Just then Jim begun to breathe heavy; next he begun to snore—and then I was pretty soon comfortable again.

Tom he made a sign to me—kind of a little noise with his mouth—and we went creeping away on our hands and knees. When we was ten foot off, Tom whispered to me and wanted to tie Jim to the tree for fun; but I said no; he might wake and make a disturbance, and then they'd find out I warn't in. Then Tom said he hadn't got candles enough, and he would slip in the kitchen and get some more. I didn't want him to try. I said Jim might wake up and come. But Tom wanted to resk it; so we slid in there and got three candles, and Tom laid five cents on the table for pay. Then we got out, and I was in a sweat to get away; but nothing would do Tom but he must crawl to where Jim was, on his hands and knees, and play something on him. I waited, and it seemed a good while, everything was so still and lonesome.

As soon as Tom was back, we cut along the path, around the garden fence, and by-and-by fetched up on the steep top of the hill the other side of the house. Tom said he slipped Jim's hat off of his head and hung it on a limb right over him, and Jim stirred a little, but he didn't wake. Afterwards Jim said the witches bewitched him and put him in a trance, and rode him all over the State, and then set him under the trees again and hung his hat on a limb to show who done it. And next time Jim told it he said they rode him down to New Orleans; and after that, every time he told it he spread it more and more, till by-and-by he said they rode him all over the world, and tired him most to death, and his back was all over saddle-boils. Jim was monstrous proud about

*how's a
celebration.*

it, and he got so he wouldn't hardly notice the other niggers. Niggers would come miles to hear Jim tell about it, and he was more looked up to than any nigger in that country. Strange niggers[9] would stand with their mouths open and look him all over, same as if he was a wonder. Niggers is always talking about witches in the dark by the kitchen fire; but whenever one was talking and letting on to know all about such things, Jim would happen in and say, "Hm! What you know 'bout witches?" and that nigger was corked up and had to take a back seat. Jim always kept that five-center piece around his neck with a string and said it was a charm the devil give to him with his own hands and told him he could cure anybody with it and fetch witches whenever he wanted to, just by saying something to it; but he never told what it was he said to it. Niggers would come from all around there and give Jim anything they had, just for a sight of the five-center piece; but they wouldn't touch it, because the devil had had his hands on it. Jim was most ruined, for a servant, because he got so stuck up on account of having seen the devil and been rode by witches.

Well, when Tom and me got to the edge of the hill-top, we looked away down into the village[1] and could see three or four lights twinkling, where there was sick folks, may be; and the stars over us was sparkling ever so fine; and down by the village was the river, a whole mile broad, and awful still and grand. We went down the hill and found Jo Harper, and Ben Rogers, and two or three more of the boys, hid in the old tanyard. So we unhitched a skiff and pulled down the river two mile and a half, to the big scar on the hillside, and went ashore.

*reflective of
MT's riverboat
days.*

We went to a clump of bushes, and Tom made everybody swear to keep the secret, and then showed them a hole in the hill, right in the thickest part of the bushes. Then we lit the candles and crawled in on our hands and knees. We went about two hundred yards, and then the cave opened up. Tom poked about amongst the passages and pretty soon ducked under a wall where you wouldn't a noticed that there was a hole. We went along a narrow place and got into a kind of room, all damp and sweaty and cold, and there we stopped. Tom says:

"Now we'll start this band of robbers and call it Tom Sawyer's Gang. Everybody that wants to join has got to take an oath, and write his name in blood."

Everybody was willing. So Tom got out a sheet of paper that he had wrote the oath on, and read it. It swore every boy to stick to the band, and never tell any of the secrets; and if anybody done anything to any boy in the band, whichever boy was ordered to kill that person and his family must do it, and he mustn't eat and he mustn't sleep till he had killed them and hacked a cross in their breasts, which was the sign of the band. And nobody that didn't belong to the band could use that mark, and if he did he must be sued; and if he done it again he must be killed. And if anybody that belonged to the band told the secrets, he must have his throat cut, and then have his carcass burnt up and the ashes scattered all around, and his name blotted off of the list with blood and never mentioned again by the gang, but have a curse put on it and be forgot, forever.

*crosses →
representing
the south?*

9. Those who did not live in the immediate area.
1. The village, called St. Petersburg here and in *Tom Sawyer*, is modeled on Hannibal, Missouri.

Everybody said it was a real beautiful oath, and asked Tom if he got it out of his own head. He said, some of it, but the rest was out of pirate books, and robber books, and every gang that was high-toned had it.

Some thought it would be good to kill the *families* of boys that told the secrets. Tom said it was a good idea, so he took a pencil and wrote it in. Then Ben Rogers says:

"Here's Huck Finn, he hain't got no family—what you going to do 'bout him?"

"Well, hain't he got a father?" says Tom Sawyer.

"Yes, he's got a father, but you can't never find him, these days. He used to lay drunk with the hogs in the tanyard, but he hain't been seen in these parts for a year or more."

They talked it over, and they was going to rule me out, because they said every boy must have a family or somebody to kill, or else it wouldn't be fair and square for the others. Well, nobody could think of anything to do—everybody was stumped, and set still. I was most ready to cry; but all at once I thought of a way, and so I offered them Miss Watson—they could kill her. Everybody said:

"Oh, she'll do, she'll do. That's all right. Huck can come in."

Then they all stuck a pin in their fingers to get blood to sign with, and I made my mark on the paper.

"Now," says Ben Rogers, "what's the line of business of this Gang?"

"Nothing only robbery and murder," Tom said.

"But who are we going to rob? houses—or cattle—or—"

"Stuff! stealing cattle and such things ain't robbery, it's burglary," says Tom Sawyer. "We ain't burglars. That ain't no sort of style. We are highwaymen. We stop stages and carriages on the road, with masks on, and kill the people and take their watches and money."

"Must we always kill the people?"

"Oh, certainly. It's best. Some authorities think different, but mostly it's considered best to kill them. Except some that you bring to the cave here and keep them till they're ransomed."

"Ransomed? What's that?"

"I don't know. But that's what they do. I've seen it in books; and so of course that's what we've got to do."

"But how can we do it if we don't know what it is?"

"Why blame it all, we've *got* to do it. Don't I tell you it's in the books? Do you want to go to doing different from what's in the books, and get things all muddled up?"

"Oh, that's all very fine to *say,* Tom Sawyer, but how in the nation[2] are these fellows going to be ransomed if we don't know how to do it to them? that's the thing I want to get at. Now what do you *reckon* it is?"

"Well I don't know. But per'aps if we keep them till they're ransomed, it means that we keep them till they're dead."

"Now, that's something *like.* That'll answer. Why couldn't you said that before? We'll keep them till they're ransomed to death—and a bothersome lot they'll be, too, eating up everything and always trying to get loose."

2. Damnation.

"How you talk, Ben Rogers. How can they get loose when there's a guard over them, ready to shoot them down if they move a peg?"

"A guard. Well, that *is* good. So somebody's got to set up all night and never get any sleep, just so as to watch them. I think that's foolishness. Why can't a body take a club and ransom them as soon as they get here?"

"Because it ain't in the books so—that's why. Now Ben Rogers, do you want to do things regular, or don't you?—that's the idea. Don't you reckon that the people that made the books knows what's the correct thing to do? Do you reckon *you* can learn 'em anything? Not by a good deal. No, sir, we'll just go on and ransom them in the regular way."

"All right. I don't mind; but I say it's a fool way, anyhow. Say—do we kill the women, too?"

"Well, Ben Rogers, if I was as ignorant as you I wouldn't let on. Kill the women? No—nobody ever saw anything in the books like that. You fetch them to the cave, and you're always as polite as pie to them; and by-and-by they fall in love with you and never want to go home any more."

"Well, if that's the way, I'm agreed, but I don't take no stock in it. Mighty soon we'll have the cave so cluttered up with women, and fellows waiting to be ransomed, that there won't be no place for the robbers. But go ahead, I ain't got nothing to say."

Little Tommy Barnes was asleep, now, and when they waked him up he was scared, and cried, and said he wanted to go home to his ma, and didn't want to be a robber any more.

So they all made fun of him, and called him cry-baby, and that made him mad, and he said he would go straight and tell all the secrets. But Tom give him five cents to keep quiet, and said we would all go home and meet next week and rob somebody and kill some people.

Ben Rogers said he couldn't get out much, only Sundays, and so he wanted to begin next Sunday; but all the boys said it would be wicked to do it on Sunday, and that settled the thing. They agreed to get together and fix a day as soon as they could, and then we elected Tom Sawyer first captain and Jo Harper second captain of the Gang, and so started home.

I clumb up the shed and crept into my window just before day was breaking. My new clothes was all greased up and clayey, and I was dog-tired.

*[handwritten marginalia: satirical perspective on the "gang"]*

### Chapter III

Well, I got a good going-over in the morning, from old Miss Watson, on account of my clothes; but the widow she didn't scold, but only cleaned off the grease and clay and looked so sorry that I thought I would behave a while if I could. Then Miss Watson she took me in the closet[3] and prayed, but nothing come of it. She told me to pray every day, and whatever I asked for I would get it. But it warn't so. I tried it. Once I got a fish-line, but no hooks. It warn't any good to me without hooks. I tried for the hooks three or four times, but somehow I couldn't make it work. By-and-by, one day, I asked Miss Watson to try for me, but she said I was a fool. She never told me why, and I couldn't make it out no way.

---

3. "But thou, when thou prayest, enter into thy closet" (Matthew 6.6) is apparently the admonition Miss Watson has in mind.

I set down, one time, back in the woods, and had a long think about it. I says to myself, if a body can get anything they pray for, why don't Deacon Winn get back the money he lost on pork? Why can't the widow get back her silver snuff-box that was stole? Why can't Miss Watson fat up? No, says I to myself, there ain't nothing in it. I went and told the widow about it, and she said the thing a body could get by praying for it was "spiritual gifts." This was too many for me, but she told me what she meant—I must help other people, and do everything I could for other people, and look out for them all the time, and never think about myself. This was including Miss Watson, as I took it. I went out in the woods and turned it over in my mind a long time, but I couldn't see no advantage about it—except for the other people—so at last I reckoned I wouldn't worry about it any more, but just let it go. Sometimes the widow would take me one side and talk about Providence in a way to make a boy's mouth water; but maybe next day Miss Watson would take hold and knock it all down again. I judged I could see that there was two Providences, and a poor chap would stand considerable show with the widow's Providence, but if Miss Watson's got him there warn't no help for him any more. I thought it all out, and reckoned I would belong to the widow's, if he wanted me, though I couldn't make out how he was agoing to be any better off then than what he was before, seeing I was so ignorant and so kind of low-down and ornery.

Pap he hadn't been seen for more than a year, and that was comfortable for me; I didn't want to see him no more. He used to always whale me when he was sober and could get his hands on me; though I used to take to the woods most of the time when he was around. Well, about this time he was found in the river drowned, about twelve mile above town, so people said. They judged it was him, anyway; said this drowned man was just his size, and was ragged, and had uncommon long hair—which was all like pap—but they couldn't make nothing out of the face, because it had been in the water so long it warn't much like a face at all. They said he was floating on his back in the water. They took him and buried him on the bank. But I warn't comfortable long, because I happened to think of something. I knowed mighty well that a drownded man don't float on his back, but on his face. So I knowed, then, that this warn't pap, but a woman dressed up in a man's clothes. So I was uncomfortable again. I judged the old man would turn up again by-and-by, though I wished he wouldn't.

We played robber now and then about a month, and then I resigned. All the boys did. We hadn't robbed nobody, we hadn't killed any people, but only just pretended. We used to hop out of the woods and go charging down on hog-drovers and women in carts taking garden stuff to market, but we never hived[4] any of them. Tom Sawyer called the hogs "ingots," and he called the turnips and stuff "julery" and we would go to the cave and pow-wow over what we had done and how many people we had killed and marked. But I couldn't see no profit in it. One time Tom sent a boy to run about town with a blazing stick, which he called a slogan (which was the sign for the Gang to get together), and then he said he had got secret news by his spies that next day a whole parcel of Spanish merchants and rich A-rabs was going to camp in Cave Hol-

4. Captured, secured.

low with two hundred elephants, and six hundred camels, and over a thousand "sumter" mules,[5] all loaded with di'monds, and they didn't have only a guard of four hundred soldiers, and so we would lay in ambuscade, as he called it, and kill the lot and scoop the things. He said we must slick up our swords and guns, and get ready. He never could go after even a turnip-cart but he must have the swords and guns all scoured up for it; though they was only lath and broom-sticks, and you might scour at them till you rotted and then they warn't worth a mouthful of ashes more than what they was before. I didn't believe we could lick such a crowd of Spaniards and A-rabs, but I wanted to see the camels and elephants, so I was on hand next day, Saturday, in the ambuscade; and when we got the word, we rushed out of the woods and down the hill. But there warn't no Spaniards and A-rabs, and there warn't no camels nor no elephants. It warn't anything but a Sunday-school picnic, and only a primer-class at that. We busted it up, and chased the children up the hollow; but we never got anything but some doughnuts and jam, though Ben Rogers got a rag doll, and Jo Harper got a hymn-book and a tract; and then the teacher charged in and made us drop everything and cut. I didn't see no di'monds, and I told Tom Sawyer so. He said there was loads of them there, anyway; and he said there was A-rabs there, too, and elephants and things. I said, why couldn't we see them, then? He said if I warn't so ignorant, but had read a book called "Don Quixote,"[6] I would know without asking. He said it was all done by enchantment. He said there was hundreds of soldiers there, and elephants and treasure, and so on, but we had enemies which he called magicians, and they had turned the whole thing into an infant Sunday school, just out of spite. I said, all right, then the thing for us to do was to go for the magicians. Tom Sawyer said I was a numskull.

"Why," says he, "a magician could call up a lot of genies, and they would hash you up like nothing before you could say Jack Robinson. They are as tall as a tree and as big around as a church."

"Well," I says, "s'pose we got some genies to help *us*—can't we lick the other crowd then?"

"How you going to get them?"

"I don't know. How do *they* get them?"

"Why they rub an old tin lamp or an iron ring, and then the genies come tearing in, with the thunder and lightning a-ripping around and the smoke a-rolling, and everything they're told to do they up and do it. They don't think nothing of pulling a shot tower[7] up by the roots, and belting a Sunday-school superintendent over the head with it—or any other man."

"Who makes them tear around so?"

"Why, whoever rubs the lamp or the ring. They belong to whoever rubs the lamp or the ring, and they've got to do whatever he says. If he tells them to build a palace forty miles long, out of di'monds, and fill it full of chewing gum, or whatever you want, and fetch an emperor's daughter from China for you to marry, they've got to do it—and they've got to do it before sun-up next morning, too. And more—they've got to waltz that palace around over the country whenever you want it, you understand."

---

5. Pack mules.
6. Tom is here alluding to stories in *The Arabian Nights Entertainments* (1838–41) and to the hero in Cervantes' *Don Quixote* (1605).
7. A device in which gunshot was formed by dripping molten lead into water.

"Well," says I, "I think they are a pack of flatheads for not keeping the palace themselves 'stead of fooling them away like that. And what's more—if I was one of them I would see a man in Jericho before I would drop my business and come to him for the rubbing of an old tin lamp."

"How you talk, Huck Finn. Why, you'd *have* to come when he rubbed it, whether you wanted to or not."

"What, and I as high as a tree and as big as a church? All right, then; I *would* come; but I lay I'd make that man climb the highest tree there was in the country."

"Shucks, it ain't no use to talk to you, Huck Finn. You don't seem to know anything, somehow—perfect sap-head."

I thought all this over for two or three days, and then I reckoned I would see if there was anything in it. I got an old tin lamp and an iron ring and went out in the woods and rubbed and rubbed till I sweat like an Injun, calculating to build a palace and sell it; but it warn't no use, none of the genies come. So then I judged that all that stuff was only just one of Tom Sawyer's lies. I reckoned he believed in the A-rabs and the elephants, but as for me I think different. It had all the marks of a Sunday school.

## Chapter IV

Well, three or four months run along, and it was well into the winter, now. I had been to school most all the time, and could spell, and read, and write just a little, and could say the multiplication table up to six times seven is thirty-five, and I don't reckon I could ever get any further than that if I was to live forever. I don't take no stock in mathematics, anyway.

At first I hated the school, but by-and-by I got so I could stand it. Whenever I got uncommon tired I played hookey, and the hiding I got next day done me good and cheered me up. So the longer I went to school the easier it got to be. I was getting sort of used to the widow's ways, too, and they warn't so raspy on me. Living in a house, and sleeping in a bed, pulled on me pretty tight, mostly, but before the cold weather I used to slide out and sleep in the woods, sometimes, and so that was a rest to me. I liked the old ways best, but I was getting so I liked the new ones, too, a little bit. The widow said I was coming along slow but sure, and doing very satisfactory. She said she warn't ashamed of me.

One morning I happened to turn over the salt-cellar at breakfast. I reached for some of it as quick as I could, to throw over my left shoulder and keep off the bad luck, but Miss Watson was in ahead of me, and crossed me off. She says, "Take your hands away, Huckleberry—what a mess you are always making." The widow put in a good word for me, but that warn't going to keep off the bad luck, I knowed that well enough. I started out, after breakfast, feeling worried and shaky, and wondering where it was going to fall on me, and what it was going to be. There is ways to keep off some kinds of bad luck, but this wasn't one of them kind; so I never tried to do anything, but just poked along low-spirited and on the watch-out.

I went down the front garden and clumb over the stile,[8] where you go through the high board fence. There was an inch of new snow on the ground,

---

8. Steps that flank and straddle a fence.

*His DAD?*

and I seen somebody's tracks. They had come up from the quarry and stood around the stile a while, and then went on around the garden fence. It was funny they hadn't come in, after standing around so. I couldn't make it out. It was very curious, somehow. I was going to follow around, but I stooped down to look at the tracks first. I didn't notice anything at first, but next I did. There was a cross in the left boot-heel made with big nails, to keep off the devil.

I was up in a second and shinning down the hill. I looked over my shoulder every now and then, but I didn't see nobody. I was at Judge Thatcher's as quick as I could get there. He said:

"Why, my boy, you are all out of breath. Did you come for your interest?"

"No sir," I says; "is there some for me?"

"Oh, yes, a half-yearly is in, last night. Over a hundred and fifty dollars. Quite a fortune for you. You better let me invest it along with your six thousand, because if you take it you'll spend it."

"No sir," I says, "I don't want to spend it. I don't want it at all—nor the six thousand, nuther. I want you to take it; I want to give it to you—the six thousand and all."

He looked surprised. He couldn't seem to make it out. He says:

"Why, what can you mean, my boy?"

I says, "Don't you ask me no questions about it, please. You'll take it—won't you?"

He says:

"Well I'm puzzled. Is something the matter?"

"Please take it," says I, "and don't ask me nothing—then I won't have to tell no lies."

He studied a while, and then he says:

"Oho-o. I think I see. You want to *sell* all your property to me—not give it. That's the correct idea."

Then he wrote something on a paper and read it over, and says:

"There—you see it says 'for a consideration.' That means I have bought it of you and paid you for it. Here's a dollar for you. Now, you sign it."

So I signed it, and left.

Miss Watson's nigger, Jim, had a hair-ball as big as your fist, which had been took out of the fourth stomach of an ox, and he used to do magic with it.[9] He said there was a spirit inside of it, and it knowed everything. So I went to him that night and told him pap was here again, for I found his tracks in the snow. What I wanted to know, was, what he was going to do, and was he going to stay? Jim got out his hair-ball, and said something over it, and then he held it up and dropped it on the floor. It fell pretty solid, and only rolled about an inch. Jim tried it again, and then another time, and it acted just the same. Jim got down on his knees and put his ear against it and listened. But it warn't no use; he said it wouldn't talk. He said sometimes it wouldn't talk without money. I told him I had an old slick counterfeit quarter that warn't no good because the brass showed through the silver a little, and it wouldn't pass nohow, even if the brass didn't show, because it was so slick it felt greasy, and so that would tell on it every time. (I reckoned I wouldn't say nothing about the dollar I got from the judge.) I said it was pretty bad money, but

9. Though most of the superstitions in *Tom Sawyer* and *Huck Finn* have been traced to European sources, belief in the magical powers of hair balls found in the stomachs of oxen seems to be African American in origin.

maybe the hair-ball would take it, because maybe it wouldn't know the difference. Jim smelt it, and bit it, and rubbed it, and said he would manage so the hair-ball would think it was good. He said he would split open a raw Irish potato and stick the quarter in between and keep it there all night, and next morning you couldn't see no brass, and it wouldn't feel greasy no more, and so anybody in town would take it in a minute, let alone a hair-ball. Well, I knowed a potato would do that, before, but I had forgot it.

Jim put the quarter under the hair-ball and got down and listened again. This time he said the hair-ball was all right. He said it would tell my whole fortune if I wanted it to. I says, go on. So the hair-ball talked to Jim, and Jim told it to me. He says:

"Yo' ole father doan' know, yit, what he's a-gwyne to do. Sometimes he spec he'll go 'way, en den agin he spec he'll stay. De bes' way is to res' easy en let de ole man take his own way. Dey's two angels hoverin' roun' 'bout him. One uv 'em is white en shiny, en 'tother one is black. De white one gits him to go right, a little while, den de black one sail in en bust it all up. A body can't tell, yit, which one gwyne to fetch him at de las'. But you is all right. You gwyne to have considable trouble in yo' life, en considable joy. Sometimes you gwyne to git hurt, en sometimes you gwyne to git sick; but every time you's gwyne to git well agin. Dey's two gals flyin' 'bout you in yo' life. One uv 'em's light en 'tother one is dark. One is rich en 'tother is po'. You's gwyne to marry de po' one fust en de rich one by-en-by. You wants to keep 'way fum de water as much as you kin, en don't run no resk, 'kase it's down in de bills dat you's gwyne to git hung."

*[handwritten margin note: Irony. Deamonizing black through a black Character]*

When I lit my candle and went up to my room that night, there set pap, his own self!

## Chapter V

I had shut the door to. Then I turned around, and there he was. I used to be scared of him all the time, he tanned me so much. I reckoned I was scared now, too; but in a minute I see I was mistaken. That is, after the first jolt, as you may say, when my breath sort of hitched—he being so unexpected; but right away after, I see I warn't scared of him worth bothering about.

He was most fifty, and he looked it. His hair was long and tangled and greasy, and hung down, and you could see his eyes shining through like he was behind vines. It was all black, no gray; so was his long, mixed-up whiskers. There warn't no color in his face, where his face showed; it was white; not like another man's white, but a white to make a body sick, a white to make a body's flesh crawl—a tree-toad white, a fish-belly white. As for his clothes—just rags, that was all. He had one ankle resting on 'tother knee; the boot on that foot was busted, and two of his toes stuck through, and he worked them now and then. His hat was laying on the floor; an old black slouch with the top caved in, like a lid.

I stood a-looking at him; he set there a-looking at me, with his chair tilted back a little. I set the candle down. I noticed the window was up; so he had clumb in by the shed. He kept a-looking me all over. By-and-by he says:

"Starchy clothes—very. You think you're a good deal of a big-bug, *don't* you?"

"Maybe I am, maybe I ain't," I says.

"Don't you give me none o' your lip," says he. "You've put on considerble many frills since I been away. I'll take you down a peg before I get done with you. You're educated, too, they say; can read and write. You think you're bet-ter'n your father, now, don't you, because he can't? *I'll* take it out of you. Who told you you might meddle with such hifalut'n foolishness, hey?—who told you you could?"

"The widow. She told me."

"The widow, hey?—and who told the widow she could put in her shovel about a thing that ain't none of her business?"

"Nobody never told her."

"Well, I'll learn her how to meddle. And looky here—you drop that school, you hear? I'll learn people to bring up a boy to put on airs over his own father and let on to be better'n what *he* is. You lemme catch you fooling around that school again, you hear? Your mother couldn't read, and she couldn't write, nuther, before she died. None of the family couldn't, before *they* died. *I* can't; and here you're a-swelling yourself up like this. I ain't the man to stand it— you hear? Say—lemme hear you read."

I took up a book and begun something about General Washington and the wars. When I'd read about a half a minute, he fetched the book a whack with his hand and knocked it across the house. He says:

"It's so. You can do it. I had my doubts when you told me. Now looky here; you stop that putting on frills. I won't have it. I'll lay for you, my smarty; and if I catch you about that school I'll tan you good. First you know you'll get reli-gion, too. I never see such a son."

He took up a little blue and yaller picture of some cows and a boy, and says: "What's this?"

"It's something they give me for learning my lessons good."

He tore it up, and says—

"I'll give you something better—I'll give you a cowhide."[1]

He set there a-mumbling and a-growling a minute, and then he says—

"*Ain't* you a sweet-scented dandy, though? A bed; and bedclothes; and a look'n-glass; and a piece of carpet on the floor—and your own father got to sleep with the hogs in the tanyard. I never see such a son. I bet I'll take some o' these frills out o' you before I'm done with you. Why there ain't no end to your airs—they say you're rich. Hey?—how's that?"

"They lie—that's how."

"Looky here—mind how you talk to me; I'm a-standing about all I can stand, now—so don't gimme no sass. I've been in town two days, and I hain't heard nothing but about you bein' rich. I heard about it away down the river, too. That's why I come. You git me that money to-morrow—I want it."

"I hain't got no money."

"It's a lie. Judge Thatcher's got it. You git it. I want it."

"I hain't got no money, I tell you. You ask Judge Thatcher; he'll tell you the same."

"All right. I'll ask him; and I'll make him pungle,[2] too, or I'll know the rea-son why. Say—how much you got in your pocket? I want it."

"I hain't got only a dollar, and I want that to—"

"It don't make no difference what you want it for—you just shell it out."

---

1. A beating with a cowhide whip.    2. Turn over the money.

He took it and bit it to see if it was good, and then he said he was going down town to get some whiskey; said he hadn't had a drink all day. When he had got out on the shed, he put his head in again, and cussed me for putting on frills and trying to be better than him; and when I reckoned he was gone, he come back and put his head in again, and told me to mind about that school, because he was going to lay for me and lick me if I didn't drop that.

Next day he was drunk, and he went to Judge Thatcher's and bullyragged him and tried to make him give up the money, but he couldn't, and then he swore he'd make the law force him.

The judge and the widow went to law to get the court to take me away from him and let one of them be my guardian; but it was a new judge that had just come, and he didn't know the old man; so he said courts mustn't interfere and separate families if they could help it; said he'd druther not take a child away from its father. So Judge Thatcher and the widow had to quit on the business.

That pleased the old man till he couldn't rest. He said he'd cowhide me till I was black and blue if I didn't raise some money for him. I borrowed three dollars from Judge Thatcher, and pap took it and got drunk and went a-blowing around and cussing and whooping and carrying on; and he kept it up all over town, with a tin pan, till most midnight; then they jailed him, and next day they had him before court, and jailed him again for a week. But he said *he* was satisfied; said he was boss of his son, and he'd make it warm for *him*.

When he got out the new judge said he was agoing to make a man of him. So he took him to his own house, and dressed him up clean and nice, and had him to breakfast and dinner and supper with the family, and was just old pie to him, so to speak. And after supper he talked to him about temperance and such things till the old man cried, and said he'd been a fool, and fooled away his life; but now he was agoing to turn over a new leaf and be a man nobody wouldn't be ashamed of, and he hoped the judge would help him and not look down on him. The judge said he could hug him for them words; so *he* cried, and his wife she cried again; pap said he'd been a man that had always been misunderstood before, and the judge said he believed it. The old man said that what a man wanted that was down, was sympathy; and the judge said it was so; so they cried again. And when it was bedtime, the old man rose up and held out his hand, and says:

"Look at it gentlemen, and ladies all; take ahold of it; shake it. There's a hand that was the hand of a hog; but it ain't so no more; it's the hand of a man that's started in on a new life, and 'll die before he'll go back. You mark them words—don't forget I said them. It's a clean hand now; shake it—don't be afeard."

So they shook it, one after the other, all around, and cried. The judge's wife she kissed it. Then the old man he signed a pledge—made his mark. The judge said it was the holiest time on record, or something like that. Then they tucked the old man into a beautiful room, which was the spare room, and in the night sometime he got powerful thirsty and clumb out onto the porch-roof and slid down a stanchion and traded his new coat for a jug of forty-rod,[3] and clumb back again and had a good old time; and towards daylight he crawled out again, drunk as a fiddler, and rolled off the porch and broke his left arm in two places and was almost froze to death when somebody found

---

3. Home-distilled whiskey strong enough to knock a person forty rods, or 220 yards.

him after sun-up. And when they come to look at that spare room, they had to take soundings before they could navigate it.

The judge he felt kind of sore. He said he reckoned a body could reform the ole man with a shot-gun, maybe, but he didn't know no other way.

### Chapter VI

Well, pretty soon the old man was up and around again, and then he went for Judge Thatcher in the courts to make him give up that money, and he went for me, too, for not stopping school. He catched me a couple of times and thrashed me, but I went to school just the same, and dodged him or out-run him most of the time. I didn't want to go to school much, before, but I reckoned I'd go now to spite pap. That law trial was a slow business; appeared like they warn't ever going to get started on it; so every now and then I'd borrow two or three dollars off of the judge for him, to keep from getting a cowhiding. Every time he got money he got drunk; and every time he got drunk he raised Cain around town; and every time he raised Cain he got jailed. He was just suited—this kind of thing was right in his line.

He got to hanging around the widow's too much, and so she told him at last, that if he didn't quit using around there she would make trouble for him. Well, *wasn't* he mad? He said he would show who was Huck Finn's boss. So he watched out for me one day in the spring, and catched me, and took me up the river about three mile, in a skiff, and crossed over to the Illinois shore where it was woody and there warn't no houses but an old log hut in a place where the timber was so thick you couldn't find it if you didn't know where it was.

He kept me with him all the time, and I never got a chance to run off. We lived in that old cabin, and he always locked the door and put the key under his head, nights. He had a gun which he had stole, I reckon, and we fished and hunted, and that was what we lived on. Every little while he locked me in and went down to the store, three miles, to the ferry, and traded fish and game for whisky and fetched it home and got drunk and had a good time, and licked me. The widow she found out where I was, by-and-by, and she sent a man over to try to get hold of me, but pap drove him off with the gun, and it warn't long after that till I was used to being where I was, and liked it, all but the cowhide part.

It was kind of lazy and jolly, laying off comfortable all day, smoking and fishing, and no books nor study. Two months or more run along, and my clothes got to be all rags and dirt, and I didn't see how I'd ever got to like it so well at the widow's, where you had to wash, and eat on a plate, and comb up, and go to bed and get up regular, and be forever bothering over a book and have old Miss Watson pecking at you all the time. I didn't want to go back no more. I had stopped cussing, because the widow didn't like it; but now I took to it again because pap hadn't no objections. It was pretty good times up in the woods there, take it all around.

But by-and-by pap got too handy with his hick'ry, and I couldn't stand it. I was all over welts. He got to going away so much, too, and locking me in. Once he locked me in and was gone three days. It was dreadful lonesome. I judged he had got drowned and I wasn't ever going to get out any more. I was scared. I made up my mind I would fix up some way to leave there. I had tried to get out of that cabin many a time, but I couldn't find no way. There warn't a window to it big enough for a dog to get through. I couldn't get up the chimbly, it was too narrow. The door was thick solid oak slabs. Pap was pretty careful not to leave a knife or anything in the cabin when he was away; I reckon I had hunted the place over as much as a hundred times; well, I was 'most all the time at it, because it was about the only way to put in the time. But this time I found something at last; I found an old rusty wood-saw without any handle; it was laid in between a rafter and the clapboards of the roof. I greased it up and went to work. There was an old horse-blanket nailed against the logs at the far end of the cabin behind the table, to keep the wind from blowing through the chinks and putting the candle out. I got under the table and raised the blanket and went to work to saw a section of the big bottom log out, big enough to let me through. Well, it was a good long job, but I was getting towards the end of it when I heard pap's gun in the woods. I got rid of the signs of my work, and dropped the blanket and hid my saw, and pretty soon pap come in.

Pap warn't in a good humor—so he was his natural self. He said he was down to town, and everything was going wrong. His lawyer said he reckoned he would win his lawsuit and get the money, if they ever got started on the trial; but then there was ways to put it off a long time, and Judge Thatcher knowed how to do it. And he said people allowed there'd be another trial to get me away from him and give me to the widow for my guardian, and they guessed it would win, this time. This shook me up considerable, because I didn't want to go back to the widow's any more and be so cramped up and sivilized, as they called it. Then the old man got to cussing, and cussed everything and everybody he could think of, and then cussed them all over again to make sure he hadn't skipped any, and after that he polished off with a kind of general cuss all round, including a considerable parcel of people which he didn't know the names of, and so called them what's-his-name, when he got to them, and went right along with his cussing.

He said he would like to see the widow get me. He said he would watch out, and if they tried to come any such game on him he knowed of a place six or seven mile off, to stow me in, where they might hunt till they dropped and they couldn't find me. That made me pretty uneasy again, but only for a minute; I reckoned I wouldn't stay on hand till he got that chance.

The old man made me go to the skiff and fetch the things he had got. There was a fifty-pound sack of corn meal, and a side of bacon, ammunition, and a four-gallon jug of whisky, and an old book and two newspapers for wadding, besides some tow.[4] I toted up a load, and went back and set down on the bow of the skiff to rest. I thought it all over, and I reckoned I would walk off with the gun and some lines, and take to the woods when I run away. I guessed I wouldn't stay in one place, but just tramp right across the country, mostly night times, and hunt and fish to keep alive, and so get so far away that the old man nor the widow couldn't ever find me any more. I judged I would saw out and leave that night if pap got drunk enough, and I reckoned he would. I got so full of it I didn't notice how long I was staying, till the old man hollered and asked me whether I was asleep or drownded.

I got the things all up to the cabin, and then it was about dark. While I was cooking supper the old man took a swig or two and got sort of warmed up, and went to ripping again. He had been drunk over in town, and laid in the

---

4. Cheap rope. "Wadding": material (here paper) used to pack the gunpowder in a rifle.

gutter all night, and he was a sight to look at. A body would a thought he was Adam, he was just all mud.[5] Whenever his liquor begun to work, he most always went for the govment. This time he says:

"Call this a govment! why, just look at it and see what it's like. Here's the law a-standing ready to take a man's son away from him—a man's own son, which he has had all the trouble and all the anxiety and all the expense of raising. Yes, just as that man has got that son raised at last, and ready to go to work and begin to do suthin' for *him* and give him a rest, the law up and goes for him. And they call *that* govment! That ain't all, nuther. The law backs that old Judge Thatcher up and helps him to keep me out o' my property. Here's what the law does. The law takes a man worth six thousand dollars and upards, and jams him into an old trap of a cabin like this, and lets him go round in clothes that ain't fitten for a hog. They call that govment! A man can't get his rights in a govment like this. Sometimes I've a mighty notion to just leave the country for good and all. Yes, and I *told* 'em so: I told old Thatcher so to his face. Lots of 'em heard me, and can tell what I said. Says I, for two cents I'd leave the blamed country and never come anear it agin. Them's the very words. I says, look at my hat—if you call it a hat—but the lid raises up and the rest of it goes down till it's below my chin, and then it ain't rightly a hat at all, but more like my head was shoved up through a jint o' stove-pipe. Look at it, says I—such a hat for me to wear—one of the wealthiest men in this town, if I could git my rights.

"Oh, yes, this is a wonderful govment, wonderful. Why, looky here. There was a free nigger there, from Ohio; a mulatter,[6] most as white as a white man. He had the whitest shirt on you ever see, too, and the shiniest hat; and there ain't a man in that town that's got as fine clothes as what he had; and he had a gold watch and chain and a silver-headed cane—the awfulest old gray-headed nabob in the State. And what do you think? they said he was a p'fessor in a college, and could talk all kinds of languages, and knowed every thing. And that ain't the wust. They said he could *vote,* when he was at home. Well, that let me out. Thinks I, what is the country a-coming to? It was 'lection day, and I was just about to go and vote, myself, if I warn't too drunk to get there; but when they told me there was a State in this country where they'd let that nigger vote, I drawed out. I says I'll never vote agin. Them's the very words I said; they all heard me; and the country may rot for all me—I'll never vote agin as long as I live. And to see the cool way of that nigger—why, he wouldn't a give me the road if I hadn't shoved him out o' the way. I says to the people, why ain't this nigger put up at auction and sold?—that's what I want to know. And what do you reckon they said? Why, they said he couldn't be sold till he'd been in the State six months, and he hadn't been there that long yet. There, now—that's a specimen. They call that a govment that can't sell a free nigger till he's been in the State six months. Here's a govment that calls itself a govment, and lets on to be a govment, and thinks it is a govment, and yet's got to set stock-still for six whole months before it can take ahold of a prowling, thieving, infernal, white-shirted free nigger, and[7]—"

5. God created Adam from earth in Genesis 2.7.
6. Mulatto, a person of mixed white and black ancestry.
7. Missouri's original constitution prohibited the entrance of freed slaves and mulattoes into the state, but the "second Missouri Compromise" of 1820 deleted the provision. In the 1830s and 1840s, however, increasingly strict antiblack laws were passed, and by 1850 a black person without freedom papers could be sold downriver with a mere sworn statement of ownership from a white man.

Pap was agoing on so, he never noticed where his old limber legs was taking him to, so he went head over heels over the tub of salt pork, and barked both shins, and the rest of his speech was all the hottest kind of language—mostly hove at the nigger and the govment, though he give the tub some, too, all along, here and there. He hopped around the cabin considerble, first on one leg and then on the other, holding first one shin and then the other one, and at last he let out with his left foot all of a sudden and fetched the tub a rattling kick. But it warn't good judgment, because that was the boot that had a couple of his toes leaking out of the front end of it; so now he raised a howl that fairly made a body's hair raise, and down he went in the dirt, and rolled there, and held his toes; and the cussing he done then laid over anything he had ever done previous. He said so his own self, afterwards. He had heard old Sowberry Hagan in his best days, and he said it laid over him, too; but I reckon that was sort of piling it on, maybe.

After supper pap took the jug, and said he had enough whiskey there for two drunks and one delirium tremens. That was always his word. I judged he would be blind drunk in about an hour, an then I would steal the key, or saw myself out, one or 'tother. He drank, and drank, and tumbled down on his blankets, by-and-by; but luck didn't run my way. He didn't go sound asleep, but was uneasy. He groaned, and moaned, and thrashed around this way and that, for a long time. At last I got so sleepy I couldn't keep my eyes open, all I could do, and so before I knowed what I was about I was sound asleep, and the candle burning.

I don't know how long I was asleep, but all of a sudden there was an awful scream and I was up. There was pap, looking wild and skipping around every which way and yelling about snakes. He said they was crawling up his legs; and then he would give a jump and scream, and say one had bit him on the cheek—but I couldn't see no snakes. He started to run round and round the cabin, hollering "take him off! take him off! he's biting me on the neck!" I never see a man look so wild in the eyes. Pretty soon he was all fagged out, and fell down panting; then he rolled over and over, wonderful fast, kicking things every which way, and striking and grabbing at the air with his hands, and screaming, and saying there was devils ahold of him. He wore out, by-and-by, and laid still a while, moaning. Then he laid stiller, and didn't make a sound. I could hear the owls and the wolves, away off in the woods, and it seemed terrible still. He was laying over by the corner. By-and-by he raised up part way, and listened, with his head to one side. He says very low:

"Tramp—tramp—tramp; that's the dead; tramp—tramp—tramp; they're coming after me; but I won't go—Oh, they're here! don't touch me—don't! hands off—they're cold; let go—Oh, let a poor devil alone!"

Then he went down on all fours and crawled off begging them to let him alone, and he rolled himself up in his blanket and wallowed in under the old pine table, still a-begging; and then he went to crying. I could hear him through the blanket.

By-and-by he rolled out and jumped up on his feet looking wild, and he see me and went for me. He chased me round and round the place, with a clasp-knife, calling me the Angel of Death and saying he would kill me and then I couldn't come for him no more. I begged, and told him I was only Huck, but he laughed *such* a screechy laugh, and roared and cussed, and kept on chasing me up. Once when I turned short and dodged under his arm he made a grab and got me by the jacket between my shoulders, and I thought I was gone; but I skid out of the jacket quick as lightning, and saved myself. Pretty soon he was all tired out, and dropped down with his back against the door, and said he would rest a minute and then kill me. He put his knife under him, and said he would sleep and get strong, and then he would see who was who.

So he dozed off, pretty soon. By-and-by I got the old split bottom[8] chair and clumb up, as easy as I could, not to make any noise, and got down the gun. I slipped the ramrod down it to make sure it was loaded, and then I laid it across the turnip barrel, pointing towards pap, and set down behind it to wait for him to stir. And how slow and still the time did drag along.

## Chapter VII

"Git up! what you 'bout!"

I opened my eyes and looked around, trying to make out where I was. It was after sun-up, and I had been sound asleep. Pap was standing over me, looking sour—and sick, too. He says—

"What you doin' with this gun?"

I judged he didn't know nothing about what he had been doing, so I says:

"Somebody tried to get in, so I was laying for him."

"Why didn't you roust me out?"

"Well I tried to, but I couldn't; I couldn't budge you."

"Well, all right. Don't stand there palavering all day, but out with you and see if there's a fish on the lines for breakfast. I'll be along in a minute."

He unlocked the door and I cleared out, up the river bank. I noticed some pieces of limbs and such things floating down, and a sprinkling of bark; so I knowed the river had begun to rise. I reckoned I would have great times, now, if I was over at the town. The June rise used to be always luck for me; because as soon as that rise begins, here comes cord-wood floating down, and pieces of log rafts—sometimes a dozen logs together; so all you have to do is to catch them and sell them to the wood yards and the sawmill.

I went along up the bank with one eye out for pap and 'tother one out for what the rise might fetch along. Well, all at once, here comes a canoe; just a beauty, too, about thirteen or fourteen foot long, riding high like a duck. I shot head first off of the bank, like a frog, clothes and all on, and struck out for the canoe. I just expected there'd be somebody laying down in it, because people often done that to fool folks, and when a chap had pulled a skiff out most to it they'd raise up and laugh at him. But it warn't so this time. It was a drift-canoe, sure enough, and I clumb in and paddled her ashore. Thinks I, the old man will be glad when he sees this—she's worth ten dollars. But when I got to shore pap wasn't in sight yet, and as I was running her into a little creek like a gully, all hung over with vines and willows, I struck another idea; I judged I'd hide her good, and then, stead of taking to the woods when I run off, I'd go down the river about fifty mile and camp in one place for good, and not have such a rough time tramping on foot.

It was pretty close to the shanty, and I thought I heard the old man coming, all the time; but I got her hid; and then I out and looked around a bunch

8. I.e., splint-bottom, made by weaving thin strips of wood.

of willows, and there was the old man down the path apiece just drawing a bead on a bird with his gun. So he hadn't seen anything.

When he got along, I was hard at it taking up a "trot" line.[9] He abused me a little for being so slow, but I told him I fell in the river and that was what made me so long. I knowed he would see I was wet, and then he would be asking questions. We got five catfish off of the lines and went home.

While we laid off, after breakfast, to sleep up, both of us being about wore out, I got to thinking that if I could fix up some way to keep pap and the widow from trying to follow me, it would be a certainer thing than trusting to luck to get far enough off before they missed me; you see, all kinds of things might happen. Well, I didn't see no way for a while, but by-and-by pap raised up a minute, to drink another barrel of water, and he says:

"Another time a man comes a-prowling round here, you roust me out, you hear? That man warn't here for no good. I'd a shot him. Next time, you roust me out, you hear?"

Then he dropped down and went to sleep again—but what he had been saying give me the very idea I wanted. I says to myself, I can fix it now so nobody won't think of following me.

About twelve o'clock we turned out and went along up the bank. The river was coming up pretty fast, and lots of drift-wood going by on the rise. By-and-by, along comes part of a log raft—nine logs fast together. We went out with the skiff and towed it ashore. Then we had dinner. Anybody but pap would a waited and seen the day through, so as to catch more stuff; but that warn't pap's style. Nine logs was enough for one time; he must shove right over to town and sell. So he locked me in and took the skiff and started off towing the raft about half-past three. I judged he wouldn't come back that night. I waited till I reckoned he had got a good start, then I out with my saw and went to work on that log again. Before he was 'tother side of the river I was out of the hole; him and his raft was just a speck on the water away off yonder.

I took the sack of corn meal and took it to where the canoe was hid, and shoved the vines and branches apart and put it in; then I done the same with the side of bacon; then the whiskey jug; I took all the coffee and sugar there was, and all the ammunition; I took the wadding; I took the bucket and gourd, I took a dipper and a tin cup, and my old saw and two blankets, and the skillet and the coffee-pot. I took fish-lines and matches and other things—everything that was worth a cent. I cleaned out the place. I wanted an axe, but there wasn't any, only the one out at the wood pile, and I knowed why I was going to leave that. I fetched out the gun, and now I was done.

I had wore the ground a good deal, crawling out of the hole and dragging out so many things. So I fixed that as good as I could from the outside by scattering dust on the place, which covered up the smoothness and the sawdust. Then I fixed the piece of log back into its place, and put two rocks under it and one against it to hold it there,—for it was bent up at the place, and didn't quite touch ground. If you stood four or five foot away and didn't know it was sawed, you wouldn't ever notice it; and besides, this was the back of the cabin and it warn't likely anybody would go fooling around there.

It was all grass clear to the canoe; so I hadn't left a track. I followed around

9. A long fishing line fastened across a stream; to this line several shorter baited lines are attached.

to see. I stood on the bank and looked out over the river. All safe. So I took the gun and went up a piece into the woods and was hunting around for some birds, when I see a wild pig; hogs soon went wild in them bottoms after they had got away from the prairie farms. I shot this fellow and took him into camp.

I took the axe and smashed in the door—I beat it and hacked it considerable, a-doing it. I fetched the pig in and took him back nearly to the table and hacked into his throat with the ax, and laid him down on the ground to bleed—I say ground, because it *was* ground—hard packed, and no boards. Well, next I took an old sack and put a lot of big rocks in it,—all I could drag— and I started it from the pig and dragged it to the door and through the woods down to the river and dumped it in, and down it sunk, out of sight. You could easy see that something had been dragged over the ground. I did wish Tom Sawyer was there, I knowed he would take an interest in this kind of business, and throw in the fancy touches. Nobody could spread himself like Tom Sawyer in such a thing as that.

Well, last I pulled out some of my hair, and bloodied the ax good, and stuck it on the back side, and slung the ax in the corner. Then I took up the pig and held him to my breast with my jacket (so he couldn't drip) till I got a good piece below the house and then dumped him into the river. Now I thought of something else. So I went and got the bag of meal and my old saw out of the canoe and fetched them to the house. I took the bag to where it used to stand, and ripped a hole in the bottom of it with the saw, for there warn't no knives and forks on the place—pap done everything with his clasp-knife, about the cooking. Then I carried the sack about a hundred yards across the grass and through the willows east of the house, to a shallow lake that was five mile wide and full of rushes—and ducks too, you might say, in the season. There was a slough or a creek leading out of it on the other side, that went miles away, I don't know where, but it didn't go to the river. The meal sifted out and made a little track all the way to the lake. I dropped pap's whetstone there too, so as to look like it had been done by accident. Then I tied up the rip in the meal sack with a string, so it wouldn't leak no more, and took it and my saw to the canoe again.

It was about dark, now; so I dropped the canoe down the river under some willows that hung over the bank, and waited for the moon to rise. I made fast to a willow; then I took a bite to eat, and by-and-by laid down in the canoe to smoke a pipe and lay out a plan. I says to myself, they'll follow the track of that sackful of rocks to the shore and then drag the river for me. And they'll follow that meal track to the lake and go browsing down the creek that leads out of it to find the robbers that killed me and took the things. They won't ever hunt the river for anything but my dead carcass. They'll soon get tired of that, and won't bother no more about me. All right; I can stop anywhere I want to. Jackson's Island[1] is good enough for me; I know that island pretty well, and nobody ever comes there. And then I can paddle over to town, nights, and slink around and pick up things I want. Jackson's Island's the place.

I was pretty tired, and the first thing I knowed, I was asleep. When I woke

---

1. The same island that serves for an adventure in *Tom Sawyer* (Ch. 13); actually known as Glasscock's Island, it has been washed away.

up I didn't know where I was, for a minute. I set up and looked around, a little scared. Then I remembered. The river looked miles and miles across. The moon was so bright I could a counted the drift logs that went a slipping along, black and still, hundreds of yards out from shore. Everything was dead quiet, and it looked late, and *smelt* late. You know what I mean—I don't know the words to put it in.

I took a good gap and a stretch, and was just going to unhitch and start, when I heard a sound away over the water. I listened. Pretty soon I made it out. It was that dull kind of a regular sound that comes from oars working in rowlocks when it's a still night. I peeped out through the willow branches, and there it was—a skiff, away across the water. I couldn't tell how many was in it. It kept a-coming, and when it was abreast of me I see there warn't but one man in it. Thinks I, maybe it's pap, though I warn't expecting him. He dropped below me, with the current, and by-and-by he come a-swinging up shore in the easy water, and he went by so close I could a reached out the gun and touched him. Well, it *was* pap, sure enough—and sober, too, by the way he laid to his oars.

I didn't lose no time. The next minute I was a-spinning down stream soft but quick in the shade of the bank. I made two mile and a half, and then struck out a quarter of a mile or more towards the middle of the river, because pretty soon I would be passing the ferry landing and people might see me and ~Peaceful~ hail me. I got out amongst the drift-wood and then laid down in the bottom of the canoe and let her float. I laid there and had a good rest and a smoke out of my pipe, looking away into the sky, not a cloud in it. The sky looks ever so deep when you lay down on your back in the moonshine; I never knowed it before. And how far a body can hear on the water such nights! I heard people talking at the ferry landing. I heard what they said, too, every word of it. One man said it was getting towards the long days and the short nights, now. 'Tother one said *this* warn't one of the short ones, he reckoned—and then they laughed, and he said it over again and they laughed again; then they waked up another fellow and told him, and laughed, but he didn't laugh; he ripped out something brisk and said let him alone. The first fellow said he 'lowed to tell it to his old woman—she would think it was pretty good; but he said that warn't nothing to some things he had said in his time. I heard one man say it was nearly three o'clock, and he hoped daylight wouldn't wait more than about a week longer. After that, the talk got further and further away, and I couldn't make out the words any more, but I could hear the mumble; and now and then a laugh, too, but it seemed a long ways off.

I was away below the ferry now. I rose up and there was Jackson's Island, about two mile and a half down stream, heavy-timbered and standing up out of the middle of the river, big and dark and solid, like a steamboat without any lights. There warn't any signs of the bar at the head—it was all under water, now.

It didn't take me long to get there. I shot past the head at a ripping rate, the current was so swift, and then I got into the dead water and landed on the side towards the Illinois shore. I run the canoe into a deep dent in the bank that I knowed about; I had to part the willow branches to get in; and when I made fast nobody could a seen the canoe from the outside.

I went up and set down on a log at the head of the island and looked out on the big river and the black driftwood, and away over to the town, three mile away, where there was three or four lights twinkling. A monstrous big lumber raft was about a mile up stream, coming along down, with a lantern in the middle of it. I watched it come creeping down, and when it was most abreast of where I stood I heard a man say, "Stern oars, there! heave her head to stab-board!"[2] I heard that just as plain as if the man was by my side.

There was a little gray in the sky, now; so I stepped into the woods and laid down for a nap before breakfast.

## Chapter VIII

The sun was up so high when I waked, that I judged it was after eight o'clock. I laid there in the grass and the cool shade, thinking about things and feeling rested and ruther comfortable and satisfied. I could see the sun out at one or two holes, but mostly it was big trees all about, and gloomy in there amongst them. There was freckled places on the ground where the light sifted down through the leaves, and the freckled places swapped about a little, showing there was a little breeze up there. A couple of squirrels set on a limb and jabbered at me very friendly.

I was powerful lazy and comfortable—didn't want to get up and cook break-fast. Well, I was dozing off again, when I thinks I hears a deep sound of "boom!" away up the river. I rouses up and rests on my elbow and listens; pretty soon I hears it again. I hopped up and went and looked out at a hole in the leaves, and I see a bunch of smoke laying on the water a long ways up—about abreast the ferry. And there was the ferry-boat full of people, floating along down. I knowed what was the matter, now. "Boom!" I see the white smoke squirt out of the ferry-boat's side. You see, they was firing cannon over the water, trying to make my carcass come to the top.

I was pretty hungry, but it warn't going to do for me to start a fire, because they might see the smoke. So I set there and watched the cannon-smoke and listened to the boom. The river was a mile wide, there, and it always looks pretty on a summer morning—so I was having a good enough time seeing them hunt for my remainders, if I only had a bite to eat. Well, then I hap-pened to think how they always put quicksilver in loaves of bread and float them off because they always go right to the drownded carcass and stop there. So says I, I'll keep a lookout, and if any of them's floating around after me, I'll give them a show. I changed to the Illinois edge of the island to see what luck I could have, and I warn't disappointed. A big double loaf come along, and I most got it, with a long stick, but my foot slipped and she floated out further. Of course I was where the current set in the closest to the shore—I knowed enough for that. But by-and-by along comes another one, and this time I won. I took out the plug and shook out the little dab of quicksilver, and set my teeth in. It was "baker's bread"—what the quality eat—none of your low-down corn-pone.[3]

I got a good place amongst the leaves, and set there on a log, munching the bread and watching the ferry-boat, and very well satisfied. And then some-thing struck me. I says, now I reckon the widow or the parson or somebody prayed that this bread would find me, and here it has gone and done it. So

2. Starboard, the right-hand side of a boat, facing forward.

3. A simple corn bread.

there ain't no doubt but there is something in that thing. That is, there's something in it when a body like the widow or the parson prays, but it don't work for me, and I reckon it don't work for only just the right kind.

I lit a pipe and had a good long smoke and went on watching. The ferry-boat was floating with the current, and I allowed I'd have a chance to see who was aboard when she come along, because she would come in close, where the bread did. When she'd got pretty well along down towards me, I put out my pipe and went to where I fished out the bread, and laid down behind a log on the bank in a little open place. Where the log forked I could peep through.

By-and-by she came along, and she drifted in so close that they could a run out a plank and walked ashore. Most everybody was on the boat. Pap, and Judge Thatcher, and Bessie Thatcher, and Jo Harper, and Tom Sawyer, and his old Aunt Polly, and Sid and Mary, and plenty more. Everybody was talking about the murder, but the captain broke in and says:

"Look sharp, now; the current sets in the closest here, and maybe he's washed ashore and got tangled amongst the brush at the water's edge. I hope so, anyway."

I didn't hope so. They all crowded up and leaned over the rails, nearly in my face, and kept still, watching with all their might. I could see them first-rate, but they couldn't see me. Then the captain sung out:

"Stand away!" and the cannon let off such a blast right before me that it made me deef with the noise and pretty near blind with the smoke, and I judged I was gone. If they'd a had some bullets in, I reckon they'd a got the corpse they was after. Well, I see I warn't hurt, thanks to goodness. The boat floated on and went out of sight around the shoulder of the island. I could hear the booming, now and then, further and further off, and by-and-by after an hour, I didn't hear it no more. The island was three mile long. I judged they had got to the foot, and was giving it up. But they didn't yet a while. They turned around the foot of the island and started up the channel on the Missouri side, under steam, and booming once in a while as they went. I crossed over to that side and watched them. When they got abreast the head of the island they quit shooting and dropped over to the Missouri shore and went home to the town.

I knowed I was all right now. Nobody else would come a-hunting after me. I got my traps out of the canoe and made me a nice camp in the thick woods. I made a kind of a tent out of my blankets to put my things under so the rain couldn't get at them. I catched a cat fish and haggled him open with my saw, and towards sundown I started my camp fire and had supper. Then I set out a line to catch some fish for breakfast.

When it was dark I set by my camp fire smoking, and feeling pretty satisfied; but by-and-by it got sort of lonesome, and so I went and set on the bank and listened to the currents washing along, and counted the stars and drift-logs and rafts that come down, and then went to bed; there ain't no better way to put in time when you are lonesome; you can't stay so, you soon get over it.

And so for three days and nights. No difference—just the same thing. But the next day I went exploring around down through the island. I was boss of it; it all belonged to me, so to say, and I wanted to know all about it; but mainly I wanted to put in the time. I found plenty strawberries, ripe and prime; and green summer-grapes, and green razberries; and the green blackberries was just beginning to show. They would all come handy by-and-by, I judged.

Well, I went fooling along in the deep woods till I judged I warn't far from the foot of the island. I had my gun along, but I hadn't shot nothing; it was for protection; thought I would kill some game nigh home. About this time I mighty near stepped on a good sized snake, and it went sliding off through the grass and flowers, and I after it, trying to get a shot at it. I clipped along, and all of sudden I bounded right on to the ashes of a camp fire that was still smoking.

My heart jumped up amongst my lungs. I never waited for to look further, but uncocked my gun and went sneaking back on my tip-toes as fast as ever I could. Every now and then I stopped a second, amongst the thick leaves, and listened; but my breath come so hard I couldn't hear nothing else. I slunk along another piece further, then listened again; and so on, and so on; if I see a stump, I took it for a man; if I trod on a stick and broke it, it made me feel like a person had cut one of my breaths in two and I only got half, and the short half, too.

When I got to camp I warn't feeling very brash, there warn't much sand in my craw;[4] but I says, this ain't no time to be fooling around. So I got all my traps into my canoe again so as to have them out of sight, and I put out the fire and scattered the ashes around to look like an old last year's camp, and then clumb a tree.

I reckon I was up in the tree two hours; but I didn't see nothing, I didn't hear nothing—I only *thought* I heard and seen as much as a thousand things. Well, I couldn't stay up there forever; so at last I got down, but I kept in the thick woods and on the lookout all the time. All I could get to eat was berries and what was left over from breakfast.

By the time it was night I was pretty hungry. So when it was good and dark, I slid out from shore before moonrise and paddled over to the Illinois bank—about a quarter of a mile. I went out in the woods and cooked a supper, and I had about made up my mind I would stay there all night, when I hear a *plunkety-plunk, plunkety-plunk,* and says to myself, horses coming; and next I hear people's voices. I got everything into the canoe as quick as I could, and then went creeping through the woods to see what I could find out. I hadn't got far when I hear a man say:

"We'd better camp here, if we can find a good place; the horses is about beat out. Let's look around."[5]

I didn't wait, but shoved out and paddled away easy. I tied up in the old place, and reckoned I would sleep in the canoe.

I didn't sleep much. I couldn't, somehow, for thinking. And every time I waked up I thought somebody had me by the neck. So the sleep didn't do me no good. By-and-by I says to myself, I can't live this way; I'm agoing to find out who it is that's here on the island with me; I'll find it out or bust. Well, I felt better, right off.

So I took my paddle and slid out from shore just a step or two, and then let the canoe drop along down amongst the shadows. The moon was shining, and outside of the shadows it made it most as light as day. I poked along well onto

---

4. Slang for not feeling very brave.
5. Apparently this episode is a vestige of an early

conception of the novel involving Pap in a murder plot and court trial.

an hour, everything still as rocks and sound asleep. Well by this time I was most down to the foot of the island. A little ripply, cool breeze begun to blow, and that was as good as saying the night was about done. I give her a turn with the paddle and brung her nose to shore; then I got my gun and slipped out and into the edge of the woods. I set down there on a log and looked out through the leaves. I see the moon go off watch and the darkness begin to blanket the river. But in a little while I see a pale streak over the tree-tops, and knowed the day was coming. So I took my gun and slipped off towards where I had run across that camp fire, stopping every minute or two to listen. But I hadn't no luck, somehow; I couldn't seem to find the place. But by-and-by, sure enough, I catched a glimpse of fire, away through the trees. I went for it, cautious and slow. By-and-by I was close enough to have a look, and there laid a man on the ground. It most give me the fan-tods.[6] He had a blanket around his head, and his head was nearly in the fire. I set there behind a clump of bushes, in about six foot of him, and kept my eyes on him steady. It was getting gray daylight, now. Pretty soon he gapped, and stretched himself, and hove off the blanket, and it was Miss Watson's Jim! I bet I was glad to see him. I says:

"Hello, Jim!" and skipped out.

He bounced up and stared at me wild. Then he drops down on his knees, and puts his hands together and says:

"Doan' hurt me—don't! I hain't ever done no harm to a ghos'. I awluz liked dead people, en done all I could for 'em. You go en git in de river agin, whah you b'longs, en doan' do nuffn to Ole Jim, 'at 'uz awluz yo' fren'."

Well, I warn't long making him understand I warn't dead. I was ever so glad to see Jim. I warn't lonesome, now. I told him I warn't afraid of *him* telling the people where I was. I talked along, but he only set there and looked at me; never said nothing. Then I says:

"It's good daylight. Let's get breakfast. Make up your camp fire good."

"What's de use er makin' up de camp fire to cook strawbries en sich truck? But you got a gun, hain't you? Den we kin git sumfn better den strawbries."

"Strawberries and such truck," I says. "Is that what you live on?"

"I couldn' git nuffn else," he says.

"Why, how long you been on the island, Jim?"

"I come heah de night arter you's killed."

"What, all that time?"

"Yes-indeedy."

"And ain't you had nothing but that kind of rubbage to eat?"

"No, sah—nuffn else."

"Well, you must be most starved, ain't you?"

"I reck'n I could eat a hoss. I think I could. How long you ben on de islan'?"

"Since the night I got killed."

"No! W'y, what has you lived on? But you got a gun. Oh, yes, you got a gun. Dat's good. Now you kill sumfn en I'll make up de fire."

So we went over to where the canoe was, and while he built a fire in a grassy open place amongst the trees, I fetched meal and bacon and coffee, and coffee-pot and frying-pan, and sugar and tin cups, and the nigger was set back considerable, because he reckoned it was all done with witchcraft. I

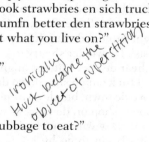

*Ironically, Huck became the object of superstition*

---

6. Slang for the hallucinatory state associated with delirium tremens, a condition that afflicts alcoholics.

catched a good big cat-fish, too, and Jim cleaned him with his knife, and fried him.

When breakfast was ready, we lolled on the grass and eat it smoking hot. Jim laid it in with all his might, for he was most about starved. Then when we had got pretty well stuffed, we laid off and lazied.

By-and-by Jim says:

"But looky here, Huck, who wuz it dat 'uz killed in dat shanty, ef it warn't you?"

Then I told him the whole thing, and he said it was smart. He said Tom Sawyer couldn't get up no better plan than what I had. Then I says:

"How do you come to be here, Jim, and how'd you get here?"

He looked pretty uneasy, and didn't say nothing for a minute. Then he says:

"Maybe I better not tell."

"Why, Jim?"

"Well, dey's reasons. But you wouldn' tell on me ef I 'uz to tell you, would you, Huck?"

"Blamed if I would, Jim."

"Well, I b'lieve you, Huck. I—I *run off.*"

"Jim!"

"But mind, you said you wouldn't tell—you know you said you wouldn't tell, Huck."

"Well, I did. I said I wouldn't, and I'll stick to it. Honest *injun* I will. People would call me a low down Ablitionist and despise me for keeping mum— but that don't make no difference. I ain't agoing to tell, and I ain't agoing back there anyways. So now, le's know all about it."

"Well, you see, it 'uz dis way. Ole Missus—dat's Miss Watson—she pecks on me all de time, en treats me pooty rough, but she awluz said she wouldn' sell me down to Orleans. But I noticed dey wuz a nigger trader roun' de place considable, lately, en I begin to git oneasy. Well, one night I creeps to de do', pooty late, en de do' warn't quite shet, en I hear ole missus tell de widder she gwyne to sell me down to Orleans, but she didn' want to, but she could git eight hund'd dollars for me,[7] en it 'uz sich a big stack o' money she couldn' resis'. De widder she try to git her to say she wouldn' do it, but I never waited to hear de res'. I lit out mighty quick, I tell you.

"I tuck out en shin down de hill en 'spec to steal a skift 'long de sho' som'ers 'bove de town, but dey wuz people a-stirrin' yit, so I hid in de ole tumble-down cooper shop on de bank to wait for everybody to go 'way. Well, I wuz dah all night. Dey wuz somebody roun' all de time. 'Long 'bout six in de mawnin', skifts begin to go by, en 'bout eight or nine every skift dat went 'long wuz talkin' 'bout how yo' pap come over to de town en say you's killed. Dese las' skifts wuz full o' ladies en genlmen agoin' over for to see de place. Sometimes dey'd pull up at de sho' en take a res' b'fo' dey started acrost, so by de talk I got to know all 'bout de killin'. I 'uz powerful sorry you's killed, Huck, but I ain't no mo', now.

"I laid dah under de shavins all day. I 'uz hungry, but I warn't afeared; bekase I knowed ole missus en de widder wuz goin' to start to de camp-meetn' right arter breakfas' en be gone all day, en dey knows I goes off wid de cattle 'bout daylight, so dey wouldn' 'spec to see me roun' de place, en so dey

---

7. A realistic price for a healthy male slave in the 1840s.

wouldn' miss me tell arter dark in de evenin'. De yuther servants wouldn' miss me, kase dey'd shin out en take holiday, soon as de ole folks 'uz out'n de way.

"Well, when it come dark I tuck out up de river road, en went 'bout two mile er more to whah dey warn't no houses. I'd made up my mind 'bout what I's agwyne to do. You see ef I kep' on tryin' to git away afoot, de dogs 'ud track me; ef I stole a skift to cross over, dey'd miss dat skift, you see, en dey'd know 'bout whah I'd lan' on de yuther side en whah to pick up my track. So I says, a raff is what I's arter; it doan' *make* no track.

"I see a light a-comin' roun' de p'int, bymeby, so I wade' in en shove' a log ahead o' me, en swum more'n half-way acrost de river, en got in 'mongst de drift-wood, en kep' my head down low, en kinder swum agin de current tell de raff come along. Den I swum to de stern uv it, en tuck aholt. It clouded up en 'uz pooty dark for a little while. So I clumb up en laid down on de planks. De men 'uz all 'way yonder in de middle,[8] whah de lantern wuz. De river wuz arisin' en dey wuz a good current; so I reck'n'd 'at by fo' in de mawnin' I'd be twenty-five mile down de river, en den I'd slip in, jis' b'fo' day-light, en swim asho' en take to de woods on de Illinoi side.[9]

"But I didn' have no luck. When we 'uz mos' down to de head er de islan', a man begin to come aft wid de lantern. I see it warn't no use fer to wait, so I slid overboad, en struck out fer de islan'. Well, I had a notion I could lan' mos' anywhers, but I couldn'—bank too bluff. I 'uz mos' to de foot er de islan' b'fo' I foun' a good place. I went into de woods en jedged I wouldn' fool wid raffs no mo', long as dey move de lantern roun' so. I had my pipe en a plug er dog-leg,[1] en some matches in my cap, en dey warn't wet, so I 'uz all right."

"And so you ain't had no meat nor bread to eat all this time? Why didn't you get mud-turkles?"

"How you gwyne to git'm? You can't slip up on um en grab um; en how's a body gwyne to hit um wid a rock? How could a body do it in de night? en I warn't gwyne to show myself on de bank in de daytime."

"Well, that's so. You've had to keep in the woods all the time, of course. Did you hear 'em shooting the cannon?"

"Oh, yes. I knowed dey was arter you. I see um go by heah; watched um thoo de bushes."

Some young birds come along, flying a yard or two at a time and lighting. Jim said it was a sign it was going to rain. He said it was a sign when young chickens flew that way, and so he reckoned it was the same way when young birds done it. I was going to catch some of them, but Jim wouldn't let me. He said it was death. He said his father laid mighty sick once, and some of them catched a bird, and his old granny said his father would die, and he did.

And Jim said you mustn't count the things you are going to cook for dinner, because that would bring bad luck. The same if you shook the table-cloth after sundown. And he said if a man owned a bee-hive, and that man died, the bees must be told about it before sun-up next morning, or else the bees would all weaken down and quit work and die. Jim said bees wouldn't sting idiots; but I didn't believe that, because I had tried them lots of times myself, and they wouldn't sting me.

---

8. A river raft would be large enough to make this easily possible.

9. Though Illinois was not a slave state, by state law any black person without freedom papers could be arrested and subjected to forced labor. Jim's chances for escape would be improved if he went down the Mississippi and then up the Ohio.

1. Cheap tobacco.

I had heard about some of these things before, but not all of them. Jim knowed all kinds of signs. He said he knowed most everything. I said it looked to me like all the signs was about bad luck, and so I asked him if there warn't any good-luck signs. He says:

"Mighty few—an' *dey* ain' no use to a body. What you want to know when good luck's a-comin' for? want to keep it off?" And he said: "Ef you's got hairy arms en a hairy breas', it's a sign dat you's agwyne to be rich. Well, dey's some use in a sign like dat, 'kase it's so fur ahead. You see, maybe you's got to be po' a long time fust, en so you might git discourage' en kill yo'sef 'f you didn' know by de sign dat you gwyne to be rich bymeby."

"Have you got hairy arms and a hairy breast, Jim?"

"What's de use to ax dat question? don' you see I has?"

"Well, are you rich?"

"No, but I ben rich wunst, and gwyne to be rich agin. Wunst I had foteen dollars, but I tuck to specalat'n', en got busted out."

"What did you speculate in, Jim?"

"Well, fust I tackled stock."

"What kind of stock?"

"Why, live stock. Cattle, you know. I put ten dollars in a cow. But I ain't gwyne to resk no mo' money in stock. De cow up 'n' died on my han's."

"So you lost the ten dollars."

"No, I didn' lose it all. I on'y los' 'bout nine of it. I sole de hide en taller for a dollar en ten cents."

"You had five dollars and ten cents left. Did you speculate any more?"

"Yes. You know dat one-laigged nigger dat b'longs to old Misto Bradish? well, he sot up a bank, en say anybody dat put in a dollar would git fo' dollars mo' at de en' er de year. Well, all de niggers went in, but dey didn' have much. I wuz de on'y one dat had much. So I stuck out for mo' dan fo' dollars, en I said 'f I didn' git it I'd start a bank myself. Well o' course dat nigger want' to keep me out er de business, bekase he say dey warn't business 'nough for two banks, so he say I could put in my five dollars en he pay me thirty-five at de en' er de year.

"So I done it. Den I reck'n'd I'd inves' de thirty-five dollars right off en keep things a-movin'. Dey wuz a nigger name' Bob, dat had ketched a wood-flat,[2] en his marster didn' know it; en I bought it off'n him en told him to take de thirty-five dollars when de en' er de year come; but somebody stole de wood-flat dat night, en nex' day de one-laigged nigger say de bank 's busted. So dey didn' none uv us git no money."

"What did you do with the ten cents, Jim?"

"Well, I 'uz gwyne to spen' it, but I had a dream, en de dream tole me to give it to a nigger name' Balum—Balum's Ass[3] dey call him for short, he's one er dem chuckle-heads, you know. But he's lucky, dey say, en I see I warn't lucky. De dream say let Balum inves' de ten cents en he'd make a raise for me. Well, Balum he tuck de money, en when he wuz in church he hear de preacher say dat whoever give to de po' len' to de Lord, en boun' to git his

_Satire._

---

2. A flat-bottomed boat used to transport timber.
3. Balaam, Old Testament prophet. God's avenging angel interrupted this prophet's journey to curse the Israelites by standing in the path of his progress. Balaam was blind to the angel's presence, but his ass saw the angel clearly and swerved off the road, much to Balaam's chagrin (Numbers 22).

money back a hund'd times. So Balum he tuck en give de ten cents to de po',
en laid low to see what wuz gwyne to come of it."

"Well, what did come of it, Jim?"

"Nuffn never come of it. I couldn' manage to k'leck dat money no way; en
Balum he couldn'. I ain' gwyne to len' no mo' money 'dout I see de security.
Boun' to git yo' money back a hund'd times, de preacher says! Ef I could git
de ten *cents* back, I'd call it squah, en be glad er de chanst."

"Well, it's all right anyway, Jim, long as you're going to be rich again some
time or other."

"Yes—en I's rich now, come to look at it. I owns mysef, en I's wuth eight
hund'd dollars. I wisht I had de money, I wouldn' want no mo'."

## Chapter IX

I wanted to go and look at a place right about the middle of the island, that
I'd found when I was exploring; so we started, and soon got to it, because the
island was only three miles long and a quarter of a mile wide.

This place was a tolerable long steep hill or ridge, about forty foot high. We
had a rough time getting to the top, the sides was so steep and the bushes so
thick. We tramped and clumb around all over it, and by-and-by found a good
big cavern in the rock, most up to the top on the side towards Illinois. The
cavern was as big as two or three rooms bunched together, and Jim could
stand up straight in it. It was cool in there. Jim was for putting our traps in
there, right away, but I said we didn't want to be climbing up and down there
all the time.

Jim said if we had the canoe hid in a good place, and had all the traps in
the cavern, we could rush there if anybody was to come to the island, and they
would never find us without dogs. And besides, he said them little birds had
said it was going to rain, and did I want the things to get wet?

So we went back and got the canoe and paddled up abreast the cavern, and
lugged all the traps up there. Then we hunted up a place close by to hide the
canoe in, amongst the thick willows. We took some fish off of the lines and
set them again, and begun to get ready for dinner.

The door of the cavern was big enough to roll a hogshead in, and on one
side of the door the floor stuck out a little bit and was flat and a good place
to build a fire on. So we built it there and cooked dinner.

We spread the blankets inside for a carpet, and eat our dinner in there. We
put all the other things handy at the back of the cavern. Pretty soon it darkened up and begun to thunder and lighten; so the birds was right about it.
Directly it begun to rain, and it rained like all fury, too, and I never see the
wind blow so. It was one of these regular summer storms. It would get so dark
that it looked all blue-black outside, and lovely; and the rain would thrash
along by so thick that the trees off a little ways looked dim and spider-webby;
and here would come a blast of wind that would bend the trees down and turn
up the pale underside of the leaves; and then a perfect ripper of a gust would
follow along and set the branches to tossing their arms as if they was just wild;
and next, when it was just about the bluest and blackest—*fst!* it was as bright
as glory and you'd have a little glimpse of tree-tops a-plunging about, away
off yonder in the storm, hundreds of yards further than you could see before;

dark as sin again in a second, and now you'd hear the thunder let go with an awful crash and then go rumbling, grumbling, tumbling down the sky towards the under side of the world, like rolling empty barrels down stairs, where it's long stairs and they bounce a good deal, you know.

"Jim, this is nice," I says. "I wouldn't want to be nowhere else but here. Pass me along another hunk of fish and some hot cornbread."

"Well, you wouldn' a ben here, 'f it hadn' a ben for Jim. You'd a ben down dah in de woods widout any dinner, en gittn' mos' drownded, too, dat you would, honey. Chickens knows when its gwyne to rain, en so do de birds, chile."

The river went on raising and raising for ten or twelve days, till at last it was over the banks. The water was three or four foot deep on the island in the low places and on the Illinois bottom. On that side it was a good many miles wide; but on the Missouri side it was the same old distance across—a half a mile— because the Missouri shore was just a wall of high bluffs.

Daytimes we paddled all over the island in the canoe. It was mighty cool and shady in the deep woods even if the sun was blazing outside. We went winding in and out amongst the trees; and sometimes the vines hung so thick we had to back away and go some other way. Well, on every old broken-down tree, you could see rabbits, and snakes, and such things; and when the island had been overflowed a day or two, they got so tame, on account of being hungry, that you could paddle right up and put your hand on them if you wanted to; but not the snakes and turtles—they would slide off in the water. The ridge our cavern was in, was full of them. We could a had pets enough if we'd wanted them.

One night we catched a little section of a lumber raft—nice pine planks. It was twelve foot wide and about fifteen or sixteen foot long, and the top stood above water six or seven inches, a solid level floor. We could see saw-logs go by in the daylight, sometimes, but we let them go; we didn't show ourselves in daylight.

Another night, when we was up at the head of the island, just before daylight, here comes a frame house down, on the west side. She was a two-story, and tilted over, considerable. We paddled out and got aboard—clumb in at an up-stairs window. But it was too dark to see yet, so we made the canoe fast and set in her to wait for daylight.

The light begun to come before we got to the foot of the island. Then we looked in at the window. We could make out a bed, and a table, and two old chairs, and lots of things around about on the floor; and there was clothes hanging against the wall. There was something laying on the floor in the far corner that looked like a man. So Jim says.

"Hello, you!"

But it didn't budge. So I hollered again, and then Jim says:

"De man ain' asleep—he's dead. You hold still—I'll go en see."

He went and bent down and looked, and says:

"It's a dead man. Yes, indeedy; naked, too. He's ben shot in de back. I reck'n he's ben dead two er three days. Come in, Huck, but doan' look at his face— it's too gashly."

I didn't look at him at all. Jim throwed some old rags over him, but he needn't done it; I didn't want to see him. There was heaps of old greasy cards scattered around over the floor, and old whisky bottles, and a couple of masks made out of black cloth; and all over the walls was the ignorantest kind of words and pictures, made with charcoal. There was two old dirty calico dresses, and a sun-bonnet, and some women's under-clothes, hanging against the wall, and some men's clothing, too. We put the lot into the canoe; it might come good. There was a boy's old speckled straw hat on the floor; I took that too. And there was a bottle that had had milk in it; and it had a rag stopper for a baby to suck. We would a took the bottle, but it was broke. There was a seedy old chest, and an old hair trunk with the hinges broke. They stood open, but there warn't nothing left in them that was any account. The way things was scattered about, we reckoned the people left in a hurry and warn't fixed so as to carry off most of their stuff.

We got an old tin lantern, and a butcher-knife without any handle, and a bran-new Barlow knife[4] worth two bits in any store, and a lot of tallow candles, and a tin candlestick, and a gourd, and a tin cup, and a ratty old bed-quilt off the bed, and a reticule with needles and pins and beeswax and buttons and thread and all such truck in it, and a hatchet and some nails, and a fish-line as thick as my little finger, with some monstrous hooks on it, and a roll of buckskin, and a leather dog-collar, and a horse-shoe, and some vials of medicine that didn't have no label on them; and just as we was leaving I found a tolerable good curry-comb, and Jim he found a ratty old fiddle-bow, and a wooden leg. The straps was broke off of it, but barring that, it was a good enough leg, though it was too long for me and not long enough for Jim, and we couldn't find the other one, though we hunted all around.

And so, take it all around, we made a good haul. When we was ready to shove off, we was a quarter of a mile below the island, and it was pretty broad day; so I made Jim lay down in the canoe and cover up with the quilt, because if he set up, people could tell he was a nigger a good ways off. I paddled over to the Illinois shore, and drifted down most a half a mile doing it. I crept up the dead water under the bank, and hadn't no accidents and didn't see nobody. We got home all safe.

## Chapter X

After breakfast I wanted to talk about the dead man and guess out how he come to be killed, but Jim didn't want to. He said it would fetch bad luck; and besides, he said, he might come and ha'nt us; he said a man that warn't buried was more likely to go a-ha'nting around than one that was planted and comfortable. That sounded pretty reasonable, so I didn't say no more; but I couldn't keep from studying over it and wishing I knowed who shot the man, and what they done it for.

We rummaged the clothes we'd got, and found eight dollars in silver sewed up in the lining of an old blanket overcoat. Jim said he reckoned the people in that house stole the coat, because if they'd a knowed the money was there they wouldn't a left it. I said I reckoned they killed him, too; but Jim didn't want to talk about that. I says:

"Now, you think it's bad luck; but what did you say when I fetched in the snake-skin that I found on the top of the ridge day before yesterday? You said it was the worst bad luck in the world to touch a snake-skin with my hands.

4. Pocketknife with one blade, named for the inventor.

Well, here's your bad luck! We've raked in all this truck and eight dollars besides. I wish we could have some bad luck like this every day, Jim."

"Never you mind, honey, never you mind. Don't you git too peart. It's a-comin'. Mind I tell you, it's a-comin'."

It did come, too. It was Tuesday that we had that talk. Well, after dinner Friday, we was laying around in the grass at the upper end of the ridge, and got out of tobacco. I went to the cavern to get some, and found a rattlesnake in there. I killed him, and curled him up on the foot of Jim's blanket, ever so natural, thinking there'd be some fun when Jim found him there. Well, by night I forgot all about the snake, and when Jim flung himself down on the blanket while I struck a light, the snake's mate was there, and bit him.

He jumped up yelling, and the first thing the light showed was the varmint curled up and ready for another spring. I laid him out in a second with a stick, and Jim grabbed pap's whiskey jug and began to pour it down.

He was barefooted, and the snake bit him right on the heel. That all comes of my being such a fool as to not remember that whenever you leave a dead snake its mate always comes there and curls around it. Jim told me to chop off the snake's head and throw it away, and then skin the body and roast a piece of it. I done it, and he eat it and said it would help cure him.[5] He made me take off the rattles and tie them around his wrist, too. He said that that would help. Then I slid out quiet and throwed the snakes clear away amongst the bushes; for I warn't going to let Jim find out it was all my fault, not if I could help it.

Jim sucked and sucked at the jug, and now and then he got out of his head and pitched around and yelled; but every time he come to himself he went to sucking at the jug again. His foot swelled up pretty big, and so did his leg; but by-and-by the drunk begun to come, and so I judged he was all right; but I'd druther been bit with a snake than pap's whiskey.

Jim was laid up for four days and nights. Then the swelling was all gone and he was around again. I made up my mind I wouldn't ever take aholt of a snake-skin again with my hands, now that I see what had come of it. Jim said he reckoned I would believe him next time. And he said that handling a snake-skin was such awful bad luck that maybe we hadn't got to the end of it yet. He said he druther see the new moon over his left shoulder as much as a thousand times than take up a snake-skin in his hand. Well, I was getting to feel that way myself, though I've always reckoned that looking at the new moon over your left shoulder is one of the carelessest and foolishest things a body can do. Old Hank Bunker done it once, and bragged about it; and in less than two years he got drunk and fell off of the shot tower and spread himself out so that he was just a kind of layer, as you may say; and they slid him edge-ways between two barn doors for a coffin, and buried him so, so they say, but I didn't see it. Pap told me. But anyway, it all come of looking at the moon that way, like a fool.

Well, the days went along, and the river went down between its banks again; and about the first thing we done was to bait one of the big hooks with a skinned rabbit and set it and catch a cat-fish that was as big as a man, being six foot two inches long, and weighed over two hundred pounds. We couldn't handle him, of course; he would a flung us into Illinois. We just set there and

---

5. Jim's homeopathic remedy is a common folk-medical practice.

watched him rip and tear around till he drowned. We found a brass button in his stomach, and a round ball, and lots of rubbage. We split the ball open with the hatchet, and there was a spool in it. Jim said he'd had it there a long time, to coat it over so and make a ball of it. It was as big a fish as was ever catched in the Mississippi, I reckon. Jim said he hadn't ever seen a bigger one. He would a been worth a good deal over at the village. They peddle out such a fish as that by the pound in the market house there; everybody buys some of him; his meat's as white as snow and makes a good fry.

Next morning I said it was getting slow and dull, and I wanted to get a stirring up, some way. I said I reckoned I would slip over the river and find out what was going on. Jim liked that notion; but he said I must go in the dark and look sharp. Then he studied it over and said, couldn't I put on some of them old things and dress up like a girl? That was a good notion, too. So we shortened up one of the calico gowns and I turned up my trowser-legs to my knees and got into it. Jim hitched it behind with the hooks, and it was a fair fit. I put on the sun-bonnet and tied it under my chin, and then for a body to look in and see my face was like looking down a joint of stove-pipe. Jim said nobody would know me, even in the daytime, hardly. I practiced around all day to get the hang of the things, and by-and-by I could do pretty well in them, only Jim said I didn't walk like a girl; and he said I must quit pulling up my gown to get at my britches pocket. I took notice, and done better.

I started up the Illinois shore in the canoe just after dark.

I started across to the town from a little below the ferry landing, and the drift of the current fetched me in at the bottom of the town. I tied up and started along the bank. There was a light burning in a little shanty that hadn't been lived in for a long time, and I wondered who had took up quarters there. I slipped up and peeped in at the window. There was a woman about forty year old in there, knitting by a candle that was on a pine table. I didn't know her face; she was a stranger, for you couldn't start a face in that town that I didn't know. Now this was lucky, because I was weakening; I was getting afraid I had come; people might know my voice and find me out. But if this woman had been in such a little town two days she could tell me all I wanted to know; so I knocked at the door, and made up my mind I wouldn't forget I was a girl.

## Chapter XI

"Come in," says the woman, and I did. She says:

"Take a cheer."

I done it. She looked me all over with her little shiny eyes, and says:

"What might your name be?"

"Sarah Williams."

"Where 'bouts do you live? In this neighborhood?"

"No'm. In Hookerville, seven mile below. I've walked all the way and I'm all tired out."

"Hungry, too, I reckon. I'll find you something."

"No'm, I ain't hungry. I was so hungry I had to stop two mile below here at a farm; so I ain't hungry no more. It's what makes me so late. My mother's down sick, and out of money and everything, and I come to tell my uncle

Abner Moore. He lives at the upper end of the town, she says. I hain't ever
been here before. Do you know him?"

"No; but I don't know everybody yet. I haven't lived here quite two weeks.
It's a considerable ways to the upper end of the town. You better stay here all
night. Take off your bonnet."

"No," I says, "I'll rest a while, I reckon, and go on. I ain't afeard of the dark."

She said she wouldn't let me go by myself, but her husband would be in by-
and-by, maybe in a hour and a half, and she'd send him along with me. Then
she got to talking about her husband, and about her relations up the river, and
her relations down the river, and how much better off they used to was, and
how they didn't know but they'd made a mistake coming to our town, instead
of letting well alone—and so on and so on, till I was afeard I had made a mistake coming to her to find out what was going on in the town; but by-and-by
she dropped onto pap and the murder, and then I was pretty willing to let her
clatter right along. She told about me and Tom Sawyer finding the six thousand dollars (only she got it ten) and all about pap and what a hard lot he was,
and what a hard lot I was, and at last she got down to where I was murdered.
I says:

"Who done it? We've heard considerable about these goings on, down in
Hookerville, but we don't know who 'twas that killed Huck Finn."

"Well, I reckon there's a right smart chance of people *here* that'd like to
know who killed him. Some thinks old Finn done it himself."

"No—is that so?"

"Most everybody thought it at first. He'll never know how nigh he come to
getting lynched. But before night they changed around and judged it was
done by a runaway nigger named Jim."

"Why he—"

I stopped. I reckoned I better keep still. She run on, and never noticed I
had put in at all.

"The nigger run off the very night Huck Finn was killed. So there's a reward
out for him—three hundred dollars. And there's a reward out for old Finn
too—two hundred dollars. You see, he come to town the morning after the
murder, and told about it, and was out with 'em on the ferry-boat hunt, and
right away after he up and left. Before night they wanted to lynch him, but
he was gone, you see. Well, next day they found out the nigger was gone; they
found out he hadn't ben seen sence ten o'clock the night the murder was
done. So then they put it on him, you see, and while they was full of it, next
day back comes old Finn and went boohooing to Judge Thatcher to get money
to hunt for the nigger all over Illinois with. The judge give him some, and that
evening he got drunk and was around till after midnight with a couple of
mighty hard looking strangers, and then went off with them. Well, he hain't
come back sence, and they ain't looking for him back till this thing blows over
a little, for people thinks now that he killed his boy and fixed things so folks
would think robbers done it, and then he'd get Huck's money without having
to bother a long time with a lawsuit. People do say he warn't any too good to
do it. Oh, he's sly, I reckon. If he don't come back for a year, he'll be all right.
You can't prove anything on him, you know; everything will be quieted down
then, and he'll walk into Huck's money as easy as nothing."

"Yes, I reckon so, 'm. I don't see nothing in the way of it. Has everybody quit
thinking the nigger done it?"

"Oh no, not everybody. A good many thinks he done it. But they'll get the nigger pretty soon, now, and maybe they can scare it out of him."

"Why, are they after him yet?"

"Well, you're innocent, ain't you! Does three hundred dollars lay round every day for people to pick up? Some folks thinks the nigger ain't far from here. I'm one of them—but I hain't talked it around. A few days ago I was talking with an old couple that lives next door in the log shanty, and they happened to say hardly anybody ever goes to that island over yonder that they call Jackson's Island. Don't anybody live there? says I. No, nobody, says they. I didn't say any more, but I done some thinking. I was pretty near certain I'd seen smoke over there, about the head of the island, a day or two before that, so I says to myself, like as not that nigger's hiding over there; anyway, says I, it's worth the trouble to give the place a hunt. I hain't seen any smoke sence, so I reckon maybe he's gone, if it was him; but husband's going over to see—him and another man. He was gone up the river; but he got back to-day and I told him as soon as he got here two hours ago."

I had got so uneasy I couldn't set still. I had to do something with my hands; so I took up a needle off of the table and went to threading it. My hands shook and I was making a bad job of it. When the woman stopped talking, I looked up, and she was looking at me pretty curious, and smiling a little. I put down the needle and thread and let on to be interested—and I was, too—and says:

"Three hundred dollars is a power of money. I wish my mother could get it. Is your husband going over there to-night?"

"Oh, yes. He went up town with the man I was telling you of, to get a boat and see if they could borrow another gun. They'll go over after midnight."

"Couldn't they see better if they was to wait till daytime?"

"Yes. And couldn't the nigger see better too? After midnight he'll likely be asleep, and they can slip around through the woods and hunt up his camp fire all the better for the dark, if he's got one."

"I didn't think of that."

The woman kept looking at me pretty curious, and I didn't feel a bit comfortable. Pretty soon she says:

"What did you say your name was, honey?"

"M—Mary Williams."

Somehow it didn't seem to me that I said it was Mary before, so I didn't look up; seemed to me I said it was Sarah; so I felt sort of cornered, and was afeared maybe I was looking it, too. I wished the woman would say something more; the longer she set still, the uneasier I was. But now she says:

"Honey, I thought you said it was Sarah when you first come in?"

"Oh, yes'm, I did. Sarah Mary Williams. Sarah's my first name. Some calls me Sarah, some calls me Mary."

"Oh, that's the way of it?"

"Yes'm."

I was feeling better, then, but I wished I was out of there, anyway. I couldn't look up yet.

Well, the woman fell to talking about how hard times was, and how poor they had to live, and how the rats was as free as if they owned the place, and so forth, and so on, and then I got easy again. She was right about the rats. You'd see one stick his nose out of a hole in the corner every little while. She said she had to have things handy to throw at them when she was alone, or they wouldn't give her no peace. She showed me a bar of lead, twisted up into a knot, and she said she was a good shot with it generly, but she'd wrenched her arm a day or two ago, and didn't know whether she could throw true, now. But she watched for a chance, and directly she banged away at a rat, but she missed him wide, and said "Ouch!" it hurt her arm so. Then she told me to try for the next one. I wanted to be getting away before the old man got back, but of course I didn't let on. I got the thing, and the first rat that showed his nose I let drive, and if he'd a stayed where he was he'd a been a tolerable sick rat. She said that that was first-rate, and she reckoned I would hive[6] the next one. She went and got the lump of lead and fetched it back and brought along a hank of yarn, which she wanted me to help her with. I held up my two hands and she put the hank over them and went on talking about her and her husband's matters. But she broke off to say:

"Keep your eye on the rats. You better have the lead in your lap, handy."

So she dropped the lump into my lap, just at that moment, and I clapped my legs together on it and she went on talking. But only about a minute. Then she took off the hank and looked me straight in the face, but very pleasant, and says:

"Come, now—what's your real name?"

"Wh-what, mum?"

"What's your real name? Is it Bill, or Tom, or Bob?—or what is it?"

I reckon I shook like a leaf, and I didn't know hardly what to do. But I says:

"Please to don't poke fun at a poor girl like me, mum. If I'm in the way, here I'll—"

"No, you won't. Set down and stay where you are. I ain't going to hurt you, and I ain't going to tell on you, nuther. You just tell me your secret, and trust me. I'll keep it; and what's more, I'll help you. So'll my old man, if you want him to. You see, you're a run-away 'prentice—that's all. It ain't anything. There ain't any harm in it. You've been treated bad, and you made up your mind to cut. Bless you, child, I wouldn't tell on you. Tell me all about it, now—that's a good boy."

So I said it wouldn't be no use to try to play it any longer, and I would just make a clean breast and tell her everything, but she mustn't go back on her promise. Then I told her my father and mother was dead, and the law had bound me out to a mean old farmer in the country thirty mile back from the river, and he treated me so bad I couldn't stand it no longer; he went away to be gone a couple of days, and so I took my chance and stole some of his daughter's old clothes, and cleared out, and I had been three nights coming the thirty miles; I traveled nights, and hid daytimes and slept, and the bag of bread and meat I carried from home lasted me all the way and I had a plenty. I said I believed my uncle Abner Moore would take care of me, and so that was why I struck out for this town of Goshen.

"Goshen, child? This ain't Goshen. This is St. Petersburg. Goshen's ten mile further up the river. Who told you this was Goshen?"

"Why, a man I met at day-break this morning, just as I was going to turn into the woods for my regular sleep. He told me when the roads forked I must take the right hand, and five mile would fetch me to Goshen."

"He was drunk I reckon. He told you just exactly wrong."

6. Get, in the sense of hit and kill.

"Well, he did act like he was drunk, but it ain't no matter now. I got to be moving along. I'll fetch Goshen before day-light."

"Hold on a minute. I'll put you up a snack to eat. You might want it."

So she put me up a snack, and says:

"Say—when a cow's laying down, which end of her gets up first? Answer up prompt, now—don't stop to study over it. Which end gets up first?"

"The hind end, mum."

"Well, then, a horse?"

"The for'rard end, mum."

"Which side of a tree does the most moss grow on?"

"North side."

"If fifteen cows is browsing on a hillside, how many of them eats with their heads pointed the same direction?"

"The whole fifteen, mum."

"Well, I reckon you *have* lived in the country. I thought maybe you was trying to hocus me again. What's your real name, now?"

"George Peters, mum."

"Well, try to remember it, George. Don't forget and tell me it's Elexander before you go, and then get out by saying it's George Elexander when I catch you. And don't go about women in that old calico. You do a girl tolerable poor, but you might fool men, maybe. Bless you, child, when you set out to thread a needle, don't hold the thread still and fetch the needle up to it; hold the needle still and poke the thread at it—that's the way a woman most always does; but a man always does 'tother way. And when you throw at a rat or anything, hitch yourself up a tip-toe, and fetch your hand up over your head as awkard as you can, and miss your rat about six or seven foot. Throw stiff-armed from the shoulder, like there was a pivot there for it to turn on—like a girl; not from the wrist and elbow, with your arm out to one side, like a boy. And mind you, when a girl tries to catch anything in her lap, she throws her knees apart; she don't clap them together, the way you did when you catched the lump of lead. Why, I spotted you for a boy when you was threading the needle; and I contrived the other things just to make certain. Now trot along to your uncle, Sarah Mary Williams George Elexander Peters, and if you get into trouble you send word to Mrs. Judith Loftus, which is me, and I'll do what I can to get you out of it. Keep the river road, all the way, and next time you tramp, take shoes and socks with you. The river road's a rocky one, and your feet 'll be in a condition when you get to Goshen, I reckon."

I went up the bank about fifty yards, and then I doubled on my tracks and slipped back to where my canoe was, a good piece below the house. I jumped in and was off in a hurry. I went up stream far enough to make the head of the island, and then started across. I took off the sun-bonnet, for I didn't want no blinders on, then. When I was about the middle, I hear the clock begin to strike; so I stops and listens; the sound come faint over the water, but clear—eleven. When I struck the head of the island I never waited to blow, though I was most winded, but I shoved right into the timber where my old camp used to be, and started a good fire there on a high-and-dry spot.

Then I jumped in the canoe and dug out for our place a mile and a half below, as hard as I could go. I landed, and slopped through the timber and up the ridge and into the cavern. There Jim laid, sound asleep on the ground. I roused him out and says.

"Git up and hump yourself, Jim! There ain't a minute to lose. They're after us!"

Jim never asked no questions, he never said a word; but the way he worked for the next half an hour showed about how he was scared. By that time everything we had in the world was on our raft and she was ready to be shoved out from the willow cove where she was hid. We put out the camp fire at the cavern the first thing, and didn't show a candle outside after that.

I took the canoe out from shore a little piece and took a look, but if there was a boat around I couldn't see it, for stars and shadows ain't good to see by. Then we got out the raft and slipped along down in the shade, past the foot of the island dead still, never saying a word.

## Chapter XII

It must a been close onto one o'clock when we got below the island at last, and the raft did seem to go mighty slow. If a boat was to come along, we was going to take to the canoe and break for the Illinois shore; and it was well a boat didn't come, for we hadn't ever thought to put the gun into the canoe, or a fishing-line or anything to eat. We was in ruther too much of a sweat to think of so many things. It warn't good judgment to put *everything* on the raft.

If the men went to the island, I just expect they found the camp fire I built, and watched it all night for Jim to come. Anyways, they stayed away from us, and if my building the fire never fooled them it warn't no fault of mine. I played it as low-down on them as I could.

When the first streak of day begun to show, we tied up to a tow-head in a big bend on the Illinois side, and hacked off cotton-wood branches with the hatchet and covered up the raft with them so she looked like there had been a cave-in in the bank there. A tow-head is a sand-bar that has cotton-woods on it as thick as harrow-teeth.

We had mountains on the Missouri shore and heavy timber on the Illinois side, and the channel was down the Missouri shore at that place, so we warn't afraid of anybody running across us. We laid there all day and watched the rafts and steamboats spin down the Missouri shore, and up-bound steamboats fight the big river in the middle. I told Jim all about the time I had jabbering with that woman; and Jim said she was a smart one, and if she was to start after us herself *she* wouldn't set down and watch a camp fire—no, sir, she'd fetch a dog. Well, then, I said, why couldn't she tell her husband to fetch a dog? Jim said he bet she did think of it by the time the men was ready to start, and he believed they must a gone up town to get a dog and so they lost all that time, or else we wouldn't be here on a tow-head sixteen or seventeen mile below the village—no, indeedy, we would be in that same old town again. So I said I didn't care what was the reason they didn't get us, as long as they didn't.

When it was beginning to come on dark, we poked our heads out of the cottonwood thicket and looked up, and down, and across; nothing in sight; so Jim took up some of the top planks of the raft and built a snug wigwam to get under in blazing weather and rainy, and to keep the things dry. Jim made a floor for the wigwam, and raised it a foot or more above the level of the raft, so now the blankets and all the traps was out of the reach of steamboat waves. Right in the middle of the wigwam we made a layer of dirt about five or six inches deep with a frame around it for to hold it to its place; this was to build a fire on in sloppy weather or chilly; the wigwam would keep it from being seen. We made an extra steering oar, too, because one of the others might get broke, on a snag or something. We fixed up a short forked stick to hang the old lantern on; because we must always light the lantern whenever we see a steamboat coming down stream, to keep from getting run over; but we wouldn't have to light it up for upstream boats unless we see we was in what they call "crossing;" for the river was pretty high yet, very low banks being still a little under water; so up-bound boats didn't always run the channel, but hunted easy water.

This second night we run between seven and eight hours, with a current that was making over four mile an hour. We catched fish, and talked, and we took a swim now and then to keep off sleepiness. It was kind of solemn, drifting down the big still river, laying on our backs looking up at the stars, and we didn't ever feel like talking loud, and it warn't often that we laughed, only a little kind of a low chuckle. We had mighty good weather, as a general thing, and nothing ever happened to us at all, that night, nor the next, nor the next.

Every night we passed towns, some of them away up on black hillsides, nothing but just a shiny bed of lights, not a house could you see. The fifth night we passed St. Louis, and it was like the whole world lit up. In St. Petersburg they used to say there was twenty or thirty thousand people in St. Louis,[7] but I never believed it till I see that wonderful spread of lights at two o'clock that still night. There warn't a sound there; everybody was asleep.

Every night now, I used to slip ashore, towards ten o'clock, at some little village, and buy ten or fifteen cents' worth of meal or bacon or other stuff to eat; and sometimes I lifted a chicken that warn't roosting comfortable, and took him along. Pap always said, take a chicken when you get a chance, because if you don't want him yourself you can easy find somebody that does, and a good deed ain't ever forgot. I never see pap when he didn't want the chicken himself, but that is what he used to say, anyway.

Mornings, before daylight, I slipped into corn fields and borrowed a watermelon, or a mushmelon, or a punkin, or some new corn, or things of that kind. Pap always said it warn't no harm to borrow things, if you was meaning to pay them back, sometime; but the widow said it warn't anything but a soft name for stealing, and no decent body would do it. Jim said he reckoned the widow was partly right and pap was partly right; so the best way would be for us to pick out two or three things from the list and say we wouldn't borrow them any more—then he reckoned it wouldn't be no harm to borrow the others. So we talked it over all one night, drifting along down the river, trying to make up our minds whether to drop the watermelons, or the cantelopes, or the mushmelons, or what. But towards daylight we got it all settled satisfactory, and concluded to drop crabapples and p'simmons. We warn't feeling just right, before that, but it was all comfortable now. I was glad the way it come out, too, because crabapples ain't ever good, and the p'simmons wouldn't be ripe for two or three months yet.

We shot a water-fowl, now and then, that got up too early in the morning or didn't go to bed early enough in the evening. Take it all around, we lived pretty high.

7. St. Louis is 170 miles down the Mississippi from Hannibal.

The fifth night below St. Louis we had a big storm after midnight, with a power of thunder and lightning, and the rain poured down in a solid sheet. We stayed in the wigwam and let the raft take care of itself. When the lightning glared out we could see a big straight river ahead, and high rocky bluffs on both sides. By-and-by says I, "Hel-*lo* Jim, looky yonder!" It was a steamboat that had killed herself on a rock. We was drifting straight down for her. The lightning showed her very distinct. She was leaning over, with part of her upper deck above water, and you could see every little chimbly-guy[8] clean and clear, and a chair by the big bell, with an old slouch hat hanging on the back of it when the flashes come.

Well, it being away in the night, and stormy, and all so mysterious-like, I felt just the way any other boy would a felt when I see that wreck laying there so mournful and lonesome in the middle of the river. I wanted to get aboard of her and slink around a little, and see what there was there. So I says:

"Le's land on her, Jim."

But Jim was dead against it, at first. He says:

"I doan' want to go fool'n 'long er no wrack. We's doin' blame' well, en we better let blame' well alone, as de good book says. Like as not dey's a watchman on dat wrack."

"Watchman your grandmother," I says; "there ain't nothing to watch but the texas[9] and the pilot-house; and do you reckon anybody's going to resk his life for a texas and a pilot-house such a night as this, when it's likely to break up and wash off down the river any minute?" Jim couldn't say nothing to that, so he didn't try. "And besides," I says, "we might borrow something worth having, out of the captain's stateroom. Seegars, *I* bet you—and cost five cents apiece, solid cash. Steamboat captains is always rich, and get sixty dollars a month, and *they* don't care a cent what a thing costs, you know, long as they want it. Stick a candle in your pocket; I can't rest, Jim, till we give her a rummaging. Do you reckon Tom Sawyer would ever go by this thing? Not for pie, he wouldn't. He'd call it an adventure—that's what he'd call it; and he'd land on that wreck if it was his last act. And wouldn't he throw style into it?— wouldn't he spread himself, nor nothing? Why, you'd think it was Christopher C'lumbus discovering Kingdom-Come. I wish Tom Sawyer *was* here."

Jim he grumbled a little, but give in. He said we mustn't talk any more than we could help, and then talk mighty low. The lightning showed us the wreck again, just in time, and we fetched the starboard derrick,[1] and made fast there.

The deck was high out, here. We went sneaking down the slope of it to labboard, in the dark, towards the texas, feeling our way slow with our feet, and spreading our hands out to fend off the guys, for it was so dark we couldn't see no sign of them. Pretty soon we struck the forward end of the skylight, and clumb onto it; and the next step fetched us in front of the captain's door, which was open, and by Jimminy, away down through the texas-hall we see a light! and all in the same second we seem to hear low voices in yonder!

Jim whispered and said he was feeling powerful sick, and told me to come along. I says, all right; and was going to start for the raft; but just then I heard a voice wail out and say:

"Oh, please don't, boys; I swear I won't ever tell!"

---

8. Wires used to steady the chimney stacks.
9. The large cabin on the top deck located just behind or beneath the pilothouse; it serves as officers' quarters.
1. Boom for lifting cargo.

Another voice said, pretty loud:

"It's a lie, Jim Turner. You've acted this way before. You always want more'n your share of the truck and you've always got it, too, because you've swore 't if you didn't you'd tell. But this time you've said it jest one time too many. You're the meanest, treacherousest hound in this country."

By this time Jim was gone for the raft. I was just a-biling with curiosity; and I says to myself, Tom Sawyer wouldn't back out now, and so I won't either; I'm agoing to see what's going on here. So I dropped on my hands and knees, in the little passage, and crept aft in the dark, till there warn't but about one stateroom betwixt me and the cross-hall of the texas. Then, in there I see a man stretched on the floor and tied hand and foot, and two men standing over him, and one of them had a dim lantern in his hand, and the other one had a pistol. This one kept pointing the pistol at the man's head on the floor and saying—

"I'd *like* to! And I orter, too, a mean skunk!"

The man on the floor would shrivel up, and say: "Oh, please don't, Bill—I hain't ever goin' to tell."

And every time he said that, the man with the lantern would laugh and say:

" 'Deed you *ain't!* You never said no truer thing 'n that, you bet you." And once he said, "Hear him beg! and yit if we hadn't got the best of him and tied him, he'd a killed us both. And what *for?* Jist for noth'n. Jist because we stood on our *rights*—that's what for. But I lay you ain't agoin' to threaten nobody any more, Jim Turner. Put *up* that pistol, Bill."

Bill says:

"I don't want to, Jake Packard. I'm for killin' him—and didn't he kill old Hatfield jist the same way—and don't he deserve it?"

"But I don't *want* him killed, and I've got my reasons for it."

"Bless yo' heart for them words, Jake Packard! I'll never forget you, long's I live!" says the man on the floor, sort of blubbering.

Packard didn't take no notice of that, but hung up his lantern on a nail, and started towards where I was, there in the dark, and motioned Bill to come. I crawfished[2] as fast as I could, about two yards, but the boat slanted so that I couldn't make very good time; so to keep from getting run over and catched I crawled into a stateroom on the upper side. The man come a-pawing along in the dark, and when Packard got to my stateroom, he says:

"Here—come in here."

And in he come, and Bill after him. But before they got in, I was up in the upper berth, cornered, and sorry I come. Then they stood there, with their hands on the ledge of the berth, and talked. I couldn't see them, but I could tell where they was, by the whisky they'd been having. I was glad I didn't drink whisky; but it wouldn't made much difference, anyway, because most of the time they couldn't a treed me because I didn't breathe. I was too scared. And besides, a body *couldn't* breathe, and hear such talk. They talked low and earnest. Bill wanted to kill Turner. He says:

"He's said he'll tell, and he will. If we was to give both our shares to him *now*, it wouldn't make no difference after the row, and the way we've served him. Shore's you're born, he'll turn State's evidence; now you hear *me*. I'm for putting him out of his troubles."

---

2. Crept backward on all fours.

"So'm I," says Packard, very quiet.

"Blame it, I'd sorter begun to think you wasn't. Well, then, that's all right. Les' go and do it."

"Hold on a minute; I hain't had my say yit. You listen to me. Shooting's good, but there's quieter ways if the thing's *got* to be done. But what I say, is this; it ain't good sense to go court'n around after a halter,[3] if you can git at what you're up to in some way that's jist as good and at the same time don't bring you into no resks. Ain't that so?"

"You bet it is. But how you goin' to manage it this time?"

"Well, my idea is this: we'll rustle around and gether up whatever pickins we've overlooked in the staterooms, and shove for shore and hide the truck. Then we'll wait. Now I say it ain't agoin' to be more 'n two hours befo' this wrack breaks up and washes off down the river. See? He'll be drownded, and won't have nobody to blame for it but his own self. I reckon that's a considerble sight better'n killin' of him. I'm unfavorable to killin' a man as long as you can git around it; it ain't good sense, it ain't good morals. Ain't I right?"

"Yes—I reck'n you are. But s'pose she *don't* break up and wash off?"

"Well, we can wait the two hours, anyway, and see, can't we?"

"All right, then; come along."

So they started, and I lit out, all in a cold sweat, and scrambled forward. It was dark as pitch there; but I said in a kind of a coarse whisper, "Jim!" and he answered up, right at my elbow, with a sort of a moan, and I says:

"Quick, Jim, it ain't no time for fooling around and moaning; there's a gang of murderers in yonder, and if we don't hunt up their boat and set her drifting down the river so these fellows can't get away from the wreck, there's one of 'em going to be in a bad fix. But if we find their boat we can put *all* of 'em in a bad fix—for the Sheriff 'll get 'em. Quick—hurry! I'll hunt the labboard side, you hunt the stabboard. You start at the raft, and—"

"Oh, my lordy, lordy! *Raf'*? Dey ain' no raf' no mo', she done broke loose en gone!—'en here we is!"

## Chapter XIII

Well, I catched my breath and most fainted. Shut up on a wreck with such a gang as that! But it warn't no time to be sentimentering. We'd *got* to find that boat, now—had to have it for ourselves. So we went a-quaking and down the stabboard side, and slow work it was, too—seemed a week before we got to the stern. No sign of a boat. Jim said he didn't believe he could go any further—so scared he hadn't hardly any strength left, he said. But I said come on, if we get left on this wreck, we are in a fix, sure. So on we prowled, again. We struck for the stern of the texas, and found it, and then scrabbled along forwards on the skylight, hanging on from shutter to shutter, for the edge of the skylight was in the water. When we got pretty close to the cross-hall door there was the skiff, sure enough! I could just barely see her. I felt ever so thankful. In another second I would a been aboard of her; but just then the door opened. One of the men stuck his head out, only about a couple of foot from me, and I thought I was gone; but he jerked it in again, and says:

3. Hangman's noose.

"Heave that blame lantern out o' sight, Bill!"

He flung a bag of something into the boat, and then got in himself, and set down. It was Packard. Then Bill *he* come out and got in. Packard says, in a low voice:

"All ready—shove off!"

I couldn't hardly hang onto the shutters, I was so weak. But Bill says:

"Hold on—'d you go through him?"

"No. Didn't you?"

"No. So he's got his share o' the cash, yet."

"Well, then, come along—no use to take truck and leave money."

"Say—won't he suspicion what we're up to?"

"Maybe he won't. But we got to have it anyway. Come along." So they got out and went in.

The door slammed to, because it was on the careened side; and in a half second I was in the boat, and Jim come a tumbling after me. I out with my knife and cut the rope, and away we went!

We didn't touch an oar, and we didn't speak nor whisper, nor hardly even breathe. We went gliding swift along, dead silent, past the tip of the paddle-box, and past the stern; then in a second or two more we was a hundred yards below the wreck, and the darkness soaked her up, every last sign of her, and we was safe, and knowed it.

When we was three or four hundred yards down stream, we see the lantern show like a little spark at the texas door, for a second, and we knowed by that that the rascals had missed their boat, and was beginning to understand that they was in just as much trouble, now, as Jim Turner was.

Then Jim manned the oars, and we took out after our raft. Now was the first time that I begun to worry about the men—I reckon I hadn't had time to before. I begun to think how dreadful it was, even for murderers, to be in such a fix. I says to myself, there ain't no telling but I might come to be a murderer myself, yet, and then how would I like it? So says I to Jim:

"The first light we see, we'll land a hundred yards below it or above it, in a place where it's a good hiding-place for you and the skiff, and then I'll go and fix up some kind of a yarn, and get somebody to go for that gang and get them out of their scrape, so they can be hung when their time comes."

But that idea was a failure; for pretty soon it begun to storm again, and this time worse than ever. The rain poured down, and never a light showed; everybody in bed, I reckon. We boomed along down the river, watching for lights and watching for our raft. After a long time the rain let up, but the clouds staid, and the lightning kept whimpering, and by-and-by a flash showed us a black thing ahead, floating, and we made for it.

It was the raft, and mighty glad was we to get aboard of it again. We seen a light, now, away down to the right, on shore. So I said I would go for it. The skiff was half full of plunder which that gang had stole, there on the wreck. We hustled it onto the raft in a pile, and I told Jim to float along down, and show a light when he judged he had gone about two mile, and keep it burning till I come; then I manned my oars and shoved for the light. As I got down towards it, three or four more showed—up on a hillside. It was a village. I closed in above the shore-light, and laid on my oars and floated. As I went by, I see it was a lantern hanging on the jackstaff of a double-hull ferry-boat. I skimmed around for the watchman, a-wondering whereabouts he slept; and by-and-by I found him roosting on the bitts,[4] forward, with his head down between his knees. I give his shoulder two or three little shoves, and begun to cry.

He stirred up, in a kind of startlish way; but when he see it was only me, he took a good gap and stretch, and then he says:

"Hello, what's up? Don't cry, bub. What's the trouble?"

I says:

"Pap, and mam, and sis, and—"

Then I broke down. He says:

"Oh, dang it, now, *don't* take on so, we all has to have our troubles and this'n 'll come out all right. What's the matter with 'em?"

"They're—they're—are you the watchman of the boat?"

"Yes," he says, kind of pretty-well-satisfied like. "I'm the captain and the owner, and the mate, and the pilot, and watchman, and head deck-hand; and sometimes I'm the freight and passengers. I ain't as rich as old Jim Hornback, and I can't be so blame' generous and good to Tom, Dick and Harry as what he is, and slam around money the way he does; but I've told him a many a time 't I wouldn't trade places with him; for, says I, a sailor's life's the life for me, and I'm derned if I'd live two mile out o' town, where there ain't nothing ever goin' on, not for all his spondulicks and as much more on top of it. Says I—"

I broke in and says:

"They're in an awful peck of trouble, and—"

"*Who* is?"

"Why, pap, and mam, and sis, and Miss Hooker; and if you'd take your ferry-boat and go up there—"

"Up where? Where are they?"

"On the wreck."

"What wreck?"

"Why, there ain't but one."

"What, you don't mean the *Walter Scott?*"[5]

"Yes."

"Good land! what are they doin' *there,* for gracious sakes?"

"Well, they didn't go there a-purpose."

"I bet they didn't! Why, great goodness, there ain't no chance for 'em if they don't git off mighty quick! Why, how in the nation did they ever git into such a scrape?"

"Easy enough. Miss Hooker was a-visiting, up there to the town—"

"Yes, Booth's Landing—go on."

"She was a-visiting, there at Booth's Landing, and just in the edge of the evening she started over with her nigger woman in the horse-ferry,[6] to stay all night at her friend's house, Miss What-you-may-call her, I disremember her name, and they lost their steering-oar, and swung around and went a-floating

---

4. Vertical wooden posts to which cables can be secured.
5. Twain held Sir Walter Scott's romantic adventure novels set in feudal England responsible for the distorted antidemocratic notions held by so many Southerners and thus for the false ideology they were willing to fight and die for in the Civil War. Twain expressed himself most vividly on this subject in *Life on the Mississippi* (Ch. 46), where he observes: "Sir Walter had so large a hand in making Southern character, as it existed before the war, that he is in great measure responsible for the war."
6. A ferry large enough to take horses and wagons.

down, stern-first, about two mile, and saddle-baggsed[7] on the wreck, and the ferry man and the nigger woman and the horses was all lost, but Miss Hooker she made a grab and got aboard the wreck. Well, about an hour after dark, we come along down in our trading-scow, and it was so dark we didn't notice the wreck till we was right on it; and so *we* saddle-baggsed; but all of us was saved but Bill Whipple—and oh, he *was* the best cretur!—I most wish't it had been me, I do."

"My George! It's the beatenest thing I ever struck. And *then* what did you all do?"

"Well, we hollered and took on, but it's so wide there, we couldn't make nobody hear. So pap said somebody got to get ashore and get help somehow. I was the only one that could swim, so I made a dash for it, and Miss Hooker she said if I didn't strike help sooner, come here and hunt up her uncle, and he'd fix the thing. I made the land about a mile below, and been fooling along ever since, trying to get people to do something, but they said, 'What, in such a night and such a current? there ain't no sense in it; go for the steam-ferry.' Now if you'll go, and—"

"By Jackson, I'd *like* to, and blame it I don't know but I will; but who in the dingnation's agoin' to *pay* for it? Do you reckon your pap—"

"Why *that's* all right. Miss Hooker she told me, *particular,* that her uncle Hornback—"

"Great guns! is *he* her uncle? Look here, you break for that light over yonder-way, and turn out west when you git there, and about a quarter of a mile out you'll come to the tavern; tell 'em to dart you out to Jim Hornback's and he'll foot the bill. And don't you fool around any, because he'll want to know the news. Tell him I'll have his niece all safe before he can get to town. Hump yourself, now; I'm agoing up around the corner here, to roust out my engineer."

I struck for the light, but as soon as he turned the corner I went back and got into my skiff and bailed her out and then pulled up shore in the easy water about six hundred yards, and tucked myself in among some woodboats; for I couldn't rest easy till I could see the ferry-boat start. But take it all around, I was feeling ruther comfortable on accounts of taking all this trouble for that gang, for not many would a done it. I wished the widow knowed about it. I judged she would be proud of me for helping these rapscallions, because rapscallions and dead beats is the kind the widow and good people takes the most interest in.

Well, before long, here comes the wreck, dim and dusky, sliding along down! A kind of cold shiver went through me, and then I struck out for her. She was very deep, and I see in a minute there warn't much chance for anybody being alive in her. I pulled all around her and hollered a little, but there wasn't any answer; all dead still. I felt a little bit heavy-hearted about the gang, but not much, for I reckoned if they could stand it, I could.

Then here comes the ferry-boat; so I shoved for the middle of the river on a long down-stream slant; and when I judged I was out of eye-reach, I laid on my oars, and looked back and see her go and smell around the wreck for Miss Hooker's remainders, because the captain would know her uncle Hornback would want them; and then pretty soon the ferry-boat give it up and went for shore, and I laid into my work and went a-booming down the river.

---

7. Broken and doubled around the wreck.

It did seem a powerful long time before Jim's light showed up; and when it did show, it looked like it was a thousand mile off. By the time I got there the sky was beginning to get a little gray in the east; so we struck for an island, and hid the raft, and sunk the skiff, and turned in and slept like dead people.

## Chapter XIV

By-and-by, when we got up, we turned over the truck the gang had stole off of the wreck, and found boots, and blankets, and clothes, and all sorts of other things, and a lot of books, and a spyglass, and three boxes of seegars. We hadn't ever been this rich before, in neither of our lives. The seegars was prime. We laid off all the afternoon in the woods talking, and me reading the books, and having a general good time. I told Jim all about what happened inside the wreck, and at the ferry-boat; and I said these kinds of things was adventures; but he said he didn't want no more adventures. He said that when I went in the texas and he crawled back to get on the raft and found her gone, he nearly died; because he judged it was all up with *him*, anyway it could be fixed; for if he didn't get saved he would get drownded; and if he did get saved, whoever saved him would send him back home so as to get the reward, and then Miss Watson would sell him South, sure. Well, he was right; he was most always right; he had an uncommon level head, for a nigger.

I read considerable to Jim about kings, and dukes, and earls, and such, and how gaudy they dressed, and how much style they put on, and called each other your majesty, and your grace, and your lordship, and so on, 'stead of mister; and Jim's eyes bugged out, and he was interested. He says:

"I didn't know dey was so many un um. I hain't hearn 'bout none un um, skasely, but ole King Sollermun, onless you counts dem kings dat's in a pack er k'yards. How much do a king git?"

"Get?" I says; "why, they get a thousand dollars a month if they want it; they can have just as much as they want; everything belongs to them."

"*Ain'* dat gay? En what dey got to do, Huck?"

"*They* don't do nothing! Why how you talk. They just set around."

"No—is dat so?"

"Of course it is. They just set around. Except maybe when there 's a war; then they go to the war. But other times they just lazy around; or go hawking—just hawking and sp—Sh!—d' you hear a noise?"

We skipped out and looked; but it warn't nothing but the flutter of a steamboat's wheel, away down coming around the point; so we come back.

"Yes," says I, "and other times, when things is dull, they fuss with the parlyment; and if everybody don't go just so he whacks their heads off. But mostly they hang round the harem."

"Roun' de which?"

"Harem."

"What's de harem?"

"The place where he keep his wives. Don't you know about the harem? Solomon had one; he had about a million wives."

"Why, yes, dat's so; I—I'd done forgot it. A harem's a bo'd'n-house, I reck'n. Mos' likely dey has rackety times in de nussery. En I reck'n de wives quarrels considable; en dat 'crease de racket. Yit dey say Sollermun de wises' man dat ever live.' I doan' take no stock in dat. Bekase why: would a wise man want to live in de mids' er sich a blimblammin' all de time? No—'deed he wouldn't. A wise man 'ud take en buil' a biler-factry; en den he could shet *down* de biler-factry when he want to res'."

"Well, but he *was* the wisest man, anyway; because the widow she told me so, her own self."

"I doan k'yer what de widder say, he *warn'* no wise man, nuther. He had some er de dad-fetchedes' ways I ever see. Does you know 'bout dat chile dat he 'uz gwyne to chop in two?"[8]

"Yes, the widow told me all about it."

"*Well*, den! Warn' dat de beatenes' notion in de worl'? You jes' take en look at it a minute. Dah's de stump, dah—dat's one er de women; heah's you—dat's de yuther one; I's Sollermun; en dish-yer dollar bill's de chile. Bofe un you claims it. What does I do? Does I shin aroun' mongs' de neighbors en fine out which un you de bill do b'long to, en han' it over to de right one, all safe en soun', de way dat anybody dat had any gumption would? No—I take en whack de bill in *two*, en give half un it to you, en de yuther half to de yuther woman. Dat's de way Sollermun was gwyne to do wid de chile. Now I want to ask you: what's de use er dat half a bill?—can't buy noth'n wid it. En what use is a half a chile? I wouldn' give a dern for a million un um."

"But hang it, Jim, you've clean missed the point—blame it, you've missed it a thousand mile."

"Who? Me? Go 'long. Doan' talk to *me* 'bout yo' pints. I reck'n I knows sense when I sees it; en dey ain' no sense in sich doin's as dat. De 'spute warn't 'bout a half a chile, de 'spute was 'bout a whole chile; en de man dat think he kin settle a 'spute 'bout a whole chile wid a half a chile, doan' know enough to come in out'n de rain. Doan' talk to me 'bout Sollermun, Huck, I knows him by de back."

"But I tell you you don't get the point."

"Blame de pint! I reck'n I knows what I knows. En mine you, de *real* pint is down furder—it's down deeper. It lays in de way Sollermun was raised. You take a man dat's got on'y one er two children; is dat man gwyne to be wase-ful o' chillen? No, he ain't; he can't 'ford it. *He* know how to value 'em. But you take a man dat's got 'bout five million chillen runnin' roun' de house, en it's diffunt. *He* as soon chop a chile in two as a cat. Dey's plenty mo'. A chile er two, mo' er less, warn't no consekens to Sollermun, dad fetch him!"

I never see such a nigger. If he got a notion in his head once, there warn't no getting it out again. He was the most down on Solomon of any nigger I ever see. So I went to talking about other kings, and let Solomon slide. I told about Louis Sixteenth that got his head cut off in France long time ago; and about his little boy the dolphin,[9] that would a been a king, but they took and shut him up in jail, and some say he died there.

"Po' little chap."

"But some says he got out and got away, and come to America."

"Dat's good! But he'll be pooty lonesome—dey ain' no kings here, is dey, Huck?"

"No."

8. In 1 Kings 3.16–28. When two women appeared before him claiming to be the mother of the same infant, Solomon ordered the child cut in two. The real mother pleaded with him to save the baby and to give it to the other woman, who maliciously agreed to Solomon's original plan.

9. The Dauphin, Louis Charles, next in line of the succession to the throne, was eight years old when his father, Louis XVI, was beheaded (1793). Though the boy died in prison, probably in 1795, legends of his escape to America (and elsewhere) persisted, and Twain owned a book on the subject by Horace W. Fuller: *Imposters and Adventurers, Noted French Trials* (1882).

"Den he cain't git no situation. What he gwyne to do?"

"Well, I don't know. Some of them gets on the police, and some of them learns people how to talk French."

"Why, Huck, doan' de French people talk de same way we does?"

"No, Jim; you couldn't understand a word they said—not a single word."

"Well now, I be ding-busted! How do dat come?"

"I don't know; but it's so. I got some of their jabber out of a book. Spose a man was to come to you and say *Polly-voo-franzy*—what would you think?"

"I wouldn' think nuff'n; I'd take en bust him over de head. Dat is, if he warn't white. I wouldn't 'low no nigger to call me dat."

"Shucks, it ain't calling you anything. It's only saying do you know how to talk French?"

"Well, den, why couldn't he *say* it?"

"Why, he *is* a-saying it. That's a Frenchman's *way* of saying it."

"Well, it's a blame' ridicklous way, en I doan' want to hear no mo' 'bout it. Dey ain' no sense in it."

"Looky here, Jim; does a cat talk like we do?"

"No, a cat don't."

"Well, does a cow?"

"No, a cow don't, nuther."

"Does a cat talk like a cow, or a cow talk like a cat?"

"No, dey don't."

"It's natural and right for 'em to talk different from each other, ain't it?"

" 'Course."

"And ain't it natural and right for a cat and a cow to talk different from *us*?"

"Why, mos' sholy it is."

"Well, then, why ain't it natural and right for a *Frenchman* to talk different from us? You answer me that."

"Is a cat a man, Huck?"

"No."

"Well, den, dey ain't no sense in a cat talkin' like a man. Is a cow a man?—er is a cow a cat?"

"No, she ain't either of them."

"Well, den, she ain' got no business to talk like either one er the yuther of 'em. Is a Frenchman a man?"

"Yes."

"*Well*, den! Dad blame it, why doan' he *talk* like a man? You answer me *dat*!"

I see it warn't no use wasting words—you can't learn a nigger to argue. So I quit.

## Chapter XV

We judged that three nights more would fetch us to Cairo,[1] at the bottom of Illinois, where the Ohio River comes in, and that was what we was after. We would sell the raft and get on a steamboat and go way up the Ohio amongst the free States, and then be out of trouble.[2]

1. Pronounced *Cair-ō*, the town is 364 miles from Hannibal, 194 miles from St. Louis.
2. Southern Illinois was proslavery in sentiment. The state, moreover, had a system of indentured labor, not unlike slavery, to which a black person without proof of free status might be subjected. Although even in the "free" states there were similar dangers for Jim, the chances of his making his way to freedom and safety in Canada from Ohio or Pennsylvania would be much greater.

Well, the second night a fog begun to come on, and we made for a tow-head to tie to, for it wouldn't do to try to run in fog; but when I paddled ahead in the canoe, with the line, to make fast, there warn't anything but little saplings to tie to. I passed the line around one of them right on the edge of the cut bank, but there was a stiff current, and the raft come booming down so lively she tore it out by the roots and away she went. I see the fog closing down, and it made me so sick and scared I couldn't budge for most a half a minute it seemed to me—and then there warn't no raft in sight; you couldn't see twenty yards. I jumped into the canoe and run back to the stern and grabbed the paddle and set her back a stroke. But she didn't come. I was in such a hurry I hadn't untied her. I got up and tried to untie her, but I was so excited my hands shook so I couldn't hardly do anything with them.

As soon as I got started I took out after the raft, hot and heavy, right down the tow-head. That was all right as far as it went, but the tow-head warn't sixty yards long, and the minute I flew by the foot of it I shot out into the solid white fog, and hadn't no more idea which way I was going than a dead man.

Thinks I, it won't do to paddle; first I know I'll run into the bank or a tow-head or something; I got to set still and float, and yet it's mighty fidgety business to have to hold your hands still at such a time. I whooped and listened. Away down there, somewheres, I hears a small whoop, and up comes my spirits. I went tearing after it, listening sharp to hear it again. The next time it come, I see I warn't heading for it but heading away to the right of it. And the next time, I was heading away to the left of it—and not gaining on it much, either, for I was flying around, this way and that and 'tother, but it was going straight ahead all the time.

I did wish the fool would think to beat a tin pan, and beat it all the time, but he never did, and it was the still places between the whoops that was making the trouble for me. Well, I fought along, and directly I hears the whoops *behind* me. I was tangled good, now. That was somebody's else's whoop, or else I was turned around.

I throwed the paddle down. I heard the whoop again; it was behind me yet, but in a different place; it kept coming, and kept changing its place, and I kept answering, till by-and-by it was in front of me again and I knowed the current had swung the canoe's head down stream and I was all right, if that was Jim and not some other raftsman hollering. I couldn't tell nothing about voices in a fog, for nothing don't look natural nor sound natural in a fog.

The whooping went on, and in about a minute I come a booming down on a cut bank[3] with smoky ghosts of big trees on it, and the current throwed me off to the left and shot by, amongst a lot of snags that fairly roared, the current was tearing by them so swift.

In another second or two it was solid white and still again. I set perfectly still, then, listening to my heart thump, and I reckon I didn't draw a breath while it thumped a hundred.

I just give up, then. I knowed what the matter was. That cut bank was an island, and Jim had gone down 'tother side of it. It warn't no tow-head, that you could float by in ten minutes. It had the big timber of a regular island; it might be five or six mile long and more than a half a mile wide.

I kept quiet, with my ears cocked, about fifteen minutes, I reckon. I was

---

3. Steep bank carved out by the force of the current.

floating along, of course, four or five mile an hour; but you don't ever think of that. No, you *feel* like you are laying dead still on the water; and if a little glimpse of a snag slips by, you don't think to yourself how fast *you're* going, but you catch your breath and think, my! how that snag's tearing along. If you think it ain't dismal and lonesome out in a fog that way, by yourself, in the night, you try it once—you'll see.

Next, for about a half an hour, I whoops now and then; at last I hears the answer a long ways off, and tries to follow it, but I couldn't do it, and directly I judged I'd got into a nest of tow-heads, for I had little dim glimpses of them on both sides of me, sometimes just a narrow channel between; and some that I couldn't see, I knowed was there, because I'd hear the wash of the current against the old dead brush and trash that hung over the banks. Well, I warn't long losing the whoops, down amongst the tow-heads; and I only tried to chase them a little while, anyway, because it was worse than chasing a Jack-o-lantern. You never knowed a sound dodge around so, and swap places so quick and so much.

I had to claw away from the bank pretty lively, four or five times, to keep from knocking the islands out of the river; and so I judged the raft must be butting into the bank every now and then, or else it would get further ahead and clear out of hearing—it was floating a little faster than what I was.

Well, I seemed to be in the open river again, by-and-by, but I couldn't hear no sign of a whoop nowheres. I reckoned Jim had fetched up on a snag, maybe, and it was all up with him. I was good and tired, so I laid down in the canoe and said I wouldn't bother no more. I didn't want to go to sleep, of course; but I was so sleepy I couldn't help it; so I thought I would take just one little cat-nap.

But I reckon it was more than a cat-nap, for when I waked up the stars was shining bright, the fog was all gone, and I was spinning down a big bend stern first. First I didn't know where I was; I thought I was dreaming; and when things begun to come back to me, they seemed to come up dim out of last week.

It was a monstrous big river here, with the tallest and the thickest kind of timber on both banks; just a solid wall, as well as I could see, by the stars. I looked away down stream, and seen a black speck on the water. I took out after it; but when I got to it it warn't nothing but a couple of saw-logs made fast together. Then I see another speck, and chased that; then another, and this time I was right. It was the raft.

When I got to it Jim was setting there with his head down between his knees, asleep, with his right arm hanging over the steering oar. The other oar was smashed off, and the raft was littered up with leaves and branches and dirt. So she'd had a rough time.

I made fast and laid down under Jim's nose on the raft, and begun to gap, and stretch my fists out against Jim, and says:

"Hello, Jim, have I been asleep? Why didn't you stir me up?"

"Goodness gracious, is dat you, Huck? En you ain' dead—you ain' drownded—you's back agin? It's too good for true, honey, it's too good for true. Lemme look at you, chile, lemme feel o' you. No, you ain' dead? you's back agin, 'live en soun', jis de same ole Huck—de same ole Huck, thanks to goodness!"

"What's the matter with you, Jim? You been a drinking?"

"Drinkin'? Has I ben a drinkin'? Has I had a chance to be a drinkin'?"

"Well, then, what makes you talk so wild?"

"How does I talk wild?"

"*How?* why, haint you been talking about my coming back, and all that stuff, as if I'd been gone away?"

"Huck—Huck Finn, you look me in de eye; look me in de eye. *Hain't* you ben gone away?"

"Gone away? Why, what in the nation do you mean? *I* hain't been gone anywhere. Where would I go to?"

"Well, looky here, boss, dey's sumf'n wrong, dey is. Is I *me*, or who *is* I? Is I heah, or whah *is* I? Now dat's what I wants to know?"

"Well, I think you're here, plain enough, but I think you're a tangle-headed old fool, Jim."

"I is, is I? Well you answer me dis. Didn't you tote out de line in de canoe, fer to make fas' to de tow-head?"

"No, I didn't. What tow-head? I hain't seen no tow-head."

"You hain't seen no tow-head? Looky here—didn't de line pull loose en de raf' go a hummin' down de river, en leave you en de canoe behine in de fog?"

"What fog?"

"Why *de* fog. De fog dat's ben aroun' all night. En didn't you whoop, en didn't I whoop, tell we got mix' up in de islands en one un us got 'los' en 'tother one was jis' as good as los', 'kase he didn' know whah he wuz? En didn't I bust up agin a lot er dem islands en have a turrible time en mos' git drownded? Now ain' dat so, boss—ain't it so? You answer me dat."

"Well, this is too many for me, Jim. I hain't seen no fog, nor no islands, nor no troubles, nor nothing. I been setting here talking with you all night till you went to sleep about ten minutes ago, and I reckon I done the same. You couldn't a got drunk in that time, so of course you've been dreaming."

"Dad fetch it, how is I gwyne to dream all dat in ten minutes?"

"Well, hang it all, you did dream it, because there didn't any of it happen."

"But Huck, it's all jis' as plain to me as—"

"It don't make no difference how plain it is, there ain't nothing in it. I know, because I've been here all the time."

Jim didn't say nothing for about five minutes, but set there studying over it. Then he says:

"Well, den, I reck'n I did dream it, Huck; but dog my cats ef it ain't de powerfullest dream I ever see. En I hain't ever had no dream b'fo' dat's tired me like dis one."

"Oh, well, that's all right, because a dream does tire a body like everything, sometimes. But this one was a staving[4] dream—tell me all about it, Jim."

So Jim went to work and told me the whole thing right through, just as it happened, only he painted it up considerable. Then he said he must start in and " 'terpret" it, because it was sent for a warning. He said the first tow-head stood for a man that would try to do us some good, but the current was another man that would get us away from him. The whoops was warnings that would come to us every now and then, and if we didn't try hard to make out to understand them they'd just take us into bad luck, 'stead of keeping us out of it. The lot of tow-heads was troubles we was going to get into with quar-

---

4. Vivid, compelling.

relsome people and all kinds of mean folks, but if we minded our business and didn't talk back and aggravate them, we would pull through and get out of the fog and into the big clear river, which was the free States, and wouldn't have no more trouble.

It had clouded up pretty dark just after I got onto the raft, but it was clearing up again, now.

"Oh, well, that's all interpreted well enough, as far as it goes, Jim," I says; "but what does *these* things stand for?"

It was the leaves and rubbish on the raft, and the smashed oar. You could see them first rate, now.

Jim looked at the trash, and then looked at me, and back at the trash again. He had got the dream fixed so strong in his head that he couldn't seem to shake it loose and get the facts back into its place again, right away. But when he did get the thing straightened around, he looked at me steady, without ever smiling, and says:

"What do dey stan' for? I's gwyne to tell you. When I got all wore out wid work, en wid de callin' for you, en went to sleep, my heart wuz mos' broke bekase you wuz los', en I didn' k'yer no mo' what become er me en de raf'. En when I wake up en fine you back agin', all safe en soun', de tears come en I could a got down on my knees en kiss' yo' foot I's so thankful. En all you wuz thinkin' 'bout wuz how you could make a fool uv ole Jim wid a lie. Dat truck dah is *trash*; en trash is what people is dat puts dirt on de head er dey fren's en makes 'em ashamed."

Then he got up slow, and walked to the wigwam, and went in there, without saying anything but that. But that was enough. It made me feel so mean I could almost kissed *his* foot to get him to take it back.

It was fifteen minutes before I could work myself up to go and humble myself to a nigger—but I done it, and I warn't ever sorry for it afterwards, neither. I didn't do him no more mean tricks, and I wouldn't done that one if I'd a knowed it would make him feel that way.

### Chapter XVI

We slept most all day, and started out at night, a little ways behind a monstrous long raft that was as long going by as a procession. She had four long sweeps[5] at each end, so we judged she carried as many as thirty men, likely. She had five big wigwams aboard, wide apart, and an open camp fire in the middle, and a tall flagpole at each end. There was a power of style about her. It *amounted* to something being a raftsman on such a craft as that.

We went drifting down into a big bend, and the night clouded up and got hot. The river was very wide, and was walled with solid timber on both sides; you couldn't see a break in it hardly ever, or a light. We talked about Cairo, and wondered whether we would know it when we got to it. I said likely we wouldn't, because I had heard say there warn't but about a dozen houses there, and if they didn't happen to have them lit up, how was we going to know we was passing a town? Jim said if the two big rivers joined together there, that would show. But I said maybe we might think we was passing the foot of an island and coming into the same old river again. That disturbed

---

5. Long oars used chiefly for steering.

Jim—and me too. So the question was, what to do? I said, paddle ashore the first time a light showed, and tell them pap was behind, coming along with a trading-scow, and was a green hand at the business, and wanted to know how far it was to Cairo. Jim thought it was a good idea, so we took a smoke on it and waited.[6]

But you know a young person can't wait very well when he is impatient to find a thing out. We talked it over, and by and by Jim said it was such a black night, now, that it wouldn't be no risk to swim down to the big raft and crawl aboard and listen—they would talk about Cairo, because they would be calculating to go ashore there for a spree, maybe; or anyway they would send boats ashore to buy whisky or fresh meat or something. Jim had a wonderful level head, for a nigger: he could most always start a good plan when you wanted one.

I stood up and shook my rags off and jumped into the river, and struck out for the raft's light. By and by, when I got down nearly to her, I eased up and went slow and cautious. But everything was all right—nobody at the sweeps. So I swum down along the raft till I was most abreast the camp fire in the middle, then I crawled aboard and inched along and got in among some bundles of shingles on the weather side of the fire. There was thirteen men there— they was the watch on deck of course. And a mighty rough-looking lot, too. They had a jug, and tin cups, and they kept the jug moving. One man was singing—roaring, you may say; and it wasn't a nice song—for a parlor, anyway. He roared through his nose, and strung out the last word of every line very long. When he was done they all fetched a kind of Injun war-whoop, and then another was sung. It begun:

> "There was a woman in our towdn,
>     In our towdn did dwed'l [dwell],
> She loved her husband dear-i-lee,
>     But another man twyste as wed'l.

> "Singing too, riloo, riloo, riloo,
>     Ri-too, riloo, rilay—e,
> She loved her husband dear-i-lee,
>     But another man twyste as wed'l."

And so on—fourteen verses. It was kind of poor, and when he was going to start on the next verse one of them said it was the tune the old cow died on; and another one said: "Oh, give us a rest!" And another one told him to take a walk. They made fun of him till he got mad and jumped up and begun to cuss the crowd, and said he could lam any thief in the lot.

They was all about to make a break for him, but the biggest man there jumped up and says:

"Set whar you are, gentlemen. Leave him to me; he's my meat."

Then he jumped up in the air three times, and cracked his heels together

6. The passage that follows was part of the final autograph manuscript for *Huck Finn* that Twain sent to his nephew-publisher Charles L. Webster in April 1884. Though Twain acquiesced to the cutting of this "Raft Passage" (on a suggestion made initially by W. D. Howells), the cut was made to save space and not on literary or aesthetic grounds, and the passage is, therefore, reinstated in this text. The raft material had already appeared—with an introductory note explaining that it was part of a book in progress—as part of Ch. 3 of *Life on the Mississippi* (1883). For a further discussion of this textual crux see Walter Blair, *Mark Twain and "Huck Finn"* (1960), and Peter G. Beidler, "The Raft Episode in *Huckleberry Finn*," *Modern Fiction Studies* 14 (Spring 1965): 11–20. See also Victor Doyno's *Writing "Huck Finn": Mark Twain's Creative Process* (1991).

every time. He flung off a buckskin coat that was all hung with fringes, and says, "You lay thar tell the chawin-up's done"; and flung his hat down, which was all over ribbons, and says, "You lay thar tell his sufferin's is over."

Then he jumped up in the air and cracked his heels together again, and shouted out:

"Whoo-oop! I'm the old original iron-jawed, brass-mounted, copper-bellied corpse-maker from the wilds of Arkansaw. Look at me! I'm the man they call Sudden Death and General Desolation! Sired by a hurricane, dam'd by an earthquake, half-brother to the cholera, nearly related to the smallpox on the mother's side! Look at me! I take nineteen alligators and a bar'l of whisky for breakfast when I'm in robust health, and a bushel of rattlesnakes and a dead body when I'm ailing. I split the everlasting rocks with my glance, and I squench[7] the thunder when I speak! Whoo-oop! Stand back and give me room according to my strength! Blood's my natural drink, and the wails of the dying is music to my ear. Cast your eye on me, gentlemen! and lay low and hold your breath, for I'm 'bout to turn myself loose![8]

All the time he was getting this off, he was shaking his head and looking fierce, and kind of swelling around in a little circle, tucking up his wristbands, and now and then straightening up and beating his breast with his fist, saying, "Look at me, gentlemen!" When he got through, he jumped up and cracked his heels together three times, and let off a roaring "Whoo-oop! I'm the bloodiest son of a wildcat that lives!"

Then the man that had started the row tilted his old slouch hat down over his right eye; then he bent stooping forward, with his back sagged and his south end sticking out far, and his fists a-shoving out and drawing in in front of him, and so went around in a little circle about three times, swelling himself up and breathing hard. Then he straightened, and jumped up and cracked his heels together three times before he lit again (that made them cheer), and he began to shout like this:

"Whoo-oop! bow you neck and spread, for the kingdom of sorrow's a-coming! Hold me down to the earth, for I feel my powers a-working! whoo-oop! I'm a child of sin, *don't* let me get a start! Smoked glass, here, for all! Don't attempt to look at me with the naked eye, gentlemen! When I'm playful I use the meridians of longitude and parallels of latitude for a seine, and drag the Atlantic Ocean for whales! I scratch my head with the lightning and purr myself to sleep with the thunder! When I'm cold, I bile the Gulf of Mexico and bathe in it; when I'm hot I fan myself with an equinoctial storm; when I'm thirsty I reach up and suck a cloud dry like a sponge; when I range the earth hungry, famine follows in my tracks! Whoo-oop! Bow your neck and spread! I put my hand on the sun's face and make it night in the earth; I bite a piece out of the moon and hurry the seasons; I shake myself and crumble the mountains! Contemplate me through leather—*don't* use the naked eye! I'm the man with a petrified heart and biler-iron bowels! The massacre of isolated communities is the pastime of my idle moments, the destruction of nationalities the serious business of my life! The boundless vastness of the great American desert is my inclosed property, and I bury my dead on my own premises!" He jumped up and cracked his heels together three times before

---

7. Outdo, overpower.
8. Twain here immortalizes the ritual boasting of the "ring-tailed roarers," chiefly associated with Kentucky but familiar both in the oral traditions of the frontier and in the writings of the southwestern humorists, in whose tradition Twain follows.

he lit (they cheered him again), and as he come down he shouted out: "Whoo-oop! bow your neck and spread, for the Pet Child of Calamity's a-coming!"

Then the other one went to swelling around and blowing again—the first one—the one they called Bob; next, the Child of Calamity chipped in again, bigger than ever; then they both got at it at the same time, swelling round and round each other and punching their fists most into each other's faces, and whooping and jawing like Injuns; then Bob called the Child names, and the Child called him names back again; next, Bob called him a heap rougher names, and the Child come back at him with the very worst kind of language; next, Bob knocked the Child's hat off, and the Child picked it up and kicked Bob's ribbony hat about six foot; Bob went and got it and said never mind, this warn't going to be the last of this thing, because he was a man that never forgot and never forgive, and so the Child better look out, for there was a time a-coming, just as sure as he was a living man, that he would have to answer to him with the best blood in his body. The Child said no man was willinger than he for that time to come, and he would give Bob fair warning, *now*, never to cross his path again, for he could never rest till he had waded in his blood, for such was his nature, though he was sparing him now on account of his family, if he had one.

Both of them was edging away in different directions, growling and shaking their heads and going on about what they was going to do; but a little black-whiskered chap skipped up and says:

"Come back here, you couple of chicken-livered cowards, and I'll thrash the two of ye!"

And he done it, too. He snatched them, he jerked them his way and that, he booted them around, he knocked them sprawling faster than they could get up. Why, it warn't two minutes till they begged like dogs—and how the other lot did yell and laugh and clap their hands all the way through, and shout "Sail in, Corpse-Maker!" "Hit at him again, Child of Calamity!" "Bully for you, little Davy!" Well, it was a perfect pow-wow for a while. Bob and the Child had red noses and black eyes when they got through. Little Davy made them own up that they were sneaks and cowards and not fit to eat with a dog or drink with a nigger; then Bob and the Child shook hands with each other, very solemn, and said they had always respected each other and was willing to let bygones be bygones. So then they washed their faces in the river; and just then there was a loud order to stand by for a crossing, and some of them went forward to man the sweeps there, and the rest went aft to handle the after sweeps.

I laid still and waited for fifteen minutes, and had a smoke out of a pipe that one of them left in reach; then the crossing was finished, and they stumped back and had a drink around and went to talking and singing again. Next they got out an old fiddle, and one played, and another patted juba, and the rest turned themselves loose on a regular old-fashioned keelboat break-down.[9] They couldn't keep that up very long without getting winded, so by and by they settled around the jug again.

They sung "Jolly, Jolly Raftsman's the Life for Me," with a rousing chorus, and then they got to talking about differences betwixt hogs, and their differ-

9. As the name suggests, a wild dance with a rapid rhythm. The "juba" is a strongly rhythmical dance that originated among southern blacks about 1830; to "pat a juba" would be to clap the hands or tap the feet to make the rhythm.

ent kind of habits, and next about women and their different ways; and next
about the best ways to put out houses that was afire; and next about what
ought to be done with the Injuns; and next about what a king had to do, and
how much he got; and next about how to make cats fight; and next about what
to do when a man has fits; and next about differences betwixt clear-water
rivers and muddy-water ones. The man they called Ed said the muddy Mississippi water was wholesomer to drink than the clear water of the Ohio; he
said if you let a pint of this yaller Mississippi water settle, you would have
about a half to three-quarters of an inch of mud in the bottom, according to
the stage of the river, and then it warn't no better than Ohio water—what you
wanted to do was to keep it stirred up—and when the river was low, keep mud
on hand to put in and thicken the water up the way it ought to be.

The Child of Calamity said that was so; he said there was nutritiousness in
the mud, and a man that drunk Mississippi water could grow corn in his
stomach if he wanted to. He says:

"You look at the graveyards; that tells the tale. Trees won't grow worth
shucks in a Cincinnati graveyard, but in a Sent Louis graveyard they grow
upwards of eight hundred foot high. It's all on account of the water the people drunk before they laid up. A Cincinnati corpse don't richen a soil any."

And they talked about how Ohio water didn't like to mix with Mississippi
water. Ed said if you take the Mississippi on a rise when the Ohio is low, you'll
find a wide band of clear water all the way down the east side of the Mississippi for a hundred miles or more, and the minute you get out a quarter of a
mile from shore and pass the line, it is all thick and yaller the rest of the way
across. Then they talked about how to keep tobacco from getting moldy, and
from that they went into ghosts and told about a lot that other folks had seen;
but Ed says:

"Why don't you tell something that you've seen yourselves? Now let me
have a say. Five years ago I was on a raft as big as this, and right along here
it was a bright moonshiny night, and I was on watch and boss of the stabboard
oar forrard, and one of my pards was a man named Dick Allbright, and he
come along to where I was sitting, forrard—gaping and stretching, he was—
and stooped down on the edge of the raft and washed his face in the river,
and come and set down by me and got out his pipe, and had just got it filled,
when he looks up and says:

" 'Why looky-here,' he says, 'ain't that Buck Miller's place, over yander in
the bend?"

" 'Yes,' says I, 'it is—why?' He laid his pipe down and leaned his head on his
hand, and says:

" 'I thought we'd be furder down.' I says:

" 'I thought it, too, when I went off watch'—we was standing six hours on
and six off—'but the boys told me,' I says, 'that the raft didn't seem to hardly
move, for the last hour,' says I, 'though she's a-slipping along all right now,'
says I. He give a kind of a groan, and says:

" 'I've seed a raft act so before, along here,' he says. 'Pears to me the current has most quit above the head of this bend durin' the last two years,' he
says.

"Well, he raised up two or three times, and looked away off and around on
the water. That started me at it, too. A body is always doing what he sees
somebody else doing, though there mayn't be no sense in it. Pretty soon I see

a black something floating on the water away off to stabboard and quartering behind us. I see he was looking at it, too. I says:

" 'What's that?' He says, sort of pettish:

" ' 'Tain't nothing but an old empty bar'l.'

" 'An empty bar'l!' says I, 'why,' says I, 'a spy-glass is a fool to *your* eyes. How can you tell it's an empty bar'l?' He says:

" 'I don't know; I reckon it ain't a bar'l, but I thought it might be,' says he.

" 'Yes,' I says, 'so it might be, and it might be anything else too; a body can't tell nothing about it, such a distance as that,' I says.

"We hadn't nothing else to do, so we kept on watching it. By and by I says:

" 'Why, looky-here, Dick Allbright, that thing's a-gaining on us, I believe.'

"He never said nothing. The thing gained and gained, and I judged it must be a dog that was about tired out. Well, we swung down into the crossing, and the thing floated across the bright streak of the moonshine, and by George, it *was* a bar'l. Says I:

" 'Dick Allbright, what made you think that thing was a bar'l, when it was half a mile off?' says I. Says he:

" 'I don't know.' Says I:

" 'You tell me, Dick Allbright.' Says he:

" 'Well, I knowed it was a bar'l; I've seen it before; lots has seen it; they says it's a ha'nted bar'l.'

"I called the rest of the watch, and they come and stood there, and I told them what Dick said. It floated right along abreast, now, and didn't gain any more. It was about twenty foot off. Some was for having it aboard, but the rest didn't want to. Dick Allbright said rafts that had fooled with it had got bad luck by it. The captain of the watch said he didn't believe in it. He said he reckoned the bar'l gained on us because it was in a little better current than what we was. He said it would leave by and by.

"So then we went to talking about other things, and we had a song, and then a breakdown; and after that the captain of the watch called for another song; but it was clouding up now, and the bar'l stuck right thar in the same place, and the song didn't seem to have much warm-up to it, somehow, and so they didn't finish it, and there warn't any cheers, but it sort of dropped flat, and nobody said anything for a minute. Then everybody tried to talk at once, and one chap got off a joke, but it warn't no use, they didn't laugh, and even the chap that made the joke didn't laugh at it, which ain't usual. We all just settled down glum, and watched the bar'l, and was oneasy and oncomfortable. Well, sir, it shut down black and still, and then the wind began to moan around, and next the lightning began to play and the thunder to grumble. And pretty soon there was a regular storm, and in the middle of it a man that was running aft stumbled and fell and sprained his ankle so that he had to lay up. This made the boys shake their heads. And every time the lightning come, there was that bar'l, with the blue lights winking around it. We was always on the lookout for it. But by and by, toward dawn, she was gone. When the day come we couldn't see her anywhere, and we warn't sorry, either.

"But next night about half-past nine, when there was songs and high jinks going on, here she comes again, and took her old roost on the stabboard side. There warn't no more high jinks. Everybody got solemn; nobody talked; you couldn't get anybody to do anything but set around moody and look at the bar'l. It begun to cloud up again. When the watch changed, the off watch stayed up, 'stead of turning in. The storm ripped and roared around all night, and in the middle of it another man tripped and sprained his ankle, and had to knock off. The bar'l left toward day, and nobody see it go.

"Everybody was sober and down in the mouth all day. I don't mean the kind of sober that comes of leaving liquor alone—not that. They was quiet, but they all drunk more than usual—not together, but each man sidled off and took it private, by himself.

"After dark the off watch didn't turn in; nobody sung, nobody talked; the boys didn't scatter around, neither; they sort of huddled together, forrard; and for two hours they set there, perfectly still, looking steady in the one direction, and heaving a sigh once in a while. And then, here comes the bar'l again. She took up her old place. She stayed there all night; nobody turned in. The storm come on again, after midnight. It got awful dark; the rain poured down; hail, too; the thunder boomed and roared and bellowed; the wind blowed a hurricane; and the lightning spread over everything in big sheets of glare, and showed the whole raft as plain as day; and the river lashed up white as milk as far as you could see for miles, and there was that bar'l jiggering along, same as ever. The captain ordered the watch to man the after sweeps for a crossing, and nobody would go—no more sprained ankles for them, they said. They wouldn't even *walk* aft. Well, then, just then the sky split wide open, with a crash, and the lightning killed two men of the after watch, and crippled two more. Crippled them how, say you? Why, *sprained their ankles!*

"The bar'l left in the dark betwixt lightnings, toward dawn. Well, not a body eat a bite at breakfast that morning. After that the men loafed around, in twos and threes, and talked low together. But none of them herded with Dick Allbright. They all give him the cold shake. If he come around where any of the men was, they split up and sidled away. They wouldn't man the sweeps with him. The captain had all the skiffs hauled up on the raft, alongside of his wigwam, and wouldn't let the dead men be took ashore to be planted; he didn't believe a man that got ashore would come back: and he was right.

"After night come, you could see pretty plain that there was going to be trouble if that bar'l come again; there was such a muttering going on. A good many wanted to kill Dick Allbright, because he'd seen the bar'l on other trips, and that had an ugly look. Some wanted to put him ashore. Some said: 'Let's all go ashore in a pile, if the bar'l comes again.'

"This kind of whispers was still going on, the men being bunched together forrard watching for the bar'l, when lo and behold you! here she comes again. Down she comes, slow and steady, and settles into her old tracks. You could 'a' heard a pin drop. Then up comes the captain, and says:

" 'Boys, don't be a pack of children and fools; I don't want this bar'l to be dogging us all the way to Orleans, and *you* don't: Well, then, how's the best way to stop it? Burn it up—that's the way. I'm going to fetch it aboard,' he says. And before anybody could say a word, in he went.

"He swum to it, and as he come pushing it to the raft, the men spread to one side. But the old man got it aboard and busted in the head, and there was a baby in it! Yes, sir; a stark-naked baby. It was Dick Allbright's baby; he owned up and said so.

" 'Yes,' he says, a-leaning over it, 'yes, it is my own lamented darling, my poor lost Charles William Allbright deceased,' says he—for he could curl his tongue around the bulliest words in the language when he was a mind to, and lay them before you without a jint started anywheres.[1] Yes, he said, he used to live up at the head of this bend, and one night he choked his child, which was crying, not intending to kill it—which was prob'ly a lie—and then he was scared, and buried it in a bar'l, before his wife got home, and off he went, and struck the northern trail and went to rafting; and this was the third year that the bar'l had chased him. He said the bad luck always begun light, and lasted till four men was killed, and then the bar'l didn't come any more after that. He said if the men would stand it one more night—and was a-going on like that—but the men had got enough. They started to get out a boat to take him ashore and lynch him, but he grabbed the little child all of a sudden and jumped overboard with it, hugged up to his breast and shedding tears, and we never see him again in this life, poor old suffering soul, nor Charles William neither."

"*Who* was shedding tears?" says Bob; "was it Allbright or the baby?"

"Why, Allbright, of course; didn't I tell you the baby was dead? Been dead three years—how could it cry?"

"Well, never mind how it could cry—how could it *keep* all that time?" says Davy. "You answer me that."

"I don't know how it done it," says Ed. "It done it, though—that's all I know about it."

"Say—what did they do with the bar'l?" says the Child of Calamity.

"Why, they hove it overboard, and it sunk like a chunk of lead."

"Edward, did the child look like it was choked?" says one.

"Did it have its hair parted?" says another.

"What was the brand on that bar'l, Eddy?" says a fellow they called Bill.

"Have you got the papers for them statistics, Edmund?" says Jimmy.

"Say, Edwin, was you one of the men that was killed by the lightning?" says Davy.

"Hm? Oh, no! he was both of 'em," says Bob. Then they all haw-hawed.

"Say, Edward, don't you reckon you'd better take a pill? You look bad—don't you feel pale?" says the Child of Calamity.

"Oh, come now, Eddy," says Jimmy, "show up; you must 'a' kept part of that bar'l to prove the thing by. Show us the bung-hole—*do*—and we'll all believe you."

"Say, boys," says Bill, "less divide it up. Thar's thirteen of us. I can swaller a thirteenth of the yarn, if you can worry down the rest."

Ed got up mad and said they could all go to some place which he ripped out pretty savage, and then walked off aft, cussing to himself, and they yelling and jeering at him, and roaring and laughing so you could hear them a mile.

"Boys, we'll split a watermelon on that," says the Child of Calamity; and he came rummaging around in the dark amongst the shingle bundles where I was, and put his hand on me. I was warm and soft and naked; so he says "Ouch!" and jumped back.

"Fetch a lantern or a chunk of fire here, boys—there's a snake here as big as a cow!"

So they run there with a lantern, and crowded up and looked in on me.

"Come out of that, you beggar!" says one.

"Who are you?" says another.

1. Without cracking open joints; i.e., perfectly smoothly and eloquently.

"What are you after here? Speak up prompt, or overboard you go."

"Snake him out, boys. Snatch him out by the heels."

I began to beg, and crept out amongst them trembling. They looked me over, wondering, and the Child of Calamity says:

"A cussed thief! Lend a hand and less heave him overboard!"

"No," says Big Bob, "less get out the paint-pot and paint him a sky-blue all over from head to heel, and *then* heave him over."

"Good! that's it. Go for the paint, Jimmy."

When the paint come, and Bob took the brush and was just going to begin, the others laughing and rubbing their hands. I begun to cry, and that sort of worked on Davy, and he says:

" 'Vast there. He's nothing but a cub. I'll paint the man that teches him!"

So I looked around on them, and some of them grumbled and growled, and Bob put down the paint, and the others didn't take it up.

"Come here to the fire, and less see what you're up to here," says Davy. "Now set down there and give an account of yourself. How long have you been aboard here?"

"Not over a quarter of a minute, sir," says I.

"How did you get dry so quick?"

"I don't know, sir. I'm always that way, mostly."

"Oh, you are, are you? What's your name?"

I warn't going to tell my name. I didn't know what to say, so I just says:

"Charles William Allbright, sir."

Then they roared—the whole crowd; and I was mighty glad I said that, because, maybe, laughing would get them in a better humor.

When they got done laughing, Davy says:

"It won't hardly do, Charles William. You couldn't have growed this much in five year, and you was a baby when you come out of the bar'l, you know, and dead at that. Come, now, tell a straight story, and nobody'll hurt you, if you ain't up to anything wrong. What is your name?"

"Aleck Hopkins, sir. Aleck James Hopkins."

"Well, Aleck, where did you come from, here?"

"From a trading-scow. She lays up the bend yonder. I was born on her. Pap has traded up and down here all his life; and he told me to swim off here, because when you went by he said he would like to get some of you to speak to a Mr. Jonas Turner, in Cairo, and tell him—"

"Oh, come!"

"Yes, sir, it's as true as the world. Pap he says—"

"Oh, your grandmother!"

They all laughed, and I tried again to talk, but they broke in on me and stopped me.

"Now, looky-here," says Davy; "you're scared, and so you talk wild. Honest, now, do you live in a scow, or is it a lie?"

"Yes, sir, in a trading-scow. She lays up at the head of the bend. But I warn't born in her. It's our first trip."

"Now you're talking! What did you come aboard here for? To steal?"

"No sir, I didn't. It was only to get a ride on the raft. All boys does that."

"Well, I know that. But what did you hide for?"

"Sometimes they drive the boys off."

"So they do. They might steal. Looky-here; if we let you off this time, will you keep out of these kind of scrapes hereafter?"

" 'Deed I will, boss. You try me."

"All right, then. You ain't but little ways from shore. Overboard with you, and don't you make a fool of yourself another time this way. Blast it, boy, some raftsmen would rawhide you till you were black and blue!"

I didn't wait to kiss good-by, but went overboard and broke for shore. When Jim come along by and by, the big raft was away out of sight around the point. I swum out and got aboard, and was mighty glad to see home again.[2]

There warn't nothing to do, now, but to look out sharp for the town, and not pass it without seeing it. He said he'd be mighty sure to see it, because he'd be a free man the minute he seen it, but if he missed it he'd be in the slave country again and no more show for freedom. Every little while he jumps up and says:

"Dah she is!"

But it warn't. It was Jack-o-lanterns, or lightning-bugs; so he set down again, and went to watching, same as before. Jim said it made him all over trembly and feverish to be so close to freedom. Well, I can tell you it made me all over trembly and feverish, too, to hear him, because I begun to get it through my head that he *was* most free—and who was to blame for it? Why, *me*. I couldn't get that out of my conscience, no how nor no way. It got to troubling me so I couldn't rest; I couldn't stay still in one place. It hadn't ever come home to me before, what this thing was that I was doing. But now it did; and it staid with me, and scorched me more and more. I tried to make out to myself that *I* warn't to blame, because I didn't run Jim off from his rightful owner; but it warn't no use, conscience up and says, every time, "But you knowed he was running for his freedom, and you could a paddled ashore and told somebody." That was so—I couldn't get around that, noway. That was where it pinched. Conscience says to me, "What had poor Miss Watson done to you, that you could see her nigger go off right under your eyes and never say one single word? What did that poor old woman do to you, that you could treat her so mean? Why, she tried to learn you your book, she tried to learn you your manners, she tried to be good to you every way she knowed how. *That's* what she done."

I got to feeling so mean and so miserable I most wished I was dead. I fidgeted up and down the raft, abusing myself to myself, and Jim was fidgeting up and down past me. We neither of us could keep still. Every time he danced around and says, "Dah's Cairo!" it went through me like a shot, and I thought if it *was* Cairo I reckoned I would die of miserableness.

Jim talked out loud all the time while I was talking to myself. He was saying how the first thing he would do when he got to a free State he would go to saving up money and never spend a single cent, and when he got enough he would buy his wife, which was owned on a farm close to where Miss Watson lived; and then they would both work to buy the two children, and if their master wouldn't sell them, they'd get an Ab'litionist to go and steal them.

It most froze me to hear such talk. He wouldn't ever dared to talk such talk in his life before. Just see what a difference it made in him the minute he

*[handwritten marginalia: Struggling w/ the idea he helped Jim run away.]*

2. End of the interpolated passage.

judged he was about free. It was according to the old saying, "give a nigger an inch and he'll take an ell." Thinks I, this is what comes of my not thinking. Here was this nigger which I had as good as helped to run away, coming right out flat-footed and saying he would steal his children—children that belonged to a man I didn't even know; a man that hadn't ever done me no harm.

I was sorry to hear Jim say that, it was such a lowering of him. My conscience got to stirring me up hotter than ever, until at last I says to it, "Let up on me—it ain't too late, yet—I'll paddle ashore at the first light, and tell." I felt easy, and happy, and light as a feather, right off. All my troubles was gone. I went to looking out sharp for a light, and sort of singing to myself. By-and-by one showed. Jim sings out:

"We's safe, Huck, we's safe! Jump up and crack yo' heels, dat's de good ole Cairo at las', I jis knows it!"

I says:

"I'll take the canoe and go see, Jim. It mightn't be, you know."

He jumped and got the canoe ready, and put his old coat in the bottom for me to set on, and give me the paddle; and as I shoved off, he says:

"Pooty soon I'll be a-shout'n for joy, en I'll say, it's all on accounts o' Huck; I's a free man, en I couldn't ever ben free ef it hadn' ben for Huck; Huck done it. Jim won't ever forget you, Huck; you's de bes' fren' Jim's ever had; en you's de *only* fren' ole Jim's got now."

I was paddling off, all in a sweat to tell on him; but when he says this, it seemed to kind of take the tuck all out of me. I went along slow then, and I warn't right down certain whether I was glad I started or whether I warn't. When I was fifty yards off, Jim says:

"Dah you goes, de ole true Huck; de on'y white genlman dat ever kep' his promise to ole Jim."

Well, I just felt sick. But I says, I *got* to do it—I can't get *out* of it. Right then, along comes a skiff with two men in it, with guns, and they stopped and I stopped. One of them says:

"What's that, yonder?"

"A piece of raft," I says.

"Do you belong on it?"

"Yes, sir."

"Any men on it?"

"Only one, sir."

"Well, there's five niggers run off to-night, up yonder above the head of the bend. Is your man white or black?"

I didn't answer up prompt. I tried to, but the words wouldn't come. I tried, for a second or two, to brace up and out with it, but I warn't man enough—hadn't the spunk of a rabbit. I see I was weakening; so I just give up trying, and up and says—

"He's white."

"I reckon we'll go and see for ourselves."

"I wish you would," says I, "because it's pap that's there, and maybe you'd help me tow the raft ashore where the light is. He's sick—and so is mam and Mary Ann."

"Oh, the devil! we're in a hurry, boy. But I s'pose we've got to. Come—buckle to your paddle, and let's get along."

I buckled to my paddle and they laid to their oars. When we had made a stroke or two, I says:

"Pap'll be mighty much obleeged to you, I can tell you. Everybody goes away when I want them to help me tow the raft ashore, and I can't do it myself."

"Well, that's infernal mean. Odd, too. Say, boy, what's the matter with your father?"

"It's the—a—the—well, it ain't anything, much."

They stopped pulling. It warn't but a mighty little ways to the raft, now. One says:

"Boy, that's a lie. What *is* the matter with your pap? Answer up square, now, and it'll be the better for you."

"I will, sir, I will, honest—but don't leave us, please. It's the—the—gentlemen, if you'll only pull ahead, and let me heave you the head-line you won't have to come a-near the raft—please do."

"Set her back, John, set her back!" says one. They backed water. "Keep away, boy—keep to looard.[3] Confound it, I just expect the wind has blowed it to us. Your pap's got the small-pox,[4] and you know it precious well. Why didn't you come out and say so? Do you want to spread it all over?"

"Well," says I, a-blubbering, "I've told everybody before, and then they just went away and left us."

"Poor devil, there's something in that. We are right down sorry for you, but we—well, hang it, we don't want the small-pox, you see. Look here, I'll tell you what to do. Don't you try to land by yourself, or you'll smash everything to pieces. You float along down about twenty miles and you'll come to a town on the left-hand side of the river. It will be long after sun-up, then, and when you ask for help, you tell them your folks are all down with chills and fever. Don't be a fool again, and let people guess what is the matter. Now we're trying to do you a kindness; so you just put twenty miles between us, that's a good boy. It wouldn't do any good to land yonder where the light is—it's only a wood-yard. Say—I reckon your father's poor, and I'm bound to say he's in pretty hard luck. Here—I'll put a twenty dollar gold piece on this board, and you get it when it floats by. I feel mighty mean to leave you, but my kingdom! it won't do to fool with small-pox, don't you see?"

"Hold on, Parker," says the other man, "here's a twenty to put on the board for me. Good-bye boy, you do as Mr. Parker told you, and you'll be all right."

"That's so, my boy—good-bye, good-bye. If you see any runaway niggers, you get help and nab them, and you can make some money by it."

"Good-bye, sir," says I, "I won't let no runaway niggers get by me if I can help it."

They went off, and I got aboard the raft, feeling bad and low, because I knowed very well I had done wrong, and I see it warn't no use for me to try to learn to do right; a body that don't get *started* right when he's little, ain't got no show—when the pinch comes there ain't nothing to back him up and keep him to his work, and so he gets beat. Then I thought a minute, and says to myself, hold on,—s'pose you'd a done right and give Jim up; would you felt better than what you do now? No, says I, I'd feel bad—I'd feel just the same way I do now. Well, then, says I, what's the use you learning to do right, when it's

internal
conflict

3. I.e., leeward.

4. A highly infectious, often fatal disease.

troublesome to do right and ain't no trouble to do wrong, and the wages is just the same? I was stuck. I couldn't answer that. So I reckoned I wouldn't bother no more about it, but after this always do whichever come handiest at the time.

I went into the wigwam; Jim warn't there. I looked all around; he warn't anywhere. I says:

"Jim!"

"Here I is, Huck. Is dey out o' sight yit? Don't talk loud."

He was in the river, under the stern oar, with just his nose out. I told him they was out of sight, so he come aboard. He says:

"I was a-listenin' to all de talk, en I slips into de river en was gwyne to shove for sho' if dey come aboard. Den I was gwyne to swim to de raf' agin when dey was gone. But lawsy, how you did fool 'em, Huck! Dat *wuz* de smartes' dodge! I tell you, chile, I 'speck it save' ole Jim—ole Jim ain' gwyne to forgit you for dat, honey."

Then we talked about the money. It was a pretty good raise, twenty dollars apiece. Jim said we could take deck passage on a steamboat now, and the money would last us as far as we wanted to go in the free States. He said twenty mile more warn't far for the raft to go, but he wished we was already there.

Towards daybreak we tied up, and Jim was mighty particular about hiding the raft good. Then he worked all day fixing things in bundles, and getting all ready to quit rafting.

That night about ten we hove in sight of the lights of a town away down in a left-hand bend.

I went off in the canoe, to ask about it. Pretty soon I found a man out in the river with a skiff, setting a trot-line. I ranged up and says:

"Mister, is that town Cairo?"

"Cairo? no. You must be a blame' fool."

"What town is it, mister?"

"If you want to know, go and find out. If you stay here botherin' around me for about a half a minute longer, you'll get something you won't want."

I paddled to the raft. Jim was awful disappointed, but I said never mind, Cairo would be the next place, I reckoned.

We passed another town before daylight, and I was going out again; but it was high ground, so I didn't go. No high ground about Cairo, Jim said. I had forgot it. We laid up for the day, on a tow-head tolerable close to the left-hand bank. I begun to suspicion something. So did Jim. I says:

"Maybe we went by Cairo in the fog that night."

He says:

"Doan' less' talk about it, Huck. Po' niggers can't have no luck. I awluz 'spected dat rattle-snake skin warn't done wid it's work."

"I wish I'd never seen that snake-skin, Jim—I do wish I'd never laid eyes on it."

"It ain't yo' fault, Huck; you didn't know. Don't you blame yo'sef 'bout it."

When it was daylight, here was the clear Ohio water in shore, sure enough, and outside was the old regular Muddy! So it was all up with Cairo.[5]

---

5. Because Cairo is located at the confluence of the Ohio and Mississippi rivers, which in turn lies below the confluence of the Missouri (Big Muddy) and Mississippi, they know that they have passed Cairo and lost the opportunity to sell the raft and travel up the Ohio by steamboat to freedom.

We talked it all over. It wouldn't do to take to the shore; we couldn't take the raft up the stream, of course. There warn't no way but to wait for dark, and start back in the canoe and take the chances. So we slept all day amongst the cotton-wood thicket, so as to be fresh for the work, and when we went back to the raft about dark the canoe was gone!

We didn't say a word for a good while. There warn't anything to say. We both knowed well enough it was some more work of the rattle-snake skin; so what was the use to talk about it? It would only look like we was finding fault, and that would be bound to fetch more bad luck—and keep on fetching it, too, till we knowed enough to keep still.

By-and-by we talked about what we better do, and found there warn't no way but just to go along down with the raft till we got a chance to buy a canoe to go back in. We warn't going to borrow it when there warn't anybody around, the way pap would do, for that might set people after us.

So we shoved out, after dark, on the raft.[6]

Anybody that don't believe yet, that it's foolishness to handle a snake-skin, after all that that snake-skin done for us, will believe it now, if they read on and see what more it done for us.

The place to buy canoes is off of rafts laying up at shore. But we didn't see no rafts laying up; so we went along during three hours and more. Well, the night got gray, and ruther thick, which is the next meanest thing to fog. You can't tell the shape of the river, and you can't see no distance. It got to be very late and still, and then along comes a steamboat up the river. We lit the lantern, and judged she would see it. Up-stream boats didn't generly come close to us; they go out and follow the bars and hunt for easy water under the reefs; but nights like this they bull right up the channel against the whole river.

We could hear her pounding along, but we didn't see her good till she was close. She aimed right for us. Often they do that and try to see how close they can come without touching; sometimes the wheel bites off a sweep, and then the pilot sticks his head out and laughs, and thinks he's mighty smart. Well, here she comes, and we said she was going to try to shave us; but she didn't seem to be sheering off a bit. She was a big one, and she was coming in a hurry, too, looking like a black cloud with rows of glow-worms around it; but all of a sudden she bulged out, big and scary, with a long row of wide-open furnace doors shining like red-hot teeth, and her monstrous bows and guards hanging right over us. There was a yell at us, and a jingling of bells to stop the engines, a pow-wow of cussing, and whistling of steam—and as Jim went overboard on one side and I on the other, she come smashing straight through the raft.

I dived—and I aimed to find the bottom, too, for a thirty-foot wheel had got to go over me, and I wanted it to have plenty of room. I could always stay under water a minute; this time I reckon I staid under water a minute and a

---

6. Twain was "stuck" at this point in the writing of the novel and put the 400-page manuscript aside for approximately three years. In the winter of 1879–80 he added the two chapters dealing with the feud (XVII and XVIII) and then the three chapters (XIX–XXI) in which the king and duke enter the story and for a time dominate the action. The novel was not completed until 1883, when Twain wrote the last half of it in a few months of concentrated work. As late as 1882, he was not confident he would ever complete the book. See Walter Blair, *Mark Twain and "Huck Finn"* (1960); Victor Doyno, *Writing "Huck Finn": Mark Twain's Creative Process* (1991); and Doyno's Foreword and Textual Addendum to the 1996 Random House edition of *Adventures of Huckleberry Finn*.

half. Then I bounced for the top in a hurry, for I was nearly busting. I popped out to my arm-pits and blowed the water out of my nose, and puffed a bit. Of course there was a booming current; and of course that boat started her engines again ten seconds after she stopped them, for they never cared much for raftsmen; so now she was churning along up the river, out of sight in the thick weather, though I could hear her.

I sung out for Jim about a dozen times, but I didn't get any answer; so I grabbed a plank that touched me while I was "treading water," and struck out for shore, shoving it ahead of me. But I made out to see that the drift of the current was towards the left-hand shore,[7] which meant that I was in a crossing; so I changed off and went that way.

It was one of these long, slanting, two-mile crossings; so I was a good long time in getting over. I made a safe landing, and clum up the bank. I couldn't see but a little ways, but I went poking along over rough ground for a quarter of a mile or more, and then I run across a big old-fashioned double log house before I noticed it. I was going to rush by and get away, but a lot of dogs jumped out and went to howling and barking at me, and I knowed better than to move another peg.

### Chapter XVII

In about half a minute somebody spoke out of a window, without putting his head out, and says:

"Be done, boys! Who's there?"

I says:

"It's me."

"Who's me?"

"George Jackson, sir."

"What do you want?"

"I don't want nothing, sir. I only want to go along by, but the dogs won't let me."

"What are you prowling around here this time of night, for—hey?"

"I warn't prowling around, sir; I fell overboard off of the steamboat."

"Oh, you did, did you? Strike a light there, somebody. What did you say your name was?"

"George Jackson, sir. I'm only a boy."

"Look here; if you're telling the truth, you needn't be afraid—nobody'll hurt you. But don't try to budge; stand right where you are. Rouse our Bob and Tom, some of you, and fetch the guns. George Jackson, is there anybody with you?"

"No, sir, nobody."

I heard the people stirring around in the house, now, and see a light. The man sung out:

"Snatch that light away, Betsy, you old fool—ain't you got any sense? Put it on the floor behind the front door. Bob, if you and Tom are ready, take your places."

"All ready."

"Now, George Jackson, do you know the Shepherdsons?"

---

7. Kentucky, where the feud in Chs. XVII and XVIII is set.

"No, sir—I never heard of them."

"Well, that may be so, and it mayn't. Now, all ready. Step forward, George Jackson. And mind, don't you hurry—come mighty slow. If there's anybody with you, let him keep back—if he shows himself he'll be shot. Come along, now. Come slow; push the door open, yourself—just enough to squeeze in, d' you hear?"

I didn't hurry, I couldn't if I'd a wanted to. I took one slow step at a time, and there warn't a sound, only I thought I could hear my heart. The dogs were as still as the humans, but they followed a little behind me. When I got to the three log door-steps, I heard them unlocking and unbarring and unbolting. I put my hand on the door and pushed it a little and a little more, till somebody said, "There, that's enough—put your head in." I done it, but I judged they would take it off.

The candle was on the floor, and there they all was, looking at me, and me at them, for about a quarter of a minute. Three big men with guns pointed at me, which made me wince, I tell you; the oldest, gray and about sixty, the other two thirty or more—all of them fine and handsome—and the sweetest old gray-headed lady, and back of her two young women which I couldn't see right well. The old gentleman says:

"There—I reckon it's all right. Come in."

As soon as I was in, the old gentleman he locked the door and barred it and bolted it, and told the young men to come in with their guns, and they all went in a big parlor that had a new rag carpet on the floor, and got together in a corner that was out of range of the front windows—there warn't none on the side. They held the candle, and took a good look at me, and all said, "Why *he* ain't a Shepherdson—no, there ain't any Shepherdson about him." Then the old man said he hoped I wouldn't mind being searched for arms, because he didn't mean no harm by it—it was only to make sure. So he didn't pry into my pockets, but only felt outside with his hands, and said it was all right. He told me to make myself easy and at home, and tell all about myself; but the old lady says:

"Why bless you, Saul, the poor thing's as wet as he can be; and don't you reckon it may be he's hungry?"

"True for you, Rachel—I forgot."

So the old lady says:

"Betsy" (this was a nigger woman), "you fly around and get him something to eat, as quick as you can, poor thing; and one of you girls go and wake up Buck and tell him—Oh, here he is himself. Buck, take this little stranger and get the wet clothes off from him and dress him up in some of yours that's dry."

Buck looked about as old as me—thirteen or fourteen[8] or along there, though he was a little bigger than me. He hadn't on anything but a shirt, and he was very frowsy-headed. He come in gaping and digging one fist into his eyes, and he was dragging a gun along with the other one. He says:

"Ain't they no Shepherdsons around?"

They said, no, 'twas a false alarm.

"Well," he says, "if they'd a ben some, I reckon I'd a got one."

They all laughed, and Bob says:

"Why, Buck, they might have scalped us all, you've been so slow in coming."

---

8. Twain identifies Huck as "a boy of 14" in a notebook.

"Well, nobody come after me, and it ain't right. I'm always kep' down; I don't get no show."

"Never mind, Buck, my boy," says the old man, "you'll have show enough, all in good time, don't you fret about that. Go 'long with you now, and do as your mother told you."

When we got up stairs to his room, he got me a coarse shirt and a round-about[9] and pants of his, and I put them on. While I was at it he asked me what my name was, but before I could tell him, he started to telling me about a blue jay and a young rabbit he had catched in the woods day before yesterday, and he asked me where Moses was when the candle went out. I said I didn't know; I hadn't heard about it before, no way.

"Well, guess," he says.

"How'm I going to guess," says I, "when I never heard tell about it before?"

"But you can guess, can't you? It's just as easy."

"*Which* candle?" I says.

"Why, any candle," he says.

"I don't know where he was," says I; "where was he?"

"Why he was in the *dark!* That's where he was!"

"Well, if you knowed where he was, what did you ask me for?"

"Why, blame it, it's a riddle, don't you see? Say, how long are you going to stay here? You got to stay always. We can just have booming times—they don't have no school now. Do you own a dog? I've got a dog—and he'll go in the river and bring out chips that you throw in. Do you like to comb up, Sundays, and all that kind of foolishness? You bet I don't, but ma she makes me. Confound these ole britches, I reckon I'd better put 'em on, but I'd ruther not, it's so warm. Are you all ready? All right—come along, old hoss."

Cold corn-pone, cold corn-beef, butter and butter-milk—that is what they had for me down there, and there ain't nothing better that ever I've come across yet. Buck and his ma and all of them smoked cob pipes, except the nigger woman, which was gone, and the two young women. They all smoked and talked, and I eat and talked. The young women had quilts around them, and their hair down their backs. They all asked me questions, and I told them how pap and me and all the family was living on a little farm down at the bottom of Arkansaw, and my sister Mary Ann run off and got married and never was heard of no more, and Bill went to hunt them and he warn't heard of no more, and Tom and Mort died, and then there warn't nobody but just me and pap left, and he was just trimmed down to nothing, on account of his troubles; so when he died I took what there was left, because the farm didn't belong to us, and started up the river, deck passage, and fell overboard; and that was how I come to be here. So they said I could have a home there as long as I wanted it. Then it was most daylight, and everybody went to bed, and I went to bed with Buck, and when I waked up in the morning, drat it all, I had forgot what my name was. So I laid there about an hour trying to think and when Buck waked up, I says:

"Can you spell, Buck?"

"Yes," he says.

"I bet you can't spell my name," says I.

"I bet you what you dare I can," says he.

"All right," says I, "go ahead."

9. Short, close-fitting jacket.

"G-o-r-g-e J-a-x-o-n—there now," he says.

"Well," says I, "you done it, but I didn't think you could. It ain't no slouch of a name to spell—right off without studying."

I set it down, private, because somebody might want *me* to spell it, next, and so I wanted to be handy with it and rattle it off like I was used to it.

It was a mighty nice family, and a mighty nice house, too. I hadn't seen no house out in the country before that was so nice and had so much style.[1] It didn't have an iron latch on the front door, nor a wooden one with a buckskin string, but a brass knob to turn, the same as houses in a town. There warn't no bed in the parlor, not a sign of a bed; but heaps of parlors in towns has beds in them. There was a big fireplace that was bricked on the bottom, and the bricks was kept clean and red by pouring water on them and scrubbing them with another brick; sometimes they washed them over with red water-paint that they call Spanish-brown, same as they do in town. They had big brass dog-irons that could hold up a saw-log.[2] There was a clock on the middle of the mantel-piece, with a picture of a town painted on the bottom half of the glass front, and a round place in the middle of it for the sun, and you could see the pendulum swing behind it. It was beautiful to hear that clock tick; and sometimes when one of these peddlers had been along and scoured her up and got her in good shape, she would start in and strike a hundred and fifty before she got tuckered out. They wouldn't took any money for her.

Well, there was a big outlandish parrot on each side of the clock, made out of something like chalk, and painted up gaudy. By one of the parrots was a cat made of crockery, and a crockery dog by the other; and when you pressed down on them they squeaked, but didn't open their mouths nor look different nor interested. They squeaked through underneath. There was a couple of big wild-turkey-wing fans spread out behind those things. On a table in the middle of the room was a kind of a lovely crockery basket that had apples and oranges and peaches and grapes piled up in it which was much redder and yellower and prettier than real ones is, but they warn't real because you could see where pieces had got chipped off and showed the white chalk or whatever it was, underneath.

This table had a cover made out of beautiful oil-cloth, with a red and blue spread-eagle painted on it, and a painted border all around. It come all the way from Philadelphia, they said. There was some books too, piled up perfectly exact, on each corner of the table. One was a big family Bible, full of pictures. One was "Pilgrim's Progress," about a man that left his family it didn't say why. I read considerable in it now and then. The statements was interesting, but tough. Another was "Friendship's Offering," full of beautiful stuff and poetry; but I didn't read the poetry. Another was Henry Clay's Speeches, and another was Dr. Gunn's Family Medicine, which told you all about what to do if a body was sick or dead. There was a Hymn Book, and a lot of other books.[3] And there was nice split-bottom chairs, and perfectly sound, too—not bagged down in the middle and busted, like an old basket.

They had pictures hung on the walls—mainly Washingtons and Lafayettes,

1. Every detail of the furniture, furnishing, and decorations as well as the dress, speech, manners, and mores of the Grangerford household is carefully selected to satirically epitomize pre–Civil War culture of the lower Mississippi Valley.
2. A log large enough to be sawed into planks.
3. The neatly stacked, unread books are meant to define the values and tastes of the time and place. The Bible, Bunyan's *Pilgrim's Progress*, and the hymn book establish Calvinistic piety. Clay's speeches suggest political orthodoxy. Gunn's *Domestic Medicine* suggests popular notions of science and medical practice. *Friendship's Offering* was a popular gift book.

and battles, and Highland Marys,[4] and one called "Signing the Declaration." There was some that they called crayons, which one of the daughters which was dead made her own self when she was only fifteen years old. They was different from any pictures I ever see before; blacker, mostly, than is common. One was a woman in a slim black dress, belted small under the armpits, with bulges like a cabbage in the middle of the sleeves, and a large black scoop-shovel bonnet with a black veil, and white slim ankles crossed about with black tape, and very wee black slippers, like a chisel, and she was leaning pensive on a tombstone on her right elbow, under a weeping willow, and her other hand hanging down her side holding a white handkerchief and a reticule, and underneath the picture it said "Shall I Never See Thee More Alas." Another one was a young lady with her hair all combed up straight to the top of her head, and knotted there in front of a comb like a chair-back, and she was crying into a handkerchief and had a dead bird laying on its back in her other hand with its heels up, and underneath the picture it said "I Shall Never Hear Thy Sweet Chirrup More Alas." There was one where a young lady was at a window looking up at the moon, and tears running down her cheeks; and she had an open letter in one hand with black sealing-wax showing on one edge of it, and she was mashing a locket with a chain to it against her mouth, and underneath the picture it said "And Art Thou Gone Yes Thou Art Gone Alas." These was all nice pictures, I reckon, but I didn't somehow seem to take to them, because if ever I was down a little, they always give me the fan-tods. Everybody was sorry she died, because she had laid out a lot more of these pictures to do, and a body could see by what she had done what they had lost. But I reckoned, that with her disposition, she was having a better time in the graveyard. She was at work on what they said was her greatest picture when she took sick, and every day and every night it was her prayer to be allowed to live till she got it done, but she never got the chance. It was a picture of a young woman in a long white gown, standing on the rail of a bridge all ready to jump off, with her hair all down her back, and looking up to the moon, with the tears running down her face, and she had two arms folded across her breast, and two arms stretched out in front, and two more reaching up towards the moon—and the idea was, to see which pair would look best and then scratch out all the other arms; but, as I was saying, she died before she got her mind made up, and now they kept this picture over the head of the bed in her room, and every time her birthday come they hung flowers on it. Other times it was hid with a little curtain. The young woman in the picture had a kind of a nice sweet face, but there was so many arms it made her look too spidery, seemed to me.

This young girl kept a scrap-book when she was alive, and used to paste obituaries and accidents and cases of patient suffering in it out of the *Presbyterian Observer*, and write poetry after them out of her own head. It was very good poetry.[5] This is what she wrote about a boy by the name of Stephen Dowling Bots that fell down a well and was drownded:

4. The pictures similarly typify the culture of the region in the 1840s and 1850s. "Highland Mary" depicts poet Robert Burns's first love, who died a few months after they met. He memorialized her in several poems, especially "To Mary in Heaven."
5. This parody derives in particular from two poems by "The Sweet Singer of Michigan," Julia A. Moore (1847–1920), whose sentimental poetry was popular at the time Twain was writing *Huck Finn*. In one of the two poems, "Little Libbie," the heroine "was choken on a piece of beef." The graveyard and obituary (or "sadful") schools of popular poetry are much older and more widespread. See Walter Blair, *Mark Twain and "Huck Finn"* (1960).

### ODE TO STEPHEN DOWLING BOTS, DEC'D

And did young Stephen sicken,
   And did young Stephen die?
And did the sad hearts thicken,
   And did the mourners cry?

No; such was not the fate of
   Young Stephen Dowling Bots;
Though sad hearts round him thickened,
   'Twas not from sickness' shots.

No whooping-cough did rack his frame,
   Nor measles drear, with spots;
Not these impaired the sacred name
   Of Stephen Dowling Bots.

Despised love struck not with woe
   That head of curly knots,
Nor stomach troubles laid him low,
   Young Stephen Dowling Bots.

O no. Then list with tearful eye,
   Whilst I his fate do tell.
His soul did from this cold world fly,
   By falling down a well.

They got him out and emptied him;
   Alas it was too late;
His spirit was gone for to sport aloft
   In the realms of the good and great.

If Emmeline Grangerford could make poetry like that before she was four-teen, there ain't no telling what she could a done by-and-by. Buck said she could rattle off poetry like nothing. She didn't ever have to stop to think. He said she would slap down a line, and if she couldn't find anything to rhyme with it she would just scratch it out and slap down another one, and go ahead. She warn't particular, she could write about anything you choose to give her to write about, just so it was sadful. Every time a man died, or a woman died, or a child died, she would be on hand with her "tribute" before he was cold. She called them tributes. The neighbors said it was the doctor first, then Emmeline, then the undertaker—the undertaker never got in ahead of Emmeline but once, and then she hung fire on a rhyme for the dead person's name, which was Whistler. She warn't ever the same, after that; she never complained, but she kind of pined away and did not live long. Poor thing, many's the time I made myself go up to the little room that used to be hers and get out her poor old scrapbook and read in it when her pictures had been aggravating me and I had soured on her a little. I liked all the family, dead ones and all, and warn't going to let anything come between us. Poor Emme-line made poetry about all the dead people when she was alive, and it didn't seem right that there warn't nobody to make some about her, now she was gone; so I tried to sweat out a verse or two myself, but I couldn't seem to make it go, somehow. They kept Emmeline's room trim and nice and all the things fixed in it just the way she liked to have them when she was alive, and nobody ever slept there. The old lady took care of the room herself, though there was plenty of niggers, and she sewed there a good deal and read her Bible there, mostly.

Well, as I was saying about the parlor, there was beautiful curtains on the windows: white, with pictures painted on them, of castles with vines all down the walls, and cattle coming down to drink. There was a little old piano, too, that had tin pans in it, I reckon, and nothing was ever so lovely as to hear the young ladies sing, "The Last Link is Broken" and play "The Battle of Prague"[6] on it. The walls of all the rooms was plastered, and most had carpets on the floors, and the whole house was whitewashed on the outside.

It was a double house, and the big open place betwixt them was roofed and floored, and sometimes the table was set there in the middle of the day, and it was a cool, comfortable place. Nothing couldn't be better. And warn't the cooking good, and just bushels of it too!

### Chapter XVIII

Col. Grangerford was a gentleman, you see. He was a gentleman all over; and so was his family. He was well born, as the saying is, and that's worth as much in a man as it is in a horse, so the Widow Douglas said, and nobody ever denied that she was of the first aristocracy in our town; and pap he always said it, too, though he warn't no more quality than a mudcat,[7] himself. Col. Grangerford was very tall and very slim, and had a darkish-paly complexion, not a sign of red in it anywheres; he was clean-shaved every morning, all over his thin face, and he had the thinnest kind of lips, and the thinnest kind of nostrils, and a high nose, and heavy eyebrows, and the blackest kind of eyes, sunk so deep back that they seemed like they was looking out of caverns at you, as you may say. His forehead was high, and his hair was black and straight, and hung to his shoulders. His hands was long and thin, and every day of his life he put on a clean shirt and a full suit from head to foot made out of linen so white it hurt your eyes to look at it; and on Sundays he wore a blue tail-coat with brass buttons on it. He carried a mahogany cane with a silver head to it. There warn't no frivolishness about him, not a bit, and he warn't ever loud. He was as kind as he could be—you could feel that, you know, and so you had confidence. Sometimes he smiled, and it was good to see; but when he straightened himself up like a liberty-pole,[8] and the lightning begun to flicker out from under his eyebrows you wanted to climb a tree first, and find out what the matter was afterwards. He didn't ever have to tell anybody to mind their manners—everybody was always good mannered where he was. Everybody loved to have him around, too; he was sunshine most always—I mean he made it seem like good weather. When he turned into a cloud-bank it was awful dark for a half a minute and that was enough; there wouldn't nothing go wrong again for a week.

When him and the old lady come down in the morning, all the family got up out of their chairs and give them good-day, and didn't set down again till they had set down. Then Tom and Bob went to the sideboard where the

---

6. A bloody story told in clichéd style, written by the Czech composer Franz Kotswara in about 1788; Twain first heard it in 1878. William Clifton's *The Last Link Is Broken* was published about 1840; it is the musical equivalent of Moore's poetry.
7. General term for a number of species of catfish; in this context the lowliest and least esteemed.
8. Flagpole.

decanters was, and mixed a glass of bitters and handed it to him, and he held it in his hand and waited till Tom's and Bob's was mixed, and then they bowed and said "Our duty to you, sir, and madam;" and *they* bowed the least bit in the world and said thank you, and so they drank, all three, and Bob and Tom poured a spoonful of water on the sugar and the mite of whisky or apple brandy in the bottom of their tumblers, and give it to me and Buck, and we drank to the old people too.

Bob was the oldest, and Tom next. Tall, beautiful men with very broad shoulders and brown faces, and long black hair and black eyes. They dressed in white linen from head to foot, like the old gentleman, and wore broad Panama hats.

Then there was Miss Charlotte, she was twenty-five, and tall and proud and grand, but as good as she could be, when she warn't stirred up; but when she was, she had a look that would make you wilt in your tracks, like her father. She was beautiful.

So was her sister, Miss Sophia, but it was a different kind. She was gentle and sweet, like a dove, and she was only twenty.

Each person had their own nigger to wait on them—Buck, too. My nigger had a monstrous easy time, because I warn't used to having anybody do any-thing for me, but Buck's was on the jump most of the time.

This was all there was of the family, now; but there used to be more—three sons; they got killed; and Emmeline that died.

The old gentleman owned a lot of farms, and over a hundred niggers. Sometimes a stack of people would come there, horseback, from ten or fif-teen miles around, and stay five or six days, and have such junketings round about and on the river, and dances and picnics in the woods, day-times, and balls at the house, nights. These people was mostly kin-folks of the family. The men brought their guns with them. It was a handsome lot of quality, I tell you.

There was another clan of aristocracy around there—five or six families— mostly of the name of Shepherdson. They was as high-toned, and well born, and rich and grand, as the tribe of Grangerfords. The Shepherdsons and the Grangerfords used the same steamboat landing, which was about two mile above our house; so sometimes when I went up there with a lot of our folks I used to see a lot of Shepherdsons there, on their fine horses.

One day Buck and me was away out in the woods, hunting, and heard a horse coming. We was crossing the road. Buck says:

"Quick! Jump for the woods!"

We done it, and then peeped down the woods through the leaves. Pretty soon a splendid young man come galloping down the road, setting his horse easy and looking like a soldier. He had his gun across his pommel. I had seen him before. It was young Harney Shepherdson. I heard Buck's gun go off at my ear, and Harney's hat tumbled off from his head. He grabbed his gun and rode straight to the place where we was hid. But we didn't wait. We started through the woods on a run. The woods warn't thick, so I looked over my shoulder, to dodge the bullet, and twice I seen Harney cover Buck with his gun; and then he rode away the way he come—to get his hat, I reckon, but I couldn't see. We never stopped running till we got home. The old gentleman's eyes blazed a minute—'twas pleasure, mainly, I judged—then his face sort of smoothed down, and he says, kind of gentle:

"I don't like that shooting from behind a bush. Why didn't you step into the road, my boy?"

"The Shepherdsons don't, father. They always take advantage."

Miss Charlotte she held her head up like a queen while Buck was telling his tale, and her nostrils spread and her eyes snapped. The two young men looked dark, but never said nothing. Miss Sophia she turned pale, but the color come back when she found the man warn't hurt.

Soon as I could get Buck down by the corn-cribs under the trees by ourselves, I says:

"Did you want to kill him, Buck?"

"Well, I bet I did."

"What did he do to you?"

"Him? He never done nothing to me."

"Well, then, what did you want to kill him for?"

"Why nothing—only it's on account of the feud."

"What's a feud?"

"Why, where was you raised? Don't you know what a feud is?"

"Never heard of it before—tell me about it."

"Well," says Buck, "a feud is this way. A man has a quarrel with another man, and kills him; then that other man's brother kills *him*; then the other brothers, on both sides, goes for one another; then the *cousins* chip in—and by-and-by everybody's killed off, and there ain't no more feud. But it's kind of slow, and takes a long time."

"Has this one been going on long, Buck?"

"Well I should *reckon!* it started thirty year ago, or som'ers along there. There was trouble 'bout something and then a lawsuit to settle it; and the suit went agin one of the men, and so he up and shot the man that won the suit—which he would naturally do, of course. Anybody would."

"What was the trouble about, Buck?—land?"

"I reckon maybe—I don't know."

"Well, who done the shooting?—was it a Grangerford or a Shepherdson?"

"Laws, how do *I* know? it was so long ago."

"Don't anybody know?"

"Oh, yes, pa knows, I reckon, and some of the other old folks; but they don't know, now, what the row was about in the first place."

"Has there been many killed, Buck?"

"Yes—right smart chance of funerals. But they don't always kill. Pa's got a few buck-shot in him; but he don't mind it 'cuz he don't weigh much anyway. Bob's been carved up some with a bowie, and Tom's been hurt once or twice."

"Has anybody been killed this year, Buck?"

"Yes, we got one and they got one. 'Bout three months ago, my cousin Bud, fourteen year old, was riding through the woods, on t'other side of the river, and didn't have no weapon with him, which was blame' foolishness, and in a lonesome place he hears a horse a-coming behind him, and sees old Baldy Shepherdson a-linkin' after him with his gun in his hand and his white hair a-flying in the wind; and 'stead of jumping off and taking to the brush, Bud 'lowed he could outrun him; so they had it, nip and tuck, for five mile or more, the old man a-gaining all the time; so at last Bud seen it warn't any use, so he stopped and faced around so as to have the bullet holes in front, you know, and the old man he rode up and shot him down. But he didn't git much chance to enjoy his luck, for inside of a week our folks laid *him* out."

"I reckon that old man was a coward, Buck."

"I reckon he *warn't* a coward. Not by a blame' sight. There ain't a coward amongst them Shepherdsons—not a one. And there ain't no cowards amongst the Grangerfords, either. Why, that old man kep' up his end in a fight one day, for a half an hour, against three Grangerfords, and come out winner. They was all a-horseback; he lit off of his horse and got behind a little wood-pile, and kep' his horse before him to stop the bullets; but the Grangerfords staid on their horses and capered around the old man, and peppered away at him, and he peppered away at them. Him and his horse both went home pretty leaky and crippled, but the Grangerfords had to be *fetched* home—and one of 'em was dead, and another died the next day. No, sir, if a body's out hunting for cowards, he don't want to fool away any time amongst them Shepherdsons, becuz they don't breed any of that *kind*."

Next Sunday we all went to church, about three mile, everybody a-horseback. The men took their guns along, so did Buck, and kept them between their knees or stood them handy against the wall. The Shepherdsons done the same. It was pretty ornery preaching—all about brotherly love, and such-like tiresomeness; but everybody said it was a good sermon, and they all talked it over going home, and had such a powerful lot to say about faith, and good works, and free grace, and preforeordestination,[9] and I don't know what all, that it did seem to me to be one of the roughest Sundays I had run across yet.

About an hour after dinner everybody was dozing around, some in their chairs and some in their rooms, and it got to be pretty dull. Buck and a dog was stretched out on the grass in the sun, sound asleep. I went up to our room, and judged I would take a nap myself. I found that sweet Miss Sophia standing in her door, which was next to ours, and she took me in her room and shut the door very soft, and asked me if I liked her, and I said I did; and she asked me if I would do something for her and not tell anybody, and I said I would. Then she said she'd forgot her Testament, and left it in the seat at church, between two other books and would I slip out quiet and go there and fetch it to her, and not say nothing to nobody. I said I would. So I slid out and slipped off up the road, and there warn't anybody at the church, except maybe a hog or two, for there warn't any lock on the door, and hogs like a puncheon floor[1] in summer-time because it's cool. If you notice, most folks don't go to church only when they've got to; but a hog is different.

Says I to myself something's up—it ain't natural for a girl to be in such a sweat about a Testament; so I give it a shake, and out drops a little piece of paper with "*Half-past two*" wrote on it with a pencil. I ransacked it, but couldn't find anything else. I couldn't make anything out of that, so I put the paper in the book again, and when I got home and up stairs, there was Miss Sophia in her door waiting for me. She pulled me in and shut the door; then she looked in the Testament till she found the paper, and as soon as she read it she looked glad; and before a body could think, she grabbed me and give me a squeeze, and said I was

9. Huck combines the closely related Presbyterian terms *predestination* and *foreordination*.

1. A crude floor made from log slabs in which the flat side is turned up and the rounded side is set in the dirt.

the best boy in the world, and not to tell anybody. She was mighty red in the face, for a minute, and her eyes lighted up and it made her powerful pretty. I was a good deal astonished, but when I got my breath I asked her what the paper was about, and she asked me if I had read it, and I said no, and she asked me if I could read writing, and I told her "no, only coarse-hand,"[2] and then she said the paper warn't anything but a book-mark to keep her place, and I might go and play now.

I went off down to the river, studying over this thing, and pretty soon I noticed that my nigger was following along behind. When we was out of sight of the house, he looked back and around a second, and then comes a-running, and says:

"Mars Jawge, if you'll come down into de swamp, I'll show you a whole stack o' water-moccasins."

Thinks I, that's mighty curious; he said that yesterday. He oughter know a body don't love water-moccasins enough to go around hunting for them. What is he up to anyway? So I says—

"All right, trot ahead."

I followed a half a mile, then he struck out over the swamp and waded ankle deep as much as another half mile. We come to a little flat piece of land which was dry and very thick with trees and bushes and vines, and he says—

"You shove right in dah, jist a few steps, Mars Jawge, dah's whah dey is. I's seed 'm befo', I don't k'yer to see 'em no mo'."

Then he slopped right along and went away, and pretty soon the trees hid him. I poked into the place a-ways, and come to a little open patch as big as a bedroom, all hung around with vines, and found a man laying there asleep—and by jings it was my old Jim!

I waked him up, and I reckoned it was going to be a grand surprise to him to see me again, but it warn't. He nearly cried, he was so glad, but he warn't surprised. Said he swum along behind me, that night, and heard me yell every time, but dasn't answer, because he didn't want nobody to pick *him* up, and take him into slavery again. Says he—

"I got hurt a little, en couldn't swim fas', so I wuz a considable ways behine you, towards de las'; when you landed I reck'ned I could ketch up wid you on de lan' 'dout havin' to shout at you, but when I see dat house I begin to go slow. I 'uz off too fur to hear what dey say to you—I wuz 'fraid o' de dogs— but when it 'uz all quiet again, I knowed you's in de house, so I struck out for de woods to wait for day. Early in de mawnin' some er de niggers come along, gwyne to de fields, en dey tuck me en showed me dis place, whah de dogs can't track me on accounts o' de water, en dey brings me truck to eat every night, en tells me how you's a gitt'n along."

"Why didn't you tell my Jack to fetch me here sooner, Jim?"

"Well, 'twarn't no use to 'sturb you, Huck, tell we could do sumfn—but we's all right, now. I ben a-buyin' pots en pans en vittles, as I got a chanst, en a patchin' up de raf', nights, when—"

"*What* raft, Jim?"

"Our ole raf'."

"You mean to say our old raft warn't smashed all to flinders?"

---

2. Block printing.

"No, she warn't. She was tore up a good deal—one en' of her was—but dey warn't no great harm done, on'y our traps was mos' all los'. Ef we hadn' dive' so deep en swum so fur under water, en de night hadn' ben so dark, en we warn't so sk'yerd, en ben sich punkin-heads, as de sayin' is, we'd a seed de raf'. But it's jis' as well we didn't, 'kase now she's all fixed up agin mos' as good as new, en we's got a new lot o' stuff, too, in de place o' what 'uz los'."

"Why, how did you get hold of the raft again, Jim—did you catch her?"

"How I gwyne to ketch her, en I out in de woods? No, some er de niggers foun' her ketched on a snag, along heah in de ben', en dey hid her in a crick, 'mongst de willows, en dey wuz so much jawin' 'bout which un 'um she b'long to de mos', dat I come to heah 'bout it pooty soon, so I ups en settles de trouble by tellin' um she don't b'long to none uv um, but to you en me; en I ast 'm if dey gwyne to grab a young white genlman's propaty, en git a hid'n for it? Den I gin 'm ten cents apiece, en dey 'uz mighty well satisfied, en wisht some mo' raf's 'ud come along en make 'm rich agin. Dey's mighty good to me, dese niggers is, en whatever I wants 'm to do fur me, I doan' have to ast 'm twice, honey. Dat Jack's a good nigger, en pooty smart."

"Yes, he is. He ain't ever told me you was here; told me to come, and he'd show me a lot of water-moccasins. If anything happens, *he* ain't mixed up in it. He can say he never seen us together, and it'll be the truth."

I don't want to talk much about the next day. I reckon I'll cut it pretty short. I waked up about dawn, and was agoing to turn over and go to sleep again, when I noticed how still it was—didn't seem to be anybody stirring. That warn't usual. Next I noticed that Buck was up and gone. Well, I gets up, a-wondering, and goes down stairs—nobody around; everything as still as a mouse. Just the same outside; thinks I, what does it mean? Down by the wood-pile I comes across my Jack, and says:

"What's it all about?"

Says he:

"Don't you know, Mars Jawge?"

"No," says I, "I don't."

"Well, den, Miss Sophia's run off! 'deed she has. She run off in de night, sometime—nobody don't know jis' when—run off to git married to dat young Harney Shepherdson, you know—leastways, so dey 'spec. De fambly foun' it out, 'bout half an hour ago—maybe a little mo'—en' I *tell* you dey warn't no time los'. Sich another hurryin' up guns en hosses *you* never see! De women folks has gone for to stir up de relations, en ole Mars Saul en de boys tuck dey guns en rode up de river road for to try to ketch dat young man en kill him 'fo' he kin git acrost de river wid Miss Sophia. I reck'n dey's gwyne to be mighty rough times."

"Buck went off 'thout waking me up."

"Well I reck'n he *did!* Dey warn't gwyne to mix you up in it. Mars Buck he loaded up his gun en 'lowed he's gwyne to fetch home a Shepherdson or bust. Well, dey'll be plenty un 'm dah, I reck'n, en you bet you he'll fetch one ef he gits a chanst."

I took up the river road as hard as I could put. By-and-by I begin to hear guns a good ways off. When I come in sight of the log store and the wood-pile where the steamboats lands, I worked along under the trees and brush till I got to a good place, and then I clumb up into the forks of a cotton-wood that was out of reach, and watched. There was a wood-rank four foot high,[3] a little ways in front of the tree, and first I was going to hide behind that; but maybe it was luckier I didn't.

There was four or five men cavorting around on their horses in the open place before the log store, cussing and yelling, and trying to get at a couple of young chaps that was behind the wood-rank alongside of the steamboat landing—but they couldn't come it. Every time one of them showed himself on the river side of the wood-pile he got shot at. The two boys was squatting back to back behind the pile, so they could watch both ways.

By-and-by the men stopped cavorting around and yelling. They started riding towards the store; then up gets one of the boys, draws a steady bead over the wood-rank, and drops one of them out of his saddle. All the men jumped off of their horses and grabbed the hurt one and started to carry him to the store; and that minute the two boys started on the run. They got half-way to the tree I was in before the men noticed. Then the men see them, and jumped on their horses and took out after them. They gained on the boys, but it didn't do no good, the boys had too good a start; they got to the wood-pile that was in front of my tree, and slipped in behind it, and so they had the bulge[4] on the men again. One of the boys was Buck, and the other was a slim young chap about nineteen years old.

The men ripped around awhile, and then rode away. As soon as they was out of sight, I sung out to Buck and told him. He didn't know what to make of my voice coming out of the tree, at first. He was awful surprised. He told me to watch out sharp and let him know when the men come in sight again; said they was up to some devilment or other—wouldn't be gone long. I wished I was out of that tree, but I dasn't come down. Buck began to cry and rip, and 'lowed that him and his cousin Joe (that was the other young chap) would make up for this day, yet. He said his father and his two brothers was killed, and two or three of the enemy. Said the Shepherdsons laid for them, in ambush. Buck said his father and brothers ought to waited for their relations—the Shepherdsons was too strong for them. I asked him what was become of young Harney and Miss Sophia. He said they'd got across the river and was safe. I was glad of that; but the way Buck did take on because he didn't manage to kill Harney that day he shot at him—I hain't ever heard anything like it.

All of a sudden, bang! bang! bang! goes three or four guns—the men had slipped around through the woods and come in from behind without their horses! The boys jumped for the river—both of them hurt—and as they swum down the current the men run along the bank shooting at them and singing out, "Kill them, kill them!" It made me so sick I most fell out of the tree. I ain't agoing to tell *all* that happened!—it would make me sick again if I was to do that. I wished I hadn't ever come ashore that night, to see such things. I ain't ever going to get shut of them—lots of times I dream about them.

I staid in the tree till it begun to get dark, afraid to come down. Sometimes I heard guns away off in the woods; and twice I seen little gangs of men gallop past the log store with guns; so I reckoned the trouble was still agoing on. I was mighty downhearted; so I made up my mind I wouldn't ever go anear that house again, because I reckoned I was to blame, somehow. I judged that

---

3. Half a cord of stacked firewood.    4. Upper hand.

that piece of paper meant that Miss Sophia was to meet Harney somewheres at half-past two and run off; and I judged I ought to told her father about that paper and the curious way she acted, and then maybe he would a locked her up and this awful mess wouldn't ever happened.

When I got down out of the tree, I crept along down the river bank a piece, and found the two bodies laying in the edge of the water, and tugged at them till I got them ashore; then I covered up their faces, and got away as quick as I could. I cried a little when I was covering up Buck's face, for he was mighty good to me.

It was just dark, now. I never went near the house, but struck through the woods and made for the swamp. Jim warn't on his island, so I tramped off in a hurry for the crick, and crowded through the willows, red-hot to jump aboard and get out of that awful country—the raft was gone! My souls, but I was scared! I couldn't get my breath for most a minute. Then I raised a yell. A voice not twenty-five foot from me, says—

"Good lan'! is dat you, honey? Doan' make no noise."

It was Jim's voice—nothing ever sounded so good before. I run along the bank a piece and got aboard, and Jim he grabbed me and hugged me, he was so glad to see me. He says—

"Laws bless you, chile, I 'uz right down sho' you's dead agin. Jack's been heah, he say he reck'n you's ben shot, kase you didn' come home no mo'; so I's jes' dis minute a startin' de raf' down towards de mouf er de crick, so's to be all ready for to shove out en leave soon as Jack comes agin en tells me for certain you *is* dead. Lawsy, I's mighty glad to git you back agin, honey."

I says—

"All right—that's mighty good; they won't find me, and they'll think I've been killed, and floated down the river—there's something up there that'll help them to think so—so don't you lose no time, Jim, but just shove off for the big water as fast as ever you can."

I never felt easy till the raft was two mile below there and out in the middle of the Mississippi. Then we hung up our signal lantern, and judged that we was free and safe once more. I hadn't had a bite to eat since yesterday; so Jim he got out some corn-dodgers[5] and buttermilk, and pork and cabbage, and greens—there ain't nothing in the world so good, when it's cooked right—and whilst I eat my supper we talked, and had a good time. I was powerful glad to get away from the feuds, and so was Jim to get away from the swamp. We said there warn't no home like a raft, after all. Other places do seem so cramped up and smothery, but a raft don't. You feel mighty free and easy and comfortable on a raft.

## Chapter XIX

Two or three days and nights went by; I reckon I might say they swum by, they slid along so quiet and smooth and lovely. Here is the way we put in the time. It was a monstrous big river down there—sometimes a mile and a half wide; we run nights, and laid up and hid day-times; soon as night was most gone, we stopped navigating and tied up—nearly always in the dead water under a tow-head; and then cut young cottonwoods and willows and hid the

5. Hard cornmeal rolls or cakes.

raft with them. Then we set out the lines. Next we slid into the river and had a swim, so as to freshen up and cool off; then we set down on the sandy bottom where the water was about knee deep, and watched the daylight come. Not a sound, anywheres—perfectly still—just like the whole world was asleep, only sometimes the bull-frogs a-cluttering, maybe. The first thing to see, looking away over the water, was a kind of dull line—that was the woods on t'other side—you couldn't make nothing else out; then a pale place in the sky; then more paleness, spreading around; then the river softened up, away off, and warn't black any more, but gray; you could see little dark spots drifting along, ever so far away—trading scows, and such things; and long black streaks—rafts; sometimes you could hear a sweep screaking; or jumbled up voices, it was so still, and sounds come so far; and by-and-by you could see a streak on the water which you know by the look of the streak that there's a snag there in a swift current which breaks on it and makes that streak look that way; and you see the mist curl up off of the water, and the east reddens up, and the river, and you make out a log cabin in the edge of the woods, away on the bank on t'other side of the river, being a wood-yard, likely, and piled by them cheats so you can throw a dog through it anywheres;[6] then the nice breeze springs up, and comes fanning you from over there, so cool and fresh, and sweet to smell, on account of the woods and the flowers; but sometimes not that way, because they've left dead fish laying around, gars, and such, and they do get pretty rank; and next you've got the full day, and everything smiling in the sun, and the song-birds just going it!

A little smoke couldn't be noticed, now, so we would take some fish off of the lines, and cook up a hot breakfast. And afterwards we would watch the lonesomeness of the river, and kind of lazy along, and by-and-by lazy off to sleep. Wake up, by-and-by, and look to see what done it, and maybe see a steamboat coughing along up stream, so far off towards the other side you couldn't tell nothing about her only whether she was stern-wheel or side-wheel; then for about an hour there wouldn't be nothing to hear nor nothing to see—just solid lonesomeness. Next you'd see a raft sliding by, away off yonder, and maybe a galoot on it chopping, because they're almost always doing it on a raft; you'd see the ax flash, and come down—you don't hear nothing; you see that ax go up again, and by the time it's above the man's head, then you hear the *k'chunk!*—it had took all that time to come over the water. So we would put in the day, lazying around, listening to the stillness. Once there was a thick fog, and the rafts and things that went by was beating tin pans so the steamboats wouldn't run over them. A scow or a raft went by so close we could hear them talking and cussing and laughing—heard them plain; but we couldn't see no sign of them; it made you feel crawly, it was like spirits carrying on that way in the air. Jim said he believed it was spirits; but I says:

"No, spirits wouldn't say, 'dern the dern fog.' "

Soon as it was night, out we shoved; when we got her out to about the middle, we let her alone, and let her float wherever the current wanted her to; then we lit the pipes, and dangled our legs in the water and talked about all kinds of things—we was always naked, day and night, whenever the mosquitoes would let us—the new clothes Buck's folks made for me was too good to be comfortable, and besides I didn't go much on clothes, nohow.

---

6. Stacks of wood in this yard were sold by their volume, gappage included.

Sometimes we'd have that whole river all to ourselves for the longest time. Yonder was the banks and the islands, across the water; and maybe a spark— which was a candle in a cabin window—and sometimes on the water you could see a spark or two—on a raft or a scow, you know; and maybe you could hear a fiddle or a song coming over from one of them crafts. It's lovely to live on a raft. We had the sky, up there, all speckled with stars, and we used to lay on our backs and look up at them, and discuss about whether they was made, or only just happened—Jim he allowed they was made, but I allowed they happened; I judged it would have took too long to *make* so many. Jim said the moon could a *laid* them; well, that looked kind of reasonable, so I didn't say nothing against it, because I've seen a frog lay most as many, so of course it could be done. We used to watch the stars that fell, too, and see them streak down. Jim allowed they'd got spoiled and was hove out of the nest.

Once or twice of a night we would see a steamboat slipping along in the dark, and now and then she would belch a whole world of sparks up out of her chimbleys, and they would rain down in the river and look awful pretty; then she would turn a corner and her lights would wink out and her pow-wow shut off and leave the river still again; and by-and-by her waves would get to us, a long time after she was gone, and joggle the raft a bit, and after that you wouldn't hear nothing for you couldn't tell how long, except maybe frogs or something.

After midnight the people on shore went to bed, and then for two or three hours the shores was black—no more sparks in the cabin windows. These sparks was our clock—the first one that showed again meant morning was coming, so we hunted a place to hide and tie up, right away.

One morning about day-break, I found a canoe and crossed over a chute[7] to the main shore—it was only two hundred yards—and paddled about a mile up a crick amongst the cypress woods, to see if I couldn't get some berries. Just as I was passing a place where a kind of a cow-path crossed the crick, here comes a couple of men tearing up the path as tight as they could foot it. I thought I was a goner, for whenever anybody was after anybody I judged it was *me*—or maybe Jim. I was about to dig out from there in a hurry, but they was pretty close to me then, and sung out and begged me to save their lives— said they hadn't been doing nothing, and was being chased for it—said there was men and dogs a-coming. They wanted to jump right in, but I says—

"Don't you do it. I don't hear the dogs and horses yet; you've got time to crowd through the brush and get up the crick a little ways; then you take to the water and wade down to me and get in—that'll throw the dogs off the scent."

They done it, and soon as they was aboard I lit out for our tow-head, and in about five or ten minutes we heard the dogs and the men away off, shouting. We heard them come along towards the crick, but couldn't see them; they seemed to stop and fool around a while; then, as we got further and further away all the time, we couldn't hardly hear them at all; by the time we had left a mile of woods behind us and struck the river, everything was quiet, and we paddled over to the tow-head and hid in the cotton-woods and was safe.

One of these fellows was about seventy, or upwards, and had a bald head and very gray whiskers. He had an old battered-up slouch hat on, and a greasy

7. A narrow channel with swift-flowing water.

blue woolen shirt, and ragged old blue jeans britches stuffed into his boot tops, and home-knit galluses[8]—no, he only had one. He had an old long-tailed blue jeans coat with slick brass buttons, flung over his arm, and both of them had big fat ratty-looking carpet-bags.

The other fellow was about thirty and dressed about as ornery. After breakfast we all laid off and talked, and the first thing that come out was that these chaps didn't know one another.

"What got you into trouble?" says the baldhead to t'other chap.

"Well, I'd been selling an article to take the tartar off the teeth—and it does take it off, too, and generly the enamel along with it—but I staid about one night longer than I ought to, and was just in the act of sliding out when I ran across you on the trail this side of town, and you told me they were coming, and begged me to help you to get off. So I told you I was expecting trouble myself and would scatter out *with* you. That's the whole yarn—what's yourn?"

"Well, I'd ben a-runnin' a little temperance revival thar, 'bout a week, and was the pet of the women-folks, big and little, for I was makin' it mighty warm for the rummies, I *tell* you, and takin' as much as five or six dollars a night— ten cents a head, children and niggers free—and business a growin' all the time; when somehow or another a little report got around, last night, that I had a way of puttin' in my time with a private jug, on the sly. A nigger rousted me out this mornin', and told me the people was getherin' on the quiet, with their dogs and horses, and they'd be along pretty soon and give me 'bout half an hour's start, and then run me down, if they could; and if they got me they'd tar and feather me and ride me on a rail, sure. I didn't wait for no breakfast— I warn't hungry."

"Old man," says the young one, "I reckon we might double-team it together; what do you think?"

"I ain't undisposed. What's your line—mainly?"

"Jour printer,[9] by trade; do a little in patent medicines; theatre-actor— tragedy, you know; take a turn at mesmerism and phrenology,[1] when there's a chance; teach singing-geography school for a change; sling a lecture, sometimes—oh, I do lots of things—most anything that comes handy, so it ain't work. What's your lay?"[2]

"I've done considerable in the doctoring way in my time. Layin' on o' hands is my best holt—for cancer, and paralysis, and sich things; and I k'n tell a fortune pretty good, when I've got somebody along to find out the facts for me. Preachin's my line, too; and workin' camp-meetin's; and missionaryin' around."

Nobody never said anything for a while; then the young man hove a sigh and says—

"Alas!"

"What 're you alassin' about?" says the baldhead.

"To think I should have lived to be leading such a life, and be degraded down into such company." And he begun to wipe the corner of his eye with a rag.

"Dern your skin, ain't the company good enough for you?" says the baldhead, pretty pert and uppish.

---

8. Suspenders.
9. A journeyman printer, not yet a salaried master-printer, who worked by the day.
1. The study of the shape of the skull as an indi-

cator of intelligence and character. "Mesmerism": hypnotic induction involving animal magnetism— broadly, hypnotism.
2. Work, in the sense here of hustle or scheme.

"Yes, it *is* good enough for me; it's as good as I deserve; for who fetched me so low, when I was so high? *I* did myself. I don't blame *you,* gentlemen—far from it; I don't blame anybody. I deserve it all. Let the cold world do its worst; one thing I know—there's a grave somewhere for me. The world may go on just as its always done, and take everything from me—loved ones, property, everything—but it can't take that. Some day I'll lie down in it and forget it all, and my poor broken heart will be at rest." He went on a-wiping.

"Drot your pore broken heart," says the baldhead; "what are you heaving your pore broken heart at *us* f'r? *We* hain't done nothing."

"No, I know you haven't. I ain't blaming you, gentlemen. I brought myself down—yes, I did it myself. It's right I should suffer—perfectly right—I don't make any moan."

"Brought you down from whar? Whar was you brought down from?"

"Ah, you would not believe me; the world never believes—let it pass—'tis no matter. The secret of my birth—"

"The secret of your birth? Do you mean to say—"

"Gentlemen," says the young man, very solemn, "I will reveal it to you, for I feel I may have confidence in you. By rights I am a duke!"

Jim's eyes bugged out when he heard that; and I reckon mine did, too. Then the baldhead says: "No! you can't mean it?"

"Yes. My great-grandfather, eldest son of the Duke of Bridgewater, fled to this country about the end of the last century, to breathe the pure air of freedom; married here, and died, leaving a son, his own father dying about the same time. The second son of the late duke seized the title and estates—the infant real duke was ignored. I am the lineal descendant of that infant—I am the rightful Duke of Bridgewater; and here am I, forlorn, torn from my high estate, hunted of men, despised by the cold world, ragged, worn, heart-broken, and degraded to the companionship of felons on a raft!"

Jim pitied him ever so much, and so did I. We tried to comfort him, but he said it warn't much use, he couldn't be much comforted; said if we was a mind to acknowledge him, that would do him more good than most anything else; so we said we would, if he would tell us how. He said we ought to bow, when we spoke to him, and say "Your Grace," or "My Lord," or "Your Lordship"—and he wouldn't mind it if we called him plain "Bridgewater," which he said was a title, anyway, and not a name; and one of us ought to wait on him at dinner, and do any little thing for him he wanted done.

Well, that was all easy, so we done it. All through dinner Jim stood around and waited on him, and says, "Will yo' Grace have some o' dis, or some o' dat?" and so on, and a body could see it was mighty pleasing to him.

But the old man got pretty silent, by-and-by—didn't have much to say, and didn't look pretty comfortable over all that petting that was going on around that duke. He seemed to have something on his mind. So, along in the afternoon, he says:

"Looky here, Bilgewater," he says, "I'm nation sorry for you, but you ain't the only person that's had troubles like that."

"No?"

"No, you ain't. You ain't the only person that's ben snaked down wrongfully out'n a high place."

"Alas!"

"No, you ain't the only person that's had a secret of his birth." And by jings, *he* begins to cry.

"Hold! What do you mean?"

"Bilgewater, kin I trust you?" says the old man, still sort of sobbing.

"To the bitter death!" He took the old man by the hand and squeezed it, and says, "The secret of your being: speak!"

"Bilgewater, I am the late Dauphin!"[3]

You bet you Jim and me stared, this time. Then the duke says:

"You are what?"

"Yes, my friend, it is too true—your eyes is lookin' at this very moment on the pore disappeared Dauphin, Looy the Seventeen, son of Looy the Sixteen and Marry Antonette."

"You! At your age! No! You mean you're the late Charlemagne;[4] you must be six or seven hundred years old, at the very least."

"Trouble has done it, Bilgewater, trouble has done it; trouble has brung these gray hairs and this premature balditude. Yes, gentlemen, you see before you, in blue jeans and misery, the wanderin', exiled, trampled-on and sufferin' rightful King of France."

Well, he cried and took on so, that me and Jim didn't know hardly what to do, we was so sorry—and so glad and proud we'd got him with us, too. So we set in, like we done before with the duke, and tried to comfort *him*. But he said it warn't no use, nothing but to be dead and done with it all could do him any good; though he said it often made him feel easier and better for a while if people treated him according to his rights, and got down on one knee to speak to him, and always called him "Your Majesty," and waited on him first at meals, and didn't set down in his presence till he asked them. So Jim and me set to majestying him, and doing this and that and t'other for him, and standing up till he told us we might set down. This done him heaps of good, and so he got cheerful and comfortable. But the duke kind of soured on him, and didn't look a bit satisfied with the way things was going; still, the king acted real friendly towards him, and said the duke's great-grandfather and all the other Dukes of Bilgewater was a good deal thought of by *his* father and was allowed to come to the palace considerable; but the duke staid huffy a good while, till by-and-by the king says:

"Like as not we got to be together a blamed long time, on this h-yer raft, Bilgewater, and so what's the use o' your bein' sour? It'll only make things oncomfortable. It ain't my fault I warn't born a duke, it ain't your fault you warn't born a king—so what's the use to worry? Make the best o' things the way you find 'em, says I—that's my motto. This ain't no bad thing that we've struck here—plenty grub and an easy life—come, give us your hand, Duke, and less all be friends."

The duke done it, and Jim and me was pretty glad to see it. It took away all the uncomfortableness, and we felt mighty good over it, because it would a been a miserable business to have any unfriendliness on the raft; for what you want, above all things, on a raft, is for everybody to be satisfied, and feel right and kind towards the others.

It didn't take me long to make up my mind that these liars warn't no kings nor dukes, at all, but just low-down humbugs and frauds. But I never said nothing, never let on; kept it to myself; it's the best way; then you don't have

---

3. The Dauphin, born in 1785, would have been in his mid-fifties or sixties had he survived.

4. Charlemagne (742–814), emperor of the West (800–814).

no quarrels, and don't get into no trouble. If they wanted us to call them kings and dukes, I hadn't no objections, 'long as it would keep peace in the family; and it warn't no use to tell Jim, so I didn't tell him. If I never learnt nothing else out of pap, I learnt that the best way to get along with his kind of people is to let them have their own way.

## Chapter XX

They asked us considerable many questions; wanted to know what we covered up the raft that way for, and laid by in the daytime instead of running—was Jim a runaway nigger? Says I—

"Goodness sakes, would a runaway nigger run *south?*"

No, they allowed he wouldn't. I had to account for things some way, so I says:

"My folks was living in Pike County, in Missouri, where I was born, and they all died off but me and pa and my brother Ike. Pa, he 'lowed he'd break up and go down and live with Uncle Ben, who's got a little one-horse place on the river, forty-four mile below Orleans. Pa was pretty poor, and had some debts; so when he'd squared up there warn't nothing left but sixteen dollars and our nigger, Jim. That warn't enough to take us fourteen hundred mile, deck passage nor no other way. Well, when the river rose, pa had a streak of luck one day; he ketched this piece of a raft; so we reckoned we'd go down to Orleans on it. Pa's luck didn't hold out; a steamboat run over the forrard corner of the raft, one night, and we all went overboard and dove under the wheel; Jim and me come up, all right, but pa was drunk, and Ike was only four years old, so they never come up no more. Well, for the next day or two we had considerable trouble, because people was always coming out in skiffs and trying to take Jim away from me, saying they believed he was a runaway nigger. We don't run day-times no more, now; nights they don't bother us."

The duke says—

"Leave me alone to cipher out a way so we can run in the daytime if we want to. I'll think the thing over—I'll invent a plan that'll fix it. We'll let it alone for to-day, because of course we don't want to go by that town yonder in daylight—it mightn't be healthy."

Towards night it begun to darken up and look like rain; the heat lightning was squirting around, low down in the sky, and the leaves was beginning to shiver—it was going to be pretty ugly, it was easy to see that. So the duke and the king went to overhauling our wigwam, to see what the beds was like. My bed was a straw tick[5]—better than Jim's, which was a corn-shuck tick; there's always cobs around about in a shuck tick, and they poke into you and hurt; and when you roll over, the dry shucks sound like you was rolling over in a pile of dead leaves; it makes such a rustling that you wake up. Well, the duke allowed he would take my bed; but the king allowed he wouldn't. He says—

"I should a reckoned the difference in rank would a sejested to you that a corn-shuck bed warn't just fitten for me to sleep on. Your Grace'll take the shuck bed yourself."

Jim and me was in a sweat again, for a minute, being afraid there was going

5. Mattress.

to be some more trouble amongst them; so we was pretty glad when the duke says—

" 'Tis my fate to be always ground into the mire under the iron heel of oppression. Misfortune has broken my once haughty spirit; I yield, I submit; 'tis my fate. I am alone in the world—let me suffer; I can bear it."

We got away as soon as it was good and dark. The king told us to stand well out towards the middle of the river, and not show a light till we got a long ways below the town. We come in sight of the little bunch of lights by-and-by— that was the town, you know—and slid by, about a half a mile out, all right. When we was three-quarters of a mile below, we hoisted up our signal lantern; and about ten o'clock it come on to rain and blow and thunder and lighten like everything; so the king told us to both stay on watch till the weather got better; then him and the duke crawled into the wigwam and turned in for the night. It was my watch below, till twelve, but I wouldn't a turned in, anyway, if I'd had a bed; because a body don't see such a storm as that every day in the week, not by a long sight. My souls, how the wind did scream along! And every second or two there'd come a glare that lit up the white-caps for a half a mile around, and you'd see the islands looking dusty through the rain, and the trees thrashing around in the wind; then comes a *h-wack!*—bum! bum! bumble-umble-um-bum-bum-bum-bum—and the thunder would go rumbling and grumbling away, and quit—and then *rip* comes another flash and another sock-dolager.[6] The waves most washed me off the raft, sometimes, but I hadn't any clothes on, and didn't mind. We did-n't have no trouble about snags; the lightning was glaring and flittering around so constant that we could see them plenty soon enough to throw her head this way or that and miss them.

I had the middle watch, you know, but I was pretty sleepy by that time, so Jim he said he would stand the first half of it for me; he was always mighty good, that way, Jim was. I crawled into the wigwam, but the king and the duke had their legs sprawled around so there warn't no show for me; so I laid out-side—I didn't mind the rain, because it was warm, and the waves warn't run-ning so high, now. About two they come up again, though, and Jim was going to call me, but he changed his mind because he reckoned they warn't high enough yet to do any harm; but he was mistaken about that, for pretty soon all of a sudden along comes a regular ripper, and washed me overboard. It most killed Jim a-laughing. He was the easiest nigger to laugh that ever was, anyway.

I took the watch, and Jim he laid down and snored away; and by-and-by the storm let up for good and all; and the first cabin-light that showed, I rousted him out and we slid the raft into hiding-quarters for the day.

The king got out an old ratty deck of cards, after breakfast, and him and the duke played seven-up a while, five cents a game. Then they got tired of it, and allowed they would "lay out a campaign," as they called it. The duke went down into his carpet-bag and fetched up a lot of little printed bills, and read them out loud. One bill said "The celebrated Dr. Armand de Montalban of Paris," would "lecture on the Science of Phrenology" at such and such a place, on the blank day of blank, at ten cents admission, and "furnish charts of character at twenty-five cents apiece." The duke said that was *him*. In

6. Something exceptionally strong or climactic.

another bill he was the "world renowned Shaksperean tragedian, Garrick the Younger,[7] of Drury Lane, London." In other bills he had a lot of other names and done other wonderful things, like finding water and gold with a "divining rod," "dissipating witch-spells," and so on. By-and-by he says—

"But the histrionic muse is the darling. Have you ever trod the boards, Royalty?"

"No," says the king.

"You shall, then, before you're three days older, Fallen Grandeur," says the duke. "The first good town we come to, we'll hire a hall and do the sword-fight in Richard III. and the balcony scene in Romeo and Juliet. How does that strike you?"

"I'm in, up to the hub, for anything that will pay, Bilgewater, but you see I don't know nothing about play-actn', and hain't ever seen much of it. I was too small when pap used to have 'em at the palace. Do you reckon you can learn me?"

"Easy!"

"All right. I'm jist a-freezn' for something fresh, anyway. Less commence, right away."

So the duke he told him all about who Romeo was, and who Juliet was, and said he was used to being Romeo, so the king could be Juliet.

"But if Juliet's such a young gal, Duke, my peeled head and my white whiskers is goin' to look oncommon odd on her, maybe."

"No, don't you worry—these country jakes won't ever think of that. Besides, you know, you'll be in costume, and that makes all the difference in the world; Juliet's in a balcony, enjoying the moonlight before she goes to bed, and she's got on her night-gown and her ruffled night-cap. Here are the costumes for the parts."

He got out two or three curtain-calico suits, which he said was meedyevil armor for Richard III. and t'other chap, and a long white cotton night-shirt and a ruffled night-cap to match. The king was satisfied; so the duke got out his book and read the parts over in the most splendid spread-eagle way, prancing around and acting at the same time, to show how it had got to be done; then he give the book to the king and told him to get his part by heart.

There was a little one-horse town about three mile down the bend, and after dinner the duke said he had ciphered out his idea about how to run in daylight without it being dangersome for Jim; so he allowed he would go down to the town and fix that thing. The king allowed he would go too, and see if he couldn't strike something. We was out of coffee, so Jim said I better go along with them in the canoe and get some.

When we got there, there warn't nobody stirring; streets empty, and perfectly dead and still, like Sunday. We found a sick nigger sunning himself in a back yard, and he said everybody that warn't too young or too sick or too old, was gone to camp-meeting, about two mile back in the woods. The king got the directions, and allowed he'd go and work that camp-meeting for all it was worth, and I might go, too.[8]

7. David Garrick (1717–1779) was a famous tragedian at the Theatre Royal in Drury Lane, London.
8. Notoriously easy pickings for confidence men, camp meetings are extended outdoor evangelical meetings. Families camp nearby for the duration of the event. One of the best-known literary renderings of this stock situation is Johnson J. Hooper's "The Captain Attends a Camp-Meeting."

The duke said what he was after was a printing office. We found it; a little bit of a concern, up over a carpenter shop—carpenters and printers all gone to the meeting, and no doors locked. It was a dirty, littered-up place, and had ink marks, and handbills with pictures of horses and runaway niggers on them, all over the walls. The duke shed his coat and said he was all right, now. So me and the king lit out for the camp-meeting.

We got there in about a half an hour, fairly dripping, for it was a most awful hot day. There was as much as a thousand people there, from twenty mile around. The woods was full of teams and wagons, hitched everywheres, feeding out of the wagon troughs and stomping to keep off the flies. There was sheds made out of poles and roofed over with branches, where they had lemonade and gingerbread to sell, and piles of watermelons and green corn and such-like truck.

The preaching was going on under the same kinds of sheds, only they was bigger and held crowds of people. The benches was made out of outside slabs of logs, with holes bored in the round side to drive sticks into for legs. They didn't have no backs. The preachers had high platforms to stand on, at one end of the sheds. The women had on sunbonnets; and some had linsey-woolsey frocks, some gingham ones, and a few of the young ones had on calico. Some of the young men was barefooted, and some of the children didn't have on any clothes but just a tow-linen[9] shirt. Some of the old women was knitting, and some of the young folks was courting on the sly.

The first shed we come to, the preacher was lining out a hymn. He lined out two lines, everybody sung it, and it was kind of grand to hear it, there was so many of them and they done it in such a rousing way; then he lined out two more for them to sing—and so on. The people woke up more and more, and sung louder and louder; and towards the end, some begun to groan, and some begun to shout. Then the preacher begun to preach; and begun in earnest, too; and went weaving first to one side of the platform and then the other, and then a leaning down over the front of it, with his arms and his body going all the time, and shouting his words out with all his might; and every now and then he would hold up his Bible and spread it open, and kind of pass it around this way and that, shouting, "It's the brazen serpent in the wilderness! Look upon it and live!" And people would shout out, "Glory!—A-*a-men!*" And so he went on, and the people groaning and crying and saying amen:

"Oh, come to the mourners' bench![1] come, black with sin! (*amen!*) come, sick and sore! (*amen!*) come, lame and halt, and blind! (*amen!*) come, pore and needy, sunk in shame! (*a-a-men!*) come all that's worn, and soiled, and suffering!—come with a broken spirit! come with a contrite heart! come in your rags and sin and dirt! the waters that cleanse is free, the door of heaven stands open—oh, enter in and be at rest!" (*a-a-men! glory, glory hallelujah!*)

And so on. You couldn't make out what the preacher said, any more, on account of the shouting and crying. Folks got up, everywheres in the crowd, and worked their way, just by main strength, to the mourners' bench, with the tears running down their faces; and when all the mourners had got up there to the front benches in a crowd, they sung, and shouted, and flung themselves down on the straw, just crazy and wild.

9. Coarse linen cloth. "Linsey-woolsey": cheap, often homespun, unpatterned cloth composed of wool and flax. "Gingham" and "calico" are inex- pensive, store-bought printed cotton.
1. Front-row pews filled by penitents.

Well, the first I knowed, the king got agoing; and you could hear him over everybody; and next he went a-charging up on to the platform and the preacher he begged him to speak to the people, and he done it. He told them he was a pirate—been a pirate for thirty years, out in the Indian Ocean, and his crew was thinned out considerable, last spring, in a fight, and he was home now, to take out some fresh men, and thanks to goodness he'd been robbed last night, and put ashore off of a steamboat without a cent, and he was glad of it, it was the blessedest thing that ever happened to him, because he was a changed man now, and happy for the first time in his life; and poor as he was, he was going to start right off and work his way back to the Indian Ocean and put in the rest of his life trying to turn the pirates into the true path; for he could do it better than anybody else, being acquainted with all the pirate crews in that ocean; and though it would take him a long time to get there, without money, he would get there anyway, and every time he convinced a pirate he would say to him, "Don't you thank me, don't you give me no credit, it all belongs to them dear people in Pokeville camp-meeting, natural brothers and benefactors of the race—and that dear preacher there, the truest friend a pirate ever had!"

And then he busted into tears, and so did everybody. Then somebody sings out, "Take up a collection for him, take up a collection!" Well, a half a dozen made a jump to do it, but somebody sings out, "Let *him* pass the hat around!" Then everybody said it, the preacher too.

So the king went all through the crowd with his hat, swabbing his eyes, and blessing the people and praising them and thanking them for being so good to the poor pirates away off there; and every little while the prettiest kind of girls, with the tears running down their cheeks, would up and ask him would he let them kiss him, for to remember him by; and he always done it; and some of them he hugged and kissed as many as five or six times—and he was invited to stay a week; and everybody wanted him to live in their houses, and said they'd think it was an honor; but he said as this was the last day of the camp-meeting he couldn't do no good, and besides he was in a sweat to get to the Indian Ocean right off and go to work on the pirates.

When we got back to the raft and he come to count up, he found he had collected eighty-seven dollars and seventy-five cents. And then he had fetched away a three-gallon jug of whisky, too, that he found under a wagon when we was starting home through the woods. The king said, take it all around, it laid over any day he'd ever put in in the missionarying line. He said it warn't no use talking, heathens don't amount to shucks, alongside of pirates, to work a camp-meeting with.

The duke was thinking *he'd* been doing pretty well, till the king come to show up, but after that he didn't think so so much. He had set up and printed off two little jobs for farmers, in that printing office—horse bills—and took the money, four dollars. And he had got in ten dollars worth of advertisements for the paper, which he said he would put in for four dollars if they would pay in advance—so they done it. The price of the paper was two dollars a year, but he took in three subscriptions for half a dollar apiece on condition of them paying him in advance; they were going to pay in cord-wood and onions, as usual, but he said he had just bought the concern and knocked down the price as low as he could afford it, and was going to run it for cash. He set up a little piece of poetry, which he made, himself, out of his own head—three

verses—kind of sweet and saddish—the name of it was, "Yes, crush, cold
world, this breaking heart"—and he left that all set up and ready to print in
the paper and didn't charge nothing for it. Well, he took in nine dollars and
a half, and said he'd done a pretty square day's work for it.

Then he showed us another little job he'd printed and hadn't charged for,
because it was for us. It had a picture of a runaway nigger, with a bundle on
a stick, over his shoulder, and "$200 reward" under it. The reading was all
about Jim, and just described him to a dot. It said he run away from St.
Jacques' plantation, forty mile below New Orleans, last winter, and likely
went north, and whoever would catch him and send him back, he could have
the reward and expenses.

"Now," says the duke, "after to-night we can run in the daytime if we want
to. Whenever we see anybody coming, we can tie Jim hand and foot with a
rope, and lay him in the wigwam and show this handbill and say we captured
him up the river, and were too poor to travel on a steamboat, so we got this
little raft on credit from our friends and are going down to get the reward.
Handcuffs and chains would look still better on Jim, but it wouldn't go well
with the story of us being so poor. Too much like jewelry. Ropes are the correct thing—we must preserve the unities,[2] as we say on the boards."

We all said the duke was pretty smart, and there couldn't be no trouble
about running daytimes. We judged we could make miles enough that night
to get out of the reach of the pow-wow we reckoned the duke's work in the
printing office was going to make in that little town—then we could boom
right along, if we wanted to.

We laid low and kept still, and never shoved out till nearly ten o'clock; then
we slid by, pretty wide away from the town, and didn't hoist our lantern till
we was clear out of sight of it.

When Jim called me to take the watch at four in the morning, he says—

"Huck, does you reck'n we gwyne to run acrost any mo' kings on dis trip?"

"No," I says, "I reckon not."

"Well," says he, "dat's all right, den. I doan' mine one er two kings, but dat's
enough. Dis one's powerful drunk, en de duke ain' much better."

I found Jim had been trying to get him to talk French, so he could hear
what it was like; but he said he had been in this country so long, and had so
much trouble, he'd forgot it.

## Chapter XXI

It was after sun-up, now, but we went right on, and didn't tie up. The king
and the duke turned out, by-and-by, looking pretty rusty; but after they'd
jumped overboard and took a swim, it chippered them up a good deal. After
breakfast the king he took a seat on a corner of the raft, and pulled off his
boots and rolled up his britches, and let his legs dangle in the water, so as to
be comfortable, and lit his pipe, and went to getting his Romeo and Juliet by
heart. When he had got it pretty good, him and the duke begun to practice it
together. The duke had to learn him over and over again, how to say every
speech; and he made him sigh, and put his hand on his heart, and after while
he said he done it pretty well; "only," he says, "you mustn't bellow out *Romeo!*

---

2. Of time, place, and action in classical drama; here the duke is using the term to mean "consistent with
the rest of our story."

that way, like a bull—you must say it soft, and sick, and languishy, so—R-o-o-meo! that is the idea; for Juliet's a dear sweet mere child of a girl, you know, and she don't bray like a jackass."

Well, next they got out a couple of long swords that the duke made out of oak laths, and begun to practice the sword-fight—the duke called himself Richard III.; and the way they laid on, and pranced around the raft was grand to see. But by-and-by the king tripped and fell overboard, and after that they took a rest, and had a talk about all kinds of adventures they'd had in other times along the river.

After dinner, the duke says:

"Well, Capet,³ we'll want to make this a first-class show, you know, so I guess we'll add a little more to it. We want a little something to answer encores with, anyway."

"What's onkores, Bilgewater?"

The duke told him, and then says:

"I'll answer by doing the Highland fling or the sailor's hornpipe; and you—well, let me see—oh, I've got it—you can do Hamlet's soliloquy."

"Hamlet's which?"

"Hamlet's soliloquy, you know; the most celebrated thing in Shakespeare. Ah, it's sublime, sublime! Always fetches the house. I haven't got it in the book—I've only got one volume—but I reckon I can piece it out from memory. I'll just walk up and down a minute, and see if I can call it back from recollection's vaults."

So he went to marching up and down, thinking, and frowning horrible every now and then; then he would hoist up his eyebrows; next he would squeeze his hand on his forehead and stagger back and kind of moan; next he would sigh, and next he'd let on to drop a tear. It was beautiful to see him. By-and-by he got it. He told us to give attention. Then he strikes a most noble attitude, with one leg shoved forwards, and his arms stretched away up, and his head tilted back, looking up at the sky; and then he begins to rip and rave and grit his teeth; and after that, all through his speech he howled, and spread around, and swelled up his chest, and just knocked the spots out of any acting ever *I* see before. This is the speech—I learned it, easy enough, while he was learning it to the king:⁴

To be, or not to be; that is the bare bodkin
That makes calamity of so long life;
For who would fardels bear, till Birnam Wood do come to Dunsinane,
But that the fear of something after death
Murders the innocent sleep,
Great nature's second course,
And makes us rather sling the arrows of outrageous fortune
Than fly to others that we know not of.
There's the respect must give us pause:
Wake Duncan with thy knocking! I would thou couldst;
For who would bear the whips and scorns of time,
The oppressor's wrong, the proud man's contumely,

---

3. The family name of Louis VI–X.
4. The comical garbling of Shakespeare was another stock-in-trade of the southwestern humorists in whose tradition Twain follows. The soliloquy is composed chiefly of phrases from *Hamlet* and *Macbeth*, but Twain also draws on several other plays.

The law's delay, and the quietus which his pangs might take,
In the dead waste and middle of the night, when churchyards yawn
In customary suits of solemn black,
But that the undiscovered country from whose bourne no traveler returns,
Breathes forth contagion on the world,
And thus the native hue of resolution, like the poor cat i' the adage,
Is sicklied o'er with care,
And all the clouds that lowered o'er our housetops,
With this regard their currents turn awry,
And lose the name of action.
'Tis a consummation devoutly to be wished. But soft you, the fair Ophelia:
Ope not thy ponderous and marble jaws,
But get thee to a nunnery—go!

Well, the old man he liked that speech, and he mighty soon got it so he could do it first rate. It seemed like he was just born for it; and when he had his hand in and was excited, it was perfectly lovely the way he would rip and tear and rair up behind when he was getting it off.

The first chance we got, the duke he had some show bills printed; and after that, for two or three days as we floated along, the raft was a most uncommon lively place, for there warn't nothing but sword-fighting and rehearsing—as the duke called it—going on all the time. One morning, when we was pretty well down the State of Arkansaw, we come in sight of a little one-horse town[5] in a big bend; so we tied up about three-quarters of a mile above it, in the mouth of a crick which was shut in like a tunnel by the cypress trees, and all of us but Jim took the canoe and went down there to see if there was any chance in that place for our show.

We struck it mighty lucky; there was going to be a circus there that afternoon, and the country people was already beginning to come in, in all kinds of old shackly wagons, and on horses. The circus would leave before night, so our show would have a pretty good chance. The duke he hired the court house, and we went around and stuck up our bills. They read like this:

Shaksperean Revival! ! !
Wonderful Attraction!
For One Night Only!
The world renowned tragedians,
David Garrick the younger, of Drury Lane Theatre, London,
and
Edmund Kean the elder,[6] of the Royal Haymarket Theatre, White-
chapel, Pudding Lane, Piccadilly, London, and the
Royal Continental Theatres, in their sublime
Shaksperean Spectacle entitled
The Balcony Scene
in
Romeo and Juliet! ! !

Romeo . . . . . . . . . . . . . . . . . . . . . . . . . . . . . . . . . . . . . . . . . . . . Mr. Garrick.
Juliet . . . . . . . . . . . . . . . . . . . . . . . . . . . . . . . . . . . . . . . . . . . . . . . Mr. Kean.

---

5. Twain's Bricksville is apparently modeled after Napoleon, Arkansas, although certain unattractive elements of Bricksville and its inhabitants were common to most river towns—including Hannibal.

6. Here, as elsewhere, the duke garbles the facts. Garrick, Edmund Kean (1787–1833), and Charles John Kean (1811–1868) were all famous tragedians at the Theatre Royal in Drury Lane, London.

Assisted by the whole strength of the company!
New costumes, new scenery, new appointments!
Also:
The thrilling, masterly, and blood-curdling
Broad-sword conflict
In Richard III.!!!
Richard III . . . . . . . . . . . . . . . . . . . . . . . . . . . . . . . . . . . . Mr. Garrick.
Richmond . . . . . . . . . . . . . . . . . . . . . . . . . . . . . . . . . . . . . . Mr. Kean.
also:
(by special request,)
Hamlet's Immortal Soliloquy! !
By the Illustrious Kean!
Done by him 300 consecutive nights in Paris!
For One Night Only,
On account of imperative European engagements!
Admission 25 cents; children and servants, 10 cents.

Then we went loafing around the town. The stores and houses was most all old shackly dried-up frame concerns that hadn't ever been painted; they was set up three or four foot above ground on stilts, so as to be out of reach of the water when the river was overflowed. The houses had little gardens around them, but they didn't seem to raise hardly anything in them but jimpson weeds, and sunflowers, and ash-piles, and old curled-up boots and shoes, and pieces of bottles, and rags, and played-out tin-ware. The fences was made of different kinds of boards, nailed on at different times; and they leaned every which-way, and had gates that didn't generly have but one hinge—a leather one. Some of the fences had been whitewashed, some time or another, but the duke said it was in Clumbus's time, like enough. There was generly hogs in the garden, and people driving them out.

All the stores was along one street. They had white-domestic awnings[7] in front, and the country people hitched their horses to the awning-posts. There was empty dry-goods boxes under the awnings, and loafers roosting on them all day long, whittling them with their Barlow knives; and chawing tobacco, and gaping and yawning and stretching—a mighty ornery lot. They generly had on yellow straw hats most as wide as an umbrella, but didn't wear no coats nor waistcoats; they called one another Bill, and Buck, and Hank, and Joe, and Andy, and talked lazy and drawly, and used considerable many cuss-words. There was as many as one loafer leaning up against every awning-post, and he most always had his hands in his britches pockets, except when he fetched them out to lend a chaw of tobacco or scratch. What a body was hearing amongst them, all the time was—

"Gimme a chaw 'v tobacker, Hank."

"Cain't—I hain't got but one chaw left. Ask Bill."

Maybe Bill he gives him a chaw; maybe he lies and says he ain't got none. Some of them kinds of loafers never has a cent in the world, nor a chaw of tobacco of their own. They get all their chawing by borrowing—they say to a fellow, "I wisht you'd len' me a chaw, Jack, I jist this minute give Ben Thompson the last chaw I had"—which is a lie, pretty much every time; it don't fool anybody but a stranger; but Jack ain't no stranger, so he says—

7. Awnings made from crude canvas.

"*You* give him a chaw, did you? so did your sister's cat's grandmother. You pay me back the chaws you've awready borry'd off'n me, Lafe Buckner, then I'll loan you one or two ton of it, and won't charge you no back intrust, nuther."

"Well, I *did* pay you back some of it wunst."

"Yes, you did—'bout six chaws. You borry'd store tobacker and paid back nigger-head."

Store tobacco is flat black plug, but these fellows mostly chaws the natural leaf twisted. When they borrow a chaw, they don't generly cut it off with a knife, but they set the plug in between their teeth, and gnaw with their teeth and tug at the plug with their hands till they get it in two—then sometimes the one that owns the tobacco looks mournful at it when it's handed back, and says, sarcastic—

"Here, gimme the *chaw*, and you take the *plug*."

All the streets and lanes was just mud, they warn't nothing else *but* mud—as black as tar, and nigh about a foot deep in some places; and two or three inches deep in *all* the places. The hogs loafed and grunted around, everywheres. You'd see a muddy sow and a litter of pigs come lazying along the street and whollop herself right down in the way, where folks had to walk around her, and she'd stretch out, and shut her eyes, and wave her ears, whilst the pigs was milking her, and look as happy as if she was on salary. And pretty soon you'd hear a loafer sing out, "Hi! *so* boy! sick him, Tige!" and away the sow would go, squealing most horrible, with a dog or two swinging to each ear, and three or four dozen more a-coming; and then you would see all the loafers get up and watch the thing out of sight, and laugh at the fun and look grateful for the noise. Then they'd settle back again till there was a dog-fight. There couldn't anything wake them up all over, and make them happy all over, like a dog-fight—unless it might be putting turpentine on a stray dog and setting fire to him, or tying a tin pan to his tail and see him run himself to death.

On the river front some of the houses was sticking out over the bank, and they was bowed and bent, and about ready to tumble in. The people had moved out of them. The bank was caved away under one corner of some others, and that corner was hanging over. People lived in them yet, but it was dangersome, because sometimes a strip of land as wide as a house caves in at a time. Sometimes a belt of land a quarter of a mile deep will start in and cave along and cave along till it all caves into the river in one summer. Such a town as that has to be always moving back, and back, and back, because the river's always gnawing at it.

The nearer it got to noon that day, the thicker and thicker was the wagons and horses in the streets, and more coming all the time. Families fetched their dinners with them, from the country, and eat them in the wagons. There was considerable whiskey drinking going on, and I seen three fights. By-and-by somebody sings out—

"Here comes old Boggs!—in from the country for his little old monthly drunk—here he comes, boys!"

All the loafers looked glad—I reckoned they was used to having fun out of Boggs. One of them says—

"Wonder who he's a gwyne to chaw up this time. If he'd a chawed up all the men he's ben a gwyne to chaw up in the last twenty year, he'd have considerable ruputation, now."

Another one says, "I wisht old Boggs'd threaten me, 'cuz then I'd know I warn't gwyne to die for a thousan' year."

Boggs comes a-tearing along on his horse, whooping and yelling like an Injun, and singing out—

"Cler the track, thar. I'm on the war-path, and the price uv coffins is a gwyne to raise."

He was drunk, and weaving about in his saddle; he was over fifty year old, and had a very red face. Everybody yelled at him, and laughed at him, and sassed him, and he sassed back, and said he'd attend to them and lay them out in their regular turns, but he couldn't wait now, because he'd come to town to kill old Colonel Sherburn, and his motto was, "meat first, and spoon vittles to top off on."

He see me, and rode up and says—

"Whar'd you come f'm, boy? You prepared to die?"

Then he rode on. I was scared; but a man says—

"He don't mean nothing; he's always a carryin' on like that, when he's drunk. He's the best-naturedest old fool in Arkansaw—never hurt nobody, drunk nor sober."

Boggs rode up before the biggest store in town and bent his head down so he could see under the curtain of the awning, and yells—

"Come out here, Sherburn! Come out and meet the man you've swindled. You're the houn' I'm after, and I'm a gwyne to have you, too!"

And so he went on, calling Sherburn everything he could lay his tongue to, and the whole street packed with people listening and laughing and going on. By-and-by a proud-looking man about fifty-five—and he was a heap the best dressed man in that town, too—steps out of the store, and the crowd drops back on each side to let him come. He says to Boggs, mighty ca'm and slow— he says:

"I'm tired of this; but I'll endure it till one o'clock. Till one o'clock, mind— no longer. If you open your mouth against me only once, after that time, you can't travel so far but I will find you."

Then he turns and goes in. The crowd looked mighty sober; nobody stirred, and there warn't no more laughing. Boggs rode off blackguarding Sherburn as loud as he could yell, all down the street; and pretty soon back he comes and stops before the store, still keeping it up. Some men crowded around him and tried to get him to shut up, but he wouldn't; they told him it would be one o'clock in about fifteen minutes, and so he *must* go home—he must go right away. But it didn't do no good. He cussed away, with all his might, and throwed his hat down in the mud and rode over it, and pretty soon away he went a-raging down the street again, with his gray hair a-flying. Everybody that could get a chance at him tried their best to coax him off of his horse so they could lock him up and get him sober; but it warn't no use—up the street he would tear again, and give Sherburn another cussing. By-and-by somebody says—

"Go for his daughter!—quick, go for his daughter; sometimes he'll listen to her. If anybody can persuade him, she can."

So somebody started on a run. I walked down street a ways, and stopped. In about five or ten minutes, here comes Boggs again—but not on his horse. He was a-reeling across the street towards me, bareheaded, with a friend on both sides of him aholt of his arms and hurrying him along. He was quiet, and looked uneasy; and he warn't hanging back any, but was doing some of the hurrying himself. Somebody sings out—

"Boggs!"

I looked over there to see who said it, and it was that Colonel Sherburn. He was standing perfectly still, in the street, and had a pistol raised in his right hand—not aiming it, but holding it out with the barrel tilted up towards the sky. The same second I see a young girl coming on the run, and two men with her. Boggs and the men turned round, to see who called him, and when they see the pistol the men jumped to one side, and the pistol barrel come down slow and steady to a level—both barrels cocked. Boggs throws up both of his hands, and says, "O Lord, don't shoot!" Bang! goes the first shot, and he staggers back clawing at the air—bang! goes the second one, and he tumbles backwards onto the ground, heavy and solid, with his arms spread out. That young girl screamed out, and comes rushing, and down she throws herself on her father, crying, and saying, "Oh, he's killed him, he's killed him!" The crowd closed up around them, and shouldered and jammed one another, with their necks stretched, trying to see, and people on the inside trying to shove them back, and shouting, "Back, back! give him air, give him air!"

Colonel Sherburn he tossed his pistol onto the ground, and turned around on his heels and walked off.

They took Boggs to a little drug store, the crowd pressing around, just the same, and the whole town following, and I rushed and got a good place at the window, where I was close to him and could see in. They laid him on the floor, and put one large Bible under his head, and opened another one and spread it on his breast—but they tore open his shirt first, and I seen where one of the bullets went in. He made about a dozen long gasps, his breast lifting the Bible up when he drawed in his breath, and letting it down again when he breathed it out—and after that he laid still; he was dead.[8] Then they pulled his daughter away from him, screaming and crying, and took her off. She was about sixteen, and very sweet and gentle-looking, but awful pale and scared.

Well, pretty soon the whole town was there, squirming and scrouging and pushing and shoving to get at the window and have a look, but people that had the places wouldn't give them up, and folks behind them was saying all the time, "Say, now, you've looked enough, you fellows; 'taint right and 'taint fair, for you to stay thar all the time, and never give nobody a chance; other folks has their rights as well as you."

There was considerable jawing back, so I slid out, thinking maybe there was going to be trouble. The streets was full, and everybody was excited. Everybody that seen the shooting was telling how it happened, and there was a big crowd packed around each one of these fellows, stretching their necks and listening. One long lanky man, with long hair and a big white fur stovepipe hat on the back of his head, and a crooked-handled cane, marked out the places on the ground where Boggs stood, and where Sherburn stood, and the people following him around from one place to t'other and watching everything he done, and bobbing their heads to show they understood, and stooping a little and resting their hands on their thighs to watch him mark the places on the ground with his cane; and then he stood up straight and stiff

8. Twain had witnessed a shooting very much like this one when he was ten years old. His father was the presiding judge at the trial, which ended in acquittal. Only the Bibles under the victim's head and on his chest seem to have been added by Twain, who seldom could resist ironies at the expense of institutionalized religion.

where Sherburn had stood, frowning and having his hat-brim down over his eyes, and sung out, "Boggs!" and then fetched his cane down slow to a level, and says "Bang!" staggered backwards, says "Bang!" again, and fell down flat on his back. The people that had seen the thing said he done it perfect; said it was just exactly the way it all happened. Then as much as a dozen people got out their bottles and treated him.

Well, by-and-by somebody said Sherburn ought to be lynched. In about a minute everybody was saying it; so away they went, mad and yelling, and snatching down every clothes-line they come to, to do the hanging with.

## Chapter XXII

They swarmed up the street towards Sherburn's house, a-whooping and yelling and raging like Injuns, and everything had to clear the way or get run over and tromped to mush, and it was awful to see. Children was heeling it ahead of the mob, screaming and trying to get out of the way; and every window along the road was full of women's heads, and there was nigger boys in every tree, and bucks and wenches looking over every fence; and as soon as the mob would get nearly to them they would break and skaddle back out of reach. Lots of the women and girls was crying and taking on, scared most to death.

They swarmed up in front of Sherburn's palings as thick as they could jam together, and you couldn't hear yourself think for the noise. It was a little twenty-foot yard. Some sung out "Tear down the fence! tear down the fence!" Then there was a racket of ripping and tearing and smashing, and down she goes, and the front wall of the crowd begins to roll in like a wave.

Just then Sherburn steps out on to the roof of his little front porch, with a double-barrel gun in his hand, and takes his stand, perfectly ca'm and deliberate, not saying a word. The racket stopped, and the wave sucked back.

Sherburn never said a word—just stood there, looking down. The stillness was awful creepy and uncomfortable. Sherburn run his eye slow along the crowd; and wherever it struck, the people tried a little to outgaze him, but they couldn't; they dropped their eyes and looked sneaky. Then pretty soon Sherburn sort of laughed; not the pleasant kind, but the kind that makes you feel like when you are eating bread that's got sand in it.

Then he says, slow and scornful:

"The idea of *you* lynching anybody! It's amusing. The idea of you thinking you had pluck enough to lynch a *man!* Because you're brave enough to tar and feather poor friendless cast-out women that come along here, did that make you think you had grit enough to lay your hands on a *man?* Why, a *man's* safe in the hands of ten thousand of your kind—as long as it's day-time and you're not behind him.

"Do I know you? I know you clear through. I was born and raised in the South, and I've lived in the North; so I know the average all around. The average man's a coward. In the North he lets anybody walk over him that wants to, and goes home and prays for a humble spirit to bear it. In the South one man, all by himself, has stopped a stage full of men, in the day-time, and robbed the lot. Your newspapers call you a brave people so much that you think you *are* braver than any other people—whereas you're just *as* brave, and no braver. Why don't your juries hang murderers? Because they're afraid the man's friends will shoot them in the back, in the dark—and it's just what they *would* do.

"So they always acquit; and then a *man* goes in the night, with a hundred masked cowards at his back, and lynches the rascal. Your mistake is, that you didn't bring a man with you; that's one mistake, and the other is that you didn't come in the dark, and fetch your masks. You brought *part* of a man—Buck Harkness, there—and if you hadn't had him to start you, you'd a taken it out in blowing.

"You didn't want to come. The average man don't like trouble and danger. *You* don't like trouble and danger. But if only *half* a man—like Buck Harkness, there—shouts 'Lynch him, lynch him!' you're afraid to back down—afraid you'll be found out to be what you are—*cowards*—and so you raise a yell, and hang yourselves onto that half-a-man's coat tail, and come raging up here, swearing what big things you're going to do. The pitifulest thing out is a mob; that's what an army is—a mob; they don't fight with courage that's born in them, but with courage that's borrowed from their mass, and from their officers. But a mob without any *man* at the head of it, is *beneath* pitifulness. Now the thing for *you* to do, is to droop your tails and go home and crawl in a hole. If any real lynching's going to be done, it will be done in the dark, Southern fashion; and when they come they'll bring their masks, and fetch a *man* along. Now *leave*—and take your half-a-man with you"—tossing his gun up across his left arm and cocking it, when he says this.

The crowd washed back sudden, and then broke all apart and went tearing off every which way, and Buck Harkness he heeled it after them, looking tolerable cheap. I could a staid, if I'd a wanted to, but I didn't want to.

I went to the circus, and loafed around the back side till the watchman went by, and then dived in under the tent. I had my twenty-dollar gold piece and some other money, but I reckoned I better save it, because there ain't no telling how soon you are going to need it, away from home and amongst strangers, that way. You can't be too careful. I ain't opposed to spending money on circuses, when there ain't no other way, but there ain't no use in *wasting* it on them.

It was a real bully circus. It was the splendidest sight that ever was, when they all come riding in, two and two, a gentleman and lady, side by side, the men just in their drawers and under-shirts, and no shoes nor stirrups, and resting their hands on their thighs, easy and comfortable—there must a' been twenty of them—and every lady with a lovely complexion, and perfectly beautiful, and looking just like a gang of real sure-enough queens, and dressed in clothes that cost millions of dollars, and just littered with diamonds. It was a powerful fine sight; I never see anything so lovely. And then one by one they got up and stood, and went a-weaving around the ring so gentle and wavy and graceful, the men looking ever so tall and airy and straight, with their heads bobbing and skimming along, away up there under the tent-roof, and every lady's rose-leafy dress flapping soft and silky around her hips, and she looking like the most loveliest parasol.

And then faster and faster they went, all of them dancing, first one foot stuck out in the air and then the other, the horses leaning more and more, and the ring-master going round and round the centre-pole, cracking his whip and shouting "hi!—hi!" and the clown cracking jokes behind him; and by-and-by all hands dropped the reins, and every lady put her knuckles on her hips and every gentlemen folded his arms, and then how the horses did lean over and hump themselves! And so, one after the other they all skipped off into the ring, and made the sweetest bow I ever see, and then scampered out, and everybody clapped their hands and went just about wild.

Well, all through the circus they done the most astonishing things; and all the time that clown carried on so it most killed the people. The ring-master couldn't ever say a word to him but he was back at him quick as a wink with the funniest things a body ever said; and how he ever *could* think of so many of them, and so sudden and so pat, was what I couldn't noway understand. Why, I couldn't a thought of them in a year. And by-and-by a drunk man tried to get into the ring—said he wanted to ride; said he could ride as well as anybody that ever was. They argued and tried to keep him out, but he wouldn't listen, and the whole show come to a standstill. Then the people begun to holler at him and make fun of him, and that made him mad, and he begun to rip and tear; so that stirred up the people, and a lot of men began to pile down off of the benches and swarm towards the ring, saying "Knock him down! throw him out!" and one or two women begun to scream. So, then, the ring-master he made a little speech, and said he hoped there wouldn't be no disturbance, and if the man would promise he wouldn't make no more trouble, he would let him ride, if he thought he could stay on the horse. So everybody laughed and said all right, and the man got on. The minute he was on, the horse begun to rip and tear and jump and cavort around, with two circus men hanging onto his bridle trying to hold him, and the drunk man hanging onto his neck, and his heels flying in the air every jump, and the whole crowd of people standing up shouting and laughing till the tears rolled down. And at last, sure enough, all the circus men could do, the horse broke loose, and away he went like the very nation, round and round the ring, with that sot laying down on him and hanging to his neck, with first one leg hanging most to the ground on one side, and then t'other one on t'other side, and the people just crazy. It warn't funny to me, though; I was all of a tremble to see his danger. But pretty soon he struggled up astraddle and grabbed the bridle, a-reeling this way and that; and the next minute he sprung up and dropped the bridle and stood! and the horse agoing like a house afire too. He just stood up there, a-sailing around as easy and comfortable as if he warn't ever drunk in his life—and then he begun to pull off his clothes and sling them. He shed them so thick they kind of clogged up the air, and altogether he shed seventeen suits. And then, there he was, slim and handsome, and dressed the gaudiest and prettiest you ever saw, and he lit into that horse with his whip and made him fairly hum—and finally skipped off, and made his bow and danced off to the dressing-room, and everybody just a-howling with pleasure and astonishment.

Then the ring-master he see how he had been fooled, and he *was* the sickest ring-master you ever see, I reckon. Why, it was one of his own men! He had got up that joke all out of his own head, and never let on to nobody. Well, I felt sheepish enough, to be took in so, but I wouldn't a been in that ring-master's place, not for a thousand dollars. I don't know; there may be bullier circuses than what that one was, but I never struck them yet. Anyways it was plenty good enough for *me*; and wherever I run across it, it can have all of *my* custom, everytime.

Well, that night we had *our* show; but there warn't only about twelve people there; just enough to pay expenses. And they laughed all the time, and that made the duke mad; and everybody left, anyway, before the show was over, but one boy which was asleep. So the duke said these Arkansaw lunkheads couldn't come up to Shakspeare; what they wanted was low comedy—and may be something ruther worse than low comedy, he reckoned. He said he could size their style. So next morning he got some big sheets of wrapping-paper and some black paint, and drawed off some handbills and stuck them up all over the village. The bills said:

AT THE COURT HOUSE!

FOR 3 NIGHTS ONLY!

*The World-Renowned Tragedians*

DAVID GARRICK THE YOUNGER

AND

EDMUND KEAN THE ELDER!

*Of the London and Continental*
*Theatres,*

In their Thrilling Tragedy of

THE KING'S CAMELOPARD[9]

OR

THE ROYAL NONESUCH! ! !

*Admission 50 cents.*

Then at the bottom was the biggest line of all—which said:

LADIES AND CHILDREN NOT ADMITTED.

"There," says he, "if that line don't fetch them, I don't know Arkansaw!"

## Chapter XXIII

Well, all day him and the king was hard at it, rigging up a stage, and a curtain, and a row of candles for footlights; and that night the house was jam full of men in no time. When the place couldn't hold no more, the duke he quit tending door and went around the back way and come onto the stage and stood up before the curtain, and made a little speech, and praised up this tragedy, and said it was the most thrillingest one that ever was; and so he went on a-bragging about the tragedy and about Edmund Kean the Elder, which was to play the main principal part in it; and at last when he'd got everybody's expectations up high enough, he rolled up the curtain, and the next minute the king come a-prancing out on all fours, naked; and he was painted all over, ring-streaked-and-striped, all sorts of colors, as splendid as a rainbow. And—but never mind the rest of his outfit, it was just wild, but it was awful funny. The people most killed themselves laughing; and when the king got done capering, and capered off behind the scenes, they roared and clapped and stormed and haw-hawed till he come back and done it over again; and after that, they made him do it another time. Well, it would a made a cow laugh to see the shines that old idiot cut.

Then the duke he lets the curtain down, and bows to the people, and says the great tragedy will be performed only two nights more, on accounts of pressing London engagements, where the seats is all sold aready for it in Drury Lane; and then he makes them another bow, and says if he has succeeded in pleasing them and instructing them, he will be deeply obleeged if they will mention it to their friends and get them to come and see it.

---

9. An archaic name for a giraffe, but also describes a legendary spotted beast the size of a camel. This hoax performance was a popular subject of comic stories, and Twain had heard a version he referred to as "The Burning Shame" from his friend Jim Gillis in his California newspaper days.

Twenty people sings out:

"What, is it over? Is that *all?*"

The duke says yes. Then there was a fine time. Everybody sings out "sold," and rose up mad, and was agoing for that stage and them tragedians. But a big fine-looking man jumps up on a bench, and shouts:

"Hold on! Just a word, gentlemen." They stopped to listen. "We are sold—mighty badly sold. But we don't want to be the laughing-stock of this whole town, I reckon, and never hear the last of this thing as long as we live. *No.* What we want, is to go out of here quiet, and talk this show up, and sell the *rest* of the town! Then we'll all be in the same boat. Ain't that sensible?" ("You bet it is!—the jedge is right!" everybody sings out.) "All right, then—not a word about any sell. Go along home, and advise everybody to come and see the tragedy."

Next day you couldn't hear nothing around that town but how splendid that show was. House was jammed again, that night, and we sold this crowd the same way. When me and the king and the duke got home to the raft, we all had a supper; and by-and-by, about midnight, they made Jim and me back her out and float her down the middle of the river and fetch her in and hide her about two mile below town.

The third night the house was crammed again—and they warn't new-comers, this time, but people that was at the show the other two nights. I stood by the duke at the door, and I see that every man that went in had his pockets bulging, or something muffled up under his coat—and I see it warn't no perfumery neither, not by a long sight. I smelt sickly eggs by the barrel, and rotten cabbages, and such things; and if I know the signs of a dead cat being around, and I bet I do, there was sixty-four of them went in. I shoved in there for a minute, but it was too various for me, I couldn't stand it. Well, when the place couldn't hold no more people, the duke he give a fellow a quarter and told him to tend door for him a minute, and then he started around for the stage door, I after him; but the minute we turned the corner and was in the dark, he says:

"Walk fast, now, till you get away from the houses, and then shin for the raft like the dickens was after you!"

I done it, and he done the same. We struck the raft at the same time, and in less than two seconds we was gliding down stream, all dark and still, and edging towards the middle of the river, nobody saying a word. I reckoned the poor king was in for a gaudy time of it with the audience; but nothing of the sort; pretty soon he crawls out from under the wigwam, and says:

"Well, how'd the old thing pan out this time, Duke?"

He hadn't been up town at all.

We never showed a light till we was about ten mile below that village. Then we lit up and had a supper, and the king and the duke fairly laughed their bones loose over the way they'd served them people. The duke says:

"Greenhorns, flatheads! *I* knew the first house would keep mum and let the rest of the town get roped in; and I knew they'd lay for us the third night, and consider it was *their* turn now. Well, it *is* their turn, and I'd give something to know how much they'd take for it. I *would* just like to know how they're putting in their opportunity. They can turn it into a picnic, if they want to—they brought plenty provisions."

Them rapscallions took in four hundred and sixty-five dollars in that three nights. I never see money hauled in by the wagon-load like that, before.

By-and-by, when they was asleep and snoring, Jim says:

"Don't it 'sprise you, de way dem kings carries on, Huck?"

"No," I says, "it don't."

"Why don't it, Huck?"

"Well, it don't, because it's in the breed. I reckon they're all alike."

"But, Huck, dese kings o' ourn is reglar rapscallions; dat's jist what dey is; dey's reglar rapscallions."

"Well, that's what I'm a-saying; all kings is mostly rapscallions, as fur as I can make out."

"Is dat so?"

"You read about them once—you'll see. Look at Henry the Eight; this'n 's a Sunday-School Superintendent to *him*. And look at Charles Second, and LouisFourteen, and Louis Fifteen, and James Second, and Edward Second, and Richard Third, and forty more; besides all them Saxon heptarchies that used to rip around so in old times and raise Cain. My, you ought to seen old Henry the Eight when he was in bloom. He *was* a blossom. He used to marry a new wife every day, and chop off her head next morning. And he would do it just as indifferent as if he was ordering up eggs. 'Fetch up Nell Gwynn,' he says. They fetch her up. Next morning, 'Chop off her head!' And they chop it off. 'Fetch up Jane Shore,' he says; and up she comes. Next morning 'Chop off her head'—and they chop it off. 'Ring up Fair Rosamun.' Fair Rosamun answers the bell. Next morning, 'Chop off her head.' And he made every one of them tell him a tale every night; and he kept that up till he had hogged a thousand and one tales that way, and then he put them all in a book, and called it Domesday Book—which was a good name and stated the case. You don't know kings, Jim, but I know them; and this old rip of ourn is one of the cleanest I've struck in history. Well, Henry he takes a notion he wants to get up some trouble with this country. How does he go at it—give notice?—give the country a show? No. All of sudden he heaves all the tea in Boston Harbor overboard, and whacks out a declaration of independence, and dares them to come on. That was *his* style—he never give anybody a chance. He had suspicions of his father, the Duke of Wellington. Well, what did he do?—ask him to show up? No—drownded him in a butt of mamsey, like a cat. Spose people left money laying around where he was—what did he do? He collared it. Spose he contracted to do a thing; and you paid him, and didn't set down there and see that he done it—what did he do? He always done the other thing. Spose he opened his mouth—what then? If he didn't shut it up powerful quick, he'd lose a lie, every time. That's the kind of a bug Henry was; and if we'd a had him along 'stead of our kings, he'd a fooled that town a heap worse than ourn done.[1] I don't say that ourn is lambs, because they ain't, when you come right down to the cold facts; but they ain't nothing to *that* old ram, anyway. All I say is, kings is kings, and you

1. Huck's "history" of kingly behavior is a hodge-podge of fact and fiction. Henry VIII, king of England from 1509 to 1547, did execute two of his wives and divorced two others. Nell Gwynn, however, was the mistress of Charles II (r. 1660–85). Jane Shore was mistress to Edward IV (r. 15th century). Rosamund Clifford was mistress to Henry II in the 12th century. The Anglo-Saxon heptarchy (seven friendly kingdoms) ruled England from 449 to 829. The Domesday Book, in which William the Conqueror of England recorded all landowners and the value of their holdings, was completed in 1086; Huck confuses it with *The Arabian Nights*. The duke of Wellington is a 19th-century personage. The duke of Clarence was reportedly drowned in a cask of wine in the late 15th century. The Boston Tea Party took place in 1773, and the Declaration of Independence was adopted in 1776; neither event, of course, has any connection with Henry VIII.

got to make allowances. Take them all around, they're a mighty o
It's the way they're raised."

"But dis one do *smell* so like de nation, Huck."

"Well, they all do, Jim. *We* can't help the way a king smells; history don't
tell no way."

"Now de duke, he's a tolerable likely man, in some ways."

"Yes, a duke's different. But not very different. This's a middling hard
lot, for a duke. When he's drunk, there ain't no near-sighted man could tell
him from a king."

"Well, anyways, I doan' hanker for no mo' un um, Huck. Dese is all I kin
stan'."

"It's the way I feel, too, Jim. But we've got them on our hands, and we got
to remember what they are, and make allowances. Sometimes I wish we could
hear of a country that's out of kings."

What was the use to tell Jim these warn't real kings and dukes? It wouldn't
a done no good; and besides, it was just as I said; you couldn't tell them from
the real kind.

I went to sleep, and Jim didn't call me when it was my turn. He often done
that. When I waked up, just at day-break, he was setting there with his head
down betwixt his knees, moaning and mourning to himself. I didn't take
notice, nor let on. I knowed what it was about. He was thinking about his wife
and his children, away up yonder, and he was low and homesick; because he
hadn't ever been away from home before in his life; and I do believe he cared
just as much for his people as white folks does for their'n. It don't seem natural, but I reckon it's so. He was often moaning and mourning that way,
nights, when he judged I was asleep, and saying "Po' little 'Lizabeth! po' little
Johnny! its mighty hard; I spec' I ain't ever gwyne to see you no mo', no mo'!"
He was a mighty good nigger, Jim was.

But this time I somehow got to talking to him about his wife and young
ones; and by-and-by he says:

"What makes me feel so bad dis time, 'uz bekase I hear sumpn over yonder
on de bank like a whack, er a slam, while ago, en it mine me er de time I treat
my little 'Lizabeth so ornery. She warn't on'y 'bout fo' year ole, en she tuck de
sk'yarlet-fever, en had a powful rough spell; but she got well, en one day she
was a-stannin' aroun', en I says to her, I says:

" 'Shet de do'.'

"She never done it; jis' stood dar, kiner smilin' up at me. It make me mad;
en I says agin, mighty loud, I says:

" 'Doan' you hear me?—shet de do'!'

"She jis' stood de same way, kiner smilin' up. I was a-bilin'! I says:

" 'I lay I *make* you mine!'

"En wid dat I fetch' her a slap side de head dat sont her a-sprawlin'. Den I
went into de yuther room, en 'uz gone 'bout ten minutes; en when I come
back, dah was dat do' a-stannin' open *yit*, en dat chile stannin' mos' right in
it, a-lookin' down and mournin', en de tears runnin' down. My, but I *wuz* mad,
I was agwyne for de chile, but jis' den—it was a do' dat open innerds—jis' den,
'long come de wind en slam it to, behine de chile, *ker-blam!*—en my lan', de
chile never move'! My breff mos' hop outer me; en I feel so—so—I doan' know
*how* I feel. I crope out, all a-tremblin', en crope aroun' en open de do' easy en
slow, en poke my head in behine de chile, sof' en still, en all uv a sudden, I

says *pow!* jis' as loud as I could yell. *She never budge!* Oh, Huck, I bust out a-cryin' en grab her up in my arms, en say, 'Oh, de po' little thing! de Lord God Amighty fogive po' ole Jim, kaze he never gwyne to fogive hisself as long's he live!' Oh, she was plumb deef en dumb, Huck, plumb deef en dumb—en I'd ben a'treat'n her so!"

## Chapter XXIV

Next day, towards night, we laid up under a little willow tow-head out in the middle, where there was a village on each side of the river, and the duke and the king begun to lay out a plan for working them towns. Jim he spoke to the duke, and said he hoped it wouldn't take but a few hours, because it got mighty heavy and tiresome to him when he had to lay all day in the wigwam tied with the rope. You see, when we left him all alone we had to tie him, because if anybody happened on him all by himself and not tied, it wouldn't look much like he was a runaway nigger, you know. So the duke said it *was* kind of hard to have to lay roped all day, and he'd cipher out some way to get around it.

He was uncommon bright, the duke was, and he soon struck it. He dressed Jim up in King Lear's outfit—it was a long curtain-calico gown, and a white horse-hair wig and whiskers; and then he took his theatre-paint and painted Jim's face and hands and ears and neck all over a dead dull solid blue, like a man that's been drownded nine days. Blamed if he warn't the horriblest looking outrage I ever see. Then the duke took and wrote out a sign on a shingle so—

*Sick Arab—but harmless when not out of his head.*

And he nailed that shingle to a lath, and stood the lath up four or five foot in front of the wigwam. Jim was satisfied. He said it was a sight better than laying tied a couple of years every day and trembling all over every time there was a sound. The duke told him to make himself free and easy, and if anybody ever come meddling around, he must hop out of the wigwam, and carry on a little, and fetch a howl or two like a wild beast, and he reckoned they would light out and leave him alone. Which was sound enough judgment; but you take the average man, and he wouldn't wait for him to howl. Why, he didn't only look like he was dead, he looked considerable more than that.

These rapscallions wanted to try the Nonesuch again, because there was so much money in it, but they judged it wouldn't be safe, because maybe the news might a worked along down by this time. They couldn't hit no project that suited, exactly; so at last the duke said he reckoned he'd lay off and work his brains an hour or two and see if he couldn't put up something on the Arkansaw village; and the king he allowed he would drop over to t'other village, without any plan, but just trust in Providence to lead him the profitable way—meaning the devil, I reckon. We had all bought store clothes where we stopped last; and now the king put his'n on, and he told me to put mine on. I done it, of course. The king's duds was all black, and he did look real swell and starchy. I never knowed how clothes could change a body before. Why, before, he looked like the orneriest old rip that ever was; but now, when he'd take off his new white beaver and make a bow and do a smile, he looked that grand and good and pious that you'd say he had walked right out of the ark, and maybe was old Leviticus[2] himself. Jim cleaned up the canoe, and I got my paddle ready. There was a big steamboat laying at the shore away up under the point, about three mile above town—been there a couple of hours, taking on freight. Says the king:

"Seein' how I'm dressed, I reckon maybe I better arrive down from St. Louis or Cincinnati, or some other big place. Go for the steamboat, Huckleberry; we'll come down to the village on her."

I didn't have to be ordered twice, to go and take a steamboat ride. I fetched the shore a half a mile above the village, and then went scooting along the bluff bank in the easy water. Pretty soon we come to a nice innocent-looking young country jake setting on a log swabbing the sweat off of his face, for it was powerful warm weather; and he had a couple of big carpet-bags by him.

"Run her nose in shore," says the king. I done it. "Wher' you bound for, young man?"

"For the steamboat; going to Orleans."

"Git aboard," says the king. "Hold on a minute, my servant 'll he'p you with them bags. Jump out and he'p the gentleman, Adolphus"—meaning me, I see.

I done so, and then we all three started on again. The young chap was mighty thankful; said it was tough work toting his baggage such weather. He asked the king where he was going, and the king told him he'd come down the river and landed at the other village this morning, and now he was going up a few mile to see an old friend on a farm up there. The young fellow says:

"When I first see you, I says to myself, 'It's Mr. Wilks, sure, and he come mighty near getting here in time.' But then I says again, 'No, I reckon it ain't him, or else he wouldn't be paddling up the river.' You *ain't* him, are you?"

"No, my name's Blodgett—Elexander Blodgett—*Reverend* Elexander Blodgett, I spose I must say, as I'm one o' the Lord's poor servants. But still I'm jist as able to be sorry for Mr. Wilks for not arriving in time, all the same, if he's missed anything by it—which I hope he hasn't."

"Well, he don't miss any property by it, because he'll get that all right; but he's missed seeing his brother Peter die—which he mayn't mind, nobody can tell as to that—but his brother would a give anything in this world to see *him* before he died; never talked about nothing else all these three weeks; hadn't seen him since they was boys together—and hadn't ever seen his brother William at all—that's the deef and dumb one—William ain't more than thirty or thirty-five. Peter and George was the only ones that come out here; George was the married brother; him and his wife both died last year. Harvey and William's the only ones that's left now; and, as I was saying, they haven't got here in time."

"Did anybody send 'em word?"

"Oh, yes; a month or two ago, when Peter was first took; because Peter said then that he sorter felt like he warn't going to get well this time. You see, he was pretty old, and George's g'yirls was too young to be much company for him, except Mary Jane the red-headed one; and so he was kinder lonesome after George and his wife died, and didn't seem to care much to live. He most desperately wanted to see Harvey—and William too, for that matter—because he was one of them kind that can't bear to make a will. He left a let-

2. The third book of the Old Testament is here confused with Noah.

ter behind for Harvey, and said he'd told in it where his money was hid, and how he wanted the rest of the property divided up so George's g'yirls would be all right—for George didn't leave nothing. And that letter was all they could get him to put a pen to."

"Why do you reckon Harvey don't come? Wher' does he live?"

"Oh, he lives in England—Sheffield—preaches there—hasn't ever been in this country. He hasn't had any too much time—and besides he mightn't a got the letter at all, you know."

"Too bad, too bad he couldn't a lived to see his brothers, poor soul. You going to Orleans, you say?"

"Yes, but that ain't only a part of it. I'm going in a ship, next Wednesday, for Ryo Janeero, where my uncle lives."

"It's a pretty long journey. But it'll be lovely; I wisht I was agoing. Is Mary Jane the oldest? How old is the others?"

"Mary Jane's nineteen, Susan's fifteen, and Joanna's about fourteen—that's the one that gives herself to good works and has a hare-lip."

"Poor things! to be left alone in the cold world so."

"Well, they could be worse off. Old Peter had friends, and they ain't going to let them come to no harm. There's Hobson, the Babtis' preacher; and Deacon Lot Hovey, and Ben Rucker, and Abner Shackleford, and Levi Bell, the lawyer; and Dr. Robinson, and their wives, and the widow Bartley, and—well, there's a lot of them; but these are the ones that Peter was thickest with, and used to write about sometimes, when he wrote home; so Harvey'll know where to look for friends when he gets here."

Well, the old man he went on asking questions till he just fairly emptied that young fellow. Blamed if he didn't inquire about everybody and everything in that blessed town, and all about all the Wilkses; and about Peter's business—which was a tanner; and about George's—which was a carpenter; and about Harvey's—which was a dissentering[3] minister, and so on, and so on. Then he says:

"What did you want to walk all the way up to the steamboat for?"

"Because she's a big Orleans boat, and I was afeard she mightn't stop there. When they're deep they won't stop for a hail. A Cincinnati boat will, but this is a St. Louis one."

"Was Peter Wilks well off?"

"Oh, yes, pretty well off. He had houses and land, and it's reckoned he left three or four thousand in cash hid up som'ers."

"When did you say he died?"

"I didn't say, but it was last night."

"Funeral to-morrow, likely?"

"Yes, 'bout the middle of the day."

"Well, it's all terrible sad; but we've all got to go, one time or another. So what we want to do is to be prepared; then we're all right."

"Yes, sir, it's the best way. Ma used to always say that."

When we struck the boat, she was about done loading, and pretty soon she got off. The king never said nothing about going aboard, so I lost my ride, after all. When the boat was gone, the king made me paddle up another mile to a lonesome place, and then he got ashore, and says:

3. Dissenting.

"Now hustle back, right off, and fetch the duke up here, and the new carpet-bags. And if he's gone over to t'other side, go over there and git him. And tell him to git himself up regardless. Shove along, now."

I see what *he* was up to; but I never said nothing, of course. When I got back with the duke, we hid the canoe and then they set down on a log, and the king told him everything, just like the young fellow had said it—every last word of it. And all the time he was a doing it, he tried to talk like an Englishman; and he done it pretty well too, for a slouch. I can't imitate him, and so I ain't agoing to try to; but he really done it pretty good. Then he says:

"How are you on the deef and dumb, Bilgewater?"

The duke said, leave him alone for that; said he had played a deef and dumb person on the histrionic boards. So then they waited for a steamboat.

About the middle of the afternoon a couple of little boats come along, but they didn't come from high enough up the river; but at last there was a big one, and they hailed her. She sent out her yawl, and we went aboard, and she was from Cincinnati; and when they found we only wanted to go four or five mile, they was booming mad, and give us a cussing, and said they wouldn't land us. But the king was ca'm. He says:

"If gentlemen kin afford to pay a dollar a mile apiece, to be took on and put off in a yawl, a steamboat kin afford to carry 'em, can't it?"

So they softened down and said it was all right; and when we got to the village, they yawled us ashore. About two dozen men flocked down, when they see the yawl a coming; and when the king says—

"Kin any of you gentlemen tell me wher' Mr. Peter Wilks lives?" they give a glance at one another, and nodded their heads, as much as to say, "What d' I tell you?" Then one of them says, kind of soft and gentle:

"I'm sorry, sir, but the best we can do is to tell you where he *did* live yesterday evening."

Sudden as winking, the ornery old cretur went all to smash, and fell up against the man, and put his chin on his shoulder, and cried down his back, and says:

"Alas, alas, our poor brother—gone, and we never got to see him; oh, it's too, *too* hard!"

Then he turns around, blubbering, and makes a lot of idiotic signs to the duke on his hands, and blamed if *he* didn't drop a carpet-bag and bust out a-crying. If they warn't the beatenest lot, them two frauds, that ever I struck.

Well, the men gethered around, and sympathized with them, and said all sorts of kind things to them, and carried their carpet-bags up the hill for them, and let them lean on them and cry, and told the king all about his brother's last moments, and the king he told it all over again on his hands to the duke, and both of them took on about that dead tanner like they'd lost the twelve disciples. Well, if ever I struck anything like it, I'm a nigger. It was enough to make a body ashamed of the human race.

## Chapter XXV

The news was all over town in two minutes, and you could see the people tearing down on the run, from every which way, some of them putting on their coats as they come. Pretty soon we was in the middle of a crowd, and the noise of the tramping was like a soldier-march. The windows and dooryards was full; and every minute somebody would say, over a fence:

"Is it *them!*"

And somebody trotting along with the gang would answer back and say. "You bet it is."

When we got to the house, the street in front of it was packed, and the three girls was standing in the door. Mary Jane *was* red-headed, and that don't make no difference, she was most awful beautiful, and her face and her eyes was all lit up like glory, she was so glad her uncles was come. The king he spread his arms, and Mary Jane she jumped for them, and the hare-lip jumped for the duke, and there they *had* it! Everybody most, leastways women, cried for joy to see them meet again at last and have such good times.

Then the king he hunched the duke, private—I see him do it—and then he looked around and see the coffin, over in the corner on two chairs; so then, him and the duke, with a hand across each other's shoulder, and t'other hand to their eyes, walked slow and solemn over there, everybody dropping back to give them room, and all the talk and noise stopping, people saying "Sh!" and all the men taking their hats off and drooping their heads, so you could a heard a pin fall. And when they got there, they bent over and looked in the coffin, and took one sight, and then they bust out a crying so you could a heard them to Orleans, most; and then they put their arms around each other's necks, and hung their chins over each other's shoulders; and then for three minutes, or maybe four, I never see two men leak the way they done. And mind you, everybody was doing the same; and the place was that damp I never see anything like it. Then one of them got on one side of the coffin, and t'other on t'other side, and they kneeled down and rested their foreheads on the coffin, and let on to pray all to theirselves. Well, when it come to that, it worked the crowd like you never see anything like it, and so everybody broke down and went to sobbing right out loud—the poor girls, too; and every woman, nearly, went up to the girls, without saying a word, and kissed them, solemn, on the forehead, and then put their hand on their head, and looked up towards the sky, with the tears running down, and then busted out and went off sobbing and swabbing, and give the next woman a show. I never see anything so disgusting.

Well, by-and-by the king he gets up and comes forward a little, and works himself up and slobbers out a speech, all full of tears and flapdoodle about its being a sore trial for him and his poor brother to lose the diseased, and to miss seeing diseased alive, after the long journey of four thousand mile, but it's a trial that's sweetened and sanctified to us by this dear sympathy and these holy tears, and so he thanks them out of his heart and out of his brother's heart, because out of their mouths they can't, words being too weak and cold, and all that kind of rot and slush, till it was just sickening; and then he blubbers out a pious goody-goody Amen, and turns himself loose and goes to crying fit to bust.

And the minute the words was out of his mouth somebody over in the crowd struck up the doxolojer,[4] and everybody joined in with all their might, and it just warmed you up and made you feel as good as church letting out.

---

4. I.e., doxology, or hymn of praise to God. The particular doxology referred to here begins "Praise God, from whom all blessings flow."

Music *is* a good thing; and after all that soul-butter and hogwash, I never see it freshen up things so, and sound so honest and bully.

Then the king begins to work his jaw again, and says how him and his nieces would be glad if a few of the main principal friends of the family would take supper here with them this evening, and help set up with the ashes of the diseased; and says if his poor brother laying yonder could speak, he knows who he would name, for they was names that was very dear to him, and mentioned often in his letters; and so he will name the same, to-wit, as follows, vizz:—Rev. Mr. Hobson, and Deacon Lot Hovey, and Mr. Ben Rucker, and Abner Shackleford, and Levi Bell, and Dr. Robinson, and their wives, and the widow Bartley.

Rev. Hobson and Dr. Robinson was down to the end of the town, a-hunting together; that is, I mean the doctor was shipping a sick man to t'other world, and the preacher was pinting him right. Lawyer Bell was away up to Louisville on some business. But the rest was on hand, and so they all come and shook hands with the king and thanked him and talked to him; and then they shook hands with the duke, and didn't say nothing but just kept a-smiling and bobbing their heads like a passel of sapheads whilst he made all sorts of signs with his hands and said "Goo-goo—goo-goo-goo," all the time, like a baby that can't talk.

So the king he blatted along, and managed to inquire about pretty much everybody and dog in town, by his name, and mentioned all sorts of little things that happened one time or another in the town, or to George's family, or to Peter; and he always let on that Peter wrote him the things, but that was a lie, he got every blessed one of them out of that young flathead that we canoed up to the steamboat.

Then Mary Jane she fetched the letter her father left behind, and the king he read it out loud and cried over it. It give the dwelling-house and three thousand dollars, gold, to the girls; and it give the tanyard (which was doing a good business), along with some other houses and land (worth about seven thousand), and three thousand dollars in gold to Harvey and William, and told where the six thousand cash was hid, down cellar. So these two frauds said they'd go and fetch it up, and have everything square and above-board; and told me to come with a candle. We shut the cellar door behind us, and when they found the bag they spilt it out on the floor, and it was a lovely sight, all them yallerboys.[5] My, the way the king's eyes did shine! He slaps the duke on the shoulder, and says:

"Oh, *this* ain't bully, nor noth'n! Oh, no, I reckon not! Why, Biljy, it beats the Nonesuch, *don't* it!"

The duke allowed it did. They pawed the yaller-boys, and sifted them through their fingers and let them jingle down on the floor; and the king says:

"It ain't no use talkin'; bein' brothers to a rich dead man, and representatives of furrin heirs that's got left, is the line for you and me, Bilge. Thish-yer comes of trust'n to Providence. It's the best way, in the long run. I've tried 'em all, and ther' ain't no better way."

Most everybody would a been satisfied with the pile, and took it on trust; but no, they must count it. So they counts it, and it comes out four hundred and fifteen dollars short. Says the king:

5. Gold coins.

"Dern him, I wonder what he done with that four hundred and fifteen dollars?"

They worried over that a while, and ransacked all around for it. Then the duke says:

"Well, he was a pretty sick man, and likely he made a mistake—I reckon that's the way of it. The best way's to let it go, and keep still about it. We can spare it."

"Oh, shucks, yes, we can *spare* it. I don't k'yer noth'n 'bout that—it's the *count* I'm thinkin' about. We want to be awful square and open and aboveboard, here, you know. We want to lug this h'yer money up stairs and count it before everybody—then ther' ain't noth'n suspicious. But when the dead man says ther's six thous'n dollars, you know, we don't want to—"

"Hold on," says the duke. "Less make up the deffisit"—and he begun to haul out yallerboys out of his pocket.

"It's a most amaz'n good idea, duke—you *have* got a rattlin' clever head on you," says the king. "Blest if the old Nonesuch ain't a heppin' us out agin"—and *he* begun to haul out yallerjackets and stack them up.

It most busted them, but they made up the six thousand clean and clear.

"Say," says the duke, "I got another idea. Le's go up stairs and count this money, and then take and *give it to the girls.*"

"Good land, duke, lemme hug you! It's the most dazzling idea 'at ever a man struck. You have cert'nly got the most astonishin' head I ever see. Oh, this is the boss dodge,[6] ther' ain't no mistake 'bout it. Let 'em fetch along their suspicions now, if they want to—this'll lay 'em out."

When we got up stairs, everybody gathered around the table, and the king he counted it and stacked it up, three hundred dollars in a pile—twenty elegant little piles. Everybody looked hungry at it, and licked their chops. Then they raked it into the bag again, and I see the king begin to swell himself up for another speech. He says:

"Friends all, my poor brother that lays yonder, has done generous by them that's left behind in the vale of sorrers. He has done generous by these-yer poor little lambs that he loved and sheltered, and that's left fatherless and motherless. Yes, and we that knowed him, knows that he would a done *more* generous by 'em if he hadn't been afeard o' woundin' his dear William and me. Now, *wouldn't* he? Ther' ain't no question 'bout it, in *my* mind. Well, then— what kind o' brothers would it be, that 'd stand in his way at sech a time? And what kind o' uncles would it be that 'd rob—yes, *rob*—sech poor sweet lambs as these 'at he loved so, at sech a time? If I know William—and I *think* I do— he—well, I'll jest ask him." He turns around and begins to make a lot of signs to the duke with his hands; and the duke he looks at him stupid and leatherheaded a while, then all of sudden he seems to catch his meaning, and jumps for the king, goo-gooing with all his might for joy, and hugs him about fifteen times before he lets up. Then the king says, "I knowed it; I reckon *that* 'll convince anybody the way *he* feels about it. Here, Mary Jane, Susan, Joanner, take the money—take it *all*. It's the gift of him that lays yonder, cold but joyful."

Mary Jane she went for him, Susan and the hare-lip went for the duke, and then such another hugging and kissing I never see yet. And everybody

6. Best confidence trick.

crowded up with the tears in their eyes, and most shook the hands off of them frauds, saying all the time:

"You *dear* good souls!—how *lovely!*—how *could* you!"

Well, then, pretty soon all hands got to talking about the diseased again, and how good he was, and what a loss he was, and all that; and before long a big iron-jawed man worked himself in there from outside, and stood a listening and looking, and not saying anything; and nobody saying anything to him either, because the king was talking and they was all busy listening. The king was saying—in the middle of something he'd started in on—

"—they bein' partickler friends o' the diseased. That's why they're invited here this evenin'; but to-morrow we want *all* to come—everybody; for he respected everybody, he liked everybody, and so it's fitten that his funeral orgies sh'd be public."

And so he went a-mooning on and on, liking to hear himself talk, and every little while he fetched in his funeral orgies again, till the duke he couldn't stand it no more; so he writes on a little scrap of paper, "*obsequies,* you old fool," and folds it up and goes to goo-gooing and reaching it over people's heads to him. The king he reads it, and puts it in his pocket, and says:

"Poor William, afflicted as he is, his *heart's* aluz right. Asks me to invite everybody to come to the funeral—wants me to make 'em all welcome. But he needn't a worried—it was jest what I was at."

Then he weaves along again, perfectly ca'm, and goes to dropping in his funeral orgies again every now and then, just like he done before. And when he done it the third time, he says:

"I say orgies, not because it's the common term, because it ain't—obsequies bein' the common term—but because orgies is the right term. Obsequies ain't used in England no more, now—it's gone out. We say orgies now, in England. Orgies is better, because it means the thing you're after, more exact. It's a word that's made up out'n the Greek *orgo,* outside, open, abroad; and the Hebrew *jeesum,* to plant, cover up; hence in*ter.* So, you see, funeral orgies is an open er public funeral."[7]

He was the *worst* I ever struck. Well, the iron-jawed man he laughed right in his face. Everybody was shocked. Everybody says, "Why *doctor!*" and Abner Shackleford says:

"Why, Robinson, hain't you heard the news? This is Harvey Wilks."

The king he smiled eager, and shoved out his flapper, and says:

"*Is* it my poor brother's dear good friend and physician? I—"

"Keep your hands off of me!" says the doctor. "*You* talk like an Englishman—*don't* you? It's the worse imitation I ever heard. *You* Peter Wilks's brother. You're a fraud, that's what you are!"

Well, how they all took on! They crowded around the doctor, and tried to quiet him down, and tried to explain to him, and tell him how Harvey'd showed in forty ways that he *was* Harvey, and knowed everybody by name, and the names of the very dogs, and begged and *begged* him not to hurt Harvey's feelings and the poor girls' feelings, and all that; but it warn't no use, he stormed right along, and said any man that pretended to be an Englishman and couldn't imitate the lingo no better than what he did, was a fraud and a

---

7. The comic etymology was a stock-in-trade of the southwestern humorists and is still popular in comedy routines.

liar. The poor girls was hanging to the king and crying; and all of a sudden the doctor ups and turns on *them*. He says:

"I was your father's friend, and I'm your friend; and I warn you *as* a friend, and an honest one, that wants to protect you and keep you out of harm and trouble, to turn your backs on that scoundrel, and have nothing to do with him, the ignorant tramp, with his idiotic Greek and Hebrew as he calls it. He is the thinnest kind of an impostor—has come here with a lot of empty names and facts which he has picked up somewheres, and you take them for *proofs*, and are helped to fool yourselves by these foolish friends here, who ought to know better. Mary Jane Wilks, you know me for your friend, and for your unselfish friend, too. Now listen to me; turn this pitiful rascal out—I *beg* you to do it. Will you?"

Mary Jane straightened herself up, and my, but she was handsome! She says:

"*Here* is my answer." She hove up the bag of money and put it in the king's hands, and says, "Take this six thousand dollars, and invest it for me and my sisters any way you want to, and don't give us no receipt for it."

Then she put her arm around the king on one side, and Susan and the hare-lip done the same on the other. Everybody clapped their hands and stomped on the floor like a perfect storm, whilst the king held up his head and smiled proud. The doctor says:

"All right, I wash *my* hands of the matter. But I warn you all that a time's coming when you're going to feel sick whenever you think of this day"—and away he went.

"All right, doctor," says the king, kinder mocking him, "we'll try and get 'em to send for you"—which made them all laugh, and they said it was a prime good hit.

## Chapter XXVI

Well, when they was all gone, the king he asks Mary Jane how they was off for spare rooms, and she said she had one spare room, which would do for Uncle William, and she'd give her own room to Uncle Harvey, which was a little bigger, and she would turn into the room with her sisters and sleep on a cot; and up garret was a little cubby, with a pallet in it. The king said the cubby would do for his valley—meaning me.

So Mary Jane took us up, and she showed them their rooms, which was plain but nice. She said she'd have her frocks and a lot of other traps took out of her room if they was in Uncle Harvey's way, but he said they warn't. The frocks was hung along the wall, and before them was a curtain made out of calico that hung down to the floor. There was an old hair trunk in one corner, and a guitar box in another, and all sorts of little knickknacks and jimcracks around, like girls brisken up a room with. The king said it was all the more homely and more pleasanter for these fixings, and so don't disturb them. The duke's room was pretty small, but plenty good enough, and so was my cubby.

That night they had a big supper, and all them men and women was there, and I stood behind the king and the duke's chairs and waited on them, and the niggers waited on the rest. Mary Jane she set at the head of the table, with Susan along side of her, and said how bad the biscuits was, and how mean the preserves was, and how ornery and tough the fried chickens was—and all that kind of rot, the way women always do for to force out compliments; and the people all knowed everything was tip-top, and said so—said "How *do* you get biscuits to brown so nice?" and "Where, for the land's sake *did* you get these amaz'n pickles?" and all that kind of humbug talky-talk, just the way people always does at a supper, you know.

And when it was all done, me and the hare-lip had supper in the kitchen off of the leavings, whilst the others was helping the niggers clean up the things. The hare-lip she got to pumping me about England, and blest if I didn't think the ice was getting mighty thin, sometimes. She says:

"Did you ever see the king?"

"Who? William Fourth? Well, I bet I have—he goes to our church." I knowed he was dead years ago, but I never let on. So when I says he goes to our church, she says:

"What—regular?"

"Yes—regular. His pew's right over opposite ourn—on 'tother side the pulpit."

"I thought he lived in London?"

"Well, he does. Where *would* he live?"

"But I thought *you* lived in Sheffield?"

I see I was up a stump. I had to let on to get choked with a chicken bone, so as to get time to think how to get down again. Then I says:

"I mean he goes to our church regular when he's in Sheffield. That's only in the summer-time, when he comes there to take the sea baths."

"Why, how you talk—Sheffield ain't on the sea."

"Well, who said it was?"

"Why, you did."

"I *didn't*, nuther."

"You did!"

"I didn't."

"You did."

"I never said nothing of the kind."

"Well, what *did* you say, then?"

"Said he come to take the sea *baths*—that's what I said."

"Well, then! how's he going to take the sea baths if it ain't on the sea?"

"Looky here," I says, "did you ever see any Congress water?"[8]

"Yes."

"Well, did you have to go to Congress to get it?"

"Why, no."

"Well, neither does William Fourth have to go to the sea to get a sea bath."

"How does he get it, then?"

"Gets it the way people down here gets Congress water—in barrels. There in the palace at Sheffield they've got furnaces, and he wants his water hot. They can't bile that amount of water away off there at the sea. They haven't got no conveniences for it."

"Oh, I see, now. You might a said that in the first place and saved time."

When she said that, I see I was out of the woods again, and so I was comfortable and glad. Next, she says:

---

8. Famous mineral water from the Congress Spring in Saratoga Springs, New York.

"Do you go to church, too?"

"Yes—regular."

"Where do you set?"

"Why, in our pew."

"*Whose* pew?"

"Why, *ourn*—your Uncle Harvey's."

"His'n? What does *he* want with a pew?"

"Wants it to set in. What did you *reckon* he wanted with it?"

"Why, I thought he'd be in the pulpit."

Rot him, I forgot he was a preacher. I see I was up a stump again, so I played another chicken bone and got another think. Then I says:

"Blame it, do you suppose there ain't but one preacher to a church?"

"Why, what do they want with more?"

"What!—to preach before a king? I never see such a girl as you. They don't have no less than seventeen."

"Seventeen! My land! Why, I wouldn't set out such a string as that, not if I *never* got to glory. It must take 'em a week."

"Shucks, they don't *all* of 'em preach the same day—only *one* of 'em."

"Well, then, what does the rest of 'em do?"

"Oh, nothing much. Loll around, pass the plate—and one thing or another. But mainly they don't do nothing."

"Well, then, what are they *for?*"

"Why, they're for *style.* Don't you know nothing?"

"Well, I don't *want* to know no such foolishness as that. How is servants treated in England? Do they treat 'em better 'n we treat our niggers?"

"*No!* A servant ain't nobody there. They treat them worse than dogs."

"Don't they give 'em holidays, the way we do, Christmas and New Year's week, and Fourth of July?"

"Oh, just listen! A body could tell *you* hain't ever been to England, by that. Why, Hare-l—why, Joanna, they never see a holiday from year's end to year's end; never go to the circus, nor theatre, nor nigger shows, nor nowheres."

"Nor church?"

"Nor church."

"But *you* always went to church."

Well, I was gone up again. I forgot I was the old man's servant. But next minute I whirled in on a kind of an explanation how a valley was different from a common servant, and *had* to go to church whether he wanted to or not, and set with the family, on account of it's being the law. But I didn't do it pretty good, and when I got done I see she warn't satisfied. She says:

"Honest injun, now, hain't you been telling me a lot of lies?"

"Honest injun," says I.

"None of it at all?"

"None of it at all. Not a lie in it," says I.

"Lay your hand on this book and say it."

I see it warn't nothing but a dictionary, so I laid my hand on it and said it. So then she looked a little better satisfied, and says:

"Well, then, I'll believe some of it; but I hope to gracious if I'll believe the rest."

"What is it you won't believe, Joe?" says Mary Jane, stepping in with Susan behind her. "It ain't right nor kind for you to talk so to him, and him a stranger and so far from his people. How would you like to be treated so?"

"That's always your way, Maim—always sailing in to help somebody before they're hurt. I hain't done nothing to him. He's told some stretchers, I reckon; and I said I wouldn't swallow it all; and that's every bit and grain I *did* say. I reckon he can stand a little thing like that, can't he?"

"I don't care whether 'twas little or whether 'twas big, he's here in our house and a stranger, and it wasn't good of you to say it. If you was in his place, it would make you feel ashamed; and so you ought'nt to say a thing to another person that will make *them* feel ashamed."

"Why, Maim, he said—"

"It don't make no difference what he *said*—that ain't the thing. The thing is for you to treat him *kind*, and not be saying things to make him remember he ain't in his own country and amongst his own folks."

I says to myself, *this* is a girl that I'm letting that old reptle rob her of her money!

Then Susan *she* waltzed in; and if you'll believe me, she did give Hare-lip hark from the tomb![9]

Says I to myself, And this is *another* one that I'm letting him rob her of her money!

Then Mary Jane she took another inning, and went in sweet and lovely again—which was her way—but when she got done there warn't hardly anything left o' poor Hare-lip. So she hollered.

"All right, then," says the other girls, "you just ask his pardon."

She done it, too. And she done it beautiful. She done it so beautiful it was good to hear; and I wished I could tell her a thousand lies, so she could do it again.

I says to myself, this is *another* one that I'm letting him rob her of her money. And when she got through, they all jest laid theirselves out to make me feel at home and know I was amongst friends. I felt so ornery and low down and mean, that I says to myself, My mind's made up; I'll hive that money for them or bust.

So then I lit out—for bed, I said, meaning some time or another. When I got by myself, I went to thinking the thing over. I says to myself, shall I go to that doctor, private, and blow on these frauds? No—that won't do. He might tell who told him; then the king and the duke would make it warm for me. Shall I go, private, and tell Mary Jane? No—I dasn't do it. Her face would give them a hint, sure; they've got the money, and they'd slide right out and get away with it. If she was to fetch in help, I'd get mixed up in the business, before it was done with, I judge. No, there ain't no good way but one. I got to steal that money, somehow; and I got to steal it some way that they won't suspicion that I done it. They've got a good thing, here; and they ain't agoing to leave till they've played this family and this town for all they're worth, so I'll find a chance time enough. I'll steal it, and hide it; and by-and-by, when I'm away down the river, I'll write a letter and tell Mary Jane where it's hid. But I better hive it to-night, if I can, because the doctor maybe hasn't let up as much as he lets on he has; he might scare them out of here, yet.

So, thinks I, I'll go and search them rooms. Up stairs the hall was dark, but I found the duke's room, and started to paw around it with my hands; but I recollected it wouldn't be much like the king to let anybody else take care of that money but his own self; so then I went to his room and begun to paw

9. A chewing out.

around there. But I see I couldn't do nothing without a candle, and I dasn't light one, of course. So I judged I'd got to do the other thing—lay for them, and eavesdrop. About that time, I hears their footsteps coming, and was going to skip under the bed; I reached for it, but it wasn't where I thought it would be; but I touched the curtain that hid Mary Jane's frocks, so I jumped in behind that and snuggled in amongst the gowns, and stood there perfectly still.

They come in and shut the door; and the first thing the duke done was to get down and look under the bed. Then I was glad I hadn't found the bed when I wanted it. And yet, you know, it's kind of natural to hide under the bed when you are up to anything private. They sets down, then, and the king says:

"Well, what is it? and cut it middlin' short, because it's better for us to be down there a whoopin'-up the mournin', than up here givin' 'em a chance to talk us over."

"Well, this is it, Capet. I ain't easy; I ain't comfortable. That doctor lays on my mind. I wanted to know your plans. I've got a notion, and I think it's a sound one."

"What is it, duke?"

"That we better glide out of this, before three in the morning, and clip it down the river with what we've got. Specially, seeing we got it so easy—*given* back to us, flung at our heads, as you may say, when of course we allowed to have to steal it back. I'm for knocking off and lighting out."

That made me feel pretty bad. About an hour or two ago, it would a been a little different, but now it made me feel bad and disappointed. The king rips out and says:

"What! And not sell out the rest o' the property? March off like a passel o' fools and leave eight or nine thous'n dollars' worth o' property layin' around jest sufferin' to be scooped in?—and all good salable stuff, too."

The duke he grumbled; said the bag of gold was enough, and he didn't want to go no deeper—didn't want to rob a lot of orphans of *everything* they had.

"Why, how you talk!" says the king. "We shan't rob 'em of nothing at all but jest this money. The people that *buys* the property is the suff'rers; because as soon's it's found out 'at we didn't own it—which won't be long after we've slid—the sale won't be valid, and it'll all go back to the estate. These-yer orphans 'll git their house back agin, and that's enough for *them*; they're young and spry, and k'n easy earn a livin'. *They* ain't agoing to suffer. Why, jest think—there's thous'n's and thous'n's that ain't nigh so well off. Bless you, *they* ain't got noth'n to complain of."

Well, the king he talked him blind; so at last he give in, and said all right, but said he believed it was blame foolishness to stay, and that doctor hanging over them. But the king says:

"Cuss the doctor! What do we k'yer for *him*? Hain't we got all the fools in town on our side? and ain't that a big enough majority in any town?"

So they got ready to go down stairs again. The duke says:

"I don't think we put that money in a good place."

That cheered me up. I'd begun to think I warn't going to get a hint of no kind to help me. The king says:

"Why?"

"Because Mary Jane 'll be in mourning from this out; and first you know the nigger that does up the rooms will get an order to box these duds up and

put 'em away; and do you reckon a nigger can run across money and not borrow some of it?"

"Your head's level, agin, duke," says the king; and he come a fumbling
under the curtain two or three foot from where I was. I stuck tight to the wall,
and kept mighty still, though quivery; and I wondered what them fellows
would say to me if they catched me; and I tried to think what I'd better do if
they did catch me. But the king he got the bag before I could think more than
about a half a thought, and he never suspicioned I was around. They took and
shoved the bag through a rip in the straw tick that was under the feather bed,
and crammed it in a foot or two amongst the straw and said it was all right,
now, because a nigger only makes up the feather bed, and don't turn over the
straw tick only about twice a year, and so it warn't in no danger of getting
stole, now.

But I knowed better. I had it out of there before they was halfway down
stairs. I groped along up to my cubby, and hid it there till I could get a chance
to do better. I judged I better hide it outside of the house somewheres, because
if they missed it they would give the house a good ransacking. I knowed that
very well. Then I turned in, with my clothes all on; but I couldn't a gone to
sleep, if I'd a wanted to, I was in such a sweat to get through with the business. By-and-by I heard the king and the duke come up; so I rolled off of my
pallet and laid with my chin at the top of my ladder and waited to see if anything was going to happen. But nothing did.

So I held on till all the late sounds had quit and the early ones hadn't
begun, yet; and then I slipped down the ladder.

### Chapter XXVII

I crept to their doors and listened; they was snoring, so I tip-toed along, and
got down stairs all right. There warn't a sound anywheres. I peeped through
a crack of the dining-room door, and see the men that was watching the
corpse all sound asleep on their chairs. The door was open into the parlor,
where the corpse was laying, and there was a candle in both rooms, I passed
along, and the parlor door was open; but I see there warn't nobody in there
but the remainders of Peter; so I shoved on by; but the front door was locked,
and the key wasn't there. Just then I heard somebody coming down the stairs,
back behind me. I run in the parlor, and took a swift look around, and the only
place I see to hide the bag was in the coffin. The lid was shoved along about
a foot, showing the dead man's face down in there, with a wet cloth over it,
and his shroud on. I tucked the money-bag in under the lid, just down beyond
where his hands was crossed, which made me creep, they was so cold, and
then I run back across the room and in behind the door.

The person coming was Mary Jane. She went to the coffin, very soft, and
kneeled down and looked in; then she put up her handkerchief and I see she
begun to cry, though I couldn't hear her, and her back was to me. I slid out, and
as I passed the dining-room I thought I'd make sure them watchers hadn't seen
me; so I looked through the crack and everything was all right. They hadn't
stirred.

I slipped up to bed, feeling ruther blue, on accounts of the thing playing
out that way after I had took so much trouble and run so much resk about it.
Says I, if it could stay where it is, all right; because when we get down the

river a hundred mile or two, I could write back to Mary Jane, and she could dig him up again and get it; but that ain't the thing that's going to happen; the thing that's going to happen is, the money 'll be found when they come to screw on the lid. Then the king 'll get it again, and it 'll be a long day before he gives anybody another chance to smouch it from him. Of course I *wanted* to slide down and get it out of there, but I dasn't try it. Every minute it was getting earlier, now, and pretty soon some of them watchers would begin to stir, and I might get catched—catched with six thousand dollars in my hands that nobody hadn't hired me to take care of. I don't wish to be mixed up in no such business as that, I says to myself.

When I got down stairs in the morning, the parlor was shut up, and the watchers was gone. There warn't nobody around but the family and the widow Bartley and our tribe. I watched their faces to see if anything had been happening, but I couldn't tell.

Towards the middle of the day the undertaker come, with his man, and they set the coffin in the middle of the room on a couple of chairs, and then set all our chairs in rows, and borrowed more from the neighbors till the hall and the parlor and the dining-room was full. I see the coffin lid was the way it was before, but I dasn't go to look in under it, with folks around.

Then the people begun to flock in, and the beats and the girls took seats in the front row at the head of the coffin, and for a half an hour the people filed around slow, in single rank, and looked down at the dead man's face a minute, and some dropped in a tear, and it was all very still and solemn, only the girls and the beats holding handkerchiefs to their eyes and keeping their heads bent, and sobbing a little. There warn't no other sound but the scraping of the feet on the floor, and blowing noses—because people always blows them more at a funeral than they do at other places except church.

When the place was packed full, the undertaker he slid around in his black gloves with his softy soothering ways, putting on the last touches, and getting people and things all shipshape and comfortable, and making no more sound than a cat. He never spoke; he moved people around, he squeezed in late ones, he opened up passage-ways, and done it all with nods, and signs with his hands. Then he took his place over against the wall. He was the softest, glidingest, stealthiest man I ever see; and there warn't no more smile to him than there is to a ham.

They had borrowed a melodeum[1]—a sick one; and when everything was ready, a young woman set down and worked it, and it was pretty skreeky and colicky, and everybody joined in and sung, and Peter was the only one that had a good thing, according to my notion. Then the Reverend Hobson opened up, slow and solemn, and begun to talk; and straight off the most outrageous row busted out in the cellar a body ever heard; it was only one dog, but he made a most powerful racket, and he kept it up, right along; the parson he had to stand there, over the coffin, and wait—you couldn't hear yourself think. It was right down awkward, and nobody didn't seem to know what to do. But pretty soon they see that long-legged undertaker make a sign to the preacher as much as to say, "Don't you worry—just depend on me." Then he stooped down and begun to glide along the wall, just his shoulders showing

---

1. A melodeon, small keyboard organ.

over the people's heads. So he glided along, and the pow-wow and racket getting more and more outrageous all the time; and at last, when he had gone around two sides of the room, he disappears down cellar. Then, in about two seconds we heard a whack, and the dog he finished up with a most amazing howl or two, and then everything was dead still, and the parson begun his solemn talk where he left off. In a minute or two here comes this undertaker's back and shoulders gliding along the wall again; and so he glided, and glided, around three sides of the room, and then rose up, and shaded his mouth with his hands, and stretched his neck out towards the preacher, over the people's heads, and says, in a kind of a coarse whisper, *"He had a rat!"* Then he drooped down and glided along the wall again to his place. You could see it was a great satisfaction to the people, because naturally they wanted to know. A little thing like that don't cost nothing, and it's just the little things that makes a man to be looked up to and liked. There warn't no more popular man in town than what that undertaker was.

Well, the funeral sermon was very good, but pison long and tiresome; and then the king he shoved in and got off some of his usual rubbage, and at last the job was through, and the undertaker begun to sneak up on the coffin with his screw-driver. I was in a sweat then, and watched him pretty keen. But he never meddled at all; just slid the lid along, as soft as mush, and screwed it down tight and fast. So there I was! I didn't know whether the money was in there, or not. So, says I, spose somebody has hogged that bag on the sly?—now how do *I* know whether to write to Mary Jane or not? 'Spose she dug him up and didn't find nothing—what would she think of me? Blame it, I says, I might get hunted up and jailed; I'd better lay low and keep dark, and not write at all; the thing's awful mixed, now; trying to better it, I've worsened it a hundred times, and I wish to goodness I'd just let it alone, dad fetch the whole business!

They buried him, and we come back home, and I went to watching faces again—I couldn't help it, and I couldn't rest easy. But nothing come of it; the faces didn't tell me nothing.

The king he visited around, in the evening, and sweetened every body up, and made himself ever so friendly; and he give out the idea that his congregation over in England would be in a sweat about him, so he must hurry and settle up the estate right away, and leave for home. He was very sorry he was so pushed, and so was everybody; they wished he could stay longer, but they said they could see it couldn't be done. And he said of course him and William would take the girls home with them; and that pleased everybody too, because then the girls would be well fixed, and amongst their own relations; and it pleased the girls, too—tickled them so they clean forgot they ever had a trouble in the world; and told him to sell out as quick as he wanted to, they would be ready. Them poor things was that glad and happy it made my heart ache to see them getting fooled and lied to so, but I didn't see no safe way for me to chip in and change the general tune.

Well, blamed if the king didn't bill the house and the niggers and all the property for auction straight off—sale two days after the funeral; but anybody could buy private beforehand if they wanted to.

So the next day after the funeral, along about noontime, the girls' joy got the first jolt; a couple of nigger traders come along, and the king sold them the niggers reasonable, for three-day drafts[2] as they called it, and away they went, the two sons up the river to Memphis, and their mother down the river to Orleans. I thought them poor girls and them niggers would break their hearts for grief; they cried around each other, and took on so it most made me down sick to see it. The girls said they hadn't ever dreamed of seeing the family separated or sold away from the town. I can't ever get it out of my memory, the sight of them poor miserable girls and niggers hanging around each other's necks and crying; and I reckon I couldn't a stood it all but would a had to bust out and tell on our gang if I hadn't knowed the sale warn't no account and the niggers would be back home in a week or two.

The thing made a big stir in the town, too, and a good many come out flat-footed and said it was scandalous to separate the mother and the children that way. It injured the frauds some; but the old fool he bulled right along, spite of all the duke could say or do, and I tell you the duke was powerful uneasy.

Next day was auction day. About broad-day in the morning, the king and the duke come up in the garret and woke me up, and I see by their look that there was trouble. The king says:

"Was you in my room night before last?"

"No, your majesty"—which was the way I always called him when nobody but our gang warn't around.

"Was you in there yesterday er last night?"

"No, your majesty."

"Honor bright, now—no lies."

"Honor bright, your majesty, I'm telling you the truth. I hain't been anear your room since Miss Mary Jane took you and the duke and showed it to you."

The duke says:

"Have you seen anybody else go in there?"

"No, your grace, not as I remember, I believe."

"Stop and think."

I studied a while, and see my chance, then I says:

"Well, I see the niggers go in there several times."

Both of them give a little jump; and looked like they hadn't ever expected it, and then like they *had*. Then the duke says:

"What, *all* of them?"

"No—leastways not all at once. That is, I don't think I ever see them all come *out* at once but just one time."

"Hello—when was that?"

"It was the day we had the funeral. In the morning. It warn't early, because I overslept. I was just starting down the ladder, and I see them."

"Well, go on, *go on*—what did they do? How'd they act?"

"They didn't do nothing. And they didn't act anyway, much, as fur as I see. They tip-toed away; so I seen, easy enough, that they'd shoved in there to do up your majesty's room, or something, sposing you was up; and found you *warn't* up, and so they was hoping to slide out of the way of trouble without waking you up, if they hadn't already waked you up."

"Great guns, *this* is a go!" says the king; and both of them looked pretty sick, and tolerable silly. They stood there a thinking and scratching their heads, a

---

2. Bank drafts or checks payable three days later.

minute, and then the duke he bust into a kind of a little raspy chuckle, and says:

"It does beat all, how neat the niggers played their hand. They let on to be *sorry* they was going out of this region! and I believed they *was* sorry. And so did you, and so did everybody. Don't ever tell *me* any more that a nigger ain't got any histrionic talent. Why, the way they played that thing, it would fool *anybody.* In my opinion there's a fortune in 'em. If I had capital and a theatre, I wouldn't want a better lay out than that—and here we've gone and sold 'em for a song. Yes, and ain't privileged to sing the song, yet. Say, where *is* that song?—that draft."

"In the bank for to be collected. Where *would* it be?"

"Well, *that's* all right then, thank goodness."

Says I, kind of timid-like:

"Is something gone wrong?"

The king whirls on me and rips out:

"None o' your business! You keep your head shet, and mind y'r own affairs—if you got any. Long as you're in this town, don't you forget *that,* you hear?" Then he says to the duke, "We got to jest swaller it, and say noth'n: mum's the word for *us.*"

As they was starting down the ladder, the duke he chuckles again, and says:

"Quick sales *and* small profits! It's a good business—yes."

The king snarls around on him and says,

"I was trying to do for the best, in sellin' 'm out so quick. If the profits has turned out to be none, lackin' considable, and none to carry, is it my fault any more'n it's yourn?"

"Well, *they'd* be in this house yet, and we *wouldn't* if I could a got my advice listened to."

The king sassed back, as much as was safe for him, and then swapped around and lit into *me* again. He give me down the banks[3] for not coming and *telling* him I see the niggers come out of his room acting that way—said any fool would a *knowed* something was up. And then waltzed in and cussed *himself* a while; and said it all come of him not laying late and taking his natural rest that morning, and he'd be blamed if he'd ever do it again. So they went off a jawing; and I felt dreadful glad I'd worked it all off onto the niggers and yet hadn't done the niggers no harm by it.

## Chapter XXVIII

By-and-by it was getting-up time; so I come down the ladder and started for down stairs, but as I come to the girls' room, the door was open, and I see Mary Jane setting by her old hair trunk, which was open and she'd been packing things in it—getting ready to go to England. But she had stopped now, with a folded gown in her lap, and had her face in her hands, crying. I felt awful bad to see it; of course anybody would. I went in there, and says:

"Miss Mary Jane, you can't abear to see people in trouble, and *I* can't—most always. Tell me about it."

So she done it. And it was the niggers—I just expected it. She said the beautiful trip to England was most about spoiled for her; she didn't know *how*

3. A cussing out.

she was ever going to be happy there, knowing the mother and the children warn't ever going to see each other no more—and then busted out bitterer than ever, and flung up her hands, and says

"Oh, dear, dear, to think they ain't *ever* going to see each other any more!"

"But they *will*—and inside of two weeks—and I *know* it!" says I.

Laws it was out before I could think!—and before I could budge, she throws her arms around my neck, and told me to say it *again*, say it *again*, say it *again!*

I see I had spoke too sudden, and said too much, and was in a close place. I asked her to let me think a minute; and she set there, very impatient and excited, and handsome, but looking kind of happy and eased-up, like a person that's had a tooth pulled out. So I went to studying it out. I says to myself, I reckon a body that ups and tells the truth when he is in a tight place, is taking considerable many resks, though I ain't had no experience, and can't say for certain; but it looks so to me, anyway; and yet here's a case where I'm blest if it don't look to me like the truth is better, and actuly *safer,* than pa lie. I must lay it by in my mind, and think it over some time or other, it's so kind of strange and unregular. I never see nothing like it. Well, I says to myself at last, I'm agoing to chance it; I'll up and tell the truth this time, though it does seem most like setting down on a kag of powder and touching it off just to see where you'll go to. Then I says:

"Miss Mary Jane, is there any place out of town a little ways, where you could go and stay three or four days?"

"Yes—Mr. Lothrop's. Why?"

"Never mind why, yet. If I'll tell you how I know the niggers will see each other again—inside of two weeks—here in this house—and *prove* how I know it—will you go to Mr. Lothrop's and stay four days?"

"Four days!" she says; "I'll stay a year!"

"All right," I says, "I don't want nothing more out of *you* than just your word—I druther have it than another man's kiss-the-Bible." She smiled, and reddened up very sweet, and I says, "If you don't mind it, I'll shut the door—and bolt it."

Then I come back and set down again, and says:

"Don't you holler. Just set still, and take it like a man. I got to tell the truth, and you want to brace up, Miss Mary, because it's a bad kind, and going to be hard to take, but there ain't no help for it. These uncles of yourn ain't no uncles at all—they're a couple of frauds—regular dead-beats. There, now we're over the worst of it—you can stand the rest middling easy."

It jolted her up like everything, of course; but I was over the shoal water now, so I went right along, her eyes a blazing higher and higher all the time, and told her every blame thing, from where we first struck that young fool going up to the steamboat, clear through to where she flung herself onto the king's breast at the front door and he kissed her sixteen or seventeen times—and then up she jumps, with her face afire like sunset, and says:

"The brute! Come—don't waste a minute—not a *second*—we'll have them tarred and feathered, and flung in the river!"[4]

4. The victim of this fairly commonplace mob punishment was tied to a rail, smeared with hot tar, and covered with feathers. Then the victim would be ridden out of town on the rail to the jeers of the mob.

Says I;

"Cert'nly. But do you mean, *before* you go to Mr. Lothrop's, or—"

"Oh," she says, "what am I *thinking* about!" she says, and set right down again. "Don't mind what I said—please don't—you *won't*, now, *will* you?" Laying her silky hand on mine in that kind of a way that I said I would die first. "I never thought, I was so stirred up," she says; "now go on, and I won't do so any more. You tell me what to do, and whatever you say, I'll do it."

"Well," I says, "it's a rough gang, them two frauds, and I'm fixed so I got to travel with them a while longer, whether I want to or not—I druther not tell you why—and if you was to blow on them this town would get me out of their claws, and *I'd* be all right, but there'd be another person that you don't know about who'd be in big trouble. Well, we got to save *him*, hain't we? Of course. Well, then, we won't blow on them."

Saying them words put a good idea in my head. I see how maybe I could get me and Jim rid of the frauds; get them jailed here, and then leave. But I didn't want to run the raft in day-time, without anybody aboard to answer questions but me; so I didn't want the plan to begin working till pretty late to-night. I says:

"Miss Mary Jane, I'll tell you what we'll do—and you won't have to stay at Mr. Lothrop's so long, nuther. How fur is it?"

"A little short of four miles—right out in the country, back here."

"Well, that'll answer. Now you go along out there, and lay low till nine or half-past, to-night, and then get them to fetch you home again—tell them you've thought of something. If you get here before eleven, put a candle in this window, and if I don't turn up, wait *till* eleven, and *then* if I don't turn up it means I'm gone, and out of the way, and safe. Then you come out and spread the news around, and get these beats jailed."

"Good," she says, "I'll do it."

"And if it just happens so that I don't get away, but get took up along with them, you must up and say I told you the whole thing beforehand, and you must stand by me all you can."

"Stand by you, indeed I will. They sha'n't touch a hair of your head!" she says, and I see her nostrils spread and her eyes snap when she said it, too.

"If I get away, I sha'n't be here," I says, "to prove these rapscallions ain't your uncles, and I couldn't do it if I *was* here. I could swear they was beats and bummers, that's all; though that's worth something. Well, there's others can do that better than what I can—and they're people that ain't going to be doubted as quick as I'd be. I'll tell you how to find them. Gimme a pencil and a piece of paper. There—'*Royal Nonesuch, Bricksville.*' Put it away, and don't lose it. When the court wants to find out something about these two, let them send up to Bricksville and say they've got the men that played the Royal Nonesuch, and ask for some witnesses—why, you'll have that entire town down here before you can hardly wink, Miss Mary. And they'll come a-biling, too."

I judged we had got everything fixed about right, now. So I says:

"Just let the auction go right along, and don't worry. Nobody don't have to pay for the things they buy till a whole day after the auction, on accounts of the short notice, and they ain't going out of this till they get that money—and the way we've fixed it the sale ain't going to count, and they ain't going to *get* no money. It's just like the way it was with the niggers—it warn't no sale, and the niggers will be back before long. Why, they can't collect the money for the *niggers,* yet—they're in the worst kind of a fix, Miss Mary."

"Well," she says, "I'll run down to breakfast now, and then I'll start straight for Mr. Lothrop's."

" 'Deed, *that* ain't the ticket, Miss Mary Jane," I says, "by no manner of means; go *before* breakfast."

"Why?"

"What did you reckon I wanted you to go at all for, Miss Mary?"

"Well, I never thought—and come to think, I don't know. What was it?"

"Why, it's because you ain't one of these leather-face people. I don't want no better book than what your face is. A body can set down and read it off like coarse paint. Do you reckon you can go and face your uncles, when they come to kiss you good-morning, and never—"

"There, there, don't! Yes, I'll go before breakfast—I'll be glad to. And leave my sisters with them?"

"Yes—never mind about them. They've got to stand it yet a while. They might suspicion something if all of you was to go. I don't want you to see them, nor your sisters, nor nobody in this town—if a neighbor was to ask how is your uncles this morning, your face would tell something. No, you go right along, Miss Mary Jane, and I'll fix it with all of them. I'll tell Miss Susan to give your love to your uncles and say you've went away for a few hours for to get a little rest and change, or to see a friend, and you'll be back to-night or early in the morning."

"Gone to see a friend is all right, but I won't have my love given to them."

"Well, then, it sha'n't be." It was well enough to tell *her* so—no harm in it. It was only a little thing to do, and no trouble; and it's the little things that smoothes people's roads the most, down here below; it would make Mary Jane comfortable, and it wouldn't cost nothing. Then I says: "There's one more thing—that bag of money."

"Well, they've got that; and it makes me feel pretty silly to think *how* they got it."

"No, you're out, there. They hain't got it."

"Why, who's got it?"

"I wish I knowed, but I don't. I *had* it, because I stole it from them: and I stole it to give to you; and I know where I hid it, but I'm afraid it ain't there no more. I'm awful sorry, Miss Mary Jane, I'm just as sorry as I can be; but I done the best I could; I did, honest. I come nigh getting caught, and I had to shove it into the first place I come to, and run—and it warn't a good place."

"Oh, stop blaming yourself—it's too bad to do it, and I won't allow it—you couldn't help it; it wasn't your fault. Where did you hide it?"

I didn't want to set her to thinking about her troubles again; and I couldn't seem to get my mouth to tell her what would make her see that corpse laying in the coffin with that bag of money on his stomach. So for a minute I didn't say nothing—then I says:

"I'd rather not *tell* you where I put it, Miss Mary Jane, if you don't mind letting me off; but I'll write it for you on a piece of paper, and you can read it along the road to Mr. Lothrop's; if you want to. Do you reckon that'll do?"

"Oh, yes."

So I wrote: "I put it in the coffin. It was in there when you was crying there, away in the night. I was behind the door, and I was mighty sorry for you, Miss Mary Jane."

It made my eyes water a little, to remember her crying there all by herself in the night, and them devils laying there right under her own roof, shaming her and robbing her; and when I folded it up and give it to her, I see the water come into her eyes, too; and she shook me by the hand, hard, and says:

"*Good*-bye—I'm going to do everything just as you've told me; and if I don't ever see you again, I sha'n't ever forget you, and I'll think of you a many and a many a time, and I'll *pray* for you, too!"—and she was gone.

Pray for me! I reckoned if she knowed me she'd take a job that was more nearer her size. But I bet she done it, just the same—she was just that kind. She had the grit to pray for Judus if she took the notion—there warn't no backdown to her, I judge. You may say what you want to, but in my opinion she had more sand in her than any girl I ever see; in my opinion she was just full of sand.[5] It sounds like flattery, but it ain't no flattery. And when it comes to beauty—and goodness too—she lays over them all. I hain't ever seen her since that time that I see her go out of that door; no, I hain't ever seen her since, but I reckon I've thought of her a many and a many a million times, and of her saying she would pray for me; and if ever I'd a thought it would do any good for me to pray for *her,* blamed if I wouldn't a done it or bust.

Well, Mary Jane she lit out the back way, I reckon; because nobody see her go. When I struck Susan and the hare-lip, I says:

"What's the name of them people over on t'other side of the river that you all goes to see sometimes?"

They says:

"There's several; but it's the Proctors, mainly."

"That's the name," I says; "I most forgot it. Well, Miss Mary Jane she told me to tell you she's gone over there in a dreadful hurry—one of them's sick."

"Which one?"

"I don't know; leastways I kinder forget; but I think it's—"

"Sakes alive, I hope it ain't *Hanner?*"

"I'm sorry to say it," I says, "but Hanner's the very one."

"My goodness—and she so well only last week! Is she took bad?"

"It ain't no name for it. They set up with her all night, Miss Mary Jane said, and they don't think she'll last many hours."

"Only think of that, now! What's the matter with her!"

I couldn't think of anything reasonable, right off that way, so I says:

"Mumps."

"Mumps your granny! They don't set up with people that's got the mumps."

"They don't, don't they? You better bet they do with *these* mumps. These mumps is different. It's a new kind, Miss Mary Jane said."

"How's it a new kind?"

"Because it's mixed up with other things."

"What other things?"

"Well, measles, and whooping-cough, and erysiplas, and consumption, and yaller janders, and brain fever, and I don't know what all."

5. Courage, guts.

"My land! And they call it the *mumps*?"

"That's what Miss Mary Jane said."

"Well, what in the nation do they call it the *mumps* for?"

"Why, because it *is* the mumps. That's what it starts with."

"Well, ther' ain't no sense in it. A body might stump his toe, and take pison, and fall down the well, and break his neck, and bust his brains out, and somebody come along and ask what killed him, and some numskull up and say, 'Why, he stumped his *toe*.' Would ther' be any sense in that? *No*. And ther' ain't no sense in *this*, nuther. Is it ketching?"

"Is it *ketching*? Why, how you talk. Is a *harrow* catching?—in the dark? If you don't hitch onto one tooth, you're bound to on another, ain't you? And you can't get away with that tooth without fetching the whole harrow along, can you? Well, these kind of mumps is a kind of a harrow, as you may say— and it ain't no slouch of a harrow, nuther, you come to get it hitched on good."

"Well, it's awful, *I* think," says the hare-lip. "I'll go to Uncle Harvey and—"

"Oh, yes," I says, "I *would*. Of *course* I would. I wouldn't lose no time."

"Well, why wouldn't you?"

"Just look at it a minute, and maybe you can see. Hain't your uncles obleeged to get along home to England as fast as they can? And do you reckon they'd be mean enough to go off and leave you to go all that journey by yourselves? *You* know they'll wait for you. So fur, so good. Your uncle Harvey's a preacher, ain't he? Very well, then; is a *preacher* going to deceive a steamboat clerk? is he going to deceive a *ship clerk?*—so as to get them to let Miss Mary Jane go aboard? Now *you* know he ain't. What *will* he do, then? Why, he'll say, 'It's a great pity, but my church matters has got to get along the best way they can; for my niece has been exposed to the dreadful pluribus-unum[6] mumps, and so it's my bounden duty to set down here and wait the three months it takes to show on her if she's got it.' But never mind, if you think it's best to tell your uncle Harvey—"

"Shucks, and stay fooling around here when we could all be having good times in England whilst we was waiting to find out whether Mary Jane's got it or not? Why, you talk like a muggins."[7]

"Well, anyway, maybe you better tell some of the neighbors."

"Listen at that, now. You do beat all, for natural stupidity. Can't you *see* that *they'd* go and tell? Ther' ain't no way but just to not tell anybody at *all*."

"Well, maybe you're right—yes, I judge you *are* right."

"But I reckon we ought to tell Uncle Harvey she's gone out a while, anyway, so he wont be uneasy about her?"

"Yes, Miss Mary Jane she wanted you to do that. She says, 'Tell them to give Uncle Harvey and William my love and a kiss, and say I've run over the river to see Mr.—Mr.—what *is* the name of that rich family your uncle Peter used to think so much of?—I mean the one that—"

"Why, you must mean the Apthorps, ain't it?"

"Of course; bother them kind of names, a body can't ever seem to remember them, half the time, somehow. Yes, she said, say she has run over for to ask the Apthorps to be sure and come to the auction and buy this house,

---

6. Huck reaches for the handiest Latin phrase he could be expected to know; meaning "out of many, one," the phrase is appropriate.

7. A fool.

because she allowed her uncle Peter would ruther they had it than anybody else; and she's going to stick to them till they say they'll come, and then, if she ain't too tired, she's coming home; and if she is, she'll be home in the morning anyway. She said, don't say nothing about the Proctors, but only about the Apthorps—which'll be perfectly true, because she *is* going there to speak about their buying the house; I know it, because she told me so, herself."

"All right," they said, and cleared out to lay for their uncles, and give them the love and the kisses, and tell them the message.

Everything was all right now. The girls wouldn't say nothing because they wanted to go to England; and the king and the duke would ruther Mary Jane was off working for the auction than around in reach of Doctor Robinson. I felt very good; I judged I had done it pretty neat—I reckoned Tom Sawyer couldn't a done it no neater himself. Of course he would a throwed more style into it, but I can't do that very handy, not being brung up to it.

Well, they held the auction in the public square, along towards the end of the afternoon, and it strung along, and strung along, and the old man he was on hand and looking his level piousest, up there longside of the auctioneer, and chipping in a little Scripture, now and then, or a little goody-goody saying, of some kind, and the duke he was around goo-gooing for sympathy all he knowed how, and just spreading himself generly.

But by-and-by the thing dragged through, and everything was sold. Everything but a little old trifling lot in the graveyard. So they'd got to work *that* off—I never see such a girafft as the king was for wanting to swallow *everything*. Well, whilst they was at it, a steamboat landed, and in about two minutes up comes a crowd a whooping and yelling and laughing and carrying on, and singing out:

"*Here's* your opposition line! here's your two sets o' heirs to old Peter Wilks—and you pays your money and you takes your choice!"

### Chapter XXIX

They was fetching a very nice looking old gentleman along, and a nice looking younger one, with his right arm in a sling. And my souls, how the people yelled, and laughed, and kept it up. But I didn't see no joke about it, and I judged it would strain the duke and the king some to see any. I reckoned they'd turn pale. But no, nary a pale did *they* turn. The duke he never let on he suspicioned what was up, but just went a goo-gooing around, happy and satisfied, like a jug that's googling out buttermilk; and as for the king, he just gazed and gazed down sorrowful on them newcomers like it give him the stomach-ache in his very heart to think there could be such frauds and rascals in the world. Oh, he done it admirable. Lots of the principal people gethered around the king, to let him see they was on his side. That old gentleman that had just come looked all puzzled to death. Pretty soon he begun to speak, and I see, straight off, he pronounced *like* an Englishman, not the king's way, though the king's *was* pretty good, for an imitation. I can't give the old gent's words, nor I can't imitate him; but he turned around to the crowd, and says, about like this:

"This is a surprise to me which I wasn't looking for; and I'll acknowledge, candid and frank, I ain't very well fixed to meet it and answer it; for my brother and me has had misfortunes, he's broke his arm, and our baggage got put off at a town above here, last night in the night by a mistake. I am Peter Wilks's brother Harvey, and this is his brother William, which can't hear nor speak—and can't even make signs to amount to much, now 't he's only got one hand to work them with. We are who we say we are; and in a day or two, when I get the baggage, I can prove it. But, up till then, I won't say nothing more, but go to the hotel and wait."

So him and the new dummy started off; and the king he laughs, and blethers out:

"Broke his arm—*very* likely *ain't* it?—and very convenient, too, for a fraud that's got to make signs, and hain't learnt how. Lost their baggage! That's *mighty* good!—and mighty ingenious—under the *circumstances!*"

So he laughed again; and so did everybody else, except three or four, or maybe half a dozen. One of these was that doctor; another one was a sharp looking gentleman, with a carpet-bag of the old-fashioned kind made out of carpet-stuff, that had just come off of the steamboat and was talking to him in a low voice, and glancing towards the king now and then and nodding their heads—it was Levi Bell, the lawyer that was gone up to Louisville; and another one was a big rough husky that come along and listened to all the old gentleman said, and was listening to the king now. And when the king got done, this husky up and says:

"Say, looky here; if you are Harvey Wilks, when'd you come to this town?"

"The day before the funeral, friend," says the king.

"But what time o' day?"

"In the evenin'—'bout an hour er two before sundown."

"*How'd* you come?"

"I come down on the *Susan Powell,* from Cincinnati."

"Well, then, how'd you come to be up at the Pint in the *mornin'*—in a canoe?"

"I warn't up at the Pint in the mornin'."

"It's a lie."

Several of them jumped for him and begged him not to talk that way to an old man and a preacher.

"Preacher be hanged, he's a fraud and a lair. He was up at the Pint that mornin'. I live up there, don't I? Well, I was up there, and he was up there. I *see* him there. He come in a canoe, along with Tim Collins and a boy."

The doctor he up and says:

"Would you know the boy again if you was to see him, Hines?"

"I reckon I would, but I don't know. Why, yonder he is, now. I know him perfectly easy."

It was me he pointed at. The doctor says:

"Neighbors. I don't know whether the new couple is frauds or not; but if *these* two ain't frauds, I am an idiot, that's all. I think it's our duty to see that they don't get away from here till we've looked into this thing. Come along, Hines; come along, the rest of you. We'll take these fellows to the tavern and affront them with t'other couple, and I reckon we'll find out *something* before we get through."

It was nuts for the crowd, though maybe not for the king's friends; so we all started. It was about sundown. The doctor he led me along by the hand, and was plenty kind enough, but he never let *go* my hand.

We all got in a big room in the hotel, and lit up some candles, and fetched in the new couple. First, the doctor says:

"I don't wish to be too hard on these two men, but *I* think they're frauds, and they may have complices that we don't know nothing about. If they have, won't the complices get away with that bag of gold Peter Wilks left? It ain't unlikely. If these men ain't frauds, they won't object to sending for that money and letting us keep it till they prove they're all right—ain't that so?"

Everybody agreed to that. So I judged they had our gang in a pretty tight place, right at the outstart. But the king he only looked sorrowful, and says:

"Gentlemen, I wish the money was there, for I ain't got no disposition to throw anything in the way of a fair, open, out-and-out investigation o' this misable business; but alas, the money ain't there; you k'n send and see, if you want to."

"Where is it, then?"

"Well, when my niece give it to me to keep for her, I took and hid it inside o' the straw tick o' my bed, not wishin' to bank it for the few days we'd be here, and considerin' the bed a safe place, we not bein' used to niggers, and suppos'n' 'em honest, like servants in England. The niggers stole it the very next mornin' after I had went down stairs; and when I sold 'em, I hadn't missed the money yit, so they got clean away with it. My servant here k'n tell you 'bout it gentlemen."

The doctor and several said "Shucks!" and I see nobody didn't altogether believe him. One man asked me if I see the niggers steal it. I said no, but I see them sneaking out of the room and hustling away, and I never thought nothing, only I reckoned they was afraid they had waked up my master and was trying to get away before he made trouble with them. That was all they asked me. Then the doctor whirls on me and says:

"Are *you* English too?"

I says yes; and him and some others laughed, and said, "Stuff!"

Well, then they sailed in on the general investigation, and there we had it, up and down, hour in, hour out, and nobody never said a word about supper, nor ever seemed to think about it—and so they kept it up, and kept it up; and it *was* the worst mixed-up thing you ever see. They made the king tell his yarn, and they made the old gentleman tell his'n; and anybody but a lot of prejudiced chuckleheads would a *seen* that the old gentleman was spinning truth and t'other one lies. And by-and-by they had me up to tell what I knowed. The king he give me a left-handed look out of the corner of his eye, and so I knowed enough to talk on the right side. I begun to tell about Sheffield, and how we lived there, and all about the English Wilkses, and so on; but I didn't get pretty fur till the doctor begun to laugh; and Levi Bell, the lawyer says:

"Set down, my boy, I wouldn't strain myself, if I was you. I reckon you ain't used to lying, it don't seem to come handy; what you want is practice. You do it pretty awkward."

I didn't care nothing for the compliment, but I was glad to be let off, anyway.

The doctor he started to say something, and turns and says:

"If you'd been in town at first, Levi Bell—"

The king broke in and reached out his hand, and says:

"Why, is this my poor dead brother's old friend that he's wrote so often about?"

The lawyer and him shook hands, and the lawyer smiled and looked pleased, and they talked right along a while, and then got to one side and talked low; and at last the lawyer speaks up and says:

"That'll fix it. I'll take the order and send it, along with your brother's, and then they'll know it's all right."

So they got some paper and a pen, and the king he set down and twisted his head to one side, and chawed his tongue, and scrawled off something; and then they give the pen to the duke—and then for the first time, the duke looked sick. But he took the pen and wrote. So then the lawyer turns to the new old gentleman and says:

"You and your brother please write a line or two and sign your names."

The old gentleman wrote, but nobody couldn't read it. The lawyer looked powerful astonished, and says:

"Well, it beats *me*"—and snaked a lot of old letters out of his pocket, and examined them, and then examined the old man's writing, and then *them* again; and then says: "These old letters is from Harvey Wilks; and here's *these* two's handwritings, and anybody can see *they* didn't write them" (the king and the duke looked sold and foolish, I tell you, to see how the lawyer had took them in), "and here's *this* old gentleman's handwriting, and anybody can tell, easy enough, *he* didn't write them—fact is, the scratches he makes ain't properly *writing,* at all. Now here's some letters from—"

The new old gentleman says:

"If you please, let me explain. Nobody can read my hand but my brother there—so he copies for me. It's *his* hand you've got there, not mine."

"*Well!*" says the lawyer, "this *is* a state of things. I've got some of William's letters too; so if you'll get him to write a line or so we can com—"

"He *can't* write with his left hand," says the old gentleman. "If he could use his right hand, you would see that he wrote his own letters and mine too. Look at both, please—they're by the same hand."

The lawyer done it, and says:

"I believe it's so—and if it ain't so, there's a heap stronger resemblance than I'd noticed before, anyway. Well, well, well! I thought we was right on the track of a slution, but it's gone to grass, partly. But anyway, *one* thing is proved—*these* two ain't either of 'em Wilkses"—and he wagged his head towards the king and the duke.

Well, what do you think?—that muleheaded old fool wouldn't give in *then!* Indeed he wouldn't. Said it warn't no fair test. Said his brother William was the cussedest joker in the world, and hadn't *tried* to write—*he* see William was going to play one of his jokes the minute he put the pen to paper. And so he warmed up and went warbling and warbling right along, till he was actuly beginning to believe what he was saying, *himself*—but pretty soon the new old gentleman broke in, and says:

"I've thought of something. Is there anybody here that helped to lay out my br—helped to lay out the late Peter Wilks for burying?"

"Yes," says somebody, "me and Ab Turner done it. We're both here."

Then the old man turns towards the king, and says:

"Peraps this gentleman can tell me what was tatooed on his breast?"

Blamed if the king didn't have to brace up mighty quick, or he'd a squshed down like a bluff bank that the river has cut under, it took him so sudden—and mind you, it was a thing that was calculated to make most *anybody* sqush to get fetched such a solid one as that without any notice—because how was *he* going to know what was tatooed on the man? He whitened a little; he couldn't help it; and it was mighty still in there, and everybody bending a little forwards and gazing at him. Says I to myself, *Now* he'll throw up the sponge—there ain't no more use. Well, did he? A body can't hardly believe it, but he didn't. I reckon he thought he'd keep the thing up till he tired them people out, so they'd thin out, and him and the duke could break loose and get away. Anyway, he set there, and pretty soon he begun to smile, and says:

"Mf! It's a *very* tough question, *ain't* it! *Yes,* sir, I k'n tell you what's tatooed on his breast. It's jest a small, thin, blue arrow—that's what it is; and if you don't look clost, you can't see it. *Now* what do you say—hey?"

Well, *I* never see anything like that old blister for clean out-and-out cheek.

The new old gentleman turns brisk towards Ab Turner and his pard, and his eye lights up like he judged he'd got the king *this* time, and says:

"There—you've heard what he said! Was there any such mark on Peter Wilks's breast?"

Both of them spoke up and says:

"We didn't see no such mark."

"Good!" says the old gentleman. "Now, what you *did* see on his breast was a small dim P, and a B (which is an initial he dropped when he was young), and a W, with dashes between them, so: P—B—W"—and he marked them that way on a piece of paper. "Come—ain't that what you saw?"

Both of them spoke up again, and says:

"No, we *didn't.* We never seen any marks at all."

Well, everybody *was* in a state of mind, now; and they sings out:

"The whole *bilin'* of 'm 's frauds! Le's duck 'em! le's drown 'em! le's ride 'em on a rail!" and everybody was whooping at once, and there was a rattling pow-wow. But the lawyer he jumps on the table and yells, and says:

"Gentlemen—gentle*men*! Hear me just a word—just a *single* word—if you PLEASE! There's one way yet—let's go and dig up the corpse and look."

That took them.

"Hooray!" they all shouted, and was starting right off; but the lawyer and the doctor sung out:

"Hold on, hold on! Collar all these four men and the boy, and fetch *them* along, too!"

"We'll do it!" they all shouted: "and if we don't find them marks we'll lynch the whole gang!"

I *was* scared, now, I tell you. But there warn't no getting away, you know. They gripped us all, and marched us right along, straight for the graveyard, which was a mile and a half down the river, and the whole town at our heels, for we made noise enough, and it was only nine in the evening.

As we went by our house I wished I hadn't sent Mary Jane out of town; because now if I could tip her the wink, she'd light out and save me, and blow on our dead-beats.

Well, we swarmed along down the river road, just carrying on like wild-cats; and to make it more scary, the sky was darking up, and the lightning beginning to wink and flitter, and the wind to shiver amongst the leaves. This was the most awful trouble and most dangersome I ever was in; and I was kinder stunned; everything was going so different from what I had allowed for; stead of being fixed so I could take my own time, if I wanted to, and see all the fun, and have Mary Jane at my back to save me and set me free when the close-fit come, here was nothing in the world betwixt me and sudden death but just them tatoo-marks. If they didn't find them—

I couldn't bear to think about it; and yet, somehow, I couldn't think about nothing else. It got darker and darker, and it was a beautiful time to give the crowd the slip; but that big husky had me by the wrist—Hines—and a body might as well try to give Goliar[8] the slip. He dragged me right along, he was so excited; and I had to run to keep up.

When they got there they swarmed into the graveyard and washed over it like an overflow. And when they got to the grave, they found they had about a hundred times as many shovels as they wanted, but nobody hadn't thought to fetch a lantern. But they sailed into digging, anyway, by the flicker of the lightning, and sent a man to the nearest house a half a mile off, to borrow one.

So they dug and dug, like everything; and it got awful dark, and the rain started, and the wind swished and swushed along, and the lightning come brisker and brisker, and the thunder boomed; but them people never took no notice of it, they was so full of this business; and one minute you could see everything and every face in that big crowd, and the shovelfuls of dirt sailing up out of the grave, and the next second the dark wiped it all out, and you couldn't see nothing at all.

At last they got out the coffin, and begun to unscrew the lid, and then such another crowding, and shouldering, and shoving as there was, to scrouge in and get a sight, you never see; and in the dark, that way, it was awful. Hines he hurt my wrist dreadful, pulling and tugging so, and I reckon he clean forgot I was in the world, he was so excited and panting.

All of a sudden the lightning let go a perfect sluice of white glare, and somebody sings out:

"By the living jingo, here's the bag of gold on his breast!"

Hines let out a whoop, like everybody else, and dropped my wrist and give a big surge to bust his way in and get a look, and the way I lit out and shinned for the road in the dark, there ain't nobody can tell.

I had the road all to myself, and I fairly flew—leastways I had it all to myself except the solid dark, and the now-and-then glares, and the buzzing of the rain, and the thrashing of the wind, and the splitting of the thunder; and sure as you are born I did clip it along!

When I struck the town, I see there warn't nobody out in the storm, so I never hunted for no back streets, but humped it straight through the main one; and when I begun to get towards our house I aimed my eye and set it. No light there; the house all dark—which made me feel sorry and disappointed, I didn't know why. But at last, just as I was sailing by, *flash* comes the light in Mary Jane's window! and my heart swelled up sudden, like to bust; and the same second the house and all was behind me in the dark, and wasn't ever going to be before me no more in this world. She *was* the best girl I ever see, and had the most sand.

The minute I was far enough above the town to see I could make the tow-head, I begun to look sharp for a boat to borrow; and the first time the light-

8. Goliath, a Philistine giant who challenged the Israelites. David, a young shepherd, accepted his challenge and killed him with a stone thrown from a sling.

ning showed me one that wasn't chained, I snatched it and shoved. It was a canoe, and warn't fastened with nothing but a rope. The tow-head was a rattling big distance off, away out there in the middle of the river, but I didn't lose no time; and when I struck the raft at last, I was so fagged I would a just laid down to blow and gasp if I could afforded it. But I didn't. As I sprung aboard I sung out:

"Out with you Jim, and set her loose! Glory be to goodness, we're shut of them!"

Jim lit out, and was a coming for me with both arms spread, he was so full of joy; but when I glimpsed him in the lightning, my heart shot up in my mouth, and I went overboard backwards; for I forgot he was old King Lear and a drownded A-rab all in one, and it most scared the livers and lights out of me. But Jim fished me out, and was going to hug me and bless me, and so on, he was so glad I was back and we was shut of the king and the duke, but I says:

"Not now—have it for breakfast, have it for breakfast! Cut loose and let her slide!"

So, in two seconds, away we went, a sliding down the river, and it *did* seem so good to be free again and all by ourselves on the big river and nobody to bother us. I had to skip around a bit, and jump up and crack my heels a few times, I couldn't help it; but about the third crack, I noticed a sound that I knowed mighty well—and held my breath and listened and waited—and sure enough, when the next flash busted out over the water, here they come!—and just a laying to their oars and making their skiff hum! It was the king and the duke.

So I wilted right down onto the planks, then, and give up; and it was all I could do to keep from crying.

## Chapter XXX

When they got aboard, the king went for me, and shook me by the collar, and says:

"Tryin' to give us the slip, was ye, you pup! Tired of our company—hey!" I says:

"No, your majesty, we warn't—*please* don't, your majesty!"

"Quick, then, and tell us what *was* your idea, or I'll shake the insides out o' you!"

"Honest, I'll tell you everything, just as it happened, your majesty. The man that had aholt of me was very good to me, and kept saying he had a boy about as big as me that died last year, and he was sorry to see a boy in such a dangerous fix; and when they was all took by surprise by finding the gold, and made a rush for the coffin, he lets go of me and whispers, 'Heel it, now, or they'll hang ye, sure!' and I lit out. It didn't seem no good for *me* to stay—I couldn't do nothing, and I didn't want to be hung if I could get away. So I never stopped running till I found the canoe; and when I got here I told Jim to hurry, or they'd catch me and hang me yet, and said I was afeard you and the duke wasn't alive, now, and I was awful sorry, and so was Jim, and was awful glad when we see you coming, you may ask Jim if I didn't."

Jim said it was so; and the king told him to shut up, and said, "Oh, yes, it's *mighty* likely!" and shook me up again, and said he reckoned he'd drownded me. But the duke says:

"Leggo the boy, you old idiot! Would *you* a done any different? Did you inquire around for *him,* when you got loose? *I* don't remember it."

So the king let go of me, and begun to cuss that town and everybody in it. But the duke says:

"You better a blame sight give *yourself* a good cussing, for you're the one that's entitled to it most. You hain't done a thing, from the start, that had any sense in it, except coming out so cool and cheeky with that imaginary blue-arrow mark. That *was* bright—it was right down bully; and it was the thing that saved us. For if it hadn't been for that, they'd a jailed us till them Englishmen's baggage come—and then—the penitentiary, you bet! But that trick took 'em to the graveyard, and the gold done us a still bigger kindness; for if the excited fools hadn't let go all holts and made that rush to get a look, we'd a slept in our cravats to-night—cravats warranted to *wear,* too—longer than *we'd* need 'em."

They was still a minute—thinking—then the king says, kind of absent-minded like:

"Mf! And we reckoned the *niggers* stole it!"

That made me squirm!

"Yes," says the duke, kinder slow, and deliberate, and sarcastic, "*We* did."

After about a half a minute, the king drawls out:

"Leastways—*I* did."

The duke says, the same way:

"On the contrary—*I* did."

The king kind of ruffles up, and says:

"Looky here, Bilgewater, what'r you referrin' to?"

The duke says, pretty brisk:

"When it comes to that, maybe you'll let me ask, what was *you* referring to?"

"Shucks!" says the king, very sarcastic; "but *I* don't know—maybe you was asleep, and didn't know what you was about."

The duke bristles right up, now, and says:

"Oh, let *up* on this cussed nonsense—do you take me for a blame' fool? Don't you reckon *I* know who hid that money in that coffin?"

"*Yes,* sir! I know you *do* know—because you done it yourself!"

"It's a lie!"—and the duke went for him. The king sings out:

"Take y'r hands off!—leggo my throat!—I take it all back!"

The duke says:

"Well, you just own up, first, that you *did* hide that money there, intending to give me the slip one of these days, and come back and dig it up, and have it all to yourself."

"Wait jest a minute, duke—answer me this one question, honest and fair; if you didn't put the money there, say it, and I'll b'lieve you, and take back everything I said."

"You old scoundrel, I didn't, and you know I didn't. There, now!"

"Well, then, I b'lieve you. But answer me only jest this one more—now *don't* git mad; didn't you have it in your *mind* to hook the money and hide it?"

The duke never said nothing for a little bit; then he says:

"Well—I don't care if I *did*, I didn't *do* it, anyway. But you not only had it in mind to do it, but you *done* it."

"I wisht I may never die if I done it, duke, and that's honest. I won't say I warn't *goin'* to do it, because I *was*; but you—I mean somebody—got in ahead o' me."

"It's a lie! You done it, and you got to *say* you done it, or—"

The king begun to gurgle, and then he gasps out:

" 'Nough!—I *own up!*"

I was very glad to hear him say that, it made me feel much more easier than what I was feeling before. So the duke took his hands off, and says:

"If you ever deny it again, I'll drown you. It's *well* for you to set there and blubber like a baby—it's fitten for you, after the way you've acted. I never see such an old ostrich for wanting to gobble everything—and I a trusting you all the time, like you was my own father. You ought to be ashamed of yourself to stand by and hear it saddled onto a lot of poor niggers and you never say a word for 'em. It makes me feel ridiculous to think I was soft enough to *believe* that rubbage. Cuss you, I can see, now, why you was so anxious to make up the deffesit—you wanted to get what money I'd got out of the Nonesuch and one thing or another, and scoop it *all!*"

The king says, timid, and still a snuffling:

"Why, duke, it was you that said make up the deffersit, it warn't me."

"Dry up! I don't want to hear no more *out* of you!" says the duke. "And *now* you see what you *got* by it. They've got all their own money back, and all of *ourn* but a shekel or two, *besides.* G'long to bed—and don't you deffersit *me* no more deffersits, long 's *you* live!"

So the king sneaked into the wigwam, and took to his bottle for comfort; and before long the duke tackled *his* bottle; and so in about a half an hour they was as thick as thieves again, and the tighter they got, the lovinger they got; and went off a snoring in each other's arms. They both got powerful mellow, but I noticed the king didn't get mellow enough to forget to remember to not deny about hiding the money-bag again. That made me feel easy and satisfied. Of course when they got to snoring, we had a long gabble, and I told Jim everything.

## Chapter XXXI

We dasn't stop again at any town, for days and days; kept right along down the river. We was down south in the warm weather, now, and a mighty long ways from home. We begun to come to trees with Spanish moss on them, hanging down from the limbs like long gray beards. It was the first I ever see it growing, and it made the woods look solemn and dismal. So now the frauds reckoned they was out of danger, and they begun to work the villages again.

First they done a lecture on temperance; but they didn't make enough for them both to get drunk on. Then in another village they started a dancing school; but they didn't know no more how to dance than a kangaroo does; so the first prance they made, the general public jumped in and pranced them out of town. Another time they tried a go at yellocution; but they didn't yellocute long till the audience got up and give them a solid good cussing and made them skip out. They tackled missionarying, and

mesmerizering, and doctoring, and telling fortunes, and a little of everything; but they couldn't seem to have no luck. So at last they got just about
dead broke, and laid around the raft, as she floated along, thinking, and
thinking, and never saying nothing, by the half a day at a time, and dreadful blue and desperate.

And at last they took a change, and begun to lay their heads together in the
wigwam and talk low and confidential two or three hours at a time. Jim and
me got uneasy. We didn't like the look of it. We judged they was studying up
some kind of worse deviltry than ever. We turned it over and over, and at last
we made up our minds they was going to break into somebody's house or
store, or was going into the counterfeit-money business, or something. So
then we was pretty scared, and made up an agreement that we wouldn't have
nothing in the world to do with such actions, and if we ever got the least show
we would give them the cold shake, and clear out and leave them behind.
Well, early one morning we hid the raft in a good safe place about two mile
below a little bit of a shabby village, named Pikesville, and the king he went
ashore, and told us all to stay hid whilst he went up to town and smelt around
to see if anybody had got any wind of the Royal Nonesuch there yet. ("House
to rob, you *mean*," says I to myself; "and when you get through robbing it
you'll come back here and wonder what's become of me and Jim and the
raft—and you'll have to take it out in wondering.") And he said if he warn't
back by midday, the duke and me would know it was all right, and we was to
come along.

So we staid where we was. The duke he fretted and sweated around, and
was in a mighty sour way. He scolded us for everything, and we couldn't seem
to do nothing right; he found fault with every little thing. Something was a-
brewing, sure. I was good and glad when midday come and no king; we could
have a change, anyway—and maybe a chance for *the* change, on top of it. So
me and the duke went up to the village, and hunted around there for the king,
and by-and-by we found him in the back room of a little low doggery,[9] very
tight, and a lot of loafers bullyragging him for sport, and he a cussing and
threatening with all his might, and so tight he couldn't walk, and couldn't do
nothing to them. The duke he begun to abuse him for an old fool, and the
king begun to sass back; and the minute they was fairly at it, I lit out, and
shook the reefs out of my hind legs, and spun down the river road like a
deer—for I see our chance; and I made up my mind that it would be a long
day before they ever see me and Jim again. I got down there all out of breath
but loaded up with joy, and sung out—

"Set her loose, Jim, we're all right, now!"

But there warn't no answer, and nobody come out of the wigwam. Jim was
gone! I set up a shout—and then another—and then another one; and run
this way and that in the woods, whooping and screeching; but it warn't no
use—old Jim was gone. Then I set down and cried; I couldn't help it. But I
couldn't set still long. Pretty soon I went out on the road, trying to think what
I better do, and I run across a boy walking, and asked him if he'd seen a
strange nigger, dressed so and so, and he says:

"Yes."

"Whereabouts?" says I.

9. Cheap barroom.

"Down to Silas Phelps's place, two mile below here. He's
and they've got him. Was you looking for him?"

"You bet I ain't! I run across him in the woods about
and he said if I hollered he'd cut my livers out—and told
stay where I was; and I done it. Been there ever since; afearu

"Well," he says, "you needn't be afraid no more, becuz they've got
run off f'm down South, som'ers."

"It's a good job they got him."

"Well, I *reckon!* There's two hundred dollars reward on him. It's like picking up money out'n the road."

"Yes, it is—and *I* could a had it if I'd been big enough; I see him *first*. Who
nailed him?"

"It was an old fellow—a stranger—and he sold out his chance in him for
forty dollars, becuz he's got to go up the river and can't wait. Think o' that,
now! You bet *I'd* wait, if it was seven year."

"That's me, every time," says I. "But maybe his chance ain't worth no more
than that, if he'll sell it so cheap. Maybe there's something ain't straight about
it."

"But it *is*, though—straight as a string. I see the handbill myself. It tells all
about him, to a dot—paints him like a picture, and tells the plantation he's
frum, below New*rleans*. No-siree-*bob*, they ain't no trouble 'bout *that* speculation, you bet you. Say, gimme a chaw tobacker, won't ye?"

I didn't have none, so he left. I went to the raft, and set down in the wigwam to think. But I couldn't come to nothing. I thought till I wore my head
sore, but I couldn't see no way out of the trouble. After all this long journey,
and after all we'd done for them scoundrels, here was it all come to nothing,
everything all busted up and ruined, because they could have the heart to
serve Jim such a trick as that, and make him a slave again all his life, and
amongst strangers, too, for forty dirty dollars.

Once I said to myself it would be a thousand times better for Jim to be a
slave at home where his family was, as long as he'd *got* to be a slave, and so
I'd better write a letter to Tom Sawyer and tell him to tell Miss Watson where
he was. But I soon give up that notion, for two things: she'd be mad and disgusted at his rascality and ungratefulness for leaving her, and so she'd sell him
straight down the river again; and if she didn't, everybody naturally despises
an ungrateful nigger, and they'd make Jim feel it all the time, and so he'd feel
ornery and disgraced. And then think of *me*! It would get all around, that
Huck Finn helped a nigger to get his freedom; and if I was to ever see anybody from that town again, I'd be ready to get down and lick his boots for
shame. That's just the way: a person does a low-down thing, and then he don't
want to take no consequences of it. Thinks as long as he can hide it, it ain't
no disgrace. That was my fix exactly. The more I studied about this, the more
my conscience went to grinding me, and the more wicked and low-down and
ornery I got to feeling. And at last, when it hit me all of a sudden that here
was the plain hand of Providence slapping me in the face and letting me know
my wickedness was being watched all the time from up there in heaven,
whilst I was stealing a poor old woman's nigger that hadn't ever done me no
harm, and now was showing me there's One that's always on the lookout, and
ain't agoing to allow no such miserable doings to go only just so fur and no
further, I most dropped in my tracks I was so scared. Well, I tried the best I

ıld to kinder soften it up somehow for myself, by saying I was brung up ıicked, and so I warn't so much to blame; but something inside of me kept saying, "There was the Sunday school, you could a gone to it; and if you'd a done it they'd a learnt you, there, that people that acts as I'd been acting about the nigger goes to everlasting fire."

It made me shiver. And I about made up my mind to pray; and see if I couldn't try to quit being the kind of a boy I was, and be better. So I kneeled down. But the words wouldn't come. Why wouldn't they? It warn't no use to try and hide it from Him. Nor from *me*, neither. I knowed very well why they wouldn't come. It was because my heart warn't right; it was because I warn't square; it was because I was playing double. I was letting *on* to give up sin, but away inside of me I was holding on to the biggest one of all. I was trying to make my mouth *say* I would do the right thing and the clean thing, and go and write to that nigger's owner and tell where he was; but deep down in me I knowed it was a lie—and He knowed it. You can't pray a lie—I found that out.

So I was full of trouble, full as I could be; and didn't know what to do. At last I had an idea; and I says, I'll go and write the letter—and *then* see if I can pray. Why, it was astonishing, the way I felt as light as a feather, right straight off, and my troubles all gone. So I got a piece of paper and a pencil, all glad and excited, and set down and wrote:

> Miss Watson your runaway nigger Jim is down here two mile below Pikesville and Mr. Phelps has got him and he will give him up for the reward if you send.
>
> Huck Finn.

I felt good and all washed clean of sin for the first time I had ever felt so in my life, and I knowed I could pray now. But I didn't do it straight off, but laid the paper down and set there thinking—thinking how good it was all this happened so, and how near I come to being lost and going to hell. And went on thinking. And got to thinking over our trip down the river; and I see Jim before me, all the time, in the day, and in the night-time, sometimes moonlight, sometimes storms, and we a floating along, talking, and singing, and laughing. But somehow I couldn't seem to strike no places to harden me against him, but only the other kind. I'd see him standing my watch on top of his'n, stead of calling me, so I could go on sleeping; and see him how glad he was when I come back out of the fog; and when I come to him again in the swamp, up there where the feud was; and such-like times; and would always call me honey, and pet me, and do everything he could think of for me, and how good he always was; and at last I struck the time I saved him by telling the men we had small-pox aboard, and he was so grateful, and said I was the best friend old Jim ever had in the world, and the *only* one he's got now; and then I happened to look around, and see that paper.

It was a close place. I took it up, and held it in my hand. I was a trembling, because I'd got to decide, forever, betwixt two things, and I knowed it. I studied a minute, sort of holding my breath, and then says to myself:

"All right, then, I'll *go* to hell"—and tore it up.

It was awful thoughts, and awful words, but they was said. And I let them stay said; and never thought no more about reforming. I shoved the whole thing out of my head; and said I would take up wickedness again, which was in my line, being brung up to it, and the other warn't. And for a starter, I would go to work and steal Jim out of slavery again; and if I could think up anything worse, I would do that, too; because as long as I was in, and in for good, I might as well go the whole hog. ⟶

Then I set to thinking over how to get at it, and turned over considerable many ways in my mind; and at last fixed up a plan that suited me. So then I took the bearings of a woody island that was down the river a piece, and as soon as it was fairly dark I crept out with my raft and went for it, and hid it there, and then turned in. I slept the night through, and got up before it was light, and had my breakfast, and put on my store clothes, and tied up some others and one thing or another in a bundle, and took the canoe and cleared for shore. I landed below where I judged was Phelps's place, and hid my bundle in the woods, and then filled up the canoe with water, and loaded rocks into her and sunk her where I could find her again when I wanted her, about a quarter of a mile below a little steam sawmill that was on the bank.

Then I struck up the road, and when I passed the mill I see a sign on it, "Phelps's Sawmill," and when I come to the farmhouses, two or three hundred yards further along, I kept my eyes peeled, but didn't see nobody around, though it was good daylight, now. But I didn't mind, because I didn't want to see nobody just yet—I only wanted to get the lay of the land. According to my plan, I was going to turn up there from the village, not from below. So I just took a look, and shoved along, straight for town. Well, the very first man I see, when I got there, was the duke. He was sticking up a bill for the Royal Nonesuch—three-night performance—like that other time. *They* had the cheek, them frauds! I was right on him, before I could shirk. He looked astonished, and says:

"Hel-*lo!* Where'd *you* come from?" Then he says, kind of glad and eager, "Where's the raft?—got her in a good place?"

I says:

"Why, that's just what I was agoing to ask your grace."

Then he didn't look so joyful—and says:

"What was your idea for asking *me?*" he says.

"Well," I says, "when I see the king in that doggery yesterday, I says to myself, we can't get him home for hours, till he's soberer; so I went a loafing around town to put in the time, and wait. A man up and offered me ten cents to help him pull a skiff over the river and back to fetch a sheep, and so I went along; but when we was dragging him to the boat, and the man left me aholt of the rope and went behind him to shove him along, he was too strong for me, and jerked loose and run, and we after him. We didn't have no dog, and so we had to chase him all over the country till we tired him out. We never got him till dark, then we fetched him over, and I started down for the raft. When I got there and see it was gone, I says to myself, 'they've got into trouble and had to leave; and they've took my nigger, which is the only nigger I've got in the world, and now I'm in a strange country, and ain't got no property no more, nor nothing, and no way to make my living;' so I set down and cried. I slept in the woods all night. But what *did* become of the raft then?—and Jim, poor Jim!"

"Blamed if *I* know—that is, what's become of the raft. That old fool had made a trade and got forty dollars, and when we found him in the doggery the loafers had matched half dollars with him and got every cent but what he'd spent for whisky; and when I got him home late last night and found the raft gone, we said, 'That little rascal has stole our raft and shook us, and run off down the river.' "

"I wouldn't shake my *nigger*, would I?—the only nigger I had in the world, and the only property."

"We never thought of that. Fact is, I reckon we'd come to consider him *our* nigger; yes, we did consider him so—goodness knows we had trouble enough for him. So when we see the raft was gone, and we flat broke, there warn't anything for it but to try the Royal Nonesuch another shake. And I've pegged along ever since, dry as a powderhorn. Where's that ten cents? Give it here."

I had considerable money, so I give him ten cents, but begged him to spend it for something to eat, and give me some, because it was all the money I had, and I hadn't had nothing to eat since yesterday. He never said nothing. The next minute he whirls on me and says:

"Do you reckon that nigger would blow on us? We'd skin him if he done that!"

"How can he blow? Hain't he run off?"

"No! That old fool sold him, and never divided with me, and the money's gone."

"*Sold* him?" I says, and begun to cry; "why, he was *my* nigger, and that was my money. Where is he?—I want my nigger."

"Well, you can't *get* your nigger, that's all—so dry up your blubbering. Looky here—do you think *you'd* venture to blow on us? Blamed if I think I'd trust you. Why, if you *was* to blow on us—"

He stopped, but I never see the duke look so ugly out of his eyes before. I went on a-whimpering, and says:

"I don't want to blow on nobody; and I ain't got no time to blow, nohow. I got to turn out and find my nigger."

He looked kinder bothered, and stood there with his bills fluttering on his arm, thinking, and wrinkling up his forehead. At last he says:

"I'll tell you something. We got to be here three days. If you'll promise you won't blow, and won't let the nigger blow, I'll tell you where to find him."

So I promised, and he says:

"A farmer by the name of Silas Ph—" and then he stopped. You see he started to tell me the truth; but when he stopped, that way, and begun to study and think again, I reckoned he was changing his mind. And so he was. He wouldn't trust me; he wanted to make sure of having me out of the way the whole three days. So pretty soon he says: "The man that bought him is named Abram Foster—Abram G. Foster—and he lives forty mile back here in the country, on the road to Lafayette."

"All right," I says, "I can walk it in three days. And I'll start this very afternoon."

"No you won't, you'll start *now*; and don't you lose any time about it, neither, nor do any gabbling by the way. Just keep a tight tongue in your head and move right along, and then you won't get into trouble with *us*, d'ye hear?"

That was the order I wanted, and that was the one I played for. I wanted to be left free to work my plans.

"So clear out," he says; "and you can tell Mr. Foster whatever you want to. Maybe you can get him to believe that Jim *is* your nigger—some idiots don't require documents—leastways I've heard there's such down South here. And when you tell him the handbill and the reward's bogus, maybe he'll believe you when you explain to him what the idea was for getting 'em out. Go 'long, now, and tell him anything you want to; but mind you don't work your jaw any *between* here and there."

So I left, and struck for the back country. I didn't look around, but I kinder felt like he was watching me. But I knowed I could tire him out at that. I went straight out in the country as much as a mile, before I stopped; then I doubled back through the woods towards Phelps's. I reckoned I better start in on my plan straight off, without fooling around, because I wanted to stop Jim's mouth till these fellows could get away. I didn't want no trouble with their kind. I'd seen all I wanted to of them, and wanted to get entirely shut of them.

## Chapter XXXII

When I got there it was all still and Sunday-like, and hot and sunshiny—the hands was gone to the fields; and there was them kind of faint dronings of bugs and flies in the air that makes it seem so lonesome and like everybody's dead and gone; and if a breeze fans along and quivers the leaves, it makes you feel mournful, because you feel like it's spirits whispering—spirits that's been dead ever so many years—and you always think they're talking about *you.* As a general thing it makes a body wish *he* was dead, too, and done with it all.

Phelps's was one of these little one-horse cotton plantations; and they all look alike. A rail fence round a two-acre yard; a stile, made out of logs sawed off and up-ended, in steps, like barrels of a different length, to climb over the fence with, and for the women to stand on when they are going to jump onto a horse; some sickly grass-patches in the big yard, but mostly it was bare and smooth, like an old hat with the nap rubbed off; big double log house for the white folks—hewed logs, with the chinks stopped up with mud or mortar, and these mud-stripes been whitewashed some time or another; round-log kitchen, with a big broad, open but roofed passage joining it to the house; log smoke-house back of the kitchen; three little log nigger-cabins in a row t'other side the smokehouse; one little hut all by itself away down against the back fence, and some outbuildings down a piece the other side; ash-hopper,[1] and big kettle to bile soap in, by the little hut; bench by the kitchen door, with bucket of water and a gourd; hound asleep there, in the sun; more hounds asleep, round about; about three shade-trees away off in a corner; some currant bushes and gooseberry bushes in one place by the fence; outside of the fence a garden and a water-melon patch; then the cotton fields begins; and after the fields, the woods.

I went around and clumb over the back stile by the ash-hopper, and started for the kitchen. When I got a little ways, I heard the dim hum of a spinning-wheel wailing along up and sinking along down again; and then I knowed for certain I wished I was dead—for that *is* the lonesomest sound in the whole world.[2]

I went right along, not fixing up any particular plan, but just trusting to Providence to put the right words in my mouth when the time come; for I'd

1. A container for lye used in making soap.
2. For the details of the Phelps plantation, Twain drew on memories of vacations at his uncle John
Quarles's farm near Hannibal. See Twain's *Autobiography* for his vivid evocation of the farm.

noticed that Providence always did put the right words in my mouth, if I left it alone.

When I got half-way, first one hound and then another got up and went for me, and of course I stopped and faced them, and kept still. And such another pow-wow as they made! In a quarter of a minute I was a kind of a hub of a wheel, as you may say—spokes made out of dogs—circle of fifteen of them packed together around me, with their necks and noses stretched up towards me, a barking and howling; and more a coming; you could see them sailing over fences and around corners from everywheres.

A nigger woman come tearing out of the kitchen with a rolling-pin in her hand, singing out, "Begone! *you* Tige! you Spot! begone, sah!" and she fetched first one and then another of them a clip and sent him howling, and then the rest followed; and the next second, half of them come back, wagging their tails around me and making friends with me. There ain't no harm in a hound, nohow.

And behind the woman comes a little nigger girl and two little nigger boys, without anything on but tow-linen shirts, and they hung onto their mother's gown, and peeped out from behind her at me, bashful, the way they always do. And here comes the white woman running from the house, about forty-five or fifty year old, bare-headed, and her spinning-stick in her hand; and behind her comes her little white children, acting the same way the little niggers was doing. She was smiling all over so she could hardly stand—and says:

"It's *you*, at last!—*ain't* it?"

I out with a "Yes'm," before I thought.

She grabbed me and hugged me tight; and then gripped me by both hands and shook and shook; and the tears come in her eyes, and run down over; and she couldn't seem to hug and shake enough, and kept saying, "You don't look as much like your mother as I reckoned you would, but law sakes, I don't care for that, I'm *so* glad to see you! Dear, dear, it does seem like I could eat you up! Children, it's your cousin Tom!—tell him howdy."

But they ducked their heads, and put their fingers in their mouths, and hid behind her. So she run on:

"Lize, hurry up and get him a hot breakfast, right away—or did you get your breakfast on the boat?"

I said I had got it on the boat. So then she started for the house, leading me by the hand, and the children tagging after. When we got there, she set me down in a split-bottomed chair, and set herself down on a little low stool in front of me, holding both of my hands, and says:

"Now I can have a *good* look at you; and laws-a-me, I've been hungry for it a many and a many a time, all these long years, and it's come at last! We been expecting you a couple of days and more. What's kep' you?—boat get aground?"

"Yes'm—she—"

"Don't say yes'm—say Aunt Sally. Where'd she get aground?"

I didn't rightly know what to say, because I didn't know whether the boat would be coming up the river or down. But I go a good deal on instinct; and my instinct said she would be coming up—from down toward Orleans. That didn't help me much, though; for I didn't know the names of bars down that way. I see I'd got to invent a bar, or forget the name of the one we got aground on—or—Now I struck an idea, and fetched it out:

*Commentary on the Culture*

"It warn't the grounding—that didn't keep us back but a little. We blowed out a cylinder-head."

"Good gracious! anybody hurt?"

"No'm. Killed a nigger."

"Well, it's lucky; because sometimes people do get hurt. Two years ago last Christmas, your uncle Silas was coming up from Newrleans on the old *Lally Rook*,[3] and she blowed out a cylinder-head and crippled a man. And I think he died afterwards. He was a Babtist. Your uncle Silas knowed a family in Baton Rouge that knowed his people very well. Yes, I remember, now he *did* die. Mortification[4] set in, and they had to amputate him. But it didn't save him. Yes, it was mortification—that was it. He turned blue all over, and died in the hope of a glorious resurrection. They say he was a sight to look at. Your uncle's been up to the town every day to fetch you. And he's gone again, not more'n an hour ago; he'll be back any minute, now. You must a met him on the road, didn't you?—oldish man, with a—"

"No, I didn't see nobody, Aunt Sally. The boat landed just at daylight, and I left my baggage on the wharf-boat and went looking around the town and out a piece in the country, to put in the time and not get here too soon; and so I come down the back way."

"Who'd you give the baggage to?"

"Nobody."

"Why, child, it'll be stole!"

"Not where *I* hid it I reckon it won't," I says.

"How'd you get your breakfast so early on the boat?"

It was kinder thin ice, but I says:

"The captain see me standing around, and told me I better have something to eat before I went ashore; so he took me in the texas to the officers' lunch, and give me all I wanted."

I was getting so uneasy I couldn't listen good. I had my mind on the children all the time; I wanted to get them out to one side, and pump them a little, and find out who I was. But I couldn't get no show, Mrs. Phelps kept it up and run on so. Pretty soon she made the cold chills streak all down my back, because she says:

"But here we're a running on this way, and you hain't told me a word about Sis, nor any of them. Now I'll rest my works a little, and you start up yourn; just tell me *everything*—tell me all about 'm all—every one of 'm; and how they are, and what they're doing, and what they told you to tell me; and every last thing you can think of."

Well, I see I was up a stump—and up it good. Providence had stood by me this fur, all right, but I was hard and tight aground, now. I see it warn't a bit of use to try to go ahead—I'd *got* to throw up my hand. So I says to myself, here's another place where I got to resk the truth. I opened my mouth to begin; but she grabbed me and hustled me in behind the bed, and says:

"Here he comes! stick your head down lower—there, that'll do; you can't be seen, now. Don't you let on you're here. I'll play a joke on him. Children, don't you say a word."

I see I was in a fix, now. But it warn't no use to worry; there warn't nothing

<hr>

3. "Lalla Rookh" (1817), a popular Romantic poem by Thomas Moore.

4. Gangrene.

to do but just hold still, and try to be ready to stand from under when the lightning struck.

I had just one little glimpse of the old gentleman when he come in, then the bed hid him. Mrs. Phelps she jumps for him and says:

"Has he come?"

"No," says her husband.

"Good-*ness* gracious!" she says, "what in the world *can* have become of him?"

"I can't imagine," says the old gentleman; "and I must say, it makes me dreadful uneasy."

"Uneasy!" she says, "I'm ready to go distracted! He *must* a come; and you've missed him along the road. I *know* it's so—something *tells* me so."

"Why Sally, I *couldn't* miss him along the road—*you* know that."

"But oh, dear, dear, what *will* Sis say! He must a come! You must a missed him. He—"

"Oh, don't distress me any more'n I'm already distressed. I don't know what in the world to make of it. I'm at my wit's end, and I don't mind acknowledging 't I'm right down scared. But there's no hope that he's come; for he couldn't come and me miss him. Sally, it's terrible—just terrible—something's happened to the boat, sure!"

"Why, Silas! Look yonder!—up the road!—ain't that somebody coming?"

He sprung to the window at the head of the bed, and that give Mrs. Phelps the chance she wanted. She stooped down quick, at the foot of the bed, and give me a pull, and out I come; and when he turned back from the window, there she stood, a-beaming and a-smiling like a house afire, and I standing pretty meek and sweaty alongside. The old gentleman stared, and says:

"Why, who's that?"

"Who do you reckon 't is?"

"I hain't no idea. Who *is* it?"

"It's *Tom Sawyer!*"[5]

By jings, I most slumped through the floor. But there warn't no time to swap knives;[6] the old man grabbed me by the hand and shook, and kept on shaking; and all the time, how the woman did dance around and laugh and cry; and then how they both did fire off questions about Sid, and Mary, and the rest of the tribe.

But if they was joyful, it warn't nothing to what I was; for it was like being born again, I was so glad to find out who I was. Well, they froze to me for two hours; and at last when my chin was so tired it couldn't hardly go, any more, I had told them more about my family—I mean the Sawyer family—than ever happened to any six Sawyer families. And I explained all about how we blowed out a cylinder-head at the mouth of the White River and it took us three days to fix it. Which was all right, and worked first rate; because *they* didn't know but what it would take three days to fix it. If I'd a called it a bolt-head it would a done just as well.

Now I was feeling pretty comfortable all down one side, and pretty uncomfortable all up the other. Being Tom Sawyer was easy and comfortable; and it

---

5. Huck's being mistaken for Tom is seen by many critics as a sardonic comment on Huck's seeming to forget his loyalty to Jim and once again falling under Tom's sway in tormenting Jim at the Phelps farm.

6. Change plans.

stayed easy and comfortable till by-and-by I hear a steamboat coughing along down the river—then I says to myself, spose Tom Sawyer come down on that boat?—and spose he steps in here, any minute, and sings out my name before I can throw him a wink to keep quiet? Well, I couldn't *have* it that way—it wouldn't do at all. I must go up the road and waylay him. So I told the folks I reckoned I would go up to the town and fetch down my baggage. The old gentleman was for going along with me, but I said no, I could drive the horse myself, and I druther he wouldn't take no trouble about me.

## Chapter XXXIII

So I started for town, in the wagon, and when I was half-way I see a wagon coming, and sure enough it was Tom Sawyer, and I stopped and waited till he come along. I says "Hold on!" and it stopped alongside, and his mouth opened up like a trunk, and staid so; and he swallowed two or three times like a person that's got a dry throat, and then says:

"I hain't ever done you no harm. You know that. So then, what you want to come back and ha'nt *me* for?"

I says:

"I hain't come back—I hain't been *gone*."

When he heard my voice, it righted him up some, but he warn't quite satisfied yet. He says:

"Don't you play nothing on me, because I wouldn't on you. Honest injun, now, you ain't a ghost?"

"Honest injun, I ain't," I says.

"Well—I—I—well, that ought to settle it, of course; but I can't somehow seem to understand it, no way. Looky here, warn't you ever murdered *at all?*"

"No. I warn't ever murdered at all—I played it on them. You come in here and feel of me if you don't believe me."

So he done it; and it satisfied him; and he was that glad to see me again, he didn't know what to do. And he wanted to know all about it right off; because it was a grand adventure, and mysterious, and so it hit him where he lived. But I said, leave it along till by-and-by; and told his driver to wait, and we drove off a little piece, and I told him the kind of a fix I was in, and what did he reckon we better do? He said, let him alone a minute, and don't disturb him. So he thought and thought, and pretty soon he says:

"It's all right, I've got it. Take my trunk in your wagon, and let on it's your'n; and you turn back and fool along slow, so as to get to the house about the time you ought to; and I'll go towards town a piece, and take a fresh start, and get there a quarter or a half an hour after you; and you needn't let on to know me, at first."

I says:

"All right; but wait a minute. There's one more thing—a thing that *nobody* don't know but me. And that is, there's a nigger here that I'm trying to steal out of slavery—and his name is *Jim*—old Miss Watson's Jim."

He says:

"What! Why Jim is—"

He stopped and went to studying. I says:

"*I* know what you'll say. You'll say it's dirty low-down business; but what if it is?—I'm low down; and I'm agoing to steal him, and I want you to keep mum and not let on. Will you?"

His eye lit up, and he says:

"I'll *help* you steal him!"

Well, I let go all holts then, like I was shot. It was the most astonishing speech I ever heard—and I'm bound to say Tom Sawyer fell, considerable, in my estimation. Only I couldn't believe it. Tom Sawyer a *nigger stealer!*

"Oh, shucks," I says, "you're joking."

"I ain't joking, either."

"Well, then," I says, "joking or no joking, if you hear anything said about a runaway nigger, don't forget to remember that *you* don't know nothing about him, and *I* don't know nothing about him."

Then we took the trunk and put it in my wagon, and he drove off his way, and I drove mine. But of course I forgot all about driving slow, on accounts of being glad and full of thinking; so I got home a heap too quick for that length of trip. The old gentleman was at the door, and he says.

"Why, this is wonderful. Who ever would a thought it was in that mare to do it. I wish we'd a timed her. And she hain't sweated a hair—not a hair. It's wonderful. Why, I wouldn't take a hundred dollars for that horse now; I wouldn't, honest; and yet I'd a sold her for fifteen before, and thought 'twas all she was worth."

That's all he said. He was the innocentest, best old soul I ever see. But it warn't surprising; because he warn't only just a farmer, he was a preacher, too, and had a little one-horse log church down back of the plantation, which he built it himself at his own expense, for a church and school-house, and never charged nothing for his preaching, and it was worth it, too. There was plenty other farmer-preachers like that, and done the same way, down South.

In about half an hour Tom's wagon drove up to the front stile, and Aunt Sally she see it through the window because it was only about fifty yards, and says:

"Why, there's somebody come! I wonder who 'tis? Why, I do believe it's a stranger. Jimmy" (that's one of the children), "run and tell Lize to put on another plate for dinner."

Everybody made a rush for the front door, because, of course, a stranger don't come *every* year, and so he lays over the yaller fever, for interest, when he does come. Tom was over the stile and starting for the house; the wagon was spinning up the road for the village, and we was all bunched in the front door. Tom had his store clothes on, and an audience—and that was always nuts for Tom Sawyer. In them circumstances it warn't no trouble to him to throw in an amount of style that was suitable. He warn't a boy to meeky along up that yard like a sheep; no, he come ca'm and important, like the ram. When he got afront of us, he lifts his hat ever so gracious and dainty, like it was the lid of a box that had butterflies asleep in it and he didn't want to disturb them, and says:

"Mr. Archibald Nichols, I presume?"

"No, my boy," says the old gentleman, "I'm sorry to say 't your driver has deceived you; Nichols's place is down a matter of three mile more. Come in, come in."

Tom he took a look back over his shoulder, and says, "Too late—he's out of sight."

"Yes, he's gone, my son, and you must come in and eat your dinner with us; and then we'll hitch up and take you down to Nichols's."

"Oh, I *can't* make you so much trouble; I couldn't think of it. I'll walk—I don't mind the distance."

"But we won't *let* you walk—it wouldn't be Southern hospitality to do it. Come right in."

"Oh, *do,*" says Aunt Sally; "it ain't a bit of trouble to us, not a bit in the world. You *must* stay. It's a long, dusty three mile, and we *can't* let you walk. And besides, I've already told 'em to put on another plate, when I see you coming; so you mustn't disappoint us. Come right in, and make yourself at home."

So Tom he thanked them very hearty and handsome, and let himself be persuaded, and come in; and when he was in, he said he was a stranger from Hicksville, Ohio, and his name was William Thompson—and he made another bow.

Well, he run on, and on, and on, making up stuff about Hicksville and everybody in it he could invent, and I getting a little nervous, and wondering how this was going to help me out of my scrape; and at last, still talking along, he reached over and kissed Aunt Sally right on the mouth, and then settled back again in his chair, comfortable, and was going on talking; but she jumped up and wiped it off with the back of her hand, and says:

"You owdacious puppy!"

He looked kind of hurt, and says:

"I'm surprised at you, m'am."

"You're s'rp—Why, what do you reckon *I* am? I've a good notion to take and—say, what do you mean by kissing me?"

He looked kind of humble, and says:

"I didn't mean nothing, m'am. I didn't mean no harm. I—I—thought you'd like it."

"Why, you born fool!" She took up the spinning-stick, and it looked like it was all she could do to keep from giving him a crack with it. "What made you think I'd like it?"

"Well, I don't know. Only, they—they—told me you would."

"*They* told you I would. Whoever told you's *another* lunatic. I never heard the beat of it. Who's *they?*"

"Why—everybody. They all said so, m'am."

It was all she could do to hold in; and her eyes snapped, and her fingers worked like she wanted to scratch him; and she says:

"Who's everybody?' Out with their names—or ther'll be an idiot short."

He got up and looked distressed, and fumbled his hat, and says:

"I'm sorry, and I warn't expecting it. They told me to. They all told me to. They all said kiss her; and said she'll like it. They all said it—every one of them. But I'm sorry, m'am, and I won't do it no more—I won't, honest."

"You won't, won't you? Well, I sh'd *reckon* you won't!"

"No'm, I'm honest about it; I won't ever do it again. Till you ask me."

"Till I *ask* you! Well, I never see the beat of it in my born days! I lay you'll be the Methusalem-numskull[7] of creation before ever *I* ask you—or the likes of you."

---

7. Methuselah was a biblical patriarch said to have lived 969 years.

"Well," he says, "it does surprise me so. I can't make it out, somehow. They said you would, and I thought you would. But—" He stopped and looked around slow, like he wished he could run across a friendly eye, somewhere's; and fetched up on the old gentleman's, and says, "Didn't *you* think she'd like me to kiss her, sir?"

"Why, no, I—I—well, no, I b'lieve I didn't."

Then he looks on around, the same way, to me—and says:

"Tom, didn't *you* think Aunt Sally 'd open out her arms and say, 'Sid Sawyer—' "

"My land!" she says, breaking in and jumping for him, "you impudent young rascal, to fool a body so—" and was going to hug him, but he fended her off, and says:

"No, not till you've asked me, first."

So she didn't lose no time, but asked him; and hugged him and kissed him, over and over again, and then turned him over to the old man, and he took what was left. And after they got a little quiet again, she says:

"Why, dear me, I never see such a surprise. We warn't looking for *you*, at all, but only Tom. Sis never wrote to me about anybody coming but him."

"It's because it warn't *intended* for any of us to come but Tom," he says; "but I begged and begged, and at the last minute she let me come, too; so, coming down the river, me and Tom thought it would be a first-rate surprise for him to come here to the house first, and for me to by-and-by tag along and drop in and let on to be a stranger. But it was a mistake, Aunt Sally. This ain't no healthy place for a stranger to come."

"No—not impudent whelps, Sid. You ought to had your jaws boxed; I hain't been so put out since I don't know when. But I don't care, I don't mind the terms—I'd be willing to stand a thousand such jokes to have you here. Well, to think of that performance! I don't deny it, I was most putrified[8] with astonishment when you give me that smack."

We had dinner out in that broad open passage betwixt the house and the kitchen; and there was things enough on that table for seven families—and all hot, too; none of your flabby tough meat that's laid in a cupboard in a damp cellar all night and tastes like a hunk of old cold cannibal in the morning. Uncle Silas he asked a pretty long blessing over it, but it was worth it; and it didn't cool it a bit, neither, the way I've seen them kind of interruptions do, lots of times.

There was a considerable good deal of talk, all the afternoon, and me and Tom was on the lookout all the time, but it warn't no use, they didn't happen to say nothing about any runaway nigger, and we was afraid to try to work up to it. But at supper, at night, one of the little boys says:

"Pa, mayn't Tom and Sid and me go to the show?"

"No," says the old man, "I reckon there ain't going to be any; and you couldn't go if there was; because the runaway nigger told Burton and me all about that scandalous show, and Burton said he would tell the people; so I reckon they've drove the owdacious loafers out of town before this time."

So there it was!—but *I* couldn't help it. Tom and me was to sleep in the same room and bed; so, being tired, we bid good-night and went up to bed, right after supper, and clumb out of the window and down the lightning-rod,

---

8. Petrified or stunned.

and shoved for the town; for I didn't believe anybody was going to give the king and the duke a hint, and so, if I didn't hurry up and give them one they'd get into trouble sure.

On the road Tom he told me all about how it was reckoned I was murdered, and how pap disappeared, pretty soon, and didn't come back no more, and what a stir there was when Jim run away; and I told Tom all about our Royal Nonesuch rapscallions, and as much of the raft-voyage as I had time to; and as we struck into the town and up through the middle of it—it was as much as half-after eight, then—here comes a raging rush of people, with torches, and an awful whooping and yelling, and banging tin pans and blowing horns; and we jumped to one side to let them go by; and as they went by, I see they had the king and the duke astraddle of a rail—that is, I knowed it *was* the king and the duke, though they was all over tar and feathers, and didn't look like nothing in the world that was human—just looked like a couple of monstrous big soldier-plumes. Well, it made me sick to see it; and I was sorry for them poor pitiful rascals, it seemed like I couldn't ever feel any hardness against them any more in the world. It was a dreadful thing to see. Human beings *can* be awful cruel to one another.

We see we was too late—couldn't do no good. We asked some stragglers about it, and they said everybody went to the show looking very innocent; and laid low and kept dark till the poor old king was in the middle of his cavortings on the stage; then somebody give a signal, and the house rose up and went for them.

So we poked along back home, and I warn't feeling so brash as I was before, but kind of ornery, and humble, and to blame, somehow—though *I* hadn't done anything. But that's always the way; it don't make no difference whether you do right or wrong, a person's conscience ain't got no sense, and just goes for him *anyway*. If I had a yaller dog that didn't know no more than a person's conscience does, I would pison him. It takes up more room than all the rest of a person's insides, and yet ain't no good, nohow. Tom Sawyer he says the same.

## Chapter XXXIV

We stopped talking, and got to thinking. By-and-by Tom says:

"Looky here, Huck, what fools we are, to not think of it before! I bet I know where Jim is."

"No! Where?"

"In that hut down by the ash-hopper. Why, looky here. When we was at dinner, didn't you see a nigger man go in there with some vittles?"

"Yes."

"What did you think the vittles was for?"

"For a dog."

"So'd I. Well, it wasn't for a dog."

"Why?"

"Because part of it was watermelon."

"So it was—I noticed it. Well, it does beat all, that I never thought about a dog not eating watermelon. It shows how a body can see and don't see at the same time."

"Well, the nigger unlocked the padlock when he went in, and he locked it again when he come out. He fetched uncle a key, about the time we got up from table—same key, I bet. Watermelon shows man, lock shows prisoner; and it ain't likely there's two prisoners on such a little plantation, and where the people's all so kind and good. Jim's the prisoner. All right—I'm glad we found it out detective fashion; I wouldn't give shucks for any other way. Now you work your mind and study out a plan to steal Jim, and I will study out one, too; and we'll take the one we like the best."

What a head for just a boy to have! If I had Tom Sawyer's head, I wouldn't trade it off to be a duke, nor mate of a steamboat, nor clown in a circus, nor nothing I can think of. I went to thinking out a plan, but only just to be doing something; I knowed very well where the right plan was going to come from. Pretty soon, Tom says:

"Ready?"

"Yes," I says.

"All right—bring it out."

"My plan is this," I says. "We can easy find out if it's Jim in there. Then get up my canoe to-morrow night, and fetch my raft over from the island. Then the first dark night that comes, steal the key out of the old man's britches, after he goes to bed, and shove off down the river on the raft, with Jim, hiding daytimes and running nights, the way me and Jim used to do before. Wouldn't that plan work?"

"*Work?* Why cert'nly, it would work, like rats a fighting. But it's too blame' simple; there ain't nothing *to* it. What's the good of a plan that ain't no more trouble than that? It's as mild as goose-milk. Why, Huck, it wouldn't make no more talk than breaking into a soap factory."

I never said nothing, because I warn't expecting nothing different; but I knowed mighty well that whenever he got *his* plan ready it wouldn't have none of them objections to it.

And it didn't. He told me what it was, and I see in a minute it was worth fifteen of mine, for style, and would make Jim just as free a man as mine would, and maybe get us all killed besides. So I was satisfied, and said we would waltz in on it. I needn't tell what it was, here, because I knowed it wouldn't stay the way it was. I knowed he would be changing it around, every which way, as we went along, and heaving in new bullinesses wherever he got a chance. And that is what he done.

Well, one thing was dead sure; and that was, that Tom Sawyer was in earnest and was actuly going to help steal that nigger out of slavery. That was the thing that was too many for me. Here was a boy that was respectable, and well brung up; and had a character to lose; and folks at home that had characters; and he was bright and not leather-headed; and knowing and not ignorant; and not mean, but kind; and yet here he was, without any more pride, or rightness, or feeling, than to stoop to this business, and make himself a shame, and his family a shame, before everybody. I *couldn't* understand it, no way at all. It was outrageous, and I knowed I ought to just up and tell him so; and so be his true friend, and let him quit the thing right where he was, and save himself. And I *did* start to tell him; but he shut me up, and says:

"Don't you reckon I know what I'm about? Don't I generly know what I'm about?"

"Yes."

"Didn't I *say* I was going to help steal the nigger?"

"Yes."

"*Well* then."

That's all he said, and that's all I said. It warn't no use to say any more; because when he said he'd do a thing, he always done it. But *I* couldn't make out how he was willing to go into this thing; so I just let it go, and never bothered no more about it. If he was bound to have it so, I couldn't help it.

When we got home, the house was all dark and still; so we went on down to the hut by the ash-hopper, for to examine it. We went through the yard, so as to see what the hounds would do. They knowed us, and didn't make no more noise than country dogs is always doing when anything comes by in the night. When we got to the cabin, we took a look at the front and the two sides; and on the side I warn't acquainted with—which was the north side—we found a square window-hole, up tolerable high, with just one stout board nailed across it. I says:

"Here's the ticket. This hole's big enough for Jim to get through, if we wrench off the board."

Tom says:

"It's as simple as tit-tat-toe, three-in-a-row, and as easy as playing hooky. I should *hope* we can find a way that's a little more complicated than *that,* Huck Finn."

"Well, then," I says, "how'll it do to saw him out, the way I done before I was murdered, that time?"

"That's more *like,*" he says, "It's real mysterious, and troublesome, and good," he says; "but I bet we can find a way that's twice as long. There ain't no hurry; le's keep on looking around."

Betwixt the hut and the fence, on the back side, was a lean-to, that joined the hut at the eaves, and was made out of plank. It was as long as the hut, but narrow—only about six foot wide. The door to it was at the south end, and was padlocked. Tom he went to the soap kettle, and searched around and fetched back the iron thing they lift the lid with; so he took it and prized out one of the staples. The chain fell down, and we opened the door and went in, and shut it, and struck a match, and see the shed was only built against the cabin and hadn't no connection with it; and there warn't no floor to the shed, nor nothing in it but some old rusty played-out hoes, and spades, and picks, and a crippled plow. The match went out, and so did we, and shoved in the staple again, and the door was locked as good as ever. Tom was joyful. He says:

"Now we're all right. We'll *dig* him out. It'll take about a week!"

Then we started for the house, and I went in the back door—you only have to pull a buckskin latch-string, they don't fasten the doors—but that warn't romantical enough for Tom Sawyer: no way would do him but he must climb up the lightning-rod. But after he got up half-way about three times, and missed fire and fell every time, and the last time most busted his brains out, he thought he'd got to give it up; but after he rested, he allowed he would give her one more turn for luck, and this time he made the trip.

In the morning we was up at break of day, and down to the nigger cabins to pet the dogs and make friends with the nigger that fed Jim—if it *was* Jim

that was being fed. The niggers was just getting through breakfast and starting for the fields; and Jim's nigger was piling up a tin pan with bread and meat
and things; and whilst the other was leaving, the key come from the house.

This nigger had a good-natured, chuckle-headed face, and his wool was all
tied up in little bunches with thread. That was to keep witches off. He said
the witches was pestering him awful, these nights, and making him see all
kinds of strange things, and hear all kinds of strange words and noises, and
he didn't believe he was ever witched so long, before, in his life. He got so
worked up, and got to running on so about his troubles, he forgot all about
what he'd been agoing to do. So Tom says:

"What's the vittles for? Going to feed the dogs?"

The nigger kind of smiled around gradly over his face, like when you
heave a brickbat in a mud puddle, and he says:

"Yes, Mars Sid, *a* dog. Cur'us dog too. Does you want to go en look at 'im?"

"Yes."

I hunched Tom, and whispers:

"You going, right here in the day-break? *That* warn't the plan."

"No, it warn't—but it's the plan *now.*"

So, drat him, we went along, but I didn't like it much. When we got in, we
couldn't hardly see anything, it was so dark; but Jim was there, sure enough,
and could see us; and he sings out:

"Why, *Huck!* En good *lan'!* ain' dat Misto Tom?"

I just knowed how it would be; I just expected it. *I* didn't know nothing to
do; and if I had, I couldn't done it; because that nigger busted in and says:

"Why, de gracious sakes! do he know you genlmen?"

We could see pretty well, now. Tom he looked at the nigger, steady and kind
of wondering, and says:

"Does *who* know us?"

"Why, dish-yer runaway nigger."

"I don't reckon he does; but what put that into your head?"

"What *put* it dar? Didn' he jis' dis minute sing out like he knowed you?"

Tom says, in a puzzled-up kind of way:

"Well, that's mighty curious. *Who* sung out? *When* did he sing out? *What*
did he sing out?" And turns to me, perfectly ca'm, and says, "Did *you* hear anybody sing out?"

Of course there warn't nothing to be said but the one thing; so I says:

"No; *I* ain't heard nobody say nothing."

Then he turns to Jim, and looks him over like he never see him before; and
says:

"Did you sing out?"

"No, sah," says Jim; "*I* hain't said nothing, sah."

"Not a word?"

"No, sah, I hain't said a word."

"Did you ever see us before?"

"No, sah; not as *I* knows on."

So Tom turns to the nigger, which was looking wild and distressed, and
says, kind of severe:

"What do you reckon's the matter with you, anyway? What made you think
somebody sung out?"

"Oh, it's de dad-blame' witches, sah, en I wisht I was dead, I do. Dey's awluz at it, sah, en dey do mos' kill me, dey sk'yers me so. Please to don't tell nobody 'bout it sah, er old Mars Silas he'll scole me; 'kase he say dey *ain't* no witches. I jis' wish to goodness he was heah now—*den* what would he say! I jis' bet he couldn' fine no way to git aroun' it *dis* time. But it's awluz jis' so; people dat's *sot*, stays sot; dey won't look into nothn' en fine it out f'r deyselves, en when *you* fine it out en tell um 'bout it, dey doan' b'lieve you."

Tom give him a dime, and said we wouldn't tell nobody; and told him to buy some more thread to tie up his wool with; and then looks at Jim, and says:

"I wonder if Uncle Silas is going to hang this nigger. If I was to catch a nigger that was ungrateful enough to run away, *I* wouldn't give him up, I'd hang him." And whilst the nigger stepped to the door to look at the dime and bite it to see if it was good, he whispers to Jim and says:

"Don't ever let on to know us. And if you hear any digging going on nights, it's us: we're going to set you free."

Jim only had time to grab us by the hand and squeeze it, then the nigger come back, and we said we'd come again some time if the nigger wanted us to; and he said he would, more particular if it was dark, because the witches went for him mostly in the dark, and it was good to have folks around then.

## Chapter XXXV

It would be most an hour, yet, till breakfast, so we left, and struck down into the woods; because Tom said we got to have *some* light to see how to dig by, and a lantern makes too much, and might get us into trouble; what we must have was a lot of them rotten chunks that's called fox-fire[9] and just makes a soft kind of a glow when you lay them in a dark place. We fetched an armful and hid it in the weeds, and set down to rest, and Tom says, kind of dissatisfied:

"Blame it, this whole thing is just as easy and awkard as it can be. And so it makes it so rotten difficult to get up a difficult plan. There ain't no watchman to be drugged—now there *ought* to be a watchman. There ain't even a dog to give a sleeping-mixture to. And there's Jim chained by one leg, with a ten-foot chain, to the leg of his bed; why, all you got to do is to lift up the bedstead and slip off the chain. And Uncle Silas he trusts everybody; sends the key to the punkin-headed nigger, and don't send nobody to watch the nigger. Jim could a got out of that window hole before this, only there wouldn't be no use trying to travel with a ten-foot chain on his leg. Why, drat it, Huck, it's the stupidest arrangement I ever see. You got to invent *all* the difficulties. Well, we can't help it, we got to do the best we can with the materials we've got. Anyhow, there's one thing—there's more honor in getting him out through a lot of difficulties and dangers, where there warn't one of them furnished to you by the people who it was their duty to furnish them, and you had to contrive them all out of your own head. Now look at just that one thing of the lantern. When you come down to the cold facts, we simply got to *let on* that a lantern's resky. Why, we could work with a torchlight procession if we wanted to, I believe. Now, whilst I think of it, we got to hunt up something to make a saw out of, the first chance we get."

"What do we want of a saw?"

9. Phosphorescent glow of fungus on rotting wood.

"What do we *want* of it? Hain't we got to saw the leg of Jim's bed off, so as to get the chain loose?"

"Why, you just said a body could lift up the bedstead and slip the chain off."

"Well, if that ain't just like you, Huck Finn. You *can* get up the infant-schooliest ways of going at a thing. Why, hain't you ever read any books at all?—Baron Trenck, nor Casanova, nor Benvenuto Chelleeny, nor Henri IV.,[1] nor none of them heroes? Whoever heard of getting a prisoner loose in such an old-maidy way as that? No; the way all the best authorities does, is to saw the bedleg in two, and leave it just so, and swallow the sawdust, so it can't be found, and put some dirt and grease around the sawed place so the very keen-est seneskal[2] can't see no sign of it's being sawed, and thinks the bed-leg is perfectly sound. Then, the night you're ready, fetch the leg a kick, down she goes; slip off your chain, and there you are. Nothing to do but hitch your rope-ladder to the battlements, shin down it, break your leg in the moat—because a rope-ladder is nineteen foot too short, you know—and there's your horses and your trusty vassles, and they scoop you up and fling you across a saddle and away you go, to your native Langudoc, or Navarre,[3] or wherever it is. It's gaudy, Huck. I wish there was a moat to this cabin. If we get time, the night of the escape, we'll dig one."

I says:

"What do we want of a moat, when we're going to snake him out from under the cabin?"

But he never heard me. He had forgot me and everything else. He had his chin in his hand, thinking. Pretty soon, he sighs, and shakes his head; then sighs again, and says:

"No, it wouldn't do—there ain't necessity enough for it."

"For what?" I says.

"Why, to saw Jim's leg off," he says.

"Good land!" I says, "why, there ain't *no* necessity for it. And what would you want to saw his leg off for, anyway?"

"Well, some of the best authorities has done it. They couldn't get the chain off, so they just cut their hand off, and shoved. And a leg would be better still. But we got to let that go. There ain't necessity enough in this case; and besides, Jim's a nigger and wouldn't understand the reasons for it, and how it's the custom in Europe, so we'll let it go. But there's one thing—he can have a rope-ladder; we can tear up our sheets and make him a rope-ladder easy enough. And we can send it to him in a pie; it's mostly done that way. And I've et worse pies."

"Why, Tom Sawyer, how you talk," I says; "Jim ain't got no use for a rope-ladder."

"He *has* got use for it. How *you* talk, you better say; you don't know nothing about it. He's *got* to have a rope ladder; they all do."

"What in the nation can he *do* with it?"

"*Do* with it? He can hide it in his bed, can't he? That's what they all do; and he's got to, too. Huck, you don't ever seem to want to do anything that's reg-

---

1. Baron Friedrich von der Trenck (1726–1794), an Austrian soldier, and Henry IV of France (1553–1610), military heroes. Benvenuto Cellini (1500–1571), an artist, and Giovanni Jacopo Casanova (1725–1798) were both famous lovers. All four were involved in daring escape attempts.
2. Seneschal, powerful official in the service of medieval nobles.
3. Provinces in France and Spain, respectively.

ular; you want to be starting something fresh all the time. Spose he *don't* do nothing with it? ain't it there in his bed, for a clew, after he's gone? and don't you reckon they'll want clews? Of course they will. And you wouldn't leave them any? That would be a *pretty* howdy-do *wouldn't* it! I never heard of such a thing."

"Well," I says, "if it's in the regulations, and he's got to have it, all right, let him have it; because I don't wish to go back on no regulations; but there's one thing, Tom Sawyer—if we go tearing up our sheets to make Jim a rope-ladder, we're going to get into trouble with Aunt Sally, just as sure as you're born. Now, the way I look at it, a hickry-bark ladder don't cost nothing, and don't waste nothing, and is just as good to load up a pie with, and hide in a straw tick, as any rag ladder you can start; and as for Jim, he hain't had no experience, and so *he* don't care what kind of a—"

"Oh, shucks, Huck Finn, if I was as ignorant as you, I'd keep still—that's what *I'd* do. Who ever heard of a state prisoner escaping by a hickry-bark ladder? Why, it's perfectly ridiculous."

"Well, all right, Tom, fix it your own way; but if you'll take my advice, you'll let me borrow a sheet off of the clothes-line."

He said that would do. And that give him another idea, and he says:

"Borrow a shirt, too."

"What do we want of a shirt, Tom?"

"Want it for Jim to keep a journal on."

"Journal your granny—*Jim* can't write."

"Spose he *can't* write—he can make marks on the shirt, can't he, if we make him a pen out of an old pewter spoon or a piece of an old iron barrel-hoop?"

"Why, Tom, we can pull a feather out of a goose and make him a better one; and quicker, too."

"*Prisoners* don't have geese running around the donjon-keep to pull pens out of, you muggins. They *always* make their pens out of the hardest, toughest, troublesomest piece of old brass candlestick or something like that they can get their hands on; and it takes them weeks and weeks, and months and months to file it out, too, because they've got to do it by rubbing it on the wall. *They* wouldn't use a goose-quill if they had it. It ain't regular."

"Well, then, what'll we make him the ink out of?"

"Many makes it out of iron-rust and tears; but that's the common sort and women; the best authorities uses their own blood. Jim can do that; and when he wants to send any little common ordinary mysterious message to let the world know where he's captivated, he can write it on the bottom of a tin plate with a fork and throw it out of the window. The Iron Mask[4] always done that, and it's a blame' good way, too."

"Jim ain't got no tin plates. They feed him in a pan."

"That ain't anything; we can get him some."

"Can't nobody *read* his plates."

"That ain't got nothing to *do* with it, Huck Finn. All *he's* got to do is to write on the plate and throw it out. You don't *have* to be able to read it. Why, half the time you can't read anything a prisoner writes on a tin plate, or anywhere else."

"Well, then, what's the sense in wasting the plates?"

---

4. The chief character in Alexandre Dumas's novel *Le Vicomte de Bragelonne* (1848–50), part of which was translated into English as *The Man in the Iron Mask*.

"Why, blame it all, it ain't the *prisoner's* plates."

"But it's *somebody's* plates, ain't it?"

"Well, spos'n it is? What does the *prisoner* care whose—"

He broke off there, because we heard the breakfast-horn blowing. So we cleared out for the house.

Along during that morning I borrowed a sheet and a white shirt off of the clothes-line; and I found an old sack and put them in it, and we went down and got the fox-fire, and put that in too. I called it borrowing, because that was what pap always called it; but Tom said it warn't borrowing, it was stealing. He said we was representing prisoners; and prisoners don't care how they get a thing so they get it, and nobody don't blame them for it, either. It ain't no crime in a prisoner to steal the thing he needs to get away with, Tom said; it's his right; and so, as long as we was representing a prisoner, we had a perfect right to steal anything on this place we had the least use for, to get ourselves out of prison with. He said if we warn't prisoners it would be a very different thing, and nobody but a mean ornery person would steal when he warn't a prisoner. So we allowed we would steal everything there was that come handy. And yet he made a mighty fuss, one day, after that, when I stole a watermelon out of the nigger patch and eat it; and he made me go and give the niggers a dime, without telling them what it was for. Tom said that what he meant was, we could steal anything we *needed*. Well, I says, I needed the watermelon. But he said I didn't need it to get out of prison with, there's where the difference was. He said if I'd a wanted it to hide a knife in, and smuggle it to Jim to kill the seneskal with, it would a been all right. So I let it go at that, though I couldn't see no advantage in my representing a prisoner, if I got to set down and chaw over a lot of gold-leaf distinctions like that, every time I see a chance to hog a watermelon.

Well, as I was saying, we waited that morning till everybody was settled down to business, and nobody in sight around the yard; then Tom he carried the sack into the lean-to whilst I stood off a piece to keep watch. By-and-by he come out, and we went and set down on the wood-pile, to talk. He says:

"Everything's all right, now, except tools; and that's easy fixed."

"Tools?" I says.

"Yes."

"Tools for what?"

"Why, to dig with. We ain't agoing to *gnaw* him out, are we?"

"Ain't them old crippled picks and things in there good enough to dig a nigger out with?" I says.

He turns on me looking pitying enough to make a body cry, and says:

"Huck Finn, did you *ever* hear of a prisoner having picks and shovels, and all the modern conveniences in his wardrobe to dig himself out with? Now I want to ask you—if you got any reasonableness in you at all—what kind of a show would *that* give him to be a hero? Why, they might as well lend him the key, and done with it. Picks and shovels—why they wouldn't furnish 'em to a king."

"Well, then," I says, "if we don't want the picks and shovels, what do we want?"

"A couple of case-knives."[5]

---

5. Ordinary kitchen knives.

"To dig the foundations out from under that cabin with?"

"Yes."

"Confound it, it's foolish, Tom."

"It don't make no difference how foolish it is, it's the *right way*—and it's the regular way. And there ain't no *other* way, that ever *I* heard of, and I've read all the books that gives any information about these things. They always dig out with a case-knife—and not through dirt, mind you; generly it's through solid rock. And it takes them weeks and weeks and weeks, and for ever and ever. Why, look at one of them prisoners in the bottom dungeon of the Castle Deef,[6] in the harbor of Marseilles, that dug himself out that way; how long was *he* at it, you reckon?"

"I don't know."

"Well, guess."

"I don't know. A month and a half?"

"*Thirty-seven year*—and he come out in China. *That's* the kind. I wish the bottom of *this* fortress was solid rock."

"*Jim* don't know nobody in China."

"What's *that* got to do with it? Neither did that other fellow. But you're always a-wandering off on a side issue. Why can't you stick to the main point?"

"All right—*I* don't care where he comes out, so he *comes* out; and Jim don't, either, I reckon. But there's one thing, anyway—Jim's too old to be dug out with a case-knife. He won't last."

"Yes he will *last*, too. You don't reckon it's going to take thirty-seven years to dig out through a *dirt* foundation, do you?"

"How long will it take, Tom?"

"Well, we can't resk being as long as we ought to, because it mayn't take very long for Uncle Silas to hear from down there by New Orleans. He'll hear Jim ain't from there. Then his next move will be to advertise Jim, or something like that. So we can't resk being as long digging him out as we ought to. By rights I reckon we ought to be a couple of years; but we can't. Things being so uncertain, what I recommend is this: that we really dig right in, as quick as we can; and after that, we can *let on*, to ourselves, that we was at it thirty-seven years. Then we can snatch him out and rush him away the first time there's an alarm. Yes, I reckon that'll be the best way."

"Now, there's *sense* in that," I says. "Letting on don't cost nothing; letting on ain't no trouble; and if it's any object, I don't mind letting on we was at it a hundred and fifty year. It wouldn't strain me none, after I got my hand in. So I'll mosey along now, and smouch a couple of case-knives."

"Smouch three," he says; "we want one to make a saw out of."

"Tom, if it ain't unregular and irreligious to sejest it," I says, "there's an old rusty saw-blade around yonder sticking under the weatherboarding behind the smoke-house."

He looked kind of weary and discouraged-like, and says:

"It ain't no use to try to learn you nothing, Huck. Run along and smouch the knives—three of them." So I done it.

6. The hero of Alexandre Dumas's popular Romantic novel *The Count Château of Monte Cristo* (1844) was held prisoner at the Chateau d'If, a castle built by Francis I in 1524 on a small island in Marseilles harbor and used for many years as a state prison.

## Chapter XXXVI

As soon as we reckoned everybody was asleep, that night, we went down the lightning-rod, and shut ourselves up in the lean-to, and got out our pile of fox-fire, and went to work. We cleared everything out of the way, about four or five foot along the middle of the bottom log. Tom said he was right behind Jim's bed now, and we'd dig in under it, and when we got through there couldn't nobody in the cabin ever know there was any hole there, because Jim's counterpin[7] hung down most to the ground, and you'd have to raise it up and look under to see the hole. So we dug and dug, with case-knives, till most midnight; and then we was dog-tired, and our hands was blistered, and yet you couldn't see we'd done anything, hardly. At last I says:

"This ain't no thirty-seven year job, this is a thirty-eight year job, Tom Sawyer."

He never said nothing. But he sighed, and pretty soon he stopped digging, and then for a good little while I knowed he was thinking. Then he says:

"It ain't no use, Huck, it ain't agoing to work. If we was prisoners it would, because then we'd have as many years as we wanted, and no hurry; and we wouldn't get but a few minutes to dig, every day, while they was changing watches, and so our hands wouldn't get blistered, and we could keep it up right along, year in and year out, and do it right, and the way it ought to be done. But we can't fool along, we got to rush; we ain't got no time to spare. If we was to put in another night this way, we'd have to knock off for a week to let our hands get well—couldn't touch a case-knife with them sooner."

"Well, then, what we going to do, Tom?"

"I'll tell you. It ain't right, and it ain't moral, and I wouldn't like it to get out—but there ain't only just the one way; we got to dig him out with the picks, and let on it's case-knives."

"Now you're talking!" I says; "your head gets leveler and leveler all the time, Tom Sawyer," I says. "Picks is the thing, moral or no moral; and as for me, I don't care shucks for the morality of it, nohow. When I start in to steal a nigger, or a watermelon, or a Sunday-school book, I ain't no ways particular how it's done so it's done. What I want is my nigger; or what I want is my watermelon; or what I want is my Sunday-school book; and if a pick's the handiest thing, that's the thing I'm agoing to dig that nigger or that watermelon or that Sunday-school book out with; and I don't give a dead rat what the authorities thinks about it nuther."

"Well," he says, "there's excuse for picks and letting-on in a case like this; if it warn't so, I wouldn't approve of it, nor I wouldn't stand by and see the rules broke—because right is right, and wrong is wrong, and a body ain't got no business doing wrong when he ain't ignorant and knows better. It might answer for you to dig Jim out with a pick, without any letting-on, because you don't know no better; but it wouldn't for me, because I do know better. Gimme a case-knife."

He had his own by him, but I handed him mine. He flung it down, and says: "Gimme a case-knife."

I didn't know just what to do—but then I thought. I scratched around

---

7. Counterpane or bedspread.

amongst the old tools, and got a pick-ax and give it to him, and he took it and went to work, and never said a word.

He was always just that particular. Full of principle.

So then I got a shovel, and then we picked and shoveled, turn about, and made the fur fly. We stuck to it about a half an hour, which was as long as we could stand up; but we had a good deal of a hole to show for it. When I got up stairs, I looked out at the window and see Tom doing his level best with the lightning-rod, but he couldn't come it, his hands was so sore. At last he says:

"It ain't no use, it can't be done. What you reckon I better do? Can't you think up no way?"

"Yes," I says, "but I reckon it ain't regular. Come up the stairs, and let on it's a lightning-rod."

So he done it.

Next day Tom stole a pewter spoon and a brass candlestick in the house, for to make some pens for Jim out of, and six tallow candles; and I hung around the nigger cabins, and laid for a chance, and stole three tin plates. Tom said it wasn't enough; but I said nobody wouldn't ever see the plates that Jim throwed out, because they'd fall in the dog-fennel and jimpson weeds under the window-hole—then we could tote them back and he could use them over again. So Tom was satisfied. Then he says:

"Now, the thing to study out is, how to get the things to Jim."

"Take them in through the hole," I says, "when we get it done."

He only just looked scornful, and said something about nobody ever heard of such an idiotic idea, and then he went to studying. By-and-by he said he had ciphered out two or three ways, but there warn't no need to decide on any of them yet. Said we'd got to post Jim first.

That night we went down the lightning-rod a little after ten, and took one of the candles along, and listened under the window-hole, and heard Jim snoring; so we pitched it in, and it didn't wake him. Then we whirled in with the pick and shovel, and in about two hours and a half the job was done. We crept in under Jim's bed and into the cabin, and pawed around and found the candle and lit it, and stood over Jim a while, and found him looking hearty and healthy, and then we woke him up gentle and gradual. He was so glad to see us he most cried; and called us honey, and all the pet names he could think of; and was for having us hunt up a cold chisel to cut the chain off of his leg with, right away, and clearing out without losing any time. But Tom he showed him how unregular it would be, and set down and told him all about our plans, and how we could alter them in a minute any time there was an alarm; and not to be the least afraid, because we would see he got away, *sure*. So Jim he said it was all right, and we set there and talked over old times a while, and then Tom asked a lot of questions, and when Jim told him Uncle Silas come in every day or two to pray with him, and Aunt Sally come in to see if he was comfortable and had plenty to eat, and both of them was kind as they could be, Tom says:

"*Now* I know how to fix it. We'll send you some things by them."

I said, "Don't do nothing of the kind; it's one of the most jackass ideas I ever struck;" but he never paid no attention to me; went right on. It was his way when he'd got his plans set.

So he told Jim how we'd have to smuggle in the rope-ladder pie, and other large things, by Nat, the nigger that fed him, and he must be on the lookout, and not be surprised, and not let Nat see him open them; and we would put small things in uncle's coat pockets and he must steal them out; and we would tie things to aunt's apron strings or put them in her apron pocket, if we got a chance; and told him what they would be and what they was for. And told him how to keep a journal on the shirt with his blood, and all that. He told him everything. Jim he couldn't see no sense in the most of it, but he allowed we was white folks and knowed better than him; so he was satisfied, and said he would do it all just as Tom said.

Jim had plenty corn-cob pipes and tobacco; so we had a right down good sociable time; then we crawled out through the hole, and so home to bed, with hands that looked like they'd been chawed. Tom was in high spirits. He said it was the best fun he ever had in his life, and the most intellectural; and said if he only could see his way to it we would keep it up all the rest of our lives and leave Jim to our children to get out; for he believed Jim would come to like it better and better the more he got used to it. He said that in that way it could be strung out to as much as eighty year, and would be the best time on record. And he said it would make us all celebrated that had a hand in it.

In the morning we went out to the wood-pile and chopped up the brass candlestick into handy sizes, and Tom put them and the pewter spoon in his pocket. Then we went to the nigger cabins, and while I got Nat's notice off, Tom shoved a piece of candlestick into the middle of a corn-pone that was in Jim's pan, and we went along with Nat to see how it would work, and it just worked noble; when Jim bit into it it most mashed all his teeth out; and there warn't ever anything could a worked better. Tom said so himself. Jim he never let on but what it was only just a piece of rock or something like that that's always getting into bread, you know; but after that he never bit into nothing but what he jabbed his fork into it in three or four places, first.

And whilst we was a standing there in the dimmish light, here comes a couple of the hounds bulging in, from under Jim's bed; and they kept on piling in till there was eleven of them, and there warn't hardly room in there to get your breath. By jings, we forgot to fasten that lean-to door. The nigger Nat he only just hollered "witches!" once, and kneeled over onto the floor amongst the dogs, and begun to groan like he was dying. Tom jerked the door open and flung out a slab of Jim's meat, and the dogs went for it, and in two seconds he was out himself and back again and shut the door, and I knowed he'd fixed the other door too. Then he went to work on the nigger, coaxing him and petting him, and asking him if he'd been imagining he saw something again. He raised up, and blinked his eyes around, and says:

"Mars Sid, you'll say I's a fool, but if I didn't b'lieve I see most a million dogs, er devils, er some'n, I wisht I may die right heah in dese tracks. I did, mos' sholy. Mars Sid, I *felt* um—I *felt* um, sah; dey was all over me. Dad fetch it, I jis' wisht I could git my han's on one er dem witches jis' wunst—on'y jis' wunst—it's all I'd ast. But mos'ly I wisht dey'd lemme 'lone, I does."

Tom says:

"Well, I tell you what I think. What makes them come here just at this runaway nigger's breakfast-time? It's because they're hungry; that's the reason. You make them a witch pie; that's the thing for *you* to do."

"But my lan', Mars Sid, how's I gwyne to make 'm a witch pie? I doan' know how to make it. I hain't ever hearn er sich a thing b'fo.' "

"Well, then, I'll have to make it myself."

"Will you do it, honey?—will you? I'll wusshup de groun' und' yo' foot, I will!"

"All right, I'll do it, seeing it's you, and you've been good to us and showed us the runaway nigger. But you got to be mighty careful. When we come around, you turn your back; and then whatever we've put in the pan, don't you let on you see it at all. And don't you look, when Jim unloads the pan—something might happen, I don't know what. And above all, don't you *handle* the witch-things."

"*Hannel* 'm Mars Sid? What *is* you a talkin' 'bout? I wouldn' lay de weight er my finger on um, not f'r ten hund'd thous'n' billion dollars, I wouldn't."

## Chapter XXXVII

That was all fixed. So then we went away and went to the rubbage-pile in the back yard where they keep the old boots, and rags, and pieces of bottles, and wore-out tin things, and all such truck, and scratched around and found an old tin washpan and stopped up the holes as well as we could, to bake the pie in, and took it down cellar and stole it full of flour, and started for breakfast and found a couple of shingle-nails that Tom said would be handy for a prisoner to scrabble his name and sorrows on the dungeon walls with, and dropped one of them in Aunt Sally's apron pocket which was hanging on a chair, and t'other we stuck in the band of Uncle Silas's hat, which was on the bureau, because we heard the children say their pa and ma was going to the runaway nigger's house this morning, and then went to breakfast, and Tom dropped the pewter spoon in Uncle Silas's coat pocket, and Aunt Sally wasn't come yet, so we had to wait a little while.

And when she come she was hot, and red, and cross, and couldn't hardly wait for the blessing; and then she went to sluicing out coffee with one hand and cracking the handiest child's head with her thimble with the other, and says:

"I've hunted high, and I've hunted low, and it does beat all, what *has* become of your other shirt."

My heart fell down amongst my lungs and livers and things, and a hard piece of corn-crust started down my throat after it and got met on the road with a cough and was shot across the table and took one of the children in the eye and curled him up like a fishing-worm, and let a cry out of him the size of a war-whoop, and Tom he turned kinder blue around the gills, and it all amounted to a considerable state of things for about a quarter of a minute or as much as that, and I would a sold out for half price if there was a bidder. But after that we was all right again—it was the sudden surprise of it that knocked us so kind of cold. Uncle Silas he says:

"It's most uncommon curious, I can't understand it. I know perfectly well I took it *off*, because——"

"Because you hain't got but one on. Just *listen* at the man! I know you took it off, and know it by a better way than your wool-gethering memory, too, because it was on the clo'es-line yesterday—I see it there myself. But it's gone—that's the long and the short of it, and you'll just have to change to a red flann'l one till I can get time to make a new one. And it'll be the third I've made in two years; it just keeps a body on the jump to keep you in shirts; and whatever you do manage to *do* with 'm all, is more'n I can make out. A body'd think you *would* learn to take some sort of care of 'em, at your time of life."

"I know it, Sally, and I do try all I can. But it oughtn't to be altogether my fault, because you know I don't see them nor have nothing to do with them except when they're on me; and I don't believe I've ever lost one of them *off* of me."

"Well, it ain't *your* fault if you haven't, Silas—you'd a done it if you could, I reckon. And the shirt ain't all that's gone, nuther. Ther's a spoon gone; and *that* ain't all. There was ten, and now ther's only nine. The calf got the shirt I reckon, but the calf never took the spoon, *that's* certain."

"Why, what else is gone, Sally?"

"Ther's six *candles* gone—that's what. The rats could a got the candles, and I reckon they did; I wonder they don't walk off with the whole place, the way you're always going to stop their holes and don't do it; and if they warn't fools they'd sleep in your hair, Silas—*you'd* never find it out; but you can't lay the *spoon* on the rats, and that I *know*."

"Well, Sally, I'm in fault, and I acknowledge it; I've been remiss; but I won't let to-morrow go by without stopping up them holes."

"Oh, I wouldn't hurry, next year'll do. Matilda Angelina Araminta *Phelps!*"

Whack comes the thimble, and the child snatches her claws out of the sugar-bowl without fooling around any. Just then, the nigger woman steps onto the passage, and says:

"Missus, dey's a sheet gone."

"A *sheet* gone! Well, for land's sake!"

"I'll stop up them holes *to-day*," says Uncle Silas, looking sorrowful.

"Oh, *do* shet up!—spose the rats took the *sheet? Where's* it gone, Lize?"

"Clah to goodness I hain't no notion, Miss Sally. She wuz on de clo's-line yistiddy, but she done gone; she ain' dah no mo', now."

"I reckon the world *is* coming to an end. I *never* see the beat of it, in all my born days. A shirt, and a sheet, and a spoon, and six can—"

"Missus," comes a young yaller wench, "dey's a brass candlestick miss'n."

"Cler out from here, you hussy, er I'll take a skillet to ye!"

Well, she was just a biling. I begun to lay for a chance; I reckoned I would sneak out and go for the woods till the weather moderated. She kept a raging right along, running her insurrection all by herself, and everybody else mighty meek and quiet; and at last Uncle Silas, looking kind of foolish, fishes up that spoon out of his pocket. She stopped, with her mouth open and her hands up, and as for me, I wished I was in Jerusalem or somewheres. But not long; because she says:

"It's *just* as I expected. So you had it in your pocket all the time; and like as not you've got the other things there, too. How'd it get there?"

"I reely don't know, Sally," he says, kind of apologizing, "or you know I would tell. I was a-studying over my text in Acts Seventeen, before breakfast, and I reckon I put it in there, not noticing, meaning to put my Testament in, and it must be so, because my Testament ain't in, but I'll go and see, and if the Testament is where I had it, I'll know I didn't put it in, and that will show that I laid the Testament down and took up the spoon, and——"

"Oh, for the land's sake! Give a body a rest! Go 'long now, the whole kit and biling of ye; and don't come nigh me again till I've got back my peace of mind."

*I'd* a heard her, if she'd a said it to herself, let alone speaking it out; and I'd a got up and obeyed her, if I'd a been dead. As we was passing through the setting-room, the old man he took up his hat, and the shingle-nail fell out on the floor, and he just merely picked it up and laid it on the mantel-shelf, and never said nothing, and went out. Tom see him do it, and remembered about the spoon, and says:

"Well, it ain't no use to send things by *him* no more, he ain't reliable." Then he says: "But he done us a good turn with the spoon, anyway, without knowing it, and so we'll go and do him one without *him* knowing it—stop up his rat-holes."

There was a noble good lot of them, down cellar, and it took us a whole hour, but we done the job tight and good, and ship-shape. Then we heard steps on the stairs, and blowed out our light, and hid; and here comes the old man, with a candle in one hand and a bundle of stuff in t'other, looking as absent-minded as year before last. He went a mooning around, first to one rat-hole and then another, till he'd been to them all. Then he stood about five minutes, picking tallow-drip off of his candle and thinking. Then he turns off slow and dreamy towards the stairs, saying:

"Well, for the life of me I can't remember when I done it. I could show her now that I warn't to blame on account of the rats. But never mind—let it go. I reckon it wouldn't do no good."

And so he went on a mumbling up stairs, and then we left. He was a mighty nice old man. And always is.

Tom was a good deal bothered about what to do for a spoon, but he said we'd got to have it; so he took a think. When he had ciphered it out, he told me how we was to do; then we went and waited around the spoon-basket till we see Aunt Sally coming, and then Tom went to counting the spoons and laying them out to one side, and I slip one of them up my sleeve, and Tom says:

"Why, Aunt Sally, there ain't but nine spoons, *yet.*"

She says:

"Go 'long to your play, and don't bother me. I know better, I counted 'm myself."

"Well, I've counted them twice, Aunty, and *I* can't make but nine."

She looked out of all patience, but of course she come to count—anybody would.

"I declare to gracious ther' *ain't* but nine!" she says. "Why, what in the world—plague *take* the things, I'll count 'm again."

So I slipped back the one I had, and when she got done counting, she says:

"Hang the troublesome rubbage, ther's *ten* now!" and she looked huffy and bothered both. But Tom says:

"Why, Aunty *I* don't think there's ten."

"You numskull, didn't you see me *count* 'm?"

"I know, but—"

"Well, I'll count 'm *again.*"

So I smouched one, and they come out nine same as the other time. Well, she *was* in a tearing way—just a trembling all over, she was so mad. But she counted and counted, till she got that addled she'd start to count-in the *bas-*

*ket* for a spoon, sometimes; and so, three times they come out right, and three times they come out wrong. Then she grabbed up the basket and slammed it across the house and knocked the cat galley-west;[8] and she said cle'r out and let her have some peace, and if we come bothering around her again betwixt that and dinner, she'd skin us. So we had the odd spoon; and dropped it in her apron pocket whilst she was giving us our sailing-orders, and Jim got it all right, along with her shingle-nail, before noon. We was very well satisfied with the business, and Tom allowed it was worth twice the trouble it took, because he said *now* she couldn't ever count them spoons twice alike again to save her life; and wouldn't believe she'd counted them right, if she *did*; and said that after she'd about counted her head off, for the last three days, he judged she'd give it up and offer to kill anybody that wanted her to ever count them any more.

So we put the sheet back on the line, that night, and stole one out of her closet; and kept on putting it back and stealing it again, for a couple of days, till she didn't know how many sheets she had, any more, and said she didn't *care*, and warn't agoing to bullyrag[9] the rest of her soul out about it, and wouldn't count them again not to save her life, she druther die first.

So we was all right now, as to the shirt and the sheet and the spoon and the candles, by the help of the calf and the rats and the mixed-up counting; and as to the candlestick, it warn't no consequence, it would blow over by-and-by.

But that pie was a job; we had no end of trouble with that pie. We fixed it up away down in the woods, and cooked it there; and we got it done at last, and very satisfactory, too; but not all in one day; and we had to use up three wash-pans full of flour, before we got through, and we got burnt pretty much all over, in places, and eyes put out with the smoke; because, you see, we didn't want nothing but a crust, and we couldn't prop it up right, and she would always cave in. But of course we thought of the right way at last; which was to cook the ladder, too, in the pie. So then we laid in with Jim, the second night, and tore up the sheet all in little strings, and twisted them together, and long before daylight we had a lovely rope, that you could a hung a person with. We let on it took nine months to make it.

And in the forenoon we took it down to the woods, but it wouldn't go in the pie. Being made of a whole sheet, that way, there was rope enough for forty pies, if we'd a wanted them, and plenty left over for soup, or sausage, or anything you choose. We could a had a whole dinner.

But we didn't need it. All we needed was just enough for the pie, and so we throwed the rest away. We didn't cook none of the pies in the washpan, afraid the solder would melt; but Uncle Silas he had a noble brass warming-pan which he thought considerable of, because it belonged to one of his ancestors with a long wooden handle that come over from England with William the Conqueror in the *Mayflower*[1] or one of them early ships and was hid away up garret with a lot of other old pots and things that was valuable, not on account of being any account because they warn't, but on account of them being relicts, you know, and we snaked her out, private, and took her down there, but she failed on the first pies, because we didn't know how, but

---

8. Knocked the cat out completely.
9. To nag mercilessly.

1. William the Conqueror lived in the 11th century. The *Mayflower* made its crossing in 1620.

she come up smiling on the last one. We took and lined her with dough, and set her in the coals, and loaded her up with rag-rope, and put on a dough roof, and shut down the lid, and put hot embers on top, and stood off five foot, with the long handle, cool and comfortable, and in fifteen minutes she turned out a pie that was a satisfaction to look at. But the person that et it would want to fetch a couple of kags of toothpicks along, for if that rope-ladder wouldn't cramp him down to business, I don't know nothing what I'm talking about, and lay him in enough stomach-ache to last him till next time, too.

Nat didn't look, when we put the witch-pie in Jim's pan; and we put the three tin plates in the bottom of the pan under the vittles; and so Jim got everything all right, and as soon as he was by himself he busted into the pie and hid the rope-ladder inside of his straw tick, and scratched some marks on a tin plate and throwed it out of the window-hole.

## Chapter XXXVIII

Making them pens was a distressid-tough job, and so was the saw; and Jim allowed the inscription was going to be the toughest of all. That's the one which the prisoner has to scrabble on the wall. But we had to have it; Tom said we'd *got* to; there warn't no case of a state prisoner not scrabbling his inscription to leave behind, and his coat of arms.

"Look at Lady Jane Grey," he says; "look at Gilford Dudley; look at old Northumberland![2] Why, Huck, spose it *is* considerable trouble?—what you going to do?—how you going to get around it? Jim's *got* to do his inscription and coat of arms. They all do."

Jim says:

"Why, Mars Tom, I hain't got no coat o' arms; I hain't got nuffn but dish-yer old shirt, en you knows I got to keep de journal on dat."

"Oh, you don't understand, Jim; a coat of arms is very different."

"Well," I says, "Jim's right, anyway, when he says he hain't got no coat of arms, because he hain't."

"I reckon *I* knowed that," Tom says, "but you bet he'll have one before he goes out of this—because he's going out *right*, and there ain't going to be no flaws in his record."

So whilst me and Jim filed away at the pens on a brickbat[3] apiece, Jim a making his'n out of the brass and I making mine out of the spoon, Tom set to work to think out the coat of arms. By-and-by he said he'd struck so many good ones he didn't hardly know which to take, but there was one which he reckoned he'd decide on. He says:

"On the scutcheon[4] we'll have a bend *or* in the dexter base, a saltire *murrey* in the fess, with a dog, couchant, for common charge, and under his foot a chain embattled, for slavery, with a chevron *vert* in a chief engrailed, and three invected lines on a field *azure,* with the nombril points rampant on a dancette indented; crest, a runaway nigger, *sable,* with his bundle over his shoulder on a bar sinister: and a couple of gules for supporters, which is you

2. The story of Lady Jane Grey (1537–1554), her husband, Guildford Dudley, and his father, the duke of Northumberland, was told in W. H. Ainsworth's romance *The Tower of London* (1840). The duke was at work carving a poem on the wall of his cell when the executioners came for him.
3. A fragment of brick.
4. An escutcheon is the shield-shaped surface on which a coat of arms is inscribed. The details are expressed in the technical terminology of heraldry.

and me; motto, *Maggiore fretta, minore atto.* Got it out of a book—means, the more haste, the less speed."

"Geewhillikins," I says, "but what does the rest of it mean?"

"We ain't got no time to bother over that," he says, "we got to dig in like all git-out."

"Well, anyway," I says, "what's *some* of it? What's a fess?"

"A fess—a fess is—*you* don't need to know what a fess is. I'll show him how to make it when he gets to it."

"Shucks, Tom," I says, "I think you might tell a person. What's a bar sinister?"

"Oh, *I* don't know. But he's got to have it. All the nobility does."

That was just his way. If it didn't suit him to explain a thing to you, he wouldn't do it. You might pump at him a week, it wouldn't make no difference.

He'd got all that coat of arms business fixed, so now he started in to finish up the rest of that part of the work, which was to plan out a mournful inscription—said Jim got to have one, like they all done. He made up a lot, and wrote them out on a paper, and read them off, so:

1. *Here a captive heart busted.*

2. *Here a poor prisoner, forsook by the world and friends, fretted out his sorrowful life.*

3. *Here a lonely heart broke, and a worn spirit went to its rest, after thirty-seven years of solitary captivity.*

4. *Here, homeless and friendless, after thirty-seven years of bitter captivity, perished a noble stranger, natural son of Louis XIV.*

Tom's voice trembled, whilst he was reading them, and he most broke down. When he got done, he couldn't no way make up his mind which one for Jim to scrabble onto the wall, they was all so good; but at last he allowed he would let him scrabble them all on. Jim said it would take him a year to scrabble such a lot of truck onto the logs with a nail, and he didn't know how to make letters, besides; but Tom said he would block them out for him, and then he wouldn't have nothing to do but just follow the lines. Then pretty soon he says:

"Come to think, the logs ain't agoing to do; they don't have log walls in a dungeon: we got to dig the inscriptions into a rock. We'll fetch a rock."

Jim said the rock was worse than the logs; he said it would take him such a pison long time to dig them into a rock, he wouldn't ever get out. But Tom said he would let me help him do it. Then he took a look to see how me and Jim was getting along with the pens. It was most pesky tedious hard work and slow, and didn't give my hands no show to get well of the sores, and we didn't seem to make no headway, hardly. So Tom says:

"I know how to fix it. We got to have a rock for the coat of arms and mournful inscriptions, and we can kill two birds with that same rock. There's a gaudy big grindstone down at the mill, and we'll smouch it, and carve the things on it, and file out the pens and the saw on it, too."

It warn't no slouch of an idea; and it warn't no slouch of a grindstone nuther; but we allowed we'd tackle it. It warn't quite midnight, yet, so we cleared out for the mill, leaving Jim at work. We smouched the grindstone, and set out to roll her home, but it was a most nation tough job. Sometimes, do what we could, we couldn't keep her from falling over, and she come mighty near mashing us, every time. Tom said she was going to get one of us, sure, before we got through. We got her half way; and then we was plumb played out, and most drownded with sweat. We see it warn't no use, we got to go and fetch Jim. So he raised up his bed and slid the chain off of the bed-leg, and wrapt it round and round his neck, and we crawled out through our hole and down there, and Jim and me laid into that grindstone and walked her along like nothing; and Tom superintended. He could out-superintend any boy I ever see. He knowed how to do everything.

Our hole was pretty big, but it warn't big enough to get the grindstone through; but Jim he took the pick and soon made it big enough. Then Tom marked out them things on it with the nail, and set Jim to work on them, with the nail for a chisel and an iron bolt from the rubbage in the lean-to for a hammer, and told him to work till the rest of his candle quit on him, and then he could go to bed, and hide the grindstone under his straw tick and sleep on it. Then we helped him fix his chain back on the bed-leg, and was ready for bed ourselves. But Tom thought of something, and says:

"You got any spiders in here, Jim?"

"No, sah, thanks to goodness I hain't, Mars Tom."

"All right, we'll get you some."

"But bless you, honey, I doan' *want* none. I's afeard un um. I jis' 's soon have rattlesnakes aroun'."

Tom thought a minute or two, and says:

"It's a good idea. And I reckon it's been done. It *must* a been done; it stands to reason. Yes, it's a prime good idea. Where could you keep it?"

"Keep what, Mars Tom?"

"Why, a rattlesnake."

"De goodness gracious alive, Mars Tom! Why, if dey was a rattlesnake to come in heah, I'd take en bust right out thoo dat log wall, I would, wid my head."

"Why, Jim, you wouldn't be afraid of it, after a little. You could tame it."

"*Tame* it!"

"Yes—easy enough. Every animal is grateful for kindness and petting, and they wouldn't *think* of hurting a person that pets them. Any book will tell you that. You try—that's all I ask; just try for two or three days. Why, you can get him so, in a little while, that he'll love you; and sleep with you; and won't stay away from you a minute; and will let you wrap him round your neck and put his head in your mouth."

"*Please*, Mars Tom—*doan'* talk so! I can't *stan'* it! He'd *let* me shove his head in my mouf—fer a favor, hain't it? I lay he'd wait a pow'ful long time 'fo' I *ast* him. En mo' en dat, I doan' *want* him to sleep wid me."

"Jim, don't act so foolish. A prisoner's *got* to have some kind of a dumb pet, and if a rattlesnake hain't ever been tried, why, there's more glory to be gained in your being the first to ever try it than any other way you could ever think of to save your life."

"Why, Mars Tom, I doan' *want* no sich glory. Snake take 'n bite Jim's chin off, den *whah* is de glory? No, sah, I doan' want no sich doin's."

"Blame it, can't you *try*? I only *want* you to try—you needn't keep it up if it don't work."

"But de trouble all *done,* ef de snake bite me while I's a tryin' him. Mars Tom, I's willin' to tackle mos' anything 'at ain't onreasonable, but ef you en Huck fetches a rattlesnake in heah for me to tame, I's gwyne to *leave,* dat's *shore.*"

"Well, then, let it go, let it go, if you're so bullheaded about it. We can get you some garter-snakes and you can tie some buttons on their tails, and let on they're rattlesnakes, and I reckon that'll have to do."

"I k'n stan' *dem,* Mars Tom, but blame' 'f I couldn't get along widout um, I tell you dat. I never knowed b'fo', 't was so much bother and trouble to be a prisoner."

"Well, it *always* is, when it's done right. You got any rats around here?"

"No, sah, I hain't seed none."

"Well, we'll get you some rats."

"Why, Mars Tom, I doan' *want* no rats. Dey's de dad-blamedest creturs to sturb a body, en rustle roun' over 'im, en bite his feet, when he's tryin' to sleep, I ever see. So, sah, gimme g'yarter-snakes, 'f I's got to have 'm, but doan' gimme no rats. I ain' got not use f'r um, skasely."

"But Jim, you *got* to have 'em—they all do. So don't make no more fuss about it. Prisoners ain't ever without rats. There ain't no instance of it. And they train them, and pet them, and learn them tricks, and they get to be as sociable as flies. But you got to play music to them. You got anything to play music on?"

"I ain't got nuffn but a coase comb en a piece o' paper, en a juice-harp; but I reck'n dey wouldn't take no stock in a juice-harp."

"Yes, they would. *They* don't care what kind of music 'tis. A jews-harp's plenty good enough for a rat. All animals likes music—in a prison they dote on it. Specially, painful music; and you can't get no other kind out of a jews-harp. It always interests them; they come out to see what's the matter with you. Yes, you're all right; you're fixed very well. You want to set on your bed, nights, before you go to sleep, and early in the mornings, and play your jews-harp; play The Last Link is Broken—that's the thing that'll scoop a rat, quicker'n anything else: and when you've played about two minutes, you'll see all the rats, and the snakes, and spiders, and things begin to feel worried about you, and come. And they'll just fairly swarm over you, and have a noble good time."

"Yes, *dey* will, I reck'n, Mars Tom, but what kine er time is *Jim* havin'? Blest if I kin see de pint. But I'll do it ef I got to. I reck'n I better keep de animals satisfied, en not have no trouble in de house."

Tom waited to think over, and see if there wasn't nothing else; and pretty soon he says:

"Oh—there's one thing I forgot. Could you raise a flower here, do you reckon?"

"I doan' know but maybe I could, Mars Tom; but it's tolable dark in heah, en I ain' got no use f'r no flower, nohow, en she'd be a pow'ful sight o' trouble."

"Well, you try it, anyway. Some other prisoners has done it."

"One er dem big cat-tail-lookin' mullen-stalks would grow in heah, Mars Tom, I reck'n, but she wouldn' be wuth half de trouble she'd coss."

"Don't you believe it. We'll fetch you a little one, and you plant it in the corner, over there, and raise it. And don't call it mullen, call it Pitchiola—that's its right name, when it's in a prison.⁵ And you want to water it with your tears."

"Why, I got plenty spring water, Mars Tom."

"You don't *want* spring water; you want to water it with your tears. It's the way they always do."

"Why, Mars Tom, I lay I kin raise one er dem mullen-stalks twyste wid spring water whiles another man's a *start'n* one wid tears."

"That ain't the idea. You *got* to do it with tears."

"She'll die on my han's, Mars Tom, she sholy will; kase I doan' skasely ever cry."

So Tom was stumped. But he studied it over, and then said Jim would have to worry along the best he could with an onion. He promised he would go to the nigger cabins and drop one, private, in Jim's coffee-pot, in the morning. Jim said he would "jis' 's soon have tobacker in his coffee;" and found so much fault with it, and with the work and bother of raising the mullen, and jews-harping the rats, and petting and flattering up the snakes and spiders and things, on top of all the other work he had to do on pens, and inscriptions, and journals, and things, which made it more trouble and worry and responsibility to be a prisoner than anything he ever undertook, that Tom most lost all patience with him; and said he was just loadened down with more gaudier chances than a prisoner ever had in the world to make a name for himself, and yet he didn't know enough to appreciate them, and they was just about wasted on him. So Jim he was sorry, and said he wouldn't behave so no more, and then me and Tom shoved for bed.

## Chapter XXXIX

In the morning we went up to the village and bought a wire rat trap and fetched it down, and unstopped the best rat hole, and in about an hour we had fifteen of the bulliest kind of ones; and then we took it and put it in a safe place under Aunt Sally's bed. But while we was gone for spiders, little Thomas Franklin Benjamin Jefferson Elexander Phelps found it there, and opened the door of it to see if the rats would come out, and they did; and Aunt Sally she come in, and when we got back she was standing on top of the bed raising Cain, and the rats was doing what they could to keep off the dull times for her. So she took and dusted us both with the hickry, and we was as much as two hours catching another fifteen or sixteen, drat that meddlesome cub, and they warn't the likeliest, nuther, because the first haul was the pick of the flock. I never see a likelier lot of rats than what that first haul was.

We got a splendid stock of sorted spiders, and bugs, and frogs, and caterpillars, and one thing or another; and we like-to got a hornet's nest, but we didn't. The family was at home. We didn't give it right up, but staid with them as long as we could; because we allowed we'd tire them out or they'd got to tire us out, and they done it. Then we got allycumpain⁶ and rubbed on the places, and was pretty near all right again, but couldn't set down convenient. And so we went for the snakes, and grabbed a couple of dozen garters and house-snakes, and put them in a bag, and put it in our room, and by that time

---

5. *Picciola* (1836) was a popular romantic story by Xavier Saintine (pseudonym for Joseph Xavier Boniface, 1798–1865), in which a plant helps a prisoner survive.
6. Elecampane is an herb that Tom and Huck are using to relieve the pain of the hornet stings.

it was supper time, and a rattling good honest day's work; and hungry?—oh, no I reckon not! And there warn't a blessed snake up there, when we went back—we didn't half tie the sack, and they worked out, somehow, and left. But it didn't matter much, because they was still on the premises some-wheres. So we judged we could get some of them again. No, there warn't no real scarcity of snakes about the house for a considerble spell. You'd see them dripping from the rafters and places, every now and then; and they generly landed in your plate, or down the back of your neck, and most of the time where you didn't want them. Well, they was handsome, and striped, and there warn't no harm in a million of them; but that never made no difference to Aunt Sally, she despised snakes, be the breed what they might, and she couldn't stand them no way you could fix it; and every time one of them flopped down on her, it didn't make no difference what she was doing, she would just lay that work down and light out. I never see such a woman. And you could hear her whoop to Jericho. You couldn't get her to take aholt of one of them with the tongs. And if she turned over and found one in bed, she would scramble out and lift a howl that you would think the house was afire. She disturbed the old man so, that he said he could most wish there hadn't ever been no snakes created. Why, after every last snake had been gone clear out of the house for as much as a week, Aunt Sally warn't over it yet; she warn't near over it; when she was setting thinking about something, you could touch her on the back of her neck with a feather and she would jump right out of her stockings. It was very curious. But Tom said all women was just so. He said they was made that way; for some reason or other.

We got a licking every time one of our snakes come in her way; and she allowed these lickings warn't nothing to what she would do if we ever loaded up the place again with them. I didn't mind the lickings, because they didn't amount to nothing; but I minded the trouble we had, to lay in another lot. But we got them laid in, and all the other things; and you never see a cabin as blithesome as Jim's was when they'd all swarm out for music and go for him. Jim didn't like the spiders, and the spiders didn't like Jim; and so they'd lay for him and make it mighty warm for him. And he said that between the rats, and the snakes, and the grindstone, there warn't no room in bed for him, skasely; and when there was, a body couldn't sleep, it was so lively, and it was always lively, he said, because *they* never all slept at one time, but took turn about, so when the snakes was asleep the rats was on deck, and when the rats turned in the snakes come on watch, so he always had one gang under him, in his way, and t'other gang having a circus over him, and if he got up to hunt a new place, the spiders would take a chance at him as he crossed over. He said if he ever got out, this time, he wouldn't ever be a prisoner again, not for a salary.

Well, by the end of three weeks, everything was in pretty good shape. The shirt was sent in early, in a pie, and every time a rat bit Jim he would get up and write a little in his journal whilst the ink was fresh; the pens was made, the inscriptions and so on was all carved on the grindstone; the bed-leg was sawed in two, and we had et up the sawdust, and it give us a most amazing stomach-ache. We reckoned we was all going to die, but didn't. It was the most undigestible sawdust I ever see; and Tom said the same. But as I was saying, we'd got all the work done, now, at last; and we was all pretty much fagged out, too, but mainly Jim. The old man had wrote a couple of times to the plantation below Orleans to come and get their runaway nigger, but hadn't got no answer, because there warn't no such plantation; so he allowed he would advertise Jim in the St. Louis and New Orleans papers; and when he mentioned the St. Louis ones, it give me the cold shivers, and I see we hadn't no time to lose. So Tom said, now for the nonnamous letters.

"What's them?" I says.

"Warnings to the people that something is up. Sometimes it's done one way, sometimes another. But there's always somebody spying around, that gives notice to the governor of the castle. When Louis XVI was going to light out of the Tooleries,[7] a servant girl done it. It's a very good way, and so is the nonnamous letters. We'll use them both. And it's usual for the prisoner's mother to change clothes with him, and she stays in, and he slides out in her clothes. We'll do that too."

"But looky here, Tom, what do we want to *warn* anybody for, that something's up? Let them find it out for themselves—it's their lookout."

"Yes, I know; but you can't depend on them. It's the way they've acted from the very start—left us to do *everything*. They're so confiding and mullet-headed they don't take notice of nothing at all. So if we don't *give* them notice, there won't be nobody nor nothing to interfere with us, and so after all our hard work and trouble this escape 'll go off perfectly flat: won't amount to nothing—won't be nothing *to* it."

"Well, as for me, Tom, that's the way I'd like."

"Shucks," he says, and looked disgusted. So I says:

"But I ain't going to make no complaint. Anyway that suits you suits me. What you going to do about the servant-girl?"

"You'll be her. You slide in, in the middle of the night, and hook that yaller girl's frock."

"Why, Tom, that'll make trouble next morning; because of course she prob'bly hain't got any but that one."

"I know; but you don't want it but fifteen minutes, to carry the nonnamous letter and shove it under the front door."

"All right, then, I'll do it; but I could carry it just as handy in my own togs."

"You wouldn't look like a servant-girl *then*, would you?"

"No, but there won't be nobody to see what I look like, *anyway*."

"That ain't got nothing to do with it. The thing for us to do, is just to do our *duty*, and not worry about whether anybody *sees* us do it or not. Hain't you got no principle at all?"

"All right, I ain't saying nothing; I'm the servant-girl. Who's Jim's mother?"

"I'm his mother. I'll hook a gown from Aunt Sally."

"Well, then, you'll have to stay in the cabin when me and Jim leaves."

"Not much. I'll stuff Jim's clothes full of straw and lay it on his bed to represent his mother in disguise: and Jim 'll take Aunt Sally's gown off of me and wear it, and we'll all evade together. When a prisoner of style escapes, it's called an evasion. It's always called so when a king escapes, f'rinstance. And the same with a king's son; it don't make no difference whether he's a natural one or an unnatural one."

So Tom he wrote the nonnamous letter, and I smouched the yaller wench's

---

7. Twain probably read this episode of the Tuileries, a palace in Paris, in Thomas Carlyle's *French Revolution* (1837).

frock, that night, and put it on, and shoved it under the front door, the way Tom told me to. It said:

> Beware, Trouble is brewing. Keep a sharp lookout.
> UNKNOWN FRIEND.

Next night we stuck a picture which Tom drawed in blood, of a skull and crossbones, on the front door; and next night another one of a coffin, on the back door. I never see a family in such a sweat. They couldn't a been worse scared if the place had a been full of ghosts laying for them behind everything and under the beds and shivering through the air. If a door banged, Aunt Sally she jumped, and said "ouch!" if anything fell, she jumped and said "ouch!" if you happened to touch her, when she warn't noticing, she done the same; she couldn't face noway and be satisfied, because she allowed there was something behind her every time—so she was always a whirling around, sudden, and saying "ouch," and before she'd get two-thirds around, she'd whirl back again, and say it again; and she was afraid to go to bed, but she dasn't set up. So the thing was working very well, Tom said; he said he never see a thing work more satisfactory. He said it showed it was done right.

So he said, now for the grand bulge! So the very next morning at the streak of dawn we got another letter ready, and was wondering what we better do with it, because we heard them say at supper they was going to have a nigger on watch at both doors all night. Tom he went down the lightning-rod to spy around; and the nigger at the back door was asleep, and he stuck it in the back of his neck and come back. This letter said:

> Don't betray me, I wish to be your friend. There is a desprate gang of cut-throats from over in the Ingean Territory[8] going to steal your runaway nigger to-night, and they have been trying to scare you so as you will stay in the house and not bother them. I am one of the gang, but have got religgion and wish to quit it and lead a honest life again, and will betray the helish design. They will sneak down from northards, along the fence, at midnight exact, with a false key, and go in the nigger's cabin to get him. I am to be off a piece and blow a tin horn if I see any danger; but stead of that, I will BA like a sheep soon as they get in and not blow at all; then whilst they are getting his chains loose, you slip there and lock them in, and can kill them at your leasure. Don't do anything but just the way I am telling you, if you do they will suspicion something and raise whoopjam-boreehoo. I do not wish any reward but to know I have done the right thing.
> UNKNOWN FRIEND.

## Chapter XL

We was feeling pretty good, after breakfast, and took my canoe and went over the river a fishing, with a lunch, and had a good time, and took a look at the raft and found her all right, and got home late to supper, and found them in such a sweat and worry they didn't know which end they was standing on, and made us go right off to bed the minute we was done supper, and wouldn't tell us what the trouble was, and never let on a word about the new letter, but didn't need to,

---

8. The area now the state of Oklahoma was granted to displaced Native Americans in the 1830s and was a base of operations for outlaws for most of the 19th century.

because we knowed as much about it as anybody did, and as soon as we was half up stairs and her back was turned, we slid for the cellar cupboard and loaded up a good lunch and took it up to our room and went to bed, and got up about half-past eleven, and Tom put on Aunt Sally's dress that he stole and was going to start with the lunch, but says:

"Where's the butter?"

"I laid out a hunk of it," I says, "on a piece of a corn-pone."

"Well, you *left* it laid out, then—it ain't here."

"We can get along without it," I says.

"We can get along *with* it, too," he says; "just you slide down cellar and fetch it. And then mosey right down the lightning-rod and come along. I'll go and stuff the straw into Jim's clothes to represent his mother in disguise, and be ready to *ba* like a sheep and shove soon as you get there."

So out he went, and down cellar went I. The hunk of butter, big as a person's fist, was where I had left it, so I took up the slab of corn-pone with it on, and blowed out my light, and started up stairs, very stealthy, and got up to the main floor all right, but here comes Aunt Sally with a candle, and I clapped the truck in my hat, and clapped my hat on my head, and the next second she see me; and she says:

"You been down cellar?"

"Yes'm."

"What you been doing down there?"

"Noth'n."

"*Noth'n!*"

"No'm."

"Well, then, what possessed you to go down there, this time of night?"

"I don't know'm."

"You don't *know?* Don't answer me that way, Tom, I want to know what you been *doing* down there?"

"I hain't been doing a single thing, Aunt Sally, I hope to gracious if I have."

I reckoned she'd let me go, now, and as a generl thing she would; but I spose there was so many strange things going on she was just in a sweat about every little thing that warn't yard-stick straight; so she says, very decided:

"You just march into that setting-room and stay there till I come. You been up to something you no business to, and I lay I'll find out what it is before *I'm* done with you."

So she went away as I opened the door and walked into the setting-room. My, but there was a crowd there! Fifteen farmers, and every one of them had a gun. I was most powerful sick, and slunk to a chair and set down. They was setting around, some of them talking a little, in a low voice, and all of them fidgety and uneasy, but trying to look like they warn't; but I knowed they was, because they was always taking off their hats, and putting them on, and scratching their heads, and changing their seats, and fumbling with their buttons. I warn't easy myself, but I didn't take my hat off, all the same.

I did wish Aunt Sally would come, and get done with me, and lick me, if she wanted to, and let me get away and tell Tom how we'd overdone this thing, and what a thundering hornet's nest we'd got ourselves into, so we could stop fooling around, straight off, and clear out with Jim before these rips got out of patience and come for us.

At last she come, and begun to ask me questions, but I *couldn't* answer them straight, I didn't know which end of me was up; because these men was in such a fidget now, that some was wanting to start right *now* and lay for them desperadoes, and saying it warn't but a few minutes to midnight; and others was trying to get them to hold on and wait for the sheep-signal; and here was aunty pegging away at the questions, and me a shaking all over and ready to sink down in my tracks I was that scared; and the place getting hotter and hotter, and the butter beginning to melt and run down my neck and behind my ears: and pretty soon, when one of them says, "*I'm* for going and getting in the cabin *first,* and right *now,* and catching them when they come," I most dropped; and a streak of butter came a trickling down my forehead, and Aunt Sally she see it, and turns white as a sheet, and says:

"For the land's sake what *is* the matter with the child!—he's got the brain fever as shore as you're born, and they're oozing out!"

And everybody runs to see, and she snatches off my hat, and out comes the bread, and what was left of the butter, and she grabbed me, and hugged me, and says:

"Oh, what a turn you did give me! and how glad and grateful I am it ain't no worse; for luck's against us, and it never rains but it pours, and when I see that truck I thought we'd lost you, for I knowed by the color and all, it was just like your brains would be if—Dear, dear, whyd'nt you *tell* me that was what you'd been down there for, *I* wouldn't a cared. Now cler out to bed, and don't lemme see no more of you till morning!"

I was up stairs in a second, and down the lightning-rod in another one, and shinning through the dark for the lean-to. I couldn't hardly get my words out, I was so anxious; but I told Tom as quick as I could, we must jump for it, now, and not a minute to lose—the house full of men, yonder, with guns!

His eyes just blazed; and he says:

"No!—is that so? *Ain't* it bully! Why, Huck, if it was to do over again, I bet I could fetch two hundred! If we could put it off till—"

"Hurry! *hurry!*" I says. "Where's Jim?"

"Right at your elbow; if you reach out your arm you can touch him. He's dressed, and everything's ready. Now we'll slide out and give the sheep-signal."

But then we heard the tramp of men, coming to the door, and heard them begin to fumble with the padlock; and heard a man say:

"I *told* you we'd be too soon; they haven't come—the door is locked. Here, I'll lock some of you into the cabin and you lay for 'em in the dark and kill 'em when they come; and the rest scatter around a piece, and listen if you can hear 'em coming."

So in they come, but couldn't see us in the dark, and most trod on us whilst we was hustling to get under the bed. But we got under all right, and out through the hole, swift but soft—Jim first, me next, and Tom last, which was according to Tom's orders. Now we was in the lean-to, and heard trampings close by outside. So we crept to the door, and Tom stopped us there and put his eye to the crack, but couldn't make out nothing, it was so dark; and whispered and said he would listen for the steps to get further, and when he nudged us Jim must glide out first, and him last. So he set his ear to the crack and listened, and listened, and listened, and the steps a scraping around, out there, all the time; and at last he nudged us, and we slid out, and stooped down, not breathing, and not making the least noise, and slipped stealthy towards the fence, in Injun file, and got to it, all right, and me and Jim over it; but Tom's britches catched fast on a splinter on the top rail, and then he hear the steps coming, so he had to pull loose, which snapped the splinter and made a noise; and as he dropped in our tracks and started, somebody sings out:

"Who's that? Answer, or I'll shoot!"

But we didn't answer; we just unfurled our heels and shoved. Then there was a rush, and a *bang, bang, bang!* and the bullets fairly whizzed around us! We heard them sing out:

"Here they are! They've broke for the river! after 'em, boys! And turn loose the dogs!"

So here they come, full tilt. We could hear them, because they wore boots, and yelled, but we didn't wear no boots, and didn't yell. We was in the path to the mill; and when they got pretty close onto us, we dodged into the bush and let them go by, and then dropped in behind them. They'd had all the dogs shut up, so they wouldn't scare off the robbers; but by this time somebody had let them loose, and here they come, making pow-wow enough for a million; but they was our dogs; so we stopped in our tracks till they catched up; and when they see it warn't nobody but us, and no excitement to offer them, they only just said howdy, and tore right ahead towards the shouting and clattering; and then we up steam again and whizzed along after them till we was nearly to the mill, and then struck up through the bush to where my canoe was tied, and hopped in and pulled for dear life towards the middle of the river, but didn't make no more noise than we was obleeged to. Then we struck out, easy and comfortable, for the island where my raft was; and we could hear them yelling and barking at each other all up and down the bank, till we was so far away the sounds got dim and died out. And when we stepped onto the raft, I says:

"*Now,* old Jim, you're a free man *again,* and I bet you won't ever be a slave no more."

"En a mighty good job it wuz, too, Huck. It 'uz planned beautiful, en it 'uz *done* beautiful; en dey aint' *nobody* kin git up a plan dat's mo' mixed-up en splendid den what dat one wuz."

We was all as glad as we could be, but Tom was the gladdest of all, because he had a bullet in the calf of his leg.

When me and Jim heard that, we didn't feel so brash as what we did before. It was hurting him considerble, and bleeding; so we laid him in the wigwam and tore up one of the duke's shirts for to bandage him, but he says:

"Gimme the rags, I can do it myself. Don't stop, now; don't fool around here, and the evasion booming along so handsome; man the sweeps, and set her loose! Boys, we done it elegant!—'deed we did. I wish *we'd* a had the handling of Louis XVI, there wouldn't a been no 'Son of Saint Louis, ascend to heaven!'[9] wrote down in *his* biography: no, sir, we'd a whooped him over the *border*—that's what we'd a done with *him*—and done it just as slick as nothing at all, too. Man the sweeps—man the sweeps!"

But me and Jim was consulting—and thinking. And after we'd thought a minute, I says:

"Say it, Jim."

So he says:

9. Taken from Carlyle's rendering of the king's execution in *The French Revolution* (1837).

"Well, den, dis is de way it look to me, Huck. Ef it wuz *him* dat 'uz bein' sot free, en one er de boys wuz to git shot, would he say, 'Go on en save me, nem-mine 'bout a doctor f'r to save dis one?' Is dat like Mars Tom Sawyer? Would he say dat? You *bet* he wouldn't! *Well*, den, is *Jim* gwyne to say it? No, sah—I doan' budge a step out'n dis place, 'dout a *doctor*; not if its forty year!"

I knowed he was white inside, and I reckoned he'd say what he did say—so it was all right, now, and I told Tom I was agoing for a doctor. He raised considerble row about it, but me and Jim stuck to it and wouldn't budge; so he was for crawling out and setting the raft loose himself; but we wouldn't let him. Then he give us a piece of his mind—but it didn't do no good.

So when he see me getting the canoe ready, he says:

"Well, then, if you're bound to go, I'll tell you the way to do, when you get to the village. Shut the door, and blindfold the doctor tight and fast, and make him swear to be silent as the grave, and put a purse full of gold in his hand, and then take and lead him all around the back alleys and everywheres, in the dark, and then fetch him here in the canoe, in a roundabout way amongst the islands, and search him and take his chalk away from him, and don't give it back to him till you get him back to the village, or else he will chalk this raft so he can find it again. It's the way they all do."

So I said I would, and left, and Jim was to hide in the woods when he see the doctor coming, till he was gone again.

### Chapter XLI

The doctor was an old man; a very nice, kind-looking old man, when I got him up. I told him me and my brother was over on Spanish Island hunting, yesterday afternoon, and camped on a piece of a raft we found, and about midnight he must a kicked his gun in his dreams, for it went off and shot him in the leg, and we wanted him to go over there and fix it and not say nothing about it, nor let anybody know, because we wanted to come home this evening, and surprise the folks.

"Who is your folks?" he says.

"The Phelpses, down yonder."

"Oh," he says. And after a minute, he says: "How'd you say he got shot?"

"He had a dream," I says, "and it shot him."

"Singular dream," he says.

So he lit up his lantern, and got his saddle-bags, and we started. But when he see the canoe, he didn't like the look of her—said she was big enough for one, but didn't look pretty safe for two. I says:

"Oh, you needn't be afeard, sir, she carried the three of us, easy enough."

"What three?"

"Why, me and Sid, and—and—and *the guns*; that's what I mean."

"Oh," he says.

But he put his foot on the gunnel, and rocked her; and shook his head, and said he reckoned he'd look around for a bigger one. But they was all locked and chained; so he took my canoe, and said for me to wait till he come back, or I could hunt around further, or maybe I better go down home and get them ready for the surprise, if I wanted to. But I said I didn't; so I told him just how to find the raft, and then he started.

I struck an idea, pretty soon. I says to myself, spos'n he can't fix that leg just in three shakes of a sheep's tail, as the saying is? spos'n it takes him three or four days? What are we going to do?—lay around there till he lets the cat out of the bag? No, sir, I know what *I'll* do. I'll wait, and when he comes back, if he says he's got to go any more, I'll get him down there, too, if I swim; and we'll take and tie him, and keep him, and shove out down the river; and when Tom's done with him, we'll give him what it's worth, or all we got, and then let him get shore.

So then I crept into a lumber pile to get some sleep; and next time I waked up the sun was away up over my head! I shot out and went for the doctor's house, but they told me he'd gone away in the night, some time or other, and warn't back yet. Well, thinks I, that looks powerful bad for *Tom,* and I'll dig out for the island, right off. So away I shoved, and turned the corner, and nearly rammed my head into Uncle Silas's stomach! He says:

"Why, Tom! Where you been, all this time, you rascal?"

"*I* hain't been nowheres," I says, "only just hunting for the runaway nigger—me and Sid."

"Why, where ever did you go?" he says. "Your aunt's been mighty uneasy."

"She needn't," I says, "because we was all right. We followed the men and the dogs, but they out-run us, and we lost them; but we thought we heard them on the water, so we got a canoe and took out after them, and crossed over but couldn't find nothing of them; so we cruised along up-shore till we got kind of tired and beat out; and tied up the canoe and went to sleep, and never waked up till about an hour ago, then we paddled over here to hear the news, and Sid's at the post-office to see what he can hear, and I'm a branching out to get something to eat for us, and then we're going home."

So then we went to the post-office to get "Sid"; but just as I suspicioned, he warn't there; so the old man he got a letter out of the office, and we waited a while longer but Sid didn't come; so the old man said come along, let Sid foot it home, or canoe-it, when he got done fooling around—but we would ride. I couldn't get him to let me stay and wait for Sid; and he said there warn't no use in it, and I must come along, and let Aunt Sally see we was all right.

When we got home, Aunt Sally was that glad to see me she laughed and cried both, and hugged me, and give me one of them lickings of hern that don't amount to shucks, and said she'd serve Sid the same when he come.

And the place was plumb full of farmers and farmers' wives, to dinner; and such another clack a body never heard. Old Mrs. Hotchkiss was the worst; her tongue was agoing all the time. She says:

"Well, Sister Phelps, I've ransacked that-air cabin over an' I b'lieve the nigger was crazy. I says so to Sister Damrell—didn't I, Sister Damrell?—s'I, he's crazy, s'I—them's the very words I said. You all hearn me: he's crazy, s'I; everything shows it, s'I. Look at that-air grindstone, s'I; want to tell *me*'t any cretur 'ts in his right mind 's agoin' to scrabble all them crazy things onto a grindstone, s'I? Here sich 'n' sich a person busted his heart; 'n' here so 'n' so pegged along for thirty-seven year, 'n' all that—natcherl son o' Louis somebody, 'n' sich everlast'n rubbage. He's plumb crazy, s'I; it's what I says in the fust place, it's what I says in the middle, 'n' it's what I says last 'n' all the time—the nigger's crazy—crazy's Nebokoodneezer,[1] s'I."

---

1. Nebuchadnezzar (605–562 B.C.E.), king of Babylon, is described in Daniel 4.33 as going mad and eating grass.

"An' look at that-air ladder made out'n rags, Sister Hotchkiss," says old Mrs. Damrell, "what in the name o'goodness *could* he ever want of—"

"The very words I was a-sayin' no longer ago th'n this minute to Sister Utterback, 'n' she'll tell you so herself. Sh-she, look at that-air rag ladder, sh-she; 'n' s'I, yes, *look* at it, s'I—what *could* he a wanted of it, s'I. Sh-she, Sister Hotchkiss, sh-she—"

"But how in the nation'd they ever *git* that grindstone *in* there, *anyway*? 'n' who dug that-air *hole*? 'n' who—"

"My very *words*, Brer Penrod! I was a-sayin'—pass that-air sasser o' m'lasses, won't ye?—I was a-sayin' to Sister Dunlap, jist this minute, how *did* they git that grindstone in there, s'I. Without *help*, mind you—'thout *help*! *Thar's* wher' tis. Don't tell *me*, s'I; there *wuz* help, s'I; 'n' ther' wuz a *plenty* help, too, s'I; ther's ben a *dozen* a-helpin' that nigger, 'n' I lay I'd skin every last nigger on this place, but *I'd* find out who done it, s'I; 'n' moreover, s'I—"

"A *dozen* says you!—*forty* couldn't a done everything that's been done. Look at them case-knife saws and things, how tedious they've been made; look at that bed-leg sawed off with 'em, a week's work for six men; look at that nigger made out'n straw on the bed; and look at—"

"You may *well* say it, Brer Hightower! It's jist as I was a-sayin' to Brer Phelps, his own self. S'e, what do *you* think of it, Sister Hotchkiss, s'e? think o' what, Brer Phelps, s'I? think o' that bed-leg sawed off that a way, s'e? *think* of it, s'I? I lay it never sawed *itself* off, s'I—somebody sawed it, s'I; that's my opinion, take it or leave it, it mayn't be no 'count, s'I, but sich as 't is, it's my opinion, s'I, 'n' if anybody k'n start a better one, s'I, let him *do* it, s'I, that's all. I says to Sister Dunlap, s'I—"

"Why, dog my cats, they must a ben a house-full o' niggers in there every night for four weeks, to a done all that work, Sister Phelps. Look at that shirt—every last inch of it kivered over with secret African writ'n done with blood! Must a ben a raft uv 'm at it right along, all the time, amost. Why, I'd give two dollars to have it read to me; 'n' as for the niggers that wrote it, I 'low I'd take 'n' lash 'm t'll—"

"People to *help* him, Brother Marples! Well, I reckon you'd *think* so, if you'd a been in this house for a while back. Why, they've stole everything they could lay their hands on—and we a watching, all the time, mind you. They stole that shirt right off o' the line! and as for that sheet they made the rag ladder out of ther' ain't no telling how many times they *didn't* steal that; and flour, and candles, and candlesticks, and spoons, and the old-warming-pan, and most a thousand things that I disremember, now, and my new calico dress; and me, and Silas, and my Sid and Tom on the constant watch day *and* night, as I was a telling you, and not a one of us could catch hide nor hair, nor sight nor sound of them; and here at the last minute, lo and behold you, they slides right in under our noses, and fools us, and not only fools *us* but the Injun Territory robbers too, and actly gets *away* with that nigger, safe and sound, and that with sixteen men and twenty-two dogs right on their very heels at that very time! I tell you, it just bangs anything I ever *heard* of. Why, *sperits* couldn't a done better, and been no smarter. And I reckon they must a *been* sperits—because, *you* know our dogs, and ther' ain't no better; well, them dogs never even got on the *track* of 'm, once! You explain *that* to me, if you can!—*any* of you!"

"Well, it does beat—"

"Laws alive, I never—"

"So help me, I wouldn't a be—"

"*House* thieves as well as—"

"Goodnessgracioussakes, I'd a ben afeard to *live* in sich a—"

" 'Fraid to *live!*—why, I was that scared I dasn't hardly go to bed, or get up, or lay down, or *set* down, Sister Ridgeway. Why, they'd steal the very—why, goodness sakes, you can guess what kind of a fluster *I* was in by the time midnight come, last night. I hope to gracious if I warn't afraid they'd steal some o' the family! I was just to that pass, I didn't have no reasoning faculties no more. It looks foolish enough, *now,* in the day-time; but I says to myself, there's my two poor boys asleep, 'way up stairs in that lonesome room, and I declare to goodness I was that uneasy 't I crep' up there and locked 'em in! I *did.* And anybody would. Because, you know, when you get scared, that way, and it keeps running on, and getting worse and worse, all the time, and your wits gets to addling, and you get to doing all sorts o' wild things, and by-and-by you think to yourself, spos'n *I* was a boy, and was away up there, and the door ain't locked, and you—" She stopped, looking kind of wondering, and then she turned her head around slow, and when her eye lit on me—I got up and took a walk.

Says I to myself, I can explain better how we come to not be in that room this morning, if I go out to one side and study over it a little. So I done it. But I dasn't go fur, or she'd a sent for me. And when it was late in the day, the people all went, and then I come in and told her the noise and shooting waked up me and "Sid," and the door was locked, and we wanted to see the fun, so we went down the lightning-rod, and both of us got hurt a little, and we didn't never want to try *that* no more. And then I went on and told her all what I told Uncle Silas before; and then she said she'd forgive us, and maybe it was all right enough anyway, and about what a body might expect of boys, for all boys was a pretty harum-scarum lot, as fur as she could see; and so, as long as no harm hadn't come of it, she judged she better put in her time being grateful we was alive and well and she had us still, stead of fretting over what was past and done. So then she kissed me, and patted me on the head, and dropped into a kind of a brown study; and pretty soon jumps up, and says:

"Why, lawsamercy, it's most night, and Sid not come yet! What *has* become of that boy?"

I see my chance; so I skips up and says:

"I'll run right up to town and get him," I says.

"No, you won't," she says. "You'll stay right wher' you are; *one's* enough to be lost at a time. If he ain't here to supper, your uncle 'll go."

Well, he warn't there to supper; so right after supper uncle went.

He come back about ten, a little bit uneasy; hadn't run across Tom's track. Aunt Sally was a good *deal* uneasy; but Uncle Silas he said there warn't no occasion to be—boys will be boys, he said, and you'll see this one turn up in the morning, all sound and right. So she had to be satisfied. But she said she'd set up for him a while, anyway, and keep a light burning, so he could see it.

And then when I went up to bed she come up with me and fetched her candle, and tucked me in, and mothered me so good I felt mean, and like I couldn't look her in the face; and she set down on the bed and talked with me a long time, and said what a splendid boy Sid was, and didn't seem to want to ever stop talking about him; and kept asking me every now and then, if I reckoned he could a got lost, or hurt, or maybe drownded, and might be laying at this minute, some-wheres, suffering or dead, and she not by him to help him, and so the tears would drip down, silent, and I would tell her that Sid was all right, and would be home in the morning, sure; and she would squeeze my hand, or maybe kiss me, and tell me to say it again, and keep on saying it, because it done her good, and she was in so much trouble. And when she was going away, she looked down in my eyes, so steady and gentle, and says:

"The door ain't going to be locked, Tom; and there's the window and the rod; but you'll be good, *won't* you? And you won't go? For *my* sake."

Laws knows I *wanted* to go, bad enough, to see about Tom, and was all intending to go; but after that, I wouldn't a went, not for kingdoms.

But she was on my mind, and Tom was on my mind; so I slept very restless. And twice I went down the rod, away in the night, and slipped around front, and see her setting there by her candle in the window with her eyes towards the road and the tears in them; and I wished I could do something for her, but I couldn't, only to swear that I wouldn't never do nothing to grieve her any more. And the third time, I waked up at dawn, and slid down, and she was there yet, and her candle was most out, and her old gray head was rest-ing on her hand, and she was asleep.

## Chapter XLII

The old man was up town again, before breakfast, but couldn't get no track of Tom; and both of them set at the table, thinking, and not saying nothing, and looking mournful, and their coffee getting cold, and not eating anything. And by-and-by the old man says:

"Did I give you the letter?"

"What letter?"

"The one I got yesterday out of the post-office."

"No, you didn't give me no letter."

"Well, I must a forgot it."

So he rummaged his pockets, and then went off somewheres where he had laid it down, and fetched it, and give it to her. She says:

"Why, it's from St. Petersburg—it's from Sis."

I allowed another walk would do me good; but I couldn't stir. But before she could break it open, she dropped it and run—for she see something. And so did I. It was Tom Sawyer on a mattress; and that old doctor; and Jim, in *her* calico dress, with his hands tied behind him; and a lot of people. I hid the letter behind the first thing that come handy, and rushed. She flung herself at Tom, crying, and says:

"Oh, he's dead, he's dead, I know he's dead!"

And Tom he turned his head a little, and muttered something or other, which showed he warn't in his right mind; then she flung up her hands and says:

"He's alive, thank God! And that's enough!" and she snatched a kiss of him, and flew for the house to get the bed ready, and scattering orders right and left at the niggers and everybody else, as fast as her tongue could go, every jump of the way.

I followed the men to see what they was going to do with Jim; and the old doctor and Uncle Silas followed after Tom into the house. The men was very huffy, and some of them wanted to hang Jim, for an example to all the other niggers around there, so they wouldn't be trying to run away, like Jim done, and making such a raft of trouble, and keeping a whole family scared most to death for days and nights. But the others said, don't do it, it wouldn't answer at all, he ain't our nigger, and his owner would turn up and make us pay for him, sure. So that cooled them down a little, because the people that's always the most anxious for to hang a nigger that hain't done just right, is always the very ones that ain't the most anxious to pay for him when they've got their satisfaction out of him.

They cussed Jim considerble, though, and give him a cuff or two, side the head, once in a while, but Jim never said nothing, and he never let on to know me, and they took him to the same cabin, and put his own clothes on him, and chained him again, and not to no bed-leg, this time, but to a big staple drove into the bottom log, and chained his hands, too, and both legs, and said he warn't to have nothing but bread and water to eat, after this, till his owner come or he was sold at auction, because he didn't come in a certain length of time, and filled up our hole, and said a couple of farmers with guns must stand watch around about the cabin every night, and a bull-dog tied to the door in the day time; and about this time they was through with the job and was tapering off with a kind of generl good-bye cussing, and then the old doctor comes and takes a look and says:

"Don't be no rougher on him than you're obleeged to, because he ain't a bad nigger. When I got to where I found the boy, I see I couldn't cut the bullet out without some help, and he warn't in no condition for me to leave, to go and get help; and he got a little worse and a little worse, and after a long time he went out of his head, and wouldn't let me come anigh him, any more, and said if I chalked his raft he'd kill me, and no end of wild foolishness like that, and I see I couldn't do anything at all with him; so I says, I got to have *help,* somehow; and the minute I says it, out crawls this nigger from somewheres, and says he'll help, and he done it, too, and done it very well. Of course I judged he must be a runaway nigger, and there I *was!* and there I had to stick, right straight along all the rest of the day, and all night. It was a fix, I tell you! I had a couple of patients with the chills, and of course I'd of liked to run up to town and see them, but I dasn't, because the nigger might get away, and then I'd be to blame; and yet never a skiff come close enough for me to hail. So there I had to stick, plumb till daylight this morning; and I never see a nigger that was a better nuss or faithfuller, and yet he was resking his freedom to do it, and was all tired out, too, and I see plain enough he'd been worked main hard, lately. I liked the nigger for that; I tell you, gentlemen, a nigger like that is worth a thousand dollars—and kind treatment, too. I had everything I needed, and the boy was doing as well there as he would a done at home—better, maybe, because it was so quiet; but there I *was,* with both of 'm on my hands; and there I had to stick, till about dawn this morning; then some men in a skiff come by, and as good luck would have it, the nigger was setting by the pallet with his head propped on his knees, sound asleep; so I motioned them in, quiet, and they slipped up on him and grabbed him and tied him before he knowed what he was about, and we never had no trouble. And the boy being in a kind of a flighty sleep, too, we muffled the oars and hitched the raft on, and towed her over very nice and quiet, and the nigger never made the least row nor said a word, from the start. He ain't no bad nigger, gentlemen; that's what I think about him."

Somebody says:

"Well, it sounds very good, doctor, I'm obleeged to say."

Then the others softened up a little, too, and I was mighty thankful to that old doctor for doing Jim that good turn; and I was glad it was according to my judgment of him, too; because I thought he had a good heart in him and was a good man, the first time I see him. Then they all agreed that Jim had acted very well, and was deserving to have some notice took of it, and reward. So every one of them promised, right out and hearty, that they wouldn't cuss him no more.

Then they come out and locked him up. I hoped they was going to say he could have one or two of the chains took off, because they was rotten heavy, or could have meat and greens with his bread and water, but they didn't think of it, and I reckoned it warn't best for me to mix in, but I judged I'd get the doctor's yarn to Aunt Sally, somehow or other, as soon as I'd got through the breakers that was laying just ahead of me. Explanations, I mean, of how I forgot to mention about Sid being shot, when I was telling how him and me put in that dratted night paddling around hunting the runaway nigger.

But I had plenty time. Aunt Sally she stuck to the sick-room all day and all night; and every time I see Uncle Silas mooning around, I dodged him.

Next morning I heard Tom was a good deal better, and they said Aunt Sally was gone to get a nap. So I slips to the sick-room, and if I found him awake I reckoned we could put up a yarn for the family that would wash. But he was sleeping, and sleeping very peaceful, too; and pale, not fire-faced the way he was when he come. So I set down and laid for him to wake. In about a half an hour, Aunt Sally comes gliding in, and there I was, up a stump again! She motioned me to be still, and set down by me, and begun to whisper, and said we could all be joyful now, because all the symptoms was first rate, and he'd been sleeping like that for ever so long, and looking better and peacefuller all the time, and ten to one he'd wake up in his right mind.

So we set there watching, and by-and-by he stirs a bit, and opened his eyes very natural, and takes a look, and says:

"Hello, why I'm at *home*! How's that? Where's the raft?"

"It's all right," I says.

"And *Jim*?"

"The same," I says, but couldn't say it pretty brash. But he never noticed, but says:

"Good! Splendid! *Now* we're all right and safe! Did you tell Aunty?"

I was about to say yes; but she chipped in and says:

"About what, Sid?"

"Why, about the way the whole thing was done."

"What whole thing?"

"Why, *the* whole thing. There ain't but one; how we set the runaway nigger free—me and Tom."

"Good land! Set the run—What *is* the child talking about! Dear, dear, out of his head again!"

"*No*, I ain't out of my HEAD; I know all what I'm talking about. We *did* set him free—me and Tom. We laid out to do it, and we *done* it. And we done it elegant, too." He'd got a start, and she never checked him up, just set and stared and stared, and let him clip along, and I see it warn't no use for *me* to put in. "Why, Aunty, it cost us a power of work—weeks of it—hours and hours, every night, whilst you was all asleep. And we had to steal candles, and the sheet, and the shirt, and your dress, and spoons, and tin plates, and case-knives, and the warming-pan, and the grindstone, and flour, and just no end of things, and you can't think what work it was to make the saws, and pens, and inscriptions, and one thing or another, and you can't think *half* the fun it was. And we had to make up the pictures of coffins and things, and non-namous letters from the robbers, and get up and down the lightning-rod, and dig the hole into the cabin, and make the rope-ladder and send it in cooked up in a pie, and send in spoons and things to work with, in your apron pocket"—

"Mercy sakes!"

—"and load up the cabin with rats and snakes and so on, for company for Jim; and then you kept Tom here so long with the butter in his hat that you come near spiling the whole business, because the men come before we was out of the cabin, and we had to rush, and they heard us and let drive at us, and I got my share, and we dodged out of the path and let them go by, and when the dogs come they warn't interested in us, but went for the most noise, and we got our canoe, and made for the raft, and was all safe, and Jim was a free man, and we done it all by ourselves, and *wasn't* it bully, Aunty!"

"Well, I never heard the likes of it in all my born days! So it was *you*, you little rapscallions, that's been making all this trouble, and turn everybody's wits clean inside out and scared us all most to death. I've as good a notion as ever I had in my life, to take it out o' you this very minute. To think, here I've been, night after night, a—*you* just get well once, you young scamp, and I lay I'll tan the Old Harry out o' both o' ye!"

But Tom, he *was* so proud and joyful, he just *couldn't* hold in, and his tongue just *went* it—she a-chipping in, and spitting fire all along, and both of them going it at once, like a cat-convention; and she says:

"*Well,* you get all the enjoyment you can out of it *now*, for mind I tell you if I catch you meddling with him again—"

"Meddling with *who*?" Tom says, dropping his smile and looking surprised.

"With *who*? Why, the runaway nigger, of course. Who'd you reckon?"

Tom looks at me very grave, and says:

"Tom, didn't you just tell me he was all right? Hasn't he got away?"

"*Him?*" says Aunt Sally; "the runaway nigger? 'Deed he hasn't. They've got him back, safe and sound, and he's in that cabin again, on bread and water, and loaded down with chains, till he's claimed or sold!"

Tom rose square up in bed, with his eye hot, and his nostrils opening and shutting like gills, and sings out to me:

"They hain't no *right* to shut him up! *Shove!*—and don't you lose a minute. Turn him loose! he ain't no slave; he's as free as any cretur that walks this earth!"

"What *does* the child mean?"

"I mean every word I *say*, Aunt Sally, and if somebody don't go, *I'll* go. I've knowed him all his life, and so has Tom, there. Old Miss Watson died two months ago, and she was ashamed she ever was going to sell him down the river, and *said* so; and she set him free in her will."

"Then what on earth did *you* want to set him free for, seeing he was already free?"

"Well, that *is* a question, I must say; and *just* like women! Why, I wanted the *adventure* of it; and I'd a waded neck-deep in blood to—goodness alive, AUNT POLLY!"[2]

If she warn't standing right there, just inside the door, looking as sweet and contented as an angel half-full of pie, I wish I may never!

Aunt Sally jumped for her, and most hugged the head off of her, and cried over her, and I found a good enough place for me under the bed, for it was getting pretty sultry for *us*, seemed to me. And I peeped out, and in a little while Tom's Aunt Polly shook herself loose and stood there looking across at Tom over her spectacles—kind of grinding him into the earth, you know. And then she says:

"Yes, you *better* turn y'r head away—I would if I was you, Tom."

"Oh, deary me!" says Aunt Sally; "*is* he changed so? Why, that ain't *Tom* it's Sid; Tom's—Tom's—why, where is Tom? He was here a minute ago."

"You mean where's Huck *Finn*—that's what you mean! I reckon I hain't raised such a scamp as my Tom all these years, not to know him when I *see* him. That *would* be a pretty howdy-do. Come out from under the bed, Huck Finn."

So I done it. But not feeling brash.

Aunt Sally she was one of the mixed-upest looking persons I ever see; except one, and that was Uncle Silas, when he come in, and they told it all to him. It kind of made him drunk, as you may say, and he didn't know nothing at all the rest of the day, and preached a prayer-meeting sermon that night that give him a rattling ruputation, because the oldest man in the world couldn't a understood it. So Tom's Aunt Polly, she told all about who I was, and what; and I had to up and tell how I was in such a tight place that when Mrs. Phelps took me for Tom Sawyer—she chipped in and says, "Oh, go on and call me Aunt Sally, I'm used to it, now, and 'tain't no need to change"— that when Aunt Sally took me for Tom Sawyer, I had to stand it—that warn't no other way, and I knowed he wouldn't mind, because it would be nuts for him, being a mystery, and he'd make an adventure out of it and be perfectly satisfied. And so it turned out, and he let on to be Sid, and made things as soft as he could for me.

And his Aunt Polly she said Tom was right about old Miss Watson setting Jim free in her will; and so, sure enough, Tom Sawyer had gone and took all that trouble and bother to set a free nigger free! and I couldn't ever understand, before, until that minute and that talk, how he *could* help a body set a nigger free, with his bringing-up.

Well, Aunt Polly she said that when Aunt Sally wrote to her that Tom and *Sid* had come, all right and safe, she says to herself:

"Look at that, now! I might have expected it, letting him go off that way without anybody to watch him. So now I got to go and trapse all the way down the river, eleven hundred mile,[3] and find out what that creetur's up to, *this* time; as long as I couldn't seem to get any answer out of you about it."

"Why, I never heard nothing from you," says Aunt Sally.

---

2. Tom Sawyer's aunt and guardian.
3. This distance from Hannibal would place the Phelps plantation in northern Louisiana.

"Well, I wonder! Why, I wrote to you twice, to ask you what you could mean by Sid being here."

"Well, I never got 'em, Sis."

Aunt Polly, she turns around slow and severe, and says:

"You, Tom!"

"Well—*what?*" he says, kind of pettish.

"Don't you what *me*, you impudent thing—hand out them letters."

"What letters?"

"*Them* letters. I be bound, if I have to take aholt of you I'll—"

"They're in the trunk. There, now. And they're just the same as they was when I got them out of the office. I hain't looked into them, I hain't touched them. But I knowed they'd make trouble, and I thought if you warn't in no hurry, I'd—"

"Well, you *do* need skinning, there ain't no mistake about it. And I wrote another one to tell you I was coming; and I spose he—"

"No, it come yesterday; I hain't read it yet, but *it's* all right, I've got that one."

I wanted to offer to bet two dollars she hadn't, but I reckoned maybe it was just as safe to not to. So I never said nothing.

## Chapter the Last

The first time I catched Tom, private, I asked him what was his idea, time of the evasion?—what it was he'd planned to do if the evasion worked all right and he managed to set a nigger free that was already free before? And he said, what he had planned in his head, from the start, if we got Jim out all safe, was for us to run him down the river, on the raft, and have adventures plumb to the mouth of the river, and then tell him about his being free, and take him back up home on a steamboat, in style, and pay him for his lost time, and write word ahead and get out all the niggers around, and have them waltz him into town with a torchlight procession and a brass band, and then he would be a hero, and so would we. But I reckoned it was about as well the way it was.

We had Jim out of the chains in no time, and when Aunt Polly and Uncle Silas and Aunt Sally found out how good he helped the doctor nurse Tom, they made a heap of fuss over him, and fixed him up prime, and give him all he wanted to eat, and a good time, and nothing to do. And we had him up to the sickroom; and had a high talk; and Tom give Jim forty dollars for being prisoner for us so patient, and doing it up so good, and Jim was pleased most to death, and busted out, and says:

"*Dah,* now, Huck, what I tell you?—what I tell you up dah on Jackson islan'? I *tole* you I got a hairy breas', en what's de sign un it; en I *tole* you I ben rich wunst, en gwineter to be rich *agin;* en it's come true; en heah she *is! Dah,* now! doan' talk to *me*—signs is *signs,* mine I tell you; en I knowed jis' 's well 'at I 'uz gwineter be rich agin as I's a stannin' heah dis minute!"

And then Tom he talked along, and talked along, and says, le's all three slide out of here, one of these nights, and get an outfit, and go for howling adventures amongst the Injuns, over in the Territory, for a couple of weeks or two; and I says, all right, that suits me, but I ain't got no money for to buy the outfit, and I reckon I couldn't get none from home, because it's likely pap's been back before now, and got it all away from Judge Thatcher and drunk it up.

"No he hain't," Tom says; "it's all there, yet—six thousand dollars and more; and your pap hain't ever been back since. Hadn't when I come away, anyhow."

Jim says, kind of solemn:

"He ain't a comin' back no mo', Huck."

I says:

"Why, Jim?"

"Nemmine why, Huck—but he ain't comin' back no mo'."

But I kept at him; so at last he says:

"Doan' you 'member de house dat was float'n down de river, en dey wuz a man in dah, kivered up, en I went in en unkivered him and didn' let you come in? Well, den, you k'n git yo' money when you wants it; kase dat wuz him."

Tom's most well, now, and got his bullet around his neck on a watch-guard for a watch, and is always seeing what time it is, and so there ain't nothing more to write about, and I am rotten glad of it, because if I'd a knowed what a trouble it was to make a book I wouldn't a tackled it and ain't agoing to no more. But I reckon I got to light out for the Territory ahead of the rest, because Aunt Sally she's going to adopt me and sivilize me and I can't stand it. I been there before.

THE END. YOURS TRULY, HUCK FINN.

1876–83                                                                            1884

## Fenimore Cooper's Literary Offences[1]

*The Pathfinder* and *The Deerslayer* stand at the head of Cooper's novels as artistic creations. There are others of his works which contain parts as perfect as are to be found in these, and scenes even more thrilling. Not one can be compared with either of them as a finished whole.

The defects in both of these tales are comparatively slight. They were pure works of art.—*Prof. Lounsbury.*

The five tales reveal an extraordinary fulness of invention.

. . . One of the very greatest characters in fiction, "Natty Bumppo." . . .

The craft of the woodsman, the tricks of the trapper, all the delicate art of the forest, were familiar to Cooper from his youth up.—*Prof. Brander Matthews.*

Cooper is the greatest artist in the domain of romantic fiction yet produced by America.—*Wilkie Collins.*[2]

It seems to me that it was far from right for the Professor of English Literature in Yale, the Professor of English Literature in Columbia, and Wilkie

1. James Fenimore Cooper (1789–1851) is best known for his series of historical novels in which the hero is variously called Leatherstocking, Natty Bumppo, Hawkeye, and Deerslayer. The novels are *The Pioneers* (1823), *The Last of the Mohicans* (1826), *The Prairie* (1827), *The Pathfinder* (1840), and *The Deerslayer* (1841). This essay was first published in July 1895 in *North American Review,* the source of the text, and later in the collection *How to Tell a Story and Other Essays* (1897).
2. William Wilkie Collins (1824–1889), English novelist. Thomas Raynesford Lounsbury (1838–1915), American scholar and editor; professor at Yale University. James Brander Matthews (1852–1929), American educator and author, professor at Columbia University.

Collins, to deliver opinions on Cooper's literature without having read some of it. It would have been much more decorous to keep silent and let persons talk who have read Cooper.

Cooper's art has some defects. In one place in *Deerslayer,* and in the restricted space of two-thirds of a page, Cooper has scored 114 offences against literary art out of a possible 115. It breaks the record.

There are nineteen rules governing literary art in the domain of romantic fiction—some say twenty-two. In *Deerslayer* Cooper violated eighteen of them. These eighteen require:

1. That a tale shall accomplish something and arrive somewhere. But the *Deerslayer* tale accomplishes nothing and arrives in the air.

2. They require that the episodes of a tale shall be necessary parts of the tale, and shall help to develop it. But as the *Deerslayer* tale is not a tale, and accomplishes nothing and arrives nowhere, the episodes have no rightful place in the work, since there was nothing for them to develop.

3. They require that the personages in a tale shall be alive, except in the case of corpses, and that always the reader shall be able to tell the corpses from the others. But this detail has often been overlooked in the *Deerslayer* tale.

4. They require that the personages in a tale, both dead and alive, shall exhibit a sufficient excuse for being there. But this detail also has been overlooked in the *Deerslayer* tale.

5. They require that when the personages of a tale deal in conversation, the talk shall sound like human talk, and be talk such as human beings would be likely to talk in the given circumstances, and have a discoverable meaning, also a discoverable purpose, and a show of relevancy, and remain in the neighborhood of the subject in hand, and be interesting to the reader, and help out the tale, and stop when the people cannot think of anything more to say. But this requirement has been ignored from the beginning of the *Deerslayer* tale to the end of it.

6. They require that when the author describes the character of a personage in his tale, the conduct and conversation of that personage shall justify said description. But this law gets little or no attention in the *Deerslayer* tale, as "Natty Bumppo's" case will amply prove.

7. They require that when a personage talks like an illustrated, gilt-edged, tree-calf, hand-tooled, seven-dollar Friendship's Offering[3] in the beginning of a paragraph, he shall not talk like a negro minstrel in the end of it. But this rule is flung down and danced upon in the *Deerslayer* tale.

8. They require that crass stupidities shall not be played upon the reader as "the craft of the woodsman, the delicate art of the forest," by either the author or the people in the tale. But this rule is persistently violated in the *Deerslayer* tale.

9. They require that the personages of a tale shall confine themselves to possibilities and let miracles alone; or, if they venture a miracle, the author must so plausibly set it forth as to make it look possible and reasonable. But these rules are not respected in the *Deerslayer* tale.

10. They require that the author shall make the reader feel a deep interest in the personages of his tale and in their fate; and that he shall make the

---

3. I.e., like one of the then-popular, expensive, illustrated literary miscellanies, or collections of writings on various subjects ("tree-calf" was leather chemically treated to produce a treelike design).

reader love the good people in the tale and hate the bad ones. But the reader of the *Deerslayer* tale dislikes the good people in it, is indifferent to the others, and wishes they would all get drowned together.

11. They require that the characters in a tale shall be so clearly defined that the reader can tell beforehand what each will do in a given emergency. But in the *Deerslayer* tale this rule is vacated.

In addition to these large rules there are some little ones. These require that the author shall

12. *Say* what he is proposing to say, not merely come near it.
13. Use the right word, not its second cousin.
14. Eschew surplusage.
15. Not omit necessary details.
16. Avoid slovenliness of form.
17. Use good grammar.
18. Employ a simple and straightforward style.

Even these seven are coldly and persistently violated in the *Deerslayer* tale.

Cooper's gift in the way of invention was not a rich endowment; but such as it was he liked to work it, he was pleased with the effects, and indeed he did some quite sweet things with it. In his little box of stage properties he kept six or eight cunning devices, tricks, artifices for his savages and woodsmen to deceive and circumvent each other with, and he was never so happy as when he was working these innocent things and seeing them go. A favorite one was to make a moccasined person tread in the tracks of the moccasined enemy, and thus hide his own trail. Cooper wore out barrels and barrels of moccasins in working that trick. Another stage-property that he pulled out of his box pretty frequently was his broken twig. He prized his broken twig above all the rest of his effects, and worked it the hardest. It is a restful chapter in any book of his when somebody doesn't step on a dry twig and alarm all the reds and whites for two hundred yards around. Every time a Cooper person is in peril, and absolute silence is worth four dollars a minute, he is sure to step on a dry twig. There may be a hundred handier things to step on, but that wouldn't satisfy Cooper. Cooper requires him to turn out and find a dry twig; and if he can't do it, go and borrow one. In fact the Leather Stocking Series ought to have been called the Broken Twig Series.

I am sorry there is not room to put in a few dozen instances of the delicate art of the forest, as practiced by Natty Bumppo and some of the other Cooperian experts. Perhaps we may venture two or three samples. Cooper was a sailor—a naval officer; yet he gravely tells us how a vessel, driving toward a lee shore[4] in a gale, is steered for a particular spot by her skipper because he knows of an *undertow* there which will hold her back against the gale and save her. For just pure woodcraft, or sailor-craft, or whatever it is, isn't that neat? For several years Cooper was daily in the society of artillery, and he ought to have noticed that when a cannon ball strikes the ground it either buries itself or skips a hundred feet or so; skips again a hundred feet or so—and so on, till it finally gets tired and rolls. Now in one place he loses some "females"—as he always calls women—in the edge of a wood near a plain at night in a fog, on purpose to give Bumppo a chance to show off the delicate art of the forest before the reader. These mislaid people are hunting

---

4. Shore that is protected from the wind.

for a fort. They hear a cannon-blast, and a cannon-ball presently comes rolling into the wood and stops at their feet. To the females this suggests nothing. The case is very different with the admirable Bumppo. I wish I may never know peace again if he doesn't strike out promptly and *follow the track* of that cannon-ball across the plain through the dense fog and find the fort. Isn't it a daisy? If Cooper had any real knowledge of Nature's ways of doing things, he had a most delicate art in concealing the fact. For instance: one of his acute Indian experts, Chingachgook[5] (pronounced Chicago, I think), has lost the trail of a person he is tracking through the forest. Apparently that trail is hopelessly lost. Neither you nor I could ever have guessed out the way to find it. It was very different with Chicago. Chicago was not stumped for long. He turned a running stream out of its course, and there, in the slush in its old bed, were that person's moccasin-tracks. The current did not wash them away, as it would have done in all other like cases—no, even the eternal laws of Nature have to vacate when Cooper wants to put up a delicate job of wood-craft on the reader.

We must be a little wary when Brander Matthews tells us that Cooper's books "reveal an extraordinary fulness of invention." As a rule, I am quite willing to accept Brander Matthews's literary judgments and applaud his lucid and graceful phrasing of them; but that particular statement needs to be taken with a few tons of salt. Bless your heart, Cooper hadn't any more invention than a horse; and I don't mean a high-class horse, either; I mean a clothes-horse. It would be very difficult to find a really clever "situation" in Cooper's books; and still more difficult to find one of any kind which he has failed to render absurd by his handling of it. Look at the episodes of "the caves;" and at the celebrated scuffle between Maqua and those others on the table-land a few days later; and at Hurry Harry's queer water-transit from the castle to the ark; and at Deerslayer's half hour with his first corpse; and at the quarrel between Hurry Harry and Deerslayer later; and at—but choose for yourself; you can't go amiss.

If Cooper had been an observer, his inventive faculty would have worked better, not more interestingly, but more rationally, more plausibly. Cooper's proudest creations in the way of "situations" suffer noticeably from the absence of the observer's protecting gift. Cooper's eye was splendidly inaccurate. Cooper seldom saw anything correctly. He saw nearly all things as through a glass eye, darkly.[6] Of course a man who cannot see the commonest little everyday matters accurately is working at a disadvantage when he is constructing a "situation." In the *Deerslayer* tale Cooper has a stream which is fifty feet wide, where it flows out of a lake; it presently narrows to twenty as it meanders along for no given reason, and yet, when a stream acts like that it ought to be required to explain itself. Fourteen pages later the width of the brook's outlet from the lake has suddenly shrunk thirty feet, and become "the narrowest part of the stream." This shrinkage is not accounted for. The stream has bends in it, a sure indication that it has alluvial banks, and cuts them; yet these bends are only thirty and fifty feet long. If Cooper had been a nice[7] and punctilious observer he would have noticed that the bends were oftener nine hundred feet long than short of it.

5. Natty Bumppo's Indian friend.
6. Humorous turn of the biblical "through a glass,

darkly" (1 Corinthians 13.12).
7. I.e., meticulous.

Cooper made the exit of that stream fifty feet wide in the first place, for no particular reason; in the second place, he narrowed it to less than twenty to accommodate some Indians. He bends a "sapling" to the form of an arch over this narrow passage, and conceals six Indians in its foliage. They are "laying" for a settler's scow or ark which is coming up the stream on its way to the lake; it is being hauled against the stiff current by a rope whose stationary end is anchored in the lake; its rate of progress cannot be more than a mile an hour. Cooper describes the ark, but pretty obscurely. In the matter of dimensions "it was little more than a modern canal boat." Let us guess, then, that it was about 140 feet long. It was of "greater breadth than common." Let us guess, then, that it was about sixteen feet wide. This leviathan had been prowling down bends which were but a third as long as itself, and scraping between banks where it had only two feet of space to spare on each side. We cannot too much admire this miracle. A low-roofed log dwelling occupies "two-third's of the ark's length"—a dwelling ninety feet long and sixteen feet wide, let us say—a kind of vestibule train. The dwelling has two rooms—each forty-five feet long and sixteen feet wide, let us guess. One of them is the bed-room of the Hutter girls, Judith and Hetty; the other is the parlor, in the day time, at night it is papa's bed chamber. The ark is arriving at the stream's exit, now, whose width has been reduced to less than twenty feet to accommodate the Indians—say to eighteen. There is a foot to spare on each side of the boat. Did the Indians notice that there was going to be a tight squeeze there? Did they notice that they could make money by climbing down out of that arched sapling and just stepping aboard when the ark scraped by? No; other Indians would have noticed these things, but Cooper's Indians never notice anything. Cooper thinks they are marvellous creatures for noticing, but he was almost always in error about his Indians. There was seldom a sane one among them.

The ark is 140 feet long; the dwelling is 90 feet long. The idea of the Indians is to drop softly and secretly from the arched sapling to the dwelling as the ark creeps along under it at the rate of a mile an hour, and butcher the family. It will take the ark a minute and a half to pass under. It will take the 90-foot dwelling a minute to pass under. Now, then, what did the six Indians do? It would take you thirty years to guess, and even then you would have to give it up, I believe. Therefore, I will tell you what the Indians did. Their chief, a person of quite extraordinary intellect for a Cooper Indian, warily watched the canal boat as it squeezed along under him, and when he had got his calculations fined down to exactly the right shade, as he judged, he let go and dropped. And *missed the house!* That is actually what he did. He missed the house, and landed in the stern of the scow. It was not much of a fall, yet it knocked him silly. He lay there unconscious. If the house had been 97 feet long, he would have made the trip. The fault was Cooper's, not his. The error lay in the construction of the house. Cooper was no architect.

There still remained in the roost five Indians. The boat has passed under and is now out of their reach. Let me explain what the five did—you would not be able to reason it out for yourself. No. 1 jumped for the boat, but fell in the water astern of it. Then No. 2 jumped for the boat, but fell in the water still further astern of it. Then No. 3 jumped for the boat, and fell a good way astern of it. Then No. 4 jumped for the boat, and fell in the water *away* astern. Then even No. 5 made a jump for the boat—for he was a Cooper Indian. In the matter of intellect, the difference between a Cooper Indian and the

Indian that stands in front of the cigar shop is not spacious. The scow episode is really a sublime burst of invention; but it does not thrill, because the inaccuracy of the details throws a sort of air of fictitiousness and general improbability over it. This comes of Cooper's inadequacy as an observer.

The reader will find some examples of Cooper's high talent for inaccurate observation in the account of the shooting match in *The Pathfinder*. "A common wrought nail was driven lightly into the target, its head having been first touched with paint." The color of the paint is not stated—an important omission, but Cooper deals freely in important omissions. No, after all, it was not an important omission; for this nail head is *a hundred yards* from the marksmen and could not be seen by them at that distance no matter what its color might be. How far can the best eyes see a common house fly? A hundred yards? It is quite impossible. Very well, eyes that cannot see a house fly that is a hundred yards away cannot see an ordinary nail head at that distance, for the size of the two objects is the same. It takes a keen eye to see a fly or a nail head at fifty yards—one hundred and fifty feet. Can the reader do it?

The nail was lightly driven, its head painted, and game called. Then the Cooper miracles began. The bullet of the first marksman chipped an edge of the nail head; the next man's bullet drove the nail a little way into the target—and removed all the paint. Haven't the miracles gone far enough now? Not to suit Cooper; for the purpose of this whole scheme is to show off his prodigy, Deerslayer-Hawkeye-Long-Rifle-Leather-Stocking-Pathfinder-Bumppo before the ladies.

> "Be all ready to clench it, boys!" cried out Pathfinder, stepping into his friend's tracks the instant they were vacant. "Never mind a new nail; I can see that, though the paint is gone, and what I can see, I can hit at a hundred yards, though it were only a mosquitos's eye. Be ready to clench!"
>
> The rifle cracked, the bullet sped its way and the head of the nail was buried in the wood, covered by the piece of flattened lead.

There, you see, is a man who could hunt flies with a rifle, and command a ducal salary in a Wild West show to-day, if we had him back with us.

The recorded feat is certainly surprising, just as it stands; but it is not surprising enough for Cooper. Cooper adds a touch. He has made Pathfinder do this miracle with another man's rifle, and not only that, but Pathfinder did not have even the advantage of loading it himself. He had everything against him, and yet he made that impossible shot, and not only made it, but did it with absolute confidence, saying, "Be ready to clench." Now a person like that would have undertaken that same feat with a brickbat, and with Cooper to help he would have achieved it, too.

Pathfinder showed off handsomely that day before the ladies. His very first feat was a thing which no Wild West show can touch. He was standing with the group of marksmen, observing—a hundred yards from the target, mind: one Jasper raised his rifle and drove the centre of the bull's-eye. Then the quartermaster fired. The target exhibited no result this time. There was a laugh. "It's a dead miss," said Major Lundie. Pathfinder waited an impressive moment or two, then said in that calm, indifferent, know-it-all way of his, "No, Major—he has covered Jasper's bullet, as will be seen if any one will take the trouble to examine the target."

Wasn't it remarkable! How *could* he see that little pellet fly through the air and enter that distant bullet-hole? Yet that is what he did; for nothing is impossible to a Cooper person. Did any of those people have any deep-seated doubts about this thing? No; for that would imply sanity, and these were all Cooper people.

> The respect for Pathfinder's skill and for his *quickness and accuracy of sight* (the italics are mine) was so profound and general, that the instant he made this declaration the spectators began to distrust their own opinions, and a dozen rushed to the target in order to ascertain the fact. There, sure enough, it was found that the quartermaster's bullet had gone through the hole made by Jasper's, and that, too, so accurately as to require a minute examination to be certain of the circumstance, which, however, was soon clearly established by discovering one bullet over the other in the stump against which the target was placed.

They made a "minute" examination; but never mind, how could they know that there were two bullets in that hole without digging the latest one out? for neither probe nor eyesight could prove the presence of any more than one bullet. Did they dig? No; as we shall see. It is the Pathfinder's turn now; he steps out before the ladies, takes aim, and fires.

But alas! here is a disappointment; an incredible, an unimaginable disappointment—for the target's aspect is unchanged; there is nothing there but that same old bullet hole!

> "If one dared to hint at such a thing," cried Major Duncan, "I should say that the Pathfinder has also missed the target."

As nobody had missed it yet, the "also" was not necessary; but never mind about that, for the Pathfinder is going to speak.

> "No, no, Major," said he, confidently, "that *would* be a risky declaration. I didn't load the piece, and can't say what was in it, but if it was lead, you will find the bullet driving down those of the Quartermaster and Jasper, else is not my name Pathfinder."
> A shout from the target announced the truth of this assertion.

Is the miracle sufficient as it stands? Not for Cooper. The Pathfinder speaks again, as he "now slowly advances towards the stage occupied by the females:"

> "That's not all, boys, that's not all; if you find the target touched at all, I'll own to a miss. The Quartermaster cut the wood, but you'll find no wood cut by that last messenger."

The miracle is at last complete. He knew—doubtless *saw*—at the distance of a hundred yards—that his bullet had passed into the hole *without fraying the edges*. There were now three bullets in that one hole—three bullets imbedded processionally in the body of the stump back of the target. Everybody knew this—somehow or other—and yet nobody had dug any of them out to make sure. Cooper is not a close observer, but he is interesting. He is certainly always that, no matter what happens. And he is more interesting when he is not noticing what he is about than when he is. This is a considerable merit.

The conversations in the Cooper books have a curious sound in our modern ears. To believe that such talk really ever came out of people's mouths would be to believe that there was a time when time was of no value to a person who thought he had something to say; when it was the custom to spread a two-minute remark out to ten; when a man's mouth was a rolling-mill, and busied itself all day long in turning four-foot pigs[8] of thought into thirty-foot bars of conversational railroad iron by attenuation; when subjects were seldom faithfully stuck to, but the talk wandered all around and arrived nowhere; when conversations consisted mainly of irrelevances, with here and there a relevancy, a relevancy with an embarrassed look, as not being able to explain how it got there.

Cooper was certainly not a master in the construction of dialogue. Inaccurate observation defeated him here as it defeated him in so many other enterprises of his. He even failed to notice that the man who talks corrupt English six days in the week must and will talk it on the seventh, and can't help himself. In the *Deerslayer* story he lets Deerslayer talk the showiest kind of book talk sometimes, and at other times the basest of base dialects. For instance, when some one asks him if he has a sweetheart, and if so, where she abides, this is his majestic answer:

> "She's in the forest—hanging from the boughs of the trees, in a soft rain—in the dew on the open grass—the clouds that float about in the blue heavens—the birds that sing in the woods—the sweet springs where I slake my thirst—and in all the other glorious gifts that come from God's Providence!"

And he preceded that, a little before, with this:

> "It consarns me as all things that touches a fri'nd consarns a fri'nd."

And this is another of his remarks:

> "If I was Injun born, now, I might tell of this, or carry in the scalp and boast of the expl'ite afore the whole tribe; or if my inimy had only been a bear"—and so on.

We cannot imagine such a thing as a veteran Scotch Commander-in-Chief, comporting himself in the field like a windy melodramatic actor, but Cooper could. On one occasion Alice and Cora were being chased by the French through a fog in the neighborhood of their father's fort:

> *"Point de quartier aux coquins!"*[9] cried an eager pursuer, who seemed to direct the operations of the enemy.
>
> "Stand firm and be ready, my gallant 60ths!" suddenly exclaimed a voice above them; "wait to see the enemy; fire low, and sweep the glacis."[1]
>
> "Father! father!" exclaimed a piercing cry from out the mist; "it is I! Alice! thy own Elsie! spare, O! save your daughters!"
>
> "Hold!" shouted the former speaker, in the awful tones of parental agony, the sound reaching even to the woods, and rolling back in solemn

8. Crudely molded pieces of iron.
9. No quarter for the rascals! (French).

1. Slope that runs downward from a fortification.

echo. " 'Tis she! God has restored me my children! Throw open the sally-port;[2] to the field, 60ths, to the field; pull not a trigger, lest ye kill my lambs! Drive off these dogs of France with your steel."

Cooper's word-sense was singularly dull. When a person has a poor ear for music he will flat and sharp right along without knowing it. He keeps near the tune, but it is *not* the tune. When a person has a poor ear for words, the result is a literary flatting and sharping; you perceive what he is intending to say, but you also perceive that he doesn't *say* it. This is Cooper. He was not a word-musician. His ear was satisfied with the *approximate* word. I will furnish some circumstantial evidence in support of this charge. My instances are gathered from half a dozen pages of the tale called *Deerslayer*. He uses "verbal," for "oral"; "precision," for "facility"; "phenomena," for "marvels"; "necessary," for "predetermined"; "unsophisticated," for "primitive"; "preparation," for "expectancy"; "rebuked," for "subdued"; "dependent on," for "resulting from"; "fact," for "condition"; "fact," for "conjecture"; "precaution," for "caution"; "explain," for "determine"; "mortified," for "disappointed"; "meretricious," for "factitious"; "materially," for "considerably"; "decreasing," for "deepening"; "increasing," for "disappearing"; "embedded," for "enclosed"; "treacherous," for "hostile"; "stood," for "stooped"; "softened," for "replaced"; "rejoined," for "remarked"; "situation," for "condition"; "different," for "differing"; "insensible," for "unsentient"; "brevity," for "celerity"; "distrusted," for "suspicious"; "mental imbecility," for "imbecility"; "eyes," for "sight"; "counteracting," for "opposing"; "funeral obsequies," for "obsequies."

There have been daring people in the world who claimed that Cooper could write English, but they are all dead now—all dead but Lounsbury. I don't remember that Lounsbury makes the claim in so many words, still he makes it, for he says that *Deerslayer* is a "pure work of art." Pure, in that connection, means faultless—faultless in all details—and language is a detail. If Mr. Lounsbury had only compared Cooper's English with the English which he writes himself—but it is plain that he didn't; and so it is likely that he imagines until this day that Cooper's is as clean and compact as his own. Now I feel sure, deep down in my heart, that Cooper wrote about the poorest English that exists in our language, and that the English of *Deerslayer* is the very worst than even Cooper ever wrote.

I may be mistaken, but it does seem to me that *Deerslayer* is not a work of art in any sense; it does seem to me that it is destitute of every detail that goes to the making of a work of art; in truth, it seems to me that *Deerslayer* is just simply a literary *delirium tremens*.

A work of art? It has no invention; it has no order, system, sequence, or result; it has no lifelikeness, no thrill, no stir, no seeming of reality; its characters are confusedly drawn, and by their acts and words they prove that they are not the sort of people the author claims that they are; its humor is pathetic; its pathos is funny; its conversations are—oh! indescribable; its love-scenes odious; its English a crime against the language.

Counting these out, what is left is Art. I think we must all admit that.

1895

2. Gate or passage in a fortified place for use by troops making a raid or other expedition.

# *From* Roughing It[1]

## Chapter 23

If there is any life that is happier than the life we led on our timber ranch[2] for the next two or three weeks, it must be a sort of life which I have not read of in books or experienced in person. We did not see a human being but ourselves during the time, or hear any sounds but those that were made by the wind and the waves, the sighing of the pines, and now and then the far-off thunder of an avalanche. The forest about us was dense and cool, the sky above us was cloudless and brilliant with sunshine, the broad lake before us was glassy and clear, or rippled and breezy, or black and storm-tossed, according to Nature's mood; and its circling border of mountain domes, clothed with forests, scarred with land-slides, cloven by cañons and valleys, and helmeted with glittering snow, fitly framed and finished the noble picture. The view was always fascinating, bewitching, entrancing. The eye was never tired of gazing, night or day, in calm or storm; it suffered but one grief and that was that it could not look always, but must close sometimes in sleep.

We slept in the sand close to the water's edge, between two protecting boulders, which took care of the stormy night-winds for us. We never took any paregorre[3] to make us sleep. At the first break of dawn we were always up and running foot-races to tone down excess of physical vigor and exuberance of spirits. That is, Johnny[4] was—but I held his hat. While smoking the pipe of peace after breakfast we watched the sentinel peaks put on the glory of the sun, and followed the conquering light as it swept down among the shadows, and set the captive crags and forests free. We watched the tinted pictures grow and brighten upon the water till every little detail of forest, precipice and pinnacle was wrought in and finished, and the miracle of the enchanter complete. Then to "business."

That is, drifting around in the boat. We were on the north shore. There, the rocks on the bottom are sometimes gray, sometimes white. This gives the marvelous transparency of the water a fuller advantage than it has elsewhere on the lake. We usually pushed out a hundred yards or so from shore, and then lay down on the thwarts,[5] in the sun, and let the boat drift by the hour whither it would. We seldom talked. It interrupted the Sabbath stillness, and marred the dreams the luxurious rest and indolence brought. The shore all along was indented with deep, curved bays and coves, bordered by narrow sand-beaches; and where the sand ended, the steep mountain sides rose right up aloft into space—rose up like a vast wall a little out of the perpendicular, and thickly wooded with tall pines.

1. Based on experiences from 1861–66, *Roughing It* was first published with illustrations by True Williams, Edward F. Mullen, and others in Hartford, Connecticut, by the American Publishing Company in 1872. It was reprinted by the Mark Twain Project of the Bancroft Library at the University of California, Berkeley, in 1993, edited by Harriet Elinor Smith and Edgar Marquess Browning, the source of the present text.
2. Having failed at silver mining in Nevada, Twain and a friend start what they believe will be a profitable timber ranch near Lake Tahoe.
3. Paregoric, a morphine mixture prescribed for diarrhea and pain; it caused drowsiness.
4. "Johnny" or "Johnny K" was the "young son of an Ohio nabob and . . . out there for recreation" (Ch. 22).
5. Cross-pieces in a boat upon which a rower may sit.

So singularly clear was the water, that where it was only twenty or thirty feet deep the bottom was so perfectly distinct that the boat seemed floating in the air![6] Yes, where it was even *eighty* feet deep. Every little pebble was distinct, every speckled trout, every hand's-breadth of sand. Often, as we lay on our faces, a granite boulder, as large as a village church, would start out of the bottom apparently, and seem climbing up rapidly to the surface, till presently it threatened to touch our faces, and we could not resist the impulse to seize an oar and avert the danger. But the boat would float on, and the boulder descend again, and then we could see that when we had been exactly above it, it must still have been twenty or thirty feet below the surface. Down through the transparency of these great depths, the water was not *merely* transparent, but dazzlingly, brilliantly so. All objects seen through it had a bright, strong vividness, not only of outline, but of every minute detail, which they would not have had when seen simply through the same depth of atmosphere. So empty and airy did all spaces seem below us, and so strong was the sense of floating high aloft in mid-nothingness, that we called these boat-excursions "balloon-voyages."

We fished a good deal, but we did not average one fish a week. We could see trout by the thousand winging about in the emptiness under us, or sleeping in shoals on the bottom, but they would not bite—they could see the line too plainly, perhaps. We frequently selected the trout we wanted, and rested the bait patiently and persistently on the end of his nose at a depth of eighty feet, but he would only shake it off with an annoyed manner, and shift his position.

We bathed occasionally, but the water was rather chilly, for all it looked so sunny. Sometimes we rowed out to the "blue water," a mile or two from shore. It was as dead blue as indigo there, because of the immense depth.[7] By official measurement the lake in its centre is one thousand five hundred and twenty-five feet deep!

Sometimes, on lazy afternoons, we lolled on the sand in camp, and smoked pipes and read some old well-worn novels. At night, by the camp-fire, we played euchre and seven-up[8] to strengthen the mind—and played them with cards so greasy and defaced that only a whole summer's acquaintance with them could enable the student to tell the ace of clubs from the jack of diamonds.

We never slept in our "house."[9] It never recurred to us, for one thing; and besides, it was built to hold the ground, and that was enough. We did not wish to strain it.

By and by our provisions began to run short, and we went back to the old camp and laid in a new supply. We were gone all day, and reached home again about nightfall, pretty tired and hungry. While Johnny was carrying the main bulk of the provisions up to our "house" for future use, I took the loaf of

---

6. Though today Lake Tahoe is cloudier due to added sediments, in some places it is still so clear that objects can be seen to depths of seventy-five feet.
7. Lake Tahoe has an average depth of a thousand feet.

8. A plain-trick card game usually for four players in which the object is to win at least three of the five tricks. "Seven-up": a card game for two to four players.
9. They had built a brush and timber lean-to.

"Fire at Lake Tahoe." By True Williams (1839–1937).
From *Roughing It* (1872), American Publishing Company (Hartford).

bread, some slices of bacon, and the coffee-pot, ashore, set them down by a tree, lit a fire, and went back to the boat to get the frying pan. While I was at this, I heard a shout from Johnny, and looking up I saw that my fire was galloping all over the premises!

Johnny was on the other side of it. He had to run through the flames to get to the lake shore, and then we stood helpless and watched the devastation.

The ground was deeply carpeted with dry pine-needles, and the fire touched them off as if they were gunpowder. It was wonderful to see with what fierce speed the tall sheet of flame traveled! My coffee-pot was gone, and everything with it. In a minute and a half the fire seized upon a dense growth of dry manzanita chaparral[1] six or eight feet high, and then the roaring and popping and crackling was something terrific. We were driven to the boat by the intense heat, and there we remained, spell-bound.

Within half an hour all before us was a tossing, blinding tempest of flame! It went surging up adjacent ridges—surmounted them and disappeared in the cañons beyond—burst into view upon higher and farther ridges, presently— shed a grander illumination abroad, and dove again—flamed out again, directly, higher and still higher up the mountain side—threw out skirmishing parties of fire here and there, and sent them trailing their crimson spirals away among remote ramparts and ribs and gorges, till as far as the eye could reach the lofty mountain-fronts were webbed as it were with a tangled network of red lava streams. Away across the water the crags and domes were lit with a ruddy glare, and the firmament above was a reflected hell!

Every feature of the spectacle was repeated in the glowing mirror of the lake! Both pictures were sublime, both were beautiful, but that in the lake had a bewildering richness about it that enchanted the eye and held it with the stronger fascination.

We sat absorbed and motionless through four long hours. We never thought of supper, and never felt fatigue. But at eleven o'clock the conflagration had traveled beyond our range of vision, and then darkness stole down upon the landscape again.

Hunger asserted itself now, but there was nothing to eat. The provisions were all cooked, no doubt, but we did not go to see. We were homeless wanderers again, without any property. Our fence was gone, our house burned down; no insurance. Our pine forest was well scorched, the dead trees all burned up, and our broad acres of manzanita swept away Our blankets were on our usual sandbed, however, and so we lay down and went to sleep. The next morning we started back to the old camp, but while out a long way from shore, so great a storm came up that we dared not try to land. So I baled out the seas we shipped, and Johnny pulled heavily through the billows till we had reached a point three or four miles beyond the camp. The storm was increasing, and it became evident that it was better to take the hazard of beaching the boat than go down in a hundred fathoms of water; so we ran in, with tall whitecaps following, and I sat down in the stern-sheets[2] and pointed her head on to the shore. The instant the bow struck, a wave came over the stern that washed crew and cargo ashore, and saved a deal of trouble. We shivered in the lee of a boulder all the rest of the day, and froze all the night through. In the morning the tempest had gone down, and we paddled down to the camp without any unnecessary delay. We were so starved that we ate up the rest of the Brigade's provisions,[3] and then set out to Carson to tell them about it and ask their forgiveness. It was accorded, upon payment of damages.

1. Manzanita is a characteristic tree of northern California, with red bark, gray-green leaves, and white flower clusters. "Chaparral": a dense thicket of trees and brush.
2. The stern (or rear) portion of an open boat.
3. In Chapter 22, Twain describes the "Brigade" as

"principally voluntary camp-followers of the Governor, who had joined his retinue by their own election at New York and San Francisco and came along, feeling that in the scuffle for little territorial crumbs and offices they could not make their condition more precarious than it was, and might

We made many trips to the lake after that, and had many a hair-breadth escape and blood-curdling adventure which will never be recorded in any history.

1861–66                                                           1872

## *From* Letters from the Earth[1]

The Creator sat upon the throne, thinking. Behind him stretched the illimitable continent of heaven, steeped in a glory of light and color; before him rose the black night of Space, like a wall. His mighty bulk towered rugged and mountain-like into the zenith, and His divine head blazed there like a distant sun. At His feet stood three colossal figures, diminished to extinction, almost, by contrast—archangels—their heads level with His ankle-bone.

When the Creator had finished thinking, He said, "I have thought. Behold!"

He lifted His hand, and from it burst a fountain-spray of fire, a million stupendous suns, which clove the blackness and soared, away and away and away, diminishing in magnitude and intensity as they pierced the far frontiers of Space, until at last they were but as diamond nailheads sparkling under the domed vast roof of the universe.

At the end of an hour the Grand Council was dismissed.

They left the Presence impressed and thoughtful, and retired to a private place, where they might talk with freedom. None of the three seemed to want to begin, though all wanted somebody to do it. Each was burning to discuss the great event, but would prefer not to commit himself till he should know how the others regarded it. So there was some aimless and halting conversation about matters of no consequence, and this dragged tediously along, arriving nowhere, until at last the archangel Satan gathered his courage together—of which he had a very good supply—and broke ground. He said: "We know what we are here to talk about, my lords, and we may as well put pretense aside, and begin. If this is the opinion of the Council—"

"It is, it is!" said Gabriel and Michael, gratefully interrupting.

"Very well, then, let us proceed. We have witnessed a wonderful thing; as to that, we are necessarily agreed. As to the value of it—if it has any—that is a matter which does not personally concern us. We can have as many opinions about it as we like, and that is our limit. We have no vote. I think Space was well enough, just at it was, and useful, too. Cold and dark—a restful place, now and then, after a season of the overdelicate climate and trying

reasonably expect to make it better. They were popularly known as the 'Irish Brigade,' though there were only four or five Irishmen among all the Governor's retainers." The Secretary (Twain's brother Orion) put them to work as surveyors: "which will provide you with recreation amid noble landscapes, and afford you never ceasing opportunities for enriching your minds by observation and study."
1. Though the *Letters from the Earth* date back to 1909, they were published only posthumously in a volume by Harper & Row in 1961, edited by Bernard DeVoto, the source of the text here. Twain believed that "This book will never be published[;] . . . in fact, it couldn't be, because it would be a felony." When DeVoto became literary editor of Twain's estate in 1938, he decided to publish manuscripts that he deemed worthy of the public's attention, and so in 1939, he presented twenty writings to the estate's trustees, seeking approval for publication of *Letters from the Earth*. Clara Clemens, Twain's daughter, objected, feeling that the letters misrepresented her father's beliefs about religion; as a result, publication was delayed until shortly after Clara's death.

splendors of heaven. But these are details of no considerable moment; the new feature, the immense feature, is—what, gentlemen?"

"The invention and introduction of automatic, unsupervised, self-regulating *law* for the government of those myriads of whirling and racing suns and worlds!"

"That is it!" said Satan. "You perceive that it is a stupendous idea. Nothing approaching it has been evolved from the Master Intellect before. Law—*Automatic* Law—exact and unvarying Law—requiring no watching, no correcting, no readjusting while the eternities endure! He said those countless vast bodies would plunge through the wastes of Space ages and ages, at unimaginable speed, around stupendous orbits, yet never collide, and never lengthen nor shorten their orbital periods by so much as the hundredth part of a second in two thousand years! That is the new miracle, and the greatest of all—*Automatic Law!* And He gave it a name—the LAW OF NATURE—and said Natural Law is the LAW OF GOD—interchangeable names for one and the same thing."

"Yes," said Michael, "and He said He would establish Natural Law—the Law of God—throughout His dominions, and its authority should be supreme and inviolable."

"Also," said Gabriel, "He said He would by and by create animals, and place them, likewise, under the authority of that Law."

"Yes," said Satan, "I heard Him, but did not understand. What *is* animals, Gabriel?"

"Ah, how should I know? How should any of us know? It is a new word."

[*Interval of three centuries, celestial time—the equivalent of a hundred million years, earthly time. Enter a Messenger-Angel.*]

"My lords, He is making animals. Will it please you to come and see?"

They went, they saw, and were perplexed. Deeply perplexed—and the Creator noticed it, and said, "Ask. I will answer."

"Divine One," said Satan, making obeisance, "what are they for?"

"They are an experiment in Morals and Conduct. Observe them, and be instructed."

There were thousands of them. They were full of activities. Busy, all busy—mainly in persecuting each other. Satan remarked—after examining one of them through a powerful microscope: "This large beast is killing weaker animals, Divine One."

"The tiger—yes. The law of his nature is ferocity. The law of his nature is the Law of God. He cannot disobey it."

"Then in obeying it he commits no offense, Divine One?"

"No, he is blameless."

"This other creature, here, is timid, Divine One, and suffers death without resisting."

"The rabbit—yes. He is without courage. It is the law of his nature—the Law of God. He must obey it."

"Then he cannot honorably be required to go counter to his nature and resist, Divine One?"

"No. No creature can be honorably required to go counter to the law of his nature—the Law of God."

After a long time and many questions, Satan said, "The spider kills the fly, and eats it; the bird kills the spider and eats it; the wildcat kills the goose;

the—well, they all kill each other. It is murder all along the line. Here are countless multitudes of creatures, and they all kill, kill, kill, they are all murderers. And they are not to blame, Divine One?"

"They are not to blame. It is the law of their nature. And always the law of nature is the Law of God. Now—observe—behold! A new creature—and the masterpiece—*Man!*"

Men, women, children, they came swarming in flocks, in droves, in millions.

"What shall you do with them, Divine One?"

"Put into each individual, in differing shades and degrees, all the various Moral Qualities, in mass, that have been distributed, a single distinguishing characteristic at a time, among the non-speaking animal world—courage, cowardice, ferocity, gentleness, fairness, justice, cunning, treachery, magnanimity, cruelty, malice, malignity, lust, mercy, pity, purity, selfishness, sweetness, honor, love, hate, baseness, nobility, loyalty, falsity, veracity, untruthfulness—each human being shall have *all* of these in him, and they will constitute his nature. In some, there will be high and fine characteristics which will submerge the evil ones, and those will be called good men; in others the evil characteristics will have dominion, and those will be called bad men. Observe—behold—they vanish!"

"Whither are they gone, Divine One?"

"To the earth—they and all their fellow animals."

"What is the earth?"

"A small globe I made, a time, two times and a half ago. You saw it, but did not notice it in the explosion of worlds and suns that sprayed from my hand. Man is an experiment, the other animals are another experiment. Time will show whether they were worth the trouble. The exhibition is over; you may take your leave, my lords."

Several days passed by.

This stands for a long stretch of (our) time, since in heaven a day is as a thousand years.

Satan had been making admiring remarks about certain of the Creator's sparkling industries—remarks which, being read between the lines, were sarcasms. He had made them confidentially to his safe friends the other archangels, but they had been overheard by some ordinary angels and reported at Headquarters.

He was ordered into banishment for a day—the celestial day. It was a punishment he was used to, on account of his too flexible tongue. Formerly he had been deported into Space, there being nowhither else to send him, and had flapped tediously around there in the eternal night and the Arctic chill; but now it occurred to him to push on and hunt up the earth and see how the Human-Race experiment was coming along.

By and by he wrote home—very privately—to St. Michael and St. Gabriel about it.

### Satan's Letter

This is a strange place, an extraordinary place, and interesting. There is nothing resembling it at home. The people are all insane, the other animals are all insane, the earth is insane, Nature itself is insane. Man is a marvelous curiosity. When he is at his very very best he is a sort of low grade nickel-plated angel; at his worst he is unspeakable, unimaginable; and first and last and all the time he is a sarcasm. Yet he blandly and in all sincerity calls himself the "noblest work of God." This is the truth I am telling you. And this is not a new idea with him, he has talked it through all the ages, and believed it. Believed it, and found nobody among all his race to laugh at it.

Moreover—if I may put another strain upon you—he thinks he is the Creator's pet. He believes the Creator is proud of him; he even believes the Creator loves him; has a passion for him; sits up nights to admire him; yes, and watch over him and keep him out of trouble. He prays to Him, and thinks He listens. Isn't it a quaint idea? Fills his prayers with crude and bald and florid flatteries of Him, and thinks He sits and purrs over these extravagancies and enjoys them. He prays for help, and favor, and protection, every day; and does it with hopefulness and confidence, too, although no prayer of his has ever been answered. The daily affront, the daily defeat, do not discourage him, he goes on praying just the same. There is something almost fine about this perseverance. I must put one more strain upon you: he thinks he is going to heaven!

He has salaried teachers who tell him that. They also tell him there is a hell, of everlasting fire, and that he will go to it if he doesn't keep the Commandments. What are the Commandments? They are a curiosity. I will tell you about them by and by.

### Letter II

"I have told you nothing about man that is not true." You must pardon me if I repeat that remark now and then in these letters; I want you to take seriously the things I am telling you, and I feel that if I were in your place and you in mine, I should need that reminder from time to time, to keep my credulity from flagging.

For there is nothing about man that is not strange to an immortal. He looks at nothing as we look at it, his sense of proportion is quite different from ours, and his sense of values is so widely divergent from ours, that with all our large intellectual powers it is not likely that even the most gifted among us would ever be quite able to understand it.

For instance, take this sample: he has imagined a heaven, and has left entirely out of it the supremest of all his delights, the one ecstasy that stands first and foremost in the heart of every individual of his race—and of ours—sexual intercourse!

It is as if a lost and perishing person in a roasting desert should be told by a rescuer he might choose and have all longed-for things but one, and he should elect to leave out water!

His heaven is like himself: strange, interesting, astonishing, grotesque. I give you my word, it has not a single feature in it that he *actually values*. It consists—utterly and entirely—of diversions which he cares next to nothing about, here in the earth, yet is quite sure he will like in heaven. Isn't it curious? Isn't it interesting? You must not think I am exaggerating, for it is not so. I will give you details.

Most men do not sing, most men cannot sing, most men will not stay where others are singing if it be continued more than two hours. Note that.

Only about two men in a hundred can play upon a musical instrument, and not four in a hundred have any wish to learn how. Set that down.

Many men pray, not many of them like to do it. A few pray long, the others make a short cut.

More men go to church than want to.

To forty-nine men in fifty the Sabbath Day is a dreary, dreary bore.

Of all the men in a church on a Sunday, two-thirds are tired when the service is half over, and the rest before it is finished.

The gladdest moment for all of them is when the preacher uplifts his hands for the benediction. You can hear the soft rustle of relief that sweeps the house, and you recognize that it is eloquent with gratitude.

All nations look down upon all other nations.

All nations dislike all other nations.

All white nations despise all colored nations, of whatever hue, and oppress them when they can.

White men will not associate with "niggers," nor marry them.

They will not allow them in their schools and churches.

All the world hates the Jew, and will not endure him except when he is rich.

I ask you to note all those particulars.

Further. All sane people detest noise.

All people, sane or insane, like to have variety in their life. Monotony quickly wearies them.

Every man, according to the mental equipment that has fallen to his share, exercises his intellect constantly, ceaselessly, and this exercise makes up a vast and valued and essential part of his life. The lowest intellect, like the highest, possesses a skill of some kind and takes a keen pleasure in testing it, proving it, perfecting it. The urchin who is his comrade's superior in games is as diligent and as enthusiastic in his practice as are the sculptor, the painter, the pianist, the mathematician and the rest. Not one of them could be happy if his talent were put under an interdict.

Now then, you have the facts. You know what the human race enjoys, and what it doesn't enjoy. It has invented a heaven, out of its own head, all by itself: guess what it is like! In fifteen hundred eternities you couldn't do it. The ablest mind known to you or me in fifty million aeons couldn't do it. Very well, I will tell you about it.

1. First of all, I recall to your attention the extraordinary fact with which I began. To wit, that the human being, like the immortals, naturally places sexual intercourse far and away above all other joys—yet he has left it out of his heaven! The very thought of it excites him; opportunity sets him wild; in this state he will risk life, reputation, everything—even his queer heaven itself—to make good that opportunity and ride it to the overwhelming climax. From youth to middle age all men and all women prize copulation above all other pleasures combined, yet it is actually as I have said: it is not in their heaven; prayer takes its place.

They prize it thus highly; yet, like all their so-called "boons," it is a poor thing. At its very best and longest the act is brief beyond imagination—the imagination of an immortal, I mean. In the matter of repetition the man is limited—oh, quite beyond immortal conception. We who continue the act and its supremest ecstasies unbroken and without withdrawal for centuries, will never be able to understand or adequately pity the awful poverty of these people in that rich gift which, possessed as we possess it, makes all other possessions trivial and not worth the trouble of invoicing.

2. In man's heaven *everybody sings!* The man who did not sing on earth sings there; the man who could not sing on earth is able to do it there. This universal singing is not casual, not occasional, not relieved by intervals of quiet; it goes on, all day long, and every day, during a stretch of twelve hours. And *everybody stays;* whereas in the earth the place would be empty in two hours. The singing is of hymns alone. Nay, it is of *one* hymn alone. The words are always the same, in number they are only about a dozen, there is no rhyme, there is no poetry: "Hosannah, hosannah, hosannah, Lord God of Sabaoth, 'rah! 'rah! 'rah! siss!—boom! . . . a-a-ah!"

3. Meantime, every person is playing on a harp—those millions and millions!—whereas not more than twenty in the thousand of them could play an instrument in the earth, or ever wanted to.

Consider the deafening hurricane of sound—millions and millions of voices screaming at once and millions and millions of harps gritting their teeth at the same time! I ask you: is it hideous, is it odious, is it horrible?

Consider further: it is a *praise* service; a service of compliment, of flattery, of adulation! Do you ask who it is that is willing to endure this strange compliment, this insane compliment; and who not only endures it, but likes it, enjoys it, requires it, *commands* it? Hold your breath!

It is God! This race's God, I mean. He sits on his throne, attended by his four and twenty elders and some other dignitaries pertaining to his court, and looks out over his miles and miles of tempestuous worshipers, and smiles, and purrs, and nods his satisfaction northward, eastward, southward; as quaint and naïve a spectacle as has yet been imagined in this universe, I take it.

It is easy to see that the inventor of the heaven did not originate the idea, but copied it from the show-ceremonies of some sorry little sovereign State up in the back settlements of the Orient somewhere.

All sane white people hate noise; yet they have tranquilly accepted this kind of a heaven—without thinking, without reflection, without examination—and they actually want to go to it! Profoundly devout old gray-headed men put in a large part of their time dreaming of the happy day when they will lay down the cares of this life and enter into the joys of that place. Yet you can see how unreal it is to them, and how little it takes a grip upon them as being fact, for they make no practical preparation for the great change: you never see one of them with a harp, you never hear one of them sing.

As you have seen, that singular show is a service of praise: praise by hymn, praise by prostration. It takes the place of "church." Now then, in the earth these people cannot stand much church—an hour and a quarter is the limit, and they draw the line at once a week. That is to say, Sunday. One day in seven; and even then they do not look forward to it with longing. And so—consider what their heaven provides for them:"church" that lasts forever, and a Sabbath that has no end! They quickly weary of this brief hebdomadal[2] Sabbath here; yet they long for that eternal one; they dream of it, they talk about it, they *think* they think they are going to enjoy it—with all their simple hearts they think they think they are going to be happy in it!

It is because they do not think at all; they only think they think. Whereas

*(handwritten margin note: they don't really believe it)*

they can't think; not two human beings in ten thousand have anything to think with. And as to imagination—oh, well, look at their heaven! They accept it, they approve it, they admire it. That gives you their intellectual measure.

4. The inventor of their heaven empties into it all the nations of the earth, in one common jumble. All are on an equality absolute, no one of them ranking another; they have to be "brothers"; they have to mix together, pray together, harp together, hosannah together—whites, niggers, Jews, everybody—there's no distinction. Here in the earth all nations hate each other, and every one of them hates the Jew. Yet every pious person adores that heaven and wants to get into it. He really does. And when he is in a holy rapture he thinks he thinks that if he were only there he would take all the populace to his heart, and hug, and hug, and hug!

He is a marvel—man is! I would I knew who invented him.

5. Every man in the earth possesses some share of intellect, large or small; and be it large or be it small he takes a pride in it. Also his heart swells at mention of the names of the majestic intellectual chiefs of his race, and he loves the tale of their splendid achievements. For he is of their blood, and in honoring themselves they have honored him. Lo, what the mind of man can do! he cries; and calls the roll of the illustrious of all the ages; and points to the imperishable literatures they have given to the world, and the mechanical wonders they have invented, and the glories wherewith they have clothed science and the arts; and to them he uncovers, as to kings, and gives to them the profoundest homage, and the sincerest, his exultant heart can furnish—thus exalting intellect above all things else in his world, and enthroning it there under the arching skies in a supremacy unapproachable. And then he contrives a heaven that hasn't a rag of intellectuality in it anywhere!

Is it odd, is it curious, is it puzzling? It is exactly as I have said, incredible as it may sound. This sincere adorer of intellect and prodigal rewarder of its mighty services here in the earth has invented a religion and a heaven which pay no compliments to intellect, offer it no distinctions, fling to it no largess: in fact, never even mention it.

By this time you will have noticed that the human being's heaven has been thought out and constructed upon an absolutely definite plan; and that this plan is, that it shall contain, in labored detail, each and every imaginable thing that is repulsive to a man, and not a single thing he likes!

Very well, the further we proceed the more will this curious fact be apparent.

Make a note of it: in man's heaven there are no exercises for the intellect, nothing for it to live upon. It would rot there in a year—rot and stink. Rot and stink—and at that stage become holy. A blessed thing: for only the holy can stand the joys of that bedlam.

\* \* \*

## Letter IV

So the First Pair went forth from the Garden under a curse—a permanent one. They had lost every pleasure they had possessed before "The Fall"; and yet they were rich, for they had gained one worth all the rest: they knew the Supreme Art.

They practiced it diligently and were filled with contentment. The Deity ordered them to practice it. They obeyed, this time. But it was just as well it was not forbidden, for they would have practiced it anyhow, if a thousand Deities had forbidden it.

Results followed. By the name of Cain and Abel. And these had some sisters; and knew what to do with them. And so there were some more results: Cain and Abel begot some nephews and nieces. These, in their turn, begot some second cousins. At this point classification of relationships began to get difficult, and the attempt to keep it up was abandoned.

The pleasant labor of populating the world went on from age to age, and with prime efficiency; for in those happy days the sexes were still competent for the Supreme Art when by rights they ought to have been dead eight hundred years. The sweeter sex, the dearer sex, the lovelier sex was manifestly at its very best, then, for it was even able to attract gods. Real gods. They came down out of heaven and had wonderful times with those hot young blossoms. The Bible tells about it.[3]

By help of those visiting foreigners the population grew and grew until it numbered several millions. But it was a disappointment to the Deity. He was dissatisfied with its morals; which in some respects were not any better than his own. Indeed they were an unflatteringly close imitation of his own. They were a very bad people, and as he knew of no way to reform them, he wisely concluded to abolish them. This is the only really enlightened and superior idea his Bible has credited him with, and it would have made his reputation for all time if he could only have kept to it and carried it out. But he was always unstable—except in his advertisements—and his good resolution broke down. He took a pride in man; man was his finest invention; man was his pet, after the housefly, and he could not bear to lose him wholly; so he finally decided to save a sample of him and drown the rest.

Nothing could be more characteristic of him. He created all those infamous people, and he alone was responsible for their conduct. Not one of them deserved death, yet it was certainly good policy to extinguish them; especially since in creating them the master crime had already been committed, and to allow them to go on procreating would be a distinct addition to the crime. But at the same time there could be no justice, no fairness, in any favoritism—all should be drowned or none.

No, he would not have it so; he would save half a dozen and try the race over again. He was not able to foresee that it would go rotten again, for he is only the Far-Sighted One in his advertisements.

He saved out Noah and his family, and arranged to exterminate the rest. He planned an Ark, and Noah built it. Neither of them had ever built an Ark before, nor knew anything about Arks; and so something out of the common was to be expected. It happened. Noah was a farmer, and although he knew what was required of the Ark he was quite incompetent to say whether this one would be large enough to meet the requirements or not (which it wasn't), so he ventured no advice. The Deity did not know it wasn't large enough, but took the chances and made no adequate measurements. In the end the ship fell far short of the necessities, and to this day the world still suffers for it.

3. See Genesis 6.4, in which, depending on the translation, either fallen angels or giants copulate with human women; in the Hebrew sources these beings are called the "Nephilim." This behavior angers God and leads him to send the Flood to destroy most of humankind.

Noah built the Ark. He built it the best he could, but left out most of the essentials. It had no rudder, it had no sails, it had no compass, it had no pumps, it had no charts, no lead-lines, no anchors, no log, no light, no ventilation, and as for cargo room—which was the main thing—the less said about that the better. It was to be at sea eleven months, and would need fresh water enough to fill two Arks of its size—yet the additional Ark was not provided. Water from outside could not be utilized: half of it would be salt water, and men and land animals could not drink it.

For not only was a sample of man to be saved, but business samples of the other animals, too. You must understand that when Adam ate the apple in the Garden and learned how to multiply and replenish, the other animals learned the Art, too, by watching Adam. It was cunning of them, it was neat; for they got all that was worth having out of the apple without tasting it and afflicting themselves with the disastrous Moral Sense, the parent of all the immoralities.

\* \* \*

## Letter VI

On the third day, about noon, it was found that a fly had been left behind. The return voyage turned out to be long and difficult, on account of the lack of chart and compass, and because of the changed aspects of all coasts, the steadily rising water having submerged some of the lower landmarks and given to higher ones an unfamiliar look; but after sixteen days of earnest and faithful seeking, the fly was found at last, and received on board with hymns of praise and gratitude, the Family standing meanwhile uncovered, out of reverence for its divine origin. It was weary and worn, and had suffered somewhat from the weather, but was otherwise in good estate. Men and their families had died of hunger on barren mountain tops, but it had not lacked for food, the multitudinous corpses furnishing it in rank and rotten richness. Thus was the sacred bird providentially preserved.

Providentially. That is the word. For the fly had not been left behind by accident. No, the hand of Providence was in it. There are no accidents. All things that happen, happen for a purpose. They are foreseen from the beginning of time, they are ordained from the beginning of time. From the dawn of Creation the Lord had foreseen that Noah, being alarmed and confused by the invasion of the prodigious brevet fossils,[4] would prematurely fly to sea unprovided with a certain invaluable disease. He would have all the other diseases, and could distribute them among the new races of men as they appeared in the world, but he would lack one of the very best—typhoid fever; a malady which, when the circumstances are especially favorable, is able to utterly wreck a patient without killing him; for it can restore him to his feet with a long life in him, and yet deaf, dumb, blind, crippled, and idiotic. The

4. The first scientific identification of fossils (freshwater mollusks) in the American West resulted from an Oregon Trail expedition led by Brevet Captain J. C. Frémont in Wyoming, Idaho, and Utah, from 1842 to 1844. A brevet rank was an honorary promotion given to an officer (or occasionally, an enlisted man) in recognition of meritorious service, serving much the same purpose that medals play today. A brevet rank advanced the man during wartime to the responsibilities of his new rank, but after the war became a title without rank responsibilities. What Twain means by "brevet fossils" is that the animals on the Ark have been promoted; that is, had they not been taken on the Ark, they would have merely been fossils.

housefly is its main disseminator, and is more competent and more calamitously effective than all the other distributors of the dreaded scourge put together. And so, by foreordination from the beginning of time, this fly was left behind to seek out a typhoid corpse and feed upon its corruptions and gaum[5] its legs with the germs and transmit them to the repeopled world for permanent business. From that one housefly, in the ages that have since elapsed, billions of sickbeds have been stocked, billions of wrecked bodies sent tottering about the earth, and billions of cemeteries recruited with the dead.

It is most difficult to understand the disposition of the Bible God, it is such a confusion of contradictions; of watery instabilities and iron firmnesses; of goody-goody abstract morals made out of words, and concreted hell-born ones made out of acts; of fleeting kindnesses repented of in permanent malignities.

However, when after much puzzling you get at the key to his disposition, you do at last arrive at a sort of understanding of it. With a most quaint and juvenile and astonishing frankness he has furnished that key himself. It is jealousy!

I expect that to take your breath away. You are aware—for I have already told you in an earlier letter—that among human beings jealousy ranks distinctly as a weakness; a trade-mark of small minds; a property of *all* small minds, yet a property which even the smallest is ashamed of; and when accused of its possession will lyingly deny it and resent the accusation as an insult.

Jealousy. Do not forget it, keep it in mind. It is the key. With it you will come to partly understand God as we go along; without it nobody can understand him. As I have said, he has openly held up this treasonous key himself, for all to see. He says, naïvely, outspokenly, and without suggestion of embarrassment: "I the Lord thy God am a jealous God."

You see, it is only another way of saying, "I the Lord thy God am a small God; a small God, and fretful about small things."

He was giving a warning: he could not bear the thought of any other God getting some of the Sunday compliments of this comical little human race—he wanted all of them for himself. He valued them. To him they were riches; just as tin money is to a Zulu.

But wait—I am not fair; I am misrepresenting him; prejudice is beguiling me into saying what is not true. He did not say he wanted all of the adulations; he said nothing about not being willing to share them with his fellow gods; what he said was, "Thou shalt have no other gods *before* me."

It is a quite different thing, and puts him in a much better light—I confess it. There was an abundance of gods, the woods were full of them, as the saying is, and all he demanded was that he should be ranked as high as the others—not above any of them, but not below any of them. He was willing that they should fertilize earthly virgins, but not on any better terms than he could have for himself in his turn. He wanted to be held their equal. This he insisted upon, in the clearest language: he would have no other gods *before* him. They could march abreast with him, but none of them could head the procession, and he did not claim the right to head it himself.

---

5. To smudge or smear.

Do you think he was able to stick to that upright and creditable position? No. He could keep to a bad resolution forever, but he couldn't keep to a good one a month. By and by he threw this one aside and calmly claimed to be the only God in the entire universe.

As I was saying, jealousy is the key; all through his history it is present and prominent. It is the blood and bone of his disposition, it is the basis of his character. How small a thing can wreck his composure and disorder his judgment if it touches the raw of his jealousy! And nothing warms up this trait so quickly and so surely and so exaggeratedly as a suspicion that some competition with the god-Trust is impending. The fear that if Adam and Eve ate of the fruit of the Tree of Knowledge they would "be as gods" so fired his jealousy that his reason was affected, and he could not treat those poor creatures either fairly or charitably, or even refrain from dealing cruelly and criminally with their blameless posterity.

To this day his reason has never recovered from that shock; a wild nightmare of vengefulness has possessed him ever since, and he has almost bankrupted his native ingenuities in inventing pains and miseries and humiliations and heartbreaks wherewith to embitter the brief lives of Adam's descendants. Think of the diseases he has contrived for them! They are multitudinous; no book can name them all. And each one is a trap, set for an innocent victim.

The human being is a machine. An automatic machine. It is composed of thousands of complex and delicate mechanisms, which perform their functions harmoniously and perfectly, in accordance with laws devised for their governance, and over which the man himself has no authority, no mastership, no control. For each one of these thousands of mechanisms the Creator has planned an enemy, whose office is to harass it, pester it, persecute it, damage it, afflict it with pains, and miseries, and ultimate destruction. Not one has been overlooked.

From cradle to grave these enemies are always at work; they know no rest, night or day. They are an army: an organized army; a besieging army; an assaulting army; an army that is alert, watchful, eager, merciless; an army that never relents, never grants a truce.

It moves by squad, by company, by battalion, by regiment, by brigade, by division, by army corps; upon occasion it masses its parts and moves upon mankind with its whole strength. It is the Creator's Grand Army, and he is the Commander-in-Chief. Along its battlefront its grisly banners wave their legends in the face of the sun: Disaster, Disease, and the rest.

Disease! That is the main force, the diligent force, the devastating force! It attacks the infant the moment it is born; it furnishes it one malady after another: croup, measles, mumps, bowel troubles, teething pains, scarlet fever, and other childhood specialties. It chases the child into youth and furnishes it some specialties for that time of life. It chases the youth into maturity, maturity into age, and age into the grave.

With these facts before you will you now try to guess man's chiefest pet name for this ferocious Commander-in-Chief? I will save you the trouble— but you must not laugh. It is Our Father in Heaven!

It is curious—the way the human mind works. The Christian begins with this straight proposition, this definite proposition, this inflexible and uncompromising proposition: *God is all-knowing, and all-powerful.*

This being the case, nothing can happen without his knowing beforehand that it is going to happen; nothing happens without his permission; nothing can happen that he chooses to prevent.

That is definite enough, isn't it? It makes the Creator distinctly responsible for everything that happens, doesn't it?

The Christian concedes it in that italicized sentence. Concedes it with feeling, with enthusiasm.

Then, having thus made the Creator responsible for all those pains and diseases and miseries above enumerated, and which he could have prevented, the gifted Christian blandly calls him Our Father!

It is as I tell you. He equips the Creator with every trait that goes to the making of a fiend, and then arrives at the conclusion that a fiend and a father are the same thing! Yet he would deny that a malevolent lunatic and a Sunday school superintendent are essentially the same. What do you think of the human mind? I mean, in case you think there is a human mind.

## Letter to the Earth

OFFICE OF THE RECORDING ANGEL
Department of Petitions, Jan. 20

*Abner Scofield*
*Coal Dealer*
*Buffalo, New York*

I have the honor, as per command, to inform you that your recent act of benevolence and self-sacrifice has been recorded upon a page of the Book called *Golden Deeds of Men*; a distinction, I am permitted to remark, which is not merely extraordinary, it is unique.

As regards your prayers, for the week ending the 19th, I have the honor to report as follows:

1. For weather to advance hard coal 15 cents a ton. Granted.
2. For influx of laborers to reduce wages 10 percent. Granted.
3. For a break in rival soft-coal prices. Granted.
4. For a visitation upon the man, or upon the family of the man, who has set up a competing retail coal-yard in Rochester. Granted, as follows: diphtheria, 2, 1 fatal; scarlet fever, 1, to result in deafness and imbecility. NOTE. This prayer should have been directed against this subordinate's principals, the N.Y. Central R. R. Co.
5. For deportation to Sheol[6] of annoying swarms of persons who apply daily for work, or for favors of one sort or another. Taken under advisement for later decision and compromise, this petition appearing to conflict with another one of same date, which will be cited further along.
6. For application of some form of violent death to neighbor who threw brick at family cat, whilst the same was serenading. Reserved for consideration and compromise because of conflict with a prayer of even date to be cited further along.
7. To "damn the missionary cause." Reserved also—as above.
8. To increase December profits of $22,230 to $45,000 for January, and

---

6. Hell.

perpetuate a proportionate monthly increase thereafter—"which will satisfy you." The prayer granted; the added remark accepted with reservations.

9. For cyclone, to destroy the works and fill up the mine of the North Pennsylvania Co. NOTE: Cyclones are not kept in stock in the winter season. A reliable article of fire-damp can be furnished upon application.

Especial note is made of the above list, they being of particular moment. The 298 remaining supplications classifiable under the head of Special Providences, Schedule A, for week ending 19th, are granted in a body, except that 3 of the 32 cases requiring immediate death have been modified to incurable disease.

This completes the week's invoice of petitions known to this office under the technical designation of Secret Supplications of the Heart, and which, for a reason which may suggest itself, always receive our first and especial attention.

The remainder of the week's invoice falls under the head of what we term Public Prayers, in which classification we place prayers uttered in Prayer Meeting, Sunday School, Class Meeting, Family Worship, etc. These kinds of prayers have value according to classification of Christian uttering them. By rule of this office, Christians are divided into two grand classes, to wit: (1) Professing Christians; (2) Professional Christians. These, in turn, are minutely subdivided and classified by Size, Species, and Family; and finally, Standing is determined by carats, the minimum being 1, the maximum 1,000.

As per balance sheet for quarter ending Dec. 31st, 1847, you stood classified as follows:

*Grand Classification*: Professing Christian.

*Size*: one-fourth of maximum.

*Species*: Human-Spiritual.

*Family*: A of the Elect, Division 16.

*Standing*: 322 carats fine.

As per balance sheet for quarter just ended—that is to say, forty years later—you stand classified as follows:

*Grand Classification*: Professional Christian.

*Size*: six one-hundredths of maximum.

*Species*: Human-Animal.

*Family*: W of the Elect, Division 1547.

*Standing*: 3 carats fine.

I have the honor to call your attention to the fact that you seem to have deteriorated.

To resume report upon your Public Prayers—with the side remark that in order to encourage Christians of your grade and of approximate grades, it is the custom of this office to grant many things to them which would not be granted to Christians of a higher grade—partly because they would not be asked for:

Prayer for weather mercifully tempered to the needs of the poor and the naked. Denied. This was a Prayer-Meeting prayer. It conflicts with Item 1 of this report, which was a Secret Supplication of the Heart. By a rigid rule of this office, certain sorts of Public Prayers of Professional Christians are forbidden to take precedence of Secret Supplications of the Heart.

Prayer for better times and plentier food "for the hard-handed son of toil whose patient and exhausting labors make comfortable the homes, and pleasant the ways, of the more fortunate, and entitle him to our vigilant and effective protection from the wrongs and injustices which grasping avarice would do him, and to the tenderest offices of our grateful hearts." Prayer-Meeting prayer. Refused. Conflicts with Secret Supplication of the Heart No. 2.

Prayer "that such as in any way obstruct our preferences may be generously blessed, both themselves and their families, we here calling our hearts to witness that in their worldly prosperity we are spiritually blessed, and our joys made perfect." Prayer-Meeting prayer. Refused. Conflicts with Secret Supplications of the Heart Nos. 3 and 4.

"Oh, let none fall heir to the pains of perdition through words or acts of ours." Family Worship. Received fifteen minutes in advance of Secret Supplication of the Heart No. 5, with which it distinctly conflicts. It is suggested that one or the other of these prayers be withdrawn, or both of them modified.

"Be mercifully inclined toward all who would do us offense in our persons or our property." Includes man who threw brick at cat. Family Prayer. Received some minutes in advance of No. 6, Secret Supplications of the Heart. Modification suggested, to reconcile discrepancy.

"Grant that the noble missionary cause, the most precious labor entrusted to the hands of men, may spread and prosper without let or limit in all heathen lands that do as yet reproach us with their spiritual darkness." Uninvited prayer shoved in at meeting of American Board.[7] Received nearly half a day in advance of No. 7, Secret Supplications of the Heart. This office takes no stock in missionaries, and is not connected in any way with the American Board. We should like to grant one of these prayers, but cannot grant both. It is suggested that the American Board one be withdrawn.

This office desires for the twentieth time to call urgent attention to your remark appended to No. 8. It is a chestnut.

Of the 464 specifications contained in your Public Prayers for the week, and not previously noted in this report, we grant 2, and deny the rest. To wit: Granted, (1) "that the clouds may continue to perform their office; (2) and the sun his." It was the divine purpose anyhow; it will gratify you to know that you have not disturbed it. Of the 462 details refused, 61 were uttered in Sunday School. In this connection I must once more remind you that we grant no Sunday School Prayers of Professional Christians of the classification technically known in this office as the John Wanamaker grade.[8] We merely enter them as "words," and they count to his credit according to number uttered within certain limits of time; 3,000 per quarter-minute required, or no score; 4,200 in a possible 5,000 is a quite common Sunday School score, among experts, and counts the same as two hymns and a bouquet furnished by young ladies in the assassin's cell, execution morning. Your remaining 401 details count for wind only. We bunch them and use them for head winds in retarding the ships of improper people, but it takes so many of them to make an impression that we cannot allow anything for their use.

7. Chartered in 1812 during the religious revival of the Second Great Awakening, the American Board of Commissioners for Foreign Missions was the first American Christian foreign mission agency. Congregationalist in origin, it became the leading missionary society in the United States.
8. John Wanamaker (1838–1922), Pennsylvania businessman, is considered the father of the department store and of modern advertising. Wanamaker became very wealthy and owned several mansions, living by his motto, "The customer is always right." Twain evidently sees him as a model of the (rich) Professional Christian.

I desire to add a word of my own to this report. When certain sorts of people do a sizable good deed, we credit them up a thousand-fold more for it than we would in the case of a better man—on account of the strain. You stand far away above your classification record here, because of certain self-sacrifices of yours which greatly exceed what could have been expected of you. Years ago, when you were worth only $100,000, and sent $2 to your impoverished cousin the widow when she appealed to you for help, there were many in heaven who were not able to believe it, and many more who believed that the money was counterfeit. Your character went up many degrees when it was shown that these suspicions were unfounded. A year or two later, when you sent the poor girl $4 in answer to another appeal, everybody believed it, and you were all the talk here for days together. Two years later you sent $6, upon supplication, when the widow's youngest child died, and that act made perfect your good fame. Everybody in heaven said, "Have you heard about Abner?"—for you are now affectionately called Abner here. Your increasing donation, every two or three years, has kept your name on all lips, and warm in all hearts. All heaven watches you Sundays, as you drive to church in your handsome carriage; and when your hand retires from the contribution plate, the glad shout is heard even to the ruddy walls of remote Sheol, "Another nickel from Abner!"

But the climax came a few days ago, when the widow wrote and said she could get a school in a far village to teach if she had $50 to get herself and her two surviving children over the long journey; and you counted up last month's clear profit from your three coal mines—$22,230—and added to it the certain profit for the current month—$45,000 and a possible fifty—and then got down your pen and your checkbook and mailed her *fifteen whole dollars!* Ah, heaven bless and keep you forever and ever, generous heart! There was not a dry eye in the realms of bliss; and amidst the hand-shakings, and embracings, and praisings, the decree was thundered forth from the shining mount, that this deed should outhonor all the historic self-sacrifices of men and angels, and be recorded by itself upon a page of its own, for that the strain of it upon you had been heavier and bitterer than the strain it costs ten thousand martyrs to yield up their lives at the fiery stake; and all said, "What is the giving up of life, to a noble soul, or to ten thousand noble souls, compared with the giving up of fifteen dollars out of the greedy grip of the meanest white man that ever lived on the face of the earth?"

And it was a true word. And Abraham, weeping, shook out the contents of his bosom and pasted the eloquent label there, "RESERVED"; and Peter, weeping, said, "He shall be received with a torchlight procession when he comes"; and then all heaven boomed, and was glad you were going there. And so was hell.

[Signed]

THE RECORDING ANGEL [SEAL]

By command

1909                                                                                              1961

# The War Prayer[1]

It was a time of great and exalting excitement. The country was up in arms, the war was on, in every breast burned the holy fire of patriotism; the drums were beating, the bands playing, the toy pistols popping, the bunched fire-crackers hissing and spluttering; on every hand and far down the receding and fading spread of roofs and balconies a fluttering wilderness of flags flashed in the sun; daily the young volunteers marched down the wide avenue gay and fine in their new uniforms, the proud fathers and mothers and sisters and sweethearts cheering them with voices choked with happy emotion as they swung by; nightly the packed mass meetings listened, panting, to patriot oratory which stirred the deepest deeps of their hearts, and which they interrupted at briefest intervals with cyclones of applause, the tears running down their cheeks the while; in the churches the pastors preached devotion to flag and country, and invoked the God of Battles, beseeching His aid in our good cause in outpouring of fervid eloquence which moved every listener. It was indeed a glad and gracious time, and the half dozen rash spirits that ventured to disapprove of the war and cast a doubt upon its righteousness straightway got such a stern and angry warning that for their personal safety's sake they quickly shrank out of sight and offended no more in that way.

Sunday morning came—next day the battalions would leave for the front; the church was filled; the volunteers were there, their young faces alight with martial dreams—visions of the stern advance, the gathering momentum, the rushing charge, the flashing sabers, the flight of the foe, the tumult, the enveloping smoke, the fierce pursuit, the surrender!—them home from the war, bronzed heroes, welcomed, adored, submerged in golden seas of glory! With the volunteers sat their dear ones, proud, happy, and envied by the neighbors and friends who had no sons and brothers to send forth to the field of honor, there to win for the flag, or, failing, die the noblest of noble deaths. The service proceeded; a war chapter from the Old Testament was read; the first prayer was said; it was followed by an organ burst that shook the building, and with one impulse the house rose, with glowing eyes and beating hearts, and poured out that tremendous invocation—

> "God the all-terrible! Thou who ordainest,
> Thunder thy clarion and lightning thy sword!"

Then came the "long" prayer. None could remember the like of it for passionate pleading and moving and beautiful language. The burden of its supplication was, that an ever-merciful and benignant Father of us all would watch over our noble young soldiers, and aid, comfort, and encourage them in their patriotic work; bless them, shield them in the day of battle and the hour of peril, bear them in His mighty hand, make them strong and confident, invincible in the bloody onset; help them to crush the foe, grant to them and to their flag and country imperishable honor and glory—

An aged stranger entered and moved with slow and noiseless step up the main aisle, his eyes fixed upon the minister, his long body clothed in a robe

---

1. Written as early as 1905, during the Philippine-American War, but considered unsuitable for publication in Twain's day, "The War Prayer" first appeared posthumously in Albert Bigelow Paine's collection of Twain's writings, *Europe and Elsewhere* (1923), published by Harper & Brothers.

that reached to his feet, his head bare, his white hair descending in a frothy cataract to his shoulders, his seamy face unnaturally pale, pale even to ghast-liness. With all eyes following him and wondering, he made his silent way; without pausing, he ascended to the preacher's side and stood there, waiting. With shut lids the preacher, unconscious of his presence, continued his moving prayer, and at last finished it with the words, uttered in fervent appeal, "Bless our arms, grant us the victory, O Lord our God, Father and Protector of our land and flag!"

The stranger touched his arm, motioned him to step aside—which the startled minister did—and took his place. During some moments he surveyed the spellbound audience with solemn eyes, in which burned an uncanny light; then in a deep voice he said:

"I come from the Throne—bearing a message from Almighty God!" The words smote the house with a shock; if the stranger perceived it he gave no attention. "He has heard the prayer of His servant your shepherd, and will grant it if such shall be your desire after I, His messenger, shall have explained to you its import—that is to say, its full import. For it is like unto many of the prayers of men, in that it asks for more than he who utters it is aware of—except he pause and think.

"God's servant and yours has prayed his prayer. Has he paused and taken thought? Is it one prayer? No, it is two—one uttered, the other not. Both have reached the ear of Him Who heareth all supplications, the spoken and the unspoken. Ponder this—keep it in mind. If you would beseech a blessing upon yourself, beware! lest without intent you invoke a curse upon a neighbor at the same time. If you pray for the blessing of rain upon your crop which needs it, by that act you are possibly praying for a curse upon some neighbor's crop which may not need rain and can be injured by it.

"You have heard your servant's prayer—the uttered part of it. I am commissioned of God to put into words the other part of it—that part which the pastor—and also you in your hearts—fervently prayed silently. And ignorantly and unthinkingly? God grant that it was so! You heard these words: 'Grant us the victory, O Lord our God!' That is sufficient. The *whole* of the uttered prayer is compact into those pregnant words. Elaborations were not necessary. When you have prayed for victory you have prayed for many unmentioned results which follow victory—*must* follow it, cannot help but follow it. Upon the listening spirit of God the Father fell also the unspoken part of the prayer. He commandeth me to put it into words. Listen!

"O Lord our Father, our young patriots, idols of our hearts, go forth to battle—be Thou near them! With them—in spirit—we also go forth from the sweet peace of our beloved firesides to smite the foe. O Lord our God, help us to tear their soldiers to bloody shreds with our shells; help us to cover their smiling fields with the pale forms of their patriot dead; help us to drown the thunder of the guns with the shrieks of their wounded, writhing in pain; help us to lay waste their humble homes with a hurricane of fire; help us to wring the hearts of their unoffending widows with unavailing grief; help us to turn them out roofless with their little children to wander unfriended the wastes of their desolated land in rags and hunger and thirst, sports of the sun flames of summer and the icy winds of winter, broken in spirit, worn with travail, imploring Thee for the refuge of the grave and denied it—for our sakes who adore Thee, Lord, blast their hopes, blight their lives, protract their bitter pilgrimage, make heavy their steps, water their way with their tears, stain the white snow with the blood of their wounded feet! We ask it, in the spirit of love, of Him Who is the Source of Love, and Who is the ever-faithful refuge and friend of all that are sore beset and seek His aid with humble and contrite hearts. Amen."

(*After a pause.*) "Ye have prayed it; if ye still desire it, speak! The messenger of the Most High waits."

It was believed afterward that the man was a lunatic, because there was no sense in what he said.

1905                                                                                    1923

---

# BRET HARTE
## 1836–1902

Francis Bret[t] Harte was born August 25, 1836, in Albany, New York, of English, Dutch, and Jewish descent. His father, Henry, a schoolteacher, died in 1845, and four years later Harte left school to work in a lawyer's office and then in the counting room of a merchant. In 1854 he followed his mother, Elizabeth Rebecca, and his elder sister and brother to Oakland, California, and for a year lived with his mother and stepfather, Colonel Andrew Williams, the first mayor of Oakland. When he turned twenty-one, he left to seek employment further north in California, where he worked for a time for Wells Fargo (he claimed that he "rode shotgun") and also as a miner, teacher, tutor, pharmacist's clerk, and in the printing room of the *Humboldt Times*. From 1858 to 1860 he set type and served as an editorial assistant on the staff of the Uniontown *Northern Californian*. In late February 1860, while the editor-in-chief was out of town, Harte wrote an editorial expressing outrage over the massacre in nearby Eureka of sixty Native Americans, mostly women and children, by a small gang of white vigilantes. After the appearance of the editorial, his life was apparently threatened, and within a month he left for San Francisco.

Harte quickly found a job setting type for *The Golden Era* and soon began contributing poems, stories, and sketches to the paper, many under the pseudonym "The Bohemian." Several of these pieces became part of the collection *"The Luck of Roaring Camp" and Other Sketches* (1870), his best-known book, which Kate Chopin called "the first resounding note" in the development of a distinctive western American literature; in it Harte "reached across the continent and startled the Academists on the Atlantic Coast. . . . They opened their eyes and ears at the sound and awoke to the fact that there might some day be a literary West." Like his fellow westerners Mark Twain, Joaquin Miller, Ambrose Bierce, Ina Coolbrith, and later, Jack London, Harte challenged genteel assumptions about the West and presented a first-hand view of its variety, both romantic and realistic.

Jessie Benton Frémont, daughter of John C. Frémont, a former presidential candidate, befriended Harte and helped him obtain a series of government appointments that culminated in 1863 in his being named secretary to the superintendent in the U.S. Branch Mint in San Francisco, a position that left him free to write nearly full time. Harte's career as a writer was confirmed in 1868 when he became the first editor of the newly established and quickly influential *Overland Monthly*, for which he wrote the works that made him and other western writers famous. In the second issue appeared "The Luck of Roaring Camp," which made him a national celebrity. In this story, as elsewhere, Harte's success rested on his ability to combine features of regional writing—distinctive characters and realistically described settings—with romantic and sentimentalized settings and characters. But perhaps what most distinguishes him from other writers who exploited the myths of the Wild West is an ironic perspective that often went undetected by readers unfamiliar with California, who wished to believe in noble gamblers and prostitutes with hearts of gold. The strange tale "Miggles," for its time quite a challenge to American sexual and gender mores, takes this ironic perspective on the "mystery" of the title character.

Harte focused on character types, such as schoolmarms, stagedrivers, and whores, to give readers a feel for what he called "a heterogeneous and remarkable population" drawn to the Pacific coast by the discovery of gold and remaining there to make their fortunes. There, "men were accepted for what they actually were" and what they could contribute to camp or settlement, and "distinction of previous position or advantages were unknown." If he condescended to these subjects in order to appeal to eastern readers, he also immortalized them. As the critic Gary Scharnhorst has noted, "[I]n his best Western writing Harte challenged the dime-novelized treatment of the frontier. His gamblers may be libertines, but they are also chivalrous; his redshirt miners may be coarse, but they are also charitable; and his fallen women may be 'easy,' but they are also self-sacrificial."

Harte often parodied biblical texts in order to challenge accepted beliefs and ridicule religious hypocrisy. If, as Scharnhorst has also pointed out, "The Luck of Roaring Camp" is a retelling of the gospel story of the Nativity, the Madonna is a mixed-blood prostitute named Cherokee Sal, and her son Tommy (the name of the doubting Apostle) is a false Messiah. The name "Luck" denotes merely chance, not faith; in the end all is swept away by a flood of biblical proportions. "The Luck of Roaring Camp," turns out to be all bad.

Harte, who had married Anna Griswold in 1862, left San Francisco early in 1871 at the height of his fame in hopes that in the East his literary reputation would grow even more. After a journey cross-country that was covered by the daily press, the Hartes were entertained in Boston by the new editor of the *Atlantic Monthly*, William Dean Howells. James T. Fields, who owned the *Atlantic Monthly* and the firm of J. R. Osgood and Company, Harte's publisher, offered Harte the unheard-of sum of ten thousand dollars to write twelve or more poems and sketches to be published in the *Atlantic* and *Every Saturday* during the course of the year. Unfortunately, Harte did not produce much writing in the twelve months following, and his contract was not renewed. At the same time, his drinking was harming his lecturing career, which was already shaky due to performances that some saw as "dandified" and not at all those of a rugged western character. Whenever Harte departed from his standard western stories, he was castigated by critics, and so remained trapped in formula and self-parody. During the winter of 1877–78, his contract with Osgood having ended, Harte became nearly penniless.

The last three decades of Harte's life constitute a decline in his personal and literary fortunes. His novel *Gabriel Conroy* (1876) sold well but was slammed by the critics, and though his two plays, *Two Men of Sandy Bar* (1876) and (with Mark Twain) *Ah Sin* (1877), were produced, neither was successful. Harte was appointed consul to Crefield, Prussia, in 1878 and to Glasgow, Scotland, in 1880, and moved to Europe. But when Grover Cleveland became president in 1885, Harte lost his consulship. Though his American audience waned, Harte's English readers continued to receive his work favorably until his death, from throat cancer, in May 1902.

Harte should be remembered as a literary pioneer for his use of local color, his bringing of California and western subjects to readers in the East, and his encouragement of western writers. He spawned a host of imitators, including Damon Runyon and O. Henry. Like his friend Buffalo Bill Cody, Harte helped create the West as a place of adventure and romance, injecting a characteristic note of gritty realism and irony. On the side of the San Francisco Bohemian Club is a bronze memorial commemorating Harte's life and featuring Cherokee Sal, Colonel Starbottle, and Miggles, among other of his most memorable characters.

# The Luck of Roaring Camp[1]

There was commotion in Roaring Camp. It could not have been a fight, for in 1850 that was not novel enough to have called together the entire settlement. The ditches and claims were not only deserted, but "Tuttle's grocery" had contributed its gamblers, who, it will be remembered, calmly continued their game the day that French Pete and Kanaka Joe[2] shot each other to death over the bar in the front room. The whole camp was collected before a rude cabin on the outer edge of the clearing. Conversation was carried on in a low tone, but the name of a woman was frequently repeated. It was a name familiar enough in the camp,—"Cherokee Sal."

Perhaps the less said of her the better. She was a coarse and, it is to be feared, a very sinful woman. But at that time she was the only woman in Roaring Camp, and was just then lying in sore extremity, when she most needed the ministration of her own sex. Dissolute, abandoned, and irreclaimable, she was yet suffering a martyrdom hard enough to bear even when veiled by sympathizing womanhood, but now terrible in her loneliness. The primal curse had come to her in that original isolation which must have made the punishment of the first transgression so dreadful. It was, perhaps, part of the expiation of her sin that, at a moment when she most lacked her sex's intuitive tenderness and care, she met only the half-contemptuous faces of her masculine associates. Yet a few of the spectators were, I think, touched by her sufferings. Sandy Tipton thought it was "rough on Sal," and, in the contemplation of her condition, for a moment rose superior to the fact that he had an ace and two bowers[3] in his sleeve.

It will be seen also that the situation was novel. Deaths were by no means uncommon in Roaring Camp, but a birth was a new thing. People had been dismissed the camp effectively, finally, and with no possibility of return; but this was the first time that anybody had been introduced *ab initio*.[4] Hence the excitement.

"You go in there, Stumpy," said a prominent citizen known as "Kentuck," addressing one of the loungers. "Go in there, and see what you kin do. You've had experience in them things."

Perhaps there was a fitness in the selection. Stumpy, in other climes, had been the putative head of two families; in fact, it was owing to some legal informality in these proceedings that Roaring Camp—a city of refuge—was indebted to his company. The crowd approved the choice, and Stumpy was wise enough to bow to the majority. The door closed on the extempore surgeon and midwife, and Roaring Camp sat down outside, smoked its pipe, and awaited the issue.

1. First appearing in 1868 in *Overland Monthly*, the tale was reprinted by Osgood of Boston in 1870 in *"The Luck of Roaring Camp" and Other Sketches* and by Houghton Mifflin in 1878 in *"The Luck of Roaring Camp" and Other Tales*; the present text is taken from the 1878 revision.

2. Hawai'ian word for adult man, used (nonpejoratively) by both Hawaiians and Americans at the time.

3. In the card game euchre, jacks of the trump suit or the other suit of the same color.

4. From the beginning (Latin).

The assemblage numbered about a hundred men. One or two of these were actual fugitives from justice, some were criminal, and all were reckless. Physically they exhibited no indication of their past lives and character. The greatest scamp had a Raphael[5] face, with a profusion of blonde hair; Oakhurst, a gambler, had the melancholy air and intellectual abstraction of a Hamlet; the coolest and most courageous man was scarcely over five feet in height, with a soft voice and an embarrassed, timid manner. The term "roughs" applied to them was a distinction rather than a definition. Perhaps in the minor details of fingers, toes, ears, etc., the camp may have been deficient, but these slight omissions did not detract from their aggregate force. The strongest man had but three fingers on his right hand; the best shot had but one eye.

Such was the physical aspect of the men that were dispersed around the cabin. The camp lay in a triangular valley between two hills and a river. The only outlet was a steep trail over the summit of a hill that faced the cabin, now illuminated by the rising moon. The suffering woman might have seen it from the rude bunk whereon she lay,—seen it winding like a silver thread until it was lost in the stars above.

A fire of withered pine boughs added sociability to the gathering. By degrees the natural levity of Roaring Camp returned. Bets were freely offered and taken regarding the result. Three to five that "Sal would get through with it;" even that the child would survive; side bets as to the sex and complexion of the coming stranger. In the midst of an excited discussion an exclamation came from those nearest the door, and the camp stopped to listen. Above the swaying and moaning of the pines, the swift rush of the river, and the crackling of the fire rose a sharp, querulous cry,—a cry unlike anything heard before in the camp. The pines stopped moaning, the river ceased to rush, and the fire to crackle. It seemed as if Nature had stopped to listen too.

The camp rose to its feet as one man! It was proposed to explode a barrel of gunpowder; but in consideration of the situation of the mother, better counsels prevailed, and only a few revolvers were discharged; for whether owing to the rude surgery of the camp, or some other reason, Cherokee Sal was sinking fast. Within an hour she had climbed, as it were, that rugged road that led to the stars, and so passed out of Roaring Camp, its sin and shame, forever. I do not think that the announcement disturbed them much, except in speculation as to the fate of the child. "Can he live now?" was asked of Stumpy. The answer was doubtful. The only other being of Cherokee Sal's sex and maternal condition in the settlement was an ass. There was some conjecture as to fitness, but the experiment was tried. It was less problematical than the ancient treatment of Romulus and Remus,[6] and apparently as successful.

When these details were completed, which exhausted another hour, the door was opened, and the anxious crowd of men, who had already formed themselves into a queue, entered in single file. Beside the low bunk or shelf, on which the figure of the mother was starkly outlined below the blankets,

5. Raffaello Sanzio (1483–1520), painter and architect of the Italian High Renaissance, best known for his Madonnas.
6. Twin brothers Romulus and Remus, traditional founders of Rome, were sons of Mars and Rhea, daughter of King Numitor of Alba Longa. When Numitor's brother Amulius deposed him, he made Rhea a Vestal Virgin (and thus forbidden to marry). But when Mars fell in love with her and she bore him the twins, Amulius, fearing they would grow up to overthrow him, left them by the banks of the River Tiber to fend for themselves; they were found by a she-wolf who took pity on them and fed them with her milk.

stood a pine table. On this a candle-box was placed, and within it, swathed in staring red flannel, lay the last arrival at Roaring Camp. Beside the candle-box was placed a hat. Its use was soon indicated. "Gentlemen," said Stumpy, with a singular mixture of authority and *ex officio*[7] complacency,—"gentlemen will please pass in at the front door, round the table, and out at the back door. Them as wishes to contribute anything toward the orphan will find a hat handy." The first man entered with his hat on; he uncovered, however, as he looked about him, and so unconsciously set an example to the next. In such communities good and bad actions are catching. As the procession filed in comments were audible,—criticisms addressed perhaps rather to Stumpy in the character of showman: "Is that him?" "Mighty small specimen;" "Hasn't more'n got the color;" "Ain't bigger nor a derringer." The contributions were as characteristic: A silver tobacco box; a doubloon; a navy revolver, silver mounted; a gold specimen; a very beautifully embroidered lady's handkerchief (from Oakhurst the gambler); a diamond breastpin; a diamond ring (suggested by the pin, with the remark from the giver that he "saw that pin and went two diamonds better"); a slung-shot; a Bible (contributor not detected); a golden spur; a silver teaspoon (the initials: I regret to a say, were not the giver's); a pair of surgeon's shears; a lancet;[8] Bank of England note for £5; and about $200 in loose gold and silver coin. During these proceedings Stumpy maintained a silence as impassive as the dead on his left, a gravity as inscrutable as that of the newly born on his right. Only one incident occurred to break the monotony of the curious procession. As Kentuck bent over the candle-box half curiously, the child turned, and, in a spasm of pain, caught at his groping finger, and held it fast for a moment. Kentuck looked foolish and embarrassed. Something like a blush tried to assert itself in his weather-beaten cheek. "The d—d little cuss!" he said, as he extricated his finger, with perhaps more tenderness and care than he might have been deemed capable of showing. He held that finger a little apart from its fellows as he went out, and examined it curiously. The examination provoked the same original remark in regard to the child. In fact, he seemed to enjoy repeating it. "He rastled with my finger," he remarked to Tipton, holding up the member, "the d—d little cuss!"

It was four o'clock before the camp sought repose. A light burnt in the cabin where the watchers sat, for Stumpy did not go to bed that night. Nor did Kentuck. He drank quite freely, and related with great gusto his experience, invariably ending with his characteristic condemnation of the newcomer. It seemed to relieve him of any unjust implication of sentiment, and Kentuck had the weaknesses of the nobler sex. When everybody else had gone to bed, he walked down to the river and whistled reflectingly. Then he walked up the gulch past the cabin, still whistling with demonstrative unconcern. At a large redwood-tree he paused and retraced his steps, and again passed the cabin. Halfway down to the river's bank he again paused, and then returned and knocked at the door. It was opened by Stumpy. "How goes it?" said Kentuck, looking past Stumpy toward the candle-box. "All serene!" replied Stumpy. "Anything up?" "Nothing." There was a pause—an embarrassing one—Stumpy still holding the door. Then Kentuck had recourse to his fin-

---

7. By virtue of one's office, or position (Latin).      8. A small surgical knife.

ger, which he held up to Stumpy. "Rastled with it,—the d—d little cuss," he said, and retired.

The next day Cherokee Sal had such rude sepulture as Roaring Camp afforded. After her body had been committed to the hillside, there was a formal meeting of the camp to discuss what should be done with her infant. A resolution to adopt it was unanimous and enthusiastic. But an animated discussion in regard to the manner and feasibility of providing for its wants at once sprang up. It was remarkable that the argument partook of none of those fierce personalities with which discussions were usually conducted at Roaring Camp. Tipton proposed that they should send the child to Red Dog,—a distance of forty miles,—where female attention could be procured. But the unlucky suggestion met with fierce and unanimous opposition. It was evident that no plan which entailed parting from their new acquisition would for a moment be entertained. "Besides," said Tom Ryder, "them fellows at Red Dog would swap it, and ring in somebody else on us."⁹ A disbelief in the honesty of other camps prevailed at Roaring Camp, as in other places.

The introduction of a female nurse in the camp also met with objection. It was argued that no decent woman could be prevailed to accept Roaring Camp as her home, and the speaker urged that "they did n't want any more of the other kind." This unkind allusion to the defunct mother, harsh as it may seem, was the first spasm of propriety,—the first symptom of the camp's regeneration. Stumpy advanced nothing. Perhaps he felt a certain delicacy in interfering with the selection of a possible successor in office. But when questioned, he averred stoutly that he and "Jinny"—the mammal before alluded to—could manage to rear the child. There was something original, independent, and heroic about the plan that pleased the camp. Stumpy was retained. Certain articles were sent for to Sacramento. "Mind," said the treasurer, as he pressed a bag of gold-dust into the expressman's hand, "the best that can be got,—lace, you know, and filigree-work and frills,—d—n the cost!"

Strange to say, the child thrived. Perhaps the invigorating climate of the mountain camp was compensation for material deficiencies. Nature took the foundling to her broader breast. In that rare atmosphere of the Sierra foothills,—that air pungent with balsamic odor, that ethereal cordial at once bracing and exhilarating,—he may have found food and nourishment, or a subtle chemistry that transmuted ass's milk to lime and phosphorus.¹ Stumpy inclined to the belief that it was the latter and good nursing. "Me and that ass," he would say, "has been father and mother to him! Don't you," he would add, apostrophizing the helpless bundle before him, "never go back on us."

By the time he was a month old the necessity of giving him a name became apparent. He had generally been known as "The Kid," "Stumpy's Boy," "The Coyote" (an allusion to his vocal powers), and even by Kentuck's endearing diminutive of "The d—d little cuss." But these were felt to be vague and unsatisfactory, and were at last dismissed under another influence. Gamblers and adventurers are generally superstitious, and Oakhurst one day declared that the baby had brought "the luck" to Roaring Camp. It was certain that of

9. Tom fears that the men of Red Dog might substitute another baby for theirs.
1. Both lime and phosphorus are used as fertilizer and both are generally white; the suggestion is that the ass's milk would help the child's bones grow strong.

late they had been successful. "Luck" was the name agreed upon, with the prefix of Tommy for greater convenience. No allusion was made to the mother, and the father was unknown. "It's better," said the philosophical Oakhurst, "to take a fresh deal all round. Call him Luck, and start him fair." A day was accordingly set apart for the christening. What was meant by this ceremony the reader may imagine who has already gathered some idea of the reckless irreverence of Roaring Camp. The master of ceremonies was one "Boston," a noted wag, and the occasion seemed to promise the greatest face-tiousness. This ingenious satirist had spent two days in preparing a burlesque of the Church service, with pointed local allusions. The choir was properly trained, and Sandy Tipton was to stand godfather. But after the procession had marched to the grove with music and banners, and the child had been deposited before a mock altar, Stumpy stepped before the expectant crowd. "It ain't my style to spoil fun, boys," said the little man, stoutly eying the faces around him, "but it strikes me that this thing ain't exactly on the squar. It's playing it pretty low down on this yer baby to ring in fun on him that he ain't goin' to understand. And ef there's goin' to be any godfathers round, I'd like to see who's got any better rights than me." A silence followed Stumpy's speech. To the credit of all humorists be it said that the first man to acknowl-edge its justice was the satirist thus stopped of his fun. "But," said Stumpy, quickly following up his advantage, "we're here for a christening, and we'll have it. I proclaim you Thomas Luck, according to the laws of the United States and the State of California, so help me God." It was the first time that the name of the Deity had been otherwise uttered than profanely in the camp. The form of christening was perhaps even more ludicrous than the satirist had conceived; but strangely enough, nobody saw it and nobody laughed. "Tommy" was christened as seriously as he would have been under a Christ-ian roof, and cried and was comforted in as orthodox fashion.

And so the work of regeneration began in Roaring Camp. Almost imper-ceptibly a change came over the settlement. The cabin assigned to "Tommy Luck"—or "The Luck," as he was more frequently called—first showed signs of improvement. It was kept scrupulously clean and whitewashed. Then it was boarded, clothed, and papered. The rosewood cradle, packed eighty miles by mule, had, in Stumpy's way of putting it, "sorter killed the rest of the fur-niture." So the rehabilitation of the cabin became a necessity. The men who were in the habit of lounging in at Stumpy's to see "how 'The Luck' got on" seemed to appreciate the change, and in self-defense the rival establishment of "Tuttle's grocery" bestirred itself and imported a carpet and mirrors. The reflections of the latter on the appearance of Roaring Camp tended to pro-duce stricter habits of personal cleanliness. Again Stumpy imposed a kind of quarantine upon those who aspired to the honor and privilege of holding The Luck. It was a cruel mortification to Kentuck—who, in the carelessness of a large nature and the habits of frontier life, had begun to regard all garments as a second cuticle, which, like a snake's, only sloughed off through decay—to be debarred this privilege from certain prudential reasons. Yet such was the subtle influence of innovation that he thereafter appeared regularly every afternoon in a clean shirt and face still shining from his ablutions. Nor were moral and social sanitary laws neglected. "Tommy," who was supposed to spend his whole existence in a persistent attempt to repose, must not be dis-turbed by noise. The shouting and yelling, which had gained the camp its infelicitous title, were not permitted within hearing distance of Stumpy's. The men conversed in whispers or smoked with Indian gravity. Profanity was tacitly given up in these sacred precincts, and throughout the camp a popular form of expletive, known as "D—n the luck!" and "Curse the luck!" was abandoned, as having a new personal bearing. Vocal music was not interdicted, being supposed to have a soothing, tranquilizing quality; and one song, sung by "Man-o'-War Jack," an English sailor from her Majesty's Australian colonies, was quite popular as a lullaby. It was a lugubrious recital of the exploits of "the Arethusa, Seventy-four," in a muffled minor, ending with a prolonged dying fall at the burden of each verse, "On b-oo-o-ard of the Arethusa." It was a fine sight to see Jack holding The Luck, rocking from side to side as if with the motion of a ship, and crooning forth this naval ditty. Either through the peculiar rocking of Jack or the length of his song,—it contained ninety stanzas, and was continued with conscientious deliberation to the bitter end,—the lullaby generally had the desired effect. At such times the men would lie at full length under the trees in the soft summer twilight, smoking their pipes and drinking in the melodious utterances. An indistinct idea that this was pastoral happiness pervaded the camp. "This 'ere kind o' think," said the Cockney Simmons, meditatively reclining on his elbow, "is 'evingly." It reminded him of Greenwich.[2]

On the long summer days The Luck was usually carried to the gulch from whence the golden store of Roaring Camp was taken. There, on a blanket spread over pine boughs, he would lie while the men were working in the ditches below. Latterly there was a rude attempt to decorate this bower with flowers and sweet-smelling shrubs, and generally some one would bring him a cluster of wild honeysuckles, azaleas, or the painted blossoms of Las Mariposas. The men had suddenly awakened to the fact that there were beauty and significance in these trifles, which they had so long trodden carelessly beneath their feet. A flake of glittering mica, a fragment of variegated quartz, a bright pebble from the bed of the creek, became beautiful to eyes thus cleared and strengthened, and were invariably put aside for The Luck. It was wonderful how many treasures the woods and hillsides yielded that "would do for Tommy." Surrounded by playthings such as never child out of fairyland had before, it is to be hoped that Tommy was content. He appeared to be serenely happy, albeit there was an infantine gravity about him, a contemplative light in his round gray eyes, that sometimes worried Stumpy. He was always tractable and quiet, and it is recorded that once, having crept beyond his "corral,"—a hedge of tessellated pine boughs, which surrounded his bed,—he dropped over the bank on his head in the soft earth, and remained with his mottled legs in the air in that position for at least five minutes with unflinching gravity. He was extricated without a murmur. I hesitate to record the many other instances of his sagacity, which rest, unfortunately, upon the statements of prejudiced friends. Some of them were not without a tinge of superstition. "I crep' up the bank just now," said Kentuck one day, in a breathless state of excitement, "and dern my skin if he wasn't a-talking to a jaybird as was a-sittin' on his lap. There they was, just as free and sociable as anything you please, a-jawin' at each other just like two cherrybums." Howbeit,

---

2. A town on the Thames River in England, birthplace of Henry VIII and site of the Royal Naval College, venerated by seafarers for its keeping of official, or Greenwich Mean, time.

whether creeping over the pine boughs or lying lazily on his back blinking at the leaves above him, to him the birds sang, the squirrels chattered, and the flowers bloomed. Nature was his nurse and playfellow. For him she would let slip between the leaves golden shafts of sunlight that fell just within his grasp; she would send wandering breezes to visit him with the balm of bay and resinous gum; to him the tall redwoods nodded familiarly and sleepily, the bumblebees buzzed, and the rooks cawed a slumbrous accompaniment.

Such was the golden summer of Roaring Camp. They were "flush times," and the luck was with them. The claims had yielded enormously. The camp was jealous of its privileges and looked suspiciously on strangers. No encouragement was given to immigration, and, to make their seclusion more perfect, the land on either side of the mountain wall that surrounded the camp they duly preëmpted. This, and a reputation for singular proficiency with the revolver, kept the reserve of Roaring Camp inviolate. The expressman—their only connecting link with the surrounding world—sometimes told wonderful stories of the camp. He would say, "They've a street up there in 'Roaring' that would lay over any street in Red Dog. They've got vines and flowers round their houses, and they wash themselves twice a day. But they're mighty rough on strangers, and they worship an Ingin baby."

With the prosperity of the camp came a desire for further improvement. It was proposed to build a hotel in the following spring, and to invite one or two decent families to reside there for the sake of The Luck, who might perhaps profit by female companionship. The sacrifice that this concession to the sex cost these men, who were fiercely skeptical in regard to its general virtue and usefulness, can only be accounted for by their affection for Tommy. A few still held out. But the resolve could not be carried into effect for three months, and the minority meekly yielded in the hope that something might turn up to prevent it. And it did.

The winter of 1851 will long be remembered in the foothills. The snow lay deep on the Sierras, and every mountain creek became a river, and every river a lake. Each gorge and gulch was transformed into a tumultuous watercourse that descended the hillsides, tearing down giant trees and scattering its drift and débris along the plain. Red Dog had been twice under water, and Roaring Camp had been forewarned. "Water put the gold into them gulches," said Stumpy. "It's been here once and will be here again!" And that night the North Fork suddenly leaped over its banks and swept up the triangular valley of Roaring Camp.

In the confusion of rushing water, crashing trees, and crackling timber, and the darkness which seemed to flow with the water and blot out the fair valley, but little could be done to collect the scattered camp. When the morning broke, the cabin of Stumpy, nearest the river-bank, was gone. Higher up the gulch they found the body of its unlucky owner; but the pride, the hope, the joy, The Luck, of Roaring Camp had disappeared. They were returning with sad hearts when a shout from the bank recalled them.

It was a relief-boat from down the river. They had picked up, they said, a man and an infant, nearly exhausted, about two miles below. Did anybody know them, and did they belong here?

It needed but a glance to show them Kentuck lying there, cruelly crushed and bruised, but still holding The Luck of Roaring Camp in his arms. As they bent over the strangely assorted pair, they saw that the child was cold and pulseless. "He is dead," said one. Kentuck opened his eyes. "Dead?" he repeated feebly. "Yes, my man, and you are dying too." A smile lit the eyes of the expiring Kentuck. "Dying!" he repeated; "he's a-taking me with him. Tell the boys I've got The Luck with me now;" and the strong man, clinging to the frail babe as a drowning man is said to cling to a straw, drifted away into the shadowy river that flows forever to the unknown sea.

1868                                                                                          1870, 1878

## Miggles[1]

We were eight including the driver. We had not spoken during the passage of the last six miles, since the jolting of the heavy vehicle over the roughening road had spoiled the Judge's last poetical quotation. The tall man beside the Judge was asleep, his arm passed through the swaying strap and his head resting upon it,—altogether a limp, helpless looking object, as if he had hanged himself and been cut down too late. The French lady on the back seat was asleep too, yet in a half-conscious propriety of attitude, shown even in the disposition of the handkerchief which she held to her forehead and which partially veiled her face. The lady from Virginia City, traveling with her husband, had long since lost all individuality in a wild confusion of ribbons, veils, furs, and shawls. There was no sound but the rattling of wheels and the dash of rain upon the roof. Suddenly the stage stopped and we became dimly aware of voices. The driver was evidently in the midst of an exciting colloquy with some one in the road,—a colloquy of which such fragments as "bridge gone," "twenty feet of water," "can't pass," were occasionally distinguishable above the storm. Then came a lull, and a mysterious voice from the road shouted the parting adjuration—

"Try Miggles's."

We caught a glimpse of our leaders as the vehicle slowly turned, of a horseman vanishing through the rain, and we were evidently on our way to Miggles's.

Who and where was Miggles? The Judge, our authority, did not remember the name, and he knew the country thoroughly. The Washoe[2] traveler thought Miggles must keep a hotel. We only knew that we were stopped by high water in front and rear, and that Miggles was our rock of refuge. A ten minutes' splashing through a tangled byroad, scarcely wide enough for the stage, and we drew up before a barred and boarded gate in a wide stone wall or fence about eight feet high. Evidently Miggles's, and evidently Miggles did not keep a hotel.

The driver got down and tried the gate. It was securely locked.

"Miggles! O Miggles!"

No answer.

---

1. First appearing in 1869 in the *Overland Monthly*, the story was reprinted in *"The Luck of Roaring Camp" and Other Sketches* by Osgood in 1870 and then in *"The Luck of Roaring Camp" and Other Tales* by Houghton Mifflin in 1878; the present text is taken from the 1878 revision.

2. Washoe, the name of an Indian tribe and later a county in Nevada, in general refers to the gold-mining region of Nevada. Reno is now the major city, but in Harte's day the mining towns of Virginia City, Carson City, and Gold Hill were the primary settlements.

"Migg-ells! You Miggles!" continued the driver, with rising wrath.

"Migglesy!" joined in the expressman persuasively. "O Miggy! Mig!"

But no reply came from the apparently insensate Miggles. The Judge, who had finally got the window down, put his head out and propounded a series of questions, which if answered categorically would have undoubtedly elucidated the whole mystery, but which the driver evaded by replying that "if we didn't want to sit in the coach all night we had better rise up and sing out for Miggles."

So we rose up and called on Miggles in chorus, then separately. And when we had finished, a Hibernian[3] fellow passenger from the roof called for "Maygells!" whereat we all laughed. While we were laughing the driver cried, "Shoo!"

We listened. To our infinite amazement the chorus of "Miggles" was repeated from the other side of the wall, even to the final and supplemental "Maygells."

"Extraordinary echo!" said the Judge.

"Extraordinary d—d skunk!" roared the driver contemptuously. "Come out of that, Miggles, and show yourself! Be a man, Miggles! Don't hide in the dark; I wouldn't if I were you, Miggles," continued Yuba Bill, now dancing about in an excess of fury.

"Miggles!" continued the voice, "O Miggles!"

"My good man! Mr. Myghail!" said the Judge, softening the asperities of the name as much as possible. "Consider the inhospitality of refusing shelter from the inclemency of the weather to helpless females. Really, my dear sir"— But a succession of "Miggles," ending in a burst of laughter, drowned his voice.

Yuba Bill hesitated no longer. Taking a heavy stone from the road, he battered down the gate, and with the expressman entered the inclosure. We followed. Nobody was to be seen. In the gathering darkness all that we could distinguish was that we were in a garden—from the rose bushes that scattered over us a minute spray from their dripping leaves—and before a long, rambling wooden building.

"Do you know this Miggles?" asked the Judge of Yuba Bill.

"No, nor don't want to," said Bill shortly, who felt the Pioneer Stage Company insulted in his person by the contumacious Miggles.

"But, my dear sir," expostulated the Judge, as he thought of the barred gate.

"Lookee here," said Yuba Bill, with fine irony, "hadn't you better go back and sit in the coach till yer introduced? I'm going in," and he pushed open the door of the building.

A long room, lighted only by the embers of a fire that was dying on the large hearth at its farther extremity; the walls curiously papered, and the flickering firelight bringing out its grotesque pattern; somebody sitting in a large armchair by the fireplace. All this we saw as we crowded together into the room after the driver and expressman.

"Hello! be you Miggles?" said Yuba Bill to the solitary occupant.

The figure neither spoke nor stirred. Yuba Bill walked wrathfully toward it and turned the eye of his coach-lantern upon its face. It was a man's face, prematurely old and wrinkled, with very large eyes, in which there was that

---

3. Poetic name for a citizen of Ireland (Latin).

expression of perfectly gratuitous solemnity which I had sometimes seen in an owl's. The large eyes wandered from Bill's face to the lantern, and finally fixed their gaze on that luminous object without further recognition.

Bill restrained himself with an effort.

"Miggles! be you deaf? You ain't dumb anyhow, you know," and Yuba Bill shook the insensate figure by the shoulder.

To our great dismay, as Bill removed his hand, the venerable stranger apparently collapsed, sinking into half his size and an undistinguishable heap of clothing.

"Well, dern my skin," said Bill, looking appealingly at us, and hopelessly retiring from the contest.

The Judge now stepped forward, and we lifted the mysterious invertebrate back into his original position. Bill was dismissed with the lantern to reconnoitre outside, for it was evident that, from the helplessness of this solitary man, there must be attendants near at hand, and we all drew around the fire. The Judge, who had regained his authority, and had never lost his conversational amiability,—standing before us with his back to the hearth,—charged us, as an imaginary jury, as follows:—

"It is evident that either our distinguished friend here has reached that condition described by Shakespeare as 'the sere and yellow leaf,'[4] or has suffered some premature abatement of his mental and physical faculties. Whether he is really the Miggles"—

Here he was interrupted by "Miggles! O Miggles! Migglesy! Mig!" and, in fact, the whole chorus of Miggles in very much the same key as it had once before been delivered unto us.

We gazed at each other for a moment in some alarm. The Judge, in particular, vacated his position quickly, as the voice seemed to come directly over his shoulder. The cause, however, was soon discovered in a large magpie who was perched upon a shelf over the fireplace, and who immediately relapsed into a sepulchral silence, which contrasted singularly with his previous volubility. It was, undoubtedly, his voice which we had heard in the road, and our friend in the chair was not responsible for the discourtesy. Yuba Bill, who reëntered the room after an unsuccessful search, was loth to accept the explanation, and still eyed the helpless sitter with suspicion. He had found a shed in which he had put up his horses, but he came back dripping and skeptical. "Thar ain't nobody but him within ten mile of the shanty, and that ar d—d old skeesicks[5] knows it."

But the faith of the majority proved to be securely based. Bill had scarcely ceased growling before we heard a quick step upon the porch, the trailing of a wet skirt, the door was flung open, and with a flash of white teeth, a sparkle of dark eyes, and an utter absence of ceremony or diffidence, a young woman entered, shut the door, and, panting, leaned back against it.

"Oh, if you please, I'm Miggles!"

And this was Miggles! this bright-eyed, full-throated young woman, whose wet gown of coarse blue stuff could not hide the beauty of the feminine curves to which it clung; from the chestnut crown of whose head, topped by a man's oil-skin sou'wester,[6] to the little feet and ankles, hidden somewhere

---

4. *Macbeth* 5.3.23.
5. American slang for "good-for-nothing, a rascal, a rogue" (*Oxford English Dictionary*).

6. A waterproof hat of plastic, oilskin, or canvas, with a broad brim to protect the neck.

in the recesses of her boy's brogans,[7] all was grace,—this was Miggles, laughing at us, too, in the most airy, frank, off-hand manner imaginable.

"You see, boys," said she, quite out of breath, and holding one little hand against her side, quite unheeding the speechless discomfiture of our party or the complete demoralization of Yuba Bill, whose features had relaxed into an expression of gratuitous and imbecile cheerfulness,—"you see, boys, I was mor'n two miles away when you passed down the road. I thought you might pull up here, and so I ran the whole way, knowing nobody was home but Jim,—and—and—I'm out of breath—and—that lets me out." And here Miggles caught her dripping oilskin hat from her head, with a mischievous swirl that scattered a shower of raindrops over us; attempted to put back her hair; dropped two hairpins in the attempt; laughed, and sat down beside Yuba Bill, with her hands crossed lightly on her lap.

The Judge recovered himself first and essayed an extravagant compliment.

"I'll trouble you for that ha'rpin," said Miggles gravely. Half a dozen hands were eagerly stretched forward; the missing hairpin was restored to its fair owner; and Miggles, crossing the room, looked keenly in the face of the invalid. The solemn eyes looked back at hers with an expression we had never seen before. Life and intelligence seemed to struggle back into the rugged face. Miggles laughed again,—it was a singularly eloquent laugh,—turned her black eyes and white teeth once more towards us.

"This afflicted person is"—hesitated the Judge.

"Jim!" said Miggles.

"Your father?"

"No!"

"Brother?"

"No!"

"Husband?"

Miggles darted a quick, half-defiant glance at the two lady passengers, who I had noticed did not participate in the general masculine admiration of Miggles, and said gravely, "No; it's Jim!"

There was an awkward pause. The lady passengers moved closer to each other; the Washoe husband looked abstractedly at the fire, and the tall man apparently turned his eyes inward for self-support at this emergency. But Miggles's laugh, which was very infectious, broke the silence.

"Come," she said briskly, "you must be hungry. Who'll bear a hand to help me get tea?"

She had no lack of volunteers. In a few moments Yuba Bill was engaged like Caliban in bearing logs for this Miranda;[8] the expressman was grinding coffee on the veranda; to myself the arduous duty of slicing bacon was assigned; and the Judge lent each man his good-humored and voluble counsel. And when Miggles, assisted by the Judge and our Hibernian "deck-passenger," set the table with all the available crockery, we had become quite joyous, in spite of the rain that beat against the windows, the wind that whirled down the chimney, the two ladies who whispered together in the corner, or the magpie, who uttered a satirical and croaking commentary on their conversation from his perch above. In the now bright, blazing fire we could see that the walls

7. Heavy, ankle-high work shoes.
8. Characters in Shakespeare's *Tempest* (1611)—Caliban is a monster created by the magician Prospero to do his bidding; Miranda is Prospero's daughter.

were papered with illustrated journals, arranged with feminine taste and discrimination. The furniture was extemporized and adapted from candle-boxes and packing-cases, and covered with gay calico or the skin of some animal. The armchair of the helpless Jim was an ingenious variation of a flour-barrel. There was neatness, and even a taste for the picturesque, to be seen in the few details of the long, low room.

The meal was a culinary success. But more, it was a social triumph,—chiefly, I think, owing to the rare tact of Miggles in guiding the conversation, asking all the questions herself, yet bearing throughout a frankness that rejected the idea of any concealment on her own part, so that we talked of ourselves, of our prospects, of the journey, of the weather, of each other,—of everything but our host and hostess. It must be confessed that Miggles's conversation was never elegant, rarely grammatical, and that at times she employed expletives the use of which had generally been yielded to our sex. But they were delivered with such a lighting up of teeth and eyes, and were usually followed by a laugh—a laugh peculiar to Miggles—so frank and honest that it seemed to clear the moral atmosphere.

Once during the meal we heard a noise like the rubbing of a heavy body against the outer walls of the house. This was shortly followed by a scratching and sniffling at the door. "That's Joaquin," said Miggles, in reply to our questioning glances; "would you like to see him?" Before we could answer she had opened the door, and disclosed a half-grown grizzly, who instantly raised himself on his haunches, with his fore paws hanging down in the popular attitude of mendicancy, and looked admiringly at Miggles, with a very singular resemblance in his manner to Yuba Bill. "That's my watch-dog," said Miggles, in explanation. "Oh, he don't bite," she added, as the two lady passengers fluttered into a corner. "Does he, old Toppy?" (the latter remark being addressed directly to the sagacious Joaquin). "I tell you what, boys," continued Miggles, after she had fed and closed the door on Ursa Minor, "you were in big luck that Joaquin wasn't hanging round when you dropped in to-night."

"Where was he?" asked the Judge.

"With me," said Miggles. "Lord love you! he trots round with me nights like as if he was a man."

We were silent for a few moments, and listened to the wind. Perhaps we all had the same picture before us,—of Miggles walking through the rainy woods with her savage guardian at her side. The Judge, I remember, said something about Una and her lion;[9] but Miggles received it, as she did other compliments, with quiet gravity. Whether she was altogether unconscious of the admiration she excited,—she could hardly have been oblivious of Yuba Bill's adoration,—I know not; but her very frankness suggested a perfect sexual equality that was cruelly humiliating to the younger members of our party.

The incident of the bear did not add anything in Miggles's favor to the opinions of those of her own sex who were present. In fact, the repast over, a chillness radiated from the two lady passengers that no pine boughs brought in by Yuba Bill and cast as a sacrifice upon the hearth could wholly overcome. Miggles felt it; and suddenly declaring that it was time to "turn in," offered

9. The hero Redcrosse's future wife, and the other major protagonist in Book I of Edmund Spenser's epic poem *The Faerie Queene* (1590). Una is meek, humble, and beautiful, but strong when necessary, representing Truth, which Redcrosse must find in order to be a true Christian. A lion once tried to devour her, but, struck by her beauty, became her protector and constant companion.

to show the ladies to their bed in an adjoining room. "You, boys, will have to camp out here by the fire as well as you can," she added, "for thar ain't but the one room."

Our sex—by which, my dear sir, I allude of course to the stronger portion of humanity—has been generally relieved from the imputation of curiosity or a fondness for gossip. Yet I am constrained to say, that hardly had the door closed on Miggles than we crowded together, whispering, snickering, smiling, and exchanging suspicions, surmises, and a thousand speculations in regard to our pretty hostess and her singular companion. I fear that we even hustled that imbecile paralytic, who sat like a voiceless Memnon[1] in our midst, gazing with the serene indifference of the Past in his passionless eyes upon our wordy counsels. In the midst of an exciting discussion the door opened again and Miggles reëntered.

But not, apparently, the same Miggles who a few hours before had flashed upon us. Her eyes were downcast, and as she hesitated for a moment on the threshold, with a blanket on her arm, she seemed to have left behind her the frank fearlessness which had charmed us a moment before. Coming into the room, she drew a low stool beside the paralytic's chair, sat down, drew the blanket over her shoulders, and saying, "If it's all the same to you, boys, as we're rather crowded, I'll stop here to-night," took the invalid's withered hand in her own, and turned her eyes upon the dying fire. An instinctive feeling that this was only premonitory to more confidential relations, and perhaps some shame at our previous curiosity, kept us silent. The rain still beat upon the roof, wandering gusts of wind stirred the embers into momentary brightness, until, in a lull of the elements, Miggles suddenly lifted up her head, and, throwing her hair over her shoulder, turned her face upon the group and asked,—

"Is there any of you that knows me?"

There was no reply.

"Think again! I lived at Marysville in '53. Everybody knew me there, and everybody had the right to know me. I kept the Polka Saloon until I came to live with Jim. That's six years ago. Perhaps I've changed some."

The absence of recognition may have disconcerted her. She turned her head to the fire again, and it was some seconds before she again spoke, and then more rapidly—

"Well, you see I thought some of you must have known me. There's no great harm done anyway. What I was going to say was this: Jim here"—she took his hand in both of hers as she spoke—"used to know me, if you didn't, and spent a heap of money upon me. I reckon he spent all he had. And one day—it's six years ago this winter—Jim came into my back room, sat down on my sofy, like as you see him in that chair, and never moved again without help. He was struck all of a heap, and never seemed to know what ailed him. The doctors came and said as how it was caused all along of his way of life,—for Jim was mighty free and wild-like,—and that he would never get better, and couldn't last long anyway. They advised me to send him to Frisco to the hospital, for

---

1. King of Ethiopia, son of Eos (Greek goddess of dawn) and Tithonos; he fought with the Trojans in the Trojan War, and when he was killed by Achilles, Zeus made him immortal for his mother's sake. Among the most imposing monuments on the West Bank of the Nile at Luxor in Egypt are the "Colossi of Memnon," massive statues that once flanked the entrance to Pharaoh Amenhotep III's mortuary. A fissure ran through one, and when the stone was warmed by early morning rays it gave an eerie moan, which the Greeks thought was Memnon greeting his mother.

he was no good to any one and would be a baby all his life. Perhaps it was something in Jim's eye, perhaps it was that I never had a baby, but I said 'No.' I was rich then, for I was popular with everybody,—gentlemen like yourself, sir, came to see me,—and I sold out my business and bought this yer place, because it was sort of out of the way of travel, you see, and I brought my baby here."

With a woman's intuitive tact and poetry, she had, as she spoke, slowly shifted her position so as to bring the mute figure of the ruined man between her and her audience, hiding in the shadow behind it, as if she offered it as a tacit apology for her actions. Silent and expressionless, it yet spoke for her; helpless, crushed, and smitten with the Divine thunderbolt, it still stretched an invisible arm around her.

Hidden in the darkness, but still holding his hand, she went on:—

"It was a long time before I could get the hang of things about yer, for I was used to company and excitement. I could n't get any woman to help me, and a man I durs n't trust; but what with the Indians hereabout, who'd do odd jobs for me, and having everything sent from the North Fork, Jim and I managed to worry through. The Doctor would run up from Sacramento once in a while. He'd ask to see 'Miggles's baby,' as he called Jim, and when he'd go away, he'd say, 'Miggles, you're a trump,—God bless you,' and it did n't seem so lonely after that. But the last time he was here he said, as he opened the door to go, 'Do you know, Miggles, your baby will grow up to be a man yet and an honor to his mother; but not here, Miggles, not here!' And I thought he went away sad,—and—and"—and here Miggles's voice and head were somehow both lost completely in the shadow.

"The folks about here are very kind," said Miggles, after a pause, coming a little into the light again. "The men from the Fork used to hang around here, until they found they was n't wanted, and the women are kind, and don't call. I was pretty lonely until I picked up Joaquin in the woods yonder one day, when he was n't so high, and taught him to beg for his dinner; and then thar's Polly—that's the magpie—she knows no end of tricks, and makes it quite sociable of evenings with her talk, and so I don't feel like as I was the only living being about the ranch. And Jim here," said Miggles, with her old laugh again, and coming out quite into the firelight,—"Jim—Why, boys, you would admire to see how much he knows for a man like him. Sometimes I bring him flowers, and he looks at 'em just as natural as if he knew 'em; and times, when we're sitting alone, I read him those things on the wall. Why, Lord!" said Miggles, with her frank laugh, "I've read him that whole side of the house this winter. There never was such a man for reading as Jim."

"Why," asked the Judge, "do you not marry this man to whom you have devoted your youthful life?"

"Well, you see," said Miggles, "it would be playing it rather low down on Jim to take advantage of his being so helpless. And then, too, if we were man and wife, now, we'd both know that I was *bound* to do what I do now of my own accord."

"But you are young yet and attractive"—

"It's getting late," said Miggles gravely, "and you'd better all turn in. Goodnight, boys;" and throwing the blanket over her head, Miggles laid herself down beside Jim's chair, her head pillowed on the low stool that held his feet, and spoke no more. The fire slowly faded from the hearth; we each sought our blankets in silence; and presently there was no sound in the long room but the pattering of the rain upon the roof and the heavy breathing of the sleepers.

It was nearly morning when I awoke from a troubled dream. The storm had passed, the stars were shining, and through the shutterless window the full moon, lifting itself over the solemn pines without, looked into the room. It touched the lonely figure in the chair with an infinite compassion, and seemed to baptize with a shining flood the lowly head of the woman whose hair, as in the sweet old story, bathed the feet of him she loved. It even lent a kindly poetry to the rugged outline of Yuba Bill, half reclining on his elbow between them and his passengers, with savagely patient eyes keeping watch and ward. And then I fell asleep and only woke at broad day, with Yuba Bill standing over me, and "All aboard" ringing in my ears.

Coffee was waiting for us on the table, but Miggles was gone. We wandered about the house and lingered long after the horses were harnessed, but she did not return. It was evident that she wished to avoid a formal leave-taking, and had so left us to depart as we had come. After we had helped the ladies into the coach, we returned to the house and solemnly shook hands with the paralytic Jim, as solemnly setting him back into position after each handshake. Then we looked for the last time around the long low room, at the stool where Miggles had sat, and slowly took our seats in the waiting coach. The whip cracked, and we were off!

But as we reached the highroad, Bill's dexterous hand laid the six horses back on their haunches, and the stage stopped with a jerk. For there, on a little eminence beside the road, stood Miggles, her hair flying, her eyes sparkling, her white handkerchief waving, and her white teeth flashing a last "good-by." We waved our hats in return. And then Yuba Bill, as if fearful of further fascination, madly lashed his horses forward, and we sank back in our seats.

We exchanged not a word until we reached the North Fork and the stage drew up at the Independence House. Then, the Judge leading, we walked into the bar-room and took our places gravely at the bar.

"Are your glasses charged, gentlemen?" said the Judge, solemnly taking off his white hat.

They were.

"Well, then, here's to *Miggles*—GOD BLESS HER!"

Perhaps He had. Who knows?

1869                                                                                     1870, 1878

## Tennessee's Partner[1]

I do not think that we ever knew his real name. Our ignorance of it certainly never gave us any social inconvenience, for at Sandy Bar[2] in 1854 most men

1. First published in *Overland Monthly and Out West Magazine* in October 1869; rpt. in *"The Luck of Roaring Camp," and Other Sketches*, from which the present text is taken.
2. Harte uses a number of place-names for California gold-mining sites. "Sandy Bar" alludes to an actual place called Sandy Gulch in northeastern

Calaveras County; it was a trading center for miners, established in 1849. Later, "Poker Flat" may refer to the O'Byrne Ferry area, with its chain cable bridge; in late 1849, there was a large camp here, with miners washing gold out on both banks of the Stanislaus River.

were christened anew. Sometimes these appellatives were derived from some distinctiveness of dress, as in the case of "Dungaree Jack"; or from some peculiarity of habit, as shown in "Saleratus Bill,"[3] so called from an undue proportion of that chemical in his daily bread; or from some unlucky slip, as exhibited in "The Iron Pirate," a mild, inoffensive man, who earned that baleful title by his unfortunate mispronunciation of the term "iron pyrites."[4] Perhaps this may have been the beginning of a rude heraldry; but I am constrained to think that it was because a man's real name in that day rested solely upon his own unsupported statement. "Call yourself Clifford, do you?" said Boston, addressing a timid new-comer with infinite scorn; "hell is full of such Cliffords!" He then introduced the unfortunate man, whose name happened to be really Clifford, as "Jay-bird Charley,"—an unhallowed inspiration of the moment that clung to him ever after.

But to return to Tennessee's Partner, whom we never knew by any other than this relative title; that he had ever existed as a separate and distinct individuality we only learned later. It seems that in 1853 he left Poker Flat to go to San Francisco, ostensibly to procure a wife. He never got any farther than Stockton. At that place he was attracted by a young person who waited upon the table at the hotel where he took his meals. One morning he said something to her which caused her to smile not unkindly, to somewhat coquettishly break a plate of toast over his upturned, serious, simple face, and to retreat to the kitchen. He followed her, and emerged a few moments later, covered with more toast and victory. That day week they were married by a Justice of the Peace, and returned to Poker Flat. I am aware that something more might be made of this episode, but I prefer to tell it as it was current at Sandy Bar,—in the gulches and bar-rooms,—where all sentiment was modified by a strong sense of humor.

Of their married felicity but little is known, perhaps for the reason that Tennessee, then living with his partner, one day took occasion to say something to the bride on his own account, at which, it is said, she smiled not unkindly and chastely retreated,—this time as far as Marysville, where Tennessee followed her, and where they went to housekeeping without the aid of a Justice of the Peace. Tennessee's Partner took the loss of his wife simply and seriously, as was his fashion. But to everybody's surprise, when Tennessee one day returned from Marysville, without his partner's wife,—she having smiled and retreated with somebody else,—Tennessee's Partner was the first man to shake his hand and greet him with affection. The boys who had gathered in the cañon to see the shooting were naturally indignant. Their indignation might have found vent in sarcasm but for a certain look in Tennessee's Partner's eye that indicated a lack of humorous appreciation. In fact, he was a grave man, with a steady application to practical detail which was unpleasant in a difficulty.

Meanwhile a popular feeling against Tennessee had grown up on the Bar. He was known to be a gambler; he was suspected to be a thief. In these suspicions Tennessee's Partner was equally compromised; his continued intimacy with Tennessee after the affair above quoted could only be accounted for on the hypothesis of a copartnership of crime. At last Tennessee's guilt became flagrant. One day he overtook a stranger on his way to Red Dog. The

---

3. "Saleratus" is sodium bicarbonate, or baking powder. Miners had to make their own bread—hence those experienced at taking care of such needs in the Northland were called "sourdoughs." 4. Sulfide mineral sometimes mistaken for gold.

stranger afterward related that Tennessee beguiled the time with interesting anecdote and reminiscence, but illogically concluded the interview in the following words: "And now, young man, I'll trouble you for your knife, your pistols, and your money. You see your weppings might get you into trouble at Red Dog, and your money's a temptation to the evilly disposed. I think you said your address was San Francisco. I shall endeavor to call." It may be stated here that Tennessee had a fine flow of humor, which no business preoccupation could wholly subdue.

This exploit was his last. Red Dog and Sandy Bar made common cause against the highwayman. Tennessee was hunted in very much the same fashion as his prototype, the grizzly. As the toils closed around him, he made a desperate dash through the Bar, emptying his revolver at the crowd before the Arcade Saloon, and so on up Grizzly Cañon; but at its farther extremity he was stopped by a small man on a gray horse. The men looked at each other a moment in silence. Both were fearless, both self-possessed and independent; and both types of a civilization that in the seventeenth century would have been called heroic, but, in the nineteenth, simply "reckless." "What have you got there?—I call," said Tennessee, quietly. "Two bowers and an ace," said the stranger, as quietly, showing two revolvers and a bowie-knife. "That takes me," returned Tennessee; and with this gamblers' epigram, he threw away his useless pistol, and rode back with his captor.

It was a warm night. The cool breeze which usually sprang up with the going down of the sun behind the *chaparral*-crested mountain was that evening withheld from Sandy Bar. The little cañon was stifling with heated resinous odors, and the decaying drift-wood on the Bar sent forth faint, sickening exhalations. The feverishness of day, and its fierce passions, still filled the camp. Lights moved restlessly along the bank of the river, striking no answering reflection from its tawny current. Against the blackness of the pines the windows of the old loft above the express-office stood out staringly bright; and through their curtainless panes the loungers below could see the forms of those who were even then deciding the fate of Tennessee. And above all this, etched on the dark firmament, rose the Sierra, remote and passionless, crowned with remoter passionless stars.

The trial of Tennessee was conducted as fairly as was consistent with a judge and jury who felt themselves to some extent obliged to justify, in their verdict, the previous irregularities of arrest and indictment. The law of Sandy Bar was implacable, but not vengeful. The excitement and personal feeling of the chase were over; with Tennessee safe in their hands they were ready to listen patiently to any defence, which they were already satisfied was insufficient. There being no doubt in their own minds, they were willing to give the prisoner the benefit of any that might exist. Secure in the hypothesis that he ought to be hanged, on general principles, they indulged him with more latitude of defence than his reckless hardihood seemed to ask. The Judge appeared to be more anxious than the prisoner, who, otherwise unconcerned, evidently took a grim pleasure in the responsibility he had created. "I don't take any hand in this yer game," had been his invariable, but good-humored reply to all questions. The Judge—who was also his captor—for a moment vaguely regretted that he had not shot him "on sight," that morning, but presently dismissed this human weakness as unworthy of the judicial mind.

Nevertheless, when there was a tap at the door, and it was said that Tennessee's Partner was there on behalf of the prisoner, he was admitted at once without question. Perhaps the younger members of the jury, to whom the proceedings were becoming irksomely thoughtful, hailed him as a relief.

For he was not, certainly, an imposing figure. Short and stout, with a square face, sunburned into a preternatural redness, clad in a loose duck "jumper," and trousers streaked and splashed with red soil, his aspect under any circumstances would have been quaint, and was now even ridiculous. As he stooped to deposit at his feet a heavy carpet-bag he was carrying, it became obvious, from partially developed legends and inscriptions, that the material with which his trousers had been patched had been originally intended for a less ambitious covering. Yet he advanced with great gravity, and after having shaken the hand of each person in the room with labored cordiality, he wiped his serious, perplexed face on a red bandanna handkerchief, a shade lighter than his complexion, laid his powerful hand upon the table to steady himself, and thus addressed the Judge:—

"I was passin' by," he began, by way of apology, "and I thought I'd just step in and see how things was gittin' on with Tennessee thar,—my pardner. It's a hot night. I disremember any sich weather before on the Bar."

He paused a moment, but nobody volunteering any other meteorological recollection, he again had recourse to his pocket-handkerchief, and for some moments mopped his face diligently.

"Have you anything to say in behalf of the prisoner?" said the Judge, finally.

"Thet's it," said Tennessee's Partner, in a tone of relief. "I come yar as Tennessee's pardner,—knowing him nigh on four year, off and on, wet and dry, in luck and out o' luck. His ways ain't allers my ways, but thar ain't any p'ints in that young man, thar ain't any liveliness as he's been up to, as I don't know. And you sez to me, sez you,—confidential-like, and between man and man,—sez you, 'Do you know anything in his behalf?' and I sez to you, sez I,—confidential-like, as between man and man,—'What should a man know of his pardner?'"

"Is this all you have to say?" asked the Judge, impatiently, feeling, perhaps, that a dangerous sympathy of humor was beginning to humanize the Court.

"Thet's so," continued Tennessee's Partner. "It ain't for me to say anything agin' him. And now, what's the case? Here's Tennessee wants money, wants it bad, and doesn't like to ask it of his old pardner. Well, what does Tennessee do? He lays for a stranger, and he fetches that stranger. And you lays for *him*, and you fetches *him*; and the honors is easy. And I put it to you, bein' a far-minded man, and to you, gentlemen, all, as far-minded men, ef this isn't so."

"Prisoner," said the Judge, interrupting, "have you any questions to ask this man?"

"No! no!" continued Tennessee's Partner, hastily. "I play this yer hand alone. To come down to the bed-rock, it's just this: Tennessee, thar, has played it pretty rough and expensive-like on a stranger, and on this yer camp. And now, what's the fair thing? Some would say more; some would say less. Here's seventeen hundred dollars in coarse gold and a watch,—it's about all my pile,—and call it square!" And before a hand could be raised to prevent him, he had emptied the contents of the carpet-bag upon the table.

For a moment his life was in jeopardy. One or two men sprang to their feet, several hands groped for hidden weapons, and a suggestion to "throw him from the window" was only overridden by a gesture from the Judge. Tennessee laughed. And apparently oblivious of the excitement, Tennessee's Partner improved the opportunity to mop his face again with his handkerchief.

When order was restored, and the man was made to understand, by the use of forcible figures and rhetoric, that Tennessee's offence could not be condoned by money, his face took a more serious and sanguinary hue, and those who were nearest to him noticed that his rough hand trembled slightly on the table. He hesitated a moment as he slowly returned the gold to the carpet-bag, as if he had not yet entirely caught the elevated sense of justice which swayed the tribunal, and was perplexed with the belief that he had not offered enough. Then he turned to the Judge, and saying, "This yer is a lone hand, played alone, and without my pardner," he bowed to the jury and was about to withdraw, when the Judge called him back. "If you have anything to say to Tennessee, you had better say it now." For the first time that evening the eyes of the prisoner and his strange advocate met. Tennessee smiled, showed his white teeth, and, saying, "Euchred, old man!" held out his hand. Tennessee's Partner took it in his own, and saying, "I just dropped in as I was passin' to see how things was gettin' on," let the hand passively fall, and adding that "it was a warm night," again mopped his face with his handkerchief, and without another word withdrew.

The two men never again met each other alive. For the unparalleled insult of a bribe offered to Judge Lynch—who, whether bigoted, weak, or narrow, was at least incorruptible—firmly fixed in the mind of that mythical personage any wavering determination of Tennessee's fate; and at the break of day he was marched, closely guarded, to meet it at the top of Marley's Hill.

How he met it, how cool he was, how he refused to say anything, how perfect were the arrangements of the committee, were all duly reported, with the addition of a warning moral and example to all future evil-doers, in the Red Dog Clarion, by its editor, who was present, and to whose vigorous English I cheerfully refer the reader. But the beauty of that midsummer morning, the blessed amity of earth and air and sky, the awakened life of the free woods and hills, the joyous renewal and promise of Nature, and above all, the infinite Serenity that thrilled through each, was not reported, as not being a part of the social lesson. And yet, when the weak and foolish deed was done, and a life, with its possibilities and responsibilities, had passed out of the misshapen thing that dangled between earth and sky, the birds sang, the flowers bloomed, the sun shone, as cheerily as before; and possibly the Red Dog Clarion was right.

Tennessee's Partner was not in the group that surrounded the ominous tree. But as they turned to disperse attention was drawn to the singular appearance of a motionless donkey-cart halted at the side of the road. As they approached, they at once recognized the venerable "Jenny" and the two-wheeled cart as the property of Tennessee's Partner,—used by him in carrying dirt from his claim; and a few paces distant the owner of the equipage himself, sitting under a buckeye-tree, wiping the perspiration from his glowing face. In answer to an inquiry, he said he had come for the body of the "diseased," "if it was all the same to the committee." He didn't wish to "hurry anything"; he could "wait." He was not working that day; and when the gentlemen were done with the "diseased," he would take him. "Ef thar is any present," he added, in his simple, serious way, "as would care to jine in the fun'l. They kin come." Perhaps it was from a sense of humor, which I have already intimated was a feature of Sandy Bar,—perhaps it was from something even better than that; but two thirds of the loungers accepted the invitation at once.

It was noon when the body of Tennessee was delivered into the hands of his partner. As the cart drew up to the fatal tree, we noticed that it contained a rough, oblong box,—apparently made from a section of sluicing[5]— and half filled with bark and the tassels of pine. The cart was further decorated with slips of willow, and made fragrant with buckeye-blossoms. When the body was deposited in the box, Tennessee's Partner drew over it a piece of tarred canvas, and gravely mounting the narrow seat in front, with his feet upon the shafts, urged the little donkey forward. The equipage moved slowly on, at that decorous pace which was habitual with "Jenny" even under less solemn circumstances. The men—half curiously, half jestingly, but all good-humoredly—strolled along beside the cart; some in advance, some a little in the rear of the homely catafalque.[6] But, whether from the narrowing of the road or some present sense of decorum, as the cart passed on, the company fell to the rear in couples, keeping step, and otherwise assuming the external show of a formal procession. Jack Folinsbee, who had at the outset played a funeral march in dumb show upon an imaginary trombone, desisted, from a lack of sympathy and appreciation,— not having, perhaps, your true humorist's capacity to be content with the enjoyment of his own fun.

The way led through Grizzly Cañon,—by this time clothed in funereal drapery and shadows. The redwoods, burying their moccasined feet in the red soil, stood in Indian-file along the track, trailing an uncouth benediction from their bending boughs upon the passing bier. A hare, surprised into helpless inactivity, sat upright and pulsating in the ferns by the roadside, as the *cortège* went by. Squirrels hastened to gain a secure outlook from higher boughs; and the blue-jays, spreading their wings, fluttered before them like outriders, until the outskirts of Sandy Bar were reached, and the solitary cabin of Tennessee's Partner.

Viewed under more favorable circumstances, it would not have been a cheerful place. The unpicturesque site, the rude and unlovely outlines, the unsavory details, which distinguish the nest-building of the California miner, were all here, with the dreariness of decay superadded. A few paces from the cabin there was a rough enclosure, which, in the brief days of Tennessee's Partner's matrimonial felicity, had been used as a garden, but was now overgrown with fern. As we approached it we were surprised to find that what we had taken for a recent attempt at cultivation was the broken soil about an open grave.

The cart was halted before the enclosure; and rejecting the offers of assistance with the same air of simple self-reliance he had displayed throughout, Tennessee's Partner lifted the rough coffin on his back, and deposited it, unaided, within the shallow grave. He then nailed down the board which served as a lid; and mounting the little mound of earth beside it, took off his hat, and slowly mopped his face with his handkerchief. This the crowd felt

---

5. A "sluice box" was used to separate gold from gravel.

6. A raised bier or platform, often movable, used to support the coffin at a funeral.

was a preliminary to speech; and they disposed themselves variously on stumps and boulders, and sat expectant.

"When a man," began Tennessee's Partner, slowly, "has been running free all day, what's the natural thing for him to do? Why, to come home. And if he ain't in a condition to go home, what can his best friend do? Why, bring him home! And here's Tennessee has been running free, and we brings him home from his wandering." He paused, and picked up a fragment of quartz, rubbed it thoughtfully on his sleeve, and went on: "It ain't the first time that I've packed him on my back, as you see'd me now. It ain't the first time that I brought him to this yer cabin when he couldn't help himself; it ain't the first time that I and 'Jinny' have waited for him on yon hill, and picked him up and so fetched him home, when he couldn't speak, and didn't know me. And now that it's the last time, why—" he paused, and rubbed the quartz gently on his sleeve—"you see it's sort of rough on his pardner. And now, gentlemen," he added, abruptly, picking up his long-handled shovel, "the fun'l 's over; and my thanks, and Tennessee's thanks, to you for your trouble."

Resisting any proffers of assistance, he began to fill in the grave, turning his back upon the crowd, that after a few moments' hesitation gradually withdrew. As they crossed the little ridge that hid Sandy Bar from view, some, looking back, thought they could see Tennessee's Partner, his work done, sitting upon the grave, his shovel between his knees, and his face buried in his red bandanna handkerchief. But it was argued by others that you couldn't tell his face from his handkerchief at that distance; and this point remained undecided.

In the reaction that followed the feverish excitement of that day, Tennessee's Partner was not forgotten. A secret investigation had cleared him of any complicity in Tennessee's guilt, and left only a suspicion of his general sanity. Sandy Bar made a point of calling on him, and proffering various uncouth, but well-meant kindnesses. But from that day his rude health and great strength seemed visibly to decline; and when the rainy season fairly set in, and the tiny grass-blades were beginning to peep from the rocky mound above Tennessee's grave, he took to his bed.

One night, when the pines beside the cabin were swaying in the storm, and trailing their slender fingers over the roof, and the roar and rush of the swollen river were heard below, Tennessee's Partner lifted his head from the pillow, saying, "It is time to go for Tennessee; I must put 'Jinny' in the cart"; and would have risen from his bed but for the restraint of his attendant. Struggling, he still pursued his singular fancy: "There, now, steady, 'Jinny,'— steady, old girl. How dark it is! Look out for the ruts,—and look out for him, too, old gal. Sometimes, you know, when he's blind drunk, he drops down right in the trail. Keep on straight up to the pine on the top of the hill. Thar— I told you so!—thar he is,—coming this way, too,—all by himself, sober, and his face a-shining. Tennessee! Pardner!"

And so they met.

1869, 1870

# HENRY ADAMS
## 1838–1918

Henry Adams's great-grandfather John was second president of the United States; his grandfather John Quincy was sixth president; and his father, Charles Francis, was a distinguished political leader and diplomat. Despite Henry's lifelong penchant for self-deprecation, his own achievements as scholar, teacher, novelist, editor, and cultural historian are worthy of his eminent forebears, for they earn him an important place in American intellectual and literary history. Indeed, it could be argued that Adams's claim in *The Education of Henry Adams* that he was unworthy of the family name has kept him more alive in history than those formidable relatives who achieved greater celebrity in their own day.

Adams was born in Boston, on Beacon Hill, and spent his happy childhood in the constant presence of renowned politicians, artists, and intellectuals; the index to his autobiography, *The Education of Henry Adams,* is virtually an "International Who Was Who" of the time. He was to claim that his studies at Harvard College in the 1850s prepared him neither for a career nor for the extraordinary intellectual, technological, and social transformations of the last half of the century, but the records reveal that he was a good student, and his disparagement of his college experience should be understood as an example of Adams's persistent self-irony. After graduation, he studied and traveled in Europe before he returned to America in 1860 to become private secretary to his father, a position he held for nine years, first in Washington, when the elder Adams was elected to Congress, then in London, where his father served as U.S. Ambassador to the Court of St. James.

In 1870, after a brief career as a freelance journalist, he rather reluctantly accepted a position as assistant professor of medieval history at Harvard, doubting his own fitness for the job. In the same period he undertook the editorship of the *North American Review,* using this position to criticize both of the major political parties of this period concerning uncontrolled expansion and widespread government corruption. He sardonically remarked of his two vocations that "a professor commonly became a pedagogue or a pedant; an editor an authority on advertising." By all accounts other than his own, however, he served the college and the journal well before he gave up both positions in the late 1870s to settle in Washington to devote his time to historical research.

Adams's new career as historian did not begin auspiciously. His biography (1879) of Albert Gallatin, Thomas Jefferson's secretary of the treasury, and his subsequent biography of the flamboyant congressman John Randolph, were successful neither with his professional colleagues nor with the public. The research in original documents Adams had undertaken to write these biographies, however, brought him to the grander subject of which they were a part: *The History of the United States of America during the Administrations of Thomas Jefferson and James Madison* (1889–91). The nine-volume work (which took almost nine years to complete) is still a standard account of this crucial period of transition from Old to New World dominance. During these years Adams also published two novels rich in social detail: *Democracy* in 1880, and *Esther* in 1884. Both novels stirred considerable interest when they were published and continue to attract readers who find, in the first work, a contemporary account of the corruption of government by business interests and, in the second, a representation of the effect of scientific thought on traditional religious belief.

Adams's life was profoundly changed by the suicide, in 1885, of his much-loved wife, Marian Hooper, who was despondent over her father's death. The publication of the *History* also left Adams physically drained and intellectually depleted after a decade of mourning. But a trip to northern France in the summer of 1895 with Mrs. Henry Cabot Lodge, the wife of his friend the senator from Massachusetts, stirred his intellectual curiosity and re-ignited his creative energies. What most struck the world-weary Adams that summer was the severe and majestic harmony of the twelfth- and thirteenth-century Norman and Gothic cathedrals they visited, particularly the one at Chartres. *Mont-Saint-Michel and Chartres* (privately printed in 1904; published 1913) not only provided illuminating discussions of the literary and architectural monuments of the period but penetrated to the powerful spiritual forces that lay behind those achievements. Paradoxically, the insights that allowed Adams to represent what he considered a historical decline from this medieval unity to his own period of confusion and immanent disaster served to renew his spirits and brought his mind and work to the attention of a wider public, not unlike in some ways T. S. Eliot's immersion in the Grail legend in his modernist lament *The Waste Land* (1922).

*The Education of Henry Adams*, begun as a kind of sequel to *Mont-Saint-Michel*, was privately printed early in 1907 and distributed to nearly one hundred friends and prominent people mentioned in the text. In it, Adams rehearses his own miseducation by his family, by schools, and by his experience of various social institutions; ironically offers his own "failures" as a negative example to young men of the time; and describes the increasingly rapid collapse of Western culture in the era after the twelfth century, during which the Virgin Mary (the spiritually unifying) gave way to the Industrial Dynamo (the scientifically disunifying) as the object of humankind's worship.

The Virgin and the Dynamo were presented not only as historical facts but also as what are now enduring symbols. In fact, the *Education* is primarily a literary, not a biographical or historical, work. This book, because it shows imaginatively how the major intellectual, social, political, military, and economic issues and developments of Adams's day are interrelated, is now considered by many critics to be an indispensable text for those seeking to understand the period between the Civil War and World War I. The perspective taken by Adams in the *Education* used to seem excessively pessimistic; its final chapter (dated 1905) prophesied that the disintegrative forces unleashed by science threatened to destroy the world within a generation. This prophecy has not been borne out literally, but the sense of imminent global disaster has come to be widely shared. "Naturally," as Adams went on to observe in this chapter, "such an attitude of an umpire is apt to infuriate the spectators. Above all, it was profoundly unmoral, and tended to discourage effort. On the other hand, it tended to encourage foresight and to economize waste of mind. If this was not itself education, it pointed out the economies necessary for the education of the new American. There, the duty stopped."

The *Education* has grown in interest in recent years for two major reasons: for what it tells us about its complex, elusive, and paradoxical author and for what it tells us about the technology-dominated, dehumanized world whose major power alignments, political and material, Adams foresaw the development of so clearly. As a prophet, he was, as social analyst Daniel Bell observed, the first American writer who "caught a sense of the quickening change of pace that drives all our lives." As a historian of his own time, he was also, as historian Richard Hofstadter noted, "singular not only for the quality of his prose and the sophistication of his mind but also for the unparalleled mixture of his detachment and involvement."

# *From* The Education of Henry Adams[1]

## Editor's Preface

This volume, written in 1905 as a sequel to the same author's "Mont-Saint-Michel and Chartres," was privately printed, to the number of one hundred copies, in 1906, and sent to the persons interested, for their assent, correction, or suggestion. The idea of the two books was thus explained at the end of Chapter XXIX:—

"Any schoolboy could see that man as a force must be measured by motion from a fixed point. Psychology helped here by suggesting a unit—the point of history when man held the highest idea of himself as a unit in a unified universe. Eight or ten years of study had led Adams to think he might use the century 1150–1250, expressed in Amiens Cathedral and the Works of Thomas Aquinas, as the unit from which he might measure motion down to his own time, without assuming anything as true or untrue, except relation. The movement might be studied at once in philosophy and mechanics. Setting himself to the task, he began a volume which he mentally knew as 'Mont-Saint-Michel and Chartres: A Study of Thirteenth-Century Unity.' From that point he proposed to fix a position for himself, which he could label: 'The Education of Henry Adams: A Study of Twentieth-Century Multiplicity.' With the help of these two points of relation, he hoped to project his lines forward and backward indefinitely, subject to correction from any one who should know better."

The "Chartres" was finished and privately printed in 1904. The "Education" proved to be more difficult. The point on which the author failed to please himself, and could get no light from readers or friends, was the usual one of literary form. Probably he saw it in advance, for he used to say, half in jest, that his great ambition was to complete St. Augustine's "Confessions,"[2] but that St. Augustine, like a great artist, had worked from multiplicity to unity, while he, like a small one, had to reverse the method and work back from unity to multiplicity. The scheme became unmanageable as he approached his end.

Probably he was, in fact, trying only to work into it his favorite theory of history, which now fills the last three or four chapters of the "Education," and he could not satisfy himself with his workmanship. At all events, he was still pondering over the problem in 1910, when he tried to deal with it in another way which might be more intelligible to students. He printed a small volume called "A Letter to American Teachers," which he sent to his associates in the American Historical Association, hoping to provoke some response. Before he

1. The selections from the *Education* reprint the Houghton Mifflin Riverside Edition text established by Ernest Samuels. For the notes to these selections we are indebted to Samuels's annotations for that volume. The "Editor's Preface" was written by Adams in 1916; his friend Lodge simply agreed to have his name used. It rationalizes the process of composition of the *Education*, which actually grew out of the earlier book on Chartres. The *Education* was begun in 1903, essentially completed in 1905, and privately printed in 1907.

Adams suffered a stroke on April 24, 1912; his reference to midsummer 1914 is to the beginning of World War I, which confirmed his worst views as to the eventual outcome of the force unleashed by science. Adams made a gift of the book's copyright to the Massachusetts Historical Society in 1918, the year the first edition of the book was publicly sold.
2. Written c. 400, the *Confessions* is Augustine's account of his life and the events leading to his conversion to Christianity.

could satisfy himself even on this minor point, a severe illness in the spring of 1912 put an end to his literary activity forever.

The matter soon passed beyond his control. In 1913 the Institute of Architects published the "Mont-Saint-Michel and Chartres." Already the "Education" had become almost as well known, as the "Chartres," and was freely quoted by every book whose author requested it. The author could no longer withdraw either volume; he could no longer rewrite either, and he could not publish that which he thought unprepared and unfinished, although in his opinion the other was historically purposeless without its sequel. In the end, he preferred to leave the "Education" unpublished, avowedly incomplete, trusting that it might quietly fade from memory. According to his theory of history as explained in Chapters XXXIII and XXXIV, the teacher was at best helpless, and, in the immediate future, silence next to good temper was the mark of sense. After midsummer, 1914, the rule was made absolute.

The Massachusetts Historical Society now publishes the "Education" as it was printed in 1907 with only such marginal corrections as the author made, and it does this, not in opposition to the author's judgment, but only to put both volumes equally within reach of students who have occasion to consult them.

Henry Cabot Lodge

September, 1918

## Preface

Jean Jacques Rousseau[3] began his famous "Confessions" by a vehement appeal to the Deity: "I have shown myself as I was; contemptible and vile when I was so; good, generous, sublime when I was so; I have unveiled my interior such as Thou thyself hast seen it, Eternal Father! Collect about me the innumerable swarm of my fellows; let them hear my confessions; let them groan at my unworthiness; let them blush at my meannesses! Let each of them discover his heart in his turn at the foot of thy throne with the same sincerity; and then let any one of them tell thee if he dares: 'I was a better man!' "

Jean Jacques was a very great educator in the manner of the eighteenth century, and has been commonly thought to have had more influence than any other teacher of his time; but his peculiar method of improving human nature has not been universally admired. Most educators of the nineteenth century have declined to show themselves before their scholars as objects more vile or contemptible than necessary, and even the humblest teacher hides, if possible, the faults with which nature has generously embellished us all, as it did Jean Jacques, thinking, as most religious minds are apt to do, that the Eternal Father himself may not feel unmixed pleasure at our thrusting under his eyes chiefly the least agreeable details of his creation.

As an unfortunate result the twentieth century finds few recent guides to avoid, or to follow. American literature offers scarcely one working model for high education. The student must go back, beyond Jean Jacques, to Benjamin Franklin,[4] to find a model even of self-teaching. Except in the abandoned

---

3. French philosopher (1712–1778) who contended that humans are good by nature and corrupted by the institutions of society. His *Confessions* was published posthumously. Adams's translation is apparently his own.

4. Franklin's *Autobiography* was first published in 1818; it was immediately popular and has become a classic.

sphere of the dead languages, no one has discussed what part of education has, in his personal experience, turned out to be useful, and what not. This volume attempts to discuss it.

As educator, Jean Jacques was, in one respect, easily first; he erected a monument of warning against the Ego. Since his time, and largely thanks to him, the Ego has steadily tended to efface itself, and, for purposes of model, to become a manikin on which the toilet[5] of education is to be draped in order to show the fit or misfit of the clothes. The object of study is the garment, not the figure. The tailor adapts the manikin as well as the clothes to his patron's wants. The tailor's object, in this volume, is to fit young men, in universities or elsewhere, to be men of the world, equipped for any emergency; and the garment offered to them is meant to show the faults of the patchwork fitted on their fathers.

At the utmost, the active-minded young man should ask of his teacher only mastery of his tools. The young man himself, the subject of education, is a certain form of energy; the object to be gained is economy of his force; the training is partly the clearing away of obstacles, partly the direct application of effort. Once acquired, the tools and models may be thrown away.

The manikin, therefore, has the same value as any other geometrical figure of three or more dimensions, which is used for the study of relation. For that purpose it cannot be spared; it is the only measure of motion, of proportion, of human condition; it must have the air of reality; must be taken for real; must be treated as though it had life. Who knows? Possibly it had![6] February 16, 1907[7]

## Chapter XXV. The Dynamo and the Virgin

Until the Great Exposition of 1900[8] closed its doors in November, Adams haunted it, aching to absorb knowledge, and helpless to find it. He would have liked to know how much of it could have been grasped by the best-informed man in the world. While he was thus meditating chaos, Langley[9] came by, and showed it to him. At Langley's behest, the Exhibition dropped its superfluous rags and stripped itself to the skin, for Langley knew what to study, and why, and how; while Adams might as well have stood outside in the night, staring at the Milky Way. Yet Langley said nothing new, and taught nothing that one might not have learned from Lord Bacon,[1] three hundred years before; but though one should have known the "Advancement of Science" as well as one knew the "Comedy of Errors,"[2] the literary knowledge counted for nothing until some teacher should show how to apply it. Bacon took a vast deal of trouble in teaching King James I[3] and his subjects, American or other, towards the year 1620, that true science was the development or economy of forces; yet an elderly American in 1900 knew neither the formula nor the forces; or even so much as to say to himself that his historical

5. Fashionable style of dress.
6. Paraphrase of an observation by Ralph Waldo Emerson in his essay "Experience": "Let us treat the men and women well; treat them as if they were real: perhaps they are."
7. Adams's sixty-ninth birthday.
8. The World's Fair held in Paris from April through November.

9. Samuel P. Langley (1834–1906), American astronomer and inventor, in 1896, of the first airplane to fly successfully.
1. Sir Francis Bacon (1561–1626), English natural philosopher, author of The Advancement of Learning (1605).
2. Early Shakespearean comedy (1594).
3. King of England (1603–25).

business in the Exposition concerned only the economics or developments of force since 1893, when he began to study at Chicago.[4]

Nothing in education is so astonishing as the amount of ignorance it accumulates in the form of inert facts. Adams had looked at most of the accumulations of art in the storehouses called Art Museums; yet he did not know how to look at the art exhibits of 1900. He had studied Karl Marx[5] and his doctrines of history with profound attention, yet he could not apply them at Paris. Langley, with the ease of a great master of experiment, threw out of the field every exhibit that did not reveal a new application of force, and naturally threw out, to begin with, almost the whole art exhibit. Equally, he ignored almost the whole industrial exhibit. He led his pupil directly to the forces. His chief interest was in new motors to make his airship feasible, and he taught Adams the astonishing complexities of the new Daimler[6] motor, and of the automobile, which, since 1893, had become a nightmare at a hundred kilometres an hour, almost as destructive as the electric tram which was only ten years older; and threatening to become as terrible as the locomotive steam-engine itself, which was almost exactly Adams's own age.

Then he showed his scholar the great hall of dynamos, and explained how little he knew about electricity or force of any kind, even of his own special sun, which spouted heat in inconceivable volume, but which, as far as he knew, might spout less or more, at any time, for all the certainty he felt in it. To him, the dynamo itself was but an ingenious channel for conveying somewhere the heat latent in a few tons of poor coal hidden in a dirty engine-house carefully kept out of sight; but to Adams the dynamo became a symbol of infinity. As he grew accustomed to the great gallery of machines, he began to feel the forty-foot dynamos as a moral force, much as the early Christians felt the Cross. The planet itself seemed less impressive, in its old-fashioned, deliberate, annual or daily revolution, than this huge wheel, revolving within arm's-length at some vertiginous speed, and barely murmuring—scarcely humming an audible warning to stand a hair's-breadth further for respect of power—while it would not wake the baby lying close against its frame. Before the end, one began to pray to it; inherited instinct taught the national expression of man before silent and infinite force. Among the thousand symbols of ultimate energy, the dynamo was not so human as some, but it was the most expressive.

Yet the dynamo, next to the steam-engine, was the most familiar of exhibits. For Adams's object its value lay chiefly in its occult mechanism. Between the dynamo in the gallery of machines and the engine-house outside, the break of continuity amounted to abysmal fracture for a historian's objects. No more relation could he discover between the steam and the electric current than between the Cross and the cathedral. The forces were interchangeable if not reversible, but he could see only an absolute *fiat* in electricity as in faith. Langley could not help him. Indeed, Langley seemed to be worried by the same trouble, for he constantly repeated that the new forces were anarchical, and especially that he was not responsible for the new rays, that were little short

4. The subject of Ch. 22 of the *Education*. The Chicago Exposition of 1893 first stimulated Adams's interest in the "economy of forces."
5. German social philosopher (1818–1883) and architect of modern socialism and communism; he formulated his theories on the principle of "dialectical materialism."
6. Gottlieb Daimler (1834–1900), German engineer, inventor of the high-speed internal combustion engine and an early developer of the automobile.

of parricidal in their wicked spirit towards science. His own rays,[7] with which he had doubled the solar spectrum, were altogether harmless and beneficent; but Radium denied its God[8]—or, what was to Langley the same thing, denied the truths of his Science. The force was wholly new.

A historian who asked only to learn enough to be as futile as Langley or Kelvin,[9] made rapid progress under this teaching, and mixed himself up in the tangle of ideas until he achieved a sort of Paradise of ignorance vastly consoling to his fatigued senses. He wrapped himself in vibrations and rays which were new, and he would have hugged Marconi and Branly[1] had he met them, as he hugged the dynamo; while he lost his arithmetic in trying to figure out the equation between the discoveries and the economies of force. The economies, like the discoveries, were absolute, supersensual, occult; incapable of expression in horse-power. What mathematical equivalent could he suggest as the value of a Branly coherer? Frozen air, or the electric furnace, had some scale of measurement, no doubt, if somebody could invent a thermometer adequate to the purpose; but X-rays[2] had played no part whatever in man's consciousness, and the atom itself had figured only as a fiction of thought. In these seven years man had translated himself into a new universe which had no common scale of measurement with the old. He had entered a supersensual world, in which he could measure nothing except by chance collisions of movements imperceptible to his senses, perhaps even imperceptible to his instruments, but perceptible to each other, and so to some known ray at the end of the scale. Langley seemed prepared for anything, even for an indeterminable number of universes interfused—physics stark mad in metaphysics.

Historians undertake to arrange sequences,—called stories, or histories—assuming in silence a relation of cause and effect. These assumptions, hidden in the depths of dusty libraries, have been astounding, but commonly unconscious and childlike; so much so, that if any captious critic were to drag them to light, historians would probably reply, with one voice, that they had never supposed themselves required to know what they were talking about. Adams, for one, had toiled in vain to find out what he meant. He had even published a dozen volumes of American history for no other purpose than to satisfy himself whether, by the severest process of stating, with the least possible comment, such facts as seemed sure, in such order as seemed rigorously consequent, he could fix for a familiar moment a necessary sequence of human movement. The result had satisfied him as little as at Harvard College. Where he saw sequence, other men saw something quite different, and no one saw the same unit of measure. He cared little about his experiments and less about his statesmen, who seemed to him quite as ignorant as himself and, as a rule, no more honest; but he insisted on a relation of sequence, and if he could not reach it by one method, he would try as many methods as science knew. Satisfied that the sequence of men led to nothing and that the

7. Langley had invented the bolometer, with which he was able to measure intensities of invisible heat rays in the infrared spectrum.
8. Because radium, first isolated by the Curies in 1898, underwent spontaneous transformation through radioactive emission, it did not fit prevailing scientific distinctions between matter and energy.
9. William Thomson, Baron Kelvin (1824–1907),

English mathematician and physicist known especially for his work in thermodynamics and electrodynamics.
1. Édouard Branly (1844–1940), French physicist and inventor, in 1890, of the Branly "coherer" for detecting radio waves. Guglielmo Marconi (1874–1937), Italian inventor of radio telegraphy in 1895.
2. Wilhelm Roentgen (1845–1923) discovered X-rays in 1895.

sequence of their society could lead no further, while the mere sequence of time was artificial, and the sequence of thought was chaos, he turned at last to the sequence of force; and thus it happened that, after ten years' pursuit, he found himself lying in the Gallery of Machines at the Great Exposition of 1900, his historical neck broken by the sudden irruption of forces totally new.

Since no one else showed much concern, an elderly person without other cares had no need to betray alarm. The year 1900 was not the first to upset schoolmasters. Copernicus and Galileo[3] had broken many professorial necks about 1600; Columbus had stood the world on its head towards 1500; but the nearest approach to the revolution of 1900 was that of 310, when Constantine set up the Cross.[4] The rays that Langley disowned, as well as those which he fathered, were occult, supersensual, irrational; they were a revelation of mysterious energy like that of the Cross; they were what, in terms of mediæval science, were called immediate modes of the divine substance.

The historian was thus reduced to his last resources. Clearly if he was bound to reduce all these forces to a common value, this common value could have no measure but that of their attraction on his own mind. He must treat them as they had been felt; as convertible, reversible, interchangeable attractions on thought. He made up his mind to venture it; he would risk translating rays into faith. Such a reversible process would vastly amuse a chemist, but the chemist could not deny that he, or some of his fellow physicists, could feel the force of both. When Adams was a boy in Boston, the best chemist in the place had probably never heard of Venus except by way of scandal, or of the Virgin except as idolatry;[5] neither had he heard of dynamos or automobiles or radium; yet his mind was ready to feel the force of all, thought the rays were unborn and the women were dead.

Here opened another totally new education, which promised to be by far the most hazardous of all. The knife-edge along which he must crawl, like Sir Lancelot[6] in the twelfth century, divided two kingdoms of force which had nothing in common but attraction. They were as different as a magnet is from gravitation, supposing one knew what a magnet was, or gravitation, or love. The force of the Virgin was still felt at Lourdes,[7] and seemed to be as potent as X-rays; but in America neither Venus nor Virgin ever had value as force— at most as sentiment. No American had ever been truly afraid of either.

This problem in dynamics gravely perplexed an American historian. The Woman had once been supreme; in France she still seemed potent, not merely as a sentiment, but as a force. Why was she unknown in America? For evidently America was ashamed of her, and she was ashamed of herself, otherwise they would not have strewn fig-leaves so profusely all over her.[8] When she was a true force, she was ignorant of fig-leaves, but the monthly-magazine-made American female had not a feature that would have been recognized by

3. Galileo (1564–1642), Italian astronomer and developer of the refracting telescope, was condemned by the Inquisition for espousing Copernican heliocentric theory. Copernicus (1473–1543), Polish astronomer, proved that the earth rotated around the sun and not vice versa.
4. Constantine the Great (288?–337), Roman emperor, issued the Edict of Milan in 313 proclaiming toleration of Christians, which paved the way for the ascendancy of Christianity.
5. That is, the druggist knew of Venus only

through selling medication for venereal disease, and because Boston was largely Protestant, he would have heard of the Virgin only as the object of idolatrous worship.
6. In Chrétien de Troyes's *Lancelot*, the hero had to crawl across a bridge made of a knife to enter a castle and rescue Guinevere.
7. A famous shrine in France known for its miraculous cures; the Virgin Mary was said to have appeared to a peasant girl there in 1858.
8. I.e., to conceal sexual organs and sensuality.

rait was notorious, and often humorous, but any one brought up
tans knew that sex was sin. In any previous age, sex was strength.
nor beauty was needed. Every one, even among Puritans, knew
r Diana of the Ephesians[9] nor any of the Oriental goddesses was
d for her beauty. She was goddess because of her force; she was the
dynamo; she was reproduction—the greatest and most mysterious
rgies; all she needed was to be fecund. Singularly enough, not one of
many schools of education had ever drawn his attention to the open-
s of Lucretius,[1] though they were perhaps the finest in all Latin liter-
where the poet invoked Venus exactly as Dante invoked the Virgin:—

"Quae quoniam rerum naturam *sola* gubernas."

The Venus of Epicurean philosophy survived in the Virgin of the Schools:—

"Donna, sei tanto grande, e tanto vali,
Che qual vuol grazia, e a te non ricorre,
Sua disianza vuol volar senz' ali."[2]

All this was to American thought as though it had never existed. The true American knew something of the facts, but nothing of the feelings; he read the letter, but he never felt the law. Before this historical chasm, a mind like that of Adams felt itself helpless; he turned from the Virgin to the Dynamo as though he were a Branly coherer. On one side, at the Louvre and at Chartres, as he knew by the record of work actually done and still before his eyes, was the highest energy ever known to man, the creator of four-fifths of his noblest art, exercising vastly more attraction over the human mind than all the steam-engines and dynamos ever dreamed of; and yet this energy was unknown to the American mind. An American Virgin would never dare command; an American Venus would never dare exist.

The question, which to any plain American of the nineteenth century seemed as remote as it did to Adams, drew him almost violently to study, once it was posed; and on this point Langleys were as useless as though they were Herbert Spencers[3] or dynamos. The idea survived only as art. There one turned as naturally as though the artist were himself a woman. Adams began to ponder, asking himself whether he knew of any American artist who had ever insisted on the power of sex, as every classic had always done; but he could think only of Walt Whitman; Bret Harte,[4] as far as the magazines would let him venture; and one or two painters, for the flesh-tones. All the rest had used sex for sentiment, never for force; to them, Eve was a tender flower, and Herodias[5] an unfeminine horror. American art, like the American language

9. The shrine at Ephesus on the west coast of Asia Minor was dedicated to Artemis, a virgin goddess and mother figure.
1. Lucretius (c. 99–55 B.C.E.), in "On the Nature of Things" 1.21: "And since 'tis *thou* / Venus alone / Guidest the Cosmos" (trans. W. E. Leonard).
2. The Virgin of the Schools is a reference to medieval scholastic philosophers. The lines from Dante translate as follows:

Lady, thou art so great and hath such worth, that if there be who would have grace yet betaketh not himself to thee, his longing seeketh to fly without wings (*Paradiso* 33, trans. Carlyle-Wicksteed).

3. Nineteenth-century English philosopher and popularizer of Darwinian evolutionary principles. Adams ironically suggests that Spencer's explanations were too general and abstract to explain this primal force.
4. Harte (1836–1902) sympathetically portrayed prostitutes in such stories as "The Outcasts of Poker Flat," "Cressy," and "The Pupil of Chestnut Ridge." Whitman's *Leaves of Grass* (1855) treated sex boldly and was much criticized on that account.
5. The wife of King Herod; she collaborated with her daughter Salome in arranging the beheading of John the Baptist.

and American education, was as far as possible sexless.[6] Society reg
victory over sex as its greatest triumph, and the historian readily adn
since the moral issue, for the moment, did not concern one who was
ing the relations of unmoral force. He cared nothing for the sex o
dynamo until he could measure its energy.

Vaguely seeking a clue, he wandered through the art exhibit, and, in
stroll, stopped almost every day before St. Gaudens's[7] General Shermar
which had been given the central post of honor. St. Gaudens himself was in
Paris, putting on the work his usual interminable last touches, and listening
to the usual contradictory suggestions of brother sculptors. Of all the American artists who gave to American art whatever life it breathed in the seven-
ties, St. Gaudens was perhaps the most sympathetic, but certainly the most
inarticulate. General Grant or Don Cameron[8] had scarcely less instinct of
rhetoric than he. All the others—the Hunts, Richardson, John La Farge,
Stanford White[9]—were exuberant; only St. Gaudens could never discuss or
dilate on an emotion, or suggest artistic arguments for giving to his work the
forms that he felt. He never laid down the law, or affected the despot, or
became brutalized like Whistler[1] by the brutalities of his world. He required
no incense; he was no egoist; his simplicity of thought was excessive; he could
not imitate, or give any form but his own to the creations of his hand. No one
felt more strongly than he the strength of other men, but the idea that they
could affect him never stirred an image in his mind.

This summer his health was poor and his spirits were low. For such a temper, Adams was not the best companion, since his own gaiety was not *folle*;[2]
but he risked going now and then to the studio on Mont Parnasse to draw him
out for a stroll in the Bois de Boulogne,[3] or dinner as pleased his moods, and
in return St. Gaudens sometimes let Adams go about in his company.

Once St. Gaudens took him down to Amiens, with a party of Frenchmen,
to see the cathedral. Not until they found themselves actually studying the
sculpture of the western portal, did it dawn on Adams's mind that, for his purposes, St. Gaudens on the spot had more interest to him than the cathedral
itself. Great men before great monuments express great truths, provided they
are not taken too solemnly. Adams never tired of quoting the supreme phrase
of his idol Gibbon, before the Gothic cathedrals: "I darted a contemptuous
look on the stately monuments of superstition."[4] Even in the footnotes of his
history, Gibbon had never inserted a bit of humor more human than this, and
one would have paid largely for a photograph of the fat little historian, on the
background of Notre Dame of Amiens, trying to persuade his readers—perhaps himself—that he was darting a contemptuous look on the stately monument, for which he felt in fact the respect which every man of his vast study
and active mind always feels before objects worthy of it; but besides the

6. Just as the American language is not inflected
for gender, so American education was coeduca-
tional and in Adams's day entirely excluded sex as
a subject from the curriculum.
7. Augustus Saint-Gaudens (1848–1907), American sculptor.
8. Senator James Donald Cameron (1833–1918),
secretary of war under President Grant.
9. Architect (1853–1906). William Morris Hunt
(1824–1879), painter, and his younger brother
Richard Morris Hunt (1828–1895), architect.

Henry Hobson Richardson (1838–1886), architect. La Farge (1835–1910), muralist and maker of
stained-glass windows.
1. James Abbott McNeill Whistler (1834–1903),
American painter and lithographer.
2. Excessive (French).
3. A large wooded park on the outskirts of Paris.
"Mont Parnasse": a Paris Left Bank district frequented by artists and writers.
4. Apparently Adams's adaptation of a passage in
Gibbon's French journal for February 21, 1763.

humor, one felt also the relation. Gibbon ignored in Virgin, because in 1789 religious monuments were out of fashion. In 1900 his remark sounded fresh and simple as the green fields to ears that had heard a hundred years of other remarks, mostly no more fresh and certainly less simple. Without malice, one might find it more instructive than a whole lecture of Ruskin.[5] One sees what one brings, and at that moment Gibbon brought the French Revolution. Ruskin brought reaction against the Revolution. St. Gaudens had passed beyond all. He liked the Stately monuments much more than he liked Gibbon or Ruskin; he loved their dignity; their unity; their scale; their lines; their lights and shadows; their decorative sculpture; but he was even less conscious than they of the force that created it all—the Virgin, the Woman—by whose genius "the stately monuments of superstition" were built, through which she was expressed. He would have seen more meaning in Isis[6] with the cow's horns, at Edfoo, who expressed the same thought. The art remained, but the energy was lost even upon the artist.

Yet in mind and person St. Gaudens was a survival of the 1500s; he bore the stamp of the Renaissance, and should have carried an image of the Virgin round his neck, or stuck in his hat, like Louis XI.[7] In mere time he was a lost soul that had strayed by chance into the twentieth century, and forgotten where it came from. He writhed and cursed at his ignorance, much as Adams did at his own, but in the opposite sense. St. Gaudens was a child of Benvenuto Cellini,[8] smothered in an American cradle. Adams was a quintessence of Boston, devoured by curiosity to think like Benvenuto. St. Gaudens's art was starved from birth, and Adams's instinct was blighted from babyhood. Each had but half of a nature, and when they came together before the Virgin of Amiens they ought both to have felt in her the force that made them one; but it was not so. To Adams she became more than ever a channel of force; to St Gaudens she remained as before a channel of taste.

For a symbol of power St. Gaudens instinctively preferred the horse, as was plain in his horse and Victory of the Sherman monument. Doubtless Sherman also felt it so. The attitude was so American that, for at least forty years, Adams had never realized that any other could be in sound taste. How many years had he taken to admit a notion of what Michael Angelo and Rubens[9] were driving at? He could not say; but he knew that only since 1895 had he begun to feel the Virgin or Venus as force, and not everywhere even so. At Chartres—perhaps at Lourdes—possibly at Cnidos[1] if one could still find there the divinely naked Aphrodite of Praxiteles—but otherwise one must look for force to the goddesses of Indian mythology. The idea died out long ago in the German and English stock. St. Gaudens at Amiens was hardly less sensitive to the force of the female energy than Matthew Arnold at the Grande Chartreuse.[2] Neither of them felt goddesses as power—only as

5. John Ruskin (1819–1900), English art critic and social reformer, famous for his highly imaginative interpretations of great works of the Italian Renaissance.
6. Egyptian earth-mother goddess. Adams visited Edfu, the site of the best-preserved temple in Egypt, in 1872–73 and in 1893.
7. A pious French king (1423–1483) who often disguised himself as a pilgrim and wore an old felt hat decorated with the lead statuette of a saint.
8. Italian sculptor and goldsmith (1500–1571), author of a famous autobiography.

9. Peter Paul Rubens (1577–1640), 17th-century Flemish painter. Michelangelo Buonarroti (1475–1564), Italian sculptor, painter, architect, and poet of the High Renaissance. Both are known for their exceptional renderings of the human body.
1. Cnidos, or Cnidus, is an ancient city in Asia Minor, site of the most famous of the statues of Aphrodite by Praxiteles (c. 370–330 B.C.E.); only a copy survives, in the Vatican.
2. Arnold's poem "Stanzas from the Grande Chartreuse" invokes the Virgin Mary in mourning the loss of faith formerly held by ascetic Carthusian monks.

reflected emotion, human expression, beauty, purity, taste, scarcely even as sympathy. They felt a railway train as power; yet they, and all other artists, constantly complained that the power embodied in a railway train could never be embodied in art. All the steam in the world could not, like the Virgin, build Chartres.

Yet in mechanics, whatever the mechanicians might think, both energies acted as interchangeable forces on man, and by action on man all known force may be measured. Indeed, few men of science measured force in any other way. After once admitting that a straight line was the shortest distance between two points, no serious mathematician cared to deny anything that suited his convenience, and rejected no symbol, unproved or unproveable, that helped him to accomplish work. The symbol was force, as a compass-needle or a triangle was force, as the mechanist might prove by losing it, and nothing could be gained by ignoring their value. Symbol or energy, the Virgin had acted as the greatest force the Western world ever felt, and had drawn man's activities to herself more strongly than any other power, natural or supernatural, had ever done; the historian's business was to follow the track of the energy; to find where it came from and where it went to; its complex source and shifting channels; its values, equivalents, conversions. It could scarcely be more complex than radium; it could hardly be deflected, diverted, polarized, absorbed more perplexingly than other radiant matter. Adams knew nothing about any of them, but as a mathematical problem of influence on human progress, though all were occult, all reacted on his mind, and he rather inclined to think the Virgin easiest to handle.

The pursuit turned out to be long and tortuous, leading at last into the vast forests of scholastic science. From Zeno to Descartes, hand in hand with Thomas Aquinas, Montaigne, and Pascal,[3] one stumbled as stupidly as though one were still a German student of 1860. Only with the instinct of despair could one force one's self into this old thicket of ignorance after having been repulsed at a score of entrances more promising and more popular. Thus far, no path had led anywhere, unless perhaps to an exceedingly modest living. Forty-five years of study had proved to be quite futile for the pursuit of power; one controlled no more force in 1900 than in 1850, although the amount of force controlled by society had enormously increased. The secret of education still hid itself somewhere behind ignorance, and one fumbled over it as feebly as ever. In such labyrinths, the staff is a force almost more necessary than the legs; the pen becomes a sort of blind-man's dog, to keep him from falling into the gutters. The pen works for itself, and acts like a hand, modelling the plastic material over and over again to the form that suits it best. The form is never arbitrary, but is a sort of growth like crystallization, as any artist knows too well; for often the pencil or pen runs into side-paths and shapelessness, loses its relations, stops or is bogged. Then it has to return on its trail, and recover, if it can, its line of force. The result of a year's work depends more on what is struck out than on what is left in; on the sequence of the main lines of thought, than on their play or variety. Com-

3. Blaise Pascal (1623–1662), French philosopher. Probably Zeno of Citium (c. 366–264 B.C.E.), Greek philosopher. René Descartes (1596–1650), French philosopher. Aquinas (1225?–1274), Italian philosopher and theologian who is the subject of the last chapter of Adams's *Mont-Saint-Michel and Chartres*. Michel Eyquem de Montaigne (1533–1592), French essayist and skeptical philosopher.

pelled once more to lean heavily on this support, Adams covered more thousands of pages with figures as formal as though they were algebra, laboriously striking out, altering, burning, experimenting, until the year had expired, the Exposition had long been closed, and winter drawing to its end, before he sailed from Cherbourg, on January 19, 1901, for home.

1907, 1918

# AMBROSE BIERCE
## 1842–1914?

Ambrose Gwinnett Bierce was born on June 24, 1842, in Meigs County, Ohio, the last of nine children of strongly religious parents. Bierce's childhood was unhappy, and as an adult he cut himself off from his parents and all but one of his siblings. Perhaps the fascination with the supernatural that he displays in his fiction is similarly an attempt to escape the ordinary society of humanity he claimed to detest. In any case, from his earliest days "Bitter Bierce," as he came to be called, seemed disappointed with what had been, displeased with his present condition, and pessimistic about what lay ahead.

Not long after he spent one year at a military academy in Kentucky—his only formal schooling—the Civil War broke out and Bierce volunteered for the Union Army. After being involved in several battles, he was mustered out a lieutenant. Bierce later defined war (in his *Devil's Dictionary*) as a "by-product of the arts of peace" and peace as "a period of cheating between two periods of fighting," and it is hard to accept his own testimony that he was a zealous soldier. The Civil War, however, was an important source of some of his best fiction, including the suspenseful "An Occurrence at Owl Creek Bridge" (1890) and the equally bitter war narrative "Chickamauga" (1889).

After the war, Bierce moved to San Francisco. By 1866 he was working as a journalist, the career he pursued for the rest of his life. He began as a columnist for the *News Letter* and in 1868 became its editor. Among his writer friends in San Francisco were Mark Twain, Bret Harte, Joaquin Miller, Jack London, and George Sterling, all of whom were involved as journalists, lecturers, and writers in establishing San Francisco as a literary center. Bierce married in 1872 and with his wife traveled to England, where they lived until 1876. There, under the influence of literary sophisticates such as George Augustus Sala and Thomas Hood, he developed from a crude western humorist into a satirist of elegance and bite. His best early work appeared in his "Prattler" columns written first for the *Argonaut* (1877–79) and then for the *Wasp* (1880–86). In that year the popular column was picked up by William Randolph Hearst's *San Francisco Sunday Examiner*, where it continued until 1896. A mixture of reviews, gossip, and political and social commentary, the "Prattler" also served as an outlet for a number of Bierce's best short stories.

Bierce's personal life was a series of disasters. His definition of marriage—"the state or condition of a community consisting of a master, a mistress, and two slaves, making in all, two"—reflected his views on his own marriage (which ended in divorce in 1891). In 1889 his elder son was shot to death during a fight over a girl; in 1901 his younger son died of alcoholism. In 1913, Bierce went to Mexico and disappeared without a trace, although there is a story that he was killed in the Mexican Revolution, which pitted Pancho Villa, whom Bierce had planned to join, and Venustiano Carranza against General Victoriano Huerta, the dictator of Mexico. His time in Mexico was retold in Carlos Fuentes's novel *The Old Gringo* (1985), which was made into a film starring Gregory Peck.

Bierce's pessimism, cynicism, nihilism, and gallows humor, as well as his publicized spats with fellow writers, are in the American tradition of naysaying, which runs from Herman Melville to Thomas Pynchon. It is not the mordant wit of the *Devil's Dictionary* (first published in 1906 as *The Cynic's Word Book*) or Bierce's penchant for the grotesque, however, that finally makes him significant. In his best work, such as *Tales of Soldiers and Civilians* (1891; later retitled *In the Midst of Life*), Bierce, like Stephen Crane and Ernest Hemingway after him, converted the disordered experience of war into resonant and dramatic fictional revelations with strong moral and ethical messages.

## An Occurrence at Owl Creek Bridge[1]

### I

A man stood upon a railroad bridge in northern Alabama, looking down into the swift water twenty feet below. The man's hands were behind his back, the wrists bound with a cord. A rope closely encircled his neck. It was attached to a stout cross-timber above his head and the slack fell to the level of his knees. Some loose boards laid upon the sleepers[2] supporting the metals of the railway supplied a footing for him and his executioners—two private soldiers of the Federal army, directed by a sergeant who in civil life may have been a deputy sheriff. At a short remove upon the same temporary platform was an officer in the uniform of his rank, armed. He was a captain. A sentinel at each end of the bridge stood with his rifle in the position known as "support," that is to say, vertical in front of the left shoulder, the hammer resting on the forearm thrown straight across the chest—a formal and unnatural position, enforcing an erect carriage of the body. It did not appear to be the duty of these two men to know what was occurring at the centre of the bridge; they merely blockaded the two ends of the foot planking that traversed it.

Beyond one of the sentinels nobody was in sight; the railroad ran straight away into a forest for a hundred yards, then, curving, was lost to view. Doubtless there was an outpost farther along. The other bank of the stream was open ground—a gentle acclivity topped with a stockade of vertical tree trunks, loopholed for rifles, with a single embrasure through which protruded the muzzle of a brass cannon commanding the bridge. Midway of the slope between bridge and fort were the spectators—a single company of infantry in line, at "parade rest," the butts of the rifles on the ground, the barrels inclining slightly backward against the right shoulder, the hands crossed upon the stock. A lieutenant stood at the right of the line, the point of his sword upon the ground, his left hand resting upon his right. Excepting the group of four at the centre of the bridge, not a man moved. The company faced the bridge, staring stonily, motionless. The sentinels, facing the banks of the stream, might have been statues to adorn the bridge. The captain stood with folded arms, silent, observing the work of his subordinates, but making no sign.

1. First published in the *San Francisco Examiner* on July 13, 1890, this story was subsequently reprinted as part of the collection *Tales of Soldiers and Civilians* (1891; retitled *In the Midst of Life* in 1898) and in Volume II of *The Collected Works of* *Ambrose Bierce* (1909–12), the basis of the text printed here.
2. Pieces of timber, stone, or steel on or near the ground to keep railroad rails in place.

Death is a dignitary who when he comes announced is to be received with formal manifestations of respect, even by those most familiar with him. In the code of military etiquette silence and fixity are forms of deference.

The man who was engaged in being hanged was apparently about thirty-five years of age. He was a civilian, if one might judge from his habit, which was that of a planter. His features were good—a straight nose, firm mouth, broad forehead, from which his long, dark hair was combed straight back, falling behind his ears to the collar of his well-fitting frock-coat. He wore a mustache and pointed beard, but no whiskers; his eyes were large and dark gray, and had a kindly expression which one would hardly have expected in one whose neck was in the hemp. Evidently this was no vulgar assassin. The liberal military code makes provision for hanging many kinds of persons, and gentlemen are not excluded.

The preparations being complete, the two private soldiers stepped aside and each drew away the plank upon which he had been standing. The sergeant turned to the captain, saluted and placed himself immediately behind that officer, who in turn moved apart one pace. These movements left the condemned man and the sergeant standing on the two ends of the same plank, which spanned three of the cross-ties of the bridge. The end upon which the civilian stood almost, but not quite, reached a fourth. This plank had been held in place by the weight of the captain; it was now held by that of the sergeant. At a signal from the former the latter would step aside, the plank would tilt and the condemned man go down between two ties. The arrangement commended itself to his judgment as simple and effective. His face had not been covered nor his eyes bandaged. He looked a moment at his "unsteadfast footing," then let his gaze wander to the swirling water of the stream racing madly beneath his feet. A piece of dancing driftwood caught his attention and his eyes followed it down the current. How slowly it appeared to move! What a sluggish stream!

He closed his eyes in order to fix his last thoughts upon his wife and children. The water, touched to gold by the early sun, the brooding mists under the banks at some distance down the stream, the fort, the soldiers, the piece of drift—all had distracted him. And now he became conscious of a new disturbance. Striking through the thought of his dear ones was a sound which he could neither ignore nor understand, a sharp, distinct, metallic percussion like the stroke of a blacksmith's hammer upon the anvil; it had the same ringing quality. He wondered what it was, and whether immeasurably distant or near by—it seemed both. Its recurrence was regular, but as slow as the tolling of a death knell. He awaited each stroke with impatience and—he knew not why—apprehension. The intervals of silence grew progressively longer; the delays became maddening. With their greater infrequency the sounds increased in strength and sharpness. They hurt his ear like the thrust of a knife; he feared he would shriek. What he heard was the ticking of his watch.

He unclosed his eyes and saw again the water below him. "If I could free my hands," he thought, "I might throw off the noose and spring into the stream. By diving I could evade the bullets and, swimming vigorously, reach the bank, take to the woods and get away home. My home, thank God, is as yet outside their lines; my wife and little ones are still beyond the invader's farthest advance."

As these thoughts, which have here to be set down in words, were flashed into the doomed man's brain rather than evolved from it the captain nodded to the sergeant. The sergeant stepped aside.

## II

Peyton Farquhar was a well-to-do planter, of an old and highly respected Alabama family. Being a slave owner and like other slave owners a politician he was naturally an original secessionist and ardently devoted to the Southern cause. Circumstances of an imperious nature, which it is unnecessary to relate here, had prevented him from taking service with the gallant army that had fought the disastrous campaigns ending with the fall of Corinth,[3] and he chafed under the inglorious restraint, longing for the release of his energies, the larger life of the soldier, the opportunity for distinction. That opportunity, he felt, would come, as it comes to all in war time. Meanwhile he did what he could. No service was too humble for him to perform in aid of the South, no adventure too perilous for him to undertake if consistent with the character of a civilian who was at heart a soldier, and who in good faith and without too much qualification assented to at least a part of the frankly villainous dictum that all is fair in love and war.

One evening while Farquhar and his wife were sitting on a rustic bench near the entrance to his grounds, a gray-clad soldier rode up to the gate and asked for a drink of water. Mrs. Farquhar was only too happy to serve him with her own white hands. While she was fetching the water her husband approached the dusty horseman and inquired eagerly for news from the front.

"The Yanks are repairing the railroads," said the man, "and are getting ready for another advance. They have reached the Owl Creek bridge, put it in order and built a stockade on the north bank. The commandant has issued an order, which is posted everywhere, declaring that any civilian caught interfering with the railroad, its bridges, tunnels or trains will be summarily hanged. I saw the order."

"How far is it to the Owl Creek bridge?" Farquhar asked.

"About thirty miles."

"Is there no force on this side the creek?"

"Only a picket post[4] half a mile out, on the railroad, and a single sentinel at this end of the bridge."

"Suppose a man—a civilian and student of hanging—should elude the picket post and perhaps get the better of the sentinel," said Farquhar, smiling, "what could he accomplish?"

The soldier reflected. "I was there a month ago," he replied. "I observed that the flood of last winter had lodged a great quantity of driftwood against the wooden pier at this end of the bridge. It is now dry and would burn like tow."

The lady had now brought the water, which the soldier drank. He thanked her ceremoniously, bowed to her husband and rode away. An hour later, after nightfall, he repassed the plantation, going northward in the direction from which he had come. He was a Federal scout.

---

3. Corinth, Mississippi, fell to the Union forces on April 6 and 7, 1862, under General Ulysses S.    Grant in the Battle of Shiloh.
4. Guard post.

### III

As Peyton Farquhar fell straight downward through the bridge he lost consciousness and was as one already dead. From this state he was awakened—ages later, it seemed to him—by the pain of a sharp pressure upon his throat, followed by a sense of suffocation. Keen, poignant agonies seemed to shoot from his neck downward through every fibre of his body and limbs. These pains appeared to flash along well-defined lines of ramification and to beat with an inconceivably rapid periodicity. They seemed like streams of pulsating fire heating him to an intolerable temperature. As to his head, he was conscious of nothing but a feeling of fulness—of congestion. These sensations were unaccompanied by thought. The intellectual part of his nature was already effaced; he had power only to feel, and feeling was torment. He was conscious of motion. Encompassed in a luminous cloud, of which he was now merely the fiery heart, without material substance, he swung through unthinkable arcs of oscillation, like a vast pendulum. Then all at once, with terrible suddenness, the light about him shot upward with the noise of a loud plash; a frightful roaring was in his ears, and all was cold and dark. The power of thought was restored; he knew that the rope had broken and he had fallen into the stream. There was no additional strangulation; the noose about his neck was already suffocating him and kept the water from his lungs. To die of hanging at the bottom of a river!—the idea seemed to him ludicrous. He opened his eyes in the darkness and saw above him a gleam of light, but how distant, how inaccessible! He was still sinking, for the light became fainter and fainter until it was a mere glimmer. Then it began to grow and brighten, and he knew that he was rising toward the surface—knew it with reluctance, for he was now very comfortable. "To be hanged and drowned," he thought, "that is not so bad; but I do not wish to be shot. No; I will not be shot; that is not fair."

He was not conscious of an effort, but a sharp pain in his wrist apprised him that he was trying to free his hands. He gave the struggle his attention, as an idler might observe the feat of a juggler, without interest in the outcome. What splendid effort!—what magnificent, what superhuman strength! Ah, that was a fine endeavor! Bravo! The cord fell away; his arms parted and floated upward, the hands dimly seen on each side in the growing light. He watched them with a new interest as first one and then the other pounced upon the noose at his neck. They tore it away and thrust it fiercely aside, its undulations resembling those of a water-snake. "Put it back, put it back!" He thought he shouted these words to his hands, for the undoing of the noose had been succeeded by the direst pang that he had yet experienced. His neck ached horribly; his brain was on fire; his heart, which had been fluttering faintly, gave a great leap, trying to force itself out at his mouth. His whole body was racked and wrenched with an insupportable anguish! But his disobedient hands gave no heed to the command. They beat the water vigorously with quick, downward strokes, forcing him to the surface. He felt his head emerge; his eyes were blinded by the sunlight; his chest expanded convulsively, and with a supreme and crowning agony his lungs engulfed a great draught of air, which instantly he expelled in a shriek!

He was now in full possession of his physical senses. They were, indeed, preternaturally keen and alert. Something in the awful disturbance of his organic system had so exalted and refined them that they made record of things never before perceived. He felt the ripples upon his face and heard their separate sounds as they struck. He looked at the forest on the bank of the stream, saw the individual trees, the leaves and the veining of each leaf— saw the very insects upon them: the locusts, the brilliant-bodied flies, the gray spiders stretching their webs from twig to twig. He noted the prismatic colors in all the dewdrops upon a million blades of grass. The humming of the gnats that danced above the eddies of the stream, the beating of the dragonflies' wings, the strokes of the water-spiders' legs, like oars which had lifted their boat—all these made audible music. A fish slid along beneath his eyes and he heard the rush of its body parting the water.

He had come to the surface facing down the stream; in a moment the visible world seemed to wheel slowly round, himself the pivotal point, and he saw the bridge, the fort, the soldiers upon the bridge, the captain, the sergeant, the two privates, his executioners. They were in silhouette against the blue sky. They shouted and gesticulated, pointing at him. The captain had drawn his pistol, but did not fire; the others were unarmed. Their movements were grotesque and horrible, their forms gigantic.

Suddenly he heard a sharp report and something struck the water smartly within a few inches of his head, spattering his face with spray. He heard a second report, and saw one of the sentinels with his rifle at his shoulder, a light cloud of blue smoke rising from the muzzle. The man in the water saw the eye of the man on the bridge gazing into his own through the sights of the rifle. He observed that it was a gray eye and remembered having read that gray eyes were keenest, and that all famous marksmen had them. Nevertheless, this one had missed.

A counter-swirl had caught Farquhar and turned him half round; he was again looking into the forest on the bank opposite the fort. The sound of a clear, high voice in a monotonous singsong now rang out behind him and came across the water with a distinctness that pierced and subdued all other sounds, even the beating of the ripples in his ears. Although no soldier, he had frequented camps enough to know the dread significance of that deliberate, drawling, aspirated chant; the lieutenant on shore was taking a part in the morning's work. How coldly and pitilessly—with what an even, calm intonation, presaging, and enforcing tranquillity in the men—with what accurately measured intervals fell those cruel words:

"Attention, company! . . . Shoulder arms! . . . Ready! . . . Aim! . . . Fire!"

Farquhar dived—dived as deeply as he could. The water roared in his ears like the voice of Niagara, yet he heard the dulled thunder of the volley and, rising again toward the surface, met shining bits of metal, singularly flattened, oscillating slowly downward. Some of them touched him on the face and hands, then fell away, continuing their descent. One lodged between his collar and neck; it was uncomfortably warm and he snatched it out.

As he rose to the surface, gasping for breath, he saw that he had been a long time under water; he was perceptibly farther down stream—nearer to safety. The soldiers had almost finished reloading; the metal ramrods flashed all at once in the sunshine as they were drawn from the barrels, turned in the air, and thrust into their sockets. The two sentinels fired again, independently and ineffectually.

The hunted man saw all this over his shoulder; he was now swimming vigorously with the current. His brain was as energetic as his arms and legs; he thought with the rapidity of lightning.

"The officer," he reasoned, "will not make that martinet's error a second time. It is as easy to dodge a volley as a single shot. He has probably already given the command to fire at will. God help me, I cannot dodge them all!"

An appalling plash within two yards of him was followed by a loud, rushing sound, *diminuendo*,[5] which seemed to travel back through the air to the fort and died in an explosion which stirred the very river to its deeps! A rising sheet of water curved over him, fell down upon him, blinded him, strangled him! The cannon had taken a hand in the game. As he shook his head free from the commotion of the smitten water he heard the deflected shot humming through the air ahead, and in an instant it was cracking and smashing the branches in the forest beyond.

"They will not do that again," he thought; "the next time they will use a charge of grape.[6] I must keep my eye upon the gun; the smoke will apprise me—the report arrives too late; it lags behind the missile. That is a good gun."

Suddenly he felt himself whirled round and round—spinning like a top. The water, the banks, the forests, the now distant bridge, fort and men—all were commingled and blurred. Objects were represented by their colors only; circular horizontal streaks of color—that was all he saw. He had been caught in a vortex and was being whirled on with a velocity of advance and gyration that made him giddy and sick. In a few moments he was flung upon the gravel at the foot of the left bank of the stream—the southern bank—and behind a projecting point which concealed him from his enemies. The sudden arrest of his motion, the abrasion of one of his hands on the gravel, restored him, and he wept with delight. He dug his fingers into the sand, threw it over himself in handfuls and audibly blessed it. It looked like diamonds, rubies, emeralds; he could think of nothing beautiful which it did not resemble. The trees upon the bank were giant garden plants; he noted a definite order in their arrangement, inhaled the fragrance of their blooms. A strange, roseate light shone through the spaces among their trunks and the wind made in their branches the music of aeolian harps.[7] He had no wish to perfect his escape—was content to remain in that enchanting spot until retaken.

A whiz and rattle of grapeshot among the branches high above his head roused him from his dream. The baffled cannoneer had fired him a random farewell. He sprang to his feet, rushed up the sloping bank, and plunged into the forest.

All that day he traveled, laying his course by the rounding sun. The forest seemed interminable; nowhere did he discover a break in it, not even a woodman's road. He had not known that he lived in so wild a region. There was something uncanny in the revelation.

By nightfall he was fatigued, footsore, famishing. The thought of his wife and children urged him on. At last he found a road which led him in what he knew to be the right direction. It was as wide and straight as a city street, yet it seemed untraveled. No fields bordered it, no dwelling anywhere. Not so

5. Diminishing.
6. Grapeshot, a cluster of small iron balls used as a cannon charge.

7. Stringed instruments activated by the wind (Aeolus was the keeper of the winds in classical mythology).

much as the barking of a dog suggested human habitation. The black bodies of the trees formed a straight wall on both sides, terminating on the horizon in a point, like a diagram in a lesson in perspective. Overhead, as he looked up through this rift in the wood, shone great golden stars looking unfamiliar and grouped in strange constellations. He was sure they were arranged in some order which had a secret and malign significance. The wood on either side was full of singular noises, among which—once, twice, and again—he distinctly heard whispers in an unknown tongue.

His neck was in pain and lifting his hand to it he found it horribly swollen. He knew that it had a circle of black where the rope had bruised it. His eyes felt congested; he could no longer close them. His tongue was swollen with thirst; he relieved its fever by thrusting it forward from between his teeth into the cold air. How softly the turf had carpeted the untraveled avenue—he could no longer feel the roadway beneath his feet!

Doubtless, despite his suffering, he had fallen asleep while walking, for now he sees another scene—perhaps he has merely recovered from a delirium. He stands at the gate of his own home. All is as he left it, and all bright and beautiful in the morning sunshine. He must have traveled the entire night. As he pushes open the gate and passes up the wide white walk, he sees a flutter of female garments; his wife, looking fresh and cool and sweet, steps down from the veranda to meet him. At the bottom of the steps she stands waiting, with a smile of ineffable joy, an attitude of match less grace and dignity. Ah, how beautiful she is! He springs forward with extended arms. As he is about to clasp her he feels a stunning blow upon the back of the neck; a blinding white light blazes all about him with a sound like the shock of a cannon—then all is darkness and silence!

Peyton Farquhar was dead; his body, with a broken neck, swung gently from side to side beneath the timbers of the Owl Creek bridge.

1890, 1891

# Chickamauga[1]

One sunny autumn afternoon a child strayed away from its rude home in a small field and entered a forest unobserved. It was happy in a new sense of freedom from control, happy in the opportunity of exploration and adventure; for this child's spirit, in bodies of its ancestors, had for thousands of years been trained to memorable feats of discovery and conquest—victories in battles whose critical moments were centuries, whose victors' camps were cities of hewn stone. From the cradle of its race it had conquered its way through two continents and passing a great sea had penetrated a third, there to be born to war and dominion as a heritage.

The child was a boy aged about six years, the son of a poor planter. In his younger manhood the father had been a soldier, had fought against naked

1. First published on January 20, 1889, in the *San Francisco Examiner*, the story was reprinted in 1946 in *The Collected Writings of Ambrose Bierce*, edited by Clifton Fadiman, from which the present text is taken. Chickamauga, September 19, 1863, was one of the bloodiest single-day battles of the Civil War, a costly Union defeat along a creek south of Chattanooga, Tennessee.

savages and followed the flag of his country into the capital of a civilized race to the far South. In the peaceful life of a planter the warrior-fire survived; once kindled, it is never extinguished. The man loved military books and pictures and the boy had understood enough to make himself a wooden sword, though even the eye of his father would hardly have known it for what it was. This weapon he now bore bravely, as became the son of an heroic race, and pausing now and again in the sunny space of the forest assumed, with some exaggeration, the postures of aggression and defense that he had been taught by the engraver's art. Made reckless by the ease with which he overcame invisible foes attempting to stay his advance, he committed the common enough military error of pushing the pursuit to a dangerous extreme, until he found himself upon the margin of a wide but shallow brook, whose rapid waters barred his direct advance against the flying foe that had crossed with illogical ease. But the intrepid victor was not to be baffled; the spirit of the race which had passed the great sea burned unconquerable in that small breast and would not be denied. Finding a place where some bowlders in the bed of the stream lay but a step or a leap apart, he made his way across and fell again upon the rear-guard of his imaginary foe, putting all to the sword.

Now that the battle had been won, prudence required that he withdraw to his base of operations. Alas; like many a mightier conqueror, and like one, the mightiest, he could not

> curb the lust for war,
> Nor learn that tempted Fate will leave the loftiest star.[2]

Advancing from the bank of the creek he suddenly found himself confronted with a new and more formidable enemy: in the path that he was following, sat, bolt upright, with ears erect and paws suspended before it, a rabbit! With a startled cry the child turned and fled, he knew not in what direction, calling with inarticulate cries for his mother, weeping, stumbling, his tender skin cruelly torn by brambles, his little heart beating hard with terror—breathless, blind with tears—lost in the forest! Then, for more than an hour, he wandered with erring feet through the tangled undergrowth, till at last, overcome by fatigue, he lay down in a narrow space between two rocks, within a few yards of the stream and still grasping his toy sword, no longer a weapon but a companion, sobbed himself to sleep. The wood birds sang merrily above his head; the squirrels, whisking their bravery of tail, ran barking from tree to tree, unconscious of the pity of it, and somewhere far away was a strange, muffled thunder, as if the partridges were drumming in celebration of nature's victory over the son of her immemorial enslavers. And back at the little plantation, where white men and black were hastily searching the fields and hedges in alarm, a mother's heart was breaking for her missing child.

Hours passed, and then the little sleeper rose to his feet. The chill of the evening was in his limbs, the fear of the gloom in his heart. But he had rested, and he no longer wept. With some blind instinct which impelled to action he struggled through the undergrowth about him and came to a more open ground—on his right the brook, to the left a gentle acclivity studded with

2. From Canto 3 of Byron's long narrative poem *Childe Harold's Pilgrimage*, these lines refer to Napoleon at the Battle of Waterloo.

infrequent trees; over all, the gathering gloom of twilight. A thin, ghostly mist rose along the water. It frightened and repelled him; instead of recrossing, in the direction whence he had come, he turned his back upon it, and went forward toward the dark inclosing wood. Suddenly he saw before him a strange moving object which he took to be some large animal—a dog, a pig—he could not name it; perhaps it was a bear. He had seen pictures of bears, but knew of nothing to their discredit and had vaguely wished to meet one. But something in form or movement of this object—something in the awkwardness of its approach—told him that it was not a bear, and curiosity was stayed by fear. He stood still and as it came slowly on gained courage every moment, for he saw that at least it had not the long, menacing ears of the rabbit. Possibly his impressionable mind was half conscious of something familiar in its shambling, awkward gait. Before it had approached near enough to resolve his doubts he saw that it was followed by another and another. To right and to left were many more; the whole open space about him was alive with them— all moving toward the brook.

They were men. They crept upon their hands and knees. They used their hands only, dragging their legs. They used their knees only, their arms hanging idle at their sides. They strove to rise to their feet, but fell prone in the attempt. They did nothing naturally, and nothing alike, save only to advance foot by foot in the same direction. Singly, in pairs and in little groups, they came on through the gloom, some halting now and again while others crept slowly past them, then resuming their movement. They came by dozens and by hundreds; as far on either hand as one could see in the deepening gloom they extended and the black wood behind them appeared to be inexhaustible. The very ground seemed in motion toward the creek. Occasionally one who had paused did not again go on, but lay motionless. He was dead. Some, pausing, made strange gestures with their hands, erected their arms and lowered them again, clasped their heads; spread their palms upward, as men are sometimes seen to do in public prayer.

Not all of this did the child note; it is what would have been noted by an elder observer; he saw little but that these were men, yet crept like babes. Being men, they were not terrible, though unfamiliarly clad. He moved among them freely, going from one to another and peering into their faces with childish curiosity. All their faces were singularly white and many were streaked and gouted with red. Something in this—something too, perhaps, in their grotesque attitudes and movements—reminded him of the painted clown whom he had seen last summer in the circus, and he laughed as he watched them. But on and ever on they crept, these maimed and bleeding men, as heedless as he of the dramatic contrast between his laughter and their own ghastly gravity. To him it was a merry spectacle. He had seen his father's Negroes creep upon their hands and knees for his amusement—had ridden them so, "making believe" they were his horses. He now approached one of these crawling figures from behind and with an agile movement mounted it astride. The man sank upon his breast, recovered, flung the small boy fiercely to the ground as an unbroken colt might have done, then turned upon him a face that lacked a lower jaw—from the upper teeth to the throat was a great red gap fringed with hanging shreds of flesh and splinters of bone. The unnatural prominence of nose, the absence of chin, the fierce eyes, gave this man the appearance of a great bird of prey crimsoned in throat and breast by the blood of its quarry. The man rose to his knees, the child to his feet. The man shook his fist at the child; the child, terrified at last, ran to a tree near by, got upon the farther side of it and took a more serious view of the situation. And so the clumsy multitude dragged itself slowly and painfully along in hideous pantomime—moved forward down the slope like a swarm of great black beetles, with never a sound of going—in silence profound, absolute.

Instead of darkening, the haunted landscape began to brighten. Through the belt of trees beyond the brook shone a strange red light, the trunks and branches of the trees making a black lacework against it. It struck the creeping figures and gave them monstrous shadows, which caricatured their movements on the lit grass. It fell upon their faces, touching their whiteness with a ruddy tinge, accentuating the stains with which so many of them were freaked and maculated.[3] It sparkled on buttons and bits of metal in their clothing. Instinctively the child turned toward the growing splendor and moved down the slope with his horrible companions; in a few moments had passed the foremost of the throng—not much of a feat, considering his advantages. He placed himself in the lead, his wooden sword still in hand, and solemnly directed the march, conforming his pace to theirs and occasionally turning as if to see that his forces did not straggle. Surely such a leader never before had such a following.

Scattered about upon the ground now slowly narrowing by the encroachment of this awful march to water, were certain articles to which, in the leader's mind, were coupled no significant associations: an occasional blanket, tightly rolled lengthwise, doubled and the ends bound together with a string; a heavy knapsack here, and there a broken rifle—such things, in short, as are found in the rear of retreating troops, the "spoor"[4] of men flying from their hunters. Everywhere near the creek, which here had a margin of lowland, the earth was trodden into mud by the feet of men and horses. An observer of better experience in the use of his eyes would have noticed that these footprints pointed in both directions; the ground had been twice passed over—in advance and in retreat. A few hours before, these desperate, stricken men, with their more fortunate and now distant comrades, had penetrated the forest in thousands. Their successive battalions, breaking into swarms and reforming in lines, had passed the child on every side—had almost trodden on him as he slept. The rustle and murmur of their march had not awakened him. Almost within a stone's throw of where he lay they had fought a battle; but all unheard by him were the roar of the musketry, the shock of the cannon, "the thunder of the captains and the shouting."[5] He had slept through it all, grasping his little wooden sword with perhaps a tighter clutch in unconscious sympathy with his martial environment, but as heedless of the grandeur of the struggle as the dead who had died to make the glory.

The fire beyond the belt of woods on the farther side of the creek, reflected to earth from the canopy of its own smoke, was now suffusing the whole landscape. It transformed the sinuous line of mist to the vapor of gold. The water

3. Spotted, blemished. "Freaked": streaked or flecked.

4. The track, trail, or droppings of a wild animal.

5. Job 39.25.

gleamed with dashes of red, and red, too, were many of the stones protruding above the surface. But that was blood; the less desperately wounded had stained them in crossing. On them, too, the child now crossed with eager steps; he was going to the fire. As he stood upon the farther bank he turned about to look at the companions of his march. The advance was arriving at the creek. The stronger had already drawn themselves to the brink and plunged their faces into the flood. Three or four who lay without motion appeared to have no heads. At this the child's eyes expanded with wonder; even his hospitable understanding could not accept a phenomenon implying such vitality as that. After slaking their thirst these men had not had the strength to back away from the water, nor to keep their heads above it. They were drowned. In rear of these, the open spaces of the forest showed the leader as many formless figures of his grim command as at first; but not nearly so many were in motion. He waved his cap for their encouragement and smilingly pointed with his weapon in the direction of the guiding light—a pillar of fire to this strange exodus.

Confident of the fidelity of his forces, he now entered the belt of woods, passed through it easily in the red illumination, climbed a fence, ran across a field, turning now and again to coquet with his responsive shadow, and so approached the blazing ruin of a dwelling. Desolation everywhere! In all the wide glare not a living thing was visible. He cared nothing for that; the spectacle pleased, and he danced with glee in imitation of the wavering flames. He ran about, collecting fuel, but every object that he found was too heavy for him to cast in from the distance to which the heat limited his approach. In despair he flung in his sword—a surrender to the superior forces of nature. His military career was at an end.

Shifting his position, his eyes fell upon some outbuildings which had an oddly familiar appearance, as if he had dreamed of them. He stood considering them with wonder, when suddenly the entire plantation, with its inclosing forest, seemed to turn as if upon a pivot. His little world swung half around; the points of the compass were reversed. He recognized the blazing building as his own home!

For a moment he stood stupefied by the power of the revelation, then ran with stumbling feet, making a half-circuit of the ruin. There, conspicuous in the light of the conflagration, lay the dead body of a woman—the white face turned upward, the hands thrown out and clutched full of grass, the clothing deranged, the long dark hair in tangles and full of clotted blood. The greater part of the forehead was torn away, and from the jagged hole the brain protruded, overflowing the temple, a frothy mass of gray, crowned with clusters of crimson bubbles—the work of a shell.

The child moved his little hands, making wild, uncertain gestures. He uttered a series of inarticulate and indescribable cries—something between the chattering of an ape and the gobbling of a turkey—a startling, soulless, unholy sound, the language of a devil. The child was a deaf mute.

Then he stood motionless, with quivering lips, looking down upon the wreck.

1889

NATIVE AMERICAN CHANTS AND SONGS

# THE NAVAJO NIGHT CHANT

The Navajos migrated to the American Southwest from points further north some five hundred years ago. Once settled, the Navajos learned farming and weaving from the Pueblo peoples; they later acquired livestock from the Spanish and developed silver-working skills from contact with Mexicans. When the United States took possession of the southwestern territories in 1848 after the Mexican war, it inherited the problem of raiding Navajos. In 1863, the government hired the well-known scout Kit Carson to subdue the Navajos by destroying their crops and livestock. The following year, starving Navajo people began to make their way into Fort Defiance. Later that year, some eight thousand Navajos were forced to make the Long Walk from Fort Defiance in western Arizona three hundred miles to Fort Sumner in east-central New Mexico, where they were imprisoned. This traumatic event is remembered by Navajos much as the Trail of Tears is remembered by Cherokees and Wounded Knee by the Sioux. In 1868 a new treaty established a three-million-acre reservation for the Navajos in New Mexico and Arizona—and the people began to return to their homes. Despite food shortages, drought, and further land cessions, the Navajos gradually grew in number. Today they are the most populous American Indian nation in the United States.

Ceremonies are a central part of Navajo culture. They are used to enhance life—to promote a successful hunt and good crops—to cure physical illness, and to remedy misfortunes of all kinds—a fire or miscarriage, lightning striking sheep. Although songs, dances, and sand paintings are important parts of Navajo ceremonies, it was the intoning of long, complex prayers that led the first recorders of these ceremonies to call them chants. An individual desiring that a ceremony be performed first consults with a seer, a ritual diagnostician who determines which chant is likely to address the problem at hand. The initiator of the ceremony is referred to as the "patient," regardless of whether she or he is sick in the Western sense. The chants may last from one to nine nights. They are conducted by an expert in a particular ceremonial, a person endowed not so much with special power (as is the seer) as with special knowledge. Each ceremonial requires elaborate preparation by the chanter and the patient's family. The chanter must renew or refresh ritual objects to be used during the ceremony—masks, prayer sticks, and the like—and the family must provide such things as the baskets used as drums that the chanter requires and food for the many invited guests.

The Night Chant is one of the most elaborate of Navajo ceremonials, taking nine nights to perform. It begins at sunset, when the chanter enters the house of the patient and a crier, standing at the door, calls, *Biké hatáli hakú* ("Come on the trail of song"), enjoining both the patient and the guests to participate. The patient seats himself or herself west of a fire that has been kindled for the ceremony: the place of honor. At sunrise on the ninth day, after an elaborate series of songs, dances, and chanted prayers, the patient is invited to look eastward and greet the dawn in newfound health and wholeness.

The earliest and still most detailed version of the Navajo Night Chant was published in 1902 by Washington Matthews (1843–1905), an army surgeon assigned to Fort Wingate, New Mexico, in the 1880s. Drawn to the culture of the Navajos, Matthews learned their language and published his first study of a Navajo ceremonial, *The Mountain Chant,* in 1887. After witnessing a Night Chant in the fall of 1884, Matthews devoted the last twenty years of his life to its study. Although he worked with many priests of the Night Chant, one in particular, Hatali Natloi (Laughing Chanter), contributed to the version Matthews published in 1902. Today, the chants are commonly referred to in English as *ways:* Night Way, Mountain Way, Enemy Way, Blessing Way, Red Ant Way, and so on. The change of name points to the fact that these are dramatic *acts* not limited to chanting alone. We retain the name Night Chant, originally used by Matthews and still used by John Bierhorst, whose edition of Matthews's version we print here.

# The Night Chant[1]

## *Concluding Rite, First Day*

### THE SACRED MOUNTAINS

Sprinkling dry pigments on the floor of the lodge, the chanter prepares a small sand painting featuring the four sacred mountains of the Navajo world; a trail leads into their midst. At the doorway the crier issues his usual call: *Biké hatáli hakú.*[2] The patient enters, walking slowly along the "trail" to the "mountains," followed by Hastshéyalti.[3] The singers begin:

> In a holy place with a god I walk,
> In a holy place with a god I walk,
> On Tsisnadzhíni with a god I walk,
> On a chief of mountains with a god I walk,
> In old age wandering with a god I walk,                    5
> On a trail of beauty with a god I walk.

The stanza is repeated three times, changing the name of the mountain, in turn, to Tsótsil, Dokoslíd, and Depéntsa.[4] The patient reaches the center of the picture; the chanter recites:

> From the base of the east.
> From the base of Tsisnadzhíni.
> From the house made of mirage,
> From the story[5] made of mirage,                          10
> From the doorway of rainbow,
> The path out of which is the rainbow,
> The rainbow passed out with me.
> The rainbow raised up with me
> Through the middle of broad fields,                         15
> The rainbow returned with me.
> To where my house is visible,
> The rainbow returned with me.
> To the roof of my house,
> The rainbow returned with me.                               20
> To the entrance of my house,
> The rainbow returned with me.

1. From John Bierhorst's *Four Masterworks of American Indian Literature: Quetzalcoatl, The Ritual of Condolence, Cuceb, The Night Chant* (1974, 1984). Bierhorst's version of Washington Matthews's text condenses it somewhat and slightly alters the original spelling. The descriptions of ritual procedure are also condensed from Matthews.
2. Come on the trail of song (Navajo).
3. The Talking God, principal figure of the Night Chant.
4. Probably Pelado Peak, New Mexico, the mountain marking the eastern point of the Navajo world. Tsótil is Mt. Taylor, NM, and marks the south; Dokoslíd is Humphrey's Peak, Arizona, and marks the west; while Depéntsa is probably Hesperus Peak, Colorado, and marks the north. The patient symbolically follows a holy trail that takes him to each of these mountains, homes of the gods [Bierhorst's note].
5. Matthews's poetic "story" is misleading. "Base," or "lower part," would be more correct [Bierhorst's note].

To just within my house,
The rainbow returned with me.
To my fireside,                                                          25
The rainbow returned with me.
To the center of my house,
The rainbow returned with me.
At the fore part of my house with the dawn,[6]
The Talking God sits with me.                                           30
The House God sits with me.
Pollen Boy sits with me.
Grasshopper Girl sits with me.
In beauty Estsánatlehi, my mother, for her I return.[7]
Beautifully my fire to me is restored.                                  35
Beautifully my possessions are to me restored.
Beautifully my soft goods to me are restored.
Beautifully my hard goods to me are restored.
Beautifully my horses to me are restored.
Beautifully my sheep to me are restored.                                40
Beautifully my old men to me are restored.
Beautifully my old women to me are restored.
Beautifully my young men to me are restored.
Beautifully my young women to me are restored.
Beautifully my children to me are restored.                             45
Beautifully my wife to me is restored.
Beautifully my chiefs to me are restored.
Beautifully my country to me is restored.
Beautifully my fields to me are restored.
Beautifully my house to me is restored.                                 50
Talking God sits with me.
House God sits with me.
Pollen Boy sits with me.
Grasshopper Girl sits with me.
Beautifully white corn to me is restored.                               55
Beautifully yellow corn to me is restored.
Beautifully blue corn to me is restored.
Beautifully corn of all kinds to me is restored.
In beauty may I walk.
All day long may I walk.                                                60
Through the returning seasons may I walk.
[*line untranslated*][8]
Beautifully . . . will I possess again.
[*line untranslated*]
Beautifully birds . . .                                                 65
Beautifully joyful birds . . .
On the trail marked with pollen may I walk.
With grasshoppers about my feet may I walk.

---

6. I.e., the front ("forepart") of all Navajo houses,
or hogans, faces east.
7. Estsánatlehi is Changing Woman, a personification of the earth. The return to the mother (or
grandmother) is a motif typical of Navajo myths.
Pollen Boy symbolizes male generative power and

Grasshopper Girl, female generative power
[adapted from Bierhorst's note].
8. Matthews's 1902 publication gives the Navajo
for these lines, because he could not arrive at a satisfactory translation of them.

With dew about my feet may I walk.
With beauty may I walk.                                                    70
With beauty before me, may I walk.
With beauty behind me, may I walk.
With beauty above me, may I walk.
With beauty below me, may I walk.
With beauty all around me, may I walk.                                    75
In old age wandering on a trail of beauty, lively, may I walk.
In old age wandering on a trail of beauty, living again, may I walk.
It is finished in beauty.
It is finished in beauty.

The prayer is thrice repeated, substituting in turn the names of the other three directions (south, west, north) and their corresponding mountains (Tsótsil, Dokoslíd, Depéntsa). Kneeling, Hastshéyalti takes sand from each of the "mountains" and applies it to the patient. The patient kneels: coals are removed from the fire and placed before him; over these the chanter sprinkles a powder of feathers and resin, giving rise to an incense inhaled by the patient. The coals are extinguished, the picture obliterated. The party withdraws.

### Concluding Rite, Ninth Day

Four great fires are kindled on either side of the level space, or "dancing ground," in front of the lodge. Facing the lodge at a distance of some hundred paces stands the newly constructed "arbor," a circle of evergreen boughs to be used as the performers' changing room. Spectators, numbering in the hundreds, gather just beyond the fires along both sides of the dancing ground.

#### DANCE OF THE ATSÁLEI, THUNDERBIRDS

The chanter's assistants paint with white earth the bodies of dancers who will represent the four thunderbirds (of corn, of child-rain, of vegetation, and of pollen). The chanter sings:

Now the holy one paints his form,
The Wind Boy,[9] the holy one, paints his form,
All over his body, he paints his form,
With the dark cloud he paints his form,
With the misty rain he paints his form,                                   5
With the rainy bubbles he paints his form,
To the ends of his toes he paints his form,
To fingers and rattle he paints his form,
To the plume on his head he paints his form.

As the dancers repair to the arbor, the basket is turned down [overturned, used as a drum] and singing begins anew. Fully costumed, the thunderbirds, led by Hastshéyalti, approach the dancing ground. A crier calls: Come on the trail of song [Biké hatáli hakú]. The patient emerges from the lodge and sprinkles the dancers with meal. (Singing within the lodge continues unabated.)

---

9. Wind is the precursor of rain. Before he becomes rain, the dancer must be wind (or "Wind Boy," emphasizing his youthfulness) [Bierhorst's note].

Addressing the thunderbird of pollen, the patient recites after the chanter, line by line:[1]

In Tsegíhi,[2]                                                                    10
In the house made of the dawn,
In the house made of the evening twilight,
In the house made of the dark cloud,
In the house made of the he-rain,
In the house made of the dark mist,                                15
In the house made of the she-rain,
In the house made of pollen,
In the house made of grasshoppers,
Where the dark mist curtains the doorway,
The path to which is on the rainbow,                              20
Where the zigzag lightning stands high on top,
Where the he-rain stands high on top,
Oh, male divinity!
With your moccasins of dark cloud, come to us.
With your leggings of dark cloud, come to us.                25
With your shirt of dark cloud, come to us.
With your headdress of dark cloud, come to us.
With your mind enveloped in dark cloud, come to us.
With the dark thunder above you, come to us soaring.
With the shapen cloud at your feet, come to us soaring.    30
With the far darkness made of the dark cloud over your
    head, come to us soaring.
With the far darkness made of the he-rain over your
    head, come to us soaring.
With the far darkness made of the dark mist over your
    head, come to us soaring.
With the far darkness made of the she-rain over your
    head, come to us soaring.
With the zigzag lightning flung out on high over your
    head, come to us soaring.                                          35
With the rainbow hanging high over your head, come
    to us soaring.
With the far darkness made of the dark cloud on the
    ends of your wings, come to us soaring.
With the far darkness made of the he-rain on the ends
    of your wings, come to us soaring.
With the far darkness made of the dark mist on the
    ends of your wings, come to us soaring.
With the far darkness made of the she-rain on the ends
    of your wings, come to us soaring.                             40
With the zigzag lightning flung out on high on the ends
    of your wings, come to us soaring.
With the rainbow hanging high on the ends of your
    wings, come to us soaring.

1. In the great prayer that follows, the Night Chant reaches its climax; the prayer for rain is the prayer for salvation [Bierhorst's note].
2. Tsegíhi is a distant canyon, site of the shrine known as House Made of Dawn (cf. N. Scott Momaday's novel of that name), considered to be the dwelling place of the sun on earth.

With the near darkness made of the dark cloud, of the
    he-rain, of the dark mist, and of the she-rain, come
    to us.
With the darkness on the earth, come to us.
With these I wish the foam floating on the flowing
    water over the roots of the great corn.          45
I have made your sacrifice.
I have prepared a smoke for you.
My feet restore for me.
My limbs restore for me.
My body restore for me.          50
My mind restore for me.
My voice restore for me.
Today, take out your spell for me.
Today, take away your spell for me.
Away from me you have taken it.          55
Far off from me it is taken.
Far off you have done it.
Happily I recover.
Happily my interior becomes cool.
Happily my eyes regain their power.          60
Happily my head becomes cool.
Happily my limbs regain their power.
Happily I hear again.
Happily for me *the spell* is taken off.
Happily may I walk.          65
Impervious to pain, may I walk.
Feeling light within, may I walk.
With lively feelings, may I walk.
Happily abundant dark clouds I desire.
Happily abundant dark mists I desire.          70
Happily abundant passing showers I desire.
Happily an abundance of vegetation I desire.
Happily an abundance of pollen I desire.
Happily abundant dew I desire.
Happily may fair white corn, to the ends of the earth,
    come with you.          75
Happily may fair yellow corn, to the end of the earth,
    come with you.
Happily may fair blue corn, to the ends of the earth,
    come with you.
Happily may fair corn of all kinds, to the ends of the
    earth, come with you.
Happily may fair plants of all kinds, to the ends of the
    earth, come with you.
Happily may fair goods of all kinds, to the ends of the
    earth, come with you.          80
Happily may fair jewels of all kinds, to the ends of the
    earth, come with you.
With these before you, happily may they come with you.
With these behind you, happily may they come with you.
With these below you, happily may they come with you.
With these above you, happily may they come with you.          85

With these all around you, happily may they come with you.
Thus happily you accomplish your tasks.
Happily the old men will regard you.
Happily the old women will regard you.
Happily the young men will regard you.                                    90
Happily the young women will regard you.
Happily the boys will regard you.
Happily the girls will regard you.
Happily the children will regard you.
Happily the chiefs will regard you.                                       95
Happily, as they scatter in different directions, they will
     regard you.
Happily, as they approach their homes, they will regard you.
Happily may their roads home be on the trail of pollen.
Happily may they all get back.
In beauty I walk.                                                        100
With beauty before me, I walk.
With beauty behind me, I walk.
With beauty below me, I walk.
With beauty above me, I walk.
With beauty all around me, I walk.                                      105
It is finished in beauty,
It is finished in beauty,
It is finished in beauty,
It is finished in beauty.

\*  \*  \*

The grand ceremonial concludes: The basket [used as a drum] is turned up
and the drumstick (of twisted yucca leaves) taken outside by an assistant, who
pulls it apart, sprinkling pollen on the shreds, repeating in a low voice the
benediction:

> Thus will it be beautiful,
> Thus walk in beauty, my grandchild.

The patient, facing east, inhales the breath of dawn.[3]

3. The description of the patient's gesture as the very last action of the Night Chant, Bierhorst notes, is *not* from Matthews, who probably never witnessed it in the late-19th- and early-20th- century performances he attended. Later writers note the patient's inhalation of the breath of dawn as typical of the Night Chant's conclusion.

# CHIPPEWA SONGS

The Chippewa, one of the largest Indian groups in North America, are also known as
the Ojibwe or, in their own Algonquian language, the Anishinabe. Their territories once
ranged along the shores of Lake Huron and Lake Superior, across Minnesota, and west
to the Turtle Mountains of North Dakota. In summer Chippewa bands gathered into
villages where they fished, planted small gardens, and collected wild foods. In fall
Chippewas living on the lakes cultivated large wild rice fields, paddling the lakes in
their canoes and harvesting the rice by striking the plants with a stick. In winter, bands
moved to their hunting grounds in pursuit of deer, moose, bear, and small animals,

like rabbits, otter, and beaver. The most important ceremonial organization of the Woodlands Chippewa was the Mide'wiwin, or Medicine Lodge Society, whose central ritual, the Medicine Dance, like the Navajo Night Chant, lasted several days and was predominantly a curing ceremony.

Frances Densmore (1867–1957) was born in Chippewa country, in the small town of Red Wing, Minnesota. At an early age, she became interested in a wide range of American Indian music, eventually devoting her life to its study and publishing on Chippewa, Teton Sioux, Mandan, Northern Ute, Papago, Yaqui, Nootka, Quileute, and Seminole music. Deeply interested in the importance of the Mide'wiwin to the Chippewa, Densmore published in 1910 an elaborate account of the Mide', or Medicine Society songs, and in 1913 issued the second part of her study of Chippewa music. The songs printed here were collected by Densmore between 1907 and 1909 on the White Earth, Leech Lake, and Red Lake reservations, all west of Lake Superior in Minnesota.

"Every phase of Chippewa life," Densmore wrote, "is expressed in music." Many Chippewa songs offer an individual yet culturally patterned response to the concerns of Chippewa life—love, war, a change in the weather, and the like; these songs often pass, with great interest and respect, from reservation to reservation. Traditionally, the songs were said to be "given" in dreams by some spirit power or animal. Singers frequently prefaced their performances with short speeches announcing the origin of the song and its relation to other songs. The usual accompaniment for Mide' and other medicine songs was the drum and rattle; love songs would often include the music of a flute. As will be apparent, Chippewa songs are quite short, with few words and brief melodies. But phrases could be repeated many times, with the drum sometimes continuing during the pauses in between the sets of repetitions. In the "Love-Charm Song" of the Mide'wiwin sung by Na'waji'bigo'kwe, printed here, the first word, translated as "What are you saying to me?" is repeated seven times before the second word, translated as "I am arrayed like the roses," is sung. The third word, translated as "And beautiful as they," does not conclude the song, as the translation seems to suggest, because another five repetitions of the first word follow.

These songs may be read simply as poems; indeed, the contemporary Chippewa writer Gerald Vizenor has compared them to Japanese haiku. Nonetheless, because the Chippewa songs were meant to be sung, we have in two cases included the music. Also included here are the Chippewa language texts as transcribed by Densmore.

## Song of the Crows[1]

*Sung by Henry Selkirk*

Be'bani'gani'
Nin'digog'
Binĕsiwûg'
Nin'wĕndjigi'miwûñ'
Andeg'nindigo'

### TRANSLATION

The first to come
I am called
Among the birds
I bring the rain
Crow is my name

---

1. From *Chippewa Music* (1910). Densmore notes that crows are said to have given this song to a young man who was fasting. The crow then became his *manido*, or spirit power. As crows are the first birds to return to the Chippewa lands in spring, they are thought to bring the welcome spring rains.

# My Love Has Departed[2]

*Sung by Mrs. Mary English*

VOICE ♩ = 132; RECORDED WITHOUT DRUM

Man-go-dûg-win nǐn-dǐ-nĕn-dûm mang-go-dûg-win nǐn-di-nĕn-dûm,

mi-gwe-na-wǐn nǐn-ǐ-mu-ce ĕ-ni-wa-wa-sa-bo-ye-zud.

Ba-wi-tǐñ gi-nǐ-madja nǐn-ǐ-mu-ce a-ni-madja

ka-wǐn-i-na-wa nǐn-da-wa-ba-ma-si *Si* Man-go-dûg-win

nǐn-dǐ-nĕn-dum man-go-dûg-win nǐn-dǐ-nĕn-dum,

mi-gwe-na-wǐn ka-wǐn-i-mu-ce, ĕ-ni-wa-wa-sa-bo-ye-zud.

## TRANSLATION

### I

A loon
I thought it was
But it was
My love's
Splashing oar

### 2

To Sault Ste. Marie[3]
He has departed
My love
Has gone on before me
Never again
Can I see him

2. From *Chippewa Music* (1910). Densmore notes that the song recalls a time when the city of Duluth, Minnesota, at the western end of Lake Superior, was a camping ground for the Chippewa.
3. Sault Ste. Marie marks the eastern end of Lake Superior.

# Love-Charm Song[4]

*Sung by Na'waji'bigo'kwe*

VOICE ♩ = 88; RECORDED WITHOUT DRUM

A - ni - na - ji - a - ne a - ni - na - ji - a - ne

a - ni - na - ji - a - ne a - ni - na - ji - a - ne

a - ni - na - ji - a - ne a - ni - na - ji - a - ne

a - ni - na - ji - a - ne o - gĭ - ni - ba - uñ e

a - ji - na - go - o - yăn a - ni - na - ji - a - ne

a - ni - na - ji - a - ne a - ni - na - ji - a - ne

a - ni - na - ji - a - ne a - ni - na - ji - a - ne

**TRANSLATION**

What are you saying to me?
I am arrayed like the roses
And beautiful as they

---

4. From *Chippewa Music* (1910) by Frances Densmore. Densmore notes that love-charm songs were considered very powerful.

# The Approach of the Storm[5]

*Sung by Ga'Gandac'*

Abitû'
Gicĭguñ'
Ebigwĕn'
Kabide'bwewiduñ'

### TRANSLATION

From the half of the sky
That which lives there
Is coming, and makes a noise

# The Sioux Women Gather Up Their Wounded[6]

*Sung by Odjib'we*

Oma'mikweg'
Paba'made'mowûg'
Ona'djida'bamawûn'
O'dinini'miwûn
Ani'mûde'mûwug'

### TRANSLATION

The Sioux women
Pass to and fro wailing
As they gather up
Their wounded men
The voice of their weeping comes back to us

# The Sioux Woman Defends Her Children[7]

*Sung by Odjib'we*

Neta'gica'wasosig'
Wape'toñ
Biäpi'sika'dug
Go'cawin'
Bigica'wasud'

---

5. From *Chippewa Music* (1910). The thunder, understood as a *manido*, or spirit, of the storm, makes its noise to warn people that severe weather is on the way. Upon hearing thunder, the Chippewas would put tobacco on the fire, offering the smoke to the *manido*, in gratitude for the warning [adapted from Densmore's note].
6. From *Chippewa Music—II* (1913) by Frances Densmore. The Sioux were traditional enemies of the Chippewas, and there are many war songs relating to engagements with the Sioux.
7. From *Chippewa Music—II* (1913). Densmore notes that "the following two songs were composed about a war expedition which occurred when Odjib'we [the singer] was a young man."

TRANSLATION

Once careless of her children[8]
She of the Wapeton Sioux
Now comes in haste
Surely
To their defense

## Song of the Captive Sioux Woman[9]

*Sung by Odjib'we*

Kaka'tawû[1]
Waya'bamagin'
Nin'gaödji'ma
Kegĕt'
Nin'jawe'nimĭg'

TRANSLATION

Any Chippewa
Whenever I see
I will greet with a kiss
Truly
He pities me

8. This may reflect Chippewa views of Sioux child care in general.
9. From *Chippewa Music—II* (1913). The woman referred to here was taken captive in a battle and was to be shot. First, she was given the opportunity to sing. The song she sang there is not known, but as Densmore notes, "It moved the elder brother of Odjib'we so strongly that he rushed forward and rescued her." Later, the captive woman thanked the warriors for sparing her and sang this song.
1. The Sioux word for "Chippewa."

---

# NATIVE AMERICAN ORATORY

American Indian oratory marked significant occasions in the calendrical and ceremonial year and responded to notable events in daily life. Speeches might be given to greet a victorious war party or, as in the case of some Hopi chants, addressed to the people of the village to mobilize participation in a house-building project. Today, traditional rhetorical practices continue to govern formal speeches given, for example, to dedicate a new local fish hatchery or gaming casino or to bless a museum exhibit of Indian art and craftswork.

We do know that Chief Seatthl's celebrated speech, delivered in the 1850s and first published in English in 1887, in the form in which it usually appears today, derives from a version composed by the poet William Arrowsmith in the 1960s and substantially revised by Professor Ted Perry in the 1970s! Whatever speech Seatthl may have delivered, it is certainly not the one widely reprinted. The English-language texts of the speeches of Cochise and Charlot given here have considerably better claim actually to represent what these men said on these occasions, but there is no way to know for sure. The best we can do for Native American oratory from the ages before the tape recorder is to note both the circumstances under which the speech was delivered and the circumstances by which it was translated and brought to the printed page.

# COCHISE

## ca. 1812–1874

The man we know as Cochise was a leader of the Chiricahua Apaches, one of the four main Apache groups. (The others are the Mescalero, the Lipan, and the Jicarilla.) The Apaches, who frequently were raiders of sheep, cattle, and horses, became the concern of the Americans when, after the end of the Mexican war in 1848, they took control of their homelands in Arizona and New Mexico. As the ever-advancing whites increasingly moved into Apache territory, a series of "wars" between the settlers and the various Apache groups broke out around 1860 and did not end until the capture in 1886 of the great Chiricahua leader Geronimo.

In 1871, Colonel George Crook, an experienced Indian fighter, was given command of the U.S. Army in Arizona. Employing a number of Native scouts, Crook tracked Cochise and persuaded him to negotiate a peace settlement. But when Cochise learned that his people were to be placed on a harsh reservation at Fort Tularosa, New Mexico, he renounced the agreement. President Grant then sent General O. O. Howard, another experienced Indian fighter, as his envoy to the Apaches. With the aid of Thomas Jeffords (or Jefferds), a former captain of the California volunteer cavalry who had established a friendship with Cochise, Howard arranged a meeting between Cochise and General Gordon Granger, commander of the district of New Mexico. After eleven days of negotiations, it was agreed that Cochise and his people might live on a reservation along Apache Pass, in southeastern Arizona, where Jeffords would serve as Indian agent.

It was during these negotiations that Cochise made a speech to the Americans that has since been anthologized (though incorrectly dated) in three important collections of Native American oratory. One of these accounts, all of which are based on A. N. Ellis's *Recollections of an Interview with Cochise* (1913), mentions another account, "presumably of the same occasion, by Henry Stuart Turrill," a retired brigadier general of the U.S. Army, who, as a young soldier, was present at the parley between Cochise, Granger, and Jeffords.

In an extraordinary talk called "A Vanished Race of Aboriginal Founders," delivered on February 14, 1907, to the New York Society of the Founders and Patriots of America, Turrill gives the history of the Apaches and the Southwest and calls Cochise "the strongest Indian I had ever seen"—no small praise inasmuch as Turrill had encountered the eminent Lakota warriors Red Cloud, Spotted Tail, and Gall, and the illustrious Chief Joseph of the Nez Perce. Much as he admired these men, said Turrill, "I do not hesitate in naming Cochise as the greatest Indian that I have ever met."

While he admits that he can do no more than attempt to recreate Cochise's speech "after a lapse of thirty-five years," Turrill offers the account of a witness aware of the complexity of the communication he was hearing. Cochise, according to Turrill, began in Apache and then shifted to Spanish, in which he was quite fluent. While the A. N. Ellis version conventionally anthologized is more "poetic" than Turrill's, Turrill conveys more sharply the historical and political basis of Cochise's bargain with "your great father in Washington."

## [I am alone][1]

This for a very long time has been the home of my people; they came from the darkness, few in numbers and feeble. The country was held by a much

---

1. From Brigadier General Henry Stuart Turrill, "A Vanished Race of Aboriginal Founders," address delivered before the New York Society of the Order of the Founders and Patriots of America (1907).

stronger and more numerous people, and from their stone houses[2] we were quickly driven. We were a hunting people, living on the animals that we could kill. We came to these mountains about us; no one lived here, and so we took them for our home and country. Here we grew from the first feeble band to be a great people, and covered the whole country as the clouds cover the mountains. Many people came to our country. First the Spanish, with their horses and their iron shirts, their long knives[3] and guns, great wonders to my simple people. We fought some, but they never tried to drive us from our homes in these mountains. After many years the Spanish soldiers were driven away and the Mexican ruled the land. With these little wars came many, but we were now a strong people and we did not fear them. At last in my youth came the white man, your people. Under the counsels of my grandfather, who had for a very long time been the head of the Apaches, they were received with friendship. Soon their numbers increased and many passed through my country to the great waters of the setting sun.[4] Your soldiers came and their strong houses were all through my country.[5] I received favors from your people and did all that I could in return and we lived at peace. At last your soldiers did me a very great wrong, and I and my whole people went to war with them. At first we were successful and your soldiers were driven away and your people killed and we again possessed our land. Soon many soldiers came from the north and from the west, and my people were driven to the mountain hiding places; but these did not protect us, and soon my people were flying from one mountain to another, driven by the soldiers, even as the wind is now driving the clouds. I have fought long and as best I could against you. I have destroyed many of your people, but where I have destroyed one white man many have come in his place; but where an Indian has been killed, there has been none to come in his place, so that the great people that welcomed you with acts of kindness to this land are now but a feeble band that fly before your soldiers as the deer before the hunter, and must all perish if this war continues. I have come to you, not from any love for you or for your great father in Washington, or from any regard for his or your wishes, but as a conquered chief, to try to save alive the few people that still remain to me. I am the last of my family, a family that for very many years have been the leaders of this people, and on me depends their future, whether they shall utterly vanish from the land or that a small remnant remain for a few years to see the sun rise over these mountains, their home. I here pledge my word, a word that has never been broken, that if your great father will set aside a part of my own country, where I and my little band can live, we will remain at peace with your people forever. If from his abundance he will give food for my women and children, whose protectors his soldiers have killed, with blankets to cover their nakedness, I will receive them with gratitude. If not, I will do my best to feed and clothe them, in peace with the white man. I have spoken.

1907                                                                                          1872

---

2. In keeping with the early-20th-century belief that the most substantial archaeological ruins of the Southwest were remnants of the Aztec civilization, Turrill believed the people of the stone houses were Aztecs.

3. I.e., swords. The horse was introduced in the Americas by the Spaniards. "Iron shirts": the breast armor of the Spanish.

4. I.e., the Pacific Ocean. Cochise is referring to the westward migration in the wake of the discovery of gold in California in 1848.

5. The military forts established throughout the Southwest.

# CHARLOT

## ca. 1831–1900

Slemhakkah, or Bear Claw, known as Charlot, succeeded his father as a principal chief of the Kalispel band of the Flathead Indians, whose traditional homelands were in present-day Idaho, northwest Montana, and northeast Washington.

In 1855, Charlot's father signed a treaty with the federal government ceding a large portion of Flathead land on the condition that the Bitterroot Valley in western Montana be the site of his people's reservation. The government, however, assigned them land elsewhere. Some Flathead people agreed to settle on the Kalispel and Colville reservations in Washington and the Jocko reservation in Montana. Charlot refused to go and continued to live with his people in the Bitterroot region. In 1872, under government pressure, some of the Bitterroot Kalispels moved to the Jocko reservation, but Charlot continued to resist nonviolently. Charlot held out peacefully against the whites until 1890, when troops were sent in to force the last of his band onto the Jocko reservation, where Charlot died ten years later.

In 1876, it was proposed that reservation Indians in Montana be required to pay taxes. Charlot spoke to this issue, and his speech, a strong condemnation of the white people's greed, was reported in the *Missoula* (Montana) *Missoulian*. The text below is the entirety of Charlot's speech (translated, with what accuracy it is not possible to say, from the Salish language) as reported under the headline "Indian Taxation, Recent Speech of a Flathead Chief Presenting the Question from an Indian Standpoint." That this powerful critique of the white people's ways found its way into print on the western frontier in the year of the centennial celebration of American independence (and two months short of the defeat of Custer on the Little Bighorn) is in itself extraordinary.

## [He has filled graves with our bones][1]

Yes, my people, the white man wants us to pay him. He comes in his intent, and says we must pay him—pay him for our own—for the things we have from our God and our forefathers; for things he never owned, and never gave us. What law or right is that? What shame or what charity? The Indian says that a woman is more shameless than a man;[2] but the white man has less shame than our women. Since our forefathers first beheld him, more than seven times ten winters have snowed and melted. Most of them like those snows have dissolved away. Their spirits went whither they came; his, they say, go there too. Do they meet and see us here[?] Can he blush before his Maker, or is he forever dead[?] Is his prayer his promise—a trust of the wind? Is it a sound without sense? Is it a thing whose life is a foul thing? And is he not foul? He has filled graves with our bones. His horses, his cattle, his sheep, his men, his women have a rot. Does not his breath, his gums, stink? His jaws lose their teeth, and he stamps them with false ones; yet he is not ashamed. No, no; his course is destruction; he spoils what the Spirit who gave us this country made beautiful and clean. But that is not enough; he wants us to pay

---

1. From the *Missoula* (Montana) *Missoulian* (1876).
2. A statement fairly typical of male-centered cul-

tures, Indian and non-Indian, vaguely parallel to such Western proverbial wisdom as "Vanity thy name is woman."

him besides his enslaving our country. Yes, and our people, besides, that degradation of a tribe who never were his enemies. What is he? Who sent him here? We were happy when he first came; since then we often saw him, always heard him and of him. We first thought he came from the light;[3] but he comes like the dusk of the evening now, not like the dawn of the morning. He comes like a day that has passed, and night enters our future with him.

To take and to lie should be burnt on his forehead, as he burns the sides of my stolen horses with his own name. Had Heaven's Chief burnt him with some mark[4] to refuse him, we might have refused him[.] No; we did not refuse him in his weakness; in his poverty we fed, we cherished him—yes, befriended him, and showed [him] the fords and defiles of our lands. Yet we did think his face was concealed with hair, and that he often smiled like a rabbit in his own beard. A long-tailed, skulking thing, fond of flat lands, and soft grass and woods.

Did he not feast us with our own cattle, on our own land, yes, on our own plain by the cold spring? Did he not invite our hands to his papers;[5] did he not promise before the sun, and before the eye that put fire in it,[6] and to the name of both, and in the name of his own Chief,[7] promise us what he promised— to give us what he has not given; to do what he knew he would never do. Now, because he lied, and because he yet lies, without friendship, manhood, justice, or charity, he wants us to give him money—pay him more. When shall he be satisfied? A roving skulk,[8] first; a natural liar, next; and, withal, a murderer, a tyrant.

To confirm his purpose; to make the trees and stones and his own people hear him, he whispers soldiers, lock houses and iron chains.[9] My people, we are poor; we are fatherless. The white man fathers this doom—yes, this curse on us and on the few that may yet see a few days more. He, the cause of our ruin, is his own snake, which he says stole on his mother in her own country to lie to her.[1] He says his story is that man was rejected and cast off. Why did we not reject him forever? He says one of his virgins had a son nailed to death on two cross sticks to save him. Were all of them dead then when that young man died, we would be all safe now and our country our own.

But he lives to persist; yes, the rascal is also an unsatisfied beggar, and his hangman and swine[2] follow his walk. Pay him money! Did he inquire, how? No, no; his meanness ropes his charity, his avarice wives[3] his envy, his race breeds to extort. Did he speak at all like a friend? He saw a few horses and some cows, and many tens of rails,[4] with the few of us that own them. His

---

3. I.e., from the east, where the sun rises.
4. References both to the Euro-American practice of branding horses and cattle and, perhaps, to Cain, who bore a mark that would identify him as a murderer (of his brother Abel).
5. Ask that the Flatheads make their mark on treaties.
6. Possibly a reference to the God of Genesis, who created the sun.
7. Probably the president of the United States, the "chief" of the whites.
8. One who "skulked" about Indian lands. In violation of treaties, settlers encroached on Indian lands, and when the Native Americans retaliated, the state and / or federal government usually inter-

vened to protect the settlers who were violating laws negotiated and passed by that same government.
9. I.e., the white people threaten by hinting at the intervention of soldiers and at imprisonment in chains.
1. Reference to the story of Eve's temptation in the Garden of Eden.
2. Pig farming, a practice introduced by the Euro-Americans, was apparently as strange and repugnant to some American Indians as death by hanging, also introduced by Euro-Americans.
3. I.e., is married to. "Ropes": constrains.
4. Fence rails.

envy thereon baited to the quick. Why thus? Because he himself says he is in a big debt, and wants us to help him pay it. His avarice put him in debt, and he wants us to pay him for it and be his fools. Did he ask how many a helpless widow, how many a fatherless child, how many a blind and naked thing fare a little of that little we have[?] Did he—in a destroying night when the mountains and the firmaments [*sic*] put their faces together to freeze us—did he inquire if we had a spare rag of a blanket to save his lost and perishing steps to our fires? No, no; cold he is, you know, and merciless. Four times in one shivering night I last winter knew the old one-eyed Indian, Keneth [*sic*], that gray man of full seven tens of winters, was refused shelter in four of the white man's houses on his way in that bad night; yet the aged, blinded man was turned out to his fate. No, no; he is cold and merciless, haughty and overbearing. Look at him, and he looks at you—how? His fishy eye scans you as the why-oops[5] do the shelled blue cock. He is cold, and stealth and envy are with him, and fit him as do his hands and feet. We owe him nothing; he owes us more than he will pay, yet says there is a God.

I know another aged Indian, with his only daughter and wife alone in their lodge. He had a few beaver skins and four or five poor horses—all he had. The light [? print unclear] was bad, and held every stream in thick ice; the earth was white; the stars burned nearer us as if to pity us, but the more they burned the more stood the hair of the deer on end with cold, nor heeded they the frost-bursting barks of the willows. Two of the white man's people came to the lodge, lost and freezing pitifully. They fared well inside that lodge. The old wife and only daughter unbound and put [? print unclear] off their frozen shoes; gave them new ones, and crushed sage bark rind to put therein to keep their feet smooth and warm. She gave them warm soup; boiled deer meat, and boiled beaver. They were saved; their safety returned to make them live. After a while they would not stop; they would go. They went away. Mind you; remember well: at midnight they returned. [M]urdered the old father, and his daughter and her mother asleep, took the beaver skins and horses, and left. Next day, the first and only Indian they met, a fine young man, they killed, put his body under the ice and rode away on his horse.

Yet, they say we are not good. Will he tell his own crimes? No, no; his crimes to us are left untold. But the Desolator bawls and cries the dangers of the country from us, the few left of us. Other tribes kill and ravish his women and stake his children, and eat his steers, and he gives them blankets and sugar for it. We, the poor Flatheads, who never troubled him, he wants now to distress and make poorer.

I have more to say, my people; but this much I have said, and chose [close?] to hear your minds about this payment. We never begot laws or rights to ask it. His laws never gave us a blade nor a tree, nor a duck; nor a grouse, nor a trout. No; like the wolverine that steals your *cache,* how often does he come: You know he comes as long as he lives, and takes more and more, and dirties what he leaves.

1876

---

5. Unidentified, but probably a Salish word for an animal that preys on the blue cock.

# HENRY JAMES
## 1843–1916

As a young man Henry James set out to be a "literary master" in the European sense. Even though the highly cultivated characters in his fiction ran counter to the vernacular tradition popularized by Mark Twain, James attracted, in his own lifetime, a select company of admirers and made a good living from his writings. His writings, the product of more than half a century as a publishing author, include tales, novellas, novels, plays, autobiographies, criticism, travel pieces, letters, reviews, and biographies—altogether perhaps as many as one hundred volumes, a prodigious output even by late-nineteenth-century standards. The recognition of his importance as well as his wide influence as novelist and critic increased in the years between the world wars, when American literary taste reached a new level of sophistication. Since that time James has been firmly established as one of America's greatest novelists and critics, a subtle psychological realist and an unsurpassed literary stylist and craftsman.

Henry James was born in New York City on April 15, 1843. His father was an eccentric, independently wealthy philosopher and religious visionary; his mother, Mary Robertson Walsh James, had enormous influence on her children—James once said of her, "She was our life, she was the house, she was the keystone of the arch." His slightly older brother, William, was America's first notable psychologist and perhaps its most influential philosopher. There were also two younger brothers and a sister, Alice, herself a perceptive observer and diarist, to complete this remarkable American family. First taken to Europe as an infant, James spent his boyhood in a then almost bucolic Washington Square in New York City before the family once again left for the Continent when he was twelve. His father wanted the children to have a rich, "sensuous education," and during the next four years, with stays in England, Switzerland, and France, they were taken to galleries, libraries, museums, and (of special interest to Henry) theaters. Henry's formal schooling was unsystematic, but he mastered French well enough to begin a lifelong study of its literature, and from childhood on he was aware of the intricate network of institutions and traditions in Europe that he later lamented (in *Hawthorne* [1879], his first book and the first book-length critical study of an American author) American novelists had to do without. Two of his earliest memories were of the Place Vendome in Paris, with its huge monument to Napoleonic grandeur, and the Louvre's Galerie d'Apollon.

James early developed what he described in *A Small Boy and Others* (1913) as the "practice of wondering and dawdling and gaping." This memoir also tells about an "obscure hurt" to his back that, disqualifying him from service in the Civil War, must have reinforced his inclination to observe rather than participate. In his later teens, his interest in literature and in writing intensified, and by the time he was twenty-one he was publishing reviews and stories in some of the leading American journals—*Atlantic Monthly, North American Review, Galaxy,* and *Nation*. He settled permanently in England in 1876 (after much shuttling back and forth between America and Europe and after trial residences in France and Italy). James never married. He maintained close ties with his family, including William's children. He kept up a large correspondence, was extremely sociable, and knew most of his great contemporaries in the arts, many intimately. Still, James lived and worked alone. His emotional life and prodigious creative energy were invested for more than fifty years in what he called the "sacred rage" of his art.

Leon Edel, James's biographer, divides the writer's mature career into three parts. In the first, which culminated with *The Portrait of a Lady* (1881), he felt his way toward and appropriated the so-called international theme—the drama, comic and tragic, of Americans in Europe and occasionally of Europeans in America. In the tripartite second period, he experimented with diverse themes and forms—initially in novels dealing explicitly with the social and political currents of the 1870s and 1880s, then in writing for the theater, and finally in shorter fictions exploring the relationship of artists to society and the troubled psyches of oppressed children, as in *What Maisie Knew* (1908), and haunted or obsessed adults, as in "The Beast in the Jungle" (1903, 1909). Surprisingly, James the bachelor wrote some of the finest characterizations of the child or adolescent mind in American literature. In his last period, the so-called major phase, which culminated with *The Golden Bowl* (1904), he returned to international and cosmopolitan subjects in elaborately complex narratives of great epistemological and moral challenge to readers.

Three of his earliest books, *A Passionate Pilgrim* (stories), *Transatlantic Sketches* (travel pieces), and *Roderick Hudson* (a novel), were published in 1875. *The American* (1877) was his first successful extended treatment of the naïve young American in conflict with the traditions, customs, and values of the Old World. "Daisy Miller" (1878), with its portrayal of the "new" American girl, brought him widespread popularity. In this "study," as it was originally subtitled, a dangerously naïve American girl willfully resists European (and American) social mores. These works show James as neither a chauvinist for America nor a resentful émigré but a true cosmopolitan concerned with exploring American national character as it is tested by cultural displacement.

Despite their appeal, the relatively simple characters of Christopher Newman (*The American*) and Daisy Miller present romance, melodrama, and pathos more than psychological complexity and genuine tragedy, which required for James a broader canvas. In the character and career of Isabel Archer he found the focus for his first masterpiece of the international theme, *The Portrait of a Lady*. Here, the complex inner lives of his American characters are fully and realistically projected. Yet in "Daisy Miller" these complexities are already hinted at. In this work James's skillful use of the limited point of view, which seems to be largely from Winterbourne's perspective but actually is not, projects a character who is himself limited by self-absorption and class position and who is thus unable to see Daisy for who she is. This device, described by Percy Lubbock as the use of a "focal character" somewhere over the protagonist's left shoulder, became an increasingly important part of James's technique. In these early works James was already developing the hallmarks of his later greatness. He was also beginning to make problems of knowledge, whether characters' knowledge of each other or readers' struggles with deliberately limited information, the central problems of his texts.

From 1885 to 1890 James was largely occupied by writing three novels in the naturalistic mode—*The Bostonians* (1886), *The Princess Casamassima* (1886), and *The Tragic Muse* (1889). These stories of reformers, radicals, and revolutionaries are better appreciated, perhaps, in our time than they were in his. Out of a sense of artistic challenge as well as financial need, James attempted to regain the popularity of "Daisy Miller" and earn money by turning dramatist. Between 1890 and 1895 he wrote seven plays; two were produced, and both were painful public failures for their author, leading him into a period of intense self-doubt. Between 1895 and 1900 he returned to fiction, especially to experimental works with three dominant subjects, which he often combined: misunderstood or troubled writers and artists, ghosts and apparitions, and doomed or threatened children and adolescents. Emotionally close to home, "The Beast in the Jungle" projects the life of an egocentric man whose obsessive concern over the vague prospect of personal disaster destroys his chances for love and life in the present. James's biographers trace the guilt in this tale to the suicide of Constance Fenimore Woolson in 1894, which she may have resorted to partly out of unrequited (and entirely unrecognized) love for James.

Following his own advice to other novelists to "dramatize, dramatize, dramatize," James increasingly removed himself as controlling narrator; in T. S. Eliot's phrase, he became invisible in his work. The benefits of this heightened emphasis on showing rather than telling were compression or intensification and enhanced opportunity for ambiguity. The more the author withdrew—not telling what was said, not analyzing a character's responses—the more the reader was forced to enter the process of creating meaning. Though we are accustomed today to having our fiction thus "objectified," it is James who was largely responsible for the development of this narrative technique. The major works in which he developed such realism were his last three great novels, *The Wings of the Dove* (1902), *The Ambassadors* (1903), and *The Golden Bowl* (1904). All three return to the international theme, but with a new and remorseless insight into how people make their own realities through their perceptions, impressions, and inner motivations. American innocence, at this point, becomes only a willful refusal to see, while awareness of one's own character as well as others' provides the wisdom to escape the designs that lead to disaster—though disaster is rarely thwarted in time and we are usually left both with insight and with the knowledge that it has come "too late." James's remedy for unhappiness is sometimes more unhappiness, but more importantly the willingness to entertain diverse points of view on moral struggles. His treatment of such an extraordinarily complex theme allows him an unparalleled richness of syntax, sentence structure, metaphoric webs, symbols, characterization, point of view, and organizing rhythms. The world of these novels is the one James defined in "The Art of Fiction" (1884) as representing "the very atmosphere of the mind." These late dramas of perception are widely considered to be James's most influential contribution to the craft of fiction.

When James was not writing fiction, he often wrote about it—either his own or others'. He was, as he noted in a letter, "a critical, a *non-naif*, a questioning, worrying reader." If he was somewhat narrow in his reading—restricting himself chiefly to nineteenth-century fiction—he made his limited experience count for as much in criticism as it did in fiction. His inquiries into the achievement of other writers—preserved in such volumes as *French Poets and Novelists* (1878), *Partial Portraits* (1888), and *Notes on Novelists* (1914)—are remarkable for their breadth, balance, and acuteness. More broadly theoretical than his reviews or essays on individual writers, "The Art of Fiction" (an excerpt from which appears later in this volume, fairly represents James's central aesthetic conceptions. Calling attention to the unparalleled opportunities open to the artist of fiction and the beauty of the novel form, James also insists that "the deepest quality of a work of art will always be the quality of the mind of the producer" and that "no good novel will ever proceed from a superficial mind." James left no better record than this essay of his always twinned concerns over the moral and formal qualities of fiction, of the relationship between aesthetic and moral perception.

James was an extremely self-conscious writer, and his *Complete Notebooks,* edited and published in 1987 with an introduction by Leon Edel and Lyall Powers, reveal a subtle, intense mind in the act of discovering subjects, methods, and principles. The prefaces he wrote for Scribner's lavish twenty-four-volume New York Edition (1907–09) of his extensively revised novels and tales, gathered and published in 1934 with an introduction by R. P. Blackmur as *The Art of the Novel*, contain James's final analyses of the works he considered to best represent his achievement—not to mention the extensive revisions themselves. As the culmination of a lifetime of reflection on the craft of fiction, they provide extraordinary accounts of the origins and growth of his major writings and exquisite analyses of the fictional problems each work posed. These prefaces lent both vocabulary and example for the close textual analysis of prose fiction dominant in English departments following World War II.

During his 1904–05 visit to the United States, the first after nearly twenty years, James traveled extensively and lectured in his native land and in Canada. The chief result of this visit was *The American Scene* (1907). This "absolutely personal" book is a vivid account of the profound changes that occurred in America between the Civil War and World War I, the period James characterized as the "Age of the Mistake." His views of turn-of-the-century America seem quite inadequate, however, when he deals with race and immigration in prejudicial terms. The same richness of personal rumination is found in three other autobiographical reminiscences he wrote later in life: *A Small Boy and Others* (1913), *Notes of a Son and Brother* (1914), and the fragmentary and posthumously published *The Middle Years* (1917).

Henry James became a naturalized British subject out of impatience with America's reluctance to enter World War I. He had involved himself in war-relief work starting in 1915. In 1916, he was awarded the British Order of Merit. Despite their considerable difficulty, most of James's novels and tales have remained in print. The rich depth of his work—especially his incisive psychological renderings of *why* people do the things they do—has continued to attract literary scholars and critics, as well as millions of readers around the world.

# Daisy Miller: A Study[1]

## I

At the little town of Vevey, in Switzerland, there is a particularly comfortable hotel. There are, indeed, many hotels; for the entertainment of tourists is the business of the place, which, as many travelers will remember, is seated upon the edge of a remarkably blue lake[2]—a lake that it behoves every tourist to visit. The shore of the lake presents an unbroken array of establishments of this order, of every category, from the "grand hotel" of the newest fashion, with a chalk-white front, a hundred balconies, and a dozen flags flying from its roof, to the little Swiss *pension* of an elder day, with its name inscribed in German-looking lettering upon a pink or yellow wall, and an awkward summer-house in the angle of the garden. One of the hotels at Vevey, however, is famous, even classical, being distinguished from many of its upstart neighbors by an air both of luxury and of maturity. In this region, in the month of June, American travelers are extremely numerous; it may be said, indeed, that Vevey assumes at this period some of the characteristics of an American watering-place. There are sights and sounds which evoke a vision, an echo, of Newport and Saratoga.[3] There is a flitting hither and thither of "stylish" young girls, a rustling of muslin flounces, a rattle of dance-music in the morning hours, a sound of high-pitched voices at all times. You receive an impression of these things at the excellent inn of the "Trois Couronnes,"[4] and are transported in fancy to the Ocean House or to Congress Hall. But at the "Trois Couronnes," it must be added, there are other features that are much at variance with these suggestions: neat German waiters, who look like secretaries of legation; Russian princesses sitting in the garden; little Polish boys walking about, held by the hand, with their governors; a view of the snowy crest of the Dent du Midi and the picturesque towers of the Castle of Chillon.[5]

I hardly know whether it was the analogies or the differences that were uppermost in the mind of a young American, who, two or three years ago, sat in the garden of the "Trois Couronnes," looking about him, rather idly, at some of the graceful objects I have mentioned. It was a beautiful summer morning, and in whatever fashion the young American looked at things, they must have seemed to him charming. He had come from Geneva the day

1. First published in the *Cornhill Magazine* 37 (June–July 1878). The text reprinted here follows the first British book edition, published by Macmillan in 1879. Punctuation and spelling have been Americanized. The editor was Sir Leslie Stephen, Virginia Woolf's father and an editor willing to take on this then-scandalous story, vilified in America as slandering American womanhood. Of course, the "scandal," once the story was published at home, made for James's rapid fame.

2. Lac Léman, or Lake of Geneva.
3. Newport, Rhode Island, and Saratoga, New York, resort areas for the rich, where the Ocean House and Congress Hall (below) are located.
4. Three Crowns (French).
5. The romantic setting for Byron's poem "The Prisoner of Chillon" (1816). "Dent du Midi": the highest peak in the Dents du Midi, a mountain group in the Alps in southwest Switzerland.

before, by the little steamer, to see his aunt, who was staying at the hotel—Geneva having been for a long time his place of residence. But his aunt had a headache—his aunt had almost always a headache—and now she was shut up in her room, smelling camphor,[6] so that he was at liberty to wander about. He was some seven-and-twenty years of age; when his friends spoke of him, they usually said that he was at Geneva, "studying." When his enemies spoke of him they said—but, after all, he had no enemies; he was an extremely amiable fellow, and universally liked. What I should say is, simply, that when certain persons spoke of him they affirmed that the reason of his spending so much time at Geneva was that he was extremely devoted to a lady who lived there—a foreign lady—a person older than himself. Very few Americans—indeed I think none—had ever seen this lady, about whom there were some singular stories. But Winterbourne had an old attachment for the little metropolis of Calvinism;[7] he had been put to school there as a boy, and he had afterwards gone to college there—circumstances which had led to his forming a great many youthful friendships. Many of these he had kept, and they were a source of great satisfaction to him.

After knocking at his aunt's door and learning that she was indisposed, he had taken a walk about the town, and then he had come in to his breakfast. He had now finished his breakfast, but he was drinking a small cup of coffee, which had been served to him on a little table in the garden by one of the waiters who looked like an _attaché._[8] At last he finished his coffee and lit a cigarette. Presently a small boy came walking along the path—an urchin of nine or ten. The child, who was diminutive for his years, had an aged expression of countenance, a pale complexion, and sharp little features. He was dressed in knickerbockers, with red stockings, which displayed his poor little spindle-shanks; he also wore a brilliant red cravat. He carried in his hand a long alpenstock, the sharp point of which he thrust into everything that he approached—the flower-beds, the garden-benches, the trains of the ladies' dresses. In front of Winterbourne he paused, looking at him with a pair of bright, penetrating little eyes.

"Will you give me a lump of sugar?" he asked, in a sharp, hard little voice—a voice immature, and yet, somehow, not young.

Winterbourne glanced at the small table near him, on which his coffee-service rested, and saw that several morsels of sugar remained. "Yes, you may take one," he answered; "but I don't think sugar is good for little boys."

This little boy stepped forward and carefully selected three of the coveted fragments, two of which he buried in the pocket to his knickerbockers, depositing the other as promptly in another place. He poked his alpenstock, lance-fashion, into Winterbourne's bench, and tried to crack the lump of sugar with his teeth.

"Oh, blazes; it's har-r-d!" he exclaimed, pronouncing the adjective in a peculiar manner.

Winterbourne had immediately perceived that he might have the honor of claiming him as a fellow-countryman. "Take care you don't hurt your teeth," he said, paternally.

6. An aromatic substance from the bark and wood of the camphor laurel; made into oils and liniments, it was used as a light topical anesthetic and also administered in small amounts for minor heart symptoms and fatigue.
7. Geneva, where John Calvin (1509–1564) centered his Protestant regime.
8. I.e., like a member of the diplomatic corps.

"I haven't got any teeth to hurt. They have all come out. I have only got seven teeth. My mother counted them last night, and one came out right afterwards. She said she'd slap me if any more came out. I can't help it. It's this old Europe. It's the climate that makes them come out. In America they didn't come out. It's these hotels."

Winterbourne was much amused. "If you eat three lumps of sugar, your mother will certainly slap you," he said.

"She's got to give me some candy, then," rejoined his young interlocutor. "I can't get any candy here—any American candy. American candy's the best candy."

"And are American little boys the best little boys?" asked Winterbourne.

"I don't know. I'm an American boy," said the child.

"I see you are one of the best!" laughed Winterbourne.

"Are you an American man?" pursued this vivacious infant. And then, on Winterbourne's affirmative reply—"American men are the best," he declared.

His companion thanked him for the compliment; and the child, who had now got astride of his alpenstock, stood looking about him, while he attacked a second lump of sugar. Winterbourne wondered if he himself had been like this in his infancy, for he had been brought to Europe at about this age.

*Parallel to the man?*

"Here comes my sister!" cried the child, in a moment. "She's an American girl."

Winterbourne looked along the path and saw a beautiful young lady advancing. "American girls are the best girls," he said, cheerfully, to his young companion.

"My sister ain't the best!" the child declared. "She's always blowing at me."

"I imagine that is your fault, not hers," said Winterbourne. The young lady meanwhile had drawn near. She was dressed in white muslin, with a hundred frills and flounces, and knots of pale-colored ribbon. She was bare-headed; but she balanced in her hand a large parasol, with a deep border of embroidery; and she was strikingly, admirably pretty. "How pretty they are!" thought Winterbourne, straightening himself in his seat, as if he were prepared to rise.

The young lady paused in front of his bench, near the parapet of the garden, which overlooked the lake. The little boy had now converted his alpenstock into a vaulting-pole, by the aid of which he was springing about in the gravel, and kicking it up not a little.

"Randolph," said the young lady, "what *are* you doing?"

"I'm going up the Alps," replied Randolph. "This is the way!" And he gave another little jump, scattering the pebbles about Winterbourne's ears.

"That's the way they come down," said Winterbourne.

"He's an American man!" cried Randolph, in his little hard voice.

The young lady gave no heed to this announcement, but looked straight at her brother. "Well, I guess you had better be quiet," she simply observed.

It seemed to Winterbourne that he had been in a manner presented. He got up and stepped slowly towards the young girl, throwing away his cigarette. "This little boy and I have made acquaintance," he said, with great civility. In Geneva, as he had been perfectly aware, a young man was not at liberty to speak to a young unmarried lady except under certain rarely-occurring conditions; but here at Vevey, what conditions could be better than these?—a pretty American girl coming and standing in front of you in a garden. This pretty American girl, however, on hearing Winterbourne's observation, simply glanced at him;

she then turned her head and looked over the parapet, at the lake and the opposite mountains. He wondered whether he had gone too far; but he decided that he must advance farther, rather than retreat. While he was thinking of something else to say, the young lady turned to the little boy again.

"I should like to know where you got that pole," she said.

"I bought it!" responded Randolph.

"You don't mean to say you're going to take it to Italy!"

"Yes, I am going to take it to Italy!" the child declared.

The young girl glanced over the front of her dress, and smoothed out a knot or two of ribbon. Then she rested her eyes upon the prospect again. "Well, I guess you had better leave it somewhere," she said, after a moment.

"Are you going to Italy?" Winterbourne inquired, in a tone of great respect.

The young lady glanced at him again.

"Yes, sir," she replied. And she said nothing more.

"Are you—a—going over the Simplon?"[9] Winterbourne pursued, a little embarrassed.

"I don't know," she said, "I suppose it's some mountain. Randolph, what mountain are we going over?"

"Going where?" the child demanded.

"To Italy," Winterbourne explained.

"I don't know," said Randolph. "I don't want to go to Italy. I want to go to America."

"Oh, Italy is a beautiful place!" rejoined the young man.

"Can you get candy there?" Randolph loudly inquired.

"I hope not," said his sister. "I guess you have had enough candy, and mother thinks so too."

"I haven't had any for ever so long—for a hundred weeks!" cried the boy, still jumping about.

The young lady inspected her flounces and smoothed her ribbons again; and Winterbourne presently risked an observation upon the beauty of the view. He was ceasing to be embarrassed, for he had begun to perceive that she was not in the least embarrassed herself. There had not been the slightest alteration in her charming complexion; she was evidently neither offended nor fluttered. If she looked another way when he spoke to her, and seemed not particularly to hear him, this was simply her habit, her manner. Yet, as he talked a little more, and pointed out some of the objects of interest in the view, with which she appeared quite unacquainted, she gradually gave him more of the benefit of her glance; and then he saw that this glance was perfectly direct and unshrinking. It was not, however, what would have been called an immodest glance, for the young girl's eyes were singularly honest and fresh. They were wonderfully pretty eyes; and, indeed, Winterbourne had not seen for a long time anything prettier than his fair countrywoman's various features—her complexion, her nose, her ears, her teeth. He had a great relish for feminine beauty; he was addicted to observing and analyzing it; and as regards this young lady's face he made several observations. It was not at all insipid, but it was not exactly expressive; and though it was eminently delicate, Winterbourne mentally accused it—very forgivingly—of a want of fin-

9. A pass in the Alps between Switzerland and Italy.

ish. He thought it very possible that Master Randolph's sister was a coquette; he was sure she had a spirit of her own; but in her bright, sweet, superficial little visage there was no mockery, no irony. Before long it became obvious that she was much disposed towards conversation. She told him that they were going to Rome for the winter—she and her mother and Randolph. She asked him if he was a "real American"; she wouldn't have taken him for one; he seemed more like a German—this was said after a little hesitation, especially when he spoke. Winterbourne, laughing, answered that he had met Germans who spoke like Americans; but that he had not, so far as he remembered, met an American who spoke like a German. Then he asked her if she would not be more comfortable in sitting upon the bench which he had just quitted. She answered that she liked standing up and walking about; but she presently sat down. She told him she was from New York State—"if you know where that is." Winterbourne learned more about her by catching hold of her small, slippery brother and making him stand a few minutes by his side.

"Tell me your name, my boy," he said.

"Randolph C. Miller," said the boy, sharply. "And I'll tell you her name"; and he leveled his alpenstock at his sister.

"You had better wait till you are asked!" said this young lady, calmly.

"I should like very much to know your name," said Winterbourne.

"Her name is Daisy Miller!" cried the child. "But that isn't her real name; that isn't her name on her cards."

"It's a pity you haven't got one of my cards!" said Miss Miller.

"Her real name is Annie P. Miller," the boy went on.

"Ask him *his* name," said his sister, indicating Winterbourne.

But on this point Randolph seemed perfectly indifferent; he continued to supply information with regard to his own family. "My father's name is Ezra B. Miller," he announced. "My father ain't in Europe; my father's in a better place than Europe."

Winterbourne imagined for a moment that this was the manner in which the child had been taught to intimate that Mr. Miller had been removed to the sphere of celestial rewards. But Randolph immediately added, "My father's in Schenectady. He's got a big business. My father's rich, you bet."

"Well!" ejaculated Miss Miller, lowering her parasol and looking at the embroidered border. Winterbourne presently released the child, who departed, dragging his alpenstock along the path. "He doesn't like Europe," said the young girl. "He wants to go back."

"To Schenectady, you mean?"

"Yes; he wants to go right home. He hasn't got any boys here. There is one boy here, but he always goes round with a teacher; they won't let him play."

"And your brother hasn't any teacher?" Winterbourne inquired.

"Mother thought of getting him one, to travel round with us. There was a lady told her of a very good teacher; an American lady—perhaps you know her—Mrs. Sanders. I think she came from Boston. She told her of this teacher, and we thought of getting him to travel round with us. But Randolph said he didn't want a teacher traveling round with us. He said he wouldn't have lessons when he was in the cars.[1] And we *are* in the cars about half the time. There was an English lady we met in the cars—I think her name was

1. Railway cars.

Miss Featherstone; perhaps you know her. She wanted to know why I didn't give Randolph lessons—give him 'instruction,' she called it. I guess he could give me more instruction than I could give him. He's very smart."

"Yes," said Winterbourne; "he seems very smart."

"Mother's going to get a teacher for him as soon as we get to Italy. Can you get good teachers in Italy?"

"Very good, I should think," said Winterbourne.

"Or else she's going to find some school. He ought to learn some more. He's only nine. He's going to college." And in this way Miss Miller continued to converse upon the affairs of her family, and upon other topics. She sat there with her extremely pretty hands, ornamented with very brilliant rings, folded in her lap, and with her pretty eyes now resting upon those of Winterbourne, now wandering over the garden, the people who passed by, and the beautiful view. She talked to Winterbourne as if she had known him a long time. He found it very pleasant. It was many years since he heard a young girl talk so much. It might have been said of this unknown young lady, who had come and sat down beside him upon a bench, that she chattered. She was very quiet, she sat in a charming tranquil attitude; but her lips and her eyes were constantly moving. She had a soft, slender, agreeable voice, and her tone was decidedly sociable. She gave Winterbourne a history of her movements and intentions, and those of her mother and brother, in Europe, and enumerated, in particular, the various hotels at which they had stopped. "That English lady in the cars," she said—"Miss Featherstone—asked me if we didn't all live in hotels in America. I told her I had never been in so many hotels in my life as since I came to Europe. I have never seen so many—it's nothing but hotels." But Miss Miller did not make this remark with a querulous accent; she appeared to be in the best humor with everything. She declared that the hotels were very good, when once you got used to their ways, and that Europe was perfectly sweet. She was not disappointed—not a bit. Perhaps it was because she had heard so much about it before. She had ever so many intimate friends that had been there ever so many times. And then she had had ever so many dresses and things from Paris. Whenever she put on a Paris dress she felt as if she were in Europe.

"It was a kind of wishing-cap," said Winterbourne.

"Yes," said Miss Miller, without examining this analogy; "it always made me wish I was here. But I needn't have done that for dresses. I am sure they send all the pretty ones to America; you see the most frightful things here. The only thing I don't like," she proceeded, "is the society. There isn't any society; or, if there is, I don't know where it keeps itself. Do you? I suppose there is some society somewhere, but I haven't seen anything of it. I'm very fond of society, and I have always had a great deal of it. I don't mean only in Schenectady, but in New York. I used to go to New York every winter. In New York I had lots of society. Last winter I had seventeen dinners given me; and three of them were by gentlemen," added Daisy Miller. "I have more friends in New York than in Schenectady—more gentlemen friends; and more young lady friends too," she resumed in a moment. She paused again for an instant; she was looking at Winterbourne with all her prettiness in her lively eyes and in her light, slightly monotonous smile. "I have always had," she said, "a great deal of gentlemen's society."

*materialism?*

Poor Winterbourne was amused, perplexed, and decidedly charmed. He had never yet heard a young girl express herself in just this fashion; never, at least, save in cases where to say such things seemed a kind of demonstrative evidence of a certain laxity of deportment. And yet was he to accuse Miss Daisy Miller of actual or potential *inconduite*,[2] as they said at Geneva? He felt that he had lived at Geneva so long that he had lost a good deal; he had become dishabituated to the American tone. Never, indeed, since he had grown old enough to appreciate things, had he encountered a young American girl of so pronounced a type as this. Certainly she was very charming; but how deucedly sociable! Was she simply a pretty girl from New York State— were they all like that, the pretty girls who had a good deal of gentlemen's society? Or was she also a designing, an audacious, an unscrupulous young person? Winterbourne had lost his instinct in this matter, and his reason could not help him. Miss Daisy Miller looked extremely innocent. Some people had told him that, after all, American girls were exceedingly innocent; and others had told him that, after all, they were not. He was inclined to think Miss Daisy Miller was a flirt—a pretty American flirt. He had never, as yet, had any relations with young ladies of this category. He had known, here in Europe, two or three women—persons older than Miss Daisy Miller, and provided, for respectability's sake, with husbands—who were great coquettes— dangerous, terrible women, with whom one's relations were liable to take a serious turn. But this young girl was not a coquette in that sense; she was very unsophisticated; she was only a pretty American flirt. Winterbourne was almost grateful for having found the formula that applied to Miss Daisy Miller. He leaned back in his seat; he remarked to himself that she had the most charming nose he had ever seen; he wondered what were the regular conditions and limitations of one's intercourse with a pretty American flirt. It presently became apparent that he was on the way to learn.

"Have you been to that old castle?" asked the young girl, pointing with her parasol to the far-gleaming walls of the Château de Chillon.

"Yes, formerly, more than once," said Winterbourne. "You too, I suppose, have seen it?"

"No; we haven't been there. I want to go there dreadfully. Of course I mean to go there. I wouldn't go away from here without having seen that old castle."

"It's a very pretty excursion," said Winterbourne, "and very easy to make. You can drive, you know, or you can go by the little steamer."

"You can go in the cars," said Miss Miller.

"Yes; you can go in the cars," Winterbourne assented.

"Our courier[3] says they take you right up to the castle," the young girl continued. "We were going last week; but my mother gave out. She suffers dreadfully from dyspepsia. She said she couldn't go. Randolph wouldn't go either; he says he doesn't think much of old castles. But I guess we'll go this week, if we can get Randolph."

"Your brother is not interested in ancient monuments?" Winterbourne inquired, smiling.

2. Misconduct (French).    3. Social guide.

"He says he don't care much about old castles. He's only nine. He wants to stay at the hotel. Mother's afraid to leave him alone, and the courier won't stay with him; so we haven't been to many places. But it will be too bad if we don't go up there." And Miss Miller pointed again at the Château de Chillon.

"I should think it might be arranged," said Winterbourne. "Couldn't you get some one to stay—for the afternoon—with Randolph?"

Miss Miller looked at him a moment; and then, very placidly—"I wish *you* would stay with him!" she said.

Winterbourne hesitated a moment. "I would much rather go to Chillon with you."

"With me?" asked the young girl, with the same placidity.

She didn't rise, blushing, as a young girl at Geneva would have done; and yet Winterbourne, conscious that he had been very bold, thought it possible she was offended. "With your mother," he answered very respectfully.

But it seemed that both his audacity and his respect were lost upon Miss Daisy Miller. "I guess my mother won't go, after all," she said. "She don't like to ride round in the afternoon. But did you really mean what you said just now; that you would like to go up there?"

"Most earnestly," Winterbourne declared.

"Then we may arrange it. If mother will stay with Randolph, I guess Eugenio will."

"Eugenio?" the young man inquired.

"Eugenio's our courier. He doesn't like to stay with Randolph; he's the most fastidious man I ever saw. But he's a splendid courier. I guess he'll stay at home with Randolph if mother does, and then we can go to the castle."

Winterbourne reflected for an instant as lucidly as possible—"we" could only mean Miss Daisy Miller and himself. This programme seemed almost too agreeable for credence; he felt as if he ought to kiss the young lady's hand. Possibly he would have done so—and quite spoiled the project; but at this moment another person—presumably Eugenio—appeared. A tall, handsome man, with superb whiskers, wearing a velvet morning-coat and a brilliant watch-chain, approached Miss Miller, looking sharply at her companion. "Oh, Eugenio!" said Miss Miller, with the friendliest accent.

Eugenio had looked at Winterbourne from head to foot; he now bowed gravely to the young lady. "I have the honor to inform mademoiselle that luncheon is upon the table."

Miss Miller slowly rose. "See here, Eugenio," she said. "I'm going to that old castle, any way."

"To the Château de Chillon, mademoiselle?" the courier inquired. "Mademoiselle had made arrangements?" he added, in a tone which struck Winterbourne as very impertinent.

Eugenio's tone apparently threw, even to Miss Miller's own apprehension, a slightly ironical light upon the young girl's situation. She turned to Winterbourne, blushing a little—a very little. "You won't back out?" she said.

"I shall not be happy till we go!" he protested.

"And you are staying in this hotel?" she went on. "And you are really an American?"

The courier stood looking at Winterbourne, offensively. The young man, at least, thought his manner of looking an offence to Miss Miller; it conveyed an imputation that she "picked up" acquaintances. "I shall have the honor of presenting to you a person who will tell you all about me," he said smiling, and referring to his aunt.

"Oh well, we'll go some day," said Miss Miller. And she gave him a smile and turned away. She put up her parasol and walked back to the inn beside Eugenio. Winterbourne stood looking after her; and as she moved away, drawing her muslin furbelows over the gravel, said to himself that she had the *tournure*[4] of a princess.

## II

He had, however, engaged to do more than proved feasible, in promising to present his aunt, Mrs. Costello, to Miss Daisy Miller. As soon as the former lady had got better of her headache he waited upon her in her apartment; and, after the proper inquiries in regard to her health, he asked her if she had observed, in the hotel, an American family—a mamma, a daughter, and a little boy.

"And a courier?" said Mrs. Costello. "Oh, yes, I have observed them. Seen them—heard them—and kept out of their way." Mrs. Costello was a widow with a fortune; a person of much distinction, who frequently intimated that, if she were not so dreadfully liable to sick-headaches, she would probably have left a deeper impress upon her time. She had a long pale face, a high nose, and a great deal of very striking white hair, which she wore in large puffs and *rouleaux*[5] over the top of her head. She had two sons married in New York, and another who was now in Europe. This young man was amusing himself at Homburg,[6] and, though he was on his travels, was rarely perceived to visit any particular city at the moment selected by his mother for her own appearance there. Her nephew, who had come up to Vevey expressly to see her, was therefore more attentive than those who, as she said, were nearer to her. He had imbibed at Geneva the idea that one must always be attentive to one's aunt. Mrs. Costello had not seen him for many years, and she was greatly pleased with him, manifesting her approbation by initiating him into many of the secrets of that social sway which, as she gave him to understand, she exerted in the American capital. She admitted that she was very exclusive; but, if he were acquainted with New York, he would see that one had to be. And her picture of the minutely hierarchical constitution of the society of that city, which she presented to him in many different lights, was, to Winterbourne's imagination, almost oppressively striking.

He immediately perceived, from her tone, that Miss Daisy Miller's place in the social scale was low. "I am afraid you don't approve of them," he said.

"They are very common," Mrs. Costello declared. "They are the sort of Americans that one does one's duty by not—not accepting."

"Ah, you don't accept them?" said the young man.

"I can't, my dear Frederick. I would if I could, but I can't."

"The young girl is very pretty," said Winterbourne, in a moment.

"Of course she's pretty. But she is very common."

"I see what you mean, of course," said Winterbourne, after another pause.

"She has that charming look that they all have," his aunt resumed. "I can't

---

4. Grace, poise, expression (French).
5. Small rolls, especially of coins wrapped in
paper, but in this case of hair.
6. A resort in Germany.

think where they pick it up; and she dresses in perfection—no, you don't know how well she dresses. I can't think where they get their taste."

"But, my dear aunt, she is not, after all, a Comanche savage."

"She is a young lady," said Mrs. Costello, "who has an intimacy with her mamma's courier?"

"An intimacy with the courier?" the young man demanded.

"Oh, the mother is just as bad! They treat the courier like a familiar friend—like a gentleman. I shouldn't wonder if he dines with them. Very likely they have never seen a man with such good manners, such fine clothes, so like a gentleman. He probably corresponds to the young lady's idea of a Count. He sits with them in the garden, in the evening. I think he smokes."

Winterbourne listened with interest to these disclosures; they helped him to make up his mind about Miss Daisy. Evidently she was rather wild. "Well," he said, "I am not a courier, and yet she was very charming to me."

"You had better have said at first," said Mrs. Costello with dignity, "that you had made her acquaintance."

"We simply met in the garden, and we talked a bit."

"*Tout bonnement!*[7] And pray what did you say?"

"I said I should take the liberty of introducing her to my admirable aunt."

"I am much obliged to you."

"It was to guarantee my respectability," said Winterbourne.

"And pray who is to guarantee hers?"

"Ah, you are cruel!" said the young man. "She's a very nice girl."

"You don't say that as if you believed it," Mrs. Costello observed.

"She is completely uncultivated," Winterbourne went on. "But she is wonderfully pretty, and, in short, she is very nice. To prove that I believe it, I am going to take her to the Château de Chillon."

"You two are going off there together? I should say it proved just the contrary. How long had you known her, may I ask, when this interesting project was formed. You haven't been twenty-four hours in the house."

"I had known her half-an-hour!" said Winterbourne, smiling.

"Dear me!" cried Mrs. Costello. "What a dreadful girl!"

Her nephew was silent for some moments.

"You really think, then," he began earnestly, and with a desire for trustworthy information—"you really think that—" But he paused again.

"Think what, sir," said his aunt.

"That she is the sort of young lady who expects a man—sooner or later—to carry her off?"

"I haven't the least idea what such young ladies expect a man to do. But I really think that you had better not meddle with little American girls that are uncultivated, as you call them. You have lived too long out of the country. You will be sure to make some great mistake. You are too innocent."

"My dear aunt, I am not so innocent," said Winterbourne, smiling and curling his moustache.

"You are too guilty, then?"

Winterbourne continued to curl his moustache, meditatively. "You won't let the poor girl know you then?" he asked at last.

"Is it literally true that she is going to the Château de Chillon with you?"

7. Quite simply the best! (French).

"I think that she fully intends it."

"Then, my dear Frederick," said Mrs. Costello, "I must decline the honor of her acquaintance. I am an old woman, but I am not too old—thank Heaven—to be shocked!"

"But don't they all do these things—the young girls in America?" Winterbourne inquired.

Mrs. Costello stared a moment. "I should like to see my granddaughters do them!" she declared, grimly.

This seemed to throw some light upon the matter, for Winterbourne remembered to have heard that his pretty cousins in New York were "tremendous flirts." If, therefore, Miss Daisy Miller exceeded the liberal license allowed to these young ladies, it was probable that anything might be expected of her. Winterbourne was impatient to see her again, and he was vexed with himself that, by instinct, he should not appreciate her justly.

Though he was impatient to see her, he hardly knew what he should say to her about his aunt's refusal to become acquainted with her; but he discovered, promptly enough, that with Miss Daisy Miller there was no great need of walking on tiptoe. He found her that evening in the garden, wandering about in the warm starlight, like an indolent sylph, and swinging to and fro the largest fan he had ever beheld. It was ten o'clock. He had dined with his aunt, had been sitting with her since dinner, and had just taken leave of her till the morrow. Miss Daisy Miller seemed very glad to see him; she declared it was the longest evening she had ever passed.

"Have you been all alone?" he asked.

"I have been walking round with mother. But mother gets tired walking round," she answered.

"Has she gone to bed?"

"No; she doesn't like to go to bed," said the young girl. "She doesn't sleep—not three hours. She says she doesn't know how she lives. She's dreadfully nervous. I guess she sleeps more than she thinks. She's gone somewhere after Randolph; she wants to try to get him to go to bed. He doesn't like to go to bed."

"Let us hope she will persuade him," observed Winterbourne.

"She will talk to him all she can; but he doesn't like her to talk to him," said Miss Daisy, opening her fan. "She's going to try to get Eugenio to talk to him. But he isn't afraid of Eugenio. Eugenio's a splendid courier, but he can't make much impression on Randolph! I don't believe he'll go to bed before eleven." It appeared that Randolph's vigil was in fact triumphantly prolonged, for Winterbourne strolled about with the young girl for some time without meeting her mother. "I have been looking round for that lady you want to introduce me to," his companion resumed. "She's your aunt." Then, on Winterbourne's admitting the fact, and expressing some curiosity as to how she had learned it, she said she had heard all about Mrs. Costello from the chambermaid. She was very quiet and very *comme il faut*; she wore white puffs; she spoke to no one, and she never dined at the *table d'hôte*.[8] Every two days she had a headache. "I think that's a lovely description, headache and all!" said Miss Daisy, chattering along in her thin, gay voice. "I want to know her ever so much. I know just what *your* aunt would be; I know I should like her. She

---

8. A common table for guests in a restaurant or hotel (French). "*Comme il faut*": well mannered (French).

would be very exclusive. I like a lady to be exclusive; I'm dying to be exclusive myself. Well, we *are* exclusive, mother and I. We don't speak to every one— or they don't speak to us. I suppose it's about the same thing. Any way, I shall be ever so glad to know your aunt."

Winterbourne was embarrassed. "She would be most happy," he said, "but I am afraid those headaches will interfere."

The young girl looked at him through the dusk. "But I suppose she doesn't have a headache every day," she said, sympathetically.

Winterbourne was silent a moment. "She tells me she does," he answered at last—not knowing what to say.

Miss Daisy Miller stopped and stood looking at him. Her prettiness was still visible in the darkness; she was opening and closing her enormous fan. "She doesn't want to know me!" she said suddenly. "Why don't you say so? You needn't be afraid. I'm not afraid!" And she gave a little laugh.

Winterbourne fancied there was a tremor in her voice; he was touched, shocked, mortified by it. "My dear young lady," he protested, "she knows no one. It's her wretched health."

The young girl walked on a few steps, laughing still. "You needn't be afraid," she repeated. "Why should she want to know me?" Then she paused again; she was close to the parapet of the garden, and in front of her was the starlit lake. There was a vague sheen upon its surface, and in the distance were dimly-seen mountain forms. Daisy Miller looked out upon the mysterious prospect, and then she gave another little laugh. "Gracious! she *is* exclusive!" she said. Winterbourne wondered whether she was seriously wounded, and for a moment almost wished that her sense of injury might be such as to make it becoming in him to attempt to reassure and comfort her. He had a pleasant sense that she would be very approachable for consolatory purposes. He felt then, for the instant, quite ready to sacrifice his aunt, conversationally; to admit that she was a proud, rude woman, and to declare that they needn't mind her. But before he had time to commit himself to this perilous mixture of gallantry and impiety, the young lady, resuming her walk, gave an exclamation in quite another tone. "Well; here's mother! I guess she hasn't got Randolph to go to bed." The figure of a lady appeared, at a distance, very indistinct in the darkness, and advancing with a slow and wavering movement. Suddenly it seemed to pause.

"Are you sure it is your mother? Can you distinguish her in this thick dusk?" Winterbourne asked.

"Well!" cried Miss Daisy Miller, with a laugh, "I guess I know my own mother. And when she has got on my shawl, too! She is always wearing my things."

The lady in question, ceasing to advance, hovered vaguely about the spot at which she had checked her steps.

"I am afraid your mother doesn't see you," said Winterbourne. "Or perhaps," he added—thinking, with Miss Miller, the joke permissible—"perhaps she feels guilty about your shawl."

"Oh, it's a fearful old thing!" the young girl replied, serenely. "I told her she could wear it. She won't come here, because she sees you."

"Ah, then," said Winterbourne, "I had better leave you."

"Oh, no; come on!" urged Miss Daisy Miller.

"I'm afraid your mother doesn't approve of my walking with you."

Miss Miller gave him a serious glance. "It isn't for me; it's for you—that is, it's for *her*. Well; I don't know who it's for! But mother doesn't like any of my gentlemen friends. She's right down timid. She always makes a fuss if I introduce a gentleman. But I *do* introduce them—almost always. If I didn't introduce my gentlemen friends to mother," the young girl added, in her little soft, flat monotone, "I shouldn't think I was natural."

"To introduce me," said Winterbourne, "you must know my name." And he proceeded to pronounce it.

"Oh, dear; I can't say all that!" said his companion, with a laugh. But by this time they had come up to Mrs. Miller, who, as they drew near, walked to the parapet of the garden and leaned upon it, looking intently at the lake and turning her back upon them. "Mother!" said the young girl, in a tone of decision. Upon this the elderly lady turned round. "Mr. Winterbourne," said Miss Daisy Miller, introducing the young man very frankly and prettily. "Common" she was, as Mrs. Costello had pronounced her; yet it was a wonder to Winterbourne that, with her commonness, she had a singularly delicate grace.

Her mother was a small, spare, light person, with a wandering eye, a very exiguous nose, and a large forehead, decorated with a certain amount of thin, much-frizzled hair. Like her daughter, Mrs. Miller was dressed with extreme elegance; she had enormous diamonds in her ears. So far as Winterbourne could observe, she gave him no greeting—she certainly was not looking at him. Daisy was near her, pulling her shawl straight. "What are you doing, poking round here?" this young lady inquired; but by no means with that harshness of accent which her choice of words may imply.

"I don't know," said her mother, turning towards the lake again.

"I shouldn't think you'd want that shawl!" Daisy exclaimed.

"Well—I do!" her mother answered, with a little laugh.

"Did you get Randolph to go to bed?" asked the young girl.

"No; I couldn't induce him," said Mrs. Miller, very gently. "He wants to talk to the waiter. He likes to talk to that waiter."

"I was telling Mr. Winterbourne," the young girl went on; and to the young man's ear her tone might have indicated that she had been uttering his name all her life.

"Oh, yes!" said Winterbourne; "I have the pleasure of knowing your son."

Randolph's mamma was silent; she turned her attention to the lake. But at last she spoke. "Well, I don't see how he lives!"

"Anyhow, it isn't so bad as it was at Dover," said Daisy Miller.

"And what occurred at Dover?" Winterbourne asked.

"He wouldn't go to bed at all. I guess he sat up all night—in the public parlour. He wasn't in bed at twelve o'clock: I know that."

"It was half-past twelve," declared Mrs. Miller, with mild emphasis.

"Does he sleep much during the day?" Winterbourne demanded.

"I guess he doesn't sleep much," Daisy rejoined.

"I wish he would!" said her mother. "It seems as if he couldn't."

"I think he's real tiresome," Daisy pursued.

Then, for some moments, there was silence. "Well, Daisy Miller," said the elder lady, presently, "I shouldn't think you'd want to talk against your own brother!"

"Well, he *is* tiresome, mother," said Daisy, quite without the asperity of a retort.

"He's only nine," urged Mrs. Miller.

"Well, he wouldn't go to that castle," said the young girl. "I'm going there with Mr. Winterbourne."

To this announcement, very placidly made, Daisy's mamma offered no response. Winterbourne took for granted that she deeply disapproved of the projected excursion; but he said to himself that she was a simple, easily managed person, and that a few deferential protestations would take the edge from her displeasure. "Yes," he began; "your daughter has kindly allowed me the honor of being her guide."

Mrs. Miller's wandering eyes attached themselves, with a sort of appealing air, to Daisy, who, however, strolled a few steps farther, gently humming to herself. "I presume you will go in the cars," said her mother.

"Yes; or in the boat," said Winterbourne.

"Well, of course, I don't know," Mrs. Miller rejoined. "I have never been to that castle."

"It is a pity you shouldn't go," said Winterbourne, beginning to feel reassured as to her opposition. And yet he was quite prepared to find that, as a matter of course, she meant to accompany her daughter.

"We've been thinking ever so much about going," she pursued; "but it seems as if we couldn't. Of course Daisy—she wants to go round. But there's a lady here—I don't know her name—she says she shouldn't think we'd want to go to see castles *here*; she should think we'd want to wait till we got to Italy. It seems as if there would be so many there," continued Mrs. Miller, with an air of increasing confidence. "Of course, we only want to see the principal ones. We visited several in England," she presently added.

"Ah, yes! in England there are beautiful castles," said Winterbourne. "But Chillon, here, is very well worth seeing."

"Well, if Daisy feels up to it—," said Mrs. Miller, in a tone impregnated with a sense of the magnitude of the enterprise. "It seems as if there was nothing she wouldn't undertake."

"Oh, I think she'll enjoy it!" Winterbourne declared. And he desired more and more to make it a certainty that he was to have the privilege of a *tête-à-tête* with the young lady, who was still strolling along in front of them, softly vocalizing. "You are not disposed, madam," he inquired, "to undertake it yourself?"

Daisy's mother looked at him, an instant, askance, and then walked forward in silence. Then—"I guess she had better go alone," she said, simply.

Winterbourne observed to himself that this was a very different type of maternity from that of the vigilant matrons who massed themselves in the forefront of social intercourse in the dark old city at the other end of the lake. But his meditations were interrupted by hearing his name very distinctly pronounced by Mrs. Miller's unprotected daughter.

"Mr. Winterbourne!" murmured Daisy.

"Mademoiselle!" said the young man.

"Don't you want to take me out in a boat?"

"At present?" he asked.

"Of course!" said Daisy.

"Well, Annie Miller!" exclaimed her mother.

"I beg you, madam, to let her go," said Winterbourne, ardently; for he had never yet enjoyed the sensation of guiding through the summer starlight a skiff freighted with a fresh and beautiful young girl.

"I shouldn't think she'd want to," said her mother. "I should think she'd rather go indoors."

"I'm sure Mr. Winterbourne wants to take me," Daisy declared. "He's so awfully devoted!"

"I will row you over to Chillon, in the starlight."

"I don't believe it!" said Daisy.

"Well!" ejaculated the elderly lady again.

"You haven't spoken to me for half-an-hour," her daughter went on.

"I have been having some very pleasant conversation with your mother," said Winterbourne.

"Well; I want you to take me out in a boat!" Daisy repeated. They had all stopped, and she had turned round and was looking at Winterbourne. Her face wore a charming smile, her pretty eyes were gleaming, she was swinging her great fan about. No; it's impossible to be prettier than that, thought Winterbourne.

"There are half-a-dozen boats moored at that landing-place," he said, pointing to certain steps which descended from the garden to the lake. "If you will do me the honor to accept my arm, we will go and select one of them."

Daisy stood there smiling; she threw back her head and gave a little light laugh. "I like a gentleman to be formal!" she declared.

"I assure you it's a formal offer."

"I was bound I would make you say something," Daisy went on.

"You see it's not very difficult," said Winterbourne. "But I am afraid you are chaffing me."

"I think not, sir," remarked Mrs. Miller, very gently.

"Do, then, let me give you a row," he said to the young girl.

"It's quite lovely, the way you say that!" said Daisy.

"It will be still more lovely to do it."

"Yes, it would be lovely!" said Daisy. But she made no movement to accompany him; she only stood there laughing.

"I should think you had better find out what time it is," interposed her mother.

"It is eleven o'clock, madam," said a voice, with a foreign accent, out of the neighboring darkness; and Winterbourne, turning, perceived the florid personage who was in attendance upon the two ladies. He had apparently just approached.

"Oh, Eugenio," said Daisy, "I am going out in a boat!"

Eugenio bowed. "At eleven o'clock, mademoiselle?"

"I am going with Mr. Winterbourne. This very minute."

"Do tell her she can't," said Mrs. Miller to the courier.

"I think you had better not go out in a boat, mademoiselle," Eugenio declared.

Winterbourne wished to Heaven this pretty girl were not so familiar with her courier; but he said nothing.

"I suppose you don't think it's proper!" Daisy exclaimed, "Eugenio doesn't think anything's proper."

"I am at your service," said Winterbourne.

"Does mademoiselle propose to go alone?" asked Eugenio of Mrs. Miller.

"Oh, no; with this gentleman!" answered Daisy's mamma.

The courier looked for a moment at Winterbourne—the latter thought he was smiling—and then, solemnly, with a bow, "As mademoiselle pleases!" he said.

"Oh, I hoped you would make a fuss!" said Daisy. "I don't care to go now."

"I myself shall make a fuss if you don't go," said Winterbourne.

"That's all I want—a little fuss!" And the young girl began to laugh again.

"Mr. Randolph has gone to bed!" the courier announced, frigidly.

"Oh, Daisy; now we can go!" said Mrs. Miller.

Daisy turned away from Winterbourne, looking at him, smiling and fanning herself. "Good night," she said; "I hope you are disappointed, or disgusted, or something!"

He looked at her, taking the hand she offered him. "I am puzzled," he answered.

"Well; I hope it won't keep you awake!" she said, very smartly; and, under the escort of the privileged Eugenio, the two ladies passed towards the house.

Winterbourne stood looking after them; he was indeed puzzled. He lingered beside the lake for a quarter of an hour, turning over the mystery of the young girl's sudden familiarities and caprices. But the only very definite conclusion he came to was that he should enjoy deucedly "going off" with her somewhere.

Two days afterwards he went off with her to the Castle of Chillon. He waited for her in the large hall of the hotel, where the couriers, the servants, the foreign tourists were lounging about and staring. It was not the place he would have chosen, but she had appointed it. She came tripping downstairs, buttoning her long gloves, squeezing her folded parasol against her pretty figure, dressed in the perfection of a soberly elegant travelling-costume. Winterbourne was a man of imagination and, as our ancestors used to say, of sensibility; as he looked at her dress and, on the great staircase, her little rapid, confiding step, he felt as if there were something romantic going forward. He could have believed he was going to elope with her. He passed out with her among all the idle people that were assembled there; they were all looking at her very hard; she had begun to chatter as soon as she joined him. Winterbourne's preference had been that they should be conveyed to Chillon in a carriage; but she expressed a lively wish to go in the little steamer; she declared that she had a passion for steamboats. There was always such a lovely breeze upon the water, and you saw such lots of people. The sail was not long, but Winterbourne's companion found time to say a great many things. To the young man himself their little excursion was so much of an escapade—an adventure—that, even allowing for her habitual sense of freedom, he had some expectation of seeing her regard it in the same way. But it must be confessed that, in this particular, he was disappointed. Daisy Miller was extremely animated, she was in charming spirits; but she was apparently not at all excited; she was not fluttered; she avoided neither his eyes nor those of any one else; she blushed neither when she looked at him nor when she saw that people were looking at her. People continued to look at her a great deal, and Winterbourne took much satisfaction in his pretty companion's distinguished air. He had been a little afraid that she would talk loud, laugh overmuch, and even, perhaps, desire to move about the boat a good deal. But he quite forgot his fears; he sat smiling, with his eyes upon her face, while, without moving from her place, she delivered herself of a great number of original reflections. It was the most charming garrulity he had ever heard. He had assented to the idea that she was "common"; but was she so, after all, or was he simply getting used to her commonness? Her conversation was chiefly of what metaphysicians term the objective cast; but every now and then it took a subjective turn.

"What on *earth* are you so grave about?" she suddenly demanded, fixing her agreeable eyes upon Winterbourne's.

"Am I grave?" he asked. "I had an idea I was grinning from ear to ear."

"You look as if you were taking me to a funeral. If that's a grin, your ears are very near together."

"Should you like me to dance a hornpipe[9] on the deck?"

"Pray do, and I'll carry round your hat. It will pay the expenses of our journey."

"I never was better pleased in my life," murmured Winterbourne.

She looked at him a moment, and then burst into a little laugh. "I like to make you say those things! You're a queer mixture!"

In the castle, after they had landed, the subjective element decidedly prevailed. Daisy tripped about the vaulted chambers, rustled her skirts in the corkscrew staircases, flirted back with a pretty little cry and a shudder from the edge of the *oubliettes*,[1] and turned a singularly well-shaped ear to everything that Winterbourne told her about the place. But he saw that she cared very little for feudal antiquities, and that the dusky traditions of Chillon made but a slight impression upon her. They had the good fortune to have been able to walk about without other companionship than that of the custodian; and Winterbourne arranged with this functionary that they should not be hurried—that they should linger and pause wherever they chose. The custodian interpreted the bargain generously—Winterbourne, on his side, had been generous—and ended by leaving them quite to themselves. Miss Miller's observations were not remarkable for logical consistency; for anything she wanted to say she was sure to find a pretext. She found a great many pretexts in the rugged embrasures of Chillon for asking Winterbourne sudden questions about himself—his family, his previous history, his tastes, his habits, his intentions—and for supplying information upon corresponding points in her own personality. Of her own tastes, habits, and intentions Miss Miller was prepared to give the most definite, and indeed the most favourable, account.

"Well; I hope you know enough!" she said to her companion, after he had told her the history of the unhappy Bonivard.[2] "I never saw a man that knew so much!" The history of Bonivard had evidently, as they say, gone into one ear and out of the other. But Daisy went on to say that she wished Winterbourne would travel with them and "go round" with them; they might know something, in that case. "Don't you want to come and teach Randolph?" she asked. Winterbourne said that nothing could possibly please him so much; but that he had unfortunately other occupations. "Other occupations? I don't

---

9. An English dance similar to the jig, popular with sailors from the 16th through the 19th centuries.
1. Secret pitlike dungeons with an opening only at the top; places where one is forgotten (French).

2. Hero of Byron's poem "The Prisoner of Chillon"; François de Bonivard (1496–1570), Swiss patriot and martyr, was confined for seven years in the Castle of Chillon.

believe it!" said Miss Daisy. "What do you mean? You are not in business." The young man admitted that he was not in business; but he had engagements which, even within a day or two, would force him to go back to Geneva. "Oh, bother!" she said. "I don't believe it!" and she began to talk about something else. But a few moments later, when he was pointing out to her the pretty design of an antique fireplace, she broke out irrelevantly, "You don't mean to say you are going back to Geneva?"

"It is a melancholy fact that I shall have to return to Geneva to-morrow."

"Well, Mr. Winterbourne," said Daisy; "I think you're horrid!"

"Oh, don't say such dreadful things!" said Winterbourne—"just at the last."

"The last!" cried the young girl; "I call it the first. I have half a mind to leave you here and go straight back to the hotel alone." And for the next ten minutes she did nothing but call him horrid. Poor Winterbourne was fairly bewildered; no young lady had as yet done him the honor to be so agitated by the announcement of his movements. His companion, after this, ceased to pay any attention to the curiosities of Chillon or the beauties of the lake; she opened fire upon the mysterious charmer in Geneva, whom she appeared to have instantly taken it for granted that he was hurrying back to see. How did Miss Daisy Miller know that there was a charmer in Geneva? Winterbourne, who denied the existence of such a person, was quite unable to discover; and he was divided between amazement at the rapidity of her induction and amusement at the frankness of her *persiflage*.[3] She seemed to him, in all this, an extraordinary mixture of innocence and crudity. "Does she never allow you more than three days at a time?" asked Daisy, ironically. "Doesn't she give you a vacation in summer? There's no one so hard worked but they can get leave to go off somewhere at this season. I suppose, if you stay another day, she'll come after you in the boat. Do wait over till Friday, and I will go down to the landing to see her arrive!" Winterbourne began to think he had been wrong to feel disappointed in the temper in which the young lady had embarked. If he had missed the personal accent, the personal accent was now making its appearance. It sounded very distinctly, at last, in her telling him she would stop "teasing" him if he would promise her solemnly to come down to Rome in the winter.

"That's not a difficult promise to make," said Winterbourne. "My aunt has taken an apartment in Rome for the winter, and has already asked me to come and see her."

"I don't want you to come for your aunt," said Daisy; "I want you to come for me." And this was the only allusion that the young man was ever to hear her make to his invidious kinswoman. He declared that, at any rate, he would certainly come. After this Daisy stopped teasing. Winterbourne took a carriage, and they drove back to Vevey in the dusk; the young girl was very quiet.

In the evening Winterbourne mentioned to Mrs. Costello that he had spent the afternoon at Chillon, with Miss Daisy Miller.

"The Americans—of the courier?" asked this lady.

"Ah, happily," said Winterbourne, "the courier stayed at home."

"She went with you all alone?"

"All alone."

3. Frivolous or bantering talk.

Mrs. Costello sniffed a little at her smelling-bottle. "And that," she exclaimed, "is the young person you wanted me to know!"

### III

Winterbourne, who had returned to Geneva the day after his excursion to Chillon, went to Rome towards the end of January. His aunt had been established there for several weeks, and he had received a couple of letters from her. "Those people you were so devoted to last summer at Vevey have turned up here, courier and all," she wrote. "They seem to have made several acquaintances, but the courier continues to be the most *intime*. The young lady, however, is also very intimate with some third-rate Italians, with whom she rackets about in a way that makes much talk. Bring me that pretty novel of Cherbuliez's[4]—'Paule Méré'—and don't come later than the 23rd."

In the natural course of events, Winterbourne, on arriving in Rome, would presently have ascertained Mrs. Miller's address at the American banker's and have gone to pay his compliments to Miss Daisy. "After what happened at Vevey I certainly think I may call upon them," he said to Mrs. Costello.

"If, after what happens—at Vevey and everywhere—you desire to keep up the acquaintance, you are very welcome. Of course a man may know every one. Men are welcome to the privilege!"

"Pray what is it that happens—here, for instance?" Winterbourne demanded.

"The girl goes about alone with her foreigners. As to what happens farther, you must apply elsewhere for information. She has picked up half-a-dozen of the regular Roman fortune-hunters, and she takes them about to people's houses. When she comes to a party she brings with her a gentleman with a good deal of manner and a wonderful moustache."

"And where is the mother?"

"I haven't the least idea. They are very dreadful people."

Winterbourne meditated a moment. "They are very ignorant—very innocent only. Depend upon it they are not bad."

"They are hopelessly vulgar," said Mrs. Costello. "Whether or no being hopelessly vulgar is being 'bad' is a question for the metaphysicians. They are bad enough to dislike, at any rate; and for this short life that is quite enough."

The news that Daisy Miller was surrounded by half-a-dozen wonderful moustaches checked Winterbourne's impulse to go straightway to see her. He had perhaps not definitely flattered himself that he had made an ineffaceable impression upon her heart, but he was annoyed at hearing of a state of affairs so little in harmony with an image that had lately flitted in and out of his own meditations; the image of a very pretty girl looking out of an old Roman window and asking herself urgently when Mr. Winterbourne would arrive. If, however, he determined to wait a little before reminding Miss Miller of his claims to her consideration, he went very soon to call upon two or three other friends. One of these friends was an American lady who had spent several winters at Geneva, when she had placed her children at school. She was a very accomplished woman and she lived in the Via Gregoriana. Winterbourne

4. Victor Cherbuliez (1829–1899), which James spelled "Cherbuliex," a minor French novelist of Swiss origin.

found her in a little crimson drawing-room, on a third floor; the room was filled with southern sunshine. He had not been there ten minutes when the servant came in, announcing "Madame Mila!" This announcement was presently followed by the entrance of little Randolph Miller, who stopped in the middle of the room and stood staring at Winterbourne. An instant later his pretty sister crossed the threshold; and then, after a considerable interval, Mrs. Miller slowly advanced.

"I know you!" said Randolph.

"I'm sure you know a great many things," exclaimed Winterbourne, taking him by the hand. "How is your education coming on?"

Daisy was exchanging greetings very prettily with her hostess; but when she heard Winterbourne's voice she quickly turned her head. "Well, I declare!" she said.

"I told you I should come, you know," Winterbourne rejoined smiling.

"Well—I didn't believe it," said Miss Daisy.

"I am much obliged to you," laughed the young man.

"You might have come to see me!" said Daisy.

"I arrived only yesterday."

"I don't believe that!" the young girl declared.

Winterbourne turned with a protesting smile to her mother; but this lady evaded his glance, and seating herself, fixed her eyes upon her son. "We've got a bigger place than this," said Randolph. "It's all gold on the walls."

Mrs. Miller turned uneasily in her chair. "I told you if I were to bring you, you would say something!" she murmured.

"I told *you*!" Randolph exclaimed. "I tell *you*, sir!" he added jocosely, giving Winterbourne a thump on the knee. "It *is* bigger, too!"

Daisy had entered upon a lively conversation with her hostess; Winterbourne judged it becoming to address a few words to her mother. "I hope you have been well since we parted at Vevey," he said.

Mrs. Miller now certainly looked at him—at his chin. "Not very well, sir," she answered.

"She's got the dyspepsia," said Randolph. "I've got it too. Father's got it. I've got it worst!"

This announcement, instead of embarrassing Mrs. Miller, seemed to relieve her. "I suffer from the liver," she said. "I think it's the climate; it's less bracing than Schenectady, especially in the winter season. I don't know whether you know we reside at Schenectady. I was saying to Daisy that I certainly hadn't found any one like Dr. Davis, and I didn't believe I should. Oh, at Schenectady, he stands first; they think everything of him. He has so much to do, and yet there was nothing he wouldn't do for me. He said he never saw anything like my dyspepsia, but he was bound to cure it. I'm sure there was nothing he wouldn't try. He was just going to try something new when we came off. Mr. Miller wanted Daisy to see Europe for herself. But I wrote to Mr. Miller that it seems as if I couldn't get on without Dr. Davis. At Schenectady he stands at the very top; and there's a great deal of sickness there, too. It affects my sleep."

Winterbourne had a good deal of pathological gossip with Dr. Davis's patient, during which Daisy chattered unremittingly to her own companion. The young man asked Mrs. Miller how she was pleased with Rome. "Well, I must say I am disappointed," she answered. "We had heard so much about it;

I suppose we had heard too much. But we couldn't help that. We had been led to expect something different."

"Ah, wait a little, and you will become very fond of it," said Winterbourne.

"I hate it worse and worse every day!" cried Randolph.

"You are like the infant Hannibal,"[5] said Winterbourne.

"No, I ain't!" Randolph declared, at a venture.

"You are not much like an infant," said his mother. "But we have seen places," she resumed, "that I should put a long way before Rome." And in reply to Winterbourne's interrogation, "There's Zurich," she observed; "I think Zurich is lovely; and we hadn't heard half so much about it."

"The best place we've seen is the City of Richmond!" said Randolph.

"He means the ship," his mother explained. "We crossed in that ship. Randolph had a good time on the City of Richmond."

"It's the best place I've seen," the child repeated. "Only it was turned the wrong way."

"Well, we've got to turn the right way some time," said Mrs. Miller, with a little laugh. Winterbourne expressed the hope that her daughter at least found some gratification in Rome, and she declared that Daisy was quite carried away. "It's on account of the society—the society's splendid. She goes round everywhere; she has made a great number of acquaintances. Of course she goes round more than I do. I must say they have been very sociable; they have taken her right in. And then she knows a great many gentlemen. Oh, she thinks there's nothing like Rome. Of course, it's a great deal pleasanter for a young lady if she knows plenty of gentlemen."

By this time Daisy had turned her attention again to Winterbourne. "I've been telling Mrs. Walker how mean you were!" the young girl announced.

"And what is the evidence you have offered?" asked Winterbourne, rather annoyed at Miss Miller's want of appreciation of the zeal of an admirer who on his way down to Rome had stopped neither at Bologna nor at Florence, simply because of a certain sentimental impatience. He remembered that a cynical compatriot had once told him that American women—the pretty ones, and this gave a largeness to the axiom—were at once the most exacting in the world and the least endowed with a sense of indebtedness.

"Why, you were awfully mean at Vevey," said Daisy. "You wouldn't do anything. You wouldn't stay there when I asked you."

"My dearest young lady," cried Winterbourne, with eloquence, "have I come all the way to Rome to encounter your reproaches?"

"Just hear him say that!" said Daisy to her hostess, giving a twist to a bow on this lady's dress. "Did you ever hear anything so quaint?"

"So quaint, my dear?" murmured Mrs. Walker, in the tone of a partisan of Winterbourne.

"Well, I don't know," said Daisy, fingering Mrs. Walker's ribbons. "Mrs. Walker, I want to tell you something."

"Motherr," interposed Randolph, with his rough ends to his words, "I tell you you've got to go. Eugenio'll raise something!"

"I'm not afraid of Eugenio," said Daisy, with a toss of her head. "Look here, Mrs. Walker," she went on, "you know I'm coming to your party."

"I am delighted to hear it."

5. The Carthaginian general (247–183 B.C.E.) was sworn at his birth to an eternal hatred of Rome.

"I've got a lovely dress."

"I am very sure of that."

"But I want to ask a favor—permission to bring a friend."

"I shall be happy to see any of your friends," said Mrs. Walker, turning with a smile to Mrs. Miller.

"Oh, they are not my friends," answered Daisy's mamma, smiling shyly, in her own fashion. "I never spoke to them!"

"It's an intimate friend of mine—Mr. Giovanelli," said Daisy, without a tremor in her clear little voice or a shadow on her brilliant little face.

Mrs. Walker was silent a moment, she gave a rapid glance at Winterbourne. "I shall be glad to see Mr. Giovanelli," she then said.

"He's an Italian," Daisy pursued, with the prettiest serenity. "He's a great friend of mine—he's the handsomest man in the world—except Mr. Winterbourne! He knows plenty of Italians, but he wants to know some Americans. He thinks ever so much of Americans. He's tremendously clever. He's perfectly lovely!"

It was settled that this brilliant personage should be brought to Mrs. Walker's party, and then Mrs. Miller prepared to take her leave. "I guess we'll go back to the hotel," she said.

"You may go back to the hotel, mother, but I'm going to take a walk," said Daisy.

"She's going to walk with Mr. Giovanelli," Randolph proclaimed.

"I am going to the Pincio," said Daisy, smiling.

"Alone, my dear at this hour?" Mrs. Walker asked. The afternoon was drawing to a close—it was the hour for the throng of carriages and of contemplative pedestrians. "I don't think it's safe, my dear," said Mrs. Walker.

"Neither do I," subjoined Mrs. Miller. "You'll get the fever[6] as sure as you live. Remember what Dr. Davis told you!"

"Give her some medicine before she goes," said Randolph.

The company had risen to its feet; Daisy, still showing her pretty teeth, bent over and kissed her hostess. "Mrs. Walker, you are too perfect," she said. "I'm not going alone; I am going to meet a friend."

"Your friend won't keep you from getting the fever," Mrs. Miller observed.

"Is it Mr. Giovanelli?" asked the hostess.

Winterbourne was watching the girl; at this question his attention quickened. She stood there smiling and smoothing her bonnet-ribbons; she glanced at Winterbourne. Then, while she glanced and smiled, she answered without a shade of hesitation, "Mr. Giovanelli—the beautiful Giovanelli."

"My dear young friend," said Mrs. Walker, taking her hand, pleadingly, "don't walk off to the Pincio at this hour to meet a beautiful Italian."

"Well, he speaks English," said Mrs. Miller.

"Gracious me!" Daisy exclaimed, "I don't want to do anything improper. There's an easy way to settle it." She continued to glance at Winterbourne. "The Pincio is only a hundred yards distant, and if Mr. Winterbourne were as polite as he pretends he would offer to walk with me!"

Winterbourne's politeness hastened to affirm itself, and the young girl gave

---

6. What is meant is malaria, whose means of transmission (the mosquito) was unknown in James's day, but which was associated with damp, dark places.

him gracious leave to accompany her. They passed downstairs before her mother, and at the door Winterbourne perceived Mrs. Miller's carriage drawn up, with the ornamental courier whose acquaintance he had made at Vevey seated within. "Good-bye, Eugenio!" cried Daisy, "I'm going to take a walk." The distance from the Via Gregoriana to the beautiful garden at the other end of the Pincian Hill is, in fact, rapidly traversed. As the day was splendid, however, and the concourse of vehicles, walkers, and loungers numerous, the young Americans found their progress much delayed. This fact was highly agreeable to Winterbourne, in spite of his consciousness of his singular situation. The slow-moving, idly-gazing Roman crowd bestowed much attention upon the extremely pretty young foreign lady who was passing through it upon his arm; and he wondered what on earth had been in Daisy's mind when she proposed to expose herself, unattended, to its appreciation. His own mission, to her sense, apparently, was to consign her to the hands of Mr. Giovanelli; but Winterbourne, at once annoyed and gratified, resolved that he would do no such thing.

"Why haven't you been to see me?" asked Daisy. "You can't get out of that."

"I have had the honor of telling you that I have only just stepped out of the train."

"You must have stayed in the train a good while after it stopped!" cried the young girl, with her little laugh. "I suppose you were asleep. You have had time to go to see Mrs. Walker."

"I knew Mrs. Walker—" Winterbourne began to explain.

"I knew where you knew her. You knew her at Geneva. She told me so. Well, you knew me at Vevey. That's just as good. So you ought to have come." She asked him no other question than this; she began to prattle about her own affairs. "We've got splendid rooms at the hotel; Eugenio says they're the best rooms in Rome. We are going to stay all winter—if we don't die of the fever; and I guess we'll stay then. It's a great deal nicer than I thought; I thought it would be fearfully quiet; I was sure it would be awfully poky. I was sure we should be going round all the time with one of those dreadful old men that explain about the pictures and things. But we only had about a week of that, and now I'm enjoying myself. I know ever so many people, and they are all so charming. The society's extremely select. There are all kinds—English, and Germans, and Italians. I think I like the English best. I like their style of conversation. But there are some lovely Americans. I never saw anything so hospitable. There's something or other every day. There's not much dancing; but I must say I never thought dancing was everything. I was always fond of conversation. I guess I shall have plenty at Mrs. Walker's—her rooms are so small." When they had passed the gate of the Pincian Gardens, Miss Miller began to wonder where Mr. Giovanelli might be. "We had better go straight to that place in front," she said, "where you look at the view."

"I certainly shall not help you to find him," Winterbourne declared.

"Then I shall find him without you," said Miss Daisy.

"You certainly won't leave me!" cried Winterbourne.

She burst into her little laugh. "Are you afraid you'll get lost—or run over? But there's Giovanelli, leaning against that tree. He's staring at the women in the carriages: did you ever see anything so cool?"

Winterbourne perceived at some distance a little man standing with folded arms, nursing his cane. He had a handsome face, an artfully poised hat, a glass in one eye, and a nosegay in his button-hole. Winterbourne looked at him a moment and then said, "Do you mean to speak to that man?"

"Do I mean to speak to him? Why, you don't suppose I mean to communicate by signs?"

"Pray understand, then," said Winterbourne, "that I intend to remain with you."

 Daisy stopped and looked at him, without a sign of troubled consciousness in her face; with nothing but the presence of her charming eyes and her happy dimples. "Well, she's a cool one!" thought the young man.

"I don't like the way you say that," said Daisy. "It's too imperious."

"I beg your pardon if I say it wrong. The main point is to give you an idea of my meaning."

The young girl looked at him more gravely, but with eyes that were prettier than ever. "I have never allowed a gentleman to dictate to me, or to interfere with anything I do."

"I think you have made a mistake," said Winterbourne. "You should sometimes listen to a gentleman—the right one?"

Daisy began to laugh again, "I do nothing but listen to gentlemen!" she exclaimed. "Tell me if Mr. Giovanelli is the right one?"

The gentleman with the nosegay in his bosom had now perceived our two friends, and was approaching the young girl with obsequious rapidity. He bowed to Winterbourne as well as to the latter's companion; he had a brilliant smile, an intelligent eye; Winterbourne thought him not a bad-looking fellow. But he nevertheless said to Daisy—"No, he's not the right one."

Daisy evidently had a natural talent for performing introductions; she mentioned the name of each of her companions to the other. She strolled along with one of them on each side of her; Mr. Giovanelli, who spoke English very cleverly—Winterbourne afterwards learned that he had practiced the idiom upon a great many American heiresses—addressed her a great deal of very polite nonsense; he was extremely urbane, and the young American, who said nothing, reflected upon that profundity of Italian cleverness which enables people to appear more gracious in proportion as they are more acutely disappointed. Giovanelli, of course, had counted upon something more intimate; he had not bargained for a party of three. But he kept his temper in a manner which suggested far-stretching intentions. Winterbourne flattered himself that he had taken his measure. "He is not a gentleman," said the young American; "he is only a clever imitation of one. He is a music-master, or a penny-a-liner, or a third-rate artist. Damn his good looks!" Mr. Giovanelli had certainly a very pretty face; but Winterbourne felt a superior indignation at his own lovely fellow-countrywoman's not knowing the difference between a spurious gentleman and a real one. Giovanelli chattered and jested and made himself wonderfully agreeable. It was true that if he was an imitation the imitation was very skillful. "Nevertheless," Winterbourne said to himself, "a nice girl ought to know!" And then he came back to the question whether this was in fact a nice girl. Would a nice girl—even allowing for her being a little American flirt—make a rendezvous with a presumably low-lived foreigner? The rendezvous in this case, indeed, had been in broad daylight, and in the most crowded corner of Rome; but was it not impossible to regard the choice of these circumstances as a proof of extreme cynicism? Singular though it may seem, Winterbourne was vexed that the young girl, in joining her *amoroso,*[7] should not appear more impatient of his own company, and he was vexed because of his inclination. It was impossible to regard her as a perfectly well-conducted young lady; she was wanting in a certain indispensable delicacy. It would therefore simplify matters greatly to be able to treat her as the object of one of those sentiments which are called by romancers "lawless passions." That she should seem to wish to get rid of him would help him to think more lightly of her, and to be able to think more lightly of her would make her much less perplexing. But Daisy, on this occasion, continued to present herself as an inscrutable combination of audacity and innocence.

She had been walking some quarter of an hour, attended by her two cavaliers, and responding in a tone of very childish gaiety, as it seemed to Winterbourne, to the pretty speeches of Mr. Giovanelli, when a carriage that had detached itself from the revolving train drew up beside the path. At the same moment Winterbourne perceived that his friend Mrs. Walker—the lady whose house he had lately left—was seated in the vehicle and was beckoning to him. Leaving Miss Miller's side, he hastened to obey her summons. Mrs. Walker was flushed; she wore an excited air. "It is really too dreadful," she said. "That girl must not do this sort of thing. She must not walk here with you two men. Fifty people have noticed her."

Winterbourne raised his eyebrows. "I think it's a pity to make too much fuss about it."

"It's a pity to let the girl ruin herself!"

"She is very innocent," said Winterbourne.

"She's very crazy!" cried Mrs. Walker. "Did you ever see anything so imbecile as her mother? After you had all left me, just now, I could not sit still for thinking of it. It seemed too pitiful, not even to attempt to save her. I ordered the carriage and put on my bonnet, and came here as quickly as possible. Thank heaven I have found you!"

"What do you propose to do with us?" asked Winterbourne, smiling.

"To ask her to get in, to drive her about here for half-an-hour, so that the world may see she is not running absolutely wild, and then to take her safely home."

"I don't think it's a very happy thought," said Winterbourne; "but you can try."

Mrs. Walker tried. The young man went in pursuit of Miss Miller, who had simply nodded and smiled at his interlocutrix in the carriage and had gone her way with her own companion. Daisy, on learning that Mrs. Walker wished to speak to her, retraced her steps with a perfect good grace and with Mr. Giovanelli at her side. She declared that she was delighted to have a chance to present this gentleman to Mrs. Walker. She immediately achieved the introduction, and declared that she had never in her life seen anything so lovely as Mrs. Walker's carriage-rug.

"I am glad you admire it," said this lady, smiling sweetly. "Will you get in and let me put it over you?"

"Oh, no, thank you," said Daisy. "I shall admire it much more as I see you driving round with it."

"Do get in and drive with me," said Mrs. Walker.

7. Lover (Italian).

"That would be charming, but it's so enchanting just as I am!" and Daisy gave a brilliant glance at the gentlemen on either side of her.

"It may be enchanting, dear child, but it is not the custom here," urged Mrs. Walker, leaning forward in her victoria[8] with her hands devoutly clasped.

"Well, it ought to be, then!" said Daisy. "If I didn't walk I should expire."

"You should walk with your mother, dear," cried the lady from Geneva, losing patience.

"With my mother dear!" exclaimed the young girl. Winterbourne saw that she scented interference. "My mother never walked ten steps in her life. And then, you know," she added with a laugh, "I am more than five years old."

"You are old enough to be more reasonable. You are old enough, dear Miss Miller, to be talked about."

Daisy looked at Mrs. Walker, smiling intensely. "Talked about? What do you mean?"

"Come into my carriage and I will tell you."

Daisy turned her quickened glance again from one of the gentlemen beside her to the other. Mr. Giovanelli was bowing to and fro, rubbing down his gloves and laughing very agreeably; Winterbourne thought it a most unpleasant scene. "I don't think I want to know what you mean," said Daisy presently. "I don't think I should like it."

Winterbourne wished that Mrs. Walker would tuck in her carriage-rug and drive away; but this lady did not enjoy being defied, as she afterwards told him. "Should you prefer being thought a very reckless girl?" she demanded.

"Gracious me!" exclaimed Daisy. She looked again at Mr. Giovanelli, then she turned to Winterbourne. There was a little pink flush in her check; she was tremendously pretty. "Does Mr. Winterbourne think," she asked slowly, smiling, throwing back her head and glancing at him from head to foot, "that—to save my reputation—I ought to get into the carriage?"

Winterbourne colored; for an instant he hesitated greatly. It seemed so strange to hear her speak that way of her "reputation." But he himself, in fact, must speak in accordance with gallantry. The finest gallantry, here, was simply to tell her the truth; and the truth, for Winterbourne, as the few indications I have been able to give have made him known to the reader, was that Daisy Miller should take Mrs. Walker's advice. He looked at her exquisite prettiness; and then he said very gently, "I think you should get into the carriage."

Daisy gave a violent laugh. "I never heard anything so stiff! If this is improper, Mrs. Walker," she pursued, "then I am all improper, and you must give me up. Good-bye; I hope you'll have a lovely ride!" and, with Mr. Giovanelli, who made a triumphantly obsequious salute, she turned away.

Mrs. Walker sat looking after her, and there were tears in Mrs. Walker's eyes. "Get in here, sir," she said to Winterbourne, indicating the place beside her. The young man answered that he felt bound to accompany Miss Miller; whereupon Mrs. Walker declared that if he refused her this favor she would never speak to him again. She was evidently in earnest. Winterbourne overtook Daisy and her companion and, offering the young girl his hand, told her that Mrs. Walker had made an imperious claim upon his society. He expected that in answer she would say something rather free, something to commit

---

8. A horse-drawn carriage for two with a raised seat in front for the driver.

herself still farther to that "recklessness" from which Mrs. Walker had so charitably endeavored to dissuade her. But she only shook his hand, hardly looking at him, while Mr. Giovanelli bade him farewell with a too emphatic flourish of the hat.

Winterbourne was not in the best possible humor as he took his seat in Mrs. Walker's victoria. "That was not clever of you," he said candidly, while the vehicle mingled again with the throng of carriages.

"In such a case," his companion answered, "I don't wish to be clever, I wish to be *earnest!*"

"Well, your earnestness has only offended her and put her off."

"It has happened very well," said Mrs. Walker. "If she is so perfectly determined to compromise herself, the sooner one knows it the better; one can act accordingly."

"I suspect she meant no harm," Winterbourne rejoined.

"So I thought a month ago. But she has been going too far."

"What has she been doing?"

"Everything that is not done here. Flirting with any man she could pick up; sitting in corners with mysterious Italians; dancing all the evening with the same partners; receiving visits at eleven o'clock at night. Her mother goes away when visitors come."

"But her brother," said Winterbourne, laughing, "sits up till midnight."

"He must be edified by what he sees. I'm told that at their hotel every one is talking about her, and that a smile goes round among the servants when a gentleman comes and asks for Miss Miller."

"The servants be hanged!" said Winterbourne angrily. "The poor girl's only fault," he presently added, "is that she is very uncultivated."

"She is naturally indelicate," Mrs. Walker declared. "Take that example this morning. How long had you known her at Vevey?"

"A couple of days."

"Fancy, then, her making it a personal matter that you should have left the place!"

Winterbourne was silent for some moments; then he said, "I suspect, Mrs. Walker, that you and I have lived too long at Geneva!" And he added a request that she should inform him with what particular design she had made him enter her carriage.

"I wished to beg you to cease your relations with Miss Miller—not to flirt with her—to give her no farther opportunity to expose herself—to let her alone, in short."

"I'm afraid I can't do that," said Winterbourne. "I like her extremely."

"All the more reason that you shouldn't help her to make a scandal."

"There shall be nothing scandalous in my attentions to her."

"There certainly will be in the way she takes them. But I have said what I had on my conscience," Mrs. Walker pursued. "If you wish to rejoin the young lady I will put you down. Here, by-the-way, you have a chance."

The carriage was traversing that part of the Pincian Garden which overhangs the wall of Rome and overlooks the beautiful Villa Borghese. It is bordered by a large parapet, near which there are several seats. One of the seats, at a distance, was occupied by a gentleman and a lady, towards whom Mrs. Walker gave a toss of her head. At the same moment these persons rose and walked towards the parapet. Winterbourne had asked the coachman to stop;

he now descended from the carriage. His companion looked at him a moment in silence; then, while he raised his hat, she drove majestically away. Winterbourne stood there; he had turned his eyes towards Daisy and her cavalier. They evidently saw no one; they were too deeply occupied with each other. When they reached the low garden-wall they stood a moment looking off at the great flat-topped pine-clusters of the Villa Borghese; then Giovanelli seated himself familiarly upon the broad ledge of the wall. The western sun in the opposite sky sent out a brilliant shaft through a couple of cloud-bars; whereupon Daisy's companion took her parasol out of her hands and opened it. She came a little nearer and he held the parasol over her; then, still holding it, he let it rest upon her shoulder, so that both of their heads were hidden from Winterbourne. This young man lingered a moment, then he began to walk. But he walked—not towards the couple with the parasol; towards the residence of his aunt, Mrs. Costello.

## IV

He flattered himself on the following day that there was no smiling among the servants when he, at least, asked for Mrs. Miller at her hotel. This lady and her daughter, however, were not at home; and on the next day, after repeating his visit, Winterbourne again had the misfortune not to find them. Mrs. Walker's party took place on the evening of the third day, and in spite of the frigidity of his last interview with the hostess, Winterbourne was among the guests. Mrs. Walker was one of those American ladies who, while residing abroad, make a point, in their own phrase, of studying European society; and she had on this occasion collected several specimens of her diversely-born fellow-mortals to serve, as it were, as text-books. When Winterbourne arrived Daisy Miller was not there; but in a few moments he saw her mother come in alone, very shyly and ruefully. Mrs. Miller's hair, above her exposed-looking temples, was more frizzled than ever. As she approached Mrs. Walker, Winterbourne also drew near.

"You see I've come all alone," said poor Mrs. Miller. "I'm so frightened; I don't know what to do; it's the first time I've ever been to a party alone—especially in this country. I wanted to bring Randolph or Eugenio, or someone, but Daisy just pushed me off by myself. I ain't used to going round alone."

"And does not your daughter intend to favor us with her society?" demanded Mrs. Walker, impressively.

"Well, Daisy's all dressed," said Mrs. Miller, with that accent of the dispassionate, if not of the philosophic, historian with which she always recorded the current incidents of her daughter's career. "She's got dressed on purpose before dinner. But she's got a friend of hers there; that gentleman—the Italian—that she wanted to bring. They've got going at the piano; it seems as if they couldn't leave off. Mr. Giovanelli sings splendidly. But I guess they'll come before very long," concluded Mrs. Miller hopefully.

"I'm sorry she should come—in that way," said Mrs. Walker.

"Well, I told her that there was no use in her getting dressed before dinner if she was going to wait three hours," responded Daisy's mamma. "I didn't see the use of her putting on such a dress as that to sit round with Mr. Giovanelli."

"This is most horrible!" said Mrs. Walker, turning away and addressing herself to Winterbourne. *"Elle s'affiche.*[9] It's her revenge for my having ventured to remonstrate with her. When she comes I shall not speak to her."

Daisy came after eleven o'clock, but she was not, on such an occasion, a young lady to wait to be spoken to. She rustled forward in radiant loveliness, smiling and chattering, carrying a large bouquet and attended by Mr. Giovanelli. Every one stopped talking, and turned and looked at her. She came straight to Mrs. Walker. "I'm afraid you thought I never was coming, so I sent mother off to tell you. I wanted to make Mr. Giovanelli practice some things before he came; you know he sings beautifully, and I want you to ask him to sing. This is Mr. Giovanelli; you know I introduced him to you; he's got the most lovely voice and he knows the most charming set of songs. I made him go over them this evening, on purpose; we had the greatest time at the hotel." Of all this Daisy delivered herself with the sweetest, brightest audibleness, looking now at her hostess and now round the room, while she gave a series of little pats, round her shoulders, to the edges of her dress. "Is there anyone I know?" she asked.

"I think every one knows you!" said Mrs. Walker pregnantly, and she gave a very cursory greeting to Mr. Giovanelli. This gentleman bore himself gallantly. He smiled and bowed and showed his white teeth, he curled his moustaches and rolled his eyes, and performed all the proper functions of a handsome Italian at an evening party. He sang, very prettily, half-a-dozen songs, though Mrs. Walker afterwards declared that she had been quite unable to find out who asked him. It was apparently not Daisy who had given him his orders. Daisy sat at a distance from the piano, and though she had publicly, as it were, professed a high admiration for his singing, talked, not inaudibly, while it was going on.

"It's a pity these rooms are so small; we can't dance," she said to Winterbourne, as if she had seen him five minutes before.

"I am not sorry we can't dance," Winterbourne answered; "I don't dance."

"Of course you don't dance; you're too stiff," said Miss Daisy. "I hope you enjoyed your drive with Mrs. Walker."

"No, I didn't enjoy it; I preferred walking with you."

"We paired off, that was much better," said Daisy. "But did you ever hear anything so cool as Mrs. Walker's wanting me to get into her carriage and drop poor Mr. Giovanelli; and under the pretext that it was proper? People have different ideas! It would have been most unkind; he had been talking about that walk for ten days."

"He should not have talked about it at all," said Winterbourne; "he would never have proposed to a young lady of this country to walk about the streets with him."

"About the streets?" cried Daisy, with her pretty stare. "Where then would he have proposed to her to walk? The Pincio is not the streets, either; and I, thank goodness, am not a young lady of this country. The young ladies of this country have a dreadfully pokey time of it, so far as I can learn; I don't see why I should change my habits for *them.*"

"I am afraid your habits are those of a flirt," said Winterbourne gravely.

"Of course they are," she cried, giving him her little smiling stare again.

9. She's making a spectacle of herself (French).

"I'm a fearful, frightful flirt! Did you ever hear of a nice girl that was not? But I suppose you will tell me now that I am not a nice girl."

"You're a very nice girl, but I wish you would flirt with me, and me only," said Winterbourne.

"Ah! thank you, thank you very much; you are the last man I should think of flirting with. As I have had the pleasure of informing you, you are too stiff."

"You say that too often," said Winterbourne.

Daisy gave a delighted laugh. "If I could have the sweet hope of making you angry, I would say it again."

"Don't do that; when I am angry I'm stiffer than ever. But if you won't flirt with me, do cease at least to flirt with your friend at the piano; they don't understand that sort of thing here."

"I thought they understood nothing else!" exclaimed Daisy.

"Not in young unmarried women."

"It seems to me much more proper in young unmarried women than in old married ones," Daisy declared.

"Well," said Winterbourne, "when you deal with natives you must go by the custom of the place. Flirting is a purely American custom; it doesn't exist here. So when you show yourself in public with Mr. Giovanelli and without your mother—"

"Gracious! Poor mother!" interposed Daisy.

"Though you may be flirting, Mr. Giovanelli is not; he means something else."

"He isn't preaching, at any rate," said Daisy with vivacity. "And if you want very much to know, we are neither of us flirting; we are too good friends for that; we are very intimate friends."

"Ah," rejoined Winterbourne, "if you are in love with each other it is another affair."

She had allowed him up to this point to talk so frankly that he had no expectation of shocking her by this ejaculation; but she immediately got up, blushing visibly, and leaving him to exclaim mentally that little American flirts were the queerest creatures in the world. "Mr. Giovanelli, at least," she said, giving her interlocutor a single glance, "never says such very disagreeable things to me."

Winterbourne was bewildered; he stood staring. Mr. Giovanelli had finished singing; he left the piano and came over to Daisy. "Won't you come into the other room and have some tea?" he asked, bending before her with his decorative smile.

Daisy turned to Winterbourne, beginning to smile again. He was still more perplexed, for this inconsequent smile made nothing clear, though it seemed to prove, indeed, that she had a sweetness and softness that reverted instinctively to the pardon of offences. "It has never occurred to Mr. Winterbourne to offer me any tea," she said, with her little tormenting manner.

"I have offered you advice," Winterbourne rejoined.

"I prefer weak tea!" cried Daisy, and she went off with the brilliant Giovanelli. She sat with him in the adjoining room, in the embrasure of the window, for the rest of the evening. There was an interesting performance at the piano, but neither of these young people gave heed to it. When Daisy came to take leave of Mrs. Walker, this lady conscientiously repaired the weakness of which she had been guilty at the moment of the young girl's arrival. She turned her back straight upon Miss Miller and left her to depart with what grace she might. Winterbourne was standing near the door; he saw it all. Daisy turned very pale and looked at her mother, but Mrs. Miller was humbly unconscious of any violation of the usual social forms. She appeared, indeed, to have felt an incongruous impulse to draw attention to her own striking observance of them. "Good night, Mrs. Walker," she said; "we've had a beautiful evening. You see if I let Daisy come to parties without me, I don't want her to go away without me." Daisy turned away, looking with a pale, grave face at the circle near the door; Winterbourne saw that, for the first moment, she was too much shocked and puzzled even for indignation. He on his side was greatly touched.

"That was very cruel," he said to Mrs. Walker.

"She never enters my drawing-room again," replied his hostess.

Since Winterbourne was not to meet her in Mrs. Walker's drawing-room, he went as often as possible to Mrs. Miller's hotel. The ladies were rarely at home, but when he found them the devoted Giovanelli was always present. Very often the polished little Roman was in the drawing-room with Daisy alone, Mrs. Miller being apparently constantly of the opinion that discretion is the better part of surveillance. Winterbourne noted, at first with surprise, that Daisy on these occasions was never embarrassed or annoyed by his own entrance; but he very presently began to feel that she had no more surprises for him; the unexpected in her behavior was the only thing to expect. She showed no displeasure at her *tête-à-tête* with Giovanelli being interrupted; she could chatter as freshly and freely with two gentlemen as with one; there was always, in her conversation, the same odd mixture of audacity and puerility. Winterbourne remarked to himself that if she was seriously interested in Giovanelli it was very singular that she should not take more trouble to preserve the sanctity of their interviews, and he liked her the more for her innocent-looking indifference and her apparently inexhaustible good humor. He could hardly have said why, but she seemed to him a girl who would never be jealous. At the risk of exciting a somewhat derisive smile on the reader's part, I may affirm that with regard to the women who had hitherto interested him it very often seemed to Winterbourne among the possibilities that, given certain contingencies, he should be afraid—literally afraid—of these ladies. He had a pleasant sense that he should never be afraid of Daisy Miller. It must be added that this sentiment was not altogether flattering to Daisy; it was part of his conviction, or rather of his apprehension, that she would prove a very light young person.

But she was evidently very much interested in Giovanelli. She looked at him whenever he spoke; she was perpetually telling him to do this and to do that; she was constantly "chaffing" and abusing him. She appeared completely to have forgotten that Winterbourne had said anything to displease her at Mrs. Walker's little party. One Sunday afternoon, having gone to St. Peter's with his aunt, Winterbourne perceived Daisy strolling about the great church in company with the inevitable Giovanelli. Presently he pointed out the young girl and her cavalier to Mrs. Costello. This lady looked at them a moment through her eyeglasses, and then she said:

"That's what makes you so pensive in these days, eh?"

"I had not the least idea I was pensive," said the young man.

"You are very much preoccupied, you are thinking of something."

"And what is it," he asked, "that you accuse me of thinking of?"

"Of that young lady's, Miss Baker's, Miss Chandler's—what's her name?—Miss Miller's intrigue with that little barber's block."

"Do you call it an intrigue," Winterbourne asked—"an affair that goes on with such peculiar publicity?"

"That's their folly," said Mrs. Costello, "it's not their merit."

"No," rejoined Winterbourne, with something of that pensiveness to which his aunt had alluded. "I don't believe that there is anything to be called an intrigue."

"I have heard a dozen people speak of it; they say she is quite carried away by him."

"They are certainly very intimate," said Winterbourne.

Mrs. Costello inspected the young couple again with her optical instrument. "He is very handsome. One easily sees how it is. She thinks him the most elegant man in the world, the finest gentleman. She has never seen anything like him; he is better even than the courier. It was the courier probably who introduced him, and if he succeeds in marrying the young lady, the courier will come in for a magnificent commission."

"I don't believe she thinks of marrying him," said Winterbourne, "and I don't believe he hopes to marry her."

"You may be very sure she thinks of nothing. She goes on from day to day, from hour to hour, as they did in the Golden Age. I can imagine nothing more vulgar. And at the same time," added Mrs. Costello, "depend upon it that she may tell you any moment that she is 'engaged.' "

"I think that is more than Giovanelli expects," said Winterbourne.

"Who is Giovanelli?"

"The little Italian. I have asked questions about him and learned something. He is apparently a perfectly respectable little man. I believe he is in a small way a *cavaliere avvocato*.[1] But he doesn't move in what are called the first circles. I think it is really not absolutely impossible that the courier introduced him. He is evidently immensely charmed with Miss Miller. If she thinks him the finest gentleman in the world, he, on his side, has never found himself in personal contact with such splendor, such opulence, such expensiveness, as this young lady's. And then she must seem to him wonderfully pretty and interesting. I rather doubt whether he dreams of marrying her. That must appear to him too impossible a piece of luck. He has nothing but his handsome face to offer, and there is a substantial Mr. Miller in that mysterious land of dollars. Giovanelli knows that he hasn't a title to offer. If he were only a count or a *marchese*![2] He must wonder at his luck at the way they have taken him up."

"He accounts for it by his handsome face, and thinks Miss Miller a young lady *qui se passe ses fantaisies*!"[3] said Mrs. Costello.

"It is very true," Winterbourne pursued, "that Daisy and her mamma have not yet risen to that stage of—what shall I call it?—of culture, at which the idea of catching a count or a *marchese* begins. I believe that they are intellectually incapable of that conception."

"Ah! but the *cavalier* can't believe it," said Mrs. Costello.

1. Lawyer (Italian). *"Cavaliere"*: an honorific.   3. Who is indulging her whims (French).
2. Marquis (Italian).

Of the observation excited by Daisy's "intrigue," Winterbourne gathered that day at St. Peter's sufficient evidence. A dozen of the American colonists in Rome came to talk with Mrs. Costello, who sat on a little portable stool at the base of one of the great pilasters. The vesper-service was going forward in splendid chants and organ-tones in the adjacent choir, and meanwhile, between Mrs. Costello and her friends, there was a great deal said about poor little Miss Miller's going really "too far." Winterbourne was not pleased with what he heard; but when, coming out upon the great steps of the church, he saw Daisy, who had emerged before him, get into an open cab with her accomplice and roll away through the cynical streets of Rome, he could not deny to himself that she was going very far indeed. He felt very sorry for her—not exactly that he believed that she had completely lost her head, but because it was painful to hear so much that was pretty and undefended and natural assigned to a vulgar place among the categories of disorder. He made an attempt after this to give a hint to Mrs. Miller. He met one day in the Corso a friend—a tourist like himself—who had just come out of the Doria Palace, where he had been walking through the beautiful gallery. His friend talked for a moment about the superb portrait of Innocent X. by Velasquez,[4] which hangs in one of the cabinets of the palace, and then said, "And in the same cabinet, by-the-way, I had the pleasure of contemplating a picture of a different kind—that pretty American girl whom you pointed out to me last week." In answer to Winterbourne's inquiries, his friend narrated that the pretty American girl—prettier than ever—was seated with a companion in the secluded nook in which the great papal portrait is enshrined.

"Who was her companion?" asked Winterbourne.

"A little Italian with a bouquet in his button-hole. The girl is delightfully pretty, but I thought I understood from you the other day that she was a young lady *du meilleur monde*."[5]

"So she is!" answered Winterbourne; and having assured himself that his informant had seen Daisy and her companion but five minutes before, he jumped into a cab and went to call on Mrs. Miller. She was at home; but she apologized to him for receiving him in Daisy's absence.

"She's gone out somewhere with Mr. Giovanelli," said Mrs. Miller. "She's always going round with Mr. Giovanelli."

"I have noticed that they are very intimate," Winterbourne observed.

"Oh! it seems as if they couldn't live without each other!" said Mrs. Miller. "Well, he's a real gentleman, anyhow. I keep telling Daisy she's engaged!"

"And what does Daisy say?"

"Oh, she says she isn't engaged. But she might as well be!" this impartial parent resumed. "She goes on as if she was. But I've made Mr. Giovanelli promise to tell me, if *she* doesn't. I should want to write to Mr. Miller about it—shouldn't you?"

Winterbourne replied that he certainly should; and the state of mind of Daisy's mamma struck him as so unprecedented in the annals of parental vigilance that he gave up as utterly irrelevant the attempt to place her upon her guard.

After this Daisy was never at home, and Winterbourne ceased to meet her

---

4. Diego Rodríguez de Silva y Velázque (1599–1660), Spanish painter.

5. Of the better society (French).

at the houses of their common acquaintances, because, as he perceived, these shrewd people had quite made up their minds that she was going too far. They ceased to invite her, and they intimated that they desired to express to observant Europeans the great truth that, though Miss Daisy Miller was a young American lady, her behavior was not representative—was regarded by her compatriots as abnormal. Winterbourne wondered how she felt about all the cold shoulders that were turned towards her, and sometimes it annoyed him to suspect that she did not feel at all. He said to himself that she was too light and childish, too uncultivated and unreasoning, too provincial, to have reflected upon her ostracism or even to have perceived it. Then at other moments he believed that she carried about in her elegant and irresponsible little organism a defiant, passionate, perfectly observant consciousness of the impression she produced. He asked himself whether Daisy's defiance came from the consciousness of innocence or from her being, essentially, a young person of the reckless class. It must be admitted that holding oneself to a belief in Daisy's "innocence" came to seem to Winterbourne more and more a matter of fine-spun gallantry. As I have already had occasion to relate, he was angry at finding himself reduced to chopping logic about this young lady; he was vexed at his want of instinctive certitude as to how far her eccentricities were generic, national, and how far they were personal. From either view of them he had somehow missed her, and now it was too late. She was "carried away" by Mr. Giovanelli.

A few days after his brief interview with her mother, he encountered her in that beautiful abode of flowering desolation known as the Palace of the Cæsars. The early Roman spring had filled the air with bloom and perfume, and the rugged surface of the Palatine was muffled with tender verdure. Daisy was strolling along the top of one of those great mounds of ruin that are embanked with mossy marble and paved with monumental inscriptions. It seemed to him that Rome had never been so lovely as just then. He stood looking off at the enchanting harmony of line and color that remotely encircles the city, inhaling the softly humid odors and feeling the freshness of the year and the antiquity of the place reaffirm themselves in mysterious interfusion. It seemed to him also that Daisy had never looked so pretty; but this had been an observation of his whenever he met her. Giovanelli was at her side, and Giovanelli, too, wore an aspect of even unwonted brilliancy.

"Well," said Daisy, "I should think you would be lonesome!"

"Lonesome?" asked Winterbourne.

"You are always going round by yourself. Can't you get any one to walk with you?"

"I am not so fortunate," said Winterbourne, "as your companion."

Giovanelli, from the first, had treated Winterbourne with distinguished politeness; he listened with a deferential air to his remarks; he laughed, punctiliously, at his pleasantries; he seemed disposed to testify to his belief that Winterbourne was a superior young man. He carried himself in no degree like a jealous wooer; he had obviously a great deal of tact; he had no objection to your expecting a little humility of him. It even seemed to Winterbourne at times that Giovanelli would find a certain mental relief in being able to have a private understanding with him—to say to him, as an intelligent man, that, bless you, *he* knew how extraordinary was this young lady, and didn't flatter himself with delusive—or at least *too* delusive—hopes of matrimony and dol-

lars. On this occasion he strolled away from his companion to pluck a sprig
of almond blossom, which he carefully arranged in his button-hole.

"I know why you say that," said Daisy, watching Giovanelli. "Because you
think I go round too much with *him*!" And she nodded at her attendant.

"Everyone thinks so—if you care to know," said Winterbourne.

"Of course I care to know!" Daisy exclaimed seriously. "But I don't believe
it. They are only pretending to be shocked. They don't really care a straw what
I do. Besides, I don't go round so much."

"I think you will find they do care. They will show it—disagreeably."

Daisy looked at him a moment. "How—disagreeably?"

"Haven't you noticed anything?" Winterbourne asked.

"I have noticed you. But I noticed you were as stiff as an umbrella the first
time I saw you."

"You will find I am not so stiff as several others," said Winterbourne, smiling.

"How shall I find it?"

"By going to see the others."

"What will they do to me?"

"They will give you the cold shoulder. Do you know what that means?"

Daisy was looking at him intently; she began to color. "Do you mean as
Mrs. Walker did the other night?"

"Exactly!" said Winterbourne.

She looked away at Giovanelli, who was decorating himself with his
almond-blossom. Then looking back at Winterbourne—"I shouldn't think you
would let people be so unkind!" she said.

"How can I help it?" he asked.

"I should think you would say something."

"I do say something"; and he paused a moment. "I say that your mother
tells me that she believes you are engaged."

"Well, she does," said Daisy very simply.

Winterbourne began to laugh. "And does Randolph believe it?" he asked.

"I guess Randolph doesn't believe anything," said Daisy. Randolph's scep-
ticism excited Winterbourne to farther hilarity, and he observed that Giovanelli was coming back to them. Daisy, observing it too, addressed herself
again to her countryman. "Since you have mentioned it," she said, "I *am*
engaged." . . . Winterbourne looked at her; he had stopped laughing. "You
don't believe it!" she added.

He was silent a moment; and then, "Yes, I believe it!" he said.

"Oh, no, you don't," she answered. "Well, then—I am not!"

The young girl and her cicerone[6] were on their way to the gate of the enclosure, so that Winterbourne, who had but lately entered, presently took leave
of them. A week afterwards he went to dine at a beautiful villa on the Cælian
Hill, and, on arriving, dismissed his hired vehicle. The evening was charming, and he promised himself the satisfaction of walking home beneath the
Arch of Constantine and past the vaguely-lighted monuments of the Forum.
There was a waning moon in the sky, and her radiance was not brilliant, but
she was veiled in a thin cloud-curtain which seemed to diffuse and equalize
it. When, on his return from the villa (it was eleven o'clock), Winterbourne

6. Chaperone (Italian).

approached the dusky circle of the Colosseum, it occurred to him, as a lover of the picturesque, that the interior, in the pale moonshine, would be well worth a glance. He turned aside and walked to one of the empty arches, near which, as he observed, an open carriage—one of the little Roman street-cabs— was stationed. Then he passed in among the cavernous shadows of the great structure, and emerged upon the clear and silent arena. The place had never seemed to him more impressive. One-half of the gigantic circus was in deep shade; the other was sleeping in the luminous dusk. As he stood there he began to murmur Byron's famous lines, out of "Manfred";[7] but before he had finished his quotation he remembered that if nocturnal meditations in the Colosseum are recommended by the poets, they are deprecated by the doctors. The historic atmosphere was there, certainly; but the historic atmosphere, scientifically considered, was not better than a villainous miasma. Winterbourne walked to the middle of the arena, to take a more general glance, intending thereafter to make a hasty retreat. The great cross in the center was covered with shadow; it was only as he drew near it that he made it out distinctly. Then he saw that two persons were stationed upon the low steps which formed its base. One of these was a woman, seated; her companion was standing in front of her.

Presently the sound of the woman's voice came to him distinctly in the warm night air. "Well, he looks at us as one of the old lions or tigers may have looked at the Christian martyrs!" These were the words he heard, in the familiar accent of Miss Daisy Miller.

"Let us hope he is not very hungry," responded the ingenious Giovanelli. "He will have to take me first; you will serve for dessert!"

Winterbourne stopped, with a sort of horror; and, it must be added, with a sort of relief. It was as if a sudden illumination had been flashed upon the ambiguity of Daisy's behavior and the riddle had become easy to read. She was a young lady whom a gentleman need no longer be at pains to respect. He stood there looking at her—looking at her companion, and not reflecting that though he saw them vaguely, he himself must have been more brightly visible. He felt angry with himself that he had bothered so much about the right way of regarding Miss Daisy Miller. Then, as he was going to advance again, he checked himself; not from the fear that he was doing her injustice, but from a sense of the danger of appearing unbecomingly exhilarated by this sudden revulsion from cautious criticism. He turned away towards the entrance of the place; but as he did so he heard Daisy speak again.

"Why, it was Mr. Winterbourne! He saw me—and he cuts me!"

What a clever little reprobate she was, and how smartly she played an injured innocence! But he wouldn't cut her. Winterbourne came forward again, and went towards the great cross. Daisy had got up; Giovanelli lifted his hat. Winterbourne had now begun to think simply of the craziness, from a sanitary point of view, of a delicate young girl lounging away the evening in this nest of malaria. What if she *were* a clever little reprobate? that was no

7. Byron's 1817 dramatic poem contains the following lines: ". . . the night / Hath been to me a more familiar face / Than that of man; and in her starry shade / Of dim and solitary loveliness, / I learn'd the language of another world. / I do remember me, that in my youth, / When I was wandering,—upon such a night / I stood within the Colosseum's wall, / 'Midst the chief relics of almighty Rome; / The trees which grew along the broken arches / Waved dark in the blue midnight, and the stars / Shone through the rents of ruin. . . ."

reason for her dying of the *perniciosa*.[8] "How long have you been there?" he asked, almost brutally.

Daisy, lovely in the flattering moonlight, looked at him a moment. Then— "All the evening," she answered gently. . . . "I never saw anything so pretty."

"I am afraid," said Winterbourne, "that you will not think Roman fever very pretty. This is the way people catch it. I wonder," he added, turning to Giovanelli, "that you, a native Roman, should countenance such a terrible indiscretion."

"Ah," said the handsome native, "for myself, I am not afraid."

"Neither am I—for you! I am speaking for this young lady."

Giovanelli lifted his well-shaped eyebrows and showed his brilliant teeth. But he took Winterbourne's rebuke with docility. "I told the Signorina it was a grave indiscretion; but when was the Signorina ever prudent?"

"I never was sick, and I don't mean to be!" the Signorina declared. "I don't look like much, but I'm healthy! I was bound to see the Colosseum by moonlight; I shouldn't have wanted to go home without that; and we have had the most beautiful time, haven't we, Mr. Giovanelli! If there has been any danger, Eugenio can give me some pills. He has got some splendid pills."

"I should advise you," said Winterbourne, "to drive home as fast as possible and take one!"

"What you say is very wise," Giovanelli rejoined. "I will go and make sure the carriage is at hand." And he went forward rapidly.

Daisy followed with Winterbourne. He kept looking at her; she seemed not in the least embarrassed. Winterbourne said nothing; Daisy chattered about the beauty of the place. "Well, I *have* seen the Colosseum by moonlight!" she exclaimed. "That's one good thing." Then, noticing Winterbourne's silence, she asked him why he didn't speak. He made no answer; he only began to laugh. They passed under one of the dark archways; Giovanelli was in front with the carriage. Here Daisy stopped a moment, looking at the young American. "*Did* you believe I was engaged the other day?" she asked.

"It doesn't matter what I believed the other day," said Winterbourne, still laughing.

"Well, what do you believe now?"

"I believe that it makes very little difference whether you are engaged or not!"

He felt the young girl's pretty eyes fixed upon him through the thick gloom of the archway; she was apparently going to answer. But Giovanelli hurried her forward. "Quick, quick," he said; "if we get in by midnight we are quite safe."

Daisy took her seat in the carriage, and the fortunate Italian placed himself beside her. "Don't forget Eugenio's pills!" said Winterbourne, as he lifted his hat.

"I don't care," said Daisy, in a little strange tone, "whether I have Roman fever or not!" Upon this the cab-driver cracked his whip, and they rolled away over the desultory patches of the antique pavement.

Winterbourne—to do him justice, as it were—mentioned to no one that he had encountered Miss Miller, at midnight, in the Colosseum with a gentleman; but nevertheless, a couple of days later, the fact of her having been there

8. Malaria (Italian).

under these circumstances was known to every member of the little American circle, and commented accordingly. Winterbourne reflected that they had of course known it at the hotel, and that, after Daisy's return, there had been an exchange of jokes between the porter and the cab-driver. But the young man was conscious at the same moment that it had ceased to be a matter of serious regret to him that the little American flirt should be "talked about" by low-minded menials. These people, a day or two later, had serious information to give: the little American flirt was alarmingly ill. Winterbourne, when the rumor came to him, immediately went to the hotel for more news. He found that two or three charitable friends had preceded him, and that they were being entertained in Mrs. Miller's salon by Randolph.

"It's going round at night," said Randolph—"that's what made her sick. She's always going round at midnight. I shouldn't think she'd want to—it's so plaguey dark. You can't see anything here at night, except when there's a moon. In America there's always a moon!" Mrs. Miller was invisible; she was now, at least, giving her daughter the advantage of her society. It was evident that Daisy was dangerously ill.

Winterbourne went often to ask for news of her, and once he saw Mrs. Miller, who, though deeply alarmed, was—rather to his surprise—perfectly composed, and, as it appeared, a most efficient and judicious nurse. She talked a good deal about Dr. Davis, but Winterbourne paid her the compliment of saying to himself that she was not, after all, such a monstrous goose. "Daisy spoke of you the other day," she said to him. "Half the time she doesn't know what she's saying, but that time I think she did. She gave me a message: she told me to tell you. She told me to tell you that she never was engaged to that handsome Italian. I am sure I am very glad; Mr. Giovanelli hasn't been near us since she was taken ill. I thought he was so much of a gentleman; but I don't call that very polite! A lady told me that he was afraid I was angry with him for taking Daisy round at night. Well, so I am; but I suppose he knows I'm a lady. I would scorn to scold him. Any way, she says she's not engaged. I don't know why she wanted you to know; but she said to me three times—'Mind you tell Mr. Winterbourne.' And then she told me to ask if you remembered the time you went to that castle, in Switzerland. But I said I wouldn't give any such messages as that. Only, if she is not engaged, I'm sure I'm glad to know it."

But, as Winterbourne had said, it mattered very little. A week after this the poor girl died; it had been a terrible case of the fever. Daisy's grave was in the little Protestant cemetery, in an angle of the wall of imperial Rome, beneath the cypresses and the thick spring-flowers. Winterbourne stood there beside it, with a number of other mourners; a number larger than the scandal excited by the young lady's career would have led you to expect. Near him stood Giovanelli, who came nearer still before Winterbourne turned away. Giovanelli was very pale; on this occasion he had no flower in his button-hole; he seemed to wish to say something. At last he said, "She was the most beautiful young lady I ever saw, and the most amiable." And then he added in a moment, "And she was the most innocent."

Winterbourne looked at him, and presently repeated his words, "And the most innocent?"

"The most innocent!"

Winterbourne felt sore and angry. "Why the devil," he asked, "did you take her to that fatal place?"

Mr. Giovanelli's urbanity was apparently imperturbable. He looked on the ground a moment, and then he said, "For myself, I had no fear; and she wanted to go."

"That was no reason!" Winterbourne declared.

The subtle Roman again dropped his eyes. "If she had lived, I should have got nothing. She would never have married me, I am sure."

"She would never have married you?"

"For a moment I hoped so. But no, I am sure."

Winterbourne listened to him; he stood staring at the raw protuberance among the April daisies. When he turned away again Mr. Giovanelli, with his light slow step, had retired.

Winterbourne almost immediately left Rome; but the following summer he again met his aunt, Mrs. Costello, at Vevey. Mrs. Costello was fond of Vevey. In the interval Winterbourne had often thought of Daisy Miller and her mystifying manners. One day he spoke of her to his aunt—said it was on his conscience that he had done her injustice.

"I am sure I don't know," said Mrs. Costello. "How did your injustice affect her?"

"She sent me a message before her death which I didn't understand at the time. But I have understood it since. She would have appreciated one's esteem."

"Is that a modest way," asked Mrs. Costello, "of saying that she would have reciprocated one's affection?"

Winterbourne offered no answer to this question; but he presently said, "You were right in that remark that you made last summer. I was booked to make a mistake. I have lived too long in foreign parts."

Nevertheless, he went back to live at Geneva, whence there continue to come the most contradictory accounts of his motives of sojourn: a report that he is "studying" hard—an intimation that he is much interested in a very clever foreign lady.

1878, 1879

## The Real Thing[1]

### I

When the porter's wife, who used to answer the house-bell, announced "A gentleman and a lady, sir" I had, as I often had in those days—the wish being father to the thought—an immediate vision of sitters. Sitters my visitors in this case proved to be; but not in the sense I should have preferred. There was nothing at first however to indicate that they mightn't have come for a portrait. The gentleman, a man of fifty, very high and very straight, with a mous-

---

1. This "little gem of bright, quick vivid form," as James called it, first appeared in Black and White on April 16, 1892; in "The Real Thing" and Other Tales (1893); and finally in Vol. 18 (1909) of the New York edition, the source of the text printed here.

tache slightly grizzled and a dark grey walking-coat admirably fitted, both of which I noted professionally—I don't mean as a barber or yet as a tailor—would have struck me as a celebrity if celebrities often were striking. It was a truth of which I had for some time been conscious that a figure with a good deal of frontage was, as one might say, almost never a public institution. A glance at the lady helped to remind me of this paradoxical law: she also looked too distinguished to be a "personality." Moreover one would scarcely come across two variations together.

Neither of the pair immediately spoke—they only prolonged the preliminary gaze suggesting that each wished to give the other a chance. They were visibly shy; they stood there letting me take them in—which, as I afterwards perceived, was the most practical thing they could have done. In this way their embarrassment served their cause. I had seen people painfully reluctant to mention that they desired anything so gross as to be represented on canvas; but the scruples of my new friends appeared almost insurmountable. Yet the gentleman might have said "I should like a portrait of my wife," and the lady might have said "I should like a portrait of my husband." Perhaps they weren't husband and wife—this naturally would make the matter more delicate. Perhaps they wished to be done together—in which case they ought to have brought a third person to break the news.

"We come from Mr. Rivet," the lady finally said with a dim smile that had the effect of a moist sponge passed over a "sunk"[2] piece of painting, as well as of a vague allusion to vanished beauty. She was as tall and straight, in her degree, as her companion, and with ten years less to carry. She looked as sad as a woman could look whose face was not charged with expression; that is her tinted oval mask showed waste as an exposed surface shows friction. The hand of time had played over her freely, but to an effect of elimination. She was slim and stiff, and so well-dressed, in dark blue cloth, with lappets and pockets and buttons, that it was clear she employed the same tailor as her husband. The couple had an indefinable air of prosperous thrift—they evidently got a good deal of luxury for their money. If I was to be one of their luxuries it would behove me to consider my terms.

"Ah Claude Rivet recommended me?" I echoed; and I added that it was very kind of him, though I could reflect that, as he only painted landscape, this wasn't a sacrifice.

The lady looked very hard at the gentleman, and the gentleman looked round the room. Then staring at the floor a moment and stroking his moustache, he rested his pleasant eyes on me with the remark: "He said you were the right one."

"I try to be, when people want to sit."

"Yes, we should like to," said the lady anxiously.

"Do you mean together?"

My visitors exchanged a glance. "If you could do anything with *me* I suppose it would be double," the gentleman stammered.

"Oh yes, there's naturally a higher charge for two figures than for one."

"We should like to make it pay," the husband confessed.

"That's very good of you," I returned, appreciating so unwonted a sympathy—for I supposed he meant pay the artist.

---

2. When colors lose their brilliance after they have dried on the canvas, they are said to have "sunk in."

A sense of strangeness seemed to draw on the lady.

"We mean for the illustrations—Mr. Rivet said you might put one in."

"Put in—an illustration?" I was equally confused.

"Sketch her off, you know," said the gentleman, colouring.

It was only then that I understood the service Claude Rivet had rendered me; he had told them how I worked in black-and-white, for magazines, for storybooks, for sketches of contemporary life, and consequently had copious employment for models. These things were true, but it was not less true—I may confess it now; whether because the aspiration was to lead to everything or to nothing I leave the reader to guess—that I couldn't get the honours, to say nothing of the emoluments, of a great painter of portraits out of my head. My "illustrations" were my pot-boilers; I looked to a different branch of art— far and away the most interesting it had always seemed to me—to perpetuate my fame. There was no shame in looking to it also to make my fortune; but that fortune was by so much further from being made from the moment my visitors wished to be "done" for nothing. I was disappointed; for in the pictorial sense I had immediately *seen* them. I had seized their type—I had already settled what I would do with it. Something that wouldn't absolutely have pleased them, I afterwards reflected.

"Ah you're—you're—a—?" I began as soon as I had mastered my surprise. I couldn't bring out the dingy word "models": it seemed so little to fit the case.

"We haven't had much practice," said the lady.

"We've got to *do* something, and we've thought that an artist in your line might perhaps make something of us," her husband threw off. He further mentioned that they didn't know many artists and that they had gone first, on the off-chance—he painted views of course, but sometimes put in figures; perhaps I remembered—to Mr. Rivet, whom they had met a few years before at a place in Norfolk where he was sketching.

"We used to sketch a little ourselves," the lady hinted.

"It's very awkward, but we absolutely *must* do something," her husband went on.

"Of course we're not so *very* young," she admitted with a wan smile.

With the remark that I might as well know something more about them the husband had handed me a card extracted from a neat new pocket-book— their appurtenances were all of the freshest—and inscribed with the words "Major Monarch." Impressive as these words were they didn't carry my knowledge much further; but my visitor presently added: "I've left the army and we've had the misfortune to lose our money. In fact our means are dreadfully small."

"It's awfully trying—a regular strain," said Mrs. Monarch.

They evidently wished to be discreet—to take care not to swagger because they were gentlefolk. I felt them willing to recognise this as something of a drawback, at the same time that I guessed at an underlying sense—their consolation in adversity—that they *had* their points. They certainly had; but these advantages struck me as preponderantly social; such for instance as would help to make a drawing-room look well. However, a drawing-room was always, or ought to be, a picture.

In consequence of his wife's allusion to their age Major Monarch observed: "Naturally it's more for the figure that we thought of going in. We can still hold ourselves up." On the instant I saw that the figure was indeed their strong point. His "naturally" didn't sound vain, but it lighted up the question. "*She* has the best one," he continued, nodding at his wife with a pleasant after-dinner absence of circumlocution. I could only reply, as if we were in fact sitting over our wine, that this didn't prevent his own from being very good; which led him in turn to make answer: "We thought that if you ever have to do people like us we might be something like it. *She* particularly—for a lady in a book, you know."

I was so amused by them that, to get more of it, I did my best to take their point of view; and though it was an embarrassment to find myself appraising physically, as if they were animals on hire or useful blacks, a pair whom I should have expected to meet only in one of the relations in which criticism is tacit, I looked at Mrs. Monarch judicially enough to be able to exclaim after a moment with conviction: "Oh yes, a lady in a book!" She was singularly like a bad illustration.

"We'll stand up, if you like," said the Major; and he raised himself before me with a really grand air.

I could take his measure at a glance—he was six feet two and a perfect gentleman. It would have paid any club in process of formation and in want of a stamp to engage him at a salary to stand in the principal window. What struck me at once was that in coming to me they had rather missed their vocation; they could surely have been turned to better account for advertising purposes. I couldn't of course see the thing in detail, but I could see them make somebody's fortune—I don't mean their own. There was something in them for a waistcoat-maker, an hotel-keeper or a soap-vendor. I could imagine "We always use it" pinned on their bosoms with the greatest effect; I had a vision of the brilliancy with which they would launch a table d'hôte.[3]

Mrs. Monarch sat still, not from pride but from shyness, and presently her husband said to her: "Get up, my dear, and show how smart you are." She obeyed, but she had no need to get up to show it. She walked to the end of the studio and then came back blushing, her fluttered eyes on the partner of her appeal. I was reminded of an incident I had accidentally had a glimpse of in Paris—being with a friend there, a dramatist about to produce a play, when an actress came to him to ask to be entrusted with a part. She went through her paces before him, walked up and down as Mrs. Monarch was doing. Mrs. Monarch did it quite as well, but I abstained from applauding. It was very odd to see such people apply for such poor pay. She looked as if she had ten thousand a year. Her husband had used the word that described her: she was in the London current jargon essentially and typically "smart." Her figure was, in the same order of ideas, conspicuously and irreproachably "good." For a woman of her age her waist was surprisingly small; her elbow moreover had the orthodox crook. She held her head at the conventional angle, but why did she come to *me*? She ought to have tried on jackets at a big shop. I feared my visitors were not only destitute but "artistic"—which would be a great complication. When she sat down again I thanked her, observing that what a draughtsman most valued in his model was the faculty of keeping quiet.

"Oh *she* can keep quiet," said Major Monarch. Then he added jocosely: "I've always kept her quiet."

---

3. A common table for guests at a hotel.

"I'm not a nasty fidget, am I?" It was going to wring tears from me, I felt, the way she hid her head, ostrich-like, in the other broad bosom.

The owner of this expanse addressed his answer to me. "Perhaps it isn't out of place to mention—because we ought to be quite business-like, oughtn't we?—that when I married her she was known as the Beautiful Statue."

"Oh dear!" said Mrs. Monarch ruefully.

"Of course I should want a certain amount of expression," I rejoined.

"Of *course!*"—and I had never heard such unanimity.

"And then I suppose you know that you'll get awfully tired."

"Oh we *never* get tired!" they eagerly cried.

"Have you had any kind of practice?"

They hesitated—they looked at each other. "We've been photographed—*immensely,*" said Mrs. Monarch.

"She means the fellows have asked us themselves," added the Major.

"I see—because you're so good-looking."

"I don't know what they thought, but they were always after us."

"We always got our photographs for nothing," smiled Mrs. Monarch.

"We might have brought some, my dear," her husband remarked.

"I'm not sure we have any left. We've given quantities away," she explained to me.

"With our autographs and that sort of thing," said the Major.

"Are they to be got in the shops?" I enquired as a harmless pleasantry.

"Oh yes, *hers*—they used to be."

"Not now," said Mrs. Monarch with her eyes on the floor.

## II

I could fancy the "sort of thing" they put on the presentation copies of their photographs, and I was sure they wrote a beautiful hand. It was odd how quickly I was sure of everything that concerned them. If they were now so poor as to have to earn shillings and pence they could never have had much of a margin. Their good looks had been their capital, and they had good-humouredly made the most of the career that this resource marked out for them. It was in their faces, the blankness, the deep intellectual repose of the twenty years of country-house visiting that had given them pleasant intonations. I could see the sunny drawing-rooms, sprinkled with periodicals she didn't read, in which Mrs. Monarch had continuously sat; I could see the wet shrubberies in which she had walked, equipped to admiration for either exercise. I could see the rich covers[4] the Major had helped to shoot and the wonderful garments in which, late at night, he repaired to the smoking-room to talk about them. I could imagine their leggings and waterproofs, their knowing tweeds and rugs, their rolls of sticks and cases of tackle and neat umbrellas; and I could evoke the exact appearance of their servants and the compact variety of their luggage on the platforms of country stations.

They gave small tips, but they were liked; they didn't do anything themselves, but they were welcome. They looked so well everywhere; they gratified the general relish for stature, complexion and "form." They knew it

4. I.e., successful bagging of game birds.

without fatuity or vulgarity, and they respected themselves in consequence. They weren't superficial; they were thorough and kept themselves up—it had been their line. People with such a taste for activity had to have some line. I could feel how even in a dull house they could have been counted on for the joy of life. At present something had happened—it didn't matter what, their little income had grown less, it had grown least—and they had to do something for pocket-money. Their friends could like them, I made out, without liking to support them. There was something about them that represented credit—their clothes, their manners, their type; but if credit is a large empty pocket in which an occasional chink reverberates, the chink at least must be audible. What they wanted of me was to help to make it so. Fortunately they had no children—I soon divined that. They would also perhaps wish our relations to be kept secret: this was why it was "for the figure"—the reproduction of the face would betray them.

I liked them—I felt, quite as their friends must have done—they were so simple; and I had no objection to them if they would suit. But somehow with all their perfections I didn't easily believe in them. After all they were amateurs, and the ruling passion of my life was the detestation of the amateur. Combined with this was another perversity—an innate preference for the represented subject over the real one: the defect of the real one was so apt to be a lack of representation. I liked things that appeared; then one was sure. Whether they *were* or not was a subordinate and almost always a profitless question. There were other considerations, the first of which was that I already had two or three recruits in use, notably a young person with big feet, in alpaca, from Kilburn, who for a couple of years had come to me regularly for my illustrations and with whom I was still—perhaps ignobly—satisfied. I frankly explained to my visitors how the case stood, but they had taken more precautions than I supposed. They had reasoned out their opportunity, for Claude Rivet had told them of the projected *édition de luxe* of one of the writers of our day—the rarest of the novelists—who, long neglected by the multitudinous vulgar and dearly prized by the attentive (need I mention Philip Vincent?)[5] had had the happy fortune of seeing, late in life, the dawn and then the full light of a higher criticism; an estimate in which on the part of the public there was something really of expiation. The edition preparing, planned by a publisher of taste, was practically an act of high reparation; the wood-cuts with which it was to be enriched were the homage of English art to one of the most independent representatives of English letters. Major and Mrs. Monarch confessed to me they had hoped I might be able to work *them* into my branch of the enterprise. They knew I was to do the first of the books, "Rutland Ramsay," but I had to make clear to them that my participation in the rest of the affair—this first book was to be a test—must depend on the satisfaction I should give. If this should be limited my employers would drop me with scarce common forms. It was therefore a crisis for me, and naturally I was making special preparations, looking about for new people, should they be necessary, and securing the best types. I admitted however that I should like to settle down to two or three good models who would do for everything.

"Should we have often to—a—put on special clothes?" Mrs. Monarch timidly demanded.

---

5. Obviously James, here indulging in some good-natured complaining and fantasizing.

"Dear yes—that's half the business."

"And should we be expected to supply our own costumes?"

"Oh no; I've got a lot of things. A painter's models put on—or put off—anything he likes."

"And you mean—a—the same?"

"The same?"

Mrs. Monarch looked at her husband again.

"Oh she was just wondering," he explained, "if the costumes are in *general* use." I had to confess that they were, and I mentioned further that some of them—I had a lot of genuine greasy last-century things—had served their time, a hundred years ago, on living world-stained men and women; on figures not perhaps so far removed, in that vanished world, from *their* type, the Monarchs', *quoi!*[6] of a breeched and bewigged age. "We'll put on anything that *fits*," said the Major.

"Oh I arrange that—they fit in the pictures."

"I'm afraid I should do better for the modern books. I'd come as you like," said Mrs. Monarch.

"She has got a lot of clothes at home: they might do for contemporary life," her husband continued.

"Oh I can fancy scenes in which you'd be quite natural." And indeed I could see the slipshod rearrangements of stale properties—the stories I tried to produce pictures for without the exasperation of reading them—whose sandy tracts the good lady might help to people. But I had to return to the fact that for this sort of work—the daily mechanical grind—I was already equipped: the people I was working with were fully adequate.

"We only thought we might be more like *some* characters," said Mrs. Monarch mildly, getting up.

Her husband also rose; he stood looking at me with a dim wistfulness that was touching in so fine a man. "Wouldn't it be rather a pull sometimes to have—a—to have—?" He hung fire; he wanted me to help him by phrasing what he meant. But I couldn't—I didn't know. So he brought it out awkwardly: "The *real* thing; a gentleman, you know, or a lady." I was quite ready to give a general assent—I admitted that there was a great deal in that. This encouraged Major Monarch to say, following up his appeal with an unacted gulp: "It's awfully hard—we've tried everything." The gulp was communicative; it proved too much for his wife. Before I knew it Mrs. Monarch had dropped again upon a divan and burst into tears. Her husband sat down beside her, holding one of her hands; whereupon she quickly dried her eyes with the other, while I felt embarrassed as she looked up at me. "There isn't a confounded job I haven't applied for—waited for—prayed for. You can fancy we'd be pretty bad first. Secretaryships and that sort of thing? You might as well ask for a peerage. I'd be *anything*—I'm strong; a messenger or a coal-heaver. I'd put on a gold-laced cap and open carriage-doors in front of the haberdasher's; I'd hang about a station to carry portmanteaux; I'd be a post-man. But they won't *look* at you; there are thousands as good as yourself already on the ground. *Gentlemen,* poor beggars, who've drunk their wine, who've kept their hunters!"

I was as reassuring as I knew how to be, and my visitors were presently on

6. What! (French).

their feet again while, for the experiment, we agreed on an hour. We were discussing it when the door opened and Miss Churm came in with a wet umbrella. Miss Churm had to take the omnibus to Maida Vale and then walk half a mile. She looked a trifle blowsy and slightly splashed. I scarcely ever saw her come in without thinking afresh how odd it was that, being so little in herself, she should yet be so much in others. She was a meagre little Miss Churm, but was such an ample heroine of romance. She was only a freckled cockney,[7] but she could represent everything, from a fine lady to a shepherdess; she had the faculty as she might have had a fine voice or long hair. She couldn't spell and she loved beer, but she had two or three "points," and practice, and a knack, and mother-wit, and a whimsical sensibility, and a love of the theatre, and seven sisters, and not an ounce of respect, especially for the *h*. The first thing my visitors saw was that her umbrella was wet, and in their spotless perfection they visibly winced at it. The rain had come on since their arrival.

"I'm all in a soak; there *was* a mess of people in the 'bus. I wish you lived near a stytion," said Miss Churm. I requested her to get ready as quickly as possible, and she passed into the room in which she always changed her dress. But before going out she asked me what she was to get into this time.

"It's the Russian princess, don't you know?" I answered; "the one with the 'golden eyes,' in black velvet, for the long thing in the *Cheapside*."[8]

"Golden eyes? I *say!*" cried Miss Churm, while my companions watched her with intensity as she withdrew. She always arranged herself, when she was late, before I could turn around; and I kept my visitors a little on purpose, so that they might get an idea, from seeing her, what would be expected of themselves. I mentioned that she was quite my notion of an excellent model—she was really very clever.

"Do you think she looks like a Russian princess?" Major Monarch asked with lurking alarm.

"When I make her, yes."

"Oh if you have to *make* her—!" he reasoned, not without point.

"That's the most you can ask. There are so many who are not makeable."

"Well now, *here's* a lady"—and with a persuasive smile he passed his arm into his wife's—"who's already made!"

"Oh I'm not a Russian princess," Mrs. Monarch protested a little coldly. I could see she had known some and didn't like them. There at once was a complication of a kind I never had to fear with Miss Churm.

This young lady came back in black velvet—the gown was rather rusty and very low on her lean shoulders—and with a Japanese fan in her red hands. I reminded her that in the scene I was doing she had to look over some one's head. "I forget whose it is; but it doesn't matter. Just look over a head."

"I'd rather look over a stove," said Miss Churm; and she took her station near the fire. She fell into position, settled herself into a tall attitude, gave a certain backward inclination to her head and a certain forward droop to her fan, and looked, at least to my prejudiced sense, distinguished and charming, foreign and dangerous. We left her looking so while I went downstairs with Major and Mrs. Monarch.

---

7. Native of London, especially the East End. The cockney dialect is known for dropping *h*'s; e.g., *hair* would be pronounced *air*.

8. Imaginary magazine named after a main business street in London.

"I believe I could come about as near it as that," said Mrs. Monarch.

"Oh, you think she's shabby, but you must allow for the alchemy of art."

However, they went off with an evident increase of comfort founded on their demonstrable advantage in being the real thing. I could fancy them shuddering over Miss Churm. She was very droll about them when I went back, for I told her what they wanted.

"Well, if *she* can sit I'll tyke to bookkeeping," said my model.

"She's very ladylike," I replied as an innocent form of aggravation.

"So much the worse for *you*. That means she can't turn round."

"She'll do for the fashionable novels."

"Oh yes, she'll *do* for them!" my model humorously declared. "Ain't they bad enough without her?" I had often sociably denounced them to Miss Churm.

### III

It was for the elucidation of a mystery in one of these works that I first tried Mrs. Monarch. Her husband came with her, to be useful if necessary—it was sufficiently clear that as a general thing he would prefer to come with her. At first I wondered if this were for "propriety's" sake—if he were going to be jealous and meddling. The idea was too tiresome, and if it had been confirmed it would speedily have brought our acquaintance to a close. But I soon saw there was nothing in it and that if he accompanied Mrs. Monarch it was—in addition to the chance of being wanted—simply because he had nothing else to do. When they were separate his occupation was gone and they never *had* been separate. I judged rightly that in their awkward situation their close union was their main comfort and that this union had no weak spot. It was a real marriage, an encouragement to the hesitating, a nut for pessimists to crack. Their address was humble—I remember afterwards thinking it had been the only thing about them that was really professional—and I could fancy the lamentable lodgings in which the Major would have been left alone. He could sit there more or less grimly with his wife—he couldn't sit there anyhow without her.

He had too much tact to try and make himself agreeable when he couldn't be useful; so when I was too absorbed in my work to talk he simply sat and waited. But I liked to hear him talk—it made my work, when not interrupting it, less mechanical, less special. To listen to him was to combine the excitement of going out with the economy of staying at home. There was only one hindrance—that I seemed not to know any of the people this brilliant couple had known. I think he wondered extremely, during the term of our intercourse, whom the deuce I *did* know. He hadn't a stray sixpence of an idea to fumble for, so we didn't spin it very fine; we confined ourselves to questions of leather and even of liquor—saddlers and breeches-makers and how to get excellent claret cheap—and matters like "good trains" and the habits of small game. His lore on these last subjects was astonishing—he managed to interweave the station-master with the ornithologist. When he couldn't talk about greater things he could talk cheerfully about smaller, and since I couldn't accompany him into reminiscences of the fashionable world he could lower the conversation without a visible effort to my level.

So earnest a desire to please was touching in a man who could so easily have knocked one down. He looked after the fire and had an opinion on the draught of the stove without my asking him, and I could see that he thought many of my arrangements not half knowing. I remember telling him that if I were only rich I'd offer him a salary to come and teach me how to live. Sometimes he gave a random sigh of which the essence might have been: "Give me even such a bare old barrack as *this*, and I'd do something with it!" When I wanted to use him he came alone; which was an illustration of the superior courage of women. His wife could bear her solitary second floor, and she was in general more discreet; showing by various small reserves that she was alive to the propriety of keeping our relations markedly professional—not letting them slide into sociability. She wished it to remain clear that she and the Major were employed, not cultivated, and if she approved of me as a superior, who could be kept in his place, she never thought me quite good enough for an equal.

She sat with great intensity, giving the whole of her mind to it, and was capable of remaining for an hour almost as motionless as before a photographer's lens. I could see she had been photographed often, but somehow the very habit that made her good for that purpose unfitted her for mine. At first I was extremely pleased with her ladylike air, and it was a satisfaction, on coming to follow her lines, to see how good they were and how far they could lead the pencil. But after a little skirmishing I began to find her too insurmountably stiff; do what I would with it my drawing looked like a photograph or a copy of a photograph. Her figure had no variety of expression—she herself had no sense of variety. You may say that this was my business and was only a question of placing her. Yet I placed her in every conceivable position and she managed to obliterate their differences. She was always a lady certainly, and into the bargain was always the same lady. She was the real thing, but always the same thing. There were moments when I rather writhed under the serenity of her confidence that she *was* the real thing. All her dealings with me and all her husband's were an implication that this was lucky for *me*. Meanwhile I found myself trying to invent types that approached her own, instead of making her own transform itself—in the clever way that was not impossible for instance to poor Miss Churm. Arrange as I would and take the precautions I would, she always came out, in my pictures, too tall—landing me in the dilemma of having represented a fascinating woman as seven feet high, which (out of respect perhaps to my own very much scantier inches) was far from my idea of such a personage.

The case was worse with the Major—nothing I could do would keep *him* down, so that he became useful only for representation of brawny giants. I adored variety and range, I cherished human accidents, the illustrative note; I wanted to characterise closely, and the thing in the world I most hated was the danger of being ridden by a type. I had quarrelled with some of my friends about it; I had parted company with them for maintaining that one *had* to be, and that if the type was beautiful—witness Raphael and Leonardo[9]—the servitude was only a gain. I was neither Leonardo nor Raphael—I might only be a presumptuous young modern searcher; but I held that everything was to be sacrificed sooner than character. When they claimed that the obsessional

---

9. Leonardo da Vinci (1452–1519), Florentine painter, sculptor, architect, and engineer. Raffaello Santi or Sanzio (1483–1520), Italian painter.

form could easily *be* character I retorted, perhaps superficially, "Whose?" It couldn't be everybody's—it might end in being nobody's.

After I had drawn Mrs. Monarch a dozen times I felt surer even than before that the value of such a model as Miss Churm resided precisely in the fact that she had no positive stamp, combined of course with the other fact that what she did have was a curious and inexplicable talent for imitation. Her usual appearance was like a curtain which she could draw up at request for a capital performance. This performance was simply suggestive; but it was a word to the wise—it was vivid and pretty. Sometimes even I thought it, though she was plain herself, too insipidly pretty; I made it a reproach to her that the figures drawn from her were monotonously (*bêtement*,[1] as we used to say) graceful. Nothing made her more angry: it was so much her pride to feel she could sit for characters that had nothing in common with each other. She would accuse me at such moments of taking away her "reputytion."

It suffered a certain shrinkage, this queer quantity, from the repeated visits of my new friends. Miss Churm was greatly in demand, never in want of employment, so I had no scruple in putting her off occasionally, to try them more at my ease. It was certainly amusing at first to do the real thing—it was amusing to do Major Monarch's trousers. There *were* the real thing, even if he did come out colossal. It was amusing to do his wife's back hair—it was so mathematically neat—and the particular "smart" tension of her tight stays. She lent herself especially to positions in which the face was somewhat averted or blurred; she abounded in ladylike back views and *profils perdus*.[2] When she stood erect she took naturally one of the attitudes in which court-painters represent queens and princesses; so that I found myself wondering whether, to draw out this accomplishment, I couldn't get the editor of the *Cheapside* to publish a really royal romance, "A Tale of Buckingham Palace." Sometimes however the real thing and the make-believe came into contact; by which I mean that Miss Churm, keeping an appointment or coming to make one on days when I had much work in hand, encountered her invidious rivals. The encounter was not on their part, for they noticed her no more than if she had been the housemaid; not from intentional loftiness, but simply because as yet, professionally, they didn't know how to fraternise, as I could imagine they would have liked—or at least that the Major would. They couldn't talk about the omnibus—they always walked; and they didn't know what else to try—she wasn't interested in good trains or cheap claret. Besides, they must have felt—in the air—that she was amused at them, secretly derisive of their ever knowing how. She wasn't a person to conceal the limits of her faith if she had had a chance to show them. On the other hand Mrs. Monarch didn't think her tidy; for why else did she take pains to say to me— it was going out of the way, for Mrs. Monarch—that she didn't like dirty women?

One day when my young lady happened to be present with my other sitters— she even dropped in, when it was convenient, for a chat—I asked her to be so good as to lend a hand in getting tea, a service with which she was familiar and which was one of a class that, living as I did in a small way, with slender domestic resources, I often appealed to my models to render. They liked to lay hands on my property, to break the sitting, and sometimes the

---

1. Foolishly (French).      2. Averted glances (French).

china—it made them feel Bohemian. The next time I saw Miss Churm after this incident she surprised me greatly by making a scene about it—she accused me of having wished to humiliate her. She hadn't resented the outrage at the time, but had seemed obliging and amused, enjoying the comedy of asking Mrs. Monarch, who sat vague and silent, whether she would have cream and sugar, and putting an exaggerated simper into the question. She had tried intonations—as if she too wished to pass for the real thing—till I was afraid my other visitors would take offence.

Oh they were determined not to do this, and their touching patience was the measure of their great need. They would sit by the hour, uncomplaining, till I was ready to use them; they would come back on the chance of being wanted and would walk away cheerfully if it failed. I used to go to the door with them to see in what magnificent order they retreated. I tried to find other employment for them—I introduced them to several artists. But they didn't "take," for reasons I could appreciate, and I became rather anxiously aware that after such disappointments they fell back upon me with a heavier weight. They did me the honour to think me most *their* form. They weren't romantic enough for the painters, and in those days there were few serious workers in black-and-white. Besides, they had an eye to the great job I had mentioned to them—they had secretly set their hearts on supplying the right essence for my pictorial vindication of our fine novelist. They knew that for this undertaking I should want no costume-effects, none of the frippery of past ages—that it was a case in which everything would be contemporary and satirical and presumably genteel. If I could work them into it their future would be assured, for the labour would of course be long and the occupation steady.

One day Mrs. Monarch came without her husband—she explained his absence by his having had to go to the City.[3] While she sat there in her usual relaxed majesty there came at the door a knock which I immediately recognised as the subdued appeal of a model out of work. It was followed by the entrance of a young man whom I at once saw to be a foreigner and who proved in fact an Italian acquainted with no English word but my name, which he uttered in a way that made it seem to include all others. I hadn't then visited his country, nor was I proficient in his tongue; but as he was not so meanly constituted—what Italian is?—as to depend only on that member for expression he conveyed to me, in familiar but graceful mimicry, that he was in search of exactly the employment in which the lady before me was engaged. I was not struck with him at first, and while I continued to draw I dropped few signs of interest or encouragement. He stood his ground however—not importunately, but with a dumb dog-like fidelity in his eyes that amounted to innocent impudence, the manner of a devoted servant—he might have been in the house for years—unjustly suspected. Suddenly it struck me that this very attitude and expression made a picture; whereupon I told him to sit down and wait till I should be free. There was another picture in the way he obeyed me, and I observed as I worked that there were others still in the way he looked wonderingly, with his head thrown back, about the high studio. He might have been crossing himself in Saint Peter's. Before

3. London. The "City" also specifically means the old part of London around St. Paul's Cathedral, especially the financial and legal institutions there.

I finished I said to myself "The fellow's a bankrupt orange-monger, but a treasure."

When Mrs. Monarch withdrew he passed across the room like a flash to open the door for her, standing there with the rapt pure gaze of the young Dante spellbound by the young Beatrice.[4] As I never insisted, in such situations, on the blankness of the British domestic, I reflected that he had the making of a servant—and I needed one, but couldn't pay him to be only that—as well as of a model; in short I resolved to adopt my bright adventurer if he would agree to officiate in the double capacity. He jumped at my offer, and in the event my rashness—for I had really known nothing about him— wasn't brought home to me. He proved a sympathetic though a desultory ministrant, and had in a wonderful degree the *sentiment de la pose*.[5] It was uncultivated, instinctive, a part of the happy instinct that had guided him to my door and helped him to spell out my name on the card nailed to it. He had had no other introduction to me than a guess, from the shape of my high north window, seen outside, that my place was a studio and that as a studio it would contain an artist. He had wandered to England in search of fortune, like other itinerants, and had embarked, with a partner and a small green hand-cart, on the sale of penny ices. The ices had melted away and the partner had dissolved in their train. My young man wore tight yellow trousers with reddish stripes and his name was Oronte. He was sallow but fair, and when I put him into some old clothes of my own he looked like an Englishman. He was as good as Miss Churm, who could look, when requested, like an Italian.

## IV

I thought Mrs. Monarch's face slightly convulsed when, on her coming back with her husband, she found Oronte installed. It was strange to have to recognise in a scrap of a lazzarone[6] a competitor to her magnificent Major. It was she who scented danger first, for the Major was anecdotically unconscious. But Oronte gave us tea, with a hundred eager confusions—he had never been concerned in so queer a process—and I think she thought better of me for having at last an "establishment." They saw a couple of drawings that I had made of the establishment, and Mrs. Monarch hinted that it never would have struck her he had sat for them. "Now the drawings you make from *us*, they look exactly like us," she reminded me, smiling in triumph; and I recognised that this was indeed just their defect. When I drew the Monarchs I couldn't anyhow get away from them—get into the character I wanted to represent; and I hadn't the least desire my model should be discoverable in my picture. Miss Churm never was, and Mrs. Monarch thought I hid her, very properly, because she was vulgar; whereas if she was lost it was only as the dead who go to heaven are lost—in the gain of an angel the more.

By this time I had got a certain start with "Rutland Ramsay," the first novel in the great projected series; that is I had produced a dozen drawings, several with the help of the Major and his wife, and I had sent them in for approval.

4. Dante Alighieri (1265–1321), Italian poet, first saw Beatrice Portinari when they were both nine. Though he saw her only a few times, she made a lasting impression on him and became his ideal, his life's inspiration, and the direct agent of his sal- vation (as his greatest work, *The Divine Comedy*, makes clear).
5. Instinct for striking poses (French).
6. Beggar (Italian).

My understanding with the publishers, as I have already hinted, had been that I was to be left to do my work, in this particular case, as I liked, with the whole book committed to me; but my connexion with the rest of the series was only contingent. There were moments when, frankly, it *was* a comfort to have the real thing under one's hand; for there were characters in "Rutland Ramsay" that were very much like it. There were people presumably as erect as the Major and women of as good a fashion as Mrs. Monarch. There was a great deal of country-house life—treated, it is true, in a fine fanciful ironical generalised way—and there was a considerable implication of knickerbockers and kilts.[7] There were certain things I had to settle at the outset; such things for instance as the exact appearance of the hero and the particular bloom and figure of the heroine. The author of course gave me a lead, but there was a margin for interpretation. I took the Monarchs into my confidence, I told them frankly what I was about, I mentioned my embarrassments and alternatives. "Oh take *him!*" Mrs. Monarch murmured sweetly, looking at her husband; and "What could you want better than my wife?" the Major enquired with the comfortable candour that now prevailed between us.

I wasn't obliged to answer these remarks—I was only obliged to place my sitters. I wasn't easy in mind, and I postponed a little timidly perhaps the solving of my question. The book was a large canvas, the other figures were numerous, and I worked off at first some of the episodes in which the hero and the heroine were not concerned. When once I had set *them* up I should have to stick to them—I couldn't make my young man seven feet high in one place and five feet nine in another. I inclined on the whole to the latter measurement, though the Major more than once reminded me that *he* looked about as young as any one. It was indeed quite possible to arrange him, for the figure, so that it would have been difficult to detect his age. After the spontaneous Oronte had been with me a month, and after I had given him to understand several times over that his native exuberance would presently constitute an insurmountable barrier to our further intercourse, I waked to a sense of his heroic capacity. He was only five feet seven, but the remaining inches were latent. I tried him almost secretly at first, for I was really rather afraid of the judgment my other models would pass on such a choice. If they regarded Miss Churm as little better than a snare what would they think of the representation by a person so little the real thing as an Italian street-vendor of a protagonist formed by a public school?

If I went a little in fear of them it wasn't because they bullied me, because they had got an oppressive foothold, but because in their really pathetic decorum and mysteriously permanent newness they counted on me so intensely. I was therefore very glad when Jack Hawley came home: he was always of such good counsel. He painted badly himself, but there was no one like him for putting his finger on the place. He had been absent from England for a year; he had been somewhere—I don't remember where—to get a fresh eye. I was in a good deal of dread of any such organ, but we were old friends; he had been away for months and a sense of emptiness was creeping into my life. I hadn't dodged a missile for a year.

He came back with a fresh eye, but with the same old black velvet blouse,

7. Knickerbockers (close-fitting short pants gathered at the knee) and kilts (knee-length pleated skirts, usually of tartan, worn by Scottish men) suggest a rural, outdoor attire.

and the first evening he spent in my studio we smoked cigarettes till the small hours. He had done no work himself, he had only got the eye; so the field was clear for the production of my little things. He wanted to see what I had produced for the *Cheapside,* but he was disappointed in the exhibition. That at least seemed the meaning of two or three comprehensive groans which, as he lounged on my big divan, his leg folded under him, looking at my latest drawings, issued from his lips with the smoke of the cigarette.

"What's the matter with you?" I asked.

"What's the matter with *you?*"

"Nothing save that I'm mystified."

"You are indeed. You're quite off the hinge. What's the meaning of this new fad?" And he tossed me, with visible irreverence, a drawing in which I happened to have depicted both my elegant models. I asked if he didn't think it good, and he replied that it struck him as execrable, given the sort of thing I had always represented myself to him as wishing to arrive at; but I let that pass—I was so anxious to see exactly what he meant. The two figures in the picture looked colossal, but I supposed this was *not* what he meant, inasmuch as, for aught he knew the contrary, I might have been trying for some such effect. I maintained that I was working exactly in the same way as when he last had done me the honour to tell me I might do something some day. "Well, there's a screw loose somewhere," he answered; "wait a bit and I'll discover it." I depended upon him to do so: where else was the fresh eye? But he produced at last nothing more luminous than "I don't know—I don't like your types." This was lame for a critic who had never consented to discuss with me anything but the question of execution, the direction of strokes and the mystery of values.

"In the drawings you've been looking at I think my types are very handsome."

"Oh they won't do!"

"I've been working with new models."

"I see you have. *They* won't do."

"Are you very sure of that?"

"Absolutely—they're stupid."

"You mean *I* am—for I ought to get round that."

"You *can't*—with such people. Who are they?"

I told him, so far as was necessary, and he concluded heartlessly: "Ce sont des gens qu'il faut mettre à la porte."[8]

"You've never seen them; they're awfully good"—I flew to their defence.

"Not seen them? Why all this recent work of yours drops to pieces with them. It's all I want to see of them."

"No one else has said anything against it—the *Cheapside* people are pleased."

"Everyone else is an ass, and the *Cheapside* people the biggest asses of all. Come, don't pretend at this time of day to have pretty illusions about the public, especially about publishers and editors. It's not for *such* animals you work—it's for those who know, *coloro che sanno*;[9] so keep straight for *me* if you can't keep straight for yourself. There was a certain sort of thing you used

8. Such people should be shown the door (French).

9. A misquotation of a phrase Dante applied to Aristotle in *The Divine Comedy,* "Inferno," 4.131, which reads, *"el maestro di color che sanno,"* literally, "the master of those who know."

to try for—and a very good thing it was. But this twaddle isn't *in* it." When I talked with Hawley later about "Rutland Ramsay" and its possible successors he declared that I must get back into my boat again or I should go to the bottom. His voice in short was the voice of warning.

I noted the warning, but I didn't turn my friends out of doors. They bored me a good deal; but the very fact that they bored me admonished me not to sacrifice them—if there was anything to be done with them—simply to irritation. As I look back at this phase they seem to me to have pervaded my life not a little. I have a vision of them as most of the time in my studio, seated against the wall on an old velvet bench to be out of the way, and resembling the while a pair of patient courtiers in a royal ante-chamber. I'm convinced that during the coldest weeks of the winter they held their ground because it saved them fire. Their newness was losing its gloss, and it was impossible not to feel them objects of charity. Whenever Miss Churm arrived they went away, and after I was fairly launched in "Rutland Ramsay" Miss Churm arrived pretty often. They managed to express to me tacitly that they supposed I wanted her for the low life of the book, and I let them suppose it, since they had attempted to study the work—it was lying about the studio—without discovering that it dealt only with the highest circles. They had dipped into the most brilliant of our novelists without deciphering many passages. I still took an hour from them, now and again, in spite of Jack Hawley's warning: it would be time enough to dismiss them, if dismissal should be necessary, when the rigour of the season was over. Hawley had made their acquaintance—he had met them at my fireside—and thought them a ridiculous pair. Learning that he was a painter they tried to approach him, to show him too that they were the real thing; but he looked at them, across the big room, as if they were miles away: they were a compendium of everything he most objected to in the social system of his country. Such people as that, all convention and patent-leather, with ejaculations that stopped conversation, had no business in a studio. A studio was a place to learn to see, and how could you see through a pair of feather-beds?

The main inconvenience I suffered at their hands was that at first I was shy of letting it break upon them that my artful little servant had begun to sit to me for "Rutland Ramsay." They knew I had been odd enough—they were prepared by this time to allow oddity to artists—to pick a foreign vagabond out of the streets when I might have had a person with whiskers and credentials, but it was some time before they learned how high I rated his accomplishments. They found him in an attitude more than once, but they never doubted I was doing him as an organ-grinder. There were several things they never guessed, and one of them was that for a striking scene in the novel, in which a footman briefly figured, it occurred to me to make use of Major Monarch as the menial. I kept putting this off, I didn't like to ask him to don the livery—besides the difficulty of finding a livery to fit him. At last, one day late in the winter, when I was at work on the despised Oronte, who caught one's idea on the wing, and was in the glow of feeling myself go very straight, they came in, the Major and his wife, with their society laugh about nothing (there was less and less to laugh at); came in like country-callers—they always reminded me of that—who have walked across the park after church and are presently persuaded to stay to luncheon. Luncheon was over, but they could stay to tea—I knew they wanted it. The fit was on me, however, and I couldn't let my ardour cool and my work wait, with the fading daylight, while my model prepared it. So I asked Mrs. Monarch if she would mind laying it out— a request which for an instant brought all the blood to her face. Her eyes were on her husband's for a second, and some mute telegraphy passed between them. Their folly was over the next instant; his cheerful shrewdness put an end to it. So far from pitying their wounded pride, I must add, I was moved to give it as complete a lesson as I could. They bustled about together and got out the cups and saucers and made the kettle boil. I know they felt as if they were waiting on my servant, and when the tea was prepared I said: "He'll have a cup, please—he's tired." Mrs. Monarch brought him one where he stood, and he took it from her as if had been a gentleman at a party squeezing a crush-hat with an elbow.

Then it came over me that she had made a great effort for me—made it with a kind of nobleness—and that I owed her a compensation. Each time I saw her after this I wondered what the compensation could be. I couldn't go on doing the wrong thing to oblige them. Oh it *was* the wrong thing, the stamp of the work for which they sat—Hawley was not the only person to say it now. I sent in a large number of the drawings I had made for "Rutland Ramsay," and I received a warning that was more to the point than Hawley's. The artistic adviser of the house for which I was working was of opinion that many of my illustrations were not what had been looked for. Most of these illustrations were the subjects in which the Monarchs had figured. Without going into the question of what *had* been looked for, I had to face the fact that at this rate I shouldn't get the other books to do. I hurled myself in despair on Miss Churm—I put her through all her paces. I not only adopted Oronte publicly as my hero, but one morning when the Major looked in to see if I didn't require him to finish a *Cheapside* figure for which he had begun to sit the week before, I told him I had changed my mind—I'd do the drawing from my man. At this my visitor turned pale and stood looking at me. "Is *he* your idea of an English gentleman?" he asked.

I was disappointed, I was nervous, I wanted to get on with my work; so I replied with irritation: "Oh my dear Major—I can't be ruined for *you!*"

It was a horrid speech, but he stood another moment—after which, without a word, he quitted the studio. I drew a long breath, for I said to myself that I shouldn't see him again. I hadn't told him definitely that I was in danger of having my work rejected, but I was vexed at his not having felt the catastrophe in the air, read with me the moral of our fruitless collaboration, the lesson that in the deceptive atmosphere of art even the highest respectability may fail of being plastic.

I didn't owe my friends money, but I did see them again. They reappeared together three days later, and, given all the other facts, there was something tragic in that one. It was a clear proof they could find nothing else in life to do. They had threshed the matter out in a dismal conference—they had digested the bad news that they were not in for the series. If they weren't useful to me even for the *Cheapside* their function seemed difficult to determine, and I could only judge at first that they had come, forgivingly, decorously, to take a last leave. This made me rejoice in secret that I had little leisure for a scene; for I had placed both my other models in position together and I was pegging away at a drawing from which I hoped to derive glory. It had been suggested by the passage in which Rutland Ramsay, drawing up a chair to

Artemisia's piano-stool, says extraordinary things to her while she ostensibly fingers out a difficult piece of music. I had done Miss Churm at the piano before—it was an attitude in which she knew how to take on an absolutely poetic grace. I wished the two figures to "compose" together with intensity, and my little Italian had entered perfectly into my conception. The pair were vividly before me, the piano had been pulled out; it was a charming show of blended youth and murmured love, which I had only to catch and keep. My visitors stood and looked at it, and I was friendly to them over my shoulder.

They made no response, but I was used to silent company and went on with my work, only a little disconcerted—even though exhilarated by the sense that *this* was at least the ideal thing—at not having got rid of them after all. Presently I heard Mrs. Monarch's sweet voice beside or rather above me: "I wish her hair were a little better done." I looked up and she was staring with a strange fixedness at Miss Churm, whose back was turned to her. "Do you mind my just touching it?" she went on—a question which made me spring up for an instant as with the instinctive fear that she might do the young lady a harm. But she quieted me with a glance I shall never forget—I confess I should like to have been able to paint *that*—and went for a moment to my model. She spoke to her softly, laying a hand on her shoulder and bending over her; and as the girl, understanding, gratefully assented, she disposed her rough curls, with a few quick passes, in such a way as to make Miss Churm's head twice as charming. It was one of the most heroic personal services I've ever seen rendered. Then Mrs. Monarch turned away with a low sigh and, looking about her as if for something to do, stooped to the floor with a noble humility and picked up a dirty rag that had dropped out of my paint-box.

The Major meanwhile had also been looking for something to do, and, wandering to the other end of the studio, saw before him my breakfast-things neglected, unremoved. "I say, can't I be useful *here*?" he called out to me with an irrepressible quaver. I assented with a laugh that I fear was awkward, and for the next ten minutes, while I worked, I heard the light clatter of china and the tinkle of spoons and glass. Mrs. Monarch assisted her husband—they washed up my crockery, they put it away. They wandered off into my little scullery, and I afterwards found that they had cleaned my knives and that my slender stock of plate had an unprecedented surface. When it came over me, the latent eloquence of what they were doing, I confess that my drawing was blurred for a moment—the picture swam. They had accepted their failure, but they couldn't accept their fate. They had bowed their heads in bewilderment to the perverse and cruel law in virtue of which the real thing could be so much less precious than the unreal; but they didn't want to starve. If my servants were my models, then my models might be my servants. They would reverse the parts—the others would sit for the ladies and gentlemen and *they* would do the work. They would still be in the studio—it was an intense dumb appeal to me not to turn them out. "Take us on," they wanted to say—"we'll do *anything*."

My pencil dropped from my hand; my sitting was spoiled and I got rid of my sitters, who were also evidently rather mystified and awestruck. Then, alone with the Major and his wife I had a most uncomfortable moment. He put their prayer into a single sentence: "I say, you know—just let *us* do for you, can't you?" I couldn't—it was dreadful to see them emptying my slops; but I pretended I could, to oblige them, for about a week. Then I gave them a sum of money to go away, and I never saw them again. I obtained the remaining books, but my friend Hawley repeats that Major and Mrs. Monarch did me a permanent harm, got me into false ways. If it be true I'm content to have paid the price—for the memory.

1892, 1909

# The Beast in the Jungle[1]

## I

What determined the speech that startled him in the course of their encounter scarcely matters, being probably but some words spoken by himself quite without intention—spoken as they lingered and slowly moved together after their renewal of acquaintance. He had been conveyed by friends an hour or two before to the house at which she was staying; the party of visitors at the other house, of whom he was one, and thanks to whom it was his theory, as always, that he was lost in the crowd, had been invited over to luncheon. There had been after luncheon much dispersal, all in the interest of the original motive, a view of Weatherend itself and the fine things, intrinsic features, pictures, heirlooms, treasures of all the arts, that made the place almost famous; and the great rooms were so numerous that guests could wander at their will, hang back from the principal group and in cases where they took such matters with the last seriousness give themselves up to mysterious appreciations and measurements. There were persons to be observed, singly or in couples, bending toward objects in out-of-the-way corners with their hands on their knees and their heads nodding quite as with the emphasis of an excited sense of smell. When they were two they either mingled their sounds of ecstasy or melted into silences of even deeper import, so that there were aspects of the occasion that gave it for Marcher much the air of the "look round," previous to a sale highly advertised, that excites or quenches, as may be, the dream of acquisition. The dream of acquisition at Weatherend would have had to be wild indeed, and John Marcher found himself, among such suggestions, disconcerted almost equally by the presence of those who knew too much and by that of those who knew nothing. The great rooms caused so much poetry and history to press upon him that he needed some straying apart to feel in a proper relation with them, though this impulse was not, as happened, like the gloating of some of his companions, to be compared to the movements of a dog sniffing a cupboard. It had an issue promptly enough in a direction that was not to have been calculated.

It led, briefly, in the course of the October afternoon, to his closer meeting with May Bartram, whose face, a reminder, yet not quite a remembrance, as they sat much separated at a very long table, had begun merely by troubling him rather pleasantly. It affected him as the sequel of something of which he had lost the beginning. He knew it, and for the time quite welcomed

---

1. James initially recorded the germ for this story in 1895, but it first appeared in the collection *The Better Sort* (1903). It was reprinted, with minor revisions, in the *Altar of the Dead* volume of the New York edition, Vol. 17 (1909), the source of the text printed here.

it, as a continuation, but didn't know what it continued, which was an interest or an amusement the greater as he was also somehow aware—yet without a direct sign from her—that the young woman herself hadn't lost the thread. She hadn't lost it, but she wouldn't give it back to him, he saw, without some putting forth of his hand for it; and he not only saw that, but saw several things more, things odd enough in the light of the fact that at the moment some accident of grouping brought them face to face he was still merely fumbling with the idea that any contact between them in the past would have had no importance. If it had had no importance he scarcely knew why his actual impression of her should so seem to have so much; the answer to which, however, was that in such a life as they all appeared to be leading for the moment one could but take things as they came. He was satisfied, without in the least being able to say why, that this young lady might roughly have ranked in the house as a poor relation; satisfied also that she was not there on a brief visit, but was more or less a part of the establishment—almost a working, a remunerated part. Didn't she enjoy at periods a protection that she paid for by helping, among other services, to show the place and explain it, deal with the tiresome people, answer questions about the dates of the building, the styles of the furniture, the authorship of the pictures, the favourite haunts of the ghost? It wasn't that she looked as if you could have given her shillings—it was impossible to look less so. Yet when she finally drifted toward him, distinctly handsome, though ever so much older—older than when he had seen her before—it might have been as an effect of her guessing that he had, within the couple of hours, devoted more imagination to her than to all the others put together, and had thereby penetrated to a kind of truth that the others were too stupid for. She *was* there on harder terms than any one; she was there as a consequence of things suffered, one way and another, in the interval of years; and she remembered him very much as she was remembered—only a good deal better.

By the time they at last thus came to speech they were alone in one of the rooms—remarkable for a fine portrait over the chimney-place—out of which their friends had passed, and the charm of it was that even before they had spoken they had practically arranged with each other to stay behind for talk. The charm, happily, was in other things too—partly in there being scarce a spot at Weatherend without something to stay behind for. It was in the way the autumn day looked into the high windows as it waned; the way the red light, breaking at the close from under a low sombre sky, reached out in a long shaft and played over old wainscots, old tapestry, old gold, old colour. It was most of all perhaps in the way she came to him as if, since she had been turned on to deal with the simpler sort, he might, should he choose to keep the whole thing down, just take her mild attention for a part of her general business. As soon as he heard her voice, however, the gap was filled up and the missing link supplied; the slight irony he divined in her attitude lost its advantage. He almost jumped at it to get there before her. "I met you years and years ago in Rome. I remember all about it." She confessed to disappointment—she had been so sure he didn't; and to prove how well he did he began to pour forth the particular recollections that popped up as he called for them. Her face and her voice, all at his service now, worked the miracle—the impression operating like the torch of a lamplighter who touches into flame, one by one, a long row of gas-jets. Marcher flattered himself the illumination was brilliant, yet he was really still more pleased on her showing him, with amusement, that in his haste to make everything right he had got most things rather wrong. It hadn't been at Rome—it had been at Naples; and it hadn't been eight years before—it had been more nearly ten. She hadn't been, either, with her uncle and aunt, but with her mother and her brother; in addition to which it was not with the Pembles *he* had been, but with the Boyers, coming down in their company from Rome—a point on which she insisted, a little to his confusion, and as to which she had her evidence in hand. The Boyers she had known, but didn't know the Pembles, though she had heard of them, and it was the people he was with who had made them acquainted. The incident of the thunderstorm that had raged round them with such violence as to drive them for refuge into an excavation—this incident had not occurred at the Palace of the Cæsars, but at Pompeii,[2] on an occasion when they had been present there at an important find.

He accepted her amendments, he enjoyed her corrections, though the moral of them was, she pointed out, that he *really* didn't remember the least thing about her; and he only felt it as a drawback that when all was made strictly historic there didn't appear much of anything left. They lingered together still, she neglecting her office—for from the moment he was so clever she had no proper right to him—and both neglecting the house, just waiting as to see if a memory or two more wouldn't again breathe on them. It hadn't taken them many minutes, after all, to put down on the table, like the cards of a pack, those that constituted their respective hands; only what came out was that the pack was unfortunately not perfect—that the past, invoked, invited, encouraged, could give them, naturally, no more than it had. It had made them anciently meet—her at twenty, him at twenty-five; but nothing was so strange, they seemed to say to each other, as that, while so occupied, it hadn't done a little more for them. They looked at each other as with the feeling of an occasion missed; the present would have been so much better if the other, in the far distance, in the foreign land, hadn't been so stupidly meagre. There weren't apparently, all counted, more than a dozen little old things that had succeeded in coming to pass between them; trivialities of youth, simplicities of freshness, stupidities of ignorance, small possible germs, but too deeply buried—too deeply (didn't it seem?) to sprout after so many years. Marcher could only feel he ought to have rendered her some service—saved her from a capsized boat in the Bay or at least recovered her dressing-bag, filched from her cab in the streets of Naples by a lazzarone[3] with a stiletto. Or it would have been nice if he could have been taken with fever all alone at his hotel, and she could have come to look after him, to write to his people, to drive him out in convalescence. *Then* they would be in possession of the something or other that their actual show seemed to lack. It yet somehow presented itself, this show, as too good to be spoiled; so that they were reduced for a few minutes more to wondering a little helplessly why—since they seemed to know a certain number of the same people—their reunion had been so long averted. They didn't use that name for it, but their delay from minute to minute to join the others was a kind of confession that they didn't quite want it to be a failure. Their attempted supposition of reasons for their not having met but showed how little they knew of each other.

---

2. Pompeii is near Naples, not Rome.

3. Beggar (Italian).

There came in fact a moment when Marcher felt a positive pang. It was vain to pretend she was an old friend, for all the communities were wanting, in spite of which it was as an old friend that he saw she would have suited him. He had new ones enough—was surrounded with them for instance on the stage of the other house; as a new one he probably wouldn't have so much as noticed her. He would have liked to invent something, get her to make-believe with him that some passage of a romantic or critical kind *had* originally occurred. He was really almost reaching out in imagination—as against time—for something that would do, and saying to himself that if it didn't come this sketch of a fresh start would show for quite awkwardly bungled. They would separate, and now for no second or no third chance. They would have tried and not succeeded. Then it was, just at the turn, as he afterwards made it out to himself, that, everything else failing, she herself decided to take up the case and, as it were, save the situation. He felt as soon as she spoke that she had been consciously keeping back what she said and hoping to get on without it; a scruple in her that immensely touched him when, by the end of three or four minutes more, he was able to measure it. What she brought out, at any rate, quite cleared the air and supplied the link—the link it was so odd he should frivolously have managed to lose.

"You know you told me something I've never forgotten and that again and again has made me think of you since; it was that tremendously hot day when we went to Sorrento,[4] across the bay, for the breeze. What I allude to was what you said to me, on the way back, as we sat under the awning of the boat enjoying the cool. Have you forgotten?"

He had forgotten and was even more surprised than ashamed. But the great thing was that he saw in this no vulgar reminder of any "sweet" speech. The vanity of women had long memories, but she was making no claim on him of a compliment or a mistake. With another woman, a totally different one, he might have feared the recall possibly of even some imbecile "offer." So, in having to say that he had indeed forgotten, he was conscious rather of a loss than of a gain; he already saw an interest in the matter of her mention. "I try to think—but I give it up. Yet I remember the Sorrento day."

"I'm not very sure you do," May Bartram after a moment said; "and I'm not very sure I ought to want you to. It's dreadful to bring a person back at any time to what he was ten years before. If you've lived away from it," she smiled, "so much the better."

"Ah if *you* haven't why should I?" he asked.

"Lived away, you mean, from what I myself was?"

"From what *I* was. I was of course an ass," Marcher went on; "but I would rather know from you just the sort of ass I was than—from the moment you have something in your mind—not know anything."

Still, however, she hesitated. "But if you've completely ceased to be that sort—?"

"Why I can then all the more bear to know. Besides, perhaps I haven't."

"Perhaps. Yet if you haven't," she added. "I should suppose you'd remember. Not indeed that *I* in the least connect with my impression the invidious name you use. If I had only thought you foolish," she explained, "the thing I

---

4. Across the bay from Naples.

speak of wouldn't so have remained with me. It was about yourself." She waited as if it might come to him; but as, only meeting her eyes in wonder, he gave no sign, she burnt her ships. "Has it ever happened?"

Then it was that, while he continued to stare, a light broke for him and the blood slowly came to his face, which began to burn with recognition. "Do you mean I told you—?" But he faltered, lest what came to him shouldn't be right, lest he should only give himself away.

"It was something about yourself that it was natural one shouldn't forget— that is if one remembered you at all. That's why I ask you," she smiled, "if the thing you then spoke of has ever come to pass?"

Oh then he saw, but he was lost in wonder and found himself embarrassed. This, he also saw, made her sorry for him, as if her allusion had been a mistake. It took him but a moment, however, to feel it hadn't been, much as it had been a surprise. After the first little shock of it her knowledge on the contrary began, even if rather strangely, to taste sweet to him. She was the only other person in the world then who would have it, and she had had it all these years, while the fact of his having so breathed his secret had unaccountably faded from him. No wonder they couldn't have met as if nothing had happened. "I judge," he finally said, "that I know what you mean. Only I had strangely enough lost any sense of having taken you so far into my confidence."

"Is it because you've taken so many others as well?"

"I've taken nobody. Not a creature since then."

"So that I'm the only person who knows?"

"The only person in the world."

"Well," she quickly replied, "I myself have never spoken. I've never, never repeated of you what you told me." She looked at him so that he perfectly believed her. Their eyes met over it in such a way that he was without a doubt. "And I never will."

She spoke with an earnestness that, as if almost excessive, put him at ease about her possible derision. Somehow the whole question was a new luxury to him—that is from the moment she was in possession. If she didn't take the sarcastic view she clearly took the sympathetic, and that was what he had had, in all the long time, from no one whomsoever. What he felt was that he couldn't at present have begun to tell her, and yet could profit perhaps exquisitely by the accident of having done so of old. "Please don't then. We're just right as it is."

"Oh I am," she laughed, "if you are!" To which she added: "Then you do still feel in the same way?"

It was impossible he shouldn't take to himself that she was really interested, though it all kept coming as perfect surprise. He had thought of himself so long as abominably alone, and lo he wasn't alone a bit. He hadn't been, it appeared, for an hour—since those moments on the Sorrento boat. It was *she* who had been, he seemed to see as he looked at her—she who had been made so by the graceless fact of his lapse of fidelity. To tell her what he had told her—what had it been but to ask something of her? something that she had given, in her charity, without his having, by a remembrance, by a return of the spirit, failing another encounter, so much as thanked her. What he had asked of her had been simply at first not to laugh at him. She had beautifully not done so for ten years, and she was not doing so now. So he had endless gratitude to make up. Only for that he must see just how he had figured to her. "What, exactly, was the account I gave——?"

"Of the way you did feel? Well, it was very simple. You said you had had from your earliest time, as the deepest thing within you, the sense of being kept for something rare and strange, possibly prodigious and terrible, that was sooner or later to happen to you, that you had in your bones the foreboding and the conviction of, and that would perhaps overwhelm you."

"Do you call that very simple?" John Marcher asked.

She thought a moment. "It was perhaps because I seemed, as you spoke, to understand it."

"You do understand it?" he eagerly asked.

Again she kept her kind eyes on him. "You still have the belief?"

"Oh!" he exclaimed helplessly. There was too much to say.

"Whatever it's to be," she clearly made out, "it hasn't yet come."

He shook his head in complete surrender now. "It hasn't yet come. Only, you know, it isn't anything I'm to *do,* to achieve in the world, to be distinguished or admired for. I'm not such an ass as *that.* It would be much better, no doubt, if I were."

"It's to be something you're merely to suffer?"

"Well, say to wait for—to have to meet, to face, to see suddenly break out in my life; possibly destroying all further consciousness, possibly annihilating me; possibly, on the other hand, only altering everything, striking at the root of all my world and leaving me to the consequences, however they shape themselves."

She took this in, but the light in her eyes continued for him not to be that of mockery. "Isn't what you describe perhaps but the expectation—or at any rate the sense of danger, familiar to so many people—of falling in love?"

John Marcher wondered. "Did you ask me that before?"

"No—I wasn't so free-and-easy then. But it's what strikes me now."

"Of course," he said after a moment, "it strikes you. Of course it strikes *me.* Of course what's in store for me may be no more than that. The only thing is," he went on, "that I think if it had been that I should by this time know."

"Do you mean because you've *been* in love?" And then as he but looked at her in silence: "You've been in love, and it hasn't meant such a cataclysm, hasn't proved the great affair?"

"Here I am, you see. It hasn't been overwhelming."

"Then it hasn't been love," said May Bartram.

"Well, I at least thought it was. I took it for that—I've taken it till now. It was agreeable, it was delightful, it was miserable," he explained. "But it wasn't strange. It wasn't what *my* affair's to be."

"You want something all to yourself—something that nobody else knows or *has* known?"

"It isn't a question of what I 'want'—God knows I don't want anything. It's only a question of the apprehension that haunts me—that I live with day by day."

He said this so lucidly and consistently that he could see it further impose itself. If she hadn't been interested before she'd have been interested now. "Is it a sense of coming violence?"

Evidently now too again he liked to talk of it. "I don't think of it as—when it does come—necessarily violent. I only think of it as natural and as of course above all unmistakeable. I think of it simply as *the* thing. *The* thing will of itself appear natural."

"Then how will it appear strange?"

Marcher bethought himself. "It won't—to *me*."

"To whom then?"

"Well," he replied, smiling at last, "say to you."

"Oh then I'm to be present?"

"Why you *are* present—since you know."

"I see." She turned it over. "But I mean at the catastrophe."

At this, for a minute, their lightness gave way to their gravity; it was as if the long look they exchanged held them together. "It will only depend on yourself—if you'll watch with me."

"Are you afraid?" she asked.

"Don't leave me *now*," he went on.

"Are you afraid?" she repeated.

"Do you think me simply out of my mind?" he pursued instead of answering. "Do I merely strike you as a harmless lunatic?"

"No," said May Bartram. "I understand you. I believe you."

"You mean you feel how my obsession—poor old thing!—may correspond to some possible reality?"

"To some possible reality."

"Then you *will* watch with me?"

She hesitated, then for the third time put her question. "Are you afraid?"

"Did I tell you I was—at Naples?"

"No, you said nothing about it."

"Then I don't know. And I should *like* to know," said John Marcher. "You'll tell me yourself whether you think so. If you'll watch with me you'll see."

"Very good then." They had been moving by this time across the room, and at the door, before passing out, they paused as for the full wind-up of their understanding. "I'll watch with you," said May Bartram.

## II

The fact that she "knew"—knew and yet neither chaffed him nor betrayed him—had in a short time begun to constitute between them a goodly bond, which became more marked when, within the year that followed their afternoon at Weatherend, the opportunities for meeting multiplied. The event that thus promoted these occasions was the death of the ancient lady her great-aunt, under whose wing, since losing her mother, she had to such an extent found shelter, and who, though but the widowed mother of the new successor to the property, had succeeded—thanks to a high tone and a high temper—in not forfeiting the supreme position at the great house. The deposition of this personage arrived but with her death, which, followed by many changes, made in particular a difference for the young woman in whom Marcher's expert attention had recognised from the first a dependent with a pride that might ache though it didn't bristle. Nothing for a long time had made him easier than the thought that the aching must have been much soothed by Miss Bartram's now finding herself able to set up a small home in London. She had acquired property, to an amount that made that luxury just possible, under her aunt's extremely complicated will, and when the whole matter began to be straightened out, which indeed took time, she let him know that the happy issue was at last in view. He had seen her again before that day, both because she had more than once accompanied the ancient lady to town and because he had paid another visit to the friends who so conveniently made of Weatherend one of the charms of their own hospitality. These friends had taken him back there; he had achieved there again with Miss Bartram some quiet detachment; and he had in London succeeded in persuading her to more than one brief absence from her aunt. They went together, on these latter occasions, to the National Gallery and the South Kensington Museum, where, among vivid reminders, they talked of Italy at large—not now attempting to recover, as at first, the taste of their youth and their ignorance. That recovery, the first day at Weatherend, had served its purpose well, had given them quite enough; so that they were, to Marcher's sense, no longer hovering about the headwaters of their stream, but had felt their boat pushed sharply off and down the current.

They were literally afloat together; for our gentleman this was marked, quite as marked as that the fortunate cause of it was just the buried treasure of her knowledge. He had with his own hands dug up this little hoard, brought to light—that is to within reach of the dim day constituted by their discretions and privacies—the object of value the hiding-place of which he had, after putting it into the ground himself, so strangely, so long forgotten. The rare luck of his having again just stumbled on the spot made him indifferent to any other question; he would doubtless have devoted more time to the odd accident of his lapse of memory if he hadn't been moved to devote so much to the sweetness, the comfort, as he felt, for the future, that this accident itself had helped to keep fresh. It had never entered into his plan that any one should "know," and mainly for the reason that it wasn't in him to tell any one. That would have been impossible, for nothing but the amusement of a cold world would have waited on it. Since, however, a mysterious fate had opened his mouth betimes, in spite of him, he would count that a compensation and profit by it to the utmost. That the right person *should* know tempered the asperity of his secret more even than his shyness had permitted him to imagine; and May Bartram was clearly right, because—well, because there she was. Her knowledge simply settled it; he would have been sure enough by this time had she been wrong. There was that in his situation, no doubt, that disposed him too much to see her as a mere confidant, taking all her light for him from the fact—the fact only—of her interest in his predicament; from her mercy, sympathy, seriousness, her consent not to regard him as the funniest of the funny. Aware, in fine, that her price for him was just in her giving him this constant sense of his being admirably spared, he was careful to remember that she had also a life of her own, with things that might happen to *her*, things that in friendship one should likewise take account of. Something fairly remarkable came to pass with him, for that matter, in this connexion—something represented by a certain passage of his consciousness, in the suddenest way, from one extreme to the other.

He had thought himself, so long as nobody knew, the most disinterested person in the world, carrying his concentrated burden, his perpetual sus-

*seclusive. unsettled.*

pense, ever so quietly, holding his tongue about it, giving others no glimpse of it nor of its effect upon his life, asking of them no allowance and only making on his side all those that were asked. He hadn't disturbed people with the queerness of their having to know a haunted man, though he had had moments of rather special temptation on hearing them say they were forsooth "unsettled." If they were as unsettled as he was—he who had never been settled for an hour in his life—they would know what it meant. Yet it wasn't, all the same, for him to make them, and he listened to them civilly enough. This was why he had such good—though possibly such rather colourless—manners; this was why, above all, he could regard himself, in a greedy world, as decently—as in fact perhaps even a little sublimely—unselfish. Our point is accordingly that he valued this character quite sufficiently to measure his present danger of letting it lapse, against which he promised himself to be much on his guard. He was quite ready, none the less, to be selfish just a little, since surely no more charming occasion for it had come to him. "Just a little," in a word, was just as much as Miss Bartram, taking one day with another, would let him. He never would be in the least coercive, and would keep well before him the lines on which consideration for her—the very highest—ought to proceed. He would thoroughly establish the heads under which her affairs, her requirements, her peculiarities—he went so far as to give them the latitude of that name—would come into their intercourse. All this naturally was a sign of how much he took the intercourse itself for granted. There was nothing more to be done about *that*. It simply existed; had sprung into being with her first penetrating question to him in the autumn light there at Weatherend. The real form it should have taken on the basis that stood out large was the form of their marrying. But the devil in this was that the very basis itself put marrying out of the question. His conviction, his apprehension, his obsession, in short, wasn't a privilege he could invite a woman to share; and that consequence of it was precisely what was the matter with him. Something or other lay in wait for him, amid the twists and the turns of the months and the years, like a crouching beast in the jungle. It signified little whether the crouching beast were destined to slay him or to be slain. The definite point was the inevitable spring of the creature; and the definite lesson from that was that a man of feeling didn't cause himself to be accompanied by a lady on a tiger-hunt. Such was the image under which he had ended by figuring his life.

They had at first, none the less, in the scattered hours spent together, made no allusion to that view of it; which was a sign he was handsomely alert to give that he didn't expect, that he in fact didn't care, always to be talking about it. Such a feature in one's outlook was really like a hump on one's back. The difference it made every minute of the day existed quite independently of discussion. One discussed of course *like* a hunchback, for there was always, if nothing else, the hunchback face. That remained, and she was watching him; but people watched best, as a general thing, in silence, so that such would be predominantly the manner of their vigil. Yet he didn't want, at the same time, to be tense and solemn; tense and solemn was what he imagined he too much showed for with other people. The thing to be, with the one person who knew, was easy and natural—to make the reference rather than be seeming to avoid it, to avoid it rather than be seeming to make it, and to keep it, in any case, familiar, facetious even, rather than pedantic and por-

*sexual. intercourse / penetrating*

*foreshadowing?* *may're connected - foreshadowing - foreshadowing*

tentous. Some such consideration as the latter was doubtless in his mind for instance when he wrote pleasantly to Miss Bartram that perhaps the great thing he had so long felt as in the lap of the gods was no more than this circumstance, which touched him so nearly, of her acquiring a house in London. It was the first allusion they had yet again made, needing any other hitherto so little; but when she replied, after having given him the news, that she was by no means satisfied with such a trifle as the climax to so special a suspense, she almost set him wondering if she hadn't even a larger conception of singularity for him than he had for himself. He was at all events destined to become aware little by little, as time went by, that she was all the while looking at his life, judging it, measuring it, in the light of the thing she knew, which grew to be at last, with the consecration of the years, never mentioned between them save as "the real truth" about him. That had always been his own form of reference to it, but she adopted the form so quietly that, looking back at the end of a period, he knew there was no moment at which it was traceable that she had, as he might say, got inside his idea, or exchanged the attitude of beautifully indulging for that of still more beautifully believing him.

It was always open to him to accuse her of seeing him but as the most harmless of maniacs, and this, in the long run—since it covered so much ground—was his easiest description of their friendship. He had a screw loose for her, but she liked him in spite of it and was practically, against the rest of the world, his kind wise keeper, unremunerated but fairly amused and, in the absence of other near ties, not disreputably occupied. The rest of the world of course thought him queer, but she, she only, knew how, and above all why, queer; which was precisely what enabled her to dispose the concealing veil in the right folds. She took his gaiety from him—since it had to pass with them for gaiety—as she took everything else; but she certainly so far justified by her unerring touch his finer sense of the degree to which he had ended by convincing her. *She* at least never spoke of the secret of his life except as "the real truth about you," and she had in fact a wonderful way of making it seem, as such, the secret of her own life too. That was in fine how he so constantly felt her as allowing for him; he couldn't on the whole call it anything else. He allowed for himself, but she, exactly, allowed still more; partly because, better placed for a sight of the matter, she traced his unhappy perversion through reaches of its course into which he could scarce follow it. He knew how he felt, but, besides knowing that, she knew how he *looked* as well; he knew each of the things of importance he was insidiously kept from doing, but she could add up the amount they made, understand how much, with a lighter weight on his spirit, he might have done, and thereby establish how, clever as he was, he fell short. Above all she was in the secret of the difference between the forms he went through—those of his little office under Government, those of caring for his modest patrimony, for his library, for his garden in the country, for the people in London whose invitations he accepted and repaid—and the detachment that reigned beneath them and that made of all behaviour, all that could in the least be called behaviour, a long act of dissimulation. What it had come to was that he wore a mask painted with the social simper, out of the eyeholes of which there looked eyes of an expression not in the least matching the other features. This the stupid world, even after years, had never more than half-discovered. It was only May

Bartram who had, and she achieved, by an art indescribable, the feat of at once—or perhaps it was only alternately—meeting the eyes from in front and mingling her own vision, as from over his shoulder, with their peep through the apertures. *eyes. Symbolic.*

So while they grew older together she did watch with him, and so she let this association give shape and colour to her own existence. Beneath *her* forms as well detachment had learned to sit, and behaviour had become for her, in the social sense, a false account of herself. There was but one account of her that would have been true all the while and that she could give straight to nobody, least of all to John Marcher. Her whole attitude was a virtual statement, but the perception of that only seemed called to take its place for him as one of the many things necessarily crowded out of his consciousness. If she had moreover, like himself, to make sacrifices to their real truth, it was to be granted that her compensation might have affected her as more prompt and more natural. They had long periods, in this London time, during which, when they were together, a stranger might have listened to them without in the least pricking up his ears; on the other hand the real truth was equally liable at any moment to rise to the surface, and the auditor would then have wondered indeed what they were talking about. They had from an early hour made up their mind that society was, luckily, unintelligent, and the margin allowed them by this had fairly become one of their commonplaces. Yet there were still moments when the situation turned almost fresh—usually under the effect of some expression drawn from herself. Her expressions doubtless repeated themselves, but her intervals were generous. "What saves us, you know, is that we answer so completely to so usual an appearance: that of the man and woman whose friendship has become such a daily habit—or almost—as to be at last indispensable." That for instance was a remark she had frequently enough had occasion to make, though she had given it at different times different developments. What we are especially concerned with is the turn it happened to take from her one afternoon when he had come to see her in honour of her birthday. This anniversary had fallen on a Sunday, at a season of thick fog and general outward gloom; but he had brought her his customary offering, having known her now long enough to have established a hundred small traditions. It was one of his proofs to himself, the present he made her on her birthday, that he hadn't sunk into real selfishness. It was mostly nothing more than a small trinket, but it was always fine of its kind, and he was regularly careful to pay for it more than he thought he could afford. "Our habit saves you at least, don't you see? because it makes you, after all, for the vulgar, indistinguishable from other men. What's the most inveterate mark of men in general? Why the capacity to spend endless time with dull women—to spend it I won't say without being bored, but without minding that they are, without being driven off at a tangent by it; which comes to the same thing. I'm your dull woman, a part of the daily bread for which you pray at church. That covers your tracks more than anything."

"And what covers yours?" asked Marcher, whom his dull woman could mostly to this extent amuse. "I see of course what you mean by your saving me, in this way and that, so far as other people are concerned—I've seen it all along. Only what is it that saves *you?* I often think, you know, of that."

She looked as if she sometimes thought of that too, but rather in a different way. "Where other people, you mean, are concerned?"

"Well, you're really so in ^love^ with me, you know—as a sort of result of my being so in with yourself. I mean of my having such an immense regard for you, being so tremendously mindful of all you've done for me. I sometimes ask myself if it's quite fair. Fair I mean to have so involved and—since one may say it—interested you. I almost feel as if you hadn't really had time to do anything else."

"Anything else but be interested?" she asked. "Ah what else does one ever want to be? If I've been 'watching' with you, as we long ago agreed I was to do, watching's always in itself an absorption."

"Oh certainly," John Marcher said, "if you hadn't had your curiosity—! Only doesn't it sometimes come to you as time goes on that your curiosity isn't being particularly repaid?"

May Bartram had a pause. "Do you ask that, by any chance, because you feel at all that yours isn't? I mean because you have to wait so long."

Oh he understood what she meant! "For the thing to happen that never does happen? For the beast to jump out? No, I'm just where I was about it. It isn't a matter as to which I can *choose*, I can decide for a change. It isn't one as to which there *can* be a change. It's in the lap of the gods. One's in the hands of one's law—there one is. As to the form the law will take, the way it will operate, that's its own affair."

"Yes," Miss Bartram replied; "of course one's fate's coming, of course it *has* come in its own form and its own way, all the while. Only, you know, the form and the way in your case were to have been—well, something so exceptional and, as one may say, so particularly *your* own."

Something in this made him look at her with suspicion. "You say 'were to *have* been,' as if in your heart you had begun to doubt."

"Oh!" she vaguely protested.

"As if you believed," he went on, "that nothing will now take place."

She shook her head slowly but rather inscrutably. "You're far from my thought."

He continued to look at her. "What then is the matter with you?"

"Well," she said after another wait, "the matter with me is simply that I'm more sure than ever my curiosity, as you call it, will be but too well repaid."

They were frankly grave now; he had got up from his seat, had turned once more about the little drawing-room to which, year after year, he brought his inevitable topic; in which he had, as he might have said, tasted their intimate community with every sauce, where every object was as familiar to him as the things of his own house and the very carpets were worn with his fitful walk very much as the desks in old counting-houses are worn by the elbows of generations of clerks. The generations of his nervous moods had been at work there, and the place was the written history of his whole middle life. Under the impression of what his friend had just said he knew himself, for some reason, more aware of these things; which made him, after a moment, stop again before her. "Is it possibly that you've grown afraid?"

"Afraid?" He thought, as she repeated the word, that his question had made her, a little, change colour; so that, lest he should have touched on a truth, he explained very kindly: "You remember that that was what you asked *me* long ago—that first day at Weatherend."

"Oh yes, and you told me you didn't know—that I was to see for myself. We've said little about it since, even in so long a time."

"Precisely," Marcher interposed—"quite as if it were too delicate a matter for us to make free with. Quite as if we might find, on pressure, that I *am* afraid. For then," he said, "we shouldn't, should we? quite know what to do."

She had for the time no answer to his question. "There have been days when I thought you were. Only, of course," she added, "there have been days when we have thought almost anything."

"Everything. Oh!" Marcher softly groaned as with a gasp, half-spent, at the face, more uncovered just then than it had been for a long while, of the imagination always with them. It had always had its incalculable moments of glaring out, quite as with the very eyes of the very Beast, and, used as he was to them, they could still draw from him the tribute of a sigh that rose from the depths of his being. All they had thought, first and last, rolled over him; the past seemed to have been reduced to mere barren speculation. This in fact was what the place had just struck him as so full of—the simplification of everything but the state of suspense. That remained only by seeming to hang in the void surrounding it. Even his original fear, if fear it had been, had lost itself in the desert. "I judge, however," he continued, "that you see I'm not afraid now."

"What I see, as I make it out, is that you've achieved something almost unprecedented in the way of getting used to danger. Living with it so long and so closely you've lost your sense of it; you know it's there, but you're indifferent, and you cease even, as of old, to have to whistle in the dark. Considering what the danger is," May Bartram wound up, "I'm bound to say I don't think your attitude could well be surpassed."

John Marcher faintly smiled. "It's heroic?"

"Certainly—call it that."

It was what he would have liked indeed to call it. "I *am* then a man of courage?"

"That's what you were to show me."

He still, however, wondered. "But doesn't the man of courage know what he's afraid of—or *not* afraid of? I don't know *that*, you see. I don't focus it. I can't name it. I only know I'm exposed."

"Yes, but exposed—how shall I say?—so directly. So intimately. That's surely enough."

"Enough to make you feel then—as what we may call the end and the upshot of our watch—that I'm not afraid?"

"You're not afraid. But it isn't," she said, "the end of our watch. That is it isn't the end of yours. You've everything still to see."

"Then why haven't *you*?" he asked. He had had, all along, to-day, the sense of her keeping something back, and he still had it. As this was his first impression of that it quite made a date. The case was the more marked as she didn't at first answer; which in turn made him go on. "You know something I don't." Then his voice, for that of a man of courage, trembled a little. "You know what's to happen." Her silence, with the face she showed, was almost a confession—it made him sure. "You know, and you're afraid to tell me. It's so bad that you're afraid I'll find out."

All this might be true, for she did look as if, unexpectedly to her, he had crossed some mystic line that she had secretly drawn round her. Yet she might, after all, not have worried; and the real climax was that he himself, at all events, needn't. "You'll never find out."

### III

It was all to have made, none the less, as I have said, a date; which came out in the fact that again and again, even after long intervals, other things that passed between them wore in relation to this hour but the character of recalls and results. Its immediate effect had been indeed rather to lighten insistence—almost to provoke a reaction; as if their topic had dropped by its own weight and as if moreover, for that matter, Marcher had been visited by one of his occasional warnings against egotism. He had kept up, he felt, and very decently on the whole, his consciousness of the importance of not being selfish, and it was true that he had never sinned in that direction without promptly enough trying to press the scales the other way. He often repaired his fault, the season permitting, by inviting his friend to accompany him to the opera; and it not infrequently thus happened that, to show he didn't wish her to have but one sort of food for her mind, he was the cause of her appearing there with him a dozen nights in the month. It even happened that, seeing her home at such times, he occasionally went in with her to finish, as he called it, the evening, and, the better to make his point, sat down to the frugal but always careful little supper that awaited his pleasure. His point was made, he thought, by his not eternally insisting with her on himself; made for instance, at such hours, when it befell that, her piano at hand and each of them familiar with it, they went over passages of the opera together. It chanced to be on one of these occasions, however, that he reminded her of her not having answered a certain question he had put to her during the talk that had taken place between them on her last birthday. "What is it that saves *you?*"—saved her, he meant, from that appearance of variation from the usual human type. If he had practically escaped remark, as she pretended, by doing, in the most important particular, what most men do—find the answer to life in patching up an alliance of a sort with a woman no better than himself—how had she escaped it, and how could the alliance, such as it was, since they must suppose it had been more or less noticed, have failed to make her rather positively talked about?

"I never said," May Bartram replied, "that it hadn't made me a good deal talked about."

"Ah well then you're not 'saved.' "

"It hasn't been a question for me. If you've had your woman I've had," she said, "my man."

"And you mean that makes you all right?"

Oh it was always as if there were so much to say! "I don't know why it shouldn't make me—humanly, which is what we're speaking of—as right as it makes you."

"I see," Marcher returned. " 'Humanly,' no doubt, as showing that you're living for something. Not, that is, just for me and my secret."

May Bartram smiled. "I don't pretend it exactly shows that I'm not living for you. It's my intimacy with you that's in question."

He laughed as he saw what she meant. "Yes, but since, as you say, I'm only, so far as people make out, ordinary, you're—aren't you?—no more than ordinary either. You help me to pass for a man like another. So if I *am*, as I understand you, you're not compromised. Is that it?"

She had another of her waits, but she spoke clearly enough. "That's it. It's all that concerns me—to help you to pass for a man like another."

He was careful to acknowledge the remark handsomely. "How kind, how beautiful, you are to me! How shall I ever repay you?"

She had her last grave pause, as if there might be a choice of ways. But she chose. "By going on as you are."

It was into this going on as he was that they relapsed, and really for so long a time that the day inevitably came for a further sounding of their depths. These depths, constantly bridged over by a structure firm enough in spite of its lightness and of its occasional oscillation in the somewhat vertiginous air, invited on occasion, in the interest of their nerves, a dropping of the plummet and a measurement of the abyss. A difference had been made moreover, once for all, by the fact that she had all the while not appeared to feel the need of rebutting his charge of an idea within her that she didn't dare to express—a charge uttered just before one of the fullest of their later discussions ended. It had come up for him then that she "knew" something and that what she knew was bad—too bad to tell him. When he had spoken of it as visibly so bad that she was afraid he might find it out, her reply had left the matter too equivocal to be let alone and yet, for Marcher's special sensibility, almost too formidable again to touch. He circled about it at a distance that alternately narrowed and widened and that still wasn't much affected by the consciousness in him that there was nothing she could "know," after all, any better than he did. She had no source of knowledge he hadn't equally—except of course that she might have finer nerves. That was what women had where they were interested; they made out things, where people were concerned, that the people often couldn't have made out for themselves. Their nerves, their sensibility, their imagination, were conductors and revealers, and the beauty of May Bartram was in particular that she had given herself so to his case. He felt in these days what, oddly enough, he had never felt before, the growth of a dread of losing her by some catastrophe—some catastrophe that yet wouldn't at all be *the* catastrophe: partly because she had almost of a sudden begun to strike him as more useful to him than ever yet, and partly by reason of an appearance of uncertainty in her health, coincident and equally new. It was characteristic of the inner detachment he had hitherto so successfully cultivated and to which our whole account of him is a reference, it was characteristic that his complications, such as they were, had never yet seemed so as at this crisis to thicken about him, even to the point of making him ask himself if he were, by any chance, of a truth, within sight or sound, within touch or reach, within the immediate jurisdiction, of the thing that waited.

When the day came, as come it had to, that his friend confessed to him her fear of a deep disorder in her blood, he felt somehow the shadow of a change and the chill of a shock. He immediately began to imagine aggravations and disasters, and above all to think of her peril as the direct menace for himself of personal privation. This indeed gave him one of those partial recoveries of equanimity that were agreeable to him—it showed him that what was still first in his mind was the loss she herself might suffer. "What if she should have to die before knowing, before seeing—?" It would have been brutal, in the early stages of her trouble, to put that question to her; but it had immediately sounded for him to his own concern, and the possibility was what most made him sorry for her. If she did "know," moreover, in the sense of her having had some—what should he think?—mystical irresistible light, this would make the matter not better, but worse, inasmuch as her original adoption of his own curiosity had quite become the basis of her life. She had been living to see what would *be* to be seen, and it would quite lacerate her to have to give up before the accomplishment of the vision. These reflexions, as I say, quickened his generosity; yet, make them as he might, he saw himself, with the lapse of the period, more and more disconcerted. It lapsed for him with a strange steady sweep, and the oddest oddity was that it gave him, independently of the threat of much inconvenience, almost the only positive surprise his career, if career it could be called, had yet offered him. She kept the house as she had never done; he had to go to her to see her—she could meet him nowhere now, though there was scarce a corner of their loved old London in which she hadn't in the past, at one time or another, done so; and he found her always seated by her fire in the deep old-fashioned chair she was less and less able to leave. He had been struck one day, after an absence exceeding his usual measure, with her suddenly looking much older to him than he had ever thought of her being; then he recognised that the suddenness was all on his side—he had just simply and suddenly noticed. She looked older because inevitably, after so many years, she *was* old, or almost; which was of course true in still greater measure of her companion. If she was old, or almost, John Marcher assuredly was, and yet it was her showing of the lesson, not his own, that brought the truth home to him. His surprises began here; when once they had begun they multiplied; they came rather with a rush: it was as if, in the oddest way in the world, they had all been kept back, sown in a thick cluster, for the late afternoon of life, the time at which for people in general the unexpected has died out.

One of them was that he should have caught himself—for he *had* so done—*really* wondering if the great accident would take form now as nothing more than his being condemned to see this charming woman, this admirable friend, pass away from him. He had never so unreservedly qualified her as while confronted in thought with such a possibility; in spite of which there was small doubt for him that as an answer to his long riddle the mere effacement of even so fine a feature of his situation would be an abject anti-climax. It would represent, as connected with his past attitude, a drop of dignity under the shadow of which his existence could only become the most grotesque of failures. He had been far from holding it a failure—long as he had waited for the appearance that was to make it a success. He had waited for quite another thing, not for such a thing as that. The breath of his good faith came short, however, as he recognised how long he had waited, or how long at least his companion had. That she, at all events, might be recorded as having waited in vain—this affected him sharply, and all the more because of his at first having done little more than amuse himself with the idea. It grew more grave as the gravity of her condition grew, and the state of mind it produced in him, which he himself ended by watching as if it had been some definite disfigurement of his outer person, may pass for another of his surprises. This conjoined itself still with another, the really stupefying consciousness of a question that he would have allowed to shape itself had he dared. What did everything mean—what, that is, did *she* mean, she and her

vain waiting and her probable death and the soundless admonition of it all—
unless that, at this time of day, it was simply, it was overwhelmingly too late?
He had never at any stage of his queer consciousness admitted the whisper
of such a correction; he had never till within these last few months been so
false to his conviction as not to hold that what was to come to him had time,
whether *he* struck himself as having it or not. That at last, at last, he certainly
hadn't it, to speak of, or had it but in the scantiest measure—such, soon
enough, as things went with him, became the inference with which his old
obsession had to reckon: and this it was not helped to do by the more and
more confirmed appearance that the great vagueness casting the long shadow
in which he had lived had, to attest itself, almost no margin left. Since it was
in Time that he was to have met his fate, so it was in Time that his fate was
to have acted; and as he waked up to the sense of no longer being young,
which was exactly the sense of being stale, just as that, in turn, was the sense
of being weak, he waked up to another matter beside. It all hung together;
they were subject, he and the great vagueness, to an equal and indivisible law.
When the possibilities themselves had accordingly turned stale, when the
secret of the gods had grown faint, had perhaps even quite evaporated, that,
and that only, was failure. It wouldn't have been failure to be bankrupt, dis-
honoured, pilloried, hanged; it was failure not to be anything. And so, in the
dark valley into which his path had taken its unlooked-for twist, he wondered
not a little as he groped. He didn't care what awful crash might overtake him,
with what ignominy or what monstrosity he might yet be associated—since
he wasn't after all too utterly old to suffer—if it would only be decently proportionate to the posture he had kept, all his life, in the threatened presence
of it. He had but one desire left—that he shouldn't have been "sold."

## IV

Then it was that, one afternoon, while the spring of the year was young and
new she met all in her own way his frankest betrayal of these alarms. He had
gone in late to see her, but evening hadn't settled and she was presented to
him in that long fresh light of waning April days which affects us often with
a sadness sharper than the greyest hours of autumn. The week had been
warm, the spring was supposed to have begun early, and May Bartram sat, for
the first time in the year, without a fire; a fact that, to Marcher's sense, gave
the scene of which she formed part a smooth and ultimate look, an air of
knowing, in its immaculate order and cold meaningless cheer, that it would
never see a fire again. Her own aspect—he could scarce have said why—
intensified this note. Almost as white as wax, with the marks and signs in her
face as numerous and as fine as if they had been etched by a needle, with soft
white draperies relieved by a faded green scarf on the delicate tone of which
the years had further refined, she was the picture of a serene and exquisite
but impenetrable sphinx, whose head, or indeed all whose person, might have
been powdered with silver. She was a sphinx, yet with her white petals and
green fronds she might have been a lily too—only an artificial lily, wonderfully imitated and constantly kept, without dust or stain, though not exempt
from a slight droop and a complexity of faint creases, under some clear glass
bell. The perfection of household care, of high polish and finish, always

reigned in her rooms, but they now looked most as if everything had been wound up, tucked in, put away, so that she might sit with folded hands and with nothing more to do. She was "out of it," to Marcher's vision; her work was over; she communicated with him as across some gulf or from some island of rest that she had already reached, and it made him feel strangely abandoned. Was it—or rather wasn't it—that if for so long she had been watching with him the answer to their question must have swum into her ken and taken on its name, so that her occupation was verily gone? He had as much as charged her with this in saying to her, many months before, that she even then knew something she was keeping from him. It was a point he had never since ventured to press, vaguely fearing as he did that it might become a difference, perhaps a disagreement, between them. He had in this later time turned nervous, which was what he in all the other years had never been; and the oddity was that his nervousness should have waited till he had begun to doubt, should have held off so long as he was sure. There was something, it seemed to him, that the wrong word would bring down on his head, something that would so at least ease off his tension. But he wanted not to speak the wrong word; that would make everything ugly. He wanted the knowledge he lacked to drop on him, if drop it could, by its own august weight. If she was to forsake him it was surely for her to take leave. This was why he didn't directly ask her again what she knew; but it was also why, approaching the matter from another side, he said to her in the course of his visit: "What do you regard as the very worst that at this time of day *can* happen to me?"

He had asked her that in the past often enough; they had, with the odd irregular rhythm of their intensities and avoidances, exchanged ideas about it and then had seen the ideas washed away by cool intervals, washed like figures traced in sea-sand. It had ever been the mark of their talk that the oldest allusions in it required but a little dismissal and reaction to come out again, sounding for the hour as new. She could thus at present meet his enquiry quite freshly and patiently. "Oh yes, I've repeatedly thought, only it always seemed to me of old that I couldn't quite make up my mind. I thought of dreadful things, between which it was difficult to choose; and so must you have done."

"Rather! I feel now as if I had scarce done anything else. I appear to myself to have spent my life in thinking of nothing *but* dreadful things. A great many of them I've at different times named to you, but there were others I couldn't name."

"They were too, too dreadful?"

"Too, too dreadful—some of them."

She looked at him a minute, and there came to him as he met it an inconsequent sense that her eyes, when one got their full clearness, were still as beautiful as they had been in youth, only beautiful with a strange cold light— a light that somehow was a part of the effect, if it wasn't rather a part of the cause, of the pale hard sweetness of the season and the hour. "And yet," she said at last, "there are horrors we've mentioned."

It deepened the strangeness to see her, as such a figure in such a picture, talk of "horrors," but she was to do in a few minutes something stranger yet— though even of this he was to take the full measure but afterwards—and the note of it already trembled. It was, for the matter of that, one of the signs that her eyes were having again the high flicker of their prime. He had to admit, however, what she said. "Oh yes, there were times when we did go far." He caught himself in the act of speaking as if it all were over. Well, he wished it were; and the consummation depended for him clearly more and more on his friend.

But she had now a soft smile. "Oh far—!"

It was oddly ironic. "Do you mean you're prepared to go further?"

She was frail and ancient and charming as she continued to look at him, yet it was rather as if she had lost the thread. "Do you consider that we went far?"

"Why I thought it the point you were just making—that we *had* looked most things in the face."

"Including each other?" She still smiled. "But you're quite right. We've had together great imaginations, often great fears; but some of them have been unspoken."

"Then the worst—we haven't faced that. I *could* face it, I believe, if I knew what you think it. I feel," he explained, "as if I had lost my power to conceive such things." And he wondered if he looked as blank as he sounded. "It's spent."

"Then why do you assume," she asked, "that mine isn't?"

"Because you've given me signs to the contrary. It isn't a question for you of conceiving, imagining, comparing. It isn't a question now of choosing." At last he came out with it. "You know something I don't. You've shown me that before."

These last words had affected her, he made out in a moment, exceedingly, and she spoke with firmness. "I've shown you, my dear, nothing."

He shook his head. "You can't hide it."

"Oh, oh!" May Bartram sounded over what she couldn't hide. It was almost a smothered groan.

"You admitted it months ago, when I spoke of it to you as of something you were afraid I should find out. Your answer was that I couldn't, that I wouldn't, and I don't pretend I have. But you had something therefore in mind, and I now see how it must have been, how it still is, the possibility that, of all possibilities, has settled itself for you as the worst. This," he went on, "is why I appeal to you. I'm only afraid of ignorance to-day—I'm not afraid of knowledge." And then as for a while she said nothing: "What makes me sure is that I see in your face and feel here, in this air and amid these appearances, that you're out of it. You've done. You've had your experience. You leave me to my fate."

Well, she listened, motionless and white in her chair, as on a decision to be made, so that her manner was fairly an avowal, though still, with a small fine inner stiffness, an imperfect surrender. "It *would* be the worst," she finally let herself say. "I mean the thing I've never said."

It hushed him a moment. "More monstrous than all the monstrosities we've named?"

"More monstrous. Isn't that what you sufficiently express," she asked, "in calling it the worst?"

Marcher thought. "Assuredly—if you mean, as I do, something that includes all the loss and all the shame that are thinkable."

"It would if it *should* happen," said May Bartram. "What we're speaking of, remember, is only my idea."

"It's your belief," Marcher returned. "That's enough for me. I feel your beliefs are right. Therefore if, having this one, you give me no more light on it, you abandon me."

"No, no!" she repeated. "I'm with you—don't you see?—still." And as to make it more vivid to him she rose from her chair—a movement she seldom risked in these days—and showed herself, all draped and all soft, in her fairness and slimness. "I haven't forsaken you."

It was really, in its effort against weakness, a generous assurance, and had the success of the impulse not, happily, been great, it would have touched him to pain more than to pleasure. But the cold charm in her eyes had spread, as she hovered before him, to all the rest of her person, so that it was for the minute almost a recovery of youth. He couldn't pity her for that; he could only take her as she showed—as capable even yet of helping him. It was as if, at the same time, her light might at any instant go out; wherefore he must make the most of it. There passed before him with intensity the three or four things he wanted most to know; but the question that came of itself to his lips really covered the others. "Then tell me if I shall consciously suffer."

She promptly shook her head. "Never!"

It confirmed the authority he imputed to her, and it produced on him an extraordinary effect. "Well, what's better than that? Do you call that the worst?"

"You think nothing is better?" she asked.

She seemed to mean something so special that he again sharply wondered, though still with the dawn of a prospect of relief. "Why not, if one doesn't *know?*" After which, as their eyes, over his question, met in a silence, the dawn deepened and something to his purpose came prodigiously out of her very face. His own, as he took it in, suddenly flushed to the forehead, and he gasped with the force of a perception to which, on the instant, everything fitted. The sound of his gasp filled the air; then he became articulate. "I see—if I don't suffer!"

In her own look, however, was doubt. "You see what?"

"Why what you mean—what you've always meant."

She again shook her head. "What I mean isn't what I've always meant. It's different."

"It's something new?"

She hung back from it a little. "Something new. It's not what you think. I see what you think."

His divination drew breath then; only her correction might be wrong. "It isn't that I *am* a blockhead?" he asked between faintness and grimness. "It isn't that it's all a mistake."

"A mistake?" she pityingly echoed. *That* possibility, for her, he saw, would be monstrous; and if she guaranteed him the immunity from pain it would accordingly not be what she had in mind. "Oh no," she declared; "it's nothing of that sort. You've been right."

Yet he couldn't help asking himself if she weren't, thus pressed, speaking but to save him. It seemed to him he should be most in a hole if his history should prove all a platitude. "Are you telling me the truth, so that I shan't have been a bigger idiot than I can bear to know? I *haven't* lived with a vain imagination, in the most besotted illusion? I haven't waited but to see the door shut in my face?"

She shook her head again. "However the case stands *that* isn't the truth. Whatever the reality, it *is* a reality. The door isn't shut. The door's open," said May Bartram.

"Then something's to come?"

She waited once again, always with her cold sweet eyes on him. "It's never too late." She had, with her gliding step, diminished the distance between them, and she stood nearer to him, close to him, a minute, as if still charged with the unspoken. Her movement might have been for some finer emphasis of what she was at once hesitating and deciding to say. He had been standing by the chimney-piece, fireless and sparely adorned, a small perfect old French clock and two morsels of rosy Dresden[5] constituting all its furniture; and her hand grasped the shelf while she kept him waiting, grasped it a little as for support and encouragement. She only kept him waiting, however; that is he only waited. It had become suddenly, from her movement and attitude, beautiful and vivid to him that she had something more to give him; her wasted face delicately shone with it—it glittered almost as with the white lustre of silver in her expression. She was right, incontestably, for what he saw in her face was the truth, and strangely, without consequence, while their talk of it as dreadful was still in the air, she appeared to present it as inordinately soft. This, prompting bewilderment, made him but gape the more gratefully for her revelation, so that they continued for some minutes silent, her face shining at him, her contact imponderably pressing, and his stare all kind but all expectant. The end, none the less, was that what he had expected failed to come to him. Something else took place instead, which seemed to consist at first in the mere closing of her eyes. She gave way at the same instant to a slow fine shudder, and though he remained staring—though he stared in fact but the harder—turned off and regained her chair. It was the end of what she had been intending, but it left him thinking only of that.

"Well, you don't say—?"

She had touched in her passage a bell near the chimney and had sunk back strangely pale. "I'm afraid I'm too ill."

"Too ill to tell me?" It sprang up sharp to him, and almost to his lips, the fear she might die without giving him light. He checked himself in time from so expressing his question, but she answered as if she had heard the words.

"Don't you know—now?"

" 'Now'—?" She had spoken as if some difference had been made within the moment. But her maid, quickly obedient to her bell, was already with them. "I know nothing." And he was afterwards to say to himself that he must have spoken with odious impatience, such an impatience as to show that, supremely disconcerted, he washed his hands of the whole question.

"Oh!" said May Bartram.

"Are you in pain?" he asked as the woman went to her.

"No," said May Bartram.

Her maid, who had put an arm round her as if to take her to her room, fixed on him eyes that appealingly contradicted her; in spite of which, however, he showed once more his mystification. "What then has happened?"

5. Fine German porcelain.

She was once more, with her companion's help, on her feet, and, feeling withdrawal imposed on him, he had blankly found his hat and gloves and had reached the door. Yet he waited for her answer. "What *was* to," she said.

## V

He came back the next day, but she was then unable to see him, and as it was literally the first time this had occurred in the long stretch of their acquaintance he turned away, defeated and sore, almost angry—or feeling at least that such a break in their custom was really the beginning of the end—and wandered alone with his thoughts, especially with the one he was least able to keep down. She was dying and he would lose her; she was dying and his life would end. He stopped in the Park, into which he had passed, and stared before him at his recurrent doubt. Away from her the doubt pressed again; in her presence he had believed her, but as he felt his forlornness he threw himself into the explanation that, nearest at hand, had most of a miserable warmth for him and least of a cold torment. She had deceived him to save him—to put him off with something in which he should be able to rest. What could the thing that was to happen to him be, after all, but just this thing that had begun to happen? Her dying, her death, his consequent solitude—*that* was what he had figured as the Beast in the Jungle, that was what had been in the lap of the gods. He had had her word for it as he left her—what else on earth could she have meant? It wasn't a thing of a monstrous order; not a fate rare and distinguished; not a stroke of fortune that overwhelmed and immortalised; it had only the stamp of the common doom. But poor Marcher at this hour judged the common doom sufficient. It would serve his turn, and even as the consummation of infinite waiting he would bend his pride to accept it. He sat down on a bench in the twilight. He hadn't been a fool. Something had *been*, as she had said, to come. Before he rose indeed it had quite struck him that the final fact really matched with the long avenue through which he had had to reach it. As sharing his suspense and as giving herself all, giving her life, to bring it to an end, she had come with him every step of the way. He had lived by her aid, and to leave her behind would be cruelly, damnably to miss her. What could be more overwhelming than that?

Well, he was to know within the week, for though she kept him a while at bay, left him restless and wretched during a series of days on each of which he asked about her only again to have to turn away, she ended his trial by receiving him where she had always received him. Yet she had been brought out at some hazard into the presence of so many of the things that were, consciously, vainly, half their past, and there was scant service left in the gentleness of her mere desire, all too visible, to check his obsession and wind up his long trouble. That was clearly what she wanted, the one thing more for her own peace while she could still put out her hand. He was so affected by her state that, once seated by her chair, he was moved to let everything go; it was she herself therefore who brought him back, took up again, before she dismissed him, her last word of the other time. She showed how she wished to leave their business in order. "I'm not sure you understood. You've nothing to wait for more. It *has* come."

Oh how he looked at her! "Really?"

"Really."

"The thing that, as you said, *was* to?"

"The thing that we began in our youth to watch for."

Face to face with her once more he believed her; it was a claim to which he had so abjectly little to oppose. "You mean that it has come as a positive definite occurrence, with a name and a date?"

"Positive. Definite. I don't know about the 'name,' but oh with a date!"

He found himself again too helplessly at sea. "But come in the night—come and passed me by?"

May Bartram had her strange faint smile. "Oh no, it hasn't passed you by!"

"But if I haven't been aware of it and it hasn't touched me—?"

"Ah your not being aware of it"—and she seemed to hesitate an instant to deal with this—"your not being aware of it is the strangeness *in* the strangeness. It's the wonder *of* the wonder." She spoke as with the softness almost of a sick child, yet now at last, at the end of all, with the perfect straightness of a sibyl. She visibly knew that she knew, and the effect on him was of something co-ordinate, in its high character, with the law that had ruled him. It was the true voice of the law; so on her lips would the law itself have sounded. "It *has* touched you," she went on. "It has done its office. It has made you all its own."

"So utterly without my knowing it?"

"So utterly without your knowing it." His hand, as he leaned to her, was on the arm of her chair, and, dimly smiling always now, she placed her own on it. "It's enough if *I* know it."

"Oh!" he confusedly breathed, as she herself of late so often had done.

"What I long ago said is true. You'll never know now, and I think you ought to be content. You've *had* it," said May Bartram.

"But had what?"

"Why what was to have marked you out. The proof of your law. It has acted. I'm too glad," she then bravely added, "to have been able to see what it's *not*."

He continued to attach his eyes to her, and with the sense that it was all beyond him, and that *she* was too, he would still have sharply challenged her hadn't he so felt it an abuse of her weakness to do more than take devoutly what she gave him, take it hushed as to a revelation. If he did speak, it was out of the foreknowledge of his loneliness to come. "If you're glad of what it's 'not' it might then have been worse?"

She turned her eyes away, she looked straight before her; with which after a moment: "Well, you know our fears."

He wondered. "It's something then we never feared?"

On this slowly she turned to him. "Did we ever dream, with all our dreams, that we should sit and talk of it thus?"

He tried for a little to make out that they had; but it was as if their dreams, numberless enough, were in solution in some thick cold mist through which thought lost itself. "It might have been that we couldn't talk?"

"Well"—she did her best for him—"not from this side. This, you see," she said, "is the *other* side."

"I think," poor Marcher returned, "that all sides are the same to me." Then, however, as she gently shook her head in correction: "We mightn't, as it were, have got across—?"

"To where we are—no. We're *here*"—she made her weak emphasis.

"And much good does it do us!" was her friend's frank comment.

"It does us the good it can. It does us the good that *it* isn't here. It's past. It's behind," said May Bartram. "Before—" but her voice dropped.

He had got up, not to tire her, but it was hard to combat his yearning. She after all told him nothing but that his light had failed—which he knew well enough without her. "Before—?" he blankly echoed.

"Before, you see, it was always to *come*. That kept it present."

"Oh I don't care what comes now! Besides," Marcher added, "it seems to me I liked it better present, as you say, than I can like it absent with *your* absence."

"Oh mine!"—and her pale hands made light of it.

"With the absence of everything." He had a dreadful sense of standing there before her for—so far as anything but this proved, this bottomless drop was concerned—the last time of their life. It rested on him with a weight he felt he could scarce bear, and this weight it apparently was that still pressed out what remained in him of speakable protest. "I believe you; but I can't begin to pretend I understand. *Nothing*, for me, is past; nothing *will* pass till I pass myself, which I pray my stars may be as soon as possible. Say, however," he added, "that I've eaten my cake, as you contend, to the last crumb—how can the thing I've never felt at all be the thing I was marked out to feel?"

She met him perhaps less directly, but she met him unperturbed. "You take your 'feelings' for granted. You were to suffer your fate. That was not necessarily to know it."

"How in the world—when what is such knowledge but suffering?"

She looked up at him a while in silence. "No—you don't understand."

"I suffer," said John Marcher.

"Don't, don't!"

"How can I help at least *that?*"

"*Don't!*" May Bartram repeated.

She spoke it in a tone so special, in spite of her weakness, that he stared an instant—stared as if some light, hitherto hidden, had shimmered across his vision. Darkness again closed over it, but the gleam had already become for him an idea. "Because I haven't the right—?"

"Don't *know*—when you needn't," she mercifully urged. "You needn't—for we shouldn't."

"Shouldn't?" If he could but know what she meant!

"No—it's too much."

"Too much?" he still asked but, with a mystification that was the next moment of a sudden to give way. Her words, if they meant something, affected him in this light—the light also of her wasted face—as meaning *all*, and the sense of what knowledge had been for herself came over him with a rush which broke through into a question. "Is it of that then you're dying?"

She but watched him, gravely at first, as to see, with this, where he was, and she might have seen something or feared something that moved her sympathy. "I would live for you still—if I could." Her eyes closed for a little, as if, withdrawn into herself, she were for a last time trying. "But I can't!" she said as she raised them again to take leave of him.

She couldn't indeed, as but too promptly and sharply appeared, and he had no vision of her after this that was anything, but darkness and doom. They had parted for ever in that strange talk; access to her chamber of pain, rigidly guarded, was almost wholly forbidden him; he was feeling now moreover, in the face of doctors, nurses, the two or three relatives attracted doubtless by the presumption of what she had to "leave," how few were the rights, as they were called in such cases, that he had to put forward, and how odd it might even seem that their intimacy shouldn't have given him more of them. The stupidest fourth cousin had more, even though she had been nothing in such a person's life. She had been a feature of features in *his,* for what else was it to have been so indispensable? Strange beyond saying were the ways of existence, baffling for him the anomaly of his lack, as he felt it to be, of producible claim. A woman might have been, as it were, everything to him, and it might yet present him in no connexion that any one seemed held to recognise. If this was the case in these closing weeks it was the case more sharply on the occasion of the last offices rendered, in the great grey London cemetery, to what had been mortal, to what had been precious, in his friend. The concourse at her grave was not numerous, but he saw himself treated as scarce more nearly concerned with it than if there had been a thousand others. He was in short from this moment face to face with the fact that he was to profit extraordinarily little by the interest May Bartram had taken in him. He couldn't quite have said what he expected, but he hadn't surely expected this approach to a double privation. Not only had her interest failed him, but he seemed to feel himself unattended—and for a reason he couldn't seize— by the distinction, the dignity, the propriety, if nothing else, of the man markedly bereaved. It was as if in the view of society he had not *been* markedly bereaved, as if there still failed some sign or proof of it, and as if none the less his character could never be affirmed nor the deficiency ever made up. There were moments as the weeks went by when he would have liked, by some almost aggressive act, to take his stand on the intimacy of his loss, in order that it *might* be questioned and his retort, to the relief of his spirit, so recorded; but the moments of an irritation more helpless followed fast on these, the moments during which, turning things over with a good conscience but with a bare horizon, he found himself wondering if he oughtn't to have begun, so to speak, further back.

He found himself wondering at many things, and this last speculation had others to keep it company. What could he have done, after all, in her lifetime, without giving them both, as it were, away? He couldn't have made known she was watching him, for that would have published the superstition of the Beast. This was what closed his mouth now—now that the Jungle had been threshed to vacancy and that the Beast had stolen away. It sounded too foolish and too flat; the difference for him in this particular, the extinction in his life of the element of suspense, was such as in fact to surprise him. He could scarce have said what the effect resembled; the abrupt cessation, the positive prohibition, of music perhaps, more than anything else, in some place all adjusted and all accustomed to sonority and to attention. If he could at any rate have conceived lifting the veil from his image at some moment of the past (what had he done, after all, if not lift it to *her?*) so to do this today, to talk to people at large of the Jungle cleared and confide to them that he now felt it as safe, would have been not only to see them listen as to a goodwife's tale, but really to hear himself tell one. What it presently came to in truth was that poor Marcher waded through his beaten grass, where no life stirred, where no breath sounded, where no evil eye seemed to gleam from a possible lair,

very much as if vaguely looking for the Beast, and still more as if acutely missing it. He walked about in an existence that had grown strangely more spacious, and, stopping fitfully in places where the undergrowth of life struck
him as closer, asked himself yearningly, wondered secretly and sorely, if it
would have lurked here or there. It would have at all events *sprung*; what was
at least complete was his belief in the truth of the assurance given him. The
change from his old sense to his new was absolute and final: what was to happen *had* so absolutely and finally happened that he was as little able to know
a fear for his future as to know a hope; so absent in short was any question
of anything still to come. He was to live entirely with the other question, that
of his unidentified past, that of his having to see his fortune impenetrably
muffled and masked.

The torment of this vision became then his occupation; he couldn't perhaps have consented to live but for the possibility of guessing. She had told
him, his friend, not to guess; she had forbidden him, so far as he might, to
know, and she had even in a sort denied the power in him to learn: which
were so many things, precisely, to deprive him of rest. It wasn't that he
wanted, he argued for fairness, that anything past and done should repeat
itself; it was only that he shouldn't, as an anticlimax, have been taken sleeping so sound as not to be able to win back by an effort of thought the lost stuff
of consciousness. He declared to himself at moments that he would either
win it back or have done with consciousness for ever; he made this idea his
one motive in fine, made it so much his passion that none other, to compare
with it, seemed ever to have touched him. The lost stuff of consciousness
became thus for him as a strayed or stolen child to an unappeasable father;
he hunted it up and down very much as if he were knocking at doors and
enquiring of the police. This was the spirit in which, inevitably, he set himself to travel; he started on a journey that was to be as long as he could make
it; it danced before him that, as the other side of the globe couldn't possibly
have less to say to him, it might, by a possibility of suggestion, have more.
Before he quitted London, however, he made a pilgrimage to May Bartram's
grave, took his way to it through the endless avenues of the grim suburban
metropolis, sought it out in the wilderness of tombs, and, though he had
come but for the renewal of the act of farewell, found himself, when he had
at last stood by it, beguiled into long intensities. He stood for an hour, powerless to turn away and yet powerless to penetrate the darkness of death; fixing with his eyes her inscribed name and date, beating his forehead against
the fact of the secret they kept, drawing his breath, while he waited, as if
some sense would in pity of him rise from the stones. He kneeled on the
stones, however, in vain; they kept what they concealed; and if the face of the
tomb did become a face for him it was because her two names became a pair
of eyes that didn't know him. He gave them a last long look, but no palest light
broke.

## VI

He stayed away, after this, for a year; he visited the depths of Asia, spending himself on scenes of romantic interest, of superlative sanctity; but what
was present to him everywhere was that for a man who had known what *he*
had known the world was vulgar and vain. The state of mind in which he had

lived for so many years shone out to him, in reflexion, as a light that coloured and refined, a light beside which the glow of the East was garish cheap and thin. The terrible truth was that he had lost—with everything else—a distinction as well; the things he saw couldn't help being common when he had become common to look at them. He was simply now one of them himself—he was in the dust, without a peg for the sense of difference; and there were hours when, before the temples of gods and the sepulchres of kings, his spirit turned for nobleness of association to the barely discriminated slab in the London suburb. That had become for him, and more intensely with time and distance, his one witness of a past glory. It was all that was left to him for proof or pride, yet the past glories of Pharaohs were nothing to him as he thought of it. Small wonder then that he came back to it on the morrow of his return. He was drawn there this time as irresistibly as the other, yet with a confidence, almost, that was doubtless the effect of the many months that had elapsed. He had lived, in spite of himself, into his change of feeling, and in wandering over the earth had wandered, as might be said, from the circumference to the centre of his desert. He had settled to his safety and accepted perforce his extinction; figuring to himself, with some colour, in the likeness of certain little old men he remembered to have seen, of whom, all meagre and wizened as they might look, it was related that they had in their time fought twenty duels or been loved by ten princesses. They indeed had been wondrous for others while he was but wondrous for himself; which, however, was exactly the cause of his haste to renew the wonder by getting back, as he might put it, into his own presence. That had quickened his steps and checked his delay. If his visit was prompt it was because he had been separated so long from the part of himself that alone he now valued.

It's accordingly not false to say that he reached his goal with a certain elation and stood there again with a certain assurance. The creature beneath the sod *knew* of his rare experience, so that, strangely now, the place had lost for him its mere blankness of expression. It met him in mildness—not, as before, in mockery; it wore for him the air of conscious greeting that we find, after absence, in things that have closely belonged to us and which seem to confess of themselves to the connexion. The plot of ground, the graven tablet, the tended flowers affected him so as belonging to him that he resembled for the hour a contented landlord reviewing a piece of property. Whatever had happened—well, had happened. He had not come back this time with the vanity of that question, his former worrying "What, *what?*" now practically so spent. Yet he would none the less never again so cut himself off from the spot; he would come back to it every month, for if he did nothing else by its aid he at least held up his head. It thus grew for him, in the oddest way, a positive resource; he carried out his idea of periodical returns, which took their place at last among the most inveterate of his habits. What it all amounted to, oddly enough, was that in his finally so simplified world this garden of death gave him the few square feet of earth on which he could still most live. It was as if, being nothing anywhere else for any one, nothing even for himself, he were just everything here, and if not for a crowd of witnesses or indeed for any witness but John Marcher, then by clear right of the register that he could scan like an open page. The open page was the tomb of his friend, and *there* were the facts of the past, there the truth of his life, there the backward reaches in which he could lose himself. He did this from time to time with such effect that he seemed to wander through the old years with his hand in the arm of a companion who was, in the most extraordinary manner, his other, his younger self; and to wander, which was more extraordinary yet, round and round a third presence—not wandering she, but stationary, still, whose eyes, turning with his revolution, never ceased to follow him, and whose seat was his point, so to speak, of orientation. Thus in short he settled to live—feeding all on the sense that he once *had* lived, and dependent on it not alone for a support but for an identity.

It sufficed him in its way for months and the year elapsed; it would doubtless even have carried him further but for an accident, superficially slight, which moved him, quite in another direction, with a force beyond any of his impressions of Egypt or of India. It was a thing of the merest chance—the turn, as he afterwards felt, of a hair, though he was indeed to live to believe that if light hadn't come to him in this particular fashion it would still have come in another. He was to live to believe this, I say, though he was not to live, I may not less definitely mention, to do much else. We allow him at any rate the benefit of the conviction, struggling up for him at the end, that, whatever might have happened or not happened, he would have come round of himself to the light. The incident of an autumn day had put the match to the train laid from of old by his misery. With the light before him he knew that even of late his ache had only been smothered. It was strangely drugged, but it throbbed; at the touch it began to bleed. And the touch, in the event, was the face of a fellow mortal. This face, one grey afternoon when the leaves were thick in the alleys, looked into Marcher's own, at the cemetery, with an expression like the cut of a blade. He felt it, that is, so deep down that he winced at the steady thrust. The person who so mutely assaulted him was a figure he had noticed, on reaching his own goal, absorbed by a grave a short distance away, a grave apparently fresh, so that the emotion of the visitor would probably match it for frankness. This face alone forbade further attention, though during the time he stayed he remained vaguely conscious of his neighbour, a middle-aged man apparently, in mourning, whose bowed back, among the clustered monuments and mortuary yews, was constantly presented. Marcher's theory that these were elements in contact with which he himself revived, had suffered, on this occasion, it may be granted, a marked, an excessive check. The autumn day was dire for him as none had recently been, and he rested with a heaviness he had not yet known on the low stone table that bore May Bartram's name. He rested without power to move, as if some spring in him, some spell vouchsafed, had suddenly been broken for ever. If he could have done that moment as he wanted he would simply have stretched himself on the slab that was ready to take him, treating it as a place prepared to receive his last sleep. What in all the wide world had he now to keep awake for? He stared before him with the question, and it was then that, as one of the cemetery walks passed near him, he caught the shock of the face.

His neighbour at the other grave had withdrawn, as he himself, with force enough in him, would have done by now, and was advancing along the path on his way to one of the gates. This brought him close, and his pace was slow, so that—and all the more as there was a kind of hunger in his look—the two men were for a minute directly confronted. Marcher knew him at once for one of the deeply stricken—a perception so sharp that nothing else in the picture comparatively lived, neither his dress, his age, nor his presumable character and class; nothing lived but the deep ravage of the features he showed. He *showed* them—that was the point; he was moved, as he passed, by some impulse that was either a signal for sympathy or, more possibly, a challenge to an opposed sorrow. He might already have been aware of our friend, might at some previous hour have noticed in him the smooth habit of the scene, with which the state of his own senses so scantly consorted, and might thereby have been stirred as by an overt discord. What Marcher was at all events conscious of was in the first place that the image of scarred passion presented to him was conscious too—of something that profaned the air; and in the second that, roused, startled, shocked, he was yet the next moment looking after it, as it went, with envy. The most extraordinary thing that had happened to him—though he had given that name to other matters as well—took place, after his immediate vague stare, as a consequence of this impression. The stranger passed, but the raw glare of his grief remained, making our friend wonder in pity what wrong, what wound it expressed, what injury not to be healed. What had the man *had,* to make him by the loss of it so bleed and yet live?

Something—and this reached him with a pang—that *he,* John Marcher, hadn't; the proof of which was precisely John Marcher's arid end. No passion had ever touched him, for this was what passion meant; he had survived and maundered and pined, but where had been *his* deep ravage? The extraordinary thing we speak of was the sudden rush of the result of this question. The sight that had just met his eyes named to him, as in letters of quick flame, something he had utterly, insanely missed, and what he had missed made these things a train of fire, made them mark themselves in an anguish of inward throbs. He had seen *outside* of his life, not learned it within, the way a woman was mourned when she had been loved for herself: such was the force of his conviction of the meaning of the stranger's face, which still flared for him as a smoky torch. It hadn't come to him, the knowledge, on the wings of experience; it had brushed him, jostled him, upset him, with the disrespect of chance, the insolence of accident. Now that the illumination had begun, however, it blazed to the zenith, and what he presently stood there gazing at was the sounded void of his life. He gazed, he drew breath, in pain; he turned in his dismay, and, turning, he had before him in sharper incision than ever the open page of his story. The name on the table smote him as the passage of his neighbour had done, and what it said to him, full in the face, was that *she* was what he had missed. This was the awful thought, the answer to all the past, the vision at the dread clearness of which he grew as cold as the stone beneath him. Everything fell together, confessed, explained, overwhelmed; leaving him most of all stupefied at the blindness he had cherished. The fate he had been marked for he had met with a vengeance—he had emptied the cup to the lees; he had been the man of his time, *the* man, to whom nothing on earth was to have happened. That was the rare stroke—that was his visitation. So he saw it, as we say, in pale horror, while the pieces fitted and fitted. So *she* had seen it while he didn't, and so she served at this hour to drive the truth home. It was the truth, vivid and monstrous, that all the while he had waited the wait was itself his portion. This the companion of his vigil had at a given moment made out, and she had then offered him the chance to baffle his doom. One's doom, however, was never baffled, and on the day she told him his own had come down she had seen him but stupidly stare at the escape she offered him.

The escape would have been to love her; then, *then* he would have lived. *She* had lived—who could say now with what passion?—since she had loved him for himself; whereas he had never thought of her (ah, how it hugely glared at him!) but in the chill of his egotism and the light of her use. Her spoken words came back to him—the chain stretched and stretched. The Beast had lurked indeed, and the Beast, at its hour, had sprung; it had sprung in that twilight of the cold April when, pale, ill, wasted, but all beautiful, and perhaps even then recoverable, she had risen from her chair to stand before him and let him imaginably guess. It had sprung as he didn't guess; it had sprung as she hopelessly turned from him, and the mark, by the time he left her, had fallen where it *was* to fall. He had justified his fear and achieved his fate; he had failed, with the last exactitude, of all he was to fail of; and a moan now rose to his lips as he remembered she had prayed he mightn't know. This horror of waking—*this* was knowledge, knowledge under the breath of which the very tears in his eyes seemed to freeze. Through them, none the less, he tried to fix it and hold it; he kept it there before him so that he might feel the pain. That at least, belated and bitter, had something of the taste of life. But the bitterness suddenly sickened him, and it was as if, horribly, he saw, in the truth, in the cruelty of his image, what had been appointed and done. He saw the Jungle of his life and saw the lurking Beast; then, while he looked, perceived it, as by a stir of the air, rise, huge and hideous, for the leap that was to settle him. His eyes darkened—it was close; and, instinctively turning, in his hallucination, to avoid it, he flung himself, face down, on the tomb.

1901                                                                              1903, 1909

## The Figure in the Carpet[1]

### I

I had done a few things and earned a few pence—I had perhaps even had time to begin to think I was finer than was perceived by the patronising; but when I take the little measure of my course (a fidgety habit, for it's none of the longest yet) I count my real start from the evening George Corvick, breathless and worried, came in to ask me a service. He had done more things than I, and earned more pence, though there were chances for cleverness I thought he sometimes missed. I could only however that evening declare to him that he never missed one for kindness. There was almost rapture in hearing it proposed to me to prepare for *The Middle*, the organ of our lucubrations,[2] so called from the position in the week of its day of appearance, an article for which he had made himself responsible and of which, tied up with a stout string, he laid on my table the subject. I pounced upon my opportunity—that is on the first volume of it—and paid scant attention to my friend's explanation of his appeal. What explanation could be more to the point than

1. First published in *Cosmopolis* 1 (January 1896), the story was revised by James and included in the Macmillan New York edition of 1907–09 (vol. 15), from which the present text is taken.
2. Intense study.

my obvious fitness for the task? I had written on Hugh Vereker, but never a word in *The Middle*, where my dealings were mainly with the ladies and the minor poets. This was his new novel, an advance copy, and whatever much or little it should do for his reputation I was clear on the spot as to what it should do for mine. Moreover if I always read him as soon as I could get hold of him I had a particular reason for wishing to read him now: I had accepted an invitation to Bridges for the following Sunday, and it had been mentioned in Lady Jane's note that Mr. Vereker was to be there. I was young enough for a flutter at meeting a man of his renown, and innocent enough to believe the occasion would demand the display of an acquaintance with his "last."

Corvick, who had promised a review of it, had not even had time to read it; he had gone to pieces in consequence of news requiring—as on precipitate reflexion he judged—that he should catch the nightmail to Paris.[3] He had had a telegram from Gwendolen Erme in answer to his letter offering to fly to her aid. I knew already about Gwendolen Erme; I had never seen her, but I had my ideas, which were mainly to the effect that Corvick would marry her if her mother would only die. That lady seemed now in a fair way to oblige him; after some dreadful mistake about a climate or a "cure" she had suddenly collapsed on the return from abroad. Her daughter, unsupported and alarmed, desiring to make a rush for home but hesitating at the risk, had accepted our friend's assistance, and it was my secret belief that at sight of him Mrs. Erme would pull round. His own belief was scarcely to be called secret; it discernibly at any rate differed from mine. He had showed me Gwendolen's photograph with the remark that she wasn't pretty but was awfully interesting; she had published at the age of nineteen a novel in three volumes, "Deep Down," about which, in *The Middle*, he had been really splendid. He appreciated my present eagerness and undertook that the periodical in question should do no less; then at the last, with his hand on the door, he said to me: "Of course you'll be all right, you know." Seeing I was a trifle vague he added: "I mean you won't be silly."

"Silly—about Vereker! Why what do I ever find him but awfully clever?"

"Well, what's that but silly? What on earth does 'awfully clever' mean? For God's sake try to get *at* him. Don't let him suffer by our arrangement. Speak of him, you know, if you can, as *I* should have spoken of him."

I wondered an instant. "You mean as far and away the biggest of the lot—that sort of thing?"

Corvick almost groaned. "Oh you know, I don't put them back to back that way; it's the infancy of art! But he gives me a pleasure so rare; the sense of"—he mused a little—"something or other."

I wondered again. "The sense, pray, of what?"

"My dear man, that's just what I want *you* to say!"

Even before he had banged the door I had begun, book in hand, to prepare myself to say it. I sat up with Vereker half the night; Corvick couldn't have done more than that. He was awfully clever—I stuck to that, but he wasn't a bit the biggest of the lot. I didn't allude to the lot, however; I flattered myself that I emerged on this occasion from the infancy of art. "It's all right," they declared vividly at the office; and when the number appeared I felt there was a basis on which I could meet the great man. It gave me confidence for a day

---

3. Evening train to Paris.

or two—then that confidence dropped. I had fancied him reading it with relish, but if Corvick wasn't satisfied how could Vereker himself be? I reflected indeed that the heat of the admirer was sometimes grosser even than the appetite of the scribe. Corvick at all events wrote me from Paris a little ill-humouredly. Mrs. Erme was pulling round, and I hadn't at all said what Vereker gave him the sense of.

## II

The effect of my visit to Bridges was to turn me out for more profundity. Hugh Vereker, as I saw him there, was of a contact so void of angles that I blushed for the poverty of imagination involved in my small precautions. If he was in spirits it wasn't because he had read my review; in fact on the Sunday morning I felt sure he hadn't read it, though *The Middle* had been out three days and bloomed, I assured myself, in the stiff garden of periodicals which gave one of the ormolu[4] tables the air of a stand at a station. The impression he made on me personally was such that I wished him to read it, and I corrected to this end with a surreptitious hand what might be wanting in the careless conspicuity of the sheet. I'm afraid I even watched the result of my manœuvre, but up to luncheon I watched in vain.

When afterwards, in the course of our gregarious walk, I found myself for half an hour, not perhaps without another manœuvre, at the great man's side, the result of his affability was a still livelier desire that he shouldn't remain in ignorance of the peculiar justice I had done him. It wasn't that he seemed to thirst for justice; on the contrary I hadn't yet caught in his talk the faintest grunt of a grudge—a note for which my young experience had already given me an ear. Of late he had had more recognition, and it was pleasant, as we used to say in *The Middle*, to see how it drew him out. He wasn't of course popular, but I judged one of the sources of his good humour to be precisely that his success was independent of that. He had none the less become in a manner the fashion; the critics at least had put on a spurt and caught up with him. We had found out at last how clever he was, and he had had to make the best of the loss of his mystery. I was strongly tempted, as I walked beside him, to let him know how much of that unveiling was my act; and there was a moment when I probably should have done so had not one of the ladies of our party, snatching a place at his other elbow, just then appealed to him in a spirit comparatively selfish. It was very discouraging: I almost felt the liberty had been taken with myself.

I had had on my tongue's end, for my own part, a phrase or two about the right word at the right time; but later on I was glad not to have spoken, for when on our return we clustered at tea I perceived Lady Jane, who had not been out with us, brandishing *The Middle* with her longest arm. She had taken it up at her leisure; she was delighted with what she had found, and I saw that, as a mistake in a man may often be a felicity in a woman, she would practically do for me what I hadn't been able to do for myself. "Some sweet little truths that needed to be spoken," I heard her declare, thrusting the paper at rather a bewildered couple by the fireplace. She grabbed it away from

4. Any of several copper and zinc or tin alloys resembling gold and used to ornament furniture, moldings, architectural details, and jewelry.

them again on the reappearance of Hugh Vereker, who after our walk had
been upstairs to change something. "I know you don't in general look at this
kind of thing, but it's an occasion really for doing so. You *haven't* seen it? Then
you must. The man has actually got *at* you, at what *I* always feel, you know."
Lady Jane threw into her eyes a look evidently intended to give an idea of what
she always felt; but she added that she couldn't have expressed it. The man
in the paper expressed it in a striking manner. "Just see there, and there,
where I've dashed it, how he brings it out." She had literally marked for him
the brightest patches of my prose, and if I was a little amused Vereker himself may well have been. He showed how much he was when before us all
Lady Jane wanted to read something aloud. I liked at any rate the way he
defeated her purpose by jerking the paper affectionately out of her clutch.
He'd take it upstairs with him and look at it on going to dress. He did this half
an hour later—I saw it in his hand when he repaired to his room. That was
the moment at which, thinking to give her pleasure, I mentioned to Lady Jane
that I was the author of the review. I did give her pleasure, I judged, but perhaps not quite so much as I had expected. If the author was "only me" the
thing didn't seem quite so remarkable. Hadn't I had the effect rather of
diminishing the lustre of the article than of adding to my own? Her ladyship
was subject to the most extraordinary drops. It didn't matter; the only effect
I cared about was the one it would have on Vereker up there by his bedroom
fire.

At dinner I watched for the signs of this impression, tried to fancy some
happier light in his eyes; but to my disappointment Lady Jane gave me no
chance to make sure. I had hoped she'd call triumphantly down the table,
publicly demand if she hadn't been right. The party was large—there were people from outside as well, but I had never seen a table long enough to deprive
Lady Jane of a triumph. I was just reflecting in truth that this interminable
board[5] would deprive *me* of one when the guest next me, dear woman—
she was Miss Poyle, the vicar's sister, a robust unmodulated person—had the
happy inspiration and the unusual courage to address herself across it to
Vereker, who was opposite, but not directly, so that when he replied they were
both leaning forward. She enquired, artless body, what he thought of Lady
Jane's "panegyric," which she had read—not connecting it however with her
right-hand neighbour; and while I strained my ear for his reply I heard him,
to my stupefaction, call back gaily, his mouth full of bread: "Oh it's all right—
the usual twaddle!"

I had caught Vereker's glance as he spoke, but Miss Poyle's surprise was a
fortunate cover for my own. "You mean he doesn't do you justice?" said the
excellent woman.

Vereker laughed out, and I was happy to be able to do the same. "It's a
charming article," he tossed us.

Miss Poyle thrust her chin half across the cloth. "Oh you're so deep!" she
drove home.

"As deep as the ocean! All I pretend is that the author doesn't see—" But
a dish was at this point passed over his shoulder, and we had to wait while he
helped himself.

5. Table of food.

"Doesn't see what?" my neighbour continued.

"Doesn't see anything."

"Dear me—how very stupid!"

"Not a bit," Vereker laughed again. "Nobody does."

The lady on his further side appealed to him and Miss Poyle sank back to myself. "Nobody sees anything!" she cheerfully announced; to which I replied that I had often thought so too, but had somehow taken the thought for a proof on my own part of a tremendous eye. I didn't tell her the article was mine; and I observed that Lady Jane, occupied at the end of the table, had not caught Vereker's words.

I rather avoided him after dinner, for I confess he struck me as cruelly conceited, and the revelation was a pain. "The usual twaddle"—my acute little study! That one's admiration should have had a reserve or two could gall him to that point? I had thought him placid, and he was placid enough; such a surface was the hard polished glass that encased the bauble of his vanity. I was really ruffled, and the only comfort was that if nobody saw anything George Corvick was quite as much out of it as I. This comfort however was not sufficient, after the ladies had dispersed, to carry me in the proper manner—I mean in a spotted jacket[6] and humming an air—into the smoking-room. I took my way in some dejection to bed; but in the passage I encountered Mr. Vereker, who had been up once more to change, coming out of his room. *He* was humming an air and had on a spotted jacket, and as soon as he saw me his gaiety gave a start.

"My dear young man," he exclaimed, "I'm so glad to lay hands on you! I'm afraid I most unwittingly wounded you by those words of mine at dinner to Miss Poyle. I learned but half an hour ago from Lady Jane that you're the author of the little notice in *The Middle*."

I protested that no bones were broken; but he moved with me to my own door, his hand, on my shoulder, kindly feeling for a fracture; and on hearing that I had come up to bed he asked leave to cross my threshold and just tell me in three words what his qualification of my remarks had represented. It was plain he really feared I was hurt, and the sense of his solicitude suddenly made all the difference to me. My cheap review fluttered off into space, and the best things I had said in it became flat enough beside the brilliancy of his being there. I can see him there still, on my rug, in the firelight and his spotted jacket, his fine clear face all bright with the desire to be tender to my youth. I don't know what he had at first meant to say, but I think the sight of my relief touched him, excited him, brought up words to his lips from far within. It was so these words presently conveyed to me something that, as I afterwards knew, he had never uttered to any one. I've always done justice to the generous impulse that made him speak; it was simply compunction for a snub unconsciously administered to a man of letters in a position inferior to his own, a man of letters moreover in the very act of praising him. To make the thing right he talked to me exactly as an equal and on the ground of what we both loved best. The hour, the place, the unexpectedness deepened the impression: he couldn't have done anything more intensely effective.

6. A leopardskin jacket. The spotted jacket worn by James's narrator alludes to a moment in the first book of Virgil's *Aeneid*, where Venus, the Roman goddess of beauty and love, is described as a huntress wearing a lynx's hide "varied with spots."

## III

"I don't quite know how to explain it to you," he said, "but it was the very fact that your notice of my book had a spice of intelligence, it was just your exceptional sharpness, that produced the feeling—a very old story with me, I beg you to believe—under the momentary influence of which I used in speaking to that good lady the words you so naturally resent. I don't read the things in the newspapers unless they're thrust upon me as that one was—it's always one's best friend who does it! But I used to read them sometimes—ten years ago. I dare say they were in general rather stupider then; at any rate it always struck me they missed my little point with a perfection exactly as admirable when they patted me on the back as when they kicked me in the shins. Whenever since I've happened to have a glimpse of them they were still blazing away—still missing it, I mean, deliciously. You miss it, my dear fellow, with inimitable assurance; the fact of your being awfully clever and your article's being awfully nice doesn't make a hair's breadth of difference. It's quite with you rising young men," Vereker laughed, "that I feel most what a failure I am!"

I listened with keen interest; it grew keener as he talked. "You a failure—heavens! What then may your 'little point' happen to be?"

"Have I got to *tell* you, after all these years and labours?" There was something in the friendly reproach of this—jocosely exaggerated—that made me, as an ardent young seeker for truth, blush to the roots of my hair. I'm as much in the dark as ever, though I've grown used in a sense to my obtuseness; at that moment, however, Vereker's happy accent made me appear to myself, and probably to him, a rare dunce. I was on the point of exclaiming "Ah yes, don't tell me: for my honour, for that of the craft, don't!" when he went on in a manner that showed he had read my thought and had his own idea of the probability of our some day redeeming ourselves. "By my little point I mean—what shall I call it?—the particular thing I've written my books most *for*. Isn't there for every writer a particular thing of that sort, the thing that most makes him apply himself, the thing without the effort to achieve which he wouldn't write at all, the very passion of his passion, the part of the business in which, for him, the flame of art burns most intensely? Well, it's *that!*"

I considered a moment—that is I followed at a respectful distance, rather gasping. I was fascinated—easily, you'll say; but I wasn't going after all to be put off my guard. "Your description's certainly beautiful, but it doesn't make what you describe very distinct."

"I promise you it would be distinct if it should dawn on you at all." I saw that the charm of our topic overflowed for my companion into an emotion as lively as my own. "At any rate," he went on, "I can speak for myself: there's an idea in my work without which I wouldn't have given a straw for the whole job. It's the finest fullest intention of the lot, and the application of it has been, I think, a triumph of patience, of ingenuity. I ought to leave that to somebody else to say; but that nobody does say it is precisely what we're talking about. It stretches, this little trick of mine, from book to book, and everything else, comparatively, plays over the surface of it. The order, the form, the texture of my books will perhaps some day constitute for the initiated a complete representation of it. So it's naturally the thing for the critic to look for. It strikes me," my visitor added, smiling, "even as the thing for the critic to find."

This seemed a responsibility indeed. "You call it a little trick?"

"That's only my little modesty. It's really an exquisite scheme."

"And you hold that you've carried the scheme out?"

"The way I've carried it out is the thing in life I think a bit well of myself for."

I had a pause. "Don't you think you ought—just a trifle—to assist the critic?"

"Assist him? What else have I done with every stroke of my pen? I've shouted my intention in his great blank face!" At this, laughing out again, Vereker laid his hand on my shoulder to show the allusion wasn't to my personal appearance.

"But you talk about the initiated. There must therefore, you see, *be* initiation."

"What else in heaven's name is criticism supposed to be?" I'm afraid I coloured at this too; but I took refuge in repeating that his account of his silver lining was poor in something or other that a plain man knows things by. "That's only because you've never had a glimpse of it," he returned. "If you had had one the element in question would soon have become practically all you'd see. To me it's exactly as palpable as the marble of this chimney. Besides, the critic just *isn't* a plain man: if he were, pray, what would he be doing in his neighbour's garden? You're anything but a plain man yourself, and the very *raison d'être* of you all is that you're little demons of subtlety. If my great affair's a secret, that's only because it's a secret in spite of itself— the amazing event has made it one. I not only never took the smallest precaution to keep it so, but never dreamed of any such accident. If I had I shouldn't in advance have had the heart to go on. As it was, I only became aware little by little, and meanwhile I had done my work."

"And now you quite like it?" I risked.

"My work?"

"Your secret. It's the same thing."

"Your guessing that," Vereker replied, "is a proof that you're as clever as I say!" I was encouraged by this to remark that he would clearly be pained to part with it, and he confessed that it was indeed with him now the great amusement of life. "I live almost to see if it will ever be detected." He looked at me for a jesting challenge; something far within his eyes seemed to peep out. "But I needn't worry—it won't!"

"You fire me as I've never been fired," I declared; "you make me determined to do or die." Then I asked: "Is it a kind of esoteric message?"

His countenance fell at this—he put out his hand as if to bid me good-night. "Ah my dear fellow, it can't be described in cheap journalese!"

I knew of course he'd be awfully fastidious, but our talk had made me feel how much his nerves were exposed. I was unsatisfied—I kept hold of his hand. "I won't make use of the expression then," I said, "in the article in which I shall eventually announce my discovery, though I dare say I shall have hard work to do without it. But meanwhile, just to hasten that difficult birth, can't you give a fellow a clue?" I felt much more at my ease.

"My whole lucid effort gives him the clue—every page and line and letter. The thing's as concrete there as a bird in a cage, a bait on a hook, a piece of cheese in a mouse-trap. It's stuck into every volume as your foot is stuck into your shoe. It governs every line, it chooses every word, it dots every i, it places every comma."

I scratched my head. "Is it something in the style or something in the thought? An element of form or an element of feeling?"

He indulgently shook my hand again, and I felt my questions to be crude and my distinctions pitiful. "Good-night, my dear boy—don't bother about it. After all, you do like a fellow."

"And a little intelligence might spoil it?" I still detained him.

He hesitated. "Well, you've got a heart in your body. Is that an element of form or an element of feeling? What I contend that nobody has ever mentioned in my work is the organ of life."

"I see—it's some idea *about* life, some sort of philosophy. Unless it be," I added with the eagerness of a thought perhaps still happier, "some kind of game you're up to with your style, something you're after in the language. Perhaps it's a preference for the letter P!" I ventured profanely to break out. "Papa, potatoes, prunes—that sort of thing?" He was suitably indulgent: he only said I hadn't got the right letter. But his amusement was over; I could see he was bored. There was nevertheless something else I had absolutely to learn. "Should you be able, pen in hand, to state it clearly yourself—to name it, phrase it, formulate it?"

"Oh," he almost passionately sighed, "if I were only, pen in hand, one of *you* chaps!"

"That would be a great chance for you of course. But why should you despise us chaps for not doing what you can't do yourself?"

"Can't do?" He opened his eyes. "Haven't I done it in twenty volumes? I do it in my way," he continued. "Go *you* and don't do it in yours."

"Ours is so devilish difficult," I weakly observed.

"So's mine! We each choose our own. There's no compulsion. You won't come down and smoke?"

"No. I want to think this thing out."

"You'll tell me then in the morning that you've laid me bare?"

"I'll see what I can do; I'll sleep on it. But just one word more," I added. We had left the room—I walked again with him a few steps along the passage. "This extraordinary 'general intention,' as you call it—for that's the most vivid description I can induce you to make of it—is then, generally, a sort of buried treasure?"

His face lighted. "Yes, call it that, though it's perhaps not for me to do so."

"Nonsense!" I laughed. "You know you're hugely proud of it."

"Well, I didn't propose to tell you so; but it *is* the joy of my soul!"

"You mean it's a beauty so rare, so great?"

He waited a little again. "The loveliest thing in the world!" We had stopped, and on these words he left me; but at the end of the corridor, while I looked after him rather yearningly, he turned and caught sight of my puzzled face. It made him earnestly, indeed I thought quite anxiously, shake his head and wave his finger. "Give it up—give it up!"

This wasn't a challenge—it was fatherly advice. If I had had one of his books at hand I'd have repeated my recent act of faith—I'd have spent half the night with him. At three o'clock in the morning, not sleeping, remembering moreover how indispensable he was to Lady Jane, I stole down to the library with a candle. There wasn't, so far as I could discover, a line of his writing in the house.

## IV

Returning to town I feverishly collected them all; I picked out each in its order and held it up to the light. This gave me a maddening month, in the course of which several things took place. One of these, the last, I may as well immediately mention, was that I acted on Vereker's advice: I renounced my ridiculous attempt. I could really make nothing of the business; it proved a dead loss. After all I had always, as he had himself noted, liked him; and what now occurred was simply that my new intelligence and vain preoccupation damaged my liking. I not only failed to run a general intention to earth, I found myself missing the subordinate intentions I had formerly enjoyed. His books didn't even remain the charming things they had been for me; the exasperation of my search put me out of conceit of them. Instead of being a pleasure the more they became a resource the less; for from the moment I was unable to follow up the author's hint I of course felt it a point of honour not to make use professionally of my knowledge of them. I *had* no knowledge—nobody had any. It was humiliating, but I could bear it—they only annoyed me now. At last they even bored me, and I accounted for my confusion—perversely, I allow—by the idea that Vereker had made a fool of me. The buried treasure was a bad joke, the general intention a monstrous *pose*.

The great point of it all is, however, that I told George Corvick what had befallen me and that my information had an immense effect on him. He had at last come back, but so, unfortunately, had Mrs. Erme, and there was as yet, I could see, no question of his nuptials. He was immensely stirred up by the anecdote I had brought from Bridges; it fell in so completely with the sense he had had from the first that there was more in Vereker than met the eye. When I remarked that the eye seemed what the printed page had been expressly invented to meet he immediately accused me of being spiteful because I had been foiled. Our commerce had always that pleasant latitude. The thing Vereker had mentioned to me was exactly the thing he, Corvick, had wanted me to speak of in my review. On my suggesting at last that with the assistance I had now given him he would doubtless be prepared to speak of it himself he admitted freely that before doing this there was more he must understand. What he would have said, had he reviewed the new book, was that there was evidently in the writer's inmost art something to *be* understood. I hadn't so much as hinted at that: no wonder the writer hadn't been flattered! I asked Corvick what he really considered he meant by his own supersubtlety, and, unmistakeably kindled, he replied: "It isn't for the vulgar—it isn't for the vulgar!" He had hold of the tail of something: he would pull hard, pull it right out. He pumped me dry on Vereker's strange confidence and, pronouncing me the luckiest of mortals, mentioned half a dozen questions he wished to goodness I had had the gumption to put. Yet on the other hand he didn't want to be told too much—it would spoil the fun of seeing what would come. The failure of *my* fun was at the moment of our meeting not complete, but I saw it ahead, and Corvick saw that I saw it. I, on my side, saw likewise that one of the first things he would do would be to rush off with my story to Gwendolen.

On the very day after my talk with him I was surprised by the receipt of a note from Hugh Vereker, to whom our encounter at Bridges had been recalled, as he mentioned, by his falling, in a magazine, on some article to which my signature was attached. "I read it with great pleasure," he wrote, "and remembered under its influence our lively conversation by your bedroom fire. The consequence of this has been that I begin to measure the temerity of my having saddled you with a knowledge that you may find something of a burden. Now that the fit's over I can't imagine how I came to be moved so much beyond my wont. I had never before mentioned, no matter in what state of expansion, the fact of my little secret, and I shall never speak of that mystery again. I was accidentally so much more explicit with you than it had ever entered into my game to be, that I find this game—I mean the pleasure of playing it—suffers considerably. In short, if you can understand it, I've rather spoiled my sport. I really don't want to give anybody what I believe you clever young men call the tip. That's of course a selfish solicitude, and I name it to you for what it may be worth to you. If you're disposed to humour me don't repeat my revelation. Think me demented—it's your right; but don't tell anybody why."

The sequel to this communication was that as early on the morrow as I dared I drove straight to Mr. Vereker's door. He occupied in those years one of the honest old houses in Kensington Square. He received me immediately, and as soon as I came in I saw I hadn't lost my power to minister to his mirth. He laughed out at sight of my face, which doubtless expressed my perturbation. I had been indiscreet—my compunction was great. "I *have* told somebody," I panted, "and I'm sure that person will by this time have told somebody else! It's a woman, into the bargain."

"The person you've told?"

"No, the other person. I'm quite sure he must have told her."

"For all the good it will do her—or do *me!* A woman will never find out."

"No, but she'll talk all over the place: she'll do just what you don't want."

Vereker thought a moment, but wasn't so disconcerted as I had feared: he felt that if the harm was done it only served him right. "It doesn't matter—don't worry."

"I'll do my best, I promise you, that your talk with me shall go no further."

"Very good; do what you can."

"In the meantime," I pursued, "George Corvick's possession of the tip may, on his part, really lead to something."

"That will be a brave day."

I told him about Corvick's cleverness, his admiration, the intensity of his interest in my anecdote; and without making too much of the divergence of our respective estimates mentioned that my friend was already of opinion that he saw much further into a certain affair than most people. He was quite as fired as I had been at Bridges. He was moreover in love with the young lady: perhaps the two together would puzzle something out.

Vereker seemed struck with this. "Do you mean they're to be married?"

"I dare say that's what it will come to."

"That may help them," he conceded, "but we must give them time!"

I spoke of my own renewed assault and confessed my difficulties; whereupon he repeated his former advice: "Give it up, give it up!" He evidently didn't think me intellectually equipped for the adventure. I stayed half an hour, and he was most good-natured, but I couldn't help pronouncing him a man of unstable moods. He had been free with me in a mood, he had repented in a mood, and now in a mood he had turned indifferent. This general levity helped me to believe that, so far as the subject of the tip went, there wasn't much in it. I contrived however to make him answer a few more questions about it, though he did so with visible impatience. For himself, beyond doubt, the thing we were all so blank about was vividly there. It was something, I guessed, in the primal plan; something like a complex figure in a Persian carpet. He highly approved of this image when I used it, and he used another himself. "It's the very string," he said, "that my pearls are strung on!" The reason of his note to me had been that he really didn't want to give us a grain of succour—our density was a thing too perfect in its way to touch. He had formed the habit of depending on it, and if the spell was to break it must break by some force of its own. He comes back to me from that last occasion—for I was never to speak to him again—as a man with some safe preserve for sport. I wondered as I walked away where he had got *his* tip.

## V

When I spoke to George Corvick of the caution I had received he made me feel that any doubt of his delicacy would be almost an insult. He had instantly told Gwendolen, but Gwendolen's ardent response was in itself a pledge of discretion. The question would now absorb them and would offer them a pastime too precious to be shared with the crowd. They appeared to have caught instinctively at Vereker's high idea of enjoyment. Their intellectual pride, however, was not such as to make them indifferent to any further light I might throw on the affair they had in hand. They were indeed of the "artistic temperament," and I was freshly struck with my colleague's power to excite himself over a question of art. He'd call it letters, he'd call it life, but it was all one thing. In what he said I now seemed to understand that he spoke equally for Gwendolen, to whom, as soon as Mrs. Erme was sufficiently better to allow her a little leisure, he made a point of introducing me. I remember our going together one Sunday in August to a huddled house in Chelsea, and my renewed envy of Corvick's possession of a friend who had some light to mingle with his own. He could say things to her that I could never say to him. She had indeed no sense of humour and, with her pretty way of holding her head on one side, was one of those persons whom you want, as the phrase is, to shake, but who have learnt Hungarian by themselves. She conversed perhaps in Hungarian with Corvick; she had remarkably little English for his friend. Corvick afterwards told me that I had chilled her by my apparent indisposition to oblige them with the detail of what Vereker had said to me. I allowed that I felt I had given thought enough to that indication: hadn't I even made up my mind that it was vain and would lead nowhere? The importance they attached to it was irritating and quite envenomed my doubts.

That statement looks unamiable, and what probably happened was that I felt humiliated at seeing other persons deeply beguiled by an experiment that had brought me only chagrin. I was out in the cold while, by the evening fire, under the lamp, they followed the chase for which I myself had sounded the horn. They did as I had done, only more deliberately and sociably—they went over their author from the beginning. There was no hurry, Corvick said—the future was before them and the fascination could only grow; they would take him page by page, as they would take one of the classics, inhale him in slow draughts and let him sink all the way in. They would scarce have got so wound up, I think, if they hadn't been in love: poor Vereker's inner meaning gave them endless occasion to put and to keep their young heads together. None the less it represented the kind of problem for which Corvick had a special aptitude, drew out the particular pointed patience of which, had he lived, he would have given more striking and, it is to be hoped, more fruitful examples. He at least was, in Vereker's words, a little demon of subtlety. We had begun by disputing, but I soon saw that without my stirring a finger his infatuation would have its bad hours. He would bound off on false scents as I had done— he would clap his hands over new lights and see them blown out by the wind of the turned page. He was like nothing, I told him, but the maniacs who embrace some bedlamitical[7] theory of the cryptic character of Shakespeare. To this he replied that if we had had Shakespeare's own word for his being cryptic he would at once have accepted it. The case there was altogether different—we had nothing but the word of Mr. Snooks. I returned that I was stupefied to see him attach such importance even to the word of Mr. Vereker. He wanted thereupon to know if I treated Mr. Vereker's word as a lie. I wasn't perhaps prepared, in my unhappy rebound, to go so far as that, but I insisted that till the contrary was proved I should view it as too fond an imagination. I didn't, I confess, say—I didn't at that time quite know—all I felt. Deep down, as Miss Erme would have said, I was uneasy, I was expectant. At the core of my disconcerted state—for my wonted curiosity lived in its ashes—was the sharpness of a sense that Corvick would at last probably come out some-where. He made, in defence of his credulity, a great point of the fact that from of old, in his study of this genius, he had caught whiffs and hints of he did-n't know what, faint wandering notes of a hidden music. That was just the rar-ity, that was the charm: it fitted so perfectly into what I reported.

If I returned on several occasions to the little house in Chelsea I dare say it was as much for news of Vereker as for news of Miss Erme's ailing parent. The hours spent there by Corvick were present to my fancy as those of a chessplayer bent with a silent scowl, all the lamplit winter, over his board and his moves. As my imagination filled it out the picture held me fast. On the other side of the table was a ghostlier form, the faint figure of an antagonist good-humouredly but a little wearily secure—an antagonist who leaned back in his chair with his hands in his pockets and a smile on his fine clear face. Close to Corvick, behind him, was a girl who had begun to strike me as pale and wasted and even, on more familiar view, as rather handsome, and who rested on his shoulder and hung on his moves. He would take up a chessman and hold it poised a while over one of the little squares, and then would put it back in its place with a long sigh of disappointment. The young lady, at this, would slightly but uneasily shift her position and look across, very hard, very long, very strangely, at their dim participant. I had asked them at an early stage of the business if it mightn't contribute to their success to have some closer communication with him. The special circumstances would surely be held to have given me a right to introduce them. Corvick immediately replied

---

7. Insane—the reference is to the Bethlem Royal Hospital (founded in London in 1247), popularly known as "Bedlam," the world's oldest institution for people with mental disorders.

that he had no wish to approach the altar before he had prepared the sacrifice. He quite agreed with our friend both as to the delight and as to the honour of the chase—he would bring down the animal with his own rifle. When I asked him if Miss Erme were as keen a shot he said after thinking: "No, I'm ashamed to say she wants to set a trap. She'd give anything to see him; she says she requires another tip. She's really quite morbid about it. But she must play fair—she *shan't* see him!" he emphatically added. I wondered if they hadn't even quarrelled a little on the subject—a suspicion not corrected by the way he more than once exclaimed to me: "She's quite incredibly literary, you know—quite fantastically!" I remember his saying of her that she felt in italics and thought in capitals. "Oh when I've run him to earth," he also said, "then, you know, I shall knock at his door. Rather—I beg you to believe. I'll have it from his own lips: 'Right you are, my boy; you've done it this time!' He shall crown me victor—with the critical laurel."

Meanwhile he really avoided the chances London life might have given him of meeting the distinguished novelist; a danger, however, that disappeared with Vereker's leaving England for an indefinite absence, as the newspapers announced—going to the south for motives connected with the health of his wife, which had long kept her in retirement. A year—more than a year—had elapsed since the incident at Bridges, but I had had no further sight of him. I think I was at bottom rather ashamed—I hated to remind him that, though I had irremediably missed his point, a reputation for acuteness was rapidly overtaking me. This scruple led me a dance; kept me out of Lady Jane's house, made me even decline, when in spite of my bad manners she was a second time so good as to make me a sign, an invitation to her beautiful seat. I once became aware of her under Vereker's escort at a concert, and was sure I was seen by them, but I slipped out without being caught. I felt, as on that occasion I splashed along in the rain, that I couldn't have done anything else; and yet I remember saying to myself that it was hard, was even cruel. Not only had I lost the books, but I had lost the man himself: they and their author had been alike spoiled for me. I knew too which was the loss I most regretted. I had taken to the man still more than I had ever taken to the books.

## VI

Six months after our friend had left England George Corvick, who made his living by his pen, contracted for a piece of work which imposed on him an absence of some length and a journey of some difficulty, and his undertaking of which was much of a surprise to me. His brother-in-law had become editor of a great provincial paper, and the great provincial paper, in a fine flight of fancy, had conceived the idea of sending a "special commissioner" to India. Special commissioners had begun, in the "metropolitan press," to be the fashion, and the journal in question must have felt it had passed too long for a mere country cousin. Corvick had no hand, I knew, for the big brush of the correspondent, but that was his brother-in-law's affair, and the fact that a particular task was not in his line was apt to be with himself exactly a reason for accepting it. He was prepared to out-Herod[8] the metropolitan press; he took

---

8. That is, to perform an action to excess; the actor who played King Herod in English medieval mystery plays often roared ferociously and stomped around the stage (cf. *Hamlet* 3.2.15).

solemn precautions against priggishness, he exquisitely outraged taste. Nobody ever knew it—that offended principle was all his own. In addition to his expenses he was to be conveniently paid, and I found myself able to help him, for the usual fat book, to a plausible arrangement with the usual fat publisher. I naturally inferred that his obvious desire to make a little money was not unconnected with the prospect of a union with Gwendolen Erme. I was aware that her mother's opposition was largely addressed to his want of means and of lucrative abilities, but it so happened that, on my saying the last time I saw him something that bore on the question of his separation from our young lady, he brought out with an emphasis that startled me: "Ah I'm not a bit engaged to her, you know!"

"Not overtly," I answered, "because her mother doesn't like you. But I've always taken for granted a private understanding."

"Well, there *was* one. But there isn't now." That was all he said save something about Mrs. Erme's having got on her feet again in the most extraordinary way—a remark pointing, as I supposed, the moral that private understandings were of little use when the doctor didn't share them. What I took the liberty of more closely inferring was that the girl might in some way have estranged him. Well, if he had taken the turn of jealousy for instance it could scarcely be jealousy of me. In that case—over and above the absurdity of it—he wouldn't have gone away just to leave us together. For some time before his going we had indulged in no allusion to the buried treasure, and from his silence, which my reserve simply emulated, I had drawn a sharp conclusion. His courage had dropped, his ardour had gone the way of mine—this appearance at least he left me to scan. More than that he couldn't do; he couldn't face the triumph with which I might have greeted an explicit admission. He needn't have been afraid, poor dear, for I had by this time lost all need to triumph. In fact I considered I showed magnanimity in not reproaching him with his collapse, for the sense of his having thrown up the game made me feel more than ever how much I at last depended on him. If Corvick had broken down I should never know; no one would be of any use if *he* wasn't. It wasn't a bit true I had ceased to care for knowledge; little by little my curiosity not only had begun to ache again, but had become the familiar torment of my days and my nights. There are doubtless people to whom torments of such an order appear hardly more natural than the contortions of disease; but I don't after all know why I should in this connexion so much as mention them. For the few persons, at any rate, abnormal or not, with whom my anecdote is concerned, literature was a game of skill, and skill meant courage, and courage meant honour, and honour meant passion, meant life. The stake on the table was of a special substance and our roulette the revolving mind, but we sat round the green board as intently as the grim gamblers at Monte Carlo. Gwendolen Erme, for that matter, with her white face and her fixed eyes, was of the very type of the lean ladies one had met in the temples of chance. I recognised in Corvick's absence that she made this analogy vivid. It was extravagant, I admit, the way she lived for the art of the pen. Her passion visibly preyed on her, and in her presence I felt almost tepid. I got hold of "Deep Down" again: it was a desert in which she had lost herself, but in which too she had dug a wonderful hole in the sand—a cavity out of which Corvick had still more remarkably pulled her.

Early in March I had a telegram from her, in consequence of which I repaired immediately to Chelsea, where the first thing she said to me was: "He has got it, he has got it!"

She was moved, as I could see, to such depths that she must mean the great thing. "Vereker's idea?"

"His general intention. George has cabled from Bombay."

She had the missive open there; it was emphatic though concise. "Eureka. Immense." That was all—he had saved the cost of the signature. I shared her emotion, but I was disappointed. "He doesn't say what it is."

"How could he—in a telegram? He'll write it."

"But how does he know?"

"Know it's the real thing? Oh I'm sure that when you see it you do know. *Vera incessu patuit dea!*"[9]

"It's you, Miss Erme, who are a 'dear' for bringing me such news!"—I went all lengths in my high spirits. "But fancy finding our goddess in the temple of Vishnu! How strange of George to have been able to go into the thing again in the midst of such different and such powerful solicitations!"

"He hasn't gone into it, I know; it's the thing itself, let severely alone for six months, that has simply sprung out at him like a tigress out of the jungle. He didn't take a book with him—on purpose; indeed he wouldn't have needed to—he knows every page, as I do, by heart. They all worked in him together, and some day somewhere, when he wasn't thinking, they fell, in all their superb intricacy, into the one right combination. The figure in the carpet came out. That's the way he knew it would come and the real reason—you didn't in the least understand, but I suppose I may tell you now—why he went and why I consented to his going. We knew the change would do it—that the difference of thought, of scene, would give the needed touch, the magic shake. We had perfectly, we had admirably calculated. The elements were all in his mind, and in the *secousse*[1] of a new and intense experience they just struck light. She positively struck light herself—she was literally, facially luminous. I stammered something about unconscious cerebration, and she continued: "He'll come right home—this will bring him."

"To see Vereker, you mean?"

"To see Vereker—and to see *me*. Think what he'll have to tell me!"

I hesitated. "About India?"

"About fiddlesticks! About Vereker—about the figure in the carpet."

"But, as you say, we shall surely have that in a letter."

She thought like one inspired, and I remembered how Corvick had told me long before that her face was interesting. "Perhaps it can't be got into a letter if it's 'immense.' "

"Perhaps not if it's immense bosh. If he has hold of something that can't be got into a letter he hasn't hold of *the* thing. Vereker's own statement to me was exactly that the 'figure' *would* fit into a letter."

"Well, I cabled to George an hour ago—two words," said Gwendolen.

"Is it indiscreet of me to ask what they were?"

She hung fire, but at last brought them out. " 'Angel, write.' "

"Good!" I cried. "I'll make it sure—I'll send him the same."

---

9. Virgil's introduction of Venus in Book 1 of *The Aeneid* describes how "by her graceful walk, the Queen of Love is known."
1. Concussion, or shock.

## VII

My words however were not absolutely the same—I put something instead of "angel"; and in the sequel my epithet seemed the more apt, for when eventually we heard from our traveller it was merely, it was thoroughly to be tantalised. He was magnificent in his triumph, he described his discovery as stupendous; but his ecstasy only obscured it—there were to be no particulars till he should have submitted his conception to the supreme authority. He had thrown up his commission, he had thrown up his book, he had thrown up everything but the instant need to hurry to Rapallo,[2] on the Genoese shore, where Vereker was making a stay. I wrote him a letter which was to await him at Aden[3]—I besought him to relieve my suspense. That he had found my letter was indicated by a telegram which, reaching me after weary days and in the absence of any answer to my laconic dispatch to him at Bombay, was evidently intended as a reply to both communications. Those few words were in familiar French, the French of the day, which Corvick often made use of to show he wasn't a prig. It had for some persons the opposite effect, but his message may fairly be paraphrased. "Have patience; I want to see, as it breaks on you, the face you'll make!" "Tellement envie de voir ta tête!"[4]—that was what I had to sit down with. I can certainly not be said to have sat down, for I seem to remember myself at this time as rattling constantly between the little house in Chelsea and my own. Our impatience, Gwendolen's and mine, was equal, but I kept hoping her light would be greater. We all spent during this episode, for people of our means, a great deal of money in telegrams and cabs, and I counted on the receipt of news from Rapallo immediately after the junction of the discoverer with the discovered. The interval seemed an age, but late one day I heard a hansom precipitated to my door with the crash engendered by a hint of liberality. I lived with my heart in my mouth and accordingly bounded to the window—a movement which gave me a view of a young lady erect on the footboard of the vehicle and eagerly looking up at my house. At sight of me she flourished a paper with a movement that brought me straight down, the movement with which, in melodramas, handkerchiefs and reprieves are flourished at the foot of the scaffold.

"Just seen Vereker—not a note wrong. Pressed me to bosom—keeps me a month." So much I read on her paper while the cabby dropped a grin from his perch. In my excitement I paid him profusely and in hers she suffered it; then as he drove away we started to walk about and talk. We had talked, heaven knows, enough before, but this was a wondrous lift. We pictured the whole scene at Rapallo, where he would have written, mentioning my name, for permission to call; that is I pictured it, having more material than my companion, whom I felt hang on my lips as we stopped on purpose before shop-windows we didn't look into. About one thing we were clear: if he was staying on for fuller communication we should at least have a letter from him that would help us through the dregs of delay. We understood his staying on, and yet each of us saw, I think, that the other hated it. The letter we were clear about arrived; it was for Gwendolen, and I called on her in time to save

2. An ancient Roman city in Italy, favored in the 19th century by writers such as Guy de Maupassant and philosophers such as Friedrich Nietzsche.

3. Port area in Yemen.
4. "So much desire for the sight of your head" (or "face") (French).

her the trouble of bringing it to me. She didn't read it out, as was natural enough; but she repeated to me what it chiefly embodied. This consisted of the remarkable statement that he'd tell her after they were married exactly what she wanted to know.

"Only *then*, when I'm his wife—not before," she explained. "It's tantamount to saying—isn't it?—that I must marry him straight off!" She smiled at me while I flushed with disappointment, a vision of fresh delay that made me at first unconscious of my surprise. It seemed more than a hint that on me as well he would impose some tiresome condition. Suddenly, while she reported several more things from his letter, I remembered what he had told me before going away. He had found Mr. Vereker deliriously interesting and his own possession of the secret a real intoxication. The buried treasure was all gold and gems. Now that it was there it seemed to grow and grow before him; it would have been, through all time and taking all tongues, one of the most wonderful flowers of literary art. Nothing, in especial, once you were face to face with it, could show for more consummately *done*. When once it came out it came out, was there with a splendour that made you ashamed; and there hadn't been, save in the bottomless vulgarity of the age, with every one tasteless and tainted, every sense stopped, the smallest reason why it should have been overlooked. It was great, yet so simple, was simple, yet so great, and the final knowledge of it was an experience quite apart. He intimated that the charm of such an experience, the desire to drain it, in its freshness, to the last drop, was what kept him there close to the source. Gwendolen, frankly radiant as she tossed me these fragments, showed the elation of a prospect more assured than my own. That brought me back to the question of her marriage, prompted me to ask if what she meant by what she had just surprised me with was that she was under an engagement.

"Of course I am!" she answered. "Didn't you know it?" She seemed astonished, but I was still more so, for Corvick had told me the exact contrary. I didn't mention this, however; I only reminded her how little I had been on that score in her confidence, or even in Corvick's, and that moreover I wasn't in ignorance of her mother's interdict. At bottom I was troubled by the disparity of the two accounts; but after a little I felt Corvick's to be the one I least doubted. This simply reduced me to asking myself if the girl had on the spot improvised an engagement—vamped up an old one or dashed off a new—in order to arrive at the satisfaction she desired. She must have had resources of which I was destitute, but she made her case slightly more intelligible by returning presently: "What the state of things has been is that we felt of course bound to do nothing in mamma's lifetime."

"But now you think you'll just dispense with mamma's consent?"

"Ah it mayn't come to that!" I wondered what it might come to, and she went on: "Poor dear, she may swallow the dose. In fact, you know," she added with a laugh, "she really *must!*"—a proposition of which, on behalf of every one concerned, I fully acknowledged the force.

## VIII

Nothing more vexatious had ever happened to me than to become aware before Corvick's arrival in England that I shouldn't be there to put him through. I found myself abruptly called to Germany by the alarming illness of my younger brother, who, against my advice, had gone to Munich to study, at the feet indeed of a great master, the art of portraiture in oils. The near relative who made him an allowance had threatened to withdraw it if he should, under specious pretexts, turn for superior truth to Paris—Paris being somehow, for a Cheltenham[5] aunt, the school of evil, the abyss. I deplored this prejudice at the time, and the deep injury of it was now visible—first in the fact that it hadn't saved the poor boy, who was clever frail and foolish, from congestion of the lungs, and second in the greater break with London to which the event condemned me. I'm afraid that what was uppermost in my mind during several anxious weeks was the sense that if we had only been in Paris I might have run over to see Corvick. This was actually out of the question from every point of view: my brother, whose recovery gave us both plenty to do, was ill for three months, during which I never left him and at the end of which we had to face the absolute prohibition of a return to England. The consideration of climate imposed itself, and he was in no state to meet it alone. I took him to Meran[6] and there spent the summer with him, trying to show him by example how to get back to work and nursing a rage of another sort that I tried *not* to show him.

The whole business proved the first of a series of phenomena so strangely interlaced that, taken all together—which was how I had to take them—they form as good an illustration as I can recall of the manner in which, for the good of his soul doubtless, fate sometimes deals with a man's avidity. These incidents certainly had larger bearings than the comparatively meagre consequence we are here concerned with—though I feel that consequence also a thing to speak of with some respect. It's mainly in such a light, I confess, at any rate, that the ugly fruit of my exile is at this hour present to me. Even at first indeed the spirit in which my avidity, as I have called it, made me regard that term owed no element of ease to the fact that before coming back from Rapallo George Corvick addressed me in a way I objected to. His letter had none of the sedative action I must today profess myself sure he had wished to give it, and the march of occurrences was not so ordered as to make up for what it lacked. He had begun on the spot, for one of the quarterlies, a great last word on Vereker's writings, and this exhaustive study, the only one that would have counted, have existed, was to turn on the new light, to utter—oh so quietly!—the unimagined truth. It was in other words to trace the figure in the carpet through every convolution, to reproduce it in every tint. The result, according to my friend, would be the greatest literary portrait ever painted, and what he asked of me was just to be so good as not to trouble him with questions till he should hang up his masterpiece before me. He did me the honour to declare that, putting aside the great sitter himself, all aloft in his indifference, I was individually the connoisseur he was most working for. I was therefore to be a good boy and not try to peep under the curtain before the show was ready: I should enjoy it all the more if I sat very still.

I did my best to sit very still, but I couldn't help giving a jump on seeing in *The Times*, after I had been a week or two in Munich and before, as I knew, Corvick had reached London, the announcement of the sudden death of poor Mrs. Erme. I instantly, by letter, appealed to Gwendolen for particulars, and

---

5. An early Anglo-Saxon settlement that, from the 18th century on, became known as a popular spa and as a town with a conservative social climate.
6. City in the Trentino-South Tyrol area of Italy.

she wrote me that her mother had yielded to long-threatened failure of the heart. She didn't say, but I took the liberty of reading into her words, that from the point of view of her marriage and also of her eagerness, which was quite a match for mine, this was a solution more prompt than could have been expected and more radical than waiting for the old lady to swallow the dose. I candidly admit indeed that at the time—for I heard from her repeatedly— I read some singular things into Gwendolen's words and some still more extraordinary ones into her silences. Pen in hand, this way, I live the time over, and it brings back the oddest sense of my having been, both for months and in spite of myself, a kind of coerced spectator. All my life had taken refuge in my eyes, which the procession of events appeared to have committed itself to keep astare. There were days when I thought of writing to Hugh Vereker and simply throwing myself on his charity. But I felt more deeply that I hadn't fallen quite so low—besides which, quite properly, he would send me about my business. Mrs. Erme's death brought Corvick straight home, and within the month he was united "very quietly"—as quietly, I seemed to make out, as he meant in his article to bring out his *trouvaille*[7]—to the young lady he had loved and quitted. I use this last term, I may parenthetically say, because I subsequently grew sure that at the time he went to India, at the time of his great news from Bombay, there had been no positive pledge between them whatever. There had been none at the moment she was affirming to me the very opposite. On the other hand he had certainly become engaged the day he returned. The happy pair went down to Torquay for their honeymoon, and there, in a reckless hour, it occurred to poor Corvick to take his young bride a drive. He had no command of that business: this had been brought home to me of old in a little tour we had once made together in a dogcart. In a dog-cart he perched his companion for a rattle over Devonshire[8] hills, on one of the likeliest of which he brought his horse, who, it was true, had bolted, down with such violence that the occupants of the cart were hurled forward and that he fell horribly on his head. He was killed on the spot; Gwendolen escaped unhurt.

I pass rapidly over the question of this unmitigated tragedy, of what the loss of my best friend meant for me, and I complete my little history of my patience and my pain by the frank statement of my having, in a postscript to my very first letter to her after the receipt of the hideous news, asked Mrs. Corvick whether her husband mightn't at least have finished the great article on Vereker. Her answer was as prompt as my question: the article, which had been barely begun, was a mere heartbreaking scrap. She explained that our friend, abroad, had just settled down to it when interrupted by her mother's death, and that then, on his return, he had been kept from work by the engrossments into which that calamity was to plunge them. The opening pages were all that existed; they were striking, they were promising, but they didn't unveil the idol. That great intellectual feat was obviously to have formed his climax. She said nothing more, nothing to enlighten me as to the state of her own knowledge—the knowledge for the acquisition of which I had fancied her prodigiously acting. This was above all what I wanted to know: had *she* seen the idol unveiled? Had there been a private ceremony for

---

7. Lucky find (French).
8. This town in the southern English county of

Devon was a fashionable 19th-century seaside resort renowned for its healthy climate.

a palpitating audience of one? For what else but that ceremony had the nuptials taken place? I didn't like as yet to press her, though when I thought of
what had passed between us on the subject in Corvick's absence her reticence
surprised me. It was therefore not till much later, from Meran, that I risked
another appeal, risked it in some trepidation, for she continued to tell me
nothing. "Did you hear in those few days of your blighted bliss," I wrote,
"what we desired so to hear?" I said "we" as a little hint; and she showed me
she could take a little hint. "I heard everything," she replied, "and I mean to
keep it to myself!"

## IX

It was impossible not to be moved with the strongest sympathy for her, and
on my return to England I showed her every kindness in my power. Her
mother's death had made her means sufficient, and she had gone to live in a
more convenient quarter. But her loss had been great and her visitation cruel;
it never would have occurred to me moreover to suppose she could come to
feel the possession of a technical tip, of a piece of literary experience, a coun-
terpoise to her grief. Strange to say, none the less, I couldn't help believing
after I had seen her a few times that I caught a glimpse of some such oddity.
I hasten to add that there had been other things I couldn't help believing, or
at least imagining; and as I never felt I was really clear about these, so, as to
the point I here touch on, I give her memory the benefit of the doubt.
Stricken and solitary, highly accomplished and now, in her deep mourning,
her maturer grace and her uncomplaining sorrow, incontestably handsome,
she presented herself as leading a life of singular dignity and beauty. I had at
first found a way to persuade myself that I should soon get the better of the
reserve formulated, the week after the catastrophe, in her reply to an appeal
as to which I was not unconscious that it might strike her as mistimed. Certainly that reserve was something of a shock to me—certainly it puzzled me
the more I thought of it and even though I tried to explain it (with moments
of success) by an imputation of exalted sentiments, of superstitious scruples,
of a refinement of loyalty. Certainly it added at the same time hugely to the
price of Vereker's secret, precious as this mystery already appeared. I may as
well confess abjectly that Mrs. Corvick's unexpected attitude was the final tap
on the nail that was to fix fast my luckless idea, convert it into the obsession
of which I'm for ever conscious.

But this only helped me the more to be artful, to be adroit, to allow time
to elapse before renewing my suit. There were plenty of speculations for the
interval, and one of them was deeply absorbing. Corvick had kept his information from his young friend till after the removal of the last barrier to their
intimacy—then only had he let the cat out of the bag. Was it Gwendolen's
idea, taking a hint from him, to liberate this animal only on the basis of the
renewal of such a relation? Was the figure in the carpet traceable or describ-
able only for husbands and wives—for lovers supremely united? It came back
to me in a mystifying manner that in Kensington Square, when I mentioned
that Corvick would have told the girl he loved, some word had dropped from
Vereker that gave colour to this possibility. There might be little in it, but
there was enough to make me wonder if I should have to marry Mrs. Corvick
to get what I wanted. Was I prepared to offer her this price for the blessing

of her knowledge? Ah that way madness lay!—so I at least said to myself in bewildered hours. I could see meanwhile the torch she refused to pass on flame away in her chamber of memory—pour through her eyes a light that shone in her lonely house. At the end of six months I was fully sure of what this warm presence made up to her for. We had talked again and again of the man who had brought us together—of his talent, his character, his personal charm, his certain career, his dreadful doom, and even of his clear purpose in that great study which was to have been a supreme literary portrait, a kind of critical Vandyke or Velasquez.[9] She had conveyed to me in abundance that she was tongue-tied by her perversity, by her piety, that she would never break the silence it had not been given to the "right person," as she said, to break. The hour however finally arrived. One evening when I had been sitting with her longer than usual I laid my hand firmly on her arm. "Now at last what *is* it?"

She had been expecting me and was ready. She gave a long slow soundless headshake, merciful only in being inarticulate. This mercy didn't prevent its hurling at me the largest finest coldest "Never!" I had yet, in the course of a life that had known denials, had to take full in the face. I took it and was aware that with the hard blow the tears had come into my eyes. So for a while we sat and looked at each other; after which I slowly rose. I was wondering if some day she would accept me; but this was not what I brought out. I said as I smoothed down my hat: "I know what to think then. It's nothing!"

A remote disdainful pity for me gathered in her dim smile; then she spoke in a voice that I hear at this hour. "It's my *life*!" As I stood at the door she added: "You've insulted him!"

"Do you mean Vereker?"

"I mean the Dead!"

I recognised when I reached the street the justice of her charge. Yes, it was her life—I recognised that too; but her life none the less made room with the lapse of time for another interest. A year and a half after Corvick's death she published in a single volume her second novel, "Overmastered," which I pounced on in the hope of finding in it some tell-tale echo or some peeping face. All I found was a much better book than her younger performance, showing I thought the better company she had kept. As a tissue tolerably intricate it was a carpet with a figure of its own; but the figure was not the figure I was looking for. On sending a review of it to *The Middle* I was surprised to learn from the office that a notice was already in type. When the paper came out I had no hesitation in attributing this article, which I thought rather vulgarly overdone, to Drayton Deane, who in the old days had been something of a friend of Corvick's, yet had only within a few weeks made the acquaintance of his widow. I had had an early copy of the book, but Deane had evidently had an earlier. He lacked all the same the light hand with which Corvick had gilded the gingerbread—he laid on the tinsel in splotches.

## X

Six months later appeared "The Right of Way," the last chance, though we didn't know it, that we were to have to redeem ourselves. Written wholly dur-

---

9. Diego Rodriguez de Silva Velasquez (1599–1660), court painter to Philip IV of Spain. Anthony Van Dyke (1599–1641), Flemish painter who became court painter for James I and Charles I.

ing Vereker's sojourn abroad, the book had been heralded, in a hundred paragraphs, by the usual ineptitudes. I carried it, as early a copy as any, I this time flattered myself, straightway to Mrs. Corvick. This was the only use I had for it; I left the inevitable tribute of *The Middle* to some more ingenious mind and some less irritated temper. "But I already have it," Gwendolen said. "Drayton Deane was so good as to bring it to me yesterday, and I've just finished it."

"Yesterday? How did he get it so soon?"

"He gets everything so soon! He's to review it in *The Middle*."

"He—Drayton Deane—review Vereker?" I couldn't believe my ears.

"Why not? One fine ignorance is as good as another."

I winced but I presently said: "You ought to review him yourself!"

"I don't 'review,' " she laughed. "I'm reviewed!"

Just then the door was thrown open. "Ah yes, here's your reviewer!" Drayton Deane was there with his long legs and his tall forehead: he had come to see what she thought of "The Right of Way," and to bring news that was singularly relevant. The evening papers were just out with a telegram on the author of that work, who, in Rome, had been ill for some days with an attack of malarial fever. It had at first not been thought grave, but had taken, in consequence of complications, a turn that might give rise to anxiety. Anxiety had indeed at the latest hour begun to be felt.

I was struck in the presence of these tidings with the fundamental detachment that Mrs. Corvick's overt concern quite failed to hide: it gave me the measure of her consummate independence. That independence rested on her knowledge, the knowledge which nothing now could destroy and which nothing could make different. The figure in the carpet might take on another twist or two, but the sentence had virtually been written. The writer might go down to his grave: she was the person in the world to whom—as if she had been his favoured heir—his continued existence was least of a need. This reminded me how I had observed at a particular moment—after Corvick's death—the drop of her desire to see him face to face. She had got what she wanted without that. I had been sure that if she hadn't got it she wouldn't have been restrained from the endeavour to sound him personally by those superior reflexions, more conceivable on a man's part than on a woman's, which in my case had served as a deterrent. It wasn't however, I hasten to add, that my case, in spite of this invidious comparison, wasn't ambiguous enough. At the thought that Vereker was perhaps at that moment dying there rolled over me a wave of anguish—a poignant sense of how inconsistently I still depended on him. A delicacy that it was my one compensation to suffer to rule me had left the Alps and the Apennines between us, but the sense of the waning occasion suggested that I might in my despair at last have gone to him. Of course I should really have done nothing of the sort. I remained five minutes, while my companions talked of the new book, and when Drayton Deane appealed to me for my opinion of it I made answer, getting up, that I detested Hugh Vereker and simply couldn't read him. I departed with the moral certainty that as the door closed behind me Deane would brand me for awfully superficial. His hostess wouldn't contradict *that* at least.

I continue to trace with a briefer touch our intensely odd successions. Three weeks after this came Vereker's death, and before the year was out the death of his wife. That poor lady I had never seen, but I had had a futile theory that, should she survive him long enough to be decorously accessible, I might approach her with the feeble flicker of my plea. Did she know and if she knew would she speak? It was much to be presumed that for more reasons than one she would have nothing to say; but when she passed out of all reach I felt renouncement indeed my appointed lot. I was shut up in my obsession for ever—my gaolers had gone off with the key. I find myself quite as vague as a captive in a dungeon about the time that further elapsed before Mrs. Corvick became the wife of Drayton Deane. I had foreseen, through my bars, this end of the business, though there was no indecent haste and our friendship had rather fallen off. They were both so "awfully intellectual" that it struck people as a suitable match, but I had measured better than any one the wealth of understanding the bride would contribute to the union. Never, for a marriage in literary circles—so the newspapers described the alliance— had a lady been so bravely dowered. I began with due promptness to look for the fruit of the affair—that fruit, I mean, of which the premonitory symptoms would be peculiarly visible in the husband. Taking for granted the splendour of the other party's nuptial gift, I expected to see him make a show commensurate with his increase of means. I knew what his means had been—his article on "The Right of Way" had distinctly given one the figure. As he was now exactly in the position in which still more exactly I was not I watched from month to month, in the likely periodicals, for the heavy message poor Corvick had been unable to deliver and the responsibility of which would have fallen on his successor. The widow and wife would have broken by the rekindled hearth the silence that only a widow and wife might break, and Deane would be as aflame with the knowledge as Corvick in his own hour, as Gwendolen in hers, had been. Well, he was aflame doubtless, but the fire was apparently not to become a public blaze. I scanned the periodicals in vain: Drayton Deane filled them with exuberant pages, but he withheld the page I most feverishly sought. He wrote on a thousand subjects, but never on the subject of Vereker. His special line was to tell truths that other people either "funked," as he said, or overlooked, but he never told the only truth that seemed to me in these days to signify. I met the couple in those literary circles referred to in the papers: I have sufficiently intimated that it was only in such circles we were all constructed to revolve. Gwendolen was more than ever committed to them by the publication of her third novel, and I myself definitely classed by holding the opinion that this work was inferior to its immediate predecessor. Was it worse because she had been keeping worse company? If her secret was, as she had told me, her life—a fact discernible in her increasing bloom, an air of conscious privilege that, cleverly corrected by pretty charities, gave distinction to her appearance—it had yet not a direct influence on her work. That only made one—everything only made one— yearn the more for it; only rounded it off with a mystery finer and subtler.

## XI

It was therefore from her husband I could never remove my eyes: I beset him in a manner that might have made him uneasy. I went even so far as to engage him in conversation. *Didn't* he know, hadn't he come into it as a matter of course?—that question hummed in my brain. Of course he knew; otherwise he wouldn't return my stare so queerly. His wife had told him what I wanted and he was amiably amused at my impotence. He didn't laugh—he wasn't a laugher: his system was to present to my irritation, so that I should crudely expose myself, a conversational blank as vast as his big bare brow. It always happened that I turned away with a settled conviction from these unpeopled expanses, which seemed to complete each other geographically and to symbolise together Drayton Deane's want of voice, want of form. He simply hadn't the art to use what he knew; he literally was incompetent to take up the duty where Corvick had left it. I went still further—it was the only glimpse of happiness I had. I made up my mind that the duty didn't appeal to him. He wasn't interested, he didn't care. Yes, it quite comforted me to believe him too stupid to have joy of the thing I lacked. He was as stupid after as he had been before, and that deepened for me the golden glory in which the mystery was wrapped. I had of course none the less to recollect that his wife might have imposed her conditions and exactions. I had above all to remind myself that with Vereker's death the major incentive dropped. He was still there to be honoured by what might be done—he was no longer there to give it his sanction. Who alas but he had the authority?

Two children were born to the pair, but the second cost the mother her life. After this stroke I seemed to see another ghost of a chance. I jumped at it in thought, but I waited a certain time for manners, and at last my opportunity arrived in a remunerative way. His wife had been dead a year when I met Drayton Deane in the smoking-room of a small club of which we both were members, but where for months—perhaps because I rarely entered it—I hadn't seen him. The room was empty and the occasion propitious. I deliberately offered him, to have done with the matter for ever, that advantage for which I felt he had long been looking.

"As an older acquaintance of your late wife's than even you were," I began, "you must let me say to you something I have on my mind. I shall be glad to make any terms with you that you see fit to name for the information she must have had from George Corvick—the information, you know, that had come to *him*, poor chap, in one of the happiest hours of his life, straight from Hugh Vereker."

He looked at me like a dim phrenological bust.[1] "The information—?"

"Vereker's secret, my dear man—the general intention of his books: the string the pearls were strung on, the buried treasure, the figure in the carpet."

He began to flush—the numbers on his bumps to come out. "Vereker's books had a general intention?"

I stared in my turn. "You don't mean to say you don't know it?" I thought for a moment he was playing with me. "Mrs. Deane knew it; she had it, as I say, straight from Corvick, who had, after infinite search and to Vereker's own delight, found the very mouth of the cave. Where *is* the mouth? He told after their marriage—and told alone—the person who, when the circumstances were reproduced, must have told *you*. Have I been wrong in taking for granted that she admitted you, as one of the highest privileges of the relation in which you stood to her, to the knowledge of which she was after Corvick's death the

---

1. A model of a human head used in phrenological "readings" of skulls; phrenology was a 19th-century pseudo-science that held that the shapes of skulls contained clues to personality.

sole depositary? All *I* know is that that knowledge is infinitely precious, and what I want you to understand is that if you'll in your turn admit me to it you'll do me a kindness for which I shall be lastingly grateful."

He had turned at last very red; I dare say he had begun by thinking I had lost my wits. Little by little he followed me; on my own side I stared with a livelier surprise. Then he spoke. "I don't know what you're talking about."

He wasn't acting—it was the absurd truth. "She *didn't* tell you—?"

"Nothing about Hugh Vereker."

I was stupefied; the room went round. It had been too good even for that! "Upon your honour?"

"Upon my honour. What the devil's the matter with you?" he growled.

"I'm astounded—I'm disappointed. I wanted to get it out of you."

"It isn't *in* me!" he awkwardly laughed. "And even if it were—"

"If it were you'd let me have it—oh yes, in common humanity. But I believe you. I see—I see!" I went on, conscious, with the full turn of the wheel, of my great delusion, my false view of the poor man's attitude. What I saw, though I couldn't say it, was that his wife hadn't thought him worth enlightening. This struck me as strange for a woman who had thought him worth marrying. At last I explained it by the reflexion that she couldn't possibly have married him for his understanding. She had married him for something else.

He was to some extent enlightened now, but he was even more astonished, more disconcerted: he took a moment to compare my story with his quickened memories. The result of his meditation was his presently saying with a good deal of rather feeble form: "This is the first I hear of what you allude to. I think you must be mistaken as to Mrs. Drayton Deane's having had any unmentioned, and still less any unmentionable, knowledge of Hugh Vereker. She'd certainly have wished it—should it have borne on his literary character—to be used."

"It *was* used. She used it herself. She told me with her own lips that she 'lived' on it."

I had no sooner spoken than I repented of my words; he grew so pale that I felt as if I had struck him. "Ah 'lived'—!" he murmured, turning short away from me.

My compunction was real; I laid my hand on his shoulder. "I beg you to forgive me—I've made a mistake. You *don't* know what I thought you knew. You could, if I had been right, have rendered me a service; and I had my reasons for assuming that you'd be in a position to meet me."

"Your reasons?" he echoed. "What were your reasons?"

I looked at him well; I hesitated; I considered. "Come and sit down with me here and I'll tell you." I drew him to a sofa, I lighted another cigar and, beginning with the anecdote of Vereker's one descent from the clouds, I recited to him the extraordinary chain of accidents that had, in spite of the original gleam, kept me till that hour in the dark. I told him in a word just what I've written out here. He listened with deepening attention, and I became aware, to my surprise, by his ejaculations, by his questions, that he would have been after all not unworthy to be trusted by his wife. So abrupt an experience of her want of trust had now a disturbing effect on him; but I saw the immediate shock throb away little by little and then gather again into waves of wonder and curiosity—waves that promised, I could perfectly judge, to break in the end with the fury of my own highest tides. I may say that to-day as victims of unappeased desire there isn't a pin to choose between us. The poor man's state is almost my consolation; there are really moments when I feel it to be quite my revenge.

1896                                                                                      1907–09

# SARAH WINNEMUCCA
## ca. 1844–1891

Sarah Winnemucca, or Thocmetony ("shell flower"), was a northern Paiute woman born about 1844 in western Nevada. Her mother, Tuboitony ("lettuce flower"), was the daughter of Captain Truckee, a prominent man among his people whose friendly attitude toward white settlers was based on a belief in traditional stories the Paiutes shared with other desert peoples regarding a "lost white brother" who would one day return. Sarah's father, known as Old Winnemucca, was a Paiute chief. When Captain Truckee traveled to California in the 1850s to find work on Spanish-owned ranches, he insisted that Sarah and her mother come with him. It was in California that Sarah learned some Spanish and became fluent enough in English to serve later as an interpreter for the American military. Throughout her adult life, Sarah Winnemucca worked on behalf of her people, negotiating with the Americans by means of her lectures, her writing, and her direct encounters with government officials. She was a controversial figure in her time, and, as scholar LaVonne Ruoff notes, "a courageous and eloquent spokeswoman for her people."

Sarah Winnemucca first gained public notice in 1864 when she appeared with her father and other family members on the streets of Virginia City, Nevada, in theatrical performances designed to alert white citizens to the dire situation of Paiutes who had been displaced by the Virginia City gold rush of 1859. These performances soon led her to become known, admiringly or scornfully, as "Princess Sarah." Sarah's first publication was a letter describing Paiute suffering that appeared in *Harper's Weekly* in 1870. She attracted a national audience in 1878, at the end of the Bannock War. The Bannock Indians of the California Sierras, whose territory was adjacent to that of the Paiutes, had taken up arms against the encroaching whites. Many Paiutes joined with the Bannocks. But at the conclusion of hostilities, many Paiutes who had not fought were nonetheless imprisoned with the Bannocks and their Paiute allies on the Yakima Reservation in Washington. Winnemucca lectured on the Paiute cause in San Francisco, and even made the long trip to Washington D.C. to plead the case with President Rutherford B. Hayes and Secretary of the Interior Carl Schurz. Despite her efforts, years passed and conditions for the Paiutes only worsened. Finally, in 1883, Winnemucca embarked on a lecture tour to the East on behalf of her people, speaking in New York, Baltimore, and Boston, where her audience included the poet John Greenleaf Whittier and the senator from Massachusetts, Henry Dawes. (Although it has many times been said that Ralph Waldo Emerson was among her audience, this is wrong—Emerson had died the year before.)

In Boston, Winnemucca met Mary Mann, widow of the prominent educator Horace Mann, and her sister, Elizabeth Palmer Peabody, an active reformer (years before she had taken a stand against Cherokee removal). It was while staying in Boston with the sisters that she wrote most of her autobiography, which Mary Mann edited. *Life Among the Piutes: Their Wrongs and Claims* was privately printed in 1883. In it, Winnemucca recounts the events of her life in the context of Paiute culture and history.

The book has been called an "autoethnography" (Ruoff), a "coup tale" in which she relates her brave deeds (Brumble), and a document of feminist resistance (Georgi-Findlay). She published the book under the name of Sarah Winnemucca Hopkins. Lewis Hopkins, Sarah's husband (they had married in 1881, in San Francisco, although California had a law prohibiting Indian-white unions), had accompanied her on her lecture tour and was with her in Boston. Hopkins, who had been discharged by the Army as a person of "no character," was addicted to gambling and apparently drank heavily. These unsavory qualities, and the fact that Winnemucca had had more than one white husband before him, made it possible for her opponents to attack her morals. Thus her book concludes with an "Appendix" containing testimonials to her character (the first, from Major General O. O. Howard, for whom she had worked during the Bannock War, affirms that Winnemucca's "conduct was always good"), as well as testimonials to the justice and accuracy of her accounts of and pleas for the Paiute people.

The book's authenticity has also been questioned, for it has been suggested that it was mostly written by Mary Mann, though in many places it uses material from Sarah Winnemucca's own lectures. This sort of charge has often been raised in connection with African American and Native American autobiographies, whether by Frederick Douglass and Harriet Jacobs, or by Black Hawk and Sarah Winnemucca. In her preface to *Life Among the Piutes*, Mary Mann states that her editing consisted of no more than "copying the original manuscript in correct orthography and punctuation, with occasional emendations by the author"; she called the book "an heroic act on the part of the writer." Mary Mann's judgment that *Life Among the Piutes* was "the first outbreak of the American Indian in human literature . . . *to tell the truth*" holds up quite well today.

Near the end of her life, Winnemucca, with her brother Natchez, opened a school for Indian children in Nevada called the Peabody Indian School, supported, as the name would indicate, by Elizabeth Palmer Peabody, with whom Winnemucca had developed a deep friendship. But not even Peabody could persuade eastern senators to vote an appropriation for Indian education, and the school closed in 1888. Winnemucca then went to live with her sister, Elma, at Henry's Lake, Idaho, where she died in 1891.

Our selections from *Life Among the Piutes* are from chapter I, "First Meeting of Piutes and Whites," chapter II, "Domestic and Social Moralities," and the lengthy chapter VIII, "The Yakima Affair," which ends the book. It is in this last chapter that Winnemucca's role as an activist on behalf of her Paiute people may be seen especially clearly.

## *From* Life Among the Piutes

### From *Chapter I. First Meeting of Piutes and Whites*

I was born somewhere near 1844, but am not sure of the precise time. I was a very small child when the first white people came into our country. They came like a lion, yes, like a roaring lion, and have continued so ever since, and I have never forgotten their first coming. My people were scattered at that time over nearly all the territory now known as Nevada. My grandfather was chief of the entire Piute nation, and was camped near Humboldt Lake, with a small portion of his tribe, when a party travelling eastward from California was seen coming. When the news was brought to my grandfather, he asked what they looked like? When told that they had hair on their faces, and were white, he jumped up and clasped his hands together, and cried aloud,—

"My white brothers,—my long-looked for white brothers have come at last!"

He immediately gathered some of his leading men, and went to the place where the party had gone into camp. Arriving near them, he was commanded to halt in a manner that was readily understood without an interpreter. Grandpa at once made signs of friendship by throwing down his robe and throwing up his arms to show them he had no weapons; but in vain,—they kept him at a distance. He knew not what to do. He had expected so much pleasure in welcoming his white brothers to the best in the land, that after looking at them sorrowfully for a little while, he came away quite unhappy. But he would not give them up so easily. He took some of his most trustworthy men and followed them day after day, camping near them at night, and travelling in sight of them by day, hoping in this way to gain their confidence. But he was disappointed, poor dear old soul!

I can imagine his feelings, for I have drank deeply from the same cup. When I think of my past life, and the bitter trials I have endured, I can scarcely believe I live, and yet I do; and, with the help of Him who notes the sparrow's fall, I mean to fight for my down-trodden race while life lasts.

Seeing they would not trust him, my grandfather left them, saying, "Perhaps they will come again next year." Then he summoned his whole people, and told them this tradition:—

"In the beginning of the world there were only four, two girls and two boys. Our forefather and mother were only two, and we are their children. You all know that a great while ago there was a happy family in this world. One girl and one boy were dark and the others were white. For a time they got along together without quarrelling, but soon they disagreed, and there was trouble. They were cross to one another and fought, and our parents were very much grieved. They prayed that their children might learn better, but it did not do any good; and afterwards the whole household was made so unhappy that the father and mother saw that they must separate their children; and then our father took the dark boy and girl, and the white boy and girl, and asked them, 'Why are you so cruel to each other?' They hung down their heads, and would not speak. They were ashamed. He said to them, 'Have I not been kind to you all, and given you everything your hearts wished for? You do not have to hunt and kill your own game to live upon. You see, my dear children, I have power to call whatsoever kind of game we want to eat; and I also have the power to separate my dear children, if they are not good to each other.' So he separated his children by a word. He said, 'Depart from each other, you cruel children;— go across the mighty ocean and do not seek each other's lives.'

"So the light girl and boy disappeared by that one word, and their parents saw them no more, and they were grieved, although they knew their children were happy. And by-and-by the dark children grew into a large nation; and we believe it is the one we belong to, and that the nation that sprung from the white children will some time send some one to meet us and heal all the old trouble. Now, the white people we saw a few days ago must certainly be our white brothers, and I want to welcome them. I want to love them as I love all of you. But they would not let me; they were afraid. But they will come again, and I want you one and all to promise that, should I not live to welcome them myself, you will not hurt a hair on their heads, but welcome them as I tried to do."

How good of him to try and heal the wound, and how vain were his efforts! My people had never seen a white man, and yet they existed, and were a strong race. The people promised as he wished, and they all went back to their work.

\* \* \*

That same fall, after my grandfather came home, he told my father to take charge of his people and hold the tribe, as he was going back to California with as many of his people as he could get to go with him. So my father took his place as Chief of the Piutes, and had it as long as he lived. Then my grandfather started back to California again with about thirty families. That same fall, very late, the emigrants kept coming. It was this time that our white brothers first came amongst us. They could not get over the mountains, so they had to live with us. It was on Carson River, where the great Carson City stands now. You call my people bloodseeking. My people did not seek to kill them, nor did they steal their horses,—no, no, far from it. During the winter my people helped them. They gave them such as they had to eat. They did not hold out their hands and say:—

"You can't have anything to eat unless you pay me." No,—no such word was used by us savages at that time; and the persons I am speaking of are living yet; they could speak for us if they choose to do so.

The following spring, before my grandfather returned home, there was a great excitement among my people on account of fearful news coming from different tribes, that the people whom they called their white brothers were killing everybody that came in their way, and all the Indian tribes had gone into the mountains to save their lives. So my father told all his people to go into the mountains and hunt and lay up food for the coming winter. Then we all went into the mountains. There was a fearful story they told us children. Our mothers told us that the whites were killing everybody and eating them.[1] So we were all afraid of them. Every dust that we could see blowing in the valleys we would say it was the white people. In the late fall my father told his people to go to the rivers and fish, and we all went to Humboldt River, and the women went to work gathering wild seed, which they grind between the rocks. The stones are round, big enough to hold in the hands. The women did this when they got back, and when they had gathered all they could they put it in one place and covered it with grass, and then over the grass mud. After it is covered it looks like an Indian wigwam.

Oh, what a fright we all got one morning to hear some white people were coming. Every one ran as best they could. My poor mother was left with my little sister and me. Oh, I never can forget it. My poor mother was carrying my little sister on her back, and trying to make me run; but I was so frightened I could not move my feet, and while my poor mother was trying to get me along my aunt overtook us, and she said to my mother: "Let us bury our

---

1. The reference is to a group of emigrants to California known as the Donner Party. Cut off by a storm in the Sierra Nevada Mountains in mid-December of 1846, with their rations almost gone, the group sent a party on snowshoes to seek help. Several of the party died, and the survivors resorted to cannibalism; cannibalism also occurred among those who had stayed behind. Captain Truckee knew of these events. Winnemucca refers to them later in the chapter as well.

girls, or we shall all be killed and eaten up." So they went to work and buried us, and told us if we heard any noise not to cry out, for if we did they would surely kill us and eat us. So our mothers buried me and my cousin, planted sage bushes over our faces to keep the sun from burning them, and there we were left all day.

Oh, can any one imagine my feelings *buried alive*, thinking every minute that I was to be unburied and eaten up by the people that my grandfather loved so much? With my heart throbbing, and not daring to breathe, we lay there all day. It seemed that the night would never come. Thanks be to God! the night came at last. Oh, how I cried and said: "Oh, father, have you forgotten me? Are you never coming for me?" I cried so I thought my very heart-strings would break.

At last we heard some whispering. We did not dare to whisper to each other, so we lay still. I could hear their footsteps coming nearer and nearer. I thought my heart was coming right out of my mouth. Then I heard my mother say, " 'T is right here!" Oh, can any one in this world ever imagine what were my feelings when I was dug up by my poor mother and father? My cousin and I were once more happy in our mothers' and fathers' care, and we were taken to where all the rest were.

I was once buried alive; but my second burial shall be for ever, where no father or mother will come and dig me up. It shall not be with throbbing heart that I shall listen for coming footsteps. I shall be in the sweet rest of peace,— I, the chieftain's weary daughter.

Well, while we were in the mountains hiding, the people that my grandfather called our white brothers came along to where our winter supplies were. They set everything we had left on fire. It was a fearful sight. It was all we had for the winter, and it was all burnt during that night. My father took some of his men during the night to try and save some of it, but they could not; it had burnt down before they got there.

These were the last white men that came along that fall. My people talked fearfully that winter about those they called our white brothers. My people said they had something like awful thunder and lightning, and with that they killed everything that came in their way.

This whole band of white people perished in the mountains, for it was too late to cross them. We could have saved them, only my people were afraid of them. We never knew who they were, or where they came from. So, poor things, they must have suffered fearfully, for they all starved there. The snow was too deep.

Early in the following spring, my father told all his people to go to the mountains, for there would be a great emigration that summer. He told them he had had a wonderful dream, and wanted to tell them all about it.

He said, "Within ten days come together at the sink of Carson, and I will tell you my dream."

The sub-chiefs went everywhere to tell their people what my father had told them to say; and when the time came we all went to the sink of Carson.

Just about noon, while we were on the way, a great many of our men came to meet us, all on their horses. Oh, what a beautiful song they sang for my father as they came near us! We passed them, and they followed us, and as we came near to the encampment, every man, woman, and child were out looking for us. They had a place all ready for us. Oh, how happy everybody was! One could hear laughter everywhere, and songs were sung by happy women and children.

My father stood up and told his people to be merry and happy for five days. It is a rule among our people always to have five days to settle anything.[2] My father told them to dance at night, and that the men should hunt rabbits and fish, and some were to have games of football, or any kind of sport or play-things they wished, and the women could do the same, as they had nothing else to do. My people were so happy during the five days,—the women ran races, and the men ran races on foot and on horses.

My father got up very early one morning, and told his people the time had come,—that we could no longer be happy as of old, as the white people we called our brothers had brought a great trouble and sorrow among us already. He went on and said,—

"These white people must be a great nation, as they have houses that move.[3] It is wonderful to see them move along. I fear we will suffer greatly by their coming to our country; they come for no good to us, although my father said they were our brothers, but they do not seem to think we are like them. What do you all think about it? Maybe I am wrong. My dear children, there is something telling me that I am not wrong, because I am sure they have minds like us, and think as we do; and I know that they were doing wrong when they set fire to our winter supplies. They surely knew it was our food."

And this was the first wrong done to us by our white brothers.

Now comes the end of our merrymaking.

Then my father told his people his fearful dream, as he called it. He said,—

"I dreamt this same thing three nights,—the very same. I saw the greatest emigration that has yet been through our country. I looked North and South and East and West, and saw nothing but dust, and I heard a great weeping. I saw women crying, and I also saw my men shot down by the white people. They were killing my people with something that made a great noise like thunder and lightning, and I saw the blood streaming from the mouths of my men that lay all around me. I saw it as if it was real. Oh, my dear children! You may all think it is only a dream,—nevertheless, I feel that it will come to pass. And to avoid bloodshed, we must all go to the mountains during the summer, or till my father comes back from California. He will then tell us what to do. Let us keep away from the emigrant roads and stay in the moun-tains all summer. There are to be a great many pine-nuts this summer, and we can lay up great supplies for the coming winter, and if the emigrants don't come too early, we can take a run down and fish for a month, and lay up dried fish. I know we can dry a great many in a month, and young men can go into the valleys on hunting excursions, and kill as many rabbits as they can. In that way we can live in the mountains all summer and all winter too."

So ended my father's dream. During that day one could see old women getting together talking over what they had heard my father say. They said,—

"It is true what our great chief has said, for it was shown to him by a higher power. It is not a dream. Oh, it surely will come to pass. We shall no longer

2. Five is the pattern number for Winnemucca's people, although a few paragraphs below an impor-tant dream of her father's takes place not on five but on three nights.

3. The reference might be to covered wagons but is more likely to railway cars.

be a happy people, as we now are; we shall no longer go here and there as of old; we shall no longer build our big fires as a signal to our friends, for we shall always be afraid of being seen by those bad people."

"Surely they don't eat people?"

"Yes, they do eat people, because they ate each other up in the mountains last winter."

This was the talk among the old women during the day.

"Oh, how grieved we are! Oh, where will it end?"

\* \* \*

## From *Chapter II. Domestic and Social Moralities*

Our children are very carefully taught to be good. Their parents tell them stories, traditions of old times, even of the first mother of the human race; and love stories, stories of giants, and fables; and when they ask if these last stories are true, they answer, "Oh, it is only coyote," which means that they are make-believe stories. Coyote is the name of a mean, crafty little animal, half wolf, half dog, and stands for everything low. It is the greatest term of reproach one Indian has for another. Indians do not swear,—they have no words for swearing till they learn them of white men. The worst they call each is bad or coyote; but they are very sincere with one another, and if they think each other in the wrong they say so.

We are taught to love everybody. We don't need to be taught to love our fathers and mothers. We love them without being told to. Our tenth cousin is as near to us as our first cousin; and we don't marry into our relations. Our young women are not allowed to talk to any young man that is not their cousin, except at the festive dances, when both are dressed in their best clothes, adorned with beads, feathers or shells, and stand alternately in the ring and take hold of hands. These are very pleasant occasions to all the young people.

Many years ago, when my people were happier than they are now, they used to celebrate the Festival of Flowers in the spring. I have been to three of them only in the course of my life.

Oh, with what eagerness we girls used to watch every spring for the time when we could meet with our hearts' delight, the young men, whom in civilized life you call beaux. We would all go in company to see if the flowers we were named for were yet in bloom, for almost all the girls are named for flowers. We talked about them in our wigwams, as if we were the flowers, saying, "Oh, I saw myself today in full bloom!" We would talk all the evening in this way in our families with such delight, and such beautiful thoughts of the happy day when we should meet with those who admired us and would help us to sing our flower-songs which we made up as we sang. But we were always sorry for those that were not named after some flower, because we knew they could not join in the flower-songs like ourselves, who were named for flowers of all kinds.

At last one evening came a beautiful voice, which made every girl's heart throb with happiness. It was the chief, and every one hushed to hear what he said to-day.

"My dear daughters, we are told that you have seen yourselves in the hills and in the valleys, in full bloom. Five days from to-day your festival day will come. I know every young man's heart stops beating while I am talking. I know how it was with me many years ago. I used to wish the Flower Festival would come every day. Dear young men and young women, you are saying, 'Why put it off five days?' But you all know that is our rule. It gives you time to think, and to show your sweetheart your flower."

All the girls who have flower-names dance along together, and those who have not go together also. Our fathers and mothers and grandfathers and grandmothers make a place for us where we can dance. Each one gathers the flower she is named for, and then all weave them into wreaths and crowns and scarfs, and dress up in them.

Some girls are named for rocks and are called rock-girls, and they find some pretty rocks which they carry; each one such a rock as she is named for, or whatever she is named for. If she cannot, she can take a branch of sage-brush, or a bunch of rye-grass, which have no flower.

They all go marching along, each girl in turn singing of herself; but she is not a girl any more,—she is a flower singing. She sings of herself, and her sweetheart, dancing along by her side, helps her sing the song she makes.

I will repeat what we say of ourselves. "I, Sarah Winnemucca, am a shell-flower, such as I wear on my dress. My name is Thocmetony. I am so beautiful! Who will come and dance with me while I am so beautiful? Oh, come and be happy with me! I shall be beautiful while the earth lasts. Somebody will always admire me; and who will come and be happy with me in the Spirit-land? I shall be beautiful forever there. Yes, I shall be more beautiful than my shell-flower, my Thocmetony! Then, come, oh come, and dance and be happy with me!" The young men sing with us as they dance beside us.

Our parents are waiting for us somewhere to welcome us home. And then we praise the sage-brush and the rye-grass that have no flower, and the pretty rocks that some are named for; and then we present our beautiful flowers to these companions who could carry none. And so all are happy; and that closes the beautiful day.

My people have been so unhappy for a long time they wish now to *disincrease*, instead of multiply. The mothers are afraid to have more children, for fear they shall have daughters, who are not safe even in their mother's presence.

*     *     *

Our boys are introduced to manhood by their hunting of deer and mountain-sheep. Before they are fifteen or sixteen, they hunt only small game, like rabbits, hares, fowls, etc. They never eat what they kill themselves, but only what their father or elder brothers kill. When a boy becomes strong enough to use larger bows made of sinew, and arrows that are ornamented with eagle-feathers, for the first time, he kills game that is large, a deer or an antelope, or a mountain-sheep. Then he brings home the hide, and his father cuts it into a long coil which is wound into a loop, and the boy takes his quiver and throws it on his back as if he was going on a hunt, and takes his bow and arrows in his hand. Then his father throws the loop over him, and he jumps through it. This he does five times. Now for the first time he eats the flesh of

the animal he has killed, and from that time he eats whatever he kills but he
has always been faithful to his parents' command not to eat what he has killed
before. He can now do whatever he likes, for now he is a man, and no longer
considered a boy. If there is a war he can go to it; but the Piutes, and other
tribes west of the Rocky Mountains, are not fond of going to war. I never saw
a war-dance but once. It is always the whites that begin the wars, for their
own selfish purposes. The government does not take care to send the good
men; there are a plenty who would take pains to see and understand the
chiefs and learn their characters, and their good will to the whites. But the
whites have not waited to find out how good the Indians were, and what ideas
they had of God, just like those of Jesus, who called him Father, just as my
people do, and told men to do to others as they would be done by, just as my
people teach their children to do. My people teach their children never to
make fun of any one, no matter how they look. If you see your brother or sister doing something wrong, look away, or go away from them. If you make fun
of bad persons, you make yourself beneath them. Be kind to all, both poor and
rich, and feed all that come to your wigwam, and your name can be spoken
of by every one far and near. In this way you will make many friends for yourself. Be kind both to bad and good, for you don't know your own heart. This
is the way my people teach their children. It was handed down from father
to son for many generations. I never in my life saw our children rude as I have
seen white children and grown people in the streets.

The chief's tent is the largest tent, and it is the council-tent, where every
one goes who wants advice. In the evenings the head men go there to discuss
everything, for the chiefs do not rule like tyrants; they discuss everything with
their people, as a father would in his family. Often they sit up all night. They
discuss the doings of all, if they need to be advised. If a boy is not doing well
they talk that over, and if the women are interested they can share in the talks.
If there is not room enough inside, they all go out of doors, and make a great
circle. The men are in the inner circle, for there would be too much smoke
for the women inside. The men never talk without smoking first. The women
sit behind them in another circle, and if the children wish to hear, they can
be there too. The women know as much as the men do, and their advice is
often asked. We have a republic as well as you. The council-tent is our Congress, and anybody can speak who has anything to say, women and all. They
are always interested in what their husbands are doing and thinking about.
And they take some part even in the wars. They are always near at hand when
fighting is going on, ready to snatch their husbands up and carry them off if
wounded or killed. One splendid woman that my brother Lee married after
his first wife died, went out into the battle-field after her uncle was killed, and
went into the front ranks and cheered the men on. Her uncle's horse was
dressed in a splendid robe made of eagles' feathers and she snatched it off and
swung it in the face of the enemy, who always carry off everything they find,
as much as to say, "You can't have that—I have it safe"; and she staid and took
her uncle's place, as brave as any of the men. It means something when the
women promise their fathers to make their husbands *themselves*. They faithfully keep with them in all the dangers they can share. They not only take care
of their children together, but they do everything together; and when they
grow blind, which I am sorry to say is very common, for the smoke they live

in destroys their eyes at last, they take sweet care of one another. Marriage is a sweet thing when people love each other. If women could go into your Congress I think justice would soon be done to the Indians.

* * *

From Chapter VIII. The Yakima Affair

* * *

We then went down, and Major Cochran met us at the door and said, "Sarah, are you sick? You look so badly."

I said, "No."

He then replied, "Sarah, I am heartily sorry for you, but we cannot help it. We are ordered to take your people to Yakima Reservation."[4]

It was just a little before Christmas. My people were only given one week to get ready in.

I said, "What! In this cold winter and in all this snow, and my people have so many little children? Why, they will all die. Oh, what can the President be thinking about? Oh, tell me, what is he? Is he man or beast? Yes, he must be a beast; if he has no feeling for my people, surely he ought to have some for the soldiers."

"I have never seen a president in my life and I want to know whether he is made of wood or rock, for I cannot for once think that he can be a human being. No human being would do such a thing as that,—send people across a fearful mountain in midwinter."

I was told not to say anything till three days before starting. Every night I imagined I could see the thing called President. He had long ears, he had big eyes and long legs, and a head like a bull-frog or something like that. I could not think of anything that could be so inhuman as to do such a thing,—send people across mountains with snow so deep.

Mattie and I got all the furs we could; we had fur caps, fur gloves, and fur overshoes.

At last the time arrived. The commanding-officer told me to tell Leggins to come to him.[5] I did so. He came, and Major Cochrane told me to tell him that he wanted him to tell which of the Bannock men were the worst, or which was the leader in the war. Leggins told him, and counted out twelve men to him. After this talk, Major Cochrane asked me to go and tell these men to come up to the office. They were Oytes, Bannock Joe, Captain Bearskin, Paddy Cap, Boss, Big John, Eagle Eye, Charley, D. E. Johnson, Beads, and Oytes' son-in-law, called Surger. An officer was sent with me. I called out the men by their names. They all came out to me. I said to Oytes,—

"Your soldier-father wants you all to go up to see him."

<hr />

4. This is Captain (not Major) M. A. Cochran (Winnemucca spells it "Cochrane" just below), who is the post commander at Fort Harney, Oregon. Sarah is with her close friend, Mattie, whom she will refer to as her "sister" a few paragraphs below. A number of Paiute people had been taken to Fort Harney after the conclusion of the Bannock War in 1878. They were expecting to be returned

to the Malheur Reservation in Oregon, where many had been for some time. Here, Winnemucca learns that her people are to be sent far away, to the Yakima Reservation in Washington State.
5. Leggins was the leader of Winnemucca's father's band. These Paiutes did not join the Bannocks. They were nonetheless sent to Washington.

We went up, and Oytes asked me many things.

We had to go right by the guard-house. Just as we got near it, the soldier on guard came out and headed us off and took the men and put them into the guard-house. After they were put in there the soldiers told me to tell them they must not try to get away, or they would be shot.

"We put you in here for safe-keeping," they said. "The citizens are coming over here from Canyon City to arrest you all, and we don't want them to take you; that is why we put you in here."

Ten soldiers were sent down to guard the whole encampment,—not Leggins' band, only Oytes' and the Bannocks. I was then ordered to tell them to get ready to go to Yakima Reservation.

Oh, how sad they were! Women cried and blamed their husbands for going with the Bannocks; but Leggins and his band were told they were not going with the prisoners of war, and that he was not going at all.

Then Leggins moved down the creek about two miles. At night some would get out and go off. Brother Lee[6] and Leggins were sent out to bring them back again. One afternoon Mattie and I were sent out to get five women who got away during the night, and an officer was sent with us. We were riding very fast, and my sister Mattie's horse jumped on one side and threw her off and hurt her. The blood ran out of her mouth, and I thought she would die right off; but, poor dear, she went on, for an ambulance was at our command. She had great suffering during our journey.

Oh, for shame! You who are educated by a Christian government in the art of war; the practice of whose profession makes you natural enemies of the savages, so called by you. Yes, you, who call yourselves the great civilization; you who have knelt upon Plymouth Rock, covenanting with God to make this land the home of the free and the brave. Ah, then you rise from your bended knees and seizing the welcoming hands of those who are the owners of this land, which you are not, your carbines rise upon the bleak shore, and your so-called civilization sweeps inland from the ocean wave; but, oh, my God! leaving its pathway marked by crimson lines of blood, and strewed by the bones of two races, the inheritor and the invader; and I am crying out to you for justice,—yes, pleading for the far-off plains of the West, for the dusky mourner, whose tears of love are pleading for her husband, or for their children, who are sent far away from them. Your Christian minister will hold my people against their will; not because he loves them,—no, far from it,—but because it puts money in his pockets.

Now we are ready to start for Yakima. Fifty wagons were brought, and citizens were to take us there. Some of the wagons cost the government from ten dollars to fifteen dollars per day. We got to Canyon City, and while we camped there Captain Winters got a telegram from Washington, telling him he must take Leggins' band too. So we had to wait for them to overtake us. While we were waiting, our dear good father and mother, Mr. Charles W. Parrish,[7] came with his wife and children to see us. My people threw their arms round him and his wife, crying, "Oh, our father and mother, if you had staid with us we would not suffer this."

---

6. Winnemucca's half-brother.
7. Charles Parrish had been the government Indian agent at the Malheur Reservation. As is apparent, Winnemucca thought extremely well of Parrish and his wife.

Poor Mrs. Parrish could not stop her tears at seeing the people who once loved her, the children whom she had taught,—yes, the savage children who once called her their white-lily mother, the children who used to bring her wild flowers, with happy faces, now ragged, no clothes whatever. They all cried out to him and his wife, saying, "Oh, good father and mother, talk for us! Don't let them take us away; take us back to our home!" He told them he could do nothing for them. They asked him where his brother, Sam Parrish, was. He told them he was a long way off; and then they bade us good-by, and that was the last they saw of him.

✻   ✻   ✻

1883

---

# JOEL CHANDLER HARRIS
## 1848–1908

Joel Chandler Harris was born in Eatonville, Georgia, on December 9, 1848. His mother, Mary Harris, came from a middle-class family in a neighboring county; his father was a day laborer who abandoned mother and child shortly after Joe, as he came to be called, was born. One of Eatonville's leading citizens, Andrew Reid, provided a small cottage for Mary Harris and her infant son, and soon Mary's mother and grandmother joined them. Mary went into business as a seamstress and seems to have been wholeheartedly accepted by the community. The author later claimed that he first became interested in writing when his mother read Oliver Goldsmith's *The Vicar of Wakefield* to him as a child.

As a schoolboy Harris was something of a mischief-maker; and as is often the case with class clowns, his pranks were in some measure an attempt to compensate for what his biographers agree was the most distinctive feature of his personality—his nearly pathological modesty and self-consciousness. Though later in life he stood to make a small fortune as a public reader of his immensely popular writings, he declined virtually every invitation to do so. Like Nathaniel Hawthorne, he was apparently secure and comfortable only when he was with his family, and his life as a journalist was unusual in its reclusiveness. As leading Harris scholar R. Bruce Bickley Jr. has observed, Harris hid behind his pen.

In 1862, at age fourteen, Harris went to work on Joseph Addison Turner's newly established newspaper, the *Countryman*. Turner owned Turnwold, a thousand-acre plantation nine miles from Eatonville, and was intensely loyal to plantation life and to the Confederacy, which had formed not long before Harris came to work for him as a printer's apprentice. But Turner's deepest ambitions were literary rather than political; he wanted to become a force in establishing Georgia and the South as an important center for letters. Turner encouraged Harris to make use of his large library, which included classic English writers as well as such southern authors as Edgar Allan Poe and Henry Timrod. He also served as a kind of tutor as Harris began to graduate from setting type to making contributions to the *Countryman*, at first in the form of short punning pieces and, later, reviews.

As much influence as Turner doubtless had on Harris's formation as a writer, the considerable time Harris spent with the slaves on the plantation is what left the most lasting imprint on him. It was at the feet of "Uncle" George Terrell and other older slaves that Harris listened to folk tales and developed a finely tuned ear for the rhythms and inflections of black speech he was to use so skillfully a decade later when he published his first Uncle Remus story.

Before he began to exploit this material, he pursued his career as a journalist. In 1866 he worked briefly as a printer at the *Macon Telegraph* before becoming private secretary to William Evelyn, publisher of the *New Orleans Crescent Monthly*. In the fall of 1870 he accepted a position as associate editor of the *Savannah Morning News;* there his comic writings and his daily column on Georgia affairs earned him the reputation of Georgia's foremost newspaper humorist.

On April 20, 1873, Harris married Esther La Rose. To avoid a yellow fever epidemic, he took his family to Atlanta in 1876 in what turned out to be a permanent move. He went to work for the *Atlanta Constitution* as an associate editor and started a column called "Round About in Georgia," similar to the one he had written for the *Savannah Morning News*. In time Harris became one of the leading editorial voices promoting the "New South" that was emerging from the ruin of the Civil War. More significantly, he wrote his first Uncle Remus story for the issue of October 26, 1876; others followed during the next three years.

Harris's first Uncle Remus book, *Uncle Remus: His Songs and His Sayings,* was published in 1881, and over the next twenty-five years five other collections of Remus stories and poems were published. For these hugely popular stories, Harris drew on his Turnwold experience as a fascinated listener to black folklore and storytelling, a tradition that in turn drew on a mixture of mostly African and some European sources. It is Harris's painstaking reshaping and retelling of these stories through the shrewd and inventive persona of Uncle Remus that is his most important contribution to American letters. As any number of critics have pointed out, in the Uncle Remus collections Harris typically sentimentalized plantation life and slavery more generally. Uncle Remus himself is a stereotype of the happy slave. There is no question, however, that the gallery of characters Harris's collections introduced to a wide readership have reappeared as individuals and as types in both high and popular culture in America. Such animal tricksters as Brer Rabbit symbolize the motif of the clever slave who outwits the master, a staple of late-nineteenth-century African American folklore, based on West African and Caribbean versions of tricksters. Trickster figures—some benevolent though most malicious, clever, subversive, and often violent—abound in the tales together with would-be victims. It is easy to recognize Brer Rabbit and Brer Fox in such animated cartoon antagonists as Bugs Bunny and Elmer Fudd. Other figures—Brer Bear, Brer Wolf, and Tar Baby among them—appear in the writings of such distinguished African American writers as Ralph Ellison and Toni Morrison. Nor is there any doubt that Paul Laurence Dunbar, Charles W. Chesnutt, and other turn-of-the-century writers who used African American dialect in their writings were aware of Harris's contribution to the preservation of black voices and narrative techniques. Though it is less frequently acknowledged, Harris was a pioneer in creating convincing poor white characters—and in preserving their distinctive voices, forerunner to such modern southern writers as Flannery O'Connor and Eudora Welty.

Harris's Remus volumes were not simply the product of a good ear and a good memory for what he had heard at Turnwold; he was a charter member of the American Folklore Society established in 1888 and was an active collector of oral tales. Increasingly, he depended on "informants" for tales he would then adapt to his purposes. In the twenty-five years between 1881 and 1906, Harris published twenty more volumes of tales, sketches, novels, and children's stories featuring a wide range of characters both fanciful and real. Best known among these works is *Free Joe and Other Georgian Sketches* (1887). Even though Harris was a working journalist for forty years and wrote editorials and essays on the issues of his day—especially on the need for the North and South to put the Civil War behind them—little of his fiction or journalism currently compels the attention of large numbers of readers. However, the tales of Uncle Remus—the stories, the human and animal characters who populate them, and the mode of their telling—are as much a part of American culture as the work of his contemporary and admirer Mark Twain. More recently, in yet another demonstration of their shape-shifting permanance, Julius Lester rewrote Harris's stories in contemporary black U.S. dialect in *The Complete Tales of Uncle Remus* (1999).

# The Wonderful Tar-Baby Story[1]

"Didn't the fox *never* catch the rabbit, Uncle Remus?" asked the little boy the next evening.

"He come mighty nigh it, honey, sho's you bawn—Brer Fox did. One day atter Brer Rabbit fool 'im wid dat calamus root, Brer Fox went ter wuk en got 'im some tar, en mix it wid some turkentime, en fix up a contrapshun wat he call a Tar-Baby, en he tuck dish yer Tar-Baby en he sot 'er in de big road, en den he lay off in de bushes fer ter see wat de news wuz gwineter be. En he didn't hatter wait long, nudder, kaze bimeby here come Brer Rabbit pacin' down de road—lippity-clippity, clippity-lippity—dez ez sassy ez a jay-bird. Brer Fox, he lay low. Brer Rabbit come prancin' 'long twel he spy de Tar-Baby, en den he fotch up on his behime legs like he wuz 'stonished. De Tar-Baby, she sot dar, she did, en Brer Fox, he lay low.

" 'Mawnin'!' sez Brer Rabbit, sezee—'nice wedder dis mawnin',' sezee.

"Tar-Baby ain't sayin' nothin', en Brer Fox, he lay low.

" 'How duz yo' sym'tums seem ter segashuate?' sez Brer Rabbit, sezee.

"Brer Fox, he wink his eye slow, en lay low, en de Tar-Baby, she ain't sayin' nothin'.

" 'How you come on, den? Is you deaf?' sez Brer Rabbit, sezee. 'Kaze if you is, I kin holler louder,' sezee.

"Tar-Baby stay still, en Brer Fox, he lay low.

" 'Youer stuck up, dat's w'at you is,' says Brer Rabbit, sezee, 'en I'm gwineter kyore you, dat's w'at I'm a gwineter do,' sezee.

"Brer Fox, he sorter chuckle in his stummuck, he did, but Tar-Baby ain't sayin' nothin'.

" 'I'm gwineter larn you howter talk ter 'specttubble fokes ef hit's de las' ack', sez Brer Rabbit, sezee. 'Ef you don't take off dat hat en tell me howdy, I'm gwineter bus' you wide open,' sezee.

"Tar-Baby stay still, en Brer Fox, he lay low.

"Brer Rabbit keep on axin' 'im, en de Tar-Baby, she keep on sayin' nothin', twel present'y Brer Rabbit draw back wid his fis', he did, en blip he tuck 'er side er de head. Right dar's whar he broke his merlasses jug. His fis' stuck, en he can't pull loose. De tar hilt 'im. But Tar-Baby, she stay still, en Brer Fox, he lay low.

" 'Ef you don't lemme loose, I'll knock you agin,' sez Brer Rabbit, sezee, en wid dat he fotch 'er a wipe wid de udder han', en dat stuck. Tar-Baby, she ain't sayin' nothin', en Brer Fox, he lay low.

" 'Tu'n me loose, fo' I kick de natal stuffin' outen you,' sez Brer Rabbit, sezee, but de Tar-Baby, she ain't sayin' nothin. She des hilt on, en den Brer Rabbit lose de use er his feet in de same way. Brer Fox, he lay low. Den Brer

---

1. First published in *Uncle Remus, His Songs and His Sayings* (New York: D. Appleton, 1881) and reprinted in a modern edition edited by Robert Hemenway (Penguin, 1982), the source of the present texts.

Rabbit squall out dat ef de Tar-Baby don't tu'n 'im loose he butt 'er cranksided. En den he butted, en his head got stuck. Den Brer Fox, he sa'ntered fort', lookin' des ez innercent ez wunner yo' mammy's mockin'-birds.

" 'Howdy, Brer Rabbit,' sez Brer Fox, sezee. 'You look sorter stuck up dis mawnin',' sezee, en den he rolled on de groun', en laughed en laughed twel he couldn't laugh no mo'. 'I speck you'll take dinner wid me dis time, Brer Rabbit. I done laid in some calamus root, en I ain't gwineter take no skuse,' sez Brer Fox, sezee."

Here Uncle Remus paused, and drew a two-pound yam out of the ashes.

"Did the fox eat the rabbit?" asked the little boy to whom the story had been told.

"Dat's all de fur de tale goes," replied the old man. "He mout, en den agin he moutent. Some say Jedge B'ar come 'long en loosed 'im—some say he didn't. I hear Miss Sally callin'. You better run 'long."

1881

## How Mr. Rabbit Was Too Sharp for Mr. Fox[1]

"Uncle Remus," said the little boy one evening, when he had found the old man with little or nothing to do, "did the fox kill and eat the rabbit when he caught him with the Tar-Baby?"

"Law, honey, ain't I tell you 'bout dat?" replied the old darkey, chuckling slyly. "I 'clar ter grashus I ought er tole you dat, but ole man Nod[2] wuz ridin' on my eyeleds 'twel a leetle mo'n I'd a dis'member'd my own name, en den on to dat here come yo' mammy hollerin' atter you.

"W'at I tell you w'en I fus' begin? I tole you Brer Rabbit wuz a monstus soon[3] beas'; leas'ways dat's w'at I laid out fer ter tell you. Well, den, honey, don't you go en make no udder kalkalashuns, kaze in dem days Brer Rabbit en his fambly wuz at de head er de gang w'en enny racket wuz on han', en dar dey stayed. 'Fo' you begins fer ter wipe yo' eyes 'bout Brer Rabbit, you wait en see whar'bouts Brer Rabbit gwineter fetch up at. But dat's needer yer ner dar.

"W'en Brer Fox fine Brer Rabbit mixt up wid de Tar-Baby, he feel mighty good, en he roll on de groun' en laff. Bimeby he up'n say, sezee:

" 'Well, I speck I got you dis time, Brer Rabbit,' sezee; 'maybe I ain't, but I speck I is. You been runnin' roun' here sassin' atter me a mighty long time, but I speck you done come ter de een' er de row. You bin cuttin' up yo' capers en bouncin' 'roun' in dis naberhood ontwel you come ter b'leeve yo'se'f de boss er de whole gang. En den youer allers some'rs whar you got no bizness,' sez Brer Fox, sezee. 'Who ax you fer ter come en strike up a 'quaintence wid dish yer Tar-Baby? En who stuck you up dar whar you iz? Nobody in de roun' worril. You des tuck en jam yo'se'f on dat Tar-Baby widout waitin' fer enny invite,' sez Brer Fox, sezee, 'en dar you is, en dar you'll stay twel I fixes up a bresh-pile and fires her up, kaze I'm gwineter bobbycue you dis day, sho,' sez Brer Fox, sezee.

1. This tale takes up where "The Wonderful Tar-Baby Story" left off; in the earlier story Brer Fox coaxes Brer Rabbit into being trapped in the sticky surface of a doll Brer Fox has molded from tar and set in the road.
2. Folk image of Sleep.
3. Dialect for quick or fast, speedy.

"Den Brer Rabbit talk mighty 'umble.

" 'I don't keer w'at you do wid me, Brer Fox,' sezee, 'so you don't fling me in dat brier-patch. Roas' me, Brer Fox,' sezee, 'but don't fling me in dat brier-patch,' sezee.

" 'Hit's so much trouble fer ter kindle a fire,' sez Brer Fox, sezee, 'dat I speck I'll hatter hang you,' sezee.

" 'Hang me des ez high ez you please, Brer Fox,' sez Brer Rabbit, sezee, 'but do fer de Lord's sake don't fling me in that brier-patch,' sezee.

" 'I ain't got no string,' sez Brer Fox, sezee, 'en now I speck I'll hatter drown you,' sezee.

" 'Drown me des ez deep ez you please, Brer Fox,' sez Brer Rabbit, sezee, 'but do don't fling me in dat brier-patch,' sezee.

" 'Dey ain't no water nigh,' sez Brer Fox, sezee, 'en now I speck I'll hatter skin you,' sezee.

" 'Skin me, Brer Fox,' sez Brer Rabbit, sezee, 'snatch out my eyeballs, t'ar out my years by de roots, en cut off my legs,' sezee, 'but do please, Brer Fox, don't fling me in dat brier-patch,' sezee.

"Co'se Brer Fox wanter hurt Brer Rabbit bad ez he kin, so he cotch 'im by de behime legs en slung 'im right in de middle er de brier-patch. Dar was a considerbul flutter whar Brer Rabbit struck de bushes, en Brer Fox sorter hang 'roun' fer ter see w'at wuz gwineter happen. Bimeby he hear somebody call 'im, en way up de hill he see Brer Rabbit settin' cross-legged on a chinkapin log[4] koamin' de pitch outen his har wid a chip. Den Brer Fox know dat he bin swop off mighty bad. Brer Rabbit wuz bleedzed[5] fer ter fling back some er his sass, en he holler out:

" 'Bred en bawn in a brier-patch, Brer Fox—bred en bawn in a brier-patch!' en wid dat he skip out des ez lively ez a cricket in de embers."

1881

---

4. Log of a dwarf chestnut tree.    5. Obliged.

---

# EMMA LAZARUS
## 1849–1887

There are worse fates for a writer than being remembered mainly for one poem of historic importance. Almost all Americans know some of Emma Lazarus's words, for her sonnet "The New Colossus" has been on public view, since 1903, inside the base of the Statue of Liberty, and its last several lines, especially the phrase "huddled masses yearning to breathe free," have entered the national consciousness. Lazarus's role in promoting the Statue of Liberty was unlikely because famous writers like James Russell Lowell scorned the statue as an ostentatious boondoggle. As a woman and Jewish—the first Jewish writer to make a mark in American literary history—Lazarus's perspectives on America challenge mainstream literary views.

Emma Lazarus was born in New York City on July 22, 1849, to Moses Lazarus, a wealthy sugar refiner, and Esther Nathan Lazarus, both from families long resident in New York. Her father's family were Sephardic Jews who had settled in New York while it was New Amsterdam. She grew up in luxury in Manhattan and summered at a fine home, the Beeches, in fashionable Newport, Rhode Island. Educated by tutors in three modern languages and literatures besides English, Lazarus was precocious, and when her father paid for the publication of *Poems and Translations . . . Written between the Ages of Fourteen and Sixteen* in 1866, she sent copies to poets, among them Ralph Waldo Emerson, who politely offered to be her "professor" in stylistic matters. Their cordial relationship survived her resentment that he did not include her in his 1874 anthology *Parnassus*. In addition to Emerson, Lazarus came to know other American literati of the time. While visiting the Emersons in Concord in 1876, she made a pilgrimage to the site of Henry David Thoreau's cabin, guided by Thoreau's grieving friend Ellery Channing. Corresponding with the nature writer John Burroughs, she shared an excitement over both Thoreau and Walt Whitman. In this interest in the prose and poetry of the United States, Lazarus was remarkably independent, akin not to her American contemporaries but to younger British literary people, who were already rediscovering three neglected American writers, Thoreau, Whitman, and Melville.

Lazarus's short manifesto "American Literature" in the New York *Critic* (June 18, 1881) was a retort to a critic who had deplored the lack of a "continuous tradition" in American literature. Emerson, according to this writer, had "left no lineage," only, like Irving, imitators who came to nothing. From the 1830s to the 1850s, American literary nationalism had been passionately contested, but Lazarus engaged the battle afresh, sure that Emerson's ideas had been developed by "the poet-naturalist, Henry Thoreau" as well as by Whitman and Burroughs. Daringly, she ranked Poe higher as a poet than Longfellow and mocked the efforts of "the lion hunters of London" who tried to tell Americans that they were neglecting "a certain poet"—Joaquin Miller (1841?–1913), whom she confidently declared to be nothing higher than a "second-rate singer."

Early in her literary life, Lazarus identified with the German-Jewish poet Heinrich Heine, who had felt both at home in and estranged from a Christian society and non-Hebraic literature. But, though Lazarus had written such poems as "In the Jewish Synagogue at Newport," her intellectual efforts into the early 1880s focused mainly on the continuities and distinctions between American and English literature and little on either her own Jewish heritage or the situation of Jews worldwide. In 1882, horrified that newspapers were minimizing Russian atrocities against Jews, Lazarus confronted herself, a wealthy metropolitan woman for whom being an American poet had been more important than being an American Jew. With rigor and determination, she fashioned herself into a Jewish spokeswoman on international themes as they affected American national policy on immigration. Her "Russian Christianity *versus* Modern Judaism" (*Century* [May 1882]) describes the reign of "murder, rape, arson" during which tens of thousands of Jewish families in Eastern Europe had been reduced "to homeless beggary." That November, playing on Paul's New Testament letter, she began serial publication in the *American Hebrew* of "An Epistle to the Hebrew." There she urged American Jews to become more, not less, " 'tribal,' " to recognize that their freedom depended upon the freedom of Jews in Russia and elsewhere. In "The Jewish Problem" (*Century* [February 1883]), she spoke out as an early Zionist, echoing the fervent determination of George Eliot's title character in *Daniel Deronda* to make the Jews "a nation again." And she began visiting the "undesirable" new immigrants detained on Ward's Island in the East River, those deemed too destitute or too infirm to be disembarked into American society. In 1883 she founded the Society for the Improvement and Colonization of Eastern European Jews.

Also in 1883, Lazarus wrote "The New Colossus" to raise money for the Bartholdi Pedestal Fund. The Statue of Liberty itself was to be a gift from France to the United States, and Americans had the task of erecting the expensive base such a colossal statue required. The statue had been conceived as a memorial to France's aid of the colonies during the American Revolution. In hailing the female figure as the "Mother of Exiles," Lazarus brilliantly, merely by her words, redefined the "mighty woman with a torch" into the national welcomer of "huddled masses" seeking refuge. Building on her own knowledge of immigrants arriving in the bay, she deflected the significance of the statue away from the past and toward the future.

Lazarus traveled to Europe in 1883 and 1885, meeting several famous poets, among them Robert Browning and William Morris. She died in New York on November 19, 1887. The next year, 1888, her sisters published *The Poems of Emma Lazarus*.

## In the Jewish Synagogue at Newport[1]

Here, where the noises of the busy town,
    The ocean's plunge and roar can enter not,
We stand and gaze around with tearful awe,
    And muse upon the consecrated spot.

No signs of life are here: the very prayers          5
    Inscribed around are in a language dead;[2]
The light of the "perpetual lamp"[3] is spent
    That an undying radiance was to shed.

What prayers were in this temple offered up,
    Wrung from sad hearts that knew no joy on earth,     10
By these lone exiles of a thousand years,[4]
    From the fair sunrise land that gave them birth!

Now as we gaze, in this new world of light,[5]
    Upon this relic of the days of old,
The present vanishes, and tropic bloom     15
    And Eastern towns and temples we behold.

Again we see the patriarch[6] with his flocks,
    The purple seas, the hot blue sky o'erhead,
The slaves of Egypt,—omens, mysteries,—
    Dark fleeing hosts by flaming angels led,[7]     20

A wondrous light upon a sky-kissed mount,[8]
    A man who reads Jehovah's written law,
'Midst blinding glory and effulgence rare,
    Unto a people prone with reverent awe.

1. The text is from *Admetus and Other Poems* (1871), where it is dated "July 1867." It is a companion piece to Henry Wadsworth Longfellow's similarly meditative "The Jewish Cemetery at Newport," about the cemetery attached to the Touro Synagogue, the oldest in the United States, dating from 1763. Services were no longer held there in 1852, when Longfellow visited it, and the synagogue remained closed during the years that Lazarus summered in Newport at her family's country house.
2. Lazarus calls Hebrew a dead language because at that time it was not used in everyday life.
3. In a synagogue, the light above the ark which holds the Torah (the first five books of the Hebrew scriptures—Genesis, Exodus, Leviticus, Numbers, Deuteronomy).
4. Poetically vague: Jews were expelled from

Jerusalem early in the 6th century B.C.E. and again late in the first century C.E. Most of the Newport Jews were, like Lazarus's father, Sephardic Jews, descended from Jews expelled from Spain in 1492.
5. The United States.
6. Abraham (Genesis 24.35), his son Isaac, or Isaac's sons. Lazarus is not striving for specificity but evoking images of Jewish history.
7. The enslavement of Jews in Egypt is described in Exodus 1. In Genesis 3.24, after Adam and Eve are expelled from Eden, the tree of life is protected by cherubims and a flaming sword that turns "every way." After the Hebrews crossed the Red Sea, a pillar of cloud by day and a pillar of fire by night led them through the desert (Exodus 13.21–22).
8. Mount Sinai, where God gave Moses the Ten Commandments, which he then read to the children of Israel (Exodus 34).

The pride of luxury's barbaric pomp, 25
    In the rich court of royal Solomon—[9]
Alas! we wake: one scene alone remains,—
    The exiles by the streams of Babylon.[1]

Our softened voices send us back again
    But mournful echoes through the empty hall; 30
Our footsteps have a strange unnatural sound,
    And with unwonted gentleness they fall.

The weary ones, the sad, the suffering,
    All found their comfort in the holy place,
And children's gladness and men's gratitude 35
    Took voice and mingled in the chant of praise.

The funeral and the marriage, now, alas!
    We know not which is sadder to recall;
For youth and happiness have followed age,
    And green grass lieth gently over all. 40

Nathless[2] the sacred shrine is holy yet,
    With its lone floors where reverent feet once trod.
Take off your shoes as by the burning bush,
    Before the mystery of death and God.

1867                                                     1871

## 1492[1]

Thou two-faced year, Mother of Change and Fate,
Didst weep when Spain cast forth with flaming sword,
The children of the prophets of the Lord,
Prince, priest, and people, spurned by zealot hate.
Hounded from sea to sea, from state to state, 5
The West[2] refused them, and the East abhorred.
No anchorage the known world could afford,
Close-locked was every port, barred every gate.[3]
Then smiling, thou unveil'dst, O two-faced year,
A virgin world where doors of sunset part, 10
Saying, "Ho, all who weary, enter here!
There falls each ancient barrier that the art

9. Solomon's magnificence is described in 1 Kings 4; the building of the First Temple (in Jerusalem) is described in 1 Kings 5–8.
1. The First Temple was destroyed around 588–586 B.C.E. and the Jews exiled to Babylon, the site of the modern Hilla, in Iraq, south of Baghdad.
2. Nevertheless, notwithstanding (poetic archaism).
1. This poem, reprinted from *Poems* (1888), acknowledges two events in Spain in 1492. Early in the year King Ferdinand and Queen Isabella drove from Spain all Jews who would not convert to Catholicism. A few months later they invested in Christopher Columbus's voyage into the Atlantic in the hope of establishing a new trade route to the East Indies.
2. Northern Europe, as opposed to the eastern Mediterranean.
3. The Jews expelled from Spain spread out over the Mediterranean region, many being robbed, many dying of the plague, some being enslaved, some murdered.

Of race or creed or rank devised, to rear
Grim bulwarked hatred between heart and heart!"

1883                                                                                          1888


## The New Colossus[1]

Not like the brazen giant of Greek fame,[2]
With conquering limbs astride from land to land;
Here at our sea-washed, sunset gates shall stand
A mighty woman with a torch, whose flame
Is the imprisoned lightning, and her name                                      5
Mother of Exiles. From her beacon-hand
Glows world-wide welcome; her mild eyes command
The air-bridged harbor that twin cities[3] frame.
"Keep, ancient lands, your storied pomp!" cries she
With silent lips. "Give me your tired, your poor,                            10
Your huddled masses yearning to breathe free,
The wretched refuse of your teeming shore.[4]
Send these, the homeless, tempest-tost to me,
I lift my lamp beside the golden door!"

1883                                                                                          1888

1. The footnote to the 1888 *Poems of Emma Lazarus*, the source of the present text, reads "Written in aid of Bartholdi Pedestal Fund, 1883." The sculpture by Frédéric-Auguste Bartholdi (1834–1904) was a gift from the French people, but Americans, led by the newspaper mogul Joseph Pulitzer, raised money to pay for the massive pedestal required by such a huge, heavy statue. During the mid-1870s thousands of Americans saw just how colossal the Statue of Liberty would be, for part of the statue, the hand of Liberty holding aloft the torch, was displayed for months in Madison Square in Manhattan and also displayed at the great Centennial exhibition in Philadelphia. (The statue is some 305 feet from ground to tip of torch, 151 feet from top of the pedestal to the tip of the torch.) Fittingly, in 1903 this entire poem by Emma Lazarus was engraved on a bronze tablet and affixed to an interior wall of the pedestal.
2. The gigantic statue of the sun god, Helios, created by the sculptor Chares of Lindos, loomed over the harbor of the Greek island of Rhodes for several decades before being destroyed in an earthquake in 225 B.C.E. Later reports exaggerated the size, saying that the legs of the statue straddled the harbor.
3. New York City and Jersey City, New Jersey.
4. In the early 1880s Lazarus personally knew the plight of Jews trying to take refuge in the United States after fleeing pogroms in Russia. "Huddled masses" accurately describes emigrants arriving the cheapest way, as steerage passengers.

---

# SARAH ORNE JEWETT
## 1849–1909

When Sarah Orne Jewett was born in South Berwick, Maine, in 1849, the town and region she was to memorialize in her fiction were already changing rapidly. Her grandfather had been a sea captain, shipowner, and merchant; and as a child she was exposed to the bustle of this small inland port. By the end of the Civil War, however, textile mills and a cannery had largely replaced agriculture, shipbuilding, and logging as the economic base of the community, and the arrival of French Canadian and Irish immigrants brought ethnic diversity to the area. The stable, secure, and remote small town Jewett knew and loved as a child was experiencing the economic, technological, and demographic pressures that transformed much of America in her lifetime.

Jewett's family life was steady and affectionate; she and her two sisters led happy and generally carefree childhoods. Their father was a kindly, hardworking obstetrician who indulged all three of his daughters, but Sarah most of all. He encouraged her reading, and even as a small child she accompanied him on his horse-and-buggy rounds, meeting the rural people who would later populate her fiction. Jewett loved her father deeply, and some of her strong feelings for him are invested in *A Country Doctor* (1884), a novel that celebrates the competence and independence of its female protagonist. Jewett's relationship with her mother was less intense; it was not until her mother became an invalid in the 1880s that mother and daughter became close. As Jewett admitted in a letter to editor and friend Thomas Bailey Aldrich: "I never felt so near to my mother . . . as I have since she died."

In part inspired by Harriet Beecher Stowe's novel about Maine seacoast life, *The Pearl of Orr's Island* (1862), Jewett began to write and publish verse and stories in her teens. One of her first efforts was accepted in 1869 by the influential editor William Dean Howells for publication in the prestigious *Atlantic Monthly*. In her early twenties, encouraged by Howells, she wrote a group of stories and sketches about a fictional coastal town in Maine to which she gave the name Deephaven; under that title she published her first collection of short pieces in 1877. With the publication of this book, she entered the company of George Washington Cable, Harriet Beecher Stowe, and other regional writers who were depicting the topographies, people, speech patterns, and modes of life of many distinctive regions of the country. At their best, the "regionalists" created works whose themes transcended regionality, as with Jewett's treatment of the courageous response of women to frustration and loneliness in the post–Civil War years.

From the late 1870s on, Jewett was a member of a circle of prominent women writers and artists who lived in or near Boston. This group included Cecilia Thaxter, Sarah Wyman Whitman, Sara Norton, and Marie Thérèsa Blanc. Without question, the relationship between Jewett and Annie Adams Fields, the wife of editor and publisher James T. Fields, was the most important of the many friendships Jewett formed with both men and women. Though they had known each other since the late 1870s, it was not until Annie Fields's husband died in 1881 that they established a bond that was to sustain both women until Jewett's death in 1909. During the winter months, Jewett lived at Fields's house in Boston and in the spring and summer was often to be found at Fields's oceanside home a few miles north of Boston in Manchester-by-the-Sea. Jewett maintained her residence in South Berwick, and she and Mrs. Fields would spend time together there as well. Their relationship was of a kind not uncommon at the turn of the century; indeed, such connections between women were called "Boston marriages," a term that implied shared living quarters and a partnership that paralleled ordinary marriage in its intimacy and exclusiveness. In recent years their relationship—and those of other prominent female couples of the period—has been the subject of much historical and biographical commentary. What is most central and significant about the Jewett-Fields relationship is that in their lives together in America and in the course of extended trips they took to England, the Continent, and other places, they found companionship and mutual support in a loving, caring relationship based on shared interests. Annie Fields grieved deeply at the death of her husband; when Jewett died seven years after she was seriously injured in a carriage accident, Annie Fields's grief was of the same order of magnitude.

Jewett reached artistic maturity with the publication of the collection *A White Heron* in 1886; later collections of sketches and stories include *The King of Folly Island* (1888), *A Native of Winby* (1893), and *The Life of Nancy* (1895). In these works the careful documentary record of landscape, people, and dialect is described with understanding and sympathy. In "A White Heron," reprinted here, a young girl's conflicted loyalties to her conception of herself in nature and to the world of men she will soon encounter are memorably and sensitively drawn. Jewett's most enduring work is *The Country of the Pointed Firs* (1896), a collection of linked sketches filtered through the consciousness of a summer visitor, much like the person Jewett had become. In this work, bits and pieces of the lives of a small group of men and women are quilted into a unified impression of life in a once-prosperous shipping village. The strong older women who survive in the region form a female community that, for many critics, is a hallmark of New England regionalism.

# A White Heron[1]

## I

The woods were already filled with shadows one June evening, just before eight o'clock, though a bright sunset still glimmered faintly among the trunks of the trees. A little girl was driving home her cow, a plodding, dilatory, provoking creature in her behavior, but a valued companion for all that. They were going away from whatever light there was, and striking deep into the woods, but their feet were familiar with the path, and it was no matter whether their eyes could see it or not.

There was hardly a night the summer through when the old cow could be found waiting at the pasture bars; on the contrary, it was her greatest pleasure to hide herself away among the high huckleberry bushes, and though she wore a loud bell she had made the discovery that if one stood perfectly still it would not ring. So Sylvia had to hunt for her until she found her, and call Co'! Co'! with never an answering Moo, until her childish patience was quite spent. If the creature had not given good milk and plenty of it, the case would have seemed very different to her owners. Besides, Sylvia had all the time there was, and very little use to make of it. Sometimes in pleasant weather it was a consolation to look upon the cow's pranks as an intelligent attempt to play hide and seek, and as the child had no playmates she lent herself to this amusement with a good deal of zest. Though this chase had been so long that the wary animal herself had given an unusual signal of her whereabouts, Sylvia had only laughed when she came upon Mistress Moolly at the swamp-side, and urged her affectionately homeward with a twig of birch leaves. The old cow was not inclined to wander farther, she even turned in the right direction for once as they left the pasture, and stepped along the road at a good pace. She was quite ready to be milked now, and seldom stopped to browse. Sylvia wondered what her grandmother would say because they were so late. It was a great while since she had left home at half past five o'clock, but everybody knew the difficulty of making this errand a short one. Mrs. Tilley had chased the hornéd torment too many summer evenings herself to blame any one else for lingering, and was only thankful as she waited that she had Sylvia, nowadays, to give such valuable assistance. The good woman suspected that Sylvia loitered occasionally on her own account; there never was such a child for straying about out-of-doors since the world was made! Everybody said that it was a good change for a little maid who had tried to grow for eight years in a crowded

---

1. First published in book form in *"A White Heron" and Other Stories* (1886), the source of the text printed here.

manufacturing town, but, as for Sylvia herself, it seemed as if she never had been alive at all before she came to live at the farm. She thought often with wistful compassion of a wretched geranium that belonged to a town neighbor.

" 'Afraid of folks,' " old Mrs. Tilley said to herself, with a smile, after she had made the unlikely choice of Sylvia from her daughter's houseful of children, and was returning to the farm. " 'Afraid of folks,' they said! I guess she won't be troubled no great with 'em up to the old place!" When they reached the door of the lonely house and stopped to unlock it, and the cat came to purr loudly, and rub against them, a deserted pussy, indeed, but fat with young robins, Sylvia whispered that this was a beautiful place to live in, and she never should wish to go home.

The companions followed the shady woodroad, the cow taking slow steps, and the child very fast ones. The cow stopped long at the brook to drink, as if the pasture were not half a swamp, and Sylvia stood still and waited, letting her bare feet cool themselves in the shoal water, while the great twilight moths struck softly against her. She waded on through the brook as the cow moved away, and listened to the thrushes with a heart that beat fast with pleasure. There was a stirring in the great boughs overhead. They were full of little birds and beasts that seemed to be wide awake, and going about their world, or else saying good-night to each other in sleepy twitters. Sylvia herself felt sleepy as she walked along. However, it was not much farther to the house, and the air was soft and sweet. She was not often in the woods so late as this, and it made her feel as if she were a part of the gray shadows and the moving leaves. She was just thinking how long it seemed since she first came to the farm a year ago, and wondering if everything went on in the noisy town just the same as when she was there; the thought of the great red-faced boy who used to chase and frighten her made her hurry along the path to escape from the shadow of the trees.

Suddenly this little woods-girl is horror-stricken to hear a clear whistle not very far away. Not a bird's whistle, which would have a sort of friendliness, but a boy's whistle, determined, and somewhat aggressive. Sylvia left the cow to whatever sad fate might await her, and stepped discreetly aside into the bushes, but she was just too late. The enemy had discovered her, and called out in a very cheerful and persuasive tone, "Halloa, little girl, how far is it to the road?" and trembling Sylvia answered almost inaudibly, "A good ways."

She did not dare to look boldly at the tall young man, who carried a gun over his shoulder, but she came out of her bush and again followed the cow, while he walked alongside.

"I have been hunting for some birds," the stranger said kindly, "and I have lost my way, and need a friend very much. Don't be afraid," he added gallantly. "Speak up and tell me what your name is, and whether you think I can spend the night at your house, and go out gunning early in the morning."

Sylvia was more alarmed than before. Would not her grandmother consider her much to blame? But who could have foreseen such an accident as this? It did not seem to be her fault, and she hung her head as if the stem of it were broken, but managed to answer "Sylvy," with much effort when her companion again asked her name.

Mrs. Tilley was standing in the doorway when the trio came into view. The cow gave a loud moo by way of explanation.

"Yes, you'd better speak up for yourself, you old trial! Where'd she tucked herself away this time, Sylvy?" But Sylvia kept an awed silence; she knew by instinct that her grandmother did not comprehend the gravity of the situation. She must be mistaking the stranger for one of the farmer-lads of the region.

The young man stood his gun beside the door, and dropped a lumpy game-bag beside it; then he bade Mrs. Tilley good-evening, and repeated his way-farer's story, and asked if he could have a night's lodging.

"Put me anywhere you like," he said. "I must be off early in the morning, before day; but I am very hungry, indeed. You can give me some milk at any rate, that's plain."

"Dear sakes, yes," responded the hostess, whose long slumbering hospitality seemed to be easily awakened. "You might fare better if you went out to the main road a mile or so, but you're welcome to what we've got. I'll milk right off, and you make yourself at home. You can sleep on husks or feathers," she proffered graciously. "I raised them all myself. There's good pasturing for geese just below here towards the ma'sh. Now step round and set a plate for the gentleman, Sylvy!" And Sylvia promptly stepped. She was glad to have something to do, and she was hungry herself.

It was a surprise to find so clean and comfortable a little dwelling in this New England wilderness. The young man had known the horrors of its most primitive housekeeping, and the dreary squalor of that level of society which does not rebel at the companionship of hens. This was the best thrift of an old-fashioned farmstead, though on such a small scale that it seemed like a hermitage. He listened eagerly to the old woman's quaint talk, he watched Sylvia's pale face and shining gray eyes with ever growing enthusiasm, and insisted that this was the best supper he had eaten for a month, and afterward the new-made friends sat down in the door-way together while the moon came up.

Soon it would be berry-time, and Sylvia was a great help at picking. The cow was a good milker, though a plaguy thing to keep track of, the hostess gossiped frankly, adding presently that she had buried four children, so Sylvia's mother, and a son (who might be dead) in California were all the children she had left. "Dan, my boy, was a great hand to go gunning," she explained sadly. "I never wanted for pa'tridges or gray squer'ls while he was to home. He's been a great wand'rer, I expect, and he's no hand to write letters. There, I don't blame him, I'd ha' seen the world myself if it had been so I could.

"Sylvia takes after him," the grandmother continued affectionately, after a minute's pause. "There ain't a foot o' ground she don't know her way over, and the wild creaturs counts her one o' themselves. Squer'ls she'll tame to come an' feed right out o' her hands, and all sorts o' birds. Last winter she got the jay-birds to bangeing[2] here, and I believe she'd 'a' scanted herself of her own meals to have plenty to throw out amongst 'em, if I hadn't kep' watch. Anything but crows, I tell her, I'm willin' to help support—though Dan he had a tamed one o' them that did seem to have reason same as folks. It was round here a good spell after he went away. Dan an' his father they didn't hitch,—but he never held up his head ag'in after Dan had dared him an' gone off."

2. Hanging around.

The guest did not notice this hint of family sorrows in his eager interest in something else.

"So Sylvy knows all about birds, does she?" he exclaimed, as he looked round at the little girl who sat, very demure but increasingly sleepy, in the moonlight. "I am making a collection of birds myself. I have been at it ever since I was a boy." (Mrs. Tilley smiled.) "There are two or three very rare ones I have been hunting for these five years. I mean to get them on my own ground if they can be found."

"Do you cage 'em up?" asked Mrs. Tilley doubtfully, in response to this enthusiastic announcement.

"Oh, no, they're stuffed and preserved, dozens and dozens of them," said the ornithologist, "and I have shot or snared every one myself. I caught a glimpse of a white heron three miles from here on Saturday, and I have followed it in this direction. They have never been found in this district at all. The little white heron, it is," and he turned again to look at Sylvia with the hope of discovering that the rare bird was one of her acquaintances.

But Sylvia was watching a hop-toad in the narrow footpath.

"You would know the heron if you saw it," the stranger continued eagerly. "A queer tall white bird with soft feathers and long thin legs. And it would have a nest perhaps in the top of a high tree, made of sticks, something like a hawk's nest."

Sylvia's heart gave a wild beat; she knew that strange white bird, and had once stolen softly near where it stood in some bright green swamp grass, away over at the other side of the woods. There was an open place where the sunshine always seemed strangely yellow and hot, where tall, nodding rushes grew, and her grandmother had warned her that she might sink in the soft black mud underneath and never be heard of more. Not far beyond were the salt marshes just this side the sea itself, which Sylvia wondered and dreamed about, but never had seen, whose great voice could sometimes be heard above the noise of the woods on stormy nights.

"I can't think of anything I should like so much as to find that heron's nest," the handsome stranger was saying. "I would give ten dollars to anybody who could show it to me," he added desperately, "and I mean to spend my whole vacation hunting for it if need be. Perhaps it was only migrating, or had been chased out of its own region by some bird of prey."

Mrs. Tilley gave amazed attention to all this, but Sylvia still watched the toad, not divining, as she might have done at some calmer time, that the creature wished to get to its hole under the door-step, and was much hindered by the unusual spectators at that hour of the evening. No amount of thought, that night, could decide how many wished-for treasures the ten dollars, so lightly spoken of, would buy.

The next day the young sportsman hovered about the woods, and Sylvia kept him company, having lost her first fear of the friendly lad, who proved to be most kind and sympathetic. He told her many things about the birds and what they knew and where they lived and what they did with themselves. And he gave her a jack-knife, which she thought as great a treasure as if she were a desert-islander. All day long he did not once make her troubled or afraid except when he brought down some unsuspecting singing creature from its bough. Sylvia would have liked him vastly better without his gun; she could not understand why he killed the very birds he seemed to like so much. But as they day waned, Sylvia still watched the young man with loving admiration. She had never seen anybody so charming and delightful; the woman's heart, asleep in the child, was vaguely thrilled by a dream of love. Some premonition of that great power stirred and swayed these young creatures who traversed the solemn woodlands with soft-footed silent care. They stopped to listed to a bird's song; they pressed forward again eagerly, parting the branches,—speaking to each other rarely and in whispers; the young man going first and Sylvia following, fascinated, a few steps behind, with her gray eyes dark with excitement.

She grieved because the longed-for white heron was elusive, but she did not lead the guest, she only followed, and there was no such thing as speaking first. The sound of her own unquestioned voice would have terrified her,—it was hard enough to answer yes or no when there was need of that. At last evening began to fall, and they drove the cow home together, and Sylvia smiled with pleasure when they came to the place where she heard the whistle and was afraid only the night before.

## II

Half a mile from home, at the farther edge of the woods, where the land was highest, a great pine-tree stood, the last of its generation. Whether it was left for a boundary mark, or for what reason, no one could say; the woodchoppers who had felled its mates were dead and gone long ago, and a whole forest of sturdy trees, pines and oaks and maples, had grown again. But the stately head of this old pine towered above them all and made a landmark for sea and shore miles and miles away. Sylvia knew it well. She had always believed that whoever climbed to the top of it could see the ocean; and the little girl had often laid her hand on the great rough trunk and looked up wistfully at those dark boughs that the wind always stirred, no matter how hot and still the air might be below. Now she thought of the tree with a new excitement, for why, if one climbed it at break of day, could not one see all the world, and easily discover from whence the white heron flew, and mark the place, and find the hidden nest?

What a spirit of adventure, what wild ambition! What fancied triumph and delight and glory for the later morning when she could make known the secret! It was almost too real and too great for the childish heart to bear.

All night the door of the little house stood open and the whippoorwills came and sang upon the very step. The young sportsman and his old hostess were sound asleep, but Sylvia's great design kept her broad awake and watching. She forgot to think of sleep. The short summer night seemed as long as the winter darkness, and at last when the whippoorwills ceased, and she was afraid the morning would after all come too soon, she stole out of the house and followed the pasture path through the woods, hastening toward the open ground beyond, listening with a sense of comfort and companionship to the drowsy twitter of a half-awakened bird, whose perch she had jarred in passing. Alas, if the great wave of human interest which flooded for the first time this dull little life should sweep away the satisfactions of an existence heart to heart with nature and the dumb life of the forest!

There was the huge tree asleep yet in the paling moonlight, and small and silly Sylvia began with utmost bravery to mount to the top of it, with tingling, eager blood coursing the channels of her whole frame, with her bare feet and fingers, that pinched and held like bird's claws to the monstrous ladder reaching up, up, almost to the sky itself. First she must mount the white oak tree that grew alongside, where she was almost lost among the dark branches and the green leaves heavy and wet with dew; a bird fluttered off its nest, and a red squirrel ran to and fro and scolded pettishly at the harmless housebreaker. Sylvia felt her way easily. She had often climbed there, and knew that higher still one of the oak's upper branches chafed against the pine trunk, just where its lower boughs were set close together. There, when she made the dangerous pass from one tree to the other, the great enterprise would really begin.

She crept out along the swaying oak limb at last, and took the daring step across into the old pine-tree. The way was harder than she thought; she must reach far and hold fast, the sharp dry twigs caught and held her and scratched her like angry talons, the pitch made her thin little fingers clumsy and stiff as she went round and round the tree's great stem, higher and higher upward. The sparrows and robins in the woods below were beginning to wake and twitter to the dawn, yet it seemed much lighter there aloft in the pine-tree, and the child knew that she must hurry if her project were to be of any use.

The tree seemed to lengthen itself out as she went up, and to reach farther and farther upward. It was like a great main-mast to the voyaging earth; it must truly have been amazed that morning through all its ponderous frame as it felt this determined spark of human spirit winding its way from higher branch to branch. Who knows how steadily the least twigs held themselves to advantage this light, weak creature on her way! The old pine must have loved his new dependent. More than all the hawks, and bats, and moths, and even the sweet voiced thrushes, was the brave, beating heart of the solitary gray-eyed child. And the tree stood still and frowned away the winds that June morning while the dawn grew bright in the east.

Sylvia's face was like a pale star, if one had seen it from the ground, when the last thorny bough was past, and she stood trembling and tired but wholly triumphant, high in the tree-top. Yes, there was the sea with the dawning sun making a golden dazzle over it, and toward that glorious east flew two hawks with slow-moving pinions. How low they looked in the air from that height when one had only seen them before far up, and dark against the blue sky. Their gray feathers were as soft as moths; they seemed only a little way from the tree, and Sylvia felt as if she too could go flying away among the clouds. Westward, the woodlands and farms reached miles and miles into the distance; here and there were church steeples, and white villages; truly it was a vast and awesome world!

The birds sang louder and louder. At last the sun came up bewilderingly bright. Sylvia could see the white sails of ships out at sea, and the clouds that were purple and rose-colored and yellow at first began to fade away. Where was the white heron's nest in the sea of green branches, and was this wonderful sight and pageant of the world the only reward for having climbed to such a giddy height? Now look down again, Sylvia, where the green marsh is set among the shining birches and dark hemlocks; there where you saw the white heron once you will see him again; look, look! a white spot of him like a single floating feather comes up from the dead hemlock and grows larger, and rises, and comes close at last, and goes by the landmark pine with steady sweep of wing and outstretched slender neck and crested head. And wait! wait! do not move a foot or a finger, little girl, do not send an arrow of light and consciousness from your two eager eyes, for the heron has perched on a pine bough not far beyond yours, and cries back to his mate on the nest, and plumes his feathers for the new day!

The child gives a long sigh a minute later when a company of shouting cat-birds comes also to the tree, and vexed by their fluttering and lawlessness the solemn heron goes away. She knows his secret now, the wild, light, slender bird that floats and wavers, and goes back like an arrow presently to his home in the green world beneath. Then Sylvia, well satisfied, makes her perilous way down again, not daring to look far below the branch she stands on, ready to cry sometimes because her fingers ache and her lamed feet slip. Wondering over and over again what the stranger would say to her, and what he would think when she told him how to find his way straight to the heron's nest.

"Sylvy, Sylvy!" called the busy old grandmother again and again, but nobody answered, and the small husk bed was empty and Sylvia had disappeared.

The guest waked from a dream, and remembering his day's pleasure hurried to dress himself that might it sooner begin. He was sure from the way the shy little girl looked once or twice yesterday that she had at least seen the white heron, and now she must really be made to tell. Here she comes now, paler than ever, and her worn old frock is torn and tattered, and smeared with pine pitch. The grandmother and the sportsman stand in the door together and question her, and the splendid moment has come to speak of the dead hemlock-tree by the green marsh.

But Sylvia does not speak after all, though the old grandmother fretfully rebukes her, and the young man's kind, appealing eyes are looking straight in her own. He can make them rich with money; he has promised it, and they are poor now. He is so well worth making happy, and he waits to hear the story she can tell.

No, she must keep silence! What is it that suddenly forbids her and makes her dumb? Has she been nine years growing and now, when the great world for the first time puts out a hand to her, must she thrust it aside for a bird's sake? The murmur of the pine's green branches is in her ears, she remembers how the white heron came flying through the golden air and how they watched the sea and the morning together, and Sylvia cannot speak; she cannot tell the heron's secret and give its life away.

Dear loyalty, that suffered a sharp pang as the guest went away disappointed later in the day, that could have served and followed him and loved him as a dog loves! Many a night Sylvia heard the echo of his whistle haunting the pasture path as she came home with the loitering cow. She forgot even her sorrow at the sharp report of his gun and the sight of thrushes and sparrows dropping silent to the ground, their songs hushed and their pretty feathers stained and wet with blood. Were the birds better friends than their hunter might have been,—who can tell? Whatever treasures were lost to her, woodlands and summer-time, remember! Bring your gifts and graces and tell your secrets to this lonely country child!

1886

# KATE CHOPIN
## 1850–1904

Katherine O'Flaherty seemed more likely as a young woman to become a consumer of literature than a producer of it. Her Irish immigrant father was a successful business-man who died in a train wreck when his daughter was four years old. The family enjoyed a high place in St. Louis society; and her mother, grandmother, and great-grandmother were active, pious Catholics of French heritage. Without doubt Kate O'Flaherty grew up in the company of loving, intelligent, independent women. Particularly important was her strong-willed great-grandmother, a compelling and tireless storyteller whose influence may have been central to Chopin's becoming a significant regional writer and the author of a remarkable novel, *The Awakening* (1899), that speaks radically to issues of gender, sexuality, and the American family.

Chopin was nine years old before she entered St. Louis Academy of the Sacred Heart, but she was already well-read in English and French authors, and by the time she graduated from the academy in 1868 she had absorbed Cervantes, Dante, Goethe, and many English novelists and poets of the eighteenth and nineteenth centuries—Austen, the Brontës, and Coleridge among them. But it was French writers who most strongly influenced her sense of life and her craft as a writer. She read and admired French classical authors as well as more contemporary figures such as Gustave Flaubert and Madame de Staël; but it was Émile Zola and Guy de Maupassant who provided philosophical perspective and fictional method when she began to write in earnest in her late thirties. What she said of Maupassant she might have said of her-self: "Here was a man who had escaped from tradition and authority, who had entered into himself and looked out upon life through his own being and with his own eyes; and who in a direct and simple way, told us what he saw." Though Chopin is sometimes praised for her symbolic, imagistic prose, she was able to see and to narrate a new real-ity indeed. What she saw, whether in St. Louis, New Orleans, or the Louisiana coun-tryside, was the tension between individual erotic inclination and the constraints placed on desire—especially on women's sexual desire—by traditional social mores. What she told directly—and without moral judgment—was how certain women were beginning to challenge the patriarchal rules that sought not only to confine them to well-defined social, economic, and vocational domains but to control their inner life as well. Her new, modern perspectives, especially on female sexuality, paralleled those of Edith Wharton and Theodore Dreiser.

At the age of nineteen she married Oscar Chopin and spent the next decade in New Orleans, where her husband first prospered, then failed, in the cotton business. After a few years in Cloutierville, a village in northwest Louisiana near Natchitoches, where her husband opened a general store and managed a family cotton plantation, she returned to St. Louis permanently in 1884, a year after her husband's death from swamp fever (probably malaria). A year later her mother died, and at the age of thirty-five Chopin was left essentially alone to raise her six young children. Having recog-nized the ready market for "local color," or regional, fiction, Chopin decided to fashion a literary career out of her experience of the Creole and Cajun cultures she had come to know.

Chopin had the gift of equanimity and wrote on a lapboard in the midst of a busy household. Many of her stories were written in a single day. She claimed that she wrote on impulse, that she was "completely at the mercy of unconscious selection" of subject, and that "the polishing up process . . . always proved disastrous." This method, although it ensured freshness and sincerity, made some of her stories anec-dotal or thin. Though a score of the best of them have endured, it is remarkable that in the relatively few years of her writing career—scarcely more than a decade—she completed three novels; more than 150 stories and sketches; and a substantial body of poetry, reviews, and criticism. A first novel, *At Fault*, was self-published in 1890, but it was her stories of Louisiana rural life, especially in the collection *Bayou Folk* (1894), that won her national recognition as a practitioner of local-color fiction. She made the Catholic Creoles and Cajuns with their old-fashioned European customs, their polyglot, witty speech, their sensuous and seemingly unself-conscious lives, and their rich agricultural landscape in picturesque Natchitoches Parish familiar to Americans, as Sarah Orne Jewett was making known the severe Protestant towns of rocky, coastal Maine. A second collection of stories, *A Night in Acadie*, was published three years later and increased her reputation as a local colorist. Nina Baym has argued persuasively that local-color writing, which flourished after the Civil War, was in part the product of anxiety over the loss of the familiar in a period of rapid change and dislocation (literal and figurative), nostalgia for more stable times, and the emergence of a homogenized national society. The trauma of America's most destructive war up until that time made antebellum America seem like a golden age to many. Yet Chopin does not idealize the Old South; to the contrary, she often presents it from a critical or oppositional view, especially as concerns gender and race. Chopin managed to be recognized as a regionalist while subtly critiquing southern values, in many ways anticipating the early Faulkner.

Chopin was skilled in the depiction of characters and advancement of plot through distinctive dialogue. She was able to create with great economy a believable physical world in which climate, culture, community, and individual personalities exist in subtle reciprocal relations. Sexuality is often a part of this scene; what Chopin notices and portrays of such undercurrents challenged conventional limits in fiction. In her explicit and unapologetic eroticism, as in "The Storm" (1898), it was not so much that adultery is committed under the steamiest of conditions, but that in the end no one is left feeling guilty or unhappy that almost certainly kept Chopin from submitting the story for publication. In any event, it was not published until 1969 as part of Per Seyersted's edition of *The Complete Works of Kate Chopin*.

Chopin's major work, *The Awakening*, influenced by Gustave Flaubert's *Madame Bovary* (1856), was published in 1899. The novel, which traces the sensual and sexual coming to consciousness of a young woman, predictably aroused hostility among contemporary reviewers, just as Whitman's *Leaves of Grass*, which Chopin admired, had half a century earlier. The "new woman"—demanding social, economic, and political equality—was already a common topic of public discussion and subject of fiction. But the depiction of such an unrepentant (if ultimately deeply psychologically confused) sensualist as Edna Pontellier was more than many of the critics of the time could allow to pass. The book was called "trite and sordid," "essentially vulgar," and "unhealthily introspective and morbid in feeling." Chopin was dropped from her St. Louis clubs and snubbed by friends. But in objecting to Edna's behavior, these readers missed what is more disturbing about *The Awakening*; Chopin presented nothing less than a "waste land" for women of her generation, describing not only Edna's desire for individual freedom but also the naturalistic forces that made her quest futile. It should have been Chopin's essential pessimism and not her racy scenes that unnerved the critics. Though some commentators found much to praise in *The Awakening*, Chopin's only published response to her reviews was to claim, tongue in cheek, "I never dreamed of Mrs. Pontellier making such a mess of things and working out her own damnation as she did. If I had had the slightest intimation of such a thing I would have excluded her from the company." After the book was published, Chopin's health began to deteriorate, and she wrote little. Though the novel and its author fell into obscurity for half a century, since the 1970s and particularly since the publication of the Norton Critical Edition, which helped bring Chopin into the canon, they have now secured an honored place in American literary history. Wharton and Chopin were among the first women authors after Emily Dickinson to be added to many American literature syllabi. In recent years, critics have begun to explore the intricacies of race, class, and ethnicity as subjects and contexts in this remarkable novel that once was thought to be only, or at least primarily, aimed at exploring Edna's sexuality.

In *The Awakening*, more impressively because on a grander scale than in her shorter fiction, Chopin demonstrates her unusual capacity to make the exotic worlds of New Orleans and the Louisiana Gulf Coast real and to fill those worlds with complex and often baffled men and women—not unlike T. S. Eliot's Prufrock—whose humanity she confirms by refusing to judge them or use them to support a thesis. Some critics have accordingly found the novel's feminist argument to be complicated by the fatal weaknesses in Edna's psyche.

The notes to *The Awakening* printed here owe much to the second Norton Critical Edition, edited by Margo Culley.

# The Storm

### A Sequel to "The 'Cadian Ball"[1]

#### I

The leaves were so still that even Bibi thought it was going to rain. Bobinôt, who was accustomed to converse on terms of perfect equality with his little son, called the child's attention to certain sombre clouds that were rolling with sinister intention from the west, accompanied by a sullen, threatening roar. They were at Friedheimer's store and decided to remain there till the storm had passed. They sat within the door on two empty kegs. Bibi was four years old and looked very wise.

"Mama'll be 'fraid, yes," he suggested with blinking eyes.

"She'll shut the house. Maybe she got Sylvie helpin' her this evenin'," Bobinôt responded reassuringly.

"No; she ent got Sylvie. Sylvie was helpin' her yistiday," piped Bibi.

Bobinôt arose and going across to the counter purchased a can of shrimps, of which Calixta was very fond. Then he returned to his perch on the keg and sat stolidly holding the can of shrimps while the storm burst. It shook the wooden store and seemed to be ripping furrows in the distant field. Bibi laid his little hand on his father's knee and was not afraid.

#### II

Calixta, at home, felt no uneasiness for their safety. She sat at a side window sewing furiously on a sewing machine. She was greatly occupied and did not notice the approaching storm. But she felt very warm and often stopped to mop her face on which the perspiration gathered in beads. She unfastened her white sacque at the throat. It began to grow dark, and suddenly realizing the situation she got up hurriedly and went about closing windows and doors.

Out on the small front gallery she had hung Bobinôt's Sunday clothes to dry and she hastened out to gather them before the rain fell. As she stepped outside, Alcée Laballière rode in at the gate. She had not seen him very often

---

1. Chopin's notebooks show that this story was written on July 18, 1898, just six months after she had submitted *The Awakening* to a publisher. As its subtitle indicates, it was intended as a sequel to her tale "At the 'Cadian Ball." "The Storm" was appar-ently never submitted for publication and did not see print until the publication of Per Seyersted's edition of *The Complete Works of Kate Chopin* in 1969, the basis for the text printed here.

since her marriage, and never alone. She stood there with Bobinôt's coat in her hands, and the big rain drops began to fall. Alcée rode his horse under the shelter of a side projection where the chickens had huddled and there were plows and a harrow piled up in the corner.

"May I come and wait on your gallery till the storm is over, Calixta?" he asked.

"Come 'long in, M'sieur Alcée."

His voice and her own startled her as if from a trance, and she seized Bobinôt's vest. Alcée, mounting to the porch, grabbed the trousers and snatched Bibi's braided jacket that was about to be carried away by a sudden gust of wind. He expressed an intention to remain outside, but it was soon apparent that he might as well have been out in the open: the water beat in upon the boards in driving sheets, and he went inside, closing the door after him. It was even necessary to put something beneath the door to keep the water out.

"My! what a rain! It's good two years sence it rain' like that," exclaimed Calixta as she rolled up a piece of bagging and Alcée helped her to thrust it beneath the crack.

She was a little fuller of figure than five years before when she married; but she had lost nothing of her vivacity. Her blue eyes still retained their melting quality; and her yellow hair, disheveled by the wind and rain, kinked more stubbornly than ever about her ears and temples.

The rain beat upon the low, shingled roof with a force and clatter that threatened to break an entrance and deluge them there. They were in the dining room—the sitting room—the general utility room. Adjoining was her bed room, with Bibi's couch along side her own. The door stood open, and the room with its white, monumental bed, its closed shutters, looked dim and mysterious.

Alcée flung himself into a rocker and Calixta nervously began to gather up from the floor the lengths of a cotton sheet which she had been sewing.

"If this keeps up, *Dieu sait*[2] if the levees goin' to stan' it!" she exclaimed.

"What have you got to do with the levees?"

"I got enough to do! An' there's Bobinôt with Bibi out in that storm—if he only didn' left Friedheimer's!"

"Let us hope, Calixta, that Bobinôt's got sense enough to come in out of a cyclone."

She went and stood at the window with a greatly disturbed look on her face. She wiped the frame that was clouded with moisture. It was stiflingly hot. Alcée got up and joined her at the window, looking over her shoulder. The rain was coming down in sheets obscuring the view of far-off cabins and enveloping the distant wood in a gray mist. The playing of the lightning was incessant. A bolt struck a tall chinaberry tree at the edge of the field. It filled all visible space with a blinding glare and the crash seemed to invade the very boards they stood upon.

Calixta put her hands to her eyes, and with a cry, staggered backward. Alcée's arm encircled her, and for an instant he drew her close and spasmodically to him.

---

2. Built-up earth banks designed to keep the river from flooding the surrounding land. *"Dieu sait"*: God knows (French).

"*Bonté!*"[3] she cried, releasing herself from his encircling arm and retreating from the window, "the house'll go next! If I only knew w'ere Bibi was!" She would not compose herself; she would not be seated. Alcée clasped her shoulders and looked into her face. The contact of her warm, palpitating body when he had unthinkingly drawn her into his arms, had aroused all the old-time infatuation and desire for her flesh.

"Calixta," he said, "don't be frightened. Nothing can happen. The house is too low to be struck, with so many tall trees standing about. There! aren't you going to be quiet? say, aren't you?" He pushed her hair back from her face that was warm and steaming. Her lips were as red and moist as pomegranate seed. Her white neck and a glimpse of her full, firm bosom disturbed him powerfully. As she glanced up at him the fear in her liquid blue eyes had given place to a drowsy gleam that unconsciously betrayed a sensuous desire. He looked down into her eyes and there was nothing for him to do but to gather her lips in a kiss. It reminded him of Assumption.[4]

"Do you remember—in Assumption, Calixta?" he asked in a low voice broken by passion. Oh! she remembered; for in Assumption he had kissed her and kissed and kissed her; until his senses would well nigh fail, and to save her he would resort to a desperate flight. If she was not an immaculate dove in those days, she was still inviolate; a passionate creature whose very defenselessness had made her defense, against which his honor forbade him to prevail. Now—well, now—her lips seemed in a manner free to be tasted, as well as her round, white throat and her whiter breasts.

They did not heed the crashing torrents, and the roar of the elements made her laugh as she lay in his arms. She was a revelation in that dim, mysterious chamber; as white as the couch she lay upon. Her firm, elastic flesh that was knowing for the first time its birthright, was like a creamy lily that the sun invites to contribute its breath and perfume to the undying life of the world.

The generous abundance of her passion, without guile or trickery, was like a white flame which penetrated and found response in depths of his own sensuous nature that had never yet been reached.

When he touched her breasts they gave themselves up in quivering ecstasy, inviting his lips. Her mouth was a fountain of delight. And when he possessed her, they seemed to swoon together at the very borderland of life's mystery.

He stayed cushioned upon her, breathless, dazed, enervated, with his heart beating like a hammer upon her. With one hand she clasped his head, her lips lightly touching his forehead. The other hand stroked with a soothing rhythm his muscular shoulders.

The growl of the thunder was distant and passing away. The rain beat softly upon the shingles, inviting them to drowsiness and sleep. But they dared not yield.

### III

The rain was over; and the sun was turning the glistening green world into a palace of gems. Calixta, on the gallery, watched Alcée ride away. He turned and smiled at her with a beaming face; and she lifted her pretty chin in the air and laughed aloud.

3. Goodness! (French).
4. I.e., Assumption Parish, Louisiana, the setting for "At the 'Cadian Ball."

Bobinôt and Bibi, trudging home, stopped without at the cistern to make themselves presentable.

"My! Bibi, w'at will yo' mama say! You ought to be ashame'. You oughta' put on those good pants. Look at 'em! An' that mud on yo' collar! How you got that mud on yo' collar, Bibi? I never saw such a boy!" Bibi was the picture of pathetic resignation. Bobinôt was the embodiment of serious solicitude as he strove to remove from his own person and his son's the signs of their tramp over heavy roads and through wet fields. He scraped the mud off Bibi's bare legs and feet with a stick and carefully removed all traces from his heavy brogans. Then, prepared for the worst—the meeting with an over-scrupulous housewife, they entered cautiously at the back door.

Calixta was preparing supper. She had set the table and was dripping coffee at the hearth. She sprang up as they came in.

"Oh, Bobinôt! You back! My! but I was uneasy. W'ere you been during the rain? An' Bibi? he ain't wet? he ain't hurt?" She had clasped Bibi and was kissing him effusively. Bobinôt's explanations and apologies which he had been composing all along the way, died on his lips as Calixta felt him to see if he were dry, and seemed to express nothing but satisfaction at their safe return.

"I brought you some shrimps, Calixta," offered Bobinôt, hauling the can from his ample side pocket and laying it on the table.

"Shrimps! Oh, Bobinôt! you too good fo' anything!" and she gave him a smacking kiss on the cheek that resounded, "*J'vous réponds,*[5] we'll have a feas' to night! umph-umph!"

Bobinôt and Bibi began to relax and enjoy themselves, and when the three seated themselves at table they laughed much and so loud that anyone might have heard them as far away as Laballière's.

IV

Alcée Laballière wrote to his wife, Clarisse, that night. It was a loving letter, full of tender solicitude. He told her not to hurry back, but if she and the babies liked it at Biloxi, to stay a month longer. He was getting on nicely; and though he missed them, he was willing to bear the separation a while longer—realizing that their health and pleasure were the first things to be considered.

V

As for Clarisse, she was charmed upon receiving her husband's letter. She and the babies were doing well. The society was agreeable; many of her old friends and acquaintances were at the bay. And the first free breath since her marriage seemed to restore the pleasant liberty of her maiden days. Devoted as she was to her husband, their intimate conjugal life was something which she was more than willing to forego for a while.

So the storm passed and every one was happy.

1898                                                                                          1969

---

5. I promise you (French).

# The Awakening

## I

A green and yellow parrot, which hung in a cage outside the door, kept repeating over and over:

"*Allez vous-en! Allez vous-en! Sapristi!*[1] That's all right!"

He could speak a little Spanish, and also a language which nobody understood, unless it was the mocking-bird that hung on the other side of the door, whistling his fluty notes out upon the breeze with maddening persistence.

Mr. Pontellier, unable to read his newspaper with any degree of comfort, arose with an expression and an exclamation of disgust. He walked down the gallery and across the narrow "bridges" which connected the Lebrun cottages one with the other. He had been seated before the door of the main house. The parrot and the mocking-bird were the property of Madame Lebrun, and they had the right to make all the noise they wished. Mr. Pontellier had the privilege of quitting their society when they ceased to be entertaining.

He stopped before the door of his own cottage, which was the fourth one from the main building and next to the last. Seating himself in a wicker rocker which was there, he once more applied himself to the task of reading the newspaper. The day was Sunday; the paper was a day old. The Sunday papers had not yet reached Grand Isle.[2] He was already acquainted with the market reports, and he glanced restlessly over the editorials and bits of news which he had not had time to read before quitting New Orleans the day before.

Mr. Pontellier wore eye-glasses. He was a man of forty, of medium height and rather slender build; he stooped a little. His hair was brown and straight, parted on one side. His beard was neatly and closely trimmed.

Once in a while he withdrew his glance from the newspaper and looked about him. There was more noise than ever over at the house. The main building was called "the house," to distinguish it from the cottages. The chattering and whistling birds were still at it. Two young girls, the Farival twins, were playing a duet from "Zampa"[3] upon the piano. Madame Lebrun was bustling in and out, giving orders in a high key to a yard-boy whenever she got inside the house, and directions in an equally high voice to a dining-room servant whenever she got outside. She was a fresh, pretty woman, clad always in white with elbow sleeves. Her starched skirts crinkled as she came and went. Farther down, before one of the cottages, a lady in black was walking demurely up and down, telling her beads. A good many persons of the *pension* had gone over to the *Chênière Caminada* in Beaudelet's lugger[4] to hear mass. Some young people were out under the water-oaks playing croquet. Mr. Pontellier's two children were there—sturdy little fellows of four and five. A quadroon[5] nurse followed them about with a far-away, meditative air.

Mr. Pontellier finally lit a cigar and began to smoke, letting the paper drag idly from his hand. He fixed his gaze upon a white sunshade[6] that was advanc-

1. Go away! Go away! For God's sake! (French).
2. A resort island, fifty miles south of New Orleans, between the Gulf of Mexico and Caminada Bay.
3. Romantic opera by Louis Hérold (1791–1833).
4. Passenger boat. *"Pension"*: a bed-and-board hotel. *"Chênière Caminada"*: an island between Grande Isle and the Louisiana coast.
5. A person with one-quarter ("quad") black ancestry.
6. I.e., parasol.

ing at snail's pace from the beach. He could see it plainly between the gaunt trunks of the water-oaks and across the stretch of yellow camomile. The gulf looked far away, melting hazily into the blue of the horizon. The sunshade continued to approach slowly. Beneath its pink-lined shelter were his wife, Mrs. Pontellier, and young Robert Lebrun. When they reached the cottage, the two seated themselves with some appearance of fatigue upon the step of the porch, facing each other, each leaning against a supporting post.

"What folly! to bathe at such an hour in such heat!" exclaimed Mr. Pontellier. He himself had taken a plunge at daylight. That was why the morning seemed long to him.

"You are burnt beyond recognition," he added, looking at his wife as one looks at a valuable piece of personal property which has suffered some damage. She held up her hands, strong, shapely hands, and surveyed them critically, drawing up her lawn[7] sleeves above the wrists. Looking at them reminded her of her rings, which she had given to her husband before leaving for the beach. She silently reached out to him, and he, understanding, took the rings from his vest pocket and dropped them into her open palm. She slipped them upon her fingers; then clasping her knees, she looked across at Robert and began to laugh. The rings sparkled upon her fingers. He sent back an answering smile.

"What is it?" asked Pontellier, looking lazily and amused from one to the other. It was some utter nonsense; some adventure out there in the water, and they both tried to relate it at once. It did not seem half so amusing when told. They realized this, and so did Mr. Pontellier. He yawned and stretched himself. Then he got up, saying he had half a mind to go over to Klein's hotel[8] and play a game of billiards.

"Come go along, Lebrun," he proposed to Robert. But Robert admitted quite frankly that he preferred to stay where he was and talk to Mrs. Pontellier.

"Well, send him about his business when he bores you, Edna," instructed her husband as he prepared to leave.

"Here, take the umbrella," she exclaimed, holding it out to him. He accepted the sunshade, and lifting it over his head descended the steps and walked away.

"Coming back to dinner?" his wife called after him. He halted a moment and shrugged his shoulders. He felt in his vest pocket; there was a ten-dollar bill there. He did not know; perhaps he would return for the early dinner and perhaps he would not. It all depended upon the company which he found over at Klein's and the size of "the game." He did not say this, but she understood it, and laughed, nodding good-by to him.

Both children wanted to follow their father when they saw him starting out. He kissed them and promised to bring them back bonbons and peanuts.

## II

Mrs. Pontellier's eyes were quick and bright; they were a yellowish brown, about the color of her hair. She had a way of turning them swiftly upon an

7. Fine linen or sheer muslin.
8. Probably based on Krantz's Hotel, a well-known establishment of the time.

object and holding them there as if lost in some inward maze of contemplation or thought.

Her eyebrows were a shade darker than her hair. They were thick and almost horizontal, emphasizing the depth of her eyes. She was rather handsome than beautiful. Her face was captivating by reason of a certain frankness of expression and a contradictory subtle play of features. Her manner was engaging.

Robert rolled a cigarette. He smoked cigarettes because he could not afford cigars, he said. He had a cigar in his pocket which Mr. Pontellier had presented him with, and he was saving it for his after-dinner smoke.

This seemed quite proper and natural on his part. In coloring he was not unlike his companion. A clean-shaven face made the resemblance more pronounced than it would otherwise have been. There rested no shadow of care upon his open countenance. His eyes gathered in and reflected the light and languor of the summer day.

Mrs. Pontellier reached over for a palmleaf fan that lay on the porch and began to fan herself, while Robert sent between his lips light puffs from his cigarette. They chatted incessantly: about the things around them; their amusing adventure out in the water—it had again assumed its entertaining aspect; about the wind, the trees, the people who had gone to the *Chênière*; about the children playing croquet under the oaks, and the Farival twins, who were now performing the overture to "The Poet and the Peasant."[9]

Robert talked a good deal about himself. He was very young, and did not know any better. Mrs. Pontellier talked a little about herself for the same reason. Each was interested in what the other said. Robert spoke of his intention to go to Mexico in the autumn, where fortune awaited him. He was always intending to go to Mexico, but some way never got there. Meanwhile he held on to his modest position in a mercantile house in New Orleans, where an equal familiarity with English, French and Spanish gave him no small value as a clerk and correspondent.

He was spending his summer vacation, as he always did, with his mother at Grand Isle. In former times, before Robert could remember, "the house" had been a summer luxury of the Lebruns. Now, flanked by its dozen or more cottages, which were always filled with exclusive visitors from the *"Quartier Français,"*[1] it enabled Madame Lebrun to maintain the easy and comfortable existence which appeared to be her birthright.

Mrs. Pontellier talked about her father's Mississippi plantation and her girlhood home in the old Kentucky blue-grass country. She was an American woman, with a small infusion of French which seemed to have been lost in dilution. She read a letter from her sister, who was away in the East, and who had engaged herself to be married. Robert was interested, and wanted to know what manner of girls the sisters were, what the father was like, and how long the mother had been dead.

When Mrs. Pontellier folded the letter it was time for her to dress for the early dinner.

"I see Léonce isn't coming back," she said, with a glance in the direction

9. An operetta by Franz von Suppé (1819–1895).
1. The French Quarter of New Orleans, settled by the French in the early 1700s and occupied by wealthy, older families.

whence her husband had disappeared. Robert supposed he was not, as there were a good many New Orleans club men over at Klein's.

When Mrs. Pontellier left him to enter her room, the young man descended the steps and strolled over toward the croquet players, where, during the half-hour before dinner, he amused himself with the little Pontellier children, who were very fond of him.

## III

It was eleven o'clock that night when Mr. Pontellier returned from Klein's hotel. He was in an excellent humor, in high spirits, and very talkative. His entrance awoke his wife, who was in bed and fast asleep when he came in. He talked to her while he undressed, telling her anecdotes and bits of news and gossip that he had gathered during the day. From his trousers pockets he took a fistful of crumpled bank notes and a good deal of silver coin, which he piled on the bureau indiscriminately with keys, knife, handkerchief, and whatever else happened to be in his pockets. She was overcome with sleep, and answered him with little half utterances.

He thought it very discouraging that his wife, who was the sole object of his existence, evinced so little interest in things which concerned him and valued so little his conversation.

Mr. Pontellier had forgotten the bonbons and peanuts for the boys. Notwithstanding he loved them very much, and went into the adjoining room where they slept to take a look at them and make sure that they were resting comfortably. The result of his investigation was far from satisfactory. He turned and shifted the youngsters about in bed. One of them began to kick and talk about a basket full of crabs.

Mr. Pontellier returned to his wife with the information that Raoul had a high fever and needed looking after. Then he lit a cigar and went and sat near the open door to smoke it.

Mrs. Pontellier was quite sure Raoul had no fever. He had gone to bed perfectly well, she said, and nothing had ailed him all day. Mr. Pontellier was too well acquainted with fever symptoms to be mistaken. He assured her the child was consuming[2] at that moment in the next room.

He reproached his wife with her inattention, her habitual neglect of the children. If it was not a mother's place to look after children, whose on earth was it? He himself had his hands full with his brokerage business. He could not be in two places at once; making a living for his family on the street, and staying at home to see that no harm befell them. He talked in a monotonous, insistent way.

Mrs. Pontellier sprang out of bed and went into the next room. She soon came back and sat on the edge of the bed, leaning her head down on the pillow. She said nothing, and refused to answer her husband when he questioned her. When his cigar was smoked out he went to bed, and in half a minute he was fast asleep.

Mrs. Pontellier was by that time thoroughly awake. She began to cry a little, and wiped her eyes on the sleeve of her *peignoir*. Blowing out the candle, which her husband had left burning, she slipped her bare feet into a pair of

2. I.e., feverish.

satin *mules* at the foot of the bed and went out on the porch, where she sat down in the wicker chair and began to rock gently to and fro.

It was then past midnight. The cottages were all dark. A single faint light gleamed out from the hallway of the house. There was no sound abroad except the hooting of an old owl in the top of a water-oak, and the everlasting voice of the sea, that was not uplifted at that soft hour. It broke like a mournful lullaby upon the night.

The tears came so fast to Mrs. Pontellier's eyes that the damp sleeve of her *peignoir* no longer served to dry them. She was holding the back of her chair with one hand; her loose sleeve had slipped almost to the shoulder of her uplifted arm. Turning, she thrust her face, steaming and wet, into the bend of her arm, and she went on crying there, not caring any longer to dry her face, her eyes, her arms. She could not have told why she was crying. Such experiences as the foregoing were not uncommon in her married life. They seemed never before to have weighed much against the abundance of her husband's kindness and a uniform devotion which had come to be tacit and self-understood.

An indescribable oppression, which seemed to generate in some unfamiliar part of her consciousness, filled her whole being with a vague anguish. It was like a shadow, like a mist passing across her soul's summer day. It was strange and unfamiliar; it was a mood. She did not sit there inwardly upbraiding her husband, lamenting at Fate, which had directed her footsteps to the path which they had taken. She was just having a good cry all to herself. The mosquitoes made merry over her, biting her firm, round arms and nipping at her bare insteps.

The little stinging, buzzing imps succeeded in dispelling a mood which might have held her there in the darkness half a night longer.

The following morning Mr. Pontellier was up in good time to take the rockaway[3] which was to convey him to the steamer at the wharf. He was returning to the city to his business, and they would not see him again at the Island till the coming Saturday. He had regained his composure, which seemed to have been somewhat impaired the night before. He was eager to be gone, as he looked forward to a lively week in Carondelet Street.[4]

Mr. Pontellier gave his wife half the money which he had brought away from Klein's hotel the evening before. She liked money as well as most women, and accepted it with no little satisfaction.

"It will buy a handsome wedding present for Sister Janet!" she exclaimed, smoothing out the bills as she counted them one by one.

"Oh! we'll treat Sister Janet better than that, my dear," he laughed, as he prepared to kiss her good-by.

The boys were tumbling about, clinging to his legs, imploring that numerous things be brought back to them. Mr. Pontellier was a great favorite, and ladies, men, children, even nurses, were always on hand to say good-by to him. His wife stood smiling and waving, the boys shouting, as he disappeared in the old rockaway down the sandy road.

A few days later a box arrived for Mrs. Pontellier from New Orleans. It was from her husband. It was filled with *friandises,* with luscious and toothsome

---

3. A four-wheeled carriage (manufactured in Rockaway, New Jersey).

4. New Orleans's equivalent of Wall Street, and the location of the Cotton Exchange.

bits—the finest of fruits, *patés*, a rare bottle or two, delicious syrups, and bonbons in abundance.

Mrs. Pontellier was always very generous with the contents of such a box; she was quite used to receiving them when away from home. The *patés* and fruit were brought to the dining-room; the bonbons were passed around. And the ladies, selecting with dainty and discriminating fingers and a little greedily, all declared that Mr. Pontellier was the best husband in the world. Mrs. Pontellier was forced to admit that she knew of none better.

## IV

It would have been a difficult matter for Mr. Pontellier to define to his own satisfaction or any one else's wherein his wife failed in her duty toward their children. It was something which he felt rather than perceived, and he never voiced the feeling without subsequent regret and ample atonement.

If one of the little Pontellier boys took a tumble whilst at play, he was not apt to rush crying to his mother's arms for comfort; he would more likely pick himself up, wipe the water out of his eyes and the sand out of his mouth, and go on playing. Tots as they were, they pulled together and stood their ground in childish battles with doubled fists and uplifted voices, which usually prevailed against the other mother-tots. The quadroon nurse was looked upon as a huge encumbrance, only good to button up waists and panties and to brush and part hair; since it seemed to be a law of society that hair must be parted and brushed.

In short, Mrs. Pontellier was not a mother-woman. The mother-women seemed to prevail that summer at Grand Isle. It was easy to know them, fluttering about with extended, protecting wings when any harm, real or imaginary, threatened their precious brood. They were women who idolized their children, worshiped their husbands, and esteemed it a holy privilege to efface themselves as individuals and grow wings as ministering angels.

Many of them were delicious in the rôle; one of them was the embodiment of every womanly grace and charm. If her husband did not adore her, he was a brute, deserving of death by slow torture. Her name was Adèle Ratignolle. There are no words to describe her save the old ones that have served so often to picture the bygone heroine of romance and the fair lady of our dreams. There was nothing subtle or hidden about her charms; her beauty was all there, flaming and apparent: the spun-gold hair that comb nor confining pin could restrain; the blue eyes that were like nothing but sapphires; two lips that pouted, that were so red one could only think of cherries or some other delicious crimson fruit in looking at them. She was growing a little stout, but it did not seem to detract an iota from the grace of every step, pose, gesture. One would not have wanted her white neck a mite less full or her beautiful arms more slender. Never were hands more exquisite than hers, and it was a joy to look at them when she threaded her needle or adjusted her gold thimble to her taper[5] middle finger as she sewed away on the little night-drawers or fashioned a bodice or a bib.

Madame Ratignolle was very fond of Mrs. Pontellier, and often she took her sewing and went over to sit with her in the afternoons. She was sitting there

5. I.e., tapered.

the afternoon of the day the box arrived from New Orleans. She had possession of the rocker, and she was busily engaged in sewing upon a diminutive pair of night-drawers.

She had brought the pattern of the drawers for Mrs. Pontellier to cut out—a marvel of construction, fashioned to enclose a baby's body so effectually that only two small eyes might look out from the garment, like an Eskimo's. They were designed for winter wear, when treacherous drafts came down chimneys and insidious currents of deadly cold found their way through keyholes.

Mrs. Pontellier's mind was quite at rest concerning the present material needs of her children, and she could not see the use of anticipating and making winter night garments the subject of her summer meditations. But she did not want to appear unamiable and uninterested, so she had brought forth newspapers which she spread upon the floor of the gallery, and under Madame Ratignolle's directions she had cut a pattern of the impervious garment.

Robert was there, seated as he had been the Sunday before, and Mrs. Pontellier also occupied her former position on the upper step, leaning listlessly against the post. Beside her was a box of bonbons, which she held out at intervals to Madame Ratignolle.

That lady seemed at a loss to make a selection, but finally settled upon a stick of nugat, wondering if it were not too rich; whether it could possibly hurt her. Madame Ratignolle had been married seven years. About every two years she had a baby. At that time she had three babies, and was beginning to think of a fourth one. She was always talking about her "condition." Her "condition" was in no way apparent, and no one would have known a thing about it but for her persistence in making it the subject of conversation.

Robert started to reassure her, asserting that he had known a lady who had subsisted upon nugat during the entire—but seeing the color mount into Mrs. Pontellier's face he checked himself and changed the subject.

Mrs. Pontellier, though she had married a Creole,[6] was not thoroughly at home in the society of Creoles; never before had she been thrown so intimately among them. There were only Creoles that summer at Lebrun's. They all knew each other, and felt like one large family, among whom existed the most amicable relations. A characteristic which distinguished them and which impressed Mrs. Pontellier most forcibly was their entire absence of prudery. Their freedom of expression was at first incomprehensible to her, though she had no difficulty in reconciling it with a lofty chastity which in the Creole woman seems to be inborn and unmistakable.

Never would Edna Pontellier forget the shock with which she heard Madame Ratignolle relating to old Monsieur Farival the harrowing story of one of her *accouchements*,[7] withholding no intimate detail. She was growing accustomed to like shocks, but she could not keep the mounting color back from her cheeks. Oftener than once her coming had interrupted the droll story with which Robert was entertaining some amused group of married women.

A book had gone the rounds of the *pension*. When it came her turn to read

---

6. A person descended from the original French and Spanish settlers of New Orleans, thus, at this time, an aristocrat.
7. The birth of one of her children.

it, she did so with profound astonishment. She felt moved to read the book in secret and solitude, though none of the others had done so—to hide it from view at the sound of approaching footsteps. It was openly criticised and freely discussed at table. Mrs. Pontellier gave over being astonished, and concluded that wonders would never cease.

## V

They formed a congenial group sitting there that summer afternoon—Madame Ratignolle sewing away, often stopping to relate a story or incident with much expressive gesture of her perfect hands; Robert and Mrs. Pontellier sitting idle, exchanging occasional words, glances or smiles which indicated a certain advanced stage of intimacy and *camaraderie*.

He had lived in her shadow during the past month. No one thought anything of it. Many had predicted that Robert would devote himself to Mrs. Pontellier when he arrived. Since the age of fifteen, which was eleven years before, Robert each summer at Grand Isle had constituted himself the devoted attendant of some fair dame or damsel. Sometimes it was a young girl, again a widow; but as often as not it was some interesting married woman.

For two consecutive seasons he lived in the sunlight of Mademoiselle Duvigné's presence. But she died between summers; then Robert posed as an inconsolable, prostrating himself at the feet of Madame Ratignolle for whatever crumbs of sympathy and comfort she might be pleased to vouchsafe.

Mrs. Pontellier liked to sit and gaze at her fair companion as she might look upon a faultless Madonna.

"Could any one fathom the cruelty beneath that fair exterior?" murmured Robert. "She knew that I adored her once, and she let me adore her. It was 'Robert, come; go; stand up; sit down; do this; do that; see if the baby sleeps; my thimble, please, that I left God knows where. Come and read Daudet[8] to me while I sew.' "

"*Par exemple!*[9] I never had to ask. You were always there under my feet, like a troublesome cat."

"You mean like an adoring dog. And just as soon as Ratignolle appeared on the scene, then it *was* like a dog. '*Passez! Adieu! Allez vous-en!*' "[1]

"Perhaps I feared to make Alphonse jealous," she interjoined, with excessive naïveté. That made them all laugh. The right hand jealous of the left! The heart jealous of the soul! But for that matter, the Creole husband is never jealous; with him the gangrene passion is one which has become dwarfed by disuse.

Meanwhile Robert, addressing Mrs. Pontellier, continued to tell of his one time hopeless passion for Madame Ratignolle; of sleepless nights, of consuming flames till the very sea sizzled when he took his daily plunge. While the lady at the needle kept up a little running, contemptuous comment:

"*Blagueur—farceur—gros bête, va!*"[2]

He never assumed this serio-comic tone when alone with Mrs. Pontellier. She never knew precisely what to make of it; at that moment it was impossi-

---

8. Alphonse Daudet (1840–1887), French novelist.
9. For example (French, literal trans.); here, "For goodness' sake!"
1. Go on! Good-bye! Go away! (French).
2. Liar—comedian—silly, come off it! (French).

ble for her to guess how much of it was jest and what proportion was earnest. It was understood that he had often spoken words of love to Madame Ratignolle, without any thought of being taken seriously. Mrs. Pontellier was glad he had not assumed a similar rôle toward herself. It would have been unacceptable and annoying.

Mrs. Pontellier had brought her sketching materials, which she sometimes dabbled with in an unprofessional way. She liked the dabbling. She felt in it satisfaction of a kind which no other employment afforded her.

She had long wished to try herself on Madame Ratignolle. Never had that lady seemed a more tempting subject than at that moment, seated there like some sensuous Madonna, with the gleam of the fading day enriching her splendid color.

Robert crossed over and seated himself upon the step below Mrs. Pontellier, that he might watch her work. She handled her brushes with a certain ease and freedom which came, not from long and close acquaintance with them, but from a natural aptitude. Robert followed her work with close attention, giving forth little ejaculatory expressions of appreciation in French, which he addressed to Madame Ratignolle.

*"Mais ce n'est pas mal! Elle s'y connait, elle a de la force, oui."*[3]

During his oblivious attention he once quietly rested his head against Mrs. Pontellier's arm. As gently she repulsed him. Once again he repeated the offense. She could not but believe it to be thoughtlessness on his part; yet that was no reason she should submit to it. She did not remonstrate, except again to repulse him quietly but firmly. He offered no apology.

The picture completed bore no resemblance to Madame Ratignolle. She was greatly disappointed to find that it did not look like her. But it was a fair enough piece of work, and in many respects satisfying.

Mrs. Pontellier evidently did not think so. After surveying the sketch critically she drew a broad smudge of paint across its surface, and crumpled the paper between her hands.

The youngsters came tumbling up the steps, the quadroon following at the respectful distance which they required her to observe. Mrs. Pontellier made them carry her paints and things into the house. She sought to detain them for a little talk and some pleasantry. But they were greatly in earnest. They had only come to investigate the contents of the bonbon box. They accepted without murmuring what she chose to give them, each holding out two chubby hands scoop-like, in the vain hope that they might be filled; and then away they went.

The sun was low in the west, and the breeze soft and languorous that came up from the south, charged with the seductive odor of the sea. Children, freshly befurbeloved,[4] were gathering for their games under the oaks. Their voices were high and penetrating.

Madame Ratignolle folded her sewing, placing thimble, scissors and thread all neatly together in the roll, which she pinned securely. She complained of faintness. Mrs. Pontellier flew for the cologne water and a fan. She bathed Madame Ratignolle's face with cologne, while Robert plied the fan with unnecessary vigor.

3. Not bad at all! She knows what she's doing, she has talent (French).

4. Dressed up in petticoats.

The spell was soon over, and Mrs. Pontellier could not help wondering if there were not a little imagination responsible for its origin, for the rose tint had never faded from her friend's face.

She stood watching the fair woman walk down the long line of galleries with the grace and majesty which queens are sometimes supposed to possess. Her little ones ran to meet her. Two of them clung about her white skirts, the third she took from its nurse and with a thousand endearments bore it along in her own fond, encircling arms. Though, as everybody well knew, the doctor had forbidden her to lift so much as a pin!

"Are you going bathing?" asked Robert of Mrs. Pontellier. It was not so much a question as a reminder.

"Oh, no," she answered, with a tone of indecision. "I'm tired; I think not." Her glance wandered from his face away toward the Gulf, whose sonorous murmur reached her like a loving but imperative entreaty.

"Oh, come!" he insisted. "You mustn't miss your bath. Come on. The water must be delicious; it will not hurt you. Come."

He reached up for her big, rough straw hat that hung on a peg outside the door, and put it on her head. They descended the steps, and walked away together toward the beach. The sun was low in the west and the breeze was soft and warm.

## VI

Edna Pontellier could not have told why, wishing to go to the beach with Robert, she should in the first place have declined, and in the second place have followed in obedience to one of the two contradictory impulses which impelled her.

A certain light was beginning to dawn dimly within her,—the light which, showing the way, forbids it.

At that early period it served but to bewilder her. It moved her to dreams, to thoughtfulness, to the shadowy anguish which had overcome her the midnight when she had abandoned herself to tears.

In short, Mrs. Pontellier was beginning to realize her position in the universe as a human being, and to recognize her relations as an individual to the world within and about her. This may seem like a ponderous weight of wisdom to descend upon the soul of a young woman of twenty-eight—perhaps more wisdom than the Holy Ghost is usually pleased to vouchsafe to any woman.

But the beginning of things, of a world especially, is necessarily vague, tangled, chaotic, and exceedingly disturbing. How few of us ever emerge from such beginning! How many souls perish in its tumult!

The voice of the sea is seductive; never ceasing, whispering, clamoring, murmuring, inviting the soul to wander for a spell in abysses of solitude; to lose itself in mazes of inward contemplation.

The voice of the sea speaks to the soul. The touch of the sea is sensuous, enfolding the body in its soft, close embrace.

## VII

Mrs. Pontellier was not a woman given to confidences, a characteristic hitherto contrary to her nature. Even as a child she had lived her own small life all within herself. At a very early period she had apprehended instinctively the dual life—that outward existence which conforms, the inward life which questions.

That summer at Grand Isle she began to loosen a little the mantle of reserve that had always enveloped her. There may have been—there must have been—influences, both subtle and apparent, working in their several ways to induce her to do this; but the most obvious was the influence of Adèle Ratignolle. The excessive physical charm of the Creole had first attracted her, for Edna had a sensuous susceptibility to beauty. Then the candor of the woman's whole existence, which every one might read, and which formed so striking a contrast to her own habitual reserve—this might have furnished a link. Who can tell what metals the gods use in forging the subtle bond which we call sympathy, which we might as well call love.

The two women went away one morning to the beach together, arm in arm, under the huge white sunshade. Edna had prevailed upon Madame Ratignolle to leave the children behind, though she could not induce her to relinquish a diminutive roll of needlework, which Adèle begged to be allowed to slip into the depths of her pocket. In some unaccountable way they had escaped from Robert.

The walk to the beach was no inconsiderable one, consisting as it did of a long, sandy path, upon which a sporadic and tangled growth that bordered it on either side made frequent and unexpected inroads. There were acres of yellow camomile reaching out on either hand. Further away still, vegetable gardens abounded, with frequent small plantations of orange or lemon trees intervening. The dark green clusters glistened from afar in the sun.

The women were both of goodly height, Madame Ratignolle possessing the more feminine and matronly figure. The charm of Edna Pontellier's physique stole insensibly upon you. The lines of her body were long, clean and symmetrical; it was a body which occasionally fell into splendid poses; there was no suggestion of the trim, stereotyped fashion-plate about it. A casual and indiscriminating observer, in passing, might not cast a second glance upon the figure. But with more feeling and discernment he would have recognized the noble beauty of its modeling, and the graceful severity of poise and movement, which made Edna Pontellier different from the crowd.

She wore a cool muslin that morning—white, with a waving vertical line of brown running through it; also a white linen collar and the big straw hat which she had taken from the peg outside the door. The hat rested any way on her yellow-brown hair, that waved a little, was heavy, and clung close to her head.

Madame Ratignolle, more careful of her complexion, had twined a gauze veil about her head. She wore doeskin gloves, white gauntlets that protected her wrists. She was dressed in pure white, with a fluffiness of ruffles that became her. The draperies and fluttering things which she wore suited her rich, luxuriant beauty as a greater severity of line could not have done.

There were a number of bath-houses along the beach, of rough but solid construction, built with small, protecting galleries facing the water. Each house consisted of two compartments, and each family at Lebrun's possessed a compartment for itself, fitted out with all the essential paraphernalia of the bath and whatever other conveniences the owners might desire. The two women had no intention of bathing; they had just strolled down to the beach for a walk and to be alone and near the water. The Pontellier and Ratignolle compartments adjoined one another under the same roof.

Mrs. Pontellier had brought down her key through force of habit. Unlocking the door of her bath-room she went inside, and soon emerged, bringing a rug,[5] which she spread upon the floor of the gallery, and two huge hair pillows covered with crash,[6] which she placed against the front of the building.

The two seated themselves there in the shade of the porch, side by side, with their backs against the pillows and their feet extended. Madame Ratignolle removed her veil, wiped her face with a rather delicate handkerchief, and fanned herself with the fan which she always carried suspended somewhere about her person by a long, narrow ribbon. Edna removed her collar and opened her dress at the throat. She took the fan from Madame Ratignolle and began to fan both herself and her companion. It was very warm, and for a while they did nothing but exchange remarks about the heat, the sun, the glare. But there was a breeze blowing, a choppy stiff wind that whipped the water into froth. It fluttered the skirts of the two women and kept them for a while engaged in adjusting, readjusting, tucking in, securing hair-pins and hat-pins. A few persons were sporting some distance away in the water. The beach was very still of human sound at that hour. The lady in black was reading her morning devotions on the porch of a neighboring bath-house. Two young lovers were exchanging their hearts' yearnings beneath the children's tent, which they had found unoccupied.

Edna Pontellier, casting her eyes about had finally kept them at rest upon the sea. The day was clear and carried the gaze out as far as the blue sky went; there were a few white clouds suspended idly over the horizon. A lateen[7] sail was visible in the direction of Cat Island, and others to the south seemed almost motionless in the far distance.

"Of whom—of what are you thinking?" asked Adèle of her companion, whose countenance she had been watching with a little amused attention, arrested by the absorbed expression which seemed to have seized and fixed every feature into a statuesque repose.

"Nothing," returned Mrs. Pontellier, with a start, adding at once: "How stupid! But it seems to me it is the reply we make instinctively to such a question. Let me see," she went on, throwing back her head and narrowing her fine eyes till they shone like two vivid points of light. "Let me see. I was really not conscious of thinking of anything; but perhaps I can retrace my thoughts."

"Oh! never mind!" laughed Madame Ratignolle. "I am not quite so exacting. I will let you off this time. It is really too hot to think, especially to think about thinking."

"But for the fun of it," persisted Edna. "First of all, the sight of the water stretching so far away, those motionless sails against the blue sky, made a delicious picture that I just wanted to sit and look at. The hot wind beating in my face made me think—without any connection that I can trace—of a summer day in Kentucky, of a meadow that seemed as big as the ocean to the very little girl walking through the grass, which was higher than her waist. She threw

5. Blanket.
6. Heavy linen fabric.

7. Triangular sail extended by a long spar that is slung to a usually low mast.

out her arms as if swimming when she walked, beating the tall grass as one strikes out in the water. Oh, I see the connection now!"

"Where were you going that day in Kentucky, walking through the grass?"

"I don't remember now. I was just walking diagonally across a big field. My sun-bonnet obstructed the view. I could see only the stretch of green before me, and I felt as if I must walk on forever, without coming to the end of it. I don't remember whether I was frightened or pleased. I must have been entertained."

"Likely as not it was Sunday," she laughed; "and I was running away from prayers, from the Presbyterian service, read in a spirit of gloom by my father that chills me yet to think of."

"And have you been running away from prayers ever since, *ma chère?*" asked Madame Ratignolle, amused.

"No! oh, no!" Edna hastened to say. "I was a little unthinking child in those days, just following a misleading impulse without question. On the contrary, during one period of my life religion took a firm hold upon me; after I was twelve and until—until—why, I suppose until now, though I never thought much about it—just driven along by habit. But do you know," she broke off, turning her quick eyes upon Madame Ratignolle and leaning forward a little so as to bring her face quite close to that of her companion, "sometimes I feel this summer as if I were walking through the green meadow again; idly, aimlessly, unthinking and unguided."

Madame Ratignolle laid her hand over that of Mrs. Pontellier, which was near her. Seeing that the hand was not withdrawn, she clasped it firmly and warmly. She even stroked it a little, fondly, with the other hand, murmuring in an undertone, *"Pauvre chérie."*[8]

The action was at first a little confusing to Edna, but she soon lent herself readily to the Creole's gentle caress. She was not accustomed to an outward and spoken expression of affection, either in herself or in others. She and her younger sister, Janet, had quarreled a good deal through force of unfortunate habit. Her older sister, Margaret, was matronly and dignified, probably from having assumed matronly and house-wifely responsibilities too early in life, their mother having died when they were quite young. Margaret was not effusive; she was practical. Edna had had an occasional girl friend, but whether accidentally or not, they seemed to have been all of one type—the self-contained. She never realized that the reserve of her own character had much, perhaps everything, to do with this. Her most intimate friend at school had been one of rather exceptional intellectual gifts, who wrote fine-sounding essays, which Edna admired and strove to imitate; and with her she talked and glowed over the English classics, and sometimes held religious and political controversies.

Edna often wondered at one propensity which sometimes had inwardly disturbed her without causing any outward show or manifestation on her part. At a very early age—perhaps it was when she traversed the ocean of waving grass—she remembered that she had been passionately enamored of a dignified and sad-eyed cavalry officer who visited her father in Kentucky. She could not leave his presence when he was there, nor remove her eyes from

8. Poor dear (French).

his face, which was something like Napoleon's, with a lock of black hair falling across the forehead. But the cavalry officer melted imperceptibly out of her existence.

At another time her affections were deeply engaged by a young gentleman who visited a lady on a neighboring plantation. It was after they went to Mississippi to live. The young man was engaged to be married to the young lady, and they sometimes called upon Margaret, driving over of afternoons in a buggy. Edna was a little miss, just merging into her teens; and the realization that she herself was nothing, nothing, nothing to the engaged young man was a bitter affliction to her. But he, too, went the way of dreams.

She was a grown young woman when she was overtaken by what she supposed to be the climax of her fate. It was when the face and figure of a great tragedian[9] began to haunt her imagination and stir her senses. The persistence of the infatuation lent it an aspect of genuineness. The hopelessness of it colored it with the lofty tones of a great passion.

The picture of the tragedian stood enframed upon her desk. Any one may possess the portrait of a tragedian without exciting suspicion or comment. (This was a sinister reflection which she cherished.) In the presence of others she expressed admiration for his exalted gifts, as she handed the photograph around and dwelt upon the fidelity of the likeness. When alone she sometimes picked it up and kissed the cold glass passionately.

Her marriage to Léonce Pontellier was purely an accident, in this respect resembling many other marriages which masquerade as the decrees of Fate. It was in the midst of her secret great passion that she met him. He fell in love, as men are in the habit of doing, and pressed his suit with an earnestness and an ardor which left nothing to be desired. He pleased her; his absolute devotion flattered her. She fancied there was a sympathy of thought and taste between them, in which fancy she was mistaken. Add to this the violent opposition of her father and her sister Margaret to her marriage with a Catholic, and we need seek no further for the motives which led her to accept Monsieur Pontellier for her husband.

The acme of bliss, which would have been a marriage with the tragedian, was not for her in this world. As the devoted wife of a man who worshiped her, she felt she would take her place with a certain dignity in the world of reality, closing the portals forever behind her upon the realm of romance and dreams.

But it was not long before the tragedian had gone to join the cavalry officer and the engaged young man and a few others; and Edna found herself face to face with the realities. She grew fond of her husband, realizing with some unaccountable satisfaction that no trace of passion or excessive and fictitious warmth colored her affection, thereby threatening its dissolution.

She was fond of her children in an uneven, impulsive way. She would sometimes gather them passionately to her heart; she would sometimes forget them. The year before they had spent part of the summer with their grandmother Pontellier in Iberville. Feeling secure regarding their happiness and welfare, she did not miss them except with an occasional intense longing. Their absence was a sort of relief, though she did not admit this, even to

9. Perhaps Edwin Booth (1833–1893), the Shakespearean actor particularly acclaimed for his Hamlet.

eemed to free her of a responsibility which she had blindly
ed for which Fate had not fitted her.

herself
as
d not reveal so much as all this to Madame Ratignolle that sum-
when they sat with faces turned to the sea. But a good part of it
her. She had put her head down on Madame Ratignolle's shoulder.
s flushed and felt intoxicated with the sound of her own voice and the
astomed taste of candor. It muddled her like wine, or like a first breath
edom.

here was the sound of approaching voices. It was Robert, surrounded by
oop of children, searching for them. The two little Pontelliers were with
him, and he carried Madame Ratignolle's little girl in his arms. There were
other children beside, and two nursemaids followed, looking disagreeable and
resigned.

The women at once rose and began to shake out their draperies and relax
their muscles. Mrs. Pontellier threw the cushions and rug into the bath-
house. The children all scampered off to the awning, and they stood there in
a line, gazing upon the intruding lovers, still exchanging their vows and sighs.
The lovers got up, with only a silent protest, and walked slowly away somewhere else.

The children possessed themselves of the tent, and Mrs. Pontellier went
over to join them.

Madame Ratignolle begged Robert to accompany her to the house; she
complained of cramp in her limbs and stiffness of the joints. She leaned drag-
gingly upon his arm as they walked.

## VIII

"Do me a favor, Robert," spoke the pretty woman at his side, almost as soon
as she and Robert had started on their slow, homeward way. She looked up
in his face, leaning on his arm beneath the encircling shadow of the umbrella
which he had lifted.

"Granted; as many as you like," he returned, glancing down into her eyes
that were full of thoughtfulness and some speculation.

"I only ask for one; let Mrs. Pontellier alone."

"*Tiens!*" he exclaimed, with a sudden, boyish laugh. "*Voilà que Madame
Ratignolle est jalouse!*"[1]

"Nonsense! I'm in earnest; I mean what I say. Let Mrs. Pontellier alone."

"Why?" he asked; himself growing serious at his companion's solicitation.

"She is not one of us; she is not like us. She might make the unfortunate
blunder of taking you seriously."

His face flushed with annoyance, and taking off his soft hat he began to
beat it impatiently against his leg as he walked. "Why shouldn't she take me
seriously?" he demanded sharply. "Am I a comedian, a clown, a jack-in-the-
box? Why shouldn't she? You Creoles! I have no patience with you! Am I
always to be regarded as a feature of an amusing programme? I hope Mrs.
Pontellier does take me seriously. I hope she has discernment enough to find
in me something besides the *blagueur*.[2] If I thought there was any doubt—"

1. So, Madame Ratignolle is jealous! (French).   2. Joker (French).

"Oh, enough, Robert!" she broke into his heated outburst. "Yo thinking of what you are saying. You speak with about as little refle we might expect from one of those children down there playing in the If your attentions to any married women here were ever offered with intention of being convincing, you would not be the gentleman we all kn you to be, and you would be unfit to associate with the wives and daughter of the people who trust you."

Madame Ratignolle had spoken what she believed to be the law and the gospel. The young man shrugged his shoulders impatiently.

"Oh! well! That isn't it," slamming his hat down vehemently upon his head. "You ought to feel that such things are not flattering to say to a fellow."

"Should our whole intercourse consist of an exchange of compliments? *Ma foi!*"[3]

"It isn't pleasant to have a woman tell you—" he went on, unheedingly, but breaking off suddenly: "Now if I were like Arobin—you remember Alcée Arobin and that story of the consul's wife at Biloxi?"[4] And he related the story of Alcée Arobin and the consul's wife; and another about the tenor of the French Opera,[5] who received letters which should never have been written; and still other stories, grave and gay, till Mrs. Pontellier and her possible propensity for taking young men seriously was apparently forgotten.

Madame Ratignolle, when they had regained her cottage, went in to take the hour's rest which she considered helpful. Before leaving her, Robert begged her pardon for the impatience—he called it rudeness—with which he had received her well-meant caution.

"You made one mistake, Adèle," he said, with a light smile; "there is no earthly possibility of Mrs. Pontellier ever taking me seriously. You should have warned me against taking myself seriously. Your advice might then have carried some weight and given me subject for some reflection. *Au revoir*. But you look tired," he added, solicitously. "Would you like a cup of bouillon? Shall I stir you a toddy? Let me mix you a toddy with a drop of Angostura."[6]

She acceded to the suggestion of bouillon, which was grateful and acceptable. He went himself to the kitchen, which was a building apart from the cottages and lying to the rear of the house. And he himself brought her the golden-brown bouillon, in a dainty Sèvres[7] cup, with a flaky cracker or two on the saucer.

She thrust a bare, white arm from the curtain which shielded her open door, and received the cup from his hands. She told him he was a *bon garcon*,[8] and she meant it. Robert thanked her and turned away toward "the house."

The lovers were just entering the grounds of the *pension*. They were leaning toward each other as the water-oaks bent from the sea. There was not a particle of earth beneath their feet. Their heads might have been turned upside-down, so absolutely did they tread upon blue ether. The lady in black, creeping behind them, looked a trifle paler and more jaded than usual. There was no sign of Mrs. Pontellier and the children. Robert scanned the distance

3. For heaven's sake! (French).
4. A coastal resort town in Mississippi near New Orleans.
5. The French Opera in New Orleans, perhaps the most distinguished opera company in 19th-century America.
6. Aromatic bitters.
7. Fine porcelain made in Sèvres, France.
8. The French phrase means both "nice fellow" and "good waiter."

for any such apparition. They would doubtless remain away till the dinner hour. The young man ascended to his mother's room. It was situated at the top of the house, made up of odd angles and a queer, sloping ceiling. Two broad dormer windows looked out toward the Gulf, and as far across it as a man's eye might reach. The furnishings of the room were light, cool, and practical.

Madame Lebrun was busily engaged at the sewing-machine. A little black girl sat on the floor, and with her hands worked the treadle of the machine. The Creole woman does not take any chances which may be avoided of imperiling her health.

Robert went over and seated himself on the broad sill of one of the dormer windows. He took a book from his pocket and began energetically to read it, judging by the precision and frequency with which he turned the leaves. The sewing-machine made a resounding clatter in the room; it was of a ponderous, by-gone make. In the lulls, Robert and his mother exchanged bits of desultory conversation.

"Where is Mrs. Pontellier?"

"Down at the beach with the children."

"I promised to lend her the Goncourt.[9] Don't forget to take it down when you go; it's there on the bookshelf over the small table." Clatter, clatter, clatter, bang! for the next five or eight minutes.

"Where is Victor going with the rockaway?"

"The rockaway? Victor?"

"Yes; down there in front. He seems to be getting ready to drive away somewhere."

"Call him." Clatter, clatter!

Robert uttered a shrill, piercing whistle which might have been heard back at the wharf.

"He won't look up."

Madame Lebrun flew to the window. She called "Victor!" She waved a handkerchief and called again. The young fellow below got into the vehicle and started the horse off at a gallop.

Madame Lebrun went back to the machine, crimson with annoyance. Victor was the younger son and brother—a *tête montée*,[1] with a temper which invited violence and a will which no ax could break.

"Whenever you say the word I'm ready to thrash any amount of reason into him that he's able to hold."

"If your father had only lived!" Clatter, clatter, clatter, clatter, bang! It was a fixed belief with Madame Lebrun that the conduct of the universe and all things pertaining thereto would have been manifestly of a more intelligent and higher order had not Monsieur Lebrun been removed to other spheres during the early years of their married life.

"What do you hear from Montel?" Montel was a middle-aged gentleman whose vain ambition and desire for the past twenty years had been to fill the void which Monsieur Lebrun's taking off had left in the Lebrun household. Clatter, clatter, bang, clatter!

"I have a letter somewhere," looking in the machine drawer and finding the

---

9. A novel by the French writer Edmond de Goncourt (1822–1896).

1. Impulsive character (French).

letter in the bottom of the work-basket. "He says to tell you he will be in Vera Cruz[2] the beginning of next month"—clatter, clatter!—"and if you still have the intention of joining him"—bang! clatter, clatter, bang!

"Why didn't you tell me so before, mother? You know I wanted—" Clatter, clatter, clatter!

"Do you see Mrs. Pontellier starting back with the children? She will be in late to luncheon again. She never starts to get ready for luncheon till the last minute." Clatter, clatter! "Where are you going?"

"Where did you say the Goncourt was?"

## IX

Every light in the hall was ablaze; every lamp turned as high as it could be without smoking the chimney or threatening explosion. The lamps were fixed at intervals against the wall, encircling the whole room. Some one had gathered orange and lemon branches and with these fashioned graceful festoons between. The dark green of the branches stood out and glistened against the white muslin curtains which draped the windows, and which puffed, floated, and flapped at the capricious will of a stiff breeze that swept up from the Gulf.

It was Saturday night a few weeks after the intimate conversation held between Robert and Madame Ratignolle on their way from the beach. An unusual number of husbands, fathers, and friends had come down to stay over Sunday; and they were being suitably entertained by their families, with the material help of Madame Lebrun. The dining tables had all been removed to one end of the hall, and the chairs ranged about in rows and in clusters. Each little family group had had its say and exchanged its domestic gossip earlier in the evening. There was now an apparent disposition to relax; to widen the circle of confidences and give a more general tone to the conversation.

Many of the children had been permitted to sit up beyond their usual bedtime. A small band of them were lying on their stomachs on the floor looking at the colored sheets of the comic papers which Mr. Pontellier had brought down. The little Pontellier boys were permitting them to do so, and making their authority felt.

Music, dancing, and a recitation or two were the entertainments furnished, or rather, offered. But there was nothing systematic about the programme, no appearance of prearrangement nor even premeditation.

At an early hour in the evening the Farival twins were prevailed upon to play the piano. They were girls of fourteen, always clad in the Virgin's colors, blue and white, having been dedicated to the Blessed Virgin at their baptism. They played a duet from "Zampa," and at the earnest solicitation of every one present followed it with the overture to "The Poet and the Peasant."[3]

"Allez vous-en! Sapristi!" shrieked the parrot outside the door. He was the only being present who possessed sufficient candor to admit that he was not listening to these gracious performances for the first time that summer. Old Monsieur Farival, grandfather of the twins, grew indignant over the interruption, and insisted upon having the bird removed and consigned to regions of darkness. Victor Lebrun objected; and his decrees were as immutable as

2. City in the state of Vera Cruz, Mexico, on the Gulf of Mexico.

3. Comic operetta by Austrian composer Franz von Suppé (1819–1895).

those of Fate. The parrot fortunately offered no further interruption to the entertainment, the whole venom of his nature apparently having been cherished up and hurled against the twins in that one impetuous outburst.

Later a young brother and sister gave recitations, which every one present had heard many times at winter evening entertainments in the city.

A little girl performed a skirt dance in the center of the floor. The mother played her accompaniments and at the same time watched her daughter with greedy admiration and nervous apprehension. She need have had no apprehension. The child was mistress of the situation. She had been properly dressed for the occasion in black tulle and black silk tights. Her little neck and arms were bare, and her hair, artificially crimped, stood out like fluffy black plumes over her head. Her poses were full of grace, and her little black-shod toes twinkled as they shot out and upward with a rapidity and a suddenness which were bewildering.

But there was no reason why every one should not dance. Madame Ratignolle could not, so it was she who gaily consented to play for the others. She played very well, keeping excellent waltz time and infusing an expression into the strains which was indeed inspiring. She was keeping up her music on account of the children, she said; because she and her husband both considered it a means of brightening the home and making it attractive.

Almost every one danced but the twins, who could not be induced to separate during the brief period when one or the other should be whirling around the room in the arms of a man. They might have danced together, but they did not think of it.

The children were sent to bed. Some went submissively; others with shrieks and protests as they were dragged away. They had been permitted to sit up till after the ice-cream, which naturally marked the limit of human indulgence.

The ice-cream was passed around with cake—gold and silver cake arranged on platters in alternate slices; it had been made and frozen during the afternoon back of the kitchen by two black women, under the supervision of Victor. It was pronounced a great success—excellent if it had only contained a little less vanilla or a little more sugar, if it had been frozen a degree harder, and if the salt might have been kept out of portions of it. Victor was proud of his achievement, and went about recommending it and urging every one to partake of it to excess.

After Mrs. Pontellier had danced twice with her husband, once with Robert, and once with Monsieur Ratignolle, who was thin and tall and swayed like a reed in the wind when he danced, she went out on the gallery and seated herself on the low window-sill, where she commanded a view of all that went on in the hall and could look out toward the Gulf. There was a soft effulgence in the east. The moon was coming up, and its mystic shimmer was casting a million lights across the distant, restless water.

"Would you like to hear Mademoiselle Reisz play?" asked Robert, coming out on the porch where she was. Of course Edna would like to hear Mademoiselle Reisz play; but she feared it would be useless to entreat her.

"I'll ask her," he said. "I'll tell her that you want to hear her. She likes you. She will come." He turned and hurried away to one of the far cottages, where Mademoiselle Reisz was shuffling away. She was dragging a chair in and out of her room, and at intervals objecting to the crying of a baby, which a nurse in the adjoining cottage was endeavoring to put to sleep. She was a disagreeable little woman, no longer young, who had quarreled with almost every one, owing to a temper which was self-assertive and a disposition to trample upon the rights of others. Robert prevailed upon her without any too great difficulty.

She entered the hall with him during a lull in the dance. She made an awkward, imperious little bow as she went in. She was a homely woman, with a small weazened face and body and eyes that glowed. She had absolutely no taste in dress, and wore a batch of rusty black lace with a bunch of artificial violets pinned to the side of her hair.

"Ask Mrs. Pontellier what she would like to hear me play," she requested of Robert. She sat perfectly still before the piano, not touching the keys, while Robert carried her message to Edna at the window. A general air of surprise and genuine satisfaction fell upon every one as they saw the pianist enter. There was a settling down, and a prevailing air of expectancy everywhere. Edna was a trifle embarrassed at being thus signaled out for the imperious little woman's favor. She would not dare to choose, and begged that Mademoiselle Reisz would please herself in her selections.

Edna was what she herself called very fond of music. Musical strains, well rendered, had a way of evoking pictures in her mind. She sometimes liked to sit in the room of mornings when Madame Ratignolle played or practiced. One piece which that lady played Edna had entitled "Solitude."[4] It was a short, plaintive, minor strain. The name of the piece was something else, but she called it "Solitude." When she heard it there came before her imagination the figure of a man standing beside a desolate rock on the seashore. He was naked. His attitude was one of hopeless resignation as he looked toward a distant bird winging its flight away from him.

Another piece called to her mind a dainty young woman clad in an Empire gown, taking mincing dancing steps as she came down a long avenue between tall hedges. Again, another reminded her of children at play, and still another of nothing on earth but a demure lady stroking a cat.

The very first chords which Mademoiselle Reisz struck upon the piano sent a keen tremor down Mrs. Pontellier's spinal column. It was not the first time she had heard an artist at the piano. Perhaps it was the first time she was ready, perhaps the first time her being was tempered to take an impress of the abiding truth.

She waited for the material pictures which she thought would gather and blaze before her imagination. She waited in vain. She saw no pictures of solitude, of hope, of longing, or of despair. But the very passions themselves were aroused within her soul, swaying it, lashing it, as the waves daily beat upon her splendid body. She trembled, she was choking, and the tears blinded her.

Mademoiselle had finished. She arose, and bowing her stiff, lofty bow, she went away, stopping for neither thanks nor applause. As she passed along the gallery she patted Edna upon the shoulder.

"Well, how did you like my music?" she asked. The young woman was unable to answer; she pressed the hand of the pianist convulsively. Mademoiselle Reisz perceived her agitation and even her tears. She patted her again upon the shoulder as she said:

---

4. In "Solitude" (1884), by Guy de Maupassant (1850–1893), which Chopin translated for a St. Louis magazine, a character notes, "Whatever we may do or attempt, despite the embrace and transports of love, the hunger of the lips, we are always alone."

"You are the only one worth playing for. Those others? Bah!" and she went shuffling and sidling on down the gallery toward her room.

But she was mistaken about "those others." Her playing had aroused a fever of enthusiasm. "What passion!" "What an artist!" "I have always said no one could play Chopin[5] like Mademoiselle Reisz!" "That last prelude! Bon Dieu! It shakes a man!"

It was growing late, and there was a general disposition to disband. But some one, perhaps it was Robert, thought of a bath at that mystic hour and under that mystic moon.

X

At all events Robert proposed it, and there was not a dissenting voice. There was not one but was ready to follow when he led the way. He did not lead the way, however, he directed the way; and he himself loitered behind with the lovers, who had betrayed a disposition to linger and hold themselves apart. He walked between them, whether with malicious or mischievous intent was not wholly clear, even to himself.

The Pontelliers and Ratignolles walked ahead; the women leaning upon the arms of their husbands. Edna could hear Robert's voice behind them, and could sometimes hear what he said. She wondered why he did not join them. It was unlike him not to. Of late he had sometimes held away from her for an entire day, redoubling his devotion upon the next and the next, as though to make up for hours that had been lost. She missed him the days when some pretext served to take him away from her, just as one misses the sun on a cloudy day without having thought much about the sun when it was shining.

The people walked in little groups toward the beach. They talked and laughed; some of them sang. There was a band playing down at Klein's hotel, and the strains reached them faintly, tempered by the distance. There were strange, rare odors abroad—a tangle of the sea smell and of weeds and damp, new-plowed earth, mingled with the heavy perfume of a field of white blossoms somewhere near. But the night sat lightly upon the sea and the land. There was no weight of darkness; there were no shadows. The white light of the moon had fallen upon the world like the mystery and the softness of sleep.

Most of them walked into the water as though into a native element. The sea was quiet now, and swelled lazily in broad billows that melted into one another and did not break except upon the beach in little foamy crests that coiled back like slow, white serpents.

Edna had attempted all summer to learn to swim. She had received instructions from both the men and women; in some instances from the children. Robert had pursued a system of lessons almost daily; and he was nearly at the point of discouragement in realizing the futility of his efforts. A certain ungovernable dread hung about her when in the water, unless there was a hand near by that might reach out and reassure her.

But that night she was like the little tottering, stumbling, clutching child, who of a sudden realizes its powers, and walks for the first time alone, boldly and with over-confidence. She could have shouted for joy. She did shout for

5. Frédéric Chopin (1810–1849), Polish composer.

joy, as with a sweeping stroke or two she lifted her body to the surface of the water.

A feeling of exultation overtook her, as if some power of significant import had been given her soul. She grew daring and reckless, overestimating her strength. She wanted to swim far out, where no woman had swum before.

Her unlooked-for achievement was the subject of wonder, applause, and admiration. Each one congratulated himself that his special teachings had accomplished this desired end.

"How easy it is!" she thought. "It is nothing," she said aloud; "why did I not discover before that it was nothing. Think of the time I have lost splashing about like a baby!" She would not join the groups in their sports and bouts, but intoxicated with her newly conquered power, she swam out alone.

She turned her face seaward to gather in an impression of space and solitude, which the vast expanse of water, meeting and melting with the moon-lit sky, conveyed to her excited fancy. As she swam she seemed to be reaching out for the unlimited in which to lose herself.

Once she turned and looked toward the shore, toward the people she had left there. She had not gone any great distance—that is, what would have been a great distance for an experienced swimmer. But to her unaccustomed vision the stretch of water behind her assumed the aspect of a barrier which her unaided strength would never be able to overcome.

A quick vision of death smote her soul, and for a second of time appalled and enfeebled her senses. But by an effort she rallied her staggering faculties and managed to regain the land.

She made no mention of her encounter with death and her flash of terror, except to say to her husband, "I thought I should have perished out there alone."

"You were not so very far, my dear; I was watching you," he told her.

Edna went at once to the bath-house, and she had put on her dry clothes and was ready to return home before the others had left the water. She started to walk away alone. They all called to her and shouted to her. She waved a dissenting hand, and went on, paying no further heed to their renewed cries which sought to detain her.

"Sometimes I am tempted to think that Mrs. Pontellier is capricious," said Madame Lebrun, who was amusing herself immensely and feared that Edna's abrupt departure might put an end to the pleasure.

"I know she is," assented Mr. Pontellier; "sometimes, not often."

Edna had not traversed a quarter of the distance on her way home before she was overtaken by Robert.

"Did you think I was afraid?" she asked him, without a shade of annoyance.

"No; I knew you weren't afraid."

"Then why did you come? Why didn't you stay out there with the others?"

"I never thought of it."

"Thought of what?"

"Of anything. What difference does it make?"

"I'm very tired," she uttered, complainingly.

"I know you are."

"You don't know anything about it. Why should you know? I never was so exhausted in my life. But it isn't unpleasant. A thousand emotions have swept through me to-night. I don't comprehend half of them. Don't mind what I'm saying; I am just thinking aloud. I wonder if I shall ever be stirred again as Mademoiselle Reisz's playing moved me to-night. I wonder if any night on earth will ever again be like this one. It is like a night in a dream. The people about me are like some uncanny, half-human beings. There must be spirits abroad to-night."

"There are," whispered Robert. "Didn't you know this was the twenty-eighth of August?"

"The twenty-eighth of August?"

"Yes. On the twenty-eighth of August, at the hour of midnight, and if the moon is shining—the moon must be shining—a spirit that has haunted these shores for ages rises up from the Gulf. With its own penetrating vision the spirit seeks some one mortal worthy to hold him company, worthy of being exalted for a few hours into realms of the semi-celestials. His search has always hitherto been fruitless, and he has sunk back, disheartened, into the sea. But to-night he found Mrs. Pontellier. Perhaps he will never wholly release her from the spell. Perhaps she will never again suffer a poor, unworthy earthling to walk in the shadow of her divine presence."

"Don't banter me," she said, wounded at what appeared to be his flippancy. He did not mind the entreaty, but the tone with its delicate note of pathos was like a reproach. He could not explain; he could not tell her that he had penetrated her mood and understood. He said nothing except to offer her his arm, for, by her own admission, she was exhausted. She had been walking alone with her arms hanging limp, letting her white skirts trail along the dewy path. She took his arm, but she did not lean upon it. She let her hand lie listlessly, as though her thoughts were elsewhere—somewhere in advance of her body, and she was striving to overtake them.

Robert assisted her into the hammock which swung from the post before her door out to the trunk of a tree.

"Will you stay out here and wait for Mr. Pontellier?" he asked.

"I'll stay out here. Good-night."

"Shall I get you a pillow?"

"There's one here," she said, feeling about, for they were in the shadow.

"It must be soiled; the children have been tumbling it about."

"No matter." And having discovered the pillow, she adjusted it beneath her head. She extended herself in the hammock with a deep breath of relief. She was not a supercilious or an over-dainty woman. She was not much given to reclining in the hammock, and when she did so it was with no catlike suggestion of voluptuous ease, but with a beneficent repose which seemed to invade her whole body.

"Shall I stay with you till Mr. Pontellier comes?" asked Robert, seating himself on the outer edge of one of the steps and taking hold of the hammock rope which was fastened to the post.

"If you wish. Don't swing the hammock. Will you get my white shawl which I left on the window-sill over at the house?"

"Are you chilly?"

"No; but I shall be presently."

"Presently?" he laughed. "Do you know what time it is? How long are you going to stay out here?"

"I don't know. Will you get the shawl?"

"Of course I will," he said, rising. He went over to the house, walking along the grass. She watched his figure pass in and out of the strips of moonlight. It was past midnight. It was very quiet.

When he returned with the shawl she took it and kept it in her hand. She did not put it around her.

"Did you say I should stay till Mr. Pontellier came back?"

"I said you might if you wished to."

He seated himself again and rolled a cigarette, which he smoked in silence. Neither did Mrs. Pontellier speak. No multitude of words could have been more significant than those moments of silence, or more pregnant with the first-felt throbbings of desire.

When the voices of the bathers were heard approaching, Robert said goodnight. She did not answer him. He thought she was asleep. Again she watched his figure pass in and out of the strips of moonlight as he walked away.

## XI

"What are you doing out here, Edna? I thought I should find you in bed," said her husband, when he discovered her lying there. He had walked up with Madame Lebrun and left her at the house. His wife did not reply.

"Are you asleep?" he asked, bending down close to look at her.

"No." Her eyes gleamed bright and intense, with no sleepy shadows, as they looked into his.

"Do you know it is past one o'clock? Come on," and he mounted the steps and went into their room.

"Edna!" called Mr. Pontellier from within, after a few moments had gone by.

"Don't wait for me," she answered. He thrust his head through the door.

"You will take cold out there," he said, irritably. "What folly is this? Why don't you come in?"

"It isn't cold; I have my shawl."

"The mosquitoes will devour you."

"There are no mosquitoes."

She heard him moving about the room; every sound indicating impatience and irritation. Another time she would have gone in at his request. She would, through habit, have yielded to his desire; not with any sense of submission or obedience to his compelling wishes, but unthinkingly, as we walk, move, sit, stand, go through the daily treadmill of the life which has been portioned out to us.

"Edna, dear, are you not coming in soon?" he asked again, this time fondly, with a note of entreaty.

"No; I am going to stay out here."

"This is more than folly," he blurted out. "I can't permit you to stay out there all night. You must come in the house instantly."

With a writhing motion she settled herself more securely in the hammock. She perceived that her will had blazed up, stubborn and resistant. She could not at that moment have done other than denied and resisted. She wondered if her husband had ever spoken to her like that before, and if she had submitted to his command. Of course she had; she remembered that she had. But she could not realize why or how she should have yielded, feeling as she then did.

"Léonce, go to bed," she said. "I mean to stay out here. I don't wish to go in, and I don't intend to. Don't speak to me like that again; I shall not answer you."

Mr. Pontellier had prepared for bed, but he slipped on an extra garment. He opened a bottle of wine, of which he kept a small and select supply in a buffet of his own. He drank a glass of the wine and went out on the gallery and offered a glass to his wife. She did not wish any. He drew up the rocker, hoisted his slippered feet on the rail, and proceeded to smoke a cigar. He smoked two cigars; then he went inside and drank another glass of wine. Mrs. Pontellier again declined to accept a glass when it was offered to her. Mr. Pontellier once more seated himself with elevated feet, and after a reasonable interval of time smoked some more cigars.

Edna began to feel like one who awakens gradually out of a dream, a delicious, grotesque, impossible dream, to feel again the realities pressing into her soul. The physical need for sleep began to overtake her; the exuberance which had sustained and exalted her spirit left her helpless and yielding to the conditions which crowded her in.

The stillest hour of the night had come, the hour before dawn, when the world seems to hold its breath. The moon hung low, and had turned from silver to copper in the sleeping sky. The old owl no longer hooted, and the water-oaks had ceased to moan as they bent their heads.

Edna arose, cramped from lying so long and still in the hammock. She tottered up the steps, clutching feebly at the post before passing into the house.

"Are you coming in, Léonce?" She asked, turning her face toward her husband.

"Yes, dear," he answered, with a glance following a misty puff of smoke. "Just as soon as I have finished my cigar."

## XII

She slept but a few hours. They were troubled and feverish hours, disturbed with dreams that were intangible, that eluded her, leaving only an impression upon her half-awakened senses of something unattainable. She was up and dressed in the cool of the early morning. The air was invigorating and steadied somewhat her faculties. However, she was not seeking refreshment or help from any source, either external or from within. She was blindly following whatever impulse moved her, as if she had placed herself in alien hands for direction, and freed her soul of responsibility.

Most of the people at that early hour were still in bed and asleep. A few, who intended to go over to the *Chênière* for mass, were moving about. The lovers, who had laid their plans the night before, were already strolling toward the wharf. The lady in black, with her Sunday prayer book, velvet and gold-clasped, and her Sunday silver beads, was following them at no great distance. Old Monsieur Farival was up, and was more than half inclined to do anything that suggested itself. He put on his big straw hat, and taking his umbrella from the stand in the hall, followed the lady in black, never overtaking her.

The little negro girl who worked Madame Lebrun's sewing-machine was sweeping the galleries with long, absent-minded strokes of the broom. Edna sent her up into the house to awaken Robert.

"Tell him I am going to the *Chênière*. The boat is ready; tell him to hurry."

He had soon joined her. She had never sent for him before. She had never asked for him. She had never seemed to want him before. She did not appear conscious that she had done anything unusual in commanding his presence. He was apparently equally unconscious of anything extraordinary in the situation. But his face was suffused with a quiet glow when he met her.

They went together back to the kitchen to drink coffee. There was no time to wait for any nicety of service. They stood outside the window and the cook passed them their coffee and a roll, which they drank and ate from the window-sill. Edna said it tasted good. She had not thought of coffee nor of anything. He told her he had often noticed that she lacked forethought.

"Wasn't it enough to think of going to the *Chênière* and waking you up?" she laughed. "Do I have to think of everything?—as Léonce says when he's in a bad humor. I don't blame him; he'd never be in a bad humor if it weren't for me."

They took a short cut across the sands. At a distance they could see the curious procession moving toward the wharf—the lovers, shoulder to shoulder, creeping; the lady in black, gaining steadily upon them; old Monsieur Farival, losing ground inch by inch, and a young barefooted Spanish girl, with a red kerchief on her head and a basket on her arm, bringing up the rear.

Robert knew the girl, and he talked to her a little in the boat. No one present understood what they said. Her name was Mariequita. She had a round, sly, piquant face and pretty black eyes. Her hands were small, and she kept them folded over the handle of her basket. Her feet were broad and coarse. She did not strive to hide them. Edna looked at her feet, and noticed the sand and slime between her brown toes.

Beaudelet grumbled because Mariequita was there, taking up so much room. In reality he was annoyed at having old Monsieur Farival, who considered himself the better sailor of the two. But he would not quarrel with so old a man as Monsieur Farival, so he quarreled with Mariequita. The girl was deprecatory at one moment, appealing to Robert. She was saucy the next, moving her head up and down, making "eyes" at Robert and making "mouths" at Beaudelet.

The lovers were all alone. They saw nothing, they heard nothing. The lady in black was counting her beads for the third time. Old Monsieur Farival talked incessantly of what he knew about handling a boat, and of what Beaudelet did not know on the same subject.

Edna liked it all. She looked Mariequita up and down, from her ugly brown toes to her pretty black eyes, and back again.

"Why does she look at me like that?" inquired the girl of Robert.

"Maybe she thinks you are pretty. Shall I ask her?"

"No. Is she your sweetheart?"

"She's a married lady, and has two children."

"Oh! well! Francisco ran away with Sylvano's wife, who had four children. They took all his money and one of the children and stole his boat."

"Shut up!"

"Does she understand?"

"Oh, hush!"

"Are those two married over there—leaning on each other?"

"Of course not," laughed Robert.

"Of course not," echoed Mariequita, with a serious, confirmatory bob of the head.

The sun was high up and beginning to bite. The swift breeze seemed to Edna to bury the sting of it into the pores of her face and hands. Robert held his umbrella over her.

As they went cutting sidewise through the water, the sails bellied taut, with the wind filling and overflowing them. Old Monsieur Farival laughed sardonically at something as he looked at the sails, and Beaudelet swore at the old man under his breath.

Sailing across the bay to the *Chênière Caminada,* Edna felt as if she were being borne away from some anchorage which had held her fast, whose chains had been loosening—had snapped the night before when the mystic spirit was abroad, leaving her free to drift whithersoever she chose to set her sails. Robert spoke to her incessantly; he no longer noticed Mariequita. The girl had shrimps in her bamboo basket. They were covered with Spanish moss. She beat the moss impatiently, and muttered to herself sullenly.

"Let us go to Grande Terre[6] to-morrow?" said Robert in a low voice.

"What shall we do there?"

"Climb up the hill to the old fort and look at the little wriggling gold snakes, and watch the lizards sun themselves."

She gazed away toward Grande Terre and thought she would like to be alone there with Robert, in the sun, listening to the ocean's roar and watching the slimy lizards writhe in and out among the ruins of the old fort.

"And the next day or the next we can sail to the Bayou Brulow,"[7] he went on.

"What shall we do there?"

"Anything—cast bait for fish."

"No; we'll go back to Grande Terre. Let the fish alone."

"We'll go wherever you like," he said. "I'll have Tonie come over and help me patch and trim my boat. We shall not need Beaudelet nor any one. Are you afraid of the pirogue?"[8]

"Oh, no."

"Then I'll take you some night in the pirogue when the moon shines. Maybe your Gulf spirit will whisper to you in which of these islands the treasures are hidden—direct you to the very spot, perhaps."

"And in a day we should be rich!" she laughed. "I'd give it all to you, the pirate gold and every bit of treasure we could dig up. I think you would know how to spend it. Pirate gold isn't a thing to be hoarded or utilized. It is something to squander and throw to the four winds, for the fun of seeing the golden specks fly."

"We'd share it, and scatter it together," he said. His face flushed.

They all went together up to the quaint little Gothic church of Our Lady of Lourdes, gleaming all brown and yellow with paint in the sun's glare.

Only Beaudelet remained behind, tinkering at his boat, and Mariequita walked away with her basket of shrimps, casting a look of childish ill-humor and reproach at Robert from the corner of her eye.

---

6. An island adjacent to Grand Isle.
7. Bayou Brulow (or Bruleau) was the nearest to Grand Isle of a series of villages built on stilts or platforms in large marshy areas called *bayous.*

Inhabited by Acadians, descendants of French Canadians expelled from Nova Scotia in 1755.
8. Canoe.

## XIII

A feeling of oppression and drowsiness overcame Edna during the service. Her head began to ache, and the lights on the altar swayed before her eyes. Another time she might have made an effort to regain her composure; but her one thought was to quit the stifling atmosphere of the church and reach the open air. She arose, climbing over Robert's feet with a muttered apology. Old Monsieur Farival, flurried, curious, stood up, but upon seeing that Robert had followed Mrs. Pontellier, he sank back into his seat. He whispered an anxious inquiry of the lady in black, who did not notice him or reply, but kept her eyes fastened upon the pages of her velvet prayer-book.

"I felt giddy and almost overcome," Edna said, lifting her hands instinctively to her head and pushing her straw hat up from her forehead. "I couldn't have stayed through the service." They were outside in the shadow of the church. Robert was full of solicitude.

"It was folly to have thought of going in the first place, let alone staying. Come over to Madame Antoine's; you can rest there." He took her arm and led her away, looking anxiously and continuously down into her face.

How still it was, with only the voice of the sea whispering through the reeds that grew in the salt-water pools! The long line of little gray, weather-beaten houses nestled peacefully among the orange trees. It must always have been God's day on that low, drowsy island, Edna thought. They stopped, leaning over a jagged fence made of sea-drift, to ask for water. A youth, a mild-faced Acadian, was drawing water from the cistern, which was nothing more than a rusty buoy, with an opening on one side, sunk in the ground. The water which the youth handed to them in a tin pail was not cold to taste, but it was cool to her heated face, and it greatly revived and refreshed her.

Madame Antoine's cot[9] was at the far end of the village. She welcomed them with all the native hospitality, as she would have opened her door to let the sunlight in. She was fat, and walked heavily and clumsily across the floor. She could speak no English, but when Robert made her understand that the lady who accompanied him was ill and desired to rest, she was all eagerness to make Edna feel at home and to dispose of her comfortably.

The whole place was immaculately clean, and the big, four-posted bed, snow-white, invited one to repose. It stood in a small side room which looked out across a narrow grass plot toward the shed, where there was a disabled boat lying keel upward.

Madame Antoine had not gone to mass. Her son Tonie had, but she supposed he would soon be back, and she invited Robert to be seated and wait for him. But he went and sat outside the door and smoked. Madame Antoine busied herself in the large front room preparing dinner. She was boiling mullets[1] over a few red coals in the huge fireplace.

Edna, left alone in the little side room, loosened her clothes, removing the greater part of them. She bathed her face, her neck and arms in the basin that stood between the windows. She took off her shoes and stockings and stretched herself in the very center of the high, white bed. How luxurious it felt to rest thus in a strange, quaint bed, with its sweet country odor of laurel lingering about the sheets and mattress! She stretched her strong limbs

---

9. Cottage.     1. Small fish.

that ached a little. She ran her fingers through her loosened hair for a while. She looked at her round arms as she held them straight up and rubbed them one after the other, observing closely, as if it were something she saw for the first time, the fine, firm quality and texture of her flesh. She clasped her hands easily above her head, and it was thus she fell asleep.

She slept lightly at first, half awake and drowsily attentive to the things about her. She could hear Madame Antoine's heavy, scraping tread as she walked back and forth on the sanded floor. Some chickens were clucking outside the windows, scratching for bits of gravel in the grass. Later she half heard the voices of Robert and Tonie talking under the shed. She did not stir. Even her eyelids rested numb and heavily over her sleepy eyes. The voices went on—Tonie's slow, Acadian drawl, Robert's quick, soft, smooth French. She understood French imperfectly unless directly addressed, and the voices were only part of the other drowsy, muffled sounds lulling her senses.

When Edna awoke it was with the conviction that she had slept long and soundly. The voices were hushed under the shed. Madame Antoine's step was no longer to be heard in the adjoining room. Even the chickens had gone elsewhere to scratch and cluck. The mosquito bar was drawn over her; the old woman had come in while she slept and let down the bar. Edna arose quietly from the bed, and looking between the curtains of the window, she saw by the slanting rays of the sun that the afternoon was far advanced. Robert was out there under the shed, reclining in the shade against the sloping keel of the overturned boat. He was reading from a book. Tonie was no longer with him. She wondered what had become of the rest of the party. She peeped out at him two or three times as she stood washing herself in the little basin between the windows.

Madame Antoine had laid some coarse, clean towels upon a chair, and had placed a box of *poudre de riz*[2] within easy reach. Edna dabbed the powder upon her nose and cheeks as she looked at herself closely in the little distorted mirror which hung on the wall above the basin. Her eyes were bright and wide awake and her face glowed.

When she had completed her toilet she walked into the adjoining room. She was very hungry. No one was there. But there was a cloth spread upon the table that stood against the wall, and a cover was laid for one, with a crusty brown loaf and a bottle of wine beside the plate. Edna bit a piece from the brown loaf, tearing it with her strong, white teeth. She poured some of the wine into the glass and drank it down. Then she went softly out of doors, and plucking an orange from the low-hanging bough of a tree, threw it at Robert, who did not know she was awake and up.

An illumination broke over his whole face when he saw her and joined her under the orange tree.

"How many years have I slept?" she inquired. "The whole island seems changed. A new race of beings must have sprung up, leaving only you and me as past relics. How many ages ago did Madame Antoine and Tonie die? and when did our people from Grand Isle disappear from the earth?"

He familiarly adjusted a ruffle upon her shoulder.

"You have slept precisely one hundred years. I was left here to guard your slumbers; and for one hundred years I have been out under the shed reading

2. Talcum powder (French).

a book. The only evil I couldn't prevent was to keep a broiled fowl from drying up."

"If it had turned to stone, still will I eat it," said Edna, moving with him into
the house. "But really, what has become of Monsieur Farival and the others?"

"Gone hours ago. When they found that you were sleeping they thought it
best not to awake you. Any way, I wouldn't have let them. What was I here
for?"

"I wonder if Léonce will be uneasy!" she speculated, as she seated herself
at table.

"Of course not; he knows you are with me," Robert replied, as he busied
himself among sundry pans and covered dishes which had been left standing
on the hearth.

"Where are Madame Antoine and her son?" asked Edna.

"Gone to Vespers,[3] and to visit some friends, I believe. I am to take you back
in Tonie's boat whenever you are ready to go."

He stirred the smoldering ashes till the broiled fowl began to sizzle afresh.
He served her with no mean repast, dripping the coffee anew and sharing it
with her. Madame Antoine had cooked little else than the mullets, but while
Edna slept Robert had foraged the island. He was childishly gratified to discover her appetite, and to see the relish with which she ate the food which
he had procured for her.

"Shall we go right away?" she asked, after draining her glass and brushing
together the crumbs of the crusty loaf.

"The sun isn't as low as it will be in two hours," he answered.

"The sun will be gone in two hours."

"Well, let it go; who cares!"

They waited a good while under the orange trees, till Madame Antoine
came back, panting, waddling, with a thousand apologies to explain her
absence. Tonie did not dare to return. He was shy, and would not willingly
face any woman except his mother.

It was very pleasant to stay there under the orange trees, while the sun
dipped lower and lower, turning the western sky to flaming copper and gold.
The shadows lengthened and crept out like stealthy, grotesque monsters
across the grass.

Edna and Robert both sat upon the ground—that is, he lay upon the
ground beside her, occasionally picking at the hem of her muslin gown.

Madame Antoine seated her fat body, broad and squat, upon a bench
beside the door. She had been talking all the afternoon, and had wound herself up to the story-telling pitch.

And what stories she told them! But twice in her life she had left the
Chênière Caminada, and then for the briefest span. All her years she had
squatted and waddled there upon the island, gathering legends of the
Baratarians[4] and the sea. The night came on, with the moon to lighten it.
Edna could hear the whispering voices of dead men and the click of muffled
gold.

When she and Robert stepped into Tonie's boat, with the red lateen sail,

3. Evening church service.
4. Pirates, most notably the legendary Jean Lafitte, who operated in the area of Barataria Bay.

misty spirit forms were prowling in the shadows and among the reeds, and upon the water were phantom ships, speeding to cover.

## XIV

The youngest boy, Etienne, had been very naughty, Madame Ratignolle said, as she delivered him into the hands of his mother. He had been unwilling to go to bed and had made a scene; whereupon she had taken charge of him and pacified him as well as she could. Raoul had been in bed and asleep for two hours.

The youngster was in his long white nightgown, that kept tripping him up as Madame Ratignolle led him along by the hand. With the other chubby fist he rubbed his eyes, which were heavy with sleep and ill humor. Edna took him in her arms, and seating herself in the rocker, began to coddle and caress him, calling him all manner of tender names, soothing him to sleep.

It was not more than nine o'clock. No one had yet gone to bed but the children.

Léonce had been very uneasy at first, Madame Ratignolle said, and had wanted to start at once for the *Chênière*. But Monsieur Farival had assured him that his wife was only overcome with sleep and fatigue, that Tonie would bring her safely back later in the day; and he had thus been dissuaded from crossing the bay. He had gone over to Klein's, looking up some cotton broker whom he wished to see in regard to securities, exchanges, stocks, bonds, or something of the sort, Madame Ratignolle did not remember what. He said he would not remain away late. She herself was suffering from heat and oppression, she said. She carried a bottle of salts and a large fan. She would not consent to remain with Edna, for Monsieur Ratignolle was alone, and he detested above all things to be left alone.

When Etienne had fallen asleep Edna bore him into the back room, and Robert went and lifted the mosquito bar that she might lay the child comfortably in his bed. The quadroon had vanished. When they emerged from the cottage Robert bade Edna good-night.

"Do you know we have been together the whole livelong day, Robert—since early this morning?" she said at parting.

"All but the hundred years when you were sleeping. Good-night."

He pressed her hand and went away in the direction of the beach. He did not join any of the others, but walked alone toward the Gulf.

Edna stayed outside, awaiting her husband's return. She had no desire to sleep or to retire; nor did she feel like going over to sit with the Ratignolles, or to join Madame Lebrun and a group whose animated voices reached her as they sat in conversation before the house. She let her mind wander back over her stay at Grand Isle; and she tried to discover wherein this summer had been different from any and every other summer of her life. She could only realize that she herself—her present self—was in some way different from the other self. That she was seeing with different eyes and making the acquaintance of new conditions in herself that colored and changed her environment, she did not yet suspect.

She wondered why Robert had gone away and left her. It did not occur to her to think he might have grown tired of being with her the livelong day. She was not tired, and she felt that he was not. She regretted that he had gone. It was so much more natural to have him stay, when he was not absolutely required to leave her.

As Edna waited for her husband she sang low a little song that Robert had sung as they crossed the bay. It began with "Ah! *Si tu savais*," and every verse ended with *"si tu savais."*[5]

Robert's voice was not pretentious. It was musical and true. The voice, the notes, the whole refrain haunted her memory.

*XV*

When Edna entered the dining-room one evening a little late, as was her habit, an unusually animated conversation seemed to be going on. Several persons were talking at once, and Victor's voice was predominating, even over that of his mother. Edna had returned late from her bath, had dressed in some haste, and her face was flushed. Her head, set off by her dainty white gown, suggested a rich, rare blossom. She took her seat at table between old Monsieur Farival and Madame Ratignolle.

As she seated herself and was about to begin to eat her soup, which had been served when she entered the room, several persons informed her simultaneously that Robert was going to Mexico. She laid her spoon down and looked about her bewildered. He had been with her, reading to her all the morning, and had never even mentioned such a place as Mexico. She had not seen him during the afternoon; she had heard some one say he was at the house, upstairs with his mother. This she had thought nothing of, though she was surprised when he did not join her later in the afternoon, when she went down to the beach.

She looked across at him, where he sat beside Madame Lebrun, who presided. Edna's face was a blank picture of bewilderment, which she never thought of disguising. He lifted his eyebrows with the pretext of a smile as he returned her glance. He looked embarrassed and uneasy.

"When is he going?" she asked of everybody in general, as if Robert were not there to answer for himself.

"To-night!" "This very evening!" "Did you ever!" "What possesses him!" some of the replies she gathered, uttered simultaneously in French and English.

"Impossible!" she exclaimed. "How can a person start off from Grand Isle to Mexico at a moment's notice, as if he were going over to Klein's or to the wharf or down to the beach?"

"I said all along I was going to Mexico; I've been saying so for years!" cried Robert, in an excited and irritable tone, with the air of a man defending himself against a swarm of stinging insects.

Madame Lebrun knocked on the table with her knife handle.

"Please let Robert explain why he is going, and why he is going to-night," she called out. "Really, this table is getting to be more and more like Bedlam[6] every day, with everybody talking at once. Sometimes—I hope God will forgive me—but positively, sometimes I wish Victor would lose the power of speech."

<hr>

5. "Couldst Thou But Know" (French), a song written by Michael William Balfe (1808–1870), does not contain the quoted words.
6. Notorious lunatic asylum in London.

Victor laughed sardonically as he thanked his mother for her holy wish, of which he failed to see the benefit to anybody, except that it might afford her a more ample opportunity and license to talk herself.

Monsieur Farival thought that Victor should have been taken out in mid-ocean in his earliest youth and drowned. Victor thought there would be more logic in thus disposing of old people with an established claim for making themselves universally obnoxious. Madame Lebrun grew a trifle hysterical; Robert called his brother some sharp, hard names.

"There's nothing much to explain, mother," he said: though he explained, nevertheless—looking chiefly at Edna—that he could only meet the gentleman whom he intended to join at Vera Cruz by taking such and such a steamer, which left New Orleans on such a day; that Beaudelet was going out with his lugger-load of vegetables that night, which gave him an opportunity of reaching the city and making his vessel in time.

"But when did you make up your mind to all this?" demanded Monsieur Farival.

"This afternoon," returned Robert, with a shade of annoyance.

"At what time this afternoon?" persisted the old gentleman, with nagging determination, as if he were cross-questioning a criminal in a court of justice.

"At four o'clock this afternoon, Monsieur Farival," Robert replied, in a high voice and with a lofty air, which reminded Edna of some gentleman on the stage.

She had forced herself to eat most of her soup, and now she was picking the flaky bits of a *court bouillon*[7] with her fork.

The lovers were profiting by the general conversation on Mexico to speak in whispers of matters which they rightly considered were interesting to no one but themselves. The lady in black had once received a pair of prayer-beads of curious workmanship from Mexico, with very special indulgence[8] attached to them, but she had never been able to ascertain whether the indulgence extended outside the Mexican border. Father Fochel of the Cathedral had attempted to explain it; but he had not done so to her satisfaction. And she begged that Robert would interest himself, and discover, if possible, whether she was entitled to the indulgence accompanying the remarkably curious Mexican prayer-beads.

Madame Ratignolle hoped that Robert would exercise extreme caution in dealing with the Mexicans, who, she considered, were a treacherous people, unscrupulous and revengeful. She trusted she did them no injustice in thus condemning them as a race. She had known personally but one Mexican, who made and sold excellent tamales, and whom she would have trusted implicitly, so soft-spoken was he. One day he was arrested for stabbing his wife. She never knew whether he had been hanged or not.

Victor had grown hilarious, and was attempting to tell an anecdote about a Mexican girl who served chocolate one winter in a restaurant in Dauphine Street.[9] No one would listen to him but old Monsieur Farival, who went into convulsions over the droll story.

Edna wondered if they had all gone mad, to be talking and clamoring at

7. Broth in which fish is poached (French).
8. According to a Roman Catholic belief, some religious articles, through contact with a holy person or a special blessing, had the power to take away part of the punishment that would otherwise be meted out to the sinner after death.
9. In the French Quarter.

that rate. She herself could think of nothing to say about Mexico or the Mexicans.

"At what time do you leave?" she asked Robert.

"At ten," he told her. "Beaudelet wants to wait for the moon."

"Are you all ready to go?"

"Quite ready. I shall only take a handbag, and shall pack my trunk in the city."

He turned to answer some question put to him by his mother, and Edna, having finished her black coffee, left the table.

She went directly to her room. The little cottage was close and stuffy after leaving the outer air. But she did not mind; there appeared to be a hundred different things demanding her attention indoors. She began to set the toilet-stand to rights, grumbling at the negligence of the quadroon, who was in the adjoining room putting the children to bed. She gathered together stray garments that were hanging on the backs of chairs, and put each where it belonged in closet or bureau drawer. She changed her gown for a more comfortable and commodious wrapper. She rearranged her hair, combing and brushing it with unusual energy. Then she went in and assisted the quadroon in getting the boys to bed.

They were very playful and inclined to talk—to do anything but lie quiet and go to sleep. Edna sent the quadroon away to her supper and told her she need not return. Then she sat and told the children a story. Instead of soothing it excited them, and added to their wakefulness. She left them in heated argument, speculating about the conclusion of the tale which their mother promised to finish the following night.

The little black girl came in to say that Madame Lebrun would like to have Mrs. Pontellier go and sit with them over at the house till Mr. Robert went away. Edna returned answer that she had already undressed, that she did not feel quite well, but perhaps she would go over to the house later. She started to dress again, and got as far advanced as to remove her *peignoir*. But changing her mind once more she resumed the *peignoir,* and went outside and sat down before her door. She was overheated and irritable, and fanned herself energetically for a while. Madame Ratignolle came down to discover what was the matter.

"All that noise and confusion at the table must have upset me," replied Edna, "and moreover, I hate shocks and surprises. The idea of Robert starting off in such a ridiculously sudden and dramatic way! As if it were a matter of life and death! Never saying a word about it all morning when he was with me."

"Yes," agreed Madame Ratignolle. "I think it was showing us all—you especially—very little consideration. It wouldn't have surprised me in any of the others; those Lebruns are all given to heroics. But I must say I should never have expected such a thing from Robert. Are you not coming down? Come on, dear; it doesn't look friendly."

"No," said Edna, a little sullenly. "I can't go to the trouble of dressing again; I don't feel like it."

"You needn't dress; you look all right; fasten a belt around your waist. Just look at me!"

"No," persisted Edna; "but you go on. Madame Lebrun might be offended if we both stayed away."

Madame Ratignolle kissed Edna good-night, and went away, being in truth rather desirous of joining in the general and animated conversation which was still in progress concerning Mexico and the Mexicans.

Somewhat later Robert came up, carrying his hand-bag.

"Aren't you feeling well?" he asked.

"Oh, well enough. Are you going right away?"

He lit a match and looked at his watch. "In twenty minutes," he said. The sudden and brief flare of the match emphasized the darkness for a while. He sat down upon a stool which the children had left out on the porch.

"Get a chair," said Edna.

"This will do," he replied. He put on his soft hat and nervously took it off again, and wiping his face with his handkerchief, complained of the heat.

"Take the fan," said Edna, offering it to him.

"Oh, no! Thank you. It does no good; you have to stop fanning some time, and feel all the more uncomfortable afterward."

"That's one of the ridiculous things which men always say. I have never known one to speak otherwise of fanning. How long will you be gone?"

"Forever, perhaps. I don't know. It depends upon a good many things."

"Well, in case it shouldn't be forever, how long will it be?"

"I don't know."

"This seems to me perfectly preposterous and uncalled for. I don't like it. I don't understand your motive for silence and mystery, never saying a word to me about it this morning." He remained silent, not offering to defend himself. He only said, after a moment:

"Don't part from me in an ill-humor. I never knew you to be out of patience with me before."

"I don't want to part in any ill-humor," said she. "But can't you understand? I've grown used to seeing you, to having you with me all the time, and your action seems unfriendly, even unkind. You don't even offer an excuse for it. Why, I was planning to be together, thinking of how pleasant it would be to see you in the city next winter."

"So was I," he blurted. "Perhaps that's the—" He stood up suddenly and held out his hand. "Good-by, my dear Mrs. Pontellier; good-by. You won't—I hope you won't completely forget me." She clung to his hand, striving to detain him.

"Write to me when you get there, won't you, Robert?" she entreated.

"I will, thank you. Good-by."

How unlike Robert! The merest acquaintance would have said something more emphatic than "I will, thank you; good-by," to such a request.

He had evidently already taken leave of the people over at the house, for he descended the steps and went to join Beaudelet, who was out there with an oar across his shoulder waiting for Robert. They walked away in the darkness. She could only hear Beaudelet's voice; Robert had apparently not even spoken a word of greeting to his companion.

Edna bit her handkerchief convulsively, striving to hold back and to hide, even from herself as she would have hidden from another, the emotion which was troubling—tearing—her. Her eyes were brimming with tears.

For the first time she recognized anew the symptoms of infatuation which she felt incipiently as a child, as a girl in her earliest teens, and later as a young woman. The recognition did not lessen the reality, the poignancy of the revelation by any suggestion or promise of instability. The past was nothing to her; offered no lesson which she was willing to heed. The future was a mystery which she never attempted to penetrate. The present alone was significant; was hers, to torture her as it was doing then with the biting conviction that she had lost that which she had held, that she had been denied that which her impassioned, newly awakened being demanded.

### XVI

"Do you miss your friend greatly?" asked Mademoiselle Reisz one morning as she came creeping up behind Edna, who had just left her cottage on her way to the beach. She spent much of her time in the water since she had acquired finally the art of swimming. As their stay at Grand Isle drew near its close, she felt that she could not give too much time to a diversion which afforded her the only real pleasurable moments that she knew. When Mademoiselle Reisz came and touched her upon the shoulder and spoke to her, the woman seemed to echo the thought which was ever in Edna's mind; or, better, the feeling which constantly possessed her.

Robert's going had some way taken the brightness, the color, the meaning out of everything. The conditions of her life were in no way changed, but her whole existence was dulled, like a faded garment which seems to be no longer worth wearing. She sought him everywhere—in others whom she induced to talk about him. She went up in the mornings to Madame Lebrun's room, braving the clatter of the old sewing-machine. She sat there and chatted at intervals as Robert had done. She gazed around the room at the pictures and photographs hanging upon the wall, and discovered in some corner an old family album, which she examined with the keenest interest, appealing to Madame Lebrun for enlightenment concerning the many figures and faces which she discovered between its pages.

There was a picture of Madame Lebrun with Robert as a baby, seated in her lap, a round-faced infant with a fist in his mouth. The eyes alone in the baby suggested the man. And that was he also in kilts, at the age of five, wearing long curls and holding a whip in his hand. It made Edna laugh, and she laughed, too, at the portrait in his first long trousers; while another interested her, taken when he left for college, looking thin, long-faced, with eyes full of fire, ambition and great intentions. But there was no recent picture, none which suggested the Robert who had gone away five days ago, leaving a void and wilderness behind him.

"Oh, Robert stopped having his pictures taken when he had to pay for them himself! He found wiser use for his money, he says," explained Madame Lebrun. She had a letter from him, written before he left New Orleans. Edna wished to see the letter, and Madame Lebrun told her to look for it either on the table or the dresser, or perhaps it was on the mantelpiece.

The letter was on the bookshelf. It possessed the greatest interest and attraction for Edna; the envelope, its size and shape, the postmark, the handwriting. She examined every detail of the outside before opening it. There were only a few lines, setting forth that he would leave the city that afternoon, that he had packed his trunk in good shape, that he was well, and sent her his love and begged to be affectionately remembered to all. There was no special message to Edna except a postscript saying that if Mrs. Pontellier desired to finish the book which he had been reading to her, his mother would find it in his room, among other books there on the table. Edna experienced a pang of jealousy because he had written to his mother rather than to her.

Every one seemed to take for granted that she missed him. Even her husband, when he came down the Saturday following Robert's departure, expressed regret that he had gone.

"How do you get on without him, Edna?" he asked.

"It's very dull without him," she admitted. Mr. Pontellier had seen Robert in the city, and Edna asked him a dozen questions or more. Where had they met? On Carondelet Street, in the morning. They had gone "in" and had a drink and a cigar together. What had they talked about? Chiefly about his prospects in Mexico, which Mr. Pontellier thought were promising. How did he look? How did he seem—grave, or gay, or how? Quite cheerful, and wholly taken up with the idea of his trip, which Mr. Pontellier found altogether natural in a young fellow about to seek fortune and adventure in a strange, queer country.

Edna tapped her foot impatiently, and wondered why the children persisted in playing in the sun when they might be under the trees. She went down and led them out of the sun, scolding the quadroon for not being more attentive.

It did not strike her as in the least grotesque that she should be making of Robert the object of conversation and leading her husband to speak of him. The sentiment which she entertained for Robert in no way resembled that which she felt for her husband, or had ever felt, or ever expected to feel. She had all her life long been accustomed to harbor thoughts and emotions which never voiced themselves. They had never taken the form of struggles. They belonged to her and were her own, and she entertained the conviction that she had a right to them and that they concerned no one but herself. Edna had once told Madame Ratignolle that she would never sacrifice herself for her children, or for any one. Then had followed a rather heated argument; the two women did not appear to understand each other or to be talking the same language. Edna tried to appease her friend, to explain.

"I would give up the unessential; I would give my money, I would give my life for my children; but I wouldn't give myself. I can't make it more clear; it's only something which I am beginning to comprehend, which is revealing itself to me."

"I don't know what you would call the essential, or what you mean by the unessential," said Madame Ratignolle, cheerfully; "but a woman who would give her life for her children could do no more than that—your Bible tells you so. I'm sure I couldn't do more than that."

"Oh, yes you could!" laughed Edna.

She was not surprised at Mademoiselle Reisz's question the morning that lady, following her to the beach, tapped her on the shoulder and asked if she did not greatly miss her young friend.

"Oh, good morning, Mademoiselle; it is you? Why, of course I miss Robert. Are you going down to bathe?"

"Why should I go down to bathe at the very end of the season when I haven't been in the surf all summer?" replied the woman, disagreeably.

"I beg your pardon," offered Edna, in some embarrassment, for she should have remembered that Mademoiselle Reisz's avoidance of the water had furnished a theme for much pleasantry. Some among them thought it was on account of her false hair, or the dread of getting the violets wet, while others attributed it to the natural aversion for water sometimes believed to accompany the artistic temperament. Mademoiselle offered Edna some chocolates in a paper bag, which she took from her pocket, by way of showing that she bore no ill feeling. She habitually ate chocolates for their sustaining quality; they contained much nutriment in small compass, she said. They saved her from starvation, as Madame Lebrun's table was utterly impossible; and no one save so impertinent a woman as Madame Lebrun could think of offering such food to people and requiring them to pay for it.

"She must feel very lonely without her son," said Edna, desiring to change the subject. "Her favorite son, too. It must have been quite hard to let him go."

Mademoiselle laughed maliciously.

"Her favorite son! Oh dear! Who could have been imposing such a tale upon you? Aline Lebrun lives for Victor, and for Victor alone. She has spoiled him into the worthless creature he is. She worships him and the ground he walks on. Robert is very well in a way, to give up all the money he can earn to the family, and keep the barest pittance for himself. Favorite son, indeed! I miss the poor fellow myself, my dear. I liked to see him and to hear him about the place—the only Lebrun who is worth a pinch of salt. He comes to see me often in the city. I like to play to him. That Victor! hanging would be too good for him. It's a wonder Robert hasn't beaten him to death long ago."

"I thought he had great patience with his brother," offered Edna, glad to be talking about Robert, no matter what was said.

"Oh! he thrashed him well enough a year or two ago," said Mademoiselle. "It was about a Spanish girl, whom Victor considered that he had some sort of claim upon. He met Robert one day talking to the girl, or walking with her, or bathing with her, or carrying her basket—I don't remember what;—and he became so insulting and abusive that Robert gave him a thrashing on the spot that has kept him comparatively in order for a good while. It's about time he was getting another."

"Was her name Mariequita?" asked Edna.

"Mariequita—yes, that was it. Mariequita. I had forgotten. Oh, she's a sly one, and a bad one, that Mariequita!"

Edna looked down at Mademoiselle Reisz and wondered how she could have listened to her venom so long. For some reason she felt depressed, almost unhappy. She had not intended to go into the water; but she donned her bathing suit, and left Mademoiselle alone, seated under the shade of the children's tent. The water was growing cooler as the season advanced. Edna plunged and swam about with an abandon that thrilled and invigorated her. She remained a long time in the water, half hoping that Mademoiselle Reisz would not wait for her.

But Mademoiselle waited. She was very amiable during the walk back, and raved much over Edna's appearance in her bathing suit. She talked about music. She hoped that Edna would go to see her in the city, and wrote her address with the stub of a pencil on a piece of card which she found in her pocket.

"When do you leave?" asked Edna.

"Next Monday; and you?"

"The following week," answered Edna, adding, "It has been a pleasant summer, hasn't it, Mademoiselle?"

"Well," agreed Mademoiselle Reisz, with a shrug, "rather pleasant, if it hadn't been for the mosquitoes and the Farival twins."

## XVII

The Pontelliers possessed a very charming home on Esplanade Street[1] in New Orleans. It was a large, double cottage, with a broad front veranda, whose round, fluted columns supported the sloping roof. The house was painted a dazzling white; the outside shutters, or jalousies, were green. In the yard, which was kept scrupulously neat, were flowers and plants of every description which flourishes in South Louisiana. Within doors the appointments were perfect after the conventional type. The softest carpets and rugs covered the floors; rich and tasteful draperies hung at doors and windows. There were paintings, selected with judgment and discrimination, upon the walls. The cut glass, the silver, the heavy damask which daily appeared upon the table were the envy of many women whose husbands were less generous than Mr. Pontellier.

Mr. Pontellier was very fond of walking about his house examining its various appointments and details, to see that nothing was amiss. He greatly valued his possessions, chiefly because they were his, and derived genuine pleasure from contemplating a painting, a statuette, a rare lace curtain—no matter what—after he had bought it and placed it among his household goods.

On Tuesday afternoons—Tuesday being Mrs. Pontellier's reception day[2]—there was a constant stream of callers—women who came in carriages or in the street cars, or walked when the air was soft and distance permitted. A light-colored mulatto boy, in dress coat and bearing a diminutive silver tray for the reception of cards, admitted them. A maid, in white fluted cap, offered the callers liqueur, coffee, or chocolate, as they might desire. Mrs. Pontellier, attired in a handsome reception gown, remained in the drawing-room the entire afternoon receiving her visitors. Men sometimes called in the evening with their wives.

This had been the programme which Mrs. Pontellier had religiously followed since her marriage, six years before. Certain evenings during the week she and her husband attended the opera or sometimes the play.

Mr. Pontellier left his home in the mornings between nine and ten o'clock, and rarely returned before half-past six or seven in the evening—dinner being served at half-past seven.

He and his wife seated themselves at table on Tuesday evening, a few weeks after their return from Grand Isle. They were alone together. The boys were being put to bed; the patter of their bare, escaping feet could be heard occasionally, as well as the pursuing voice of the quadroon, lifted in mild protest and entreaty. Mrs. Pontellier did not wear her usual Tuesday reception gown;

1. The most exclusive address of the Creole aristocracy; it was a street of palatial homes shaded by oaks, palms, and magnolias.

2. A day once a week when a woman was expected to be "at home" to receive visitors.

she was in ordinary house dress. Mr. Pontellier, who was observant about such things, noticed it, as he served the soup and handed it to the boy in waiting.

"Tired out, Edna? Whom did you have? Many callers?" he asked. He tasted his soup and began to season it with pepper, salt, vinegar, mustard—everything within reach.

"There were a good many," replied Edna, who was eating her soup with evident satisfaction. "I found their cards when I got home; I was out."

"Out!" exclaimed her husband, with something like genuine consternation in his voice as he laid down the vinegar cruet and looked at her through his glasses. "Why, what could have taken you out on Tuesday? What did you have to do?"

"Nothing. I simply felt like going out, and I went out."

"Well, I hope you left some suitable excuse," said her husband, somewhat appeased, as he added a dash of cayenne pepper to the soup.

"No, I left no excuse. I told Joe to say I was out, that was all."

"Why, my dear, I should think you'd understand by this time that people don't do such things; we've got to observe *les convenances*[3] if we ever expect to get on and keep up with the procession. If you felt that you had to leave home this afternoon, you should have left some suitable explanation for your absence.

"This soup is really impossible; it's strange that woman hasn't learned yet to make a decent soup. Any free-lunch stand in town serves a better one. Was Mrs. Belthrop here?"

"Bring the tray with the cards, Joe. I don't remember who was here."

The boy retired and returned after a moment, bringing the tiny silver tray, which was covered with ladies' visiting cards. He handed it to Mrs. Pontellier.

"Give it to Mr. Pontellier," she said.

Joe offered the tray to Mr. Pontellier, and removed the soup.

Mr. Pontellier scanned the names of his wife's callers, reading some of them aloud, with comments as he read.

" 'The Misses Delasidas.' I worked a big deal in futures[4] for their father this morning; nice girls; it's time they were getting married. 'Mrs. Belthrop.' I tell you what it is, Edna; you can't afford to snub Mrs. Belthrop. Why, Belthrop could buy and sell us ten times over. His business is worth a good, round sum to me. You'd better write her a note. 'Mrs. James Highcamp.' Hugh! the less you have to do with Mrs. Highcamp, the better. 'Madame Laforcé.' Came all the way from Carrolton,[5] too, poor old soul. 'Miss Wiggs,' 'Mrs. Eleanor Boltons.' " He pushed the cards aside.

"Mercy!" exclaimed Edna, who had been fuming. "Why are you taking the thing so seriously and making such a fuss over it?"

"I'm not making any fuss over it. But it's just such seeming trifles that we've got to take seriously; such things count."

The fish was scorched. Mr. Pontellier would not touch it. Edna said she did not mind a little scorched taste. The roast was in some way not to his fancy, and he did not like the manner in which the vegetables were served.

---

3. Proprieties, social conventions (French).
4. Commodities bought and sold for delivery at a future time and thus a form of speculation.

5. Village to the west of New Orleans, later absorbed by the city.

"It seems to me," he said, "we spend money enough in this house to procure at least one meal a day which a man could eat and retain his self-respect."

"You used to think the cook was a treasure," returned Edna, indifferently.

"Perhaps she was when she first came; but cooks are only human. They need looking after, like any other class of persons that you employ. Suppose I didn't look after the clerks in my office, just let them run things their own way; they'd soon make a nice mess of me and my business."

"Where are you going?" asked Edna, seeing that her husband arose from table without having eaten a morsel except a taste of the highly-seasoned soup.

"I'm going to get my dinner at the club. Good night." He went into the hall, took his hat and stick from the stand, and left the house.

She was somewhat familiar with such scenes. They had often made her very unhappy. On a few previous occasions she had been completely deprived of any desire to finish her dinner. Sometimes she had gone into the kitchen to administer a tardy rebuke to the cook. Once she went to her room and studied the cookbook during an entire evening, finally writing out a menu for the week, which left her harrassed with a feeling that, after all, she had accomplished no good that was worth the name.

But that evening Edna finished her dinner alone, with forced deliberation. Her face was flushed and her eyes flamed with some inward fire that lighted them. After finishing her dinner she went to her room, having instructed the boy to tell any other callers that she was indisposed.

It was a large, beautiful room, rich and picturesque in the soft, dim light which the maid had turned low. She went and stood at an open window and looked out upon the deep tangle of the garden below. All the mystery and witchery of the night seemed to have gathered there amid the perfumes and the dusky and tortuous outlines of flowers and foliage. She was seeking herself and finding herself in just such sweet, half-darkness which met her moods. But the voices were not soothing that came to her from the darkness and the sky above and the stars. They jeered and sounded mournful notes without promise, devoid even of hope. She turned back into the room and began to walk to and fro down its whole length, without stopping, without resting. She carried in her hands a thin handkerchief, which she tore into ribbons, rolled into a ball, and flung from her. Once she stopped, and taking off her wedding ring, flung it upon the carpet. When she saw it lying there, she stamped her heel upon it, striving to crush it. But her small boot heel did not make an indenture, not a mark upon the little glittering circlet.

In a sweeping passion she seized a glass vase from the table and flung it upon the tiles of the hearth. She wanted to destroy something. The crash and clatter were what she wanted to hear.

A maid, alarmed at the din of breaking glass, entered the room to discover what was the matter.

"A vase fell upon the hearth," said Edna. "Never mind; leave it till morning."

"Oh! you might get some of the glass in your feet, ma'am," insisted the young woman, picking up bits of the broken vase that were scattered upon the carpet. "And here's your ring, ma'am, under the chair."

Edna held out her hand, and taking the ring, slipped it upon her finger.

## XVIII

The following morning Mr. Pontellier, upon leaving for his office, asked Edna if she would not meet him in town in order to look at some new fixtures for the library.

"I hardly think we need new fixtures, Léonce. Don't let us get anything new; you are too extravagant. I don't believe you ever think of saving or putting by."

"The way to become rich is to make money, my dear Edna, not to save it," he said. He regretted that she did not feel inclined to go with him and select new fixtures. He kissed her good-by, and told her she was not looking well and must take care of herself. She was unusually pale and very quiet.

She stood on the front veranda as he quitted the house, and absently picked a few sprays of jessamine[6] that grew upon a trellis near by. She inhaled the odor of the blossoms and thrust them into the bosom of her white morning gown. The boys were dragging along the banquette[7] a small "express wagon," which they had filled with blocks and sticks. The quadroon was following them with little quick steps, having assumed a fictitious animation and alacrity for the occasion. A fruit vender was crying his wares in the street.

Edna looked straight before her with a self-absorbed expression upon her face. She felt no interest in anything about her. The street, the children, the fruit vender, the flowers growing there under her eyes, were all part and parcel of an alien world which had suddenly become antagonistic.

She went back into the house. She had thought of speaking to the cook concerning her blunders of the previous night; but Mr. Pontellier had saved her that disagreeable mission, for which she was so poorly fitted. Mr. Pontellier's arguments were usually convincing with those whom he employed. He left home feeling quite sure that he and Edna would sit down that evening, and possibly a few subsequent evenings, to a dinner deserving of the name.

Edna spent an hour or two in looking over some of her old sketches. She could see their shortcomings and defects, which were glaring in her eyes. She tried to work a little, but found she was not in the humor. Finally she gathered together a few of the sketches—those which she considered the least discreditable; and she carried them with her when, a little later, she dressed and left the house. She looked handsome and distinguished in her street gown. The tan of the seashore had left her face, and her forehead was smooth, white, and polished beneath her heavy, yellow-brown hair. There were a few freckles on her face, and a small, dark mole near the under lip and one on the temple, half-hidden in her hair.

As Edna walked along the street she was thinking of Robert. She was still under the spell of her infatuation. She had tried to forget him, realizing the inutility of remembering. But the thought of him was like an obsession, ever pressing itself upon her. It was not that she dwelt upon details of their acquaintance, or recalled in any special or peculiar way his personality; it was his being, his existence, which dominated her thought, fading sometimes as if it would melt into the mist of the forgotten, reviving again with an intensity which filled her with an incomprehensible longing.

6. Jasmine.  7. Sidewalk.

Edna was on her way to Madame Ratignolle's. Their intimacy, begun at Grand Isle, had not declined, and they had seen each other with some frequency since their return to the city. The Ratignolles lived at no great distance from Edna's home, on the corner of a side street, where Monsieur Ratignolle owned and conducted a drug store which enjoyed a steady and prosperous trade. His father had been in the business before him, and Monsieur Ratignolle stood well in the community and bore an enviable reputation for integrity and clear-headedness. His family lived in commodious apartments over the store, having an entrance on the side within the *porte cochère*.[8] There was something which Edna thought very French, very foreign, about their whole manner of living. In the large and pleasant salon which extended across the width of the house, the Ratignolles entertained their friends once a fortnight with a *soirée musicale*,[9] sometimes diversified by card-playing. There was a friend who played upon the 'cello. One brought his flute and another his violin, while there were some who sang and a number who performed upon the piano with various degrees of taste and agility. The Ratignolles' *soirées musicales* were widely known, and it was considered a privilege to be invited to them.

Edna found her friend engaged in assorting the clothes which had returned that morning from the laundry. She at once abandoned her occupation upon seeing Edna, who had been ushered without ceremony into her presence.

" 'Cité can do it as well as I; it is really her business," she explained to Edna, who apologized for interrupting her. And she summoned a young black woman, whom she instructed, in French, to be very careful in checking off the list which she handed her. She told her to notice particularly if a fine linen handkerchief of Monsieur Ratignolle's, which was missing last week, had been returned; and to be sure to set to one side such pieces as required mending and darning.

Then placing an arm around Edna's waist, she led her to the front of the house, to the salon, where it was cool and sweet with the odor of great roses that stood upon the hearth in jars.

Madame Ratignolle looked more beautiful than ever there at home, in a negligé which left her arms almost wholly bare and exposed the rich, melting curves of her white throat.

"Perhaps I shall be able to paint your picture some day," said Edna with a smile when they were seated. She produced the roll of sketches and started to unfold them. "I believe I ought to work again. I feel as if I wanted to be doing something. What do you think of them? Do you think it worth while to take it up again and study some more? I might study for a while with Laidpore."

She knew that Madame Ratignolle's opinion in such a matter would be next to valueless, that she herself had not alone decided, but determined; but she sought the words and praise and encouragement that would help her to put heart into her venture.

"Your talent is immense, dear!"

"Nonsense!" protested Edna, well pleased.

"Immense, I tell you," persisted Madame Ratignolle, surveying the

---

8. In America, a porch under which a car or carriage may be driven to protect travelers alighting or boarding (French).

9. An evening of music (French).

sketches one by one, at close range, then holding then at arm's length, narrowing her eyes, and dropping her head on one side. "Surely, this Bavarian peasant is worthy of framing; and this basket of apples! never have I seen anything more lifelike. One might almost be tempted to reach out a hand and take one."

Edna could not control a feeling which bordered upon complacency at her friend's praise, even realizing, as she did, its true worth. She retained a few of the sketches, and gave all the rest to Madame Ratignolle, who appreciated the gift far beyond its value and proudly exhibited the pictures to her husband when he came up from the store a little later for his midday dinner.

Mr. Ratignolle was one of those men who are called the salt of the earth. His cheerfulness was unbounded, and it was matched by his goodness of heart, his broad charity, and common sense. He and his wife spoke English with an accent which was only discernible through its un-English emphasis and a certain carefulness and deliberation. Edna's husband spoke English with no accent whatever. The Ratignolles understood each other perfectly. If ever the fusion of two human beings into one has been accomplished on this sphere it was surely in their union.

As Edna seated herself at table with them she thought, "Better a dinner of herbs,"[1] though it did not take her long to discover that was no dinner of herbs, but a delicious repast, simple, choice, and in every way satisfying.

Monsieur Ratignolle was delighted to see her, though he found her looking not so well as at Grand Isle, and he advised a tonic. He talked a good deal on various topics, a little politics, some city news and neighborhood gossip. He spoke with an animation and earnestness that gave an exaggerated importance to every syllable he uttered. His wife was keenly interested in everything he said, laying down her fork the better to listen, chiming in, taking the words out of his mouth.

Edna felt depressed rather than soothed after leaving them. The little glimpse of domestic harmony which had been offered her, gave her no regret, no longing. It was not a condition of life which fitted her, and she could see in it but an appalling and hopeless ennui. She was moved by a kind of commiseration for Madame Ratignolle,—a pity for that colorless existence which never uplifted its possessor beyond the region of blind contentment, in which no moment of anguish ever visited her soul, in which she would never have the taste of life's delirium. Edna vaguely wondered what she meant by "life's delirium." It had crossed her thought like some unsought, extraneous impression.

## XIX

Edna could not help but think that it was very foolish, very childish, to have stamped upon her wedding ring and smashed the crystal vase upon the tiles. She was visited by no more outbursts, moving her to such futile expedients. She began to do as she liked and to feel as she liked. She completely abandoned her Tuesdays at home, and did not return the visits of those who had called upon her. She made no ineffectual efforts to conduct her household *en bonne ménagère,*[2] going and coming as it suited her fancy, and, so far as she was able, lending herself to any passing caprice.

1. "Better is a dinner of herbs where love is, than a stalled [fattened] ox and hatred therewith" (Proverbs 15.7).
2. As a good housewife (French).

Mr. Pontellier had been a rather courteous husband so long as he met a certain tacit submissiveness in his wife. But her new and unexpected line of conduct completely bewildered him. It shocked him. Then her absolute disregard for her duties as a wife angered him. When Mr. Pontellier became rude, Edna grew insolent. She had resolved never to take another step backward.

"It seems to me the utmost folly for a woman at the head of a household, and the mother of children, to spend in an atelier[3] days which would be better employed contriving for the comfort of her family."

"I feel like painting," answered Edna. "Perhaps I shan't always feel like it."

"Then in God's name paint! but don't let the family go to the devil. There's Madame Ratignolle; because she keeps up her music, she doesn't let everything go else to chaos. And she's more of a musician than you are a painter."

"She isn't a musician, and I'm not a painter. It isn't on account of painting that I let things go."

"On account of what, then?"

"Oh! I don't know. Let me alone; you bother me."

It sometimes entered Mr. Pontellier's mind to wonder if his wife were not growing a little unbalanced mentally. He could see plainly that she was not herself. That is, he could not see that she was becoming herself and daily casting aside that fictitious self which we assume like a garment with which to appear before the world.

Her husband let her alone as she requested, and went away to his office. Edna went up to her atelier—a bright room in the top of the house. She was working with great energy and interest, without accomplishing anything, however, which satisfied her even in the smallest degree. For a time she had the whole household enrolled in the service of art. The boys posed for her. They thought it amusing at first, but the occupation soon lost its attractiveness when they discovered that it was not a game arranged especially for their entertainment. The quadroon sat for hours before Edna's palette, patient as a savage, while the housemaid took charge of the children, and the drawing-room went undusted. But the house-maid, too, served her term as model when Edna perceived that the young woman's back and shoulders were molded on classic lines, and that her hair, loosened from its confining cap, became an inspiration. While Edna worked she sometimes sang low the little air, *"Ah! si tu savais!"*

It moved her with recollections. She could hear again the ripple of the water, the flapping sail. She could see the glint of the moon upon the bay, and could feel the soft, gusty beating of the hot south wind. A subtle current of desire passed through her body, weakening her hold upon the brushes and making her eyes burn.

There were days when she was very happy without knowing why. She was happy to be alive and breathing, when her whole being seemed to be one with the sunlight, the color, the odors, the luxuriant warmth of some perfect Southern day. She liked then to wander alone into strange and unfamiliar places. She discovered many a sunny, sleepy corner, fashioned to dream in. And she found it good to dream and to be alone and unmolested.

There were days when she was unhappy, she did not know why,—when it did not seem worth while to be glad or sorry, to be alive or dead; when life

3. Studio.

appeared to her like a grotesque pandemonium and humanity like worms struggling blindly toward inevitable annihilation. She could not work on such a day, nor weave fancies to stir her pulses and warm her blood.

## XX

It was during such a mood that Edna hunted up Mademoiselle Reisz. She had not forgotten the rather disagreeable impression left upon her by their last interview; but she nevertheless felt a desire to see her—above all, to listen while she played upon the piano. Quite early in the afternoon she started upon her quest for the pianist. Unfortunately she had mislaid or lost Mademoiselle Reisz's card, and looking up her address in the city directory, she found that the woman lived on Bienville Street,[4] some distance away. The directory which fell into her hands was a year or more old, however, and upon reaching the number indicated, Edna discovered that the house was occupied by a respectable family of mulattoes who had *chambres garnies*[5] to let. They had been living there for six months, and knew absolutely nothing of a Mademoiselle Reisz. In fact, they knew nothing of any of their neighbors; their lodgers were all people of the highest distinction, they assured Edna. She did not linger to discuss class distinctions with Madame Pouponne, but hastened to a neighboring grocery store, feeling sure that Mademoiselle would have left her address with the proprietor.

He knew Mademoiselle Reisz a good deal better than he wanted to know her, he informed his questioner. In truth, he did not want to know her at all, anything concerning her—the most disagreeable and unpopular woman who ever lived in Bienville Street. He thanked heaven she had left the neighborhood, and was equally thankful that he did not know where she had gone.

Edna's desire to see Mademoiselle Reisz had increased tenfold since these unlooked-for obstacles had arisen to thwart it. She was wondering who could give her the information she sought, when it suddenly occurred to her that Madame Lebrun would be the one most likely to do so. She knew it was useless to ask Madame Ratignolle, who was on the most distant terms with the musician, and preferred to know nothing concerning her. She had once been almost as emphatic in expressing herself upon the subject as the corner grocer.

Edna knew that Madame Lebrun had returned to the city, for it was the middle of November. And she also knew where the Lebruns lived, on Chartres Street.[6]

Their home from the outside looked like a prison, with iron bars before the door and lower windows. The iron bars were a relic of the old *régime*,[7] and no one had ever thought of dislodging them. At the side was a high fence enclosing the garden. A gate or door opening upon the street was locked. Edna rang the bell at this side garden gate, and stood upon the banquette, waiting to be admitted.

It was Victor who opened the gate for her. A black woman, wiping her hands upon her apron, was close at his heels. Before she saw them Edna

4. On the opposite side of the French Quarter from the Pontelliers' house.
5. Furnished rooms (French).

6. In the heart of the French Quarter.
7. The Spanish regime (1766–1803).

could hear them in altercation, the woman—plainly an anomaly—claiming the right to be allowed to perform her duties, one of which was to answer the bell.

Victor was surprised and delighted to see Mrs. Pontellier, and he made no attempt to conceal either his astonishment or his delight. He was a dark-browed, good-looking youngster of nineteen, greatly resembling his mother, but with ten times her impetuosity. He instructed the black woman to go at once and inform Madame Lebrun that Mrs. Pontellier desired to see her. The woman grumbled a refusal to do part of her duty when she had not been permitted to do it all, and started back to her interrupted task of weeding the garden. Whereupon Victor administered a rebuke in the form of a volley of abuse, which owing to its rapidity and incoherence, was all but incomprehensible to Edna. Whatever it was, the rebuke was convincing, for the woman dropped her hoe and went mumbling into the house.

Edna did not wish to enter. It was very pleasant there on the side porch, where there were chairs, a wicker lounge, and a small table. She seated herself, for she was tired from her long tramp; and she began to rock gently and smooth out the folds of her silk parasol. Victor drew up his chair beside her. He at once explained that the black woman's offensive conduct was all due to imperfect training, as he was not there to take her in hand. He had only come up from the island the morning before, and expected to return next day. He stayed all winter at the island; he lived there, and kept the place in order and got things ready for the summer visitors.

But a man needed occasional relaxation, he informed Mrs. Pontellier, and every now and again he drummed up a pretext to bring him to the city. My! but he had had a time of it the evening before! He wouldn't want his mother to know, and he began to talk in a whisper. He was scintillant with recollections. Of course, he couldn't think of telling Mrs. Pontellier all about it, she being a woman and not comprehending such things. But it all began with a girl peeping and smiling at him through the shutters as he passed by. Oh! but she was a beauty! Certainly he smiled back, and went up and talked to her. Mrs. Pontellier did not know him if she supposed he was one to let an opportunity like that escape him. Despite herself, the youngster amused her. She must have betrayed in her look some degree of interest or entertainment. The boy grew more daring, and Mrs. Pontellier might have found herself, in a little while, listening to a highly colored story but for the timely appearance of Madame Lebrun.

That lady was still clad in white, according to her custom of the summer. Her eyes beamed an effusive welcome. Would not Mrs. Pontellier go inside? Would she partake of some refreshment? Why had she not been there before? How was that dear Mr. Pontellier and how were those sweet children? Has Mrs. Pontellier ever known such a warm November?

Victor went and reclined on the wicker lounge behind his mother's chair, where he commanded a view of Edna's face. He had taken her parasol from her hands while he spoke to her, and he now lifted it and twirled it above him as he lay on his back. When Madame Lebrun complained that it was so dull coming back to the city; that she saw so few people now; that even Victor, when he came up from the island for a day or two, had so much to occupy him and engage his time, then it was that the youth went into contortions on the lounge and winked mischievously at Edna. She somehow felt like a confederate in crime, and tried to look severe and disapproving.

There had been but two letters from Robert, with little in them, they told her. Victor said it was really not worth while to go inside for the letters, when his mother entreated him to go in search of them. He remembered the contents, which in truth he rattled off very glibly when put to the test.

One letter was written from Vera Cruz and the other from the City of Mexico. He had met Montel, who was doing everything toward his advancement. So far, the financial situation was no improvement over the one he had left in New Orleans, but of course the prospects were vastly better. He wrote of the City of Mexico, the buildings, the people and their habits, the conditions of life which he found there. He sent his love to the family. He inclosed a check to his mother, and hoped she would affectionately remember him to all his friends. That was about the substance of the two letters. Edna felt that if there had been a message for her, she would have received it. The despondent frame of mind in which she had left home began again to overtake her, and she remembered that she wished to find Mademoiselle Reisz.

Madame Lebrun knew where Mademoiselle Reisz lived. She gave Edna the address, regretting that she would not consent to stay and spend the remainder of the afternoon, and pay a visit to Mademoiselle Reisz some other day. The afternoon was already well advanced.

Victor escorted her out upon the banquette, lifted her parasol, and held it over her while he walked to the car with her. He entreated her to bear in mind that the disclosures of the afternoon were strictly confidential. She laughed and bantered him a little, remembering too late that she should have been dignified and reserved.

"How handsome Mrs. Pontellier looked!" said Madame Lebrun to her son.

"Ravishing!" he admitted. "The city atmosphere has improved her. Some way she doesn't seem like the same woman."

## XXI

Some people contended that the reason Mademoiselle Reisz always chose apartments up under the roof was to discourage the approach of beggars, peddlars and callers. There were plenty of windows in her little front room. They were for the most part dingy, but as they were nearly always open it did not make so much difference. They often admitted into the room a good deal of smoke and soot; but at the same time all the light and air that there was came through them. From her windows could be seen the crescent of the river, the masts of ships and the big chimneys of the Mississippi steamers. A magnificent piano crowded the apartment. In the next room she slept, and in the third and last she harbored a gasoline stove on which she cooked her meals when disinclined to descend to the neighboring restaurant. It was there also that she ate, keeping her belongings in a rare old buffet, dingy and battered from a hundred years of use.

When Edna knocked at Mademoiselle Reisz's front room door and entered, she discovered that person standing beside the window, engaged in mending or patching an old prunella gaiter.[8] The little musician laughed all over when

8. A cloth button shoe with leather soles.

she saw Edna. Her laugh consisted of a contortion of the face and all the muscles of the body. She seemed strikingly homely, standing there in the afternoon light. She still wore the shabby lace and the artificial bunch of violets on the side of her head.

"So you remembered me at last," said Mademoiselle. "I had said to myself, 'Ah, bah! she will never come.' "

"Did you want me to come?" asked Edna with a smile.

"I had not thought much about it," answered Mademoiselle. The two had seated themselves on a little bumpy sofa which stood against the wall. "I am glad, however, that you came. I have the water boiling back there, and was just about to make some coffee. You will drink a cup with me. And how is *la belle dame?*[9] Always handsome! always healthy! always contented!" She took Edna's hand between her strong wiry fingers, holding it loosely without warmth, and executing a sort of double theme upon the back and palm.

"Yes," she went on; "I sometimes thought: 'She will never come. She promised as those women in society always do, without meaning it. She will not come.' For I really don't believe you like me, Mrs. Pontellier."

"I don't know whether I like you or not," replied Edna, gazing down at the little woman with a quizzical look.

The candor of Mrs. Pontellier's admission greatly pleased Mademoiselle Reisz. She expressed her gratification by repairing forthwith to the region of the gasoline stove and rewarding her guest with the promised cup of coffee. The coffee and the biscuit accompanying it proved very acceptable to Edna, who had declined refreshment at Madame Lebrun's and was now beginning to feel hungry. Mademoiselle set the tray which she brought in upon a small table near at hand, and seated herself once again on the lumpy sofa.

"I have had a letter from your friend," she remarked, as she poured a little cream into Edna's cup and handed it to her.

"My friend?"

"Yes, your friend Robert. He wrote to me from the City of Mexico."

"Wrote to *you?*" repeated Edna in amazement, stirring her coffee absently.

"Yes, to me. Why not? Don't stir all the warmth out of your coffee; drink it. Though the letter might as well have been sent to you; it was nothing but Mrs. Pontellier from beginning to end."

"Let me see it," requested the young woman, entreatingly.

"No; a letter concerns no one but the person who writes it and the one to whom it is written."

"Haven't you just said it concerned me from beginning to end?"

"It was written about you, not to you. 'Have you seen Mrs. Pontellier? How is she looking?' he asks. 'As Mrs. Pontellier says,' or 'as Mrs. Pontellier once said.' 'If Mrs. Pontellier should call upon you, play for her that Impromptu of Chopin's, my favorite. I heard it here a day or two ago, but not as you play it. I should like to know how it affects her,' and so on, as if he supposed we were constantly in each other's society."

"Let me see the letter."

"Oh, no."

"Have you answered it?"

"No."

9. The lovely lady (French).

"Let me see the letter."

"No, and again, no."

"Then play the Impromptu for me."

"It is growing late; what time do you have to be home?"

"Time doesn't concern me. Your question seems a little rude. Play the Impromptu."

"But you have told me nothing of yourself. What are you doing?"

"Painting!" laughed Edna. "I am becoming an artist. Think of it!"

"Ah! an artist! You have pretensions, Madame."

"Why pretensions? Do you think I could not become an artist?"

"I do not know you well enough to say. I do not know your talent or your temperament. To be an artist includes much; one must possess many gifts—absolute gifts—which have not been acquired by one's own effort. And, moreover, to succeed, the artist must possess the courageous soul."

"What do you mean by the courageous soul?"

"Courageous, *ma foi!* The brave soul. The soul that dares and defies."

"Show me the letter and play for me the Impromptu. You see that I have persistence. Does that quality count for anything in art?"

"It counts with a foolish old woman whom you have captivated," replied Mademoiselle, with her wriggling laugh.

The letter was right there at hand in the drawer of the little table upon which Edna had just placed her coffee cup. Mademoiselle opened the drawer and drew forth the letter, the topmost one. She placed it in Edna's hands, and without further comment arose and went to the piano.

Mademoiselle played a soft interlude. It was an improvisation. She sat low at the instrument, and the lines of her body settled into ungraceful curves and angles that gave it an appearance of deformity. Gradually and imperceptibly the interlude melted into the soft opening minor chords of the Chopin Impromptu.

Edna did not know when the Impromptu began or ended. She sat in the sofa corner reading Robert's letter by the fading light. Mademoiselle had glided from the Chopin into the quivering love-notes of Isolde's song,[1] and back again to the Impromptu with its soulful and poignant longing.

The shadows deepened in the little room. The music grew strange and fantastic—turbulent, insistent, plaintive and soft with entreaty. The shadows grew deeper. The music filled the room. It floated out upon the night, over the housetops, the crescent of the river, losing itself in the silence of the upper air.

Edna was sobbing, just as she had wept one midnight at Grand Isle when strange, new voices awoke in her. She arose in some agitation to take her departure. "May I come again, Mademoiselle?" she asked at the threshold.

"Come whenever you feel like it. Be careful; the stairs and landings are dark; don't stumble."

Mademoiselle reëntered and lit a candle. Robert's letter was on the floor. She stooped and picked it up. It was crumpled and damp with tears. Mademoiselle smoothed the letter out, restored it to the envelope, and replaced it in the table drawer.

1. From Richard Wagner's opera *Tristan und Isolde* (1857–59), based on a medieval legend of ill-fated love. Isolde's *Liebestod* (Love-death) is sung as she bids her dead lover farewell and falls dead herself in his arms.

## XXII

One morning on his way into town Mr. Pontellier stopped at the house of his old friend and family physician, Doctor Mandelet. The Doctor was a semi-retired physician, resting, as the saying is, upon his laurels. He bore a reputation for wisdom rather than skill—leaving the active practice of medicine to his assistants and younger contemporaries—and was much sought for in matters of consultation. A few families, united to him by bonds of friendship, he still attended when they required the services of a physician. The Pontelliers were among these.

Mr. Pontellier found the Doctor reading at the open window of his study. His house stood rather far back from the street, in the center of a delightful garden, so that it was quiet and peaceful at the old gentleman's study window. He was a great reader. He stared up disapprovingly over his eye-glasses as Mr. Pontellier entered, wondering who had the temerity to disturb him at that hour of the morning.

"Ah, Pontellier! Not sick, I hope. Come and have a seat. What news do you bring this morning?" He was quite portly, with a profusion of gray hair, and small blue eyes which age had robbed of much of their brightness but none of their penetration.

"Oh! I'm never sick, Doctor. You know that I come of tough fiber—of that old Creole race of Pontelliers that dry up and finally blow away. I came to consult—no, not precisely to consult—to talk to you about Edna. I don't know what ails her."

"Madame Pontellier not well?" marveled the Doctor. "Why I saw her—I think it was a week ago—walking along Canal Street,[2] the picture of health, it seemed to me."

"Yes, yes; she seems quite well," said Mr. Pontellier, leaning forward and whirling his stick between his two hands; "but she doesn't act well. She's odd, she's not like herself. I can't make her out, and I thought perhaps you'd help me."

"How does she act?" inquired the doctor.

"Well, it isn't easy to explain," said Mr. Pontellier, throwing himself back in his chair. "She lets the housekeeping go to the dickens."

"Well, well; women are not all alike, my dear Pontellier. We've got to consider—"

"I know that; I told you I couldn't explain. Her whole attitude—toward me and everybody and everything—has changed. You know I have a quick temper, but I don't want to quarrel or be rude to a woman, especially my wife; yet I'm driven to it, and feel like ten thousand devils after I've made a fool of myself. She's making it devilishly uncomfortable for me," he went on nervously. "She's got some sort of notion in her head concerning the eternal rights of women; and—you understand—we meet in the morning at the breakfast table."

The old gentleman lifted his shaggy eyebrows, protruded his thick nether lip, and tapped the arms of his chair with his cushioned finger-tips.

"What have you been doing to her, Pontellier?"

---

2. The main street of downtown New Orleans, separating the old French city from the new American section.

"Doing! *Parbleu!*"[3]

"Has she," asked the Doctor, with a smile, "has she been associating of late with a circle of pseudo-intellectual women[4]—superspiritual superior beings? My wife has been telling me about them."

"That's the trouble," broke in Mr. Pontellier, "she hasn't been associating with any one. She has abandoned her Tuesdays at home, has thrown over all her acquaintances, and goes tramping about by herself, moping in the street-cars, getting in after dark. I tell you she's peculiar. I don't like it; I feel a little worried over it."

This was a new aspect for the Doctor. "Nothing hereditary?" he asked, seriously. "Nothing peculiar about her family antecedents, is there?"

"Oh, no, indeed! She comes of sound old Presbyterian Kentucky stock. The old gentleman, her father, I have heard, used to atone for his week-day sins with his Sunday devotions. I know for a fact, that his race horses literally ran away with the prettiest bit of Kentucky farming land I ever laid eyes upon. Margaret—you know Margaret—she has all the Presbyterianism undiluted. And the youngest is something of a vixen. By the way, she gets married in a couple of weeks from now."

"Send your wife up to the wedding," exclaimed the Doctor, foreseeing a happy solution. "Let her stay among her own people for a while; it will do her good."

"That's what I want her to do. She won't go to the marriage. She says a wedding is one of the most lamentable spectacles on earth. Nice thing for a woman to say to her husband!" exclaimed Mr. Pontellier, fuming anew at the recollection.

"Pontellier," said the Doctor, after a moment's reflection, "let your wife alone for a while. Don't bother her, and don't let her bother you. Woman, my dear friend, is a very peculiar and delicate organism—a sensitive and highly organized woman, such as I know Mrs. Pontellier to be, is especially peculiar. It would require an inspired psychologist to deal successfully with them. And when ordinary fellows like you and me attempt to cope with their idiosyncrasies the result is bungling. Most women are moody and whimsical. This is some passing whim of your wife, due to some cause or causes which you and I needn't try to fathom. But it will pass happily over, especially if you let her alone. Send her around to see me."

"Oh! I couldn't do that; there'd be no reason for it," objected Mr. Pontellier.

"Then I'll go around and see her," said the Doctor. "I'll drop in to dinner some evening *en bon ami.*"[5]

"Do! by all means," urged Mr. Pontellier. "What evening will you come? Say Thursday. Will you come Thursday?" he asked, rising to take his leave.

"Very well; Thursday. My wife may possibly have some engagement for me Thursday. In case she has, I shall let you know. Otherwise, you may expect me."

Mr. Pontellier turned before leaving to say:

---

3. For heaven's sake! (French).
4. Women's clubs flourished during the late nineteenth century in America. They were a source of education for women as well as an arena for polit- ical organization. As the doctor's remark indicates, the club movement was met with scorn in some quarters [Culley's note].
5. As a friend (French).

"I am going to New York on business very soon. I have a big scheme on hand, and want to be on the field proper to pull the ropes and handle the ribbons.[6] We'll let you in on the inside if you say so, Doctor," he laughed.

"No, I thank you, my dear sir," returned the Doctor. "I leave such ventures to you younger men with the fever of life still in your blood."

"What I wanted to say," continued Mr. Pontellier, with his hand on the knob; "I may have to be absent a good while. Would you advise me to take Edna along?"

"By all means, if she wishes to go. If not, leave her here. Don't contradict her. The mood will pass, I assure you. It may take a month, two, three months—possibly longer, but it will pass; have patience."

"Well, good-by, *à jeudi*,"[7] said Mr. Pontellier, as he let himself out.

The Doctor would have liked during the course of conversation to ask, "Is there any man in the case?" but he knew his Creole too well to make such a blunder as that.

He did not resume his book immediately, but sat for a while meditatively looking out into the garden.

## XXIII

Edna's father was in the city, and had been with them several days. She was not very warmly or deeply attached to him, but they had certain tastes in common, and when together they were companionable. His coming was in the nature of a welcome disturbance; it seemed to furnish a new direction for her emotions.

He had come to purchase a wedding gift for his daughter, Janet, and an outfit for himself in which he might make a creditable appearance at her marriage. Mr. Pontellier had selected the bridal gift, as every one immediately connected with him always deferred to his taste in such matters. And his suggestions on the question of dress—which too often assumes the nature of a problem—were of inestimable value to his father-in-law. But for the past few days the old gentleman had been upon Edna's hands, and in his society she was becoming acquainted with a new set of sensations. He had been a colonel in the Confederate army, and still maintained, with the title, the military bearing which had always accompanied it. His hair and mustache were white and silky, emphasizing the rugged bronze of his face. He was tall and thin, and wore his coats padded, which gave a fictitious breadth and depth to his shoulders and chest. Edna and her father looked very distinguished together, and excited a good deal of notice during their perambulations. Upon his arrival she began by introducing him to her atelier and making a sketch of him. He took the whole matter very seriously. If her talent had been ten-fold greater than it was, it would not have surprised him, convinced as he was that he had bequeathed to all of his daughters the germs of a masterful capability, which only depended upon their own efforts to be directed toward successful achievement.

Before her pencil he sat rigid and unflinching, as he had faced the cannon's mouth in days gone by. He resented the intrusion of the children, who gaped

6. I.e., the reins.                    7. Until Thursday (French).

with wondering eyes at him, sitting so stiff up there in their mother's bright atelier. When they drew near he motioned them away with an expressive action of the foot, loath to disturb the fixed lines of his countenance, his arms, or his rigid shoulders.

Edna, anxious to entertain him, invited Mademoiselle Reisz to meet him, having promised him a treat in her piano playing; but Mademoiselle declined the invitation. So together they attended a *soirée musicale* at the Ratignolles'. Monsieur and Madame Ratignolle made much of the Colonel, installing him as the guest of honor and engaging him at once to dine with them the following Sunday, or any day which he might select. Madame coquetted with him in the most captivating and naïve manner, with eyes, gestures, and a profusion of compliments, till the Colonel's old head felt thirty years younger on his padded shoulders. Edna marveled, not comprehending. She herself was almost devoid of coquetry.

There were one or two men whom she observed at the *soirée musicale*; but she would never have felt moved to any kittenish display to attract their notice—to any feline or feminine wiles to express herself toward them. Their personality attracted her in an agreeable way. Her fancy selected them, and she was glad when a lull in the music gave them an opportunity to meet her and talk with her. Often on the street the glance of strange eyes had lingered in her memory, and sometimes had disturbed her.

Mr. Pontellier did not attend these *soirée musicales*. He considered them *bourgeois*, and found more diversion at the club. To Madame Ratignolle he said the music dispensed at her *soirées* was too "heavy," too far beyond his untrained comprehension. His excuse flattered her. But she disapproved of Mr. Pontellier's club, and she was frank enough to tell Edna so.

"It's a pity Mr. Pontellier doesn't stay home more in the evenings. I think you would be more—well, if you don't mind my saying it—more united, if he did."

"Oh! dear no!" said Edna, with a blank look in her eyes. "What should I do if he stayed home? We wouldn't have anything to say to each other."

She had not much of anything to say to her father, for that matter; but he did not antagonize her. She discovered that he interested her, though she realized that he might not interest her long; and for the first time in her life she felt as if she were thoroughly acquainted with him. He kept her busy serving him and ministering to his wants. It amused her to do so. She would not permit a servant or one of the children to do anything for him which she might do herself. Her husband noticed, and thought it was the expression of a deep filial attachment which he had never suspected.

The Colonel drank numerous "toddies" during the course of the day, which left him, however, imperturbed. He was an expert at concocting strong drinks. He had even invented some, to which he had given fantastic names, and for whose manufacture he required diverse ingredients that it devolved upon Edna to procure for him.

When Doctor Mandelet dined with the Pontelliers on Thursday he could discern in Mrs. Pontellier no trace of that morbid condition which her husband had reported to him. She was excited and in a manner radiant. She and her father had been to the race course, and their thoughts when they seated themselves at table were still occupied with the events of the afternoon, and their talk was still of the track. The Doctor had not kept pace with turf affairs.

He had certain recollections of racing in what he called "the good old times" when the Lecompte stables[8] flourished, and he drew upon this fund of memories so that he might not be left out and seem wholly devoid of the modern spirit. But he failed to impose upon the Colonel, and was even far from impressing him with this trumped-up knowledge of bygone days. Edna had staked her father on his last venture, with the most gratifying results to both of them. Besides, they had met some very charming people, according to the Colonel's impressions. Mrs. Mortimer Merriman and Mrs. James Highcamp, who were there with Alcée Arobin, had joined them and had enlivened the hours in a fashion that warmed him to think of.

Mr. Pontellier himself had no particular leaning toward horse-racing, and was even rather inclined to discourage it as a pastime, especially when he considered the fate of that blue-grass farm in Kentucky. He endeavored, in a general way, to express a particular disapproval, and only succeeded in arousing the ire and opposition of his father-in-law. A pretty dispute followed, in which Edna warmly espoused her father's cause and the Doctor remained neutral.

He observed his hostess attentively from under his shaggy brows, and noted a subtle change which had transformed her from the listless woman he had known into a being who, for the moment, seemed palpitant with the forces of life. Her speech was warm and energetic. There was no repression in her glance or gesture. She reminded him of some beautiful, sleek animal waking up in the sun.

The dinner was excellent. The claret was warm and the champagne was cold, and under their beneficent influence the threatened unpleasantness melted and vanished with the fumes of the wine.

Mr. Pontellier warmed up and grew reminiscent. He told some amusing plantation experiences, recollections of old Iberville and his youth, when he hunted 'possum in company with some friendly darky; thrashed the pecan trees, shot the grosbec,[9] and roamed the woods and fields in mischievous idleness.

The Colonel, with little sense of humor and of the fitness of things, related a somber episode of those dark and bitter days, in which he had acted a conspicuous part and always formed a central figure. Nor was the Doctor happier in his selection, when he told the old, ever new and curious story of the waning of a woman's love, seeking strange, new channels, only to return to its legitimate source after days of fierce unrest. It was one of the many little human documents which had been unfolded to him during his long career as a physician. The story did not seem especially to impress Edna. She had one of her own to tell, of a woman who paddled away with her lover one night in a pirogue and never came back. They were lost amid the Baratarian Islands, and no one ever heard of them or found trace of them from that day to this. It was a pure invention. She said that Madame Antoine had related it to her. That, also, was an invention. Perhaps it was a dream she had had. But every glowing word seemed real to those who listened. They could feel the hot breath of the Southern night; they could hear the long sweep of the pirogue through the glistening moonlit water, the beating of birds' wings, rising star-

---

8. New Orleans was a celebrated racing center before the Civil War, boasting four racetracks. Lecompte was the name of a famous racehorse.

9. I.e., grosbeak, game birds distinguished by their large (*gros*) bills.

tled from among the reeds in the salt-water pools; they could see the faces of the lovers, pale, close together, rapt in oblivious forgetfulness, drifting into the unknown.

The champagne was cold, and its subtle fumes played fantastic tricks with Edna's memory that night.

Outside, away from the glow of the fire and the soft lamplight, the night was chill and murky. The Doctor doubled his old-fashioned cloak across his breast as he strode home through the darkness. He knew his fellow-creatures better than most men; knew that inner life which so seldom unfolds itself to unanointed eyes. He was sorry he had accepted Pontellier's invitation. He was growing old, and beginning to need rest and an imperturbed spirit. He did not want the secrets of other lives thrust upon him.

"I hope it isn't Arobin," he muttered to himself as he walked. "I hope to heaven it isn't Alcée Arobin."

## XXIV

Edna and her father had a warm, and almost violent dispute upon the subject of her refusal to attend her sister's wedding. Mr. Pontellier declined to interfere, to interpose either his influence or his authority. He was following Doctor Mandelet's advice, and letting her do as she liked. The Colonel reproached his daughter for her lack of filial kindness and respect, her want of sisterly affection and womanly consideration. His arguments were labored and unconvincing. He doubted if Janet would accept any excuse—forgetting that Edna had offered none. He doubted if Janet would ever speak to her again, and he was sure Margaret would not.

Edna was glad to be rid of her father when he finally took himself off with his wedding garments and his bridal gifts, with his padded shoulders, his Bible reading, his "toddies" and ponderous oaths.

Mr. Pontellier followed him closely. He meant to stop at the wedding on his way to New York and endeavor by every means which money and love could devise to atone somewhat for Edna's incomprehensible action.

"You are too lenient, too lenient by far, Léonce," asserted the Colonel. "Authority, coercion are what is needed. Put your foot down good and hard; the only way to manage a wife. Take my word for it."

The Colonel was perhaps unaware that he had coerced his own wife into her grave. Mr. Pontellier had a vague suspicion of it which he thought it needless to mention at that late day.

Edna was not so consciously gratified at her husband's leaving home as she had been over the departure of her father. As the day approached when he was to leave her for a comparatively long stay, she grew melting and affectionate, remembering his many acts of consideration and his repeated expressions of an ardent attachment. She was solicitous about his health and his welfare. She bustled around, looking after his clothing, thinking about heavy underwear, quite as Madame Ratignolle would have done under similar circumstances. She cried when he went away, calling him her dear, good friend, and she was quite certain she would grow lonely before very long and go to join him in New York.

But after all, a radiant peace settled upon her when she at last found herself alone. Even the children were gone. Old Madame Pontellier had come herself and carried them off to Iberville with their quadroon. The old madame did not venture to say she was afraid they would be neglected during Léonce's absence; she hardly ventured to think so. She was hungry for them—even a little fierce in her attachment. She did not want them to be wholly "children of the pavement," she always said when begging to have them for a space. She wished them to know the country, with its streams, its fields, its woods, its freedom, so delicious to the young. She wished them to taste something of the life their father had lived and known and loved when he, too, was a little child.

When Edna was at last alone, she breathed a big, genuine sigh of relief. A feeling that was unfamiliar but very delicious came over her. She walked all through the house, from one room to another, as if inspecting it for the first time. She tried the various chairs and lounges, as if she had never sat and reclined upon them before. And she perambulated around the outside of the house, investigating, looking to see if windows and shutters were secure and in order. The flowers were like new acquaintances; she approached them in a familiar spirit, and made herself at home among them. The garden walks were damp, and Edna called to the maid to bring out her rubber sandals. And there she stayed, and stooped, digging around the plants, trimming, picking dead, dry leaves. The children's little dog came out, interfering, getting in her way. She scolded him, laughing at him, played with him. The garden smelled so good and looked so pretty in the afternoon sunlight. Edna plucked all the bright flowers she could find, and went into the house with them, she and the little dog.

Even the kitchen assumed a sudden interesting character which she had never before perceived. She went in to give directions to the cook, to say that the butcher would have to bring much less meat, that they would require only half their usual quantity of bread, of milk and groceries. She told the cook that she herself would be greatly occupied during Mr. Pontellier's absence, and she begged her to take all thought and responsibility of the larder upon her own shoulders.

That night Edna dined alone. The candelabra, with a few candles in the center of the table, gave all the light she needed. Outside the circle of light in which she sat, the large dining-room looked solemn and shadowy. The cook, placed upon her mettle, served a delicious repast—a luscious tender-loin broiled à point.[1] The wine tasted good; the marron glacé[2] seemed to be just what she wanted. It was so pleasant, too, to dine in a comfortable peignoir.

She thought a little sentimentally about Léonce and the children, and wondered what they were doing. As she gave a dainty scrap or two to the doggie, she talked intimately to him about Etienne and Raoul. He was beside himself with astonishment and delight over these companionable advances, and showed his appreciation by his little quick, snappy barks and a lively agitation.

Then Edna sat in the library after dinner and read Emerson[3] until she grew sleepy. She realized that she had neglected her reading, and determined to start anew upon a course of improving studies, now that her time was completely her own to do with as she liked.

1. Medium rare (French).
2. Glazed chestnuts (French).

3. Ralph Waldo Emerson (1803–1882), American philosopher, essayist, and poet.

After a refreshing bath, Edna went to bed. And as she snuggled comfortably beneath the eiderdown a sense of restfulness invaded her, such as she had not known before.

## XXV

When the weather was dark and cloudy Edna could not work. She needed the sun to mellow and temper her mood to the sticking point. She had reached a stage when she seemed to be no longer feeling her way, working, when in the humor, with sureness and ease. And being devoid of ambition, and striving not toward accomplishment, she drew satisfaction from the work in itself.

On rainy or melancholy days Edna went out and sought the society of the friends she had made at Grand Isle. Or else she stayed indoors and nursed a mood with which she was becoming too familiar for her own comfort and peace of mind. It was not despair; but it seemed to her as if life were passing by, leaving its promise broken and unfulfilled. Yet there were other days when she listened, was led on and deceived by fresh promises which her youth held out to her.

She went again to the races, and again. Alcée Arobin and Mrs. Highcamp called for her one bright afternoon in Arobin's drag.[4] Mrs. Highcamp was a worldly but unaffected, intelligent, slim, tall blonde woman in the forties, with an indifferent manner and blue eyes that stared. She had a daughter who served her as a pretext for cultivating the society of young men of fashion. Alcée Arobin was one of them. He was a familiar figure at the race course, the opera, the fashionable clubs. There was a perpetual smile in his eyes, which seldom failed to awaken a corresponding cheerfulness in any one who looked into them and listened to his good-humored voice. His manner was quiet, and at times a little insolent. He possessed a good figure, a pleasing face, not overburdened with depth of thought or feeling; and his dress was that of the conventional man of fashion.

He admired Edna extravagantly, after meeting her at the races with her father. He had met her before on other occasions, but she had seemed to him unapproachable until that day. It was at his instigation that Mrs. Highcamp called to ask her to go with them to the Jockey Club[5] to witness the turf event of the season.

There were possibly a few track men out there who knew the race horse as well as Edna, but there was certainly none who knew it better. She sat between her two companions as one having authority to speak. She laughed at Arobin's pretensions, and deplored Mrs. Highcamp's ignorance. The race horse was a friend and intimate associate of her childhood. The atmosphere of the stables and the breath of the blue grass paddock revived in her memory and lingered in her nostrils. She did not perceive that she was talking like her father as the sleek geldings ambled in review before them. She played for very high stakes, and fortune favored her. The fever of the game flamed in her cheeks and eyes, and it got into her blood and into her brain like an intoxicant. People turned their heads to look at her, and more than one lent an attentive ear to her utterances, hoping thereby to secure the elusive but ever-

---

4. Heavy coach drawn by four horses.
5. The New Louisiana Jockey Club, an exclusive social club.

desired "tip." Arobin caught the contagion of excitement which drew him to Edna like a magnet. Mrs. Highcamp remained, as usual, unmoved, with her indifferent stare and uplifted eyebrows.

Edna stayed and dined with Mrs. Highcamp upon being urged to do so. Arobin also remained and sent away his drag.

The dinner was quiet and uninteresting, save for the cheerful efforts of Arobin to enliven things. Mrs. Highcamp deplored the absence of her daughter from the races, and tried to convey to her what she had missed by going to the "Dante[6] reading" instead of joining them. The girl held a geranium leaf up to her nose and said nothing, but looked knowing and noncommittal. Mr. Highcamp was a plain, bald-headed man, who only talked under compulsion. He was unresponsive. Mrs. Highcamp was full of delicate courtesy and consideration toward her husband. She addressed most of her conversation to him at table. They sat in the library after dinner and read the evening papers together under the drop-light;[7] while the younger people went into the drawing-room near by and talked. Miss Highcamp played some selections from Grieg[8] upon the piano. She seemed to have apprehended all of the composer's coldness and none of his poetry. While Edna listened she could not help wondering if she had lost her taste for music.

When the time came for her to go home, Mr. Highcamp grunted a lame offer to escort her, looking down at his slippered feet with tactless concern. It was Arobin who took her home. The car ride was long, and it was late when they reached Esplanade Street. Arobin asked permission to enter for a second to light his cigarette—his match safe[9] was empty. He filled his match safe, but did not light his cigarette until he left her, after she had expressed her willingness to go to the races with him again.

Edna was neither tired nor sleepy. She was hungry again, for the Highcamp dinner, though of excellent quality, had lacked abundance. She rummaged in the larder and brought forth a slice of "Gruyère"[1] and some crackers. She opened a bottle of beer which she found in the ice-box. Edna felt extremely restless and excited. She vacantly hummed a fantastic tune as she poked at the wood embers on the hearth and munched a cracker.

She wanted something to happen—something, anything; she did not know what. She regretted that she had not made Arobin stay a half hour to talk over the horses with her. She counted the money she had won. But there was nothing else to do, so she went to bed, and tossed there for hours in a sort of monotonous agitation.

In the middle of the night she remembered that she had forgotten to write her regular letter to her husband; and she decided to do so next day and tell him about her afternoon at the Jockey Club. She lay wide awake composing a letter which was nothing like the one which she wrote the next day. When the maid awoke her in the morning Edna was dreaming of Mr. Highcamp playing the piano at the entrance of a music store on Canal Street, while his wife was saying to Alcée Arobin, as they boarded an Esplanade Street car:

"What a pity that so much talent has been neglected! but I must go."

6. Dante Alighieri (1265–1321), Italian poet, author of *The Divine Comedy.* Highcamp's daughter preferred intellectual activities to the social frivolity of racing.
7. Gas lamp that could be lowered for reading.

8. Edvard Grieg (1843–1907), Norwegian composer.
9. Box for friction matches.
1. Cheese originally made in Gruyère, Switzerland.

When, a few days later, Alcée Arobin again called for Edna in his drag, Mrs. Highcamp was not with him. He said they would pick her up. But as the lady had not been apprised of his intention of picking her up, she was not at home. The daughter was just leaving the house to attend the meeting of a branch Folk Lore Society,[2] and regretted that she could not accompany them. Arobin appeared nonplused, and asked Edna if there were any one else she cared to ask.

She did not deem it worth while to go in search of any of the fashionable acquaintances from whom she had withdrawn herself. She thought of Madame Ratignolle, but knew that her fair friend did not leave the house, except to take a languid walk around the block with her husband after night-fall. Mademoiselle Reisz would have laughed at such a request from Edna. Madame Lebrun might have enjoyed the outing, but for some reason Edna did not want her. So they went alone, she and Arobin.

The afternoon was intensely interesting to her. The excitement came back upon her like a remittent fever. Her talk grew familiar and confidential. It was no labor to become intimate with Arobin. His manner invited easy confidence. The preliminary stage of becoming acquainted was one which he always endeavored to ignore when a pretty and engaging woman was concerned.

He stayed and dined with Edna. He stayed and sat beside the wood fire. They laughed and talked; and before it was time to go he was telling her how different life might have been if he had known her years before. With ingenuous frankness he spoke of what a wicked, ill-disciplined boy he had been, and impulsively drew up his cuff to exhibit upon his wrist the scar from a saber cut which he had received in a duel outside of Paris when he was nineteen. She touched his hand as she scanned the red cicatrice[3] on the inside of his white wrist. A quick impulse that was somewhat spasmodic impelled her fingers to close in a sort of clutch upon his hand. He felt the pressure of her pointed nails in the flesh of his palm.

She arose hastily and walked toward the mantel.

"The sight of a wound or scar always agitates and sickens me," she said. "I shouldn't have looked at it."

"I beg your pardon," he entreated, following her; "it never occurred to me that it might be repulsive."

He stood close to her, and the effrontery in his eyes repelled the old, vanishing self in her, yet drew all her awakening sensuousness. He saw enough in her face to impel him to take her hand and hold it while he said his lingering good night.

"Will you go to the races again?" he asked.

"No," she said. "I've had enough of the races. I don't want to lose all the money I've won, and I've got to work when the weather is bright, instead of—"

"Yes; work; to be sure. You promised to show me your work. What morning may I come up to your atelier? To-morrow?"

"No!"

"Day after?"

<hr />

2. The New Orleans Association of the American Folklore Society, founded by Alcée Fortier of Tulane University, was active from 1892 to 1895.
3. Scar.

"No, no."

"Oh, please don't refuse me! I know something of such things. I might help you with a stray suggestion or two."

"No. Good night. Why don't you go after you have said good night? I don't like you," she went on in a high, excited pitch, attempting to draw away her hand. She felt that her words lacked dignity and sincerity, and she knew that he felt it.

"I'm sorry you don't like me. I'm sorry I offended you. How have I offended you? What have I done? Can't you forgive me?" And he bent and pressed his lips upon her hand as if he wished never more to withdraw them.

"Mr. Arobin," she complained, "I'm greatly upset by the excitement of the afternoon; I'm not myself. My manner must have misled you in some way. I wish you to go, please." She spoke in a monotonous, dull tone. He took his hat from the table, and stood with eyes turned from her, looking into the dying fire. For a moment or two he kept an impressive silence.

"Your manner has not misled me, Mrs. Pontellier," he said finally. "My own emotions have done that. I couldn't help it. When I'm near you, how could I help it? Don't think anything of it, don't bother, please. You see, I go when you command me. If you wish me to stay away, I shall do so. If you let me come back, I—oh! you will let me come back?"

He cast one appealing glance at her, to which she made no response. Alcée Arobin's manner was so genuine that it often deceived even himself.

Edna did not care or think whether it were genuine or not. When she was alone she looked mechanically at the back of her hand which he had kissed so warmly. Then she leaned her head down on the mantelpiece. She felt somewhat like a woman who in a moment of passion is betrayed into an act of infidelity, and realizes the significance of the act without being wholly awakened from its glamour. The thought was passing vaguely through her mind, "What would he think?"

She did not mean her husband; she was thinking of Robert Lebrun. Her husband seemed to her now like a person whom she had married without love as an excuse.

She lit a candle and went up to her room. Alcée Arobin was absolutely nothing to her. Yet his presence, his manners, the warmth of his glances, and above all the touch of his lips upon her hand had acted like a narcotic upon her.

She slept a languorous sleep, interwoven with vanishing dreams.

## XXVI

Alcée Arobin wrote Edna an elaborate note of apology, palpitant with sincerity. It embarrassed her; for in a cooler, quieter moment it appeared to her absurd that she should have taken his action so seriously, so dramatically. She felt sure that the significance of the whole occurrence had lain in her own self-consciousness. If she ignored his note it would give undue importance to a trivial affair. If she replied to it in a serious spirit it would still leave in his mind the impression that she had in a susceptible moment yielded to his influence. After all, it was no great matter to have one's hand kissed. She was provoked at his having written the apology. She answered in as light and bantering a spirit as she fancied it deserved, and said she would be glad to have him look in upon her at work whenever he felt the inclination and his business gave him the opportunity.

He responded at once by presenting himself at her home with all his disarming naïveté. And then there was scarcely a day which followed that she did not see him or was not reminded of him. He was prolific in pretexts. His attitude became one of good-humored subservience and tacit adoration. He was ready at all times to submit to her moods, which were as often kind as they were cold. She grew accustomed to him. They became intimate and friendly by imperceptible degrees, and then by leaps. He sometimes talked in a way that astonished her at first and brought the crimson into her face; in a way that pleased her at last, appealing to the animalism that stirred impatiently within her.

There was nothing which so quieted the turmoil of Edna's senses as a visit to Mademoiselle Reisz. It was then, in the presence of that personality which was offensive to her, that the woman, by her divine art, seemed to reach Edna's spirit and set it free.

It was misty, with heavy, lowering atmosphere, one afternoon, when Edna climbed the stairs to the pianist's apartments under the roof. Her clothes were dripping with moisture. She felt chilled and pinched as she entered the room. Mademoiselle was poking at a rusty stove that smoked a little and warmed the room indifferently. She was endeavoring to heat a pot of chocolate on the stove. The room looked cheerless and dingy to Edna as she entered. A bust of Beethoven, covered with a hood of dust, scowled at her from the mantelpiece.

"Ah! here comes the sunlight!" exclaimed Mademoiselle, rising from her knees before the stove. "Now it will be warm and bright enough; I can let the fire alone."

She closed the stove door with a bang, and approaching, assisted in removing Edna's dripping mackintosh.

"You are cold; you look miserable. The chocolate will soon be hot. But would you rather have a taste of brandy? I have scarcely touched the bottle which you brought me for my cold." A piece of red flannel was wrapped around Mademoiselle's throat; a stiff neck compelled her to hold her head on one side.

"I will take some brandy," said Edna, shivering as she removed her gloves and overshoes. She drank the liquor from the glass as a man would have done. Then flinging herself upon the uncomfortable sofa she said, "Mademoiselle, I am going to move away from my house on Esplanade Street."

"Ah!" ejaculated the musician, neither surprised nor especially interested. Nothing ever seemed to astonish her very much. She was endeavoring to adjust the bunch of violets which had become loose from its fastening in her hair. Edna drew her down upon the sofa and taking a pin from her own hair, secured the shabby artificial flowers in their accustomed place.

"Aren't you astonished?"

"Passably. Where are you going? To New York? to Iberville? to your father in Mississippi? where?"

"Just two steps away," laughed Edna, "in a little four-room house around the corner. It looks so cozy, so inviting and restful, whenever I pass by; and it's for rent. I'm tired looking after that big house. It never seemed like mine, anyway—like home. It's too much trouble. I have to keep too many servants. I am tired bothering with them."

"That is not your true reason, *ma belle*. There is no use in telling me lies. I don't know your reason, but you have not told me the truth." Edna did not protest or endeavor to justify herself.

"The house, the money that provides for it, are not mine. Isn't that enough reason?"

"They are your husband's," returned Mademoiselle, with a shrug and a malicious elevation of the eyebrows.

"Oh! I see there is no deceiving you. Then let me tell you: It is a caprice. I have a little money of my own from my mother's estate, which my father sends me by driblets. I won a large sum this winter on the races, and I am beginning to sell my sketches. Laidpore is more and more pleased with my work; he says it grows in force and individuality. I cannot judge of that myself, but I feel that I have gained in ease and confidence. However, as I said, I have sold a good many through Laidpore. I can live in the tiny house for little or nothing, with one servant. Old Celestine, who works occasionally for me, says she will come stay with me and do my work. I know I shall like it, like the feeling of freedom and independence."

"What does your husband say?"

"I have not told him yet. I only thought of it this morning. He will think I am demented, no doubt. Perhaps you think so."

Mademoiselle shook her head slowly. "Your reason is not yet clear to me," she said.

Neither was it quite clear to Edna herself; but it unfolded itself as she sat for a while in silence. Instinct had prompted her to put away her husband's bounty in casting off her allegiance. She did not know how it would be when he returned. There would have to be an understanding, an explanation. Conditions would some way adjust themselves, she felt, but whatever came, she had resolved never again to belong to another than herself.

"I shall give a grand dinner before I leave the old house!" Edna exclaimed. "You will have to come to it, Mademoiselle. I will give you everything that you like to eat and to drink. We shall sing and laugh and be merry for once." And she uttered a sigh that came from the very depths of her being.

If Mademoiselle happened to have received a letter from Robert during the interval of Edna's visits, she would give her the letter unsolicited. And she would seat herself at the piano and play as her humor prompted her while the young woman read the letter.

The little stove was roaring; it was red-hot, and the chocolate in the tin sizzled and sputtered. Edna went forward and opened the stove door, and Mademoiselle rising, took a letter from under the bust of Beethoven and handed it to Edna.

"Another! so soon!" she exclaimed, her eyes filled with delight. "Tell me, Mademoiselle, does he know that I see his letters?"

"Never in the world! He would be angry and would never write to me again if he thought so. Does he write to you? Never a line. Does he send you a message? Never a word. It is because he loves you, poor fool, and is trying to forget you, since you are not free to listen to him or to belong to him."

"Why do you show me his letters, then?"

"Haven't you begged for them? Can I refuse you anything? Oh! you cannot deceive me," and Mademoiselle approached her beloved instrument and began to play. Edna did not at once read the letter. She sat holding it in her hand, while the music penetrated her whole being like an effulgence, warming and brightening the dark places of her soul. It prepared her for joy and exultation.

"Oh!" she exclaimed, letting the letter fall to the floor. "Why did you not tell me?" She went and grasped Mademoiselle's hands up from the keys. "Oh! unkind! malicious! Why did you not tell me?"

"That he was coming back? No great news, *ma foi.* I wonder he did not come long ago."

"But when, when?" cried Edna, impatiently. "He does not say when."

"He says, 'very soon.' You know as much about it as I do; it is all in the letter."

"But why? Why is he coming? Oh, if I thought—" and she snatched the letters from the floor and turned the pages this way and that way, looking for the reason, which was left untold.

"If I were young and in love with a man," said Mademoiselle, turning on the stool and pressing her wiry hands between her knees as she looked down at Edna, who sat on the floor holding the letter, "it seems to me he would have to be some *grand esprit,*[4] a man with lofty aims and ability to reach them; one who stood high enough to attract the notice of his fellow-men. It seems to me if I were young and in love I should never deem a man of ordinary caliber worthy of my devotion."

"Now it is you who are telling lies and seeking to deceive me, Mademoiselle; or else you have never been in love, and know nothing about it. Why," went on Edna, clasping her knees and looking up into Mademoiselle's twisted face, "do you suppose a woman knows why she loves? Does she select? Does she say to herself: 'Go to! Here is a distinguished statesman with presidential possibilities; I shall proceed to fall in love with him.' Or, 'I shall set my heart upon this musician, whose fame is on every tongue?' Or, 'This financier, who controls the world's money markets?' "

"You are purposely misunderstanding me, *ma reine.*[5] Are you in love with Robert?"

"Yes," said Edna. It was the first time she had admitted it, and a glow overspread her face, blotching it with red spots.

"Why?" asked her companion. "Why do you love him when you ought not to?"

Edna, with a motion or two, dragged herself on her knees before Mademoiselle Reisz, who took the glowing face between her two hands.

"Why? Because his hair is brown and grows away from his temples; because he opens and shuts his eyes, and his nose is a little out of drawing; because he has two lips and a square chin, and a little finger which he can't straighten from having played baseball too energetically in his youth. Because—"

"Because you do, in short," laughed Mademoiselle. "What will you do when he comes back?" she asked.

---

4. Grand spirit (French, literal trans.); here, noble soul.    5. My queen (French).

"Do? Nothing, except feel glad and happy to be alive."

She was already glad and happy to be alive at the mere thought of his return. The murky, lowering sky, which had depressed her a few hours before, seemed bracing and invigorating as she splashed through the streets on her way home.

She stopped at a confectioner's and ordered a huge box of bonbons for the children in Iberville. She slipped a card in the box, on which she scribbled a tender message and sent an abundance of kisses.

Before dinner in the evening Edna wrote a charming letter to her husband, telling him of her intention to move for a while into the little house around the block, and to give a farewell dinner before leaving, regretting that he was not there to share it, to help her out with the menu and assist her in entertaining the guests. Her letter was brilliant and brimming with cheerfulness.

## XXVII

"What is the matter with you?" asked Arobin that evening. "I never found you in such a happy mood." Edna was tired by that time, and was reclining on the lounge before the fire.

"Don't you know the weather prophet has told us we shall see the sun pretty soon?"

"Well, that ought to be reason enough," he acquiesced. "You wouldn't give me another if I sat here all night imploring you." He sat close to her on a low tabouret,[6] and as he spoke his fingers lightly touched the hair that fell a little over her forehead. She liked the touch of his fingers through her hair, and closed her eyes sensitively.

"One of these days," she said, "I'm going to pull myself together for a while and think—try to determine what character of a woman I am; for, candidly, I don't know. By all the codes which I am acquainted with, I am a devilishly wicked specimen of the sex. But some way I can't convince myself that I am. I must think about it."

"Don't. What's the use? Why should you bother thinking about it when I can tell you what manner of woman you are." His fingers strayed occasionally down to her warm, smooth cheeks and firm chin, which was growing a little full and double.

"Oh, yes! You will tell me that I am adorable; everything that is captivating. Spare yourself the effort."

"No; I shan't tell you anything of the sort, though I shouldn't be lying if I did."

"Do you know Mademoiselle Reisz?" she asked irrelevantly.

"The pianist? I know her by sight. I've heard her play."

"She says queer things sometimes in a bantering way that you don't notice at the time and you feel yourself thinking about afterward."

"For instance?"

"Well, for instance, when I left her today, she put her arms around me and felt my shoulder blades, to see if my wings were strong, she said. 'The bird that would soar above the level plain of tradition and prejudice must have strong wings. It is a sad spectacle to see the weaklings bruised, exhausted, fluttering back to earth.' "

6. Cylindrical seat or stool without arms or back.

"Whither would you soar?"

"I'm not thinking of any extraordinary flights. I only half comprehend her."

"I've heard she's partially demented," said Arobin.

"She seems to me wonderfully sane," Edna replied.

"I'm told she's extremely disagreeable and unpleasant. Why have you introduced her at a moment when I desired to talk of you?"

"Oh! talk of me if you like," cried Edna, clasping her hands beneath her head; "but let me think of something else while you do."

"I'm jealous of your thoughts to-night. They're making you a little kinder than usual; but some way I feel as if they were wandering, as if they were not here with me." She only looked at him and smiled. His eyes were very near. He leaned upon the lounge with an arm extended across her, while the other hand still rested upon her hair. They continued silently to look into each other's eyes. When he leaned forward and kissed her, she clasped his head, holding his lips to hers.

It was the first kiss of her life to which her nature had really responded. It was a flaming torch that kindled desire.

## XXVIII

Edna cried a little that night after Arobin left her. It was only one phase of the multitudinous emotions which had assailed her. There was with her an overwhelming feeling of irresponsibility. There was the shock of the unexpected and the unaccustomed. There was her husband's reproach looking at her from external things around her which he had provided for her external existence. There was Robert's reproach making itself felt by a quicker, fiercer, more overpowering love, which had awakened within her toward him. Above all, there was understanding. She felt as if a mist had been lifted from her eyes, enabling her to look upon and comprehend the significance of life, that monster made up of beauty and brutality. But among the conflicting sensations which assailed her, there was neither shame nor remorse. There was a dull pang of regret because it was not the kiss of love which had inflamed her, because it was not love which had held this cup of life to her lips.

## XXIX

Without even waiting for an answer from her husband regarding his opinion or wishes in the matter, Edna hastened her preparations for quitting her home on Esplanade Street and moving into the little house around the block. A feverish anxiety attended her every action in that direction. There was no moment of deliberation, no interval of repose between the thought and its fulfillment. Early upon the morning following those hours passed in Arobin's society, Edna set about securing her new abode and hurrying her arrangements for occupying it. Within the precincts of her home she felt like one who has entered and lingered within the portals of some forbidden temple in which a thousand muffled voices bade her begone.

Whatever was her own in the house, everything which she had acquired aside from her husband's bounty, she caused to be transported to the other house, supplying simple and meager deficiencies from her own resources.

Arobin found her with rolled sleeves, working in company with the housemaid when he looked in during the afternoon. She was splendid and robust, and had never appeared handsomer than in the old blue gown, with a red silk handkerchief knotted at random around her head to protect her hair from the dust. She was mounted upon a high stepladder, unhooking a picture from the wall when he entered. He had found the front door open, and had followed his ring by walking in unceremoniously.

"Come down!" he said. "Do you want kill yourself?" She greeted him with affected carelessness, and appeared absorbed in her occupation.

If he had expected to find her languishing, reproachful, or indulging in sentimental tears, he must have been greatly surprised.

He was no doubt prepared for any emergency, ready for any one of the foregoing attitudes, just as he bent himself easily and naturally to the situation which confronted him.

"Please come down," he insisted, holding the ladder and looking up at her.

"No," she answered; "Ellen is afraid to mount the ladder. Joe is working over at the 'pigeon house'—that's the name Ellen gives it, because it's so small and looks like a pigeon house[7]—and some one has to do this."

Arobin pulled off his coat, and expressed himself ready and willing to tempt fate in her place. Ellen brought him one of her dust-caps, and went into contortions of mirth, which she found it impossible to control, when she saw him put it on before the mirror as grotesquely as he could. Edna herself could not refrain from smiling when she fastened it at his request. So it was he who in turn mounted the ladder, unhooking pictures and curtains, and dislodging ornaments as Edna directed. When he had finished he took off his dust-cap and went out to wash his hands.

Edna was sitting on the tabouret, idly brushing the tips of a feather duster along the carpet when he came in again.

"Is there anything more you will let me do?" he asked.

"That is all," she answered. "Ellen can manage the rest." She kept the young woman occupied in the drawing-room, unwilling to be left alone with Arobin.

"What about the dinner?" he asked; "the grand event, the *coup d'état?*"

"It will be day after to-morrow. Why do you call it the *'coup d'état?'* Oh! it will be very fine; all my best of everything—crystal, silver and gold. Sèvres, flowers, music, and champagne to swim in. I'll let Léonce pay the bills. I wonder what he'll say when he sees the bills."

"And you ask me why I call it a *coup d'état?*" Arobin had put on his coat, and he stood before her and asked if his cravat was plumb. She told him it was, looking no higher than the tip of his collar.

"When do you go to the 'pigeon house?'—with all due acknowledgment to Ellen."

"Day after to-morrow, after the dinner. I shall sleep there."

"Ellen, will you very kindly get me a glass of water?" asked Arobin. "The dust in the curtains, if you will pardon me for hinting such a thing, has parched my throat to a crisp."

"While Ellen gets the water," said Edna, rising, "I will say good-by and let you go. I must get rid of this grime, and I have a million things to do and think of."

7. A house for domesticated birds kept for show or sport.

"When shall I see you?" asked Arobin, seeking to detain her, the maid having left the room.

"At the dinner, of course. You are invited."

"Not before?—not to-night or to-morrow morning or to-morrow noon or night? or the day after morning or noon? Can't you see yourself, without my telling you, what an eternity it is?"

He had followed her into the hall and to the foot of the stairway, looking up at her as she mounted with her face half turned to him.

"Not an instant sooner," she said. But she laughed and looked at him with eyes that at once gave him courage to wait and made it torture to wait.

## XXX

Though Edna had spoken of the dinner as a very grand affair, it was in truth a very small affair and very select, in so much as the guests invited were few and were selected with discrimination. She had counted upon an even dozen seating themselves at her round mahogany board, forgetting for the moment that Madame Ratignolle was to the last degree *souffrante*[8] and unpresentable, and not foreseeing that Madame Lebrun would send a thousand regrets at the last moment. So there were only ten, after all, which made a cozy, comfortable number.

There were Mr. and Mrs. Merriman, a pretty, vivacious little woman in the thirties; her husband, a jovial fellow, something of a shallow-pate, who laughed a good deal at other people's witticisms, and had thereby made himself extremely popular. Mrs. Highcamp had accompanied them. Of course, there was Alcée Arobin; and Mademoiselle Reisz had consented to come. Edna had sent her a fresh bunch of violets with black lace trimmings for her hair. Monsieur Ratignolle brought himself and his wife's excuses. Victor Lebrun, who happened to be in the city, bent upon relaxation, had accepted with alacrity. There was a Miss Mayblunt, no longer in her teens, who looked at the world through lorgnettes and with the keenest interest. It was thought and said that she was intellectual; it was suspected of her that she wrote under a *nom de guerre*.[9] She had come with a gentleman by the name of Gouvernail, connected with one of the daily papers, of whom nothing special could be said, except that he was observant and seemed quiet and inoffensive. Edna herself made the tenth, and at half-past eight they seated themselves at table, Arobin and Monsieur Ratignolle on either side of their hostess.

Mrs. Highcamp sat between Arobin and Victor Lebrun. Then came Mrs. Merriman, Mr. Gouvernail, Miss Mayblunt, Mr. Merriman, and Mademoiselle Reisz next to Monsieur Ratignolle.

There was something extremely gorgeous about the appearance of the table, an effect of splendor conveyed by a cover of pale yellow satin under strips of lace-work. There were wax candles in massive brass candelabra, burning softly under yellow silk shades; full, fragrant roses, yellow and red, abounded. There were silver and gold, as she had said there would be, and crystal which glittered like the gems which the women wore.

8. Ill (French).  9. Pseudonym (French).

The ordinary stiff dining chairs had been discarded for the occasion and replaced by the most commodious and luxurious which could be collected throughout the house. Mademoiselle Reisz, being exceedingly diminutive, was elevated upon cushions, as small children are sometimes hoisted at table upon bulky volumes.

"Something new, Edna?" exclaimed Miss Mayblunt, with lorgnette directed toward a magnificent cluster of diamonds that sparkled, that almost sputtered, in Edna's hair, just over the center of her forehead.

"Quite new; 'brand' new, in fact; a present from my husband. It arrived this morning from New York. I may as well admit that this is my birthday, and that I am twenty-nine. In good time I expect you to drink my health. Meanwhile, I shall ask you to begin with this cocktail, composed—would you say 'composed?' " with an appeal to Miss Mayblunt—"composed by my father in honor of Sister Janet's wedding."

Before each guest stood a tiny glass that looked and sparkled like a garnet gem.

"Then, all things considered," spoke Arobin, "it might not be amiss to start out by drinking the Colonel's health in the cocktail which he composed, on the birthday of the most charming of women—the daughter whom he invented."

Mr. Merriman's laugh at this sally was such a genuine outburst and so contagious that it started the dinner with an agreeable swing that never slackened.

Miss Mayblunt begged to be allowed to keep her cocktail untouched before her, just to look at. The color was marvelous! She could compare it to nothing she had ever seen, and the garnet lights which it emitted were unspeakably rare. She pronounced the Colonel an artist, and stuck to it.

Monsieur Ratignolle was prepared to take things seriously; the *mets,* and *entre-mets,*[1] the service, the decorations, even the people. He looked up from his pompono[2] and inquired of Arobin if he were related to the gentleman of that name who formed one of the firm of Laitner and Arobin, lawyers. The young man admitted that Laitner was a warm personal friend, who permitted Arobin's name to decorate the firm's letterheads and to appear upon a shingle that graced Perdido Street.

"There are so many inquisitive people and institutions abounding," said Arobin, "that one is really forced as a matter of convenience these days to assume the virtue of an occupation if he has it not."

Monsieur Ratignolle stared a little, and turned to ask Mademoiselle Reisz if she considered the symphony concerts up to the standard which had been set the previous winter. Mademoiselle Reisz answered Monsieur Ratignolle in French, which Edna thought a little rude, under the circumstances, but characteristic. Mademoiselle had only disagreeable things to say of the symphony concerts, and insulting remarks to make of all the musicians of New Orleans, singly and collectively. All her interest seemed to be centered upon the delicacies placed before her.

Mr. Merriman said that Mr. Arobin's remark about inquisitive people

---

1. Main course and side dishes (French).
2. I.e., pompano, fish of the southern Atlantic and Gulf coasts of North America.

reminded him of a man from Waco[3] the other day at the St. Charles Hotel—but as Mr. Merriman's stories were always lame and lacking point, his wife seldom permitted him to complete them. She interrupted him to ask if he remembered the name of the author whose book she had bought the week before to send to a friend in Geneva. She was talking "books" with Mr. Gouvernail and trying to draw from him his opinion upon current literary topics. Her husband told the story of the Waco man privately to Miss Mayblunt, who pretended to be greatly amused and to think it extremely clever.

Mrs. Highcamp hung with languid but unaffected interest upon the warm and impetuous volubility of her left-hand neighbor, Victor Lebrun. Her attention was never for a moment withdrawn from him after seating herself at table; and when he turned to Mrs. Merriman, who was prettier and more vivacious than Mrs. Highcamp, she waited with easy indifference for an opportunity to reclaim his attention. There was the occasional sound of music, of mandolins, sufficiently removed to be an agreeable accompaniment rather than an interruption to the conversation. Outside the soft, monotonous splash of a fountain could be heard; the sound penetrated into the room with the heavy odor of jessamine that came through the open windows.

The golden shimmer of Edna's satin gown spread in rich folds on either side of her. There was a soft fall of lace encircling her shoulders. It was the color of her skin, without the glow, the myriad living tints that one may sometimes discover in vibrant flesh. There was something in her attitude, in her whole appearance when she leaned her head against the high-backed chair and spread her arms, which suggested the regal woman, the one who rules, who looks on, who stands alone.

But as she sat there amid her guests, she felt the old ennui overtaking her; the hopelessness which so often assailed her, which came upon her like an obsession, like something extraneous, independent of volition. It was something which announced itself; a chill breath that seemed to issue from some vast cavern wherein discords wailed. There came over her the acute longing which always summoned into her spiritual vision the presence of the beloved one, overpowering her at once with a sense of the unattainable.

The moments glided on, while a feeling of good fellowship passed around the circle like a mystic cord, holding and binding these people together with jest and laughter. Monsieur Ratignolle was the first to break the pleasant charm. At ten o'clock he excused himself. Madame Ratignolle was waiting for him at home. She was *bien souffrante,*[4] and she was filled with vague dread, which only her husband's presence could allay.

Mademoiselle Reisz arose with Monsieur Ratignolle, who offered to escort her to the car. She had eaten well; she had tasted the good, rich wines, and they must have turned her head, for she bowed pleasantly to all as she withdrew from table. She kissed Edna upon the shoulder, and whispered: *"Bonne nuit, ma reine; soyez sage."*[5] She had been a little bewildered upon rising, or rather, descending from her cushions, and Monsieur Ratignolle gallantly took her arm and led her away.

Mrs. Highcamp was weaving a garland of roses, yellow and red. When she had finished the garland, she laid it lightly upon Victor's black curls. He was

---

3. A town in Texas.
4. Very ill (French).

5. Good night, my love; be good (French).

reclining far back in the luxurious chair, holding a glass of champagne to the light.

As if a magician's wand had touched him, the garland of roses transformed him into a vision of Oriental beauty. His cheeks were the color of crushed grapes, and his dusky eyes glowed with a languishing fire.

"*Sapristi!*" exclaimed Arobin. What the parrot says

But Mrs. Highcamp had one more touch to add to the picture. She took from the back of her chair a white silken scarf, with which she had covered hershoulders in the early part of the evening. She draped it across the boy in graceful folds, and in a way to conceal his black, conventional evening dress. He did not seem to mind what she did to him, only smiled, showing a faint gleam of white teeth, while he continued to gaze with narrowing eyes at the light through his glass of champagne.

"Oh! to be able to paint in color rather than in words!" exclaimed Miss Mayblunt, losing herself in a rhapsodic dream as she looked at him.

> " 'There was a graven image of Desire
> Painted with red blood on a ground of gold.' "[6]

murmured Gouvernail, under his breath.

The effect of the wine upon Victor was, to change his accustomed volubility into silence. He seemed to have abandoned himself to a reverie, and to be seeing pleasing visions in the amber bead.

"Sing," entreated Mrs. Highcamp. "Won't you sing to us?"

"Let him alone," said Arobin.

"He's posing," offered Mr. Merriman; "let him have it out."

"I believe he's paralyzed," laughed Mrs. Merriman. And leaning over the youth's chair, she took the glass from his hand and held it to his lips. He sipped the wine slowly, and when he had drained the glass she laid it upon the table and wiped his lips with her little filmy handkerchief.

"Yes, I'll sing for you," he said, turning in his chair toward Mrs. Highcamp. He clasped his hands behind his head, and looking up at the ceiling began to hum a little, trying his voice like a musician tuning an instrument. Then, looking at Edna, he began to sing:

> "Ah! si tu savais!"

"Stop!" she cried, "don't sing that. I don't want you to sing it," and she laid her glass so impetuously and blindly upon the table as to shatter it against a caraffe. The wine spilled over Arobin's legs and some of it trickled down upon Mrs. Highcamp's black gauze gown. Victor had lost all idea of courtesy, or else he thought his hostess was not in earnest, for he laughed and went on:

> "Ah! si tu savais
> Ce que tes yeux me disent"—

"Oh! you mustn't! you mustn't," exclaimed Edna, and pushing back her chair she got up, and going behind him placed her hand over his mouth. He kissed the soft palm that pressed upon his lips.

"No, no, I won't, Mrs. Pontellier. I didn't know you meant it," looking up at her with caressing eyes. The touch of his lips was like a pleasing sting to

6. Lines from the sonnet "A Cameo," by A. C. Swinburne (1837–1909).

her hand. She lifted the garland of roses from his head and flung it across the room.

"Come, Victor; you've posed long enough. Give Mrs. Highcamp her scarf."

Mrs. Highcamp undraped the scarf from about him with her own hands. Miss Mayblunt and Mr. Gouvernail suddenly conceived the notion that it was time to say good night. And Mr. and Mrs. Merriman wondered how it could be so late.

Before parting from Victor, Mrs. Highcamp invited him to call upon her daughter, who she knew would be charmed to meet him and talk French and sing French songs with him. Victor expressed his desire and intention to call upon Mrs. Highcamp at the first opportunity which presented itself. He asked if Arobin were going his way. Arobin was not.

The mandolin players had long since stolen away. A profound stillness had fallen upon the broad, beautiful street. The voices of Edna's disbanding guests jarred like a discordant note upon the quiet harmony of the night.

## XXXI

"Well?" questioned Arobin, who had remained with Edna after the others had departed.

"Well," she reiterated, and stood up, stretching her arms, and feeling the need to relax her muscles after having been so long seated.

"What next?" he asked.

"The servants are all gone. They left when the musicians did. I have dismissed them. The house has to be closed and locked, and I shall trot around to the pigeon house, and shall send Celestine over in the morning to straighten things up."

He looked around, and began to turn out some of the lights.

"What about upstairs?" he inquired.

"I think it is all right; but there may be a window or two unlatched. We had better look; you might take a candle and see. And bring me my wrap and hat on the foot of the bed in the middle room."

He went up with the light, and Edna began closing doors and windows. She hated to shut in the smoke and the fumes of the wine. Arobin found her cape and hat, which he brought down and helped her to put on.

When everything was secured and the lights put out, they left through the front door, Arobin locking it and taking the key, which he carried for Edna. He helped her down the steps.

"Will you have a spray of jessamine?" he asked, breaking off a few blossoms as he passed.

"No; I don't want anything."

She seemed disheartened, and had nothing to say. She took his arm, which he offered her, holding up the weight of her satin train with the other hand. She looked down, noticing the black line of his leg moving in and out so close to her against the yellow shimmer of her gown. There was the whistle of a railway train somewhere in the distance, and the midnight bells were ringing. They met no one in their short walk.

The "pigeon-house" stood behind a locked gate, and a shallow *parterre*[7] that had been somewhat neglected. There was a small front porch, upon

---

7. Garden (French).

which a long window and the front door opened. The door opened directly into the parlor; there was no side entry. Back in the yard was a room for servants, in which old Celestine had been ensconced.

Edna had left a lamp burning low upon the table. She had succeeded in making the room look habitable and homelike. There were some books on the table and a lounge near at hand. On the floor was a fresh matting, covered with a rug or two; and on the walls hung a few tasteful pictures. But the room was filled with flowers. These were a surprise to her. Arobin had sent them, and had had Celestine distribute them during Edna's absence. Her bedroom was adjoining, and across a small passage were the dining-room and kitchen.

Edna seated herself with every appearance of discomfort.

"Are you tired?" he asked.

"Yes, and chilled and miserable. I feel as if I had been wound up to a certain pitch—too tight—and something inside of me had snapped." She rested her head against the table upon her bare arm.

"You want to rest," he said, "and to be quiet. I'll go; I'll leave you and let you rest."

"Yes," she replied.

He stood up beside her and smoothed her hair with his soft magnetic hand. His touch conveyed to her a certain physical comfort. She could have fallen quietly asleep there if he had continued to pass his hand over her hair. He brushed the hair upward from the nape of her neck.

"I hope you will feel better and happier in the morning," he said. "You have tried to do too much in the past few days. The dinner was the last straw; you might have dispensed with it."

"Yes," she admitted; "it was stupid."

"No, it was delightful; but it has worn you out." His hand had strayed to her beautiful shoulders, and he could feel the response of her flesh to his touch. He seated himself beside her and kissed her lightly upon the shoulder.

"I thought you were going away," she said, in an uneven voice.

"I am, after I have said good night."

"Good night," she murmured.

He did not answer, except to continue to caress her. He did not say good night until she had become supple to his gentle, seductive entreaties.

## XXXII

When Mr. Pontellier learned of his wife's intention to abandon her home and take up her residence elsewhere, he immediately wrote her a letter of unqualified disapproval and remonstrance. She had given reasons which he was unwilling to acknowledge as adequate. He hoped she had not acted upon her rash impulse; and he begged her to consider first, foremost, and above all else, what people would say. He was not dreaming of scandal when he uttered this warning; that was a thing which would never have entered into his mind to consider in connection with his wife's name or his own. He was simply thinking of his financial integrity. It might get noised about that the Pontelliers had met with reverses, and were forced to conduct their *ménage*[8] on a humbler scale than heretofore. It might do incalculable mischief to his business prospects.

8. Household (French).

But remembering Edna's whimsical turn of mind of late, and foreseeing that she had immediately acted upon her impetuous determination, he grasped the situation with his usual promptness and handled it with his well-known business tact and cleverness.

The same mail which brought to Edna his letter of disapproval carried instructions—the most minute instructions—to a well-known architect concerning the remodeling of his home, changes which he had long contemplated, and which he desired carried forward during his temporary absence.

Expert and reliable packers and movers were engaged to convey the furniture, carpets, pictures—everything movable, in short—to places of security. And in an incredibly short time the Pontellier house was turned over to the artisans. There was to be an addition—a small snuggery; there was to be frescoing, and hardwood flooring was to be put into such rooms as had not yet been subjected to this improvement.

Furthermore, in one of the daily papers appeared a brief notice to the effect that Mr. and Mrs. Pontellier were contemplating a summer sojourn abroad, and that their handsome residence on Esplanade Street was undergoing sumptuous alterations, and would not be ready for occupancy until their return. Mr. Pontellier had saved appearances!

Edna admired the skill of his maneuver, and avoided any occasion to balk his intentions. When the situation as set forth by Mr. Pontellier was accepted and taken for granted, she was apparently satisfied that it should be so.

The pigeon-house pleased her. It at once assumed the intimate character of a home, while she herself invested it with a charm which it reflected like a warm glow. There was with her a feeling of having descended in the social scale, with a corresponding sense of having risen in the spiritual. Every step which she took toward relieving herself from obligations added to her strength and expansion as an individual. She began to look with her own eyes; to see and to apprehend the deeper undercurrents of life. No longer was she content to "feed upon opinion" when her own soul had invited her.

After a little while, a few days, in fact, Edna went up and spent a week with her children in Iberville. They were delicious February days, with all the summer's promise hovering in the air.

How glad she was to see the children! She wept for very pleasure when she felt their little arms clasping her; their hard, ruddy cheeks pressed against her own glowing cheeks. She looked into their faces with hungry eyes that could not be satisfied with looking. And what stories they had to tell their mother! About the pigs, the cows, the mules! About riding to the mill behind Gluglu; fishing back in the lake with their Uncle Jasper; picking pecans with Lidie's little black brood, and hauling chips in their express wagon. It was a thousand times more fun to haul real chips for old lame Susie's real fire than to drag painted blocks along the banquette on Esplanade Street!

She went with them herself to see the pigs and the cows, to look at the darkies laying the cane, to thrash the pecan trees, and catch fish in the back lake. She lived with them a whole week long, giving them all of herself, and gathering and filling herself with their young existence. They listened, breathless, when she told them the house in Esplanade Street was crowded with workmen, hammering, nailing, sawing, and filling the place with clatter. They wanted to know where their bed was; what had been done with their rocking-horse; and where did Joe sleep, and where had Ellen gone, and the cook? But, above all, they were fired with a desire to see the little house around the block. Was there any place to play? Were there any boys next door? Raoul, with pessimistic foreboding, was convinced that there were only girls next door. Where would they sleep, and where would papa sleep? She told them the fairies would fix it all right.

The old Madame was charmed with Edna's visit, and showered all manner of delicate attentions upon her. She was delighted to know that the Esplanade Street house was in a dismantled condition. It gave her the promise and pretext to keep the children indefinitely.

It was with a wrench and a pang that Edna left her children. She carried away with her the sound of their voices and the touch of their cheeks. All along the journey homeward their presence lingered with her like the memory of a delicious song. But by the time she had regained the city the song no longer echoed in her soul. She was again alone.

## XXXIII

It happened sometimes when Edna went to see Mademoiselle Reisz that the little musician was absent, giving a lesson or making some small necessary household purchase. The key was always left in a secret hiding-place in the entry, which Edna knew. If Mademoiselle happened to be away, Edna would usually enter and wait for her return.

When she knocked at Mademoiselle Reisz's door one afternoon there was no response; so unlocking the door, as usual, she entered and found the apartment deserted, as she had expected. Her day had been quite filled up, and it was for a rest, for a refuge, and to talk about Robert, that she sought out her friend.

She had worked at her canvas—a young Italian character study—all the morning, completing the work without the model; but there had been many interruptions, some incident to her modest housekeeping, and others of a social nature.

Madame Ratignolle had dragged herself over, avoiding the too public thoroughfares, she said. She complained that Edna had neglected her much of late. Besides, she was consumed with curiosity to see the little house and the manner in which it was conducted. She wanted to hear all about the dinner party; Monsieur Ratignolle had left *so* early. What had happened after he left? The champagne and grapes which Edna sent over were *too* delicious. She had so little appetite; they had refreshed and toned her stomach. Where on earth was she going to put Mr. Pontellier in that little house, and the boys? And then she made Edna promise to go to her when her hour of trial overtook her.

"At any time—any time of the day or night, dear," Edna assured her.

Before leaving Madame Ratignolle said:

"In some way you seem to me like a child, Edna. You seem to act without a certain amount of reflection which is necessary in this life. That is the reason I want to say you mustn't mind if I advise you to be a little careful while you are living here alone. Why don't you have some one come and stay with you? Wouldn't Mademoiselle Reisz come?"

"No; she wouldn't wish to come, and I shouldn't want her always with me."

"Well, the reason—you know how evil-minded the world is—some one was talking of Alcée Arobin visiting you. Of course, it wouldn't matter if Mr.

Arobin had not such a dreadful reputation. Monsieur Ratignolle was telling me that his attentions alone are considered enough to ruin a woman's name."

"Does he boast of his successes?" asked Edna, indifferently, squinting at her picture.

"No, I think not. I believe he is a decent fellow as far as that goes. But his character is so well known among the men. I shan't be able to come back and see you; it was very, very imprudent today."

"Mind the step!" cried Edna.

"Don't neglect me," entreated Madame Ratignolle; "and don't mind what I said about Arobin, or having some one to stay with you."

"Of course not," Edna laughed, "You may say anything you like to me." They kissed each other good-bye. Madame Ratignolle had not far to go, and Edna stood on the porch a while watching her walk down the street.

Then in the afternoon Mrs. Merriman and Mrs. Highcamp had made their "party call." Edna felt that they might have dispensed with the formality. They had also come to invite her to play *vingt-et-un*[9] one evening at Mrs. Merriman's. She was asked to go early, to dinner, and Mr. Merriman or Mr. Arobin would take her home. Edna accepted in a half-hearted way. She sometimes felt very tired of Mrs. Highcamp and Mrs. Merriman.

Late in the afternoon she sought refuge with Mademoiselle Reisz, and stayed there alone, waiting for her, feeling a kind of repose invade her with the very atmosphere of the shabby, unpretentious little room.

Edna sat at the window, which looked out over the house-tops and across the river. The window frame was filled with pots of flowers, and she sat and picked the dry leaves from a rose geranium. The day was warm, and the breeze which blew from the river was very pleasant. She removed her hat and laid it on the piano. She went on picking the leaves and digging around the plants with her hat pin. Once she thought she heard Mademoiselle Reisz approaching. But it was a young black girl, who came in, bringing a small bundle of laundry, which she deposited in the adjoining room, and went away.

Edna seated herself at the piano, and softly picked out with one hand the bars of a piece of music which lay open before her. A half-hour went by. There was the occasional sound of people going and coming in the lower hall. She was growing interested in her occupation of picking out the aria, when there was a second rap at the door. She vaguely wondered what these people did when they found Mademoiselle's door locked.

"Come in," she called, turning her face toward the door. And this time it was Robert Lebrun who presented himself. She attempted to rise; she could not have done so without betraying the agitation which mastered her at sight of him, so she fell back upon the stool, only exclaiming, "Why Robert!"

He came and clasped her hand, seemingly without knowing what he was saying or doing.

"Mrs. Pontellier! How do you happen—oh! how well you look! Is Mademoiselle Reisz not here? I never expected to see you."

"When did you come back?" asked Edna in an unsteady voice, wiping her face with her handkerchief. She seemed ill at ease on the piano stool, and he begged her to take the chair by the window. She did so, mechanically, while he seated himself on the stool.

---

9. Twenty-one (French), a card game.

"I returned day before yesterday," he answered, while he leaned his arm on the keys, bringing forth a crash of discordant sound.

"Day before yesterday!" she repeated, aloud, and went on thinking to herself, "day before yesterday," in a sort of an uncomprehending way. She had pictured him seeking her at the very first hour, and he had lived under the same sky since day before yesterday; while only by accident had he stumbled upon her. Mademoiselle must have lied when she said, "Poor fool, he loves you."

"Day before yesterday," she repeated, breaking off a spray of Mademoiselle's geranium; "then if you had not met me here to-day you wouldn't—when—that is, didn't you mean to come and see me?"

"Of course, I should have gone to see you. There have been so many things—" he turned the leaves of Mademoiselle's music nervously. "I started in at once yesterday with the old firm. After all there is as much chance for me here as there was there—that is, I might find it profitable some day. The Mexicans were not very congenial."

So he had come back because the Mexicans were not congenial; because business was as profitable here as there; because of any reason, and not because he cared to be near her. She remembered the day she sat on the floor, turning the pages of his letter, seeking the reason which was left untold.

She had not noticed how he looked—only feeling his presence; but she turned deliberately and observed him. After all, he had been absent but a few months, and was not changed. His hair—the color of hers—waved back from his temples in the same way as before. His skin was not more burned than it had been at Grand Isle. She found in his eyes, when he looked at her for one silent moment, the same tender caress, with an added warmth and entreaty which had not been there before—the same glance which had penetrated to the sleeping places of her soul and awakened them.

A hundred times Edna had pictured Robert's return, and imagined their first meeting. It was usually at her home, whither he had sought her out at once. She always fancied him expressing or betraying in some way his love for her. And here, the reality was that they sat ten feet apart, she at the window, crushing geranium leaves in her hand and smelling them, he twirling around on the piano stool, saying:

"I was very much surprised to hear of Mr. Pontellier's absence; it's a wonder Mademoiselle Reisz did not tell me; and your moving—mother told me yesterday. I should think you would have gone to New York with him, or to Iberville with the children, rather than be bothered here with housekeeping. And you are going abroad, too, I hear. We shan't have you at Grand Isle next summer; it won't seem—do you see much of Mademoiselle Reisz? She often spoke of you in the few letters she wrote."

"Do you remember that you promised to write to me when you went away?" A flush overspread his whole face.

"I couldn't believe that my letters would be of any interest to you."

"That is an excuse; it isn't the truth." Edna reached for her hat on the piano. She adjusted it, sticking the hat pin through the heavy coil of hair with some deliberation.

"Are you not going to wait for Mademoiselle Reisz?" asked Robert.

"No; I have found when she is absent this long, she is liable not to come back till late." She drew on her gloves, and Robert picked up his hat.

"Won't you wait for her?" asked Edna.

"Not if you think she will not be back till late," adding, as if suddenly aware of some discourtesy in his speech, "and I should miss the pleasure of walking home with you." Edna locked the door and put the key back in its hiding place.

They went together, picking their way across muddy streets and sidewalks encumbered with the cheap display of small tradesmen. Part of the distance they rode in the car, and after disembarking, passed the Pontellier mansion, which looked broken and half torn asunder. Robert had never known the house, and looked at it with interest.

"I never knew you in your home," he remarked.

"I am glad you did not."

"Why?" She did not answer. They went on around the corner, and it seemed as if her dreams were coming true after all, when he followed her into the little house.

"You must stay and dine with me, Robert. You see I am all alone, and it is so long since I have seen you. There is so much I want to ask you."

She took off her hat and gloves. He stood irresolute, making some excuse about his mother who expected him; he even muttered something about an engagement. She struck a match and lit the lamp on the table; it was growing dusk. When he saw her face in the lamplight, looking pained, with all the soft lines gone out of it, he threw his hat aside and seated himself.

"Oh! you know I want to stay if you will let me!" he exclaimed. All the softness came back. She laughed, and went and put her hand on his shoulder.

"This is the first moment you have seemed like the old Robert. I'll go tell Celestine." She hurried away to tell Celestine to set an extra place. She even sent her off in search of some added delicacy which she had not thought of for herself. And she recommended great care in dripping the coffee and having the omelet done to a proper turn.

When she reëntered, Robert was turning over magazines, sketches, and things that lay upon the table in great disorder. He picked up a photograph, and exclaimed:

"Alcée Arobin! What on earth is his picture doing here?"

"I tried to make a sketch of his head one day," answered Edna, "and he thought the photograph might help me. It was at the other house. I thought it had been left there. I must have picked it up with my drawing materials."

"I should think you would give it back to him if you have finished with it."

"Oh! I have a great many such photographs. I never think of returning them. They don't amount to anything." Robert kept on looking at the picture.

"It seems to me—do you think his head worth drawing? Is he a friend of Mr. Pontellier's? You never said you knew him."

"He isn't a friend of Mr. Pontellier's; he's a friend of mine. I always knew him—that is, it is only of late that I know him pretty well. But I'd rather talk about you, and know what you have been seeing and doing and feeling out there in Mexico." Robert threw aside the picture.

"I've been seeing the waves and the white beach of Grand Isle; the quiet, grassy street of the *Chênière*; the old fort at Grande Terre. I've been working like a machine, and feeling like a lost soul. There was nothing interesting."

She leaned her head upon her hand to shade her eyes from the light.

"And what have you been seeing and doing and feeling all these days?" he asked.

"I've been seeing the waves and the white beach of Grand Isle; the quiet, grassy street of the *Chênière Caminada;* the old sunny fort at Grande Terre. I've been working with little more comprehension than a machine, and still feeling like a lost soul. There was nothing interesting."

"Mrs. Pontellier, you are cruel," he said, with feeling, closing his eyes and resting his head back in his chair. They remained in silence till old Celestine announced dinner.

## XXXIV

The dining-room was very small. Edna's round mahogany would have almost filled it. As it was there was but a step or two from the little table to the kitchen, to the mantel, the small buffet, and the side door that opened out on the narrow brick-paved yard.

A certain degree of ceremony settled upon them with the announcement of dinner. There was no return to personalities. Robert related incidents of his sojourn in Mexico, and Edna talked of events likely to interest him, which had occurred during his absence. The dinner was of ordinary quality, except for the few delicacies which she had sent out to purchase. Old Celestine, with a bandana *tignon*[1] twisted about her head, hobbled in and out, taking a personal interest in everything; and she lingered occasionally to talk *patois*[2] with Robert, whom she had known as a boy.

He went out to a neighboring cigar stand to purchase cigarette papers, and when he came back he found that Celestine had served the black coffee in the parlor.

"Perhaps I shouldn't have come back," he said. "When you are tired of me, tell me to go."

"You never tire me. You must have forgotten the hours and hours at Grand Isle in which we grew accustomed to each other and used to being together."

"I have forgotten nothing at Grand Isle," he said, not looking at her, but rolling a cigarette. His tobacco pouch, which he laid upon the table, was a fantastic embroidered silk affair, evidently the handiwork of a woman.

"You used to carry your tobacco in a rubber pouch," said Edna, picking up the pouch and examining the needlework.

"Yes; it was lost."

"Where did you buy this one? In Mexico?"

"It was given to me by a Vera Cruz girl; they are very generous," he replied, striking a match and lighting his cigarette.

"They are very handsome, I suppose, those Mexican women; very picturesque, with their black eyes and their lace scarfs."

"Some are; others are hideous. Just as you find women everywhere."

"What was she like—the one who gave you the pouch? You must have known her very well."

"She was very ordinary. She wasn't of the slightest importance. I knew her well enough."

"Did you visit at her house? Was it interesting? I should like to know and hear about the people you met, and the impressions they made on you."

---

1. Archaic form of the word *chignon,* a "coil of hair" or a "bun." She has her hair tied up with a scarf.

2. A dialect, here of archaic French mixed with English, Spanish, German, and American Indian words spoken by the descendants of the Acadians.

"There are some people who leave impressions not so lasting as the imprint of an oar upon the water."

"Was she such a one?"

"It would be ungenerous for me to admit that she was of that order and kind." He thrust the pouch back in his pocket, as if to put away the subject with the trifle which had brought it up.

Arobin dropped in with a message from Mrs. Merriman, to say that the card party was postponed on account of the illness of one of her children.

"How do you do, Arobin?" said Robert, rising from the obscurity.

"Oh! Lebrun. To be sure! I heard yesterday you were back. How did they treat you down in Mexique?"

"Fairly well."

"But not well enough to keep you there. Stunning girls, though, in Mexico. I thought I should never get away from Vera Cruz when I was down there a couple of years ago."

"Did they embroider slippers and tobacco pouches and hat-bands and things for you?" asked Edna.

"Oh! my! no! I didn't get so deep in their regard. I fear they made more impression on me than I made on them."

"You were less fortunate than Robert, then."

"I am always less fortunate than Robert. Has he been imparting tender confidences?"

"I've been imposing myself long enough," said Robert, rising, and shaking hands with Edna. "Please convey my regards to Mr. Pontellier when you write."

He shook hands with Arobin and went away.

"Fine fellow, that Lebrun," said Arobin when Robert had gone. "I never heard you speak of him."

"I knew him last summer at Grand Isle," she replied. "Here is that photograph of yours. Don't you want it?"

"What do I want with it? Throw it away." She threw it back on the table.

"I'm not going to Mrs. Merriman's," she said. "If you see her, tell her so. But perhaps I had better write. I think I shall write now, and say that I am sorry her child is sick, and tell her not to count on me."

"It would be a good scheme," acquiesced Arobin. "I don't blame you; stupid lot!"

Edna opened the blotter, and having procured paper and pen, began to write the note. Arobin lit a cigar and read the evening paper, which he had in his pocket.

"What is the date?" she asked. He told her.

"Will you mail this for me when you go out?"

"Certainly." He read to her little bits out of the newspaper, while she straightened things on the table.

"What do you want to do?" he asked, throwing aside the paper. "Do you want to go out for a walk or a drive or anything? It would be a fine night to drive."

"No; I don't want to do anything but just be quiet. You go away and amuse yourself. Don't stay."

"I'll go away if I must; but I shan't amuse myself. You know that I only live when I am near you."

He stood up to bid her good night.

*The Modern Samson,* Thomas Nast, 1868

Known as the "Gladiator of the Political Pencil," Nast (1840–1902), a Radical Republican (liberal, progressive) supporter of the Union cause, skewered political corruption; his cartoons were said to have elected Lincoln and brought down the Tammany Hall corruption ring of "Boss" Tweed. This image, which ran in *Harper's Weekly* on October 3, 1868, drawn to expose opposition to black male suffrage, shows voting rights (Samson's hair) cut off by southern Democrats (Delilah) and their northern allies. In the left foreground the Bible and other books are burning. Among the armed figures in the left background are (second from left) Nathan Bedford Forrest, Confederate general; a squatting Robert E. Lee; presidential nominee Horatio Seymour, with demonically horned hair, wearing a Ku Klux Klan breastplate, carrying a flag that commemorates the Confederacy; vice presidential nominee Frank Blair, also wearing a Klan breastplate; and (far right) a stereotypical Irish American Catholic.

*Snap the Whip,* Winslow Homer, 1872

Homer (1836–1910), famous for his *Harper's Weekly* illustrations of Civil War battle scenes, eventually became known as the quintessential painter of a traditional and nostalgic view of American life. In this, his best-known painting, Homer fuses mountain scenery with the "little red schoolhouse" and schoolboys at recess, reminding viewers (as did much regional writing) of bygone times. Like Mark Twain's work, this painting celebrates American boyhood and the cycles of nature at the same time that it explores their fragility.

*Children Sleeping in Mulberry Street,* Jacob Riis, 1890

Riis (1825–1914) was a Danish immigrant who worked as a New York police reporter. His photographs of the Irish and Italian immigrant poor appeared in his influential book *How the Other Half Lives* (1890). Riis's composition articulates the position of homeless slum children: they sleep where they can, bunched up below street level. The photograph emphasizes their reliance on each other—they huddle together—but also shows that the space they inhabit is not "safe": the stones behind the boys seem overwhelming and the iron railing and drainpipe make it seem as if they are in a subterranean prison.

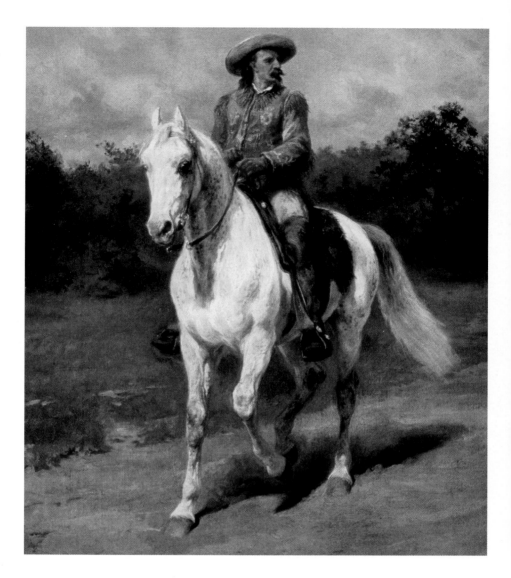

*Colonel William F. Cody,* Rosa Bonheur, 1889

Called "Buffalo Bill" because he shot buffalo to feed workers building the railroad, Cody (1845–1917) served in the Civil War on the Union side and acted as a scout during the Indian wars of the 1870s. In 1883 he organized the first Wild West show. The show, in Omaha, Nebraska, featured patriotic displays and romanticized historical reenactments involving cowboys, Indians, sharpshooters, and Mexican vaqueros. For two decades it traveled around the country and to Europe. Huge audiences made Cody's show the most significant source of imagery about the American West just as the "frontier" was closing. In Paris, Cody gave behind-the-scenes access to the French realist painter Marie-Rosalie (Rosa) Bonheur (1822–1899), who was known for her studies of animals. Grateful, Bonheur painted this picture, Cody's favorite among the innumerable images of him.

*Mrs. Elliott Fitch Shepard,* John Singer Sargent, 1888

Sargent (1856–1925), the most famous American portraitist of his day, lived in Europe and counted as influences Spanish master Diego Velásquez, the French Impressionists, and Dutch painter Franz Hals. He was in high demand among the U.S. and European wealthy and painted two American presidents and the business tycoons Rockefeller and Vanderbilt. Sargent's portraits focused on the sophistication of his subjects and conveyed the sense of a life beneath the surface, somewhat akin to the work of Henry James and Edith Wharton. This portrait of Mrs. Shepard, a Vanderbilt, announces her social position and calls attention to a certain sensuality, perhaps one projected by the artist himself.

*A Feast Day at Acoma,* Edward S. Curtis, 1904

In 1892 Curtis (1868–1952) opened a portrait studio in Washington Territory and began to photograph local Indians. Curtis traveled widely, portraying Native people and scenes in an elegiac manner, attempting to document what he understood to be the last days of the "vanishing Indian." Whatever his intentions, *A Feast Day at Acoma* shows a lively and bustling scene of Pueblo people in the Southwest.

*Hopi House,* Mary Colter, 1905

Colter (1869–1958), one of the nation's few women architects, used traditional Southwest Native American elements in buildings in Grand Canyon National Park and hotels and lodges for the Fred Harvey Company and the Santa Fe Railroad. These structures, including La Fonda in Santa Fe and the El Navajo in Gallup, New Mexico, helped introduce the Southwest to easterners, as did the writings of Willa Cather, Mary Austin, and others. The rustic style, drawing on Native American shapes and using local materials, influenced southwestern architecture for generations. Many of Colter's buildings have been torn down, but the eleven that remain are on the National Register of Historic Places, with five designated National Historic Landmarks.

*Women Watching a Sun Dance*, Amos Bad Heart Bull, undated

In the years 1890–1913 Amos Bad Heart Bull (1869–1913), an Oglala Lakota (Sioux), produced 415 paintings and drawings. Many depict aspects of the Battle of the Little Big Horn, in which General George Armstrong Custer was defeated, as well as other important events in the history and culture of his people. This painting depicts women watching a Sun Dance through a pine-bough barricade. The horseshoe shape of each woman's head, black except for the part at the center, is conventional in the art of Plains people.

*An Indian Horse Dance*, Kills Two, undated

This early-twentieth-century painting by the Lakota (Sioux) Kills Two depicts a traditional ceremony of the Horse Dance Society. The Horse Dance Society was composed of men and women who used powers granted to them in visions to heal and train horses. The markings on the horses and the men symbolize thunder and lightning, powers important to the Horse Dance Society and prominent in Black Elk's vision. Black Elk called for a Horse Dance to be performed to help distribute this power among his people.

*Both Members of This Club,* George Bellows, 1909

Bellows (1882–1925) was a member of the Ashcan school, a group of artists who advocated representing American society in all its forms, especially the crude and chaotic lives of the working class and the moral shortcomings of the wealthy, much like the naturalist writers of the time. Bellows's paintings of boxing matches are characterized by savage brushstrokes on a dark background and emphasize the motion of human figures within the confines of the ring. In *Both Members of This Club,* Bellows creates an atmosphere not of athleticism but of defeat, with both boxers reduced to mere entertainment for the grotesquely leering crowd.

*Manhattan's Misty Sunset*, Childe Hassam, 1911

Frederick Childe Hassam (1850–1935), an American Impressionist, was the premier painter of New York City. *Manhattan's Misty Sunset* captures the romantic attraction of New York as a place both of tremendous opportunity and of uncertainty and mystery. Hassam's limited color palette is organized around cool tones, as shades of green generalize the shapes of Brooklyn warehouses across the East River from Hassam's studio, punctuated by barely visible streetlights; the drizzle and fog suggest an ambivalence toward industrial America.

"Is that one of the things you always say to women?"

"I have said it before, but I don't think I ever came so near meaning it," he answered with a smile. There were no warm lights in her eyes; only a dreamy, absent look.

"Good night, I adore you. Sleep well," he said, and he kissed her hand and went away.

She stayed alone in a kind of reverie—a sort of stupor. Step by step she lived over every instant of the time she had been with Robert after he had entered Mademoiselle Reisz's door. She recalled his words, his looks. How few and meager they had been for her hungry heart! A vision—a transcendently seductive vision of a Mexican girl arose before her. She writhed with a jealous pang. She wondered when he would come back. He had not said he would come back. She had been with him, had heard his voice and touched his hand. But some way he had seemed nearer to her off there in Mexico.

## XXXV

The morning was full of sunlight and hope. Edna could see before her no denial—only the promise of excessive joy. She lay in bed awake, with bright eyes full of speculation. "He loves you, poor fool." If she could but get that conviction firmly fixed in her mind, what mattered about the rest? She felt she had been childish and unwise the night before in giving herself over to despondency. She recapitulated the motives which no doubt explained Robert's reserve. They were not insurmountable; they would not hold if he really loved her; they could not hold against her own passion, which he must come to realize in time. She pictured him going to his business that morning. She even saw how he was dressed; how he walked down one street, and turned the corner of another; saw him bending over his desk, talking to people who entered the office, going to his lunch, and perhaps watching for her on the street. He would come to her in the afternoon or evening, sit and roll his cigarette, talk a little, and go away as he had done the night before. But how delicious it would be to have him there with her! She would have no regrets, nor seek to penetrate his reserve if he still chose to wear it.

Edna ate her breakfast only half dressed. The maid brought her a delicious printed scrawl from Raoul, expressing his love, asking her to send him some bonbons, and telling her they had found that morning ten tiny white pigs all lying in a row beside Lidie's big white pig.

A letter also came from her husband, saying he hoped to be back early in March, and then they would get ready for that journey abroad which he had promised her so long, which he felt now fully able to afford; he felt able to travel as people should, without any thought of small economies—thanks to his recent speculations in Wall Street.

Much to her surprise she received a note from Arobin, written at midnight from the club. It was to say good morning to her, to hope that she had slept well, to assure her of his devotion, which he trusted she in some faintest manner returned.

All these letters were pleasing to her. She answered the children in a cheerful frame of mind, promising them bonbons, and congratulating them upon their happy find of the little pigs.

She answered her husband with friendly evasiveness,—not with any fixed design to mislead him, only because all sense of reality had gone out of her life; she had abandoned herself to Fate, and awaited the consequences with indifference.

To Arobin's note she made no reply. She put it under Celestine's stove-lid.

Edna worked several hours with much spirit. She saw no one but a picture dealer, who asked her if it were true that she was going abroad to study in Paris.

She said possibly she might, and he negotiated with her for some Parisian studies to reach him in time for the holiday trade in December.

Robert did not come that day. She was keenly disappointed. He did not come the following day, nor the next. Each morning she awoke with hope, and each night she was a prey to despondency. She was tempted to seek him out. But far from yielding to the impulse, she avoided any occasion which might throw her in his way. She did not go to Mademoiselle Reisz's nor pass by Madame Lebrun's, as she might have done if he had still been in Mexico.

When Arobin, one night, urged her to drive with him, she went—out to the lake, on the Shell Road.[3] His horses were full of mettle, and even a little unmanageable. She liked the rapid gait at which they spun along, and the quick, sharp sound of the horses' hoofs on the hard road. They did not stop anywhere to eat or to drink. Arobin was not needlessly imprudent. But they ate and they drank when they regained Edna's little dining-room—which was comparatively early in the evening.

It was late when he left her. It was getting to be more than a passing whim with Arobin to see her and be with her. He had detected the latent sensuality, which unfolded under his delicate sense of her nature's requirements like a torpid, torrid, sensitive blossom.

There was no despondency when she fell asleep that night; nor was there hope when she awoke in the morning.

## XXXVI

There was a garden out in the suburbs; a small, leafy corner, with a few green tables under the orange trees. An old cat slept all day on the stone step in the sun, and an old *mulatresse*[4] slept her idle hours away in her chair at the open window, till some one happened to knock on one of the green tables. She had milk and cream cheese to sell, and bread and butter. There was no one who could make such excellent coffee or fry a chicken so golden brown as she.

The place was too modest to attract the attention of people of fashion, and so quiet as to have escaped the notice of those in search of pleasure and dissipation. Edna had discovered it accidentally one day when the high-board gate stood ajar. She caught sight of a little green table, blotched with the checkered sunlight that filtered through the quivering leaves overhead. Within she had found the slumbering *mulatresse*, the drowsy cat, and a glass of milk which reminded her of the milk she had tasted in Iberville.

She often stopped there during her perambulations; sometimes taking a book with her, and sitting an hour or two under the trees when she found the

---

3. A road along Lake Pontchartrain, a favorite for testing the speed of horses.

4. A woman of mixed African American and Caucasian ancestry.

place deserted. Once or twice she took a quiet dinner there alone, having instructed Celestine beforehand to prepare no dinner at home. It was the last place in the city where she would have expected to meet any one she knew.

Still she was not astonished when, as she was partaking of a modest dinner late in the afternoon, looking into an open book, stroking the cat, which had made friends with her—she was not greatly astonished to see Robert come in at the tall garden gate.

"I am destined to see you only by accident," she said, shoving the cat off the chair beside her. He was surprised, ill at ease, almost embarrassed at meeting her thus so unexpectedly.

"Do you come here often?" he asked.

"I almost live here," she said.

"I used to drop in very often for a cup of Catiche's good coffee. This is the first time since I came back."

"She'll bring you a plate, and you will share my dinner. There's always enough for two—even three." Edna had intended to be indifferent and as reserved as he when she met him; she had reached the determination by a laborious train of reasoning, incident to one of her despondent moods. But her resolve melted when she saw him before her, seated there beside her in the little garden, as if a designing Providence had led him into her path.

"Why have you kept away from me, Robert?" she asked, closing the book that lay open upon the table.

"Why are you so personal, Mrs. Pontellier? Why do you force me to idiotic subterfuges?" he exclaimed with sudden warmth. "I suppose there's no use telling you I've been very busy, or that I've been sick, or that I've been to see you and not found you at home. Please let me off with any one of those excuses."

"You are the embodiment of selfishness," she said. "You save yourself something—I don't know what—but there is some selfish motive, and in sparing yourself you never consider for a moment what I think, or how I feel your neglect and indifference. I suppose this is what you would call unwomanly; but I have got into a habit of expressing myself. It doesn't matter to me, and you may think me unwomanly if you like."

"No; I only think you cruel, as I said the other day. Maybe not intentionally cruel; but you seem to be forcing me into disclosures which can result in nothing; as if you would have me bare a wound for the pleasure of looking at it, without the intention or power of healing it."

"I'm spoiling your dinner, Robert; never mind what I say. You haven't eaten a morsel."

"I only came in for a cup of coffee." His sensitive face was all disfigured with excitement.

"Isn't this a delightful place?" she remarked. "I am so glad it has never actually been discovered. It is so quiet, so sweet here. Do you notice there is scarcely a sound to be heard? It's so out of the way; and a good walk from the car. However, I don't mind walking. I always feel so sorry for women who don't like to walk; they miss so much—so many rare little glimpses of life; and we women learn so little of life on the whole.

"Catiche's coffee is always hot. I don't know how she manages it, here in the open air. Celestine's coffee gets cold bringing it from the kitchen to the dining-room. Three lumps! How can you drink it so sweet? Take some of the cress with your chop; it's so biting and crisp. Then there's the advantage of being able to smoke with your coffee out here. Now, in the city—aren't you going to smoke?"

"After a while," he said, laying a cigar on the table.

"Who gave it to you?" she laughed.

"I bought it. I suppose I'm getting reckless; I bought a whole box." She was determined not to be personal again and make him uncomfortable.

The cat made friends with him, and climbed into his lap when he smoked his cigar. He stroked her silky fur, and talked a little about her. He looked at Edna's book, which he had read; and he told her the end, to save her the trouble of wading through it, he said.

Again he accompanied her back to her home; and it was after dusk when they reached the little "pigeon-house." She did not ask him to remain, which he was grateful for, as it permitted him to stay without the discomfort of blundering through an excuse which he had no intention of considering. He helped her to light the lamp; then she went into her room to take off her hat and to bathe her face and hands.

When she came back Robert was not examining the pictures and magazines as before; he sat off in the shadow, leaning his head back on the chair as if in a reverie. Edna lingered a moment beside the table, arranging the books there. Then she went across the room to where he sat. She bent over the arm of his chair and called his name.

"Robert," she said, "are you asleep?"

"No," he answered, looking up at her.

She leaned over and kissed him—a soft, cool, delicate kiss, whose voluptuous sting penetrated his whole being—then she moved away from him. He followed, and took her in his arms, just holding her close to him. She put her hand up to his face and pressed his cheek against her own. The action was full of love and tenderness. He sought her lips again. Then he drew her down upon the sofa beside him and held her hand in both of his.

"Now you know," he said, "now you know what I have been fighting against since last summer at Grand Isle; what drove me away and drove me back again."

"Why have you been fighting against it?" she asked. Her face glowed with soft lights.

"Why? Because you were not free; you were Léonce Pontellier's wife. I couldn't help loving you if you were ten times his wife, but so long as I went away from you and kept away I could help telling you so." She put her free hand up to his shoulder, and then against his cheek, rubbing it softly. He kissed her again. His face was warm and flushed.

"There in Mexico I was thinking of you all the time, and longing for you."

"But not writing to me," she interrupted.

"Something put into my head that you cared for me; and I lost my senses. I forgot everything but a wild dream of your some way becoming my wife."

"Your wife!"

"Religion, loyalty, everything would give way if only you cared."

"Then you must have forgotten that I was Léonce Pontellier's wife."

"Oh! I was demented, dreaming of wild, impossible things, recalling men who had set their wives free, we have heard of such things."

"Yes, we have heard of such things."

"I came back full of vague, mad intentions. And when I got here—"

"When you got here you never came near me!" She was still caressing his cheek.

"I realized what a cur I was to dream of such a thing, even if you had been willing."

She took his face between her hands and looked into it as if she would never withdraw her eyes more. She kissed him on the forehead, the eyes, the cheeks, and the lips.

"You have been a very, very foolish boy, wasting your time dreaming of impossible things when you speak of Mr. Pontellier setting me free! I am no longer one of Mr. Pontellier's possessions to dispose of or not. I give myself where I choose. If he were to say, 'Here, Robert, take her and be happy; she is yours,' I should laugh at you both."

His face grew a little white. "What do you mean?" he asked.

There was a knock at the door. Old Celestine came in to say that Madame Ratignolle's servant had come around the back way with a message that Madame had been taken sick and begged Mrs. Pontellier to go to her immediately.

"Yes, yes," said Edna, rising: "I promised. Tell her yes—to wait for me. I'll go back with her."

"Let me walk over with you," offered Robert.

"No," she said; "I will go with the servant." She went into her room to put on her hat, and when she came in again she sat once more upon the sofa beside him. He had not stirred. She put her arms about his neck.

"Good-by, my sweet Robert. Tell me good-by." He kissed her with a degree of passion which had not before entered into his caress, and strained her to him.

"I love you," she whispered, "only you; no one but you. It was you who awoke me last summer out of a life-long, stupid dream. Oh! you have made me so unhappy with your indifference. Oh! I have suffered, suffered! Now you are here we shall love each other, my Robert. We shall be everything to each other. Nothing else in the world is of any consequence. I must go to my friend; but you will wait for me? No matter how late; you will wait for me, Robert?"

"Don't go; don't go! Oh! Edna, stay with me," he pleaded. "Why should you go? Stay with me, stay with me."

"I shall come back as soon as I can; I shall find you here." She buried her face in his neck, and said good-by again. Her seductive voice, together with his great love for her, had enthralled his senses, had deprived him of every impulse but the longing to hold her and keep her.

## XXXVII

Edna looked in at the drug store. Monsieur Ratignolle was putting up a mixture himself, very carefully, dropping a red liquid into a tiny glass. He was grateful to Edna for having come; her presence would be a comfort to his wife. Madame Ratignolle's sister, who had always been with her at such trying times, had not been able to come up from the plantation, and Adèle had been inconsolable until Mrs. Pontellier so kindly promised to come to her. The nurse had been with them at night for the past week, as she lived a great distance away. And Dr. Mandelet had been coming and going all the afternoon. They were then looking for him any moment.

Edna hastened upstairs by a private stairway that led from the rear of the store to the apartments above. The children were all sleeping in a back room. Madame Ratignolle was in the salon, whither she had strayed in her suffering impatience. She sat on the sofa, clad in an ample white *peignoir,* holding a handkerchief tight in her hand with a nervous clutch. Her face was drawn and pinched, her sweet blue eyes haggard and unnatural. All her beautiful hair had been drawn back and plaited. It lay in a long braid on the sofa pillow, coiled like a golden serpent. The nurse, a comfortable looking *Griffe* woman[5] in white apron and cap, was urging her to return to her bedroom.

"There is no use, there is no use," she said at once to Edna. "We must get rid of Mandelet; he is getting too old and careless. He said he would be here at half-past seven; now it must be eight. See what time it is, Joséphine."

The woman was possessed of a cheerful nature, and refused to take any situation too seriously, especially a situation with which she was so familiar. She urged Madame to have courage and patience. But Madame only set her teeth hard into her under lip, and Edna saw the sweat gather in beads on her white forehead. After a moment or two she uttered a profound sigh and wiped her face with the handkerchief rolled in a ball. She appeared exhausted. The nurse gave her a fresh handkerchief, sprinkled with cologne water.

"This is too much!" she cried. "Mandelet ought to be killed! Where is Alphonse? Is it possible I am to be abandoned like this—neglected by every one!"

"Neglected, indeed!" exclaimed the nurse. Wasn't she there? And here was Mrs. Pontellier leaving, no doubt, a pleasant evening at home to devote to her? And wasn't Monsieur Ratignolle coming that very instant through the hall? And Joséphine was quite sure she had heard Doctor Mandelet's coupé. Yes, there it was, down at the door.

Adèle consented to go back to her room. She sat on the edge of a little low couch next to her bed.

Doctor Mandelet paid no attention to Madame Ratignolle's upbraidings. He was accustomed to them at such times, and was too well convinced of her loyalty to doubt it.

He was glad to see Edna, and wanted her to go with him into the salon and entertain him. But Madame Ratignolle would not consent that Edna should leave her for an instant. Between agonizing moments, she chatted a little, and said it took her mind off her sufferings.

Edna began to feel uneasy. She was seized with a vague dread. Her own like experiences seemed far away, unreal, and only half remembered. She recalled faintly an ecstasy of pain, the heavy odor of chloroform, a stupor which had deadened sensation, and an awakening to find a little new life to which she had given being, added to the great unnumbered multitude of souls that come and go.

She began to wish she had not come; her presence was not necessary. She might have invented a pretext for staying away; she might even invent a pretext now for going. But Edna did not go. With an inward agony, with a flam-

5. The daughter of a mulatto and a black or of a mulatto and an American Indian.

ing, outspoken revolt against the ways of Nature, she witnessed the scene of torture.

She was still stunned and speechless with emotion when later she leaned over her friend to kiss her and softly say good-by. Adèle, pressing her cheek, whispered in an exhausted voice: "Think of the children, Edna. Oh think of the children! Remember them!"

## XXXVIII

Edna still felt dazed when she got outside in the open air. The Doctor's coupé had returned for him and stood before the *porte cochère*. She did not wish to enter the coupé, and told Doctor Mandelet she would walk; she was not afraid, and would go alone. He directed his carriage to meet him at Mrs. Pontellier's, and he started to walk home with her.

Up—away up, over the narrow street between the tall houses, the stars were blazing. The air was mild and caressing, but cool with the breath of spring and the night. They walked slowly, the Doctor with a heavy, measured tread and his hands behind him; Edna, in an absent-minded way, as she had walked one night at Grand Isle, as if her thoughts had gone ahead of her and she was striving to overtake them.

"You shouldn't have been there, Mrs. Pontellier," he said. "That was no place for you. Adèle is full of whims at such times. There were a dozen women she might have had with her, unimpressionable women. I felt that it was cruel, cruel. You shouldn't have gone."

"Oh, well!" she answered, indifferently. "I don't know that it matters after all. One has to think of the children some time or other; the sooner the better."

"When is Léonce coming back?"

"Quite soon. Some time in March."

"And you are going abroad?"

"Perhaps—no, I am not going. I'm not going to be forced into doing things. I don't want to go abroad. I want to be let alone. Nobody has any right—except children, perhaps—and even then, it seems to me—or it did seem—" She felt that her speech was voicing the incoherency of her thoughts, and stopped abruptly.

"The trouble is," sighed the Doctor, grasping her meaning intuitively, "that youth is given up to illusions. It seems to be a provision of Nature; a decoy to secure mothers for the race. And Nature takes no account of moral consequences, of arbitrary conditions which we create, and which we feel obliged to maintain at any cost."

"Yes," she said. "The years that are gone seem like dreams—if one might go on sleeping and dreaming—but to wake up and find—oh! well! perhaps it is better to wake up after all, even to suffer, rather than to remain a dupe to illusions all one's life."

"It seems to me, my dear child," said the Doctor at parting, holding her hand, "you seem to me to be in trouble. I am not going to ask for your confidence. I will only say that if ever you feel moved to give it to me, perhaps I might help you. I know I would understand, and I tell you there are not many who would—not many, my dear."

"Some way I don't feel moved to speak of things that trouble me. Don't think I am ungrateful or that I don't appreciate your sympathy. There are periods of despondency and suffering which take possession of me. But I don't want anything but my own way. That is wanting a good deal, of course, when you have to trample upon the lives, the hearts, the prejudices of others—but no matter—still, I shouldn't want to trample upon the little lives. Oh! I don't know what I'm saying, Doctor. Good night. Don't blame me for anything."

"Yes, I will blame you if you don't come and see me soon. We will talk of things you never have dreamt of talking about before. It will do us both good. I don't want you to blame yourself, whatever comes. Good night, my child."

She let herself in at the gate, but instead of entering she sat upon the step of the porch. The night was quiet and soothing. All the tearing emotion of the last few hours seemed to fall away from her like a somber, uncomfortable garment, which she had but to loosen to be rid of. She went back to that hour before Adèle had sent for her; and her senses kindled afresh in thinking of Robert's words, the pressure of his arms, and the feeling of his lips upon her own. She could picture at that moment no greater bliss on earth than possession of the beloved one. His expression of love had already given him to her in part. When she thought that he was there at hand, waiting for her, she grew numb with the intoxication of expectancy. It was so late; he would be asleep perhaps. She would awaken him with a kiss. She hoped he would be asleep that she might arouse him with her caresses.

Still, she remembered Adèle's voice whispering, "Think of the children, think of them." She meant to think of them; that determination had driven into her soul like a death wound—but not to-night. To-morrow would be time to think of everything.

Robert was not waiting for her in the little parlor. He was nowhere at hand. The house was empty. But he had scrawled on a piece of paper that lay in the lamplight:

"I love you. Good-by—because I love you."

Edna grew faint when she read the words. She went and sat on the sofa. Then she stretched herself out there, never uttering a sound. She did not sleep. She did not go to bed. The lamp sputtered and went out. She was still awake in the morning, when Celestine unlocked the kitchen door and came in to light the fire.

## XXXIX

Victor, with hammer and nails and scraps of scantling,[6] was patching a corner of one of the galleries. Mariequita sat near by, dangling her legs, watching him work, and handing him nails from the tool-box. The sun was beating down upon them. The girl had covered her head with her apron folded into a square pad. They had been talking for an hour or more. She was never tired of hearing Victor describe the dinner at Mrs. Pontellier's. He exaggerated every detail, making it appear a veritable Lucillean[7] feast. The flowers were in tubs, he said. The champagne was quaffed from huge golden goblets. Venus[8] rising from the foam could have presented no more entrancing a spec-

6. Small pieces of lumber.
7. After the 1st-century Roman general Lucius Licinius Lucullus, who was noted for his banquets.

8. Roman goddess of love and beauty, daughter of Jupiter and Dione, sprang from the foam at birth.

tacle than Mrs. Pontellier, blazing with beauty and diamonds at the head of the board, while the other women were all of them youthful houris[9] possessed of incomparable charms.

She got it into her head that Victor was in love with Mrs. Pontellier, and he gave her evasive answers, framed so as to confirm her belief. She grew sullen and cried a little, threatening to go off and leave him to his fine ladies. There were a dozen men crazy about her at the *Chênière*; and since it was the fashion to be in love with married people, why, she could run away any time she liked to New Orleans with Célina's husband.

Célina's husband was a fool, a coward, and a pig, and to prove it to her, Victor intended to hammer his head into a jelly the next time he encountered him. This assurance was very consoling to Mariequita. She dried her eyes, and grew cheerful at the prospect.

They were still talking of the dinner and the allurements of city life when Mrs. Pontellier herself slipped around the corner of the house. The two youngsters stayed dumb with amazement before what they considered to be an apparition. But it was really she in flesh and blood, looking tired and a little travel-stained.

"I walked up from the wharf," she said, "and heard the hammering. I supposed it was you, mending the porch. It's a good thing. I was always tripping over those loose planks last summer. How dreary and deserted everything looks!"

It took Victor some little time to comprehend that she had come in Beaudelet's lugger, that she had come alone, and for no purpose but to rest.

"There's nothing fixed up yet, you see. I'll give you my room; it's the only place."

"Any corner will do," she assured him.

"And if you can stand Philomel's cooking," he went on, "though I might try to get her mother while you are here. Do you think she would come?" turning to Mariequita.

Mariequita thought that perhaps Philomel's mother might come for a few days, and money enough.

Beholding Mrs. Pontellier make her appearance, the girl had at once suspected a lovers' rendezvous. But Victor's astonishment was so genuine, and Mrs. Pontellier's indifference so apparent, that the disturbing notion did not lodge long in her brain. She contemplated with the greatest interest this woman who gave the most sumptuous dinners in America, and who had all the men in New Orleans at her feet.

"What time will you have dinner?" asked Edna. "I'm very hungry; but don't get anything extra."

"I'll have it ready in little or no time," he said, bustling and packing away his tools. "You may go to my room to brush up and rest yourself. Mariequita will show you."

"Thank you," said Edna. "But, do you know, I have a notion to go down to the beach and take a good wash and even a little swim, before dinner?"

"The water is too cold!" they both exclaimed. "Don't think of it."

"Well, I might go down and try—dip my toes in. Why, it seems to me the sun is hot enough to have warmed the very depths of the ocean. Could you

---

9. Virgin nymphs, everlastingly young and beautiful.

get me a couple of towels? I'd better go right away, so as to be back in time. It would be a little too chilly if I waited till this afternoon."

Mariequita ran over to Victor's room, and returned with some towels, which she gave to Edna.

"I hope you have fish for dinner," said Edna, as she started to walk away; "but don't do anything extra if you haven't."

"Run and find Philomel's mother," Victor instructed the girl. "I'll go to the kitchen and see what I can do. By Gimminy! Women have no consideration! She might have sent me word."

Edna walked on down to the beach rather mechanically, not noticing anything special except that the sun was hot. She was not dwelling upon any particular train of thought. She had done all the thinking which was necessary after Robert went away, when she lay awake upon the sofa till morning.

She had said over and over to herself: "To-day it is Arobin; to-morrow it will be some one else. It makes no difference to me, it doesn't matter about Léonce Pontellier—but Raoul and Etienne!" She understood now clearly what she had meant long ago when she said to Adèle Ratignolle that she would give up the unessential, but she would never sacrifice herself for her children.

Despondency had come upon her there in the wakeful night, and had never lifted. There was no one thing in the world that she desired. There was no human being whom she wanted near her except Robert; and she even realized that the day would come when he, too, and the thought of him would melt out of her existence, leaving her alone. The children appeared before her like antagonists who had overcome her; who had overpowered and sought to drag her into the soul's slavery for the rest of her days. But she knew a way to elude them. She was not thinking of these things when she walked down to the beach.

The water of the Gulf stretched out before her, gleaming with the million lights of the sun. The voice of the sea is seductive, never ceasing, whispering, clamoring, murmuring, inviting the soul to wander in abysses of solitude. All along the white beach, up and down, there was no living thing in sight. A bird with a broken wing was beating the air above, reeling, fluttering, circling disabled down, down to the water.

Edna had found her old bathing suit still hanging, faded, upon its accustomed peg.

She put it on, leaving her clothing in the bath-house. But when she was there beside the sea, absolutely alone, she cast the unpleasant, pricking garments from her, and for the first time in her life she stood naked in the open air, at the mercy of the sun, the breeze that beat upon her, and the waves that invited her.

How strange and awful it seemed to stand naked under the sky! how delicious! She felt like some new-born creature, opening its eyes in a familiar world that it had never known.

The foamy wavelets curled up to her white feet, and coiled like serpents about her ankles. She walked out. The water was chill, but she walked on. The water was deep, but she lifted her white body and reached out with a long, sweeping stroke. The touch of the sea is sensuous, enfolding the body in its soft, close embrace.

She went on and on. She remembered the night she swam far out, and recalled the terror that seized her at the fear of being unable to regain the shore. She did not look back now, but went on and on, thinking of the blue-grass meadow that she had traversed when a little child, believing that it had no beginning and no end.

Her arms and legs were growing tired.

She thought of Léonce and the children. They were a part of her life. But they need not have thought that they could possess her, body and soul. How Mademoiselle Reisz would have laughed, perhaps sneered, if she knew! "And you call yourself an artist! What pretensions, Madame! The artist must possess the courageous soul that dares and defies."

Exhaustion was pressing upon and over-powering her.

"Good-by—because, I love you." He did not know; he did not understand. He would never understand. Perhaps Doctor Mandelet would have understood if she had seen him—but it was too late; the shore was far behind her, and her strength was gone.

She looked into the distance, and the old terror flamed up for an instant, then sank again. Edna heard her father's voice and her sister Margaret's. She heard the barking of an old dog that was chained to the sycamore tree. The spurs of the cavalry officer clanged as he walked across the porch. There was the hum of bees, and the musky odor of pinks filled the air.

*remembering what she's leaving behind*

1899

---

# MARY E. WILKINS FREEMAN
## 1852–1930

Mary E. Wilkins Freeman, best known for her depiction of New England village life, was born on October 31, 1852, in Randolph, Massachusetts, a small town twenty miles south of Boston. She was not a strong child, and two other Wilkins children died before they reached three years of age; her sister Anne lived to be seventeen. Freeman's parents were orthodox Congregationalists, and she was subject to a strict code of behavior. The constraints of religious belief, and the effect of these constraints on character formation and behavior, is one of her chief subjects.

In 1867 Freeman's father became part owner of a dry-goods store in Brattleboro, Vermont, where she graduated from high school. In 1870, she entered Mount Holyoke Female Seminary, which Emily Dickinson had attended two decades earlier. Like Dickinson, Freeman left after a year in which she resisted the school's pressure on all students to offer public testimony as to their Christian commitment. She finished her formal education with a year at West Brattleboro Seminary, though the reading and discussion with her friend Evelyn Sawyer of Johann Wolfgang von Goethe, Ralph Waldo Emerson, Henry David Thoreau, Charles Dickens, William Makepeace Thackeray, Edgar Allan Poe, Nathaniel Hawthorne, Harriet Beecher Stowe, and Sarah Orne Jewett were probably more important than her schoolwork in developing her literary taste.

After the failure of her father's business in 1876, Freeman's family moved into the Brattleboro home of the Reverend Thomas Pickman Tyler, where her mother became housekeeper. Poverty was hard for the Wilkinses to bear, especially because their Puritan heritage led them to believe that poverty was a punishment for sin. Freeman's mother died in 1880, her father three years later, leaving Freeman alone at the age of twenty-eight, with a legacy of less than one thousand dollars.

Fortunately, by this time she had begun to sell poems and stories to such leading magazines as *Harper's Bazaar,* and by the mid-1880s she had a ready market for her work. As soon as she achieved a measure of economic independence, she returned to Randolph, where she lived with her childhood friend Mary Wales. Her early stories, especially those gathered and published in *A Humble Romance* (1887), are set in the Vermont countryside, but as she put it in a preface to an edition of these stories published in Edinburgh, the characters are generalized "studies of the descendants of the Massachusetts Bay colonists, in whom can still be seen traces of those features of will and conscience, so strong as to be almost exaggerations and deformities, which characterized their ancestors." More specifically, the title story dramatizes a theme Freeman was to return to frequently: the potential for unpredictable revolt in outwardly meek and downtrodden natures, such as the central character in "The Revolt of 'Mother.'"

*"A New England Nun" and Other Stories,* which appeared in 1891, contains several of her best stories, most notably the title story, which treats (with particular dramatic success) the pervasive theme of the psychic oppression and rebellion of women. At the same time as she provides a vivid sense of place, local dialect, and personality type, Freeman also offers in her best work insight into the individual psychology and interior life produced when confining, inherited codes of village life are subject to the pressure of a rapidly changing secular and urban world. This is a world in which, as the critic Marjorie Pryse argued, women begin to assert, individually and collectively, their vision and power against an exhausted Puritan patriarchy.

Freeman continued to write for another three decades. Although she is best known today for her stories, she also wrote plays and a number of successful novels on diverse topics from local history to labor unrest, but always with a focus on women. Among these novels are *Pembroke* (1894) and *The Shoulders of Atlas* (1908). She married Dr. Charles Freeman in 1902, when she was forty-nine, and moved to Metuchen, New Jersey; after a few happy years, her husband's drinking developed into destructive alcoholism, and he had to be institutionalized in 1920. In 1926, she was awarded the W. D. Howells medal for fiction by the American Academy of Arts and Letters and elected to the National Institute of Arts and Letters—both these honors were seldom given to women writers in those days. She died of a heart attack four years later.

# A New England Nun[1]

It was late in the afternoon, and the light was waning. There was a difference in the look of the tree shadows out in the yard. Somewhere in the distance cows were lowing and a little bell was tinkling; now and then a farm-wagon tilted by, and the dust flew; some blue-shirted laborers with shovels over their shoulders plodded past; little swarms of flies were dancing up and down before the peoples' faces in the soft air. There seemed to be a gentle stir arising over everything for the mere sake of subsidence—a very premonition of rest and hush and night.

This soft diurnal commotion was over Louisa Ellis also. She had been peacefully sewing at her sitting-room window all the afternoon. Now she quilted her needle carefully into her work, which she folded precisely, and

---

1. From *"A New England Nun" and Other Stories* (1891), the source of the text printed here.

laid in a basket with her thimble and thread and scissors. Louisa Ellis could
not remember that ever in her life she had mislaid one of these little feminine appurtenances, which had become, from long use and constant association, a very part of her personality.

Louisa tied a green apron round her waist, and got out a flat straw hat with
a green ribbon. Then she went into the garden with a little blue crockery
bowl, to pick some currants for her tea. After the currants were picked she
sat on the back door-step and stemmed them, collecting the stems carefully
in her apron, and afterwards throwing them into the hen-coop. She looked
sharply at the grass beside the step to see if any had fallen there.

Louisa was slow and still in her movements; it took her a long time to prepare her tea; but when ready it was set forth with as much grace as if she had
been a veritable guest to her own self. The little square table stood exactly in
the centre of the kitchen, and was covered with a starched linen cloth whose
border pattern of flowers glistened. Louisa had a damask napkin on her tea-
tray, where were arranged a cut-glass tumbler full of teaspoons, a silver
cream-pitcher, a china sugar-bowl, and one pink china cup and saucer.
Louisa used china every day—something which none of her neighbors did.
They whispered about it among themselves. Their daily tables were laid with
common crockery, their sets of best china stayed in the parlor closet, and
Louisa Ellis was no richer nor better bred than they. Still she would use the
china. She had for her supper a glass dish full of sugared currants, a plate of
little cakes, and one of light white biscuits. Also a leaf or two of lettuce, which
she cut up daintily. Louisa was very fond of lettuce, which she raised to perfection in her little garden. She ate quite heartily, though in a delicate, pecking way; it seemed almost surprising that any considerable bulk of the food
should vanish.

After tea she filled a plate with nicely baked thin corn-cakes, and carried
them out into the back-yard.

"Cæsar!" she called. "Cæsar! Cæsar!"

There was a little rush, and the clank of a chain, and a large yellow-and-
white dog appeared at the door of his tiny hut, which was half hidden among
the tall grasses and flowers. Louisa patted him and gave him the corn-cakes.
Then she returned to the house and washed the tea-things, polishing the
china carefully. The twilight had deepened; the chorus of the frogs floated in
at the open window wonderfully loud and shrill, and once in a while a long
sharp drone from a tree-toad pierced it. Louisa took off her green gingham
apron, disclosing a shorter one of pink and white print. She lighted her lamp,
and sat down again with her sewing.

In about half an hour Joe Dagget came. She heard his heavy step on the
walk, and rose and took off her pink-and-white apron. Under that was still
another—white linen with a little cambric edging on the bottom; that was
Louisa's company apron. She never wore it without her calico sewing apron
over it unless she had a guest. She had barely folded the pink and white one
with methodical haste and laid it in a table-drawer when the door opened and
Joe Dagget entered.

He seemed to fill up the whole room. A little yellow canary that had been
asleep in his green cage at the south window woke up and fluttered wildly,
beating his little yellow wings against the wires. He always did so when Joe
Dagget came into the room.

"Good-evening," said Louisa. She extended her hand with a kind of solemn cordiality.

"Good-evening, Louisa," returned the man, in a loud voice.

She placed a chair for him, and they sat facing each other, with the table between them. He sat bolt-upright, toeing out his heavy feet squarely, glancing with a good-humored uneasiness around the room. She sat gently erect, folding her slender hands in her white-linen lap.

"Been a pleasant day," remarked Dagget.

"Real pleasant," Louisa assented, softly. "Have you been haying?" she asked, after a little while.

"Yes, I've been haying all day, down in the ten-acre lot. Pretty hot work."

"It must be."

"Yes, it's pretty hot work in the sun."

"Is your mother well to-day?"

"Yes, mother's pretty well."

"I suppose Lily Dyer's with her now?"

Dagget colored. "Yes, she's with her," he answered, slowly.

He was not very young, but there was a boyish look about his large face. Louisa was not quite as old as he, her face was fairer and smoother, but she gave people the impression of being older.

"I suppose she's a good deal of help to your mother," she said, further.

"I guess she is; I don't know how mother'd get along without her," said Dagget, with a sort of embarrassed warmth.

"She looks like a real capable girl. She's pretty-looking too," remarked Louisa.

"Yes, she is pretty fair looking."

Presently Dagget began fingering the books on the table. There was a square red autograph album, and a Young Lady's Gift-Book[2] which had belonged to Louisa's mother. He took them up one after the other and opened them; then laid them down again, the album on the Gift-Book.

Louisa kept eying them with mild uneasiness. Finally she rose and changed the position of the books, putting the album underneath. That was the way they had been arranged in the first place.

Dagget gave an awkward little laugh. "Now what difference did it make which book was on top?" said he.

Louisa looked at him with a deprecating smile. "I always keep them that way," murmured she.

"You do beat everything," said Dagget, trying to laugh again. His large face was flushed.

He remained about an hour longer, then rose to take leave. Going out, he stumbled over a rug, and trying to recover himself, hit Louisa's work-basket on the table, and knocked it on the floor.

He looked at Louisa, then at the rolling spools; he ducked himself awkwardly toward them, but she stopped him. "Never mind," said she; "I'll pick them up after you're gone."

She spoke with a mild stiffness. Either she was a little disturbed, or his nervousness affected her, and made her seem constrained in her effort to reassure him.

---

2. Gift books (ca. 1825–65) were popular annual miscellanies, containing stories, essays, and poems, usually with a polite or moral tone. They were lavishly printed and decorated for use as Christmas or New Year's gifts.

When Joe Dagget was outside he drew in the sweet evening air with a sigh, and felt much as an innocent and perfectly well-intentioned bear might after his exit from a china shop.

Louisa, on her part, felt much as the kind-hearted, long-suffering owner of the china shop might have done after the exit of the bear.

She tied on the pink, then the green apron, picked up all the scattered treasures and replaced them in her work-basket, and straightened the rug. Then she set the lamp on the floor, and began sharply examining the carpet. She even rubbed her fingers over it, and looked at them.

"He's tracked in a good deal of dust," she murmured. "I thought he must have."

Louisa got a dust-pan and brush, and swept Joe Dagget's track carefully.

If he could have known it, it would have increased his perplexity and uneasiness, although it would not have disturbed his loyalty in the least. He came twice a week to see Louisa Ellis, and every time, sitting there in her delicately sweet room, he felt as if surrounded by a hedge of lace. He was afraid to stir lest he should put a clumsy foot or hand through the fairy web, and he had always the consciousness that Louisa was watching fearfully lest he should.

Still the lace and Louisa commanded perforce his perfect respect and patience and loyalty. They were to be married in a month, after a singular courtship which had lasted for a matter of fifteen years. For fourteen out of the fifteen years the two had not once seen each other, and they had seldom exchanged letters. Joe had been all those years in Australia, where he had gone to make his fortune, and where he had stayed until he made it. He would have stayed fifty years if it had taken so long, and come home feeble and tottering, or never come home at all, to marry Louisa.

But the fortune had been made in the fourteen years, and he had come home now to marry the woman who had been patiently and unquestioningly waiting for him all that time.

Shortly after they were engaged he had announced to Louisa his determination to strike out into new fields, and secure a competency before they should be married. She had listened and assented with the sweet serenity which never failed her, not even when her lover set forth on that long and uncertain journey. Joe, buoyed up as he was by his sturdy determination, broke down a little at the last, but Louisa kissed him with a mild blush, and said good-by.

"It won't be for long," poor Joe had said, huskily; but it was for fourteen years.

In that length of time much had happened. Louisa's mother and brother had died, and she was all alone in the world. But greatest happening of all— a subtle happening which both were too simple to understand—Louisa's feet had turned into a path, smooth maybe under a calm, serene sky, but so straight and unswerving that it could only meet a check at her grave, and so narrow that there was no room for any one at her side.

Louisa's first emotion when Joe Dagget came home (he had not apprised her of his coming) was consternation, although she would not admit it to herself, and he never dreamed of it. Fifteen years ago she had been in love with him—at least she considered herself to be. Just at that time, gently acquiescing with and falling into the natural drift of girlhood, she had seen marriage ahead as a reasonable feature and a probable desirability of life. She had listened with calm docility to her mother's views upon the subject. Her mother was remarkable for her cool sense and sweet, even temperament. She talked wisely to her daughter when Joe Dagget presented himself, and Louisa accepted him with no hesitation. He was the first lover she had ever had.

She had been faithful to him all these years. She had never dreamed of the possibility of marrying any one else. Her life, especially for the last seven years, had been full of a pleasant peace, she had never felt discontented nor impatient over her lover's absence; still she had always looked forward to his return and their marriage as the inevitable conclusion of things. However, she had fallen into a way of placing it so far in the future that it was almost equal to placing it over the boundaries of another life.

When Joe came she had been expecting him, and expecting to be married for fourteen years, but she was as much surprised and taken aback as if she had never thought of it.

Joe's consternation came later. He eyed Louisa with an instant confirmation of his old admiration. She had changed but little. She still kept her pretty manner and soft grace, and was, he considered, every whit as attractive as ever. As for himself, his stent was done; he had turned his face away from fortune-seeking, and the old winds of romance whistled as loud and sweet as ever through his ears. All the song which he had been wont to hear in them was Louisa; he had for a long time a loyal belief that he heard it still, but finally it seemed to him that although the winds sang always that one song, it had another name. But for Louisa the wind had never more than murmured; now it had gone down, and everything was still. She listened for a little while with half-wistful attention; then she turned quietly away and went to work on her wedding clothes.

Joe had made some extensive and quite magnificent alterations in his house. It was the old homestead; the newly-married couple would live there, for Joe could not desert his mother, who refused to leave her old home. So Louisa must leave hers. Every morning, rising and going about among her neat maidenly possessions, she felt as one looking her last upon the faces of dear friends. It was true that in a measure she could take them with her, but, robbed of their old environments, they would appear in such new guises that they would almost cease to be themselves. Then there were some peculiar features of her happy solitary life which she would probably be obliged to relinquish altogether. Sterner tasks than these graceful but half-needless ones would probably devolve upon her. There would be a large house to care for; there would be company to entertain; there would be Joe's rigours and feeble old mother to wait upon; and it would be contrary to all thrifty village traditions for her to keep more than one servant. Louisa had a little still, and she used to occupy herself pleasantly in summer weather with distilling the sweet and aromatic essences from roses and peppermint and spearmint. By-and-by her still must be laid away. Her store of essences was already considerable, and there would be no time for her to distil for the mere pleasure of it. Then Joe's mother would think it foolishness; she had already hinted her opinion in the matter. Louisa dearly loved to sew a linen seam, not always for use, but for the simple, mild pleasure which she took in it. She would have been loath to confess how more than once she had ripped a seam for the mere delight of sewing it together again. Sitting at her window during long sweet afternoons, drawing her needle gently through the dainty fabric, she was peace itself. But there was small chance of such foolish comfort in the future. Joe's mother, domineering, shrewd old matron that she was even in her old age, and very likely even Joe himself, with his honest masculine rudeness, would laugh and frown down all these pretty but senseless old maiden ways.

Louisa had almost the enthusiasm of an artist over the mere order and cleanliness of her solitary home. She had throbs of genuine triumph at the sight of the window-panes which she had polished until they shone like jewels. She gloated gently over her orderly bureau-drawers, with their exquisitely folded contents redolent with lavender and sweet clover and very purity. Could she be sure of the endurance of even this? She had visions, so startling that she half repudiated them as indelicate, of coarse masculine belongings strewn about in endless litter; of dust and disorder arising necessarily from a coarse masculine presence in the midst of all this delicate harmony.

Among her forebodings of disturbance, not the least was with regard to Cæsar. Cæsar was a veritable hermit of a dog. For the greater part of his life he had dwelt in his secluded hut, shut out from the society of his kind and all innocent canine joys. Never had Cæsar since his early youth watched at a woodchuck's hole; never had he known the delights of a stray bone at a neighbor's kitchen door. And it was all on account of a sin committed when hardly out of his puppyhood. No one knew the possible depth of remorse of which this mild-visaged, altogether innocent-looking old dog might be capable; but whether or not he had encountered remorse, he had encountered a full measure of righteous retribution. Old Cæsar seldom lifted up his voice in a growl or a bark; he was fat and sleepy; there were yellow rings which looked like spectacles around his dim old eyes; but there was a neighbor who bore on his hand the imprint of several of Cæsar's sharp white youthful teeth, and for that he had lived at the end of a chain, all alone in a little hut, for fourteen years. The neighbor, who was choleric and smarting with the pain of his wound, had demanded either Cæsar's death or complete ostracism. So Louisa's brother, to whom the dog had belonged, had built him his little kennel and tied him up. It was now fourteen years since, in a flood of youthful spirits, he had inflicted that memorable bite, and with the exception of short excursions, always at the end of the chain, under the strict guardianship of his master or Louisa, the old dog had remained a close prisoner. It is doubtful if, with his limited ambition, he took much pride in the fact, but it is certain that he was possessed of considerable cheap fame. He was regarded by all the children in the village and by many adults as a very monster of ferocity. St. George's dragon[3] could hardly have surpassed in evil repute Louisa Ellis's old yellow dog. Mothers charged their children with solemn emphasis not to go too near him, and the children listened and believed greedily, with a fascinated appetite for terror, and ran by Louisa's house stealthily, with many sidelong and backward glances at the terrible dog. If perchance he sounded a hoarse bark, there was a panic. Wayfarers chancing into Louisa's yard eyed him with respect, and inquired if the chain were stout. Cæsar at large might have seemed a very ordinary dog, and excited no comment whatever; chained, his reputation overshadowed him, so that he lost his own proper outlines and looked darkly vague and enormous. Joe Dagget, however,

---

3. The story of St. George (patron saint of England) and the Dragon is an allegorical expression of the triumph of the Christian hero over evil.

with his good-humored sense and shrewdness, saw him as he was. He strode valiantly up to him and patted him on the head, in spite of Louisa's soft clamor of warning, and even attempted to set him loose. Louisa grew so alarmed that he desisted, but kept announcing his opinion in the matter quite forcibly at intervals. "There ain't a better-natured dog in town," he would say, "and it's downright cruel to keep him tied up there. Some day I'm going to take him out."

Louisa had very little hope that he would not, one of these days, when their interests and possessions should be more completely fused in one. She pictured to herself Cæsar on the rampage through the quiet and unguarded village. She saw innocent children bleeding in his path. She was herself very fond of the old dog, because he had belonged to her dead brother, and he was always very gentle with her; still she had great faith in his ferocity. She always warned people not to go too near him. She fed him on ascetic fare of corn-mush and cakes, and never fired his dangerous temper with heating and san-guinary diet of flesh and bones. Louisa looked at the old dog munching his simple fare, and thought of her approaching marriage and trembled. Still no anticipation of disorder and confusion in lieu of sweet peace and harmony, no forebodings of Cæsar on the rampage, no wild fluttering of her little yel-low canary, were sufficient to turn her a hair's-breadth. Joe Dagget had been fond of her and working for her all these years. It was not for her, whatever came to pass, to prove untrue and break his heart. She put the exquisite lit-tle stitches into her wedding-garments, and the time went on until it was only a week before her wedding-day. It was a Tuesday evening, and the wedding was to be a week from Wednesday.

There was a full moon that night. About nine o'clock Louisa strolled down the road a little way. There were harvest-fields on either hand, bordered by low stone walls. Luxuriant clumps of bushes grew beside the wall, and trees—wild cherry and old apple-trees—at intervals. Presently Louisa sat down on the wall and looked about her with mildly sorrowful reflectiveness. Tall shrubs of blueberry and meadow-sweet, all woven together and tangled with blackberry vines and horsebriers, shut her in on either side. She had a little clear space between. Opposite her, on the other side of the road, was a spreading tree; the moon shone between its boughs, and the leaves twinkled like silver. The road was bespread with a beautiful shifting dapple of silver and shadow; the air was full of a mysterious sweetness. "I wonder if it's wild grapes?" murmured Louisa. She sat there some time. She was just thinking of rising, when she heard footsteps and low voices, and remained quiet. It was a lonely place, and she felt a little timid. She thought she would keep still in the shadow and let the persons, whoever they might be, pass her.

But just before they reached her the voices ceased, and the footsteps. She understood that their owners had also found seats upon the stone wall. She was wondering if she could not steal away unobserved, when the voice broke the stillness. It was Joe Dagget's. She sat still and listened.

The voice was announced by a loud sigh, which was as familiar as itself. "Well," said Dagget, "you've made up your mind, then, I suppose?"

"Yes," returned another voice; "I'm going day after to-morrow."

"That's Lily Dyer," thought Louisa to herself. The voice embodied itself in her mind. She saw a girl tall and full-figured, with a firm, fair face, looking fairer and firmer in the moonlight, her strong yellow hair braided in a close knot. A girl full of a calm rustic strength and bloom, with a masterful way which might have beseemed a princess. Lily Dyer was a favorite with the village folk; she had just the qualities to arouse the admiration. She was good and handsome and smart. Louisa had often heard her praises sounded.

"Well," said Joe Dagget, "I ain't got a word to say."

"I don't know what you could say," returned Lily Dyer.

"Not a word to say," repeated Joe, drawing out the words heavily. Then there was silence. "I ain't sorry," he began at last, "that that happened yesterday—that we kind of let on how we felt to each other. I guess it's just as well we knew. Of course I can't do anything any different. I'm going right on an' get married next week. I ain't going back on a woman that's waited for me fourteen years, an' break her heart."

"If you should jilt her to-morrow, I wouldn't have you," spoke up the girl, with sudden vehemence.

"Well, I ain't going to give you the chance," said he; "but I don't believe you would, either."

"You'd see I wouldn't. Honor's honor, an' right's right. An' I'd never think anything of any man that went against 'em for me or any other girl; you'd find that out, Joe Dagget."

"Well, you'll find out fast enough that I ain't going against 'em for you or any other girl," returned he. Their voices sounded almost as if they were angry with each other. Louisa was listening eagerly.

"I'm sorry you feel as if you must go away," said Joe, "but I don't know but it's best."

"Of course it's best. I hope you and I have got common-sense."

"Well, I suppose you're right." Suddenly Joe's voice got an undertone of tenderness. "Say, Lily," said he, "I'll get along well enough myself, but I can't bear to think—You don't suppose you're going to fret much over it?"

"I guess you'll find out I sha'n't fret much over a married man."

"Well, I hope you won't—I hope you won't, Lily. God knows I do. And—I hope—one of these days—you'll—come across somebody else—"

"I don't see any reason why I shouldn't." Suddenly her tone changed. She spoke in a sweet, clear voice, so loud that she could have been heard across the street. "No, Joe Dagget," said she, "I'll never marry any other man as long as I live. I've got good sense, an' I ain't going to break my heart nor make a fool of myself; but I'm never going to be married, you can be sure of that. I ain't that sort of a girl to feel this way twice."

Louisa heard an exclamation and a soft commotion behind the bushes; then Lily spoke again—the voice sounded as if she had risen. "This must be put a stop to," said she. "We've stayed here long enough. I'm going home."

Louisa sat there in a daze, listening to their retreating steps. After a while she got up and slunk softly home herself. The next day she did her housework methodically; that was as much a matter of course as breathing; but she did not sew on her wedding-clothes. She sat at her window and meditated. In the evening Joe came. Louisa Ellis had never known that she had any diplomacy in her, but when she came to look for it that night she found it, although meek of its kind, among her little feminine weapons. Even now she could hardly believe that she had heard aright, and that she would not do Joe a terrible injury should she break her troth-plight. She wanted to sound him without betraying too soon her own inclinations in the matter. She did it successfully, and they finally came to an understanding; but it was a difficult thing, for he was as afraid of betraying himself as she.

She never mentioned Lily Dyer. She simply said that while she had no cause of complaint against him, she had lived so long in one way that she shrank from making a change.

"Well, I never shrank, Louisa," said Dagget. "I'm going to be honest enough to say that I think maybe it's better this way; but if you'd wanted to keep on, I'd have stuck to you till my dying day. I hope you know that."

"Yes, I do," said she.

That night she and Joe parted more tenderly than they had done for a long time. Standing in the door, holding each other's hands, a last great wave of regretful memory swept over them.

"Well, this ain't the way we've thought it was all going to end, is it, Louisa?" said Joe.

She shook her head. There was a little quiver on her placid face.

"You let me know if there's ever anything I can do for you," said he. "I ain't ever going to forget you, Louisa." Then he kissed her, and went down the path.

Louisa, all alone by herself that night, wept a little, she hardly knew why; but the next morning, on waking, she felt like a queen who, after fearing lest her domain be wrested away from her, sees it firmly insured in her possession.

Now the tall weeds and grasses might cluster around Cæsar's little hermit hut, the snow might fall on its roof year in and year out, but he never would go on a rampage through the unguarded village. Now the little canary might turn itself into a peaceful yellow ball night after night, and have no need to wake and flutter with wild terror against its bars. Louisa could sew linen seams, and distil roses, and dust and polish and fold away in lavender, as long as she listed. That afternoon she sat with her needle-work at the window, and felt fairly steeped in peace. Lily Dyer, tall and erect and blooming, went past; but she felt no qualm. If Louisa Ellis had sold her birthright she did not know it, the taste of the pottage[4] was so delicious, and had been her sole satisfaction for so long. Serenity and placid narrowness had become to her as the birthright itself. She gazed ahead through a long reach of future days strung together like pearls in a rosary, every one like the others, and all smooth and flawless and innocent, and her heart went up in thankfulness. Outside was the fervid summer afternoon; the air was filled with the sounds of the busy harvest of men and birds and bees; there were halloos, metallic clatterings, sweet calls, and long hummings. Louisa sat, prayerfully numbering her days, like an uncloistered nun.

1891

---

4. In Genesis 25, Esau sells his birthright as oldest son of Isaac and Rebekah to his younger brother Jacob for a bowl of pottage (lentil stew).

# The Revolt of "Mother"[1]

"Father!"

"What is it?"

"What are them men diggin' over there in the field for?"

There was a sudden dropping and enlarging of the lower part of the old man's face, as if some heavy weight had settled therein; he shut his mouth tight, and went on harnessing the great bay mare. He hustled the collar on to her neck with a jerk.

"Father!"

The old man slapped the saddle upon the mare's back.

"Look here, father, I want to know what them men are diggin' over in the field for, an' I'm goin' to know."

"I wish you'd go into the house, mother, an' 'tend to your own affairs," the old man said then. He ran his words together, and his speech was almost as inarticulate as a growl.

But the woman understood; it was her most native tongue. "I ain't goin' into the house till you tell me what them men are doin' over there in the field," said she.

Then she stood waiting. She was a small woman, short and straight-waisted like a child in her brown cotton gown. Her forehead was mild and benevolent between the smooth curves of gray hair; there were meek downward lines about her nose and mouth; but her eyes, fixed upon the old man, looked as if the meekness had been the result of her own will, never of the will of another.

They were in the barn, standing before the wide open doors. The spring air, full of the smell of growing grass and unseen blossoms, came in their faces. The deep yard in front was littered with farm wagons and piles of wood; on the edges, close to the fence and the house, the grass was a vivid green, and there were some dandelions.

The old man glanced doggedly at his wife as he tightened the last buckles on the harness. She looked as immovable to him as one of the rocks in his pasture-land, bound to the earth with generations of blackberry vines. He slapped the reins over the horse, and started forth from the barn.

"*Father!*" said she.

The old man pulled up. "What is it?"

"I want to know what them men are diggin' over there in that field for."

"They're diggin' a cellar, I s'pose, if you've got to know."

"A cellar for what?"

"A barn."

"A barn? You ain't goin' to build a barn over there where we was goin' to have a house, father?"

The old man said not another word. He hurried the horse into the farm wagon, and clattered out of the yard, jouncing as sturdily on his seat as a boy.

The woman stood a moment looking after him, then she went out of the barn across a corner of the yard to the house. The house, standing at right angles with the great barn and a long reach of sheds and out-buildings, was infinitesimal compared with them. It was scarcely as commodious for people as the little boxes under the barn eaves were for doves.

---

1. First published in *"A New England Nun" and Other Stories* (1891), the source of the text printed here.

A pretty girl's face, pink and delicate as a flower, was looking out of one of the house windows. She was watching three men who were digging over in the field which bounded the yard near the road line. She turned quietly when the woman entered.

"What are they digging for, mother?" said she. "Did he tell you?"

"They're diggin' for—a cellar for a new barn."

"Oh, mother, he ain't going to build another barn?"

"That's what he says."

A boy stood before the kitchen glass combing his hair. He combed slowly and painstakingly, arranging his brown hair in a smooth hillock over his forehead. He did not seem to pay any attention to the conversation.

"Sammy, did you know father was going to build a new barn?" asked the girl.

The boy combed assiduously.

"Sammy!"

He turned, and showed a face like his father's under his smooth crest of hair. "Yes, I s'pose I did," he said, reluctantly.

"How long have you known it?" asked his mother.

" 'Bout three months, I guess."

"Why didn't you tell of it?"

"Didn't think 'twould do no good."

"I don't see what father wants another barn for," said the girl, in her sweet, slow voice. She turned again to the window, and stared out at the digging men in the field. Her tender, sweet face was full of a gentle distress. Her forehead was as bald and innocent as a baby's, with the light hair strained back from it in a row of curl-papers. She was quite large, but her soft curves did not look as if they covered muscles.

Her mother looked sternly at the boy. "Is he goin' to buy more cows?" said she.

The boy did not reply; he was tying his shoes.

"Sammy, I want you to tell me if he's goin' to buy more cows."

"I s'pose he is."

"How many?"

"Four, I guess."

His mother said nothing more. She went up into the pantry, and there was a clatter of dishes. The boy got his cap from a nail behind the door, took an old arithmetic from the shelf, and started for school. He was lightly built, but clumsy. He went out of the yard with a curious spring in his hips, that made his loose home-made jacket tilt up in the rear.

The girl went to the sink, and began to wash the dishes that were piled up there. Her mother came promptly out of the pantry, and shoved her aside. "You wipe 'em," said she; "I'll wash. There's a good many this mornin'."

The mother plunged her hands vigorously into the water, the girl wiped the plates slowly and dreamily. "Mother," said she, "don't you think it's too bad father's going to build that new barn, much as we need a decent house to live in?"

Her mother scrubbed a dish fiercely. "You ain't found out yet we're women-folks, Nanny Penn," said she. "You ain't seen enough of men-folks yet to. One of these days you'll find it out, an' then you'll know that we know only what men-folks think we do, so far as any use of it goes, an' how we'd ought to reckon men-folks in with Providence, an' not complain of what they do any more than we do of the weather."

"I don't care; I don't believe George is anything like that, anyhow," said Nanny. Her delicate face flushed pink, her lips pouted softly, as if she were going to cry.

"You wait an' see. I guess George Eastman ain't no better than other men. You hadn't ought to judge father, though. He can't help it, 'cause he don't look at things jest the way we do. An' we've been pretty comfortable here, after all. The roof don't leak—ain't never but once—that's one thing. Father's kept it shingled right up."

"I do wish we had a parlor."

"I guess it won't hurt George Eastman any to come to see you in a nice clean kitchen. I guess a good many girls don't have as good a place as this. Nobody's ever heard me complain."

"I ain't complained either, mother."

"Well, I don't think you'd better, a good father an' a good home as you've got. S'pose your father made you go out an' work for your livin'? Lots of girls have to that ain't no stronger an' better able to than you be."

Sarah Penn washed the frying-pan with a conclusive air. She scrubbed the outside of it as faithfully as the inside. She was a masterly keeper of her box of a house. Her one living-room never seemed to have in it any of the dust which the friction of life with inanimate matter produces. She swept, and there seemed to be no dirt to go before the broom; she cleaned, and one could see no difference. She was like an artist so perfect that he has apparently no art. To-day she got out a mixing bowl and a board, and rolled some pies, and there was no more flour upon her than upon her daughter who was doing finer work. Nanny was to be married in the fall, and she was sewing on some white cambric and embroidery. She sewed industriously while her mother cooked, her soft milk-white hands and wrists showed whiter than her delicate work.

"We must have the stove moved out in the shed before long," said Mrs. Penn. "Talk about not havin' things, it's been a real blessin' to be able to put a stove up in that shed in hot weather. Father did one good thing when he fixed that stove-pipe out there."

Sarah Penn's face as she rolled her pies had that expression of meek vigor which might have characterized one of the New Testament saints. She was making mince-pies. Her husband, Adoniram Penn, liked them better than any other kind. She baked twice a week. Adoniram often liked a piece of pie between meals. She hurried this morning. It had been later than usual when she began, and she wanted to have a pie baked for dinner. However deep a resentment she might be forced to hold against her husband, she would never fail in sedulous attention to his wants.

Nobility of character manifests itself at loop-holes when it is not provided with large doors. Sarah Penn's showed itself to-day in flaky dishes of pastry. So she made the pies faithfully, while across the table she could see, when she glanced up from her work, the sight that rankled in her patient and stead-fast soul—the digging of the cellar of the new barn in the place where Adoniram forty years ago had promised her their new house should stand.

The pies were done for dinner. Adoniram and Sammy were home a few minutes after twelve o'clock. The dinner was eaten with serious haste. There was never much conversation at the table in the Penn family. Adoniram asked a blessing, and they ate promptly, then rose up and went about their work.

Sammy went back to school, taking soft sly lopes out of the yard like a rab-bit. He wanted a game of marbles before school, and feared his father would give him some chores to do. Adoniram hastened to the door and called after him, but he was out of sight.

"I don't see what you let him go for, mother," said he. "I wanted him to help me unload that wood."

Adoniram went to work out in the yard unloading wood from the wagon. Sarah put away the dinner dishes, while Nanny took down her curl-papers and changed her dress. She was going down to the store to buy some more embroidery and thread.

When Nanny was gone, Mrs. Penn went to the door. "Father!" she called. "Well, what is it!"

"I want to see you jest a minute, father."

"I can't leave this wood nohow. I've got to git it unloaded an' go for a load of gravel afore two o'clock. Sammy had ought to helped me. You hadn't ought to let him go to school so early."

"I want to see you jest a minute."

"I tell ye I can't, nohow, mother."

"Father, you come here." Sarah Penn stood in the door like a queen; she held her head as if it bore a crown; there was that patience which makes authority royal in her voice. Adoniram went.

Mrs. Penn led the way into the kitchen, and pointed to a chair. "Sit down, father," said she; "I've got somethin' I want to say to you."

He sat down heavily; his face was quite stolid, but he looked at her with restive eyes. "Well, what is it, mother?"

"I want to know what you're buildin' that new barn for, father?"

"I ain't got nothin' to say about it."

"It can't be you think you need another barn?"

"I tell ye I ain't got nothin' to say about it, mother; an' I ain't goin' to say nothin'."

"Be you goin' to buy more cows?"

Adoniram did not reply; he shut his mouth tight.

"I know you be, as well as I want to. Now, father, look here"—Sarah Penn had not sat down; she stood before her husband in the humble fashion of a Scripture woman[2]—"I'm goin' to talk real plain to you; I never have sence I married you, but I'm goin' to now. I ain't never complained, an' I ain't goin' to complain now, but I'm goin' to talk plain. You see this room here, father; you look at it well. You see there ain't no carpet on the floor, an' you see the paper is all dirty, an' droppin' off the walls. We ain't had no new paper on it for ten year, an' then I put it on myself, an' it didn't cost but ninepence a roll. You see this room, father; it's all the one I've had to work in an' eat in an' sit in sence we was married. There ain't another woman in the whole town whose husband ain't got half the means you have but what's got better. It's all the room Nanny's got to have her company in; an' there ain't one of her mates but what's got better, an' their fathers not so able as hers is. It's all the room she'll have to be married in. What would you have thought, father, if we had had our weddin' in a room no better than this? I was married in my mother's parlor, with a carpet on the floor, an' stuffed furniture, an' a mahogany card-table. An' this is all the room my daughter will have to be married in. Look here, father!"

Sarah Penn went across the room as though it were a tragic stage. She flung open a door and disclosed a tiny bedroom, only large enough for a bed and bureau, with a path between. "There, father," said she—"there's all the

---

2. I.e., a woman, like Ruth, patient and obedient to her husband.

room I've had to sleep in forty year. All my children were born there—the two that died, an' the two that's livin'. I was sick with a fever there."

She stepped to another door and opened it. It led into the small, ill-lighted pantry. "Here," said she, "is all the buttery[3] I've got—every place I've got for my dishes, to set away my victuals in, an' to keep my milk-pans in. Father, I've been takin' care of the milk of six cows in this place, an' now you're goin' to build a new barn, an' keep more cows, an' give me more to do in it."

She threw open another door. A narrow crooked flight of stairs wound upward from it. "There, father," said she, "I want you to look at the stairs that go up to them two unfinished chambers that are all the places our son an' daughter have had to sleep in all their lives. There ain't a prettier girl in town nor a more ladylike one than Nanny, an' that's the place she has to sleep in. It ain't so good as your horse's stall; it ain't so warm an' tight."

Sarah Penn went back and stood before her husband. "Now, father," said she, "I want to know if you think you're doin' right an' accordin' to what you profess. Here, when we was married, forty year ago, you promised me faithful that we should have a new house built in that lot over in the field before the year was out. You said you had money enough, an' you wouldn't ask me to live in no such place as this. It is forty year now, an' you've been makin' more money, an' I've been savin' of it for you ever since, an' you ain't built no house yet. You've built sheds an' cow-houses an' one new barn, an' now you're goin' to build another. Father, I want to know if you think it's right. You're lodgin' your dumb beasts better than you are your own flesh an' blood. I want to know if you think it's right."

"I ain't got nothin' to say."

"You can't say nothin' without ownin' it ain't right, father. An' there's another thing—I ain't complained; I've got along forty year, an' I s'pose I should forty more, if it wa'n't for that—if we don't have another house. Nanny she can't live with us after she's married. She'll have to go somewheres else to live away from us, an' it don't seem as if I could have it so, noways, father. She wa'n't ever strong. She's got considerable color, but there wa'n't never any backbone to her. I've always took the heft of everything off her, an' she ain't fit to keep house an' do everything herself. She'll be all worn out inside a year. Think of her doin' all the washin' an' ironin' an' bakin' with them soft white hands an' arms, an' sweepin'! I can't have it so, noways, father."

Mrs. Penn's face was burning; her mild eyes gleamed. She had pleaded her little cause like a Webster;[4] she had ranged from severity to pathos; but her opponent employed that obstinate silence which makes eloquence futile with mocking echoes. Adoniram arose clumsily.

"Father, ain't you got nothin' to say?" said Mrs. Penn.

"I've got to go off after that load of gravel. I can't stan' here talkin' all day."

"Father, won't you think it over, an' have a house built there instead of a barn?"

"I ain't got nothin' to say."

Adoniram shuffled out. Mrs. Penn went into her bedroom. When she came out, her eyes were red. She had a roll of unbleached cotton cloth. She spread it out on the kitchen table, and began cutting out some shirts for her husband. The men over in the field had a team to help them this afternoon; she could hear their halloos. She had a scanty pattern for the shirts; she had to plan and piece the sleeves.

---

3. Pantry.
4. I.e., like Daniel Webster (1782–1852), American statesman and celebrated orator.

Nanny came home with her embroidery, and sat down with her needle-work. She had taken down her curl-papers, and there was a soft roll of fair hair like an aureole over her forehead; her face was as delicately fine and clear as porcelain. Suddenly she looked up, and the tender red flamed all over her face and neck. "Mother," said she.

"What say?"

"I've been thinking—I don't see how we're goin' to have any—wedding in this room. I'd be ashamed to have his folks come if we didn't have anybody else."

"Mebbe we can have some new paper before then; I can put it on. I guess you won't have no call to be ashamed of your belongin's."

"We might have the wedding in the new barn," said Nanny, with gentle pet-tishness. "Why, mother, what makes you look so?"

Mrs. Penn had started, and was staring at her with a curious expression. She turned again to her work, and spread out a pattern carefully on the cloth. "Nothin'," said she.

Presently Adoniram clattered out of the yard in his two-wheeled dump cart, standing as proudly upright as a Roman charioteer.[5] Mrs. Penn opened the door and stood there a minute looking out; the halloos of the men sounded louder.

It seemed to her all through the spring months that she heard nothing but the halloos and the noises of the saws and hammers. The new barn grew fast. It was a fine edifice for this little village. Men came on pleasant Sundays, in their meeting suits and clean shirt bosoms, and stood around it admiringly. Mrs. Penn did not speak of it, and Adoniram did not mention it to her, although sometimes, upon a return from inspecting it, he bore himself with injured dignity.

"It's a strange thing how your mother feels about the new barn," he said, confidentially, to Sammy one day.

Sammy only grunted after an odd fashion for a boy; he had learned it from his father.

The barn was all completed ready for use by the third week in July. Adoniram had planned to move his stock in on Wednesday; on Tuesday he received a letter which changed his plans. He came in with it early in the morning. "Sammy's been to the post-office," said he, "an' I've got a letter from Hiram." Hiram was Mrs. Penn's brother, who lived in Vermont.

"Well," said Mrs. Penn, "what does he say about the folks?"

"I guess they're all right. He says he thinks if I come up country right off there's a chance to buy jest the kind of horse I want." He stared reflectively out of the window at the new barn.

Mrs. Penn was making pies. She went on clapping the rolling-pin into the crust, although she was very pale, and her heart beat loudly.

"I dun' know but what I'd better go," said Adoniram. "I hate to go off jest now, right in the midst of hayin', but the ten-acre lot's cut, an' I guess Rufus an' the others can git along without me three or four days. I can't get a horse round here to suit me, nohow, an' I've got to have another for all the wood-haulin' in the fall. I told Hiram to watch out, an' if he got wind of a good horse to let me know. I guess I'd better go."

"I'll get out your clean shirt an' collar," said Mrs. Penn calmly.

---

5. Roman charioteers raced standing in their chariots.

She laid out Adoniram's Sunday suit and his clean clothes on the bed in the little bedroom. She got his shaving-water and razor ready. At last she buttoned on his collar and fastened his black cravat.

Adoniram never wore his collar and cravat except on extra occasions. He held his head high, with a rasped dignity. When he was all ready, with his coat and hat brushed, and a lunch of pie and cheese in a paper bag, he hesitated on the threshold of the door. He looked at his wife, and his manner was defiantly apologetic. "*If* them cows come to-day, Sammy can drive 'em into the new barn," said he; "an' when they bring the hay up, they can pitch it in there."

"Well," replied Mrs. Penn.

Adoniram set his shaven face ahead and started. When he had cleared the door-step, he turned and looked back with a kind of nervous solemnity. "I shall be back by Saturday if nothin' happens," said he.

"Do be careful, father," returned his wife.

She stood in the door with Nanny at her elbow and watched him out of sight. Her eyes had a strange, doubtful expression in them; her peaceful forehead was contracted. She went in, and about her baking again. Nanny sat sewing. Her wedding-day was drawing nearer, and she was getting pale and thin with her steady sewing. Her mother kept glancing at her.

"Have you got that pain in your side this mornin'?" she asked.

"A little."

Mrs. Penn's face, as she worked, changed, her perplexed forehead smoothed, her eyes were steady, her lips firmly set. She formed a maxim for herself, although incoherently with her unlettered thoughts. "Unsolicited opportunities are the guide-posts of the Lord to the new roads of life," she repeated in effect, and she made up her mind to her course of action.

"S'posin' I *had* wrote to Hiram," she muttered once, when she was in the pantry—"s'posin' I had wrote, an' asked him if he knew of any horse? But I didn't, an' father's goin' wa'n't none of my doin'. It looks like a providence." Her voice rang out quite loud at the last.

"What you talkin' about, mother?" called Nanny.

"Nothin'."

Mrs. Penn hurried her baking; at eleven o'clock it was all done. The load of hay from the west field came slowly down the cart track, and drew up at the new barn. Mrs. Penn ran out. "Stop!" she screamed—"stop!"

The men stopped and looked; Sammy upreared from the top of the load, and stared at his mother.

"Stop!" she cried out again. "Don't you put the hay in that barn; put it in the old one."

"Why, he said to put it in here," returned one of the haymakers, wonderingly. He was a young man, a neighbor's son, whom Adoniram hired by the year to help on the farm.

"Don't you put the hay in the new barn; there's room enough in the old one, ain't there?" said Mrs. Penn.

"Room enough," returned the hired man, in his thick, rustic tones. "Didn't need the new barn, nohow, far as room's concerned. Well, I s'pose he changed his mind." He took hold of the horses' bridles.

Mrs. Penn went back to the house. Soon the kitchen windows were darkened, and a fragrance like warm honey came into the room.

Nanny laid down her work. "I thought father wanted them to put the hay into the new barn?" she said, wonderingly.

"It's all right," replied her mother.

Sammy slid down from the load of hay, and came in to see if dinner was ready.

"I ain't goin' to get a regular dinner to-day, as long as father's gone," said his mother. "I've let the fire go out. You can have some bread an' milk an' pie. I thought we could get along." She set out some bowls of milk, some bread, and a pie on the kitchen table. "You'd better eat your dinner now," said she. "You might jest as well get through with it. I want you to help me afterward."

Nanny and Sammy stared at each other. There was something strange in their mother's manner. Mrs. Penn did not eat anything herself. She went into the pantry, and they heard her moving dishes while they ate. Presently she came out with a pile of plates. She got the clothes-basket out of the shed, and packed them in it. Nanny and Sammy watched. She brought out cups and saucers, and put them in with the plates.

"What you goin' to do, mother?" inquired Nanny, in a timid voice. A sense of something unusual made her tremble, as if it were a ghost. Sammy rolled his eyes over his pie.

"You'll see what I'm goin' to do," replied Mrs. Penn. "If you're through, Nanny, I want you to go up-stairs an' pack up your things; an' I want you, Sammy, to help me take down the bed in the bedroom."

"Oh, mother, what for?" gasped Nanny.

"You'll see."

During the next few hours a feat was performed by this simple, pious New England mother which was equal in its way to Wolfe's storming of the Heights of Abraham.[6] It took no more genius and audacity of bravery for Wolfe to cheer his wondering soldiers up those steep precipices, under the sleeping eyes of the enemy, than for Sarah Penn, at the head of her children, to move all their little household goods into the new barn while her husband was away.

Nanny and Sammy followed their mother's instructions without a murmur; indeed, they were overawed. There is a certain uncanny and superhuman quality about all such purely original undertakings as their mother's was to them. Nanny went back and forth with her light loads, and Sammy tugged with sober energy.

At five o'clock in the afternoon the little house in which the Penns had lived for forty years had emptied itself into the new barn.

Every builder builds somewhat for unknown purposes, and is in a measure a prophet. The architect of Adoniram Penn's barn, while he designed it for the comfort of four-footed animals, had planned better than he knew for the comfort of humans. Sarah Penn saw at a glance its possibilities. Those great box-stalls, with quilts hung before them, would make better bedrooms than the one she had occupied for forty years, and there was a tight carriage-room. The harness room, with its chimney and shelves, would make a kitchen of her dreams. The great middle space would make a parlor, by-and-by, fit for a palace. Up stairs there was as much room as down. With partitions and windows, what a house would there be! Sarah looked at the row of stanchions[7]

---

6. James Wolfe (1727–1759), British general, led the arduous expedition to capture Quebec from the French. He died in his hour of victory on September 13, 1759, after he scaled the steep cliffs onto the Plains of Abraham near Quebec and defeated the French.

7. Upright supports that fit loosely around a cow's neck and limit the animal's forward and backward movement.

before the allotted space for cows, and reflected that she would have her front entry there.

At six o'clock the stove was up in the harness-room, the kettle was boiling, and the table set for tea. It looked almost as homelike as the abandoned house across the yard had ever done. The young hired man milked, and Sarah directed him calmly to bring the milk to the new barn. He came gaping, dropping little blots of foam from the brimming pails on the grass. Before the next morning he had spread the story of Adoniram Penn's wife moving into the new barn all over the little village. Men assembled in the store and talked it over, women with shawls over their heads scuttled into each other's houses before their work was done. Any deviation from the ordinary course of life in this quiet town was enough to stop all progress in it. Everybody paused to look at the staid, independent figure on the side track.[8] There was a difference of opinion with regard to her. Some held her to be insane; some, of lawless and rebellious spirit.

Friday the minister went to see her. It was in the forenoon, and she was at the barn door shelling pease for dinner. She looked up and returned his salutation with dignity, then she went on with her work. She did not invite him in. The saintly expression of her face remained fixed, but there was an angry flush over it.

The minister stood awkwardly before her, and talked. She handled the pease as if they were bullets. At last she looked up, and her eyes showed the spirit that her meek front had covered for a lifetime.

"There ain't no use talkin', Mr. Hersey," said she. "I've thought it all over an' over, an' I believe I'm doin' what's right. I've made it the subject of prayer, an' it's betwixt me an' the Lord an' Adoniram. There ain't no call for nobody else to worry about it."

"Well, of course, if you have brought it to the Lord in prayer, and feel satisfied that you are doing right, Mrs. Penn," said the minister, helplessly. His thin gray-bearded face was pathetic. He was a sickly man; his youthful confidence had cooled; he had to scourge himself up to some of his pastoral duties as relentlessly as a Catholic ascetic, and then he was prostrated by the smart.

"I think it's right jest as much as I think it was right for our forefathers to come over from the old country 'cause they didn't have what belonged to 'em," said Mrs. Penn. She arose. The barn threshold might have been Plymouth Rock from her bearing. "I don't doubt you mean well, Mr. Hersey," said she, "but there are things people hadn't ought to interfere with. I've been a member of the church for over forty year. I've got my own mind an' my own feet, an' I'm goin' to think my own thoughts an' go my own ways, an' nobody but the Lord is goin' to dictate to me unless I've a mind to have him. Won't you come in an' set down? How is Mis' Hersey?"

"She is well, I thank you," replied the minister. He added some more perplexed apologetic remarks; then he retreated.

He could expound the intricacies of every character study in the Scriptures, he was competent to grasp the Pilgrim Fathers and all historical innovators, but Sarah Penn was beyond him. He could deal with primal cases, but parallel ones worsted him. But, after all, although it was aside from his

8. A short, side railroad track connected with the main track.

province, he wondered more how Adoniram Penn would deal with his wife than how the Lord would. Everybody shared the wonder. When Adoniram's four new cows arrived, Sarah ordered three to be put in the old barn, the other in the house shed where the cooking-stove had stood. That added to the excitement. It was whispered that all four cows were domiciled in the house.

Towards sunset on Saturday, when Adoniram was expected home, there was a knot of men in the road near the new barn. The hired man had milked, but he still hung around the premises. Sarah Penn had supper all ready. There was brown-bread and baked beans and a custard pie; it was the supper that Adoniram loved on a Saturday night. She had on a clean calico, and she bore herself imperturbably. Nanny and Sammy kept close at her heels. Their eyes were large, and Nanny was full of nervous tremors. Still there was to them more pleasant excitement than anything else. An inborn confidence in their mother over their father asserted itself.

Sammy looked out of the harness-room window. "There he is," he announced, in an awed whisper. He and Nanny peeped around the casing. Mrs. Penn kept on about her work. The children watched Adoniram leave the new horse standing in the drive while he went to the house door. It was fastened. Then he went around to the shed. That door was seldom locked, even when the family was away. The thought how her father would be confronted by the cow flashed upon Nanny. There was a hysterical sob in her throat. Adoniram emerged from the shed and stood looking about in a dazed fashion. His lips moved; he was saying something, but they could not hear what it was. The hired man was peeping around a corner of the old barn, but nobody saw him.

Adoniram took the new horse by the bridle and led him across the yard to the new barn. Nanny and Sammy slunk close to their mother. The barn doors rolled back, and there stood Adoniram, with the long mild face of the great Canadian farm horse looking over his shoulder.

Nanny kept behind her mother, but Sammy stepped suddenly forward, and stood in front of her.

Adoniram stared at the group. "What on airth you all down here for?" said he. "What's the matter over to the house?"

"We've come here to live, father," said Sammy. His shrill voice quavered out bravely.

"What"—Adoniram sniffed—"what is it smells like cookin?" said he. He stepped forward and looked in the open door of the harness-room. Then he turned to his wife. His old bristling face was pale and frightened. "What on airth does this mean, mother?" he gasped.

"You come in here, father," said Sarah. She led the way into the harness-room and shut the door. "Now, father," said she, "you needn't be scared. I ain't crazy. There ain't nothin' to be upset over. But we've come here to live, an' we're goin' to live here. We've got jest as good a right here as new horses an' cows. The house wa'n't fit for us to live in any longer, an' I made up my mind I wa'n't goin' to stay there. I've done my duty by you forty year, an' I'm goin' to do it now; but I'm goin' to live here. You've got to put in some windows and partitions; an' you'll have to buy some furniture."

"Why, mother!" the old man gasped.

"You'd better take your coat off an' get washed—there's the wash-basin—an' then we'll have supper."

"Why, mother!"

Sammy went past the window, leading the new horse to the old barn. The old man saw him, and shook his head speechlessly. He tried to take off his coat, but his arms seemed to lack the power. His wife helped him. She poured some water into the tin basin, and put in a piece of soap. She got the comb and brush, and smoothed his thin gray hair after he had washed. Then she put the beans, the hot bread, and tea on the table. Sammy came in, and the family drew up. Adoniram sat looking dazedly at his plate, and they waited.

"Ain't you goin' to ask a blessin', father?" said Sarah.

And the old man bent his head and mumbled.

All through the meal he stopped eating at intervals, and stared furtively at his wife; but he ate well. The home food tasted good to him, and his old frame was too sturdily healthy to be affected by his mind. But after supper he went out, and sat down on the step of the smaller door at the right of the barn, through which he had meant his Jerseys to pass in stately file, but which Sarah designed for her front house door, and he leaned his head on his hands.

After the supper dishes were cleared away and the milk-pans washed, Sarah went out to him. The twilight was deepening. There was a clear green glow in the sky. Before them stretched the smooth level of field; in the distance was a cluster of hay-stacks like the huts of a village; the air was very cool and calm and sweet. The landscape might have been an ideal one of peace.

Sarah bent over and touched her husband on one of his thin, sinewy shoulders. "Father!"

The old man's shoulders heaved: he was weeping.

"Why, don't do so, father," said Sarah.

"I'll—put up the—partitions, an'—everything you—want, mother."

Sarah put her apron up to her face; she was overcome by her own triumph.

Adoniram was like a fortress whose walls had no active resistance, and went down the instant the right besieging tools were used. "Why, mother," he said, hoarsely, "I hadn't no idee you was so set on't as all this comes to."

1891

---

# ANNA JULIA COOPER
## 1858–1964

Anna Julia Cooper's commitment to her African American students and to black Americans in general is reflected in a distinguished career fueled by the continuing determination to teach and write on racial reform. She strongly believed that the key to social reform and progress lay with women—black and white.

Cooper was born into slavery to Hannah Stanley Haywood and her master, George Washington Haywood, in Raleigh, North Carolina. At the age of nine she enrolled in the Episcopal St. Augustine's Normal School and Collegiate Institute for free blacks. In 1877 she married George C. Cooper, a Bahamaian teacher of Greek and candidate for the ministry. His sudden death in 1879 led Cooper to pursue further education and a teaching career. She received bachelor's and master's degrees from Oberlin College in Ohio, finishing in 1884, and began to teach math and science at M Street High School, at that time Washington D.C.'s only black high school (later known as Paul Laurence Dunbar High School). She became principal in 1902. Interrupting her doctoral studies at Columbia University in 1915, she adopted the five orphaned grandchildren of her half-brother. In 1925, at the age of sixty-five, Cooper received her Ph.D. from the University of Paris (the Sorbonne), only the fourth African American woman to receive the degree. Her writing and lecturing, which she continued until she was ninety, reflected her strong social concerns, including the education of underprivileged children and, especially, the fight against racism and sexism. Her dissertation, translated by Frances Richardson Keller and published in 1988 as *Slavery and the French Revolutionists (1788–1805)*, argues that the revolutions in France and in Haiti (then called Saint-Domingue) were intertwined; it investigates the efforts of a group of abolitionists in France, *Les Amis des Noir*.

Cooper's best-known book, *A Voice from the South by a Black Woman from the South* (1892), argued that women were the keys to racial reform. Perhaps because of its focus on women, her work was largely ignored, even by such black leaders as Frederick Douglass and W. E. B. Du Bois, whom she publicly supported. She openly resisted Booker T. Washington's efforts to steer blacks into technical education for manual labor, arguing that black students should be prepared for academic colleges and professional work. She had been dismissed from M Street High School in 1905 on trumped-up charges, in all likelihood because, defying stated goals, she was sending black students to such colleges as Harvard, Brown, Oberlin, and Yale. Having spoken at the World's Congress of Representative Women in 1893 and the Pan-African Congress in 1900, in 1905 Cooper helped found the Colored Women's YMCA. She was once again invited to teach Latin at the M Street High School by a new principal in 1910, and continued in this position until her retirement in 1930. The year of her retirement she became president of Frelinghuysen University in D.C., an institution designed to serve working-class black students. At one point, when the institution was in peril, she moved its operations into her own home. Anna Julia Cooper died of a heart attack at the age of 105 on February 27, 1964, her heroic life having spanned the years from the Civil War through the Civil Rights Movement.

The essay included here, "Woman versus the Indian," decries the neglect of women's issues in favor of those of minority groups such as Native Americans, who were sentimentalized as "noble" during Cooper's time, and calls on white women to set the tone for equal rights for all people, especially women, appealing to their belief in good manners. Cooper was not against Indian rights, but felt that women's rights in general were not as popular a cause. Cooper saw women's cause as "the cause of the weak," and her essay includes many sharp insights into racial and gender issues of her day. She calls on women to proclaim "that every interest in this world is entitled at least to a respectful hearing, that every sentiency is worthy of its own gratification." All her life Cooper believed that "The cause of freedom is not the cause of a race or a sect, a party or a class—it is the cause of humankind, the very birthright of humanity."

# Woman versus the Indian[1]

In the National Woman's Council convened at Washington in February 1891,[2] among a number of thoughtful and suggestive papers read by eminent women, was one by the Rev. Anna Shaw,[3] bearing the above title.

That Miss Shaw is broad and just and liberal in principal is proved beyond contradiction. Her noble generosity and womanly firmness are unimpeachable. The unwavering stand taken by herself and Miss Anthony[4] in the subsequent color ripple in Wimodaughsis ought to be sufficient to allay forever any doubts as to the pure gold of these two women.

Of Wimodaughsis (which, being interpreted for the uninitiated, is a woman's culture club whose name is made up of the first few letters of the four words wives, mothers, daughters, and sisters)[5] Miss Shaw is president, and a lady from the Blue Grass State[6] *was* secretary.

Pandora's box is opened in the ideal harmony of this modern Eden without an Adam when a colored lady, a teacher in one of our schools, applies for admission to its privileges and opportunities.

The Kentucky secretary, a lady zealous in good works and one who, I can't help imagining, belongs to that estimable class who daily thank the Lord that He made the earth that they may have the job of superintending its rotations, and who really would like to help "elevate" the colored people (in her own way of course and so long as they understand their places) is filled with grief and horror that any persons of Negro extraction should aspire to learn typewriting or languages or to enjoy any other advantages offered in the sacred halls of Wimodaughsis. Indeed, she had not calculated that there were any wives, mothers, daughters, and sisters, except white ones; and she is really convinced that *Whimodaughsis* would sound just as well, and then it need mean just *white mothers, daughters and sisters.* In fact, so far as there is anything in a name, nothing would be lost by omitting for the sake of euphony, from this unique mosaic, the letters that represent wives. *Whiwimodaughsis* might be a little startling, and on the whole wives would better yield to white; since clearly all women are not wives, while surely all wives are daughters. The daughters therefore could represent the wives and this immaculate assembly for propagating liberal and progressive ideas and disseminating a broad and humanizing culture might be spared the painful possibility of the sight of a black man coming in the future to escort from an evening class this solitary cream-colored applicant. Accordingly the Kentucky secretary took the cream-colored applicant aside, and, with emotions befitting such an epoch-making crisis, told her, "as kindly as she could," that colored people were not

1. First published in *A Voice from the South* (1892). The essay argues for putting women's rights on the public agenda at a time when Indian rights had become "the" political issue of the day, perhaps explaining why, despite its title, the essay includes so little on "the Indian."
2. Cooper refers to the first meeting of this organization, founded in 1888, at Albaugh's Opera House in Washington D.C.
3. Recipient of a medical degree and ordained a Methodist minister in 1880, Anna Shaw Curtis (1838–1927) organized and lectured throughout the world on behalf of temperance, women's suf-

frage, and peace, leading to the founding of the League of Women Voters.
4. Susan B. Anthony (1820–1906) was a leading activist for the causes of temperance, abolition, and women's rights, including especially the vote. She organized the International Council of Women in 1888 and the International Woman Suffrage Alliance in 1904.
5. Club founded by Emma Gillett (1852–1927), a prominent attorney and one of the first women to argue before the U.S. Supreme Court.
6. Kentucky.

admitted to the classes, at the same time refunding the money which said cream-colored applicant had paid for lessons in type-writing.

When this little incident came to the knowledge of Miss Shaw, she said firmly and emphatically, NO. As a minister of the gospel and as a Christian woman, she could not lend her influence to such unreasonable and uncharitable discrimination; and she must resign the honor of president of Wimodaughsis if persons were to be proscribed solely on account of their color.

To the honor of the board of managers, be it said, they sustained Miss Shaw; and the Kentucky secretary, and those whom she succeeded in inoculating with her prejudices, resigned.

'Twas only a ripple,—some bewailing of lost opportunity on the part of those who could not or would not seize God's opportunity for broadening and enlarging their own souls—and then the work flowed on as before.

Susan B. Anthony and Anna Shaw are evidently too noble to be held in thrall by the provincialisms of women who seem never to have breathed the atmosphere beyond the confines of their grandfathers' plantations. It is only from the broad plateau of light and love that one can see petty prejudice and narrow priggishness in their true perspective; and it is on this high ground, as I sincerely believe, these two grand women stand.

As leaders in the woman's movement of today, they have need of clearness of vision as well as firmness of soul in adjusting recalcitrant forces, and wheeling into line the thousand and one none-such, never-to-be-modified, won't-be-dictated-to banners of their somewhat mottled array.

The black woman and the southern woman, I imagine, often get them into the predicament of the befuddled man who had to take singly across a stream a bag of corn, a fox and a goose. There was no one to help, and to leave the goose with the fox was death—with the corn, destruction. To re-christen the animals, the lion could not be induced to lie down with the lamb unless the lamb would take the inside berth.

The black woman appreciates the situation and can even sympathize with the actors in the serio-comic dilemma.

But, may it not be that, as women, the very lessons which seem hardest to master now, are possibly the ones most essential for our promotion to a higher grade of work?

We assume to be leaders of thought and guardians of society. Our country's manners and morals are under our tutoring. Our standards are law in our several little worlds. However tenaciously men may guard some prerogatives, they are our willing slaves in that sphere which they have always conceded to be woman's. Here, no one dares demur when her fiat has gone forth. The man would be mad who presumed, however inexplicable and past finding out any reason for her action might be, to attempt to open a door in her kingdom officially closed and regally sealed by her.

The American woman of to-day not only gives tone directly to her immediate world, but her tiniest pulsation ripples out and out, down and down, till the outermost circles and the deepest layers of society feel the vibrations. It is pre-eminently an age of organizations. The "leading woman," the preacher, the reformer, the organizer "enthuses" her lieutenants and captains, the literary women, the thinking women, the strong, earnest, irresistible women; these in turn touch their myriads of church clubs, social clubs, culture clubs, pleasure clubs and charitable clubs, till the same lecture has been duly administered to every married man in the land (not to speak of sons and brothers) from the President in the White House to the stone-splitter of the ditches. And so woman's lightest whisper is heard as in Dionysius' ear,[7] by quick relays and endless reproductions, through every recess and cavern as well as on every hill-top and mountain in her vast domain. And her mandates are obeyed. When she says "thumbs up," woe to the luckless thumb that falters in its rising. They may be little things, the amenities of life, the little nothings which cost nothing and come to nothing, and yet can make a sentient being so comfortable or so miserable in this life, the oil of social machinery, which we call the courtesies of life, all are under the magic key of woman's permit.

The American woman then is responsible for American manners. Not merely the right ascension and declination of the satellites of her own drawing room; but the rising and the setting of the pestilential or life-giving orbs which seem to wander afar in space, all are governed almost wholly through her magnetic polarity. The atmosphere of street cars and parks and boulevards, of cafés and hotels and steamboats is charged and surcharged with her sentiments and restrictions. Shop girls and serving maids, cashiers and accountant clerks, scribblers and drummers, whether wage earner, salaried toiler, or proprietress, whether laboring to instruct minds, to save souls, to delight fancies, or to win bread,—the working women of America in whatever station or calling they may be found, are subjects, officers, or rulers of a strong centralized government, and bound together by a system of codes and countersigns, which, though unwritten, forms a network of perfect subordination and unquestioning obedience as marvelous as that of the Jesuits. At the head and center in this regime stands the Leading Woman in the principality. The one talismanic word that plays along the wires from palace to cook-shop, from imperial Congress to the distant plain, is *Caste*. With all her vaunted independence, the American woman of to-day is as fearful of losing caste as a Brahmin in India. That is the law under which she lives, the precepts which she binds as frontlets[8] between her eyes and writes on the door-posts of her homes, the lesson which she instils into her children with their first baby breakfasts, the injunction she lays upon husband and lover with direst penalties attached.

The queen of the drawing room is absolute ruler under this law. Her pose gives the cue. The microscopic angle at which her pencilled brows are elevated, signifies who may be recognized and who are beyond the pale. The delicate intimation is, quick as electricity, telegraphed down. Like the wonderful transformation in the House that Jack Built (or regions thereabouts) when the rat began to gnaw the rope, the rope to hang the butcher, the butcher to kill the ox, the ox to drink the water, the water to quench the fire, the fire to burn the stick, the stick to beat the dog, and the dog to worry the cat, and on, and on, and on,—when miladi causes the inner arch over her matchless orbs to ascend the merest trifle, *presto*! the Miss at the notions counter grows curt and pert, the dress goods clerk becomes indifferent and taciturn, hotel waiters and ticket dispensers look the other way, the Irish street laborer snarls and scowls, conductors, policemen and park superintendents jostle and push and

---

7. That is, the ear of the Greek soldier and ruler of Syracuse (405–367 B.C.E.), not to be confused with the Greek god of wine.
8. Ornamental bands, particularly "phylacteries," or small leather cases holding slips inscribed with scriptural passages, fastened to the forehead by Orthodox or Conservative Jewish men during morning weekday prayer. Cooper also refers to the marking of doorposts for Passover. "Brahmin": a member of the highest caste in Indian society; also used to describe the elite of Boston.

threaten, and society suddenly seems transformed into a band of organized adders, snapping, and striking and hissing just because they like it on general principles. The tune set by the head singer, sung through all keys and registers, with all qualities of tone,—the smooth, flowing, and gentle, the creaking, whizzing, grating, screeching, growling—according to ability, taste, and temperament of the singers. Another application of like master, like man. In this case, like mistress, like nation.

It was the good fortune of the Black Woman of the South to spend some weeks, not long since, in a land over which floated the Union Jack. The Stars and Stripes were not the only familiar experiences missed. A uniform, matter-of-fact courtesy, a genial kindliness, quick perception of opportunities for rendering any little manly assistance, a readiness to give information to strangers,—a hospitable, thawing-out atmosphere everywhere—in shops and waiting rooms, on cars and in the streets, actually seemed to her chilled little soul to transform the commonest boor in the service of the public into one of nature's noblemen, and when the old whipped-cur feeling was taken up and analyzed she could hardly tell whether it consisted mostly of self pity for her own wounded sensibilities, or of shame for her country and mortification that her countrymen offered such an unfavorable contrast.

Some American girls, I noticed recently, in search of novelty and adventure, were taking an extended trip through our country unattended by gentleman friends; their wish was to write up for a periodical or lecture the ease and facility, the comfort and safety of American travel, even for the weak and unprotected, under our well-nigh perfect railroad systems and our gentlemanly and efficient corps of officials and public servants. I have some material I could furnish these young ladies, though possibly it might not be just on the side they wish to have illuminated. The Black Woman of the South has to do considerable travelling in this country, often unattended. She thinks she is quiet and unobtrusive in her manner, simple and inconspicuous in her dress, and can see no reason why in any chance assemblage of *ladies*, or even a promiscuous gathering of ordinarily well-bred and dignified individuals, she should be signaled out for any marked consideration. And yet she has seen these same "gentlemanly and efficient" railroad conductors, when their cars had stopped at stations having no raised platforms, making it necessary for passengers to take the long and trying leap from the car step to the ground or step on the narrow little stool placed under by the conductor, after standing at their posts and handing woman after woman from the steps to the stool, thence to the ground, or else relieving her of satchels and bags and enabling her to make the descent easily, deliberately fold their arms and turn round when the Black Woman's turn came to alight—bearing her satchel, and bearing besides another unnamable burden inside the heaving bosom and tightly compressed lips. The feeling of slighted womanhood is unlike every other emotion of the soul. Happily for the human family, it is unknown to many and indescribable to all. Its poignancy, compared with which even Juno's *spretae injuria formae* is earthly and vulgar,[9] is holier than that of jealousy, deeper than indignation, tenderer than rage. Its first impulse of wrathful protest and

---

9. "The wrong offered her slighted beauty" (Latin; Virgil, *Aeneid* 1.26)—a reference to the judgment of Paris, in which the Trojan Paris picked Aphrodite, goddess of beauty and love, as more beautiful than Athena, goddess of wisdom and war, and Hera (the Roman Juno), goddess of married women and sister of Zeus.

proud self vindication is checked and shamed by the consciousness that self
assertion would outrage still further the same delicate instinct. Were there a
brutal attitude of hate or of ferocious attack, the feminine response of fear
or repulsion is simple and spontaneous. But when the keen sting comes
through the finer sensibilities, from a hand which, by all known traditions and
ideals of propriety, should have been trained to reverence and respect them,
the condemnation of man's inhumanity to woman is increased and embittered by the knowledge of personal identity with a race of beings so fallen.

I purposely forbear to mention instances of personal violence to colored
women travelling in less civilized sections of our country, where women have
been forcibly ejected from cars, thrown out of seats, their garments rudely
torn, their person wantonly and cruelly injured. America is large and must for
some time yet endure its out-of-the-way jungles of barbarism as Africa its
uncultivated tracts of marsh and malaria. There are murderers and thieves
and villains in both London and Paris. Humanity from the first has had its
vultures and sharks, and representatives of the fraternity who prey upon
mankind may be expected no less in America than elsewhere. That this virulence breaks out most readily and commonly against colored persons in this
country, is due of course to the fact that they are, generally speaking, weak
and can be imposed upon with impunity. Bullies are always cowards at heart
and may be credited with a pretty safe instinct in scenting their prey. Besides,
society, where it has not exactly said to its dogs "s-s-sik him!" has at least
engaged to be looking in another direction or studying the rivers on Mars. It
is not of the dogs and their doings, but of society holding the leash that I shall
speak. It is those subtile exhalations of atmospheric odors for which woman
is accountable, the indefinable, unplaceable aroma which seems to exude
from the very pores in her finger tips like the delicate sachet so dexterously
hidden and concealed in her linens; the essence of her teaching, guessed
rather than read, so adroitly is the lettering and wording manipulated; it is the
undertones of the picture laid finely on by woman's own practiced hand, the
reflection of the lights and shadows on her own brow; it is, in a word, the reputation of our nation for general politeness and good manners and of our fellow citizens to be somewhat more than cads or snobs that shall engage our
present study. There can be no true test of national courtesy without travel.
Impressions and conclusions based on provincial traits and characteristics
can thus be modified and generalized. Moreover, the weaker and less influential the experimenter, the more exact and scientific the deductions. Courtesy "for revenue only" is not politeness, but diplomacy. Any rough can
assume civility toward those of "his set," and does not hesitate to carry it even
to servility toward those in whom he recognizes a possible patron or his master in power, wealth, rank, or influence. But, as the chemist prefers distilled
$H_2O$ in testing solutions to avoid complications and unwarranted reactions,
so the Black Woman holds that her femininity linked with the impossibility
of popular affinity or unexpected attraction through position and influence
in her case makes her a touchstone of American courtesy exceptionally pure
and singularly free from extraneous modifiers. The man who is courteous to
her is so, not because of anything he hopes or fears or sees, but because *he
is a gentleman.*

I would eliminate also from the discussion all uncharitable reflections
upon the orderly execution of laws existing in certain states of this Union,

requiring persons known to be colored to ride in one car, and persons supposed to be white in another. A good citizen may use his influence to have existing laws and statutes changed or modified, but a public servant must not be blamed for obeying orders. A railroad conductor is not asked to dictate measures, nor to make and pass laws. His bread and butter are conditioned on his managing his part of the machinery as he is told to do. If, therefore, I found myself in that compartment of a train designated by the sovereign law of the state for presumable Caucasians, and for colored persons only when traveling in the capacity of nurses and maids, should a conductor inform me, as a gentleman might, that I had made a mistake, and offer to show me the proper car for black ladies; I might wonder at the expensive arrangements of the company and of the state in providing special and separate accommodations for the transportation of the various hues of humanity, but I certainly could not take it as a want of courtesy on the conductor's part that he gave the information. It is true, public sentiment precedes and begets all laws, good or bad; and on the ground I have taken, our women are to the credited largely as teachers and moulders of public sentiment. But when a law has passed and received the sanction of the land, there is nothing for our officials to do but enforce it till repealed; and I for one, as a loyal American citizen, will give those officials cheerful support and ready sympathy in the discharge of their duty. But when a great burly six feet of masculinity with sloping shoulders and unkempt beard swaggers in, and, throwing a roll of tobacco into one corner of his jaw, growls out at me over the paper I am reading, "Here gurl," (I am past thirty) "you better git out 'n dis kyar 'f yer don't, I'll put yer out,"—my mental annotation is *Here's an American citizen who has been badly trained. He is sadly lacking in both 'sweetness' and 'light'*;[1] and when in the same section of our enlightened and progressive country, I see from the car window, working on private estates, convicts from the state penitentiary, among them squads of boys from fourteen to eighteen years of age in a chaingang, their feet chained together and heavy blocks attached—not in 1850, but in 1890, '91 and '92, I make a note on the fly-leaf of my memorandum, *The women in this section should organize a Society for the Prevention of Cruelty to Human Beings, and disseminate civilizing tracts, and send throughout the region apostles of anti-barbarism for the propagation of humane and enlightened ideas.* And when farther on in the same section our train stops at a dilapidated station, rendered yet more unsightly by dozens of loafers with their hands in their pockets while a productive soil and inviting climate beckon in vain to industry; and when, looking a little more closely, I see two dingy little rooms with "FOR LADIES" swinging over one and "FOR COLORED PEOPLE" over the other; while wondering under which head I come, I notice a little way off the only hotel proprietor of the place whittling a pine stick as he sits with one leg thrown across an empty goods box; and as my eye falls on a sample room next door which seems to be driving the only wide-awake and popular business of the commonwealth, I cannot help ejaculating under my breath, "What a field for the missionary woman." I know that if by any fatality I should be obliged to lie over at that station, and, driven by hunger, should be compelled to seek refreshments or the bare necessaries of

1. According to English social critic Matthew Arnold (1822–1888), in *Culture and Anarchy* (1882), "sweetness" (moral righteousness) and "light" (intellectual power and truth) are touchstones of a culture's worth.

life at the only public accommodation in the town, that same stick-whittler would coolly inform me, without looking up from his pine splinter, "We doan uccommodate no niggers hyur." And yet we are so scandalized at Russia's barbarity and cruelty to the Jews! We pay a man a thousand dollars a night just to make us weep, by a recital of such heathenish inhumanity as is practiced on Sclavonic[2] soil.

A recent writer on Eastern nations says: "If we take through the earth's temperate zone, a belt of country whose northern and southern edges are determined by certain limiting isotherms, not more than half the width of the zone apart, we shall find that we have included in a relatively small extent of surface almost all the nations of note in the world, past or present. Now, if we examine this belt and compare the different parts of it with one another, we shall be struck by a remarkable fact. *The peoples inhabiting it grow steadily more personal as we go west.* So unmistakable is this gradation, that one is almost tempted to ascribe it to cosmical rather than to human causes. It is as marked as the change in color of the human complexion observable along any meridian, which ranges from black at the equator to blonde toward the pole. In like manner the sense of self grows more intense as we follow in the wake of the setting sun, and fades steadily as we advance into the dawn. America, Europe, the Levant,[3] India, Japan, each is less personal than the one before. . . . *That politeness should be one of the most marked results of impersonality* may appear surprising, yet a slight examination will show it to be a fact. Considered *a priori*, the connection is not far to seek. Impersonality by lessening the interest in one's self, induces one to take an interest in others. Looked at *a posteriori*, we find that where the one trait exists the other is most developed, while an absence of the second seems to prevent the full growth of the first. This is true both in general and in detail. *Courtesy increases as we travel eastward round the world, coincidently with a decrease in the sense of self.* Asia is more courteous than Europe, Europe than America. Particular races show the same concomitance of characteristics. France, the most impersonal nation of Europe, is at the same time the most polite." And by inference, Americans, the most personal, are the least courteous nation on the globe.

The Black Woman had reached this same conclusion by an entirely different route; but it is gratifying to vanity, nevertheless, to find one's self sustained by both science and philosophy in a conviction, wrought in by hard experience, and yet too apparently audacious to be entertained even as a stealthy surmise. In fact the Black Woman was emboldened some time since by a well put and timely article from an Editor's Drawer on the "Mannerless Sex," to give the world the benefit of some of her experience with the *"Mannerless Race"*; but since Mr. Lowell[4] shows so conclusively that the entire Land of the West is a *mannerless continent*, I have determined to plead with our women, the mannerless sex on this mannerless continent, to institute a reform by placing immediately in our national curricula a department for teaching GOOD MANNERS.

Now, am I right in holding the American Woman responsible? Is it true that the exponents of woman's advancement, the leaders in woman's thought, the

---

2. Slavic.
3. Term used at the time to refer to the Middle East in general.

4. James Russell Lowell (1819–1891), American poet, critic, essayist, editor, and diplomat.

preachers and teachers of all woman's reforms, can teach this nation to be courteous, to be pitiful, having compassion one of another, not rendering evil for inoffensiveness, and railing in proportion to the improbability of being struck back; but contrariwise, being *all* of one mind, to love as brethren?

I think so.

It may require some heroic measures, and like all revolutions will call for a determined front and a courageous, unwavering, stalwart heart on the part of the leaders of the reform.

The "*all*" will inevitably stick in the throat of the Southern woman. She must be allowed, please, to except the 'darkey' from the 'all'; it is too bitter a pill with black people in it. You must get the Revised Version to put it, "*love all white people* as brethren." She really could not enter any society on earth, or in heaven above, or in—the waters under the earth, on such unpalatable conditions.

The Black Woman has tried to understand the Southern woman's difficulties; to put herself in her place, and to be as fair, as charitable, and as free from prejudice in judging her antipathies, as she would have others in regard to her own. She has honestly weighed the apparently sincere excuse, "But you must remember that these people were once our slaves"; and that other, "But civility towards the Negroes will bring us on *social equality* with them."

These are the two bugbears; or rather, the two humbugbears: for, though each is founded on a most glaring fallacy, one would think they were words to conjure with, so potent and irresistible is their spell as an argument at the North as well as in the South.

One of the most singular facts about the unwritten history of this country is the consummate ability with which Southern influence, Southern ideas and Southern ideals, have from the very beginning even up to the present day, dictated to and domineered over the brain and sinew of this nation. Without wealth, without education, without inventions, arts, sciences, or industries, without well-nigh every one of the progressive ideas and impulses which have made this country great, prosperous and happy, personally indolent and practically stupid, poor in everything but bluster and self-esteem, the Southerner has nevertheless with Italian finesse and exquisite skill, uniformly and invariably, so manipulated Northern sentiment as to succeed sooner or later in carrying his point and shaping the policy of this government to suit his purposes. Indeed, the Southerner is a magnificent manager of men, a born educator. For two hundred and fifty years he trained to his hand a people whom he made absolutely his own, in body, mind, and sensibility. He so insinuated differences and distinctions among them, that their personal attachment for him was stronger than for their own brethren and fellow sufferers. He made it a crime for two or three of them to be gathered together in Christ's name without a white man's supervision, and a felony for one to teach them to read even the Word of Life; and yet they would defend his interest with their life blood; his smile was their happiness, a pat on the shoulder from him their reward. The slightest difference among themselves in condition, circumstances, opportunities, became barriers of jealousy and disunion. He sowed his blood broadcast among them, then pitted mulatto against black, bond against free, house slave against plantation slave, even the slave of one clan against like slave of another clan; till, wholly oblivious of their ability for mutual succor and defense, all became centers of myriad systems of repel-

lent forces, having but one sentiment in common, and that their entire subjection to that master hand.

And he not only managed the black man, he also hoodwinked the white
man, the tourist and investigator who visited his lordly estates. The slaves
were doing well, in fact couldn't be happier,—plenty to eat, plenty to drink,
comfortably housed and clothed—they wouldn't be free if they could; in
short, in his broad brimmed plantation hat and easy aristocratic smoking
gown, he made you think him a veritable patriarch in the midst of a lazy, well
fed, good natured, over-indulged tenantry.

Then, too, the South represented blood—not red blood, but blue blood.
The difference is in the length of the stream and your distance from its
source. If your own father was a pirate, a robber, a murderer, his hands are
dyed in red blood, and you don't say very much about it. But if your great great
great grandfather's grandfather stole and pillaged and slew, and you can prove
it, your blood has become blue and you are at great pains to establish the relationship. So the South had neither silver nor gold, but she had blood; and she
paraded it with so much gusto that the substantial little Puritan maidens of
the North, who had been making bread and canning currants and not thinking of blood the least bit, began to hunt up the records of the Mayflower to
see if some of the passengers thereon could not claim the honor of having
been one of William the Conqueror's brigands, when he killed the last of the
Saxon kings and, red-handed, stole his crown and his lands. Thus the ideal
from out the Southland brooded over the nation and we sing less lustily than
of yore

> 'Kind hearts are more than coronets
> And simple faith than Norman blood.'[5]

In politics, the two great forces, commerce and empire, which would otherwise have shaped the destiny of the country, have been made to pander and
cater to Southern notions. "Cotton is King" meant the South must be allowed
to dictate or there would be no fun. Every statesman from 1830 to 1860
exhausted his genius in persuasion and compromises to smooth out her ruffled temper and gratify her petulant demands. But like a sullen younger sister, the South has pouted and sulked and cried: "I won't play with you now;
so there!" and the big brother at the North has coaxed and compromised and
given in, and—ended by letting her have her way. Until 1860 she had as her
pet an institution which it was death by the law to say anything about, except
that it was divinely instituted, inaugurated by Noah, sanctioned by Abraham,
approved by Paul, and just ideally perfect in every way. And when, to preserve
the autonomy of the family arrangements, in '61, '62 and '63, it became necessary for the big brother to administer a little wholesome correction and set
the obstreperous Miss vigorously down in her seat again, she assumed such
an air of injured innocence, and melted away so lugubriously, the big brother
has done nothing since but try to sweeten and pacify and laugh her back into
a companionable frame of mind.

Father Lincoln[6] did all he could to get her to repent of her petulance and
behave herself. He even promised she might keep her pet, so disagreeable to
all the neighbors and hurtful even to herself, and might manage it at home

---

5. From Alfred Lord Tennyson's 1842 poem "Lady
Clara Vere de Vere."

6. President Abraham Lincoln (1809–1865).

to suit herself, if she would only listen to reason and be just tolerably nice. But, no—she was going to leave and set up for herself; she didn't propose to be meddled with; and so, of course, she had to be spanked. Just a little at first—didn't mean to hurt, merely to teach her who was who. But she grew so ugly, and kicked and fought and scratched so outrageously, and seemed so determined to smash up the whole business, the head of the family got red in the face, and said: "Well, now, he couldn't have any more of that foolishness. Arabella[7] must just behave herself or take the consequences." And after the spanking, Arabella sniffed and whimpered and pouted, and the big brother bit his lip, looked half ashamed, and said: "Well, I didn't want to hurt you. You needn't feel so awfully bad about it, I only did it for your good. You know I wouldn't do anything to displease you if I could help it; but you would insist on making the row, and so I just had to. Now, there—there—let's be friends!" and he put his great strong arms about her and just dared anybody to refer to that little unpleasantness—he'd show them a thing or two. Still Arabella sulked,—till the rest of the family decided she might just keep her pets, and manage her own affairs and nobody should interfere.

So now, if one intimates that some clauses of the Constitution are a dead letter at the South and that only the name and support of that pet institution are changed while the fact and essence, minus the expense and responsibility, remain, he is quickly told to mind his own business and informed that he is waving the bloody shirt.[8]

Even twenty-five years after the fourteenth and fifteenth amendments to our Constitution,[9] a man who has been most unequivocal in his outspoken condemnation of the wrongs regularly and systematically heaped on the oppressed race in this country, and on all even most remotely connected with them—a man whom we had thought our staunchest friend and most noble champion and defender—after a two weeks' trip in Georgia and Florida immediately gives signs of the fatal inception of the virus. Not even the chance traveller from England or Scotland escapes. The arch-manipulator takes him under his special watch-care and training, uses up his stock arguments and gives object lessons with his choicest specimens of Negro depravity and worthlessness; takes him through what, in New York, would be called "the slums," and would predicate there nothing but the duty of enlightened Christians to send out their light and emulate their Master's aggressive labors of love; but in Georgia is denominated "our terrible problem, which people of the North so little understand, yet vouchsafe so much gratuitous advice about." With an injured air he shows the stupendous and atrocious mistake of reasoning about these people as if they were just ordinary human beings, and amenable to the tenets of the Gospel; and not long after the inoculation begins to work, you hear this old-time friend of the oppressed delivering himself something after this fashion: "Ah, well, the South must be left to manage the Negro. She is most directly concerned and must understand her

7. A name Cooper associates with an upper-class southern woman, whom she here makes a symbol for the feminized South.
8. That is, he is waving something to anger others or inspire them to retaliatory action. In 1866, a northern congressman displayed to Congress the bloody shirt of an Ohio carpetbagger said to have been beaten in Mississippi, with the idea of fan-

ning postwar bitterness and stirring up sectional animosity.
9. The Fourteenth Amendment provided that all males born in the United States were citizens; the Fifteenth Amendment declared that the right of U.S. citizens to vote could "not be abridged or denied" by any state "on account of race, color, or previous condition of servitude."

problem better than outsiders. We must not meddle. We must be very careful not to widen the breaches. The Negro is not worth a feud between brothers and sisters."

Lately a great national and international movement characteristic of this age and country, a movement based on the inherent right of every soul to its own highest development, I mean the movement making for Woman's full, free, and complete emancipation, has, after much courting, obtained the gracious smile of the Southern woman—I beg her pardon—the Southern *lady*.

She represents blood, and of course could not be expected to leave that out; and firstly and foremostly she must not, in any organization she may deign to grace with her presence, be asked to associate with "these people who were once her slaves."

Now the Southern woman (I may be pardoned, being one myself) was never renowned for her reasoning powers, and it is not surprising that just a little picking will make her logic fall to pieces even here.

In the first place she imagines that because her grandfather had slaves who were black, all the blacks in the world of every shade and tint were once in the position of her slaves. This is as bad as the Irishman who was about to kill a peaceable Jew in the streets of Cork,—having just learned that Jews slew his Redeemer. The black race constitutes one-seventh the known population of the globe; and there are representatives of it here as elsewhere who were never in bondage at any time to any man,—whose blood is as blue and lineage as noble as any, even that of the white lady of the South. That her slaves were black and she despises her slaves, should no more argue antipathy to all dark people and peoples, than that Guiteau,[1] an assassin, was white, and I hate assassins, should make me hate all persons more or less white. The objection shows a want of clear discrimination.

The second fallacy in the objection grows out of the use of an ambiguous middle, as the logicians would call it, or assigning a double signification to the term "*Social equality.*"

Civility to the Negro implies social equality. I am opposed to *associating* with dark persons on terms of social equality. Therefore, I abrogate civility to the Negro. This is like

> Light is opposed to darkness.
> Feathers are light.
> *Ergo*, Feathers are opposed to darkness.

The "social equality" implied by civility to the Negro is a very different thing from forced association with him socially. Indeed it seems to me that the mere application of a little cold common sense would show that uncongenial social environments could by no means be forced on any one. I do not, and cannot be made to associate with all dark persons, simply on the ground that I am dark; and I presume the Southern lady can imagine some whose faces are white, with whom she would no sooner think of chatting unreservedly than, were it possible, with a veritable 'darkey.' Such things must and will always be left to individual election. No law, human or divine, can legislate for or against them. Like seeks like; and I am sure with the Southern lady's antipathies at their present temperature, she might enter ten thousand

---

1. Charles Julius Guiteau (1841–1882), a mentally ill American lawyer who assassinated President James Garfield on July 2, 1881.

organizations besprinkled with colored women without being any more deflected by them than by the proximity of a stone. The social equality scare then is all humbug, conscious or unconscious, I know not which. And were it not too bitter a thought to utter here, I might add that the overtures for forced association in the past history of these two races were not made by the manacled black man, nor by *the silent and suffering black woman!*

When I seek food in a public café or apply for first-class accommodations on a railway train, I do so because my physical necessities are identical with those of other human beings of like constitution and temperament, and crave satisfaction. I go because I want food, or I want comfort—not because I want association with those who frequent these places; and I can see no more "social equality" in buying lunch at the same restaurant, or riding in a common car, than there is in paying for dry goods at the same counter or walking on the same street.

The social equality which means forced or unbidden association would be as much deprecated and as strenuously opposed by the circle in which I move as by the most hide-bound Southerner in the land. Indeed I have been more than once annoyed by the inquisitive white interviewer, who, with spectacles on nose and pencil and note-book in hand, comes to get some "points" about "*your people.*" My "people" are just like other people—indeed, too like for their own good. They hate, they love, they attract and repel, they climb or they grovel, struggle or drift, aspire or despair, endure in hope or curse in vexation, exactly like all the rest of unregenerate humanity. Their likes and dislikes are as strong; their antipathies—and prejudices too I fear, are as pronounced as you will find anywhere; and the entrance to the inner sanctuary of their homes and hearts is as jealously guarded against profane intrusion.

What the dark man wants then is merely to live his own life, in his own world, with his own chosen companions, in whatever of comfort, luxury, or emoluments his talent or his money can in an impartial market secure. Has he wealth, he does not want to be forced into inconvenient or unsanitary sections of cities to buy a home and rear his family. Has he art, he does not want to be cabined and cribbed into emulation with the few who merely happen to have his complexion. His talent aspires to study without proscription the masters of all ages and to rub against the broadest and fullest movements of his own day.

Has he religion, he does not want to be made to feel that there is a white Christ and a black Christ, a white Heaven and a black Heaven, a white Gospel and a black Gospel,—but the one ideal of perfect manhood and womanhood, the one universal longing for development and growth, the one desire for being, and being better, the one great yearning, aspiring, outreaching, in all the heartthrobs of humanity in whatever race or clime.

A recent episode in the Corcoran art gallery[2] at the American capital is to the point. A colored woman who had shown marked ability in drawing and coloring, was advised by her teacher, himself an artist of no mean rank, to apply for admission to the Corcoran school in order to study the models and to secure other advantages connected with the organization. She accordingly sent a written application accompanied by specimens of her drawings, the usual *modus operandi* in securing admission.

---

2. Located in Washington D.C., the Corcoran Gallery of Art was founded by William Wilson Corcoran (1798–1888), a leading patron of American art.

The drawings were examined by the best critics and pronounced excellent, and a ticket of admission was immediately issued together with a highly complimentary reference to her work.

The next day my friend, congratulating her country and herself that at least in the republic of art no caste existed, presented her ticket of admission *in propria persona*.[3] There was a little preliminary side play in Delsarte pantomine,[4]—aghast—incredulity—wonder; then the superintendent told her in plain unartistic English that of course he had not dreamed a colored person could do such work, and had he suspected the truth he would never have issued the ticket of admission; that, to be right frank, the ticket would have to be cancelled,—she could under no condition be admitted to the studio.

Can it be possible that even art in America is to be tainted by this shrivelling caste spirit? If so, what are we coming to? Can any one conceive a Shakespeare, a Michael Angelo, or a Beethoven putting away any fact of simple merit because the thought, or the suggestion, or the creation emanated from a soul with an unpleasing exterior?

What is it that makes the great English bard pre-eminent as the photographer of the human soul? Where did he learn the universal language, so that Parthians, Medes and Elamites, and the dwellers in Mesopotamia, in Egypt and Libya, in Crete and Arabia do hear every one in our own tongue the wonderful revelations of this myriad mind? How did he learn our language? Is it not that his own soul was infinitely receptive to Nature, the dear old nurse, in all her protean forms? Did he not catch and reveal her own secret by his sympathetic listening as she "would constantly sing a more wonderful song or tell a more marvellous tale" in the souls he met around him?

"Stand off! I am better than thou!" has never yet painted a true picture, nor written a thrilling song, nor given a pulsing, a soul-burning sermon. 'Tis only sympathy, another name for love,—that one poor word which, as George Eliot[5] says, "expresses so much of human insight"—that can interpret either man or matter.

It was Shakespeare's own all-embracing sympathy, that infinite receptivity of his, and native, all-comprehending appreciation, which proved a key to unlock and open every soul that came within his radius. And *he received as much as he gave*. His own stores were infinitely enriched thereby. For it is decreed

> Man like the vine supported lives,
> The strength he gains is from th' embrace he gives.[6]

It is only through clearing the eyes from bias and prejudice, and becoming one with the great all pervading soul of the universe that either art or science can

> "Read what is still unread
> In the manuscripts of God."[7]

No true artist can allow himself to be narrowed and provincialized by deliberately shutting out any class of facts or subjects through prejudice against exter-

3. Acting on behalf of oneself (Latin).
4. That is, in the system of recitation and gesture for public performance devised by François Delsarte (1811–1871), a French elocution teacher.
5. English novelist (1819–1880).
6. Slight misquotation from Epistle III of Alexan-

der Pope's 1734 poem *Essay on Man*.
7. From "The Fiftieth Birthday of Agassiz," by Henry Wadsworth Longfellow (1807–1882), the most popular American poet of the 19th century; the Swiss-born émigré Louis Agassiz (1807–1873) was a well-known scientist.

nals. And American art, American science, American literature can never be founded in truth, the universal beauty; can never learn to speak a language intelligible in all climes and for all ages, till this paralyzing grip of caste prejudice is loosened from its vitals, and the healthy sympathetic eye is taught to look out on the great universe as holding no favorites and no black beasts, but bearing in each plainest or loveliest feature the handwriting of its God.

And this is why, as it appears to me, woman in her lately acquired vantage ground for speaking an earnest helpful word, can do this country no deeper and truer and more lasting good than by bending all her energies to thus broadening, humanizing, and civilizing her native land.

"Except ye become as little children"[8] is not a pious precept, but an inexorable law of the universe. God's kingdoms are all sealed to the seedy, moss-grown mind of self-satisfied maturity. Only the little child in spirit, the simple, receptive, educable mind can enter. Preconceived notions, blinding prejudices, and shrivelling antipathies must be wiped out, and the cultivable soul made a *tabula rasa* for whatever lesson great Nature has to teach.

This, too, is why I conceive the subject to have been unfortunately worded which was chosen by Miss Shaw at the Woman's Council and which stands at the head of this chapter.

Miss Shaw is one of the most powerful of our leaders, and we feel her voice should give no uncertain note. Woman should not, even by inference, or for the sake of argument, seem to disparage what is weak. For woman's cause is the cause of the weak; and when all the weak shall have received their due consideration, then woman will have her "rights," and the Indian will have his rights, and the Negro will have his rights, and all the strong will have learned at last to deal justly, to love mercy, and to walk humbly; and our fair land will have been taught the secret of universal courtesy which is after all nothing but the art, the science, and the religion of regarding one's neighbor as one's self, and to do for him as we would, were conditions swapped, that he do for us.

It cannot seem less than a blunder, whenever the exponents of a great reform or the harbingers of a noble advance in thought and effort allow themselves to seem distorted by a narrow view of their own aims and principles. All prejudices, whether of race, sect or sex, class pride and caste distinctions are the belittling inheritance and badge of snobs and prigs.

The philosophic mind sees that its own "rights" are the rights of humanity. That in the universe of God nothing trivial is or mean; and the recognition it seeks is not through the robber and wild beast adjustment of the survival of the bullies but through the universal application ultimately of the Golden Rule.

Not unfrequently has it happened that the impetus of a mighty thought wave has done the execution meant by its Creator in spite of the weak and distorted perception of its human embodiment. It is not strange if reformers, who, after all, but think God's thoughts after him, have often "builded more wisely than they knew;" and while fighting consciously for only a narrow gateway[9] for themselves, have been driven forward by that irresistible "Power not ourselves which makes for righteousness" to open a high road for humanity.

---

8. In Matthew 18.3, Jesus tells the disciples, who have asked which among them will be the greatest in Heaven, that unless they become like little children none of them will enter Heaven.

9. Reference to Matthew 7.14: "Because strait is the gate, and narrow is the way, which leadeth unto life, and few there be that find it."

It was so with our sixteenth century reformers. The fathers of the Reformation had no idea that they were inciting an insurrection of the human mind against all domination. None would have been more shocked than they at our nineteenth-century deductions from their sixteenth-century premises. Emancipation of mind and freedom of thought would have been as appalling to them as it was distasteful to the pope. They were right, they argued, to rebel against Romish absolutism—because Romish preaching and Romish practicing were wrong. They denounced popes for hacking heretics and forthwith began themselves to roast witches. The Spanish Inquisition in the hands of Philip and Alva was an institution of the devil;[1] wielded by the faithful, it would become quite another thing. The only "rights" they were broad enough consciously to fight for was the right to substitute the absolutism of their conceptions, their party, their 'ism' for an authority whose teaching they conceived to be corrupt and vicious. Persecution for a belief was wrong only when the persecutors were wrong and the persecuted right. The sacred prerogative of the individual to decide on matters of belief they did not dream of maintaining. Universal tolerance and its twin, universal charity, were not conceived yet. The broad foundation stone of all human rights, the great democratic principle "A man's a man, *and his own sovereign* for a' that"[2] they did not dare enunciate. They were incapable of drawing up a Declaration of Independence for humanity. The Reformation to the Reformers meant one bundle of authoritative opinions vs. another bundle of authoritative opinions. Justification by faith, vs. justification by ritual. Submission to Calvin[3] vs. submission to the Pope. English and Germans vs. the Italians.

To our eye, viewed through a vista of three centuries, it was the death wrestle of the principle of thought enslavement in the throttling grasp of personal freedom; it was the great Emancipation Day of human belief, man's intellectual Independence Day, prefiguring and finally compelling the world-wide enfranchisement of his body and all its activities. Not Protestant vs. Catholic, then; not Luther vs. Leo, not Dominicans vs. Augustinians, nor Geneva vs. Rome;[4]—but humanity rationally free, vs. the clamps of tradition and superstition which had manacled and muzzled it.

The cause of freedom is not the cause of a race or a sect, a party or a class,—it is the cause of human kind, the very birthright of humanity. Now unless we are greatly mistaken the Reform of our day, known as the Woman's Movement, is essentially such an embodiment, if its pioneers could only realize it, of the universal good. And specially important is it that there be no confusion of ideas among its leaders as to its scope and universality. All mists must be cleared from the eyes of woman if she is to be a teacher of morals and manners: the former strikes its roots in the individual and its training and pruning may be accomplished by classes; but the latter is to lubricate the joints and minimize the friction of society, and it is important and funda-

---

1. The Spanish Inquisition was the rigorous identification, torture, and execution of heretics begun in 1481 during the reign of Ferdinand and Isabella. "Alva" refers to Fernando Alvarez, who was sent by Philip II of Spain to punish the Netherlands in 1557.
2. Paraphrase of Robert Burns's poem "For a' that and a' that" (1795).
3. John Calvin (1509–1564), French Christian theologian during the Protestant Reformation, founder of Calvinism; he settled in Geneva in 1541.
4. That is, Calvinism vs. the pope (Roman Catholicism). Martin Luther (1483–1546), German leader of the Protestant Reformation. Leo X, born Giovanni di Lorenzo de' Medici (1475–1521), pope from 1513 to his death. Dominicans and Augustinians: major orders of Catholic priests.

mental that there be no chromatic or other aberration when the teacher is settling the point, "Who is my neighbor?"[5]

It is not the intelligent woman vs. the ignorant woman; nor the white woman vs. the black, the brown, and the red,—it is not even the cause of woman vs. man. Nay, 'tis woman's strongest vindication for speaking that *the world needs to hear her voice.* It would be subversive of every human interest that the cry of one-half the human family be stifled. Woman in stepping from the pedestal of statue-like inactivity in the domestic shrine, and daring to think and move and speak,—to undertake to help shape, mold, and direct the thought of her age, is merely completing the circle of the world's vision. Hers is every interest that has lacked an interpreter and a defender. Her cause is linked with that of every agony that has been dumb—every wrong that needs a voice.

It is no fault of man's that he has not been able to see truth from her standpoint. It does credit both to his head and heart that no greater mistakes have been committed or even wrongs perpetrated while she sat making tatting and snipping paper flowers. Man's own innate chivalry and the mutual interdependence of their interests have insured his treating her cause, in the main at least, as his own. And he is pardonably surprised and even a little chagrined, perhaps, to find his legislation not considered "perfectly lovely" in every respect. But in any case his work is only impoverished by her remaining dumb. The world has had to limp along with the wobbling gait and one-sided hesitancy of a man with one eye. Suddenly the bandage is removed from the other eye and the whole body is filled with light. It sees a circle where before it saw a segment. The darkened eye restored, every member rejoices with it.

What a travesty of its case for this eye to become plaintiff in a suit, *Eye vs. Foot.* "There is that dull clod, the foot, allowed to roam at will, free and untrammelled; while I, the source and medium of light, brilliant and beautiful, am fettered in darkness and doomed to desuetude." The great burly black man, ignorant and gross and depraved, is allowed to vote; while the franchise is withheld from the intelligent and refined, the pure-minded and lofty souled white woman. Even the untamed and untamable Indian of the prairie, who can answer nothing but 'ugh' to great economic and civic questions is thought by some worthy to wield the ballot which is still denied the Puritan maid and the first lady of Virginia.

Is not this hitching our wagon to something much lower than a star? Is not woman's cause broader, and deeper, and grander, than a blue stocking debate or an aristocratic pink tea?[6] Why should woman become plaintiff in a suit versus the Indian, or the Negro or any other race or class who have been crushed under the iron heel of Anglo-Saxon power and selfishness? If the Indian has been wronged and cheated by the puissance of this American government, it is woman's mission to plead with her country to cease to do evil and to pay its honest debts. If the Negro has been deceitfully cajoled or inhumanly cuffed according to selfish expediency or capricious antipathy, let it be woman's mission to plead that he be met as a man and honestly given half the road. If woman's own happiness has been ignored or misunderstood in our country's legislating for bread winners, for rum sellers, for property holders,

---

5. From Luke 10.29, where Jesus explains that all people are one's neighbors.

6. A suffrage-sponsored women's tea party. "Blue stocking": a learned, bookish woman.

for the family relations, for any or all the interests that touch her vitally, let her rest her plea, not on Indian inferiority, nor on Negro depravity, but on the obligation of legislators to do for her as they would have others do for them were relations reversed. Let her try to teach her country that every interest in this world is entitled at least to a respectful hearing, that every sentiency is worthy of its own gratification, that a helpless cause should not be trampled down, nor a bruised reed broken; and when the right of the individual is made sacred, when the image of God in human form, whether in marble or in clay, whether in alabaster or in ebony, is consecrated and inviolable, when men have been taught to look beneath the rags and grime, the pomp and pageantry of mere circumstance and have regard unto the celestial kernel uncontaminated at the core,—when race, color, sex, condition, are realized to be the accidents, not the substance of life, and consequently as not obscuring or modifying the inalienable title to life, liberty, and pursuit of happiness,—then is mastered the science of politeness, the art of courteous contact, which is naught but the practical application of the principal of benevolence, the back bone and marrow of all religion; then woman's lesson is taught and woman's cause is won—not the white woman nor the black woman nor the red woman, but the cause of every man or woman who has writhed silently under a mighty wrong. The pleading of the American woman for the right and the opportunity to employ the American method of influencing the disposal to be made of herself, her property, her children in civil, economic, or domestic relations is thus seen to be based on a principle as broad as the human race and as old as human society. Her wrongs are thus indissolubly linked with all undefended woe, all helpless suffering, and the plenitude of her "rights" will mean the final triumph of all right over might, the supremacy of the moral forces of reason and justice and love in the government of the nation.

God hasten the day.

1892

# BOOKER T. WASHINGTON
## 1856–1915

Between the last decade of the nineteenth century and the beginning of World War I, no one exercised more influence over race relations in the United States than did Booker Taliaferro Washington; some contemporary historians of the African American experience in America call the period the "Era of Booker T. Washington." Washington's influence continues to the present day. He wanted to help African Americans enter mainstream white society with the least possible violence and thus advocated an educational program of vocational rather than intellectual or professional training. His works have been contrasted with the dynamic and militant efforts of Frederick Douglass (whose successor as African American leader Washington wished to be) and the intellectual and professional initiatives of the fiercely independent W. E. B. Du Bois, but Washington was able to institutionalize his power to a far greater degree than either of these two. He owed no small part of his power to extraordinary skill with written and spoken language. To his sense of calling Washington added the command of memory and the detail of living as a racial "other," all of which he expressed in an unforgettable voice.

Washington's birth date is uncertain; as an adult he selected April 5, 1856. His mother was born a slave in Hale's Ford, Virginia; his father was a white man whose identity is unknown. As a boy, he had, like most slaves, only a first name, and it was not until he entered school that he adopted the surname Washington, which was the first name of Washington Ferguson, a slave whom his mother had married. Washington's account of his early life is a catalog of deprivation and struggle. At the end of the Civil War, when he was nine years old, he accompanied his mother to Malden, West Virginia, to join his stepfather, who had found work there in a salt furnace. From 1865 to 1872, Washington worked as a salt packer, coal miner, and house servant while attending school in the off hours and thus beginning to satisfy his "intense longing" to learn to read and write. In 1872, he set out on a five hundred–mile, month-long journey by rail, cart, and foot to reach Hampton, Virginia, where he would attend the Hampton Normal and Agricultural Institute, a school established by the American Missionary Association to train African Americans as teachers. There Washington paid his way by working as a janitor. In the quasi-military atmosphere of the school, he was drilled in the goals of cleanliness, thrift, and hard work that became central to his life and educational philosophy.

After graduating from Hampton in 1875 with honors and a certificate to teach in a trade school, Washington returned to Malden and found work with a local school. He studied for a while at Wayland Seminary and in 1878 was hired by Samuel Armstrong, the principal of Hampton, to teach in a program for Native Americans. Then, in 1881, he became the first principal of what was to become the Tuskegee Institute, a school established by the Alabama legislature to train African American men and women in agricultural and mechanical trades and teaching. Tuskegee began with thirty students, and Washington, the staff, and the students constructed the school buildings from bricks they made themselves. But through his considerable powers as a conciliator and fund-raiser, and aided by publicity over his goals of instilling Christian virtues and encouraging simple, disciplined living among the students, Washington soon developed Tuskegee into a thriving institution.

Despite this success on the education front, it was not until 1895 that Washington emerged as a national figure. His emergence was the result of a short speech, included below, to a crowd of two thousand at the Atlanta Exposition of 1895. In the speech, popularly known as the "Atlanta Compromise," Washington agreed to defer equal rights for African Americans in return for low-level economic opportunities. This approach appealed to the majority of southern African Americans as well as most whites in the North and the South. A modern reader must understand its appeal in the context of the years between 1885 and 1910, when some thirty-five hundred African Americans were lynched and when, following the end of Reconstruction, most southern states effectively disenfranchised African Americans. Even such militant African American leaders as T. Thomas Fortune and Du Bois praised the speech and supported the philosophy of conciliation that was its pragmatic basis. Their opposition to Washington did not develop until several years later, when they felt it was time to insist on civil, social, and political equality for all African Americans.

In the years following the Atlanta speech, Washington consolidated his position as the "Moses of his race." Nothing did more to enhance this mythic stature than his own brilliant autobiography, *Up from Slavery* (1901), a masterpiece of the genre that was widely praised in the United States and popular in translation around the world. The early chapters included here reveal the physical and psychological realities of Washington's origins, realities that were shared by so many millions of the slaves set "free" at the conclusion of the Civil War. Later chapters show Washington at the peak of his success as an African American spokesperson, particularly as a master of rhetoric that allowed him to appear both as sincerely humble and as a force to be reckoned with, both as a man of selfless industry and as one of considerable political know-how.

Washington believed in rewarding deserving individuals rather than asking for policies treating African Americans as a population. His writings argue that success should be measured not so much by the position a person has reached as by the obstacles overcome while trying to succeed. In his work he urges African Americans to emulate the proverbial ship captain who urged his crew to "cast down your buckets where you are" even though they were still at sea, and who thus found fresh water at the mouth of a river. "Cast down your bucket where you are" was what he said to urge African Americans to start from wherever they happened to be rather than waiting for times to change. He argued that by seeking improvement African Americans would inevitably rise as individuals. Yet he also urged whites not to judge African American children against white children until they had had a chance to catch up in school. In short, Washington proposed a middle ground wherein African Americans would raise themselves by individual effort and white Americans would appreciate the efforts being made and judge accordingly.

*Up from Slavery* is as important as a literary production as it is as a record of a time, place, and person. Washington's skillful use of metaphor and symbol, his deftly masked ironies, and the art of his artlessness have been addressed by such critics as William L. Andrews, Houston A. Baker, Jr., and James M. Cox. Over the years, his assimilationist position has drawn criticism, most recently from Baker, but his legacy lives on and continues to inspire readers.

Washington was awarded an honorary degree by Harvard University, was invited to dine by President Theodore Roosevelt, was widely consulted on policy questions by white political and business leaders, effectively influenced the press, and controlled areas of public and private patronage. On November 5, 1915, Washington was taken ill and entered St. Luke's Hospital in New York City; diagnosed with arteriosclerosis, he was told that he did not have long to live. He traveled to Tuskegee, where he died on November 14. Over eight thousand people attended his funeral, which was held in the Tuskegee Institute Chapel.

## *From* Up from Slavery[1]

### Chapter I. A Slave among Slaves

I was born a slave on a plantation in Franklin County, Virginia. I am not quite sure of the exact place or exact date of my birth, but at any rate I suspect I must have been born somewhere and at some time. As nearly as I have been able to learn, I was born near a cross-roads post-office called Hale's Ford, and the year was 1858 or 1859.[2] I do not know the month or the day. The earliest impressions I can now recall are of the plantation and the slave quarters—the latter being the part of the plantation where the slaves had their cabins.

My life had its beginning in the midst of the most miserable, desolate, and discouraging surroundings. This was so, however, not because my owners were especially cruel, for they were not, as compared with many others. I was born in a typical log cabin, about fourteen by sixteen feet square. In this cabin I lived with my mother and a brother and sister till after the Civil War, when we were all declared free.

Of my ancestry I know almost nothing. In the slave quarters, and even later, I heard whispered conversations among the coloured people of the tortures which the slaves, including, no doubt, my ancestors on my mother's side, suffered in the middle passage of the slave ship while being conveyed from Africa

1. Published serially in *Outlook* from November 3, 1900, to February 23, 1901, *Up from Slavery* was first published in book form by Doubleday, Page and Company (1901), the source of the text printed here.

2. The first volume of Louis H. Harlan's biography, *Booker T. Washington: The Making of a Black Leader, 1856–1901*, establishes Washington's date of birth as 1856.

to America. I have been unsuccessful in securing any information that would throw any accurate light upon the history of my family beyond my mother. She, I remember, had a half-brother and a half-sister. In the days of slavery not very much attention was given to family history and family records—that is, black family records. My mother, I suppose, attracted the attention of a purchaser who was afterward my owner and hers. Her addition to the slave family attracted about as much attention as the purchase of a new horse or cow. Of my father I know even less than of my mother. I do not even know his name. I have heard reports to the effect that he was a white man who lived on one of the near-by plantations. Whoever he was, I never heard of his taking the least interest in me or providing in any way for my rearing. But I do not find especial fault with him. He was simply another unfortunate victim of the institution which the Nation unhappily had engrafted upon it at that time.

The cabin was not only our living-place, but was also used as the kitchen for the plantation. My mother was the plantation cook. The cabin was without glass windows; it had only openings in the side which let in the light, and also the cold, chilly air of winter. There was a door to the cabin—that is, something that was called a door—but the uncertain hinges by which it was hung, and the large cracks in it, to say nothing of the fact that it was too small, made the room a very uncomfortable one. In addition to these openings there was, in the lower right-hand corner of the room, the "cat-hole,"—a contrivance which almost every mansion or cabin in Virginia possessed during the ante-bellum period. The "cat-hole" was a square opening, about seven by eight inches, provided for the purpose of letting the cat pass in and out of the house at will during the night. In the case of our particular cabin I could never understand the necessity for this convenience, since there were at least a half-dozen other places in the cabin that would have accommodated the cats. There was no wooden floor in our cabin, the naked earth being used as a floor. In the centre of the earthen floor there was a large, deep opening covered with boards, which was used as a place in which to store sweet potatoes during the winter. An impression of this potato-hole is very distinctly engraved upon my memory, because I recall that during the process of putting the potatoes in or taking them out I would often come into possession of one or two, which I roasted and thoroughly enjoyed. There was no cooking-stove on our plantation, and all the cooking for the whites and slaves my mother had to do over an open fireplace, mostly in pots and "skillets." While the poorly built cabin caused us to suffer with cold in the winter, the heat from the open fireplace in summer was equally trying.

The early years of my life, which were spent in the little cabin, were not very different from those of thousands of other slaves. My mother, of course, had little time in which to give attention to the training of her children during the day. She snatched a few moments for our care in the early morning before her work began, and at night after the day's work was done. One of my earliest recollections is that of my mother cooking a chicken late at night, and awakening her children for the purpose of feeding them. How or where she got it I do not know. I presume, however, it was procured from our owner's farm. Some people may call this theft. If such a thing were to happen now, I should condemn it as theft myself. But taking place at the time it did, and for the reason that it did, no one could ever make me believe that my mother was guilty of thieving. She was simply a victim of the system of slavery. I cannot remember having slept in a bed until after our family was declared free by the Emancipation Proclamation.[3] Three children—John, my older brother, Amanda, my sister, and myself—had a pallet on the dirt floor, or, to be more correct, we slept in and on a bundle of filthy rags laid upon the dirt floor.

I was asked not long ago to tell something about the sports and pastimes that I engaged in during my youth. Until that question was asked it had never occurred to me that there was no period of my life that was devoted to play. From the time that I can remember anything, almost every day of my life has been occupied in some kind of labour; though I think I would now be a more useful man if I had had time for sports. During the period that I spent in slavery I was not large enough to be of much service, still I was occupied most of the time in cleaning the yards, carrying water to the men in the fields, or going to the mill, to which I used to take the corn, once a week, to be ground. The mill was about three miles from the plantation. This work I always dreaded. The heavy bag of corn would be thrown across the back of the horse, and the corn divided about evenly on each side; but in some way, almost without exception, on these trips, the corn would so shift as to become unbalanced and would fall off the horse, and often I would fall with it. As I was not strong enough to reload the corn upon the horse, I would have to wait, sometimes for many hours, till a chance passer-by came along who would help me out of my trouble. The hours while waiting for some one were usually spent in crying. The time consumed in this way made me late in reaching the mill, and by the time I got my corn ground and reached home it would be far into the night. The road was a lonely one, and often led through dense forests. I was always frightened. The woods were said to be full of soldiers who had deserted from the army, and I had been told that the first thing a deserter did to a Negro boy when he found him alone was to cut off his ears. Besides, when I was late in getting home I knew I would always get a severe scolding or a flogging.

I had no schooling whatever while I was a slave, though I remember on several occasions I went as far as the schoolhouse door with one of my young mistresses to carry her books. The picture of several dozen boys and girls in a schoolroom engaged in study made a deep impression upon me, and I had the feeling that to get into a schoolhouse and study in this way would be about the same as getting into paradise.

So far as I can now recall, the first knowledge that I got of the fact that we were slaves, and that freedom of the slaves was being discussed, was early one morning before day, when I was awakened by my mother kneeling over her children and fervently praying that Lincoln and his armies might be successful, and that one day she and her children might be free. In this connection I have never been able to understand how the slaves throughout the South, completely ignorant as were the masses so far as books or newspapers were concerned, were able to keep themselves so accurately and completely

3. Issued, after a long and complex birth, on January 1, 1863, the Emancipation Proclamation declared free all slaves in states in rebellion against the United States but exempted border slave states and all or part of three Confederate states controlled by the Union Army. These exceptions, which run contrary to popular understanding of the proclamation, suggest just how carefully President Lincoln felt obliged to proceed on the issue of slavery before and during the Civil War.

informed about the great National questions that were agitating the country. From the time that Garrison, Lovejoy,[4] and others began to agitate for freedom, the slaves throughout the South kept in close touch with the progress of the movement. Though I was a mere child during the preparation for the Civil War and during the war itself, I now recall the many late-at-night whispered discussions that I heard my mother and the other slaves on the plantation indulge in. These discussions showed that they understood the situation, and that they kept themselves informed of events by what was termed the "grape-vine" telegraph.

During the campaign when Lincoln was first a candidate for the Presidency, the slaves on our far-off plantation, miles from any railroad or large city or daily newspaper, knew what the issues involved were. When war was begun between the North and the South, every slave on our plantation felt and knew that, though other issues were discussed, the primal one was that of slavery. Even the most ignorant members of my race on the remote plantations felt in their hearts, with a certainty that admitted of no doubt, that the freedom of the slaves would be the one great result of the war, if the Northern armies conquered. Every success of the Federal armies and every defeat of the Confederate forces was watched with the keenest and most intense interest. Often the slaves got knowledge of the results of great battles before the white people received it. This news was usually gotten from the coloured man who was sent to the post-office for the mail. In our case the post-office was about three miles from the plantation, and the mail came once or twice a week. The man who was sent to the office would linger about the place long enough to get the drift of the conversation from the group of white people who naturally congregated there, after receiving their mail, to discuss the latest news. The mail-carrier on his way back to our master's house would as naturally retail the news that he had secured among the slaves, and in this way they often heard of important events before the white people at the "big house," as the master's house was called.

I cannot remember a single instance during my childhood or early boyhood when our entire family sat down to the table together, and God's blessing was asked, and the family ate a meal in a civilized manner. On the plantation in Virginia, and even later, meals were gotten by the children very much as dumb animals get theirs. It was a piece of bread here and a scrap of meat there. It was a cup of milk at one time and some potatoes at another. Sometimes a portion of our family would eat out of the skillet or pot, while some one else would eat from a tin plate held on the knees, and often using nothing but the hands with which to hold the food. When I had grown to sufficient size, I was required to go to the "big house" at meal-times to fan the flies from the table by means of a large set of paper fans operated by a pulley. Naturally much of the conversation of the white people turned upon the subject of freedom and the war, and I absorbed a good deal of it. I remember that at one time I saw two of my young mistresses and some lady visitors eating ginger-cakes, in the yard. At that time those cakes seemed to me to be absolutely the most tempting and desirable things that I had ever seen; and I then and there resolved that, if I ever got free, the height of my ambition would be reached if I could

4. Elijah P. Lovejoy (1802–1837), antislavery editor who was murdered by a mob while attempting to defend his press in Alton, Illinois. William Lloyd Garrison (1805–1879), editor of the *Liberator*—the leading antislavery newspaper—and leader of the American Anti-Slavery Society.

get to the point where I could secure and eat ginger-cakes in the way that I saw those ladies doing.

Of course as the war was prolonged the white people, in many cases, often found it difficult to secure food for themselves. I think the slaves felt the deprivation less than the whites, because the usual diet for the slaves was corn bread and pork, and these could be raised on the plantation; but coffee, tea, sugar, and other articles which the whites had been accustomed to use could not be raised on the plantation, and the conditions brought about by the war frequently made it impossible to secure these things. The whites were often in great straits. Parched corn was used for coffee, and a kind of black molasses was used instead of sugar. Many times nothing was used to sweeten the so-called tea and coffee.

The first pair of shoes that I recall wearing were wooden ones. They had rough leather on the top, but the bottoms, which were about an inch thick, were of wood. When I walked they made a fearful noise, and besides this they were very inconvenient, since there was no yielding to the natural pressure of the foot. In wearing them one presented an exceedingly awkward appearance. The most trying ordeal that I was forced to endure as a slave boy, however, was the wearing of a flax[5] shirt. In the portion of Virginia where I lived it was common to use flax as part of the clothing for the slaves. That part of the flax from which our clothing was made was largely the refuse, which of course was the cheapest and roughest part. I can scarcely imagine any torture, except, perhaps, the pulling of a tooth, that is equal to that caused by putting on a new flax shirt for the first time. It is almost equal to the feeling that one would experience if he had a dozen or more chestnut burrs, or a hundred small pin-points, in contact with his flesh. Even to this day I can recall accurately the tortures that I underwent when putting on one of these garments. The fact that my flesh was soft and tender added to the pain. But I had no choice. I had to wear the flax shirt or none; and had it been left to me to choose, I should have chosen to wear no covering. In connection with the flax shirt, my brother John, who is several years older than I am, performed one of the most generous acts that I ever heard of one slave relative doing for another. On several occasions when I was being forced to wear a new flax shirt, he generously agreed to put it on in my stead and wear it for several days, till it was "broken in." Until I had grown to be quite a youth this single garment was all that I wore.

One may get the idea, from what I have said, that there was bitter feeling toward the white people on the part of my race, because of the fact that most of the white population was away fighting in a war which would result in keeping the Negro in slavery if the South was successful. In the case of the slaves on our place this was not true, and it was not true of any large portion of the slave population in the South where the Negro was treated with anything like decency. During the Civil War one of my young masters was killed, and two were severely wounded. I recall the feeling of sorrow which existed among the slaves when they heard of the death of "Mars' Billy." It was no sham sorrow, but real. Some of the slaves had nursed "Mars' Billy"; others had played with him when he was a child. "Mars' Billy" had begged for mercy in

5. An ancient vegetable source for cloth and rope and the chief material of clothing in the United States until cotton came into widespread use in the early 19th century with the introduction of the cotton gin and industrial textile manufacturing methods.

the case of others when the overseer or master was thrashing them. The sorrow in the slave quarter was only second to that in the "big house." When the two young masters were brought home wounded, the sympathy of the slaves was shown in many ways. They were just as anxious to assist in the nursing as the family relatives of the wounded. Some of the slaves would even beg for the privilege of sitting up at night to nurse their wounded masters. This tenderness and sympathy on the part of those held in bondage was a result of their kindly and generous nature. In order to defend and protect the women and children who were left on the plantations when the white males went to war, the slaves would have laid down their lives. The slave who was selected to sleep in the "big house" during the absence of the males was considered to have the place of honour. Any one attempting to harm "young Mistress" or "old Mistress" during the night would have had to cross the dead body of the slave to do so. I do not know how many have noticed it, but I think that it will be found to be true that there are few instances, either in slavery or freedom, in which a member of my race has been known to betray a specific trust.

As a rule, not only did the members of my race entertain no feelings of bitterness against the whites before and during the war, but there are many instances of Negroes tenderly caring for their former masters and mistresses who for some reason have become poor and dependent since the war. I know of instances where the former masters of slaves have for years been supplied with money by their former slaves to keep them from suffering. I have known of still other cases in which the former slaves have assisted in the education of the descendants of their former owners. I know of a case on a large plantation in the South in which a young white man, the son of the former owner of the estate, has become so reduced in purse and self-control by reason of drink that he is a pitiable creature; and yet, notwithstanding the poverty of the coloured people themselves on this plantation, they have for years supplied this young white man with the necessities of life. One sends him a little coffee or sugar, another a little meat, and so on. Nothing that the coloured people possess is too good for the son of "old Mars' Tom," who will perhaps never be permitted to suffer while any remain on the place who knew directly or indirectly of "old Mars' Tom."

I have said that there are few instances of a member of my race betraying a specific trust. One of the best illustrations of this which I know of is in the case of an ex-slave from Virginia whom I met not long ago in a little town in the state of Ohio. I found that this man had made a contract with his master, two or three years previous to the Emancipation Proclamation, to the effect that the slave was to be permitted to buy himself, by paying so much per year for his body; and while he was paying for himself, he was to be permitted to labour where and for whom he pleased. Finding that he could secure better wages in Ohio, he went there. When freedom came, he was still in debt to his master some three hundred dollars. Notwithstanding that the Emancipation Proclamation freed him from any obligation to his master, this black man walked the greater portion of the distance back to where his old master lived in Virginia, and placed the last dollar, with interest, in his hands. In talking to me about this, the man told me that he knew that he did not have to pay the debt, but that he had given his word to his master, and his word he had never broken. He felt that he could not enjoy his freedom till he had fulfilled his promise.

From some things that I have said one may get the idea that some of the slaves did not want freedom. This is not true. I have never seen one who did not want to be free, or one who would return to slavery.

I pity from the bottom of my heart any nation or body of people that is so unfortunate as to get entangled in the net of slavery. I have long since ceased to cherish any spirit of bitterness against the Southern white people on account of the enslavement of my race. No one section of our country was wholly responsible for its introduction, and, besides, it was recognized and protected for years by the General Government. Having once got its tentacles fastened on to the economic and social life of the Republic, it was no easy matter for the country to relieve itself of the institution. Then, when we rid ourselves of prejudice, or racial feeling, and look facts in the face, we must acknowledge that, notwithstanding the cruelty and moral wrong of slavery, the ten million Negroes inhabiting this country, who themselves or whose ancestors went through the school of American slavery, are in a stronger and more hopeful condition, materially, intellectually, morally, and religiously, than is true of an equal number of black people in any other portion of the globe. This is so to such an extent that Negroes in this country, who themselves or whose forefathers went through the school of slavery, are constantly returning to Africa as missionaries to enlighten those who remained in the fatherland. This I say, not to justify slavery—on the other hand, I condemn it as an institution, as we all know that in America it was established for selfish and financial reasons, and not from a missionary motive—but to call attention to a fact, and to show how Providence so often uses men and institutions to accomplish a purpose. When persons ask me in these days how, in the midst of what sometimes seem hopelessly discouraging conditions, I can have such faith in the future of my race in this country, I remind them of the wilderness through which and out of which, a good Providence has already led us.

Ever since I have been old enough to think for myself, I have entertained the idea that, notwithstanding the cruel wrongs inflicted upon us, the black man got nearly as much out of slavery as the white man did. The hurtful influences of the institution were not by any means confined to the Negro. This was fully illustrated by the life upon our own plantation. The whole machinery of slavery was so constructed as to cause labour, as a rule, to be looked upon as a badge of degradation, of inferiority. Hence labour was something that both races on the slave plantation sought to escape. The slave system on our place, in a large measure, took the spirit of self-reliance and self-help out of the white people. My old master had many boys and girls, but not one, so far as I know, ever mastered a single trade or special line of productive industry. The girls were not taught to cook, sew, or to take care of the house. All of this was left to the slaves. The slaves, of course, had little personal interest in the life of the plantation, and their ignorance prevented them from learning how to do things in the most improved and thorough manner. As a result of the system, fences were out of repair, gates were hanging half off the hinges, doors creaked, window-panes were out, plastering had fallen but was not replaced, weeds grew in the yard. As a rule, there was food for whites and blacks, but inside the house, and on the dining-room table, there was wanting that delicacy and refinement of touch and finish which can make a home the most convenient, comfortable, and attractive place in the world. Withal there was a waste of food and other materials which was sad. When freedom came, the slaves were almost as well fitted to begin life anew as the master, except in the matter of book-learning and ownership of property. The slave owner and his sons had mastered no special industry. They unconsciously had imbibed the feeling that manual labour was not the proper thing for them. On the other hand, the slaves, in many cases, had mastered some handicraft, and none were ashamed, and few unwilling, to labour.

Finally the war closed, and the day of freedom came. It was a momentous and eventful day to all upon our plantation. We had been expecting it. Freedom was in the air, and had been for months. Deserting soldiers returning to their homes were to be seen every day. Others who had been discharged, or whose regiments had been paroled, were constantly passing near our place. The "grape-vine telegraph" was kept busy night and day. The news and mutterings of great events were swiftly carried from one plantation to another. In the fear of "Yankee" invasions, the silverware and other valuables were taken from the "big house," buried in the woods, and guarded by trusted slaves. Woe be to any one who would have attempted to disturb the buried treasure. The slaves would give the Yankee soldiers food, drink, clothing—anything but that which had been specifically intrusted to their care and honour. As the great day drew nearer, there was more singing in the slave quarters than usual. It was bolder, had more ring, and lasted later into the night. Most of the verses of the plantation songs had some reference to freedom. True, they had sung those same verses before, but they had been careful to explain that the "freedom" in these songs referred to the next world, and had no connection with life in this world. Now they gradually threw off the mask, and were not afraid to let it be known that the "freedom" in their songs meant freedom of the body in this world. The night before the eventful day, word was sent to the slave quarters to the effect that something unusual was going to take place at the "big house" the next morning. There was little, if any, sleep that night. All was excitement and expectancy. Early the next morning word was sent to all the slaves, old and young, to gather at the house. In company with my mother, brother, and sister, and a large number of other slaves, I went to the master's house. All of our master's family were either standing or seated on the veranda of the house, where they could see what was to take place and hear what was said. There was a feeling of deep interest, or perhaps sadness, on their faces, but not bitterness. As I now recall the impression they made upon me, they did not at the moment seem to be sad because of the loss of property, but rather because of parting with those whom they had reared and who were in many ways very close to them. The most distinct thing that I now recall in connection with the scene was that some man who seemed to be a stranger (a United States officer, I presume) made a little speech and then read a rather long paper—the Emancipation Proclamation, I think. After the reading we were told that we were all free, and could go when and where we pleased. My mother, who was standing by my side, leaned over and kissed her children, while tears of joy ran down her cheeks. She explained to us what it all meant, that this was the day for which she had been so long praying, but fearing that she would never live to see.

For some minutes there was great rejoicing, and thanksgiving, and wild scenes of ecstasy. But there was no feeling of bitterness. In fact, there was pity among the slaves for our former owners. The wild rejoicing on the part of the emancipated coloured people lasted but for a brief period, for I noticed that by the time they returned to their cabins there was a change in their feelings. The great responsibility of being free, of having charge of themselves, of having to think and plan for themselves and their children, seemed to take possession of them. It was very much like suddenly turning a youth of ten or twelve years out into the world to provide for himself. In a few hours the great questions with which the Anglo-Saxon race had been grappling for centuries had been thrown upon these people to be solved. These were the questions of a home, a living, the rearing of children, education, citizenship, and the establishment and support of churches. Was it any wonder that within a few hours the wild rejoicing ceased and a feeling of deep gloom seemed to pervade the slave quarters? To some it seemed that, now that they were in actual possession of it, freedom was a more serious thing than they had expected to find it. Some of the slaves were seventy or eighty years old; their best days were gone. They had no strength with which to earn a living in a strange place and among strange people, even if they had been sure where to find a new place of abode. To this class the problem seemed especially hard. Besides, deep down in their hearts there was a strange and peculiar attachment to "old Marster" and "old Missus," and to their children, which they found it hard to think of breaking off. With these they had spent in some cases nearly a half-century, and it was no light thing to think of parting. Gradually, one by one, stealthily at first, the older slaves began to wander from the slave quarters back to the "big house" to have a whispered conversation with their former owners as to the future.

## Chapter II. Boyhood Days

After the coming of freedom there were two points upon which practically all the people on our place were agreed, and I find that this was generally true throughout the South: that they must change their names, and that they must leave the old plantation for at least a few days or weeks in order that they might really feel sure that they were free.

In some way a feeling got among the coloured people that it was far from proper for them to bear the surname of their former owners, and a great many of them took other surnames. This was one of the first signs of freedom. When they were slaves, a coloured person was simply called "John" or "Susan." There was seldom occasion for more than the use of the one name. If "John" or "Susan" belonged to a white man by the name of "Hatcher," sometimes he was called "John Hatcher," or as often "Hatcher's John." But there was a feeling that "John Hatcher" or "Hatcher's John" was not the proper title by which to denote a freeman; and so in many cases "John Hatcher" was changed to "John S. Lincoln" or "John S. Sherman," the initial "S" standing for no name, it being simply a part of what the coloured man proudly called his "entitles."

As I have stated, most of the coloured people left the old plantation for a short while at least, so as to be sure, it seemed, that they could leave and try their freedom on to see how it felt. After they had remained away for a time, many of the older slaves, especially, returned to their old homes and made some kind of contract with their former owners by which they remained on the estate.

My mother's husband, who was the stepfather of my brother John and myself, did not belong to the same owners as did my mother. In fact, he seldom came to our plantation. I remember seeing him there perhaps once a year, that being about Christmas time. In some way, during the war, by running away and following the Federal soldiers, it seems, he found his way into the new state of West Virginia. As soon as freedom was declared, he sent for my mother to come to the Kanawha Valley, in West Virginia. At that time a journey from Virginia over the mountains to West Virginia was rather a tedious and in some cases a painful undertaking. What little clothing and few household goods we had were placed in a cart, but the children walked the greater portion of the distance, which was several hundred miles.

I do not think any of us ever had been very far from the plantation, and the taking of a long journey into another state was quite an event. The parting from our former owners and the members of our own race on the plantation was a serious occasion. From the time of our parting till their death we kept up a correspondence with the older members of the family, and in later years we have kept in touch with those who were the younger members. We were several weeks making the trip, and most of the time we slept in the open air and did our cooking over a log fire out-of-doors. One night I recall that we camped near an abandoned log cabin, and my mother decided to build a fire in that for cooking, and afterward to make a "pallet" on the floor for our sleeping. Just as the fire had gotten well started a large black snake fully a yard and a half long dropped down the chimney and ran out on the floor. Of course we at once abandoned that cabin. Finally we reached our destination—a little town called Malden, which is about five miles from Charleston, the present capital of the state.

At that time salt-mining was the great industry in that part of West Virginia, and the little town of Malden was right in the midst of the salt-furnaces. My stepfather had already secured a job at a salt-furnace, and he had also secured a little cabin for us to live in. Our new house was no better than the one we had left on the old plantation in Virginia. In fact, in one respect it was worse. Notwithstanding the poor condition of our plantation cabin, we were at all times sure of pure air. Our new home was in the midst of a cluster of cabins crowded closely together, and as there were no sanitary regulations, the filth about the cabins was often intolerable. Some of our neighbours were coloured people, and some were the poorest and most ignorant and degraded white people. It was a motley mixture. Drinking, gambling, quarrels, fights, and shockingly immoral practices were frequent. All who lived in the little town were in one way or another connected with the salt business. Though I was a mere child, my stepfather put me and my brother at work in one of the furnaces. Often I began work as early as four o'clock in the morning.

The first thing I ever learned in the way of book knowledge was while working in this salt-furnace. Each salt-packer had his barrels marked with a certain number. The number allotted to my stepfather was "18." At the close of the day's work the boss of the packers would come around and put "18" on each of our barrels, and I soon learned to recognize that figure wherever I saw it, and after a while got to the point where I could make that figure, though I knew nothing about any other figures or letters.

From the time that I can remember having any thoughts about anything, I recall that I had an intense longing to learn to read. I determined, when quite a small child, that, if I accomplished nothing else in life, I would in some way get enough education to enable me to read common books and newspapers. Soon after we got settled in some manner in our new cabin in West Virginia, I induced my mother to get hold of a book for me. How or where she got it I do not know, but in some way she procured an old copy of Webster's[6] "blue-back" spelling-book, which contained the alphabet, followed by such meaningless words as "ab," "ba," "ca," "da." I began at once to devour this book, and I think that it was the first one I ever had in my hands. I had learned from somebody that the way to begin to read was to learn the alphabet, so I tried in all the ways I could think of to learn it,—all of course without a teacher, for I could find no one to teach me. At that time there was not a single member of my race anywhere near us who could read, and I was too timid to approach any of the white people. In some way, within a few weeks, I mastered the greater portion of the alphabet. In all my efforts to learn to read my mother shared fully my ambition, and sympathized with me and aided me in every way that she could. Though she was totally ignorant, so far as mere book knowledge was concerned, she had high ambitions for her children, and a large fund of good, hard, common sense which seemed to enable her to meet and master every situation. If I have done anything in life worth attention, I feel sure that I inherited the disposition from my mother.

In the midst of my struggles and longing for an education, a young coloured boy who had learned to read in the state of Ohio came to Malden. As soon as the coloured people found out that he could read, a newspaper was secured, and at the close of nearly every day's work this young man would be surrounded by a group of men and women who were anxious to hear him read the news contained in the papers. How I used to envy this man! He seemed to me to be the one young man in all the world who ought to be satisfied with his attainments.

About this time the question of having some kind of a school opened for the coloured children in the village began to be discussed by members of the race. As it would be the first school for Negro children that had ever been opened in that part of Virginia, it was, of course, to be a great event, and the discussion excited the widest interest. The most perplexing question was where to find a teacher. The young man from Ohio who had learned to read the papers was considered, but his age was against him. In the midst of the discussion about a teacher, another young coloured man from Ohio, who had been a soldier, in some way found his way into town. It was soon learned that he possessed considerable education, and he was engaged by the coloured people to teach their first school. As yet no free schools had been started for coloured people in that section, hence each family agreed to pay a certain amount per month, with the understanding that the teacher was to "board 'round"—that is, spend a day with each family. This was not bad for the teacher, for each family tried to provide the very best on the day the teacher was to be its guest. I recall that I looked forward with an anxious appetite to the "teacher's day" at our little cabin.

This experience of a whole race beginning to go to school for the first time, presents one of the most interesting studies that has ever occurred in

6. Noah Webster (1758–1843), famous orator and politician, was the author of the most widely used spelling books in the United States.

connection with the development of any race. Few people who were not right in the midst of the scenes can form any exact idea of the intense desire which the people of my race showed for an education. As I have stated, it was a whole race trying to go to school. Few were too young, and none too old, to make the attempt to learn. As fast as any kind of teachers could be secured, not only were day-schools filled, but night-schools as well. The great ambition of the older people was to try to learn to read the Bible before they died. With this end in view, men and women who were fifty or seventy-five years old would often be found in the night-school. Sunday-schools were formed soon after freedom, but the principal book studied in the Sunday-school was the spelling-book. Day-school, night-school, Sunday-school, were always crowded, and often many had to be turned away for want of room.

The opening of the school in the Kanawha Valley, however, brought to me one of the keenest disappointments that I ever experienced. I had been working in a salt-furnace for several months, and my stepfather had discovered that I had a financial value, and so, when the school opened, he decided that he could not spare me from my work. This decision seemed to cloud my every ambition. The disappointment was made all the more severe by reason of the fact that my place of work was where I could see the happy children passing to and from school, mornings and afternoons. Despite this disappointment, however, I determined that I would learn something, anyway. I applied myself with greater earnestness than ever to the mastering of what was in the "blue-back" speller.

My mother sympathized with me in my disappointment, and sought to comfort me in all the ways she could, and to help me find a way to learn. After a while I succeeded in making arrangements with the teacher to give me some lessons at night, after the day's work was done. These night lessons were so welcome that I think I learned more at night than the other children did during the day. My own experiences in the night-school gave me faith in the night-school idea, with which, in after years, I had to do both at Hampton and Tuskegee. But my boyish heart was still set upon going to the day-school, and I let no opportunity slip to push my case. Finally I won, and was permitted to go to the school in the day for a few months, with the understanding that I was to rise early in the morning and work in the furnace till nine o'clock, and return immediately after school closed in the afternoon for at least two more hours of work.

The schoolhouse was some distance from the furnace, and as I had to work till nine o'clock, and the school opened at nine, I found myself in a difficulty. School would always be begun before I reached it, and sometimes my class had recited. To get around this difficulty I yielded to a temptation for which most people, I suppose, will condemn me; but since it is a fact, I might as well state it. I have great faith in the power and influence of facts. It is seldom that anything is permanently gained by holding back a fact. There was a large clock in a little office in the furnace. This clock, of course, all the hundred or more workmen depended upon to regulate their hours of beginning and ending the day's work. I got the idea that the way for me to reach school on time was to move the clock hands from half-past eight up to the nine o'clock mark. This I found myself doing morning after morning, till the furnace "boss" discovered that something was wrong, and locked the clock in a case.

I did not mean to inconvenience anybody. I simply meant to reach that schoolhouse in time.

When, however, I found myself at the school for the first time, I also found myself confronted with two other difficulties. In the first place, I found that all of the other children wore hats or caps on their heads, and I had neither hat nor cap. In fact, I do not remember that up to the time of going to school I had ever worn any kind of covering upon my head, nor do I recall that either I or anybody else had even thought anything about the need of covering for my head. But, of course, when I saw how all the other boys were dressed, I began to feel quite uncomfortable. As usual, I put the case before my mother, and she explained to me that she had no money with which to buy a "store hat," which was a rather new institution at that time among the members of my race and was considered quite the thing for young and old to own, but that she would find a way to help me out of the difficulty. She accordingly got two pieces of "homespun" (jeans) and sewed them together, and I was soon the proud possessor of my first cap.

The lesson that my mother taught me in this has always remained with me, and I have tried as best I could to teach it to others. I have always felt proud, whenever I think of the incident, that my mother had strength of character enough not to be led into the temptation of seeming to be that which she was not—of trying to impress my schoolmates and others with the fact that she was able to buy me a "store hat" when she was not. I have always felt proud that she refused to go into debt for that which she did not have the money to pay for. Since that time I have owned many kinds of caps and hats, but never one of which I have felt so proud as of the cap made of the two pieces of cloth sewed together by my mother. I have noted the fact, but without satisfaction, I need not add, that several of the boys who began their careers with "store hats" and who were my schoolmates and used to join in the sport that was made of me because I had only a "homespun" cap, have ended their careers in the penitentiary, while others are not able now to buy any kind of hat.

My second difficulty was with regard to my name, or rather *a* name. From the time when I could remember anything, I had been called simply "Booker." Before going to school it had never occurred to me that it was needful or appropriate to have an additional name. When I heard the school-roll called, I noticed that all of the children had at least two names, and some of them indulged in what seemed to me the extravagance of having three. I was in deep perplexity, because I knew that the teacher would demand of me at least two names, and I had only one. By the time the occasion came for the enrolling of my name, an idea occurred to me which I thought would make me equal to the situation; and so, when the teacher asked me what my full name was, I calmly told him "Booker Washington," as if I had been called by that name all my life; and by that name I have since been known. Later in my life I found that my mother had given me the name of "Booker Taliaferro" soon after I was born, but in some way that part of my name seemed to disappear and for a long while was forgotten, but as soon as I found out about it I revived it, and made my full name "Booker Taliaferro Washington." I think there are not many men in our country who have had the privilege of naming themselves in the way that I have.

More than once I have tried to picture myself in the position of a boy or man with an honoured and distinguished ancestry which I could trace back through a period of hundreds of years, and who had not only inherited a name, but fortune and a proud family homestead; and yet I have sometimes had the feeling that if I had inherited these, and had been a member of a more popular race, I should have been inclined to yield to the temptation of depending upon my ancestry and my colour to do that for me which I should do for myself. Years ago I resolved that because I had no ancestry myself I would leave a record of which my children would be proud, and which might encourage them to still higher effort.

The world should not pass judgment upon the Negro, and especially the Negro youth, too quickly or too harshly. The Negro boy has obstacles, discouragements, and temptations to battle with that are little known to those not situated as he is. When a white boy undertakes a task, it is taken for granted that he will succeed. On the other hand, people are usually surprised if the Negro boy does not fail. In a word, the Negro youth starts out with the presumption against him.

The influence of ancestry, however, is important in helping forward any individual or race, if too much reliance is not placed upon it. Those who constantly direct attention to the Negro youth's moral weaknesses, and compare his advancement with that of white youths, do not consider the influence of the memories which cling about the old family homesteads. I have no idea, as I have stated elsewhere, who my grandmother was. I have, or have had, uncles and aunts and cousins, but I have no knowledge as to where most of them are. My case will illustrate that of hundreds of thousands of black people in every part of our country. The very fact that the white boy is conscious that, if he fails in life, he will disgrace the whole family record, extending back through many generations, is of tremendous value in helping him to resist temptations. The fact that the individual has behind and surrounding him proud family history and connection serves as a stimulus to help him to overcome obstacles when striving for success.

The time that I was permitted to attend school during the day was short, and my attendance was irregular. It was not long before I had to stop attending day-school altogether, and devote all of my time again to work. I resorted to the night-school again. In fact, the greater part of the education I secured in my boyhood was gathered through the night-school after my day's work was done. I had difficulty often in securing a satisfactory teacher. Sometimes, after I had secured some one to teach me at night, I would find, much to my disappointment, that the teacher knew but little more than I did. Often I would have to walk several miles at night in order to recite my night-school lessons. There was never a time in my youth, no matter how dark and discouraging the days might be, when one resolve did not continually remain with me, and that was a determination to secure an education at any cost.

Soon after we moved to West Virginia, my mother adopted into our family, notwithstanding our poverty, an orphan boy, to whom afterward we gave the name of James B. Washington. He has ever since remained a member of the family.

After I had worked in the salt-furnace for some time, work was secured for me in a coal-mine which was operated mainly for the purpose of securing fuel for the salt-furnace. Work in the coal-mine I always dreaded. One reason for this was that any one who worked in a coal-mine was always unclean, at least while at work, and it was a very hard job to get one's skin clean after the day's work was over. Then it was fully a mile from the opening of the coal-mine to the face of the coal, and all, of course, was in the blackest darkness. I do not believe that one ever experiences anywhere else such darkness as he does in a coal-mine. The mine was divided into a large number of different "rooms" or departments, and, as I never was able to learn the location of all these "rooms," I many times found myself lost in the mine. To add to the horror of being lost, sometimes my light would go out, and then, if I did not happen to have a match, I would wander about in the darkness until by chance I found some one to give me a light. The work was not only hard, but it was dangerous. There was always the danger of being blown to pieces by a premature explosion of powder, or of being crushed by falling slate. Accidents from one or the other of these causes were frequently occurring, and this kept me in constant fear. Many children of the tenderest years were compelled then, as is now true I fear, in most coal-mining districts, to spend a large part of their lives in these coal-mines, with little opportunity to get an education; and, what is worse, I have often noted that, as a rule, young boys who begin life in a coal-mine are often physically and mentally dwarfed. They soon lose ambition to do anything else than to continue as a coal-miner.

In those days, and later as a young man, I used to try to picture in my imagination the feelings and ambitions of a white boy with absolutely no limit placed upon his aspirations and activities. I used to envy the white boy who had no obstacles placed in the way of his becoming a Congressman, Governor, Bishop, or President by reason of the accident of his birth or race. I used to picture the way that I would act under such circumstances; how I would begin at the bottom and keep rising until I reached the highest round of success.

In later years, I confess that I do not envy the white boy as I once did. I have learned that success is to be measured not so much by the position that one has reached in life as by the obstacles which he has overcome while trying to succeed. Looked at from this standpoint, I almost reach the conclusion that often the Negro boy's birth and connection with an unpopular race is an advantage, so far as real life is concerned. With few exceptions, the Negro youth must work harder and must perform his tasks even better than a white youth in order to secure recognition. But out of the hard and unusual struggle through which he is compelled to pass, he gets a strength, a confidence, that one misses whose pathway is comparatively smooth by reason of birth and race.

From any point of view, I had rather be what I am, a member of the Negro race, than be able to claim membership with the most favoured of any other race. I have always been made sad when I have heard members of any race claiming rights and privileges, or certain badges of distinction, on the ground simply that they were members of this or that race, regardless of their own individual worth or attainments. I have been made to feel sad for such persons because I am conscious of the fact that mere connection with what is known as a superior race will not permanently carry an individual forward unless he has individual worth, and mere connection with what is regarded as an inferior race will not finally hold an individual back if he possesses intrinsic, individual merit. Every persecuted individual and race should get much consolation out of the great human law, which is universal and eternal, that merit, no matter under what skin found, is, in the long run, recognized and rewarded. This I have said here, not to call attention to myself as an individual, but to the race to which I am proud to belong.

\* \* \*

### Chapter XIV. The Atlanta Exposition Address

The Atlanta Exposition, at which I had been asked to make an address as a representative of the Negro race, as stated in the last chapter, was opened with a short address from Governor Bullock. After other interesting exercises, including an invocation from Bishop Nelson, of Georgia, a dedicatory ode by Albert Howell, Jr., and addresses by the President of the Exposition and Mrs. Joseph Thompson, the President of the Woman's Board, Governor Bullock introduced me with the words, "We have with us to-day a representative of Negro enterprise and Negro civilization."

When I arose to speak, there was considerable cheering, especially from the coloured people. As I remember it now, the thing that was uppermost in my mind was the desire to say something that would cement the friendship of the races and bring about hearty coöperation between them. So far as my outward surroundings were concerned, the only thing that I recall distinctly now is that when I got up, I saw thousands of eyes looking intently into my face. The following is the address which I delivered:—

> Mr. President and Gentlemen of the Board of Directors and Citizens:
> One-third of the population of the South is of the Negro race. No enterprise seeking the material, civil, or moral welfare of this section can disregard this element of our population and reach the highest success. I but convey to you, Mr. President and Directors, the sentiment of the masses of my race when I say that in no way have the value and manhood of the American Negro been more fittingly and generously recognized than by the managers of this magnificent Exposition at every stage of its progress. It is a recognition that will do more to cement the friendship of the two races than any occurrence since the dawn of our freedom.
>
> Not only this, but the opportunity here afforded will awaken among us a new era of industrial progress. Ignorant and inexperienced, it is not strange that in the first years of our new life we began at the top instead of at the bottom; that a seat in Congress or the state legislature was more sought than real estate or industrial skill; that the political convention or stump speaking had more attractions than starting a dairy farm or truck garden.
>
> A ship lost at sea for many days suddenly sighted a friendly vessel. From the mast of the unfortunate vessel was seen a signal, "Water, water; we die of thirst!" The answer from the friendly vessel at once came back, "Cast down your bucket where you are." A second time the signal, "Water, water; send us water!" ran up from the distressed vessel, and was answered, "Cast down your bucket where you are." And a third and fourth signal for water was answered, "Cast down your bucket where you are." The captain of the distressed vessel, at last heeding the injunction, cast down his bucket, and it came up full of fresh, sparkling water from

the mouth of the Amazon River. To those of my race who depend on bettering their condition in a foreign land or who underestimate the importance of cultivating friendly relations with the Southern white man, who is their next-door neighbour, I would say: "Cast down your bucket where you are"—cast it down in making friends in every manly way of the people of all races by whom we are surrounded.

Cast it down in agriculture, mechanics, in commerce, in domestic service, and in the professions. And in this connection it is well to bear in mind that whatever other sins the South may be called to bear, when it comes to business, pure and simple, it is in the South that the Negro is given a man's chance in the commercial world, and in nothing is this Exposition more eloquent than in emphasizing this chance. Our greatest danger is that in the great leap from slavery to freedom we may overlook the fact that the masses of us are to live by the productions of our hands, and fail to keep in mind that we shall prosper in proportion as we learn to dignify and glorify common labour and put brains and skill into the common occupations of life; shall prosper in proportion as we learn to draw the line between the superficial and the substantial, the ornamental gewgaws of life and the useful. No race can prosper till it learns that there is as much dignity in tilling a field as in writing a poem. It is at the bottom of life we must begin, and not at the top. Nor should we permit our grievances to overshadow our opportunities.

To those of the white race who look to the incoming of those of foreign birth and strange tongue and habits for the prosperity of the South, were I permitted I would repeat what I say to my own race, "Cast down your bucket where you are." Cast it down among the eight millions of Negroes whose habits you know, whose fidelity and love you have tested in days when to have proved treacherous meant the ruin of your firesides. Cast down your bucket among these people who have, without strikes and labour wars, tilled your fields, cleared your forests, builded your railroads and cities, and brought forth treasures from the bowels of the earth, and helped make possible this magnificent representation of the progress of the South. Casting down your bucket among my people, helping and encouraging them as you are doing on these grounds, and to education of head, hand, and heart, and you will find that they will buy your surplus land, make blossom the waste places in your fields, and run your factories. While doing this, you can be sure in the future, as in the past, that you and your families will be surrounded by the most patient, faithful, law-abiding, and unresentful people that the world has seen. As we have proved our loyalty to you in the past, in nursing your children, watching by the sick-bed of your mothers and fathers, and often following them with tear-dimmed eyes to their graves, so in the future, in our humble way, we shall stand by you with a devotion that no foreigner can approach, ready to lay down our lives, if need be, in defence of yours, interlacing our industrial, commercial, civil, and religious life with yours in a way that shall make the interests of both races one. In all things that are purely social we can be as separate as the fingers, yet one as the hand in all things essential to mutual progress.

There is no defence or security for any of us except in the highest intelligence and development of all. If anywhere there are efforts tending to curtail the fullest growth of the Negro, let these efforts be turned into stimulating, encouraging, and making him the most useful and intelligent citizen. Effort or means so invested will pay a thousand per cent interest. These efforts will be twice blessed—"blessing him that gives and him that takes."[7]

There is no escape through law of man or God from the inevitable:—

> "The laws of changeless justice bind
> Oppressor with oppressed;
> And close as sin and suffering joined
> We march to fate abreast."[8]

Nearly sixteen millions of hands will aid you in pulling the load upward, or they will pull against you the load downward. We shall constitute one-third and more of the ignorance and crime of the South, or one-third its intelligence and progress; we shall contribute one-third to the business and industrial prosperity of the South, or we shall prove a veritable body of death, stagnating, depressing, retarding every effort to advance the body politic.

Gentlemen of the Exposition, as we present to you our humble effort at an exhibition of our progress, you must not expect overmuch. Starting thirty years ago with ownership here and there in a few quilts and pumpkins and chickens (gathered from miscellaneous sources), remember the path that has led from these to the inventions and production of agricultural implements, buggies, steam-engines, newspapers, books, statuary, carving, paintings, the management of drug-stores and banks, has not been trodden without contact with thorns and thistles. While we take pride in what we exhibit as a result of our independent efforts, we do not for a moment forget that our part in this exhibition would fall far short of your expectations but for the constant help that has come to our educational life, not only from the Southern states, but especially from Northern philanthropists, who have made their gifts a constant stream of blessing and encouragement.

The wisest among my race understand that the agitation of questions of social equality is the extremest folly, and that progress in the enjoyment of all the privileges that will come to us must be the result of severe and constant struggle rather than of artificial forcing. No race that has anything to contribute to the markets of the world is long in any degree ostracized. It is important and right that all privileges of the law be ours, but it is vastly more important that we be prepared for the exercises of these privileges. The opportunity to earn a dollar in a factory just now is worth infinitely more than the opportunity to spend a dollar in an opera-house.

In conclusion, may I repeat that nothing in thirty years has given us more hope and encouragement, and drawn us so near to you of the white race, as this opportunity offered by the Exposition; and here bending, as it were, over the altar that represents the results of the struggles of your race and mine, both starting practically empty-handed three decades ago, I pledge that in your effort to work out the great and intricate problem which God has laid at the doors of the South, you shall have at all times

---

7. "It blesseth him that gives and him that takes" (Shakespeare, *The Merchant of Venice* 3.1.167).

8. John Greenleaf Whittier (1807–1892), "Song of Negro Boatmen."

the patient, sympathetic help of my race; only let this be constantly in mind, that, while from representations in these buildings of the product of field, of forest, of mine, of factory, letters, and art, much good will come, yet far above and beyond material benefits will be that higher good, that, let us pray God, will come, in a blotting out of sectional differences and racial animosities and suspicions, in a determination to administer absolute justice, in a willing obedience among all classes to the mandates of law. This, this, coupled with our material prosperity, will bring into our beloved South a new heaven and a new earth.

The first thing that I remember, after I had finished speaking, was that Governor Bullock rushed across the platform and took me by the hand, and that others did the same. I received so many and such hearty congratulations that I found it difficult to get out of the building. I did not appreciate to any degree, however, the impression which my address seemed to have made, until the next morning, when I went into the business part of the city. As soon as I was recognized, I was surprised to find myself pointed out and surrounded by a crowd of men who wished to shake hands with me. This was kept up on every street on to which I went, to an extent which embarrassed me so much that I went back to my boarding-place. The next morning I returned to Tuskegee. At the station in Atlanta, and at almost all of the stations at which the train stopped between the city and Tuskegee, I found a crowd of people anxious to shake hands with me.

The papers in all the parts of the United States published the address in full, and for months afterward there were complimentary editorial references to it. Mr. Clark Howell, the editor of the Atlanta *Constitution,* telegraphed to a New York paper, among other words, the following, "I do not exaggerate when I say that Professor Booker T. Washington's address yesterday was one of the most notable speeches, both as to character and as to the warmth of its reception, ever delivered to a Southern audience. The address was a revelation. The whole speech is a platform upon which blacks and whites can stand with full justice to each other."

The Boston *Transcript* said editorially: "The speech of Booker T. Washington at the Atlanta Exposition, this week, seems to have dwarfed all the other proceedings and the Exposition itself. The sensation that it has caused in the press has never been equalled."

I very soon began receiving all kinds of propositions from lecture bureaus, and editors of magazines and papers, to take the lecture platform, and to write articles. One lecture bureau offered me fifty thousand dollars, or two hundred dollars a night and expenses, if I would place my services at its disposal for a given period. To all these communications I replied that my life-work was at Tuskegee; and that whenever I spoke it must be in the interests of the Tuskegee school and my race, and that I would enter into no arrangements that seemed to place a mere commercial value upon my services.

Some days after its delivery I sent a copy of my address to the President of the United States, the Hon. Grover Cleveland.[9] I received from him the following autograph reply:—

9. Cleveland (1837–1908), twenty-second (1885–89) and twenty-fourth (1893–97) president of the United States.

Gray Gables
Buzzard's Bay, Mass., October 6, 1895

Booker T. Washington, Esq.:

My Dear Sir: I thank you for sending me a copy of your address delivered at the Atlanta Exposition.

I thank you with much enthusiasm for making the address. I have read it with intense interest, and I think the Exposition would be fully justified if it did not do more than furnish the opportunity for its delivery. Your words cannot fail to delight and encourage all who wish well for your race; and if our coloured fellow-citizens do not from your utterances father new hope and form new determinations to gain every valuable advantage offered them by their citizenship, it will be strange indeed. Yours very truly,

Grover Cleveland

Later I met Mr. Cleveland, for the first time, when, as President, he visited the Atlanta Exposition. At the request of myself and others he consented to spend an hour in the Negro Building, for the purpose of inspecting the Negro exhibit and of giving the coloured people in attendance an opportunity to shake hands with him. As soon as I met Mr. Cleveland I became impressed with his simplicity, greatness, and rugged honesty. I have met him many times since then, both at public functions and at his private residence in Princeton, and the more I see of him the more I admire him. When he visited the Negro Building in Atlanta he seemed to give himself up wholly, for that hour, to the coloured people. He seemed to be as careful to shake hands with some old coloured "auntie" clad partially in rags, and to take as much pleasure in doing so, as if he were greeting some millionaire. Many of the coloured people took advantage of the occasion to get him to write his name in a book or on a slip of paper. He was as careful and patient in doing this as if he were putting his signature to some great state document.

Mr. Cleveland has not only shown his friendship for me in many personal ways, but has always consented to do anything I have asked of him for our school. This he has done, whether it was to make a personal donation or to use his influence in securing the donations of others. Judging from my personal acquaintance with Mr. Cleveland, I do not believe that he is conscious of possessing any colour prejudice. He is too great for that. In my contact with people I find that, as a rule, it is only the little, narrow people who live for themselves, who never read good books, who do not travel, who never open up their souls in a way to permit them to come into contact with other souls— with the great outside world. No man whose vision is bounded by colour can come into contact with what is highest and best in the world. In meeting men, in many places, I have found that the happiest people are those who do the most for others; the most miserable are those who do the least. I have also found that few things, if any, are capable of making one so blind and narrow as race prejudice. I often say to our students, in the course of my talks to them on Sunday evenings in the chapel, that the longer I live and the more experience I have of the world, the more I am convinced that, after all, the one thing that is most worth living for—and dying for, if need be—is the opportunity of making some one else more happy and more useful.

The coloured people and the coloured newspapers at first seemed to be greatly pleased with the character of my Atlanta address, as well as with its reception. But after the first burst of enthusiasm began to die away, and the coloured people began reading the speech in cold type, some of them seemed to feel that they had been hypnotized. They seemed to feel that I had been too liberal in my remarks toward the Southern whites, and that I had not spoken out strongly enough for what they termed the "rights" of the race. For a while there was a reaction, so far as a certain element of my own race was concerned, but later these reactionary ones seemed to have been won over to my way of believing and acting.

While speaking of changes in public sentiment, I recall that about ten years after the school at Tuskegee was established, I had an experience that I shall never forget. Dr. Lyman Abbott, then the pastor of Plymouth Church, and also editor of the *Outlook* (then the *Christian Union*), asked me to write a letter for his paper giving my opinion of the exact condition, mental and moral of the coloured ministers in the South, as based upon my observations. I wrote the letter, giving the exact facts as I conceived them to be. The picture painted was a rather black one—or, since I am black, shall I say "white"? It could not be otherwise with a race but a few years out of slavery, a race which had not had time or opportunity to produce a competent ministry.

What I said soon reached every Negro minister in the country, I think, and the letters of condemnation which I received from them were not few. I think that for a year after the publication of this article every association and every conference or religious body of any kind, of my race, that met, did not fail before adjourning to pass a resolution condemning me, or calling upon me to retract or modify what I had said. Many of these organizations went so far in their resolutions as to advise parents to cease sending their children to Tuskegee. One association even appointed a "missionary" whose duty it was to warn the people against sending their children to Tuskegee. This missionary had a son in the school, and I noticed that, whatever the "missionary" might have said or done with regard to others, he was careful not to take his son away from the institution. Many of the coloured papers, especially those that were the organs of religious bodies, joined in the general chorus of condemnation or demands for retraction.

During the whole time of the excitement, and through all the criticism, I did not utter a word of explanation or retraction. I knew that I was right, and that time and the sober second thought of the people would vindicate me. It was not long before the bishops and other church leaders began to make a careful investigation of the conditions of the ministry, and they found out that I was right. In fact, the oldest and most influential bishop in one branch of the Methodist Church said that my words were far too mild. Very soon public sentiment began making itself felt, in demanding a purifying of the ministry. While this is not yet complete by any means, I think I may say, without egotism, and I have been told by many of our most influential ministers, that my words had much to do with starting a demand for the placing of a higher type of men in the pulpit. I have had the satisfaction of having many who once condemned me thank me heartily for my frank words.

The change of the attitude of the Negro ministry, so far as regards myself, is so complete that at the present time I have no warmer friends among any class than I have among the clergymen. The improvement in the character and life of the Negro ministers is one of the most gratifying evidences of the progress of the race. My experience with them, as well as other events in my life, convince me that the thing to do, when one feels sure that he has said or done the right thing, and is condemned, is to stand still and keep quiet. If he is right, time will show it.

In the midst of the discussion which was going on concerning my Atlanta speech, I received a letter which I give below, from Dr. Gilman, the President of Johns Hopkins University, who had been made chairman of the judges of award in connection with the Atlanta Exposition:—

> Johns Hopkins University, Baltimore
> President's Office, September 30, 1895
>
> Dear Mr. Washington: Would it be agreeable to you to be one of the Judges of Award in the Department of Education at Atlanta? If so, I shall be glad to place your name upon the list. A line by telegraph will be welcomed. Yours very truly,
>
> D. C. Gilman

I think I was even more surprised to receive this invitation than I had been to receive the invitation to speak at the opening of the Exposition. It was to be a part of my duty, as one of the jurors, to pass not only upon the exhibits of the coloured schools, but also upon those of the white schools. I accepted the position, and spent a month in Atlanta in performance of the duties which it entailed. The board of jurors was a large one, consisting in all of sixty members. It was about equally divided between Southern white people and Northern white people. Among them were college presidents, leading scientists and men of letters, and specialists in many subjects. When the group of jurors to which I was assigned met for organization, Mr. Thomas Nelson Page,[1] who was one of the number, moved that I be made secretary of that division, and the motion was unanimously adopted. Nearly half of our division were Southern people. In performing my duties in the inspection of the exhibits of white schools I was in every case treated with respect, and at the close of our labours I parted from my associates with regret.

I am often asked to express myself more freely than I do upon the political condition and the political future of my race. These recollections of my experience in Atlanta give me the opportunity to do so briefly. My own belief is, although I have never before said so in so many words, that the time will come when the Negro in the South will be accorded all the political rights which his ability, character, and material possessions entitle him to. I think, though, that the opportunity to freely exercise such political rights will not come in any large degree through outside or artificial forcing, but will be accorded to the Negro by the Southern white people themselves, and that they will protect him in the exercise of those rights. Just as soon as the South gets over the old feeling that it is being forced by "foreigners," or "aliens," to do something which it does not want to do, I believe that the change in the direction that I have indicated is going to begin. In fact, there are indications that it is already beginning in a slight degree.

Let me illustrate my meaning. Suppose that some months before the open-

---

1. American author and diplomat (1853–1922).

ing of the Atlanta Exposition there had been a general demand from the press and public platform outside the South that a Negro be given a place on the opening programme, and that a Negro be placed upon the board of jurors of award. Would any such recognition of the race have taken place? I do not think so. The Atlanta officials went as far as they did because they felt it to be a pleasure, as well as a duty, to reward what they considered merit in the Negro race. Say what we will, there is something in human nature which we cannot blot out, which makes one man, in the end, recognize and reward merit in another, regardless of colour or race.

I believe it is the duty of the Negro—as the greater part of the race is already doing—to deport himself modestly in regard to political claims, depending upon the slow but sure influences that proceed from the possession of property, intelligence, and high character for the full recognition of his political rights. I think that the according of the full exercise of political rights is going to be a matter of natural, slow growth, not an over-night, gourd-vine affair. I do not believe that the Negro should cease voting, for a man cannot learn the exercise of self-government by ceasing to vote, any more than a boy can learn to swim by keeping out of the water, but I do believe that in his voting he should more and more be influenced by those of intelligence and character who are his next-door neighbours.

I know coloured men who, through the encouragement, help, and advice of Southern white people, have accumulated thousands of dollars' worth of property, but who, at the same time, would never think of going to those same persons for advice concerning the casting of their ballots. This, it seems to me, is unwise and unreasonable, and should cease. In saying this I do not mean that the Negro should truckle, or not vote from principle, for the instant he ceases to vote from principle he loses the confidence and respect of the Southern white man even.

I do not believe that any state should make a law that permits an ignorant and poverty-stricken white man to vote, and prevents a black man in the same condition from voting. Such a law is not only unjust, but it will react, as all unjust laws do, in time; for the effect of such a law is to encourage the Negro to secure education and property, and at the same time it encourages the white man to remain in ignorance and poverty. I believe that in time, through the operation of intelligence and friendly race relations, all cheating at the ballot-box in the South will cease. It will become apparent that the white man who begins by cheating a Negro out of his ballot soon learns to cheat a white man out of his, and that the man who does this ends his career of dishonesty by the theft of property or by some equally serious crime. In my opinion, the time will come when the South will encourage all of its citizens to vote. It will see that it pays better, from every standpoint, to have healthy, vigorous life than to have that political stagnation which always results when one-half of the population has no share and no interest in the Government.

As a rule, I believe in universal, free suffrage, but I believe that in the South we are confronted with peculiar conditions that justify the protection of the ballot in many of the states, for a while at least, either by an educational test, a property test, or by both combined; but whatever tests are required, they should be made to apply with equal and exact justice to both races.

1901

# CHARLES W. CHESNUTT
## 1858–1932

Charles Waddell Chesnutt was born on June 20, 1858, in Cleveland, Ohio. His parents were free-born blacks from North Carolina; his father served in the Union Army and after the Civil War moved his family back to Fayetteville, North Carolina. Chesnutt went to a school established by the Freedman's Bureau during Reconstruction and eventually became a teacher, school principal, newspaper reporter, accountant, court stenographer, and lawyer before he first achieved success as a writer. In 1887 the *Atlantic Monthly* published "The Goophered Grapevine," the first of what was to be a group of stories in the regional-dialect folktale tradition earlier made nationally popular by Joel Chandler Harris. Most readers of the story would have supposed that, like Harris, Chesnutt was white because the stories are framed in the language of an apparently superior and bemused white narrator listening to an old black retainer's folktale. Chesnutt's Uncle Julius, though superficially like Harris's Uncle Remus, is in reality a wise old slave who has learned not only to survive but to use and defeat his supposed superiors through a mocking mask of ignorance. Most of Chesnutt's contemporaries saw the picturesque stereotype of the old slave as an easygoing, shuffling retainer and took pleasure in the authenticity of the language, customs, and settings in the stories; only in recent years, however, have readers had the added satisfaction of perceiving the ironic drama played out between "master" and "slave" underneath Chesnutt's "folktales."

With age and fame Chesnutt became more direct in his critique of "race." Chesnutt was himself very light-skinned but had never tried to hide his racial identity; it was not until 1899, however, the year he began to write full time, that he revealed himself to his readers as a black man. In that year the dialect stories set in rural North Carolina were gathered and published as *The Conjure Woman*. Conjure (or hoodoo) is the name given to a set of folk beliefs combining elements of Caribbean and West African healing and spiritual practices with elements of Christian belief. Practitioners of conjure were thought to know how to get in touch with and direct the powers of nature to make something happen—or to keep something from happening. In addition, two other books appeared: a collection of mostly nondialect and urban stories titled *"The Wife of His Youth" and Other Stories of the Color Line* and a biography, a *Life of Frederick Douglass*. A number of Chesnutt's stories written in the 1890s dealt with the usually disastrous consequences of light-skinned blacks attempting to pass as whites. "The Wife of His Youth," printed here, is, of course, an exception, telling, as it does, of the obligation of upwardly mobile blacks to remember and honor their collective past. A second story from that collection, "The Passing of Grandison," also printed here, uses biting satire to show the narrow limits of white reality.

Chesnutt's first novel, *The House behind the Cedars* (1900), explores the theme of mixed-blood marriages and the troubled psychology of people of mixed race who live in the South. His first important essay, "What Is a White Man?" (1889), points out the practical futility and moral unfairness of laws against interracial marriages. *The Marrow of Tradition* (1901), his most successful novel, exposes the violent social tensions created in a small town in the South by the entrenched traditions of white supremacy and black servitude, culminating in a massacre of blacks based on the Wilmington Riot of 1898. Chesnutt's third novel on the theme of race problems in the post–Civil War South, *The Colonel's Dream* (1905), reveals his increasing pessimism over finding a solution to the pervasive racism of the South. By then, post-Reconstruction Jim Crow practices, the disenfranchisement of black voters, and the widespread use of violence and intimidation against African Americans left scant hope for an early mitigation of racist attitudes in the South.

In 1880, Chesnutt recorded in his journal his youthful ambitions as a writer:

> The object of my writings would be not so much the elevation of the colored peo-
> ple as the elevation of the whites—for I consider the unjust spirit of caste which
> is so insidious as to pervade a whole nation, and so powerful as to subject a whole
> race and all connected with it to scorn and social ostracism—I consider this a
> barrier to the moral progress of the American people; and I would be one of the
> first to head a determined, organized crusade against it.

Chesnutt became a skillful, original, realistic regionalist who depicted both average
southern blacks and those of mixed blood who lived on the color line and were sometimes middle-class. He was also the first African American imaginative writer to be
taken seriously by the white press, including William Dean Howells, even when he did
not write mere "dialect stories"; finally, as a harbinger of the literature of the "New
South," Chesnutt did in fact lead a crusade against racism of the kind he imagined as
a young man. His many essays also contributed to his crusade against the stupidity and
injustice of racism wherever it was practiced.

Although he wrote sporadically after 1905, Chesnutt never again commanded much
of an audience during his lifetime, and by the 1920s he had lost touch both with his
white readership and with the dramatic changes being wrought in African American culture by the Harlem Renaissance. Nonetheless, among black writers and intellectuals—
and black readers more generally—he was still esteemed as the pioneering writer of
fiction who addressed racial issues seriously and sensitively, and in 1928, he received the
Spingarn Medal for his groundbreaking contribution to the literary depiction of the "life
and struggle of Americans of Negro descent." The ways in which this award was well
deserved are only now beginning to be fully understood. In the last twenty years, thanks
to the efforts of such scholars as Andrews, Werner Sollors, Joseph R. McElrath, Jr.,
Richard H. Brodhead, and Eric Sundquist, new editions of Chesnutt's works and critical essays and books on him have multiplied, emphasizing his complex artistry, acute (if
often masked) sense of irony, and modernity, whether as naturalist or as existentialist.

# The Goophered Grapevine[1]

About ten years ago my wife was in poor health, and our family doctor, in
whose skill and honesty I had implicit confidence, advised a change of climate.
I was engaged in grape-culture in northern Ohio, and decided to look for
a location suitable for carrying on the same business in some Southern State.
I wrote to a cousin who had gone into the turpentine business in central North
Carolina, and he assured me that no better place could be found in the South
than the State and neighborhood in which he lived: climate and soil were all
that could be asked for, and land could be bought for a mere song. A cordial
invitation to visit him while I looked into the matter was accepted. We found
the weather delightful at that season, the end of the summer, and were most
hospitably entertained. Our host placed a horse and buggy at our disposal, and
himself acted as guide until I got somewhat familiar with the country.

I went several times to look at a place which I thought might suit me. It
had been at one time a thriving plantation, but shiftless cultivation had well-
nigh exhausted the soil. There had been a vineyard of some extent on the
place, but it had not been attended to since the war, and had fallen into utter

1. First published in the *Atlantic Monthly* (August 1887)—the source of the text printed here—this story
was published in book form in the collection *The Conjure Woman* (1899).

neglect. The vines—here partly supported by decayed and broken-down arbors, there twining themselves among the branches of the slender saplings which had sprung up among them—grew in wild and unpruned luxuriance, and the few scanty grapes which they bore were the undisputed prey of the first comer. The site was admirably adapted to grape-raising; the soil, with a little attention, could not have been better; and with the native grape, the luscious scuppernong, mainly to rely upon, I felt sure that I could introduce and cultivate successfully a number of other varieties.

One day I went over with my wife, to show her the place. We drove between the decayed gate-posts—the gate itself had long since disappeared—and up the straight, sandy lane to the open space where a dwelling-house had once stood. But the house had fallen a victim to the fortunes of war, and nothing remained of it except the brick pillars upon which the sills had rested. We alighted, and walked about the place for a while; but on Annie's complaining of weariness I led the way back to the yard, where a pine log, lying under a spreading elm, formed a shady though somewhat hard seat. One end of the log was already occupied by a venerable-looking colored man. He held on his knees a hat full of grapes, over which he was smacking his lips with great gusto, and a pile of grape-skins near him indicated that the performance was no new thing. He respectfully rose as we approached, and was moving away, when I begged him to keep his seat.

"Don't let us disturb you," I said. "There's plenty of room for us all."

He resumed his seat with somewhat of embarrassment.

"Do you live around here?" I asked, anxious to put him at his ease.

"Yas, suh. I lives des ober yander, behine de nex' san'-hill, on de Lumberton plank-road."

"Do you know anything about the time when this vineyard was cultivated?"

"Lawd bless yer, suh, I knows all about it. Dey ain' na'er a man in dis settlement w'at won' tell yer ole Julius McAdoo 'uz bawn an' raise' on dis yer same plantation. Is you de Norv'n gemman w'at's gwine ter buy de ole vimya'd?"

"I am looking at it," I replied; "but I don't know that I shall care to buy unless I can be reasonably sure of making something out of it."

"Well, suh, you is a stranger ter me, en I is a stranger ter you, en we is bofe strangers ter one anudder, but 'f I 'uz in yo' place, I wouldn' buy dis vimya'd."

"Why not?" I asked.

"Well, I dunner whe'r you b'lieves in cunj'in er not,—some er de w'ite folks don't, er says dey don't,—but de truf er de matter is dat dis yer old vimya'd is goophered."

"Is what?" I asked, not grasping the meaning of this unfamiliar word.

"Is goophered, cunju'd, bewitch'."

He imparted this information with such solemn earnestness, and with such an air of confidential mystery, that I felt somewhat interested, while Annie was evidently much impressed, and drew closer to me.

"How do you know it is bewitched?" I asked.

"I wouldn' spec' fer you ter b'lieve me 'less you know all 'bout de fac's. But ef you en young miss dere doan' min' lis'n'in' ter a ole nigger run on a minute er two while you er restin', I kin 'splain to yer how it all happen'."

We assured him that we would be glad to hear how it all happened, and he began to tell us. At first the current of his memory—or imagination—seemed somewhat sluggish; but as his embarrassment wore off, his language flowed more freely, and the story acquired perspective and coherence. As he became more and more absorbed in the narrative, his eyes assumed a dreamy expression, and he seemed to lose sight of his auditors, and to be living over again in monologue his life on the old plantation.

"Ole Mars Dugal' McAdoo bought dis place long many years befo' de wah, en I 'member well w'en he sot out all dis yer part er de plantation in scuppernon's. De vimes growed monst'us fas', en Mars Dugal' made a thousan' gallon er scuppernon' wine eve'y year.

"Now, ef dey's an'thing a nigger lub, nex' ter 'possum, en chick'n, en watermillyums, it's scuppernon's. Dey ain' niffin dat kin stan' up side'n de scuppernon' fer sweetness; sugar ain't a suckumstance ter scuppernon'. W'en de season is nigh 'bout ober, en de grapes begin ter swivel up des a little wid de wrinkles er ole age,—w'en de skin git sof' en brown,—den de scuppernon' make you smack yo' lip en roll yo' eye en wush fer mo'; so I reckon it ain' very 'stonishin' dat niggers lub scuppernon'.

"Dey wuz a sight er niggers in de naberhood er de vimya'd. Dere wuz ole Mars Henry Brayboy's niggers, en ole Mars Dunkin McLean's niggers, en Mars Dugal's own niggers; den dey wuz a settlement er free niggers en po' buckrahs[2] down by de Wim'l'ton Road, en Mars Dugal' had de only vimya'd in de naberhood. I reckon it ain' so much so nowadays, but befo' de wah, in slab'ry times, er nigger didn' mine goin' fi' er ten mile in a night, w'en dey wuz sump'n good ter eat at de yuther een.

"So atter a w'ile Mars Dugal' begin ter miss his scuppernon's. Co'se he 'cuse' de niggers er it, but dey all 'nied it ter de las'. Mars Dugal' sot spring guns en steel traps, en he en de oberseah sot up nights once't er twice't, tel one night Mars Dugal'—he 'uz a monst'us keerless man—got his leg shot full er cow-peas. But somehow er nudder dey couldn' nebber ketch none er de niggers. I dunner how it happen, but it happen des like I tell yer, en de grapes kep' on a-goin des de same.

"But bimeby ole Mars Dugal' fix' up a plan ter stop it. Dey 'uz a cunjuh 'ooman livin' down mongs' de free niggers on de Wim'l'ton Road, en all de darkies fum Rockfish ter Beaver Crick wuz feared uv her. She could wuk de mos' powerfulles' kind er goopher,—could make people hab fits er rheumatiz, er make 'em des dwinel away en die; en dey say she went out ridin' de niggers at night, for she wuz a witch 'sides bein' a cunjuh 'ooman. Mars Dugal' hearn 'bout Aun' Peggy's doin's, en begun ter 'flect whe'r er no he couldn' git her ter he'p him keep de niggers off'n de grapevimes. One day in de spring er de year, ole miss pack' up a basket er chick'n en poun'-cake, en a bottle er scuppernon' wine, en Mars Dugal' tuk it in his buggy en driv ober ter Aun' Peggy's cabin. He tuk de basket in, en had a long talk wid Aun' Peggy. De nex' day Aun' Peggy come up ter de vimya'd. De niggers seed her slippin' 'roun', en dey soon foun' out what she 'uz doin' dere. Mars Dugal' had hi'ed her ter goopher de grapevimes. She sa'ntered 'roun' mongs' de vimes, en tuk a leaf fum dis one, en a grape-hull fum dat one, en a grape-seed fum anudder one; en den a little twig fum here, en a little pinch er dirt fum dere,—en put it all in a big black bottle, wid a snake's toof en a speckle' hen's gall en some ha'rs fum a black cat's tail, en den fill' de bottle wid scuppernon' wine. W'en she got de

2. Regionalism meaning "white men."

goopher all ready en fix', she tuk 'n went out in de woods en buried it under de root uv a red oak tree, en den come back en tole one er de niggers she done goopher de grapevimes, en a'er a nigger w'at eat dem grapes 'ud be sho ter die inside'n twel' mont's.

"Atter dat de niggers let de scuppernons' lone, en Mars Dugal' didn' hab no 'casion ter fine no mo' fault; en de season wuz mos' gone, w'en a strange gemman stop at de plantation one night ter see Mars Dugal' on some business; en his coachman, seein' de scuppernon's growin' so nice en sweet, slip 'roun behine de smoke-house, en et all de scuppernon's he could hole. Nobody didn' notice it at de time, but dat night, on de way home, de gemman's hoss runned away en kill' de coachman. W'en we hearn de noos, Aun' Lucy, de cook, she up 'n say she seed de strange nigger eat'n er de scuppernon's behind de smoke-house; en den we knowed de goopher had b'en er wukkin. Den one er de nigger chilluns runned away fum de quarters one day, en got in de scuppernon's, en died de nex' week. W'ite folks say he die' er de fevuh, but de niggers knowed it wuz de goopher. So you k'n be sho de darkies didn' hab much ter do wid dem scuppernon' vimes.

"W'en de scuppernon' season 'uz ober fer dat year, Mars Dugal' foun' he had made fifteen hund'ed gallon er wine; en one er de niggers hearn him laffin' wid de oberseah fit ter kill, en sayin' dem fifteen hund'ed gallon er wine wuz monst'us good intrus' on de ten dollars he laid out on de vimya'd. So I 'low ez he paid Aun' Peggy ten dollars fer to goopher de grapevimes.

"De goopher didn' wuk no mo' tel de nex' summer, w'en 'long to'ds de middle er de season one er de fiel' han's died; en ez dat lef' Mars Dugal' sho't er han's, he went off ter town fer ter buy anudder. He fotch de noo nigger home wid 'im. He wuz er ole nigger, er de color er a gingy-cake, en ball ez a hoss-apple on de top er his head. He wuz a peart ole nigger, do', en could do a big day's wuk.

"Now it happen dat one er de niggers on de nex' plantation, one er ole Mars Henry Brayboy's niggers, had runned away de day befo', en tuk ter de swamp, en ole Mars Dugal' en some er de yuther nabor w'ite folks had gone out wid dere guns en dere dogs fer ter he'p 'em hunt fer de nigger; en de han's on our own plantation wuz all so flusterated dat we fuhgot ter tell de noo han' 'bout de goopher on de scuppernon' vimes. Co'se he smell de grapes en see de vimes, an atter dahk de fus' thing he done wuz ter slip off ter de grapevimes 'dout sayin' nuffin ter nobody. Nex' mawnin' he tole some er de niggers 'bout de fine bait er scuppernon' he et de night befo'.

"W'en dey tole 'im 'bout de goopher on de grapevimes, he 'uz dat tarrified dat he turn pale, en look des like he gwine ter die right in his tracks. De oberseah come up en axed w'at 'uz de matter; en w'en dey tol 'im Henry be'n eatin' er de scuppernon's, en got de goopher on 'im, he gin Henry a big drink er w'iskey, en 'low dat de nex' rainy day he take 'im ober ter Aun' Peggy's, en see ef she wouldn' take de goopher off'n him, seein' ez he didn't know nuffin erbout it tel he done et de grapes.

"Sho nuff, it rain de nex' day, en de oberseah went ober ter Aun' Peggy's wid Henry. En Aun' Peggy say dat bein' ez Henry didn' know 'bout de goopher, en et de grapes in ign'ance er de quinseconces, she reckon she mought be able fer ter take de goopher off'n him. So she fotch out er bottle wid some cunjuh medicine in it, en po'd some out in a go'd fer Henry ter drink. He manage ter git it down; he say it tas'e like whiskey wid sump'n bitter in it. She

'lowed dat 'ud keep de goopher off'n him tel de spring; but w'en de sap begin
ter rise in de grapevimes he ha ter come en see her agin, en she tell him w'at
e's ter do.

"Nex' spring, w'en de sap commence' ter rise in de scuppernon' vime, Henry
tuk a ham one night. Whar'd he git de ham? *I* doan know; dey wa'nt no hams
on de plantation 'cep'n w'at 'uz in de smoke-house, but *I* never see Henry
'bout de smoke-house. But ez I wuz a-sayin', he tuk de ham ober ter Aun'
Peggy's; en Aun' Peggy tole 'im dat w'en Mars Dugal' begin ter prume de
grapevimes, he mus' go en take 'n scrape off de sap whar it ooze out'n de cut
een's er de vimes, en 'n'int his ball head wid it; en ef he do dat once't a year
de goopher wouldn' wuk agin 'im long ez he done it. En bein 'ez he fotch her
de ham, she fix' it so he kin eat all de scuppernon' he want.

"So Henry 'n'int his head wid de sap out'n de big grapevime des ha'f way
'twix' de quarters en de big house, en de goopher nebber wuk agin him dat
summer. But de beatenes' thing you eber see happen ter Henry. Up ter dat
time he wuz ez ball ez a sweeten' 'tater, but des ez soon ez de young leaves
begun ter come out on de grapevimes de ha'r begun ter grow out on Henry's
head, en by de middle er de summer he had de bigges' head er ha'r on de plantation. Befo' dat, Henry had tol'able good ha'r 'roun' de aidges, but soon ez de
young grapes begun ter come Henry's ha'r begun ter quirl all up in little balls,
des like dis yer reg'lar grapy ha'r, en by de time de grapes got ripe his head
look des like a bunch er grapes. Combin' it didn' do no good; he wuk at it ha'f
de night wid er Jim Crow,[3] en think he git it straighten' out, but in de mawnin'
de grapes 'ud be dere des de same. So he gin it up, en tried ter keep de grapes
down by havin' his ha'r cut sho't.

"But dat wa'nt de quares' thing 'bout de goopher. When Henry come ter de
plantation, he wuz gittin' a little ole an stiff in de j'ints. But dat summer he
got des ez spray en libely ez any young nigger on de plantation; fac' he got so
biggity dat Mars Jackson, de oberseah, ha' ter th'eaten ter whip 'im, ef he didn'
stop cuttin' up his didos[4] en behave hisse'f. But de mos' cur'ouses' thing happen' in de fall, when de sap begin ter go down in de grapevimes. Fus', when
de grapes 'uz gethered, de knots begun ter straighten out'n Henry's h'ar; en
w'en de leaves begin ter fall, Henry's ha'r begin ter drap out; en w'en de vimes
'uz b'ar, Henry's head wuz baller'n it wuz in de spring, en he begin ter git ole
en stiff in de j'ints ag'in, en paid no mo' tention ter de gals dyoin' er de whole
winter. En nex' spring, w'en he rub de sap on ag'in, he got young ag'in, en so
soopl en libely dat none er de young niggers on de plantation could n' jump,
ner dance, ner hoe ez much cotton ez Henry. But in de fall er de year his
grapes begun ter straighten out, en his j'ints ter git stiff, en his ha'r drap off,
en de rheumatiz begin ter wrastle wid 'im.

"Now, ef you'd a knowed ole Mars Dugal' McAdoo, you'd a knowed dat it
ha' ter be a mighty rainy day when he could n' fine sump'n fer his niggers ter
do, en it ha' ter be a mightly little hole he couldn' crawl thoo, en ha' ter be a
monst'us cloudy night w'en a dollar git by him in de dahkness; en w'en he see
how Henry git young in de spring en ole in de fall, he 'lowered ter hisse'f ez
how he could make mo' money outen Henry dan by wukkin' him in de cotton
fiel'. 'Long de nex' spring, atter de sap commence' ter rise, en Henry 'n'int 'is

3. A small card, resembling a curry-comb in construction, and used by negroes in the rural districts

instead of a comb [Chesnutt's note].
4. Behaving in a silly or mischievous way.

head en commence fer ter git young en soopl, Mars Dugal' up'n tuk Henry
ter town, en sole 'im fer fifteen hunder' dollars. Co'se de man w'at bought
Henry didn' know nuffin 'bout de goopher, en Mars Dugal' didn' see no 'casion
fer ter tell 'im. Long to'ds de fall, w'en de sap went down, Henry begin ter git
ole again same ez yuzhal, en his noo marster begin ter git skeered les'n he
gwine ter lose his fifteen-hunder'-dollar nigger. He sent fer a mighty fine doctor, but de med'cine didn' 'pear ter do no good; de goopher had a good holt.
Henry tole de doctor 'bout de goopher, but de doctor des laff at 'im.

"One day in de winter Mars Dugal' went ter town, en wuz santerin' 'long de
Main Street, when who should he meet but Henry's noo marster. Dey said
'Hoddy,' en Mars Dugal' ax 'im ter hab a seegyar; en atter dey run on awhile
'about de craps en de weather, Mars Dugal' ax 'im, sorter keerless, like ez ef
he des thought of it,—

" 'How you like de nigger I sole you las' spring?'

"Henry's marster shuck his head en knock de ashes off'n his seegyar.

" 'Spec' I made a bad bahgin when I bought dat nigger. Henry done good
wuk all de summer, but sence de fall set in he 'pears ter be sorter pinin' away.
Dey ain' nuffin pertickler de matter wid 'im—leastways de doctor ay so—
'cep'n' a tech er de rheumatiz; but his ha'r is all fell out, en ef he don't pick
up his strenk mighty soon, I spec' I'm gwine ter lose 'im.'

"Dey smoked on awhile, en bimeby ole mars say, 'Well, a bahgin's a bahgin,
but you en me is good fren's, en I doan wan' ter see you lose all de money you
paid fer dat digger; en ef w'at you say is so, en I ain't 'sputin' it, he ain't wuf
much now. I spec's you wukked him too ha'd dis summer, er e'se de swamps
down here don't agree wid de san'-hill nigger. So you des lemme know, en ef
he gits any wusser I'll be willin' ter gib yer five hund'ed dollars fer 'im, en take
my chances on his livin'.'

"Sho nuff, when Henry begun ter draw up wid de rheumatiz en it look like
he gwine ter die fer sho, his noo marster sen' fer Mars Dugal', en Mars Dugal'
gin him what he promus, en brung Henry home ag'in. He tuk good keer uv
'im dyoin' er de winter,—give 'im w'iskey ter rub his rheumatiz, en terbacker
ter smoke, en all he want ter eat,—'caze a nigger w'at he could make a thousan' dollars a year off'n didn' grow on eve'y huckleberry bush.

"Nex' spring, w'en de sap ris en Henry's ha'r commence' ter sprout, Mars
Dugal' sole 'im ag'in, down in Robeson County dis time; en he kep' dat sellin'
business up fer five year er mo'. Henry nebber say nuffin 'bout de goopher ter
his noo marsters, 'caze he knew he gwine ter be tuk good keer uv de nex' winter, w'en Mars Dugal' buy him back. En Mars Dugal' made 'nuff money off'n
Henry ter buy anudder plantation ober on Beaver Crick.

"But long 'bout de een' er dat five year dey come a stranger ter stop at de
plantation. De fus' day he 'us dere he went out wid Mars Dugal' en spent all
de mawnin' lookin' ober de vimya'd, en atter dinner dey spent all de evenin'
playin' kya'ds. De niggers soon 'skiver' dat he wuz a Yankee, en dat he come
down ter Norf C'lina fer ter learn de w'ite folks how to raise grapes en make
wine. He promus Mars Dugal' he cud make de grapevimes ba'r twice't ez
many grapes, en dat de noo wine-press he wuz a-sellin' would make mo' d'n
twice't ez many gallons er wine. En ole Mars Dugal' des drunk it all in, des
'peared ter be bewitched wid dat Yankee. W'en de darkies see dat Yankee runnin' 'roun de vimya'd en diggin' under de grapevimes, dey shuk dere heads,
en 'lowed dat dey feared Mars Dugal' losin' his min'. Mars Dugal' had all de

dirt dug away fum under de roots er all de scuppernon' vimes, an' let 'em stan' dat away fer a week er mo'. Den dat Yankee made de niggers fix up a mixtry er lime en ashes en manyo,[5] en po' it roun' de roots er de grapevimes. Den he 'vise' Mars Dugal' fer ter trim de vimes close't, en Mars Dugal' tuck 'n done eve'ything de Yankee tole him ter do. Dyoin' all er dis time, mind yer, 'e wuz libbin' off'n de fat er de lan', at de big house, en playin' kyards wid Mars Dugal' eve'y night; en dey say Mars Dugal' los' mo'n a thousan' dollars dyoin' er de week dat Yankee wuz a runnin' de grapevimes.

"W'en de sap ris nex' spring, old Henry 'n'inted his head ez yuzhal, en his ha'r commence' ter grow des de same ez it done eve'y year. De scuppernon' vimes growed monst's fas', en de leaves wuz greener en thicker dan dey eber be'n dyowin my rememb'ance; en Henry's ha'r growed out thicker dan eber, en he 'peared ter git younger 'n younger, en soopler 'n soopler; en seein' ez he wuz sho't er han's dat spring, havin' tuk in consid'able noo groun', Mars Dugal' 'cluded he would n' sell Henry 'tel he git de crap in en de cotton chop'. So he kep' Henry on de plantation.

"But 'long 'bout time fer de grapes ter come on de scuppernon' vimes, dey 'peared ter come a change ober dem; de leaves wivered en swivel' up, en de young grapes turn' yaller, en bimeby eve'ybody on de plantation could see dat de whole vimya'd wuz dyin'. Mars Dugal' tuck'n water de vimes en done all he could, but 't wan' no use: dat Yankee done bus' de watermillyum. One time de vimes picked up a bit, en Mars Dugal' thought dey wuz gwine ter come out ag'in; but dat Yankee done dug too close unde' de roots, en prune de branches too close ter de vime, en all dat lime en ashes done burn' de life outen de vimes, en dey des kep' a with'in' en a swivelin'.

"All dis time de goopher wuz a-wukkin'. W'en de vimes commence' ter wither, Henry commence' ter complain er his rheumatiz, en when de leaves begin ter dry up his ha'r commence' ter drap out. When de vimes fresh up a bit Henry 'ud git peart agin, en when de vimes wither agin Henry 'ud git ole agin, en des kep' gittin' mo' en mo' fitten fer nuffin; he des pined away, en fine'ly tuk ter his cabin; en when de big vime whar he got de sap ter 'n'int his head withered en turned yaller en died, Henry died too,—des went out sorter like a cannel. Dey didn't 'pear ter be nuffin de matter wid 'im, cep'n' de rheumatiz, but his strenk des dwinel' away, 'tel he didn' hab ernuff lef' ter draw his bref. De goopher had got de under holt, en th'owed Henry fer good en all dat time.

"Mars Dugal' tuk on might'ly 'bout losin' his vimes en his nigger in de same year; en he swo' dat ef he could git holt er dat Yankee he'd wear 'im ter a frazzle, en den chaw up de frazzle; en he'd done it, too, for Mars Dugal' 'uz a monst'us brash man w'en he once git started. He sot de vimya'd out ober agin, but it wuz th'ee er fo' year befo' de vimes got ter b'arin' any scuppernon's.

"W'en de wah broke out, Mars Dugal' raise' a comp'ny, en went off ter fight de Yankees. He say he wuz mighty glad dat wah come, en he des want ter kill a Yankee fer eve'y dollar he los' 'long er dat grape-raisin' Yankee. En I 'spec' he would a done it, too, ef de Yankees hadn' s'picioned sump'n, en killed him fus'. Atter de s'render ole miss move' ter town, de niggers all scattered 'way fum de plantation, en de vimya'd ain' be'n cultervated sence."

---

5. Mango, yam, or sweet potato; although there are differences among these starchy fruits and tubers, the names are used interchangeably.

"Is that story true?" asked Annie, doubtfully, but seriously, as the old man concluded his narrative.

"It's des ez true ez I'm a-settin' here, miss. Dey's a easy way ter prove it: I kin lead de way right ter Henry's grave ober yander in de plantation buryin'-groun'. En I tell yer w'at, marster, I wouldn' 'vise yer to buy dis yer ole vimya'd, 'caze de goopher's on it yit, en dey ain' no tellin' w'en it's gwine ter crap out."

"But I thought you said all the old vines died."

"Dey did 'pear ter die, but a few ov 'em come out ag'in, en is mixed in mongs' de yuthers. I ain' skeered ter eat de grapes, 'caze I knows de old vimes fum de noo ones; but wid strangers dey ain' no tellin' w'at might happen. I wouldn' 'vise yer ter buy dis vimya'd."

I bought the vineyard, nevertheless, and it has been for a long time in a thriving condition, and is referred to by the local press as a striking illustration of the opportunities open to Northern capital in the development of Southern industries. The luscious scuppernong holds first rank among our grapes, though we cultivate a great many other varieties, and our income from grapes packed and shipped to the Northern markets is quite considerable. I have not noticed any developments of the goopher in the vineyard, although I have a mild suspicion that our colored assistants do not suffer from want of grapes during the season.

I found, when I bought the vineyard, that Uncle Julius had occupied a cabin on the place for many years, and derived a respectable revenue from the neglected grapevines. This, doubtless, accounted for his advice to me not to buy the vineyard, though whether it inspired the goopher story I am unable to state. I believe, however, that the wages I pay him for his services are more than an equivalent for anything he lost by the sale of the vineyard.

1887, 1899

# The Wife of His Youth[1]

## I

Mr. Ryder was going to give a ball. There were several reasons why this was an opportune time for such an event.

Mr. Ryder might aptly be called the dean of the Blue Veins. The original Blue Veins were a little society of colored persons organized in a certain Northern city shortly after the war. Its purpose was to establish and maintain correct social standards among a people whose social condition presented almost unlimited room for improvement. By accident, combined perhaps with some natural affinity, the society consisted of individuals who were, generally speaking, more white than black. Some envious outsider made the suggestion that no one was eligible for membership who was not white enough to show blue veins. The suggestion was readily adopted by those who were not of the favored few, and since that time the society, though possessing a longer and more pretentious name, had been known far and wide as the "Blue Vein Society," and its members as the "Blue Veins."

---

1. First published in the *Atlantic* (July 1898); later reprinted in the collection *"The Wife of His Youth" and Other Stories of the Color Line* (1899), the source of the text printed here.

The Blue Veins did not allow that any such requirement existed for admission to their circle, but, on the contrary, declared that character and culture were the only things considered; and that if most of their members were light-colored, it was because such persons, as a rule, had had better opportunities to qualify themselves for membership. Opinions differed, too, as to the usefulness of the society. There were those who had been known to assail it violently as a glaring example of the very prejudice from which the colored race had suffered most; and later, when such critics had succeeded in getting on the inside, they had been heard to maintain with zeal and earnestness that the society was a life-boat, an anchor, a bulwark and a shield,—a pillar of cloud by day and of fire by night, to guide their people through the social wilderness. Another alleged prerequisite for Blue Vein membership was that of free birth; and while there was really no such requirement, it is doubtless true that very few of the members would have been unable to meet it if there had been. If there were one or two of the older members who had come up from the South and from slavery, their history presented enough romantic circumstances to rob their servile origin of its grosser aspects.

While there were no such tests of eligibility, it is true that the Blue Veins had their notions on these subjects, and that not all of them were equally liberal in regard to the things they collectively disclaimed. Mr. Ryder was one of the most conservative. Though he had not been among the founders of the society, but had come in some years later, his genius for social leadership was such that he had speedily become its recognized adviser and head, the custodian of its standards, and the preserver of its traditions. He shaped its social policy, was active in providing for its entertainment, and when the interest fell off, as it sometimes did, he fanned the embers until they burst again into a cheerful flame.

There were still other reasons for his popularity. While he was not as white as some of the Blue Veins, his appearance was such as to confer distinction upon them. His features were of a refined type, his hair was almost straight; he was always neatly dressed; his manners were irreproachable, and his morals above suspicion. He had come to Groveland a young man, and obtaining employment in the office of a railroad company as messenger had in time worked himself up to the position of stationery clerk, having charge of the distribution of the office supplies for the whole company. Although the lack of early training had hindered the orderly development of a naturally fine mind, it had not prevented him from doing a great deal of reading or from forming decidedly literary tastes. Poetry was his passion. He could repeat whole pages of the great English poets; and if his pronunciation was sometimes faulty, his eye, his voice, his gestures, would respond to the changing sentiment with a precision that revealed a poetic soul and disarmed criticism. He was economical, and had saved money; he owned and occupied a very comfortable house on a respectable street. His residence was handsomely furnished, containing among other things a good library, especially rich in poetry, a piano, and some choice engravings. He generally shared his house with some young couple, who looked after his wants and were company for him; for Mr. Ryder was a single man. In the early days of his connection with the Blue Veins he had been regarded as quite a catch, and young ladies and their mothers had manœuvred with much ingenuity to capture him. Not, however, until Mrs. Molly Dixon visited Groveland had any woman ever made him wish to change his condition to that of a married man.

Mrs. Dixon had come to Groveland from Washington in the spring, and before the summer was over she had won Mr. Ryder's heart. She possessed many attractive qualities. She was much younger than he; in fact, he was old enough to have been her father, though no one knew exactly how old he was. She was whiter than he, and better educated. She had moved in the best colored society of the country, at Washington, and had taught in the schools of that city. Such a superior person had been eagerly welcomed to the Blue Vein Society, and had taken a leading part in its activities. Mr. Ryder had at first been attracted by her charms of person, for she was very good looking and not over twenty-five; then by her refined manners and the vivacity of her wit. Her husband had been a government clerk, and at his death had left a considerable life insurance. She was visiting friends in Groveland, and, finding the town and the people to her liking, had prolonged her stay indefinitely. She had not seemed displeased at Mr. Ryder's attentions, but on the contrary had given him every proper encouragement; indeed, a younger and less cautious man would long since have spoken. But he had made up his mind, and had only to determine the time when he would ask her to be his wife. He decided to give a ball in her honor, and at some time during the evening of the ball to offer her his heart and hand. He had no special fears about the outcome, but, with a little touch of romance, he wanted the surroundings to be in harmony with his own feelings when he should have received the answer he expected.

Mr. Ryder resolved that this ball should mark an epoch in the social history of Groveland. He knew, of course,—no one could know better,—the entertainments that had taken place in past years, and what must be done to surpass them. His ball must be worthy of the lady in whose honor it was to be given, and must, by the quality of its guests, set an example for the future. He had observed of late a growing liberality, almost a laxity, in social matters, even among members of his own set, and had several times been forced to meet in a social way persons whose complexions and callings in life were hardly up to the standard which he considered proper for the society to maintain. He had a theory of his own.

"I have no race prejudice," he would say, "but we people of mixed blood are ground between the upper and the nether millstone. Our fate lies between absorption by the white race and extinction in the black. The one doesn't want us yet, but may take us in time. The other would welcome us, but it would be for us a backward step. 'With malice towards none, with charity for all,'[2] we must do the best we can for ourselves and those who are to follow us. Self-preservation is the first law of nature."

His ball would serve by its exclusiveness to counteract leveling tendencies, and his marriage with Mrs. Dixon would help to further the upward process of absorption he had been wishing and waiting for.

## II

The ball was to take place on Friday night. The house had been put in order, the carpets covered with canvas, the halls and stairs decorated with palms and potted plants; and in the afternoon Mr. Ryder sat on his front porch, which the shade of a vine running up over a wire netting made a cool

2. From Abraham Lincoln's second inaugural address (1865).

and pleasant lounging place. He expected to respond to the toast "The Ladies" at the supper, and from a volume of Tennyson—his favorite poet—was fortifying himself with apt quotations. The volume was open at "A Dream of Fair Women."[3] His eyes fell on these lines, and he read them aloud to judge better of their effect:—

> "At length I saw a lady within call,
>    Stiller than chisell'd marble, standing there;
> A daughter of the gods, divinely tall,
>    And most divinely fair."

He marked the verse, and turning the page read the stanza beginning,—

> "O sweet pale Margaret,
>    O rare pale Margaret."[4]

He weighed the passage a moment, and decided that it would not do. Mrs. Dixon was the palest lady he expected at the ball, and she was of a rather ruddy complexion, and of lively disposition and buxom build. So he ran over the leaves until his eye rested on the description of Queen Guinevere:[5]—

> "She seem'd a part of joyous Spring:
> A gown of grass-green silk she wore,
> Buckled with golden clasps before;
> A light-green tuft of plumes she bore
> Closed in a golden ring.

> • • • • •

> "She look'd so lovely, as she sway'd
> The rein with dainty finger-tips,
> A man had given all other bliss,
> And all his worldly worth for this,
> To waste his whole heart in one kiss
> Upon her perfect lips."

As Mr. Ryder murmured these words audibly, with an appreciative thrill, he heard the latch of his gate click, and a light foot-fall sounding on the steps. He turned his head, and saw a woman standing before his door.

She was a little woman, not five feet tall, and proportioned to her height. Although she stood erect, and looked around her with very bright and restless eyes, she seemed quite old; for her face was crossed and recrossed with a hundred wrinkles, and around the edges of her bonnet could be seen protruding here and there a tuft of short gray wool. She wore a blue calico gown of ancient cut, a little red shawl fastened around her shoulders with an old-fashioned brass brooch, and a large bonnet profusely ornamented with faded red and yellow artificial flowers. And she was very black,—so black that her toothless gums, revealed when she opened her mouth to speak, were not red, but blue. She looked like a bit of the old plantation life, summoned up from the past by the wave of a magician's wand, as the poet's fancy had called into being the gracious shapes of which Mr. Ryder had just been reading.

3. This poem, by English poet Alfred, Lord Tennyson (1809–1892), was published in 1832.
4. By Tennyson, "Margaret" was published in 1832.

5. Wife of the legendary King Arthur, described in the following quotation from Tennyson's "Sir Launcelot and Queen Guinevere" (1842).

He rose from his chair and came over to where she stood.

"Good-afternoon, madam," he said.

"Good-evenin', suh," she answered, ducking suddenly with a quaint curtsy. Her voice was shrill and piping, but softened somewhat by age. "Is dis yere whar Mistuh Ryduh lib, suh?" she asked, looking around her doubtfully, and glancing into the open windows, through which some of the preparations for the evening were visible.

"Yes," he replied, with an air of kindly patronage, unconsciously flattered by her manner, "I am Mr. Ryder. Did you want to see me?"

"Yas, suh, ef I ain't 'sturbin' of you too much."

"Not at all. Have a seat over here behind the vine, where it is cool. What can I do for you?"

" 'Scuse me, suh," she continued, when she had sat down on the edge of a chair, " 'scuse me, suh, I's lookin' for my husban'. I heerd you wuz a big man an' had libbed heah a long time, an' I 'lowed you wouldn't min' ef I'd come roun' an' ax you ef you'd ever heerd of a merlatter[6] man by de name er Sam Taylor 'quirin' roun' in de chu'ches ermongs' de people fer his wife 'Liza Jane?"

Mr. Ryder seemed to think for a moment.

"There used to be many such cases right after the war," he said, "but it has been so long that I have forgotten them. There are very few now. But tell me your story, and it may refresh my memory."

She sat back farther in her chair so as to be more comfortable, and folded her withered hands in her lap.

"My name's 'Liza," she began, " 'Liza Jane. W'en I wuz young I us'ter b'long ter Marse Bob Smif, down in ole Missoura. I wuz bawn down dere. W'en I wuz a gal I wuz married ter a man named Jim. But Jim died, an' after dat I married a merlatter man named Sam Taylor. Sam wuz free-bawn, but his mammy and daddy died, an' de w'ite folks 'prenticed him ter my marster fer ter work fer 'im 'tel he wuz growed up. Sam worked in de fiel', an' I wuz de cook. One day Ma'y Ann, ole miss's maid, came rushin' out ter de kitchen, an' says she, ' 'Liza Jane, ole marse gwine sell yo' Sam down de ribber.'

" 'Go way f'm yere,' says I; 'my husban' 's free!'

" 'Don' make no diff'ence. I heerd ole marse tell ole miss he wuz gwine take yo' Sam 'way wid 'im ter-morrow, fer he needed money, an' he knowed whar he could git a t'ousan' dollars fer Sam an' no questions axed.'

"W'en Sam come home f'm de fiel' dat night, I tole him 'bout ole marse gwine steal 'im, an' Sam run erway. His time wuz mos' up, an' he swo' dat w'en he wuz twenty-one he would come back an' he'p me run erway, er else save up de money ter buy my freedom. An' I know he'd 'a' done it, fer he thought a heap er me, Sam did. But w'en he come back he didn' fin' me, fer I wuzn' dere. Ole marse had heerd dat I warned Sam, so he had me whip' an' sol' down de ribber.

"Den de wah broke out, an' w'en it wuz ober de cullud folks wuz scattered. I went back ter de ole home; but Sam wuzn' dere, an' I couldn' l'arn nuffin' 'bout 'im. But I knowed he'd be'n dere to look for me an' hadn' foun' me, an' had gone erway ter hunt fer me.

"I's be'n lookin' fer 'im eber sence," she added simply, as though twenty-five years were but a couple of weeks, "an' I knows he's be'n lookin' fer me. Fer he

---

6. Mulatto.

sot a heap er sto' by me, Sam did, an' I know he's be'n huntin' fer me all dese years,—'less'n he's be'n sick er sump'n, so he couldn' work, er out'n his head, so he couldn' 'member his promise. I went back down de ribber, fer I 'lowed he'd gone down dere lookin' fer me. I's be'n ter Noo Orleans, an' Atlanty, an' Charleston, an' Richmon'; an' w'en I'd be'n all ober de Souf I come ter de Norf. Fer I knows I'll fin' 'im some er dese days," she added softly, "er he'll fin' me, an' den we'll bofe be as happy in freedom as we wuz in de ole days befo' de wah." A smile stole over her withered countenance as she paused a moment, and her bright eyes softened into a far-away look.

This was the substance of the old woman's story. She had wandered a little here and there. Mr. Ryder was looking at her curiously when she finished.

"How have you lived all these years?" he asked.

"Cookin', suh. I's a good cook. Does you know anybody w'at needs a good cook, suh? I's stoppin' wid a cullud fam'ly round' de corner yonder 'tel I kin git a place."

"Do you really expect to find your husband? He may be dead long ago."

She shook her head emphatically. "Oh no, he ain' dead. De signs an' de tokens tells me. I dremp three nights runnin' on'y dis las' week dat I foun' him."

"He may have married another woman. Your slave marriage would not have prevented him, for you never lived with him after the war, and without that your marriage doesn't count."

"Wouldn' make no diff'ence wid Sam. He wouldn' marry no yuther 'ooman 'tel he foun' out 'bout me. I knows it," she added. "Sump'n's be'n tellin' me all dese years dat I's gwine fin' Sam 'fo' I dies."

"Perhaps he's outgrown you, and climbed up in the world where he wouldn't care to have you find him."

"No, indeed, suh," she replied, "Sam ain' dat kin' er man. He wuz good ter me, Sam wuz, but he wuzn' much good ter nobody e'se, fer he wuz one er de triflin'es' han's on de plantation. I 'spec's ter haf ter suppo't 'im w'en I fin' 'im, fer he nebber would work 'less'n he had ter. But den he wuz free, an' he didn' git no pay fer his work, an' I don' blame 'im much. Mebbe he's done better sence he run erway, but I ain' 'spectin' much."

"You may have passed him on the street a hundred times during the twenty-five years, and not have known him; time works great changes."

She smiled incredulously. "I'd know 'im 'mongs' a hund'ed men. Fer dey wuz n' no yuther merlatter man like my man Sam, an' I couldn' be mistook. I's toted his picture roun' wid me twenty-five years."

"May I see it?" asked Mr. Ryder. "It might help me to remember whether I have seen the original."

As she drew a small parcel from her bosom he saw that it was fastened to a string that went around her neck. Removing several wrappers, she brought to light an old-fashioned daguerreotype in a black case. He looked long and intently at the portrait. It was faded with time, but the features were still distinct, and it was easy to see what manner of man it had represented.

He closed the case, and with a slow movement handed it back to her.

"I don't know of any man in town who goes by that name," he said, "nor have I heard of any one making such inquiries. But if you will leave me your address, I will give the matter some attention, and if I find out anything I will let you know."

She gave him the number of a house in the neighborhood, and went away, after thanking him warmly.

He wrote the address on the fly-leaf of the volume of Tennyson, and, when she had gone, rose to his feet and stood looking after her curiously. As she walked down the street with mincing step, he saw several persons whom she passed turn and look back at her with a smile of kindly amusement. When she had turned the corner, he went upstairs to his bedroom, and stood for a long time before the mirror of his dressing-case, gazing thoughtfully at the reflection of his own face.

### III

At eight o'clock the ballroom was a blaze of light and the guests had begun to assemble; for there was a literary programme and some routine business of the society to be gone through with before the dancing. A black servant in evening dress waited at the door and directed the guests to the dressing-rooms.

The occasion was long memorable among the colored people of the city; not alone for the dress and display, but for the high average of intelligence and culture that distinguished the gathering as a whole. There were a number of school-teachers, several young doctors, three or four lawyers, some professional singers, an editor, a lieutenant in the United States army spending his furlough in the city, and others in various polite callings; these were colored, though most of them would not have attracted even a casual glance because of any marked difference from white people. Most of the ladies were in evening costume, and dress coats and dancing pumps were the rule among the men. A band of string music, stationed in an alcove behind a row of palms, played popular airs while the guests were gathering.

The dancing began at half past nine. At eleven o'clock supper was served. Mr. Ryder had left the ballroom some little time before the intermission, but reappeared at the supper-table. The spread was worthy of the occasion, and the guests did full justice to it. When the coffee had been served, the toast-master, Mr. Solomon Sadler, rapped for order. He made a brief introductory speech, complimenting host and guests, and then presented in their order the toasts of the evening. They were responded to with a very fair display of after-dinner wit.

"The last toast," said the toast-master, when he reached the end of the list, "is one which must appeal to us all. There is no one of us of the sterner sex who is not at some time dependent upon woman,—in infancy for protection, in manhood for companionship, in old age for care and comforting. Our good host has been trying to live alone, but the fair faces I see around me to-night prove that he too is largely dependent upon the gentler sex for most that makes life worth living,—the society and love of friends,—and rumor is at fault if he does not soon yield entire subjection to one of them. Mr. Ryder will now respond to the toast,—The Ladies."

There was a pensive look in Mr. Ryder's eyes as he took the floor and adjusted his eye-glasses. He began by speaking of woman as the gift of Heaven to man, and after some general observations on the relations of the sexes he said: "But perhaps the quality which most distinguishes woman is her fidelity and devotion to those she loves. History is full of examples, but has recorded none more striking than one which only to-day came under my notice."

He then related, simply but effectively, the story told by his visitor of the afternoon. He gave it in the same soft dialect, which came readily to his lips, while the company listened attentively and sympathetically. For the story had awakened a responsive thrill in many hearts. There were some present who had seen, and others who had heard their fathers and grandfathers tell, the wrongs and sufferings of this past generation, and all of them still felt, in their darker moments, the shadow hanging over them. Mr. Ryder went on:—

"Such devotion and confidence are rare even among women. There are many who would have searched a year, some who would have waited five years, a few who might have hoped ten years; but for twenty-five years this woman has retained her affection for and her faith in a man she has not seen or heard of in all that time.

"She came to me to-day in the hope that I might be able to help her find this long-lost husband. And when she was gone I gave my fancy rein, and imagined a case I will put to you.

"Suppose that this husband, soon after his escape, had learned that his wife had been sold away, and that such inquiries as he could make brought no information of her whereabouts. Suppose that he was young, and she much older than he; that he was light, and she was black; that their marriage was a slave marriage, and legally binding only if they chose to make it so after the war. Suppose, too, that he made his way to the North, as some of us have done, and there, where he had larger opportunities, had improved them, and had in the course of all these years grown to be as different from the ignorant boy who ran away from fear of slavery as the day is from the night. Suppose, even, that he had qualified himself, by industry, by thrift, and by study, to win the friendship and be considered worthy the society of such people as these I see around me to-night, gracing my board and filling my heart with gladness; for I am old enough to remember the day when such a gathering would not have been possible in this land. Suppose, too, that, as the years went by, this man's memory of the past grew more and more indistinct, until at last it was rarely, except in his dreams, that any image of this bygone period rose before his mind. And then suppose that accident should bring to his knowledge the fact that the wife of his youth, the wife he had left behind him,—not one who had walked by his side and kept pace with him in his upward struggle, but one upon whom advancing years and a laborious life had set their mark,—was alive and seeking him, but that he was absolutely safe from recognition or discovery, unless he chose to reveal himself. My friends, what would the man do? I will presume that he was one who loved honor, and tried to deal justly with all men. I will even carry the case further, and suppose that perhaps he had set his heart upon another, whom he had hoped to call his own. What would he do, or rather what ought he to do, in such a crisis of a lifetime?

"It seemed to me that he might hesitate, and I imagined that I was an old friend, a near friend, and that he had come to me for advice; and I argued the case with him. I tried to discuss it impartially. After we had looked upon the matter from every point of view, I said to him, in words that we all know:—

"This above all: to thine own self be true,
And it must follow, as the night the day,
Thou canst not then be false to any man."[7]

Then, finally, I put the question to him, 'Shall you acknowledge her?'

"And now, ladies and gentlemen, friends and companions, I ask you, what should he have done?"

There was something in Mr. Ryder's voice that stirred the hearts of those who sat around him. It suggested more than mere sympathy with an imaginary situation; it seemed rather in the nature of a personal appeal. It was observed, too, that his look rested more especially upon Mrs. Dixon, with a mingled expression of renunciation and inquiry.

She had listened, with parted lips and streaming eyes. She was the first to speak: "He should have acknowledged her."

"Yes," they all echoed, "he should have acknowledged her."

"My friends and companions," responded Mr. Ryder, "I thank you, one and all. It is the answer I expected, for I knew your hearts."

He turned and walked toward the closed door of an adjoining room, while every eye followed him in wondering curiosity. He came back in a moment, leading by the hand his visitor of the afternoon, who stood startled and trembling at the sudden plunge into this scene of brilliant gayety. She was neatly dressed in gray, and wore the white cap of an elderly woman.

"Ladies and gentlemen," he said, "this is the woman, and I am the man, whose story I have told you. Permit me to introduce to you the wife of my youth."

1899

## The Passing of Grandison[1]

### I

When it is said that it was done to please a woman, there ought perhaps to be enough said to explain anything; for what a man will not do to please a woman is yet to be discovered. Nevertheless, it might be well to state a few preliminary facts to make it clear why young Dick Owens tried to run one of his father's negro men off to Canada.

In the early fifties, when the growth of anti-slavery sentiment and the constant drain of fugitive slaves into the North had so alarmed the slave-holders of the border states as to lead to the passage of the Fugitive Slave Law,[2] a young white man from Ohio, moved by compassion for the sufferings of a certain bondman who happened to have a "hard master," essayed to help the slave to freedom. The attempt was discovered and frustrated; the abductor was tried and convicted for slave-stealing, and sentenced to a term of imprisonment in the penitentiary. His death, after the expiration of only a small part of the sentence, from cholera contracted while nursing stricken fellow pris-

7. Shakespeare, *Hamlet* 1.3.
1. First published in *"The Wife of His Youth" and Other Stories of the Color Line* (1901); rpt. in *Southern Local Color: Stories of Region, Race, and Gender,* ed. Barbara C. Ewell and Pamela Glenn

Menke (2002), from which this text and some information from annotations are taken.
2. Part of the Compromise of 1850, the Fugitive Slave Law mandated the return to their owners of slaves who had escaped to free states.

oners, lent to the case a melancholy interest that made it famous in anti-slavery annals.

Dick Owens had attended the trial. He was a youth of about twenty-two, intelligent, handsome, and amiable, but extremely indolent, in a graceful and gentlemanly way; or, as old Judge Fenderson put it more than once, he was lazy as the Devil,—a mere figure of speech, of course, and not one that did justice to the Enemy of Mankind. When asked why he never did anything serious, Dick would good-naturedly reply, with a well-modulated drawl, that he didn't have to. His father was rich; there was but one other child, an unmarried daughter, who because of poor health would probably never marry, and Dick was therefore heir presumptive to a large estate. Wealth or social position he did not need to seek, for he was born to both. Charity Lomax had shamed him into studying law, but notwithstanding an hour or so a day spent at old Judge Fenderson's office, he did not make remarkable headway in his legal studies.

"What Dick needs," said the judge, who was fond of tropes, as became a scholar, and of horses, as was befitting a Kentuckian, "is the whip of necessity, or the spur of ambition. If he had either, he would soon need the snaffle[3] to hold him back."

But all Dick required, in fact, to prompt him to the most remarkable thing he accomplished before he was twenty-five, was a mere suggestion from Charity Lomax. The story was never really known to but two persons until after the war, when it came out because it was a good story and there was no particular reason for its concealment.

Young Owens had attended the trial of this slave-stealer, or martyr,—either or both,—and, when it was over, had gone to call on Charity Lomax, and, while they sat on the veranda after sundown, had told her all about the trial. He was a good talker, as his career in later years disclosed, and described the proceedings very graphically.

"I confess," he admitted, "that while my principles were against the prisoner, my sympathies were on his side. It appeared that he was of good family, and that he had an old father and mother, respectable people, dependent upon him for support and comfort in their declining years. He had been led into the matter by pity for a negro whose master ought to have been run out of the county long ago for abusing his slaves. If it had been merely a question of old Sam Briggs's negro, nobody would have cared anything about it. But father and the rest of them stood on the principle of the thing, and told the judge so, and the fellow was sentenced to three years in the penitentiary."

Miss Lomax had listened with lively interest.

"I've always hated old Sam Briggs," she said emphatically, "ever since the time he broke a negro's leg with a piece of cordwood. When I hear of a cruel deed it makes the Quaker blood that came from my grandmother assert itself. Personally I wish that all Sam Briggs's negroes would run away. As for the young man, I regard him as a hero. He dared something for humanity. I could love a man who would take such chances for the sake of others."

"Could you love me, Charity, if I did something heroic?"

"You never will, Dick. You're too lazy for any use. You'll never do anything harder than playing cards or fox-hunting."

3. Bit or restraint for a horse.

"Oh, come now, sweetheart! I've been courting you for a year, and it's the hardest work imaginable. Are you never going to love me?" he pleaded.

His hand sought hers, but she drew it back beyond his reach.

"I'll never love you, Dick Owens, until you have done something. When that time comes, I'll think about it."

"But it takes so long to do anything worth mentioning, and I don't want to wait. One must read two years to become a lawyer, and work five more to make a reputation. We shall both be gray by then."

"Oh, I don't know," she rejoined. "it doesn't require a lifetime for a man to prove that he is a man. This one did something, or at least tried to."

"Well, I'm willing to attempt as much as any other man. What do you want me to do, sweetheart? Give me a test."

"Oh, dear me!" said Charity, "I don't care what you *do,* so you do *something.* Really, come to think of it, why should I care whether you do anything or not?"

"I'm sure I don't know why you should, Charity," rejoined Dick humbly, "for I'm aware that I'm not worthy of it."

"Except that I do hate," she added, relenting slightly, "to see a really clever man so utterly lazy and good for nothing."

"Thank you, my dear; a word of praise from you has sharpened my wits already. I have an idea! Will you love me if *I* run a negro off to Canada?"

"What nonsense!" said Charity scornfully. "You must be losing your wits. Steal another man's slave, indeed, while your father owns a hundred!"

"Oh, there'll be no trouble about that," responded Dick lightly; "I'll run off one of the old man's; we've got too many anyway. It may not be quite as difficult as the other man found it, but it will be just as unlawful, and will demonstrate what I am capable of."

"Seeing's believing," replied Charity. "Of course, what you are talking about now is merely absurd. I'm going away for three weeks, to visit my aunt in Tennessee. If you are able to tell me, when I return, that you've done something to prove your quality, I'll—well, you may come and tell me about it."

## II

Young Owens got up about nine o'clock next morning, and while making his toilet put some questions to his personal attendant, a rather bright looking young mulatto of about his own age.

"Tom," said Dick.

"Yas, Mars Dick," responded the servant.

"I'm going on a trip North. Would you like to go with me?"

Now, if there was anything that Tom would have liked to make, it was a trip North. It was something he had long contemplated in the abstract, but had never been able to muster up sufficient courage to attempt in the concrete. He was prudent enough, however, to dissemble his feelings.

"I wouldn't min' it, Mars Dick, ez long ez you'd take keer er me an' fetch me home all right."

Tom's eyes belied his words, however, and his young master felt well assured that Tom needed only a good opportunity to make him run away. Having a comfortable home, and a dismal prospect in case of failure, Tom was not likely to take any desperate chances; but young Owens was satisfied that in a free state but little persuasion would be required to lead Tom astray. With a very logical and characteristic desire to gain his end with the least necessary expenditure of effort, he decided to take Tom with him, if his father did not object.

Colonel Owens had left the house when Dick went to breakfast, so Dick did not see his father till luncheon.

"Father," he remarked casually to the colonel over the fried chicken, "I'm feeling a trifle run down. I imagine my health would be improved somewhat by a little travel and change of scene."

"Why don't you take a trip North?" suggested his father. The colonel added to paternal affection a considerable respect for his son as the heir of a large estate. He himself had been "raised" in comparative poverty, and had laid the foundations of his fortune by hard work; and while he despised the ladder by which he had climbed, he could not entirely forget it, and unconsciously manifested, in his intercourse with his son, some of the poor man's deference toward the wealthy and well-born.

"I think I'll adopt your suggestion, sir," replied the son, "and run up to New York; and after I've been there awhile I may go on to Boston for a week or so. I've never been there, you know."

"There are some matters you can talk over with my factor[4] in New York," rejoined the colonel, "and while you are up there among the Yankees, I hope you'll keep your eyes and ears open to find out what the rascally abolitionists[5] are saying and doing. They're becoming altogether too active for our comfort, and entirely too many ungrateful niggers are running away. I hope the conviction of that fellow yesterday may discourage the rest of the breed. I'd just like to catch any one trying to run off one of my darkeys. He'd get short shrift; I don't think any Court would have a chance to try him."

"They are a pestiferous lot," assented Dick, "and dangerous to our institutions. But say, father, if I go North I shall want to take Tom with me."

Now, the colonel, while a very indulgent father, had pronounced views on the subject of negroes, having studied them, as he often said, for a great many years, and, as he asserted oftener still, understanding them perfectly. It is scarcely worth while to say, either, that he valued more highly than if he had inherited them the slaves he had toiled and schemed for.

"I don't think it safe to take Tom up North," he declared, with promptness and decision. "He's a good enough boy, but too smart to trust among those low-down abolitionists. I strongly suspect him of having learned to read, though I can't imagine how. I saw him with a newspaper the other day, and while he pretended to be looking at a woodcut, I'm almost sure he was reading the paper. I think it by no means safe to take him."

Dick did not insist, because he knew it was useless. The colonel would have obliged his son in any other matter, but his negroes were the outward and visible sign of his wealth and station, and therefore sacred to him.

"Whom do you think it safe to take?" asked Dick. "I suppose I'll have to have a body-servant."

"What's the matter with Grandison?" suggested the colonel. "He's handy enough, and I reckon we can trust him. He's too fond of good eating to risk losing his regular meals; besides, he's sweet on your mother's maid, Betty, and

---

4. An agent for the sale of goods entrusted to his possession—in this case, a cotton factor.

5. Abolitionists argued for immediate emancipation of all slaves in the United States.

I've promised to let 'em get married before long. I'll have Grandison up, and we'll talk to him. Here, you boy Jack," called the colonel to a yellow[6] youth in the next room who was catching flies and pulling their wings off to pass the time, "go down to the barn and tell Grandison to come here."

"Grandison," said the colonel, when the negro stood before him, hat in hand.

"Yas, marster."

"Haven't I always treated you right?"

"Yas, marster."

"Haven't you always got all you wanted to eat?"

"Yas, marster."

"And as much whiskey and tobacco as was good for you, Grandison?"

"Y-a-s, marster."

"I should just like to know, Grandison, whether you don't think yourself a great deal better off than those poor free negroes down by the plank road, with no kind master to look after them and no mistress to give them medicine when they're sick and—and—"

"Well, I sh'd jes' reckon I is better off, suh, dan dem low-down free niggers, suh! Ef anybody ax 'em who dey b'long ter, dey has ter say nobody, er e'se lie erbout it. Anybody ax me who I b'longs ter, I ain' got no 'casion ter be shame' ter tell 'em, no, suh, 'deed I ain', suh!"

The colonel was beaming. This was true gratitude, and his feudal heart thrilled at such appreciative homage. What cold-blooded, heartless monsters they were who would break up this blissful relationship of kindly protection on the one hand, of wise subordination and loyal dependence on the other! The colonel always became indignant at the mere thought of such wickedness.

"Grandison," the colonel continued, "your young master Dick is going North for a few weeks, and I am thinking of letting him take you along. I shall send you on this trip, Grandison, in order that you may take care of your young master. He will need some one to wait on him, and no one can ever do it so well as one of the boys brought up with him on the old plantation. I am going to trust him in your hands, and I'm sure you'll do your duty faithfully, and bring him back home safe and sound—to old Kentucky."

Grandison grinned. "Oh yas, marster, I'll take keer er young Mars Dick."

"I want to warn you, though, Grandison," continued the colonel impressively, "against these cussed abolitionists, who try to entice servants from their comfortable homes and their indulgent masters, from the blue skies, the green fields, and the warm sunlight of their southern home, and send them away off yonder to Canada, a dreary country, where the woods are full of wildcats and wolves and bears, where the snow lies up to the eaves of the houses for six months of the year, and the cold is so severe that it freezes your breath and curdles your blood; and where, when runaway niggers get sick and can't work, they are turned out to starve and die, unloved and uncared for. I reckon, Grandison, that you have too much sense to permit yourself to be led astray by any such foolish and wicked people."

" 'Deed, suh, I would n' low none er dem cussed, low-down abolitioners ter come nigh me, suh. I'd—I'd—would I be 'lowed ter hit 'em, suh?"

---

6. Refers to a light-complexioned person of mixed race who can sometimes "pass" for white.

"Certainly, Grandison," replied the colonel, chuckling, "hit 'em, as hard as you can. I reckon they'd rather like it. Begad, I believe they would! It would serve 'em right to be hit by a nigger!"

"Er ef I did n't hit 'em, suh," continued Grandison reflectively, "I'd tell Mars Dick, en *he'd* fix 'em. He'd smash de face off'n 'em, suh, I jes' knows he would."

"Oh yes, Grandison, your young master will protect you. You need fear no harm while he is near."

"Dey won't try ter steal me, will dey, marster?" asked the negro, with sudden alarm.

"I don't know, Grandison," replied the colonel, lighting a fresh cigar. "They're a desperate set of lunatics, and there's no telling what they may resort to. But if you stick close to your young master, and remember always that he is your best friend, and understands your real needs, and has your true interests at heart, and if you will be careful to avoid strangers who try to talk to you, you'll stand a fair chance of getting back to your home and your friends. And if you please your master Dick, he'll buy you a present, and a string of beads for Betty to wear when you and she get married in the fall."

"Thanky, marster, thanky, suh," replied Grandison, oozing gratitude at every pore; "you is a good marster, to be sho', suh; yas, 'deed you is. You kin jes' bet me and Mars Dick gwine git 'long jes' lack I wuz own boy ter Mars Dick. En it won't be my fault ef he don' want me fer his boy all de time, w'en we come back home ag'in."

"All right, Grandison, you may go now. You needn't work any more today, and here's a piece of tobacco for you off my own plug."

"Thanky, marster, thanky, marster! You is de bes' marster any nigger ever had in dis worl'." And Grandison bowed and scraped and disappeared round the corner, his jaws closing around a large section of the colonel's best tobacco.

"You may take Grandison," said the colonel to his son. "I allow he's abolitionist-proof."

### III

Richard Owens, Esq., and servant, from Kentucky, registered at the fashionable New York hostelry for Southerners in those days, a hotel where an atmosphere congenial to Southern institutions was sedulously maintained. But there were negro waiters in the dining-room, and mulatto bell-boys, and Dick had no doubt that Grandison, with the native gregariousness and garrulousness of his race, would foregather and palaver with them, sooner or later, and Dick hoped that they would speedily inoculate him with the virus of freedom. For it was not Dick's intention to say anything to his servant about his plan to free him, for obvious reasons. To mention one of them, if Grandison should go away, and by legal process be recaptured, his young master's part in the matter would doubtless become known, which would be embarrassing to Dick, to say the least. If, on the other hand, he should merely give Grandison sufficient latitude, he had no doubt he would eventually lose him. For while not exactly skeptical about Grandison's perfervid loyalty, Dick had been a somewhat keen observer of human nature, in his own indolent way, and based his expectations upon the force of the example and argument that his servant could scarcely fail to encounter. Grandison should have a fair chance to become free by his own initiative; if it should become necessary to adopt other measures to get rid of him, it would be time enough to act when the necessity arose; and Dick Owens was not the youth to take needless trouble.

The young master renewed some acquaintances and made others, and spent a week or two very pleasantly in the best society of the metropolis, easily accessible to a wealthy, well-bred young Southerner, with proper introductions. Young women smiled on him and young men of convivial habits pressed their hospitalities; but the memory of Charity's sweet, strong face and clear blue eyes made him proof against the blandishments of the one sex and the persuasions of the other. Meanwhile he kept Grandison supplied with pocket-money, and left him mainly to his own devices. Every night when Dick came in he hoped he might have to wait upon himself, and every morning he looked forward with pleasure to the prospect of making his toilet unaided. His hopes, however, were doomed to disappointment, for every night when he came in Grandison was on hand with a bootjack,[7] and a nightcap mixed for his young master as the colonel had taught him to mix it, and every morning Grandison appeared with his master's boots blacked and his clothes brushed, and laid his linen out for the day.

"Grandison," said Dick one morning, after finishing his toilet, "this is the chance of your life to go around among your own people and see how they live. Have you met any of them?"

"Yas, suh, I's seen some of 'em. But I don' keer nuffin fer 'em, suh. Dey're diffe'nt f'm de niggers down ou' way. Dey 'lows dey're free, but dey ain' got sense 'nuff ter know dey ain' half as well off as dey would be down Souf, whar dey'd be 'preciated."

When two weeks had passed without any apparent effect of evil example upon Grandison, Dick resolved to go on to Boston, where he thought the atmosphere might prove more favorable to his ends. After he had been at the Revere House[8] for a day or two without losing Grandison, he decided upon slightly different tactics.

Having ascertained from a city directory the addresses of several well-known abolitionists, he wrote them each a letter something like this:—

DEAR FRIEND AND BROTHER:—

> A wicked slaveholder from Kentucky, stopping at the Revere House, has dared to insult the liberty-loving people of Boston by bringing his slave into their midst. Shall this be tolerated? Or shall steps be taken in the name of liberty to rescue a fellow-man from bondage? For obvious reasons I can only sign myself,

A FRIEND OF HUMANITY.

That his letter might have an opportunity to prove effective, Dick made it a point to send Grandison away from the hotel on various errands. On one of these occasions Dick watched him for quite a distance down the street. Grandison had scarcely left the hotel when a long-haired, sharp-featured man came out behind him, followed him, soon overtook him, and kept along beside him until they turned the next corner. Dick's hopes were roused by this

7. Device for removing close-fitting boots.
8. The home of Revolutionary War hero Paul Revere.

spectacle, but sank correspondingly when Grandison returned to the hotel. As Grandison said nothing about the encounter, Dick hoped there might be some self-consciousness behind this unexpected reticence, the results of which might develop later on.

But Grandison was on hand again when his master came back to the hotel at night, and was in attendance again in the morning, with hot water, to assist at his master's toilet. Dick sent him on further errands from day to day, and upon one occasion came squarely up to him—inadvertently of course—while Grandison was engaged in conversation with a young white man in clerical garb. When Grandison saw Dick approaching, he edged away from the preacher and hastened toward his master, with a very evident expression of relief upon his countenance.

"Mars Dick," he said, "dese yer abolitioners is jes' pesterin' de life out er me tryin' ter git me ter run away. I don' pay no 'tention ter 'em, but dey riles me so sometimes dat I'm feared I'll hit some of 'em some er dese days, an' dat mought git me inter trouble. I ain' said nuffin' ter you 'bout it, Mars Dick, fer I did n' wanter 'sturb yo' min'; but I don' like it, suh; no, suh, I don'! Is we gwine back home 'fo' long, Mars Dick?"

"We'll be going back soon enough," replied Dick somewhat shortly, while he inwardly cursed the stupidity of a slave who could be free and would not, and registered a secret vow that if he were unable to get rid of Grandison without assassinating him, and were therefore compelled to take him back to Kentucky, he would see that Grandison got a taste of an article of slavery that would make him regret his wasted opportunities. Meanwhile he determined to tempt his servant yet more strongly.

"Grandison," he said next morning, "I'm going away for a day or two, but I shall leave you here. I shall lock up a hundred dollars in this drawer and give you the key. If you need any of it, use it and enjoy yourself,—spend it all if you like,—for this is probably the last chance you'll have for some time to be in a free State, and you 'd better enjoy your liberty while you may."

When he came back a couple of days later and found the faithful Grandison at his post, and the hundred dollars intact, Dick felt seriously annoyed. His vexation was increased by the fact that he could not express his feelings adequately. He did not even scold Grandison; how could he, indeed, find fault with one who so sensibly recognized his true place in the economy of civilization, and kept it with such touching fidelity?

"I can't say a thing to him," groaned Dick. "He deserves a leather medal, made out of his own hide tanned. I reckon I'll write to father and let him know what a model servant he has given me."

He wrote his father a letter which made the colonel swell with pride and pleasure. "I really think," the colonel observed to one of his friends, "that Dick ought to have the nigger interviewed by the Boston papers, so that they may see how contented and happy our darkeys really are."

Dick also wrote a long letter to Charity Lomax, in which he said, among many other things, that if she knew how hard he was working, and under what difficulties, to accomplish something serious for her sake, she would no longer keep him in suspense, but overwhelm him with love and admiration.

Having thus exhausted without result the more obvious methods of getting rid of Grandison, and diplomacy having also proved a failure, Dick was forced to consider more radical measures. Of course he might run away himself, and abandon Grandison, but this would be merely to leave him in the United States, where he was still a slave, and where, with his notions of loyalty, he would speedily be reclaimed. It was necessary, in order to accomplish the purpose of his trip to the North, to leave Grandison permanently in Canada, where he would be legally free.

"I might extend my trip to Canada," he reflected, "but that would be too palpable. I have it! I'll visit Niagara Falls on the way home, and lose him on the Canadian side. When he once realizes that he is actually free, I'll warrant that he'll stay."

So the next day saw them westward bound, and in due course of time, by the somewhat slow conveyances of the period, they found themselves at Niagara. Dick walked and drove about the Falls for several days, taking Grandison along with him on most occasions. One morning they stood on the Canadian side, watching the wild whirl of the waters below them.

"Grandison," said Dick, raising his voice above the roar of the cataract, "do you know where you are now?"

"I's wid you, Mars Dick; dat's all I keers."

"You are now in Canada, Grandison, where your people go when they run away from their masters. If you wished, Grandison, you might walk away from me this very minute, and I could not lay my hand upon you to take you back."

Grandison looked around uneasily.

"Let's go back ober de ribber, Mars Dick. I's feared I'll lose you ovuh heah, an' den I won' hab no marster, an' won't nebber be able to git back home no mo'."

Discouraged, but not yet hopeless, Dick said, a few minutes later,—

"Grandison, I'm going up the road a bit, to the inn over yonder. You stay here until I return. I'll not be gone a great while."

Grandison's eyes opened wide and he looked somewhat fearful.

"Is dey any er dem dadblasted abolitioners roun' heah, Mars Dick?"

"I don't imagine that there are," replied his master, hoping there might be. "But I'm not afraid of *your* running away, Grandison. I only wish I were," he added to himself.

Dick walked leisurely down the road to where the whitewashed inn, built of stone, with true British solidity, loomed up through the trees by the roadside. Arrived there he ordered a glass of ale and a sandwich, and took a seat at a table by a window, from which he could see Grandison in the distance. For a while he hoped that the seed he had sown might have fallen on fertile ground, and that Grandison, relieved from the restraining power of a master's eye, and finding himself in a free country, might get up and walk away; but the hope was vain, for Grandison remained faithfully at his post, awaiting his master's return. He had seated himself on a broad flat stone, and, turning his eyes away from the grand and awe-inspiring spectacle that lay close at hand, was looking anxiously toward the inn where his master sat cursing his ill-timed fidelity.

By and by a girl came into the room to serve his order, and Dick very naturally glanced at her; and as she was young and pretty and remained in attendance, it was some minutes before he looked for Grandison. When he did so his faithful servant had disappeared.

To pay his reckoning and go away without the change was a matter quickly accomplished. Retracing his footsteps toward the Falls, he saw, to his great disgust, as he approached the spot where he had left Grandison, the familiar form of his servant stretched out on the ground, his face to the sun, his mouth open, sleeping the time away, oblivious alike to the grandeur of the scenery, the thunderous roar of the cataract, or the insidious voice of sentiment.

"Grandison," soliloquized his master, as he stood gazing down at his ebony encumbrance, "I do not deserve to be an American citizen; I ought not to have the advantages I possess over you; and I certainly am not worthy of Charity Lomax, if I am not smart enough to get rid of you. I have an idea! You shall yet be free, and I will be the instrument of your deliverance. Sleep on, faithful and affectionate servitor, and dream of the blue grass and the bright skies of old Kentucky, for it is only in your dreams that you will ever see them again!"

Dick retraced his footsteps toward the inn. The young woman chanced to look out of the window and saw the handsome young gentleman she had waited on a few minutes before, standing in the road a short distance away, apparently engaged in earnest conversation with a colored man employed as hostler[9] for the inn. She thought she saw something pass from the white man to the other, but at that moment her duties called her away from the window, and when she looked out again the young gentleman had disappeared, and the hostler, with two other young men of the neighborhood, one white and one colored, were walking rapidly towards the Falls.

## IV

Dick made the journey homeward alone, and as rapidly as the conveyances of the day would permit. As he drew near home his conduct in going back without Grandison took on a more serious aspect than it had borne at any previous time, and although he had prepared the colonel by a letter sent several days ahead, there was still the prospect of a bad quarter of an hour with him; not, indeed, that his father would upbraid him, but he was likely to make searching inquiries. And notwithstanding the vein of quiet recklessness that had carried Dick through his preposterous scheme, he was a very poor liar, having rarely had occasion or inclination to tell anything but the truth. Any reluctance to meet his father was more than offset, however, by a stronger force drawing him homeward, for Charity Lomax must long since have returned from her visit to her aunt in Tennessee.

Dick got off easier than he had expected. He told a straight story, and a truthful one, so far as it went.

The colonel raged at first, but rage soon subsided into anger, and anger moderated into annoyance, and annoyance into a sort of garrulous sense of injury. The colonel thought he had been hardly used; he had trusted this negro, and he had broken faith. Yet, after all, he did not blame Grandison so much as he did the abolitionists, who were undoubtedly at the bottom of it.

As for Charity Lomax, Dick told her, privately of course, that he had run his father's man, Grandison, off to Canada, and left him there.

"Oh, Dick," she had said with shuddering alarm, "what have you done? If they knew it they'd send you to the penitentiary, like they did that Yankee."

9. Attendant for travelers' horses.

"But they don't know it," he had replied seriously; adding, with an injured tone, "you don't seem to appreciate my heroism like you did that of the Yankee; perhaps it's because I wasn't caught and sent to the penitentiary. I thought you wanted me to do it."

"Why, Dick Owens!" she exclaimed. "You know I never dreamed of any such outrageous proceeding."

"But I presume I'll have to marry you," she concluded, after some insistence on Dick's part, "if only to take care of you. You are too reckless for anything; and a man who goes chasing all over the North, being entertained by New York and Boston society and having negroes to throw away, needs some one to look after him."

"It's a most remarkable thing," replied Dick fervently, "that your views correspond exactly with my profoundest convictions. It proves beyond question that we were made for one another."

They were married three weeks later. As each of them had just returned from a journey, they spent their honeymoon at home.

A week after the wedding they were seated, one afternoon, on the piazza of the colonel's house, where Dick had taken his bride, when a negro from the yard ran down the lane and threw open the big gate for the colonel's buggy to enter. The colonel was not alone. Beside him, ragged and travel-stained, bowed with weariness, and upon his face a haggard look that told of hardship and privation, sat the lost Grandison.

The colonel alighted at the steps.

"Take the lines, Tom," he said to the man who had opened the gate, "and drive round to the barn. Help Grandison down,—poor devil, he's so stiff he can hardly move!—and get a tub of water and wash him and rub him down, and feed him, and give him a big drink of whiskey, and then let him come round and see his young master and his new mistress."

The colonel's face wore an expression compounded of joy and indignation,—joy at the restoration of a valuable piece of property; indignation for reasons he proceeded to state.

"It's astounding, the depths of depravity the human heart is capable of! I was coming along the road three miles away, when I heard some one call me from the roadside. I pulled up the mare, and who should come out of the woods but Grandison. The poor nigger could hardly crawl along, with the help of a broken limb. I was never more astonished in my life. You could have knocked me down with a feather. He seemed pretty far gone,—he could hardly talk above a whisper,—and I had to give him a mouthful of whiskey to brace him up so he could tell his story. It's just as I thought from the beginning, Dick; Grandison had no notion of running away; he knew when he was well off, and where his friends were. All the persuasions of abolition liars and runaway niggers did not move him. But the desperation of those fanatics knew no bounds; their guilty consciences gave them no rest. They got the notion somehow that Grandison belonged to a nigger-catcher, and had been brought North as a spy to help capture ungrateful runaway servants. They actually kidnapped him—just think of it!—and gagged him and bound him and threw him rudely into a wagon, and carried him into the gloomy depths of a Canadian forest, and locked him in a lonely hut, and fed him on bread and water for three weeks. One of the scoundrels wanted to kill him, and persuaded the others that it ought to be done; but they got to quarreling about how they should do it, and before they had their minds made up Grandison escaped, and, keeping his back steadily to the North Star, made his way, after suffering incredible hardships, back to the old plantation, back to his master, his friends, and his home. Why, it's as good as one of Scott's novels Mr. Simms[1] or some other one of our Southern authors ought to write it up."

"Don't you think, sir," suggested Dick, who had calmly smoked his cigar throughout the colonel's animated recital, "that that kidnapping yarn sounds a little improbable? Isn't there some more likely explanation?"

"Nonsense, Dick; it's the gospel truth! Those infernal abolitionists are capable of anything—everything! Just think of their locking the poor, faithful nigger up, beating him, kicking him, depriving him of his liberty, keeping him on bread and water for three long, lonesome weeks, and he all the time pining for the old plantation!"

There were almost tears in the colonel's eyes at the picture of Grandison's sufferings that he conjured up. Dick still professed to be slightly skeptical, and met Charity's severely questioning eye with bland unconsciousness.

The colonel killed the fatted calf[2] for Grandison, and for two or three weeks the returned wanderer's life was a slave's dream of pleasure. His fame spread through-out the county, and the colonel gave him a permanent place among the house servants, where he could always have him conveniently at hand to relate his adventures to admiring visitors.

About three weeks after Grandison's return the colonel's faith in sable humanity was rudely shaken, and its foundations almost broken up. He came near losing his belief in the fidelity of the negro to his master,—the servile virtue most highly prized and most sedulously cultivated by the colonel and his kind. One Monday morning Grandison was missing. And not only Grandison, but his wife, Betty the maid; his mother, aunt Eunice; his father, uncle Ike; his brothers, Tom and John, and his little sister Elsie, were likewise absent from the plantation: and a hurried search and inquiry in the neighborhood resulted in no information as to their whereabouts. So much valuable property could not be lost without an effort to recover it, and the wholesale nature of the transaction carried consternation to the hearts of those whose ledgers were chiefly bound in black. Extremely energetic measures were taken by the colonel and his friends. The fugitives were traced, and followed from point to point, on their northward run through Ohio. Several times the hunters were close upon their heels, but the magnitude of the escaping party begot unusual vigilance on the part of those who sympathized with the fugitives, and strangely enough, the underground railroad[3] seemed to have had its tracks cleared and signals set for this particular train. Once, twice, the colonel thought he had them, but they slipped through his fingers.

One last glimpse he caught of his vanishing property, as he stood, accompanied by a United States marshal, on a wharf at a port on the south shore

---

1. William Gilmore Simms (1806–1870), perhaps the antebellum South's most admired writer. Sir Walter Scott (1771–1832), British author whose historical novels were immensely popular in the South, particularly those about medieval feudalism.
2. When the prodigal son of Jesus' parable returned home from a life of dissipation, his joyful father butchered a calf for a special feast (Luke 15.11–32).
3. The system of safe havens in the homes of abolitionists along the dangerous escape route from the South to Canada.

of Lake Erie. On the stern of a small steamboat which was receding rapidly from the wharf, with her nose pointing toward Canada, there stood a group of familiar dark faces, and the look they cast backward was not one of longing for the fleshpots of Egypt.[4] The colonel saw Grandison point him out to one of the crew of the vessel, who waved his hand derisively toward the colonel. The latter shook his fist impotently—and the incident was closed.

1901

4. When the fleeing Israelites began to starve in the desert, they complained to Moses that they preferred the full pots of meat they had had as slaves in Egypt (Exodus 16.2–3).

---

# CHARLES ALEXANDER EASTMAN (OHIYESA)
## 1858–1939

Charles Alexander Eastman, a Santee Sioux, was born at Red Wood Falls, Minnesota, in 1858. The youngest of five children of Many Lightnings, a full-blood Sioux, and Mary Eastman, daughter of the well-known painter of Indian subjects Seth Eastman, Eastman was named Hakadah, or The Pitiful Last. This "humiliating name," as he calls it in his first book, *Indian Boyhood* (1902), was changed to Ohiyesa, The Winner, as a result of a victory in a lacrosse game. In 1862 Many Lightnings took part in the Minnesota Sioux uprising and fled with his family over the border to Canada to escape arrest by the U.S. government. Along with Little Six and Medicine Bottle, two leaders of the uprising, Many Lightnings was captured by pursuing troops, and carried back to the United States. His family assumed that he would be executed, and so they remained among the Canadian Sioux. Until his eleventh year, Ohiyesa led a traditional Sioux life.

But in 1869, Many Lightnings, now a Christian convert who had taken the name Jacob Eastman, came for his son, renamed him Charles Alexander Eastman, and set him to acquiring an education. Eastman first attended mission schools in South Dakota, where his father farmed, then Beloit and Knox colleges. He continued his formal education on scholarship at Dartmouth, before taking his M.D. at the Boston University School of Medicine. Eastman's first post was as a physician at Pine Ridge Agency in South Dakota; the year was 1890, and the acculturated Christian doctor soon found himself ministering to wounded Ghost Dancers, his fellow Sioux. This sort of situation—both-and, as it were, rather than either-or—was to be Eastman's lot all the rest of his life.

Thus he supported the 1887 Dawes Allotment Act and its aim of turning what had been tribally held lands into tracts of private property. From 1903 to 1908, he participated in a government project to assign Sioux people Anglicized names and in 1910 helped establish the Boy Scout movement in the United States so that American youth might have an outdoor "Indian" experience. No one of these actions (and others) on Eastman's part can be taken as exclusive evidence of either his commitment to "civilizing" the Indian—something he did believe necessary to the survival of Native people—or his commitment to preserving the most important values of indigenous peoples, also important to him. His brave and persistent attempt in this difficult "transition" period to bridge two worlds may be seen in the last book he was to publish. *Indian Heroes and Great Chieftains* (1918) celebrates both Native leaders who accommodated the whites or mediated between Indian and white people (e.g., American Horse, who appears in one of the accounts) and leaders like Crazy Horse, Sitting Bull, and Gall, who steadfastly resisted and rejected the religion and the culture of the Euro-Americans.

In the last years of his life, Eastman largely withdrew from public affairs, spending much of the 1930s living simply in a cabin in the woods of Ontario. This move from civilization to the deep woods brought him full circle from his most widely read book, his 1916 autobiography, *From the Deep Woods to Civilization*.

## *From* From the Deep Woods to Civilization[1]

### *Chapter VII. The Ghost Dance War*

A religious craze such as that of 1890–91 was a thing foreign to the Indian philosophy.[2] I recalled that a hundred years before, on the overthrow of the Algonquin nations, a somewhat similar faith was evolved by the astute Delaware prophet, brother to Tecumseh. It meant that the last hope of race entity had departed, and my people were groping blindly after spiritual relief in their bewilderment and misery. I believe that the first prophets of the "Red Christ" were innocent enough and that the people generally were sincere, but there were doubtless some who went into it for self-advertisement, and who introduced new and fantastic features to attract the crowd.

The ghost dancers had gradually concentrated on the Medicine Root creek and the edge of the "Bad Lands,"[3] and they were still further isolated by a new order from the agent, calling in all those who had not adhered to the new religion. Several thousand of these "friendlies" were soon encamped on the White Clay creek, close by the agency. It was near the middle of December, with weather unusually mild for that season. The dancers held that there would be no snow so long as their rites continued.

An Indian called Little had been guilty of some minor offense on the reservation and had hitherto evaded arrest. Suddenly he appeared at the agency on an issue day, for the express purpose, as it seemed, of defying the authorities. The assembly room of the Indian police, used also as a council room, opened out of my dispensary, and on this particular morning a council was in progress. I heard some loud talking, but was too busy to pay particular attention, though my assistant had gone in to listen to the speeches. Suddenly the place was in an uproar, and George burst into the inner office, crying excitedly "Look out for yourself, friend! They are going to fight!"

I went around to see what was going on. A crowd had gathered just outside the council room, and the police were surrounded by wild Indians with guns and drawn knives in their hands. "Hurry up with them!" one shouted, while another held his stone war-club over a policeman's head. The attempt to arrest Little had met with a stubborn resistance.

At this critical moment, a fine-looking Indian in citizen's clothes faced the excited throng, and spoke in a clear, steady, almost sarcastic voice.

"Stop! Think! What are you going to do? Kill these men of our own race? Then what? Kill all these helpless white men, women and children? And what

1. The text reprinted here is from the first edition (1916).
2. Contrary to Eastman's statement that movements like the Ghost Dance are "foreign to the Indian philosophy," there was a Paiute Ghost Dance in the 1870s and other messianic movements.
3. An area of stark terrain about fifty miles northwest of the Pine Ridge agency.

then? What will these brave words, brave deeds lead to in the end? How long can you hold out? Your country is surrounded with a network of railroads; thousands of white soldiers will be here within three days. What ammunition have you? what provisions? What will become of your families? Think, think, my brothers! this is a child's madness."

It was the "friendly" chief, American Horse, and it seems to me as I recall the incident that this man's voice had almost magic power. It is likely that he saved us all from massacre, for the murder of the police, who represented the authority of the Government, would surely have been followed by a general massacre. It is a fact that those Indians who upheld the agent were in quite as much danger from their wilder brethren as were the whites, indeed it was said that the feeling against them was even stronger. Jack Red Cloud, son of the chief, thrust the muzzle of a cocked revolver almost into the face of American Horse. "It is you and your kind," he shouted, "who have brought us to this pass!" That brave man never flinched. Ignoring his rash accuser, he quietly reentered the office; the door closed behind him; the mob dispersed, and for the moment the danger seemed over.

That evening I was surprised by a late call from American Horse, the hero of the day. His wife entered close behind him. Scarcely were they seated when my door again opened softly, and Captain Sword came in, followed by Lieutenant Thunder Bear and most of the Indian police. My little room was crowded. I handed them some tobacco, which I had always at hand for my guests, although I did not smoke myself. After a silence, the chief got up and shook hands with me ceremoniously. In a short speech, he asked my advice in the difficult situation that confronted them between the ghost dancers, men of their own blood, and the Government to which they had pledged their loyalty.

Thanks to Indian etiquette, I could allow myself two or three minutes to weigh my words before replying. I finally said, in substance: "There is only one thing for us to do and be just to both sides. We must use every means for a peaceful settlement of this difficulty. Let us be patient; let us continue to reason with the wilder element, even though some hotheads may threaten our lives. If the worst happens, however, it is our solemn duty to serve the United States Government. Let no man ever say that we were disloyal! Following such a policy, dead or alive, we shall have no apology to make."

After the others had withdrawn, Sword informed me confidentially that certain young men had threatened to kill American Horse while asleep in his tent, and that his friends had prevailed upon him and his wife to ask my hospitality for a few days. I showed Mrs. American Horse to a small room that I had vacant, and soon afterward came three strokes of the office bell—the signal for me to report at the agent's office.

I found there the agent, his chief clerk, and a visiting inspector, all of whom obviously regarded the situation as serious. "You see, doctor," said the agent, "the occurrence of today was planned with remarkable accuracy, so that even our alert police were taken entirely by surprise and readily overpowered. What will be the sequel we cannot tell, but we must be prepared for anything. I shall be glad to have your views," he added.

I told him that I still did not believe there was any widespread plot, or deliberate intention to make war upon the whites. In my own mind, I felt sure that the arrival of troops would be construed by the ghost dancers as a threat or a challenge, and would put them at once on the defensive. I was not in favor of that step; neither was Mr. Cook, who was also called into conference; but the officials evidently feared a general uprising, and argued that it was their duty to safeguard the lives of the employees and others by calling for the soldiers without more delay. Sword, Thunder Bear, and American Horse were sent for and their opinions appeared to be fully in accord with those of the agent and inspector, so the matter was given out as settled. As a matter of fact, the agent had telegraphed to Fort Robinson[4] for troops before he made a pretense of consulting us Indians, and they were already on their way to Pine Ridge.

I scarcely knew at the time, but gradually learned afterward, that the Sioux had many grievances and causes for profound discontent, which lay back of and were more or less closely related to the ghost dance craze and the prevailing restlessness and excitement. Rations had been cut from time to time; the people were insufficiently fed, and their protests and appeals were disregarded. Never was more ruthless fraud and graft practiced upon a defenseless people than upon these poor natives by the politicans! Never were there more worthless "scraps of paper" anywhere in the world than many of the Indian treaties and Government documents! Sickness was prevalent and the death rate alarming, especially among the children. Trouble from all these causes had for some time been developing, but might have been checked by humane and conciliatory measures. The "Messiah craze" in itself was scarcely a source of danger, and one might almost as well call upon the army to suppress Billy Sunday[5] and his hysterical followers. Other tribes than the Sioux who adopted the new religion were let alone, and the craze died a natural death in the course of a few months.

Among the leaders of the malcontents[6] at this time were Jack Red Cloud, No Water, He Dog, Four Bears, Yellow Bear, and Kicking Bear. Friendly leaders included American Horse, Young Man Afraid of his Horses, Bad Wound, Three Stars. There was still another set whose attitude was not clearly defined, and among these men was Red Cloud,[7] the greatest of them all. He who had led his people so brilliantly and with such remarkable results, both in battle and diplomacy, was now an old man of over seventy years, living in a frame house which had been built for him within a half mile of the agency. He would come to council, but said little or nothing. No one knew exactly where he stood, but it seemed that he was broken in spirit as in body and convinced of the hopelessness of his people's cause.

It was Red Cloud who asked the historic question, at a great council held in the Black Hills region with a Government commission, and after good Bishop Whipple had finished the invocation, "Which God is our brother praying to now? Is it the same God whom they have twice deceived, when they made treaties with us which they afterward broke?"

Early in the morning after the attempted arrest of Little, George rushed into my quarters and awakened me. "Come quick!" he shouted, "the soldiers

---

4. Near the White River, which runs through the Badlands in South Dakota.
5. William Ashley Sunday (1862–1935), a popular American evangelist.
6. Traditionalists opposed to accommodationist practices of "progressive" or "friendly" leaders like American Horse.
7. In 1866 Chief Red Cloud (1822–1909) led the Oglala Sioux's opposition to the expansion of the Union Pacific Railroad into Sioux country, which disturbed, among other things, the migratory patterns of buffalo herds. He gave an internationally recognized speech at the Cooper Union in New York in 1879, calling for justice for the American Indian. After gold was discovered in the Black Hills of the Dakotas in the 1870s, he led the attempt to keep fortune hunters from overrunning the region, which was sacred ground for the Sioux.

are here!" I looked along the White Clay creek toward the little railroad town of Rushville, Nebraska, twenty-five miles away, and just as the sun rose above the knife-edged ridges black with stunted pine, I perceived a moving cloud of dust that marked the trail of the Ninth Cavalry. There was instant commotion among the camps of friendly Indians. Many women and children were coming in to the agency for refuge, evidently fearing that the dreaded soldiers might attack their villages by mistake. Some who had not heard of their impending arrival hurried to the offices to ask what it meant. I assured those who appealed to me that the troops were here only to preserve order, but their suspicions were not easily allayed.

As the cavalry came nearer, we saw that they were colored troopers, wearing buffalo overcoats and muskrat caps; the Indians with their quick wit called them "buffalo soldiers."[8] They halted, and established their temporary camp in the open space before the agency enclosure. The news had already gone out through the length and breadth of the reservation, and the wildest rumors were in circulation. Indian scouts might be seen upon every hill top, closely watching the military encampment.

At this juncture came the startling news from Fort Yates, some two hundred and fifty miles to the north of us, that Sitting Bull had been killed by Indian police while resisting arrest, and a number of his men with him, as well as several of the police. We next heard that the remnant of his band had fled in our direction, and soon afterward, that they had been joined by Big Foot's band from the western part of Cheyenne River agency, which lay directly in their road. United States troops continued to gather at strategic points, and of course the press seized upon the opportunity to enlarge upon the strained situation and predict an "Indian uprising." The reporters were among us, and managed to secure much "news" that no one else ever heard of. Border towns were fortified and cowboys and militia gathered in readiness to protect them against the "red devils." Certain classes of the frontier population industriously fomented the excitement for what there was in it for them, since much money is apt to be spent at such times. As for the poor Indians, they were quite as badly scared as the whites and perhaps with more reason.

General Brooke undertook negotiations with the ghost dancers, and finally induced them to come within reach. They camped on a flat about a mile north of us and in full view, while the more tractable bands were still gathered on the south and west. The large boarding school had locked its doors and succeeded in holding its hundreds of Indian children, partly for their own sakes, and partly as hostages for the good behavior of their fathers. At the agency were now gathered all the government employees and their families, except such as had taken flight, together with traders, missionaries, and ranchmen, army officers, and newspaper men. It was a conglomerate population.

During this time of grave anxiety and nervous tension, the cooler heads among us went about our business, and still refused to believe in the tragic possibility of an Indian war. It may be imagined that I was more than busy, though I had not such long distances to cover, for since many Indians accustomed to comfortable log houses were compelled to pass the winter in tents, there was even more sickness than usual. I had access and welcome to the camps of all

8. Black cavalry began to appear in the West after the Civil War. The Indians' term "buffalo soldiers" seems to refer to their hair—which, to the gener- ally straight-haired natives, resembled the buffalo's tightly curled hair—rather than to their winter clothing.

the various groups and factions, a privilege shared by my good friend Father Jutz, the Catholic missionary, who was completely trusted by his people.

The Christmas season was fast approaching, and this is perhaps the brightest spot in the mission year. The children of the Sunday Schools, and indeed all the people, look eagerly forward to the joyous feast; barrels and boxes are received and opened, candy bags made and filled, carols practiced, and churches decorated with ropes of spicy evergreen.

Anxious to relieve the tension in every way within his power, Mr. Cook and his helpers went on with their preparations upon even a larger scale than usual. Since all of the branch stations had been closed and the people called in, it was planned to keep the Christmas tree standing in the chapel for a week, and to distribute gifts to a separate congregation each evening. I found myself pressed into the service, and passed some happy hours in the rectory. For me, at that critical time, there was inward struggle as well as the threat of outward conflict, and I could not but recall what my "white mother" had said jokingly one day, referring to my pleasant friendships with many charming Boston girls, "I know one Sioux who has not been conquered, and I shall not rest till I hear of his capture!"

I had planned to enter upon my life work unhampered by any other ties, and declared that all my love should be vested in my people and my profession. At last, however, I had met a woman whose sincerity was convincing and whose ideals seemed very like my own. Her childhood had been spent almost as much out of doors as mine, on a lonely estate high up in the Berkshire hills; her ancestry Puritan on one side, proud Tories on the other. She had been moved by the appeals of that wonderful man, General Armstrong, and had gone to Hampton as a young girl to teach the Indians there. After three years, she undertook pioneer work in the West as teacher of a new camp school among the wilder Sioux, and after much travel and study of their peculiar problems had been offered the appointment she now held. She spoke the Sioux language fluently and went among the people with the utmost freedom and confidence. Her methods of work were very simple and direct. I do not know what unseen hand had guided me to her side, but on Christmas day of 1890, Elaine Goodale and I announced our engagement.[9]

Three days later, we learned that Big Foot's band of ghost dancers from the Cheyenne river reservation north of us was approaching the agency, and that Major Whiteside was in command of troops with orders to intercept them.

Late that afternoon, the Seventh Cavalry[1] under Colonel Forsythe was called to the saddle and rode off toward Wounded Knee creek, eighteen miles away. Father Craft, a Catholic priest with some Indian blood, who knew Sitting Bull and his people, followed an hour or so later, and I was much inclined to go too, but my fiancée pointed out that my duty lay rather at home with our Indians, and I stayed.

The morning of December 29th was sunny and pleasant. We were all straining our ears toward Wounded Knee, and about the middle of the forenoon we distinctly heard the reports of the Hotchkiss guns. Two hours later, a rider was seen approaching at full speed, and in a few minutes he had dismounted from his exhausted horse and handed his message to General Brooke's orderly. The Indians were watching their own messenger, who ran

9. Married in 1891, they separated in 1921. Eastman always acknowledged his wife's contribution to his work. It has recently been suggested, however, that Elaine Goodale may have done a good deal of the actual writing of his books.
1. Also once Custer's regiment.

on foot along the northern ridges and carried the news to the so-called "hostile" camp. It was said that he delivered his message at almost the same time as the mounted officer.

The resulting confusion and excitement was unmistakable. The white teepees disappeared as if by magic and soon the caravans were in motion, going toward the natural fortress of the "Bad Lands." In the "friendly" camp there was almost as much turmoil, and crowds of frightened women and children poured into the agency. Big Foot's band had been wiped out by the troops, and reprisals were naturally looked for. The enclosure was not barricaded in any way and we had but a small detachment of troops for our protection. Sentinels were placed, and machine guns trained on the various approaches.

A few hot-headed young braves fired on the sentinels and wounded two of them. The Indian police began to answer by shooting at several braves who were apparently about to set fire to some of the outlying buildings. Every married employee was seeking a place of safety for his family, the interpreter among them. Just then General Brooke ran out into the open, shouting at the top of his voice to the police: "Stop, stop! Doctor, tell them they must not fire until ordered!" I did so, as the bullets whistled by us, and the General's coolness perhaps saved all our lives, for we were in no position to repel a large attacking force. Since we did not reply, the scattered shots soon ceased, but the situation remained critical for several days and nights.

My office was full of refugees. I called one of my good friends aside and asked him to saddle my two horses and stay by them. "When general fighting begins, take them to Miss Goodale and see her to the railroad if you can," I told him. Then I went over to the rectory. Mrs. Cook refused to go without her husband, and Miss Goodale would not leave while there was a chance of being of service. The house was crowded with terrified people, most of them Christian Indians, whom our friends were doing their best to pacify.

At dusk, the Seventh Cavalry returned with their twenty-five dead and I believe thirty-four wounded, most of them by their own comrades, who had encircled the Indians, while few of the latter had guns. A majority of the thirty or more Indian wounded were women and children, including babies in arms. As there were not tents enough for all, Mr. Cook offered us the mission chapel, in which a Christmas tree still stood, for a temporary hospital. We tore out the pews and covered the floor with hay and quilts. There we laid the poor creatures side by side in rows, and the night was devoted to caring for them as best we could. Many were frightfully torn by pieces of shells, and the suffering was terrible. General Brooke placed me in charge and I had to do nearly all the work, for although the army surgeons were more than ready to help as soon as their own men had been cared for, the tortured Indians would scarcely allow a man in uniform to touch them. Mrs. Cook, Miss Goodale, and several of Mr. Cook's Indian helpers acted as volunteer nurses. In spite of all our efforts, we lost the greater part of them, but a few recovered, including several children who had lost all their relatives and who were adopted into kind Christian families.

On the day following the Wounded Knee massacre there was a blizzard, in the midst of which I was ordered out with several Indian police, to look for a policeman who was reported to have been wounded and left some two miles from the agency. We did not find him. This was the only time during the whole affair that I carried a weapon; a friend lent me a revolver which I put in my overcoat pocket, and it was lost on the ride. On the third day it cleared, and the ground was covered with an inch or two of fresh snow. We had feared that some of the Indian wounded might have been left on the field, and a number of us volunteered to go and see. I was placed in charge of the expedition of about a hundred civilians, ten or fifteen of whom were white men. We were supplied with wagons in which to convey any whom we might find still alive. Of course a photographer and several reporters were of the party.

Fully three miles from the scene of the massacre we found the body of a woman completely covered with a blanket of snow, and from this point on we found them scattered along as they had been relentlessly hunted down and slaughtered while fleeing for their lives. Some of our people discovered relatives or friends among the dead, and there was much wailing and mourning. When we reached the spot where the Indian camp had stood, among the fragments of burned tents and other belongings we saw the frozen bodies lying close together or piled one upon another. I counted eighty bodies of men who had been in the council and who were almost as helpless as the women and babes when the deadly fire began, for nearly all their guns had been taken from them. A reckless and desperate young Indian fired the first shot when the search for weapons was well under way, and immediately the troops opened fire from all sides, killing not only unarmed men, women, and children, but their own comrades who stood opposite them, for the camp was entirely surrounded.

It took all of my nerve to keep my composure in the face of this spectacle, and of the excitement and grief of my Indian companions, nearly every one of whom was crying aloud or singing his death song. The white men became very nervous, but I set them to examining and uncovering every body to see if one were living. Although they had been lying untended in the snow and cold for two days and nights, a number had survived. Among them I found a baby of about a year old warmly wrapped and entirely unhurt. I brought her in, and she was afterward adopted and educated by an army officer. One man who was severely wounded begged me to fill his pipe. When we brought him into the chapel he was welcomed by his wife and daughters with cries of joy, but he died a day or two later.

Under a wagon I discovered an old woman, totally blind and entirely helpless. A few had managed to crawl away to some place of shelter, and we found in a log store near by several who were badly hurt and others who had died after reaching there. After we had dispatched several wagon loads to the agency, we observed groups of warriors watching us from adjacent buttes; probably friends of the victims who had come there for the same purpose as ourselves. A majority of our party, fearing an attack, insisted that some one ride back to the agency for an escort of soldiers, and as mine was the best horse, it fell to me to go. I covered the eighteen miles in quick time and was not interfered with in any way, although if the Indians had meant mischief they could easily have picked me off from any of the ravines and gulches.

All this was a severe ordeal for one who had so lately put all his faith in the Christian love and lofty ideals of the white man. Yet I passed no hasty judgment, and was thankful that I might be of some service and relieve even a small part of the suffering. An appeal published in a Boston paper brought us liberal supplies of much needed clothing, and linen for dressings. We worked on. Bishop Hare of South Dakota visited us, and was overcome by faintness when he entered his mission chapel, thus transformed into a rude hospital.

After some days of extreme tension, and weeks of anxiety, the "hostiles," so called, were at last induced to come in and submit to a general disarmament. Father Jutz, the Catholic missionary, had gone bravely among them and used all his influence toward a peaceful settlement. The troops were all recalled and took part in a grand review before General Miles, no doubt intended to impress the Indians with their superior force.

In March, all being quiet, Miss Goodale decided to send in her resignation and go East to visit her relatives, and our wedding day was set for the following June.

1916

---

# PAULINE ELIZABETH HOPKINS
## 1859–1930

Prolific African American woman writer and influential literary editor of the first decade of the twentieth century Pauline Hopkins has until recently been overshadowed by writers of the Harlem Renaissance, for whom she helped lay much groundwork. Like Anna Julia Cooper and Ida B. Wells-Barnett, Hopkins was an outspoken journalist, but she was also a gifted storyteller whose fiction mingles suspenseful story lines with forceful presentations of turn-of-the-century debates on race.

Hopkins was born in Portland, Maine. Her mother, Sarah A. Allen, had been born free in Exeter, New Hampshire, and her father, Northrup Hopkins, was either a free black or a former slave who came north from Virginia. Her forebears include the Reverends Nathaniel and Thomas Paul, founders of the first Baptist church in Boston for blacks, their activist sister Susan Paul, and the poet James M. Whitfield.

When Hopkins was ready for school, the family moved to Boston, and within the city's intellectual and social ferment Pauline grew up, performing with her family as an actress, singer, and musician, and at the age of fifteen winning first prize in a city-wide essay contest for her "Evils of Intemperance and Their Remedy." She graduated from the Girls' High School of Boston. Her play, *The Slave's Escape; or, the Underground Railroad,* was produced in Boston in 1880—Hopkins was just twenty years old.

In part Hopkins was inspired by a group of African American women whom W. E. B. Du Bois called "the New Women of Color" of the "Black Brahmin" class of Boston, an elite of land- and home-owners with money, education, cultivation, and social exclusivity. She was also influenced by the broader ideas in African American political thought surging throughout the nation. Hopkins began her writing career in earnest at the turn of the century, a time of unprecedented activity by African American artists such as Charles Chesnutt and Paul Laurence Dunbar, who started publishing regularly in the leading periodicals *Atlantic Monthly, Harper's,* and *Century Magazine,* as well as in journals such as *Colored American Magazine,* which Hopkins helped found in 1900 as a means of using literature for political advancement of African Americans. She served as literary editor in 1903–04 and there published short stories and three of her four novels: *Hagar's Daughter; A Story of Southern Caste Prejudice* (1901) (under her mother's maiden name), *Winona: A Tale of Negro Life in the South and Southwest* (1902), and *Of One Blood; or, The Hidden Self* (1902). *Contending Forces: A Romance Illustrative of Negro Life North and South* (1900), her first and best-known work, had already been published. Throughout her career Hopkins believed literature had socially transformative power.

*Contending Forces,* a family saga tracing the personal and social effects of racism in the South and North, follows the Montfort family for several generations after its move to North Carolina from Bermuda, a move undertaken by plantation owner Charles Montfort to avoid the financial repercussions of the ending of slavery in Bermuda in 1807. With seven hundred slaves, Montfort plans to emancipate them gradually—according to his own plan—in North Carolina. However, as Hopkins shows, his selfish decision leads to disaster: he is murdered by local whites, his wife is brutalized and then commits suicide, and his children become the property of the evil Anson Pollock.

The chapters printed here first tell the story of the Montforts' undoing in North Carolina and then present a debate later in the novel, occasioned by a notorious lynching, in which Hopkins's characters articulate the most powerful views on "the race problem," especially Washington's gradualism versus Du Bois's call for full identity and citizenship. One argument that emerges forcefully is that racial mixing is already a predominant feature of the United States. Recognition of this fact might temper white anxieties about "bloodlines" and in particular undermine the assumed white racist views. The novel's psychological exploration of racial "hidden selves" painfully imagines the personal implications of Du Bois's "double consciousness." Richard Yarborough finds *Contending Forces* to be a "didactic" effort full of a romance's "noble heroes and virtuous heroines, melodramatic situations, unsavory villains, exotic locations, highly emotional scenes, amazing coincidences, an alternately light-hearted and star-crossed love affair, even touches of the supernatural." In her Schomburg Library edition introduction to *The Magazine Novels of Pauline Hopkins,* Hazel Carby describes these works as "histories that rewrote definitions of American culture . . . with a pedagogic function, narratives of relations between the races that challenged racist ideologies." Its conclusion depends on a breaking down of racial barriers between characters, as long-estranged family members re-discover one another in scenes reminiscent of the ending of *Uncle Tom's Cabin* (1852).

Hopkins's association with *Colored American Magazine* reportedly ended when an ally of Washington's, who was said to disapprove of Hopkins's politics, bought the magazine and fired her. She continued to work in journalism and in 1905 co-founded her own publishing company—its only book, published the same year, was her *Primer of Facts Pertaining to the Early Greatness of the African Race and the Possibility of Restoration by Its Descendants—With an Epilogue.* Hopkins seems to have dropped out of public sight until 1916, when she co-founded the *New Era Magazine* with William Wallace, with whom she had founded the *Colored American Magazine,* but it failed. In her last years she worked as a stenographer and died unrecognized for her achievements.

## *From* Contending Forces[1]

### Chapter III. *"Coming Events Cast Their Shadows Before"*

> In sooth I know not why I am so sad:
> It wearies me; you say it, wearies you;
> But how I caught it, found it, or came by it,
> What stuff 'tis made of, whereof it is born,
> I am to learn;
> And such a wantwit sadness makes of me
> That I have much ado to know myself.
> —*Merchant of Venice*[2]

The old Pollock homestead was an exquisite spot. The house was a long, low, rambling structure, consisting of many large, airy rooms inside, and orna-

---

1. *Contending Forces: A Romance Illustrative of Negro Life North and South* was first published in *Colored American Magazine* in 1900 and then by the Colored Co-operative Publishing Company (1900), from which this text is taken.
2. Opening lines of William Shakespeare's *Merchant of Venice* (1597).

mented without by piazzas supported by huge pillars. Immense trees shaded the driveway and embowered the stately white mansion. Gay parterres of flowers ornamented the rolling lawn, which divided the great house from the Negro quarters which were picturesquely visible at a convenient distance from it.

Within the house Mr. Montfort had gathered all the treasures which could possibly add to the comfort and pleasure of his lovely wife. Beautiful rugs covered the floors, fine paintings adorned the walls, gleaming statuary flashed upon one from odd nooks and corners. In the library music had found a home in the most comfortable corner of the room. On a table one might find a volume of Goethe[3] in the original; on the grand piano the score of a then-popular opera; while a magnificent harp, standing near, hinted of musical talents highly cultivated.

Business had prospered with Montfort; his crops flourished; but a nameless trouble seemed to be halting upon the threshold of the home he loved, and to threaten those whom he cherished so fondly.

The first year of residence in Newbern[4] had been very pleasant for the Montforts. Society, such as it was, opened its arms to the family and voted the highly cultured wife and cherub children great additions. The house was a favorite resort for all the young people of the neighborhood. Mrs. Montfort had been educated in England, and had brought with her to the provincial families with whom she now associated all the refinements of the Old World. Having great wealth for the times, she had always been indulged in every whim by the doting bachelor uncle who had made her his heiress, but who had died soon after her marriage to Charles Montfort. As Grace Montfort, she found again the love her uncle had delighted to lavish upon his adopted child. Possessed of a bright, joyous nature, she liked nothing better than to gather about her the young men and women of the neighborhood and make life pleasant for them; and they in turn learned from her customs and refinements which otherwise might never have come their way. Everyone voted her the dearest and most beautiful woman they had ever known, and all would have gone merry as a marriage-bell, *but* (if it were not for the *buts* and *ifs* of this life, what a pleasant place the world would be) into this paradise of good feelings and admiration came Anson Pollock with his bitter envy and his unlawful love, and finally with his determination to possess the lovely Grace Montfort at all hazards.

Gradually the friendly relations of the neighbors turned to coldness and reserve. It was whispered about that Montfort was about to free his slaves. This in itself was a dangerous doctrine at that time in that part of the world, and a man suspected of entertaining ideas of freedom for slaves must either change his tactics or his residence, or else forfeit life and property. Then again, Bill Sampson's words to Hank Davis had somehow found a voice, and the suspicion of Negro blood in the veins of Mrs. Montfort was a deathblow to a proud spirit and social aspirations. These two serious charges had spread abroad like wildfire.

It was a hot morning, a very hot morning in early summer. There had been

---

3. Johann Wolfgang von Goethe (1749–1832), German poet, novelist, playwright, and philosopher; his most famous work is the poetic drama *Faust* (1808).
4. Charles Montfort of Bermuda has purchased Anson Pollock's large home in Newbern, North Carolina, a colonial town founded in 1710 at the confluence of the Trent and Neuse rivers and settled by Swiss and German adventurers from Bern, Switzerland.

no rain for some time. Mrs. Montfort lay in a hammock outside the breakfast-room windows. Lucy, her maid, was mending lace and children's garments a short distance away.

Lucy was Mrs. Montfort's foster sister; both were born on the same day. Their relations had always been those of inseparable friends rather than of mistress and slave.

"No rain today, Lucy. I never used to mind the heat at home (this with a sigh). How fair it must be over the blue waters of the bay; I can almost smell the cedars outside the entrance gates."

"Yas, Miss Grace" (to Lucy her mistress was always "Miss Grace"), "I do feel sort o' squeamish myself sometimes when I tink of the gals all dancin' Sundays in the square; but reckon we'll git used ter these people here arter a-while; leastwise, I hope so."

Mrs. Montfort did not reply, and her maid noticed, as she glanced anxiously at her mistress, that a frown was on her face. Lucy sighed. "Miss Grace" had been noted once for her sunny, cheerful temper. Now all was changed.

Beyond the rolling lawn fields of cotton could be seen, the leaves twisting in the heat and the steady glare of the sun. Zigzag fences separated the cotton from fields of corn; away in the distance dim aisles of pine trees stretched their dark arms towards the heavens, their dark foliage suggestive of cool shadows and quiet glades. The road wound in and out among the pines, through a woodland, and terminated in the highway just visible from the piazza. Inside the long, open windows little Jesse played at building houses with the bags of golden eagles that his father kept in a drawer of his escritoire.[5]

"Grace, Grace, Lucy," called the child, "my houses won't stay up; come in and help me."

Just then a group appeared coming around a corner of an outbuilding. Two men walked beside a pony, astride whose back sat Master Charles. As they approached the house the gentlemen swept off their wide-brimmed hats in a gallant salute to Mrs. Montfort, which she returned by rising from her recumbent position and dropping a low courtesy. The gentlemen were Mr. Montfort and Mr. Pollock. Jesse, hearing the pony's feet, came out the window and ran down the piazza steps to his father, who, as Charles sprang to the ground, lifted the excited child to the pony's back. Mrs. Montfort watched the approach of the little procession with a pleased smile. She made a fair picture in her elaborately embroidered white morning robe, her beautiful hair arranged in drooping curls at the sides of her head, as was the fashion of the time.

"See me, Mama Grace," cried Jesse, as he clapped his little hands, and dug the heels of his tiny-slippered feet into the pony's side, in imitation of his father on horseback. As Montfort watched him, the picture of his last Sunday in Bermuda arose before him: the little Negro child astride his mother's back, spurring her like a rider his horse; and in his ears rang the pleasant voice of his silver-haired pastor. At the piazza steps he called a servant to take away the pony, and turned to enter the house, followed by Mr. Pollock, with Jesse in his arms and Charles by his side. Jesse kept up an incessant chatter. They passed through the breakfast-room, where Montfort placed the child upon the floor.

"Charles, help me build my houses!" he cried, attracted to his late employ-

5. A writing desk or table (French). "Eagles": twenty-dollar gold coins.

ment at sight of the golden eagles. "See, papa, all my houses tumble down. Charles' houses don't fall down, but mine always do. Come and help me, Charles."

"You are not patient enough, my son," replied the father, smiling down upon his petulance. "You must be patient and persevere, and after awhile you will be able to make your houses stand. Isn't that right, Mr. Pollock?"

Pollock stood a little apart, gazing in amazement at the scene before him. *Golden eagles given to a child to play with* was a little beyond him. He made no direct reply to Mr. Montfort's remark, and if the latter had been an observant man, he might have been a bit puzzled at the expression on his face. But Charles Montfort was ingenuousness itself, seeing in no man an enemy. Anson Pollock was his opposite; his ruling passion was covetousness. His eyes were fairly dazzled by the sight of the gold so carelessly strewing the floor. It positively took away his breath.

"Come, Pollock, we will talk over those matters in my study," said Montfort presently. "My son," he added, as he paused at the doorway, "be careful not to lose your ducats. They are your portion to pay your college bills when you cross the ocean to finish your education."

"Going to send him abroad to study?" carelessly inquired Pollock.

"Oh, yes; America's all right for me, but bonny England for my boys."

Anson Pollock, whom Charles Montfort had chosen for his friend, was a man of dashing appearance. He carried his years jauntily, and had a good opinion of himself where women were concerned. He was made much of by the ladies in the vicinity because of his wealth. It mattered not that his wife had died mysteriously. Rumor said his ill treatment and infidelity had driven her to suicide; it had even been whispered that he had not hesitated to whip her by proxy through his overseer, Bill Sampson, in the same way he did his slaves; but rumor is a lying jade.[6] Nevertheless, his fair speech, auburn curls and deep-blue eyes, so falsely smiling, won his way, and Mr. Pollock was the popular ladies' man of two counties.

He had showered Mrs. Montfort with assiduous attention since her arrival three years before, but he soon found that he made no headway. Once he dared to tell her of his passion—that from the first moment he saw her aboard the "Island Queen" he had been maddened by her beauty.

"Why do you tell me this?" she cried, in angry amazement at his daring. "Am I so careless of my husband's honor that his friends feel at liberty to insult me?"

"Granted that I overstep the bounds of friendship in speaking thus to you, but it is from no lack of respect; rather the deed of one who risks all upon one throw of the dice. Have mercy, I pray you, and grant me your friendship— your love."

Then Grace Montfort said, while her eyes blazed with wrath: "Mr. Pollock, we are strangers here, my husband and I. He trusts you, and I have no wish to disturb that trust; but if you ever address such words to me again, I shall let Mr. Montfort know the kind of man you are. I promise you that he will know how to deal with you." This conversation had taken place one night at a grand fête, where Grace had been the belle of the assembly; they were in the conservatory at the time. Anson Pollock was not accustomed to having his

---

6. A loose or disreputable woman.

advances received in this way by any woman whom he elected to honor with his admiration. As the indignant woman swept back to the ballroom, he stood and watched her with an evil look, which meant no good. After that they met as usual, but Pollock had never ventured to speak to her again of love. Outwardly he was the same suave, genial gentleman, but within his breast was a living fire of hatred. The two men became faster friends than ever. Mrs. Montfort was pleased to have it so; they had so few friends in this alien land; she felt so lonely, so helpless. She dreaded making enemies. It was but the lull before the storm.

When the study door had closed behind the two men, Mr. Montfort dropped his pleasant, careless manner and faced Mr. Pollock with an anxious face.

"Pollock," he began abruptly, "I'm worried."

"What about?" asked Pollock, turning from the window, where he seemed to be viewing the landscape.

"Have you heard the rumors about my wife being of African descent?" Montfort asked, coming very close to Pollock, as though afraid the very air would hear him. "There are threats, too, against my life because of my desire to free my slaves."

"Nonsense!" exclaimed Pollock. "I have heard the rumors about Mrs. Montfort, but that is nothing—nothing but the malice of some malicious, jealous woman. As for the threats against your life, how can you think of such things a second time. You are among the most chivalrous people on the face of the earth, who will protect you in your home."

Montfort stood a moment before his friend, gazing at him earnestly; then he said: "Pollock, if anything happens to me, I want you to promise me to help my wife and babies to get back to Bermuda."

"Why, what can happen, man; you are nervous without a cause."

"In that safe," continued Montfort, not heeding the interruption, "you will find money and deeds; promise me that you will save them for my family."

"I promise; but it is all nonsense."

"I shall hold you to your promise," replied Montfort solemnly.

The committee on public safety[7] generally met once a month. They had a chairman, but no one knew his identity save a chosen few of the committee. Indeed very little was known positively as to the identity of any of the members; certainly no one would ever have suspected the elegant Anson Pollock of being connected with such an organization.

On this particular evening Bill Sampson lounged by the Jefferson house on the lookout for some of his friends. Anson Pollock sat on the broad steps, evidently on the watch for some one, too. "Hi, Bill!" he called, as the latter came in sight.

"Holloa! want me?" returned Bill; and at a nod from his employer, he followed him through the entrance to a small back room, generally used for the meetings of the committee.

"Anything new for the committee tonight?" asked Pollock, as he lounged

---

7. The Committee of Public Safety (French: *Comité de salut publique*) was the de facto executive government of France during the Reign of Terror (1793–94) of the French Revolution. The Jacobins centralized denunciations, trials, and executions under the supervision of this committee of twelve members. In the American South, the name denoted secret meetings of white property-owners to spy on and control African Americans, often through terror tactics and sometimes murder.

over the back of a chair. Bill took a seat on the edge of the table and began cutting circles in the air with his rawhide. Bill Sampson was a character in his way. One could not imagine Newbern without Bill, and no one could possibly imagine Bill without his rawhide.

"Wall, mabby, mabby; depends on what you call wurk. Somebody," with a sly glance at Pollock from beneath his bushy eyebrows, "somebody's been cir-clatin' a r'port about a fren' o' yourn."

"Well," replied Pollock sharply.

"Looks like we'd treed a 'possum, sho."

"Well."

"Somebody says how's Montfort's slaves is wurkin' fur part pay; leastways, every mother's son o' them'll be free inside o' five years."

"Anything else?"

"We kin' o' thought that'd do fer a spell. He's done nuff in that ar to con-vict him an' buy his halter. Thet'll do fer one pint."

"But that don't cover the case. What luck have you had in spreading the other report?"

"Wall," said Bill, as he shot a copious draught of tobacco juice over the sanded floor, "mos' the fellers think it a pity 'bout Mis' Montfort. Blamed nice 'ooman. She's been mighty good to Jeff Peterson's fam'ly, an' Jeff he feels mighty uncomf'table 'bout hurtin' on her, durned ef he don'."

"You and Jeff want to do your duty," replied Pollock. "No matter about sen-timent. Influence is great with certain people, and if niggers are tolerated in any way, it will end in weakening the law, and then good-by to our institu-tions."

"Course, course; we 'tend ter do our duty; yas, sir, our whol duty; but it beats all nater 'bout Mis' Montfort. I knowed she wuz mixed the minute I seed her, but 'ain't nuff to 'tract 'tention." He paused a moment, and then said with a sigh: "Well, Cap'n, what's yer orders?"

Pollock saw that the man's sympathy was more than half enlisted on the woman's side, and with arch diplomacy changed his tactics. He handed Bill a cigar, saying, "We may as well make ourselves comfortable"; and before the latter had fairly begun to enjoy the fragrant weed, had called for whiskey and was pressing him to help himself. Under its stimulating influence Bill soon lost what slight scruples he had felt, and was as eager for the downfall of the unfortunate family as his patron.

"Well, Bill," continued Pollock, "the first thing to be done is to put Mont-fort out of the way; then it will be plain sailing. The next question is: Who will do that job?"

"Reckon I know jes' the man—a man o' the right sperrit, who'll be glad to serve his country fer a reasun'ble consideration. An' thet remin's me, how much o' the property is to be resarved fer you?"

"The boys may have what they can get of it; I don't care for any part of the spoils; all I want is the mother and the children."

"Jes' so; wall, now, seein's I understan' the case jes' as you want it, I'll lay low, set the boys on; you keep shady an' stan' ready the minute the mine's fired. I ain't got a cuss agin Montfort myself, but the institootion[8] must be respected. Sure thar's plenty o' whiskey an' stuff in the cellur? 'Twould look kin' o' mean in Montfort not to have a full cellur. It's a big job, an' the boys'll

8. That is, slavery.

be thirsty." With this, the two worthies arose from their seats and sauntered through the door and up to the bar.

A day or two after the foregoing, Hank Davis, true to his word, formally applied to Mr. Montfort for the position of overseer on his plantation.

"What made you think that I wanted an overseer?" asked Montfort, as he pushed his hat off his face a little farther and eyed the petitioner critically, mentally vowing that he would never place even a horse in the power of such an ill-favored, beastly looking fellow.

"Wall, most Southern gentlemen don't keer ter have a nigger overseer. It spiles 'em; they gives themselves airs, an' git sot up in thar idees. Thought mabby you, bein' a stranger, mightn't know our ways. You see, it's jes' hyar, we have certain rules in this commoonity that we all mus' 'bide by ef we want t'void trouble." As Hank ventured this last remark in a cautious manner, he scraped the gravel of the walk with one foot while he slyly noted the reception of his venture by an upward cast of his eye.

Charles Montfort looked at him a moment with a slumbering wrath before he asked with dangerous coolness: "What do I understand by what you have just said, Mr. Davis? Do you mean to insinuate that a man cannot do as he will with his own property?"

"Wall, no; not eggsactly; but it's jes' hyar, to speak plainly as 'tween fren's," replied Hank, as he shifted his tobacco to the other side of his mouth, "the plain fac' is: I want the job of drivin' yer niggers, an' you'll want me to keep the commoonity fren'ly to yer now it's got out thet yer a-gwine ter set the gang free byme by."

Charles Montfort possessed one characteristic of the West Indian to a marked degree, and that was a bad temper under just provocation. Without more ado he seized the offending Hank by the collar, and with his riding whip, which he carried in his hand, he administered a sound flogging to the offender. As he released him, he said: "When you leave my grounds, don't you ever set your foot inside the gates again, or it will be the worse for you."

Hank said nothing as he raised himself from the ground where the irate man had thrown him, but as he turned to leave the place he looked at Mr. Montfort; and even in his wrath at the insolence of such a mongrel cur, as he mentally styled Davis, Charles Montfort felt a shudder of real physical fear pass over him for a moment. Surprised at himself, he turned to enter the house, dismissing the whole incident as a piece of impudence which he had done well to chastise.

Taking it all in all, Mr. Montfort was not feeling very happy on this June morning, as he sat upon the piazza thinking over the late encounter. An hour passed swiftly away; still the master of the house continued his meditations; but now he had changed his seat for a thoughtful promenade up and down the broad piazza. Finally he said softly to himself: "Yes, that is just what I will do; I'll send Gracie and the little fellows home for awhile on a visit, and there they shall stay until I know just what the trouble is here about the slaves, and certain insinuations concerning my family are cleared up." When a man makes up his mind that he has solved a difficult problem that has worried him, he generally has an air of relief which is the more pathetic, that in nine cases out of ten he does not believe that his remedy will prove effective, although he fancies that he so believes.

When Hank Davis left Mr. Montfort he moved slowly down the sun-baked road, nursing his wrath and swearing vengeance. Nothing but the life of the man who had inflicted such an insult upon him could wipe it out. He had received the same treatment that he had given hundreds of his associates, until his name and presence had become a terror in the county where he resided. Hitherto he had given his orders and they had been obeyed; but here was a man, a comparative stranger, for whom he considered that he had been willing to do a great kindness, for a consideration, and not only had he met with a refusal of his request but at the same time had received personal violence of a character that was most galling to the spirit of any free-born Southern man—an ordinary cowhiding, such as he would mete out to his slave. As he thought more and more about the matter he grew more and more filled with a desire for vengeance,—not the ordinary kind, but something extraordinary. As he gradually turned over in his mind schemes for the undoing of the Montforts, he was accosted by the voice of Bill Sampson, calling to him from across the fields. Bill was overseeing the harvesting of a great field of cotton, and the voices of the slaves could be heard droning out their weird and plaintive notes, as they sought by song movement to lighten the monotony of their heavy tasks and bring solace to their sad hearts. Some, in their simple ignorance, may not have known why they were sad, but, like the captive bird, their hearts longed for that which was ever the birthright of man— property in himself. Crushed out of sight for many years, the seed of desire for all those things which make a man, and sweeten toil, was struggling ever toward the light of civilization denied to these poor, ignorant, enslaved souls.

Hank sat down on a log by the wayside and beckoned Bill over to him. The latter came slowly across the field and seated himself astride one end of the log.

"Howdy, Hank"; "Howdy, Bill," passed in greeting between the two cronies.

" 'Pears like to me, Hank, yer a-lookin' pale," remarked Bill, as he trailed his whip backward and forward in the dust.

Hank could stand it no longer; and with a terrible imprecation, he unfolded to his friend his tale of woe and insult. Bill listened with eager curiosity, and a satisfied, knowing look might have been seen to settle about the corners of his eyes and mouth.

"Wall, wall," said he, "these ar' great times when a d—— West Ingy *half-white nigger*[9] can raise his hand agin a white man. Be yer hurt much, Hank?"

"Some in my body, but more in my feelin's."

"What ar' we a-comin' to? I tell you, Hank, it is 'bout time sumthin' was done."

"That's all well enough to talk," replied Hank, "but what kin a man do agin the money thet thet feller's got to back him up? I cayn't see a handle on him."

"Wall," replied Bill, "I *kin*."

"You *kin*!" exclaimed Hank, while a slow smile of derision covered his face; "wall, I'd jes' like to know how."

"Yer kin laugh, Hank Davis, but it's a fac'. 'Taint goin' to be no hard job, nuther, to git all thet money, all them purty trinkets and fine furniture, and the seven hundred niggers in our pockets *ef* "—(and here he paused as though to give emphasis to his words) "*ef* we wurks the thing right."

"Damn it all, man, why don't yer let out?" demanded Hank, as he rose excit-

---

9. Although nowhere in the novel is there mention of Montfort's being of mixed descent, Bill's insult here draws on the implication that there are many people of mixed blood in the West Indies, as opposed to North Carolina, another untruth.

edly from his seat on the log. "I'm the man to help on anythin' agin thet man, an' yer knows it. No need of yer bein' so infernal aggravatin' 'bout tellin' me."

Bill laughed at his companion's excitement. "Easy thar, easy, Hank. This ar' a mighty titlish[1] job, but we kin wurk it—we kin wurk it. Fust place, yer see Montfort's brought them slaves o' hisn hyar and don't tend to keep 'em only 'bout ten years, and then every one o' them will have bought hisself, accordin' to the laws thet ar' governin' them over to the West Indies. Now, yer know ther's a bad eggsample to set befo' the niggers roun' this town. Eny way, we's goin' to think so," drawled Bill, with an expressive wink at his friend. "It's a law of the United States that ef eny man is caught creatin' dissatisfacshun among the slaves he desarves death, and death he gits.[2] Now, this ar Montfort has been causin' trouble fer us by his eggsample. Every nigger roun' hyar knows all 'bout his 'rangements fer givin' his slaves thar freedom, and I tell yer, Hank, its causin' dissatisfacshun 'mong all our slaves. An' then the money, honey, the money! sech sights of it all done up in little shammy-skin bags, an' thet boy Jesse settin' on the floor amoosin' hisself buildin' houses with them gold eagles!"

Hank listened to his companion's words with open mouth. As the latter finished he said, with a look of admiration: "Wall, I'll be d——d! Now, look a-hyar, Bill Sampson, yer needn't tell me thet all thet yer have just unfolded to me is yer own idees, 'cause yer could no more hev got them thoughts through yer thick head than I could. Some one's been fixin' yer up. Out with it now, an' tell me the whole thing. Ef we's goin' inter this business, we's got to be square on the deal with our fren's. Who's the bottom o' this thing?"

Bill produced a plug of tobacco, offered his friend a chew and took one himself. "What I'm tellin' yer, Hank, is 'tween fren's," said he, chewing and crossing his legs.

"Jes' so," replied Hank.

"I wuz tellin' yer the 'riginater o' this plan, or I wuz about to." Bill paused to spit out some of his tobacco juice on the ground, so that it would not overflow the tank, so to speak, and run out of each corner of his mouth. "Beats all nater, Hank, how a man'll git dead set onter a piece o' caliker."[3]

"Meanin' by that, Bill, that Ans Pollock's got set on some gal."

"Fact!" said Bill, with a wink.

"Who's?" asked Hank.

"It mote be Mis' Montfort herself, Hank."

"Sho, you don' say, re'lly," said Hank, with a wicked look. "Don' blame him, blamed ef I do. But thet's all the good it'll do him."

Bill cut the air into imaginary circles with his whip, and without taking any notice of his friend, continued: "As I was sayin', Ans Pollock, he says ter me, 'Bill, thet's a dooced purty 'ooman o' Montfort's,' an' I tol' him what I thought 'bout her havin' black blud in her somewhar. 'Mabby,' says he, 'mabby.' An' then he says, kin' o' generous like, 'I'd take the 'ooman an' the two brats, an' the boys might hev the slaves, an' the money, an' the fixin's in the house.' I tol' him I knew the boys 'd stan' by him in enything he might do to rid a peaceful neighborhood of sech a disturbin' critter as Montfort. I tol' him I thought yer would be 'bout the very match to light on Montfort, so he wouldn't give us eny more trouble. An' so we've been waitin' fer the business ter 'velop itself

1. Ticklish.
2. Many southern states had such laws on their books at this time.

3. Calico, a common material for dresses; "a piece o' caliker" = a woman.

good an' ripe, an' I jes' think this 'tack o' Montfort's on yer will 'bout do the business fer the whole o' them.

"Bill," said Hank Davis, as he held out his hand to his friend, "we's allers been pardners, an' I reckon we allers will be."

## Chapter IV. The Tragedy

Thus man devotes his brother, and destroys him;
And worse than all, and most to be deplored
Chains him, and tasks him and exacts his sweat
With stripes that Mercy, with a bleeding heart,
Weeps when she sees inflicted on a beast.
　　　　　　　　　　　　　　　　—COWPER.[4]

"Kismet,"[5] says the Oriental, when unaccountable evils beset his path; "It is fate," says the Anglo-Saxon, under like circumstances: but fate is the will of Providence after all. Nature avenges herself upon us for every law violated in the mad rush for wealth or position or personal comfort where the rights of others of the human family are not respected. If Charles Montfort had been contented to accept the rulings of the English Parliament, and had allowed his human property to come under the new laws just made for its government, although poorer in the end, he would have spared himself and family all the horrors which were to follow his selfish flight to save that property.

The sun rose clear and resplendent a few mornings later. On this particular morning Nature outdid herself. There was a blending together of all the sweet forces—odorous air, golden sunshine, musical sounds from bird and from bush; it was pure happiness to feel the life-blood leaping in one's veins; to feel the marvelous joy of living.

Eight o'clock was the usual breakfast hour for the Montforts. The family had just assembled at the table; Aunt Cindy had brought in the great silver coffee urn and placed it beside Mrs. Montfort. Mr. Montfort had settled himself in his chair with a weekly paper, for in this rural neighborhood a newspaper once in a week was a great luxury, when his attention was caught by the sound of hoofbeats of several horses on the road. Mrs. Montfort, with usual Southern hospitality, looked over her well-appointed board to make sure that all was in order for dispensing those creature comforts so dear to the entertainer and the entertained.

The hoofbeats drew nearer and paused on the graveled walk. Montfort hastened to the door, while Mrs. Montfort turned toward the entrance of the breakfast-room with a pleasant smile of welcome on her lips. She heard a number of voices speaking together in an excited jumble, then a shot, followed by a heavy fall. Little Jesse ran from his station by his mother's side through one of the long windows opening upon the piazza. She heard his scream of "papa, papa!" and then again the jumble of excited voices. With little Charles clinging to her skirts she stumbled blindly to the entrance and faced the crowd of angry men, headed by Anson Pollock. Hank Davis had done his work well, and Charles Montfort lay dead with a bullet in his brain, sped by an unseen hand. Mrs. Montfort's arms were grasped by rude hands, and she was forcibly

4. From William Cowper, "The Time-Piece," Book II of *The Task* (1795). 　　5. "Fate" or "destiny" (Turkish).

drawn out upon the veranda, where in the sunlight of the beautiful morning she saw the body of her husband lying face downward. She was dimly conscious of hearing the cries of frightened slaves mingled with the screams of her children. Through it all she realized but two things—that the lifeless object lying there so still was the body of her husband, and that the sensual face of Anson Pollock, whom she had grown to loathe and fear, was gloating over her agony, devilish in its triumph. Then she lost consciousness.

As she lay upon the green sward, oblivious to thought and feeling, supported by her weeping maid, who had been ordered to care for her mistress by Mr. Pollock, Hank Davis came and stood for a moment looking down upon the unconscious woman. Suddenly an evil smile lighted up his countenance. He looked around, but saw nothing of Anson Pollock, who had disappeared within the house, searching for money and papers in the safe. Now was his time. This woman's husband had flogged him—he would have a sweet revenge. Those lily-like limbs, the tender flesh that had never known aught but the touch of love, should feel the lash as he had.

He called to Bill Sampson to help lift her; and despite the prayers and tears of the poor slave girl who followed her beloved mistress until Sampson knocked her senseless with the butt end of his rawhide, they bore the hapless lady to the whipping post. She revived as they reached the spot; and when she realized the fate in store for her, the sweet woman's strong soul failed her. She uttered a wild cry of agony as the rough hand of Hank Davis was laid upon her to tear her garments from her shrinking shoulders.

"Charles, my husband, save me!" she cried, and fell fainting upon the ground. There was none to answer the heartrending appeal. He who would have shed his heart's best blood for her lay cold in death. She was soon restored to consciousness, for Hank's savage instinct for revenge would only be appeased by the victim's full realization of her sufferings.

She was bound to the whipping post as the victim to the stake, and lashed with rawhides alternately by the two strong, savage men. Hank Davis drew first blood by reason of his wrongs at Mr. Montfort's hands. With all his mighty strength he brought the lash down upon the frail and shrinking form. O God! was there none to rescue her! The air whistled as the snaky leather thong curled and writhed in its rapid, vengeful descent. A shriek from the victim—a spurt of blood that spattered the torturer—a long, raw gash across a tender, white back. Hank gazed at the cut with critical satisfaction, as he compared its depth with the skin and blood that encased the long, tapering lash. It was now Bill's turn.

"I'll go you one better," he said, as he sighted the distance and exact place to make his mark with mathematical precision, at the same time shifting his tobacco from the right to the left cheek. Again the rawhide whistled through the air, falling across the other cut squarely in the center. Another shriek, a stifled sob, a long-drawn quivering sigh—then the deep stillness of unconsciousness. Again and again was the outrage repeated. Fainting fit followed fainting fit. The blood stood in a pool about her feet.

When Hank Davis had satiated his vengeful thirst he cut the ropes which bound her, and she sank upon the ground again—unconscious, bleeding, friendless, alone. Lucy had hidden in the smokehouse with the two children, that they might not witness their mother's agony.

Meantime, the committee on public safety, instigated by Anson Pollock to put down an imaginary insurrection (having no existence but in his own mind, and supposed to have originated with the slaves of Charles Montfort) and to legalize the looting of the house, took possession of the mansion. Soon the crowd had stripped it of its furniture and all the articles of value. The house itself was fired, and Grace Montfort again became conscious of her misery in time to see the dead body of her husband flung amid the burning rafters of his dwelling. Two and two the slaves were handcuffed together to be driven to the market place. Mrs. Montfort, secured to her maid, was placed in a wagon with her two children; and so the miserable woman was driven away from her outraged home.

In those old days, if accused of aiding slaves in a revolt, a white man stood no more chance than a Negro accused of the same crime. He forfeited life and property. This power of the law Anson Pollock had invoked; and to add to the devilishness of the plot, had used Bill Sampson's suggestion of black blood in Mrs. Montfort, to further his scheme for possessing the beautiful woman. So the two children and their mother fell to the lot of Anson Pollock as his portion of the spoils. Shortly after these events Grace Montfort disappeared and was never seen again. The waters of Pamlico Sound[6] tell of sweet oblivion for the broken-hearted found within their soft embrace.

After the loss of their mother the two lads clung very closely to each other. So many changes had come to them, such desperate, bloody scenes had dazed their brains and terrified them, that even the loss of their mother seemed but in keeping with the rest. Bewilderment at so much sorrow, the numbness of black despair was ever with them.

Pollock's rage was terrible when he learned that Mrs. Montfort had destroyed herself. He grew morose and unsociable, so that his society was no longer sought in the county. He seemed to have a superstitious fear of the children, and for a long time would not tolerate them in his presence. It was common talk among the slaves that Mrs. Montfort "walked," weeping and wringing her hands, night after night about the plantation.

But wonder could go no farther when Pollock elected to take Lucy in the place he had designed for Mrs. Montfort. God's mysteries are past man's understanding; and thus the poor black girl became his instrument to temper the wind to the shorn lambs. Night after night she stole away to the little attic under the eaves laden with dainties to tempt the appetite of the children. For hours she would sit hushing Jesse's sobs upon her ample breast, and speaking words of comfort in her poor, blind way to Charles.

When a year had dragged its slow length past, a stranger in the town stopped Bill Sampson on the street one day and asked him if he knew where he could hire a likely boy to go with him into the woods for a few days and help arrange specimens of the quartz in that locality. He was looking up the minerals in that section for speculators, he said. Bill promised to get him a boy, and asked Pollock's permission for Charles to go with the man.

"I don't care what you do with him, only keep him away from me. I'll sell him south soon," said Pollock.

So it happened that Charles went every day for a month with the mineralogist. The lad's appearance, education and refinement puzzled the man for a time, until he learned the tragic story.

"Charles," said he, a few weeks later, "I am about to leave this part of the

---

6. Pamlico Sound, in North Carolina, is separated from the Atlantic Ocean by the Outer Banks.

country. I don't want to leave you here. Do you think Mr. Pollock could be induced to part with you?"

"O sir!" cried Charles, throwing himself at the gentleman's feet, "for the love of God buy me and my little brother. If you will only take us to Bermuda, some one there will pay you back. My father had money there; we have friends there. O sir, for the love of God!"

The man looked at the weeping boy as through a mist. He had a tender heart.

"I will tell you something, Charles," said he kindly, as he raised the lad and drew him to a seat beside him on the grass, with his arm tenderly enfolding the child. "I am an Englishman, but it will not do to have that fact known here, for then I would be powerless to help you. Anson Pollock would never sell you to me if he knew that fact. I have been trying to buy you and Jesse, but Pollock wants to keep the boy for a valet. He intends to sell you south; you are too old to forget, and he fears you. Now I propose to buy you; and as soon as possible I shall take you to Bermuda, collect the proofs there concerning your family, and then go to England, invoke the power of the home government, and demand Jesse's freedom and indemnity from the United States government for all the outrages perpetrated against your family. Can you keep this secret, and will you try and be patient until I can accomplish my purpose?"

"I will do anything you say," replied the boy humbly, "but I hate to leave Jesse. O mama, mama, my beautiful mama!" and with a burst of grief he cast himself upon the velvet turf.

The mineralogist lost no time in completing the purchase of Charles, and in a few days they left the town. Then little Jesse, the petted darling of a luxurious home, found himself alone in the power of Anson Pollock. He must wait upon him obsequiously by day, and be ready to answer his call at any hour of the night. Under his enemy's eye by day and night, hopeless, utterly alone upon the wide waste of waters which represented his life. Oh, how black, boundless, trackless, was the unknown future to this unfortunate child! Once, after his brother was sold, he resisted his master—rebelled with all his puny strength. He was severely flogged. That night he slept in the lonely cabin kept as a sort of prison for refractory slaves. Not a sigh disturbed the silence of the night as he lay in pain, gazing up at the stars which shone so peacefully through the dilapidated roof. He thought himself delirious, or was it indeed possible that God had taken compassion on his loneliness and allowed the comfort and help of communion with the dead! He saw his murdered father and mother. Hand in hand they passed and repassed over the gaping holes in the roof of the hut. His father's noble, loving face smiled upon him; his mother's curls moved in the faint breeze, while her loving glance seemed to say: "Courage, courage, we are ever near you."

"Father, Grace, speak to me!" he shrieked in agony.

Then he seemed to feel their actual presence, tangible though viewless, beside him in the hut. Calmness came to him, and a change grand to see in that slight frame. Unconsciously he asked the question: "How long must I endure before I join you in heaven?"

It seemed to him that he was answered: "Many days, and even years; but fear not, we will never leave thee."

After that night Jesse's childhood appeared to slip from him, and he became a man in thought. He studied his master, and matched low cunning with lofty determination. He rebelled no more, was silent, not provoking Anson Pollock's wrath. The time seemed long and dreary waiting for the freedom he had resolved to have; still he was patient. Sometimes at night, when rolled in his blanket on the hard floor, he would weep over the painful past. Then he would feel the touch of a tiny hand upon his eyelids. It was his mother's hand; he knew it to be so. Then he would lose himself in sweet dreams and awaken in the morning refreshed and comforted. So the years rolled on until he was sixteen. Meantime, nothing was heard from Charles and his supposed friend. Jesse had made up his mind that Charles was either dead or else lost to him forever.

Jesse was now a man in stature, though still slender, with the same haughty bearing and distinguished appearance that had marked his father. Anson Pollock, upon whom age and the memory of dreadful crimes were making fearful inroads, began to look up to the boy and lean upon him for aid in his various plans for making money. He had spoken to him of making him the overseer, in place of Bill Sampson, and had even hinted at his taking a mate. Then Jesse knew that his probation was nearly over. That spring Pollock, as was the common practice among planters, made out passes for Jesse and sent him to New York in charge of a vessel filled with produce, and charged to bring back necessary merchandise for use on the plantation. Pollock thought the boy still too young to venture to leave him. Indeed Jesse had no such idea when he started on his trip to the North. When the vessel reached New York, Jesse performed all the necessary duties—disposed of the produce, and reloaded the ship for its homeward voyage. The night before they were to sail he sat on the wharf watching the crews of other vessels making ready for departure. His mind was engrossed with thoughts of Charles. He feared some evil had befallen him.

"At any rate," he said to himself, "I shall never see him again. And must I remain in servitude? Can I do nothing to help myself, since all hope is gone in that direction?" Just then a group of men paused in front of him. They did not know he was a slave.

"Will you give passage to two on board your vessel? You are bound for Newbern in the morning, aren't you? We'll pay you what you charge," said one of the group respectfully.

"Speak to the cap'n," called out a man standing near; "that's nuthin' but a nigger you're talkin' to."

"Well," said the one who had first addressed him, "you're a likely boy, anyhow; who do you belong to?"

Jesse arose from his seat, white with passion, and said to the man: "I am no man's property; I belong to Jesus Christ!" The question had answered itself. When the vessel sailed the next morning, Jesse was far on his road to Boston.

Traveling then was done by stage, and was a slow process; but about a week later he stood beside the stone wall that enclosed the historic Boston Common, and as he watched the cows chewing their peaceful cuds and inhaled deep draughts of freedom's air, he vowed to die rather than return to Anson Pollock.

He found work in Boston. It mattered not that it was menial work; he was happy. But fate or Providence was not done with him yet.

One day he received word that Anson Pollock was on his way to Boston in search of him. Again he made a hurried journey. This time to Exeter, N.H. In his character of a fugitive slave, the lad had from the first cast his lot with the colored people of the community, and when he left Boston he was directed to see Mr. Whitfield, a negro in Exeter, who could and would help the fugitive.

Late one afternoon, just before tea time, a comely black woman stood in her long, low-raftered kitchen preparing supper before the open fireplace. There was every indication of plenty in the homely furnishings. As the woman passed rapidly from the cupboard to the table she would touch with her foot the rockers of the little red cradle which stood in the center of the floor. The baby in it was crying in a fretful way. "Oh, hush, Lizzie," said the mother; "don't be so cross." There came a low rap at the open door, and in answer to her "Come in," Jesse stepped into the room.

"Is Mr. Whitfield in?" he asked, as he doffed his hat respectfully.

"No," was the reply, "but I expect him every minute. Sit down, won't you? He'll soon be in to his supper, I guess."

Mrs. Whitfield thought him a white man, come on business with her husband. "A handsome lad," she thought. Jesse seated himself; and then as the child continued to cry, said: "Shall I rock the cradle for you, ma'am? The child seems fretful."

Fifteen years later Jesse married Elizabeth Whitfield, the baby he had rocked to sleep the first night of his arrival in Exeter. By her he had a large family.

Thus he was absorbed into that unfortunate race, of whom it is said that a man had better be born dead than to come into the world as part and parcel of it.

✳   ✳   ✳

### Chapter XIII. The American Colored League

> Shall tongues be mute when deeds are wrought
>    Which well might shame extremest hell?
> Shall Pity's bosom cease to swell?
>    Shall Honor bleed?—shall Truth succumb?
> Shall pen and press and soul be dumb?
>
> No;—by each spot of haunted ground
>    Where Freedom weeps her children's fall,—
> By Plymouth's rock and Bunker's mound,
>    By Griswold's stained and shattered wall,
> By Warren's ghost, by Langdon's shade,
>    By all the memories of our dead!
>
> By their enlarging souls, which burst
>    The bands and fetters round them set,
> By the free Pilgrim spirit nursed
>    Within our inmost bosoms, yet,
> By all above, around, below,
>    Be ours the indignant answer,—No!
>              —WHITTIER.[7]

When Judge Watson, the president of the League,[8] reached his office on that eventful March morning, he found his desk deluged with telegrams from

7. From John Greenleaf Whittier's *Stanzas for the Times* (1835), composed after a contentious meeting in Boston on slavery. In the chapters between Chapter III and this one, the Montfort children are separated—Charles is purchased by a kindly mineralogist and Jesse is owned by Anson Pollock. Jesse travels to Boston and New Hampshire and marries a mulatto woman, founding a family with the surname of "Smith," of which Will Smith is a descendant. Charles's fate is not known until the end of the novel, when a Charles Montfort-Withington arrives from England, where he has been living, and the family is reunited.

8. The American Colored League is a fictional organization, based on the many such groups forming in the Northeast at the time.

all over the country. From the South the cry was: "Can nothing be done?" "Where is Massachusetts? Has our old friend been turned against us at last?" "For God's sake help us!" "How long, O Lord, how long!" "Let the voice of the League be heard from every city, town and village in the Union. Speak, and let our voices be heard!"

Such were the messages that compelled the hoary-haired veteran of a hundred anti-slavery meetings to crush back the sobs which arose in his throat as he, too, reiterated the cry of an afflicted people: "How long, O Lord, how long!" That day the executive committee of the League met and asked themselves what could be done. "Nothing," was the final decision after debating the question, "but to *agitate*." This plan they proceeded to put into execution. Notices were sent all over New England of a gigantic public meeting to be held at the church on X Street, on the Tuesday evening following. The press, with one or two exceptions, sided either openly or secretly against the Negroes, North and South. "Ah, ah!" they cried, "see how the Negro abuses the great privileges which we have bestowed upon him." In view of this fact, the League decided that a conservative white man should be asked to address the meeting, along with men imbued with the old abolition spirit, and in this way each side could have a chance to represent the subject as seen from its point of view. "Let us, once and for all, look at the question dispassionately; if the fault be ours, let us acknowledge it like men, and seek to amend it; if it belongs to others, may God help them to do right."

The excitement among the colored people was intense: prayers were held in all the churches the Sunday preceding. Telegrams were received from the branches of the League all over the state that delegates would represent them. The meeting would be a great expression of public opinion.

Dr. Arthur Lewis was head of a large educational institution in the South devoted to the welfare of the Negroes.[9] Every year he visited the city, and assisted by a quartette of singers, who were also members of the school, collected large sums of money from the best class of philanthropic citizens, who gave to the Negro not only because they believed he was wronged, but also because they believed that in great measure his elevation would remove the stigma under which the Southern white labored. For the loyal white man there would be no greater joy in life than to see his poetic dream of superiority to all other governments realized in the "land of the free and the home of the brave." He knows that this can never be while the Negro question keeps up the line of demarkation which marks the division of the North from the South.[1] True and loyal son of his country, he would sacrifice any race, any principle, to bring about this much-desired consummation; so he contributes his money to build up manufacturing interests at the South to his own material disadvantage in the North: to develop uncultivated land there, and to educate the Negro with the hope that in the general advance the latter question may be buried from public notice, if not obliterated. Delusive hope that grasps at shadows!

That momentous Tuesday evening rolled quickly round. The committee

9. Lewis generally voices the ideas of Booker T. Washington, as Will Smith voices those of W. E. B. Du Bois.
1. Also known as "Mason and Dixon's Line," this line ran for the most part along Pennsylvania's southern boundary. After Pennsylvania began abolishing slavery in 1781, this line, and the Ohio River, became known as the border between free and slave states.

asked that the meeting should open at half-past seven, on account of the time needed by the speakers, and long before the hour appointed the large edifice was filled to overflowing. And what a crowd! They came from towns remote, from the farm, from domestic service in the homes of wealth and from among the lowly ones who earn a scanty living with scrubbing-brush and pail. Doctor, lawyer, politician, mechanic—every class sent its representative there to help protest against the wrongs of down-trodden manhood.

The platform was heavily draped in American flags supplemented by wide bands of mourning. Pictures of the anti-slavery apostles peered out at the audience from the folds of the national colors. Speakers and representative citizens were seated upon the platform, and visiting delegates occupied seats in close proximity. The choir had volunteered its services, and, after a prayer by the pastor, rendered Mrs. Julia Ward Howe's "Battle Hymn of the Republic" in masterly style.[2] In listening to the martial strains the pulse of the vast concourse of people was strained with excitement and expectation. The stillness was intense as the gray-haired president of the League and chairman of the meeting arose in his seat and passing to the desk, rapped for order.

"Fellow-citizens and men and women of my race: The occasion for this meeting is one of great solemnity. Forty years ago, when as a young man I sat at the feet of Sumner, Phillips, Garrison, Pillsbury, Charles Lenox Remond, Nell, Robert Morris, Fred Douglas and all the mighty host of anti-slavery fathers,[3] we thought that with the abolishment of slavery the black man's destiny would be accomplished, and fixed beyond a peradventure. Today a condition of affairs confronts us that they never foresaw: the systematic destruction of the Negro by every device which the fury of enlightened malevolence can invent. In whatever direction we turn, the clouds hang dark and threatening. This new birth of the black race is a mighty agony. God help us in our struggle for liberty and manhood! *Agitation and eternal vigilance in the formation of public opinion* were the weapons which broke the power of the slave-holder and gave us emancipation. I recommend these methods to you today, knowing their value in the past.

> " 'Up then and act! Thy courage wake!
> Combat intrigue, injustice, tyranny,
> And in thine efforts God will be with thee.' "

He then called upon the Hon. Herbert Clapp, as a representative of the party and of the sentiment of the best white people of the country, to address the meeting.

The political contingent gave him a hearty welcome as he moved with stately tread to the front of the platform. He said:

"The topic to be discussed is a very serious one, and I feel deeply how incompetent I am to deal with it, how incompetent most of us are to attempt the solution of the question before us. As a white man looking upon the South as my brother, and desiring to see the welfare of that section secured along with the rights of the brother in black, I feel the responsibility which rests upon me tonight to be fair and just, impartial to both sides in what I may say.

2. Julia Ward Howe's "Battle Hymn of the Republic" was published in the *Atlantic Monthly* in 1862.

3. Leaders of the abolitionist movement.

I ask you tonight as rational people to look at this question from both points of view; to be calm and logical; to be willing, as just men of intelligence and judgment, to see and acknowledge wrong wherever you find it among your own people, and to be willing to consult as to the best method of procedure to rectify mistakes which if corrected may lead to an amicable adjustment of all difficulties in the South. As a friend of both sides, I ask you to do this.

"I am not here to apologize for the South; she has her ills and her sins. What section has not? Let us thank God that sectionalism is dead.

"Now, then, let us try to appreciate the relations of the Negro at the South. All history shows that two races, approaching in any degree equality in numbers, cannot live together unless intermarriage takes place or the one is dependent and in some sense subject to the other. Miscegenation by law will never take place in the South. No matter how much we people of the North may differ with our brothers of the South, this point will always remain fixed. Miscegenation, then, being out of the question, nothing remains for the Negro but to be dominated by the white man there. I hold that the Negro in American civilization is a problem of a vast deal more import than we are inclined to believe. The problem is national, not sectional. The sin of slavery was the sin of the nation, and that sin stands before us today full of menace, full of peril to the whole people. The Southern brother claims, and with some justice I think you will allow, that under the influence of scalawags and carpet-baggers, mostly composed of unprincipled Northern white men, the Negro has opposed, politically, everything that he thinks the white man wants. Upon this subject Prof. H. M. Brown, a Negro and member of the faculty of Hampton Institute, says: 'The greatest enemy to the Negro and the greatest obstacle to his progress is the politician, and the Negro politician is the worst of all.'

"You cannot deny that the well-behaved Negro has the respect of the community in which he lives at the South. Witness the death of a highly respected Negro in Georgia a short time ago. He never dabbled in politics, and his death was deplored by white and black alike. In thirty years forty per cent of the illiteracy at the South among the colored people has disappeared, due no doubt to environment and emulation of the whites. All kinds of employment, trades, professions, etc., are open to the Negro at the South, and you know that counts for a great deal. Here at the North the pressure is so great from the white laborer that we are forced, to some extent, to bar against the colored brother. I am ashamed to say it; but let us state the case truthfully, if at all.

"To come to the case in hand, I wish it to be distinctly understood that I am absolutely opposed to mob law. But there is an unwritten law, not peculiar to any section, which demands the quickest execution, in the quickest way, of the fiend who robs a virtuous woman of her honor to gratify his hellish diabolism. Human nature is the same throughout the civilized world. If in return for all the benefits conferred upon the Negro at the South, which I have enumerated previously, they give us the heinous crime of rape, what shall we say? Where find excuses for such ingratitude? Surely as men we must have sympathy for the pure and virtuous woman who carries with her a living shame, in a living death, in a life all too long for its miseries, if it lasts but for a day."

As he finished and returned to his seat, a sigh like a broken moan seemed to come from the very heart of the multitude, but not a movement broke the stillness. The Hon. Herbert Clapp felt that his part of the exercises was a failure. After a pause, the chairman introduced Doctor Lewis as a leading representative of the race whom they would, doubtless, be glad to hear express his views upon the momentous question under consideration. He was received with liberal applause, and said:

"I agree with our friend the Hon. Herbert Clapp in about all that he has said in relation to the grievous matter before us. I think that he has stated the case as impartially as it is possible so to do. The moment there is a lynching in the South, it is made the pretext for many press comments and public meetings among ourselves, and a general agitation of the question in the wrong way. The result is that you people at the North get a wrong idea of the matter. The published accounts of your meetings here do us at the South, who are working along the best lines that we know of for the elevation of the race, an injury, and often retard us greatly in the accomplishment of our designs. Take the Black Belt, and within its circumference you will find the densest ignorance, as well as bright intelligence of no ordinary quality. Among those people you will find the vicious ones who would rather drink, carouse, and fight than do a day's work to keep themselves from the penitentiary. Such men can be bought, bribed, worked upon for the furtherance of any plan or scheme that may suggest itself to the wily brain of the unscrupulous politician. These men are dangerous to the peace of the community, and it is such men who commit the deeds of violence with which the country is horrified at short intervals. If we cannot reach these men individually, we hope to reach their children. Thus we have planned that with the aid of our universities we shall at length root out evil and ignorance, and in the future give our race a clean, pure citizenship. As our friend has stated—politics is the bane of the Negro's existence. Those of us who eschew that subject, let matters of government take care of themselves, while we look out for our own individual or collective advancement, find no difficulty in living at the South in peace and harmony with our neighbors. If we are patient, docile, harmless, we may expect to see that prosperity for which we long, in the years to come, if not for ourselves then for our children. I am an optimist in regard to the future. I have great hopes of the better class of Southern people themselves.

"Let us remember that the South was more conquered than persuaded. The Confederates did not surrender their convictions with their swords. Immediately after the war Henry W. Grady[4] would have been looked upon as a monstrosity. It was a severe blow to the South when the slave gained his liberty. As the South gains wealth and resources I think that the problem will grow less difficult. It is the idea of the Negro holding political preferment that is so hard for the North and South to swallow. But if we give them time and do not hurry them, they will grow gradually accustomed to the new era. Convince the South that we do not want social equality, neither do we wish to rule. We want nothing but our God-given rights as men.

"I believe in the humanizing influence of the dollar judiciously expended for educational advantages, 'holding it better and wiser to tend the weeds in the garden than to water the exotic in the window.' We should strive to obtain the education of the industrial school, seeking there our level, content to

---

4. Editor of the *Atlanta Constitution* and a white supremacist leader.

abide there, leaving to the white man the superiority of brain and intellect which hundreds of years have developed."

He ceased speaking and sat down amid murmurs of applause, mingled with disapprobation. Some among the audience began to grow restless. Was this what they came to hear—an apology, almost an eulogy upon the course pursued by the South toward the Negro? Other speakers—white and colored—followed; then the chairman introduced our friend John Langley. He came to the front of the platform with his usual graceful bearing. He was well known among the people, especially the younger contingent, and was received with liberal applause.

"My friends," he said, "I shall not detain you with any lengthy remarks upon the situation, because there are speakers to follow me. I am glad of the opportunity to say what I think about lynch law: It is a terrible thing to contemplate. The crime which provokes it is still more terrible, to my thinking. I utter no eulogy upon the position of the South toward the Negro, neither do I harbor undue resentment for the grievous wrongs which I feel they have, in some measure, heaped upon us. I am willing to leave the punishment of criminals, the suppression of mob violence, with the national government, being convinced that in good time the government so trusted will acquit itself with equity toward my race. You have listened to the speeches made by our friend, the Hon. Herbert Clapp, and our brother, Dr. Arthur Lewis, upon whose word we can implicitly rely, because he works, lives, and moves among the very happenings of which we know nothing save by reading. It is discretion to act coolly, calmly and deliberately; to look at all sides of a question before we jump at conclusions. I can see nothing to be gained, if, as we have been advised, we took up arms in defense of our rights of citizenship. Extermination would speedily follow. Let us not invite destruction. But we have opportunities of advancement. Let us seize them. Let us await the issue of events with patience, trusting in the fealty of our party leaders, putting faith in their sagacity to push our claims and redress whatever grievances we may have, at a seasonable time. We thoroughly understand the attitude of the whites. Let us not offend the class upon whom we depend for employment and assistance in times of emergencies. By so doing, if we cannot have amity we can have peace."

## Chapter XIV. Luke Sawyer Speaks to the League

> My ear is pained,
> My soul is sick with every day's report
> Of wrong and outrage with which earth is filled.
> There is no flesh in man's obdurate heart;
> It does not feel for man: the natural bond
> Of brotherhood is severed as the flax
> That falls asunder at the touch of fire.
> He finds his fellow guilty of a skin
> *Not colored like his own*; and, having power
> To enforce the wrong *for such a worthy cause*,
> Dooms and devotes him as a lawful prey.
> —COWPER.[5]

Scarcely had the speaker taken his seat amid suppressed murmurs of discontent, when a tall, gaunt man of very black complexion arose in his seat

5. From William Cowper's "Charity" (1782), an antislavery poem.

among the delegates, and in a sonorous bass voice uttered the solemn protest of Patrick Henry, so famous in history: "Gentlemen may cry 'Peace! peace!' but there is no peace!"[6]

In an instant confusion reigned. Women fluttered their handkerchiefs, and above waves of applause and cheers could be heard cries of "Hear, hear!" "Platform! platform!" The chairman rapped for order, and when he could make himself heard, asked the delegate to come to the platform; another speaker was waiting, but the audience would be glad to hear anything he might have to say. As he passed up the aisle and mounted the steps of the rostrum, the people saw a man of majestic frame, rugged physique and immense muscular development. His face was kindly, but withal bore the marks of superior intelligence, shrewdness and great strength of character. He might have been a Cromwell, a Robespierre, a Lincoln.[7] Men of his physiological development—when white—mould humanity, and leave their own characteristics engraved upon the pages of the history of their times.

"Friends," said he, when he stood before them, "I come from Williamstown, in the western part of this state, to be a delegate at this meeting. Here are my credentials to show that I am in good standing in the League where I belong. (He handed his papers to the chairman.) I want to impress that fact upon the minds of this assembly, because I am going to tell you some awful facts before I get through." He paused, and with his handkerchief wiped the tears and perspiration from his face. "Friends, I am thirty years old and look fifty. I want to tell you why this is so. I want to tell you what brought me *here*. I want to tell the gentlemen who have spoken here tonight that conservatism, lack of brotherly affiliation, lack of energy for the right and the power of the almighty dollar which deadens men's hearts to the sufferings of their brothers, and makes them feel that if only *they* can rise to the top of the ladder may God help the hindmost man, are the forces which are ruining the Negro in this country. It is killing him off by thousands, destroying his self-respect, and degrading him to the level of the brute. *These are the contending forces that are dooming this race to despair!*

"My name is Lycurgus Sawyer; Luke they call me for short. When I was about ten years old my father kept a large store in a little town in the state of Louisany. I had two brothers and a sister. My mother was a fine woman, somewhat better educated than my father. Through her influence he went into this business of trading, and soon had the largest business and as much money as any man in the county. Father didn't care to meddle with politics, for, with the natural shrewdness of many of us, he saw that that might be made an excuse for his destruction. When I was about ten years old, then, a white man in the village, seeing the headway my father was making in accumulating property, opened a store on the same street. Father said nothing, but his customers still continued to trade with him, and it seemed that the other man would be compelled to give up. About this time father received threatening letters ordering him to move, and saying that in case he did not do as ordered he would lose his life. Mother was frightened, and advised father to

6. Henry's 1775 speech in support of the American Revolution proclaimed, "Give me liberty, or give me death."
7. Oliver Cromwell (1599–1658), member of the British Parliament and major participant in the revolution of 1648–49, including the trial and execution of Charles I and the abolition of monarchy and the House of Lords; from 1653 until his death, he was the constitutional head of state. Maximilien Robespierre (1758–1794), a Jacobin leader of the French Revolution. Abraham Lincoln (1809–1865), 16th president of the United States.

get out of the place, but he, anxious to save some part of his hard earnings, waited to sell his stock and houses before seeking a home elsewhere. One night a posse of men came to our house and began smoking us out. You don't know anything about that up here, do you? Well, you'll get there if things keep on as they're going. My father had arms. He raised the window of his sleeping-room and fired into the mob of cowardly hounds. Thoroughly enraged, they broke open the doors back and front, seized my father and hung him to the nearest tree, whipped my mother and sister, and otherwise abused them so that they died next day. My brothers were twins, still so small that they were but babes. The mob took them by the heels and dashed their brains out against the walls of the house! Then they burned the house. I saw all this, and frenzied with horror, half-dead with fright, crept into the woods to die. I was found there by a colored planter named Beaubean, who lived in the next township. He pitied me and took me home. *That*, gentlemen, was my *first* experience of lynching. Do you think it is possible to preach 'peace' to a man like me?"

The house was filled with the cries and groans of the audience. Sobs shook the women, while the men drank in the words of the speaker with darkening brows and hands which involuntarily clinched themselves in sympathy with his words.

"But that is not the only story I can tell. Here's another. I will tell it to you, and you can digest it at your leisure.

"Monsieur Beaubean was an educated man, descended from a very wealthy family. His father had been his owner. When the father died he left to his son, born of a black mother, an equal share of the estate along with his legitimate heirs. They made no objections, so he got it.

"Monsieur Beaubean had married a quadroon[8] woman of great beauty— Louisany abounds in handsome women of color; they had two children, a boy and a girl. She was three years old when I went to live with them. I remained in the family twelve years. I learned many things there; along with the trade of blacksmithing I learned to esteem myself as a man.

"I cannot describe to you the beauty and loveliness of that child. As a boy I worshipped her, and as a man I loved her; not with the hope of ever having a return of the feeling she had aroused in me, but as a faithful dog that would lay down his life for those who shelter and care for him, so I felt to Beaubean's family, and especially to that child. When Mabelle, as we called her, was old enough, she was sent to the Colored Sisters' School in the city of New Orleans. It was my pleasant duty to drive her into the city each day and go for her at night.

"Monsieur Beaubean had a half-brother—a white man—who was very wealthy and stood very high in politics. In fact, he was in the State Senate. He was very warm in his expressions of friendship for the family, and especially so in his assumption of relationship. I noticed that he seemed extremely fond of Mabelle. One day, after she had passed her fourteenth birthday, she had a holiday from school, and went with some schoolfellows to visit a companion who lived in the city. They returned at night without her, saying that she went into a store with Monsieur Beaubean's brother, and they had not seen her since.

8. A person with one black grandparent.

"Can you imagine what a night was passed by that family? No, you cannot, unless you have been through the same experience. The father went in one direction and I in another. All night long we searched the city streets; nothing could be heard of her. Finally we went to police headquarters and secured the services of a detective. After *three weeks* of incessant searching we found her a prisoner in a house of the vilest character in the lowest portion of the city of New Orleans—a poor, ruined, half-crazed creature in whom it was almost impossible to trace a resemblance to the beautiful pet of our household. These arms bore her forth from that vile den and restored her to a broken-hearted parent. I think that I must have gone mad. If I had had the man there then that committed the crime (he raised one gaunt arm above his head, and standing in that attitude seemed the embodiment of vengeance) I would have taken him by the throat and shaken him (he hissed the words through clinched teeth), shaken him as a dog would a rat until he was *dead!* DEAD! DEAD! We took her home, but I believe that her father was a madman from the time he placed his eyes upon her until he was murdered. And who do you think had done this foul crime? Why, the father's *half-brother, uncle* of the victim!

"Crazed with grief, Monsieur Beaubean faced his brother and accused him of his crime. 'Well,' said he, 'whatever damage I have done I am willing to pay for. But your child is no better than her mother or her grandmother. What does a woman of mixed blood, or any Negress, for that matter, know of virtue? It is my belief that they were a direct creation by God to be the pleasant companions of men of my race. Now, I am willing to give you a thousand dollars and call it square.' He handed Monsieur Beaubean a roll of bills as he spoke. Beaubean seized them and hurled them into the villain's face with these words: 'I leave you to carry my case into the Federal courts and appeal for justice.' Unhappy man! That night his house was mobbed. The crowd surrounded the building after firing it, and as an inmate would show his head at a window in the struggle to escape from the burning building, someone would pick him off. So it went all that night. I seized Mabelle and wrapped her in a blanket. Watching my chance I stole from the house after the fire was well under way, and miraculously reached a place of safety. I took Mabelle to the colored convent at New Orleans, and left her there in the care of the sisters. *There she died when her child was born!*"

As the speaker stood silently contemplating his weeping, grief-convulsed audience, a woman was borne from the auditorium in a fainting condition. John Langley from his seat on the platform leaned over and asked an usher who the lady was. "Miss Sappho Clark," was his reply.

Amid universal silence, the silence which comes from feeling too deep for outward expression, the speaker concluded: "A tax too heavy placed on tea and things like that, made the American Colonies go to war with Great Britain to get their liberty. I ask you what you think the American Colonies would have done if they had suffered as we have suffered and are still suffering?

"Mr. Chairman, gentlemen call for peace, and I reply: 'Peace if possible; justice at any rate.' Where is there peace for men like me? When the grave has closed over me and my memories, I shall have peace.

"Under such conditions as I have described, contentment, amity—call it by what name you will—is impossible; justice alone remains to us."

### Chapter XV. Will Smith's Defense of His Race

Thank God for the token!
Thank God that one man as a free
Man has spoken!
—WHITTIER.[9]

Someone at this moment began to sing that grand old hymn, ever new and consoling:

"Jesus, Lover of my soul,
Let me to thy bosom fly,
While the nearer waters roll,
While the tempest still is nigh."[1]

When quiet once more reigned, amid intense silence the chairman arose and introduced Mr. William Smith as the last speaker of the evening. Tremendous applause greeted him, for he was known to be an able and eloquent debater.

"Friends," he said, "I shall not attempt a lengthy and discursive argument; I shall simply try to answer some of the arguments which have been advanced by other speakers. I have no doubt that they have spoken their honest convictions. Now let us look at the other side of the question.

"We know that the Negro question is the most important issue in the affairs of the American Republic today. We are told that there are but two ways of solving the vexed question of the equality of the two races: miscegenation by law, which can *never* take place, or complete domination by the white race— meaning by that *comparative servitude*.

"Miscegenation, either *lawful* or *unlawful*, we *do not want*. The Negro dwells less on such a social cataclysm than any other race among us. Social equality does not exist; no man is forced to receive another within the environments of intimate social life. 'Social position is not to be gained by pushing.' That much for miscegenation. The question now stands: Which race shall dominate within certain parallels of latitude south of Mason and Dixon's line?[2] The Negro, if given his full political rights, would carry the balance of power every time. This power the South has sworn that he shall never exercise. All sorts of arguments are brought forward to prove the inferiority of intellect, hopeless depravity, and God knows what not, to uphold the white man in his wanton cruelty toward the American Ishmael.[3]

"We are told that we can receive education only along certain elementary lines, and in the next breath we are taunted with not producing a genius in science or art. A Southern white man will tell you that of all politicians the Negro is the vilest, ignoring the fact that for corrupt politics no race ever can or ever will excel the venality of a certain class of whites. Let us, for the sake of illustration, glance at the position of the Irish element in politics. They come to

9. Opening of Whittier's antislavery poem "Ritner" (1836).
1. From a well-known hymn with words by Charles Wesley (1707–1788) and music by Joseph Parry (1841–1903).
2. See n. 1, p. 740, above.

3. The son of Abraham and his handmaiden Hagar, Ishmael and his mother were cast out when Abraham's wife, Sarah, gave birth to Isaac, who became Abraham's heir (Genesis 21.9–21). He is seen as the traditional progenitor of Arab peoples, and here, symbolically, of Africans as well.

this country poor, unlettered, despised. Fifty years ago Pat was as little welcome at the North as the Negro at the South. What has changed the status of his citizenship? *Politics*. The Irishman dominates politics at the North, and there is no gift within the power of the government that does not feel his influence. I remember a story I heard once of an Irishman just landed at Castle Garden.[4] A friend met him, and as they walked up the street said to him: 'Well, Pat, you are just in time to vote for the city government election.' 'Begorra,' replied Pat, 'an' is it a guvimint they have here? Sure, thin, I'll vote agin it.'

"The Irish vote, then, is massed at certain strategic points in the North, and its power is feared and respected. The result has been a rapid and dazzling advance all along the avenues of education and wealth in this country for that incisive race. To the Negro alone politics shall bring no fruit.

"To the defense of slavery in the past, and the inhuman treatment of the Negro in the present, the South has consecrated her best energies. Literature, politics, theology, history have been ransacked and perverted to prove the hopeless inferiority of the Negro and the design of God that he should serve by right of color and physique. She has convinced no one but herself. Bitterer than double-distilled gall was the Federal success which brought Negro emancipation, domination and supremacy.

"Disfranchisement is what is wanted by the South. Disfranchise the Negro and the South will be content. He, as the weaker race, can soon be crowded out.

"Many solutions of the question of Negro domination have been advanced; among them the deportation of the Negro to Africa has been most warmly advocated by public men all over the country. They argue that in this way the prophecy of the Bible will soonest be fulfilled; that 'Ethiopia shall stretch forth her hand and princes shall come out of Egypt.'[5]

"The late Henry Grady told us 'that in the wise and humane administration, in the lifting the slave to heights of which he had not dreamed in his savage home, and giving him a happiness he has not yet found in freedom— our fathers (Southern men) left their sons a saving and excellent heritage (slavery).' Another man, also a Southerner, has told us: 'In education and industrial progress this race has accomplished more than it could have achieved in centuries in different environment, without the aid of the whites. The Negro has needed the example as well as the aid of the white man. In sections where the colored population is massed and removed from contact with the whites, the Negro has retrograded. Segregate the colored population and you take away the object-lesson.' Here, then, is the testimony of two intellectual white men as to the dependence of the Negro upon his proximity to the whites for a continuance of what advancement he has made since the abolishment of slavery. Is such a race as this fit at the present time to carry enlightenment into a savage and barbarous country? Can the blind lead the blind? Would not the Negro gradually fall into the same habits of ignorance and savagery from which the white slave-trader so humanely rescued him when he transported him into the blissful lap of American slavery? The Negro cannot be deported.

---

4. Today known as Castle Clinton National Monument, this fort at the southern tip of Manhattan was America's first official immigration center.
5. Psalms 68.31.

"It is being argued that the Negro is receiving education beyond his needs or his capacity. In short, that a Negro highly educated is a Negro spoiled. I agree with the gentleman on the other side that education alone will not produce a good citizen. But, of those who would curtail his endeavors to reach the highest that may be opened to him, I would ask: Of what use has education been to you in the upbuilding of the social and political structure which you designate the United States of America? What are the uses of education anyhow?

"To those who know the constitution of the brain as the organ of the moral and intellectual powers of man, education is of the highest importance in the formation of the character of the individual, the race, the government, the social life of any community under heaven. The objects presented to the mind by education stimulate in the same manner that the physical elements of nature do the nerves and muscles—they afford the faculties scope for action. Education is knowledge of nature in all its departments. The moment the mind discovers its own constitution and discerns the importance of the natural laws, the great advantage of moral and intellectual cultivation as a means of invigorating the brain and mental faculties, and of directing the conduct in obedience to the laws of God and man, is apparent. It is important that the Negro should not be hampered in his search after knowledge if we would eliminate from his nature any tendency toward vice that he may be thought to possess, and *which has been largely increased by what he has imbibed from the example and the close*, IMMORAL ASSOCIATION *which often existed between the master and the slave*. From my own observation I should say that in this country today the science of man's whole nature—animal, moral and intellectual—was never more required to guide him than at present, when he seems to wield a giant's power, and in the application of it to display the selfish ignorance of an overgrown child.

"We come now to the crime of rape, with which the Negro is accused. For the sake of argument, we will allow that in one case out of a hundred the Negro is guilty of the crime with which he is charged; in the other ninety-nine cases the white man gratifies his lust, either of passion or vengeance. None of us will ever forget the tales told us tonight by Luke Sawyer; the wanton passions he revealed and which it has taken centuries of white civilization to develop, disclosing a dire hell to which the common crime of the untutored Negro is as white as alabaster. And it is from such men as these that the appeal comes for protection for woman's virtue! Do such examples as these render the Negro gentle and pacific? No; he sees himself traveling for years the barren Sahara of poverty, imprisonment, broken hopes and violated home ties; the ignorant, half-savage, irresponsible human animal who forms the rank and file of a race so recently emancipated from servitude, sees only revenge before his short-sighted vision.

"Rape is the outgrowth of a fiendish animus of the whites toward the blacks and of the blacks toward the whites. The Southern white is unable to view the feared domination of the blacks with the dispassionate reasoning of the unprejudiced mind. He exaggerates the nearness of that possibility, which is not desired by the blacks, and, like the physician sick of a mortal disease, is unable to prescribe for himself, and cannot realize that the simple remedy, gently applied, will lift him from his couch of pain. Lynch law prevails as the only sure cure for the ills of the South.

" 'Lynchings are justifiable on two grounds,' says a thoughtful writer: 'First, if they are consonant with the moral dignity and well-being of the people; and secondly, if they stop, and are the only sure means of stopping, the crime they avenge.' Lynching does not stop crime; it is but a subterfuge for killing men. It is a good excuse, to use a rough expression, to 'go a-gunning for niggers.'

"Lynching was instituted to crush the manhood of the enfranchised black. Rape is the crime which appeals most strongly to the heart of the home life. Merciful God! Irony of ironies! *The men who created the mulatto race, who recruit its ranks year after year by the very means which they invoked lynch law to suppress*, bewailing the sorrows of violated womanhood!

"No; it is not rape. If the Negro votes, he is shot; if he marries a white woman, he is shot; if he accumulates property, he is shot or lynched—he is a pariah whom the National Government cannot defend. But if he defends himself and his home, then is heard the tread of marching feet as the Federal troops move southward to quell a 'race riot.'

"The South declares that she is no worse than the North, and that the North would do the same under like provocation. Perhaps so, if the offender were a Negro. Take the case of Christie Warden and Frank Almy, which occurred in New Hampshire only a few years ago.[6] Where could a more atrocious crime be perpetrated? The refinement of intellectual pursuits, the elegancies of social intercourse, were the attributes which went to make up the personnel of the most brutal murderer that ever disgraced the history of crime. Centuries of culture and civilization were combined in his make-up. The community where the girl lived and was respected and beloved did not lynch the brute. The white heat of passion led men to lay aside all pursuits for days in order to hunt the criminal from his hiding-place. New Hampshire justice gave him counsel and every means to defend himself from the penalty of his horrid crime. *That was in the North!*

"Human nature is the same in everything. The characteristic traits of the master will be found in his dog. Black, devilish, brutal as they may picture the Negro to be, he but reflects the nature of his environments. *He is the Hyde who torments the Dr. Jekyll of the white man's refined civilization!*[7]

"My friends, it is going to take time to straighten out this problem; it will only be done by the formation of public opinion. Brute force will not accomplish anything. We must *agitate*. As the anti-slavery apostles went everywhere, preaching the word fifty years before emancipation, *so must we do to-day*. Appeal for the justice of our cause to every civilized nation under the heavens. Lift ourselves upward and forward in this great march of life until 'Ethiopia shall indeed stretch forth her hand, and princes shall come out of Egypt.' "

When he had finished there was not a dry eye in that vast audience. Every heart followed the words of the pastor as with broken utterance he invoked

6. Reference to a notorious murder trial in New Hanover, New Hampshire, in 1891, in which Frank Almy (aka George Abbott), accused of murdering Christie Warden, was quickly convicted and hanged.
7. Twinned good and evil personae from Robert Louis Stevenson's novel *Dr. Jekyll and Mr. Hyde* (1886).

the divine blessing upon the meeting just ended. Slowly they dispersed to their homes, filled with thoughts that burn but cannot be spoken.

The papers said next day that a very interesting meeting occurred the night before at the church on X Street.

1900

---

# HAMLIN GARLAND
## 1860–1940

Hannibal Hamlin Garland, born in rural poverty, was self-educated and ambitious; he wished to leave behind the hard life he had known as a boy and young man growing up on a succession of desolate midwestern farms from Wisconsin to the Dakotas. In 1884 he migrated to Boston, where, after a period of loneliness and economic struggle, he was befriended by such influential literary figures as Oliver Wendell Holmes and William Dean Howells and began to earn a living as a teacher, lecturer, and writer. It was not until the late 1880s, however, after a visit to his family on their farm stirred him to try to describe the pain of their mean rural condition, that Garland gained public attention with the group of stories gathered in *Main-Travelled Roads* (1891). These rather pessimistic stories unsentimentally depicted the day-to-day lives of the farmers—and especially of their wives—who lived along this metaphorical "long and wearyful" byway. Often explicit, almost always implicit, in the stories is a strong reformist impulse: the meagerness of these silently heroic lives could be made more fruitful and loving, Garland believed, if the economic system was more humane. This is the thesis of his most famous story, "Under the Lion's Paw," which Garland read without fee before tax-reform groups across the land. He devoutly believed at this time that "if you would raise the standard of art in America you must raise the standard of living." Garland's conception of realism—he called it "veritism" in "Crumbling Idols" (1904)—entailed, as this story demonstrates, an allegiance to the accurate representation of outer surfaces, however grim, and inner truths, however somber. Garland was convinced that the deepest and most realistic writer creates as a responsible and compassionate member of a social community whose end is justice.

Justice for Garland applied equally to women, and he was active in feminist reform movements, especially in this early period of his life. *Rose of Dutcher's Coolly* (1895), perhaps his best longer fiction, tells the story of a farm girl's attempt to escape the physical drudgery and spiritual emptiness of farm life by going off to college and then becoming a writer in Chicago. Unable to attract an audience for unsentimentally realistic work of this kind, from 1896 to 1916 Garland turned out popular romantic adventure novels set in the Rocky Mountains. The best of them—*The Captain of the Gray Horse Troop* (1902), *Hesper* (1903), and *Cavanaugh, Forest Ranger* (1910)—contain realistic descriptions and a muted note of reformist propaganda, but they are in essence polite and romantic.

By the late 1890s Garland had begun to mine a vein that was eventually to be an important source of his literary capital through 1930, when he moved to California from New York. The vein was autobiography, and by general agreement *A Son of the Middle Border* (1917), *A Daughter of the Middle Border* (1921), *Trail-Makers of the Middle Border* (1928), and *Roadside Meetings* (1930) constitute a permanent contribution to American letters and history. Together with Garland's early work, in which he converts his anger over the oppressive condition of people he loved into powerful fiction, these works make uniquely available to us the rural life of common people of the upper Midwest in the second half of the nineteenth century.

# Under the Lion's Paw[1]

## I

It was the last of autumn and first day of winter coming together. All day long the ploughmen on their prairie farms had moved to and fro on their wide level fields through the falling snow, which melted as it fell, wetting them to the skin—all day, notwithstanding the frequent squalls of snow, the dripping, desolate clouds, and the muck of the furrows, black and tenacious as tar.

Under their dripping harnesses the horses swung to and fro silently, with that marvelous uncomplaining patience which marks the horse. All day the wild-geese, honking wildly, as they sprawled sidewise down the wind, seemed to be fleeing from an enemy behind, and with neck out-thrust and wings extended, sailed down the wind, soon lost to sight.

Yet the ploughman behind his plough, though the snow lay on his ragged great-coat, and the cold clinging mud rose on his heavy boots, fettering him like gyves,[2] whistled in the very beard of the gale. As day passed, the snow, ceasing to melt, lay along the ploughed land, and lodged in the depth of the stubble, till on each slow round the last furrow stood out black and shining as jet between the ploughed land and the gray stubble.

When night began to fall, and the geese, flying low, began to alight invisibly in the near corn field, Stephen Council was still at work "finishing a land." He rode on his sulky-plough[3] when going with the wind, but walked when facing it. Sitting bent and cold but cheery under his slouch hat, he talked encouragingly to his weary four-in-hand.

"Come round there, boys!—round agin! We got t' finish this land. Come in there, Dan! *Stiddy*, Kate!—stiddy! None o' y'r tantrums, Kittie. It's purty tuff, but got a be did. *Tchk! tchk!* Step along, Pete! Don't let Kate git y'r single-tree[4] on the wheel. *Once* more!"

They seemed to know what he meant, and that this was the last round, for they worked with greater vigor than before.

"Once more, boys, an' sez I, oats an' a nice warm stall, an' sleep f'r all."

By the time the last furrow was turned on the land it was too dark to see the house, and the snow was changing to rain again. The tired and hungry man could see the light from the kitchen shining through the leafless hedge, and lifting a great shout, he yelled, "*Supper* f'r a half a dozen!"

It was nearly eight o'clock by the time he had finished his chores and started for supper. He was picking his way carefully through the mud, when the tall form of a man loomed up before him with a premonitory cough.

"Waddy ye want?" was the rather startled question of the farmer.

"Well, ye see," began the stranger, in a deprecating tone, "we'd like t' git in f'r the night. We've tried every house f'r the last two miles, but they hadn't any room f'r us. My wife's jest about sick, 'n' the children are cold and hungry—"

"Oh, y' want a stay all night, eh?"

"Yes, sir; it 'ud be a great accom—"

---

1. This story first appeared in *Harper's Weekly* 33 (September 7, 1889), the source of the text printed here.
2. Shackles.

3. Plow with wheels and a seat for the driver.
4. Pivoted swinging bar to which the straps of a harness are fastened and by which a vehicle or implement is drawn; also called "whiffletree."

"Waal, I don't make it a practice t' turn anybuddy away hungry, not on sech nights as this. Drive right in. We 'ain't got much, but sech as it is—"

But the stranger had disappeared. And soon his steaming, weary team, with drooping heads and swinging single-trees, moved past the well on to the block beside the path. Council stood at the side of the "schooner" and helped the children out—two little half-sleeping children—and then a small woman with a babe in her arms.

"There ye go!" he shouted, jovially, to the children. "*Now* we're all right. Run right along to the house there, an' tell Mam' Council you wants sumpthin' t' eat. Right this way, Mis'—Keep right off t' the right there. I'll go an' git a lantern. Come," he said to the dazed and silent group at his side.

"Mother," he shouted, as he neared the fragrant and warmly lighted kitchen, "here are some wayfarers an' folks who need sumpthin' t' eat an' a place t' snooze," he ended, pushing them all in.

Mrs. Council, a large, jolly, rather coarse-looking woman, took the children in her arms. "Come right in, you little rabbits. 'Most asleep, hay? Now here's a drink o' milk f'r each o' ye. I'll have s'm' tea in a minute. Take off y'r things and set up t' the fire."

While she set the children to drinking milk, Council got out his lantern and went out to the barn to help the stranger about his team, where his loud, hearty voice could be heard as it came and went between the hay-mow and the stalls.

The woman came to light as a small, timid, and discouraged-looking woman, but still pretty, in a thin and sorrowful way.

"Land sakes! An' you've travelled all the way from Clear Lake t'day in this mud! Waal! waal! No wunder you're all tired out. Don't wait f'r the men, Mis'—" She hesitated, waiting for the name.

"Haskins."

"Mis' Haskins, set right up to the table an' take a good swig o' that tea, whilst I make y' s'm' toast. It's green tea, an' it's good. I tell Council as I git older I don't seem t' enjoy Young Hyson n'r gunpowder.[5] I want the reel green tea, jest as it comes off 'n the vines. Seems t' have more heart in it some way. Don't s'pose it has. Council says it's all in m' eye."

Going on in this easy way, she soon had the children filled with bread and milk and the woman thoroughly at home, eating some toast and sweet melon pickles, and sipping the tea.

"*See* the little rats!" she laughed at the children. "They're full as they can stick now, and they want to go to bed. Now don't git up, Mis' Haskins; set right where you are, an' let me look after 'em. I know all about young ones, though I *am* all alone now. Jane went an' married last fall. But, as I tell Council, it's lucky we keep our health. Set right *there*, Mis' Haskins; I won't have you stir a finger."

It was an unmeasured pleasure to sit there in the warm, homely kitchen, the jovial chatter of the housewife driving out and holding at bay the growl of the impotent, cheated wind.

The little woman's eyes filled with tears, which fell down upon the sleeping baby in her arms. The world was not so desolate and cold and hopeless, after all.

---

5. Young Hyson and gunpowder are green teas that have been dried for export.

"Now I hope Council won't stop out there and talk politics all night. He's the greatest man to talk politics an' read the *Tribune*. How old is it?"

She broke off and peered down at the face of the babe.

"Two months 'n' five days," said the mother, with a mother's exactness.

"Ye don't say! I want t' know! The dear little pudzy-wudzy," she went on, stirring it up in the neighborhood of the ribs with her fat forefinger.

"Pooty tough on 'oo to go gallavant'n' 'cross lots this way."

"Yes, that's so; a man can't lift a mountain," said Council, entering the door. "Sarah, this is Mr. Haskins, from Kansas. He's been eat up 'n' drove out by grasshoppers."

"Glad t' see yeh! Pa, empty that wash-basin, 'n' give him a chance t' wash."

Haskins was a tall man, with a thin, gloomy face. His hair was a reddish brown, like his coat, and seemed equally faded by the wind and sun. And his sallow face, though hard and set, was pathetic somehow. You would have felt that he had suffered much by the line of his mouth showing under his thin yellow mustache.

"Hain't Ike got home yet, Sairy?"

"Hain't seen 'im."

"W-a-a-l, set right up, Mr. Haskins; wade right into what we've got; 'tain't much, but we manage t' live on it—least I do; *she* gits fat on it," laughed Council, pointing his thumb at his wife.

After supper, while the women put the children to bed, Haskins and Council talked on, seated near the huge cooking stove, the steam rising from their wet clothing. In the Western fashion Council told as much of his own life as he drew from his guest. He asked but few questions; but by-and-by the story of Haskins's struggles and defeat came out. The story was a terrible one, but he told it quietly, seated with his elbows on his knees, gazing most of the time at the hearth.

"I didn't like the looks of the country, anyhow," Haskins said, partly rising and glancing at his wife. "I was ust t' northern Ingyannie,[6] where we hav' lots of timber 'n' lots of rain, 'n' I didn't like the looks o' that dry prairie. What galled me the worst was goin' s' far away acrosst so much fine land layin' all through here vacant."

"And the 'hoppers eat ye four years hand running, did they?"

"Eat! They wiped us out. They chawed everything that was green. They jest set around waitin' f'r us to die t' eat us too. My God! I ust t' dream of 'em sitt'n' 'round on the bedpost, six feet long, workin' their jaws. They eet the fork handles. They got worse 'n' worse, till they jest rolled on one another, piled up like snow in winter. Well, it ain't no use; if I was t' talk all winter I couldn't tell nawthin'. But all the while I couldn't help thinkin' of all that land back here that nobuddy was usin, that I ought a had 'stead o' bein 'out there in that cussed country."

"Waal, why didn't ye stop an' settle here?" asked Ike, who had come in and was eating his supper.

"Fer the simple reason that you fellers wantid ten 'r fifteen dollars an acre fer the bare land, and I hadn't no money fer that kind o' thing."

"Yes, I do my own work," Mrs. Council was heard to say in the pause which followed. "I'm a-gettin' purty heavy t' be on m' laigs all day, but we can't afford

6. Indiana.

t' hire, so I keep rackin' around somehow, like a foundered horse. S'lame—I tell Council he can't tell *how* lame I am, f'r I'm jest as lame in one laig as t'other." And the good soul laughed at the joke on herself as she took a handful of flour and dusted the biscuit board to keep the dough from sticking.

"Well, I hain't *never* been very strong," said Mrs. Haskins. "Our folks was Canadians an' small-boned, and then since my last child I hain't got up again fairly. I don't like t' complain—Tim has about all he can bear now—but they was days this week when I jest wanted to lay right down an' die."

"Waal, now, I'll tell ye," said Council, from his side of the stove, silencing everybody with his good-natured roar, "I'd go down and *see* Butler *anyway,* if I was you. I guess he'd let you have his place purty cheap; the farm's all run down. He's ben anxious t' let t' somebuddy next year. It 'ud be a good chance fer you. Anyhow, you go to bed, and sleep like a babe. I've got some ploughin' t' do anyhow, an' we'll see if somethin' can't be done about your case. Ike, you go out an' see if the horses is all right, an' I'll show the folks t' bed."

When the tired husband and wife were lying under the generous quilts of the spare bed, Haskins listened a moment to the wind in the eaves, and then said, with a slow and solemn tone,

"There are people in this world who are good enough t' be angels, an' only haff t' die to *be* angels."

## II

Jim Butler was one of those men called in the West "land poor." Early in the history of Rock River he had come into the town and started in the grocery business in a small way, occupying a small building in a mean part of the town. At this period of his life he earned all he got, and was up early and late, sorting beans, working over butter, and carting his goods to and from the station. But a change came over him at the end of the second year, when he sold a lot of land for four times what he paid for it. From that time forward he believed in land speculation as the surest way of getting rich. Every cent he could save or spare from his trade he put into land at forced sale, or mortgages on land, which were "just as good as the wheat," he was accustomed to say.

Farm after farm fell into his hands, until he was recognized as one of the leading land-owners of the county. His mortgages were scattered all over Cedar County, and as they slowly but surely fell in, he sought usually to retain the former owner as tenant.

He was not ready to foreclose; indeed, he had the name of being one of the "easiest" men in the town. He let the debtor off again and again, extending the time whenever possible.

"I don't want y'r land," he said. "All I'm after is the int'rest on my money—that's all. Now if y' want 'o stay on the farm, why, I'll give y' a good chance. I can't have the land layin' vacant." And in many cases the owner remained as tenant.

In the mean time he had sold his store; he couldn't spend time in it; he was mainly occupied now with sitting around town on rainy days, smoking and "gassin' with the boys," or in riding to and from his farms. In fishing-time he fished a good deal. Doc Grimes, Ben Ashley, and Cal Cheatham were his cronies on these fishing excursions or hunting trips in the time of chickens or partridges. In winter they went to northern Wisconsin to shoot deer.

In spite of all these signs of easy life, Butler persisted in saying he "hadn't money enough to pay taxes on his land," and was careful to convey the impression that he was poor in spite of his twenty farms. At one time he was said to be worth fifty thousand dollars, but land had been a little slow of sale of late, so that he was not worth so much. A fine farm, known as the Higley place, had fallen into his hands in the usual way the previous year, and he had not been able to find a tenant for it. Poor Higley, after working himself nearly to death on it, in the attempt to lift the mortgage, had gone off to Dakota, leaving the farm and his curse to Butler.

This was the farm that Council advised Haskins to apply for, and the next day Council hitched up his team and drove down-town to see Butler.

"You jest lem *me* do the talkin'," he said. "We'll find him wearin' out his pants on some salt barrel somewears; and if he thought you *wanted* a place, he'd sock it to you hot and heavy. You jest keep quiet; I'll fix 'im."

Butler was seated in Ben Ashley's store, telling "fish yarns," when Council sauntered in casually.

"Hello, But! lyin' agin, hay?"

"Hello, Steve! how goes it?"

"Oh, so-so. Too dang much rain these days. I thought it was goin' t' freeze up f'r good last night. Tight squeak if I git m' ploughin' done. How's farmin' with *you* these days?"

"Bad. Ploughin' ain't half done."

"It 'ud be a religious idee f'r you t' go out and take a hand y'rself."

"I don't haff to," said Butler, with a wink.

"Got anybody on the Higley place?"

"No. Know of anybody?"

"Waal, no; not eggsackly. I've got a relation back t' Michigan who's ben hot an' cold on the idee o' comin' West f'r some time. *Might* come if he could git a good lay-out. What do you talk on the farm?"

"Well, I d' know. I'll rent it on shares, or I'll rent it money rent."

"Waal, how much money, say?"

"Well, say ten per cent on the price—$250."

"Waal, that ain't bad. Wait on 'im till 'e thrashes?"

Haskins listened eagerly to this important question, but Council was coolly eating a dried apple which he had speared out of a barrel with his knife. Butler studied him carefully.

"Well, knocks me out o' twenty-five dollars interest."

"My relation 'll need all he's got t' git his crops in," said Council, in the same indifferent way.

"Well, all right; *say* wait," concluded Butler.

"All right; this is the man. Haskins, this is Mr. Butler—no relation to Ben—the hardest-working man in Cedar County."

On the way home, Haskins said: "I ain't much better off. I'd like that farm; it's a good farm, but it's all run down, an' so 'm I. I could make a good farm of it if I had half a show. But I can't stock it n'r seed it."

"Waal, now, don't you worry," roared Council, in his ear. "We'll pull y' through somehow till next harvest. He's agreed t' hire it ploughed, an' you can earn a hundred dollars ploughin', an' y' c'n git the seed o' me, an' pay me back when y' can."

Haskins was silent with emotion, but at last he said, "I 'ain't got nothin' t' live on."

"Now don't you worry 'bout that. You jest make your head-quarters at ol' Steve Council's. Mother 'll take a pile o' comfort in havin' y'r wife an' children 'round. Y'see Jane's married off lately, an' Ike's away a good 'eal, so we'll be darn glad t' have ye stop with us this winter. Nex' spring we'll see if y' can't git a start agin;" and he chirruped to the team, which sprang forward with the rumbling, clattering wagon.

"Say, looky here, Council, you can't do this. I never saw—" shouted Haskins in his neighbor's ear.

Council moved about uneasily in his seat, and stopped his stammering gratitude by saying: "Hold on now; don't make such a fuss over a little thing. When I see a man down, an' things all on top of 'im, I jest like t' kick 'em off an' help 'im up. That's the kind of religion I got, an' it's about the *only* kind."

They rode the rest of the way home in silence. And when the red light of the lamp shone out into the darkness of the cold and windy night, and he thought of this refuge for his children and wife, Haskins could have put his arm around the neck of his burly companion and squeezed him like a lover; but he contented himself with saying, "Steve Council, you'll git y'r pay f'r this some day."

"Don't want any pay. My religion ain't run on such business principles."

The wind was growing colder, and the ground was covered with a white frost, as they turned into the gate of the Council farm, and the children came rushing out, shouting, "Papa's come!" They hardly looked like the same children who had sat at the table the night before. Their torpidity under the influence of sunshine and Mother Council had given way to a sort of spasmodic cheerfulness, as insects in winter revive when laid on the hearth.

### III

Haskins worked like a fiend, and his wife, like the heroic little woman that she was, bore also uncomplainingly the most terrible burdens. They rose early and toiled without intermission till the darkness fell on the plain, then tumbled into bed, every bone and muscle aching with fatigue, to rise with the sun the next morning to the same round of the same ferocity of labor.

The eldest boy, now nine years old, drove a team all through the spring, ploughing and seeding, milked the cows, and did chores innumerable, in most ways taking the place of a man; an infinitely pathetic but common figure—this boy—on the American farm, where there is no law against child labor. To see him in his coarse clothing, his huge boots, and his ragged cap, as he stogged with a pail of water from the well, or trudged in the cold and cheerless dawn out into the frosty field behind his team, gave the city-bred visitor a sharp pang of sympathetic pain. Yet Haskins loved his boy, and would have saved him from this if he could, but he could not.

By June the first year the result of such Herculean toil began to show on the farm. The yard was cleaned up and sown to grass, the garden ploughed and planted, and the house mended. Council had given them four of his cows.

"Take'em an' run 'em on shares. I don't want a milk s' many. Ike's away s' much now, Sat'd'ys an' Sund'ys, I can't stand the bother anyhow."

Other men, seeing the confidence of Council in the new-comer, had sold him tools on time; and as he was really an able farmer, he soon had round him many evidences of his care and thrift. At the advice of Council he had taken the farm for three years, with the privilege of rerenting or buying at the end of the term.

"It's a good bargain, an' y' want 'o nail it," said Council. "If you have any kind ov a crop, you can pay half y'r debts, an' keep seed an' bread."

The new hope which now sprang up in the heart of Haskins and his wife grew great almost as a pain by the time the wide field of wheat began to wave and rustle and swirl in the winds of July. Day after day he would snatch a few moments after supper to go and look at it.

"Have ye seen the wheat t'-day, Nettie?" he asked one night as he rose from supper.

"No, Tim, I 'ain't had time."

"Well, take time now. Le's go look at it."

She threw an old hat on her head—Tommy's hat—and looking almost pretty in her thin sad way, went out with her husband to the hedge.

"Ain't it grand, Nettie? Just look at it."

It was grand. Level, russet here and there, heavy-headed, wide as a lake, and full of multitudinous whispers and gleams of health, it stretched away before the gazers like the fabled field of the cloth of gold.

"Oh, I think—I *hope* we'll have a good crop, Tim; and oh, how good the people have been to us!"

"Yes; I don't know where we'd be t'-day if it hadn't a ben f'r Council and his wife."

"They're the best people in the world," said the little woman, with a great sob of gratitude.

"We'll be into that field on Monday, sure," said Haskins, griping the rail on the fence as if already at the work of the harvest.

The harvest came bounteous, glorious, but the winds came and blew it into tangles, and the rain matted it here and there close to the ground, increasing the work of gathering it threefold.

Oh, how they toiled in those glorious days! Clothing dripping with sweat, arms aching, filled with briars, fingers raw and bleeding, backs broken with the weight of heavy bundles, Haskins and his man toiled on. Tommy drove the harvester while his father and a hired man bound on the machine. In this way they cut ten acres every day, and almost every night after supper, when the hand went to bed, Haskins returned to the field, shocking[7] the bound grain in the light of the moon. Many a night he worked till he staggered with utter fatigue; worked till his anxious wife came out to call him in to rest and lunch.

At the same time she cooked for the men, took care of the children, washed and ironed, milked the cows at night, made the butter, and some-

7. Gathering and piling sheaves of grain.

times fed the horses and watered them while her husband kept at the shocking. No slave in the Roman galleys could have toiled so frightfully and lived, for this man *thought* himself a freeman, and that he was working for his wife and babes.

When he sank into his bed with a deep groan of relief, too tired to change his grimy, dripping clothing, he felt that he was getting nearer and nearer to a home of his own, and pushing the wolf of want a little further from his door.

There is no despair so deep as the despair of a homeless man or woman. To roam the roads of the country or the streets of the city, to feel there is no rood of ground on which the feet can rest, to halt weary and hungry outside lighted windows and hear laughter and song within—these are the hungers and rebellions that drive men to crime and women to shame.

It was the memory of this homelessness, and the fear of its coming again, that spurred Timothy Haskins and Nettie, his wife, to such ferocious labor during that first year.

## IV

" 'M, yes; 'm, yes; first-rate," said Butler, as his eye took in the neat garden, the pigpen, and the well-filled barn-yard. "You're git'n' quite a stock around yer. Done well, eh?"

Haskins was showing Butler around the place. He had not seen it for a year, having spent the year in Washington and Boston with Ashley, his brother-in-law, who had been elected to Congress.

"Yes, I've laid out a good deal of money during the last three years. I've paid out three hundred dollars f'r fencin'."

"Um—h'm! I see, I see," said Butler, while Haskins went on.

"The kitchen there cost two hundred; the barn 'ain't cost much in money, but I've put a lot o' time on it. I've dug a new well, and I—"

"Yes, yes. I see! You've done well. Stalk worth a thousand dollars," said Butler, picking his teeth with a straw.

"About that," said Haskins, modestly. "We begin to feel 's if we wuz git'n' a home f'r ourselves; but we've worked hard. I tell ye we begin to feel it, Mr. Butler, and we're goin' t' begin t' ease up purty soon. We've been kind o' plannin' a trip back t' *her* folks after the fall ploughin's done."

"*Eggs*-actly!" said Butler, who was evidently thinking of something else. "I suppose you've kind o' kalklated on stayin' here three years more?"

"Well, yes. Fact is, I think I c'n buy the farm this fall, if you'll give me a reasonable show."

"Um—m! What do you call a reasonable show?"

"Waal; say a quarter down and three years' time."

Butler looked at the huge stacks of wheat which filled the yard, over which the chickens were fluttering and crawling, catching grasshoppers, and out of which the crickets were singing innumerably. He smiled in a peculiar way as he said, "Oh, I won't be hard on yeh. But what did you expect to pay f'r the place?"

"Why, about what you offered it for before, twenty-five hundred dollars, or *possibly* three thousand," he added, quickly, as he saw the owner shake his head.

"This farm is worth five thousand and five hundred dollars," said Butler, in a careless but decided voice.

*"What!"* almost shrieked the astounded Haskins. "What's that? Five thousand? Why, that's double what you offered it for three years ago."

"Of course; and its worth it. It was all run down then; now it's in good shape. You've laid out fifteen hundred dollars in improvements, according to your own story."

"But *you* had nothin' t' do about that. It's my work an' my money."

"You bet it was; but it's my land."

"But what's to pay me for all?"

" 'Ain't you had the use of 'em?" replied Butler, smiling calmly into his face.

Haskins was like a man struck on the head with a sand-bag; he couldn't think, he stammered as he tried to say: "But—I never 'd git the use. You'd rob me. More'n that: you agreed—you promised that I could buy or rent at the end of three years at—"

"That's all right. But I didn't say I'd let you carry off the improvements, nor that I'd go on renting the farm at two-fifty. The land is doubled in value, it don't matter how; it don't enter into the question; an' now you can pay me five hundred dollars a year rent, or take it on your own terms at fifty-five hundred, or—git out."

He was turning away, when Haskins, the sweat pouring from his face, fronted him, saying again:

"But *you've* done nothing to make it so. You hain't added a cent. I put it all there myself, expectin' to buy. I worked an' sweat to improve it. I was workin' f'r myself an' babes."

"Well, why didn't you buy when I offered to sell? What y' kickin' about?"

"I'm kickin' about payin' you twice f'r my own things—my own fences, my own kitchen, my own garden."

Butler laughed. "You're too green t' eat, young feller. *Your* improvements! The law will sing another tune."

"But I trusted your word."

"Never trust anybody, my friend. Besides, I didn't promise not to do this thing. Why, man, don't look at me like that. Don't take me for a thief. It's the law. The reg'lar thing. Everybody does it."

"I don't care if they do. It's stealin' jest the same. You take three thousand dollars of my money. The work o' my hands and my wife's." He broke down at this point. He was not a strong man mentally. He could face hardship, ceaseless toil, but he could not face the cold and sneering face of Butler.

"But I don't take it," said Butler, coolly. "All you've got to do is to go on jest as you've been a-doin', or give me a thousand dollars down, and a mortgage at ten percent on the rest."

Haskins sat down blindly on a bundle of oats near by, and with staring eyes and drooping head went over the situation. He was under the lion's paw. He felt a horrible numbness in his heart and limbs. He was hid in a mist, and there was no path out.

Butler walked about, looking at the huge stacks of grain, and pulling now and again a few handfuls out, shelling the heads in his hands and blowing the chaff away. He hummed a little tune as he did so. He had an accommodating air of waiting.

Haskins was in the midst of the terrible toil of the last year. He was walking again in the rain and the mud behind his plough, he felt the dust and dirt of the threshing. The ferocious husking-time, with its cutting wind and biting, clinging snows, lay hard upon him. Then he thought of his wife, how she had cheerfully cooked and baked, without holiday and without rest.

"Well, what do you think of it?" inquired the cool, mocking, insinuating voice of Butler.

"I think you're a thief and a liar," shouted Haskins, leaping up. "A black-hearted houn'!" Butler's smile maddened him; with a sudden leap he caught a fork in his hands, and whirled it in the air. "You'll never rob another man, damn ye!" he grated through his teeth, a look of pitiless ferocity in his aching eyes.

Butler shrank and quivered, expecting the blow; stood, held hypnotized by the eyes of the man he had a moment before despised—a man transformed into an avenging demon. But in the deadly hush between the lift of the weapon and its fall there came a gush of faint, childish laughter, and then across the range of his vision, far away and dim, he saw the sun-bright head of his baby girl, as, with the pretty tottering run of a two-year-old, she moved across the grass of the door-yard. His hands relaxed; the fork fell to the ground; his head lowered.

"Make out y'r deed an' morgige, an' git off'n my land, an' don't ye never cross my line again; if y' do, I'll kill ye."

Butler backed away from the man in wild haste, and climbing into his buggy with trembling limbs, drove off down the road, leaving Haskins seated dumbly on the sunny pile of sheaves, his head sunk into his hands.

1889                                                                                        1891

---

# ABRAHAM CAHAN
## 1860–1951

One of the central subjects of turn-of-the-twentieth-century U.S. literature is the (usually painful) process of "Americanization" or assimilation of immigrants from all corners of the world. Such assimilation is at the heart of the work of Abraham Cahan, both as a prolific journalist and as the author of a relatively small but important body of fiction.

Cahan was born into an Orthodox Jewish family in a village a few miles from Vilna, Lithuania, then a part of the Russian Empire. He was educated as a youth first in Hebrew schools and then in a *yeshiva*—a seminary for studies in Jewish law and commentaries on it. His absorption in traditional Jewish studies gave way in his teens to a comparably passionate engagement with secular subjects, especially literature and social theory. As a student at the Vilna Teacher Training Institute, he was among a small group of young men who, like self-described intellectuals in other Russian cities, read and discussed such subversive works as Nikolai Chernishevsky's radical utopian novel *What Is to Be Done?* (1863). Of more lasting importance to him was the reading of Tolstoi and other Russian writers; of these, Chekhov, a brilliant short-story writer, became his favorite. Although Cahan was neither a leader nor an active conspirator in efforts to overthrow the czarist regime, his room was searched twice during his first year as a teacher, and he had good reason to be concerned about the possibilities of arrest and imprisonment.

The intensified attempt to suppress dissent that brought Cahan and other intellectuals under suspicion (it was considered a revolutionary act simply to be in possession of prohibited writings) was one consequence of the assassination of Czar Alexander II in March 1881. More important historically was intensified Russian anti-Semitism and an unprecedented series of murderous pogroms unleashed against Russian Jews with at least the tacit approval of local police and other government officials. There had been pogroms before and in other regions, but these pogroms led almost immediately to the massive emigration, starting in 1882, of Russian and Eastern European Jews to Palestine and, in much greater numbers, to America (two million by 1924).

Within two months of his arrival in the United States in 1882, Cahan gave the first socialist speech to be delivered in the country in Yiddish—a language that combined Middle High German dialects with vocabularies from Hebrew, Slavic, and European languages and as time went on a distinctively Jewish American vocabulary. Cahan soon helped organize the first Jewish tailors' union; taught English at night to immigrants at the Young Men's Hebrew Association; and began his careers as editor and journalist with Yiddish, Russian, and English papers.

In 1897 Cahan was active in founding the *Jewish Daily Forward*, a Yiddish-language newspaper he edited, with some short interruptions, for nearly fifty years. As critic Jules Chametsky observed: "[Cahan] took a sectarian journal of the Social Democratic Party with 6,000 subscribers and made it the most successful foreign-language newspaper in America and the leading Yiddish paper in the world." At its height the *Forward* had a circulation of a quarter of a million (and was read by perhaps a million people altogether). Cahan's editorial policy was designed to help Jewish immigrants make the transition from the often medieval conditions of the urban ghettos and *shtetls* to the new realities of a rapidly industrializing democracy. The *Forward* combined news, information, cultural commentary, and reviews with short stories, including work of I.J. Singer and Sholem Asch. It included features such as *"A Bintel Brief"* (A Bundle of Letters), which printed anonymous letters from subscribers together with authoritative advice from the editor.

For twenty-five years—from 1892 until 1917—Cahan turned his attention to writing fiction in English. Encouraged by novelist and critic William Dean Howells, Cahan published his first novel, *Yekl: A Tale of the New York Ghetto*, in 1896. Encouraged further by the generally favorable reception of this work (later made more popular by Joan Micklen Silver's film adaptation, released in 1975 under the title *Hester Street*), Cahan wrote short stories that he published in 1898 as *"The Imported Bridegroom" and Other Stories of the New York Ghetto*. In the title story and throughout the volume, Yiddish and heavily accented English are largely absorbed and "translated" into the perceptive but lucid language of an omniscient third-person narrator. This change in presentational mode was a sign of Cahan's mastery of English and sophistication of technique, as well as developing control of irony. In this story, his sharp eye and sensitive ear for language—as well as his culturally rich and complex sense of his characters' identities—are at the service of mood and characterization.

Cahan's masterpiece was his novel *The Rise of David Levinsky* (1917), a powerful depiction of the garment industry and the people who work in it. This book established Cahan as a progenitor of Jewish American writers as diverse as Michael Gold, Henry Roth, Saul Bellow, and Alfred Kazin. The rich tapestry of this intensely realistic account of turn-of-the-twentieth-century New York is at once a Jewish novel, a novel about the always difficult process of Americanization, and a more universal story of self-estrangement and social alienation. Both as a journalist and as a writer of fiction, Abraham Cahan was influential in his own time. He remains one of the central chroniclers of American immigrant life.

# The Imported Bridegroom[1]

## I

Flora was alone in the back parlor, which she had appropriated for a sort of boudoir. She sat in her rocker, in front of the parlor stove, absorbed in "Little Dorrit."[2] Her well-groomed girlish form was enveloped in a kindly warmth whose tender embrace tinged her interest in the narrative with a triumphant consciousness of the snowstorm outside.

Little by little the rigid afternoon light began to fade into a melancholy gray. Dusk was creeping into the room in almost visible waves. Flora let the book rest on her lap and fixed her gaze on the twinkling scarlet of the stove-glass. The thickening twilight, the warmth of the apartment, and the atmosphere of the novel blended together, and for some moments Flora felt far away from herself.

She was the only girl of her circle who would read Dickens, Scott, or Thackeray in addition to the "Family Story Paper" and the "Fireside Companion,"[3] which were the exclusive literary purveyors to her former classmates at the Chrystie Street Grammar School.[4] There were a piano and a neat little library in her room.

She was rather tall and well formed. Her oblong ivory face, accentuated by a mass of unruly hair of a lustreless black, was never deserted by a faint glimmer of a smile, at once pensive and arch. When she broke into one of her hearty, good-natured laughs, her deep, dark, appealing eyes would seem filled with grief. Her nose, a trifle too precipitous, gave an unexpected tone to the extreme picturesqueness of the whole effect, and, when she walked, partook of the dignity of her gait.

A month or two before we make Flora's acquaintance she had celebrated her twentieth birthday, having been born in this little private house on Mott Street, which was her father's property.

A matchmaker[5] had recently called, and he had launched into a eulogy[6] of a young Jewish physician; but old Stroon had cut him short, in his blunt way: his only child was to marry a God-fearing business man, and no fellow deep in Gentile lore and shaving his beard[7] need apply. As to Flora, she was burning to be a doctor's wife. A rising young merchant, a few years in the country, was the staple matrimonial commodity in her set. Most of her married girl friends, American-born themselves, like Flora, had husbands of this class—queer fellows, whose broken English had kept their own sweethearts chuckling. Flora hated the notion of marrying as the other Mott or Bayard Street girls did. She was accustomed to use her surroundings

1. First published in "The Imported Bridegroom" and Other Stories of the New York Ghetto (1898), from which this text is taken.
2. Novel (1857) by Charles Dickens (1812–1870), set for the most part in an English debtors' prison.
3. Charles Dickens, Sir Walter Scott (1771–1832), and William Makepeace Thackeray (1811–1863)—British novelists. "Family Story Paper" and "Fireside Companion": The New York Family Story Paper (as it was first known) published popular fiction from 1873 through 1921; the Fireside Companion was a series of cheap reprints of popular

books.
4. Chrystie Street, like other New York City locations mentioned in the story, is on the Lower East Side of Manhattan, home at that time to the majority of Jewish immigrants.
5. Arranged marriages were traditional among Orthodox Jews at this time.
6. Speech or writing in praise of a person, not necessarily a deceased person.
7. Orthodox Jewish practice dictates that men not shave, and frequently not trim, their beards. "Gentile": non-Jewish.

for a background, throwing her own personality into high relief. But apart from this, she craved a more refined atmosphere than her own, and the vague ideal she had was an educated American gentleman, like those who lived uptown.

Accordingly, when the word "doctor" had left the matchmaker's lips, she seized upon it as a great discovery. In those days—the early eighties—a match of this kind was an uncommon occurrence in the New York Ghetto.

Flora pictured a clean-shaven, high-hatted, spectacled gentleman jumping out of a buggy, and the image became a fixture in her mind. "I won't marry anybody except a doctor," she would declare, with conscious avoidance of bad grammar, as it behooved a doctor's wife.

But what was to be done with father's opposition? Asriel Stroon had never been the man to yield, and now that he grew more devout every day, her case seemed hopeless. But then Flora was her father's daughter, and when she took a resolve she could not imagine herself otherwise than carrying it out, sooner or later.

Flora's thoughts were flowing in this direction when her father's gruff voice made itself heard from the dining-room below. It was the anniversary of his father's death. In former years he would have contented himself with obit services, at the synagogue; this time, however, he had passed the day in fasting and chanting psalms at home, in addition to lighting his own candle in front of the cantor's desk and reciting Kaddish[8] for the departed soul, at the house of prayer. It touched Flora's heart to think of him fasting and praying all day, and, with her book in her hand, she ran down to meet him.

"Just comin' from the synagogue, papa?" she greeted him affectionately, in English. "This settles your fast, don't it?"

"It is not so easy to settle with Him, my daughter," he returned, in Yiddish,[9] pointing to the ceiling. "You can never be through serving the Uppermost. Hurry up, Tamara!" he added, in the direction of the adjoining kitchen.

"You ain' goin' to say more Thilim[1] tonight, are you, pa?"

"Why, does it cost you too much?" he snarled good humoredly.

"Yes it does—your health. I won't let you sing again. You are weak and you got enough."

"Hush! It is not potato-soup; you can never have enough of it." He fell to tugging nervously at his white beard, which grew in a pair of tiny imperials.[2] "Tamara! It's time to break the fast, isn't it?"

"You can wash your hands. Supper is ready," came the housekeeper's pleasant voice.

He took off his brown derby, and covered his steel-gray hair with a velvet skull-cap; and as he carried his robust, middle-sized body into the kitchen, to perform his ablutions, his ruddy, gnarled face took on an air of piety.

When supper was over and Asriel and Tamara were about to say grace, Flora resumed the reading of her novel.

8. A mourner's prayer, recited regularly for eleven months following the death of a parent. "Obit services": the Yarzheit is observed on the day a person died according to the Jewish calendar. "Cantor": a *chazzan* (cantor) leads the synagogue's congregation in prayer.
9. A language derived from Middle High German, spoken by Eastern European Jews and their descendants in other countries; it is written in the Hebrew alphabet and borrows vocabulary from Hebrew, Russian, Polish, English, and other languages. "Yiddish" is the Yiddish word for "Jewish."
1. Psalms.
2. Pointed tufts of beard on the lower lip and chin—named after Emperor Louis Napoleon of France, who set this fashion.

"Off with that lump of Gentile nastiness while holy words are being said!" the old man growled.

Flora obeyed, in amazement. Only a few months before she had seldom seen him intone grace at all. She was getting used to his new habits, but such rigor as he now displayed was unintelligible to her, and she thought it unbearable.

"You can read your book a little after. The wisdom of it will not run away," chimed in Tamara, with good-natured irony. She was a poor widow of forty. Asriel had engaged her for her piety and for the rabbinical learning of her late husband, as much as for her culinary fame in the Ghetto.

Asriel intoned grace in indistinct droning accents. By degrees, however, as he warmed up to the Hebrew prayer, whose words were a conglomeration of incomprehensible sounds to him, he fell to swaying to and fro, and his voice broke into an exalted, heart-rending sing-song, Tamara accompanying him in whispers, and dolefully nodding her bewigged head all the while.

Flora was moved. The scene was novel to her, and she looked on with the sympathetic reverence of a Christian visiting a Jewish synagogue on the Day of Atonement.[3]

At last the fervent tones died away in a solemn murmur. Silence fell over the cosy little room. Asriel sat tugging at his scanty beard as if in an effort to draw it into a more venerable growth.

"Flora!" he presently growled. "I am going to Europe."

When Asriel Stroon thought he spoke, and when he spoke he acted.

"Goin' to Europe! Are you crazy, papa? What are you talkin' about?"

"Just what you hear. After Passover I am going to Europe. I must take a look at Pravly."[4]

"But you ain't been there over thirty-five years. You don't remember not'in' at all."

"I don't remember Pravly? Better than Mott Street; better than my nose. I was born there, my daughter," he added, as he drew closer to her and began to stroke her glossless black hair. This he did so seldom that the girl felt her heart swelling in her throat. She was yearning after him in advance.

Tamara stared in beaming amazement at the grandeur of the enterprise. "Are you really going?" she queried, with a touch of envy.

"What will you do there?—It's so far away!" Flora resumed, for want of a weightier argument at hand.

"Never mind, my child; I won't have to walk all the way."

"But the Russian police will arrest you for stayin' away so long. Didn't you say they would?"

"The kernel of a hollow nut!" he replied, extemporizing an equivalent of "Fiddlesticks!" Flora was used to his metaphors, although they were at times rather vague, and set one wondering how they came into his head at all. "The kernel of a hollow nut! Show a *treif*[5] gendarme a *kosher*[6] coin, and he will be shivering with ague. Long live the American dollar!"

She gave him a prolonged, far-away look, and said, peremptorily:—

"Mister, you ain' goin' nowheres."

"Tamara, hand me my Psalter, will you?" the old man grumbled.

---

3. Yom Kippur, or the Day of Atonement, the most important holiday of the Jewish year.
4. Fictional town in Poland where Asriel was born.

5. Impure; *treif* refers specifically to food not prepared according to the laws of Moses.
6. The opposite of *treif*.

When the girl was gone, the housekeeper inquired:—

"And Flora—will you take her along?"

"What for? That she might make fun of our ways there, or that the pious people should point their fingers at her and call her Gentile girl, hey? She will stay with you and collect rent. I did not have her in Pravly, and I want to be there as I used to. I feel like taking a peep at the graves of my folks. It is pulling me by the heart, Tamara," he added, in a grave undertone, as he fell to turning over the leaves of his Psalter.

## II

When Asriel Stroon had retired from business, he suddenly grew fearful of death. Previously he had had no time for that. What with his flour store, two bakeries, and some real estate, he had been too busy to live, much less to think of death. He had never been seen at the synagogue on weekdays; and on the Sabbath, when, enveloped in his praying-shawl, he occupied a seat at the East Wall,[7] he would pass the time drowsing serenely and nodding unconscious approval of the cantor's florid improvisations, or struggling to keep flour out of his mind, where it clung as pertinaciously as it did to his long Sabbath coat.

The first sermon that failed to lull him to sleep was delivered by a newly landed preacher, just after Asriel had found it more profitable to convert his entire property into real estate. The newcomer dwelt, among other things, upon the fate of the wicked after death and upon their forfeited share in the World to Come. As Asriel listened to the fiery exhortation it suddenly burst upon him that he was very old and very wicked. "I am as full of sins as a watermelon is of seeds," he said to himself, on coming out of the synagogue. "You may receive notice to move at any time, Asriel. And where is your baggage? Got anything to take along to the other world, as the preacher said, hey?"

Alas! he had been so taken up with earthly title deeds that he had given but little thought to such deeds as would entitle him to a "share in the World to Come;" and while his valuable papers lay secure between the fireproof walls of his iron safe, his soul was left utterly exposed to the flames of Sheol.[8]

Then it was that he grew a pair of bushy sidelocks, ceased trimming his twin goatees, and, with his heart divided between yearning after the business he had sold and worrying over his sins, spent a considerable part of his unlimited leisure reading psalms.

What a delight it was to wind off chapter after chapter! And how smoothly it now came off, in his father's (peace upon him!) sing-song, of which he had not even thought for more than thirty years, but which suddenly came pouring out of his throat, together with the first verse he chanted! Not that Asriel Stroon could have told you the meaning of what he was so zestfully intoning, for in his boyhood he had scarcely gone through the Pentateuch[9] when he was set to work by his father's side, at flax heckling.[1] But then the very sounds of the words and the hereditary intonation, added to the consciousness that

---

7. A place for the Ark was usually kept in the eastern wall of a synagogue. "Sabbath": or *Shabbat*, is the seventh day of the week in Jewish tradition, celebrated from sundown Friday to sundown Saturday, during which time no work is done. "Praying-shawl": a white woollen shawl with sacred fringes in each corner, worn by Jewish men after marriage, during certain devotional exercises.

8. The underworld.

9. The first five books of the Bible.

1. The removal of impurities from flax so that it can be made into linen.

it was psalms he was reciting, "made every line melt like sugar in his mouth," as he once described it to the devout housekeeper.

He grew more pious and exalted every day, and by degrees fell prey to a feeling to which he had been a stranger for more than three decades.

Asriel Stroon grew homesick.

It was thirty-five years since he had left his birthplace; thirty years or more since, in the whirl of his American successes, he had lost all interest in it. Yet now, in the fifty-eighth year of his life, he suddenly began to yearn and pine for it.

Was it the fervor of his religious awakening which resoldered the long-broken link? At all events, numerous as were the examples of piety within the range of his American acquaintance, his notion of genuine Judaism was somehow inseparably associated with Pravly. During all the years of his life in New York he had retained a vague but deep-rooted feeling that American piety was as tasteless an article as American cucumbers and American fish— the only things in which his ecstasy over the adopted country admitted its hopeless inferiority to his native town.

### III

On a serene afternoon in May, Asriel drove up to Pravly in a peasant's wagon. He sat listlessly gazing at the unbroken line of wattle-fences and running an imaginary stick along the endless zigzag of their tops. The activity of his senses seemed suspended.

Presently a whiff of May aroma awakened his eye to a many-colored waving expanse, and his ear to the languorous whisper of birds. He recognized the plushy clover knobs in the vast array of placid magnificence, and the dandelions and the golden buttercups, although his poor mother-tongue could not afford a special name for each flower, and he now addressed them collectively as *tzatzkes*[2]—a word he had not used for thirty-five years. He looked at the tzatzkes, as they were swaying thoughtfully hither and thither, and it somehow seemed to him that it was not the birds but the clover blossoms which did the chirping. The whole scene appealed to his soul as a nodding, murmuring congregation engrossed in the solemnity of worship. He felt as though there were no such flowers in America, and that he had not seen any since he had left his native place.

Echoes of many, many years ago called to Asriel from amid the whispering host. His soul burst into song. He felt like shutting his eyes and trusting himself to the caressing breath of the air, that it might waft him whithersoever it chose. His senses were in confusion: he beheld a sea of fragrance; he inhaled heavenly music; he listened to a symphony of hues.

"What a treat to breathe! What a paradise!" he exclaimed in his heart. "The cholera take it, how delicious! Do you deserve it, old sinner you? Ten plagues[3] you do! But hush! the field is praying"—

With a wistful babyish look he became absorbed in a gigantic well-sweep[4] suspended from the clear sky, and then in the landscape it overhung. The woody mass darkling in the distance was at once racing about and standing

---

2. Decorative items.
3. Referring to the ten plagues God visited on Egypt before Pharaoh released the Hebrews to

Moses.
4. A source or fountain.

still. Fleecy clouds crawled over a hazy hill-top. And yonder—behold! a long, broad streak of silver gleaming on the horizon! Is it a lake? Asriel's eyes are riveted and memories stir in his breast. He recalls not the place itself, but he can remember his reminiscences of it. During his first years in America, at times when he would surrender himself to the sweet pangs of home-sickness and dwell, among other things, on the view that had seen him off to the unknown land, his mind would conjure up something like the effect now before his eyes. As a dream does it come back to him now. The very shadows of thirty-five years ago are veiled.

Asriel gazes before him in deep reverence. The sky is letting itself down with benign solemnity, its measureless trough filled with melody, the peasant's wagon creaking an accompaniment to it all—to every speck of color, as well as to every sound of the scene.

At one moment he felt as though he had strayed into the other world; at another, he was seized with doubt as to his own identity. "Who are you?" he almost asked himself, closing and reopening his hand experimentally. "Who or what is that business which you call life? Are you alive, Asriel?" Whereupon he somehow remembered Flora's photograph, and, taking it out of his bosom pocket, fell to contemplating it.

The wagon turned into a side-road, and the Polish peasant, leaning forward, cursed and whipped the animal into a peevish trot. Presently something gray hove in sight. Far away, below, hazy blotches came creeping from behind the sky. The wagon rolls downhill. Asriel is in a flurry. He feels like one on the eve of a great event, he knows not exactly what.

The wagon dashes on. Asriel's heart is all of a flutter. Suddenly—O Lord of the Universe! Why, there glistens the brook—what do you call it? 'Repka?' " he asks the driver.

"Repka!" the other replies, without facing about.

"Repka, a disease into her heart! Repka, dear, may she live long! Who could beat Asriel in swimming?" Over there, on the other side, it was where Asriel's father once chased him for bathing during Nine Days.[5] He bumped his head against the angle of a rock, did the little scamp, and got up with a deep, streaming gash in his lower lip. The mark is still there, and Asriel delights to feel it with his finger now. As he does so the faces of some of his playmates rise before him. Pshaw! he could whip every one of them! Was he not a dare-devil of a loafer! But how many of those fellow truants of his will he find alive? he asks himself, and the question wrings his heart.

Asriel strains his eyes at the far distance till, behold! smoke is spinning upward against the blue sky. He can make out the chimney-pots. His soul overflows. Sobs choke his breath. "Say!" he begins, addressing himself to the driver. But "Say" is English. "*Sloukhai!*" he shouts, with delight in the Polish word. He utters the names of the surrounding places, and the dull peasant's nods of assent thrill him to the core. He turns this way and that, and in his paroxysm of impatience all but leaps out of the wagon.

The rambling groups of houses define their outlines. Asriel recognizes the Catholic church. His heart bounds with joy. "Hush, wicked thing! It's a church of Gentiles." But the wicked thing surreptitiously resumes its greeting. And over there, whitening at some distance from the other dwellings—

---

5. Days of intense mourning, the first nine days of the Jewish month of Av.

what is it? "The nobleman's palace, as sure as I am a Jew!" He had forgotten all about it, as sure as he was a Jew! But what is the nobleman's name? Is he alive?—And there is the mill—the same mill! "I'll swoon away!" he says to himself audibly.

Asriel regains some composure.

Half an hour later he made his entry into his native town. Here he had expected his agitation to pass the bounds of his physical strength; but it did not. At this moment he was solemnly serene.

The town had changed little, and he recognized it at once. Every spot greeted him, and his return of the salutation was a speechless devotional pathos. He found several things which had faded out of his enshrined picture of the place, and the sight of these moved his soul even more powerfully than those he had looked forward to. Only in one instance was he taken aback. Sure enough, this is Synagogue Lane, as full of puddles as ever; but what has come over him? He well remembers that little alley in the rear; and yet it runs quite the other way. Length has turned into width.

And here is Leizer Poisner's inn. "But how rickety it has become!" Asriel's heart exclaims with a pang, as though at sight of a friend prematurely aged and run to seed. He can almost smell the stable occupying the entire length of the little building, and he remembers every room—Hello! The same market place, the same church with the bailiff's office by its side! The sparse row of huts on the river-bank, the raft bridge, the tannery,—everything was the same as he had left it; and yet it all had an odd, mysterious, far-away air— like things seen in a cyclorama.[6] It was Pravly and at the same time it was not; or, rather, it certainly was the same dear old Pravly, but added to it was something else, through which it now gazed at Asriel. Thirty-five years lay wrapped about the town.

Still, Stroon feels like Asrielke Thirteen Hairs,[7] as his nickname had been here. Then he relapses into the Mott Street landlord, and for a moment he is an utter stranger in his birthplace. Why, he could buy it all up now! He could discount all the rich men in town put together; and yet there was a time when he was of the meanest hereabout. An overpowering sense of triumph surged into his breast. Hey, there! Where are your bigbugs—Zorach Latozky, Reb Lippe, Reb Nochum? Are they alive? Thirty-five years ago Asrielke considered it an honor to shake their palm branch on the Feast of Tabernacles, while now—out with your purses, you proud magnates, measure fortunes with Asrielke the heckler, if you dare! His heart swells with exultation. And yet— the black year take it!—it yearns and aches, does Asriel's heart. He looks at Pravly, and his soul is pining for Pravly—for the one of thirty-five years ago, of which this is only a reflection,—for the one in which he was known as a crack-brained rowdy of a mechanic, a poor devil living on oatmeal and herring.

With the townspeople of his time Asriel's experience was somewhat different from what he felt in the case of inanimate Pravly. As he confronted them some faces lighted up with their identity at once; and there were even some younger people in whom he instantly recognized the transcribed images of

---

6. A series of large pictures, as of a landscape, put on the wall of a circular room so as to appear in natural perspective to a spectator standing in the center.

7. In the Jewish mystical tradition of Kabbalah, the thirteenth disposition refers to men's hair and beards.

their deceased parents. But many a countenance was slow to catch the reflection of the past which shone out of his eyes; and in a few instances it was not until the name was revealed to Asriel that the retrospective likeness would begin to struggle through the unfamiliar features before him.

"Shmulke!" he shrieked, the moment he caught sight of an old crony, as though they had been parted for no more than a month. Shmulke is not the blooming, sprightly young fellow of yore. He has a white beard and looks somewhat decrepit. Asriel, however, feels as if the beard were only glued to the smooth face he had known. But how Asriel's heart does shrink in his bosom! The fever of activity in which he had passed the thirty-five years had kept him deaf to the departing footsteps of Time. Not until recently had he realized that the words "old man" applied to him; but even then the fact never came home to him with such convincing, with such terrible force, as it did now that he stood face to face with Shmulke. Shmulke was his mirror.

"Shmulke, Angel of Death, an inflammation into your bones!" he shouted, as he suddenly remembered his playmate's by-name and fell on his shoulder.

Shmulke feels awkward. He is ashamed of the long-forgotten nickname, and is struggling to free himself from the unwelcome embrace; but Asriel is much the stronger of the two, and he continues to squeeze him and pat him, grunting and puffing for emotion as he does so.

Aunt Sarah-Rachel, whom Asriel had left an elderly but exceedingly active and clever tradeswoman, he found a bag of bones and in her dotage.

"Don't you know me, auntie?" he implored her. She made no reply, and went on munching her lips. "Can it be that you don't know Asrielke, who used to steal raisins from your grocery?"

"She does not understand anything!" Asriel whispered, in consternation.

## IV

Asriel's first Sabbath in the native place he was revisiting was destined to be a memorable day in the annals of that peaceful little town.

At the synagogue, during the morning service, he was not the only object of interest. So far as the furtive glances that came through the peepholes of the women's compartment were concerned, a much younger guest, from a hamlet near by, had even greater magnetism than he. Reb[8] Lippe, for forty years the "finest householder" of the community, expected to marry his youngest daughter to an *Illoui* (a prodigy of Talmudic lore), and he now came to flaunt him, and the five-thousand rouble dowry he represented, before the congregation.

Only nineteen and a poor orphan, the fame of the prospective bridegroom, as a marvel of acumen and memory, reached far and wide. Few of the subtlest rabbinical minds in the district were accounted his match in debate, and he was said to have some two thousand Talmudical folios literally at his finger's ends. This means that if you had placed the tip of your finger on some word of a volume, he could have told you the word which came under your pressure on any other page you might name. As we shall have to cultivate the young man's acquaintance, let it be added that he was quite boyish of figure, and that had it not been for an excess of smiling frankness, his pale, blue-eyed

---

8. Abbreviation of Rabbi; used as the equivalent of Mister.

face would have formed the nearest Semitic approach to the current portraits of Lord Byron.[9] His admirers deplored his lack of staidness. While visiting at Pravly, in a manner, as the guest of the town, he was detected giving snuff to a pig, and then participating with much younger boys in a race over the bridge.

His betrothment to Reb Lippe's daughter was still the subject of negotiation, and there were said to be serious obstacles in the way. The prodigy's relatives were pleased with Reb Lippe's pedigree and social rank, but thought that the boy could marry into a wealthier family and get a prettier girl into the bargain. Nevertheless Reb Lippe's manner at the synagogue was as though the engagement were an accomplished fact, and he kept the young man by his side, his own seat being next the rabbi's, which was by the Holy Ark.

Asriel, as a newcomer, and out of respect for his fabulous wealth, was also accorded a seat of honor on the other side of the Ark. Before he had expatriated himself his place used to be near the door—a circumstance which was fresh in the mind of Reb Lippe, who chafed to see him divert attention from the prodigy and his purchaser. Now Reb Lippe was a proud old gentleman, too jealous of the memory of his rabbinical ancestry and of his own time-honored dignity to give way to a mere boor[1] of a heckler, no matter how much American gold he had to atone for his antecedents. Accordingly, when his fellow trustee suggested that the American ought to be summoned to the reading of the Third Section in the week's portion of the Pentateuch,—the highest honor connected with the reading of the Law, and one for which the visiting nabob was sure to pay a liberal donation,—the venerable countenance turned crimson.

"Let the sections be auctioned off!" he jerked out.

The proceeding was seldom practiced on an ordinary Sabbath; but Reb Lippe's will was law, as peremptory and irresistible as the Law of Moses, with which it was now concerned. And so the worshipers presently found themselves converted into so many eye-witnesses of a battle of purses.

"Five gildens[2] for the Third!" called out the weazen-faced little sexton[3] from the reading-platform, in the traditional sing-song that became his draggling black beard so well. As a bona-fide business transaction is not allowed on the holy day, even though the house of God be the sole gainer by it, the sexton's figures were fictitious—in so far, at least, as they were understood to represent double the actual amount to be paid to the synagogue by the purchaser of the good deed.

"Six gildens for the Third!" he went on in interpretation of a frowning nod from Reb Lippe.

A contemptuous toss of Asriel's head threw another gilden on top of the sum. Two other members signaled to the auctioneer, and, warming up to his task, he sang out with gusto, "Eight gildens for the Third!"

Then came in rapid succession: "Nine gildens for the Third! Ten gildens for the Third! Eleven gildens, twelve, thirteen, fourteen gildens for the Third!"

---

9. George Gordon, Lord Byron (1788–1824), English Romantic poet, renowned for his handsomeness.
1. Original meaning was simply a peasant or farmer, from Dutch roots suggesting "fellow

dweller" and "to build or cultivate."
2. Gold pieces.
3. Officer in charge of church or synagogue maintenance.

The other bidders, one by one, dropped out of the race, and when the sum reached sixty gildens the field was left to Reb Lippe and Asriel.

The congregation was spellbound. Some with gaping mouths, others with absorbed simpers on their faces, but all with sportsman-like fire in their eyes, the worshipers craned their necks in the direction of the two contestants alternately.

The prodigy had edged away from his seat to a coign of vantage.[4] He was repeatedly called back by winks from his uncle, but was too deeply interested in the progress of the auction to heed them.

"Seventy gildens for the Third! Seventy-one, seventy-two, three, four, five, seventy-six, seventy-seven, eight, nine, eighty gildens for the Third!"

The skirmish waxed so hot, shots flew so thick and so fast, that the perspiring sexton, and with him some of the spectators, was swiveling his head from right to left and from left to right with the swift regularity of gymnastic exercise.

It must be owned that so far as mute partisanship was concerned, Asriel had the advantage of his adversary, for even some of Reb Lippe's stanchest friends and admirers had a lurking relish for seeing it brought home to their leading citizen that there were wealthier people than he in the world.

The women, too, shared in the excitement of the morning. Their windows were glistening with eyes, and the reports of their lucky occupants to the anxious knots in the rear evoked hubbubs of conflicting interjections which came near involving the matronly assemblage in civil war.

The Third Section brought some twenty-eight rubles, net. Asriel was certain that the last bid had been made by him, and that the honor and the good deed were accordingly his. When it came to the reading, however, and the Third Section was reached, the reader called out Reb Lippe's name.

Asriel was stupefied.

"Hold on! That won't do!" he thundered, suddenly feeling himself an American citizen. "I have bought it and I mean to have it." His face was fire; his eyes looked havoc.

A wave of deprecation swept over the room. Dozens of reading-desks were slapped for order. Reb Lippe strode up to the platform, pompous, devout, resplendent in the gold lace of his praying-shawl and the flowing silver of his beard, as though the outburst of indignation against Asriel were only an ovation to himself. He had the cunning of a fox, the vanity of a peacock, and the sentimentality of a woman during the Ten Days of Penance.[5] There were many skeptics as to the fairness of the transaction, but these were too deeply impressed by the grandeur of his triumphal march to whisper an opinion. The prodigy alone spoke his mind.

"Why, I do think the other man was the last to nod—may I be ill if he was not," the *enfant terrible* said quite audibly, and was hushed by his uncle.

"Is he really going to get it?" Asriel resumed, drowning all opposition with his voice. "Milk a billy-goat! You can't play that trick on me! Mine was the last

---

4. Archaic expression meaning an advantageous position for observation or action.
5. Beginning with Rosh Hashanah, the ten days of repentance leading up to Yom Kippur. On Rosh Hashanah, all are judged by God for the actions of the previous year; thus a person's future is deter-

mined for the following year, but is not yet sealed and can still be changed for ten days. God waits until Yom Kippur to seal the book for the year. A person can change the judgment through repentance, prayer, and charity.

bid. Twenty-eight scurvy rubles! Pshaw! I am willing to pay a hundred, two hundred, five hundred. I can buy up all Pravly, Reb Lippe, his gold lace and all, and sell him at a loss, too!" He made a dash at the reading-platform, as if to take the Third Section by force, but the bedlam which his sally called forth checked him.

"Is this a market-place?" cried the second trustee, with conscious indignation.

"Shut the mouth of that boor!" screamed a member, in sincere disgust.

"Put him out!" yelled another, with relish in the scene.

"If he can't behave in a holy place let him go back to his America!" exclaimed a third, merely to be in the running. But his words had the best effect: they reminded Asriel that he was a stranger and that the noise might attract the police.

At the same moment he saw the peaked face of the aged rabbi by his side. Taking him by the arm, the old man begged him not to disturb the Sabbath.

Whether the mistake was on Asriel's side or on the sexton's, or whether there was any foul play in the matter, is not known; but Asriel relented and settled down at his desk to follow the remainder of the reading in his Peutateuch, although the storm of revenge which was raging in his breast soon carried off his attention, and he lost track.

The easy success of his first exhortation brought the rabbi to Asriel's side once again.

"I knew your father,—peace upon him! He was a righteous Jew," he addressed him in a voice trembling and funereal with old age. "Obey me, my son, ascend the platform, and offer the congregation a public apology. The Holy One—blessed be He—will help you."

The rabbi's appeal moved Asriel to tears, and tingling with devout humility he was presently on the platform, speaking in his blunt, gruff way.

"Do not take it hard, my rabbis! I meant no offense to any one, though there was a trick—as big as a fat bull. Still, I donate two hundred rubles, and let the cantor recite 'God full of Mercy' for the souls of my father and mother,—peace upon them."

It was quite a novel way of announcing one's contribution, and the manner of his apology, too, had at once an amusing and a scandalizing effect upon the worshipers, but the sum took their breath away and silenced all hostile sentiment.

The reading over, and the scrolls restored, amid a tumultuous acclaim, to the Holy Ark, the cantor resumed his place at the Omud,[6] chanting a hurried Half-Kaddish. "And say ye Amen!" he concluded abruptly, as if startled, together with his listeners, into sudden silence.

Nodding or shaking their heads, or swaying their forms to and fro, some, perhaps mechanically, others with composed reverence, still others in a convulsion of religious fervor, the two or three hundred men were joined in whispering chorus, offering the solemn prayer of Mussaff.[7] Here and there a sigh made itself heard amid the monotony of speechless, gesticulating ardor; a pair of fingers snapped in an outburst of ecstasy, a sob broke from some corner, or a lugubrious murmur from the women's room. The prodigy, his eyes

6. Altar.     7. Additional offering or prayer.

shut, and his countenance stern with unfeigned rapture, was violently working his lips as if to make up for the sounds of the words which they dared not
utter. Asriel was shaking and tossing about. His face was distorted with the
piteous, reproachful mien of a neglected child about to burst into tears, his
twin imperials dancing plaintively to his whispered intonations. He knew not
what his lips said, but he did know that his soul was pouring itself forth before
Heaven, and that his heart might break unless he gave way to his restrained
sobs.

At last the silent devotions were at an end. One after another the worshipers retreated, each three paces from his post. Only three men were still
absorbed in the sanctity of the great prayer: the rabbi, for whom the cantor
was respectfully waiting with the next chant, Reb Lippe, who would not
"retreat" sooner than the rabbi, and Asriel, who, in his frenzy of zeal, was
repeating the same benediction for the fifth time.

When Asriel issued forth from the synagogue he found Pravly completely
changed. It was as if, while he was praying and battling, the little town had
undergone a trivializing process. All the poetry of thirty-five years' separation
had fled from it, leaving a heap of beggarly squalor. He felt as though he had
never been away from the place, and were tired to death of it, and at the same
time his heart was contracted with homesickness for America. The only interest the town now had for him was that of a medium to be filled with the rays
of his financial triumph. "I'll show them who they are and who Asriel is," he
comforted himself.

The afternoon service was preceded by a sermon. The "town preacher" took
his text, as usual, from the passage in the "Five Books" which had been read
in the morning. But he contrived to make it the basis of an allusion to the all-
absorbing topic of gossip. Citing the Talmud and the commentaries[8] with
ostentatious profuseness, he laid particular stress on the good deed of procur-
ing a scholar of sacred lore for one's son-in-law.

"It is a well-known saying in tractate *Psohim*," he said, "that 'one should be
ready to sell his all in order to marry his daughter to a scholar.' On the other
hand, 'to give your daughter in marriage to a boor is like giving her to a lion.'
Again, in tractate *Berochath* we learn that 'to give shelter to a scholar bent
upon sacred studies, and to sustain him from your estates, is like offering sacrifices to God;' and 'to give wine to such a student is,' according to a passage
in tractate *Sota*, 'tantamount to pouring it out on an altar.' "

Glances converged on Reb Lippe and the prodigy by his side.

Proceeding with his argument, the learned preacher, by an ingenious chain
of quotations and arithmetical operations upon the numerical value of letters,
arrived at the inference that compliance with the above teachings was one of
the necessary conditions of securing a place in the Garden of Eden.

All of which filled Asriel's heart with a new dread of the world to come and
with a rankling grudge against Reb Lippe. He came away from the synagogue
utterly crushed, and when he reached his inn the prodigy was the prevailing
subject of his chat with the landlord.

8. The Talmud is a record of rabbinic discussions
on Jewish law, ethics, customs, legends, and stories, and a fundamental source of legislation, case
histories, and moral exhortations. References in
the next paragraph and elsewhere in the story are
to parts of the Talmud.

## V

In the evening of the same day, at the conclusion of the Sabbath, the auction of another good deed took place, and once more the purses of Reb Lippe and Asriel clashed in desperate combat.

This time the good deed assumed the form of a prodigy of Talmudic learning in the character of a prospective son-in-law.

The room (at the residence of one of the young man's uncles) was full of bearded Jews, tobacco smoke, and noise. There were Shaya, the prodigy himself, his two uncles, Reb Lippe, his eldest son, and two of his lieutenants, Asriel, his landlord, and a match-maker. A live broad-shouldered samovar,[9] its air-holes like so many glowing eyes, stood in the centre of the table. Near it lay Flora's photograph, representing her in all the splendor of Grand Street millinery.

The youthful hero of the day eyed the portrait with undisguised, open-mouthed curiosity, till, looked out of countenance by the young lady's doleful, penetrating eyes, he turned from it, but went on viewing it with furtive interest.

His own formula of a bride was a hatless image. The notion, therefore, of this princess becoming his wife both awed him and staggered his sense of decorum. Then the smiling melancholy of the Semitic face upset his image of himself in his mind and set it afloat in a haze of phantasy. "I say you need not look at me like that," he seemed to say to the picture. "Pshaw! you are a Jewish girl after all, and I am not afraid of you a bit. But what makes you so sad? Can I do anything for you? Why don't you answer? Do take off that hat, will you?"

Reb Lippe's daughter did not wear a hat, but she was not to his liking, and he now became aware of it. On the other hand, the word "America" had a fascinating ring, and the picture it conjured was a blend of Talmudic and modern glory.

Reb Lippe's venerable beard was rippled with a nervous smile.

"Yes, I am only a boor!" roared Asriel, with a touch of Bounderby[1] ostentation. "But you know it is not myself I want the boy to marry. Twenty thousand rubles, spot cash, then, and when the old boor takes himself off, Shaya will inherit ten times as much. She is my only child, and when I die—may I be choked if I take any of my houses into the grave. Worms don't eat houses, you know."

The quality of his unhackneyed phrase vexed the sedate old talmudists, and one of them remarked, as he pointed a sarcastic finger at the photograph:—

"Your girl looks like the daughter of some titled Gentile. Shaya is a Jewish boy."

"You don't like my girl, don't you?" Asriel darted back. "And why, pray? Is it because she is not a lump of ugliness and wears a hat? The grand rabbi of Wilna is as pious as any of you, isn't he? Well, when I was there, on my way here, I saw his daughter, and she also wore a hat and was also pretty. Twenty thousand rubles!"

By this time the prodigy was so absorbed in the proceedings that he forgot

---

9. A metal urn with a spigot and an internal tube for heating water to make tea; used especially in Russia.

1. Character in Charles Dickens's *Hard Times* (1854) who boasts about rising from childhood poverty to become a banker and factory owner.

the American photograph, as well as the bearing which the auction in progress had upon himself. Leaning over the table as far as the samovar would allow, and propping up his face with both arms, he watched the scene with thrilling but absolutely disinterested relish.

After a great deal of whispering and suppressed excitement in the camp of Asriel's foe, Reb Lippe's son announced:—

"Ten thousand rubles and five years' board." This, added to Reb Lippe's advantages over his opponent by virtue of his birth, social station, and learning, as well as of his residing in Russia, was supposed to exceed the figure named by Asriel. In point of fact, everybody in the room knew that the old talmudist's bid was much beyond his depth; but the assemblage had no time to be surprised by his sum, for no sooner had it been uttered than Asriel yelled out, with impatient sarcasm:—

"Thirty thousand rubles, and life-long board, and lodging, and bath money, and stocking darning, and cigarettes, and matches, and mustard, and soap— and what else?"

The prodigy burst into a chuckle, and was forthwith pulled down to his chair. He took a liking to the rough-and-ready straightforwardness of the American.

There was a pause. Shaya and his uncles were obviously leaning toward the "boor." Asriel was clearly the master of the situation.

At last Reb Lippe and his suite rose from their seats.

"You can keep the bargain!" he said to Asriel, with a sardonic smile.

"And be choked with it!" added his son.

"What is your hurry, Reb Lippe?" said one of the uncles, rushing to the old man's side with obsequious solicitude. "Why, the thing is not settled yet. We don't know whether"—

"*You* don't, but I do. I won't take that boy if *he* brings twenty thousand rubles to *his* marriage portion. Good-night!"

"Good-night and good-year!" Asriel returned. "Why does the cat hate the cream? Because it is locked up."

An hour afterward the remainder of the gathering were touching glasses and interchanging *mazol-tovs* (congratulations) upon the engagement of Flora Stroon to Shaya Golub.

"And now receive my *mazol-tov!*" said Asriel, pouncing upon the prodigy and nearly crushing him in his mighty embrace. "*Mazol-tov* to you, Flora's bridegroom! *Mazol-tov* to you, Flora's predestinated one! My child's dear little bridegroom!" he went on, hiding his face on the young man's shoulder. "I am only a boor, but you shall be my son-in-law. I'll dine you and wine you, as the preacher commanded, pearls will I strew on your righteous path, a crown will I place on your head—I am only a boor!"

Sobs rang in the old man's voice. The bystanders looked on in smiling, pathetic silence.

"A boor, but an honest man," some one whispered to the uncles.

"A heart of gold!" put in the innkeeper.

"And what will Flora say?" something whispered to Asriel, from a corner of his overflowing heart. "Do you mean to tell me that the American young lady will marry this old-fashioned, pious fellow?" "Hold your tongue, fool you!" Asriel snarled inwardly. "She will have to marry him, and that settles it, and don't you disturb my joy. It's for her good as well as for mine."

With a sudden movement he disengaged his arms, and, taking off his enormous gold watch and chain, he put it on Shaya, saying:—

"Wear it in good health, my child. This is your first present from your sweetheart. But wait till we come to America!"

The next morning Asriel visited the cemetery, and was overawed by its size. While living Pravly had increased by scarcely a dozen houses, the number of dwellings in silent Pravly had nearly doubled.

The headstones, mostly of humble size and weatherworn, were a solemn minority in a forest of plain wooden monuments, from which hung, for identification, all sorts of unceremonious tokens, such as old tin cans, bottomless pots, cast-off hats, shoes, and what not. But all this, far from marring the impressiveness of the place, accentuated and heightened the inarticulate tragedy of its aspect. The discarded utensils or wearing apparel seemed to be brooding upon the days of their own prime, when they had participated in the activities of the living town yonder. They had an effect of mysterious muteness, as of erstwhile animated beings,—comrades of the inmates of the overgrown little mounds underneath, come to join them in the eternal rest of the city of death.

"Father! Father!" Asriel began, in a loud synagogue intonation, as he prostrated himself upon an old grave, immediately after the cantor had concluded his prayer and withdrawn from his side. "It is I, Asriel, your son—do you remember? I have come all the way from America to ask you to pray for me and my child. She is a good girl, father, and I am trying to lead her on the path of righteousness. She is about to marry the greatest scholar of God's Law hereabouts. Do pray that the boy may find favor in her eyes, father! You know, father dear, that I am only a boor, and woe is me! I am stuffed full of sins. But now I am trying to make up and to be a good Jew. Will you pray the Uppermost to accept my penance?" he besought, with growing pathos in his voice. "You are near Him, father, so do take pity upon your son and see to it that his sins are forgiven. Will you pray for me? Will you? But, anyhow, I care more for Flora—Bloome, her Yiddish name is. What am I? A rusty lump of nothing. But Flora—she is a flower. Do stand forth before the High Tribunal and pray that no ill wind blow her away from me, that no evil eye injure my treasure. She lost her mother when she was a baby, poor child, and she is the only consolation I have in the world. But you are her grandfather—do pray for her!"

Asriel's face shone, his heavy voice rang in a dismal, rapturous, devotional sing-song. His eyes were dry, but his soul was full of tears and poetry, and he poured it forth in passionate, heart-breaking cadences.

"What is the difference between this grass blade and myself?" he asked, a little after. "Why should you give yourself airs, Asriel? Don't kick, be good, be pious, carry God in your heart, and make no fuss! Be as quiet as this grass, for hark! the hearse is coming after you, the contribution boxes are jingling, the Angel of Death stands ready with his knife—Oh, do pray for your son, father!" he shrieked, in terror.

He paused. A bee, droning near by, seemed to be praying like himself, and its company stirred Asriel's heart.

"Oh, father! I have not seen you for thirty-five years. Thirty-five years!" he repeated in deliberate tones and listening to his own voice.

"We are the thirty-five!" some distant tombstones responded, and Asriel could not help pausing to look about, and then he again repeated, "Thirty-five years! Can I never see you again, father? Can't I see your dear face and talk to you, as of old, and throw myself into fire or water for you? Can't I? Can't I? Do you remember how you used to keep me on your knees or say prayers with me at the synagogue, and box my ears so that the black year[2] took me when you caught me skipping in the prayer-book? Has it all flown away? Has it really?"

He paused as though for an answer, and then resumed, with a bitter, malicious laugh at his own expense: "Your father is silent, Asriel! Not a word, even if you tear yourself to pieces. All is gone, Asrielke! All, all, all is lost forever!"

His harsh voice collapsed. His speech died away in a convulsion of subdued sobbing. His soul went on beseeching his father to admit him to the restful sanctity of his company.

When Asriel rose to his feet and his eye fell upon a tombstone precisely like his father's, he frowned upon it, with a sense of jealousy. On his way to his mother's grave, in the older part of the cemetery, he ever and anon turned to look back. His father's tombstone was rapidly becoming merged in a forest of other monuments. His dead father, his poor father, was losing his individuality, till he was a mere speck in this piebald medley of mounds, stones, boards, and all sorts of waste. Asriel felt deeply hurt. He retraced his steps till his father's resting-place once more became the centre of the world.

Then he went to pay his respects and tears to the graves of his mother, sisters, brothers, uncles. At last, completely exhausted, he took to walking among the other headstones. As he stopped to make out their Hebrew inscriptions, he would now hang his head, in heart-wringing reminiscence, now heave a sigh, or clap his hands, in grievous surprise.

The tombstones and tomb-boards were bathed in the reddish gold of the late afternoon sun. Asriel had not yet broken his fast, but although shattered in body and spirit he felt no hunger and was reluctant to leave the graveyard. He found here more of his contemporaries that he well remembered, more of the Pravly of his time, than in the town a verst[3] or two away. The place asserted a stronger claim upon him and held him by the force of its unearthly fascination.

When he reached town at last, he felt new-born. Pravly was again dear to his heart, although Flora and America drew him to them with more magnetism than ever. He strove to speak in soft accents, and went about the houses of his relatives and the poor of the town, distributing various sums and begging the recipients of his gifts "to have pity and not to thank him," lest it should detract from the value of his good deed.

Then he went to make peace with Reb Lippe.

"You are going to stay here, so you can get another prodigy," he pleaded humbly. "But one cannot get such goods in America. Besides, you can read Talmud yourself, while I am only a boor, and what have I done to make sure of my share in the world to come? Here are three hundred rubles for charity. Do forgive me, Reb Lippe, will you? What will you lose by it?"

There were others in the room, and the unique pathos of the plea touched and amused them at once. Reb Lippe was moved to the point of tears. Moreover, the present situation took the venom out of his defeat.

2. Reference to the Black Plague that swept Europe in 1348–49, for which Jews were blamed and persecuted.

3. An old Russian unit of linear measure, equal to .663 miles.

"I forgive you with all my heart," he said impulsively, patting "the boor" as he would a child. "Be seated. May the Uppermost bring you home in peace and bless the union. There is another young man who is worthy of my daughter; and Shaya—may the Holy One—blessed be He—grant him the will and the power to spread His Law in America. The Jews there want a young man like him, and I am glad he is going with you. You are taking a precious stone with you, Reb Asriel. Hold it dear."

"You bet I will," Asriel replied gleefully.

## VI

The nearer Asriel, with the prodigy in tow, came to New York, the deeper did Pravly sink into the golden mist of romance, and the more real did the great American city grow in his mind. Every mile added detail to the picture, and every new bit of detail made it dearer to his heart.

He was going home. He felt it more keenly, more thrillingly every day, every hour, every minute.

Sandy Hook[4] hove in sight.

Can there be anything more beautiful, more sublime, and more uplifting than the view, on a clear summer morning, of New York harbor from an approaching ship? Shaya saw in the enchanting effect of sea, verdure, and sky a new version of his visions of paradise, where, ensconced behind luxuriant foliage, the righteous—venerable old men with silvery beards—were nodding and swaying over gold-bound tomes of the Talmud. Yet, overborne with its looming grandeur, his heart grew heavy with suspense, and he clung close to Asriel.

All was bustle and expectation on board. The little deck engines never ceased rumbling, and the passengers, spruced up as if for church, were busy about their baggage, or promenading with a festive, nervous air.

Asriel twitched and bit his lip in rapture.

"Oh, how blue the water is!" said Shaya wistfully.

"America is a fine country, is it not?" the old man rejoined. "But it can't hold a candle to Flora. Wait till you see her. You just try to be a good boy," he kept murmuring; "stick to your Talmud, and don't give a *peper*[5] for anything else, and all God has given me shall be yours. I have no son to say *Kaddish* for my soul when I am dead. Will you be my Kaddish, Shaya? Will you observe the anniversary of my death?" he queried, in a beseeching tone which the young man had never heard from him.

"Of course I will," Shaya returned, like a dutiful child.

"Will you? May you live long for it. In palaces will I house you, like the eye in my head will I cherish you. I am only a boor, but she is my daughter, my only child, and my whole life in this world."

Asriel kept Flora unadvised as to the name of the steamer or the date of his arrival. Upon landing he did not go directly to his residence, but first took his importation into a large "clothing and gents' furnishing store" on Broadway, from which the *illoui* emerged completely transformed. Instead of his uncouth cap and the draggling coat which had hidden his top-boots from

4. Point of land in New Jersey, the first land to be sighted by ships coming from Europe.

5. Dutch for "pepper."

view, he was now arrayed in the costliest "Prince Albert,"[6] the finest summer derby, and the most elegant button-shoes the store contained. This and a starched shirt-front, a turned-down collar, and a gaudy puff-tie set into higher relief the Byronic effect of his intellectual, winsome face.

Asriel snapped his fingers for delight. He thought him easily the handsomest and best-dressed man on Broadway. "It is the Divine Presence shining upon him!" he murmured to himself, dragging the young man by the hand, as if he were a truant schoolboy. Barring the prodigy's sidelocks (badges of divine learning and piety), which were tightly curled into two little cushions in front of his ears, he now thought him thoroughly Americanized.

The prodigy, however, felt tied and fettered in the garb of Gentile civilization, and as he trudged along by his convoy's side, he viewed his transformed self in the store windows, or stared, rabbit-like, at the lumbering stagecoaches and the hurrying noble-men.

Asriel let himself and his charge in noiselessly with the latchkey, which had accompanied him, together with a bunch of other keys, on his tour. They entered the hallway on tiptoe.

The little house rang with the voluminous tones of Flora's piano, through which trickled the doleful tremolo of her subdued contralto. Since her father had left her pining for his return, "Home, Sweet Home" had become her favorite tune.

Flora was alone in the house, and her unconscious welcome was all the sweeter to Asriel's soul for the grieving note which ran through it. His heart throbbed with violence. Shaya's sank in awe. He had never heard a piano except through the window of some nobleman's house.

"Hush! Do you hear?" the old man whispered. "That's your predestined bride." With that he led the way downstairs. There they paused to kiss the divine name on the *Mezuzah*[7] of the door-post.

"Tamara!" Asriel called, under his breath, looking for the pious housekeeper in the dining-room and in the kitchen. "She is not in. Must be out marketing or about her good deeds. A dear soul she! Oh, it's her fast day; she fasts Mondays and Thursdays."

Then he stepped up in front of a tin box that was nailed to one of the kitchen doors and took out his pocket-book. It was one of the contribution-boxes of the "Meyer-the-Wonder-worker Fund," which is devoted to the support of pious old European Jews who go to end their days in the Land of Israel. Every orthodox Jew in the world keeps a similar box in his house and drops a coin into it whenever he escapes some danger. Asriel had safely crossed the wide ocean, and his offering was a handful of silver.

"Well, you stay here, Shaya, and don't budge till you are called," he said; and leaving the young man to his perplexity he betook himself upstairs, to surprise his daughter.

Flora burst into tears of joy, and hugged him again and again, while he stroked her black hair or stood scowling and grinning for admiration.

"Ah, you dear, cranky papa!" she burst out, for the fourth time realizing that he was actually come back to her, and for the fourth time attacking him.

---

6. Albert of Saxe-Coburg and Gotha (1819–1861), the Consort of Queen Victoria, popularized a formal coat that became known by his name.

7. A small case fastened to a home's doorpost as a reminder of God's commands; the case contains a parchment on which are inscribed two sections from the Torah.

At last he thought they had had enough. He was dying to protract the scene, but there was that troublesome job to get rid of, and Asriel was not the man to put such things off. Whenever he felt somewhat timid he would grow facetious. This was the case at the present juncture.

"Well, Flora, guess what sort of present your papa has brought you," he said, reddening to his ears. "I'll bet you you won't hit if you keep on guessing till to-morrow. No girl has ever got such a present as long as America is America."

Flora's eyes danced with joyous anticipation. Her mind was ablaze with diamonds, rubies, emeralds, sapphires, pearls.

"I have got a bridegroom for you—a fifteen-thousand-dollar one. Handsomest and smartest fellow on earth. He is an *illoui*."

"A what?" she asked, in amazement.

"Oh, a wonderful chap, you know, deep in the Talmud and the other holy books. He could knock all the rabbis of Europe to smithereens. The biggest bug in Pravly was after him, but I beat him clean out of his boots. Shaya! Come right up!"

The girl gazed at her father in bewilderment. Was he joking or was he in dead, terrific earnest?

Shaya made his appearance, with his eyes on the floor, and wringing the index finger of his right hand, as he was wont to do whenever he felt ill at ease, which was seldom, however.

Flora's brain was in a whirl.

"This is your predestined bridegroom, my daughter. A fine present, is it not? Did you ever expect such a raisin of a sweetheart, hey? Well, children, I must go around to see about the baggage. Have a chat and be acquainted." With that he advanced to the door.

"Papa! Papa!" Flora frantically called to him. But he never turned his head and went his way.

In her despair she rushed at the young stranger, who was still wringing his finger, as he stood in the middle of the parlor, eyeing the carpet, and snapped out:—

"Mister, you had better go. If you think you are going to be my bridegroom, you are sadly mistaken."

She spoke in Yiddish, but her pronunciation, particularly of the letter "r," was so decidedly American that to Shaya it sounded at once like his native tongue and the language of Gentiles. However, it was Yiddish enough, and the fact of this imposing young lady speaking it gave him the feeling of being in the presence of a Jewish princess of biblical times.

"Where shall I go? I don't know anybody here." He said it with an air of naïve desperation which touched the girl's heart. "Where is my fault?" he added pleadingly.

She gave him a close look, and, taking him by his clean-cut beardless chin, opened her eyes wide at him, and broke into a hearty laugh.

"My father has really brought you over to marry me?" she questioned, for the first time awakening to the humorous side of the situation, and again she burst out laughing.

Shaya blushed and took hold of his finger, but he forthwith released it and also broke into a giggle. Her merriment set him at his ease, and her labored Yiddish struck him as the prattle of a child.

Flora was amused and charmed as with a baby. Shaya felt as if he were playing with another boy.

Of all the immigrants who had married or were engaged to marry some of her girl friends, none had, just after landing, been so presentable, so sweet-faced, and so droll as this scholarly-looking fellow. There would have been nothing odd in her marrying him a year or two later, after he had picked up some broken English and some of the customs of the country. But then her mind was firmly made up, and she had boasted to her friends that she was bound to marry a doctor, and here this boy was not even going to be a business man, but an orthodox rabbi or something of the sort. The word "rabbi" was associated in her mind with the image of an unkempt, long-skirted man who knew nothing of the world, took snuff, and made life a nuisance to himself and to others. Is she going to be a *rabbitzen* (a rabbi's wife)? No! No! No! Come what may, none but a refined American gentleman shall lead her under the nuptial canopy! And in her rage she fled from the parlor and went to nurse her misery on the dining-room lounge.

Presently, as she lay with her hands clasped under her head, abandoned to her despair and fury, and yet unable to realize that it was all in real earnest, a fretting sensation settled somewhere in her heart. At first it was only like a grain of sand, but it kept growing till it lay a heavy, unbearable lump. She could not stand the idea of that poor, funny dear being left alone and scared out of his wits. Still, she would not stir. Let papa take him away or she will leave the house and go to work in a factory.

"Tamara!" she suddenly raised herself to say, the moment the housekeeper came into the room. "There is a man upstairs. He must be hungry."

"Then why don't *you* give him something to eat?" Tamara responded tartly. "You know it is Monday and I am faint. But who is he and what is he doing upstairs? Let him come down."

"Go and see him for yourself," snapped Flora. "You will find him one of your set—a Talmudical scholar, a pious soul," she added, with a venomous laugh.

Tamara bent upon her a look full of resentment as well as of devout reproach, and betook herself upstairs.

When Asriel came he explained that Shaya was not going to be a rabbi, nor dress otherwise than as an American gentleman, but that he would lead a life of piety and spend his time studying the Talmud, partly at home and partly at some synagogue. "What, then, have I worked all my life for?" he pleaded. "I am only a boor, my daughter, and how long does a fellow live? Don't darken my days, Flora."

Tamara kept nodding pious assent. "In the old country a girl like you would be glad to marry such a child of the Law," she expostulated with the girl. "It is only here that we are sinners and girls marry none but worldly men. May every daughter of Israel be blessed with such a match."

"Mind your own business!" Flora exploded. She understood her father's explanation but vaguely, and it had the opposite of the desired effect upon her.

"Leave her alone. The storm will blow over," Asriel whispered.

When Asriel's baggage arrived it proved to include a huge box full of Hebrew books. They were of various sizes, but twenty-five of them were large, uniform, leather-bound folio volumes, portly and resplendent in a superabundance of gilding and varnish. Of these, twenty contained the whole of the Babylonian Talmud together with the various commentaries, the remaining five comprising the Alphos. After a little a walnut bookcase made its appearance. It was accorded a place of honor in the front parlor, and Asriel, Tamara, and Shaya busied themselves with arranging the sacred books on its shelves.

Flora sat eyeing them sarcastically, till, sobs rising to her throat, she retired to the seclusion of her bedroom, on the top floor, and burst out crying as if her heart would break. The contents of all those books, which her father had imported as accessories of her would-be bridegroom, were Chinese to her. She had never seen so many of them nor given a moment's attention to the occasional talks which she had chanced to overhear concerning such books and the men who spent their lives reading them. They now frightened her, as if they were filled with weird incantations and Shaya were the master of some uncanny art.

The prodigy was busy arranging his library, now and then opening a book to examine its print. Presently, as he was squatting down before a chair upon which he was turning over the leaves of a bulky volume, his attention was arrested by a celebrated passage. Without changing his posture, he proceeded to glance it over, until, completely absorbed, he fell to humming the words, in that peculiar sing-song, accompanied by indescribable controversial gesticulations, which seem to be as indispensable in reading Talmud as a pair of eyes.

"Look, look!" Tamara nudged Asriel, whom she was helping to transfer the remaining books to the marble table. Asriel turned his head toward the prodigy, and for a few moments the two stood staring at the odd, inspiring spectacle with gaping admiration. Then the housekeeper and her employer exchanged a glance of intelligence, she nodding her bewigged head piously, as much as to say: "What a find Heaven has placed in your way!"

"The Uppermost has blessed you," she added in whispers.

"May he enjoy long life with us!" Asriel returned, with a sigh.

"Flora does not know what a treasure the Lord of the Universe has sent her."

"She will," he rejoined curtly.

### VII

It was at the head of a dozen venerable Talmudists, including the rabbi of the congregation, that Asriel returned from the synagogue next Saturday morning. The learned company was entertained with wine, cold fish, and some of the lemon pie and genuine Yiddish pastry for which Tamara was famous.

"Here is life, Mr. Stroon! Here is life, Shaya!" each of the guests said, raising his glass.

"Life and peace! Life and peace!" was the uniform response.

"God bless the union and let them live a hundred and twenty years," pursued Reb Mendele, a little man with luxuriant red side-locks, as he reached for a piece of Sabbath cake.

"And grant that they give birth to children and bring them up to the Law, the Bridal Canopy, and deeds of righteousness," chimed in another, whose ear-locks were two sorry corkscrew-like appendages, as he held up a slice of fish on the points of his fork.

"And Shaya continue a child of the Law and study it with never-failing zeal," came from between a dangling pair of tubes.

"That's the point!" emphasized a chorus of munching mouths.

"But where is the bride?" somebody demanded. "She must show herself! she must show herself!"

"That's right," Reb Mendele seconded heartily. "Out with the bride! 'And the daughters of Jerusalem come out dancing,' " he quoted; " 'and what do they say? "Lift thine eyes, young man, and behold the maiden thou choosest. Do not set thine eye on beauty, but' ' "—[8] He broke off abruptly, reddening. The remainder of the quoted passage runs as follows: "Set thine eye (the maidens say to the young man) on good family connections, as is written in Proverbs: 'False is grace and vain is beauty: a woman that feareth the Lord shall indeed be praised.' " It would have been anything but appropriate to the occasion, and while the Chaldaic[9] and the Hebrew of the citation were Greek to Asriel, there was the prodigy to resent it.

Another hoary-headed child of the Law interposed: " 'Go forth and look, O ye daughters of Zion, on King Solomon, with the crown wherewith his mother hath crowned him on the day of his espousals, and on the day of the joy of his heart.'[1] Saith the Talmud: 'By "the day of his espousals" is meant the day of the Giving of the Law.' Accordingly, when Shaya's wedding takes place, if God be pleased, it will be an espousal in the literal as well as in the Talmudic sense, for is he not full of Law? It will therefore be the Giving of the Law in marriage to Reb Asriel's daughter, will it not?"

"Never mind blushing, Shaya," said the rabbi, although the prodigy, engrossed with the "paradise taste" of the lemon pie,—a viand he had never dreamed of,—and keeping a sharp eye on the dwindling contents of the tart-dish, was too busy to blush.

Flora was in her bedroom, the place of her voluntary exile most of the time that her compulsory sweetheart was in the house. Her father was kind and attentive to her, as usual, and never mentioned Shaya's name to her. But she knew that he was irrevocably bent upon the marriage, and her mood often verged on suicide. Could it really be that after all her cherished dreams of afternoon drives in Central Park, in a doctor's buggy and with the doctor himself by her side, she was doomed to be the wife of that clumsy rustic, who did not even know how to shake hands or to bow to a lady, and who could not say a word without performing some grotesque gesture or curling his horrid side-locks? Oh, what would the girls say! She had twitted them on the broken English of their otherwise worldly and comparatively well-mannered sweethearts, and now she herself was matched with that wretch of a holy soul!

And yet Shaya was never in her mind invested in the image of a "clumsy rustic" nor of a "holy soul." Whenever she saw him she would screw up a

---

8. "Young man, lift up your eyes and see what you would choose for yourself: set not your eyes upon beauty, but set your eyes on family; for Grace is deceitful and beauty is vain, but a woman that fears the Lord she shall be praised" (Proverbs 31.30).
9. Of Chaldea, an ancient region along the lower Tigris and Euphrates Rivers, part of Babylonia, and home to a Semitic people related to Babylonians.
1. "Go forth you daughters of Zion, and behold king Solomon with the crown wherewith his mother hath crowned him in the day of his espousals and in the day of the gladness of his heart" (Song of Songs 3.11).

frown, but on one occasion, when their eyes met across the supper-table, they could not help smiling to each other, like children at church.

"Flora dear, I want to speak to you," Asriel said, knocking at the locked door of her hiding-place.

"Leave me alone, papa, will you? I've got a headache," she responded.

"That's all right, but unlock the door. I won't eat you up."

She was burning to have her father broach the painful subject, so that she might have it out with him. With that end in view, she set her teeth and turned the key. But Asriel came in so unaggressive, so meek, in a pleading attitude so utterly unlike him, that he took her by surprise, as it were, and she stood completely disarmed.

"I beg you, my daughter, do not shorten my days, and come down-stairs," he entreated with heartfelt ardor. "I have so little to live, and the Uppermost has sent me a piece of comfort so that I may die a righteous Jew,—will you take it away from me? Will you put me to shame before God and man?"

The words and the pathos with which they were delivered so oddly contrasted with all she knew of her father that she felt as if he were really praying for his life. She was deeply touched and dazed, and before she knew what she was about, found herself in the crowded little dining-room below.

"Good Sabbath, Flora, good Sabbath!" the venerable assemblage greeted her.

"Good Sabbath!" she returned, bowing gracefully, and blushing.

"May your guest be pleasing to you," one of the company went on in time-honored phrase; "and, if God be pleased, we shall live to make merry at your wedding."

Flora's face turned a deeper red.

Several of the Talmudists were itching for some banter at the expense of the young pair, but the American girl's dignified bearing and her commanding figure and dress bore down every tendency in that direction, so that the scholarly old gentlemen turned their overflowing spirits in other channels.

"Give us some Law, Shaya!" said Reb Mendele, with a Talmudic wave of both hands.

"That's right," the others concurred. "Your prospective father-in-law is feasting us upon fare of the earth, and it is meet that you should regale us with Words of Law."

Shaya, his face as red as Flora's, was eyeing the tablecloth as he murmured,—

" 'No conversing during repast.' "

"Words of Law are no converse," Reb Mendele retorted.

"The Commentary adds: 'Not so much as to quote the precept about silence during repast,' " Shaya rejoined reluctantly, without raising his eyes. "Now the precept is Words of the Law, is it not? Which means that the prohibition does extend to Words of Law."

Apart from his embarrassment, the prodigy was somehow loath to engage in a spiritual discussion in the presence of the stylish young lady.

"Why did you quote it then?" Reb Mendele pursued aggressively. He referred to two other passages, in support of his position; and Shaya, with his eyes still on the tablecloth, and refraining from all gesticulation, could not help showing the irrelevance of both. It was a "knock-out blow," but his red-bearded opponent cleverly extricated himself from the ignominy of his defeat by assuming an amused air, as if it had all been mere bait to decoy the prodigy to a display of his erudition and mental powers; and retaining his smile against further emergency, Reb Mendele hazarded another assault. Some of the other Talmudists took a hand. The battle waxed hot, though Shaya, fighting single-handed against half a dozen elders remained calm, and parried their blows with a shamefaced but contemptuous look, never raising a finger nor his eyes from the tablecloth. Once in the fray, he would not have Flora see him get the worst of it.

She, on her part, could not help a growing interest in the debate, and finally accepted the chair which Tamara had tenderly placed by her side five minutes before. To be sure, she understood not a word of the controversy. To her it was something like a boxing-match, with every exciting element of the sport, but without any of its violence (which alone kept Flora from attending pugilistic performances), though the arms and fingers of our venerable combatants were even more active than are the arms and fists of two athletes in a modern ring. As she watched the progress of the discussion she became conscious of a decided partisan feeling in favor of the younger man. "It ain't fair a bit!" she said to herself. "Six old-timers against one boy—I declare!"

Asriel and Tamara, to both of whom the contest was as unintelligible as it was to Flora, were so abandoned to their admiration of the youthful disputant that they omitted to notice the girl's undisguised interest in the scene and to congratulate themselves upon it. The host followed the controversy with a sheepish look of reverence, as if the company were an assemblage of kings. The housekeeper looked on with a beaming face, and every time one of the patriarchs made a bold attack, she would nod her head as if she understood it all, and conceded the strength of his contention.

Egged on by Flora's presence as well as by the onslaughts of his adversaries, Shaya gradually warmed up to the debate, until, having listened, with sardonic patience, to a lengthy and heated argument by a fleshy child of the Law, he suddenly leaped upon his man.

"Is this the way you understand the passage?" he shouted, with a vicious chuckle. Then, thrusting his curly head in his opponent's face, and savagely gesticulating, he poured forth a veritable cataract of the most intricate syllogisms and quotations.

It was quite a new Shaya. His blue eyes flashed fire, his whole countenance gleamed, his sing-song rang with tuneful ferocity.

"But it seems to me that Rabbi Yohanon does not say that," the portly Talmudist objected. "I am afraid you have misquoted him."

It was the drowning man's straw. Even Flora, who understood the Yiddish of the retort, could see that; and her heart bounded with cruel delight.

"Have I? You are sure, are you?" Shaya demanded, with boyish virulence. "All right. We shall see!" With which he darted out of the room and upstairs.

"The boy is a *gaon*," the corpulent old man remarked humbly. "What a head! What a memory, what a *chariff!*"

"Yes, and what a *bokki!*"[2] chimed in the rabbi. "One cannot help wondering when he had time to study up so much."

---

2. Man of erudition; "*gaon*": a genius, after Gaon, head of a Jewish academy in Babylonia between the 7th and 11th centuries C.E.; "*chariff*": acute intellect—all Yiddish.

"He'll just take a peep at a book and then he knows it all by heart," put in Asriel. "He licked all the rabbis around Pravly."

The boorish remark disposed some of the listeners to laugh, but they did not.

"You have got a treasure, Mr. Stroon," said Reb Mendele.

"You bet!" the host answered with a blissful simper, as he took to stroking his daughter's hair.

"You know what the Talmud says, Mr. Stroon?" resumed the rabbi. "That he who supports a scholar of the Law is like unto him who offers sacrifices."

"I know," Asriel returned exultingly. At the Pravly synagogue the preacher had applied the same quotation to Reb Lippe.

Presently Shaya returned with a pile of huge volumes in his arms. His citation proved correct, and meeting with no further opposition, but too far carried away by the subject to quit it so soon, he volunteered an extemporaneous discourse. His face was now wrapped in genial, infantile ecstasy and his intonation was a soft, impassioned melody. The old man followed him with paternal admiration.

When he concluded and leaned back in his chair, he gave Flora a triumphant smile. The color mounted to her cheeks and she dropped her gaze. At the same moment Asriel flung himself upon the young hero.

"Oh, you dear little sparrow!" he exclaimed, lifting Shaya in his arms like a baby, and passionately kissing him.

Tamara wiped her eyes with her apron. Flora had a mind to flee for safety, but she forthwith saw herself out of danger, for her father seemed unmindful of her presence, and the first thing he did as he let the prodigy down was to invite his guests upstairs to show them the newly imported library.

As the patriarchal company was filing out of the dining-room, Shaya, passing by Flora, said to her gleefully:—

"I gave it to them, didn't I?"

"Tell me now," said Tamara, when the two women found themselves alone in the room; "ought you not to thank God for such a treasure of a sweetheart?"

"He is nothing of the kind to me," Flora burst out, "and he never will be, either. I don't care how long papa is going to keep him in the house."

## VIII

"Oh, papa!" sobbed Flora; "will you ever put an end to it? You know I'll never marry him."

"Do I compel you to?" he replied. "What do you care if he is in the house? He does not take away your dinner, does he? Imagine that he is your brother and don't bother your head about him. The boy has become so dear to me that I feel as if he were my own son. Will *you* recite Kaddish for my soul? Will you play for me at the anniversary of my death? God thought I was not good enough to have a son, but he sent me this holy child to take the place of one. As I hear him read his holy books," he went on, with mounting pathos, "it melts like ice-cream in my heart. It pleased the Uppermost to make a boor of your papa. Well, I suppose He knows his business, and I am not going to poke my nose in, and ask questions; but He seems to have taken pity on me after all, and in my old age he has sent me an angel, so that I may get the credit of supporting him. Did you hear what the wise men said? That to support a man who does nothing but study sacred books is as good as offering sacrifices. Yes, my daughter, God has put this boy in my hands; He sent me all the way to Pravly for him—all to give me a chance to make up for my sins. Do you want me to kick him out? Not if New York turned upside down."

"But, father"—

"Hold on! Let me talk the heart out of myself. It's no use asking me to send him away. He is God's gift. He is as holy as a Purity (the scrolls of the Law). You are my daughter, and he is my son. I don't chase you under the bridal canopy with a strap, do I? If God does not wish the match, it won't come off, that's all."

The conversation took place about a fortnight after the great debate. Asriel lived in the hope that when Shaya had learned some English and the ways of Flora's circle, she would get to like him. He could not see how it was possible to withstand the charms of the young man whom he sincerely thought the handsomest fellow in the Jewish colony. He provided him with a teacher, and trusted the rest to time and God.

"Just fix him up in English and a little figuring, and that's all," he instructed the teacher. "But mind you, don't take him too far into those Gentile books of yours. He does not want any of the monkey tricks they teach the children at college. Do you understand?"

Flora was getting used to Shaya's presence in the house, as if he actually were a newly discovered brother of hers, brought up in a queer way which she could not understand, and it was only occasionally and at growing intervals that the situation would burst upon her, and she would plead with her father as she had done.

The two young people frequently found themselves alone. The door between the front parlor, which was now Shaya's study, and Flora's boudoir was most of the time open. They often talked together, and she quizzed him about his manners, and once or twice even went over his English lessons with him, laughing at his mispronunciations, and correcting them in the imposing manner of her former school-teachers.

"Why do you work your fingers like that?" she once said, with a pained look. "Can't you try and read without them?"

"I am used to it from the Talmud-he-he-he!" he tittered, as if acknowledging a compliment.

Her piano did not disturb him in his studies, for in the synagogues, where he had grown up, he had been used to read in a turmoil of other voices; but he loved the instrument, and he would often pause to listen to Flora's energetic strokes through the door. When the tune was a melancholy one its first accords would make him start, with a thrill; and as he proceeded to listen his heart would contract with a sharp feeling of homesickness, and at the same time he would be longing for still more familiarity in the performer's manner toward him. Sometimes he would cross over to her room and quietly stand behind her while she was playing.

"Ah, it is so nice!" he once said, feeling himself in a paradise on earth.

"What are you doing here?" she exclaimed, facing about toward him, in affected surprise. "Music ain't for a 'holy child' like yourself." She mocked a favorite expression of her father's.

"Don't say that," he reproached her. "You always like to tease me. Why don't I tease you?"

Upon the whole, Shaya took the situation quite recklessly. He studied his Talmud and his English, let Tamara cloy him with all sorts of tidbits, and roamed about the streets and public buildings. In less than six months he knew the city and its suburbs much better than Flora, and could tell the meaning of thousands of printed English words, although he neither knew how to use them himself nor recognized them in the speech of others. Flora was amazed by his rapid progress, and the facility with which he mastered his Arithmetic and English Grammar—in neither of which she had been strong at school—even piqued her ambition. It was as if she had been beaten by the "holy soul" on her own ground.

The novelty of studying things so utterly out of his rut was like a newly discovered delicacy to his mental palate. He knew by heart a considerable part of the English translation in his Hebrew prayer-book and Old Testament, and his greatest pleasure, when Asriel was not about, was to do arithmetical problems. But the problems were all child's play to him, and he craved some higher grade of intellectual food in the same Gentile line. This he knew from his Talmud to be contained in the "Wisdom of Measuring," which he had learned of his teacher to call Geometry.

"Bring me a Geometry, please," he whispered to his instructor.

"I will, but don't say a word to Mr. Stroon about it."

The forbidden fruit was furnished, and the prodigy of sacred lore applied himself to it with voracity.

"How cunning!" he said to the teacher, in a transport of enthusiasm. "Of course, it is not as deep as Talmud, but I never dreamed there were such subtle things in the Gentile books at all—may I be ill if I did."

"This is only the beginning of it," the other returned, in whispered exultation. "Wait till you get deeper into it. And then there are other books, far more interesting."

"Say, young fellow!" Asriel said to Shaya's teacher a week or so later; "you need not trouble your righteous legs to bring you here any more. You are getting too thick with the boy."

Shaya now found no difficulty in plodding through the theorems and problems unaided. But he yearned after his teacher and friend, and for several days could relish neither his Talmud nor his contraband Geometry. He grew restless. His soul was languishing with thirst.

"Guess where I have been," he confidentially said to Flora, coming from the street one afternoon. He spoke in Yiddish, and she answered in English, interspersed with the same dialect.

"Not in the synagogue, studying?" she queried.

"No—at the Astor Library,"[3] he whispered. "They have such a lot of books there, Flora! Upstairs and downstairs—large rooms like rich synagogues, with shelves all over the walls, and all full of books. Have you ever been there, Flora?"

"N-no!" she owned, with reluctance. The "holy soul" was clearly forging

---

3. The Astor Library, forerunner of the New York Public Library, opened its doors in 1849 with a bequest from John Jacob Astor (1763–1848).

ahead of her in a world which she considered all her own; and she hated the idea of it, and liked it at the same time. "What did you there?"

"I just looked at the books—oh, what a lot!—and then I found out how to get a Geometry,—they have everything in the world, I tell you,—and I did some problems. Don't tell your father I was there."

"Of course I won't," she said intimately. "Can ladies come in?"

"Certainly; they have a separate place for them, though; will you go there with me?"

"Some day," she rejoined evasively.

"Will you? Oh, it's so nice to be sitting and reading there! Only you must sit still. I forgot myself, and as I was figuring out some nice point, I began to reason aloud, so a fine old gentleman stepped up to my side and touched me on the shoulder. Oh, I got so scared, Flora! But he did not do me anything— may I be ill if he did. He only told me to be quiet."

Flora burst out laughing.

"I'll bet you, you was singing in that funny way you have when you are studying the Talmud."

"Yes," he admitted joyfully.

"And working your hands and shaking the life out of yourself," she pursued, mimicking his gestures.

"No, I was not—may I not live till tomorrow if I was," he protested vehemently, with a touch of resentment. "Oh, it is so nice to be there! I never knew there were so many Gentile books in the world at all. I wonder what they are all about. Only I am so troubled about my English." He interrupted himself, with a distressed air. "When I asked them for the book, and how to get it, they could not understand me."

"*I* can understand everything you say when you speak English. You're all right," she comforted him. His troubled, childlike smile and his shining clear blue eyes, as he spoke, went to her heart.

"*You* can, but other people can't. I so wish I could speak it like you, Flora. Do read a page or two with me, will you? I'll get my Reader—shall I?"

"What's your hurry? Can't you wait?"

He could not wait. He was in a fever of impatience to inhale the whole of the Gentile language—definitions, spelling, pronunciation, and all— with one desperate effort. It was the one great impediment that seemed to stand between him and the enchanted new world that had revealed itself to him.

"Oh, do hear me read—may you live long, Flora! It somehow draws me as with a kind of impure force. Will you?"

"All right," she yielded, with kindly curiosity at the fervor of his request, and feeling flattered.

He had been reading perhaps a quarter of an hour when he grew absent-minded.

"You must have skipped a line again," she said, in an awkward undertone.

"Oh, yes!"

They were seated at a respectful distance, with the corner of the marble table between them, her full, well-modeled bust erect and stately against the pier-glass. She wore a waist of dark-blue silk, trimmed with red, and there was a red ribbon in her shock of inky hair. Presently she leaned forward to see a mispronounced word for herself. Their heads found themselves close together. Her ivory cheek almost touched his.

"Where is it?" she questioned, under her breath.

He made no reply. His glance was riveted to her raven eyelashes. A dash of scarlet lurking under her chin dazed his brain. After a slight pause he said, as he timidly stroked her burning cheek:—

"It is so smooth!"

She had an impulse to withdraw her face, but felt benumbed. He went on patting her, until, meeting with no resistance, his lips touched her cheek, in a gingerly kiss. Both lowered their eyes. They were silent, but their hearts, each conscious of the other's beatings, throbbed wildly.

"Bad boy!" she then whispered, without raising her head.

After another silence, as their eyes met, they burst into a subdued, nervous titter.

"You must not do that again," she said. "Is this the kind of pious man you are?"

"Don't say that, Flora—pray don't. You know it hurts my feelings when you speak like that," he implored her. And impelled by the embarrassed, affectionate sadness of her mien, he seized her hand and fell to kissing first her fingers and then her eyes, as though beseeching them to reveal the meaning of their sombre look. Their lips met and clung together in a trance of passion. When they parted Shaya felt ten years older, and as his eye fell upon the bookcase, he wondered what those glittering, massive tomes were doing there.

"Will you tell your father that you want to be my sweetheart?" he asked after a while.

His voice and his features appeared to her in a novel aspect.

"How do you know I do?" she said, with playful defiance, hiding a burst of admiration which was lost upon the unworldly young man.

"Why—don't you?" he demanded solicitously.

Then, a sudden light of inspiration coming in her eyes, Flora said,—

"Hol' on! How would you like to be a doctor, Shayie?"

"But your father would turn me out if I began to study for it."

She grew thoughtful. "But suppose he had no objection?" she queried, her bashfulness suddenly returning to her face.

"Oh, then I should be dying to study doctor books—any kind of Gentile books you wanted me to, Flora. But Reb Asriel won't let me."

"Listen! Can you keep a secret?" she asked like a conspiring little school-girl.

"You mean about your being my sweetheart?"

"No!" she rejoined impatiently. "I mean the other thing—your studyin'. Papa needn't get wind of it till it's too late—you understand? If you are smart, we can fix that."

"That's all right. I am awful clever at keeping a secret," he boasted.

"Well, I want you to be a doctor, Shayie," she resumed, with matronly tenderness. "If you are, I'll care for you, and you'll be my birdie boy, an' all; if not, you won't. Oh, won't it be lovely when everybody knows that you go to college and study together with nice, educated up-town fellows! We would go to theatres together and read different books. You'll make a daisy of a college boy, too—you bet. Would you like to wear a high hat, and spec's, and ride in a buggy, with a little nigger for a driver?—would you, would you, bad boy, you? Hello, Doctor Golub! How are you?"

She presented her lips, and they kissed again and again.

"You know what, Shayie? When papa comes I'll go out somewheres, so you can tell him—you know what I mean. It'll make it so much easier to fool him. Will you tell him?"

"I am ashamed."

"*I* won't tell him."

"Don't be angry—I will. I shall always do everything you tell me, Flora," he said, looking into her black gleaming eyes,—"always, always!" And in the exuberance of his delight he once again felt himself a little boy, and broke out into a masterly imitation of the crow of a cock, jumping up and flapping his arms for a pair of wings.

When Asriel and Shaya were alone in the parlor, the young man said, as he fell to wringing his index finger,—

"Flora wants me to tell you that she is satisfied."

"Satisfied with what?" the old man demanded, leaping to his feet.

"To be my sweetheart."

"Is she? Did she say so? When?—Tamara!" he yelled, rushing downstairs and dragging the prodigy along,—"Tamara! May you live long! The Uppermost has taken pity upon me after all. Floraly has come around—blessed be the Uppermost."

"Blessed be the Uppermost!" Tamara echoed, her pleasant, swarthy face beaming with heartfelt delight. "When He wills, walls of iron must give way. It is a divine match—any one can see it is. May they live a hundred and twenty years together. Mazol-tov!"[4]

"Mazol-tov to you and to all of us," Asriel responded. "But where is Flora? Fetch some drink, Tamara."

He stepped up to the "Wonder-worker box," and deposited a silver coin for the support of the pilgrims at Palestine, saying as he did so:—

"I thank and praise thee, O Lord of the Universe, for thy mercy toward me. Mayest Thou grant the children long years, and keep up in Shaya his love for thy sacred Law. You know the match is all of your own making, and you must take care of it. I am only your slave, that's all."

## IX

"Is Shayaly in?" inquired old Asriel on entering Flora's room one morning in midsummer. It was four months after his daughter's betrothal to the Talmudist had been celebrated by a solemn ceremony and a sumptuous feast, the wedding having been set for a later date. The crowning glory of his achievement Stroon postponed, like a rare bottle of wine, for some future day. He dreaded to indulge himself in such a rapid succession of This World joys lest he might draw upon his Share in the World-to-come. Will the Uppermost let him live to see his daughter and the "holy child," standing side by side under the Canopy? Asriel was now confident that He would. "Is Shayaly in?"

4. Congratulations or best wishes.

"Of course he is—papa," Flora answered, raising her face from her book. Her "papa" was added aloud, and as if upon afterthought.

The parlor door stood ajar. Asriel stationed himself near by and listened to the young man's habitual sing-song. The old man's face gradually became radiant with bliss.

"My crown, my Messiah, my Kaddish! My Share in the World-to-come!" he muttered.

"Did you have breakfast, papa?" Flora demanded, speaking still louder than before.

At this moment Shaya's sing-song broke out with fresh enthusiasm and his Hebrew words became distinct. Asriel waved her away fiercely. After a little he remarked in a subdued voice, as he pointed to the front parlor,—

"*This* is my breakfast. This is for the soul, my child; the worms of the grave cannot touch it, and you take it along to the other world. Everything else is a lot of rubbish."

He made to leave, but could not help pausing, in fresh admiration, and then, softly opening the parlor door he entered the sanctum, on tiptoe, in order to feast his eye as well as his ear on the thrilling scene. He found Shaya rapturously swaying and singing over a Talmud volume. Flora watched her father with roguish delight.

"I am afraid I must not be gloating over him like this," Asriel rebuked himself in his heart. "I may give him the evil eye." When he regained the back parlor he said, under his breath: "Floraly, I am afraid your company may disturb him sometimes. A pretty sweetheart is apt to stir a fellow's brains, you know, and take him away from the Law. He had better study more at the synagogues."

The girl blushed to her charcoal hair and dropped her glance. But her father had scarcely gained his room, on the floor above, when she flew into the front parlor with a ringing giggle.

"Now you can go right on, dearie," she said, encircling Shaya's neck with one arm, and producing with the other an English textbook on Natural Philosophy, which had lain open under the huge Hebrew volume.

"You heard me holler, didn't you?"

"Of course I did," Shaya answered beamingly. "He interrupted me in the middle of such a cunning explanation!"

"Did he? What was it about? All about sounds—the same as before?"

"Yes, but it is even more brainy than what I told you."

He proceeded to expound, in Yiddish, what he had been reading on Acoustics, she listening to his enthusiastic popularization with docile, loving inattention.

The young man made a pretense of spending his afternoons, and sometimes also mornings, at the various synagogues of the Jewish quarter. His proud guardian encouraged this habit, in order that his "daughter's bridegroom" might disseminate his sacred knowledge among other congregations than his own. "Your learning is the gift of God, Shayaly," he would say, "and you needn't be ashamed to peddle it around. Reb Lippe said America wanted a man like you to spread the holy Law here. Go and do it, my son, and the Uppermost will help us all for your sake."

The prodigy and his importer were the talk of the orthodox colony, and nothing was more pleasing to Asriel than to hear the praises of his daughter's fiancé sounded by the Talmudists. There came a time, however, when, in his own synagogue, at least, these encomiums ceased. Asriel missed them keenly and pestered the learned men of the congregation with incessant talks about Shaya, for the purpose of worrying out some acknowledgment of his phenomenal talents. But the concession was mostly made in a half-hearted way, and poor Asriel would be left hungrier than ever. Particularly was his heart longing for the warm eulogies of Reb Tzalel, a poor, sickly old peddler, who was considered one of the most pious and learned men in the neighborhood. Asriel liked the man for his nervous sincerity and uncompromising self-respect. He often asked him to his house, but the tattered, underfed peddler invariably declined the invitation.

"What will I do there, Reb Asriel?" he would say, with the pained sort of smile which would light up his ghastly old face whenever he spoke. "Look at your costly carpet and furniture, and bear in mind that you are a landlord and I a poor peddler! At the synagogue I like you better, for here we are equals. Saith the verse in the Book of Job: 'Whereas He is one that shows no favor to chieftains, and distinguishes not the rich before the indigent, for all of them are the work of his hands.' "[5] Reb Tzalel translated the verse into Yiddish for the benefit of his listener, whereupon Asriel felt a much wealthier man than he was, and at the same time he had a sense of humiliation, as though his money were something to be ashamed of.

This man's unusual reticence on the point of Shaya's merits chagrined Asriel sorely, and his mind even began to be troubled by some vague misgivings on that score.

One evening Asriel sat by Reb Tzalel's side in the study rooms of his synagogue. It was in the latter part of November, and Shaya's wedding was to take place during the Feast of Hanuccah,[6] some few weeks later. The evening services, which on week days were held in these rooms, were over, and the "learners" could now give themselves to their divine studies undisturbed, save for the possible and unwelcome advent of some belated Ten Worshipers.[7] The two spacious, dingy rooms, their connecting doors wide open, were dimly lighted with candles placed upon the plain long deal tables ranged against their discolored walls. The open bookcases were filled with dilapidated old volumes, many more being in use or strewn about, in chaotic heaps, on the tables, benches, or window-sills.

In one room, around one of the long tables, were gathered the members of the daily Mishnah class. There were about a dozen of them, mostly poor peddlers or artisans,—a humble, seedy, pitiable lot, come after a hard day's work or freezing, to "take a holy word into their mouths." Hardly one of these was up to the Gemarah part of the Talmud, and even the Mishnah only few could brave single-handed. They sat at their open books following their voluntary teacher, a large, heavy, middle-aged man,—a mass of unkempt beard, flesh,

---

5. Job 34.19.
6. Hanukkah, the festival of lights, an eight-day celebration, usually in December, commemorating the rededication of the Temple in Jerusalem after a successful revolt against the Selucid Greeks.

7. It is considered a *mitzvah* (good deed performed out of religious duty) and a blessing to be one of the first ten to arrive at synagogue, especially to be the tenth—the one to complete the *minyan*, or community.

and rags, ablaze with the intellectual fury of his enormous black eyes. He was reading aloud, with ferocious appetite, swaying and jerking his disheveled bulk, as he ever and anon tossed up his head to interpret the Mishnah to his pupils, and every little while breaking off in the middle of a sentence, or even a word, to let his class shout the other half as a guaranty of proficiency. Some of his listeners plodded along the lines of their books, in humble silence, with their index fingers for fescues; the brighter ones boldly interrupted the ponderous man, joyously anticipating his explanations or pointing out some discrepancy; one old dissembler repeated unintelligible half-sentences with well-acted gusto; another little old fellow betrayed the fog in his mind by timid nods of assent, while still another was bravely kept from dozing off on his holy book by frequent neighborly nudges from the man next him. Standing behind the members of the class were some envying "boors," like our poor Asriel, to whom even the Mishnah was a luxury beyond their intellectual means.

One of the long tables in the adjoining room was covered with the open folios of the daily Gemarah class,—some fifteen men of all ages and economical conditions from the doddering apple-vender, to whom the holy books are the only source of pleasure in this life as well as in the other, to the well-fed, overdressed young furniture-dealer, with whom the Talmud is a second nature, contracted in the darker days of his existence in Russia. There were several "keen brains" in the group, and a former "prodigy" or two, like Shaya. The class needed no guide, but one old man with a boyish face framed in snow-white hair, and wearing a sea of unstarched linen collar about his emaciated neck, was their chosen reader. He also left many sentences unuttered, but he did it merely because he thought them too well-known to need repetition. Whenever he had something to add to the text, he would address himself to the man by his side, snapping his fingers at him genially, and at times all but pinching him for ecstasy. The others participated now by a twirl of a finger, now by the swift repetition of a whole syllogism, now by an indescribable system of gestures, enacting, in dumb show, the whole logical process involved in a nice point. All at once the whole class would burst into a bedlam of voices and gesticulations. When the whirlwind of enthusiasm subsided, it might be followed by a bit of pleasantry,—from the exuberance of good spirits at having got the better of a difficult point,—and, upon the whole the motley company looked like a happy family at the Sabbath table.

The other long tables in both rooms were occupied by *lomdim* (learned men), each intent upon the good deed of studying "for study's sake" by himself: some humming to their musty folios melodiously; others smiling and murmuring to them, like a fond mother to her babe; still others wailing or grumbling or expostulating with their books, or slapping them and yelling for delight, or roaring like a lion in a cage. A patriarch teaching his ten-year-old grandson and both shouting at the top of their voices, in an entanglement of pantomime; a swarthy little grammar-school boy going it on his own hook over a volume bigger than himself; a "fine householder" in reduced circumstances dignifiedly swinging his form and twirling his side-lock as if he were confiding a secret to his immense golden beard; one or two of the hollow-voiced *prooshim*,[8] who had come to America in search of fortune, but who

---

8. Plural of *poresh*, a recluse, one who devotes himself to the study of the Jewish sacred books.

were now supported by the congregation for giving all their time to "the law and the service"; a knot of men engaged in a mixed discussion of "words of law" and "words of every-day life"—all these voices and murmurs mingled in one effervescence of the sublime and the ridiculous, with tragedy for a keynote,—twenty centuries thrown pell-mell in a chaos of sound and motion.

Asriel could have lived on the spectacle, and although unable to participate in it himself, he now, since the advent of the prodigy, looked upon it as a world in which he was not without a voice. He was seated in a remote corner of the Gemarah room, now watching the noisy scenes with openmouthed reverence, now turning to admire Reb Tzalel by his side. The cadaverous face and burning eyes of the peddler were sneering at the drab-colored page before him, while his voice sounded melancholy, like a subdued bugle call.

Presently Reb Tzalel paused, and the two engaged in converse. As Asriel was boasting of Shaya's genius and kindliness of disposition, vainly courting his friend for a word of assent, the peddler, suddenly reddening in the face, interrupted him:—

"What's the use of playing cat and rat, Mr. Stroon?" he burst out with his ghastly smile. "I may as well tell you what lies like a heavy stone on my heart. Your Shaya is going to the bad. He is an *appikoros*."[9]

"An appikoros!" Asriel demanded, as if the word had suddenly acquired a new meaning.

"Yes, an appikoros, and a Jeroboam the son of Nebat[1]—he sins, and leads others to sin," the Talmudist declared tartly. "I hated to cause you the pain, Mr. Stroon, but he has gone too far in Gentile books, and when he is here and you are not about he talks to everybody he can get hold of concerning the way the world swings around the sun, how rain and thunder, day and night—everything—can be explained as a matter of common sense, and that there is no God in heaven, and all that sort of vile stuff that you hear from every appikoros—may they all be hurled from one end of the world to the other! Everything can be explained—may the Angel of Death explain it to them, may they"—

"Hold on, Reb Tzalel!" Asriel shouted: "You need not curse him: you don't feed him, do you? And what you say is a lie!—as big a lie as Og the King of Bashan!"[2] he concluded with calm ferocity, raising his burly figure from the bench.

"A lie, is it? Very well, then—you shall know all. Little Mendele saw your imported decoration smoking a cigarette last Sabbath."

"Shaya smoke on the Sabbath!" Asriel echoed. The practical, concrete nature of this sin came home to him with a more forceful blow than all the peddler had said about Shaya's ungodly theories. "Begone!" the surrounding chaos seemed to say to the "boor." "From now on you have nothing to do here!"

"Shaya smoke a cigarette on the Sabbath!" he repeated. "Well, and I have this to say, that Mendele, and yourself, and the whole lot of you are nothing but a set of first-class liars and begrudging gossip-mongers. It must give him a belly-ache to think that he could not afford such a bridegroom for his girl and that I could. Well, I have got a prodigy for my daughter and he has licked

9. Atheist.
1. Originally in the service of King Solomon, he became king of a new nation and fell when he tried

to start his own religion. See 1 Kings 11.26–14.20.
2. Defeated by the Israelites under Moses (Numbers 21.33–37).

the whole lot of you learned fellows to ground coffee. I have got him,—see?—
and let all my enemies and the boy's enemies burst for envy." He clicked his
tongue and snapped his fingers, and for a moment stood glaring witheringly
at his interlocutor.

"Well, I am not going to argue with a boor," said Reb Tzalel, in utter disgust.

His words were drowned in the noise, but the "boor" reached Asriel's ear
and touched him on the raw. "Shut up, Reb Tzalel!" he said, paling.

"Why should I? This is not your house. It is God's dwelling. Here I am
richer than you. I only wanted to say that it is not you I pity. You have been a
boor, and that's what you are and will be. But the boy was about to become a
great man in Israel, and you have brought him over here for bedeviled America to turn him into an appikoros. Woe! woe! woe!"

"Keep still, Reb Tzalel; take pity," Asriel implored, in a squeaking voice.
"Don't spill any salt over my wounds. Forgive me,—you know I am a boor. Do
take pity and say no more; but all you have said—they have said—is a lie—
the cholera choke me if it is not." And gasping for breath, he ran out of the
synagogue.

When he found himself in the street he was conscious of some terrific blow
having just been dealt him, but did not clearly realize its full meaning; and
what had transpired a minute before, between him and Reb Tzalel, seemed
to have occurred in the remote past. The clamor of the street peddlers, and
the whole maze of squalor and noise through which he was now scurrying,
he appeared to hear and to view at a great distance, as if it all were on the
other side of a broad river, he hurrying on his lonely way along the deserted
bank opposite.

"An appikoros! an appikoros!" he said to himself, vainly trying to grasp the
meaning of the word which he knew but too well. "An appikoros, smoking on
the Sabbath!" The spectacle smote him in cold blood. "Shaya smoke on the
holy Sabbath! It's a lie!"

He started in the direction of Mendele's residence, bent upon thrashing the
red-haired talebearer to death. Soon, however, he halted and turned homeward. The courage failed Asriel Stroon to face the man who had seen his
daughter's fiancé smoke a cigarette on a Saturday. Then Shaya appeared to
his mind as something polluted, sacrilegious, and although this something
had nothing in common with his beloved prodigy, save the name, and the
young man whitened in the distance, pure and lovely as ever, Asriel's rage
surged in the direction of his home, and he mended pace to storm the house
as soon as he could get there.

When he collected his wits he decided to wait till he found out everything
for himself. For the first time, perhaps, he felt himself a coward. He quailed
before the thought that what he had heard from the learned peddler might
prove true, and he cringingly begged his own mind to put off the culminating agony of believing it.

Nevertheless, when he saw Shaya, at the supper-table, his heart whispered
to him, in dismay: "An appikoros!" and the unuttered word enveloped the
prodigy in a forbidding, sinister atmosphere.

He now hated Shaya; he felt as though he feared him.

"Where have you been so late, papa?" Flora inquired.

"Deep in the earth. You care much where your papa is, do you?" he snarled.

"Papa!" she said deprecatingly; "are you mad?"

He made no response.

"Have you been to the Mariv[3] service?" Shaya intervened. "I studied at the Souvalk Synagogue to-day."

Asriel remained grimly uncommunicative.

The young people, reinforced by Tamara, made several other attempts at conversation, but the dogged taciturnity of the head of the family cast a spell of misery over them all, and the meal passed in unsupportable silence.

"See if papa ain't getting on to what you are doing, Shayie," Flora said, when the two were alone.

"Pshaw! is it the first time you see him out of humor? He must have had some trouble with a tenant or janitor."

"He must have," she assented gloomily. "But what if he gets wind? I'm worrying the life out of myself about it."

"So am I. I love your father just the same as if he were my own papa. I wish the wedding were over, don't you?" he asked in his childish way.

X

On the following morning Asriel repaired to the Souvalk Synagogue to attend the service (his usual place of worship he had not the heart to visit), and, incidentally, to ascertain how Shaya had spent his time there the day before.

To his consternation he learned that his "daughter's bridegroom" had not been seen there for weeks.

Asriel held his counsel, and took to shadowing the young man.

He now had no doubt as to the accuracy of Reb Tzalel's story. But it gave him no pain. It was Shaya no longer; it was not his daughter's bridegroom; it was not the prodigy he had imported,—it was an appikoros. But then Asriel's heart withered at the notion of being the victim of systematic deception. Shaya was an appikoros and a secret, sneaking enemy.

"That youngster trick Asriel Stroon!" He panted with hatred and thrilled with a detective-like passion to catch Shaya in the act of some grave violation of the Mosaic Law.

He went about the various synagogues where the young man was supposed to study the Talmud, with a keen foretaste of his vicious joy at finding that he had been playing truant. Yet each time his fervent expectations were realized he would, instead of triumph, experience an overpowering sense of defeat.

"You have been cheated out of your boots by a stripling, Asrielke—woe to your foolish head!" he tortured himself, reveling in an agony of fury. "Ah, a cholera into him! I'll show him how to fool Asriel Stroon!"

He discovered that Shaya's frequent companion was his former teacher of English, whom he often visited in his attic room on Clinton Street, and he impatiently awaited the next Saturday to raid the atheistic resort and to overtake Shaya smoking or writing on the holy day. But the climax came a day or two sooner.

After tracing Shaya to the Clinton Street house Asriel stood waiting around a corner, at a vantage point from which he could see the windows of the two

3. Evening prayers.

garret rooms one of which was the supposed scene of the young man's ungodly pursuits. He had no definite purpose in view, for it was not Sabbath, and he would not spoil his game by apprehending his man in the mere act of reading Gentile books. Yet he was rooted to the place, and remained aimlessly waiting, with his eyes riveted to the windows which they could not penetrate. Tired at last, and overcome with a sense of having been engaged in a fool's errand, he returned home, and, reaching his bedroom, sank on the bed in a prostration of hurt pride and impotent rage.

On the following morning he returned to his post. The attic windows drew him like the evil one, as he put it to himself.

He had been keeping watch for some minutes when, to his fierce joy, Shaya and his accomplice sallied forth into the street. He dogged their steps to Grand Street, and thence, through the Bowery, to Lafayette Place, where they disappeared behind the massive doors of an imposing structure, apparently neither a dwelling-place nor an office building.

"Dis a choych?" Asriel asked a passer-by.

"A church? No, it's a library—the Astor Library," the stranger explained.

"Ah, a lot of Gentile books!" he exclaimed to himself, disappointed in one way and triumphant in another. The unaccustomed neighborhood and the novelty of his impressions increased the power of the "evil one" over him. He took up a position whence he could observe without being observed, and waited for the two young men to come out. What he would gain by tracing them back to the Jewish quarter he never asked himself. He waited because the "evil one" would not let him stir from the spot.

An hour passed. He was growing faint with hunger; yet he never moved. "He has not had his lunch, either," he thought. "Still, he can stand it. It's the witchcraft of the Gentile books—may he be burned to death!—keeping up his strength. They'll come out in a minute or two."

Many more minutes elapsed, and still Asriel waited. At last "Here, they are, the convert Jews! Look at them—how jolly! It's the Black Year shining out of their faces—may they shine on their death-beds! That beggar of a teacher I shall have arrested."

He followed them through Fourth Street back to the Bowery and down the rumbling thoroughfare, till—"a lamentation!"—they entered a Christian restaurant!

A terrific pang smote Asriel's heart. It was as if he saw his temple, the embodiment of many years of labor, the object of his fondest cares, just completed and ready to be dedicated, suddenly enveloped in flames. The prodigy, *his* prodigy, his Kaddish, his glory in this and the other world, plunged into the very thick of impurity!

He made to rush after them, but checked himself to wait till the *treife* food was served them. A few minutes later he made his entry, cool and collected as a regular customer.

Each of the two young men was bent on a veal cutlet. The collegian was dispatching his with the nonchalant appetite and ease of manner of an habitué, whereas poor Shaya looked like one affecting to relish his first plate of raw oysters. The smells proceeding from the kitchen made him dizzy, and the cutlet itself, partly because he was accustomed to meat of a better quality, but mainly through the consciousness of eating treife, inclined him to nausea.

Asriel took a vacant chair at the same table.

"Bless the sitter,[4] Shaya!" he said.

The two young men were petrified.

"How is the pork—does it taste well?" Asriel pursued.

"It is not pork. It is veal cutlet," the teacher found tongue to retort.

"I am not speaking to you, am I?" Asriel hissed out. Murder was swelling in his heart. But at this point the waiter came up to his side.

"Vot'll ye have?"

"Notink!" Asriel replied, suddenly rising from his seat and rushing out, as if this were the most terrible sort of violence he could conceive.

## XI

Asriel found his daughter playing.

"Stop that or I'll smash your Gentile piano to pieces!" he commanded her, feeling as though the instrument had all along been in the conspiracy and were now bidding him defiance.

"Why, what's the matter?" she questioned, getting up from her stool in stupefaction.

"Matter? Bluff a dead rooster, not me—my head is still on my shoulders. Here it is, you see?" he added, taking himself by the head. "It's all up, Flora."

"What do you mean?" she made out to inquire.

"I mean that if Shayke[5] ever enters this house I'll murder both of you. You thought your papa was a fool, didn't you? Well, you are a poor hand at figuring, Flora. I knew everything, but I wanted some particulars. I have got them all now here, in my pocket, and a minute ago I took the pleasure of bidding him 'bless the sitter' in a Gentile restaurant—may he be choked with his treife gorge!"

"You've got no business to curse him like that!" she flamed out, coloring violently.

"*I* have no business? And who is to stop me, pray?"

"*I* am. It ain't my fault. You know I did not care at first."

The implication that he had only himself to blame threw him into a new frenzy. But he restrained himself, and said with ghastly deliberation:—

"Flora, you are not going to marry him."

"I *am*. I can't live without him," she declared with quiet emphasis.

Asriel left her room.

"It's all gone, Tamara! My candle is blown out," he said, making his way from the dining-room to the kitchen. "There is no Shaya any longer."

"A weeping, a darkness to me! Has an accident—mercy and peace!— befallen the child?"

"Yes, he is 'dead and buried, and gone from the market-place.' Worse than that: a convert Jew is worse than a dead one. It's all gone, Tamara!" he repeated gravely. "I have just seen him eating treife in a Gentile restaurant. America has robbed me of my glory."

---

4. Form of greeting when the host is found at table.

5. Contemptuous diminutive of Shaya.

"Woe is me!" the housekeeper gasped, clutching at her wig. "Treife! Does he not get enough to eat here?" She then burst out, "Don't I serve him the best food there is in the world? Any king would be glad to get such dinners."

"Well, it seems treife tastes better," Asriel rejoined bitterly.

"A calamity upon my sinful head! We must have evil-eyed the child; we have devoured him with our admiring looks."

While Asriel was answering her volley of questions, Flora stealthily left the house.

When Stroon missed her he hurried off to Clinton Street. There he learned of the landlady that her lodger had left a short while before, in the company of his friend and a young lady whom the two young men had found waiting in her parlor. In his despair Asriel betook himself to the Astor Library, to some of Flora's friends, and even to the Bowery restaurant.

When he reached home, exhausted with fatigue and rage, he found his daughter in her room.

"Where have you been?" he demanded, sternly.

"I'll tell you where, but don't aggravate yourself, papaly," she replied in beseeching, tearful accents.

"Where have you been?"

"I am going to tell you, but don't blame Shaya. He is awful fond of you. It's all my fault. He didn't want to go, but I couldn't help it, papaly. We've been to the city court and got married by a judge. Shaya didn't want to."

"You married!"

"Yes, but don't be angry, papaly darlin'. We'll do everything to please you. If you don't want him to be a doctor, he won't."

"A doctor!" he resumed, still speaking like one in a daze. "Is that what you have been up to? I see—you have got the best of me, after all. You married, Flora?" he repeated, unable to apply the meaning of the word to his daughter. "In court—without Canopy and Dedication—like Gentiles? What have you done, Flora?" He sank into a chair, gnashing his teeth and tearing at his sidelocks.

"Papaly, papaly, don't!" she sobbed, hugging and kissing him. "You know I ain't to blame for it all."

It dawned upon him that no serious wrong had been committed, after all, and that it could all be mended by a Jewish marriage ceremony; and so great was his relief at the thought that it took away all his anger, and he even felt as if he were grateful to his daughter for not being guilty of a graver transgression than she was.

"I know you are not to blame," he said, tragic in his calmness. "America has done it all. But what is the use talking! It's gone, and I am not going to take another sin upon my soul. I won't let you be his wife without Canopy and Dedication. Let the Jewish wedding come off at once—this week—to-morrow. You have got the best of me and I don't kick, do I? It seems God does not want Asrielke the boor to have some joy in his old age, nor a Kaddish for his soul, when the worms will be feasting upon his silly bones"—

"Oh, don't say that, papa. It'll break my heart if you do. You know Shaya is as good as a son to you."

"An appikoros my son? An appikoros my Kaddish? No," he rejoined, shaking his head pensively.

As he said it he felt as if Flora, too, were a stranger to him.

He descended to the basement in a state of mortal indifference.

"I have lost everything, Tamara," he said. "I have no daughter, either. I am all alone in the world—alone as a stone."

He had no sooner closed the kitchen door behind him, than Flora was out and away to Clinton Street to surprise her bridegroom with the glad news of her father's surrender.

The housekeeper was in the kitchen, sewing upon some silk vestments for the scrolls of her synagogue. Asriel stood by her side, leaning against the cupboard door, in front of the Palestine box. Speaking in a bleak, resigned undertone, he told her of Flora's escapade and of his determination to make the best of it by precipitating the Jewish ceremony. A gorgeous celebration was now, of course, out of the question. The proposed fête which was to have been the talk of the synagogues and which had been the centre of his sweetest dreams had suddenly turned in his imagination to something like a funeral feast. Tamara bade him be of good cheer, and cited Rabbi Nochum And-This-Too, who would hail the severest blows of fate with the words: "And this, too, is for the best." But Asriel would not be comforted.

"Yes, Tamara, it is gone, all gone," he murmured forlornly. "It was all a dream,—a last year's lemon pie. It has flown away and you can't catch it. Gone, and that's all. You know how I feel? As if some fellow had played a joke on me."

The pious woman was moved.

"But it is a sin to take things so close to heart," she said impetuously. "You must take care of your health. Bear up under your affliction like a righteous Jew, Reb Asriel. Trust to the Uppermost, and you will live to rejoice in your child and in her children, if God be pleased."

Asriel heaved a sigh and fell silent. He stood with his eyes upon the pilgrim box, listening to the whisper of her needle.

"You know what; let us go to the Land of Israel," he presently said, as though continuing an interrupted sentence. "They have got the best of me. I cannot change the world. Let them live as they please and be responsible to the Uppermost for themselves. I don't care the kernel of a hollow nut. I shall give Flora half my property and the rest I'll sell. You are a righteous woman, Tamara. Why not marry and end our days serving God in the Holy Land together?"

Tamara plied her needle with redoubled zeal. He could see only her glossy black wig and the flaming dusk of her cheek.

"We'll have a comfortable living and plenty of money for deeds of charity," he pursued. "I know I am only a boor. Do I say I am not? But is a boor no human being at all? Can't I die a righteous Jew?" he pleaded piteously.

The glossy wig bent lower and the silk rustled busily.

"You know that I have on my tongue what I have on my lung, Tamara. I mean what I say, and we want no match-makers. America is now treife to me. I can't show my head. The world is dark and empty to me. All is gone, gone, gone. I am a little baby, Tamara. Come, take pity. I shall see Flora married according to the laws of Moses and Israel, and then let us put up a canopy and set out on our journey. I want to be born again. Well?"

There was no response.

"Well, Tamara?"

"Since it is the will of God," she returned resignedly, without raising her head from the vestments.

## XII

Flora was all of a flutter with impatience to share her joy with Shaya, and yearning for his presence. She had not seen him since he had become her legal husband, and the two or three hours seemed a week.

When the German landlady of the little Clinton Street house told her that neither her lodger nor his friend were in the attic room the young woman's heart sank within her. Her message seemed to be bubbling over and her over-wrought mind too weak to bear it another minute. She mentally berated her absent bridegroom, and not knowing whither to bend her steps in quest of him she repaired to some girl friends to while away the time and to deliver herself of part of her burden to them.

"When he comes tell him he da's not leave for one second till I come back. Tell him I've got some grand news for him," she instructed the landlady, struggling hard against a wild temptation to unbosom herself to the stranger.

It was about eight o'clock when she returned. Shaya met her in the hallway.

"Well?" he inquired anxiously.

"Well?" she mocked him. "You are a daisy! Why didn't you wait? Couldn't you guess I'd come?"

"How should I? But tell me what your father says. Why should you torment me?"

"He says he don't want you," she replied. But her look told even a more encouraging tale than the one she had to deliver, and they flew into mutual embrace in an outburst of happiness which seemed to both of them unlike any they had ever experienced before.

"A life into your little eyes! A health into your little hands and feet!" he muttered, stroking her arm sheepishly. "You shall see how fine it will all come out. You don't know me yet. I tell you you don't begin to know me," he kept repeating with some braggadocio and without distinctly knowing what he meant.

They were to return home at once and to try to pacify Asriel as best they could. When Flora pressed him to take his hat and overcoat, however, he looked reluctant and then said:—

"Floraly, you know what; come upstairs for just one minute. We are reading the nicest book you ever saw, and there is a lot of such nice gentlemen there!—several genuine Americans—Christians. Do come, Floraly." He drew her up the two flights of stairs almost by force. "Don't be afraid: the landlady knows all about it," he whispered. "You'll see what nice people. I tell you they are so educated, and they love Jews so much! A Jew is the same as a Gentile to them—even better."

Flora felt a lump growing in her heart. The notion of Shaya being at this minute interested in anything outside of herself and their mutual happiness literally dazed her, and before she had time to recover from her shock she was in the over-crowded attic.

There were some ten or twelve men in the room, some seated—two on chairs, two on the host's trunk, and three on his bed—the others standing by the window or propping the sloping wall with their heads. They were clustered about a round table, littered with books, papers, and cigarette stumps. A tin can was hissing on the flat top of a little parlor stove, and some of the company were sipping Russian tea from tumblers, each with a slice of lemon floating in it. The group was made up of a middle-aged man with a handsome and intensely intellectual Scotch face, who was a laborer by day and a philosopher by night; a Swedish tailor with the face of a Catholic priest; a Zurich Ph.D. in blue eyeglasses; a young Hindoo who eked out a wretched existence by selling first-rate articles to second-rate weeklies, and several Russian Jews, all of them insatiable debaters and most of them with university or gymnasium diplomas. The group met every Thursday to read and discuss Harriet Martineau's "Auguste Comte," under the guidance of the Scotchman, who was a leading spirit in positivist circles.[6]

The philosopher surrendered his chair to the lady, in a flurry of chivalry, but a seat was made for him on the trunk, and he forthwith resumed his reading with well-bred impetuosity, the kerosene lamp in the centre of the table casting a halo upon his frank, pleasant face.

His auditors were now listening with conscious attention, some of the younger men affecting an absorbed mien or interrupting the reader with unnecessary questions. Shaya's eyes were traveling between Flora and the Scotchman's audience. "Did you ever see such a beautiful and stylish young lady?" he seemed to be saying. "She is my bride—mine and nobody else's in the world," and, "Look at these great men, Flora—I am their chum." Presently, however, he became engrossed in the reading; and only half-conscious of Flora's presence, he sat leaning forward, his mouth wide open, his face rapt, and his fingers quietly reproducing the mental gymnastics of Comte's system in the air.

The young woman gazed about her in perplexity. The Scotchman and his reading inspired her with respect, but the rest of the company and the *tout ensemble*[7] of the scene impressed her as the haunt of queer individuals, meeting for some sinister purpose. It was anything but the world of intellectual and physical elegance into which she had dreamed to be introduced by marriage to a doctor. Any society of "custom peddlers" was better dressed than these men, who appeared to her more like some of the grotesque and uncouth characters in Dickens's novels than an assemblage of educated people. For a moment even Shaya seemed a stranger and an enemy. Overcome by the stuffy, overheated atmosphere of the misshapen apartment, she had a sense of having been kidnaped into the den of some terrible creatures, and felt like crying for help. Next she was wondering what her Shaya could have in common with these shabby beings and what it all had to do with becoming a doctor and riding in a buggy.

"Shaya!" she whispered, tugging him by the coat-sleeve.

"Just one moment, Floraly," he begged her. "Ah, it's so deep!"

A discussion engaged itself. The Russians fell to greedily. One of them, in particular, a young man with a dignified bass, was hateful to Flora. She could

---

6. Harriet Martineau (1802–1876), an English writer and scholar, was an early sociologist. "Positivism" is a system of philosophy that bases knowledge solely on the data of sense experience, rejecting speculation about or search for ultimate origins; it was originated by Auguste Comte (1798–1857), a French thinker and sociologist.
7. The total impression or effect of something made up of individual parts (French).

not have told you why, but his voice, coupled with the red embroidery of his Little-Russian shirt-front, cut her to the quick.

The room was full of smoke and broken English.

Shaya was brimful of arguments and questions which he had not the courage to advance; and so he sat, now making a vehement gesture of despair at somebody else's absurdities, now nodding violent approval, and altogether fidgeting about in a St. Vitus's dance[8] of impotent pugnacity.

"Shaya, it is getting late, and papa"—

"One second, do please, Floraly, may you live long," he implored her, with some irritation; and taking the book from the Scotchman's hand, he fell to turning over its leaves in a feverish search of what struck him as a misinterpreted passage.

Flora was going to protest and to threaten to leave without him, but she could neither speak nor stir from her seat. A nightmare of desolation and jealousy choked her—jealousy of the Scotchman's book, of the Little-Russian shirt, of the empty tea-glasses with the slices of lemon on their bottoms, of the whole excited crowd, and of Shaya's entire future, from which she seemed excluded.

1898

8. Acute disturbance of the central nervous system characterized by involuntary muscular movements of the face and extremities.

---

# CHARLOTTE PERKINS GILMAN
## 1860–1935

Charlotte Perkins Gilman lived her life, for the most part, on the margins of a society whose economic assumptions about and social definitions of women she vigorously repudiated. Out of this resistance to conventional values and what she later characterized as "masculinist" ideals, Gilman produced the large body of polemical writings and what we would call today self-consciously feminist fiction that made her the leading theoretician, speaker, and writer on women's issues of her time.

Charlotte Anna Perkins was born in Hartford, Connecticut, on July 3, 1860. Her father, Frederic Beecher Perkins, was a minor literary figure, grandson of the theologian Lyman Beecher, and nephew of the preacher Henry Ward Beecher and of Harriet Beecher Stowe. Her mother was Mary A. Fitch, whose family had lived in Rhode Island since the middle of the seventeenth century. Gilman's father deserted his family and left for San Francisco shortly after her birth, and she spent many years trying, without success, to establish some intimacy with him. She received from him only occasional letters with lists of books she should read. Her mother returned to Providence, Rhode Island, where she supported herself and her two children with great difficulty; she withheld from them all physical expressions of love, hoping to prevent their later disillusionment over broken relationships. It is easy to understand why in her autobiography Gilman described her childhood as painful and lonely.

Between 1880 and her marriage in May 1884 to Charles Stetson, a promising Providence artist, Gilman supported herself in Providence as a governess, art teacher, and designer of greeting cards. During those years she had increasingly become aware of the injustices inflicted on women, and she had begun to write poems—one in defense of prostitutes—in which she developed her own views on women's rights. She entered into the marriage reluctantly, anticipating the difficulties of reconciling her ambition to be a writer with the demands of being a wife, housekeeper, and mother. Within eleven months, their only child, Katharine, was born; following the birth, Gilman became increasingly despondent, and marital tensions increased. Her husband and her mother were convinced that Gilman needed rest and willpower to overcome her depression; they persuaded her to go to Philadelphia for treatment by Dr. S. Weir Mitchell, the most famous American neurologist of the day. A specialist in women's "nervous" disorders, Mitchell usually prescribed a "rest cure" consisting of total bedrest for several weeks and limited intellectual activity thereafter. In those days, postpartum depression was not widely understood. As Gilman put it in "Why I Wrote 'The Yellow Wall-paper'?" (1913), the doctor "sent me home [after six weeks] with the solemn advice to 'live as domestic a life as . . . possible,' to 'have but two hours' intellectual life a day,' and 'never to touch pen, brush, or pencil again' as long as I lived." The patient returned to Providence and obeyed these instructions for three months "and came so near the borderline of utter mental ruin that I could see over." She drew back from the edge of madness by resuming her life as a reluctant wife and mother and as an enthusiastic writer and frequent contributor to the Boston *Woman's Journal*. A few years later she wrote her most famous story. As she concluded: "It was not intended to drive people crazy, but to save people from being driven crazy, and it worked." Writing "The Yellow Wall-paper" (1892), however, did not keep Gilman from suffering all her life with extended periods of depression.

In 1888, after a trial separation, convinced that her marriage threatened her sanity, Gilman moved with her daughter to Pasadena, California, and in 1892 was granted a divorce. Her former husband promptly married her best friend, the writer Grace Ellery Channing, and not long thereafter Gilman sent her daughter east to live with them. Such actions generated much publicity and hostile criticism in the press, but nothing kept Gilman from pursuing her double career as writer and lecturer on women, labor, and social organization. In these years she was particularly influenced by the sociologist Lester Ward and the utopian novelist Edward Bellamy.

In 1898 Gilman published *Women and Economics*, the book that earned her immediate celebrity and that is still considered her most important nonfiction work. This powerful "feminist manifesto" argues a thesis Gilman was to develop and refine for the rest of her life: women's economic dependency on men stunts not only the growth of women but that of the whole human species. More particularly, she argued that because of the dependency of women on men for food and shelter the sexual and maternal aspects of their personalities had been developed excessively and to the detriment of their other productive capacities. To free women to develop in a more balanced and socially constructive way, Gilman urged such reforms as centralized nurseries (in *Concerning Children,* 1900) and professionally staffed collective kitchens (in *The Home,* 1904).

In 1911 she published *The Man-Made World,* which contrasted the competitiveness and aggressiveness of men with the cooperativeness and nurturance of women and posited that until women played a larger part in national and international life, social injustice and war would characterize industrialized societies. In this same year her short story "Turned" appeared, taking on similar gender issues. Similarly, in *His Religion and Hers* (1923) Gilman predicted that only when women influenced theology would the fear of death and punishment cease to be central to religious institutions and practices.

Gilman's poetry and fiction, most written when she was well past forty, must be seen, as the critic Ann J. Lane has observed, as "part of her ideological world view, and therein lies its interest and power." Therein, also, lie its limits, for as Lane also says, "She wrote quickly, carelessly, to make a point." Still, many of Gilman's stories and her utopian novels—such as *Moving the Mountain* (1911), *Herland* (1915), and *With Her in Ourland* (1916)—offer vivid dramatizations of the social ills (and their potential remedies) that result from a competitive economic system in which women are subordinate to men and accept their subordination. In *Herland*, for instance, Gilman offers a vision of an all-female society in which caring women raise children (reproduced by parthenogenesis) collectively in a world that is both prosperous and ecologically sound.

In 1900, after a long courtship, she married her first cousin George Houghton Gilman. They lived together happily, first in New York, then in Norwich, Connecticut, until he died suddenly in 1934. Gilman then moved to Pasadena to live with her daughter's family. The next year, suffering from breast cancer and convinced that her productive life was over, she committed suicide with chloroform she had long been accumulating.

# The Yellow Wall-paper[1]

It is very seldom that mere ordinary people like John and myself secure ancestral halls for the summer.

A colonial mansion, a hereditary estate, I would say a haunted house, and reach the height of romantic felicity—but that would be asking too much of fate!

Still I will proudly declare that there is something queer about it.

Else, why should it be let so cheaply? And why have stood so long untenanted?

John laughs at me, of course, but one expects that in marriage.

John is practical in the extreme. He has no patience with faith, an intense horror of superstition, and he scoffs openly at any talk of things not to be felt and seen and put down in figures.

John is a physician, and *perhaps*—(I would not say it to a living soul, of course, but this is dead paper and a great relief to my mind)—*perhaps* that is one reason I do not get well faster.

You see he does not believe I am sick!

And what can one do?

If a physician of high standing, and one's own husband, assures friends and relatives that there is really nothing the matter with one but temporary nervous depression—a slight hysterical tendency[2]—what is one to do?

My brother is also a physician, and also of high standing, and he says the same thing.

So I take phosphates or phosphites—whichever it is—and tonics, and journeys, and air, and exercise, and am absolutely forbidden to "work" until I am well again.

Personally, I disagree with their ideas.

1. The complete and complex textual history of the extant fair copy manuscript and seven editions of the story during Gilman's lifetime is available in Julie Bates Dock's *Charlotte Perkins Gilman's "The Yellow Wall-paper" and the History of Its Publication and Reception: A Critical Edition and Documentary Casebook* (Pennsylvania State University Press, 1998). Dock's volume also contains a detailed textual apparatus and notes, a variety of background material, early reviews, and other commentary. Professor Dock and Pennsylvania State University Press have kindly granted permission to use her eclectic critical edition of this story.
2. At the time this story was written, *hysteria* was a term used to describe a wide variety of symptoms, thought to be particularly prevalent among women, that indicated emotional disturbance or dysfunction. Depression, anxiety, excitability, and vague somatic complaints were among the conditions treated as "hysteria." As the words *uterus* and *hysteria* came from the same Greek root, so the medical profession blamed women's reproductive systems for their "sick" mentalities; hysterectomies were increasingly performed.

Personally, I believe that congenial work, with excitement and change, would do me good.

But what is one to do?

I did write for a while in spite of them; but it *does* exhaust me a good deal—having to be so sly about it, or else meet with heavy opposition.

I sometimes fancy that in my condition if I had less opposition and more society and stimulus—but John says the very worst thing I can do is to think about my condition, and I confess it always makes me feel bad.

So I will let it alone and talk about the house.

The most beautiful place! It is quite alone, standing well back from the road, quite three miles from the village. It makes me think of English places that you read about, for there are hedges and walls and gates that lock, and lots of separate little houses for the gardeners and people.

There is a *delicious* garden! I never saw such a garden—large and shady, full of box-bordered paths, and lined with long grape-covered arbors with seats under them.

There were greenhouses, too, but they are all broken now.

There was some legal trouble, I believe, something about the heirs and co-heirs; anyhow, the place has been empty for years.

That spoils my ghostliness, I am afraid, but I don't care—there is something strange about the house—I can feel it.

I even said so to John one moonlight evening, but he said what I felt was a *draught,* and shut the window.

I get unreasonably angry with John sometimes. I'm sure I never used to be so sensitive. I think it is due to this nervous condition.

But John says if I feel so, I shall neglect proper self-control; so I take pains to control myself—before him, at least, and that makes me very tired.

I don't like our room a bit. I wanted one downstairs that opened on the piazza and had roses all over the window, and such pretty old-fashioned chintz hangings! But John would not hear of it.

He said there was only one window and not room for two beds, and no near room for him if he took another.

He is very careful and loving, and hardly lets me stir without special direction.

I have a schedule prescription for each hour in the day; he takes all care from me, and so I feel basely ungrateful not to value it more.

He said we came here solely on my account, that I was to have perfect rest and all the air I could get. "Your exercise depends on your strength, my dear," said he, "and your food somewhat on your appetite; but air you can absorb all the time." So we took the nursery at the top of the house.

It is a big, airy room, the whole floor nearly, with windows that look all ways, and air and sunshine galore. It was nursery first and then playroom and gymnasium, I should judge; for the windows are barred for little children, and there are rings and things in the walls.

The paint and paper look as if a boys' school had used it. It is stripped off—the paper—in great patches all around the head of my bed, about as far as I can reach, and in a great place on the other side of the room low down. I never saw a worse paper in my life.

One of those sprawling flamboyant patterns committing every artistic sin.

It is dull enough to confuse the eye in following, pronounced enough to constantly irritate and provoke study, and when you follow the lame uncertain curves for a little distance they suddenly commit suicide—plunge off at outrageous angles, destroy themselves in unheard of contradictions.

The color is repellent, almost revolting; a smouldering unclean yellow, strangely faded by the slow-turning sunlight.

It is a dull yet lurid orange in some places, a sickly sulphur tint in others.

No wonder the children hated it! I should hate it myself if I had to live in this room long.

There comes John, and I must put this away—he hates to have me write a word.

•　•　•　•　•　•

We have been here two weeks, and I haven't felt like writing before, since that first day.

I am sitting by the window now, up in this atrocious nursery, and there is nothing to hinder my writing as much as I please, save lack of strength.

John is away all day, and even some nights when his cases are serious.

I am glad my case is not serious!

But these nervous troubles are dreadfully depressing.

John does not know how much I really suffer. He knows there is no *reason* to suffer, and that satisfies him.

Of course it is only nervousness. It does weigh on me so not to do my duty in any way!

I meant to be such a help to John, such a real rest and comfort, and here I am a comparative burden already!

Nobody would believe what an effort it is to do what little I am able—to dress and entertain, and order things.

It is fortunate Mary is so good with the baby. Such a dear baby!

And yet I *cannot* be with him, it makes me so nervous.

I suppose John never was nervous in his life. He laughs at me so about this wall-paper!

At first he meant to repaper the room, but afterwards he said that I was letting it get the better of me, and that nothing was worse for a nervous patient than to give way to such fancies.

He said that after the wall-paper was changed it would be the heavy bedstead, and then the barred windows, and then that gate at the head of the stairs, and so on.

"You know the place is doing you good," he said, "and really, dear, I don't care to renovate the house just for a three months' rental."

"Then do let us go downstairs," I said, "there are such pretty rooms there."

Then he took me in his arms and called me a blessed little goose, and said he would go down cellar, if I wished, and have it whitewashed into the bargain.

But he is right enough about the beds and windows and things.

It is as airy and comfortable a room as any one need wish, and, of course, I would not be so silly as to make him uncomfortable just for a whim.

I'm really getting quite fond of the big room, all but that horrid paper.

Out of one window I can see the garden, those mysterious deep-shaded arbors, the riotous old-fashioned flowers, and bushes and gnarly trees.

Out of another I get a lovely view of the bay and a little private wharf belonging to the estate. There is a beautiful shaded lane that runs down there from the house. I always fancy I see people walking in these numerous paths and arbors, but John has cautioned me not to give way to fancy in the least. He says that with my imaginative power and habit of story-making, a nervous weakness like mine is sure to lead to all manner of excited fancies, and that I ought to use my will and good sense to check the tendency. So I try.

I think sometimes that if I were only well enough to write a little it would relieve the press of ideas and rest me.

But I find I get pretty tired when I try.

It is so discouraging not to have any advice and companionship about my work. When I get really well, John says we will ask Cousin Henry and Julia down for a long visit; but he says he would as soon put fireworks in my pillowcase as to let me have those stimulating people about now.

I wish I could get well faster.

But I must not think about that. This paper looks to me as if it *knew* what a vicious influence it had!

There is a recurrent spot where the pattern lolls like a broken neck and two bulbous eyes stare at you upside down.

I get positively angry with the impertinence of it and the everlastingness. Up and down and sideways they crawl, and those absurd, unblinking eyes are everywhere. There is one place where two breadths didn't match, and the eyes go all up and down the line, one a little higher than the other.

I never saw so much expression in an inanimate thing before, and we all know how much expression they have! I used to lie awake as a child and get more entertainment and terror out of blank walls and plain furniture than most children could find in a toy-store.

I remember what a kindly wink the knobs of our big, old bureau used to have, and there was one chair that always seemed like a strong friend.

I used to feel that if any of the other things looked too fierce I could always hop into that chair and be safe.

The furniture in this room is no worse than inharmonious, however, for we had to bring it all from downstairs. I suppose when this was used as a playroom they had to take the nursery things out, and no wonder! I never saw such ravages as the children have made here.

The wall-paper, as I said before, is torn off in spots, and it sticketh closer than a brother[3]—they must have had perseverance as well as hatred.

Then the floor is scratched and gouged and splintered, the plaster itself is dug out here and there, and this great heavy bed, which is all we found in the room, looks as if it had been through the wars.

But I don't mind it a bit—only the paper.

There comes John's sister. Such a dear girl as she is, and so careful of me! I must not let her find me writing.

She is a perfect and enthusiastic housekeeper, and hopes for no better profession. I verily believe she thinks it is the writing which made me sick!

But I can write when she is out, and see her a long way off from these windows.

There is one that commands the road, a lovely shaded winding road, and one that just looks off over the country. A lovely country, too, full of great elms and velvet meadows.

---

3. Proverbs 18.24: "There is a friend that sticketh closer than a brother."

This wall-paper has a kind of sub-pattern in a different shade, a particularly irritating one, for you can only see it in certain lights, and not clearly then.

But in the places where it isn't faded and where the sun is just so—I can see a strange, provoking, formless sort of figure, that seems to skulk about behind that silly and conspicuous front design.

There's sister on the stairs!

• • • • • •

Well, the Fourth of July is over! The people are all gone and I am tired out. John thought it might do me good to see a little company, so we just had mother and Nellie and the children down for a week.

Of course I didn't do a thing. Jennie sees to everything now.

But it tired me all the same.

John says if I don't pick up faster he shall send me to Weir Mitchell[4] in the fall.

But I don't want to go there at all. I had a friend who was in his hands once, and she says he is just like John and my brother, only more so!

Besides, it is such an undertaking to go so far.

I don't feel as if it was worth while to turn my hand over for anything, and I'm getting dreadfully fretful and querulous.

I cry at nothing, and cry most of the time.

Of course I don't when John is here, or anybody else, but when I am alone.

And I am alone a good deal just now. John is kept in town very often by serious cases, and Jennie is good and lets me alone when I want her to.

So I walk a little in the garden or down that lovely lane, sit on the porch under the roses, and lie down up here a good deal.

I'm getting really fond of the room in spite of the wall-paper. Perhaps *because* of the wall-paper.

It dwells in my mind so!

I lie here on this great immovable bed—it is nailed down, I believe—and follow that pattern about by the hour. It is as good as gymnastics, I assure you. I start, we'll say, at the bottom, down in the corner over there where it has not been touched, and I determine for the thousandth time that I *will* follow that pointless pattern to some sort of a conclusion.

I know a little of the principle of design, and I know this thing was not arranged on any laws of radiation, or alternation, or repetition, or symmetry, or anything else that I ever heard of.

It is repeated, of course, by the breadths, but not otherwise.

Looked at in one way each breadth stands alone, the bloated curves and flourishes—a kind of "debased Romanesque"[5] with *delirium tremens*—go waddling up and down in isolated columns of fatuity.

But, on the other hand, they connect diagonally, and the sprawling outlines run off in great slanting waves of optic horror, like a lot of wallowing seaweeds in full chase.

---

4. Silas Weir Mitchell (1829–1914), American physician, novelist, and specialist in nerve disorders, popularized the "rest cure" in the management of hysteria, nervous breakdowns, and related disorders. A friend of W. D. Howells, he was the model for the nerve specialist in Howells's *The Shadow of a Dream* (1890).
5. The style is here associated with ornamental complexity and repeated motifs and figures.

The whole thing goes horizontally, too, at least it seems so, and I exhaust myself in trying to distinguish the order of its going in that direction.

They have used a horizontal breadth for a frieze,[6] and that adds wonderfully to the confusion.

There is one end of the room where it is almost intact, and there, when the crosslights fade and low sun shines directly upon it, I can almost fancy radiation after all—the interminable grotesques seem to form around a common centre and rush off in headlong plunges of equal distraction.

It makes me tired to follow it. I will take a nap I guess.

• • • • • •

I don't know why I should write this.

I don't want to.

I don't feel able.

And I know John would think it absurd. But I *must* say what I feel and think in some way—it is such a relief!

But the effort is getting to be greater than the relief.

Half the time now I am awfully lazy, and lie down ever so much.

John says I mustn't lose my strength, and has me take cod liver oil and lots of tonics and things, to say nothing of ale and wine and rare meat.

Dear John! He loves me very dearly, and hates to have me sick. I tried to have a real earnest reasonable talk with him the other day, and tell him how I wish he would let me go and make a visit to Cousin Henry and Julia.

But he said I wasn't able to go, nor able to stand it after I got there; and I did not make out a very good case for myself, for I was crying before I had finished.

It is getting to be a great effort for me to think straight. Just this nervous weakness I suppose.

And dear John gathered me up in his arms, and just carried me upstairs and laid me on the bed, and sat by me and read to me till it tired my head.

He said I was his darling and his comfort and all he had, and that I must take care of myself for his sake, and keep well.

He says no one but myself can help me out of it, that I must use my will and self-control and not let any silly fancies run away with me.

There's one comfort, the baby is well and happy, and does not have to occupy this nursery with the horrid wall-paper.

If we had not used it, that blessed child would have! What a fortunate escape! Why, I wouldn't have a child of mine, an impressionable little thing, live in such a room for worlds.

I never thought of it before, but it is lucky that John kept me here after all, I can stand it so much easier than a baby, you see.

Of course I never mention it to them any more—I am too wise—but I keep watch of it all the same.

There are things in that paper that nobody knows but me, or ever will.

Behind that outside pattern the dim shapes get clearer every day.

It is always the same shape, only very numerous.

And it is like a woman stooping down and creeping about behind that pat-

---

6. An ornamental border at the top of the wall.

tern. I don't like it a bit. I wonder—I begin to think—I wish John would take me away from here!

• • • • •

It is so hard to talk with John about my case, because he is so wise, and because he loves me so.

But I tried it last night.

It was moonlight. The moon shines in all around just as the sun does.

I hate to see it sometimes, it creeps so slowly, and always comes in by one window or another.

John was asleep and I hated to waken him, so I kept still and watched the moonlight on that undulating wall-paper till I felt creepy.

The faint figure behind seemed to shake the pattern, just as if she wanted to get out.

I got up softly and went to feel and see if the paper *did* move, and when I came back John was awake.

"What is it, little girl?" he said. "Don't go walking about like that—you'll get cold."

I thought it was a good time to talk, so I told him that I really was not gaining here, and that I wished he would take me away.

"Why, darling!" said he, "our lease will be up in three weeks, and I can't see how to leave before.

"The repairs are not done at home, and I cannot possibly leave town just now. Of course if you were in any danger, I could and would, but you really are better, dear, whether you can see it or not. I am a doctor, dear, and I know. You are gaining flesh and color, your appetite is better, I feel really much easier about you."

"I don't weigh a bit more," said I, "nor as much; and my appetite may be better in the evening when you are here, but it is worse in the morning when you are away!"

"Bless her little heart!" said he with a big hug, "she shall be as sick as she pleases! But now let's improve the shining hours[7] by going to sleep, and talk about it in the morning!"

"And you won't go away?" I asked gloomily.

"Why, how can I, dear? It is only three weeks more and then we will take a nice little trip of a few days while Jennie is getting the house ready. Really, dear, you are better!"

"Better in body perhaps—" I began, and stopped short, for he sat up straight and looked at me with such a stern, reproachful look that I could not say another word.

"My darling," said he, "I beg of you, for my sake and for our child's sake, as well as for your own, that you will never for one instant let that idea enter your mind! There is nothing so dangerous, so fascinating, to a temperament like yours. It is a false and foolish fancy. Can you not trust me as a physician when I tell you so?"

---

7. In his poem "Against Idleness and Mischief," Issac Watts (1674–1748) writes:

> How doth the little busy bee
> Improve each shining hour,
> And gather honey all the day
> From every opening flower!

These lines are parodied in Lewis Carroll's *Alice's Adventures in Wonderland* (1865), when Alice eats a cake that makes her grow larger—in her transformation, she finds she has forgotten, or scrambled her knowledge of poems, history, mathematics, and other information.

So of course I said no more on that score, and we went to sleep before long. He thought I was asleep first, but I wasn't, and lay there for hours trying to decide whether that front pattern and the back pattern really did move together or separately.

• • • • • •

On a pattern like this, by daylight, there is a lack of sequence, a defiance of law, that is a constant irritant to a normal mind.

The color is hideous enough, and unreliable enough, and infuriating enough, but the pattern is torturing.

You think you have mastered it, but just as you get well underway in following, it turns a back-somersault and there you are. It slaps you in the face, knocks you down, and tramples upon you. It is like a bad dream.

The outside pattern is a florid arabesque, reminding one of a fungus. If you can imagine a toadstool in joints, an interminable string of toadstools, budding and sprouting in endless convolutions—why, that is something like it.

That is, sometimes!

There is one marked peculiarity about this paper, a thing nobody seems to notice but myself, and that is that it changes as the light changes.

When the sun shoots in through the east window—I always watch for that first long, straight ray—it changes so quickly that I never can quite believe it.

That is why I watch it always.

By moonlight—the moon shines in all night when there is a moon—I wouldn't know it was the same paper.

At night in any kind of light, in twilight, candlelight, lamplight, and worst of all by moonlight, it becomes bars! The outside pattern, I mean, and the woman behind it is as plain as can be.

I didn't realize for a long time what the thing was that showed behind, that dim sub-pattern, but now I am quite sure it is a woman.

By daylight she is subdued, quiet. I fancy it is the pattern that keeps her so still. It is so puzzling. It keeps me quiet by the hour.

I lie down ever so much now. John says it is good for me, and to sleep all I can.

Indeed he started the habit by making me lie down for an hour after each meal.

It is a very bad habit, I am convinced, for you see I don't sleep.

And that cultivates deceit, for I don't tell them I'm awake—O no!

The fact is I am getting a little afraid of John.

He seems very queer sometimes, and even Jennie has an inexplicable look.

It strikes me occasionally, just as a scientific hypothesis, that perhaps it is the paper!

I have watched John when he did not know I was looking, and come into the room suddenly on the most innocent excuses, and I've caught him several times *looking at the paper!* And Jennie too. I caught Jennie with her hand on it once.

She didn't know I was in the room, and when I asked her in a quiet, a very quiet voice, with the most restrained manner possible, what she was doing with the paper—she turned around as if she had been caught stealing, and looked quite angry—asked me why I should frighten her so!

Then she said that the paper stained everything it touched, that she had found yellow smooches on all my clothes and John's, and she wished we would be more careful!

Did not that sound innocent? But I know she was studying that pattern, and I am determined that nobody shall find it out but myself!

• • • • • •

Life is very much more exciting now than it used to be. You see I have something more to expect, to look forward to, to watch. I really do eat better, and am more quiet than I was.

John is so pleased to see me improve! He laughed a little the other day, and said I seemed to be flourishing in spite of my wall-paper.

I turned it off with a laugh. I had no intention of telling him it was *because* of the wall-paper—he would make fun of me. He might even want to take me away.

I don't want to leave now until I have found it out. There is a week more, and I think that will be enough.

• • • • • •

I'm feeling ever so much better! I don't sleep much at night, for it is so interesting to watch developments; but I sleep a good deal in the daytime.

In the daytime it is tiresome and perplexing.

There are always new shoots on the fungus, and new shades of yellow all over it. I cannot keep count of them, though I have tried conscientiously.

It is the strangest yellow, that wall-paper! It makes me think of all the yellow things I ever saw—not beautiful ones like buttercups, but old foul, bad yellow things.

But there is something else about that paper—the smell! I noticed it the moment we came into the room, but with so much air and sun it was not bad. Now we have had a week of fog and rain, and whether the windows are open or not, the smell is here.

It creeps all over the house.

I find it hovering in the dining-room, skulking in the parlor, hiding in the hall, lying in wait for me on the stairs.

It gets into my hair.

Even when I go to ride, if I turn my head suddenly and surprise it—there is that smell!

Such a peculiar odor, too! I have spent hours in trying to analyze it, to find what it smelled like.

It is not bad—at first—and very gentle, but quite the subtlest, most enduring odor I ever met.

In this damp weather it is awful, I wake up in the night and find it hanging over me.

It used to disturb me at first. I thought seriously of burning the house—to reach the smell.

But now I am used to it. The only thing I can think of that it is like is the *color* of the paper! A yellow smell.

There is a very funny mark on this wall, low down, near the mopboard. A streak that runs round the room. It goes behind every piece of furniture, except the bed, a long, straight, even *smooch*, as if it had been rubbed over and over.

I wonder how it was done and who did it, and what they did it for. Round and round and round—round and round and round—it makes me dizzy!

. . . . . .

I really have discovered something at last.

Through watching so much at night, when it changes so, I have finally found out.

The front pattern *does* move—and no wonder! The woman behind shakes it!

Sometimes I think there are a great many women behind, and sometimes only one, and she crawls around fast, and her crawling shakes it all over.

Then in the very bright spots she keeps still, and in the very shady spots she just takes hold of the bars and shakes them hard.

And she is all the time trying to climb through. But nobody could climb through that pattern—it strangles so; I think that is why it has so many heads.

They get through, and then the pattern strangles them off and turns them upside down, and makes their eyes white!

If those heads were covered or taken off it would not be half so bad.

. . . . . .

I think that woman gets out in the daytime!

And I'll tell you why—privately—I've seen her!

I can see her out of every one of my windows!

It is the same woman, I know, for she is always creeping, and most women do not creep by daylight.

I see her in that long shaded lane, creeping up and down. I see her in those dark grape arbors, creeping all around the garden.

I see her on that long road under the trees, creeping along, and when a carriage comes she hides under the blackberry vines.

I don't blame her a bit. It must be very humiliating to be caught creeping by daylight!

I always lock the door when I creep by daylight. I can't do it at night, for I know John would suspect something at once.

And John is so queer now, that I don't want to irritate him. I wish he would take another room! Besides, I don't want anybody to get that woman out at night but myself.

I often wonder if I could see her out of all the windows at once.

But, turn as fast as I can, I can only see out of one at one time.

And though I always see her, she *may* be able to creep faster than I can turn!

I have watched her sometimes away off in the open country, creeping as fast as a cloud shadow in a high wind.

. . . . . .

If only that top pattern could be gotten off from the under one! I mean to try it, little by little.

I have found out another funny thing, but I shan't tell it this time! It does not do to trust people too much.

There are only two more days to get this paper off, and I believe John is beginning to notice. I don't like the look in his eyes.

And I heard him ask Jennie a lot of professional questions about me. She had a very good report to give.

She said I slept a good deal in the daytime.

John knows I don't sleep very well at night, for all I'm so quiet!

He asked me all sorts of questions, too, and pretended to be very loving and kind.

As if I couldn't see through him!

Still, I don't wonder he acts so, sleeping under this paper for three months.

It only interests me, but I feel sure John and Jennie are secretly affected by it.

• • • • •

Hurrah! This is the last day, but it is enough. John had to stay in town over night, and won't be out until this evening.

Jennie wanted to sleep with me—the sly thing!—but I told her I should undoubtedly rest better for a night all alone.

That was clever, for really I wasn't alone a bit! As soon as it was moonlight and that poor thing began to crawl and shake the pattern, I got up and ran to help her.

I pulled and she shook, I shook and she pulled, and before morning we had peeled off yards of that paper.

A strip about as high as my head and half around the room.

And then when the sun came and that awful pattern began to laugh at me, I declared I would finish it to-day!

We go away to-morrow, and they are moving all my furniture down again to leave things as they were before.

Jennie looked at the wall in amazement, but I told her merrily that I did it out of pure spite at the vicious thing.

She laughed and said she wouldn't mind doing it herself, but I must not get tired.

How she betrayed herself that time!

But I am here, and no person touches this paper but me—not *alive!*

She tried to get me out of the room—it was too patent! But I said it was so quiet and empty and clean now that I believed I would lie down again and sleep all I could; and not to wake me even for dinner—I would call when I woke.

So now she is gone, and the servants are gone, and the things are gone, and there is nothing left but that great bedstead nailed down, with the canvas mattress we found on it.

We shall sleep downstairs to-night, and take the boat home to-morrow.

I quite enjoy the room, now it is bare again.

How those children did tear about here!

This bedstead is fairly gnawed!

But I must get to work.

I have locked the door and thrown the key down into the front path.

I don't want to go out, and I don't want to have anybody come in, till John comes.

I want to astonish him.

I've got a rope up here that even Jennie did not find. If that woman does get out, and tries to get away, I can tie her!

But I forgot I could not reach far without anything to stand on!

This bed will *not* move!

I tried to lift and push it until I was lame, and then I got so angry I bit off a little piece at one corner—but it hurt my teeth.

Then I peeled off all the paper I could reach standing on the floor. It sticks horribly and the pattern just enjoys it! All those strangled heads and bulbous eyes and waddling fungus growths just shriek with derision!

I am getting angry enough to do something desperate. To jump out of the window would be admirable exercise, but the bars are too strong even to try.

Besides, I wouldn't do it. Of course not. I know well enough that a step like that is improper and might be misconstrued.

I don't like to *look* out of the windows even—there are so many of those creeping women, and they creep so fast.

I wonder if they all come out of that wall-paper as I did?

But I am securely fastened now by my well-hidden rope—you don't get *me* out in the road there!

I suppose I shall have to get back behind the pattern when it comes night, and that is hard!

It is so pleasant to be out in this great room and creep around as I please!

I don't want to go outside. I won't, even if Jennie asks me to.

For outside you have to creep on the ground, and everything is green instead of yellow.

But here I can creep smoothly on the floor, and my shoulder just fits in that long smooch around the wall, so I cannot lose my way.

Why, there's John at the door!

It is no use, young man, you can't open it!

How he does call and pound!

Now he's crying for an axe.

It would be a shame to break down that beautiful door!

"John, dear!" said I in the gentlest voice, "the key is down by the front steps, under a plantain leaf!"

That silenced him for a few moments.

Then he said—very quietly indeed—"Open the door, my darling!"

"I can't," said I. "The key is down by the front door under a plantain leaf!"

And then I said it again, several times, very gently and slowly, and said it so often that he had to go and see, and he got it of course, and came in. He stopped short by the door.

"What is the matter?" he cried. "For God's sake, what are you doing!"

I kept on creeping just the same, but I looked at him over my shoulder.

"I've got out at last," said I, "in spite of you and Jane! And I've pulled off most of the paper, so you can't put me back!"

Now why should that man have fainted? But he did, and right across my path by the wall, so that I had to creep over him every time!

1892

## Why I Wrote "The Yellow Wall-paper"?[1]

Many and many a reader has asked that. When the story first came out, in the *New England Magazine* about 1891,[2] a Boston physician made protest in *The Transcript.* Such a story ought not to be written, he said; it was enough to drive anyone mad to read it.

Another physician, in Kansas I think, wrote to say that it was the best description of incipient insanity he had ever seen, and—begging my pardon—had I been there?

Now the story of the story is this:

For many years I suffered from a severe and continuous nervous breakdown tending to melancholia—and beyond. During about the third year of this trouble I went, in devout faith and some faint stir of hope, to a noted specialist[3] in nervous diseases, the best known in the country. This wise man put me to bed and applied the rest cure, to which a still good physique responded so promptly that he concluded there was nothing much the matter with me, and sent me home with solemn advice to "live as domestic a life as far as possible," to "have but two hours' intellectual life a day," and "never to touch pen, brush or pencil again as long as I lived." This was in 1887.

I went home and obeyed those directions for some three months, and came so near the border line of utter mental ruin that I could see over.

Then, using the remnants of intelligence that remained, and helped by a wise friend,[4] I cast the noted specialist's advice to the winds and went to work again—work, the normal life of every human being; work, in which is joy and growth and service, without which one is a pauper and a parasite; ultimately recovering some measure of power.

Being naturally moved to rejoicing by this narrow escape, I wrote "The Yellow Wall-paper," with its embellishments and additions to carry out the ideal (I never had hallucinations or objections to my mural decorations) and sent a copy to the physician who so nearly drove me mad. He never acknowledged it.

The little book is valued by alienists[5] and as a good specimen of one kind of literature. It has to my knowledge saved one woman from a similar fate—so terrifying her family that they let her out into normal activity and she recovered.

But the best result is this. Many years later I was told that the great specialist had admitted to friends of his that he had altered his treatment of neurasthenia since reading "The Yellow Wall-paper."

It was not intended to drive people crazy, but to save people from being driven crazy, and it worked.

1913

---

1. First published in the *Forerunner* (October 1913), the source of the text printed here.
2. The correct date is January 1892.
3. Silas Weir Mitchell (1829–1914), a specialist in nerve disorders (and a novelist) who popularized the "rest cure" for women. See n. 4, p. 812.

4. This is almost certainly the writer Grace Channing (1862–1937). Channing and Gilman had been friends since they were teenagers; in 1894, after Gilman and Charles Stetson were divorced, Channing and Stetson married.
5. Those who treat diseases of the mind.

# To the Indifferent Women[1]

### A Sestina

You who are happy in a thousand homes,
Or overworked therein, to a dumb peace;
Whose souls are wholly centered in the life
Of that small group you personally love—
Who told you that you need not know or care          5
About the sin and sorrow of the world?

Do you believe the sorrow of the world
Does not concern you in your little homes?
That you are licensed to avoid the care
And toil for human progress, human peace,          10
And the enlargement of our power of love
Until it covers every field of life?

The one first duty of all human life
Is to promote the progress of the world
In righteousness, in wisdom, truth and love;          15
And you ignore it, hidden in your homes,
Content to keep them in uncertain peace,
Content to leave all else without your care.

Yet you are mothers! And a mother's care
Is the first step towards friendly human life,          20
Life where all nations in untroubled peace
Unite to raise the standard of the world
And make the happiness we seek in homes
Spread everywhere in strong and fruitful love.

You are content to keep that mighty love          25
In its first steps forever; the crude care
Of animals for mate and young and homes,
Instead of pouring it abroad in life,
Its mighty current feeding all the world
Till every human child shall grow in peace.          30

You cannot keep your small domestic peace,
Your little pool of undeveloped love,
While the neglected, starved, unmothered world
Struggles and fights for lack of mother's care,
And its tempestuous, bitter, broken life          35
Beats in upon you in your selfish homes.

We all may have our homes in joy and peace
When woman's life, in its rich power of love
Is joined with man's to care for all the world.

1911

---

1. First published in *Woman's Journal* (February 1904); rpt. in *Suffrage Songs and Verses* by Charlotte Perkins Gilman (1911), from which this text is taken.

## She Walketh Veiled and Sleeping[1]

She walketh veiled and sleeping,
For she knoweth not her power;
She obeyeth but the pleading
Of her heart, and the high leading
Of her soul, unto this hour.                          5
Slow advancing, halting, creeping,
Comes the Woman to the hour!—
She walketh veiled and sleeping,
For she knoweth not her power.

1911

## Turned[1]

In her soft-carpeted, thick-curtained, richly furnished chamber, Mrs. Marroner lay sobbing on the wide, soft bed.

She sobbed bitterly, chokingly, despairingly; her shoulders heaved and shook convulsively; her hands were tight-clenched; she had forgotten her elaborate dress, the more elaborate bedcover; forgotten her dignity, her self-control, her pride. In her mind was an overwhelming, unbelievable horror, an immeasurable loss, a turbulent, struggling mass of emotion.

In her reserved, superior, Bostonbred life she had never dreamed that it would be possible for her to feel so many things at once, and with such trampling intensity.

She tried to cool her feelings into thoughts; to stiffen them into words; to control herself—and could not. It brought vaguely to her mind an awful moment in the breakers at York Beach, one summer in girlhood, when she had been swimming under water and could not find the top.

In her uncarpeted, thin-curtained, poorly furnished chamber on the top floor, Gerta Petersen lay sobbing on the narrow, hard bed.

She was of larger frame than her mistress, grandly built and strong; but all her proud young womanhood was prostrate now, convulsed with agony dissolved in tears. She did not try to control herself. She wept for two.

If Mrs. Marroner suffered more from the wreck and ruin of a longer love— perhaps a deeper one; if her tastes were finer, her ideals loftier; if she bore the pangs of bitter jealousy and outraged pride, Gerta had personal shame to meet, a hopeless future, and a looming present which filled her with unreasoning terror.

She had come like a meek young goddess into that perfectly ordered house,

1. First appeared in *Suffrage Songs and Verses* by Charlotte Perkins Gilman (1911), from which this text is taken.

1. "Turned" first appeared in the September 1911 issue of *The Forerunner*.

strong, beautiful, full of good will and eager obedience, but ignorant and childish—a girl of eighteen.

Mr. Marroner had frankly admired her, and so had his wife. They discussed her visible perfections and as visible limitations with that perfect confidence which they had so long enjoyed. Mrs. Marroner was not a jealous woman. She had never been jealous in her life—till now.

Gerta had stayed and learned their ways. They had both been fond of her. Even the cook was fond of her. She was what is called "willing," was unusually teachable and plastic; and Mrs. Marroner, with her early habits of giving instruction, tried to educate her somewhat.

"I never saw anyone so docile," Mrs. Marroner had often commented. "It is perfection in a servant, but almost a defect in character. She is so helpless and confiding."

She was precisely that: a tall, rosy-cheeked baby; rich womanhood without, helpless infancy within. Her braided wealth of dead-gold hair, her grave blue eyes, her mighty shoulders and long, firmly moulded limbs seemed those of a primal earth spirit; but she was only an ignorant child, with a child's weakness.

When Mr. Marroner had to go abroad for his firm, unwillingly, hating to leave his wife, he had told her he felt quite safe to leave her in Gerta's hands—she would take care of her.

"Be good to your mistress, Gerta," he told the girl that last morning at breakfast. "I leave her to you to take care of. I shall be back in a month at latest."

Then he turned, smiling, to his wife. "And you must take care of Gerta, too," he said. "I expect you'll have her ready for college when I get back."

This was seven months ago. Business had delayed him from week to week, from month to month. He wrote to his wife, long, loving, frequent letters, deeply regretting the delay, explaining how necessary, how profitable it was, congratulating her on the wide resources she had, her well-filled, well-balanced mind, her many interests.

"If I should be eliminated from your scheme of things, by any of those 'acts of God' mentioned on the tickets, I do not feel that you would be an utter wreck," he said. "That is very comforting to me. Your life is so rich and wide that no one loss, even a great one, would wholly cripple you. But nothing of the sort is likely to happen, and I shall be home again in three weeks—if this thing gets settled. And you will be looking so lovely, with that eager light in your eyes and the changing flush I know so well—and love so well! My dear wife! We shall have to have a new honeymoon—other moons come every month, why shouldn't the mellifluous kind?"

He often asked after "little Gerta," sometimes enclosed a picture postcard to her, joked his wife about her laborious efforts to educate "the child," was so loving and merry and wise—

All this was racing through Mrs. Marroner's mind as she lay there with the broad, hemstitched border of fine linen sheeting crushed and twisted in one hand, and the other holding a sodden handkerchief.

She had tried to teach Gerta, and had grown to love the patient, sweet-natured child, in spite of her dullness. At work with her hands, she was clever, if not quick, and could keep small accounts from week to week. But to the woman who held a Ph.D., who had been on the faculty of a college, it was like baby-tending.

Perhaps having no babies of her own made her love the big child the more, though the years between them were but fifteen.

To the girl she seemed quite old, of course; and her young heart was full of grateful affection for the patient care which made her feel so much at home in this new land.

And then she had noticed a shadow on the girl's bright face. She looked nervous, anxious, worried. When the bell rang, she seemed startled, and would rush hurriedly to the door. Her peals of frank laughter no longer rose from the area gate as she stood talking with the always admiring tradesmen.

Mrs. Marroner had labored long to teach her more reserve with men, and flattered herself that her words were at last effective. She suspected the girl of homesickness, which was denied. She suspected her of illness, which was denied also. At last she suspected her of something which could not be denied.

For a long time she refused to believe it, waiting. Then she had to believe it, but schooled herself to patience and understanding. "The poor child," she said. "She is here without a mother—she is so foolish and yielding—I must not be too stern with her." And she tried to win the girl's confidence with wise, kind words.

But Gerta had literally thrown herself at her feet and begged her with streaming tears not to turn her away. She would admit nothing, explain nothing, but frantically promised to work for Mrs. Marroner as long as she lived— if only she would keep her.

Revolving the problem carefully in her mind, Mrs. Marroner thought she would keep her, at least for the present. She tried to repress her sense of ingratitude in one she had so sincerely tried to help, and the cold, contemptuous anger she had always felt for such weakness.

"The thing to do now," she said to herself, "is to see her through this safely. The child's life should not be hurt any more than is unavoidable. I will ask Dr. Bleet about it—what a comfort a woman doctor is! I'll stand by the poor, foolish thing till it's over, and then get her back to Sweden somehow with her baby. How they do come where they are not wanted—and don't come where they are wanted!" And Mrs. Marroner, sitting alone in the quiet, spacious beauty of the house, almost envied Gerta.

Then came the deluge.

She had sent the girl out for needed air toward dark. The late mail came; she took it in herself. One letter for her—her husband's letter. She knew the postmark, the stamp, the kind of typewriting. She impulsively kissed it in the dim hall. No one would suspect Mrs. Marroner of kissing her husband's letters—but she did, often.

She looked over the others. One was for Gerta, and not from Sweden. It looked precisely like her own. This struck her as a little odd, but Mr. Marroner had several times sent messages and cards to the girl. She laid the letter on the hall table and took hers to her room.

"My poor child," it began. What letter of hers had been sad enough to warrant that?

"I am deeply concerned at the news you send." What news to so concern him had she written? "You must bear it bravely, little girl. I shall be home soon, and will take care of you, of course. I hope there is not immediate anxiety—you do not say. Here is money, in case you need it. I expect to get home in a month at latest. If you have to go, be sure to leave your address at my office. Cheer up—be brave—I will take care of you."

The letter was typewritten, which was not unusual. It was unsigned, which was unusual. It enclosed an American bill—fifty dollars. It did not seem in the least like any letter she had ever had from her husband, or any letter she could imagine him writing. But a strange, cold feeling was creeping over her, like a flood rising around a house.

She utterly refused to admit the ideas which began to bob and push about outside her mind, and to force themselves in. Yet under the pressure of these repudiated thoughts she went downstairs and brought up the other letter— the letter to Gerta. She laid them side by side on a smooth dark space on the table; marched to the piano and played, with stern precision, refusing to think, till the girl came back. When she came in, Mrs. Marroner rose quietly and came to the table. "Here is a letter for you," she said.

The girl stepped forward eagerly, saw the two lying together there, hesitated, and looked at her mistress.

"Take yours, Gerta. Open it, please."

The girl turned frightened eyes upon her.

"I want you to read it, here," said Mrs. Marroner.

"Oh, ma'am—No! Please don't make me!"

"Why not?"

There seemed to be no reason at hand, and Gerta flushed more deeply and opened her letter. It was long; it was evidently puzzling to her; it began "My dear wife." She read it slowly.

"Are you sure it is your letter?" asked Mrs. Marroner. "Is not this one yours? Is not that one—mine?"

She held out the other letter to her.

"It is a mistake," Mrs. Marroner went on, with a hard quietness. She had lost her social bearings somehow, lost her usual keen sense of the proper thing to do. This was not life; this was a nightmare.

"Do you not see? Your letter was put in my envelope and my letter was put in your envelope. Now we understand it."

But poor Gerta had no antechamber to her mind; no trained forces to preserve order while agony entered. The thing swept over her, resistless, overwhelming. She cowered before the outraged wrath she expected; and from some hidden cavern that wrath arose and swept over her in pale flame.

"Go and pack your trunk," said Mrs. Marroner. "You will leave my house to-night. Here is your money."

She laid down the fifty-dollar bill. She put with it a month's wages. She had no shadow of pity for those anguished eyes, those tears which she heard drop on the floor.

"Go to your room and pack," said Mrs. Marroner. And Gerta, always obedient, went.

Then Mrs. Marroner went to hers, and spent a time she never counted, lying on her face on the bed.

But the training of the twenty-eight years which had elapsed before her marriage; the life at college, both as student and teacher; the independent growth which she had made, formed a very different background for grief from that in Gerta's mind.

After a while Mrs. Marroner arose. She administered to herself a hot bath, a cold shower, a vigorous rubbing. "Now I can think," she said.

First she regretted the sentence of instant banishment. She went upstairs to see if it had been carried out. Poor Gerta! The tempest of her agony had worked itself out at last as in a child, and left her sleeping, the pillow wet, the lips still grieving, a big sob shuddering itself off now and then.

Mrs. Marroner stood and watched her, and as she watched she considered the helpless sweetness of the face; the defenseless, unformed character; the docility and habit of obedience which made her so attractive—and so easily a victim. Also she thought of the mighty force which had swept over her; of the great process now working itself out through her; of how pitiful and futile seemed any resistance she might have made.

She softly returned to her own room, made up a little fire, and sat by it, ignoring her feelings now, as she had before ignored her thoughts.

Here were two women and a man. One woman was a wife; loving, trusting, affectionate. One was a servant; loving, trusting, affectionate: a young girl, an exile, a dependent; grateful for any kindness; untrained, uneducated, childish. She ought, of course, to have resisted temptation; but Mrs. Marroner was wise enough to know how difficult temptation is to recognize when it comes in the guise of friendship and from a source one does not suspect.

Gerta might have done better in resisting the grocer's clerk; had, indeed, with Mrs. Marroner's advice, resisted several. But where respect was due, how could she criticize? Where obedience was due, how could she refuse—with ignorance to hold her blinded—until too late?

As the older, wiser woman forced herself to understand and extenuate the girl's misdeed and foresee her ruined future, a new feeling rose in her heart, strong, clear, and overmastering; a sense of measureless condemnation for the man who had done this thing. He knew. He understood. He could fully foresee and measure the consequences of his act. He appreciated to the full the innocence, the ignorance, the grateful affection, the habitual docility, of which he deliberately took advantage.

Mrs. Marroner rose to icy peaks of intellectual apprehension, from which her hours of frantic pain seemed far indeed removed. He had done this thing under the same roof with her—his wife. He had not frankly loved the younger woman, broken with his wife, made a new marriage. That would have been heart-break pure and simple. This was something else.

That letter, that wretched, cold, carefully guarded, unsigned letter: that bill—far safer than a check—these did not speak of affection. Some men can love two women at one time. This was not love.

Mrs. Marroner's sense of pity and outrage for herself, the wife, now spread suddenly into a perception of pity and outrage for the girl. All that splendid, clean young beauty, the hope of a happy life, with marriage and motherhood; honorable independence, even—these were nothing to that man. For his own pleasure he had chosen to rob her of her life's best joys.

He would "take care of her" said the letter? How? In what capacity?

And then, sweeping over both her feelings for herself, the wife, and Gerta, his victim, came a new flood, which literally lifted her to her feet. She rose and walked, her head held high. "This is the sin of man against woman," she said. "The offense is against womanhood. Against motherhood. Against—the child."

She stopped.

The child. His child. That, too, he sacrificed and injured—doomed to degradation.

Mrs. Marroner came of stern New England stock. She was not a Calvinist,[2] hardly even a Unitarian, but the iron of Calvinism was in her soul: of that grim faith which held that most people had to be damned "for the glory of God."

Generations of ancestors who both preached and practiced stood behind her; people whose lives had been sternly moulded to their highest moments of religious conviction. In sweeping bursts of feeling they achieved "conviction," and afterward they lived and died according to that conviction.

When Mr. Marroner reached home, a few weeks later, following his letters too soon to expect an answer to either, he saw no wife upon the pier, though he had cabled; and found the house closed darkly. He let himself in with his latch-key, and stole softly upstairs, to surprise his wife.

No wife was there.

He rang the bell. No servant answered it.

He turned up light after light; searched the house from top to bottom; it was utterly empty. The kitchen wore a clean, bald, unsympathetic aspect. He left it and slowly mounted the stair, completely dazed. The whole house was clean, in perfect order, wholly vacant.

One thing he felt perfectly sure of—she knew.

Yet was he sure? He must not assume too much. She might have been ill. She might have died. He started to his feet. No, they would have cabled him. He sat down again.

For any such change, if she had wanted him to know, she would have written. Perhaps she had, and he, returning so suddenly, had missed the letter. The thought was some comfort. It must be so. He turned to the telephone, and again hesitated. If she had found out—if she had gone—utterly gone, without a word—should he announce it himself to friends and family?

He walked the floor; he searched everywhere for some letter, some word of explanation. Again and again he went to the telephone—and always stopped. He could not bear to ask: "Do you know where my wife is?"

The harmonious, beautiful rooms reminded him in a dumb, helpless way of her; like the remote smile on the face of the dead. He put out the lights; could not bear the darkness; turned them all on again.

It was a long night——

In the morning he went early to the office. In the accumulated mail was no letter from her. No one seemed to know of anything unusual. A friend asked after his wife—"Pretty glad to see you, I guess?" He answered evasively.

About eleven a man came to see him; John Hill, her lawyer. Her cousin, too. Mr. Marroner had never liked him. He liked him less now, for Mr. Hill merely handed him a letter, remarked, "I was requested to deliver this to you personally," and departed, looking like a person who is called on to kill something offensive.

"I have gone. I will care for Gerta. Good-bye. Marion."

---

2. Calvinists were followers of the theology of John Calvin (1509–1564), which stresses the Absolute Sovereignty of God and the inability of humans to affect their chances of salvation through their own behavior; Unitarians deny the idea of the Trinity and tend to see Jesus not as a God but as the highest expression of humanity.

That was all. There was no date, no address, no postmark; nothing but that.

In his anxiety and distress he had fairly forgotten Gerta and all that. Her name aroused in him a sense of rage. She had come between him and his wife. She had taken his wife from him. That was the way he felt.

At first he said nothing, did nothing; lived on alone in his house, taking meals where he chose. When people asked him about his wife he said she was traveling—for her health. He would not have it in the newspapers. Then, as time passed, as no enlightenment came to him, he resolved not to bear it any longer, and employed detectives. They blamed him for not having put them on the track earlier, but set to work, urged to the utmost secrecy.

What to him had been so blank a wall of mystery seemed not to embarrass them in the least. They made careful inquiries as to her "past," found where she had studied, where taught, and on what lines; that she had some little money of her own, that her doctor was Josephine L. Bleet, M.D., and many other bits of information.

As a result of careful and prolonged work, they finally told him that she had resumed teaching under one of her old professors; lived quietly, and apparently kept boarders; giving him town, street, and number, as if it were a matter of no difficulty whatever.

He had returned in early spring. It was autumn before he found her.

A quiet college town in the hills, a broad, shady street, a pleasant house standing in its own lawn, with trees and flowers about it. He had the address in his hand, and the number showed clear on the white gate. He walked up the straight gravel path and rang the bell. An elderly servant opened the door.

"Does Mrs. Marroner live here?"

"No, sir."

"This is number twenty-eight?"

"Yes, sir."

"Who does live here?"

"Miss Wheeling, sir."

Ah! Her maiden name. They had told him, but he had forgotten.

He stepped inside. "I would like to see her," he said.

He was ushered into a still parlor, cool and sweet with the scent of flowers, the flowers she had always loved best. It almost brought tears to his eyes. All their years of happiness rose in his mind again; the exquisite beginnings; the days of eager longing before she was really his; the deep, still beauty of her love.

Surely she would forgive him—she must forgive him. He would humble himself; he would tell her of his honest remorse—his absolute determination to be a different man.

Through the wide doorway there came in to him two women. One like a tall Madonna, bearing a baby in her arms.

Marion, calm, steady, definitely impersonal; nothing but a clear pallor to hint of inner stress.

Gerta, holding the child as a bulwark, with a new intelligence in her face, and her blue, adoring eyes fixed on her friend—not upon him.

He looked from one to the other dumbly.

And the woman who had been his wife asked quietly:

"What have you to say to us?"

1911

# EDITH WHARTON
## 1862–1937

Edith Wharton began to write as a very young woman, published some fifty varied volumes in her lifetime, and left a number of unpublished manuscripts and a voluminous correspondence at her death. *The House of Mirth* (1905), her second novel, was a bestseller; another novel, *The Age of Innocence* (1920), won the Pulitzer Prize; in 1930 she was awarded the gold medal of the National Institute of Arts and Letters, the first woman to be so honored.

Edith Newbold Jones was born in New York City on January 24, 1862, into a patriarchal, monied, cultivated, and rather rigid family that, like others in its small circle, disdained and feared the drastic social, cultural, and economic changes brought on by post–Civil War expansionism and immigration. It is small wonder, then, that her work, like Henry James's, deals with what she described as the tragic psychic and moral effects on its members of a frivolous society under pressure. She was educated by tutors and governesses, much of the time while the family resided in Europe. In 1885 she married the Bostonian Edward Wharton, a social equal thirteen years her senior. Though they lived together (in New York; Newport; Lenox, Massachusetts; and Paris) for twenty-eight years, their marriage was not happy. That Wharton did not seek a divorce until 1913 (on grounds of her husband's adultery) is more a tribute to what her biographer R. W. B. Lewis characterized as her "moral conservatism and her devotion to family ties and the sanctities of tradition" than to personal affection.

The social circle in which Edith Wharton moved was not given to artistic or intellectual pursuits, and any career—especially a career as a writer—was frowned on. A young woman from Wharton's background received little formal schooling. Her purpose in life—to find a marriage partner from her own social class—required constant attendance at balls and large parties from adolescence on, as well as much attention to fashion and etiquette. After marriage she took her place as a leisure-class wife. Wharton rejected these values even as a young girl; she spent as much time as she could in her father's library at home—and in similar libraries of her friends. By the time she was fifteen she had written—in secret—a thirty-thousand-word novella titled *Fast and Loose*; at this time she also wrote a great deal of lyric poetry—with what she later described as a "lamentable facility." When she was sixteen, two of her poems were published, one in the *Atlantic Monthly*. Although her intense interest in literature, ideas, and the arts never abated, she was not to publish again until 1889, when three recently composed poems were sent out to *Scribner's, Harper's,* and the *Century*—and all were accepted. The next year, a sketch of hers was published by *Scribner's.*

It was not until the late 1890s, however, that Wharton, then in her late thirties, fully embraced authorship as a career. The decision was motivated partly by her increasing marital discontent and, perhaps, partly by the fact that she was childless. The first significant product of that commitment was a collection of stories titled *The Greater Inclination* (1899). With the publication in 1905 of *The House of Mirth* Wharton confirmed her unconventional choice to be a writer and immediately found an appreciative public. Although she was later to write about other subjects, she discovered in *The House of Mirth* her central settings, plots, and themes: the old aristocracy of New York in conflict with the nouveau riche, the futile struggle of characters trapped by social forces larger and individuals morally smaller than themselves. Two novels that embody these themes are among those most critically acclaimed. *The House of Mirth* tells the story of the beautiful but hapless Lily Bart, trained to be a decorative upper-class wife but unable to sell herself as merchandise. In *The Custom of the Country* (1913), which Wharton considered her "masterpiece," the ruthless Undine Spragg from Ohio makes her way up the social ladder, stepping on Americans and Europeans alike in her pursuit of money and the power that goes with it.

In 1911 Wharton separated from her husband and took up residence in France, where she spent the rest of her life. Altogether she produced more than eighty short stories and twenty-two novellas and novels, including three very different but distinguished books: *Ethan Frome* (1911), *Summer* (1917), and *The Age of Innocence* (1920). Her autobiography, *A Backward Glance,* was published in 1934. During World War I, Wharton organized relief efforts for the refugees and orphans displaced by the advance of the German Army and was active in many other committees and organizations dealing with the devastation wrought by the war. She also wrote extensively about her visits to the front line, and a collection of these dispatches was published as *Fighting France, from Dunkerque to Belfort* (1915). In recognition of her brave and generous effort on behalf of French citizens and soldiers alike, she was awarded the highest honor given by the French government to foreigners—the Chevalier of the Legion of Honor.

Wharton's early social training persisted throughout her life in the form of a constant sociability. She made and kept numerous friends, especially among the leading male intellectuals of her day. Some of them, Egerton Winthrop, Paul Bourget, and Walter Berry to name three, were important to her as she found her way to her profession as a writer. Others, including Henry James and art critics Bernard Berenson and Kenneth Clark, she met as intellectual equals. Still others, including Jean Cocteau and Sinclair Lewis (who dedicated *Babbitt* to her), became her admirers late in her life. In this capacity for friendships among the most distinguished people of her time, Wharton is like Gertrude Stein and Willa Cather, also among the most important American writers of the early twentieth century. Her reputation continues to grow; along with James she is considered a major contributor to the practice of psychological realism. In view of the inability of her characters, despite their high social status, to control their destinies, Wharton is increasingly included by critics such as Donna M. Campbell among such naturalists as Jack London and Theodore Dreiser. Her scathing analyses of human behavior and (often base) motivation, as well as her social criticism, present struggles for power and survival no less dangerous than and sometimes as deadly as those faced by naturalist characters in the wilderness. In this respect, she also compares interestingly with Kate Chopin.

# The Other Two[1]

## I

Waythorn, on the drawing-room hearth, waited for his wife to come down to dinner.

It was their first night under his own roof, and he was surprised at his thrill of boyish agitation. He was not so old, to be sure—his glass gave him little more than the five-and-thirty years to which his wife confessed—but he had fancied himself already in the temperate zone; yet here he was listening for her step with a tender sense of all it symbolized, with some old trail of verse about the garlanded nuptial doorposts floating through his enjoyment of the pleasant room and the good dinner just beyond it.

They had been hastily recalled from their honeymoon by the illness of Lily Haskett, the child of Mrs. Waythorn's first marriage. The little girl, at Waythorn's desire, had been transferred to his house on the day of her mother's wedding, and the doctor, on their arrival, broke the news that she was ill with typhoid, but declared that all the symptoms were favorable. Lily could show twelve years of unblemished health, and the case promised to be

1. First appeared in *Collier's Weekly* (February 1904).

a light one. The nurse spoke as reassuringly, and after a moment of alarm Mrs. Waythorn had adjusted herself to the situation. She was very fond of Lily—her affection for the child had perhaps been her decisive charm in Waythorn's eyes—but she had the perfectly balanced nerves which her little girl had inherited, and no woman ever wasted less tissue in unproductive worry. Waythorn was therefore quite prepared to see her come in presently, a little late because of a last look at Lily, but as serene and well-appointed as if her good-night kiss had been laid on the brow of health. Her composure was restful to him; it acted as ballast to his somewhat unstable sensibilities. As he pictured her bending over the child's bed he thought how soothing her presence must be in illness: her very step would prognosticate recovery.

His own life had been a gray one, from temperament rather than circumstance, and he had been drawn to her by the unperturbed gaiety which kept her fresh and elastic at an age when most women's activities are growing either slack or febrile. He knew what was said about her; for, popular as she was, there had always been a faint undercurrent of detraction. When she had appeared in New York, nine or ten years earlier, as the pretty Mrs. Haskett whom Gus Varick had unearthed somewhere—was it in Pittsburgh or Utica?—society, while promptly accepting her, had reserved the right to cast a doubt on its own indiscrimination. Inquiry, however, established her undoubted connection with a socially reigning family, and explained her recent divorce as the natural result of a runaway match at seventeen; and as nothing was known of Mr. Haskett it was easy to believe the worst of him.

Alice Haskett's remarriage with Gus Varick was a passport to the set whose recognition she coveted, and for a few years the Varicks were the most popular couple in town. Unfortunately the alliance was brief and stormy, and this time the husband had his champions. Still, even Varick's stanchest supporters admitted that he was not meant for matrimony, and Mrs. Varick's grievances were of a nature to bear the inspection of the New York courts. A New York divorce is in itself a diploma of virtue, and in the semiwidowhood of this second separation Mrs. Varick took on an air of sanctity, and was allowed to confide her wrongs to some of the most scrupulous ears in town. But when it was known that she was to marry Waythorn there was a momentary reaction. Her best friends would have preferred to see her remain in the role of the injured wife, which was as becoming to her as crepe to a rosy complexion. True, a decent time had elapsed, and it was not even suggested that Waythorn had supplanted his predecessor. People shook their heads over him, however, and one grudging friend, to whom he affirmed that he took the step with his eyes open, replied oracularly: "Yes—and with your ears shut."

Waythorn could afford to smile at these innuendoes. In the Wall Street phrase, he had "discounted" them. He knew that society has not yet adapted itself to the consequences of divorce, and that till the adaptation takes place every woman who uses the freedom the law accords her must be her own social justification. Waythorn had an amused confidence in his wife's ability to justify herself. His expectations were fulfilled, and before the wedding took place Alice Varick's group had rallied openly to her support. She took it all imperturbably: she had a way of surmounting obstacles without seeming to be aware of them, and Waythorn looked back with wonder at the trivialities over which he had worn his nerves thin. He had the sense of having found refuge in a richer, warmer nature than his own, and his satisfaction, at the moment, was humorously summed up in the thought that his wife, when she had done all she could for Lily, would not be ashamed to come down and enjoy a good dinner.

The anticipation of such enjoyment was not, however, the sentiment expressed by Mrs. Waythorn's charming face when she presently joined him. Though she had put on her most engaging tea gown she had neglected to assume the smile that went with it, and Waythorn thought he had never seen her look so nearly worried.

"What is it?" he asked. "Is anything wrong with Lily?"

"No; I've just been in and she's still sleeping." Mrs. Waythorn hesitated. "But something tiresome has happened."

He had taken her two hands, and now perceived that he was crushing a paper between them.

"This letter?"

"Yes—Mr. Haskett has written—I mean his lawyer has written."

Waythorn felt himself flush uncomfortably. He dropped his wife's hands. "What about?"

"About seeing Lily. You know the courts—"

"Yes, yes," he interrupted nervously.

Nothing was known about Haskett in New York. He was vaguely supposed to have remained in the outer darkness from which his wife had been rescued, and Waythorn was one of the few who were aware that he had given up his business in Utica and followed her to New York in order to be near his little girl. In the days of his wooing, Waythorn had often met Lily on the doorstep, rosy and smiling, on her way "to see papa."

"I am so sorry," Mrs. Waythorn murmured.

He roused himself. "What does he want?"

"He wants to see her. You know she goes to him once a week."

"Well—he doesn't expect her to go to him now, does he?"

"No—he has heard of her illness; but he expects to come here."

"*Here?*"

Mrs. Waythorn reddened under his gaze. They looked away from each other.

"I'm afraid he has the right. . . . You'll see. . . ." She made a proffer of the letter.

Waythorn moved away with a gesture of refusal. He stood staring about the softly-lighted room, which a moment before had seemed so full of bridal intimacy.

"I'm so sorry," she repeated. "If Lily could have been moved—"

"That's out of the question," he returned impatiently.

"I suppose so."

Her lip was beginning to tremble, and he felt himself a brute.

"He must come, of course," he said. "When is—his day?"

"I'm afraid—tomorrow."

"Very well. Send a note in the morning."

The butler entered to announce dinner.

Waythorn turned to his wife. "Come—you must be tired. It's beastly, but try to forget about it," he said, drawing her hand through his arm.

"You're so good, dear. I'll try," she whispered back.

Her face cleared at once, and as she looked at him across the flowers, between the rosy candleshades, he saw her lips waver back into a smile.

"How pretty everything is!" she sighed luxuriously.

He turned to the butler. "The champagne at once, please. Mrs. Waythorn is tired."

In a moment or two their eyes met above the sparkling glasses. Her own were quite clear and untroubled: he saw that she had obeyed his injunction and forgotten.

## II

Waythorn, the next morning, went downtown earlier than usual. Haskett was not likely to come till the afternoon, but the instinct of flight drove him forth. He meant to stay away all day—he had thoughts of dining at his club. As his door closed behind him he reflected that before he opened it again it would have admitted another man who had as much right to enter it as himself, and the thought filled him with a physical repugnance.

He caught the elevated at the employees' hour, and found himself crushed between two layers of pendulous humanity. At Eighth Street the man facing him wriggled out, and another took his place. Waythorn glanced up and saw that it was Gus Varick. The men were so close together that it was impossible to ignore the smile of recognition on Varick's handsome overblown face. And after all—why not? They had always been on good terms, and Varick had been divorced before Waythorn's attentions to his wife began. The two exchanged a word on the perennial grievance of the congested trains, and when a seat at their side was miraculously left empty the instinct of self-preservation made Waythorn slip into it after Varick.

The latter drew the stout man's breath of relief. "Lord—I was beginning to feel like a pressed flower." He leaned back, looking unconcernedly at Waythorn. "Sorry to hear that Sellers is knocked out again."

"Sellers?" echoed Waythorn, starting at his partner's name.

Varick looked surprised. "You didn't know he was laid up with the gout?"

"No. I've been away—I only got back last night." Waythorn felt himself reddening in anticipation of the other's smile.

"Ah—yes; to be sure. And Sellers' attack came on two days ago. I'm afraid he's pretty bad. Very awkward for me, as it happens, because he was just putting through a rather important thing for me."

"Ah?" Waythorn wondered vaguely since when Varick had been dealing in "important things." Hitherto he had dabbled only in the shallow pools of speculation, with which Waythorn's office did not usually concern itself.

It occurred to him that Varick might be talking at random, to relieve the strain of their propinquity. That strain was becoming momentarily more apparent to Waythorn, and when, at Cortlandt Street, he caught sight of an acquaintance and had a sudden vision of the picture he and Varick must present to an initiated eye, he jumped up with a muttered excuse.

"I hope you'll find Sellers better," said Varick civilly, and he stammered back: "If I can be of any use to you—" and let the departing crowd sweep him to the platform.

At his office he heard that Sellers was in fact ill with the gout, and would probably not be able to leave the house for some weeks.

"I'm sorry it should have happened so, Mr. Waythorn," the senior clerk said with affable significance. "Mr. Sellers was very much upset at the idea of giving you such a lot of extra work just now."

"Oh, that's no matter," said Waythorn hastily. He secretly welcomed the pressure of additional business, and was glad to think that, when the day's work was over, he would have to call at his partner's on the way home.

He was late for luncheon, and turned in at the nearest restaurant instead of going to his club. The place was full, and the waiter hurried him to the back of the room to capture the only vacant table. In the cloud of cigar smoke Waythorn did not at once distinguish his neighbors: but presently, looking about him, he saw Varick seated a few feet off. This time, luckily, they were too far apart for conversation, and Varick, who faced another way, had probably not even seen him; but there was an irony in their renewed nearness.

Varick was said to be fond of good living, and as Waythorn sat dispatching his hurried luncheon he looked across half enviously at the other's leisurely degustation of his meal. When Waythorn first saw him he had been helping himself with critical deliberation to a bit of Camembert at the ideal point of liquefaction, and now, the cheese removed, he was just pouring his *café double* from its little two-storied earthen pot. He poured slowly, his ruddy profile bent over the task, and one beringed white hand steadying the lid of the coffeepot; then he stretched his other hand to the decanter of cognac at his elbow, filled a liqueur glass, took a tentative sip, and poured the brandy into his coffee cup.

Waythorn watched him in a kind of fascination. What was he thinking of—only of the flavor of the coffee and the liqueur? Had the morning's meeting left no more trace in his thoughts than on his face? Had his wife so completely passed out of his life that even this odd encounter with her present husband, within a week after her remarriage, was no more than an incident in his day? And as Waythorn mused, another idea struck him: had Haskett ever met Varick as Varick and he had just met? The recollection of Haskett perturbed him, and he rose and left the restaurant, taking a circuitous way out to escape the placid irony of Varick's nod.

It was after seven when Waythorn reached home. He thought the footman who opened the door looked at him oddly.

"How is Miss Lily?" he asked in haste.

"Doing very well, sir. A gentleman—"

"Tell Barlow to put off dinner for half an hour," Waythorn cut him off, hurrying upstairs.

He went straight to his room and dressed without seeing his wife. When he reached the drawing room she was there, fresh and radiant. Lily's day had been good; the doctor was not coming back that evening.

At dinner Waythorn told her of Sellers' illness and of the resulting complications. She listened sympathetically, adjuring him not to let himself be overworked, and asking vague feminine questions about the routine of the office. Then she gave him the chronicle of Lily's day; quoted the nurse and doctor, and told him who had called to inquire. He had never seen her more serene and unruffled. It struck him, with a curious pang, that she was very happy in being with him, so happy that she found a childish pleasure in rehearsing the trivial incidents of her day.

After dinner they went to the library, and the servant put the coffee and liqueurs on a low table before her and left the room. She looked singularly soft and girlish in her rosy-pale dress, against the dark leather of one of his bachelor armchairs. A day earlier the contrast would have charmed him.

He turned away now, choosing a cigar with affected deliberation.

"Did Haskett come?" he asked, with his back to her.

"Oh, yes—he came."

"You didn't see him, of course?"

She hesitated a moment. "I let the nurse see him."

That was all. There was nothing more to ask. He swung round toward her, applying a match to his cigar. Well, the thing was over for a week, at any rate. He would try not to think of it. She looked up at him, a trifle rosier than usual, with a smile in her eyes.

"Ready for your coffee, dear?"

He leaned against the mantelpiece, watching her as she lifted the coffeepot. The lamplight struck a gleam from her bracelets and tipped her soft hair with brightness. How light and slender she was, and how each gesture flowed into the next! She seemed a creature all compact of harmonies. As the thought of Haskett receded, Waythorn felt himself yielding again to the joy of possessorship. They were his, those white hands with their flitting motions, his the light haze of hair, the lips and eyes. . . .

She set down the coffeepot, and reaching for the decanter of cognac, measured off a liqueur glass and poured it into his cup.

Waythorn uttered a sudden exclamation.

"What is the matter?" she said, startled.

"Nothing; only—I don't take cognac in my coffee."

"Oh, how stupid of me," she cried.

Their eyes met, and she blushed a sudden agonized red.

### III

Ten days later, Mr. Sellers, still housebound, asked Waythorn to call on his way downtown.

The senior partner, with his swaddled foot propped up by the fire, greeted his associate with an air of embarrassment.

"I'm sorry, my dear fellow; I've got to ask you to do an awkward thing for me."

Waythorn waited, and the other went on, after a pause apparently given to the arrangement of his phrases: "The fact is, when I was knocked out I had just gone into a rather complicated piece of business for—Gus Varick."

"Well?" said Waythorn, with an attempt to put him at his ease.

"Well—it's this way: Varick came to me the day before my attack. He had evidently had an inside tip from somebody, and had made about a hundred thousand. He came to me for advice, and I suggested his going in with Vanderlyn."

"Oh, the deuce!" Waythorn exclaimed. He saw in a flash what had happened. The investment was an alluring one, but required negotiation. He listened quietly while Sellers put the case before him, and, the statement ended, he said: "You think I ought to see Varick?"

"I'm afraid I can't as yet. The doctor is obdurate. And this thing can't wait. I hate to ask you, but no one else in the office knows the ins and outs of it."

Waythorn stood silent. He did not care a farthing for the success of Varick's venture, but the honor of the office was to be considered, and he could hardly refuse to oblige his partner.

"Very well," he said, "I'll do it."

That afternoon, apprised by telephone, Varick called at the office. Waythorn, waiting in his private room, wondered what the others thought of it. The newspapers, at the time of Mrs. Waythorn's marriage, had acquainted their readers with every detail of her previous matrimonial ventures, and Waythorn could fancy the clerks smiling behind Varick's back as he was ushered in.

Varick bore himself admirably. He was easy without being undignified, and Waythorn was conscious of cutting a much less impressive figure. Varick had no experience of business, and the talk prolonged itself for nearly an hour while Waythorn set forth with scrupulous precision the details of the proposed transaction.

"I'm awfully obliged to you," Varick said as he rose. "The fact is I'm not used to having much money to look after, and I don't want to make an ass of myself—" He smiled, and Waythorn could not help noticing that there was something pleasant about his smile. "It feels uncommonly queer to have enough cash to pay one's bills. I'd have sold my soul for it a few years ago!"

Waythorn winced at the allusion. He had heard it rumored that a lack of funds had been one of the determining causes of the Varick separation, but it did not occur to him that Varick's words were intentional. It seemed more likely that the desire to keep clear of embarrassing topics had fatally drawn him into one. Waythorn did not wish to be outdone in civility.

"We'll do the best we can for you," he said. "I think this is a good thing you're in."

"Oh, I'm sure it's immense. It's awfully good of you—" Varick broke off, embarrassed. "I suppose the thing's settled now—but if—"

"If anything happens before Sellers is about, I'll see you again," said Waythorn quietly. He was glad, in the end, to appear the more self-possessed of the two.

The course of Lily's illness ran smooth, and as the days passed Waythorn grew used to the idea of Haskett's weekly visit. The first time the day came round, he stayed out late, and questioned his wife as to the visit on his return. She replied at once that Haskett had merely seen the nurse downstairs, as the doctor did not wish anyone in the child's sickroom till after the crisis.

The following week Waythorn was again conscious of the recurrence of the day, but had forgotten it by the time he came home to dinner. The crisis of the disease came a few days later, with a rapid decline of fever, and the little girl was pronounced out of danger. In the rejoicing which ensued the thought of Haskett passed out of Waythorn's mind, and one afternoon, letting himself into the house with a latchkey, he went straight to his library without noticing a shabby hat and umbrella in the hall.

In the library he found a small effaced-looking man with a thinnish gray beard sitting on the edge of a chair. The stranger might have been a piano tuner, or one of those mysteriously efficient persons who are summoned in emergencies to adjust some detail of the domestic machinery. He blinked at Waythorn through a pair of gold-rimmed spectacles and said mildly: "Mr. Waythorn, I presume? I am Lily's father."

Waythorn flushed. "Oh—" he stammered uncomfortably. He broke off, disliking to appear rude. Inwardly he was trying to adjust the actual Haskett to the image of him projected by his wife's reminiscences. Waythorn had been allowed to infer that Alice's first husband was a brute.

"I am sorry to intrude," said Haskett, with his over-the-counter politeness.

"Don't mention it," returned Waythorn, collecting himself. "I suppose the nurse has been told?"

"I presume so. I can wait," said Haskett. He had a resigned way of speaking, as though life had worn down his natural powers of resistance.

Waythorn stood on the threshold, nervously pulling off his gloves.

"I'm sorry you've been detained. I will send for the nurse," he said; and as he opened the door he added with an effort: "I'm glad we can give you a good report of Lily." He winced as the *we* slipped out, but Haskett seemed not to notice it.

"Thank you, Mr. Waythorn, It's been an anxious time for me."

"Ah, well, that's past. Soon she'll be able to go to you." Waythorn nodded and passed out.

In his own room he flung himself down with a groan. He hated the womanish sensibility which made him suffer so acutely from the grotesque chances of life. He had known when he married that his wife's former husbands were both living, and that amid the multiplied contacts of modern existence there were a thousand chances to one that he would run against one or the other, yet he found himself as much disturbed by his brief encounter with Haskett as though the law had not obligingly removed all difficulties in the way of their meeting.

Waythorn sprang up and began to pace the room nervously. He had not suffered half as much from his two meetings with Varick. It was Haskett's presence in his own house that made the situation so intolerable. He stood still, hearing steps in the passage.

"This way, please," he heard the nurse say. Haskett was being taken upstairs, then: not a corner of the house but was open to him. Waythorn dropped into another chair, staring vaguely ahead of him. On his dressing table stood a photograph of Alice, taken when he had first known her. She was Alice Varick then—how fine and exquisite he had thought her! Those were Varick's pearls about her neck. At Waythorn's instance they had been returned before her marriage. Had Haskett ever given her any trinkets—and what had become of them, Waythorn wondered? He realized suddenly that he knew very little of Haskett's past or present situation; but from the man's appearance and manner of speech he could reconstruct with curious precision the surroundings of Alice's first marriage. And it startled him to think that she had, in the background of her life, a phase of existence so different from anything with which he had connected her. Varick, whatever his faults, was a gentleman, in the conventional, traditional sense of the term: the sense which at that moment seemed, oddly enough, to have most meaning to Waythorn. He and Varick had the same social habits, spoke the same language, understood the same allusions. But this other man . . . it was grotesquely uppermost in Waythorn's mind that Haskett had worn a made-up tie attached with an elastic. Why should that ridiculous detail symbolize the whole man? Waythorn was exasperated by his own paltriness, but the fact of the tie expanded, forced itself on him, became as it were the key to Alice's past. He could see her, as Mrs. Haskett, sitting in a "front parlor" furnished in plush, with a pianola, and copy of *Ben Hur*[2] on the center table. He could see her going to the theater with Haskett—or perhaps even to a "Church Sociable"—she in a "picture hat" and Haskett in a black frock coat, a little creased, with the made-up tie on an elastic. On the way home they would stop and look at the illuminated shop windows, lingering over the photographs of New York actresses. On Sunday afternoons Haskett would take her for a walk, pushing Lily ahead of them in a white enameled perambulator, and Waythorn had a vision of the people they would stop and talk to. He could fancy how pretty Alice must have looked, in a dress adroitly constructed from the hints of a New York fashion paper, and how she must have looked down on the other women, chafing at her life, and secretly feeling that she belonged in a bigger place.

For the moment his foremost thought was one of wonder at the way in which she had shed the phase of existence which her marriage with Haskett implied. It was as if her whole aspect, every gesture, every inflection, every allusion, were a studied negation of that period of her life. If she had denied being married to Haskett she could hardly have stood more convicted of duplicity than in this obliteration of the self which had been his wife.

Waythorn started up, checking himself in the analysis of her motives. What right had he to create a fantastic effigy of her and then pass judgment on it? She had spoken vaguely of her first marriage as unhappy, had hinted, with becoming reticence, that Haskett had wrought havoc among her young illusions. . . . It was a pity for Waythorn's peace of mind that Haskett's very inoffensiveness shed a new light on the nature of those illusions. A man would rather think that his wife has been brutalized by her first husband than that the process has been reversed.

IV

"Mr. Waythorn, I don't like that French governess of Lily's."

Haskett, subdued and apologetic, stood before Waythorn in the library, revolving his shabby hat in his hand.

Waythorn, surprised in his armchair over the evening paper, stared back perplexedly at his visitor.

"You'll excuse my asking to see you," Haskett continued. "But this is my last visit, and I thought if I could have a word with you it would be a better way than writing to Mrs. Waythorn's lawyer."

Waythorn rose uneasily. He did not like the French governess either; but that was irrelevant.

"I am not so sure of that," he returned stiffly; "but since you wish it I will give your message to—my wife." He always hesitated over the possessive pronoun in addressing Haskett.

The latter sighed. "I don't know as that will help much. She didn't like it when I spoke to her."

Waythorn turned red. "When did you see her?" he asked.

---

2. *Ben Hur: A Tale of Christ* (1880) was a best-selling novel by Lew Wallace (1827–1905).

"Not since the first day I came to see Lily—right after she was taken sick. I remarked to her then that I didn't like the governess."

Waythorn made no answer. He remembered distinctly that, after that first visit, he had asked his wife if she had seen Haskett. She had lied to him then, but she had respected his wishes since; and the incident cast a curious light on her character. He was sure she would not have seen Haskett that first day if she had divined that Waythorn would object, and the fact that she did not divine it was almost as disagreeable to the latter as the discovery that she had lied to him.

"I don't like the woman," Haskett was repeating with mild persistency. "She ain't straight, Mr. Waythorn—she'll teach the child to be underhand. I've noticed a change in Lily—she's too anxious to please—and she don't always tell the truth. She used to be the straightest child, Mr. Waythorn—" He broke off, his voice a little thick. "Not but what I want her to have a stylish education," he ended.

Waythorn was touched. "I'm sorry, Mr. Haskett; but frankly, I don't quite see what I can do."

Haskett hesitated. Then he laid his hat on the table, and advanced to the hearthrug, on which Waythorn was standing. There was nothing aggressive in his manner, but he had the solemnity of a timid man resolved on a decisive measure.

"There's just one thing you can do, Mr. Waythorn," he said. "You can remind Mrs. Waythorn that, by the decree of the courts, I am entitled to have a voice in Lily's bringing-up." He paused, and went on more deprecatingly: "I'm not the kind to talk about enforcing my rights, Mr. Waythorn. I don't know as I think a man is entitled to rights he hasn't known how to hold on to; but this business of the child is different. I've never let go there—and I never mean to."

The scene left Waythorn deeply shaken. Shamefacedly, in indirect ways, he had been finding out about Haskett; and all that he had learned was favorable. The little man, in order to be near his daughter, had sold out his share in a profitable business in Utica, and accepted a modest clerkship in a New York manufacturing house. He boarded in a shabby street and had few acquaintances. His passion for Lily filled his life. Waythorn felt that this exploration of Haskett was like groping about with a dark lantern in his wife's past; but he saw now that there were recesses his lantern had not explored. He had never inquired into the exact circumstances of his wife's first matrimonial rupture. On the surface all had been fair. It was she who had obtained the divorce, and the court had given her the child. But Waythorn knew how many ambiguities such a verdict might cover. The mere fact that Haskett retained a right over his daughter implied an unsuspected compromise. Waythorn was an idealist. He always refused to recognize unpleasant contingencies till he found himself confronted with them, and then he saw them followed by a spectral train of consequences. His next days were thus haunted, and he determined to try to lay the ghosts by conjuring them up in his wife's presence.

When he repeated Haskett's request a flame of anger passed over her face; but she subdued it instantly and spoke with a slight quiver of outraged motherhood.

"It is very ungentlemanly of him," she said.

The word grated on Waythorn. "That is neither here nor there. It's a bare question of rights."

She murmured: "It's not as if he could ever be a help to Lily—"

Waythorn flushed. This was even less to his taste. "The question is," he repeated, "what authority has he over her?"

She looked downward, twisting herself a little in her seat. "I am willing to see him—I thought you objected," she faltered.

In a flash he understood that she knew the extent of Haskett's claims. Perhaps it was not the first time she had resisted them.

"My objecting has nothing to do with it," he said coldly; "if Haskett has a right to be consulted you must consult him."

She burst into tears, and he saw that she expected him to regard her as a victim.

Haskett did not abuse his rights. Waythorn had felt miserably sure that he would not. But the governess was dismissed, and from time to time the little man demanded an interview with Alice. After the first outburst she accepted the situation with her usual adaptability. Haskett had once reminded Waythorn of the piano tuner, and Mrs. Waythorn, after a month or two, appeared to class him with that domestic familiar. Waythorn could not but respect the father's tenacity. At first he had tried to cultivate the suspicion that Haskett might be "up to" something, that he had an object in securing a foothold in the house. But in his heart Waythorn was sure of Haskett's single-mindedness; he even guessed in the latter a mild contempt for such advantages as his relation with the Waythorns might offer. Haskett's sincerity of purpose made him invulnerable, and his successor had to accept him as a lien on the property.

Mr. Sellers was sent to Europe to recover from his gout, and Varick's affairs hung on Waythorn's hands. The negotiations were prolonged and complicated; they necessitated frequent conferences between the two men, and the interests of the firm forbade Waythorn's suggesting that his client should transfer his business to another office.

Varick appeared well in the transaction. In moments of relaxation his coarse streak appeared, and Waythorn dreaded his geniality; but in the office he was concise and clear-headed, with a flattering deference to Waythorn's judgment. Their business relations being so affably established, it would have been absurd for the two men to ignore each other in society. The first time they met in a drawing room, Varick took up their intercourse in the same easy key, and his hostess' grateful glance obliged Waythorn to respond to it. After that they ran across each other frequently, and one evening at a ball Waythorn, wandering through the remoter rooms, came upon Varick seated beside his wife. She colored a little, and faltered in what she was saying; but Varick nodded to Waythorn without rising, and the latter strolled on.

In the carriage, on the way home, he broke out nervously: "I didn't know you spoke to Varick."

Her voice trembled a little. "It's the first time—he happened to be standing near me; I didn't know what to do. It's so awkward, meeting everywhere—and he said you had been very kind about some business."

"That's different," said Waythorn.

She paused a moment. "I'll do just as you wish," she returned pliantly. "I thought it would be less awkward to speak to him when we meet."

Her pliancy was beginning to sicken him. Had she really no will of her own—no theory about her relation to these men? She had accepted Haskett—did she mean to accept Varick? It was "less awkward," as she had said, and her instinct was to evade difficulties or to circumvent them. With sudden vividness Waythorn saw how the instinct had developed. She was "as easy as an old shoe"—a shoe that too many feet had worn. Her elasticity was the result of tension in too many different directions. Alice Haskett—Alice Varick—Alice Waythorn—she had been each in turn, and had left hanging to each name a little of her privacy, a little of her personality, a little of the inmost self where the unknown god abides.

"Yes—it's better to speak to Varick," said Waythorn wearily.

<h2 style="text-align:center">V</h2>

The winter wore on, and society took advantage of the Waythorns' acceptance of Varick. Harassed hostesses were grateful to them for bridging over a social difficulty, and Mrs. Waythorn was held up as a miracle of good taste. Some experimental spirits could not resist the diversion of throwing Varick and his former wife together, and there were those who thought he found a zest in the propinquity. But Mrs. Waythorn's conduct remained irreproachable. She neither avoided Varick nor sought him out. Even Waythorn could not but admit that she had discovered the solution of the newest social problem.

He had married her without giving much thought to that problem. He had fancied that a woman can shed her past like a man. But now he saw that Alice was bound to hers both by the circumstances which forced her into continued relation with it, and by the traces it had left on her nature. With grim irony Waythorn compared himself to a member of a syndicate. He held so many shares in his wife's personality and his predecessors were his partners in the business. If there had been any element of passion in the transaction he would have felt less deteriorated by it. The fact that Alice took her change of husbands like a change of weather reduced the situation to mediocrity. He could have forgiven her for blunders, for excesses; for resisting Haskett, for yielding to Varick; for anything but her acquiescence and her tact. She reminded him of a juggler tossing knives; but the knives were blunt and she knew they would never cut her.

And then, gradually, habit formed a protecting surface for his sensibilities. If he paid for each day's comfort with the small change of his illusions, he grew daily to value the comfort more and set less store upon the coin. He had drifted into a dulling propinquity with Haskett and Varick and he took refuge in the cheap revenge of satirizing the situation. He even began to reckon up the advantages which accrued from it, to ask himself if it were not better to own a third of a wife who knew how to make a man happy than a whole one who had lacked opportunity to acquire the art. For it *was* an art, and made up, like all others, of concessions, eliminations and embellishments; of lights judiciously thrown and shadows skillfully softened. His wife knew exactly how to manage the lights, and he knew exactly to what training she owed her skill. He even tried to trace the source of his obligations, to discriminate between the influences which had combined to produce his domestic happiness: he perceived that Haskett's commonness had made Alice worship good breeding, while Varick's liberal construction of the marriage bond had taught her to value the conjugal virtues; so that he was directly indebted to his predecessors for the devotion which made his life easy if not inspiring.

From this phase he passed into that of complete acceptance. He ceased to satirize himself because time dulled the irony of the situation and the joke lost its humor with its sting. Even the sight of Haskett's hat on the hall table had ceased to touch the springs of epigram. The hat was often seen there now, for it had been decided that it was better for Lily's father to visit her than for the little girl to go to his boardinghouse. Waythorn, having acquiesced in this arrangement, had been surprised to find how little difference it made. Haskett was never obtrusive, and the few visitors who met him on the stairs were unaware of his identity. Waythorn did not know how often he saw Alice, but with himself Haskett was seldom in contact.

One afternoon, however, he learned on entering that Lily's father was waiting to see him. In the library he found Haskett occupying a chair in his usual provisional way. Waythorn always felt grateful to him for not leaning back.

"I hope you'll excuse me, Mr. Waythorn," he said rising. "I wanted to see Mrs. Waythorn about Lily, and your man asked me to wait here till she came in."

"Of course," said Waythorn, remembering that a sudden leak had that morning given over the drawing room to the plumbers.

He opened his cigar case and held it out to his visitor, and Haskett's acceptance seemed to mark a fresh stage in their intercourse. The spring evening was chilly, and Waythorn invited his guest to draw up his chair to the fire. He meant to find an excuse to leave Haskett in a moment; but he was tired and cold, and after all the little man no longer jarred on him.

The two were enclosed in the intimacy of their blended cigar smoke when the door opened and Varick walked into the room. Waythorn rose abruptly. It was the first time that Varick had come to the house, and the surprise of seeing him, combined with the singular inopportuneness of his arrival, gave a new edge to Waythorn's blunted sensibilities. He stared at his visitor without speaking.

Varick seemed too preoccupied to notice his host's embarrassment.

"My dear fellow," he exclaimed in his most expansive tone, "I must apologize for tumbling in on you in this way, but I was too late to catch you downtown, and so I thought—"

He stopped short, catching sight of Haskett, and his sanguine color deepened to a flush which spread vividly under his scant blond hair. But in a moment he recovered himself and nodded slightly. Haskett returned the bow in silence, and Waythorn was still groping for speech when the footman came in carrying a tea table.

The intrusion offered a welcome vent to Waythorn's nerves. "What the deuce are you bringing this here for?" he said sharply.

"I beg your pardon, sir, but the plumbers are still in the drawing room, and Mrs. Waythorn said she would have tea in the library." The footman's perfectly respectful tone implied a reflection on Waythorn's reasonableness.

"Oh, very well," said the latter resignedly, and the footman proceeded to open the folding tea table and set out its complicated appointments. While this interminable process continued the three men stood motionless, watching it with a fascinated stare, till Waythorn, to break the silence, said to Varick, "Won't you have a cigar?"

He held out the case he had just tendered to Haskett, and Varick helped himself with a smile. Waythorn looked about for a match, and finding none, proffered a light from his own cigar. Haskett, in the background, held his ground mildly, examining his cigar tip now and then, and stepping forward at the right moment to knock its ashes into the fire.

The footman at last withdrew, and Varick immediately began: "If I could just say half a word to you about this business—"

"Certainly," stammered Waythorn; "in the dining room—"

But as he placed his hand on the door it opened from without, and his wife appeared on the threshold.

She came in fresh and smiling, in her street dress and hat, shedding a fragrance from the boa which she loosened in advancing.

"Shall we have tea in here, dear?" she began; and then she caught sight of Varick. Her smile deepened, veiling a slight tremor of surprise.

"Why, how do you do?" she said with a distinct note of pleasure.

As she shook hands with Varick she saw Haskett standing behind him. Her smile faded for a moment, but she recalled it quickly, with a scarcely perceptible side glance at Waythorn.

"How do you do, Mr. Haskett?" she said, and shook hands with him a shade less cordially.

The three men stood awkwardly before her, till Varick, always the most self-possessed, dashed into an explanatory phrase.

"We—I had to see Waythorn a moment on business," he stammered, brick-red from chin to nape.

Haskett stepped forward with his air of mild obstinacy. "I am sorry to intrude; but you appointed five o'clock—" he directed his resigned glance to the timepiece on the mantel.

She swept aside their embarrassment with a charming gesture of hospitality.

"I'm so sorry—I'm always late; but the afternoon was so lovely." She stood drawing off her gloves, propitiatory and graceful, diffusing about her a sense of ease and familiarity in which the situation lost its grotesqueness. "But before talking business," she added brightly, "I'm sure everyone wants a cup of tea."

She dropped into her low chair by the tea table, and the two visitors, as if drawn by her smile, advanced to receive the cups she held out.

She glanced about for Waythorn, and he took the third cup with a laugh.

1904

# Roman Fever[1]

## I

From the table at which they had been lunching two American ladies of ripe but well-cared-for middle age moved across the lofty terrace of the Roman restaurant and, leaning on its parapet, looked first at each other, and then

1. First printed in *Liberty* magazine in 1934.

down on the outspread glories of the Palatine[2] and the Forum, with the same expression of vague but benevolent approval.

As they leaned there a girlish voice echoed up gaily from the stairs leading to the court below. "Well, come along, then," it cried, not to them but to an invisible companion, "and let's leave the young things to their knitting"; and a voice as fresh laughed back: "Oh, look here, Babs, not actually *knitting*—" "Well, I mean figuratively," rejoined the first. "After all, we haven't left out poor parents much else to do. . . ." and at that point the turn of the stairs engulfed the dialogue.

The two ladies looked at each other again, this time with a tinge of smiling embarrassment, and the smaller and paler one shook her head and colored slightly.

"Barbara!" she murmured, sending an unheard rebuke after the mocking voice in the stairway.

The other lady, who was fuller, and higher in color, with a small determined nose supported by vigorous black eyebrows, gave a good-humored laugh. "That's what our daughters think of us!"

Her companion replied by a deprecating gesture. "Not of us individually. We must remember that. It's just the collective modern idea of Mothers. And you see—" Half-guiltily she drew from her handsomely mounted black hand-bag a twist of crimson silk run through by two fine knitting needles. "One never knows," she murmured. "The new system has certainly given us a good deal of time to kill; and sometimes I get tired just looking—even at this." Her gesture was now addressed to the stupendous scene at their feet.

The dark lady laughed again, and they both relapsed upon the view, con-templating it in silence, with a sort of diffused serenity which might have been borrowed from the spring effulgence of the Roman skies. The luncheon hour was long past, and the two had their end of the vast terrace to them-selves. At its opposite extremity a few groups, detained by a lingering look at the outspread city, were gathering up guidebooks and fumbling for tips. The last of them scattered, and the two ladies were alone on the air-washed height.

"Well, I don't see why we shouldn't just stay here," said Mrs. Slade, the lady of the high color and energetic brows. Two derelict basket chairs stood near, and she pushed them into the angle of the parapet, and settled herself in one, her gaze upon the Palatine. "After all, it's still the most beautiful view in the world."

"It always will be, to me," assented her friend Mrs. Ansley, with so slight a stress on the "me" that Mrs. Slade, though she noticed it, wondered if it were not merely accidental, like the random underlinings of old-fashioned letter writers.

"Grace Ansley was always old-fashioned," she thought; and added aloud, with a retrospective smile: "It's a view we've both been familiar with for a good many years. When we first met here we were younger than our girls are now. You remember?"

"Oh, yes, I remember," murmured Mrs. Ansley, with the same undefinable stress. "There's that headwaiter wondering," she interpolated. She was evi-

---

2. The Palatine Hill is located between the Forum and the Circus Maximus in Rome; it is the former site of imperial palaces and a major tourist attraction.

dently far less sure than her companion of herself and of her rights in the world.

"I'll cure him of wondering," said Mrs. Slade, stretching her hand toward a bag as discreetly opulent-looking as Mrs. Ansley's. Signing to the head-waiter, she explained that she and her friend were old lovers of Rome, and would like to spend the end of the afternoon looking down on the view—that is, if it did not disturb the service? The headwaiter, bowing over her gratuity, assured her that the ladies were most welcome, and would be still more so if they would condescend to remain for dinner. A full-moon night, they would remember. . . .

Mrs. Slade's black brows drew together, as though references to the moon were out of place and even unwelcome. But she smiled away her frown as the headwaiter retreated. "Well, why not? We might do worse. There's no know-ing, I suppose, when the girls will be back. Do you even know back from *where*? I don't!"

Mrs. Ansley again colored slightly. "I think those young Italian aviators we met at the Embassy invited them to fly to Tarquinia[3] for tea. I suppose they'll want to wait and fly back by moonlight."

"Moonlight—moonlight! What a part it still plays. Do you suppose they're as sentimental as we were?"

"I've come to the conclusion that I don't in the least know what they are," said Mrs. Ansley. "And perhaps we didn't know much more about each other."

"No; perhaps we didn't."

Her friend gave her a shy glance. "I never should have supposed you were sentimental, Alida."

"Well, perhaps I wasn't." Mrs. Slade drew her lids together in retrospect; and for a few moments the two ladies, who had been intimate since childhood, reflected how little they knew each other. Each one, of course, had a label ready to attach to the other's name; Mrs. Delphin Slade, for instance, would have told herself, or anyone who asked her, that Mrs. Horace Ansley, twenty-five years ago, had been exquisitely lovely—no, you wouldn't believe it, would you? . . . though, of course, still charming, distinguished. . . . Well, as a girl she had been exquisite; far more beautiful than her daughter Barbara, though certainly Babs, according to the new standards at any rate, was more effective—had more *edge*, as they say. Funny where she got it, with those two nullities as parents. Yes; Horace Ansley was—well, just the duplicate of his wife. Museum specimens of old New York. Good-looking, irreproachable, exemplary. Mrs. Slade and Mrs. Ansley had lived opposite each other—actually as well as figuratively—for years. When the drawing-room curtains in No. 20 East 73rd Street were renewed, No. 23, across the way, was always aware of it. And of all the movings, buyings, travels, anniversaries, illnesses—the tame chronicle of an estimable pair. Little of it escaped Mrs. Slade. But she had grown bored with it by the time her husband made his big *coup* in Wall Street, and when they bought in upper Park Avenue had already begun to think: "I'd rather live opposite a speakeasy for a change; at least one might see it raided." The idea of seeing Grace raided was so amusing that (before the move) she launched it at a woman's lunch. It made a hit, and went the rounds—she sometimes wondered if it had crossed the street, and reached Mrs. Ansley. She hoped not, but didn't much mind.

---

3. An ancient Etruscan city in the province of Viterbo, Lazio, Italy, famous for resisting Roman rule.

Those were the days when respectability was at a discount, and it did the irreproachable no harm to laugh at them a little.

A few years later, and not many months apart, both ladies lost their husbands. There was an appropriate exchange of wreaths and condolences, and a brief renewal of intimacy in the half-shadow of their mourning; and now, after another interval, they had run across each other in Rome, at the same hotel, each of them the modest appendage of a salient daughter. The similarity of their lot had again drawn them together, lending itself to mild jokes, and the mutual confession that, if in old days it must have been tiring to "keep up" with daughters, it was now, at times, a little dull not to.

No doubt, Mrs. Slade reflected, she felt her unemployment more than poor Grace ever would. It was a big drop from being the wife of Delphin Slade to being his widow. She had always regarded herself (with a certain conjugal pride) as his equal in social gifts, as contributing her full share to the making of the exceptional couple they were: but the difference after his death was irremediable. As the wife of the famous corporation lawyer, always with an international case or two on hand, every day brought its exciting and unexpected obligation: the impromptu entertaining of eminent colleagues from abroad, the hurried dashes on legal business to London, Paris or Rome, where the entertaining was so handsomely reciprocated; the amusement of hearing in her wake: "What, that handsome woman with the good clothes and the eyes is Mrs. Slade—*the* Slade's wife? Really? Generally the wives of celebrities are such frumps."

Yes; being *the* Slade's widow was a dullish business after that. In living up to such a husband all her faculties had been engaged; now she had only her daughter to live up to, for the son who seemed to have inherited his father's gifts had died suddenly in boyhood. She had fought through that agony because her husband was there, to be helped and to help; now, after the father's death, the thought of the boy had become unbearable. There was nothing left but to mother her daughter; and dear Jenny was such a perfect daughter that she needed no excessive mothering. "Now with Babs Ansley I don't know that I *should* be so quiet," Mrs. Slade sometimes half-enviously reflected; but Jenny, who was younger than her brilliant friend, was that rare accident, an extremely pretty girl who somehow made youth and prettiness seem as safe as their absence. It was all perplexing—and to Mrs. Slade a little boring. She wished that Jenny would fall in love—with the wrong man, even; that she might have to be watched, out-maneuvered, rescued. And instead, it was Jenny who watched her mother, kept her out of drafts, made sure that she had taken her tonic. . . .

Mrs. Ansley was much less articulate than her friend, and her mental portrait of Mrs. Slade was slighter, and drawn with fainter touches. "Alida Slade's awfully brilliant; but not as brilliant as she thinks," would have summed it up; though she would have added, for the enlightenment of strangers, that Mrs. Slade had been an extremely dashing girl; much more so than her daughter, who was pretty, of course, and clever in a way, but had none of her mother's— well, "vividness," someone had once called it. Mrs. Ansley would take up current words like this, and cite them in quotation marks, as unheard-of audacities. No; Jenny was not like her mother. Sometimes Mrs. Ansley thought Alida Slade was disappointed; on the whole she had had a sad life. Full of failures and mistakes; Mrs. Ansley had always been rather sorry for her. . . .

So these two ladies visualized each other, each through the wrong end of her little telescope.

## II

FOR a long time they continued to sit side by side without speaking. It seemed as though, to both, there was a relief in laying down their somewhat futile activities in the presence of the vast Memento Mori which faced them. Mrs. Slade sat quite still, her eyes fixed on the golden slope of the Palace of the Caesars,[4] and after a while Mrs. Ansley ceased to fidget with her bag, and she too sank into meditation. Like many intimate friends, the two ladies had never before had occasion to be silent together, and Mrs. Ansley was slightly embarrassed by what seemed, after so many years, a new stage in their intimacy, and one with which she did not yet know how to deal.

Suddenly the air was full of that deep clangor of bells which periodically covers Rome with a roof of silver. Mrs. Slade glanced at her wristwatch. "Five o'clock already," she said, as though surprised.

Mrs. Ansley suggested interrogatively: "There's bridge at the Embassy at five." For a long time Mrs. Slade did not answer. She appeared to be lost in contemplation, and Mrs. Ansley thought the remark had escaped her. But after a while she said, as if speaking out of a dream: "Bridge, did you say? Not unless you want to. . . . But I don't think I will, you know."

"Oh, no," Mrs. Ansley hastened to assure her. "I don't care to at all. It's so lovely here; and so full of old memories, as you say." She settled herself in her chair, and almost furtively drew forth her knitting. Mrs. Slade took sideway note of this activity, but her own beautifully cared-for hands remained motionless on her knee.

"I was just thinking," she said slowly, "what different things Rome stands for to each generation of travelers. To our grandmothers, Roman fever[5] to our mothers, sentimental dangers—how we used to be guarded!—to our daughters, no more dangers than the middle of Main Street. They don't know it—but how much they're missing!"

The long golden light was beginning to pale, and Mrs. Ansley lifted her knitting a little closer to her eyes. "Yes; how we were guarded!"

"I always used to think," Mrs. Slade continued, "that our mothers had a much more difficult job than our grandmothers. When Roman fever stalked the streets it must have been comparatively easy to gather in the girls at the danger hour; but when you and I were young, with such beauty calling us, and the spice of disobedience thrown in, and no worse risk than catching cold during the cool hour after sunset, the mothers used to be put to it to keep us in—didn't they?"

She turned again toward Mrs. Ansley, but the latter had reached a delicate point in her knitting. "One, two, three—slip two; yes, they must have been," she assented, without looking up.

Mrs. Slade's eyes rested on her with a deepened attention. "She can knit—in the face of *this!* How like her. . . ."

4. Complex begun by Augustus Caesar on the Palatine Hill in Rome. "Momento Mori": "Remember you will die" (Latin).
5. Malaria.

Mrs. Slade leaned back, brooding, her eyes ranging from the ruins which faced her to the long green hollow of the Forum, the fading glow of the church fronts beyond it, and the outlying immensity of the Colosseum.[6] Suddenly she thought: "It's all very well to say that our girls have done away with sentiment and moonlight. But if Babs Ansley isn't out to catch that young aviator—the one who's a Marchese[7]—then I don't know anything. And Jenny has no chance beside her. I know that too. I wonder if that's why Grace Ansley likes the two girls to go everywhere together? My poor Jenny as a foil—!" Mrs. Slade gave a hardly audible laugh, and at the sound Mrs. Ansley dropped her knitting.

"Yes—?"

"I—oh, nothing. I was only thinking how your Babs carries everything before her. That Campolieri boy is one of the best matches in Rome. Don't look so innocent, my dear—you know he is. And I was wondering, ever so respectfully, you understand . . . wondering how two such exemplary characters as you and Horace had managed to produce anything quite so dynamic." Mrs. Slade laughed again, with a touch of asperity.

Mrs. Ansley's hands lay inert across her needles. She looked straight out at the great accumulated wreckage of passion and splendor at her feet. But her small profile was almost expressionless. At length she said: "I think you overrate Babs, my dear."

Mrs. Slade's tone grew easier. "No; I don't. I appreciate her. And perhaps envy you. Oh, my girl's perfect; if I were a chronic invalid I'd—well, I think I'd rather be in Jenny's hands. There must be times . . . but there! I always wanted a brilliant daughter . . . and never quite understood why I got an angel instead."

Mrs. Ansley echoed her laugh in a faint murmur. "Babs is an angel too."

"Of course—of course! But she's got rainbow wings. Well, they're wandering by the sea with their young men; and here we sit . . . and it all brings back the past a little too acutely."

Mrs. Ansley had resumed her knitting. One might almost have imagined (if one had known her less well, Mrs. Slade reflected) that, for her also, too many memories rose from the lengthening shadows of those august ruins. But no; she was simply absorbed in her work. What was there for her to worry about? She knew that Babs would almost certainly come back engaged to the extremely eligible Campolieri. "And she'll sell the New York house, and settle down near them in Rome, and never be in their way . . . she's much too tactful. But she'll have an excellent cook, and just the right people in for bridge and cocktails . . . and a perfectly peaceful old age among her grandchildren."

Mrs. Slade broke off this prophetic flight with a recoil of self-disgust. There was no one of whom she had less right to think unkindly than of Grace Ansley. Would she never cure herself of envying her? Perhaps she had begun too long ago.

She stood up and leaned against the parapet, filling her troubled eyes with the tranquilizing magic of the hour. But instead of tranquilizing her the sight

---

6. Roman amphitheater constructed between 72 and 81 C.E., capable of holding 50,000 spectators and used for gladiatorial events.
7. A member of Italian nobility.

seemed to increase her exasperation. Her gaze turned toward the Colosseum. Already its golden flank was drowned in purple shadow, and above it the sky curved crystal clear, without light or color. It was the moment when afternoon and evening hang balanced in mid-heaven.

Mrs. Slade turned back and laid her hand on her friend's arm. The gesture was so abrupt that Mrs. Ansley looked up, startled.

"The sun's set. You're not afraid, my dear?"

"Afraid—?"

"Of Roman fever or pneumonia? I remember how ill you were that winter. As a girl you had a very delicate throat, hadn't you?"

"Oh, we're all right up here. Down below, in the Forum, it does get deathly cold, all of a sudden . . . but not here."

"Ah, of course you know because you had to be so careful." Mrs. Slade turned back to the parapet. She thought: "I must make one more effort not to hate her." Aloud she said: "Whenever I look at the Forum from up here, I remember that story about a great-aunt of yours, wasn't she? A dreadfully wicked great-aunt?"

"Oh, yes; great-aunt Harriet. The one who was supposed to have sent her young sister out to the Forum after sunset to gather a night-blooming flower for her album. All our great-aunts and grandmothers used to have albums of dried flowers."

Mrs. Slade nodded. "But she really sent her because they were in love with the same man—"

"Well, that was the family tradition. They said Aunt Harriet confessed it years afterward. At any rate, the poor little sister caught the fever and died. Mother used to frighten us with the story when we were children."

"And you frightened *me* with it, that winter when you and I were here as girls. The winter I was engaged to Delphin."

Mrs. Ansley gave a faint laugh. "Oh, did I? Really frightened you? I don't believe you're easily frightened."

"Not often; but I was then. I was easily frightened because I was too happy. I wonder if you know what that means?"

"I—yes . . ." Mrs. Ansley faltered.

"Well, I suppose that was why the story of your wicked aunt made such an impression on me. And I thought: 'There's no more Roman fever, but the Forum is deathly cold after sunset—especially after a hot day. And the Colosseum's even colder and damper'."

"The Colosseum—?"

"Yes. It wasn't easy to get in, after the gates were locked for the night. Far from easy. Still, in those days it could be managed; it *was* managed, often. Lovers met there who couldn't meet elsewhere. You knew that?"

"I—I dare say. I don't remember."

"You don't remember? You don't remember going to visit some ruins or other one evening, just after dark, and catching a bad chill? You were supposed to have gone to see the moon rise. People always said that expedition was what caused your illness."

There was a moment's silence; then Mrs. Ansley rejoined: "Did they? It was all so long ago."

"Yes. And you got well again—so it didn't matter. But I suppose it struck your friends—the reason given for your illness, I mean—because everybody knew you were so prudent on account of your throat, and your mother took such care of you. . . . You *had* been out late sight-seeing, hadn't you, that night?"

"Perhaps I had. The most prudent girls aren't always prudent. What made you think of it now?"

Mrs. Slade seemed to have no answer ready. But after a moment she broke out: "Because I simply can't bear it any longer—!"

Mrs. Ansley lifted her head quickly. Her eyes were wide and very pale. "Can't bear what?"

"Why—your not knowing that I've always known why you went."

"Why I went—?"

"Yes. You think I'm bluffing, don't you? Well, you went to meet the man I was engaged to—and I can repeat every word of the letter that took you there."

While Mrs. Slade spoke Mrs. Ansley had risen unsteadily to her feet. Her bag, her knitting and gloves, slid in a panic-stricken heap to the ground. She looked at Mrs. Slade as though she were looking at a ghost.

"No, no—don't," she faltered out.

"Why not? Listen, if you don't believe me. 'My one darling, things can't go on like this. I must see you alone. Come to the Colosseum immediately after dark tomorrow. There will be somebody to let you in. No one whom you need fear will suspect'—but perhaps you've forgotten what the letter said?"

Mrs. Ansley met the challenge with an unexpected composure. Steadying herself against the chair she looked at her friend, and replied: "No; I know it by heart too."

"And the signature? 'Only *your* D.S.' Was that it? I'm right, am I? That was the letter that took you out that evening after dark?"

Mrs. Ansley was still looking at her. It seemed to Mrs. Slade that a slow struggle was going on behind the voluntarily controlled mask of her small quiet face. "I shouldn't have thought she had herself so well in hand," Mrs. Slade reflected, almost resentfully. But at this moment Mrs. Ansley spoke. "I don't know how you knew. I burnt that letter at once."

"Yes; you would, naturally—you're so prudent!" The sneer was open now. "And if you burnt the letter you're wondering how on earth I know what was in it. That's it, isn't it?"

Mrs. Slade waited, but Mrs. Ansley did not speak.

"Well, my dear, I know what was in that letter because I wrote it!"

"You wrote it?"

"Yes."

The two women stood for a minute staring at each other in the last golden light. Then Mrs. Ansley dropped back into her chair. "Oh," she murmured, and covered her face with her hands.

Mrs. Slade waited nervously for another word or movement. None came, and at length she broke out: "I horrify you."

Mrs. Ansley's hands dropped to her knee. The face they uncovered was streaked with tears. "I wasn't thinking of you. I was thinking—it was the only letter I ever had from him!"

"And I wrote it. Yes; I wrote it! But I was the girl he was engaged to. Did you happen to remember that?"

Mrs. Ansley's head drooped again. "I'm not trying to excuse myself . . . I remembered. . . ."

"And still you went?"

"Still I went."

Mrs. Slade stood looking down on the small bowed figure at her side. The flame of her wrath had already sunk, and she wondered why she had ever thought there would be any satisfaction in inflicting so purposeless a wound on her friend. But she had to justify herself.

"You do understand? I'd found out—and I hated you, hated you. I knew you were in love with Delphin—and I was afraid; afraid of you, of your quiet ways, your sweetness . . . your . . . well, I wanted you out of the way, that's all. Just for a few weeks; just till I was sure of him. So in a blind fury I wrote that letter . . . I don't know why I'm telling you now."

"I suppose," said Mrs. Ansley slowly, "it's because you've always gone on hating me."

"Perhaps. Or because I wanted to get the whole thing off my mind." She paused. "I'm glad you destroyed the letter. Of course I never thought you'd die."

Mrs. Ansley relapsed into silence, and Mrs. Slade, leaning above her, was conscious of a strange sense of isolation, of being cut off from the warm current of human communion. "You think me a monster!"

"I don't know. . . . It was the only letter I had, and you say he didn't write it?"

"Ah, how you care for him still!"

"I cared for that memory," said Mrs. Ansley.

Mrs. Slade continued to look down on her. She seemed physically reduced by the blow—as if, when she got up, the wind might scatter her like a puff of dust. Mrs. Slade's jealousy suddenly leapt up again at the sight. All these years the woman had been living on that letter. How she must have loved him, to treasure the mere memory of its ashes! The letter of the man her friend was engaged to. Wasn't it she who was the monster?

"You tried your best to get him away from me, didn't you? But you failed; and I kept him. That's all."

"Yes. That's all."

"I wish now I hadn't told you. I'd no idea you'd feel about it as you do; I thought you'd be amused. It all happened so long ago, as you say; and you must do me the justice to remember that I had no reason to think you'd ever taken it seriously. How could I, when you were married to Horace Ansley two months afterward? As soon as you could get out of bed your mother rushed you off to Florence and married you. People were rather surprised—they wondered at its being done so quickly; but I thought I knew. I had an idea you did it out of *pique*—to be able to say you'd got ahead of Delphin and me. Girls have such silly reasons for doing the most serious things. And your marrying so soon convinced me that you'd never really cared."

"Yes. I suppose it would," Mrs. Ansley assented.

The clear heaven overhead was emptied of all its gold. Dusk spread over it, abruptly darkening the Seven Hills.[8] Here and there lights began to twin-

---

8. The Seven Hills of Rome east of the Tiber River form the heart of the city.

kle through the foliage at their feet. Steps were coming and going on the deserted terrace—waiters looking out of the doorway at the head of the stairs, then reappearing with trays and napkins and flasks of wine. Tables were moved, chairs straightened. A feeble string of electric lights flickered out. Some vases of faded flowers were carried away, and brought back replenished. A stout lady in a dust coat suddenly appeared, asking in broken Italian if anyone had seen the elastic band which held together her tattered Baedeker. She poked with her stick under the table at which she had lunched, the waiters assisting.

The corner where Mrs. Slade and Mrs. Ansley sat was still shadowy and deserted. For a long time neither of them spoke. At length Mrs. Slade began again: "I suppose I did it as a sort of joke—"

"A joke?"

"Well, girls are ferocious sometimes, you know. Girls in love especially. And I remember laughing to myself all that evening at the idea that you were waiting around there in the dark, dodging out of sight, listening for every sound, trying to get in—Of course I was upset when I heard you were so ill afterward."

Mrs. Ansley had not moved for a long time. But now she turned slowly toward her companion. "But I didn't wait. He'd arranged everything. He was there. We were let in at once," she said.

Mrs. Slade sprang up from her leaning position. "Delphin there? They let you in?—Ah, now you're lying!" she burst out with violence.

Mrs. Ansley's voice grew clearer, and full of surprise. "But of course he was there. Naturally he came—"

"Came? How did he know he'd find you there? You must be raving!"

Mrs. Ansley hesitated, as though reflecting. "But I answered the letter. I told him I'd be there. So he came."

Mrs. Slade flung her hands up to her face. "Oh, God—you answered! I never thought of your answering. . . ."

"It's odd you never thought of it, if you wrote the letter."

"Yes. I was blind with rage."

Mrs. Ansley rose, and drew her fur scarf about her. "It is cold here. We'd better go . . . I'm sorry for you," she said, as she clasped the fur about her throat.

The unexpected words sent a pang through Mrs. Slade. "Yes; we'd better go." She gathered up her bag and cloak. "I don't know why you should be sorry for me," she muttered.

Mrs. Ansley stood looking away from her toward the dusky secret mass of the Colosseum. "Well—because I didn't have to wait that night."

Mrs. Slade gave an unquiet laugh. "Yes; I was beaten there. But I oughtn't to begrudge it to you, I suppose. At the end of all these years. After all, I had everything; I had him for twenty-five years. And you had nothing but that one letter that he didn't write."

Mrs. Ansley was again silent. At length she turned toward the door of the terrace. She took a step, and turned back, facing her companion.

"I had Barbara," she said, and began to move ahead of Mrs. Slade toward the stairway.

1934

# IDA B. WELLS-BARNETT
## 1862–1931

Ida Belle Wells was born to slave parents in Holly Springs, Mississippi, fifty miles southeast of Memphis. Her father's carpentry skills and her mother's fame as a cook gave them high status among slave workers. After Emancipation, they had eight children, of which Ida was the second. Both parents and two of the children died in the yellow fever epidemic of 1878, a moment Wells describes in her autobiography, *Crusade for Justice* (not published until 1970), as when "life became a reality to me." Though friends and relatives planned to separate the children through apprenticeships, adoption, and the "poor house," sixteen-year-old Ida was determined to keep the family together and honor her parents' memory, which she did by going to work as a teacher and raising all five siblings.

Wells attended Shaw University (now called Rust College) and in 1884 moved to Memphis to help her aunt raise her youngest sisters and take teacher-training courses at Fisk University. Soon after her arrival she was told by a conductor on the Chesapeake & Ohio Railroad to give up her seat in the ladies' car for a white man, and ordered into the smoky, crowded "Jim Crow" car. She refused, whereupon he seized her. As she recalls in her autobiography, "I fastened my teeth in the back of his hand . . . and he didn't try it again by himself. He went forward and got the baggageman and another man to help him and of course they succeeded in dragging me out." As the white passengers applauded, Wells was forcibly removed from the train. She filed a lawsuit against the railroad, which she lost, but this incident was the spark that ignited her journalistic self. She wrote of her ordeal in Christian and African American newspapers across the country, and gained a large following. Wells was on her way to becoming a suffragist and fearless crusader against lynching.

In 1889 Wells became a partner in a newspaper called the *Free Speech and Headlight*. The last two decades of the nineteenth century were a terrifying time for southern blacks. In 1892 three of Wells's black friends, who owned a small grocery, were lynched by white men seeking to protect the business of their own grocery stores. Wells helped organize a boycott of white-owned businesses and denounced the lynch mob in *Free Speech*, but had to leave Memphis for Chicago. There she continued her attacks on Southern injustices, and focused especially on exposing the fraudulent "reasons" why black men and women were lynched. Her pamphlet *Southern Horrors: Lynch Law in All Its Phases* (1892) was followed by *A Red Record* (1894) and "Mob Rule in New Orleans" (1900). "Mob Rule in New Orleans" is a lengthy but trenchant account of a notorious riot and lynchings in New Orleans in 1900, using the very words of the white-controlled New Orleans newspapers to condemn white violence and injustice to black citizens. Despite threats on her life, she persisted in writing and speaking at home and abroad. She participated in national suffragist marches and, with Jane Addams, founder of the social settlement Hull-House on Chicago's Near West Side, she successfully blocked the establishment of segregated schools in Chicago. Their partnership reflects the way women white and black worked together for social reform.

In 1895 Wells married the editor of the *Conservator*, one of Chicago's early black newspapers, Ferdinand L. Barnett. The couple had several children. In 1906, Wells was one of two African American women to help found the NAACP, and in 1910, she formed the Negro Fellowship League on Chicago's South Side, a refuge for travelers from the South. In her autobiography Wells wrote that everything she had done was "because our youth are entitled to the facts of race history which only the participants can give. . . ." In 1930, she ran for the Illinois State Legislature and lost. She died a year later, after a lifetime of crusading for social justice.

## From Mob Rule in New Orleans[1]

### Shot an Officer

The bloodiest week which New Orleans has known since the massacre of the Italians in 1892[2] was ushered in Monday, July 24th, by the inexcusable and unprovoked assault upon two colored men by police officers of New Orleans. Fortified by the assurance born of long experience in the New Orleans service, three policemen, Sergeant Aucoin, Officer Mora and Officer Cantrelle, observing two colored men sitting on doorsteps on Dryades street, between Washington avenue and 6th streets,[3] determined, without a shadow of authority, to arrest them. One of the colored men was named Robert Charles, the other was a lad of nineteen named Leonard Pierce. The colored men had left their homes, a few blocks distant, about an hour prior, and had been sitting upon the doorsteps for a short time talking together. They had not broken the peace in any way whatever, no warrant was in the policemen's hands justifying their arrest, and no crime had been committed of which they were the suspects. The policemen, however, secure in the firm belief that they could do anything to a Negro that they wished, approached the two men, and in less than three minutes from the time they accosted them attempted to put both colored men under arrest. The younger of the two men, Pierce, submitted to arrest, for the officer, Cantrelle, who accosted him, put his gun in the young man's face ready to blow his brains out if he moved. The other colored man, Charles, was made the victim of a savage attack by Officer Mora, who used a billet[4] and then drew a gun and tried to kill Charles. Charles drew his gun nearly as quickly as the policeman, and began a duel in the street, in which both participants were shot. The policeman got the worst of the duel, and fell helpless to the sidewalk, Charles made his escape. Cantrelle took Pierce, his captive, to the police station, to which place Mora, the wounded officer, was also taken, and a man hunt at once instituted for Charles, the wounded fugitive.

In any law-abiding community Charles would have been justified in delivering himself up immediately to the properly constituted authorities and asking a trial by a jury of his peers. He could have been certain that in resisting an unwarranted arrest he had a right to defend his life, even to the point of taking one in that defense, but Charles knew that his arrest in New Orleans, even for defending his life, meant nothing short of a long term in the penitentiary, and still more probable death by lynching at the hands of a cowardly mob. He very bravely determined to protect his life as long as he had breath in his body and strength to draw a hair trigger on his would-be murderers. How well he was justified in that belief is well shown by the newspaper accounts which were given of this transaction. Without a single line of evidence to justify the assertion, the New Orleans daily papers at once declared that both Pierce and Charles were desperadoes, that they were contemplat-

---

1. "Mob Rule in New Orleans: Robert Charles and His Fight to Death, the Story of His Life, Burning Human Beings Alive, Other Lynching Statistics" was first published as a pamphlet by Wells-Barnett in Chicago in 1900. Rpt. in *On Lynchings: Southern Horrors, A Red Record, Mob Rule in New Orleans* (1969), from which this text is taken.

2. On March 14, 1891, in New Orleans, eleven Italian immigrants were killed by a lynch mob of more than 6,000 after a court found them not guilty in the murder of a police superintendent.
3. The streets named in Barnett's article are all in downtown New Orleans.
4. Billy club.

ing a burglary and that they began the assault upon the policemen. It is interesting to note how the two leading papers of New Orleans, the *Picayune* and the *Times-Democrat,* exert themselves to justify the policemen in the absolutely unprovoked attack upon the two colored men. As these two papers did all in their power to give an excuse for the action of the policemen, it is interesting to note their versions. The *Times-Democrat* of Tuesday morning, the 25th, says:

Two blacks, who are desperate men, and no doubt will be proven burglars, made it interesting and dangerous for three bluecoats on Dryades street, between Washington avenue and Sixth street, the Negroes using pistols first and dropping Patrolman Mora. But the desperate darkies did not go free, for the taller of the two, Robinson, is badly wounded and under cover, while Leonard Pierce is in jail.

For a long time that particular neighborhood has been troubled with bad Negroes, and the neighbors were complaining to the Sixth Precinct police about them. But of late Pierce and Robinson had been camping on a door step on the street, and the people regarded their actions as suspicious. It got to such a point that some of the residents were afraid to go to bed, and last night this was told Sergeant Aucoin, who was rounding up his men. He had just picked up Officers Mora and Cantrell, on Washington avenue and Dryades street, and catching a glimpse of the blacks on the steps, he said he would go over and warn the men to get away from the street. So the patrolmen followed, and Sergeant Aucoin asked the smaller fellow, Pierce, if he lived there. The answer was short and impertinent, the black saying he did not, and with that both Pierce and Robinson drew up to their full height.

For the moment the sergeant did not think that the Negroes meant to fight, and he was on the point of ordering them away when Robinson slipped his pistol from his pocket. Pierce had his revolver out, too, and he fired twice, point blank at the sergeant, and just then Robinson began shooting at the patrolmen. In a second or so the policemen and blacks were fighting with their revolvers, the sergeant having a duel with Pierce, while Cantrell and Mora drew their line of fire on Robinson, who was working his revolver for all he was worth. One of his shots took Mora in the right hip, another caught his index finger on the right hand, and a third struck the small finger of the left hand. Poor Mora was done for; he could not fight any more, but Cantrell kept up his fire, being answered by the big black. Pierce's revolver broke down, the cartridges snapping, and he threw up his hands, begging for quarter.

The sergeant lowered his pistol and some citizens ran over to where the shooting was going on. One of the bullets that went at Robinson caught him in the breast and he began running, turning on Sixth street, with Cantrell behind him, shooting every few steps. He was loading his revolver again, but did not use it after the start he took, and in a little while, Officer Cantrell lost the man in the darkness.

Pierce was made a prisoner and hurried to the Sixth Precinct police station, where he was charged with shooting and wounding. The sergeant sent for an ambulance, and Mora was taken to the hospital, the wound in the hip being serious.

A search was made for Robinson, but he could not be found, and even at 2 o'clock this morning Captain Day, with Sergeant Aucoin and Corporals Perrier and Trenchard, with a good squad of men, were beating the weeds for the black.

The New Orleans *Picayune* of the same date described the occurrence, and from its account one would think it was an entirely different affair. Both of the two accounts cannot be true, and the unquestioned fact is that neither of them sets out the facts as they occurred. Both accounts attempt to fix the beginning of hostilities upon the colored men, but both were compelled to admit that the colored men were sitting on the doorsteps quietly conversing with one another when the three policemen went up and accosted them. The *Times-Democrat* unguardedly states that one of the two colored men tried to run away; that Mora seized him and then drew his billy and struck him on the head; that Charles broke away from him and started to run, after which the shooting began. The *Picayune,* however, declares that Pierce began the firing and that his two shots point blank at Aucoin were the first shots of the fight. As a matter of fact, Pierce never fired a single shot before he was covered by Aucoin's revolver. Charles and the officers did all the shooting. The *Picayune's* account is as follows:

Patrolman Mora was shot in the right hip and dangerously wounded last night at 11:30 o'clock in Dryades street, between Washington and Sixth, by two Negroes, who were sitting on a door step in the neighborhood.

The shooting of Patrolman Mora brings to memory the fact that he was one of the partners of Patrolman Trimp, who was shot by a Negro soldier of the United States government during the progress of the Spanish-American war. The shooting of Mora by the Negro last night is a very simple story. At the hour mentioned, three Negro women noticed two suspicious men sitting on a door step in the above locality. The women saw the two men making an apparent inspection of the building. As they told the story, they saw the men look over the fence and examine the window blinds, and they paid particular attention to the make-up of the building, which was a two-story affair. About that time Sergeant J. C. Aucoin and Officers Mora and J. D. Cantrell hove in sight. The women hailed them and described to them the suspicious actions of the two Negroes, who were still sitting on the step. The trio of bluecoats, on hearing the facts, at once crossed the street and accosted the men. The latter answered that they were waiting for a friend whom they were expecting. Not satisfied with this answer, the sergeant asked them where they lived, and they replied "down town," but could not designate the locality. To other questions put by the officers the larger of the two Negroes replied that they had been in town just three days.

As this reply was made, the larger man sprang to his feet, and Patrolman Mora, seeing that he was about to run away, seized him. The Negro took a firm hold on the officer, and a scuffle ensued. Mora, noting that he was not being assisted by his brother officers, drew his billy and struck the Negro on the head. The blow had but little effect upon the man, for he broke away and started down the street. When about ten feet away, the Negro drew his revolver and opened fire on the officer, firing three or four shots. The third shot struck Mora in the right hip, and was subsequently found to have taken an upward course. Although badly wounded, Mora drew his pistol and returned the fire. At his third shot the Negro was noticed to stagger, but he did not fall. He continued his flight. At this moment Sergeant Aucoin seized the other Negro, who proved to be a youth, Leon Pierce. As soon as Officer Mora was shot he sank to the sidewalk, and the other officer ran to the nearest telephone, and sent in a call for the ambulance. Upon its arrival the wounded officer was placed in it and conveyed to the hospital. An examination by the house surgeon revealed the fact that the bullet had taken an upward course. In the opinion of the surgeon the wound was a dangerous one.

But the best proof of the fact that the officers accosted the two colored men and without any warrant or other justification attempted to arrest them, and did actually seize and begin to club one of them, is shown by Officer Mora's own statement. The officer was wounded and had every reason in the world to make his side of the story as good as possible. His statement was made to a *Picayune* reporter and the same was published on the 25th inst., and is as follows:

> I was in the neighborhood of Dryades and Washington streets, with Sergeant Aucoin and Officer Cantrell, when three Negro women came up and told us that there were two suspicious-looking Negroes sitting on a step on Dryades street, between Washington and Sixth. We went to the place indicated and found two Negroes. We interrogated them as to who they were, what they were doing and how long they had been here. They replied that they were working for some one and had been in town three days. At about this stage the larger of the two Negroes got up and I grabbed him. The Negro pulled, but I held fast, and he finally pulled me into the street. Here I began using my billet, and the Negro jerked from my grasp and ran. He then pulled a gun and fired. I pulled my gun and returned the fire, each of us firing about three shots. I saw the Negro stumble several times, and I thought I had shot him, but he ran away and I don't know whether any of my shots took effect. Sergeant Aucoin in the meantime held the other man fast. The man was about ten feet from me when he fired, and the three Negresses who told us about the men stood away about twenty-five feet from the shooting.

Thus far in the proceeding the Monday night episode results in Officer Mora lying in the station wounded in the hip; Leonard Pierce, one of the colored men, locked up in the station, and Robert Charles, the other colored man, a fugitive, wounded in the leg and sought for by the entire police force of New Orleans. Not sought for, however, to be placed under arrest and given a fair trial and punished if found guilty according to the law of the land, but sought for by a host of enraged, vindictive and fearless officers, who were coolly ordered to kill him on sight. This order is shown by the *Picayune* of the 26th inst., in which the following statement appears:

> In talking to the sergeant about the case, the captain asked about the Negro's fighting ability, and the sergeant answered that Charles, though he called him Robinson then, was a desperate man, and it would be best to shoot him before he was given a chance to draw his pistol upon any of the officers.

This instruction was given before anybody had been killed, and the only evidence that Charles was a desperate man lay in the fact that he had refused to be beaten over the head by Officer Mora for sitting on a step quietly conversing with a friend. Charles resisted an absolutely unlawful attack, and a gun fight followed. Both Mora and Charles were shot, but because Mora was white and Charles was black, Charles was at once declared to be a desperado, made an outlaw, and subsequently a price put upon his head and the mob authorized to shoot him like a dog, on sight.

The New Orleans *Picayune* of Wednesday morning said:

> But he has gone, perhaps to the swamps, and the disappointment of the bluecoats in not getting the murderer is expressed in their curses, each man swearing that the signal to halt that will be offered Charles will be a shot.

In that same column of the *Picayune* it was said:

> Hundreds of policemen were about; each corner was guarded by a squad, commanded either by a sergeant or a corporal, and every man had the word to shoot the Negro as soon as he was sighted. He was a desperate black and would be given no chance to take more life.

Legal sanction was given to the mob or any man of the mob to kill Charles at sight by the Mayor of New Orleans, who publicly proclaimed a reward of two hundred and fifty dollars, not for the arrest of Charles, not at all, but the reward was offered for Charles' body, "dead or alive." The advertisement was as follows:

> "$250 REWARD.
>
> "Under the authority vested in me by law, I hereby offer, in the name of the city of New Orleans, $250 reward for the capture and delivery, dead or alive, to the authorities of the city, the body of the Negro murderer,
>
> "ROBERT CHARLES,
>
> who, on Tuesday morning, July 24, shot and killed
> "Police Captain John T. Day and Patrolman Peter J. Lamb, and wounded
> "Patrolman August T. Mora.
>
> "PAUL CAPDEVIELLE, Mayor."

This authority, given by the sergeant to kill Charles on sight, would have been no news to Charles, nor to any colored man in New Orleans, who, for any purpose whatever, even to save his life, raised his hand against a white man. It is now, even as it was in the days of slavery, an unpardonable sin for a Negro to resist a white man, no matter how unjust or unprovoked the white man's attack may be. Charles knew this, and knowing to be captured meant to be killed, he resolved to sell his life as dearly as possible.

The next step in the terrible tragedy occurred between 2:30 and 5 o'clock Tuesday morning, about four hours after the affair on Dryades street. The man hunt, which had been inaugurated soon after Officer Mora had been carried to the station, succeeded in running down Robert Charles, the wounded fugitive, and located him at 2023 4th street. It was nearly 2 o'clock in the morning when a large detail of police surrounded the block with the intent to kill Charles on sight. Capt. Day had charge of the squad of police. Charles, the wounded man, was in his house when the police arrived, fully prepared, as results afterward showed, to die in his own home. Capt. Day started for Charles' room. As soon as Charles got sight of him there was a flash, a report, and Day fell dead in his tracks. In another instant Charles was standing in the door, and seeing Patrolman Peter J. Lamb, he drew his gun, and Lamb fell dead. Two other officers, Sergeant Aucoin and Officer Trenchard, who were in the squad, seeing their comrades, Day and Lamb, fall dead, concluded to raise the siege, and both disappeared into an adjoining house, where they blew out their lights so that their cowardly carcasses could be safe from Charles' deadly aim. The calibre of their courage is well shown by the fact that they concluded to save themselves from any harm by remaining prisoners in that dark room until daybreak, out of reach of Charles' deadly rifle. Sergeant Aucoin, who had been so brave a few hours before when seeing the two colored men sitting on the steps talking together on Dryades street, and supposing that neither was armed, now showed his true calibre. Now he knew that Charles had a gun and was brave enough to use it, so he hid himself in a room two hours while Charles deliberately walked out of his room and into the street after killing both Lamb and Day. It is also shown, as further evidence of the bravery of some of New Orleans' "finest," that one of them, seeing Capt. Day fall, ran seven blocks before he stopped, afterwards giving the excuse that he was hunting for a patrol box.

At daybreak the officers felt safe to renew the attack upon Charles, so they broke into his room, only to find that—what they probably very well knew—he had gone. It appears that he made his escape by crawling through a hole in the ceiling to a little attic in his house. Here he found that he could not escape except by a window which led into an alley which had no opening on 4th street. He scaled the fence and was soon out of reach.

It was now 5 o'clock Tuesday morning, and a general alarm was given. Sergeant Aucoin and Corporal Trenchard, having received a new supply of courage by returning daylight, renewed their effort to capture the man that they had allowed to escape in the darkness. Citizens were called upon to participate in the man hunt and New Orleans was soon the scene of terrible excitement. Officers were present everywhere, and colored men were arrested on all sides upon the pretext that they were impertinent and "game niggers." An instance is mentioned in the *Times-Democrat* of the 25th and shows the treatment which unoffending colored men received at the hands of some of the officers. This instance shows Corporal Trenchard, who displayed such remarkable bravery on Monday night in dodging Charles' revolver, in his true light. It shows how brave a white man is when he has a gun attacking a Negro who is a helpless prisoner. The account is as follows:

> The police made some arrests in the neighborhood of the killing of the two officers. Mobs of young darkies gathered everywhere. These Negroes talked and joked about the affair, and many of them were for starting a race war on the spot. It was not until several of these little gangs amalgamated and started demonstrations that the police commenced to act.

Nearly a dozen arrests were made within an hour, and everybody in the vicinity was in a tremor of excitement.

It was about 1 o'clock that the Negroes on Fourth street became very noisy, and George Meyers, who lives on Sixth street, near Rampart, appeared to be one of the prime movers in a little riot that was rapidly developing. Policeman Exnicios and Sheridan placed him under arrest, and owing to the fact that the patrol wagon had just left with a number of prisoners, they walked him toward St. Charles avenue in order to get a conveyance to take him to the Sixth Precinct station.

A huge crowd of Negroes followed the officers and their prisoners. Between Dryades and Baronne, on Sixth, Corporal Trenchard met the trio. He had his pistol in his hand and he came on them running. The Negroes in the wake of the officers and prisoner took to flight immediately. Some disappeared through gates and some over fences and into yards, for Trenchard, visibly excited, was waving his revolver in the air and was threatening to shoot. He joined the officers in their walk toward St. Charles street, and the way he acted led the white people who were witnessing the affair to believe that his prisoner was the wanted Negro. At every step he would punch him or hit him with the barrel of his pistol, and the onlookers cried, "Lynch him!" "Kill him!" and other expressions until the spectators were thoroughly wrought up. At St. Charles street Trenchard desisted, and, calling an empty ice wagon, threw the Negro into the body of the vehicle and ordered Officer Exnicios to take him to the Sixth Precinct station.

The ride to the station was a wild one. Exnicios had all he could do to watch his prisoner. A gang climbed into the wagon and administered a terrible thrashing to the black en route. It took a half hour to reach the police station, for the mule that was drawing the wagon was not overly fast. When the station was reached a mob of nearly 200 howling white youths was awaiting it. The noise they made was something terrible. Meyers was howling for mercy before he reached the ground. The mob dragged him from the wagon, the officer with him. Then began a torrent of abuse for the unfortunate prisoner.

The station door was but thirty feet away, but it took Exnicios nearly five minutes to fight his way through the mob to the door. There were no other officers present, and the station seemed to be deserted. Neither the doorman nor the clerk paid any attention to the noise on the outside. As the result, the maddened crowd wrought their vengeance on the Negro. He was punched, kicked, bruised and torn. The clothes were ripped from his back, while his face after that few minutes was unrecognizable.

This was the treatment accorded and permitted to a helpless prisoner because he was black. All day Wednesday the man hunt continued. The excitement caused by the deaths of Day and Lamb became intense. The officers of the law knew they were trailing a man whose aim was deadly and whose courage they had never seen surpassed. Commenting upon the marksmanship of the man which the paper styled a fiend, the *Times-Democrat* of Wednesday said:

One of the extraordinary features of the tragedy was the marksmanship displayed by the Negro desperado. His aim was deadly and his coolness must have been something phenomenal. The two shots that killed Captain Day and Patrolman Lamb struck their victims in the head, a circumstance remarkable enough in itself, considering the suddenness and fury of the onslaught and the darkness that reigned in the alley way.

Later on Charles fired at Corporal Perrier, who was standing at least seventy-five yards away. The murderer appeared at the gate, took lightning aim along the side of the house, and sent a bullet whizzing past the officer's ear. It was a close shave, and a few inches' deflection would no doubt have added a fourth victim to the list.

At the time of the affray there is good reason to believe that Charles was seriously wounded, and at any event he had lost quantities of blood. His situation was as critical as it is possible to imagine, yet he shot like an expert in a target range. The circumstance shows the desperate character of the fiend, and his terrible dexterity with weapons makes him one of the most formidable monsters that has ever been loose upon the community.

Wednesday New Orleans was in the hands of a mob. Charles, still sought for and still defending himself, had killed four policemen, and everybody knew that he intended to die fighting. Unable to vent its vindictiveness and bloodthirsty vengeance upon Charles, the mob turned its attention to other colored men who happened to get in the path of its fury. Even colored women, as has happened many times before, were assaulted and beaten and killed by the brutal hoodlums who thronged the streets. The reign of absolute lawlessness began about 8 o'clock Wednesday night. The mob gathered near the Lee statue[5] and was soon making its way to the place where the officers had been shot by Charles.

                         ✻   ✻   ✻

The first colored man to meet death at the hands of the mob was a passenger on a street car. The mob had broken itself into fragments after its disappointment at the jail, each fragment looking for a Negro to kill. The bloodthirsty cruelty of one crowd is thus described by the *Times-Democrat*:

> "We will get a Nigger down here, you bet!" was the yelling boast that went up from a thousand throats, and for the first time the march of the mob was directed toward the downtown sections. The words of the rioters were prophetic, for just as Canal street was reached a car on the Villere line came along.
>
> "Stop that car!" cried half a hundred men. The advance guard, heeding the injunction, rushed up to the slowly moving car, and several, seizing the trolley, jerked it down.
>
> "Here's a Negro!' said half a dozen men who sprang upon the car.
>
> "The car was full of passengers at the time, among them several women. When the trolley was pulled down and the car thrown in total darkness, the latter began to scream, and for a moment or so it looked as if the life of every person in the car was in peril, for some of the crowd with demoniacal yells of "There he goes!" began to fire their weapons indiscriminately. The passengers in the car hastily jumped to the ground and joined the crowd, as it was evidently the safest place to be.
>
> "Where's that Nigger?" was the query passed along the line, and with that the search began in earnest. The Negro, after jumping off the car,

5. In central New Orleans, a statue in honor of Robert E. Lee.

lost himself for a few moments in the crowd, but after a brief search he was again located. The slight delay seemed, if possible, only to whet the desire of the bloodthirsty crowd, for the reappearance of the Negro was the signal for a chorus of screams and pistol shots directed at the fugitive. With the speed of a deer, the man ran straight from the corner of Canal and Villere to Customhouse street. The pursuers, closely following, kept up a running fire, but notwithstanding the fact that they were right at the Negro's heels their aim was poor and their bullets went wide of the mark.

The Negro, on reaching Customhouse street, darted from the sidewalk out into the middle of the street. This was the worst maneuver that he could have made, as it brought him directly under the light from an arc lamp, located on a nearby corner. When the Negro came plainly in view of the foremost of the closely following mob they directed a volley at him. Half a dozen pistols flashed simultaneously, and one of the bullets evidently found its mark, for the Negro stopped short, threw up his hands, wavered for a moment, and then started to run again. This stop, slight as it was, proved fatal to the Negro's chances, for he had not gotten twenty steps farther when several of the men in advance of the others reached his side. A burly fellow, grabbing him with one hand, dealt him a terrible blow on the head with the other. The wounded man sank to the ground. The crowd pressed around him and began to beat him and stamp him. The men in the rear pressed forward and those beating the man were shoved forward. The half-dead Negro, when he was freed from his assailants, crawled over to the gutter. The men behind, however, stopped pushing when those in front yelled, "We've got him," and then it was that the attack on the bleeding Negro was resumed. A vicious kick directed at the Negro's head sent him into the gutter, and for a moment the body sank from view beneath the muddy, slimy water. "Pull him out; don't let him drown," was the cry, and instantly several of the men around the half-drowned Negro bent down and drew the body out. Twisting the body around they drew the head and shoulders up on the street, while from the waist down the Negro's body remained under the water. As soon as the crowd saw that the Negro was still alive they again began to beat and kick him. Every few moments they would stop and striking matches look into the man's face to see if he still lived. To better see if he was dead they would stick lighted matches to his eyes. Finally, believing he was dead, they left him and started out to look for other Negroes. Just about this time some one yelled, "He ain't dead," and the men came back and renewed the attack. While the men were beating and pounding the prostrate form with stones and sticks a man in the crowd ran up, and crying, "I'll fix the d—— Negro," poked the muzzle of a pistol almost against the body and fired. This shot must have ended the man's life, for he lay like a stone, and realizing that they were wasting energy in further attacks, the men left their victim lying in the street.

The same paper, on the same day, July 26th, describes the brutal butchery of an aged colored man early in the morning:

> Baptiste Philo, a Negro, 75 years of age, was a victim of mob violence at Kerlerec and North Peters streets about 2:30 o'clock this morning. The

old man is employed about the French Market, and was on his way there when he was met by a crowd and desperately shot. The old man found his way to the Third Precinct police station, where it was found that he had received a ghastly wound in the abdomen. The ambulance was summoned and he was conveyed to the Charity Hospital. The students pronounced the wound fatal after a superficial examination.

Mob rule continued Thursday, its violence increasing every hour, until 2 p.m., when the climax seemed to be reached. The fact that colored men and women had been made the victims of brutal mobs, chased through the streets, killed upon the highways and butchered in their homes, did not call the best element in New Orleans to active exertion in behalf of law and order. The killing of a few Negroes more or less by irresponsible mobs does not cut much figure in Louisiana. But when the reign of mob law exerts a depressing influence upon the stock market and city securities begin to show unsteady standing in money centers, then the strong arm of the good white people of the South asserts itself and order is quickly brought out of chaos.

It was so with New Orleans on that Thursday. The better element of the white citizens began to realize that New Orleans in the hands of a mob would not prove a promising investment for Eastern capital, so the better element began to stir itself, not for the purpose of punishing the brutality against the Negroes who had been beaten, or bringing to justice the murderers of those who had been killed, but for the purpose of saving the city's credit.

\* \* \*

With the financial credit of the city at stake, the good citizens rushed to the rescue, and soon the Mayor was able to mobilize a posse of 1,000 willing men to assist the police in maintaining order, but rioting still continued in different sections of the city. Colored men and women were beaten, chased and shot whenever they made their appearance upon the street. Late in the night a most despicable piece of villainy occurred on Rousseau street, where an aged colored woman was killed by the mob. The *Times-Democrat* thus describes the murder:

> Hannah Mabry, an old Negress, was shot and desperately wounded shortly after midnight this morning while sleeping in her home at No. 1929 Rousseau street. It was the work of a mob, and was evidently well planned so far as escape was concerned, for the place was reached by police officers and a squad of the volunteer police within a very short time after the reports of the shots, but not a prisoner was secured. The square was surrounded, but the mob had scattered in several directions, and, the darkness of the neighborhood aiding them, not one was taken.
>
> At the time the mob made the attack on the little house there were also in it David Mabry, the 62-year-old husband of the wounded woman; her son, Harry Mabry; his wife, Fannie, and an infant child. The young couple with their babe could not be found after the whole affair was over, and they either escaped or were hustled off by the mob. A careful search of the whole neighborhood was made, but no trace of them could be found.
>
> The little place occupied by the Mabry family is an old cottage on the swamp side of Rousseau street. It is furnished with slat shutters to both

doors and windows. These shutters had been pulled off by the mob and the volleys fired through the glass doors. The younger Mabrys, father, mother and child, were asleep in the first room at the time. Hannah Mabry and her old husband were sleeping in the next room. The old couple occupied the same bed, and it is miraculous that the old man did not share the fate of his spouse.

Officer Bitterwolf, who was one of the first on the scene, said that he was about a block and a half away with Officers Fordyce and Sweeney. There were about twenty shots fired, and the trio raced to the cottage. They saw twenty or thirty men running down Rousseau street. Chase was given and the crowd turned toward the river and scattered into several vacant lots in the neighborhood.

The volunteer police stationed at the Sixth Precinct had about five blocks to run before they arrived. They also moved on the reports of the firing, and in a remarkably short time the square was surrounded, but no one could be taken. As they ran to the scene they were assailed on every hand with vile epithets and the accusation of "Nigger lovers."

Rousseau street, where the cottage is situated, is a particularly dark spot, and no doubt the members of the mob were well acquainted with the neighborhood, for the officers said that they seemed to sink into the earth, so completely and quickly did they disappear after they had completed their work, which was complete with the firing of the volley.

Hannah Mabry was taken to the Charity Hospital in the ambulance, where it was found on examination that she had been shot through the right lung, and that the wound was a particularly serious one.

Her old husband was found in the little wrecked home well nigh distracted with fear and grief. It was he who informed the police that at the time of the assault the younger Mabrys occupied the front room. As he ran about the little home as well as his feeble condition would permit he severely lacerated his feet on the glass broken from the windows and door. He was escorted to the Sixth Precinct station, where he was properly cared for. He could not realize why his little family had been so murderously attacked, and was inconsolable when his wife was driven off in the ambulance piteously moaning in her pain.

*　*　*

### Death of Charles

Friday witnessed the final act in the bloody drama begun by the three police officers, Aucoin, Mora and Cantrelle. Betrayed into the hands of the police, Charles, who had already sent two of his would-be murderers to their death, made a last stand in a small building, 1210 Saratoga street, and, still defying his pursuers, fought a mob of twenty thousand people, single-handed and alone, killing three more men, mortally wounding two more and seriously wounding nine others. Unable to get to him in his stronghold, the besiegers set fire to his house of refuge. While the building was burning Charles was shooting, and every crack of his death-dealing rifle added another victim to the price which he had placed upon his own life. Finally, when fire and smoke became too much for flesh and blood to stand, the long sought for fugitive appeared in the door, rifle in hand, to charge the countless guns that were drawn upon him. With a courage which was indescribable, he raised his gun to fire again, but this time it failed, for a hundred shots riddled his body, and he fell dead face fronting to the mob. This last scene in the terrible drama is thus described in the *Times-Democrat* of July 26th:

Early yesterday afternoon, at 3 o'clock or thereabouts, Police Sergeant Gabriel Porteus was instructed by Chief Gaster to go to a house at No. 1210 Saratoga street, and search it for the fugitive murderer, Robert Charles. A private 'tip' had been received at the headquarters that the fiend was hiding somewhere on the premises.

Sergeant Porteus took with him Corporal John R. Lally and Officers Zeigel and Essey. The house to which they were directed is a small, double frame cottage, standing flush with Saratoga street, near the corner of Clio. It has two street entrances and two rooms on each side, one in front and one in the rear. It belongs to the type of cheap little dwellings commonly tenanted by Negroes.

"Sergeant Porteus left Zeigel and Essey to guard the outside and went with Corporal Lally to the rear house, where he found Jackson and his wife in the large room on the left. What immediately ensued is only known by the Negroes. They say the sergeant began to question them about their lodgers and finally asked them whether they knew anything about Robert Charles. They strenuously denied all knowledge of his whereabouts.

The Negroes lied. At that very moment the hunted and desperate murderer lay concealed not a dozen feet away. Near the rear, left-hand corner of the room is a closet or pantry, about three feet deep, and perhaps eight feet long. The door was open and Charles was crouching, Winchester[6] in hand, in the dark further end.

Near the closet door was a bucket of water, and Jackson says that Sergeant Porteous walked toward it to get a drink. At the next moment a shot rang out and the brave officer fell dead. Lally was shot directly afterward. Exactly how and where will never be known, but the probabilities are that the black fiend sent a bullet into him before he recovered from his surprise at the sudden onslaught. Then the murderer dashed out of the back door and disappeared.

The neighborhood was already agog with the tragic events of the two preceding days, and the sound of the shots was a signal for wild and instant excitement. In a few moments a crowd had gathered and people were pouring in by the hundred from every point of the compass. Jackson and his wife had fled and at first nobody knew what had happened, but the surmise that Charles had recommenced his bloody work was on every tongue and soon some of the bolder found their way to the house in the rear. There the bleeding forms of the two policemen told the story.

Lally was still breathing, and a priest was sent for to administer the last rites. Father Fitzgerald responded, and while he was bending over the dying man the outside throng was rushing wildly through the surrounding yards and passageways searching for the murderer. "Where is he?" "What has become of him?" were the questions on every lip.

"Suddenly the answer came in a shot from the room directly overhead. It was fired through a window facing Saratoga street, and the bullet struck down a young man named Alfred J. Bloomfield, who was standing

6. A hunting rifle.

in the narrow passage-way between the two houses. He fell on his knees and a second bullet stretched him dead.

When he fled from the closet Charles took refuge in the upper story of the house. There are four windows on that floor, two facing toward Saratoga street and two toward Rampart. The murderer kicked several breaches in the frail central partition, so he could rush from side to side, and like a trapped beast, prepared to make his last stand.

Nobody had dreamed that he was still in the house, and when Bloomfield was shot there was a headlong stampede. It was some minutes before the exact situation was understood. Then rifles and pistols began to speak, and a hail of bullets poured against the blind frontage of the old house. Every one hunted some coign of vantage, and many climbed to adjacent roofs. Soon the glass of the four upper windows was shattered by flying lead. The fusillade sounded like a battle, and the excitement upon the streets was indescribable.

Throughout all this hideous uproar Charles seems to have retained a certain diabolical coolness. He kept himself mostly out of sight, but now and then he thrust the gleaming barrel of his rifle through one of the shattered window panes and fired at his besiegers. He worked the weapon with incredible rapidity, discharging from three to five cartridges each time before leaping back to a place of safety. These replies came from all four windows indiscriminately, and showed that he was keeping a close watch in every direction. His wonderful marksmanship never failed him for a moment, and when he missed it was always by the narrowest margin only.

On the Rampart street side of the house there are several sheds, commanding an excellent range of the upper story. Detective Littleton, Andrew Van Kuren of the Workhouse force and several others climbed upon one of these and opened fire on the upper windows, shooting whenever they could catch a glimpse of the assassin. Charles responded with his rifle, and presently Van Kuren climbed down to find a better position. He was crossing the end of the shed when he was killed.

Another of Charles' bullets found its billet in the body of Frank Evans, an ex-member of the police force. He was on the Rampart street side firing whenever he had an opportunity. Officer J. W. Bofill and A. S. Leclerc were also wounded in the fusillade.

While the events thus briefly outlined were transpiring time was a-wing, and the cooler-headed in the crowd began to realize that some quick and desperate expedient must be adopted to insure the capture of the fiend and to avert what might be a still greater tragedy than any yet enacted. For nearly two hours the desperate monster had held his besiegers at bay, darkness would soon be at hand and no one could predict what might occur if he made a dash for liberty in the dark.

At this critical juncture it was suggested that the house be fired. The plan came as an inspiration, and was adopted as the only solution of the situation. The wretched old rookery counted for nothing against the possible continued sacrifice of human life, and steps were immediately taken to apply the torch. The fire department had been summoned to the scene soon after the shooting began; its officers were warned to be ready to prevent a spread of the conflagration, and several men rushed into the lower right-hand room and started a blaze in one corner.

They first fired an old mattress, and soon smoke was pouring out in dense volumes. It filled the interior of the ramshackle structure, and it was evident that the upper story would soon become untenable. An interval of tense excitement followed, and all eyes were strained for a glimpse of the murderer when he emerged.

Then came the thrilling climax. Smoked out of his den, the desperate fiend descended the stairs and entered the lower room. Some say he dashed into the yard, glaring around vainly for some avenue of escape; but, however that may be, he was soon a few moments later moving about behind the lower windows. A dozen shots were sent through the wall in the hope of reaching him, but he escaped unscathed. Then suddenly the door on the right was flung open and he dashed out. With head lowered and rifle raised ready to fire on the instant, Charles dashed straight for the rear door of the front cottage. To reach it he had to traverse a little walk shaded by a vine-clad arbor. In the back room, with a cocked revolver in his hand, was Dr. C. A. Noiret, a young medical student, who was aiding the citizens' posse. As he sprang through the door Charles fired a shot, and the bullet whizzed past the doctor's head. Before it could be repeated Noiret's pistol cracked and the murderer reeled, turned half around and fell on his back. The doctor sent another ball into his body as he struck the floor, and half a dozen men, swarming into the room from the front, riddled the corpse with bullets.

Private Adolph Anderson of the Connell Rifles was the first man to announce the death of the wretch. He rushed to the street door, shouted the news to the crowd, and a moment later the bleeding body was dragged to the pavement and made the target of a score of pistols. It was shot, kicked and beaten almost out of semblance to humanity.

The limp dead body was dropped at the edge of the sidewalk and from there dragged to the muddy roadway by half a hundred hands. There in the road more shots were fired into the body. Corporal Trenchard, a brother-in-law of Porteus, led the shooting into the inanimate clay. With each shot there was a cheer for the work that had been done and curses and imprecations on the inanimate mass of riddled flesh that was once Robert Charles.

Cries of "Burn him! Burn him!" were heard from Clio street all the way to Erato street, and it was with difficulty that the crowd was restrained from totally destroying the wretched dead body. Some of those who agitated burning even secured a large vessel of kerosene, which had previously been brought to the scene for the purpose of firing Charles' refuge, and for a time it looked as though this vengeance might be wreaked on the body. The officers, however, restrained this move, although they were powerless to prevent the stamping and kicking of the body by the enraged crowd.

After the infuriated citizens had vented their spleen on the body of the dead Negro it was loaded into the patrol wagon. The police raised the body of the heavy black from the ground and literally chucked it into the space on the floor of the wagon between the seats. They threw it with a curse hissed more than uttered and born of the bitterness which was rankling in their breasts at the thought of Charles having taken so wantonly the lives of four of the best of their fellow-officers.

When the murderer's body landed in the wagon it fell in such a position that the hideously mutilated head, kicked, stamped and crushed, hung over the end.

As the wagon moved off, the followers, who were protesting against its being carried off, declaring that it should be burned, poked and struck it with sticks, beating it into such a condition that it was utterly impossible to tell what the man ever looked like.

As the patrol wagon rushed through the rough street, jerking and swaying from one side of the thoroughfare to the other, the gory, mud-smeared head swayed and swung and jerked about in a sickening manner, the dark blood dripping on the steps and spattering the body of the wagon and the trousers of the policemen standing on the step.

### Mob Brutality

The brutality of the mob was further shown by the unspeakable cruelty with which it beat, shot and stabbed to death an unoffending colored man, name unknown, who happened to be walking on the street with no thought that he would be set upon and killed simply because he was a colored man. The *Times-Democrat*'s description of the outrage is as follows:

> While the fight between the Negro desperado and the citizens was in progress yesterday afternoon at Clio and Saratoga streets another tragedy was being enacted downtown in the French quarter, but it was a very one-sided affair. The object of the white man's wrath was, of course, a Negro, but, unlike Charles, he showed no fight, but tried to escape from the furious mob which was pursuing him, and which finally put an end to his existence in a most cruel manner.
>
> The Negro, whom no one seemed to know—at any rate no one could be found in the vicinity of the killing who could tell who he was—was walking along the levee, as near as could be learned, when he was attacked by a number of white longshoremen or screwmen.[7] For what reason, if there was any reason other than the fact that he was a Negro, could not be learned, and immediately they pounced upon him he broke ground and started on a desperate run for his life.
>
> The hunted Negro started off the levee toward the French Vegetable Market, changed his course out the sidewalk toward Gallatin street. The angry, yelling mob was close at his heels, and increasing steadily as each block was traversed. At Gallatin street he turned up that thoroughfare, doubled back into North Peters street and ran into the rear of No. 1216 of that street, which is occupied by Chris Reuter as a commission store and residence.
>
> He rushed frantically through the place and out on to the gallery on the Gallatin street side. From this gallery he jumped to the street and fell flat on his back on the sidewalk. Springing to his feet as soon as possible, with a leaden hail fired by the angry mob whistling about him, he turned to his merciless pursuers in an appealing way, and, throwing up one hand, told them not to shoot any more, that they could take him as he was.
>
> But the hail of lead continued, and the unfortunate Negro finally

---

7. Longshoremen loaded and unloaded ships. Screwmen were longshoremen who loaded and unloaded bales of cotton.

dropped to the sidewalk, mortally wounded. The mob then rushed upon him, still continuing the fusillade, and upon reaching his body a number of Italians, who had joined the howling mob, reached down and stabbed him in the back and buttock with big knives. Others fired shots into his head until his teeth were shot out, three shots having been fired into his mouth. There were bullet wounds all over his body.

Others who witnessed the affair declared that the man was fired at as he was running up the stairs leading to the living apartments above the store, and that after jumping to the sidewalk and being knocked down by a bullet he jumped up and ran across the street, then ran back and tried to get back into the commission store. The Italians, it is said, were all drunk, and had been shooting firecrackers. Tiring of this, they began shooting at Negroes, and when the unfortunate man who was killed ran by they joined in the chase.

No one was arrested for the shooting, the neighborhood having been deserted by the police, who were sent up to the place where Charles was fighting so desperately. No one could or would give the names of any of those who had participated in the chase and the killing, nor could any one be found who knew who the Negro was. The patrol wagon was called and the terribly mutilated body sent to the morgue and the coroner notified.

The murdered Negro was copper colored, about 5 feet 11 inches in height, about 35 years of age, and was dressed in blue overalls and a brown slouch hat. At 10:30 o'clock the vicinity of the French Market was very quiet. Squads of special officers were patrolling the neighborhood, and there did not seem to be any prospects of disorder.

During the entire time the mob held the city in its hands and went about holding up street cars and searching them, taking from them colored men to assault, shoot and kill, chasing colored men upon the public square, through alleys and into houses of anybody who would take them in, breaking into the homes of defenseless colored men and women and beating aged and decrepit men and women to death, the police and the legally-constituted authorities showed plainly where their sympathies were, for in no case reported through the daily papers does there appear the arrest, trial and conviction of one of the mob for any of the brutalities which occurred. The ringleaders of the mob were at no time disguised. Men were chased, beaten and killed by white brutes, who boasted of their crimes, and the murderers still walk the streets of New Orleans, well known and absolutely exempt from prosecution. Not only were they exempt from prosecution by the police while the town was in the hands of the mob, but even now that law and order is supposed to resume control, these men, well known, are not now, nor ever will be, called to account for the unspeakable brutalities of that terrible week. On the other hand, the colored men who were beaten by the police and dragged into the station for purposes of intimidation, were quickly called up before the courts and fined or sent to jail upon the statement of the police.

\* \* \*

### Shocking Brutality

The whole city was at the mercy of the mob and the display of brutality was a disgrace to civilization. One instance is described in the *Picayune* as follows:

A smaller party detached itself from the mob at Washington and Rampart streets, and started down the latter thoroughfare. One of the foremost spied a Negro, and immediately there was a rush for the unfortunate black man. With the sticks they had torn from fences on the line of march the young outlaws attacked the black and clubbed him unmercifully, acting more like demons than human beings. After being severely beaten over the head, the Negro started to run with the whole gang at his heels. Several revolvers were brought into play and pumped their lead at the refugee. The Negro made rapid progress and took refuge behind the blinds of a little cottage in Rampart street, but he had been seen, and the mob hauled him from his hiding place and again commenced beating him. There were more this time, some twenty or thirty, all armed with sticks and heavy clubs, and under their incessant blows the Negro could not last long. He begged for mercy, and his cries were most pitiful, but a mob has no heart, and his cries were only answered with more blows.

"For God's sake, boss, I ain't done nothin'. Don't kill me. I swear I ain't done nothin'."

The white brutes turned

### A DEAF EAR TO THE PITYING CRIES

of the black wretch and the drubbing continued. The cries subsided into moans, and soon the black swooned away into unconsciousness. Still not content with their heartless work, they pulled the Negro out and kicked him into the gutter. For the time those who had beaten the black seemed satisfied and left him groaning in the gutter, but others came up, and, regretting that they had not had a hand in the affair, they determined to evidence their bravery to their fellows and beat the man while he was in the gutter, hurling rocks and stones at his black form. One thoughtless white brute, worse even than the black slayer of the police officers, thought to make himself a hero in the eyes of his fellows and fired his revolver repeatedly into the helpless wretch. It was dark and the fellow probably aimed carelessly. After firing three or four shots he also left without knowing what extent of injury he inflicted on the black wretch who was left lying in the gutter."

\* \* \*

### A Gray-Haired Victim

The bloodthirsty barbarians, having tasted blood, continued their hunt and soon ran across an old man of 75 years. His life had been spent in hard work about the French market, and he was well known as an unoffending, peaceable and industrious old man.

But that made no difference to the mob. He was a Negro, and with a fiendishness that was worse than that of cannibals they beat his life out. The report says:

There was another gang of men parading the streets in the lower part of the city, looking for any stray Negro who might be on the streets. As they neared the corner of Dauphine and Kerlerec, a square below

Esplanade avenue, they came upon Baptiste Thilo, an aged Negro, who works in the French Market.

Thilo for years has been employed by the butchers and fish merchants to carry baskets from the stalls to the wagons, and unload the wagons as they arrive in the morning. He was on his way to the market, when the mob came upon him. One of the gang struck the old Negro, and as he fell, another in the crowd, supposed to be a young fellow, fired a shot. The bullet entered the body just below the right nipple.

As the Negro fell the crowd looked into his face and they discovered then that the victim was very old. The young man who did the shooting said: 'Oh, he is an old Negro. I'm sorry that I shot him.'

This is all the old Negro received in the way of consolation.

He was left where he fell, but later staggered to his feet and made his way to the third precinct station. There the police summoned the ambulance and the students pronounced the wound very dangerous. He was carried to the hospital as rapidly as possible.

There was no arrest.

Just before daybreak the mob found another victim. He, too, was on his way to market, driving a meat wagon. But little is told of his treatment, nothing more than the following brief statement:

> At nearly 3 o'clock this morning a report was sent to the Third Precinct station that a Negro was lying on the sidewalk at the corner of Decatur and St. Philip. The man had been pulled off of a meat wagon and riddled with bullets.
>
> When the police arrived he was insensible and apparently dying. The ambulance students attended the Negro and pronounced the wounds fatal.
>
> There was nothing found which would lead to the discovery of his identity.

✳   ✳   ✳

### Was Charles a Desperado?

The press of the country has united in declaring that Robert Charles was a desperado. As usual, when dealing with a Negro, he is assumed to be guilty because he is charged. Even the most conservative of journals refuse to ask evidence to prove that the dead man was a criminal, and that his life had been given over to law-breaking. The minute that the news was flashed across the country that he had shot a white man it was at once declared that he was a fiend incarnate, and that when he was killed the community would be ridden of a black-hearted desperado.

The reporters of the New Orleans papers, who were in the best position to trace the record of this man's life, made every possible effort to find evidence to prove that he was a villain unhung. With all the resources at their command, and inspired by intense interest to paint him as black a villain as possible, these reporters signally failed to disclose a single indictment which charged Robert Charles with a crime. Because they failed to find any legal evidence that Charles was a lawbreaker and desperado his accusers gave full license to their imagination and distorted the facts that they had obtained, in every way possible, to prove a course of criminality, which the records absolutely refuse to show.

Charles had his first encounter with the police Monday night, in which he was shot in the street duel which was begun by the police after Officer Mora had beaten Charles three or four times over the head with his billy in an attempt to make an illegal arrest. In defending himself against the combined attack of two officers with a billy and their guns upon him, Charles shot Officer Mora and escaped.

Early Tuesday morning Charles was traced to Dryades street by officers who were instructed to kill him on sight. There, again defending himself, he shot and killed two officers. This, of course, in the eyes of the American press, made him a desperado. The New Orleans press, in substantiating the charges that he was a desperado, make statements which will be interesting to examine.

In the first place the New Orleans *Times-Democrat,* of July 25th, calls Charles a "ravisher and a daredevil." It says that from all sources that could be searched "the testimony was cumulative that the character of the murderer, Robert Charles, is that of a daredevil and a fiend in human form." Then in the same article it says:

> The belongings of Robert Charles which were found in his room were a complete index to the character of the man. Although the room and its contents were in a state of chaos on account of the frenzied search for clews by officers and citizens, an examination of his personal effects revealed the mental state of the murderer and the rancor in his heart toward the Caucasian race. Never was the adage, "A little learning is a dangerous thing," better exemplified than in the case of the negro who shot to death the two officers.

His room was searched, and the evidence upon which the charge that he was a desperado consisted of pamphlets in support of Negro emigration to Liberia.[8] On his mantel-piece there was found a bullet mold and an outfit for reloading cartridges. There were also two pistol scabbards and a bottle of cocaine. The other evidences that Charles was a desperado the writer described as follows:

> In his room were found negro periodicals and other "race" propaganda, most of which was in the interest of the negro's emigration to Liberia. There were *Police Gazettes* strewn about his room and other papers of a similar character. Well-worn text-books, bearing his name written in his own scrawling handwriting, and well-filled copybooks found in his trunk showed that he had burnt the midnight oil, and was desirous of improving himself intellectually in order that he might conquer the hated white race. Much of the literature found among his chattels was of a superlatively vituperative character, and attacked the white race in unstinted language and asserted the equal rights of the Negro.
>
> Charles was evidently the local agent of the "Voice of Missions," a "reli-

8. Founded by Marcus Garvey (1887–1940), a Jamaican-born publisher, journalist, entrepreneur, crusader for black nationalism, and founder of the Universal Negro Improvement Association and African Communities League, the "back-to-Africa" movement encouraged people of African ancestry to return to their ancestral homeland. Liberia was one of the main countries Garvey and his followers aimed to live in.

gious" paper, published at Atlanta, as great bundles of that sheet were found. It is edited by one Bishop Turner,[9] and seems to be the official organ of all haters of the white race. Its editorials are anarchistic in the extreme, and urge upon the negro that the sooner he realizes that he is as good as the white man the better it will be for him. The following verses were clipped from the journal; they were marked "till forbidden," and appeared in several successive numbers:

### OUR SENTIMENTS.

#### H. M. T.

My country, 'tis of thee,
Dear land of Africa,
    Of thee we sing.
Land where our fathers died,
Land of the Negro's pride,
    God's truth shall ring.

My native country, thee,
Land of the black and free,
    Thy name I love;
To see thy rocks and rills,
Thy woods and matchless hills,
    Like that above.

When all thy slanderous ghouls,
In the bosom of sheol,[1]
    Forgotten lie,
Thy monumental name shall live,
And suns thy royal brow shall gild,
    Upheaved to heaven high,
    O'ertopping thrones.

There were no valuables in his room, and if he was a professional thief he had his headquarters for storing his plunder at some other place than his room on Fourth street. Nothing was found in his room that could lead to the belief that he was a thief, except fifty or more small bits of soap. The inference was that every place he visited he took all of the soap lying around, as all of the bits were well worn and had seen long service on the washstand.

His wearing apparel was little more than rags, and financially he was evidently not in a flourishing condition. He was in no sense a skilled workman, and his room showed, in fact, that he was nothing more than a laborer.

9. African Methodist Episcopal bishop and former chaplain to the Union Army, Henry M. Turner (1834–1915) criticized U.S. imperialism and racism as an outspoken African emigrationist. He was the editor of the Voice of Missions, which disseminated his views on the need for the international solidarity of blacks, urged actions to redress their common grievances, and counseled the necessity for defensive violence. The Voice often contained graphic accounts of the outrages committed against blacks by whites. Bishop Turner established dozens of AME churches in the United States and in Africa.
1. In the Old Testament, place in the depths of the Earth where the dead go.

The "philosopher in the garret" was a dirty wretch, and his room, his bedding and his clothing were nasty and filthy beyond belief. His object in life seemed to have been the discomfiture of the white race, and to this purpose he devoted himself with zeal. He declared himself to be a "patriot," and wished to be the Moses of his race.

Under the title of "The Making of a Monster," the reporter attempts to give "something of the personality of the arch-fiend, Charles." Giving his imagination full vent, the writer says:

It is only natural that the deepest interest should attach to the personality of Robert Charles. What manner of man was this fiend incarnate? What conditions developed him? Who were his preceptors? From what ancestral strain, if any, did he derive his ferocious hatred of the whites, his cunning, his brute courage, the apostolic zeal which he displayed in spreading the propaganda of African equality? These are questions involving one of the most remarkable psychological problems of modern times.

\* \* \*

According to the further investigations of this reporter, Charles was also agent for Bishop Turner's "Voice of Missions," the colored missionary organ of the African Methodist Church, edited by H. M. Turner, of Atlanta, Georgia. Concerning his service as agent for the "Voice of Missions," the reporter says:

He secured a number of subscribers and visited them once a month to collect the installments. In order to insure regular payments it was necessary to keep up enthusiasm, which was prone to wane, and Charles consequently became an active and continual preacher of the propaganda of hatred. Whatever may have been his private sentiments at the outset, this constant harping on one string must eventually have had a powerful effect upon his own mind.

Exactly how he received his remuneration is uncertain, but he told several of his friends that he got a "big commission." Incidentally he solicited subscribers for a Negro paper called the Voice of the Missions, and when he struck a negro who did not want to go to Africa himself, he begged contributions for the "good of the cause."

In the course of time Charles developed into a fanatic on the subject of the Negro oppression and neglected business to indulge in wild tirades whenever he could find a listener. He became more anxious to make converts than to obtain subscribers, and the more conservative darkies began to get afraid of him. Meanwhile he got into touch with certain agitators in the North and made himself a distributing agent for their literature, a great deal of which he gave away. Making money was a secondary consideration to "the cause."

One of the most enthusiastic advocates of the Liberian scheme is the colored Bishop H. M. Turner, of Atlanta. Turner is a man of unusual ability, has been over to Africa personally several times, and has made himself conspicuous by denouncing laws which he claimed discriminated against the blacks. Charles was one of the bishop's disciples and evidence has been found that seems to indicate they were in correspondence.

This was all that the *Times-Democrat*'s reporters could find after the most diligent search to prove that Charles was the fiend incarnate which the press of New Orleans and elsewhere declared him to be.

The reporters of the New Orleans *Picayune* were no more successful than their brethren of the *Times-Democrat*. They, too, were compelled to substitute fiction for facts in their attempt to prove Charles a desperado. In the issue of the 26th of July it was said that Charles was well-known in Vicksburg, and was there a consort of thieves. They mentioned that a man named Benson Blake was killed in 1894 or 1895, and that four Negroes were captured, and two escaped. Of the two escaped they claim that Charles was one. The four Negroes who were captured were put in jail, and as usual, in the high state of civilization which characterizes Mississippi, the right of the person accused of crime to an indictment by legal process and a legal trial by jury was considered an useless formality if the accused happened to be black. A mob went to the jail that night, the four colored men were delivered to the mob, and all four were hanged in the court-house yard. The reporters evidently assumed that Charles was guilty, if, in fact, he was ever there, because the other four men were lynched. They did not consider it was a fact of any importance that Charles was never indicted. They called him a murderer on general principles.

### Died in Self-Defense

The life, character and death of Robert Charles challenges the thoughtful consideration of all fair-minded people. In the frenzy of the moment, when nearly a dozen men lay dead, the victims of his unerring and death-dealing aim, it was natural for a prejudiced press and for citizens in private life to denounce him as a desperado and a murderer. But sea depths are not measured when the ocean rages, nor can absolute justice be determined while public opinion is lashed into fury. There must be calmness to insure correctness of judgment. The fury of the hour must abate before we can deal justly with any man or any cause.

That Charles was not a desperado is amply shown by the discussion in the preceding chapter. The darkest pictures which the reporters could paint of Charles were quoted freely, so that the public might find upon what grounds the press declared him to be a lawbreaker. Unquestionably the grounds are wholly insufficient. Not a line of evidence has been presented to prove that Charles was the fiend which the first reports of the New Orleans [press] charge him to be.

Nothing more should be required to establish his good reputation, for the rule is universal that a reputation must be assumed to be good until it is proved bad. But that rule does not apply to the Negro, for as soon as he is suspected the public judgment immediately determines that he is guilty of whatever crime he stands charged. For this reason, as a matter of duty to the race, and the simple justice to the memory of Charles, an investigation has been made of the life and character of Charles before the fatal affray which led to his death.

Robert Charles was not an educated man. He was a student who faithfully investigated all the phases of oppression from which his race has suffered. That he was a student is amply shown by the *Times-Democrat* report of the 25th, which says:

"Well-worn text-books, bearing his name written in his own scrawling handwriting, and well-filled copy-books found in his trunk, showed that he had burned the midnight oil, and desired to improve himself intellectually in order that he might conquer the hated white race." From this quotation it will be seen that he spent the hours after days of hard toil in trying to improve himself, both in the study of text-books and in writing.

He knew that he was a student of a problem which required all the intelligence that a man could command, and he was burning his midnight oil gathering knowledge that he might better be able to come to an intelligent solution. To his aid in the study of this problem he sought the aid of a Christian newspaper, *The Voice of Missions,* the organ of the African Methodist Episcopal Church. He was in communication with its editor, who is a bishop, and is known all over this country as a man of learning, a lover of justice and the defender of law and order. Charles could receive from Bishop Turner not a word of encouragement to be other than an earnest, tireless and God-fearing student of the complex problems which affected the race.

For further help and assistance in his studies, Charles turned to an organization which has existed and flourished for many years, at all times managed by men of high Christian standing and absolute integrity. These men believe and preach a doctrine that the best interests of the Negro will be subserved by an emigration from America back to the Fatherland, and they do all they can to spread the doctrine of emigration and to give material assistance to those who desire to leave America and make their future homes in Africa. This organization is known as "The International Migration Society." It has its headquarters in Birmingham, Alabama. From this place it issues pamphlets, some of which were found in the home of Robert Charles, and which pamphlets the reporters of the New Orleans papers declare to be incendiary and dangerous in their doctrine and teaching.

Nothing could be further from the truth. Copies of any and all of them may be secured by writing to D. J. Flummer,[2] who is President and in charge of the home office in Birmingham, Alabama. Three of the pamphlets found in Charles' room are named respectively:

First, "Prospectus of the Liberian Colonization Society;" which pamphlet in a few brief pages tells of the work of the society, plans, prices and terms of transportation of colored people who choose to go to Africa. These pages are followed by a short, conservative discussion of the Negro question, and close with an argument that Africa furnishes the best asylum for the oppressed Negroes in this country.

The second pamphlet is entitled "Christian Civilization of Africa." This is a brief statement of the advantages of the Republic of Liberia, and an argument in support of the superior conditions which colored people may attain to by leaving the South and settling in Liberia.

The third pamphlet is entitled "The Negro and Liberia." This is a larger document than the other two, and treats more exhaustively the question of emigration, but from the first page to the last there is not an incendiary line or sentence. There is not even a suggestion of violence in all of its thirty-two pages, and not a word which could not be preached from every pulpit in the land.

---

2. In 1895, under the auspices of the International Migration Society, Flummer chartered a steamer to sail from Savannah with two hundred southern blacks planning to be colonists in Monrovia, Liberia.

If it is true that the workman is known by his tools, certainly no harm could ever come from the doctrines which were preached by Charles or the papers and pamphlets distributed by him. Nothing ever written in the "Voice of Missions," and nothing ever published in the pamphlets above alluded to in the remotest way suggest that a peaceable man should turn lawbreaker, or that any man should dye his hands in his brother's blood.

In order to secure as far as possible positive information about the life and character of Robert Charles, it was plain that the best course to pursue was to communicate with those with whom he had sustained business relations. Accordingly a letter was forwarded to Mr. D. J. Flummer, who is president of the colonization society, in which letter he was asked to state in reply what information he had of the life and character of Robert Charles. The result was a very prompt letter in response, the text of which is as follows:

Birmingham, Ala., Aug. 21, 1900.

Mrs. Ida B. Wells Barnett, Chicago, Ill.:

Dear Madam—Replying to your favor of recent date requesting me to write you giving such information as I may have concerning the life, habits and character of Robert Charles, who recently shot and killed police officers in New Orleans, I wish to say that my knowledge of him is only such as I have gained from his business connection with the International Migration Society during the past five or six years, during which time I was president of the society.

He having learned that the purpose of this society was to colonize the colored people in Liberia, West Africa, and thereby lessen or destroy the friction and prejudice existing in this country between the two races, set about earnestly and faithfully distributing the literature that we issued from time to time. He always appeared to be mild but earnest in his advocacy of emigration, and never to my knowledge used any method or means that would in the least appear unreasonable, and had always kept within the bounds of law and order in advocating emigration.

The work he performed for this society was all gratuitous, and apparently prompted from his love of humanity, and desires to be instrumental in building up a Negro Nationality in Africa.

If he ever violated a law before the killing of the policemen, I do not know of it. Yours very truly,

D. J. Flummer.

Besides this statement, Mr. Flummer enclosed a letter received by the Society two days before the tragedy at New Orleans. This letter was written by Robert Charles, and it attests his devotion to the cause of emigration which he had espoused. Memoranda on the margin of the letter show that the order was filled by mailing the pamphlets. It is very probable that these were the identical pamphlets which were found by the mob which broke into the room of Robert Charles and seized upon these harmless documents and declared they were sufficient evidence to prove Charles a desperado. In the light of subsequent events the letter of Charles, which follows, sounds like a voice from the tomb:

New Orleans, July 30, 1900.

Mr. D. J. Flummer:

Dear Sir—I received your last pamphlets and they are all given out. I want you to send me some more, and I enclose you the stamps. I think I will go over in Greenville, Miss., and give my people some pamphlets over there. Yours truly,

Robert Charles.

The latest word of information comes from New Orleans from a man who knew Charles intimately for six years. For obvious reasons, his name is withheld. In answer to a letter sent him he answers as follows:

New Orleans, Aug. 23, 1900.

Mrs. Ida B. Wells Barnett:

Dear Madam—It affords me great pleasure to inform you as far as I know of Robert Charles. I have been acquainted with him about six years in this city. He never has, as I know, given any trouble to anyone. He was quiet and a peaceful man and was very frank in speaking. He was too much of a hero to die; few can be found to equal him. I am very sorry to say that I do not know anything of his birthplace, nor his parents, but enclosed find letter from his uncle, from which you may find more information. You will also find one of the circulars in which Charles was in possession of which was styled as a crazy document. Let me say, until our preachers preach this document we will always be slaves. If you can help circulate this "crazy" doctrine I would be glad to have you do so, for I shall never rest until I get to that heaven on earth; that is, the west coast of Africa, in Liberia.

With best wishes to you I still remain, as always, for the good of the race,

By only those whose anger and vindictiveness warp their judgment is Robert Charles a desperado. Their word is not supported by the statement of a single fact which justifies their judgment, and no criminal record shows that he was ever indicted for any offense, much less convicted of crime. On the contrary, his work for many years had been with Christian people, circulating emigration pamphlets and active as agent for a mission publication. Men who knew him say that he was a law-abiding, quiet, industrious, peaceable man. So he lived.

So he lived and so he would have died had not he raised his hand to resent unprovoked assault and unlawful arrest that fateful Monday night. That made him an outlaw, and being a man of courage he decided to die with his face to the foe. The white people of this country may charge that he was a desperado, but to the people of his own race Robert Charles will always be regarded as the hero of New Orleans.

* * *

1900

# SUI SIN FAR (EDITH MAUD EATON)
## 1865–1914

Sui Sin Far was the first Eurasian writer to transform the experiences of late-nineteenth-century Chinese immigrants to North America into enduring art. As scholars Elizabeth Ammons, Amy Ling, and Annette White-Parks, among others, have demonstrated, Sui Sin Far—especially in her only book, *Mrs. Spring Fragrance* (1912)—deserves our attention not simply because she was the first to record the manifold wrongs done to the Chinese in North America but also because she wrote with skill and imaginative power.

Much remains unknown about Sui Sin Far, though a sense of both her vulnerability and her toughness can be strongly felt in such late autobiographical accounts as "Leaves from the Mental Portfolio of an Eurasian" (1909) and "Sui Sin Far, the Half-Chinese Writer, Tells of Her Career" (1912). The second of sixteen children, fourteen of whom lived to adulthood, Far was born Edith Maud Eaton in Macclesfield, England, to a Chinese mother raised in England and an English father from a well-to-do family. Her father, Edward Eaton, formerly a merchant, became alienated from his English family not long after his marriage to Grace Trefusus and struggled thereafter to earn a living as a landscape painter. In this rather bohemian atmosphere, as critic Amy Ling puts it, "Artistic endeavors, as well as early financial independence, were encouraged." When Far was seven the family moved first to New York State and then to Montreal. The family's fortunes entered a long period of decline when Far was eleven, and along with other siblings she was withdrawn from school to help support her parents and the younger children by selling on the street her father's paintings and her own crocheted lace. She continued to support family members for the rest of her life, though her income as a stenographer and freelance journalist barely covered her own modest needs and though her health was always fragile, partly as a result of childhood rheumatic fever. Still, it is important to know that from the time she left her Montreal home as a young woman until she returned there shortly before her death, Sui Sin Far was strongly attached to her large family and Montreal was the only place she ever thought of as home though she spent most of her adult life in the United States.

Sui Sin Far and her sister Winnifred were published while they were teenagers; two other sisters became painters, and another sister became the first Chinese American lawyer in Chicago. Winnifred, who wrote under the Japanese-sounding pseudonym Onoto Watanna, published the first Asian American novel, *Miss Nume of Japan,* in 1899, and was popular for many years as the author of sentimental and melodramatic novels.

Though Sui Sin Far began her writing career in Montreal, it was not until 1896 that she adopted her pseudonym, a literal translation of the symbol for waterlily as water fairy flower, or, more generally, bulbs that can sprout and bloom in water. That same year she published her first story, in the American literary magazine *Fly Leaf*. From 1898 to 1909 she lived chiefly in Seattle, with shorter stays in San Francisco and other U.S. West Coast cities. She spent her last years in Boston, where she produced her mature work.

"Mrs. Spring Fragrance" was first published in *Hampton's Magazine* in January 1910. In 1912 it became the title story for the only book Sui Sin Far published. The thirty-seven stories, articles, and sketches brought together in this volume provide a clear sense of Sui Sin Far's commitment to expose the racial, political, social, and economic abuses ordinary Chinese immigrants experienced in late-nineteenth-century America. Often the characters must find a balance between cultures, generations, and genders. However, they are not to be "either-or" but "both-and" figures—sympathetic to traditional Chinese values *and* to new ideas about love and marriage, among many other contested beliefs and perspectives. In many of Sui Sin Far's journalistic and fictional writings she vigorously and openly defends Chinese immigrants—especially women and working-class immigrants—with an ironic stance, as in "In the Land of the Free."

It is hard to know with certainty why Sui Sin Far published only short fiction rather than longer works. Surely her health and the need to support herself would be part of any explanation. A more positive answer is offered by Elizabeth Ammons, who places Sui Sin Far in the company of other late-nineteenth-century American women writers, such as Sarah Orne Jewett and Kate Chopin, who helped establish what scholars now call the "composite novel"—a form that, like a quilt, allows for both variety and unifying design. The collection titled *Mrs. Spring Fragrance*, in any case, tells the story of a community that has flowered literarily. Maxine Hong Kingston, Amy Tan, and David Henry Hwang, among other contemporary writers of Chinese American descent, continue to examine many of the issues Sui Sin Far first introduced to American readers.

# In the Land of the Free[1]

## I

"See, Little One—the hills in the morning sun. There is thy home for years to come. It is very beautiful and thou wilt be very happy there."

The Little One looked up into his mother's face in perfect faith. He was engaged in the pleasant occupation of sucking a sweetmeat; but that did not prevent him from gurgling responsively.

"Yes, my olive bud; there is where thy father is making a fortune for thee. Thy father! Oh, wilt thou not be glad to behold his dear face. 'Twas for thee I left him."

The Little One ducked his chin sympathetically against his mother's knee. She lifted him on to her lap. He was two years old, a round, dimple-cheeked boy with bright brown eyes and a sturdy little frame.

"Ah! Ah! Ah! Ooh! Ooh! Ooh!" puffed he, mocking a tugboat steaming by.

San Francisco's waterfront was lined with ships and steamers, while other craft, large and small, including a couple of white transports from the Philippines, lay at anchor here and there off shore. It was some time before the *Eastern Queen* could get docked, and even after that was accomplished, a lone Chinaman who had been waiting on the wharf for an hour was detained that much longer by men with the initials U. S. C.[2] on their caps, before he could board the steamer and welcome his wife and child.

"This is thy son," announced the happy Lae Choo.

Hom Hing lifted the child, felt of his little body and limbs, gazed into his face with proud and joyous eyes; then turned inquiringly to a customs officer at his elbow.

"That's a fine boy you have there," said the man. "Where was he born?"

"In China," answered Hom Hing, swinging the Little One on his right shoulder, preparatory to leading his wife off the steamer.

"Ever been to America before?"

"No, not he," answered the father with a happy laugh.

The customs officer beckoned to another.

---

1. First published in *Mrs. Spring Fragrance* (1912).     2. Initials stand for *United States Customs*.

"This little fellow," said he, "is visiting America for the first time."

The other customs officer stroked his chin reflectively.

"Good day," said Hom Hing.

"Wait!" commanded one of the officers. "You cannot go just yet."

"What more now?" asked Hom Hing.

"I'm afraid," said the first customs officer, "that we cannot allow the boy to go ashore. There is nothing in the papers that you have shown us—your wife's papers and your own—having any bearing upon the child."

"There was no child when the papers were made out," returned Hom Hing. He spoke calmly; but there was apprehension in his eyes and in his tightening grip on his son.

"What is it? What is it?" quavered Lae Choo, who understood a little English.

The second customs officer regarded her pityingly.

"I don't like this part of the business," he muttered.

The first officer turned to Hom Hing and in an official tone of voice, said:

"Seeing that the boy has no certificate entitling him to admission to this country you will have to leave him with us."

"Leave my boy!" exclaimed Hom Hing.

"Yes; he will be well taken care of, and just as soon as we can hear from Washington he will be handed over to you."

"But," protested Hom Hing, "he is my son."

"We have no proof," answered the man with a shrug of his shoulders; "and even if so we cannot let him pass without orders from the Government."

"He is my son," reiterated Hom Hing, slowly and solemnly. "I am a Chinese merchant and have been in business in San Francisco for many years. When my wife told to me one morning that she dreamed of a green tree with spreading branches and one beautiful red flower growing thereon, I answered her that I wished my son to be born in our country, and for her to prepare to go to China. My wife complied with my wish. After my son was born my mother fell sick and my wife nursed and cared for her; then my father, too, fell sick, and my wife also nursed and cared for him. For twenty moons my wife care for and nurse the old people, and when they die they bless her and my son, and I send for her to return to me. I had no fear of trouble. I was a Chinese merchant and my son was my son."

"Very good, Hom Hing," replied the first officer. "Nevertheless, we take your son."

"No, you not take him; he my son too."

It was Lae Choo. Snatching the child from his father's arms she held and covered him with her own.

The officers conferred together for a few moments; then one drew Hom Hing aside and spoke in his ear.

Resignedly Hom Hing bowed his head, then approached his wife. " 'Tis the law," said he, speaking in Chinese, "and 'twill be but for a little while—until tomorrow's sun arises."

"You, too," reproached Lae Choo in a voice eloquent with pain. But accustomed to obedience she yielded the boy to her husband, who in turn delivered him to the first officer. The Little One protested lustily against the transfer; but his mother covered her face with her sleeve and his father silently led her away. Thus was the law of the land complied with.

*II*

Day was breaking. Lae Choo, who had been awake all night, dressed herself, then awoke her husband.

" 'Tis the morn," she cried. "Go, bring our son."

The man rubbed his eyes and arose upon his elbow so that he could see out of the window. A pale star was visible in the sky. The petals of a lily in a bowl on the window-sill were unfurled.

" 'Tis not yet time," said he, laying his head down again.

"Not yet time. Ah, all the time that I lived before yesterday is not so much as the time that has been since my little one was taken from me."

The mother threw herself down beside the bed and covered her face.

Hom Hing turned on the light, and touching his wife's bowed head with a sympathetic hand inquired if she had slept.

"Slept!" she echoed, weepingly. "Ah, how could I close my eyes with my arms empty of the little body that has filled them every night for more than twenty moons! You do not know—man—what it is to miss the feel of the little fingers and the little toes and the soft round limbs of your little one. Even in the darkness his darling eyes used to shine up to mine, and often have I fallen into slumber with his pretty babble at my ear. And now, I see him not; I touch him not; I hear him not. My baby, my little fat one!"

"Now! Now! Now!" consoled Hom Hing, patting his wife's shoulder reassuringly; "there is no need to grieve so; he will soon gladden you again. There cannot be any law that would keep a child from its mother!"

Lae Choo dried her tears.

"You are right, my husband," she meekly murmured. She arose and stepped about the apartment, setting things to rights. The box of presents she had brought for her California friends had been opened the evening before; and silks, embroideries, carved ivories, ornamental lacquer-ware, brasses, camphor-wood boxes, fans, and chinaware were scattered around in confused heaps. In the midst of unpacking the thought of her child in the hands of strangers had overpowered her, and she had left everything to crawl into bed and weep.

Having arranged her gifts in order she stepped out on to the deep balcony.

The star had faded from view and there were bright streaks in the western sky. Lae Choo looked down the street and around. Beneath the flat occupied by her and her husband were quarters for a number of bachelor Chinamen,[3] and she could hear them from where she stood, taking their early morning breakfast. Below their dining-room was her husband's grocery store. Across the way was a large restaurant. Last night it had been resplendent with gay colored lanterns and the sound of music. The rejoicings over "the completion of the moon,"[4] by Quong Sum's firstborn, had been long and loud, and had caused her to tie a handkerchief over her ears. She, a bereaved mother, had it not in her heart to rejoice with other parents. This morning the place was more in accord with her mood. It was still and quiet. The revellers had dispersed or were asleep.

---

3. At this time, Chinese men were allowed to enter the country with work permits but were not allowed to bring their wives and children.
4. The baby is one month old.

A roly-poly woman in black sateen, with long pendant earrings in her ears, looked up from the street below and waved her a smiling greeting. It was her old neighbor, Kuie Hoe, the wife of the gold embosser, Mark Sing. With her was a little boy in yellow jacket and lavender pantaloons. Lae Choo remembered him as a baby. She used to like to play with him in those days when she had no child of her own. What a long time ago that seemed! She caught her breath in a sigh, and laughed instead.

"Why are you so merry?" called her husband from within.

"Because my Little One is coming home," answered Lae Choo. "I am a happy mother—a happy mother."

She pattered into the room with a smile on her face.

The noon hour had arrived. The rice was steaming in the bowls and a fragrant dish of chicken and bamboo shoots was awaiting Hom Hing. Not for one moment had Lae Choo paused to rest during the morning hours; her activity had been ceaseless. Every now and again, however, she had raised her eyes to the gilded clock on the curiously carved mantelpiece. Once, she had exclaimed:

"Why so long, oh! why so long?" Then apostrophizing herself: "Lae Choo, be happy. The Little One is coming! The Little One is coming!" Several times she burst into tears and several times she laughed aloud.

Hom Hing entered the room; his arms hung down by his side.

"The Little One!" shrieked Lae Choo.

"They bid me call tomorrow."

With a moan the mother sank to the floor.

The noon hour passed. The dinner remained on the table.

### III

The winter rains were over: the spring had come to California, flushing the hills with green and causing an ever-changing pageant of flowers to pass over them. But there was no spring in Lae Choo's heart, for the Little One remained away from her arms. He was being kept in a mission. White women were caring for him, and though for one full moon he had pined for his mother and refused to be comforted he was now apparently happy and contented. Five moons or five months had gone by since the day he had passed with Lae Choo through the Golden Gate; but the great Government at Washington still delayed sending the answer which would return him to his parents.

Hom Hing was disconsolately rolling up and down the balls in his abacus box when a keen-faced young man stepped into his store.

"What news?" asked the Chinese merchant.

"This!" The young man brought forth a typewritten letter. Hom Hing read the words:

"Re Chinese child, alleged to be the son of Hom Hing, Chinese merchant, doing business at 425 Clay street, San Francisco.

"Same will have attention as soon as possible."

Hom Hing returned the letter, and without a word continued his manipulation of the counting machine.

"Have you anything to say?" asked the young man.

"Nothing. They have sent the same letter fifteen times before. Have you not yourself showed it to me?"

"True!" The young man eyed the Chinese merchant furtively. He had a proposition to make and he was pondering whether or not the time was opportune.

"How is your wife?" he inquired solicitously—and diplomatically.

Hom Hing shook his head mournfully.

She seems less every day," he replied. "Her food she takes only when I bid her and her tears fall continually. She finds no pleasure in dress or flowers and cares not to see her friends. Her eyes stare all night. I think before another moon she will pass into the land of spirits."

"No!" exclaimed the young man, genuinely startled.

"If the boy not come home I lose my wife sure," continued Hom Hing with bitter sadness.

"It's not right," cried the young man indignantly. Then he made his proposition.

The Chinese father's eyes brightened exceedingly.

"Will I like you to go to Washington and make them give you the paper to restore my son?" cried he. "How can you ask when you know my heart's desire?"

"Then, said the young fellow, "I will start next week. I am anxious to see this thing through if only for the sake of your wife's peace of mind."

"I will call her. To hear what you think to do will make her glad," said Hom Hing.

He called a message to Lae Choo upstairs through a tube in the wall.

In a few moments she appeared, listless, wan, and hollow-eyed; but when her husband told her the young lawyer's suggestion she became as one electrified; her form straightened, her eyes glistened; the color flushed to her cheeks.

"Oh," she cried, turning to James Clancy, "You are a hundred man good!"

The young man felt somewhat embarrassed; his eyes shifted a little under the intense gaze of the Chinese mother.

"Well, we must get your boy for you," he responded. "Of course"—turning to Hom Hing—"it will cost a little money. You can't get fellows to hurry the Government for you without gold in your pocket."

Hom Hing stared blankly for a moment. Then: "How much do you want, Mr. Clancy?" he asked quietly.

"Well, I will need at least five hundred to start with."

Hom Hing cleared his throat.

"I think I told to you the time I last paid you for writing letters for me and seeing the Custom boss here that nearly all I had was gone!"

"Oh, well then we won't talk about it, old fellow. It won't harm the boy to stay where he is, and your wife may get over it all right."

"What that you say?" quavered Lae Choo.

James Clancy looked out of the window.

"He says," explained Hom Hing in English, "that to get our boy we have to have much money."

"Money! Oh, yes."

Lae Choo nodded her head.

"I have not got the money to give him."

For a moment Lae Choo gazed wonderingly from one face to the other; then, comprehension dawning upon her, with swift anger, pointing to the lawyer, she cried: "You not one hundred man good; you just common white man."

"Yes, ma'am," returned James Clancy, bowing and smiling ironically.

Hom Hing pushed his wife behind him and addressed the lawyer again: "I might try," said he, "to raise something; but five hundred—it is not possible."

"What about four?"

"I tell you I have next to nothing left and my friends are not rich."

"Very well!"

The lawyer moved lesiurely toward the door, pausing on its threshold to light a cigarette.

"Stop, white man; white man, stop!"

Lae Choo, panting and terrified, had started forward and now stood beside him, clutching his sleeve excitedly.

"You say you can go to get paper to bring my Little One to me if Hom Hing give you five hundred dollars?"

The lawyer nodded carelessly; his eyes were intent upon the cigarette which would not take the fire from the match.

"Then you go get paper. If Hom Hing not can give you five hundred dollars—I give you perhaps what more that much."

She slipped a heavy gold bracelet from her wrist and held it out to the man. Mechanically he took it.

"I go get more!"

She scurried away, disappearing behind the door through which she had come.

"Oh, look here, I can't accept this," said James Clancy, walking back to Hom Hing and laying down the bracelet before him.

"It's all right," said Hom Hing, seriously, "pure China gold. My wife's parent give it to her when we married."

"But I can't take it anyway," protested the young man.

"It is all same as money. And you want money to go to Washington," replied Hom Hing in a matter of fact manner.

"See, my jade earrings—my gold buttons—my hairpins—my comb of pearl and my rings—one, two, three, four, five rings; very good—very good—all same much money. I give them all to you. You take and bring me paper for my Little One."

Lae Choo piled up her jewels before the lawyer.

Hom Hing laid a restraining hand upon her shoulder. "Not all, my wife," he said in Chinese. He selected a ring—his gift to Lae Choo when she dreamed of the tree with the red flower. The rest of the jewels he pushed toward the white man.

"Take them and sell them," said he. "They will pay your fare to Washington and bring you back with the paper."

For one moment James Clancy hesitated. He was not a sentimental man; but something within him arose against accepting such payment for his services.

"They are good, good," pleadingly asserted Lae Choo, seeing his hesitation.

Whereupon he seized the jewels, thrust them into his coat pocket, and walked rapidly away from the store.

### IV

Lae Choo followed after the missionary woman through the mission nursery school. Her heart was beating so high with happiness that she could scarcely breathe. The paper had come at last—the precious paper which gave Hom Hing and his wife the right to the possession of their own child. It was ten months now since he had been taken from them—ten months since the sun had ceased to shine for Lae Choo.

The room was filled with children—most of them wee tots, but none so wee as her own. The mission woman talked as she walked. She told Lae Choo that little Kim, as he had been named by the school, was the pet of the place, and that his little tricks and ways amused and delighted every one. He had been rather difficult to manage at first and had cried much for his mother; "but children so soon forget, and after a month he seemed quite at home and played around as bright and happy as a bird."

"Yes," responded Lae Choo. "Oh, yes, yes!"

But she did not hear what was said to her. She was walking in a maze of anticipatory joy.

"Wait here, please," said the mission woman, placing Lae Choo in a chair. "The very youngest ones are having their breakfast."

She withdrew for a moment—it seemed like an hour to the mother—then she reappeared leading by the hand a little boy dressed in blue cotton overalls and white-soled shoes. The little boy's face was round and dimpled and his eyes were very bright.

"Little One, ah, my Little One!" cried Lae Choo.

She fell on her knees and stretched her hungry arms toward her son.

But the Little One shrunk from her and tried to hide himself in the folds of the white woman's skirt.

"Go'way, go'way!" he bade his mother.

1912

---

# MARY HUNTER AUSTIN
## 1868–1934

The author of numerous novels and collections of sketches and short stories, Mary Hunter Austin was one of her time's best-known nature and regionalist writers, speaking in particular for the redemptive power of nature in the Far West. She was born in Carlinville, Illinois, in 1868. When she was ten, her father died, her mother went to work as a nurse, and Mary—who had already begun to write and collect fossils—took on all household duties, including the care of a brother and sister. She graduated from Blackburn College, in Carlinville, in 1888. Lured by images of a land of plenty, the Austins, like many Midwesterners, moved to California only to find themselves settled in as subsistence farmers in the parched San Joaquin Valley. Austin, however, found beauty in the aridity and soon began to write about the landscapes and people she encountered while teaching to make ends meet. In 1891 she married Stafford Wallace Austin, a would-be vinyardist. Ruth Austin, who was mentally disabled, was born in 1892. With Ruth in a backpack, Austin wandered the desert, learning the lore of the local Native women and observing the plants, animals, and seasonal change around her.

With the help of Charles Lummis, editor of *Out West*—a journal devoted to writing about the beauties of California and the Southwest—Austin launched a literary career and became acquainted with authors hoping to establish a lively literary scene in California such as Charlotte Perkins Stetson (later Gilman) and poet Edwin Markham. Her *Land of Little Rain* (1903), containing sketches and stories, followed the nature-based philosophical tradition of Henry David Thoreau and John Muir; it was immediately successful and is still her best-known work. Many other books followed, including *The Basket Woman* (1904) and *Lost Borders* (1909), whose stories and sketches described and praised the cultural integrity of indigenous Americans and the history of California's diverse ethnic groups. These books demonstrated a sense of unity with nature and advocated environmental preservation. In 1905, her marriage ended, and Austin made the difficult decision to institutionalize her daughter. She continued to write and opened her home in Independence, California, Casa Querida (Beloved Home), to her writer friends, also joining the bohemian gatherings in Carmel of writers such as Jack London, George Sterling, Upton Sinclair, Ambrose Bierce, and Gertrude Atherton. She helped lead the protests—ultimately unsuccessful—over the draining of the Owens Valley to supply water for Los Angeles. Her novel, *A Woman of Genius* (1912), locates her clearly in the tradition of eco-feminism, a position arguing that women are inherently closer to and better advocates for the natural world than men.

Austin moved to Santa Fe in 1923 and became part of the circle of Mabel Dodge Luhan, a wealthy socialite who had gathered a group of artists and writers around her home in Taos. Austin's most important discovery there was Pueblo culture and its ancestors, known as the Anasazi. She became an activist for American Indians and was consulted on the Southwest through associations with geologists, botanists, Sierra Clubs, collectors of Indian artifacts, and explorers. In 1930 she collaborated with photographer Ansel Adams on *Taos Pueblo*, a book depicting the strength of Taos Indian women and expressing Austin's belief that the Southwest was the true center of "the Americas," a place where modernity could develop and mature in contact with "native" societies. She celebrated the solitude of the "indwellers" of the deserts and showed how the Indians' songs and rituals to influence nature made their lives beautiful. Urging modern men and women to become aware of such creative forces, she advocated ideas that made the desert Southwest a tourist destination. Her autobiography, *Earth Horizon* (1932), further portrays Mexican Americans, American Indians, and Anglo newcomers together in the land of "lost borders."

As Austin notes in *The Land of Little Rain*: "To understand the fashion of any life one must know the land it is lived in and the procession of the year," an idea at the heart of her lifelong commitment to regionalism.

## The Walking Woman[1]

The first time of my hearing of her was at Temblor.[2] We had come all one day between blunt, whitish bluffs rising from mirage water, with a thick, pale wake of dust billowing from the wheels, all the dead wall of the foothills slid-

---

1. First published in *Lost Borders: The People of the Desert* (1909), from which this text is taken.

2. Mountain range in the southwestern San Joaquin Valley of California.

ing and shimmering with heat, to learn that the Walking Woman had passed us somewhere in the dizzying dimness, going down to the Tulares[3] on her own feet. We heard of her again in the Carrisal, and again at Adobe Station, where she had passed a week before the shearing, and at last I had a glimpse of her at the Eighteen-Mile House as I went hurriedly northward on the Mojave stage:[4] and afterward, sheepherders at whose camps she slept, and cowboys at rodeos, told me as much of her way of life as they could understand. Like enough they told her as much of mine. That was very little. She was the Walking Woman, and no one knew her name, but because she was a sort of whom men speak respectfully, they called her to her face Mrs. Walker, and she answered to it if she was so inclined. She came and went about our western world on no discoverable errand, and whether she had some place of refuge where she lay by in the interim, or whether between her seldom, unaccountable appearances in our quarter she went on steadily walking, was never learned. She came and went, oftenest in a kind of muse of travel which the untrammelled space begets, or at rare intervals flooding wondrously with talk, never of herself, but of things she had known and seen. She must have seen some rare happenings, too—by report. She was at Maverick the time of the Big Snow, and at Tres Piños[5] when they brought home the body of Morena; and if anybody could have told whether De Borba killed Mariana for spite or defence, it would have been she, only she could not be found when most wanted. She was at Tunawai[6] at the time of the cloud-burst, and if she had cared for it could have known most desirable things of the ways of trail-making, burrow-habiting small things.

All of which should have made her worth meeting, though it was not, in fact, for such things I was wishful to meet her; and as it turned out, it was not of these things we talked when at last we came together. For one thing, she was a woman, not old, who had gone about alone in a country where the number of women is as one in fifteen. She had eaten and slept at the herder's camps, and laid by for days at one-man stations whose masters had no other touch of human kind than the passing of chance prospectors, or the halting of the tri-weekly stage. She had been set on her way by teamsters who lifted her out of white, hot desertness and put her down at the crossing of unnamed ways, days distant from anywhere. And through all this she passed unarmed and unoffended. I had the best testimony to this, the witness of the men themselves. I think they talked of it because they were so much surprised at it. It was not, on the whole, what they expected of themselves.

Well I understand that nature which wastes its borders with too eager burning, beyond which rim of desolation it flares forever quick and white, and have had some inkling of the isolating calm of a desire too high to stoop to satisfaction. But you could not think of these things pertaining to the Walk-

---

3. Spanish name for swampy areas of the San Joaquin Valley containing vast numbers of *tulés*, a species of North American freshwater sedge.
4. Carrisal, Adobe Station, Eighteen-Mile House, Mojave stage: stops along the Bradshaw Desert Trail stage route, a "gold road" connecting Los Angeles to Arizona in one direction and to San Francisco in another. Other named places in California are Warm Spring (in what is now the Silicon Valley) and Little Antelope, an area of the eastern Sierras.

5. In Austin's time, an important trade center along the Southern Pacific Railroad—now, a small rural community south of Hollister, California. "Maverick": ghost town in the White Mountain Apache reservation in southeastern Arizona with arid conditions in the summer and snowfall in the winter.
6. Indian word for a desert storm of violent thunder, lightning, and quick, torrential rain. *Tunawai* may also refer to a ruined town on today's Tejon Indian reservation.

ing Woman; and if there were ever any truth in the exemption from offence residing in a frame of behavior called ladylike, it should have been inoperative here. What this really means is that you get no affront so long as your behavior in the estimate of the particular audience invites none. In the estimate of the immeadte audience—conduct which affords protection in Mayfair[7] gets you no consideration in Maverick. And by no canon could it be considered ladylike to go about on your own feet, with a blanket and a black bag and almost no money in your purse, in and about the haunts of rude and solitary men.

There were other things that pointed the wish for a personal encounter with the Walking Woman. One of them was the contradiction of reports of her—as to whether she was comely, for example. Report said yes, and again, plain to the point of deformity. She had a twist to her face, some said; a hitch to one shoulder; they averred she limped as she walked. But by the distance she covered she should have been straight and young. As to sanity, equal incertitude. On the mere evidence of her way of life she was cracked; not quite broken, but unserviceable. Yet in her talk there was both wisdom and information, and the word she brought about trails and water-holes was as reliable as an Indian's.

By her own account she had begun by walking off an illness. There had been an invalid to be taken care of for years, leaving her at last broken in body, and with no recourse but her own feet to carry her out of that predicament. It seemed there had been, besides the death of her invalid, some other worrying affairs, upon which, and the nature of her illness, she was never quite clear, so that it might very well have been an unsoundness of mind which drove her to the open, sobered and healed at last by the large soundness of nature. It must have been about that time that she lost her name. I am convinced that she never told it because she did not know it herself. She was the Walking Woman, and the country people called her Mrs. Walker. At the time I knew her, though she wore short hair and a man's boots, and had a fine down over all her face from exposure to the weather, she was perfectly sweet and sane.

I had met her occasionally at ranch-houses and road-stations, and had got as much acquaintance as the place allowed; but for the things I wished to know there wanted a time of leisure and isolation. And when the occasion came we talked altogether of other things.

It was at Warm Spring in the Little Antelope I came upon her in the heart of a clear forenoon. The spring lies off a mile from the main trail, and has the only trees about it known in that country. First you come upon a pool of waste full of weeds of a poisonous dark green, every reed ringed about the water-level with a muddy white incrustation. Then the three oaks appear staggering on the slope, and the spring sobs and blubbers below them in ashy-colored mud. All the hills of that country have the down plunge toward the desert and back abruptly toward the Sierra. The grass is thick and brittle and bleached straw-color toward the end of the season. As I rode up the swale of the spring I saw the Walking Woman sitting where the grass was deepest, with her black bag and blanket, which she carried on a stick, beside her. It was one of those days when the genius of talk flows as smoothly as the rivers of mirage through the blue hot desert morning.

7. Elite neighborhood in London, England.

You are not to suppose that in my report of a Borderer I give you the words only, but the full meaning of the speech. Very often the words are merely the punctuation of thought; rather, the crests of the long waves of intercommunicative silences. Yet the speech of the Walking Woman was fuller than most.

The best of our talk that day began in some dropped word of hers from which I inferred that she had had a child. I was surprised at that, and then wondered why I should have been surprised, for it is the most natural of all experiences to have children. I said something of that purport, and also that it was one of the perquisites of living I should be least willing to do without. And that led to the Walking Woman saying that there were three things which if you had known you could cut out all the rest, and they were good any way you got them, but best if, as in her case, they were related to and grew each one out of the others. It was while she talked that I decided that she really did have a twist to her face, a sort of natural warp or skew into which it fell when it was worn merely as a countenance, but which disappeared the moment it became the vehicle of thought or feeling.

The first of the experiences the Walking Woman had found most worth while had come to her in a sand-storm on the south slope of Tehachapi in a dateless spring. I judged it should have been about the time she began to find herself, after the period of worry and loss in which her wandering began. She had come, in a day pricked full of intimations of a storm, to the camp of Filon Geraud, whose companion shepherd had gone a three days' *pasear*[8] to Mojave for supplies. Geraud was of great hardihood, red-blooded, of a full laughing eye, and an indubitable spark for women. It was the season of the year when there is a soft bloom on the days, but the nights are cowering cold and the lambs tender, not yet flockwise. At such times a sand-storm works incalculable disaster. The lift of the wind is so great that the whole surface of the ground appears to travel upon it slantwise, thinning out miles high in air. In the intolerable smother the lambs are lost from the ewes; neither dogs nor man make headway against it.

The morning flared through a horizon of yellow smudge, and by mid-forenoon the flock broke.

"There were but the two of us to deal with the trouble," said the Walking Woman. "Until that time I had not known how strong I was, nor how good it is to run when running is worth while. The flock travelled down the wind, the sand bit our faces; we called, and after a time heard the words broken and beaten small by the wind. But after a little we had not to call. All the time of our running in the yellow dusk of day and the black dark of night, I knew where Filon was. A flock-length away, I knew him. Feel? What should I feel? I knew. I ran with the flock and turned it this way and that as Filon would have.

"Such was the force of the wind that when we came together we held by one another and talked a little between pantings. We snatched and ate what we could as we ran. All that day and night until the next afternoon the camp kit was not out of the cayaques.[9] But we held the flock. We herded them under a butte when the wind fell off a little, and the lambs sucked; when the storm rose they broke, but we kept upon their track and brought them

---

8. Walk (Spanish). Filon Geraud was a sheep rancher.　　9. Packs.

together again. At night the wind quieted, and we slept by turns; at least Filon slept. I lay on the ground when my turn was and beat with the storm. I was no more tired than the earth was. The sand filled in the creases of the blanket, and where I turned, dripped back upon the ground. But we saved the sheep. Some ewes there were that would not give down their milk because of the worry of the storm, and the lambs died. But we kept the flock together. And I was not tired."

The Walking Woman stretched out her arms and clasped herself, rocking in them as if she would have hugged the recollection to her breast.

"For you see," said she, "I worked with a man, without excusing, without any burden on me of looking or seeming. Not fiddling or fumbling as women work, and hoping it will all turn out for the best. It was not for Filon to ask, Can you, or Will you. He said, Do, and I did. And my work was good. We held the flock. And that," said the Walking Woman, the twists coming in her face again, "is one of the things that make you able to do without the others."

"Yes," I said; and then, "What others?"

"Oh," she said, as if it pricked her, "the looking and the seeming."

And I had not thought until that time that one who had the courage to be the Walking Woman would have cared! We sat and looked at the pattern of the thick crushed grass on the slope, wavering in the fierce noon like the waterings in the coat of a tranquil beast; the ache of a world-old bitterness sobbed and whispered in the spring. At last—

"It is by the looking and the seeming," said I, "that the opportunity finds you out."

"Filon found out," said the Walking Woman. She smiled; and went on from that to tell me how, when the wind went down about four o'clock and left the afternoon clear and tender, the flock began to feed, and they had out the kit from the cayaques, and cooked a meal. When it was over, and Filon had his pipe between his teeth, he came over from his side of the fire, of his own notion, and stretched himself on the ground beside her. Of his own notion. There was that in the way she said it that made it seem as if nothing of the sort had happened before to the Walking Woman, and for a moment I thought she was about to tell me one of the things I wished to know; but she went on to say what Filon had said to her of her work with the flock. Obvious, kindly things, such as any man in sheer decency would have said, so that there must have something more gone with the words to make them so treasured of the Walking Woman.

"We were very comfortable," said she, "and not so tired as we expected to be. Filon leaned up on his elbow. I had not noticed until then how broad he was in the shoulders, and how strong in the arms. And we had saved the flock together. We felt that. There was something that said together, in the slope of his shoulders toward me. It was around his mouth and on the cheek high up under the shine of his eyes. And under the shine the look—the look that said, 'We are of one sort and one mind'—his eyes that were the color of the flat water in the tulares—do you know the look?"

"I know it."

"The wind was stopped and all the earth smelled of dust, and Filon understood very well that what I had done with him I could not have done so well with another. And the look—the look in the eyes—"

"Ah-ah—!"

I have always said, I will say again, I do not know why at this point the Walking Woman touched me. If it were merely a response to my unconscious throb of sympathy, or the unpremeditated way of her heart to declare that this, after all, was the best of all indispensable experiences; or if in some flash of forward vision, encompassing the unimpassioned years, the stir, the movement of tenderness were for *me*—but no; as often as I have thought of it, I have thought of a different reason, but no conclusive one, why the Walking Woman should have put out her hand and laid it on my arm.

"To work together, to love together," said the Walking Woman, withdrawing her hand again; "there you have two of the things; the other you know."

"The mouth at the breast," said I.

"The lips and the hands," said the Walking Woman. "The little, pushing hands and the small cry." There ensued a pause of fullest understanding, while the land before us swam in the noon, and a dove in the oaks behind the spring began to call. A little red fox came out of the hills and lapped delicately at the pool.

"I stayed with Filon until the fall," said she. "All that summer in the Sierra, until it was time to turn south on the trail. It was a good time, and longer than he could be expected to have loved one like me. And besides, I was no longer able to keep the trail. My baby was born in October."

Whatever more there was to say to this, the Walking Woman's hand said it, straying with remembering gesture to her breast. There are so many ways of loving and working, but only one way of the first-born. She added after an interval, that she did not know if she would have given up her walking to keep at home and tend him, or whether the thought of her son's small feet running beside her in the trails would have driven her to the open again. The baby had not stayed long enough for that. "And whenever the wind blows in the night," said the Walking Woman, "I wake and wonder if he is well covered."

She took up her black bag and her blanket; there was the ranch-house of Dos Palos[1] to be made before night, and she went as outliers do, without a hope expressed of another meeting and no word of good-bye. She was the Walking Woman. That was it. She had walked off all sense of society-made values, and, knowing the best when the best came to her, was able to take it. Work—as I believed; love—as the Walking Woman had proved it; a child—as you subscribe to it. But look you: it was the naked thing the Walking Woman grasped, not dressed and tricked out, for instance, by prejudices in favor of certain occupations; and love, man love, taken as it came, not picked over and rejected if it carried no obligation of permanency; and a child; *any* way you get it, a child is good to have, say nature and the Walking Woman; to have it and not to wait upon a proper concurrence of so many decorations that the event may not come at all.

At least one of us is wrong. To work and to love and to bear children. *That* sounds easy enough. But the way we live establishes so many things of much more importance.

Far down the dim, hot valley I could see the Walking Woman with her blanket and black bag over her shoulder. She had a queer, sidelong gait, as if in fact she had a twist all through her.

---

1. Today a city near Merced, California.

Recollecting suddenly that people called her lame, I ran down to the open space below the spring where she had passed. There in the bare, hot sand the track of her two feet bore evenly and white.

1909

# W. E. B. DU BOIS
## 1868–1963

William Edward Burghardt Du Bois was born on February 23, 1868, in Great Barrington, Massachusetts. His childhood was happy; but with the approach of adolescence Du Bois discovered that what made him different from his schoolmates was not so much his superior academic achievement as his brown skin. Looking back on his rejection by a white girl in grade school, Du Bois wrote, "It dawned on me with a certain suddenness, that I was . . . shut out from their world by a vast veil," a veil beyond which he claimed to have no desire to force his way. Du Bois's entire career, nonetheless, may be understood as an unremitting struggle for civil and political rights for African Americans and for human rights around the world.

Du Bois was educated at Fisk, Harvard, and the University of Berlin. His doctoral dissertation, *The Suppression of the African Slave Trade to the United States of America, 1638–1870,* was published as the first volume in the Harvard Historical Studies series. By the time Du Bois completed his graduate studies his accomplishments were already considerable, but he could not secure an appointment at a major research university. He taught first instead at Wilberforce College in Ohio, at that time a small, poor, black college. There he offered Greek, Latin, German, and English—subjects far removed from his real interest in the emerging field of sociology.

After spending a year at the University of Pennsylvania, where he produced his first major work, *The Philadelphia Negro,* Du Bois moved to Atlanta University in 1897. There, over the following thirteen years, he produced a steady stream of important studies of African American life. Dedicated to the rigorous, scholarly examination of the so-called Negro problem, Du Bois soon had to face up to the violent realities of the lives he proposed to study. On his way to present an appeal for reason in the case of a black man accused of murder and rape, Du Bois was met by the news that a lynch mob had dismembered and burned the man at the stake and that "his knuckles were on exhibition at a grocery store." Though Du Bois never ceased being a scholar, from this time on he increasingly became an activist and sought a wider audience for his writings.

Du Bois first came to national attention with the publication of *The Souls of Black Folk* (1903), characterized by scholar Eric J. Sundquist as "the preeminent text of African American cultural consciousness." Several chapters explore the implications of this extraordinary book's dramatic and prophetic announcement in its "Forethought" that "the problem of the Twentieth Century is the problem of the color-line." In the first chapter, "Of Our Spiritual Strivings," Du Bois introduces another concept that would inform his thinking for the rest of his career—the notion of the "twoness" of African Americans: "One ever feels his twoness," Du Bois asserts, "an American, a Negro; two souls, two thoughts, two unreconciled strivings; two warring ideals in one dark body, whose dogged strength alone keeps it from being torn asunder." This foundational observation hit on what Du Bois named "double-consciousness." (Another of Du Bois's important ideas was the Talented Tenth, the title of an essay he published as the second chapter of *The Negro Problem* (1903). By this he meant college-educated African Americans who could provide leadership for African Americans after Reconstruction.) Du Bois offers a concise overview of the Negro in America cast in the highly charged rhetoric of the orator who wishes to move as well as inform his audience. But the chapter that particularly caused a stir when the volume was first published was the one that challenged—coolly and without rancor—the enormous authority and power that had accumulated in the hands of one black spokesman, Booker T. Washington. Washington had founded Tuskegee Institute in Alabama to train African Americans in basic agricultural and mechanical skills and had gained national prominence with his Atlanta Exposition speech in 1895. His address seemed to many people to accept disenfranchisement and segregation and settle for a low level of education in exchange for white "toleration" and economic cooperation. Although Du Bois had initially joined in the general approval of this "separate and unequal" philosophy, by the early 1900s he had begun to reject Washington's position, and with the publication of *Souls of Black Folk* his public defiance of Washington put the two men in lasting opposition. The almost immediate repudiation of *Souls of Black Folk* by Washington's allies reinforced Du Bois's emerging radicalism; he became a leader in the Niagara Movement (1905), a movement aggressively demanding for African Americans the same civil rights enjoyed by white Americans.

In 1910 Du Bois left Atlanta for New York, where he served for the next quarter of a century as editor of *Crisis,* the official publication of the newly formed National Association for the Advancement of Colored People (NAACP), an organization he helped create. Through this publication Du Bois reached an increasingly large audience—one hundred thousand by 1919—with powerful messages that argued the need for black development and white social enlightenment.

Frustrated by the lack of fundamental change and progress in the condition of African Americans, from 1920 on Du Bois shifted his attention from the reform of race relations in America through research and political legislation to the search for longer-range worldwide economic solutions to the international problems of inequity among the races. He began a steady movement toward Pan-African and socialist perspectives that led to his joining the U.S. Communist Party in 1961 and, in the year of his death, becoming a citizen of Ghana. During these forty years he was extremely active as politician, organizer, and diplomat, and he continued as a powerful writer of poetry, fiction, autobiography, essays, and scholarly works. When, in his last major speech, Martin Luther King Jr. spoke of Du Bois as "one of the most remarkable men of our time," he was uttering the verdict of history.

## *From* The Souls of Black Folk[1]

### *The Forethought*

Herein lie buried many things which if read with patience may show the strange meaning of being black here in the dawning of the Twentieth Century. This meaning is not without interest to you, Gentle Reader; for the problem of the Twentieth Century is the problem of the color-line.

I pray you, then, receive my little book in all charity, studying my words with me, forgiving mistake and foible for sake of the faith and passion that is in me, and seeking the grain of truth hidden there.

I have sought here to sketch, in vague, uncertain outline, the spiritual world in which ten thousand thousand Americans live and strive. First, in two chapters I have tried to show what Emancipation meant to them, and what

---

1. *The Souls of Black Folk,* a compilation of nine previously printed and five unpublished essays, appeared first as a book in 1903, the source of the text printed here.

was its aftermath. In a third chapter I have pointed out the slow rise of personal leadership, and criticised candidly the leader who bears the chief burden of his race to-day. Then, in two other chapters I have sketched in swift outline the two worlds within and without the Veil, and thus have come to the central problem of training men for life. Venturing now into deeper detail, I have in two chapters studied the struggles of the massed millions of the black peasantry, and in another have sought to make clear the present relations of the sons of master and man.

Leaving, then, the world of the white man, I have stepped within the Veil, raising it that you may view faintly its deeper recesses,—the meaning of its religion, the passion of its human sorrow, and the struggle of its greater souls. All this I have ended with a tale twice told but seldom written.

Some of these thoughts of mine have seen the light before in other guise. For kindly consenting to their republication here, in altered and extended form, I must thank the publishers of *The Atlantic Monthly, The World's Work, The Dial, The New World,* and the *Annals of the American Academy of Political and Social Science.*

Before each chapter, as now printed, stands a bar of the Sorrow Songs,[2]—some echo of haunting melody from the only American music which welled up from black souls in the dark past. And, finally, need I add that I who speak here am bone of the bone and flesh of the flesh of them that live within the Veil?

W. E. B. Du B.

ATLANTA, GA., Feb. 1, 1903.

### I. Of Our Spiritual Strivings

O water, voice of my heart, crying in the sand,
    All night long crying with a mournful cry,
As I lie and listen, and cannot understand
        The voice of my heart in my side or the voice of the sea,
    O water, crying for rest, is it I, is it I?
        All night long the water is crying to me.

Unresting water, there shall never be rest
    Till the last moon droop and the last tide fail,
And the fire of the end begin to burn in the west;
        And the heart shall be weary and wonder and cry like the sea,
    All life long crying without avail,
        As the water all night long is crying to me.

ARTHUR SYMONS[3]

Between me and the other world there is ever an unasked question: unasked by some through feelings of delicacy; by others through the difficulty

2. Du Bois's term for spirituals composed by southern slaves.
3. English poet (1865–1945); the quotation is from "The Crying of Water."
4. For a rich discussion of the book as a whole and particularly of the bars of music that serve as epigraphs for each chapter, see Eric J. Sundquist's *To Wake the Nations: Race in the Making of American Literature* (1993).

of rightly framing it. All, nevertheless, flutter round it. They approach me in a half-hesitant sort of way, eye me curiously or compassionately, and then, instead of saying directly, How does it feel to be a problem? they say, I know an excellent colored man in my town; or, I fought at Mechanicsville;[5] or, Do not these Southern outrages make your blood boil? At these I smile, or am interested, or reduce the boiling to a simmer, as the occasion may require. To the real question, How does it feel to be a problem? I answer seldom a word.

And yet, being a problem is a strange experience,—peculiar even for one who has never been anything else, save perhaps in babyhood and in Europe. It is in the early days of rollicking boyhood that the revelation first bursts upon one, all in a day, as it were. I remember well when the shadow swept across me. I was a little thing, away up in the hills of New England, where the dark Housatonic winds between Hoosac and Taghkanic[6] to the sea. In a wee wooden schoolhouse, something put it into the boys' and girls' heads to buy gorgeous visiting-cards—ten cents a package—and exchange. The exchange was merry, till one girl, a tall newcomer, refused my card,—refused it peremptorily, with a glance. Then it dawned upon me with a certain suddenness that I was different from the others; or like, mayhap, in heart and life and longing, but shut out from their world by a vast veil. I had thereafter no desire to tear down that veil, to creep through; I held all beyond it in common contempt, and lived above it in a region of blue sky and great wandering shadows. That sky was bluest when I could beat my mates at examination-time, or beat them at a foot-race, or even beat their stringy heads. Alas, with the years all this fine contempt began to fade; for the worlds I longed for, and all their dazzling opportunities, were theirs, not mine. But they should not keep these prizes, I said; some, all, I would wrest from them. Just how I would do it I could never decide: by reading law, by healing the sick, by telling the wonderful tales that swam in my head,—some way. With other black boys the strife was not so fiercely sunny: their youth shrunk into tasteless sycophancy, or into silent hatred of the pale world about them and mocking distrust of everything white; or wasted itself in a bitter cry, Why did God make me an outcast and a stranger in mine own house? The shades of the prison-house closed round about us all: walls strait and stubborn to the whitest, but relentlessly narrow, tall, and unscalable to sons of night who must plod darkly on in resignation, or beat unavailing palms against the stone, or steadily, half hopelessly, watch the streak of blue above.

After the Egyptian and Indian, the Greek and Roman, the Teuton and Mongolian, the Negro is a sort of seventh son, born with a veil, and gifted with second-sight in this American world,—a world which yields him no true self-consciousness, but only lets him see himself through the revelation of the other world. It is a peculiar sensation, this double-consciousness, this sense of always looking at one's self through the eyes of others, of measuring one's soul by the tape of a world that looks on in amused contempt and pity. One ever feels his two-ness,—an American, a Negro; two souls, two thoughts, two unreconciled strivings; two warring ideals in one dark body, whose dogged strength alone keeps it from being torn asunder.

5. Civil War battle in Virginia, June 26, 1862, resulting in heavy Confederate losses.
6. Mountain ranges partly in Massachusetts, partly in Vermont. The Housatonic is a river in western Massachussetts.

The history of the American Negro is the history of this strife,—this long-ing to attain self-conscious manhood, to merge his double self into a better and truer self. In this merging he wishes neither of the older selves to be lost. He would not Africanize America, for America has too much to teach the world and Africa. He would not bleach his Negro soul in a flood of white Americanism, for he knows that Negro blood has a message for the world. He simply wishes to make it possible for a man to be both a Negro and an Amer-ican, without being cursed and spit upon by his fellows, without having the doors of Opportunity closed roughly in his face.

This, then, is the end of his striving: to be a co-worker in the kingdom of culture, to escape both death and isolation, to husband and use his best pow-ers and his latent genius. These powers of body and mind have in the past been strangely wasted, dispersed, or forgotten. The shadow of a mighty Negro past flits through the tale of Ethiopia the Shadowy and of Egypt the Sphinx. Throughout history, the powers of single black men flash here and there like falling stars, and die sometimes before the world has rightly gauged their brightness. Here in America, in the few days since Emancipation, the black man's turning hither and thither in hesitant and doubtful striving has often made his very strength to lose effectiveness, to seem like absence of power, like weakness. And yet it is not weakness,—it is the contradiction of double aims. The double-aimed struggle of the black artisan—on the one hand to escape white contempt for a nation of mere hewers of wood and drawers of water, and on the other hand to plough and nail and dig for a poverty-stricken horde—could only result in making him a poor craftsman, for he had but half a heart in either cause. By the poverty and ignorance of his people, the Negro minister or doctor was tempted toward quackery and demagogy; and by the criticism of the other world, toward ideals that made him ashamed of his lowly tasks. The would-be black *savant*[7] was confronted by the paradox that the knowledge his people needed was a twice-told tale to his white neighbors, while the knowledge which would teach the white world was Greek to his own flesh and blood. The innate love of harmony and beauty that set the ruder souls of his people a-dancing and a-singing raised but confusion and doubt in the soul of the black artist; for the beauty revealed to him was the soul-beauty of a race which his larger audience despised, and he could not articulate the message of another people. This waste of double aims, this seeking to satisfy two unreconciled ideals, has wrought sad havoc with the courage and faith and deeds of ten thousand thousand people,—has sent them often wooing false gods and invoking false means of salvation, and at times has even seemed about to make them ashamed of themselves.

Away back in the days of bondage they thought to see in one divine event the end of all doubt and disappointment; few men ever worshipped Freedom with half such unquestioning faith as did the American Negro for two cen-turies. To him, so far as he thought and dreamed, slavery was indeed the sum of all villainies, the cause of all sorrow, the root of all prejudice; Emancipa-tion was the key to a promised land of sweeter beauty than ever stretched before the eyes of wearied Israelites. In song and exhortation swelled one refrain—Liberty; in his tears and curses the God he implored had Freedom

---

7. Learned person.

in his right hand. At last it came,—suddenly, fearfully, like a dream. With one wild carnival of blood and passion came the message in his own plaintive cadences:—

> "Shout, O children!
> Shout, you're free!
> For God has bought your liberty!"[8]

Years have passed away since then,—ten, twenty, forty; forty years of national life, forty years of renewal and development, and yet the swarthy spectre sits in its accustomed seat at the Nation's feast. In vain do we cry to this our vastest social problem:—

> "Take any shape but that, and my firm nerves
> Shall never tremble!"[9]

The Nation has not yet found peace from its sins; the freedman has not yet found in freedom his promised land. Whatever of good may have come in these years of change, the shadow of a deep disappointment rests upon the Negro people,—a disappointment all the more bitter because the unattained ideal was unbounded save by the simple ignorance of a lowly people.

The first decade was merely a prolongation of the vain search for freedom, the boon that seemed ever barely to elude their grasp,—like a tantalizing will-o'-the-wisp, maddening and misleading the headless host. The holocaust of war, the terrors of the Ku-Klux Klan, the lies of carpetbaggers,[1] the disorganization of industry, and the contradictory advice of friends and foes, left the bewildered serf with no new watchword beyond the old cry for freedom. As the time flew, however, he began to grasp a new idea. The ideal of liberty demanded for its attainment powerful means, and these the Fifteenth Amendment[2] gave him. The ballot, which before he had looked upon as a visible sign of freedom, he now regarded as the chief means of gaining and perfecting the liberty with which war had partially endowed him. And why not? Had not votes made war and emancipated millions? Had not votes enfranchised the freedmen? Was anything impossible to a power that had done all this? A million black men started with renewed zeal to vote themselves into the kingdom. So the decade flew away, the revolution of 1876[3] came, and left the half-free serf weary, wondering, but still inspired. Slowly but steadily, in the following years, a new vision began gradually to replace the dream of political power,—a powerful movement, the rise of another ideal to guide the unguided, another pillar of fire by night after a clouded day. It was the ideal of "book-learning"; the curiosity, born of compulsory ignorance, to know and test the power of the cabalistic[4] letters of the white man, the longing to know. Here at last seemed to have been discovered the mountain path to Canaan;[5] longer than the highway of Emancipation and law, steep and rugged, but straight, leading to heights high enough to overlook life.

---

8. Source unidentified.
9. Shakespeare, *Macbeth* 3.2.99.
1. Used as an epithet in the South to describe Northerners who came to the South during Reconstruction to make money by exploiting conditions created by the devastation of the Civil War. Many carried luggage made of carpet materials.
2. Amendment to the Constitution passed in 1870 to guarantee and protect the voting rights of African American men.
3. Congressional opposition to the continuation of Reconstruction policies and programs after the national elections of 1876.
4. Indecipherable and mystical.
5. The Promised Land of the Israelites.

Up the new path the advance guard toiled, slowly, heavily, doggedly; only those who have watched and guided the faltering feet, the misty minds, the dull understandings, of the dark pupils of these schools know how faithfully, how piteously, this people strove to learn. It was weary work. The cold statistician wrote down the inches of progress here and there, noted also where here and there a foot had slipped or some one had fallen. To the tired climbers, the horizon was ever dark, the mists were often cold, the Canaan was always dim and far away. If, however, the vistas disclosed as yet no goal, no resting-place, little but flattery and criticism, the journey at least gave leisure for reflection and self-examination; it changed the child of Emancipation to the youth with dawning self-consciousness, self-realization, self-respect. In those sombre forests of his striving his own soul rose before him, and he saw himself,—darkly as through a veil; and yet he saw in himself some faint revelation of his power, of his mission. He began to have a dim feeling that, to attain his place in the world, he must be himself, and not another. For the first time he sought to analyze the burden he bore upon his back, that dead-weight of social degradation partially masked behind a half-named Negro problem. He felt his poverty; without a cent, without a home, without land, tools, or savings, he had entered into competition with rich, landed, skilled neighbors. To be a poor man is hard, but to be a poor race in a land of dollars is the very bottom of hardships. He felt the weight of his ignorance,— not simply of letters, but of life, of business, of the humanities; the accumulated sloth and shirking and awkwardness of decades and centuries shackled his hands and feet. Nor was his burden all poverty and ignorance. The red stain of bastardy, which two centuries of systematic legal defilement of Negro women had stamped upon his race, meant not only the loss of ancient African chastity, but also the hereditary weight of a mass of corruption from white adulterers, threatening almost the obliteration of the Negro home.

A people thus handicapped ought not to be asked to race with the world, but rather allowed to give all its time and thought to its own social problems. But alas! while sociologists gleefully count his bastards and his prostitutes, the very soul of the toiling, sweating black man is darkened by the shadow of a vast despair. Men call the shadow prejudice, and learnedly explain it as the natural defence of culture against barbarism, learning against ignorance, purity against crime, the "higher" against the "lower" races. To which the Negro cries Amen! and swears that to so much of this strange prejudice as is founded on just homage to civilization, culture, righteousness, and progress, he humbly bows and meekly does obeisance. But before that nameless prejudice that leaps beyond all this he stands helpless, dismayed, and well-nigh speechless; before that personal disrespect and mockery, the ridicule and systematic humiliation, the distortion of fact and wanton license of fancy, the cynical ignoring of the better and the boisterous welcoming of the worse, the all-pervading desire to inculcate disdain for everything black, from Toussaint[6] to the devil,—before this there rises a sickening despair that would disarm and discourage any nation save that black host to whom "discouragement" is an unwritten word.

---

6. François Dominique Toussaint L'Ouverture (1743–1803), slave-born Haitian soldier, patriot, and martyr to the liberation of Haiti from foreign control.

But the facing of so vast a prejudice could not but bring the inevitable self-questioning, self-disparagement, and lowering of ideals which ever accompany repression and breed in an atmosphere of contempt and hate. Whisperings and portents came borne upon the four winds: Lo! we are diseased and dying, cried the dark hosts; we cannot write, our voting is vain; what need of education, since we must always cook and serve? And the Nation echoed and enforced this self-criticism, saying: Be content to be servants, and nothing more; what need of higher culture for half-men? Away with the black man's ballot, by force or fraud,—and behold the suicide of a race! Nevertheless, out of the evil came something of good,—the more careful adjustment of education to real life, the clearer perception of the Negroes' social responsibilities, and the sobering realization of the meaning of progress.

So dawned the time of *Sturm und Drang:*[7] storm and stress to-day rocks our little boat on the mad waters of the world-sea; there is within and without the sound of conflict, the burning of body and rending of soul; inspiration strives with doubt, and faith with vain questionings. The bright ideals of the past,—physical freedom, political power, the training of brains and the training of hands,—all these in turn have waxed and waned, until even the last grows dim and overcast. Are they all wrong,—all false? No, not that, but each alone was over-simple and incomplete,—the dreams of a credulous race-childhood, or the fond imaginings of the other world which does not know and does not want to know our power. To be really true, all these ideals must be melted and welded into one. The training of the schools we need to-day more than ever,—the training of deft hands, quick eyes and ears, and above all the broader, deeper, higher culture of gifted minds and pure hearts. The power of the ballot we need in sheer self-defence,—else what shall save us from a second slavery? Freedom, too, the long-sought, we still seek,—the freedom of life and limb, the freedom to work and think, the freedom to love and aspire. Work, culture, liberty,—all these we need, not singly but together, not successively but together, each growing and aiding each, and all striving toward that vaster ideal that swims before the Negro people, the ideal of human brotherhood, gained through the unifying ideal of Race; the ideal of fostering and developing the traits and talents of the Negro, not in opposition to or contempt for other races, but rather in large conformity to the greater ideals of the American Republic, in order that some day on American soil two world-races may give each to each those characteristics both so sadly lack. We the darker ones come even now not altogether empty-handed: there are to-day no truer exponents of the pure human spirit of the Declaration of Independence than the American Negroes; there is no true American music but the wild sweet melodies of the Negro slave; the American fairy tales and folk-lore are Indian and African; and, all in all, we black men seem the sole oasis of simple faith and reverence in a dusty desert of dollars and smartness. Will America be poorer if she replace her brutal dyspeptic blundering with light-hearted but determined Negro humility? or her coarse and cruel wit with loving jovial good-humor? or her vulgar music with the soul of the Sorrow Songs?

Merely a concrete test of the underlying principles of the great republic is the Negro Problem, and the spiritual striving of the freedmen's sons is the travail of souls whose burden is almost beyond the measure of their strength,

7. Storm and stress (German).

but who bear it in the name of an historic race, in the name of this the land of their fathers' fathers, and in the name of human opportunity.

And now what I have briefly sketched in large outline let me on coming pages tell again in many ways, with loving emphasis and deeper detail, that men may listen to the striving in the souls of black folk.

\* \* \*

### III. Of Mr. Booker T. Washington and Others[8]

From birth till death enslaved; in word, in deed, unmanned!

• • • • • • • •

Hereditary bondsmen! Know ye not
Who would be free themselves must strike the blow?
—BYRON[9]

Easily the most striking thing in the history of the American Negro since 1876[1] is the ascendancy of Mr. Booker T. Washington. It began at the time when war memories and ideals were rapidly passing; a day of astonishing commercial development was dawning; a sense of doubt and hesitation overtook the freedmen's sons,—then it was that his leading began. Mr. Washington came, with a simple definite programme, at the psychological moment when the nation was a little ashamed of having bestowed so much sentiment on Negroes, and was concentrating its energies on Dollars. His programme of industrial education, conciliation of the South, and submission and silence as to civil and political rights, was not wholly original; the Free Negroes from 1830 up to war-time had striven to build industrial schools, and the American Missionary Association had from the first taught various trades; and Price[2] and others had sought a way of honorable alliance with the best of the Southerners. But Mr. Washington first indissolubly linked these things; he put enthusiasm, unlimited energy, and perfect faith into this programme, and changed it from a by-path into a veritable Way of Life. And the tale of the methods by which he did this is a fascinating study of human life.

8. *Of Mr. Booker T. Washington and Others* was first published in *Guardian*, July 27, 1902, and then collected in *The Souls of Black Folk*. Booker T. Washington (1856?–1915) founded and helped build Tuskegee Institute, a black college in Alabama, and became a powerful leader of and spokesman for black Americans, especially after his address at the Atlanta Exposition in 1895.
9. The epigraph is from *Childe Harold's Pilgrimage,* Canto 2, 74.710, 76.720–21. The music is from the refrain of a black spiritual titled "A Great Camp-Meetin' in de Promised Land" (also called "There's a Great Camp Meeting" and "Walk Together Children"). The words of the refrain set to this music are

> Going to mourn and never tire—
> mourn and never tire, mourn and never tire.

1. Reconstruction ended in 1876; federal troops were withdrawn from the South, and black political power was essentially destroyed.
2. Thomas Frederick Price (1860–1919), American editor, missionary, and Roman Catholic priest; one of the founders of the American Missionary Association.

It startled the nation to hear a Negro advocating such a programme after many decades of bitter complaint; it startled and won the applause of the South, it interested and won the admiration of the North; and after a confused murmur of protest, it silenced if it did not convert the Negroes themselves.

To gain the sympathy and cooperation of the various elements comprising the white South was Mr. Washington's first task; and this, at the time Tuskegee was founded, seemed, for a black man, well-nigh impossible. And yet ten ten years later it was done in the word spoken at Atlanta: "In all things purely social we can be as separate as the five fingers, and yet one as the hand in all things essential to mutual progress." This "Atlanta Compromise"[3] is by all odds the most notable thing in Mr. Washington's career. The South interpreted it in different ways: the radicals received it as a complete surrender of the demand for civil and political equality; the conservatives, as a generously conceived working basis for mutual understanding. So both approved it, and to-day its author is certainly the most distinguished Southerner since Jefferson Davis, and the one with the largest personal following.

Next to this achievement comes Mr. Washington's work in gaining place and consideration in the North. Others less shrewd and tactful had formerly essayed to sit on these two stools and had fallen between them; but as Mr. Washington knew the heart of the South from birth and training, so by singular insight he intuitively grasped the spirit of the age which was dominating the North. And so thoroughly did he learn the speech and thought of triumphant commercialism, and the ideals of material prosperity, that the picture of a lone black boy poring over a French grammar amid the weeds and dirt of a neglected home soon seemed to him the acme of absurdities.[4] One wonders what Socrates and St. Francis of Assisi would say to this.

And yet this very singleness of vision and thorough oneness with his age is a mark of the successful man. It is as though Nature must needs make men narrow in order to give them force. So Mr. Washington's cult has gained unquestioning followers, his work has wonderfully prospered, his friends are legion, and his enemies are confounded. To-day he stands as the one recognized spokesman of his ten million fellows, and one of the most notable figures in a nation of seventy millions. One hesitates, therefore, to criticise a life which, beginning with so little, has done so much. And yet the time is come when one may speak in all sincerity and utter courtesy of the mistakes and shortcomings of Mr. Washington's career, as well as of his triumphs, without being thought captious or envious, and without forgetting that it is easier to do ill than well in the world.

The criticism that has hitherto met Mr. Washington has not always been of this broad character. In the South especially has he had to walk warily to avoid the harshest judgments,—and naturally so, for he is dealing with the

---

3. In a speech at the Atlanta Exposition of 1895, Washington in effect traded political, civil, and social rights for blacks for the promise of vocational-training schools and jobs. His purpose was to reduce racial tension in the South while providing a stable black labor force whose skills would provide job security.
4. In Washington's *Up from Slavery* (1901), ch. 8, "Teaching School in a Stable and a Hen-House," there is a passage on the absurdity of knowledge not practically useful:

> In fact, one of the saddest things I saw during the month of travel which I have described was a young man, who had attended some high school, sitting down in a one-room cabin, with grease on his clothing, filth all around him, and weeds in the yard and garden, engaged in studying French grammar.

one subject of deepest sensitiveness to that section. Twice—once when at the Chicago celebration of the Spanish-American War he alluded to the color-prejudice that is "eating away the vitals of the South," and once when he dined with President Roosevelt[5]—has the resulting Southern criticism been violent enough to threaten seriously his popularity. In the North the feeling has several times forced itself into words, that Mr. Washington's counsels of submission overlooked certain elements of true manhood, and that his educational programme was unnecessarily narrow. Usually, however, such criticism has not found open expression, although, too, the spiritual sons of the Abolitionists have not been prepared to acknowledge that the schools founded before Tuskegee, by men of broad ideals and self-sacrificing spirit, were wholly failures or worthy of ridicule. While, then, criticism has not failed to follow Mr. Washington, yet the prevailing public opinion of the land has been but too willing to deliver the solution of a wearisome problem into his hands, and say, "If that is all you and your race ask, take it."

Among his own people, however, Mr. Washington has encountered the strongest and most lasting opposition, amounting at times to bitterness, and even to-day continuing strong and insistent even though largely silenced in outward expression by the public opinion of the nation. Some of this opposition is, of course, mere envy; the disappointment of displaced demagogues and the spite of narrow minds. But aside from this, there is among educated and thoughtful colored men in all parts of the land a feeling of deep regret, sorrow, and apprehension at the wide currency and ascendancy which some of Mr. Washington's theories have gained. These same men admire his sincerity of purpose, and are willing to forgive much to honest endeavor which is doing something worth the doing. They coöperate with Mr. Washington as far as they conscientiously can; and, indeed, it is no ordinary tribute to this man's tact and power that, steering as he must between so many diverse interests and opinions, he so largely retains the respect of all.

But the hushing of the criticism of honest opponents is a dangerous thing. It leads some of the best of the critics to unfortunate silence and paralysis of effort, and others to burst into speech so passionately and intemperately as to lose listeners. Honest and earnest criticism from those whose interests are most nearly touched,—criticism of writers by readers, of government by those governed, of leaders by those led,—this is the soul of democracy and the safeguard of modern society. If the best of the American Negroes receive by outer pressure a leader whom they had not recognized before, manifestly there is here a certain palpable gain. Yet there is also irreparable loss,—a loss of that peculiarly valuable education which a group receives when by search and criticism it finds and commissions its own leaders. The way in which this is done is at once the most elementary and the nicest problem of social growth. History is but the record of such group-leadership; and yet how infinitely changeful is its type and character! And of all types and kinds, what can be more instructive than the leadership of a group within a group?—that curious double movement where real progress may be negative and actual advance be relative retrogression. All this is the social student's inspiration and despair.

<hr />

5. Theodore Roosevelt (1858–1919), twenty-sixth president of the United States (1901–09). Washington's dining with him at the White House in 1901 caused controversy around the country.

Now in the past the American Negro has had instructive experience in the choosing of group leaders, founding thus a peculiar dynasty which in the light of present conditions is worth while studying. When sticks and stones and beasts form the sole environment of a people, their attitude is largely one of determined opposition to and conquest of natural forces. But when to earth and brute is added an environment of men and ideas, then the attitude of the imprisoned group may take three main forms,—a feeling of revolt and revenge; an attempt to adjust all thought and action to the will of the greater group; or, finally, a determined effort at self-realization and self-development despite environing opinion. The influence of all of these attitudes at various times can be traced in the history of the American Negro, and in the evolution of his successive leaders.

Before 1750, while the fire of African freedom still burned in the veins of the slaves, there was in all leadership or attempted leadership but the one motive of revolt and revenge,—typified in the terrible Maroons, the Danish blacks, and Cato[6] of Stono, and veiling all the Americas in fear of insurrection. The liberalizing tendencies of the latter half of the eighteenth century brought, along with kindlier relations between black and white, thoughts of ultimate adjustment and assimilation. Such aspiration was especially voiced in the earnest songs of Phyllis, in the martyrdom of Attucks, the fighting of Salem and Poor, the intellectual accomplishments of Banneker and Derham, and the political demands of the Cuffes.[7]

Stern financial and social stress after the war cooled much of the previous humanitarian ardor. The disappointment and impatience of the Negroes at the persistence of slavery and serfdom voiced itself in two movements. The slaves in the South, aroused undoubtedly by vague rumors of the Haytian revolt, made three fierce attempts at insurrection,—in 1800 under Gabriel in Virginia, in 1822 under Vesey in Carolina, and in 1831 again in Virginia under the terrible Nat Turner.[8] In the Free States, on the other hand, a new and curious attempt at self-development was made. In Philadelphia and New York color-prescription led to a withdrawal of Negro communicants from white churches and the formation of a peculiar socio-religious institution among the Negroes known as the African Church,—an organization still living and controlling in its various branches over a million of men.

Walker's wild appeal[9] against the trend of the times showed how the world was changing after the coming of the cotton-gin. By 1830 slavery seemed

6. The leader of the Stono, South Carolina, slave revolt of September 9, 1739, in which twenty-five whites were killed. "Maroons": fugitive slaves from the West Indies and Guiana in the 17th and 18th centuries, or their descendants. Many of the slaves in the Danish West Indies revolted in 1733 because of the lack of sufficient food.
7. Paul Cuffe (1759–1817) organized to resettle free blacks in African colonies. A champion of civil rights for free blacks in Massachusetts, he took thirty-eight blacks to Africa in 1815 at his own expense. Phyllis (or Phillis) Wheatley (c. 1753–1784), black slave and poet. Crispus Attucks (c. 1723–1770) was killed in the Boston massacre. Peter Salem (d. 1816), black patriot who killed Major Pitcairn in the battle of Bunker Hill. Salem Poor (b. 1747), a black soldier who fought at Bunker Hill, Valley Forge, and White Plains. Benjamin Banneker (1731–1806), a black mathematician who also studied astronomy. James Derham

(b. 1762), the first recognized black physician in America; born a slave, he learned medicine from his physician master, bought his freedom in 1783, and by 1788 was one of the foremost physicians of New Orleans.
8. A slave (1800–1831), he led the Southampton insurrection in 1831, during which sixty-one whites and more than a hundred slaves were killed or executed. Gabriel (1775?–1800) conspired to attack Richmond, Virginia, with a thousand other slaves on August 30, 1800; but a storm forced a suspension of the mission and two slaves betrayed the conspiracy. On October 7, Gabriel and fifteen others were hanged. Denmark Vesey (c. 1767–1822), a mulatto rebel, purchased his freedom in 1800; he led an unsuccessful uprising in 1822 and was hanged.
9. An inflammatory and eloquent antislavery pamphlet by David Walker (1785–1830), black leader.

hopelessly fastened on the South, and the slaves thoroughly cowed into submission. The free Negroes of the North, inspired by the mulatto immigrants from the West Indies, began to change the basis of their demands; they recognized the slavery of slaves, but insisted that they themselves were freemen, and sought assimilation and amalgamation with the nation on the same terms with other men. Thus, Forten and Purvis of Philadelphia, Shad of Wilmington, Du Bois of New Haven, Barbadoes[1] of Boston, and others, strove singly and together as men, they said, not as slaves; as "people of color," not as "Negroes." The trend of the times, however, refused them recognition save in individual and exceptional cases, considered them as one with all the despised blacks, and they soon found themselves striving to keep even the rights they formerly had of voting and working and moving as freemen. Schemes of migration and colonization arose among them; but these they refused to entertain, and they eventually turned to the Abolition movement as a final refuge.

Here, led by Remond, Nell, Wells-Brown, and Douglass,[2] a new period of self-assertion and self-development dawned. To be sure, ultimate freedom and assimilation was the ideal before the leaders, but the assertion of the manhood rights of the Negro by himself was the main reliance, and John Brown's raid was the extreme of its logic. After the war and emancipation, the great form of Frederick Douglass, the greatest of American Negro leaders, still led the host. Self-assertion, especially in political lines, was the main programme, and behind Douglass came Elliot, Bruce, and Langston, and the Reconstruction politicians, and, less conspicuous but of greater social significance Alexander Crummell and Bishop Daniel Payne.[3]

Then came the Revolution of 1876, the suppression of the Negro votes, the changing and shifting of ideals, and the seeking of new lights in the great night. Douglass, in his old age, still bravely stood for the ideals of his early manhood,—ultimate assimilation *through* self-assertion, and on no other terms. For a time Price arose as a new leader, destined, it seemed, not to give up, but to re-state the old ideals in a form less repugnant to the white South. But he passed away in his prime. Then came the new leader. Nearly all the former ones had become leaders by the silent suffrage of their fellows, had sought to lead their own people alone, and were usually, save Douglass, little known outside their race. But Booker T. Washington arose as essentially the leader not of one race but of two,—a compromiser between the South, the

1. James G. Barbadoes was one of those present at the first National Negro Convention along with Forten, Purvis, Shadd, and others. James Forten (1766–1842), black civic leader and philanthropist. Robert Purvis (1810–1898), abolitionist, helped found the American Anti-Slavery Society in 1833 and was the president of the Underground Railway. Abraham Shadd, abolitionist, was on the first board of managers of the American Anti-Slavery Society, a delegate from Delaware for the first National Negro Convention (1830), and president of the third one in 1833. Alexander Du Bois (1803–1887), paternal grandfather of W. E. B. Du Bois, helped form the Negro Episcopal Parish of St. Luke in 1847 and was the senior warden there. 2. Frederick Douglass (1817–1895), abolitionist and orator and born a slave, was U.S. minister to Haiti and U.S. marshal of the District of Columbia. Charles Lenox Remond (1810–1873), black leader. William Cooper Nell (1816–1874), abolitionist, writer, and first African American to hold

office under the government of the United States (clerk in the post office). Through his efforts equal school privileges were obtained for black children in Boston. William Wells Brown (1816?–1884) published *Clotel* in 1853, the first novel by a black American, and *The Escape* in 1858, the first play by a black American. 3. Daniel Alexander Payne (1811–1893), bishop of the African Methodist Episcopal church and president of Wilberforce University (1863–76). Robert Brown Elliot (1842–1884), black politician, graduate of Eton, South Carolina congressman in the U.S. House of Representatives. Blanche K. Bruce (1841–1898), born a slave, first black man to serve a full term in the U.S. Senate (1875–81). John Mercer Langston (1829–1897), congressman, lawyer, diplomat, educator, born a slave. Crummell (1819–1898), clergyman of the Protestant Episcopal church, missionary in Liberia for twenty years and then in Washington, D.C.

North, and the Negro. Naturally the Negroes resented, at first bitterly, signs of compromise which surrendered their civil and political rights, even though this was to be exchanged for larger chances of economic development. The rich and dominating North, however, was not only weary of the race problem, but was investing largely in Southern enterprises, and welcomed any method of peaceful coöperation. Thus, by national opinion, the Negroes began to recognize Mr. Washington's leadership; and the voice of criticism was hushed.

Mr. Washington represents in Negro thought the old attitude of adjustment and submission; but adjustment at such a peculiar time as to make his programme unique. This is an age of unusual economic development, and Mr. Washington's programme naturally takes an economic cast, becoming a gospel of Work and Money to such an extent as apparently almost completely to overshadow the higher aims of life. Moreover, this is an age when the more advanced races are coming in closer contact with the less developed races, and the race-feeling is therefore intensified; and Mr. Washington's programme practically accepts the alleged inferiority of the Negro races. Again, in our own land, the reaction from the sentiment of war time has given impetus to race-prejudice against Negroes, and Mr. Washington withdraws many of the high demands of Negroes as men and American citizens. In other periods of intensified prejudice all the Negro's tendency to self-assertion has been called forth; at this period a policy of submission is advocated. In the history of nearly all other races and peoples the doctrine preached at such crises has been that manly self-respect is worth more than lands and houses, and that a people who voluntarily surrender such respect, or cease striving for it, are not worth civilizing.

In answer to this, it has been claimed that the Negro can survive only through submission. Mr. Washington distinctly asks that black people give up, at least for the present, three things,—

First, political power,

Second, insistence on civil rights,

Third, higher education of Negro youth,—

and concentrate all their energies on industrial education, the accumulation of wealth, and the conciliation of the South. This policy has been courageously and insistently advocated for over fifteen years, and has been triumphant for perhaps ten years. As a result of this tender of the palm-branch, what has been the return? In these years there have occurred:

1. The disfranchisement of the Negro.

2. The legal creation of a distinct status of civil inferiority for the Negro.

3. The steady withdrawal of aid from institutions for the higher training of the Negro.

These movements are not, to be sure, direct results of Mr. Washington's teachings; but his propaganda has, without a shadow of doubt, helped their speedier accomplishment. The question then comes: Is it possible, and probable, that nine millions of men can make effective progress in economic lines if they are deprived of political rights, made a servile caste, and allowed only the most meagre chance for developing their exceptional men? If history and reason give any distinct answer to these questions, it is an emphatic *No.* And Mr. Washington thus faces the triple paradox of his career:

1. He is striving nobly to make Negro artisans business men and property-owners; but it is utterly impossible, under modern competitive methods, for

workingmen and property-owners to defend their rights and exist without the right of suffrage.

2. He insists on thrift and self-respect, but at the same time counsels a silent submission to civic inferiority such as is bound to sap the manhood of any race in the long run.

3. He advocates common-school[4] and industrial training, and depreciates institutions of higher learning; but neither the Negro common-schools, nor Tuskegee itself, could remain open a day were it not for teachers trained in Negro colleges, or trained by their graduates.

This triple paradox in Mr. Washington's position is the object of criticism by two classes of colored Americans. One class is spiritually descended from Toussaint the Savior,[5] through Gabriel, Vesey, and Turner, and they represent the attitude of revolt and revenge; they hate the white South blindly and distrust the white race generally, and so far as they agree on definite action, think that the Negro's only hope lies in emigration beyond the borders of the United States. And yet, by the irony of fate, nothing has more effectually made this programme seem hopeless than the recent course of the United States toward weaker and darker peoples in the West Indies, Hawaii, and the Philippines,—for where in the world may we go and be safe from lying and brute force?

The other class of Negroes who cannot agree with Mr. Washington has hitherto said little aloud. They deprecate the sight of scattered counsels, of internal disagreement; and especially they dislike making their just criticism of a useful and earnest man an excuse for a general discharge of venom from small-minded opponents. Nevertheless, the questions involved are so fundamental and serious that it is difficult to see how men like the Grimkes, Kelly Miller, J. W. E. Bowen,[6] and other representatives of this group, can much longer be silent. Such men feel in conscience bound to ask of this nation three things:

1. The right to vote.
2. Civic equality.
3. The education of youth according to ability.

They acknowledge Mr. Washington's invaluable service in counselling patience and courtesy in such demands; they do not ask that ignorant black men vote when ignorant whites are debarred, or that any reasonable restrictions in the suffrage should not be applied; they know that the low social level of the mass of the race is responsible for much discrimination against it, but they also know, and the nation knows, that relentless color-prejudice is more often a cause than a result of the Negro's degradation; they seek the abatement of this relic of barbarism, and not its systematic encouragement and pampering by all agencies of social power from the Associated Press to the Church of Christ. They advocate, with Mr. Washington, a broad system of Negro common schools supplemented by thorough industrial training; but they are surprised that a man of Mr. Washington's insight cannot see that no such educational system ever has rested or can rest on any other basis than

4. A free public school offering courses at precollege level.
5. Pierre Dominique Toussaint (1743–1803); see p. 899, n. 6.
6. John Wesley Edward Bowen (1855–?), Methodist clergyman and educator, president of

Gammon Theological Seminary of Atlanta. Archibald Grimké (1849–1930) and Francis Grimké (1850–1937), American civic leaders concerned with African American affairs. Miller (1863–1939), dean of Howard University, lectured on the race problem.

that of the well-equipped college and university, and they insist that there is a demand for a few such institutions throughout the South to train the best of the Negro youth as teachers, professional men, and leaders.

This group of men honor Mr. Washington for his attitude of conciliation toward the white South; they accept the "Atlanta Compromise" in its broadest interpretation; they recognize, with him, many signs of promise, many men of high purpose and fair judgment, in this section; they know that no easy task has been laid upon a region already tottering under heavy burdens. But, nevertheless, they insist that the way to truth and right lies in straightforward honesty, not in indiscriminate flattery; in praising those of the South who do well and criticising uncompromisingly those who do ill; in taking advantage of the opportunities at hand and urging their fellows to do the same, but at the same time in remembering that only a firm adherence to their higher ideals and aspirations will ever keep those ideals within the realm of possibility. They do not expect that the free right to vote, to enjoy civic rights, and to be educated, will come in a moment; they do not expect to see the bias and prejudices of years disappear at the blast of a trumpet; but they are absolutely certain that the way for a people to gain their reasonable rights is not by voluntarily throwing them away and insisting that they do not want them; that the way for a people to gain respect is not by continually belittling and ridiculing themselves; that, on the contrary, Negroes must insist continually, in season and out of season, that voting is necessary to modern manhood, that color discrimination is barbarism, and that black boys need education as well as white boys.

In failing thus to state plainly and unequivocally the legitimate demands of their people, even at the cost of opposing an honored leader, the thinking classes of American Negroes would shirk a heavy responsibility,—a responsibility to themselves, a responsibility to the struggling masses, a responsibility to the darker races of men whose future depends so largely on this American experiment, but especially a responsibility to this nation,—this common Fatherland. It is wrong to encourage a man or a people in evil-doing; it is wrong to aid and abet a national crime simply because it is unpopular not to do so. The growing spirit of kindliness and reconciliation between the North and South after the frightful differences of a generation ago ought to be a source of deep congratulation to all, and especially to those whose mistreatment caused the war; but if that reconciliation is to be marked by the industrial slavery and civic death of those same black men, with permanent legislation into a position of inferiority, then those black men, if they are really men, are called upon by every consideration of patriotism and loyalty to oppose such a course by all civilized methods, even though such opposition involves disagreement with Mr. Booker T. Washington. We have no right to sit silently by while the inevitable seeds are sown for a harvest of disaster to our children, black and white.

First, it is the duty of black men to judge the South discriminatingly. The present generation of Southerners are not responsible for the past, and they should not be blindly hated or blamed for it. Furthermore, to no class is the indiscriminate endorsement of the recent course of the South toward Negroes more nauseating than to the best thought of the South. The South is not "solid"; it is a land in the ferment of social change, wherein forces of all kinds are fighting for supremacy; and to praise the ill the South is to-day perpetrating is just as wrong as to condemn the good. Discriminating and broad-minded criticism is what the South needs,—needs it for the sake of her own white sons and daughters, and for the insurance of robust, healthy mental and moral development.

To-day even the attitude of the Southern whites toward the blacks is not, as so many assume, in all cases the same; the ignorant Southerner hates the Negro, the workingmen fear his competition, the money-makers wish to use him as a laborer, some of the educated see a menace in his upward development, while others—usually the sons of the masters—wish to help him to rise. National opinion has enabled this last class to maintain the Negro common schools, and to protect the Negro partially in property, life, and limb. Through the pressure of the money-makers, the Negro is in danger of being reduced to semi-slavery, especially in the country districts; the workingmen, and those of the educated who fear the Negro, have united to disfranchise him, and some have urged his deportation; while the passions of the ignorant are easily aroused to lynch and abuse any black man. To praise this intricate whirl of thought and prejudice is nonsense; to inveigh indiscriminately against "the South" is unjust; but to use the same breath in praising Governor Aycock, exposing Senator Morgan, arguing with Mr. Thomas Nelson Page, and denouncing Senator Ben Tillman,[7] is not only sane, but the imperative duty of thinking black men.

It would be unjust to Mr. Washington not to acknowledge that in several instances he has opposed movements in the South which were unjust to the Negro; he sent memorials to the Louisiana and Alabama constitutional conventions, he has spoken against lynching, and in other ways has openly or silently set his influence against sinister schemes and unfortunate happenings. Notwithstanding this, it is equally true to assert that on the whole the distinct impression left by Mr. Washington's propaganda is, first, that the South is justified in its present attitude toward the Negro because of the Negro's degradation; secondly, that the prime cause of the Negro's failure to rise more quickly is his wrong education in the past; and, thirdly, that his future rise depends primarily on his own efforts. Each of these propositions is a dangerous half-truth. The supplementary truths must never be lost sight of: first, slavery and race-prejudice are potent if not sufficient causes of the Negro's position; second, industrial and common-school training were necessarily slow in planting because they had to await the black teachers trained by higher institutions,—it being extremely doubtful if any essentially different development was possible, and certainly a Tuskegee was unthinkable before 1880; and, third, while it is a great truth to say that the Negro must strive and strive mightily to help himself, it is equally true that unless his striving be not simply seconded, but rather aroused and encouraged, by the ini-

7. Benjamin Ryan Tillman (1847–1918), governor of South Carolina (1890–94) and U.S. Senator (1895–1918), served as the chairman on the committee on suffrage (during the South Carolina constitutional convention) and framed the article providing for an educational and property qualification for voting, thus eliminating the black vote. He presented the views of the southern extremists on the race question, justified lynching in cases of rape and the use of force to disenfranchise blacks, and advocated the repeal of the Fifteenth Amendment. Charles Brantley Aycock (1859–1912), governor of North Carolina (1901–05). Edwin Denison Morgan (1811–1883), governor of New York (1859–63) and U.S. Senator (1863–69), voted with the minority in President Johnson's veto of the Freedman's Bureau bill and for Johnson's conviction. Page (1853–1922), American novelist and diplomat, did much to build up romantic legends of the southern plantation.

tiative of the richer and wiser environing group, he cannot hope for great success.

In his failure to realize and impress this last point, Mr. Washington is especially to be criticised. His doctrine has tended to make the whites, North and South, shift the burden of the Negro problem to the Negro's shoulders and stand aside as critical and rather pessimistic spectators; when in fact the burden belongs to the nation, and the hands of none of us are clean if we bend not our energies to righting these great wrongs.

The South ought to be led, by candid and honest criticism, to assert her better self and do her full duty to the race she has cruelly wronged and is still wronging. The North—her co-partner in guilt—cannot salve her conscience by plastering it with gold. We cannot settle this problem by diplomacy and suaveness, by "policy" alone. If worse come to worst, can the moral fibre of this country survive the slow throttling and murder of nine millions of men?

The black men of America have a duty to perform, a duty stern and delicate,—a forward movement to oppose a part of the work of their greatest leader. So far as Mr. Washington preaches Thrift, Patience, and Industrial Training for the masses, we must hold up his hands and strive with him, rejoicing in his honors and glorying in the strength of this Joshua called of God and of man to lead the headless host. But so far as Mr. Washington apologizes for injustice, North or South, does not rightly value the privilege and duty of voting, belittles the emasculating effects of caste distinctions, and opposes the higher training and ambition of our brighter minds,—so far as he, the South, or the Nation, does this,—we must unceasingly and firmly oppose them. By every civilized and peaceful method we must strive for the rights which the world accords to men, clinging unwaveringly to those great words which the sons of the Fathers would fain forget: "We hold these truths to be self-evident: That all men are created equal; that they are endowed by their Creator with certain unalienable rights; that among these are life, liberty, and the pursuit of happiness."

1903

# Realism and Naturalism

*Realism* and *naturalism* are closely related but disputed terms in American literary history, used interchangeably and also as opposites. Is naturalism merely realism with an emphasis on pessimistic determinism? Or is naturalism something separate from realism and at odds with it, an idealistic form of romance? As cultural conditions changed rapidly in mid-nineteenth-century America, artists of all types turned to realist styles to address such new concerns as the rise of the middle class and the struggles of the working class. Literary realism, then naturalism at the start of the new century, gave voice to Americans' changing awareness of the meaning of such concepts as "Nature"—including human nature—in such new environments as the frontier and fast-growing cities.

Realism as a movement in novel-writing developed in early nineteenth-century Europe and the United States. Writers as seemingly different as William Dean Howells and Mark Twain offered objective, detached views of everyday life appropriate for middle-class readers. Critic George J. Becker's definition of the realist novel as a substantial work in prose that offers verisimilitude of detail, a norm of experience, and an objective view of human nature fits not only the work of early realist authors but also that of their literary descendants. By the mid-nineteenth century, realism was simply considered modern, and readers assumed that contemporary fiction would aspire to offer verisimilitude.

The heights of American realism were reached in the work of Howells, Twain, Henry James, and Edith Wharton. Howell's *The Rise of Silas Lapham* (1885) transformed the novel of manners into a critique of the American Dream, as a family is nearly undone by the father's unexamined desire for high society—yet all is mostly well in the end, lessons learned. Regarded as "the father of American Realism," Howells, like Twain, rejected romanticism (if not sentiment) and its distortions. More significant for literary history than Howells's fiction were his editorships at prestigious magazines such as *Harper's* and *Atlantic Monthly*, in which he published Twain, James, and other innovators, including Charles Chesnutt and naturalist Frank Norris. If not for Howells in his editorial dimension, Twain's publishing career might never have taken off.

Though Twain and James represented two very different instances of American realism (and disliked each others' writing), Howells championed both of them. As Twain pushed realism toward satirical exaggeration and developed the vernacular voice in his fiction, James used the voice of high culture and pushed realism toward premodern psychological realism, particularly in *The Portrait of a Lady* (1882) and his other novels of Americans unprepared for situations they encounter in Europe. In later novels, such as *The Wings of the Dove* (1902), James developed realism into an absorbing, complex interior discourse, his narrator evolving into an ironic blend of first- and third-person points of view, a perspective described by critic Percy Lubbock as hovering somewhere over the shoulder of the "focal character." Wharton's satiric and often tragic novels and stories of Gilded Age New York society extend the penetrating insights of Howells and James, but move more toward naturalism; the laws of Darwinian survival are not, in her work, in operation only among the poor or along the frontier, but in the upper-crust drawing rooms and summer homes she knew from birth.

Realism was a broader movement than naturalism, and of course helped give rise to naturalism. But they present sharp differences. The realist novels of the nineteenth century attacked social mores and manners but were rarely critical of the political foundations of society itself. With its clearer doctrines, more restricted time period (1890–1920), and proving grounds mainly in France and the United States, naturalism more specifically critiqued the industrial wealth of the bourgeoisie. Naturalist novels had extreme settings, in contrast to the everyday, believable locales of realist novels. Realistic characters were usually middle class; naturalistic ones lower-class. Realist plots worked toward the restoration of order and characters' proper location in class hierarchies. Minor crises lead to a major confrontation, followed by resolution. In naturalist novels, the characters confront major crises and are destroyed by them. A realist might suggest that good will ultimately prevails, but in naturalist novels humans are doomed by their own (animalistic) shortcomings. Naturalist heroes never have a chance.

By the end of the nineteenth century, naturalism, with its "scientific" point of view, had developed narrative techniques that reflected this orientation, embracing such new technologies as photography and grappling with Freud's theories of a primitive "id" and the Unconscious, a new inner landscape. But the most important force behind naturalism was Darwin. Life as a series of events governed by natural selection, as proposed in Darwin's *Origin of Species* (1859) and *The Descent of Man* (1871), suggested that the strong survive and the weak are destroyed: this scientific "law of life," as its adherents thought of it, ran counter to religion and genteel morality.

In France, novelist and social critic Émile Zola wrote naturalist novels of the lives of poor people at the mercy of biology and class, featuring themes of power and survival. In the preface to *Thérèse Raquin* (1867), Zola compares the naturalist to a surgeon dissecting a corpse—the novel exposes social conditions in a way that might ultimately help right political and economic wrongs.

American literary naturalists—most born after the Civil War—grew up in a different world than did the realists, one dominated by what critic Donald Pizer calls a "struggle to survive materially rather than to prevail morally." Between the economic panics of the 1890s, which put masses of people out of work, and World War I, there developed naturalist literature of great diversity. Naturalist subject matter ranges from Crane's awed and terrified Union soldier in *The Red Badge of Courage* (1895), to Norris's and Upton Sinclair's exposés of the power of capitalism in *The Octopus* (1901) and *The Jungle* (1906), to the portraits of psychopathological characters in Norris's *McTeague* (1899) and London's *The Sea-Wolf* (1904). Naturalism thus appeared in many forms. Like *The Octopus*, London's *The Call of the Wild* (1903) was at once a profoundly naturalistic novel and an intensely romantic fable; in London's fiction, though human nature seems inevitably to go wrong, it may be saved in rugged environments where "civilized" notions such as self-gain are no longer useful. Later, Richard Wright and Américo Paredes would use such themes in urban settings. Despite its often brutal subject matter, naturalism "reflects an affirmative ethical conception of life," as Pizer expresses it, by endowing even the lowest characters with moral complexity.

# WILLIAM DEAN HOWELLS

Enormously influential as author, editor, and critic, William Dean Howells (1837–1920) was one of the prime innovators of American realism; his novels and even more so his editorial work shaped American fiction of his day. When Howells left his editorship at *The Atlantic Monthly* in 1881, he had already established himself as a "literary Columbus," as *Cosmopolitan* editor Perriton Maxwell called him, having discovered "a flock of brilliant essayists, poets, and storytellers whose voices would have died . . . had he not been the conscientious listener for the newer notes borne Bostonward from everywhere in these broad States of ours." Increasingly as his career progressed Howells felt American writing should be "simple, natural, and honest" and should refrain from "romantic exaggeration." Unlike Henry James or Mark Twain, his fellow realist innovators, Howells was not interested in the unconscious and irrational in humankind. Though he was criticized by Frank Norris among others for his "teacup tragedies" that take place in front parlors, as an editor and critic Howells responded deeply and sensitively to novelistic complexity. In his essay "Henry James, Jr.," Howells praises James's "impartiality" as that which leaves conclusions about characters up to the reader: "We must take him on his own ground, for clearly he will not come to ours."

"Novel-Writing and Novel-Reading" was not published until well after Howells's death; in his day it was a widely praised lecture he gave on a tour through the East and Midwest in 1899. In the essay Howells shows a change from the "Boston" Howells to the "New York" Howells. Moving to New York in 1891, Howells developed a growing concern with "social" and "race" questions in literature. He came to see novel-reading as a more serious endeavor than ever. And for novelists, he felt, "construction and criticism go hand-in-hand." From his new column in *Harper's Magazine*, Howells campaigned for the importance of realism in the novel, arguing that the reader's own "experience of life" was the only test of " 'realism.' " But, in the end, realism is less "picturesque" than historical and ethical. In his earlier career, Howells had insisted on eliding those passions that could not be revealed in polite novels; by this point, he had come to believe that "realism excludes nothing that is true," and that *truth* is synonymous with *beauty*. He argues that the novel is a vehicle of social reform and advances those who write toward that goal, such as Charles Chesnutt. Howells ties in the American realists of the day with the tradition of the novel in Europe. "The truth," he decides, "may be indecent, but it cannot be vicious, it can never corrupt or deprave" in its "material honesty."

## *From* Henry James, Jr.[1]

\* \* \*

That artistic impartiality which puzzled so many in the treatment of Daisy Miller[2] is one of the qualities most valuable in the eyes of those who care how things are done, and I am not sure that it is not Mr. James's most characteristic quality. As "frost performs the effect of fire," this impartiality comes at last to the same result as sympathy. We may be quite sure that Mr. James does not like the peculiar phase of our civilization typified in Henrietta Stackpole:[3] but he treats her with such exquisite justice that he lets *us* like her. It is an extreme case, but I confidently allege it in proof.

1. First published in *The Century* 25.1 (November 1882), from which this excerpt is taken.
2. Title character of James's 1878 novella.

3. Character in James's 1881 novel *The Portrait of a Lady*.

His impartiality is part of the reserve with which he works in most respects, and which at first glance makes us say that he is wanting in humor. But I feel pretty certain that Mr. James has not been able to disinherit himself to this degree. We Americans are terribly in earnest about making ourselves, individually and collectively; but I fancy that our prevailing mood in the face of all problems is that of an abiding faith which can afford to be funny. He has himself indicated that we have, as a nation, as a people, our joke, and every one of us is in the joke more or less. We may, some of us, dislike it extremely, disapprove it wholly, and even abhor it, but we are in the joke all the same, and no one of us is safe from becoming the great American humorist at any given moment. The danger is not apparent in Mr. James's case, and I confess that I read him with a relief in the comparative immunity that he affords from the national facetiousness. Many of his people are humorously imagined, or rather humorously *seen*, like Daisy Miller's mother, but these do not give a dominant color; the business in hand is commonly serious, and the droll people are subordinated. They abound, nevertheless, and many of them are perfectly new finds * * *. But though Mr. James portrays the humorous in character, he is decidedly not on humorous terms with his reader; he ignores rather than recognizes the fact that they are both in the joke.

If we take him at all we must take him on his own ground, for clearly he will not come to ours. We must make concessions to him, not in this respect only, but in several others, chief among which is the motive for reading fiction. By example, at least, he teaches that it is the pursuit and not the end which should give us pleasure; for he often prefers to leave us to our own conjectures in regard to the fate of the people in whom he has interested us. There is no question, of course, but he could tell the story of Isabel[4] in "The Portrait of a Lady" to the end, yet he does not tell it. We must agree, then, to take what seems a fragment instead of a whole, and to find, when we can, a name for this new kind of fiction. Evidently it is the character, not the fate, of his people which occupies him; when he has fully developed their character he leaves them to what destiny the reader pleases.

* * *

The art of fiction has, in fact, become a finer art in our day than it was with Dickens and Thackeray. We could not suffer the confidential attitude of the latter now, nor the mannerism of the former, any more than we could endure the prolixity of Richardson or the coarseness of Fielding. These great men are of the past—they and their methods and interests; even Trollope and Reade are not of the present. The new school derives from Hawthorne and George Eliot rather than any others;[5] but it studies human nature much more in its wonted aspects, and finds its ethical and dramatic examples in the operation of lighter but not really less vital motives.

* * *

---

4. Protagonist of *The Portrait of a Lady*.
5. Charles Dickens (1812–1870), William Makepeace Thackeray (1811–1863), Anthony Trollope (1815–1882), Charles Reade (1814–1884), and George Eliot (pseud. Mary Ann Evans) (1819– 1880): 19th-century British novelists. Samuel Richardson (1689–1761) and Henry Fielding (1707–1754): 18th-century British novelists. Nathaniel Hawthorne (1804–1864): 19th-century American short-story writer and novelist.

Will the reader be content to accept a novel which is an analytic study rather than a story, which is apt to leave him arbiter of the destiny of the author's creations? Will he find his account in the unflagging interest of their development? Mr. James's growing popularity seems to suggest that this may be the case; but the work of Mr. James's imitators will have much to do with the final result.

\* \* \*

His style is, upon the whole, better than that of any other novelist I know; it is always easy, without being trivial, and it is often stately, without being stiff; it gives a charm to everything he writes.

\* \* \*

I own that I like a finished story; but then also I like those which Mr. James seems not to finish. This is probably the position of most of his readers, who cannot very logically account for either preference. We can only make sure that we have here an annalist, or analyst, as we choose, who fascinates us from his first page to his last, whose narrative or whose comment may enter into any minuteness of detail without fatiguing us, and can only truly grieve us when it ceases.

1882

## *From* Novel-Writing and Novel-Reading: An Impersonal Explanation[1]

\* \* \*

By beauty of course I mean truth, for the one involves the other; it is only the false in art which is ugly, and it is only the false which is universal. The truth may be indecent, but it cannot be vicious, it can never corrupt or deprave; and I should say this in defense of the grossest material honestly treated in modern novels as against the painted and perfumed meretricious-ness of the novels that went before them. I conceive that apart from all the clamor about schools of fiction is the *quiet* question of truth, how to get it in, so that it may get itself out again as beauty, the divinely living thing which all men love and worship. So I make truth the prime test of a novel. If I do not find that it is like life, then it does not exist for me as art; it is ugly, it is ludi-crous, it is impossible. I do not expect a novel to be wholly true. I have never read one that seemed to me so except Tolstoy's novels:[2] but I expect it to be a constant endeavor for the truth, and I perceive beauty in it so far as it ful-fills this endeavor. I am quite willing to recognize and enjoy whatever meas-ure of truth I find in a novel that is partly or mainly false; only, if I come upon the falsehood at the outset I am apt not to read that novel. But I do not bear

1. From *Howells and James: A Double Billing: Novel-Writing and Novel-Reading, An Impersonal Explanation,* ed. William M. Gibson, Leon Edel, and Lyall H. Powers (1958), from which this excerpt is taken.
2. Russian realist Leo Tolstoy's (1828–1910) most famous works are *Anna Karenina, The Death of Ivan Ilych,* and *War and Peace.*

such a grudge against it as I do against the novel which lures me on with a fair face of truth, and drops the mask midway. If you ask me for illustrations, I am somewhat at a loss, but if you ask me for examples, they are manifold. In English I should say the truthful novelists or those working with an ideal of truth were Jane Austen, George Eliot, Anthony Trollope, Thomas Hardy, Mrs. Humphrey Ward, George Moore; in French, Flaubert, Maupassant, the Goncourts, Daudet and Zola; in Russian, Tourguenief and Tolstoy; in Spanish, Valdés, Galdós and Pardo-Bazan; in Norwegian, Björnson, Lie, and Kielland. In English, some untruthful novelists, or those working from an ideal of effect, are Thackeray, Dickens, Bulwer, Reade, and all their living followers; in French, Dumas, Feuillet, Ohnet; in Spanish Valera; in Russian, measurably Doystoyevsky;[3] in Norwegian, none that I know of. It is right to say, however, of some of the untruthful novelists, and notably of Thackeray, that they were the victims of their period. If Thackeray had been writing in our time, I have no question but he would have been one of its most truthful artists.

The truth which I mean, the truth which is the only beauty, is truth to human experience, and human experience is so manifold and so recondite, that no scheme can be too remote, too airy for the test. It is a well ascertained fact concerning the imagination that it can work only with the stuff of experience. It can absolutely create nothing; it can only compose. The most fantastic extravagance comes under the same law that exacts likeness to the known as well as the closest and severest study of life. Once for all, then, obedience to this law is the creed of the realist, and rebellion is the creed of the romanticist. Both necessarily work under it, but one willingly, to beautiful effect, and the other unwillingly to ugly effect.

For the reader, whether he is an author too, or not, the only test of a novel's truth is his own knowledge of life. Is it like what he has seen or felt? Then it is true, and for him it cannot otherwise be true, that is to say beautiful. It will not avail that it has style, learning, thinking, feeling; it is no more beautiful without truth than the pretty statue which cannot stand on its feet. It is very astonishing to me that any sort of people can find pleasure in such a thing; but I know that there are many who do; and I should not think of consigning them to the police for their bad taste so long as their taste alone is bad. At the same time I confess that I should suspect an unreality, an insincerity in a mature and educated person whom I found liking an unreal, an insincere novel. You see, I take novels rather seriously, and I would hold them to a much stricter account than they are commonly held to. If I could, I would have them all subject to the principles that govern an honest man, and do not suffer him to tell lies of any sort. I think the novelist is rarely the victim of such a possession, or obsession, that he does not know when he is representing and

3. Among the 19th-century novelists that Howells mentions are Jane Austen (1775–1817), Thomas Hardy (1840–1928), Mrs. Humphrey Ward (1851–1920), George Moore (1852–1933), Gustave Flaubert (1821–1880), Guy de Maupassant (1850–1893), Edmund de Goncourt (1822–1896), Jules de Goncourt (1830–1870), Alphonse Daudet (1840–1897), Émile Zola (1840–1902), Ivan Turgenev (1818–1883), Armando Palacio Valdés (1853–1938), Benito Pérez Galdós (1843–1920), Emilia Pardo-Bazan (1851–1921), Björnstjerne Martinus Björnson (1832–1910), Jonas Lie (1833–1908), Alexander Kielland (1849–1906), Edward Bulwer-Lytton (1831–1891), Alexandre Dumas, pére (1802–1870), Octave Feuillet (1821–1890), Georges Ohnet (1848–1918), Juan Valera (1824–1905), and Fyodor Dostoyevsky (1821–1881). Howells divides them into two camps: realists and idealists.

when he is misrepresenting life. If he does not know it fully at the time, he cannot fail to be aware of it upon review of his work. In the frenzy of inspiration, he may not know that he has been lying; but a time will quickly come to him, if he is at all an artist, when he will know it, and will see that the work he has done is ugly because of it. That is the time for him to tear up his work and to begin anew.

Of course, there are several ways of regarding life in fiction, and in order to do justice to the different kinds we ought to distinguish very clearly between them. There are three forms which I think of, and which I will name in the order of their greatness: the novel, the romance, and the romanticistic novel.

The novel I take to be the sincere and conscientious endeavor to picture life just as it is, to deal with character as we witness it in living people, and to record the incidents that grow out of character. This is the supreme form of fiction, and I offer as supreme examples of it, Pride and Prejudice, Middlemarch, Anna Karenina, Fathers and Sons, Doña Perfecta and Marta y Maria,[4] sufficiently varied in their origin and material and method, but all of the same absolute honesty in their intention. They all rely for their moral effect simply and solely upon their truth to nature.

The novel is easily first among books that people read willingly and it is rightfully first. It has known how to keep the charm of the story, and to add to it the attraction of almost every interest. It still beguiles, as in the hands of the Byzantine romancers,[5] not to go unnumbered centuries back to the Greek novel of Homer, the Odyssey;[6] and it has learnt how to warm, to question, to teach in every concern of life. Scarcely any predicament, moral or psychological, has escaped its study, and it has so refined and perfected its methods that antiseptic surgery itself has hardly made a more beneficent advance. It began with the merest fable, excluding from the reader's interest all but the fortunes of princes and other dignified personages for whose entertainment it existed, until now it includes all sorts and conditions of men, who turn to it for instruction, inspiration, consolation. It has broadened and deepened down and out till it compasses the whole of human nature; and no cause important to the race has been unfriended of it. Sometimes I have been vexed at its vicious pandering to passion, but I cannot think, after all, of any great modern novel which has not been distinctly moral in effect. I am not sorry to have had it go into the dark places of the soul, the filthy and squalid places of society, high and low, and shed there its great light. Let us know with its help what we are, and where we are. Let all the hidden things be brought into the sun, and let every day be the day of judgment. If the sermon cannot any longer serve this end, let the novel do it.

---

4. *Pride and Prejudice* (1813) by Jane Austen, *Middlemarch* (1872) by George Eliot, *Anna Karenina* (1877) by Leo Tolstoy, *Fathers and Sons* (1861) by Ivan Turgenev, *Doña Perfecta* (1876) by Benito Pérez Galdós, and *Marta y Maria* (1883) by Armando Palacio Valdés are 19th-century novels that represent "realism" as defined by Howells. 5. Erotic novels thrived in the Byzantine Empire from the late 5th century until the fall of Constantinople in 1453; their hero was often Alexander the Great. 6. Homer is the blind poet of ancient Greek tradition who is said to have composed both of the great Greek epics, *The Iliad* and *The Odyssey*, probably in the 8th century B.C.E. The latter depicts the trials of Odysseus and his family as he struggles to return from Troy.

# HENRY JAMES

Perhaps the most famous description of realism in the novel is Henry James's essay "The Art of Fiction," in which James (1843–1916) dismisses all prescriptions for novelistic success. A well-known traditionalist critic, Walter Besant, proposed that the good novel had to be overtly moral. James offered a rebuttal of radical realism, rejecting *a priori* requirements of the novel: "I am quite at a loss to imagine anything (at any rate in this matter of fiction) that people *ought* to like or to dislike. Selection will be sure to take care of itself, for it has a constant motive behind it. That motive is simply experience." James urges the novelist to observe not only environment but more importantly its *meaning*: "[to catch] the very note and trick, the strange irregular rhythm of life, that is the attempt whose strenuous force keeps Fiction upon her feet." James matches the desire to reflect the incomplete realities of characters—who never seem to "know" until it is too late—with his own tacit pledge not to make designs on the opinions of his readers. Though readers may observe that either nothing seems to happen in a James novel or no conclusion is arrived at, this ambiguity *is* James's design—*not* to "know" people in any certain, reductive, sense. James's idea of consciousness—a sort of spiderweb of "the very atmosphere of the mind"—means that the question of the "moral" is a false one. He finds that "the deepest quality of a work of art will always be the quality of the mind of the producer. . . . No good novel will ever proceed from a superficial mind."

## *From* The Art of Fiction[1]

*       *       *

It goes without saying that you will not write a good novel unless you possess the sense of reality; but it will be difficult to give you a recipe for calling that sense into being. Humanity is immense, and reality has a myriad forms; the most one can affirm is that some of the flowers of fiction have the odour of it, and others have not; as for telling you in advance how your nosegay should be composed, that is another affair. It is equally excellent and inconclusive to say that one must write from experience; to our suppositious aspirant such a declaration might savour of mockery. What kind of experience is intended, and where does it begin and end? Experience is never limited, and it is never complete; it is an immense sensibility, a kind of huge spider-web of the finest silken threads suspended in the chamber of consciousness, and catching every air-borne particle in its tissue. It is the very atmosphere of the mind; and when the mind is imaginative—much more when it happens to be that of a man of genius—it takes to itself the faintest hints of life, it converts the very pulses of the air into revelations. The young lady living in a village has only to be a damsel upon whom nothing is lost to make it quite unfair (as it seems to me) to declare to her that she shall have nothing to say about the military. Greater miracles have been seen than that, imagination assisting, she should speak the truth about some of these gentlemen. I remember an English novelist, a woman of genius, telling me that she was much commended for the impression she had managed to give in one of her tales of the nature and way

1. First published in *Longman's Magazine* 4 (September 1884), then in James's *Partial Portraits* (1888); rpt. in *Selected Literary Criticism* by Henry James (1968), from which this text is taken.

of life of the French Protestant youth. She had been asked where she learned so much about this recondite being, she had been congratulated on her peculiar opportunities. These opportunities consisted in her having once, in Paris, as she ascended a staircase, passed an open door where, in the household of a *pasteur*, some of the young Protestants were seated at table round a finished meal. The glimpse made a picture; it lasted only a moment, but that moment was experience. She had got her direct personal impression, and she turned out her type. She knew what youth was, and what Protestantism; she also had the advantage of having seen what it was to be French, so that she converted these ideas into a concrete image and produced a reality. Above all, however, she was blessed with the faculty which when you give it an inch takes an ell, and which for the artist is a much greater source of strength than any accident of residence or of place in the social scale. The power to guess the unseen from the seen, to trace the implication of things, to judge the whole piece by the pattern, the condition of feeling life in general so completely that you are well on your way to knowing any particular corner of it—this cluster of gifts may almost be said to constitute experience, and they occur in country and in town and in the most differing stages of education. If experience consists of impressions, it may be said that impressions *are* experience, just as (have we not seen it?) they are the very air we breathe. Therefore, if I should certainly say to a novice, 'Write from experience and experience only', I should feel that this was rather a tantalizing monition if I were not careful immediately to add, 'Try to be one of the people on whom nothing is lost!'

\* \* \*

A novel is a living thing, all one and continuous, like any other organism, and in proportion as it lives will it be found, that in each of the parts there is something of each of the other parts. The critic who over the close texture of a finished work shall pretend to trace a geography of items will mark some frontiers as artificial, I fear, as any that have been known to history. There is an old-fashioned distinction between the novel of character and the novel of incident which must have cost many a smile to the intending fabulist who was keen about his work. It appears to me as little to the point as the equally celebrated distinction between the novel and the romance—to answer as little to any reality. There are bad novels and good novels, as there are bad pictures and good pictures; but that is the only distinction in which I see any meaning, and I can as little imagine speaking of a novel of character as I can imagine speaking of a picture of character. When one says picture one says of character, when one says novel one says of incident, and the terms may be transposed at will. What is character but the determination of incident? What is incident but the illustration of character? What is either a picture or a novel that is *not* of character? What else do we seek in it and find in it? It is an incident for a woman to stand up with her hand resting on a table and look out at you in a certain way; or if it be not an incident I think it will be hard to say what it is. At the same time it is an expression of character. If you say you don't see it (character in *that*—*allons donc!*),[2] this is exactly what the artist who has reason of his own for thinking he *does* see it undertakes to show you.

2. Thus let us go! (French).

When a young man makes up his mind that he has not faith enough after all to enter the church as he intended, that is an incident, though you may not hurry to the end of the chapter to see whether perhaps he doesn't change once more. I do not say that these are extraordinary or startling incidents. I do not pretend to estimate the degree of interest proceeding from them, for this will depend upon the skill of the painter. It sounds almost puerile to say that some incidents are intrinsically much more important than others, and I need not take this precaution after having professed my sympathy for the major ones in remarking that the only classification of the novel that I can understand is into that which has life and that which has it not.

\* \* \*

There is one point at which the moral sense and the artistic sense lie very near together; that is in the light of the very obvious truth that the deepest quality of a work of art will always be the quality of the mind of the producer. In proportion as that intelligence is fine will the novel, the picture, the statue partake of the substance of beauty and truth. To be constituted of such elements is, to my vision, to have purpose enough. No good novel will ever proceed from a superficial mind; that seems to me an axiom which, for the artist in fiction, will cover all needful moral ground: if the youthful aspirant take it to heart it will illuminate for him many of the mysteries of 'purpose'.

\* \* \*

1884

# FRANK NORRIS

As a rule, naturalist novelists were not also critics. Jack London wrote essays on Poe and other writers from a naturalist point of view, but Frank Norris (1870–1902) was the only literary theorist of naturalism, though his death at the age of thirty-two robbed his readers of his full critical development. Critic Joseph R. McElrath, Jr., observes that Norris, like Stephen Crane, Henry Adams, and Kate Chopin, "registered dramatically the transition from the age of Emerson, Thoreau, and Whitman to that of Fitzgerald and Steinbeck." As such a bridge, Norris "signaled the movement away from Victorian social values" to more "positivistic and pragmatic modern" concerns. He is thus a member of the Progressive Era who painstakingly melds the realism of Balzac and Flaubert with the naturalistic demands of the modern American world, and adds a theory of romance in which he distinguishes between mere "accuracy" and "truth" and emphasizes the difference between surface commonplaces and the truth beneath the surfaces. In such works as *McTeague* (1899) Norris's anti-hero falls prey to bad heredity, a stressful environment, and the unpredictable developments of life. Norris troubled his readers by showing that the virtues of Victorian culture were of questionable value when forces beyond the individual's control rendered free will and benign intentions irrelevant. He rejects the Victorian question "Who is to blame?" in favor of dramatizing a character's deterministic state. Yet rather than promoting Zola's uncompromising exactitude or marrying Zola's naturalism with the New England realism of Howells, Norris gravitated toward Zola's more romantic and idealistic naturalism.

In "Zola as a Romantic Writer" (1896), Norris discounts Howells's realism as that of people "who live across the street from us," people of "small passions, restricted emotions, dramas of the reception-room, tragedies of an afternoon call, crises involving cups of tea." For Norris, Howells's novels of manners are uninteresting insofar as they are not passionate or romantic. The antidote is naturalism: "Terrible things must happen to the characters of the naturalistic tale." Characters may be "common," but what happens to them cannot be.

In "A Plea for Romantic Fiction," first published in 1901, Norris seeks to redefine romance and naturalism. For Norris "realism" is confined to what is generally agreed on by middle-class readers to be "normal life," while naturalism, in its romantic identity, penetrates "the surface of things." Norris again describes Howells's realism as the "drama of a broken teacup." He calls on realism to do the "entertaining," while naturalism, as romance, does the "teaching."

## Zola as a Romantic Writer[1]

It is curious to notice how persistently M. Zola[2] is misunderstood. How strangely he is misinterpreted even by those who conscientiously admire the novels of the "man of the iron pen." For most people Naturalism has a vague meaning. It is a sort of inner circle of realism—a kind of diametric opposite of romanticism, a theory of fiction wherein things are represented "as they really are," inexorably, with the truthfulness of a camera. This idea can be shown to be far from right, that Naturalism, as understood by Zola, is but a form of romanticism after all.

Observe the methods employed by the novelists who profess and call themselves "realists"—Mr. Howells,[3] for instance. Howells's characters live across the street from us, they are "on our block." We know all about them, about their affairs, and the story of their lives. One can go even further. We ourselves are Mr. Howells's characters, so long as we are well behaved and ordinary and bourgeois, so long as we are not adventurous or not rich or not unconventional. If we are otherwise, if things commence to happen to us, if we kill a man or two, or get mixed up in a tragic affair, or do something on a large scale, such as the amassing of enormous wealth or power or fame, Mr. Howells cuts our acquaintance at once. He will none of us if we are out of the usual.

This is the real Realism. It is the smaller details of every-day life, things that are likely to happen between lunch and supper, small passions, restricted emotions, dramas of the reception-room, tragedies of an afternoon call, crises involving cups of tea.[4] Every one will admit there is no romance here. The novel is interesting—which is after all the main point—but it is the commonplace tale of commonplace people made into a novel of far more than commonplace charm. Mr. Howells is not uninteresting; he is simply not romantic. But that Zola should be quoted as a realist, and as a realist of realists, is a strange perversion.

1. First published in the San Francisco *Wave* 15 (June 27, 1896); rpt. in *The Literary Criticism of Frank Norris* (1964), from which this text is taken.
2. Émile Zola (1840–1902), naturalistic French novelist.
3. William Dean Howells (1837–1920), American novelist, critic, and proponent of realism.
4. Norris's characterization of Howells's preoccupation with crises involving cups of tea became (and remains for some) a byword for Howells's lack of relevance for readers then and now.

Reflect a moment upon his choice of subject and character and episode. The Rougon-Macquart[5] live in a world of their own; they are not of our lives any more than are the Don Juans, the Jean Valjeans, the Gil Blases, the Marmions, or the Ivanhoes. We, the bourgeois, the commonplace, the ordinary, have no part nor lot in the *Rougon-Macquart*, in *Lourdes*, or in *Rome*;[6] it is not our world, not because our social position is different, but because we are *ordinary*. To be noted of M. Zola we must leave the rank and the file, either run to the forefront of the marching world, or fall by the roadway; we must separate ourselves; we must become individual, unique. The naturalist takes no note of common people, common in so far as their interests, their lives, and the things that occur in them are common, are ordinary. Terrible things must happen to the characters of the naturalistic tale. They must be twisted from the ordinary, wrenched out from the quiet, uneventful round of every-day life, and flung into the throes of a vast and terrible drama that works itself out in unleashed passions, in blood, and in sudden death. The world of M. Zola is a world of big things; the enormous, the formidable, the terrible, is what counts; no teacup tragedies here. Here Nana holds her monstrous orgies, and dies horribly, her face distorted to a frightful mask; Etienne Lantier, carried away by the strike of coal miners of *Le Voreux*, (the strike that is almost war), is involved in the vast and fearful catastrophe that comes as a climax of the great drama; Claude Lantier, disappointed, disillusioned, acknowledging the futility of his art after a life of effort, hangs himself on his huge easel; Jacques Lantier, haunted by an hereditary insanity, all his natural desires hideously distorted, cuts the throat of the girl he loves, and is ground to pieces under the wheels of his own locomotive; Jean Macquart, soldier and tiller of the fields, is drawn into the war of 1870, passes through the terrible scenes of Sedan and the Siege of Paris only to bayonet to death his truest friend and sworn brother-at-arms in the streets of the burning capital.[7]

Everything is extraordinary, imaginative, grotesque even, with a vague note of terror quivering throughout like the vibration of an ominous and low-pitched diapason. It is all romantic, at times unmistakably so, as in *Le Rêve* or *Rome*, closely resembling the work of the greatest of all modern romanticists, Hugo.[8] We have the same huge dramas, the same enormous scenic effects, the same love of the extraordinary, the vast, the monstrous, and the tragic.

5. Between 1870 and 1893, Zola wrote twenty novels about the intertwined and multigenerational Rougon-Macquart families.

6. Don Juan: a legendary fictional libertine who seduces a young woman and ends up in hell. Jean Valjean: protagonist of Victor Hugo's 1862 novel *Les Misérables*. Gil Blas: 1862 novel by Alain-Rene Lesage. Marmion: deceptive antagonist in Sir Walter Scott's 1808 epic poem of the same name. Wilfred of Ivanhoe: protagonist of Scott's 1819 novel, *Ivanhoe*. Lourdes: a town in southwest France, where it was claimed the Virgin Mary appeared to a 14-year-old girl in 1858; the largest Catholic pilgrimage in France. Rome: present-day capital of Italy, the seat of the Roman Catholic Church, and the historical center of the Roman Empire. *Lourdes* and *Rome* are also titles of Zola novels.

7. Nana: title character of Zola's 1880 novel, in which a prostitute rises from humble beginnings to destroy enemies among the Parisian elite. Etienne Lantier: protagonist of Zola's 1885 *Germinal*. Le Voreux: Fr., "the voracious one," and also the

mining-town setting for *Germinal*. Claude Lantier: tortured protagonist of Zola's 1886 *L'Oeuvre* ("The Masterpiece"). Jacques Lantier: a central character in Zola's 1890 novel, *La Bete Humaine* ("The Human Beast"). Jean Macquart: protagonist of Zola's 1892 novel, *La Debacle*, the final installment of the twenty-volume *Rougon-Macquart* series. War of 1870: War between Prussia and France which resulted in the defeat of France and the dissolution of its imperial power, and the unification of German states under the Prussian king. Sedan: battle in the War of 1870 in which Napoleon III of France, along with his army, surrendered to Prussian forces. The Siege of Paris: battle of the French capital from September 1870 to January 1871, when the armistice was signed.

8. *Le Rêve* or *Rome*: *Rougon-Macquart* novels published in 1888; the second installment of *Les Trois Villes* was published in 1896. Victor-Marie Hugo (1802–1885), 19th-century French Romantic writer best known for his novels *Les Misérables* (1862) and *Notre-Dame de Paris* (1831).

Naturalism is a form of romanticism, not an inner circle of realism. Where is the realism in the *Rougon-Macquart*? Are such things likely to happen between lunch and supper? That Zola's work is not purely romantic as was Hugo's, lies chiefly in the choice of Milieu. These great, terrible dramas no longer happen among the personnel of a feudal and Renaissance nobility, those who are in the fore-front of the marching world, but among the lower—almost the lowest—classes; those who have been thrust or wrenched from the ranks, who are falling by the roadway. This is not romanticism—this drama of the people, working itself out in blood and ordure. It is not realism. It is a school by itself, unique, somber, powerful beyond words. It is naturalism.

1896

# A Plea for Romantic Fiction[1]

Let us at the start make a distinction. Observe that one speaks of Romanticism and not of sentimentalism. One claims that the latter is as distinct from the former as is that other form of art which is called Realism. Romance has been often put upon and overburdened by being forced to bear the onus of abuse that by right should fall to sentiment; but the two should be kept very distinct, for a very high and illustrious place will be claimed for Romance, while sentiment will be handed down the scullery stairs.

Many people today are composing mere sentimentalism, and calling it and causing it to be called Romance, so with those who are too busy to think much upon these subjects, but who none the less love honest literature, Romance has fallen into disrepute. Consider now the cut-and-thrust stories. They are labelled Romances, and it is very easy to get the impression that Romance must be an affair of cloaks and daggers, or moonlight and golden hair. But this is not so at all. The true Romance is a more serious business than this. It is not merely a conjurer's trick box, full of flimsy quackeries, tinsel and clap traps, meant only to amuse, and relying upon deception to do even that. Is it not something better than this? Can we not see in it an instrument, keen, finely tempered, flawless—an instrument with which we may go straight through the clothes and tissues and wrappings of flesh down deep into the red, living heart of things?

Is all this too subtle, too merely speculative and intrinsic, too *précieuse* and nice and "literary"?[2] Devoutly one hopes the contrary. So much is made of so-called Romanticism in present-day fiction, that the subject seems worthy of discussion, and a protest against the misuse of a really noble and honest formula of literature appears to be timely—misuse, that is, in the sense of limited use. Let us suppose for the moment that a Romance can be made out of the cut-and-thrust business. Good Heavens, are there no other things that are romantic, even in this—falsely, falsely called—humdrum world of today? Why should it be that so soon as the novelist addresses himself—seriously—

1. First published in the *Boston Evening Transcript*, December 18, 1901; rpt. in *McTeague: A Story of San Francisco* by Frank Norris, 2nd ed. (1997), from which this text is taken.
2. That is, too affected and careful.

to the consideration of contemporary life he must abandon Romance and take up that harsh, loveless, colorless, blunt tool called Realism?

Now, let us understand at once what is meant by Romance and what by Realism. Romance—I take it—is the kind of fiction that takes cognizance of variations from the type of normal life. Realism is the kind of fiction that confines itself to the type of normal life. According to this definition, then, Romance may even treat of the sordid, the unlovely—as for instance, the novels of M. Zola.[3] (Zola has been dubbed a Realist, but he is, on the contrary, the very head of Romanticists.) Also, Realism, used as it sometimes is as a term of reproach, need not be in the remotest sense or degree offensive, but on the other hand respectable as a church and proper as a deacon—as, for instance, the novels of Mr. Howells.[4]

The reason why one claims so much for Romance, and quarrels so pointedly with Realism, is that Realism stultifies itself. It notes only the surface of things. For it Beauty is not even skin-deep, but only a geometrical plane, without dimensions of depth, a mere outside. Realism is very excellent so far as it goes, but it goes no farther than the Realist himself can actually see, or actually hear. Realism is minute, it is the drama of a broken teacup, the tragedy of a walk down the block, the excitement of an afternoon call, the adventure of an invitation to dinner. It is the visit to my neighbor's house, a formal visit, from which I may draw no conclusions. I see my neighbor and his friends—very, oh, such very! probable people—and that is all. Realism bows upon the doormat and goes away and says to me, as we link arms on the sidewalk: "That is life." And I say it is not. It is not, as you would very well see if you took Romance with you to call upon your neighbor.

Lately you have been taking Romance a weary journey across the water—ages and the flood of years—and haling her into the fusty, musty, worm-eaten, moth-riddled, rust-corroded "Grandes Salles"[5] of the Middle Ages and the Renaissance, and she has found the drama of a bygone age for you there. But would you take her across the street to your neighbor's front parlor (with the bisque fisher boy[6] on the mantel and the photograph of Niagara Falls on glass hanging in the front window); would you introduce her there? Not you. Would you take a walk with her on Fifth avenue, or Beacon street, or Michigan avenue? No indeed. Would you choose her for a companion of a morning spent in Wall Street, or an afternoon in the Waldorf-Astoria?[7] You just guess you would not.

She would be out of place, you say, inappropriate. She might be awkward in my neighbor's front parlor, and knock over the little bisque fisher boy. Well, she might. If she did, you might find underneath the base of the statuette, hidden away, tucked away—what? God knows. But something which would be a complete revelation of my neighbor's secretest life.

So you think Romance would stop in the front parlor and discuss medicated flannels and mineral waters with the ladies?[8] Not for more than five

3. French naturalist novelist Émile Zola (1840–1902).

4. William Dean Howells (1837–1920), American novelist, critic, and proponent of realism.

5. "Large" or "prominent" "halls," "auditoriums," or "theatres" (French).

6. Bisque-glazed figurines were popular among the rising classes in the late 19th and early 20th

centuries, intended to emulate the more expensive pieces owned by the wealthy.

7. Luxury hotel in New York City.

8. Flannels were used to apply warm liquors to the body for the purpose of easing pain by relaxing the skin. Mineral waters were bathed in or drunk as curatives for many medical conditions at this time.

minutes. She would be off upstairs with you, prying, peeping, peering into the closets of the bedrooms, into the nursery, into the sitting-room; yes, and into that little iron box screwed to the lower shelf of the closet in the library; and into those compartments and pigeonholes of the *secrétaire*[9] in the study. She would find a heartache (maybe) between the pillows of the mistress's bed, and a memory carefully secreted in the master's deedbox.[1] She would come upon a great hope amid the books and papers of the study table of the young man's room, and—perhaps—who knows—an affair, or, great heavens, an intrigue, in the scented ribbons and gloves and hairpins of the young lady's bureau. And she would pick here a little and there a little, making up a bag of hopes and fears, and a package of joys and sorrows—great ones, mind you—and then come down to the front door, and stepping out into the street, hand you the bags and package, and say to you—"That is Life!"

Romance does very well in the castles of the Middle Ages and the Renaissance chateaux, and she has the entrée there and is very well received. That is all well and good. But let us protest against limiting her to such places and such times. You will find her, I grant you, in the chatelaine's[2] chamber and the dungeon of the man-at-arms; but, if you choose to look for her, you will find her equally at home in the brownstone house on the corner and in the office building downtown. And this very day, in this very hour, she is sitting among the rags and wretchedness, the dirt and despair of the tenements of the East Side[3] of New York.

"What?" I hear you say, "look for Romance—the lady of the silken robes and golden crown, our beautiful, chaste maiden of soft voice and gentle eyes—look for her among the vicious ruffians, male and female, of Allen Street and Mulberry Bend?"[4] I tell you she is there, and to your shame be it said you will not know her in those surroundings. You, the aristocrats, who demand the fine linen and the purple in your fiction; you, the sensitive, the delicate, who will associate with your Romance only so long as she wears a silken gown. You will not follow her to the slums, for you believe that Romance should only amuse and entertain you, singing you sweet songs and touching the harp of silver strings with rosy-tipped fingers. If haply she should call to you from the squalor of a dive, or the awful degradation of a disorderly house,[5] crying: "Look! listen! This, too, is life. These, too, are my children, look at them, know them and, knowing, help!" Should she call thus, you would stop your ears; you would avert your eyes, and you would answer, "Come from there, Romance. Your place is not there!" And you would make of her a harlequin, a tumbler,[6] a sword dancer, when, as a matter of fact, she should be by right divine a teacher sent from God.

She will not always wear a robe of silk, the gold crown, the jeweled shoon,[7] will not always sweep the silver harp. An iron note is hers if so she choose, and coarse garments, and stained hands; and, meeting her thus, it

---

9. Desk (French).
1. Lockbox for money or valuables.
2. Female estate owner (French).
3. One of the oldest neighborhoods of New York City, situated along the East River from the Manhattan Bridge to 14th Street and bounded on the west by Broadway, a working-class neighborhood

defined by immigrant populations and tenements.
4. Streets in Manhattan's Lower East Side associated with the "Five Points Slum," known during Norris's time as a center of violence and crime.
5. A house of prostitution.
6. Clown or buffoon; acrobat or gymnast.
7. Archaic plural of "shoe."

is for you to know her as she passes—know her for the same young queen of the blue mantle and lilies.[8] She can teach you, if you will be humble to learn. Teach you by showing. God help you, if at last you take from Romance her mission of teaching, if you do not believe that she has a purpose, a nobler purpose and a mightier than mere amusement, mere entertainment. Let Realism do the entertaining with its meticulous presentation of teacups, rag carpets, wall paper and haircloth sofas, stopping with these, going no deeper than it sees, choosing the ordinary, the untroubled, the commonplace.[9]

But to Romance belongs the wide world for range, and the unplumbed depths of the human heart, and the mystery of sex, and the problems of life, and the black, unsearched penetralia of the soul of man. You, the indolent, must not always be amused. What matter the silken clothes, what matter the prince's houses? Romance, too, is a teacher, and if—throwing aside the purple—she wears the camel's hair and feeds upon the locusts,[1] it is to cry aloud unto the people, "Prepare ye the way of the Lord; make straight his path."

1901

---

8. Details frequently seen in depictions of the Virgin Mary.
9. Items of Victorian domesticity are often depicted in painstaking detail in realist texts.

1. Reference to John the Baptist's self-imposed exile in the wilderness and prophecies of the future (see especially Matthew 3, 11, 14).

---

# THEODORE DREISER

Theodore Dreiser (1871–1945) has been called "the American Zola" by critic George J. Becker, who writes that Dreiser found "that the official descriptions of life from pulpit, rostrum, or printed page did not square with life as he had experienced or observed it." Dreiser's *Sister Carrie* (1900), perhaps the finest of all naturalist novels, is a turn-of-the-century portrait of actress Carrie Meeber and her urban milieu that continues to be relevant today, not least because of its naturalist style of not preaching about immoral behavior but rather inquiring dispassionately into it. Despite a barrage of criticism when it was published, largely because the title character is a nice farm girl who goes bad in the city and yet prospers, the book succeeded. Dreiser called it "a picture of conditions," in its sociology, theatricality, exposé of "love" within the urban struggle for survival, and blunt portrayal of desire. Literary critic Philip Gerber points to its focus on celebrityhood and performance, casting of Carrie as an immigrant seeking the American Dream, identification of money as the *lingua franca*, theme of mobility, and dualistic version of womanhood as significant contributions to American naturalism. "True Art Speaks Plainly," first published in 1903, is a rejoinder by the author to the criticism that greeted the book on publication. Dreiser argues that the essence of morality is to "tell the truth. . . . [to] express what we see honestly and without subterfuge. . . ." Defending himself and other naturalists against charges of lewdness, Dreiser characterizes the conventional critic's version of "the mental virtue of the reader" as false. The novelist must tell the truth no matter the consequences. Despite his clear statements about truth, morality, and fiction, Dreiser struggled for acceptance of his work on its own grounds until the great success of *An American Tragedy* in 1925.

## True Art Speaks Plainly[1]

The sum and substance of literary as well as social morality may be expressed in three words—tell the truth. It matters not how the tongues of the critics may wag, or the voices of a partially developed and highly conventionalized society may complain, the business of the author, as well as of other workers upon this earth, is to say what he knows to be true, and, having said as much, to abide the result with patience.

Truth is what is; and the seeing of what is, the realization of truth. To express what we see honestly and without subterfuge: this is morality as well as art.

What the so-called judges of the truth or morality are really inveighing against most of the time is not the discussion of mere sexual lewdness, for no work with that as a basis could possibly succeed, but the disturbing and destroying of their own little theories concerning life, which in some cases may be nothing more than a quiet acceptance of things as they are without any regard to the well-being of the future. Life for them is made up of a variety of interesting but immutable forms and any attempt either to picture any of the wretched results of modern social conditions or to assail the critical defenders of the same is naturally looked upon with contempt or aversion.

It is true that the rallying cry of the critics against so-called immoral literature is that the mental virtue of the reader must be preserved; but this has become a house of refuge to which every form of social injustice hurries for protection. The influence of intellectual ignorance and physical and moral greed upon personal virtue produces the chief tragedies of the age, and yet the objection to the discussion of the sex question is so great as to almost prevent the handling of the theme entirely.

Immoral! Immoral! Under this cloak hide the vices of wealth as well as the vast unspoken blackness of poverty and ignorance; and between them must walk the little novelist, choosing neither truth nor beauty, but some half-conceived phase of life that bears no honest relationship to either the whole of nature or to man.

The impossibility of any such theory of literature having weight with the true artist must be apparent to every clear reasoning mind. Life is not made up of any one phase or condition of being, nor can man's interest possibly be so confined.

The extent of all reality is the realm of the author's pen, and a true picture of life, honestly and reverentially set down, is both moral and artistic whether it offends the conventions or not.

1903

---

1. First published in *Booklovers Magazine* (February 1903); rpt. in *Documents of Modern Literary Realism* (1963), from which this text is taken.

# JACK LONDON

Jack London's essay "What Life Means to Me" was published in *Cosmopolitan* in March 1906 as part of a series in which the magazine challenged prominent American writers to contribute articles on this theme. London (1876–1916) had been warned by the socialist and poet Edwin Markham that the Hearst Corporation, which owned *Cosmopolitan,* would never publish an attack on American capitalism, but the article appeared as London wrote it. London wryly remarked to Markham that "special writers like myself are paid well for expanding their own untrammeled views," with the understanding that these views would sell magazines. His second wife, Charmian Kittredge London, later described this essay as his "most impassioned committal of himself as a rebel toward the shames and uncleanness of the capitalist system." "What Life Means to Me" is one of London's strongest expressions of the relation between the naturalistic elements of his fiction and his gritty origins and struggles for survival within urban poverty and an exploitative class system. To fulfill "the life within me," he wrote, he had to escape the social pit. "Scared into thinking," London realized that by becoming a "vendor of brains" he could make a difference for himself and for the disenfranchised working class around him.

Even at the height of his success, London never abandoned his working-class roots and consciousness; the year he died, 1916, found him busy in various socialist endeavors, including the Pan-Pacific movement he helped found in Hawai'i. Though London had been touted in Hearst papers for his essay "The Yellow Peril," his renewed socialistic worldviews, including brother- and sisterhood with Asian workers, were not so much rebuttals of his earlier views but reflective of his education out of racism via socialism, and reminders of his identity as a lower-class émigré to the status of successful writer and idealist.

# *From* What Life Means to Me[1]

I was born in the working-class. Early I discovered enthusiasm, ambition, and ideals; and to satisfy these became the problem of my child-life. My environment was crude and rough and raw. I had no outlook, but an uplook rather. My place in society was at the bottom. Here life offered nothing but sordidness and wretchedness, both of the flesh and the spirit; for here flesh and spirit were alike starved and tormented.

Above me towered the colossal edifice of society, and to my mind the only way out was up. Into this edifice I early resolved to climb. Up above, men wore black clothes and boiled shirts, and women dressed in beautiful gowns. Also, there were good things to eat, and there was plenty to eat. This much for the flesh. Then there were the things of the spirit. Up above me, I knew, were unselfishnesses of the spirit, clean and noble thinking, keen intellectual living. I knew all this because I read "Seaside Library" novels,[2] in which, with the exception of the villains and adventuresses, all men and women thought beautiful thoughts, spoke a beautiful tongue, and performed glorious deeds. In short, as I accepted the rising of the sun, I accepted that up above me was all that was fine and noble and gracious, all that gave decency and dignity to

---

1. First published in *Cosmopolitan* 41 (March 1906); rpt. in *Revolution and Other Essays* by Jack London (1909), from which this text is taken.

2. Cheap novel series published by George Munro, New York, from 1877 to 1882.

life, all that made life worth living and that remunerated one for his travail and misery.

\* \* \*

I was a sailor before the mast, a longshoreman, a roustabout;[3] I worked in canneries, and factories, and laundries; I mowed lawns, and cleaned carpets, and washed windows. And I never got the full product of my toil. I looked at the daughter of the cannery owner, in her carriage, and knew that it was my muscle, in part, that helped drag along that carriage on its rubber tires. I looked at the son of the factory owner, going to college, and knew that it was my muscle that helped, in part, to pay for the wine and good fellowship he enjoyed.

But I did not resent this. It was all in the game. They were the strong. Very well, I was strong. I would carve my way to a place amongst them and make money out of the muscles of other men. I was not afraid of work. I loved hard work. I would pitch in and work harder than ever and eventually become a pillar of society.

And just then, as luck would have it, I found an employer that was of the same mind. I was willing to work, and he was more than willing that I should work. I thought I was learning a trade. In reality, I had displaced two men. I thought he was making an electrician out of me; as a matter of fact, he was making fifty dollars per month out of me. The two men I had displaced had received forty dollars each per month; I was doing the work of both for thirty dollars per month.

This employer worked me nearly to death. A man may love oysters, but too many oysters will disincline him toward that particular diet. And so with me. Too much work sickened me. I did not wish ever to see work again. I fled from work. I became a tramp, begging my way from door to door, wandering over the United States and sweating bloody sweats in slums and prisons.

I had been born in the working-class, and I was now, at the age of eighteen, beneath the point at which I had started. I was down in the cellar of society, down in the subterranean depths of misery about which it is neither nice nor proper to speak. I was in the pit, the abyss, the human cesspool, the shambles and the charnel-house of our civilization. This is the part of the edifice of society that society chooses to ignore. Lack of space compels me here to ignore it, and I shall say only that the things I there saw gave me a terrible scare.

I was scared into thinking. I saw the naked simplicities of the complicated civilization in which I lived. Life was a matter of food and shelter. In order to get food and shelter men sold things. The merchant sold shoes, the politician sold his manhood, and the representative of the people, with exceptions, of course, sold his trust; while nearly all sold their honor. Women, too, whether on the street or in the holy bond of wedlock, were prone to sell their flesh. All things were commodities, all people bought and sold. The one commodity that labor had to sell was muscle. The honor of labor had no price in the market-place. Labor had muscle, and muscle alone, to sell.

But there was a difference, a vital difference. Shoes and trust and honor had a way of renewing themselves. They were imperishable stocks. Muscle, on the other hand, did not renew. As the shoe merchant sold shoes, he con-

3. A dock worker who loads ships.

tinued to replenish his stock. But there was no way of replenishing the laborer's stock of muscle. The more he sold of his muscle, the less of it remained to him. It was his one commodity, and each day his stock of it diminished. In the end, if he did not die before, he sold out and put up his shutters. He was a muscle bankrupt, and nothing remained to him but to go down into the cellar of society and perish miserably.

I learned, further, that brain was likewise a commodity. It, too, was different from muscle. A brain seller was only at his prime when he was fifty or sixty years old, and his wares were fetching higher prices than ever. But a laborer was worked out or broken down at forty-five or fifty. I had been in the cellar of society, and I did not like the place as a habitation. The pipes and drains were unsanitary, and the air was bad to breathe. If I could not live on the parlor floor of society, I could, at any rate, have a try at the attic. It was true, the diet there was slim, but the air at least was pure. So I resolved to sell no more muscle, and to become a vender of brains.

Then began a frantic pursuit of knowledge. I returned to California and opened the books. While thus equipping myself to become a brain merchant, it was inevitable that I should delve into sociology. There I found, in a certain class of books, scientifically formulated, the simple sociological concepts I had already worked out for myself. Other and greater minds, before I was born, had worked out all that I had thought and a vast deal more. I discovered that I was a socialist.

The socialists were revolutionists, inasmuch as they struggled to overthrow the society of the present, and out of the material to build the society of the future. I, too, was a socialist and a revolutionist. I joined the groups of working-class and intellectual revolutionists, and for the first time came into intellectual living. Here I found keen-flashing intellects and brilliant wits; for here I met strong and alert-brained, withal horny-handed, members of the working-class; unfrocked preachers too wide in their Christianity for any congregation of Mammon-worshippers; professors broken on the wheel of university subservience to the ruling class and flung out because they were quick with knowledge which they strove to apply to the affairs of mankind.

Here I found, also, warm faith in the human, glowing idealism, sweetnesses of unselfishness, renunciation, and martyrdom—all the splendid, stinging things of the spirit. Here life was clean, noble, and alive. Here life rehabilitated itself, became wonderful and glorious; and I was glad to be alive. I was in touch with great souls who exalted flesh and spirit over dollars and cents, and to whom the thin wail of the starved slum child meant more than all the pomp and circumstance of commercial expansion and world empire. All about me were nobleness of purpose and heroism of effort, and my days and nights were sunshine and starshine, all fire and dew, with before my eyes, ever burning and blazing, the Holy Grail, Christ's own Grail, the warm human, long-suffering and maltreated, but to be rescued and saved at the last.

* * *

1906, 1909

# FRANK NORRIS
## 1870–1902

Frank Norris, along with other literary naturalists, including Jack London, Theodore Dreiser, and Stephen Crane, insisted that American writers should not portray only the middle classes—which he criticized William Dean Howells and other "realists" for doing—but also the struggles for power and survival among working people and the outcasts of capitalist society. He was born Benjamin Franklin Norris in Chicago; his well-to-do family moved to San Francisco when he was fourteen. After attending school in Paris, the University of California (1890–94), and Harvard, Norris served as a war correspondent for *McClure's Magazine* in South Africa (1895–96) and Cuba (1898). He wrote for and helped edit the San Francisco literary magazine *The Wave* (1896–97), becoming a member of San Francisco's exclusive Bohemian Club, which brought together businessmen and artists. In 1899 he moved to New York City and joined the publishing firm of Doubleday & Page as an editor.

Norris's first literary success was his grimly psychopathologic novel *McTeague: A Story of San Francisco* (1899), which was influenced by the naturalist ideas of French novelist Émile Zola. His most impressive novels were the two completed books in his proposed trilogy, "The Epic of Wheat"—*The Octopus: A Story of California* (1901), which depicts the brutal land struggle between wheat farmers and the Southern Pacific Railroad, and *The Pit* (1903), about speculation on the Chicago grain market. *The Responsibilities of the Novelist* (1903), a collection of essays, contains his idealistic views on the role of the naturalist writer.

Like many of his contemporaries, Norris was profoundly influenced by Darwinism, rejecting Victorian mores for new examinations of individual survival in modern society. Many of his novels, notably *McTeague*, feature a supposedly civilized man struggling against and failing to overcome the inner "brute," an animalistic self. Norris also works with this theme in what is thought to be an early story—"Fantaisie Printanière" (reprinted here), which uses characters who will later appear in *McTeague*. His work shows the influence of the early criminologist Cesare Lombroso, who believed in criminal "types" that could be immediately recognized by a skilled investigator. Norris saw naturalism not merely as a more intense form of realism or as mere scientific determinism but as akin to romanticism, with characters struggling against extreme challenges from forces beyond their control: class, race, gender, biology, and capitalism. Norris melded the realism of Honore de Balzac and Gustave Flaubert with the demands of the American and West Coast modern world. Despite its gruesome subject matter, Norris saw naturalism as a distinctly positive attempt to better society as a whole. Like Crane and Dreiser, Norris often seeks to disorient readers as a means of helping them toward a new sensibility. Yes, the situation of the women in "Fantaisie Printanière" is desperate, but their quarrel over their husbands' wife-beating skills showcases not only Norris's unsparing depiction of the results of poverty and ignorance but also his shockingly humorous point of view on their struggles. Norris's lack of disapproval does not minimize the situation but instead pokes fun at Victorian moral smugness and sentimentalism toward helping the poor.

Norris died of peritonitis from a ruptured appendix in 1902, leaving his trilogy unfinished. He was thirty-two years old. During his short career, his powerful works addressed the coming of age of the diverse classes of the modern United States and warned of the growing threat of monopolies and systematic urban poverty.

# Fantaisie Printanière[1]

The McTeagues and the Ryers lived at the disreputable end of Polk street,[2] away down in the squalid neighborhood by the huge red drum[3] of the gas works. The drum leaked, of course, and the nasty brassy foulness of the leak mingled with the odors of cooking from the ill-kept kitchens, and the reek of garbage in the vacant lots did not improve the locality.

McTeague had once been a dentist, and had had "parlors" up at the respectable end of the street. But after a while the license office[4] discovered that he had no diploma; in fact, had never attended a college of any sort, and had forbidden him to practice. So McTeague had taken to drink.

Ryer, some years back, had been a sort of small stock-dealer on the out-skirts of Butchertown,[5] and had done fairly well until the Health Board reported him to the Supervisors because he had fattened his hogs on poul-tices[6] obtained from the City and County Hospital. The result was a lamen-table scandal, which finally drove him out of business. So Ryer had taken to drink.

The Ryers' home (or let us say, the house in which the Ryers ate and slept), adjoined the house in which the McTeagues ate and slept. You would have thought that this propinquity, joined with the coincidence of their common misfortunes—both victims of governmental persecution—would have insured a certain degree of friendship between the two men. But this was not so at all, a state of feud existed between Montague Ryer and Capulet McTeague.[7] The feud had originated some year or so previous to the time of this tale, in the back room of Gerstle's "Wein Stube"[8] on the corner opposite the drum. A discussion had arisen between the two men, both far gone in whiskey, as to the lines of longitude on the surface of the globe. Capulet claimed they were parallel throughout their whole extent—Montague main-tained they converged at the poles. They discussed this question at length—first with heady words and vociferation, next with hurled pony glasses[9] and uplifted chairs, and finally, after their ejection from the "Stube," with fists clenched till the knuckles whitened, crooked elbows, and the soles of heavy-shod boots. They arrived at no definite conclusion. Twice since then had they fought. Their original difference of opinion had been speedily forgotten. They fought now, they knew not why—merely for the sake of fighting. The quarrel between them came to be recognized by the "block" as part of the existing order of things, like the reek from the drum and the monthly visit of the rent-collector.

---

1. First published in *The Wave* (San Francisco) 16 (Nov. 6, 1897); rpt. in *The Apprenticeship Writings of Frank Norris, 1896–1898.* Vol. II, 1897–1898, (1996), from which this text is taken. "Fantaisie Printaniere": Springtime Fantasy (French).
2. San Francisco street.
3. Container holding the by-products of coal gas manufacturing.
4. Governmental agency responsible for making sure medical practitioners met minimum educa-tional and training requirements.

5. Area of San Francisco where slaughterhouses, meat packers, tanneries, and saddle shops were located.
6. Soft adhesive masses usually made of meal or clay that was heated, spread on cloth, and applied to an aching or inflamed part of the body.
7. The Capulets and Montagues are the feuding families in Shakespeare's *Romeo and Juliet* (1597).
8. Tavern or wine room.
9. Small glass for a single measure of liquor, also known as a "shot glass."

Ryer had something the worst of it in these fights. He was a small, lean, pinkish creature, like a split carrot, his mouth a mere long slit beneath his nose. When he was angry his narrow eyes glistened like streaks of bitumen.

McTeague was a huge blonde giant, carrying his enormous fell of yellow hair, six feet and more above his ponderous, slow-moving feet. His hands, hard as wooden mallets, dangled from arms that suggested twisted cables. His jaw was that of the carnivora.

Both men thrashed their wives, McTeague on the days when he was drunk, which were many, Ryer on the days when he was sober, which were few. They went about it, each in his own peculiar fashion. Ryer found amusement in whipping Missis Ryer with a piece of rubber hose filled with gravel, or (his nature demanded variety of sensation), with a long, thin rawhide, which he kept hidden between the mattresses. He never used fists or boots; such methods revolted him. "What! am I a drayman, am I a hod-carrier!"[1] exclaimed Mister Ryer. When McTeague did not use the fist or the foot, he used the club. Refinement, such as characterized Ryer, was foreign to the ex-dentist. He struck out blindly, savagely, and with a colossal, clumsy force that often spent itself upon the air. The difference between the men could be seen in the different modes of punishment they affected. Ryer preferred the lash of the whip, McTeague the butt. Ryer was cruel, McTeague only brutal.

While common grievance had not made friends of the two men, mutual maltreatment had drawn their wives together, until no two women on the "block" were more intimate than Trina McTeague and Ryer's wife. They made long visits to each other in the morning in their wrappers and curl papers, talking for hours over a cuppa tea, served upon the ledge of the sink or a corner of the laundry table. During these visits they avoided speaking of their husbands, because, although the whole "block" knew of the occasional strained relations of their families, the two women feigned to keep the secret from each other. And this in the face of the fact that Missis Ryer would sometimes come over to see Trina with a thin welt across her neck, or Trina return the visit with a blackened eye or a split lip.

Once, however, only once, they broke in upon their reticence. Many things came of the infringement. Among others this *fantaisie*.

During that particular night three dandelions had bloomed in the vacant lot behind the gas works, the unwonted warmth of the last few days had brought back the familiar odor of the garbage heaps, an open car had appeared on the cross town cable line and Bock beer was on draught at the "Wein Stube," and Polk street knew that Spring was at hand.

About nine o'clock Trina McTeague appeared on the back steps of her house, rolling her washtub before her, preparing to do her monthly washing in the open air on that fine morning. She and Ryer's wife usually observed this hated rite at the same time, calling shrilly to one another as their backs bent and straightened over the scrubbing-boards. But that morning Trina looked long for Missis Ryer and at last fell a-wondering.

1. One who carries a hod, a trough slung over the shoulder for transporting bricks or mortar. "Drayman": driver of a small, sideless, horse-drawn cart.

The fact of the matter was that the night before Ryer had come home sober and had found occasion to coerce Missis Ryer with a trunk-strap. By a curious coincidence McTeague had come home drunk the same evening, and for two hours Trina had been hard put to it to dodge his enormous fists and his hurled boots. (Nor had she been invariably successful.)

At that moment the ex-dentist was sleeping himself sober under the stairs in the front hall, and the whilom[2] stock-dealer was drinking himself drunk in the "Wein Stube" across the street.

When eleven o'clock had struck and Missis Ryer had not appeared, Trina dried her smoking arms on her skirt, and, going through the hole in the back-yard fence, entered the kitchen of the Ryer's house and called. Missis Ryer came into the kitchen in a blue cotton wrapper and carpet slippers. Her hair was hanging down her back (it was not golden). Evidently she had just arisen.

"Ain't you goin' to wash this mornin', Missis Ryer?" asked Trina McTeague.

"Good Mornin', Trina," said the other, adding doggedly, as she sat down hard in a broken chair: "I'm *sick* and *tired* a-washin' an' workin' for Ryer."

She drew up instinctively to the cold stove, and propped her chin upon her knuckles. The loose sleeve of the wrapper fell away from her forearm, and Trina saw the fresh marks of the trunk-strap. Evidently Ryer had not held that strap by the buckle-end.

This was the first time Missis Ryer had ever mentioned her husband to Trina.

"Hoh!" ejaculated Trina, speaking before she thought. "It ain't alwus such fun workin' for Mac, either."

There was a brief silence. Both the women remained for a moment looking vaguely out of the kitchen door, absorbed in thought, very curious, each wondering what next the other would say. The conversation, almost without their wishing it, had suddenly begun upon untried and interesting ground. Missis Ryer said:

"I'll make a cuppa tea."

She made the tea, slovening languidly about the dirty kitchen, her slippers clap-clapping under her bare heels. Then the two drew up to the washboard of the sink, drinking the tea from the saucers, wiping their lips slowly from time to time with the side of their hands. Each was waiting for the other to speak. Suddenly Missis Ryer broke out:

"It's best not to fight him, or try to git away—hump your back and it's soonest over."

"You couldn't do that with Mac," answered Trina, shaking her head with decision; "if I didunt dodge, if I let um have his own way he'd sure kill me. Mac's that strong, he could break me in two."

"Oh, *Ryer's* strong all-right-all-right," returned Missis Ryer, "an' then he's sober when he fights an' knows what he's about, an' that makes it worse. Look there what he did last night." She rolled up her sleeve and Trina glanced at the arm with the critical glance of a connoisseur.

"Hoh," she said scornfully, "that ain't a circumstance. I had a row with Mac last night meself, and this is what he did with his fist. Just his fist, mind you, and it only grazed me as it was." She slipped a discolored shoulder out of her calico gown. The two critically compared bruises. Missis Ryer was forced to

2. Former.

admit that Trina's bruise was the worse. She was vexed and disappointed but rallied with:

"Yes, that's pirty bad, but I'll show you somethin' that'll open your eyes," and she thrust the blue wrapper down from the nape of the neck. "See that scar there," she said, "that's the kind of work Ryer can do when he puts his mind to it; got that nearly four months ago and it's sore yet."

"Ah, yes," said Trina loftily, "little scars, little flesh wounds like that! You never had any bones brokun. Just look at that thumb," she went on proudly, "Mac did that with just a singul grip of his fist. I can't nevur bend it again."

Then the interminable discussion began.

"Look at that, just look at *that*, will you?"

"Ah, that ain't nuthun. How about *that?* there's a lick for you."

"Why, Mac's the strongest man you ever *saw*."

"Ah-h, you make me tired, it ain't a strong man, always, that can hurt the most. It's the fellah that knows how and where to hit. It's a whip that hurts the most."

"But it's a club that does the most damage."

"Huh! wait till you git hit with a rubber hose filled with gravel."

"Why, Mac can knock me the length of the house with his left fist. He's done it plenty a times."

Then they came to reminiscences.

"Why, one time when Mac came home from a picnic at Schuetzen Park,[3] he picked me right up offun the ground with one hand and held me right up in the air like that, and let me have it with a kitchun chair. Huh! talk to *me* about Ryer's little whips, Ryer ain't a patch on my man. *You* don't know what a good thrashun *is*."

"I *don't*, hey? you can just listen to what I tell you, Trina McTeague, when I say that Ryer can lay all over your man. You jest ought a been here one night when I sassed Ryer back, I tell you I'll never do *that* again. Why the worst lickin' Mister McTeague ever gave you was just little love taps to what I got. Besides I don' *believe* your man ever held you up with one hand and banged you like that with a chair, you wouldn't a lived if he had."

"Oh, I ain't *lyun* to you," cried Trina, with shrill defiance, getting to her feet. Missis Ryer rose likewise and clapped her arms akimbo.

"Why," she cried, "you just said as much yourself, that if you didn't dodge and get away he'd kill you."

"An' I'll say it again. I ain't gowun to eat my words for the best woman that ever wore shoes, an' you can chew on that, Missus Ryer. *I* tell you Mac's the hardust hittun husband a woman ever had."

"I just like to have you live here with Ryer a week or so, you'd soon find out who was the best man, an'——" here Missis Ryer came close to Trina and shouted the words in her face. "An' don't you sass me either, an' talk about eatin' words, or I'll show you right here the kind a whalin' Ryer's taught me."

"I guess Ryer, himself, knows who's the best man of the two, he or Mac," exclaimed Trina, loftily. "How about that last scrap o' theirs? If Mac got hold a you once and gave you one lick, like the kind I get twenty of evury week, you wouldunt be as well off as your man was when Mac got through with um

3. Former park in Oakland, California, established by the Schuetzen Verein, a 19th-century German fraternal organization.

the time they fought last Washingtun's burthday, behind the brick kiln. Why Mac could do for the whole three of us, you an' Ryer an' I, yes he could, with one hand."

"Ah, talk sense, will you?" shouted Missis Ryer, as she moved the previous question. "Ain't Mister McTeague drunk when he dresses you down, and don't it stand to reason that he *can't* give it to you as hard as Ryer gives it to me when he's *sober?*"

"Do you know anything about it anyways?" said Trina, excitedly, "I tell you he's a deal worse to me than Ryer ever *thought* of be-un to you. Ain't he twysut, *three* times as strong?"

"That's a lie," retorted Ryer's wife, vindicating her absent husband with astonishing vehemence.

"Don't you tell me I lie again," shouted Trina, her cheeks flaming, her chin thrust out.

"I guess I'll say what I please in my own kitchin, you dirty little drab,"[4] screamed the other. Their faces were by this time close together, neither would draw back an inch.

"No you won't, no you won't," panted Trina, "an' don't you dare call me a drab. Drab yourself; best go back to the pigs your man used to fatten on old poultices, go back to your sty, I guess it won't be any dirtier than this here kitchun."

"Git out of it then."

"Not till I get ready."

"An' I'll call you drab till I'm black in the face, drab, *drab*, damn' nasty, dirty little drab. Git out uv my kitchin."

"Ah-h, let me see you put me out."

"Ah, dirty little drab."

"Ah, slattern,[5] ah, pig-feeder."

Suddenly they tore at each other like infuriated cats. A handful of black and gray hair came away from Missis Ryer's head. Fingernail marks, long red lines appeared on the curve of Trina's cheeks, very like McTeague's conception of the parallels upon a globe. Missis Ryer, hustling Trina toward the door, pushed her into the arms of McTeague himself. At the same time Ryer, warned of this war of wives, entered the kitchen from the front of the house. He had come over hastily from the "Wein Stube" and was half drunk. McTeague had partially slept off his intoxication and was about half sober.

"Here, here, here," cried the ex-dentist over his wife's shoulder, "you two women fightin', quit it, what the bloody Hell!"

"Scrappin'" shouted Ryer from the doorway, "choke off, ol' woman, if there's any scrappin' to be done, I'll do it meself."

"She called me a drab," gasped Trina, glaring at her enemy from under the protection of her gigantic husband.

"An' she said my kitchin wasn't a place for pigs to live in," retorted Missis Ryer, without taking her eyes from Trina.

The men had not yet looked at each other. They were unwilling to fight this morning, because each one of them was half drunk or half sober (either way you chose to put it), and because Ryer preferred to fight when he had all his

4. Slang for a promiscuous woman or a prostitute.    5. Vulgar, slovenly woman.

wits about him, while McTeague was never combative until he had lost *his* wits entirely.

"What started the row, whatcha been fightin' about?" demanded the ex-dentist.

"Yes, sure," put in Ryer, "whatcha been scrappin' about, what started the row?"

The women looked at each other, unable to answer. Then Trina began awkwardly:

"Well I—well—well—a—well she told me—she said—well, she run you down, Mac, an' I didunt figure on puttun up with it."

"She tried to make small of you, Ryer," said his wife, "an' I called her down, an'—that's all, she tried to make small of you."

"Hey? What'd she say?" demanded McTeague, "out with it."

"Well, *this* is what she said," exclaimed Trina suddenly. "She said Ryer could give her a worse dressing down than you ever gave me, an' I wouldn't stand it."

"Well," declared Missis Ryer, turning to her husband. "I ain't goin' to let every dirty little drab that comes along say—say—throw mud at my man, am I? I guess," added Missis Ryer, defiantly, facing Trina and the ex-dentist. "I guess Ryer can do what he likes in his own house. I ain't goin' to let any woman tell me that her man is better'n mine, in any way."

"An' that's what you two fought over?" exclaimed the husbands in the same breath.

"Well, suppose we did?" said Trina with defiance.

"I guess I can quarrel about what I like," observed Missis Ryer, sullenly.

For the first time since they had entered the room the eyes of the two men met, and for fully half a dozen seconds they looked squarely at each other. Then the corners of the slit under Ryer's nose began to twitch, and McTeague's huge jaws to widen to a grin in nut-cracker fashion. Suddenly a roar of laughter shook him; he sank into a chair, rocking back and forth, smiting his knee with his palm. Ryer cackled shrilly, crying out between peals of laughter: "Well, if this ain't the greatest jolly I've struck yet."

"Fightin' over our fightin' *them*," bellowed McTeague.

"I've seen queer bugs in my time," gasped Ryer, "but the biggest curios yet are women, oh Lord, but this does beat the Dutch."[6]

"Say, ain't this great, Ryer?"

"Mac, this does beat the carpet, sure."

"Look here old man, about them parallel lines, *I* say let's call it off. I ain't got no quarrel against *you*."

"That's a go, Mac, you're a good fellah, sure, put it there."

They shook hands upon their reconciliation, their breasts swelling with magnanimity. They felt that they liked one another hugely, and they slapped each other tremendous blows on the back, exclaiming at intervals "*put* it there," and gripping hands with a cordiality that was effusive beyond words. All at once Ryer had an inspiration.

"Say, Mac, come over to the Stube and have a drink on it."

"Well, I just guess I will," vociferated the ex-dentist.

6. Slang phrase meaning "to beat all," from a popular joke involving ethnic rivalries in New York.

Bewildered and raging at the unexpected reconciliation of their husbands, the two women had disappeared, Trina slamming the door of the kitchen with a parting cry of "pig feeder," which Missis Ryer immediately answered by thrusting her head out of a second story window and screaming at the top of her voice to the neighborhood in general, "dirty little drab."

Meanwhile the two men strode out of the house and across the street, their arms affectionately locked; the swing doors of the "Stube" flapped after them like a pair of silent wings.

That day settled the matter. Heretofore it had been the men who were enemies and their wives who were friends. Now the two men are fast friends, while the two women maintain perpetual feud. The "block" has come to recognize their quarrel as part of the existing order of things, like the leak from the gas-works and the collector's visits. Occasionally the women fight, and Missis Ryer, who is the larger and heavier, has something the best of it.

However, one particular custom common to both households remains unchanged—both men continue to thrash their wives in the old ratio—McTeague on the days when he is drunk (which are many), Ryer on the days when he is sober (which are few).

1897

---

# THEODORE DREISER
## 1871–1945

Theodore Herman Albert Dreiser was born in Terre Haute, Indiana, on August 17, 1871, the eleventh of thirteen children. His severe, emotionally distant father was, in Dreiser's view, "mentally a little weak"; he was in any event not very successful in providing for his large family, and he served as the prototype for the failed men who appear so frequently in Dreiser's novels. Dreiser's mother, by contrast, was steadfastly devoted to the well-being of her children; she was, Dreiser claimed, the only person who ever loved him enough. She, too, appears in fictionalized form in many of Dreiser's books.

Dreiser's unhappy childhood haunted him throughout his life. The large family moved from house to house in Indiana dogged by poverty, insecurity, and internal divisions. One of his brothers became a famous popular songwriter under the name Paul Dresser, but other siblings lived turbulent lives that not only defied their father's rigid morality but placed them on the margins of respectable society altogether. Dreiser as a youth was ungainly, confused, shy, and full of vague yearnings like most of his fictional protagonists, male and female. In this as in many other ways, Dreiser's novels are direct projections of his inner life as well as careful transcriptions of his experiences, especially those involving his unstable family.

From the age of fifteen Dreiser was on his own, earning meager support from a variety of menial jobs. A high-school teacher staked him to a year at Indiana University in 1889, but Dreiser's real education was to come from experience and from independent reading and thinking. This education began in 1892 when he landed by persistence and good luck his first newspaper job with the *Chicago Globe*. Over the next decade, as an itinerant journalist, Dreiser slowly groped his way to authorship, testing what he knew from his own life against what he had learned from reading, among others, Charles Darwin, Ernst Haeckel, Thomas Huxley, and Herbert Spencer, late-nineteenth-century scientists and social scientists who lent support to the view that nature and society had no divine sanction. Generally speaking, these thinkers agreed that human beings, just as much as other life forms, were participants in an evolutionary process in which only those who adapted successfully to their environments survived. Human beings, they agreed, were not the privileged creations of supernatural powers. At the same time, Spencer in particular argued that human consciousness was itself a product of evolutionary processes and that it entailed the adaptive capacity for altruism and various forms of social cooperation. This tension between deterministic "chemisms" (as Dreiser called them) and the potential for friendship and the improvement of social institutions appears in Dreiser's fiction throughout his writing career. Early on Dreiser emphasized the mechanistic side of this tension, while in later phases—in his fiction and in his social writings—he appeared to balance his more pessimistic views with belief in the possibilities of social justice.

Sister Carrie (1900), Dreiser's first novel, two chapters of which are included here, tells the story of Carrie Meeber, a country girl from Wisconsin who comes to Chicago, attracted by the excitement that rapidly growing urban centers held out for so many young people in the late 1800s, but even more by the possibility of supporting herself, especially given the meager opportunities in her small rural town. In Chicago she is seduced first by a traveling salesman, Charles Drouet, then by George Hurstwood, a married middle-aged manager of a chic saloon. After closing one night, Hurstwood steals ten thousand dollars from the safe in the bar; then he and Carrie flee to New York, where he slowly deteriorates into homelessness while she begins a successful career on the stage. They eventually part company and, unbeknownst to Carrie, Hurstwood commits suicide.

The novel depicts social transgressions by characters who feel no remorse and largely escape punishment—especially Carrie, who does not hesitate to use sex to get ahead—and it uses "strong" language and names living persons. It was virtually suppressed by its publisher, who printed but refused to promote the book. Since its reissue in 1907 it has steadily risen in popularity and scholarly acceptance. Students will find that Sister Carrie addresses many issues of significance today, often with a startling contemporary feel: class mobility, immigration, urban life, greater independence of women and control of their own sexualities, pressure to "make it" in American society, and celebrityhood.

In the first years of the twentieth century Dreiser suffered a nervous breakdown. With the help of his brother Paul, he recovered and by 1904 was on the way to several successful years as an editor, the last of them as editorial director of the Butterick Publishing Company. In 1910 he resigned to write Jennie Gerhardt (1911), one of his best novels and the first of a long succession of books that marked his turn to writing as a full-time career. This novel, about the doomed love between a rich man and a poor woman, takes seriously the reality of gentleness, selflessness, and loyalty, though in the end materialism and pressures associated with wealth and social position carry the day.

In The Financier (1912), The Titan (1914), and The Stoic (not published until 1947), Dreiser shifted from the pathos of helpless protagonists to the power of those unusual individuals who assume dominant roles in business and society. The protagonist of this "Trilogy of Desire" (as Dreiser described it), Frank Cowperwood, is modeled after the Chicago speculator Charles T. Yerkes. These novels of the businessman as buccaneer introduced, even more explicitly than had Sister Carrie, the notion that men of high sexual energy were financially successful, a theme that is carried over into the rather weak autobiographical novel The "Genius" (1915).

The identification of potency with money is at the heart of Dreiser's greatest and most successful novel, An American Tragedy (1925). The novel is based on a much-publicized murder in upper New York State in 1906. Clyde Griffiths is a poor boy from the provinces who dreams of a life of luxury and status. When his prospect for marrying the wealthy Sondra Finchley is threatened by the pregnant Roberta Alden, a factory worker with whom he has had a relationship, Clyde plans to murder her. The moment arrives, but he lacks the resolve to do so; he does, however, leave her to drown after their boat accidentally tips over during an outing on a deserted lake. Much of the novel recounts the capture of Clyde, the investigation and prosecution of the case, and the harrowing details of Clyde's imprisonment and execution. The novel was an immediate best-seller and confirmed Dreiser's status as one of the leading writers of his time.

During the last two decades of his life Dreiser turned to polemical writing, but also to other genres—poetry, travel books, and autobiography, including *Dawn* (1931), the first volume in the projected but uncompleted *A History of Myself*. He visited the Soviet Union in 1927 and published *Dreiser Looks at Russia* the following year. In the 1930s, like many American intellectuals and writers, Dreiser was increasingly attracted by the philosophical program of the Communist party. Unable to believe in traditional religious credos, yet unable to give up his strong sense of justice, he continued to seek a way to reconcile his determinism with his compassionate sense of the mystery of life.

Dreiser was more fascinated by ideas and human destinies than he was in love with language. His interest was in human motives and behavior and in the particularities of the environments that helped shape them. His writing is often blunt and ungainly, but many critics believe that his ability to structure complex narratives by manipulating point of view and by using symbols and clusters of metaphors as leitmotifs more than compensates for his sometimes awkward syntax. If, in the end, readers want from a novelist the communication of a deeply felt sense of life, continuing interest in Dreiser seems ensured.

In his lifetime Dreiser was controversial as a man and as a writer. He was accused, with some justice by conventional standards, of being immoral in his personal behavior and of being a poor thinker and a dangerous political radical. As time has passed, however, Dreiser has become recognized both as a profound and prescient critic of debased American values and as a powerful novelist.

## *From* Sister Carrie[1]

### Chapter I

When Caroline Meeber boarded the afternoon train for Chicago her total outfit consisted of a small trunk, which was checked in the baggage car, a cheap imitation alligator skin satchel holding some minor details of the toilet, a small lunch in a paper box and a yellow leather snap purse, containing her ticket, a scrap of paper with her sister's address in Van Buren Street,[2] and four dollars in money. It was in August, 1889. She was eighteen years of age, bright, timid and full of the illusions of ignorance and youth. Whatever touch of regret at parting characterized her thoughts it was certainly not for advantages now being given up. A gush of tears at her mother's farewell kiss, a touch in the throat when the cars clacked by the flour mill where her father worked by the day, a pathetic sigh as the familiar green environs of the village

---

1. First published by Doubleday & Page (1900), from which this text is taken.

2. East-west Chicago street that, roughly, divides the city in half.

passed in review, and the threads which bound her so lightly to girlhood and home were irretrievably broken.

To be sure she was not conscious of any of this. Any change, however great, might be remedied. There was always the next station where one might descend and return. There was the great city, bound more closely by these very trains which came up daily. Columbia City was not so very far away, even once she was in Chicago. What pray is a few hours—a hundred miles? She could go back. And then her sister was there. She looked at the little slip bearing the latter's address and wondered. She gazed at the green landscape now passing in swift review until her swifter thoughts replaced its impression with vague conjectures of what Chicago might be. Since infancy her ears had been full of its fame. Once the family had thought of moving there. If she secured good employment they might come now. Anyhow it was vast. There were lights and sounds and a roar of things. People were rich. There were vast depots. This on-rushing train was merely speeding to get there.

When a girl leaves her home at eighteen, she does one of two things. Either she falls into saving hands and becomes better, or she rapidly assumes the cosmopolitan standard of virtue and becomes worse. Of an intermediate balance, under the circumstances, there is no possibility. The city has its cunning wiles no less than the infinitely smaller and more human tempter. There are large forces which allure, with all the soulfulness of expression possible in the most cultured human. The gleam of a thousand lights is often as effective, to all moral intents and purposes, as the persuasive light in a wooing and fascinating eye. Half the undoing of the unsophisticated and natural mind is accomplished by forces wholly superhuman. A blare of sound, a roar of life, a vast array of human hives appeal to the astonished senses in equivocal terms. Without a counselor at hand to whisper cautious interpretations, what falsehoods may not these things breathe into the unguarded ear! Unrecognized for what they are, their beauty, like music, too often relaxes, then weakens, then perverts the simplest human perceptions.

Caroline, or "Sister Carrie" as she had been half affectionately termed by the family, was possessed of a mind rudimentary in its power of observation and analysis. Self-interest with her was high, but not strong. It was nevertheless her guiding characteristic. Warm with the fancies of youth, pretty with the insipid prettiness of the formative period, possessed of a figure which tended toward eventual shapeliness and an eye alight with certain native intelligence, she was a fair example of the middle American class—two generations removed from the emigrant. Books were beyond her interest—knowledge a sealed book. In the intuitive graces she was still crude. She could scarcely toss her head gracefully. Her hands were almost ineffectual for the same reason. The feet, though small, were set flatly. And yet she was interested in her charms, quick to understand the keener pleasures of life, ambitious to gain in material things. A half-equipped little knight she was, venturing to reconnoitre the mysterious city and dreaming wild dreams of some vague, far-off supremacy which should make it prey and subject, the proper penitent, grovelling at a woman's slipper.

"That," said a voice in her ear, "is one of the prettiest little resorts in Wisconsin."

"Is it?" she answered nervously.

The train was just pulling out of Waukesha.[3] For some time she had been conscious of a man behind. She felt him observing her mass of hair. He had been fidgeting, and with natural intuition she felt a certain interest growing in that quarter. Her maidenly reserve and a certain sense of what was conventional under the circumstances called her to forestall and deny this familiarity, but the daring and magnetism of the individual, born of past experience and triumphs, prevailed. She answered.

He leaned forward to put his elbows upon the back of her seat and proceeded to make himself volubly agreeable.

"Yes, that's a great resort for Chicago people. The hotels are swell. You are not familiar with this part of the country, are you?"

"Oh yes I am," answered Carrie. "That is, I live at Columbia City. I have never been through here though."

"And so this is your first visit to Chicago," he observed.

All the time she was conscious of certain features out of the side of her eye. Flush, colorful cheeks, a light mustache, a gray fedora hat. She now turned and looked upon him in full, the instincts of self-protection and coquetry mingling confusedly in her brain.

"I didn't say that," she said.

"Oh," he answered in a very pleasing way and with an assumed air of mistake. "I thought you did."

Here was a type of the traveling canvasser for a manufacturing house—a class which at that time was first being dubbed by the slang of the day "drummers."[4] He came within the meaning of a still newer term which had sprung into general use among Americans in 1880, and which concisely expressed the thought of one whose dress or manners are such as to impress strongly the fancy, or elicit the admiration, of susceptible young women—a "masher." His clothes were of an impressive character, the suit being cut of a striped and crossed pattern of brown wool, very popular at that time. It was what has since become known as a business suit. The low crotch of the vest revealed a stiff shirt bosom of white and pink stripes, surmounted by a high white collar about which was fastened a tie of distinct pattern. From his coat sleeves protruded a pair of linen cuffs of the same material as the shirt and fastened with large gold-plate buttons set with the common yellow agates known as "cat's-eyes." His fingers bore several rings, one the ever-enduring heavy seal, and from his vest dangled a neat gold watch chain from which was suspended the secret insignia of the Order of Elks. The whole suit was rather tight-fitting and was finished off with broad-soled tan shoes, highly polished, and the grey felt hat, then denominated "fedora," before mentioned. He was, for the order of intellect represented, attractive; and whatever he had to recommend him, you may be sure was not lost upon Carrie, in this her first glance.

Lest this order of individual should permanently pass, let me put down some of the most striking characteristics of his most successful manner and method. Good clothes of course were the first essential, the things without

---

3. A city in Wisconsin about 106 miles north of Chicago on Lake Michigan.

4. "Canvassers" and "drummers" are salesmen.

which he was nothing. A strong physical nature actuated by a keen desire for the feminine was the next. A mind free of any consideration of the problems or forces of the world and actuated not by greed but an insatiable love of variable pleasure—woman—pleasure. His method was always simple. Its principal element was daring, backed of course by an intense desire and admiration for the sex. Let him meet with a young woman twice and upon the third meeting he would walk up and straighten her necktie for her and perhaps address her by her first name. If an attractive woman should deign a glance of interest in passing him upon the street he would run up, seize her by the hand in feigned acquaintanceship and convince her that they had met before, providing of course that his pleasing way interested her in knowing him further. In the great department stores he was at his ease in capturing the attention of some young woman, while waiting for the cash boy to come back with his change. In such cases, by those little wiles common to the type, he would find out the girl's name, her favorite flower, where a note would reach her, and perhaps pursue the delicate task of friendship until it proved unpromising for the one aim in view, when it would be relinquished.

He would do very well with more pretentious women, though the burden of expense was a slight deterrent. Upon entering a parlor car at St. Paul, for instance, he would select a chair next to the most promising bit of femininity and soon inquire if she cared to have the shade lowered. Before the train cleared the yards he would have the porter bring her a footstool. At the next lull in his conversational progress he would find her something to read, and from then on by dint of compliment gently insinuated, personal narrative, exaggeration and service, he would win her tolerance and mayhap regard.

Those who have ever delved into the depths of a woman's conscience must, at some time or other, have come upon that mystery of mysteries—the moral significance, to her, of clothes. A woman should some day write the complete philosophy of that subject. No matter how young she is, it is one of the things she wholly comprehends. There is an indescribably faint line in the matter of man's apparel which somehow divides for her those who are worth glancing at and those who are not. Once an individual has passed this faint line on the way downward he will get no glance from her. There is another line at which the dress of a man will cause her to study her own. This line the individual at her elbow now marked for Carrie. She became conscious of an inequality. Her own plain blue dress with its black cotton tape trimmings realized itself to her imagination as shabby. She felt the worn state of her shoes.

He mistook this thought wave, which caused her to withdraw her glance and turn for relief to the landscape outside, for some little gain his grace had brought him.

"Let's see," he went on. "I know quite a number of people in your town—Morgenroth the clothier and Gibson the dry-goods man."

"Oh, do you," she interrupted, aroused by memories of longings the displays in the latter's establishment had cost her.

At last he had a clue to her interest and followed it up deftly. In a few minutes he had come about into her seat. He talked of sales of clothing, his travels, Chicago and the amusements of that city.

"If you are going there you will enjoy it immensely. Have you relatives?"

"I am going to visit my sister," she explained.

"You want to see Lincoln Park," he said, "and Michigan Avenue.[5] They are putting up great buildings there. It's a second New York, great. So much to see—theatres, crowds, fine houses—oh you'll like that."

There was a little ache in her fancy of all he described. Her insignificance in the presence of so much magnificence faintly affected her. She realized that hers was not to be a round of pleasure, and yet there was something promising in all the material prospect he set forth. There was something satisfactory in the attention of this individual with his good clothes. She could not help smiling as he told her of some popular actress she reminded him of. She was not silly and yet attention of this sort had its weight.

"You will be in Chicago some little time, won't you?" he observed, at one turn of the now easy conversation.

"I don't know," said Carrie vaguely—a flash vision of the possibility of her not securing employment rising in her mind.

"Several weeks anyhow," he said, looking steadily into her eyes.

There was much more passing now than the mere words indicated. He recognized the indescribable thing that made for fascination and beauty in her. She realized that she was of interest to him from the one standpoint which a woman both delights in and fears. Her manner was simple, though, for the very reason that she had not yet learned the many little affectations with which women conceal their true feelings—some things she did appeared bold. A clever companion, had she ever had one, would have warned her never to look a man in the eyes so steadily.

"Why do you ask?" she said.

"Well, I'm going to be there several weeks. I'm going to study stock at our place and get new samples. I might show you 'round."

"I don't know whether you can or not—I mean I don't know whether I can. I shall be living with my sister and—"

"Well, if she minds, we'll fix that." He took out his pencil and a little pocket note book, as if it were all settled. "What is your address there?"

She fumbled her purse, which contained the address slip.

He reached down in his hip pocket and took out a fat purse. It was filled with slips of paper, some mileage books, a roll of green-backs and so on. It impressed her deeply. Such a purse had never been carried by any man who had ever been attentive to her before. Indeed a man who traveled, who was brisk and experienced and of the world, had never come within such close range before. The purse, the shiny tan shoes, the smart new suit and the *air* with which he did things built up for her a dim world of fortune around him of which he was the centre. It disposed her pleasantly toward all he might do.

He took out a neat business card on which was engraved "Bartlett, Caryoe and Company," and down in the left-hand corner "Chas. H. Drouet."

"That's me," he said, putting the card in her hand and touching his name. "It's pronounced 'Drew-eh.' Our family was French on my father's side."

She looked at it while he put up his purse. Then he got out a letter from a bunch in his coat pocket.

"This is the house I travel for," he went on, pointing to a picture on it—

5. The "Magnificent Mile" of stores, restaurants, office buildings, hotels, and historic landmarks. "Lincoln Park": upscale Chicago neighborhood.

"corner of State and Lake." There was pride in his voice. He felt that it was something to be connected with such a place, and he made her feel that way.

"What is your address?" he began again, fixing his pencil to write.

She looked at his hand.

"Carrie Meeber," she said slowly, "354 West Van Buren St., care S. C. Hanson."

He wrote it carefully down and got out the purse again. "You'll be at home if I come around Monday night?" he said.

"I think so," she answered.

How true it is that words are but vague shadows of the volumes we mean. Little audible links they are, chaining together great inaudible feelings and purposes. Here were these two, bandying little phrases, drawing purses, looking at cards and both unconscious of how inarticulate all their real feelings were. Neither was wise enough to be sure of the working of the mind of the other. He could not tell how his luring succeeded. She could not realize that she was drifting, until he secured her address. Now she felt that she had yielded something—he, that he had gained a victory. Already they felt that they were somehow associated. Already he took control in directing the conversation. His words were easy. Her manner was relaxed.

They were nearing Chicago. Already the signs were numerous. Trains flashed by them. Across wide stretches of flat open prairie they could see lines of telegraph poles stalking across the fields toward the great city. Away off there were indications of suburban towns, some big smoke stacks towering high in the air. Frequently there were two-story frame houses standing out in the open fields, without fence or trees, outposts of the approaching army of homes.

To the child, the genius with imagination, or the wholly untraveled, the approach to a great city for the first time is a wonderful thing. Particularly if it be evening—that mystic period between the glare and the gloom of the world when life is changing from one sphere or condition to another. Ah, the promise of the night. What does it not hold for the weary. What old illusion of hope is not here forever repeated! Says the soul of the toiler to itself, "I shall soon be free. I shall be in the ways and the hosts of the merry. The streets, the lamp, the lighted chamber set for dining are for me. The theatres, the halls, the parties, the ways of rest and the paths of song—these are mine in the night." Though all humanity be still enclosed in the shops, the thrill runs abroad. It is in the air. The dullest feel something which they may not always express or describe. It is the lifting of the burden of toil.

Sister Carrie gazed out of the window. Her companion, affected by her wonder, so contagious are all things, felt anew some interest in the city and pointed out the marvels. Already vast net-works of tracks—the sign and insignia of Chicago—stretched on either hand. There were thousands of cars and a clangor of engine bells. At the sides of this traffic stream stood dingy houses, smoky mills, tall elevators.[6] Through the interstices, evidences of the stretching city could be seen. Street cars waited at crossings for the train to go by. Gatemen toiled at wooden arms which closed the streets. Bells clanged, the rails clacked, whistles sounded afar off.

6. Grain elevators.

"This is North-West Chicago," said Drouet. "This is the Chicago River," and he pointed to a little muddy creek, crowded with the huge, masted wanderers from far-off waters nosing the black, posted banks. With a puff, a clang and a clatter of rails it was gone. "Chicago is getting to be a great town," he went on. "It's a wonder. You'll find lots to see here."

She did not hear this very well. Her heart was troubled by a kind of terror. The fact that she was alone, away from home, rushing into a great sea of life and endeavor, began to tell. She could not help but feel a little choked for breath—a little sick as her heart beat so fast. She half closed her eyes and tried to think it was nothing, that Columbia City was only a little way off.

"Chicago!—Chicago!" called the brakeman, slamming open the door. They were rushing into a more crowded yard, alive with the clatter and clang of life. She began to gather up her poor little grip and closed her hand firmly upon her purse. Drouet arose, kicked his legs to straighten his trousers and seized his clean yellow grip.

"I suppose your people will be here to meet you," he said. "Let me carry your grip."

"Oh no," she said. "I'd rather you wouldn't. I'd rather you wouldn't be with me when I meet my sister."

"All right," he said in all kindness. "I'll be near, though, in case she isn't here, and take you out there safely."

"You're so kind," said Carrie, feeling the goodness of such attention in her strange situation.

"Chicago!" called the brakeman, drawing the word out long. They were under a great shadowy train shed, where lamps were already beginning to shine out, with passenger cars all about and the train moving at a snail's pace. The people in the car were all up and crowding about the door.

"Well, here we are," said Drouet, leading the way to the door. "Goodbye," he said, "till I see you Monday."

"Goodbye," she said, taking his proffered hand.

"Remember I'll be looking till you find your sister."

She smiled into his eyes.

They filed out and he affected to take no notice of her. A lean-faced, rather commonplace woman recognized Carrie on the platform and hurried forward.

"Why Sister Carrie!" she began and there was a perfunctory embrace of welcome.

Carrie realized the change of affectional atmosphere at once. Amid all the maze, uproar and novelty, she felt cold reality taking her by the hand. No world of light and merriment. No round of amusement. Her sister carried with her much of the grimness of shift and toil.

"Why, how are all the folks at home"—she began—"how is Father, and Mother?"

Carrie answered, but was looking away. Down the aisle toward the gate leading into the waiting room and the street stood Drouet. He was looking back. When he saw that she saw him and was safe with her sister he turned to go, sending back the shadow of a smile. Only Carrie saw it. She felt something lost to her when he moved away. When he disappeared she felt his absence thoroughly. With her sister she was much alone, a lone figure in a tossing, thoughtless sea.

\* \* \*

## Chapter III

Once across the river and into the wholesale district, she glanced about her for some likely door at which to apply. As she contemplated the wide windows and imposing sings, she became conscious of being gazed upon and understood for what she was—a wage-seeker. She had never done this thing before and lacked courage. To avoid conspicuity and a certain indefinable shame she felt at being caught spying about for some place where she might apply for a position, she quickened her steps and assumed an air of indifference supposedly common to one upon an errand. In this way she passed many manufacturing and wholesale houses without once glancing in. At last, after several blocks of walking, she felt that this would not do, and began to look about again, though without relaxing her pace. A little way on she saw a great door which for some reason attracted her attention. It was ornamented by a small brass sign, and seemed to be the entrance to a vast hive of six or seven floors. "Perhaps," she thought, "they may want some one" and crossed over to enter, screwing up her courage to the sticking point as she went. When she came within a score of feet of the desired goal, she observed a young gentleman in a grey check suit, fumbling his watch-charm and looking out. That he had anything to do with the concern she could not tell, but because he happened to be looking in her direction, her weakening heart misgave her and she hurried by, too overcome with shame to enter in. After several blocks of walking, in which the uproar of the streets and the novelty of the situation had time to wear away the effect of this, her first defeat, she again looked about. Over the way stood a great six-story structure labeled "Storm and King," which she viewed with rising hope. It was a wholesale dry goods concern and employed women. She could see them moving about now and then upon the upper floors. This place she decided to enter, no matter what. She crossed over and walked directly toward the entrance. As she did so two men came out and paused in the door. A telegraph messenger in blue dashed past her and up the few steps which graced the entrance and disappeared. Several pedestrians out of the hurrying throng which filled the sidewalks passed about her as she paused, hesitating. She looked helplessly around and then, seeing herself observed, retreated. It was too difficult a task. She could not go past them.

So severe a defeat told sadly upon her nerves. She could scarcely understand her weakness and yet she could not think of gazing inquiringly about upon the surrounding scene. Her feet carried her mechanically forward, every foot of her progress being a satisfactory portion of a flight which she gladly made. Block after block passed by. Upon street lamps at the various corners she read names such as Madison, Monroe, La Salle, Clark, Dearborn, State;[7] and still she went, her feet beginning to tire upon the broad stone flagging. She was pleased in part that the streets were bright and clean. The morning sun shining down with steadily increasing warmth made the shady side of the streets pleasantly cool. She looked at the blue sky overhead with more realization of its charm than had ever come to her before.

Her cowardice began to trouble her in a way. She turned back along the

---

7. Major downtown streets between the Chicago River and Lake Michigan.

street she had come, resolving to hunt up Storm and King and enter in. On the way she encountered a great wholesale shoe company, through the broad plate windows of which she saw an enclosed executive department, hidden by frosted glass. Without this enclosure, but just within the street entrance, sat a grey-haired gentleman at a small table, with a large open ledger of some kind before him. She walked by this institution several times hesitating, but finding herself unobserved she eventually gathered sufficient courage to falter past the screen door and stand humbly waiting.

"Well, young lady," observed the old gentleman looking of her somewhat kindly—"what is it you wish?"

"I am, that is, do you—I mean, do you need any help?" she stammered.

"Not just at present," he answered smiling. "Not just at present. Come in sometime next week. Occasionally we need some one."

She received the answer in silence and backed awkwardly out. The pleasant nature of her reception rather astonished her. She had expected that it would be more difficult, that something cold and harsh would be said—she knew not what. That she had not been put to shame and made to feel her unfortunate position seemed remarkable. She did not realize that it was just this which made her experience easy, but the result was the same. She felt greatly relieved.

Somewhat encouraged, she ventured into another large structure. It was a clothing company, and more people were in evidence—well-dressed men of forty and more, surrounded by brass railings and employed variously.

An office boy approached her.

"Who is it you wish to see?" he asked.

"I want to see the manager," she returned.

He ran away and spoke to one of a group of three men who were conferring together. One broke off and came towards her.

"Well?" he said, coldly. The greeting drove all courage from her at once.

"Do you need any help?" she stammered.

"No," he replied abruptly and turned upon his heel.

She went foolishly out, the office boy deferentially swinging the door for her, and gladly sank into the obscuring crowd. It was a severe set-back to her recently pleased mental state.

Now she walked quite aimlessly for a time, turning here and there, seeing one great company after another but finding no courage to prosecute her single inquiry. High noon came and with it hunger. She hunted out an unassuming restaurant and entered but was disturbed to find that the prices were exorbitant for the size of her purse. A bowl of soup was all that she could feel herself able to afford, and with this quickly eaten she went out again. It restored her strength somewhat and made her moderately bold to pursue the search.

In walking a few blocks to fix upon some probable place she again encountered the firm of Storm and King and this time managed to enter. Some gentlemen were conferring close at hand but took no notice of her. She was left standing, gazing nervously upon the floor, her confusion and mental distress momentarily increasing until at last she was ready to turn and hurry eagerly away. When the limit of her distress had been nearly reached she was beckoned to by a man at one of the many desks within the nearby railing.

"Who is it you wish to see?" he inquired.

"Why any one, if you please," she answered. "I am looking for something to do."

"Oh, you want to see Mr. McManus," he returned. "Sit down!" and he pointed to a chair against the neighboring wall. He went on leisurely writing until after a time a short stout gentleman came in from the street.

"Mr. McManus," called the man at the desk, "this young woman wants to see you."

The short gentleman turned about towards Carrie, and she arose and came forward.

"What can I do for you, Miss," he inquired surveying her curiously.

"I want to know if I can get a position," she inquired.

"As what?" he asked.

"Not as anything in particular," she faltered. "I—"

"Have you ever had any experience in the wholesale dry goods business?" he questioned.

"No sir," she replied.

"Are you a stenographer or typewriter?"

"No sir."

"Well we haven't anything here," he said. "We employ only experienced help."

She began to step backward toward the door, when something about her plaintive face attracted him.

"Have you ever worked at anything before?" he inquired.

"No sir," she said.

"Well now, it's hardly possible that you would get anything to do in a wholesale house of this kind. Have you tried the department stores?"

She acknowledged that she had not.

"Well, if I were you," he said, looking at her rather genially, "I would try the department stores. They often need young women as clerks."

"Thank you," she said, her whole nature relieved by this spark of friendly interest.

"Yes," he said, as she moved toward the door, "you try the department stores," and off he went.

At that time the department store was in its earliest form of successful operation and there were not many. The first three in the United States, established about 1884, were in Chicago. Carrie was familiar with the names of several through the advertisements in the "Daily News," and now proceeded to seek them. The words of Mr. McManus had somehow managed to restore her courage, which had fallen low, and she dared to hope that this new line would offer her something in the way of employment. Some time she spent in wandering up and down thinking to encounter the buildings by chance, so readily is the mind, bent upon prosecuting a hard but needful errand, eased by that self-deception which the semblance of search without the reality gives. At last she inquired of a police officer and was directed to proceed "two blocks up" where she would find The Fair. Following his advice she reached that institution and entered.

The nature of these vast retail combinations, should they ever permanently disappear, will form an interesting chapter in the commercial history of our nation. Such a flowering out of a modest trade principle the world had never witnessed up to that time. They were along the line of the most effective retail organization, with hundreds of stores coordinated into one, and laid out upon the most imposing and economic basis. They were handsome, bustling, successful affairs, with a host of clerks and a swarm of patrons. Carrie passed along the busy aisles, much affected by the remarkable displays of trinkets, dress goods, shoes, stationery, jewelry. Each separate counter was a show place of dazzling interest and attraction. She could not help feeling the claim of each trinket and valuable upon her personally and yet she did not stop. There was nothing there which she could not have used—nothing which she did not long to own. The dainty slippers and stockings, the delicately frilled skirts and petticoats, the laces, ribbons, hair-combs, purses, all touched her with individual desire, and she felt keenly the fact that not any of these things were in the range of her purchase. She was a work-seeker, an outcast without employment, one whom the average employé could tell at a glance was poor and in need of a situation.

It must not be thought that anyone could have mistaken her for a nervous, sensitive, high-strung nature, cast unduly upon a cold, calculating and unpoetic world. Such certainly she was not. But women are peculiarly sensitive to the personal adornment or equipment of their person, even the dullest, and particularly is this true of the young. Your bright-eyed, rosy-cheeked maiden, over whom a poet might well rave for the flowerlike expression of her countenance and the lissome and dainty grace of her body, may reasonably be dead to every evidence of the artistic and poetic in the unrelated evidences of life, and yet not lack in material appreciation. Never, it might be said, does she fail in this. With her the bloom of a rose may pass unappreciated, but the bloom of a fold of silk, never. If nothing in the heavens, or the earth, or the waters, could elicit her fancy or delight her from its spiritual or artistic side, think not that the material would be lost. The glint of a buckle, the hue of a precious stone, the faintest tints of the watered silk, these she would devine and qualify as readily as your poet if not more so. The creak, the rustle, the glow—the least and best of the graven or spun—, these she would perceive and appreciate—if not because of some fashionable or hearsay quality, then on account of their true beauty, their innate fitness in any order of harmony, their place in the magical order and sequence of dress.

Not only did Carrie feel the drag of desire for all of this which was new and pleasing in apparel for women, but she noticed, too, with a touch at the heart, the fine ladies who elbowed and ignored her, brushing past in utter disregard of her presence, themselves eagerly enlisted in the materials which the store contained. Carrie was not familiar with the appearance of her more fortunate sisters of the city. Neither had she before known the nature and appearance of the shop girls, with whom she now compared poorly. They were pretty in the main, some even handsome, with a certain independence and toss of indifference which added, in the case of the more favored, a certain piquancy. Their clothes were neat, in many instances fine, and wherever she encountered the eye of one, it was only to recognize in it a keen analysis of her own position—her individual shortcomings of dress and that shadow of *manner* which she thought must hang about her and make clear to all who and what she was. A flame of envy lighted in her heart. She realized in a dim way how much the city held—wealth, fashion, ease—every adornment for women, and she longed for dress and beauty with a whole and fulsome heart.

On the second floor were the managerial offices, to which after some inquiry she was now directed. There she found other girls ahead of her, applicants like herself, but with more of that self-satisfied and independent air which experience of the city lends—girls who scrutinized her in a painful manner. After a wait of perhaps three-quarters of an hour she was called in turn.

"Now," said a sharp, quick-mannered Jew who was sitting at a roll-top desk near the window—"have you ever worked in any other store?"

"No sir," said Carrie.

"Oh, you haven't," he said, eyeing her keenly.

"No sir," she replied.

"Well, we prefer young women just now with some experience. I guess we can't use you."

Carrie stood waiting a moment, hardly certain whether the interview had terminated.

"Don't wait!" he exclaimed. "Remember we are very busy here."

Carrie began to move quickly to the door.

"Hold on," he said, calling her back. "Give me your name and address. We want girls occasionally."

When she had gotten safely out again into the street she could scarcely restrain tears. It was not so much the particular rebuff which she had just experienced, but the whole abashing trend of the day. She was tired and rather over-played upon in the nerves. She abandoned the thought of appealing to the other department stores and now wandered on, feeling a certain safety and relief in mingling with the crowd.

In her indifferent wandering she turned into Jackson Street, not far from the river, and was keeping her way along the south side of that imposing thoroughfare, when a piece of wrapping paper written on with marking ink and tacked upon a door attracted her attention. It read "Girls wanted—wrappers and stitchers." She hesitated for the moment, thinking surely to go in, but upon further consideration the added qualifications of "wrappers and stitchers" deterred her. She had no idea of what that meant. Most probably she would need to be experienced in it. She walked on a little way, mentally balancing as to whether or not to apply. Necessity triumphed however and she returned.

The entrance, which opened into a small hall, led to an elevator shaft, the elevator of which was up. It was a dingy affair, being used both as a freight and passenger entrance, and the woodwork was marked and splintered by the heavy boxes which were tumbled in and out, at intervals. A frowzy-headed German-American, about fourteen years of age, operated the elevator in his shirt sleeves and bare feet. His face was considerably marked with grease and dirt.

When the elevator stopped, the boy leisurely raised a protecting arm of wood and by grace of his superior privilege admitted her.

"Wear do you want go?" he inquired.

"I want to see the manager," she replied.

"Wot manager?" he returned, surveying her caustically.

"Is there more than one?" she asked. "I thought it was all one firm."

"Naw," said the youth. "Der's six different people. Want to see Speigelheim?"

"I don't know," answered Carrie. She colored a little as she began to feel the necessity of explaining. "I want to see whoever put up that sign."

"Dot's Speigelheim," said the boy. "Fort floor." Therewith he proudly turned to his task of pulling the rope, and the elevator ascended.

The firm of Speigelheim and Co., makers of boys' caps, occupied one floor of fifty feet in width and some eighty feet in depth. It was a place rather dingily lighted, the darkest portions having incandescent lights, filled in part with machines and part with workbenches. At the latter labored quite a company of girls and some men. The former were drabby looking creatures, stained in face with oil and dust, clad in thin shapeless cotton dresses, and shod with more or less worn shoes. Many of them had their sleeves rolled up, revealing bare arms, and in some cases, owing to heat, their dresses were open at the neck. They were, a fair type of nearly the lowest order of shop girls,—careless, rather slouchy, and more or less pale from confinement. They were not timid however, were rich in curiosity and strong in daring and slang.

Carrie looked about her, very much disturbed and quite sure that she did not want to work here. Aside from making her uncomfortable by sidelong glances, no one paid her the least attention. She waited until the whole department was aware of her presence. Then some word was sent round and a foreman in an apron and shirt sleeves, the latter rolled up to his shoulders, approached.

"Do you want to see me?" he asked.

"Do you need any help?" said Carrie, already learning directness of address.

"Do you know how to stitch caps?" he returned.

"No sir," she replied.

"Have you ever had any experience at this kind of work?" he inquired.

She owned that she hadn't.

"Well," said the foreman, scratching his ear meditatively, "we do need a stitcher. We like experienced help though. We've hardly got time to break people in." He paused and looked away out of the window. "We might, though, put you at finishing," he concluded reflectively.

"How much do you pay a week?" ventured Carrie, emboldened by a certain softness in the man's manner and his simplicity of address.

"Three and a half," he answered.

"Oh," she was about to exclaim, but checked herself, and allowed her thoughts to die without expression.

"We're not exactly in need of anybody," he went on vaguely, looking her over as one would a package. "You can come Monday morning though," he added, "and I'll put you to work."

"Thank you," said Carrie weakly.

"If you come, bring an apron," he added.

He walked away and left her standing by the elevator, never so much as inquiring her name.

While the appearance of the shop and the announcement of the price paid per week operated very much as a blow to Carrie's fancy, the fact that work of any kind, after so rude a round of experience, was offered her, was gratifying. She could not begin to believe that she would take the place, modest as her aspirations were. She had been used to better than that. Her mere experience and the free out-of-doors life of the country caused her nature to revolt at such confinement. Dirt had never been her share. Her sister's flat was clean. This place was grimy and low; the girls were careless and hardened. They must be bad-minded and -hearted, she imagined. Still a place had been offered her. Surely Chicago was not so bad if she could find one place in one day. She might find another and better later.

Her subsequent experiences were not of a reassuring nature, however. From all the more pleasing or imposing places she was turned away abruptly with the most chilling formality. In others where she applied, only the experienced were required. She met with painful rebuffs, the most trying of which had been in a cloak manufacturing house, where she had gone to the fourth floor to inquire.

"No, no," said the foreman, a rough, heavy-built individual who looked after a miserably lighted work shop, "we don't want anyone. Don't come here."

In another factory she was leered upon by a most sensual-faced individual who endeavored to turn the natural questions of the inquiry into a personal interview, asking all sorts of embarrassing questions and endeavoring to satisfy himself evidently that she was of loose enough morals to suit his purpose. In that case she had been relieved enough to get away and found the busy, indifferent streets to be again a soothing refuge.

With the wane of the afternoon went her hopes, her courage and her strength. She had been astonishingly persistent. So earnest an effort was well deserving of a better reward. On every hand, to her fatigued senses, the great business portion grew larger, harder, more stolid in its indifference. It seemed as if it was all closed to her, that the struggle was too fierce for her to hope to do anything at all. Men and women hurried by in long, shifting lines. She felt the flow of the tide of effort and interest, felt her own helplessness without quite realizing the wisp on the tide that she was. She cast about vainly for some possible place to apply but found no door which she had the courage to enter. It would be the same thing all over. The old humiliation of her pleas rewarded by curt denial. Sick at heart and in body, she turned to the west, the direction of Minnie's flat, which she had now fixed in mind, and began that wearisome, baffled retreat which the seeker for employment at nightfall too often makes. In passing through Fifth Avenue, south towards Van Buren Street, where she intended to take a car, she passed the door of a large wholesale shoe house, through the plate glass window of which she could see a middle-aged gentleman sitting at a small desk. One of those forlorn impulses which often grow out of a fixed sense of defeat, the last sprouting of a baffled and uprooted growth of ideas, seized upon her. She walked deliberately through the door and up to the gentleman who looked at her weary face with partially awakened interest.

"What is it?" he said.

"Can you give me something to do?" asked Carrie.

"Now I really don't know," he said kindly. "What kind of work is it you want—you're not a typewriter, are you?"

"Oh, no," answered Carrie.

"Well, we only employ book keepers and typewriters here. You might go round to the side and inquire upstairs. They did want some help upstairs a few days ago. Ask for Mr. Brown."

She hastened around to the side entrance and was taken up by the elevator to the fourth floor.

"Call Mr. Brown, Willie," said the elevator man to a boy near by.

Willie went off and presently returned with the information that Mr. Brown said she should sit down and that he would be around in a little while.

It was a portion of a stock room which gave no idea of the general character of the floor, and Carrie could form no opinion of the nature of the work.

"So you want something to do," said Mr. Brown, after he inquired concerning the nature of her errand. "Have you ever been employed in a shoe factory before?"

"No sir," said Carrie.

"What is your name?" he inquired, and being informed, "Well, I don't know as I have anything for you. Would you work for four and a half a week?"

Carrie was too worn by defeat not to feel that it was considerable. She had not expected that he would offer her less than six. She acquiesced, however, and he took her name and address.

"Well," he said finally—"you report here at eight o'clock Monday morning. I think I can find something for you to do."

He left her revived by the possibilities, sure that she had found something to do at last. Instantly the blood crept warmly over her body. Her nervous tension relaxed. She walked out into the busy street and discovered a new atmosphere. Behold, the throng was moving with a lightsome step. She noticed that men and women were smiling. Scraps of conversation and notes of laughter floated to her. The air was light. People were already pouring out of the buildings, their labor ended for the day. She noticed that they were pleased, and thoughts of her sister's home, and the meal that would be awaiting her, quickened her steps. She hurried on, tired perhaps, but no longer weary of foot. What would not Minnie say! Ah, long the winter in Chicago—the lights, the crowd, the amusement. This was a great, pleasing metropolis after all. Her new firm was a goodly institution. Its windows were of huge plate glass. She could probably do well there. Thoughts of Drouet returned, of the things he had told her. She now felt that life was better. That it was livelier, sprightlier. She boarded a car in the best of sprits, feeling her blood still flowing pleasantly. She would live in Chicago, her mind kept saying to itself. She would have a better time than she ever had before—she would be happy.

1900

# STEPHEN CRANE
## 1871–1900

Stephen Crane was born November 1, 1871, and died on June 5, 1900, at the age of twenty-eight, by which time he had published enough material to fill a dozen volumes of a collected edition and had lived a legendary life that has grown in interest to scholars and readers the more the facts have come to light. His family settled in America in the mid-seventeenth century. He was the son of a Methodist minister and a social reform–minded mother; but he systematically rejected religious and social traditions, identified with the urban poor, and lived with the mistress of one "of the better houses of ill-fame" in Jacksonville, Florida. Although temperamentally gentle, Crane was attracted to—even obsessed by—war and other forms of physical and psychic violence.

He frequently lived the down-and-out life of a penniless artist; he was also ambitious and something of a snob; he was a poet and an impressionist; a journalist, a social critic, and a realist. In Crane, the contradictions and tensions present in many writers seem intensified.

Crane once explained to an editor: "After all, I cannot help vanishing and disappearing and dissolving. It is my foremost trait." This restless, peripatetic quality of Crane's life began early. The last of fourteen children, Crane moved with his family at least three times before he entered school at age seven in the small town of Port Jervis, New York. His father died in 1880, and three years later, after several temporary moves, the family settled in the coastal resort town of Asbury Park, New Jersey. Crane never took to school. At Syracuse University he distinguished himself as a baseball player but was unable to accept the routine of academic life and left after one semester. He was not sure what he would do with himself, but by 1891 he had begun to write for newspapers, and he hungered for immersion in life of the kind that his early journalistic assignments allowed him to witness at close hand.

New York City was the inevitable destination for a young man with literary ambitions and a desire to experience the fullness of life. A few jobs with New York newspapers proved abortive, and between 1891 and 1893 Crane shuttled between the seedy New York apartments of his artist friends and his brother Edmund's house in nearby Lake View, New Jersey. In these years of extreme privation, Crane developed his powers as an observer of psychological and social reality. Encouraged by Hamlin Garland, whom he had heard lecture in 1891, Crane began his first book while at Syracuse. After it had been rejected by several New York editors, he published the work—*Maggie, A Girl of the Streets* (*A Story of New York*)—at his own expense in 1893. Although Garland admired this short novel (reprinted here in its entirety) and the powerful literary arbiter William Dean Howells promoted both Crane and *Maggie* (and continued to think it his best work), the book did not sell even when, in revised form, it was published in 1896 by the respected publishing house of D. Appleton and Company. *Maggie* told, in a highly stylized way using heavy dialect, the story of a girl born in the slums of New York who during her short life is driven to prostitution. As one of the first reviewers of the 1893 edition observed: "the evident object of the writer is to show the tremendous influence of the environment on the human character and destiny." It remains Crane's fullest treatment of how the have-littles lived in the burgeoning cities of America in the 1880s and 1890s.

Crane turned next to the Civil War as a subject for *The Red Badge of Courage: An Episode of the American Civil War* (1895). Oddly, since the novel has assumed a kind of classic status, he later described the book as a "pot-boiler." The narrative, which depicts the (partial) education of Henry Fleming in the context of battle, is as old as Homer's *Odyssey* and is a dominant story type in American literature from Benjamin Franklin through Melville, Hemingway, Malcolm X, and Saul Bellow. Crane was not so much working within or against this tradition as he was departing sharply from it. That is, Crane is distinctively modern in conceiving personal identity as complex and ambiguous and in obliging his readers to judge for themselves the adequacy of Henry's responses to his experiences.

When *Red Badge* was first published in newspapers around the country starting in December 1894, Crane's fortunes began to improve. The same syndicate (an agency that buys and then sells stories to newspapers and magazines for simultaneous publication) that took *Red Badge* hired him early in 1895 as a roving reporter in the American West and Mexico, experiences that would give him the material for several of his finest tales—"The Bride Comes to Yellow Sky" and "The Blue Hotel" among them. Also, early in 1895, D. Appleton and Company agreed to issue *Red Badge* in book form. In the spring of that year, *The Black Riders and Other Lines*, his first volume of poetry, was published in Boston by Copeland and Day. Predictably, Garland and Howells responded favorably to Crane's spare, original, unflinchingly honest poetry, but it was too experimental in form and too unconventional in its dark philosophic outlook to win wide acceptance. When *Red Badge* appeared in the fall in book form, however, it won Crane international acclaim at the age of twenty-four.

Crane's poetry, journalism, and fiction clearly demonstrated his religious, social, and literary rebelliousness, while his alienated, unconventional stance also led him to direct action. After challenging the New York police force on behalf of a prostitute who claimed harassment at its hands, Crane left the city in the winter of 1896–97 to cover the insurrection against Spain in Cuba. On his way to Cuba he met Cora Howorth Taylor, the proprietor of a bordello, the Hotel de Dream in Jacksonville, Florida, with whom he lived for the last three years of his life. On January 2, 1897, Crane's ship *The Commodore* sank off the coast of Florida. His report of this harrowing adventure was published a few days later in the *New York Press*. He promptly converted this event into one of the best-known and most widely reprinted of all American stories, "The Open Boat." This story, like *Red Badge*, reveals Crane's characteristic subject matter—the physical, emotional, and intellectual responses of people under extreme pressure, the dominant themes of nature's indifference to humanity's fate, and the consequent need for compassionate collective action. Along with *Maggie*, "The Open Boat" locates Crane within American literary naturalism alongside its other practitioners, Frank Norris, Jack London, and Theodore Dreiser, but, unlike *Maggie*, it contains a certain romanticism.

In "The Open Boat" and another late story, "The Blue Hotel," Crane achieved his mature style, one characterized by irony and brevity, qualities later associated with Sherwood Anderson and Ernest Hemingway, among others. But Crane's style cannot exactly be contained by any of the terms typically used to describe it—realism, naturalism, impressionism, or expressionism. In these late stories (and before he began to write chiefly for money), Crane combines a poet's sensitivity to the sounds of words, the rhythms of language, and a highly original use of symbol, metaphor, and color with structures of action appropriate to the shifting emotional conditions of the characters he brought to life by carefully controlling point of view and skillfully blending sharply observed detail with convincing dialogue. In his works we can observe his tough-minded irony and his essential vision: a sympathetic but unflinching demand for courage, integrity, grace, and generosity in the face of a universe in which human beings, to quote from "The Blue Hotel," are so many lice clinging "to a whirling, fire-smote, ice-locked disease-stricken, space-lost bulb."

In 1897 Crane settled in England. In the last months of his life his situation became desperate; he was suffering from tuberculosis and was seriously in debt. He wrote furiously in a doomed attempt to earn money, but the effort only worsened his health. In 1899 he drafted thirteen stories set in the fictional town Whilomville for *Harper's* magazine and published his second volume of poetry, *War Is Kind,* the weak novel *Active Service,* and the American edition of *"The Monster" and Other Stories.* "The Monster" is a daring if flawed attack on racial prejudice and a recognizable attack on Howell's notions of realism. During a Christmas party that year Crane nearly died of a lung hemorrhage. Surviving only a few months, he summoned the strength to write a series of nine articles on great battles and complete the first twenty-five chapters of the novel *The O'Ruddy.* In spite of Cora's hopes for a miraculous cure and the generous assistance of Henry James and others, Crane died, at Badenweiler, Germany, on June 5, 1900.

# Maggie: A Girl of the Streets[1]

## Chapter I

A very little boy stood upon a heap of gravel for the honor of *Rum Alley*. He was throwing stones at howling urchins from Devil's Row[2] who were circling madly about the heap and pelting at him.

His infantile countenance was livid with fury. His small body was writhing in the delivery of great, crimson oaths.

"Run, Jimmie, run! Dey'll get yehs," screamed a retreating Rum Alley child.

"Naw," responded Jimmie with a valiant roar, "dese micks[3] can't make me run."

Howls of renewed wrath went up from Devil's Row throats. Tattered gamins on the right made a furious assault on the gravel heap. On their small, convulsed faces there shone the grins of true assassins. As they charged, they threw stones and cursed in shrill chorus.

The little champion of Rum Alley stumbled precipitately down the other side. His coat had been torn to shreds in a scuffle, and his hat was gone. He had bruises on twenty parts of his body, and blood was dripping from a cut in his head. His wan features wore a look of a tiny, insane demon.

On the ground, children from Devil's Row closed in on their antagonist. He crooked his left arm defensively about his head and fought with cursing fury. The little boys ran to and fro, dodging, hurling stones and swearing in barbaric trebles.

From a window of an apartment house that upreared its form from amid squat, ignorant stables, there leaned a curious woman. Some laborers, unloading a scow at a dock at the river,[4] paused for a moment and regarded the fight. The engineer of a passive tugboat hung lazily to a railing and watched. Over on the Island,[5] a worm of yellow convicts came from the shadow of a grey ominous building and crawled slowly along the river's bank.

A stone had smashed into Jimmie's mouth. Blood was bubbling over his chin and down upon his ragged shirt. Tears made furrows on his dirt-stained cheeks. His thin legs had begun to tremble and turn weak, causing his small body to reel. His roaring curses of the first part of the fight had changed to a blasphemous chatter.

In the yells of the whirling mob of Devil's Row children there were notes of joy like songs of triumphant savagery. The little boys seemed to leer gloatingly at the blood upon the other child's face.

Down the avenue came boastfully sauntering a lad of sixteen years, although the chronic sneer of an ideal manhood already sat upon his lips. His hat was tipped with an air of challenge over his eye. Between his teeth, a cigar stump was tilted at the angle of defiance. He walked with a certain swing of

1. First published in 1893, under the pseudonym Johnston Smith. Reprinted by D. Appleton and Company in 1896; and again as *Maggie: A Girl of the Streets* by Stephen Crane, ed. Thomas A. Gullason (1979), from which this text and selected notes are taken.
2. Rum Alley and Devil's Row are fictitious places; Rum Alley may have been suggested to Crane by the chapter "The Reign of Rum," in Jacob Riis's *How the Other Half Lives* (1890) and by the prohi-

bition work of his parents.
3. Derogatory slang for people of Irish descent.
4. The East River, which separates the western end of Long Island (Brooklyn and Queens) from Manhattan and the Bronx.
5. In the 1890s, the "Island," located in the East River, was known as Blackwell's Island. Here the City of New York maintained a penitentiary, various hospitals, and almshouses. Later it was called Welfare Island; now it is Roosevelt Island.

the shoulders which appalled the timid. He glanced over into the vacant lot in which the little raving boys from Devil's Row seethed about the shrieking and tearful child from Rum Alley.

"Gee!" he murmured with interest. "A scrap. Gee!"

He strode over to the cursing circle, swinging his shoulders in a manner which denoted that he held victory in his fists. He approached at the back of one of the most deeply engaged of the Devil's Row children.

"Ah, what deh hell," he said, and smote the deeply-engaged one on the back of the head. The little boy fell to the ground and gave a hoarse, tremendous howl. He scrambled to his feet, and perceiving, evidently, the size of his assailant, ran quickly off, shouting alarms. The entire Devil's Row party followed him. They came to a stand a short distance away and yelled taunting oaths at the boy with the chronic sneer. The latter, momentarily, paid no attention to them.

"What deh hell, Jimmie?" he asked of the small champion.

Jimmie wiped his blood-wet features with his sleeve.

"Well, it was dis way, Pete, see! I was goin' teh lick dat Riley kid and dey all pitched on me."

Some Rum Alley children now came forward. The party stood for a moment exchanging vainglorious remarks with Devil's Row. A few stones were thrown at long distances, and words of challenge passed between small warriors. Then the Rum Alley contingent turned slowly in the direction of their home street. They began to give, each to each, distorted versions of the fight. Causes of retreat in particular cases were magnified. Blows dealt in the fight were enlarged to catapultian power, and stones thrown were alleged to have hurtled with infinite accuracy. Valor grew strong again, and the little boys began to swear with great spirit.

"Ah, we blokies[6] kin lick deh hull damn Row," said a child, swaggering.

Little Jimmie was striving to stanch the flow of blood from his cut lips. Scowling, he turned upon the speaker.

"Ah, where deh hell was yeh when I was doin' all deh fightin'?" he demanded. "Youse kids makes me tired."

"Ah, go ahn," replied the other argumentatively.

Jimmie replied with heavy contempt. "Ah, youse can't fight, Blue Billie! I kin lick yeh wid one han'."

"Ah, go ahn," replied Billie again.

"Ah," said Jimmie threateningly.

"Ah," said the other in the same tone.

They struck at each other, clinched, and rolled over on the cobble stones.

"Smash 'im, Jimmie, kick deh damn guts out of 'im," yelled Pete, the lad with the chronic sneer, in tones of delight.

The small combatants pounded and kicked, scratched and tore. They began to weep and their curses struggled in their throats with sobs. The other little boys clasped their hands and wriggled their legs in excitement. They formed a bobbing circle about the pair.

A tiny spectator was suddenly agitated.

"Cheese it, Jimmie, cheese it! Here comes yer fader," he yelled.

The circle of little boys instantly parted. They drew away and waited in

6. Fellows (slang).

ecstatic awe for that which was about to happen. The two little boys fighting in the modes of four thousand years ago, did not hear the warning.

Up the avenue there plodded slowly a man with sullen eyes. He was carrying a dinner pail and smoking an apple-wood pipe.

As he neared the spot where the little boys strove, he regarded them l istlessly. But suddenly he roared an oath and advanced upon the rolling fighters.

"Here, you Jim, git up, now, while I belt yer life out, you damned disorderly brat."

He began to kick into the chaotic mass on the ground. The boy Billie felt a heavy boot strike his head. He made a furious effort and disentangled himself from Jimmie. He tottered away, damning.

Jimmie arose painfully from the ground and confronting his father, began to curse him. His parent kicked him. "Come home, now," he cried, "an' stop yer jawin', er I'll lam[7] the everlasting head off yehs."

They departed. The man paced placidly along with the apple-wood emblem of serenity between his teeth. The boy followed a dozen feet in the rear. He swore luridly, for he felt that it was degradation for one who aimed to be some vague soldier, or a man of blood with a sort of sublime license, to be taken home by a father.

## Chapter II

Eventually they entered into a dark region where, from a careening building, a dozen gruesome doorways gave up loads of babies to the street and the gutter. A wind of early autumn raised yellow dust from cobbles and swirled it against an hundred windows. Long streamers of garments fluttered from fire-escapes. In all unhandy places there were buckets, brooms, rags and bottles. In the street infants played or fought with other infants or sat stupidly in the way of vehicles. Formidable women, with uncombed hair and disordered dress, gossiped while leaning on railings, or screamed in frantic quarrels. Withered persons, in curious postures of submission to something, sat smoking pipes in obscure corners. A thousand odors of cooking food came forth to the street. The building quivered and creaked from the weight of humanity stamping about in its bowels.

A small ragged girl dragged a red, bawling infant along the crowded ways. He was hanging back, baby-like, bracing his wrinkled, bare legs.

The little girl cried out: "Ah, Tommie, come ahn. Dere's Jimmie and fader. Don't be a-pullin' me back."

She jerked the baby's arm impatiently. He fell on his face, roaring. With a second jerk she pulled him to his feet, and they went on. With the obstinacy of his order, he protested against being dragged in a chosen direction. He made heroic endeavors to keep on his legs, denounce his sister and consume a bit of orange peeling which he chewed between the times of his infantile orations.

As the sullen-eyed man, followed by the blood-covered boy, drew near, the little girl burst into reproachful cries. "Ah, Jimmie, youse bin fightin' agin."

The urchin swelled disdainfully.

7. Wallop, beat (slang).

"Ah, what deh hell, Mag. See?"

The little girl upbraided him. "Youse allus fightin', Jimmie, an' yeh knows it puts mudder out when yehs come home half dead, an' it's like we'll all git a poundin'."

She began to weep. The babe threw back his head and roared at his prospects.

"Ah, what deh hell!" cried Jimmie. "Shut up er I'll smack yer mout'. See?"

As his sister continued her lamentations, he suddenly swore and struck her. The little girl reeled and, recovering herself, burst into tears and quaveringly cursed him. As she slowly retreated her brother advanced dealing her cuffs. The father heard and turned about.

"Stop that, Jim, d'yeh hear? Leave yer sister alone on the street. It's like I can never beat any sense into yer damned wooden head."

The urchin raised his voice in defiance to his parent and continued his attacks. The babe bawled tremendously, protesting with great violence. During his sister's hasty manoevres, he was dragged by the arm.

Finally the procession plunged into one of the gruesome doorways. They crawled up dark stairways and along cold, gloomy halls. At last the father pushed open a door and they entered a lighted room in which a large woman was rampant.

She stopped in a career from a seething stove to a pan-covered table. As the father and children filed in she peered at them.

"Eh, what? Been fightin' agin, by Gawd!" She threw herself upon Jimmie. The urchin tried to dart behind the others and in the scuffle the babe, Tommie, was knocked down. He protested with his usual vehemence, because they had bruised his tender shins against a table leg.

The mother's massive shoulders heaved with anger. Grasping the urchin by the neck and shoulder she shook him until he rattled. She dragged him to an unholy sink, and, soaking a rag in water, began to scrub his lacerated face with it. Jimmie screamed in pain and tried to twist his shoulders out of the clasp of the huge arms.

The babe sat on the floor watching the scene, his face in contortions like that of a woman at a tragedy. The father, with a newly-ladened pipe in his mouth, crouched on a backless chair near the stove. Jimmie's cries annoyed him. He turned about and bellowed at his wife:

"Let the damned kid alone for a minute, will yeh, Mary? Yer allus poundin' 'im. When I come nights I can't git no rest 'cause yer allus poundin' a kid. Let up, d'yeh hear? Don't be allus poundin' a kid."

The woman's operations on the urchin instantly increased in violence. At last she tossed him to a corner where he limply lay cursing and weeping.

The wife put her immense hands on her hips and with a chieftainlike stride approached her husband.

"Ho," she said, with a great grunt of contempt. "An' what in the devil are you stickin' your nose for?"

The babe crawled under the table and, turning, peered out cautiously. The ragged girl retreated and the urchin in the corner drew his legs carefully beneath him.

The man puffed his pipe calmly and put his great mudded boots on the back part of the stove.

"Go teh hell," he murmured, tranquilly.

The woman screamed and shook her fists before her husband's eyes. The rough yellow of her face and neck flared suddenly crimson. She began to howl.

He puffed imperturbably at his pipe for a time, but finally arose and began to look out at the window into the darkening chaos of back yards.

"You've been drinkin', Mary," he said. "You'd better let up on the bot', ol' woman, or you'll git done."

"You're a liar. I ain't had a drop," she roared in reply.

They had a lurid altercation, in which they damned each other's souls with frequence.

The babe was staring out from under the table, his small face working in his excitement.

The ragged girl went stealthily over to the corner where the urchin lay.

"Are yehs hurted much, Jimmie?" she whispered timidly.

"Not a damn bit! See?" growled the little boy.

"Will I wash deh blood?"

"Naw!"

"Will I—"

"When I catch dat Riley kid I'll break 'is face! Dat's right! See?"

He turned his face to the wall as if resolved to grimly bide his time.

In the quarrel between husband and wife, the woman was victor. The man grabbed his hat and rushed from the room, apparently determined upon a vengeful drunk. She followed to the door and thundered at him as he made his way down-stairs.

She returned and stirred up the room until her children were bobbing about like bubbles.

"Git outa deh way," she persistently bawled, waving feet with their dishevelled shoes near the heads of her children. She shrouded herself, puffing and snorting, in a cloud of steam at the stove, and eventually extracted a frying-pan full of potatoes that hissed.

She flourished it. "Come teh yer suppers, now," she cried with sudden exasperation. "Hurry up, now, er I'll help yeh!"

The children scrambled hastily. With prodigious clatter they arranged themselves at table. The babe sat with his feet dangling high from a precarious infant chair and gorged his small stomach. Jimmie forced, with feverish rapidity, the grease-enveloped pieces between his wounded lips. Maggie, with side glances of fear of interruption, ate like a small pursued tigress.

The mother sat blinking at them. She delivered reproaches, swallowed potatoes and drank from a yellow-brown bottle. After a time her mood changed and she wept as she carried little Tommie into another room and laid him to sleep with his fists doubled in an old quilt of faded red and green grandeur. Then she came and moaned by the stove. She rocked to and fro upon a chair, shedding tears and crooning miserably to the two children about their "poor mother" and "yer fader, damn 'is soul."

The little girl plodded between the table and the chair with a dishpan on it. She tottered on her small legs beneath burdens of dishes.

Jimmie sat nursing his various wounds. He cast furtive glances at his mother. His practised eye perceived her gradually emerged from a muddled mist of sentiment until her brain burned in drunken heat. He sat breathless.

Maggie broke a plate.

The mother started to her feet as if propelled.

"Good Gawd," she howled. Her eyes glittered on her child with sudden hatred. The fervent red of her face turned almost to purple. The little boy ran to the halls, shrieking like a monk in an earthquake.

He floundered about in darkness until he found the stairs. He stumbled, panic-stricken, to the next floor. An old woman opened a door. A light behind her threw a flare on the urchin's quivering face.

"Eh, Gawd, child, what is it dis time? Is yer fader beatin' yer mudder, or yer mudder beatin' yer fader?"

### Chapter III

Jimmie and the old woman listened long in the hall. Above the muffled roar of conversation, the dismal wailings of babies at night, the thumping of feet in unseen corridors and rooms, mingled with the sound of varied hoarse shoutings in the street and the rattling of wheels over cobbles, they heard the screams of the child and the roars of the mother die away to a feeble moaning and a subdued bass muttering.

The old woman was a gnarled and leathery personage who could don, at will, an expression of great virtue. She possessed a small music box capable of one tune, and a collection of "God bless yehs" pitched in assorted keys of fervency. Each day she took a position upon the stones of Fifth Avenue,[8] where she crooked her legs under her and crouched immovable and hideous, like an idol. She received daily a small sum in pennies. It was contributed, for the most part, by persons who did not make their homes in that vicinity.

Once, when a lady had dropped her purse on the sidewalk, the gnarled woman had grabbed it and smuggled it with great dexterity beneath her cloak. When she was arrested she had cursed the lady into a partial swoon, and with her aged limbs, twisted from rheumatism, had almost kicked the stomach out of a huge policeman whose conduct upon that occasion she referred to when she said: "The police, damn 'em."

"Eh, Jimmie, it's cursed shame," she said. "Go, now, like a dear an' buy me a can, an' if yer mudder raises 'ell all night yehs can sleep here."

Jimmie took a tendered tin-pail and seven pennies and departed. He passed into the side door of a saloon and went to the bar. Straining up on his toes he raised the pail and pennies as high as his arms would let him. He saw two hands thrust down and take them. Directly the same hands let down the filled pail and he left.

In front of the gruesome doorway he met a lurching figure. It was his father, swaying about on uncertain legs.

"Give me deh can. See?" said the man, threateningly.

"Ah, come off! I got dis can fer dat ol' woman an' it 'ud be dirt teh swipe it. See?" cried Jimmie.

The father wrenched the pail from the urchin. He grasped it in both hands and lifted it to his mouth. He glued his lips to the under edge and tilted his head. His hairy throat swelled until it seemed to grow near his chin. There was a tremendous gulping movement and the beer was gone.

The man caught his breath and laughed. He hit his son on the head with

---

8. One of Manhattan's most fashionable streets.

the empty pail. As it rolled clanging into the street, Jimmie began to scream and kicked repeatedly at his father's shins.

"Look at deh dirt what yeh done me," he yelled. "Deh ol' woman 'ill be raisin' hell."

He retreated to the middle of the street, but the man did not pursue. He staggered toward the door.

"I'll club hell outa yeh when I ketch yeh," he shouted, and disappeared.

During the evening he had been standing against a bar drinking whiskies and declaring to all comers, confidentially: "My home reg'lar livin' hell! Damndes' place! Reg'lar hell! Why do I come an' drin' whisk' here thish way? 'Cause home reg'lar livin' hell!"

Jimmie waited a long time in the street and then crept warily up through the building. He passed with great caution the door of the gnarled woman, and finally stopped outside his home and listened.

He could hear his mother moving heavily about among the furniture of the room. She was chanting in a mournful voice, occasionally interjecting bursts of volcanic wrath at the father, who, Jimmie judged, had sunk down on the floor or in a corner.

"Why deh blazes don' chere try teh keep Jim from fightin'? I'll break yer jaw," she suddenly bellowed.

The man mumbled with drunken indifference. "Ah, wha' deh hell. W'a's odds? Wha' makes kick?"

"Because he tears 'is clothes, yeh damn fool," cried the woman in supreme wrath.

The husband seemed to become aroused. "Go teh hell," he thundered fiercely in reply. There was a crash against the door and something broke into clattering fragments. Jimmie partially suppressed a howl and darted down the stairway. Below he paused and listened. He heard howls and curses, groans and shrieks, confusingly in chorus as if a battle were raging. With all was the crash of splintering furniture. The eyes of the urchin glared in fear that one of them would discover him.

Curious faces appeared in doorways, and whispered comments passed to and fro. "Ol' Johnson's raisin' hell agin."

Jimmie stood until the noises ceased and the other inhabitants of the tenement had all yawned and shut their doors. Then he crawled up-stairs with the caution of an invader of a panther den. Sounds of labored breathing came through the broken door-panels. He pushed the door open and entered, quaking.

A glow from the fire threw red hues over the bare floor, the cracked and soiled plastering, and the overturned and broken furniture.

In the middle of the floor lay his mother asleep. In one corner of the room his father's limp body hung across the seat of a chair.

The urchin stole forward. He began to shiver in dread of awakening his parents. His mother's great chest was heaving painfully. Jimmie paused and looked down at her. Her face was inflamed and swollen from drinking. Her yellow brows shaded eye-lids that had grown blue. Her tangled hair tossed in waves over her forehead. Her mouth was set in the same lines of vindictive hatred that it had, perhaps, borne during the fight. Her bare, red arms were thrown out above her head in positions of exhaustion, something, mayhap, like those of a sated villain.

The urchin bended over his mother. He was fearful lest she should open her eyes, and the dread within him was so strong, that he could not forbear to stare, but hung as if fascinated over the woman's grim face.

Suddenly her eyes opened. The urchin found himself looking straight into that expression, which, it would seem, had the power to change his blood to salt. He howled piercingly and fell backward.

The woman floundered for a moment, tossed her arms about her head as if in combat, and again began to snore.

Jimmie crawled back in the shadows and waited. A noise in the next room had followed his cry at the discovery that his mother was awake. He grovelled in the gloom, the eyes from out his drawn face riveted upon the intervening door.

He heard it creak, and then the sound of a small voice came to him. "Jimmie! Jimmie! Are yehs dere?" it whispered. The urchin started. The thin, white face of his sister looked at him from the doorway of the other room. She crept to him across the floor.

The father had not moved, but lay in the same death-like sleep. The mother writhed in uneasy slumber, her chest wheezing as if she were in the agonies of strangulation. Out at the window a florid moon was peering over dark roofs, and in the distance the waters of a river glimmered pallidly.

The small frame of the ragged girl was quivering. Her features were haggard from weeping, and her eyes gleamed from fear. She grasped the urchin's arm in her little trembling hands and they huddled in a corner. The eyes of both were drawn, by some force, to stare at the woman's face, for they thought she need only to awake and all fiends would come from below.

They crouched until the ghost-mists of dawn appeared at the window, drawing close to the panes, and looking in at the prostrate, heaving body of the mother.

## Chapter IV

The babe, Tommie, died. He went away in a white, insignificant coffin, his small waxen hand clutching a flower that the girl, Maggie, had stolen from an Italian.

She and Jimmie lived.

The inexperienced fibres of the boy's eyes were hardened at an early age. He became a young man of leather. He lived some red years without laboring. During that time his sneer became chronic. He studied human nature in the gutter, and found it no worse than he thought he had reason to believe it. He never conceived a respect for the world, because he had begun with no idols that it had smashed.

He clad his soul in armor by means of happening hilariously in at a mission church where a man composed his sermons of "yous." While they got warm at the stove, he told his hearers just where he calculated they stood with the Lord. Many of the sinners were impatient over the pictured depths of their degradation. They were waiting for soup-tickets.

A reader of words of wind-demons might have been able to see the portions of a dialogue pass to and fro between the exhorter and his hearers.

"You are damned," said the preacher. And the reader of sounds might have seen the reply go forth from the ragged people: "Where's our soup?"

Jimmie and a companion sat in a rear seat and commented upon the things that didn't concern them, with all the freedom of English gentlemen. When they grew thirsty and went out their minds confused the speaker with Christ.

Momentarily, Jimmie was sullen with thoughts of a hopeless altitude where grew fruit. His companion said that if he should ever meet God he would ask for a million dollars and a bottle of beer.

Jimmie's occupation for a long time was to stand on street-corners and watch the world go by, dreaming blood-red dreams at the passing of pretty women. He menaced mankind at the intersections of streets.

On the corners he was in life and of life. The world was going on and he was there to perceive it.

He maintained a belligerent attitude toward all well-dressed men. To him fine raiment was allied to weakness, and all good coats covered faint hearts. He and his order were kings, to a certain extent, over the men of untarnished clothes, because these latter dreaded, perhaps, to be either killed or laughed at.

Above all things he despised obvious Christians and ciphers with the chrysanthemums of aristocracy in their button-holes. He considered himself above both of these classes. He was afraid of neither the devil nor the leader of society.

When he had a dollar in his pocket his satisfaction with existence was the greatest thing in the world. So, eventually, he felt obliged to work. His father died and his mother's years were divided up into periods of thirty days.

He became a truck driver. He was given the charge of a pains-taking pair of horses and a large rattling truck. He invaded the turmoil and tumble of the down-town streets and learned to breathe maledictory defiance at the police who occasionally used to climb up, drag him from his perch and beat him.

In the lower part of the city he daily involved himself in hideous tangles. If he and his team chanced to be in the rear he preserved a demeanor of serenity, crossing his legs and bursting forth into yells when foot-passengers took dangerous dives beneath the noses of his champing horses. He smoked his pipe calmly for he knew that his pay was marching on.

If in the front and the key-truck of chaos, he entered terrifically into the quarrel that was raging to and fro among the drivers on their high seats, and sometimes roared oaths and violently got himself arrested.

After a time his sneer grew so that it turned its glare upon all things. He became so sharp that he believed in nothing. To him the police were always actuated by malignant impulses and the rest of the world was composed, for the most part, of despicable creatures who were all trying to take advantage of him and with whom, in defense, he was obliged to quarrel on all possible occasions. He himself occupied a down-trodden position that had a private but distinct element of grandeur in its isolation.

The most complete cases of aggravated idiocy were, to his mind, rampant upon the front platforms of all of the street cars. At first his tongue strove with these beings, but he eventually was superior. He became immured like an African cow. In him grew a majestic contempt for those strings of street cars that followed him like intent bugs.

He fell into the habit, when starting on a long journey, of fixing his eye on a high and distant object, commanding his horses to begin, and then going into a sort of a trance of observation. Multitudes of drivers might howl in his rear, and passengers might load him with opprobrium, he would not awaken until some blue policeman turned red and began to frenziedly tear bridles and beat the soft noses of the responsible horses.

When he paused to contemplate the attitude of the police toward himself and his fellows, he believed that they were the only men in the city who had no rights. When driving about, he felt that he was held liable by the police for anything that might occur in the streets, and was the common prey of all energetic officials. In revenge, he resolved never to move out of the way of anything, until formidable circumstances, or a much larger man than himself forced him to it.

Foot-passengers were mere pestering flies with an insane disregard for their legs and his convenience. He could not conceive their maniacal desires to cross the streets. Their madness smote him with eternal amazement. He was continually storming at them from his throne. He sat aloft and denounced their frantic leaps, plunges, dives and straddles.

When they would thrust at, or parry, the noses of his champing horses, making them swing their heads and move their feet, disturbing a solid dreamy repose, he swore at the men as fools, for he himself could perceive that Providence had caused it clearly to be written, that he and his team had the unalienable right to stand in the proper path of the sun chariot, and if they so minded, obstruct its mission or take a wheel off.

And, perhaps, if the god-driver had an ungovernable desire to step down, put up his flame-colored fists and manfully dispute the right of way, he would have probably been immediately opposed by a scowling mortal with two sets of very hard knuckles.

It is possible, perhaps, that this young man would have derided, in an axle-wide alley, the approach of a flying ferry boat. Yet he achieved a respect for a fire engine. As one charged toward his truck, he would drive fearfully upon a sidewalk, threatening untold people with annihilation. When an engine would strike a mass of blocked trucks, splitting it into fragments, as a blow annihilates a cake of ice, Jimmie's team could usually be observed high and safe, with whole wheels, on the sidewalk. The fearful coming of the engine could break up the most intricate muddle of heavy vehicles at which the police had been swearing for the half of an hour.

A fire engine was enshrined in his heart as an appalling thing that he loved with a distant dog-like devotion. They had been known to overturn street cars. Those leaping horses, striking sparks from the cobbles in their forward lunge, were creatures to be ineffably admired. The clang of the gong pierced his breast like a noise of remembered war.

When Jimmie was a little boy, he began to be arrested. Before he reached a great age, he had a fair record.

He developed too great a tendency to climb down from his truck and fight with other drivers. He had been in quite a number of miscellaneous fights, and in some general barroom rows that had become known to the police. Once he had been arrested for assaulting a Chinaman. Two women in different parts of the city, and entirely unknown to each other, caused him considerable annoyance by breaking forth, simultaneously, at fateful intervals, into wailings about marriage and support and infants.

Nevertheless, he had, on a certain star-lit evening, said wonderingly and quite reverently: "Deh moon looks like hell, don't it?"

*Chapter V*

The girl, Maggie, blossomed in a mud puddle. She grew to be a most rare and wonderful production of a tenement district, a pretty girl.

None of the dirt of Rum Alley seemed to be in her veins. The philosophers up-stairs, down-stairs and on the same floor, puzzled over it.

When a child, playing and fighting with gamins in the street, dirt disguised her. Attired in tatters and grime, she went unseen.

There came a time, however, when the young men of the vicinity said: "Dat Johnson goil is a puty good looker." About this period her brother remarked to her: "Mag, I'll tell yeh dis! See? Yeh've edder got teh go teh hell or go teh work!" Whereupon she went to work, having the feminine aversion of going to hell.

By a chance, she got a position in an establishment where they made collars and cuffs. She received a stool and a machine in a room where sat twenty girls of various shades of yellow discontent. She perched on the stool and treadled at her machine all day, turning out collars, the name of whose brand could be noted for its irrelevancy to anything in connection with collars. At night she returned home to her mother.

Jimmie grew large enough to take the vague position of head of the family. As incumbent of that office, he stumbled up-stairs late at night, as his father had done before him. He reeled about the room, swearing at his relations, or went to sleep on the floor.

The mother had gradually arisen to that degree of fame that she could bandy words with her acquaintances among the police-justices. Court-officials called her by her first name. When she appeared they pursued a course which had been theirs for months. They invariably grinned and cried out: "Hello, Mary, you here again?" Her grey head wagged in many a court. She always besieged the bench with voluble excuses, explanations, apologies and prayers. Her flaming face and rolling eyes were a sort of familiar sight on the Island. She measured time by means of sprees, and was eternally swollen and dishevelled.

One day the young man, Pete, who as a lad had smitten the Devil's Row urchin in the back of the head and put to flight the antagonists of his friend, Jimmie, strutted upon the scene. He met Jimmie one day on the street, promised to take him to a boxing match in Williamsburg,[9] and called for him in the evening.

Maggie observed Pete.

He sat on a table in the Johnson home and dangled his checked legs with an enticing nonchalance. His hair was curled down over his forehead in an oiled bang. His rather pugged nose seemed to revolt from contact with a bristling moustache of short, wire-like hairs. His blue double-breasted coat, edged with black braid, buttoned close to a red puff tie, and his patent-leather shoes looked like murder-fitted weapons.

His mannerisms stamped him as a man who had a correct sense of his personal superiority. There was valor and contempt for circumstances in the glance of his eye. He waved his hands like a man of the world, who dismisses religion and philosophy, and says "Fudge."[1] He had certainly seen everything

---

9. In Brooklyn.                    1. Nonsense (slang).

and with each curl of his lip, he declared that it amounted to nothing. Maggie thought he must be a very elegant and graceful bartender.

He was telling tales to Jimmie.

Maggie watched him furtively, with half-closed eyes, lit with a vague interest.

"Hully gee! Dey makes me tired," he said. "Mos' e'ry day some farmer[2] comes in an' tries teh run deh shop. See? But dey gits t'rowed right out! I jolt dem right out in deh street before dey knows where dey is! See?"

"Sure," said Jimmie.

"Dere was a mug come in deh place deh odder day wid an idear he wus goin' teh own deh place! Hully gee, he wus goin' teh own deh place! I see he had a still on[3] an' I didn' wanna giv 'im no stuff, so I says: 'Git deh hell outa here an' don' make no trouble,' I says like dat! See? 'Git deh hell outa here an' don' make no trouble'; like dat. 'Git deh hell outa here,' I says. See?"

Jimmie nodded understandingly. Over his features played an eager desire to state the amount of his valor in a similar crisis, but the narrator proceeded.

"Well, deh blokie he says: 'T'hell wid it! I ain' lookin' for no scrap,' he says (See?), 'but' he says, 'I'm 'spectable cit'zen an' I wanna drink an' purtydamnsoon, too.' See? 'Deh hell,' I says. Like dat! 'Deh hell,' I says. See? 'Don' make no trouble,' I says. Like dat. 'Don' make no trouble.' See? Den deh mug he squared off an' said he was fine as silk wid his dukes (See?) an' he wanned a drink damnquick. Dat's what he said. See?"

"Sure," repeated Jimmie.

Pete continued. "Say, I jes' jumped deh bar an' deh way I plunked[4] dat blokie was great. See? Dat's right! In deh jaw! See? Hully gee, he t'rowed a spittoon true deh front windee. Say, I taut I'd drop dead. But deh boss, he comes in after an' he says, 'Pete, yehs done jes' right! Yeh've gota keep order an' it's all right.' See? 'It's all right,' he says. Dat's what he said."

The two held a technical discussion.

"Dat bloke was a dandy," said Pete, in conclusion, "but he hadn' oughta made no trouble. Dat's what I says teh dem: 'Don' come in here an' make no trouble,' I says, like dat. 'Don' make no trouble.' See?"

As Jimmie and his friend exchanged tales descriptive of their prowess, Maggie leaned back in the shadow. Her eyes dwelt wonderingly and rather wistfully upon Pete's face. The broken furniture, grimy walls, and general disorder and dirt of her home of a sudden appeared before her and began to take a potential aspect. Pete's aristocratic person looked as if it might soil. She looked keenly at him, occasionally, wondering if he was feeling contempt. But Pete seemed to be enveloped in reminiscence.

"Hully gee," said he, "dose mugs can't phase me. Dey knows I kin wipe up deh street wid any t'ree of dem."

When he said, "Ah, what deh hell," his voice was burdened with disdain for the inevitable and contempt for anything that fate might compel him to endure.

Maggie perceived that here was the beau ideal of a man. Her dim thoughts were often searching for far away lands where, as God says, the little hills sing together in the morning. Under the trees of her dream-gardens there had always walked a lover.[5]

---

2. A naïve or stupid person (slang).
3. Was drunk (slang).
4. Hit (slang).

5. Portions of the last two sentences of the chapter echo Psalms 98.8, 96.12, and 65.12.

## Chapter VI

Pete took note of Maggie.

"Say, Mag, I'm stuck on yer shape"[6] he said, parenthetically, with an affable grin.

As he became aware that she was listening closely, he grew still more eloquent in his descriptions of various happenings in his career. It appeared that he was invincible in fights.

"Why," he said, referring to a man with whom he had had a misunderstanding, "dat mug scrapped like a damn dago.[7] Dat's right. He was dead easy. See? He taut he was a scrapper! But he foun' out diff'ent! Hully gee."

He walked to and fro in the small room, which seemed then to grow even smaller and unfit to hold his dignity, the attribute of a supreme warrior. That swing of the shoulders that had frozen the timid when he was but a lad had increased with his growth and education at the ratio of ten to one. It, combined with the sneer upon his mouth, told mankind that there was nothing in space which could appall him. Maggie marvelled at him and surrounded him with greatness. She vaguely tried to calculate the altitude of the pinnacle from which he must have looked down upon her.

"I met a chump deh odder day way up in deh city," he said. "I was goin' teh see a frien' of mine. When I was a-crossin' deh street deh chump runned plump inteh me, an' den he turns aroun' an' says, 'Yer insolen' ruffin,' he says, like dat. 'Oh, gee,' I says, 'oh, gee, go teh hell and git off deh eart',' I says, like dat. See? 'Go teh hell an' git off deh eart',' like dat. Den deh blokie he got wild. He says I was a contempt'ble scoun'el, er somet'ing like dat, an' he says I was doom' teh everlastin' pe'dition an' all like dat. 'Gee,' I says, 'gee! Deh hell I am,' I says. 'Deh hell I am,' like dat. An' den I slugged 'im. See?"

With Jimmie in his company, Pete departed in a sort of a blaze of glory from the Johnson home. Maggie, leaning from the window, watched him as he walked down the street.

Here was a formidable man who disdained the strength of a world full of fists. Here was one who had contempt for brass-clothed power; one whose knuckles could defiantly ring against the granite of law. He was a knight.

The two men went from under the glimmering street-lamp and passed into shadows.

Turning, Maggie contemplated the dark, dust-stained walls, and the scant and crude furniture of her home. A clock, in a splintered and battered oblong box of varnished wood, she suddenly regarded as an abomination. She noted that it ticked raspingly. The almost vanished flowers in the carpet-pattern, she conceived to be newly hideous. Some faint attempts she had made with blue ribbon, to freshen the appearance of a dingy curtain, she now saw to be piteous.

She wondered what Pete dined on.

She reflected upon the collar and cuff factory. It began to appear to her mind as a dreary place of endless grinding. Pete's elegant occupation brought him, no doubt, into contact with people who had money and manners. It was probable that he had a large acquaintance of pretty girls. He must have great sums of money to spend.

---

6. Great, extraordinary (slang).
7. Derogatory term for a person of Latin, usually Italian, descent.

To her the earth was composed of hardships and insults. She felt instant admiration for a man who openly defied it. She thought that if the grim angel of death should clutch his heart, Pete would shrug his shoulders and say: "Oh, ev'ryt'ing goes."

She anticipated that he would come again shortly. She spent some of her week's pay in the purchase of flowered cretonne for a lambrequin.[8] She made it with infinite care and hung it to the slightly-careening mantel, over the stove, in the kitchen. She studied it with painful anxiety from different points in the room. She wanted it to look well on Sunday night when, perhaps, Jimmie's friend would come. On Sunday night, however, Pete did not appear.

Afterward the girl looked at it with a sense of humiliation. She was now convinced that Pete was superior to admiration for lambrequins.

A few evenings later Pete entered with fascinating innovations in his apparel. As she had seen him twice and he had different suits on each time, Maggie had a dim impression that his wardrobe was prodigiously extensive.

"Say, Mag," he said, "put on yer bes' duds Friday night an' I'll take yehs teh deh show. See?"

He spent a few moments in flourishing his clothes and then vanished, without having glanced at the lambrequin.

Over the eternal collars and cuffs in the factory Maggie spent the most of three days in making imaginary sketches of Pete and his daily environment. She imagined some half dozen women in love with him and thought he must lean dangerously toward an indefinite one, whom she pictured with great charms of person, but with an altogether contemptible disposition.

She thought he must live in a blare of pleasure. He had friends, and people who were afraid of him.

She saw the golden glitter of the place where Pete was to take her. An entertainment of many hues and many melodies where she was afraid she might appear small and mouse-colored.

Her mother drank whiskey all Friday morning. With lurid face and tossing hair she cursed and destroyed furniture all Friday afternoon. When Maggie came home at half-past six her mother lay asleep amidst the wreck of chairs and a table. Fragments of various household utensils were scattered about the floor. She had vented some phase of drunken fury upon the lambrequin. It lay in a bedraggled heap in the corner.

"Hah," she snorted, sitting up suddenly, "where deh hell yeh been? Why deh hell don' yeh come home earlier? Been loafin' 'round deh streets. Yer gettin' teh be a reg'lar devil."

When Pete arrived Maggie, in a worn black dress, was waiting for him in the midst of a floor strewn with wreckage. The curtain at the window had been pulled by a heavy hand and hung by one tack, dangling to and fro in the draft through the cracks at the sash. The knots of blue ribbons appeared like violated flowers. The fire in the stove had gone out. The displaced lids and open doors showed heaps of sullen grey ashes. The remnants of a meal, ghastly, like dead flesh, lay in a corner. Maggie's red mother, stretched on the floor, blasphemed and gave her daughter a bad name.

8. Drapery hung from a shelf or above a window or doorway. "Cretonne": colorfully printed fabric.

## Chapter VII

An orchestra of yellow silk women and bald-headed men on an elevated stage near the centre of a great green-hued hall,[9] played a popular waltz. The place was crowded with people grouped about little tables. A battalion of waiters slid among the throng, carrying trays of beer glasses and making change from the inexhaustible vaults of their trousers pockets. Little boys, in the costumes of French chefs, paraded up and down the irregular aisles vending fancy cakes. There was a low rumble of conversation and a subdued clinking of glasses. Clouds of tobacco smoke rolled and wavered high in air about the dull gilt of the chandeliers.

The vast crowd had an air throughout of having just quitted labor. Men with calloused hands and attired in garments that showed the wear of an endless trudge for a living, smoked their pipes contentedly and spent five, ten, or perhaps fifteen cents for beer. There was a mere sprinkling of kid-gloved men who smoked cigars purchased elsewhere. The great body of the crowd was composed of people who showed that all day they strove with their hands. Quiet Germans, with maybe their wives and two or three children, sat listening to the music, with the expressions of happy cows. An occasional party of sailors from a war-ship, their faces pictures of sturdy health, spent the earlier hours of the evening at the small round tables. Very infrequent tipsy men, swollen with the value of their opinions, engaged their companions in earnest and confidential conversation. In the balcony, and here and there below, shone the impassive faces of women. The nationalities of the Bowery[1] beamed upon the stage from all directions.

Pete aggressively walked up a side aisle and took seats with Maggie at a table beneath the balcony.

"Two beehs!"

Leaning back he regarded with eyes of superiority the scene before them. This attitude affected Maggie strongly. A man who could regard such a sight with indifference must be accustomed to very great things.

It was obvious that Pete had been to this place many times before, and was very familiar with it. A knowledge of this fact made Maggie feel little and new.

He was extremely gracious and attentive. He displayed the consideration of a cultured gentleman who knew what was due.

"Say, what deh hell? Bring deh lady a big glass! What deh hell use is dat pony?"[2]

"Don't be fresh, now," said the waiter, with some warmth, as he departed.

"Ah, git off deh eart'," said Pete, after the other's retreating form.

Maggie perceived that Pete brought forth all his elegance and all his knowledge of high-class customs for her benefit. Her heart warmed as she reflected upon his condescension.

The orchestra of yellow silk women and bald-headed men gave vent to a few bars of anticipatory music and a girl, in a pink dress with short skirts, galloped upon the stage. She smiled upon the throng as if in acknowledgment

---

9. Probably Atlantic Garden, a beer-garden popular with middle- and working-class Germans. Women were featured in the orchestra, which played waltz and polka tunes.
1. Located on the Lower East Side of Manhattan,

the Bowery was an area known for its saloons, concert and dance halls, dime museums, working-class theaters and dives, cheap lodging houses, and pawnshops.
2. Shot glass.

of a warm welcome, and began to walk to and fro, making profuse gesticulations and singing, in brazen soprano tones, a song, the words of which were inaudible. When she broke into the swift rattling measures of a chorus some half-tipsy men near the stage joined in the rollicking refrain and glasses were pounded rhythmically upon the tables. People leaned forward to watch her and to try to catch the words of the song. When she vanished there were long rollings of applause.

Obedient to more anticipatory bars, she reappeared amidst the half-suppressed cheering of the tipsy men. The orchestra plunged into dance music and the laces of the dancer fluttered and flew in the glare of gas jets. She divulged the fact that she was attired in some half dozen skirts. It was patent that any one of them would have proved adequate for the purpose for which skirts are intended. An occasional man bent forward, intent upon the pink stockings. Maggie wondered at the splendor of the costume and lost herself in calculations of the cost of the silks and laces.

The dancer's smile of stereotyped enthusiasm was turned for ten minutes upon the faces of her audience. In the finale she fell into some of those grotesque attitudes which were at the time popular among the dancers in the theatres up-town, giving to the Bowery public the phantasies of the aristocratic theatre-going public, at reduced rates.

"Say, Pete," said Maggie, leaning forward, "dis is great."

"Sure," said Pete, with proper complacence.

A ventriloquist followed the dancer. He held two fantastic dolls on his knees. He made them sing mournful ditties and say funny things about geography and Ireland.

"Do dose little men talk?" asked Maggie.

"Naw," said Pete, "it's some damn fake. See?"

Two girls, on the bills as sisters, came forth and sang a duet that is heard occasionally at concerts given under church auspices. They supplemented it with a dance which of course can never be seen at concerts given under church auspices.

After the duettists had retired, a woman of debatable age sang a negro melody. The chorus necessitated some grotesque waddlings supposed to be an imitation of a plantation darkey, under the influence, probably, of music and the moon. The audience was just enthusiastic enough over it to have her return and sing a sorrowful lay,[3] whose lines told of a mother's love and a sweetheart who waited and a young man who was lost at sea under the most harrowing circumstances. From the faces of a score or so in the crowd, the self-contained look faded. Many heads were bent forward with eagerness and sympathy. As the last distressing sentiment of the piece was brought forth, it was greeted by that kind of applause which rings as sincere.

As a final effort, the singer rendered some verses which described a vision of Britain being annihilated by America, and Ireland bursting her bonds. A carefully prepared crisis was reached in the last line of the last verse, where the singer threw out her arms and cried, "The star-spangled banner." Instantly a great cheer swelled from the throats of the assemblage of the masses. There was a heavy rumble of booted feet thumping the floor.

3. Narrative ballad of love or adventure.

Eyes gleamed with sudden fire, and calloused hands waved frantically in the air.

After a few moments' rest, the orchestra played crashingly, and a small fat man burst out upon the stage. He began to roar a song and stamp back and forth before the foot-lights, wildly waving a glossy silk hat and throwing leers, or smiles, broadcast. He made his face into fantastic grimaces until he looked like a pictured devil on a Japanese kite. The crowd laughed gleefully. His short, fat legs were never still a moment. He shouted and roared and bobbed his shock of red wig until the audience broke out in excited applause.

Pete did not pay much attention to the progress of events upon the stage. He was drinking beer and watching Maggie.

Her cheeks were blushing with excitement and her eyes were glistening. She drew deep breaths of pleasure. No thoughts of the atmosphere of the collar and cuff factory came to her.

When the orchestra crashed finally, they jostled their way to the sidewalk with the crowd. Pete took Maggie's arm and pushed a way for her, offering to fight with a man or two.

They reached Maggie's home at a late hour and stood for a moment in front of the gruesome doorway.

"Say, Mag," said Pete, "give us a kiss for takin' yeh teh deh show, will yer?"

Maggie laughed, as if startled, and drew away from him.

"Naw, Pete," she said, "dat wasn't in it."

"Ah, what deh hell?" urged Pete.

The girl retreated nervously.

"Ah, what deh hell?" repeated he.

Maggie darted into the hall, and up the stairs. She turned and smiled at him, then disappeared.

Pete walked slowly down the street. He had something of an astonished expression upon his features. He paused under a lamp-post and breathed a low breath of surprise.

"Gawd," he said, "I wonner if I've been played fer a duffer."[4]

### Chapter VIII

As thoughts of Pete came to Maggie's mind, she began to have an intense dislike for all of her dresses.

"What deh hell ails yeh? What makes yeh be allus fixin' and fussin'? Good Gawd," her mother would frequently roar at her.

She began to note, with more interest, the well-dressed women she met on the avenues. She envied elegance and soft palms. She craved those adornments of person which she saw every day on the street, conceiving them to be allies of vast importance to women.

Studying faces, she thought many of the women and girls she chanced to meet, smiled with serenity as though forever cherished and watched over by those they loved.

The air in the collar and cuff establishment strangled her. She knew she was gradually and surely shrivelling in the hot, stuffy room. The begrimed

4. Stupid person, fool (slang).

windows rattled incessantly from the passing of elevated trains. The place was filled with a whirl of noises and odors.

She wondered as she regarded some of the grizzled women in the room, mere mechanical contrivances sewing seams and grinding out, with heads bended over their work, tales of imagined or real girlhood happiness, past drunks, the baby at home, and unpaid wages. She speculated how long her youth would endure. She began to see the bloom upon her cheeks as valuable.

She imagined herself, in an exasperating future, as a scrawny woman with an eternal grievance. Too, she thought Pete to be a very fastidious person concerning the appearance of women.

She felt she would love to see somebody entangle their fingers in the oily beard of the fat foreigner who owned the establishment. He was a detestable creature. He wore white socks with low shoes.

He sat all day delivering orations, in the depths of a cushioned chair. His pocket-book deprived them of the power of retort.

"What een hell do you sink I pie fife dolla a week for? Play? No, py damn!"

Maggie was anxious for a friend to whom she could talk about Pete. She would have liked to discuss his admirable mannerisms with a reliable mutual friend. At home, she found her mother often drunk and always raving.

It seems that the world had treated this woman very badly, and she took a deep revenge upon such portions of it as came within her reach. She broke furniture as if she were at last getting her rights. She swelled with virtuous indignation as she carried the lighter articles of household use, one by one under the shadows of the three gilt balls, where Hebrews chained them with chains of interest.[5]

Jimmie came when he was obliged to by circumstances over which he had no control. His well-trained legs brought him staggering home and put him to bed some nights when he would rather have gone elsewhere.

Swaggering Pete loomed like a golden sun to Maggie. He took her to a dime museum[6] where rows of meek freaks astonished her. She contemplated their deformities with awe and thought them a sort of chosen tribe.

Pete, raking his brains for amusement, discovered the Central Park Menagerie and the Museum of Arts.[7] Sunday afternoons would sometimes find them at these places. Pete did not appear to be particularly interested in what he saw. He stood around looking heavy, while Maggie giggled in glee.

Once at the Menagerie he went into a trance of admiration before the spectacle of a very small monkey threatening to thrash a cageful because one of them had pulled his tail and he had not wheeled about quickly enough to discover who did it. Ever after Pete knew that monkey by sight and winked at him, trying to induce him to fight with other and larger monkeys.

At the Museum, Maggie said, "Dis is outa sight."

"Oh hell," said Pete, "wait till next summer an' I'll take yehs to a picnic."

While the girl wandered in the vaulted rooms, Pete occupied himself in returning stony stare for stony stare, the appalling scrutiny of the watch-dogs

---

5. Expressed here is the belief that the pawnshop and lending businesses were controlled by Jews.
6. Popular amusement center with wax figures, mechanized contrivances, and panoramic views.

7. The Metropolitan Museum of Art, on the east side of Central Park, is at Fifth Avenue and 82nd Street. The zoo, also on the east side of the park, is at Fifth Avenue and 64th Street.

of the treasures. Occasionally he would remark in loud tones: "Dat jay[8] has got glass eyes," and sentences of the sort. When he tired of this amusement he would go to the mummies and moralize over them.

Usually he submitted with silent dignity to all which he had to go through, but, at times, he was goaded into comment.

"What deh hell," he demanded once. "Look at all dese little jugs! Hundred jugs in a row! Ten rows in a case an' 'bout a t'ousand cases! what deh blazes use is dem?"

Evenings during the week he took her to see plays in which the brain-clutching heroine was rescued from the palatial home of her guardian, who is cruelly after her bonds, by the hero with the beautiful sentiments. The latter spent most of his time out at soak in pale-green snow storms, busy with a nickel-plated revolver, rescuing aged strangers from villains.

Maggie lost herself in sympathy with the wanderers swooning in snow storms beneath happy-hued church windows. And a choir within singing "Joy to the World." To Maggie and the rest of the audience this was transcendental realism. Joy always within, and they, like the actor, inevitably without. Viewing it, they hugged themselves in ecstatic pity of their imagined or real condition.

The girl thought the arrogance and granite-heartedness of the magnate of the play was very accurately drawn. She echoed the maledictions that the occupants of the gallery showered on this individual when his lines compelled him to expose his extreme selfishness.

Shady persons in the audience revolted from the pictured villainy of the drama. With untiring zeal they hissed vice and applauded virtue. Unmistakably bad men evinced an apparently sincere admiration for virtue.

The loud gallery was overwhelmingly with the unfortunate and the oppressed. They encouraged the struggling hero with cries, and jeered the villain, hooting and calling attention to his whiskers. When anybody died in the pale-green snow storms, the gallery mourned. They sought out the painted misery and hugged it as akin.

In the hero's erratic march from poverty in the first act, to wealth and triumph in the final one, in which he forgives all the enemies that he has left, he was assisted by the gallery, which applauded his generous and noble sentiments and confounded the speeches of his opponents by making irrelevant but very sharp remarks. Those actors who were cursed with villainy parts were confronted at every turn by the gallery. If one of them rendered lines containing the most subtle distinctions between right and wrong, the gallery was immediately aware if the actor meant wickedness, and denounced him accordingly.

The last act was a triumph for the hero, poor and of the masses, the representative of the audience, over the villain and the rich man, his pockets stuffed with bonds, his heart packed with tyrannical purposes, imperturbable amid suffering.

Maggie always departed with raised spirits from the showing places of the melodrama. She rejoiced at the way in which the poor and virtuous eventually surmounted the wealthy and wicked. The theatre made her think. She

8. Stupid, inexperienced person (slang).

wondered if the culture and refinement she had seen imitated, perhaps grotesquely, by the heroine on the stage, could be acquired by a girl who lived in a tenement house and worked in a shirt factory.

### Chapter IX

A group of urchins were intent upon the side door of a saloon. Expectancy gleamed from their eyes. They were twisting their fingers in excitement.

"Here she comes," yelled one of them suddenly.

The group of urchins burst instantly asunder and its individual fragments were spread in a wide, respectable half-circle about the point of interest. The saloon door opened with a crash, and the figure of a woman appeared upon the threshold. Her grey hair fell in knotted masses about her shoulders. Her face was crimsoned and wet with perspiration. Her eyes had a rolling glare.

"Not a damn cent more of me money will yehs ever get, not a damn cent. I spent me money here fer t'ree years an' now yehs tells me yeh'll sell me no more stuff! T'hell wid yeh, Johnnie Murckre! 'Disturbance'? Disturbance be damned! T'hell wid yeh, Johnnie—"

The door received a kick of exasperation from within and the woman lurched heavily out on the sidewalk.

The gamins in the half-circle became violently agitated. They began to dance about and hoot and yell and jeer. Wide dirty grins spread over each face.

The woman made a furious dash at a particularly outrageous cluster of little boys. They laughed delightedly and scampered off a short distance, calling out over their shoulders to her. She stood tottering on the curb-stone and thundered at them.

"Yeh devil's kids," she howled, shaking red fists. The little boys whooped in glee. As she started up the street they fell in behind and marched uproariously. Occasionally she wheeled about and made charges on them. They ran nimbly out of reach and taunted her.

In the frame of a gruesome doorway she stood for a moment cursing them. Her hair straggled, giving her crimson features a look of insanity. Her great fists quivered as she shook them madly in the air.

The urchins made terrific noises until she turned and disappeared. Then they filed quietly in the way they had come.

The woman floundered about in the lower hall of the tenement house and finally stumbled up the stairs. On an upper hall a door was opened and a collection of heads peered curiously out, watching her. With a wrathful snort the woman confronted the door, but it was slammed hastily in her face and the key was turned.

She stood for a few minutes, delivering a frenzied challenge at the panels.

"Come out in deh hall, Mary Murphy, damn yeh, if yehs want a row. Come ahn, yeh overgrown terrier, come ahn."

She began to kick the door with her great feet. She shrilly defied the universe to appear and do battle. Her cursing trebles brought heads from all doors save the one she threatened. Her eyes glared in every direction. The air was full of her tossing fists.

"Come ahn, deh hull damn gang of yehs, come ahn," she roared at the spectators. An oath or two, cat-calls, jeers and bits of facetious advice were given in reply. Missiles clattered about her feet.

"What deh hell's deh matter wid yeh?" said a voice in the gathered gloom, and Jimmie came forward. He carried a tin dinner-pail in his hand and under his arm a brown truckman's apron done in a bundle. "What deh hell's wrong?" he demanded.

"Come out, all of yehs, come out," his mother was howling. "Come ahn an' I'll stamp yer damn brains under me feet."

"Shet yer face, an' come home, yeh damned old fool," roared Jimmie at her. She strided up to him and twirled her fingers in his face. Her eyes were darting flames of unreasoning rage and her frame trembled with eagerness for a fight.

"T'hell wid yehs! An' who deh hell are yehs? I ain't givin' a snap of me fingers fer yehs," she bawled at him. She turned her huge back in tremendous disdain and climbed the stairs to the next floor.

Jimmie followed, cursing blackly. At the top of the flight he seized his mother's arm and started to drag her toward the door of their room.

"Come home, damn yeh," he gritted between his teeth.

"Take yer hands off me! Take yer hands off me," shrieked his mother.

She raised her arm and whirled her great fist at her son's face. Jimmie dodged his head and the blow struck him in the back of the neck. "Damn yeh," gritted he again. He threw out his left hand and writhed his fingers about her middle arm. The mother and the son began to sway and struggle like gladiators.

"Whoop!" said the Rum Alley tenement house. The hall filled with interested spectators.

"Hi, ol' lady, dat was a dandy!"

"T'ree to one on deh red!"

"Ah, stop yer damn scrappin'!"

The door of the Johnson home opened and Maggie looked out. Jimmie made a supreme cursing effort and hurled his mother into the room. He quickly followed and closed the door. The Rum Alley tenement swore disappointedly and retired.

The mother slowly gathered herself up from the floor. Her eyes glittered menacingly upon her children.

"Here, now," said Jimmie, "we've had enough of dis. Sit down, an' don' make no trouble."

He grasped her arm, and twisting it, forced her into a creaking chair.

"Keep yer hands off me," roared his mother again.

"Damn yer ol' hide," yelled Jimmie, madly. Maggie shrieked and ran into the other room. To her there came the sound of a storm of crashes and curses. There was a great final thump and Jimmie's voice cried: "Dere, damn yeh, stay still." Maggie opened the door now, and went warily out. "Oh, Jimmie."

He was leaning against the wall and swearing. Blood stood upon bruises on his knotty fore-arms where they had scraped against the floor or the walls in the scuffle. The mother lay screeching on the floor, the tears running down her furrowed face.

Maggie, standing in the middle of the room, gazed about her. The usual upheaval of the tables and chairs had taken place. Crockery was strewn broadcast in fragments. The stove had been disturbed on its legs, and now leaned idiotically to one side. A pail had been upset and water spread in all directions.

The door opened and Pete appeared. He shrugged his shoulders. "Oh, Gawd," he observed.

He walked over to Maggie and whispered in her ear. "Ah, what deh hell, Mag? Come ahn and we'll have a hell of a time."

The mother in the corner upreared her head and shook her tangled locks. "Teh hell wid him and you," she said, glowering at her daughter in the gloom. Her eyes seemed to burn balefully. "Yeh've gone teh deh devil, Mag Johnson, yehs knows yehs have gone teh deh devil. Yer a disgrace teh yer people, damn yeh. An' now, git out an' go ahn wid dat doe-faced jude[9] of yours. Go teh hell wid him, damn yeh, an' a good riddance. Go teh hell an' see how yeh likes it."

Maggie gazed long at her mother.

"Go teh hell now, an' see how yeh likes it. Git out. I won't have sech as yehs in me house! Get out, d'yeh hear! Damn yeh, git out!"

The girl began to tremble.

At this instant Pete came forward. "Oh, what deh hell, Mag, see," whispered he softly in her ear. "Dis all blows over. See? Deh ol' woman 'ill be all right in deh mornin'. Come ahn out wid me! We'll have a hell of a time."

The woman on the floor cursed. Jimmie was intent upon his bruised forearms. The girl cast a glance about the room filled with a chaotic mass of debris, and at the red, writhing body of her mother.

"Go teh hell an' good riddance."

She went.

## Chapter X

Jimmie had an idea it wasn't common courtesy for a friend to come to one's home and ruin one's sister. But he was not sure how much Pete knew about the rules of politeness.

The following night he returned home from work at rather a late hour in the evening. In passing through the halls he came upon the gnarled and leathery old woman who possessed the music box. She was grinning in the dim light that drifted through dust-stained panes. She beckoned to him with a smudged forefinger.

"Ah, Jimmie, what do yehs t'ink I got onto las' night. It was deh funnies' t'ing I ever saw," she cried, coming close to him and leering. She was trembling with eagerness to tell her tale. "I was by me door las' night when yer sister and her jude feller came in late, oh, very late. An' she, the dear, she was a-cryin' as if her heart would break, she was. It was deh funnies' t'ing I ever saw. An' right out here by me door she asked him did he love her, did he. An' she was a-cryin' as if her heart would break, poor t'ing. An' him, I could see by deh way what he said it dat she had been askin' orften, he says: 'Oh, hell, yes,' he says, says he, 'Oh, hell, yes.'"

---

9. Probably suggests "dude," for Pete is concerned about his appearance, but it may also be that Mary intends to label Pete as a "Jew" because he has money, or that she thinks of him as a Judas or betrayer.

Storm-clouds swept over Jimmie's face, but he turned from the leathery old woman and plodded on up-stairs.

"Oh, hell, yes," called she after him. She laughed a laugh that was like a prophetic croak. " 'Oh, hell, yes,' he says, says he, 'Oh, hell, yes.' "

There was no one in at home. The rooms showed that attempts had been made at tidying them. Parts of the wreckage of the day before had been repaired by an unskilful hand. A chair or two and the table, stood uncertainly upon legs. The floor had been newly swept. Too, the blue ribbons had been restored to the curtains, and the lambrequin, with its immense sheaves of yellow wheat and red roses of equal size, had been returned, in a worn and sorry state, to its position at the mantel. Maggie's jacket and hat were gone from the nail behind the door.

Jimmie walked to the window and began to look through the blurred glass. It occurred to him to vaguely wonder, for an instant, if some of the women of his acquaintance had brothers.

Suddenly, however, he began to swear.

"But he was me frien'! I brought im here! Dat's deh hell of it!"

He fumed about the room, his anger gradually rising to the furious pitch. "I'll kill deh jay! Dat's what I'll do! I'll kill deh jay!"

He clutched his hat and sprang toward the door. But it opened and his mother's great form blocked the passage.

"What deh hell's deh matter wid yeh?" exclaimed she, coming into the rooms.

Jimmie gave vent to a sardonic curse and then laughed heavily.

"Well, Maggie's gone teh deh devil! Dat's what! See?"

"Eh?" said his mother.

"Maggie's gone teh deh devil! Are yehs deaf?" roared Jimmie, impatiently.

"Deh hell she has," murmured the mother, astounded.

Jimmie grunted, and then began to stare out at the window. His mother sat down in a chair, but a moment later sprang erect and delivered a maddened whirl of oaths. Her son turned to look at her as she reeled and swayed in the middle of the room, her fierce face convulsed with passion, her blotched arms raised high in imprecation.

"May Gawd curse her forever," she shrieked. "May she eat nothin' but stones and deh dirt in deh street. May she sleep in deh gutter an' never see deh sun shine again. Deh damn—"

"Here, now," said her son. "Take a drop on yourself."

The mother raised lamenting eyes to the ceiling.

"She's deh devil's own chil', Jimmie," she whispered. "Ah, who would t'ink such a bad girl could grow up in our fambly, Jimmie, me son. Many deh hour I've spent in talk wid dat girl an' tol' her if she ever went on deh streets I'd see her damned. An' after all her bringin' up an' what I tol' her and talked wid her, she goes teh deh bad, like a duck teh water."

The tears rolled down her furrowed face. Her hands trembled.

"An' den when dat Sadie MacMallister next door to us was sent teh deh devil by dat feller what worked in deh soap-factory, didn't I tell our Mag dat if she—"

"Ah, dat's anudder story," interrupted the brother. "Of course, dat Sadie was nice an' all dat—but—see—it ain't dessame as if—well, Maggie was diff'ent—see—she was diff'ent."

He was trying to formulate a theory that he had always unconsciously held, that all sisters, excepting his own, could advisedly be ruined.

He suddenly broke out again. "I'll go t'ump hell outa deh mug what did her deh harm. I'll kill 'im! He t'inks he kin scrap, but when he gits me a-chasin' 'im he'll fin' out where he's wrong, deh damned duffer. I'll wipe up deh street wid 'im."

In a fury he plunged out of the doorway. As he vanished the mother raised her head and lifted both hands, entreating.

"May Gawd curse her forever," she cried.

In the darkness of the hallway Jimmie discerned a knot of women talking volubly. When he strode by they paid no attention to him.

"She allus was a bold thing," he heard one of them cry in an eager voice. "Dere wasn't a feller come teh deh house but she'd try teh mash¹ 'im. My Annie says deh shameless t'ing tried teh ketch her feller, her own feller, what we useter know his fader."

"I could a' tol' yehs dis two years ago," said a woman, in a key of triumph. "Yessir, it was over two years ago dat I says teh my ol' man, I says, 'Dat Johnson girl ain't straight,' I says. 'Oh, hell,' he says. 'Oh, hell.' 'Dat's all right,' I says, 'but I know what I knows,' I says, 'an' it 'ill come out later. You wait an' see,' I says, 'you see.' "

"Anybody what had eyes could see dat dere was somethin' wrong wid dat girl. I didn't like her actions."

On the street Jimmie met a friend. "What deh hell?" asked the latter.

Jimmie explained. "An' I'll t'ump 'im till he can't stand."

"Oh, what deh hell," said the friend. "What's deh use! Yeh'll git pulled in! Everybody ill be onto it! An' ten plunks!² Gee!"

Jimmie was determined. "He t'inks he kin scrap, but he'll fin' out diff'ent."

"Gee," remonstrated the friend. "What deh hell?"

## Chapter XI

On a corner a glass-fronted building shed a yellow glare upon the pavements. The open mouth of a saloon called seductively to passengers to enter and annihilate sorrow or create rage.

The interior of the place was papered in olive and bronze tints of imitation leather. A shining bar of counterfeit massiveness extended down the side of the room. Behind it a great mahogany-appearing sideboard reached the ceiling. Upon its shelves rested pyramids of shimmering glasses that were never disturbed. Mirrors set in the face of the sideboard multiplied them. Lemons, oranges and paper napkins, arranged with mathematical precision, sat among the glasses. Many-hued decanters of liquor perched at regular intervals on the lower shelves. A nickel-plated cash register occupied a position in the exact centre of the general effect. The elementary senses of it all seemed to be opulence and geometrical accuracy.

Across from the bar a smaller counter held a collection of plates upon which swarmed frayed fragments of crackers, slices of boiled ham, dishevelled bits of cheese, and pickles swimming in vinegar. An odor of grasping, begrimed hands and munching mouths pervaded.

---

1. To flirt with (slang).  2. Dollars (slang).

Pete, in a white jacket, was behind the bar bending expectantly toward a quiet stranger. "A beeh," said the man. Pete drew a foam-topped glassful and set it dripping upon the bar.

At this moment the light bamboo doors at the entrance swung open and crashed against the siding. Jimmie and a companion entered. They swaggered unsteadily but belligerently toward the bar and looked at Pete with bleared and blinking eyes.

"Gin," said Jimmie.

"Gin," said the companion.

Pete slid a bottle and two glasses along the bar. He bended his head sideways as he assiduously polished away with a napkin at the gleaming wood. He had a look of watchfulness upon his features.

Jimmie and his companion kept their eyes upon the bartender and conversed loudly in tones of contempt.

"He's a dindy masher, ain't he, by Gawd?" laughed Jimmie.

"Oh, hell, yes," said the companion, sneering widely. "He's great, he is. Git onto deh mug on deh blokie. Dat's enough to make a feller turn hand-springs in 'is sleep."

The quiet stranger moved himself and his glass a trifle further away and maintained an attitude of oblivion.

"Gee! ain't he hot stuff!"

"Git onto his shape! Great Gawd!"

"Hey," cried Jimmie, in tones of command. Pete came along slowly, with a sullen dropping of the under lip.

"Well," he growled, "what's eatin' yehs?"

"Gin," said Jimmie.

"Gin," said the companion.

As Pete confronted them with the bottle and the glasses, they laughed in his face. Jimmie's companion, evidently overcome with merriment, pointed a grimy forefinger in Pete's direction.

"Say, Jimmie," demanded he, "what deh hell is dat behind deh bar?"

"Damned if I knows," replied Jimmie. They laughed loudly. Pete put down a bottle with a bang and turned a formidable face toward them. He disclosed his teeth and his shoulders heaved restlessly.

"You fellers can't guy[3] me," he said. "Drink yer stuff an' git out an' don' make no trouble."

Instantly the laughter faded from the faces of the two men and expressions of offended dignity immediately came.

"Who deh hell has said anyt'ing teh you," cried they in the same breath.

The quiet stranger looked at the door calculatingly.

"Ah, come off," said Pete to the two men. "Don't pick me up for no jay. Drink yer rum an' git out an' don' make no trouble."

"Oh, deh hell," airily cried Jimmie.

"Oh, deh hell," airily repeated his companion.

"We goes when we git ready! See!" continued Jimmie.

"Well," said Pete in a threatening voice, "don' make no trouble."

Jimmie suddenly leaned forward with his head on one side. He snarled like a wild animal.

---

3. Make fun of, ridicule (slang).

"Well, what if we does? See?" said he.

Dark blood flushed into Pete's face, and he shot a lurid glance at Jimmie.

"Well, den we'll see whose deh bes' man, you or me," he said.

The quiet stranger moved modestly toward the door.

Jimmie began to swell with valor.

"Don' pick me up fer no tenderfoot. When yeh tackles me yeh tackles one of deh bes' men in deh city. See? I'm a scrapper, I am. Ain't dat right, Billie?"

"Sure, Mike," responded his companion in tones of conviction.

"Oh, hell," said Pete, easily. "Go fall on yerself."

The two men again began to laugh.

"What deh hell is dat talkin'?" cried the companion.

"Damned if I knows," replied Jimmie with exaggerated contempt.

Pete made a furious gesture. "Git outa here now, an' don' make no trouble. See? Youse fellers er lookin' fer a scrap an' it's damn likely yeh'll fin' one if yeh keeps on shootin' off yer mout's. I know yehs! See? I kin lick better men dan yehs ever saw in yer lifes. Dat's right! See? Don' pick me up fer no stuff er yeh might be jolted out in deh street before yeh knows where yeh is. When I comes from behind dis bar, I t'rows yehs bote inteh deh street. See?"

"Oh, hell," cried the two men in chorus.

The glare of a panther came into Pete's eyes. "Dat's what I said! Unnerstan'?"

He came through a passage at the end of the bar and swelled down upon the two men. They stepped promptly forward and crowded close to him.

They bristled like three roosters. They moved their heads pugnaciously and kept their shoulders braced. The nervous muscles about each mouth twitched with a forced smile of mockery.

"Well, what deh hell yer goin' teh do?" gritted Jimmie.

Pete stepped warily back, waving his hands before him to keep the men from coming too near.

"Well, what deh hell yer goin' teh do?" repeated Jimmie's ally. They kept close to him, taunting and leering. They strove to make him attempt the initial blow.

"Keep back, now! Don' crowd me," ominously said Pete.

Again they chorused in contempt. "Oh, hell!"

In a small, tossing group, the three men edged for positions like frigates contemplating battle.

"Well, why deh hell don' yeh try teh t'row us out?" cried Jimmie and his ally with copious sneers.

The bravery of bull-dogs sat upon the faces of the men. Their clenched fists moved like eager weapons.

The allied two jostled the bartender's elbows, glaring at him with feverish eyes and forcing him toward the wall.

Suddenly Pete swore redly. The flash of action gleamed from his eyes. He threw back his arm and aimed a tremendous, lightning-like blow at Jimmie's face. His foot swung a step forward and the weight of his body was behind his fist. Jimmie ducked his head, Bowery-like, with the quickness of a cat. The fierce, answering blows of him and his ally crushed on Pete's bowed head.

The quiet stranger vanished.

The arms of the combatants whirled in the air like flails. The faces of the men, at first flushed to flame-colored anger, now began to fade to the pallor of warriors in the blood and heat of a battle. Their lips curled back and stretched tightly over the gums in ghoul-like grins. Through their white, gripped teeth struggled hoarse whisperings of oaths. Their eyes glittered with murderous fire.

Each head was huddled between its owner's shoulders, and arms were swinging with marvelous rapidity. Feet scraped to and fro with a loud scratching sound upon the sanded floor. Blows left crimson blotches upon pale skin. The curses of the first quarter minute of the fight died away. The breaths of the fighters came wheezingly from their lips and the three chests were straining and heaving. Pete at intervals gave vent to low, labored hisses, that sounded like a desire to kill. Jimmie's ally gibbered at times like a wounded maniac. Jimmie was silent, fighting with the face of a sacrificial priest. The rage of fear shone in all their eyes and their blood-colored fists swirled.

At a tottering moment a blow from Pete's hand struck the ally and he crashed to the floor. He wriggled instantly to his feet and grasping the quiet stranger's beer glass from the bar, hurled it at Pete's head.

High on the wall it burst like a bomb, shivering fragments flying in all directions. Then missiles came to every man's hand. The place had heretofore appeared free of things to throw, but suddenly glass and bottles went singing through the air. They were thrown point blank at bobbing heads. The pyramid of shimmering glasses, that had never been disturbed, changed to cascades as heavy bottles were flung into them. Mirrors splintered to nothing.

The three frothing creatures on the floor buried themselves in a frenzy for blood. There followed in the wake of missiles and fists some unknown prayers, perhaps for death.

The quiet stranger had sprawled very pyrotechnically out on the sidewalk. A laugh ran up and down the avenue for the half of a block.

"Dey've t'rowed a bloke inteh deh street."

People heard the sound of breaking glass and shuffling feet within the saloon and came running. A small group, bending down to look under the bamboo doors, watching the fall of glass, and three pairs of violent legs, changed in a moment to a crowd.

A policeman came charging down the sidewalk and bounced through the doors into the saloon. The crowd bended and surged in absorbing anxiety to see.

Jimmie caught first sight of the on-coming interruption. On his feet he had the same regard for a policeman that, when on his truck, he had for a fire engine. He howled and ran for the side door.

The officer made a terrific advance, club in hand. One comprehensive sweep of the long night stick threw the ally to the floor and forced Pete to a corner. With his disengaged hand he made a furious effort at Jimmie's coattails. Then he regained his balance and paused.

"Well, well, you are a pair of pictures. What in hell yeh been up to?"

Jimmie, with his face drenched in blood, escaped up a side street, pursued a short distance by some of the more law-loving, or excited individuals of the crowd.

Later, from a corner safely dark, he saw the policeman, the ally and the bartender emerge from the saloon. Pete locked the doors and then followed up the avenue in the rear of the crowd-encompassed policeman and his charge.

On first thoughts Jimmie, with his heart throbbing at battle heat, started to go desperately to the rescue of his friend, but he halted.

"Ah, what deh hell?" he demanded of himself.

*Chapter XII*

In a hall of irregular shape sat Pete and Maggie drinking beer. A submissive orchestra dictated to by a spectacled man with frowsy hair and a dress suit, industriously followed the bobs of his head and the waves of his baton. A ballad singer, in a dress of flaming scarlet, sang in the inevitable voice of brass. When she vanished, men seated at the tables near the front applauded loudly, pounding the polished wood with their beer glasses. She returned attired in less gown, and sang again. She received another enthusiastic encore. She reappeared in still less gown and danced. The deafening rumble of glasses and clapping of hands that followed her exit indicated an overwhelming desire to have her come on for the fourth time, but the curiosity of the audience was not gratified.

Maggie was pale. From her eyes had been plucked all look of self-reliance. She leaned with a dependent air toward her companion. She was timid, as if fearing his anger or displeasure. She seemed to beseech tenderness of him.

Pete's air of distinguished valor had grown upon him until it threatened stupendous dimensions. He was infinitely gracious to the girl. It was apparent to her that his condescension was a marvel.

He could appear to strut even while sitting still and he showed that he was a lion of lordly characteristics by the air with which he spat.

With Maggie gazing at him wonderingly, he took pride in commanding the waiters who were, however, indifferent or deaf.

"Hi, you, git a russle[4] on yehs! What deh hell yehs lookin' at? Two more beehs, d'yeh hear?"

He leaned back and critically regarded the person of a girl with a straw-colored wig who upon the stage was flinging her heels in somewhat awkward imitation of a well-known danseuse.[5]

At times Maggie told Pete long confidential tales of her former home life, dwelling upon the escapades of the other members of the family and the difficulties she had to combat in order to obtain a degree of comfort. He responded in tones of philanthropy. He pressed her arm with an air of reassuring proprietorship.

"Dey was damn jays," he said, denouncing the mother and brother.

The sound of the music which, by the efforts of the frowsy-headed leader, drifted to her ears through the smoke-filled atmosphere, made the girl dream. She thought of her former Rum Alley environment and turned to regard Pete's strong protecting fists. She thought of the collar and cuff manufactory and the eternal moan of the proprietor: "What een hell do you sink I pie fife dolla a week for? Play? No, py damn." She contemplated Pete's man-subduing eyes and noted that wealth and prosperity was indicated by his clothes. She imagined a future, rose-tinted, because of its distance from all that she previously had experienced.

As to the present she perceived only vague reasons to be miserable. Her life was Pete's and she considered him worthy of the charge. She would be disturbed by no particular apprehensions, so long as Pete adored her as he now said he did. She did not feel like a bad woman. To her knowledge she had never seen any better.

---

4. Move, hustle (slang).          5. Ballerina.

At times men at other tables regarded the girl furtively. Pete, aware of it, nodded at her and grinned. He felt proud.

"Mag, yer a bloomin' good-looker," he remarked, studying her face through the haze. The men made Maggie fear, but she blushed at Pete's words as it became apparent to her that she was the apple of his eye.

Grey-headed men, wonderfully pathetic in their dissipation, stared at her through clouds. Smooth-cheeked boys, some of them with faces of stone and mouths of sin, not nearly so pathetic as the grey heads, tried to find the girl's eyes in the smoke wreaths. Maggie considered she was not what they thought her. She confined her glances to Pete and the stage.

The orchestra played negro melodies and a versatile drummer pounded, whacked, clattered and scratched on a dozen machines to make noise.

Those glances of the men, shot at Maggie from under half-closed lids, made her tremble. She thought them all to be worse men than Pete.

"Come, let's go," she said.

As they went out Maggie perceived two women seated at a table with some men. They were painted and their cheeks had lost their roundness. As she passed them the girl, with a shrinking movement, drew back her skirts.

## Chapter XIII

Jimmie did not return home for a number of days after the fight with Pete in the saloon. When he did, he approached with extreme caution.

He found his mother raving. Maggie had not returned home. The parent continually wondered how her daughter could come to such a pass. She had never considered Maggie as a pearl dropped unstained into Rum Alley from Heaven, but she could not conceive how it was possible for her daughter to fall so low as to bring disgrace upon her family. She was terrific in denunciation of the girl's wickedness.

The fact that the neighbors talked of it, maddened her. When women came in, and in the course of their conversation casually asked, "Where's Maggie dese days?" the mother shook her fuzzy head at them and appalled them with curses. Cunning hints inviting confidence she rebuffed with violence.

"An' wid all deh bringin' up she had, how could she?" moaningly she asked of her son. "Wid all deh talkin' wid her I did an' deh t'ings I tol' her to remember? When a girl is bringed up deh way I bringed up Maggie, how kin she go teh deh devil?"

Jimmie was transfixed by these questions. He could not conceive how under the circumstances his mother's daughter and his sister could have been so wicked.

His mother took a drink from a squdgy[6] bottle that sat on the table. She continued her lament.

"She had a bad heart, dat girl did, Jimmie. She was wicked teh deh heart an' we never knowed it."

Jimmie nodded, admitting the fact.

"We lived in deh same house wid her an' I brought her up an' we never knowed how bad she was."

Jimmie nodded again.

6. Squat.

"Wid a home like dis an' a mudder like me, she went teh deh bad," cried the mother, raising her eyes.

One day, Jimmie came home, sat down in a chair and began to wriggle about with a new and strange nervousness. At last he spoke shamefacedly.

"Well, look-a-here, dis t'ing queers us! See? We're queered! An' maybe it 'ud be better if I—well, I t'ink I kin look 'er up an'—maybe it 'ud be better if I fetched her home an'—"

The mother started from her chair and broke forth into a storm of passionate anger.

"What! Let 'er come an' sleep under deh same roof wid her mudder agin! Oh, yes, I will, won't I? Sure? Shame on yehs, Jimmie Johnson, fer sayin' such a t'ing teh yer own mudder—teh yer own mudder! Little did I t'ink when yehs was a babby playin' about me feet dat ye'd grow up teh say sech a t'ing teh yer mudder—yer own mudder. I never taut—"

Sobs choked her and interrupted her reproaches.

"Dere ain't nottin' teh raise sech hell about," said Jimmie. "I on'y says it 'ud be better if we keep dis t'ing dark, see? It queers us! See?"

His mother laughed a laugh that seemed to ring through the city and be echoed and re-echoed by countless other laughs. "Oh, yes, I will, won't I! Sure!"

"Well, yeh must take me fer a damn fool," said Jimmie, indignant at his mother for mocking him. "I didn't say we'd make 'er inteh a little tin angel, ner nottin', but deh way it is now she can queer us! Don' che see?"

"Aye, she'll git tired of deh life atter a while an' den she'll wanna be a-comin' home, won' she, deh beast! I'll let 'er in den, won' I?"

"Well, I didn' mean none of dis prod'gal bus'ness anyway," explained Jimmie.

"It wasn't no prod'gal dauter, yeh damn fool," said the mother. "It was prod'gal son,[7] anyhow."

"I know dat," said Jimmie.

For a time they sat in silence. The mother's eyes gloated on a scene her imagination could call before her. Her lips were set in a vindictive smile.

"Aye, she'll cry, won' she, an' carry on, an' tell how Pete, or some odder feller, beats 'er an' she'll say she's sorry an' all dat an' she ain't happy, she ain't, an' she wants to come home agin, she does."

With grim humor, the mother imitated the possible wailing notes of the daughter's voice.

"Den I'll take 'er in, won't I, deh beast. She kin cry 'er two eyes out on deh stones of deh street before I'll dirty deh place wid her. She abused an' ill-treated her own mudder—her own mudder what loved her an' she'll never git anodder chance dis side of hell."

Jimmie thought he had a great idea of women's frailty, but he could not understand why any of his kin should be victims.

"Damn her," he fervidly said.

Again he wondered vaguely if some of the women of his acquaintance had brothers. Nevertheless, his mind did not for an instant confuse himself with those brothers nor his sister with theirs. After the mother had, with great difficulty, suppressed the neighbors, she went among them and proclaimed her

7. The biblical parable of the Prodigal Son is found in Luke 15.11–32.

grief. "May Gawd forgive dat girl," was her continual cry. To attentive ears she recited the whole length and breadth of her woes.

"I bringed 'er up deh way a dauter oughta be bringed up an' dis is how she served me! She went teh deh devil deh first chance she got! May Gawd forgive her."

When arrested for drunkenness she used the story of her daughter's downfall with telling effect upon the police-justices. Finally one of them said to her, peering down over his spectacles: "Mary, the records of this and other courts show that you are the mother of forty-two daughters who have been ruined. The case is unparalleled in the annals of this court, and this court thinks—"

The mother went through life shedding large tears of sorrow. Her red face was a picture of agony.

Of course Jimmie publicly damned his sister that he might appear on a higher social plane. But, arguing with himself, stumbling about in ways that he knew not, he, once, almost came to a conclusion that his sister would have been more firmly good had she better known why. However, he felt that he could not hold such a view. He threw it hastily aside.

## Chapter XIV

In a hilarious hall there were twenty-eight tables and twenty-eight women and a crowd of smoking men.[8] Valiant noise was made on a stage at the end of the hall by an orchestra composed of men who looked as if they had just happened in. Soiled waiters ran to and fro, swooping down like hawks on the unwary in the throng; clattering along the aisles with trays covered with glasses; stumbling over women's skirts and charging two prices for everything but beer, all with a swiftness that blurred the view of the cocoanut palms and dusty monstrosities painted upon the walls of the room. A bouncer, with an immense load of business upon his hands, plunged about in the crowd, dragging bashful strangers to prominent chairs, ordering waiters here and there and quarreling furiously with men who wanted to sing with the orchestra.

The usual smoke cloud was present, but so dense that heads and arms seemed entangled in it. The rumble of conversation was replaced by a roar. Plenteous oaths heaved through the air. The room rang with the shrill voices of women bubbling o'er with drink-laughter. The chief element in the music of the orchestra was speed. The musicians played in intent fury. A woman was singing and smiling upon the stage, but no one took notice of her. The rate at which the piano, cornet and violins were going, seemed to impart wildness to the half-drunken crowd. Beer glasses were emptied at a gulp and conversation became a rapid chatter. The smoke eddied and swirled like a shadowy river hurrying toward some unseen falls. Pete and Maggie entered the hall and took chairs at a table near the door. The woman who was seated there made an attempt to occupy Pete's attention and, failing, went away.

Three weeks had passed since the girl had left home. The air of spaniel-like dependence had been magnified and showed its direct effect in the peculiar off-handedness and ease of Pete's ways toward her.

8. Probably a concert saloon, a working-class establishment usually found in basements and providing coarse music and entertainment. Crane's placing a woman at every table suggests that the waitresses who drank with customers received a percentage on the drinks they sold.

She followed Pete's eyes with hers, anticipating with smiles gracious looks from him.

A woman of brilliance and audacity, accompanied by a mere boy, came into the place and took seats near them.

At once Pete sprang to his feet, his face beaming with glad surprise.

"By Gawd, there's Nellie," he cried.

He went over to the table and held out an eager hand to the woman.

"Why, hello, Pete, me boy, how are you," said she, giving him her fingers.

Maggie took instant note of the woman. She perceived that her black dress fitted her to perfection. Her linen collar and cuffs were spotless. Tan gloves were stretched over her well-shaped hands. A hat of a prevailing fashion perched jauntily upon her dark hair. She wore no jewelry and was painted with no apparent paint. She looked clear-eyed through the stares of the men.

"Sit down, and call your lady-friend over," she said cordially to Pete. At his beckoning Maggie came and sat between Pete and the mere boy.

"I thought yeh were gone away fer good," began Pete, at once. "When did yeh git back? How did dat Buff'lo bus'ness turn out?"

The woman shrugged her shoulders. "Well, he didn't have as many stamps[9] as he tried to make out, so I shook him, that's all."

"Well, I'm glad teh see yehs back in deh city," said Pete, with awkward gallantry.

He and the woman entered into a long conversation, exchanging reminiscences of days together. Maggie sat still, unable to formulate an intelligent sentence upon the conversation and painfully aware of it.

She saw Pete's eyes sparkle as he gazed upon the handsome stranger. He listened smilingly to all she said. The woman was familiar with all his affairs, asked him about mutual friends, and knew the amount of his salary.

She paid no attention to Maggie, looking toward her once or twice and apparently seeing the wall beyond.

The mere boy was sulky. In the beginning he had welcomed with acclamations the additions.

"Let's all have a drink! What'll you take, Nell? And you, Miss what's-your-name. Have a drink, Mr.———, you, I mean."

He had shown a sprightly desire to do the talking for the company and tell all about his family. In a loud voice he declaimed on various topics. He assumed a patronizing air toward Pete. As Maggie was silent, he paid no attention to her. He made a great show of lavishing wealth upon the woman of brilliance and audacity.

"Do keep still, Freddie! You gibber like an ape, dear," said the woman to him. She turned away and devoted her attention to Pete.

"We'll have many a good time together again, eh?"

"Sure, Mike," said Pete, enthusiastic at once.

"Say," whispered she, leaning forward, "let's go over to Billie's and have a heluva time."

"Well, it's dis way! See?" said Pete. "I got dis lady frien' here."

"Oh, t'hell with her," argued the woman.

Pete appeared disturbed.

"All right," said she, nodding her head at him. "All right for you! We'll see the next time you ask me to go anywheres with you."

---

9. Money, especially paper money (slang).

Pete squirmed.

"Say," he said, beseechingly, "come wid me a minit an' I'll tell yer why."

The woman waved her hand.

"Oh, that's all right, you needn't explain, you know. You wouldn't come merely because you wouldn't come, that's all there is of it."

To Pete's visible distress she turned to the mere boy, bringing him speedily from a terrific rage. He had been debating whether it would be the part of a man to pick a quarrel with Pete, or would he be justified in striking him savagely with his beer glass without warning. But he recovered himself when the woman turned to renew her smilings. He beamed upon her with an expression that was somewhat tipsy and inexpressibly tender.

"Say, shake that Bowery jay," requested he, in a loud whisper.

"Freddie, you are so droll," she replied.

Pete reached forward and touched the woman on the arm.

"Come out a minit while I tells yeh why I can't go wid yer. Yer doin' me dirt, Nell! I never taut ye'd do me dirt, Nell. Come on, will yer?" He spoke in tones of injury.

"Why, I don't see why I should be interested in your explanations," said the woman, with a coldness that seemed to reduce Pete to a pulp.

His eyes pleaded with her. "Come out a minit while I tells yeh."

The woman nodded slightly at Maggie and the mere boy, " 'Scuse me."

The mere boy interrupted his loving smile and turned a shrivelling glare upon Pete. His boyish countenance flushed and he spoke, in a whine, to the woman:

"Oh, I say, Nellie, this ain't a square deal, you know. You aren't goin' to leave me and go off with that duffer, are you? I should think—"

"Why, you dear boy, of course I'm not," cried the woman, affectionately. She bended over and whispered in his ear. He smiled again and settled in his chair as if resolved to wait patiently.

As the woman walked down between the rows of tables, Pete was at her shoulder talking earnestly, apparently in explanation. The woman waved her hands with studied airs of indifference. The doors swung behind them, leaving Maggie and the mere boy seated at the table.

Maggie was dazed. She could dimly perceive that something stupendous had happened. She wondered why Pete saw fit to remonstrate with the woman, pleading for forgiveness with his eyes. She thought she noted an air of submission about her leonine Pete. She was astounded.

The mere boy occupied himself with cock-tails and a cigar. He was tranquilly silent for half an hour. Then he bestirred himself and spoke.

"Well," he said, sighing, "I knew this was the way it would be." There was another stillness. The mere boy seemed to be musing.

"She was pulling m'leg. That's the whole amount of it," he said, suddenly. "It's a bloomin' shame the way that girl does. Why, I've spent over two dollars in drinks to-night. And she goes off with that plug-ugly who looks as if he had been hit in the face with a coin-die.[1] I call it rocky treatment for a fellah like me. Here, waiter, bring me a cock-tail and make it damned strong."

Maggie made no reply. She was watching the doors. "It's a mean piece of business," complained the mere boy. He explained to her how amazing it was that anybody should treat him in such a manner. "But I'll get square with her,

1. Metal device for coining money.

you bet. She won't get far ahead of yours truly, you know," he added, winking. "I'll tell her plainly that it was bloomin' mean business. And she won't come it over me with any of her 'now-Freddie-dears.' She thinks my name is Freddie, you know, but of course it ain't. I always tell these people some name like that, because if they got onto your right name they might use it sometime. Understand? Oh, they don't fool me much."

Maggie was paying no attention, being intent upon the doors. The mere boy relapsed into a period of gloom, during which he exterminated a number of cock-tails with a determined air, as if replying defiantly to fate. He occasionally broke forth into sentences composed of invectives joined together in a long string.

The girl was still staring at the doors. After a time the mere boy began to see cobwebs just in front of his nose. He spurred himself into being agreeable and insisted upon her having a charlotte-russe[2] and a glass of beer.

"They's gone," he remarked, "they's gone." He looked at her through the smoke wreaths. "Shay, lil' girl, we mightish well make bes' of it. You ain't such bad-lookin' girl, y'know. Not half bad. Can't come up to Nell, though. No, can't do it! Well, I should shay not! Nell fine-lookin' girl! F—i—n—ine. You look damn bad longsider her, but by y'self ain't so bad. Have to do anyhow. Nell gone. On'y you left. Not half bad, though."

Maggie stood up.

"I'm going home," she said.

The mere boy started.

"Eh? What? Home," he cried, struck with amazement. "I beg pardon, did hear say home?"

"I'm going home," she repeated.

"Great Gawd, what hava struck," demanded the mere boy of himself, stupefied.

In a semi-comatose state he conducted her on board an up-town car, ostentatiously paid her fare, leered kindly at her through the rear window and fell off the steps.

## Chapter XV

A forlorn woman went along a lighted avenue. The street was filled with people desperately bound on missions. An endless crowd darted at the elevated station stairs and the horse cars were thronged with owners of bundles.

The pace of the forlorn woman was slow. She was apparently searching for some one. She loitered near the doors of saloons and watched men emerge from them. She scanned furtively the faces in the rushing stream of pedestrians. Hurrying men, bent on catching some boat or train, jostled her elbows, failing to notice her, their thoughts fixed on distant dinners.

The forlorn woman had a peculiar face. Her smile was no smile. But when in repose her features had a shadowy look that was like a sardonic grin, as if some one had sketched with cruel forefinger indelible lines about her mouth.

Jimmie came strolling up the avenue. The woman encountered him with an aggrieved air.

"Oh, Jimmie, I've been lookin' all over fer yehs—," she began.

2. Sponge cake with whipped cream or custard filling.

Jimmie made an impatient gesture and quickened his pace.

"Ah, don't bodder me! Good Gawd!" he said, with the savageness of a man whose life is pestered.

The woman followed him along the sidewalk in somewhat the manner of a suppliant.

"But, Jimmie," she said, "yehs told me ye'd—"

Jimmie turned upon her fiercely as if resolved to make a last stand for comfort and peace.

"Say, fer Gawd's sake, Hattie, don' foller me from one end of deh city teh deh odder. Let up, will yehs! Give me a minute's res', can't yehs? Yehs makes me tired, allus taggin' me. See? Ain' yehs got no sense? Do yehs want people teh get onto me? Go chase yerself, fer Gawd's sake."

The woman stepped closer and laid her fingers on his arm. "But, look-a-here—"

Jimmie snarled. "Oh, go teh hell."

He darted into the front door of a convenient saloon and a moment later came out into the shadows that surrounded the side door. On the brilliantly lighted avenue he perceived the forlorn woman dodging about like a scout. Jimmie laughed with an air of relief and went away.

When he arrived home he found his mother clamoring. Maggie had returned. She stood shivering beneath the torrent of her mother's wrath.

"Well, I'm damned," said Jimmie in greeting.

His mother, tottering about the room, pointed a quivering fore-finger.

"Lookut her, Jimmie, lookut her. Dere's yer sister, boy. Dere's yer sister. Lookut her! Lookut her!"

She screamed in scoffing laughter.

The girl stood in the middle of the room. She edged about as if unable to find a place on the floor to put her feet.

"Ha, ha, ha," bellowed the mother. "Dere she stands! Ain' she purty? Lookut her! Ain' she sweet, deh beast? Lookut her! Ha, ha, lookut her!"

She lurched forward and put her red and seamed hands upon her daughter's face. She bent down and peered keenly up into the eyes of the girl.

"Oh, she's jes' dessame as she ever was, ain' she? She's her mudder's purty darlin' yit, ain' she? Lookut her, Jimmie! Come here, fer Gawd's sake, and lookut her."

The loud, tremendous sneering of the mother brought the denizens of the Rum Alley tenement to their doors. Women came in the hallways. Children scurried to and fro.

"What's up? Dat Johnson party on anudder tear?"

"Naw! Young Mag's come home!"

"Deh hell yeh say?"

Through the open doors curious eyes stared in at Maggie. Children ventured into the room and ogled her, as if they formed the front row at a theatre. Women, without, bended toward each other and whispered, nodding their heads with airs of profound philosophy. A baby, overcome with curiosity concerning this object at which all were looking, sidled forward and touched her dress, cautiously, as if investigating a red-hot stove. Its mother's voice rang out like a warning trumpet. She rushed forward and grabbed her child, casting a terrible look of indignation at the girl.

Maggie's mother paced to and fro, addressing the doorful of eyes, expounding like a glib showman at a museum. Her voice rang through the building.

"Dere she stands," she cried, wheeling suddenly and pointing with dramatic finger. "Dere she stands! Lookut her! Ain' she a dindy? An' she was so good as to come home teh her mudder, she was! Ain' she a beaut'? Ain' she a dindy? Fer Gawd's sake!"

The jeering cries ended in another burst of shrill laughter.

The girl seemed to awaken. "Jimmie—"

He drew hastily back from her.

"Well, now, yer a hell of a t'ing, ain' yeh?" he said, his lips curling in scorn. Radiant virtue sat upon his brow and his repelling hands expressed horror of contamination.

Maggie turned and went.

The crowd at the door fell back precipitately. A baby falling down in front of the door, wrenched a scream like a wounded animal from its mother. Another woman sprang forward and picked it up, with a chivalrous air, as if rescuing a human being from an on-coming express train.

As the girl passed down through the hall, she went before open doors framing more eyes strangely microscopic, and sending broad beams of inquisitive light into the darkness of her path. On the second floor she met the gnarled old woman who possessed the music box.

"So," she cried, " 'ere yehs are back again, are yehs? An' dey've kicked yehs out? Well, come in an' stay wid me teh-night. I ain' got no moral standin'."

From above came an unceasing babble of tongues, over all of which rang the mother's derisive laughter.

### Chapter XVI

Pete did not consider that he had ruined Maggie. If he had thought that her soul could never smile again, he would have believed the mother and brother, who were pyrotechnic over the affair, to be responsible for it.

Besides, in his world, souls did not insist upon being able to smile. "What deh hell?"

He felt a trifle entangled. It distressed him. Revelations and scenes might bring upon him the wrath of the owner of the saloon, who insisted upon respectability of an advanced type.

"What deh hell do dey wanna raise such a smoke about it fer?" demanded he of himself, disgusted with the attitude of the family. He saw no necessity for anyone's losing their equilibrium merely because their sister or their daughter had stayed away from home.

Searching about in his mind for possible reasons for their conduct, he came upon the conclusion that Maggie's motives were correct, but that the two others wished to snare him. He felt pursued.

The woman of brilliance and audacity whom he had met in the hilarious hall showed a disposition to ridicule him.

"A little pale thing with no spirit," she said. "Did you note the expression of her eyes? There was something in them about pumpkin pie and virtue. That is a peculiar way the left corner of her mouth has of twitching, isn't it? Dear, dear, my cloud-compelling Pete, what are you coming to?"

Pete asserted at once that he never was very much interested in the girl. The woman interrupted him, laughing.

"Oh, it's not of the slightest consequence to me, my dear young man. You needn't draw maps for my benefit. Why should I be concerned about it?"

But Pete continued with his explanations. If he was laughed at for his tastes in women, he felt obliged to say that they were only temporary or indifferent ones.

The morning after Maggie had departed from home, Pete stood behind the bar. He was immaculate in white jacket and apron and his hair was plastered over his brow with infinite correctness. No customers were in the place. Pete was twisting his napkined fist slowly in a beer glass, softly whistling to himself and occasionally holding the object of his attention between his eyes and a few weak beams of sunlight that had found their way over the thick screens and into the shaded room.

With lingering thoughts of the woman of brilliance and audacity, the bartender raised his head and stared through the varying cracks between the swaying bamboo doors. Suddenly the whistling pucker faded from his lips. He saw Maggie walking slowly past. He gave a great start, fearing for the previously-mentioned eminent respectability of the place.

He threw a swift, nervous glance about him, all at once feeling guilty. No one was in the room.

He went hastily over to the side door. Opening it and looking out, he perceived Maggie standing, as if undecided, on the corner. She was searching the place with her eyes.

As she turned her face toward him Pete beckoned to her hurriedly, intent upon returning with speed to a position behind the bar and to the atmosphere of respectability upon which the proprietor insisted.

Maggie came to him, the anxious look disappearing from her face and a smile wreathing her lips.

"Oh, Pete—," she began brightly.

The bartender made a violent gesture of impatience.

"Oh, my Gawd," cried he, vehemently. "What deh hell do yeh wanna hang aroun' here fer? Do yeh wanna git me inteh trouble?" he demanded with an air of injury.

Astonishment swept over the girl's features. "Why, Pete! yehs tol' me—"

Pete glanced profound irritation. His countenance reddened with the anger of a man whose respectability is being threatened.

"Say, yehs makes me tired. See? What deh hell deh yeh wanna tag aroun' atter me fer? Yeh'll git me inteh trouble wid deh ol' man an' dey'll be hell teh pay! If he sees a woman roun' here he'll go crazy an' I'll lose me job! See? Ain' yehs got no sense? Don' be allus bodderin' me. See? Yer brudder come in here an' raised hell an' deh ol' man hada put up fer it! An' now I'm done! See? I'm done."

The girl's eyes stared into his face. "Pete, don' yeh remem—"

"Oh, hell," interrupted Pete, anticipating.

The girl seemed to have a struggle with herself. She was apparently bewildered and could not find speech. Finally she asked in a low voice: "But where kin I go?"

The question exasperated Pete beyond the powers of endurance. It was a direct attempt to give him some responsibility in a matter that did not concern him. In his indignation he volunteered information.

"Oh, go teh hell," cried he. He slammed the door furiously and returned, with an air of relief, to his respectability.

Maggie went away.

She wandered aimlessly for several blocks. She stopped once and asked aloud a question of herself: "Who?"

A man who was passing near her shoulder, humorously took the questioning word as intended for him.

"Eh? What? Who? Nobody! I didn't say anything," he laughingly said, and continued his way.

Soon the girl discovered that if she walked with such apparent aimlessness, some men looked at her with calculating eyes. She quickened her step, frightened. As a protection, she adopted a demeanor of intentness as if going somewhere.

After a time she left rattling avenues and passed between rows of houses with sternness and stolidity stamped upon their features. She hung her head for she felt their eyes grimly upon her.

Suddenly she came upon a stout gentleman in a silk hat and a chaste black coat, whose decorous row of buttons reached from his chin to his knees.[3] The girl had heard of the Grace of God and she decided to approach this man.

His beaming, chubby face was a picture of benevolence and kindheartedness. His eyes shone good-will.

But as the girl timidly accosted him, he gave a convulsive movement and saved his respectability by a vigorous side-step. He did not risk it to save a soul. For how was he to know that there was a soul before him that needed saving?

### Chapter XVII

Upon a wet evening, several months after the last chapter, two interminable rows of cars, pulled by slipping horses, jangled along a prominent side-street. A dozen cabs, with coat-enshrouded drivers, clattered to and fro. Electric lights, whirring softly, shed a blurred radiance. A flower dealer, his feet tapping impatiently, his nose and his wares glistening with rain-drops, stood behind an array of roses and chrysanthemums. Two or three theatres emptied a crowd upon the storm-swept pavements. Men pulled their hats over their eye-brows and raised their collars to their ears. Women shrugged impatient shoulders in their warm cloaks and stopped to arrange their skirts for a walk through the storm. People having been comparatively silent for two hours burst into a roar of conversation, their hearts still kindling from the glowings of the stage.

The pavements became tossing seas of umbrellas. Men stepped forth to hail cabs or cars, raising their fingers in varied forms of polite request or imperative demand. An endless procession wended toward elevated stations. An atmosphere of pleasure and prosperity seemed to hang over the throng, born, perhaps, of good clothes and of having just emerged from a place of forgetfulness.

In the mingled light and gloom of an adjacent park, a handful of wet wanderers, in attitudes of chronic dejection, was scattered among the benches.

A girl of the painted cohorts of the city went along the street. She threw changing glances at men who passed her, giving smiling invitations to men of

3. A clergyman.

rural or untaught pattern and usually seeming sedately unconscious of the men with a metropolitan seal upon their faces.

Crossing glittering avenues, she went into the throng emerging from the places of forgetfulness. She hurried forward through the crowd as if intent upon reaching a distant home, bending forward in her handsome cloak, daintily lifting her skirts and picking for her well-shod feet the dryer spots upon the pavements.

The restless doors of saloons, clashing to and fro, disclosed animated rows of men before bars and hurrying barkeepers.

A concert hall gave to the street faint sounds of swift, machinelike music, as if a group of phantom musicians were hastening.

A tall young man, smoking a cigarette with a sublime air, strolled near the girl. He had on evening dress, a moustache, a chrysanthemum, and a look of ennui, all of which he kept carefully under his eye. Seeing the girl walk on as if such a young man as he was not in existence, he looked back transfixed with interest. He stared glassily for a moment, but gave a slight convulsive start when he discerned that she was neither new, Parisian, nor theatrical. He wheeled about hastily and turned his stare into the air, like a sailor with a search-light.

A stout gentleman, with pompous and philanthropic whiskers, went stolidly by, the broad of his back sneering at the girl.

A belated man in business clothes, and in haste to catch a car, bounced against her shoulder. "Hi, there, Mary, I beg your pardon! Brace up, old girl." He grasped her arm to steady her, and then was away running down the middle of the street.

The girl walked on out of the realm of restaurants and saloons. She passed more glittering avenues and went into darker blocks than those where the crowd travelled.

A young man in light overcoat and derby hat received a glance shot keenly from the eyes of the girl. He stopped and looked at her, thrusting his hands in his pockets and making a mocking smile curl his lips. "Come, now, old lady," he said, "you don't mean to tell me that you sized me up for a farmer?"

A laboring man marched along with bundles under his arms. To her remarks, he replied: "It's a fine evenin', ain't it?"

She smiled squarely into the face of a boy who was hurrying by with his hands buried in his overcoat, his blonde locks bobbing on his youthful temples, and a cheery smile of unconcern upon his lips. He turned his head and smiled back at her, waving his hands.

"Not this eve—some other eve!"

A drunken man, reeling in her pathway, began to roar at her. "I ain' ga no money, dammit," he shouted, in a dismal voice. He lurched on up the street, wailing to himself, "Dammit, I ain' ga no money. Damn ba' luck. Ain' ga no more money."

The girl went into gloomy districts near the river, where the tall black factories shut in the street and only occasional broad beams of light fell across the pavements from saloons. In front of one of these places, from whence came the sound of a violin vigorously scraped, the patter of feet on boards and the ring of loud laughter, there stood a man with blotched features.

"Ah, there," said the girl.

"I've got a date," said the man.

Further on in the darkness she met a ragged being with shifting, blood-shot eyes and grimy hands. "Ah, what deh hell? T'ink I'm a millionaire?"

She went into the blackness of the final block. The shutters of the tall buildings were closed like grim lips. The structures seemed to have eyes that looked over her, beyond her, at other things. Afar off the lights of the avenues glittered as if from an impossible distance. Street car bells jingled with a sound of merriment.

When almost to the river the girl saw a great figure. On going forward she perceived it to be a huge fat man in torn and greasy garments. His grey hair straggled down over his forehead. His small, bleared eyes, sparkling from amidst great rolls of red fat, swept eagerly over the girl's upturned face. He laughed, his brown, disordered teeth gleaming under a grey, grizzled moustache from which beer-drops dripped. His whole body gently quivered and shook like that of a dead jelly fish. Chuckling and leering, he followed the girl of the crimson legions.

At their feet the river appeared a deathly black hue. Some hidden factory sent up a yellow glare, that lit for a moment the waters lapping oilily against timbers. The varied sounds of life, made joyous by distance and seeming unapproachableness, came faintly and died away to a silence.

## Chapter XVIII

In a partitioned-off section of a saloon sat a man with a half dozen women, gleefully laughing, hovering about him. The man had arrived at that stage of drunkenness where affection is felt for the universe.

"I'm good f'ler, girls," he said, convincingly. "I'm damn good f'ler. An'body treats me right, I allus trea's zem right! See?"

The women nodded their heads approvingly. "To be sure," they cried in hearty chorus. "You're the kind of a man we like, Pete. You're outa sight! What yeh goin' to buy this time, dear?"

"An't'ing yehs wants, damn it," said the man in an abandonment of good will. His countenance shone with the true spirit of benevolence. He was in the proper mode of missionaries. He would have fraternized with obscure Hottentots.[4] And above all, he was over-whelmed in tenderness for his friends, who were all illustrious.

"An't'ing yehs wants, damn it," repeated he, waving his hands with beneficent recklessness. "I'm good f'ler, girls, an' if an'body treats me right I— here," called he through an open door to a waiter, "bring girls drinks, damn it. What 'ill yehs have, girls? An't'ing yehs wants, damn it!"

The waiter glanced in with the disgusted look of the man who serves intoxicants for the man who takes too much of them. He nodded his head shortly at the order from each individual, and went.

"Damn it," said the man, "we're havin' heluva time. I like you girls! Damn'd if I don't! Yer right sort! See?"

He spoke at length and with feeling, concerning the excellencies of his assembled friends.

"Don' try pull man's leg, but have a heluva time! Das right! Das way teh do! Now, if I sawght yehs tryin' work me fer drinks, wouldn' buy damn t'ing! But

4. A South African people.

yer right sort, damn it! Yehs know how ter treat a f'ler, an' I stays by yehs 'til spen' las' cent! Das right! I'm good f'ler an' I knows when an'body treats me right!"

Between the times of the arrival and departure of the waiter, the man discoursed to the women on the tender regard he felt for all living things. He laid stress upon the purity of his motives in all dealings with men in the world and spoke of the fervor of his friendship for those who were amiable. Tears welled slowly from his eyes. His voice quavered when he spoke to them.

Once when the waiter was about to depart with an empty tray, the man drew a coin from his pocket and held it forth.

"Here," said he, quite magnificently, "here's quar'."

The waiter kept his hands on his tray.

"I don' want yer money," he said.

The other put forth the coin with tearful insistence.

"Here, damn it," cried he, "tak't! Yer damn goo' f'ler an' I wan' yehs tak't!"

"Come, come, now," said the waiter, with the sullen air of a man who is forced into giving advice. "Put yer mon in yer pocket! Yer loaded an' yehs on'y makes a damn fool of yerself."

As the latter passed out of the door the man turned pathetically to the women.

"He don' know I'm damn goo' f'ler," cried he, dismally.

"Never you mind, Pete, dear," said a woman of brilliance and audacity, laying her hand with great affection upon his arm. "Never you mind, old boy! We'll stay by you, dear!"

"Das ri'," cried the man, his face lighting up at the soothing tones of the woman's voice. "Das ri', I'm damn goo' f'ler an' w'en anyone trea's me ri', I treats zem ri'! Shee!"

"Sure!" cried the women. "And we're not goin' back on you, old man."

The man turned appealing eyes to the woman of brilliance and audacity. He felt that if he could be convicted of a contemptible action he would die.

"Shay, Nell, damn it, I allus trea's yehs shquare, didn' I? I allus been goo' f'ler wi' yehs, ain't I, Nell?"

"Sure you have, Pete," assented the woman. She delivered an oration to her companions. "Yessir, that's a fact. Pete's a square fellah, he is. He never goes back on a friend. He's the right kind an' we stay by him, don't we, girls?"

"Sure," they exclaimed. Looking lovingly at him they raised their glasses and drank his health.

"Girlsh," said the man, beseechingly, "I allus trea's yehs ri', didn' I? I'm goo' f'ler, ain' I, girlsh?"

"Sure," again they chorused.

"Well," said he finally, "le's have nozzer drink, zen."

"That's right," hailed a woman, "that's right. Yer no bloomin' jay! Yer spends yer money like a man. Dat's right."

The man pounded the table with his quivering fists.

"Yessir," he cried, with deep earnestness, as if someone disputed him. "I'm damn goo' f'ler, an' w'en anyone trea's me ri', I allus trea's—le's have nozzer drink."

He began to beat the wood with his glass.

"Shay," howled he, growing suddenly impatient. As the waiter did not then come, the man swelled with wrath.

"Shay," howled he again.

The waiter appeared at the door.

"Bringsh drinksh," said the man.

The waiter disappeared with the orders.

"Zat f'ler damn fool," cried the man. "He insul' me! I'm ge'man! Can' stan' be insul'! I'm goin' lickim when comes!"

"No, no," cried the women, crowding about and trying to subdue him. "He's all right! He didn't mean anything! Let it go! He's a good fellah!"

"Din' he insul' me?" asked the man earnestly.

"No," said they. "Of course he didn't! He's all right!"

"Sure he didn' insul' me?" demanded the man, with deep anxiety in his voice.

"No, no! We know him! He's a good fellah. He didn't mean anything."

"Well, zen," said the man, resolutely, "I'm go' 'pol'gize!"

When the waiter came, the man struggled to the middle of the floor.

"Girlsh shed you insul' me! I shay damn lie! I 'pol'gize!"

"All right," said the waiter.

The man sat down. He felt a sleepy but strong desire to straighten things out and have a perfect understanding with everybody.

"Nell, I allus trea's yeh shquare, din' I? Yeh likes me, don' yehs, Nell? I'm goo' f'ler?"

"Sure," said the woman of brilliance and audacity.

"Yeh knows I'm stuck on yehs, don' yehs, Nell?"

"Sure," she repeated, carelessly.

Overwhelmed by a spasm of drunken adoration, he drew two or three bills from his pocket, and, with the trembling fingers of an offering priest, laid them on the table before the woman.

"Yehs knows, damn it, yehs kin have all got, 'cause I'm stuck on yehs, Nell, damn't, I—I'm stuck on yehs, Nell—buy drinksh—damn't—we're havin' heluva time—w'en anyone trea's me ri'—I—damn't, Nell—we're havin' heluva—time."

Shortly he went to sleep with his swollen face fallen forward on his chest.

The women drank and laughed, not heeding the slumbering man in the corner. Finally he lurched forward and fell groaning to the floor.

The women screamed in disgust and drew back their skirts.

"Come ahn," cried one, starting up angrily, "let's get out of here."

The woman of brilliance and audacity stayed behind, taking up the bills and stuffing them into a deep, irregularly-shaped pocket. A guttural snore from the recumbent man caused her to turn and look down at him.

She laughed. "What a damn fool," she said, and went.

The smoke from the lamps settled heavily down in the little compartment, obscuring the way out. The smell of oil, stifling in its intensity, pervaded the air. The wine from an overturned glass dripped softly down upon the blotches on the man's neck.

## Chapter XIX

In a room a woman sat at a table eating like a fat monk in a picture.

A soiled, unshaven man pushed open the door and entered.

"Well," said he, "Mag's dead."

"What?" said the woman, her mouth filled with bread.

"Mag's dead," repeated the man.

"Deh hell she is," said the woman. She continued her meal. When she finished her coffee she began to weep.

"I kin remember when her two feet was no bigger dan yer t'umb, and she weared worsted boots," moaned she.

"Well, whata dat?" said the man.

"I kin remember when she weared worsted boots," she cried.

The neighbors began to gather in the hall, staring in at the weeping woman as if watching the contortions of a dying dog. A dozen women entered and lamented with her. Under their busy hands the rooms took on that appalling appearance of neatness and order with which death is greeted.

Suddenly the door opened and a woman in a black gown rushed in with outstretched arms. "Ah, poor Mary," she cried, and tenderly embraced the moaning one.

"Ah, what ter'ble affliction is dis," continued she. Her vocabulary was derived from mission churches. "Me poor Mary, how I feel fer yehs! Ah, what a ter'ble affliction is a disobed'ent chil'."

Her good, motherly face was wet with tears. She trembled in eagerness to express her sympathy. The mourner sat with bowed head, rocking her body heavily to and fro, and crying out in a high, strained voice that sounded like a dirge on some forlorn pipe.

"I kin remember when she weared worsted boots an' her two feets was no bigger dan yer t'umb an' she weared worsted boots, Miss Smith," she cried, raising her streaming eyes.

Ah, me poor Mary," sobbed the woman in black. With low, coddling cries, she sank on her knees by the mourner's chair, and put her arms about her. The other women began to groan in different keys.

"Yer poor misguided chil' is gone now, Mary, an' let us hope it's fer deh bes'. Yeh'll fergive her now, Mary, won't yehs, dear, all her disobed'ence? All her t'ankless behavior to her mudder an' all her badness? She's gone where her ter'ble sins will be judged."

The woman in black raised her face and paused. The inevitable sunlight came streaming in at the windows and shed ghastly cheerfulness upon the faded hues of the room. Two or three of the spectators were sniffling, and one was loudly weeping. The mourner arose and staggered into the other room. In a moment she emerged with a pair of faded baby shoes held in the hollow of her hand.

"I kin remember when she used to wear dem," cried she. The women burst anew into cries as if they had all been stabbed. The mourner turned to the soiled and unshaven man.

"Jimmie, boy, go git yer sister! Go git yer sister an' we'll put deh boots on her feets!"

"Dey won't fit her now, yeh damn fool," said the man.

"Go git yer sister, Jimmie," shrieked the woman, confronting him fiercely.

The man swore sullenly. He went over to a corner and slowly began to put on his coat. He took his hat and went out, with a dragging, reluctant step.

The woman in black came forward and again besought the mourner.

"Yeh'll fergive her, Mary! Yeh'll fergive yer bad, bad chil'! Her life was a curse an' her days were black an' yeh'll fergive yer bad girl? She's gone where her sins will be judged."

"She's gone where her sins will be judged," cried the other women, like a choir at a funeral.

"Deh Lord gives and deh Lord takes away," said the woman in black, raising her eyes to the sunbeams.

"Deh Lord gives and deh Lord takes away," responded the others.

"Yeh'll fergive her, Mary!" pleaded the woman in black. The mourner essayed to speak but her voice gave way. She shook her great shoulders frantically, in an agony of grief. Hot tears seemed to scald her quivering face. Finally her voice came and arose like a scream of pain.

"Oh, yes, I'll fergive her! I'll fergive her!"

1893

## The Open Boat[1]

#### A TALE INTENDED TO BE AFTER THE FACT, BEING THE EXPERIENCE OF FOUR MEN FROM THE SUNK STEAMER COMMODORE

### I

None of them knew the color of the sky. Their eyes glanced level, and were fastened upon the waves that swept toward them. These waves were of the hue of slate, save for the tops, which were of foaming white, and all of the men knew the colors of the sea. The horizon narrowed and widened, and dipped and rose, and at all times its edge was jagged with waves that seemed thrust up in points like rocks.

Many a man ought to have a bath-tub larger than the boat which here rode upon the sea. These waves were most wrongfully and barbarously abrupt and tall, and each froth-top was a problem in small boat navigation.

The cook squatted in the bottom and looked with both eyes at the six inches of gunwale which separated him from the ocean. His sleeves were rolled over his fat forearms, and the two flaps of his unbuttoned vest dangled as he bent to bail out the boat. Often he said: "Gawd! That was a narrow clip." As he remarked it he invariably gazed eastward over the broken sea.

The oiler,[2] steering with one of the two oars in the boat, sometimes raised himself suddenly to keep clear of water that swirled in over the stern. It was a thin little oar and it seemed often ready to snap.

The correspondent, pulling at the other oar, watched the waves and wondered why he was there.

The injured captain, lying in the bow, was at this time buried in that profound dejection and indifference which comes, temporarily at least, to even

1. Crane sailed as a correspondent on the steamer *Commodore*, which, on January 1, 1897, left Jacksonville, Florida, with munitions for the Cuban insurrectionists. Early on the morning of January 2, the steamer sank. With three others, Crane reached Daytona Beach in a ten-foot dinghy on the following morning. Under the title "Stephen Crane's Own Story," the *New York Press* on January 7 carried the details of his nearly fatal experience.

In June 1897, he published his fictional account, "The Open Boat," in *Scribner's Magazine*. The story gave the title to *"The Open Boat" and Other Tales of Adventure* (1898). The text here reprints that established for the University of Virginia edition of *The Works of Stephen Crane, Vol. 5, Tales of Adventure* (1970).

2. One who oils machinery in the engine room of a ship.

the bravest and most enduring when, willy nilly, the firm fails, the army loses, the ship goes down. The mind of the master of a vessel is rooted deep in the timbers of her, though he command for a day or a decade, and this captain had on him the stern impression of a scene in the grays of dawn of seven turned faces, and later a stump of a top-mast with a white ball on it that slashed to and fro at the waves, went low and lower, and down. Thereafter there was something strange in his voice. Although steady, it was deep with mourning, and of a quality beyond oration or tears.

"Keep'er a little more south, Billie," said he.

" 'A little more south,' sir," said the oiler in the stern.

A seat in his boat was not unlike a seat upon a bucking broncho, and, by the same token, a broncho is not much smaller. The craft pranced and reared, and plunged like an animal. As each wave came, and she rose for it, she seemed like a horse making at a fence outrageously high. The manner of her scramble over these walls of water is a mystic thing, and, moreover, at the top of them were ordinarily these problems in white water, the foam racing down from the summit of each wave, requiring a new leap, and a leap from the air. Then, after scornfully bumping a crest, she would slide, and race, and splash down a long incline and arrive bobbing and nodding in front of the next menace.

A singular disadvantage of the sea lies in the fact that after successfully surmounting one wave you discover that there is another behind it just as important and just as nervously anxious to do something effective in the way of swamping boats. In a ten-foot dingey one can get an idea of the resources of the sea in the line of waves that is not probable to the average experience, which is never at sea in a dingey. As each slaty wall of water approached, it shut all else from the view of the men in the boat, and it was not difficult to imagine that this particular wave was the final outburst of the ocean, the last effort of the grim water. There was a terrible grace in the move of the waves, and they came in silence, save for the snarling of the crests.

In the wan light, the faces of the men must have been gray. Their eyes must have glinted in strange ways as they gazed steadily astern. Viewed from a balcony, the whole thing would doubtlessly have been weirdly picturesque. But the men in the boat had no time to see it, and if they had had leisure there were other things to occupy their minds. The sun swung steadily up the sky, and they knew it was broad day because the color of the sea changed from slate to emerald-green, streaked with amber lights, and the foam was like tumbling snow. The process of the breaking day was unknown to them. They were aware only of this effect upon the color of the waves that rolled toward them.

In disjointed sentences the cook and the correspondent argued as to the difference between a life-saving station and a house of refuge. The cook had said: "There's a house of refuge just north of the Mosquito Inlet Light, and as soon as they see us, they'll come off in their boat and pick us up."

"As soon as who see us?" said the correspondent.

"The crew," said the cook.

"Houses of refuge don't have crews," said the correspondent. "As I understand them, they are only places where clothes and grub are stored for the benefit of shipwrecked people. They don't carry crews."

"Oh, yes, they do," said the cook.

"No, they don't," said the correspondent.

"Well, we're not there yet, anyhow," said the oiler, in the stern.

"Well," said the cook, "perhaps it's not a house of refuge that I'm thinking of as being near Mosquito Inlet Light. Perhaps it's a life-saving station."

"We're not there yet," said the oiler, in the stern.

## II

As the boat bounced from the top of each wave, the wind tore through the hair of the hatless men, and as the craft plopped her stern down again the spray slashed past them. The crest of each of these waves was a hill, from the top of which the men surveyed, for a moment, a broad tumultuous expanse, shining and wind-riven. It was probably splendid. It was probably glorious, this play of the free sea, wild with lights of emerald and white and amber.

"Bully good thing it's an on-shore wind," said the cook. "If not, where would we be? Wouldn't have a show."

"That's right," said the correspondent.

The busy oiler nodded his assent.

Then the captain, in the bow, chuckled in a way that expressed humor, contempt, tragedy, all in one. "Do you think we've got much of a show, now, boys?" said he.

Whereupon the three were silent, save for a trifle of hemming and hawing. To express any particular optimism at this time they felt to be childish and stupid, but they all doubtless possessed this sense of the situation in their mind. A young man thinks doggedly at such times. On the other hand, the ethics of their condition was decidedly against any open suggestion of hopelessness. So they were silent.

"Oh, well," said the captain, soothing his children, "we'll get ashore all right."

But there was that in his tone which made them think, so the oiler quoth: "Yes! If this wind holds!"

The cook was bailing. "Yes! If we don't catch hell in the surf."

Canton flannel[3] gulls flew near and far. Sometimes they sat down on the sea, near patches of brown sea-weed that rolled over the waves with a movement like carpets on a line in a gale. The birds sat comfortably in groups, and they were envied by some in the dingey, for the wrath of the sea was no more to them than it was to a covey of prairie chickens a thousand miles inland. Often they came very close and stared at the men with black bead-like eyes. At these times they were uncanny and sinister in their unblinking scrutiny, and the men hooted angrily at them, telling them to be gone. One came, and evidently decided to alight on the top of the captain's head. The bird flew parallel to the boat and did not circle, but made short sidelong jumps in the air in chicken-fashion. His black eyes were wistfully fixed upon the captain's head. "Ugly brute," said the oiler to the bird. "You look as if you were made with a jack-knife." The cook and the correspondent swore darkly at the creature. The captain naturally wished to knock it away with the end of the heavy painter, but he did not dare do it, because anything resembling an emphatic

---

3. Common name of a lightweight cotton fabric, usually white.

gesture would have capsized this freighted boat, and so with his open hand, the captain gently and carefully waved the gull away. After it had been discouraged from the pursuit the captain breathed easier on account of his hair, and others breathed easier because the bird struck their minds at this time as being somehow grewsome and ominous.

In the meantime the oiler and the correspondent rowed. And also they rowed.

They sat together in the same seat, and each rowed an oar. Then the oiler took both oars; then the correspondent took both oars; then the oiler; then the correspondent. They rowed and they rowed. The very ticklish part of the business was when the time came for the reclining one in the stern to take his turn at the oars. By the very last star of truth, it is easier to steal eggs from under a hen than it was to change seats in the dingey. First the man in the stern slid his hand along the thwart and moved with care, as if he were of Sèvres.[4] Then the man in the rowing seat slid his hand along the other thwart. It was all done with the most extraordinary care. As the two sidled past each other, the whole party kept watchful eyes on the coming wave, and the captain cried: "Look out now! Steady there!"

The brown mats of sea-weed that appeared from time to time were like islands, bits of earth. They were travelling, apparently, neither one way nor the other. They were, to all intents, stationary. They informed the men in the boat that it was making progress slowly toward the land.

The captain, rearing cautiously in the bow, after the dingey soared on a great swell, said that he had seen the light-house at Mosquito Inlet. Presently the cook remarked that he had seen it. The correspondent was at the oars, then, and for some reason he too wished to look at the light-house, but his back was toward the far shore and the waves were important, and for some time he could not seize an opportunity to turn his head. But at last there came a wave more gentle than the others, and when at the crest of it he swiftly scoured the western horizon.

"See it?" said the captain.

"No," said the correspondent, slowly, "I didn't see anything."

"Look again," said the captain. He pointed. "It's exactly in that direction."

At the top of another wave, the correspondent did as he was bid, and this time his eyes chanced on a small still thing on the edge of the swaying horizon. It was precisely like the point of a pin. It took an anxious eye to find a light-house so tiny.

"Think we'll make it, Captain?"

"If this wind holds and the boat don't swamp, we can't do much else," said the captain.

The little boat, lifted by each towering sea, and splashed viciously by the crests, made progress that in the absence of sea-weed was not apparent to those in her. She seemed just a wee thing wallowing, miraculously, top-up, at the mercy of five oceans. Occasionally, a great spread of water, like white flames, swarmed into her.

"Bail her, cook," said the captain, serenely.

"All right, Captain," said the cheerful cook.

4. Fine, often ornately decorated French porcelain.

## III

It would be difficult to describe the subtle brotherhood of men that was here established on the seas. No one said that it was so. No one mentioned it. But it dwelt in the boat, and each man felt it warm him. They were a captain, an oiler, a cook, and a correspondent, and they were friends, friends in a more curiously iron-bound degree than may be common. The hurt captain, lying against the water-jar in the bow, spoke always in a low voice and calmly, but he could never command a more ready and swiftly obedient crew than the motley three of the dingey. It was more than a mere recognition of what was best for the common safety. There was surely in it a quality that was personal and heartfelt. And after this devotion to the commander of the boat there was this comradeship that the correspondent, for instance, who had been taught to be cynical of men, knew even at the time was the best experience of his life. But no one said that it was so. No one mentioned it.

"I wish we had a sail," remarked the captain. "We might try my overcoat on the end of an oar and give you two boys a chance to rest." So the cook and the correspondent held the mast and spread wide the overcoat. The oiler steered, and the little boat made good way with her new rig. Sometimes the oiler had to scull sharply to keep a sea from breaking into the boat, but otherwise sailing was a success.

Meanwhile the light-house had been growing slowly larger. It had now almost assumed color, and appeared like a little gray shadow on the sky. The man at the oars could not be prevented from turning his head rather often to try for a glimpse of this little gray shadow.

At last, from the top of each wave the men in the tossing boat could see land. Even as the light-house was an upright shadow on the sky, this land seemed but a long black shadow on the sea. It certainly was thinner than paper. "We must be about opposite New Smyrna," said the cook, who had coasted this shore often in schooners. "Captain, by the way, I believe they abandoned that life-saving station there about a year ago."

"Did they?" said the captain.

The wind slowly died away. The cook and the correspondent were not now obliged to slave in order to hold high the oar. But the waves continued their old impetuous swooping at the dingey, and the little craft, no longer under way, struggled woundily over them. The oiler or the correspondent took the oars again.

Shipwrecks are *apropos* of nothing. If men could only train for them and have them occur when the men had reached pink condition, there would be less drowning at sea. Of the four in the dingey none had slept any time worth mentioning for two days and two nights previous to embarking in the dingey, and in the excitement of clambering about the deck of a foundering ship they had also forgotten to eat heartily.

For these reasons, and for others, neither the oiler nor the correspondent was fond of rowing at this time. The correspondent wondered ingenuously how in the name of all that was sane could there be people who thought it amusing to row a boat. It was not an amusement; it was a diabolical punishment, and even a genius of mental aberrations could never conclude that it was anything but a horror to the muscles and a crime against the back. He mentioned to the boat in general how the amusement of rowing struck him, and the weary-faced oiler smiled in full sympathy. Previously to the foundering, by the way, the oiler had worked double-watch in the engine-room of the ship.

"Take her easy, now, boys," said the captain. "Don't spend yourselves. If we have to run a surf you'll need all your strength, because we'll sure have to swim for it. Take your time."

Slowly the land arose from the sea. From a black line it became a line of black and a line of white—trees and sand. Finally, the captain said that he could make out a house on the shore. "That's the house of refuge, sure," said the cook. "They'll see us before long, and come out after us."

The distant light-house reared high. "The keeper ought to be able to make us out now, if he's looking through a glass," said the captain. "He'll notify the life-saving people."

"None of those other boats could have got ashore to give word of the wreck," said the oiler, in a low voice. "Else the life-boat would be out hunting us."

Slowly and beautifully the land loomed out of the sea. The wind came again. It had veered from the northeast to the southeast. Finally, a new sound struck the ears of the men in the boat. It was the low thunder of the surf on the shore. "We'll never be able to make the light-house now," said the captain. "Swing her head a little more north, Billie."

" 'A little more north,' sir," said the oiler.

Whereupon the little boat turned her nose once more down the wind, and all but the oarsman watched the shore grow. Under the influence of this expansion doubt and direful apprehension was leaving the minds of the men. The management of the boat was still most absorbing, but it could not prevent a quiet cheerfulness. In an hour, perhaps, they would be ashore.

Their back-bones had become thoroughly used to balancing in the boat and they now rode this wild colt of a dingey like circus men. The correspondent thought that he had been drenched to the skin, but happening to feel in the top pocket of his coat, he found therein eight cigars. Four of them were soaked with seawater; four were perfectly scatheless. After a search, somebody produced three dry matches, and thereupon the four waifs rode impudently in their little boat, and with an assurance of an impending rescue shining in their eyes, puffed at the big cigars and judged well and ill of all men. Everybody took a drink of water.


IV

"Cook," remarked the captain, "there don't seem to be any signs of life about your house of refuge."

"No," replied the cook. "Funny they don't see us!"

A broad stretch of lowly coast lay before the eyes of the men. It was of dunes topped with dark vegetation. The roar of the surf was plain, and sometimes they could see the white lip of a wave as it spun up the beach. A tiny house was blocked out black upon the sky. Southward, the slim light-house lifted its little gray length.

Tide, wind, and waves were swinging the dingey northward. "Funny they don't see us," said the men.

The surf's roar was here dulled, but its tone was, nevertheless, thunderous and mighty. As the boat swam over the great rollers, the men sat listening to this roar. "We'll swamp sure," said everybody.

It is fair to say here that there was not a life-saving station within twenty miles in either direction, but the men did not know this fact and in consequence they made dark and opprobrious remarks concerning the eyesight of the nation's life-savers. Four scowling men sat in the dingey and surpassed records in the invention of epithets.

"Funny they don't see us."

The light-heartedness of a former time had completely faded. To their sharpened minds it was easy to conjure pictures of all kinds of incompetency and blindness and, indeed, cowardice. There was the shore of the populous land, and it was bitter and bitter to them that from it came no sign.

"Well," said the captain, ultimately, "I suppose we'll have to make a try for ourselves. If we stay out here too long, we'll none of us have strength left to swim after the boat swamps."

And so the oiler, who was at the oars, turned the boat straight for the shore. There was a sudden tightening of muscles. There was some thinking.

"If we don't all get ashore—" said the captain. "If we don't all get ashore, I suppose you fellows know where to send news of my finish?"

They then briefly exchanged some addresses and admonitions. As for the reflections of the men, there was a great deal of rage in them. Perchance they might be formulated thus: "If I am going to be drowned—if I am going to be drowned—if I am going to be drowned, why, in the name of the seven mad gods who rule the sea, was I allowed to come thus far and contemplate sand and trees? Was I brought here merely to have my nose dragged away as I was about to nibble the sacred cheese of life? It is preposterous. If this old ninny-woman, Fate, cannot do better than this, she should be deprived of the management of men's fortunes. She is an old hen who knows not her intention. If she has decided to drown me, why did she not do it in the beginning and save me all this trouble. The whole affair is absurd. . . . But, no, she cannot mean to drown me. She dare not drown me. She cannot drown me. Not after all this work." Afterward the man might have had an impulse to shake his fist at the clouds. "Just you drown me, now, and then hear what I call you!"

The billows that came at this time were more formidable. They seemed always just about to break and roll over the little boat in a turmoil of foam. There was a preparatory and long growl in the speech of them. No mind unused to the sea would have concluded that the dingey could ascend these sheer heights in time. The shore was still afar. The oiler was a wily surfman. "Boys," he said, swiftly, "she won't live three minutes more and we're too far out to swim. Shall I take her to sea again, Captain?"

"Yes! Go ahead!" said the captain.

This oiler, by a series of quick miracles, and fast and steady oarsmanship, turned the boat in the middle of the surf and took her safely to sea again.

There was a considerable silence as the boat bumped over the furrowed sea to deeper water. Then somebody in gloom spoke. "Well, anyhow, they must have seen us from the shore by now."

The gulls went in slanting flight up the wind toward the gray desolate east. A squall, marked by dingy clouds, and clouds brick-red, like smoke from a burning building, appeared from the southeast.

"What do you think of those life-saving people? Ain't they peaches?"

"Funny they haven't seen us."

"Maybe they think we're out here for sport! Maybe they think we're fishin'. Maybe they think we're damned fools."

It was a long afternoon. A changed tide tried to force them southward, but wind and wave said northward. Far ahead, where coast-line, sea, and sky formed their mighty angle, there were little dots which seemed to indicate a city on the shore.

"St. Augustine?"

The captain shook his head. "Too near Mosquito Inlet."

And the oiler rowed, and then the correspondent rowed. Then the oiler rowed. It was a weary business. The human back can become the seat of more aches and pains than are registered in books for the composite anatomy of a regiment. It is a limited area, but it can become the theatre of innumerable muscular conflicts, tangles, wrenches, knots, and other comforts.

"Did you ever like to row, Billie?" asked the correspondent.

"No," said the oiler. "Hang it."

When one exchanged the rowing-seat for a place in the bottom of the boat, he suffered a bodily depression that caused him to be careless of everything save an obligation to wiggle one finger. There was cold sea-water swashing to and fro in the boat, and he lay in it. His head, pillowed on a thwart, was within an inch of the swirl of a wave crest, and sometimes a particularly obstreperous sea came inboard and drenched him once more. But these matters did not annoy him. It is almost certain that if the boat had capsized he would have tumbled comfortably out upon the ocean as if he felt sure that it was a great soft mattress.

"Look! There's a man on the shore!"

"Where?"

"There? See 'im? See 'im?"

"Yes, sure! He's walking along."

"Now he's stopped. Look! He's facing us!"

"He's waving at us!"

"So he is! By thunder!"

"Ah, now, we're all right! Now we're all right! There'll be a boat out here for us in half an hour."

"He's going on. He's running. He's going up to that house there."

The remote beach seemed lower than the sea, and it required a searching glance to discern the little black figure. The captain saw a floating stick and they rowed to it. A bath-towel was by some weird chance in the boat, and, tying this on the stick, the captain waved it. The oarsman did not dare turn his head, so he was obliged to ask questions.

"What's he doing now?"

"He's standing still again. He's looking, I think. . . . There he goes again. Toward the house. . . . Now he's stopped again."

"Is he waving at us?"

"No, not now! he was, though."

"Look! There comes another man!"

"He's running."

"Look at him go, would you."

"Why, he's on a bicycle. Now he's met the other man. They're both waving at us. Look!"

"There comes something up the beach."

"What the devil is that thing?"

"Why, it looks like a boat."

"Why, certainly it's a boat."

"No, it's on wheels."

"Yes, so it is. Well, that must be the life-boat. They drag them along shore on a wagon."

"That's the life-boat, sure."

"No, by——, it's—it's an omnibus."

"I tell you it's a life-boat."

"It is not! It's an omnibus. I can see it plain. See? One of those big hotel omnibuses."

"By thunder, you're right. It's an omnibus, sure as fate. What do you suppose they are doing with an omnibus? Maybe they are going around collecting the life-crew, hey?"

"That's it, likely. Look! There's a fellow waving a little black flag. He's standing on the steps of the omnibus. There come those other two fellows. Now they're all talking together. Look at the fellow with the flag. Maybe he ain't waving it!"

"That ain't a flag, is it? That's his coat. Why, certainly, that's his coat."

"So it is. It's his coat. He's taken it off and is waving it around his head. But would you look at him swing it!"

"Oh, say, there isn't any life-saving station there. That's just a winter resort hotel omnibus that has brought over some of the boarders to see us drown."

"What's that idiot with the coat mean? What's he signaling, anyhow?"

"It looks as if he were trying to tell us to go north. There must be a life-saving station up there."

"No! He thinks we're fishing. Just giving us a merry hand. See? Ah, there, Willie."

"Well, I wish I could make something out of those signals. What do you suppose he means?"

"He don't mean anything. He's just playing."

"Well, if he'd just signal us to try the surf again, or to go to sea and wait, or go north, or go south, or go to hell—there would be some reason in it. But look at him. He just stands there and keeps his coat revolving like a wheel. The ass!"

"There come more people."

"Now there's quite a mob. Look! Isn't that a boat?"

"Where? Oh, I see where you mean. No, that's no boat."

"That fellow is still waving his coat."

"He must think we like to see him do that. Why don't he quit it. It don't mean anything."

"I don't know. I think he is trying to make us go north. It must be that there's a life-saving station there somewhere."

"Say, he ain't tired yet. Look at 'im wave."

"Wonder how long he can keep that up. He's been revolving his coat ever since he caught sight of us. He's an idiot. Why aren't they getting men to bring a boat out. A fishing boat—one of those big yawls—could come out here all right. Why don't he do something?"

"Oh, it's all right, now."

"They'll have a boat out here for us in less than no time, now that they've seen us."

A faint yellow tone came into the sky over the low land. The shadows on the sea slowly deepened. The wind bore coldness with it, and the men began to shiver.

"Holy smoke!" said one, allowing his voice to express his impious mood, "if we keep on monkeying out here! If we've got to flounder out here all night!"

"Oh, we'll never have to stay here all night! Don't you worry. They've seen us now, and it won't be long before they'll come chasing out after us."

The shore grew dusky. The man waving a coat blended gradually into this gloom, and it swallowed in the same manner the omnibus and the group of people. The spray, when it dashed uproariously over the side, made the voyagers shrink and swear like men who were being branded.

"I'd like to catch the chump who waved the coat. I feel like socking him one, just for luck."

"Why? What did he do?"

"Oh, nothing, but then he seemed so damned cheerful."

In the meantime the oiler rowed, and then the correspondent rowed, and then the oiler rowed. Gray-faced and bowed forward, they mechanically, turn by turn, plied the leaden oars. The form of the light-house had vanished from the southern horizon, but finally a pale star appeared, just lifting from the sea. The streaked saffron in the west passed before the all-merging darkness, and the sea to the east was black. The land had vanished, and was expressed only by the low and drear thunder of the surf.

"If I am going to be drowned—if I am going to be drowned—if I am going to be drowned, why, in the name of the seven mad gods who rule the sea, was I allowed to come thus far and contemplate sand and trees? Was I brought here merely to have my nose dragged away as I was about to nibble the sacred cheese of life?"

The patient captain, drooped over the water-jar, was sometimes obliged to speak to the oarsman.

"Keep her head up! Keep her head up!"

" 'Keep her head up,' sir." The voices were weary and low.

This was surely a quiet evening. All save the oarsman lay heavily and listlessly in the boat's bottom. As for him, his eyes were just capable of noting the tall black waves that swept forward in a most sinister silence, save for an occasional subdued growl of a crest.

The cook's head was on a thwart, and he looked without interest at the water under his nose. He was deep in other scenes. Finally he spoke. "Billie," he murmured, dreamfully, "what kind of pie do you like best?"

## V

"Pie," said the oiler and the correspondent, agitatedly. "Don't talk about those things, blast you!"

"Well," said the cook, "I was just thinking about ham sandwiches, and——"

A night on the sea in an open boat is a long night. As darkness settled finally, the shine of the light, lifting from the sea in the south, changed to full gold. On the northern horizon a new light appeared, a small bluish gleam on the edge of the waters. These two lights were the furniture of the world. Otherwise there was nothing but waves.

Two men huddled in the stern, and distances were so magnificent in the dingey that the rower was enabled to keep his feet partly warmed by thrusting them under his companions. Their legs indeed extended far under the rowing-seat until they touched the feet of the captain forward. Sometimes, despite the efforts of the tired oarsman, a wave came piling into the boat, an icy wave of the night, and the chilling water soaked them anew. They would twist their bodies for a moment and groan, and sleep the dead sleep once more, while the water in the boat gurgled about them as the craft rocked.

The plan of the oiler and the correspondent was for one to row until he lost the ability, and then arouse the other from his sea-water couch in the bottom of the boat.

The oiler plied the oars until his head drooped forward, and the overpowering sleep blinded him. And he rowed yet afterward. Then he touched a man in the bottom of the boat, and called his name. "Will you spell me for a little while?" he said meekly.

"Sure, Billie," said the correspondent, awakening and dragging himself to a sitting position. They exchanged places carefully, and the oiler, cuddling down in the sea-water at the cook's side, seemed to go to sleep instantly.

The particular violence of the sea had ceased. The waves came without snarling. The obligation of the man at the oars was to keep the boat headed so that the tilt of the rollers would not capsize her, and to preserve her from filling when the crests rushed past. The black waves were silent and hard to be seen in the darkness. Often one was almost upon the boat before the oarsman was aware.

In a low voice the correspondent addressed the captain. He was not sure that the captain was awake, although this iron man seemed to be always awake. "Captain, shall I keep her making for that light north, sir?"

The same steady voice answered him. "Yes. Keep it about two points off the port bow."

The cook had tied a life-belt around himself in order to get even the warmth which this clumsy cork contrivance could donate, and he seemed almost stove-like when a rower, whose teeth invariably chattered wildly as soon as he ceased his labor, dropped down to sleep.

The correspondent, as he rowed, looked down at the two men sleeping under foot. The cook's arm was around the oiler's shoulders, and, with their fragmentary clothing and haggard faces, they were the babes of the sea, a grotesque rendering of the old babes in the wood.

Later he must have grown stupid at his work, for suddenly there was a growling of water, and a crest came with a roar and a swash into the boat, and it was a wonder that it did not set the cook afloat in his life-belt. The cook continued to sleep, but the oiler sat up, blinking his eyes and shaking with the new cold.

"Oh, I'm awful sorry, Billie," said the correspondent, contritely.

"That's all right, old boy," said the oiler, and lay down again and was asleep.

Presently it seemed that even the captain dozed, and the correspondent thought that he was the one man afloat on all the oceans. The wind had a voice as it came over the waves, and it was sadder than the end.

There was a long, loud swishing astern of the boat, and a gleaming trail of phosphorescence, like blue flame, was furrowed on the black waters. It might have been made by a monstrous knife.

Then there came a stillness, while the correspondent breathed with the open mouth and looked at the sea.

Suddenly there was another swish and another long flash of bluish light, and this time it was alongside the boat, and might almost have been reached with an oar. The correspondent saw an enormous fin speed like a shadow through the water, hurling the crystalline spray and leaving the long glowing trail.

The correspondent looked over his shoulder at the captain. His face was hidden, and he seemed to be asleep. He looked at the babes of the sea. They certainly were asleep. So, being bereft of sympathy, he leaned a little way to one side and swore softly into the sea.

But the thing did not then leave the vicinity of the boat. Ahead or astern, on one side or the other, at intervals long or short, fled the long sparkling streak, and there was to be heard the whiroo of the dark fin. The speed and power of the thing was greatly to be admired. It cut the water like a gigantic and keen projectile.

The presence of this biding thing did not affect the man with the same horror that it would if he had been a picnicker. He simply looked at the sea dully and swore in an undertone.

Nevertheless, it is true that he did not wish to be alone with the thing. He wished one of his companions to awaken by chance and keep him company with it. But the captain hung motionless over the water-jar and the oiler and the cook in the bottom of the boat were plunged in slumber.

## VI

"If I am going to be drowned—if I am going to be drowned—if I am going to be drowned, why, in the name of the seven mad gods who rule the sea, was I allowed to come thus far and contemplate sand and trees?"

During this dismal night, it may be remarked that a man would conclude that it was really the intention of the seven mad gods to drown him, despite the abominable injustice of it. For it was certainly an abominable injustice to drown a man who had worked so hard, so hard. The man felt it would be a crime most unnatural. Other people had drowned at sea since galleys swarmed with painted sails, but still——

When it occurs to a man that nature does not regard him as important, and that she feels she would not maim the universe by disposing of him, he at first wishes to throw bricks at the temple, and he hates deeply the fact that there are no bricks and no temples. Any visible expression of nature would surely be pelleted with his jeers.

Then, if there be no tangible thing to hoot he feels, perhaps, the desire to confront a personification and indulge in pleas, bowed to one knee, and with hands supplicant, saying: "Yes, but I love myself."

A high cold star on a winter's night is the word he feels that she says to him. Thereafter he knows the pathos of his situation.

The men in the dingey had not discussed these matters, but each had, no doubt, reflected upon them in silence and according to his mind. There was seldom any expression upon their faces save the general one of complete weariness. Speech was devoted to the business of the boat.

To chime the notes of his emotion, a verse mysteriously entered the correspondent's head. He had even forgotten that he had forgotten this verse, but it suddenly was in his mind.

A soldier of the Legion lay dying in Algiers,
There was lack of woman's nursing, there was dearth of woman's tears;
But a comrade stood beside him, and he took that comrade's hand,
And he said: "I never more shall see my own, my native land."[5]

In his childhood, the correspondent had been made acquainted with the fact that a soldier of the Legion lay dying in Algiers, but he had never regarded it as important. Myriads of his school-fellows had informed him of the soldier's plight, but the dinning had naturally ended by making him perfectly indifferent. He had never considered it his affair that a soldier of the Legion lay dying in Algiers, nor had it appeared to him as a matter for sorrow. It was less to him than the breaking of a pencil's point.

Now, however, it quaintly came to him as a human, living thing. It was no longer merely a picture of a few throes in the breast of a poet, meanwhile drinking tea and warming his feet at the grate; it was an actuality—stern, mournful, and fine.

The correspondent plainly saw the soldier. He lay on the sand with his feet out straight and still. While his pale left hand was upon his chest in an attempt to thwart the going of his life, the blood came between his fingers. In the far Algerian distance, a city of low square forms was set against a sky that was faint with the last sunset hues. The correspondent, plying the oars and dreaming of the slow and slower movements of the lips of the soldier, was moved by a profound and perfectly impersonal comprehension. He was sorry for the soldier of the Legion who lay dying in Algiers.

The thing which had followed the boat and waited had evidently grown bored at the delay. There was no longer to be heard the slash of the cut-water, and there was no longer the flame of the long trail. The light in the north still glimmered, but it was apparently no nearer to the boat. Sometimes the boom of the surf rang in the correspondent's ears, and he turned the craft seaward then and rowed harder. Southward, some one had evidently built a watch-fire on the beach. It was too low and too far to be seen, but it made a shimmering, roseate reflection upon the bluff back of it, and this could be discerned from the boat. The wind came stronger, and sometimes a wave suddenly raged out like a mountain-cat and there was to be seen the sheen and sparkle of a broken crest.

The captain, in the bow, moved on his water-jar and sat erect. "Pretty long night," he observed to the correspondent. He looked at the shore. "Those life-saving people take their time."

"Did you see that shark playing around?"

"Yes, I saw him. He was a big fellow, all right."

"Wish I had known you were awake."

Later the correspondent spoke into the bottom of the boat.

"Billie!" There was a slow and gradual disentanglement. "Billie, will you spell me?"

"Sure," said the oiler.

As soon as the correspondent touched the cold comfortable seawater in the bottom of the boat, and had huddled close to the cook's life-belt he was deep in sleep, despite the fact that his teeth played all the popular airs. This sleep was so good to him that it was but a moment before he heard a voice call his name in a tone that demonstrated the last stages of exhaustion. "Will you spell me?"

"Sure, Billie."

The light in the north had mysteriously vanished, but the correspondent took his course from the wide-awake captain.

Later in the night they took the boat farther out to sea, and the captain directed the cook to take one oar at the stern and keep the boat facing the seas. He was to call out if he should hear the thunder of the surf. This plan enabled the oiler and the correspondent to get respite together. "We'll give those boys a chance to get into shape again," said the captain. They curled down and, after a few preliminary chatterings and trembles, slept once more the dead sleep. Neither knew they had bequeathed to the cook the company of another shark, or perhaps the same shark.

As the boat caroused on the waves, spray occasionally bumped over the side and gave them a fresh soaking, but this had no power to break their repose. The ominous slash of the wind and the water affected them as it would have affected mummies.

"Boys," said the cook, with the notes of every reluctance in his voice, "she's drifted in pretty close. I guess one of you had better take her to sea again." The correspondent, aroused, heard the crash of the toppled crests.

As he was rowing, the captain gave him some whiskey and water, and this steadied the chills out of him. "If I ever get ashore and anybody shows me even a photograph of an oar—"

At last there was a short conversation.

"Billie. . . . Billie, will you spell me?"

"Sure," said the oiler.

## VII

When the correspondent again opened his eyes, the sea and the sky were each of the gray hue of the dawning. Later, carmine and gold was painted upon the waters. The morning appeared finally, in its splendor, with a sky of pure blue, and the sunlight flamed on the tips of the waves.

On the distant dunes were set many little black cottages, and a tall white wind-mill reared above them. No man, nor dog, nor bicycle appeared on the beach. The cottages might have formed a deserted village.

The voyagers scanned the shore. A conference was held in the boat. "Well," said the captain, "if no help is coming, we might better try a run through the surf right away. If we stay out here much longer we will be too weak to do anything for ourselves at all." The others silently acquiesced in this reasoning. The boat was headed for the beach. The correspondent wondered if none ever ascended the tall wind-tower, and if then they never looked seaward. This tower was a giant, standing with its back to the plight of the ants. It represented in a degree, to the correspondent, the serenity of nature amid the struggles of the individual—nature in the wind, and nature in the vision of men. She did not seem cruel to him then, nor beneficent, nor treacherous, nor wise. But she was indifferent, flatly indifferent. It is, perhaps, plausible that a man in this situation, impressed with the unconcern of the universe, should see the innumerable flaws of his life and have them taste wickedly in his mind and wish for another chance. A distinction between right and wrong seems absurdly clear to him, then, in this new ignorance of the grave-edge, and he understands that if he were given another opportunity he would mend his conduct and his words, and be better and brighter during an introduction, or at a tea.

"Now, boys," said the captain, "she is going to swamp sure. All we can do is to work her in as far as possible, and then when she swamps, pile out and scramble for the beach. Keep cool now, and don't jump until she swamps sure."

The oiler took the oars. Over his shoulders he scanned the surf. "Captain," he said, "I think I'd better bring her about, and keep her head-on to the seas and back her in."

"All right, Billie," said the captain. "Back her in." The oiler swung the boat then and, seated in the stern, the cook and the correspondent were obliged to look over their shoulders to contemplate the lonely and indifferent shore.

The monstrous inshore rollers heaved the boat high until the men were again enabled to see the white sheets of water scudding up the slanted beach. "We won't get in very close," said the captain. Each time a man could wrest his attention from the rollers, he turned his glance toward the shore, and in the expression of the eyes during this contemplation there was a singular quality. The correspondent, observing the others, knew that they were not afraid, but the full meaning of their glances was shrouded.

As for himself, he was too tired to grapple fundamentally with the fact. He tried to coerce his mind into thinking of it, but the mind was dominated at this time by the muscles, and the muscles said they did not care. It merely occurred to him that if he should drown it would be a shame.

There were no hurried words, no pallor, no plain agitation. The men simply looked at the shore. "Now, remember to get well clear of the boat when you jump," said the captain.

Seaward the crest of a roller suddenly fell with a thunderous crash, and the long white comber came roaring down upon the boat.

"Steady now," said the captain. The men were silent. They turned their eyes from the shore to the comber and waited. The boat slid up the incline, leaped at the furious top, bounced over it, and swung down the long back of the wave. Some water had been shipped and the cook bailed it out.

But the next crest crashed also. The tumbling boiling flood of white water caught the boat and whirled it almost perpendicular. Water swarmed in from all sides. The correspondent had his hands on the gunwale at this time, and when the water entered at that place he swiftly withdrew his fingers, as if he objected to wetting them.

The little boat, drunken with this weight of water, reeled and snuggled deeper into the sea.

"Bail her out, cook! Bail her out," said the captain.

"All right, Captain," said the cook.

"Now, boys, the next one will do for us, sure," said the oiler. "Mind to jump clear of the boat."

The third wave moved forward, huge, furious, implacable. It fairly swallowed the dingey, and almost simultaneously the men tumbled into the sea. A piece of life-belt had lain in the bottom of the boat, and as the correspondent went overboard he held this to his chest with his left hand.

The January water was icy, and he reflected immediately that it was colder than he had expected to find it off the coast of Florida. This appeared to his dazed mind as a fact important enough to be noted at the time. The coldness of the water was sad; it was tragic. This fact was somehow so mixed and confused with his opinion of his own situation that it seemed almost a proper reason for tears. The water was cold.

When he came to the surface he was conscious of little but the noisy water. Afterward he saw his companions in the sea. The oiler was ahead in the race. He was swimming strongly and rapidly. Off to the correspondent's left, the cook's great white and corked back bulged out of the water, and in the rear the captain was hanging with his one good hand to the keel of the overturned dingey.

There is a certain immovable quality to a shore, and the correspondent wondered at it amid the confusion of the sea.

It seemed also very attractive, but the correspondent knew that it was a long journey, and he paddled leisurely. The piece of life preserver lay under him, and sometimes he whirled down the incline of a wave as if he were on a hand-sled.

But finally he arrived at a place in the sea where travel was beset with difficulty. He did not pause swimming to inquire what manner of current had caught him, but there his progress ceased. The shore was set before him like a bit of scenery on a stage, and he looked at it and understood with his eyes each detail of it.

As the cook passed, much farther to the left, the captain was calling to him, "Turn over on your back, cook! Turn over on your back and use the oar."

"All right, sir." The cook turned on his back, and, paddling with an oar, went ahead as if he were a canoe.

Presently the boat also passed to the left of the correspondent with the captain clinging with one hand to the keel. He would have appeared like a man raising himself to look over a board fence, if it were not for the extraordinary gymnastics of the boat. The correspondent marvelled that the captain could still hold to it.

They passed on, nearer to the shore—the oiler, the cook, the captain—and following them went the water-jar, bouncing gayly over the seas.

The correspondent remained in the grip of this strange new enemy—a current. The shore, with its white slope of sand and its green bluff, topped with little silent cottages, was spread like a picture before him. It was very near to him then, but he was impressed as one who in a gallery looks at a scene from Brittany or Holland.

He thought: "I am going to drown? Can it be possible? Can it be possible? Can it be possible?" Perhaps an individual must consider his own death to be the final phenomenon of nature.

But later a wave perhaps whirled him out of this small deadly current, for he found suddenly that he could again make progress toward the shore. Later still, he was aware that the captain, clinging with one hand to the keel of the dingey, had his face turned away from the shore and toward him, and was calling his name. "Come to the boat! Come to the boat!"

In his struggle to reach the captain and the boat, he reflected that when one gets properly wearied, drowning must really be a comfortable arrangement, a cessation of hostilities accompanied by a large degree of relief, and he was glad of it, for the main thing in his mind for some moments had been horror of the temporary agony. He did not wish to be hurt.

Presently he saw a man running along the shore. He was undressing with most remarkable speed. Coat, trousers, shirt, everything flew magically off him.

"Come to the boat," called the captain.

"All right, Captain." As the correspondent paddled, he saw the captain let himself down to bottom and leave the boat. Then the correspondent performed his one little marvel of the voyage. A large wave caught him and flung him with ease and supreme speed completely over the boat and far beyond it. It struck him even then as an event in gymnastics, and a true miracle of the sea. An overturned boat in the surf is not a plaything to a swimming man.

The correspondent arrived in water that reached only to his waist, but his condition did not enable him to stand for more than a moment. Each wave knocked him into a heap, and the under-tow pulled at him.

Then he saw the man who had been running and undressing, and undressing and running, come bounding into the water. He dragged ashore the cook, and then waded toward the captain, but the captain waved him away, and sent him to the correspondent. He was naked, naked as a tree in winter, but a halo was about his head, and he shone like a saint. He gave a strong pull, and a long drag, and a bully heave at the correspondent's hand. The correspondent schooled in the minor formulæ, said: "Thanks, old man." But suddenly the man cried: "What's that?" He pointed a swift finger. The correspondent said: "Go."

In the shallows, face downward, lay the oiler. His forehead touched sand that was periodically, between each wave, clear of the sea.

The correspondent did not know all that transpired afterward. When he achieved safe ground he fell, striking the sand with each particular part of his body. It was as if he had dropped from a roof, but the thud was grateful to him.

It seems that instantly the beach was populated with men with blankets, clothes, and flasks, and women with coffee-pots and all the remedies sacred to their minds. The welcome of the land to the men from the sea was warm and generous, but a still and dripping shape was carried slowly up the beach, and the land's welcome for it could only be the different and sinister hospitality of the grave.

When it came night, the white waves paced to and fro in the moonlight, and the wind brought the sound of the great sea's voice to the men on shore, and they felt that they could then be interpreters.

1897, 1898

## *From* The Black Riders[1]

### VI

God fashioned the ship of the world carefully.
With the infinite skill of an all-master
Made He the hull and the sails,
Held He the rudder
Ready for adjustment.                                         5
Erect stood He, scanning His work proudly.
Then—at fateful time—a wrong called,

---

1. First published in *"The Black Riders" and Other Lines* by Stephen Crane (1896); rpt. in *Stephen Crane: Prose and Poetry* (1984), from which this text is taken.

And God turned, heeding.
Lo, the ship, at this opportunity, slipped slyly,
Making cunning noiseless travel down the ways.          10
So that, forever rudderless, it went upon the seas
Going ridiculous voyages,
Making quaint progress,
Turning as with serious purpose
Before stupid winds.                                    15
And there were many in the sky
Who laughed at this thing.

*    *    *

## XXIV

I saw a man pursuing the horizon;
Round and round they sped.
I was disturbed at this;
I accosted the man.
"It is futile," I said,                                 5
"You can never——"

"You lie," he cried,
And ran on.

1896

## *From* War Is Kind[1]

### I

Do not weep, maiden, for war is kind.
Because your lover threw wild hands toward the sky
And the affrighted steed ran on alone,
Do not weep.
War is kind.                                            5

    Hoarse, booming drums of the regiment
    Little souls who thirst for fight,
    These men were born to drill and die
    The unexplained glory flies above them
    Great is the battle-god, great, and his kingdom——     10
    A field where a thousand corpses lie.

Do not weep, babe, for war is kind.
Because your father tumbled in the yellow trenches,
Raged at his breast, gulped and died,
Do not weep.                                            15
War is kind.

1. First published in *"War Is Kind" and Other Lines* (1899); rpt. in Stephen Crane: *Prose and Poetry* (1984), from which this text is taken.

Swift, blazing flag of the regiment
Eagle with crest of red and gold,
These men were born to drill and die
Point for them the virtue of slaughter 20
Make plain to them the excellence of killing
And a field where a thousand corpses lie.

Mother whose heart hung humble as a button
On the bright splendid shroud of your son,
Do not weep. 25
War is kind.

\* \* \*

## XIX

The chatter of a death-demon from a tree-top.

Blood—blood and torn grass—
Had marked the rise of his agony——
This lone hunter.
The grey-green woods impassive 5
Had watched the threshing of his limbs.

A canoe with flashing paddle
A girl with soft searching eyes,
A call: "John!"

Come, arise, hunter! 10
Can you not hear?

The chatter of a death-demon from a tree-top.

## XX

The impact of a dollar upon the heart
Smiles warm red light
Sweeping from the hearth rosily upon the white table,
With the hanging cool velvet shadows
Moving softly upon the door. 5

The impact of a million dollars
Is a crash of flunkeys
And yawning emblems of Persia
Cheeked against oak, France and a sabre,
The outcry of old Beauty 10
Whored by pimping merchants
To submission before wine and chatter.
Silly rich peasants stamp the carpets of men,
Dead men who dreamed fragrance and light
Into their woof, their lives; 15
The rug of an honest bear
Under the feet of a cryptic slave

Who speaks always of baubles
Forgetting place, multitude, work and state,
Champing and mouthing of hats                    20
Making ratful squeak of hats,
Hats.

## XXI

A man said to the universe:
"Sir, I exist!"
"However," replied the universe,
"The fact has not created in me
"A sense of obligation."                          5

## XXII

When the prophet, a complacent fat man,
Arrived at the mountain-top
He cried: "Woe to my knowledge!
I intended to see good white lands
And bad black lands,                              5
But the scene is grey."

1899

---

# JAMES WELDON JOHNSON
## 1871–1938

Teacher, poet, songwriter, novelist, and civil rights activist, James William Johnson (he changed his middle name to Weldon in 1913) was born in Jacksonville, Florida. He was the son of James Johnson, a headwaiter, and Helen Louise Dillet, the first African American female teacher in Florida. Both parents had roots in Nassau, Bahamas. Johnson and his brother, John Rosamund, had a sheltered middle-class childhood and were encouraged to study English literature and European classical music. Johnson attended Atlanta University, his main aim being to use his education to further the interests of African Americans. While still in college, he taught in Hampton, Georgia, where he experienced life among poor African Americans, and attended the Columbian Exposition of 1893 in Chicago, where he heard speeches by Frederick Douglass and poems by Paul Laurence Dunbar. After graduating in 1894 he took a job as a high school principal at the Stanton Public School, where his mother taught; he also founded a short-lived newspaper, *The Daily American*. While working as a principal he studied law and became the first African American to gain admission to the Florida bar through open examination.

In 1900, Johnson and his brother, who had graduated from the New England Conservatory and become a composer, wrote "Lift Every Voice and Sing" on the occasion of Abraham Lincoln's birthday; the song was immensely popular and became known as the "Negro National Anthem." Johnson moved to New York in 1901 in order to collaborate further with his brother; the two had some success as Broadway songwriters. He also took courses at Columbia University. With a reference from Booker T. Washington to President Theodore Roosevelt, he was appointed U.S. Consul to Venezuela in 1906. While employed by the diplomatic corps, Johnson published poems in *Century Magazine* and *The Independent*. Fluent in Spanish, he was transferred to Nicaragua in 1909, where he met and married Grace Nail, the daughter of a real estate developer from New York.

In 1912, still in Nicaragua, Johnson published *The Autobiography of an Ex-Coloured Man* anonymously. He chose not to disclose his identity as author until 1927, when he began to write his own autobiography, *Along This Way* (1933). Johnson hoped that making *Ex-Coloured Man* anonymous would encourage readers to draw general sociological lessons from the book. This first-person novel tells of a musician who rejects his black roots for a life of material comfort in the white world, ironically critiquing racial identity, passing, and the values of the white bourgeoisie in turn-of-the-century America. It is one of the most significant renderings of the theme of the "tragic mulatto," especially as it enacts W. E. B. Du Bois's metaphors of the "veil" and "double-consciousness," thereby exploring the ways in which African Americans in a "white" culture conceal their identities and experience themselves from multiple perspectives. (Many readers believed it was not fiction but Johnson's true life story.) In 1913 Johnson left the diplomatic corps and returned to New York, where he became involved with the NAACP.

Johnson published his first book of poetry, *Fifty Years and Other Poems*, in 1917 and went on to edit *The Book of American Negro Poetry* (1922), *The Book of American Negro Spirituals* (1925), and *The Second Book of Negro Spirituals* (1926). He was a strong force behind the Harlem Renaissance in the 1920s, promoting writers such as Claude McKay and Langston Hughes. His second poetry collection, *God's Trombones: Seven Negro Sermons in Verse* (1927), was inspired by his impressions of the rural South when a student. Johnson did not support the heavy use of Negro dialect, as in the works of Zora Neale Hurston and others, instead challenging African American writers to "express the racial spirit [of African Americans] from within, rather than [through] symbols from without." His last works, including his "actual" autobiography, *Along This Way* argued for integration as the only solution to American racial problems.

When Johnson retired, he was Professor of Creative Literature and Writing at Fisk University. He continued lecturing on civil rights and in 1934 published his sociological book *Negro Americans, What Now?* and his last collection of verse, *Saint Peter Relates an Incident: Selected Poems*. He died near his summer home in Maine when his car was struck by a train. Nearly two thousand people attended his funeral in Harlem.

# Lift Every Voice and Sing[1]

Lift every voice and sing
Till earth and heaven ring,
Ring with the harmonies of Liberty;
Let our rejoicing rise
High as the listening skies,
Let it resound loud as the rolling sea.

5

---

1. From *Saint Peter Relates an Incident* (1935); rpt. in *James Weldon Johnson: Writings* (Library of America) (2004), from which this text is taken. Johnson wrote these lyrics in February 1900 for a school commemoration of Lincoln's birthday; his brother, John Rosamund, set them to music.

Sing a song full of the faith that the dark past has taught us,
Sing a song full of the hope that the present has brought us.
Facing the rising sun of our new day begun,
Let us march on till victory is won.                                    10

Stony the road we trod,
Bitter the chastening rod,
Felt in the days when hope unborn had died;
Yet with a steady beat,
Have not our weary feet                                                 15
Come to the place for which our fathers sighed?
We have come over a way that with tears has been watered,
We have come, treading our path through the blood of the slaughtered,
Out from the gloomy past,
Till now we stand at last                                               20
Where the white gleam of our bright star is cast.

God of our weary years,
God of our silent tears,
Thou who hast brought us thus far on the way;
Thou who hast by Thy might                                              25
Led us into the light,
Keep us forever in the path, we pray.
Lest our feet stray from the places, our God, where we met Thee,
Lest, our hearts drunk with the wine of the world, we forget Thee;
Shadowed beneath Thy hand,                                              30
May we forever stand.
True to our God,
True to our native land.

                                                                      1920

## *From* Autobiography of an Ex-Coloured Man[1]

### *Chapter X*

Among the first of my fellow-passengers of whom I took any particular notice
was a tall, broad-shouldered, almost gigantic, coloured man. His dark-brown
face was clean-shaven; he was well-dressed and bore a decidedly distinguished air. In fact, if he was not handsome, he at least compelled admiration for his fine physical proportions. He attracted general attention as he
strode the deck in a sort of majestic loneliness. I became curious to know who

1. First published in Boston by Sherman, French
in 1912; rpt. 1927, from which this chapter is
taken. The first nine chapters tell of the narrator's
upbringing by his mother, an African American
seamstress, with occasional visits by his father, a
wealthy white southern gentleman whose family
had employed the narrator's mother. The narrator
travels around the United States and throughout
Europe, observing how white and black people
behave within separate enclaves and with each
other. After an attempt at college and a career in
New York's music halls, he is hired by a man he
calls "the millionaire" to play piano for him as he
travels. In the chapter reprinted here, the Ex-
Coloured Man takes a trip down South. What
happens in this chapter leads him to commit himself to life as a composer who expresses traditional African American music in the form of
traditional "classical" music and convinces him to
pass as white and leave his own black identity
behind.

he was and determined to strike up an acquaintance with him at the first opportune moment. The chance came a day or two later. He was sitting in the smoking-room, with a cigar, which had gone out, in his mouth, reading a novel. I sat down beside him and, offering him a fresh cigar, said: "You don't mind my telling you something unpleasant, do you?" He looked at me with a smile, accepted the proffered cigar, and replied in a voice which comported perfectly with his size and appearance: "I think my curiosity overcomes any objections I might have." "Well," I said, "have you noticed that the man who sat at your right in the saloon during the first meal has not sat there since?" He frowned slightly without answering my question. "Well," I continued, "he asked the steward to remove him; and not only that, he attempted to persuade a number of the passengers to protest against your presence in the dining-saloon." The big man at my side took a long draw from his cigar, threw his head back, and slowly blew a great cloud of smoke toward the ceiling. Then turning to me he said: "Do you know, I don't object to anyone's having prejudices so long as those prejudices don't interfere with my personal liberty. Now, the man you are speaking of had a perfect right to change his seat if I in any way interfered with his appetite or his digestion. I should have no reason to complain if he removed to the farthest corner of the saloon, or even if he got off the ship; but when his prejudice attempts to move *me* one foot, one inch, out of the place where I am comfortably located, then I object." On the word "object" he brought his great fist down on the table in front of us with such a crash that everyone in the room turned to look. We both covered up the slight embarrassment with a laugh and strolled out on the deck.

We walked the deck for an hour or more, discussing different phases of the Negro question. In referring to the race I used the personal pronoun "we"; my companion made no comment about it, nor evinced any surprise, except to raise his eyebrows slightly the first time he caught the significance of the word. He was the broadest-minded coloured man I have ever talked with on the Negro question. He even went so far as to sympathize with and offer excuses for some white Southern points of view. I asked him what were his main reasons for being so hopeful. He replied: "In spite of all that is written, said, and done, this great, big, incontrovertible fact stands out—the Negro is progressing, and that disproves all the arguments in the world that he is incapable of progress. I was born in slavery, and at emancipation was set adrift a ragged, penniless bit of humanity. I have seen the Negro in every grade, and I know what I am talking about. Our detractors point to the increase of crime as evidence against us; certainly we have progressed in crime as in other things; what less could be expected? And yet, in this respect, we are far from the point which has been reached by the more highly civilized white race. As we continue to progress, crime among us will gradually lose much of its brutal, vulgar, I might say healthy, aspect, and become more delicate, refined, and subtile.[2] Then it will be less shocking and noticeable, although more dangerous to society." Then dropping his tone of irony, he continued with some show of eloquence: "But, above all, when I am discouraged and disheartened, I have this to fall back on: if there is a principle of right in the world, which finally prevails, and I believe that there is; if there is a merciful but justice-loving God in heaven, and I believe that there is, we shall win; for we have

2. Subtle.

right on our side, while those who oppose us can defend themselves by nothing in the moral law, nor even by anything in the enlightened thought of the present age."

For several days, together with other topics, we discussed the race problem, not only of the United States, but as it affected native Africans and Jews. Finally, before we reached Boston, our conversation had grown familiar and personal. I had told him something of my past and much about my intentions for the future. I learned that he was a physician, a graduate of Howard University, Washington, and had done post-graduate work in Philadelphia; and this was his second trip abroad to attend professional courses. He had practised for some years in the city of Washington, and though he did not say so, I gathered that his practice was a lucrative one. Before we left the ship, he had made me promise that I would stop two or three days in Washington before going on south.

We put up at a hotel in Boston for a couple of days and visited several of my new friend's acquaintances; they were all people of education and culture and, apparently, of means. I could not help being struck by the great difference between them and the same class of coloured people in the South. In speech and thought they were genuine Yankees. The difference was especially noticeable in their speech. There was none of that heavy-tongued enunciation which characterizes even the best-educated coloured people of the South. It is remarkable, after all, what an adaptable creature the Negro is. I have seen the black West Indian gentleman in London, and he is in speech and manners a perfect Englishman. I have seen natives of Haiti and Martinique in Paris, and they are more Frenchy than a Frenchman. I have no doubt that the Negro would make a good Chinaman, with exception of the pigtail.

My stay in Washington, instead of being two or three days, was two or three weeks. This was my first visit to the national capital, and I was, of course, interested in seeing the public buildings and something of the working of the government; but most of my time I spent with the doctor among his friends and acquaintances. The social phase of life among coloured people is more developed in Washington than in any other city in the country. This is on account of the large number of individuals earning good salaries and having a reasonable amount of leisure time to draw from. There are dozens of physicians and lawyers, scores of schoolteachers, and hundreds of clerks in the departments. As to the coloured department clerks, I think it fair to say that in educational equipment they average above the white clerks of the same grade; for, whereas a coloured college-graduate will seek such a job, the white university-man goes into one of the many higher vocations which are open to him.

In a previous chapter I spoke of social life among coloured people; so there is no need to take it up again here. But there is one thing I did not mention: among Negroes themselves there is the peculiar inconsistency of a colour question. Its existence is rarely admitted and hardly ever mentioned; it may not be too strong a statement to say that the greater portion of the race is unconscious of its influence; yet this influence, though silent, is constant. It is evidenced most plainly in marriage selection; thus the black men generally marry women fairer than themselves; while, on the other hand, the dark women of stronger mental endowment are very often married to light-complexioned men; the effect is a tendency toward lighter complexions, especially among the more active elements in the race. Some might claim that this is a tacit admission of coloured people among themselves of their own inferiority judged by the colour line. I do not think so. What I have termed an inconsistency is, after all, most natural; it is, in fact, a tendency in accordance with what might be called an economic necessity. So far as racial differences go, the United States puts a greater premium on colour, or, better, lack of colour, than upon anything else in the world. To paraphrase, "Have a white skin, and all things else may be added unto you." I have seen advertisements in newspapers for waiters, bell-boys, or elevator men, which read: "Light coloured man wanted." It is this tremendous pressure which the sentiment of the country exerts that is operating on the race. There is involved not only the question of higher opportunity, but often the question of earning a livelihood; and so I say it is not strange, but a natural tendency. Nor is it any more a sacrifice of self-respect that a black man should give to his children every advantage he can which complexion of the skin carries than that the new or vulgar rich should purchase for their children the advantages which ancestry, aristocracy, and social position carry. I once heard a coloured man sum it up in these words: "It's no disgrace to be black, but it's often very inconvenient."

Washington shows the Negro not only at his best, but also at his worst. As I drove round with the doctor, he commented rather harshly on those of the latter class which we saw. He remarked: "You see those lazy, loafing, good-for-nothing darkies; they're not worth digging graves for; yet they are the ones who create impressions of the race for the casual observer. It's because they are always in evidence on the street corners, while the rest of us are hard at work, and you know a dozen loafing darkies make a bigger crowd and a worse impression in this country than fifty white men of the same class. But they ought not to represent the race. We are the race, and the race ought to be judged by us, not by them. Every race and every nation should be judged by the best it has been able to produce, not by the worst."

The recollection of my stay in Washington is a pleasure to me now. In company with the doctor I visited Howard University, the public schools, the excellent coloured hospital, with which he was in some way connected, if I remember correctly, and many comfortable and even elegant homes. It was with some reluctance that I continued my journey south. The doctor was very kind in giving me letters to people in Richmond and Nashville when I told him that I intended to stop in both of these cities. In Richmond a man who was then editing a very creditable coloured newspaper gave me a great deal of his time and made my stay there of three or four days very pleasant. In Nashville I spent a whole day at Fisk University, the home of the "Jubilee Singers,"[3] and was more than repaid for my time. Among my letters of introduction was one to a very prosperous physician. He drove me about the city and introduced me to a number of people. From Nashville I went to Atlanta, where I stayed long enough to gratify an old desire to see Atlanta University again. I then continued my journey to Macon.

3. The first internationally acclaimed group of African American musicians. The singers introduced "slave songs" to the world and helped preserve this music. In 1871 and 1873, they toured the United States and Europe, and funds raised from their concerts were used to construct the school's first permanent building, Jubilee Hall.

During the trip from Nashville to Atlanta I went into the smoking-compartment of the car to smoke a cigar. I was travelling in a Pullman,[4] not because of an abundance of funds, but because through my experience with my millionaire a certain amount of comfort and luxury had become a necessity to me whenever it was obtainable. When I entered the car, I found only a couple of men there; but in a half-hour there were half a dozen or more. From the general conversation I learned that a fat Jewish-looking man was a cigar-manufacturer, and was experimenting in growing Havana tobacco in Florida; that a slender bespectacled young man was from Ohio and a professor in some State institution in Alabama; that a white-moustached, well-dressed man was an old Union soldier who had fought through the Civil War; and that a tall, raw-boned, red-faced man, who seemed bent on leaving nobody in ignorance of the fact that he was from Texas, was a cotton-planter.

In the North men may ride together for hours in a "smoker" and unless they are acquainted with each other never exchange a word; in the South men thrown together in such manner are friends in fifteen minutes. There is always present a warm-hearted cordiality which will melt down the most frigid reserve. It may be because Southerners are very much like Frenchmen in that they must talk; and not only must they talk, but they must express their opinions.

The talk in the car was for a while miscellaneous—on the weather, crops, business prospects; the old Union soldier had invested capital in Atlanta, and he predicted that that city would soon be one of the greatest in the country. Finally the conversation drifted to politics; then, as a natural sequence, turned upon the Negro question.

In the discussion of the race question the diplomacy of the Jew was something to be admired; he had the faculty of agreeing with everybody without losing his allegiance to any side. He knew that to sanction Negro oppression would be to sanction Jewish oppression and would expose him to a shot along that line from the old soldier, who stood firmly on the ground of equal rights and opportunity to all men; long traditions and business instincts told him when in Rome to act as a Roman. Altogether his position was a delicate one, and I gave him credit for the skill he displayed in maintaining it. The young professor was apologetic. He had had the same views as the G. A. R. man;[5] but a year in the South had opened his eyes, and he had to confess that the problem could hardly be handled any better than it was being handled by the Southern whites. To which the G. A. R. man responded somewhat rudely that he had spent ten times as many years in the South as his young friend and that he could easily understand how holding a position in a State institution in Alabama would bring about a change of views. The professor turned very red and had very little more to say. The Texan was fierce, eloquent, and profane in his argument, and, in a lower sense, there was a direct logic in what he said, which was convincing; it was only by taking higher ground, by dealing in what Southerners call "theories," that he could be combated. Occasionally some one of the several other men in the "smoker" would throw in a remark to reinforce what he said, but he really didn't need any help; he was sufficient in himself.

---

4. A sleeping car on a train. George Pullman founded the Pullman Palace Car Company in 1867.

5. Member of the Grand Army of the Republic, a post–Civil War veterans' organization that would become a political force in the South.

In the course of a short time the controversy narrowed itself down to an argument between the old soldier and the Texan. The latter maintained hotly that the Civil War was a criminal mistake on the part of the North and that the humiliation which the South suffered during Reconstruction could never be forgotten. The Union man retorted just as hotly that the South was responsible for the war and that the spirit of unforgetfulness on its part was the greatest cause of present friction; that it seemed to be the one great aim of the South to convince the North that the latter made a mistake in fighting to preserve the Union and liberate the slaves. "Can you imagine," he went on to say, "what would have been the condition of things eventually if there had been no war, and the South had been allowed to follow its course? Instead of one great, prosperous country with nothing before it but the conquests of peace, a score of petty republics, as in Central and South America, wasting their energies in war with each other or in revolutions."

"Well," replied the Texan, "anything—no country at all—is better than having niggers over you. But anyhow, the war was fought and the niggers were freed; for it's no use beating around the bush, the niggers, and not the Union, was the cause of it; and now do you believe that all the niggers on earth are worth the good white blood that was spilt? You freed the nigger and you gave him the ballot, but you couldn't make a citizen out of him. He don't know what he's voting for, and we buy 'em like so many hogs. You're giving 'em education, but that only makes slick rascals out of 'em."

"Don't fancy for a moment," said the Northern man, "that you have any monopoly in buying ignorant votes. The same thing is done on a larger scale in New York and Boston, and in Chicago and San Francisco; and they are not black votes either. As to education's making the Negro worse, you might just as well tell me that religion does the same thing. And, by the way, how many educated coloured men do you know personally?"

The Texan admitted that he knew only one, and added that he was in the penitentiary. "But," he said, "do you mean to claim, ballot or no ballot, education or no education, that niggers are the equals of white men?"

"That's not the question," answered the other, "but if the Negro is so distinctly inferior, it is a strange thing to me that it takes such tremendous effort on the part of the white man to make him realize it, and to keep him in the same place into which inferior men naturally fall. However, let us grant for sake of argument that the Negro is inferior in every respect to the white man; that fact only increases our moral responsibility in regard to our actions toward him. Inequalities of numbers, wealth, and power, even of intelligence and morals, should make no difference in the essential rights of men."

"If he's inferior and weaker, and is shoved to the wall, that's his own lookout," said the Texan. "That's the law of nature; and he's bound to go to the wall; for no race in the world has ever been able to stand competition with the Anglo-Saxon. The Anglo-Saxon race has always been and always will be the masters of the world, and the niggers in the South ain't going to change all the records of history."

"My friend," said the old soldier slowly, "if you have studied history, will you tell me, as confidentially between white men, what the Anglo-Saxon has ever done?"

The Texan was too much astonished by the question to venture any reply.

His opponent continued: "Can you name a single one of the great fundamental and original intellectual achievements which have raised man in the scale of civilization that may be credited to the Anglo-Saxon? The art of letters, of poetry, of music, of sculpture, of painting, of the drama, of architecture; the science of mathematics, of astronomy, of philosophy, of logic, of physics, of chemistry, the use of the metals, and the principles of mechanics, were all invented or discovered by darker and what we now call inferior races and nations. We have carried many of these to their highest point of perfection, but the foundation was laid by others. Do you know the only original contribution to civilization we can claim is what we have done in steam and electricity and in making implements of war more deadly? And there we worked largely on principles which we did not discover. Why, we didn't even originate the religion we use. We are a great race, the greatest in the world today, but we ought to remember that we are standing on a pile of past races, and enjoy our position with a little less show of arrogance. We are simply having our turn at the game, and we were a long time getting to it. After all, racial supremacy is merely a matter of dates in history. The man here who belongs to what is, all in all, the greatest race the world ever produced, is almost ashamed to own it. If the Anglo-Saxon is the source of everything good and great in the human race from the beginning, why wasn't the German forest the birthplace of civilization, rather than the valley of the Nile?"

The Texan was somewhat disconcerted, for the argument had passed a little beyond his limits, but he swung it back to where he was sure of his ground by saying: "All that may be true, but it hasn't got much to do with us and the niggers here in the South. We've got 'em here, and we've got 'em to live with, and it's a question of white man or nigger, no middle ground. You want us to treat niggers as equals. Do you want to see 'em sitting around in our parlours? Do you want to see a mulatto South? To bring it right home to you, would you let your daughter marry a nigger?"

"No, I wouldn't consent to my daughter's marrying a nigger, but that doesn't prevent my treating a black man fairly. And I don't see what fair treatment has to do with niggers sitting round in your parlours; they can't come there unless they're invited. Out of all the white men I know, only a hundred or so have the privilege of sitting round in my parlour. As to the mulatto South, if you Southerners have one boast that is stronger than another, it is your women; you put them on a pinnacle of purity and virtue and bow down in a chivalric worship before them; yet you talk and act as though, should you treat the Negro fairly and take the anti-intermarriage laws off your statute books, these same women would rush into the arms of black lovers and husbands. It's a wonder to me that they don't rise up and resent the insult."

"Colonel," said the Texan, as he reached into his handbag and brought out a large flask of whisky, "you might argue from now until hell freezes over, and you might convince me that you're right, but you'll never convince me that I'm wrong. All you say sounds very good, but it's got nothing to do with facts. You can say what men ought to be, but they ain't that; so there you are. Down here in the South we're up against facts, and we're meeting 'em like facts. We don't believe the nigger is or ever will be the equal of the white man, and we ain't going to treat him as an equal; I'll be damned if we will. Have a drink." Everybody except the professor partook of the generous Texan's flask, and the argument closed in a general laugh and good feeling.

I went back into the main part of the car with the conversation on my mind. Here I had before me the bald, raw, naked aspects of the race question in the South; and, in consideration of the step I was just taking, it was far from encouraging. The sentiments of the Texan—and he expressed the sentiments of the South—fell upon me like a chill. I was sick at heart. Yet I must confess that underneath it all I felt a certain sort of admiration for the man who could not be swayed from what he held as his principles. Contrasted with him, the young Ohio professor was indeed a pitiable character. And all along, in spite of myself, I have been compelled to accord the same kind of admiration to the Southern white man for the manner in which he defends not only his virtues, but his vices. He knows that, judged by a high standard, he is narrow and prejudiced, that he is guilty of unfairness, oppression, and cruelty, but this he defends as stoutly as he would his better qualities. This same spirit obtains in a great degree among the blacks; they, too, defend their faults and failings. This they generally do whenever white people are concerned. And yet among themselves they are their own most merciless critics. I have never heard the race so terribly arraigned as I have by coloured speakers to strictly coloured audiences. It is the spirit of the South to defend everything belonging to it. The North is too cosmopolitan and tolerant for such a spirit. If you should say to an Easterner that Paris is a gayer city than New York, he would be likely to agree with you, or at least to let you have your own way; but to suggest to a South Carolinian that Boston is a nicer city to live in than Charleston would be to stir his greatest depths of argument and eloquence.

But today, as I think over that smoking-car argument, I can see it in a different light. The Texan's position does not render things so hopeless, for it indicates that the main difficulty of the race question does not lie so much in the actual condition of the blacks as it does in the mental attitude of the whites; and a mental attitude, especially one not based on truth, can be changed more easily than actual conditions. That is to say, the burden of the question is not that the whites are struggling to save ten million despondent and moribund people from sinking into a hopeless slough of ignorance, poverty, and barbarity in their very midst, but that they are unwilling to open certain doors of opportunity and to accord certain treatment to ten million aspiring, education-and-property-acquiring people. In a word, the difficulty of the problem is not so much due to the facts presented as to the hypothesis assumed for its solution. In this it is similar to the problem of the solar system. By a complex, confusing, and almost contradictory mathematical process, by the use of zigzags instead of straight lines, the earth can be proved to be the centre of things celestial; but by an operation so simple that it can be comprehended by a schoolboy, its position can be verified among the other worlds which revolve about the sun, and its movements harmonized with the laws of the universe. So, when the white race assumes as a hypothesis that it is the main object of creation and that all things else are merely subsidiary to its well-being, sophism, subterfuge, perversion of conscience, arrogance, injustice, oppression, cruelty, sacrifice of human blood, all are required to maintain the position, and its dealings with other races become indeed a problem, a problem which, if based on a hypothesis of common humanity, could be solved by the simple rules of justice.

When I reached Macon, I decided to leave my trunk and all my surplus belongings, to pack my bag, and strike out into the interior. This I did; and by train, by mule and ox-cart, I travelled through many counties. This was my first real experience among rural coloured people, and all that I saw was interesting to me; but there was a great deal which does not require description at my hands; for log-cabins and plantations and dialect-speaking "darkies" are perhaps better known in American literature than any other single picture of our national life. Indeed, they form an ideal and exclusive literary concept of the American Negro to such an extent that it is almost impossible to get the reading public to recognize him in any other setting; so I shall endeavour to avoid giving the reader any already overworked and hackneyed descriptions. This generally accepted literary ideal of the American Negro constitutes what is really an obstacle in the way of the thoughtful and progressive element of the race. His character has been established as a happy-go-lucky, laughing, shuffling, banjo-picking being, and the reading public has not yet been prevailed upon to take him seriously. His efforts to elevate himself socially are looked upon as a sort of absurd caricature of "white civilization." A novel dealing with coloured people who lived in respectable homes and amidst a fair degree of culture and who naturally acted "just like white folks" would be taken in a comic-opera sense. In this respect the Negro is much in the position of a great comedian who gives up the lighter roles to play tragedy. No matter how well he may portray the deeper passions, the public is loath to give him up in his old character; they even conspire to make him a failure in serious work, in order to force him back into comedy. In the same respect, the public is not too much to be blamed, for great comedians are far more scarce than mediocre tragedians; every amateur actor is a tragedian. However, this very fact constitutes the opportunity of the future Negro novelist and poet to give the country something new and unknown, in depicting the life, the ambitions, the struggles, and the passions of those of their race who are striving to break the narrow limits of traditions. A beginning has already been made in that remarkable book by Dr. Du Bois, *The Souls of Black Folk*.[6]

Much, too, that I saw while on this trip, in spite of my enthusiasm, was disheartening. Often I thought of what my millionaire had said to me, and wished myself back in Europe. The houses in which I had to stay were generally uncomfortable, sometimes worse. I often had to sleep in a division or compartment with several other people. Once or twice I was not so fortunate as to find divisions; everybody slept on pallets on the floor. Frequently I was able to lie down and contemplate the stars which were in their zenith. The food was at times so distasteful and poorly cooked that I could not eat it. I remember that once I lived for a week or more on buttermilk, on account of not being able to stomach the fat bacon, the rank turnip-tops, and the heavy damp mixture of meal, salt, and water which was called corn bread. It was only my ambition to do the work which I had planned that kept me steadfast to my purpose. Occasionally I would meet with some signs of progress and uplift in even one of these backwood settlements—houses built of boards, with windows, and divided into rooms; decent food, and a fair standard of living. This condition was due to the fact that there was in the community some exceptionally capable Negro farmer whose thrift served as an example. As I went about among these dull, simple people—the great majority of them hard working, in their relations with the whites submissive, faithful, and often affectionate, negatively content with their lot—and contrasted them with those of the race who had been quickened by the forces of thought, I could

6. W. E. B. Du Bois (1868–1963), African American intellectual leader, civil rights activist, orator, author, and educator; his *Souls of Black Folks* (1903) is one of the first sociological analyses of African American culture.

not but appreciate the logic of the position held by those Southern leaders who have been bold enough to proclaim against the education of the Negro. They are consistent in their public speech with Southern sentiment and desires. Those public men of the South who have not been daring or heedless enough to defy the ideals of twentieth-century civilization and of modern humanitarianism and philanthropy, find themselves in the embarrassing situation of preaching one thing and praying for another. They are in the position of the fashionable woman who is compelled by the laws of polite society to say to her dearest enemy: "How happy I am to see you!"

And yet in this respect how perplexing is Southern character; for, in opposition to the above, it may be said that the claim of the Southern whites that they love the Negro better than the Northern whites do is in a manner true. Northern white people love the Negro in a sort of abstract way, as a race; through a sense of justice, charity, and philanthropy, they will liberally assist in his elevation. A number of them have heroically spent their lives in this effort (and just here I wish to say that when the coloured people reach the monument-building stage, they should not forget the men and women who went South after the war and founded schools for them). Yet, generally speaking, they have no particular liking for individuals of the race. Southern white people despise the Negro as a race, and will do nothing to aid in his elevation as such; but for certain individuals they have a strong affection, and are helpful to them in many ways. With these individual members of the race they live on terms of the greatest intimacy; they entrust to them their children, their family treasures, and their family secrets; in trouble they often go to them for comfort and counsel; in sickness they often rely upon their care. This affectionate relation between the Southern whites and those blacks who come into close touch with them has not been overdrawn even in fiction.

This perplexity of Southern character extends even to the intermixture of the races. That is spoken of as though it were dreaded worse than smallpox, leprosy, or the plague. Yet, when I was in Jacksonville, I knew several prominent families there with large coloured branches, which went by the same name and were known and acknowledged as blood relatives. And what is more, there seemed to exist between these black brothers and sisters and uncles and aunts a decidedly friendly feeling.

I said above that Southern whites would do nothing for the Negro as a race. I know the South claims that it has spent millions for the education of the blacks, and that it has of its own free will shouldered this awful burden. It seems to be forgetful of the fact that these millions have been taken from the public tax funds for education, and that the law of political economy which recognizes the land-owner as the one who really pays the taxes is not tenable. It would be just as reasonable for the relatively few land-owners of Manhattan to complain that they had to stand the financial burden of the education of the thousands and thousands of children whose parents pay rent for tenements and flats. Let the millions of producing and consuming Negroes be taken out of the South, and it would be quickly seen how much less of public funds there would be to appropriate for education or any other purpose.

In thus travelling about through the country I was sometimes amused on arriving at some little railroad-station town to be taken for and treated as a white man, and six hours later, when it was learned that I was stopping at the house of the coloured preacher or school-teacher, to note the attitude of the whole town change. At times this led even to embarrassment. Yet it cannot be so embarrassing for a coloured man to be taken for white as for a white man to be taken for coloured; and I have heard of several cases of the latter kind.

All this while I was gathering material for work, jotting down in my note-book themes and melodies, and trying to catch the spirit of the Negro in his relatively primitive state. I began to feel the necessity of hurrying so that I might get back to some city like Nashville to begin my compositions and at the same time earn at least a living by teaching and performing before my funds gave out. At the last settlement in which I stopped I found a mine of material. This was due to the fact that "big meeting" was in progress. "Big meeting" is an institution something like camp-meeting, the difference being that it is held in a permanent church, and not in a temporary structure. All the churches of some one denomination—of course, either Methodist or Baptist—in a county, or, perhaps, in several adjoining counties, are closed, and the congregations unite at some centrally located church for a series of meetings lasting a week. It is really a social as well as a religious function. The people come in great numbers, making the trip, according to their financial status, in buggies drawn by sleek, fleet-footed mules, in ox-carts, or on foot. It was amusing to see some of the latter class trudging down the hot and dusty road, with their shoes, which were brand-new, strung across their shoulders. When they got near the church, they sat on the side of the road and, with many grimaces, tenderly packed their feet into those instruments of torture. This furnished, indeed, a trying test of their religion. The famous preachers come from near and far and take turns in warning sinners of the day of wrath. Food, in the form of those two Southern luxuries, fried chicken and roast pork, is plentiful, and no one need go hungry. On the opening Sunday the women are immaculate in starched stiff white dresses adorned with ribbons, either red or blue. Even a great many of the men wear streamers of vari-coloured ribbons in the buttonholes of their coats. A few of them carefully cultivate a forelock of hair by wrapping it in twine, and on such festive occasions decorate it with a narrow ribbon streamer. Big meetings afford a fine opportunity to the younger people to meet each other dressed in their Sunday clothes, and much rustic courting, which is as enjoyable as any other kind, is indulged in.

This big meeting which I was lucky enough to catch was particularly well attended; the extra large attendance was due principally to two attractions, a man by the name of John Brown,[7] who was renowned as the most powerful preacher for miles around; and a wonderful leader of singing, who was known as "Singing Johnson."[8] These two men were a study and a revelation to me. They caused me to reflect upon how great an influence their types have been in the development of the Negro in America. Both these types are now looked upon generally with condescension or contempt by the progressive element among the coloured people; but it should never be forgotten that it was they who led the race from paganism and kept it steadfast to Christianity through all the long, dark years of slavery.

7. Suggestive of American abolitionist preacher John Brown (1800–1859), most famous for the raid on the federal armory at Harpers Ferry, Virginia, for which he was tried and hanged for treason.

8. A highly popular itinerant spiritual folk singer referred to by Johnson in his *Book of American Negro Spirituals* (1925).

John Brown was a jet-black man of medium size, with a strikingly intelligent head and face, and a voice like an organ peal. He preached each night after several lesser lights had successively held the pulpit during an hour or so. As far as subject-matter is concerned, all of the sermons were alike: each began with the fall of man, ran through various trials and tribulations of the Hebrew children, on to the redemption by Christ, and ended with a fervid picture of the judgment-day and the fate of the damned. But John Brown possessed magnetism and an imagination so free and daring that he was able to carry through what the other preachers would not attempt. He knew all the arts and tricks of oratory, the modulation of the voice to almost a whisper, the pause for effect, the rise through light, rapid-fire sentences to the terrific, thundering outburst of an electrifying climax. In addition, he had the intuition of a born theatrical manager. Night after night this man held me fascinated. He convinced me that, after all, eloquence consists more in the manner of saying than in what is said. It is largely a matter of tone pictures.

The most striking example of John Brown's magnetism and imagination was his "heavenly march"; I shall never forget how it impressed me when I heard it. He opened his sermon in the usual way; then, proclaiming to his listeners that he was going to take them on the heavenly march, he seized the Bible under his arm and began to pace up and down the pulpit platform. The congregation immediately began with their feet a tramp, tramp, tramp, in time with the preacher's march in the pulpit, all the while singing in an undertone a hymn about marching to Zion. Suddenly he cried: "Halt!" Every foot stopped with the precision of a company of well-drilled soldiers, and the singing ceased. The morning star had been reached. Here the preacher described the beauties of that celestial body. Then the march, the tramp, tramp, tramp, and the singing were again taken up. Another "Halt!" They had reached the evening star. And so on, past the sun and moon—the intensity of religious emotion all the time increasing—along the milky way, on up to the gates of heaven. Here the halt was longer, and the preacher described at length the gates and walls of the New Jerusalem. Then he took his hearers through the pearly gates, along the golden streets, pointing out the glories of the city, pausing occasionally to greet some patriarchal members of the church, well-known to most of his listeners in life, who had had "the tears wiped from their eyes, were clad in robes of spotless white, with crowns of gold upon their heads and harps within their hands," and ended his march before the great white throne. To the reader this may sound ridiculous, but listened to under the circumstances, it was highly and effectively dramatic. I was a more or less sophisticated and non-religious man of the world, but the torrent of the preacher's words, moving with the rhythm and glowing with the eloquence of primitive poetry, swept me along, and I, too, felt like joining in the shouts of "Amen! Hallelujah!"

John Brown's powers in describing the delights of heaven were no greater than those in depicting the horrors of hell. I saw great, strapping fellows trembling and weeping like children at the "mourners' bench." His warnings to sinners were truly terrible. I shall never forget one expression that he used, which for originality and aptness could not be excelled. In my opinion, it is more graphic and, for us, far more expressive than St. Paul's "It is hard to kick against the pricks." He struck the attitude of a pugilist and thundered out: "Young man, your arm's too short to box with God!"

Interesting as was John Brown to me, the other man, "Singing Johnson," was more so. He was a small, dark-brown, one-eyed man, with a clear, strong, high-pitched voice, a leader of singing, a maker of songs, a man who could improvise at the moment lines to fit the occasion. Not so striking a figure as John Brown, but, at "big meetings," equally important. It is indispensable to the success of the singing, when the congregation is a large one made up of people from different communities, to have someone with a strong voice who knows just what hymn to sing and when to sing it, who can pitch it in the right key, and who has all the leading lines committed to memory. Sometimes it devolves upon the leader to "sing down" a long-winded or uninteresting speaker. Committing to memory the leading lines of all the Negro spiritual songs is no easy task, for they run up into the hundreds. But the accomplished leader must know them all, because the congregation sings only the refrains and repeats; every ear in the church is fixed upon him, and if he becomes mixed in his lines or forgets them, the responsibility falls directly on his shoulders.

For example, most of these hymns are constructed to be sung in the following manner:

> *Leader.* Swing low, sweet chariot.
> *Congregation.* Coming for to carry me home.
> *Leader.* Swing low, sweet chariot.
> *Congregation.* Coming for to carry me home.
> *Leader.* I look over yonder, what do I see?
> *Congregation.* Coming for to carry me home.
> *Leader.* Two little angels coming after me.
> *Congregation.* Coming for to carry me home. . . . [9]

The solitary and plaintive voice of the leader is answered by a sound like the roll of the sea, producing a most curious effect.

In only a few of these songs do the leader and the congregation start off together. Such a song is the well-known "Steal away to Jesus."[1]

The leader and the congregation begin with part-singing:

> Steal away, steal away,
> Steal away to Jesus;
> Steal away, steal away home,
> I ain't got long to stay here.

Then the leader alone or the congregation in unison:

> My Lord he calls me,
> He calls me by the thunder,
> The trumpet sounds within-a my soul.

Then all together:

> I ain't got long to stay here.

The leader and the congregation again take up the opening refrain; then the leader sings three more leading lines alone, and so on almost *ad infinitum*. It will be seen that even here most of the work falls upon the leader, for

9. A Negro spiritual recited in traditional call-and-response form.

1. Another spiritual, in which the leader and congregation begin in unison.

the congregation sings the same lines over and over, while his memory and ingenuity are taxed to keep the songs going.

Generally the parts taken up by the congregation are sung in a three-part harmony, the women singing the soprano and a transposed tenor, the men with high voices singing the melody, and those with low voices a thundering bass. In a few of these songs, however, the leading part is sung in unison by the whole congregation, down to the last line, which is harmonized. The effect of this is intensely thrilling. Such a hymn is "Go down, Moses."[2] It stirs the heart like a trumpet-call.

"Singing Johnson" was an ideal leader, and his services were in great demand. He spent his time going about the country from one church to another. He received his support in much the same way as the preachers—part of a collection, food and lodging. All of his leisure time he devoted to originating new words and melodies and new lines for old songs. He always sang with his eyes—or, to be more exact, his eye—closed, indicating the *tempo* by swinging his head to and fro. He was a great judge of the proper hymn to sing at a particular moment; and I noticed several times, when the preacher reached a certain climax, or expressed a certain sentiment, that Johnson broke in with a line or two of some appropriate hymn. The speaker understood and would pause until the singing ceased.

As I listened to the singing of these songs, the wonder of their production grew upon me more and more. How did the men who originated them manage to do it? The sentiments are easily accounted for; they are mostly taken from the Bible; but the melodies, where did they come from? Some of them so weirdly sweet, and others so wonderfully strong. Take, for instance, "Go down, Moses." I doubt that there is a stronger theme in the whole musical literature of the world. And so many of these songs contain more than mere melody; there is sounded in them that elusive undertone, the note in music which is not heard with the ears. I sat often with the tears rolling down my cheeks and my heart melted within me. Any musical person who has never heard a Negro congregation under the spell of religious fervour sing these old songs has missed one of the most thrilling emotions which the human heart may experience. Anyone who without shedding tears can listen to Negroes sing "Nobody knows de trouble I see, Nobody knows but Jesus"[3] must indeed have a heart of stone.

As yet, the Negroes themselves do not fully appreciate these old slave songs. The educated classes are rather ashamed of them and prefer to sing hymns from books. This feeling is natural; they are still too close to the conditions under which the songs were produced; but the day will come when this slave music will be the most treasured heritage of the American Negro.

At the close of the "big meeting" I left the settlement where it was being held, full of enthusiasm. I was in that frame of mind which, in the artistic temperament, amounts to inspiration. I was now ready and anxious to get to some place where I might settle down to work, and give expression to the ideas which were teeming in my head; but I strayed into another deviation from my path of life as I had it marked out, which led me upon an entirely different road. Instead of going to the nearest and most convenient railroad

2. Spiritual in which all but the last verse is sung in unison.

3. Spiritual comparing slavery to the trial of Jesus on the cross.

station, I accepted the invitation of a young man who had been present the closing Sunday at the meeting to drive with him some miles farther to the town in which he taught school, and there take the train. My conversation with this young man as we drove along through the country was extremely interesting. He had been a student in one of the Negro colleges—strange coincidence, in the very college, as I learned through him, in which "Shiny"[4] was now a professor. I was, of course, curious to hear about my boyhood friend; and had it not been vacation time, and that I was not sure that I should find him, I should have gone out of my way to pay him a visit; but I determined to write to him as soon as the school opened. My companion talked to me about his work among the people, of his hopes and his discouragements. He was tremendously in earnest; I might say, too much so. In fact, it may be said that the majority of intelligent coloured people are, in some degree, too much in earnest over the race question. They assume and carry so much that their progress is at times impeded and they are unable to see things in their proper proportions. In many instances a slight exercise of the sense of humour would save much anxiety of soul. Anyone who marks the general tone of editorials in coloured newspapers is apt to be impressed with this idea. If the mass of Negroes took their present and future as seriously as do the most of their leaders, the race would be in no mental condition to sustain the terrible pressure which it undergoes; it would sink of its own weight. Yet it must be acknowledged that in the making of a race over-seriousness is a far lesser failing than its reverse, and even the faults resulting from it lean toward the right.

We drove into the town just before dark. As we passed a large, unpainted church, my companion pointed it out as the place where he held his school. I promised that I would go there with him the next morning and visit awhile. The town was of that kind which hardly requires or deserves description; a straggling line of brick and wooden stores on one side of the railroad track and some cottages of various sizes on the other side constituted about the whole of it. The young school-teacher boarded at the best house in the place owned by a coloured man. It was painted, had glass windows, contained "store bought" furniture, an organ, and lamps with chimneys. The owner held a job of some kind on the railroad. After supper it was not long before everybody was sleepy. I occupied the room with the school-teacher. In a few minutes after we got into the room he was in bed and asleep; but I took advantage of the unusual luxury of a lamp which gave light, and sat looking over my notes and jotting down some ideas which were still fresh in my mind. Suddenly I became conscious of that sense of alarm which is always aroused by the sound of hurrying footsteps on the silence of the night. I stopped work and looked at my watch. It was after eleven. I listened, straining every nerve to hear above the tumult of my quickening pulse. I caught the murmur of voices, then the gallop of a horse, then of another and another. Now thoroughly alarmed, I woke my companion, and together we both listened. After a moment he put out the light and softly opened the window-blind, and we cautiously peeped out. We saw men moving in one direction, and from the mutterings we vaguely caught the rumour that some terrible crime had been committed. I put on my coat and hat. My friend did all in his power to dis-

---

4. Boyhood schoolmate and friend of the narrator's.

suade me from venturing out, but it was impossible for me to remain in the house under such tense excitement. My nerves would not have stood it. Perhaps what bravery I exercised in going out was due to the fact that I felt sure my identity as a coloured man had not yet become known in the town.

I went out and, following the drift, reached the railroad station. There was gathered there a crowd of men, all white, and others were steadily arriving, seemingly from all the surrounding country. How did the news spread so quickly? I watched these men moving under the yellow glare of the kerosene lamps about the station, stern, comparatively silent, all of them armed, some of them in boots and spurs; fierce, determined men. I had come to know the type well, blond, tall, and lean, with ragged moustache and beard, and glittering grey eyes. At the first suggestion of daylight they began to disperse in groups, going in several directions. There was no extra noise or excitement, no loud talking, only swift, sharp words of command given by those who seemed to be accepted as leaders by mutual understanding. In fact, the impression made upon me was that everything was being done in quite an orderly manner. In spite of so many leaving, the crowd around the station continued to grow; at sunrise there were a great many women and children. By this time I also noticed some coloured people; a few seemed to be going about customary tasks; several were standing on the outskirts of the crowd; but the gathering of Negroes usually seen in such towns was missing.

Before noon they brought him in. Two horsemen rode abreast; between them, half dragged, the poor wretch made his way through the dust. His hands were tied behind him, and ropes round his body were fastened to the saddle horns of his double guard. The men who at midnight had been stern and silent were now emitting that terror-instilling sound known as the "rebel yell." A space was quickly cleared in the crowd, and a rope placed about his neck, when from somewhere came the suggestion, "Burn him!" It ran like an electric current. Have you ever witnessed the transformation of human beings into savage beasts? Nothing can be more terrible. A railroad tie was sunk into the ground, the rope was removed, and a chain brought and securely coiled round the victim and the stake. There he stood, a man only in form and stature, every sign of degeneracy stamped upon his countenance. His eyes were dull and vacant, indicating not a single ray of thought. Evidently the realization of his fearful fate had robbed him of whatever reasoning power he had ever possessed. He was too stunned and stupefied even to tremble. Fuel was brought from everywhere, oil, the torch; the flames crouched for an instant as though to gather strength, then leaped up as high as their victim's head. He squirmed, he writhed, strained at his chains, then gave out cries and groans that I shall always hear. The cries and groans were choked off by the fire and smoke; but his eyes, bulging from their sockets, rolled from side to side, appealing in vain for help. Some of the crowd yelled and cheered, others seemed appalled at what they had done, and there were those who turned away sickened at the sight. I was fixed to the spot where I stood, powerless to take my eyes from what I did not want to see.

It was over before I realized that time had elapsed. Before I could make myself believe that what I saw was really happening, I was looking at a scorched post, a smouldering fire, blackened bones, charred fragments sifting down through coils of chain; and the smell of burnt flesh—human flesh—was in my nostrils.

I walked a short distance away and sat down in order to clear my dazed mind. A great wave of humiliation and shame swept over me. Shame that I belonged to a race that could be so dealt with; and shame for my country, that it, the great example of democracy to the world, should be the only civilized, if not the only state on earth, where a human being would be burned alive. My heart turned bitter within me. I could understand why Negroes are led to sympathize with even their worst criminals and to protect them when possible. By all the impulses of normal human nature they can and should do nothing less.

Whenever I hear protests from the South that it should be left alone to deal with the Negro question, my thoughts go back to that scene of brutality and savagery. I do not see how a people that can find in its conscience any excuse whatever for slowly burning to death a human being, or for tolerating such an act, can be entrusted with the salvation of a race. Of course, there are in the South men of liberal thought who do not approve lynching, but I wonder how long they will endure the limits which are placed upon free speech. They still cower and tremble before "Southern opinion." Even so late as the recent Atlanta riot[5] those men who were brave enough to speak a word in behalf of justice and humanity felt called upon, by way of apology, to preface what they said with a glowing rhetorical tribute to the Anglo-Saxon's superiority and to refer to the "great and impassable gulf" between the races "fixed by the Creator at the foundation of the world." The question of the relative qualities of the two races is still an open one. The reference to the "great gulf" loses force in face of the fact that there are in this country perhaps three or four million people with the blood of both races in their veins; but I fail to see the pertinency of either statement subsequent to the beating and murdering of scores of innocent people in the streets of a civilized and Christian city.

The Southern whites are in many respects a great people. Looked at from a certain point of view, they are picturesque. If one will put oneself in a romantic frame of mind, one can admire their notions of chivalry and bravery and justice. In this same frame of mind an intelligent man can go to the theatre and applaud the impossible hero, who with his single sword slays everybody in the play except the equally impossible heroine. So can an ordinary peace-loving citizen sit by a comfortable fire and read with enjoyment of the bloody deeds of pirates and the fierce brutality of vikings. This is the way in which we gratify the old, underlying animal instincts and passions; but we should shudder with horror at the mere idea of such practices being realities in this day of enlightened and humanitarianized thought. The Southern whites are not yet living quite in the present age; many of their general ideas hark back to a former century, some of them to the Dark Ages. In the light of other days they are sometimes magnificent. Today they are often cruel and ludicrous.

How long I sat with bitter thoughts running through my mind I do not know; perhaps an hour or more. When I decided to get up and go back to the house, I found that I could hardly stand on my feet. I was as weak as a man who had lost blood. However, I dragged myself along, with the central idea of a general plan well fixed in my mind. I did not find my school-teacher

5. In 1906 white Atlantans, in response to alleged assaults of black men on white women, indiscriminately attacked black Atlantans, killing at least sixteen men.

friend at home, so I did not see him again. I swallowed a few mouthfuls of food, packed my bag, and caught the afternoon train.

When I reached Macon, I stopped only long enough to get the main part of my luggage and to buy a ticket for New York. All along the journey I was occupied in debating with myself the step which I had decided to take. I argued that to forsake one's race to better one's condition was no less worthy an action than to forsake one's country for the same purpose. I finally made up my mind that I would neither disclaim the black race nor claim the white race; but that I would change my name, raise a moustache, and let the world take me for what it would; that it was not necessary for me to go about with a label of inferiority pasted across my forehead. All the while I understood that it was not discouragement or fear or search for a larger field of action and opportunity that was driving me out of the Negro race. I knew that it was shame, unbearable shame. Shame at being identified with a people that could with impunity be treated worse than animals. For certainly the law would restrain and punish the malicious burning alive of animals.

So once again I found myself gazing at the towers of New York and wondering what future that city held in store for me.

1912

---

# PAUL LAURENCE DUNBAR
## 1872–1906

Paul Laurence Dunbar was one of the first professional African American literary figures, publishing six volumes of poetry, beginning with *Oak and Ivy* in 1893, as well as novels, librettos, songs, and essays. Dunbar's father, Joshua, who had escaped slavery in Kentucky and moved to Ohio via the Underground Railroad, served in the 55th Massachusetts Regiment of the Union Army during the Civil War. His mother, Matilda Murphy, also a former slave, separated from Joshua when Dunbar was two years old. Throughout his childhood, Matilda encouraged Paul in his education, often doing without so that he could continue in school. Though Dunbar first wanted to be a lawyer, he chose instead "to be a worthy singer of the songs of God and nature." He wanted "to interpret my own people though song and story, and prove to the many that we are more human than African."

Dunbar early on developed an ear for language and a love of Romantic poetry. Yet upon graduation from Central High School, in Dayton, Ohio, where he'd been student and class leader, the only jobs open to him were menial ones. In 1892 he was invited to read a poem at the Western Association of Writers, which was convening in Dayton. Inspired by this, he traveled in 1893 to the Columbian Exposition in Chicago, where he met Frederick Douglass and sold *Oak and Ivy* for a dollar per copy. Douglass—then U.S. minister to Haiti and Commissioner of the Haitian Exhibition—hired him as a clerk.

In 1895 Dunbar published his best-known work, *Lyrics of the Lowly Life*, from which most of the selections here are drawn. Committed to rendering the authentic voice of the black speaker, and inspired by Shakespeare, Shelley, Keats, and Tennyson, Dunbar published in such popular venues as the *New York Times, Century, Lippincott's Monthly*, and the *Saturday Evening Post*, journals with almost exclusively white readerships. Though he was celebrated by black and white literary leaders, among them

Douglass, Booker T. Washington, W. E. B. DuBois, William Dean Howells, Eugene Field, and James Whitcomb Riley, he was criticized in the 1920s by Harlem Renaissance leaders who saw him as catering to a white audience with "colorful" black folk elements and dialect. Despite this criticism, Dunbar's influence on subsequent African American writers such as Zora Neale Hurston is precisely that he presented traditional dialect, customs, and other cultural elements without apology.

Dunbar married writer Alice Moore in 1898; they lived in the Le Droit Park section of Washington, DC, an area that welcomed the new black middle class and where they enjoyed the company of black intellectuals, activists, and artists. They separated in 1902, in part due to Dunbar's alcoholism, and Dunbar's poetry after that time reflects a more somber mood. When he returned to Dayton to live with his mother, he believed that he had failed as a poet. Critical and popular attention to his work continued to grow throughout the twentieth century, however, and Dunbar is now recognized as a pioneer in creating a new black poetic diction.

# When Malindy Sings[1]

G'way an' quit dat noise, Miss Lucy—
   Put dat music book away;
What 's de use to keep on tryin'?
   Ef you practise twell you're gray,
You cain't sta't no notes a-flyin'          5
   Lak de ones dat rants and rings
F'om de kitchen to be big woods
   When Malindy sings.

You ain't got de nachel o'gans
   Fu' to make de soun' come right,         10
You ain't got de tu'ns an' twistin's
   Fu' to make it sweet an' light.
Tell you one thing now, Miss Lucy,
   An' I 'm tellin' you fu' true,
When hit comes to raal right singin',     15
   'T ain't no easy thing to do.

Easy 'nough fu' folks to hollah,
   Lookin' at de lines an' dots,
When dey ain't no one kin sence it,
   An' de chune comes in, in spots;     20
But fu' real melojous music,
   Dat jes' strikes yo' hea't and clings,
Jes' you stan' an' listen wif me
   When Malindy sings.

Ain't you nevah hyeahd Malindy?     25
   Blessed soul, tek up de cross!
Look hyeah, ain't you jokin', honey?
   Well, you don't know whut you los'.

---

1. First published in Dunbar's *Lyrics of the Lowly Life* (1897) and then in his *Complete Poems* (1903); rpt. in *The Complete Poems of Paul Laurence Dunbar* (1993), from which this text is taken.

Y' ought to hyeah dat gal a-wa'blin',
    Robins, la'ks, an' all dem things,        30
Heish dey moufs an' hides dey faces
    When Malindy sings.

Fiddlin' man jes' stop his fiddlin',
    Lay his fiddle on de she'f;
Mockin'-bird quit tryin' to whistle,        35
    'Cause he jes' so shamed hisse'f.
Folks a-playin' on de banjo
    Draps dey fingahs on de strings—
Bless yo' soul—fu'gits to move em,
    When Malindy sings.        40

She jes' spreads huh mouf and hollahs,
    "Come to Jesus," twell you hyeah
Sinnahs' tremblin' steps and voices,
    Timid-lak a-drawin' neah;
Den she tu'ns to "Rock of Ages,"        45
    Simply to de cross she clings,
An' you fin' yo' teahs a-drappin'
    When Malindy sings.

Who dat says dat humble praises
    Wif de Master nevah counts?        50
Heish yo' mouf, I hyeah dat music,
    Ez hit rises up an' mounts—
Floatin' by de hills an' valleys,
    Way above dis buryin' sod,
Ez hit makes its way in glory        55
    To de very gates of God!

Oh, hit 's sweetah dan de music
    Of an edicated band;
An' hit 's dearah dan de battle's
    Song o' triumph in de lan'.        60
It seems holier dan evenin'
    When de solemn chu'ch bell rings,
Ez I sit an' ca'mly listen
    While Malindy sings.

Towsah, stop dat ba'kin', hyeah me!        65
    Mandy, mek dat chile keep still;
Don't you hyeah de echoes callin'
    F'om de valley to de hill?
Let me listen, I can hyeah it,
    Th'oo de bresh of angels' wings,        70
Sof' an' sweet, "Swing Low, Sweet Chariot,"
    Ez Malindy sings.

                                        1897

# An Ante-Bellum Sermon[1]

We is gathahed hyeah, my brothahs,
    In dis howlin' wildaness,
Fu' to speak some words of comfo't
    To each othah in distress.
An' we chooses fu' ouah subjic'          5
    Dis—we 'll 'splain it by an' by;
"An' de Lawd said, 'Moses, Moses,'
    An' de man said, 'Hyeah am I.' "

Now ole Pher'oh, down in Egypt,
    Was de wuss man evah bo'n,          10
An' he had de Hebrew chillun
    Down dah wukin' in his co'n;
'T well de Lawd got tiahed o' his foolin',
    An' sez he: "I'll let him know—
Look hyeah, Moses, go tell Pher'oh          15
    Fu' to let dem chillun go."

"An' ef he refuse to do it,
    I will make him rue de houah,
Fu' I 'll empty down on Egypt
    All de vials of my powah."          20
Yes, he did—an' Pher'oh's ahmy
    Was n't wuth a ha'f a dime;
Fu' de Lawd will he'p his chilun,
    You kin trust him evah time.

An' yo' enemies may 'sail you          25
    In de back an' in de front;
But de Lawd is all aroun' you,
    Fu' to ba' de battle's brunt.
Dey kin fo'ge yo' chains an' shackles
    F'om de mountains to de sea;          30
But de Lawd will sen' some Moses
    Fu' to set his chillun free.

An' de lan' shall hyeah his thundah,
    Lak a blas' f'om Gab'el's ho'n,
Fu' de Lawd of hosts is mighty          35
    When he girds his ahmor on.
But fu' feah some one mistakes me,
    I will pause right hyeah to say,
Dat I 'm still a-preachin' ancient,
    I ain't talkin' 'bout to-day.         40

---

1. First published in Dunbar's *Lyrics of the Lowly Life* (1897) and then in his *Complete Poems* (1903); rpt. in *The Complete Poems of Paul Laurence Dunbar* (1993), from which this text is taken.

But I tell you, fellah christuns,
  Things 'll happen mighty strange;
Now, de Lawd done dis fu' Isrul,
  An' his ways don't nevah change,
An' de love he showed to Isrul                    45
  Was n't all on Isrul spent;
Now don't run an' tell yo' mastahs
  Dat I 's preachin' discontent.

'Cause I is n't; I 'se a-judgin'
  Bible people by deir ac's;                      50
I 'se a-givin' you de Scriptuah,
  I 'se a-handin' you de fac's.
Cose ole Pher'oh b'lieved in slav'ry,
  But de Lawd he let him see,
Dat de people he put bref in,—                    55
  Evah mothah's son was free.

An' dahs othahs thinks lak Pher'oh,
  But dey calls de Scriptuah liar,
Fu' de Bible says "a servant
  Is a-worthy of his hire."[2]                    60
An' you cain't git roun' nor thoo dat,
  An' you cain't git ovah it,
Fu' whatevah place you git in,
  Dis hyeah Bible too 'll fit.

So you see de Lawd's intention,                   65
  Evah sence de worl' began,
Was dat His almighty freedom
  Should belong to evah man,
But I think it would be bettah,
  Ef I 'd pause agin to say,                      70
Dat I 'm talkin' 'bout ouah freedom
  In a Bibleistic way.

But de Moses is a-comin',
  An' he 's comin', suah and fas'
We kin hyeah his feet a-trompin',                 75
  We kin hyeah his trumpit blas'.
But I want to wa'n you people,
  Don't you git too brigity;[3]
An' don't you git to braggin'
  'Bout dese things, you wait an' see.            80

But when Moses wif his powah
  Comes an' sets us chillun free,
We will praise de gracious Mastah

---

2. Biblical mandate against the unethical practice
of masters withholding wages from their servants,
here used to indict slavery (Leviticus 19.13,
Deuteronomy 24.15 and 25).
3. Brazen, presumptuous, or insolent.

Dat has gin us liberty;
An' we 'll shout ouah halleluyahs,                    85
On dat mighty reck'nin' day,
When we 'se reco'nised ez citiz'—
Huh uh! Chillun, let us pray!

1897

## We Wear the Mask[1]

We wear the mask that grins and lies,
It hides our cheeks and shades our eyes,—
This debt we pay to human guile;
With torn and bleeding hearts we smile,
And mouth with myriad subtleties.                    5

Why should the world be overwise,
In counting all our tears and sighs?
Nay, let them only see us, while
        We wear the mask.

We smile, but, O great Christ, our cries              10
To thee from tortured souls arise.
We sing, but oh the clay is vile
Beneath our feet, and long the mile;
But let the world dream otherwise,
        We wear the mask!                              15

1897

## Sympathy[1]

I know what the caged bird feels, alas!
    When the sun is bright on the upland slopes;
When the wind stirs soft through the springing grass,
And the river flows like a stream of glass;
    When the first bird sings and the first bud opes,  5
And the faint perfume from its chalice steals—
I know what the caged bird feels!

I know why the caged bird beats his wing
    Till its blood is red on the cruel bars;
For he must fly back to his perch and cling           10
When he fain would be on the bough a-swing;

1. First published in Dunbar's *Lyrics of the Lowly Life* (1897) and then in his *Complete Poems* (1903); rpt. in *The Complete Poems of Paul Laurence Dunbar* (1993), from which this text is taken.

1. First published in Dunbar's *Lyrics of the Hearthside* (1899) and then in his *Complete Poems* (1903); rpt. in *The Complete Poems of Paul Laurence Dunbar* (1993), from which this text is taken.

And a pain still throbs in the old, old scars
And they pulse again with a keener sting—
I know why he beats his wing!

I know why the caged bird sings, ah me,           15
   When his wing is bruised and his bosom sore,—
When he beats his bars and he would be free;
It is not a carol of joy or glee,
   But a prayer that he sends from his heart's deep core,
But a plea, that upward to Heaven he flings—      20
I know why the caged bird sings!

1899

## Harriet Beecher Stowe[1]

She told the story, and the whole world wept
   At wrongs and cruelties it had not known
   But for this fearless woman's voice alone.
She spoke to consciences that long had slept:
Her message, Freedom's clear reveille, swept      5
   From heedless hovel to complacent throne.
   Command and prophecy were in the tone
And from its sheath the sword of justice leapt.
Around two peoples swelled a fiery wave,
   But both came forth transfigured from the flame.     10
Blest be the hand that dared be strong to save,
   And blest be she who in our weakness came—
Prophet and priestess! At one stroke she gave
A race to freedom and herself to fame.

1899

## Frederick Douglass[1]

A hush is over all the teeming lists,
   And there is pause, a breath-space in the strife;
A spirit brave has passed beyond the mists
   And vapors that obscure the sun of life.
And Ethiopia, with bosom torn,[2]      5
Laments the passing of her noblest born.

1. First published in Dunbar's *Lyrics of the Hearth-side* (1899) and then in his *Complete Poems* (1903); rpt. in *The Complete Poems of Paul Laurence Dunbar* (1993), from which this text is taken. Harriet Beecher Stowe (1811–1896), abolitionist and author of many books, the most famous being *Uncle Tom's Cabin* (1852).
1. First published in Dunbar's *Lyrics of Love and Laughter* (1903), then in *The Complete Poems* (1903); rpt. in *The Complete Poems of Paul Laurence Dunbar* (1993), from which this text is taken.

Frederick Douglass (1818–1895) was the author of *Narrative of the Life of Frederick Douglass* (1845), in which he recounts his birth into slavery, escape into freedom, and eventual involvement with the abolitionist movement, through which he became the most prominent African American in the world.
2. Eastern African country whose long history as an independent nation made it a symbol of African independence for abolitionists, slaves, and, later, civil rights leaders.

She weeps for him a mother's burning tears—
    She loved him with a mother's deepest love.
He was her champion thro' direful years,
    And held her weal all other ends above. 10
When Bondage held her bleeding in the dust,
He raised her up and whispered, "Hope and Trust."

For her his voice, a fearless clarion, rung
    That broke in warning on the ears of men;
For her the strong bow of his power he strung, 15
    And sent his arrows to the very den
Where grim Oppression held his bloody place
And gloated o'er the mis'ries of a race.

And he was no soft-tongued apologist;
    He spoke straightforward, fearlessly uncowed; 20
The sunlight of his truth dispelled the mist,
    And set in bold relief each dark hued cloud;
To sin and crime he gave their proper hue,
And hurled at evil what was evil's due.

Through good and ill report he cleaved his way 25
    Right onward, with his face set toward the heights,
Nor feared to face the foeman's dread array,—
    The lash of scorn, the sting of petty spites.
He dared the lightning in the lightning's track,
And answered thunder with his thunder back. 30

When men maligned him, and their torrent wrath
    In furious imprecations o'er him broke,
He kept his counsel as he kept his path;
    'T was for his race, not for himself he spoke.
He knew the import of his Master's call, 35
And felt himself too mighty to be small.

No miser in the good he held was he,—
    His kindness followed his horizon's rim.
His heart, his talents, and his hands were free
    To all who truly needed aught of him. 40
Where poverty and ignorance were rife,
He gave his bounty as he gave his life.

The place and cause that first aroused his might
    Still proved its power until his latest day.
In Freedom's lists and for the aid of Right 45
    Still in the foremost rank he waged the fray;
Wrong lived; his occupation was not gone.
He died in action with his armor on!

We weep for him, but we have touched his hand,
    And felt the magic of his presence nigh, 50
The current that he sent throughout the land,
    The kindling spirit of his battlecry.

O'er all that holds us we shall triumph yet,
And place our banner where his hopes were set!

Oh, Douglass, thou hast passed beyond the shore,                    55
    But still thy voice is ringing o'er the gale!
Thou 'st taught thy race how high her hopes may soar,
    And bade her seek the heights, nor faint, nor fail.
She will not fail, she heeds thy stirring cry,
She knows thy guardian spirit will be nigh,                         60
And, rising from beneath the chast'ning rod,
She stretches out her bleeding hands to God!

                                                                1903

---

# JOHN M. OSKISON
## 1874–1947

John Milton Oskison was born in Vinita, Indian Territory, son of a white father and Cherokee mother. His father, John Oskison, had been born on an English tenant farm, orphaned in childhood, and brought to Illinois by an uncle whose mistreatment apparently caused him to run away. He worked at a variety of jobs, in a variety of places, coming eventually to Indian Territory (now Oklahoma), where he married a Cherokee woman, Rachel Crittenden. Although John Oskison Sr. had little formal education, he valued learning, naming his son John Milton and determining that he would have a chance to become well-educated. Oskison enrolled first at Willie Haskell College, which was a preparatory school rather than a college, in Vinita, and went on to Stanford University in 1898.

While Oskison advocated education in the white world for Indians, he was still fiercely proud of traditional Cherokee values and aware that these might be threatened by opportunistic Native people as well as by unscrupulous or overzealous whites. "The Problem of Old Harjo" reveals his sharp ear for the rhetoric of salvation and his ironic eye for the motives of whites "friendly" to the Indians.

Oskison's last published work was *Tecumseh and His Times* (1938), a biographical account of the great nineteenth-century Shawnee leader. Oskison left an autobiography unfinished at the time of his death.

## The Problem of Old Harjo[1]

The Spirit of the Lord had descended upon old Harjo. From the new missionary, just out from New York, he had learned that he was a sinner. The fire in the new missionary's eyes and her gracious appeal had convinced old Harjo that this was the time to repent and be saved. He was very much in earnest, and he assured Miss Evans that he wanted to be baptized and received into the church at once. Miss Evans was enthusiastic and went to Mrs. Rowell with the news. It was Mrs. Rowell who had said that it was no use to try to

1. First published in *Southern Workman* (April 1907).

convert the older Indians, and she, after fifteen years of work in Indian Territory[2] missions, should have known. Miss Evans was pardonably proud of her conquest.

"Old Harjo converted!" exclaimed Mrs. Rowell. "Dear Miss Evans, do you know that old Harjo has two wives?"[3] To the older woman it was as if someone had said to her "Madame, the Sultan of Turkey wishes to teach one of your mission Sabbath school classes."

"But," protested the younger woman, "he is really sincere, and—"

"Then ask him," Mrs. Rowell interrupted a bit sternly, "if he will put away one of his wives. Ask him, before he comes into the presence of the Lord, if he is willing to conform to the laws of the country in which he lives, the country that guarantees his idle existence. Miss Evans, your work is not even begun." No one who knew Mrs. Rowell would say that she lacked sincerity and patriotism. Her own cousin was an earnest crusader against Mormonism, and had gathered a goodly share of that wagonload of protests that the Senate had been asked to read when it was considering whether a certain statesman of Utah[4] should be allowed to represent his state at Washington.

In her practical, tactful way, Mrs. Rowell had kept clear of such embarrassments. At first, she had written letters of indignant protest to the Indian Office against the toleration of bigamy amongst the tribes. A wise inspector had been sent to the mission, and this man had pointed out that it was better to ignore certain things, "deplorable, to be sure," than to attempt to make over the habits of the old men. Of course, the young Indians would not be permitted to take more than one wife each.

So Mrs. Rowell had discreetly limited her missionary efforts to the young, and had exercised toward the old and bigamous only that strict charity which even a hopeless sinner might claim.

Miss Evans, it was to be regretted, had only the vaguest notions about "expediency"; so weak on matters of doctrine was she that the news that Harjo was living with two wives didn't startle her. She was young and possessed of but one enthusiasm—that for saving souls.

"I suppose," she ventured, "that old Harjo *must* put away one wife before he can join the church?"

"There can be no question about it, Miss Evans."

"Then I shall have to ask him to do it." Miss Evans regretted the necessity for forcing this sacrifice, but had no doubt that the Indian would make it an order to accept the gift of salvation which she was commissioned to bear to him.

Harjo lived in a "double" log cabin[5] three miles from the mission. His ten acres of corn had been gathered into its fence-rail crib; four hogs that were to furnish his winter's bacon had been brought in from the woods and penned conveniently near to the crib; out in a corner of the garden, a fat mound of dirt rose where the crop of turnips and potatoes had been buried against the

2. Land in present-day Oklahoma, Kansas, and Nebraska where the U.S. government had resettled the eastern Indians removed from their home lands.
3. Polygamy was common among the Creek Indians.
4. The Mormons also permitted polygamy. A Mormon Democrat elected to the House of Represen-

tatives in 1900 had been denied his seat because he was a polygamist, and in 1907 similar charges were raised against Reed Smoot, perhaps Oskison's "statesman of Utah," a Republican elected to the Senate. Smoot eventually was permitted to take his place in Congress.
5. Two cabins connected by a covered passageway.

corrupting frost; and in the hayloft of his log stable were stored many pumpkins, dried corn, onions (suspended in bunches from the rafters) and the varied forage that Mrs. Harjo number one and Mrs. Harjo number two had
thriftily provided. Three cows, three young heifers, two colts, and two patient,
capable mares bore the Harjo brand, a fantastic "**HH**" that the old man had
designed. Materially, Harjo was solvent; and if the Government had ever
come to his aid he could not recall the date.

This attempt to rehabilitate old Harjo morally, Miss Evans felt, was not one
to be made at the mission; it should be undertaken in the Creek's own home,
where the evidences of his sin should confront him as she explained.

When Miss Evans rode up to the block in front of Harjo's cabin, the old
Indian came out, slowly and with a broadening smile of welcome on his face.
A clean gray flannel shirt had taken the place of the white collarless garment,
with crackling stiff bosom, that he had worn to the mission meetings. Comfortable, well-patched moccasins had been substituted for creaking boots,
and brown corduroys, belted in at the waist, for tight black trousers. His
abundant gray hair fell down on his shoulders. In his eyes, clear and large and
black, glowed the light of true hospitality. Miss Evans thought of the patriarchs as she saw him lead her horse out to the stable; thus Abraham might
have looked and lived.

"Harjo," began Miss Evans before following the old man to the covered passageway between the disconnected cabins, "is it true that you have two
wives?" Her tone was neither stern nor accusatory. The Creek had heard that
question before, from scandalized missionaries and perplexed registry clerks
when he went to Muscogee to enroll himself and his family in one of the
many "final" records ordered to be made by the Government preparatory to
dividing the Creek lands among the individual citizens.[6]

For answer, Harjo called, first into the cabin that was used as a kitchen and
then, in a loud, clear voice, toward the small field, where Miss Evans saw a
flock of half-grown turkeys running about in the corn stubble. From the
kitchen emerged a tall, thin Indian woman of fifty-five, with a red handkerchief bound severely over her head. She spoke to Miss Evans and sat down
in the passageway. Presently, a clear, sweet voice was heard in the field; a
stout, handsome woman, about the same age as the other, climbed the rail
fence and came up to the house. She, also, greeted Miss Evans briefly. Then
she carried a tin basin to the well nearby, where she filled it to the brim. Setting it down on the horse block, she rolled back her sleeves, tucked in the collar of her gray blouse, and plunged her face in the water. In a minute she
came out of the kitchen freshened and smiling. 'Liza Harjo had been pulling
dried bean stalks at one end of the field, and it was dirty work. At last old
Harjo turned to Miss Evans and said, "These two my wife—this one 'Liza, this
one Jennie."

It was done with simple dignity. Miss Evans bowed and stammered. Three
pairs of eyes were turned upon her in patient, courteous inquiry.

It was hard to state the case. The old man was so evidently proud of his
women, and so flattered by Miss Evans' interest in them, that he would find

6. Such division of tribal lands followed from the Dawes Act of 1887. The Creek Indian Agency was located
in Muskogee, in present-day Oklahoma.

it hard to understand. Still, it had to be done, and Miss Evans took the plunge.

"Harjo, you want to come into our church?" The old man's face lighted. "Oh, yes, I would come to Jesus, please, my friend."

"Do you know, Harjo, that the Lord commanded that one man should mate with but one woman?" The question was stated again in simpler terms, and the Indian replied, "Me know that now, my friend. Long time ago"—Harjo plainly meant the whole period previous to his conversion—"me did not know. The Lord Jesus did not speak to me in that time and so I was blind. I do what blind man do."

"Harjo, you must have only one wife when you come into our church. Can't you give up one of these women?" Miss Evans glanced at the two, sitting by with smiles of polite interest on their faces, understanding nothing. They had not shared Harjo's enthusiasm either for the white man's God or his language.

"Give up my wife?" A sly smile stole over his face. He leaned closer to Miss Evans. "You tell me, my friend, which one I give up." He glanced from 'Liza to Jennie as if to weight their attractions, and the two rewarded him with their pleasantest smiles. "You tell me which one," he urged.

"Why, Harjo, how can I tell you!" Miss Evans had little sense of humor; she had taken the old man seriously.

"Then," Harjo sighed, continuing the comedy, for surely the missionary was jesting with him, " 'Liza and Jennie must say." He talked to the Indian women for a time, and they laughed heartily. 'Liza, pointing to the other, shook her head. At length Harjo explained, "My friend, they cannot say. Jennie, she would run a race to see which one stay, but 'Liza, she say no, she is fat and cannot run."

Miss Evans comprehended at last. She flushed angrily, and protested, "Harjo, you are making a mock of a sacred subject; I cannot allow you to talk like this."

"But did you not speak in fun, my friend?" Harjo queried, sobering. "Surely you have just said what your friend, the white woman at the mission (he meant Mrs. Rowell) would say, and you do not mean what you say."

"Yes, Harjo, I mean it. It is true that Mrs. Rowell raised the point first, but I agree with her. The church cannot be defiled by receiving a bigamist into its membership." Harjo saw that the young woman was serious, distressingly serious. He was silent for a long time, but at last he raised his head and spoke quietly, "It is not good to talk like that if it is not in fun."

He rose and went to the stable. As he led Miss Evans' horse up to the block it was champing a mouthful of corn, the last of a generous portion that Harjo had put before it. The Indian held the bridle and waited for Miss Evans to mount. She was embarrassed, humiliated, angry. It was absurd to be dismissed in this way by—"by an ignorant old bigamist!" Then the humor of it burst upon her, and its human aspect. In her anxiety concerning the spiritual welfare of the sinner Harjo, she had insulted the man Harjo. She began to understand why Mrs. Rowell had said that the old Indians were hopeless.

"Harjo," she begged, coming out of the passageway, "please forgive me. I do not want you to give up one of your wives. Just tell me why you took them."

"I will tell you that, my friend." The old Creek looped the reins over his arm and sat down on the block. "For thirty years Jennie has lived with me as my wife. She is of the Bear people, and she came to me when I was thirty-five and she was twenty-five. She could not come before, for her mother was old, very old, and Jennie, she stay with her and feed her.

"So, when I was thirty years old I took 'Liza for my woman. She is of the Crow people.[7] She help me make this little farm here when there was no farm for many miles around.

"Well, five years 'Liza and me, we live here and work hard. But there was no child. Then the old mother of Jennie she died, and Jennie got no family left in this part of the country. So 'Liza say to me, 'Why don't you take Jennie in here?' I say, 'You don't care?' and she say, 'No, maybe we have children here then.' But we have no children—never have children. We do not like that, but God He would not let it be. So, we have lived here thirty years very happy. Only just now you make me sad."

"Harjo," cried Miss Evans, "forget what I said. Forget that you wanted to join the church." For a young mission worker with a single purpose always before her, Miss Evans was saying a strange thing. Yet she couldn't help saying it; all of her zeal seemed to have been dissipated by a simple statement of the old man.

"I cannot forget to love Jesus, and I want to be saved." Old Harjo spoke with solemn earnestness. The situation was distracting. On one side stood a convert eager for the protection of the church, asking only that he be allowed to fulfill the obligations of humanity and on the other stood the church, represented by Mrs. Rowell, that set an impossible condition on receiving old Harjo to itself. Miss Evans wanted to cry; prayer, she felt, would be entirely inadequate as a means of expression.

"Oh! Harjo," she cried out, "I don't know what to do. I must think it over and talk to Mrs. Rowell again."

But Mrs. Rowell could suggest no way out; Miss Evans' talk with her only gave the older woman another opportunity to preach the folly of wasting time on the old and "unreasonable" Indians. Certainly the church could not listen even to a hint of a compromise in this case. If Harjo wanted to be saved, there was one way and only one—unless—

"Is either of the two women old? I mean, so old that she is—an—"

"Not at all," answered Miss Evans. "They're both strong and—yes, happy. I think they will outlive Harjo."

"Can't you appeal to one of the women to go away? I dare say we could provide for her." Miss Evans, incongruously, remembered Jennie's jesting proposal to race for the right to stay with Harjo. What could the mission provide as a substitute for the little home that 'Liza had helped to create there in the edge of the woods? What other home would satisfy Jennie?

"Mrs. Rowell, are you sure that we ought to try to take one of Harjo's women from him? I'm not sure that it would in the least advance morality amongst the tribe, but I'm certain that it would make three gentle people unhappy for the rest of their lives."

"You may be right, Miss Evans." Mrs. Rowell was not seeking to create unhappiness, for enough of it inevitably came to be pictured in the little mission building. "You may be right," she repeated, "but it is a grievous misfortune that old Harjo should wish to unite with the church."

7. The Bear ('Liza) and Crow (Jennie) are clans of the Creek.

No one was more regular in his attendance at the mission meetings than old Harjo. Sitting well forward, he was always in plain view of Miss Evans at the organ. Before the service began, and after it was over, the old man greeted the young woman. There was never a spoken question, but in the Creek's eyes was always a mute inquiry.

Once Miss Evans ventured to write to her old pastor in New York, and explain her trouble. This was what he wrote in reply: "I am surprised that you are troubled, for I should have expected you to rejoice, as I do, over this new and wonderful evidence of the Lord's reforming power. Though the church cannot receive the old man so long as he is confessedly a bigamist and viola-tor of his country's just laws, you should be greatly strengthened in your work through bringing him to desire salvation."

"Oh! it's easy to talk when you're free from responsibility!" cried out Miss Evans. "But I woke him up to a desire for this water of salvation that he can-not take. I have seen Harjo's home, and I know how cruel and useless it would be to urge him to give up what he loves—for he does love those two women who have spent half their lives and more with him. What, what can be done?"

Month after month, as old Harjo continued to occupy his seat in the mis-sion meetings, with that mute appeal in his eyes and a persistent light of hope on his face, Miss Evans repeated the question, "What can be done?" If she was sometimes tempted to say to the old man, "Stop worrying about your soul; you'll get to Heaven as surely as any of us," there was always Mrs. Row-ell to remind her that she was not a Mormon missionary. She could not run away from her perplexity. If she should secure a transfer to another station, she felt that Harjo would give up coming to the meetings, and in his despair become a positive influence for evil amongst his people. Mrs. Rowell would not waste her energy on an obstinate old man. No, Harjo was her creation, her impossible convert, and throughout the years, until death—the great sol-vent which is not always a solvent—came to one of them, would continue to haunt her.

And meanwhile, what?

1907

---

# JACK LONDON
## 1876–1916

John Griffith Chaney was born in San Francisco, California, on January 12, 1876, the son of Flora Wellman Chaney, spiritualist and common-law wife of William H. Chaney, an itinerant astrologer who abandoned Flora on learning of her pregnancy. Nine months after the child's birth, Flora married John London, a Civil War veteran and construction worker who adopted "Johnny." As a child, London escaped some of the unhappiness at home by living on and off with the Prentisses, African American neighbors who called him "Jack" and who served as surrogate parents until, at the age of fifteen, he sailed San Francisco Bay as an oyster pirate, going on to become a mem-ber of the California Fish Patrol. Drinking with the oyster pirates and the Fish Patrol, London developed the habit of what would later become full-blown alcoholism. Entranced by the sea and its possibilities, he sailed aboard the sealing ship the *Sophia*

*Sutherland* in 1893, returning home in 1893 to publish his first, prize-winning, story, "Typhoon Off the Coast of Japan," in the San Francisco *Morning Call.*

In 1894, following the Panic of 1893, London marched east with a contingent of Coxey's Army, an organized group of the unemployed planning to agitate for jobs in Washington D.C. He was arrested as a vagrant at Niagara Falls and did thirty days of hard time in the Erie County Penitentiary in Buffalo, New York. Returning home, he vowed to educate himself, and he also turned to Socialism, running for mayor of Oakland twice on the socialist ticket. At the age of twenty he was accepted to the University of California, but, lacking money, he attended for only one semester. The most important event of London's early life occurred in 1897, when, at age twenty-one, he headed to Alaska to take part in the Klondike Gold Rush. In 1900, the prestigious *Atlantic Monthly* featured his story "An Odyssey of the North" in its January issue; Houghton-Mifflin published his first book, *The Son of the Wolf;* and he married Bessie Mae Maddern, with whom he went on to have two daughters before their divorce in 1905 and his marriage to Charmian Kittredge London. In these years he also traveled to London, England, to write the sociological exposé *The People of the Abyss* (1903) and to Korea to cover the Russo-Japanese War of 1904, and he bought land in Sonoma County, experimenting with terracing and organic farming decades ahead of other California ranchers. He wrote one thousand words per day and won international acclaim with *The Call of the Wild* (1903) and *The Sea-Wolf* (1904). Later, after his extensive South Seas travels and residence in Hawai'i, he became modern America's first Pacific Rim writer.

London, though he said he wrote only for money, was a disciplined and careful craftsman, drawing from many literary, philosophical, scientific, and other sources, and writing on many subjects. His writings reflect the social and intellectual turbulence of the turn of the twentieth century, including his competing sympathies with socialism, Social Darwinism, and Nietzschean individualism; his startling combination of urban settings and characters with the pastoral and exotic; his conflicted ideas about race; his dual identity as a "literary" writer of the emerging naturalist school and a mass-market phenomenon. London was an important influence on later writers such as Ernest Hemingway, Richard Wright, and Américo Paredes for both his adventure writing and his socialist works, such as "The Mexican," "South of the Slot," and his many socialist essays.

Snubbed by the critical establishment (especially during the Cold War) as too popular and too politically unorthodox, London's writings have attracted new interest from scholars not only for their literary artistry but also for what they show about the cultural and historical issues of his era, especially race and class. By the time he died in 1916, London was the best-selling author in America and was on his way to becoming the most popular American writer in the world, a place he arguably holds today, with his works translated into over one hundred languages. In a writing career of only twenty years, London published 18 novels, 198 short stories, three plays, and hundreds of nonfiction books and articles. His ranch, now the Jack London State Historic Park in Glen Ellen, California, attracts visitors year-round.

# The Law of Life[1]

Old Koskoosh listened greedily. Though his sight had long since faded, his hearing was still acute, and the slightest sound penetrated to the glimmering intelligence which yet abode behind the withered forehead, but which no

---

1. This story was first printed in *McClure's Magazine* (March 1901) and was included in the collection *Children of the Frost* (1902), from which the present text is taken.

longer gazed forth upon the things of the world. Ah! that was Sit-cum-to-ha, shrilly anathematizing the dogs as she cuffed and beat them into the harnesses. Sit-cum-to-ha was his daughter's daughter, but she was too busy to waste a thought upon her broken grandfather, sitting alone there in the snow, forlorn and helpless. Camp must be broken. The long trail waited while the short day refused to linger. Life called her, and the duties of life, not death. And he was very close to death now.

The thought made the old man panicky for the moment, and he stretched forth a palsied hand which wandered tremblingly over the small heap of dry wood beside him. Reassured that it was indeed there, his hand returned to the shelter of his mangy furs, and he again fell to listening. The sulky crackling of half-frozen hides told him that the chief's moose-skin lodge had been struck, and even then was being rammed and jammed into portable compass. The chief was his son, stalwart and strong, head man of the tribesmen, and a mighty hunter. As the women toiled with the camp luggage, his voice rose, chiding them for their slowness. Old Koskoosh strained his ears. It was the last time he would hear that voice. There went Geehow's lodge! And Tusken's! Seven, eight, nine; only the Shaman's could be still standing. There! They were at work upon it now. He could hear the Shaman grunt as he piled it on the sled. A child whimpered, and a woman soothed it with soft, crooning gutturals. Little Koo-tee, the old man thought, a fretful child, and not over strong. It would die soon, perhaps, and they would burn a hole through the frozen tundra and pile rocks above to keep the wolverines away. Well, what did it matter? A few years at best, and as many an empty belly as a full one. And in the end, Death waited, ever-hungry and hungriest of them all.

What was that? Oh, the men lashing the sleds and drawing tight the thongs. He listened, who would listen no more. The whip-lashes snarled and bit among the dogs. Hear them whine! How they hated the work and the trail! They were off! Sled after sled churned slowly away into the silence. They were gone. They had passed out of his life, and he faced the last bitter hour alone. No. The snow crunched beneath a moccasin; a man stood beside him; upon his head a hand rested gently. His son was good to do this thing. He remembered other old men whose sons had not waited after the tribe. But his son had. He wandered away into the past, till the young man's voice brought him back.

"Is it well with you?" he asked.

And the old man answered, "It is well."

"There be wood beside you," the younger man continued, "and the fire burns bright. The morning is gray, and the cold has broken. It will snow presently. Even now is it snowing."

"Ay, even now is it snowing."

"The tribesmen hurry. Their bales are heavy, and their bellies flat with lack of feasting. The trail is long and they travel fast. I go now. It is well?"

"It is well. I am as a last year's leaf, clinging lightly to the stem. The first breath that blows, and I fall. My voice is become like an old woman's. My eyes no longer show me the way of my feet, and my feet are heavy, and I am tired. It is well."

He bowed his head in content till the last noise of the complaining snow had died away, and he knew his son was beyond recall. Then his hand crept out in haste to the wood. It alone stood betwixt him and the eternity which yawned in upon him. At last the measure of his life was a handful of fagots. One by one they would go to feed the fire, and just so, step by step, death would creep upon him. When the last stick had surrendered up its heat, the frost would begin to gather strength. First his feet would yield, then his hands; and the numbness would travel, slowly, from the extremities to the body. His head would fall forward upon his knees, and he would rest. It was easy. All men must die.

He did not complain. It was the way of life, and it was just. He had been born close to the earth, close to the earth had he lived, and the law thereof was not new to him. It was the law of all flesh. Nature was not kindly to the flesh. She had no concern for that concrete thing called the individual. Her interest lay in the species, the race. This was the deepest abstraction old Koskoosh's barbaric mind was capable of, but he grasped it firmly. He saw it exemplified in all life. The rise of the sap, the bursting greenness of the willow bud, the fall of the yellow leaf—in this alone was told the whole history. But one task did nature set the individual. Did he not perform it, he died. Did he perform it, it was all the same, he died. Nature did not care; there were plenty who were obedient, and it was only the obedience in this matter, not the obedient, which lived and lived always. The tribe of Koskoosh was very old. The old men he had known when a boy, had known old men before them. Therefore it was true that the tribe lived, that it stood for the obedience of all its members, way down into the forgotten past, whose very resting places were unremembered. They did not count; they were episodes. They had passed away like clouds from a summer sky. He also was an episode, and would pass away. Nature did not care. To life she set one task, gave one law. To perpetuate was the task of life, its law was death. A maiden was a good creature to look upon, full-breasted and strong, with spring to her step and light in her eyes. But her task was yet before her. The light in her eyes brightened, her step quickened, she was now bold with the young men, now timid, and she gave them of her own unrest. And ever she grew fairer and yet fairer to look upon, till some hunter, able no longer to withhold himself, took her to his lodge to cook and toil for him and to become the mother of his children. And with the coming of her offspring her looks left her. Her limbs dragged and shuffled, her eyes dimmed and bleared, and only the little children found joy against the withered cheek of the old squaw by the fire. Her task was done. But a little while, on the first pinch of famine or the first long trail, and she would be left, even as he had been left, in the snow, with a little pile of wood. Such was the law.

He placed a stick carefully upon the fire and resumed his meditations. It was the same everywhere, with all things. The mosquitos vanished with the first frost. The little tree-squirrel crawled away to die. When age settled upon the rabbit it became slow and heavy, and could no longer outfoot its enemies. Even the big bald-face grew clumsy and blind and quarrelsome, in the end to be dragged down by a handful of yelping huskies. He remembered how he had abandoned his own father on an upper reach of the Klondike one winter, the winter before the missionary came with his talk-books and his box of medicines. Many a time had Koskoosh smacked his lips over the recollection of that box, though now his mouth refused to moisten. The "painkiller" had been especially good. But the missionary was a bother after all, for he brought no meat into the camp, and he ate heartily, and the hunters grumbled. But he chilled his lungs on the divide by the Mayo, and the dogs after-wards nosed the stones away and fought over his bones.

Koskoosh placed another stick on the fire and harked back deeper into the past. There was the time of the Great Famine, when the old men crouched empty-bellied to the fire, and from their lips fell dim traditions of the ancient day when the Yukon ran wide open for three winters, and then lay frozen for three summers. He had lost his mother in that famine. In the summer the salmon run had failed, and the tribe looked forward to the winter and the coming of the caribou. Then the winter came, but with it there were no cari-bou. Never had the like been known, not even in the lives of the old men. But the caribou did not come, and it was the seventh year, and the rabbits had not replenished, and the dogs were naught but bundles of bones. And through the long darkness the children wailed and died, and the women, and the old men; and not one in ten of the tribe lived to meet the sun when it came back in the spring. That *was* a famine!

But he had seen times of plenty, too, when the meat spoiled on their hands, and the dogs were fat and worthless with over-eating—times when they let the game go unkilled, and the women were fertile, and the lodges were clut-tered with sprawling men-children and women-children. Then it was the men became high-stomached, and revived ancient quarrels, and crossed the divides to the south to kill the Pellys, and to the west that they might sit by the dead fires of the Tananas. He remembered, when a boy, during a time of plenty, when he saw a moose pulled down by the wolves. Zing-ha lay with him in the snow and watched—Zing-ha, who later became the craftiest of hunters, and who, in the end, fell through an air-hole on the Yukon. They found him, a month afterward, just as he had crawled half-way out and frozen stiff to the ice.

But the moose. Zing-ha and he had gone out that day to play at hunting after the manner of their fathers. On the bed of the creek they struck the fresh track of a moose, and with it the tracks of many wolves. "An old one," Zing-ha, who was quicker at reading the sign, said—"an old one who cannot keep up with the herd. The wolves have cut him out from his brothers, and they will never leave him." And it was so. It was their way. By day and by night, never resting, snarling on his heels, snapping at his nose, they would stay by him to the end. How Zing-ha and he felt the blood-lust quicken! The finish would be a sight to see!

Eager-footed, they took the trail, and even he, Koskoosh, slow of sight and an unversed tracker, could have followed it blind, it was so wide. Hot were they on the heels of the chase, reading the grim tragedy, fresh-written, at every step. Now they came to where the moose had made a stand. Thrice the length of a grown man's body, in every direction, had the snow been stamped about and uptossed. In the midst were the deep impressions of the splay-hoofed game, and all about, everywhere, were the lighter footmarks of the wolves. Some, while their brothers harried the kill, had lain to one side and rested. The full-stretched impress of their bodies in the snow was as perfect as though made the moment before. One wolf had been caught in a wild lunge of the maddened victim and trampled to death. A few bones, well picked, bore witness.

Again, they ceased the uplift of their snowshoes at a second stand. Here the great animal had fought desperately. Twice had he been dragged down, as the snow attested, and twice had he shaken his assailants clear and gained footing once more. He had done his task long since, but none the less was life dear to him. Zing-ha said it was a strange thing, a moose once down to get free again; but this one certainly had. The Shaman would see signs and wonders in this when they told him.

And yet again, they came to where the moose had made to mount the bank and gain the timber. But his foes had laid on from behind, till he reared and fell back upon them, crushing two deep into the snow. It was plain the kill was at hand, for their brothers had left them untouched. Two more stands were hurried past, brief in time-length and very close together. The trail was red now, and the clean stride of the great beast had grown short and slovenly. Then they heard the first sounds of the battle—not the full-throated chorus of the chase, but the short, snappy bark which spoke of close quarters and teeth to flesh. Crawling up the wind, Zing-ha bellied it through the snow, and with him crept he, Koskoosh, who was to be chief of the tribesmen in the years to come. Together they shoved aside the under branches of a young spruce and peered forth. It was the end they saw.

The picture, like all of youth's impressions, was still strong with him, and his dim eyes watched the end played out as vividly as in that far-off time. Koskoosh marveled at this, for in the days which followed, when he was a leader of men and a head of councilors, he had done great deeds and made his name a curse in the mouths of the Pellys, to say naught of the strange white man he had killed, knife to knife, in open fight.

For long he pondered on the days of his youth, till the fire died down and the frost bit deeper. He replenished it with two sticks this time, and gauged his grip on life by what remained. If Sit-cum-to-ha had only remembered her grandfather, and gathered a larger armful, his hours would have been longer. It would have been easy. But she was ever a careless child, and honored not her ancestors from the time the Beaver, son of the son of Zing-ha, first cast eyes upon her. Well, what mattered it? Had he not done likewise in his own quick youth? For a while he listened to the silence. Perhaps the heart of his son might soften, and he would come back with the dogs to take his old father on with the tribe to where the caribou ran thick and the fat hung heavy upon them.

He strained his ears, his restless brain for the moment stilled. Not a stir, nothing. He alone took breath in the midst of the great silence. It was very lonely, Hark! What was that? A chill passed over his body. The familiar, long-drawn howl broke the void, and it was close at hand. Then on his darkened eyes was projected the vision of the moose—the old bull moose—the torn flanks and bloody sides, the riddled mane, and the great branching horns, down low and tossing to the last. He saw the flashing forms of gray, the gleaming eyes, the lolling tongues, the slavered fangs. And he saw the inexorable circle close in till it became a dark point in the midst of the stamped snow.

A cold muzzle thrust against his cheek, and at its touch his soul leaped back to the present. His hand shot into the fire and dragged out a burning fagot. Overcome for the nonce by his hereditary fear of man, the brute retreated, raising a prolonged call to his brothers; and greedily they answered, till a ring of crouching, jaw-slobbered gray was stretched round about. The old man listened to the drawing in of this circle. He waved his brand wildly, and sniffs turned to snarls; but the panting brutes refused to scatter. Now one wormed his chest forward, dragging his haunches after, now a second, now a third; but never a one drew back. Why should he cling to life? he asked, and dropped the blazing stick into the snow. It sizzled and went out. The circle grunted uneasily, but held its own. Again he saw the last stand of the old bull moose, and Koskoosh dropped his head wearily upon his knees. What did it matter after all? Was it not the law of life?

1901, 1902

## To Build a Fire[1]

Day had broken cold and gray, exceedingly cold and gray, when the man turned aside from the main Yukon trail and climbed the high earth-bank, where a dim and little-travelled trail led eastward through the fat spruce timberland. It was a steep bank, and he paused for breath at the top, excusing the act to himself by looking at his watch. It was nine o'clock. There was no sun nor hint of sun, though there was not a cloud in the sky. It was a clear day, and yet there seemed an intangible pall over the face of things, a subtle gloom that made the day dark, and that was due to the absence of sun. This fact did not worry the man. He was used to the lack of sun. It had been days since he had seen the sun, and he knew that a few more days must pass before that cheerful orb, due south, would just peep above the sky-line and dip immediately from view.

The man flung a look back along the way he had come. The Yukon lay a mile wide and hidden under three feet of ice. On top of this ice were as many feet of snow. It was all pure white, rolling in gentle undulations where the ice-jams of the freeze-up had formed. North and south, as far as his eye could see, it was unbroken white, save for a dark hair-line that curved and twisted from around the spruce-covered island to the south, and that curved and twisted away into the north, where it disappeared behind another spruce-covered island. This dark hair-line was the trail—the main trail—that led south five hundred miles to the Chilcoot Pass, Dyea, and salt water; and that led north seventy miles to Dawson, and still on to the north a thousand miles to Nulato, and finally to St. Michael on Bering Sea, a thousand miles and half a thousand more.[2]

But all this—the mysterious, far-reaching hair-line trail, the absence of sun from the sky, the tremendous cold, and the strangeness and weirdness of it all—made no impression on the man. It was not because he was long used to it. He was a newcomer in the land, a *chechaquo,* and this was his first winter. The trouble with him was that he was without imagination. He was quick

---

1. First published in *The Youth's Companion* for May 29, 1902, in a version of 2,700 words—"for boys only," according to London. The later, widely anthologized version of 7,235 words, written while London was struggling to survive his South Seas voyage aboard his sailboat the *Snark,* was first published in *The Century Magazine* 76 (August 1908). The text here is that of the 1910 collection *Lost Face.*
2. The narrator surveys the entire length of Alaska and the Canadian Yukon, from the steep Chilcoot Pass near Skagway, which prospective miners first

scaled in the winter of 1897–98 to enter the Yukon; to Dyea, a shabby settlement where they disembarked onto a swampy beach; to Dawson, the hub of the Klondike gold rush; and finally to Nulato and St. Michael, sparse settlements on the way to the mouth of the Yukon River, from which miners would sail for home. The Yukon is one of the few rivers that flows north. London floated "up" the Yukon from Dawson to St. Michael in the spring of 1898 to return home after unsuccessfully prospecting for gold. This journey was the subject of his first Klondike writings.

and alert in the things of life, but only in the things, and not in the signifi-
cances. Fifty degrees below zero meant eighty-odd degrees of frost. Such fact
impressed him as being cold and uncomfortable, and that was all. It did not
lead him to meditate upon his frailty as a creature of temperature, and upon
man's frailty in general, able only to live within certain narrow limits of heat
and cold; and from there on it did not lead him to the conjectural field of
immortality and man's place in the universe. Fifty degrees below zero stood
for a bite of frost that hurt and that must be guarded against by the use of
mittens, ear-flaps, warm moccasins, and thick socks. Fifty degrees below zero
was to him just precisely fifty degrees below zero. That there should be anything more to it than that was a thought that never entered his head.

As he turned to go on, he spat speculatively. There was a sharp, explosive
crackle that startled him. He spat again. And again, in the air, before it could
fall to the snow, the spittle crackled. He knew that at fifty below spittle crackled on the snow, but this spittle had crackled in the air. Undoubtedly it was
colder than fifty below—how much colder he did not know. But the temperature did not matter. He was bound for the old claim on the left fork of Henderson Creek, where the boys were already. They had come over across the
divide from the Indian Creek country, while he had come the roundabout way
to take a look at the possibilities of getting out logs in the spring from the
islands in the Yukon. He would be in to camp by six o'clock; a bit after dark,
it was true, but the boys would be there, a fire would be going, and a hot supper would be ready. As for lunch, he pressed his hand against the protruding
bundle under his jacket. It was also under his shirt, wrapped up in a handkerchief and lying against the naked skin. It was the only way to keep the biscuits from freezing. He smiled agreeably to himself as he thought of those
biscuits, each cut open and sopped in bacon grease, and each enclosing a
generous slice of fried bacon.

He plunged in among the big spruce trees. The trail was faint. A foot of
snow had fallen since the last sled had passed over, and he was glad he was
without a sled, travelling light. In fact, he carried nothing but the lunch
wrapped in the handkerchief. He was surprised, however, at the cold. It certainly was cold, he concluded, as he rubbed his numb nose and cheek-bones
with his mittened hand. He was a warm-whiskered man, but the hair on his
face did not protect the high cheek-bones and the eager nose that thrust itself
aggressively into the frosty air.

At the man's heels trotted a dog, a big native husky, the proper wolf-dog,
gray-coated and without any visible or temperamental difference from its
brother, the wild wolf. The animal was depressed by the tremendous cold. It
knew that it was no time for travelling. Its instinct told it a truer tale than was
told to the man by the man's judgment. In reality, it was not merely colder
than fifty below zero; it was colder than sixty below, than seventy below. It was
seventy-five below zero. Since the freezing-point is thirty-two above zero, it
meant that one hundred and seven degrees of frost obtained. The dog did not
know anything about thermometers. Possibly in its brain there was no sharp
consciousness of a condition of very cold such as was in the man's brain. But
the brute had its instinct. It experienced a vague but menacing apprehension
that subdued it and made it slink along at the man's heels, and that made it
question eagerly every unwonted movement of the man as if expecting him
to go into camp or to seek shelter somewhere and build a fire. The dog had

learned fire, and it wanted fire, or else to burrow under the snow and cuddle its warmth away from the air.

The frozen moisture of its breathing had settled on its fur in a fine powder of frost, and especially were its jowls, muzzle, and eyelashes whitened by its crystalled breath. The man's red beard and mustache were likewise frosted, but more solidly, the deposit taking the form of ice and increasing with every warm, moist breath he exhaled. Also, the man was chewing tobacco, and the muzzle of ice held his lips so rigidly that he was unable to clear his chin when he expelled the juice. The result was that a crystal beard of the color and solidity of amber was increasing its length on his chin. If he fell down it would shatter itself, like glass, into brittle fragments. But he did not mind the appendage. It was the penalty all tobacco-chewers paid in that country, and he had been out before in two cold snaps. They had not been so cold as this, he knew, but by the spirit thermometer at Sixty Mile he knew they had been registered at fifty below and at fifty-five.

He held on through the level stretch of woods for several miles, crossed a wide flat of niggerheads,[3] and dropped down a bank to the frozen bed of a small stream. This was Henderson Creek, and he knew he was ten miles from the forks. He looked at his watch. It was ten o'clock. He was making four miles an hour, and he calculated that he would arrive at the forks at half-past twelve. He decided to celebrate that event by eating his lunch there.

The dog dropped in again at his heels, with a tail drooping discouragement, as the man swung along the creek-bed. The furrow of the old sled-trail was plainly visible, but a dozen inches of snow covered the marks of the last runners. In a month no man had come up or down that silent creek. The man held steadily on. He was not much given to thinking, and just then particularly he had nothing to think about save that he would eat lunch at the forks and that at six o'clock he would be in camp with the boys. There was nobody to talk to; and, had there been, speech would have been impossible because of the ice-muzzle on his mouth. So he continued monotonously to chew tobacco and to increase the length of his amber beard.

Once in a while the thought reiterated itself that it was very cold and that he had never experienced such cold. As he walked along he rubbed his cheek-bones and nose with the back of his mittened hand. He did this automatically, now and again changing hands. But rub as he would, the instant he stopped his cheek-bones went numb, and the following instant the end of his nose went numb. He was sure to frost his cheeks; he knew that, and experienced a pang of regret that he had not devised a nose-strap of the sort Bud wore in cold snaps. Such a strap passed across the cheeks, as well, and saved them. But it didn't matter much, after all. What were frosted cheeks? A bit painful, that was all; they were never serious.

Empty as the man's mind was of thoughts, he was keenly observant, and he noticed the changes in the creek, the curves and bends and timber-jams, and always he sharply noted where he placed his feet. Once, coming around a bend, he shied abruptly, like a startled horse, curved away from the place where he had been walking, and retreated several paces back along the trail. The creek he knew was frozen clear to the bottom,—no creek could contain

---

3. Racially charged name of a strong dark chewing tobacco of the period, applied here to large hummocks of earth under the snow that are created by centuries of alternate freezing and thawing.

water in that arctic winter,—but he knew also that there were springs that bubbled out from the hillsides and ran along under the snow and on top the ice of the creek. He knew that the coldest snaps never froze these springs, and he knew likewise their danger. They were traps. They hid pools of water under the snow that might be three inches deep, or three feet. Sometimes a skin of ice half an inch thick covered them, and in turn was covered by the snow. Sometimes there were alternate layers of water and ice-skin, so that when one broke through he kept on breaking through for a while, sometimes wetting himself to the waist.

That was why he had shied in such panic. He had felt the give under his feet and heard the crackle of snow-hidden ice-skin. And to get his feet wet in such a temperature meant trouble and danger. At the very least it meant delay, for he would be forced to stop and build a fire, and under its protection to bare his feet while he dried his socks and moccasins. He stood and studied the creek-bed and its banks, and decided that the flow of water came from the right. He reflected awhile, rubbing his nose and cheeks, then skirted to the left, stepping gingerly and testing the footing for each step. Once clear of the danger, he took a fresh chew of tobacco and swung along at his four-mile gait.

In the course of the next two hours he came upon several similar traps. Usually the snow above the hidden pools had a sunken, candied appearance that advertised the danger. Once again, however, he had a close call; and once, suspecting danger, he compelled the dog to go on in front. The dog did not want to go. It hung back until the man shoved it forward, and then it went quickly across the white, unbroken surface. Suddenly it broke through, floundered to one side, and got away to firmer footing. It had wet its forefeet and legs, and almost immediately the water that clung to it turned to ice. It made quick efforts to lick the ice off its legs, then dropped down in the snow and began to bite out the ice that had formed between the toes. This was a matter of instinct. To permit the ice to remain would mean sore feet. It did not know this. It merely obeyed the mysterious prompting that arose from the deep crypts of its being. But the man knew, having achieved a judgment on the subject, and he removed the mitten from his right hand and helped tear out the ice-particles. He did not expose his fingers more than a minute, and was astonished at the swift numbness that smote them. It certainly was cold. He pulled on the mitten hastily, and beat the hand savagely across his chest.

At twelve o'clock the day was at its brightest. Yet the sun was too far south on its winter journey to clear the horizon. The bulge of the earth intervened between it and Henderson Creek, where the man walked under a clear sky at noon and cast no shadow. At half-past twelve, to the minute, he arrived at the forks of the creek. He was pleased at the speed he had made. If he kept it up, he would certainly be with the boys by six. He unbuttoned his jacket and shirt and drew forth his lunch. The action consumed no more than a quarter of a minute, yet in that brief moment the numbness laid hold of the exposed fingers. He did not put the mitten on, but, instead, struck the fingers a dozen sharp smashes against his leg. Then he sat down on a snow-covered log to eat. The sting that followed upon the striking of his fingers against his leg ceased so quickly that he was startled. He had had no chance to take a bite of biscuit. He struck the fingers repeatedly and returned them to the mitten, baring the other hand for the purpose of eating. He tried to take a mouthful, but the ice-muzzle prevented. He had forgotten to build a fire and thaw out. He chuckled at his foolishness, and as he chuckled he noted the numbness creeping into the exposed fingers. Also, he noted that the stinging which had first come to his toes when he sat down was already passing away. He wondered whether the toes were warm or numb. He moved them inside the moccasins and decided that they were numb.

He pulled the mitten on hurriedly and stood up. He was a bit frightened. He stamped up and down until the stinging returned into the feet. It certainly was cold, was his thought. That man from Sulphur Creek[4] had spoken the truth when telling how cold it sometimes got in the country. And he had laughed at him at the time! That showed one must not be too sure of things. There was no mistake about it, it *was* cold. He strode up and down, stamping his feet and threshing his arms, until reassured by the returning warmth. Then he got out matches and proceeded to make a fire. From the undergrowth, where high water of the previous spring had lodged a supply of seasoned twigs, he got his fire-wood. Working carefully from a small beginning, he soon had a roaring fire, over which he thawed the ice from his face and in the protection of which he ate his biscuits. For the moment the cold of space was outwitted. The dog took satisfaction in the fire, stretching out close enough for warmth and far enough away to escape being singed.

When the man had finished, he filled his pipe and took his comfortable time over a smoke. Then he pulled on his mittens, settled the ear-flaps of his cap firmly about his ears, and took the creek trail up the left fork. The dog was disappointed and yearned back toward the fire. This man did not know cold. Possibly all the generations of his ancestry had been ignorant of cold, of real cold, of cold one hundred and seven degrees below freezing-point. But the dog knew; all its ancestry knew, and it had inherited the knowledge. And it knew that it was not good to walk abroad in such fearful cold. It was the time to lie snug in a hole in the snow and wait for a curtain of cloud to be drawn across the face of outer space whence this cold came. On the other hand, there was no keen intimacy between the dog and the man. The one was the toil-slave of the other, and the only caresses it had ever received were the caresses of the whip-lash and of harsh and menacing throat-sounds that threatened the whip-lash. So the dog made no effort to communicate its apprehension to the man. It was not concerned in the welfare of the man; it was for its own sake that it yearned back toward the fire. But the man whistled, and spoke to it with the sound of whip-lashes, and the dog swung in at the man's heels and followed after.

The man took a chew of tobacco and proceeded to start a new amber beard. Also, his moist breath quickly powdered with white his mustache, eyebrows, and lashes. There did not seem to be so many springs on the left fork of the Henderson, and for half an hour the man saw no signs of any. And then it happened. At a place where there were no signs, where the soft, unbroken snow seemed to advertise solidity beneath, the man broke through. It was not deep. He wet himself halfway to the knees before he floundered out to the firm crust.

He was angry, and cursed his luck aloud. He had hoped to get into camp with the boys at six o'clock, and this would delay him an hour, for he would

4. Mining area between the towns of Dawson and Granville.

have to build a fire and dry out his foot-gear. This was imperative at that low temperature—he knew that much; and he turned aside to the bank, which he climbed. On top, tangled in the underbrush about the trunks of several small spruce trees, was a high-water deposit of dry fire-wood—sticks and twigs, principally, but also larger portions of seasoned branches and fine, dry, last-year's grasses. He threw down several large pieces on top of the snow. This served for a foundation and prevented the young flame from drowning itself in the snow it otherwise would melt. The flame he got by touching a match to a small shred of birch-bark that he took from his pocket. This burned even more readily than paper. Placing it on the foundation, he fed the young flame with wisps of dry grass and with the tiniest dry twigs.

He worked slowly and carefully, keenly aware of his danger. Gradually, as the flame grew stronger, he increased the size of the twigs with which he fed it. He squatted in the snow, pulling the twigs out from their entanglement in the brush and feeding directly to the flame. He knew there must be no failure. When it is seventy-five below zero, a man must not fail in his first attempt to build a fire—that is, if his feet are wet. If his feet are dry, and he fails, he can run along the trail for half a mile and restore his circulation. But the circulation of wet and freezing feet cannot be restored by running when it is seventy-five below. No matter how fast he runs, the wet feet will freeze the harder.

All this the man knew. The old-timer on Sulphur Creek had told him about it the previous fall, and now he was appreciating the advice. Already all sensation had gone out of his feet. To build the fire he had been forced to remove his mittens, and the fingers had quickly gone numb. His pace of four miles an hour had kept his heart pumping blood to the surface of his body and to all the extremities. But the instant he stopped, the action of the pump eased down. The cold of space smote the unprotected tip of the planet, and he, being on that unprotected tip, received the full force of the blow. The blood of his body recoiled before it. The blood was alive, like the dog, and like the dog it wanted to hide away and cover itself up from the fearful cold. So long as he walked four miles an hour, he pumped that blood, willy-nilly, to the surface; but now it ebbed away and sank down into the recesses of his body. The extremities were the first to feel its absence. His wet feet froze the faster, and his exposed fingers numbed the faster, though they had not yet begun to freeze. Nose and cheeks were already freezing, while the skin of all his body chilled as it lost its blood.

But he was safe. Toes and nose and cheeks would be only touched by the frost, for the fire was beginning to burn with strength. He was feeding it with twigs the size of his finger. In another minute he would be able to feed it with branches the size of his wrist, and then he could remove his wet footgear, and, while it dried, he could keep his naked feet warm by the fire, rubbing them at first, of course, with snow. The fire was a success. He was safe. He remembered the advice of the old-timer on Sulphur Creek, and smiled. The old-timer had been very serious in laying down the law that no man must travel alone in the Klondike after fifty below. Well, here he was; he had had the accident; he was alone; and he had saved himself. Those old-timers were rather womanish, some of them, he thought. All a man had to do was to keep his head, and he was all right. Any man who was a man could travel alone. But it was surprising, the rapidity with which his cheeks and nose were freezing. And he had not thought his fingers could go lifeless in so short a time. Lifeless they were, for he could scarcely make them move together to grip a twig, and they seemed remote from his body and from him. When he touched a twig, he had to look and see whether or not he had hold of it. The wires were pretty well down between him and his finger-ends.

All of which counted for little. There was the fire, snapping and crackling and promising life with every dancing flame. He started to untie his moccasins. They were coated with ice; the thick German socks were like sheaths of iron halfway to the knees; and the moccasin strings were like rods of steel all twisted and knotted as by some conflagration. For a moment he tugged with his numb fingers, then, realizing the folly of it, he drew his sheath-knife.

But before he could cut the strings, it happened. It was his own fault or, rather, his mistake. He should not have built the fire under the spruce tree. He should have built it in the open. But it had been easier to pull the twigs from the brush and drop them directly on the fire. Now the tree under which he had done this carried a weight of snow on its boughs. No wind had blown for weeks, and each bough was fully freighted. Each time he had pulled a twig he had communicated a slight agitation to the tree—an imperceptible agitation, so far as he was concerned, but an agitation sufficient to bring about the disaster. High up in the tree one bough capsized its load of snow. This fell on the boughs beneath, capsizing them. This process continued, spreading out and involving the whole tree. It grew like an avalanche, and it descended without warning upon the man and the fire, and the fire was blotted out! Where it had burned was a mantle of fresh and disordered snow.

The man was shocked. It was as though he had just heard his own sentence of death. For a moment he sat and stared at the spot where the fire had been. Then he grew very calm. Perhaps the old-timer on Sulphur Creek was right. If he had only had a trail-mate he would have been in no danger now. The trail-mate could have built the fire. Well, it was up to him to build the fire over again, and this second time there must be no failure. Even if he succeeded, he would most likely lose some toes. His feet must be badly frozen by now, and there would be some time before the second fire was ready.

Such were his thoughts, but he did not sit and think them. He was busy all the time they were passing through his mind. He made a new foundation for a fire, this time in the open, where no treacherous tree could blot it out. Next, he gathered dry grasses and tiny twigs from the high-water flotsam. He could not bring his fingers together to pull them out, but he was able to gather them by the handful. In this way he got many rotten twigs and bits of green moss that were undesirable, but it was the best he could do. He worked methodically, even collecting an armful of the larger branches to be used later when the fire gathered strength. And all the while the dog sat and watched him, a certain yearning wistfulness in its eyes, for it looked upon him as the fire-provider, and the fire was slow in coming.

When all was ready, the man reached in his pocket for a second piece of birch-bark. He knew the bark was there, and, though he could not feel it with his fingers, he could hear its crisp rustling as he fumbled for it. Try as he would, he could not clutch hold of it. And all the time, in his consciousness, was the knowledge that each instant his feet were freezing. This thought tended to put him in a panic, but he fought against it and kept calm. He pulled on his mittens with his teeth, and threshed his arms back and forth, beating his hands with all his might against his sides. He did this sitting down, and he stood up to do it; and all the while the dog sat in the snow, its wolf-brush of a tail curled around warmly over its forefeet, its sharp wolf-ears pricked forward intently as it watched the man. And the man, as he beat and threshed with his arms and hands, he felt a great surge of envy as he regarded the creature that was warm and secure in its natural covering.

After a time he was aware of the first faraway signals of sensation in his beaten fingers. The faint tingling grew stronger till it evolved into a stinging ache that was excruciating, but which the man hailed with satisfaction. He stripped the mitten from his right hand and fetched forth the birch-bark. The exposed fingers were quickly going numb again. Next he brought out his bunch of sulphur matches. But the tremendous cold had already driven the life out of his fingers. In his effort to separate one match from the others, the whole bunch fell in the snow. He tried to pick it out of the snow, but failed. The dead fingers could neither touch nor clutch. He was very careful. He drove the thought of his freezing feet, and nose, and cheeks, out of his mind, devoting his whole soul to the matches. He watched, using the sense of vision in place of that of touch, and when he saw his fingers on each side the bunch, he closed them—that is, he willed to close them, for the wires were down, and the fingers did not obey. He pulled the mitten on the right hand, and beat it fiercely against his knee. Then, with both mittened hands, he scooped the bunch of matches, along with much snow, into his lap. Yet he was no better off.

After some manipulation he managed to get the bunch between the heels of his mittened hands. In this fashion he carried it to his mouth. The ice crackled and snapped when by a violent effort he opened his mouth. He drew the lower jaw in, curled the upper lip out of the way, and scraped the bunch with his upper teeth in order to separate a match. He succeeded in getting one, which he dropped on his lap. He was no better off. He could not pick it up. Then he devised a way. He picked it up in his teeth and scratched it on his leg. Twenty times he scratched before he succeeded in lighting it. As it flamed he held it with his teeth to the birch-bark. But the burning brimstone went up his nostrils and into his lungs, causing him to cough spasmodically. The match fell into the snow and went out.

The old-timer on Sulphur Creek was right, he thought in the moment of controlled despair that ensued: after fifty below, a man should travel with a partner. He beat his hands, but failed in exciting any sensation. Suddenly he bared both hands, removing the mittens with his teeth. He caught the whole bunch between the heels of his hands. His arm-muscles not being frozen enabled him to press the hand-heels tightly against the matches. Then he scratched the bunch along his leg. It flared into flame, seventy sulphur matches at once! There was no wind to blow them out. He kept his head to one side to escape the strangling fumes, and held the blazing bunch to the birch-bark. As he so held it, he became aware of sensation in his hand. His flesh was burning. He could smell it. Deep down below the surface he could feel it. The sensation developed into pain that grew acute. And still he endured it, holding the flame of the matches clumsily to the bark that would not light readily because his own burning hands were in the way, absorbing most of the flame.

At last, when he could endure no more, he jerked his hands apart. The blazing matches fell sizzling into the snow, but the birch-bark was alight. He began laying dry grasses and the tiniest twigs on the flame. He could not pick and choose, for he had to lift the fuel between the heels of his hands. Small pieces of rotten wood and green moss clung to the twigs, and he bit them off as well as he could with his teeth. He cherished the flame carefully and awkwardly. It meant life, and it must not perish. The withdrawal of blood from the surface of his body now made him begin to shiver, and he grew more awkward. A large piece of green moss fell squarely on the little fire. He tried to poke it out with his fingers, but his shivering frame made him poke too far, and he disrupted the nucleus of the little fire, the burning grasses and tiny twigs separating and scattering. He tried to poke them together again, but in spite of the tenseness of the effort, his shivering got away with him, and the twigs were hopelessly scattered. Each twig gushed a puff of smoke and went out. The fire-provider had failed. As he looked apathetically about him, his eyes chanced on the dog, sitting across the ruins of the fire from him, in the snow, making restless, hunching movements, slightly lifting one forefoot and then the other, shifting its weight back and forth on them with wistful eagerness.

The sight of the dog put a wild idea into his head. He remembered the tale of the man, caught in a blizzard, who killed a steer and crawled inside the carcass, and so was saved. He would kill the dog and bury his hands in the warm body until the numbness went out of them. Then he could build another fire. He spoke to the dog, calling it to him; but in his voice was a strange note of fear that frightened the animal, who had never known the man to speak in such way before. Something was the matter, and its suspicious nature sensed danger—it knew not what danger, but somewhere, somehow, in its brain arose an apprehension of the man. It flattened its ears down at the sound of the man's voice, and its restless, hunching movements and the liftings and shiftings of its forefeet became more pronounced; but it would not come to the man. He got on his hands and knees and crawled toward the dog. This unusual posture again excited suspicion, and the animal sidled mincingly away.

The man sat up in the snow for a moment and struggled for calmness. Then he pulled on his mittens, by means of his teeth, and got upon his feet. He glanced down at first in order to assure himself that he was really standing up, for the absence of sensation in his feet left him unrelated to the earth. His erect position in itself started to drive the webs of suspicion from the dog's mind; and when he spoke peremptorily, with the sound of whip-lashes in his voice, the dog rendered its customary allegiance and came to him. As it came within reaching distance, the man lost his control. His arms flashed out to the dog, and he experienced genuine surprise when he discovered that his hands could not clutch, that there was neither bend nor feeling in the fingers. He had forgotten for the moment that they were frozen and that they were freezing more and more. All this happened quickly, and before the animal could get away, he encircled its body with his arms. He sat down in the snow, and in this fashion held the dog, while it snarled and whined and struggled.

But it was all he could do, hold its body encircled in his arms and sit there. He realized that he could not kill the dog. There was no way to do it. With his helpless hands he could neither draw nor hold his sheath-knife nor throttle the animal. He released it, and it plunged wildly away, with tail between its legs, and still snarling. It halted forty feet away and surveyed him curiously, with ears sharply pricked forward. The man looked down at his hands in order to locate them, and found them hanging on the ends of his arms. It struck him as curious that one should have to use his eyes in order to find out where his hands were. He began threshing his arms back and forth, beating the mittened hands against his sides. He did this for five minutes, violently, and his heart pumped enough blood up to the surface to put a stop to his shivering. But no sensation was aroused in the hands. He had an impression that they hung like weights on the ends of his arms, but when he tried to run the impression down, he could not find it.

A certain fear of death, dull and oppressive, came to him. This fear quickly became poignant as he realized that it was no longer a mere matter of freezing his fingers and toes, or of losing his hands and feet, but that it was a matter of life and death with the chances against him. This threw him into a panic, and he turned and ran up the creek-bed along the old, dim trail. The dog joined in behind and kept up with him. He ran blindly, without intention, in fear such as he had never known in his life. Slowly, as he ploughed and floundered through the snow, he began to see things again—the banks of the creek, the old timber-jams, the leafless aspens, and the sky. The running made him feel better. He did not shiver. Maybe, if he ran on, his feet would thaw out; and, anyway, if he ran far enough, he would reach camp and the boys. Without doubt he would lose some fingers and toes and some of his face; but the boys would take care of him, and save the rest of him when he got there. And at the same time there was another thought in his mind that said he would never get to the camp and the boys; that it was too many miles away, that the freezing had too great a start on him, and that he would soon be stiff and dead. This thought he kept in the background and refused to consider. Sometimes it pushed itself forward and demanded to be heard, but he thrust it back and strove to think of other things.

It struck him as curious that he could run at all on feet so frozen that he could not feel them when they struck the earth and took the weight of his body. He seemed to himself to skim along above the surface, and to have no connection with the earth. Somewhere he had once seen a winged Mercury,[5] and he wondered if Mercury felt as he felt when skimming over the earth.

His theory of running until he reached camp and the boys had one flaw in it: he lacked the endurance. Several times he stumbled, and finally he tottered, crumpled up, and fell. When he tried to rise, he failed. He must sit and rest, he decided, and next time he would merely walk and keep on going. As he sat and regained his breath, he noted that he was feeling quite warm and comfortable. He was not shivering, and it even seemed that a warm glow had come to his chest and trunk. And yet, when he touched his nose or cheeks, there was no sensation. Running would not thaw them out. Nor would it thaw out his hands and feet. Then the thought came to him that the frozen portions of his body must be extending. He tried to keep this thought down, to forget it, to think of something else; he was aware of the panicky feeling that it caused, and he was afraid of the panic. But the thought asserted itself, and persisted, until it produced a vision of his body totally frozen. This was too much, and he made another wild run along the trail. Once he slowed down to a walk, but the thought of the freezing extending itself made him run again.

And all the time the dog ran with him, at his heels. When he fell down a second time, it curled its tail over its forefeet and sat in front of him, facing him,

5. Mercury is the Roman god of messengers, thieves, and storytellers; he flew between heaven and earth wearing winged sandals. He is also the god of healing and the courier of souls to the Underworld.

curiously eager and intent. The warmth and security of the animal angered him, and he cursed it till it flattened down its ears appeasingly. This time the shivering came more quickly upon the man. He was losing in his battle with the frost. It was creeping into his body from all sides. The thought of it drove him on, but he ran no more than a hundred feet, when he staggered and pitched headlong. It was his last panic. When he had recovered his breath and control, he sat up and entertained in his mind the conception of meeting death with dignity. However, the conception did not come to him in such terms. His idea of it was that he had been making a fool of himself, running around like a chicken with its head cut off—such was the simile that occurred to him. Well, he was bound to freeze anyway, and he might as well take it decently. With this new-found peace of mind came the first glimmerings of drowsiness. A good idea, he thought, to sleep off to death. It was like taking an anaesthetic. Freezing was not so bad as people thought. There were lots worse ways to die.

He pictured the boys finding his body next day. Suddenly he found himself with them, coming along the trail and looking for himself. And, still with them, he came around a turn in the trail and found himself lying in the snow. He did not belong with himself any more, for even then he was out of himself, standing with the boys and looking at himself in the snow. It certainly was cold, was his thought. When he got back to the States he could tell the folks what real cold was. He drifted on from this to a vision of the old-timer on Sulphur Creek. He could see him quite clearly, warm and comfortable, and smoking a pipe.

"You were right, old hoss; you were right," the man mumbled to the old-timer of Sulphur Creek.

Then the man drowsed off into what seemed to him the most comfortable and satisfying sleep he had ever known. The dog sat facing him and waiting. The brief day drew to a close in a long, slow twilight. There were no signs of a fire to be made, and, besides, never in the dog's experience had it known a man to sit like that in the snow and make no fire. As the twilight drew on, its eager yearning for the fire mastered it, and with a great lifting and shifting of forefeet, it whined softly, then flattened its ears down in anticipation of being chidden by the man. But the man remained silent. Later, the dog whined loudly. And still later it crept close to the man and caught the scent of death. This made the animal bristle and back away. A little longer it delayed, howling under the stars that leaped and danced and shone brightly in the cold sky. Then it turned and trotted up the trail in the direction of the camp it knew, where were the other food-providers and fire-providers.

1902, 1908

# The Mexican[1]

## I

Nobody knew his history—they of the Junta[2] least of all. He was their "little mystery," their "big patriot," and in his way he worked as hard for the coming

---

1. First published in the *Saturday Evening Post* (August 19, 1911); rpt. in London's *The Night Born* (1913), the source of the present text.
2. Spanish for a group of thinkers and planners

(Benjamin Franklin used it to describe his own reading club); *junta* later came to mean specifically a military dictatorship run by a committee of high-ranking officers.

Mexican Revolution as did they. They were tardy in recognizing this, for not one of the Junta liked him. The day he first drifted into their crowded, busy rooms, they all suspected him of being a spy—one of the bought tools of the Diaz secret service.[3] Too many of the comrades were in civil and military prisons scattered over the United States, and others of them, in irons, were even then being taken across the border to be lined up against adobe walls and shot.

At the first sight the boy did not impress them favorably. Boy he was, not more than eighteen and not over large for his years. He announced that he was Felipe Rivera, and that it was his wish to work for the Revolution. That was all—not a wasted word, no further explanation. He stood waiting. There was no smile on his lips, no geniality in his eyes. Big dashing Paulino Vera felt an inward shudder. Here was something forbidding, terrible, inscrutable. There was something venomous and snakelike in the boy's black eyes. They burned like cold fire, as with a vast, concentrated bitterness. He flashed them from the faces of the conspirators to the typewriter which little Mrs. Sethby was industriously operating. His eyes rested on hers but an instant—she had chanced to look up—and she, too, sensed the nameless something that made her pause. She was compelled to read back in order to regain the swing of the letter she was writing.

Paulino Vera looked questioningly at Arrellano and Ramos, and questioningly they looked back and to each other. The indecision of doubt brooded in their eyes. This slender boy was the Unknown, vested with all the menace of the Unknown. He was unrecognizable, something quite beyond the ken of honest, ordinary revolutionists whose fiercest hatred for Diaz and his tyranny after all was only that of honest and ordinary patriots. Here was something else, they knew not what. But Vera, always the most impulsive, the quickest to act, stepped into the breach.

"Very well," he said coldly. "You say you want to work for the Revolution. Take off your coat. Hang it over there. I will show you—come—where are the buckets and cloths. The floor is dirty. You will begin by scrubbing it, and by scrubbing the floors of the other rooms. The spittoons need to be cleaned. Then there are the windows."

"Is it for the Revolution?" the boy asked.

"It is for the Revolution," Vera answered.

Rivera looked cold suspicion at all of them, then proceeded to take off his coat.

"It is well," he said.

And nothing more. Day after day he came to his work—sweeping, scrubbing, cleaning. He emptied the ashes from the stoves, brought up the coal and kindling, and lighted the fires before the most energetic one of them was at his desk.

"Can I sleep here?" he asked once.

Ah, ha! So that was it—the hand of Diaz showing through! To sleep in the rooms of the Junta meant access to their secrets, to the lists of names, to the addresses of comrades down on Mexican soil. The request was denied, and

3. Porfirio Díaz (1830–1915) was a *mestizo*, or person of mixed Indian and Spanish blood, who ruled as dictator of Mexico from 1876 until 1911, when a revolution headed by Francisco I. Madero (1873–1913) forced him to flee the country. He died in Paris as an exile.

Rivera never spoke of it again. He slept they knew not where, and ate they knew not where nor how. Once, Arrellano offered him a couple of dollars. Rivera declined the money with a shake of the head. When Vera joined in and tried to press it upon him, he said:

"I am working for the Revolution."

It takes money to raise a modern revolution, and always the Junta was pressed. The members starved and toiled, and the longest day was none too long, and yet there were times when it appeared as if the Revolution stood or fell on no more than the matter of a few dollars. Once, the first time, when the rent of the house was two months behind and the landlord was threatening dispossession, it was Felipe Rivera, the scrub-boy in the poor, cheap clothes, worn and threadbare, who laid sixty dollars in gold on May Sethby's desk. There were other times. Three hundred letters, clicked out on the busy typewriters (appeals for assistance, for sanctions from the organized labor groups, requests for square news deals to the editors of newspapers, protests against the high-handed treatment of revolutionists by the United States courts), lay unmailed, awaiting postage. Vera's watch had disappeared—the old-fashioned gold repeater that had been his father's. Likewise had gone the plain gold band from May Sethby's third finger. Things were desperate. Ramos and Arrellano pulled their long mustaches in despair. The letters must go off, and the Post Office allowed no credit to purchasers of stamps. Then it was that Rivera put on his hat and went out. When he came back he laid a thousand two-cent stamps on May Sethby's desk.

"I wonder if it is the cursed gold of Diaz?" said Vera to the comrades.

They elevated their brows and could not decide. And Felipe Rivera, the scrubber for the Revolution, continued, as occasion arose, to lay down gold and silver for the Junta's use.

And still they could not bring themselves to like him. They did not know him. His ways were not theirs. He gave no confidences. He repelled all probing. Youth that he was, they could never nerve themselves to dare to question him.

"A great and lonely spirit, perhaps, I do not know, I do not know," Arrellano said helplessly.

"He is not human," said Ramos.

"His soul has been seared," said May Sethby. "Light and laughter have been burned out of him. He is like one dead, and yet he is fearfully alive."

"He has been through hell," said Vera. "No man could look like that who has not been through hell—and he is only a boy."

Yet they could not like him. He never talked, never inquired, never suggested. He would stand listening, expressionless, a thing dead, save for his eyes, coldly burning, while their talk of the Revolution ran high and warm. From face to face and speaker to speaker his eyes would turn, boring like gimlets of incandescent ice, disconcerting and perturbing.

"He is no spy," Vera confided to May Sethby. "He is a patriot—mark me, the greatest patriot of us all. I know it, I feel it, here in my heart and head I feel it. But him I know not at all."

"He has a bad temper," said May Sethby.

"I know," said Vera, with a shudder. "He has looked at me with those eyes of his. They do not love; they threaten; they are savage as a wild tiger's. I know, if I should prove unfaithful to the Cause, that he would kill me. He has no heart. He is pitiless as steel, keen and cold as frost. He is like moonshine in a winter night when a man freezes to death on some lonely mountain top. I am not afraid of Diaz and all his killers; but this boy, of him am I afraid. I tell you true. I am afraid. He is the breath of death."

Yet Vera it was who persuaded the others to give the first trust to Rivera. The line of communication between Los Angeles and Lower California[4] had broken down. Three of the comrades had dug their own graves and been shot into them. Two more were United States prisoners in Los Angeles. Juan Alvarado, the Federal commander, was a monster. All their plans did he checkmate. They could no longer gain access to the active revolutionists, and the incipient ones, in Lower California.

Young Rivera was given his instructions and dispatched south. When he returned, the line of communication was reëstablished, and Juan Alvarado was dead. He had been found in bed, a knife hilt-deep in his breast. This had exceeded Rivera's instructions, but they of the Junta knew the times of his movements. They did not ask him. He said nothing. But they looked at one another and conjectured.

"I have told you," said Vera. "Diaz has more to fear from this youth than from any man. He is implacable. He is the hand of God."

The bad temper, mentioned by May Sethby, and sensed by them all, was evidenced by physical proofs. Now he appeared with a cut lip, a blackened cheek, or a swollen ear. It was patent that he brawled, somewhere in that outside world where he ate and slept, gained money, and moved in ways unknown to them. As the time passed, he had come to set type for the little revolutionary sheet they published weekly. There were occasions when he was unable to set type, when his knuckles were bruised and battered, when his thumbs were injured and helpless, when one arm or the other hung wearily at his side while his face was drawn with unspoken pain.

"A wastrel," said Arrellano.

"A frequenter of low places," said Ramos.

"But where does he get the money?" Vera demanded. "Only today, just now, have I learned that he paid the bill for white paper—one hundred and forty dollars."

"There are his absences," said May Sethby. "He never explains them."

"We should set a spy upon him," Ramos propounded.

"I should not care to be that spy," said Vera. "I fear you would never see me again, save to bury me. He has a terrible passion. Not even God would he permit to stand between him and the way of his passion."

"I feel like a child before him," Ramos confessed.

"To me he is power—he is the primitive, the wild wolf,—the striking rattlesnake, the stinging centipede," said Arrellano.

"He is the Revolution incarnate," said Vera. "He is the flame and the spirit of it, the insatiable cry for vengeance that makes no cry but that slays noiselessly. He is a destroying angel moving through the still watches of the night."

"I could weep over him," said May Sethby. "He knows nobody. He hates all people. Us he tolerates, for we are the way of his desire. He is alone . . . lonely." Her voice broke in a half sob and there was dimness in her eyes.

---

4. Baja (Lower) California, then part of Mexico called the Territory of Baja California.

Rivera's ways and times were truly mysterious. There were periods when they did not see him for a week at a time. Once, he was away a month. These occasions were always capped by his return, when, without advertisement or speech, he laid gold coins on May Sethby's desk. Again, for days and weeks, he spent all his time with the Junta. And yet again, for irregular periods, he would disappear through the heart of each day, from early morning until late afternoon. At such times he came early and remained late. Arrellano had found him at midnight, setting type with fresh swollen knuckles, or mayhap it was his lip, new-split, that still bled.

II

The time of the crisis approached. Whether or not the Revolution would be depended upon the Junta, and the Junta was hard-pressed. The need for money was greater than ever before, while money was harder to get. Patriots had given their last cent and now could give no more. Section gang laborers—fugitive peons[5] from Mexico—were contributing half their scanty wages. But more than that was needed. The heart-breaking, conspiring, undermining toil of years approached fruition. The time was ripe. The Revolution hung on the balance. One shove more, one last heroic effort, and it would tremble across the scales to victory. They knew their Mexico. Once started, the Revolution would take care of itself. The whole Diaz machine would go down like a house of cards. The border was ready to rise. One Yankee, with a hundred I.W.W. men,[6] waited the word to cross over the border and begin the conquest of Lower California. But he needed guns. And clear across to the Atlantic, the Junta in touch with them all and all of them needing guns, mere adventurers, soldiers of fortune, bandits, disgruntled American union men, socialists, anarchists, rough-necks, Mexican exiles, peons escaped from bondage, whipped miners from the bull-pens of Cœur d' Alene and Colorado who desired only the more vindictively to fight—all the flotsam and jetsam of wild spirits from the madly complicated modern world. And it was guns and ammunition, ammunition and guns—the unceasing and eternal cry.

Fling this heterogeneous, bankrupt, vindictive mass across the border, and the Revolution was on. The custom house, the northern ports of entry, would be captured. Diaz could not resist. He dared not throw the weight of his armies against them, for he must hold the south. And through the south the flame would spread despite. The people would rise. The defenses of city after city would crumple up. State after state would totter down. And at last, from every side, the victorious armies of the Revolution would close in on the City of Mexico itself, Diaz's last stronghold.

But the money. They had the men, impatient and urgent, who would use the guns. They knew the traders who would sell and deliver the guns. But to culture the Revolution thus far had exhausted the Junta. The last dollar had been spent, the last resource and the last starving patriot milked dry, and the great adventure still trembled on the scales. Guns and ammunition! The ragged battalions must be armed. But how? Ramos lamented his confiscated estates. Arrellano wailed the spendthriftness of his youth. May Sethby wondered if it

---

5. Unskilled Mexican laborers or farm workers, usually bound in servitude to a landlord creditor.

6. Members of the International Workers of the World, a radical trade union.

would have been different had they of the Junta been more economical in the past.

"To think that the freedom of Mexico should stand or fall on a few paltry thousands of dollars," said Paulino Vera.

Despair was in all their faces. José Amarillo, their last hope, a recent convert, who had promised money, had been apprehended at his hacienda in Chihuahua and shot against his own stable wall. The news had just come through.

Rivera, on his knees, scrubbing, looked up, with suspended brush, his bare arms flecked with soapy, dirty water.

"Will five thousand do it?" he asked.

They looked their amazement. Vera nodded and swallowed. He could not speak, but he was on the instant invested with a vast faith.

"Order the guns," Rivera said, and thereupon was guilty of the longest flow of words they had ever heard him utter. "The time is short. In three weeks I shall bring you the five thousand. It is well. The weather will be warmer for those who fight. Also, it is the best I can do."

Vera fought his faith. It was incredible. Too many fond hopes had been shattered since he had begun to play the revolution game. He believed this threadbare scrubber of the Revolution, and yet he dared not believe.

"You are crazy," he said.

"In three weeks," said Rivera. "Order the guns."

He got up, rolled down his sleeves, and put on his coat.

"Order the guns," he said. "I am going now."

## III

After hurrying and scurrying, much telephoning and bad language, a night session was held in Kelly's office. Kelly was rushed with business; also, he was unlucky. He had brought Danny Ward out from New York, arranged the fight for him with Billy Carthey, the date was three weeks away, and for two days now, carefully concealed from the sporting writers, Carthey had been lying up, badly injured. There was no one to take his place. Kelly had been burning the wires East to every eligible lightweight, but they were tied up with dates and contracts. And now hope had revived, though faintly.

"You've got a hell of a nerve," Kelly addressed Rivera, after one look, as soon as they got together.

Hate that was malignant was in Rivera's eyes, but his face remained impassive.

"I can lick Ward," was all he said.

"How do you know? Ever see him fight?"

Rivera shook his head.

"He can beat you up with one hand and both eyes closed."

Rivera shrugged his shoulders.

"Haven't you got anything to say?" the fight promoter snarled.

"I can lick him."

"Who'd you ever fight, anyway?" Michael Kelly demanded. Michael was the promoter's brother, and ran the Yellowstone pool rooms where he made goodly sums on the fight game.

Rivera favored him with a bitter, unanswering stare.

The promoter's secretary, a distinctively sporty young man, sneered audibly.

"Well, you know Roberts," Kelly broke the hostile silence. "He ought to be here. I've sent for him. Sit down and wait, though from the looks of you, you haven't got a chance. I can't throw the public down with a bum fight. Ringside seats are selling at fifteen dollars, you know that."

When Roberts arrived, it was patent that he was mildly drunk. He was a tall, lean, slack-jointed individual, and his walk, like his talk, was a smooth and languid drawl.

Kelly went straight to the point.

"Look here, Roberts, you've been braggin' you discovered this little Mexican. You know Carthey's broke his arm. Well, this little yellow streak has the gall to blow in to-day and say he'll take Carthey's place. What about it?"

"It's all right, Kelly," came the slow response. "He can put up a fight."

"I suppose you'll be sayin' next that he can lick Ward," Kelly snapped.

Roberts considered judicially.

"No, I won't say that. Ward's a top-notcher and a ring general. But he can't hashhouse Rivera in short order. I know Rivera. Nobody can get his goat. He ain't got a goat that I could ever discover. And he's a two-handed fighter. He can throw in the sleep-makers from any position."

"Never mind that. What kind of a show can he put up? You've been conditioning and training fighters all your life. I take off my hat to your judgment. Can he give the public a run for its money?"

"He sure can, and he'll worry Ward a might heap on top of it. You don't know that boy. I do. I discovered him. He ain't got a goat. He's a devil. He's a wizzy-wooz if anybody should ask you. He'll make Ward sit up with a show of local talent that'll make the rest of you sit up. I won't say he'll lick Ward, but he'll put up such a show that you'll all know he's a comer."

"All right." Kelly turned to his secretary.

"Ring up Ward. I warned him to show up if I thought it worth while. He's right across at the Yellowstone, throwin' chests and doing the popular." Kelly turned back to the conditioner. "Have a drink?"

Roberts sipped his highball and unburdened himself.

"Never told you how I discovered the little cuss. It was a couple of years ago he showed up out at the quarters. I was getting Prayne ready for his fight with Delaney. Prayne's wicked. He ain't got a trickle of mercy in his make-up. He'd chopped up his pardners something cruel, and I couldn't find a willing boy that'd work with him. I'd noticed this little starved Mexican kid hanging around, and I was desperate. So I grabbed him, slammed on the gloves, and put him in. He was tougher'n rawhide, but weak. And he didn't know the first letter in the alphabet of boxing. Prayne chopped him to ribbons. But he hung on for two sickening rounds, when he fainted. Starvation, that was all. Battered? You couldn't have recognized him. I gave him half a dollar and a square meal. You oughta seen him wolf it down. He hadn't had a bite for a couple of days. That's the end of him, thinks I. But next day he showed up, stiff an' sore, ready for another half and a square meal. And he done better as time went by. Just a born fighter, and tough beyond belief. He hasn't a heart. He's a piece of ice. And he never talked eleven words in a string since I know him. He saws wood and does his work."

"I've seen 'm," the secretary said. "He's worked a lot for you."

"All the big little fellows has tried out on him," Roberts answered. "And he's learned from 'em. I've seen some of them he could lick. But his heart wasn't in it. I reckoned he never liked the game. He seemed to act that way."

"He's been fighting some before the little clubs the last few months," Kelly said.

"Sure. But I don't know what struck 'm. All of a sudden his heart got into it. He just went out like a streak and cleaned up all the little local fellows. Seemed to want the money, and he's won a bit, though his clothes don't look it. He's peculiar. Nobody knows his business. Nobody knows how he spends his time. Even when he's on the job, he plumb up and disappears most of each day soon as his work is done. Sometimes he just blows away for weeks at a time. But he don't take advice. There's a fortune in it for the fellow that gets the job of managin' him, only he won't consider it. And you watch him hold out for the cash money when you get down to terms."

It was at this stage that Danny Ward arrived. Quite a party it was. His manager and trainer were with him, and he breezed in like a gusty draught of geniality, good-nature, and all-conqueringness. Greetings flew about, a joke here, a retort there, a smile or a laugh for everybody. Yet it was his way, and only partly sincere. He was a good actor, and he had found geniality a most valuable asset in the game of getting on in the world. But down underneath he was the deliberate, cold-blooded fighter and business man. The rest was a mask. Those who knew him or trafficked with him said that when it came to brass tacks he was Danny-on-the-Spot. He was invariably present at all business discussions, and it was urged by some that his manager was a blind whose only function was to serve as Danny's mouth-piece.

Rivera's way was different. Indian blood, as well as Spanish, was in his veins, and he sat back in a corner, silent, immobile, only his black eyes passing from face to face and noting everything.

"So that's the guy," Danny said, running an appraising eye over his proposed antagonist. "How de do, old chap."

Rivera's eyes burned venomously, but he made no sign of acknowledgment. He disliked all Gringos, but this Gringo he hated with an immediacy that was unusual even in him.

"Gawd!" Danny protested facetiously to the promoter. "You ain't expectin' me to fight a deef mute." When the laughter subsided, he made another hit. "Los Angeles must be on the dink when this is the best you can scare up. What kindergarten did you get 'm from?"

"He's a good little boy, Danny, take it from me," Roberts defended. "Not as easy as he looks."

"And half the house is sold already," Kelly pleaded. "You'll have to take 'm on, Danny. It's the best we can do."

Danny ran another careless and unflattering glance over Rivera and sighed.

"I gotta be easy with 'm, I guess. If only he don't blow up."

Roberts snorted.

"You gotta be careful," Danny's manager warned. "No taking chances with a dub that's likely to sneak a lucky one across."

"Oh, I'll be careful all right, all right," Danny smiled. "I'll get 'm at the start an' nurse 'm along for the dear public's sake. What d' ye say to fifteen rounds, Kelly—An' then the hay for him?"

"That'll do," was the answer. "As long as you make it realistic."

"Then let's get down to biz." Danny paused and calculated. "Of course, sixty-five per cent. of gate receipts, same as with Carthey. But the split'll be different. Eighty will just about suit me." And to his manager, "That right?"

The manager nodded.

"Here, you, did you get that?" Kelly asked Rivera.

Rivera shook his head.

"Well, it's this way," Kelly exposited. "The purse'll be sixty-five per cent. of the gate receipts. You're a dub, and an unknown. You and Danny split, twenty per cent. goin' to you, an' eighty to Danny. That's fair, isn't it, Roberts?"

"Very fair, Rivera," Roberts agreed. "You see, you ain't got a reputation yet."

"What will sixty-five per cent. of the gate receipts be?" Rivera demanded.

"Oh, maybe five thousand, maybe as high as eight thousand," Danny broke in to explain. "Something like that. Your share'll come to something like a thousand or sixteen hundred. Pretty good for takin' a licking from a guy with my reputation. What d' ye say?"

Then Rivera took their breaths away.

"Winner takes all," he said with finality.

A dead silence prevailed.

"It's like candy from a baby," Danny's manager proclaimed.

Danny shook his head.

"I've been in the game too long," he explained. "I'm not casting reflections on the referee, or the present company, I'm not sayin' nothing about bookmakers an' frame-ups that sometimes happen. But what I do say is that it's poor business for a fighter like me. I play safe. There's no tellin'. Mebbe I break my arm, eh? Or some guy slips me a bunch of dope?" He shook his head solemnly. "Win or lose, eighty is my split. What d' ye say, Mexican?"

Rivera shook his head.

Danny exploded. He was getting down to brass tacks now.

"Why, you dirty little greaser! I've a mind to knock your block off right now."

Roberts drawled his body to interposition between hostilities.

"Winner takes all," Rivera repeated sullenly.

"Why do you stand out that way?" Danny asked.

"I can lick you," was the straight answer.

Danny half started to take off his coat. But, as his manager knew, it was a grand stand play. The coat did not come off, and Danny allowed himself to be placated by the group. Everybody sympathized with him. Rivera stood alone.

"Look here, you little fool," Kelly took up the argument. "You're nobody. We know what you've been doing the last few months—putting away little local fighters. But Danny is class. His next fight after this will be for the championship. And you're unknown. Nobody ever heard of you out of Los Angeles."

"They will," Rivera answered with a shrug, "after this fight."

"You think for a second you can lick me?" Danny blurted in.

Rivera nodded.

"Oh, come; listen to reason," Kelly pleaded. "Think of the advertising."

"I want the money," was Rivera's answer.

"You couldn't win from me in a thousand years," Danny assured him.

"Then what are you holding out for?" Rivera countered. "If the money's that easy, why don't you go after it?"

"I will, so help me!" Danny cried with abrupt conviction. "I'll beat you to death in the ring, my boy—you monkeyin' with me this way. Make out the articles, Kelly. Winner take all. Play it up in the sportin' columns. Tell 'em it's a grudge fight. I'll show this fresh kid a few."

Kelly's secretary had begun to write, when Danny interrupted.

"Hold on!" He turned to Rivera. "Weights?"

"Ringside," came the answer.

"Not on your life, Fresh Kid. If winner takes all, we weigh in at ten A.M."[7]

"And winner takes all?" Rivera queried.

Danny nodded. That settled it. He would enter the ring in his full ripeness of strength.

"Weigh in at ten," Rivera said.

The secretary's pen went on scratching.

"It means five pounds," Roberts complained to Rivera. "You've given too much away. You've thrown the fight right there. Danny'll be as strong as a bull. You're a fool. He'll lick you sure. You ain't got the chance of a dew-drop in hell."

Rivera's answer was a calculated look of hatred. Even this Gringo he despised, and him had he found the whitest Gringo of them all.[8]

## IV

Barely noticed was Rivera as he entered the ring. Only a very slight and very scattering ripple of half-hearted hand-clapping greeted him. The house did not believe in him. He was the lamb led to slaughter at the hands of the great Danny. Besides, the house was disappointed. It had expected a rushing battle between Danny Ward and Billy Carthey, and here it must put up with this poor little tyro. Still further, it had manifested its disapproval of the change by betting two, and even three, to one on Danny. And where a betting audience's money is, there is its heart.

The Mexican boy sat down in his corner and waited. The slow minutes lagged by. Danny was making him wait. It was an old trick, but ever it worked on the young, new fighters. They grew frightened, sitting thus and facing their own apprehensions and a callous, tobacco-smoking audience. But for once the trick failed. Roberts was right. Rivera had no goat. He, who was more delicately coördinated, more finely nerved and strung than any of them, had no nerves of this sort. The atmosphere of foredoomed defeat in his own corner had no effect on him. His handlers were Gringos and strangers. Also they were scrubs—the dirty driftage of the fight game, without honor, without efficiency. And they were chilled, as well, with certitude that theirs was the losing corner.

"Now you gotta be careful," Spider Hagerty warned him. Spider was his chief second. "Make it last as long as you can—them's my instructions from Kelly. If you don't, the papers'll call it another bum fight and give the game a bigger black eye in Los Angeles."

---

7. If they weigh in in the morning instead of just before the evening fight, Danny has several hours to eat and drink to put on weight that won't be counted; he knows Rivera has no resources to do the same.

8. That is, even the whitest of Gringos is worthless; Rivera's reflection mocks the white notion that the whiter a man is the better.

All of which was not encouraging. But Rivera took no notice. He despised prize fighting. It was the hated game of the hated Gringo. He had taken up with it, as a chopping block for others in the training quarters, solely because he was starving. The fact that he was marvelously made for it had meant nothing. He hated it. Not until he had come in to the Junta had he fought for money, and he had found the money easy. Not first among the sons of men had he been to find himself successful at a despised vocation.

He did not analyze. He merely knew that he must win this fight. There could be no other outcome. For behind him, nerving him to this belief, were profounder forces than any the crowded house dreamed. Danny Ward fought for money, and for the easy ways of life that money would bring. But the things Rivera fought for burned in his brain—blazing and terrible visions, that, with eyes wide open, sitting lonely in the corner of the ring and waiting for his tricky antagonist, he saw as clearly as he had lived them.

He saw the white-walled, water-power factories of Rio Blanco.[9] He saw the six thousand workers, starved and wan, and the little children, seven and eight years of age, who toiled long shifts for ten cents a day. He saw the perambulating corpses, the ghastly death's heads of men who labored in the dye-rooms. He remembered that he had heard his father call the dye-rooms the "suicide-holes," where a year was death. He saw the little patio, and his mother cooking and moiling at crude housekeeping and finding time to caress and love him. And his father he saw, large, big-moustached and deep-chested, kindly above all men, who loved all men and whose heart was so large that there was love to overflowing still left for the mother and the little muchacho playing in the corner of the patio. In those days his name had not been Felipe Rivera. It had been Fernandez, his father's and mother's name. Him had they called Juan. Later, he had changed it himself, for he had found the name of Fernandez hated by prefects of police, *jefes politicos,* and *rurales.*

Big, hearty Joaquin Fernandez! A large place he occupied in Rivera's visions. He had not understood at the time, but looking back he could understand. He could see him setting type in the little printery, or scribbling endless hasty, nervous lines on the much-cluttered desk. And he could see the strange evenings, when workmen, coming secretly in the dark like men who did ill deeds, met with his father and talked long hours where he, the muchacho, lay not always asleep in the corner.

As from a remote distance he could hear Spider Hagerty saying to him: "No layin' down at the start. Them's instructions. Take a beatin' an' earn your dough."

Ten minutes had passed, and he still sat in his corner. There were no signs of Danny, who was evidently playing the trick to the limit.

But more visions burned before the eye of Rivera's memory. The strike, or, rather, the lockout, because the workers of Rio Blanco had helped their striking brothers of Puebla.[1] The hunger, the expeditions in the hills for berries, the roots and herbs that all ate and that twisted and pained the stomachs of all of them. And then, the nightmare; the waste of ground before the com-

---

9. The Rio Blanco textile mill in Veracruz was the site of a massacre of striking workers in January 1909; dozens of workers were shot by government soldiers, an event that stiffened opposition to Diaz and helped spur the revolution not quite two years later.
1. Mexican manufacturing city about sixty miles southeast of Mexico City.

pany's store; the thousands of starving workers; General Rosalio Martinez[2] and the soldiers of Porfirio Diaz; and the death-spitting rifles that seemed never to cease spitting, while the workers' wrongs were washed and washed again in their own blood. And that night! He saw the flat cars, piled high with the bodies of the slain, consigned to Vera Cruz, food for the sharks of the bay. Again he crawled over the grisly heaps, seeking and finding, stripped and mangled, his father and his mother. His mother he especially remembered— only her face projecting, her body burdened by the weight of dozens of bodies. Again the rifles of the soldiers of Porfirio Diaz cracked, and again he dropped to the ground and slunk away like some hunted coyote of the hills.

To his ears came a great roar, as of the sea, and he saw Danny Ward, leading his retinue of trainers and seconds, coming down the center aisle. The house was in wild uproar for the popular hero who was bound to win. Everybody proclaimed him. Everybody was for him. Even Rivera's own seconds warmed to something akin to cheerfulness when Danny ducked jauntily through the ropes and entered the ring. His face continually spread to an unending succession of smiles, and when Danny smiled he smiled in every feature, even to the laughter-wrinkles of the corners of the eyes and into the depths of the eyes themselves. Never was there so genial a fighter. His face was a running advertisement of good feeling, of good fellowship. He knew everybody. He joked, and laughed, and greeted his friends through the ropes. Those farther away, unable to suppress their admiration, cried loudly: "Oh, you Danny!" It was a joyous ovation of affection that lasted a full five minutes.

Rivera was disregarded. For all that the audience noticed, he did not exist. Spider Hagerty's bloated face bent down close to his.

"No gettin' scared," the Spider warned. "An' remember instructions. You gotta last. No layin' down. If you lay down, we got instructions to beat you up in the dressing rooms. Savve? You just gotta fight."

The house began to applaud. Danny was crossing the ring to him. Danny bent over, caught Rivera's right hand in both his own and shook it with impulsive heartiness. Danny's smile-wreathed face was close to his. The audience yelled its appreciation of Danny's display of sporting spirit. He was greeting his opponent with the fondness of a brother. Danny's lips moved, and the audience, interpreting the unheard words to be those of a kindly-natured sport, yelled again. Only Rivera heard the low words.

"You little Mexican rat," hissed from between Danny's gaily smiling lips, "I'll fetch the yellow outa you."

Rivera made no move. He did not rise. He merely hated with his eyes.

"Get up, you dog!" some man yelled through the ropes from behind.

The crowd began to hiss and boo him for his unsportsmanlike conduct, but he sat unmoved. Another great outburst of applause was Danny's as he walked back across the ring.

When Danny stripped, there was ohs! and ahs! of delight. His body was perfect, alive with easy suppleness and health and strength. The skin was white as a woman's, and as smooth. All grace, and resilience, and power resided therein. He had proved it in scores of battles. His photographs were in all the physical culture magazines.

2. A fictional character.

A groan went up as Spider Hagerty peeled Rivera's sweater over his head. His body seemed leaner, because of the swarthiness of the skin. He had muscles, but they made no display like his opponent's. What the audience neglected to see was the deep chest. Nor could it guess the toughness of the fiber of the flesh, the instantaneousness of the cell explosions of the muscles, the fineness of the nerves that wired every part of him into a splendid fighting mechanism. All the audience saw was a brown-skinned boy of eighteen with what seemed the body of a boy. With Danny it was different. Danny was a man of twenty-four, and his body was a man's body. The contrast was still more striking as they stood together in the center of the ring receiving the referee's last instructions.

Rivera noticed Roberts sitting directly behind the newspaper men. He was drunker than usual, and his speech was correspondingly slower.

"Take it easy, Rivera," Roberts drawled. "He can't kill you, remember that. He'll rush you at the go-off, but don't get rattled. You just cover up, and stall, and clinch. He can't hurt you much. Just make believe to yourself that he's choppin' out on you at the trainin' quarters."

Rivera made no sign that he had heard.

"Sullen little devil," Roberts muttered to the man next to him. "He always was that way."

But Rivera forgot to look his usual hatred. A vision of countless rifles blinded his eyes. Every face in the audience, far as he could see, to the high dollar-seats, was transformed into a rifle. And he saw the long Mexican border arid and sun-washed and aching, and along it he saw the ragged bands that delayed only for the guns.

Back in his corner he waited, standing up. His seconds had crawled out through the ropes, taking the canvas stool with them. Diagonally across the squared ring, Danny faced him. The gong struck, and the battle was on. The audience howled its delight. Never had it seen a battle open more convincingly. The papers were right. It was a grudge fight. Three-quarters of the distance Danny covered in the rush to get together, his intention to eat up the Mexican lad plainly advertised. He assailed with not one blow, nor two, nor a dozen. He was a gyroscope of blows, a whirlwind of destruction. Rivera was nowhere. He was overwhelmed, buried beneath avalanches of punches delivered from every angle and position by a past master in the art. He was overborne, swept back against the ropes, separated by the referee, and swept back against the ropes again.

It was not a fight. It was a slaughter, a massacre. Any audience, save a prize fighting one, would have exhausted its emotions in that first minute. Danny was certainly showing what he could do—a splendid exhibition. Such was the certainty of the audience, as well as its excitement and favoritism, that it failed to take notice that the Mexican still stayed on his feet. It forgot Rivera. It rarely saw him, so closely was he enveloped in Danny's man-eating attack. A minute of this went by, and two minutes. Then, in a separation, it caught a clear glimpse of the Mexican. His lip was cut, his nose was bleeding. As he turned and staggered into a clinch, the welts of oozing blood, from his contacts with the ropes, showed in red bars across his back. But what the audience did not notice was that his chest was not heaving and that his eyes were coldly burning as ever. Too many aspiring champions, in the cruel welter of the training camps, had practiced this man-eating attack on him. He had learned to live through for a compensation of from half a dollar a go up to fifteen dollars a week—a hard school, and he was schooled hard.

Then happened the amazing thing. The whirling, blurring mix-up ceased suddenly. Rivera stood alone. Danny, the redoubtable Danny, lay on his back. His body quivered as consciousness strove to return to it. He had not staggered and sunk down, nor had he gone over in a long slumping fall. The right hook of Rivera had dropped him in midair with the abruptness of death. The referee shoved Rivera back with one hand, and stood over the fallen gladiator counting the seconds. It is the custom of prize-fighting audiences to cheer a clean knock-down blow. But this audience did not cheer. The thing had been too unexpected. It watched the toll of the seconds in tense silence, and through this silence the voice of Roberts rose exultantly:

"I told you he was a two-handed fighter!"

By the fifth second, Danny was rolling over on his face, and when seven was counted, he rested on one knee, ready to rise after the count of nine and before the count of ten. If his knee still touched the floor at "ten," he was considered "down," and also "out." The instant his knee left the floor, he was considered "up," and in that instant it was Rivera's right to try and put him down again. Rivera took no chances. The moment that knee left the floor he would strike again. He circled around, but the referee circled in between, and Rivera knew that the seconds he counted were very slow. All Gringos were against him, even the referee.

At "nine" the referee gave Rivera a sharp thrust back. It was unfair, but it enabled Danny to rise, the smile back on his lips. Doubled partly over, with arms wrapped about face and abdomen, he cleverly stumbled into a clinch. By all the rules of the game the referee should have broken it, but he did not, and Danny clung on like a surf-battered barnacle and moment by moment recuperated. The last minute of the round was going fast. If he could live to the end, he would have a full minute in his corner to revive. And live to the end he did, smiling through all desperateness and extremity.

"The smile that won't come off!" somebody yelled, and the audience laughed loudly in its relief.

"The kick that greaser's got is something God-awful," Danny gasped in his corner to his adviser while his handlers worked frantically over him.

The second and third rounds were tame. Danny, a tricky and consummate ring general, stalled and blocked and held on, devoting himself to recovering from that dazing first-round blow. In the fourth round he was himself again. Jarred and shaken, nevertheless his good condition had enabled him to regain his vigor. But he tried no man-eating tactics. The Mexican had proved a tartar.[3] Instead, he brought to bear his best fighting powers. In tricks and skill and experience he was the master, and though he could land nothing vital, he proceeded scientifically to chop and wear down his opponent. He landed three blows to Rivera's one, but they were punishing blows only, and not deadly. It was the sum of many of them that constituted deadliness. He was respectful of this two-handed dub with the amazing short-arm kicks in both his fists.

3. "Tartar" was a common mistake for "Tatar"—the Tatars were a Turkic Mongolian tribe known for their toughness.

In defense, Rivera developed a disconcerting straight-left. Again and again, attack after attack he straight-lefted away from him with accumulated damage to Danny's mouth and nose. But Danny was protean. That was why he was the coming champion. He could change from style to style of fighting at will. He now devoted himself to infighting.[4] In this he was particularly wicked, and it enabled him to avoid the other's straight-left. Here he set the house wild repeatedly, capping it with a marvelous lock-break and lift of an inside upper-cut that raised the Mexican in the air and dropped him to the mat. Rivera rested on one knee, making the most of the count, and in the soul of him he knew the referee was counting short seconds on him.

Again, in the seventh, Danny achieved the diabolical inside upper-cut. He succeeded only in staggering Rivera, but, in the ensuing moment of defenseless helplessness, he smashed him with another blow through the ropes. Rivera's body bounced on the heads of the newspaper men below, and they boosted him back to the edge of the platform outside the ropes. Here he rested on one knee, while the referee raced off the seconds. Inside the ropes, through which he must duck to enter the ring, Danny waited for him. Nor did the referee intervene or thrust Danny back.

The house was beside itself with delight.

"Kill 'm, Danny, kill 'm!" was the cry.

Scores of voices took it up until it was like a war-chant of wolves.

Danny did his best, but Rivera, at the count of eight, instead of nine, came unexpectedly through the ropes and safely into a clinch. Now the referee worked, tearing him away so that he could be hit, giving Danny every advantage that an unfair referee can give.

But Rivera lived, and the daze cleared from his brain. It was all of a piece. They were the hated Gringos and they were all unfair. And in the worst of it visions continued to flash and sparkle in his brain—long lines of railroad track that simmered across the desert; *rurales* and American constables; prisons and calabooses;[5] tramps at water tanks—all the squalid and painful panorama of his odyssey after Rio Blanco and the strike. And, resplendent and glorious, he saw the great, red Revolution sweeping across his land. The guns were there before him. Every hated face was a gun. It was for the guns he fought. He was the guns. He was the Revolution. He fought for all Mexico.

The audience began to grow incensed with Rivera. Why didn't he take the licking that was appointed him? Of course he was going to be licked, but why should he be so obstinate about it? Very few were interested in him, and they were the certain, definite percentage of a gambling crowd that plays long shots. Believing Danny to be the winner, nevertheless they had put their money on the Mexican at four to ten and one to three. More than a trifle was up on the point of how many rounds Rivera could last. Wild money had appeared at the ringside proclaiming that he could not last seven rounds, or even six. The winners of this, now that their cash risk was happily settled, had joined in cheering on the favorite.

4. Fighting at close range; "outfighting": fighting from more of a distance.    5. Slang for "jails."

Rivera refused to be licked. Through the eighth round his opponent strove vainly to repeat the upper-cut. In the ninth, Rivera stunned the house again. In the midst of a clinch he broke the lock with a quick, lithe movement, and in the narrow space between their bodies his right lifted from the waist. Danny went to the floor and took the safety of the count. The crowd was appalled. He was being bested at his own game. His famous right-upper-cut had been worked back on him. Rivera made no attempt to catch him as he arose at "nine." The referee was openly blocking that play, though he stood clear when the situation was reversed and it was Rivera who desired to rise.

Twice in the tenth, Rivera put through the right-upper-cut, lifted from waist to opponent's chin. Danny grew desperate. The smile never left his face, but he went back to his man-eating rushes. Whirlwind as he would, he could not damage Rivera, while Rivera, through the blur and whirl, dropped him to the mat three times in succession. Danny did not recuperate so quickly now, and by the eleventh round he was in a serious way. But from then till the fourteenth he put up the gamest exhibition of his career. He stalled and blocked, fought parsimoniously, and strove to gather strength. Also, he fought as foully as a successful fighter knows how. Every trick and device he employed, butting in the clinches with the seeming of accident, pinioning Rivera's glove between arm and body, heeling his glove on Rivera's mouth to clog his breathing. Often, in the clinches, through his cut and smiling lips he snarled insults unspeakable and vile in Rivera's ear. Everybody, from the referee to the house, was with Danny and was helping Danny. And they knew what he had in mind. Bested by this surprise-box of an unknown, he was pinning all on a single punch. He offered himself for punishment, fished, and feinted, and drew, for that one opening that would enable him to whip a blow through with all his strength and turn the tide. As another and greater fighter had done before him, he might do—a right and left, to solar plexus and across the jaw. He could do it, for he was noted for the strength of punch that remained in his arms as long as he could keep his feet.

Rivera's seconds were not half-caring for him in the intervals between rounds. Their towels made a showing, but drove little air into his panting lungs. Spider Hagerty talked advice to him, but Rivera knew it was wrong advice. Everybody was against him. He was surrounded by treachery. In the fourteenth round he put Danny down again, and himself stood resting, hands dropped at side, while the referee counted. In the other corner Rivera had been noting suspicious whisperings. He saw Michael Kelly make his way to Roberts and bend and whisper. Rivera's ears were a cat's, desert-trained, and he caught snatches of what was said. He wanted to hear more, and when his opponent arose he maneuvered the fight into a clinch over against the ropes.

"Got to," he could hear Michael, while Roberts nodded. "Danny's got to win—I stand to lose a mint—I've got a ton of money covered—my own—If he lasts the fifteenth I'm bust—The boy'll mind you. Put something across."

And thereafter Rivera saw no more visions. They were trying to job him. Once again he dropped Danny and stood resting, his hands at his side. Roberts stood up.

"That settled him," he said. "Go to your corner."

He spoke with authority, as he had often spoken to Rivera at the training quarters. But Rivera looked hatred at him and waited for Danny to rise. Back in his corner in the minute interval, Kelly, the promoter, came and talked to Rivera.

"Throw it, damn you," he rasped in a harsh low voice. "You gotta lay down, Rivera. Stick with me and I'll make your future. I'll let you lick Danny next time. But here's where you lay down."

Rivera showed with his eyes that he heard, but he made neither sign of assent nor dissent.

"Why don't you speak?" Kelly demanded angrily.

"You lose, anyway," Spider Hagerty supplemented. "The referee'll take it away from you. Listen to Kelly, and lay down."

"Lay down, kid," Kelly pleaded, "and I'll help you to the championship."

Rivera did not answer.

"I will, so help me, kid."

At the strike of the gong Rivera sensed something impending. The house did not. Whatever it was it was there inside the ring with him and very close. Danny's earlier surety seemed returned to him. The confidence of his advance frightened Rivera. Some trick was about to be worked. Danny rushed, but Rivera refused the encounter. He side-stepped away into safety. What the other wanted was a clinch. It was in some way necessary to the trick. Rivera backed and circled away, yet he knew, sooner or later, the clinch and the trick would come. Desperately he resolved to draw it. He made as if to effect the clinch with Danny's next rush. Instead, at the last instant, just as their bodies should have come together, Rivera darted nimbly back. And in the same instant Danny's corner raised a cry of foul. Rivera had fooled them. The referee paused irresolutely. The decision that trembled on his lips was never uttered, for a shrill, boy's voice from the gallery piped, "Raw work!"

Danny cursed Rivera openly, and forced him, while Rivera danced away. Also, Rivera made up his mind to strike no more blows at the body. In this he threw away half his chance of winning, but he knew if he was to win at all it was with the outfighting that remained to him. Given the least opportunity, they would lie a foul on him. Danny threw all caution to the winds. For two rounds he tore after and into the boy who dared not meet him at close quarters. Rivera was struck again and again; he took blows by the dozens to avoid the perilous clinch. During this supreme final rally of Danny's the audience rose to its feet and went mad. It did not understand. All it could see was that its favorite was winning after all.

"Why don't you fight?" it demanded wrathfully of Rivera. "You're yellow! You're yellow!" "Open up, you cur! Open up!" "Kill 'm, Danny! Kill 'm!" "You sure got 'm! Kill 'm!"

In all the house, bar none, Rivera was the only cold man. By temperament and blood he was the hottest-passioned there; but he had gone through such vastly greater heats that this collective passion of ten thousand throats, rising surge on surge, was to his brain no more than the velvet cool of a summer twilight.

Into the seventeenth round Danny carried his rally. Rivera, under a heavy blow, drooped and sagged. His hands dropped helplessly as he reeled backward. Danny thought it was his chance. The boy was at his mercy. Thus Rivera, feigning, caught him off his guard, lashing out a clean drive to the mouth. Danny went down. When he arose, Rivera felled him with a down-chop of the right on neck and jaw. Three times he repeated this. It was impossible for any referee to call these blows foul.

"Oh, Bill! Bill!" Kelly pleaded to the referee.

"I can't," that official lamented back. "He won't give me a chance."

Danny, battered and heroic, still kept coming up. Kelly and others near to the ring began to cry out to the police to stop it, though Danny's corner refused to throw in the towel. Rivera saw the fat police captain starting awkwardly to climb through the ropes, and was not sure what it meant. There were so many ways of cheating in this game of the Gringos. Danny, on his feet, tottered groggily and helplessly before him. The referee and the captain were both reaching for Rivera when he struck the last blow. There was no need to stop the fight, for Danny did not rise.

"Count!" Rivera cried hoarsely to the referee.

And when the count was finished, Danny's seconds gathered him up and carried him to his corner.

"Who wins?" Rivera demanded.

Reluctantly, the referee caught his gloved hand and held it aloft.

There were no congratulations for Rivera. He walked to his corner unattended, where his seconds had not yet placed his stool. He leaned backward on the ropes and looked his hatred at them, swept it on and about him till the whole ten thousand Gringos were included. His knees trembled under him, and he was sobbing from exhaustion. Before his eyes the hated faces swayed back and forth in the giddiness of nausea. Then he remembered they were the guns. The guns were his. The Revolution could go on.

1911, 1913

## The House of Pride[1]

Percival Ford wondered why he had come. He did not dance. He did not care much for army people. Yet he knew them all—gliding and revolving there on the broad *lanai* of the Seaside,[2] the officers in their fresh-starched uniforms of white, the civilians in white and black, and the women bare of shoulders and arms. After two years in Honolulu the Twentieth was departing to its new station in Alaska, and Percival Ford, as one of the big men of the Islands, could not help knowing the officers and their women.

But between knowing and liking was a vast gulf. The army women frightened him just a little. They were in ways quite different from the women he liked best—the elderly women, the spinsters and the bespectacled maidens, and the very serious women of all ages whom he met on church and library and kindergarten committees, who came meekly to him for contributions and advice. He ruled those women by virtue of his superior mentality, his great wealth, and the high place he occupied in the commercial baronage of Hawaii. And he was not afraid of them in the least. Sex, with them, was not obtrusive. Yes, that was it. There was in them something else, or more, than

1. First published in *Pacific Monthly* (December 1910), then in London's *The House of Pride* (1912), from which this text is taken. London takes his title from Edmund Spenser's *The Faerie Queene*.

2. A hotel on Waikiki Beach. *"Lanai"*: balcony (Hawaiian).

the assertive grossness of life. He was fastidious; he acknowledged that to himself; and these army women, with their bare shoulders and naked arms, their straight-looking eyes, their vitality and challenging femaleness, jarred upon his sensibilities.

Nor did he get on better with the army men, who took life lightly, drinking and smoking and swearing their way through life and asserting the essential grossness of flesh no less shamelessly than their women. He was always uncomfortable in the company of the army men. They seemed uncomfortable, too. And he felt, always, that they were laughing at him up their sleeves, or pitying him, or tolerating him. Then, too, they seemed, by mere contiguity, to emphasize a lack in him, to call attention to that in them which he did not possess and which he thanked God he did not possess. Faugh! They were like their women!

In fact, Percival Ford was no more a woman's man than he was a man's man. A glance at him told the reason. He had a good constitution, never was on intimate terms with sickness, nor even mild disorders; but he lacked vitality. His was a negative organism. No blood with a ferment in it could have nourished and shaped that long and narrow face, those thin lips, lean cheeks, and the small, sharp eyes. The thatch of hair, dust-colored, straight and sparse, advertised the niggard soil, as did the nose, thin, delicately modeled, and just hinting the suggestion of a beak. His meagre blood had denied him much of life, and permitted him to be an extremist in one thing only, which thing was righteousness. Over right conduct he pondered and agonized, and that he should do right was as necessary to his nature as loving and being loved were necessary to commoner clay.

He was sitting under the algaroba[3] trees between the *lanai* and the beach. His eyes wandered over the dancers and he turned his head away and gazed seaward across the mellow-sounding surf to the Southern Cross[4] burning low on the horizon. He was irritated by the bare shoulders and arms of the women. If he had a daughter he would never permit it, never. But his hypothesis was the sheerest abstraction. The thought process had been accompanied by no inner vision of that daughter. He did not see a daughter with arms and shoulders. Instead, he smiled at the remote contingency of marriage. He was thirty-five, and, having had no personal experience of love, he looked upon it, not as mythical, but as bestial. Anybody could marry. The Japanese and Chinese coolies, toiling on the sugar plantations and in the rice-fields, married. They invariably married at the first opportunity. It was because they were so low in the scale of life. There was nothing else for them to do. They were like the army men and women. But for him there were other and higher things. He was different from them—from all of them. He was proud of how he happened to be. He had come of no petty love-match. He had come of lofty conception of duty and of devotion to a cause. His father had not married for love. Love was a madness that had never perturbed Isaac Ford. When he answered the call to go to the heathen with the message of life, he had had no thought and no desire for marriage. In this they were alike, his father and he. But the Board of Missions was economical.[5] With New England thrift it weighed and measured and decided that married missionaries were less

3. Hawaiian tree related to mesquite.
4. A constellation visible in the Southern Hemisphere and used by sailors for navigation.

5. The American Board of Commissioners for Foreign Missions began sending missionaries to Hawai'i in 1819.

expensive per capita and more efficacious. So the Board commanded Isaac Ford to marry. Furthermore, it furnished him with a wife, another zealous soul with no thought of marriage, intent only on doing the Lord's work among the heathen. They saw each other for the first time in Boston. The Board brought them together, arranged everything, and by the end of the week they were married and started on the long voyage around the Horn.[6]

Percival Ford was proud that he had come of such a union. He had been born high, and he thought of himself as a spiritual aristocrat. And he was proud of his father. It was a passion with him. The erect, austere figure of Isaac Ford had burned itself upon his pride. On his desk was a miniature of that soldier of the Lord. In his bedroom hung the portrait of Isaac Ford, painted at the time when he had served under the Monarchy[7] as prime minister. Not that Isaac Ford had coveted place and worldly wealth, but that, as prime minister, and, later, as banker, he had been of greater service to the missionary cause. The German crowd, and the English crowd, and all the rest of the trading crowd, had sneered at Isaac Ford as a commercial soul-saver; but he, his son, knew different. When the natives, emerging abruptly from their feudal system, with no conception of the nature and significance of property in land, were letting their broad acres slip through their fingers, it was Isaac Ford who had stepped in between the trading crowd and its prey and taken possession of fat, vast holdings. Small wonder the trading crowd did not like his memory. But he had never looked upon his enormous wealth as his own. He had considered himself God's steward. Out of the revenues he had built schools, and hospitals, and churches. Nor was it his fault that sugar, after the slump, had paid forty per cent; that the bank he founded had prospered into a railroad; and that, among other things, fifty thousand acres of Oahu pasture land, which he had bought for a dollar an acre, grew eight tons of sugar to the acre every eighteen months. No, in all truth Isaac Ford was a heroic figure, fit, so Percival Ford thought privately, to stand beside the statue of Kamehameha I[8] in front of the Judiciary Building. Isaac Ford was gone, but he, his son, carried on the good work at least as inflexibly if not as masterfully.

He turned his eyes back to the *lanai*. What was the difference, he asked himself, between the shameless, grass-girdled *hula* dances and the decolleté dances[9] of the women of his own race? Was there an essential difference? or was it a matter of degree?

As he pondered the problem a hand rested on his shoulder.

"Hello, Ford, what are you doing here? Isn't this a bit festive?"

"I try to be lenient, Dr. Kennedy, even as I look on," Percival Ford answered gravely. "Won't you sit down?"

Dr. Kennedy sat down, clapping his palms sharply. A white-clad Japanese servant answered swiftly.

Scotch and soda was Kennedy's order; then, turning to the other, he said:—

"Of course, I don't ask you."

---

6. The southernmost tip of South America, a notoriously difficult passage for ships.
7. The Hawaiian monarchy as Westerners knew it lasted from 1795 until it was overthrown by the United States and Great Britain in 1893.

8. Kamehameha I (ca. 1758–1819), also known as Kamehameha the Great, was head of a dynasty that ruled the Hawaiian Islands for more than a century.
9. Dances at which women wore low-cut dresses.

"But I will take something," Ford said firmly. The doctor's eyes showed surprise, and the servant waited. "Boy, a lemonade, please."

The doctor laughed at it heartily, as a joke on himself, and glanced at the musicians under the *hau*[1] tree.

"Why, it's the Aloha Orchestra," he said. "I thought they were with the Hawaiian Hotel[2] on Tuesday nights. Some rumpus, I guess."

His eyes paused for a moment and dwelt upon the one who was playing a guitar and singing a Hawaiian song to the accompaniment of all the instruments. His face became grave as he looked at the singer, and it was still grave as he turned it to his companion.

"Look here, Ford, isn't it time you let up on Joe Garland? I understand you are in opposition to the Promotion Committee's[3] sending him to the States on this surf-board proposition, and I've been wanting to speak to you about it. I should have thought you'd be glad to get him out of the country. It would be a good way to end your persecution of him."

"Persecution?" Percival Ford's eyebrows lifted interrogatively.

"Call it by any name you please," Kennedy went on. "You've hounded that poor devil for years. It's not his fault. Even you will admit that."

"Not his fault?" Percival Ford's thin lips drew tightly together for the moment. "Joe Garland is dissolute and idle. He has always been a wastrel, a profligate."

"But that's no reason you should keep on after him the way you do. I've watched you from the beginning. The first thing you did when you returned from college and found him working on the plantation as outside *luna*[4] was to fire him—you with your millions, and he with his sixty dollars a month."

"Not the first thing," Percival Ford said judicially, in the tone he was accustomed to use in committee meetings. "I gave him his warning. The superintendent said he was a capable *luna*. I had no objection to him on that ground. It was what he did outside working hours. He undid my work faster than I could build it up. Of what use were the Sunday schools, the night schools, and the sewing classes, when in the evenings there was Joe Garland with his infernal and eternal tum-tumming of guitar and *ukulele*, his strong drink, and his *hula* dancing? After I warned him, I came upon him—I shall never forget it—came upon him, down at the cabins. It was evening. I could hear the *hula* songs before I saw the scene. And when I did see it, there were the girls, shameless in the moonlight and dancing—the girls upon whom I had worked to teach clean living and right conduct. And there were three girls there, I remember, just graduated from the mission school. Of course I discharged Joe Garland. I know it was the same at Hilo. People said I went out of my way when I persuaded Mason and Fitch[5] to discharge him. But it was the missionaries who requested me to do so. He was undoing their work by his reprehensible example."

"Afterwards, when he got on the railroad, your railroad, he was discharged without cause," Kennedy challenged.

---

1. Also known as the "beach hibiscus" for its bright yellow flowers, a tree indigenous to Hawai'i that can reach thirty feet tall; its spreading branches make it convenient to gather beneath.
2. The Royal Hawaiian Hotel, one of the first hotels on Waikiki Beach.
3. A group of elite *haole* (white) businessmen and leaders who protected Hawai'i's growing reputation as a tourist destination; its members objected to many of London's Hawaiian stories as too revealing about Hawai'i's problems, including racial tensions and leprosy.
4. Hawaiian field foreman.
5. Fictitious company; "Mason" and "Fitch" are old U.S. East Coast family names.

"Not so," was the quick answer. "I had him into my private office and talked with him for half an hour."

"You discharged him for inefficiency?"

"For immoral living, if you please."

Dr. Kennedy laughed with a grating sound. "Who the devil gave it to you to be judge and jury? Does landlordism give you control of the immortal souls of those that toil for you? I have been your physician. Am I to expect tomorrow your ukase[6] that I give up Scotch and soda or your patronage? Bah! Ford, you take life too seriously. Besides, when Joe got into that smuggling scrape (he wasn't in your employ, either), and he sent word to you, asked you to pay his fine, you left him to do his six months hard labor on the reef. Don't forget, you left Joe Garland in the lurch that time. You threw him down, hard; and yet I remember the first day you came to school—we boarded, you were only a day scholar—you had to be initiated. Three times under in the swimming tank—you remember, it was the regular dose every new boy got. And you held back. You denied that you could swim. You were frightened, hysterical—"

"Yes, I know," Percival Ford said slowly. "I was frightened. And it was a lie, for I could swim. . . . And I was frightened."

"And you remember who fought for you? who lied for you harder than you could lie and swore he knew you couldn't swim? Who jumped into the tank and pulled you out after the first under and was nearly drowned for it by the other boys, who had discovered by that time that you *could* swim?"

"Of course I know," the other rejoined coldly. "But a generous act as a boy does not excuse a lifetime of wrong living."

"He has never done wrong to you?—personally and directly, I mean?"

"No," was Percival Ford's answer. "That is what makes my position impregnable. I have no personal spite against him. He is bad, that is all. His life is bad—"

"Which is another way of saying that he does not agree with you in the way life should be lived," the doctor interrupted.

"Have it that way. It is immaterial. He is an idler—"

"With reason," was the interruption, "considering the jobs out of which you have knocked him."

"He is immoral—"

"Oh, hold on now, Ford. Don't go harping on that. You are pure New England stock. Joe Garland is half Kanaka.[7] Your blood is thin. His is warm. Life is one thing to you, another thing to him. He laughs and sings and dances through life, genial, unselfish, childlike, everybody's friend. You go through life like a perambulating prayer-wheel,[8] a friend of nobody but the righteous, and the righteous are those who agree with you as to what is right. And after all, who shall say? You live like an anchorite.[9] Joe Garland lives like a good fellow. Who has extracted the most from life? We are paid to live, you know. When the wages are too meagre we throw up the job, which is the cause, believe me, of all rational suicide. Joe Garland would starve to death on the

6. An order or decree.
7. Hawaiian or Polynesian.
8. A wheel on a spindle with written or encapsulated prayers or mantras. According to Tibetan

Buddhist beliefs, spinning such a wheel has the same effect as reciting the prayers.
9. Hermit or recluse who renounces wordly things for religious reasons.

wages you get from life. You see, he is made differently. So would you starve on his wages, which are singing, and love—"

"Lust, if you will pardon me," was the interruption.

Dr. Kennedy smiled.

"Love, to you, is a word of four letters and a definition which you have extracted from the dictionary. But love, real love, dewy and palpitant and tender, you do not know. If God made you and me, and men and women, believe me he made love, too. But to come back. It's about time you quit hounding Joe Garland. It is not worthy of you, and it is cowardly. The thing for you to do is to reach out and lend him a hand."

"Why I, any more than you?" the other demanded. "Why don't you reach him a hand?"

"I have. I'm reaching him a hand now. I'm trying to get you not to down the Promotion Committee's proposition of sending him away. I got him the job at Hilo with Mason and Fitch. I've got him half a dozen jobs, out of every one of which you drove him. But never mind that. Don't forget one thing—and a little frankness won't hurt you—it is not fair play to saddle another's fault on Joe Garland; and you know that you, least of all, are the man to do it. Why, man, it's not good taste. It's positively indecent."

"Now I don't follow you," Percival Ford answered. "You're up in the air with some obscure scientific theory of heredity and personal irresponsibility. But how any theory can hold Joe Garland irresponsible for his wrongdoings and at the same time hold me personally responsible for them—more responsible than any one else, including Joe Garland—is beyond me."

"It's a matter of delicacy, I suppose, or of taste, that prevents you from following me," Dr. Kennedy snapped out. "It's all very well, for the sake of society, tacitly to ignore some things, but you do more than tacitly ignore."

"What is it, pray, that I tacitly ignore!"

Dr. Kennedy was angry. A deeper red than that of constitutional Scotch and soda suffused his face, as he answered:

"Your father's son."

"Now just what do you mean?"

"Damn it, man, you can't ask me to be plainer spoken than that. But if you will, all right—Isaac's Ford's son—Joe Garland—your brother."

Percival Ford sat quietly, an annoyed and shocked expression on his face. Kennedy looked at him curiously, then, as the slow minutes dragged by, became embarrassed and frightened.

"My God!" he cried finally, "you don't mean to tell me that you didn't know!"

As in answer, Percival Ford's cheeks turned slowly gray.

"It's a ghastly joke," he said; "a ghastly joke."

The doctor had got himself in hand.

"Everybody knows it," he said. "I thought you knew it. And since you don't know it, it's time you did, and I'm glad of the chance of setting you straight. Joe Garland and you are brothers—half-brothers."

"It's a lie," Ford cried. "You don't mean it. Joe Garland's mother was Eliza Kunilio." (Dr. Kennedy nodded.) "I remember her well, with her duck pond and *taro*[1] patch. His father was Joseph Garland, the beach-comber." (Dr.

---

1. A large, tropical Asiatic plant cultivated for its edible corms (like roots), which were often made into poi, a dish of salt and pounded taro root eaten with meats.

Kennedy shook his head.) "He died only two or three years ago. He used to get drunk. There's where Joe got his dissoluteness. There's the heredity for you."

"And nobody told you," Kennedy said wonderingly, after a pause.

"Dr. Kennedy, you have said something terrible, which I cannot allow to pass. You must either prove or, or . . ."

"Prove it yourself. Turn around and look at him. You've got him in profile. Look at his nose. That's Isaac Ford's. Yours is a thin edition of it. That's right. Look. The lines are fuller, but they are all there."

Percival Ford looked at the Kanaka half-breed who played under the *hau* tree, and it seemed, as by some illumination, that he was gazing on a wraith of himself. Feature after feature flashed up an unmistakable resemblance. Or, rather, it was he who was the wraith of that other full-muscled and generously moulded man. And his features, and that other man's features, were all reminiscent of Isaac Ford. And nobody had told him. Every line of Isaac Ford's face he knew. Miniatures, portraits, and photographs of his father were passing in review through his mind, and here and there, over and again, in the face before him, he caught resemblances and vague hints of likeness. It was devil's work that could reproduce the austere features of Isaac Ford in the loose and sensuous features before him. Once, the man turned, and for one flashing instant it seemed to Percival Ford that he saw his father, dead and gone, peering at him out of the face of Joe Garland.

"It's nothing at all," he could faintly hear Dr. Kennedy saying. "They were all mixed up in the old days. You know that. You've seen it all your life. Sailors married queens and begat princesses and all the rest of it. It was the usual thing in the Islands."

"But not with my father," Percival Ford interrupted.

"There you are." Kennedy shrugged his shoulders. "Cosmic sap and smoke of life. Old Isaac Ford was straight-laced and all the rest, and I know there's no explaining it, least of all to himself. He understood it no more than you do. Smoke of life, that's all. And don't forget one thing, Ford. There was a dab of unruly blood in old Isaac Ford, and Joe Garland inherited it—all of it, smoke of life and cosmic sap; while you inherited all of old Isaac's ascetic blood. And just because your blood is cold, well-ordered, and well-disciplined, is no reason that you should frown upon Joe Garland. When Joe Garland undoes the work you do, remember that it is only old Isaac Ford on both sides, undoing with one hand what he does with the other. You are Isaac Ford's right hand, let us say; Joe Garland is his left hand."

Percival Ford made no answer, and in the silence Dr. Kennedy finished his forgotten Scotch and soda. From across the grounds an automobile hooted imperatively.

"There's the machine," Dr. Kennedy said, rising. "I've got to run. I'm sorry I've shaken you up, and at the same time I'm glad. And know one thing, Isaac Ford's dab of unruly blood was remarkably small, and Joe Garland got it all. And one other thing. If your father's left hand offend you, don't smite it off. Besides, Joe is all right. Frankly, if I could choose between you and him to live with me on a desert isle, I'd choose Joe."

Little bare-legged children ran about him, playing, on the grass; but Percival Ford did not see them. He was gazing steadily at the singer under the *hau* tree. He even changed his position once, to get closer. The clerk of the Seaside went by, limping with age and dragging his reluctant feet. He had lived forty years on the Islands. Percival Ford beckoned to him, and the clerk came respectfully, and wondering that he should be noticed by Percival Ford.

"John," Ford said, "I want you to give me some information. Won't you sit down?"

The clerk sat down awkwardly, stunned by the unexpected honor. He blinked at the other and mumbled, "Yes, sir, thank you."

"John, who is Joe Garland?"

The clerk stared at him, blinked, cleared his throat, and said nothing.

"Go on," Percival Ford commanded. "Who is he?"

"You're joking me, sir," the other managed to articulate.

"I spoke to you seriously."

The clerk recoiled from him.

"You don't mean to say you don't know?" he questioned, his question in itself the answer.

"I want to know."

"Why, he's . . ." John broke off and looked about him helplessly. "Hadn't you better ask somebody else? Everybody thought you knew. We always thought . . ."

"Yes, go ahead."

"We always thought that that was why you had it in for him."

Photographs and miniatures of Isaac Ford were trooping through his son's brain, and ghosts of Isaac Ford seemed in the air about him. "I wish you good night, sir," he could hear the clerk saying, and he saw him beginning to limp away.

"John," he called abruptly.

John came back and stood near him, blinking and nervously moistening his lips.

"You haven't told me yet, you know."

"Oh, about Joe Garland?"

"Yes, about Joe Garland. Who is he?"

"He's your brother, sir, if I say it who shouldn't."

"Thank you, John. Good night."

"And you didn't know?" the old man queried, content to linger, now that the crucial point was past.

"Thank you, John. Good night," was the response.

"Yes, sir, thank you, sir. I think it's going to rain. Good night, sir."

Out of a clear sky, filled only with stars and moonlight, fell a rain so fine and attenuated as to resemble a vapor spray. Nobody minded it; the children played on, running bare-legged over the grass and leaping into the sand; and in a few minutes it was gone. In the southeast, Diamond Head, a black blot, sharply defined, silhouetted its crater-form against the stars. At sleepy intervals the surf flung its foam across the sand to the grass, and far out could be seen the black specks of swimmers under the moon. The voices of the singers, singing a waltz, died away; and in the silence, from somewhere under the trees, arose the laugh of a woman that was a love-cry. It startled Percival Ford, and it reminded him of Dr. Kennedy's phrase. Down by the outrigger canoes,

1092 / Jack London

where they lay hauled out on the sand, he saw men and women, Kanakas, reclining languorously, like lotus-eaters, the women in white *holokus*;[2] and against one such *holoku* he saw the dark head of the steersman of the canoe resting upon the woman's shoulder. Farther down, where the strip of sand widened at the entrance to the lagoon, he saw a man and woman walking side by side. As they drew near the light *lanai*, he saw the woman's hand go down to her waist and disengage a girdling arm. And as they passed him, Percival Ford nodded to a captain he knew, and to a major's daughter. Smoke of life, that was it, an ample phrase. And again, from under the dark algaroba tree arose the laugh of a woman that was a love-cry; and past his chair, on the way to bed, a bare-legged youngster was led by a chiding Japanese nurse-maid. The voices of the singers broke softly and meltingly into a Hawaiian love song, and officers and women, with encircling arms, were gliding and whirling on the *lanai*; and once again the woman laughed under the algaroba trees.

And Percival Ford knew only disapproval of it all. He was irritated by the love-laugh of the woman, by the steersman with pillowed head on the white *holoku*, by the couples that walked on the beach, by the officers and women that danced, and by the voices of the singers singing of love, and his brother singing there with them under the *hau* tree. The woman that laughed especially irritated him. A curious train of thought was aroused. He was Isaac Ford's son, and what had happened with Isaac Ford might happen with him. He felt in his cheeks the faint heat of a blush at the thought, and experienced a poignant sense of shame. He was appalled by what was in his blood. It was like learning suddenly that his father had been a leper and that his own blood might bear the taint of that dread disease. Isaac Ford, the austere soldier of the Lord—the old hypocrite! What difference between him and any beach-comber? The house of pride that Percival Ford had builded was tumbling about his ears.

The hours passed, the army people laughed and danced, the native orchestra played on, and Percival Ford wrestled with the abrupt and overwhelming problem that had been thrust upon him. He prayed quietly, his elbow on the table, his head bowed upon his hand, with all the appearance of any tired onlooker. Between the dances the army men and women and the civilians fluttered up to him and buzzed conventionally, and when they went back to the *lanai* he took up his wrestling where he had left it off.

He began to patch together his shattered ideal of Isaac Ford, and for cement he used a cunning and subtle logic. It was of the sort that is compounded in the brain laboratories of egotists, and it worked. It was incontrovertible that his father had been made of finer clay than those about him; but still, old Isaac had been only in the process of becoming, while he, Percival Ford, had become. As proof of it, he rehabilitated his father and at the same time exalted himself. His lean little ego waxed to colossal proportions. He was great enough to forgive. He glowed at the thought of it. Isaac Ford had been great, but he was greater, for he could forgive Isaac Ford and even restore him to the holy place in his memory, though the place was not quite so holy as it

---

2. The *holoku* is a forerunner of the *muumuu*, a dress designed by missionaries to cover female bodies in Hawai'i and other Pacific island groups.

had been. Also, he applauded Isaac Ford for having ignored the outcome of his one step aside. Very well, he, too, would ignore it.

The dance was breaking up. The orchestra had finished "Aloha Oe"[3] and was preparing to go home. Percival Ford clapped his hands for the Japanese servant.

"You tell that man I want to see him," he said, pointing out Joe Garland. "Tell him come here, now."

Joe Garland approached and halted respectfully several paces away, nervously fingering the guitar which he still carried. The other did not ask him to sit down.

"You are my brother," he said.

"Why, everybody knows that," was the reply, in tones of wonderment.

"Yes, so I understand," Percival Ford said dryly. "But I did not know it till this evening."

The half-brother waited uncomfortably in the silence that followed, during which Percival Ford coolly considered his next utterance.

"You remember that first time I came to school and the boys ducked me?" he asked. "Why did you take my part."

The half-brother smiled bashfully.

"Because you knew?"

"Yes, that was why."

"But I didn't know," Percival Ford said in the same dry fashion.

"Yes," the other said.

Another silence fell. Servants were beginning to put out the lights on the *lanai*.

"You know . . . now," the half-brother said simply.

Percival Ford frowned. Then he looked the other over with a considering eye.

"How much will you take to leave the Islands and never come back?" he demanded.

"And never come back?" Joe Garland faltered. "It is the only land I know. Other lands are cold. I do not know other lands. I have many friends here. In other lands there would not be one voice to say, 'Aloha, Joe, my boy.' "

"I said never to come back," Percival Ford reiterated. "The *Alameda* sails to-morrow for San Francisco."

Joe Garland was bewildered.

"But why?" he asked. "You know now that we are brothers."

"That is why," was the retort. "As you said yourself, everybody knows. I will make it worth your while."

All awkwardness and embarrassment disappeared from Joe Garland. Birth and station were bridged and reversed.

"You want me to go?" he demanded.

"I want you to go and never to come back," Percival Ford answered.

And in that moment, flashing and fleeting, it was given him to see his brother tower above him like a mountain, and to feel himself dwindle and dwarf to microscopic insignificance. But it is not well for one to see himself truly, nor can one so see himself for long and live; and only for that flashing

---

3. "My love to you" (Hawaiian), a well-known Hawaiian song.

moment did Percival Ford see himself and his brother in true perspective. The next moment he was mastered by his meagre and insatiable ego.

"As I said, I will make it worth your while. You will not suffer. I will pay you well."

"All right," Joe Garland said. "I'll go."

He started to turn away.

"Joe," the other called. "You see my lawyer to-morrow morning. Five hundred down and two hundred a month as long as you stay away."

"You are very kind," Joe Garland answered softly. "You are too kind. And anyway, I guess I don't want your money. I go to-morrow on the *Alameda*."

He walked away, but did not say good-by.

Percival Ford clapped his hands.

"Boy," he said to the Japanese, "a lemonade."

And over the lemonade he smiled long and contentedly to himself.

1910, 1912

# Mauki[1]

He weighed one hundred and ten pounds. His hair was kinky and negroid, and he was black. He was peculiarly black. He was neither blue-black nor purple-black, but plum-black. His name was Mauki, and he was the son of a chief. He had three *tambos*. *Tambo* is Melanesian for *taboo*, and is first cousin to that Polynesian word. Mauki's three *tambos* were as follows: first, he must never shake hands with a woman, nor have a woman's hand touch him or any of his personal belongings; secondly, he must never eat clams nor any food from a fire in which clams had been cooked; thirdly, he must never touch a crocodile, nor travel in a canoe that carried any part of a crocodile even if as large as a tooth.

Of a different black were his teeth, which were deep black, or, perhaps better, *lamp*-black.[2] They had been made so in a single night, by his mother, who had compressed about them a powdered mineral which was dug from the landslide back of Port Adams. Port Adams is a salt-water village on Malaita, and Malaita is the most savage island in the Solomons—so savage that no traders nor planters have yet gained a foothold on it; while, from the time of the earliest bêche-de-mer[3] fishers and sandalwood[4] traders down to the latest labor recruiters equipped with automatic rifles and gasolene engines, scores of white adventurers have been passed out by tomahawks and soft-nosed Snider bullets.[5] So Malaita remains to-day, in the twentieth century, the stamping ground of the labor recruiters, who farm its coasts for laborers who engage and contract themselves to toil on the plantations of the neigh-

1. First published in *Hampton's Magazine* (December 1909); rpt. in London's *South Sea Tales* (1912), from which this text is taken. The story is based on the life of a Solomon Islander slave the Londons met on Lord Howe Atoll in 1908. However, the *tambos* that introduce him indicate his royal rank.
2. A black powdery substance consisting mainly of carbon; used to make pigments and ink.

3. Sea cucumber eaten in Asia and the South Pacific; an important item of trade. The name also refers to the pidgin English spoken in the South Seas, as the sea cucumber was a ready means of exchange, like language.
4. Sandalwood was one of several Hawaiian trees harvested for their fragrant wood.
5. The Snider rifle and its soft-nosed bullets were a 19th-century standard.

boring and more civilized islands for a wage of thirty dollars a year.[6] The natives of those neighboring and more civilized islands have themselves become too civilized to work on plantations.

Mauki's ears were pierced, not in one place, nor two places, but in a couple of dozen places. In one of the smaller holes he carried a clay pipe. The larger holes were too large for such use. The bowl of the pipe would have fallen through. In fact, in the largest hole in each ear he habitually wore round wooden plugs that were an even four inches in diameter. Roughly speaking, the circumference of said holes was twelve and one-half inches. Mauki was catholic in his tastes. In the various smaller holes he carried such things as empty rifle cartridges, horseshoe nails, copper screws, pieces of string, braids of sennit, strips of green leaf, and, in the cool of the day, scarlet hibiscus flowers. From which it will be seen that pockets were not necessary to his well-being. Besides, pockets were impossible, for his only wearing apparel consisted of a piece of calico several inches wide. A pocket knife he wore in his hair, the blade snapped down on a kinky lock. His most prized possession was the handle of a china cup, which he suspended from a ring of turtle-shell, which, in turn, was passed through the partition-cartilage of his nose.

But in spite of embellishments, Mauki had a nice face. It was really a pretty face, viewed by any standard, and for a Melanesian it was a remarkably good-looking face. Its one fault was its lack of strength. It was softly effeminate, almost girlish. The features were small, regular, and delicate. The chin was weak, and the mouth was weak. There was no strength nor character in the jaws, forehead, and nose. In the eyes only could be caught any hint of the unknown quantities that were so large a part of his make-up and that other persons could not understand. These unknown quantities were pluck, pertinacity, fearlessness, imagination, and cunning; and when they found expression in some consistent and striking action, those about him were astounded.

Mauki's father was chief over the village at Port Adams, and thus, by birth a salt-water man, Mauki was half amphibian. He knew the way of the fishes and oysters, and the reef was an open book to him. Canoes, also, he knew. He learned to swim when he was a year old. At seven years he could hold his breath a full minute and swim straight down to bottom through thirty feet of water. And at seven years he was stolen by the bushmen,[7] who cannot even swim and who are afraid of salt water. Thereafter Mauki saw the sea only from a distance, through rifts in the jungle and from open spaces on the high mountain sides. He became the slave of old Fanfoa, head chief over a score of scattered bush-villages on the range-lips of Malaita, the smoke of which, on calm mornings, is about the only evidence the seafaring white men have of the teeming interior population. For the whites do not penetrate Malaita. They tried it once, in the days when the search was on for gold, but they always left their heads behind to grin from the smoky rafters of the bushmen's huts.

6. Colonial Pacific field workers came from many islands and countries besides the Solomons, including China, Japan, the Philippines, and Samoa. Recruiters contracted to bring the workers to the plantations and also managed them. Sometimes workers were simply kidnapped.
7. In London's day two tribes constantly warred for control over many of the southwest Pacific islands, especially the Solomons and New Guinea—the "salt-water" men, who lived near the sea and occasionally traded with outsiders, and the "bushmen," who lived in the mountain jungles and rarely encountered outsiders.

When Mauki was a young man of seventeen, Fanfoa got out of tobacco. He got dreadfully out of tobacco. It was hard times in all his villages. He had been guilty of a mistake. Suo[8] was a harbor so small that a large schooner could not swing at anchor in it. It was surrounded by mangroves that overhung the deep water. It was a trap, and into the trap sailed two white men in a small ketch. They were after recruits, and they possessed much tobacco and trade-goods, to say nothing of three rifles and plenty of ammunition. Now there were no salt-water men living at Suo, and it was there that the bushmen could come down to the sea. The ketch did a splendid traffic. It signed on twenty recruits the first day. Even old Fanfoa signed on. And that same day the score of new recruits chopped off the two white men's heads, killed the boat's crew, and burned the ketch. Thereafter, and for three months, there was tobacco and trade-goods in plenty and to spare in all the bush-villages. Then came the man-of-war[9] that threw shells for miles into the hills, frightening the people out of their villages and into the deeper bush. Next the man-of-war sent landing parties ashore. The villages were all burned, along with the tobacco and trade-stuff. The cocoanuts and bananas were chopped down, the taro[1] gardens uprooted, and the pigs and chickens killed.

It taught Fanfoa a lesson, but in the meantime he was out of tobacco. Also, his young men were too frightened to sign on with the recruiting vessels. That was why Fanfoa ordered his slave, Mauki, to be carried down and signed on for half a case of tobacco advance, along with knives, axes, calico, and beads, which he would pay for with his toil on the plantations. Mauki was sorely frightened when they brought him on board the schooner. He was a lamb led to the slaughter. White men were ferocious creatures. They had to be, or else they would not make a practice of venturing along the Malaita coast and into all harbors, two on a schooner, when each schooner carried from fifteen to twenty blacks as boat's crew, and often as high as sixty or seventy black recruits. In addition to this, there was always the danger of the shore population, the sudden attack and the cutting off of the schooner and all hands. Truly, white men must be terrible. Besides, they were possessed of such devil-devils—rifles that shot very rapidly many times, things of iron and brass that made the schooners go when there was no wind, and boxes that talked and laughed just as men talked and laughed. Ay, and he had heard of one white man whose particular devil-devil was so powerful that he could take out all his teeth and put them back at will.

Down into the cabin they took Mauki. On deck, the one white man kept guard with two revolvers in his belt. In the cabin the other white man sat with a book before him, in which he inscribed strange marks and lines. He looked at Mauki as though he had been a pig or a fowl, glanced under the hollows of his arms, and wrote in the book. Then he held out the writing stick and Mauki just barely touched it with his hand, in so doing pledging himself to toil for three years on the plantations of the Moongleam Soap Company. It was not explained to him that the will of the ferocious white men would be

---

8. Town on the island of Malaita.
9. Armed naval vessel, particularly a sailing ship with a cannon. *Ketch:* a small two-masted sailing vessel.

1. Taro is a crop grown throughout the humid tropics for its edible corms (starchy roots) and also as a leaf vegetable. Taro root is most often made into *poi*, a soft pudding that is a dietary staple.

used to enforce the pledge, and that, behind all, for the same use, was all the power and all the warships of Great Britain.

Other blacks there were on board, from unheard-of far places, and when the white man spoke to them, they tore the long feather from Mauki's hair, cut that same hair short, and wrapped about his waist a lava-lava[2] of bright yellow calico.

After many days on the schooner, and after beholding more land and islands than he had ever dreamed of, he was landed on New Georgia,[3] and put to work in the field clearing jungle and cutting cane grass. For the first time he knew what work was. Even as a slave to Fanfoa he had not worked like this. And he did not like work. It was up at dawn and in at dark, on two meals a day. And the food was tiresome. For weeks at a time they were given nothing but sweet potatoes to eat, and for weeks at a time it would be nothing but rice. He cut out the cocoanut from the shells day after day; and for long days and weeks he fed the fires that smoked the copra,[4] till his eyes got sore and he was set to felling trees. He was a good axe-man, and later he was put in the bridge-building gang. Once, he was punished by being put in the road-building gang. At times he served as boat's crew in the whale-boats, when they brought in copra from distant beaches or when the white men went out to dynamite fish.

Among other things he learned bêche-de-mer English, with which he could talk with all white men, and with all recruits who otherwise would have talked in a thousand different dialects. Also, he learned certain things about the white men, principally that they kept their word. If they told a boy he was going to receive a stick of tobacco, he got it. If they told a boy they would knock seven bells[5] out of him if he did a certain thing, when he did that thing seven bells invariably were knocked out of him. Mauki did not know what seven bells were, but they occurred in bêche-de-mer, and he imagined them to be the blood and teeth that sometimes accompanied the process of knocking out seven bells. One other thing he learned: no boy was struck or punished unless he did wrong. Even when the white men were drunk, as they were frequently, they never struck unless a rule had been broken.

Mauki did not like the plantation. He hated work, and he was the son of a chief. Furthermore, it was ten years since he had been stolen from Port Adams by Fanfoa, and he was homesick. He was even homesick for the slavery under Fanfoa. So he ran away. He struck back into the bush, with the idea of working southward to the beach and stealing a canoe in which to go home to Port Adams. But the fever got him, and he was captured and brought back more dead than alive.

A second time he ran away, in the company of two Malaita boys. They got down the coast twenty miles, and were hidden in the hut of a Malaita freeman, who dwelt in that village. But in the dead of night two white men came, who were not afraid of all the village people and who knocked seven bells out of the three runaways, tied them like pigs, and tossed them into the whale-

2. A loincloth or skirt of printed cloth, worn by both men and women in the South Seas islands.
3. One of the larger and more rugged of the western Solomon Islands.
4. The dried meat, or kernel, of the coconut, from which oil is extracted, was developed as a commercial product in the South Seas and South Asia beginning in the 1860s.
5. Beat severely.

boat. But the man in whose house they had hidden—seven times seven bells must have been knocked out of him from the way the hair, skin, and teeth flew, and he was discouraged for the rest of his natural life from harboring runaway laborers.

For a year Mauki toiled on. Then he was made a house-boy, and had good food and easy times, with light work in keeping the house clean and serving the white men with whiskey and beer at all hours of the day and most hours of the night. He liked it, but he liked Port Adams more. He had two years longer to serve, but two years were too long for him in the throes of home-sickness. He had grown wiser with his year of service, and, being now a house-boy, he had opportunity. He had the cleaning of the rifles, and he knew where the key to the store-room was hung. He planned the escape, and one night ten Malaita boys and one boy from San Cristoval[6] sneaked from the barracks and dragged one of the whale-boats down to the beach. It was Mauki who supplied the key that opened the padlock on the boat, and it was Mauki who equipped the boat with a dozen Winchesters,[7] an immense amount of ammunition, a case of dynamite with detonators and fuse, and ten cases of tobacco.

The northwest monsoon was blowing, and they fled south in the night-time, hiding by day on detached and uninhabited islets, or dragging their whale-boat into the bush on the large islands. Thus they gained Guadalcanar, skirted halfway along it, and crossed the Indispensable Straits to Florida Island.[8] It was here that they killed the San Cristoval boy, saving his head and cooking and eating the rest of him. The Malaita coast was only twenty miles away, but the last night a strong current and baffling winds prevented them from gaining across. Daylight found them still several miles from their goal. But daylight brought a cutter, in which were two white men, who were not afraid of eleven Malaita men armed with twelve rifles. Mauki and his companions were carried back to Tulagi, where lived the great white master of all the white men. And the great white master held a court, after which, one by one, the runaways were tied up and given twenty lashes each, and sentenced to a fine of fifteen dollars. Then they were sent back to New Georgia, where the white men knocked seven bells out of them all around and put them to work. But Mauki was no longer house-boy. He was put in the road-making gang. The fine of fifteen dollars had been paid by the white men from whom he had run away, and he was told that he would have to work it out, which meant six months' additional toil. Further, his share of the stolen tobacco earned him another year of toil.

Port Adams was now three years and a half away, so he stole a canoe one night, hid on the islets in Manning Straits, passed through the Straits, and began working along the eastern coast of Ysabel, only to be captured, two-thirds of the way along, by the white men on Meringe Lagoon.[9] After a week, he escaped from them and took to the bush. There were no bush natives on Ysabel, only salt-water men, who were all Christians. The white men put up

6. Islands and ports in the western Solomon Islands.

7. Shotguns or rifles manufactured in the United States by the Winchester Arms Company.

8. Islands in the Solomon chain—*Guadalcanar* is an older version of "Guadalcanal," site of the famous World War II battle, and the Florida Islands are a small group in the central Solomons.

9. On Isabel Island. "Manning Straits": between Choiseul Island and Ysabel Island (now spelled Isabel) in the northern Solomons.

a reward of five hundred sticks of tobacco, and every time Mauki ventured down to the sea to steal a canoe he was chased by the salt-water men. Four months of this passed, when, the reward having been raised to a thousand sticks, he was caught and sent back to New Georgia and the road-building gang. Now a thousand sticks are worth fifty dollars, and Mauki had to pay the reward himself, which required a year and eight months' labor. So Port Adams was now five years away.

His homesickness was greater than ever, and it did not appeal to him to settle down and be good, work out his four years, and go home. The next time, he was caught in the very act of running away. His case was brought before Mr. Haveby, the island manager of the Moongleam Soap Company, who adjudged him an incorrigible. The Company had plantations on the Santa Cruz Islands, hundreds of miles across the sea, and there it sent its Solomon Islands' incorrigibles. And there Mauki was sent, though he never arrived. The schooner stopped at Santa Anna,[1] and in the night Mauki swam ashore, where he stole two rifles and a case of tobacco from the trader and got away in a canoe to Cristoval. Malaita was now to the north, fifty or sixty miles away. But when he attempted the passage, he was caught by a light gale and driven back to Santa Anna, where the trader clapped him in irons and held him against the return of the schooner from Santa Cruz. The two rifles the trader recovered, but the case of tobacco was charged up to Mauki at the rate of another year. The sum of years he now owed the Company was six.

On the way back to New Georgia, the schooner dropped anchor in Marau Sound, which lies at the southeastern extremity of Guadalcanar. Mauki swam ashore with handcuffs on his wrists and got away to the bush. The schooner went on, but the Moongleam trader ashore offered a thousand sticks, and to him Mauki was brought by the bushmen with a year and eight months tacked on to his account. Again, and before the schooner called in, he got away, this time in a whale-boat accompanied by a case of the trader's tobacco. But a northwest gale wrecked him upon Ugi,[2] where the Christian natives stole his tobacco and turned him over to the Moongleam trader who resided there. The tobacco the natives stole meant another year for him, and the tale was now eight years and a half.

"We'll send him to Lord Howe,"[3] said Mr. Haveby. "Bunster is there, and we'll let them settle it between them. It will be a case, I imagine, of Mauki getting Bunster, or Bunster getting Mauki, and good riddance in either event."

If one leaves Meringe Lagoon, on Ysabel, and steers a course due north, magnetic, at the end of one hundred and fifty miles he will lift the pounded coral beaches of Lord Howe above the sea. Lord Howe is a ring of land some one hundred and fifty miles in circumference, several hundred yards wide at its widest, and towering in places to a height of ten feet above sea-level. Inside this ring of sand is a mighty lagoon studded with coral patches. Lord Howe belongs to the Solomons neither geographically nor ethnologically. It is an

1. Santa Ana (as it is now spelled), with its old Port Mary, is a small island southeast of San Cristobal. The Santa Cruz Islands lie in the eastern Solomons.
2. An island in the southeastern Solomons. Marau

Sound is a harbor on Guadalcanal.
3. Atoll near the eastern coast of Australia, the northernmost part of the Solomons, sometimes called Ontong-Java.

atoll, while the Solomons are high islands; and its people and language are Polynesian, while the inhabitants of the Solomons are Melanesian. Lord Howe has been populated by the westward Polynesian drift which continues to this day, big outrigger canoes being washed upon its beaches by the southeast trade. That there has been a slight Melanesian drift in the period of the northwest monsoon is also evident.

Nobody ever comes to Lord Howe, or Ontong-Java as it is sometimes called. Thomas Cook & Son[4] do not sell tickets to it, and tourists do not dream of its existence. Not even a white missionary has landed on its shore. Its five thousand natives are as peaceable as they are primitive. Yet they were not always peaceable. The *Sailing Directions*[5] speak of them as hostile and treacherous. But the men who compile the *Sailing Directions* have never heard of the change that was worked in the hearts of the inhabitants, who, not many years ago, cut off a big bark[6] and killed all hands with the exception of the second mate. This survivor carried the news to his brothers. The captains of three trading schooners returned with him to Lord Howe. They sailed their vessels right into the lagoon and proceeded to preach the white man's gospel that only white men shall kill white men and that the lesser breeds must keep hands off. The schooners sailed up and down the lagoon, harrying and destroying. There was no escape from the narrow sand-circle, no bush to which to flee. The men were shot down at sight, and there was no avoiding being sighted. The villages were burned, the canoes smashed, the chickens and pigs killed, and the precious cocoanut-trees chopped down. For a month this continued, when the schooners sailed away; but the fear of the white man had been seared into the souls of the islanders and never again were they rash enough to harm one.

Max Bunster was the one white man on Lord Howe, trading in the pay of the ubiquitous Moongleam Soap Company. And the Company billeted him on Lord Howe, because, next to getting rid of him, it was the most out-of-the-way place to be found. That the Company did not get rid of him was due to the difficulty of finding another man to take his place. He was a strapping big German, with something wrong in his brain. Semi-madness would be a charitable statement of his condition. He was a bully and a coward, and a thrice-bigger savage than any savage on the island. Being a coward, his brutality was of the cowardly order. When he first went into the Company's employ, he was stationed on Savo.[7] When a consumptive colonial was sent to take his place, he beat him up with his fists and sent him off a wreck in the schooner that brought him.

Mr. Haveby next selected a young Yorkshire giant to relieve Bunster. The Yorkshire man had a reputation as a bruiser and preferred fighting to eating. But Bunster wouldn't fight. He was a regular little lamb—for ten days, at the end of which time the Yorkshire man was prostrated by a combined attack of dysentery and fever. Then Bunster went for him, among other things getting him down and jumping on him a score or so of times. Afraid of what would

4. Widely used travel agents of the time.
5. One of many nautical books London used.
6. A small vessel propelled by oars or sails.

7. Island in the Solomons a short distance from Guadalcanal.

happen when his victim recovered, Bunster fled away in a cutter to Guvutu, where he signalized himself by beating up a young Englishman already crippled by a Boer[8] bullet through both hips.

Then it was that Mr. Haveby sent Bunster to Lord Howe, the falling-off place. He celebrated his landing by mopping up half a case of gin and by thrashing the elderly and wheezy mate of the schooner which had brought him. When the schooner departed, he called the kanakas[9] down to the beach and challenged them to throw him in a wrestling bout, promising a case of tobacco to the one who succeeded. Three kanakas he threw, but was promptly thrown by a fourth, who, instead of receiving the tobacco, got a bullet through his lungs.

And so began Bunster's reign on Lord Howe. Three thousand people lived in the principal village; but it was deserted, even in broad day, when he passed through. Men, women, and children fled before him. Even the dogs and pigs got out of the way, while the king was not above hiding under a mat. The two prime ministers lived in terror of Bunster, who never discussed any moot subject, but struck out with his fists instead.

And to Lord Howe came Mauki, to toil for Bunster for eight long years and a half. There was no escaping from Lord Howe. For better or worse, Bunster and he were tied together. Bunster weighed two hundred pounds. Mauki weighed one hundred and ten. Bunster was a degenerate brute. But Mauki was a primitive savage. While both had wills and ways of their own.

Mauki had no idea of the sort of master he was to work for. He had had no warnings, and he had concluded as a matter of course that Bunster would be like other white men, a drinker of much whiskey, a ruler and a lawgiver who always kept his word and who never struck a boy undeserved. Bunster had the advantage. He knew all about Mauki and gloated over the coming into possession of him. The last cook was suffering from a broken arm and a dislocated shoulder, so Bunster made Mauki cook and general house-boy.

And Mauki soon learned that there were white men and white men. On the very day the schooner departed he was ordered to buy a chicken from Samisee, the native Tongan[1] missionary. But Samisee had sailed across the lagoon and would not be back for three days. Mauki returned with the information. He climbed the steep stairway (the house stood on piles twelve feet above the sand), and entered the living-room to report. The trader demanded the chicken. Mauki opened his mouth to explain the missionary's absence. But Bunster did not care for explanations. He struck out with his fist. The blow caught Mauki on the mouth and lifted him into the air. Clear through the doorway he flew, across the narrow veranda, breaking the top railing, and down to the ground. His lips were a contused, shapeless mass, and his mouth was full of blood and broken teeth.

"That'll teach you that back talk don't go with me," the trader shouted, purple with rage, peering down at him over the broken railing.

Mauki had never met a white man like this, and he resolved to walk small

---

8. "Boer" is an Afrikaans (and Dutch) word for *farmer*; it denotes white descendants of Dutch immigrants in what is now South Africa.

9. Hawaiians or Polynesians.
1. Tonga is an island in the South Pacific, west of Tahiti and south of Samoa.

and never offend. He saw the boat-boys knocked about, and one of them put in irons for three days with nothing to eat for the crime of breaking a rowlock while pulling. Then, too, he heard the gossip of the village and learned why Bunster had taken a third wife—by force, as was well known. The first and second wives lay in the graveyard, under the white coral sand, with slabs of coral rock at head and feet. They had died, it was said, from beatings he had given them. The third wife was certainly ill-used, as Mauki could see for himself.

But there was no way by which to avoid offending the white man, who seemed offended with life. When Mauki kept silent, he was struck and called a sullen brute. When he spoke, he was struck for giving back talk. When he was grave, Bunster accused him of plotting and gave him a thrashing in advance; and when he strove to be cheerful and to smile, he was charged with sneering at his lord and master and given a taste of stick. Bunster was a devil. The village would have done for him, had it not remembered the lesson of the three schooners. It might have done for him anyway, if there had been a bush to which to flee. As it was, the murder of the white men, of any white man, would bring a man-of-war that would kill the offenders and chop down the precious cocoanut-trees. Then there were the boat-boys, with minds fully made up to drown him by accident at the first opportunity to capsize the cutter. Only Bunster saw to it that the boat did not capsize.

Mauki was of a different breed, and, escape being impossible while Bunster lived, he was resolved to get the white man. The trouble was that he could never find a chance. Bunster was always on guard. Day and night his revolvers were ready to hand. He permitted nobody to pass behind his back, as Mauki learned after having been knocked down several times. Bunster knew that he had more to fear from the good-natured, even sweet-faced, Malaita boy than from the entire population of Lord Howe; and it gave added zest to the programme of torment he was carrying out. And Mauki walked small, accepted his punishments, and waited.

All other white men had respected his *tambos*, but not so Bunster. Mauki's weekly allowance of tobacco was two sticks. Bunster passed them to his woman and ordered Mauki to receive them from her hand. But this could not be, and Mauki went without his tobacco. In the same way he was made to miss many a meal, and to go hungry many a day. He was ordered to make chowder out of the big clams that grew in the lagoon. This he could not do, for clams were *tambo*. Six times in succession he refused to touch the clams, and six times he was knocked senseless. Bunster knew that the boy would die first, but called his refusal mutiny, and would have killed him had there been another cook to take his place.

One of the trader's favorite tricks was to catch Mauki's kinky locks and bat his head against the wall. Another trick was to catch Mauki unawares and thrust the live end of a cigar against his flesh. This Bunster called vaccination, and Mauki was vaccinated a number of times a week. Once, in a rage, Bunster ripped the cup handle from Mauki's nose, tearing the hole clear out of the cartilage.

"Oh, what a mug!" was his comment, when he surveyed the damage he had wrought.

The skin of a shark is like sandpaper, but the skin of a ray fish is like a rasp. In the South Seas the natives use it as a wood file in smoothing down canoes and paddles. Bunster had a mitten made of ray fish skin. The first time he tried it on Mauki, with one sweep of the hand it fetched the skin off his back from neck to armpit. Bunster was delighted. He gave his wife a taste of the mitten, and tried it out thoroughly on the boat-boys. The prime ministers came in for a stroke each, and they had to grin and take it for a joke.

"Laugh, damn you, laugh!" was the cue he gave.

"Mauki came in for the largest share of the mitten. Never a day passed without a caress from it. There were times when the loss of so much cuticle kept him awake at night, and often the half-healed surface was raked raw afresh by the facetious Mr. Bunster. Mauki continued his patient wait, secure in the knowledge that sooner or later his time would come. And he knew just what he was going to do, down to the smallest detail, when the time did come.

One morning Bunster got up in a mood for knocking seven bells out of the universe. He began on Mauki, and wound up on Mauki, in the interval knocking down his wife and hammering all the boat-boys. At breakfast he called the coffee slops and threw the scalding contents of the cup into Mauki's face. By ten o'clock Bunster was shivering with ague, and half an hour later he was burning with fever. It was no ordinary attack. It quickly became pernicious, and developed into black-water fever.[2] The days passed, and he grew weaker and weaker, never leaving his bed. Mauki waited and watched, the while his skin grew intact once more. He ordered the boys to beach the cutter, scrub her bottom, and give her a general overhauling. They thought the order emanated from Bunster, and they obeyed. But Bunster at the time was lying unconscious and giving no orders. This was Mauki's chance, but still he waited.

When the worst was past, and Bunster lay convalescent and conscious, but weak as a baby, Mauki packed his few trinkets, including the china cup handle, into his trade box. Then he went over to the village and interviewed the king and his two prime ministers.

"This fella Bunster, him good fella you like too much?" he asked.

They explained in one voice that they liked the trader not at all. The ministers poured forth a recital of all the indignities and wrongs that had been heaped upon them. The king broke down and wept. Mauki interrupted rudely.

"You savve me—me big fella marster my country. You no like 'm this fella white marster. Me no like 'm. Plenty good you put hundred cocoanut, two hundred cocoanut, three hundred cocoanut along cutter. Him finish, you go sleep 'm good fella. Altogether kanaka sleep 'm good fella. Bime by big fella noise along house, you no savve hear 'm that fella noise. You altogether sleep strong fella too much."

In like manner Mauki interviewed the boat-boys. Then he ordered Bunster's wife to return to her family house. Had she refused, he would have been in a quandary, for his *tambo* would not have permitted him to lay hands on her.

2. A complication of malaria; its symptoms include high fever, kidney failure, and internal hemorrhaging.

The house deserted, he entered the sleeping-room, where the trader lay in a doze. Mauki first removed the revolvers, then placed the ray fish mitten on his hand. Bunster's first warning was a stroke of the mitten that removed the skin the full length of his nose.

"Good fella, eh?" Mauki grinned, between two strokes, one of which swept the forehead bare and the other of which cleaned off one side of his face. "Laugh, damn you, laugh."

Mauki did his work thoroughly, and the kanakas, hiding in their houses, heard the "big fella noise" that Bunster made and continued to make for an hour or more.

When Mauki was done, he carried the boat compass and all the rifles and ammunition down to the cutter, which he proceeded to ballast with cases of tobacco. It was while engaged in this that a hideous, skinless thing came out of the house and ran screaming down the beach till it fell in the sand and mowed and gibbered under the scorching sun. Mauki looked toward it and hesitated. Then he went over and removed the head, which he wrapped in a mat and stowed in the stern-locker of the cutter.

So soundly did the kanakas sleep through that long hot day that they did not see the cutter run out through the passage and head south, close-hauled on the southeast trade. Nor was the cutter ever sighted on that long tack to the shores of Ysabel, and during the tedious head-beat from there to Malaita. He landed at Port Adams with a wealth of rifles and tobacco such as no one man had ever possessed before. But he did not stop there. He had taken a white man's head, and only the bush could shelter him. So back he went to the bush-villages, where he shot old Fanfoa and half a dozen of the chief men, and made himself the chief over all the villages. When his father died, Mauki's brother ruled in Port Adams, and, joined together, salt-water men and bushmen, the resulting combination was the strongest of the ten score fighting tribes of Malaita.

More than his fear of the British government was Mauki's fear of the all-powerful Moongleam Soap Company; and one day a message came up to him in the bush, reminding him that he owed the Company eight and one-half years of labor. He sent back a favorable answer, and then appeared the inevitable white man, the captain of the schooner, the only white man during Mauki's reign who ventured the bush and came out alive. This man not only came out, but he brought with him seven hundred and fifty dollars in gold sovereigns—the money price of eight years and a half of labor plus the cost price of certain rifles and cases of tobacco.

Mauki no longer weighs one hundred and ten pounds. His stomach is three times its former girth,[3] and he has four wives. He has many other things— rifles and revolvers, the handle of a china cup, and an excellent collection of bushmen's heads. But more precious than the entire collection is another head, perfectly dried and cured, with sandy hair and a yellowish beard, which is kept wrapped in the finest of fibre lava-lavas. When Mauki goes to war with villages beyond his realm, he invariably gets out this head, and, alone in his grass palace, contemplates it long and solemnly. At such times the hush of

3. In many of the Pacific islands, being large and heavy was considered the privilege of nobles and a sign of grandeur.

death falls on the village, and not even a pickaninny[4] dares make a noise. The head is esteemed the most powerful devil-devil on Malaita, and to the possession of it is ascribed all of Mauki's greatness.

1908

4. Though today considered an offensive term for "black child," *pickaninny* originated in West African languages and meant "belonging to the family."

# ZITKALA ŠA (GERTRUDE SIMMONS BONNIN)
## 1876–1938

Gertrude Simmons was born in 1876 on the Yankton Sioux Reservation in south-central South Dakota. Her mother was *Tate Iyohi Win*, or "Reaches the Wind Woman," otherwise known as Ellen Simmons, and her father was probably a white man named Felker who left his wife before the child's birth. Her mother later married another white man, John H. Simmons, whose surname was given to the child. Gertrude Simmons today is usually referred to as Zitkala Ša (pronounced *sha*), or Red Bird, a name she chose for herself. Zitkala Ša was an important Native American writer, orator, and debater; a singer, pianist, and violinist; and an activist on behalf of women's and Native American rights.

Eighteen hundred and seventy-six, the year of Zitkala Ša's birth, was the year in which George Armstrong Custer's Seventh Cavalry was defeated by a coalition of Sioux and Cheyenne warriors on the Little Bighorn River in Montana, after which the federal government finally drove both tribes onto reservations. In 1890, the U.S. Department of the Census announced the closing of the frontier, meaning that no more "free land" remained open for settlement; the United States had achieved its "manifest destiny," extending its dominion from "sea to shining sea." As an adult, then, Zitkala Ša lived in what has been called the "transitional" period in Native American history, a difficult time for Indian peoples, when the U.S. government pursued an official policy of "detribalization" and land-hungry whites sought access to tribal domains.

At the age of eight, Zitkala Ša declared her intention to learn the white man's ways—or, as she puts it, in her autobiographical, "Impressions of an Indian Childhood" (1900), she wanted to taste the "big red apples" missionaries promised Indian children if they would attend boarding school. She began her schooling at White's Manual Institute, a Quaker school in Indiana. As her autobiography details it, her introduction to "civilization" subjected her and the other Indian children to having their long hair cut, to having the clothing in which they had arrived discarded, and, perhaps most painful, to being forbidden to speak their Native languages. This was, in the oft-quoted dictum of Colonel Richard Henry Pratt, headmaster of the Carlisle Indian Institute, where Zitkala Ša later worked, an education intended to "Kill the Indian and save the man!"

From White's, Zitkala Ša went on to Earlham College, also in Indiana, where she began to demonstrate a wide range of talents. In the last section of "Impressions of an Indian Childhood," she tells of her appearance as the representative of the college in 1896 at a statewide oratorical competition, where some "rowdies," as she puts it, "threw out a large white flag, with a drawing of a most forlorn Indian girl on it," along with, "in bold black letters words that ridiculed the college which was represented by a 'squaw.' " This slight was somewhat assuaged by her winning second prize overall.

The following year, Zitkala Ša became "the latest addition to our force of workers," as the Carlisle Institute's publication, *The Indian Helper*, announced in its July 1897 number. Carlisle, as noted above, was committed to preparing Indians to assimilate into mainstream American life. At Carlisle, Zitkala Ša led the glee club, played the piano and violin, and became engaged to Thomas Marshall, a Sioux from the Pine Ridge Agency, a devout Christian convert, "without a peer among our students," who died rather suddenly from an undiagnosed illness.

Soon after Marshall's death, Zitkala Ša began to publish autobiography and fiction. (She also wrote poetry.) "Impressions of an Indian Childhood," "The Schooldays of an Indian Girl," and "An Indian Teacher among Indians" appeared in the *Atlantic Monthly* for January, February, and March of 1900. Her short story "The Soft-Hearted Sioux" and the essay-manifesto "Why I Am a Pagan," both reprinted here, appeared in *Harper's Monthly* in 1901. Nineteen hundred and one was also the date of publication of her first book, *Old Indian Legends*, a work that contributed to the vogue for Native folklore. Her other writings did not appear in book form until 1921, with the publication of *American Indian Stories*.

"The Soft-Hearted Sioux" makes powerfully clear that the protagonist's Christianization and "civilization" have utterly unfitted him for any relation to his traditional parents. In "Why I Am a Pagan," Zitkala Ša speaks of a "native preacher" who mouths "most strangely the jangling phrases of a bigoted creed," remarks that her mother is "a follower of the new superstition," and states her own preference for "excursions in natural gardens" rather than the "dogma" of the Christians. It is no wonder that the Carlisle publication, now called *Red Man and Helper*, reacted angrily to the latter two pieces, calling Zitkala Ša "a person of infinite conceit" and "utterly unthankful for all that has been done for her by the pale faces, which in her case is considerable."

In May 1902, Zitkala Ša married Raymond Bonnin, also a Yankton, and an employee of the U.S. Indian Service (later the Bureau of Indian Affairs). They had one son, Raymond Ohiya Bonnin (his middle name was a tribute to Charles Alexander Eastman, whose Indian name was Ohiyesa), born in 1903. Although she would occasionally publish stories and poems thereafter, and wrote the libretto for an opera, *Sun Dance*, the bulk of Zitkala Ša's writing over the second half of her life derived from her active engagement in Indian affairs. After years of work on the Uintah Ouray Ute Agency in Utah, the family moved to Washington, D.C., in 1916 so that Zitkala Ša could take up her elected position as secretary of the Society of the American Indian (SAI), an organization dedicated to improving the condition of Native people. During World War I, Bonnin served in the army as assistant to the Quartermaster General in Washington, retiring with the rank of captain. When the SAI broke up in 1920, Zitkala Ša began working with the General Federation of Women's Clubs, which established an Indian Welfare Committee in 1921 at her urging. One of the committee's achievements was an inquiry into the treatment of some of the tribes in Oklahoma, which led to the publication, in 1924, of a study of the graft, corruption, and exploitation of the tribes and spurred the formation under President Hoover of the Merriam Commission in 1928 to study these matters. In 1926, Zitkala Ša had founded her own organization, the National Council of American Indians, of which she was president, with her husband serving as counselor general, secretary-treasurer, and executive secretary. It was in 1938 that she fell into a coma and died.

Zitkala Ša is buried in Arlington National Cemetery beside her husband, Captain Raymond Bonnin.

# Impressions of an Indian Childhood[1]

## I. My Mother

A wigwam of weather-stained canvas stood at the base of some irregularly ascending hills. A footpath wound its way gently down the sloping land till it reached the broad river bottom; creeping through the long swamp grasses that bent over it on either side, it came out on the edge of the Missouri.

Here, morning, noon, and evening, my mother came to draw water from the muddy stream for our household use. Always, when my mother started for the river, I stopped my play to run along with her. She was only of medium height. Often she was sad and silent, at which times her full arched lips were compressed into hard and bitter lines, and shadows fell under her black eyes. Then I clung to her hand and begged to know what made the tears fall.

"Hush; my little daughter must never talk about my tears;" and smiling through them, she patted my head and said, "Now let me see how fast you can run to-day." Whereupon I tore away at my highest possible speed, with my long black hair blowing in the breeze.

I was a wild little girl of seven. Loosely clad in a slip of brown buckskin, and light-footed with a pair of soft moccasins on my feet, I was as free as the wind that blew my hair, and no less spirited than a bounding deer. These were my mother's pride,—my wild freedom and overflowing spirits. She taught me no fear save that of intruding myself upon others.

Having gone many paces ahead I stopped, panting for breath, and laughing with glee as my mother watched my every movement. I was not wholly conscious of myself, but was more keenly alive to the fire within. It was as if I were the activity, and my hands and feet were only experiments for my spirit to work upon.

Returning from the river, I tugged beside my mother, with my hand upon the bucket I believed I was carrying. One time, on such a return, I remember a bit of conversation we had. My grown-up cousin, Warca-Ziwin (Sunflower), who was then seventeen, always went to the river alone for water for her mother. Their wigwam was not far from ours; and I saw her daily going to and from the river. I admired my cousin greatly. So I said: "Mother, when I am tall as my cousin Warca-Ziwin, you shall not have to come for water. I will do it for you."

With a strange tremor in her voice which I could not understand, she answered, "If the paleface does not take away from us the river we drink."

"Mother, who is this bad paleface?" I asked.

"My little daughter, he is a sham,—a sickly sham! The bronzed Dakota is the only real man."

I looked up into my mother's face while she spoke; and seeing her bite her lips, I knew she was unhappy. This aroused revenge in my small soul. Stamping my foot on the earth, I cried aloud, "I hate the paleface that makes my mother cry!"

1. "Impressions of an Indian Childhood," "The School Days of an Indian Girl," and "An Indian Teacher among Indians" first appeared, respectively, in the *Atlantic Monthly* for January, February, and March of 1900.

Setting the pail of water on the ground, my mother stooped, and stretching her left hand out on the level with my eyes, she placed her other arm about me; she pointed to the hill where my uncle and my only sister lay buried.

"There is what the paleface has done! Since then your father too has been buried in a hill nearer the rising sun. We were once very happy. But the paleface has stolen our lands and driven us hither. Having defrauded us of our land, the paleface forced us away.

"Well, it happened on the day we moved camp that your sister and uncle were both very sick. Many others were ailing, but there seemed to be no help. We traveled many days and nights; not in the grand happy way that we moved camp when I was a little girl, but we were driven, my child, driven like a herd of buffalo. With every step, your sister, who was not as large as you are now, shrieked with the painful jar until she was hoarse with crying. She grew more and more feverish. Her little hands and cheeks were burning hot. Her little lips were parched and dry, but she would not drink the water I gave her. Then I discovered that her throat was swollen and red. My poor child, how I cried with her because the Great Spirit had forgotten us!

"At last, when we reached this western country, on the first weary night your sister died. And soon your uncle died also, leaving a widow and an orphan daughter, your cousin Warca-Ziwin. Both your sister and uncle might have been happy with us to-day, had it not been for the heartless paleface."

My mother was silent the rest of the way to our wigwam. Though I saw no tears in her eyes, I knew that was because I was with her. She seldom wept before me.

## II. The Legends

During the summer days, my mother built her fire in the shadow of our wigwam.

In the early morning our simple breakfast was spread upon the grass west of our tepee. At the farthest point of the shade my mother sat beside her fire, toasting a savory piece of dried meat. Near her, I sat upon my feet, eating my dried meat with unleavened bread, and drinking strong black coffee.

The morning meal was our quiet hour, when we two were entirely alone. At noon, several who chanced to be passing by stopped to rest, and to share our luncheon with us, for they were sure of our hospitality.

My uncle, whose death my mother ever lamented, was one of our nation's bravest warriors. His name was on the lips of old men when talking of the proud feats of valor; and it was mentioned by younger men, too, in connection with deeds of gallantry. Old women praised him for his kindness toward them; young women held him up as an ideal to their sweethearts. Every one loved him, and my mother worshiped his memory. Thus it happened that even strangers were sure of welcome in our lodge, if they but asked a favor in my uncle's name.

Though I heard many strange experiences related by these wayfarers, I loved best the evening meal, for that was the time old legends were told. I was always glad when the sun hung low in the west, for then my mother sent me to invite the neighboring old men and women to eat supper with us. Running all the way to the wigwams, I halted shyly at the entrances. Sometimes I stood long moments without saying a word. It was not any fear that made me so dumb when out upon such a happy errand; nor was it that I wished to withhold the invitation, for it was all I could do to observe this very proper silence. But it was a sensing of the atmosphere, to assure myself that I should not hinder other plans. My mother used to say to me, as I was almost bounding away for the old people: "Wait a moment before you invite any one. If other plans are being discussed, do not interfere, but go elsewhere."

The old folks knew the meaning of my pauses; and often they coaxed my confidence by asking, "What do you seek, little granddaughter?"

"My mother says you are to come to our tepee this evening," I instantly exploded, and breathed the freer afterwards.

"Yes, yes, gladly, gladly I shall come!" each replied. Rising at once and carrying their blankets across one shoulder, they flocked leisurely from their various wigwams toward our dwelling.

My mission done, I ran back, skipping and jumping with delight. All out of breath, I told my mother almost the exact words of the answers to my invitation. Frequently she asked, "What were they doing when you entered their tepee?" This taught me to remember all I saw at a single glance. Often I told my mother my impressions without being questioned.

While in the neighboring wigwams sometimes an old Indian woman asked me, "What is your mother doing?" Unless my mother had cautioned me not to tell, I generally answered her questions without reserve.

At the arrival of our guests I sat close to my mother, and did not leave her side without first asking her consent. I ate my supper in quiet, listening patiently to the talk of the old people, wishing all the time that they would begin the stories I loved best. At last, when I could not wait any longer, I whispered in my mother's ear, "Ask them to tell an Iktomi story,[2] mother."

Soothing my impatience, my mother said aloud, "My little daughter is anxious to hear your legends." By this time all were through eating, and the evening was fast deepening into twilight.

As each in turn began to tell a legend, I pillowed my head in my mother's lap; and lying flat upon my back, I watched the stars as they peeped down upon me, one by one. The increasing interest of the tale aroused me, and I sat up eagerly listening for every word. The old women made funny remarks, and laughed so heartily that I could not help joining them.

The distant howling of a pack of wolves or the hooting of an owl in the river bottom frightened me, and I nestled into my mother's lap. She added some dry sticks to the fire, and the bright flames heaped up into the faces of the old folks as they sat around in a great circle.

On such an evening, I remember the glare of the fire shone on a tattooed star upon the brow of the old warrior who was telling a story. I watched him curiously as he made his unconscious gestures. The blue star upon his bronzed forehead was a puzzle to me. Looking about, I saw two parallel lines on the chin of one of the old women. The rest had none. I examined my mother's face, but found no sign there.

After the warrior's story was finished, I asked the old woman the meaning of the blue lines on her chin, looking all the while out of the corners of my

2. A story about the Sioux trickster.

eyes at the warrior with the star on his forehead. I was a little afraid that he would rebuke me for my boldness.

Here the old woman began: "Why, my grandchild, they are signs,—secret signs I dare not tell you. I shall, however, tell you a wonderful story about a woman who had a cross tattooed upon each of her cheeks."

It was a long story of a woman whose magic power lay hidden behind the marks upon her face. I fell asleep before the story was completed.

Ever after that night I felt suspicious of tattooed people. Wherever I saw one I glanced furtively at the mark and round about it, wondering what terrible magic power was covered there.

It was rarely that such a fearful story as this one was told by the camp fire. Its impression was so acute that the picture still remains vividly clear and pronounced.

\*　\*　\*

## IV. The Coffee-Making

One summer afternoon, my mother left me alone in our wigwam, while she went across the way to my aunt's dwelling.

I did not much like to stay alone in our tepee, for I feared a tall, broad-shouldered crazy man, some forty years old, who walked loose among the hills. Wiyaka-Napbina (Wearer of a Feather Necklace) was harmless, and whenever he came into a wigwam he was driven there by extreme hunger. He went nude except for the half of a red blanket he girdled around his waist. In one tawny arm he used to carry a heavy bunch of wild sunflowers that he gathered in his aimless ramblings. His black hair was matted by the winds, and scorched into a dry red by the constant summer sun. As he took great strides, placing one brown bare foot directly in front of the other, he swung his long lean arm to and fro.

Frequently he paused in his walk and gazed far backward, shading his eyes with his hand. He was under the belief that an evil spirit was haunting his steps. This was what my mother told me once, when I sneered at such a silly big man. I was brave when my mother was near by, and Wiyaka-Napbina walking farther and farther away.

"Pity the man, my child. I knew him when he was a brave and handsome youth. He was overtaken by a malicious spirit among the hills, one day, when he went hither and thither after his ponies. Since then he cannot stay away from the hills," she said.

I felt so sorry for the man in his misfortune that I prayed to the Great Spirit to restore him. But though I pitied him at a distance, I was still afraid of him when he appeared near our wigwam.

Thus, when my mother left me by myself that afternoon, I sat in a fearful mood within our tepee. I recalled all I had ever heard about Wiyaka-Napbina; and I tried to assure myself that though he might pass near by, he would not come to our wigwam because there was no little girl around our grounds.

Just then, from without a hand lifted the canvas covering of the entrance; the shadow of a man fell within the wigwam, and a large roughly moccasined foot was planted inside.

For a moment I did not dare to breathe or stir, for I thought that could be no other than Wiyaka-Napbina. The next instant I sighed aloud in relief. It was an old grandfather who had often told me Iktomi legends.

"Where is your mother, my little grandchild?" were his first words.

"My mother is soon coming back from my aunt's tepee," I replied.

"Then I shall wait awhile for her return," he said, crossing his feet and seating himself upon a mat.

At once I began to play the part of a generous hostess. I turned to my mother's coffeepot.

Lifting the lid, I found nothing but coffee grounds in the bottom. I set the pot on a heap of cold ashes in the centre, and filled it half full of warm Missouri River water. During this performance I felt conscious of being watched. Then breaking off a small piece of our unleavened bread, I placed it in a bowl. Turning soon to the coffeepot, which would never have boiled on a dead fire had I waited forever, I poured out a cup of worse than muddy warm water. Carrying the bowl in one hand and cup in the other, I handed the light luncheon to the old warrior. I offered them to him with the air of bestowing generous hospitality.

"How! how!" he said, and placed the dishes on the ground in front of his crossed feet. He nibbled at the bread and sipped from the cup. I sat back against a pole watching him. I was proud to have succeeded so well in serving refreshments to a guest all by myself. Before the old warrior had finished eating, my mother entered. Immediately she wondered where I had found coffee, for she knew I had never made any, and that she had left the coffeepot empty. Answering the question in my mother's eyes, the warrior remarked, "My granddaughter made coffee on a heap of dead ashes, and served me the moment I came."

They both laughed, and mother said, "Wait a little longer, and I shall build a fire." She meant to make some real coffee. But neither she nor the warrior, whom the law of our custom had compelled to partake of my insipid hospitality, said anything to embarrass me. They treated my best judgment, poor as it was, with the utmost respect. It was not till long years afterward that I learned how ridiculous a thing I had done.

*   *   *

## VII. *The Big Red Apples*

The first turning away from the easy, natural flow of my life occurred in an early spring. It was in my eighth year; in the month of March, I afterward learned. At this age I knew but one language, and that was my mother's native tongue.

From some of my playmates I heard that two paleface missionaries were in our village. They were from that class of white men who wore big hats and carried large hearts, they said. Running direct to my mother, I began to question her why these two strangers were among us. She told me, after I had teased much, that they had come to take away Indian boys and girls to the East. My mother did not seem to want me to talk about them. But in a day or two, I gleaned many wonderful stories from my playfellows concerning the strangers.

"Mother, my friend Judéwin is going home with the missionaries. She is going to a more beautiful country than ours; the palefaces told her so!" I said wistfully, wishing in my heart that I too might go.

Mother sat in a chair, and I was hanging on her knee. Within the last two seasons my big brother Dawée had returned from a three years' education in the East, and his coming back influenced my mother to take a farther step from her native way of living. First it was a change from the buffalo skin to the white man's canvas that covered our wigwam. Now she had given up her wigwam of slender poles, to live, a foreigner, in a home of clumsy logs.

"Yes, my child, several others besides Judéwin are going away with the pale-faces. Your brother said the missionaries had inquired about his little sister," she said, watching my face very closely.

My heart thumped so hard against my breast, I wondered if she could hear it.

"Did he tell them to take me, mother?" I asked, fearing lest Dawée had forbidden the palefaces to see me, and that my hope of going to the Wonderland would be entirely blighted.

With a sad, slow smile, she answered: "There! I knew you were wishing to go, because Judéwin has filled your ears with the white men's lies. Don't believe a word they say! Their words are sweet, but, my child, their deeds are bitter. You will cry for me, but they will not even soothe you. Stay with me, my little one! Your brother Dawée says that going East, away from your mother, is too hard an experience for his baby sister."

Thus my mother discouraged my curiosity about the lands beyond our eastern horizon; for it was not yet an ambition for Letters that was stirring me. But on the following day the missionaries did come to our very house. I spied them coming up the footpath leading to our cottage. A third man was with them, but he was not my brother Dawée. It was another, a young interpreter, a paleface who had a smattering of the Indian language. I was ready to run out to meet them, but I did not dare to displease my mother. With great glee, I jumped up and down on our ground floor. I begged my mother to open the door, that they would be sure to come to us. Alas! They came, they saw, and they conquered!

Judéwin had told me of the great tree where grew red, red apples; and how we could reach out our hands and pick all the red apples we could eat. I had never seen apple trees. I had never tasted more than a dozen red apples in my life; and when I heard of the orchards of the East, I was eager to roam among them. The missionaries smiled into my eyes, and patted my head. I wondered how mother could say such hard words against them.

"Mother, ask them if little girls may have all the red apples they want, when they go East," I whispered aloud, in my excitement.

The interpreter heard me, and answered: "Yes, little girl, the nice red apples are for those who pick them; and you will have a ride on the iron horse if you go with these good people."

I had never seen a train, and he knew it.

"Mother, I'm going East! I like big red apples, and I want to ride on the iron horse! Mother, say yes!" I pleaded.

My mother said nothing. The missionaries waited in silence; and my eyes began to blur with tears, though I struggled to choke them back. The corners of my mouth twitched, and my mother saw me.

"I am not ready to give you any word," she said to them. "To-morrow I shall send you my answer by my son."

With this they left us. Alone with my mother, I yielded to my tears, and cried aloud, shaking my head so as not to hear what she was saying to me. This was the first time I had ever been so unwilling to give up my own desire that I refused to hearken to my mother's voice.

There was a solemn silence in our home that night. Before I went to bed I begged the Great Spirit to make my mother willing I should go with the missionaries.

The next morning came, and my mother called me to her side. "My daughter, do you still persist in wishing to leave your mother?" she asked.

"Oh, mother, it is not that I wish to leave you, but I want to see the wonderful Eastern land," I answered.

My dear old aunt came to our house that morning, and I heard her say, "Let her try it."

I hoped that, as usual, my aunt was pleading on my side. My brother Dawée came for mother's decision. I dropped my play, and crept close to my aunt.

"Yes, Dawée, my daughter, though she does not understand what it all means, is anxious to go. She will need an education when she is grown, for then there will be fewer real Dakotas, and many more palefaces. This tearing her away, so young, from her mother is necessary, if I would have her an educated woman. The palefaces, who owe us a large debt for stolen lands, have begun to pay a tardy justice in offering some education to our children. But I know my daughter must suffer keenly in this experiment. For her sake, I dread to tell you my reply to the missionaries. Go, tell them that they may take my little daughter, and that the Great Spirit shall not fail to reward them according to their hearts."

Wrapped in my heavy blanket, I walked with my mother to the carriage that was soon to take us to the iron horse. I was happy. I met my playmates, who were also wearing their best thick blankets. We showed one another our new beaded moccasins, and the width of the belts that girdled our new dresses. Soon we were being drawn rapidly away by the white man's horses. When I saw the lonely figure of my mother vanish in the distance, a sense of regret settled heavily upon me. I felt suddenly weak, as if I might fall limp to the ground. I was in the hands of strangers whom my mother did not fully trust. I no longer felt free to be myself, or to voice my own feelings. The tears trickled down my cheeks, and I buried my face in the folds of my blanket. Now the first step, parting me from my mother, was taken, and all my belated tears availed nothing.

Having driven thirty miles to the ferryboat, we crossed the Missouri in the evening. Then riding again a few miles eastward, we stopped before a massive brick building. I looked at it in amazement, and with a vague misgiving, for in our village I had never seen so large a house. Trembling with fear and distrust of the palefaces, my teeth chattering from the chilly ride, I crept noiselessly in my soft moccasins along the narrow hall, keeping very close to the bare wall. I was as frightened and bewildered as the captured young of a wild creature.

1900

# The School Days of an Indian Girl

## I. The Land of Red Apples

There were eight in our party of bronzed children who were going East with the missionaries. Among us were three young braves, two tall girls, and we three little ones, Judéwin, Thowin, and I.

We had been very impatient to start on our journey to the Red Apple Country, which, we were told, lay a little beyond the great circular horizon of the Western prairie. Under a sky of rosy apples we dreamt of roaming as freely and happily as we had chased the cloud shadows on the Dakota plains. We had anticipated much pleasure from a ride on the iron horse, but the throngs of staring palefaces disturbed and troubled us.

On the train, fair women, with tottering babies on each arm, stopped their haste and scrutinized the children of absent mothers. Large men, with heavy bundles in their hands, halted near by, and riveted their glassy blue eyes upon us.

I sank deep into the corner of my seat, for I resented being watched. Directly in front of me, children who were no larger than I hung themselves upon the backs of their seats, with their bold white faces toward me. Sometimes they took their forefingers out of their mouths and pointed at my moccasined feet. Their mothers, instead of reproving such rude curiosity, looked closely at me, and attracted their children's further notice to my blanket. This embarrassed me, and kept me constantly on the verge of tears.

I sat perfectly still, with my eyes downcast, daring only now and then to shoot long glances around me. Chancing to turn to the window at my side, I was quite breathless upon seeing one familiar object. It was the telegraph pole which strode by at short paces. Very near my mother's dwelling, along the edge of a road thickly bordered with wild sunflowers, some poles like these had been planted by white men. Often I had stopped, on my way down the road, to hold my ear against the pole, and, hearing its low moaning, I used to wonder what the paleface had done to hurt it. Now I sat watching for each pole that glided by to be the last one.

In this way I had forgotten my uncomfortable surroundings, when I heard one of my comrades call out my name. I saw the missionary standing very near, tossing candies and gums into our midst. This amused us all, and we tried to see who could catch the most of the sweetmeats. The missionary's generous distribution of candies was impressed upon my memory by a disastrous result which followed. I had caught more than my share of candies and gums, and soon after our arrival at the school I had a chance to disgrace myself, which, I am ashamed to say, I did.

Though we rode several days inside of the iron horse, I do not recall a single thing about our luncheons.

It was night when we reached the school grounds. The lights from the windows of the large buildings fell upon some of the icicled trees that stood beneath them. We were led toward an open door, where the brightness of the lights within flooded out over the heads of the excited palefaces who blocked the way. My body trembled more from fear than from the snow I trod upon.

Entering the house, I stood close against the wall. The strong glaring light in the large whitewashed room dazzled my eyes. The noisy hurrying of hard shoes upon a bare wooden floor increased the whirring in my ears. My only safety seemed to be in keeping next to the wall. As I was wondering in which direction to escape from all this confusion, two warm hands grasped me firmly, and in the same moment I was tossed high in midair. A rosy-cheeked paleface woman caught me in her arms. I was both frightened and insulted by such trifling. I stared into her eyes, wishing her to let me stand on my own feet, but she jumped me up and down with increasing enthusiasm. My mother had never made a plaything of her wee daughter. Remembering this I began to cry aloud.

They misunderstood the cause of my tears, and placed me at a white table loaded with food. There our party were united again. As I did not hush my crying, one of the older ones whispered to me, "Wait until you are alone in the night."

It was very little I could swallow besides my sobs, that evening.

"Oh, I want my mother and my brother Dawée! I want to go to my aunt!" I pleaded; but the ears of the palefaces could not hear me.

From the table we were taken along an upward incline of wooden boxes, which I learned afterward to call a stairway. At the top was a quiet hall, dimly lighted. Many narrow beds were in one straight line down the entire length of the wall. In them lay sleeping brown faces, which peeped just out of the coverings. I was tucked into bed with one of the tall girls, because she talked to me in my mother tongue and seemed to soothe me.

I had arrived in the wonderful land of rosy skies, but I was not happy, as I had thought I should be. My long travel and the bewildering sights had exhausted me. I fell asleep, heaving deep, tired sobs. My tears were left to dry themselves in streaks, because neither my aunt nor my mother was near to wipe them away.

## II. The Cutting of My Long Hair

The first day in the land of apples was a bitter-cold one; for the snow still covered the ground, and the trees were bare. A large bell rang for breakfast, its loud metallic voice crashing through the belfry overhead and into our sensitive ears. The annoying clatter of shoes on bare floors gave us no peace. The constant clash of harsh noises, with an undercurrent of many voices murmuring an unknown tongue, made a bedlam within which I was securely tied. And though my spirit tore itself in struggling for its lost freedom, all was useless.

A paleface woman, with white hair, came up after us. We were placed in a line of girls who were marching into the dining room. These were Indian girls, in stiff shoes and closely clinging dresses. The small girls wore sleeved aprons and shingled[1] hair. As I walked noiselessly in my soft moccasins, I felt like sinking to the floor, for my blanket had been stripped from my shoulders. I looked hard at the Indian girls, who seemed not to care that they were even more immodestly dressed than I, in their tightly fitting clothes. While we marched in, the boys entered at an opposite door. I watched for the three young braves who came in our party. I spied them in the rear ranks, looking as uncomfortable as I felt.

A small bell was tapped, and each of the pupils drew a chair from under the table. Supposing this act meant they were to be seated, I pulled out mine and at once slipped into it from one side. But when I turned my head, I saw that I was the only one seated, and all the rest at our table remained standing. Just as I began to rise, looking shyly around to see how chairs were to be used, a second bell was sounded. All were seated at last, and I had to crawl back into my chair again. I heard a man's voice at one end of the hall, and I

1. Bobbed, cut short.

looked around to see him. But all the others hung their heads over their plates. As I glanced at the long chain of tables, I caught the eyes of a paleface woman upon me. Immediately I dropped my eyes, wondering why I was so keenly watched by the strange woman. The man ceased his mutterings, and then a third bell was tapped. Every one picked up his knife and fork and began eating. I began crying instead, for by this time I was afraid to venture anything more.

But this eating by formula was not the hardest trial in that first day. Late in the morning, my friend Judéwin gave me a terrible warning. Judéwin knew a few words of English; and she had overheard the paleface woman talk about cutting our long, heavy hair. Our mothers had taught us that only unskilled warriors who were captured had their hair shingled by the enemy. Among our people, short hair was worn by mourners, and shingled hair by cowards!

We discussed our fate some moments, and when Judéwin said, "We have to submit, because they are strong," I rebelled.

"No, I will not submit! I will struggle first!" I answered.

I watched my chance, and when no one noticed I disappeared. I crept up the stairs as quietly as I could in my squeaking shoes,—my moccasins had been exchanged for shoes. Along the hall I passed, without knowing whither I was going. Turning aside to an open door, I found a large room with three white beds in it. The windows were covered with dark green curtains, which made the room very dim. Thankful that no one was there, I directed my steps toward the corner farthest from the door. On my hands and knees I crawled under the bed, and cuddled myself in the dark corner.

From my hiding place I peered out, shuddering with fear whenever I heard footsteps near by. Though in the hall loud voices were calling my name, and I knew that even Judéwin was searching for me, I did not open my mouth to answer. Then the steps were quickened and the voices became excited. The sounds came nearer and nearer. Women and girls entered the room. I held my breath, and watched them open closet doors and peep behind large trunks. Some one threw up the curtains, and the room was filled with sudden light. What caused them to stoop and look under the bed I do not know. I remember being dragged out, though I resisted by kicking and scratching wildly. In spite of myself, I was carried downstairs and tied fast in a chair.

I cried aloud, shaking my head all the while until I felt the cold blades of the scissors against my neck, and heard them gnaw off one of my thick braids. Then I lost my spirit. Since the day I was taken from my mother I had suffered extreme indignities. People had stared at me. I had been tossed about in the air like a wooden puppet. And now my long hair was shingled like a coward's! In my anguish I moaned for my mother, but no one came to comfort me. Not a soul reasoned quietly with me, as my own mother used to do; for now I was only one of many little animals driven by a herder.

\* \* \*

### V. Iron Routine

A loud-clamoring bell awakened us at half past six in the cold winter mornings. From happy dreams of Western rolling lands and unlassoed freedom we tumbled out upon chilly bare floors back again into a paleface day. We had short time to jump into our shoes and clothes, and wet our eyes with icy water, before a small hand bell was vigorously rung for roll call.

There were too many drowsy children and too numerous orders for the day to waste a moment in any apology to nature for giving her children such a shock in the early morning. We rushed downstairs, bounding over two high steps at a time, to land in the assembly room.

A paleface woman, with a yellow-covered roll book open on her arm and a gnawed pencil in her hand, appeared at the door. Her small, tired face was coldly lighted with a pair of large gray eyes.

She stood still in a halo of authority, while over the rim of her spectacles her eyes pried nervously about the room. Having glanced at her long list of names and called out the first one, she tossed up her chin and peered through the crystals of her spectacles to make sure of the answer "Here."

Relentlessly her pencil black-marked our daily records if we were not present to respond to our names, and no chum of ours had done it successfully for us. No matter if a dull headache or the painful cough of slow consumption[2] had delayed the absentee, there was only time enough to mark the tardiness. It was next to impossible to leave the iron routine after the civilizing machine had once begun its day's buzzing; and as it was inbred in me to suffer in silence rather than to appeal to the ears of one whose open eyes could not see my pain, I have many times trudged in the day's harness heavy-footed, like a dumb sick brute.

Once I lost a dear classmate. I remember well how she used to mope along at my side, until one morning she could not raise her head from her pillow. At her deathbed I stood weeping, as the paleface woman sat near her moistening the dry lips. Among the folds of the bedclothes I saw the open pages of the white man's Bible. The dying Indian girl talked disconnectedly of Jesus the Christ and the paleface who was cooling her swollen hands and feet.

I grew bitter, and censured the woman for cruel neglect of our physical ills. I despised the pencils that moved automatically, and the one teaspoon which dealt out, from a large bottle, healing to a row of variously ailing Indian children. I blamed the hard-working, well-meaning, ignorant woman who was inculcating in our hearts her superstitious ideas. Though I was sullen in all my little troubles, as soon as I felt better I was ready again to smile upon the cruel woman. Within a week I was again actively testing the chains which tightly bound my individuality like a mummy for burial.

The melancholy of those black days has left so long a shadow that it darkens the path of years that have since gone by. These sad memories rise above those of smoothly grinding school days. Perhaps my Indian nature is the moaning wind which stirs them now for their present record. But, however tempestuous this is within me, it comes out as the low voice of a curiously colored seashell, which is only for those ears that are bent with compassion to hear it.

### VI. Four Strange Summers

After my first three years of school, I roamed again in the Western country through four strange summers.

During this time I seemed to hang in the heart of chaos, beyond the touch or voice of human aid. My brother, being almost ten years my senior, did not

2. Old term for tuberculosis.

quite understand my feelings. My mother had never gone inside of a school-house, and so she was not capable of comforting her daughter who could read and write. Even nature seemed to have no place for me. I was neither a wee girl nor a tall one; neither a wild Indian nor a tame one. This deplorable situation was the effect of my brief course in the East, and the unsatisfactory "teenth" in a girl's years.

It was under these trying conditions that, one bright afternoon, as I sat restless and unhappy in my mother's cabin, I caught the sound of the spirited step of my brother's pony on the road which passed by our dwelling. Soon I heard the wheels of a light buckboard, and Dawée's familiar "Ho!" to his pony. He alighted upon the bare ground in front of our house. Tying his pony to one of the projecting corner logs of the low-roofed cottage, he stepped upon the wooden doorstep.

I met him there with a hurried greeting, and, as I passed by, he looked a quiet "What?" into my eyes.

When he began talking with my mother, I slipped the rope from the pony's bridle. Seizing the reins and bracing my feet against the dashboard, I wheeled around in an instant. The pony was ever ready to try his speed. Looking backward, I saw Dawée waving his hand to me. I turned with the curve in the road and disappeared. I followed the winding road which crawled upward between the bases of little hillocks. Deep water-worn ditches ran parallel on either side. A strong wind blew against my cheeks and fluttered my sleeves. The pony reached the top of the highest hill, and began an even race on the level lands. There was nothing moving within that great circular horizon of the Dakota prairies save the tall grasses, over which the wind blew and rolled off in long, shadowy waves.

Within this vast wigwam of blue and green I rode reckless and insignificant. It satisfied my small consciousness to see the white foam fly from the pony's mouth.

Suddenly, out of the earth a coyote came forth at a swinging trot that was taking the cunning thief toward the hills and the village beyond. Upon the moment's impulse, I gave him a long chase and a wholesome fright. As I turned away to go back to the village, the wolf sank down upon his haunches for rest, for it was a hot summer day; and as I drove slowly homeward, I saw his sharp nose pointed at me, until I vanished below the margin of the hill-tops.

In a little while I came in sight of my mother's house. Dawée stood in the yard, laughing at an old warrior who was pointing his forefinger, and again waving his whole hand, toward the hills. With his blanket drawn over one shoulder, he talked and motioned excitedly. Dawée turned the old man by the shoulder and pointed me out to him.

"Oh han!" (Oh yes) the warrior muttered, and went his way. He had climbed the top of his favorite barren hill to survey the surrounding praires, when he spied my chase after the coyote. His keen eyes recognized the pony and driver. At once uneasy for my safety, he had come running to my mother's cabin to give her warning. I did not appreciate his kindly interest, for there was an unrest gnawing at my heart.

As soon as he went away, I asked Dawée about something else.

"No, my baby sister, I cannot take you with me to the party to-night," he replied. Though I was not far from fifteen, and I felt that before long I should enjoy all the privileges of my tall cousin, Dawée persisted in calling me his baby sister.

That moonlight night, I cried in my mother's presence when I heard the jolly young people pass by our cottage. They were no more young braves in blankets and eagle plumes, nor Indian maids with prettily painted cheeks. They had gone three years to school in the East, and had become civilized. The young men wore the white man's coat and trousers, with bright neckties. The girls wore tight muslin dresses; with ribbons at neck and waist. At these gatherings they talked English. I could speak English almost as well as my brother, but I was not properly dressed to be taken along. I had no hat, no ribbons, and no close-fitting gown. Since my return from school I had thrown away my shoes, and wore again the soft moccasins.

While Dawée was busily preparing to go I controlled my tears. But when I heard him bounding away on his pony, I buried my face in my arms and cried hot tears.

My mother was troubled by my unhappiness. Coming to my side, she offered me the only printed matter we had in our home. It was an Indian Bible, given her some years ago by a missionary. She tried to console me. "Here, my child, are the white man's papers. Read a little from them," she said most piously.

I took it from her hand, for her sake; but my enraged spirit felt more like burning the book, which afforded me no help, and was a perfect delusion to my mother. I did not read it, but laid it unopened on the floor, where I sat on my feet. The dim yellow light of the braided muslin burning in a small vessel of oil flickered and sizzled in the awful silent storm which followed my rejection of the Bible.

Now my wrath against the fates consumed my tears before they reached my eyes. I sat stony, with a bowed head. My mother threw a shawl over her head and shoulders, and stepped out into the night.

After an uncertain solitude, I was suddenly aroused by a loud cry piercing the night. It was my mother's voice wailing among the barren hills which held the bones of buried warriors. She called aloud for her brothers' spirits to support her in her helpless misery. My fingers grew icy cold, as I realized that my unrestrained tears had betrayed my suffering to her, and she was grieving for me.

Before she returned, though I knew she was on her way, for she had ceased her weeping, I extinguished the light, and leaned my head on the window sill.

Many schemes of running away from my surroundings hovered about in my mind. A few more moons of such a turmoil drove me away to the Eastern school. I rode on the white man's iron steed, thinking it would bring me back to my mother in a few winters, when I should be grown tall, and there would be congenial friends awaiting me.

## VII. Incurring My Mother's Displeasure

In the second journey to the East I had not come without some precautions. I had a secret interview with one of our best medicine men, and when I left his wigwam I carried securely in my sleeve a tiny bunch of magic roots. This possession assured me of friends wherever I should go. So absolutely did I believe in its charms that I wore it through all the school routine for more than a year. Then, before I lost my faith in the dead roots, I lost the little buckskin bag containing all my good luck.

At the close of this second term of three years I was the proud owner of my first diploma. The following autumn I ventured upon a college career against my mother's will.

I had written for her approval, but in her reply I found no encouragement. She called my notice to her neighbors' children, who had completed their education in three years. They had returned to their homes, and were then talking English with the frontier settlers. Her few words hinted that I had better give up my slow attempt to learn the white man's ways, and be content to roam over the prairies and find my living upon wild roots. I silenced her by deliberate disobedience.

Thus, homeless and heavy-hearted, I began anew my life among strangers.

As I hid myself in my little room in the college dormitory, away from the scornful and yet curious eyes of the students, I pined for sympathy. Often I wept in secret, wishing I had gone West, to be nourished by my mother's love, instead of remaining among a cold race whose hearts were frozen hard with prejudice.

During the fall and winter seasons I scarcely had a real friend, though by that time several of my classmates were courteous to me at a safe distance.

My mother had not yet forgiven my rudeness to her, and I had no moment for letter-writing. By daylight and lamplight, I spun with reeds and thistles, until my hands were tired from their weaving, the magic design which promised me the white man's respect.

At length, in the spring term, I entered an oratorical contest among the various classes. As the day of competition approached, it did not seem possible that the event was so near at hand, but it came. In the chapel the classes assembled together, with their invited guests. The high platform was carpeted, and gayly festooned with college colors. A bright white light illumined the room, and outlined clearly the great polished beams that arched the domed ceiling. The assembled crowds filled the air with pulsating murmurs. When the hour for speaking arrived all were hushed. But on the wall the old clock which pointed out the trying moment ticked calmly on.

One after another I saw and heard the orators. Still, I could not realize that they longed for the favorable decision of the judges as much as I did. Each contestant received a loud burst of applause, and some were cheered heartily. Too soon my turn came, and I paused a moment behind the curtains for a deep breath. After my concluding words, I heard the same applause that the others had called out.

Upon my retreating steps, I was astounded to receive from my fellow students a large bouquet of roses tied with flowing ribbons. With the lovely flowers I fled from the stage. This friendly token was a rebuke to me for the hard feelings I had borne them.

Later, the decision of the judges awarded me the first place. Then there was a mad uproar in the hall, where my classmates sang and shouted my name at the top of their lungs; and the disappointed students howled and brayed in fearfully dissonant tin trumpets. In this excitement, happy students rushed forward to offer their congratulations. And I could not conceal a smile when they wished to escort me in a procession to the students' parlor, where all were going to calm themselves. Thanking them for the kind spirit which prompted them to make such a proposition, I walked alone with the night to my own little room.

A few weeks afterward, I appeared as the college representative in another contest. This time the competition was among orators from different colleges in our state. It was held at the state capital, in one of the largest opera houses.

Here again was a strong prejudice against my people. In the evening, as the great audience filled the house, the student bodies began warring among themselves. Fortunately, I was spared witnessing any of the noisy wrangling before the contest began. The slurs against the Indian that stained the lips of our opponents were already burning like a dry fever within my breast.

But after the orations were delivered a deeper burn awaited me. There, before that vast ocean of eyes, some college rowdies threw out a large white flag, with a drawing of a most forlorn Indian girl on it. Under this they had printed in bold black letters words that ridiculed the college which was represented by a "squaw." Such worse than barbarian rudeness embittered me. While we waited for the verdict of the judges, I gleamed fiercely upon the throngs of palefaces. My teeth were hard set, as I saw the white flag still floating insolently in the air.

Then anxiously we watched the man carry toward the stage the envelope containing the final decision.

There were two prizes given, that night, and one of them was mine!

The evil spirit laughed within me when the white flag dropped out of sight, and the hands which furled it hung limp in defeat.

Leaving the crowd as quickly as possible, I was soon in my room. The rest of the night I sat in an armchair and gazed into the crackling fire. I laughed no more in triumph when thus alone. The little taste of victory did not satisfy a hunger in my heart. In my mind I saw my mother far away on the Western plains, and she was holding a charge against me.

1900

## An Indian Teacher among Indians

### I. My First Day

Though an illness left me unable to continue my college course, my pride kept me from returning to my mother. Had she known of my worn condition, she would have said the white man's papers were not worth the freedom and health I had lost by them. Such a rebuke from my mother would have been unbearable, and as I felt then it would be far too true to be comfortable.

Since the winter when I had my first dreams about red apples I had been traveling slowly toward the morning horizon. There had been no doubt about the direction in which I wished to go to spend my energies in a work for the Indian race. Thus I had written my mother briefly, saying my plan for the year was to teach in an Eastern Indian school. Sending this message to her in the West, I started at once eastward.

Thus I found myself, tired and hot, in a black veiling of car smoke, as I stood wearily on a street corner of an old-fashioned town, waiting for a car. In a few moments more I should be on the school grounds, where a new work was ready for my inexperienced hands.

Upon entering the school campus, I was surprised at the thickly clustered buildings which made it a quaint little village, much more interesting than the town itself. The large trees among the houses gave the place a cool, refreshing shade, and the grass a deeper green. Within this large court of grass and trees stood a low green pump. The queer boxlike case had a revolving handle on its side, which clanked and creaked constantly.

I made myself known, and was shown to my room,—a small, carpeted room, with ghastly walls and ceiling. The two windows, both on the same side, were curtained with heavy muslin yellowed with age. A clean white bed was in one corner of the room, and opposite it was a square pine table covered with a black woolen blanket.

Without removing my hat from my head, I seated myself in one of the two stiff-backed chairs that were placed beside the table. For several heart throbs I sat still, looking from ceiling to floor, from wall to wall, trying hard to imagine years of contentment there. Even while I was wondering if my exhausted strength would sustain me through this undertaking, I heard a heavy tread stop at my door. Opening it, I met the imposing figure of a stately gray-haired man. With a light straw hat in one hand, and the right hand extended for greeting, he smiled kindly upon me. For some reason I was awed by his wondrous height and his strong square shoulders, which I felt were a finger's length above my head.

I was always slight, and my serious illness in the early spring had made me look rather frail and languid. His quick eye measured my height and breadth. Then he looked into my face. I imagined that a visible shadow flitted across his countenance as he let my hand fall. I knew he was no other than my employer.

"Ah ha! so you are the little Indian girl who created the excitement among the college orators!" he said, more to himself than to me. I thought I heard a subtle note of disappointment in his voice. Looking in from where he stood, with one sweeping glance, he asked if I lacked anything for my room.

After he turned to go, I listened to his step until it grew faint and was lost in the distance. I was aware that my car-smoked appearance had not concealed the lines of pain on my face.

For a short moment my spirit laughed at my ill fortune, and I entertained the idea of exerting myself to make an improvement. But as I tossed my hat off a leaden weakness came over me, and I felt as if years of weariness lay like water-soaked logs upon me. I threw myself upon the bed, and, closing my eyes, forgot my good intention.

\* \* \*

### III. My Mother's Curse upon White Settlers

One black night mother and I sat alone in the dim starlight, in front of our wigwam. We were facing the river, as we talked about the shrinking limits of the village. She told me about the poverty-stricken white settlers, who lived in caves dug in the long ravines of the high hills across the river.

A whole tribe of broad-footed white beggars had rushed hither to make claims on those wild lands. Even as she was telling this I spied a small glimmering light in the bluffs.

"That is a white man's lodge where you see the burning fire," she said. Then, a short distance from it, only a little lower than the first, was another light. As I became accustomed to the night, I saw more and more twinkling lights, here and there, scattered all along the wide black margin of the river.

Still looking toward the distant firelight, my mother continued: "My daughter, beware of the paleface. It was the cruel paleface who caused the death of your sister and your uncle, my brave brother. It is this same paleface who offers in one palm the holy papers, and with the other gives a holy baptism of firewater. He is the hypocrite who reads with one eye, 'Thou shalt not kill,' and with the other gloats upon the sufferings of the Indian race." Then suddenly discovering a new fire in the bluffs, she exclaimed, "Well, well, my daughter, there is the light of another white rascal!"

She sprang to her feet, and, standing firm beside her wigwam, she sent a curse upon those who sat around the hated white man's light. Raising her right arm forcibly into line with her eye, she threw her whole might into her doubled fist as she shot it vehemently at the strangers. Long she held her outstretched fingers toward the settler's lodge, as if an invisible power passed from them to the evil at which she aimed.

## IV. Retrospection

Leaving my mother, I returned to the school in the East. As months passed over me, I slowly comprehended that the large army of white teachers in Indian schools had a larger missionary creed than I had suspected.

It was one which included self-preservation quite as much as Indian education. When I saw an opium-eater holding a position as teacher of Indians, I did not understand what good was expected, until a Christian in power replied that this pumpkin-colored creature had a feeble mother to support. An inebriate paleface sat stupid in a doctor's chair, while Indian patients carried their ailments to untimely graves, because his fair wife was dependent upon him for her daily food.

I find it hard to count that white man a teacher who tortured an ambitious Indian youth by frequently reminding the brave changeling that he was nothing but a "government pauper."

Though I burned with indignation upon discovering on every side instances no less shameful than those I have mentioned, there was no present help. Even the few rare ones who have worked nobly for my race were powerless to choose workmen like themselves. To be sure, a man was sent from the Great Father to inspect Indian schools, but what he saw was usually the students' sample work *made* for exhibition. I was nettled by this sly cunning of the workmen who hoodwinked the Indian's pale Father at Washington.

My illness, which prevented the conclusion of my college course, together with my mother's stories of the encroaching frontier settlers, left me in no mood to strain my eyes in searching for latent good in my white co-workers.

At this stage of my own evolution, I was ready to curse men of small capacity for being the dwarfs their God had made them. In the process of my education I had lost all consciousness of the nature world about me. Thus, when a hidden rage took me to the small white-walled prison which I then called my room, I unknowingly turned away from my one salvation.

Alone in my room, I sat like the petrified Indian woman of whom my mother used to tell me. I wished my heart's burdens would turn me to unfeeling stone. But alive, in my tomb, I was destitute!

For the white man's papers I had given up my faith in the Great Spirit. For these same papers I had forgotten the healing in trees and brooks. On account of my mother's simple view of life, and my lack of any, I gave her up, also. I made no friends among the race of people I loathed. Like a slender tree, I had been uprooted from my mother, nature, and God. I was shorn of my branches, which had waved in sympathy and love for home and friends. The natural coat of bark which had protected my oversensitive nature was scraped off to the very quick.

Now a cold bare pole I seemed to be, planted in a strange earth. Still, I seemed to hope a day would come when my mute aching head, reared upward to the sky, would flash a zigzag lightning across the heavens. With this dream of vent for a long-pent consciousness, I walked again amid the crowds.

At last, one weary day in the schoolroom, a new idea presented itself to me. It was a new way of solving the problem of my inner self. I liked it. Thus I resigned my position as teacher; and now I am in an Eastern city, following the long course of study I have set for myself. Now, as I look back upon the recent past, I see it from a distance, as a whole. I remember how, from morning till evening, many specimens of civilized peoples visited the Indian school. The city folks with canes and eyeglasses, the countrymen with sunburnt cheeks and clumsy feet, forgot their relative social ranks in an ignorant curiosity. Both sorts of these Christian palefaces were alike astounded at seeing the children of savage warriors so docile and industrious.

As answer to their shallow inquiries they received the students' sample work to look upon. Examining the neatly figured pages, and gazing upon the Indian girls and boys bending over their books, the white visitors walked out of the schoolhouse well satisfied: they were educating the children of the red man! They were paying a liberal fee to the government employees in whose able hands lay the small forest of Indian timber.

In this fashion many have passed idly through the Indian schools during the last decade, afterward to boast of their charity to the North American Indian. But few there are who have paused to question whether real life or long-lasting death lies beneath this semblance of civilization.

1900

## The Soft-Hearted Sioux

### I

Beside the open fire I sat within our tepee. With my red blanket wrapped tightly about my crossed legs, I was thinking of the coming season, my sixteenth winter. On either side of the wigwam were my parents. My father was whistling a tune between his teeth while polishing with his bare hand a red stone pipe he had recently carved. Almost in front of me, beyond the center fire, my old grandmother sat near the entranceway.

She turned her face toward her right and addressed most of her words to my mother. Now and then she spoke to me, but never did she allow her eyes to rest upon her daughter's husband, my father. It was only upon rare occasions that my grandmother said anything to him. Thus his ears were open and ready to catch the smallest wish she might express. Sometimes when my grandmother had been saying things which pleased him, my father used to comment upon them. At other times, when he could not approve of what was spoken, he used to work or smoke silently.

On this night my old grandmother began her talk about me. Filling the bowl of her red stone pipe with dry willow bark, she looked across at me.

"My grandchild, you are tall and are no longer a little boy." Narrowing her old eyes, she asked, "My grandchild, when are you going to bring here a handsome young woman?" I stared into the fire rather than meet her gaze. Waiting for my answer, she stooped forward and through the long stem drew a flame into the red stone pipe.

I smiled while my eyes were still fixed upon the bright fire, but I said nothing in reply. Turning to my mother, she offered her the pipe. I glanced at my grandmother. The loose buckskin sleeve fell off at her elbow and showed a wrist covered with silver bracelets. Holding up the fingers of her left hand, she named off the desirable young women of our village.

"Which one, my grandchild, which one?" she questioned.

"Hoh!" I said, pulling at my blanket in confusion. "Not yet!" Here my mother passed the pipe over the fire to my father. Then she, too, began speaking of what I should do.

"My son, be always active. Do not dislike a long hunt. Learn to provide much buffalo meat and many buckskins before you bring home a wife." Presently my father gave the pipe to my grandmother, and he took his turn in the exhortations.

"Ho, my son, I have been counting in my heart the bravest warriors of our people. There is not one of them who won his title in his sixteenth winter. My son, it is a great thing for some brave of sixteen winters to do."

Not a word had I to give in answer. I knew well the fame of my warrior father. He had earned the right of speaking such words, though even he himself was a brave only at my age. Refusing to smoke my grandmother's pipe because my heart was too much stirred by their words, and sorely troubled with a fear lest I should disappoint them, I arose to go. Drawing my blanket over my shoulders, I said, as I stepped toward the entranceway: "I go to hobble my pony. It is now late in the night."

## II

Nine winters' snows had buried deep that night when my old grandmother, together with my father and mother, designed my future with the glow of a camp fire upon it.

Yet I did not grow up the warrior, huntsman, and husband I was to have been. At the mission school I learned it was wrong to kill. Nine winters I hunted for the soft heart of Christ, and prayed for the huntsmen who chased the buffalo on the plains.

In the autumn of the tenth year I was sent back to my tribe to preach Christianity to them. With the white man's Bible in my hand, and the white man's tender heart in my breast, I returned to my own people.

Wearing a foreigner's dress, I walked, a stranger, into my father's village.

Asking my way, for I had not forgotten my native tongue, an old man led me toward the tepee where my father lay. From my old companion I learned that my father had been sick many moons. As we drew near the tepee, I heard the chanting of a medicine-man within it. At once I wished to enter in and drive from my home the sorcerer of the plains, but the old warrior checked me. "Ho, wait outside until the medicine-man leaves your father," he said. While talking he scanned me from head to feet. Then he retraced his steps toward the heart of the camping-ground.

My father's dwelling was on the outer limits of the round-faced village. With every heartthrob I grew more impatient to enter the wigwam.

While I turned the leaves of my Bible with nervous fingers, the medicine-man came forth from the dwelling and walked hurriedly away. His head and face were closely covered with the loose robe which draped his entire figure.

He was tall and large. His long strides I have never forgot. They seemed to me then the uncanny gait of eternal death. Quickly pocketing my Bible, I went into the tepee.

Upon a mat lay my father, with furrowed face and gray hair. His eyes and cheeks were sunken far into his head. His sallow skin lay thin upon his pinched nose and high cheekbones. Stooping over him, I took his fevered hand. "How, Ate?"[1] I greeted him. A light flashed from his listless eyes and his dried lips parted. "My son!" he murmured, in a feeble voice. Then again the wave of joy and recognition receded. He closed his eyes, and his hand dropped from my open palm to the ground.

Looking about, I saw an old woman sitting with bowed head. Shaking hands with her, I recognized my mother. I sat down between my father and mother as I used to do, but I did not feel at home. The place where my old grandmother used to sit was now unoccupied. With my mother I bowed my head. Alike our throats were choked and tears were streaming from our eyes; but far apart in spirit our ideas and faiths separated us. My grief was for the soul unsaved; and I thought my mother wept to see a brave man's body broken by sickness.

Useless was my attempt to change the faith in the medicine-man to that abstract power named God. Then one day I became righteously mad with anger that the medicine-man should thus ensnare my father's soul. And when he came to chant his sacred songs I pointed toward the door and bade him go! The man's eyes glared upon me for an instant. Slowly gathering his robe about him, he turned his back upon the sick man and stepped out of our wigwam. "Ha, ha, ha! my son, I cannot live without the medicine-man!" I heard my father cry when the sacred man was gone.

### III

On a bright day, when the winged seeds of the prairie-grass were flying hither and thither, I walked solemnly toward the centre of the camping-ground. My heart beat hard and irregularly at my side. Tighter I grasped the sacred book I carried under my arm. Now was the beginning of life's work.

---

1. Hello, Father.

Though I knew it would be hard, I did not once feel that failure was to be my reward. As I stepped unevenly on the rolling ground, I thought of the warriors soon to wash off their war-paints and follow me.

At length I reached the place where the people had assembled to hear me preach. In a large circle men and women sat upon the dry red grass. Within the ring I stood, with the white man's Bible in my hand. I tried to tell them of the soft heart of Christ.

In silence the vast circle of bareheaded warriors sat under an afternoon sun. At last, wiping the wet from my brow, I took my place in the ring. The hush of the assembly filled me with great hope.

I was turning my thoughts upward to the sky in gratitude, when a stir called me to earth again.

A tall, strong man arose. His loose robe hung in folds over his right shoulder. A pair of snapping black eyes fastened themselves like the poisonous fangs of a serpent upon me. He was the medicine-man. A tremor played about my heart and a chill cooled the fire in my veins.

Scornfully he pointed a long forefinger in my direction and asked: "What loyal son is he who, returning to his father's people, wears a foreigner's dress?" He paused a moment, and then continued: "The dress of that foreigner of whom a story says he bound a native of our land, and heaping dry sticks around him, kindled a fire at his feet!" Waving his hand toward me, he exclaimed, "Here is the traitor to his people!"

I was helpless. Before the eyes of the crowd the cunning magician turned my honest heart into a vile nest of treachery. Alas! the people frowned as they looked upon me.

"Listen!" he went on. "Which one of you who have eyed the young man can see through his bosom and warn the people of the nest of young snakes hatching there? Whose ear was so acute that he caught the hissing of snakes whenever the young man opened his mouth? This one has not only proven false to you, but even to the Great Spirit who made him. He is a fool! Why do you sit here giving ear to a foolish man who could not defend his people because he fears to kill, who could not bring venison to renew the life of his sick father? With his prayers, let him drive away the enemy! With his soft heart, let him keep off starvation! We shall go elsewhere to dwell upon an untainted ground."

With this he disbanded the people. When the sun lowered in the west and the winds were quiet, the village of cone-shaped tepees was gone. The medicine-man had won the hearts of the people.

Only my father's dwelling was left to mark the fighting-ground.

## IV

From a long night at my father's bedside I came out to look upon the morning. The yellow sun hung equally between the snow-covered land and the cloudless blue sky. The light of the new day was cold. The strong breath of winter crusted the snow and fitted crystal shells over the rivers and lakes. As I stood in front of the tepee, thinking of the vast prairies which separated us from our tribe, and wondering if the high sky likewise separated the soft-hearted Son of God from us, the icy blast from the

North blew through my hair and skull. My neglected hair had grown long and fell upon my neck.

My father had not risen from his bed since the day the medicine-man led the people away. Though I read from the Bible and prayed beside him upon my knees, my father would not listen. Yet I believed my prayers were not unheeded in heaven.

"Ha, ha, ha! my son," my father groaned upon the first snowfall. "My son, our food is gone. There is no one to bring me meat! My son, your soft heart has unfitted you for everything!" Then covering his face with the buffalo-robe, he said no more. Now while I stood out in that cold winter morning, I was starving. For two days I had not seen any food. But my own cold and hunger did not harass my soul as did the whining cry of the sick old man.

Stepping again into the tepee, I untied my snow-shoes, which were fastened to the tent-poles.

My poor mother, watching by the sick one, and faithfully heaping wood upon the centre fire, spoke to me:

"My son, do not fail again to bring your father meat, or he will starve to death."

"How, Ina,"[2] I answered, sorrowfully. From the tepee I started forth again to hunt food for my aged parents. All day I tracked the white level lands in vain. Nowhere, nowhere were there any other footprints but my own! In the evening of this third fast-day I came back without meat. Only a bundle of sticks for the fire I brought on my back. Dropping the wood outside, I lifted the door-flap and set one foot within the tepee.

There I grew dizzy and numb. My eyes swam in tears. Before me lay my old gray-haired father sobbing like a child. In his horny hands he clutched the buffalo-robe, and with his teeth he was gnawing off the edges. Chewing the dry stiff hair and buffalo-skin, my father's eyes sought my hands. Upon seeing them empty, he cried out:

"My son, your soft heart will let me starve before you bring me meat! Two hills eastward stand a herd of cattle. Yet you will see me die before you bring me food!"

Leaving my mother lying with covered head upon her mat, I rushed out into the night.

With a strange warmth in my heart and swiftness in my feet, I climbed over the first hill, and soon the second one. The moonlight upon the white country showed me a clear path to the white man's cattle. With my hand upon the knife in my belt, I leaned heavily against the fence while counting the herd.

Twenty in all I numbered. From among them I chose the best-fattened creature. Leaping over the fence, I plunged my knife into it.

My long knife was sharp, and my hands, no more fearful and slow, slashed off choice chunks of warm flesh. Bending under the meat I had taken for my starving father, I hurried across the prairie.

Toward home I fairly ran with the life-giving food I carried upon my back. Hardly had I climbed the second hill when I heard sounds coming after me. Faster and faster I ran with my load for my father, but the sounds were gaining upon me. I heard the clicking of snowshoes and the squeaking of the leather straps at my heels; yet I did not turn to see what pursued me, for I

---

2. Hello, Mother.

was intent upon reaching my father. Suddenly like thunder an angry voice shouted curses and threats into my ear! A rough hand wrenched my shoulder and took the meat from me! I stopped struggling to run. A deafening whir filled my head. The moon and stars began to move. Now the white prairie was sky, and the stars lay under my feet. Now again they were turning. At last the starry blue rose up into place. The noise in my ears was still. A great quiet filled the air. In my hand I found my long knife dripping with blood. At my feet a man's figure lay prone in blood-red snow. The horrible scene about me seemed a trick of my senses, for I could not understand it was real. Looking long upon the blood-stained snow, the load of meat for my starving father reached my recognition at last. Quickly I tossed it over my shoulder and started again homeward.

Tired and haunted I reached the door of the wigwam. Carrying the food before me, I entered with it into the tepee.

"Father, here is food!" I cried, as I dropped the meat near my mother. No answer came. Turning about, I beheld my gray-haired father dead! I saw by the unsteady firelight an old gray-haired skeleton lying rigid and stiff.

Out into the open I started, but the snow at my feet became bloody.

## V

On the day after my father's death, having led my mother to the camp of the medicine-man, I gave myself up to those who were searching for the murderer of the paleface.

They bound me hand and foot. Here in this cell I was placed four days ago.

The shrieking winter winds have followed me hither. Rattling the bars, they howl unceasingly: "Your soft heart! your soft heart will see me die before you bring me food!" Hark! something is clanking the chain on the door. It is being opened. From the dark night without a black figure crosses the threshold. It is the guard. He comes to warn me of my fate. He tells me that tomorrow I must die. In his stern face I laugh aloud. I do not fear death.

Yet I wonder who shall come to welcome me in the realm of strange sight. Will the loving Jesus grant me pardon and give my soul a soothing sleep? or will my warrior father greet me and receive me as his son? Will my spirit fly upward to a happy heaven? or shall I sink into the bottomless pit, an outcast from a God of infinite love?

Soon, soon I shall know, for now I see the east is growing red. My heart is strong. My face is calm. My eyes are dry and eager for new scenes. My hands hang quietly at my side. Serene and brave, my soul awaits the men to perch me on the gallows for another flight. I go.

1901

## Why I Am a Pagan[1]

When the spirit swells my breast I love to roam leisurely among the green hills; or sometimes, sitting on the brink of the murmuring Missouri, I marvel at the great blue overhead. With half closed eyes I watch the huge cloud shadows in their noiseless play upon the high bluffs opposite me, while into my ear ripple the sweet, soft cadences of the river's song. Folded hands lie in my lap, for the time forgot. My heart and I lie small upon the earth like a grain of throbbing sand. Drifting clouds and tinkling waters, together with the warmth of a genial summer day, bespeak with eloquence the loving Mystery round about us. During the idle while I sat upon the sunny river brink, I grew somewhat, though my response be not so clearly manifest as in the green grass fringing the edge of the high bluff back of me.

At length retracing the uncertain footpath scaling the precipitous embankment, I seek the level lands where grew the wild prairie flowers. And they, the lovely little folk, soothe my soul with their perfumed breath.

Their quaint round faces of varied hue convince the heart which leaps with glad surprise that they, too, are living symbols of omnipotent thought. With a child's eager eye I drink in the myriad star shapes wrought in luxuriant color upon the green. Beautiful is the spiritual essence they embody.

I leave them nodding in the breeze, but take along with me their impress upon my heart. I pause to rest me upon a rock embedded on the side of a foothill facing the low river bottom. Here the Stone-Boy, of whom the American aborigine tells, frolics about, shooting his baby arrows and shouting aloud with glee at the tiny shafts of lightning that flash from the flying arrowbeaks. What an ideal warrior he became, baffling the siege of the pests of all the land till he triumphed over their united attack. And here he lay,—Inyan[2] our great-great-grandfather, older than the hill he rested on, older than the race of men who love to tell of his wonderful career.

Interwoven with the thread of this Indian legend of the rock, I fain would trace a subtle knowledge of the native folk which enabled them to recognize a kinship to any and all parts of this vast universe. By the leading of an ancient trail I move toward the Indian village.

With the strong, happy sense that both great and small are so surely enfolded in His magnitude that, without a miss, each has his allotted individual ground of opportunities, I am buoyant with good nature.

Yellow Breast, swaying upon the slender stem of a wild sunflower, warbles a sweet assurance of this as I pass near by. Breaking off the clear crystal song, he turns his wee head from side to side eyeing me wisely as slowly I plod with moccasined feet. Then again he yields himself to his song of joy. Flit, flit hither and yon, he fills the summer sky with his swift, sweet melody. And truly does it seem his vigorous freedom lies more in his little spirit than in his wing.

With these thoughts I reach the log cabin whither I am strongly drawn by the tie of a child to an aged mother. Out bounds my four-footed friend to meet me, frisking about my path with unmistakable delight. Chän is a black shaggy dog, "a thorough bred little mongrel" of whom I am very fond. Chän

---

1. First appeared in the *Atlantic Monthly* in December 1902.

2. Stone, or Stone-Boy.

seems to understand many words in Sioux, and will go to her mat even when I whisper the word, though generally I think she is guided by the tone of the voice. Often she tries to imitate the sliding inflection and long drawn out voice to the amusement of our guests, but her articulation is quite beyond my ear. In both my hands I hold her shaggy head and gaze into her large brown eyes. At once the dilated pupils contract into tiny black dots, as if the roguish spirit within would evade my questioning.

Finally resuming the chair at my desk I feel in keen sympathy with my fellow creatures, for I seem to see clearly again that all are akin.

The racial lines, which once were bitterly real, now serve nothing more than marking out a living mosaic of human beings. And even here men of same color are like the ivory keys of one instrument where each resembles all the rest, yet varies from them in pitch and quality of voice. And those creatures who are for a time mere echoes of another's note are not unlike the fable of the thin sick man whose distorted shadow, dressed like a real creature, came to the old master to make him follow as a shadow. Thus with a compassion for all echoes in human guise, I greet the solemn-faced "native preacher" whom I find awaiting me. I listen with respect for God's creature, though he mouth most strangely the jangling phrases of a bigoted creed.

As our tribe is one large family, where every person is related to all the others, he addressed me:—

"Cousin, I came from the morning church service to talk with you."

"Yes?" I said interrogatively, as he paused for some word from me.

Shifting uneasily about in the straight-backed chair he sat upon, he began: "Every holy day (Sunday) I look about our little God's house, and not seeing you there, I am disappointed. This is why I come to-day. Cousin, as I watch you from afar, I see no unbecoming behavior and hear only good reports of you, which all the more burns me with the wish that you were a church member. Cousin, I was taught long years ago by kind missionaries to read the holy book. These godly men taught me also the folly of our old beliefs.

"There is one God who gives reward or punishment to the race of dead men. In the upper region the Christian dead are gathered in unceasing song and prayer. In the deep pit below, the sinful ones dance in torturing flames.

"Think upon these things, my cousin, and choose now to avoid the afterdoom of hell fire!" Then followed a long silence in which he clasped tighter and unclasped again his interlocked fingers.

Like instantaneous lightning flashes came pictures of my own mother's making, for she, too, is now a follower of the new superstition.

"Knocking out the chinking of our log cabin, some evil hand thrust in a burning taper of braided dry grass, but failed of his intent, for the fire died out and the half burned brand fell inward to the floor. Directly above it, on a shelf, lay the holy book. This is what we found after our return from a several days' visit. Surely some great power is hid in the sacred book!"

Brushing away from my eyes many like pictures, I offered midday meal to the converted Indian sitting wordless and with downcast face. No sooner had he risen from the table with "Cousin, I have relished it," than the church bell rang.

Thither he hurried forth with his afternoon sermon. I watched him as he hastened along, his eyes bent fast upon the dusty road till he disappeared at the end of a quarter of a mile.

The little incident recalled to mind the copy of a missionary paper brought to my notice a few days ago, in which a "Christian" pugilist commented upon a recent article of mine, grossly perverting the spirit of my pen. Still I would not forget that the pale-faced missionary and the hoodooed aborigine are both God's creatures, though small indeed their own conceptions of Infinite Love. A wee child toddling in a wonder world, I prefer to their dogma my excursions into the natural gardens where the voice of the Great Spirit is heard in the twittering of birds, the rippling of mighty waters, and the sweet breathing of flowers. If this is Paganism, then at present, at least, I am a Pagan.

1902

# CORRIDOS

The *corrido*, a Mexican ballad or folk song, is an important literary genre of the south-western border region of the United States. From the mid-nineteenth century on, the displacement of Mexican people from their homes and land in what is now California and the southwestern United States led to border conflict, which in turn inspired bor-der *corridos*. Written and sung by those living in the former Mexican province of Nuevo Santander (currently Texas, New Mexico, Chihuahua, Coahuila, and Tamauli-pas), *corridos* articulate experiences of cultural conflict in the borderlands. Many nineteenth-century *corridos* are still sung and recorded, and Mexicans and Mexican Americans continue to compose new *corridos*. While *corridos* were sometimes printed and distributed as broadsides, their primary mode of circulation was and is through performance.

The *corrido* is a narrative ballad sung to a simple tune in fast waltz time, tradition-ally by Mexican and Mexican American men. It derives from the Andalusian *romance corrido*, a traditional Spanish ballad form with a rapidly sung narrative without refrains. (*Corridor* means "to run.") The *corrido* is usually 36 lines (6 stanzas of 6 lines each or 9 stanzas of 4 lines each), with 7 to 10 syllables per line and lines often repeated. Frequently composed within a short musical range of less than an octave, *corridos* enable the performer to sing at high volume. Singers are often accompanied by guitar or the *bajo sexto*, a twelve-string guitar popular in Texas and New Mexico. The *corrido* typically relates a story or event of local or national interest—a hero's deeds, a highwayman's exploits, a barroom shooting, or a natural disaster—in the lan-guage of the common people. Besides its traditional music, versification, and subject matter, the *corrido* uses certain formal ballad conventions, including the call of the *corridista*, or balladeer, to the public; identification of the place, time, and name of the hero of the ballad; arguments for the hero's importance; a message; a farewell to the hero; and the farewell of the *corridista*.

Border heroes such as Ignacio and Jacinto Treviño, famous for ambushing a group of Texas Rangers near San Benito, Texas, in 1910, are depicted in *corridos* defending their rights against the newcomer Americans. In early *corridos* the con-flict involves nonviolent professional rivalries between Mexican and American cowboys; later *corridos* develop a larger-than-life Mexican hero who single-handedly defies a cowardly gang of Anglo-American lawmen. In the early twentieth century, the *corrido* gave rise to a related form, the *canción*, a song with more lyrical qualities, usually about love. The *canción-corrido* hybrid emerged as a powerful cultural expression in the Hispanic Southwest during the mid-twentieth century. Around World War II a new kind of *corrido* emerged, but again featuring victims of Anglo oppression. This shift coincides with fundamental changes in Mexican American society, as Mexican American culture became more urban, modern, and diversified.

As records of injustices, *corridos* portray heroes driven to crime as a last resort or out of an honorable desire to avenge wrongs that have been perpetrated against them. Whatever their fate, the subjects of *corridos* are always celebrated as heroes because they defend their rights courageously and skillfully. Translating political ideals of protest and resistance into a popular form, *corridos* are powerful expressions of Mexican and Mexican American cultural pride.

# El Corrido de Gregorio Cortez[1]

In the county of El Carmen[2]
A great misfortune befell;
The Major Sheriff[3] is dead;
Who killed him no one can tell.

At two in the afternoon,          5
In half an hour or less,
They knew that the man who
    killed him
Had been Gregorio Cortez.

They let loose the bloodhound
    dogs;
They followed him from afar.      10
But trying to catch Cortez
Was like following a star.

All the rangers[4] of the county
Were flying, they rode so hard;
What they wanted was to get       15
The thousand-dollar reward.

And in the county of Kiansis
They cornered him after all;[5]
Though they were more than
    three hundred
He leaped out of their corral.    20

Then the Major Sheriff said,
As if he was going to cry,
"Cortez, hand over your weapons;
We want to take you alive."

Then said Gregorio Cortez,        25
And his voice was like a bell,
"You will never get my weapons
Till you put me in a cell."

Then said Gregorio Cortez,
With his pistol in his hand,      30
"Ah, so many mounted Rangers
Just to take one Mexican!"

1. There are many versions of various corridos, and one of the most famous, "Gregorio Cortez," composed in 1901, exists in two widely quoted versions. The first and shorter version is called "El Corrido de Gregorio Cortez" and was included by Américo Paredes in his novel about Cortez, *"With His Pistol in His Hand": A Border Ballad and Its Hero* (1958), from which the first text here is taken. A controversial Mexican American historical figure, Cortez is considered a folk hero by some and a cattle-thieving murderer by others. Cortez was confronted by Texas lawmen for allegedly stealing cattle, and a gunfight ensued. A Texas sheriff and Cortez's brother were both killed. Cortez evaded the Texas Rangers for ten days before being betrayed by a friend, captured, tried, and convicted for murder in 1904. He was pardoned by Texas governor Oscar B. Colquitt in 1913 and went south to join the Mexican Revolution. He died on February 28, 1916.
2. Possibly refers to a Catholic parish in Bexar County, Texas. However, the shootings of Rómaldo Cortez and Sheriff Morris actually took place in Kenedy, Texas, about sixty miles southeast of San Antonio.
3. Karnes County (Texas) sheriff W. T. "Brack" Morris, whom Cortez allegedly shot and killed.
4. Texas Rangers.
5. Cortez was captured in Webb County, Texas; there is no "Kiansis County."

## Gregorio Cortez[1]

En el con-da-do de El Car-menmi-ren lo que ha su-ce-di-do, murió el Che-ri-fe Ma-yor, que-dan-do Ro-mán he-ri-do.

En el condado de El Carmen
miren lo que ha sucedido,
murió el Cherife Mayor,
quedando Román herido.

En el condado de El Carmen   5
tal desgracia sucedió,
murió el Cherife Mayor,
no saben quién lo mató.

Se anduvieron informando
como media hora después,   10
supieron que el malhechor
era Gregorio Cortez.

Ya insortaron a Cortez
por toditito el estado,
que vivo o muerto se aprehenda   15
porque a varios ha matado.

Decía Gregorio Cortez
con su pistola en la mano:
—No siento haberlo matado,
lo que siento es a mi hermano.—   20

Decía Gregorio Cortez
con su alma muy encendida:
—No siento haberlo matado,
la defensa es permitida.—

Venían los americanos   25
más blancos que una amapola,
de miedo que le tenían
a Cortez con su pistola.

Decían los americanos,
decían con timidez:   30
—Vamos a seguir la huella
que el malhechor es Cortez.—

Soltaron los perros jaunes
pa' que siguieran la huella,
pero alcanzar a Cortez   35
era seguir a una estrella.

Tiró con rumbo a Gonzales
sin ninguna timidez:
—Síganme, rinches cobardes,
yo soy Gregorio Cortez.—   40

Se fue de Belmont al rancho,
lo alcanzaron a rodear,
poquitos más de trescientos,
y allí les brincó el corral.

Cuando les brincó el corral,   45
según lo que aquí se dice,
se agarraron a balazos
y les mató otro cherife.

Decía Gregorio Cortez
con su pistola en la mano:   50
—No corran, rinches cobardes,
con un solo mexicano.—

Salió Gregorio Cortez,
salió con rumbo a Laredo,
no lo quisieron seguir   55
porque le tuvieron miedo.

---

1. This longer version of the *corrido* is published as "Gregorio Cortez" in *A Texas-Mexican Cancionero: Folksongs of the Lower Border* (1976), from which this text is taken. A translation follows.

Decía Gregorio Cortez:
—¿Pa' qué se valen de planes?
No me pueden agarrar
ni con esos perros jaunes.                          60

Decían los americanos:
—Si lo alcanzamos ¿qué hacemos?
Si le entramos por derecho
muy poquitos volveremos.—

Allá por El Encinal,                                65
según lo que aquí se dice,
le formaron un corral
y les mató otro cherife.

Decía Gregorio Cortez
echando muchos balazos:                             70
—Me he escapado de aguaceros,
contimás de nublinazos.—

Ya se encontró a un mexicano,
le dice con altivez:
—Platícame qué hay de nuevo,                        75
yo soy Gregorio Cortez.

—Dicen que por culpa mía
han matado mucha gente,
pues ya me voy a entregar
porque eso no es conveniente.—                      80

Cortez le dice a Jesús:
—Ora sí lo vas a ver,
anda diles a los rinches
que me vengan a aprehender.—

Venían todos los rinches,                           85
venían que hasta volaban,
porque se iban a ganar
diez mil pesos que les daban.

Cuando rodearon la casa
Cortez se les presentó:                             90
—Por la buena sí me llevan
porque dc otro modo no.—

Decía el Cherife Mayor
como queriendo llorar:
—Cortez, entrega tus armas,                         95
no te vamos a matar.—

Decía Gregorio Cortez,
les gritaba en alta voz:
—Mis armas no las entrego
hasta estar en calaboz'—.                           100

Decía Gregorio Cortez,
decía en su voz divina:
—Mis armas no las entrego
hasta estar en bartolina.—

Ya agarraron a Cortez,                              105
ya terminó la cuestión,
la pobre de su familia
lo lleva en el corazón.

Ya con ésta me despido
a la sombra de un ciprés,                           110
aquí se acaba el corrido
de don Gregorio Cortez.

### Gregorio Cortez

In the county of El Carmen, look what has happened;
the Major Sheriff is dead, leaving Román[2] badly wounded.

In the county of El Carmen such a tragedy took place:
the Major Sheriff is dead; no one knows who killed him.

They went around asking questions about half an hour afterward;      5
they found out that the wrongdoer had been Gregorio Cortez.

---

2. Cortez's father. It was Cortez's brother, Rómaldo, not his father, who was killed in the exchange with Morris.

Now they have outlawed Cortez throughout the whole of the state;
let him be taken, dead or alive, for he has killed several men.

Then said Gregorio Cortez, with his pistol in his hand,
"I don't regret having killed him; what I regret is my brother's death."          10

Then said Gregorio Cortez, with his soul aflame,
"I don't regret having killed him; self-defense is permitted."

The Americans were coming; they were whiter than a poppy
from the fear that they had of Cortez and his pistol.

Then the Americans said, and they said it fearfully,                              15
"Come, let us follow the trail, for the wrongdoer is Cortez."

They let loose the bloodhounds so they could follow the trail,
but trying to overtake Cortez was like following a star.

He struck out for Gonzales[3] without showing any fear:
"Follow me, cowardly *rinches*;[4] I am Gregorio Cortez."                          20

From Belmont[5] he went to the ranch, where they succeeded in
        surrounding him,
quite a few more than three hundred, but he jumped out of their corral.

When he jumped out of their corral, according to what is said here,
they got into a gunfight, and he killed them another sheriff.

Then said Gregorio Cortez, with his pistol in his hand,                           25
"Don't run, you cowardly *rinches*, from a single Mexican."

Gregorio Cortez went out, he went out toward Laredo;[6]
they would not follow him because they were afraid of him.

Then said Gregorio Cortez, "What is the use of your scheming?
You cannot catch me, even with those bloodhounds."                                30

Then said the Americans, "If we catch up with him, what shall we do?
If we fight him man to man, very few of us will return."

Way over near El Encinal,[7] according to what is said here,
they made him a corral, and he killed them another sheriff.

Then said Gregorio Cortez, shooting out a lot of bullets,                         35
"I have weathered thunderstorms; this little mist doesn't bother me."

Now he has met a Mexican; he says to him haughtily,
"Tell me the news; I am Gregorio Cortez.

---

3. Texas town east of San Antonio.
4. Mexican pejorative for Texas Rangers.
5. Small Texas community west of Gonzales.

6. South Texas border city across the Río Grande
from Nuevo Laredo in Mexico.
7. Small Texas town forty miles north of Laredo.

"They say that because of me many people have been killed;
so now I will surrender, because such things are not right."                    40

Cortez says to Jesús, "At last you are going to see it;
go and tell the *rinches* that they can come and arrest me."[8]

All the *rinches* were coming, so fast that they almost flew,
because they were going to get the ten thousand dollars that were offered.

When they surrounded the house, Cortez appeared before them:               45
"You will take me if I'm willing but not any other way."

Then said the Major Sheriff, as if he was going to cry,
"Cortez, hand over your weapons; we do not want to kill you."

Then said Gregorio Cortez, shouting to them in a loud voice,
"I won't surrender my weapons until I am in a cell."                        50

Then said Gregorio Cortez, speaking in his godlike voice,
"I won't surrender my weapons until I'm inside a jail."

Now they have taken Cortez, and now the matter is ended;
his poor family are keeping him in their hearts.

Now with this I say farewell in the shade of a cypress;                    55
this is the end of the ballad of Don Gregorio Cortez.[9]

## Jacinto Treviño[1]

Ya con ésta van tres veces
que se ha visto lo bonito,
la primera fue en Macalen,
en Brónsvil y en San Benito.

Y en la cantina de Bekar                    5
se agarraron a balazos,
por dondequiera saltaban
botellas hechas pedazos.

8. Jesús Gonzales, who betrayed Cortez by turning
him over to the Texas Rangers.
9. Don: Spanish title equivalent to "sir," usually
reserved for heads of families.

1. Composed about 1911, "Jacinto Treviño" is
included in *A Texas-Mexican Cancionero: Folksongs of the Lower Border* (1976), the source of the
present text. A translation follows.

Esa cantina de Bekar
al momento quedó sola,                          10
nomás Jacinto Treviño
de carabina y pistola.

—Entrenle, rinches cobardes,
que el pleito no es con un niño,
querían conocer su padre,                       15
¡yo soy Jacinto Treviño!

—Entrenle, rinches cobardes,
validos de la ocasión,
no van a comer pan blanco
con tajadas de jamón.—                          20

Decía el Rinche Mayor;
como era un americano:
—¡Ah, qué Jacinto tan hombre,
no niega el ser mexicano!—

Decía Jacinto Treviño                           25
que se moría de la risa:
—A mí me hacen los ojales,
los puños de la camisa.—

Decía Jacinto Treviño,
abrochándose un zapato:                         30

—Aquí traigo más cartuchos
pa' divertirnos un rato.—

Decía Jacinto Treviño,
con su pistola en la mano:
—No corran, rinches cobardes,                   35
con un solo mexicano.—

Decía Jacinto Treviño:
—Yo ya me vo' a retirar,
me voy para Río Grande
y allá los voy a esperar.                        40

Decía Jacinto Treviño,
al bajar una bajada:
—¡Ay, qué rinches tan cobardes,
que no me haigan hecho nada!—

Decía Jacinto Treviño,                           45
andando en Nuevo Laredo:
—Yo soy Jacinto Treviño,
nacido en Montemorelos.—

Ya con ésta me despido
aquí a presencia de todos,                      50
yo soy Jacinto Treviño,
vecino de Matamoros.

### Jacinto Treviño

With this it will be three times that remarkable things have happened;
the first time was in McAllen, then in Brownsville and San Benito.[2]

They had a shoot-out at Baker's saloon;
broken bottles were popping all over the place.

Baker's saloon was immediately deserted;                                 5
only Jacinto Treviño remained, with his rifle and his pistol.

"Come on, you cowardly *rinches*,[3] you're not playing games with a child.
You wanted to meet your father? I am Jacinto Treviño!

"Come on, you cowardly *rinches*, you always like to take the advantage;
this is not like eating white bread with slices of ham."                 10

The chief of the *rinches* said, even though he was an American,
"Ah, what a brave man is Jacinto; you can see he is a Mexican!"

---

2. McAllen: Texas border town sixty miles northwest of the border town of Brownsville. San Benito: small Texas town five miles south of Harlingen
and eleven miles north of Brownsville.
3. Mexican pejorative for Texas Rangers.

Then said Jacinto Treviño, who was dying of laughter,
"All you're good for is to make the buttonholes and the cuffs on my shirt."

Then said Jacinto Treviño, as he was tying his shoe, 15
"I have more cartridges here, so we can amuse ourselves a while."

Then said Jacinto Treviño, with his pistol in his hand,
"Don't run, you cowardly *rinches*, from a single Mexican."

Then said Jacinto Treviño, "I am going to retire.
I'm going to Rio Grande City,[4] and I will wait for you there." 20

Then said Jacinto Treviño, as he came down an incline,
"Ah, what a cowardly bunch of *rinches*; they didn't do anything to me!"

Then said Jacinto Treviño, when he was in Nuevo Laredo,
"I am Jacinto Treviño, born in Montemorelos."[5]

Now with this I say farewell, here in everybody's presence; 25
I am Jacinto Treviño, a citizen of Matamoros.

## Tiempos Amargos[1]

¡Ay, qué contentos hemos llegado
a estos tiempos que ahora se ven!
Nosotros semos los agraristas,
varios amigos que ni lo creen.

Ya no es el tiempo del
    porfirista, 5
que antes lloraban por el patrón,
que lo encontraban, le dan la
    mano,
y le abrochaban el pantalón.

Y si algún día el mayordomo
se desgustaba con algún peón 10
era porque otro andaba mas cerca
a los remaches del pantalón.

Oh, how pleasant it is to live
during these times of today.
We are the *agraristas*,[2]
though some people still doubt it.

These are no longer the times of
    Porfirio (Díaz),[3] 5
when they cried for the master
when they'd meet him, they'd
    shake his hand,
and button his pants.

If one day the steward
became angry with a worker 10
it was because there was another one
closer to the snaps of his pants.

4. South Texas border town about ninety miles northwest of Brownsville.
5. Nuevo Laredo: Mexican border town across the Río Grande from Laredo, Texas. Montemorelos: town in the Mexican border state of Nuevo León.
1. "Tiempos Amargos" (Bitter Times), unknown composer; included in *The Mexican Revolution: Corridos About the Heroes and Events 1910–1920 and Beyond!* CD 7041–7044, Arhoolie Records, www.arhoolie.com.
2. Agricultural laborers who would organize under Emiliano Zapata as "Zapatistas" and oppose Díaz's capitalist government during the Mexican Revolution.
3. Dictator of Mexico from 1876 to 1911. Opposition grew in the last decade of Díaz's rule, and a revolution led by Francisco I. Madero (1873–1913) forced Diaz to flee the country.

| | | | |
|---|---|---|---|
| Y el que tenía hijas bonitas | | If someone had pretty daughters | |
| ahi se la daban de velador, | | he'd get a job as a night watchman, | |
| o se granjeaban muy buena | | or else he'd land a good job, | |
|     chamba | 15 | at least as a payroll clerk. | 15 |
| o cuando menos de rayador. | | | |

| | | | |
|---|---|---|---|
| El que tenía mujer bonita | | If someone had a pretty wife | |
| no lo dejaban ni descansar, | | they didn't let him rest, | |
| los levantaban muy de mañana | | they'd get them up very early | |
| como a los bueyes a trabajar. | 20 | to work just like the oxen. | 20 |

| | | |
|---|---|---|
| Ya me despido de mis amigos | I bid you farewell, friends, | |
| ahi me dispensan la indiscreción, | you'll forgive my frankness. | |
| tiempos amargos del porfirista | I've sung about the bitter times | |
| que aquí les canto en mi canción. | under the Porfiristas.[4] | |

4. Political supporters of Porfirio Díaz.

---

# GHOST DANCE SONGS

The songs that various Native American peoples composed to accompany the dances of the Ghost Dance religion resembled the songs that had traditionally accompanied "round dances," communal dances in which, as the following drawings from the Comanches and Sioux indicate, the dancers held hands and moved in a loose circle. Ghost Dance songs would originate when a dancer fell into a trancelike state and upon regaining consciousness expressed in a song what he or she had seen in the spirit world. As each dance would almost surely give rise to new songs, each tribe's repertoire was constantly changing—although some particularly appealing songs were repeated again and again, and in some cases made their way to other Indian nations.

Ghost Dance songs embodied what each people took to be the teachings of the Indian Messiah, Wovoka, but the songs also made mention of aspects of the daily lives and traditional customs and ceremonies of the various Native tribes. Thus references to important berries; to gambling wheels and gambling sticks involved in various games; to the sacred pipe, the crow, or the eagle; and to specific activities of the men or the women all appear in the Ghost Dance songs.

James Mooney (1861–1921) of the Bureau of American Ethnology studied the Ghost Dance religion and, in 1896, published a massive work titled *The Ghost Dance Religion and the Sioux Outbreak of 1890*. Mooney not only interviewed Wovoka but conducted extensive interviews with people from many Indian tribes who had participated in the Ghost Dance. An accomplished ethnographic observer familiar with Sioux languages (he had published *Siouan Tribes of the East* in 1894), Mooney is a careful observer and his commentary is richly descriptive.

Printed here are ghost dance songs from the Arapahos and Sioux. We have provided examples of musical notation as a reminder that these were songs sung as a circle of dancers moved slowly hand in hand. All the selections printed here are from James Mooney's *The Ghost Dance Religion and the Sioux Outbreak of 1890*, edited and abridged by Anthony F. C. Wallace (1965).

# Songs of the Arapaho[1]

## [FATHER, HAVE PITY ON ME][2]

A · ni'·qu ne'·cha·wu'·na·ni,   a · ni'·qu ne'·cha·wu'·na·ni';

a · wa'·wa bi'·qă·na'·ka·ye'·na,   a · wa'·wa bi'·qă·na'·ka·ye'·na;

i · ya·hu'h ni'·bi·thi'·ti,   i · ya·hu'h ni'·bi·thi'·ti.

### TRANSLATION

Father, have pity on me,
Father, have pity on me;
I am crying for thirst,
I am crying for thirst;
All is gone—I have nothing to eat,
All is gone—I have nothing to eat.

## [WHEN I MET HIM APPROACHING]

He'! Nä·ne'th bi'·shi·qa'·wä,   He'! Nä·ne'th bi'·shi·qa'·wä,   Nä' · ni · sa'·na,

nä' · ni · sa'·na,   Nä' · i · na'·ha't·dä'·bä'·naq, Nä' · i · na'·ha't·dä' · bä'·naq.

### TRANSLATION

*He!* When I met him approaching—
*He!* When I met him approaching—
My children, my children—
I then saw the multitude plainly,
I then saw the multitude plainly.

1. The Arapahos are an Algonquian-speaking people whose northern branch occupied the present state of Wyoming and whose southern branch lived in present-day Arkansas. The Arapahos share many of the traits of the Plains Indians and were particularly close to the Cheyennes. Unlike the Cheyennes, however, the Arapahos maintained generally friendly relations with the whites.

2. This is the most pathetic of the Ghost Dance songs. It is sung to a plaintive tune, sometimes with tears rolling down the cheeks of the dancers as the words would bring up thoughts of their present miserable and dependent condition [Mooney's note].

Native drawings of the Ghost Dance. *A*, Comanche; *B*, Sioux.

## Songs of the Sioux

### [THE FATHER SAYS SO][1]

A'te he'ye e'yayo!
A'te he'ye e'yayo!
A'te he'ye lo,
A'te he'ye lo.
Nitu'ñkañshi'la wa'ñiyegala'ke—kta' e'yayo'!          5
Nitu'ñkañshi'la wa'ñiyegala'ke—kta' e'yayo'!
A'te he'ye lo,
A'te he'ye lo.
Ni'takuye wañye'găla'ke—kta e'yayo'!
Ni'takuye wañye'găla'ke—kta e'yayo'!          10
A'te he'ye lo,
A'te he'ye lo.

### TRANSLATION

The father says so—*E'yayo!*
The father says so—*E'yayo!*
The father says so,
The father says so.
You shall see your grandfather—*E'yayo'!*          5
You shall see your grandfather—*E'yayo'!*

1. This is the opening song of the dance. While singing it, all the dancers stand motionless with hands stretched out toward the west, the country of the messiah and the quarter whence the new spirit world is to come. When it is ended, all cry together, after which they join hands and begin to circle around to the left. "Grandfather," as well as "father," is a reverential term applied to the messiah [Mooney's note].

The father says so,
The father says so.
You shall see your kindred—*E'yayo'!*
You shall see your kindred—*E'yayo'!*                    10
The father says so,
The father says so.

### [GIVE ME MY KNIFE][2]

Mila kiñ hiyu'michi'chiyana,
Mila kiñ hiyu'michi'chiyana.
Wa'waka'bla-kte—Ye'ye'!
Wa'waka'bla-kte—Ye'ye'!
Oñchi he'ye lo—Yo'yo'!                                    5
Oñchi he'ye lo—Yo'yo'!
Puye chiñyi wa'sna wakaghiñyiñ-kte,
Puye chiñyi wa'sna wakaghiñyiñ-kte,
Oñchi heye lo—Yo'yo!
Oñchi heye lo—Yo'yo!                                      10

### TRANSLATION

Give me my knife,
Give me my knife,
I shall hang up the meat to dry—*Ye'ye'!*
I shall hang up the meat to dry—*Ye'ye'!*
Says grandmother—*Yo'yo'!*                               5
Says grandmother—*Yo'yo'!*
When it is dry I shall make pemmican,[3]
When it is dry I shall make pemmican,
Says grandmother—*Yo'yo!*
Says grandmother—*Yo'yo!*                                 10

### [THE WHOLE WORLD IS COMING][4]

Maka' sito'maniyañ ukiye,
Oya'te uki'ye, oya'te uki'ye,
Wa'ñbali oya'te wañ hoshi'hi-ye lo,
Ate heye lo, ate heye lo,
Maka o'wañcha'ya uki'ye.                                  5
Pte kiñ ukiye, pte kiñ ukiye,
Kañghi oya'te wañ hoshi'hi-ye, lo,
A'te he'ye lo, a'te he'ye lo.

2. This song brings up a vivid picture of the old Indian life. In her trance vision the old grandmother whose experience it relates came upon her friends in the spirit world just as all the women of the camp were engaged in cutting up the meat for drying after a successful buffalo hunt. In her joy she calls for her knife to assist in the work, and says that as soon as the meat is dry she will make some pemmican [Mooney's note]. See note 3, following.
3. Dried beef, which is toasted and then pounded into a hash; it may be eaten with sugar, fruit, or mesquite pods.
4. This fine song summarizes the whole hope of the Ghost dance—the return of the buffalo and the departed dead, the message being brought to the people by the sacred birds, the eagle and the crow. The eagle known as *wañ'bali* is the war eagle, from which feathers are procured as war bonnets [Mooney's note].

TRANSLATION

The whole world is coming,
A nation is coming, a nation is coming,
The Eagle has brought the message to the tribe.
The father says so, the father says so.
Over the whole earth they are coming.                    5
The buffalo are coming, the buffalo are coming,
The Crow has brought the message to the tribe,
The father says so, the father says so.

---

# WOVOKA
## ca. 1856–1932

Quoitze Ow, known most commonly by his boyhood name Wovoka (the Wood Cutter) or his adoptive name Jack Wilson, was a Numu (Paiute) Indian, born in 1856 or 1857 at Walker Lake in present-day Nevada. Although he had earlier experienced trancelike states and visions, Wovoka's great revelation came to him on New Year's day of 1889 when he fell into a coma, perhaps induced by scarlet fever. On that day there was also a total eclipse of the sun. In his vision, Wovoka was transported to heaven, where he spoke to God, who assured him that the Messiah—Jesus, it would seem, although Wovoka himself began to assume the role of Messiah to many American Indians—was already on earth and that soon the buffalo would return (this was of particular importance to the Plains Indians), game animals would abound, and the Indian dead would be reunited with their kin in an earthly paradise. As for the whites, they would either disappear or somehow be assimilated into the Native American new world order.

The Ghost Dance itself was a form of the traditional round dance that was to be performed for five or six nights. Men and women, hand in hand, moved sideways and in a circular motion around a fire, singing songs that varied from group to group. Followers of the Ghost Dance religion believed that performing this dance, along with carrying out specifically peaceful, thoroughly Christian behaviors, would ensure the realization of Wovoka's vision of paradise. Also assumed by some, particularly the Plains Indians, who early on stripped away many of the religion's pacific aspects, was the impermeability to bullets of the dyed and painted, fringed muslin or buckskin garments known as Ghost Dance shirts. When asked about this belief, Wovoka himself called it a joke. But it was no joke when, in December of 1890, the Seventh Cavalry trained its guns on a band of starving Sioux, at Wounded Knee on the Pine Ridge reservation, called there because the government's Indian agent had become panicky about the activities of the Ghost Dancers.

A Minneconjou Sioux named Kicking Bear and his brother-in-law Short Bull had made the trip southwest to the land of the Fish Eaters (the Paiutes) to find out about this new religion, word of which had spread to the Plains. They met the Paiute Messiah, learned the songs and dances of the Ghost Dance religion and, upon their return, introduced them to the Sioux on the Rosebud, Cheyenne River, and Pine Ridge reservations. Sitting Bull, one of the most notable of the Sioux chiefs and a principal participant in the defeat of Custer at the Little Bighorn River, had his doubts about the power of the Ghost Dance. He was, however, willing to have the religion introduced among his people at Standing Rock reservation. James McLaughlin, the agent who was in charge of Standing Rock reservation, was particularly upset about the Ghost Dance, which he called a "pernicious system of religion," for all that much of it was clearly Christian. By November 1890 the agent at Pine Ridge reservation had telegraphed Washington: "Indians are dancing in the snow and are wild and crazy. . . . We need protection and we need it now." Sitting Bull, as one of the most visible and eminent of the Sioux, was singled out by those fearful of the Ghost Dance.

Shortly before dawn on December 15, 1890, Sitting Bull's cabin was surrounded by Indian police under the command of Lieutenant Bull Head, who attempted to take the old chief prisoner. Although Sitting Bull cooperated, outside the cabin a crowd of Ghost Dancers urged him to resist arrest. A man named Catch-the-Bear pulled out a rifle and shot at Bull Head, who, as he fell, attempted to shoot back at Catch-the-Bear. His bullet struck Sitting Bull instead; Red Tomahawk, another of the Indian police, then shot the old chief in the head, killing him.

Less than ten days after Sitting Bull's murder the call came for the arrest of Big Foot, an elderly Minneconjou Sioux, who was suffering, in the cold, from pneumonia. His people, too, had been participants in the Ghost Dance, and with little resistance possible, Big Foot led them to surrender at Wounded Knee, on the Pine Ridge reservation. Surrounded by cavalry, the Indians were halted and counted: 120 men and 230 women and children. The next morning Colonel James W. Forsyth of the Seventh Cavalry ordered the men outside and announced that they were to be disarmed. Some weapons were given up, but the soldiers persisted in their search. A young man named Black Coyote, who may have been deaf, refused to hand over his Winchester rifle. The soldiers seized him; Black Coyote's rifle discharged or was fired, and the violence began. Soldiers shot indiscriminately at the assembled men and the women who, at the sound of gunfire, had run to the scene. Then the big Hotchkiss guns positioned on the surrounding hills began to fire, and in a short time, the massacre was complete. Big Foot and most of his people, the majority women and children, were dead.

Later in the day, the soldiers returned to the scene and loaded the wounded Sioux into wagons: four men and forty-seven women and children. Because a blizzard was approaching, the Indian dead were left where they had fallen. After the storm had passed, on New Year's Day of 1891, white settlers, who were paid two dollars a corpse, gathered the Sioux dead, frozen, photographs show, into grotesque shapes, and threw them into a mass grave.

We give two versions of Wovoka's teachings, transcriptions of Native oratory addressed to Native people. First, we have a Cheyenne version (many of the tribes sent emissaries to visit the Paiute prophet), dictated, in English, by Black Short Nose to his daughter around 1891, following his visit with Wovoka. We have left uncorrected the grammatical and spelling errors in this account in the belief that Black Short Nose's hybrid English, however different from the standard, is of interest. Next follows Wovoka's own version of his message, as given in 1892 to James Mooney. Mooney produced this free rendering, which he titles "The Messiah Letter," as part of his detailed study of the Ghost Dance religion.

## The Messiah Letter: Cheyenne Version[1]

When you get home you have to make dance. You must dance for four nights and one day time. You will take bath in the same morning before you go to yours home, for every body, and give you all the same as this. Jackson Wilson[2] likes you all, he is glad to get good many things. His heart satting fully

---

1. From James Mooney's *The Ghost Dance Religion and the Sioux Outbreak of 1890* (1896, 1965).
2. Wovoka.

of gladness, after you get home, I will give you a good cloud and give you chance to make you feel good. I give you a good spirit, and give you all good paint, I want you people to come here again, want them in three months any tribs of you from there. There will be a good deal snow this year. Some time rains, in fall this year some rain, never give you any thing like that, grandfather, said, when they were die never cry, no hurt anybody, do any harm for it, not to fight. Be a good behave always. It will give a satisfaction in your life. This young man is a good father and mother. Do not tell the white people about this, Juses[3] is on the ground, he just like cloud. Every body is a live again. I don't know when he will be here, may be will be this fall or in spring. When it happen it may be this. There will be no sickness and return to young again. Do not refuse to work for white man or do not make any trouble with them until you leave them. When the earth shakes do not be afraid it will not hurt you. I want you to make dance for six weeks. Eat and wash good clean yourselves.[4]

## The Messiah Letter: Mooney's Free Rendering[1]

When you get home you must make a dance to continue five days. Dance four successive nights, and the last night keep up the dance until the morning of the fifth day, when all must bathe in the river and then disperse to their homes. You must all do in the same way.

I, Jack Wilson, love you all, and my heart is full of gladness for the gifts you have brought me. When you get home I shall give you a good cloud[2] which will make you feel good. I give you a good spirit and give you all good paint. I want you to come again in three months, some from each tribe there.[3]

There will be a good deal of snow this year and some rain. In the fall there will be such a rain as I have never given you before.

Grandfather[4] says, when your friends die you must not cry. You must not hurt anybody or do harm to anyone. You must not fight. Do right always. It will give you satisfaction in life. This young man has a good father and mother.[5]

Do not tell the white people about this. Jesus is now upon the earth. He appears like a cloud. The dead are all alive again. I do not know when they will be here; maybe this fall or in the spring. When the time comes there will be no more sickness and everyone will be young again. Do not refuse to work for the whites and do not make any trouble with them until you leave them. When the earth shakes[6] do not be afraid. It will not hurt you.

I want everyone to dance every six weeks. Make a feast at the dance and have food that everybody may eat. Then bathe in the water. That is all. You will receive good words again from me some time. Do not tell lies.

3. Jesus.
4. The rest of the letter had been erased [Mooney's note].
1. From James Mooney's *The Ghost Dance Religion and the Sioux Outbreak of 1890* (1896, 1965).
2. Rain? [Mooney's note].
3. The Indian Territory [Mooney's note].

4. A universal title of reverence among Indians and here meaning the Messiah [Mooney's note].
5. Possibly refers to Casper Edson, the young Arapaho who transcribed this message for the delegation [Mooney's note].
6. At the coming of the new world [Mooney's note].

# Debates over "Americanization"

One hundred years ago, *Americanization* was a keyword for a variety of related concerns being debated in American society. Specifically, the term referred to a concerted movement to turn immigrants into Americans, including classes, programs, and ceremonies focused on American speech, ideals, traditions, and customs, but it was also a broader term used in debates about national identity and a person's general fitness for citizenship. Beginning in the early 1880s, the number of immigrants, first from Europe and then from other locales, including Asia, grew dramatically until the start of World War I in 1914. One counterresponse to Americanization was *Nativism*, the belief held by many whites that only native-born "Anglo-Saxons" were "true" Americans, a belief fueled first by fear of Native Americans, then by fear and suspicion of ethnic newcomers as well as of post–Reconstruction free blacks. *Nationalism*, a uniting ideal that helped whites explain the destruction of Native Americans and their culture, gained strength when World War I broke out. In the build-up to the war, which the United States would not enter until 1917, Americans became increasingly suspicious of foreign-born workers and blamed them for both labor disputes and job shortages. These currents and crosscurrents of national identity were debated daily in periodicals. Inevitably, post-Darwinian "scientific" assertions of race as a true determinant of identity became a factor, and *Americanization* and *race* emerged as the twin themes of turn-of-the-century discourse about national identity.

Composed largely of immigrant pioneers in 1800, by 1900 the U.S. population had moved from farm to city, with urban growth attributable mainly to the waves of immigrants demanded by industrial production. Increasingly, despite the goals of Americanization, immigrants settled in close-knit groups in big cities, where their alien speech further segregated them from mainstream society. As Joan London, daughter of Jack London and herself a socialist critic, describes the scene, "Wage slaves were wanted now, not Americans. And so the melting pot, which had served the country well in the past, gradually ceased to function." In 1890 seventh-eighths of the population held one-eighth of the wealth, while 1 percent held all the rest. Boosterism, capitalism, *laissez-faire*, and individualism flourished in the moneyed classes, and property was routinely defended in courts against state legislation on workers' rights issues, while striking workers were increasingly disciplined with state constabularies and private guards.

Late-nineteenth-century authors grew up in an America "ripe with incongruities," as literary critic Eric Carl Link observes. Scientific and historical discoveries challenged traditional religious views, while expansions in industry and agriculture created uncontrolled growth. The working class saw little of the benefits of economic expansion, despite the lower cost of living and higher wages. Severe economic panics in 1873 and 1893, brought about by the manipulation of the economy by corporate and banking empires, resulted in mass unemployment and homelessness. In the cities, slums huddled beneath corporate skyscrapers. Then the run on the gold supply (the U.S. Treasury failed to redeem claims when the minimum gold reserve amount was reached), followed by the failure of silver redemption and the bankruptcy of the Philadelphia and Reading Railroad and other major concerns, led to at least 18 percent of the national workforce being unemployed. Not until new gold production and the issue of new notes by the Treasury in 1896, followed by the Gold Rush in 1897, did the economy get back on an even keel (though it did not stay there for long).

This era also saw the farthest reach of U.S. imperialism. Expansion meant new markets in Puerto Rico, the Panama Canal region, and the Virgin Islands. The Spanish-American War of 1898 led to new possessions, including a protectorate over Cuba. Hawai'i offered a burgeoning sugar industry for U.S. investors. Samoa was partitioned among the United States, England, and Germany in 1899. Wake and Midway Islands were soon claimed by the United States, and the Philippines were retained as a vantage point in the Orient. By 1900 the United States was second only to England and France in colonial power.

Capitalists continued, in contradiction to their nativist pronouncements, to bring in cheap foreign labor as new colonies were annexed, while labor union leaders encouraged white laborers to blame their problems on nonwhite immigrant laborers instead of the capitalists. For both, a central aim was to restrict immigration to certain racial groups. The upper classes used a linguistic argument, as the *Nation* argued for a secure modern state resting on a community of shared language, with immigrants restricted to English-speaking peoples. The new academic field of "race science," or racialism, advanced by professors at the nation's top universities, from Harvard to Johns Hopkins to Stanford, turned to the theories of Charles Darwin, in particular those of his follower Herbert Spencer, who attempted to apply Darwin's "survival of the fittest" to human society, specifically to racial differences, and to warn of future race competition. Central to the thinking of many Americans was the belief that U.S. citizenship was the birthright of a superior founding "race" descended from the Anglo-Saxon "race," or, what a character in Charles Chesnutt's *The Marrow of Tradition* [1901] refers to as "'de Angry-Saxon race.'"

David Starr Jordan (1851–1931), the first president of Stanford University, helped introduce Social Darwinism and eugenics, the improvement of the human species through control of heredity, to the United States, along with Francis Galton, a cousin of Darwin's, who was inspired by Spencer. In *The Care and Culture of Men* (1896), Jordan wrote that the United States must rely on its Anglo-Saxons, "the heart of this republic, . . . the sons and daughters of 'him that overcometh.'" This is "a lineage untainted by luxury, uncoddled by charity, uncorroded by vice, uncrushed by oppression. If it were not so, we could not be here today." Jordan's ideas were fairly benign compared to those of many of his contemporaries. Respected writers like H. G. Wells advocated sterilization of breeding "failures" in order to improve the "human stock," and a "Galton Society" at the Museum of Natural History in New York popularized presumed parallels between stock breeding and human mating.

This cluster presents leading figures of the day addressing the multiple meanings of *Americanization* and race, beginning with Frederick Jackson Turner's "frontier thesis" and Theodore Roosevelt's grand vision of "winning" the West, followed by five counterassessments of what the still-new United States of America ought to offer to all its inhabitants.

# FREDERICK JACKSON TURNER

Two opposing turn-of-the-nineteenth-century ideas of national identity were the "germ theory" and the "frontier theory." The germ theory held, as critic Donald Pizer puts it, that "American democracy had been racially transmitted through Anglo-Saxon immigration, first from northern Germany to England and then from England to America." Tribal councils of primitive Germans were naturally followed by the English "folkmoot" and the New England town meeting. Championed by Theodore Roosevelt, the germ theory gave rise to John O'Sullivan's statement (he was the *Democratic Review* editor who coined the term "Manifest Destiny") that in California "the irresistible army of Anglo-Saxon emigration" has taken over, "armed with the plough and the rifle, and marking its trail with schools and colleges, courts and representative halls, mills and meeting houses," a nationalist and nativist view of Jeffersonian yeomanry in the West. During the Mexican War (1846–48), the *Democratic Review* warned that the "very virtues of the Anglo-Saxon race made their political union with the degraded Mexican-Spanish impossible." Still, imperialist voices prevailed. Josiah Strong predicted in the 1880s that the world was about "to enter upon a new stage of its history—the final competition of the races for which the Anglo-Saxon is being schooled. If I do not read amiss, this powerful race will move down upon Mexico, down upon Central and South America, out upon the islands of the sea, over upon Africa and beyond." This race, Strong argued, "is destined to dispossess many weaker races, assimilate others, and mold the remainder until . . . it has Anglo-Saxonized mankind." Yet Americans also subscribed to a view of American destiny that opposed the germ theory, and that was of course Turner's notion of the frontier, and not heredity, as the transformative agent of Americans. For Turner (1861–1932), American democracy was "not the last flowering of a pure seed developed elsewhere," but lay within "the soil which took the mixed seeds which fell upon it and transformed them into something new and distinctive, the American race." Turner believed "The West, at bottom, is a form of society, rather than an area," a region where older institutions meet "the transforming influences of free land," creating an entirely new environment, where "freedom of opportunity is opened, the cake of custom is broken, and new activities, new lines of growth, new institutions and new ideals, are brought into existence." For him, the "history of our political institutions, our democracy, . . . is a history of the evolution and adaptation of organs in response to changed environment, . . . the origin of new political species."

## *From* The Significance of the Frontier in American History[1]

\* \* \* Up to our own day American history has been in a large degree the history of the colonization of the Great West. The existence of an area of free land, its continuous recession, and the advance of American settlement westward, explain American development.

Behind institutions, behind constitutional forms and modifications, lie the vital forces that call these organs into life and shape them to meet changing conditions. The peculiarity of American institutions is, the fact that they have been compelled to adapt themselves to the changes of an expanding people—to the changes involved in crossing a continent, in winning a wilderness, and in developing at each area of this progress out of the primitive economic and political conditions of the frontier into the complexity of city life. Said Calhoun[2] in 1817, "We are great, and rapidly—I was about to say fearfully—growing!" So saying, he touched the distinguishing feature of American life. All peoples show development; the germ theory of politics has been sufficiently emphasized. In the case of most nations, however, the development has occurred in a limited area; and if the nation has expanded, it has met other growing peoples whom it has conquered. But in the case of the United

1. Turner's address to the American Historical Association was delivered on July 12, 1893, in Chicago. It was printed in the *Proceedings of the State Historical Society of Wisconsin*, December 14, 1893, then in the *Report of the American Historical Association* for 1893. Along with various short papers of Turner's, it became part of *The*

*Frontier in American History* (1920), from which these excerpts are taken.
2. John Caldwell Calhoun (1782–1850), U.S. representative and senator from South Carolina and U.S. vice president under John Quincy Adams and Andrew Jackson. Turner cites "Abridgment of Debates of Congress," vol. V.

States we have a different phenomenon. Limiting our attention to the Atlantic coast, we have the familiar phenomenon of the evolution of institutions in a limited area, such as the rise of representative government; into complex organs; the progress from primitive industrial society, without division of labor, up to manufacturing civilization. But we have in addition to this a recurrence of the process of evolution in each western area reached in the process of expansion. Thus American development has exhibited not merely advance along a single line, but a return to primitive conditions on a continually advancing frontier line, and a new development for that area. American social development has been continually beginning over again on the frontier. This perennial rebirth, this fluidity of American life, this expansion westward with its new opportunities, its continuous touch with the simplicity of primitive society, furnish the forces dominating American character. The true point of view in the history of this nation is not the Atlantic coast, it is the Great West. Even the slavery struggle, which is made so exclusive an object of attention by writers like Professor von Holst,[3] occupies its important place in American history because of its relation to westward expansion. In this advance, the frontier is the outer edge of the wave—the meeting point between savagery and civilization. Much has been written about the frontier from the point of view of border warfare and the chase, but as a field for the serious study of the economist and the historian it has been neglected.

The American frontier is sharply distinguished from the European frontier—a fortified boundary line running through dense populations. The most significant thing about the American frontier is, that it lies at the hither edge of free land. In the census reports it is treated as the margin of that settlement which has a density of two or more to the square mile. The term is an elastic one, and for our purposes does not need sharp definition. We shall consider the whole frontier belt including the Indian country and the outer margin of the "settled area" of the census reports. This paper will make no attempt to treat the subject exhaustively; its aim is simply to call attention to the frontier as a fertile field for investigation, and to suggest some of the problems which arise in connection with it. In the settlement of America we have to observe how European life entered the continent, and how America modified and developed that life and reacted on Europe. Our early history is the study of European germs developing in an American environment. Too exclusive attention has been paid by institutional students to the Germanic origins, too little to the American factors. The frontier is the line of most rapid and effective Americanization. The wilderness masters the colonist. It finds him a European in dress, industries, tools, modes of travel, and thought. It takes him from the railroad car and puts him in the birch canoe. It strips off the garments of civilization and arrays him in the hunting shirt and the moccasin. It puts him in the log cabin of the Cherokee and Iroquois and runs an Indian palisade around him. Before long he has gone to planting Indian corn and plowing with a sharp stick, he shouts the war cry and takes the scalp in orthodox Indian fashion. In short, at the frontier the environment is at first too strong for the man. He must accept the conditions which it furnishes, or perish, and so he fits himself into the Indian clearings and follows the Indian trails. Little by little he transforms the wilderness, but the outcome is not the old Europe, not simply the development of Germanic germs, any more than the first phenomenon was a case of reversion

---

3. Early German psychologist and behaviorist Erich von Holst (1908–1962).

to the Germanic mark. The fact is, that here is a new product that is American. At first, the frontier was the Atlantic coast. It was the frontier of Europe in a very real sense. Moving westward, the frontier became more and more American. As successive terminal moraines result from successive glaciations, so each frontier leaves its traces behind it, and when it becomes a settled area the region still partakes of the frontier characteristics. Thus the advance of the frontier has meant a steady movement away from the influence of Europe, a steady growth of independence on American lines. And to study this advance, the men who grew up under these conditions, and the political, economic, and social results of it, is to study the really American part of our history.

\*  \*  \*

It was not merely in legislative action that the frontier worked against the sectionalism of the coast. The economic and social characteristics of the frontier worked against sectionalism. The men of the frontier had closer resemblances to the Middle region than to either of the other sections. Pennsylvania had been the seed plot of frontier emigration, and, although she passed on her settlers along the Great Valley into the west of Virginia and the Carolinas, yet the industrial society of these Southern frontiersmen was always more like that of the Middle region than like that of the tide water portion of the South, which later came to spread its industrial type throughout the South. The Middle region, entered by New York harbor, was an open door to all Europe. The tide-water part of the South represented typical Englishmen, modified by a warm climate and servile labor, and living in baronial fashion on great plantations; New England stood for a special English movement—Puritanism. The Middle region was less English than the other sections. It had a wide mixture of nationalities, a varied society, the mixed town and county system of local government, a varied economic life, many religious sects. In short, it was a region mediating between New England and the South, and the East and the West. It represented that composite nationality which the contemporary United States exhibits, that juxtaposition of non-English groups, occupying a valley or a little settlement, and presenting reflections of the map of Europe in their variety. It was democratic and nonsectional, if not national; "easy, tolerant, and contented"; rooted strongly in material prosperity. It was typical of the modern United States. It was least sectional, not only because it lay between North and South, but also because with no barriers to shut out its frontiers from its settled region, and with a system of connecting waterways, the Middle region mediated between East and West as well as between North and South. Thus it became the typically American region. Even the New Englander, who was shut out from the frontier by the Middle region, tarrying in New York or Pennsylvania on his westward march, lost the acuteness of his sectionalism on the way.

\*  \*  \*

So long as free land exists, the opportunity for a competency exists, and economic power secures political power. But the democracy born of free land, strong in selfishness and individualism, intolerant of administrative experience and education, and pressing individual liberty beyond its proper bounds, has its dangers as well as its benefits. Individualism in America has allowed a laxity in regard to governmental affairs which has rendered possible the spoils system and all the manifest evils that follow from the lack of a highly developed civic spirit. In this connection may be noted also the influence of frontier conditions in permitting lax business honor, inflated paper currency and wild-cat banking. The colonial and revolutionary frontier was the region whence emanated many of the worst forms of an evil currency. The West in the War of 1812 repeated the phenomenon on the frontier of that day, while the speculation and wild-cat banking of the period of the crisis of 1837 occurred on the new frontier belt of the next tier of States. Thus each one of the periods of lax financial integrity coincides with periods when a new set of frontier communities had arisen, and coincides in area with these successive frontiers for the most part. The recent Populist agitation is a case in point. Many a State that now declines any connection with the tenets of the Populists, itself adhered to such ideas in an earlier stage of the development of the State. A primitive society can hardly be expected to show the intelligent appreciation of the complexity of business interests in a developed society. The continual recurrence of these areas of paper-money agitation is another evidence that the frontier can be isolated and studied as a factor in American history of the highest importance.

*　*　*

From the conditions of frontier life came intellectual traits of profound importance. The works of travelers along each frontier from colonial days onward describe certain common traits, and these traits have, while softening down, still persisted as survivals in the place of their origin, even when a higher social organization succeeded. The result is that to the frontier the American intellect owes its striking characteristics. That coarseness and strength combined with acuteness and inquisitiveness; that practical, inventive turn of mind, quick to find expedients; that masterful grasp of material things, lacking in the artistic but powerful to effect great ends; that restless, nervous energy; that dominant individualism, working for good and for evil, and withal that buoyancy and exuberance which comes with freedom—these are traits of the frontier, or traits called out elsewhere because of the existence of the frontier. Since the days when the fleet of Columbus sailed into the waters of the New World, America has been another name for opportunity, and the people of the United States have taken their tone from the incessant expansion which has not only been open but has even been forced upon them. He would be a rash prophet who should assert that the expansive character of American life has now entirely ceased. Movement has been its dominant fact, and, unless this training has no effect upon a people, the American energy will continually demand a wider field for its exercise. But never again will such gifts of free land offer themselves. For a moment, at the frontier, the bonds of custom are broken and unrestraint is triumphant. There is not *tabula rasa*. The stubborn American environment is there with its imperious summons to accept its conditions; the inherited ways of doing things are also there; and yet, in spite of environment, and in spite of custom, each frontier did indeed furnish a new field of opportunity, a gate of escape from the bondage of the past; and freshness, and confidence, and scorn of older society, impatience of its restraints and its ideas, and indifference to its lessons, have accompanied the frontier. What the Mediterranean Sea was to the Greeks, breaking the bond of custom, offering new experiences, calling out new institutions and activities, that, and more, the ever retreating frontier has been to the United States directly, and to the nations of Europe more remotely. And now, four centuries from the discovery of America, at the end of a hundred years of life under the Constitution, the frontier has gone, and with its going has closed the first period of American history.

1893

---

# THEODORE ROOSEVELT

As a prolific writer and politician, Theodore Roosevelt (1858–1919) emphasized the romance of the American march westward, led by the Anglo-Saxon race, planting, at each stage of conquest, seeds that would flower in American democratic society. Roosevelt's rhetoric, unlike Turner's, was clearly that of conquest: "The warlike borderers who thronged across the Alleghanies, the restless and reckless hunters, the hard, dogged, frontier farmers, by dint of grim tenacity, overcame and displaced Indians, French, and Spaniards alike, exactly as, fourteen hundred years before, Saxon and Angle had overcame and displaced the . . . Celts." For Roosevelt, "the spread of the English-speaking peoples over the world's waste spaces has been not only the most striking feature in the world's history, but also the event of all others most far-reaching in its importance." Roosevelt applauded in Darwinian terms "the vigor and prowess shown by our fighting men" and the nation's "lift toward mighty things," scorning the "shortsighted and timid" people who opposed wars "for the advance of American civilization at the cost of savagery." He invokes values of manliness, self-reliance, and hard work as the essential hallmarks of the American West, no matter whether an earlier immigrant or a later one, no matter what "race." Indeed, as he observes in *American Ideals*, "We were . . . already, what we are now, a people of mixed blood" from many different countries. Roosevelt argues that immigrants should assimilate, but he does not discount the diverse strengths immigrants from around the world lend to the growing United States.

## *From* American Ideals[1]

### From *Chapter II. True Americanism*

\* \* \*

The mighty tide of immigration to our shores has brought in its train much of good and much of evil; and whether the good or the evil shall predominate depends mainly on whether these newcomers do or do not throw themselves heartily into our national life, cease to be European, and become Americans like the rest of us. More than a third of the people of the Northern States are of foreign birth or parentage. An immense number of them have become completely Americanized, and these stand on exactly the same plane as the descendants of any Puritan, Cavalier, or Knickerbocker among us,[2] and do

---

1. From the first edition, published in 1897.
2. Puritan: a Protestant religious dissenter; most puritans left England and settled in New England. Cavalier: a supporter of King Charles I during the English Civil War (1642–51). Knickerbocker: a descendant of the original Dutch settlers of Manhattan.

their full and honorable share of the nation's work. But where immigrants, or the sons of immigrants, do not heartily and in good faith throw in their lot with us, but cling to the speech, the customs, the ways of life, and the habits of thought of the Old World which they have left, they thereby harm both themselves and us. If they remain alien elements, unassimilated, and with interests separate from ours, they are mere obstructions to the current of our national life, and, moreover, can get no good from it themselves. In fact, though we ourselves also suffer from their perversity, it is they who really suffer most. It is an immense benefit to the European immigrant to change him into an American citizen. To bear the name of American is to bear the most honorable of titles; and whoever does not so believe has no business to bear the name at all, and, if he comes from Europe, the sooner he goes back there the better. Besides, the man who does not become Americanized nevertheless fails to remain a European, and becomes nothing at all. The immigrant cannot possibly remain what he was, or continue to be a member of the Old-World society. If he tries to retain his old language, in a few generations it becomes a barbarous jargon; if he tries to retain his old customs and ways of life, in a few generations he becomes an uncouth boor. He has cut himself off from the Old-World, and cannot retain his connection with it; and if he wishes ever to amount to anything he must throw himself heart and soul, and without reservation, into the new life to which he has come. It is urgently necessary to check and regulate our immigration, by much more drastic laws than now exist; and this should be done both to keep out laborers who tend to depress the labor market, and to keep out races which do not assimilate readily with our own, and unworthy individuals of all races—not only criminals, idiots, and paupers, but anarchists of the Most and O'Donovan Rossa type.[3]

From his own standpoint, it is beyond all question the wise thing for the immigrant to become thoroughly Americanized. Moreover, from our standpoint, we have a right to demand it. We freely extend the hand of welcome and of good-fellowship to every man, no matter what his creed or birthplace, who comes here honestly intent on becoming a good United States citizen like the rest of us; but we have a right, and it is our duty, to demand that he shall indeed become so, and shall not confuse the issues with which we are struggling by introducing among us Old-World quarrels and prejudices. There are certain ideas which he must give up. For instance, he must learn that American life is incompatible with the existence of any form of anarchy, or of any secret society having murder for its aim, whether at home or abroad; and he must learn that we exact full religious toleration and the complete separation of Church and State. Moreover, he must not bring in his Old-World religious race and national antipathies, but must merge them into love for our common country, and must take pride in the things which we can all take pride in. He must revere only our flag; not only must it come first, but no other flag should even come second. He must learn to celebrate Washington's birthday rather than that of the Queen or Kaiser, and the Fourth of July instead of St. Patrick's Day.

---

3. Johann Most (1846–1906) was a German anarchist who emigrated to the United States and was best known for his advocacy of armed revolt. Jeremiah O'Donovan Rossa (1831–1915) was an Irish Fenian leader who established the Irish Republican Brotherhood. Jailed numerous times, he was exiled to the United States in 1871; from New York City, he organized the first Irish republican bombings of English cities.

Our political and social questions must be settled on their own merits, and not complicated by quarrels between England and Ireland, or France and Germany, with which we have nothing to do: it is an outrage to fight an American political campaign with reference to questions of European politics. Above all, the immigrant must learn to talk and think and *be* United States.

The immigrant of to-day can learn much from the experience of the immigrants of the past, who came to America prior to the Revolutionary War. We were then already, what we are now, a people of mixed blood. Many of our most illustrious Revolutionary names were borne by men of Huguenot blood—Jay, Sevier, Marion, Laurens.[4] But the Huguenots were, on the whole, the best immigrants we have ever received; sooner than any other, and more completely, they became American in speech, conviction, and thought. The Hollanders took longer than the Huguenots to become completely assimilated; nevertheless they in the end became so, immensely to their own advantage. One of the leading Revolutionary generals, Schuyler, and one of the Presidents of the United States, Van Buren,[5] were of Dutch blood; but they rose to their positions, the highest in the land, because they had become Americans and had ceased being Hollanders. If they had remained members of an alien body, cut off by their speech and customs and belief from the rest of the American community, Schuyler would have lived his life as a boorish, provincial squire, and Van Buren would have ended his days a small tavern-keeper. So it is with the Germans of Pennsylvania. Those of them who became Americanized have furnished to our history a multitude of honorable names, from the days of the Mühlenbergs onward;[6] but those who did not become Americanized form to the present day an unimportant body, of no significance in American existence. So it is with the Irish, who gave to Revolutionary annals such names as Carroll and Sullivan, and to the Civil War men like Sheridan[7]—men who were Americans and nothing else: while the Irish who remain such, and busy themselves solely with alien politics, can have only an unhealthy influence upon American life, and can never rise as do their compatriots who become straightout Americans. Thus it has ever been with all people who have come hither, of whatever stock or blood. The same thing is true of the churches. A church which remains foreign, in language or spirit, is doomed.

4. French protestants of the 16th and 17th centuries. Among them were John Jay (1745–1829), who served as president of the Continental Congress and is considered one of the "founding fathers" of the United States; Ambrose Hundley Sevier (1801–1848), Democratic U.S. Senator from Arkansas, sent in 1848 to Mexico to negotiate the Treaty of Guadalupe Hildalgo, which ended the Mexican War. Others were Francis Marion (ca. 1732–1795), a general in the American Revolutionary War, during which he acquired the name "Swamp Fox" for his clever use of decoy and ambush tactics, and Henry Laurens (1724–1792), American merchant and South Carolina planter who became a political leader during the Revolutionary War, serving as delegate to the Continental Congress and as the third president of the Second Continental Congress (1777–78).
5. Martin Van Buren (1782–1862) was the eighth president of the United States; as a Dutch-descended American, he was the first president of

non-Anglo descent and the only one whose first language was not English.
6. An American political, religious, and military dynasty descended from Heinrich Melchior Mühlenberg (1711–1787), a German immigrant who settled in Philadelphia; Mühlenberg was a founder of the Lutheran Church in America.
7. Charles Carroll (1737–1832), delegate to the Continental Congress and U.S. Senator from Maryland; Carroll was the only Catholic signer of the Declaration of Independence. John Sullivan (1740–1795), general in the Revolutionary War, delegate to the Continental Congress, and governor of New Hampshire; famous for his campaign against Iroquois who opposed the American revolutionaries. Philip Henry Sheridan (1831–1888), Union general in the American Civil War and later involved in the Indian wars of the Great Plains; an early environmentalist and leading force behind the creation of Yellowstone National Park.

But I wish to be distinctly understood on one point. Americanism is a question of spirit, conviction, and purpose, not of creed or birthplace. The politician who bids for the Irish or German vote, or the Irishman or German who votes as an Irishman or German, is despicable, for all citizens of this commonwealth should vote solely as Americans; but he is not a whit less despicable than the voter who votes against a good American, merely because that American happens to have been born in Ireland or Germany. Know-nothingism,[8] in any form, is as utterly un-American as foreignism. It is a base outrage to oppose a man because of his religion or birthplace, and all good citizens will hold any such effort in abhorrence. A Scandinavian, a German, or an Irishman who has really become an American has the right to stand on exactly the same footing as any native-born citizen in the land, and is just as much entitled to the friendship and support, social and political, of his neighbors. Among the men with whom I have been thrown in close personal contact socially, and who have been among my staunchest friends and allies politically, are not a few Americans who happen to have been born on the other side of the water, in Germany, Ireland, Scandinavia; and there could be no better men in the ranks of our native-born citizens.

\* \* \*

1897

## *From* The Strenuous Life[1]

\* \* \*

In all the history of mankind there is nothing that quite parallels the way in which our people have filled a vacant continent with self-governing commonwealths, knit into one nation. And of all this marvelous history perhaps the most wonderful portion is that which deals with the way in which the Pacific coast and the Rocky Mountains were settled.

The men who founded these communities showed practically by their lifework that it is indeed the spirit of adventure which is the maker of commonwealths. Their traits of daring and hardihood and iron endurance are not merely indispensable traits for pioneers; they are also traits which must go to the make-up of every mighty and successful people. You and your fathers who built up the West did more even than you thought; for you shaped thereby the destiny of the whole republic, and as a necessary corollary profoundly influenced the course of events throughout the world. More and more as the years go by this republic will find its guidance in the thought and action of the West, because the conditions of development in the West have steadily tended to accentuate the peculiarly American characteristics of its people.

There was scant room for the coward and the weakling in the ranks of the adventurous frontiersmen—the pioneer settlers who first broke up the wild

---

8. A nativist American political movement of the 1850s, a popular reaction to fears that the political corruption of Irish Catholic immigrants was weakening U.S. cities. The membership, mostly middle class and Protestant, was absorbed by the Republican Party in the North.

1. *The Strenuous Life* is one of Roosevelt's most famous books, published in 1902. The excerpt is from the chapter entitled "Manhood and Statehood," an address Roosevelt gave in Colorado Springs on August 2, 1901.

prairie soil, who first hewed their way into the primeval forest, who guided their white-topped wagons across the endless leagues of Indian-haunted desolation, and explored every remote mountain-chain in the restless quest for metal wealth. Behind them came the men who completed the work they had roughly begun: who drove the great railroad systems over plain and desert and mountain pass; who stocked the teeming ranches, and under irrigation saw the bright green of the alfalfa and the yellow of the golden stubble supplant the gray of the sage-brush desert; who have built great populous cities—cities in which every art and science of civilization are carried to the highest point— on tracts which, when the nineteenth century had passed its meridian, were still known only to the grim trappers and hunters and the red lords of the wilderness with whom they waged eternal war.

Such is the record of which we are so proud. It is a record of men who greatly dared and greatly did; a record of wanderings wider and more dangerous than those of the Vikings; a record of endless feats of arms, of victory after victory in the ceaseless strife waged against wild man and wild nature. The winning of the West was the great epic feat in the history of our race.

We have then a right to meet to-day in a spirit of just pride in the past. But when we pay homage to the hardy, grim, resolute men who, with incredible toil and risk, laid deep the foundations of the civilization that we inherit, let us steadily remember that the only homage that counts is the homage of deeds—not merely of words. It is well to gather here to show that we remember what has been done in the past by the Western pioneers of our people, and that we glory in the greatness for which they prepared the way. But lip-loyalty by itself avails very little, whether it is expressed concerning a nation or an ideal. It would be a sad and evil thing for this country if ever the day came when we considered the great deeds of our forefathers as an excuse for our resting slothfully satisfied with what has been already done. On the contrary, they should be an inspiration and appeal, summoning us to show that we too have courage and strength; that we too are ready to dare greatly if the need arises; and, above all, that we are firmly bent upon that steady performance of every-day duty which, in the long run, is of such incredible worth in the formation of national character.

The old iron days have gone, the days when the weakling died as the penalty of inability to hold his own in the rough warfare against his surroundings. We live in softer times. Let us see to it that, while we take advantage of every gentler and more humanizing tendency of the age, we yet preserve the iron quality which made our forefathers and predecessors fit to do the deeds they did. It will of necessity find a different expression now, but the quality itself remains just as necessary as ever. Surely you men of the West, you men who with stout heart, cool head, and ready hand have wrought out your own success and built up these great new commonwealths, surely you need no reminder of the fact that if either man or nation wishes to play a great part in the world there must be no dallying with the life of lazy ease. In the abounding energy and intensity of existence in our mighty democratic republic there is small space indeed for the idler, for the luxury-loving man who prizes ease more than hard, triumph-crowned effort.

We hold work not as a curse but as a blessing, and we regard the idler with scornful pity. It would be in the highest degree undesirable that we should all work in the same way or at the same things, and for the sake of the real greatness of the nation we should in the fullest and most cordial way recognize the fact that some of the most needed work must, from its very nature, be unremunerative in a material sense. Each man must choose so far as the conditions allow him the path to which he is bidden by his own peculiar powers and inclinations. But if he is a man he must in some way or shape do a man's work. If, after making all the effort that his strength of body and of mind permits, he yet honorably fails, why, he is still entitled to a certain share of respect because he has made the effort. But if he does not make the effort, or if he makes it half-heartedly and recoils from the labor, the risk, or the irksome monotony of his task, why, he has forfeited all right to our respect, and has shown himself a mere cumberer of the earth. It is not given to us all to succeed, but it is given to us all to strive manfully to deserve success.

We need then the iron qualities that must go with true manhood. We need the positive virtues of resolution, of courage, of indomitable will, of power to do without shrinking the rough work that must always be done, and to persevere through the long days of slow progress or of seeming failure which always come before any final triumph, no matter how brilliant. But we need more than these qualities. This country cannot afford to have its sons less than men; but neither can it afford to have them other than good men. If courage and strength and intellect are unaccompanied by the moral purpose, the moral sense, they become merely forms of expression for unscrupulous force and unscrupulous cunning. If the strong man has not in him the lift toward lofty things his strength makes him only a curse to himself and to his neighbor. All this is true in private life, and it is no less true in public life. If Washington and Lincoln had not had in them the whipcord fiber of moral and mental strength, the soul that steels itself to endure disaster unshaken and with grim resolve to wrest victory from defeat, then the one could not have founded, nor the other preserved, our mighty federal Union. The least touch of flabbiness, of unhealthy softness, in either would have meant ruin for this nation, and therefore the downfall of the proudest hope of mankind. But no less is it true that had either been influenced by self-seeking ambition, by callous disregard of others, by contempt for the moral law, he would have dashed us down into the black gulf of failure. Woe to all of us if ever as a people we grow to condone evil because it is successful. We can no more afford to lose social and civic decency and honesty than we can afford to lose the qualities of courage and strength. It is the merest truism to say that the nation rests upon the individual, upon the family—upon individual manliness and womanliness, using the words in their widest and fullest meaning.

To be a good husband or good wife, a good neighbor and friend, to be hardworking and upright in business and social relations, to bring up many healthy children—to be and to do all this is to lay the foundations of good citizenship as they must be laid. But we cannot stop even with this. Each of us has not only his duty to himself, his family, and his neighbors, but his duty to the State and to the nation. We are in honor bound each to strive according to his or her strength to bring ever nearer the day when justice and wisdom shall obtain in public life as in private life. We cannot retain the full measure of our self-respect if we cannot retain pride in our citizenship. For the sake not only of ourselves but of our children and our children's children we must see that this nation stands for strength and honesty both at home and abroad.

In our internal policy we cannot afford to rest satisfied until all that the government can do has been done to secure fair dealing and equal justice as between man and man. In the great part which hereafter, whether we will or not, we must play in the world at large, let us see to it that we neither do wrong nor shrink from doing right because the right is difficult; that on the one hand we inflict no injury, and that on the other we have a due regard for the honor and the interest of our mighty nation; and that we keep unsullied the renown of the flag which beyond all others of the present time or of the ages of the past stands for confident faith in the future welfare and greatness of mankind.

1902

# HELEN HUNT JACKSON

In 1881 Helen Hunt Jackson (1830–1885) published *A Century of Dishonor: A Sketch of the United States Government's Dealings With Some of the Indian Tribes,* in which she reviews the many inequities perpetrated by whites against Native Americans. Following the book's publication, the U.S. Congress appointed a commission to look into Indian affairs, which resulted in the Dawes Act, dividing reservation lands into individual plots for Indian families. Ironically, the Dawes Act added to the continuing erosion of tribal identity and culture, as it broke large groups into more isolated family units. In this excerpt from *A Century of Dishonor,* Jackson details incidents leading to the demise of the Ponca Indians, using her own words, those of a Ponca chief, treaties, and reports of the Commission for Indian Affairs. The cover of the book displays a quotation from Benjamin Franklin: "Look upon your hands! They are stained with the blood of your relations."

## *From* A Century of Dishonor[1]

### From *Chapter VI. The Poncas*

In 1803 Captain Lewis and Lieutenant Clarke, of the First United States Infantry, were commissioned by Congress to explore the river Missouri from its mouth to its source, to "seek the best water communication from thence to the Pacific Ocean," and to enter into conference with all the Indian tribes on their route, with a view to the establishment of commerce with them.[2] They report the "Poncars" as "the remnant of a nation once respectable in point of numbers; they formerly resided on a branch of the Red River of Lake

1. From *A Century of Dishonor: A Sketch of the United States Government's Dealings with Some of the Indian Tribes,* first published by Harper & Brothers (1881), reprinted in 1885 and then by Roberts Brothers in 1886, from which this excerpt is taken.
2. On February 28, 1803, President Thomas Jefferson won approval from Congress for an endeavor to explore and record the land from the Missouri frontier to the Pacific. An expeditionary group was also to try to discover the "Northwest Passage" that would provide a sea lane between the east and west coasts. Called the "Corps of Discovery," the group was led by Meriwether Lewis (1774–1809) and William Clark (1770–1838), whose now-famous journals of the expedition were first published in 1814.

Winnipeg; being oppressed by Sioux, they removed to the west side of the Missouri, on Poncar River, where they built and fortified a village, and remained some years; but, being pursued by their ancient enemies, the Sioux, and reduced by continual wars, they have joined and now live with the Mahas (Omahas), whose language they speak." Their numbers are estimated by Lewis and Clarke as being only about two hundred, all told; but this small estimate is probably to be explained by the fact that at this time the tribe was away on its annual buffalo-hunt, and their village had been so long empty and quiet that a buffalo was found grazing there. A few years later the tribe is reckoned at four hundred: in a census of the Indian tribes, taken by General Porter in 1829, they are set down at six hundred. The artist Catlin,[3] who visited them a few years later, rated them a little less. He gives an interesting account of the chief of the tribe, named Shoo-de-ga-cha (Smoke), and his young and pretty wife, Hee-la'h-dee (the Pure Fountain), whose portraits he painted. He says: "The chief, who was wrapped in a buffalo-robe, is a noble specimen of native dignity and philosophy. I conversed much with him, and from his dignified manners, as well as from the soundness of his reasoning, I became fully convinced that he deserved to be the sachem of a more numerous and prosperous tribe. He related to me with great coolness and frankness the poverty and distress of his nation—and with the method of a philosopher predicted the certain and rapid extinction of his tribe, which he had not the power to avert. Poor, noble chief, who was equal to and worthy of a greater empire! He sat on the deck of the steamer, overlooking the little cluster of his wigwams mingled among the trees, and, like Caius Marius[4] weeping over the ruins of Carthage, shed tears as he was descanting on the poverty of his ill-fated little community, which he told me had 'once been powerful and happy; that the buffaloes which the Great Spirit had given them for food, and which formerly spread all over their green prairies, had all been killed or driven out by the approach of white men, who wanted their skins; that their country was now entirely destitute of game, and even of roots for food, as it was one continuous prairie; and that his young men, penetrating the countries of their enemies for buffaloes, which they were obliged to do, were cut to pieces and destroyed in great numbers. That his people had foolishly become fond of fire-water,[5] and had given away everything in their country for it; that it had destroyed many of his warriors, and would soon destroy the rest; that his tribe was too small and his warriors too few to go to war with the tribes around them; that they were met and killed by the Sioux on the north, by the Pawnees on the west, by the Osages and Konzas on the south, and still more alarmed from the constant advance of the pale faces—their enemies from the east—with whiskey and small-pox, which already had destroyed four-fifths of his tribe, and would soon impoverish and at last destroy the remainder of them.' In this way did

3. Pleasant Porter (1840–1907) was principal chief of the Creek Nation and a Confederate general; he was also an influential American Indian statesman, serving many times as Creek delegate to the U.S. Congress. Porter promoted a movement to establish a separate Native American state. George Catlin (1796–1872), whose mother was captured by Indians in Pennsylvania, gave up his law studies and devoted himself to Indian causes and to paint-

ing Indians in their native settings.
4. Also known as Gaius Marius (157–86 B.C.E.), a Roman general and consul noted for dramatic reforms of Roman armies; though he married Julius Caesar's aunt, he at one point was exiled by a rival general, Sulla, to Carthage, which would not accept him; he followed attacks there with another massacre of his enemies in Rome.
5. Alcohol.

this shrewd philosopher lament over the unlucky destiny of his tribe, and I pitied him with all my heart."

\* \* \*

The United States' first treaty with this handful of gentle and peaceable Indians was made in 1817. It was simply a treaty of peace and friendship.

In 1825 another was made, in which the Poncas admit that "they reside within the territorial limits of the United States, acknowledge their supremacy, and claim their protection." They also admit "the right of the United States to regulate all trade and intercourse with them." The United States, on their part, "agree to receive the Poncar tribe of Indians into their friendship and under their protection, and to extend to them from time to time such benefits and acts of kindness as may be convenient, and seem just and proper to the President of the United States."

After this there is little mention, in the official records of the Government, of the Poncas for some thirty years. Other tribes in the Upper Missouri region were so troublesome and aggressive that the peaceable Poncas were left to shift for themselves as they best could amidst all the warring and warring interests by which they were surrounded. In 1856 the agent of the Upper Platte mentions incidentally that their lands were being fast intruded upon by squatters; and in 1857 another agent reports having met on the banks of the Missouri a large band of Poncas, who made complaint that all the Indians on the river were receiving presents and they were overlooked; that the men from the steamboats cut their trees down, and that white settlers were taking away all their land. In 1858 the Commissioner for Indian Affairs writes: "Treaties were entered into in March and April last with the Poncas and Yankton Sioux, who reside west of Iowa, for the purpose of extinguishing their title to all the lands occupied and claimed by them, except small portions on which to colonize and domesticate them. This proceeding was deemed necessary in order to obtain such control over these Indians as to prevent their interference with our settlements, which are rapidly extending in that direction. These treaties were duly laid before the Senate at its last regular session, but were not, it is understood, finally acted on by that body.

"Relying on the ratification of their treaty, and the adoption of timely measures to carry out its provisions in their favor, the Poncas proceeded in good faith to comply with its stipulations by abandoning their settlements and hunting-grounds, and withdrawing to the small tract reserved for their future home. Being without a crop to rely upon, and having been unsuccessful in their usual summer hunt, they were reduced to a state of desperation and destitution. As nothing had been done for them under the treaty, they concluded it was void, and threatened to fall back upon their former settlements, some of the most important of which had, in the mean time, been taken possession of by numerous white persons."

The Poncas never heard of Grotius or Vattel; but, in assuming that the treaty was void because it was not fulfilled, they only acted on the natural principles of the law of nations and of treaties, as laid down by all authorities. Thucydides said: "They are not the first breakers of a league who, being deserted, seek for aid to others, but they that perform not by their deeds what they have promised to do upon their oaths."[6]

In consequence of this delay to fulfil the treaty provisions, the Government was forced to step in at the last moment and "incur a heavy expense" in furnishing the Poncas with food enough to keep them from starving; and in 1859, under this pressure, the Senate ratified the treaty. By it the Poncas ceded and relinquished to the United States all the lands they had ever owned or claimed, "wherever situate," except a small tract between the Ponca and Niobrara rivers. In consideration of this cession, the United States Government agreed "to protect the Poncas in the possession of this tract of land, and their persons and property thereon, during good behavior on their part; to pay them annuities annually for thirty years—$12,000 for the first five years, then $10,000 for ten years, then $8000 for fifteen years; to expend $20,000 for their subsistence during the first year, for building houses, etc.; to establish schools, and to build mills, mechanics' shops, etc.; to give $20,000 for the payment of the existing obligations of the tribe."

Two years later the agent newly appointed to take charge of the Poncas reports to the Department the amount of improvements made on the reservation: "One saw and grist-mill; two agency houses—story and a half houses—without inside lining or plastering, 16 by 26 and 18 by 32 feet in size; six small round log-houses (three with a small shed for a stable), a light log-corral for cattle, and a canvas shed for storing under; and about sixty acres of ground, broken, comprised all the improvements."

Evidently a very small part of the $20,000 had been spent as yet. He did not find an Indian on the reservation. From fear of the Sioux (who in 1860 had stolen from them more than half the horses they owned) they had moved down the Niobrara River, some twenty miles nearer the Missouri. It was with the greatest difficulty that the agent induced them to return; and after they did so, they huddled their tents close about the agency building, and could not be induced to go half a mile away unless accompanied by some of the white employees.

As the agent had no food to feed them with, and no money to buy any (spite of the appropriation of $20,000 for subsistence and house-building), he induced them to go off on a hunt; but in less than a month they came straggling back, "begging for provisions for their women and children, whom they had left on the plains half-starved, having been unable to find any game, or any food except wild-turnips. Some of them went to visit the Omahas, others the Pawnees, where they remained until the little corn they had planted produced roasting-ears. In the mean time those who were here subsisted mainly on wild-cherries and plums and the wild-turnip, and traded away most of their blankets and annuity goods for provisions."

In 1863 the reports are still more pitiful. "They started on their summer hunt toward the last of May, immediately after the first hoeing of their corn. At first they were successful and found buffaloes; but afterward, the ground being occupied by the Yanktons, who were sent south of the Niobrara by the

6. Hugo Grotius (1583–1645) was a jurist in the Dutch Republic whose work helped lay the foundations for international law, which he based on Enlightenment ideals of "natural law." Emer or Emerich de Vattel (1714–1767) was a Swiss political philosopher, diplomat, and expert on the law whose theories influenced the development of modern international law. Thucydides (460/455 B.C.E.–ca. 400 B.C.E.) was an ancient Greek historian and the author of the *History of the Peloponnesian War*, which recounts the 5th century B.C.E. war between Sparta and Athens.

general commanding the district, and who were about double the number, and with four times as many horses, they soon consumed what meat they had cured, and were compelled to abandon the chase. They commenced to return in the latter part of July. They went away with very high hopes, and reasonably so, of a large crop, but returned to see it all withered and dried up. In the mean time the plains had been burnt over, so that they could not discover the roots they are in the habit of digging. Even the wild-plums, which grow on bushes down in ravines and gullies, are withered and dried on the limbs. The building I occupy was constantly surrounded by a hungry crowd begging for food. . . . I am warned by military authority to keep the Poncas within the limits of the reservation; but this is an impossibility. There is nothing within its limits, nor can anything be obtained in sufficient quantity, or brought here soon enough to keep them from starving. . . . The Poncas have behaved well—quite as well, if not better than, under like circumstances, the same number of whites would have done. I have known whole families to live for days together on nothing but half-dried corn-stalks, and this when there were cattle and sheep in their sight."

At this time martial law was in force on many of the Indian reservations, owing to the presence of roving bands of hostile Sioux, driven from Minnesota after their outbreak there.

The Poncas through all these troubles remained loyal and peaceable, and were "unwavering in their fidelity to their treaty," says the Indian Commissioner.

In December of this year what the governmental reports call "a very unfortunate occurrence" took place in Nebraska. A party of Poncas, consisting of four men, six women, three boys, and two girls, returning from a visit to the Omahas, had camped for the night about twelve miles from their own reservation. In the night a party of soldiers from a military post on the Niobrara River came to their camp, and began to insult the squaws, "offering money with one hand, and presenting a revolver with the other." The Indians, alarmed, pulled up their lodge, and escaped to a copse of willows near by. The soldiers fired at them as they ran away, and then proceeded to destroy all their effects. They cut the lodge covers to pieces, burnt the saddles and blankets, cut open sacks of beans, corn, and dried pumpkin, and strewed their contents on the ground, and went away, taking with them a skin lodge-covering, beaver-skins, buffalo-robes, blankets, guns, and all the small articles. The Indians' ponies were hid in the willows. Early in the morning they returned with these, picked up all the corn which had not been destroyed, and such other articles as they could find, packed their ponies as best they might, and set off barefooted for home. After they had gone a few miles they stopped and built a fire to parch some corn to eat. Some of the women and children went to look for wild-beans, leaving three women and a child at the camp. Here the soldiers came on them again. As soon as the Indians saw them coming they fled. The soldiers fired on them, wounding one woman by a ball through her thigh; another, with a child on her back, by two balls through the child's thighs, one of which passed through the mother's side. These women were fired on as they were crossing the river on the ice. The soldiers then took possession of the six ponies and all the articles at the camp, and left. The squaws and children who were looking for beans were half a mile below; a little dog belonging to them barked and revealed their hiding-place in the willows. The soldiers immediately turned on them, dismounted, and, making up to them, deliberately shot them dead as they huddled helplessly together—three women and a little girl!

One of the boys, a youth, ran for the river, pursued by the soldiers. On reaching the river he dived into the water through a hole in the ice; as often as he lifted his head they fired at him. After they went away he crawled out and escaped to the agency. One of the murdered women, the mother of this boy, had three balls in her head and cheek, her throat cut, and her head half-severed by a sabre-thrust; another, the youngest woman, had her cloth skirt taken off and carried away, and all her other clothes torn from her body, leaving it naked!

The men who did this deed belonged to Company B of the Seventh Iowa Cavalry.

* * *

1881

# JOSÉ MARTÍ

Cuban poet, essayist, journalist, and political leader, José Martí (1853–1895) became a symbol of Cuba's fight for independence from Spain. Martí envisioned a pan-hemispheric "America" at odds with the Gilded Age mentality of an imperialistic United States powered by big business, government corruption, and worker unrest. Martí's pan-national and antiracist manifesto, "No man has any special right because he belongs to any specific race," helped define the nature of the Cuban revolution against Spain, known in the United States as the Spanish-American War, and is sharply at odds with then-prevailing Anglo-Saxon norms of American cultural identity. Martí focuses on New World nations' indigenous cultures and calls on all American republics—those in North America as well as Latin America—to embrace one "America" based on native uniqueness that would reject racism in favor of native pride. "Those born in America" should not be "ashamed of the mother who reared them, because she wears an Indian apron." Instead of setting European civilization over New World "barbarism," Martí characterizes devotion to the European tradition as a slavish, false erudition lacking direct knowledge. He demands the Americas' recognition of identities as mixed cultures, united by common humanity. Martí hoped that through understanding, without hatred or racism, "new" Americans could rise together.

Martí spent much of his life in exile. In 1881 he moved to New York City, where he worked for several magazines, including *The New York Sun, El Partido Liberal, La Opinión Nacional,* and *La Patria;* he served as consul for Uruguay, Paraguay, and Argentina; and he taught high school Spanish. Martí's articles on the North American scene introduced many Latina/o readers not only to urban poverty but also to such "American" figures as Ulysses S. Grant, Walt Whitman, Ralph Waldo Emerson, and Henry Wadsworth Longfellow. He admired Harriet Beecher Stowe and Helen Hunt Jackson, whose novel *Ramona* (1884) he translated into Spanish. Founder of the Cuban Revolutionary Party, he led a contingent of revolutionaries to Cuba from the United States and died in a skirmish with Spanish troops at Dos Rios on May 19,

1895. "He died," wrote his friend Charles A. Dana in the *New York Sun,* "as such a man might wish to die, battling for liberty and democracy."

## *From* Our America[1]

The conceited villager believes the entire world to be his village. Provided that he can be mayor, or humiliate the rival who stole his sweetheart, or add to the savings in his strong-box, he considers the universal order good, unaware of those giants with seven-league boots[2] who can crush him underfoot, or of the strife in the heavens between comets that streak through the drowsy air-devouring worlds. What remains of the village in America must rouse itself. These are not the times for sleeping in a nightcap, but with weapons for a pillow, like the warriors of Juan de Castellanos[3]—weapons of the mind, which conquer all others. Barricades of ideas are worth more than barricades of stone.

There is no prow that can cut through a cloudbank of ideas. A powerful idea, waved before the world at the proper time, can stop a squadron of iron-clad ships, like the mystical flag of the Last Judgment.[4] Nations that do not know one another should quickly become acquainted, as men who are to fight a common enemy. Those who shake their fists, like jealous brothers coveting the same tract of land, or like the modest cottager who envies the squire his mansion, should clasp hands and become one. Those who use the authority of a criminal tradition to lop off the lands of their defeated brother with a sword stained with his own blood, ought to return the lands to the brother already punished sufficiently, if they do not want the people to call them robbers. The honest man does not absolve himself of debts of honor with money, at so much a slap. We can no longer be a people of leaves living in the air, our foliage heavy with blooms and crackling or humming at the whim of the sun's caress, or buffeted and tossed by the storms. The trees must form ranks to keep the giant with seven-league boots from passing! It is the time of mobilization, of marching together, and we must go forward in close order, like silver in the veins of the Andes.

* * *

Only those born prematurely are lacking in courage. Those without faith in their country are seven-month weaklings. Because they have no courage, they deny it to others. Their puny arms—arms with bracelets and hands with painted nails, arms of Paris or Madrid—can hardly reach the bottom limb, and they claim the tall tree to be unclimbable. The ships should be loaded with those harmful insects that gnaw at the bone of the country that nour-

1. Martí published "Nuestra America" in Spanish in *La Revista Ilustrada* (January 10, 1891); rpt. in *Our America by José Martí: Writings on Latin America and the Struggle for Cuban Independence* (1977), from which this excerpt is taken.
2. Footwear of European folklore that allowed the wearer to take strides of seven leagues (a "league"=three miles), with great speed. Here, Martí refers to the great imperial strides that industrial countries were making into Latin America, especially into Cuba.

3. Spanish Renaissance poet (1522–1607) who migrated to South America with the Conquistadors and wrote about the "New World" as well as the exploits of the Spanish colonizers.
4. Biblical reference to the "last days," in which the armies of Christ and Satan engage in a final battle, with Christ emerging victorious, binding Satan in Hell for eternity, judging all humankind, and establishing the "New Jerusalem," as told in the book of Revelation.

ishes them. If they are Parisians or from Madrid, let them go to the Prado under lamplight, or to Tortoni's for a sherbet.[5] Those carpenters' sons who are ashamed that their fathers are carpenters! Those born in America who are ashamed of the mother who reared them, because she wears an Indian apron, and who disown their sick mother, the scoundrels, abandoning her on her sickbed! Then who is a real man? He who stays with his mother and nurses her in her illness, or he who puts her to work out of sight, and lives at her expense on decadent lands, sporting fancy neckties, cursing the womb that carried him, displaying the sign of the traitor on the back of his paper frock-coat? These sons of Our America, which will be saved by its Indians and is growing better; these deserters who take up arms in the armies of a North America that drowns its Indians in blood and is growing worse! These delicate creatures who are men but are unwilling to do men's work! The Washington[6] who made this land for them, did he not go to live with the English, to live with the English at a time when he saw them fighting against his own country? These "iconoclasts" of honor who drag that honor over foreign soil, like their counterparts in the French Revolution with their dancing, their affectations, their drawling speech!

For in what lands can men take more pride than in our long-suffering American republics, raised up from among the silent Indian masses by the bleeding arms of a hundred apostles, to the sounds of battle between the book and the processional candle? Never in history have such advanced and united nations been forged in so short a time from such disorganized elements.

\* \* \*

Along comes the natural man, strong and indignant, and he topples all the justice accumulated from books because he has not been governed in accordance with the obvious needs of the country. Knowing is what counts. To know one's country and govern it with that knowledge is the only way to free it from tyranny. The European university must bow to the American university. The history of America, from the Incas to the present, must be taught in clear detail and to the letter, even if the archons of Greece[7] are overlooked. Our Greece must take priority over the Greece which is not ours. We need it more. Nationalist statesmen must replace foreign statesmen. Let the world be grafted onto our republics, but the trunk must be our own. And let the vanquished pedant hold his tongue, for there are no lands in which a man may take greater pride than in our long-suffering American republics.

\* \* \*

1891

---

5. Museo del Prado: museum in Madrid, Spain, with one of the finest collections of European art. Tortoni's: fashionable café of the mid-1800s in Paris's Latin Quarter.
6. George Washington (1732–1799), commander

in chief of the Continental Army in the American Revolutionary War and the first president of the United States (1789–97).
7. Greek leaders.

# CHARLES W. CHESNUTT

Charles W. Chesnutt's scathing review of William Hannibal Thomas's *The American Negro: What He Was, What He Is, and What He May Become* (1901) and Anna Julia Cooper's pointed criticisms of William Dean Howells's novel *An Imperative Duty* (1891) in "One Phase of American Literature" are a pair of literary-critical responses to racial definitions of American-ness. Chesnutt (1858–1932) was admired (and promoted by Howells) for his nuanced portraits of whites and African Americans in novels such as *The House Behind the Cedars* (1900) and *The Marrow of Tradition* (1901) and in his short story collections *The Conjure Woman* (1899) and *"The Wife of His Youth" and Other Stories of the Color Line* (1901). Thomas was an African American author and preacher (1843–1935). In his review of Thomas's book, Chesnutt refutes some of the most pervasive myths of black unreadiness for full American citizenship and laments the fact that such untruths have emanated from black writers as well as from racist whites.

## A Defamer of His Race

The first thought that strikes the reader of this atrocious book[1] is, how did a reputable publishing house ever permit itself to become parties to its publication? The answer probably is that the readers of the publishing house knew nothing about the colored race beyond what they read in the newspapers, and therefore took it for granted that a colored man, who claimed to be a lawyer and ex-member of a legislature, would know all about his own people. It seems never to have occurred to them that a man might be all that, and yet be unworthy of credit, nor do they seem to have inquired into the antecedents of the author of a book the value of which must rest almost solely upon the writer's character, for the book is almost wholly an expression of opinion, with no statistics to support it, but based entirely upon the claimed knowledge and experience of the writer. That a reputable publishing house should have issued such a book against any other considerable class of people without such preliminary investigation is incredible.

The present reviewer during a recent extended tour of the Southern States, under circumstances which threw him mainly among the better class of the colored people, has taken pains to ascertain as far as possible the past record of Mr. Thomas, and is obliged to say that he has not heard anywhere one good word concerning him. The writer has conversed with colored bishops, college professors, and others, men of substance and character, who have known this man during his variegated career, and they are all unanimous in the statement that the book faithfully represents the man. The only parallel example to this book was one written some years ago by a renegade Jew, in which all the worst slanders against this oppressed people were gathered from the obscure and musty folios of ancient libraries, and dished up in a paper-covered volume for

---

1. Chesnutt's review of *The American Negro: What He Was, What He Is, and What He May Become,* by William Hannibal Thomas (1901), was published in *The Critic* 38.4 (April 1901), from which this text is taken.

the delectation of the nineteenth century. It must have been a satisfaction to the chosen people to note that within a year the author of the book was sent to the penitentiary for forgery, and that a year or two later the publishing house failed disastrously. This may have been a logical *non sequitur*, but it was poetic justice. Mr. Thomas may continue to escape this fate, but if it be any satisfaction to him to know that he has not a single friend or well-wisher among the whole eight or ten millions of his own people, he may rest content that such is emphatically the case.

So much for the man, if it be possible to separate the man from the book. The present reviewer once wrote a story in which a negro was transformed into a tree[2] and the tree sawed up into lumber, and built into a house, which was ever afterwards haunted by the spirit of the unfortunate victim of an untoward fate. The parallel between Thomas and this tree-man is obvious. He has transformed himself into white paper and black ink—he is a mulatto by blood—and has bound himself into a book. Nevertheless, it may be possible, by an effort, to consider the book as a separate thing.

In the first place, it is not a well-written book. That it has a certain amount of ability is beyond question; but it lacks consecutiveness. It would seem to have been compiled from a scrap-book, into which the author had pasted for twenty years or more every newspaper clipping that he had seen anywhere to the discredit of the colored race. A peculiarity of the book which bears out this view is his employment of the word "freedman," a term which is not now in common use as descriptive of the colored people, as it was twenty years ago. A full average generation has elapsed since the abolition of slavery, and fully three fourths of the colored people of the present day are free born, as a comparison of their numbers now and at the close of the civil war will demonstrate. Mr. Thomas has great fluency of language—a fondness for big words is supposed to be a trait of his race. A good command of a large vocabulary is a valuable accomplishment, and, if it be a race trait, one which may be judiciously cultivated to the enrichment of literature; but it is painfully apparent here and there that Mr. Thomas's thought has been swept away by the current of his own eloquence. One must sometimes fish long in this turbid pool to catch a minnow.

The negro has suffered a great deal, in the public estimation, from loose and hasty generalizations with reference to his intelligence, his morals, his physical characteristics, and his social efficiency. But not the worst things said about him by his most radical defamers, all put together, could surpass in untruthfulness and malignity the screed which this alleged reformer has put forth under his publisher's imprint. The slanders against the womanhood of his race are so vile as to confute themselves by their mere statement. There are several passages in the book, reflecting on the morals of colored youth, which ought to bar the volume from circulation in the United States mails. They are false on the face of them. No individual could possibly know that they were true, and they are utterly abhorrent to human nature and human experience. To believe them, one must read the negro out of the human family. If they are the fruit of this author's observation, one shudders to contemplate the depths of vice which he has fathomed.

His characterization of colored preachers is also unjust. That there are

2. "Po' Sandy," published in *The Conjure Woman* (1899).

many such preachers who might be otherwise employed with more profit to society may well be admitted; but that there are among them many good men, faithful to their trust, earnestly striving to uplift their people, and with encouraging results, is apparent to any one who will take the trouble to inquire. The greatest preacher of America did not escape calumny, if he avoided sin. Human character is a compound of good and evil. For aught we know, Judas Iscariot was a very good apostle before he betrayed his Master; we know that Benedict Arnold was a gallant soldier who had served his country well before he betrayed her. But here the parallel between these men and this author fails, for what good thing Thomas had ever done for his people before he dealt them this traitorous blow is not of record among the traditions of his people, nor in the archives of the South Carolina Legislature of which he claims to have been a valuable member. That membership in that body should be set forward by a writer and accepted by a publisher as a certificate of moral character, is the most curious feature of this whole remarkable performance.

Among the glimmerings of reason which here and there may be found in this book, is the statement that the colored people are deprived of social stimulus because the white people will not associate or intermarry with them. Granted. But with what face could any one ask a race with any self-respect, any pride of its past, any hope for its future, to consort with such moral and mental degenerates as Thomas has sought in this book to make of his own people?

The strongest argument against the negro suggested by this book is the existence of the book itself. As one of a race which has but just begun to win a hearing in the forum of letters, the author might have found a different theme. If the book were truthful, it would be without excuse as coming from such a source. But being false, as the book essentially is, it is all the more worthy of condemnation. That a man of color should write such a book is almost enough to make out his case against the negro.

1901

---

# JANE ADDAMS

Laura Jane Addams (1860–1935) was born in Cedarville, Illinois; she graduated from Rockford Seminary in 1882, her father having refused to allow her to attend Smith College and become a physician. After a period of indecision and depression, Addams found her calling and in 1889 founded the social settlement Hull-House in Chicago. From Hull-House, where she lived and worked for the rest of her life, Addams became one of the country's most famous women through her writing, settlement work, and international efforts for world peace. At Hull-House, which was located at the corner of Polk and Halsted Streets, immigrants to Chicago, including Italians, Russian and Polish Jews, Irish, Germans, Greeks, and Bohemians, could take refuge from dirty and over-crowded tenements and the dangers of life on the streets. The settlement provided services for the neighborhood, such as meals and clothes. It also had kindergarten and daycare facilities for children of working mothers, an employment bureau, an art gallery, libraries, discussion groups, crafts groups, and music and art classes. By 1900 Hull-House activities had broadened to include the Jane Club (a cooperative residence for working women), the first Little Theater in America, a labor museum, and a meeting hall for trade union groups. One of Addams's most characteristic programs at Hull-House was the promotion of the traditional crafts and cultural practices of immigrants, aimed at giving them renewed self-respect as they assimilated into U.S. society and forging bonds between older immigrants and their children, who were quickly becoming "American." Building on her work at Hull-House, Addams became involved in the peace movement, becoming an important advocate of internationalism. During World War I, which as a pacifist she opposed, she participated in the 1915 International Congress of Women at the Hague. She helped found the Women's International League for Peace and Freedom in 1919. Addams was awarded the Nobel Peace Prize in 1931.

## *From* Twenty Years at Hull-House[1]

### From *Chapter V. First Days at Hull-House*

\* \* \*

In spite of these flourishing clubs for children early established at Hull-House, and the fact that our first organized undertaking was a kindergarten, we were very insistent that the Settlement should not be primarily for the children, and that it was absurd to suppose that grown people would not respond to opportunities for education and social life. Our enthusiastic kindergartner herself demonstrated this with an old woman of ninety, who, because she was left alone all day while her daughter cooked in a restaurant, had formed such a persistent habit of picking the plaster off the walls that one landlord after another refused to have her for a tenant. It required but a few weeks' time to teach her to make large paper chains, and gradually she was content to do it all day long, and in the end took quite as much pleasure in adorning the walls as she had formerly taken in demolishing them. Fortunately the landlord had never heard the æsthetic principle that the exposure of basic construction is more desirable than gaudy decoration. In course of time it was discovered that the old woman could speak Gælic, and when one or two grave professors came to see her, the neighborhood was filled with pride that such a wonder lived in their midst. To mitigate life for a woman of ninety was an unfailing refutation of the statement that the Settlement was designed for the young.

On our first New Year's Day at Hull-House we invited the older people in the vicinity, sending a carriage for the most feeble and announcing to all of them that we were going to organize an Old Settlers' Party.

Every New Year's Day since, older people in varying numbers have come together at Hull-House to relate early hardships, and to take for the moment the place in the community to which their pioneer life entitles them. Many people who were formerly residents of the vicinity, but whom prosperity has carried into more desirable neighborhoods, come back to these meetings and often confess to each other that they have never since found such kindness

1. First published by Macmillan in 1910, from which the following excerpts are taken.

as in early Chicago when all its citizens came together in mutual enterprises. Many of these pioneers, so like the men and women of my earliest childhood that I always felt comforted by their presence in the house, were very much opposed to "foreigners," whom they held responsible for a depreciation of property and a general lowering of the tone of the neighborhood. Sometimes we had a chance for championship; I recall one old man, fiercely American, who had reproached me because we had so many "foreign views" on our walls, to whom I endeavored to set forth our hope that the pictures might afford a familiar island to the immigrants in a sea of new and strange impressions. The old settler guest, taken off his guard, replied, "I see; they feel as we did when we saw a Yankee notion from down East,"—thereby formulating the dim kinship between the pioneer and the immigrant, both "buffeting the waves of a new development." The older settlers as well as their children throughout the years have given genuine help to our various enterprises for neighborhood improvement, and from their own memories of earlier hardships have made many shrewd suggestions for alleviating the difficulties of that first sharp struggle with untoward conditions.

In those early days we were often asked why we had come to live on Halsted Street when we could afford to live somewhere else. I remember one man who used to shake his head and say it was "the strangest thing he had met in his experience," but who was finally convinced that it was "not strange but natural." In time it came to seem natural to all of us that the Settlement should be there. If it is natural to feed the hungry and care for the sick, it is certainly natural to give pleasure to the young, comfort to the aged, and to minister to the deep-seated craving for social intercourse that all men feel. Whoever does it is rewarded by something which, if not gratitude, is at least spontaneous and vital and lacks that irksome sense of obligation with which a substantial benefit is too often acknowledged.

In addition to the neighbors who responded to the receptions and classes, we found those who were too battered and oppressed to care for them. To these, however, was left that susceptibility to the bare offices of humanity which raises such offices into a bond of fellowship.

From the first it seemed understood that we were ready to perform the humblest neighborhood services. We were asked to wash the new-born babies, and to prepare the dead for burial, to nurse the sick, and to "mind the children."

Occasionally these neighborly offices unexpectedly uncovered ugly human traits. For six weeks after an operation we kept in one of our three bedrooms a forlorn little baby who, because he was born with a cleft palate, was most unwelcome even to his mother, and we were horrified when he died of neglect a week after he was returned to his home; a little Italian bride of fifteen sought shelter with us one November evening, to escape her husband who had beaten her every night for a week when he returned home from work, because she had lost her wedding ring; two of us officiated quite alone at the birth of an illegitimate child because the doctor was late in arriving, and none of the honest Irish matrons would "touch the likes of her"; we ministered at the deathbed of a young man, who during a long illness of tuberculosis had received so many bottles of whisky through the mistaken kindness of his friends, that the cumulative effect produced wild periods of exultation, in one of which he died.

We were also early impressed with the curious isolation of many of the immigrants; an Italian woman once expressed her pleasure in the red roses that she saw at one of our receptions in surprise that they had been "brought so fresh all the way from Italy." She would not believe for an instant that they had been grown in America. She said that she had lived in Chicago for six years and had never seen any roses, whereas in Italy she had seen them every summer in great profusion. During all that time, of course, the woman had lived within ten blocks of a florist's window; she had not been more than a five-cent car ride away from the public parks; but she had never dreamed of faring forth for herself, and no one had taken her. Her conception of America had been the untidy street in which she lived and had made her long struggle to adapt herself to American ways.

But in spite of some untoward experiences, we were constantly impressed with the uniform kindness and courtesy we received. Perhaps these first days laid the simple human foundations which are certainly essential for continuous living among the poor: first, genuine preference for residence in an industrial quarter to any other part of the city, because it is interesting and makes the human appeal; and second, the conviction, in the words of Canon Barnett,[2] that the things which make men alike are finer and better than the things that keep them apart, and that these basic likenesses, if they are properly accentuated, easily transcend the less essential differences of race, language, creed and tradition.

Perhaps even in those first days we made a beginning toward that object which was afterwards stated in our charter: "To provide a center for a higher civic and social life; to institute and maintain educational and philanthropic enterprises, and to investigate and improve the conditions in the industrial districts of Chicago."

### From Chapter XI. Immigrants and Their Children

\* \* \*

An overmastering desire to reveal the humbler immigrant parents to their own children lay at the base of what has come to be called the Hull-House Labor Museum. This was first suggested to my mind one early spring day when I saw an old Italian woman, her distaff against her homesick face, patiently spinning a thread by the simple stick spindle so reminiscent of all southern Europe. I was walking down Polk Street, perturbed in spirit, because it seemed so difficult to come into genuine relations with the Italian women and because they themselves so often lost their hold upon their Americanized children. It seemed to me that Hull-House ought to be able to devise some educational enterprise, which should build a bridge between European and American experiences in such wise as to give them both more meaning and a sense of relation. I meditated that perhaps the power to see life as a whole, is more needed in the immigrant quarter of a large city than anywhere else, and that the lack of this power is the most fruitful source of misunderstanding between European immigrants and their children, as it is between them and their American neighbors; and why should that chasm between

2. Samuel Augustus Barnett (1844–1913), English clergyman and social reformer associated with the establishment of the first university settlement, Toynbee Hall, in London, which inspired Addams to create Hull-House.

fathers and sons, yawning at the feet of each generation, be made so unnecessarily cruel and impassable to these bewildered immigrants? Suddenly I looked up and saw the old woman with her distaff, sitting in the sun on the steps of a tenement house. She might have served as a model for one of Michael Angelo's Fates,[3] but her face brightened as I passed and, holding up her spindle for me to see, she called out that when she had spun a little more yarn, she would knit a pair of stockings for her goddaughter. The occupation of the old woman gave me the clew that was needed. Could we not interest the young people working in the neighboring factories, in these older forms of industry, so that, through their own parents and grandparents, they would find a dramatic representation of the inherited resources of their daily occupation. If these young people could actually see that the complicated machinery of the factory had been evolved from simple tools, they might at least make a beginning towards that education which Dr. Dewey[4] defines as "a continuing reconstruction of experience." They might also lay a foundation for reverence of the past which Goethe[5] declares to be the basis of all sound progress.

* * * Within a month a room was fitted up to which we might invite those of our neighbors who were possessed of old crafts and who were eager to use them.

We found in the immediate neighborhood, at least four varieties of these most primitive methods of spinning and three distinct variations of the same spindle in connection with wheels. It was possible to put these seven into historic sequence and order and to connect the whole with the present method of factory spinning. The same thing was done for weaving, and on every Saturday evening a little exhibit was made of these various forms of labor in the textile industry. Within one room a Syrian woman, a Greek, an Italian, a Russian, and an Irishwoman enabled even the most casual observer to see that there is no break in orderly evolution if we look at history from the industrial standpoint; that industry develops similarly and peacefully year by year among the workers of each nation, heedless of differences in language, religion, and political experiences.

And then we grew ambitious and arranged lectures upon industrial history. I remember that after an interesting lecture upon the industrial revolution in England and a portrayal of the appalling conditions throughout the weaving districts of the north, which resulted from the hasty gathering of the weavers into the new towns, a Russian tailor in the audience was moved to make a speech. He suggested that whereas time had done much to alleviate the first difficulties in the transition of weaving from hand work to steam power, that in the application of steam to sewing we are still in the first stages, illustrated by the isolated woman who tries to support herself by hand needlework at home until driven out by starvation, as many of the hand weavers had been.

* * *

3. In Greek mythology, the Fates controlled human destinies, spinning and measuring out each person's life-span: Lacheses of things past, Clotho of things present, Atropos of things to come. The painting by Michelangelo portrays them as three elderly Italian women.
4. John Dewey (1859–1952), American philosopher, psychologist, and educational reformer.

Addams met Dewey when he began to teach at the University of Chicago in 1894.
5. Johann Wolfgang von Goethe (1749–1832), German poet, novelist, playwright, and natural philosopher. Among his most famous works are *The Sorrows of Young Werther* (1774) and *Faust* (1808, 1832).

There has been some testimony that the Labor Museum has revealed the charm of woman's primitive activities. I recall a certain Italian girl who came every Saturday evening to a cooking class in the same building in which her mother spun in the Labor Museum exhibit; and yet Angelina always left her mother at the front door while she herself went around to a side door because she did not wish to be too closely identified in the eyes of the rest of the cooking class with an Italian woman who wore a kerchief over her head, uncouth boots, and short petticoats. One evening, however, Angelina saw her mother surrounded by a group of visitors from the School of Education, who much admired the spinning, and she concluded from their conversation that her mother was "the best stick-spindle spinner in America." When she inquired from me as to the truth of this deduction, I took occasion to describe the Italian village in which her mother had lived, something of her free life, and how, because of the opportunity she and the other women of the village had to drop their spindles over the edge of a precipice, they had developed a skill in spinning beyond that of the neighboring towns. I dilated somewhat on the freedom and beauty of that life—how hard it must be to exchange it all for a two-room tenement, and to give up a beautiful homespun kerchief for an ugly department store hat. I intimated it was most unfair to judge her by these things alone, and that while she must depend on her daughter to learn the new ways, she also had a right to expect her daughter to know something of the old ways.

That which I could not convey to the child but upon which my own mind persistently dwelt, was that her mother's whole life had been spent in a secluded spot under the rule of traditional and narrowly localized observances, until her very religion clung to local sanctities,—to the shrine before which she had always prayed, to the pavement and walls of the low vaulted church,—and then suddenly she was torn from it all and literally put out to sea, straight away from the solid habits of her religious and domestic life, and she now walked timidly but with poignant sensibility upon a new and strange shore.

It was easy to see that the thought of her mother with any other background than that of the tenement was new to Angelina and at least two things resulted; she allowed her mother to pull out of the big box under the bed the beautiful homespun garments which had been previously hidden away as uncouth; and she openly came into the Labor Museum by the same door as did her mother, proud at least of the mastery of the craft which had been so much admired.

\* \* \*

1910

# ANNA JULIA COOPER

Cooper's *A Voice from the South* (1892) is an important framing of political and specifically antiracist and feminist arguments in a forceful subjective style. In the excerpt below, Cooper attacks William Dean Howells's reductive African American characterizations in his novel *An Imperative Duty*, even as she acknowledges that as an editor Howells has tried to promote African American writers. In his novel, at least, Cooper finds, "Mr. Howells does not know what he is talking about."

## *From* One Phase of American Literature[1]

\* \* \*

Among our artists for art's sweet sake, Mr. Howells[2] has recently tried his hand also at painting the Negro, attempting merely a side light in half tones, on his life and manners; and I think the unanimous verdict of the subject is that, in this single department at least, Mr. Howells does not know what he is talking about. And yet I do not think we should quarrel with *An Imperative Duty*[3] because it lacks the earnestness and bias of a special pleader. Mr. Howells merely meant to press the button and give one picture from American life involving racial complications. The kodak[4] does no more; it cannot preach sermons or solve problems.

Besides, the portrayal of Negro characteristics was by no means the main object of the story, which was rather meant, I judge, to be a thumb nail sketch containing a psychological study of a morbidly sensitive conscience hectoring over a weak and vacillating will and fevered into increased despotism by reading into its own life and consciousness the analyses and terrible retributions of fiction,—a product of the Puritan's uncompromising sense of *"right though the heavens fall,"* irritated and kept sore by being unequally yoked with indecision and cowardice. Of such strokes Mr. Howells is undoubtedly master. It is true there is little point and no force of character about the beautiful and irresponsible young heroine; but as that is an attainment of so many of Mr. Howells' models, it is perhaps not to be considered as illustrating any racial characteristics. I cannot help sharing, however, the indignation of those who resent the picture in the colored church,—"evidently," Mr. Howells assures us, "representing *the best colored society*"; where the horrified young prig, Rhoda Aldgate, meets nothing but the frog-like countenances and cat-fish mouths, the musky exhalations and the "bress de Lawd, Honey," of an uncultivated people. It is just here that Mr. Howells fails—and fails because he gives only a half truth, and that a partisan half truth. One feels that he had no business to attempt a subject of which he knew so little, or for which he cared so little. There is one thing I would like to say to my white fellow countrymen, and especially to those who dabble in ink and affect to discuss the Negro; and yet I hesitate because I feel it is a fact which persons of the finer sensibilities and more delicate perceptions must know instinctively: namely, that it is an insult to humanity and a sin against God to publish any such sweeping generalizations of a race on such meager and superficial information. We meet it at every turn—this obtrusive and offensive vulgarity, this gratuitous sizing up of the Negro and conclusively writing

1. Also known as "The Negro as Presented in American Literature," the essay was first published in Cooper's *A Voice from the South by a Black Woman of the South* (1892), from which this excerpt is taken.
2. William Dean Howells (1837–1920), American novelist, critic, and proponent of realism.
3. Psychological novel (1891) in which Howells explores issues of race and miscegenation.
4. Simple roll film camera produced by Eastman Dry Plate Company in the late 1800s.

down his equation, sometimes even among his ardent friends and bravest defenders. Were I not afraid of falling myself into the same error that I am condemning, I would say it seems an *Anglo Saxon characteristic* to have such overweening confidence in his own power of induction that there is no equation which he would acknowledge to be indeterminate, however many unknown quantities it may possess.

\* \* \*

1892

# Selected Bibliographies

## Reference

To learn more about American literature 1865–1914 or to begin research for a paper, students should begin in the reference section of the library, where there are many valuable resources for bibliographical and other research information about American literature. James L. Harner's *Literary Research Guide: A Guide to Reference Sources for the Study of Literatures in English and Related Topics*, 4th ed. (1993) is now updated online. Though it is now badly outdated, a still useful general guide to American literature and civilization is Clarence Gohdes and Sanford E. Marovitz's *Bibliographic Guide to the Literature of the U.S.A.*, 5th ed. (1984).

Author biographies are available in the *Dictionary of Literary Biography's* ongoing volumes, in the American National Biography volumes (1999), and also in such books as Jay Parini's *American Writers: A Collection of Literary Biographies* (2003); *Biographical Dictionary of Literary Influences: The Nineteenth Century, 1800–1914,* ed. John Powell and Derek W. Blakely (2001), which contains 271 biographical sketches of literary figures; James K. Bracken and Larry G. Hinman, *The Undergraduate's Companion to American Writers and Their Web Sites* (2003).

General resources on the period include *Twentieth-Century Literary Movements Dictionary,* ed. Helen Henderson and Jay P. Pederson (2000), a substantial and well-organized volume; *Encyclopedia of American Cultural and Intellectual History*, ed. Mary Kupiec, Peter W. Williams, Mary K. Cayton (2001); *Encyclopedia of American Studies*, ed. George T. Kurian, et al. (2000); *American Literature and Culture 1900–1960: An Introduction,* ed. Gail McDonald (2006); *A Companion to American Literature and Culture*, ed. Paul Lauter (2006); *A Companion to the American Novel*, ed. Alfred Bendixen (2006); *A Companion to American Fiction 1865–1914*, ed. Robert Paul Lamb and G. R. Thompson (2005). More specialized sources on movements of the period include Joseph B. McCullough and Robert L. Gale's *Nineteenth-Century American Western Writers* (1997); *A Companion to the Regional Literatures of America*, ed. Charles L. Crow (2003), which sets out to rehabilitate regionalism with essays by leading scholars such as Donna Campbell, Lawrence I. Berkove, and Susan Kollin; *A Companion to the Literature and Culture of the American South*, ed. Richard Gray and Owen Robinson (2006); the four-volume *American Women Writers: A Critical Reference Guide: From Colonial Times to the Present*, 2nd ed., ed. Taryn Benbow-Pfalzgraf (2000); *The Columbia Guide to Women in the Nineteenth Century*, ed. Catherine Clinton and Christine Lunardini (2000); Denise D. Knight and Emmanuel S. Nelson, eds., *Nineteenth-Century American Women Writ-*

ers: *A Bio-Bibliographical Critical Sourcebook* (1997); Elaine Showalter, Lea Baechler, and A. Walton Litz, eds., *Modern American Women Writers* (1991); Laurie Champion, ed., *American Women Writers, 1900–1945: A Bio-Bibliographical Critical Sourcebook* (2000); Sharon M. Harris, ed., *American Women Prose Writers, 1870–1920* (2000), which includes biographical information; Trudier Harris and Thadious M. Davis, eds., *Afro-American Writers before the Harlem Renaissance* (1986); Nelson's *African American Authors, 1745–1945* (2000); *African American Writers*, 2nd ed., ed. Valerie Smith (2001); *Jewish American Women Writers: A Bio-Bibliographical and Critical Sourcebook* (1994), ed. Ann R. Shapiro, which presents individually authored biographical-critical essays plus primary and secondary bibliographies on various authors; Nelson's *Asian-American Novelists, 1745–1945* (2000); *Chinese American Literature Since the 1850s* (2006), by Xiao-huang Yin, which traces the construction of Chinese American identity, especially in tales of interracial marriage in the fiction of Sui Sin Far and others; Deborah L. Madsen's *Asian American Writers* (2005); A. LaVonne Brown Ruoff, *American Indian Literatures: An Introduction, Bibliographic Review, and Selected Bibliography* (1990); *Hispanic Literature of the United States: A Comprehensive Reference*, ed. Nicolás Kannelos (2003); Francisco A. Lomelí, Carl R. Shirley, eds., *Chicano Writers: Third Series* (1999); and *Recovering the U.S. Hispanic Literary Heritage*, Volume IV, ed. José F. Aranda, Jr. and Silvio Torres-Saillant (2002), a series from Arte Público Press.

Still useful are James D. Hart's *Oxford Companion to American Literature*, now in an updated and revised edition co-edited with Phillip Leiniger (1995), and the discursive bibliographical supplements to Robert Spiller et al.'s *Literary History of the United States*, 4th ed. (1974). Richard M. Ludwig and Clifford Nault Jr.'s, *Annals of American Literature, 1602–1983* (1989) is a good source for locating major works in their cultural contexts. The annual and invaluable *American Literary Scholarship* (also online) provides critical commentary on a wide range of scholarly books and articles (including reference works) on American literature published each year in the United States and abroad.

For guidance to more recent general books on American literature in this period, see the "Themes, Topics, Criticism" and "Nineteenth-Century Literature" chapters in annual volumes of *American Literary Scholarship*. The *Modern Language Association Bibliography* should also be consulted. Up-to-date bibliographies and reviews may be found in such standard journals as *African American Review, American Literature, American Literary History, American Quarterly, American Literary Realism, 1870–1910, College Language Association Journal*, and *MELUS* as well as in the publications of societies devoted to individual authors in this period.

## Literary History

The ongoing, eight-volume *Cambridge History of American Literature* (Sacvan Bercovitch, general editor) addresses not only traditional literary genres and periods, but is self-consciously concerned with literary theory and criticism as well as recently emergent forms and contributors to literature as a form of cultural production. Given the breadth of its coverage and the distinction of its section authors, this set is indispensable. Also of great value is Bercovitch's often-cited *Reconstructing American Literary History* (1986). A useful introduction to the influence on the modern novel of this period is *A Cultural History of the American Novel: Henry James to William Faulkner*, by David L. Minter (1996). American poetry of the period is covered in David Perkins, *A History of American Poetry: From the 1890s to the High Modernist Mode* (1976); Alan Shucard, Fred Moramarco, and William Sullivan, *Modern American Poetry, 1865–1950* (1989); and Robert Shulman, *Social Criticism and Nineteenth Century American Poetry, 1865–1950* (1989). Among other one-volume reference works is the comprehensive *Cambridge Guide to American Theatre* (1996), edited by Don B. Wilmeth.

Important general studies of American history and culture as expressed in literature include *A History of American Literature*, Richard Gray (2004); Loren Glass, *Authors, Inc.: Literary Celebrity in the Modern United States, 1880–1980* (2004), which covers figures including Adams, Twain, London, Hemingway, Mailer, and Stein; Paul Lauter, *From Walden Pond to Jurassic Park: Activism, Culture, and American Studies* (2001); *Literary Culture and U.S. Imperialism: From the Revolution to World War II*, John Carlos Rowe (2000); Orm Overland, *Immigrant Minds, American Identities: Making the United States Home, 1870–1930* (2000); Michael Szalay, *New Deal Modernism: American Literature and the Invention of the Welfare State* (2000); Scott Casper, *Constructing American Lives: Biography and Culture in Nineteenth-Century America* (1999); Katherine B. Payant and Rose Toby, eds., *The Immigrant Experience in North American Literature: Carving Out a Niche* (1999); Eric J. Sundquist, To *Wake the Nations: Race in the Making of American Literature* (1993); *From Puritanism to Postmodernism: A History of American Literature*, Richard Ruland and Malcolm Bradbury (1992); Cushing Strout, *Making American Tradition: Visions and Revisions from Ben Franklin to Alice Walker* (1990); A. LaVonne Brown Ruoff and Jerry Ward, eds., *Redefining American Literary History* (1990); Werner Sollers, *Beyond Ethnicity: Consent and Descent in American Culture* (1986); Russell Reising, *The Unusable Past: Theory and the Study of American Literature* (1986); Richard Slotkin, *The Fatal Environment: The Myth of the Frontier in the Age of Industrialization, 1800–1890* (1985); Gordon O. Taylor, *Chapters of Experience: Studies in Twentieth Century American Autobiography* (1983); Alan Trachtenberg, *The Incorporation of America: Culture and Society in the Gilded Age* (1982); Ronald E. Martin, *American Literature and the Universe of Force* (1981); Annette Kolodny's *The Lay of the Land: Metaphor as Experience and History* (1975). Still of great importance are Alfred Kazin's *On Native Grounds: An Interpretation of Modern American Prose Literature* (1942) and *American Procession* (1984); Leo Marx, *The Machine in the Garden: Technology and the Pastoral Ideal in America* (1964); and Richard Poirier, *A World Elsewhere: The Place of Style in American Literature* (1966).

Histories of American women writers include *Before They Could Vote: American Women's Autobiographical Writing, 1819–1919*, ed. Sidonie A. Smith and Julia Watson (2006); *Beyond the Gibson Girl: Reimagining the American New Woman, 1895–1915* (2005) by Martha H. Patterson, which argues that contexts such as social class and geography helped define the

New Woman of the turn of the century; *Wayward Reproductions: Genealogies of Race and Nation in Transatlantic Modern Thought*, Alys Eve Weinbaum (2004) argues that racism, nationalism, and imperialism were ideologies founded in large part on what she calls "the race/reproduction bind"—the notion that race is something that is biologically reproduced, an idea that reveals the centrality of ideas about women's reproductive capacity to modernity's intellectual foundations, as in the work of Gilman and Du Bois among many others; *Feminist Forerunners: New Womanism and Feminism in the Early Twentieth Century* by Ann Heilmann (2003); Suzanne Bost's *Mulattas and Mestizas: Representing Mixed Identities in the Americas, 1850–2000* (2003); Dale M. Bauer and Philip Gould, eds., *The Cambridge Companion to Nineteenth-Century American Women's Writing* (2001); Nina Baym, *American Women of Letters and the Nineteenth-Century Sciences: Styles of Affiliation* (2002) and *Women's Fiction: A Guide to Novels By and About Women in America 1820–1870* (1978); Susan L. Roberson, ed., *Women, America, and Movement: Narratives of Relocation* (1998); Jane Missner Barstow, *One Hundred Years of American Women Writing, 1848–1948* (1997), which provides biographical summaries and surveys of scholarship on most of the women writers in this section of *NAAL*; Shirley Samuels, ed., *The Culture of Sentiment: Race, Gender, and Sentimentality in Nineteenth-Century America* (1992); Elizabeth Ammons, *Conflicting Stories: American Women Writers at the Turn of the Century* (1991); Barbara Bardes and Suzanne Gossett, *Declarations of Independence: Women and Political Power in Nineteenth Century American Fiction* (1990); Susan K. Harris, *Nineteenth-Century American Women's Novels* (1990); Nancy A. Walker, *A Very Serious Thing: Women's Humor and American Culture* (1988); Carroll Smith-Rosenberg, *Disorderly Conduct: Visions of Gender in Victorian America* (1986); Alfred Habegger, *Gender, Fantasy, and Realism in American Literature* (1982); Ann Douglas, *The Feminization of American Culture* (1977); Todd McGowan's *The Feminine "NO!": Psychoanalysis and the New Canon* (2001) offers a new perspective on such prominent rediscovered titles as Gilman's "The Yellow Wall-paper," Chesnutt's *The Marrow of Tradition*, and Chopin's *The Awakening*, in its study of why works were rejected from the canon despite their artistic value—they were set aside, he argues, because they show traumatic experiences (2001); and Elsa Nettels's *Language and Gender in American Fiction: Howells, James, Wharton, and Cather* (1997), which is of great value especially on Howells and Cather, who are under-studied and under-taught; and Jessica Bomarito, Jeffrey W. Hunter, and Amy Hudock, eds., *Feminism in Literature: A Gale Critical Companion* (2004).

African American literary history is covered by such sources as *Portraits of the New Negro Woman: Visual and Literary Culture in the Harlem Renaissance*, by Cherene Sherrard-Johnson (2006); Paul Gilmore, *The Genuine Article: Race, Mass Culture, and American Literary Manhood* (2002); *Saints, Sinners, Saviors: Strong Black Women in African American Literature*, Trudier Harris (2001); *Passing: Identity and Interpretation in Sexuality, Race, and Religion*, Maria Carla Sánchez and Linda Schlossberg, eds. (2001); William L. Andrews and Henry Louis Gates Jr., eds., *The Civitas Anthology of African American Slave Narratives* (1999); Paul Gilroy, *The Black Atlantic Modernity and Double Consciousness* (1993); Charles P. Henry, *Culture and African American Politics* (1990); *Reconstructing Womanhood: The Emergence of the*

*Afro-American Woman Novelist* (1988), by Hazel V. Carby, who sees the works of Cooper, Hopkins, and Wells as feminist historiographies with immense intellectual and political importance for the period; Henry Louis Gates Jr., *Figures in Black: Words, Signs, and the "Racial" Self* (1987) and *The Signifying Monkey: A Theory of Afro-American Literary Criticism* (1988); Bernard W. Bell, *The Afro-American Novel and Its Tradition* (1987); Wilson J. Moses, *The Golden Age of Black Nationalism, 1850–1925* (1978, reprinted 1988); Valerie Smith, *Self-Discovery and Authority in Afro-American Narrative* (1987); William L. Andrews, *To Tell a Free Story: The First Century of Afro-American Autobiography, 1760–1865* (1986); Toni Morrison, *Playing in the Dark: Whiteness and the Literary Imagination* (1992); George Frederickson, *The Black Image in the White Mind: The Debate on Afro-American Character and Destiny, 1817–1914* (1971); and Ruth Miller, *Backgrounds to Black American Literature* (1971). Asian-American writers are surveyed in Amy Ling's *Asian American Literature* (1982). New work on Latina/o literatures includes *Latina Legacies: Identity, Biography, and Community*, ed. Vicki L. Ruiz and Virginia Sánchez Korrol (2005); and *When We Arrive: A New Literary History of Mexican America*, José F. Aranda, Jr. (2003).

Realism and Naturalism, as the two most important literary movements of the period, are traced by many literary historians and critics, including Donald Pizer, ed., *The Cambridge Companion to American Realism and Naturalism: Howells to London* (1995); Pizer, ed., *Documents of American Realism and Naturalism* (1998); Tom Quirk and Gary Scharnhorst, eds., *American Realism and the Canon* (1994); David E. Shi, *Facing Facts: Realism in American Thought and Culture, 1850–1920* (1995); Tony Tanner, *Scenes of Nature, Signs of Men* (1987); and Kenneth Warren, *Black and White Strangers: Race and American Literary Realism* (1993); Michael Davitt Bell, *The Problem of American Realism: Studies in the Cultural History of a Literary Idea* (1993); Amy Kaplan, *The Social Construction of American* Realism (1988); Janet Holmgrin McKay, *Narration and Discourse in American Realistic Fiction* (1982); *The Ferment of Realism* (1965), by Warner Berthoff; John Conder, *Naturalism in American Fiction: The Classic Phase* (1984); June Howard, *Form and History in American Literary Naturalism* (1985); *Realism and Naturalism in Nineteenth-Century American Literature* (rev. ed. 1984); and Donald Pizer, *Twentieth Century American Naturalism* (1982). Also see Peter N. Skrine and Lillian R. Furst, *Naturalism* (1971). Regionalism has been "reclaimed" or at least brought into the canon by scholars such as Donna M. Campbell, in her *Resisting Regionalism: Gender and Naturalism in American Fiction, 1885–1915* (1998); Sherrie A. Inness and Diana Royer, eds., *Breaking Boundaries: New Perspectives on Women's Regional Writing* (1997), with fifteen essays on Stowe and Jewett and lesser-known writers, mostly from the nineteenth century; Carolyn Perry, Mary Louise Weaks, Mary Louise, and Doris Betts in their *History of Southern Women's Literature* (2002); Josephine Donovan, in *New England Local Color Literature: A Women's Tradition* (1983); Glen A. Love, *New Americans: The Westerner and the Modern Experience in the American Novel* (1982); Bonney MacDonald, *Updating the Literary West* (1997), which brings together essays by one hundred scholars who address a diverse range of topics from ethnicity and gender to children's literature and the environment. Also of interest is Larzar Ziff's *Return Passages: Great American Travel Writing 1780–1910* (2000).

## Literary Criticism and Theory

Critical and theoretical work in American literature has continued to benefit from lively perspectives by many scholars, especially in the recent past in the area of cultural studies involving class, race, and gender in national literary identity; at the same time perspectives on re-discovered writers previously marginalized have multiplied. What follows is a highly selective list of some of the most useful volumes. We begin with Leslie A. Fiedler, *Love and Death in the American Novel* (1960); John Carlos Rowe, *Through the Custom-House: Nineteenth Century American Fiction and Modern Theory* (1982); Eric J. Sundquist, ed., *American Realism: New Essays* (1982); Robert A. Ferguson, *Law and Letters in American Culture* (1984); Philip Fisher, *Hard Facts: Setting and Form in the American Novel* (1985); Thomas Cooley, *Educated Lives: The Rise of Modern Autobiography in America* (1986); Eric Homberger's *American Writers and Radical Politics, 1900–39: Equivocal Commitments* (1986); Frederick Crews, *The Critics Bear It Away* (1992); Robert Davidoff, *The Genteel Tradition and the Sacred Rage* (1992); Paul John Eakin, *American Autobiography: Retrospect and Prospect* (1991); *Writing Their Nations: The Tradition of Nineteenth-Century American Jewish Women Writers* (1992), by Diane Lichtenstein, surveys thirty Jewish and Jewish American female writers; *Speaking the Other Self: American Women Writers*, ed. Jeanne Campbell Reesman (1997); and *Unruly Tongue: Identity and Voice in American Women's Writing, 1850–1930* (1999), by Martha J. Cutter, an examination of how Cooper, Chopin, Gilman, and Frances Harper contested and sought to resignify male/female binaries.

In the past few years, newer readings, critical approaches, and theoretical models have been applied in such volumes as *White Liberal Identity, Literary Pedagogy, and Classic American Realism*, Phillip Barrish (2006), offering new reasons to read canonical American authors such as James, Wharton, Twain, and Chopin—using new analytical and pedagogical tools for probing contemporary liberalism and realism, using contexts including an affirmative-action court case, the liberal arts classroom, the "war on drugs," and current debates over U.S. roles in globalization; *A Companion to African-American Studies*, ed. Lewis R. Gordon and Jane Anna Gordon (2005); *Queer Cowboys and Other Erotic Male Friendships in Nineteenth-Century American Literature,* ed. Chris Packard (2005), which uses the approaches of Queer Theory to reread authors from James Fenimore Cooper, Whitman, Harris, Harte, Owen Wister, to Eugene Field; *Form and Transformation in Asian American Literature*, ed. Xiaojing Zhou and Samina Najmi (2005), a critical anthology; Jessica Bomarito, Jeffrey W. Hunter, and Amy Hudock, eds., *Feminism in Literature: A Gale Critical Companion* (2004); *Family, Kinship, and Sympathy in Nineteenth-Century American Literature* by Cindy Weinstein (2004), which notes how sentimental novels, more complex than they may appear, elaborate a family-based republican ideal; *Cosmopolitan Vistas: American Regionalism and Literary Value*, Tom Lutz (2004); Judith Fetterley and Marjorie Pryse, eds., essays that challenge traditional boundaries of regionalism in *Writing Out of Place: Regionalism, Women, and American Literary Culture* (2003); *Unsettling the Literary West: Authenticity and Authorship* (2003), in which Nathaniel Lewis claims that western literature since its inception has been

America's first postmodern literature; Jerilyn Fisher, Ellen S. Silber, and David Sadker, eds., *Women in Literature: Reading through the Lens of Gender* (2003); *The Concise Oxford Companion to African American Literature,* ed. William L. Andrews and Frances Smith Foster (2001), an abbreviated version of *The Oxford Companion to African American Literature* (1997); *West of the Border: The Multicultural Literature of the Western American Frontiers,* by Noreen Groover Lape (2000), which sees writers such as Sui Sin Far and Mary Austin in their engagements with borders not as dividing lines but as sites of cultural contact, using a trickster figure inspired by Du Bois's idea of "double consciousness"; *Public Sentiments,* Glenn Hendler (2001), which surveys Howells, Freeman, Jewett, Garland, Harold Frederic, Jacob Riis, and Alfred Henry Lewis; *Trickster Lives: Culture and Myth in American Fiction,* ed. Jeanne Campbell Reesman (2001), which offers an important set of essays on the ubiquitous trickster figure in diverse American literatures; *The Patchwork Quilt: Ideas of Community in Nineteenth-Century American Women's Fiction* (2001), in which Suzanne V. Shepard re-reads Susan B. Warner, Harriet Beecher Stowe, Sarah Hale, Mary Wilkins Freeman, Sarah Orne Jewett, and Susan Glaspell as work that sought to redefine the concept of "brotherhood," established in Winthrop's "city upon a hill," by providing an inclusive and matriarchal model for the communal experiment that was America, through realistic detail and women's metaphors of hearth, home, kitchen, garden, and quilt; *Reconstituting Authority: American Fiction in the Province of the Law, 1880–1920,* by William E. Moddelmog (2001), on how authority is established in the literature of Howells, Oliver Wendell Holmes, Jackson, Hopkins, and Chesnutt in fashions parallel to those of legal documents; *Plots and Proposals: American Women's Fiction, 1850–90* by Karen Tracey (2000). The very readable and informative essays in Tom Quirk's *Nothing Abstract: Investigations in the American Literary Imagination* (2001) employ a "genetic" approach to literary study, that is, such matters as a work's compositional history, the course of authors' careers, and the genesis of literary movements, mounting a strong argument against poststructuralist theory in favor of discoveries made through actual scholarship.

New critical approaches to realism have included Henry B. Wonham's *Playing the Races: Ethnic Caricature and American Literary Realism* (2004); Barbara Hochman, *Getting at the Author: Reimagining Books and Reading in the Age of American Realism* (2001), which furnishes interesting perspectives on Wharton, James, Cather, Norris, and Dreiser, and also Owen Wister, Winston Churchill, and Francis Crawford, for all of whom the development of realism meant distancing of the author; and Paul Hansom, ed. (2001), *Twentieth-Century American Cultural Theorists;* Phillip Barrish, *American Literary Realism, Critical Theory, and Intellectual Prestige 1880–1990* (2001), which reads Howells, James, Cahan, and Wharton as focused upon a reality beneath the surface of narrative tied to human suffering.

In naturalist studies, Bert Bender's important book *Evolution and "the Sex Problem": American Narratives during the Eclipse of Darwinism* (2004) is among the first of a growing collection of critical books on literary Darwinism or literary evolutionism—Bender analyzes American fiction from the realist through the Freudian eras, arguing that Darwin's theories of sexual selection and of the emotions are essential elements in American fiction from the late 1800s through the 1950s, in works by Norris, London, Crane, Dreiser, Gertrude Stein, Willa Cather, Sherwood Anderson, F. Scott Fitzgerald, writers of the Harlem Renaissance, John Steinbeck, and Ernest Hemingway. Mohamed Zaynani's *Reading the Symptom: Norris, Dreiser, and the Dynamics of Capitalism* (1999) offers a revision of the deterministic definition of naturalism, with emphasis upon its "ludic" character as complex and indeterminate, an especially rewarding approach to *Vandover and the Brute* and *McTeague*, as well as *Sister Carrie*.

Naturalist scholars and their students now have a new naturalism journal: *Studies in American Naturalism*, ed. Keith Newlin, Stephen Brennan; Vol. 1, 1, Summer 2006, offers articles on definitions of realism and naturalism, Stephen Crane, Frank Norris, Bret Harte, Jack London, Theodore Dreiser, Edith Wharton, John Dos Passos, Kate Chopin, and Ellen Glasgow. And a few very recent journal articles deserve mention, beginning with "Late Nineteenth-Century American Literary Naturalism: A Re-Introduction," by Donald Pizer (2006), a major new overview of the enduring themes of naturalism, especially Garland and Crane's investigative journalism for *McClure's* magazine and the roots of naturalism in the failure of the nation's industrial system and the deleterious effects of workplace conditions on lives of millions. In "Literature and Regional Production," by Hsuan L. Hsu, *American Literary History* (2005), Jewett, Norris, and Washington are examined in their engagements with regionalism and the changing economic structures of their day.

Students of American literature should generally be aware that new paperback editions of canonical as well as newly recovered works often contain, as do Norton Critical Editions, useful introductions, background material, and criticism. In addition to Norton, a number of publishers, such as Twayne, MLA, Bedford/St. Martin's, Oxford University Press, and Cambridge University Press have ongoing series on individual authors and/or works. Proceedings of conferences on authors, periods, genre, and specialized topics are frequently published. *Dissertation Abstracts International* and the often-invoked MLA annual bibliography (now online through institutional subscription) provide information on unpublished scholarship on this period and its authors. Newsletters devoted to studies of many of the writers represented in this period are published regularly. Finally, students should also inquire into the abundant—and often very useful—audiovisual resources for the study of American writers, individual works, and intellectual currents. Increasingly these supplements are available on CD-ROM and on the Internet as well as on audiocassettes and videocassettes. An excellent source for video and CD-ROM data is facets.com. Increasingly, students turn to resources on the Internet, where there are numerous excellent American literature web sites, electronic texts, concordances, and other resources; even just using Google.com and Amazon.com will yield more than enough for any student. Two Internet tips for students: First, to put it mildly, a lot of what is on the Internet posing as "facts" about American writers is not. Always check your sources with the kinds of experts listed here. Second, if you use any information from an Internet source, you must document it accordingly.

## AMERICAN LITERATURE 1865–1914

**Henry Adams**

No uniform, authoritatively edited collection of Adams's writings exists. Ernest Samuels's annotated edition of *The Education* sets a high standard for those who would undertake such a project in the future. In 1920, 1930, and 1938, Worthington C. Ford edited three volumes of Adams's letters. J. C. Levenson *et al.* subsequently edited six generous volumes of *The Letters of Henry Adams* (1982–88); more recently Ernest Samuels edited *Henry Adams: Selected Letters* (1992). Joanne Jackson's *Authority and Alliance in the Letters of Henry Adams* makes good use of this body of Adams's writing. In 1999 *The Education* was added to the Oxford World's Classics, edited by Ira Nadel. A valuable study of Adams's lesser-known works is *John Randolph: A Biography by Henry Adams: A New Edition with Primary Documents* (1996), edited by Robert McColley with a foreword by Paul Finkelman.

The standard biography has been a trilogy by Ernest Samuels: *The Young Henry Adams* (1948), *Henry Adams, The Middle Years* (1958), and *Henry Adams, the Major Phase* (1964). Edward Chalfant's three-volume biography, *Both Sides of the Ocean: A Biography of Henry Adams, His First Life, 1838–1862* (1982), *Better in Darkness: A Biography of Henry Adams: His Second Life, 1862–1891* (1997), and *Improvement of the World: A Biography of Henry Adams, His Last Life, 1891–1918* (2001) reflects research on Adams and *The Education* over forty years. Most recently, Garry Wills argues in *Henry Adams and the Making of America* (2005) that *The Education* is "a prose masterpiece" and still a model for how to research and write history, as Adams helped to revolutionize the study of history by conducting archival research at home and abroad, in London, Paris, and Madrid, though at the time provincial history was the norm.

Earl N. Harbert's *The Force So Much Closer Home: Henry Adams and the Adams Family* (1977) situates Adams within his family tradition. Other aspects of Adams are dealt with in Harold Kaplan's *Power and Order: Henry Adams and the Naturalist Tradition in American Fiction* (1981); J. C. Levenson's *The Mind and Art of Henry Adams* (1957), a difficult and distinguished work; John Carlos Rowe's *Henry Adams and Henry James: The Emergence of a Modern Consciousness* (1976); R. P. Blackmur's *Henry Adams* (1980); Joseph F. Byrne's *The Virgin of Chartres: An Intellectual and Psychological History of Henry Adams* (1981), and William Wasserstrom's *The Ironies of Progress* (1984). William Merrill Decker's *The Literary Vocation of Henry Adams* (1990) skillfully analyzes the rhetoric of Adams's major works. James P. Young's *Henry Adams: The Historian as Political*

*Theorist* (2001), sheds more light on the literary aspects of Adams's *oeuvre*, while Brooks D. Simpson's revisionist *The Political Education of Henry Adams* (1996) raises interesting questions about the effects of Adams's personality on his career.

**Mary Austin**

There has yet to be a complete works of Mary Austin or a definitive biography, though she has inspired heightened interest among critics in recent years. Her autobiographical novel, *A Woman of Genius* (1912), was reprinted in 1985 by the Feminist Press and is now seen as a precursor of Sinclair Lewis's *Main Street* and a counterpoint to Theodore Dreiser's *Sister Carrie*, as it deals poignantly with the costs of a woman's ambitions. On this see "Mary Austin's *A Woman of Genius*: The Text, the Novel, and the Problem of Male Publishers and Critics and Female Authors" by Karen S. Langlois (1992). *The Mary Austin Reader* (1996), ed. Esther Lanigan, is a collection of essays, novels, plays, short stories, poems and articles. *Literary America, 1903–1931: The Mary Austin Letters*, ed. Thomas Matthews Pearce (1979), is a collection of letters written to Austin by literary and political contemporaries, reflecting the important contributions of women writers to the socio-political climate of the time. *Beyond Borders: The Selected Essays of Mary Austin* (1995) is edited by Reuben J. Ellis: essays cover such subjects Austin's self-promotion as Native American expert and her nature advocacy and proto-feminist tracts. *The Land of Little Rain* is available in a Penguin edition edited by Terry Tempest Williams (1997); *The Land of Journeys' Ending*, ed. Melody Graulich (2003), from the University of Illinois Press; *The Flock* from University of Nevada Press (2001).

In literary criticism David Wyatt's *The Fall Into Eden: Landscape and Imagination in California* (1986) suggests that in Austin's work setting assumes a mythological significance constructed from first settlers into contemporary times, and connects her regionalism to that of John Muir, Norris, John Steinbeck, Robinson Jeffers, and Gary Snyder. *Mary Austin: Song of a Maverick* (1990) by Esther Lanigan Stineman situates Austin within the contexts of class, race, gender, and Native American advocacy, arguing that she was far ahead of her time on these issues. In *Writing the Western Landscape* (1994) Ann H. Zwinger contrasts Austin's nature writings with those of a male contemporary, John Muir; in *Dancing Ghosts: Native American and Christian Syncretism in Mary Austin's Works* (1998) Mark T. Hayer examines how Austin attempted to reconcile Native spirituality with Christianity; *Through the Window, Out the Door* (1998) by

Janis P. Stout rejects masculinist interpretations of Austin's work for more distinctly feminine conceptualizations of wayfaring, nostalgia for home, and related issues; *Exploring Lost Borders: Critical Essays on Mary Austin*, 1999, ed. Melody Fraulich and Elizabeth Klimasmith, is a collection of essays arguing for the primacy of Austin's stature in modern feminist and environmental movements; *The Wild and the Domestic: Animal Representation, Ecocriticism, and Western American Literature* (2000) by Barney Nelson uses published and unpublished Austin writings to refute the mythic image of the West as merely a wild space; Stacy Alaimo's chapter on Austin in her *Undomesticated Ground: Recasting Nature as Feminist Space* (2000) opposes Austin to "conservationist" clubwomen of the Progressive Era, as Austin saw undomesticated desert space as a "fertile ground for feminism"; "Creating Great Women: Mary Austin and Charlotte Perkins Gilman," by Melody Graulich, offers an incisive comparison of the two writers, in Cynthia J. Davis and Denise D. Knight, eds., *Charlotte Perkins Gilman and Her Contemporaries: Literary and Intellectual Contexts* (2004). *Mary Austin's Regionalism: Reflections on Gender, Genre, and Geography* (2004) by Heike Schaefer draws from unpublished materials and a full range of Austin's literary and theoretical writing to examine Austin's reworking of the traditions of nature writing and women's regionalism to imagine a sustainable and democratic American culture.

### Ida B. Wells-Barnett

The standard edition is *The Selected Works of Ida B. Wells-Barnett* from the Schomburg Library of Nineteenth-Century Black Women Writers (1991), ed. Trudier K. Harris. *The Red Record: With Southern Horrors: Lynch Law in All Its Phases* and *Mob Rule in New Orleans: Lynch Law in All Its Phases* (2006) are newly available in reprints, as is *On Lynchings*, ed. Patricia Hill Collins (2002). The autobiography is available as *Crusade for Justice: The Autobiography of Ida B. Wells* (1991), ed. Alfreda M. Duster. A useful introduction is "Ida B. Wells-Barnett (1862–1931)," by Lynn Domina, in Emmanuel S. Nelson's *African American Autobiographers: A Sourcebook* (2002), as is *To Keep the Waters Troubled: The Life of Ida B. Wells* Linda O. McMurry (1999). Like Booker T. Washington and Paul Laurence Dunbar, Wells-Barnett is the subject of many juvenile biographies.

*Ida B. Wells-Barnett and American Reform, 1880–1930* by Patricia A. Schechter appeared in 2000, a valuable full-length study. Critical analysis of Wells-Barnett has also been undertaken in journal articles and book chapters: "Style and Content in the Rhetoric of Early Afro-American Feminists," Karlyn Kohrs

Campbell, *The Quarterly Journal of Speech* (1986); Shirley W. Logan in "Rhetorical Strategies in Ida B. Wells's 'Southern Horrors': Lynch Law in All Its Phases," *SAGE: A Scholarly Journal on Black Women* (1991); Akiko Ochai in "Ida B. Wells and Her Crusade for Justice: An African American Woman's Testimonial Autobiography," *Soundings: An Interdisciplinary Journal* (1992); "Crusader for Justice: Ida B. Wells" by Joanne M. Braxton, in *African American Autobiography: A Collection of Critical Essays*, ed William L. Andres (1993); Simone W. Davis in "The 'Weak Race' and the Winchester: Political Voices in the Pamphlets of Ida B. Wells-Barnett," *Legacy* (1995), which explores Wells' attack upon binary concepts underlying racist ideologies in order to contest them; Barbara Diggs-Brown, "Ida B. Wells-Barnett: About the Business of Agitation," in *A Living of Words: American Women in Print Culture*, ed. Susan Albertine, (1995); "To Call a Thing by Its True Name: The Rhetoric of Ida B. Wells," Jacqueline Jones Royster, in Andrea A. Lunsford, ed. (1995), *Reclaiming Rhetorica: Women in the Rhetorical Tradition*; " 'On the Threshold of Woman's Era': Lynching, Empire, and Sexuality in Black Feminist Theory" by Hazel V. Carby, in *Dangerous Liaisons: Gender, Nation, and Postcolonial Perspectives*, ed. Anne McClintock, Aamir Mufti, and Ella Shohat (1997); "Missing in Action: Ida B. Wells, the NAACP, and the Historical Record," by Paula Giddings, *Meridians: Feminism, Race, Transnationalism* (2001); "The Radical Praxis of Ida B. Wells-Barnett: Telling the Truth Freely," chapter 4 of Anthony Bogues's *Black Heretics, Black Prophets: Radical Political Intellectuals* (2003).

### Ambrose Bierce

Scholarship and criticism on Ambrose Bierce has recently made significant strides in catching up to the significance and complexities of its subject, beginning with an exciting new set of editions and an authoritative critical study. *The Short Fiction of Ambrose Bierce, 2 Volumes: A Comprehensive Edition* (2006) is edited by S. T. Joshi, Lawrence I. Berkove, and David E. Schultz and fulfills a long-unmet need. *Ambrose Bierce: An Annotated Bibliography of Primary Sources*, is edited by Joshi and Schultz (1999). Joshi and Schultz have also produced *The Fall of the Republic and Other Political Stories* and *The Unabridged Devil's Dictionary* (2000) and *A Much Misunderstood Man: Selected Letters of Ambrose Bierce* (2003). *Phantoms of a Blood-Stained Period: The Complete Civil War Writings of Ambrose Bierce*, is edited by Russell Duncan and David J. Klooster (2002). Daniel Lindley edited *Ambrose Bierce Takes on the Railroad: The Journalist as Muckraker and Cynic* (1999). Robert C. Evans has brought out *Ambrose Bierce's 'An Occurrence at Owl Creek*

*Bridge': An Annotated Critical Edition* (2003) and Joshi *The Collected Fables of Ambrose Bierce* (2000). Bierce's poetry is found in *Poems of Ambrose Bierce*, ed. M. E. Grenander (1996). Robert L. Gale's carefully surveys Bierce's life and work in *An Ambrose Bierce Companion* (2001).

Lawrence I. Berkove's long-awaited critical study, *A Prescription for Adversity: The Moral Art of Ambrose Bierce* (2002), takes issue with simplistic clichés about Bierce's famous pessimism and focuses upon his complex artistry and moral argument. Bierce's war writings are the focus of another book, *Ambrose Bierce's Civilians and Soldiers in Context: A Critical Study*, by Donald T. Blume (2004). S. T. Joshi and David E. Schultz's *A Sole Survivor: Bits of Autobiography* (1999) is also useful. The fullest edition of Bierce's writings is still *Collected Works of Ambrose Bierce* (1909–12), edited by Walter Neale. The largest collection of Bierce's letters is available in Bertha C. Pope's edition of *The Letters of Ambrose Bierce* (1921). Until Berkove's *Prescription for Adversity*, the standard critical biography was Paul Fatout's *Ambrose Bierce, the Devil's Lexicographer* (1951); Mary Elizabeth Grenander's *Ambrose Bierce* (1971) is also still much worth consulting. Roy Morris Jr.'s *Ambrose Bierce: Alone in Bad Company* (1996) enriches our understanding of Bierce's Civil War experience and how he converted this experience into a group of fine short stories. Still a fine critical study of Bierce's work is Cathy N. Davidson's *The Experimental Fictions of Ambrose Bierce: Structuring the Ineffable* (1984). Davidson also edited *Critical Essays on Ambrose Bierce* (1982). Two interesting essay perspectives on stories included in NAAL are " 'A Quarter of an Hour': Hanging as Ambrose Bierce and Peyton Farquhar Knew It," by Donald T. Blume, *American Literary Realism* (2002), and " 'Chickamauga' as an Indian-Wars Narrative: The Relevance of Ambrose Bierce for a First-Nations-Centered Study of the Nineteenth Century," by Susan Kalter, *Arizona Quarterly: A Journal of American Literature, Culture, and Theory* (2000).

**Abraham Cahan**
There is no collected edition of Cahan's many writings in English, Russian, and Yiddish. Isaac Metzker edited *A Bintel Brief: Sixty Years of Letters from the Lower East Side to the Jewish Daily Forward* (1971). Moses Rischin's *Grandma Never Lived in America: The New Journalism of Abraham Cahan* (1985) also features an extensive and informative introduction. Cahan's *"The Imported Bridegroom" and Other Stories of the New York Ghetto* (1898) was reprinted with introduction by Bernard G. Richards in 1970. *The Rise of David Levinsky: A Novel* (1917) was reprinted with an introduction by John Higham (1960); it was reprinted again with a superb

introduction and notes by Jules Chametzky (1993).

No full-scale biography of Cahan has been published, but many of the critical books listed contain accounts of his very long and full life. Irving Howe's *World of Our Fathers* (1976) is an immensely well-informed cultural history of Jewish immigration and sheds much light on turn of the century Yiddish journalism in New York. Ronald Sanders's brilliant and engaging *The Downtown Jews: Portraits of an Immigrant Generation* (1969) focuses on Cahan's generation and provides information through the early 1920s. John Higham's still valuable *Strangers in the Land: Patterns of American Nativism, 1860–1925* (1955), as its subtitle suggests, calls attention to the mounting opposition to immigrations, Jewish and otherwise. Sanford Marovitz's Twayne volume *Abraham Cahan* (1996) is the best introduction to Cahan's life and work; its evaluation of the fiction is balanced and judicious.

Jules Chametsky's *From the Ghetto: The Fiction of Abraham Cahan* (1977) is by far the best critical study of Cahan's English and Yiddish fiction. David Fine's chapter on Cahan in *The City of the Immigrant and American Fiction, 1880–1920* (1977) provides a good overview. Louis Harap's *Creative Awakening: The Jewish Presence in Twentieth Century American Literature: 1900–1940s* (1987) is worth consulting, as is Allen Guttman's groundbreaking *The Jewish Writer in America: Assimilation and the Crisis of Identity* (1971).

**Charles Chesnutt**
In 2002, Werner Sollors edited the Library of America volume *Charles W. Chesnutt Stories, Novels and Essays*, a much-needed resource. The volume *Charles W. Chesnutt: Essays and Speeches*, ed. Joseph R. McElrath, Jr., Robert C. Leitz III, and Jesse S. Crisler (1999), presents all of Chesnutt's known nonfiction, 77 items in all, from 1881–1930s, on a wide range of topics: race, education, images of blacks in literature, and manners. And their collection of his letters, *An Exemplary Citizen: Letters of Charles W. Chesnutt, 1906–1932* (2002) provides another major contribution to the valuable if less comprehensive work before them. Sylvia L. Render edited *The Short Fiction of Charles W. Chesnutt* (1974). Richard H. Brodhead edited *The Journals of Charles W. Chesnutt* (1993). His introduction to *The Conjure Woman and Other Conjure Tales* (1993) locates Chesnutt's tales within the conventions of local color realism and particularly within the development of black vernacular voice and emerging fictions detailing black folk life. William L. Andrews brings his deep understanding of Chesnutt to his edition of the *Collected Stories of Charles W. Chesnutt* (1992).

The first full-length biography was written by

Chesnutt's daughter, Helen M. Chesnutt, as *Charles Waddell Chesnutt: Pioneer of the Color Line* (1952). Heermance J. Noel's *Charles W. Chesnutt: America's First Great Black Novelist* (1974) is a useful critical biography, as are William L. Andrews's *The Literary Career of Charles W. Chesnutt* (1980), Sylvia L. Render's *Charles W. Chesnutt* (1980), and Robert B. Stepto's *Charles Chesnutt: The Uncle Julius Stories* (1984); and Charles Duncan's *The Absent Man: The Narrative Craft of Charles W. Chesnutt* (1998), which explores sensitively what might be called the "rhetoric of elusiveness" in Chesnutt's career. Marjorie Pryse and Hortense J. Spillers's *Conjuring: Black Women, Fiction, and Literary Tradition* (1985) and Jane Campbell's *Mythic Black Fiction: The Transformation of History* (1986) contain useful contextual material on Chesnutt. A more specialized study is Ernestine Williams Pickens's *Charles W. Chesnutt and the Progressive Movement* (1994). Eric J. Sundquist's *To Wake the Nations* (1993) treats Chesnutt at length. Other valuable critical studies include Samira Kawash's *Dislocating the Color Line: Identity, Hybridity, and Singularity in African-American Narrative* (1997), which examines critically and historically representations of racial difference; Henry Wonham's *Charles W. Chesnutt: A Study of the Short Fiction* (1998); Dean McWilliams's *Charles W. Chesnutt and the Fictions of Race*, (2002); Matthew Wilson's *Whiteness in the Novels of Charles W. Chesnutt* (2004); *Conscience and Purpose: Fiction and Social Consciousness in Howells, Jewett, Chesnutt, and Cather* by Paul R. Petrie (2005); and Charles A. Walls's *Acts of the Imagination: Racial Sentimentalism and the Modern American Novel (Frederick Douglass, Charles Waddell Chesnutt, Nella Larsen, Richard Wright)* (2006). One of Chesnutt's best scholars is Joseph R. McElrath, Jr., whose *Critical Essays on Charles W. Chesnutt* (1999) gathers a variety of helpful essays prefaced by a thoughtful introductory essay; selections on Chesnutt's reputation range from its beginning at the turn of the century to the surge of interest in the 1960s that has continued to the present. In a recent essay, McElrath also thoughtfully contrasts Chesnutt and Howells: "Why Charles Chesnutt is Not a Realist," *American Literary Realism* (2000).

### Kate Chopin

*The Complete Works of Kate Chopin* (1969) was edited in two volumes by Per Seyersted, who also wrote the excellent *Kate Chopin: A Critical Biography* (1969). The Library of America volume *Kate Chopin: Complete Novels and Stories: At Fault / Bayou Folk / A Night in Acadie / The Awakening / Uncollected Stories* (2002) has appeared, edited by Sandra K. Gilbert. Emily Toth's landmark *Unveiling Kate Chopin* (1999) incorporates material from Chopin's recently discovered diaries and manuscripts and is now the standard biography. Per Seyersted and Emily Toth edited *A Kate Chopin Miscellany* (1980), and a collection of unpublished short fiction, poems, letters, etc.; their *Kate Chopin's Private Papers* appeared in 1998. Barbara C. Ewell's *Kate Chopin* (1986) and *Kate Chopin: A Literary Life,* by Nancy Walker (2001) are good introductions to the life and work. Emily Toth's critical biography *Kate Chopin* (1990) has established her as perhaps the leading Chopin scholar.

Bernard J. Kosloski's *Kate Chopin: A Study of the Short Fiction* (1996) is a fine survey of this large subject. Koloski also edited the pedagogical collection, *Approaches to Teaching Kate Chopin's "The Awakening"* (1988), and a welcome edition of Chopin's two most important collections of short stories in *Kate Chopin: "Bayou Folk" and "A Night in Acadie"* (1999). Lynda S. Boren and Sara deSaussure Davis edited a fresh collection of essays (with a foreword by Cathy N. Davidson), *Kate Chopin Reconsidered: Beyond the Bayou* (1992). Wendy Martin edited *New Essays on The Awakening* (1988), and Nancy A. Walker edited *Kate Chopin: The Awakening, Complete Authoritative Text with Biographical and Historical Contexts* (1993). Joyce Dyer wrote a closely argued monograph *The Awakening: A Novel of Beginnings* (1993; 2nd ed., 2000); Donald Kesey edited *Contexts for Criticism* (1994); and Margo Culley edited the second edition of the Norton Critical Edition of *The Awakening* with biographical and historical contexts and criticism (1994). *Kate Chopin's Short Fiction: A Critical Companion* by Robert C. Evans (2001) is useful, as is the comparative study *Kate Chopin, Edith Wharton and Charlotte Perkins Gilman: Studies in Short Fiction* (2005) by Janet Beer. Susan Disheroon Green, David Caudle, and Emily Toth teamed up to produce *Kate Chopin: An Annotated Bibliography of Critical Works* (1999); it provides not only annotation but discursive essays by the editors on Chopin's life, work, and reputation.

### Anna Julia Cooper

Scholarship and criticism on Anna Julia Cooper is not plentiful, but it is growing. Two noteworthy editions of her writings are *A Voice From the South* (The Schomburg Library of Nineteenth-Century Black Women Writers), edited by Mary H. Washington (1988) and *The Voice of Anna Julia Cooper: Including A Voice From the South and Other Important Essays, Papers, and Letters*, edited by Charles Lemert (1998). Cooper's Ph.D. Dissertation from her studies at the Sorbonne has been published as *Slavery and the French Revolutionists, 1788–1805*, translated by Frances Richardson Keller (1988). Karen Johnson's *Uplifting the Women and the Race: The Lives, Educational Philosophies and Social*

*Activism of Anna Julia Cooper and Nannie Helen Burroughs* (2000) is a welcome comparative volume. Noteworthy critical essays include Hazel V. Carby's " 'On the Threshold of Woman's Era': Lynching, Empire and Sexuality in Black Feminist Theory" (1985), *Critical Inquiry*, an examination of how Cooper, Wells-Barnett, and Hopkins articulated theories of patriarchy and racism that linked imperialism, sexual politics, and internal colonialism within an intellectual climate dominated by male figures, thus demonstrating how history is "differentially experienced"; this essay is reprinted in Anne McClintock, Aamir Mufti, and Ella Shohat, eds., *Dangerous Liaisons: Gender, Nation, and Postcolonial Perspectives* (1997). Also helpful are "Anna Julia Cooper: The Black Feminist Voice of the 1890s," by Mary Helen Washington, *Legacy: A Journal of American Women Writers* (1987); "The Five Million Women of My Race: Negotiations of Gender in W. E. B. Du Bois and Anna Julia Cooper," by Hanna Wallinger, in Karen L. Kilcup, ed., *Soft Canons: American Women Writers and Masculine Tradition* (1999); " 'We Must Be about Our Father's Business': Anna Julia Cooper and the In-Corporation of the Nineteenth-Century African-American Woman Intellectual," by Elizabeth Alexander, *Signs* (1995); "Anna Julia Cooper: 'Dedicated in the Name of My Slave Mother to the Education of Colored Working People,' " by Cathryn Bailey, *Hypatia: A Journal of Feminist Philosophy* (2004); and Vivian M. May's "Thinking from the Margins, Acting at the Intersections: Anna Julia Cooper's *A Voice from the South*," *Hypatia* (2004). A useful source for contextualizing Cooper is *Black Feminist Thought: Knowledge, Consciousness, and the Politics of Empowerment* by Patricia Hill Collins (2000).

## Samuel L. Clemens
See Mark Twain.

## Stephen Crane
Fredson Bowers is the textual editor of *The Works of Stephen Crane* (1969–76). The Library of America volume, *Crane: Prose and Poetry* (1996), is edited by J. C. Levenson. *Stephen Crane: Letters* (1960) was edited by R. W. Stallman and Lillian Gilkes and was later joined by *The Correspondence of Stephen Crane*, (1988), edited by Stanley Wertheim and Paul Sorrentino. Joseph Katz edited both *The Portable Stephen Crane* (1969) and *The Poems of Stephen Crane: A Critical Edition* (1966). Patrick K. Dooley compiled *Stephen Crane: An Annotated Bibliography of Secondary Scholarship* (1992), an indispensable research tool, now annually updated in *Stephen Crane Studies* by Dooley. excellent biographies are Linda H. Davis's *Badge of Courage: The Life of Stephen Crane* (1998) and *The Crane Log: A Documentary Life of Stephen Crane, 1871–*

*1900*, by Wertheim and Sorrentino (1994). Also of interest is *The Double Life of Stephen Crane: A Biography*, by Christopher Benfey (1992). Edwin H. Cady's *Stephen Crane* (1980) is an excellent critical introduction to Crane's life and work. Marston La France's *A Reading of Stephen Crane* (1971), Frank Bergon's *Stephen Crane's Artistry* (1975), James Nagel's *Stephen Crane and Literary Impressionism* (1980), Chester L. Wolford's *The Anger of Stephen Crane: Fiction and the Epic Tradition* (1983), James B. Colvert's *Stephen Crane* (1984), Bettina L. Knapp's *Stephen Crane* (1987), David Halliburton's *The Color of the Sky: A Study of Stephen Crane* (1991), Patrick K. Dooley's *The Pluralistic Philosophy of Stephen Crane* (1993), Michael Robertson's *Stephen Crane, Journalism, and the Making of Modern American Literature* (1997), Bill Brown's intriguing *The Material Unconscious: American Amusement, Stephen Crane and the Economics of Play* (1997), and George E. Monteiro's *Stephen Crane's Blue Badge of Courage* (2000) are among the best of surprisingly few significant book-length studies. Donald Pizer has edited and introduced *Critical Essays on Stephen Crane's* The Red Badge of Courage (1990). Claudia Durst Johnson compiled *Understanding the Red Badge of Courage* (1998), rich in historical documents, collateral readings, and commentary, and Stanley Wertheim compiled the comprehensive *A Stephen Crane Encyclopedia* (1997).

## Emily Dickinson
Three volumes of *The Poems of Emily Dickinson* (1955) were edited by Thomas H. Johnson; and Johnson and Theodora Ward edited three companion volumes of *The Letters of Emily Dickinson* (1958). R. W. Franklin's *The Manuscript Books of Emily Dickinson* (1981) provides, in two volumes, facsimile reproductions of the hand-sewn poems Dickinson left at her death in fascicles. R. W. Franklin's three-volume *Poems of Emily Dickinson: Variorum Edition* (1998) now supersedes Johnson's three-volume *Poems*. In 1999 Franklin published the one-volume *The Poems of Emily Dickinson: Reading Edition*. Important biographies include Richard B. Sewall's *The Life of Emily Dickinson* (1974), Cynthia Griffin Wolff's *Emily Dickinson* (1986), and Alfred Habegger's *My Wars Are Laid Away in Books: The Life of Emily Dickinson* (2001). Jay Leyda's *The Years and Hours of Emily Dickinson* (1960) is two volumes of documents, such as excerpts from family letters. Additional documents are in Vivian Pollak's *A Poet's Parents: The Courtship Letters of Emily Norcross and Edward Dickinson* (1988), Polly Longsworth's *The World of Emily Dickinson* (1990), and Ellen Louise Hart and Martha Nell Smith's *Open Me Carefully: Emily Dickinson's Intimate Letters to Susan Huntington Dickinson* (1998).

Research tools include Joseph Duchac's *The Poems of Emily Dickinson: An Annotated Guide to Commentary Published in English, 1890–1977* (1979), and the continuation (published in 1993) covering 1978–89; Karen Dandurand's *Dickinson Scholarship: An Annotated Bibliography 1969–1985* (1988), and the treasure trove compiled by Willis J. Buckingham (drawing on Mabel Loomis Todd's scrapbooks), *Emily Dickinson's Reception in the 1890s* (1989). Also useful are S. P. Rosenbaum's *A Concordance to the Poems of Emily Dickinson* (1964), Cynthia J. MacKenzie's *Concordance to the Letters of Emily Dickinson* (2000), Joel Myerson's *Emily Dickinson: A Descriptive Bibliography* (1984), and Jane Donahue Eberwein's *An Emily Dickinson Encyclopedia* (1998). *The Dickinson Electronic Archives* <www.emilydickinson.org>, directed by Martha Nell Smith with Ellen Louise Hart, Lara Vetter, and Marta Werner, offers more than access to many of Dickinson's manuscripts. Also available are many out-of-print volumes about Dickinson as well as never-before-published writings by various family members.

Edited collections of critical essays provide an excellent introduction to Dickinson studies. See Susan Juhasz's *Feminist Critics Read Emily Dickinson* (1983), Judith Farr's *Emily Dickinson: A Collection of Critical Essays* (1996), Gudrun Grabher, Roland Hagenbüchle, and Cristanne Miller's *The Emily Dickinson Handbook* (1998, 2006), Wendy Martin's *The Cambridge Companion to Emily Dickinson* (2002), and Vivian R. Pollak's *A Historical Guide to Emily Dickinson* (2004). Recent important studies include Paula Bennett's *Emily Dickinson: Woman Poet* (1990), Judith Farr's *The Passion of Emily Dickinson* (1992), Martha Nell Smith's *Rowing in Eden: Rereading Emily Dickinson* (1992), Sharon Cameron's *Choosing, Not Choosing: Dickinson's Fascicles* (1993), Domhnall Mitchell's *Emily Dickinson: Monarch of Perception* (2000), Eleanor Elson Heginbotham's *Reading the Fascicles of Emily Dickinson* (2003), and Virginia Walker Jackson's *Dickinson's Misery: A Theory of Lyric Reading* (2005).

**Theodore Dreiser**

Most of Dreiser's novels and short stories are largely in print, but his poetry, plays, and other writings often are not, and a well-edited uniform edition of Dreiser's writings is badly needed. The University of Pennsylvania has begun to satisfy this need; so far James L. W. West III, textual editor, and Neda Westlake, general editor, have overseen the publication of *American Diaries: 1902–1926* (edited and with an introduction by Thomas P. Riggio) and *Sister Carrie* (John C. Berkey and Alice M. Winters, historical editors) (1981). In 1992 West

and Riggio edited a dramatically restored edition of *Jennie Gerhardt*. Three years later West edited *Dreiser's Jennie Gerhardt: New Essays on the Restored Text* (1995). Donald Pizer made an important contribution with *Theodore Dreiser: A Selection of Uncollected Prose* (1977) and another in "The Text of *Sister Carrie*: Where We Are Now," *Dreiser Studies* (2001), an interesting exploration of the difficulty of an instructor's informed choice about an edition to teach. Pizer, Richard W. Dowell, and Frederic Rusch prepared *Theodore Dreiser: A Primary Bibliography and Reference Guide*, updated regularly in *Dreiser Studies*. Robert H. Elias edited the three volumes of *Letters of Theodore Dreiser* (1959). *Theodore Dreiser: Sister Carrie, Jennie Gerhardt, Twelve Men* (1987), a Library of America volume, was edited by Richard Lehan, while *Theodore Dreiser: Interviews* was edited by Rusch, Pizer, and Riggio (2004).

In a volume edited and introduced by Thomas R. Riggio, Yvette Eastman, in *Dearest Wilding: A Memoir with Love Letters from Theodore Dreiser* (1995), tells of her sixteen-year relationship with Dreiser; Marguerite Tjader's *Love That Will Not Let Go: My Time with Theodore Dreiser* (1998), edited by Lawrence E. Hussman, makes clear Eastman was not Dreiser's only lover. Jerome Loving's long-awaited *The Last Titan: A Life of Theodore Dreiser* (2005), is the authoritative biography; before that Richard Lingeman's two-volume biography was considered standard: *Theodore Dreiser: At the Gates of the City, 1891–1907* (1986) and *Theodore Dreiser: An American Journey, 1908–1945* (1990). Richard Lehan, *Theodore Dreiser: His World and His Novels* (1974); Pizer, *The Novels of Theodore Dreiser* (1976); Yoshinobu Hakutani, *Young Dreiser: A Critical Study* (1979); Hussman, *Dreiser and His Fiction: A Twentieth-Century Quest* (1983); Joseph Griffin, *The Small Canvas: An Introduction to Dreiser's Short Stories* (1985); Philip Gerber, *Theodore Dreiser Revisited* (1992); Miyoko Takeda, *The Quest for the Reality of Life: Dreiser's Spiritual and Esthetical Pilgrimage* (1991); Louis J. Zanine, *Mechanism and Mysticism: The Influence of Science on the Thought and Work of Theodore Dreiser* (1993); Pizer, *Literary Masters: Theodore Dreiser* (2000); and Clare Virginia Edy, *Dreiser and Veblen: Saboteurs of the Status Quo* (1999), have advanced our appreciation and understanding considerably. Miriam Gogol edited and introduced *Theodore Dreiser: Beyond Naturalism* (1995), a useful set of feminist, gender, psychoanalytic, and other perspectives. Yoshinobu Hakutani edited another useful collection of criticism: *Theodore Dreiser and American Culture: New Readings* (2000); Hakutani includes 33 reprints of Dreiser's magazine articles, 22 reprinted for the first time, along with essays on artists, musicians, and writers from Howells to Stieglitz. *The Cambridge Companion to Theodore Dreiser* is edited by Leonard Cassuto and Clare Virginia Eby (2004).

## W. E. B. Du Bois

There is no collected edition of Du Bois's prolific output, but several interesting collections of Du Bois's writings are available: Philip S. Foner's *W. E. B. DuBois Speaks: Speeches and Addresses* (1970), Meyer Weinberg's *W. E. B. DuBois: A Reader* (1970), Andrew G. Paschol, *A W. E. B. DuBois Reader* (1971), Herbert Lee Moon's *The Emerging Thought of W. E. B. DuBois: Essays and Editorials from the "Crisis"* (1972), and Dan S. Green and Edwin D. Driver's *W. E. B. DuBois on Sociology in the Black Community* (1978), which includes sixteen articles by DuBois. Herbert Aptheker edited the three volumes of *The Correspondence of W. E. B. DuBois* (1973–1978), the four volumes of *Writings by W. E. B. DuBois in Periodicals Edited by Others* (1982), *Selections form Phylon* (1980), and *Selections from the Crisis* in two volumes (1972). Phil Zuckerman's collection *Du Bois on Religion* (2000) also contains a perceptive introduction. Eric J. Sundquist's *The Oxford W. E. B. Du Bois Reader* (1996) offers a very substantial selection and features as good a biocritical introduction as any in print. *The Correspondence of W.E.B. Du Bois: Selections, 1877–1934* and *The Correspondence of W.E.B. Du Bois: Selections, 1934–1944* have been edited by Herbert Aptheker (1997). *W. E. B. Du Bois: An Encyclopedia*, edited by Gerald Horne and Mary Young (2001) contains 150 entries.

Several biographies of Du Bois are available: Leslie A. Lacey's *Cheer the Lonesome Traveler: The Life of W. E. B. DuBois* (1970), Shirley Graham's *His Day Is Marching On: A Memoir of W. E. B. DuBois* (1971), and Arnold Rampersad's perceptive critical study *The Art and Imagination of W. E. B. DuBois* (1976) as well as his chapter on Du Bois in his *Slavery and the Literary Imagination* 1989). David Levering Lewis's two-volume *W. E. B. DuBois: Biography of a Race, 1868–1919* (1993) and *W. E. B. DuBois: The Fight for Equality and the American Century, 1919–1963* (2000) are outstanding.

Significant background to Du Bois's place in American intellectual thought may be found in August Meier's *Negro Thought in America, 1880–1915* (1963) and John Hope Franklin's *From Slavery to Freedom: A History of American Negroes*, 7th ed. (1994). Jack B. Moore's *W. E. B. DuBois* (1981) provides a brief critical biography and introductory survey of his writings, while Joseph P. De Marco's *The Social Thought of W. E. B. Du Bois* (1983) is thorough and helpful on this complex topic; the collection of essays edited by Bernard W. Bell, Emily Grosholz, and James B. Stewart—*W. E. B. Du Bois on Race and Culture: Philosophy, Politics,* *and Poetics* (1966)—is also a distinguished contribution, as is the gathering of essays in *W. E. B. Du Bois, Race and the City: "The Philadelphia Negro" and Its Legacy* (1998) edited by Michael B. Katz and Thomas J. Sugrue, situating Du Bois in late his nineteenth-century intellectual milieu, exploring his influence on later writers, and assessing his relevance today. Further contexts are supplied in *W. E. B. Du Bois: The Fight for Equality and the American Century, 1919–1963* (2000) by David Levering Lewis, which won Pulitzer Prize; *Creative Conflict in African American Thought: Frederick Douglass, Alexander Crummell, Booker T. Washington, W. E. B. Du Bois, and Marcus Garvey,* by Wilson Jeremiah Moses (2004); *The Lost Promise of Patriotism: Debating American Identity, 1890–1920* by Jonathan M. Hansen, which covers Eugene V. Debs, Jane Addams, and Du Bois (2003); *Du Bois and His Rivals,* Raymond Wolters (2002), which addresses themes of civil rights and social change; and *The Color of Race in America, 1900–1940* by Mathew Prat Guterl (2001) treats racial attitudes such as biracialism in social change, comparing Du Bois to Jean Toomer, and others.

The centennial of publication of *The Philadelphia Negro* is celebrated in Dolan Hubbard's The Souls of Black Folk: *One Hundred Years Later* (2003) with reviews and contextual and interpretive essays; and *W. E. B. DuBois and Race: Essays Celebrating the Centennial Publication of* The Souls of Black Folk, is edited Chester J. Fontenot and Mary Alice Morgan (2001). Manning Marable's *W. E. B. DuBois: Black Radical Democrat* (1986) is similarly insightful on Du Bois's politics. Adolph L. Reed Jr.'s controversial *W. E. B. DuBois and American Political Thought* (1995) may also be consulted. William L. Andrews's *Critical Essays on W. E. B. DuBois* (1985) is the best such collection. Critical works of special interest include Houston A. Baker Jr.'s *Modernism and the Harlem Renaissance* (1987), Keith E. Byerman's *Seizing the World: History, Art, and Self in the Work of W. E. B. DuBois* (1994), Harold Cruse's *The Crisis of the Negro Intellectual: A Historical Analysis of the Failure of Black Leadership* (1967, 1984), Henry Louis Gates Jr.'s *Figures in Black: Words, Signs and the "Racial" Self* (1987), Sterling Stuckey's *Slave Culture: National Theory and the Foundations of Black America* (1987), Eric J. Sundquist's magisterial *To Wake the Nations: Race in the Making of American Literature* (1993), and Shannon Zamir's *W. E. B. DuBois and American Thought, 1888–1903* (1995). A special W. E. B. Du Bois issue of *Boundary 2: An International Journal of Literature and Culture* appeared in 2000.

## Paul Laurence Dunbar

In *Black Poets of the United States: From Paul Laurence Dunbar to Langston Hughes* (1973)

Jean Wagner describes Dunbar's generation as developing and influenced by the minstrel concept, popular music, and white writings, contrasting Dunbar with Harlem Renaissance poet such as Langston Hughes. Since then much new work on Dunbar has appeared, beginning with a 1999 reprint of *The Life and Works of Paul Laurence Dunbar: Containing his Complete Poetical Works, his Best Short Stories, Numerous Anecdotes, and a Complete Biography*, compiled and introduced by William Dean Howells in 1907. *The Complete Stories of Paul Laurence Dunbar* (2006) edited by Gene Andrew Jarrett and Thomas Lewis Morgan is a much-needed edition, as was *The Collected Poetry of Paul Laurence Dunbar* (1993), edited by Joanne M. Braxton, still the largest and most authoritative if not all-inclusive collection of Dunbar's poetry. *In His Own Voice: The Dramatic and Other Uncollected Works of Paul Laurence Dunbar*, edited by Herbert Woodward Martin and Ronald Primeau with a foreword by Henry Louis Gates, Jr. (2002) fills some major gaps. A 2005 reprint of Dunbar's 1904 collection of 16 short stories, *The Heart of Happy Hollow*, is available. There are dozens of juvenile biographies and collections of Dunbar's poetry for children. In 1975 E. W. Metcalf published *Paul Laurence Dunbar: A Bibliography*.

Felton O. Best's *Crossing the Color Line: A Biography of Paul Laurence Dunbar, 1872–1906* (1996) is a full-length biographical study of the author. In 1971 Addison Gayle published *Oak and Ivy: A Biography of Paul Laurence Dunbar*. A dramatic treatment of Dunbar's life is contained in *Lyrics of Sunshine and Shadow: The Tragic Courtship and Marriage of Paul Laurence Dunbar and Alice Ruth Moore* (2002) by Eleanor Alexander; though Dunbar and Moore were admired by African American literary society in their day, even compared to Robert and Elizabeth Barrett Browning, theirs was a difficult relationship, to say the least, made worse by Dunbar's sometimes violent and drunken behavior. Alexander analyzes the couple's courtship and marriage in light of the social customs of the period, both within and outside the African American community, especially the negative effects of race, class, and gender on romantic love.

Peter Revell's critical book *Paul Laurence Dunbar* (1979) locates Dunbar within the socio-political contexts of his time, dispelling criticisms that Dunbar capitulated to racist stereotypes in his art in order to pander to a white audience. *Liberating Voices* (1991) by Gayle Jones is a study of the emergence of the black literary tradition with particular emphasis on Dunbar's didactic poem, "When Malindy Sings," and his short story "They Lynching of June Benson." A new look at his relationship with Howells is " 'Entirely Black Verse from Him Would Succeed': Minstrel Realism and

William Dean Howells" by Gene Jarrett, *Nineteenth-Century Literature* (2004). Also of note are "Paul Laurence Dunbar's Literary Dialects" by Herbert Penzl, *PMLA: Publications of the Modern Language Association of America* (1993), and Marcellus Blount's "The Preacherly Text: African American Poetry and Vernacular Performance," *PMLA* (1992).

### Charles Alexander Eastman

Eastman's most important books, after *From the Deep Woods to Civilization* (1916), are his *Indian Boyhood* (1902), in spite of its original orientation toward what we now call a "young adult" audience; *The Soul of the Indian* (1911), a quasi-philosophical account of Native American thought; and his last book, *Indian Heroes and Great Chieftains* (1918), in which he meditates on the examples offered by a number of notable Native American people. Raymond Wilson's *Ohiyesa: Charles Eastman, Santee Sioux* (1983) is a sympathetic biography claiming that Eastman managed "to adjust to an alien culture and at the same time retain his Indian identity." Anna L. Stensland's "Charles Alexander Eastman," *American Indian Quarterly* 3 (1977), argues that Eastman should be considered as a storyteller who carried a good deal of Sioux tradition into his writings. The essay also offers a survey of most of his work. Another early but still useful account of Eastman exists in David R. Miller. "Charles Alexander Eastman, the 'Winner.' " *American Indian Intellectuals*, edited by Margot Liberty (1978). See also the chapters on Eastman in H. David Brumble's *American Indian Autobiography* (1988) and in Hertha D. Wong's *Sending My Heart Across the Years: Tradition and Innovation in Native American Autobiography* (1992). Philip J. Deloria's *Playing Indian* (1998) discusses Eastman in an interesting chapter called "Natural Indians and Identities of Modernity," and Elaine Goodale Eastman's *Sister to the Sioux: The Memoirs of Elaine Goodale Eastman, 1885–91* (1978) is also a valuable source.

### Sui Sin Far (Edith Maud Eaton)

The only substantial collection of Sui Sin Far's writing is in *"Mrs. Spring Fragrance" and Other Writings* (1995), edited by Amy Ling and Annette White-Parks; this volume contains "approximately three-fourths of the original title" published in 1912. Fortunately for scholars interested in the life and writings of this re-emerging author, there is an exhaustively researched critical biography by Annette White-Parks, *Sui Sin Far/Edith Maude Eaton: A Literary Biography* (1995). This volume contains a very helpful chronological listing of her writings.

Much of the best critical work on Sui Sin Far appears as articles or chapters in books; for an extensive listing, including the many contributions by Amy Ling, see White-Parks. Resources that contextualize Sui Sin Far as a turn-of-the-twentieth-century Eurasian woman writer are, chronologically: Doug Chin and Art Chin, *Uphill: The Settlement and Diffusion of the Chinese in Seattle* (1974); Elaine Kim, *Asian American Literature: An Introduction to the Writings and Their Social Context* (1982); William F. Wu, *The Yellow Peril: Chinese Americans in American Fiction, 1850–1940* (1982); Anthony B. Chan, *Gold Mountain: The Chinese in the Northwest* (1983); Judy Yung, *Chinese Women of America* (1986); Mary Dearborn, *Pocahontas's Daughters: Gender and Ethnicity in American Culture* (1986); Roger Daniels, *Asian America* (1988); Ronald Takaki, *Strangers from a Different Shore* (1989); Amy Ling, *Between Worlds: Women Writers of Chinese Ancestry* (1990), which contains a chapter on Sui Sin Far and her novelist sister Winnifred; and Susan Coultrap-McQuin, *Doing Literary Business: American Women Writers in the Nineteenth Century* (1990). Two books published in 2001 add to the scholarship on Sui Sin Far and her sister Onoto Watanna: Diana Birchall's *Onoto Watanna: The Story of Winnifred Eaton* and Dominika Ferens's *Edith and Winnifred Eaton: Chinatown Missions and Japanese Romances*.

Elizabeth Ammons's *Conflicting Stories: American Women Writers at the Turn of the Twentieth Century* (1992) consists of essays on a dozen writers and stories, including the superb "Audacious Words: Sui Sin Far's Mrs. Spring Fragrance." Julia Brown edited *Ethnicity and the American Short Story* (1997), which contains Carol-Roh Spaulding's fine essay " 'Wavering' Images: Mixed-Race Identity in the Stories of Edith Eaton/Sui Sin Far." Other useful essays include: "Sui Sin Far and the Chinese American Canon: Toward a Post-Gender-Wars Discourse," Wenxin Li, *MELUS* (2004); Min Hyoung Song's "Sentimentalism and Sui Sin Far," *Legacy* (2003), which examines the presence of Christianity in Far's fiction; "Smuggling across the Borders of Race, Gender, and Sexuality: Sui Sin Far's 'Mrs. Spring Fragrance,'" Martha J. Cutter, in *Mixed Race Literature*, ed. Jonathan Brennan (2002); "Reclaiming Sui Sin Far," Guy Beauregard, in *Re/Collecting Early Asian America: Essays in Cultural History*, ed. Josephine Lee, Imogene L. Lim, and Yuko Matsukawa (2002); "Connecting Links: The Anti-Progressivism of Sui Sin Far," Sean McCann, *Yale Journal of Criticism* (1999); "Sui Sin Far and Onoto Watanna: Two Early Chinese-Canadian Authors," James Doyle, *Canadian Literature* (1994); and "Between the East and West: Sui Sin Far-the First Chinese-American Woman Writer," Xiao-Huang Yin, *Arizona Quarterly*, (1991).

**Mary E. Wilkins Freeman**
The best collection of Freeman's work is *Selected Stories of Mary E. Wilkins Freeman*

(1983), edited and with a perceptive introduction by Marjorie Pryse. Brent L. Kendrick edited and introduced *The Infant Sphinx: Collected Letters of Mary E. Wilkins Freeman* (1985). Perry D. Westbrook's full-length study, *Mary Wilkins Freeman* (1988), is a good introduction to Freeman's life and work. Leah Blatt Glasser's *In a Closet Hidden: The Life and Work of Mary E. Wilkins Freeman* (1996) makes an important contribution to the biographical and critical scholarship. Mary R. Reichard's *Mary Wilkins Freeman: A Study of the Short Story* (1998) usefully brings together with her close readings of many of Freemans' 250 stories biographical information and a set of readings of "A New England Nun." Reichard has also edited a fine selection of twenty-eight of Freeman's stories: *A Mary Wilkins Freeman Reader* (1997). John Idol and Melinda Ponder's *The Unfortunate Fall: Women and Genteel Poverty in the Fiction of Hawthorne and Freeman* (1999) contains essays on Hawthorne and Freeman as well as Stowe, Rebecca Harding Davis, Jewett, Gilman, and other nineteenth- and early-twentieth-century women writers. Abigail Ann Hamblen's *The New England Art of Mary E. Wilkins Freeman* (1966) delivers what its title promises. The introduction to Judith Fetterley and Marjorie Pryse's anthology *American Women Regionalists: 1850–1910* (1992) helpfully contextualizes Freeman's fiction. In 1999 a special Mary E. Wilkins Freeman issue of *American Transcendental Quarterly* was guest-edited by Shirley Marchalonis and contains essays by Charles Johanningsmeier, Gregg Camfield, William J. Scheick and other leading scholars. Johanningsmeier is also the author of the excellent essay "Sarah Orne Jewett and Mary E. Wilkins (Freeman): Two Shrewd Businesswomen in Search of New Markets," *New England Quarterly* (1997).

**Hamlin Garland**
No collected edition of Garland is currently available. Donald Pizer edited *Hamlin Garland's Diaries* (1968), *The Rose of Dutcher's Coolly* (1969), and *Main-Travelled Roads* (1970). Joseph B. McCullough edited *Tales of the Middle Border* (1990) and *Main-Travelled Roads* (1995). In 1998 Dover reprinted *A Daughter of the Middle Border*. The publication of *Selected Letters of Hamlin Garland* (1998), edited by Newlin and McCullough, links Garland to a great many other writers from the 1890s through 1940. Newlin has also contributed *Hamlin Garland: A Bibliography (1896–1940), with a Checklist of Unpublished Letters* (1998).

The most comprehensive biography of Garland is in French: Robert Mane's *Hamlin Garland: l'homme et l'oeuvre* (1968). Jean Holloway's critical biography *Hamlin Garland* (1960) may be supplemented by Donald Pizer's still valuable *Hamlin Garland's Early Work and Career* (1960). Joseph B. McCullough's solid *Hamlin Garland* (1978) is a brief critical biography and survey of the writings. Robert Gish's *Hamlin Garland: The Far West* (1976) appeared in the Western Writers series of brief monographs. Extensive treatment of Garland by Ahnebrink, Walcutt, Parrington, Pizer, and Martin also appears in those authors' more general studies of the period of realism and naturalism. James Nagel's introduction and his edition of *Critical Essays on Hamlin Garland* (1982) make valuable contributions to Garland scholarship. Charles L. P. Silet, Robert E. Welch, and Richard Boudreau edited *The Critical Reception of Hamlin Garland* (1985). Tom Lutz devotes a chapter, "Hamlin Garland's Provincial Literature," to Garland in his *Cosmopolitan Vistas: American Regionalism and Literary Value* (2004), and recent journal articles add to critical discussion: Stephanie Foote, "The Value of Regional Identity: Labor, Representation, and Authorship in Hamlin Garland," *Studies in American Fiction* (1999); "Hamlin Garland's Relationship with Frank Norris," Jesse S. Crisler, *Frank Norris Studies* (2004); "Land and Literary: Hamlin Garland, Sarah Orne Jewett, and the Production of Regional Literatures," Phillip Joseph, *Studies in American Fiction* (1998); "Hamlin Garland's 'The Return of a Private' and 'Under the Lion's Paw' and the Monopoly of Money in Post-Civil War America," Quentin E. Martin, *American Literary Realism* (1996).

**Charlotte Perkins Gilman**

No collected edition of Gilman's writings exists, but the intense interest in her work has resulted in several reprints of such key titles as *The Living of Charlotte Perkins Gilman: An Autobiography* (1975); *Women and Economics* (1966), edited by Carl Degler; *Women and Economics: A Study of the Economic Relation Between Men and Women as a Factor in Social Evolution*, ed. Michael Kimmel (1998); *Herland* (1979), edited by Ann J. Lane; *The Charlotte Perkins Gilman Reader* (1980), edited by Ann J. Lane; *Herland and Selected Stories by Charlotte Perkins Gilman* (1992), edited by Barbara Solomon. Lane's full-scale critical biography, *To Herland and Beyond: The Life and Work of Charlotte Perkins Gilman* (1990), is now standard. Mary A. Hill's *Charlotte Perkins Gilman: The Making of a Radical Feminist* (1980) and her *Endure: The Diaries of Charles Walter Stetson* (1985) illuminate Gilman's early years. Hill also edited *A Journey From Within: The Love Letters of Charlotte Perkins Gilman, 1897–1900* (1995). Denise D. Knight edited the two-volume *The Diaries of Charlotte Perkins Gilman* (1994). An interesting biographical find is presented in " 'All the Facts of the Case': Gilman's

Lost Letter to Dr. S. Weir Mitchell," Denise D. Knight, *American Literary Realism* (2005).

Critical books worthy of note include the Twayne volume *Charlotte Perkins Gilman: A Study of the Short Fiction*, by Denise D. Knight (1997); Gary Scharnhorst's *Charlotte Perkins Gilman* (1985), Polly Wynn Allen's *Building Domestic Liberty: Charlotte Perkins Gilman's Architectural Feminism* (1988), Sheryl L. Meyering's *Charlotte Perkins Gilman: The Woman and Her Work* (1989), and Denise Knight's *Charlotte Perkins Gilman: A Study of the Short Fiction* (1997). Carol Farley Kessler's *Charlotte Perkins Gilman: Her Progress Toward Utopia with Selected Writings* (1994) reprints fourteen selections form Gilman's utopian writings. A useful companion volume, *Charlotte Perkins Gilman: Optimist Reformer* (1999), brings together essays, many of which address Gilman's reformist impulses as well as blind spots in her thinking. Cynthia J. Davis and Knight have edited *Charlotte Perkins Gilman and Her Contemporaries: Literary and Intellectual Contexts* (2004). Joanne B. Karpinski edited *Critical Essays on Charlotte Perkins Gilman* (1992). An interesting comparative study is *Kate Chopin, Edith Wharton and Charlotte Perkins Gilman: Studies in Short Fiction* by Janet Beer (2005). *Charlotte Perkins Gilman: Optimist Reformer* (1999), ed. Jill Rudd and Val Gough, offers thirteen original essays focused on such difficult issues as Gilman's racism, class consciousness, and essentialist view of women. *Raising the Dust: The Literary Housekeeping of Mary Ward, Sarah Grand, and Charlotte Perkins Gilman* by Beth Sutton-Ramspeck (2004) and *Wayward Reproductions: Genealogies of Race and Nation in Transatlantic Modern Thought*, Alys Eve Weinbaum (2004) devote considerable space to Gilman.

Thomas L. Erskine and Conee L. Richards edited and introduced *"The Yellow Wallpaper" Charlotte Perkins Gilman* (1993). Catherine Golden edited *The Captive Imagination: A Casebook on "The Yellow Wallpaper"* (1991). Julie Bates Dock's *The Legend of "The Yellow Wallpaper": A Documentary Casebook* (1998) and *Charlotte Perkins Gilman's "the Yellow Wallpaper" and the History of Its Publication and Reception: A Critical Edition and Documentary Casebook* (1998) established for the first time a reliable critical edition and publication history for this celebrated story and supplies a rich set of contextualizing documents illuminating the genesis, compositional and publication histories of the text as well as more than a score of contemporary reviews and other commentary. Dock's " 'But One Expects That': Charlotte Perkins Gilman's 'The Yellow Wallpaper' and the Shifting Light of Scholarship," *PMLA* (January 1996), should also be consulted. Also useful are *"The Yellow Wall-Paper" by Charlotte Perkins*

*Gilman : A Dual-Textbook Critical Edition*, ed. Shawn St. Jean(2006); *The Pedagogical Wallpaper: Teaching Charlotte Perkins Gilman's 'The Yellow Wallpaper,' "* ed. Jeffrey Andrew Weinstock (2003), consisting of ten essays; *Approaches to Teaching Gilman's "The Yellow Wall-paper," and* Herland, ed. Denise D. Knight and Cynthia J. Davis (2003); and *The Mixed Legacy of Charlotte Perkins Gilman*, ed. Catherine J. Golden and Joanna Schneider Zangrando, with fourteen essays on Gilman's life and career and especially "The Yellow Wall-Paper" (2000). Every year dozens of new essays on "The Yellow Wall-Paper" appear in academic journals.

**Joel Chandler Harris**
Richard Chase's edition of *The Complete Tales of Uncle Remus* (1955) is still the best one-volume collection of Harris's fiction, and it has been reprinted (2002). Popular among parents and children is Julius Lester's 1999 re-telling of *Uncle Remus: The Complete Tales*, using contemporary black English and references. Julia Collier Harris edited *Joel Chandler Harris, Editor and Essayist: Miscellaneous Literary, Political, and Social Writings* (1931). Hugh T. Keenan's *Dearest Chums and Partners: Joel Chandler Harris's Letters to His Children* (1993) makes available 280 letters. Three important biographies, are still useful: Robert L. Wiggins's still useful *The Life of Joel Chandler Harris from Obscurity in Boyhood to Fame in Early Manhood* (1918), Julia Collier Harris's *The Life and Letters of Joel Chandler Harris* (1918), and Paul M. Cousins's *Joel Chandler Harris: A Biography* (1968). Walter M. Brasch's illuminating *Brer Rabbit, Uncle Remus, and the "Cornfield Journalist": The Tale of Joel Chandler Harris* (2000) is a cultural biography. Harris scholars have long-awaited folklorist Bruce R. Bickley, Jr.'s *Joel Chandler Harris: A Biography and Critical Study* (2000). Stella Brooks's *Joel Chandler Harris, Folklorist* (1950) is a specialized study of continuing pertinence. Bruce R. Bickley's *Joel Chandler Harris* (1987) is a good introductory survey of the life and work, and his *Critical Essays on Joel Harris* (1981) is useful. Eric J. Sundquist's *To Wake the Nations* (1993) contains interesting material on Harris. Hugh T. Keenan's *The Library of Joel Chandler Harris: An Annotated Book List* (1997) is a welcome companion to his *Joel Chandler Harris: An Annotated Bibliography of Criticism, 1977–1996 with Supplement, 1892–1976* (1997), with Bruce R. Bickley, Jr. A couple of interesting re-appraisals of Harris are "Disney's *Song of the South* and the Birth of the White Negro," by Catherine Gunther Kodat, in *American Cold War Culture*, ed. Douglas Field (2005); and "Black Father: The Subversive Achievement of Joel Chandler Harris," by Robert Cochran, *African American Review* (2004).

**Bret Harte**
The most complete collection is *The Works of Bret Harte* in twenty-five volumes (1914). Harte's poetry may be found in *The Complete Poetical Works of Bret Harte* (1899). Charles Meeker Kozlay edited *Stories and Poems and Other Uncollected Writings* available in the Argonaut edition (1906). Geoffrey Bret Harte edited *The Letters of Bret Harte* (1926). Joseph B. Harrison edited *Bret Harte: Representative Selections* (1941). Gary Scharnhorst edited and introduced *Bret Harte's California* (1990). *Selected Letters of Bret Harte* appeared in 1997 edited by Scharnhorst and Robert L. Gale. Much editorial work remains to be done.

Gary Scharnhorst's fine critical biography *Bret Harte: Opening the American Literary West* (2000) elegantly furnishes analysis of the life, career, and reception of Harte, with the focus on Harte's writing life, joining his Twayne volume *Bret Harte* of 1992. (Also see: Scharnhorst, "A Coda to the Twain-Harte Feud," *Western American Literature* [2001].) Focusing on Harte's financial struggles, Axel Nissen's *Bret Harte: Prince and Pauper* (2000) provides a lively account of Harte's life and times. Patrick Morrow's *Bret Harte: Literary Critic* (1979) is a judicious account of Harte's sometimes injudicious criticism. Morrow's *Bret Harte* (1972) in the Boise College Western Writers Series provides an adequate brief introduction to the man and his work. The best single bibliography on Harte is Gary Scharnhorst's *Bret Harte: A Bibliography* (1995); Linda D. Barnett's *Bret Harte: A Reference Guide* (1980) is the best guide to writings about Harte.

Queer theorists and Gender Studies critics have recently taken up Harte's characters; see *Queer Cowboys and Other Erotic Male Friendships in Nineteenth-Century American Literature* by Packard, Chris (2005), which includes essays on James Fenimore Cooper, Walt Whitman, Harris, Twain, Harte, and Eugene Field; "The Queer Short Story," Axel Nissen, in *The Art of Brevity: Excursions in Short Fiction Theory and Analysis* (2004), ed. Per Winther, Jakob Lothe, and Hans H. Skei; "Rewriting the Gold Rush: Twain, Harte and Homosociality," Peter Stoneley, *Journal of American Studies* (1996); and " 'She War a Woman': Family Roles, Gender, and Sexuality in Bret Harte's Western Fiction," J. David Stevens, *American Literature* (1997).

**Pauline E. Hopkins**
Editions of Hopkins's works include *Daughter of the Revolution: The Major Nonfiction Works of Pauline E. Hopkins*, ed. Ira Dworkin (2006); *The Magazine Novels of Pauline Hopkins: (Including Hagar's Daughter, Winona, and Of One Blood)* from The Schomburg Library of Nineteenth-Century Black Women Writers, ed.

Hazel V. Carby (1990); *Contending Forces: A Romance Illustrative of Negro Life North and South* from The Schomburg Library of Nineteenth-Century Black Women Writers, ed. Richard Yarborough, 1991; and *Of One Blood: Or, the Hidden Self*: by Pauline Hopkins, ed. Deborah McDowell (2004). Hanna Wallinger's *Pauline E. Hopkins: A Literary Biography* (2005) and Carol Allen's *Black Women Intellectuals: Strategies of Nation, Family, and Neighborhood in the Works of Pauline Hopkins, Jessie Fauset, and Marita Bonner* (1998) have supplied much-needed reliable resources. John Cullen Gruesser has edited *The Unruly Voice: Rediscovering Pauline Elizabeth Hopkins* (1996). *Feminist Forerunners: Womanism and Feminism in the Early Twentieth Century*, edited by Ann Heilmann (2003), contains Sabina Matter-Seibel's "Pauline Hopkins's Portrayal of the African-American New Woman in *Contending Forces* and the *Colored American Magazine*"; Jill Berger's " 'A New Race of Colored Women': Pauline Hopkins at the *Colored American* Magazine"; and "Rape, Lynching, and *Contending Forces*: Pauline Hopkins—Forerunner of Critical Race Theorists" by Patricia D. Watkins.

### Henry James

*The Novels and Tales of Henry James* (The New York Edition) in twenty-six volumes, originally published in 1907–17, was reissued 1962–65. Other collections of James's diverse writings are available in Leon Edel's edition of *The Complete Plays of Henry James* (1949), R. P. Blackmur's *The Art of the Novel* (1935), Morris Shapiro's edition of *Selected Literary Criticism* (1963), Morton D. Zabel's edition of James's travel writings, *The Art of Travel* (1958), F. O. Matthiessen and Kenneth B. Murdoch's *The Notebooks of Henry James* (1947), F. W. Dupee's edition of the three volumes of *Henry James: Autobiography* (1956), and in various collections of essays and letters edited by Leon Edel. Multiple volumes of James's novels, short stories, and literary essays are contained in the Library of America series, for example *Complete Stories* (1999); *Henry James: Major Stories and Essays*, both edited by Leon Edel (1999). *The Portable Henry James* is edited by John Auchard (2003). Edel is also the editor of the five-volume *The Letters of Henry James*. Philip Horne has published *Henry James: A Life in Letters* (1999), with half of the nearly 300 selections previously unpublished; Susan E. Gunter and Steven H. Jobe have edited *Dearly Beloved Friends: Henry James's Letters to Younger Men* (2001), which contains 166 letters, 95 previously unpublished. *The Complete Letters of Henry James, 1855–1872* is edited by Pierre A. Walker and Greg W. Zacharias (2006), the first volume of a proposed set. *The Notebooks of Henry James* edited by F. O. Matthiessen and

Kenneth B. Murdock (1981) and *A Bibliography of Henry James* (1999) by Leon Edel, Dan H. Laurence, and James Rambeau round out the reference section.

*Henry James: The Imagination of Genius, A Biography*, by Fred Kaplan (1999) relies almost exclusively on the letters and diaries of James and his associates to convey both James's spirit and the background for his work. Though not as all-encompassing as Leon Edel's five-volume opus (*Henry James* [1953–72]), this volume is a highly recommended one-volume companion to the biographical study *The Jameses* by R. W. B. Lewis (1993). F. O. Matthiessen's classic *The James Family* (1947) also reveals Henry's relationship to this extraordinary American family, which included his brother, William, the celebrated psychologist and philosopher, and sister, Alice, whose diary has attracted considerable attention since its publication in 1964. Other biographical studies suggest that James and his remarkable family continue to fascinate scholars: Edwin Sill Fussell's *The Catholic Side of Henry James* (1993), Kenneth Graham's engaging *Henry James: A Literary Life* (1995), and Carol Holly's *Intensely Family: The Inheritance of Family Shame and the Autobiographies of Henry James* (1995), and Lyndall Gordon's *A Private Life of Henry James: Two Women and His Art* (1999), which looks freshly at James's relationships with his cousin Minny Temple and Constance Fenimore Woolson.

Since the 1940s, critical studies of James have abounded. Among the best of these, in chronological order, are Ruth Bernard Yeazell's *Language and Knowledge in the Late Novels of Henry James* (1976), Charles Robert Anderson's *Person, Place, and Thing in Henry James's Novels* (1977), Strother Purdy's *The Hole in the Fabric: Science, Contemporary Literature, and Henry James* (1977), Shlomith Rummon's *The Concept of Ambiguity: The Example of James* (1977), Sergio Perosa's *Henry James and the Experimental Novel* (1978), Daniel J. Schneider's *The Crystal Cage: Adventures of the Imagination in the Fiction of Henry James* (1978), Mary Doyle Springer's *A Rhetoric of Literary Character: Some Women of Henry James* (1978), Edward Wagenknecht's *Eve and Henry James: Portraits of Women and Girls in His Fiction* (1978), Nicola Bradbury's *Henry James: The Later Novels* (1979), Susanne Kappeler's *Writing and Reading in Henry James* (1980), Philip Sicker's *Love and the Quest for Identity in the Fiction of Henry James* (1980), Alwyn Buland's *Culture and Conduct in the Novels of Henry James* (1981), Sarah B. Daugherty's *The Literary Criticism of Henry James* (1981), Daniel Mark Fogel's *Henry James and the Structure of the Romantic Imagination* (1981), William W. Stowe's *Balzac, James, and the Realistic Novel* (1983), John Carlos Rowe's *The Theoretical Dimensions of Henry James* (1984),

Edward Wagenknecht's *The Novels of Henry James* (1983) and *The Tales of Henry James* (1984), Sharon Cameron's *Thinking in Henry James* (1989), Alfred Habegger's *Henry James and the "Woman Business"* (1989), Sarah S. Chapman's *Henry James's Portrait of the Writer as Hero* (1989), Philip Horne's *Henry James and Revision* (1990), Edwin S. Fussell's *The French Side of Henry James* (1990), Richard A. Hocks's *Henry James: A Study of the Short Fiction* (1990), Millicent Bell's *Meaning in Henry James* (1991), Susan M. Griffin's *The Historical Eye: The Texture of the Visual in Late James* (1991), Ross Posnock's *The Trial of Curiosity: Henry James, William James, and the Challeneg of Modernity* (1991), Adeline R. Tintner's *The Cosmopolitan World of Henry James: An Intertextual Study* (1991), Jeanne Campbell Reesman's philosophical and narratological study *Interest and Design: The Late Novels of James and Faulkner* (1991); Dietmar Schloss's *Culture and Criticism in Henry James* (1992), Priscilla L. Walton's *The Disruption of the Feminine in Henry James* (1992), Greg W. Zacharias's *Henry James and Morality of Fiction* (1993), Daniel Mark Fogel's edited *A Companion to Henry James Studies* (1993), Tony Tanner's *Henry James and the Art of Nonfiction* (1995), Sheila Teahan's *The Rhetorical Logic of Henry James* (1995), Eli Ben-Joseph's *Aesthetic Persuasion: Henry James, the Jews, and Race* (1996), John H. Pearson's *The Prefaces of Henry James: Framing the Modern Reader* (1997), Collin Meissner's *Henry James and the Language of Experience* (1999), Wendy Graham's *Henry James's Thwarted Love* (1999), Willie Tolliver's *A Self Among Others: Henry James as a Biographer* (2000), Robert B. Pippin's *Henry James and Modern Moral Life* (2000), Denis Flannery's *Henry James: A Certain Illusion* (2000), Jerry Tambling's, *Henry James* (2000), Christopher Greenwood's *Adapting to the Stage: Theater and the Work of Henry James* (2000), Marc McGurl's *The Novel Art: Elevations of American Fiction After Henry James* (2001), Clair Hughes's *Henry James and the Art of Dress* (2001), Donatella Izzo's *Portraying the Lady: Technologies of Gender in the Short Stories of Henry James* (2001), S. Selina Jamil's *Jamesian Centers of Consciousness as Readers and Tellers of Stories* (2001), Tessa Hadley's *Henry James and the Imagination of Pleasure* (2002), James Duban, *The Nature of True Virtue: Theology, Psychology, and Politics in the Writings of Henry James, Sr., Henry James, Jr., and William James* (2001), Clair Hughes's *Henry James and the Art of Dress* (2001), Eric Haralson's *Henry James and Queer Modernity* (2003), Leland Person's *Henry James and the Suspense of Masculinity* (2003), Rob Davidson's *The Master and the Dean: The Literary Criticism of Henry James and William Dean Howells* (2005), and J. Hillis Miller's *Literature As Conduct: Speech Acts in Henry James* (2005).

John R. Bradley edited *Henry James on Stage and Screen* (2000) and Susan M. Griffin edited *Henry James Goes to the Movies* (2001). *The Novel Art: Elevations of American Fiction after Henry James*, by Mark McGurl (2001) examines the influence of James on Crane, Howells, Wharton, O. Henry, John Dos Passos, Anita Loos, Gertrude Stein, William Faulkner, and Dashiell Hammett. An excellent pedagogical handbook is *Approaches to Teaching Henry James's Daisy Miller and The Turn of the Screw*, ed. Kimberly Capps Reed and Peter G. Beidler (2005).

There is no shortage of collections of criticism: Graham Clark edited *Henry James: Critical Assessment* (1991), Kevin J. Hayes edited *Henry James: The Contemporary Reviews* (1996), Peter Rawlings edited *Critical Essays on Henry James* (1993), and Joseph Dewey edited *The Finer Thread, The Tighter Weave: New Essays on the Short Fiction* (2001). Judith E. Funston compiled a very helpful guide to book and periodical publications in *Henry James: A Reference Guide, 1975–1987* (1991). Pierre A. Walker edited *Henry James on Culture: Collected Essays on Politics and the American Social Scene* (1999). *Questioning the Master: Gender and Sexuality in Henry James's Writings*, 2000, edited by Peggy McCormack, is a collection of nine previously published essays suggesting the need for dialogue between feminists and queer theorists. Adeline R. Tintner has published the fifth volume in her series of contextual studies, *The Twentieth-Century World of Henry James: Changes in His Work after 1900* (2000).

## Sarah Orne Jewett

There is no collected edition of Jewett's writings. Jewett's *Stories and Tales* were published in seven volumes in 1910; but a more readily available collection, *The Best Stories of Sarah Orne Jewett* (1925), was edited in two volumes with a foreword by Willa Cather. Richard Cary edited *The Uncollected Short Stories of Sarah Orne Jewett* (1971). Cary also edited *Sarah Orne Jewett Letters* (1967). The Library of America's edition of Jewett's *Novels and Stories* (1994), selected and with notes by Michael Davitt Bell, provides three novels and some thirty stories and is available in paperback.

An informative, feminist life of Jewett by an eminent biographer, *Sarah Orne Jewett: Her World and Her Work* by Paula Blanchard (2002) has drawn generated attention to Jewett's complexities. A good introductory study is Josephine Donovan's *Sarah Orne Jewett* (1980). More recently, Perry D. Westbrook's *Acres of Flint: Sarah Orne Jewett and Her Contemporaries* (1981), Louis A. Renza's *"A White Heron" and The Question of Minor Literature* and Sarah Way Sherman's *Sarah Orne Jewett: An Ameri-*

can *Persephone* (1989) have clarified and complicated our understanding of Jewett as have Marilyn Sanders Mobley's *Folk Roots and Mythic Wings in Sarah Orne Jewett and Toni Morrison: The Cultural Functions of Narrative* (1991), Joseph Church's *Transcendent Daughters in Jewett's Country of the Pointed Firs* (1995), and Margaret Roman's *Sarah Orne Jewett: Reconstructing Gender* (1997). Karen L. Kilcup and Thomas S. Edwards edited *Jewett and Her Contemporaries: Reshaping the Canon* (1999), fourteen essays on Jewett, nineteenth-century women's writing and new canon formation. *A Sarah Orne Jewett Companion*, edited by Robert L. Gale (1999) is of hellp, and the comparative study *Conscience and Purpose: Fiction and Social Consciousness in Howells, Jewett, Chesnutt, and Cather* by Paul R. Petrie (2005) supplies comparisons and contexts. Gwen L. Nagel's still-useful *Critical Essays on Sarah Orne Jewett* (1984) offers a rich selection of material. An intriguing recent reading of "A White Heron" is "Romantic Flight in Jewett's 'White Heron' " by Joseph Church, *Studies in American Fiction* (2002).

### James Weldon Johnson

Editions include William L. Andrews's *James Weldon Johnson: Writings* in the Library of America series (2004) and *Selected Writings of James Weldon Johnson* in two volumes (1995), edited by Sondra Kathryn Wilson. Volume 1 is a collection of Johnson's New York Age writings in role of "mass educator," while volume 2 offers selections of social and political writings, discussions of international affairs, collegiate writings, and literary works. Robert E. Fleming's *James Weldon Johnson and Arna Bontemps: A Reference Guide*, (1978) is still useful with its year-by-year, annotated checklist of material about the authors. *Along This Way: The Autobiography of James Weldon Johnson*, (1991) was edited by Sondra Kathryn Wilson and chronicles Johnson's career as songwriter, diplomat, activist, and professor; she has also given us an edition of Johnson's *Black Manhattan* (1991), Johnson's first-hand account of Harlem Renaissance period. *Living Our Stories, Telling Our Truths* (1995) by V. P. Franklin is a study of Du Bois and Johnson. *Critical Essays on James Weldon Johnson*, edited by Kenneth M. Price and Lawrence J. Oliver (1997) contains helpful essays, and more are appearing with greater frequency in academic journals and collections, such as "The Autobiography of an Ex-Coloured Man" in *Politics of the African-American Novel* (1991) by Richard Kostelanetz, with a focus on the "moral, political, and emotional ambiguities of passing"; "Public Acts and Private Utterances in James Weldon Johnson's *The Autobiography of an Ex-Colored Man*" by Nicholas L. Nownes *Southern Studies* (2005); and "The Cultural Matrix of Ragtime in James Weldon Johnson's *The Autobiography of an Ex-Colored Man*" by Timothy A. Spaulding, *Genre* (2004).

### Emma Lazarus

Lazarus's sisters Mary and Annie edited the two-volume *The Poems of Emma Lazarus* (1888); the first volume contains the biographical sketch they wrote for *Century Magazine*. In 1939 Ralph L. Rusk edited Letters to Emma Lazarus in the Columbia University Library, mainly from American and British writers. Morris U. Schappes edited The Letters of Emma Lazarus, 1868–1885 (1949) and Emma Lazarus: Selections from Her Poetry and Prose (1967). Newer editions include the Library of America volume *Emma Lazarus: Selected Poems*, edited by John Hollander, and *Emma Lazarus: In Her World* (1995), edited by Bette Roth-Young, an annotated collection of unpublished letters to friends and literary figures that seeks to dispel myths about Lazarus, some propagated by her sisters. Still the best biography is Daniel Vogel's *Emma Lazarus* (1980), especially in its treatment of neglected works.

Among critical works, Diane Lichtenstein's "Word and Worlds: Emma Lazarus's Conflicting Citizenships" *TWSL*, (1987) examines how Lazarus negotiates American and Jewish womanhood in an attempt to reconcile her multiple citizenships. Carole Kessner's "The Emma Lazarus-Henry James Connection: Eight Letters," *AmLH* (1991) demonstrates James' sympathies towards Jews from his own class vs. his antipathy toward recent émigrés. Max Cavitch's "Emma Lazarus and the Golem of Liberty," *American Literary History* (2006) is a recent rereading. Other important essays include "Emotion and the Jewish Historical Poems of Emma Lazarus" by Gregory Eiselein, Gregory, *Mosaic* (2004); Ranen Omer-Sherman's "Emma Lazarus, Jewish American Poetics, and the Challenge of Modernity," *Legacy: A Journal of American Women Writers* (2002); "Who Is the 'Mother of Exiles'? Jewish Aspects of Emma Lazarus's 'The New Colossus,'" by Daniel Marom, *Prooftexts: A Journal of Jewish Literary History* (2000); and "Words and Worlds: Emma Lazarus's Conflicting Citizenships," by Lichtenstein, *Tulsa Studies in Women's Literature* (1987). There is a fine web site on Lazarus maintained by the Jewish Women's Archive.

### Jack London

Though there are complete works of London's fifty-some books published in several foreign countries, including Japan, the Czech Republic, and France, there is none published in the United States. The rare (and incomplete) Sonoma edition (1928) printed twenty-eight titles in twenty-one volumes; the British Fitzroy *Works* reprinted twenty titles in the 1960s; and the Bodley Head Jack London half a dozen titles. Fortunately, London's enduring popularity ensures that his novels, short stories, dramas, and nonfiction are continually reprinted—a phenomenon both at home and abroad, as his millions of hits on Google.com attest. The two most significant current editions of London's writings for scholars and students are the three-volume *Letters of Jack London* (1988) and three-volume *The Complete Short Stories of Jack London* (1993), both edited by Earle Labor, Robert C. Leitz III, and I. Milo Shepard, published by Stanford University Press with major support from the National Endowment for the Humanities. Other handy editions of material otherwise difficult to track down are *Jack London Reports* (essays and newspaper articles), edited by King Hendricks and Irving Shepard (1970); *No Mentor But Myself: Jack London on Writers and Writing*, ed. Dale L. Walker and Jeanne Campbell Reesman (1999); *Jack London: Novels and Stories : Call of the Wild / White Fang / The Sea-Wolf / Klondike and Other Stories* and *Jack London : Novels and Social Writings*, the Library of America edition (1982), edited by Donald Pizer; and *The Portable Jack London,* edited by Earle Labor (1994), featuring a splendid introduction. London's most famous work is represented by several excellent teaching editions, including The Call of the Wild, *by Jack London, with an Illustrated Reader's Companion,* ed. Daniel Dyer (1995), and *The Call of the Wild* by Jack London, ed. Earl J. Wilcox and Elizabeth Wilcox (2003). Philip Foner's *Jack London: American Rebel—A Collection of His Social Writings Together with an Extensive Study of the Man and His Times* first appeared in 1947 and was reprinted as *The Social Writings of Jack London* in 1964. David Mike Hamilton's *"Tools of My Trade": The Annotated Books in Jack London's Library* (1986) is an outstanding source for London's thinking and artistic sources. Bibliographical work on London has languished since Joan Sherman's *Jack London: A Reference Guide* (1977) and Hensley C. Woodbridge, John London, and George H. Tweney's *Jack London: A Bibliography* (1966). The now-defunct *Jack London Newsletter,* edited by Woodbridge, and the ongoing magazine *The Call* from the Jack London Society, now edited by Kenneth K. Brandt, have occasionally published bibliographical updates.

London scholars and fans have eagerly awaited acknowledged leading expert Earle Labor's definitive biography, *Jack London: A Life* (2008). In the meantime, Russ Kingman's two volumes, *Jack London: A Definitive Chronology* (1992) and the biography *A Pictorial Life of Jack London* (1979) have been sources factually reliable if sometimes presented in a tone overly admiring of London. In his *Jack: A Biography of Jack London* (1977), Andrew Sinclair followed in the fictionalizing footsteps of Irving Stone in *Sailor on Horseback* (1938), copying the idea of London as a suicide

from Stone's now-discredited notions about London's death. One of London's earliest biographers was his daughter Joan London, in *Jack London and His Times* (1939; rpt. 1968). Clarice Stasz's *American Dreamers: Charmian and Jack London* (1988) and *Jack London's Women* (2001) explore his relationships with important women in his life.

Critical books and collections of essays include Franklin Walker's *Jack London and the Klondike: The Genesis of an American Writer* (1966; rpt. 2005); James McClintock's *White Logic: Jack London's Short Stories* (1975; rpt. 1997 as *Jack London's Strong Truths: A Study of the Short Stories*); Jacqueline Tavernier-Courbin, ed., *Critical Essays on Jack London* (1983); Charles N. Watson Jr.'s *The Novels of Jack London: A Reappraisal* (1983); Carolyn Johnston's *Jack London – An American Radical?* (1984); Earle Labor and Jeanne Campbell Reesman's *Jack London: Revised Edition* (1994) a Twayne volume that expands and updates Labor's original 1974 study with its effective combination of biography and criticism, is the best introduction to London; Jacqueline Tavernier-Courbin's *The Call of the Wild: A Naturalistic Romance* (1994); Susan Nuernberg's collection *The Critical Response to Jack London* (1995), which challenges the conventional wisdom of American critics by contrasting it to the more favorable evaluation of London internationally; *Rereading Jack London,* ed. Leonard Cassuto and Jeanne Campbell Reesman (1996); Jonathan Auerbach's *Male Call: Becoming Jack London* (1996); Reesman's *Jack London: A Study of the Short Fiction* (1998); *Jack London: One Hundred Years a Writer,* ed. Sara S. Hodson and Reesman (2002).

International conferences and exhibits, essays in scholarly journals, critical books, reprinted editions, web sites, teaching handbooks, studies of London as a photographer, and many other areas of London's work continue to appear each year.

### Native American Chants and Songs

Recognition of the potentially literary value of Native American chants and songs may be dated from the eighteenth century when Lieutenant Henry Timberlake in his 1765 *Memoirs* included a "Cherokee War Song" that he had translated in rhymed couplets! Henry Rowe Schoolcraft in the mid-nineteenth century worked out a method for the translation of songs that included a "literal" and a "literary" version of them, and this has been carefully examined by Dell Hymes in his seminal work *"In Vain I Tried to Tell You": Essays in Native American Ethnopoetics* (1981). Less literary but undoubtedly more accurate translations by amateur and government-bureau anthropologists began to appear near the end of the nineteenth century.

Specifically literary collections of these materials may be said to begin with Natalie Curtis Burlin's *The Indians' Book* (1907, 1968). Although Burlin's collection tends to museumize the literature of indigenous people as a priceless relic of the *past*, it does gather an extensive selection of songs, some of which are transcribed versions of the originals as well as translations. In *The Sky Clears: Poetry of the American Indians* (1951) A. Grove Day also emphasizes the "literary" over the "literal," but ranges widely. Margot Astrov's *American Indian Prose and Poetry* (1962, originally published as *The Winged Serpent: An Anthology of American Indian Poetry*, 1946) also is worth consulting. Several of John Bierhorst's compilations are well worth consulting, in particular *Cry from the Earth: Music of the North American Indians* (1979). Larry Evers and Felipe Molina's *Yaqui Deer Songs, Maso Bwikam* (1987) explains Yaqui culture and the song's place in it. Ruth Underhill's *Singing for Power: The Song Magic of the Papago Indians* (1938) remains useful, among older collections, as do Frances Densmore's many collections, e.g., her *Pawnee Music* (1929, 1972). David McAllester, in "Coyote's Song" (*Parabola* 4 [1980]: 28–35), presents a fascinating Navajo song attributed to Coyote. Gertrude Kurath and Antonio Garcia's *Music and Dance of the Tewa Pueblos* (1970) presents songs collected from 1957 to 1965. Leanne Hinton and Lucille Watahomigie's edited collection *Spirit Mountain: An Anthology of Yuman Story and Song* (1984) is worth consulting, along with Charlotte Heth's *Traditional Music of North American Indians* (1980), and Judith Vander's *Songprints: The Musical Experience of Five Shoshone Women* (1988), which shows how music is a part of these women's lives, and song a living, changing art form.

Brian Swann's recent *Wearing the Morning Star: Native American Song-Poems* (1996) is a valuable collection of songs. Thomas F. Johnson's *Eskimo Music by Region: A Comparative Circumpolar Study* (1976) and Paul Zolbrod's *Reading the Voice: Native American Oral Poetry on the Written Page* (1995) are useful studies of these materials.

The Navajo Night Chant was first described by Washington Matthews in 1894 and, in a posthumous publication, as late as 1907, with the fullest text dating from 1902. Berard Haile's "Navaho Chantways and Ceremonials" (*American Anthropologist* 40 (1938): 639–52) remains an important early study. James Faris's *The Nightway: A History and a History of the Documentation of a Navajo Ceremonial* (1990) usefully provides what its title promises.

Commentary on Densmore's collections of music from many tribes appears in anthropological and ethnomusicological journals, but there is no comprehensive study of her work to date. The contemporary Anishinabe

(Chippewa/Ojibwe) writer Gerald Vizenor has taken note of Densmore's Chippewa songs in his *People Named the Chippewa: Narrative Histories* (1984) and in his *Summer in the Spring: Ojibwe Lyric Poems and Tribal Stories*, edited and "re-expressed" by Vizenor (1981), which contains song lyrics and tales, and a glossary of Anishinaabemowin—Chippewa—words. The Library of Congress, Division of Music, issued a sound disc of Densmore's recorded *Songs of the Chippewa* in 1950.

The first and most indispensable source of material for the 1890 Ghost Dance is James Mooney's *Ghost-Dance Religion and the Sioux Outbreak of 1890*, first published in 1896 and available in an abridged edition with an introduction by Anthony F. C. Wallace (1965). Mooney also published "The Indian Ghost Dance" (*Proceedings and Collections of the Nebraska State Historical Society*, vol. 16) later in his life, in 1911. An informative biography of Mooney exists in *The Indian Man: A Biography of James Mooney* (1984) by L. G. Moses. Stanley Vestal's *New Sources of Indian History, 1850–1891: The Ghost Dance, the Prairie Sioux: A Miscellany* (1938) remains interesting, and Leslie Spier's *The Prophet Dance of the Northwest and Its Derivatives: The Source of the Ghost Dance* (1979) places the 1890 Ghost Dance in historical context.

Michael Hittman's *Wovoka and the Ghost Dance*, in its expanded edition of 1997 (the first edition of 1990 was specifically produced for the Yerington Paiute Tribe), is the fullest account of these matters, with appendices and bibliographies that are guides for further study. Russell Thornton's *We Shall Live Again: The 1870 and 1890 Ghost Dance Movements as Demographic Revitalization* (1986) discusses the importance of these movements for ongoing Native "revitalization."

### Native American Oratory

As early as the seventeenth century, English colonists were interested in the speeches of American Indians, at least those alleged to have been delivered as they expired, as in the missionary John Eliot's collection, *The Dying Speeches of Several Indians* (1685). A history of Indian speeches to Euro-Americans exists in Louis Thomas Jones's *Aboriginal American Oratory: The Traditions of Eloquence among the Indians of the United States* (1965), although Jones does not pay attention to issues of transcription and translation. David Murray's *Forked Tongues: Speech, Writing, and Representation in North American Indian Texts* (1991) is, however, attentive to all the many issues involved in bringing Native American Oratory to the page. General collections which may be consulted include Virginia Armstrong's *I Have Spoken: American History through the Voices of the Indians* (1971), which includes materials from 1609 to 1971, although the majority of speeches are from the nineteenth century; and W. C. Vanderwerth's *Indian Oratory: Famous Speeches by Noted Indian Chieftains* (1971). The most accurate compilations come from anthropologists and linguists both native and non-native. See, for example, Ruth Underhill, Donald Bahr, Baptisto Lopez, Jose Pancho, and David Lopez, *Rain-house and Ocean: Speeches for the Papago Year (1979)*, and Bahr's study, *Pima and Papago Ritual Oratory: A Study of Three Texts* (1975). Also valuable is Nora Marks Dauenhauer and Richard Dauenhauer, eds., *Haa Yuwunnaagu vis, For Healing Our Spirits* (1990).

## Frank Norris

There is no complete works of Frank Norris. *The Literary Criticism of Frank Norris* (1964) is edited by Donald Pizer and collects all Norris' critical work, and also offers an extensive bibliography. The Library of America *Frank Norris: Novels and Essays* (1986), is edited by Pizer. *The Apprenticeship Writings of Frank Norris, 1896–1898* (1996) edited by Joseph R. McElrath, Jr., and Douglas K. Burgess in two volumes, collects Norris' writings during stint as associate editor for the San Francisco *Wave*, spanning stories, sketches, essays, and reviews. *Frank Norris and The Wave: A Bibliography* (1988) is also provided by McElrath, as is *Frank Norris: A Descriptive Bibliography* (1992). *Frank Norris: The Critical Reception* (1981) edited by McElrath, is an interpretive compendium of all reviews, both contemporary and subsequent, of the author's works. With Jesse S. Crisler, McElrath is the co-author of the much-praised *Frank Norris: A Life* (2006), which is sure to be the definitive biography.

Among critical works, *The Novels of Frank Norris* (1966) by Donald Pizer argues that Norris was more about ideals than anything else—indeed, the great idealist of naturalism. For Norris, naturalism was a form of romanticism, and Pizer emphasizes the ethical dimension of Norris's work. In *The Art of Frank Norris, Storyteller* (1988), Barbara Hochman examines motifs in Norris' work that resist "incorporation into the pattern of meanings traditionally attributed to his work." *Frank Norris Revisited* (1992), is McElrath's Twayne volume, an excellent introduction which situates Norris "not in a reductive mechanistic or positivist tradition but in a humanist and humorous one." *Critical Essays on Frank Norris*, 1980, ed. Don Graham, is a collection of diverse perspectives. "Frank Norris's *McTeague*: Naturalism as Popular Myth," by Pizer, *ANQ: A Quarterly Journal of Short Articles, Notes, and Reviews* (2000) is a fresh reading of this startling novel.

## John M. Oskison

Good editions of Oskison's fiction, criticism, and other writings do not yet exist, nor is there much critical writing about him. Oskison's published novels are *Wild Harvest: A Novel of Transition Days in Oklahoma* (1925), *Black Jack Davy* (1926), and *Brothers Three* (1935). None of these, not even the first, deals much with Indian experience, unlike the biography, *Tecumseh and his Times: The Story of a Great Indian* (1938). Daniel Littlefield, Jr. and James Parins consider him in "Short Fiction Writers of the Indian Territory," *American Studies* 23 (1982), as does Gretchen Ronnow in "John Milton Oskison, Cherokee Journalist: Singer of the Semiotics of Power," *Native Press Research, Journal* 4 (1987). Robert Warrior's *Tribal Secrets: Recovering American Indian Intellectual Traditions* (1994) discusses Oskison briefly in the context indicated by the book's title. Daniel Heath Justice, in *Our Fire Survives the Storm: A Cherokee Literary History* (2006), has a fine section on Oskison using two important as-yet unpublished sources: Oskison's autobiographical "A Tale of the Old I. T. [Indian Territory]," in the manuscript collection of the Oklahoma Historical Society, and a novel, *The Singing Bird*, in the Western History Collection of the University of Oklahoma.

## María Amparo Ruiz de Burton

*The Squatter and the Don*, first published in San Francisco in 1885, was reprinted in 1997 as part of the Recovering the U.S. Hispanic Literary Heritage project by Arte Público Press, edited by Rosaura Sánchez and Beatrice Pita. It has also been reprinted by Modern Library (2004). Ruiz de Burton's other major work, *Who Would Have Thought It?* was also reprinted by Arte Público (1995), edited by Sánchez and Pita; it is a satire on U.S. politics and society set in Washington, DC, during and after the Civil War. *Conflicts of Interest: The Letters of María Amparo Ruiz de Burton*, edited by Sánchez and Pita, appeared in 2001. Amelia María de la Luz Montes and Anne Elizabeth Goldman edited *María Amparo Ruiz de Burton: Critical and Pedagogical Perspectives* (2004), which contains several fine essays on *The Squatter and the Don* by critics including José F. Aranda, Jr., Vincent Pérez, Jennifer S. Tuttle, and John M. González. The essays acknowledge the political complexity of Ruiz de Burton and draw connections between her and later Mexican-American women writers; the volume also includes a section on pedagogy that offers a discussion of teaching approaches, syllabi, discussion questions, and assignments. *Regions of Identity: The Construction of America in Women's Fiction, 1885–1914,* (1999) by Kate McCullough is valuable on Ruiz de Burton and Pauline Hopkins.

Because Ruiz de Burton is only a recently "recovered" writer, most work on her is appearing in essay form in scholarly journals. "Contradictory Impulses: María Amparo Ruiz de

Burton, Resistance Theory, and the Politics of Chicano/a Studies" by José F. Aranda, is included in *No More Separate Spheres! A Next Wave American Studies Reader*, ed. Cathy N. Davidson and Jessamyn Hatcher (2002); Aranda challenges critics to re-examine the assumptions of resistance theories, particularly if they unconsciously assume the preeminence of the United States or western cultural supremacy. "María Amparo Ruiz de Burton Negotiates American Literary Politics and Culture," by Amelia Maria de la Luz Montes, is in *Challenging Boundaries: Gender and Periodization* (2000), ed. Joyce W. Warren and Margaret Dickie. De la Luz Montes introduces an early Mexican American literary tradition and relates that tradition to already established Western writers. "Historical Amnesia and the Vanishing Mestiza: The Problem of Race in *The Squatter and the Don* and *Ramona*," by Jesse Alemán, appears in *Aztlán: A Journal of Chicano Studies* (2002). Finally, " 'Those Indians Are Great Thieves, I Suppose?': Historicizing the White Woman in *The Squatter and the Don*," by Peter A. Chvany, is included in Samina Najmi, Rajini Srikanth's *White Women in Racialized Spaces: Imaginative Transformation and Ethical Action in Literature* (2002).

### Mark Twain

*The Writings of Mark Twain* (1922–25), thirty-seven volumes, edited by Albert Bigelow Paine, is being superseded by the ongoing editions of *The Mark Twain Papers and Project* (1967–) at the University of California Press under the leadership of Robert Hirst. *The Mark Twain Papers* series publishes scholarly editions of previously unpublished notebooks, journals, letters, and literary manuscripts; *The Works of Mark Twain* publishes scholarly editions of previously published works; *The Mark Twain Library* consists of popularly priced editions with explanatory notes and illustrations; *Jumping Frogs: Undiscovered, Rediscovered, and Celebrated Writings of Mark Twain* has so far published *Is He Dead? A Comedy in Three Acts* and *Mark Twain's Helpful Hints for Good Living: A Handbook for the Damned Human Race*. *The Mark Twain Digital* Project makes available an electronic edition of Twain's letters 1876–1880. Six volumes of letters (through 1871) have appeared so far in the *Papers*, and other Twain letters are available in several scattered volumes, the most interesting of which is *The Correspondence of Samuel L. Clemens and William Dean Howells, 1872–1910* (1960), edited by Henry Nash Smith and William M. Gibson. Altogether some forty volumes have appeared as part of the Mark Twain Papers and Project. The Library of America has issued in two volumes *Mark Twain: Collected Tales, Sketches, Speeches and Essays* (1992) with notes by Louis Budd. A companion volume,

with notes by Susan K. Harris, *Mark Twain: Historical Romances, The Prince and the Pauper, A Connecticut Yankee in King Arthur's Court, Personal Recollections of Joan of Arc* followed in 1993. Tom Quirk edited a fine selection of *Mark Twain: Tales, Speeches, Essays and Sketches* (1993). Marlene Boyd Vallen's *Mark Twain: Propagandist for the Popular Culture* (1992) collects sixteen speeches and commentary. Louis J. Budd's *Mark Twain: The Contemporary Reviews* (1999) gives us over six hundred pages of early reviews, from 1867–1817.

Most controversial of new editions of Twain's best-known book the Mark Twain Project edition (2001) which calls itself "The Only Comprehensive Edition" of *Adventures of Huckleberry Finn*; it is edited by ed. Victor Fischer and Lin Salamo and dedicated to Walter Blair, leading scholar of the 1985 Mark Twain Project edition of the novel, who died in 1992. It contains 1164 pages with original drawings by E. W. Kemble and John Harley, but its greatest claim to fame is its use of the first half of *Huckleberry Finn* manuscript discovered in a Hollywood attic in 1990. The editors collated over 1,100 changes in spelling, punctuation, and other details and one hundred changes in wording, adding Jim's ghost story and chapter 16, "The Raftsmens' Passage," both previously left out. *Adventures of Huckleberry Finn*, New Riverside Editions, gen. ed. Paul Lauter, ed. Susan K. Harris (2005), includes the raftsmen's passage and critical essays by Victor Doyno, Shelley Fisher Fishkin, Norman Mailer, and Toni Morrison. Other new editions or publications include Twain's previously unpublished story, "A Murder, A Mystery, and a Marriage," unpublished Twain story, introduced by Roy Blount, Jr., *Atlantic Monthly* (2001); *The Best Short Stories of Mark Twain*, edited by Lawrence I. Berkove (2004); and *The Portable Mark Twain* edited by Tom Quirk (2004). A new journal, the *Mark Twain Annual*, was founded by the Mark Twain Circle in 2003; its 2005 issue featured a Special Section on *Adventures of Huckleberry Finn*. Tom Tenney supplies ongoing bibliographical updates in *American Literary Realism* and in the *Mark Twain Circular*, updating his 1977 *Mark Twain: A Reference Guide. A Companion to Mark Twain*, ed. Peter Messent and Louis Budd, (2005); an expansion of the 1981 *The Annotated* Huckleberry Finn, ed. Michael Patrick Hearn (2001); David E. E. Sloane's *Student Companion to Mark Twain* (2001); *Making Mark Twain Work in the Classroom*, ed. James M. Leonard (1999), which covers challenges that confront instructors, especially slavery, women's roles, and religious satire; and *Mark Twain A to Z: The Essential Reference to His Life and Writings* by R. Kent Rasmussen (2006), which offers nearly 1,300 entries devoted primarily to proper names relating to

Twain, round out the reference and teaching shelf.

Albert Bigelow Paine's *Mark Twain, a Biography* (1912) is vivid, unreliable, and still indispensable. Justin Kaplan's *Mr. Clemens and Mark Twain, a Biography* (1966) is a lively, popular account. Van Wyck Brooks's polemical and controversial *The Ordeal of Mark Twain* (1920) should be read together with Bernard De Voto's corrective *Mark Twain's America* (1932). De Lancey Ferguson's *Mark Twain: Man and Legend* (1943) is a fine full-length critical biography, as is Everett Emerson's *Mark Twain: A Literary Life* (2000), an expanded and updated version of his earlier *The Authentic Mark Twain: A Literary Biography of Samuel L. Clemens* (1984), a trusted guide to Twain's literary life. Jeffrey Steinbrink's *Getting to Be Mark Twain* (1991) examines the period 1868–71.

*Mark Twain: A Life* by Ron Powers (2005) gives us another biography; Powers, who wrote about Twain's Missouri childhood in *Dangerous Water: A Biography of the Boy Who Became Mark Twain* (2001) aims to define Twain as a "representative man" of his times and offer a full portrait of Twain in his many roles and phases of life. In *The Singular Mark Twain: A Biography* (2005), Fred Kaplan attempts something quite different. Kaplan sees Twain, in contrast to many biographers such as Justin Kaplan, as a singular personality (not multiple or divided), his two names indicating no deep internal division of identity. Twain's contradictions are those of any fine mind. Jason Gary Horn attempts to sort out all the current biographies in *Mark Twain: A Descriptive Guide to Biographical Sources* (1999).

Criticism on Twain is enormous in quantity, variety, and quality. Two excellent general studies are Henry Nash Smith's *Mark Twain: The Development of a Writer* (1962) and William M. Gibson's *The Art of Mark Twain* (1976). James M. Cox's perceptive *Mark Twain: The Fate of Humor* (1966), Edgar M. Branch's *The Literary Apprenticeship of Mark Twain* (1950), and Albert E. Stone's *The Innocent Eye: Childhood in Mark Twain's Imagination* (1961) are distinguished early contributions to serious Twain scholarship. More recent studies of permanent interest include Louis J. Budd's *Our Mark Twain: The Making of His Public Personality* (1983), James L. Johnson's *Mark Twain and the Limits of Power: Emerson's God in Ruins* (1982), Sherwood Cummings's excellent *Mark Twain and Science: Adventures of a Mind* (1989), Susan Gillman's *Dark Twins: Imposture and Identity in Mark Twain's America* (1991), Maria Ornella Marotti's *The Duplicating Imagination: Twain and the Twain Papers* (1991), and David E. E. Sloane's *Mark Twain as a Literary Comedian* (1979). Carl Dolmetsch's *Our Famous Guest: Mark Twain in Vienna* (1992)

argues against the conventional wisdom concerning the decline of Twain's creativity after the mid-1890s. The title of Shelley Fisher Fishkin's *Was Huck Black?: Mark Twain and African-American Voices* (1993) suggests its interesting argument that Twain's model for Huck was a young black friend of his. Fishkin's *Lighting Out for the Territory: Reflections on Mark Twain and American Culture* (1996) raises fascinating questions about race and the way Twain's writing personas have been appropriated and misappropriated by popular culture. Several volumes take a fresh look at Twain's humor: Don Florence, *Persona and Humor in Mark Twain's Early Writings* (1995); Stuart Hutchison, *Mark Twain: Humor on the Run* (1994); Patricia M. Mandia, *Comedic Pathos: Black Humor in Twain's Fiction* (1991); Bruce Michelson, *Mark Twain on the Loose: A Comic Writer and the American Self* (1995); and *Mark Twain's Humor: Critical Essays* (1992), edited by David E. E. Sloane. Several books address Twain's attitudes toward women—in and out of his writings: Laura E. Skandera-Trombley's *Mark Twain in the Company of Women* (1994), J. D. Stahl's *Mark Twain, Culture and Gender: Envisioning America Through Europe* (1993), Peter Stoneley's *Mark Twain and the Feminine Aesthetic* (1992), and Resa Willis's *Mark and Livy: The Love Story of Mark Twain and the Woman Who Almost Tamed Him* (1992). Other studies of note include Gregg Camfield's *Sentimental Twain: Samuel Clemens in the Maze of Moral Philosophy* (1994), Guy Cardwell's *The Man Who Was Mark Twain: Images and Ideologies* (1991), Randall Knoper's *Acting Naturally: Mark Twain in the Culture of Performance* (1995), and David R. Sewell's *Mark Twain's Languages: Discourse, Dialogue, and Linguistic Variety* (1987). Among the many collections of criticism, Robert Sattlemeyer and J. Donald Crowley's *One Hundred Years of "Huckleberry Finn": The Boy, His Book, and American Culture* (1985) merits special notice. Victor Doyno's painstaking study *Writing "Huck Finn": Mark Twain's Creative Process* (1991) will soon be revised to incorporate the discovery of the first half of the *Huckleberry Finn* manuscript.

More recent critical studies have included Hilton Obenzinger's *American Palestine: Melville, Twain, and the Holy Land Mania* (1999); *Black, White, and Huckleberry Finn: Reimagining the the American Dream* by Elaine Mensh and Harry Mensh (2000); *Refiguring Huckleberry Finn*, Carl F. Wieck (2000); Peter Messent's *The Short Works of Mark Twain: A Critical Study* (2001); the sequel to *Mark Twain and His Illustrators*, vol. 1 (1869–1875), by Beverly R. David, vol. 2, *Mark Twain and His Illustrators*, (1875–1883), which appeared in 2001; Louis J. Budd's 1962 *Mark Twain: Social Philosopher*, reprinted (2001) in the Mark

Twain and His Circle Series edited by Tom Quirk; *Searching for Jim: Slavery in Sam Clemens's World* by Terrell Dempsey (2003); *Mark Twain: A Short Introduction* by Stephen Railton (2003); Joseph L. Coulombe, *Mark Twain and the American West* (2003); *Mark Twain and Company: Six Literary Relations* by Leland Krauth (2003), which covers Twain's relationships with William Dean Howells, Robert Louis Stevenson, Rudyard Kipling, Bret Harte, Harriett Beecher Stowe, and Matthew Arnold; and *Mark Twain in Paradise: His Voyages to Bermuda*, Donald Hoffmann (2006).

Among the several recent collections of criticism the following warrant attention: James S. Leonard, Thomas A. Tenney and Thadious M. Davis's edited *Satire or Evasion?: Black Perspectives on Huckleberry Finn* (1996), Tom Quirk's *Coming to Grips with Huckleberry Finn: Essays on a Book, a Boy, and a Man* (1992), Eric J. Sundquist's *Mark Twain: A Collection of Critical Essays* (1994), Laurie Champion's *The Critical Response to Mark Twain's Huckleberry Finn* (1991), Forrest G. Robinson's *The Cambridge Companion to Mark Twain* (1995), Laura Skandera-Trombley and Michael J. Kiskis's *Constructing Mark Twain: New Directions in Scholarship* (2001), containing thirteen essays saluting Hamlin Hill's 1974 challenge to scholars, "Who Killed Mark Twain?" J. R. Le Master and James Wilson edited *The Mark Twain Encyclopedia* (1992), with 180 contributors and 740 entries. R. Kent Rasmussen's claim in the title of his *Mark Twain A-Z: The Essential Reference to His Life and Writings* (1996) is justified by its 1,300 factual entries.

### Booker T. Washington

Louis R. Harlan has edited *The Booker T. Washington Papers* in fourteen volumes (1972–89). William L. Andrews has edited a Norton Critical Edition of *Up From Slavery* (1996). August Meier's *Negro Thought in America, 1880–1915* (1963) and John Hope Franklin's *From Slavery to Freedom: A History of American Negroes* (1967) are two early and still useful background books. The standard critical biography is by Louis R. Harlan: *Booker T. Washington: The Making of a Black Leader, 1865–1901* (1972) and *Booker T. Washington: The Wizard of Tuskegee, 1901–1915* (1983).

Robert B. Stepto's chapter on Washington's *Up From Slavery* in his *Behind the Veil: A Study of Afro-American Narrative* (1979) is a classic analysis. James M. Cox's chapter "Autobiography and Washington" in his *Recovering Lost Ground: Essays in American Autobiography* (1989) is very perceptive. James Olney's essay on Frederick Douglass and Washington in Deborah McDowell and Arnold Rampersad's (eds.) *Slavery and the Literary Imagination* (1989) is also an important study, as is Kevern Verney's *The Art of the Possible: Booker T. Washington*

*and Black Leadership in the United States, 1881–1925* (2001). Also useful are "Strategies and Revisions of Self-Representation in Booker T. Washington's Autobiography" by Donald B. Gibson, *American Quarterly* (1993), and the essays of Gibson and Maurice Wallace in Michael Moon and Cathy N. Davidson's 1995 *Subjects and Citizens: Nation, Race, and Gender from Oroonoko to Anita Hill*. In *Turning South Again: Re-Thinking Modernism/Re-Reading Booker T.*, by Houston A. Baker, Jr. (2001) is sharply critical of Washington's relations to and ideas about whites. Related work includes *Creative Conflict in African American Thought: Frederick Douglass, Alexander Crummell, Booker T. Washington, W. E. B. Du Bois, and Marcus Garvey*, by Wilson Jeremiah Moses (2004); *Forever Free: The Story of Emancipation and Reconstruction* (2005) by Eric Foner and Joshua Brown; and *Inhuman Bondage: The Rise and Fall of Slavery in the New World* (2006) by David Brion Davis, each of which furnishes contexts for Washington's thought. *The Education of Booker T. Washington: American Democracy and the Idea of Race Relations* by Michael Rudolph West (2005) presents the "intertwined history of an idea and a man," Booker T. Washington as the very progenitor of "race relations," not simply a "black conservative" or pragmatist. *Uncle Tom or New Negro?: African Americans Reflect on Booker T. Washington and Up From Slavery 100 Years Later*, edited by Rebecca Carroll (2006), which includes the complete text of Washington's autobiography with twenty essays by various critics exploring the continuing debates over Washington and his relationship to African Americans, highlighting both his controversial ideas and his complexity. There are many juvenile biographies of Washington as well as numerous posters of him available on the internet.

### Edith Wharton

There is no uniform edition of Wharton's writings. Louis Auchincloss edited *The Edith Wharton Reader* (1965), and R. W. B. Lewis edited in two volumes *The Collected Short Stories of Edith Wharton* (1988). Frederick Wegener edited *Edith Wharton: The Uncollected Critical Writings* (1991). The Library of America has produced *Edith Wharton: Novels: The House of Mirth / The Reef / The Custom of the Country / The Age of Innocence*, ed. R. W. B. Lewis (1986); *Edith Wharton: Novellas and Other Writings: Madame De Treymes / Ethan Frome / Summer / Old New York / The Mother's Recompense / A Backward Glance*, ed. Cynthia Griffin Wolff (1990); *Edith Wharton: Vol. 1 Collected Stories: 1891–1910* and Vol. 2 *Collected Stories 1911–1937*, ed. Maureen Howard (2001); and *Edith Wharton: Selected Poems*, ed. Louis Auchincloss (2005).

R. W. B. Lewis, using the extensive Wharton

papers at Yale, prepared the definitive *Edith Wharton: A Biography* (1993). Millicent Bell's *Edith Wharton and Henry James: The Story of Their Friendship* (1965) is still useful. The fully illustrated *Edith Wharton: An Extraordinary Life* (1999) by Eleanor Dwight is an expansion of Wharton biography into her interests in architecture and house decoration. *Edith Wharton's Library: A Catalogue* (1999) has been compiled by George Ramsden to inventory more than 2,600 volumes, about half of her library at her death.

Margaret B. McDowell's *Edith Wharton* (1976) is a solid introductory study. Book-length studies of importance include Gary H. Lindberg's *Edith Wharton and the Novel of Manners* (1975); Cynthia Griffin Wolff's *A Feast of Words: The Triumph of Edith Wharton* (1977); Richard H. Lawson's *Edith Wharton* (1977); Elizabeth Ammons's *Edith Wharton's Argument with America* (1980); Geoffrey Walton's *Edith Wharton, a Critical Interpretation* (1982); Wendy Gimbel's *Edith Wharton: Orphancy and Survival* (1984); Carol Wershoven's *The Female Intruder in the Novels of Edith Wharton* (1983); Catherine M. Rae's *Edith Wharton's New York Quartet* (1984); Susan Goodman's *Edith Wharton's Women* (1990); Janet Goodwyn's *Edith Wharton: Traveller in the Land of Letters* (1990); Penelope Vita-Finzi's *Edith Wharton and the Art of Fiction* (1990); Gloria Erdich's *The Sexual Education of Edith Wharton* (1992); Susan Goodman's *Edith Wharton's Inner Circle* (1994); *The Cambridge Companion to Edith Wharton*, ed. Millicent Bell (1995); Helen Killoran's *Edith Wharton: Art and Allusion* (1996); *Displaying Women: Spectacles of Leisure in Edith Wharton's New York* by M. Montgomery (1998), which uses letters, print media sources, etiquette manuals, and the New York fiction of Wharton and James to explore womens' roles; Claire Preston's *Edith Wharton's Social Register* (2000), which shows how Wharton transformed social codes and conventions into narrative strategies; Hildegard Hoeller's *Edith Wharton's Dialogue with Realism and Sentimental Fiction* (2000), which sees Wharton's fiction as critiquing these literary movements; *The Critical Reception of Edith Wharton*, edited by Helen Killoran (2001), which contains chapters on *The House of Mirth, Ethan Frome, The Custom of the Country, Summer, The Age of Innocence*, and *Ghosts* and begins with contemporary reviews to trace main trends in criticism; Carol J. Singley's *Edith Wharton's The House of Mirth* and her *Historical Guide to Edith Wharton*, both 2003; and *The Portable Edith Wharton*, edited by Linda Wagner-Martin (2003).

Alfred Bendixen and Annette Zilversmit edited *Edith Wharton: New Critical Essays* (1992). Sarah Bird Wright and Clare Colquit's *Edith Wharton A to Z* (1998) is a cornucopia of information about Wharton's writings, life and times, as is *A Forward Glance: New Essays on Edith Wharton*, edited by Clare Colquitt, Susan Goodman, and Candace Waid (1999). Adeline R. Tintner's *Edith Wharton in Context: Essays on Intertextuality* (1999) gives us twenty-nine essays (of which twenty-one were previously unpublished) concerning Wharton's influence on and literary debts to other writers, especially James. *New Essays on The House of Mirth*, edited by Deborah Esch (2001) offers further contemporary perspectives on this important novel.

### Walt Whitman

The study of Whitman has been revolutionized by the *Walt Whitman Hypertext Archive* <www.whitman.archive.org>, directed by Kenneth M. Price and Ed Folsom. Before going to the printed sources listed below, students should work in and out of the sections of this gigantic and superbly ordered archive, which includes a lengthy and reliable biographical essay by Folsom and Price, all the known contemporary reviews, all the known photographs, and a current bibliography of scholarship and criticism.

*The Collected Writings of Walt Whitman* was under the general editorship of Gay Wilson Allen; part of this edition is *Walt Whitman: The Correspondence* (1961–69), a six-volume set with two supplements (1990–91), edited by Edwin H. Miller. The growth of *Leaves of Grass* may be studied in the *Comprehensive Reader's Edition* (1965, 1968), edited by Harold W. Blodgett and Sculley Bradley. Essential, in three volumes, is *"Leaves of Grass": A Textual Variorum of the Printed Poems* (1980), edited by Bradley, Blodgett, Golden, and William White. Michael Moon's Norton Critical Edition of *Leaves of Grass* (2002) includes discussion of textual variants and compositional development. Garland has printed three volumes containing facsimiles of Whitman manuscripts (1993). Important documents are in *Notebooks and Unpublished Prose Manuscripts* (1984), edited by Edward P. Grier in six volumes. The first volume of Whitman's *Journalism*, edited by Herbert Bergman, Douglas A. Noverr, and Edward J. Recchia, appeared in 1998.

Long the standard biography is Gay Wilson Allen's *The Solitary Singer* (1967). It should be supplemented by Roger Asselineau's *The Evolution of Walt Whitman* (1960, 1962; reissued 1999), the first biography to deal openly with Whitman's sexuality; Justin Kaplan's *Walt Whitman: A Life* (1980), David S. Reynolds's *Walt Whitman's America: A Cultural Biography* (1995), Gary Schmidgall's *Walt Whitman: A Gay Life* (1998), Jerome Loving's *Walt Whitman: The Song of Himself* (1999), and Ed Folsom and Kenneth M. Price's *Re-scripting Walt Whitman: An Introduction to His Life and Work* (2005). Joann P. Krieg's 1998 *A Whitman*

*Chronology* is useful. Contemporary context is emphasized in Betsy Erkkila's *Whitman the Political Poet* (1989), Ed Folsom's *Walt Whitman's Native Representations* (1994), and Roy Morris Jr.'s *The Better Angel: Walt Whitman in the Civil War* (2000). Valuable editions of documentary evidence include Thomas L. Brasher's *Whitman as Editor of the Brooklyn Daily Eagle* (1970), Joel Myerson's excellent *Whitman in His Own Time: A Biographical Chronicle of His Life, Drawn from Recollections, Memoirs, and Interviews, Friends and Associates* (1991, rev. 2000) and Myerson's *Walt Whitman: A Documentary Volume* (2000). The last of nine volumes of Horace Traubel's *With Walt Whitman in Camden*, edited by Jeanne Chapman and Robert Macisaac, appeared in 1996; an excellent starting place is Gary Schmidgall's *Intimate with Walt: Selections from Whitman's Conversations with Horace Traubel, 1888–1892* (2001).

Valuable collections of critical essays include Robert K. Martin's *The Continuing Presence of Walt Whitman: The Life after the Life* (1992), Geoffrey M. Sill's *Walt Whitman of Mickle Street: A Centennial Collection* (1994), Gay Wilson Allen and Ed Folsom's *Walt Whitman and the World* (1995), Ezra Greenspan's *The Cambridge Companion to Walt Whitman* (1995), Betsy Erkkila and Jay Grossman's *Breaking Bounds: Whitman and American Cultural Studies* (1996), David S. Reynolds's *A Historical Guide to Walt Whitman* (2000), and Donald D. Kummings's *A Companion to Walt Whitman* (2006). Two provocative recent critical works are Vivian R. Pollack's *The Erotic Whitman* (2000) and Jay Grossman's *Reconstituting the American Renaissance: Emerson, Whitman, and the Poetics of Representation* (2003). On Whitman's reception, see Graham Clarke's four-volume *Walt Whitman: Critical Assessments* (1996) and Kenneth M. Price's *Walt Whitman: The Contemporary Reviews* (1996). Joel Myerson prepared *Walt Whitman: A Descriptive Bibliography* (1993). Very useful is the 1998 *Walt Whitman: An Encyclopedia*, edited by J. R. LeMaster and Donald D. Kummings. *Walt Whitman: The Measure of His Song*, edited by Jim Perlman, Ed Folsom, and Dan Campion (2nd rev. ed., 1998), quotes other poets on Whitman. Kenneth M. Price's *To Walt Whitman, America* (2004) traces Whitman's continuing impact on U.S. literary culture.

### Zitkala Ša (Gertrude Simmons Bonnin)

Dexter Fisher's 1986 edition of Zitkala Ša's *American Indian Stories* (1921) includes an expert and insightful introduction to this collection of autobiography, fiction, and nonfiction prose. P. Jane Hafen helpfully edited a number of Zitkala Ša's works in *Dreams and Thunder: Stories, Poems and "The Sun Dance Opera"* (2001). Also of great interest is Zitkala Ša's "Why I Am a Pagan" (*Atlantic Monthly* 90 [102]: 801–03). Material on Zitkala Ša is still scarce, though articles and chapters in part or whole devoted to her are appearing more frequently; Dexter Fisher's *Zitkala Ša: The Evolution of a Writer* (1979) and Dorothea M. Susag's *Zitkala-Ša (Gertrude Simmons Bonnin): A Power(full) Literary Voice* (1993) are among the few critical and biographical studies. Two excellent articles published in books are D. K. Meisenheimer's "Regionalist Bodies/Embodied Regions: Sarah Orne Jewett and Zitkala-Ša," in Sherrie A. Innis and Diana Royer's collection *Breaking Boundaries: New Perspectives on Women's Regional Writing* (1997), and Patricia Okker's "Native American Literatures and the Canon" in Tom Quirk and Gary Scharnhost's collection *American Realism and the Canon* (1995). Two excellent articles published in journals are P. Jane Hafen's "Zitkala Ša: Sentimentality and Sovereignty" (*Wicazo Sa Review* 12 [1997]: 31–34) and Dexter Fisher's "Zitkala Ša: The Evolution of a Writer" (*American Indian Quarterly* 5 [1979]: 229–38). The best discursive bibliography of Native American literature is A. LaVonne Brown Ruoff's *American Indian Literatures: An Introduction, Bibliographic Review, and Selected Bibliography* (1990), a comprehensive and judicious survey of the field. Two other titles may be recommended to anyone interested in Native American autobiography: A. David Brumble III's *American Indian Autobiography* (1988) and Arnold Krupat's "Native American Autobiography and the Synecdochic Self" in Paul John Eakin's *American Autobiography: Retrospect and Prospect* (1991).

# IMAGE ACKNOWLEDGMENTS

# Index